Archie

1000 PAGE comics

BONANZA

Archie

1000 PAGE COMICS BONANZA

Published by Archie Comic Publications, Inc.
325 Fayette Avenue, Mamaroneck, New York 10543-2318.

ISBN: 978-1-61988-903-3

Publisher / Co-CEO: Jon Goldwater
Co-CEO: Nancy Silberkleit
President: Mike Pellerito
Co-President / Editor-In-Chief: Victor Gorelick
Chief Creative Officer: Roberto Aguirre-Sacasa
Senior Vice President – Sales and Business Development: Jim Sokolowski
Senior Vice President – Publishing and Operations: Harold Buchholz
Senior Vice President – Publicity & Marketing: Alex Segura
Executive Director of Editorial: Paul Kaminski
Production Manager: Stephen Oswald
Project Coordinator & Book Design: Joe Morciglio
Digest Editor: Carlos Antunes
Editorial Assistant / Proofreader: Jamie Lee Rotante

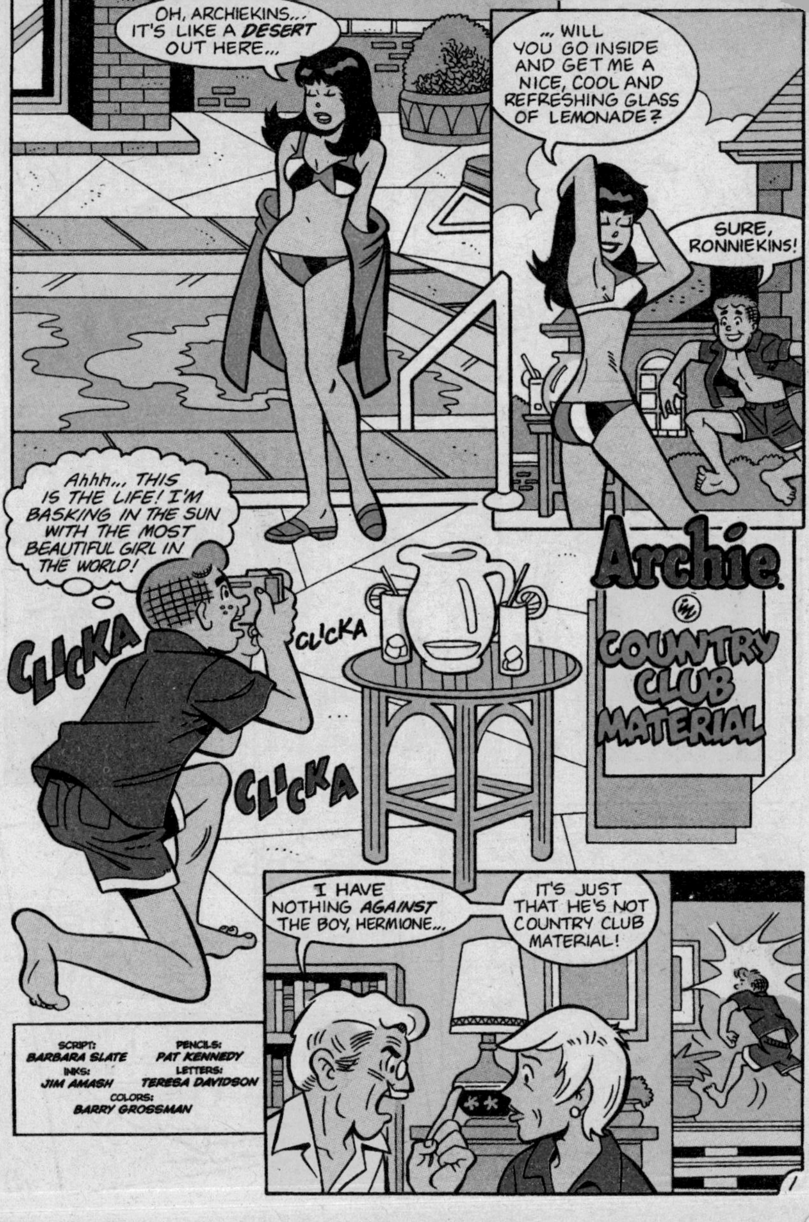

OH, ARCHIEKINS... IT'S LIKE A *DESERT* OUT HERE...
..., WILL YOU GO INSIDE AND GET ME A NICE, COOL AND REFRESHING GLASS OF LEMONADE?
SURE, RONNIEKINS!
Ahhh..., THIS IS THE LIFE! I'M BASKING IN THE SUN WITH THE MOST BEAUTIFUL GIRL IN THE WORLD!
CLICKA
CLICKA
CLICKA
Archie
in
COUNTRY CLUB MATERIAL
SCRIPT: BARBARA SLATE
PENCILS: PAT KENNEDY
INKS: JIM AMASH
LETTERS: TERESA DAVIDSON
COLORS: BARRY GROSSMAN
I HAVE NOTHING *AGAINST* THE BOY, HERMIONE...
IT'S JUST THAT HE'S NOT COUNTRY CLUB MATERIAL!
1

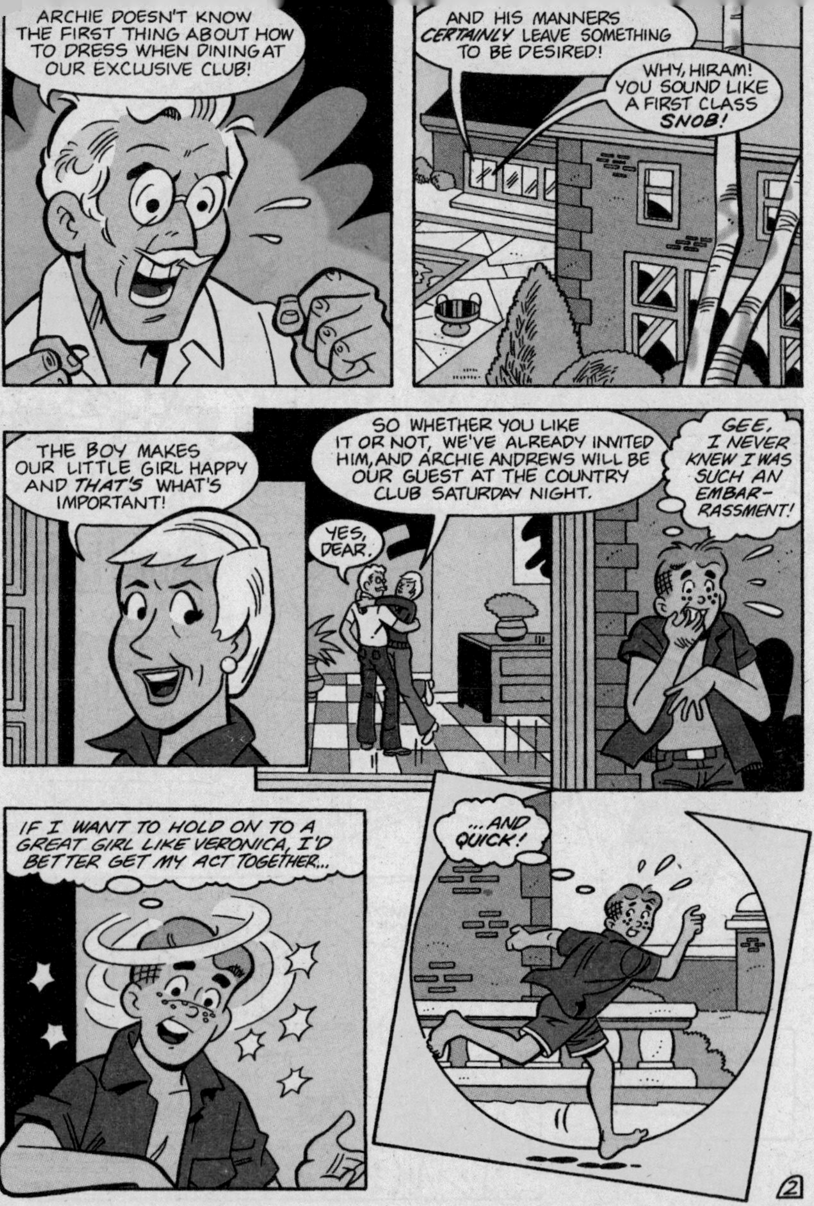
ARCHIE DOESN'T KNOW THE FIRST THING ABOUT HOW TO DRESS WHEN DINING AT OUR EXCLUSIVE CLUB!
AND HIS MANNERS CERTAINLY LEAVE SOMETHING TO BE DESIRED!
WHY, HIRAM! YOU SOUND LIKE A FIRST CLASS SNOB!
THE BOY MAKES OUR LITTLE GIRL HAPPY AND THAT'S WHAT'S IMPORTANT!
SO WHETHER YOU LIKE IT OR NOT, WE'VE ALREADY INVITED HIM, AND ARCHIE ANDREWS WILL BE OUR GUEST AT THE COUNTRY CLUB SATURDAY NIGHT.
YES, DEAR.
GEE, I NEVER KNEW I WAS SUCH AN EMBAR-RASSMENT!
IF I WANT TO HOLD ON TO A GREAT GIRL LIKE VERONICA, I'D BETTER GET MY ACT TOGETHER...
...AND QUICK!

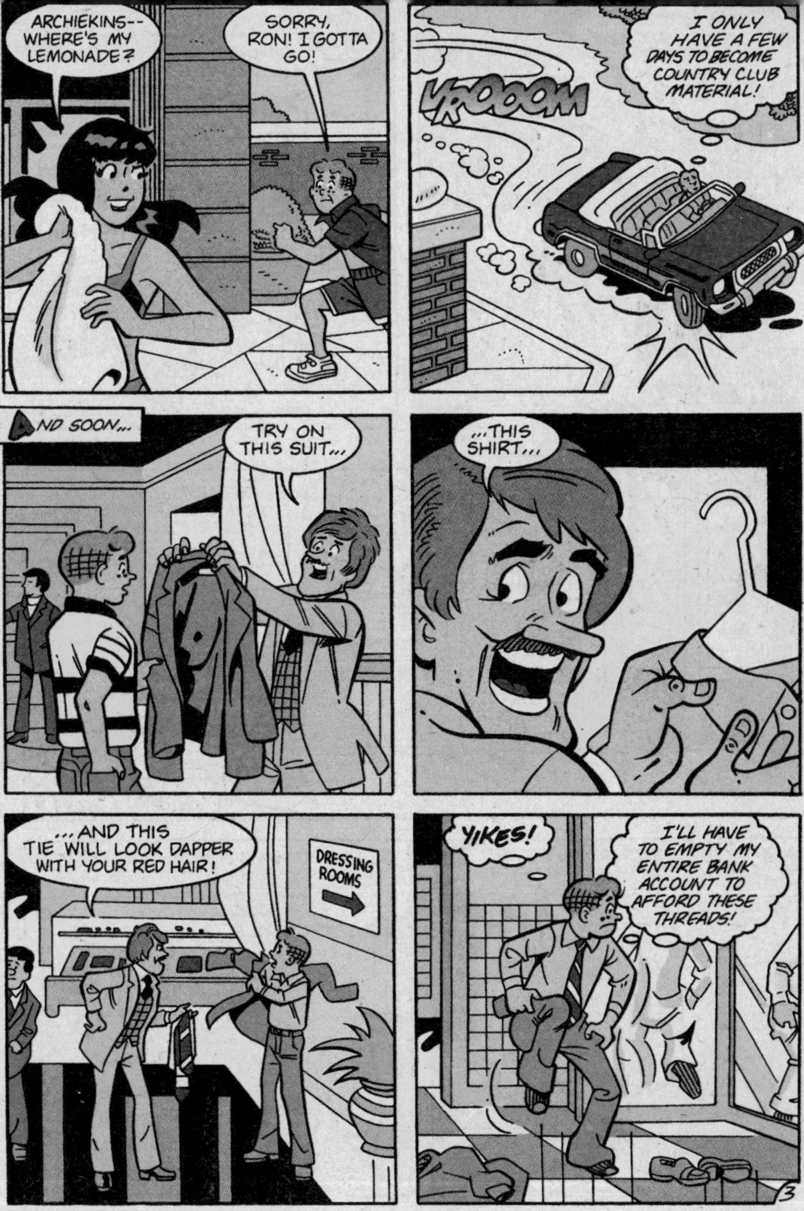
ARCHIEKINS-- WHERE'S MY LEMONADE?
SORRY, RON! I GOTTA GO!
I ONLY HAVE A FEW DAYS TO BECOME COUNTRY CLUB MATERIAL!
VROOOM
AND SOON...
TRY ON THIS SUIT...
...THIS SHIRT...
...AND THIS TIE WILL LOOK DAPPER WITH YOUR RED HAIR!
DRESSING ROOMS
YIKES!
I'LL HAVE TO EMPTY MY ENTIRE BANK ACCOUNT TO AFFORD THESE THREADS!

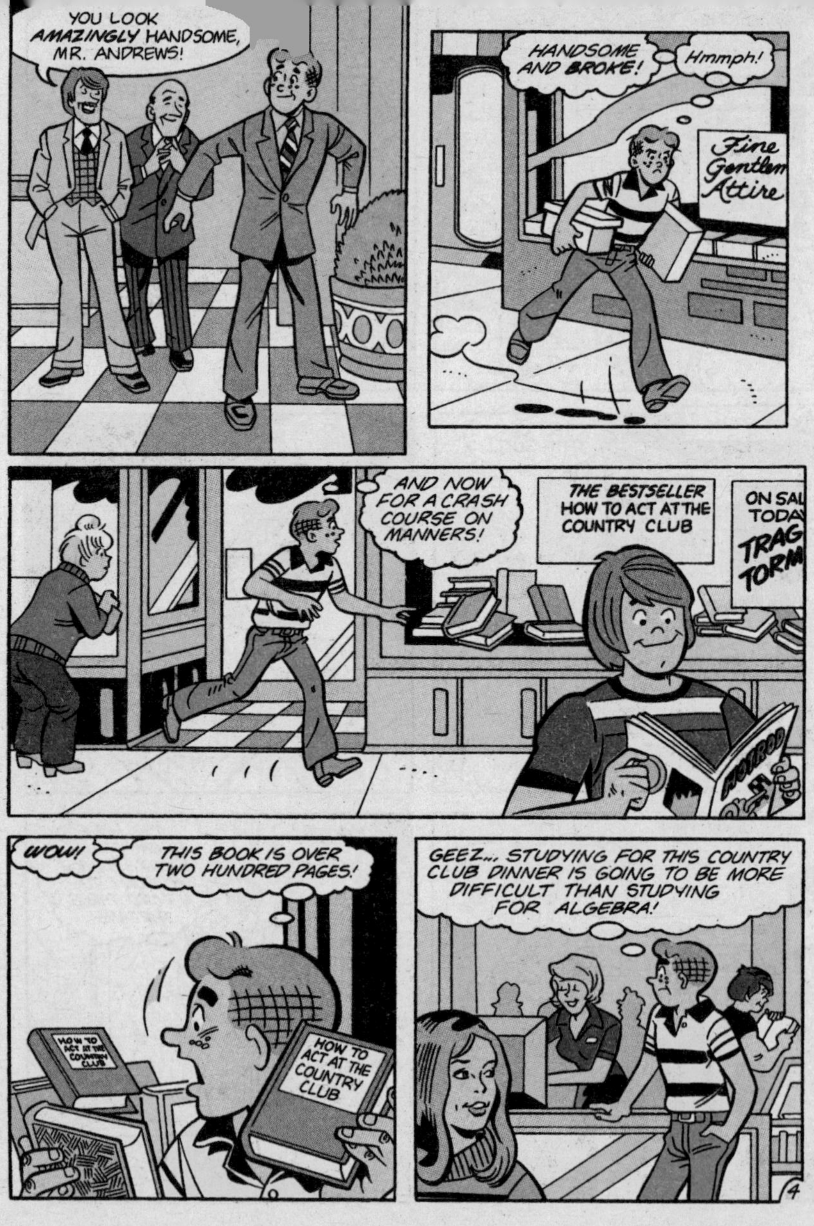
YOU LOOK AMAZINGLY HANDSOME, MR. ANDREWS!
HANDSOME AND BROKE!
Hmmph!
Fine Gentlem Attire
AND NOW FOR A CRASH COURSE ON MANNERS!
THE BESTSELLER HOW TO ACT AT THE COUNTRY CLUB
ON SAL TODAY TRAG TORM
HOTROD
WOW!
THIS BOOK IS OVER TWO HUNDRED PAGES!
HOW TO ACT AT THE COUNTRY CLUB
HOW TO ACT AT THE COUNTRY CLUB
GEEZ... STUDYING FOR THIS COUNTRY CLUB DINNER IS GOING TO BE MORE DIFFICULT THAN STUDYING FOR ALGEBRA!
4

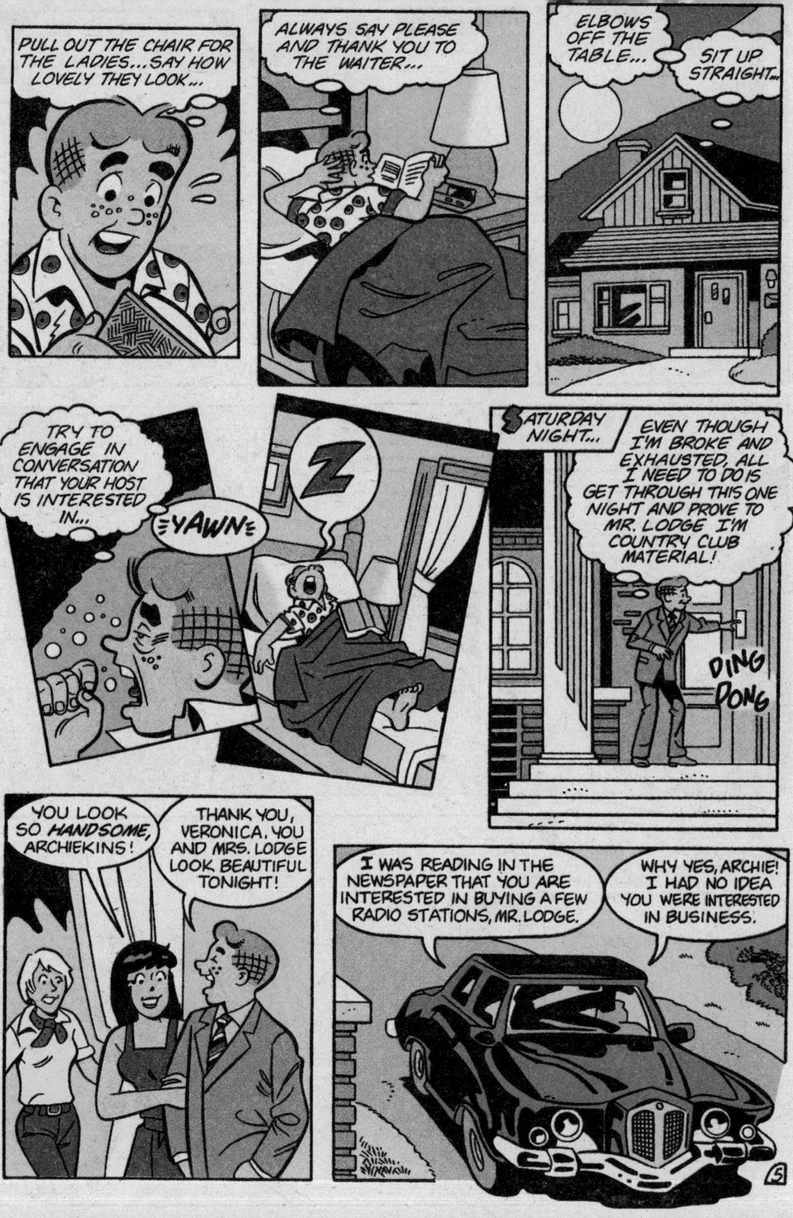
PULL OUT THE CHAIR FOR THE LADIES... SAY HOW LOVELY THEY LOOK...
ALWAYS SAY PLEASE AND THANK YOU TO THE WAITER...
ELBOWS OFF THE TABLE...
SIT UP STRAIGHT...
TRY TO ENGAGE IN CONVERSATION THAT YOUR HOST IS INTERESTED IN...
YAWN
Z
SATURDAY NIGHT...
EVEN THOUGH I'M BROKE AND EXHAUSTED, ALL I NEED TO DO IS GET THROUGH THIS ONE NIGHT AND PROVE TO MR. LODGE I'M COUNTRY CLUB MATERIAL!
DING DONG
YOU LOOK SO HANDSOME, ARCHIEKINS!
THANK YOU, VERONICA. YOU AND MRS. LODGE LOOK BEAUTIFUL TONIGHT!
I WAS READING IN THE NEWSPAPER THAT YOU ARE INTERESTED IN BUYING A FEW RADIO STATIONS, MR. LODGE.
WHY YES, ARCHIE! I HAD NO IDEA YOU WERE INTERESTED IN BUSINESS.
5

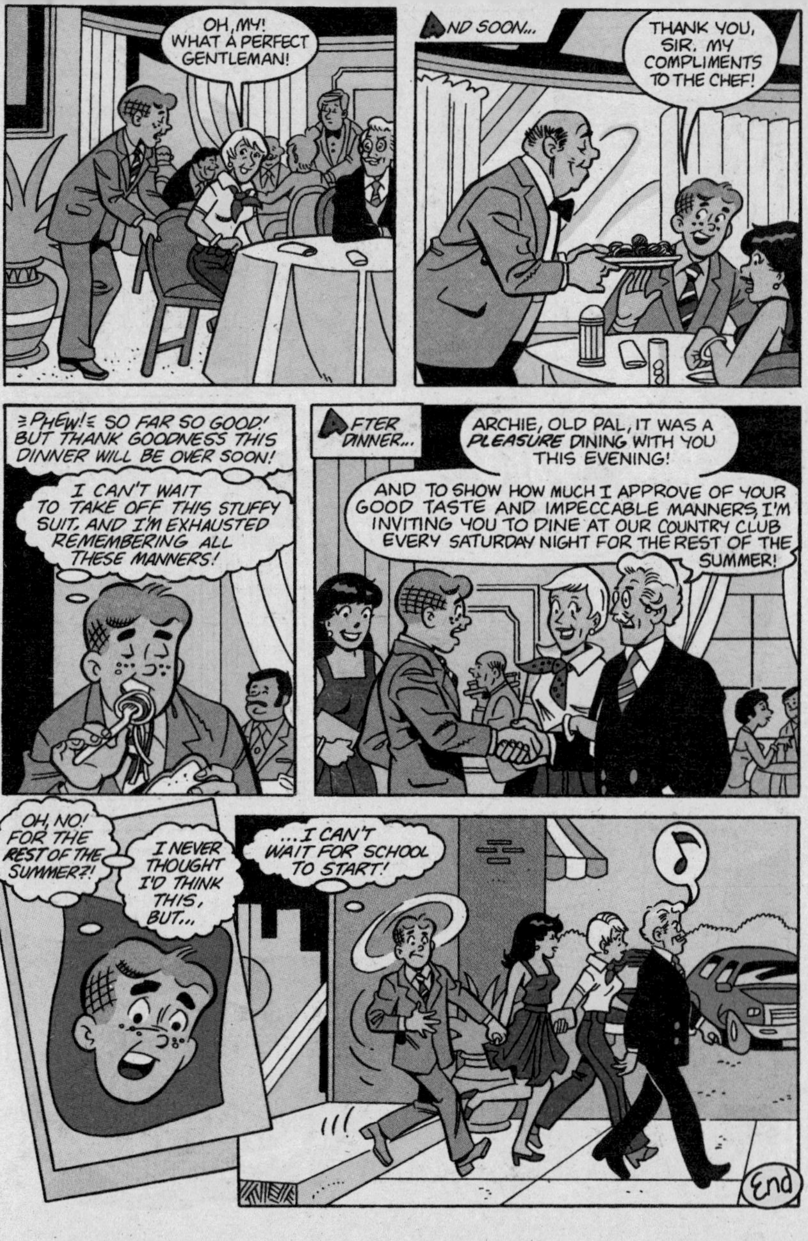
OH, MY! WHAT A PERFECT GENTLEMAN!
AND SOON...
THANK YOU, SIR. MY COMPLIMENTS TO THE CHEF!
PHEW! SO FAR SO GOOD! BUT THANK GOODNESS THIS DINNER WILL BE OVER SOON!
I CAN'T WAIT TO TAKE OFF THIS STUFFY SUIT, AND I'M EXHAUSTED REMEMBERING ALL THESE MANNERS!
AFTER DINNER...
ARCHIE, OLD PAL, IT WAS A PLEASURE DINING WITH YOU THIS EVENING!
AND TO SHOW HOW MUCH I APPROVE OF YOUR GOOD TASTE AND IMPECCABLE MANNERS, I'M INVITING YOU TO DINE AT OUR COUNTRY CLUB EVERY SATURDAY NIGHT FOR THE REST OF THE SUMMER!
OH, NO! FOR THE REST OF THE SUMMER?!
I NEVER THOUGHT I'D THINK THIS, BUT...
...I CAN'T WAIT FOR SCHOOL TO START!
End

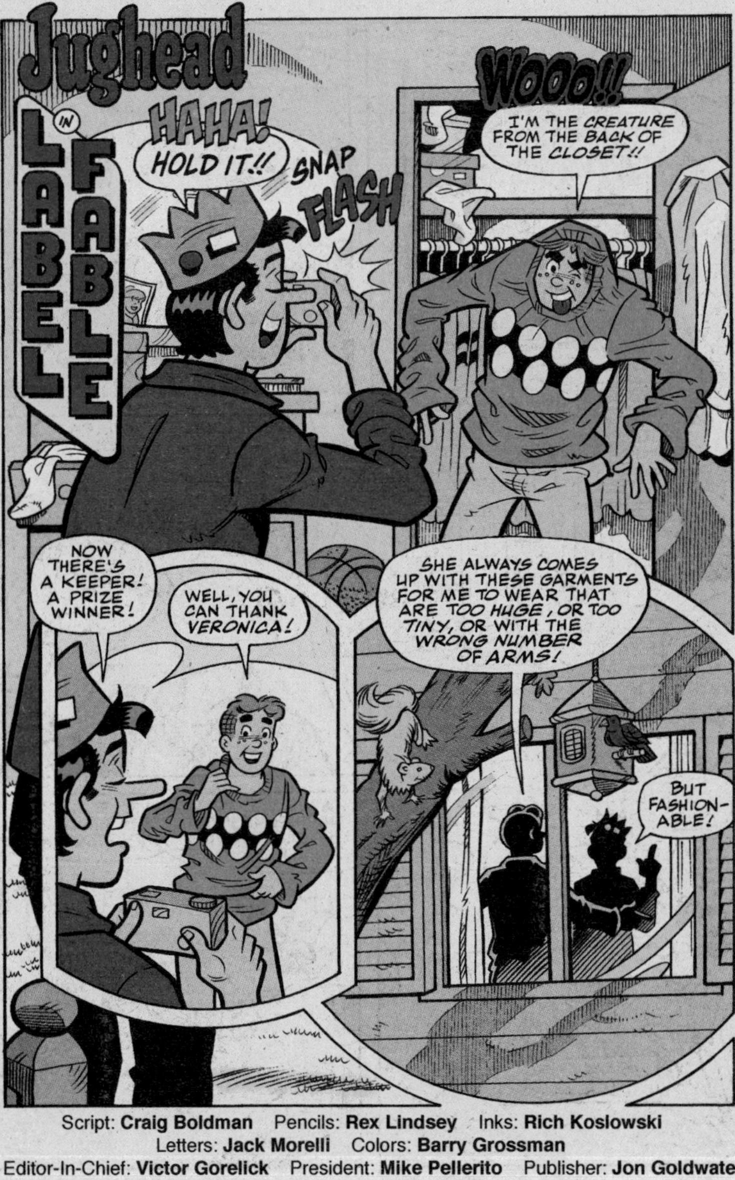
Jughead
in
LABEL FABLE
HAHA! HOLD IT!!
SNAP
FLASH
WOOO!!
I'M THE CREATURE FROM THE BACK OF THE CLOSET!!
NOW THERE'S A KEEPER! A PRIZE WINNER!
WELL, YOU CAN THANK VERONICA!
SHE ALWAYS COMES UP WITH THESE GARMENTS FOR ME TO WEAR THAT ARE TOO HUGE, OR TOO TINY, OR WITH THE WRONG NUMBER OF ARMS!
BUT FASHION-ABLE!

Script: **Craig Boldman** Pencils: **Rex Lindsey** Inks: **Rich Koslowski**
Letters: **Jack Morelli** Colors: **Barry Grossman**
Editor-In-Chief: **Victor Gorelick** President: **Mike Pellerito** Publisher: **Jon Goldwater**

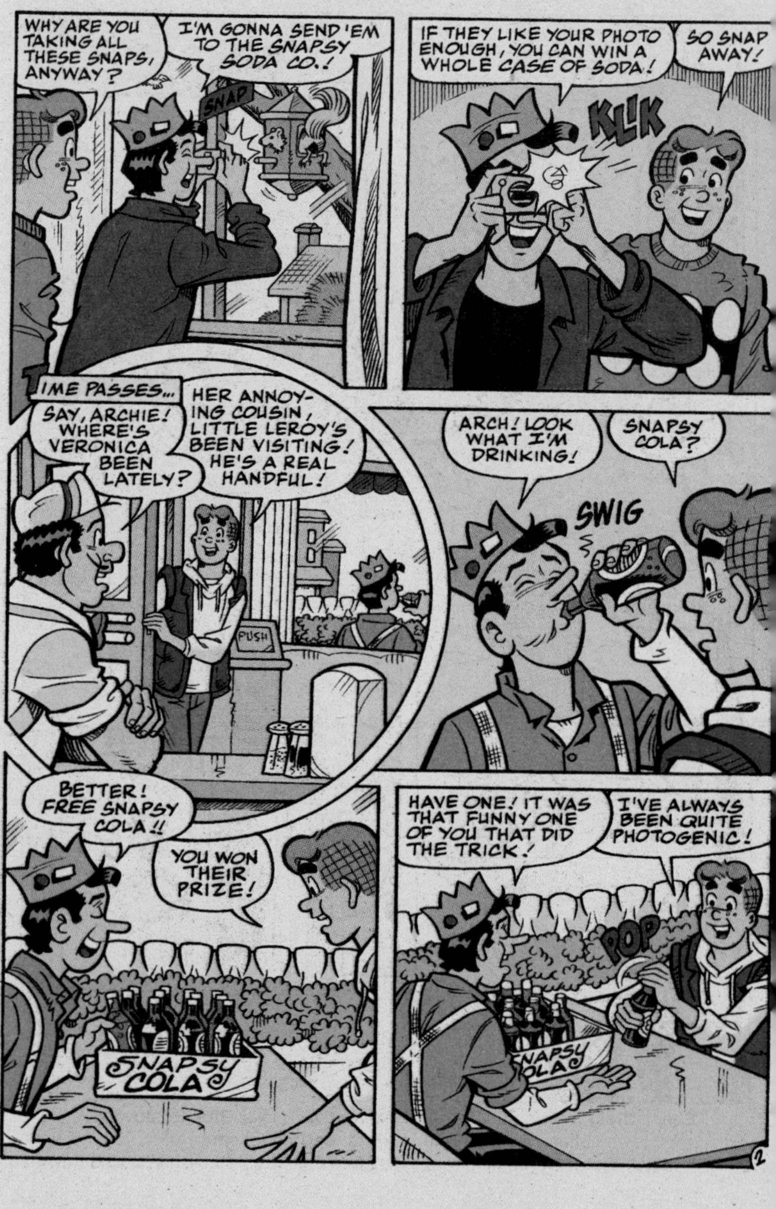
WHY ARE YOU TAKING ALL THESE SNAPS, ANYWAY?
I'M GONNA SEND 'EM TO THE SNAPSY SODA CO.!
SNAP
IF THEY LIKE YOUR PHOTO ENOUGH, YOU CAN WIN A WHOLE CASE OF SODA!
SO SNAP AWAY!
KLIK
IME PASSES...
SAY, ARCHIE! WHERE'S VERONICA BEEN LATELY?
HER ANNOYING COUSIN, LITTLE LEROY'S BEEN VISITING! HE'S A REAL HANDFUL!
PUSH
ARCH! LOOK WHAT I'M DRINKING!
SNAPSY COLA?
SWIG
BETTER! FREE SNAPSY COLA!!
YOU WON THEIR PRIZE!
SNAPSY COLA
HAVE ONE! IT WAS THAT FUNNY ONE OF YOU THAT DID THE TRICK!
I'VE ALWAYS BEEN QUITE PHOTOGENIC!
POP
SNAPSY COLA

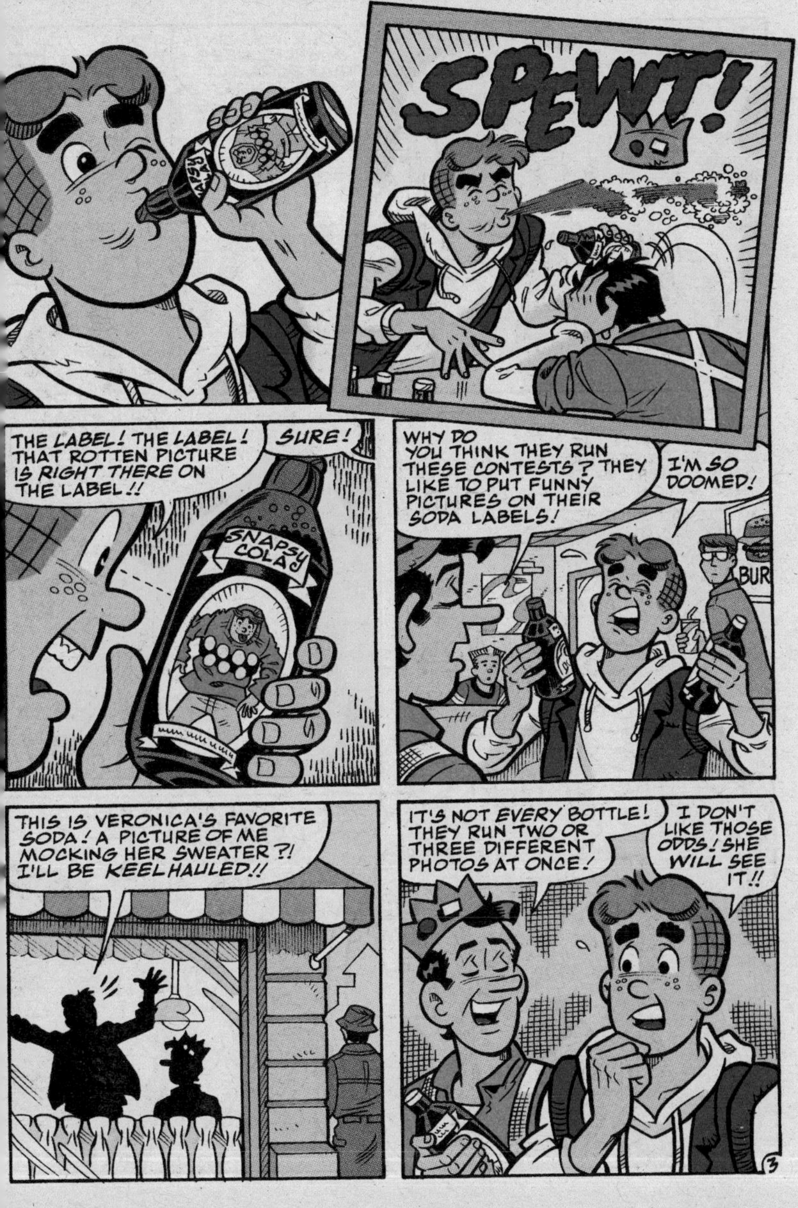

SNAPSY COLA
SPEWT!
THE LABEL! THE LABEL! THAT ROTTEN PICTURE IS RIGHT THERE ON THE LABEL!!
SURE!
SNAPSY COLA
WHY DO YOU THINK THEY RUN THESE CONTESTS? THEY LIKE TO PUT FUNNY PICTURES ON THEIR SODA LABELS!
I'M SO DOOMED!
BUR
THIS IS VERONICA'S FAVORITE SODA! A PICTURE OF ME MOCKING HER SWEATER?! I'LL BE KEELHAULED!!
IT'S NOT EVERY BOTTLE! THEY RUN TWO OR THREE DIFFERENT PHOTOS AT ONCE!
I DON'T LIKE THOSE ODDS! SHE WILL SEE IT!!

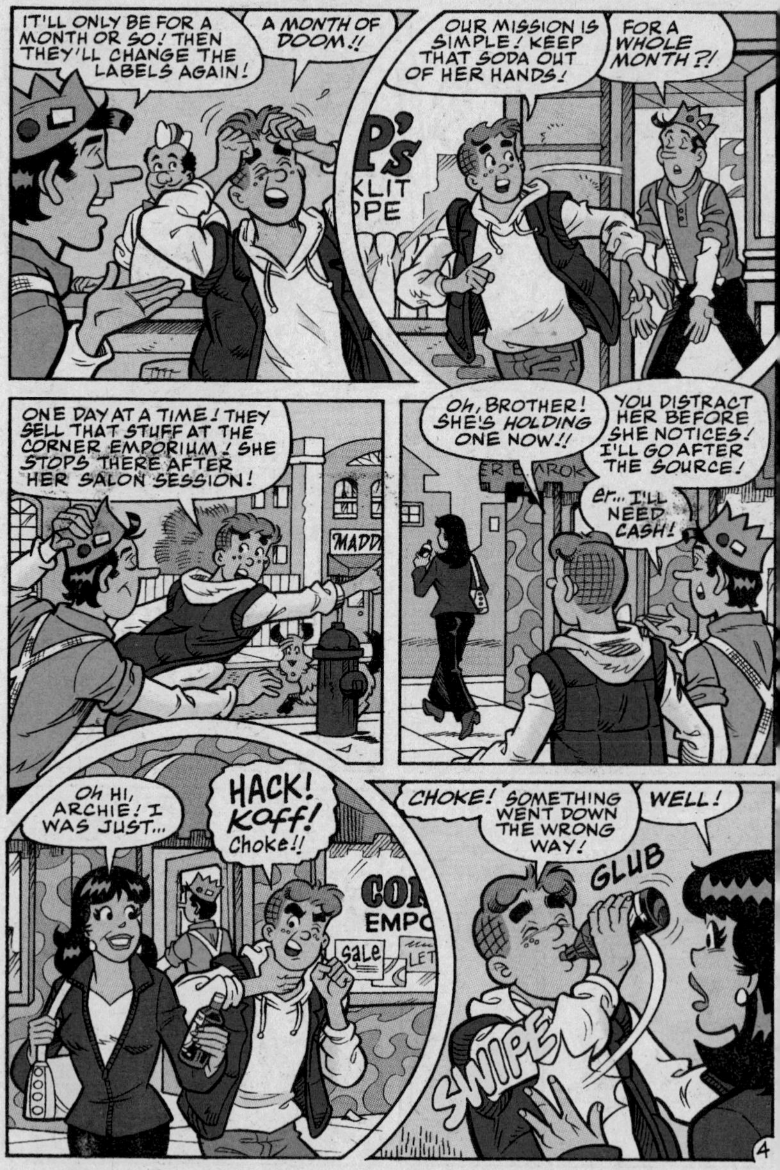
IT'LL ONLY BE FOR A MONTH OR SO! THEN THEY'LL CHANGE THE LABELS AGAIN!
A MONTH OF DOOM!!
OUR MISSION IS SIMPLE! KEEP THAT SODA OUT OF HER HANDS!
FOR A WHOLE MONTH?!
ONE DAY AT A TIME! THEY SELL THAT STUFF AT THE CORNER EMPORIUM! SHE STOPS THERE AFTER HER SALON SESSION!
Oh, BROTHER! SHE'S HOLDING ONE NOW!!
YOU DISTRACT HER BEFORE SHE NOTICES! I'LL GO AFTER THE SOURCE!
er... I'LL NEED CASH!
Oh HI, ARCHIE! I WAS JUST...
HACK! Koff! Choke!!
CHOKE! SOMETHING WENT DOWN THE WRONG WAY!
WELL!
GLUB
SWIPE
4

ER... YOU KEEP THAT ONE, ARCHIE! I'LL GET ANOTHER FOR MYSELF!

OH HI, VERONICA! DID YOU WANT ONE OF THESE? SORRY!

GUZZLE

I CAN'T BELIEVE YOU DRANK ALL THAT SODA!

URRP!!

I BELIEVE!!

MISS, I FOUND ONE MORE BOTTLE! TAKE IT BEFORE THE HUMAN SPONGE SETS HIS SIGHTS ON IT TOO!

THANKS!

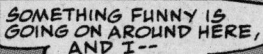

SOMETHING FUNNY IS GOING ON AROUND HERE, AND I--

eh?!

5

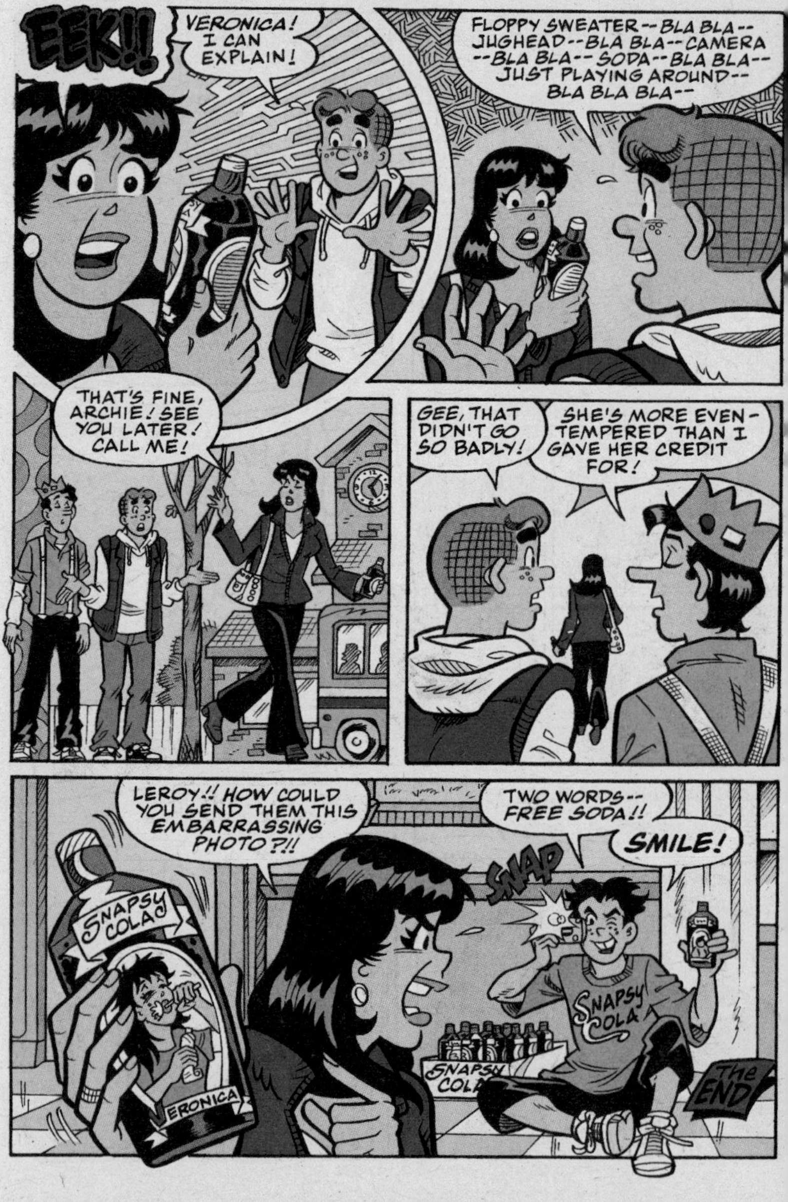
EEK!!
VERONICA! I CAN EXPLAIN!
FLOPPY SWEATER--BLA BLA--JUGHEAD--BLA BLA--CAMERA--BLA BLA--SODA--BLA BLA--JUST PLAYING AROUND--BLA BLA BLA--
THAT'S FINE, ARCHIE! SEE YOU LATER! CALL ME!
GEE, THAT DIDN'T GO SO BADLY!
SHE'S MORE EVEN-TEMPERED THAN I GAVE HER CREDIT FOR!
LEROY!! HOW COULD YOU SEND THEM THIS EMBARRASSING PHOTO?!!
SNAPSY COLA
VERONICA
SNAP
TWO WORDS--FREE SODA!!
SMILE!
SNAPSY COLA
SNAPSY COLA
The END

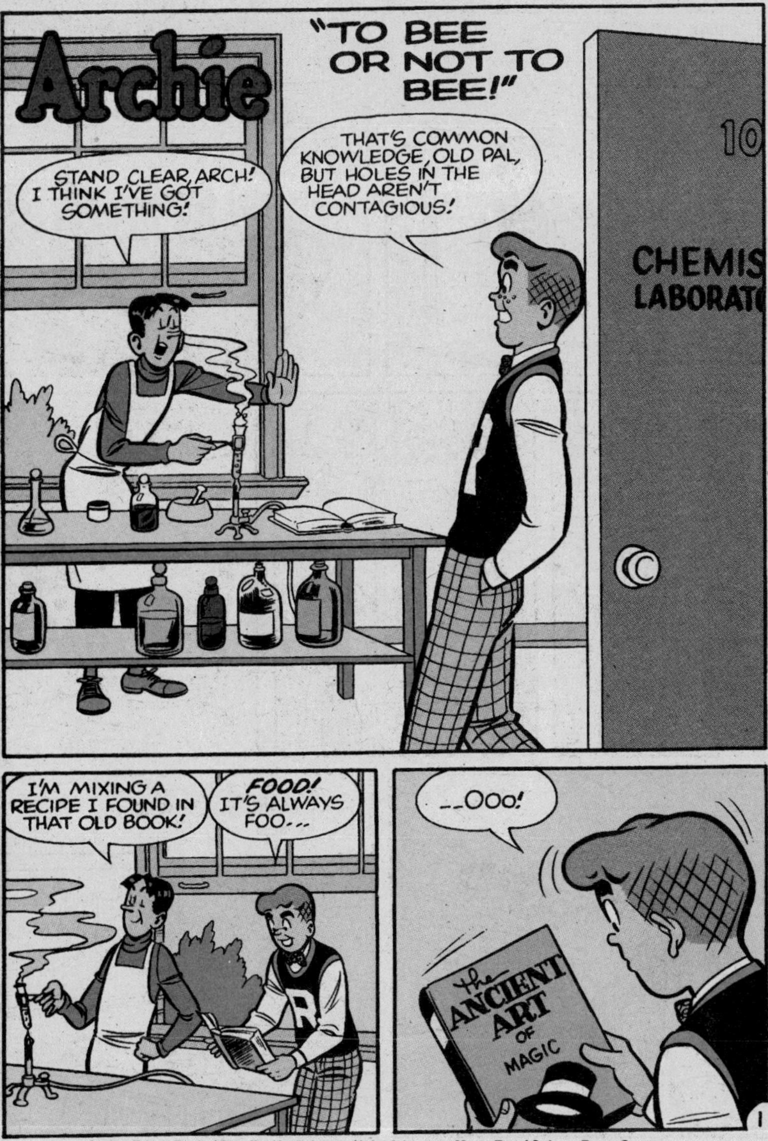
Archie
"TO BEE OR NOT TO BEE!"
STAND CLEAR, ARCH! I THINK I'VE GOT SOMETHING!
THAT'S COMMON KNOWLEDGE, OLD PAL, BUT HOLES IN THE HEAD AREN'T CONTAGIOUS!
10
CHEMIS
LABORAT
I'M MIXING A RECIPE I FOUND IN THAT OLD BOOK!
FOOD! IT'S ALWAYS FOO...
--OOO!
the ANCIENT ART OF MAGIC

Script: Frank Doyle / Pencils: Harry Lucey / Inks & Letters: Marty Epp / Colors: Barry Grossman

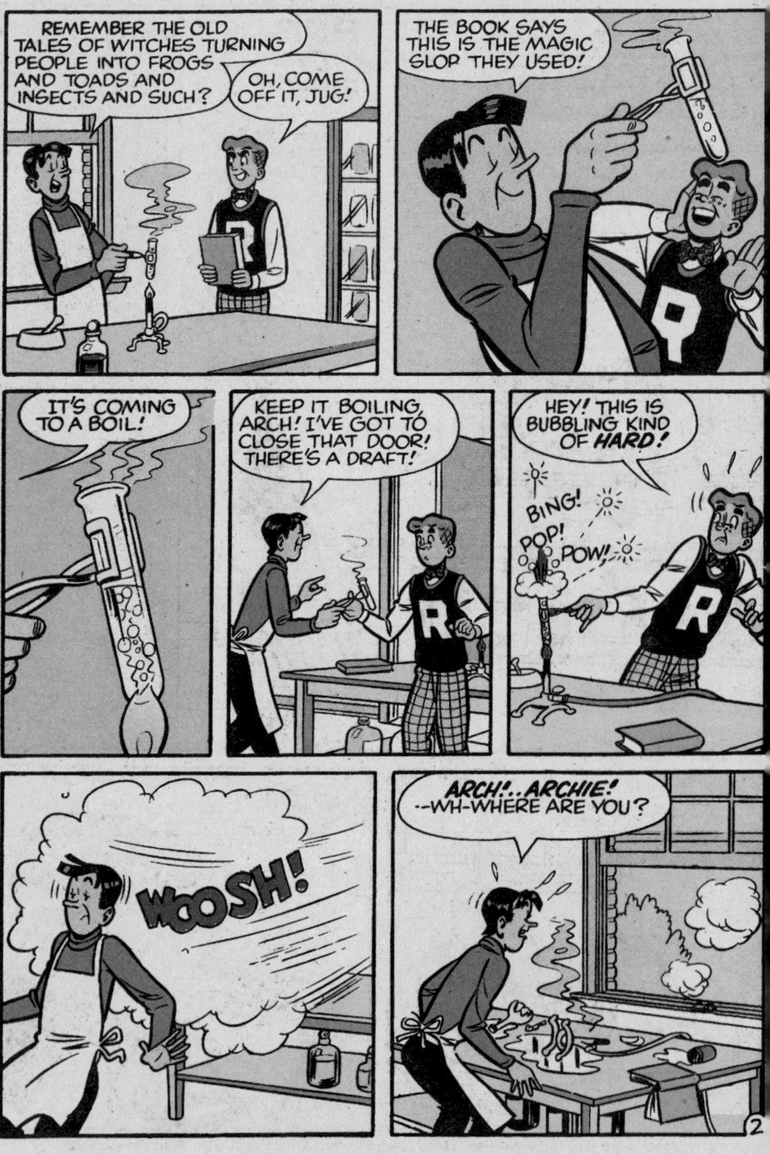
REMEMBER THE OLD TALES OF WITCHES TURNING PEOPLE INTO FROGS AND TOADS AND INSECTS AND SUCH?
OH, COME OFF IT, JUG!
THE BOOK SAYS THIS IS THE MAGIC SLOP THEY USED!
IT'S COMING TO A BOIL!
KEEP IT BOILING, ARCH! I'VE GOT TO CLOSE THAT DOOR! THERE'S A DRAFT!
HEY! THIS IS BUBBLING KIND OF HARD!
BING!
POP!
POW!
WOOSH!
ARCH!..ARCHIE! --WH-WHERE ARE YOU?
2

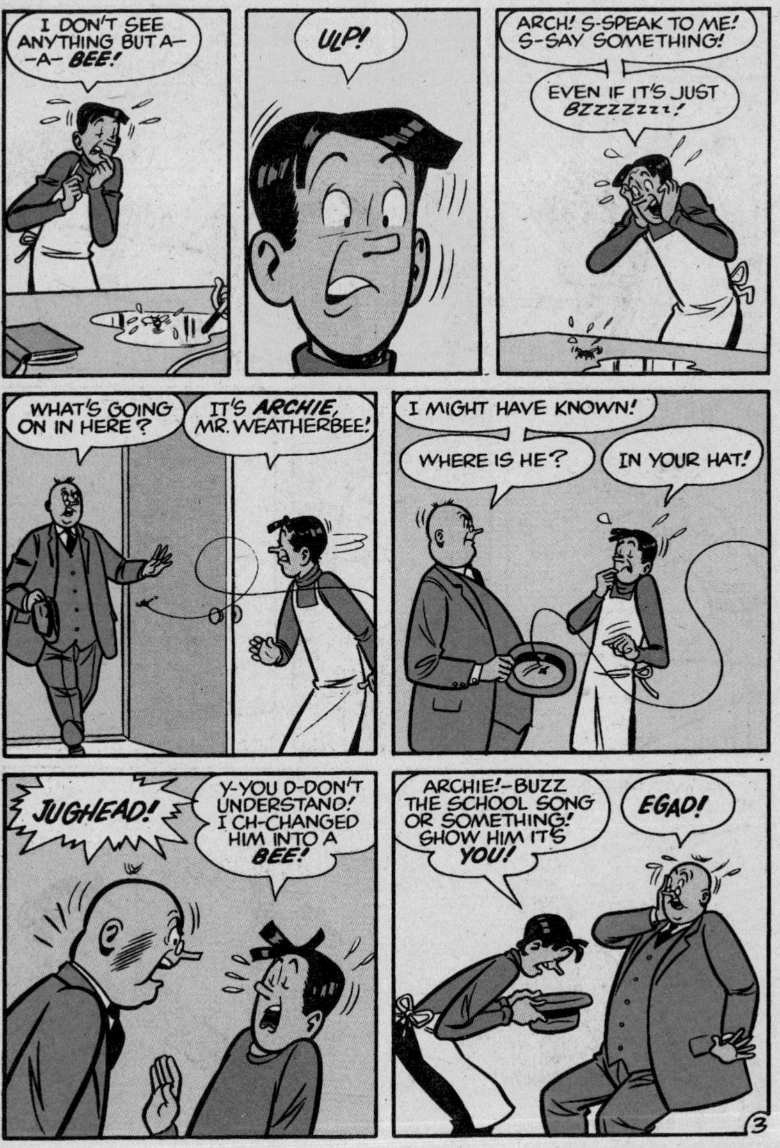

I DON'T SEE ANYTHING BUT A— —A— BEE!
ULP!
ARCH! S-SPEAK TO ME! S-SAY SOMETHING!
EVEN IF IT'S JUST BZZZZzzz!
WHAT'S GOING ON IN HERE?
IT'S ARCHIE, MR. WEATHERBEE!
I MIGHT HAVE KNOWN!
WHERE IS HE?
IN YOUR HAT!
JUGHEAD!
Y-YOU D-DON'T UNDERSTAND! I CH-CHANGED HIM INTO A BEE!
ARCHIE!—BUZZ THE SCHOOL SONG OR SOMETHING! SHOW HIM IT'S YOU!
EGAD!

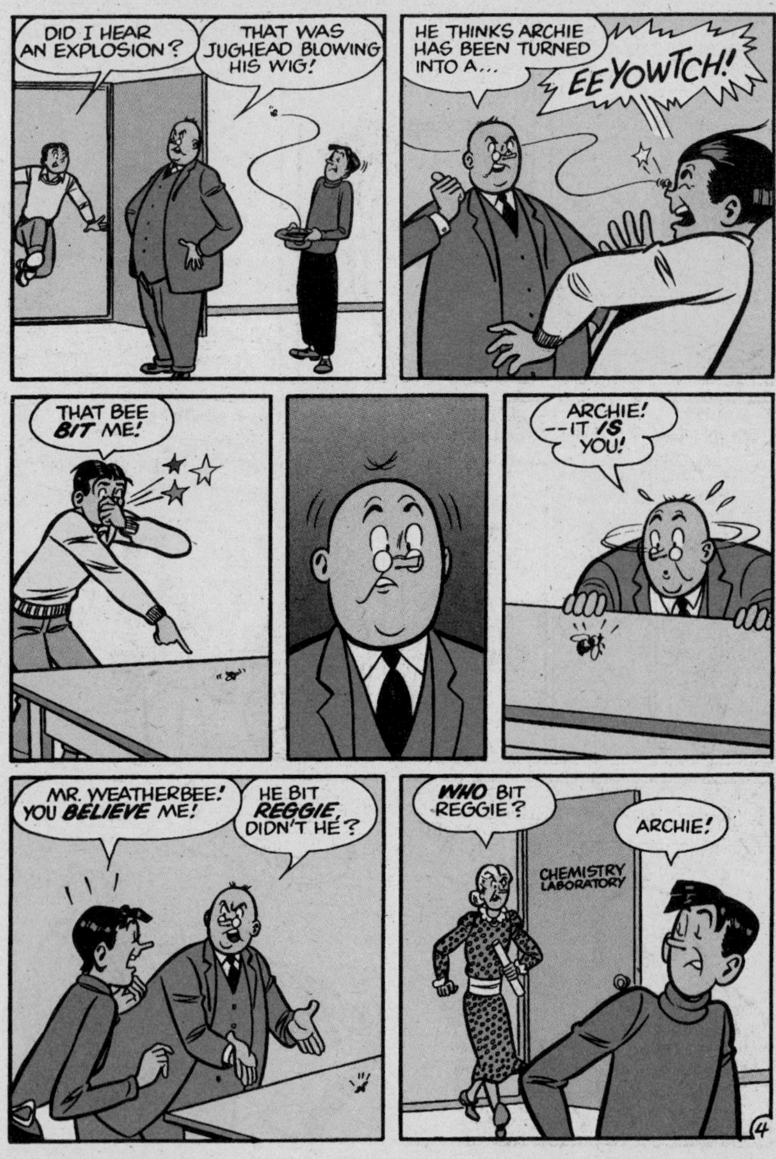
DID I HEAR AN EXPLOSION?
THAT WAS JUGHEAD BLOWING HIS WIG!
HE THINKS ARCHIE HAS BEEN TURNED INTO A...
EEYOWTCH!
THAT BEE BIT ME!
ARCHIE! --IT IS YOU!
MR. WEATHERBEE! YOU BELIEVE ME!
HE BIT REGGIE, DIDN'T HE?
WHO BIT REGGIE?
ARCHIE!
CHEMISTRY LABORATORY
4

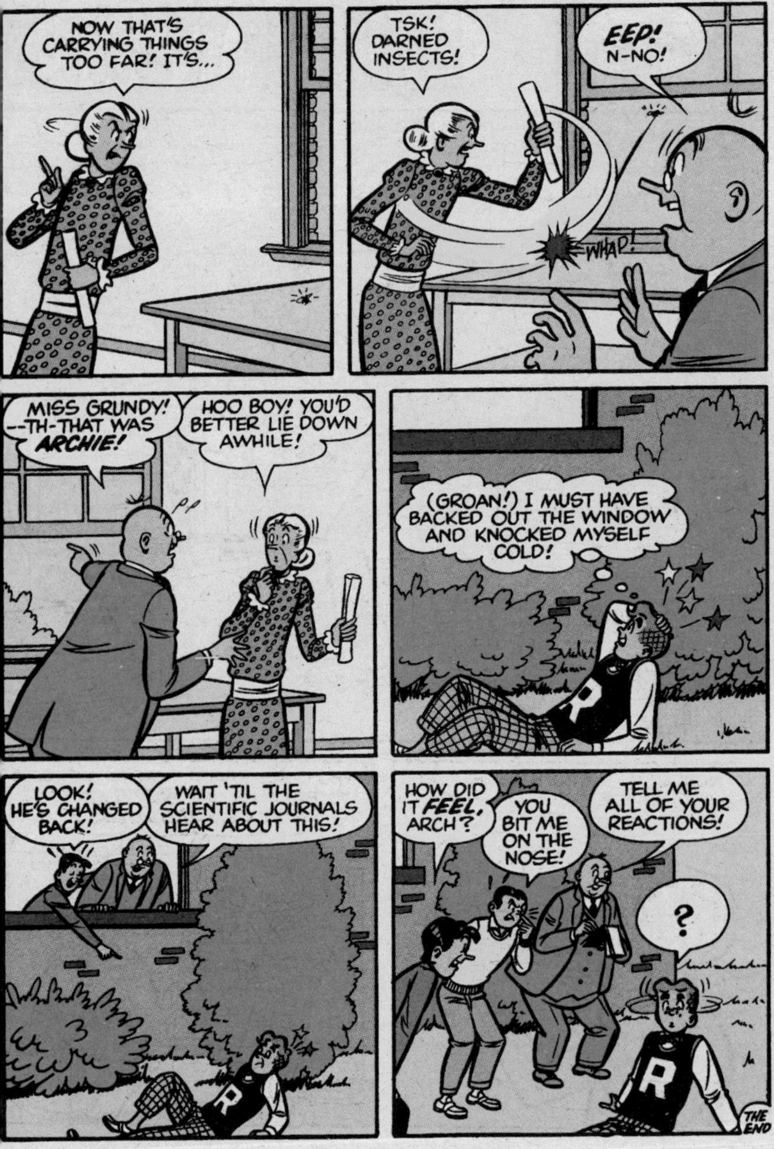
NOW THAT'S CARRYING THINGS TOO FAR! IT'S...
TSK! DARNED INSECTS!
EEP! N-NO!
WHAP!
MISS GRUNDY! --TH-THAT WAS ARCHIE!
HOO BOY! YOU'D BETTER LIE DOWN AWHILE!
(GROAN!) I MUST HAVE BACKED OUT THE WINDOW AND KNOCKED MYSELF COLD!
LOOK! HE'S CHANGED BACK!
WAIT 'TIL THE SCIENTIFIC JOURNALS HEAR ABOUT THIS!
HOW DID IT FEEL, ARCH?
YOU BIT ME ON THE NOSE!
TELL ME ALL OF YOUR REACTIONS!
?
THE END

Jughead in "NONE OF YOUR LIP"

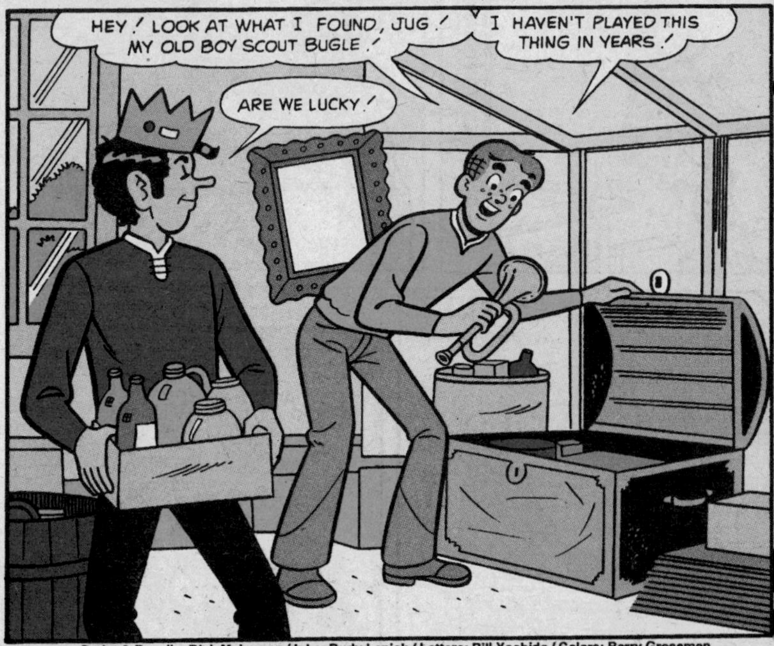
HEY! LOOK AT WHAT I FOUND, JUG! MY OLD BOY SCOUT BUGLE!
I HAVEN'T PLAYED THIS THING IN YEARS!
ARE WE LUCKY!

Script & Pencils: Dick Malmgren / Inks: Rudy Lapick / Letters: Bill Yoshida / Colors: Barry Grossman

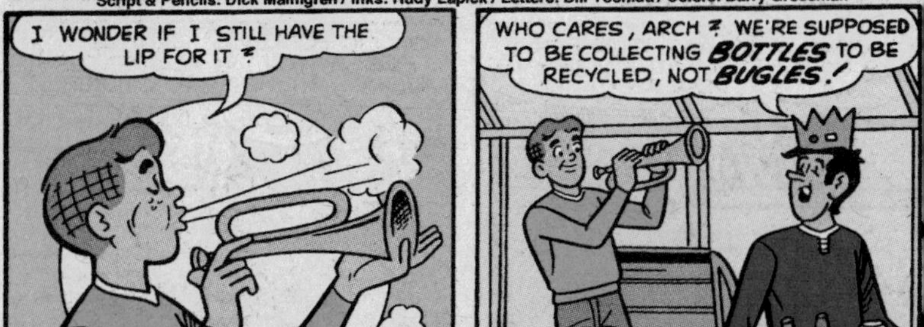
I WONDER IF I STILL HAVE THE LIP FOR IT?
WHO CARES, ARCH? WE'RE SUPPOSED TO BE COLLECTING BOTTLES TO BE RECYCLED, NOT BUGLES!

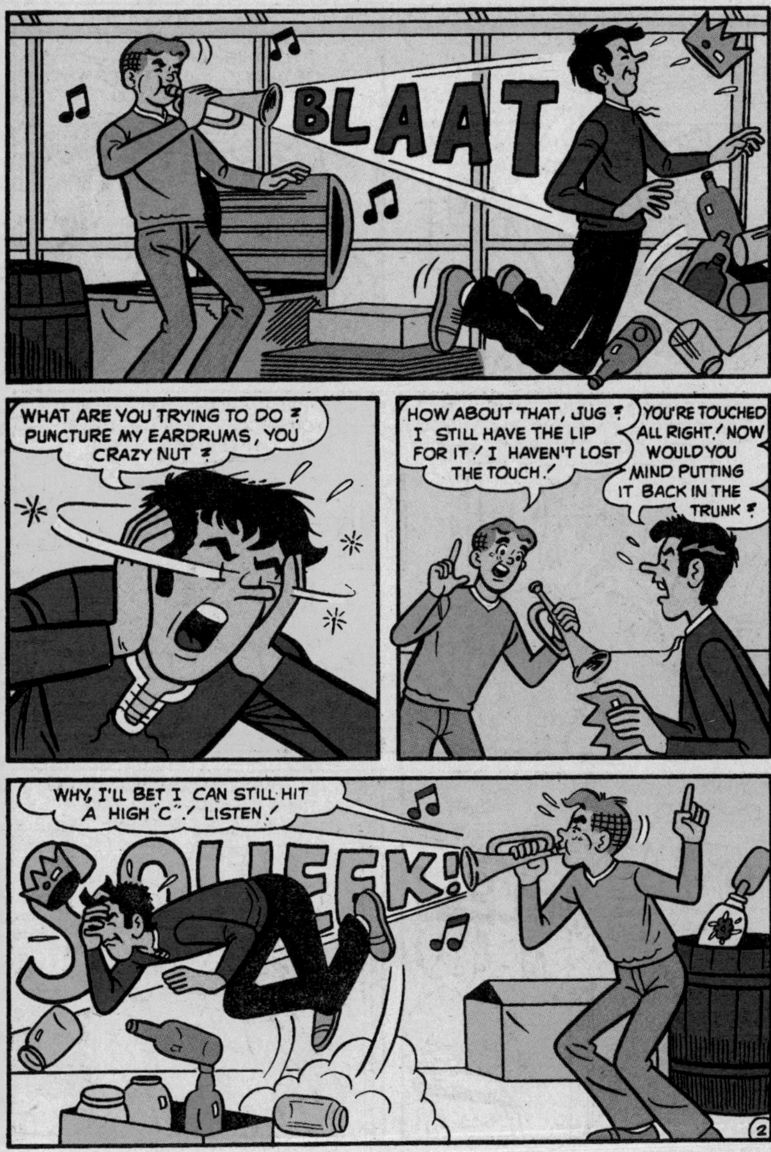
BLAAT
WHAT ARE YOU TRYING TO DO? PUNCTURE MY EARDRUMS, YOU CRAZY NUT?
HOW ABOUT THAT, JUG? I STILL HAVE THE LIP FOR IT! I HAVEN'T LOST THE TOUCH!
YOU'RE TOUCHED ALL RIGHT! NOW WOULD YOU MIND PUTTING IT BACK IN THE TRUNK?
WHY, I'LL BET I CAN STILL HIT A HIGH "C"! LISTEN!
SQUEEK!

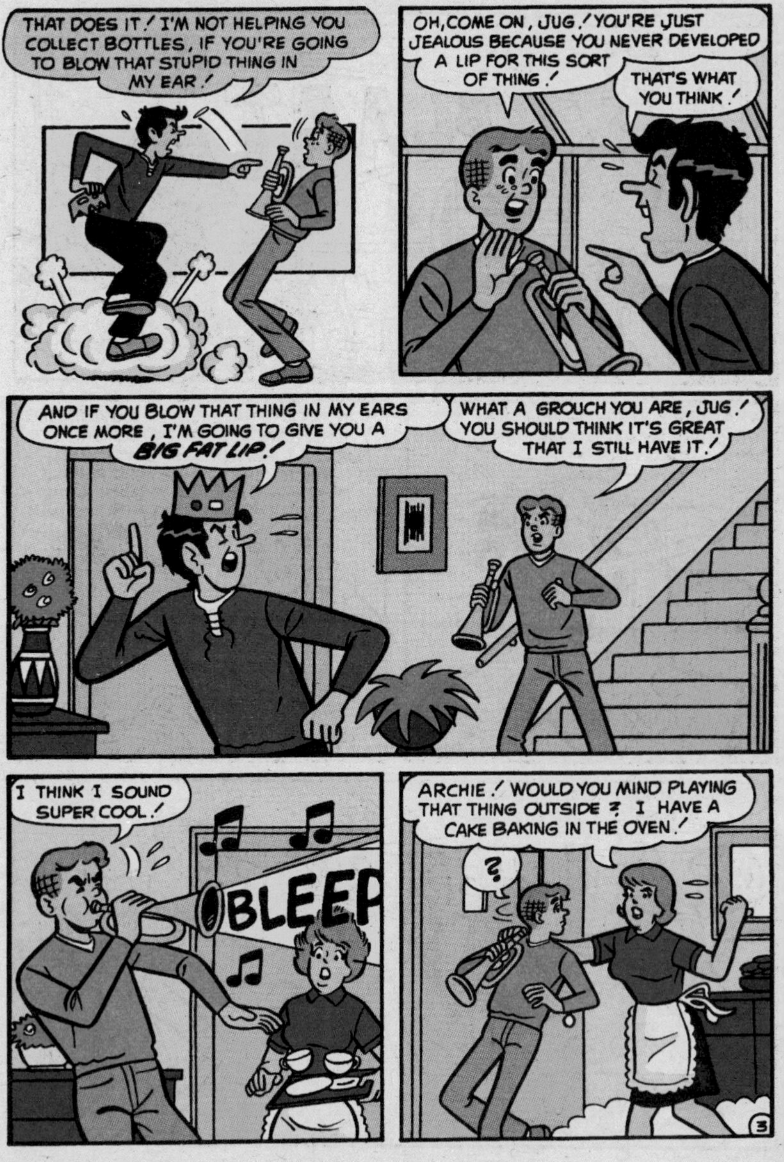
THAT DOES IT! I'M NOT HELPING YOU COLLECT BOTTLES, IF YOU'RE GOING TO BLOW THAT STUPID THING IN MY EAR!
OH, COME ON, JUG! YOU'RE JUST JEALOUS BECAUSE YOU NEVER DEVELOPED A LIP FOR THIS SORT OF THING!
THAT'S WHAT YOU THINK!
AND IF YOU BLOW THAT THING IN MY EARS ONCE MORE, I'M GOING TO GIVE YOU A BIG FAT LIP!
WHAT A GROUCH YOU ARE, JUG! YOU SHOULD THINK IT'S GREAT THAT I STILL HAVE IT!
I THINK I SOUND SUPER COOL!
BLEEP
ARCHIE! WOULD YOU MIND PLAYING THAT THING OUTSIDE? I HAVE A CAKE BAKING IN THE OVEN!
?
3

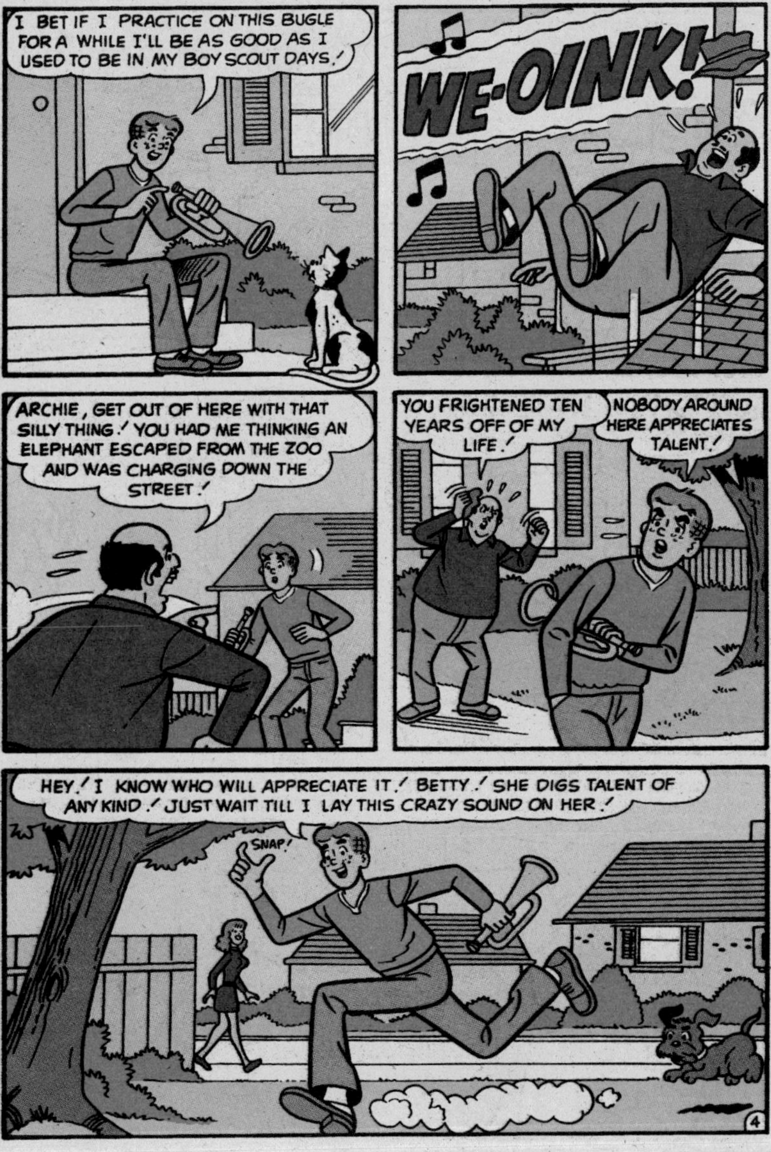

I BET IF I PRACTICE ON THIS BUGLE FOR A WHILE I'LL BE AS GOOD AS I USED TO BE IN MY BOY SCOUT DAYS!
WE-OINK!
ARCHIE, GET OUT OF HERE WITH THAT SILLY THING! YOU HAD ME THINKING AN ELEPHANT ESCAPED FROM THE ZOO AND WAS CHARGING DOWN THE STREET!
YOU FRIGHTENED TEN YEARS OFF OF MY LIFE!
NOBODY AROUND HERE APPRECIATES TALENT!
HEY! I KNOW WHO WILL APPRECIATE IT! BETTY! SHE DIGS TALENT OF ANY KIND! JUST WAIT TILL I LAY THIS CRAZY SOUND ON HER!
SNAP!
4

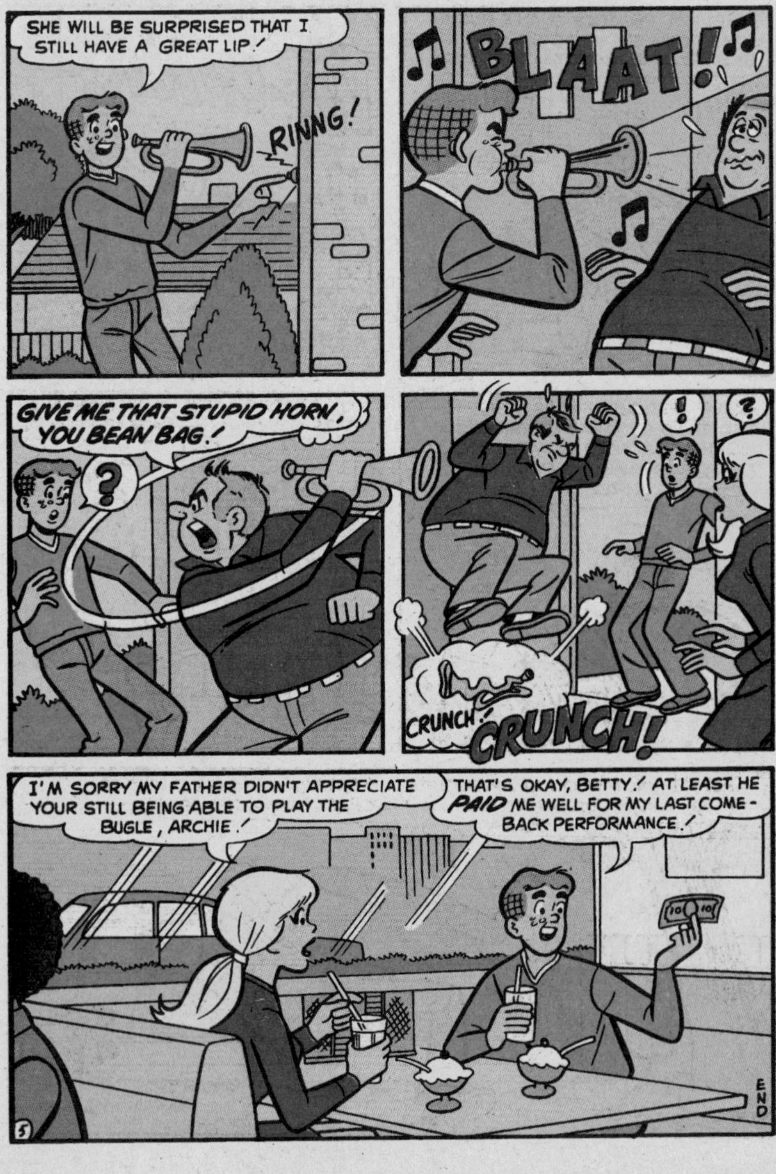
SHE WILL BE SURPRISED THAT I STILL HAVE A GREAT LIP!
RINNG!
BLAAT!
GIVE ME THAT STUPID HORN, YOU BEAN BAG!
?
!
?
CRUNCH!
CRUNCH!
I'M SORRY MY FATHER DIDN'T APPRECIATE YOUR STILL BEING ABLE TO PLAY THE BUGLE, ARCHIE!
THAT'S OKAY, BETTY! AT LEAST HE PAID ME WELL FOR MY LAST COME-BACK PERFORMANCE!
END
5

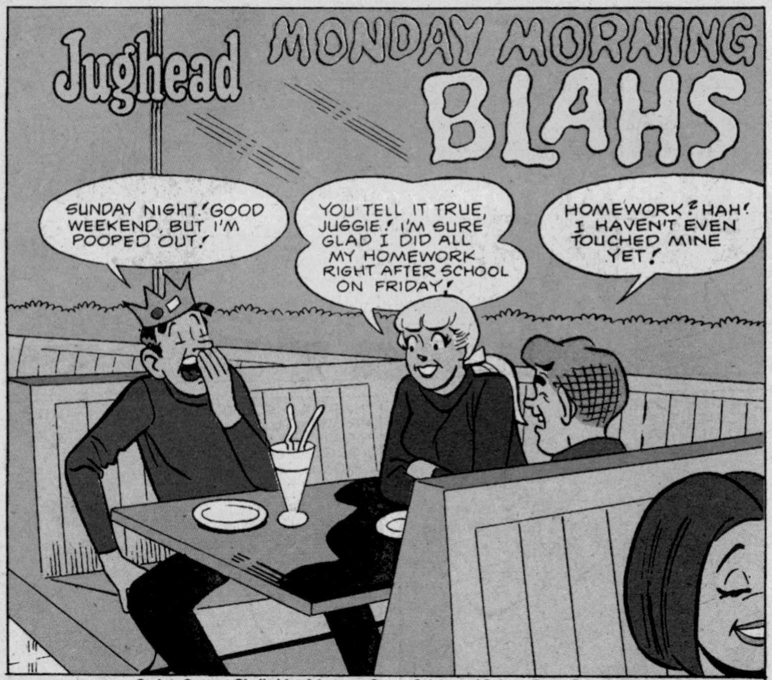
Jughead
MONDAY MORNING BLAHS
SUNDAY NIGHT! GOOD WEEKEND, BUT I'M POOPED OUT!
YOU TELL IT TRUE, JUGGIE! I'M SURE GLAD I DID ALL MY HOMEWORK RIGHT AFTER SCHOOL ON FRIDAY!
HOMEWORK? HAH! I HAVEN'T EVEN TOUCHED MINE YET!

Script: George Gladir / Art & Letters: Samm Schwartz / Colors: Barry Grossman

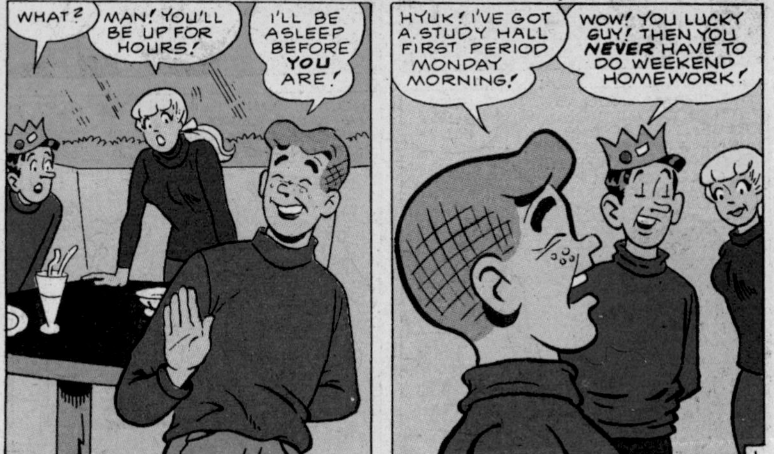
WHAT?
MAN! YOU'LL BE UP FOR HOURS!
I'LL BE ASLEEP BEFORE **YOU** ARE!
HYUK! I'VE GOT A STUDY HALL FIRST PERIOD MONDAY MORNING!
WOW! YOU LUCKY GUY! THEN YOU **NEVER** HAVE TO DO WEEKEND HOMEWORK!

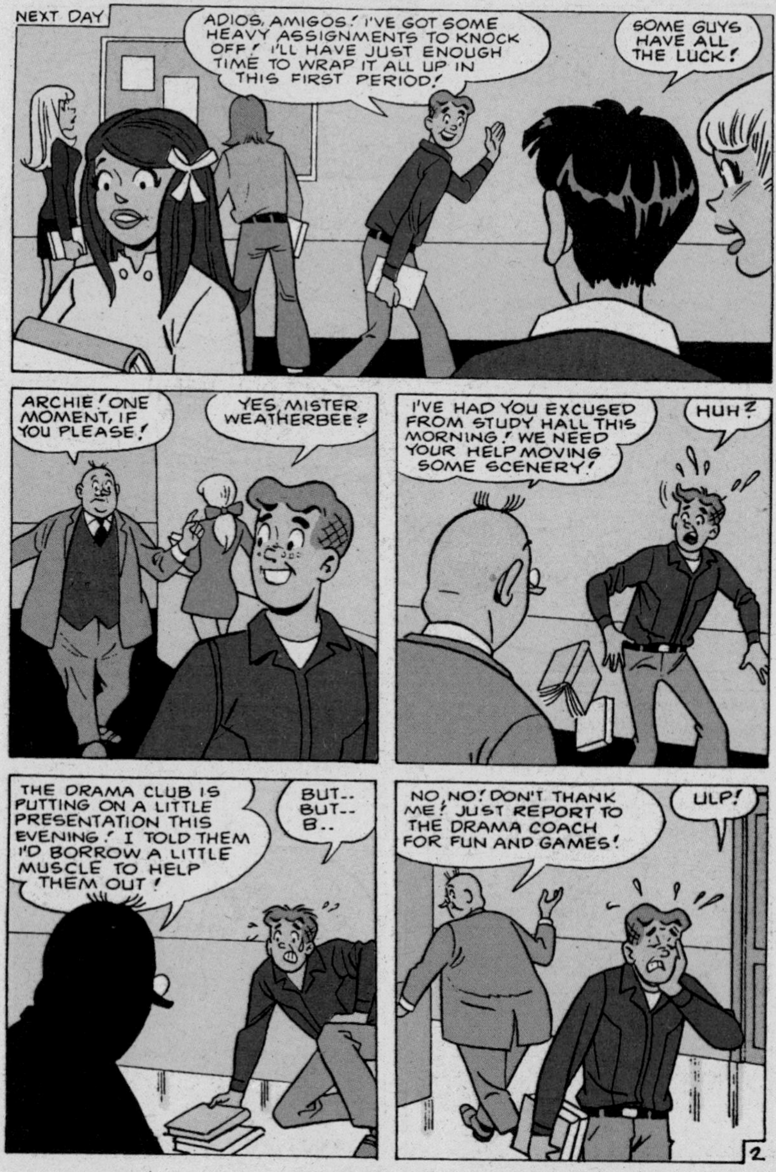
NEXT DAY
ADIOS, AMIGOS! I'VE GOT SOME HEAVY ASSIGNMENTS TO KNOCK OFF! I'LL HAVE JUST ENOUGH TIME TO WRAP IT ALL UP IN THIS FIRST PERIOD!
SOME GUYS HAVE ALL THE LUCK!
ARCHIE! ONE MOMENT, IF YOU PLEASE!
YES, MISTER WEATHERBEE?
I'VE HAD YOU EXCUSED FROM STUDY HALL THIS MORNING! WE NEED YOUR HELP MOVING SOME SCENERY!
HUH?
THE DRAMA CLUB IS PUTTING ON A LITTLE PRESENTATION THIS EVENING! I TOLD THEM I'D BORROW A LITTLE MUSCLE TO HELP THEM OUT!
BUT-- BUT-- B..
NO, NO! DON'T THANK ME! JUST REPORT TO THE DRAMA COACH FOR FUN AND GAMES!
ULP!
2

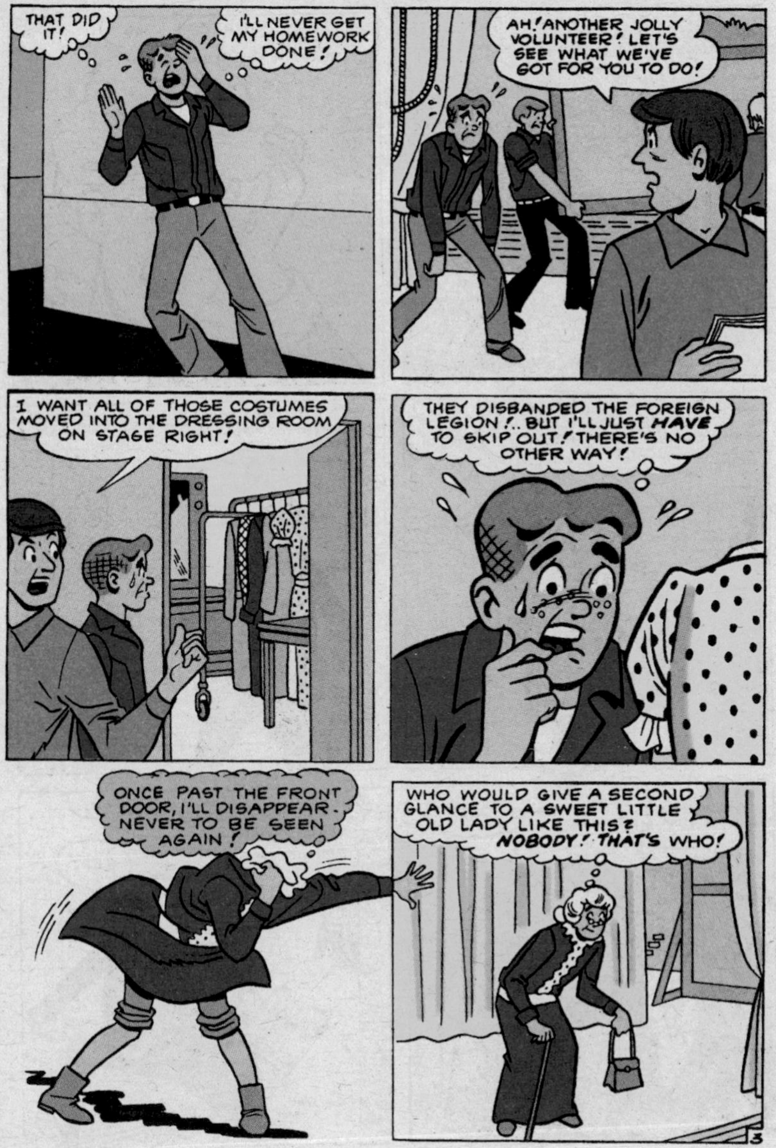
THAT DID IT!
I'LL NEVER GET MY HOMEWORK DONE!
AH! ANOTHER JOLLY VOLUNTEER! LET'S SEE WHAT WE'VE GOT FOR YOU TO DO!
I WANT ALL OF THOSE COSTUMES MOVED INTO THE DRESSING ROOM ON STAGE RIGHT!
THEY DISBANDED THE FOREIGN LEGION!.. BUT I'LL JUST HAVE TO SKIP OUT! THERE'S NO OTHER WAY!
ONCE PAST THE FRONT DOOR, I'LL DISAPPEAR. NEVER TO BE SEEN AGAIN!
WHO WOULD GIVE A SECOND GLANCE TO A SWEET LITTLE OLD LADY LIKE THIS? NOBODY! THAT'S WHO!
3

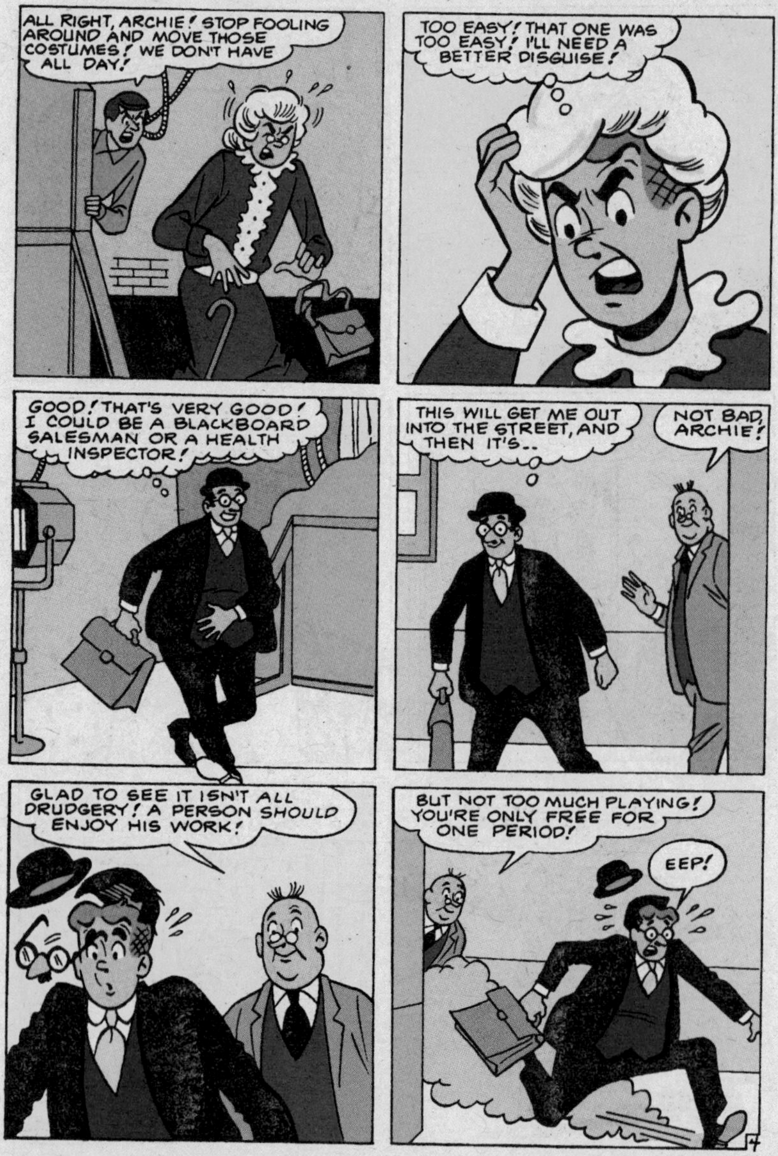
ALL RIGHT, ARCHIE! STOP FOOLING AROUND AND MOVE THOSE COSTUMES! WE DON'T HAVE ALL DAY!
TOO EASY! THAT ONE WAS TOO EASY! I'LL NEED A BETTER DISGUISE!
GOOD! THAT'S VERY GOOD! I COULD BE A BLACKBOARD SALESMAN OR A HEALTH INSPECTOR!
THIS WILL GET ME OUT INTO THE STREET, AND THEN IT'S..
NOT BAD, ARCHIE!
GLAD TO SEE IT ISN'T ALL DRUDGERY! A PERSON SHOULD ENJOY HIS WORK!
BUT NOT TOO MUCH PLAYING! YOU'RE ONLY FREE FOR ONE PERIOD!
EEP!
4

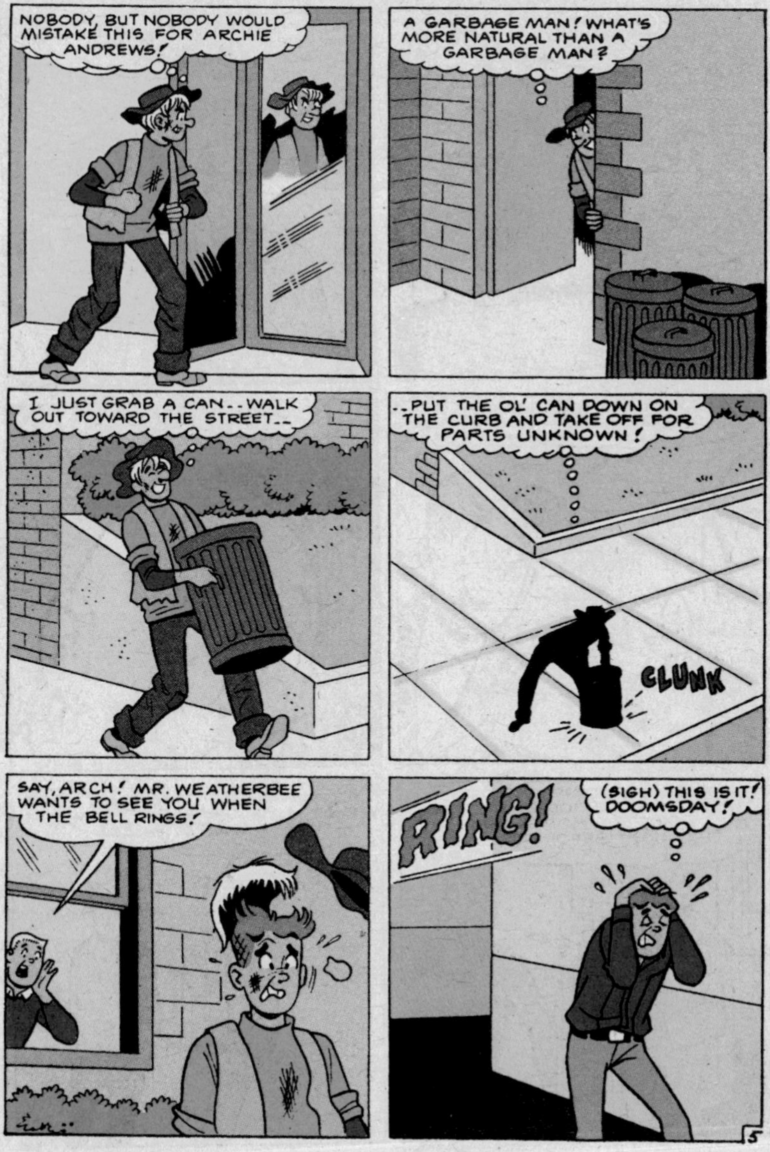
NOBODY, BUT NOBODY WOULD MISTAKE THIS FOR ARCHIE ANDREWS!
A GARBAGE MAN! WHAT'S MORE NATURAL THAN A GARBAGE MAN?
I JUST GRAB A CAN.. WALK OUT TOWARD THE STREET..
..PUT THE OL' CAN DOWN ON THE CURB AND TAKE OFF FOR PARTS UNKNOWN!
CLUNK
SAY, ARCH! MR. WEATHERBEE WANTS TO SEE YOU WHEN THE BELL RINGS!
RING!
(SIGH) THIS IS IT! DOOMSDAY!
5

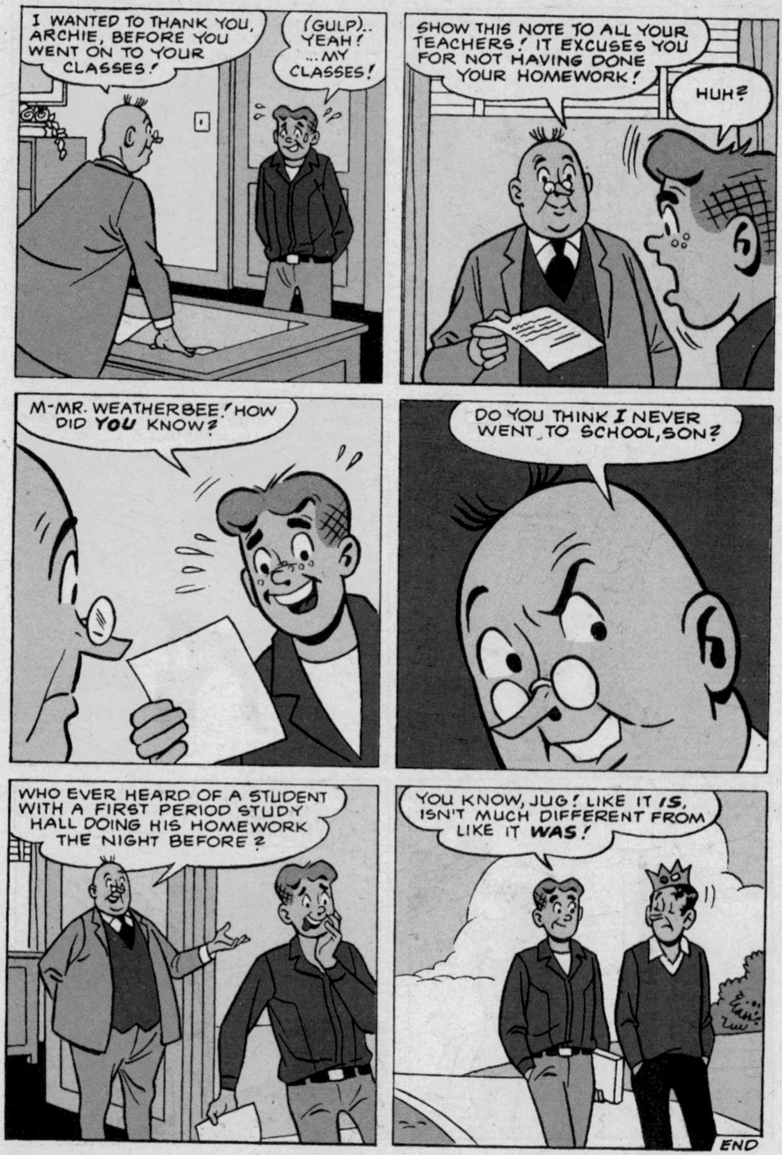
I WANTED TO THANK YOU, ARCHIE, BEFORE YOU WENT ON TO YOUR CLASSES!
(GULP).. YEAH! ...MY CLASSES!
SHOW THIS NOTE TO ALL YOUR TEACHERS! IT EXCUSES YOU FOR NOT HAVING DONE YOUR HOMEWORK!
HUH?
M-MR. WEATHERBEE! HOW DID YOU KNOW?
DO YOU THINK I NEVER WENT TO SCHOOL, SON?
WHO EVER HEARD OF A STUDENT WITH A FIRST PERIOD STUDY HALL DOING HIS HOMEWORK THE NIGHT BEFORE?
YOU KNOW, JUG! LIKE IT IS, ISN'T MUCH DIFFERENT FROM LIKE IT WAS!
END

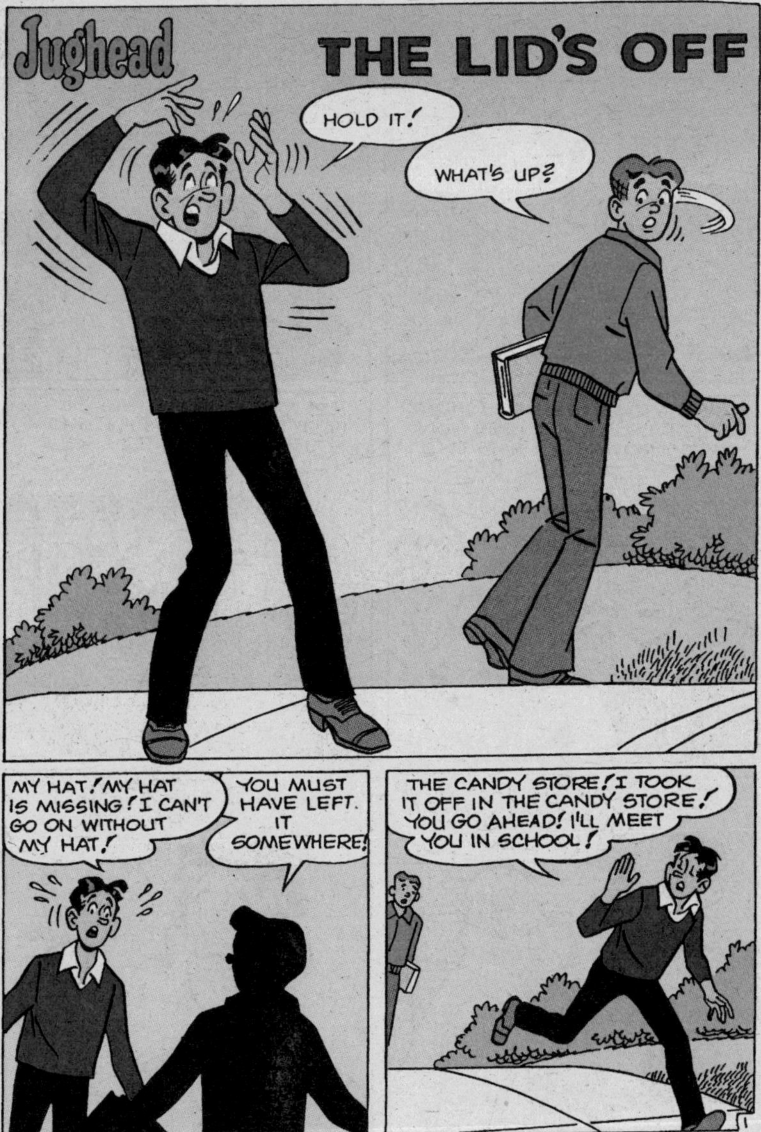
Jughead
THE LID'S OFF
HOLD IT!
WHAT'S UP?
MY HAT! MY HAT IS MISSING! I CAN'T GO ON WITHOUT MY HAT!
YOU MUST HAVE LEFT. IT SOMEWHERE!
THE CANDY STORE! I TOOK IT OFF IN THE CANDY STORE! YOU GO AHEAD! I'LL MEET YOU IN SCHOOL!

Script: Frank Doyle / Art & Letters: Samm Schwartz / Colors: Barry Grossman

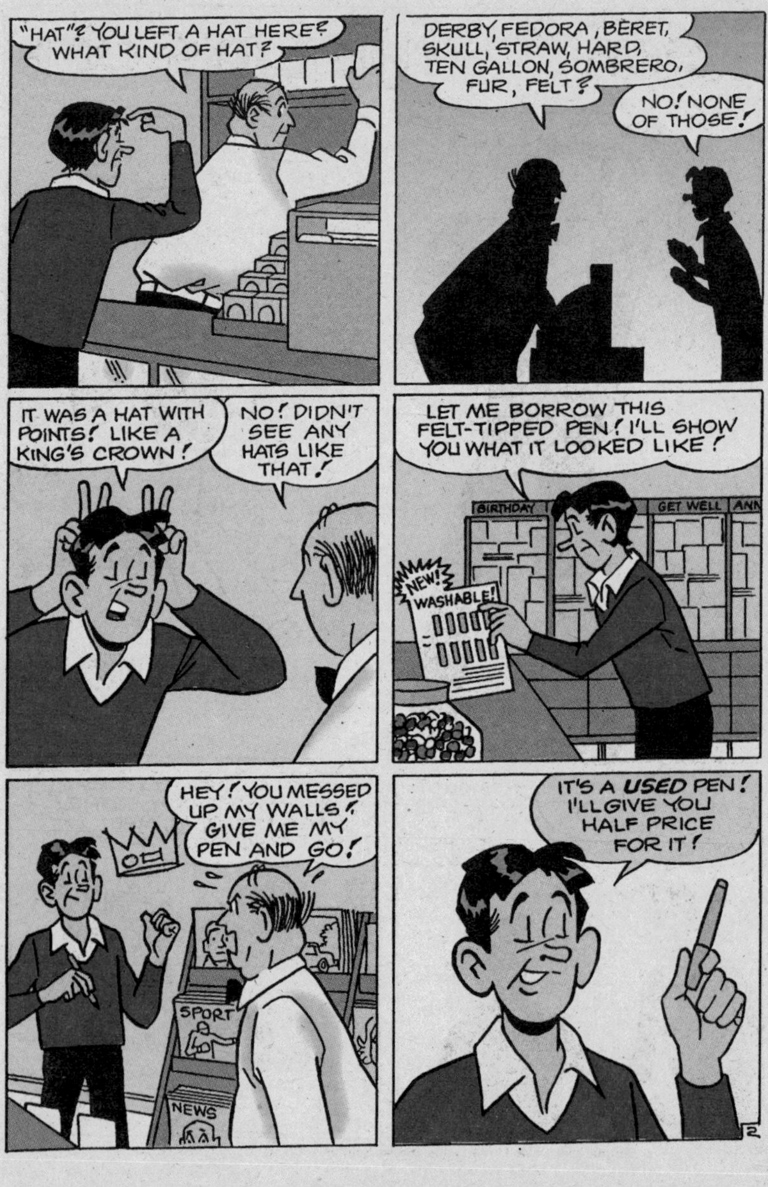
"HAT"? YOU LEFT A HAT HERE? WHAT KIND OF HAT?
DERBY, FEDORA, BERET, SKULL, STRAW, HARD, TEN GALLON, SOMBRERO, FUR, FELT?
NO! NONE OF THOSE!
IT WAS A HAT WITH POINTS! LIKE A KING'S CROWN!
NO! DIDN'T SEE ANY HATS LIKE THAT!
LET ME BORROW THIS FELT-TIPPED PEN! I'LL SHOW YOU WHAT IT LOOKED LIKE!
BIRTHDAY
GET WELL
NEW!
WASHABLE!
HEY! YOU MESSED UP MY WALLS! GIVE ME MY PEN AND GO!
SPORT
NEWS
IT'S A **USED** PEN! I'LL GIVE YOU HALF PRICE FOR IT!
2

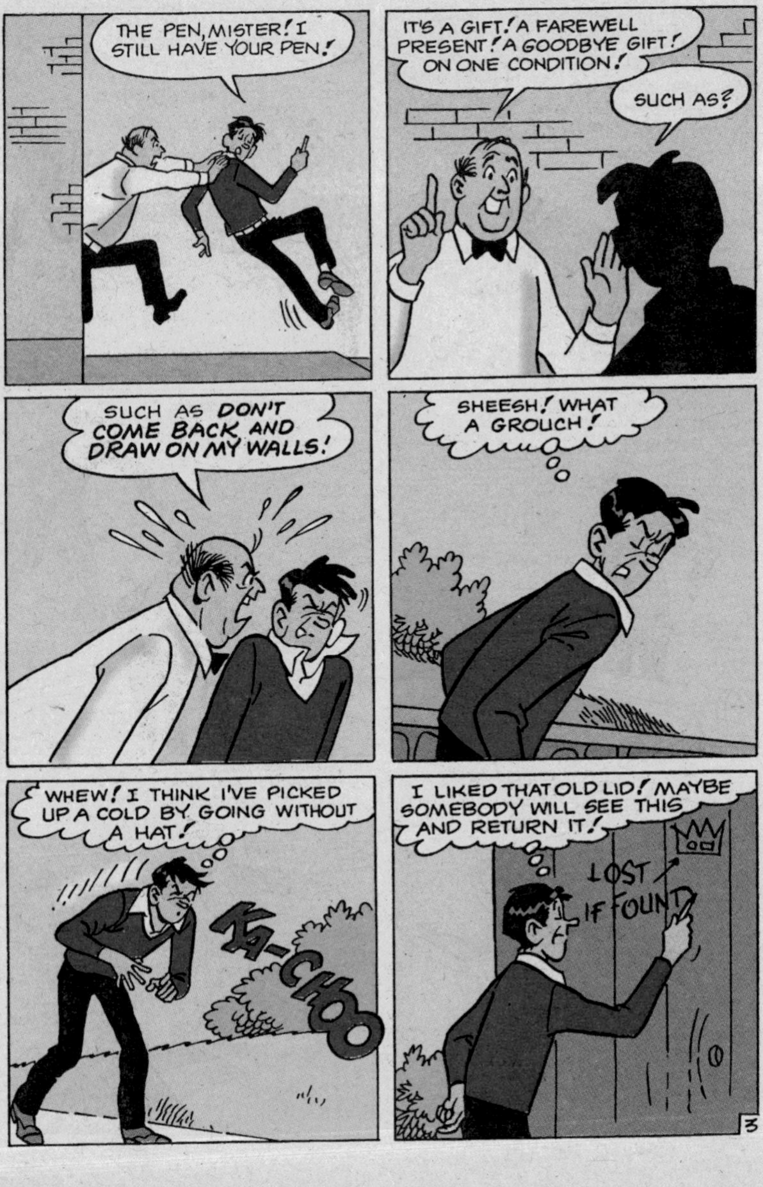
THE PEN, MISTER! I STILL HAVE YOUR PEN!
IT'S A GIFT! A FAREWELL PRESENT! A GOODBYE GIFT! ON ONE CONDITION!
SUCH AS?
SUCH AS DON'T COME BACK AND DRAW ON MY WALLS!
SHEESH! WHAT A GROUCH!
WHEW! I THINK I'VE PICKED UP A COLD BY GOING WITHOUT A HAT!
KA-CHOO
I LIKED THAT OLD LID! MAYBE SOMEBODY WILL SEE THIS AND RETURN IT!
LOST
IF FOUND
3

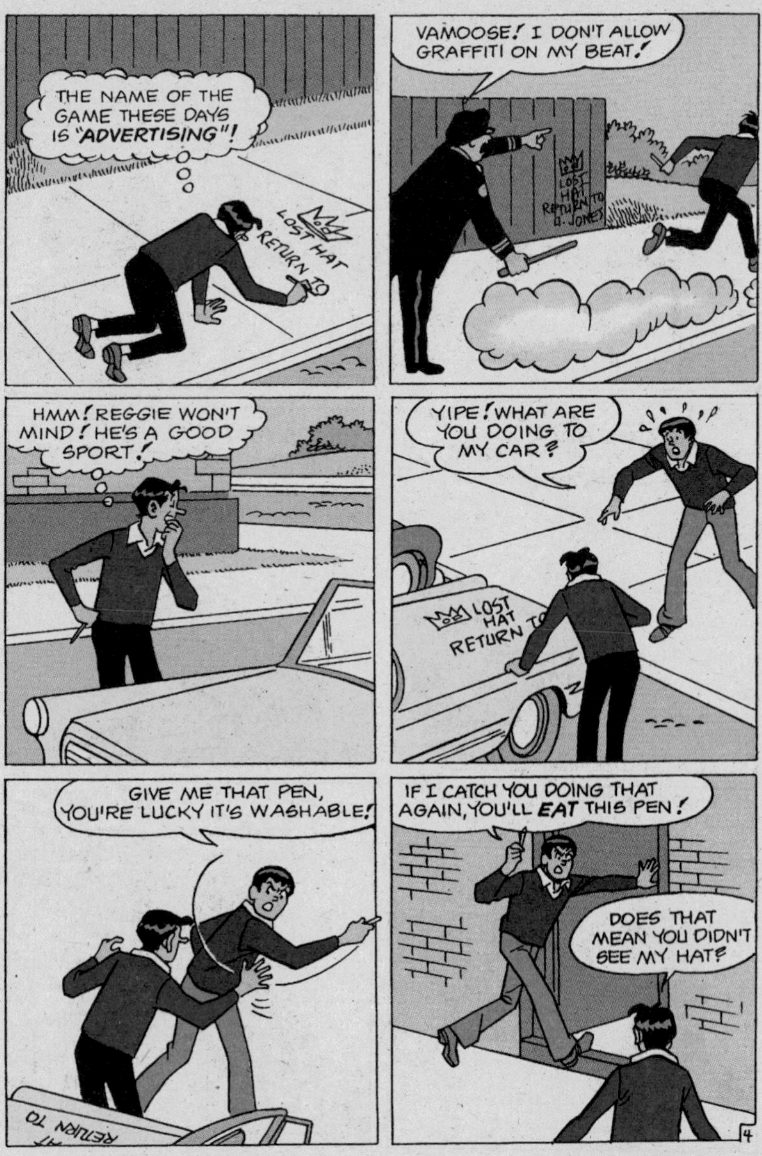
THE NAME OF THE GAME THESE DAYS IS "ADVERTISING"!
LOST HAT RETURN TO
VAMOOSE! I DON'T ALLOW GRAFFITI ON MY BEAT!
LOST HAT RETURN TO J. JONES
HMM! REGGIE WON'T MIND! HE'S A GOOD SPORT!
YIPE! WHAT ARE YOU DOING TO MY CAR?
LOST HAT RETURN TO
GIVE ME THAT PEN, YOU'RE LUCKY IT'S WASHABLE!
RETURN TO
IF I CATCH YOU DOING THAT AGAIN, YOU'LL EAT THIS PEN!
DOES THAT MEAN YOU DIDN'T SEE MY HAT?

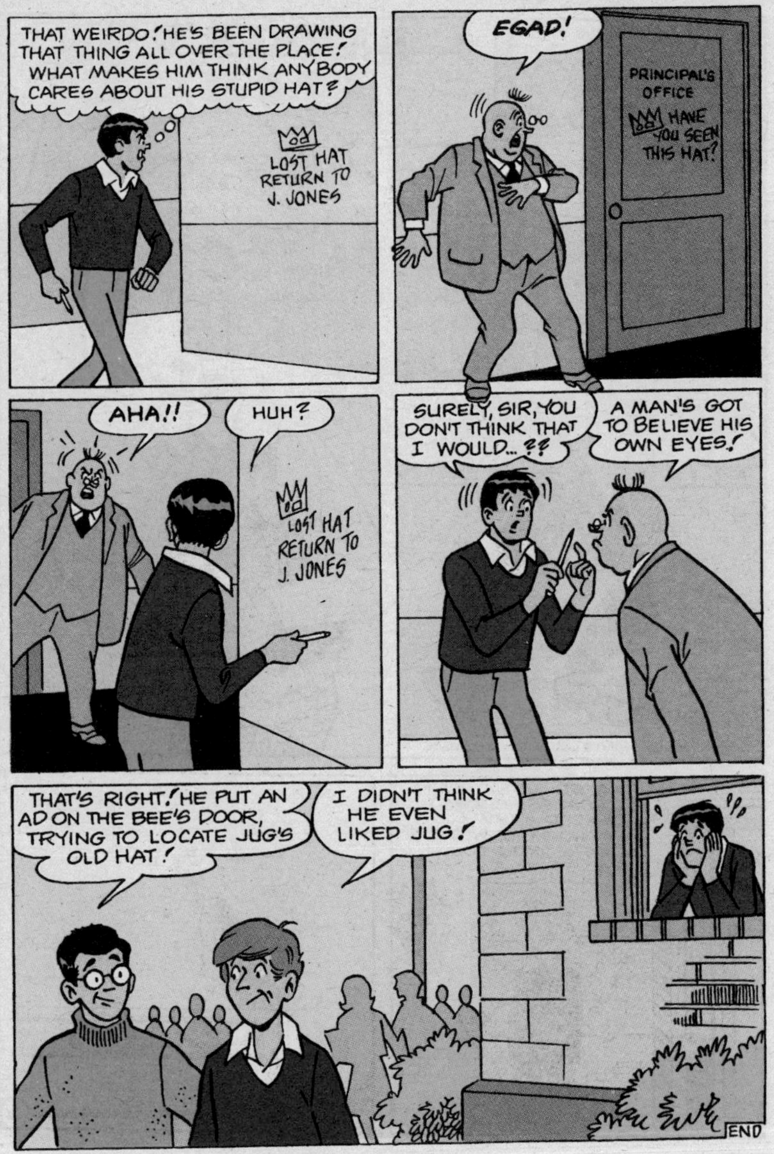
THAT WEIRDO! HE'S BEEN DRAWING THAT THING ALL OVER THE PLACE! WHAT MAKES HIM THINK ANYBODY CARES ABOUT HIS STUPID HAT?
LOST HAT RETURN TO J. JONES
EGAD!
PRINCIPAL'S OFFICE
HAVE YOU SEEN THIS HAT?
AHA!!
HUH?
LOST HAT RETURN TO J. JONES
SURELY, SIR, YOU DON'T THINK THAT I WOULD...??
A MAN'S GOT TO BELIEVE HIS OWN EYES!
THAT'S RIGHT! HE PUT AN AD ON THE BEE'S DOOR, TRYING TO LOCATE JUG'S OLD HAT!
I DIDN'T THINK HE EVEN LIKED JUG!
END

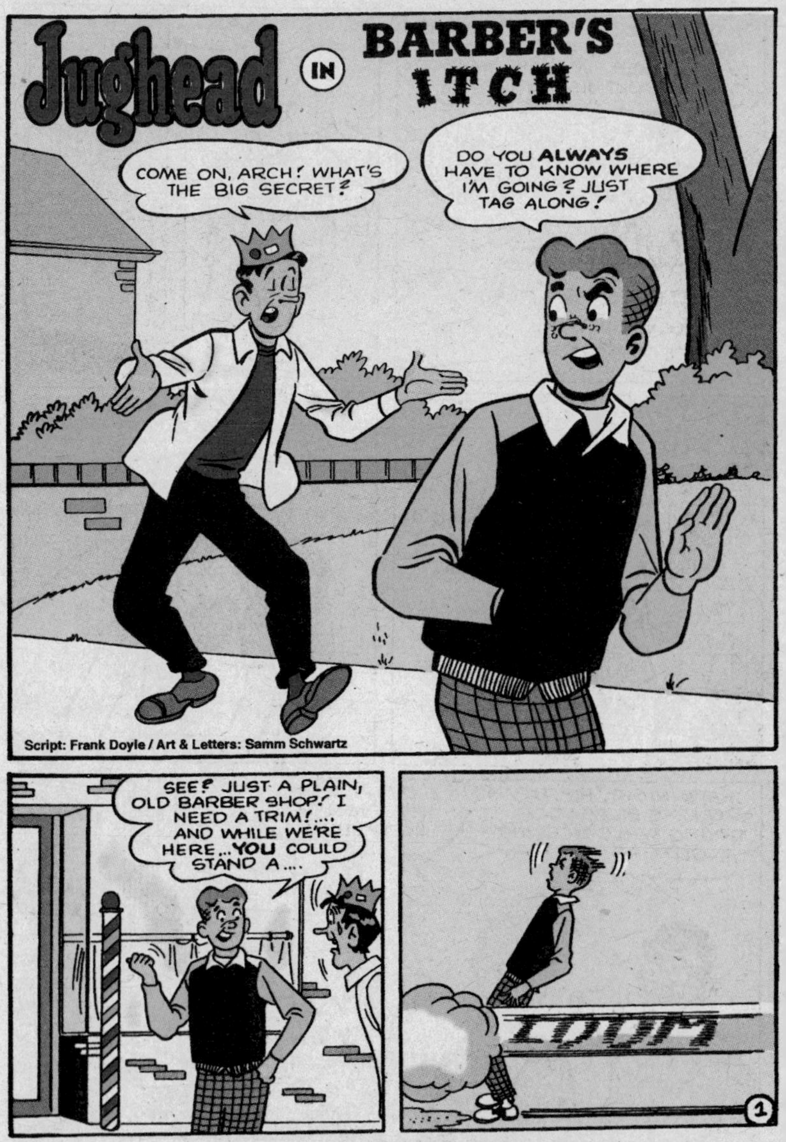
Jughead IN BARBER'S ITCH
COME ON, ARCH! WHAT'S THE BIG SECRET?
DO YOU ALWAYS HAVE TO KNOW WHERE I'M GOING? JUST TAG ALONG!
Script: Frank Doyle / Art & Letters: Samm Schwartz
SEE? JUST A PLAIN, OLD BARBER SHOP! I NEED A TRIM!.... AND WHILE WE'RE HERE...YOU COULD STAND A....
ZOOM
1

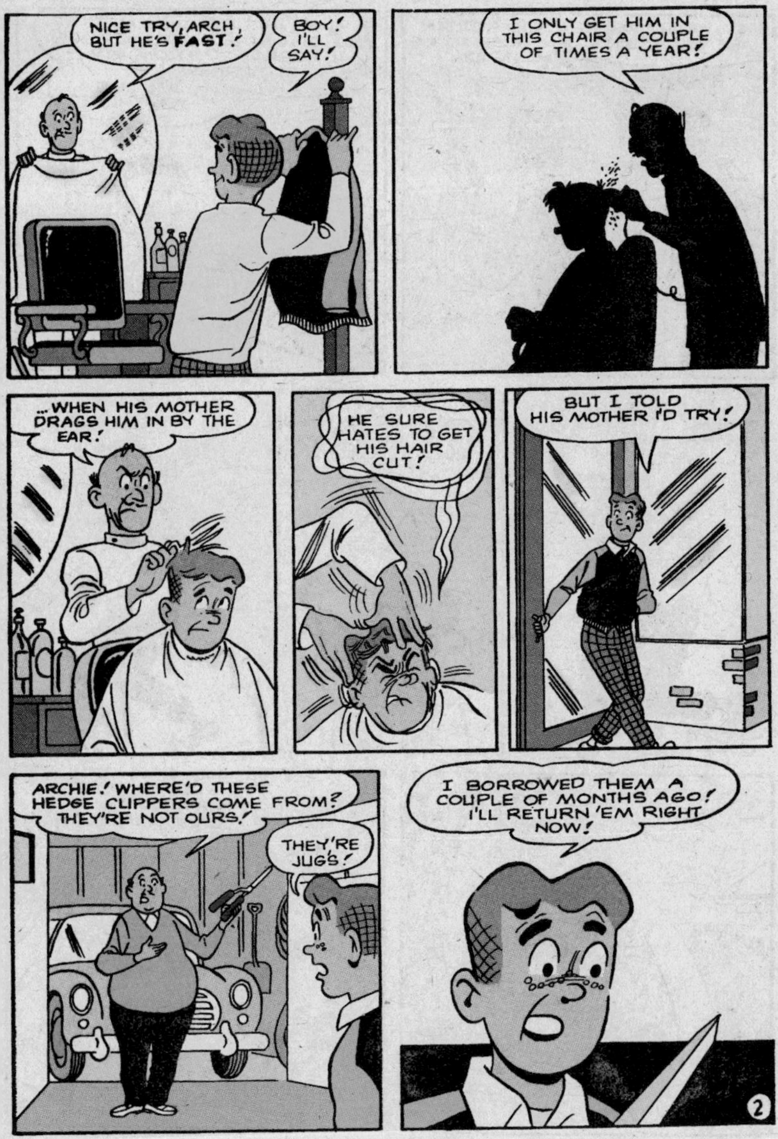

NICE TRY, ARCH, BUT HE'S **FAST**!
BOY! I'LL SAY!
I ONLY GET HIM IN THIS CHAIR A COUPLE OF TIMES A YEAR!
...WHEN HIS MOTHER DRAGS HIM IN BY THE EAR!
HE SURE HATES TO GET HIS HAIR CUT!
BUT I TOLD HIS MOTHER I'D TRY!
ARCHIE! WHERE'D THESE HEDGE CLIPPERS COME FROM? THEY'RE NOT OURS!
THEY'RE JUG'S!
I BORROWED THEM A COUPLE OF MONTHS AGO! I'LL RETURN 'EM RIGHT NOW!
2

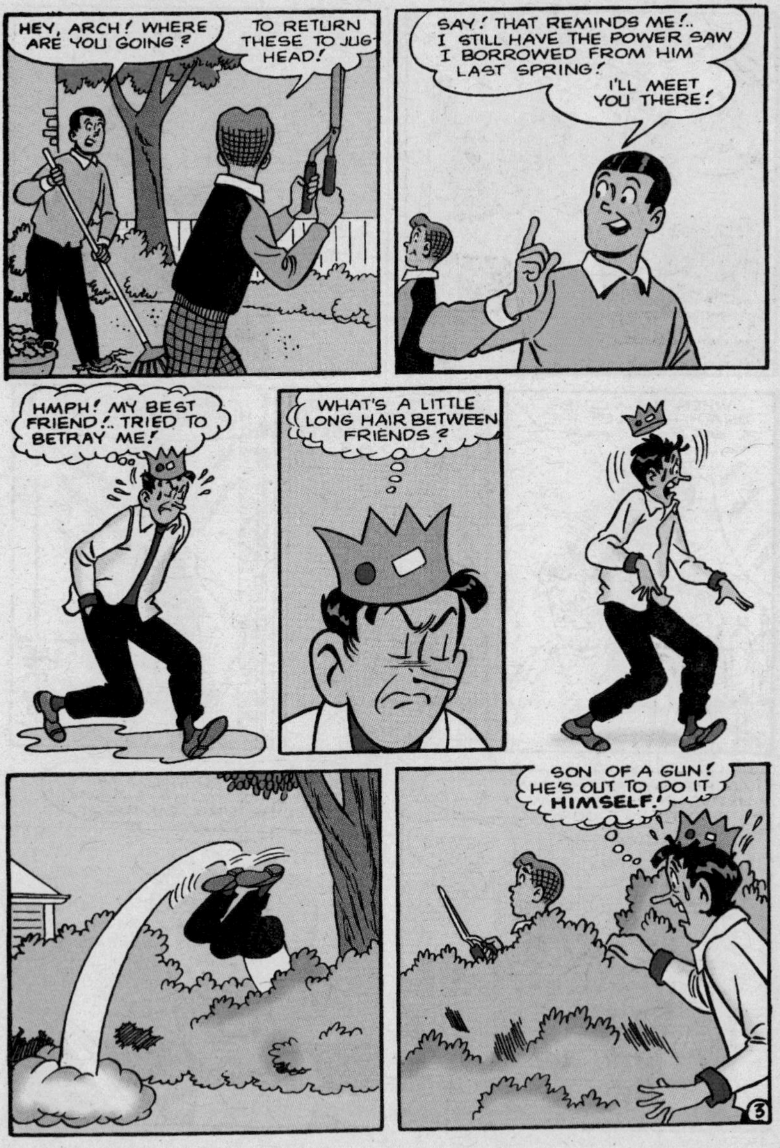
HEY, ARCH! WHERE ARE YOU GOING?
TO RETURN THESE TO JUG-HEAD!
SAY! THAT REMINDS ME!.. I STILL HAVE THE POWER SAW I BORROWED FROM HIM LAST SPRING!
I'LL MEET YOU THERE!
HMPH! MY BEST FRIEND!.. TRIED TO BETRAY ME!
WHAT'S A LITTLE LONG HAIR BETWEEN FRIENDS?
SON OF A GUN! HE'S OUT TO DO IT **HIMSELF**!
3

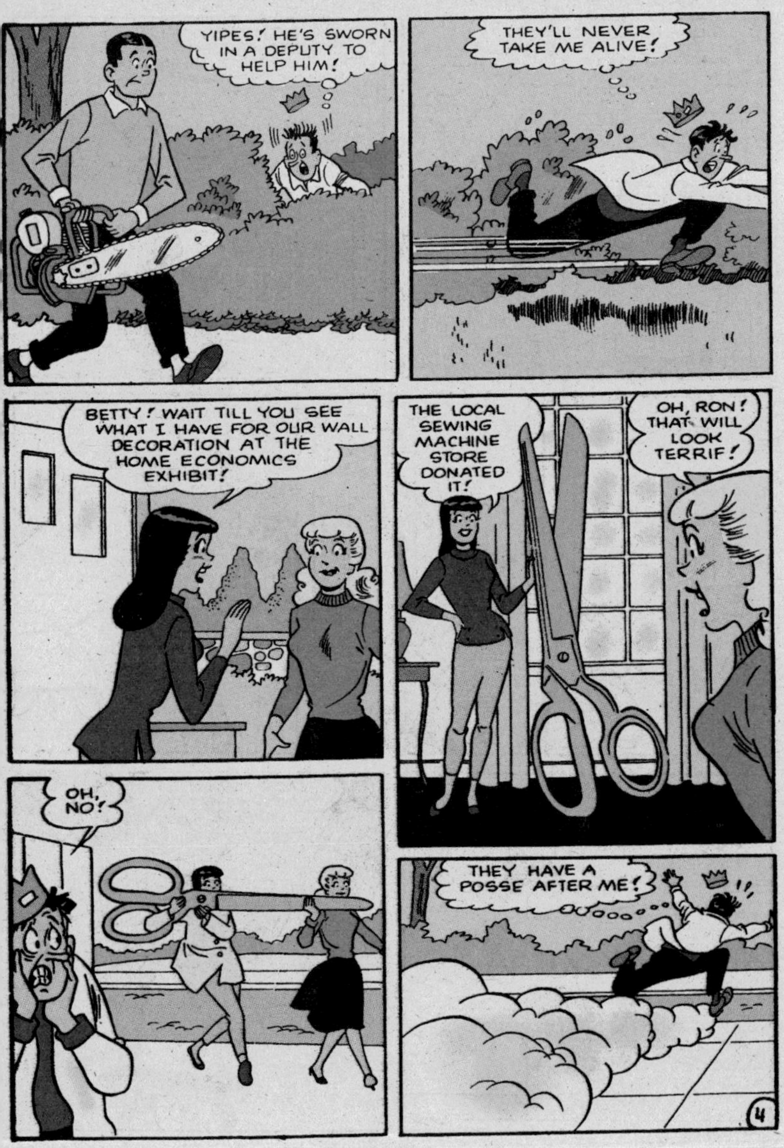
YIPES! HE'S SWORN IN A DEPUTY TO HELP HIM!
THEY'LL NEVER TAKE ME ALIVE!
BETTY! WAIT TILL YOU SEE WHAT I HAVE FOR OUR WALL DECORATION AT THE HOME ECONOMICS EXHIBIT!
THE LOCAL SEWING MACHINE STORE DONATED IT!
OH, RON! THAT WILL LOOK TERRIF!
OH, NO!
THEY HAVE A POSSE AFTER ME!
4

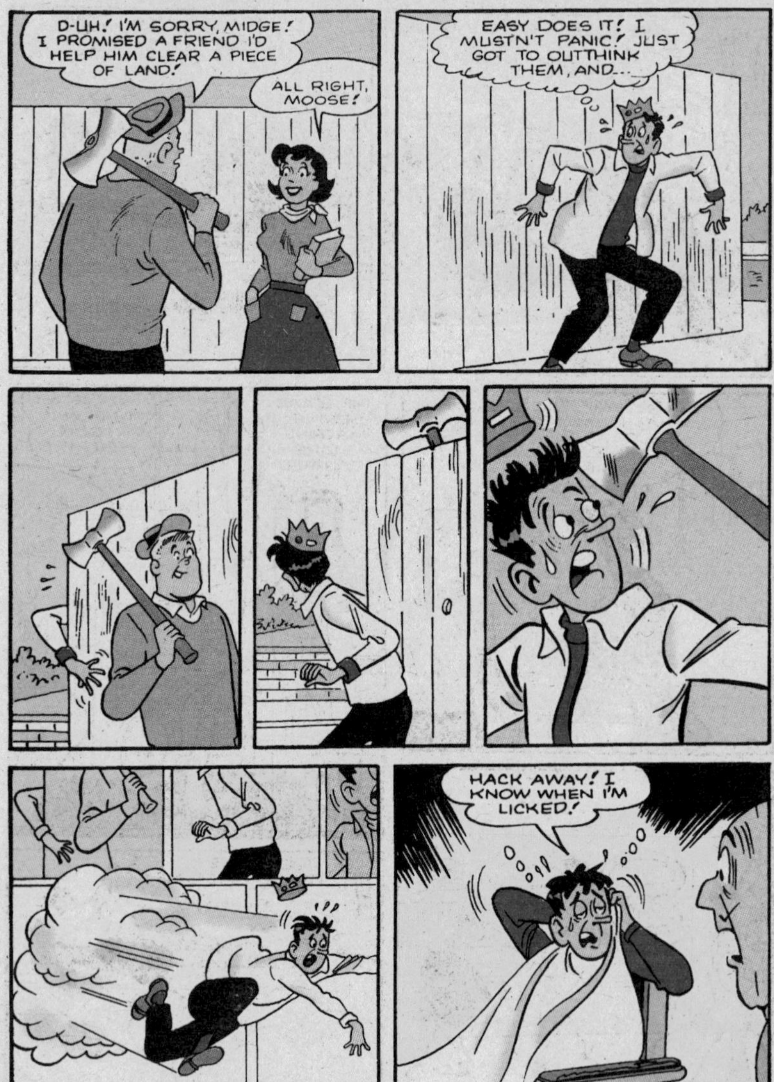
D-UH! I'M SORRY, MIDGE! I PROMISED A FRIEND I'D HELP HIM CLEAR A PIECE OF LAND!
ALL RIGHT, MOOSE!
EASY DOES IT! I MUSTN'T PANIC! JUST GOT TO OUTTHINK THEM, AND...
HACK AWAY! I KNOW WHEN I'M LICKED!
END

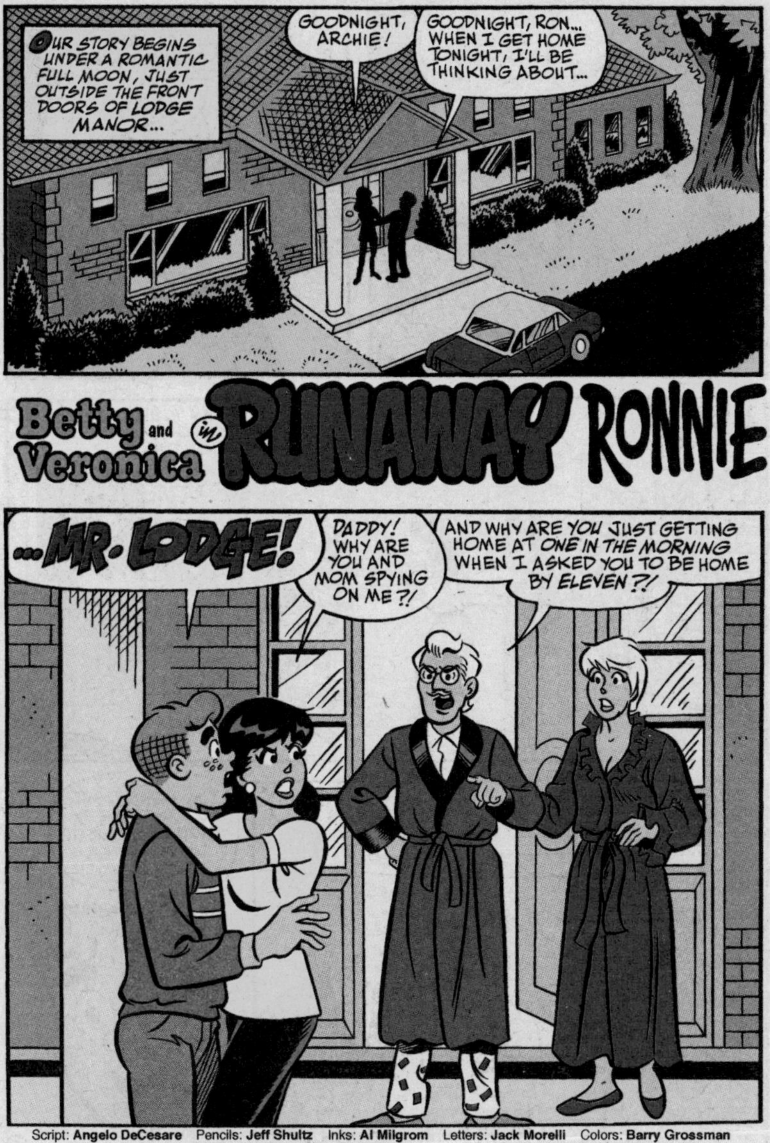
OUR STORY BEGINS UNDER A ROMANTIC FULL MOON, JUST OUTSIDE THE FRONT DOORS OF LODGE MANOR...
GOODNIGHT, ARCHIE!
GOODNIGHT, RON... WHEN I GET HOME TONIGHT, I'LL BE THINKING ABOUT...
Betty and Veronica in RUNAWAY RONNIE
...MR. LODGE!
DADDY! WHY ARE YOU AND MOM SPYING ON ME?!
AND WHY ARE YOU JUST GETTING HOME AT ONE IN THE MORNING WHEN I ASKED YOU TO BE HOME BY ELEVEN?!

Script: **Angelo DeCesare** Pencils: **Jeff Shultz** Inks: **Al Milgrom** Letters: **Jack Morelli** Colors: **Barry Grossman**
Editor-In-Chief: **Victor Gorelick** President: **Mike Pellerito** Publisher: **Jon Goldwater**

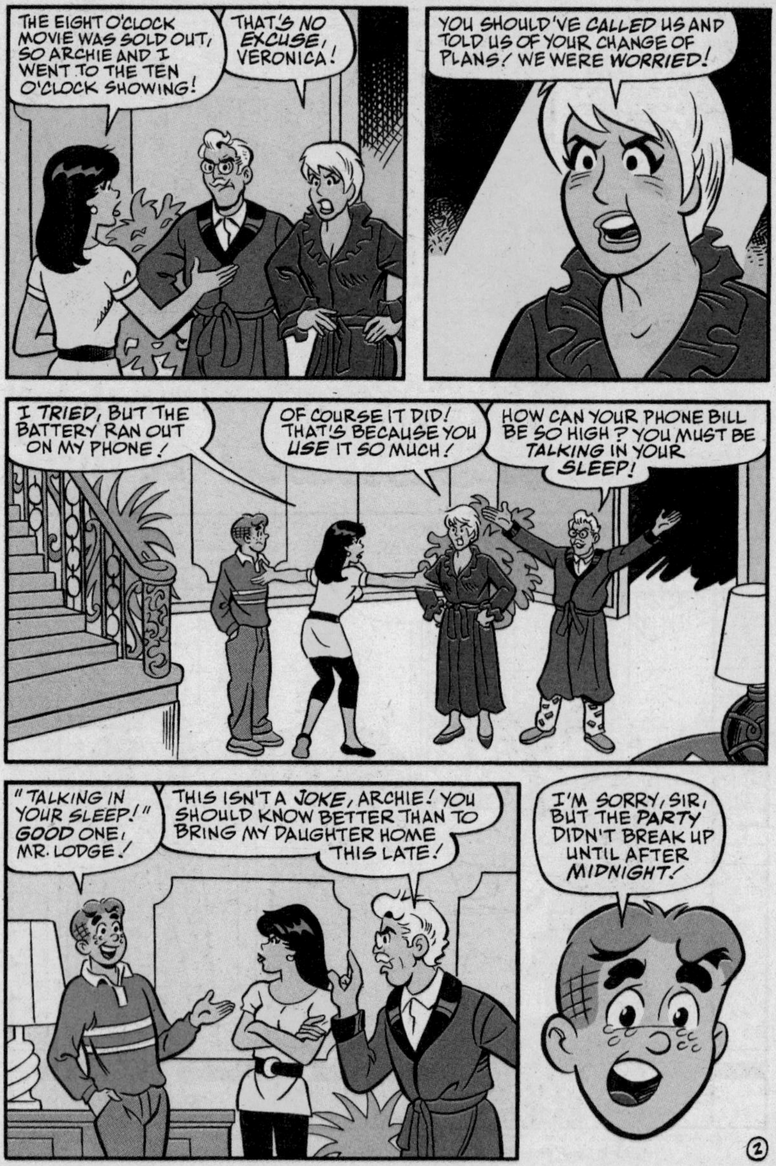
THE EIGHT O'CLOCK MOVIE WAS SOLD OUT, SO ARCHIE AND I WENT TO THE TEN O'CLOCK SHOWING!
THAT'S NO EXCUSE, VERONICA!
YOU SHOULD'VE CALLED US AND TOLD US OF YOUR CHANGE OF PLANS! WE WERE WORRIED!
I TRIED, BUT THE BATTERY RAN OUT ON MY PHONE!
OF COURSE IT DID! THAT'S BECAUSE YOU USE IT SO MUCH!
HOW CAN YOUR PHONE BILL BE SO HIGH? YOU MUST BE TALKING IN YOUR SLEEP!
"TALKING IN YOUR SLEEP!" GOOD ONE, MR. LODGE!
THIS ISN'T A JOKE, ARCHIE! YOU SHOULD KNOW BETTER THAN TO BRING MY DAUGHTER HOME THIS LATE!
I'M SORRY, SIR, BUT THE PARTY DIDN'T BREAK UP UNTIL AFTER MIDNIGHT!

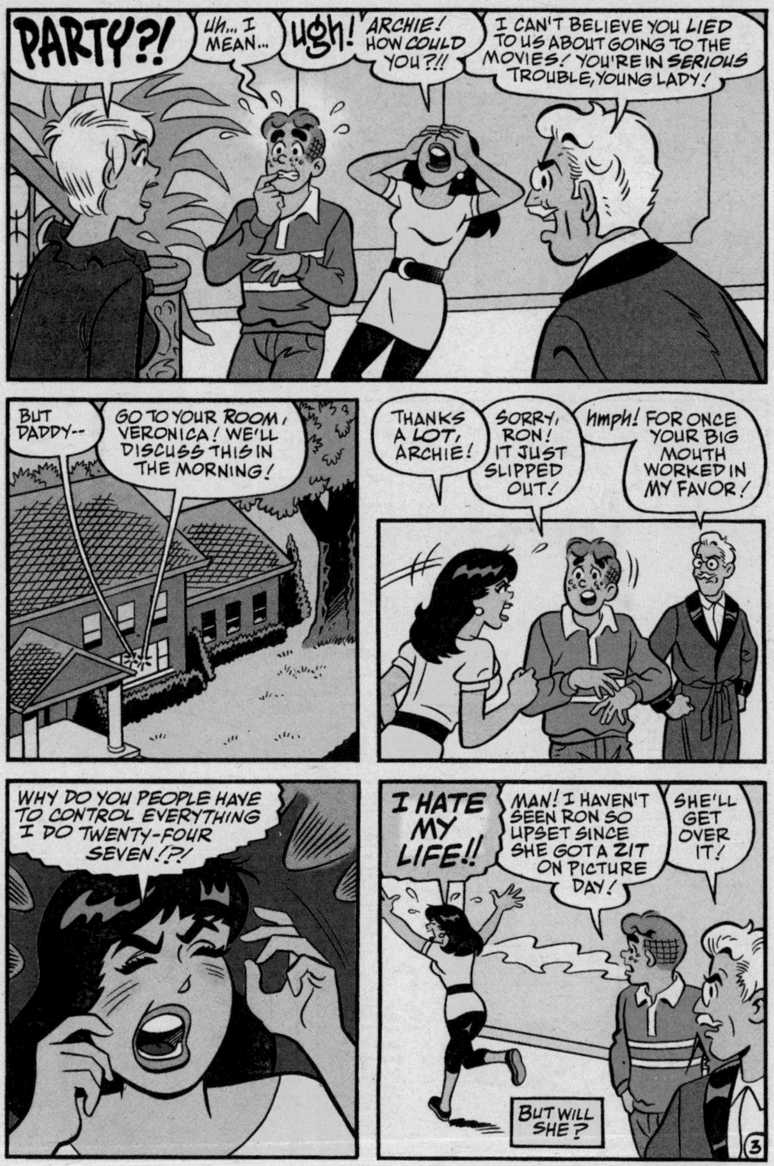
PARTY?!
uh... I MEAN...
ugh!
ARCHIE! HOW COULD YOU?!!
I CAN'T BELIEVE YOU LIED TO US ABOUT GOING TO THE MOVIES! YOU'RE IN SERIOUS TROUBLE, YOUNG LADY!
BUT DADDY--
GO TO YOUR ROOM, VERONICA! WE'LL DISCUSS THIS IN THE MORNING!
THANKS A LOT, ARCHIE!
SORRY, RON! IT JUST SLIPPED OUT!
hmph! FOR ONCE YOUR BIG MOUTH WORKED IN MY FAVOR!
WHY DO YOU PEOPLE HAVE TO CONTROL EVERYTHING I DO TWENTY-FOUR SEVEN!?!
I HATE MY LIFE!!
MAN! I HAVEN'T SEEN RON SO UPSET SINCE SHE GOT A ZIT ON PICTURE DAY!
SHE'LL GET OVER IT!
BUT WILL SHE?
3

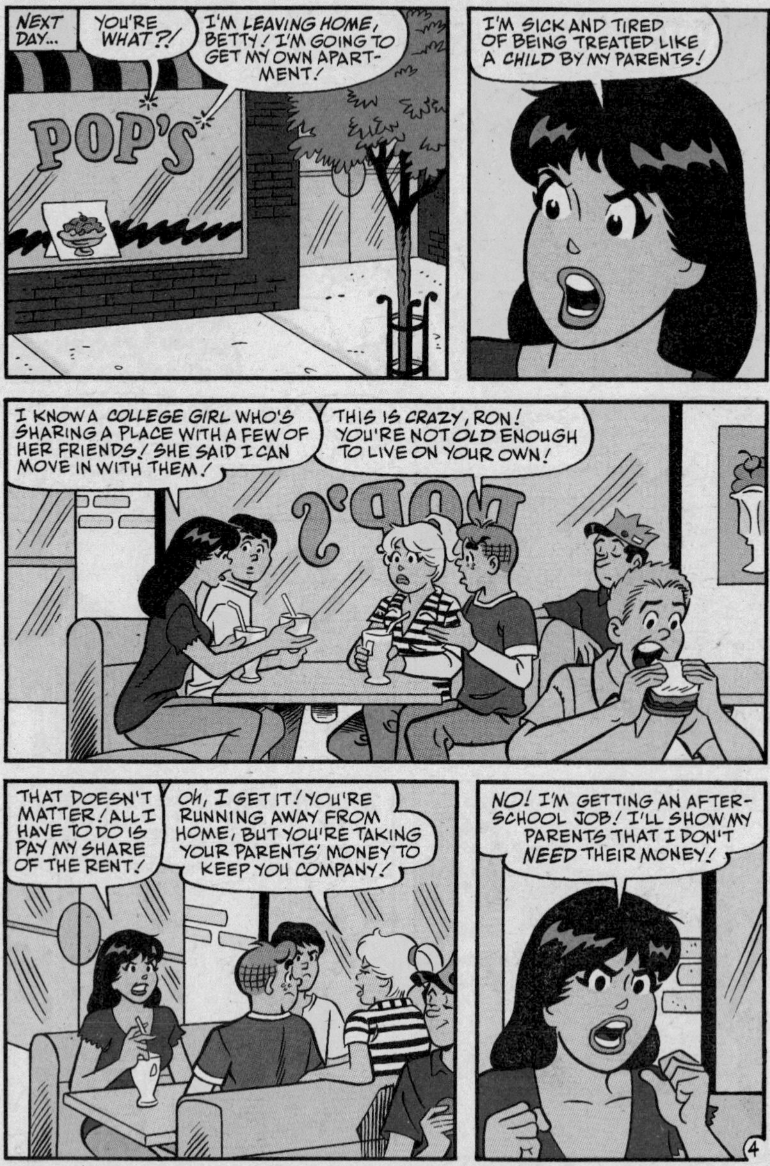
NEXT DAY...
YOU'RE WHAT?!
I'M LEAVING HOME, BETTY! I'M GOING TO GET MY OWN APARTMENT!
POP'S
I'M SICK AND TIRED OF BEING TREATED LIKE A CHILD BY MY PARENTS!
I KNOW A COLLEGE GIRL WHO'S SHARING A PLACE WITH A FEW OF HER FRIENDS! SHE SAID I CAN MOVE IN WITH THEM!
THIS IS CRAZY, RON! YOU'RE NOT OLD ENOUGH TO LIVE ON YOUR OWN!
POP'S
THAT DOESN'T MATTER! ALL I HAVE TO DO IS PAY MY SHARE OF THE RENT!
OH, I GET IT! YOU'RE RUNNING AWAY FROM HOME, BUT YOU'RE TAKING YOUR PARENTS' MONEY TO KEEP YOU COMPANY!
NO! I'M GETTING AN AFTER-SCHOOL JOB! I'LL SHOW MY PARENTS THAT I DON'T NEED THEIR MONEY!
4

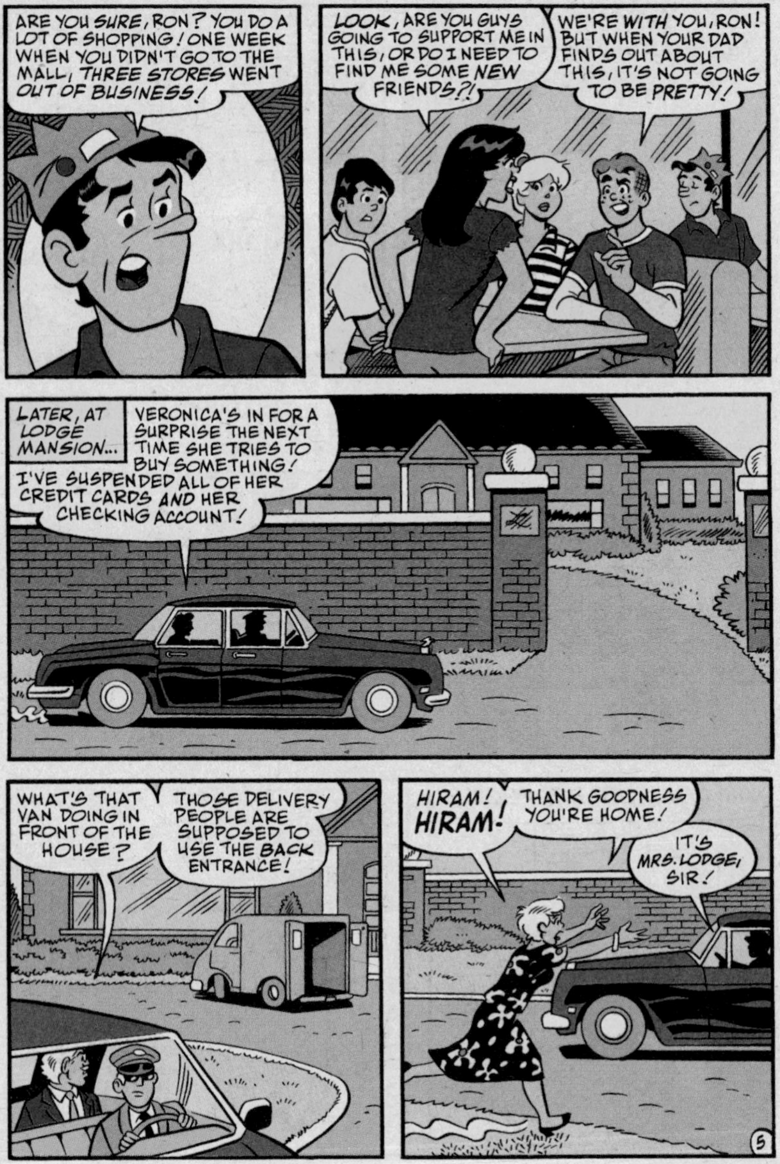
ARE YOU SURE, RON? YOU DO A LOT OF SHOPPING! ONE WEEK WHEN YOU DIDN'T GO TO THE MALL, THREE STORES WENT OUT OF BUSINESS!
LOOK, ARE YOU GUYS GOING TO SUPPORT ME IN THIS, OR DO I NEED TO FIND ME SOME NEW FRIENDS?!
WE'RE WITH YOU, RON! BUT WHEN YOUR DAD FINDS OUT ABOUT THIS, IT'S NOT GOING TO BE PRETTY!
LATER, AT LODGE MANSION...
VERONICA'S IN FOR A SURPRISE THE NEXT TIME SHE TRIES TO BUY SOMETHING! I'VE SUSPENDED ALL OF HER CREDIT CARDS AND HER CHECKING ACCOUNT!
WHAT'S THAT VAN DOING IN FRONT OF THE HOUSE?
THOSE DELIVERY PEOPLE ARE SUPPOSED TO USE THE BACK ENTRANCE!
HIRAM! HIRAM!
THANK GOODNESS YOU'RE HOME!
IT'S MRS. LODGE, SIR!
5

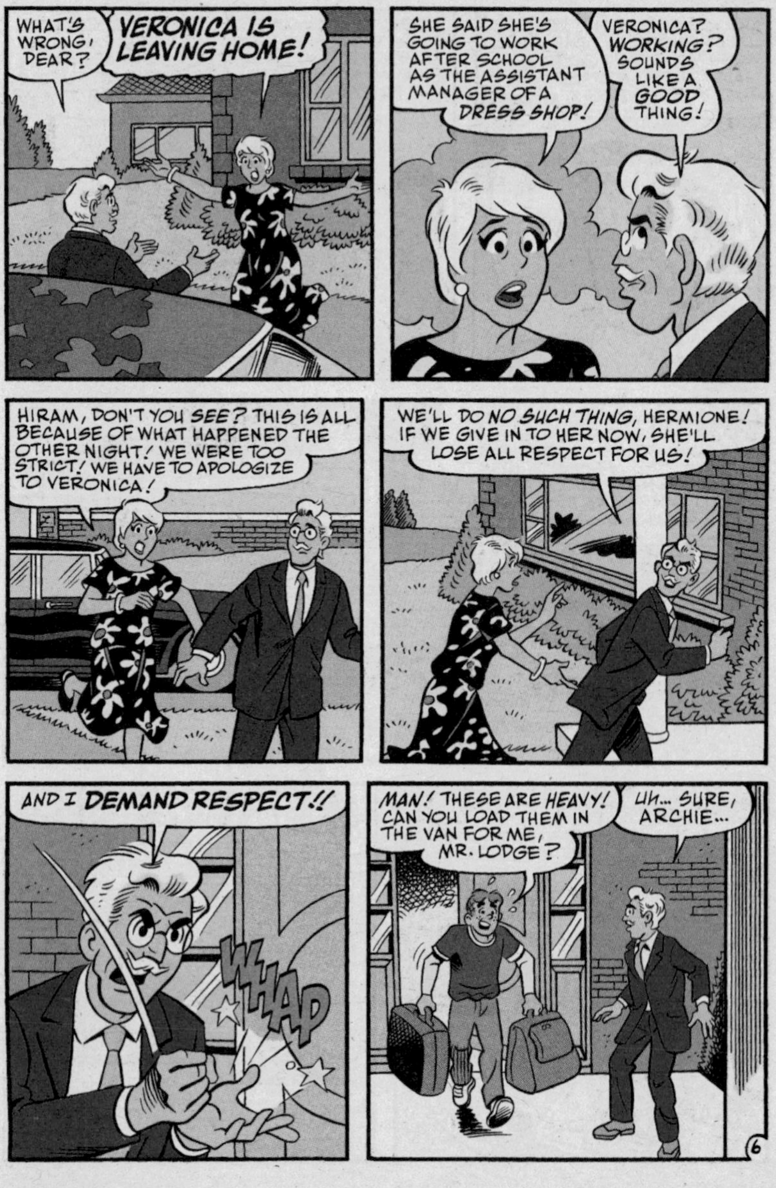
WHAT'S WRONG, DEAR?
VERONICA IS LEAVING HOME!
SHE SAID SHE'S GOING TO WORK AFTER SCHOOL AS THE ASSISTANT MANAGER OF A DRESS SHOP!
VERONICA? WORKING? SOUNDS LIKE A GOOD THING!
HIRAM, DON'T YOU SEE? THIS IS ALL BECAUSE OF WHAT HAPPENED THE OTHER NIGHT! WE WERE TOO STRICT! WE HAVE TO APOLOGIZE TO VERONICA!
WE'LL DO NO SUCH THING, HERMIONE! IF WE GIVE IN TO HER NOW, SHE'LL LOSE ALL RESPECT FOR US!
AND I DEMAND RESPECT!!
WHAP
MAN! THESE ARE HEAVY! CAN YOU LOAD THEM IN THE VAN FOR ME, MR. LODGE?
UH... SURE, ARCHIE...
6

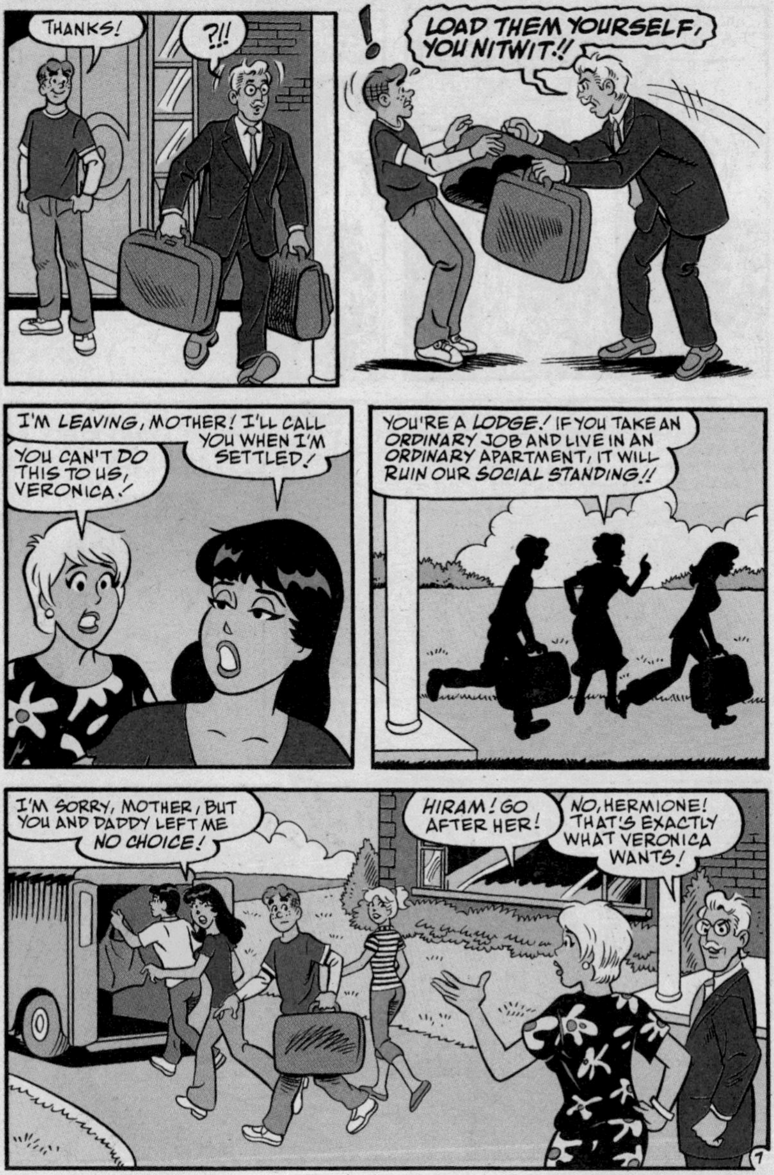
THANKS!
?!!
!
LOAD THEM YOURSELF, YOU NITWIT!!
I'M LEAVING, MOTHER! I'LL CALL YOU WHEN I'M SETTLED!
YOU CAN'T DO THIS TO US, VERONICA!
YOU'RE A LODGE! IF YOU TAKE AN ORDINARY JOB AND LIVE IN AN ORDINARY APARTMENT, IT WILL RUIN OUR SOCIAL STANDING!!
I'M SORRY, MOTHER, BUT YOU AND DADDY LEFT ME NO CHOICE!
HIRAM! GO AFTER HER!
NO, HERMIONE! THAT'S EXACTLY WHAT VERONICA WANTS!
7

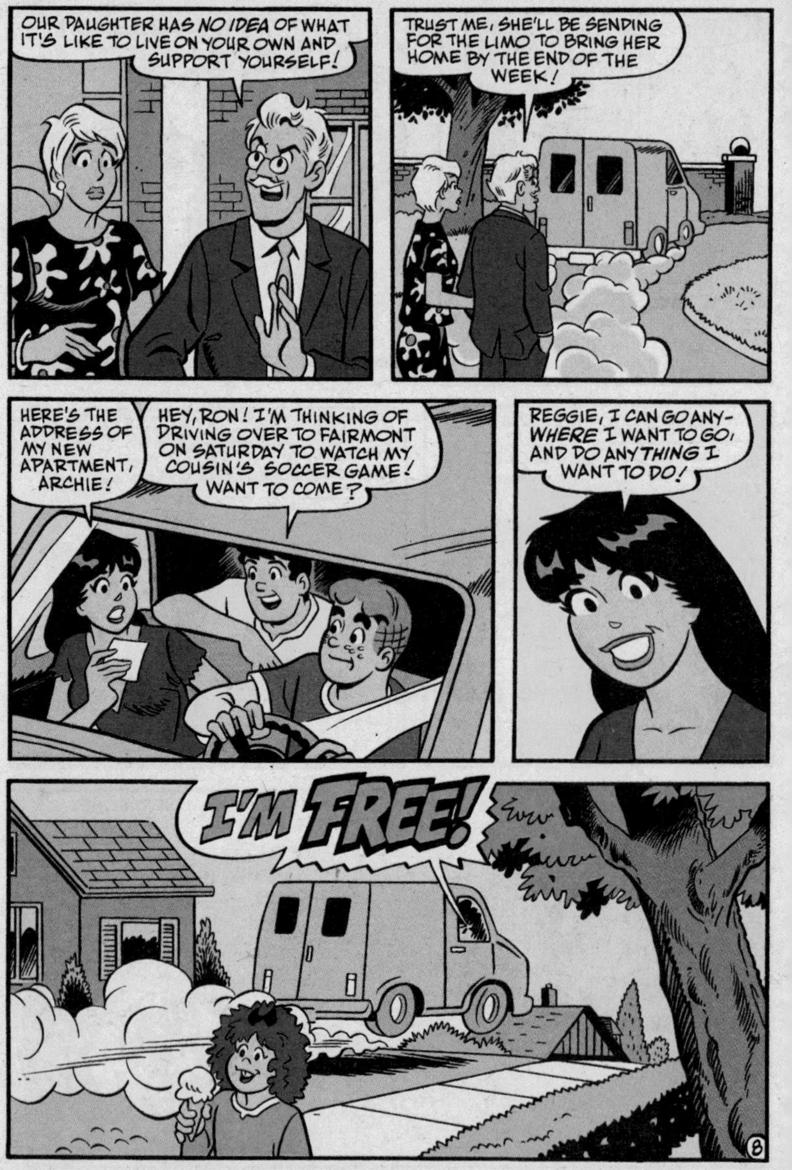
OUR DAUGHTER HAS *NO IDEA* OF WHAT IT'S LIKE TO LIVE ON YOUR OWN AND SUPPORT YOURSELF!
TRUST ME, SHE'LL BE SENDING FOR THE LIMO TO BRING HER HOME BY THE END OF THE WEEK!
HERE'S THE ADDRESS OF MY NEW APARTMENT, ARCHIE!
HEY, RON! I'M THINKING OF DRIVING OVER TO FAIRMONT ON SATURDAY TO WATCH MY COUSIN'S SOCCER GAME! WANT TO COME?
REGGIE, I CAN GO ANY*WHERE* I WANT TO GO, AND DO ANY*THING* I WANT TO DO!
I'M FREE!
8

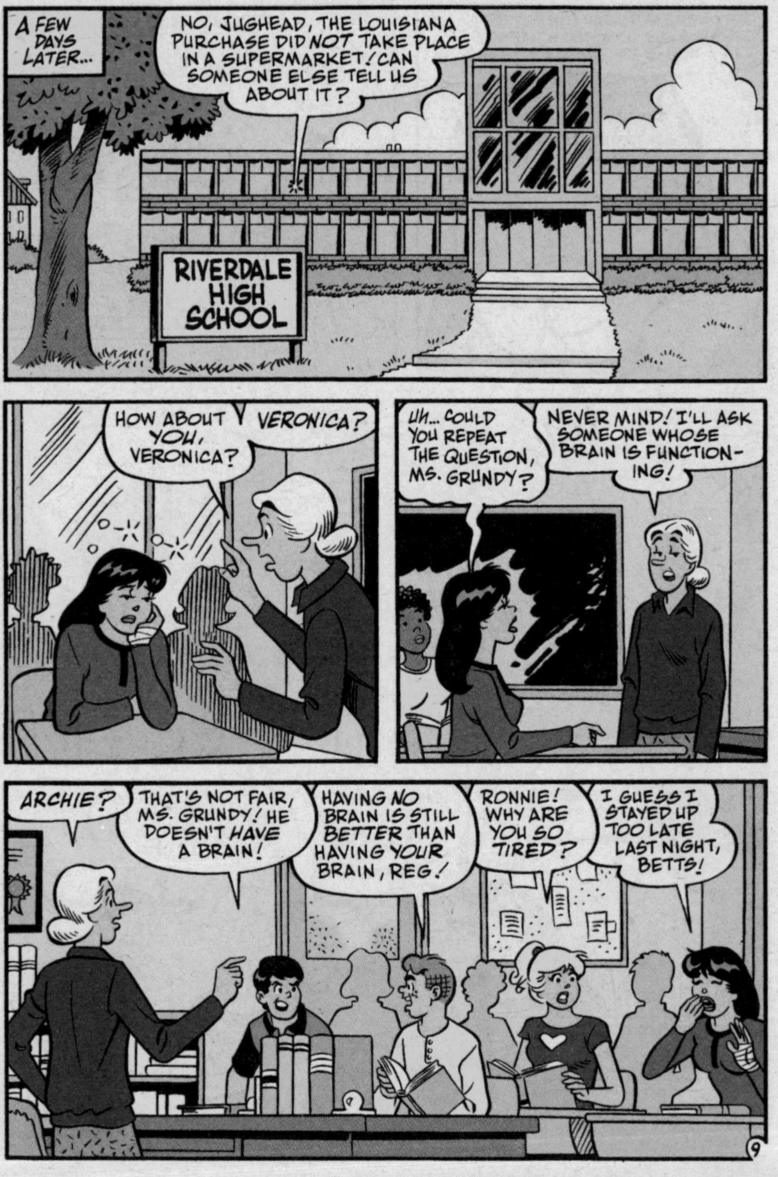
A FEW DAYS LATER...
NO, JUGHEAD, THE LOUISIANA PURCHASE DID NOT TAKE PLACE IN A SUPERMARKET! CAN SOMEONE ELSE TELL US ABOUT IT?
RIVERDALE HIGH SCHOOL
HOW ABOUT YOU, VERONICA?
VERONICA?
UH... COULD YOU REPEAT THE QUESTION, MS. GRUNDY?
NEVER MIND! I'LL ASK SOMEONE WHOSE BRAIN IS FUNCTION-ING!
ARCHIE?
THAT'S NOT FAIR, MS. GRUNDY! HE DOESN'T HAVE A BRAIN!
HAVING NO BRAIN IS STILL BETTER THAN HAVING YOUR BRAIN, REG!
RONNIE! WHY ARE YOU SO TIRED?
I GUESS I STAYED UP TOO LATE LAST NIGHT, BETTS!

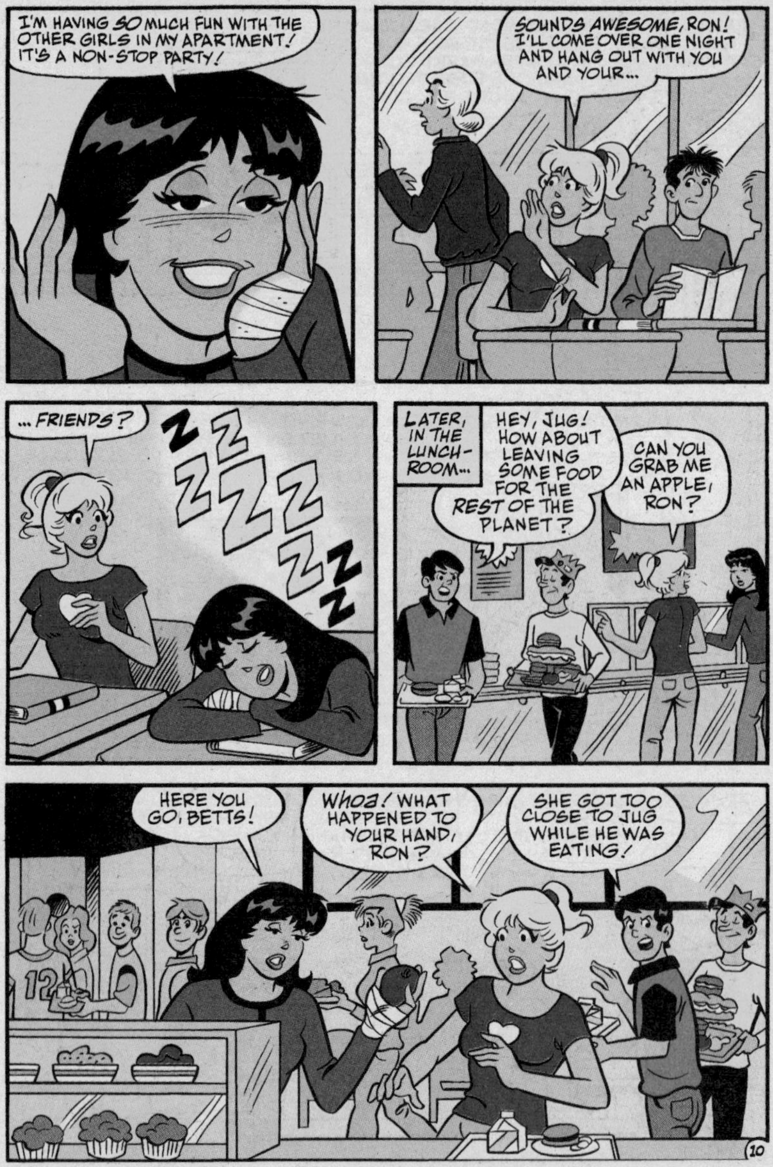
I'M HAVING SO MUCH FUN WITH THE OTHER GIRLS IN MY APARTMENT! IT'S A NON-STOP PARTY!
SOUNDS AWESOME, RON! I'LL COME OVER ONE NIGHT AND HANG OUT WITH YOU AND YOUR...
...FRIENDS?
Z Z Z Z Z Z Z Z
LATER, IN THE LUNCH-ROOM...
HEY, JUG! HOW ABOUT LEAVING SOME FOOD FOR THE REST OF THE PLANET?
CAN YOU GRAB ME AN APPLE, RON?
HERE YOU GO, BETTS!
Whoa! WHAT HAPPENED TO YOUR HAND, RON?
SHE GOT TOO CLOSE TO JUG WHILE HE WAS EATING!
12

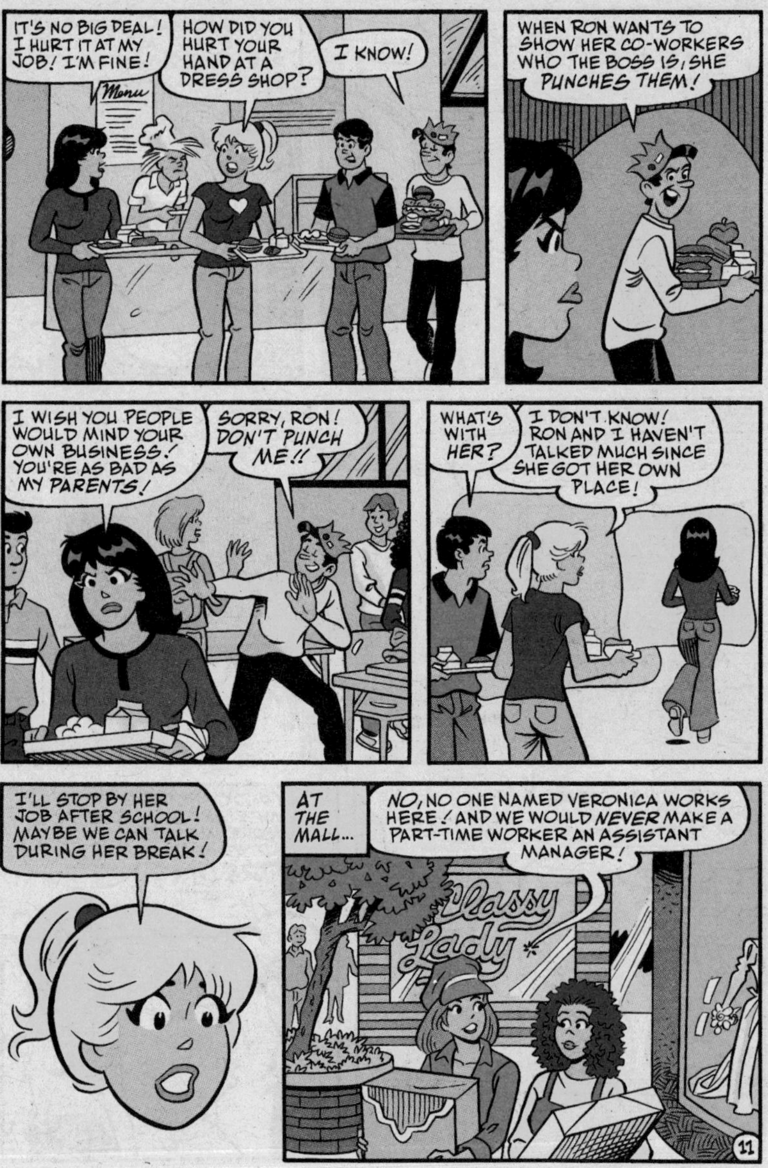
IT'S NO BIG DEAL! I HURT IT AT MY JOB! I'M FINE!
Menu
HOW DID YOU HURT YOUR HAND AT A DRESS SHOP?
I KNOW!
WHEN RON WANTS TO SHOW HER CO-WORKERS WHO THE BOSS IS, SHE PUNCHES THEM!
I WISH YOU PEOPLE WOULD MIND YOUR OWN BUSINESS! YOU'RE AS BAD AS MY PARENTS!
SORRY, RON! DON'T PUNCH ME!!
WHAT'S WITH HER?
I DON'T KNOW! RON AND I HAVEN'T TALKED MUCH SINCE SHE GOT HER OWN PLACE!
I'LL STOP BY HER JOB AFTER SCHOOL! MAYBE WE CAN TALK DURING HER BREAK!
AT THE MALL...
NO, NO ONE NAMED VERONICA WORKS HERE! AND WE WOULD NEVER MAKE A PART-TIME WORKER AN ASSISTANT MANAGER!
Classy Lady
11

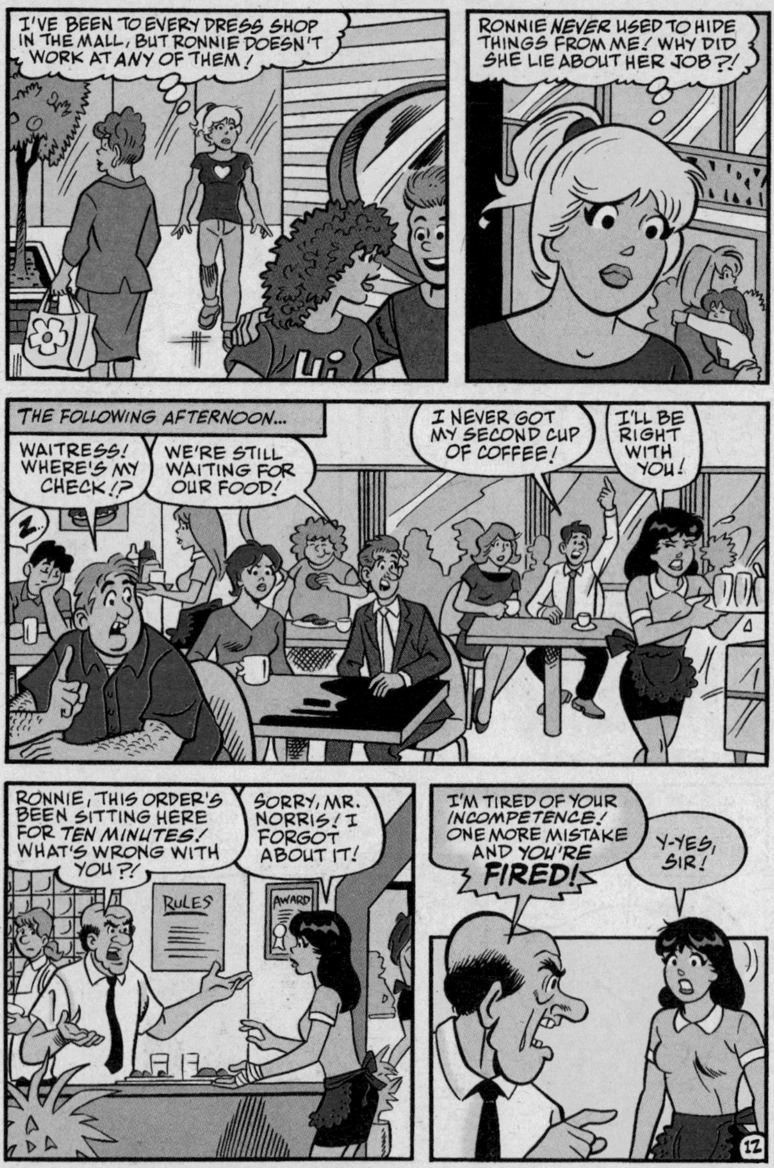

I'VE BEEN TO EVERY DRESS SHOP IN THE MALL, BUT RONNIE DOESN'T WORK AT ANY OF THEM!
RONNIE NEVER USED TO HIDE THINGS FROM ME! WHY DID SHE LIE ABOUT HER JOB?!
THE FOLLOWING AFTERNOON...
WAITRESS! WHERE'S MY CHECK!?
WE'RE STILL WAITING FOR OUR FOOD!
Z..
I NEVER GOT MY SECOND CUP OF COFFEE!
I'LL BE RIGHT WITH YOU!
RONNIE, THIS ORDER'S BEEN SITTING HERE FOR TEN MINUTES! WHAT'S WRONG WITH YOU?!
SORRY, MR. NORRIS! I FORGOT ABOUT IT!
RULES
AWARD
I'M TIRED OF YOUR INCOMPETENCE! ONE MORE MISTAKE AND YOU'RE FIRED!
Y-YES, SIR!

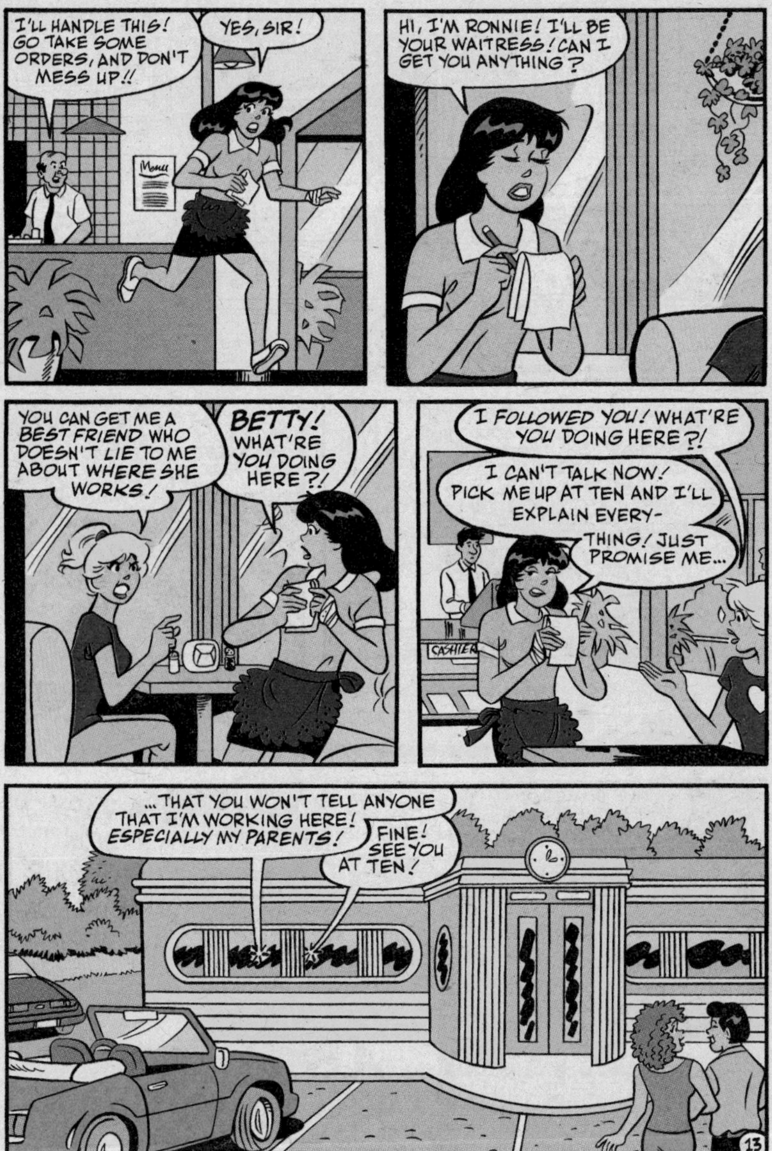
I'LL HANDLE THIS! GO TAKE SOME ORDERS, AND DON'T MESS UP!!
YES, SIR!
HI, I'M RONNIE! I'LL BE YOUR WAITRESS! CAN I GET YOU ANYTHING?
YOU CAN GET ME A BEST FRIEND WHO DOESN'T LIE TO ME ABOUT WHERE SHE WORKS!
BETTY! WHAT'RE YOU DOING HERE?!
I FOLLOWED YOU! WHAT'RE YOU DOING HERE?!
I CAN'T TALK NOW! PICK ME UP AT TEN AND I'LL EXPLAIN EVERY-
THING! JUST PROMISE ME...
CASHIER
...THAT YOU WON'T TELL ANYONE THAT I'M WORKING HERE! ESPECIALLY MY PARENTS!
FINE! SEE YOU AT TEN!

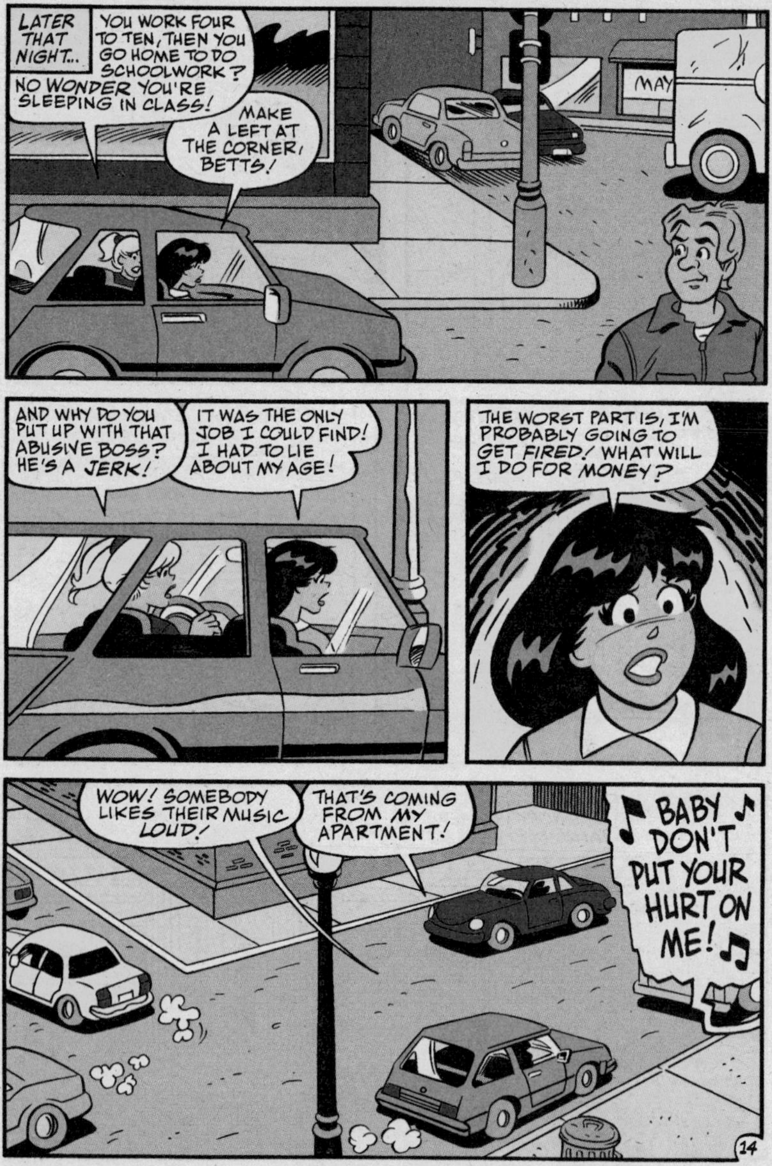
LATER THAT NIGHT...
YOU WORK FOUR TO TEN, THEN YOU GO HOME TO DO SCHOOLWORK?
NO WONDER YOU'RE SLEEPING IN CLASS!
MAKE A LEFT AT THE CORNER, BETTS!
MAY
AND WHY DO YOU PUT UP WITH THAT ABUSIVE BOSS? HE'S A JERK!
IT WAS THE ONLY JOB I COULD FIND! I HAD TO LIE ABOUT MY AGE!
THE WORST PART IS, I'M PROBABLY GOING TO GET FIRED! WHAT WILL I DO FOR MONEY?
WOW! SOMEBODY LIKES THEIR MUSIC LOUD!
THAT'S COMING FROM MY APARTMENT!
BABY DON'T PUT YOUR HURT ON ME!
14

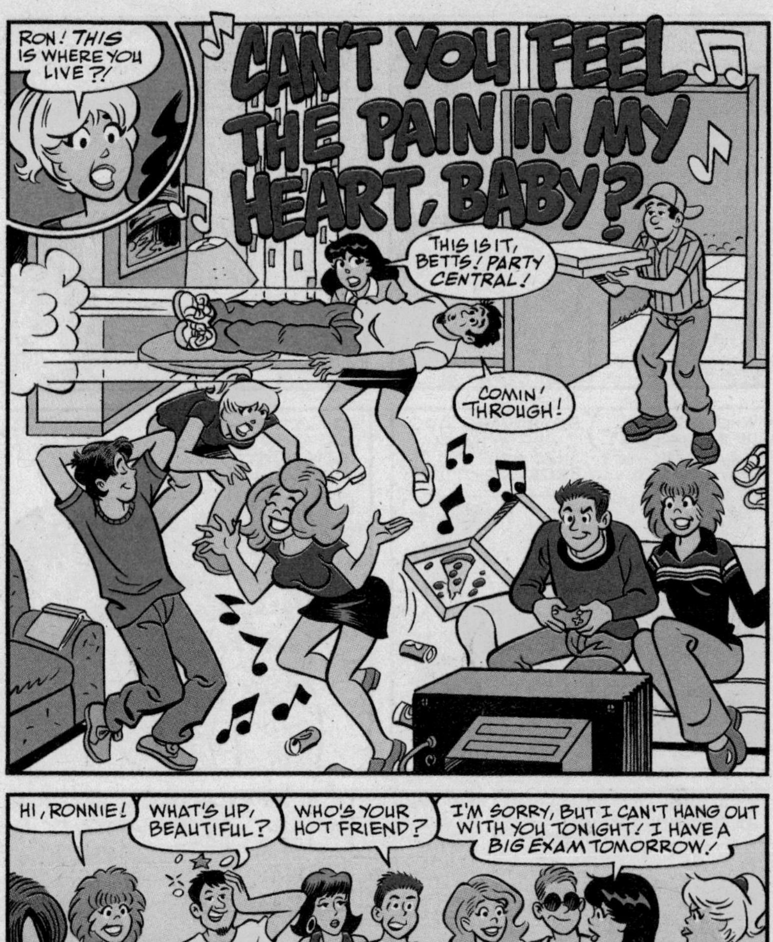
RON! THIS IS WHERE YOU LIVE?!
CAN'T YOU FEEL THE PAIN IN MY HEART, BABY?
THIS IS IT, BETTS! PARTY CENTRAL!
COMIN' THROUGH!

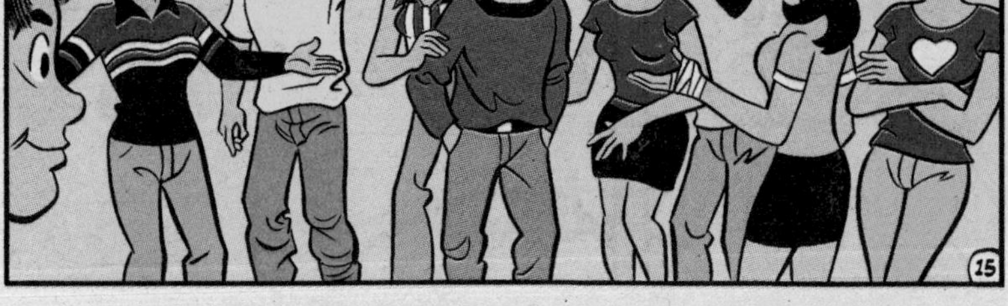
HI, RONNIE!
WHAT'S UP, BEAUTIFUL?
WHO'S YOUR HOT FRIEND?
I'M SORRY, BUT I CAN'T HANG OUT WITH YOU TONIGHT! I HAVE A BIG EXAM TOMORROW!
15

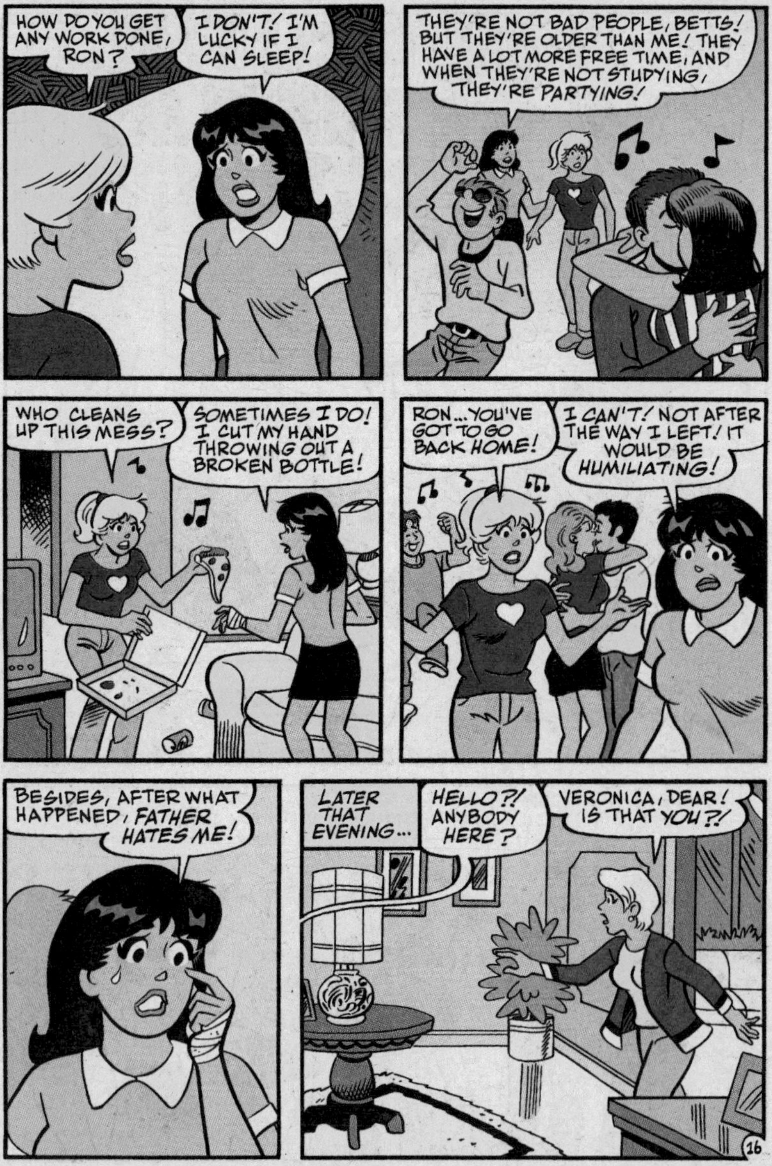
HOW DO YOU GET ANY WORK DONE, RON?
I DON'T! I'M LUCKY IF I CAN SLEEP!
THEY'RE NOT BAD PEOPLE, BETTS! BUT THEY'RE OLDER THAN ME! THEY HAVE A LOT MORE FREE TIME, AND WHEN THEY'RE NOT STUDYING, THEY'RE PARTYING!
WHO CLEANS UP THIS MESS?
SOMETIMES I DO! I CUT MY HAND THROWING OUT A BROKEN BOTTLE!
RON... YOU'VE GOT TO GO BACK HOME!
I CAN'T! NOT AFTER THE WAY I LEFT! IT WOULD BE HUMILIATING!
BESIDES, AFTER WHAT HAPPENED, FATHER HATES ME!
LATER THAT EVENING...
HELLO?! ANYBODY HERE?
VERONICA, DEAR! IS THAT YOU?!

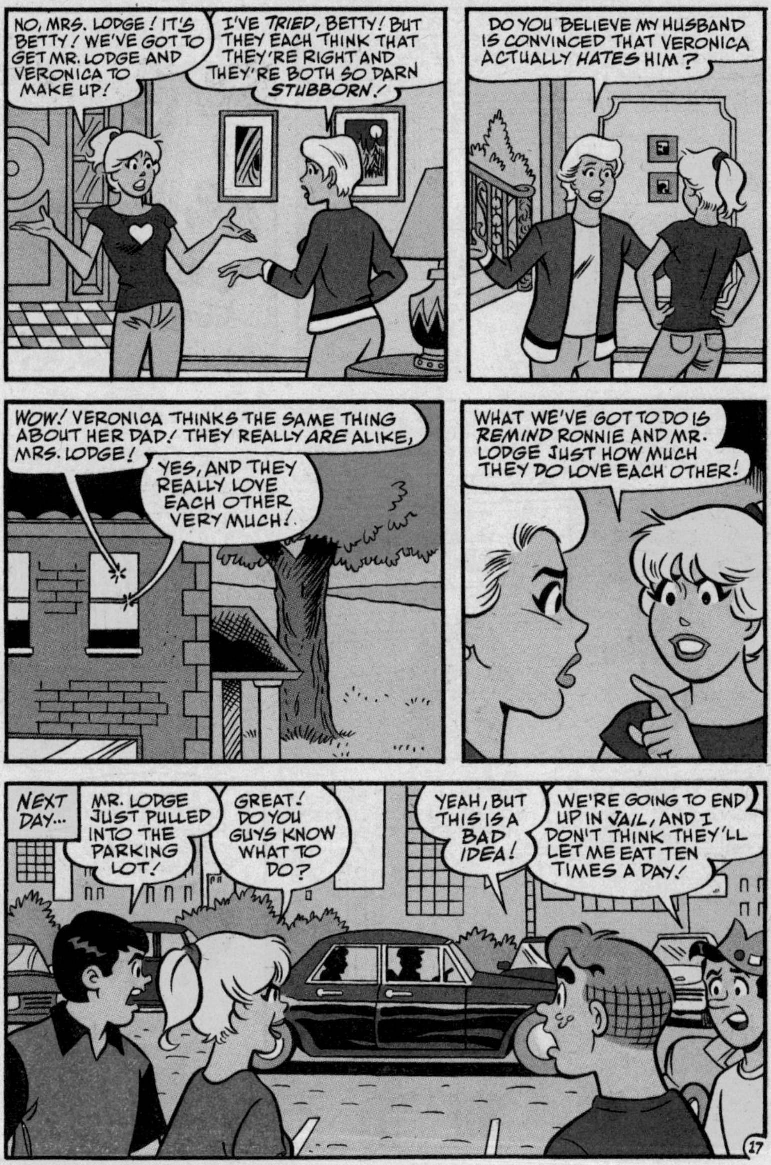
NO, MRS. LODGE! IT'S BETTY! WE'VE GOT TO GET MR. LODGE AND VERONICA TO MAKE UP!
I'VE TRIED, BETTY! BUT THEY EACH THINK THAT THEY'RE RIGHT AND THEY'RE BOTH SO DARN STUBBORN!
DO YOU BELIEVE MY HUSBAND IS CONVINCED THAT VERONICA ACTUALLY HATES HIM?
WOW! VERONICA THINKS THE SAME THING ABOUT HER DAD! THEY REALLY ARE ALIKE, MRS. LODGE!
YES, AND THEY REALLY LOVE EACH OTHER VERY MUCH!
WHAT WE'VE GOT TO DO IS REMIND RONNIE AND MR. LODGE JUST HOW MUCH THEY DO LOVE EACH OTHER!
NEXT DAY...
MR. LODGE JUST PULLED INTO THE PARKING LOT!
GREAT! DO YOU GUYS KNOW WHAT TO DO?
YEAH, BUT THIS IS A BAD IDEA!
WE'RE GOING TO END UP IN JAIL, AND I DON'T THINK THEY'LL LET ME EAT TEN TIMES A DAY!
17

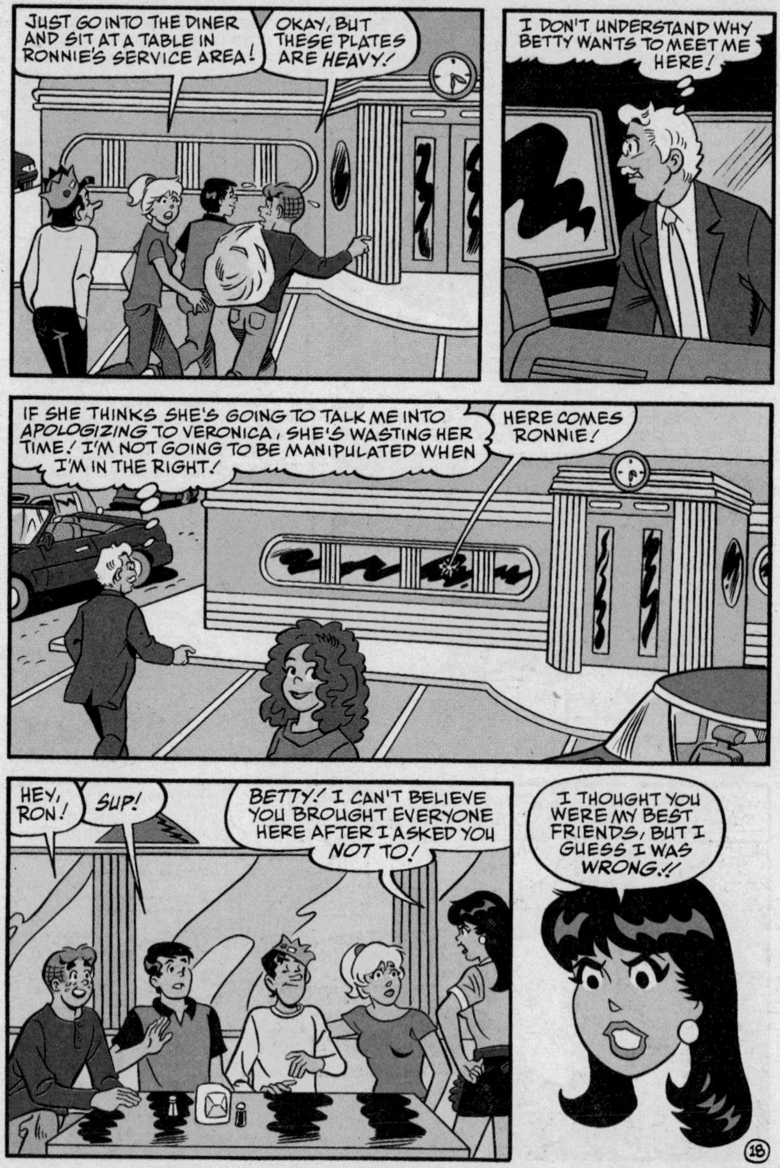
JUST GO INTO THE DINER AND SIT AT A TABLE IN RONNIE'S SERVICE AREA!
OKAY, BUT THESE PLATES ARE HEAVY!
I DON'T UNDERSTAND WHY BETTY WANTS TO MEET ME HERE!
IF SHE THINKS SHE'S GOING TO TALK ME INTO APOLOGIZING TO VERONICA, SHE'S WASTING HER TIME! I'M NOT GOING TO BE MANIPULATED WHEN I'M IN THE RIGHT!
HERE COMES RONNIE!
HEY, RON!
SUP!
BETTY! I CAN'T BELIEVE YOU BROUGHT EVERYONE HERE AFTER I ASKED YOU NOT TO!
I THOUGHT YOU WERE MY BEST FRIENDS, BUT I GUESS I WAS WRONG!!

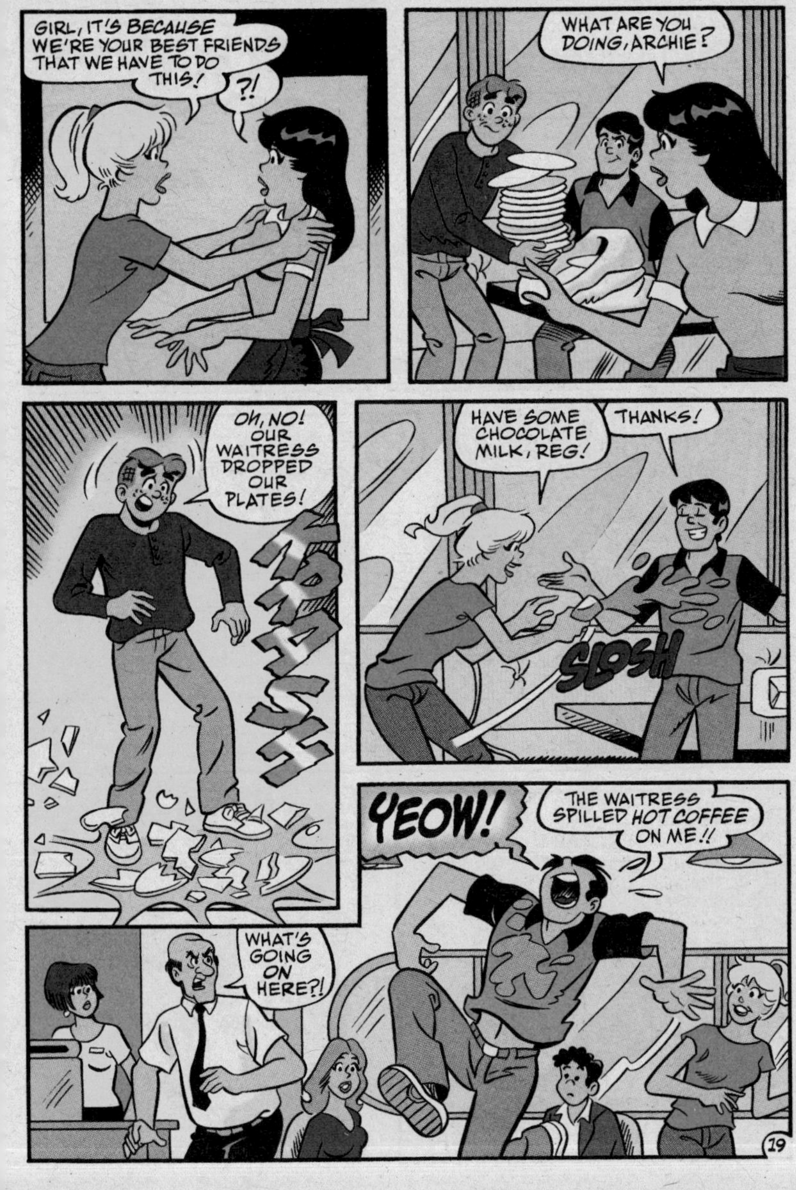
GIRL, IT'S BECAUSE WE'RE YOUR BEST FRIENDS THAT WE HAVE TO DO THIS!
?!
WHAT ARE YOU DOING, ARCHIE?
OH, NO! OUR WAITRESS DROPPED OUR PLATES!
HAVE SOME CHOCOLATE MILK, REG!
THANKS!
SLOSH
YEOW!
THE WAITRESS SPILLED HOT COFFEE ON ME!!
WHAT'S GOING ON HERE?!
19

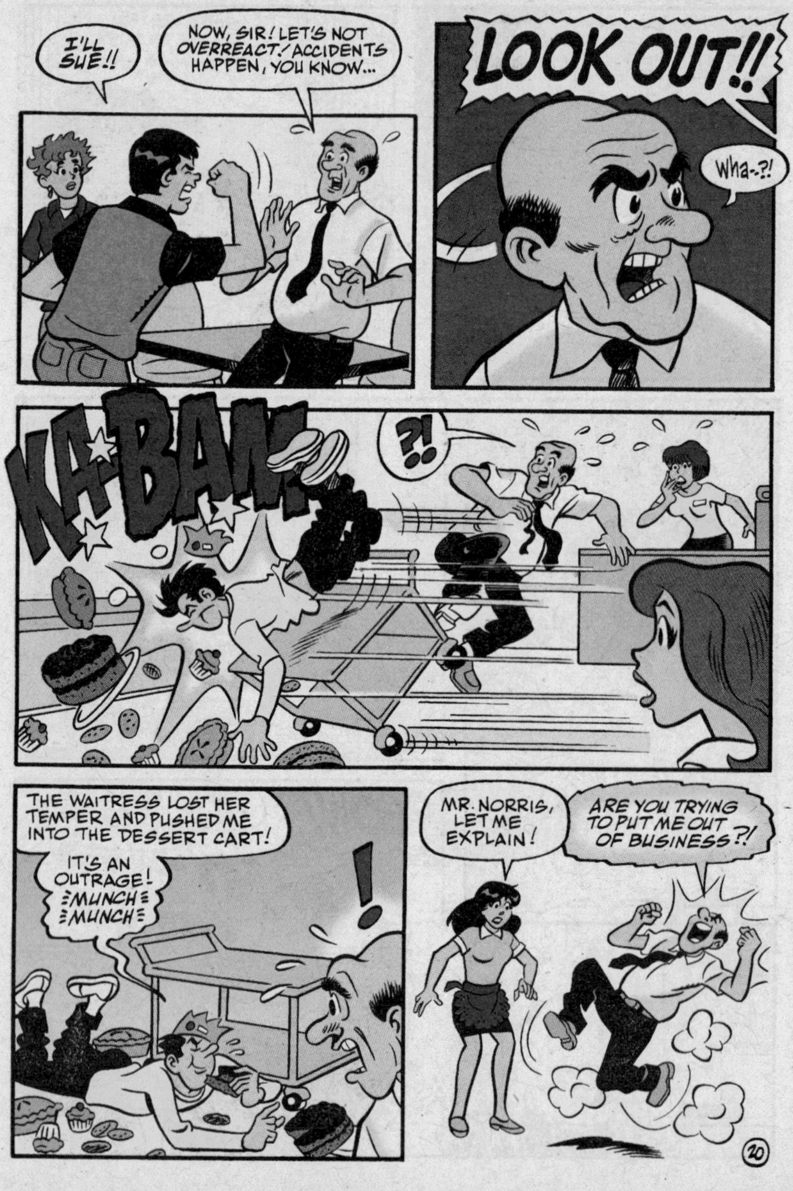
I'LL SUE!!
NOW, SIR! LET'S NOT OVERREACT! ACCIDENTS HAPPEN, YOU KNOW...
LOOK OUT!!
Wha--?!
KA-BAM!
?!
THE WAITRESS LOST HER TEMPER AND PUSHED ME INTO THE DESSERT CART!
IT'S AN OUTRAGE! MUNCH MUNCH
!
MR. NORRIS, LET ME EXPLAIN!
ARE YOU TRYING TO PUT ME OUT OF BUSINESS?!
20

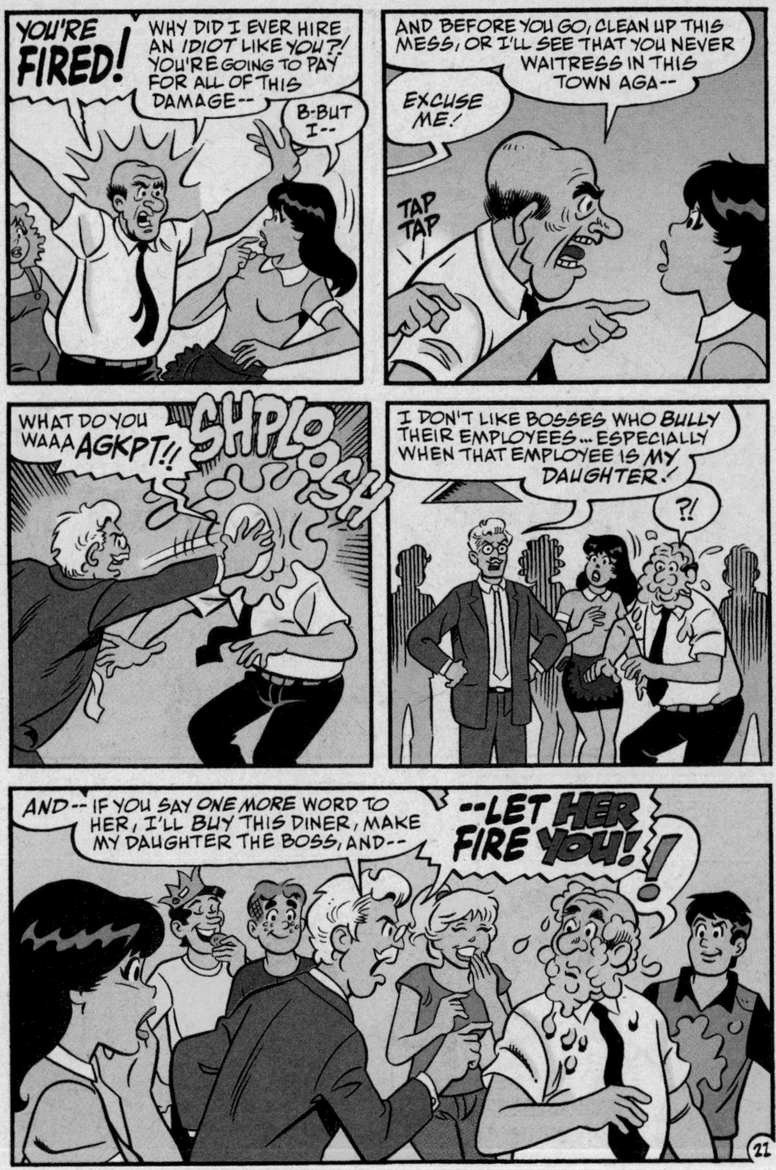
YOU'RE FIRED!
WHY DID I EVER HIRE AN IDIOT LIKE YOU?! YOU'RE GOING TO PAY FOR ALL OF THIS DAMAGE--
B-BUT I--
AND BEFORE YOU GO, CLEAN UP THIS MESS, OR I'LL SEE THAT YOU NEVER WAITRESS IN THIS TOWN AGA--
EXCUSE ME!
TAP TAP
WHAT DO YOU WAAAAGKPT!!
SHPLOOSH
I DON'T LIKE BOSSES WHO BULLY THEIR EMPLOYEES... ESPECIALLY WHEN THAT EMPLOYEE IS MY DAUGHTER!
?!
AND-- IF YOU SAY ONE MORE WORD TO HER, I'LL BUY THIS DINER, MAKE MY DAUGHTER THE BOSS, AND--
--LET HER FIRE YOU!
!
21

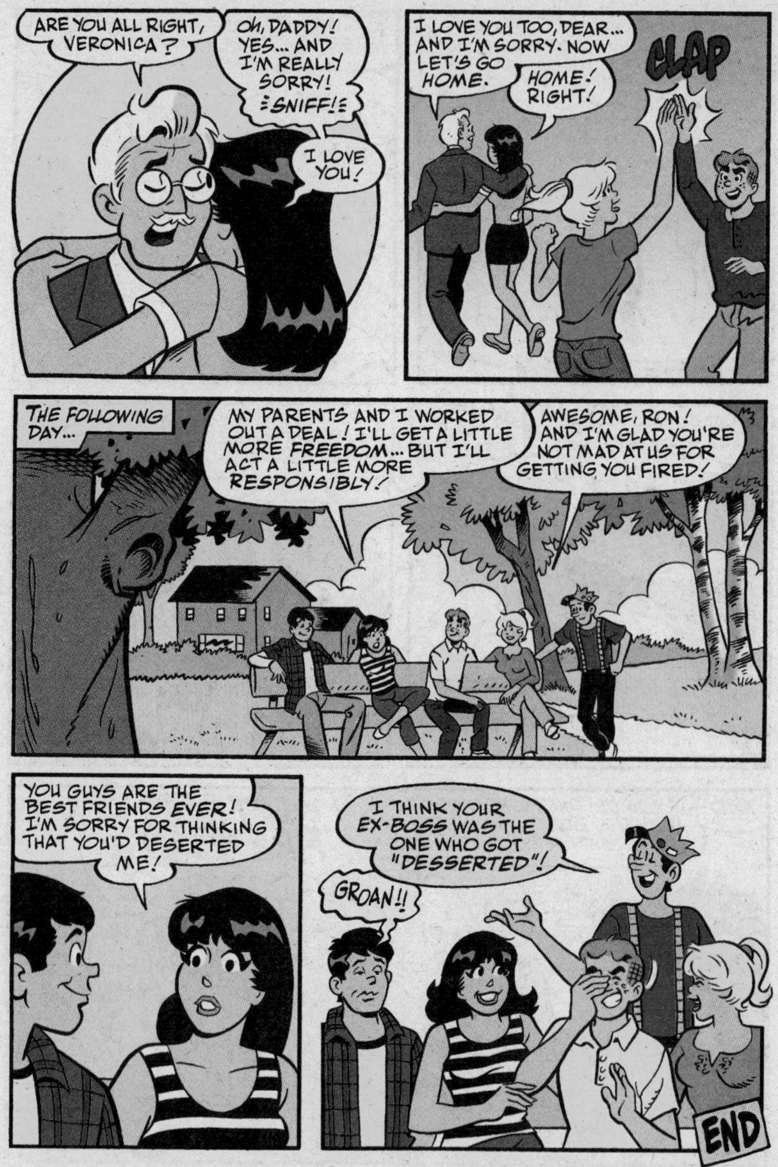
ARE YOU ALL RIGHT, VERONICA?
Oh, DADDY! YES... AND I'M REALLY SORRY! SNIFF!
I LOVE YOU!
I LOVE YOU TOO, DEAR... AND I'M SORRY. NOW LET'S GO HOME.
HOME! RIGHT!
CLAP
THE FOLLOWING DAY...
MY PARENTS AND I WORKED OUT A DEAL! I'LL GET A LITTLE MORE FREEDOM... BUT I'LL ACT A LITTLE MORE RESPONSIBLY!
AWESOME, RON! AND I'M GLAD YOU'RE NOT MAD AT US FOR GETTING YOU FIRED!
YOU GUYS ARE THE BEST FRIENDS EVER! I'M SORRY FOR THINKING THAT YOU'D DESERTED ME!
I THINK YOUR EX-BOSS WAS THE ONE WHO GOT "DESSERTED"!
GROAN!!
END

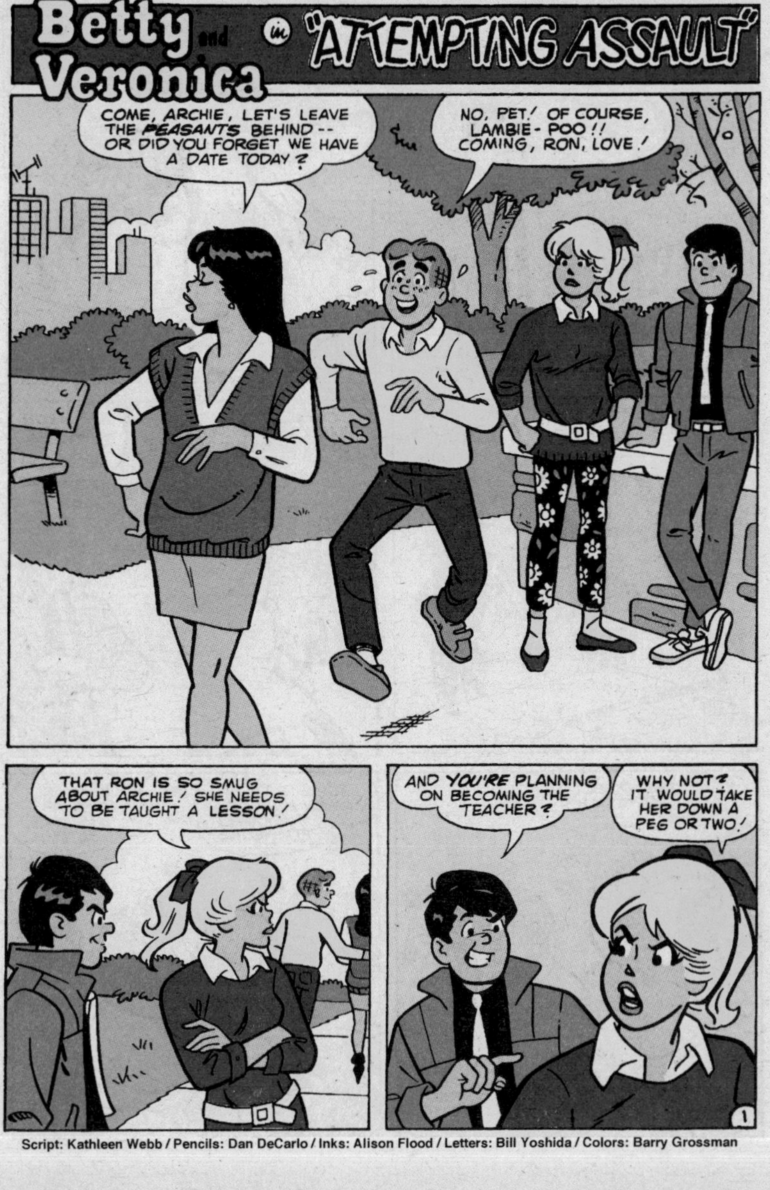
Betty and Veronica in "ATTEMPTING ASSAULT"
COME, ARCHIE, LET'S LEAVE THE PEASANTS BEHIND -- OR DID YOU FORGET WE HAVE A DATE TODAY?
NO, PET! OF COURSE, LAMBIE-POO!! COMING, RON, LOVE!
THAT RON IS SO SMUG ABOUT ARCHIE! SHE NEEDS TO BE TAUGHT A LESSON!
AND YOU'RE PLANNING ON BECOMING THE TEACHER?
WHY NOT? IT WOULD TAKE HER DOWN A PEG OR TWO!
1

Script: Kathleen Webb / Pencils: Dan DeCarlo / Inks: Alison Flood / Letters: Bill Yoshida / Colors: Barry Grossman

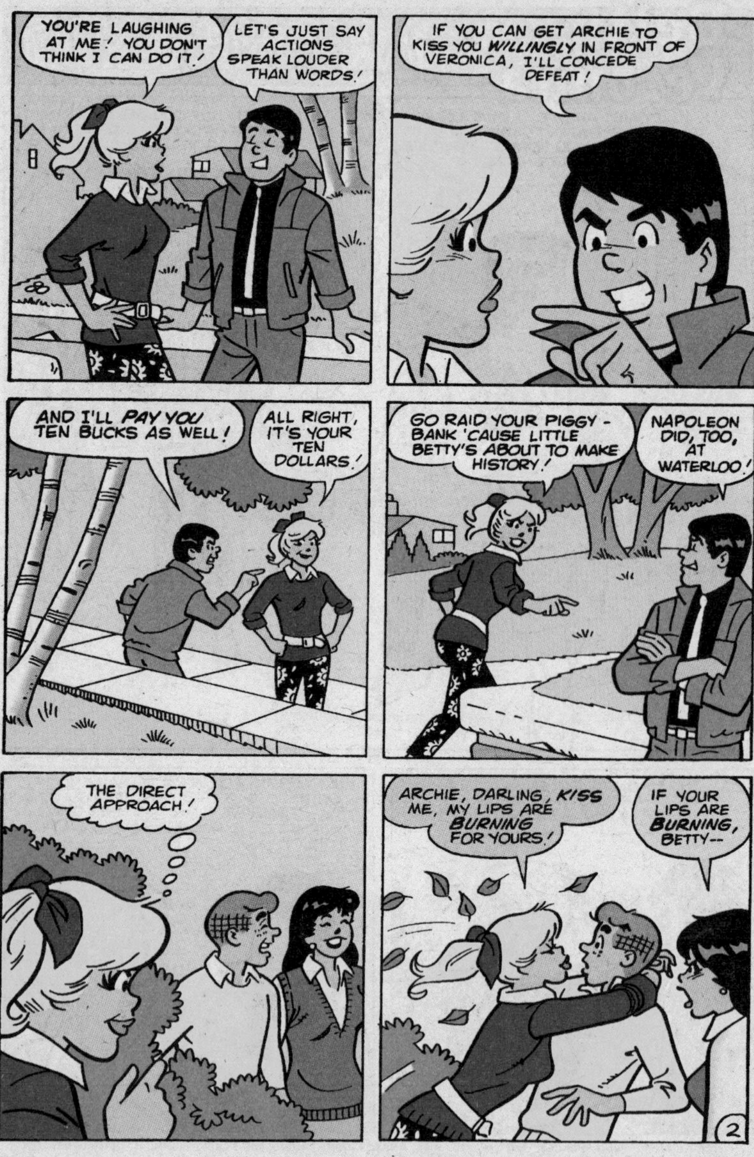
YOU'RE LAUGHING AT ME! YOU DON'T THINK I CAN DO IT!
LET'S JUST SAY ACTIONS SPEAK LOUDER THAN WORDS!
IF YOU CAN GET ARCHIE TO KISS YOU WILLINGLY IN FRONT OF VERONICA, I'LL CONCEDE DEFEAT!
AND I'LL PAY YOU TEN BUCKS AS WELL!
ALL RIGHT, IT'S YOUR TEN DOLLARS!
GO RAID YOUR PIGGY-BANK 'CAUSE LITTLE BETTY'S ABOUT TO MAKE HISTORY!
NAPOLEON DID, TOO, AT WATERLOO!
THE DIRECT APPROACH!
ARCHIE, DARLING, KISS ME, MY LIPS ARE BURNING FOR YOURS!
IF YOUR LIPS ARE BURNING, BETTY--
2

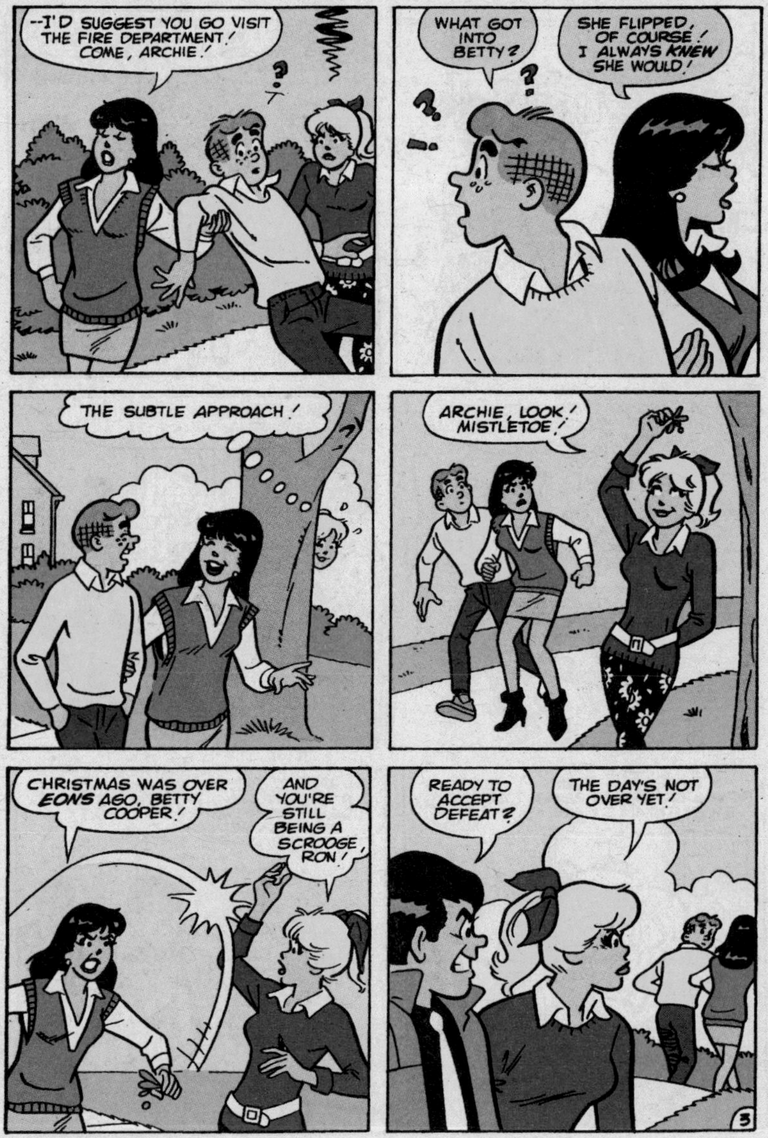
--I'D SUGGEST YOU GO VISIT THE FIRE DEPARTMENT! COME, ARCHIE!
WHAT GOT INTO BETTY?
SHE FLIPPED, OF COURSE! I ALWAYS *KNEW* SHE WOULD!
THE SUBTLE APPROACH!
ARCHIE, LOOK! MISTLETOE!
CHRISTMAS WAS OVER *EONS* AGO, BETTY COOPER!
AND YOU'RE STILL BEING A SCROOGE, RON!
READY TO ACCEPT DEFEAT?
THE DAY'S NOT OVER YET!
3

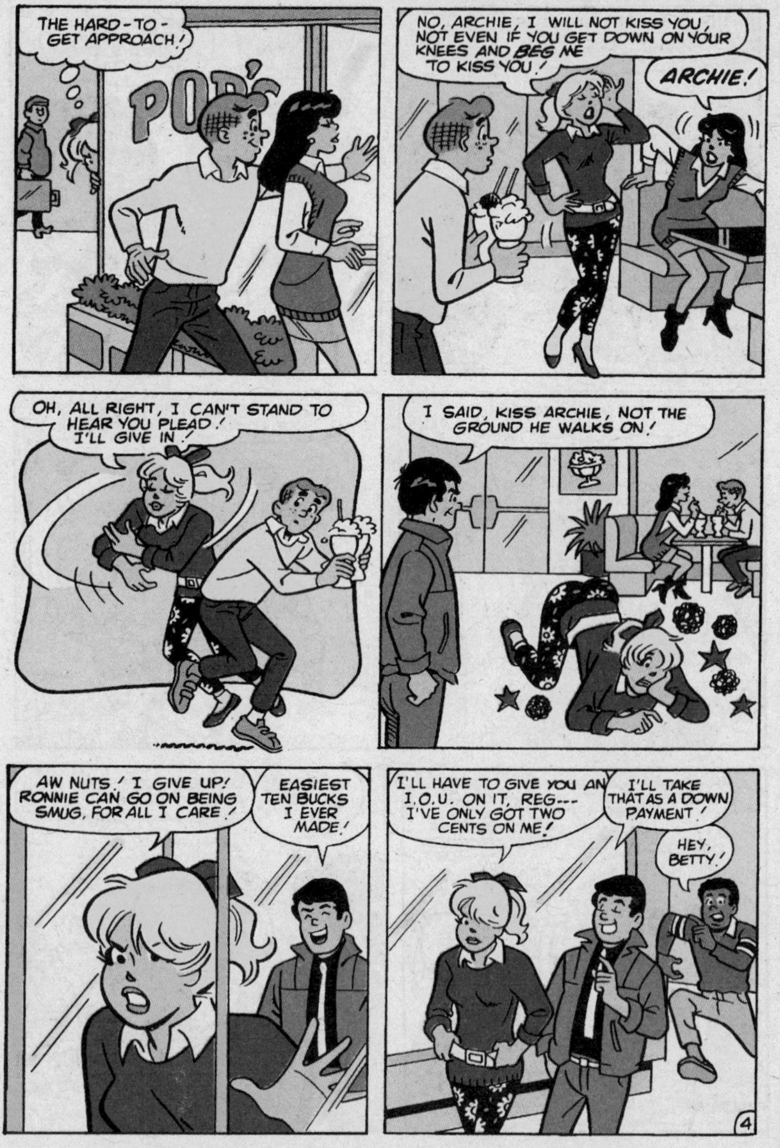
THE HARD-TO-GET APPROACH!
POP'S
NO, ARCHIE, I WILL NOT KISS YOU, NOT EVEN IF YOU GET DOWN ON YOUR KNEES AND BEG ME TO KISS YOU!
ARCHIE!
OH, ALL RIGHT, I CAN'T STAND TO HEAR YOU PLEAD! I'LL GIVE IN!
I SAID, KISS ARCHIE, NOT THE GROUND HE WALKS ON!
AW NUTS! I GIVE UP! RONNIE CAN GO ON BEING SMUG, FOR ALL I CARE!
EASIEST TEN BUCKS I EVER MADE!
I'LL HAVE TO GIVE YOU AN I.O.U. ON IT, REG--- I'VE ONLY GOT TWO CENTS ON ME!
I'LL TAKE THAT AS A DOWN PAYMENT!
HEY, BETTY!
4

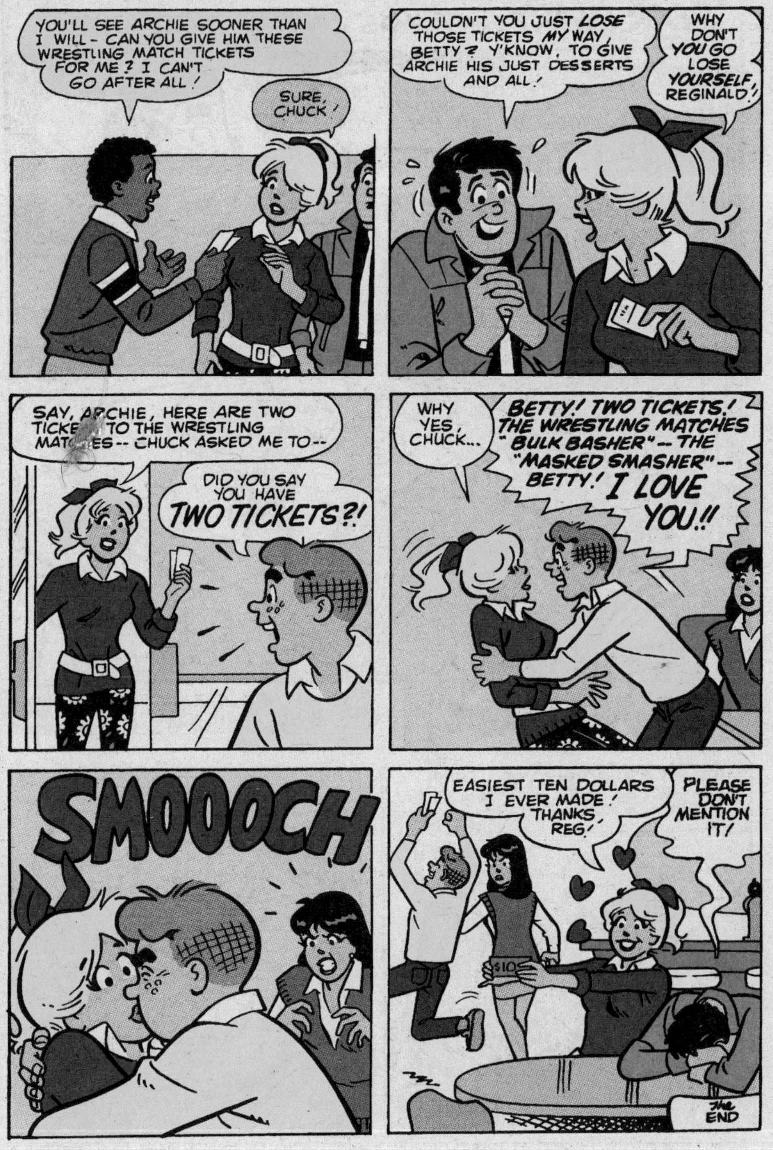
YOU'LL SEE ARCHIE SOONER THAN I WILL - CAN YOU GIVE HIM THESE WRESTLING MATCH TICKETS FOR ME? I CAN'T GO AFTER ALL!
SURE, CHUCK!
COULDN'T YOU JUST LOSE THOSE TICKETS MY WAY, BETTY? Y'KNOW, TO GIVE ARCHIE HIS JUST DESSERTS AND ALL!
WHY DON'T YOU GO LOSE YOURSELF, REGINALD!
SAY, ARCHIE, HERE ARE TWO TICKE TO THE WRESTLING MAT ES -- CHUCK ASKED ME TO--
DID YOU SAY YOU HAVE TWO TICKETS?!
WHY YES, CHUCK...
BETTY! TWO TICKETS! THE WRESTLING MATCHES "BULK BASHER" -- THE "MASKED SMASHER" -- BETTY! I LOVE YOU!!
SMOOOCH
EASIEST TEN DOLLARS I EVER MADE! THANKS, REG!
PLEASE DON'T MENTION IT!
$10
THE END

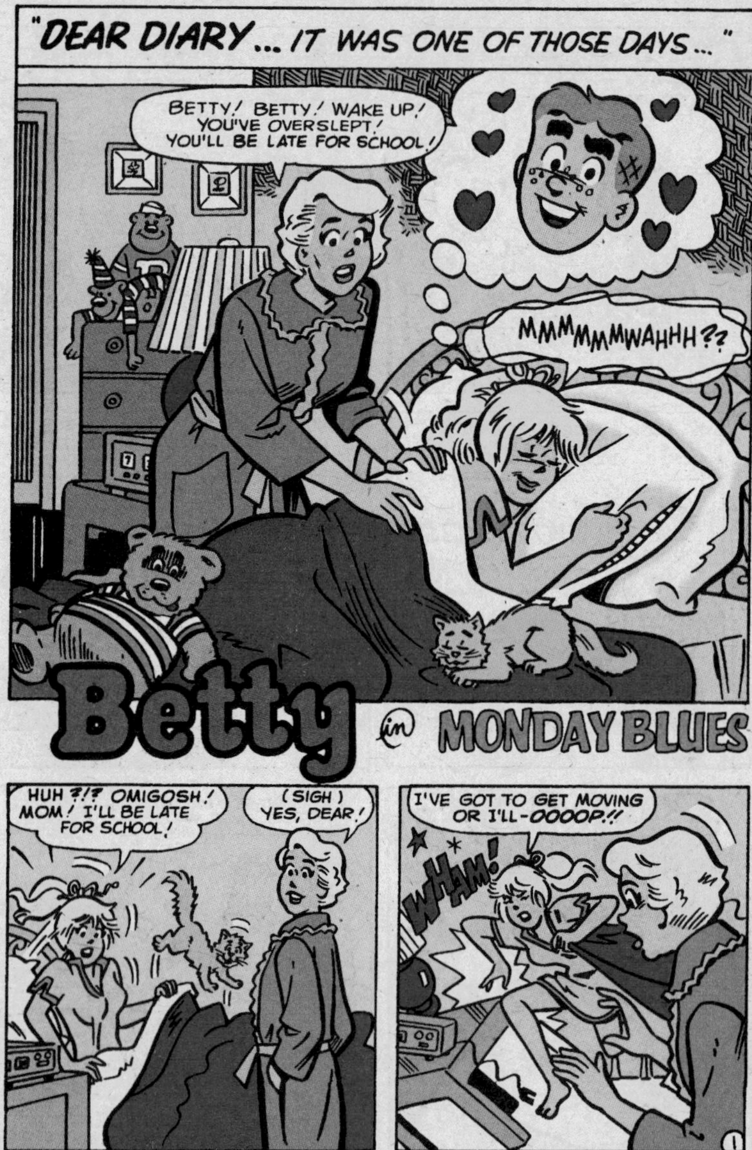
"DEAR DIARY... IT WAS ONE OF THOSE DAYS..."
BETTY! BETTY! WAKE UP! YOU'VE OVERSLEPT! YOU'LL BE LATE FOR SCHOOL!
MMMMMMMWAHHH??
Betty in MONDAY BLUES
HUH ?!? OMIGOSH! MOM! I'LL BE LATE FOR SCHOOL!
(SIGH) YES, DEAR!
I'VE GOT TO GET MOVING OR I'LL-OOOOP!!
WHAM!
1

Script: Kathleen Webb / Pencils: Stan Goldberg / Inks: Rudy Lapick / Letters: Bill Yoshida / Colors: Barry Grossman

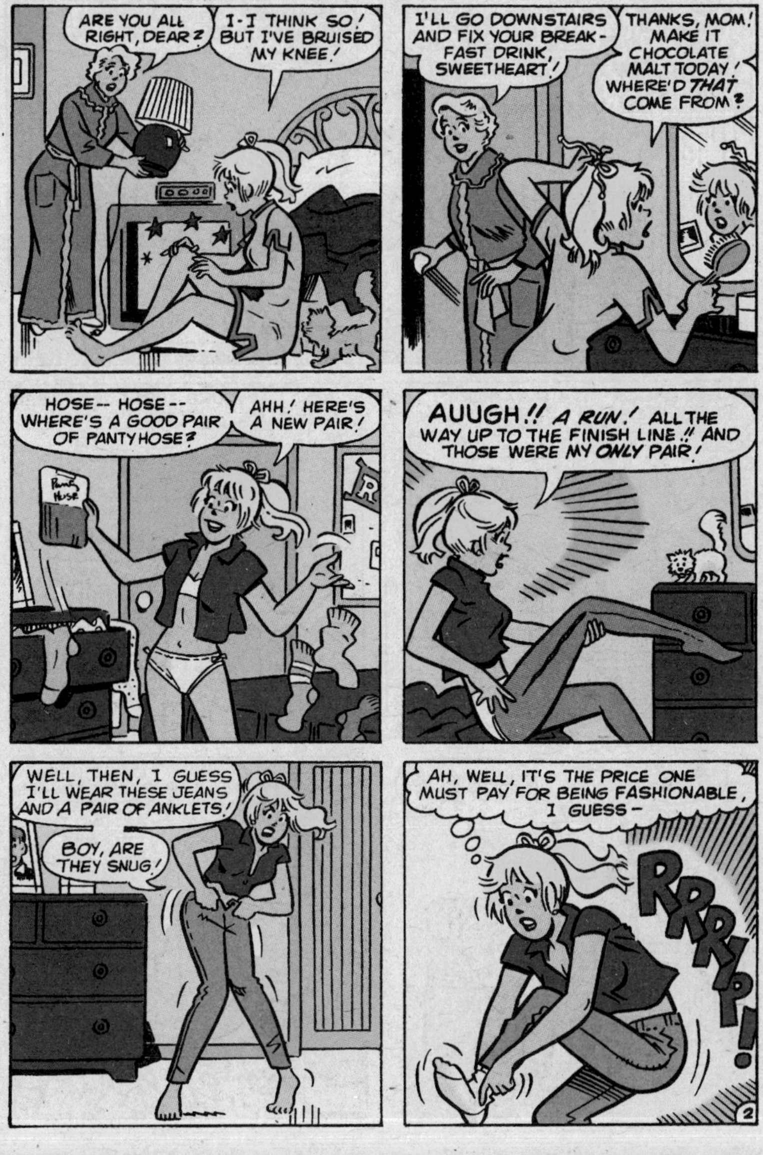
ARE YOU ALL RIGHT, DEAR?
I-I THINK SO! BUT I'VE BRUISED MY KNEE!
I'LL GO DOWNSTAIRS AND FIX YOUR BREAK-FAST DRINK, SWEETHEART!
THANKS, MOM! MAKE IT CHOCOLATE MALT TODAY! WHERE'D *THAT* COME FROM?
HOSE-- HOSE-- WHERE'S A GOOD PAIR OF PANTYHOSE?
AHH! HERE'S A NEW PAIR!
PANTY HOSE
AUUGH!! *A RUN!* ALL THE WAY UP TO THE FINISH LINE!! AND THOSE WERE MY *ONLY* PAIR!
WELL, THEN, I GUESS I'LL WEAR THESE JEANS AND A PAIR OF ANKLETS!
BOY, ARE THEY SNUG!
AH, WELL, IT'S THE PRICE ONE MUST PAY FOR BEING FASHIONABLE, I GUESS-
RRRIP!
2

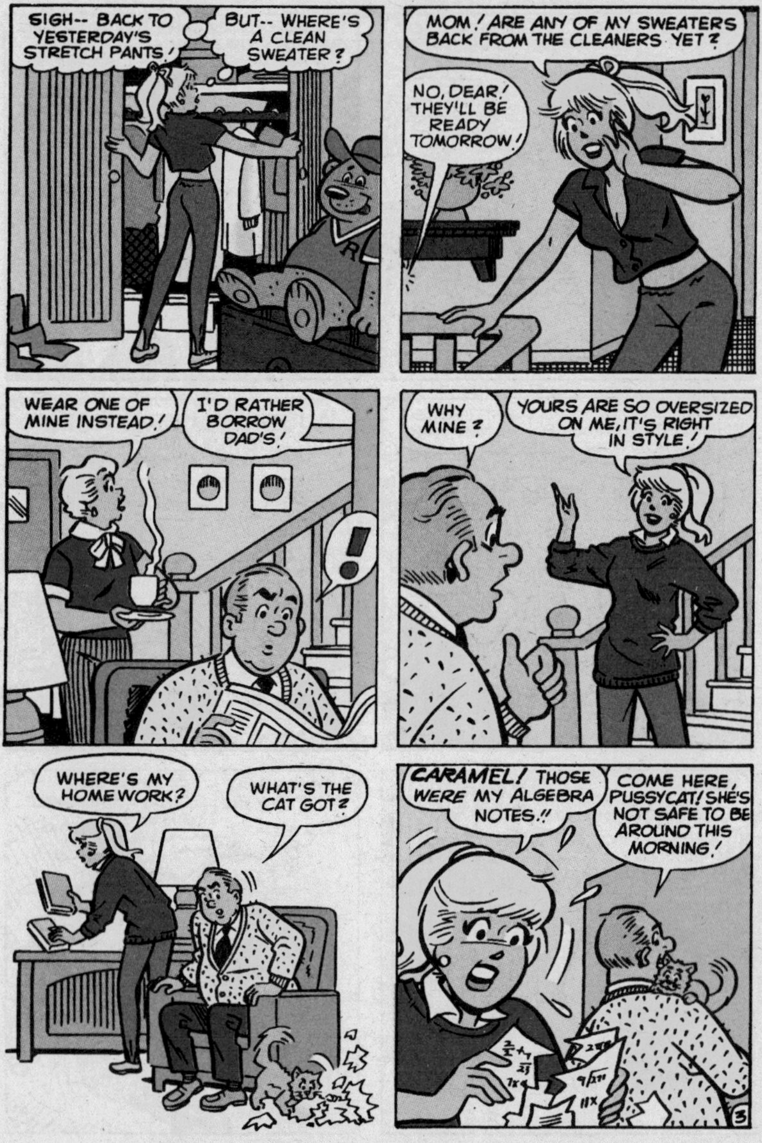
SIGH-- BACK TO YESTERDAY'S STRETCH PANTS!
BUT-- WHERE'S A CLEAN SWEATER?
MOM! ARE ANY OF MY SWEATERS BACK FROM THE CLEANERS YET?
NO, DEAR! THEY'LL BE READY TOMORROW!
WEAR ONE OF MINE INSTEAD!
I'D RATHER BORROW DAD'S!
!
WHY MINE?
YOURS ARE SO OVERSIZED ON ME, IT'S RIGHT IN STYLE!
WHERE'S MY HOMEWORK?
WHAT'S THE CAT GOT?
CARAMEL! THOSE WERE MY ALGEBRA NOTES.!!
COME HERE, PUSSYCAT! SHE'S NOT SAFE TO BE AROUND THIS MORNING!
3

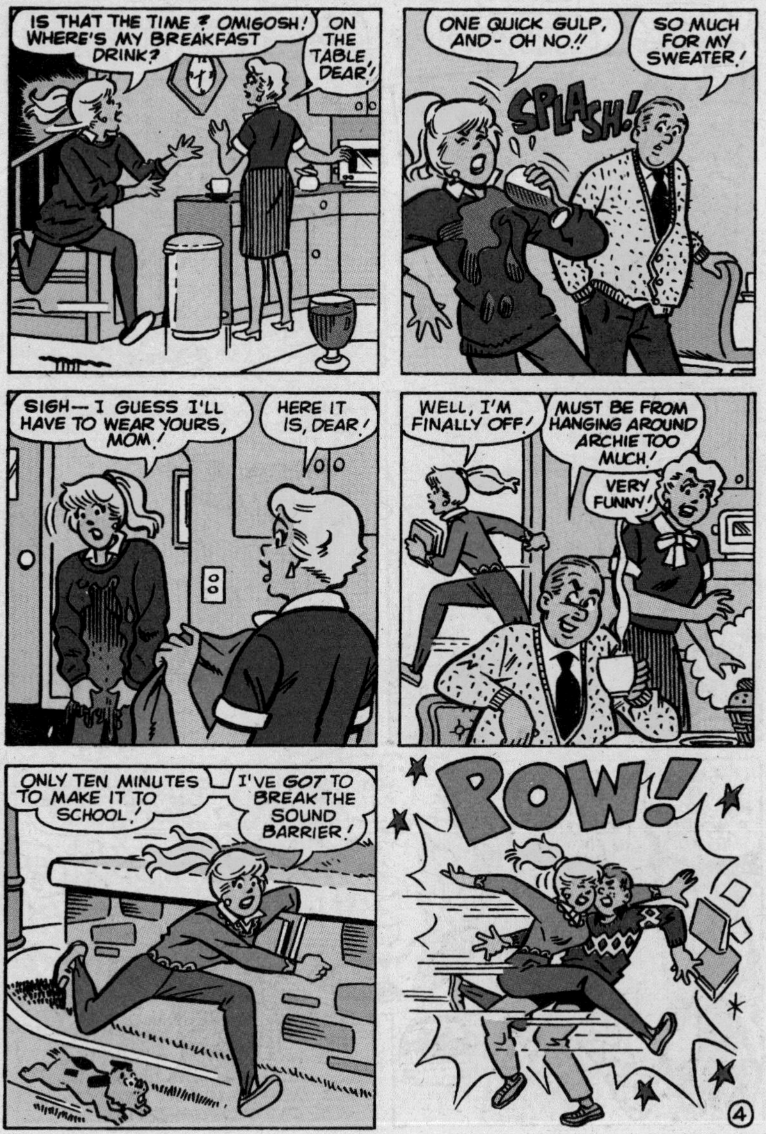
IS THAT THE TIME ? OMIGOSH! WHERE'S MY BREAKFAST DRINK?
ON THE TABLE, DEAR!
ONE QUICK GULP, AND- OH NO!!
SPLASH!
SO MUCH FOR MY SWEATER!
SIGH--- I GUESS I'LL HAVE TO WEAR YOURS, MOM!
HERE IT IS, DEAR!
WELL, I'M FINALLY OFF!
MUST BE FROM HANGING AROUND ARCHIE TOO MUCH!
VERY FUNNY!
ONLY TEN MINUTES TO MAKE IT TO SCHOOL!
I'VE GOT TO BREAK THE SOUND BARRIER!
POW!
4

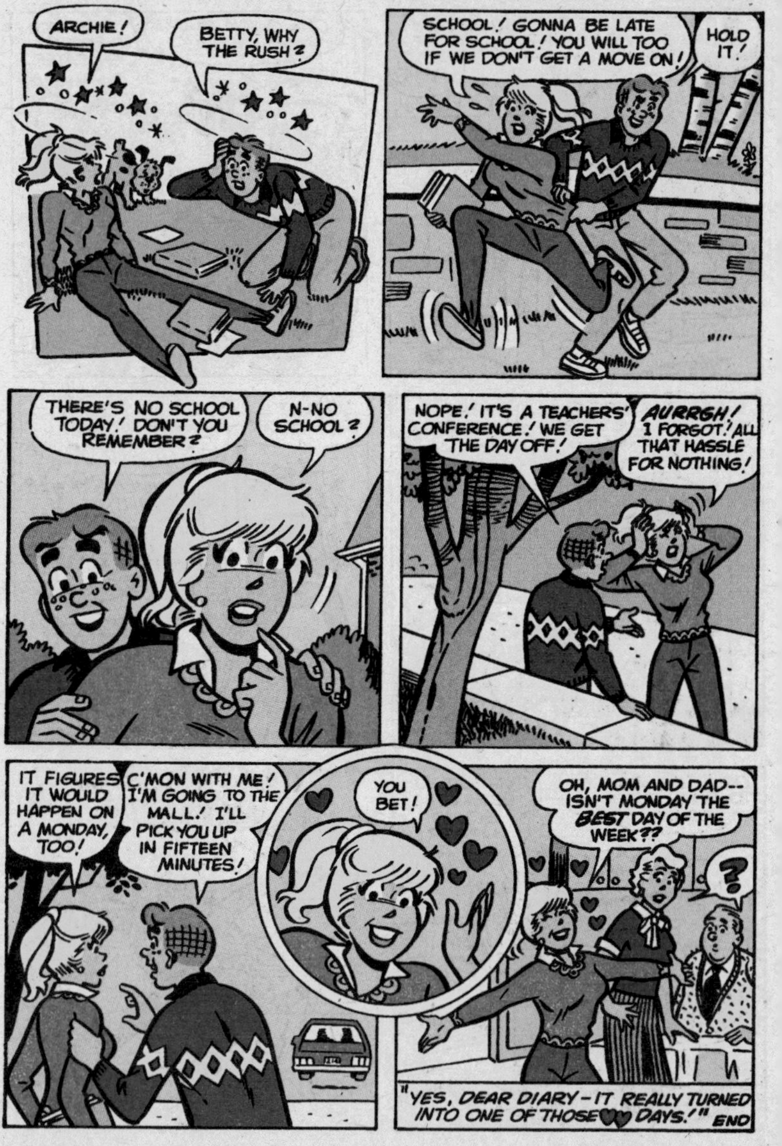
ARCHIE!
BETTY, WHY THE RUSH?
SCHOOL! GONNA BE LATE FOR SCHOOL! YOU WILL TOO IF WE DON'T GET A MOVE ON!
HOLD IT!
THERE'S NO SCHOOL TODAY! DON'T YOU REMEMBER?
N-NO SCHOOL?
NOPE! IT'S A TEACHERS' CONFERENCE! WE GET THE DAY OFF!
AURRGH! I FORGOT! ALL THAT HASSLE FOR NOTHING!
IT FIGURES IT WOULD HAPPEN ON A MONDAY, TOO!
C'MON WITH ME! I'M GOING TO THE MALL! I'LL PICK YOU UP IN FIFTEEN MINUTES!
YOU BET!
OH, MOM AND DAD-- ISN'T MONDAY THE BEST DAY OF THE WEEK??
?
"YES, DEAR DIARY - IT REALLY TURNED INTO ONE OF THOSE DAYS!" END

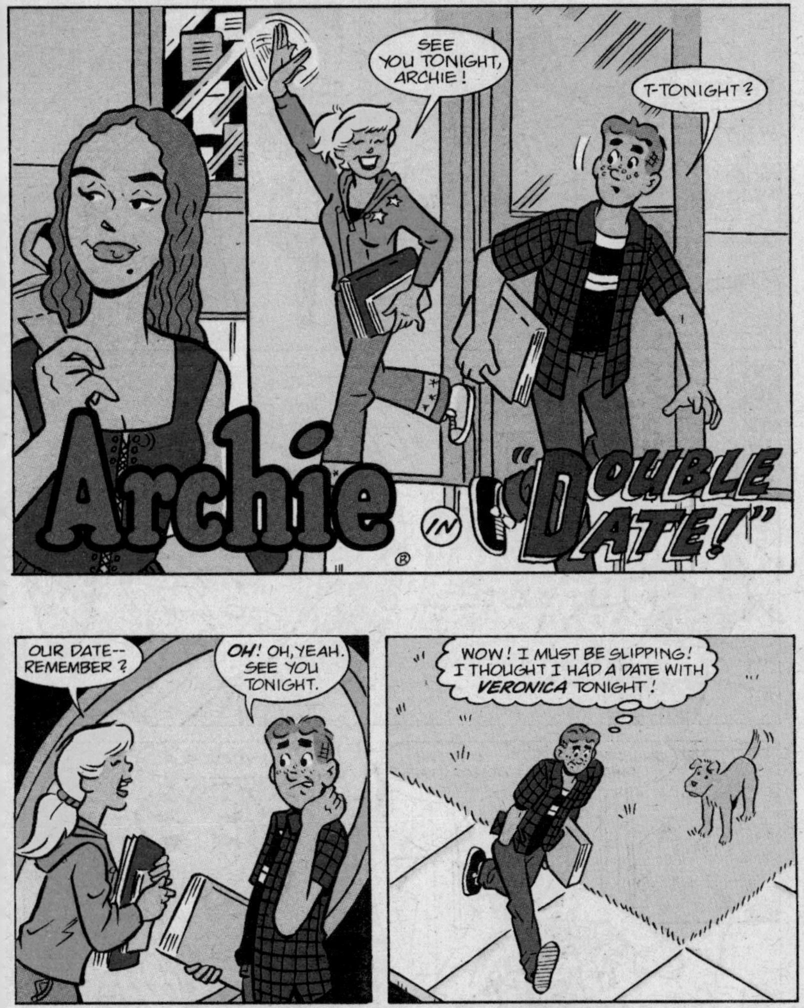
SEE YOU TONIGHT, ARCHIE!
T-TONIGHT?
Archie®
IN
"DOUBLE DATE!"
OUR DATE-- REMEMBER?
OH! OH, YEAH. SEE YOU TONIGHT.
WOW! I MUST BE SLIPPING! I THOUGHT I HAD A DATE WITH VERONICA TONIGHT!

Script: **Greg Crosby** Pencils: **Fernando Ruiz** Inks: **Rudy Lapick**
Letters: **Vickie Williams** Colors: **Barry Grossman**
Editor-In-Chief: **Victor Gorelick** President: **Mike Pellerito** Publisher: **Jon Goldwater**

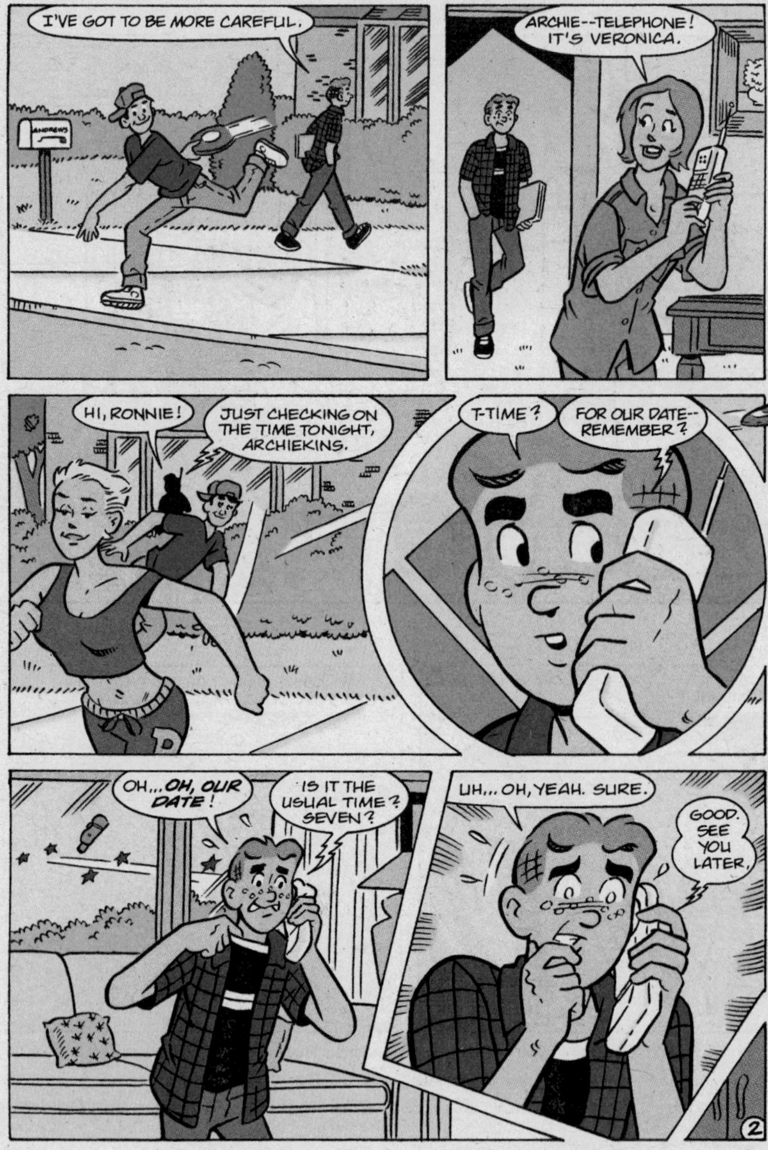
I'VE GOT TO BE MORE CAREFUL.
ANDREWS
ARCHIE--TELEPHONE! IT'S VERONICA.
HI, RONNIE!
JUST CHECKING ON THE TIME TONIGHT, ARCHIEKINS.
T-TIME?
FOR OUR DATE-- REMEMBER?
OH,... OH, OUR DATE!
IS IT THE USUAL TIME? SEVEN?
UH,... OH, YEAH. SURE.
GOOD. SEE YOU LATER.
2

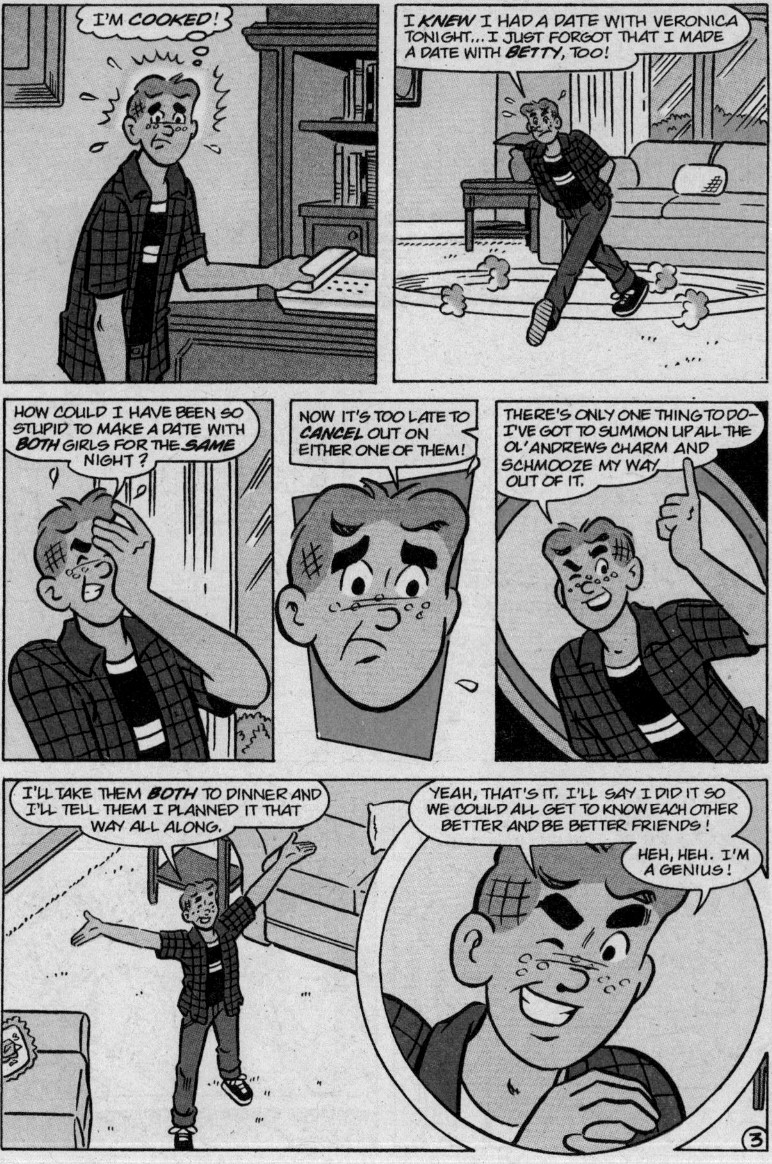
I'M COOKED!
I KNEW I HAD A DATE WITH VERONICA TONIGHT... I JUST FORGOT THAT I MADE A DATE WITH BETTY, TOO!
HOW COULD I HAVE BEEN SO STUPID TO MAKE A DATE WITH BOTH GIRLS FOR THE SAME NIGHT?
NOW IT'S TOO LATE TO CANCEL OUT ON EITHER ONE OF THEM!
THERE'S ONLY ONE THING TO DO-- I'VE GOT TO SUMMON UP ALL THE OL' ANDREWS CHARM AND SCHMOOZE MY WAY OUT OF IT.
I'LL TAKE THEM BOTH TO DINNER AND I'LL TELL THEM I PLANNED IT THAT WAY ALL ALONG.
YEAH, THAT'S IT. I'LL SAY I DID IT SO WE COULD ALL GET TO KNOW EACH OTHER BETTER AND BE BETTER FRIENDS!
HEH, HEH. I'M A GENIUS!
3

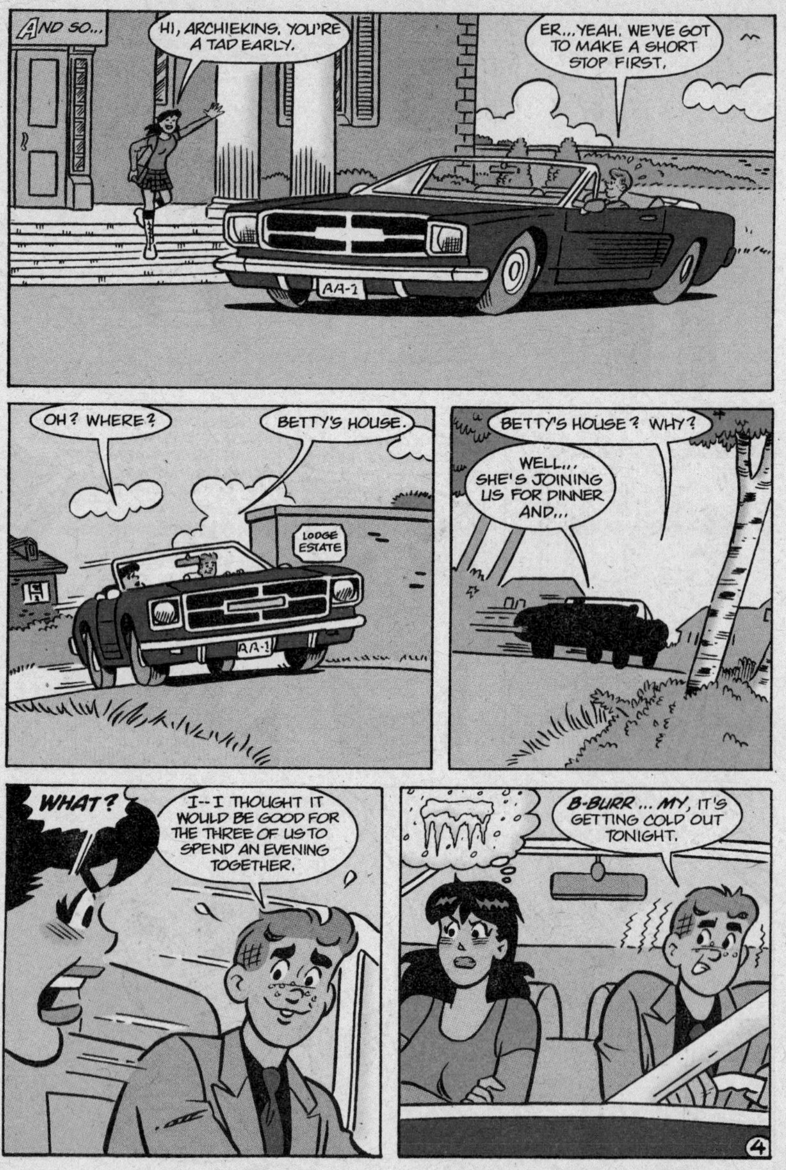
AND SO...
HI, ARCHIEKINS. YOU'RE A TAD EARLY.
ER... YEAH. WE'VE GOT TO MAKE A SHORT STOP FIRST.
AA-1
OH? WHERE?
BETTY'S HOUSE.
LODGE ESTATE
AA-1
BETTY'S HOUSE? WHY?
WELL... SHE'S JOINING US FOR DINNER AND...
WHAT?
I-- I THOUGHT IT WOULD BE GOOD FOR THE THREE OF US TO SPEND AN EVENING TOGETHER.
B-BURR... MY, IT'S GETTING COLD OUT TONIGHT.
4

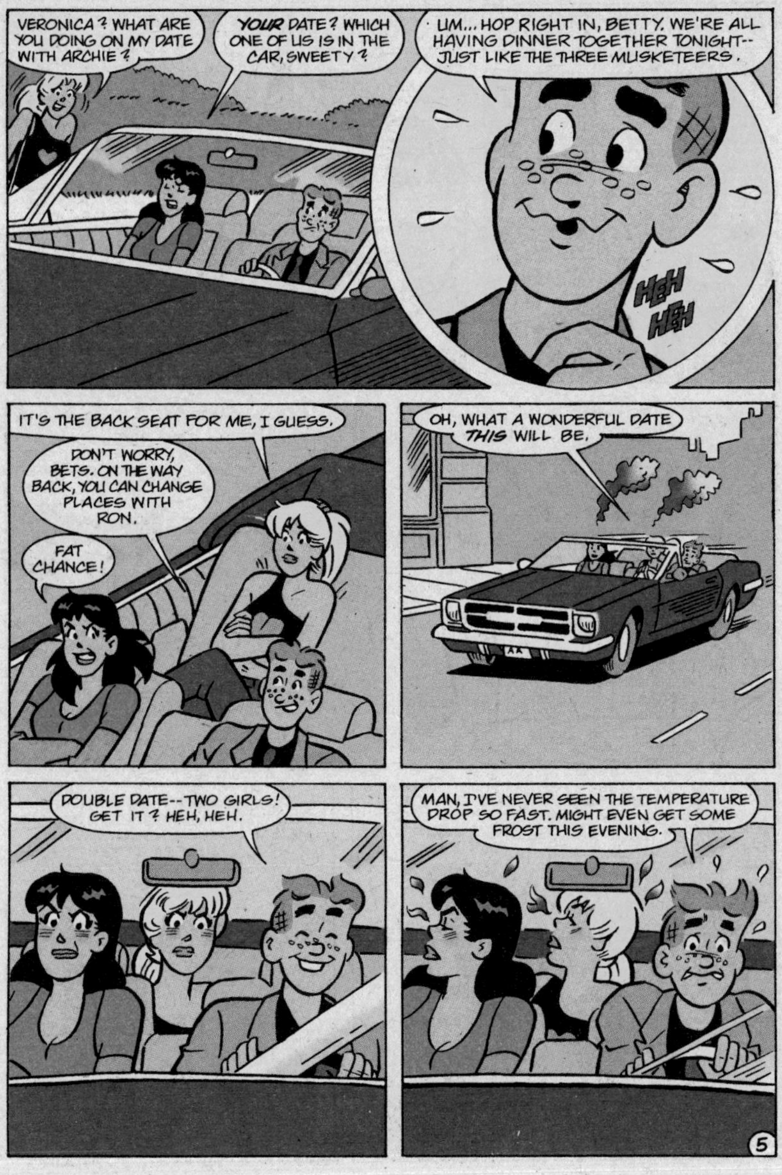
VERONICA? WHAT ARE YOU DOING ON MY DATE WITH ARCHIE?
YOUR DATE? WHICH ONE OF US IS IN THE CAR, SWEETY?
UM... HOP RIGHT IN, BETTY. WE'RE ALL HAVING DINNER TOGETHER TONIGHT-- JUST LIKE THE THREE MUSKETEERS.
HEH HEH
IT'S THE BACK SEAT FOR ME, I GUESS.
DON'T WORRY, BETS. ON THE WAY BACK, YOU CAN CHANGE PLACES WITH RON.
FAT CHANCE!
OH, WHAT A WONDERFUL DATE THIS WILL BE.
DOUBLE DATE--TWO GIRLS! GET IT? HEH, HEH.
MAN, I'VE NEVER SEEN THE TEMPERATURE DROP SO FAST. MIGHT EVEN GET SOME FROST THIS EVENING.

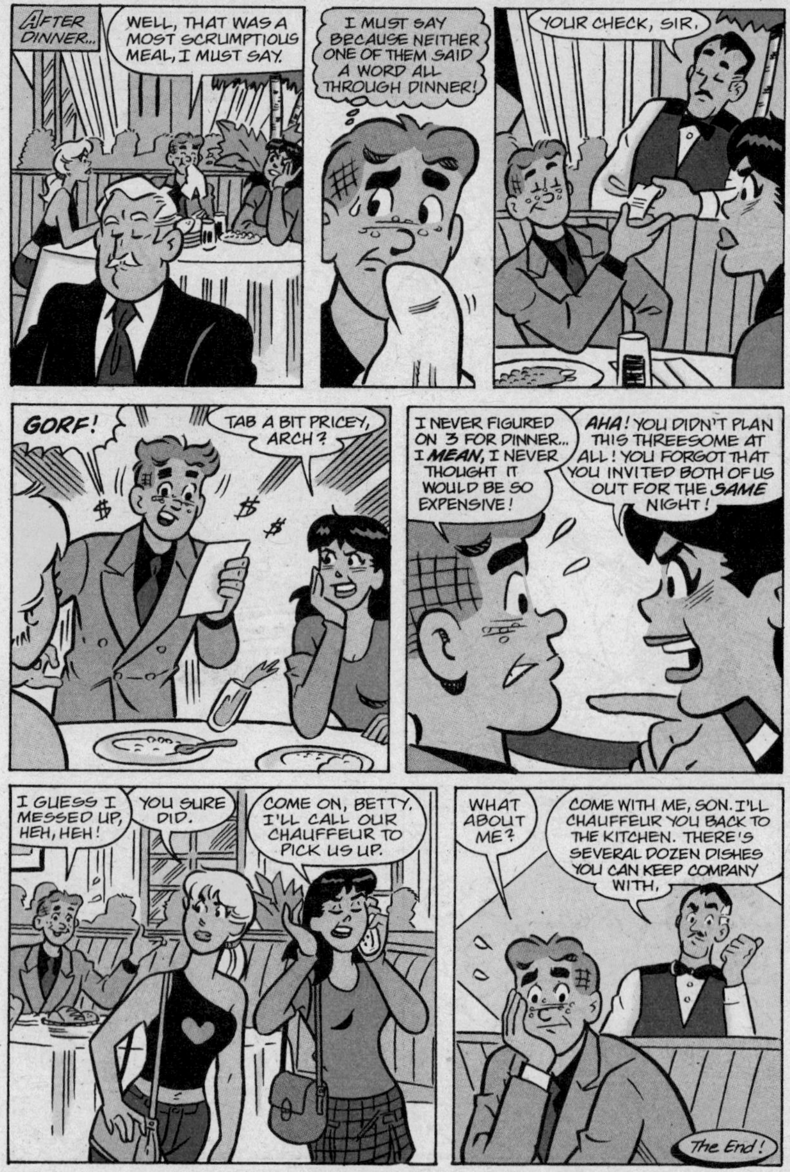

AFTER DINNER...
WELL, THAT WAS A MOST SCRUMPTIOUS MEAL, I MUST SAY.
I MUST SAY BECAUSE NEITHER ONE OF THEM SAID A WORD ALL THROUGH DINNER!
YOUR CHECK, SIR.
GORF!
TAB A BIT PRICEY, ARCH?
I NEVER FIGURED ON 3 FOR DINNER... I MEAN, I NEVER THOUGHT IT WOULD BE SO EXPENSIVE!
AHA! YOU DIDN'T PLAN THIS THREESOME AT ALL! YOU FORGOT THAT YOU INVITED BOTH OF US OUT FOR THE SAME NIGHT!
I GUESS I MESSED UP, HEH, HEH!
YOU SURE DID.
COME ON, BETTY. I'LL CALL OUR CHAUFFEUR TO PICK US UP.
WHAT ABOUT ME?
COME WITH ME, SON. I'LL CHAUFFEUR YOU BACK TO THE KITCHEN. THERE'S SEVERAL DOZEN DISHES YOU CAN KEEP COMPANY WITH.
The End!

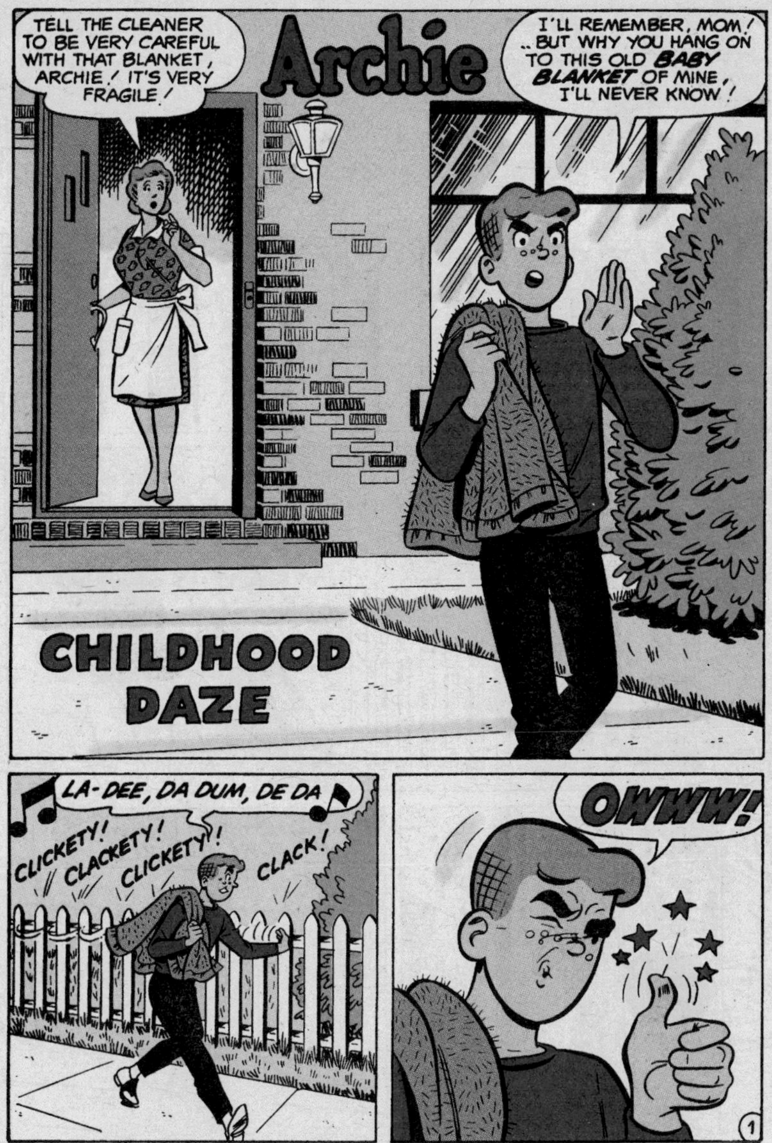
Archie
TELL THE CLEANER TO BE VERY CAREFUL WITH THAT BLANKET, ARCHIE! IT'S VERY FRAGILE!
I'LL REMEMBER, MOM! ..BUT WHY YOU HANG ON TO THIS OLD BABY BLANKET OF MINE, I'LL NEVER KNOW!
CHILDHOOD DAZE
LA-DEE, DA DUM, DE DA
CLICKETY! CLACKETY! CLICKETY! CLACK!
OWWW!
1

Script: Frank Doyle / Pencils: Harry Lucey / Letters: Bill Yoshida / Colors: Barry Grossman

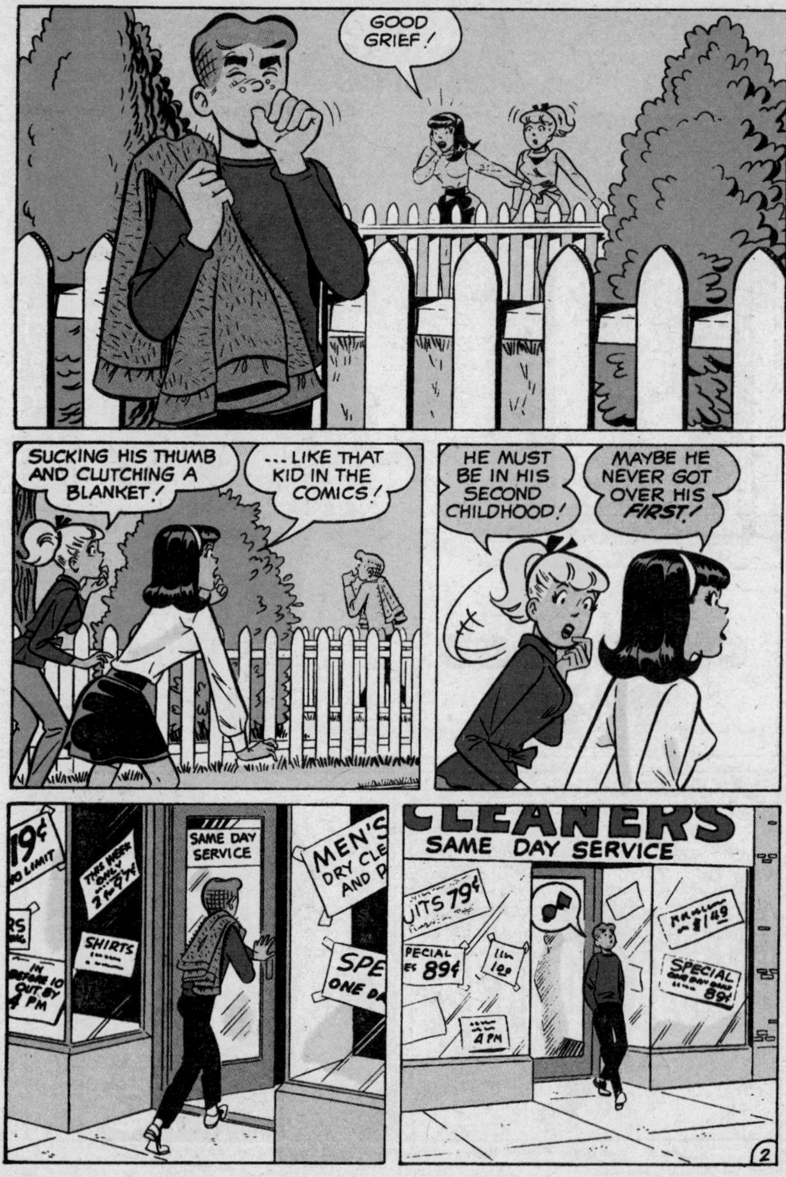
GOOD GRIEF!
SUCKING HIS THUMB AND CLUTCHING A BLANKET!
...LIKE THAT KID IN THE COMICS!
HE MUST BE IN HIS SECOND CHILDHOOD!
MAYBE HE NEVER GOT OVER HIS *FIRST!*
19¢ NO LIMIT
THIS WEEK ONLY
SAME DAY SERVICE
MEN'S DRY CLE AND P
SHIRTS
IN BEFORE 10 OUT BY 4 PM
SPE ONE DA
CLEANERS
SAME DAY SERVICE
UITS 79¢
PECIAL 89¢
4 PM
SPECIAL 89¢

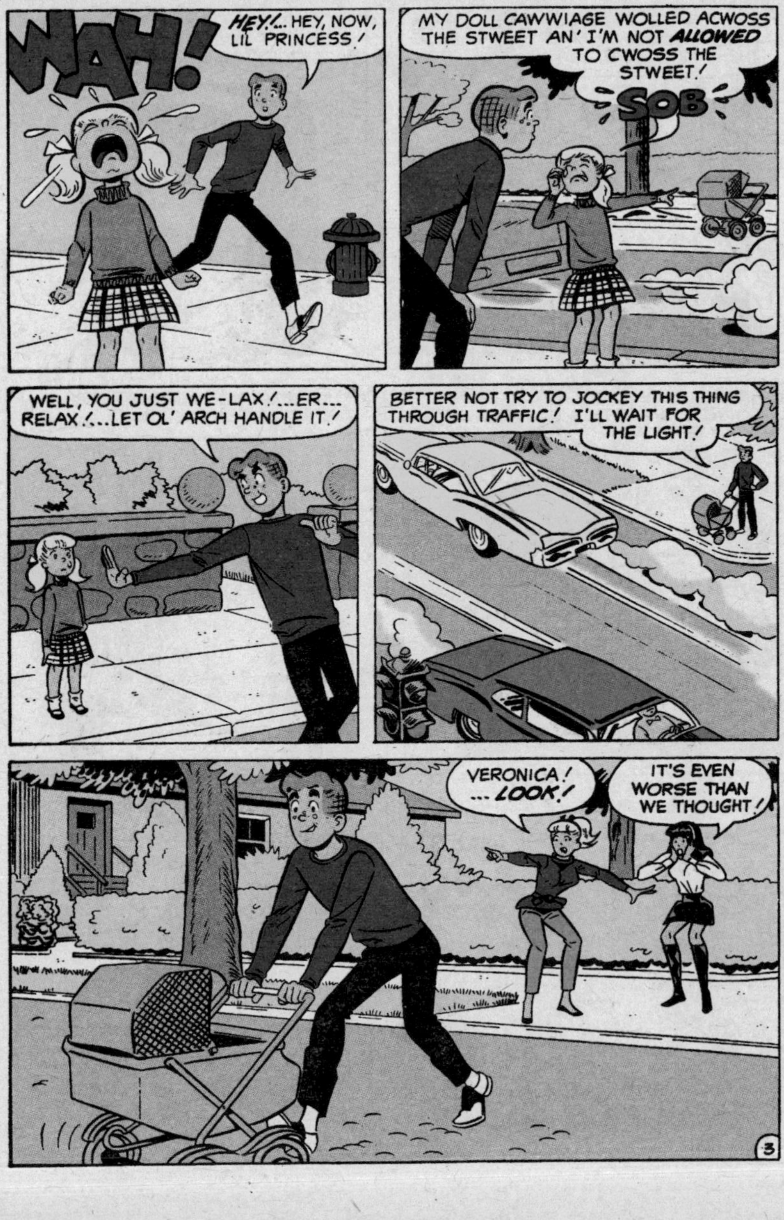
WAH!
HEY!... HEY, NOW, LIL PRINCESS!
MY DOLL CAWWIAGE WOLLED ACWOSS THE STWEET AN' I'M NOT ALLOWED TO CWOSS THE STWEET!
SOB
WELL, YOU JUST WE-LAX!...ER... RELAX!...LET OL' ARCH HANDLE IT!
BETTER NOT TRY TO JOCKEY THIS THING THROUGH TRAFFIC! I'LL WAIT FOR THE LIGHT!
VERONICA! ... LOOK!
IT'S EVEN WORSE THAN WE THOUGHT!

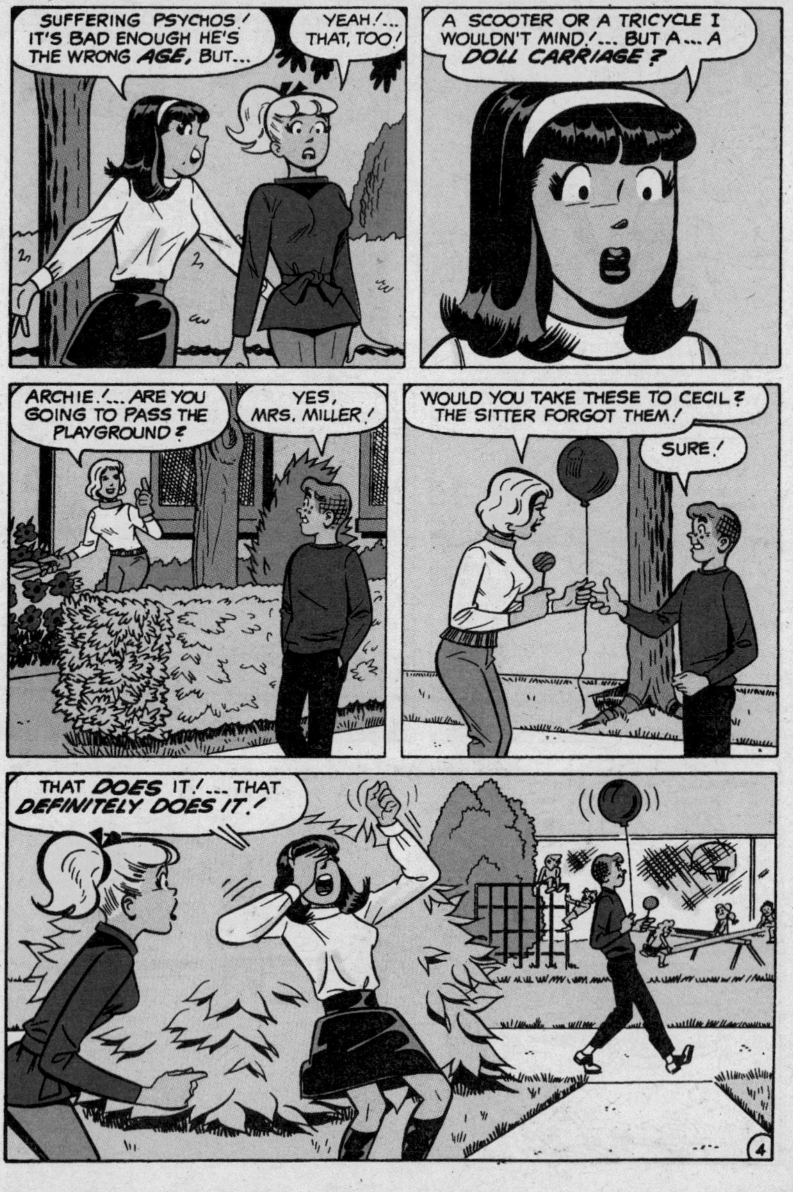
SUFFERING PSYCHOS! IT'S BAD ENOUGH HE'S THE WRONG AGE, BUT...
YEAH!... THAT, TOO!
A SCOOTER OR A TRICYCLE I WOULDN'T MIND!... BUT A... A DOLL CARRIAGE?
ARCHIE!... ARE YOU GOING TO PASS THE PLAYGROUND?
YES, MRS. MILLER!
WOULD YOU TAKE THESE TO CECIL? THE SITTER FORGOT THEM!
SURE!
THAT DOES IT!... THAT DEFINITELY DOES IT!
4

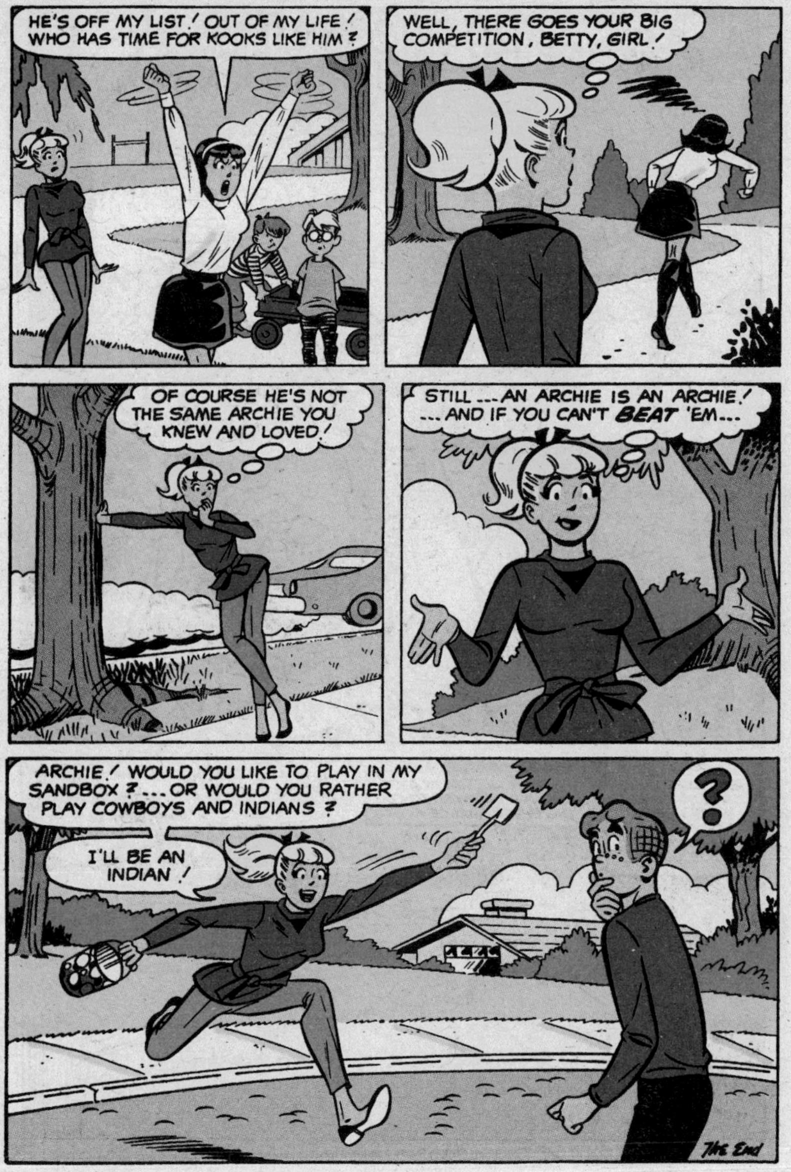
HE'S OFF MY LIST! OUT OF MY LIFE! WHO HAS TIME FOR KOOKS LIKE HIM?
WELL, THERE GOES YOUR BIG COMPETITION, BETTY, GIRL!
OF COURSE HE'S NOT THE SAME ARCHIE YOU KNEW AND LOVED!
STILL ... AN ARCHIE IS AN ARCHIE! ... AND IF YOU CAN'T BEAT 'EM ...
ARCHIE! WOULD YOU LIKE TO PLAY IN MY SANDBOX? ... OR WOULD YOU RATHER PLAY COWBOYS AND INDIANS?
I'LL BE AN INDIAN!
?
The End

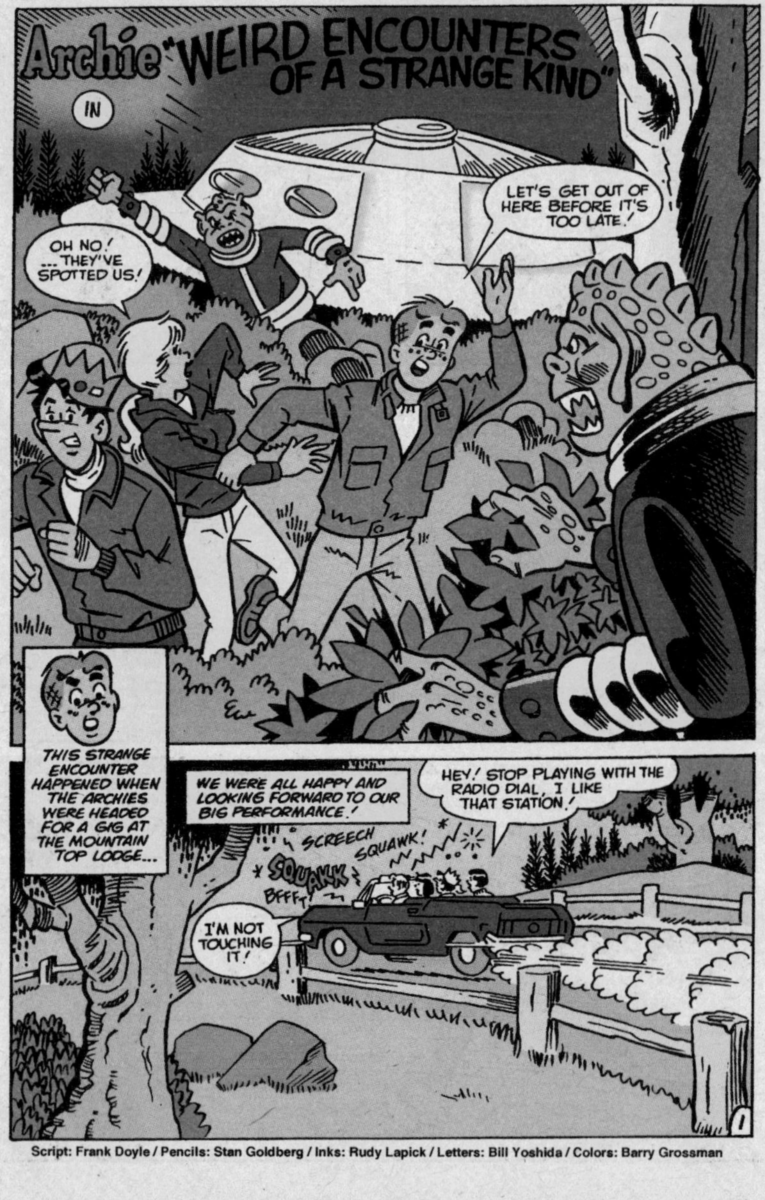
Archie IN "WEIRD ENCOUNTERS OF A STRANGE KIND"
OH NO! ... THEY'VE SPOTTED US!
LET'S GET OUT OF HERE BEFORE IT'S TOO LATE!
THIS STRANGE ENCOUNTER HAPPENED WHEN THE ARCHIES WERE HEADED FOR A GIG AT THE MOUNTAIN TOP LODGE...
WE WERE ALL HAPPY AND LOOKING FORWARD TO OUR BIG PERFORMANCE!
HEY! STOP PLAYING WITH THE RADIO DIAL, I LIKE THAT STATION!
SCREECH
SQUAWK!
SQUAWK
BFFFT
I'M NOT TOUCHING IT!
1

Script: Frank Doyle / Pencils: Stan Goldberg / Inks: Rudy Lapick / Letters: Bill Yoshida / Colors: Barry Grossman

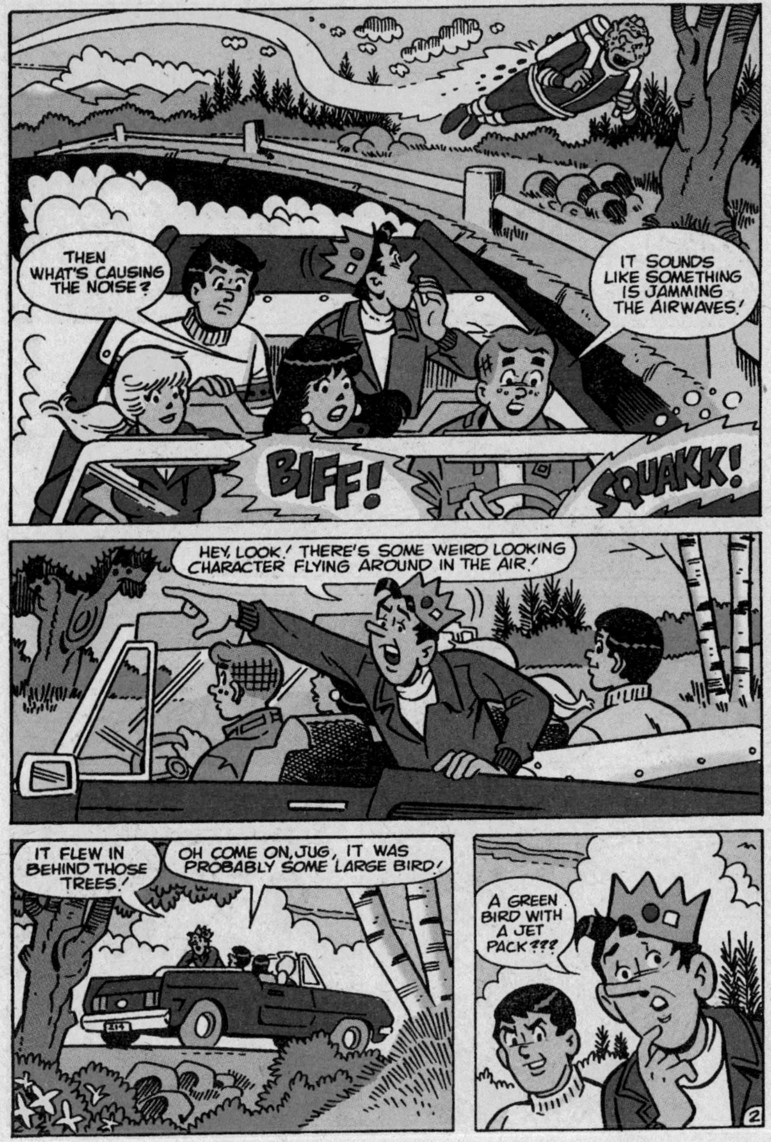
THEN WHAT'S CAUSING THE NOISE?
IT SOUNDS LIKE SOMETHING IS JAMMING THE AIRWAVES!
BIFF!
SQUAKK!
HEY, LOOK! THERE'S SOME WEIRD LOOKING CHARACTER FLYING AROUND IN THE AIR!
IT FLEW IN BEHIND THOSE TREES!
OH COME ON, JUG, IT WAS PROBABLY SOME LARGE BIRD!
A GREEN BIRD WITH A JET PACK???
2

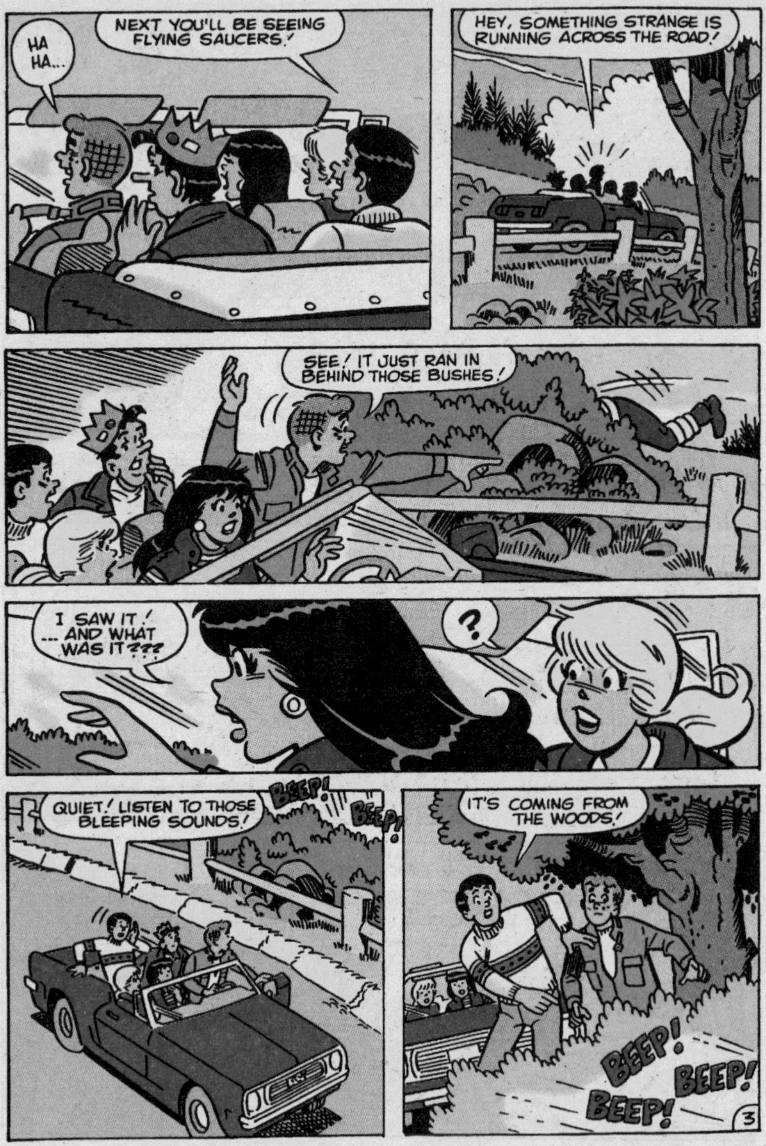
HA HA...
NEXT YOU'LL BE SEEING FLYING SAUCERS!
HEY, SOMETHING STRANGE IS RUNNING ACROSS THE ROAD!
SEE! IT JUST RAN IN BEHIND THOSE BUSHES!
I SAW IT! ... AND WHAT WAS IT???
?
QUIET! LISTEN TO THOSE BLEEPING SOUNDS!
BEEP!
BEEP!
IT'S COMING FROM THE WOODS!
BEEP!
BEEP!
BEEP!
3

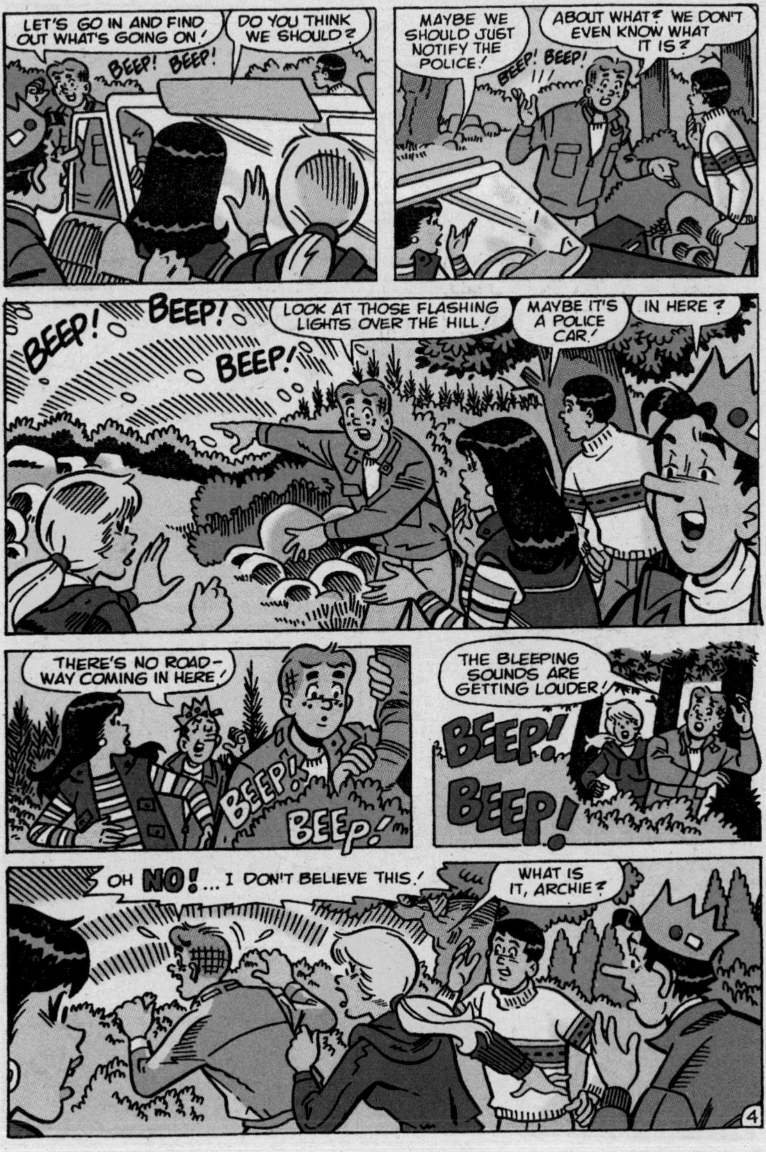
LET'S GO IN AND FIND OUT WHAT'S GOING ON!
DO YOU THINK WE SHOULD?
BEEP! BEEP!
MAYBE WE SHOULD JUST NOTIFY THE POLICE!
ABOUT WHAT? WE DON'T EVEN KNOW WHAT IT IS?
BEEP! BEEP!
BEEP! BEEP!
BEEP!
LOOK AT THOSE FLASHING LIGHTS OVER THE HILL!
MAYBE IT'S A POLICE CAR!
IN HERE?
THERE'S NO ROAD-WAY COMING IN HERE!
BEEP! BEEP!
THE BLEEPING SOUNDS ARE GETTING LOUDER!
BEEP! BEEP!
OH NO!... I DON'T BELIEVE THIS!
WHAT IS IT, ARCHIE?
4

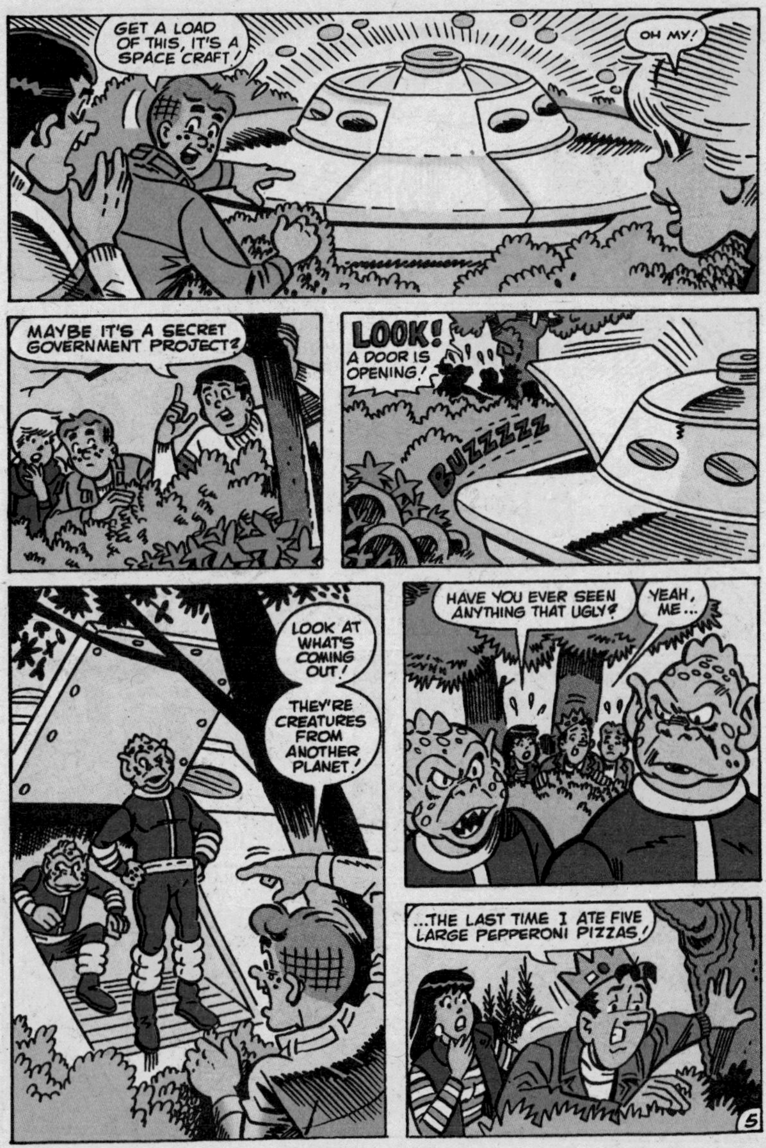
GET A LOAD OF THIS, IT'S A SPACE CRAFT!
OH MY!
MAYBE IT'S A SECRET GOVERNMENT PROJECT?
LOOK! A DOOR IS OPENING!
BUZZZZZZ
LOOK AT WHAT'S COMING OUT!
THEY'RE CREATURES FROM ANOTHER PLANET!
HAVE YOU EVER SEEN ANYTHING THAT UGLY?
YEAH, ME...
...THE LAST TIME I ATE FIVE LARGE PEPPERONI PIZZAS!
5

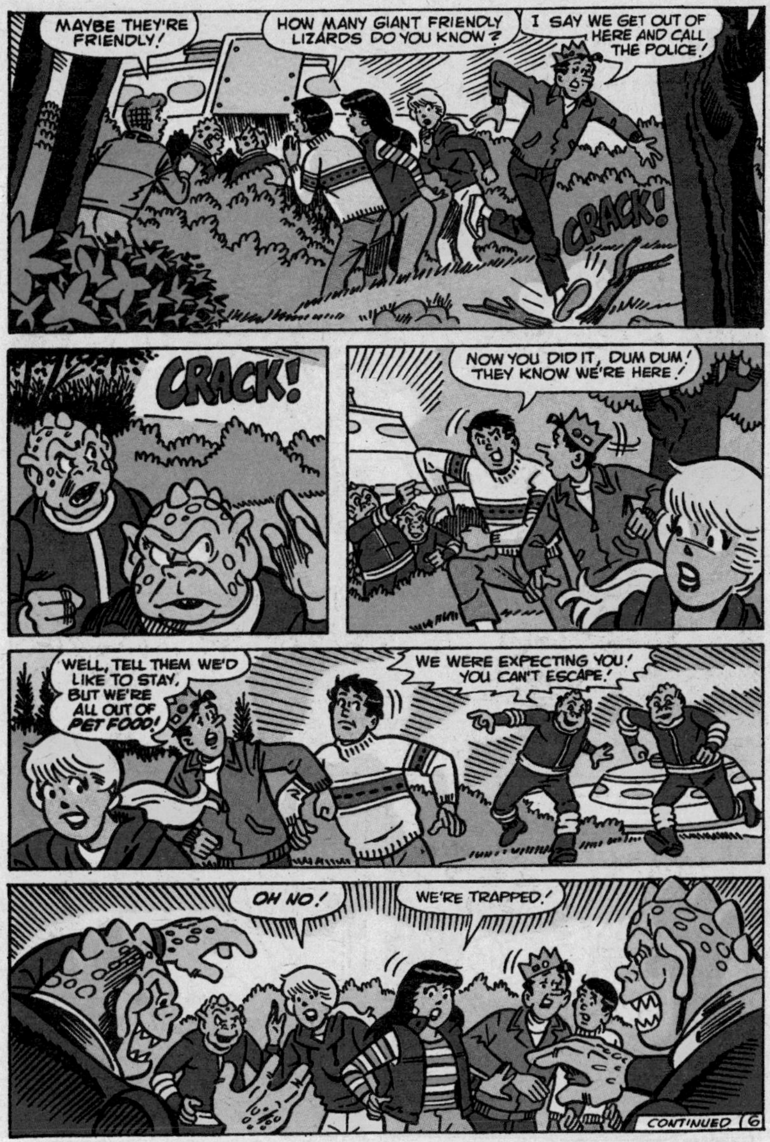
MAYBE THEY'RE FRIENDLY!
HOW MANY GIANT FRIENDLY LIZARDS DO YOU KNOW?
I SAY WE GET OUT OF HERE AND CALL THE POLICE!
CRACK!
CRACK!
NOW YOU DID IT, DUM DUM! THEY KNOW WE'RE HERE!
WELL, TELL THEM WE'D LIKE TO STAY, BUT WE'RE ALL OUT OF PET FOOD!
WE WERE EXPECTING YOU! YOU CAN'T ESCAPE!
OH NO!
WE'RE TRAPPED!
CONTINUED
6

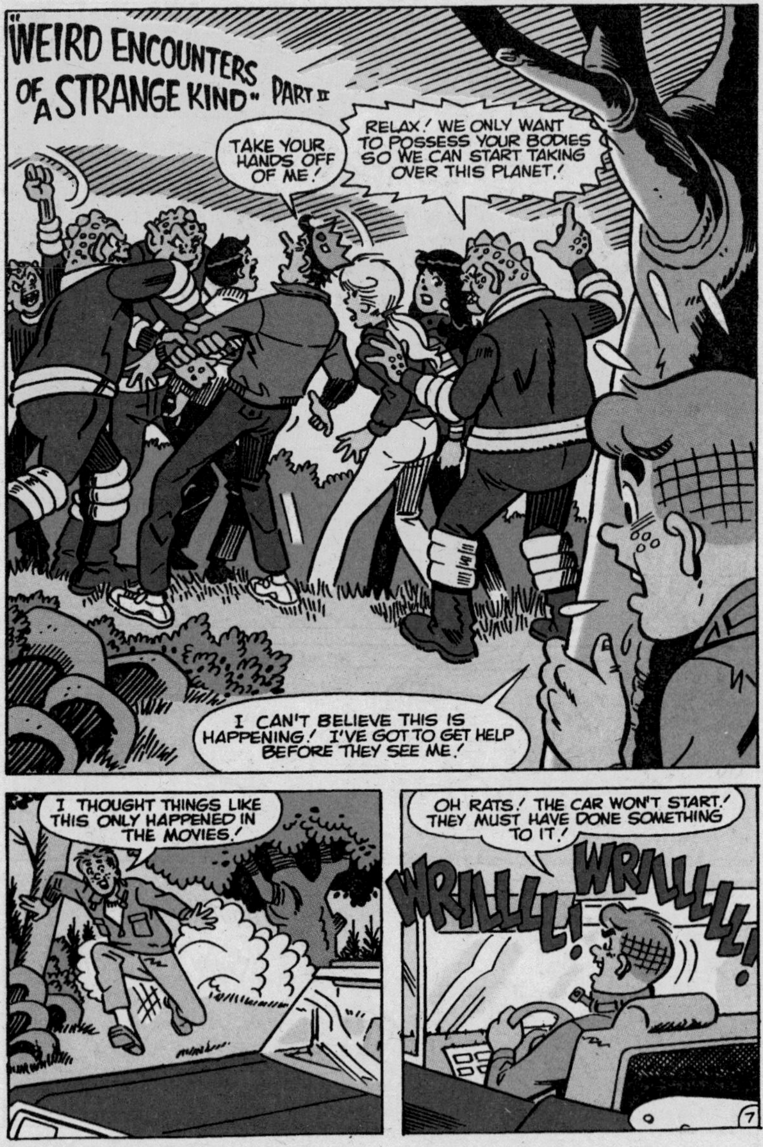
"WEIRD ENCOUNTERS OF A STRANGE KIND" PART II
TAKE YOUR HANDS OFF OF ME!
RELAX! WE ONLY WANT TO POSSESS YOUR BODIES SO WE CAN START TAKING OVER THIS PLANET!
I CAN'T BELIEVE THIS IS HAPPENING! I'VE GOT TO GET HELP BEFORE THEY SEE ME!
I THOUGHT THINGS LIKE THIS ONLY HAPPENED IN THE MOVIES!
OH RATS! THE CAR WON'T START! THEY MUST HAVE DONE SOMETHING TO IT!
WRILLLL!
WRILLLLLL!
7

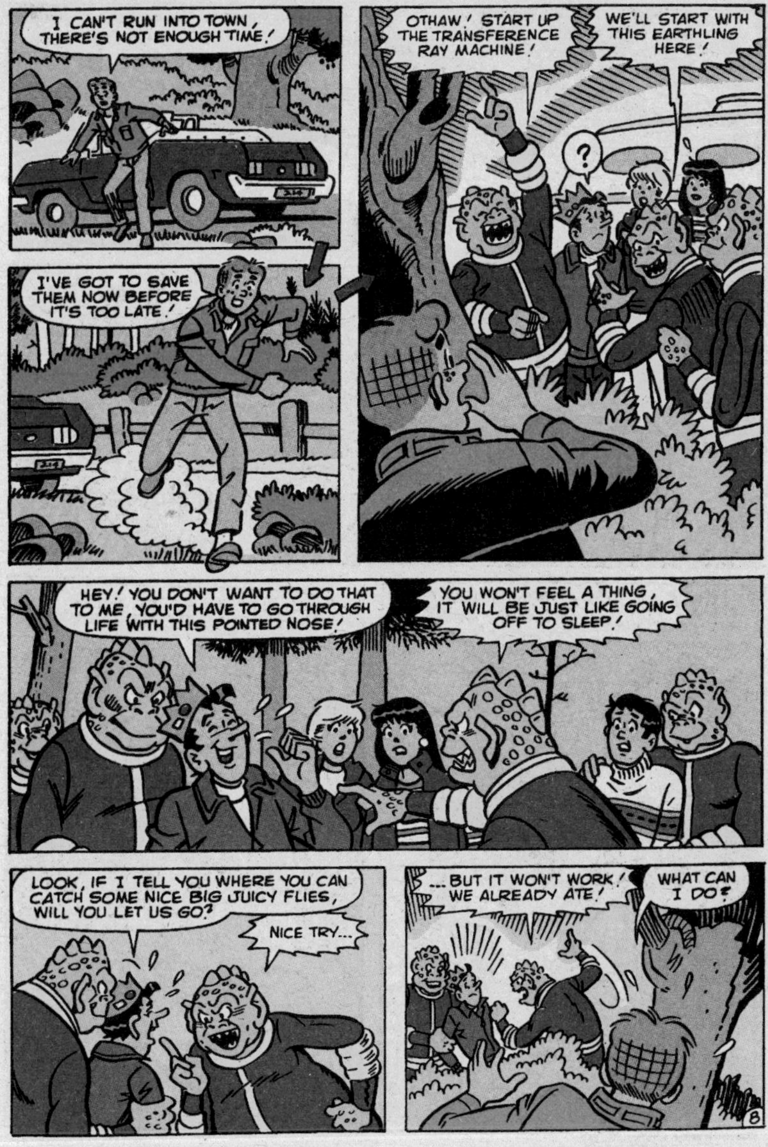
I CAN'T RUN INTO TOWN, THERE'S NOT ENOUGH TIME!
I'VE GOT TO SAVE THEM NOW BEFORE IT'S TOO LATE!
OTHAW! START UP THE TRANSFERENCE RAY MACHINE!
WE'LL START WITH THIS EARTHLING HERE!
?
HEY! YOU DON'T WANT TO DO THAT TO ME, YOU'D HAVE TO GO THROUGH LIFE WITH THIS POINTED NOSE!
YOU WON'T FEEL A THING, IT WILL BE JUST LIKE GOING OFF TO SLEEP!
LOOK, IF I TELL YOU WHERE YOU CAN CATCH SOME NICE BIG JUICY FLIES, WILL YOU LET US GO?
NICE TRY...
... BUT IT WON'T WORK! WE ALREADY ATE!
WHAT CAN I DO?
8

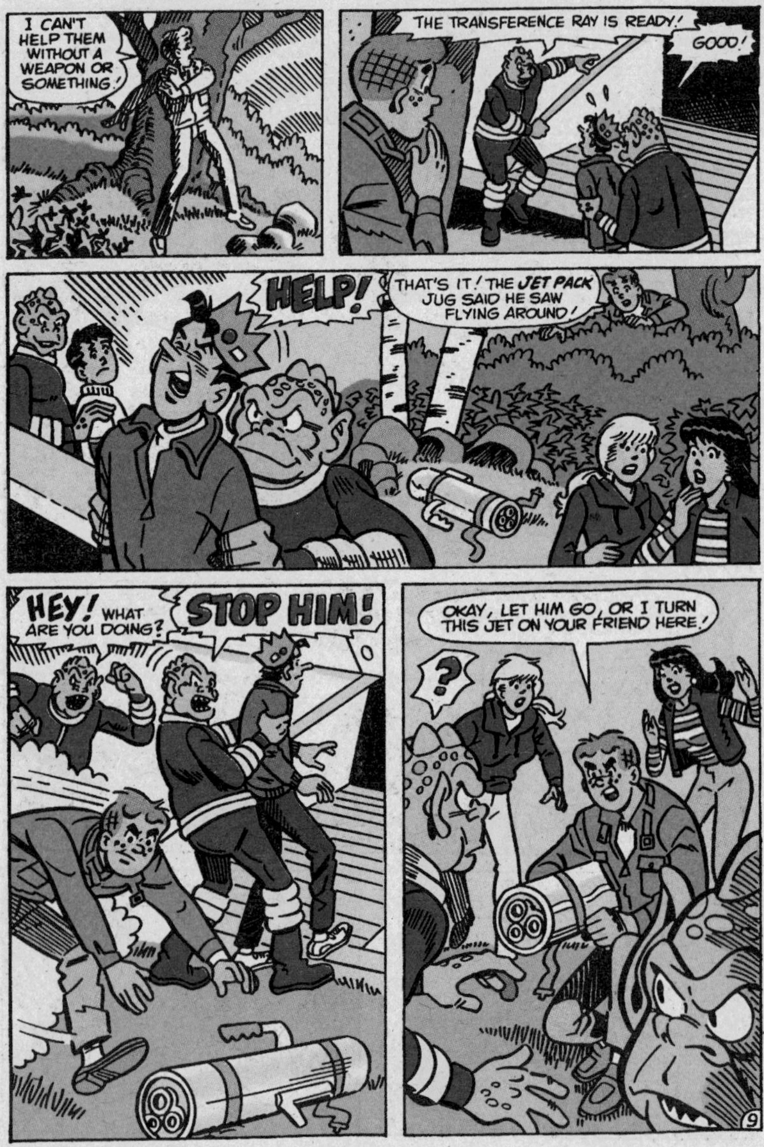
I CAN'T HELP THEM WITHOUT A WEAPON OR SOMETHING!
THE TRANSFERENCE RAY IS READY!
GOOD!
HELP!
THAT'S IT! THE JET PACK JUG SAID HE SAW FLYING AROUND!
HEY! WHAT ARE YOU DOING?
STOP HIM!
OKAY, LET HIM GO, OR I TURN THIS JET ON YOUR FRIEND HERE!
?
9

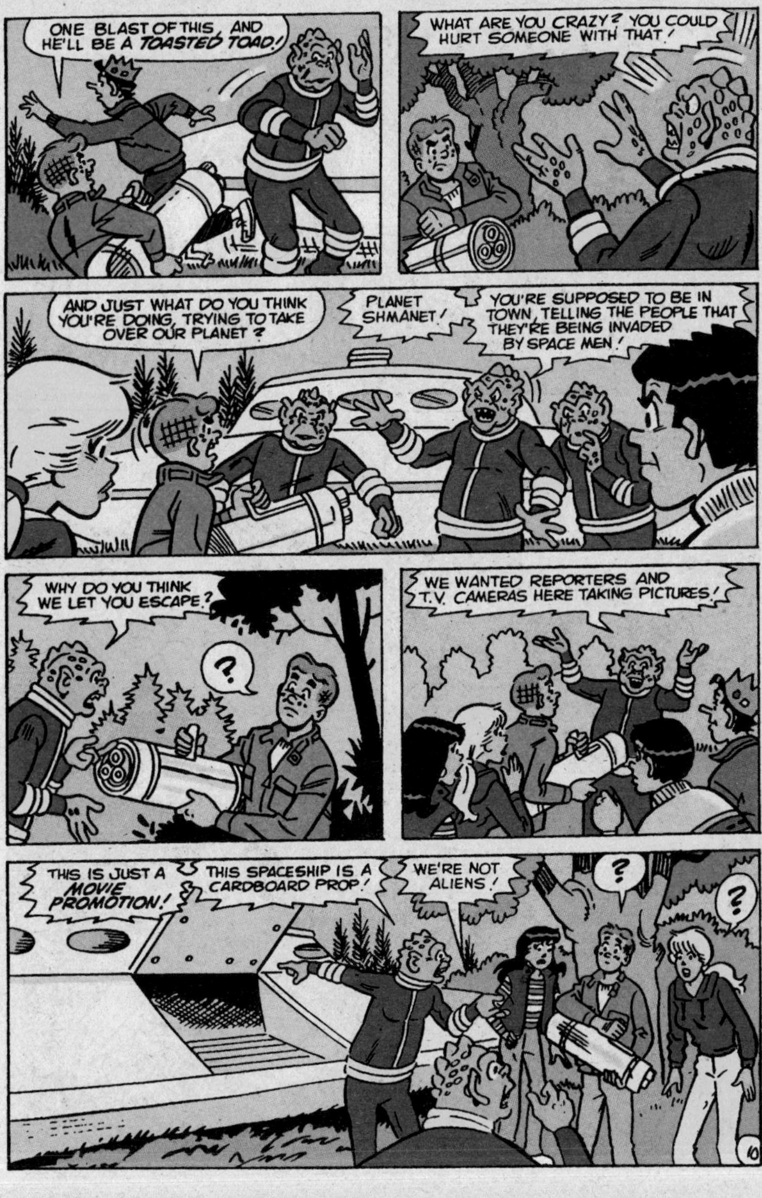
ONE BLAST OF THIS, AND HE'LL BE A TOASTED TOAD!
WHAT ARE YOU CRAZY? YOU COULD HURT SOMEONE WITH THAT!
AND JUST WHAT DO YOU THINK YOU'RE DOING, TRYING TO TAKE OVER OUR PLANET?
PLANET SHMANET!
YOU'RE SUPPOSED TO BE IN TOWN, TELLING THE PEOPLE THAT THEY'RE BEING INVADED BY SPACE MEN!
WHY DO YOU THINK WE LET YOU ESCAPE?
?
WE WANTED REPORTERS AND T.V. CAMERAS HERE TAKING PICTURES!
THIS IS JUST A MOVIE PROMOTION!
THIS SPACESHIP IS A CARDBOARD PROP!
WE'RE NOT ALIENS!
?
?
10

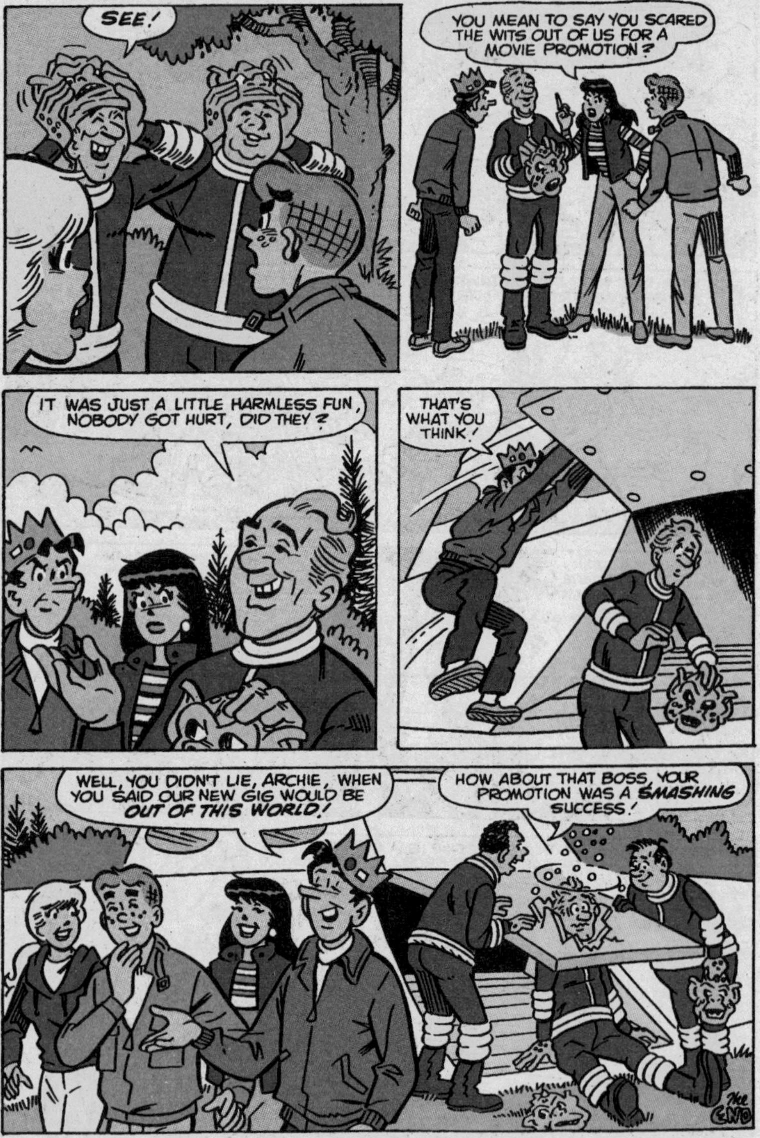
SEE!
YOU MEAN TO SAY YOU SCARED THE WITS OUT OF US FOR A MOVIE PROMOTION?
IT WAS JUST A LITTLE HARMLESS FUN, NOBODY GOT HURT, DID THEY?
THAT'S WHAT YOU THINK!
WELL, YOU DIDN'T LIE, ARCHIE, WHEN YOU SAID OUR NEW GIG WOULD BE OUT OF THIS WORLD!
HOW ABOUT THAT BOSS, YOUR PROMOTION WAS A SMASHING SUCCESS!
THE END

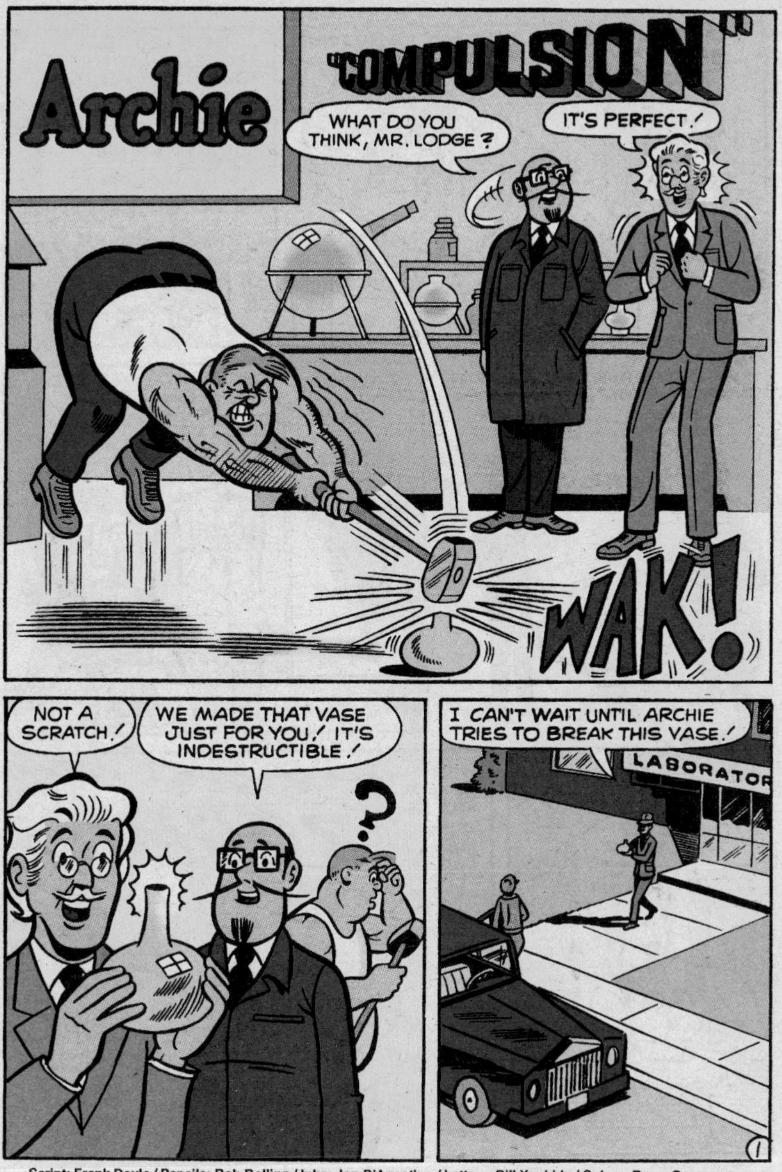
Archie
"COMPULSION"
WHAT DO YOU THINK, MR. LODGE?
IT'S PERFECT!
WAK!
NOT A SCRATCH!
WE MADE THAT VASE JUST FOR YOU! IT'S INDESTRUCTIBLE!
?
I CAN'T WAIT UNTIL ARCHIE TRIES TO BREAK THIS VASE!
LABORATOR
1

Script: Frank Doyle / Pencils: Bob Bolling / Inks: Jon D'Agostino / Letters: Bill Yoshida / Colors: Barry Grossman

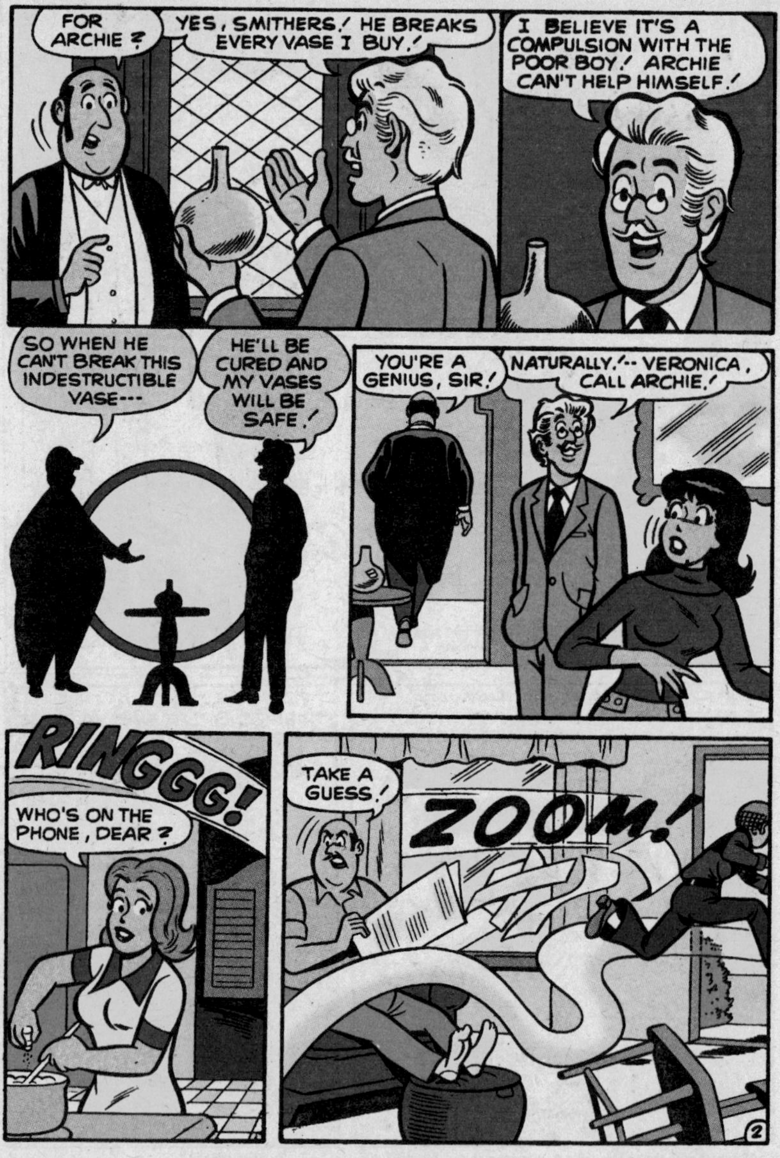
FOR ARCHIE ?
YES, SMITHERS! HE BREAKS EVERY VASE I BUY!
I BELIEVE IT'S A COMPULSION WITH THE POOR BOY! ARCHIE CAN'T HELP HIMSELF!
SO WHEN HE CAN'T BREAK THIS INDESTRUCTIBLE VASE---
HE'LL BE CURED AND MY VASES WILL BE SAFE!
YOU'RE A GENIUS, SIR!
NATURALLY!-- VERONICA, CALL ARCHIE!
RINGGG!
WHO'S ON THE PHONE, DEAR ?
TAKE A GUESS!
ZOOM!
2

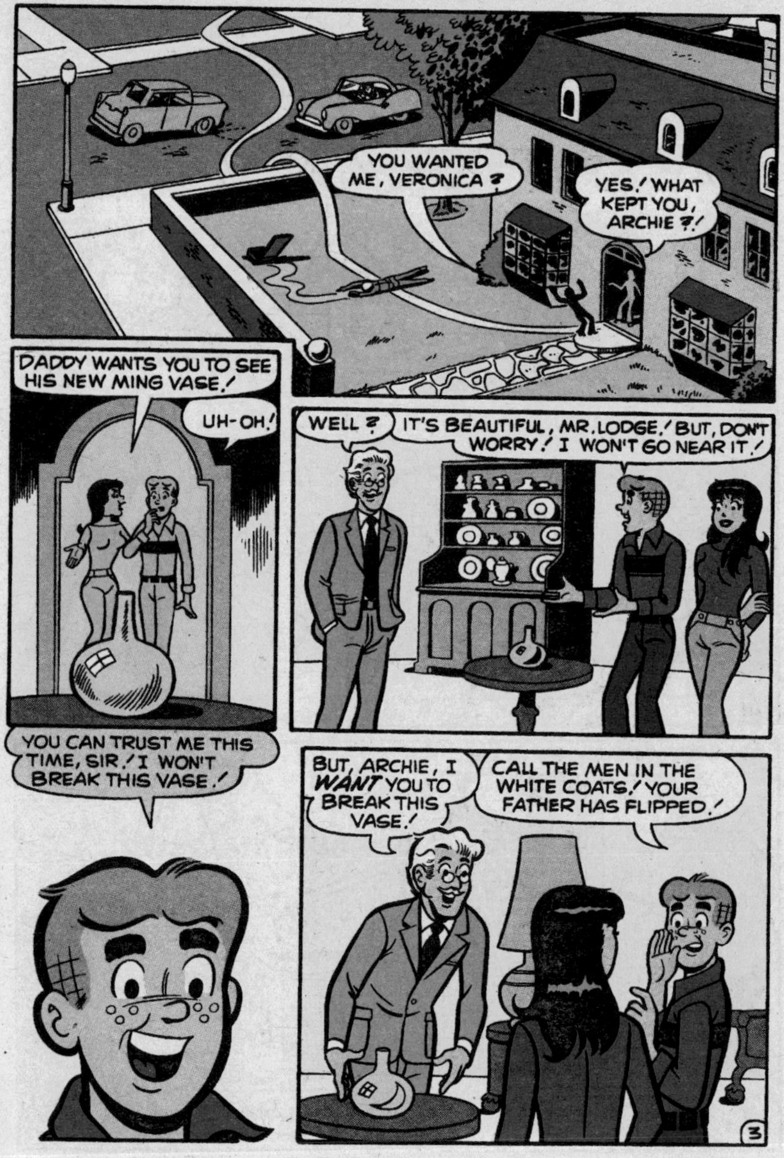

YOU WANTED ME, VERONICA ?
YES.! WHAT KEPT YOU, ARCHIE ?!
DADDY WANTS YOU TO SEE HIS NEW MING VASE.!
UH-OH!
YOU CAN TRUST ME THIS TIME, SIR.! I WON'T BREAK THIS VASE.!
WELL ?
IT'S BEAUTIFUL, MR. LODGE.! BUT, DON'T WORRY.! I WON'T GO NEAR IT.!
BUT, ARCHIE, I WANT YOU TO BREAK THIS VASE.!
CALL THE MEN IN THE WHITE COATS.! YOUR FATHER HAS FLIPPED.!
3

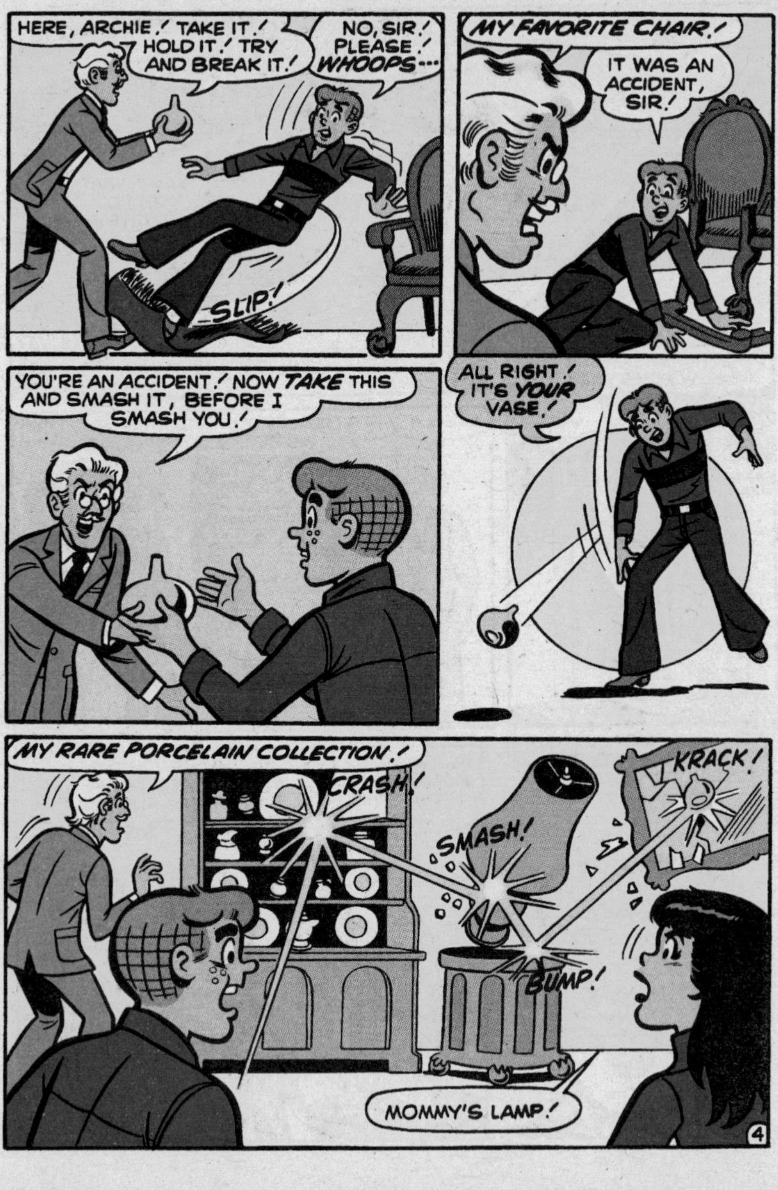
HERE, ARCHIE ! TAKE IT ! HOLD IT ! TRY AND BREAK IT !
NO, SIR ! PLEASE ! WHOOPS---
SLIP !
MY FAVORITE CHAIR !
IT WAS AN ACCIDENT, SIR !
YOU'RE AN ACCIDENT ! NOW TAKE THIS AND SMASH IT, BEFORE I SMASH YOU !
ALL RIGHT ! IT'S YOUR VASE !
MY RARE PORCELAIN COLLECTION !
CRASH !
SMASH !
KRACK !
BUMP !
MOMMY'S LAMP !
4

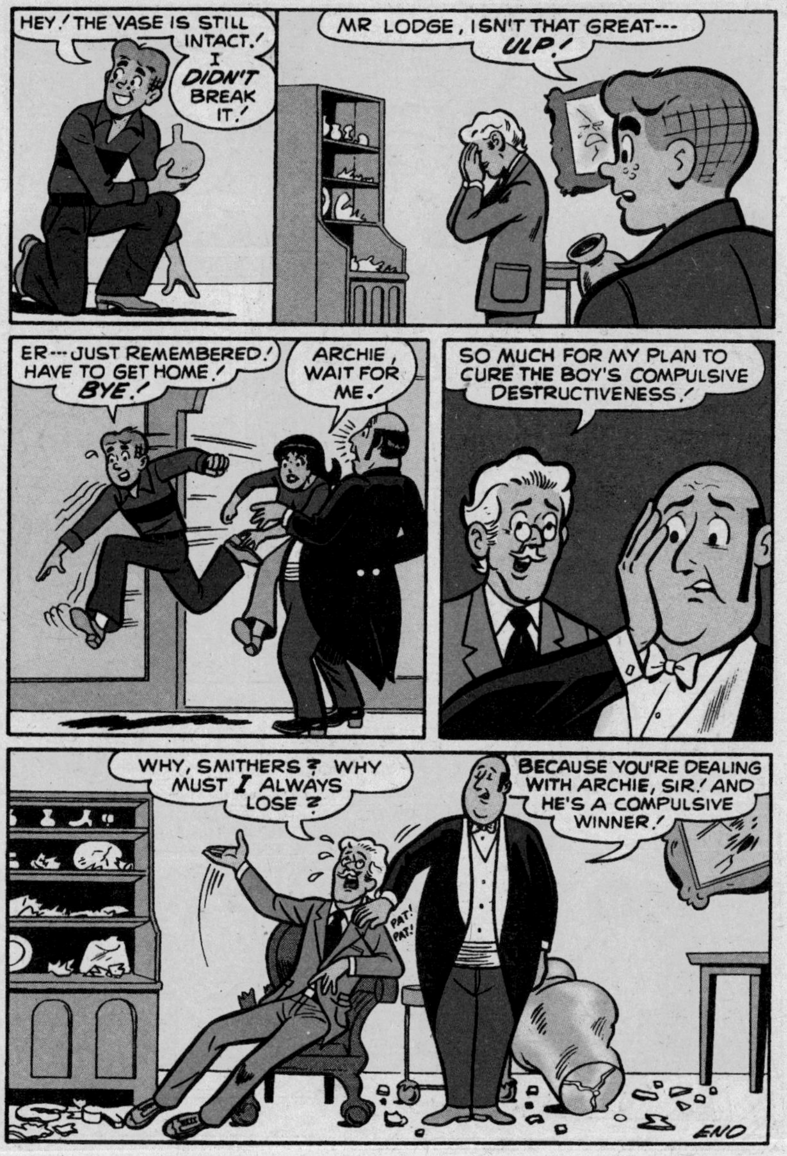
HEY.! THE VASE IS STILL INTACT.!
I DIDN'T BREAK IT.!
MR LODGE, ISN'T THAT GREAT--- ULP!
ER---JUST REMEMBERED.! HAVE TO GET HOME.! BYE.!
ARCHIE, WAIT FOR ME.!
SO MUCH FOR MY PLAN TO CURE THE BOY'S COMPULSIVE DESTRUCTIVENESS.!
WHY, SMITHERS? WHY MUST I ALWAYS LOSE?
BECAUSE YOU'RE DEALING WITH ARCHIE, SIR.! AND HE'S A COMPULSIVE WINNER.!
PAT! PAT!
END

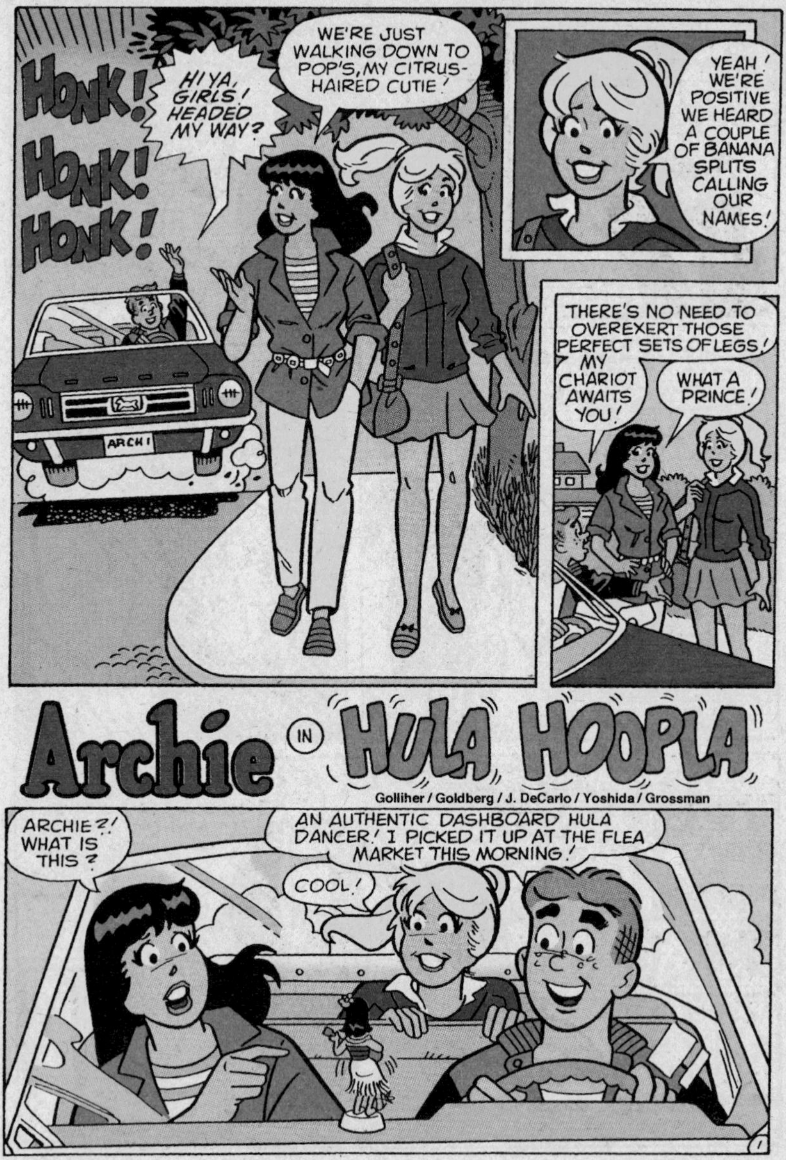
HONK! HONK! HONK!
HI YA, GIRLS! HEADED MY WAY?
WE'RE JUST WALKING DOWN TO POP'S, MY CITRUS-HAIRED CUTIE!
ARCHI
YEAH! WE'RE POSITIVE WE HEARD A COUPLE OF BANANA SPLITS CALLING OUR NAMES!
THERE'S NO NEED TO OVEREXERT THOSE PERFECT SETS OF LEGS! MY CHARIOT AWAITS YOU!
WHAT A PRINCE!
Archie IN HULA HOOPLA
Golliher / Goldberg / J. DeCarlo / Yoshida / Grossman
ARCHIE?! WHAT IS THIS?
AN AUTHENTIC DASHBOARD HULA DANCER! I PICKED IT UP AT THE FLEA MARKET THIS MORNING!
COOL!
1

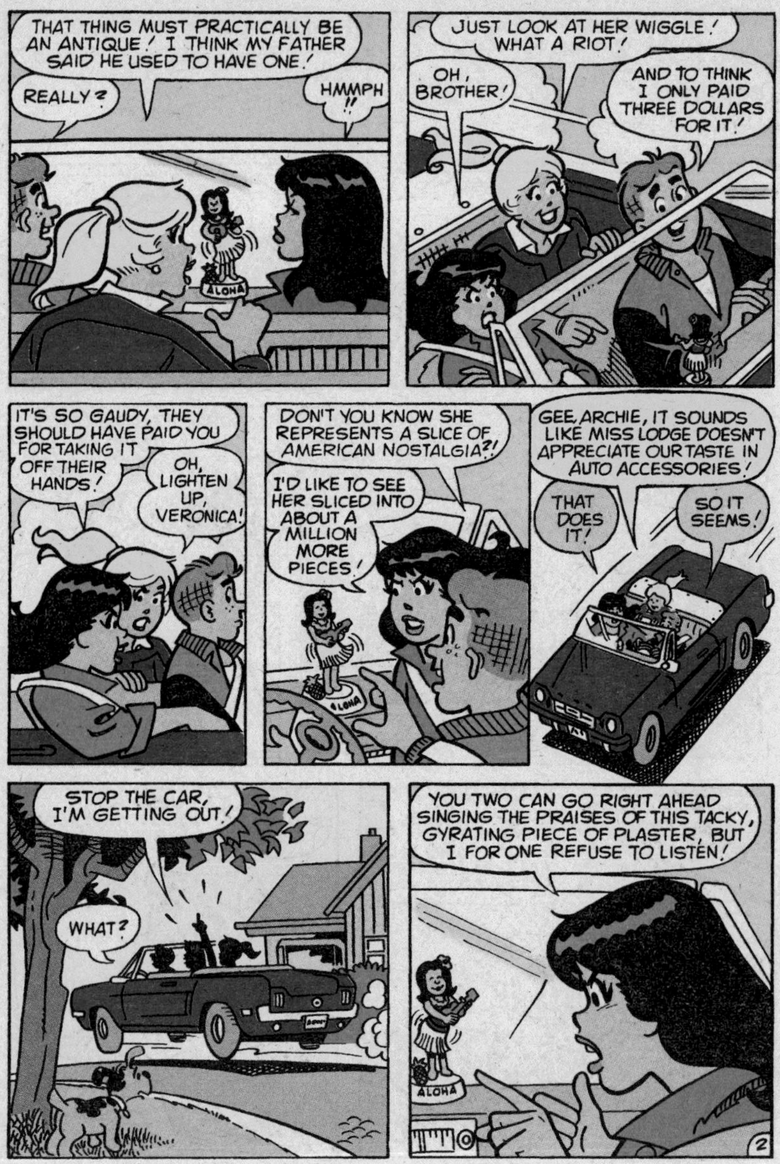
THAT THING MUST PRACTICALLY BE AN ANTIQUE! I THINK MY FATHER SAID HE USED TO HAVE ONE!
REALLY?
HMMPH!!
JUST LOOK AT HER WIGGLE! WHAT A RIOT!
OH, BROTHER!
AND TO THINK I ONLY PAID THREE DOLLARS FOR IT!
IT'S SO GAUDY, THEY SHOULD HAVE PAID YOU FOR TAKING IT OFF THEIR HANDS!
OH, LIGHTEN UP, VERONICA!
DON'T YOU KNOW SHE REPRESENTS A SLICE OF AMERICAN NOSTALGIA?!
I'D LIKE TO SEE HER SLICED INTO ABOUT A MILLION MORE PIECES!
ALOHA
GEE, ARCHIE, IT SOUNDS LIKE MISS LODGE DOESN'T APPRECIATE OUR TASTE IN AUTO ACCESSORIES!
THAT DOES IT!
SO IT SEEMS!
STOP THE CAR, I'M GETTING OUT!
WHAT?
YOU TWO CAN GO RIGHT AHEAD SINGING THE PRAISES OF THIS TACKY, GYRATING PIECE OF PLASTER, BUT I FOR ONE REFUSE TO LISTEN!
ALOHA
2

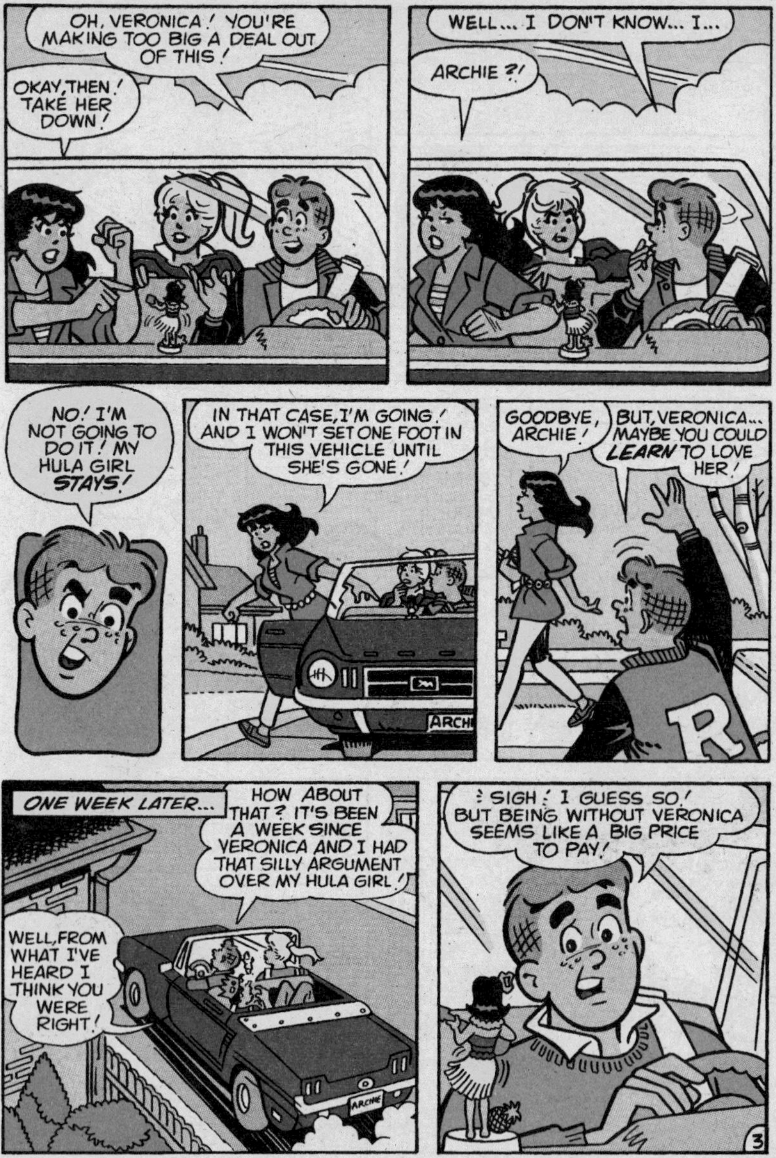
OH, VERONICA! YOU'RE MAKING TOO BIG A DEAL OUT OF THIS!
OKAY, THEN! TAKE HER DOWN!
WELL... I DON'T KNOW... I...
ARCHIE ?!
NO! I'M NOT GOING TO DO IT! MY HULA GIRL STAYS!
IN THAT CASE, I'M GOING! AND I WON'T SET ONE FOOT IN THIS VEHICLE UNTIL SHE'S GONE!
ARCHIE
GOODBYE, ARCHIE!
BUT, VERONICA... MAYBE YOU COULD LEARN TO LOVE HER!
ONE WEEK LATER...
HOW ABOUT THAT? IT'S BEEN A WEEK SINCE VERONICA AND I HAD THAT SILLY ARGUMENT OVER MY HULA GIRL!
WELL, FROM WHAT I'VE HEARD I THINK YOU WERE RIGHT!
ARCHIE
SIGH! I GUESS SO! BUT BEING WITHOUT VERONICA SEEMS LIKE A BIG PRICE TO PAY!
3

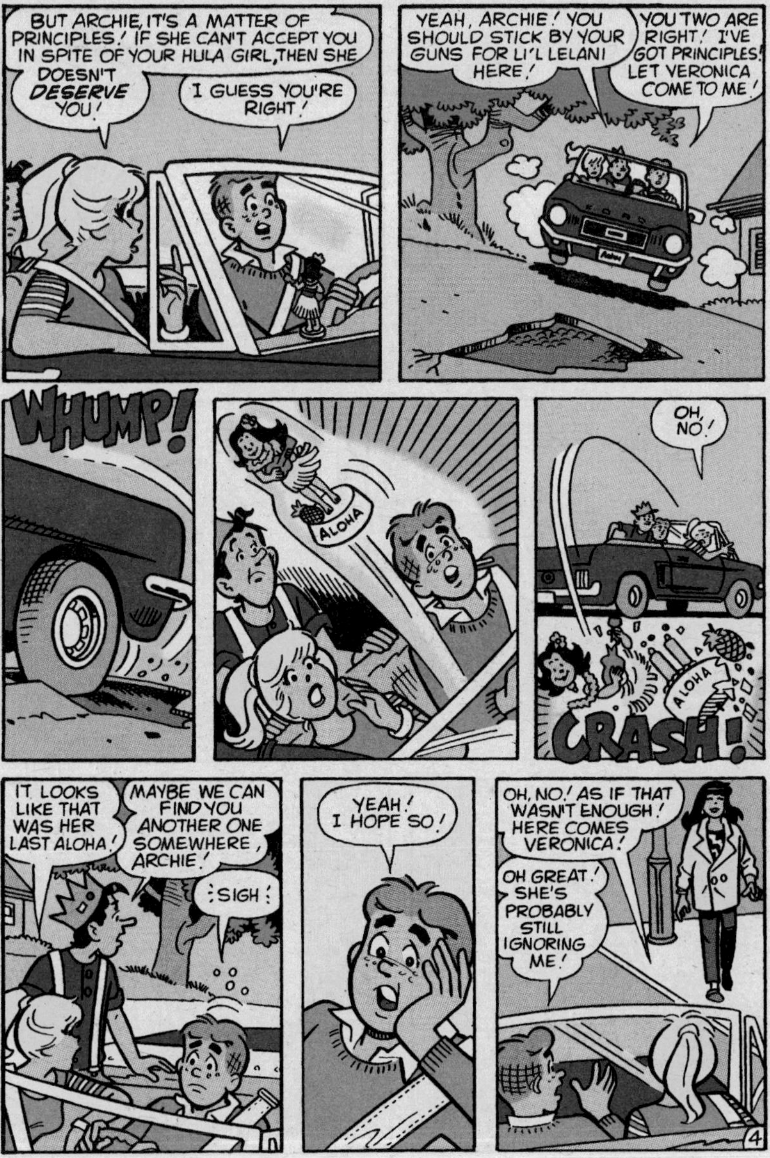
BUT ARCHIE, IT'S A MATTER OF PRINCIPLES! IF SHE CAN'T ACCEPT YOU IN SPITE OF YOUR HULA GIRL, THEN SHE DOESN'T DESERVE YOU!
I GUESS YOU'RE RIGHT!
YEAH, ARCHIE! YOU SHOULD STICK BY YOUR GUNS FOR LI'L LELANI HERE!
YOU TWO ARE RIGHT! I'VE GOT PRINCIPLES! LET VERONICA COME TO ME!
WHUMP!
ALOHA
OH, NO!
ALOHA
CRASH!
IT LOOKS LIKE THAT WAS HER LAST ALOHA!
MAYBE WE CAN FIND YOU ANOTHER ONE SOMEWHERE, ARCHIE!
SIGH
YEAH! I HOPE SO!
OH, NO! AS IF THAT WASN'T ENOUGH! HERE COMES VERONICA!
OH GREAT! SHE'S PROBABLY STILL IGNORING ME!
4

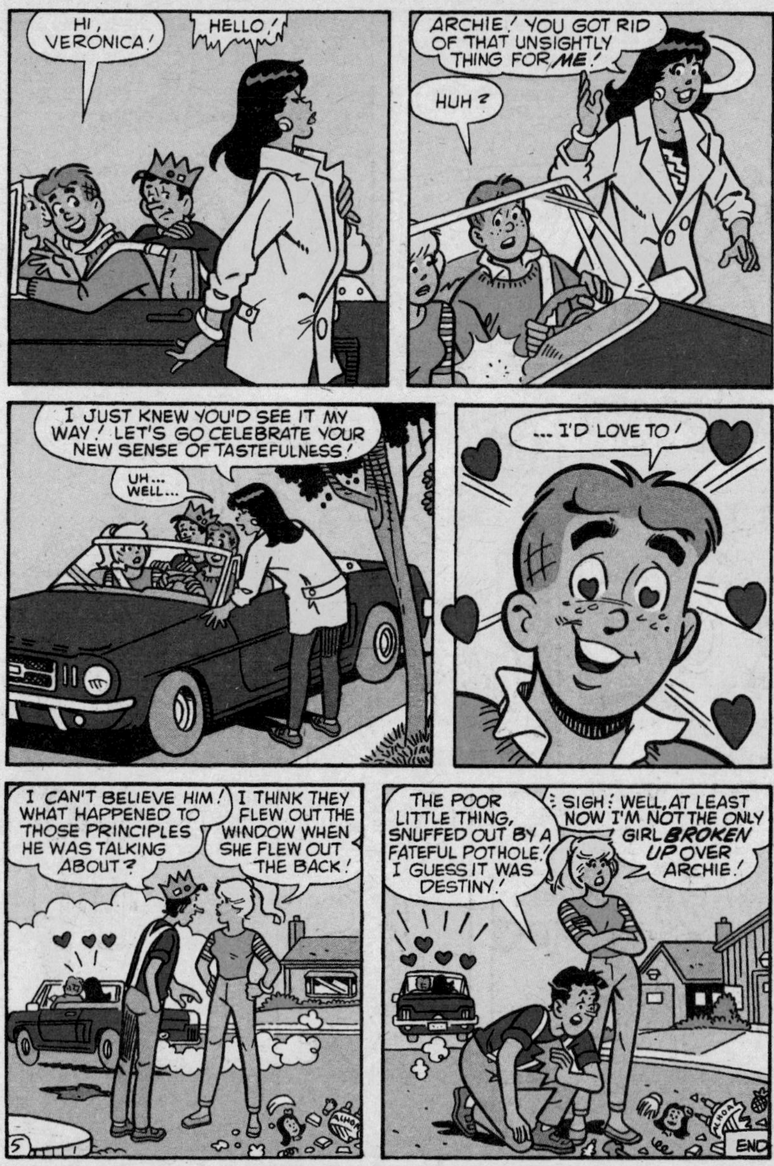
HI, VERONICA!
HELLO!
ARCHIE! YOU GOT RID OF THAT UNSIGHTLY THING FOR ME!
HUH?
I JUST KNEW YOU'D SEE IT MY WAY! LET'S GO CELEBRATE YOUR NEW SENSE OF TASTEFULNESS!
UH... WELL...
... I'D LOVE TO!
I CAN'T BELIEVE HIM! WHAT HAPPENED TO THOSE PRINCIPLES HE WAS TALKING ABOUT?
I THINK THEY FLEW OUT THE WINDOW WHEN SHE FLEW OUT THE BACK!
5
THE POOR LITTLE THING, SNUFFED OUT BY A FATEFUL POTHOLE! I GUESS IT WAS DESTINY!
SIGH! WELL, AT LEAST NOW I'M NOT THE ONLY GIRL BROKEN UP OVER ARCHIE!
END

Archie in "DOLLAR DILEMMA"

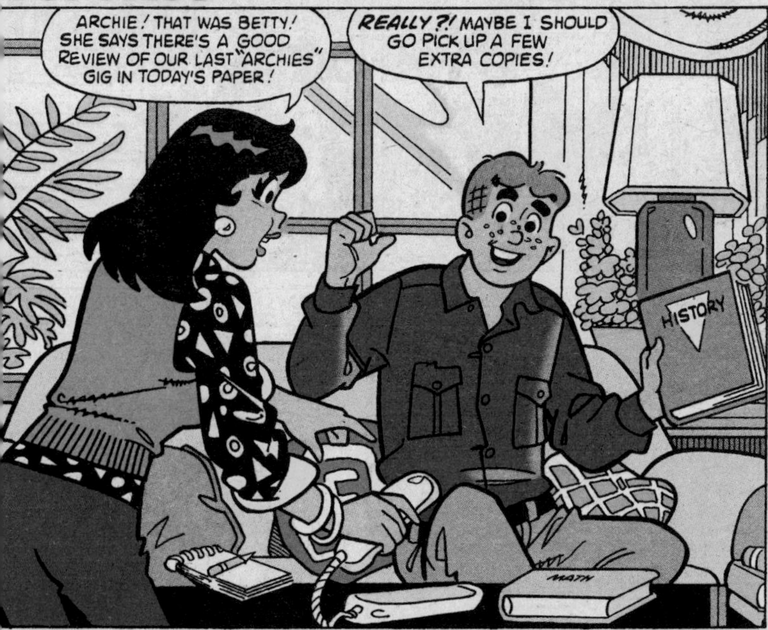

ARCHIE! THAT WAS BETTY! SHE SAYS THERE'S A GOOD REVIEW OF OUR LAST "ARCHIES" GIG IN TODAY'S PAPER!
REALLY?! MAYBE I SHOULD GO PICK UP A FEW EXTRA COPIES!
HISTORY
MATH

Script: George Gladir / Pencils: Stan Goldberg / Inks: Henry Scarpelli / Letters: Bill Yoshida / Colors: Barry Grossman

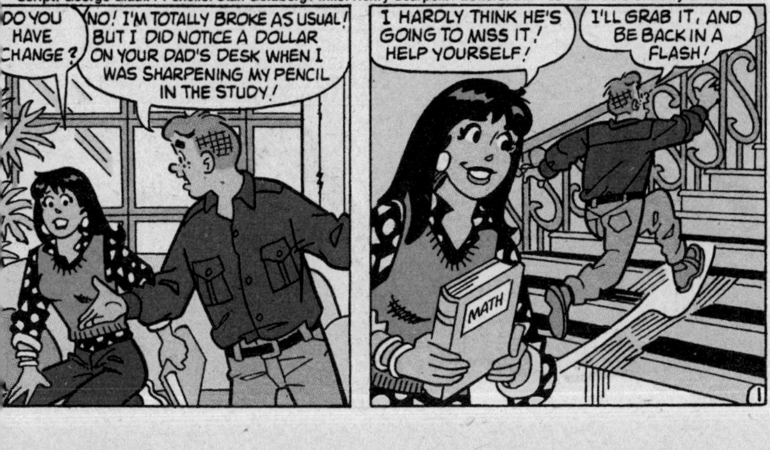

DO YOU HAVE CHANGE?
NO! I'M TOTALLY BROKE AS USUAL! BUT I DID NOTICE A DOLLAR ON YOUR DAD'S DESK WHEN I WAS SHARPENING MY PENCIL IN THE STUDY!
I HARDLY THINK HE'S GOING TO MISS IT! HELP YOURSELF!
I'LL GRAB IT, AND BE BACK IN A FLASH!
MATH
1

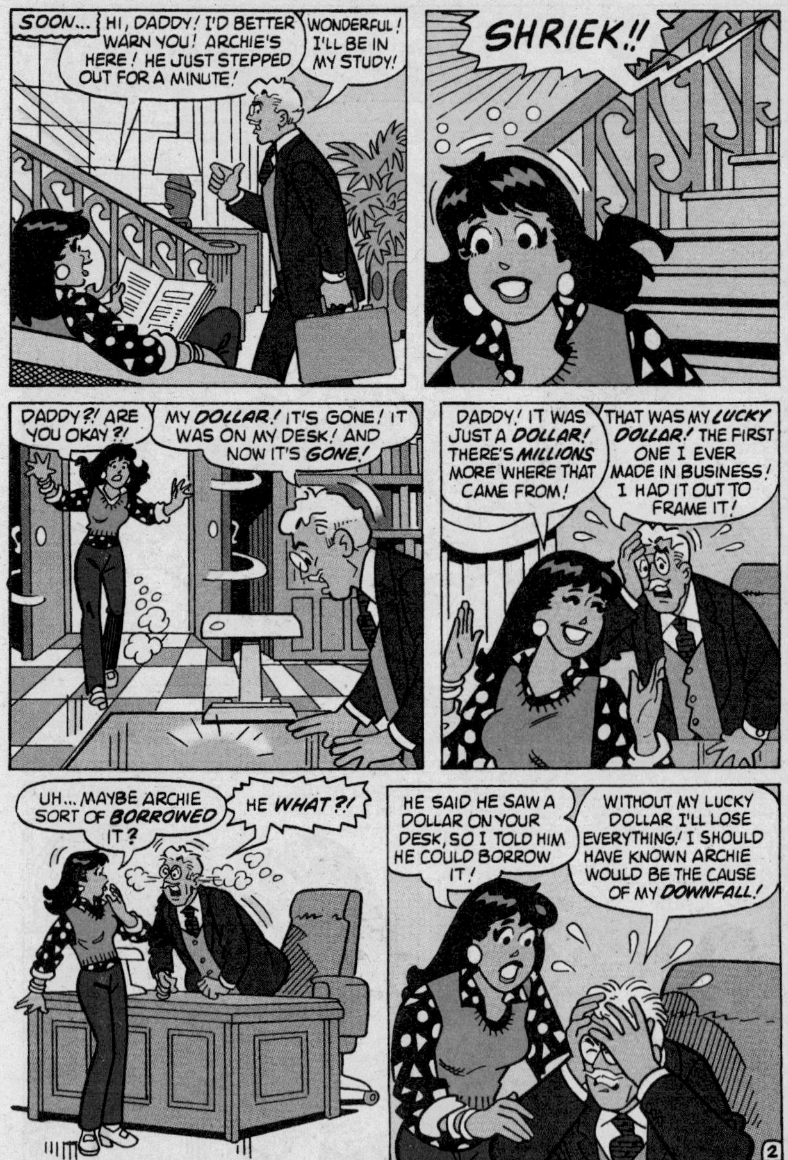
SOON...
HI, DADDY! I'D BETTER WARN YOU! ARCHIE'S HERE! HE JUST STEPPED OUT FOR A MINUTE!
WONDERFUL! I'LL BE IN MY STUDY!
SHRIEK!!
DADDY?! ARE YOU OKAY?!
MY DOLLAR! IT'S GONE! IT WAS ON MY DESK! AND NOW IT'S GONE!
DADDY! IT WAS JUST A DOLLAR! THERE'S MILLIONS MORE WHERE THAT CAME FROM!
THAT WAS MY LUCKY DOLLAR! THE FIRST ONE I EVER MADE IN BUSINESS! I HAD IT OUT TO FRAME IT!
UH... MAYBE ARCHIE SORT OF BORROWED IT?
HE WHAT?!
HE SAID HE SAW A DOLLAR ON YOUR DESK, SO I TOLD HIM HE COULD BORROW IT!
WITHOUT MY LUCKY DOLLAR I'LL LOSE EVERYTHING! I SHOULD HAVE KNOWN ARCHIE WOULD BE THE CAUSE OF MY DOWNFALL!
2

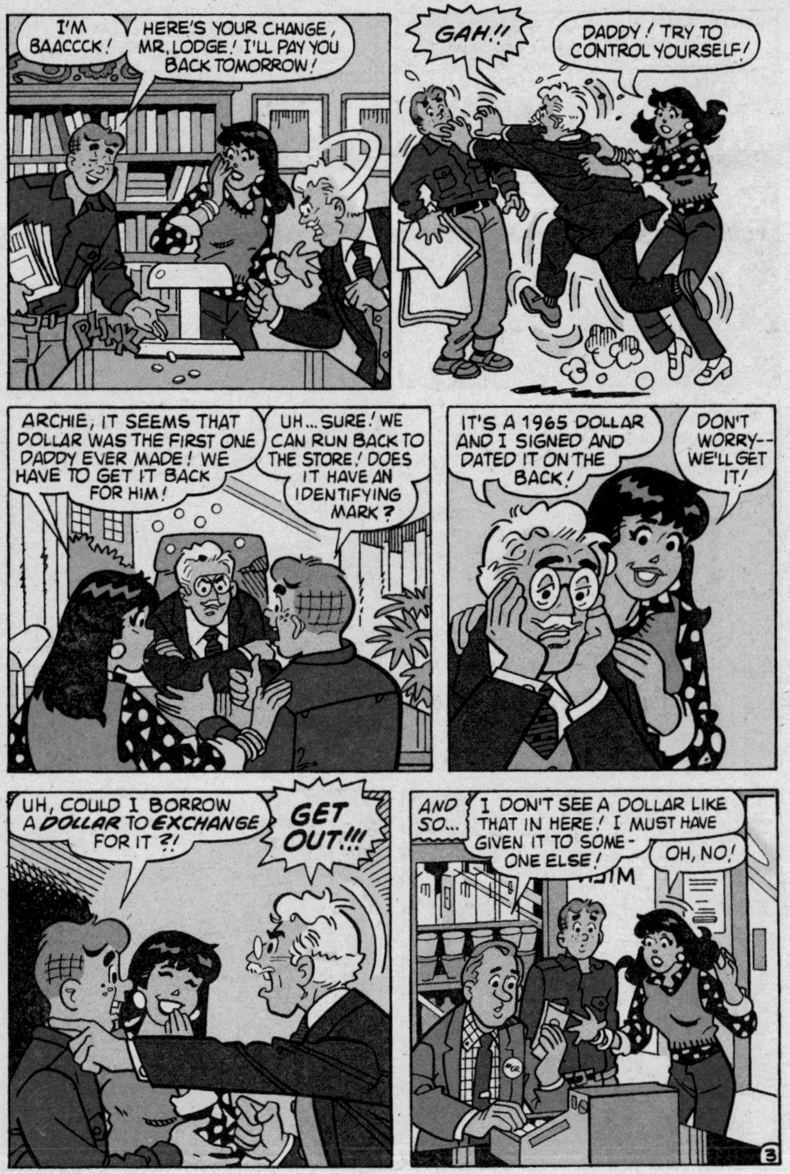

I'M BAACCCK!
HERE'S YOUR CHANGE, MR. LODGE! I'LL PAY YOU BACK TOMORROW!
PLINK
GAH!!
DADDY! TRY TO CONTROL YOURSELF!
ARCHIE, IT SEEMS THAT DOLLAR WAS THE FIRST ONE DADDY EVER MADE! WE HAVE TO GET IT BACK FOR HIM!
UH... SURE! WE CAN RUN BACK TO THE STORE! DOES IT HAVE AN IDENTIFYING MARK?
IT'S A 1965 DOLLAR AND I SIGNED AND DATED IT ON THE BACK!
DON'T WORRY-- WE'LL GET IT!
UH, COULD I BORROW A DOLLAR TO EXCHANGE FOR IT?!
GET OUT!!!
AND SO...
I DON'T SEE A DOLLAR LIKE THAT IN HERE! I MUST HAVE GIVEN IT TO SOME-ONE ELSE!
OH, NO!
3

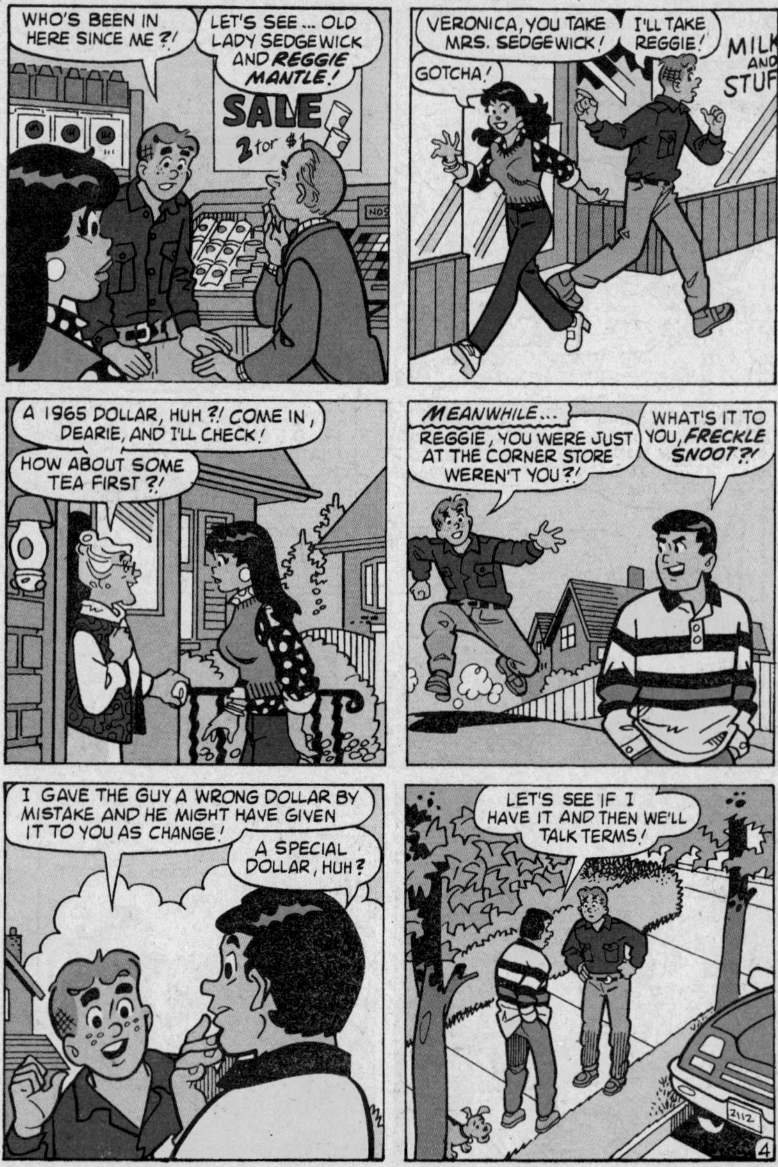
WHO'S BEEN IN HERE SINCE ME ?!
LET'S SEE ... OLD LADY SEDGEWICK AND REGGIE MANTLE!
SALE 2 for $1
VERONICA, YOU TAKE MRS. SEDGEWICK!
I'LL TAKE REGGIE!
GOTCHA!
MILK AND STUF
A 1965 DOLLAR, HUH ?! COME IN, DEARIE, AND I'LL CHECK!
HOW ABOUT SOME TEA FIRST ?!
MEANWHILE...
REGGIE, YOU WERE JUST AT THE CORNER STORE WEREN'T YOU ?!
WHAT'S IT TO YOU, FRECKLE SNOOT ?!
I GAVE THE GUY A WRONG DOLLAR BY MISTAKE AND HE MIGHT HAVE GIVEN IT TO YOU AS CHANGE!
A SPECIAL DOLLAR, HUH?
LET'S SEE IF I HAVE IT AND THEN WE'LL TALK TERMS!
4

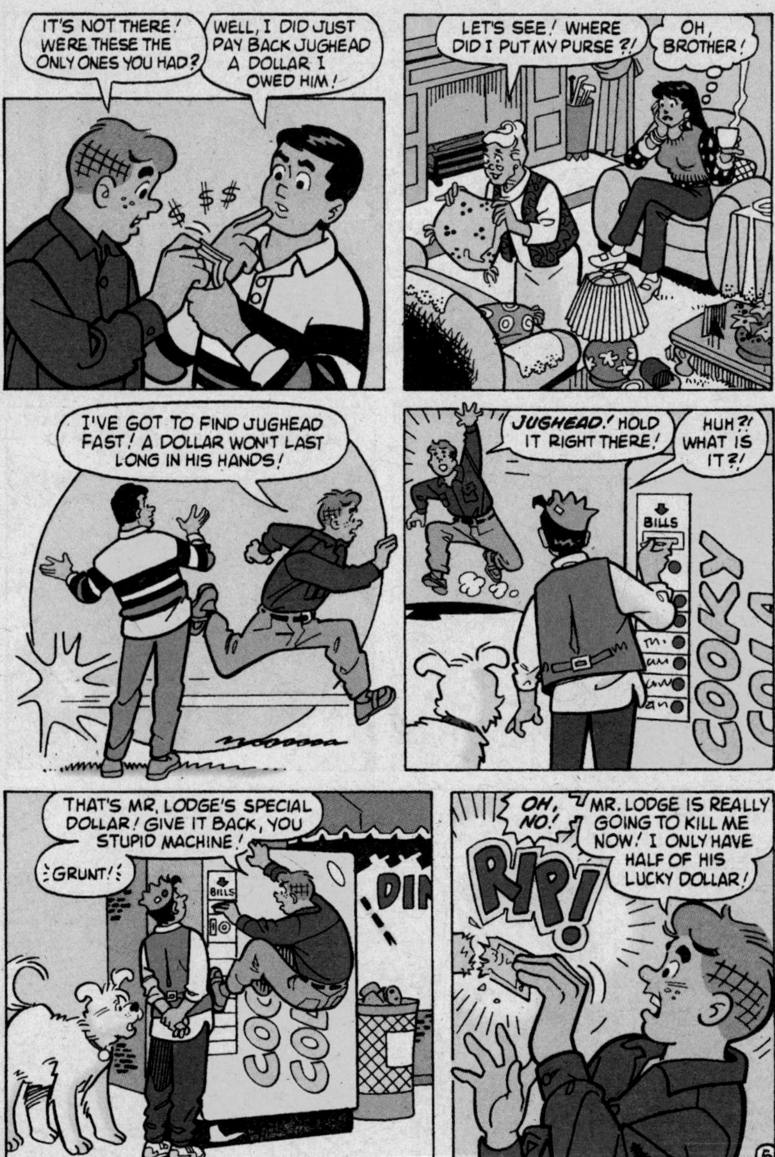
IT'S NOT THERE! WERE THESE THE ONLY ONES YOU HAD?
WELL, I DID JUST PAY BACK JUGHEAD A DOLLAR I OWED HIM!
$ $ $
LET'S SEE! WHERE DID I PUT MY PURSE?!
OH, BROTHER!
I'VE GOT TO FIND JUGHEAD FAST! A DOLLAR WON'T LAST LONG IN HIS HANDS!
JUGHEAD! HOLD IT RIGHT THERE!
HUH?! WHAT IS IT?!
BILLS
COOKY COLA
THAT'S MR. LODGE'S SPECIAL DOLLAR! GIVE IT BACK, YOU STUPID MACHINE!
GRUNT!
BILLS
DI
OH, NO!
MR. LODGE IS REALLY GOING TO KILL ME NOW! I ONLY HAVE HALF OF HIS LUCKY DOLLAR!
RIP!
5

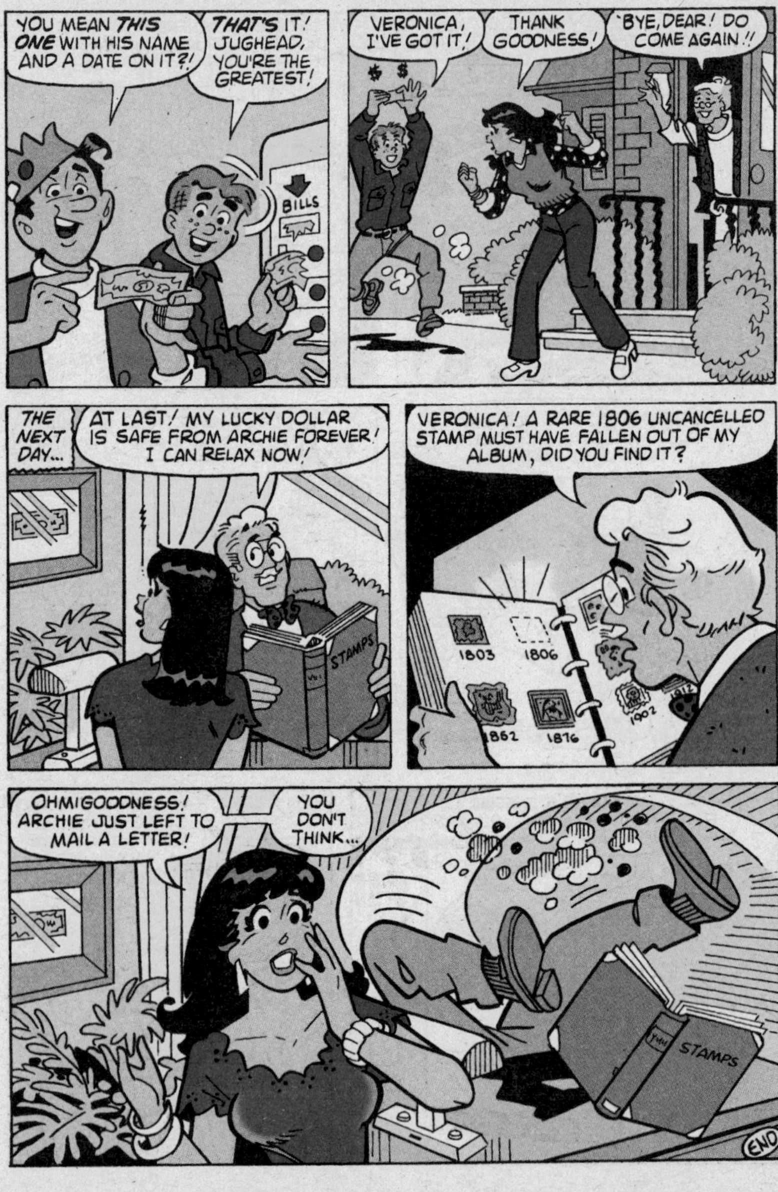
YOU MEAN THIS ONE WITH HIS NAME AND A DATE ON IT?!
THAT'S IT! JUGHEAD, YOU'RE THE GREATEST!
BILLS
VERONICA, I'VE GOT IT!
THANK GOODNESS!
'BYE, DEAR! DO COME AGAIN!!
THE NEXT DAY...
AT LAST! MY LUCKY DOLLAR IS SAFE FROM ARCHIE FOREVER! I CAN RELAX NOW!
STAMPS
VERONICA! A RARE 1806 UNCANCELLED STAMP MUST HAVE FALLEN OUT OF MY ALBUM, DID YOU FIND IT?
1803
1806
1862
1876
1902
1912
OHMIGOODNESS! ARCHIE JUST LEFT TO MAIL A LETTER!
YOU DON'T THINK...
STAMPS
END

Mr. Weatherbee in FREAKY FRACAS

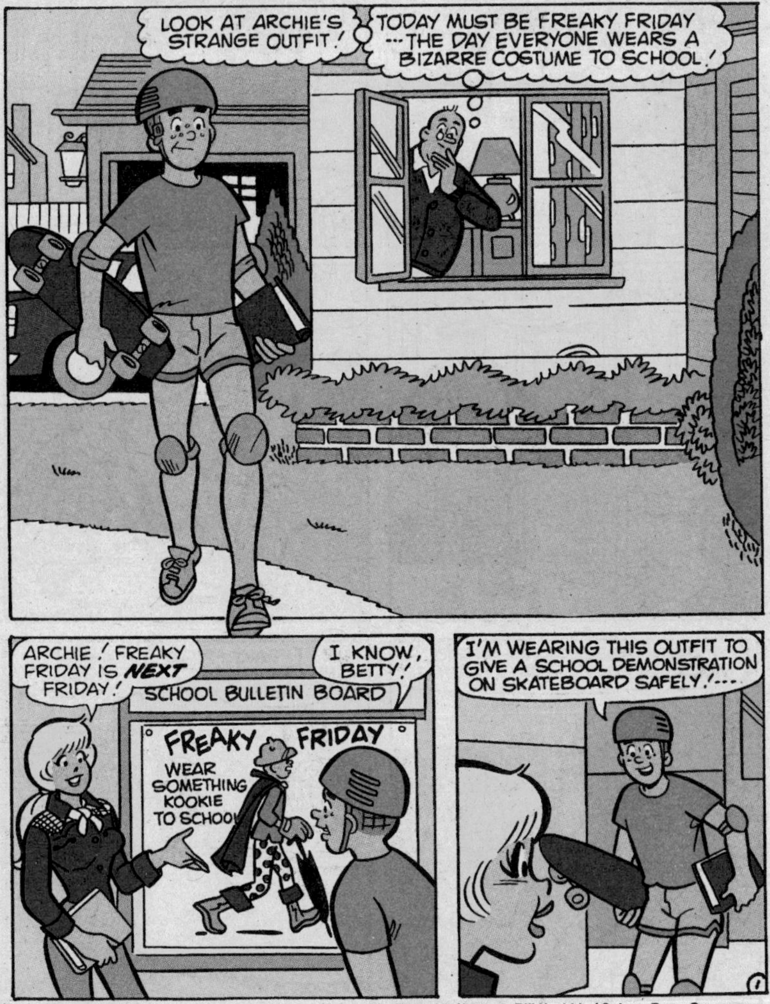

LOOK AT ARCHIE'S STRANGE OUTFIT!
TODAY MUST BE FREAKY FRIDAY ---THE DAY EVERYONE WEARS A BIZARRE COSTUME TO SCHOOL!
ARCHIE! FREAKY FRIDAY IS ***NEXT*** FRIDAY!
SCHOOL BULLETIN BOARD
I KNOW, BETTY!
FREAKY FRIDAY
WEAR SOMETHING KOOKIE TO SCHOOL
I'M WEARING THIS OUTFIT TO GIVE A SCHOOL DEMONSTRATION ON SKATEBOARD SAFELY!---
1

Script: George Gladir / Pencils: Stan Goldberg / Inks: Mike Esposito / Letters: Bill Yoshida / Colors: Barry Grossman

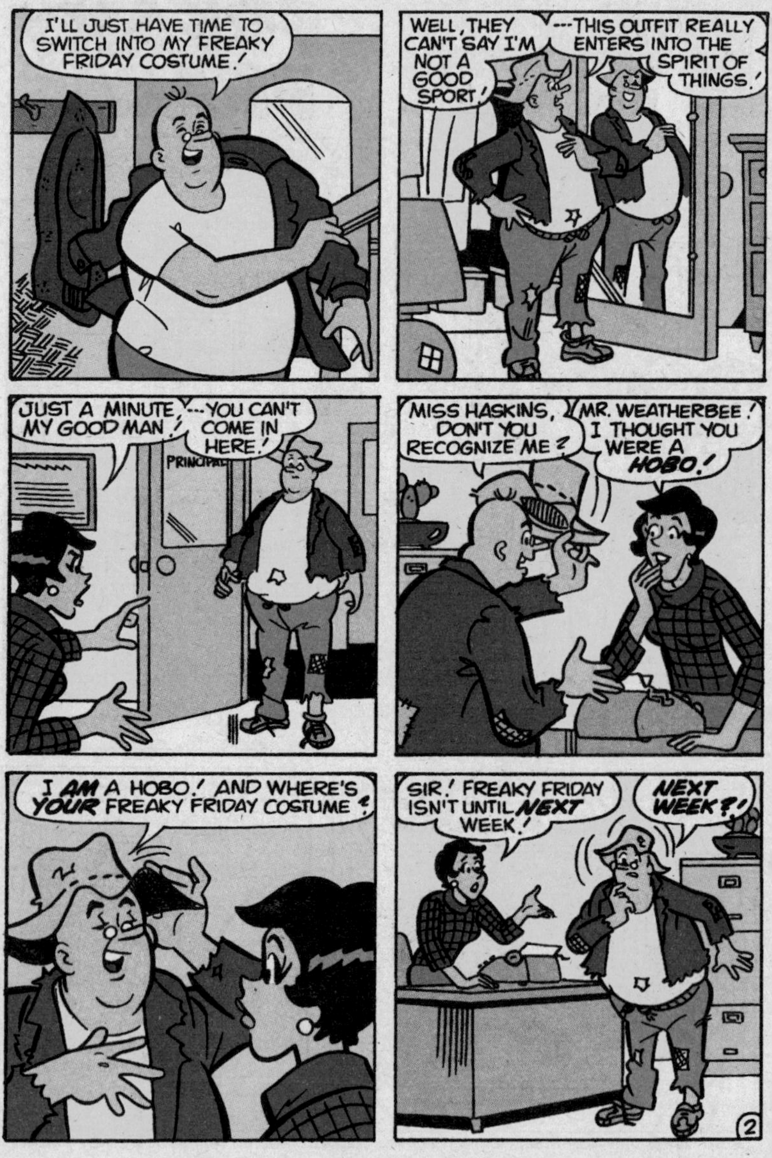
I'LL JUST HAVE TIME TO SWITCH INTO MY FREAKY FRIDAY COSTUME!
WELL, THEY CAN'T SAY I'M NOT A GOOD SPORT!
---THIS OUTFIT REALLY ENTERS INTO THE SPIRIT OF THINGS!
JUST A MINUTE, MY GOOD MAN!
---YOU CAN'T COME IN HERE!
PRINCIPAL
MISS HASKINS, DON'T YOU RECOGNIZE ME?
MR. WEATHERBEE! I THOUGHT YOU WERE A HOBO!
I AM A HOBO! AND WHERE'S YOUR FREAKY FRIDAY COSTUME?
SIR! FREAKY FRIDAY ISN'T UNTIL NEXT WEEK!
NEXT WEEK?!
2

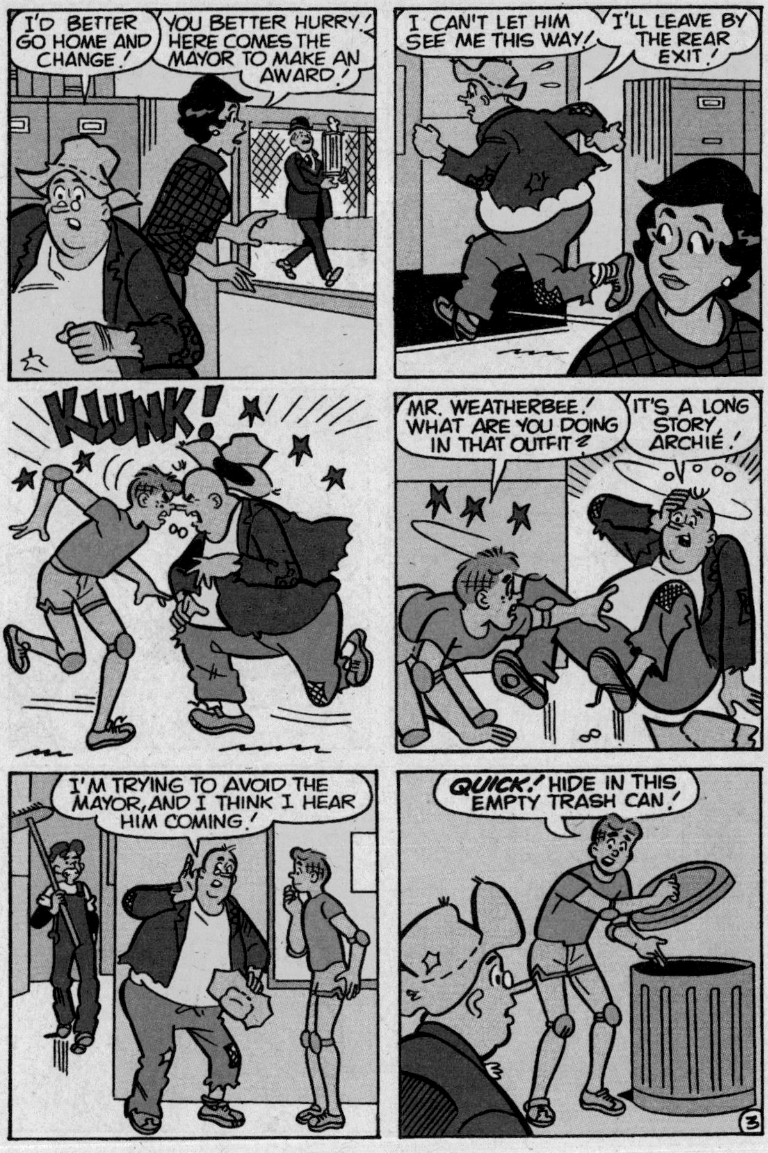
I'D BETTER GO HOME AND CHANGE!
YOU BETTER HURRY! HERE COMES THE MAYOR TO MAKE AN AWARD!
I CAN'T LET HIM SEE ME THIS WAY!
I'LL LEAVE BY THE REAR EXIT!
KLUNK!
MR. WEATHERBEE! WHAT ARE YOU DOING IN THAT OUTFIT?
IT'S A LONG STORY, ARCHIE!
I'M TRYING TO AVOID THE MAYOR, AND I THINK I HEAR HIM COMING!
QUICK! HIDE IN THIS EMPTY TRASH CAN!
3

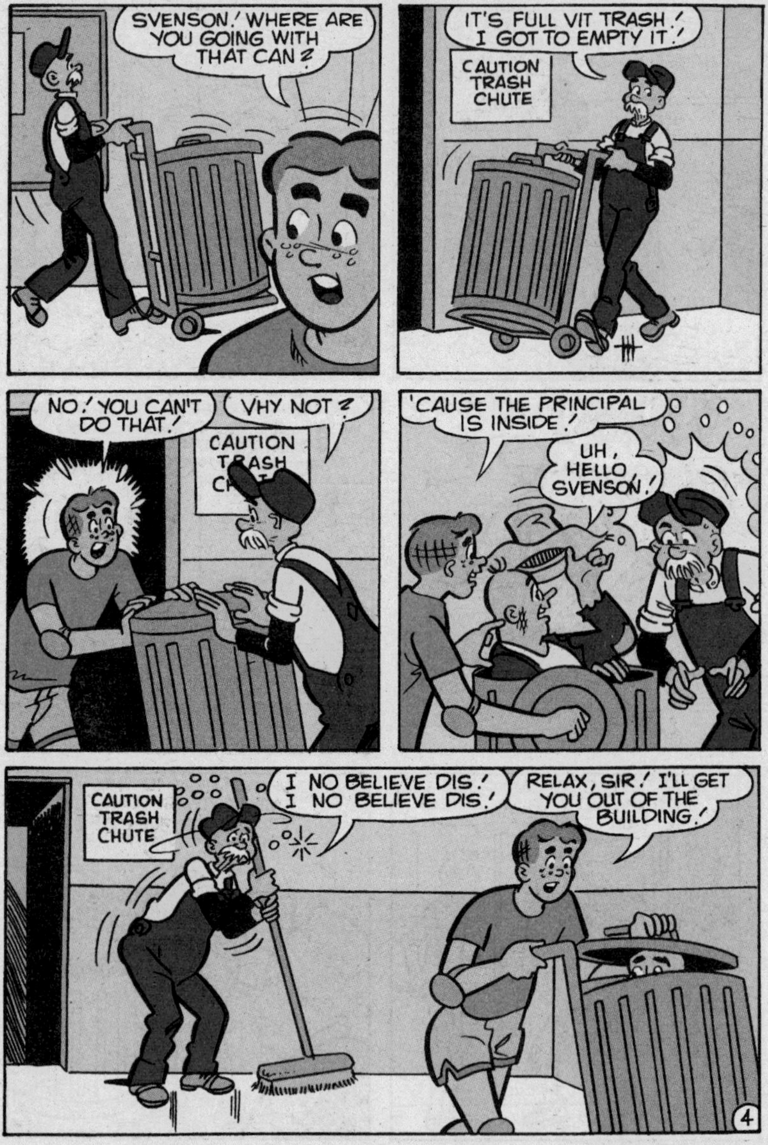
SVENSON! WHERE ARE YOU GOING WITH THAT CAN?
IT'S FULL VIT TRASH! I GOT TO EMPTY IT!
CAUTION TRASH CHUTE
NO! YOU CAN'T DO THAT!
VHY NOT?
'CAUSE THE PRINCIPAL IS INSIDE!
UH, HELLO SVENSON!
CAUTION TRASH CHUTE
I NO BELIEVE DIS! I NO BELIEVE DIS!
RELAX, SIR! I'LL GET YOU OUT OF THE BUILDING!
4

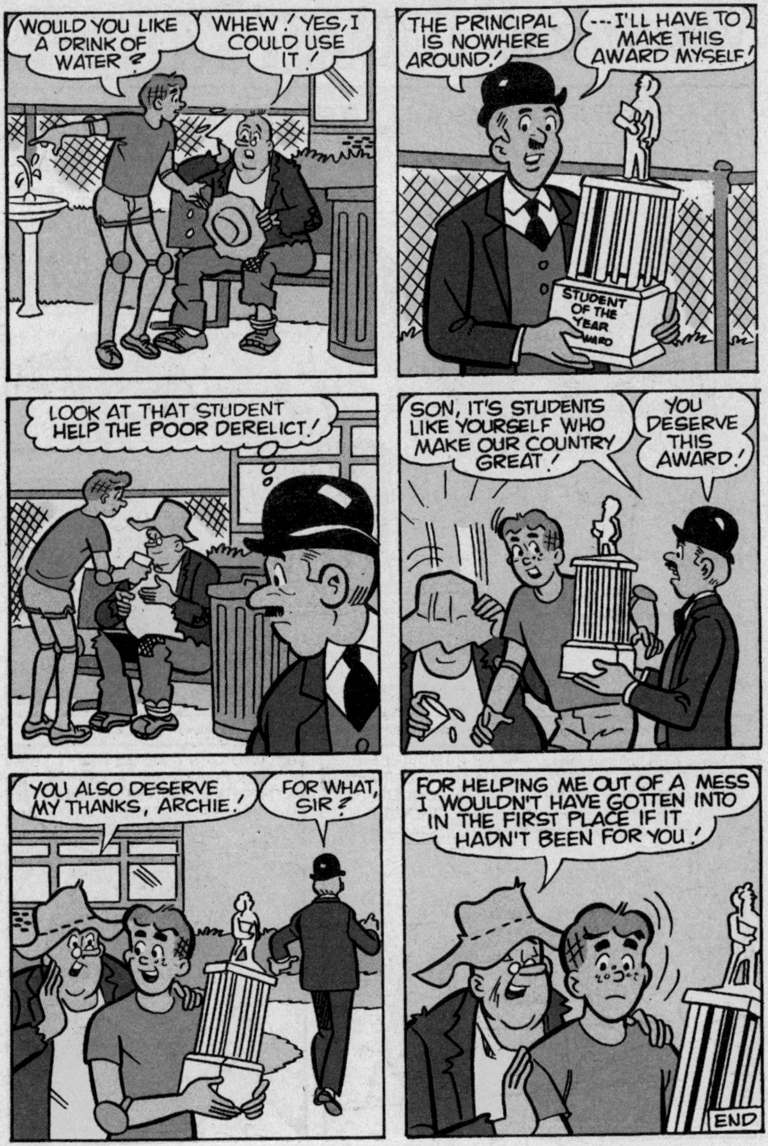
WOULD YOU LIKE A DRINK OF WATER ?
WHEW ! YES, I COULD USE IT !
THE PRINCIPAL IS NOWHERE AROUND !
--- I'LL HAVE TO MAKE THIS AWARD MYSELF !
STUDENT OF THE YEAR
LOOK AT THAT STUDENT HELP THE POOR DERELICT !
SON, IT'S STUDENTS LIKE YOURSELF WHO MAKE OUR COUNTRY GREAT !
YOU DESERVE THIS AWARD !
YOU ALSO DESERVE MY THANKS, ARCHIE !
FOR WHAT, SIR ?
FOR HELPING ME OUT OF A MESS I WOULDN'T HAVE GOTTEN INTO IN THE FIRST PLACE IF IT HADN'T BEEN FOR YOU !
END

Veronica in "CONSTANT COMPAINIONS"

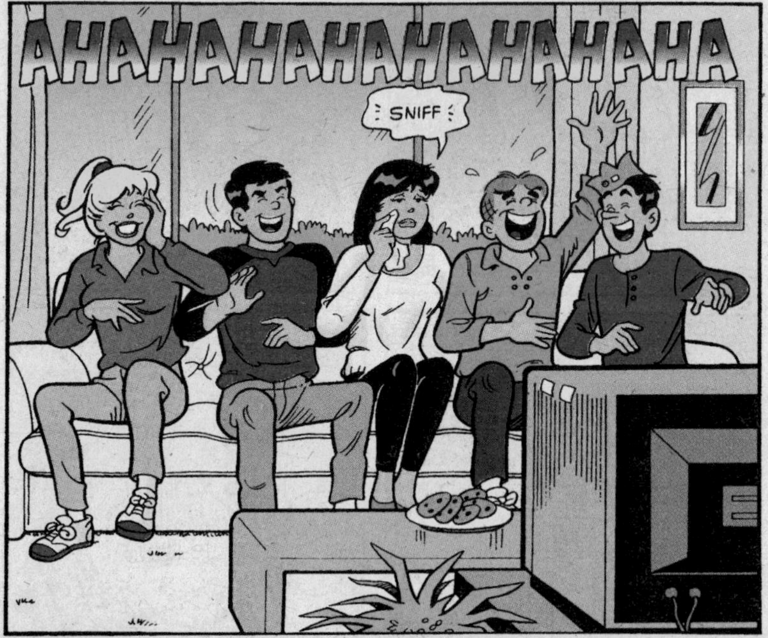
AHAHAHAHAHAHAHAHAHAHA
SNIFF

Script: Mike Pellowski / Pencils: Jeff Shultz / Inks: Rich Koslowski / Letters: Bill Yoshida / Colors: Barry Grossman

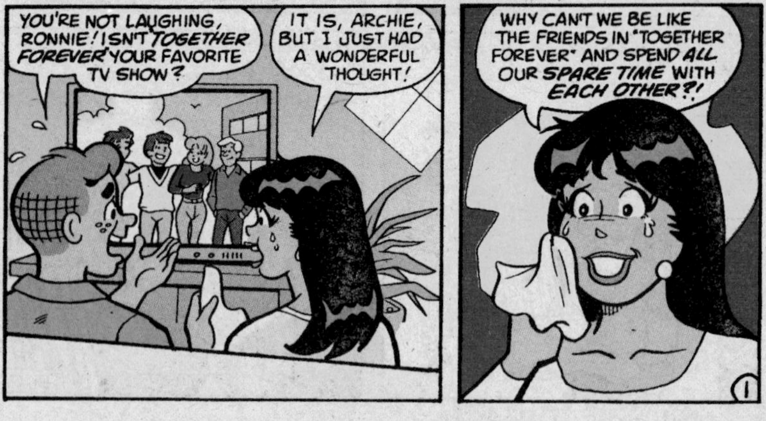
YOU'RE NOT LAUGHING, RONNIE! ISN'T TOGETHER FOREVER YOUR FAVORITE TV SHOW?
IT IS, ARCHIE, BUT I JUST HAD A WONDERFUL THOUGHT!
WHY CAN'T WE BE LIKE THE FRIENDS IN "TOGETHER FOREVER" AND SPEND ALL OUR SPARE TIME WITH EACH OTHER?!
1

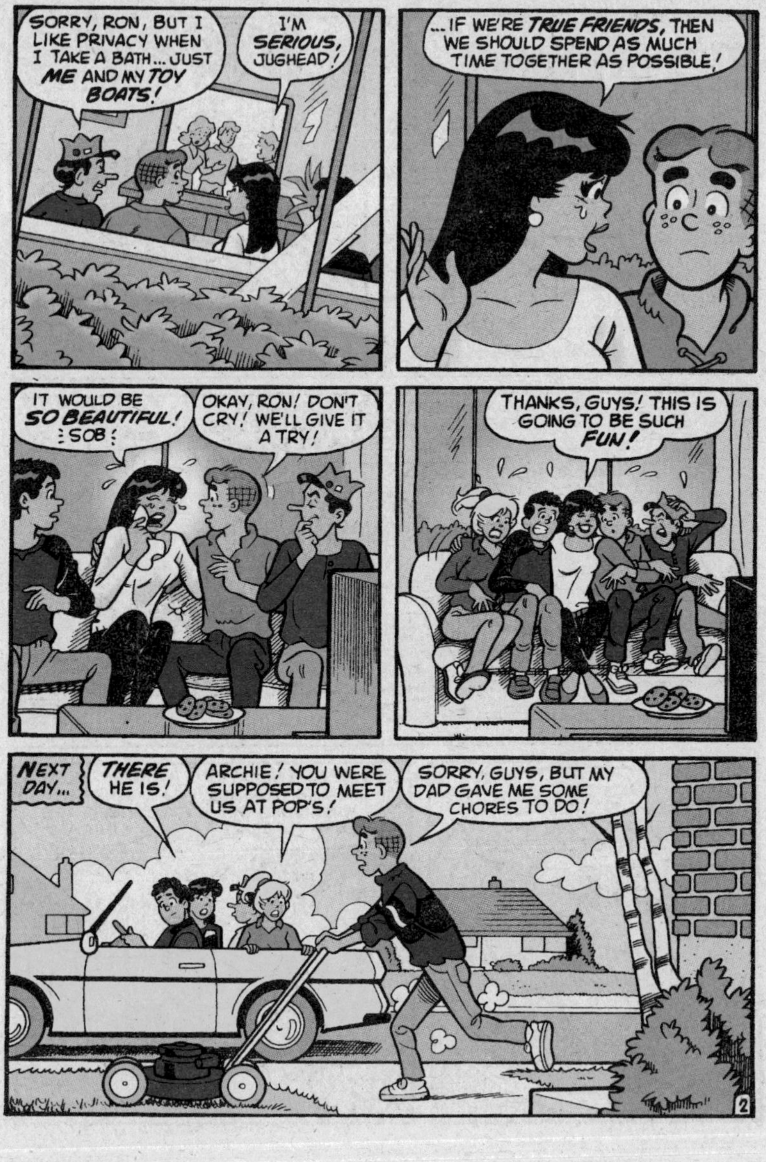

SORRY, RON, BUT I LIKE PRIVACY WHEN I TAKE A BATH... JUST ME AND MY TOY BOATS!
I'M SERIOUS, JUGHEAD!
...IF WE'RE TRUE FRIENDS, THEN WE SHOULD SPEND AS MUCH TIME TOGETHER AS POSSIBLE!
IT WOULD BE SO BEAUTIFUL! SOB
OKAY, RON! DON'T CRY! WE'LL GIVE IT A TRY!
THANKS, GUYS! THIS IS GOING TO BE SUCH FUN!
NEXT DAY...
THERE HE IS!
ARCHIE! YOU WERE SUPPOSED TO MEET US AT POP'S!
SORRY, GUYS, BUT MY DAD GAVE ME SOME CHORES TO DO!
2

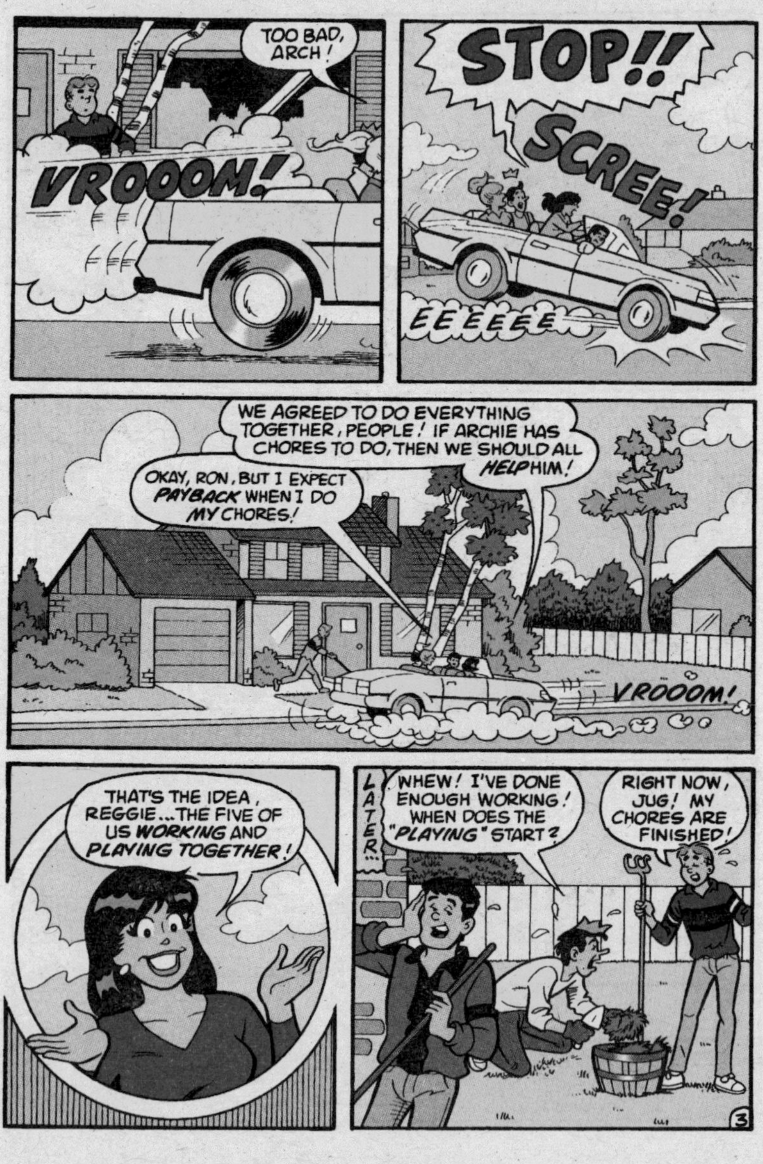
TOO BAD, ARCH!
VROOOM!
STOP!!
SCREE!
EEEEEE
WE AGREED TO DO EVERYTHING TOGETHER, PEOPLE! IF ARCHIE HAS CHORES TO DO, THEN WE SHOULD ALL HELP HIM!
OKAY, RON, BUT I EXPECT PAYBACK WHEN I DO MY CHORES!
VROOOM!
THAT'S THE IDEA, REGGIE... THE FIVE OF US WORKING AND PLAYING TOGETHER!
LATER...
WHEW! I'VE DONE ENOUGH WORKING! WHEN DOES THE "PLAYING" START?
RIGHT NOW, JUG! MY CHORES ARE FINISHED!
3

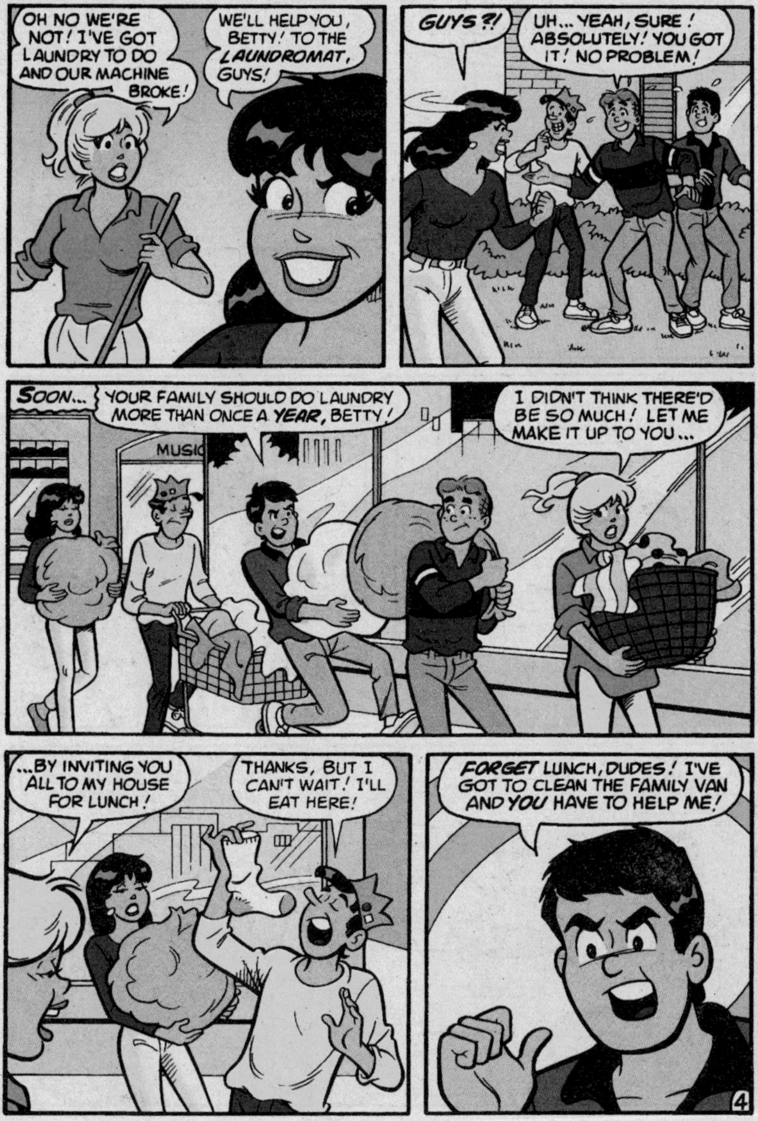

OH NO WE'RE NOT! I'VE GOT LAUNDRY TO DO AND OUR MACHINE BROKE!
WE'LL HELP YOU, BETTY! TO THE LAUNDROMAT, GUYS!
GUYS?!
UH... YEAH, SURE! ABSOLUTELY! YOU GOT IT! NO PROBLEM!
SOON...
YOUR FAMILY SHOULD DO LAUNDRY MORE THAN ONCE A YEAR, BETTY!
MUSIC
I DIDN'T THINK THERE'D BE SO MUCH! LET ME MAKE IT UP TO YOU...
...BY INVITING YOU ALL TO MY HOUSE FOR LUNCH!
THANKS, BUT I CAN'T WAIT! I'LL EAT HERE!
FORGET LUNCH, DUDES! I'VE GOT TO CLEAN THE FAMILY VAN AND YOU HAVE TO HELP ME!
4

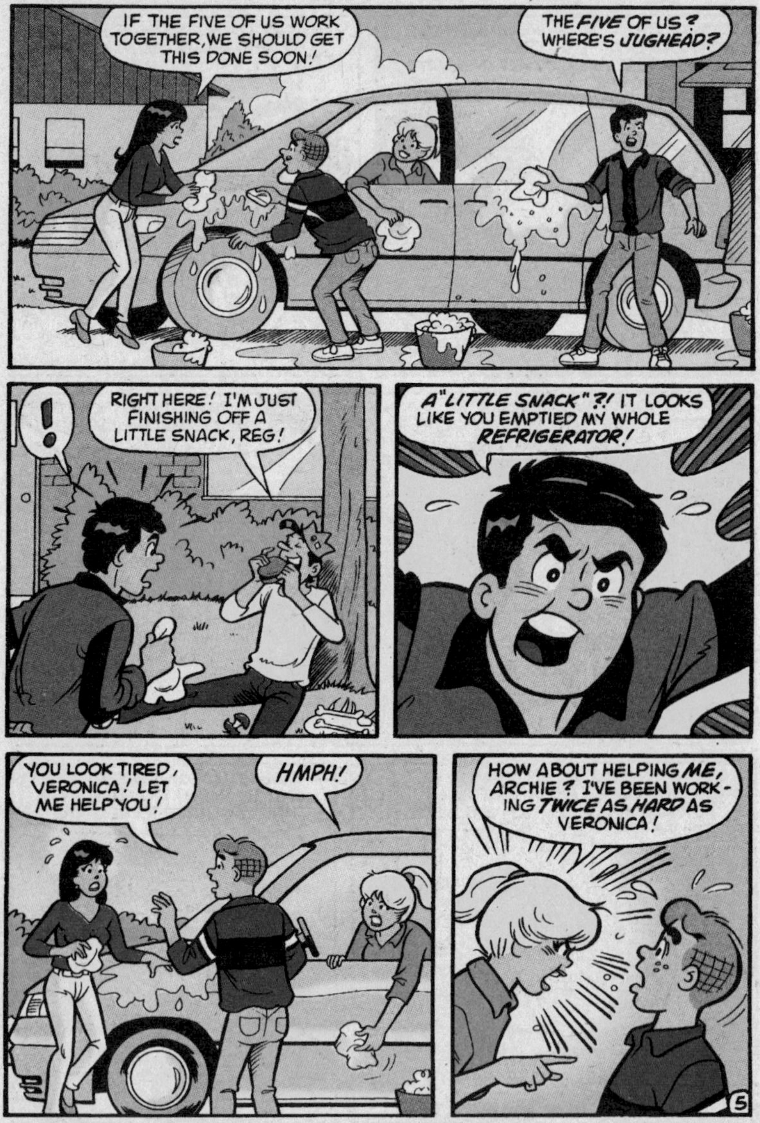
IF THE FIVE OF US WORK TOGETHER, WE SHOULD GET THIS DONE SOON!
THE FIVE OF US? WHERE'S JUGHEAD?
!
RIGHT HERE! I'M JUST FINISHING OFF A LITTLE SNACK, REG!
A "LITTLE SNACK"?! IT LOOKS LIKE YOU EMPTIED MY WHOLE REFRIGERATOR!
YOU LOOK TIRED, VERONICA! LET ME HELP YOU!
HMPH!
HOW ABOUT HELPING ME, ARCHIE? I'VE BEEN WORKING TWICE AS HARD AS VERONICA!
5

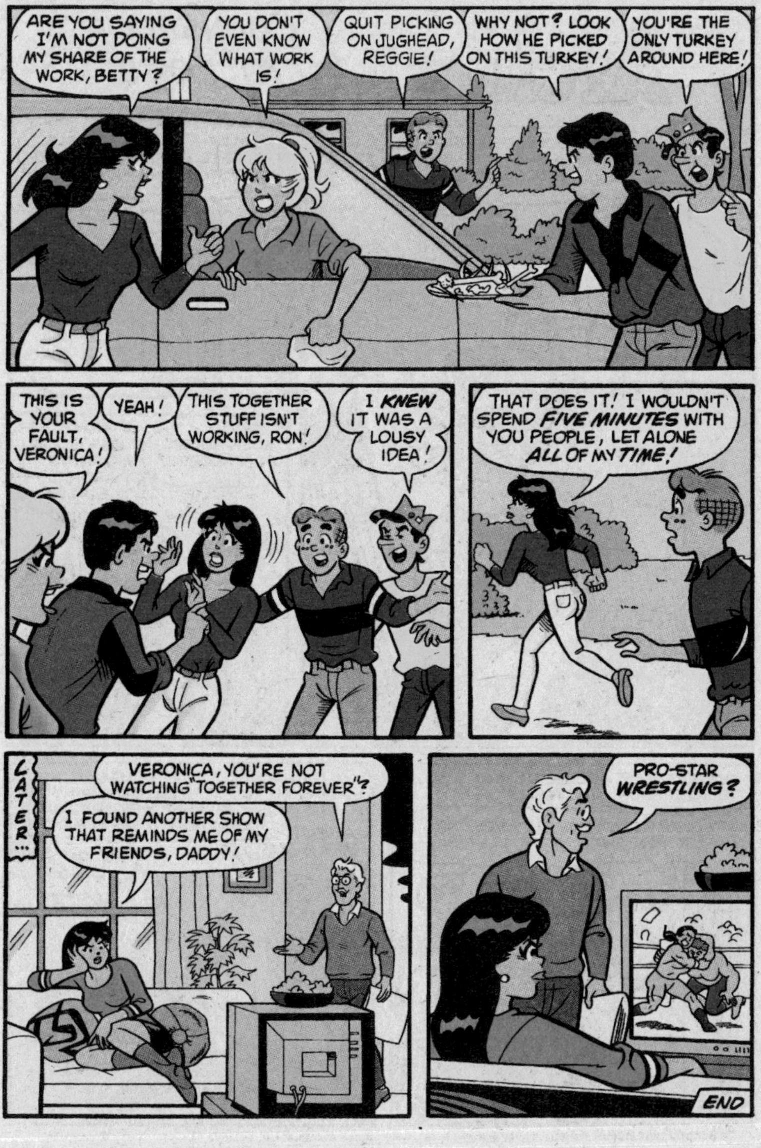
ARE YOU SAYING I'M NOT DOING MY SHARE OF THE WORK, BETTY?
YOU DON'T EVEN KNOW WHAT WORK IS!
QUIT PICKING ON JUGHEAD, REGGIE!
WHY NOT? LOOK HOW HE PICKED ON THIS TURKEY!
YOU'RE THE ONLY TURKEY AROUND HERE!
THIS IS YOUR FAULT, VERONICA!
YEAH!
THIS TOGETHER STUFF ISN'T WORKING, RON!
I KNEW IT WAS A LOUSY IDEA!
THAT DOES IT! I WOULDN'T SPEND FIVE MINUTES WITH YOU PEOPLE, LET ALONE ALL OF MY TIME!
LATER...
VERONICA, YOU'RE NOT WATCHING "TOGETHER FOREVER"?
I FOUND ANOTHER SHOW THAT REMINDS ME OF MY FRIENDS, DADDY!
PRO-STAR WRESTLING?
END

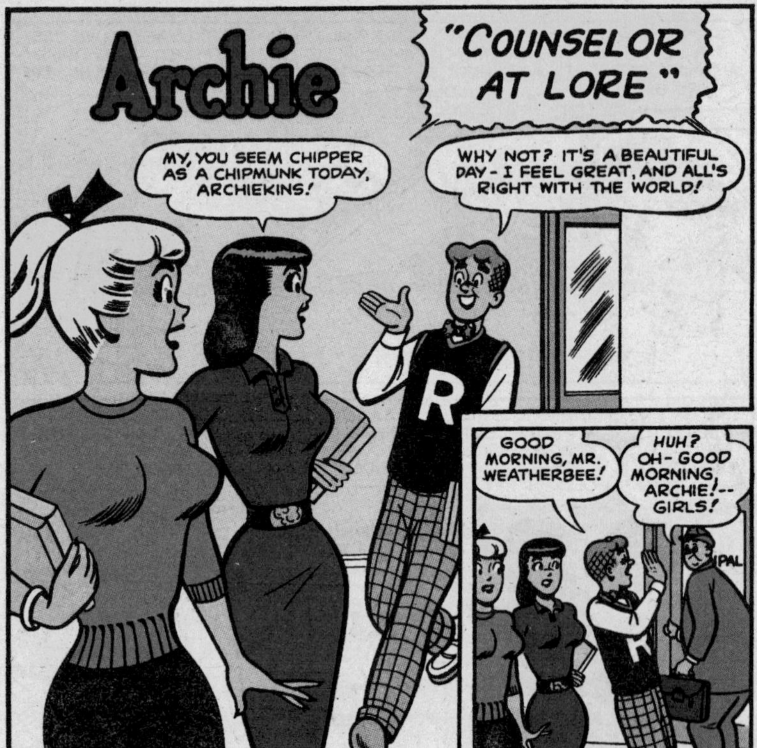
Archie
"COUNSELOR AT LORE"
MY, YOU SEEM CHIPPER AS A CHIPMUNK TODAY, ARCHIEKINS!
WHY NOT? IT'S A BEAUTIFUL DAY - I FEEL GREAT, AND ALL'S RIGHT WITH THE WORLD!
GOOD MORNING, MR. WEATHERBEE!
HUH? OH - GOOD MORNING, ARCHIE!-- GIRLS!
INCIDENTALLY, ARCHIE -- I WANT TO SEE YOUR FATHER!
TELL HIM I'LL STOP OVER TONIGHT!
YES, SIR! I'LL TELL ---
PRINCIPAL
YII! WHAT HAPPENED TO HIM?
DELAYED REACTION!
SEE IF YOU CAN BRING HIM TO, REGGIE! BETTY AND I HAVE TO GET READY FOR CLASS!
1

Script: Frank Doyle / Pencils: Harry Lucey / Inks: Rudy Lapick / Letters: Bill Yoshida / Colors: Barry Grossman

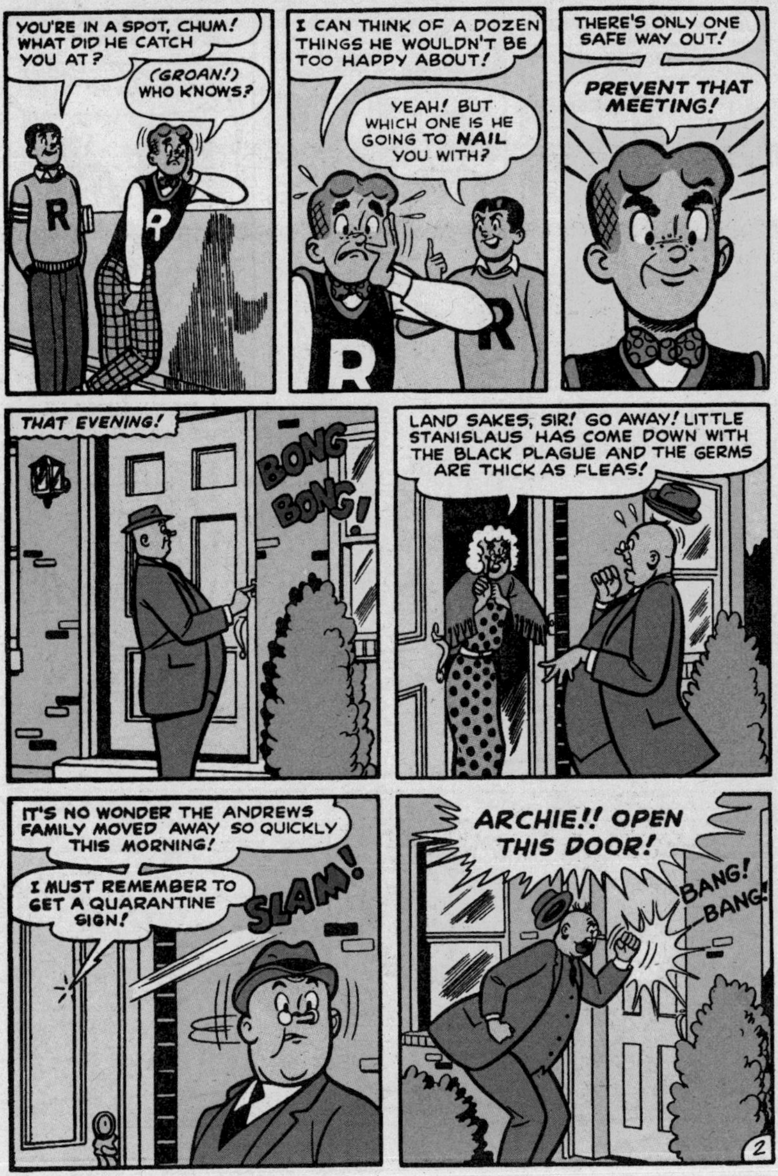
YOU'RE IN A SPOT, CHUM! WHAT DID HE CATCH YOU AT?
(GROAN!) WHO KNOWS?
I CAN THINK OF A DOZEN THINGS HE WOULDN'T BE TOO HAPPY ABOUT!
YEAH! BUT WHICH ONE IS HE GOING TO NAIL YOU WITH?
THERE'S ONLY ONE SAFE WAY OUT!
PREVENT THAT MEETING!
THAT EVENING!
BONG BONG!
LAND SAKES, SIR! GO AWAY! LITTLE STANISLAUS HAS COME DOWN WITH THE BLACK PLAGUE AND THE GERMS ARE THICK AS FLEAS!
IT'S NO WONDER THE ANDREWS FAMILY MOVED AWAY SO QUICKLY THIS MORNING!
I MUST REMEMBER TO GET A QUARANTINE SIGN!
SLAM!
ARCHIE!! OPEN THIS DOOR!
BANG! BANG!
2

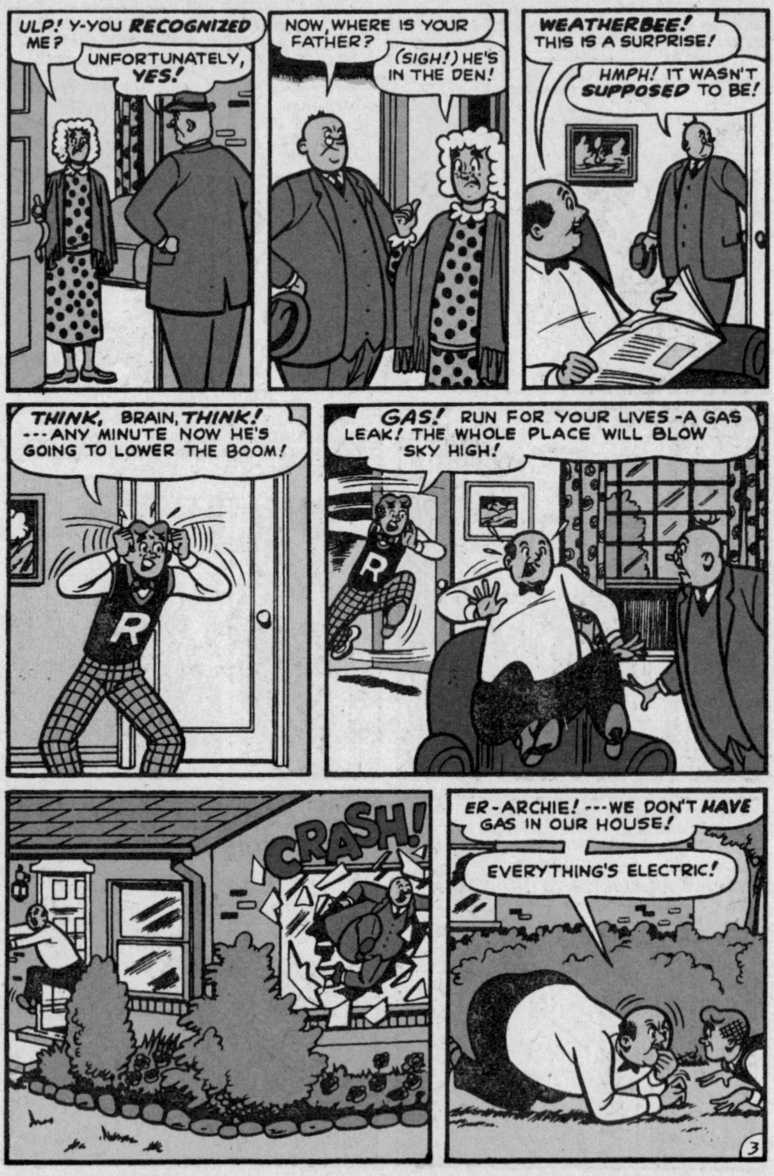
ULP! Y-YOU RECOGNIZED ME?
UNFORTUNATELY, YES!
NOW, WHERE IS YOUR FATHER?
(SIGH!) HE'S IN THE DEN!
WEATHERBEE! THIS IS A SURPRISE!
HMPH! IT WASN'T SUPPOSED TO BE!
THINK, BRAIN, THINK! ---ANY MINUTE NOW HE'S GOING TO LOWER THE BOOM!
GAS! RUN FOR YOUR LIVES -A GAS LEAK! THE WHOLE PLACE WILL BLOW SKY HIGH!
CRASH!
ER-ARCHIE! ---WE DON'T HAVE GAS IN OUR HOUSE!
EVERYTHING'S ELECTRIC!
3

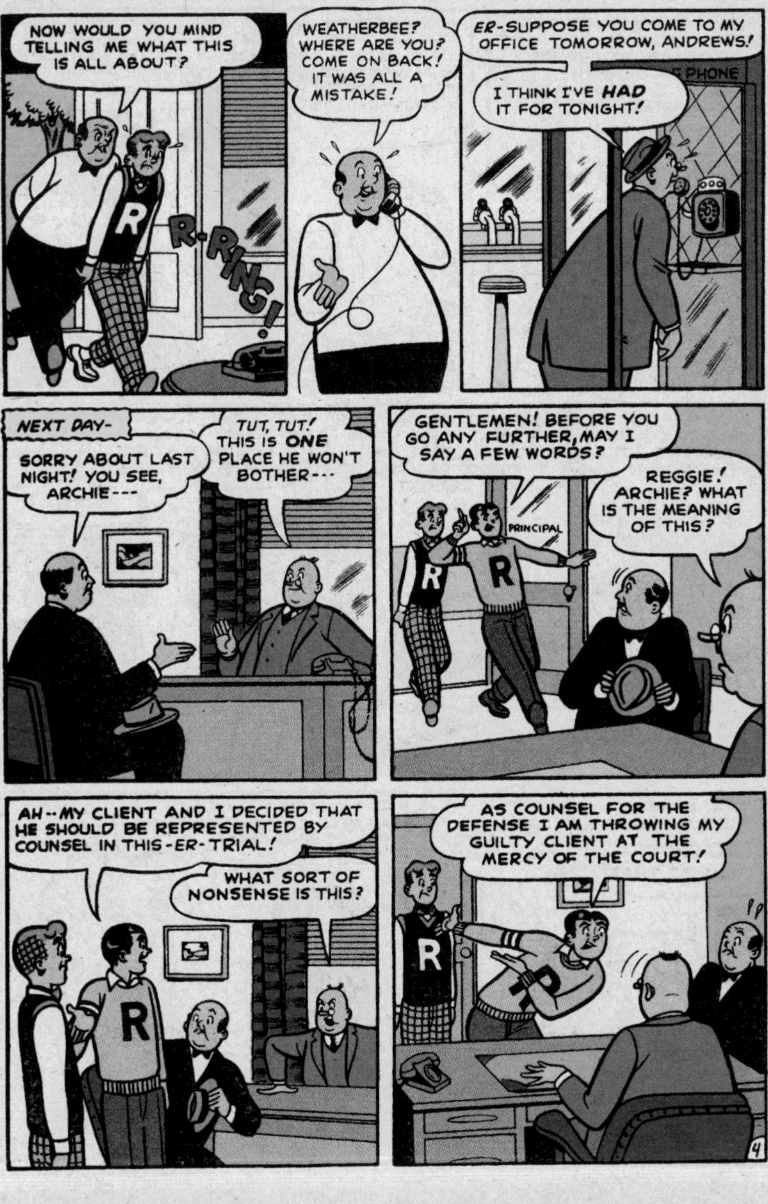
NOW WOULD YOU MIND TELLING ME WHAT THIS IS ALL ABOUT?
R-RING!
WEATHERBEE? WHERE ARE YOU? COME ON BACK! IT WAS ALL A MISTAKE!
ER-SUPPOSE YOU COME TO MY OFFICE TOMORROW, ANDREWS!
I THINK I'VE HAD IT FOR TONIGHT!
NEXT DAY-
SORRY ABOUT LAST NIGHT! YOU SEE, ARCHIE---
TUT, TUT! THIS IS ONE PLACE HE WON'T BOTHER---
GENTLEMEN! BEFORE YOU GO ANY FURTHER, MAY I SAY A FEW WORDS?
PRINCIPAL
REGGIE! ARCHIE? WHAT IS THE MEANING OF THIS?
AH--MY CLIENT AND I DECIDED THAT HE SHOULD BE REPRESENTED BY COUNSEL IN THIS-ER-TRIAL!
WHAT SORT OF NONSENSE IS THIS?
AS COUNSEL FOR THE DEFENSE I AM THROWING MY GUILTY CLIENT AT THE MERCY OF THE COURT!
4

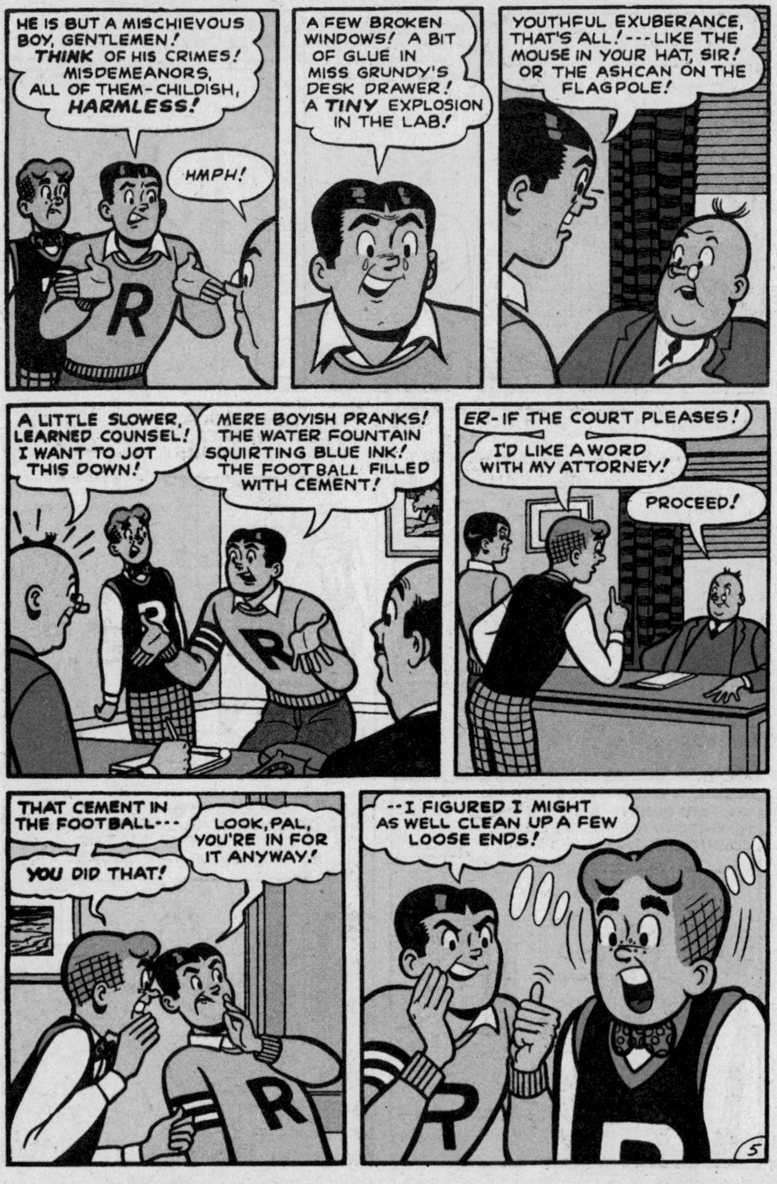
HE IS BUT A MISCHIEVOUS BOY, GENTLEMEN! THINK OF HIS CRIMES! MISDEMEANORS, ALL OF THEM- CHILDISH, HARMLESS!
HMPH!
A FEW BROKEN WINDOWS! A BIT OF GLUE IN MISS GRUNDY'S DESK DRAWER! A TINY EXPLOSION IN THE LAB!
YOUTHFUL EXUBERANCE, THAT'S ALL!---LIKE THE MOUSE IN YOUR HAT, SIR! OR THE ASHCAN ON THE FLAGPOLE!
A LITTLE SLOWER, LEARNED COUNSEL! I WANT TO JOT THIS DOWN!
MERE BOYISH PRANKS! THE WATER FOUNTAIN SQUIRTING BLUE INK! THE FOOTBALL FILLED WITH CEMENT!
ER- IF THE COURT PLEASES!
I'D LIKE A WORD WITH MY ATTORNEY!
PROCEED!
THAT CEMENT IN THE FOOTBALL---
YOU DID THAT!
LOOK, PAL, YOU'RE IN FOR IT ANYWAY!
--I FIGURED I MIGHT AS WELL CLEAN UP A FEW LOOSE ENDS!

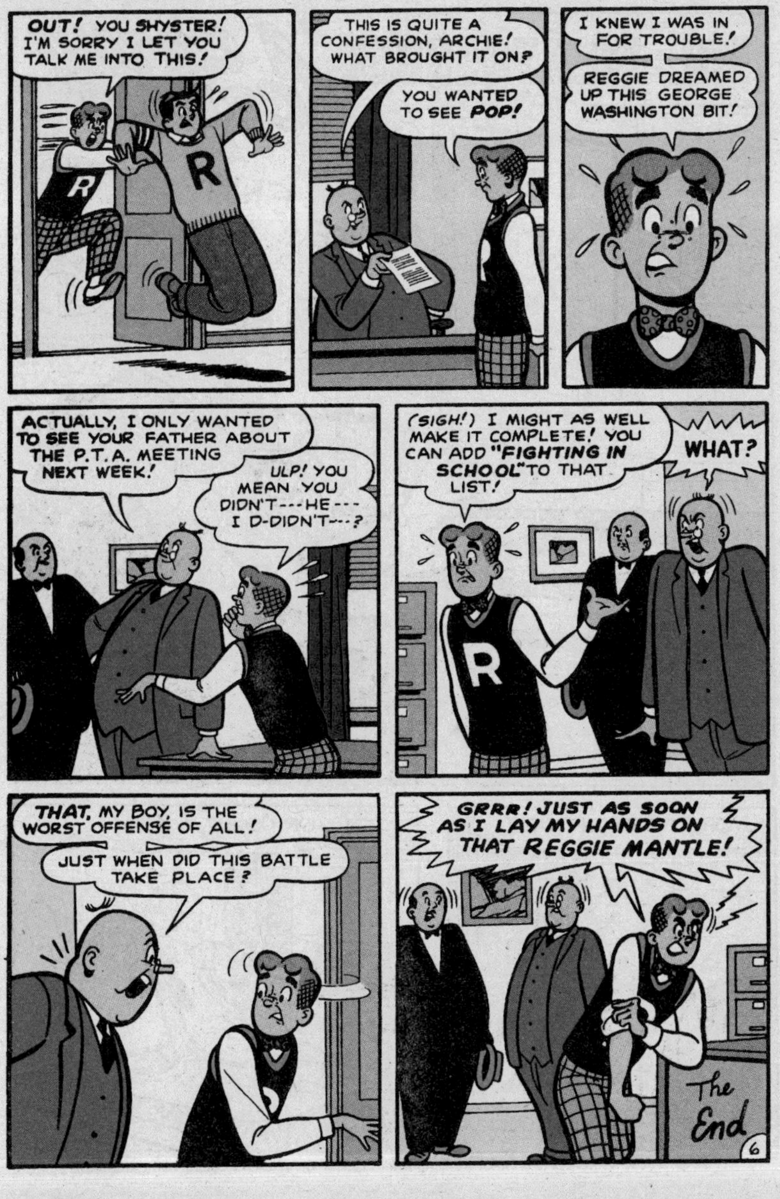
OUT! YOU SHYSTER! I'M SORRY I LET YOU TALK ME INTO THIS!
THIS IS QUITE A CONFESSION, ARCHIE! WHAT BROUGHT IT ON?
YOU WANTED TO SEE POP!
I KNEW I WAS IN FOR TROUBLE!
REGGIE DREAMED UP THIS GEORGE WASHINGTON BIT!
ACTUALLY, I ONLY WANTED TO SEE YOUR FATHER ABOUT THE P.T.A. MEETING NEXT WEEK!
ULP! YOU MEAN YOU DIDN'T---HE--- I D-DIDN'T---?
(SIGH!) I MIGHT AS WELL MAKE IT COMPLETE! YOU CAN ADD "FIGHTING IN SCHOOL" TO THAT LIST!
WHAT?
THAT, MY BOY, IS THE WORST OFFENSE OF ALL!
JUST WHEN DID THIS BATTLE TAKE PLACE?
GRRR! JUST AS SOON AS I LAY MY HANDS ON THAT REGGIE MANTLE!
The End
6

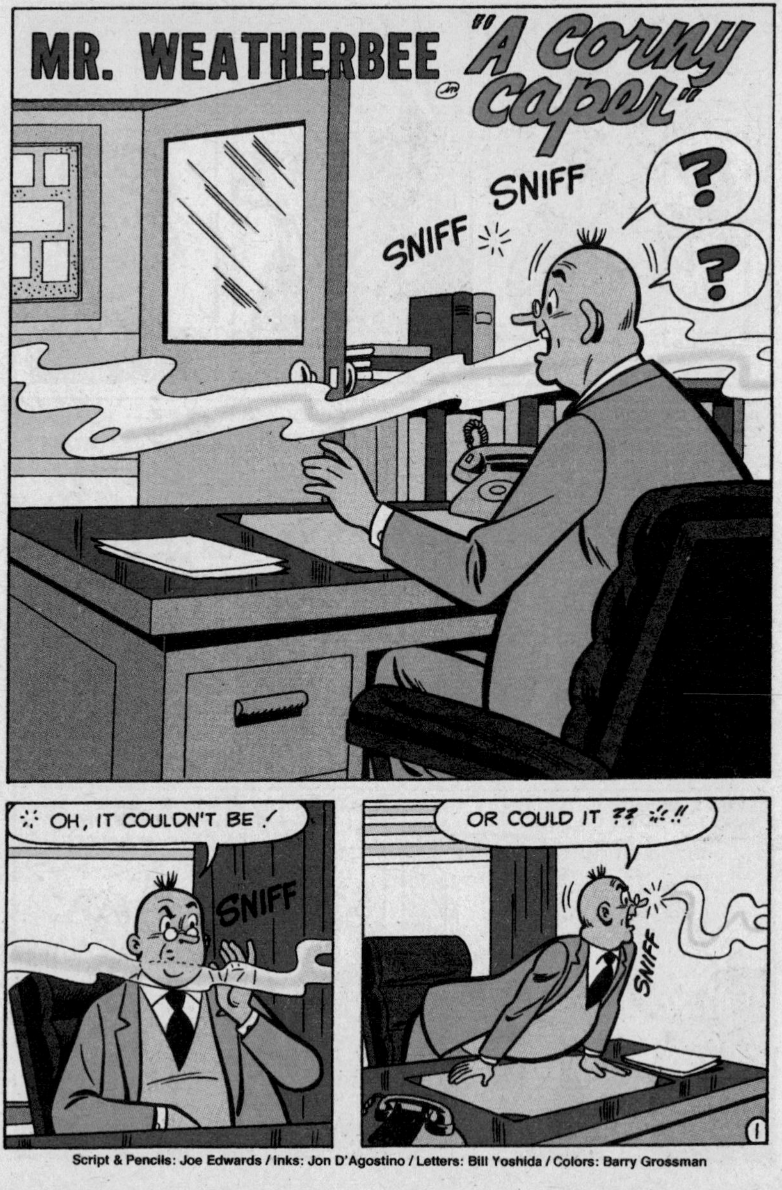
MR. WEATHERBEE in "A Corny Caper"
SNIFF SNIFF
?
?
OH, IT COULDN'T BE!
SNIFF
OR COULD IT ?? !!
SNIFF
1

Script & Pencils: Joe Edwards / Inks: Jon D'Agostino / Letters: Bill Yoshida / Colors: Barry Grossman

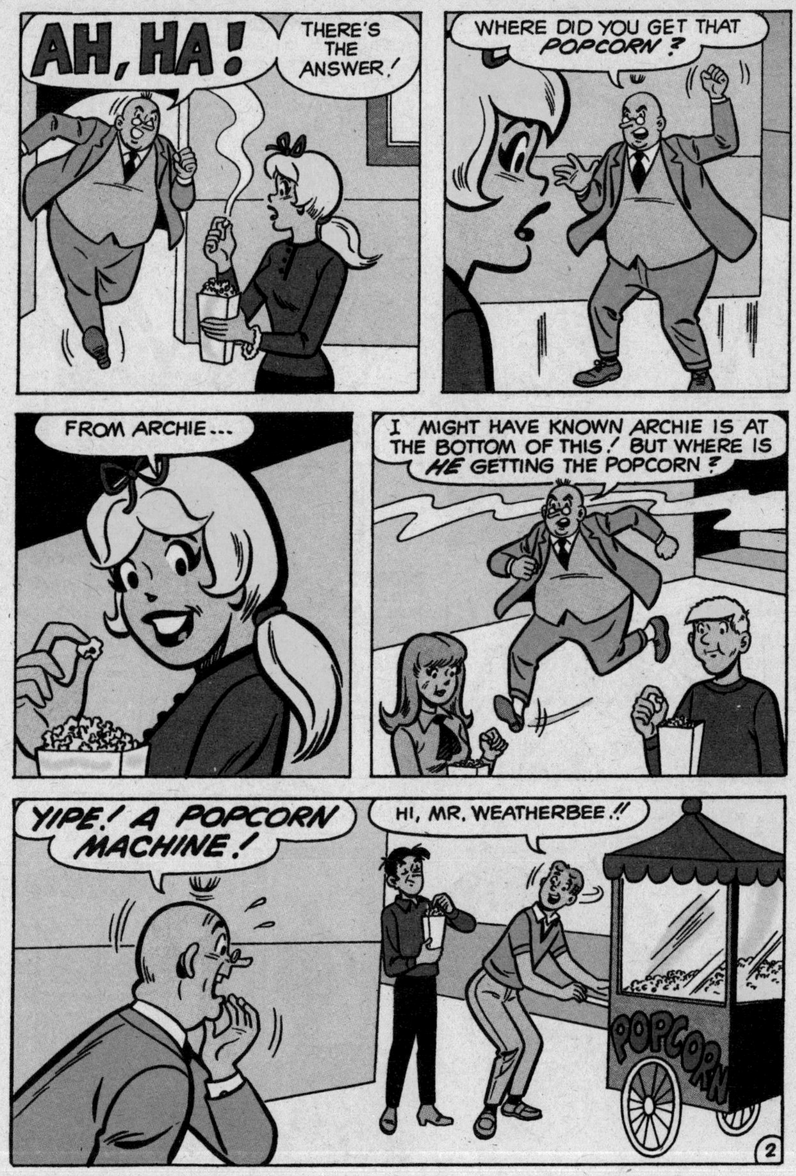
AH, HA!
THERE'S THE ANSWER!
WHERE DID YOU GET THAT POPCORN?
FROM ARCHIE...
I MIGHT HAVE KNOWN ARCHIE IS AT THE BOTTOM OF THIS! BUT WHERE IS HE GETTING THE POPCORN?
YIPE! A POPCORN MACHINE!
HI, MR. WEATHERBEE!!
POPCORN
2

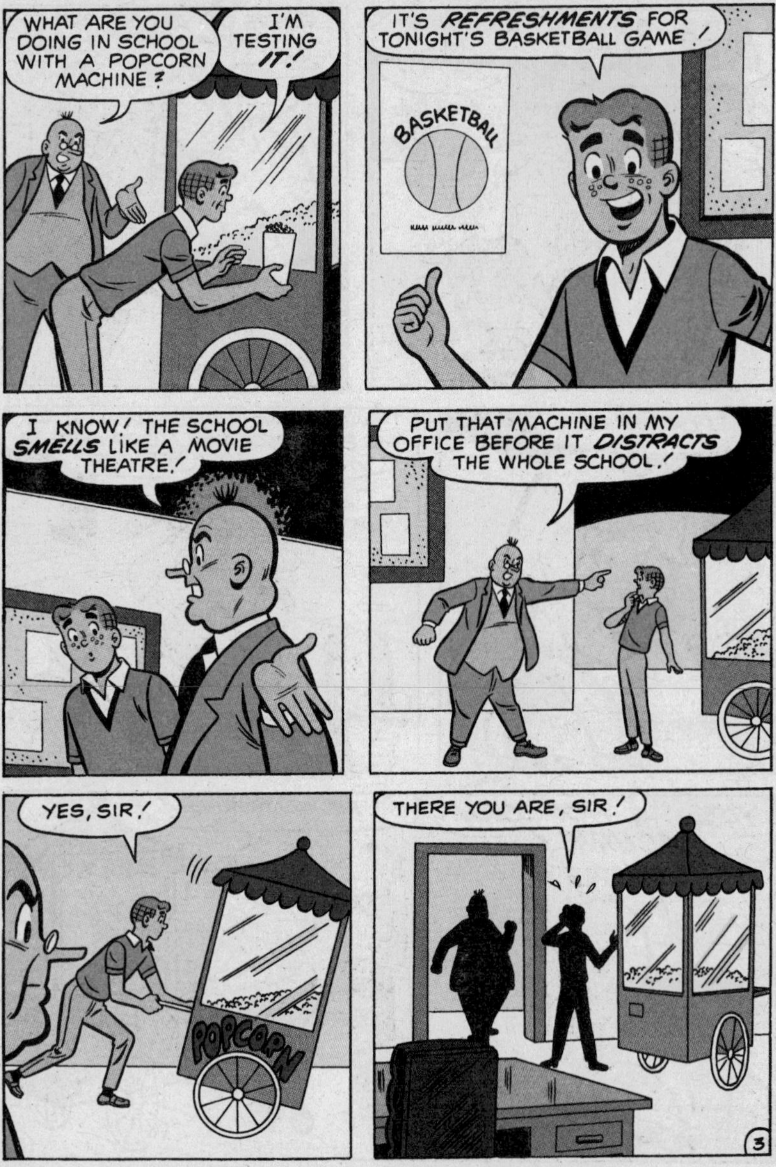
WHAT ARE YOU DOING IN SCHOOL WITH A POPCORN MACHINE?
I'M TESTING IT!
IT'S REFRESHMENTS FOR TONIGHT'S BASKETBALL GAME!
BASKETBALL
I KNOW! THE SCHOOL SMELLS LIKE A MOVIE THEATRE!
PUT THAT MACHINE IN MY OFFICE BEFORE IT DISTRACTS THE WHOLE SCHOOL!
YES, SIR!
POPCORN
THERE YOU ARE, SIR!
3

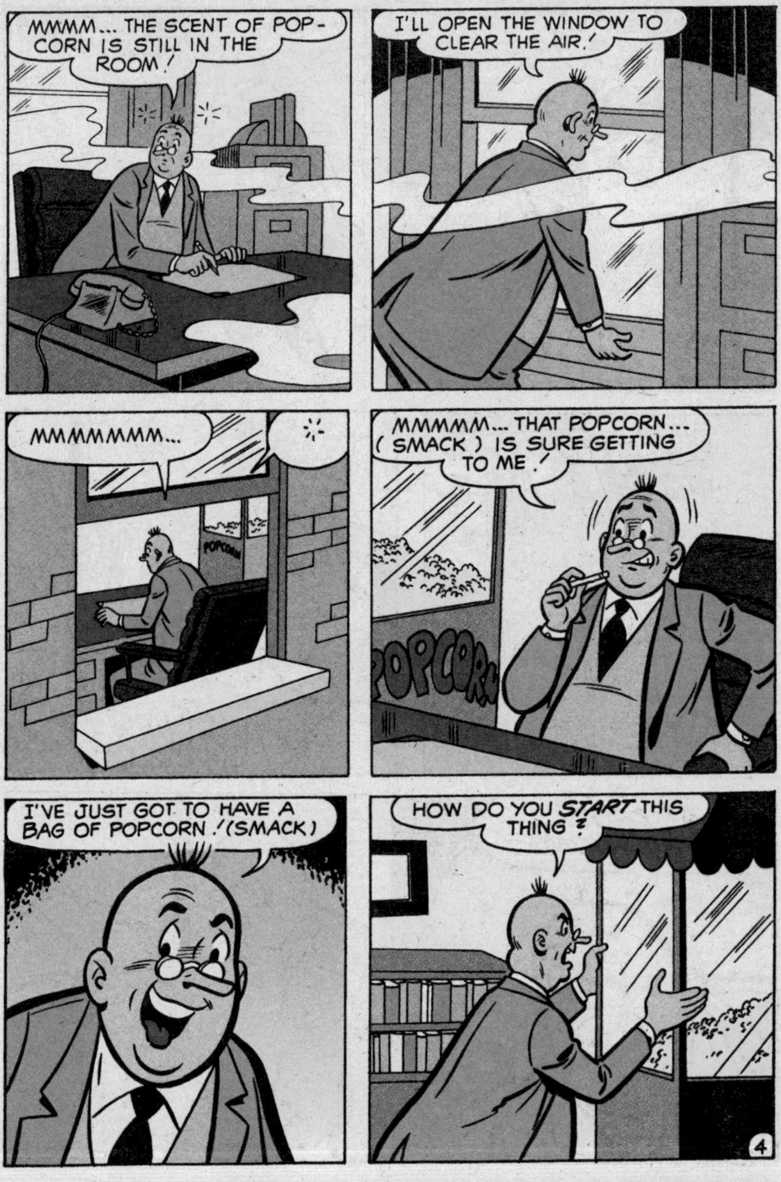
MMMM... THE SCENT OF POP-CORN IS STILL IN THE ROOM!
I'LL OPEN THE WINDOW TO CLEAR THE AIR!
MMMMMMM...
POPCORN
MMMMM... THAT POPCORN... (SMACK) IS SURE GETTING TO ME!
POPCORN
I'VE JUST GOT TO HAVE A BAG OF POPCORN!(SMACK)
HOW DO YOU START THIS THING?
4

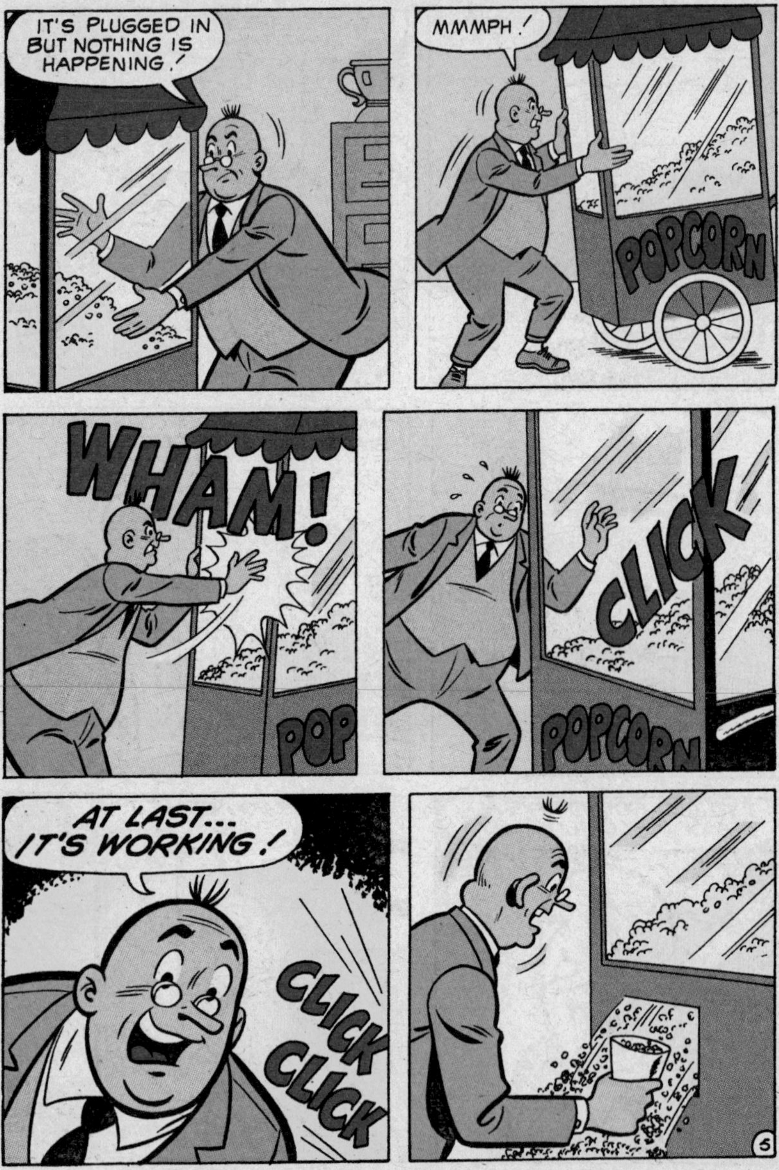
IT'S PLUGGED IN BUT NOTHING IS HAPPENING.!
MMMPH!
POPCORN
WHAM!
POP
CLICK
POPCORN
AT LAST... IT'S WORKING!
CLICK CLICK
5

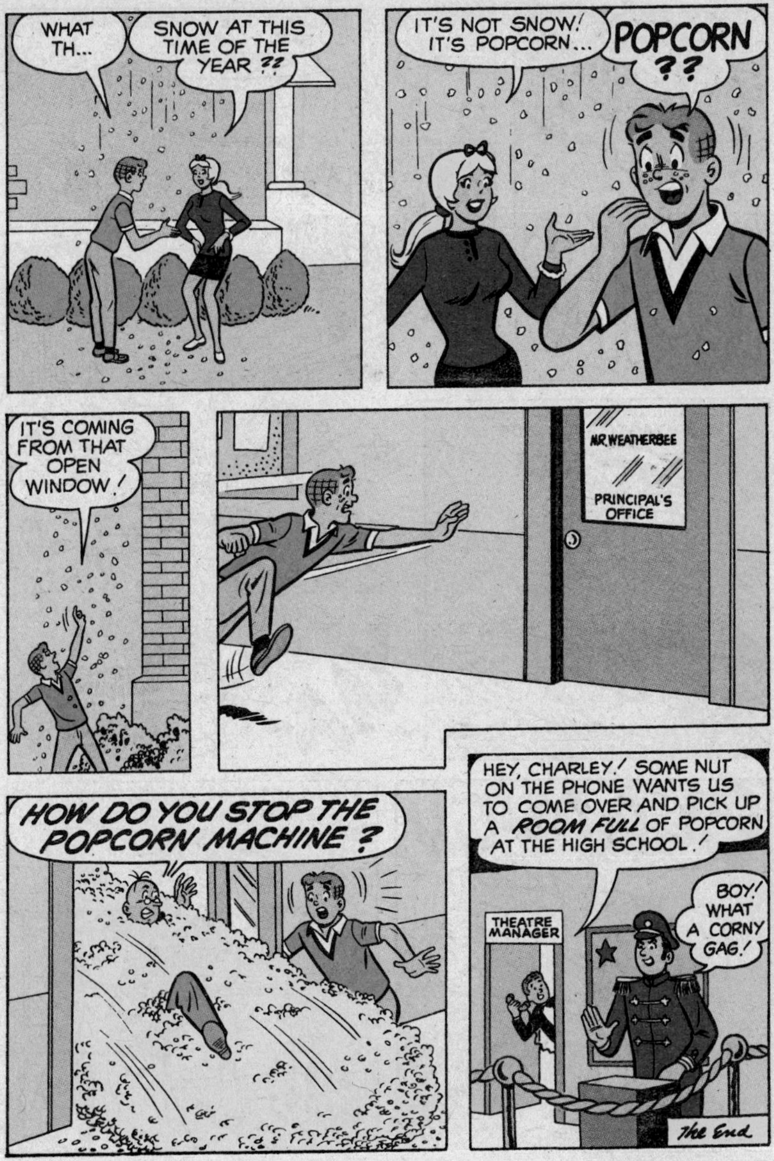
WHAT TH...
SNOW AT THIS TIME OF THE YEAR ??
IT'S NOT SNOW! IT'S POPCORN...
POPCORN ??
IT'S COMING FROM THAT OPEN WINDOW!
MR. WEATHERBEE
PRINCIPAL'S OFFICE
HOW DO YOU STOP THE POPCORN MACHINE ?
HEY, CHARLEY! SOME NUT ON THE PHONE WANTS US TO COME OVER AND PICK UP A ROOM FULL OF POPCORN AT THE HIGH SCHOOL!
THEATRE MANAGER
BOY! WHAT A CORNY GAG!
The End

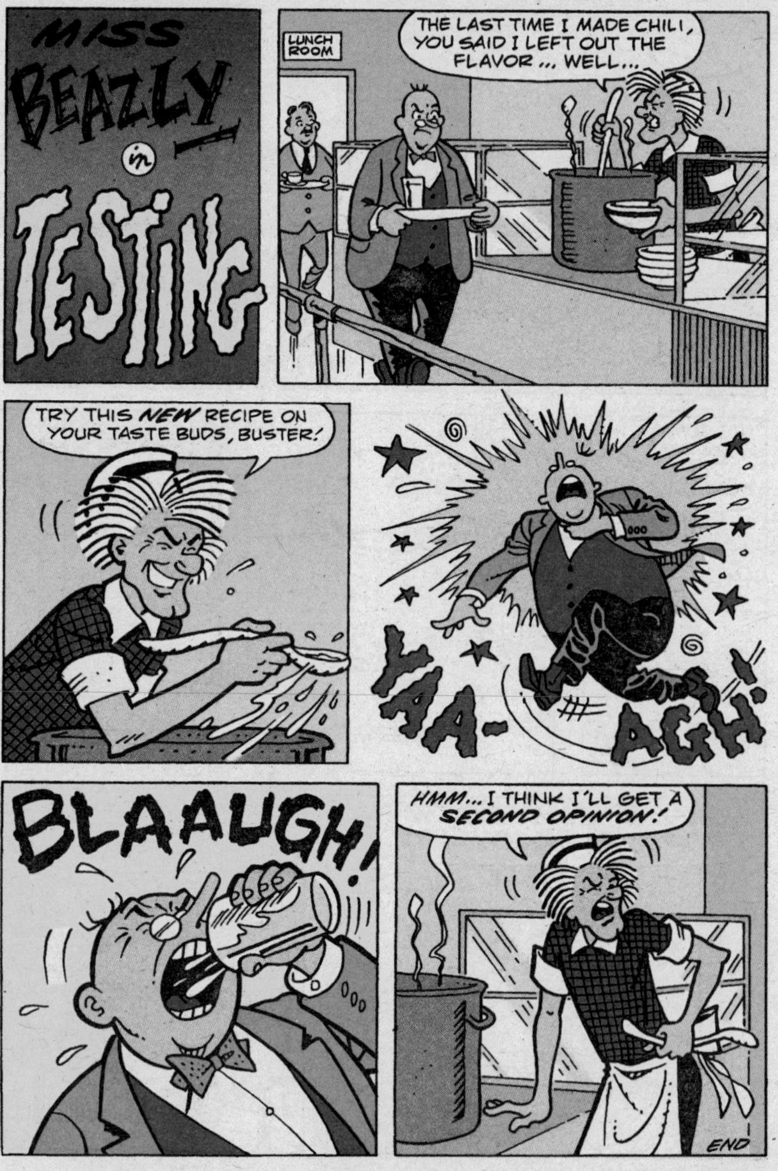
MISS BEAZLY in TESTING
LUNCH ROOM
THE LAST TIME I MADE CHILI, YOU SAID I LEFT OUT THE FLAVOR ... WELL...
TRY THIS *NEW* RECIPE ON YOUR TASTE BUDS, BUSTER!
YAA-AGH!
BLAAUGH!
HMM... I THINK I'LL GET A *SECOND OPINION*!
END

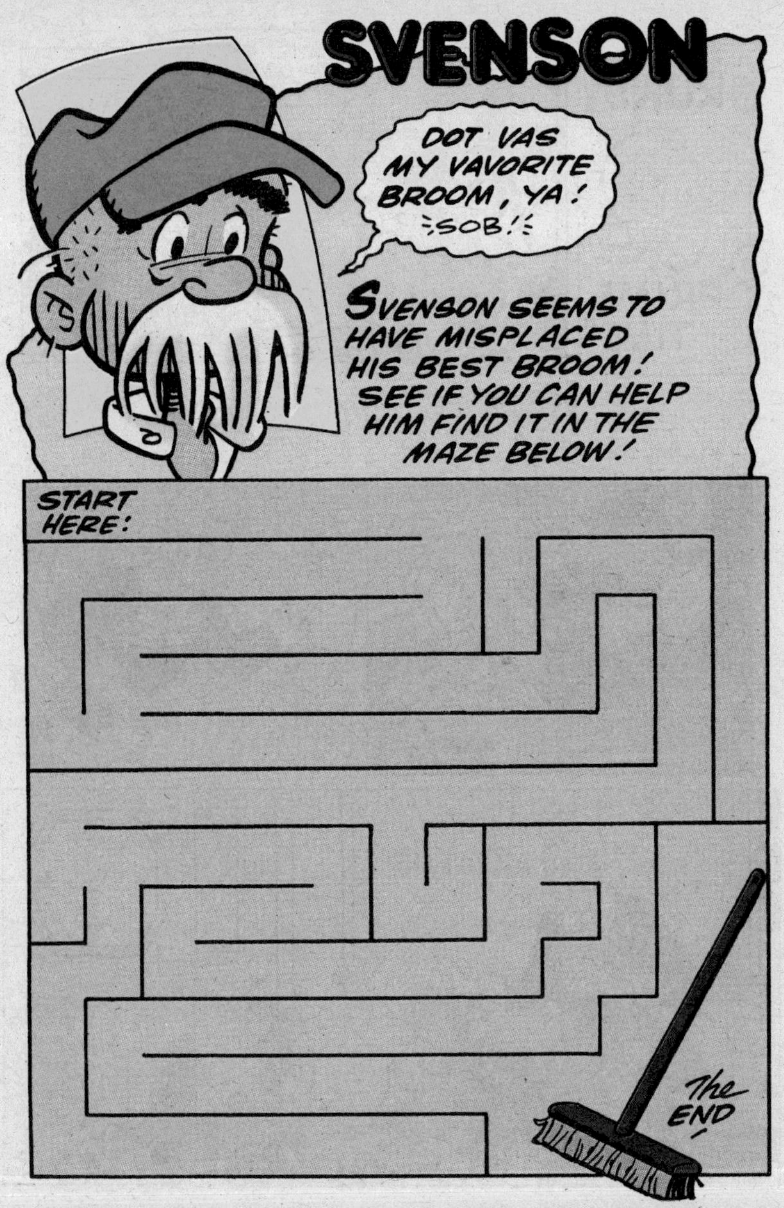
SVENSON
DOT VAS MY VAVORITE BROOM, YA! SOB!
SVENSON SEEMS TO HAVE MISPLACED HIS BEST BROOM! SEE IF YOU CAN HELP HIM FIND IT IN THE MAZE BELOW!
START HERE:
The END!

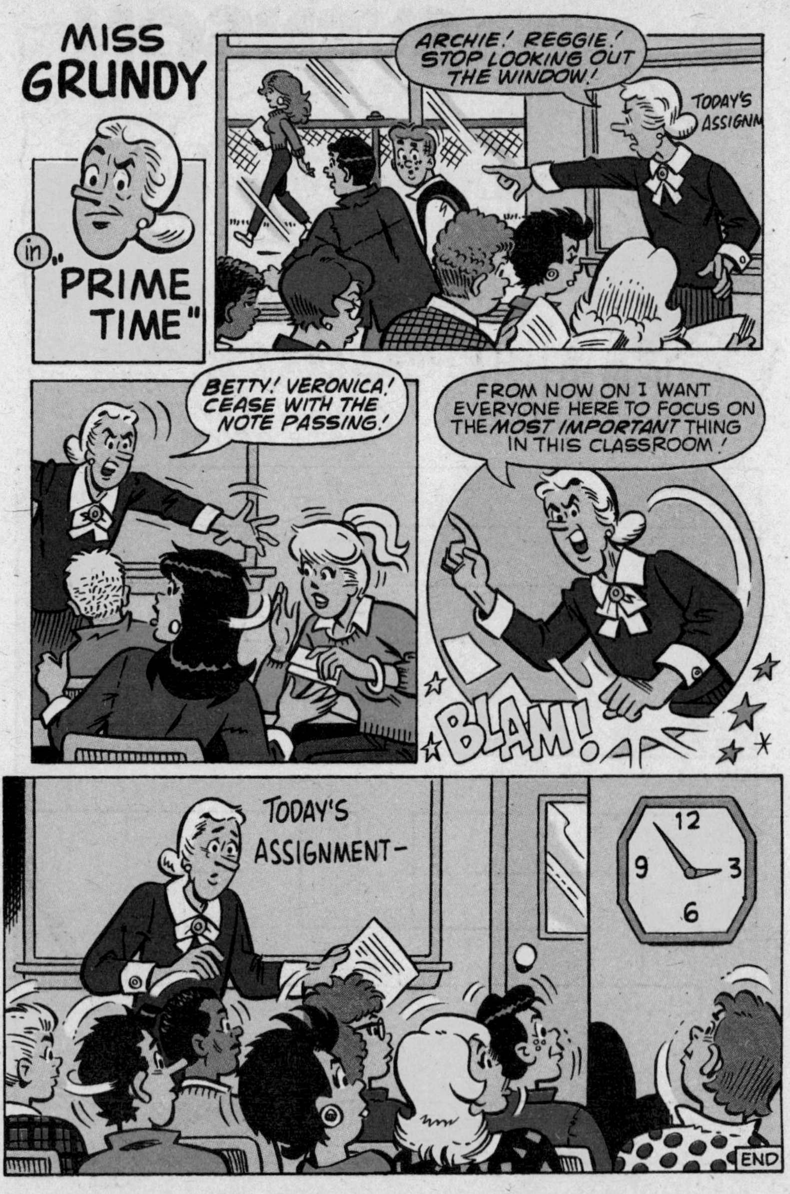
MISS GRUNDY
in "PRIME TIME"
ARCHIE! REGGIE! STOP LOOKING OUT THE WINDOW!
TODAY'S ASSIGNM
BETTY! VERONICA! CEASE WITH THE NOTE PASSING!
FROM NOW ON I WANT EVERYONE HERE TO FOCUS ON THE MOST IMPORTANT THING IN THIS CLASSROOM!
BLAM!
TODAY'S ASSIGNMENT-
12
9
3
6
END

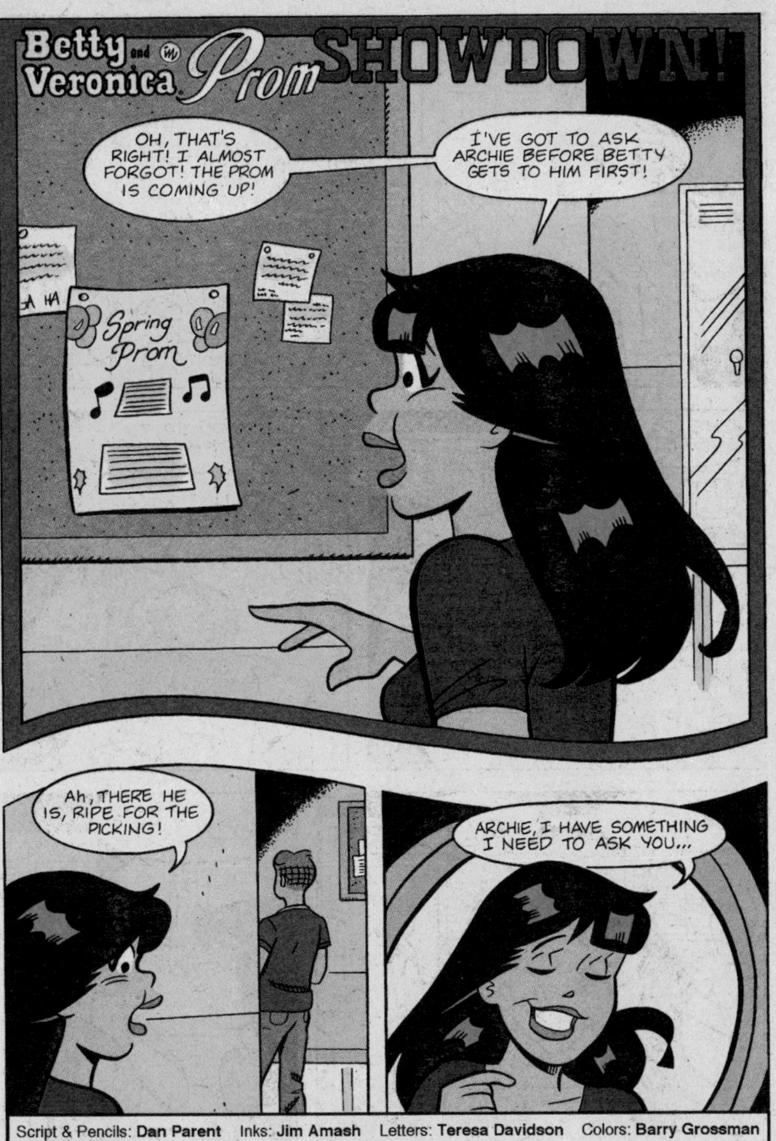
Betty and Veronica in Prom SHOWDOWN!
OH, THAT'S RIGHT! I ALMOST FORGOT! THE PROM IS COMING UP!
I'VE GOT TO ASK ARCHIE BEFORE BETTY GETS TO HIM FIRST!
Spring Prom
Ah, THERE HE IS, RIPE FOR THE PICKING!
ARCHIE, I HAVE SOMETHING I NEED TO ASK YOU...

Script & Pencils: **Dan Parent** Inks: **Jim Amash** Letters: **Teresa Davidson** Colors: **Barry Grossman**
Editor-In-Chief: **Victor Gorelick** President: **Mike Pellerito** Publisher: **Jon Goldwater**

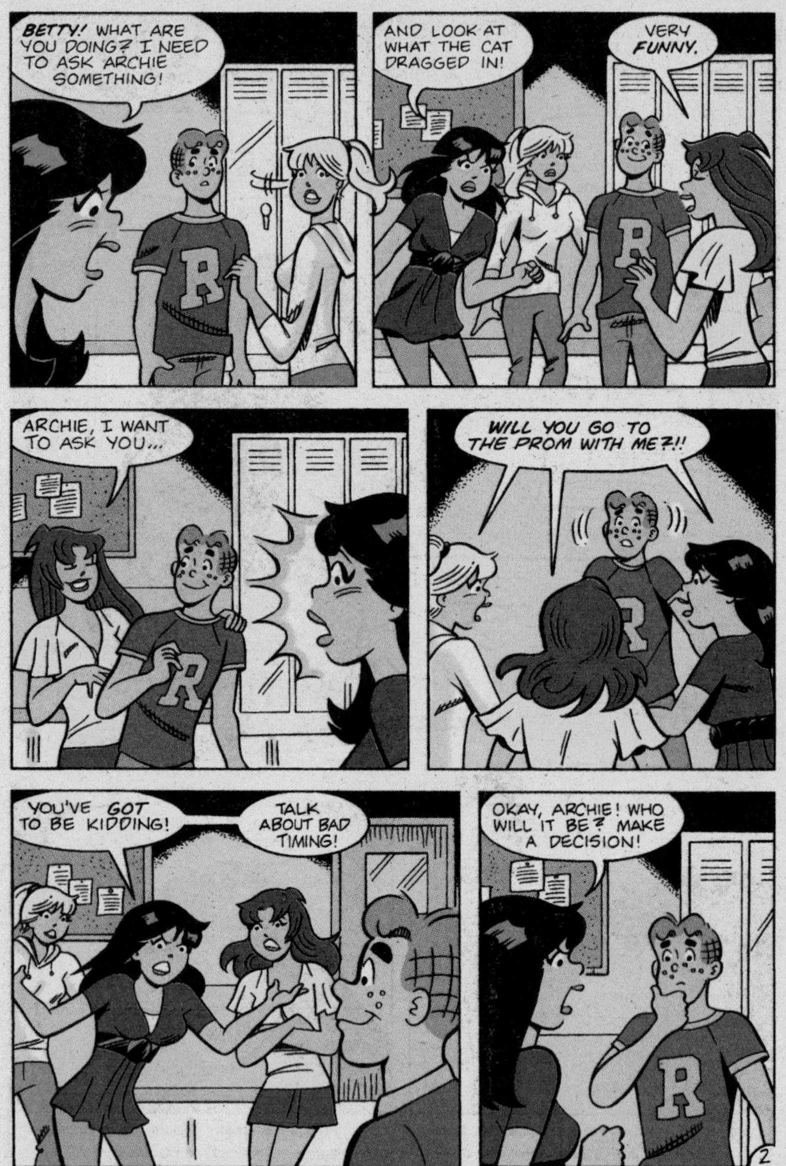
BETTY! WHAT ARE YOU DOING? I NEED TO ASK ARCHIE SOMETHING!
AND LOOK AT WHAT THE CAT DRAGGED IN!
VERY FUNNY.
ARCHIE, I WANT TO ASK YOU...
WILL YOU GO TO THE PROM WITH ME?!!
YOU'VE GOT TO BE KIDDING!
TALK ABOUT BAD TIMING!
OKAY, ARCHIE! WHO WILL IT BE? MAKE A DECISION!
2

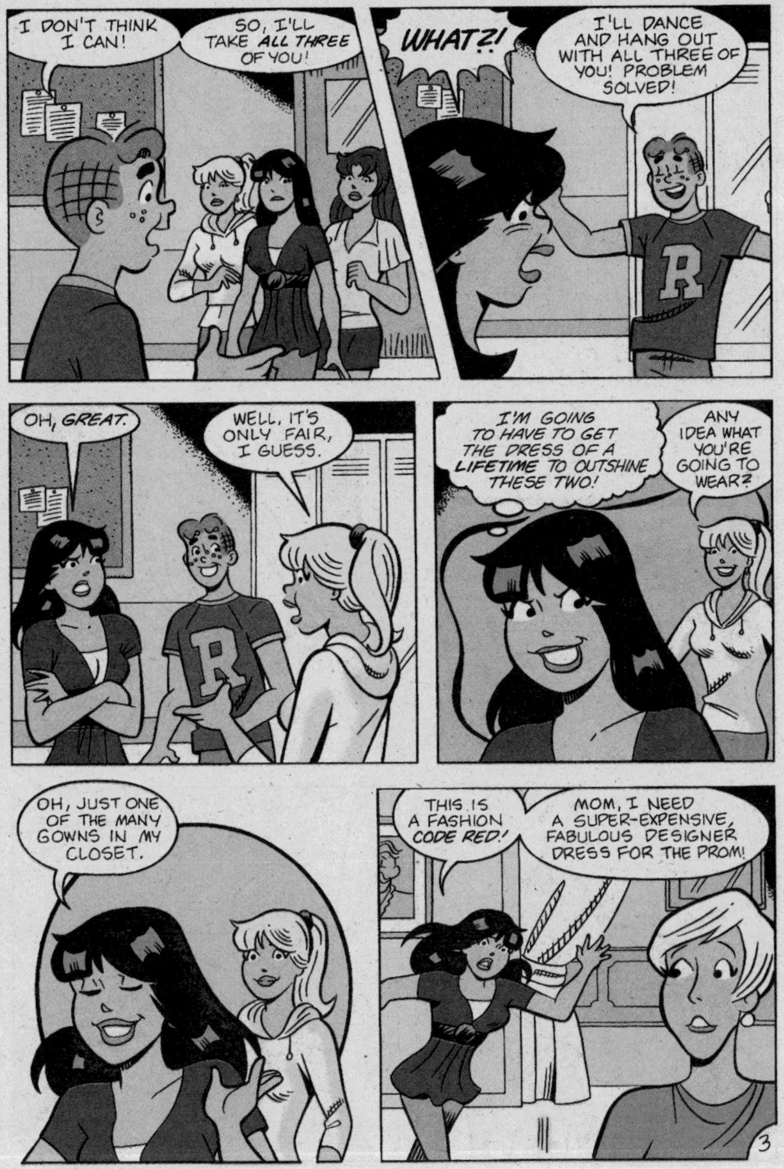
I DON'T THINK I CAN!
SO, I'LL TAKE ALL THREE OF YOU!
WHAT?!
I'LL DANCE AND HANG OUT WITH ALL THREE OF YOU! PROBLEM SOLVED!
OH, GREAT.
WELL, IT'S ONLY FAIR, I GUESS.
I'M GOING TO HAVE TO GET THE DRESS OF A LIFETIME TO OUTSHINE THESE TWO!
ANY IDEA WHAT YOU'RE GOING TO WEAR?
OH, JUST ONE OF THE MANY GOWNS IN MY CLOSET.
THIS IS A FASHION CODE RED!
MOM, I NEED A SUPER-EXPENSIVE, FABULOUS DESIGNER DRESS FOR THE PROM!
3

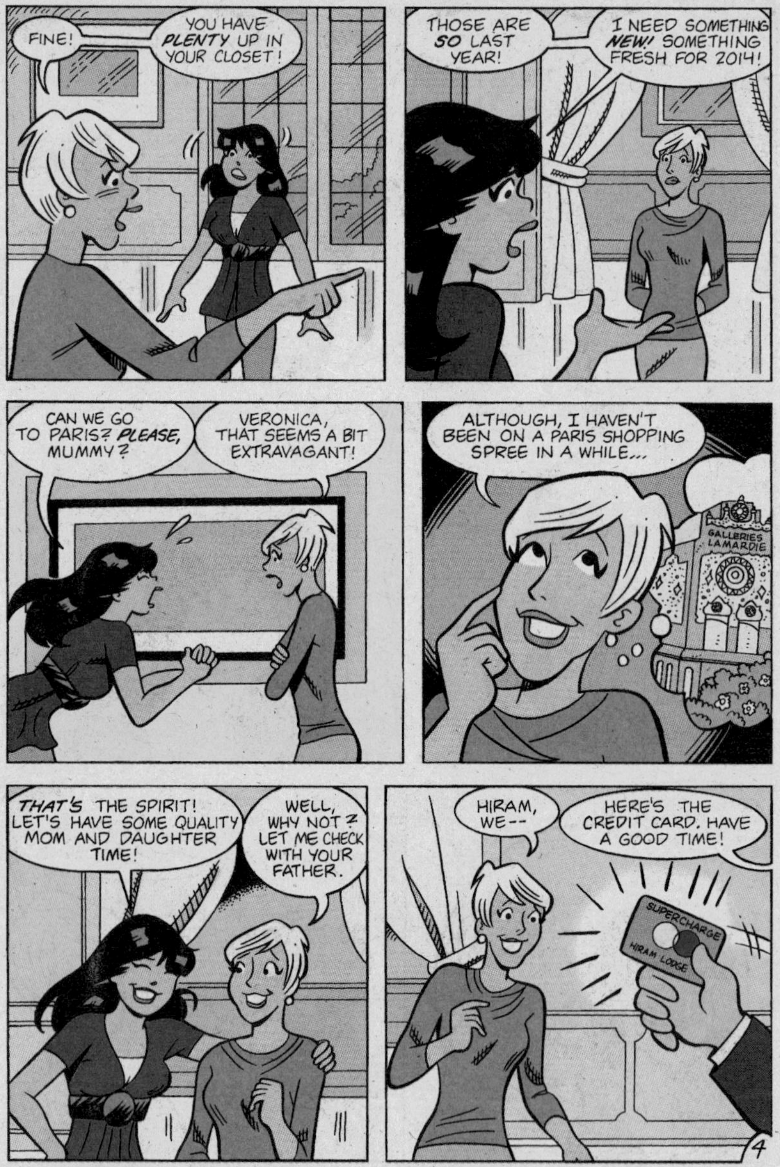
FINE!
YOU HAVE PLENTY UP IN YOUR CLOSET!
THOSE ARE SO LAST YEAR!
I NEED SOMETHING NEW! SOMETHING FRESH FOR 2014!
CAN WE GO TO PARIS? PLEASE, MUMMY?
VERONICA, THAT SEEMS A BIT EXTRAVAGANT!
ALTHOUGH, I HAVEN'T BEEN ON A PARIS SHOPPING SPREE IN A WHILE...
GALLERIES LAMARDIE
THAT'S THE SPIRIT! LET'S HAVE SOME QUALITY MOM AND DAUGHTER TIME!
WELL, WHY NOT? LET ME CHECK WITH YOUR FATHER.
HIRAM, WE--
HERE'S THE CREDIT CARD. HAVE A GOOD TIME!
SUPERCHARGE
HIRAM LODGE
4

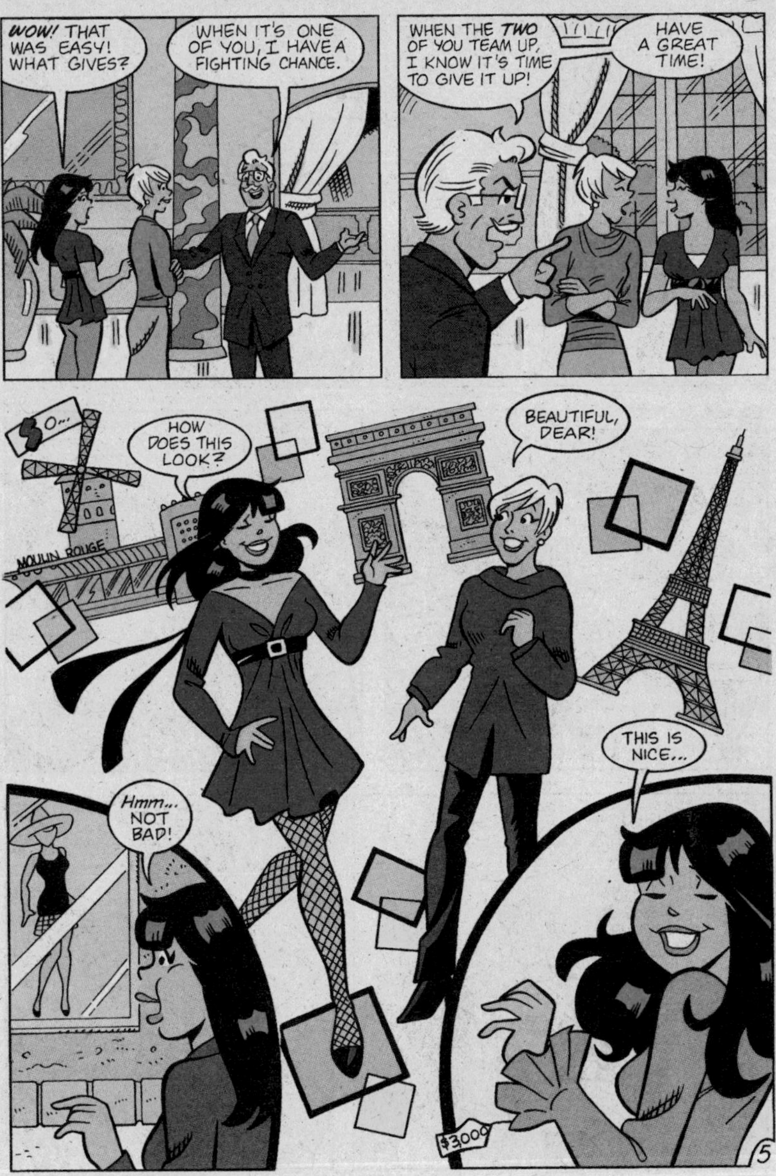
WOW! THAT WAS EASY! WHAT GIVES?
WHEN IT'S ONE OF YOU, I HAVE A FIGHTING CHANCE.
WHEN THE TWO OF YOU TEAM UP, I KNOW IT'S TIME TO GIVE IT UP!
HAVE A GREAT TIME!
MOULIN ROUGE
HOW DOES THIS LOOK?
BEAUTIFUL, DEAR!
Hmm... NOT BAD!
THIS IS NICE...
$3000
5

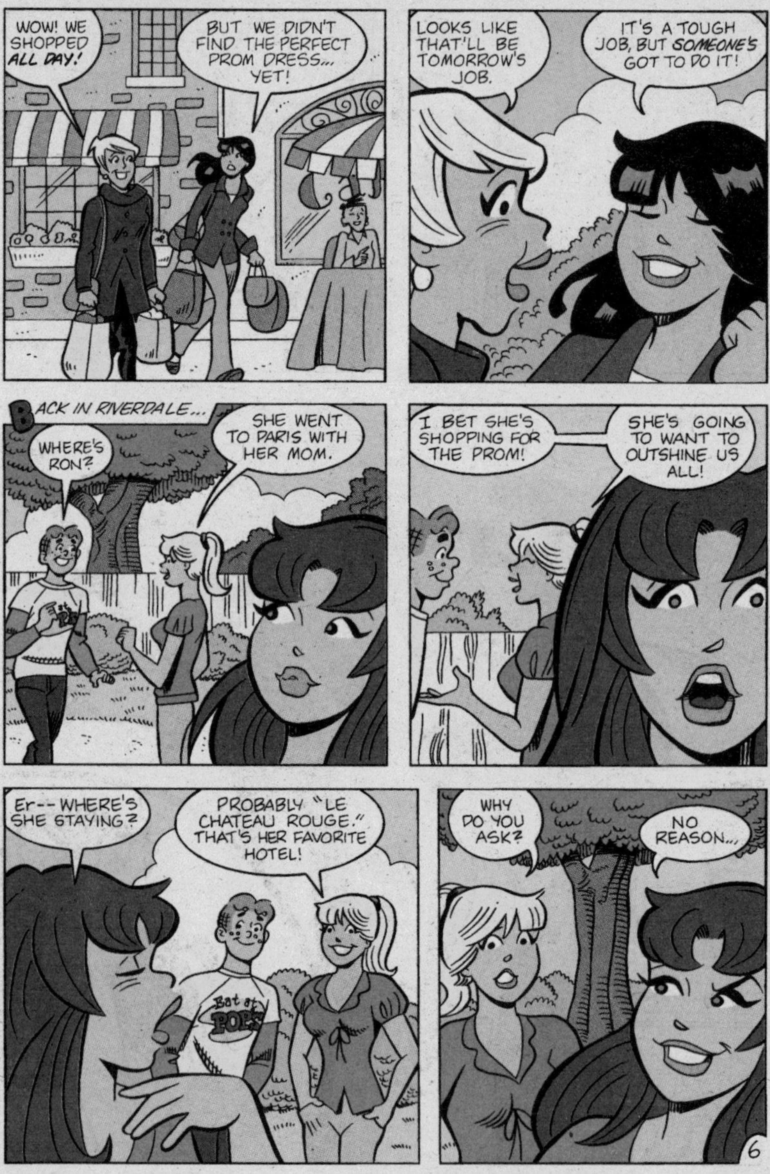
WOW! WE SHOPPED ALL DAY!
BUT WE DIDN'T FIND THE PERFECT PROM DRESS... YET!
LOOKS LIKE THAT'LL BE TOMORROW'S JOB.
IT'S A TOUGH JOB, BUT SOMEONE'S GOT TO DO IT!
BACK IN RIVERDALE...
WHERE'S RON?
SHE WENT TO PARIS WITH HER MOM.
I BET SHE'S SHOPPING FOR THE PROM!
SHE'S GOING TO WANT TO OUTSHINE US ALL!
Er-- WHERE'S SHE STAYING?
PROBABLY "LE CHATEAU ROUGE." THAT'S HER FAVORITE HOTEL!
Eat at POP'S
WHY DO YOU ASK?
NO REASON...
6

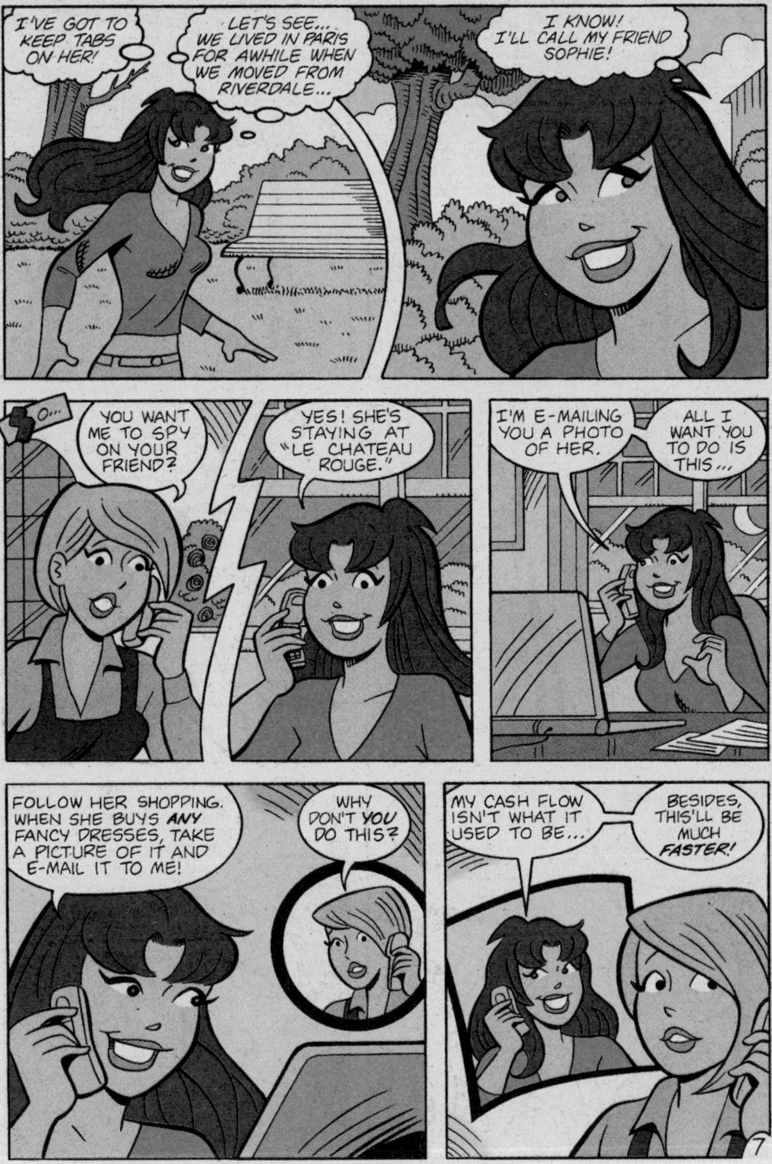
I'VE GOT TO KEEP TABS ON HER!
LET'S SEE... WE LIVED IN PARIS FOR AWHILE WHEN WE MOVED FROM RIVERDALE...
I KNOW! I'LL CALL MY FRIEND SOPHIE!
SO...
YOU WANT ME TO SPY ON YOUR FRIEND?
YES! SHE'S STAYING AT "LE CHATEAU ROUGE."
I'M E-MAILING YOU A PHOTO OF HER.
ALL I WANT YOU TO DO IS THIS...
FOLLOW HER SHOPPING. WHEN SHE BUYS ANY FANCY DRESSES, TAKE A PICTURE OF IT AND E-MAIL IT TO ME!
WHY DON'T YOU DO THIS?
MY CASH FLOW ISN'T WHAT IT USED TO BE...
BESIDES, THIS'LL BE MUCH FASTER!

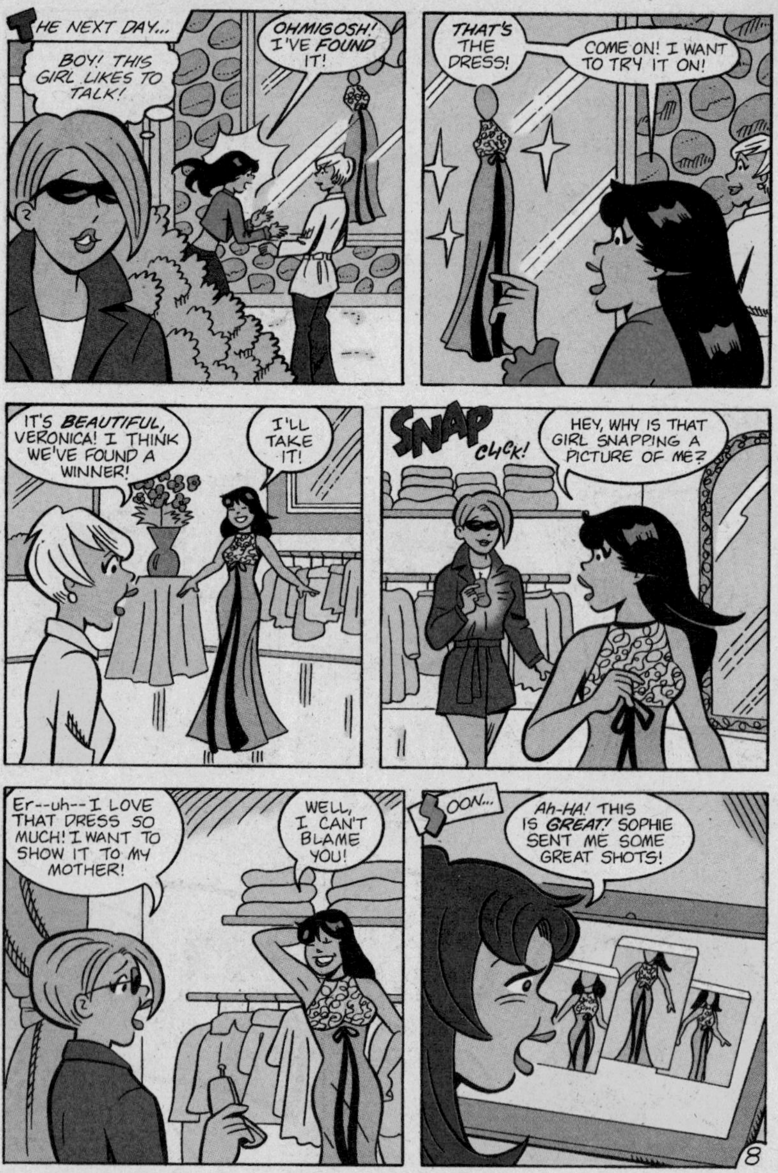
THE NEXT DAY...
BOY! THIS GIRL LIKES TO TALK!
OHMIGOSH! I'VE FOUND IT!
THAT'S THE DRESS!
COME ON! I WANT TO TRY IT ON!
IT'S BEAUTIFUL, VERONICA! I THINK WE'VE FOUND A WINNER!
I'LL TAKE IT!
SNAP
CLICK!
HEY, WHY IS THAT GIRL SNAPPING A PICTURE OF ME?
Er--uh--I LOVE THAT DRESS SO MUCH! I WANT TO SHOW IT TO MY MOTHER!
WELL, I CAN'T BLAME YOU!
SOON...
Ah-HA! THIS IS GREAT! SOPHIE SENT ME SOME GREAT SHOTS!

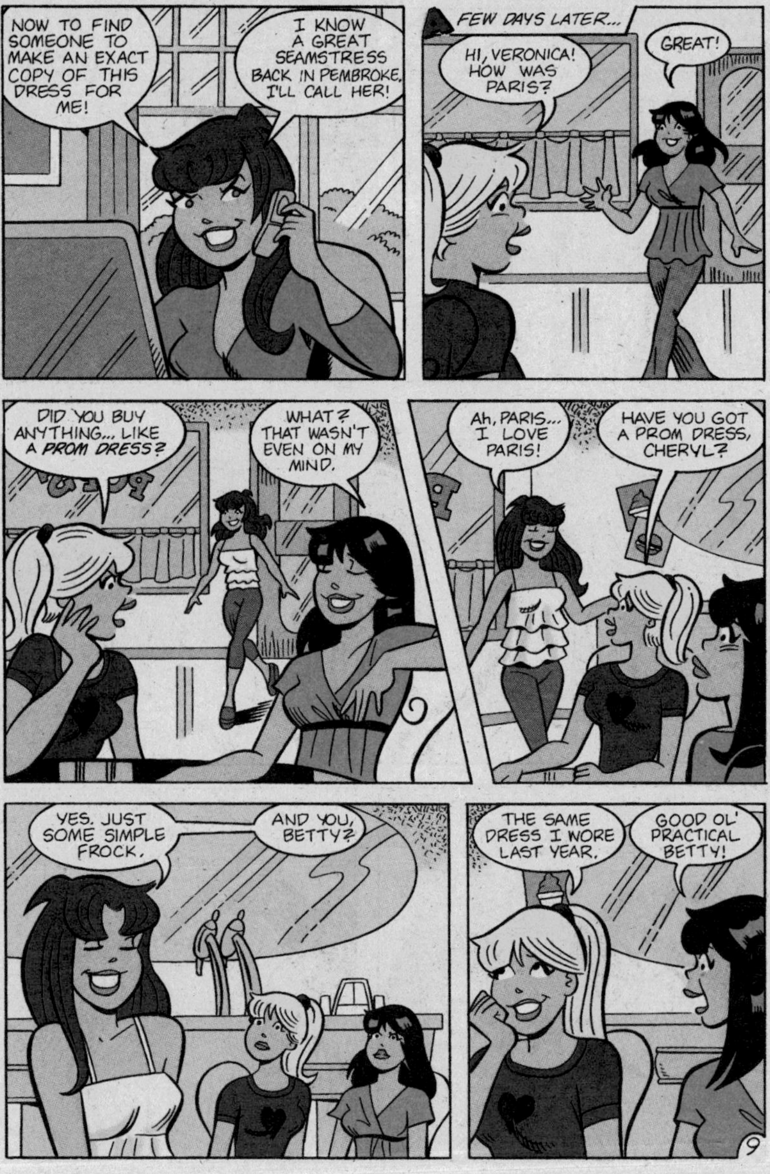
NOW TO FIND SOMEONE TO MAKE AN EXACT COPY OF THIS DRESS FOR ME!
I KNOW A GREAT SEAMSTRESS BACK IN PEMBROKE. I'LL CALL HER!
A FEW DAYS LATER...
HI, VERONICA! HOW WAS PARIS?
GREAT!
DID YOU BUY ANYTHING... LIKE A PROM DRESS?
WHAT? THAT WASN'T EVEN ON MY MIND.
Ah, PARIS... I LOVE PARIS!
HAVE YOU GOT A PROM DRESS, CHERYL?
YES. JUST SOME SIMPLE FROCK.
AND YOU, BETTY?
THE SAME DRESS I WORE LAST YEAR.
GOOD OL' PRACTICAL BETTY!
9

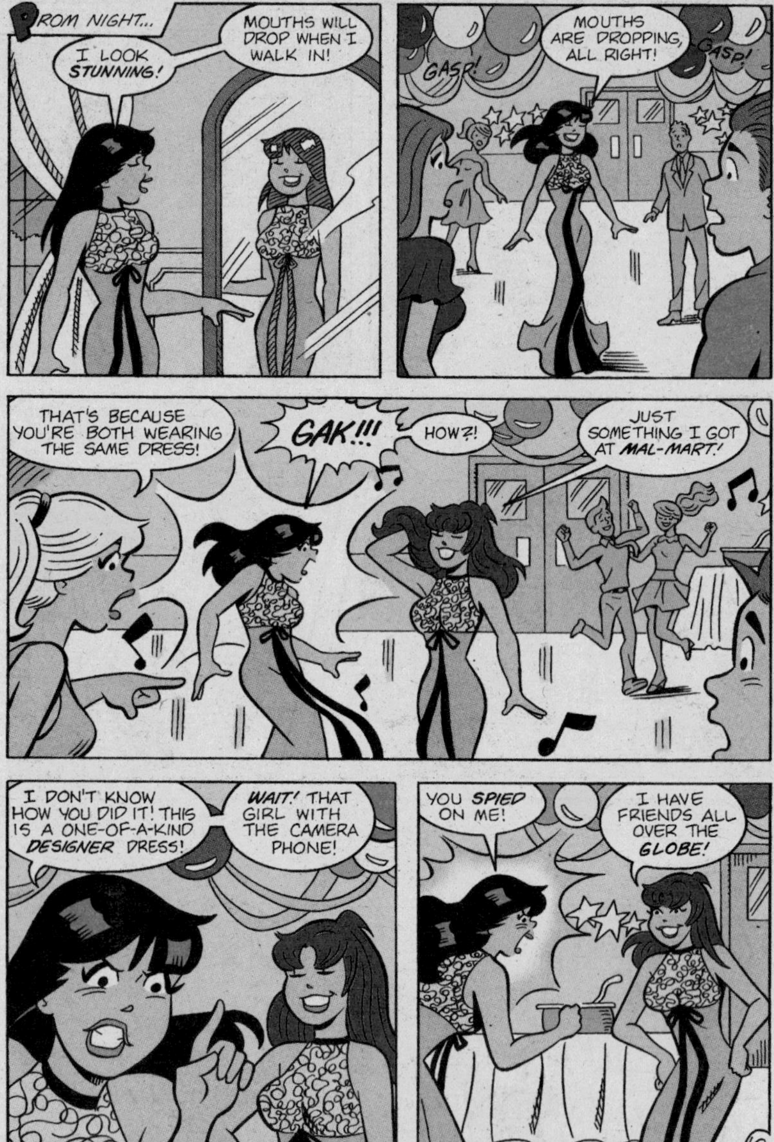
PROM NIGHT...
I LOOK STUNNING!
MOUTHS WILL DROP WHEN I WALK IN!
GASP!
MOUTHS ARE DROPPING, ALL RIGHT!
GASP!
THAT'S BECAUSE YOU'RE BOTH WEARING THE SAME DRESS!
GAK!!!
HOW?!
JUST SOMETHING I GOT AT MAL-MART!
I DON'T KNOW HOW YOU DID IT! THIS IS A ONE-OF-A-KIND DESIGNER DRESS!
WAIT! THAT GIRL WITH THE CAMERA PHONE!
YOU SPIED ON ME!
I HAVE FRIENDS ALL OVER THE GLOBE!

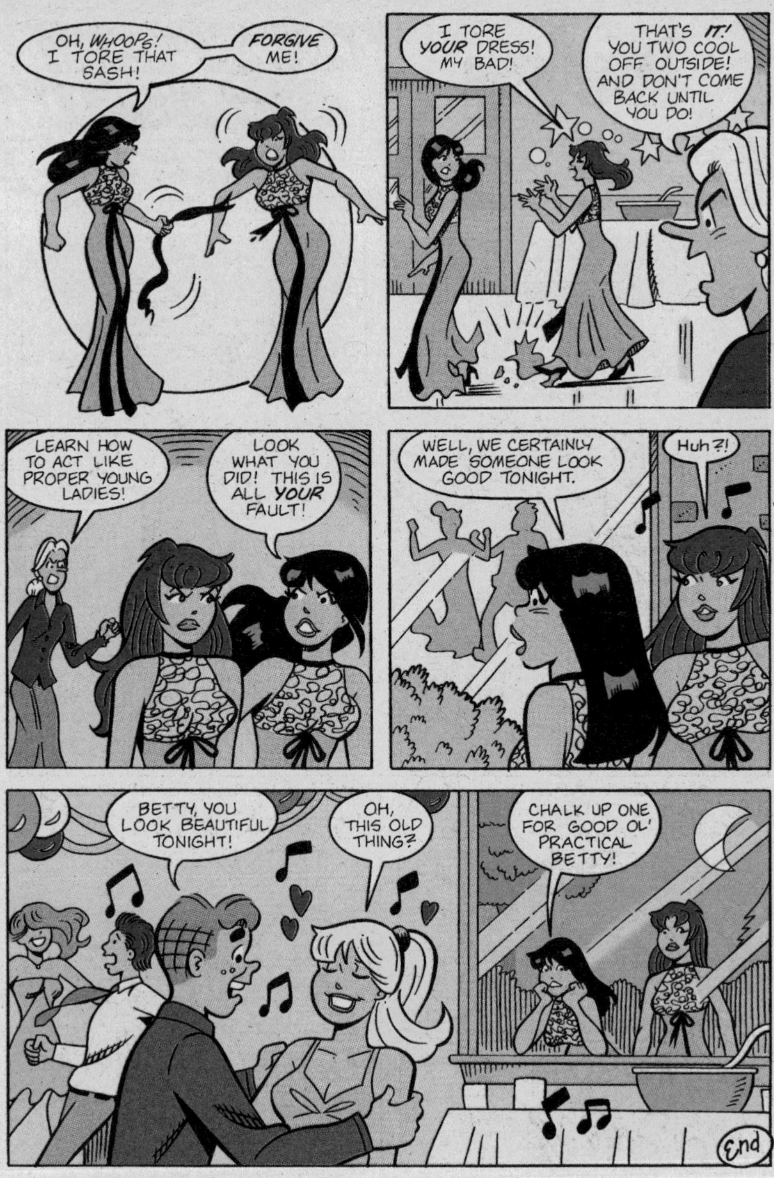
OH, WHOOPS! I TORE THAT SASH!
FORGIVE ME!
I TORE YOUR DRESS! MY BAD!
THAT'S IT! YOU TWO COOL OFF OUTSIDE! AND DON'T COME BACK UNTIL YOU DO!
LEARN HOW TO ACT LIKE PROPER YOUNG LADIES!
LOOK WHAT YOU DID! THIS IS ALL YOUR FAULT!
WELL, WE CERTAINLY MADE SOMEONE LOOK GOOD TONIGHT.
Huh?!
BETTY, YOU LOOK BEAUTIFUL TONIGHT!
OH, THIS OLD THING?
CHALK UP ONE FOR GOOD OL' PRACTICAL BETTY!
End

Betty in "OH, SPLISH SPLASH!"

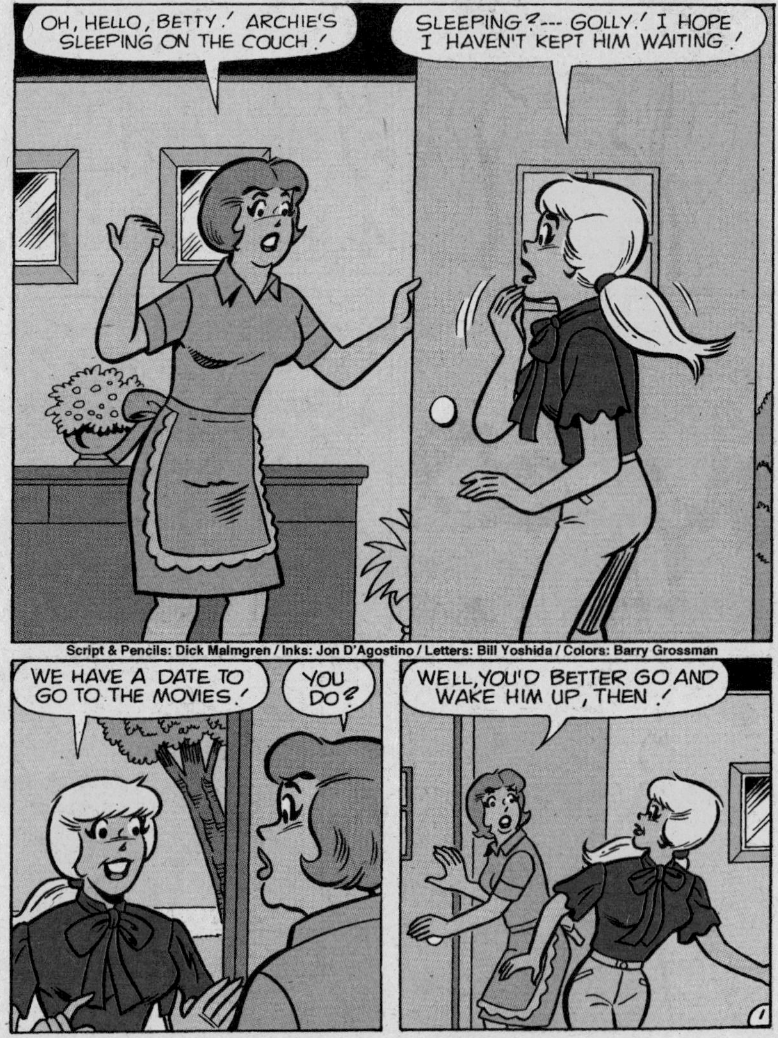
OH, HELLO, BETTY! ARCHIE'S SLEEPING ON THE COUCH!
SLEEPING?--- GOLLY! I HOPE I HAVEN'T KEPT HIM WAITING!
Script & Pencils: Dick Malmgren / Inks: Jon D'Agostino / Letters: Bill Yoshida / Colors: Barry Grossman
WE HAVE A DATE TO GO TO THE MOVIES!
YOU DO?
WELL, YOU'D BETTER GO AND WAKE HIM UP, THEN!
1

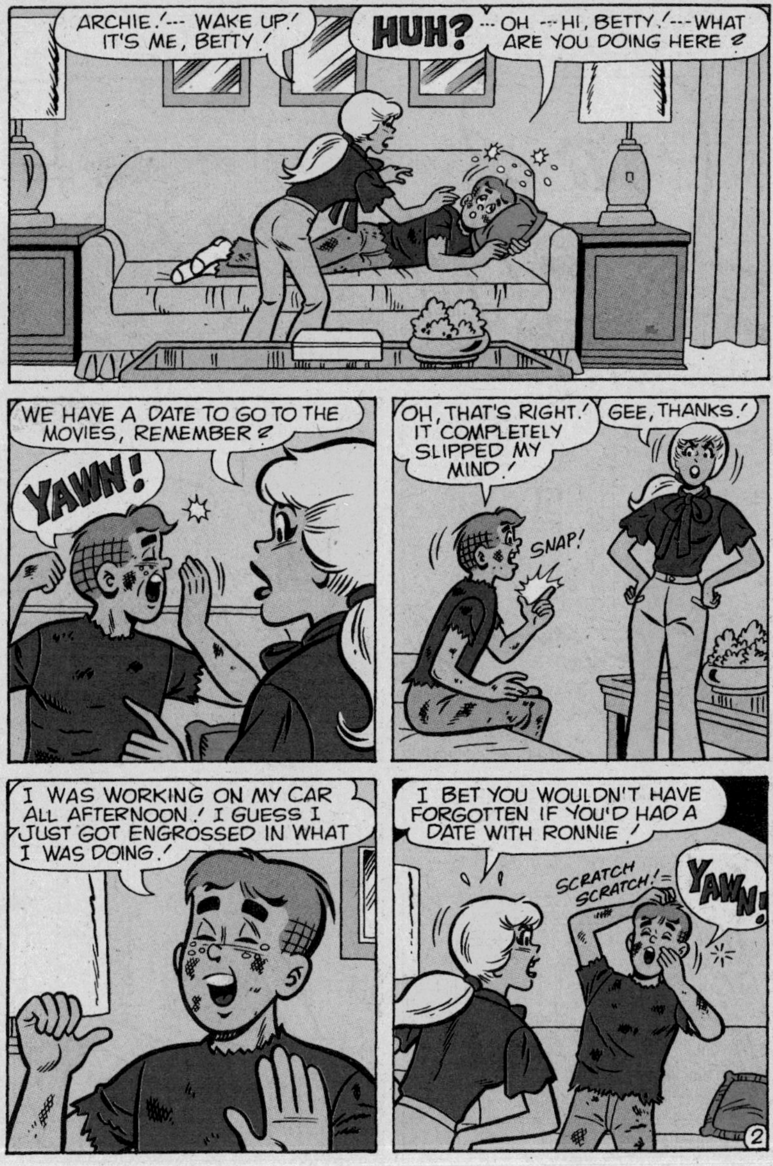
ARCHIE!--- WAKE UP! IT'S ME, BETTY!
HUH? --- OH --- HI, BETTY!---WHAT ARE YOU DOING HERE ?
WE HAVE A DATE TO GO TO THE MOVIES, REMEMBER ?
YAWN!
OH, THAT'S RIGHT! IT COMPLETELY SLIPPED MY MIND!
SNAP!
GEE, THANKS!
I WAS WORKING ON MY CAR ALL AFTERNOON! I GUESS I JUST GOT ENGROSSED IN WHAT I WAS DOING!
I BET YOU WOULDN'T HAVE FORGOTTEN IF YOU'D HAD A DATE WITH RONNIE!
SCRATCH SCRATCH!
YAWN!
2

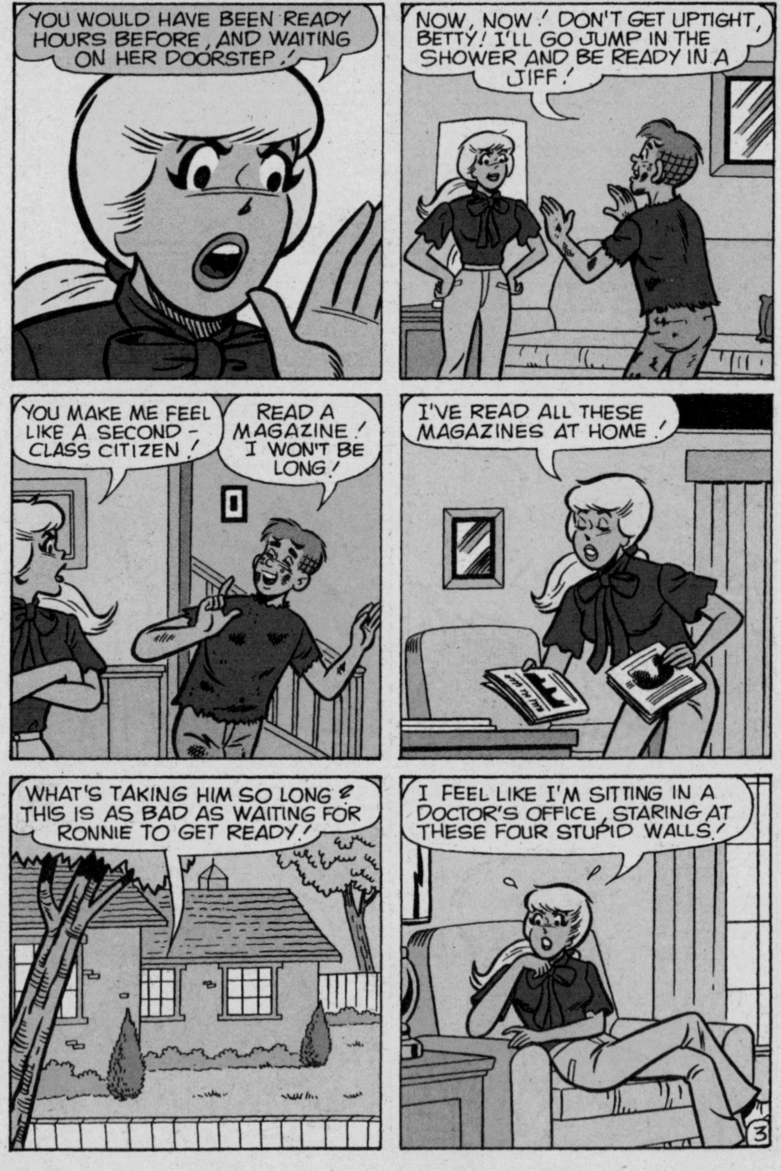
YOU WOULD HAVE BEEN READY HOURS BEFORE, AND WAITING ON HER DOORSTEP!
NOW, NOW! DON'T GET UPTIGHT, BETTY! I'LL GO JUMP IN THE SHOWER AND BE READY IN A JIFF!
YOU MAKE ME FEEL LIKE A SECOND-CLASS CITIZEN!
READ A MAGAZINE! I WON'T BE LONG!
I'VE READ ALL THESE MAGAZINES AT HOME!
WHAT'S TAKING HIM SO LONG? THIS IS AS BAD AS WAITING FOR RONNIE TO GET READY!
I FEEL LIKE I'M SITTING IN A DOCTOR'S OFFICE, STARING AT THESE FOUR STUPID WALLS!
3

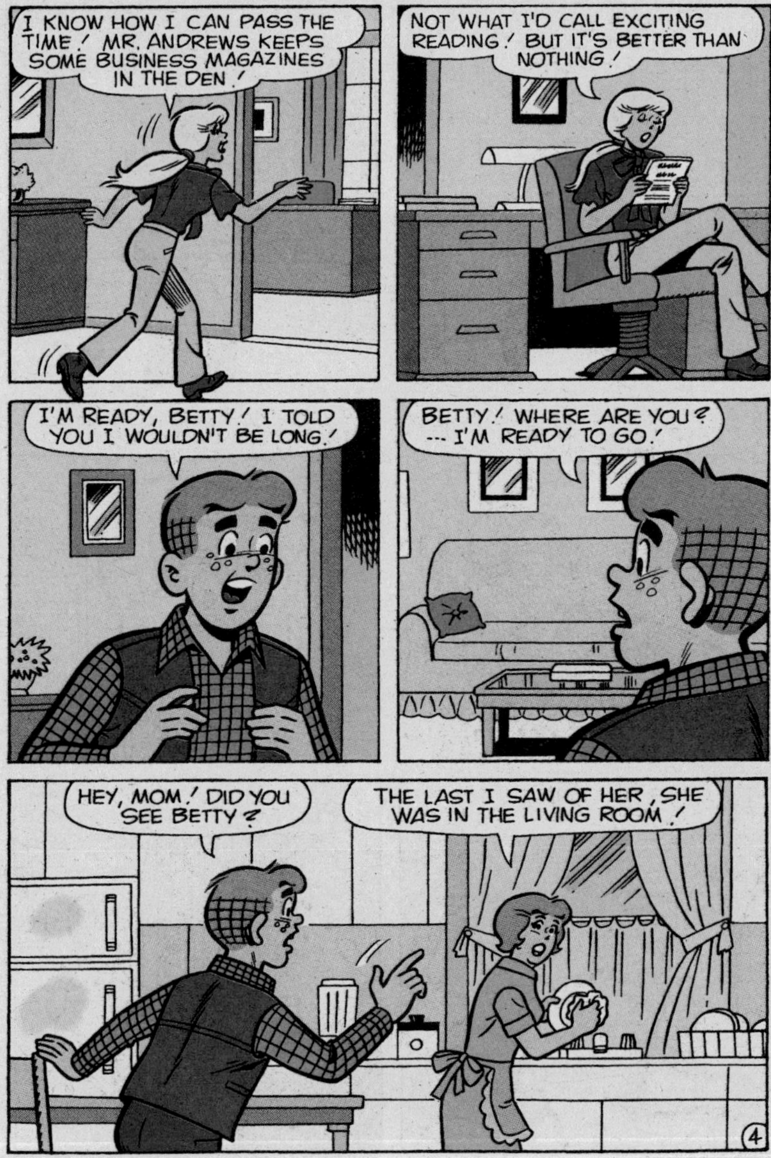
I KNOW HOW I CAN PASS THE TIME! MR. ANDREWS KEEPS SOME BUSINESS MAGAZINES IN THE DEN!
NOT WHAT I'D CALL EXCITING READING! BUT IT'S BETTER THAN NOTHING!
I'M READY, BETTY! I TOLD YOU I WOULDN'T BE LONG!
BETTY! WHERE ARE YOU? --- I'M READY TO GO!
HEY, MOM! DID YOU SEE BETTY?
THE LAST I SAW OF HER, SHE WAS IN THE LIVING ROOM!
4

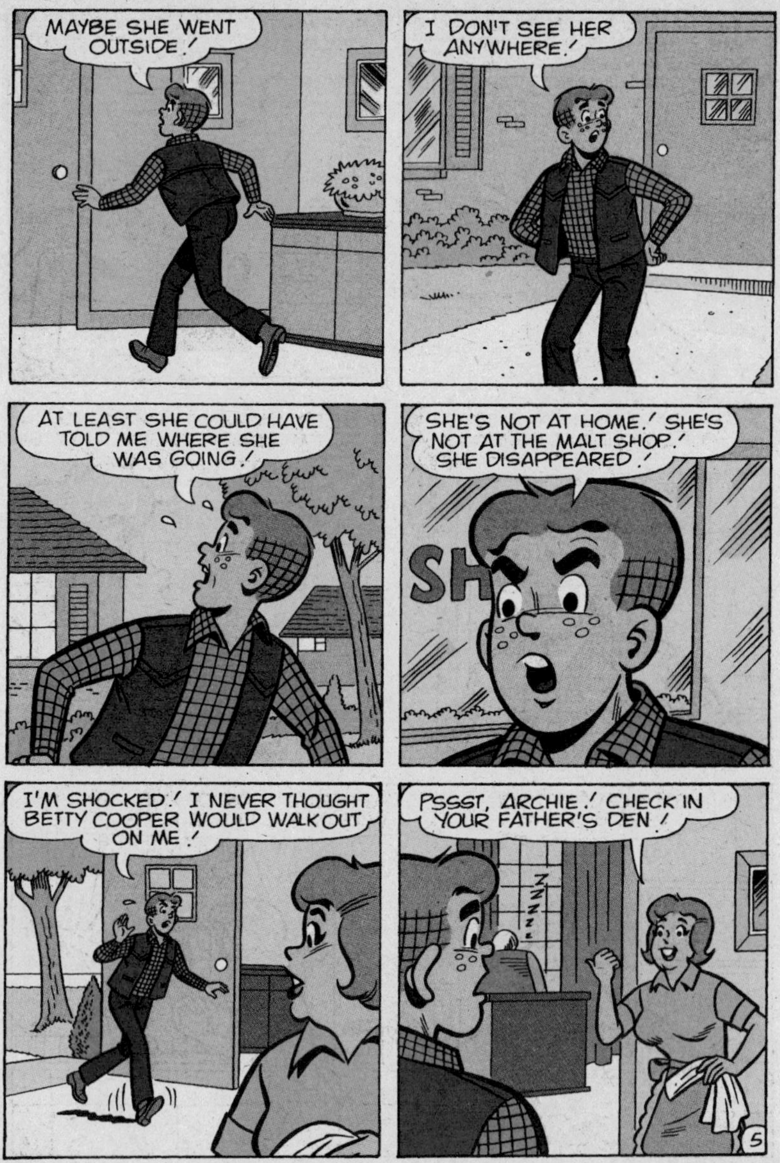
MAYBE SHE WENT OUTSIDE!
I DON'T SEE HER ANYWHERE!
AT LEAST SHE COULD HAVE TOLD ME WHERE SHE WAS GOING!
SHE'S NOT AT HOME! SHE'S NOT AT THE MALT SHOP! SHE DISAPPEARED!
I'M SHOCKED! I NEVER THOUGHT BETTY COOPER WOULD WALK OUT ON ME!
PSSST, ARCHIE! CHECK IN YOUR FATHER'S DEN!
ZZZZ
5

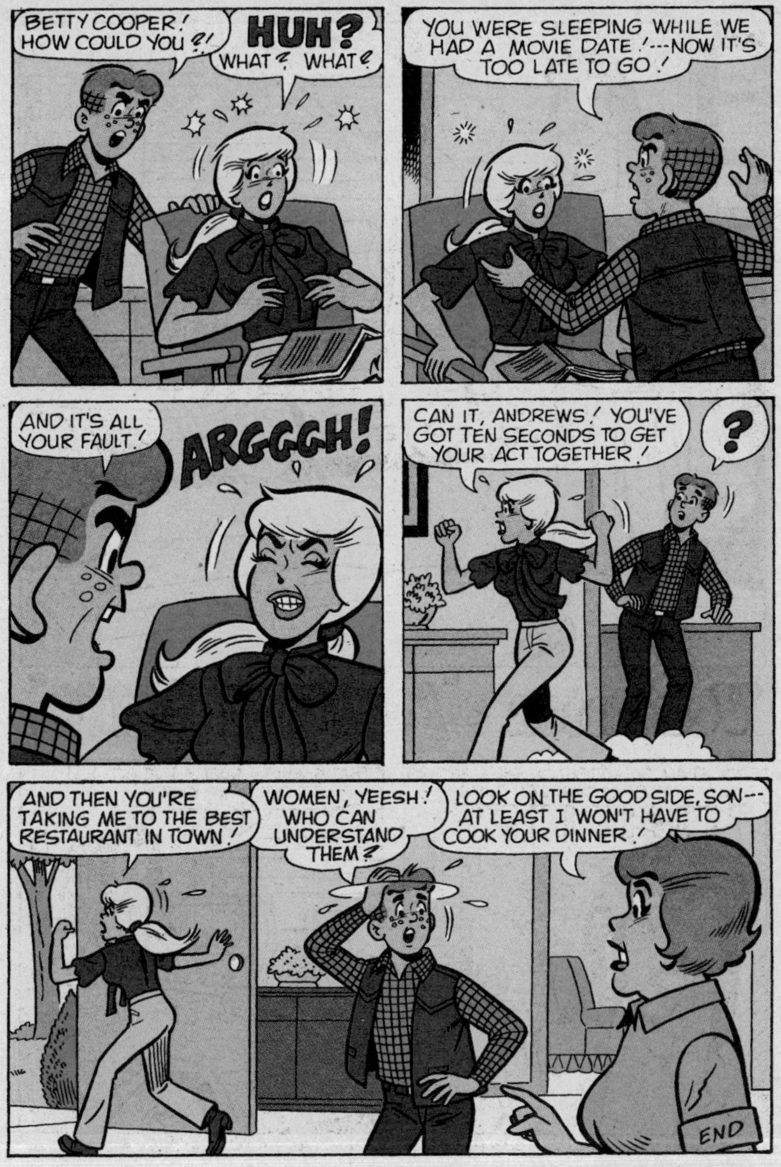
BETTY COOPER! HOW COULD YOU ?!
HUH?
WHAT? WHAT?
YOU WERE SLEEPING WHILE WE HAD A MOVIE DATE!---NOW IT'S TOO LATE TO GO!
AND IT'S ALL YOUR FAULT!
ARGGGH!
CAN IT, ANDREWS! YOU'VE GOT TEN SECONDS TO GET YOUR ACT TOGETHER!
?
AND THEN YOU'RE TAKING ME TO THE BEST RESTAURANT IN TOWN!
WOMEN, YEESH! WHO CAN UNDERSTAND THEM?
LOOK ON THE GOOD SIDE, SON--- AT LEAST I WON'T HAVE TO COOK YOUR DINNER!
END

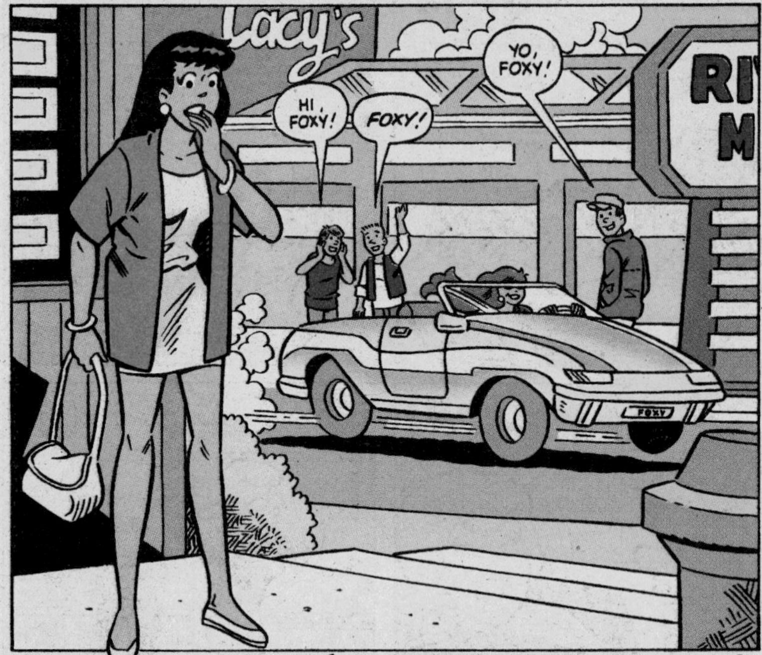
Lacy's
HI, FOXY!
FOXY!
YO, FOXY!
FOXY

Veronica in "A GREAT PLATE"

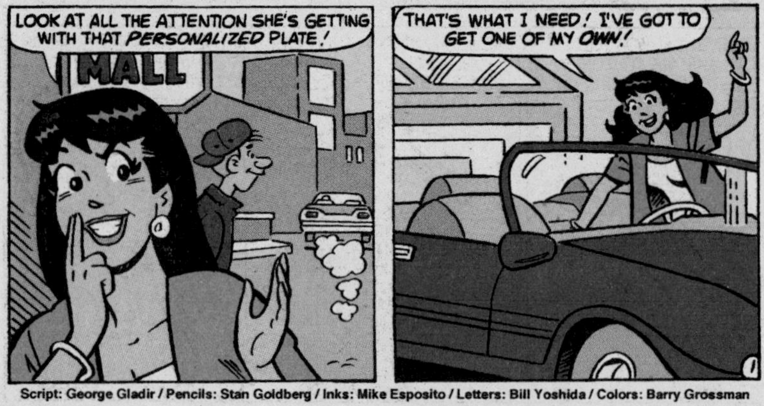
LOOK AT ALL THE ATTENTION SHE'S GETTING WITH THAT *PERSONALIZED* PLATE!
MALL
THAT'S WHAT I NEED! I'VE GOT TO GET ONE OF MY *OWN*!
1

Script: George Gladir / Pencils: Stan Goldberg / Inks: Mike Esposito / Letters: Bill Yoshida / Colors: Barry Grossman

ALL THE GOOD ONES ARE ALREADY TAKEN!

DOLL

CUTIE

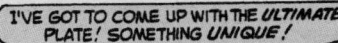

I'VE GOT TO COME UP WITH THE *ULTIMATE* PLATE! SOMETHING *UNIQUE!*

I'VE ONLY GOT SIX MONTHS TO COME UP WITH ONE!

BUT WHAT COULD TOP "FOXY"? IT *FITS* ME *PERFECTLY!*

AUGUST

BEAUTIFUL? NO! TOO MANY LETTERS!

GORGEOUS? FASHIONABLE? REALLY RAD?

I'VE GOT TO COME UP WITH SOMETHING! TIME IS RUNNING OUT!

DECEMBER

OCTOBER

②

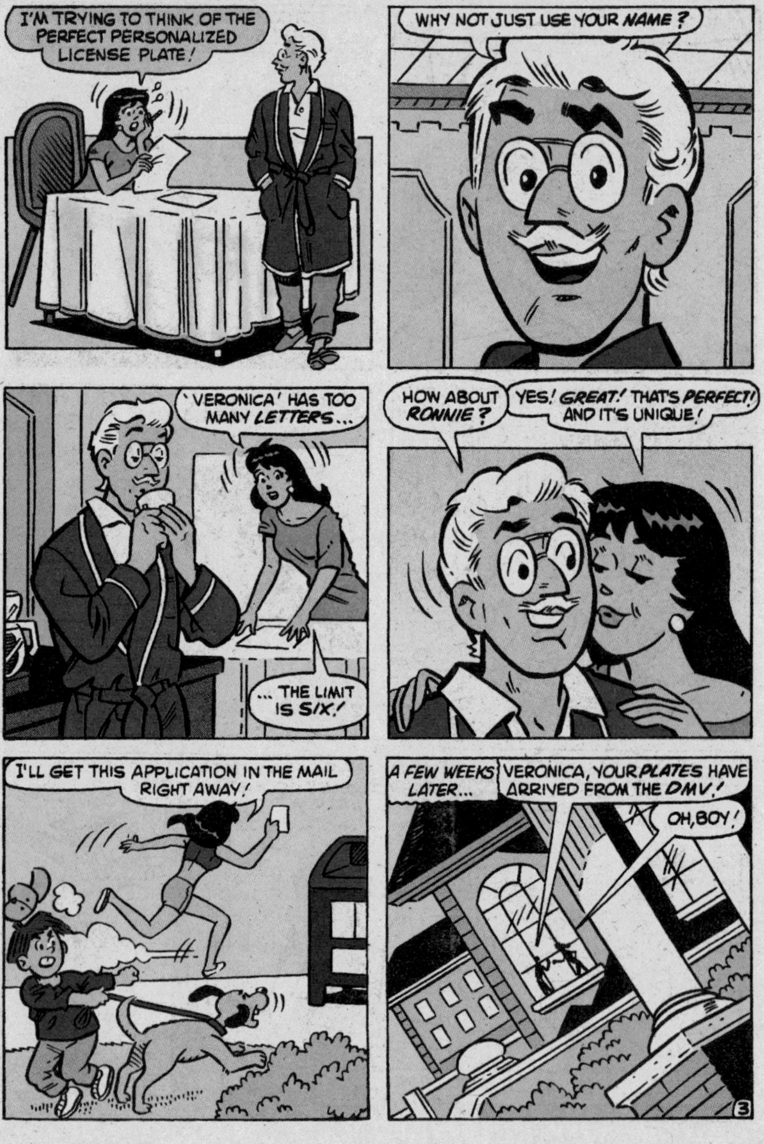
I'M TRYING TO THINK OF THE PERFECT PERSONALIZED LICENSE PLATE!
WHY NOT JUST USE YOUR *NAME*?
'VERONICA' HAS TOO MANY *LETTERS*...
... THE LIMIT IS *SIX*!
HOW ABOUT *RONNIE*?
YES! *GREAT!* THAT'S *PERFECT!* AND IT'S UNIQUE!
I'LL GET THIS APPLICATION IN THE MAIL RIGHT AWAY!
A FEW WEEKS LATER...
VERONICA, YOUR *PLATES* HAVE ARRIVED FROM THE *DMV*!
OH, BOY!
3

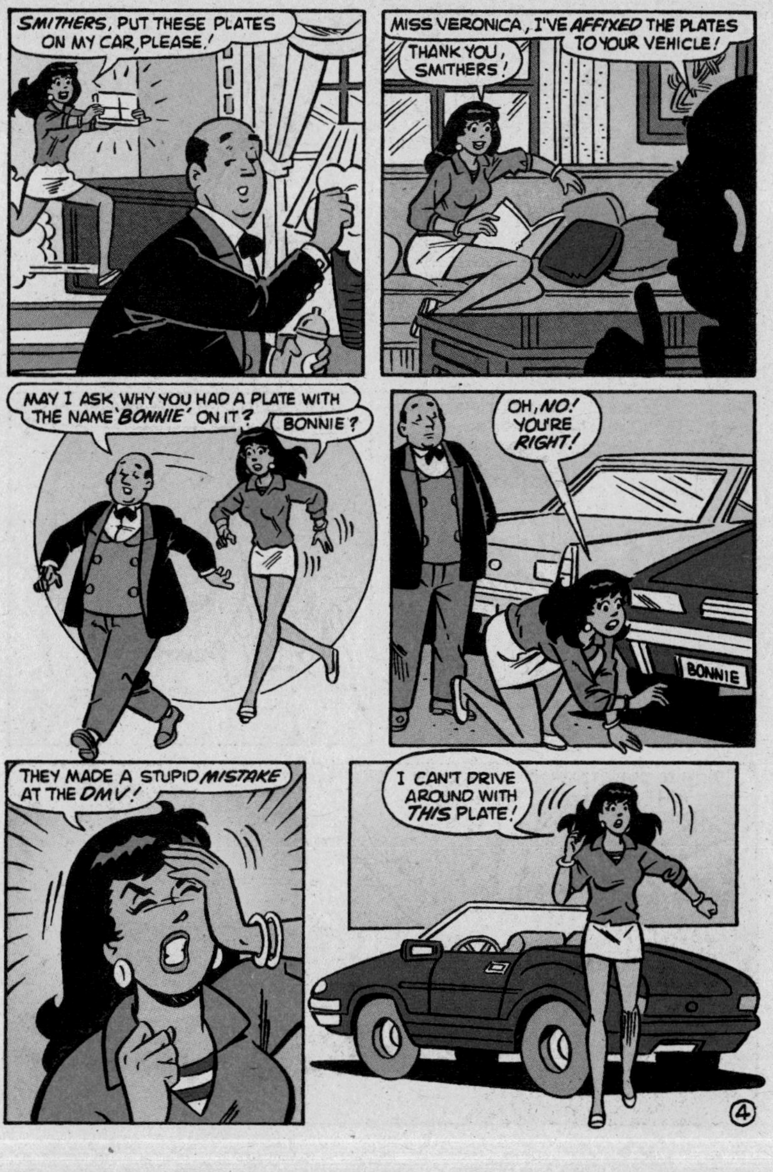
SMITHERS, PUT THESE PLATES ON MY CAR, PLEASE!
MISS VERONICA, I'VE AFFIXED THE PLATES TO YOUR VEHICLE!
THANK YOU, SMITHERS!
MAY I ASK WHY YOU HAD A PLATE WITH THE NAME 'BONNIE' ON IT?
BONNIE?
OH, NO! YOU'RE RIGHT!
BONNIE
THEY MADE A STUPID MISTAKE AT THE DMV!
I CAN'T DRIVE AROUND WITH THIS PLATE!
4

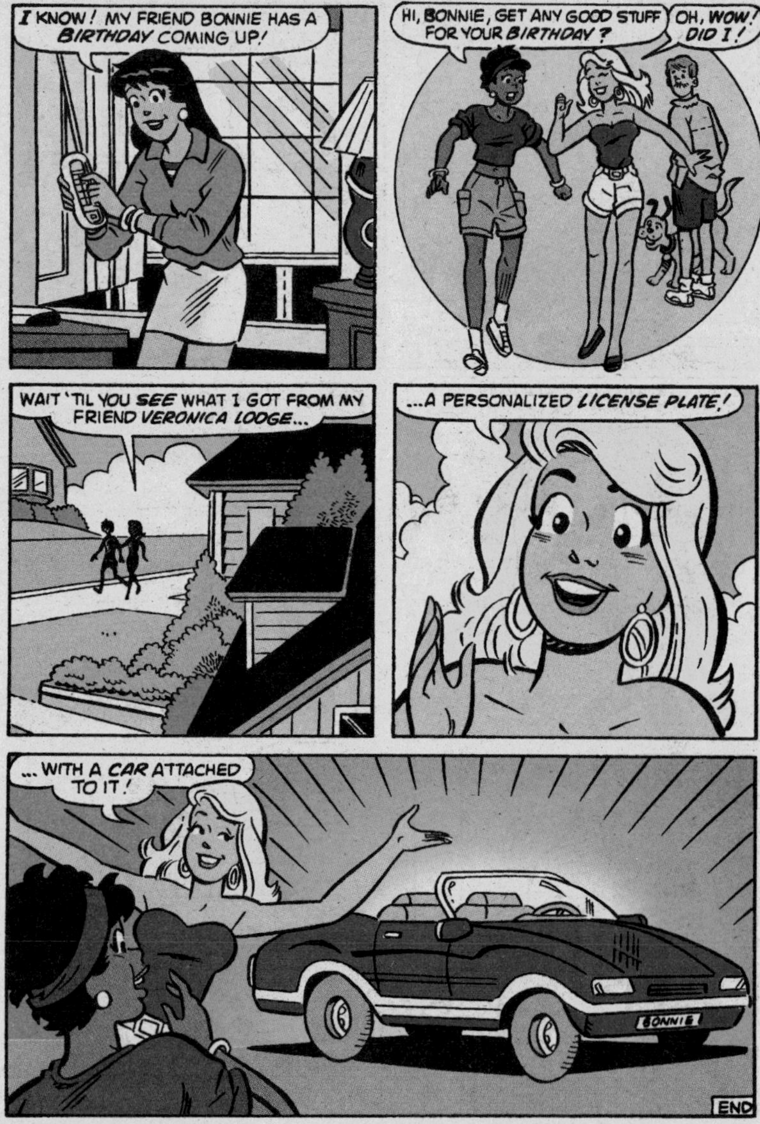
I KNOW! MY FRIEND BONNIE HAS A BIRTHDAY COMING UP!
HI, BONNIE, GET ANY GOOD STUFF FOR YOUR BIRTHDAY?
OH, WOW! DID I!
WAIT 'TIL YOU SEE WHAT I GOT FROM MY FRIEND VERONICA LODGE...
...A PERSONALIZED LICENSE PLATE!
...WITH A CAR ATTACHED TO IT!
BONNIE
END

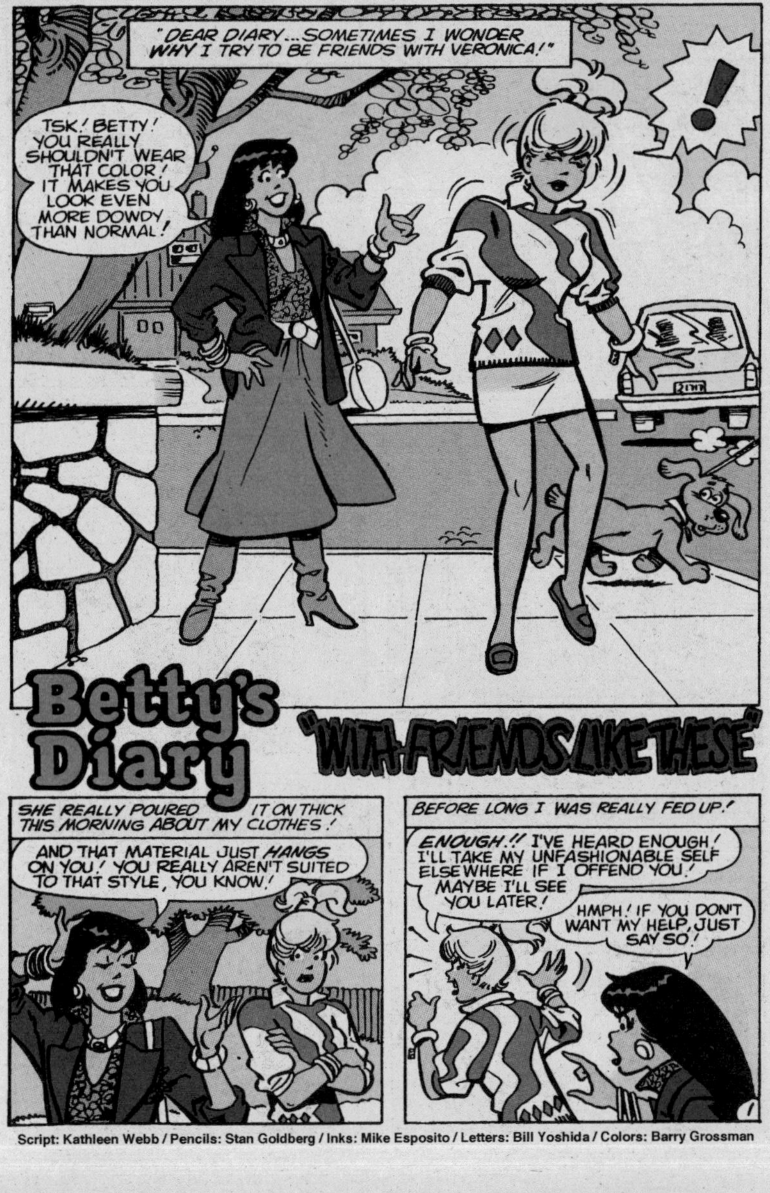
"DEAR DIARY...SOMETIMES I WONDER WHY I TRY TO BE FRIENDS WITH VERONICA!"
TSK! BETTY! YOU REALLY SHOULDN'T WEAR THAT COLOR! IT MAKES YOU LOOK EVEN MORE DOWDY THAN NORMAL!
!
Betty's Diary
"WITH FRIENDS LIKE THESE"
SHE REALLY POURED IT ON THICK THIS MORNING ABOUT MY CLOTHES!
AND THAT MATERIAL JUST HANGS ON YOU! YOU REALLY AREN'T SUITED TO THAT STYLE, YOU KNOW!
BEFORE LONG I WAS REALLY FED UP!
ENOUGH!! I'VE HEARD ENOUGH! I'LL TAKE MY UNFASHIONABLE SELF ELSEWHERE IF I OFFEND YOU! MAYBE I'LL SEE YOU LATER!
HMPH! IF YOU DON'T WANT MY HELP, JUST SAY SO!
1

Script: Kathleen Webb / Pencils: Stan Goldberg / Inks: Mike Esposito / Letters: Bill Yoshida / Colors: Barry Grossman

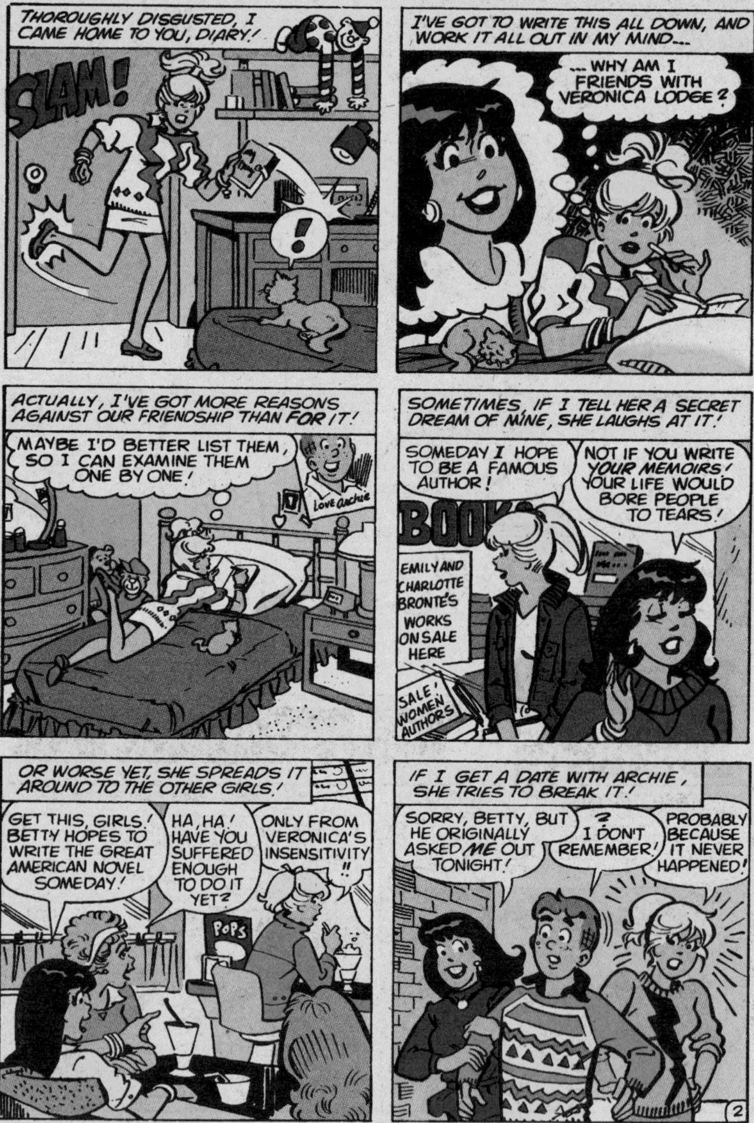

THOROUGHLY DISGUSTED, I CAME HOME TO YOU, DIARY!
SLAM!
!
I'VE GOT TO WRITE THIS ALL DOWN, AND WORK IT ALL OUT IN MY MIND...
... WHY AM I FRIENDS WITH VERONICA LODGE?
ACTUALLY, I'VE GOT MORE REASONS AGAINST OUR FRIENDSHIP THAN FOR IT!
MAYBE I'D BETTER LIST THEM, SO I CAN EXAMINE THEM ONE BY ONE!
Love Archie
SOMETIMES, IF I TELL HER A SECRET DREAM OF MINE, SHE LAUGHS AT IT!
SOMEDAY I HOPE TO BE A FAMOUS AUTHOR!
NOT IF YOU WRITE YOUR MEMOIRS! YOUR LIFE WOULD BORE PEOPLE TO TEARS!
BOOK
EMILY AND CHARLOTTE BRONTE'S WORKS ON SALE HERE
SALE! WOMEN AUTHORS
OR WORSE YET, SHE SPREADS IT AROUND TO THE OTHER GIRLS!
GET THIS, GIRLS! BETTY HOPES TO WRITE THE GREAT AMERICAN NOVEL SOMEDAY!
HA, HA! HAVE YOU SUFFERED ENOUGH TO DO IT YET?
ONLY FROM VERONICA'S INSENSITIVITY!!
POP'S
IF I GET A DATE WITH ARCHIE, SHE TRIES TO BREAK IT!
SORRY, BETTY, BUT HE ORIGINALLY ASKED ME OUT TONIGHT!
? I DON'T REMEMBER!
PROBABLY BECAUSE IT NEVER HAPPENED!
2

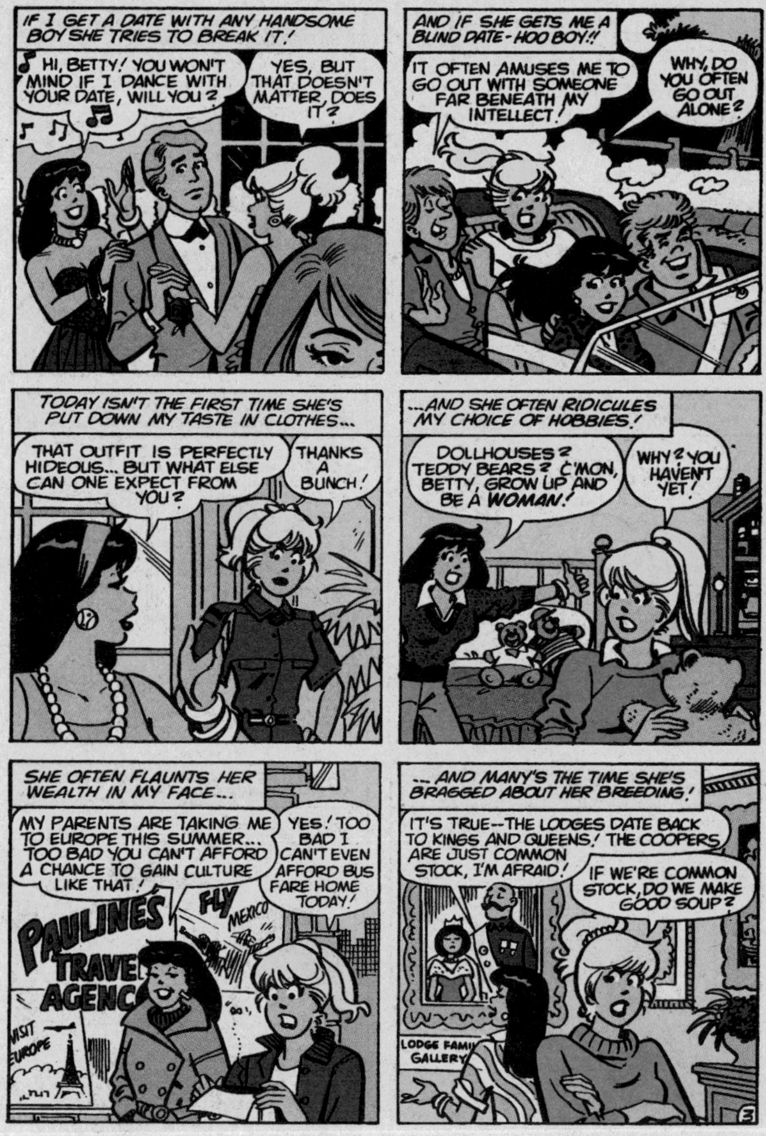
IF I GET A DATE WITH ANY HANDSOME BOY SHE TRIES TO BREAK IT!
HI, BETTY! YOU WON'T MIND IF I DANCE WITH YOUR DATE, WILL YOU?
YES, BUT THAT DOESN'T MATTER, DOES IT?
AND IF SHE GETS ME A BLIND DATE - HOO BOY!!
IT OFTEN AMUSES ME TO GO OUT WITH SOMEONE FAR BENEATH MY INTELLECT!
WHY, DO YOU OFTEN GO OUT ALONE?
TODAY ISN'T THE FIRST TIME SHE'S PUT DOWN MY TASTE IN CLOTHES...
THAT OUTFIT IS PERFECTLY HIDEOUS... BUT WHAT ELSE CAN ONE EXPECT FROM YOU?
THANKS A BUNCH!
...AND SHE OFTEN RIDICULES MY CHOICE OF HOBBIES!
DOLLHOUSES? TEDDY BEARS? C'MON, BETTY, GROW UP AND BE A WOMAN!
WHY? YOU HAVEN'T YET!
SHE OFTEN FLAUNTS HER WEALTH IN MY FACE...
MY PARENTS ARE TAKING ME TO EUROPE THIS SUMMER... TOO BAD YOU CAN'T AFFORD A CHANCE TO GAIN CULTURE LIKE THAT!
YES! TOO BAD I CAN'T EVEN AFFORD BUS FARE HOME TODAY!
PAULINE'S TRAVEL AGENCY
FLY
MEXICO
VISIT EUROPE
... AND MANY'S THE TIME SHE'S BRAGGED ABOUT HER BREEDING!
IT'S TRUE--THE LODGES DATE BACK TO KINGS AND QUEENS! THE COOPERS ARE JUST COMMON STOCK, I'M AFRAID!
IF WE'RE COMMON STOCK, DO WE MAKE GOOD SOUP?
LODGE FAMILY GALLERY
3

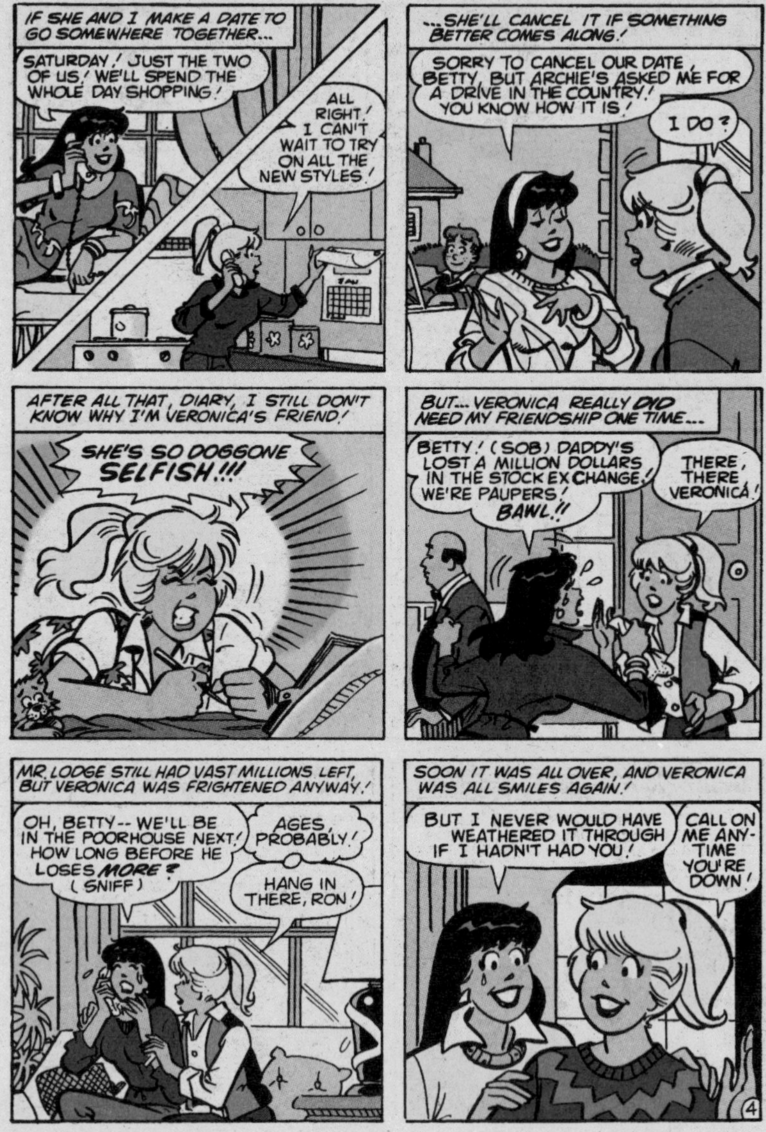
IF SHE AND I MAKE A DATE TO GO SOMEWHERE TOGETHER...
SATURDAY! JUST THE TWO OF US! WE'LL SPEND THE WHOLE DAY SHOPPING!
ALL RIGHT! I CAN'T WAIT TO TRY ON ALL THE NEW STYLES!
...SHE'LL CANCEL IT IF SOMETHING BETTER COMES ALONG!
SORRY TO CANCEL OUR DATE, BETTY, BUT ARCHIE'S ASKED ME FOR A DRIVE IN THE COUNTRY! YOU KNOW HOW IT IS!
I DO?
AFTER ALL THAT, DIARY, I STILL DON'T KNOW WHY I'M VERONICA'S FRIEND!
SHE'S SO DOGGONE SELFISH!!!
BUT... VERONICA REALLY DID NEED MY FRIENDSHIP ONE TIME...
BETTY! (SOB) DADDY'S LOST A MILLION DOLLARS IN THE STOCK EXCHANGE! WE'RE PAUPERS! BAWL!!
THERE, THERE VERONICA!
MR. LODGE STILL HAD VAST MILLIONS LEFT, BUT VERONICA WAS FRIGHTENED ANYWAY!
OH, BETTY-- WE'LL BE IN THE POORHOUSE NEXT! HOW LONG BEFORE HE LOSES MORE? (SNIFF)
AGES, PROBABLY!
HANG IN THERE, RON!
SOON IT WAS ALL OVER, AND VERONICA WAS ALL SMILES AGAIN!
BUT I NEVER WOULD HAVE WEATHERED IT THROUGH IF I HADN'T HAD YOU!
CALL ON ME ANY-TIME YOU'RE DOWN!
4

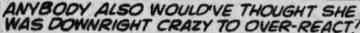

ANYBODY ALSO WOULD'VE THOUGHT SHE WAS DOWNRIGHT CRAZY TO OVER-REACT!

ONLY I UNDERSTOOD HER ECCENTRIC FEARS!

IF IT WASN'T FOR ME, VERONICA WOULDN'T HAVE ANY FRIENDS AT ALL!

NONE OF THE OTHER GIRLS WANT TO BOTHER PUTTING UP WITH HER! I'M THE ONLY ONE WHO TRIES TO UNDERSTAND HER!

AND SHE DOES HAVE HER GOOD MOMENTS!

THERE'VE BEEN LOTS OF TIMES VERONICA HAS TAKEN ME ALONG TRAVELLING WITH HER FAMILY... GIVEN ME NICE CLOTHES... SHARED BOY TALK....!

AND MOST OF THE HURT SHE DOES TO ME IS CAUSED BY HER PAMPERED, SPOILED, SELFISH LIFESTYLE... SHE CAN'T HELP HER UPBRINGING!

FUR SALE

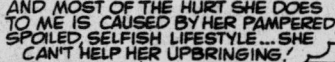

WHY AM I FRIENDS WITH VERONICA, DIARY...?

BECAUSE *MORE* THAN I NEED HER FRIENDSHIP... *SHE* NEEDS MINE...

... AND I THINK... THAT'S WHAT *TRUE* FRIENDSHIP... IS ALL ABOUT!

END

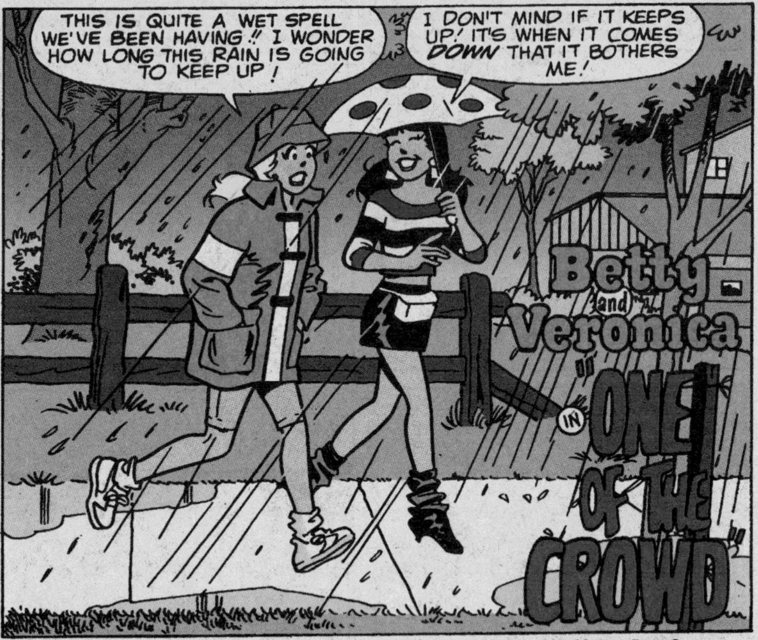
THIS IS QUITE A WET SPELL WE'VE BEEN HAVING!! I WONDER HOW LONG THIS RAIN IS GOING TO KEEP UP!
I DON'T MIND IF IT KEEPS UP! IT'S WHEN IT COMES *DOWN* THAT IT BOTHERS ME!
Betty and Veronica
IN "ONE OF THE CROWD"

Script: Mike Pellowski / Pencils: Dan DeCarlo / Inks: Alison Flood / Letters: Bill Yoshida / Colors: Barry Grossman

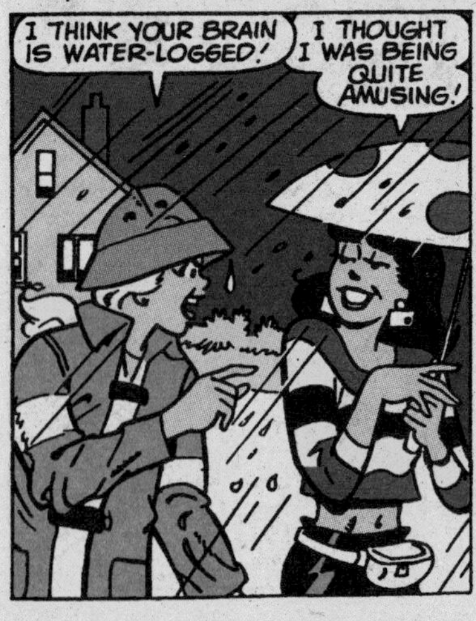
I THINK YOUR BRAIN IS WATER-LOGGED!
I THOUGHT I WAS BEING QUITE AMUSING!

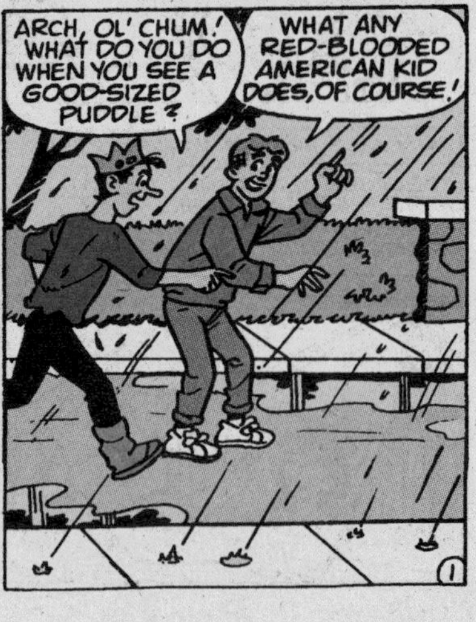
ARCH, OL' CHUM! WHAT DO YOU DO WHEN YOU SEE A GOOD-SIZED PUDDLE?
WHAT ANY RED-BLOODED AMERICAN KID DOES, OF COURSE!
1

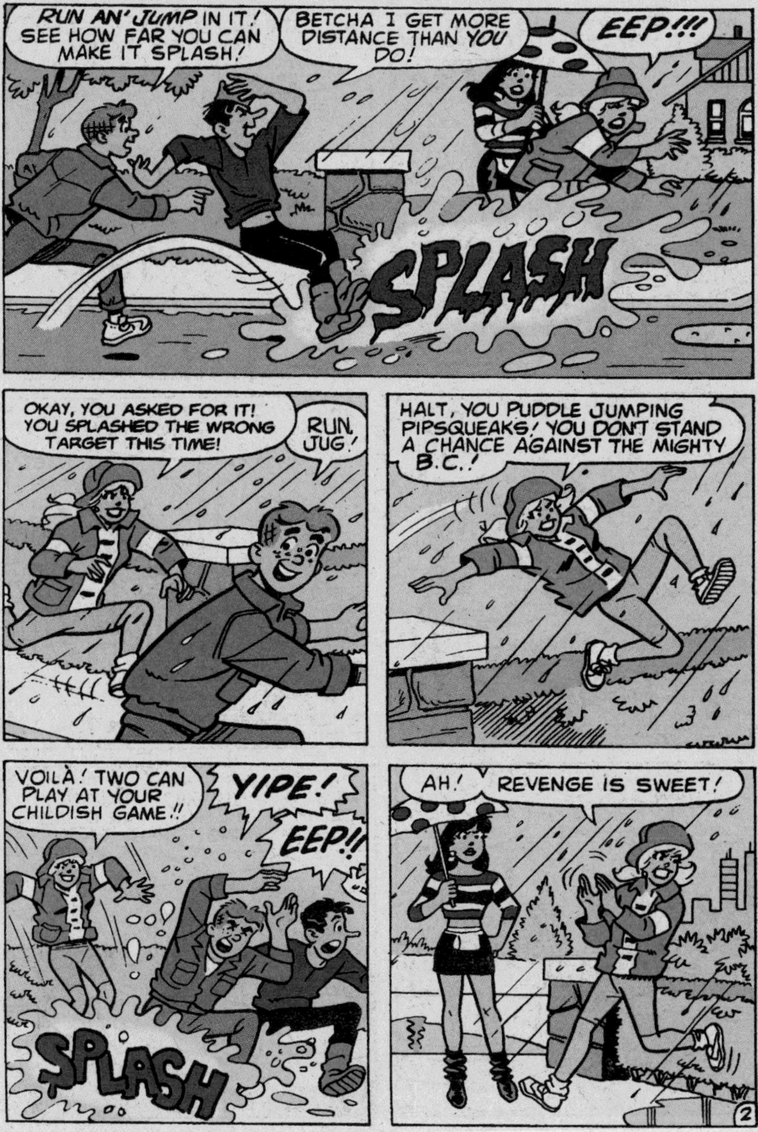
RUN AN' JUMP IN IT! SEE HOW FAR YOU CAN MAKE IT SPLASH!
BETCHA I GET MORE DISTANCE THAN YOU DO!
EEP!!!
SPLASH
OKAY, YOU ASKED FOR IT! YOU SPLASHED THE WRONG TARGET THIS TIME!
RUN, JUG!
HALT, YOU PUDDLE JUMPING PIPSQUEAKS! YOU DON'T STAND A CHANCE AGAINST THE MIGHTY B.C.!
VOILÀ! TWO CAN PLAY AT YOUR CHILDISH GAME!!
YIPE!
EEP!!
SPLASH
AH!
REVENGE IS SWEET!
2

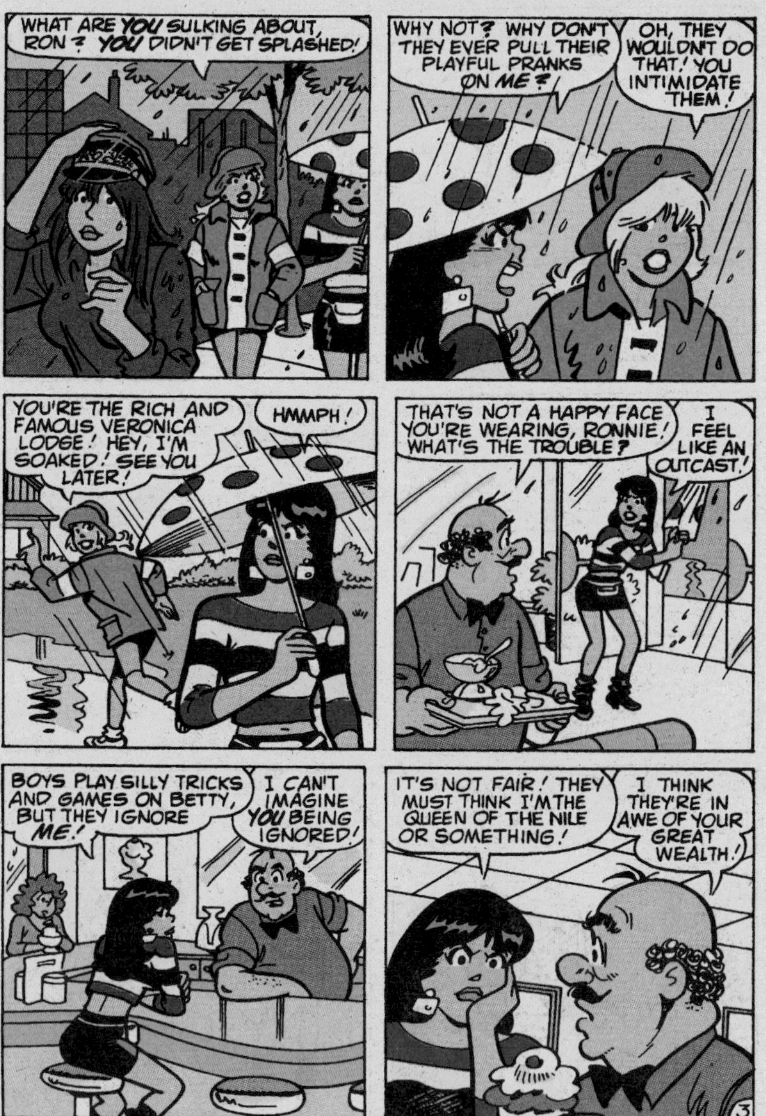
WHAT ARE YOU SULKING ABOUT, RON? YOU DIDN'T GET SPLASHED!
WHY NOT? WHY DON'T THEY EVER PULL THEIR PLAYFUL PRANKS ON ME?
OH, THEY WOULDN'T DO THAT! YOU INTIMIDATE THEM!
YOU'RE THE RICH AND FAMOUS VERONICA LODGE! HEY, I'M SOAKED! SEE YOU LATER!
HMMPH!
THAT'S NOT A HAPPY FACE YOU'RE WEARING, RONNIE! WHAT'S THE TROUBLE?
I FEEL LIKE AN OUTCAST!
BOYS PLAY SILLY TRICKS AND GAMES ON BETTY, BUT THEY IGNORE ME!
I CAN'T IMAGINE YOU BEING IGNORED!
IT'S NOT FAIR! THEY MUST THINK I'M THE QUEEN OF THE NILE OR SOMETHING!
I THINK THEY'RE IN AWE OF YOUR GREAT WEALTH!
3

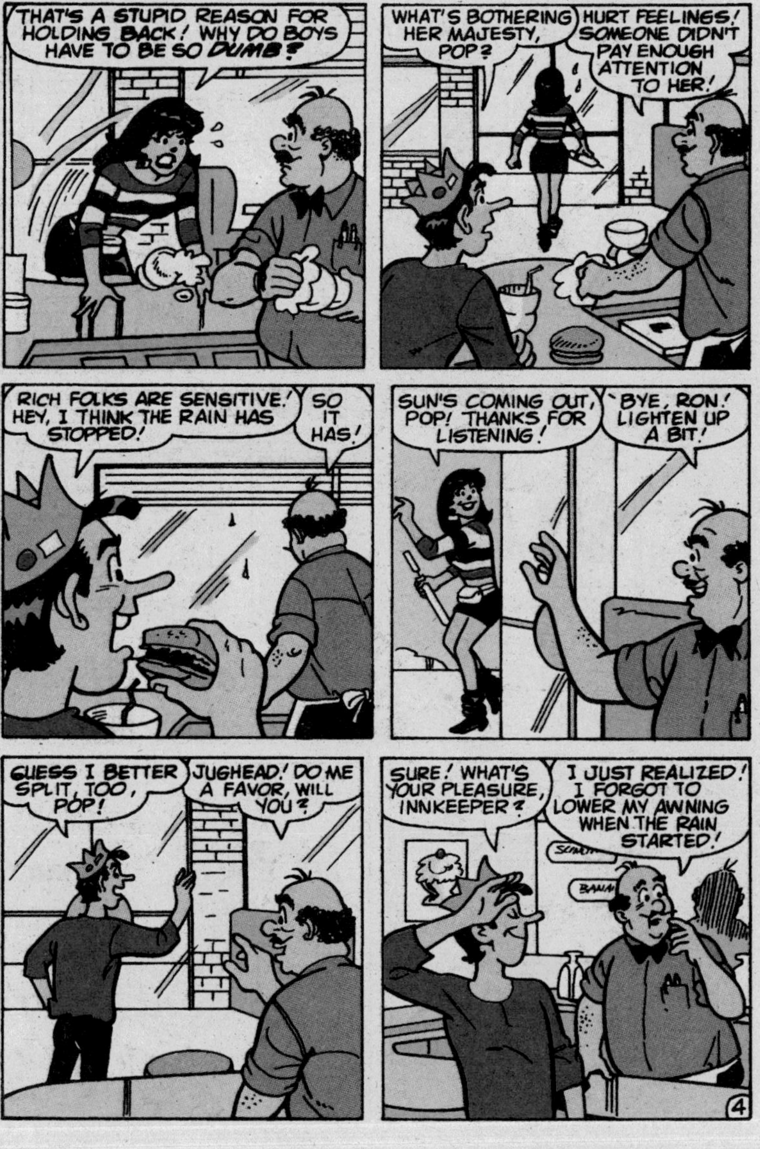
THAT'S A STUPID REASON FOR HOLDING BACK! WHY DO BOYS HAVE TO BE SO DUMB?
WHAT'S BOTHERING HER MAJESTY, POP?
HURT FEELINGS! SOMEONE DIDN'T PAY ENOUGH ATTENTION TO HER!
RICH FOLKS ARE SENSITIVE! HEY, I THINK THE RAIN HAS STOPPED!
SO IT HAS!
SUN'S COMING OUT, POP! THANKS FOR LISTENING!
'BYE, RON! LIGHTEN UP A BIT!
GUESS I BETTER SPLIT, TOO, POP!
JUGHEAD! DO ME A FAVOR, WILL YOU?
SURE! WHAT'S YOUR PLEASURE, INNKEEPER?
I JUST REALIZED! I FORGOT TO LOWER MY AWNING WHEN THE RAIN STARTED!
4

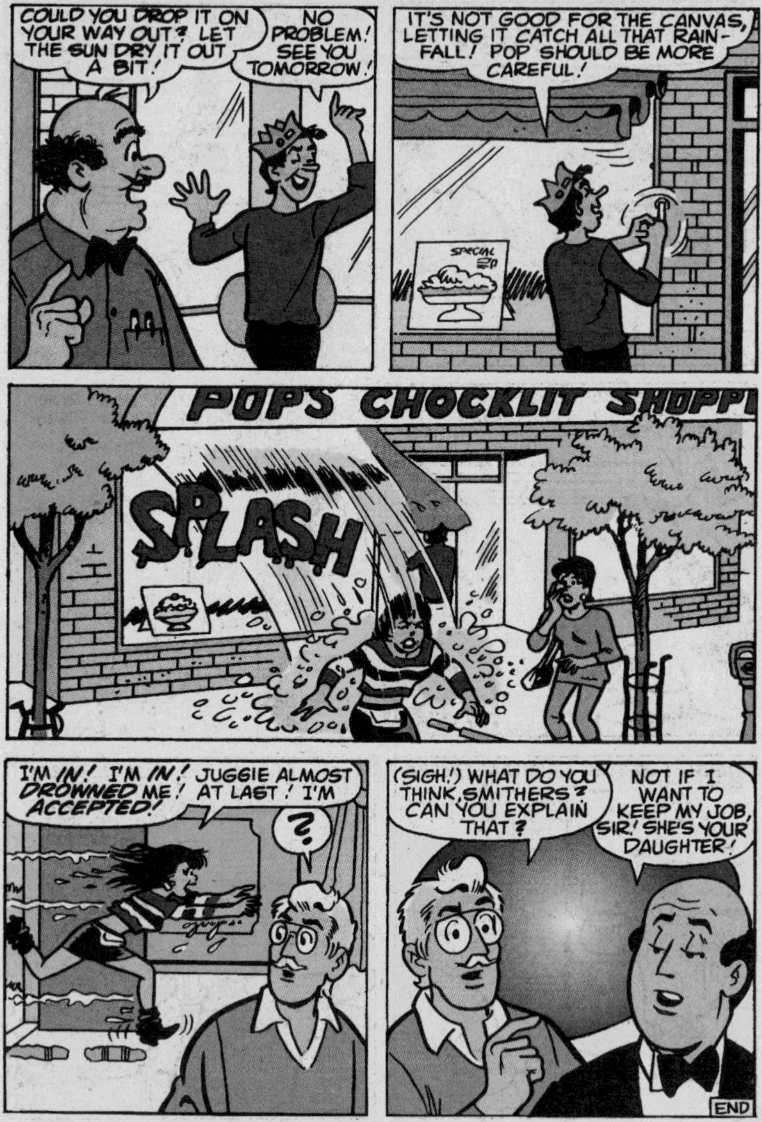
COULD YOU DROP IT ON YOUR WAY OUT? LET THE SUN DRY IT OUT A BIT!
NO PROBLEM! SEE YOU TOMORROW!
IT'S NOT GOOD FOR THE CANVAS, LETTING IT CATCH ALL THAT RAIN-FALL! POP SHOULD BE MORE CAREFUL!
SPECIAL
POP'S CHOCKLIT SHOPP
SPLASH
I'M IN! I'M IN! JUGGIE ALMOST DROWNED ME! AT LAST! I'M ACCEPTED!
?
(SIGH!) WHAT DO YOU THINK, SMITHERS? CAN YOU EXPLAIN THAT?
NOT IF I WANT TO KEEP MY JOB, SIR! SHE'S YOUR DAUGHTER!
END

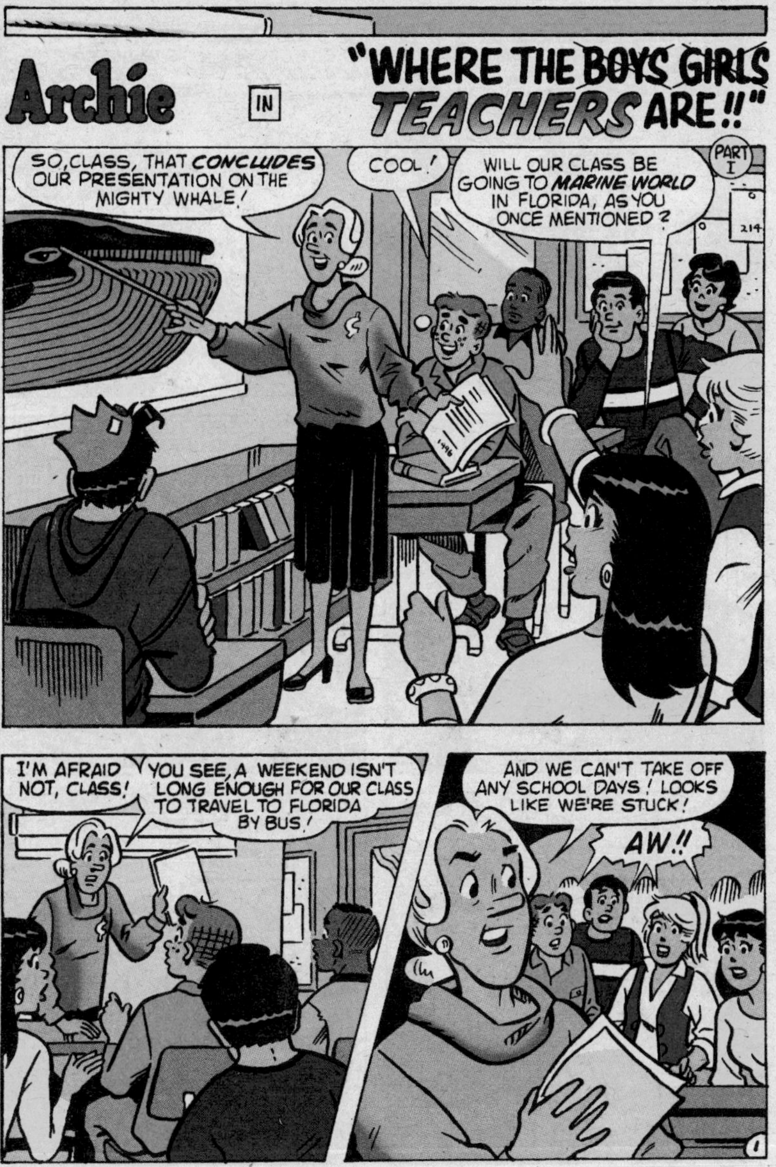
Archie
IN
"WHERE THE BOYS GIRLS TEACHERS ARE!!"
PART I
SO, CLASS, THAT CONCLUDES OUR PRESENTATION ON THE MIGHTY WHALE!
COOL!
WILL OUR CLASS BE GOING TO MARINE WORLD IN FLORIDA, AS YOU ONCE MENTIONED?
I'M AFRAID NOT, CLASS!
YOU SEE, A WEEKEND ISN'T LONG ENOUGH FOR OUR CLASS TO TRAVEL TO FLORIDA BY BUS!
AND WE CAN'T TAKE OFF ANY SCHOOL DAYS! LOOKS LIKE WE'RE STUCK!
AW!!
1

Script: Rich Margopoulos / Pencils: Stan Goldberg / Inks: Rudy Lapick / Letters: Bill Yoshida / Colors: Barry Grossman

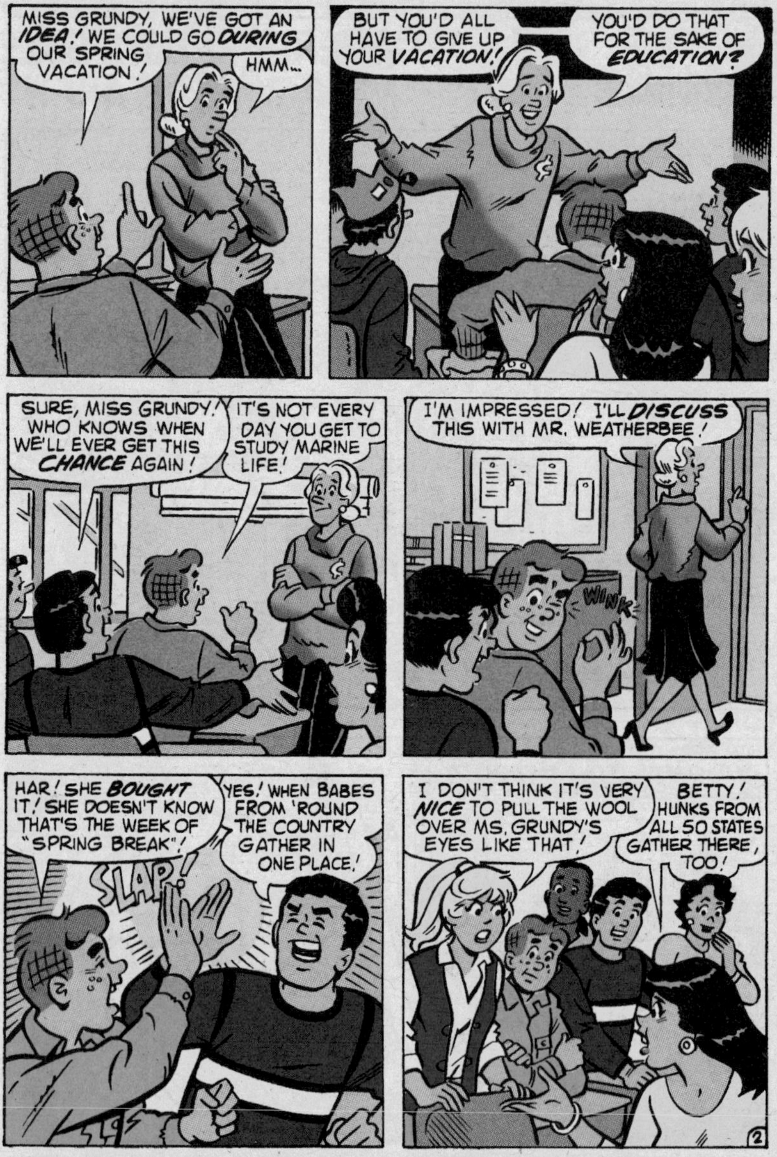
MISS GRUNDY, WE'VE GOT AN IDEA! WE COULD GO DURING OUR SPRING VACATION!
HMM...
BUT YOU'D ALL HAVE TO GIVE UP YOUR VACATION!
YOU'D DO THAT FOR THE SAKE OF EDUCATION?
SURE, MISS GRUNDY! WHO KNOWS WHEN WE'LL EVER GET THIS CHANCE AGAIN!
IT'S NOT EVERY DAY YOU GET TO STUDY MARINE LIFE!
I'M IMPRESSED! I'LL DISCUSS THIS WITH MR. WEATHERBEE!
WINK
HAR! SHE BOUGHT IT! SHE DOESN'T KNOW THAT'S THE WEEK OF "SPRING BREAK"!
YES! WHEN BABES FROM 'ROUND THE COUNTRY GATHER IN ONE PLACE!
SLAP!
I DON'T THINK IT'S VERY NICE TO PULL THE WOOL OVER MS. GRUNDY'S EYES LIKE THAT!
BETTY! HUNKS FROM ALL 50 STATES GATHER THERE, TOO!
2

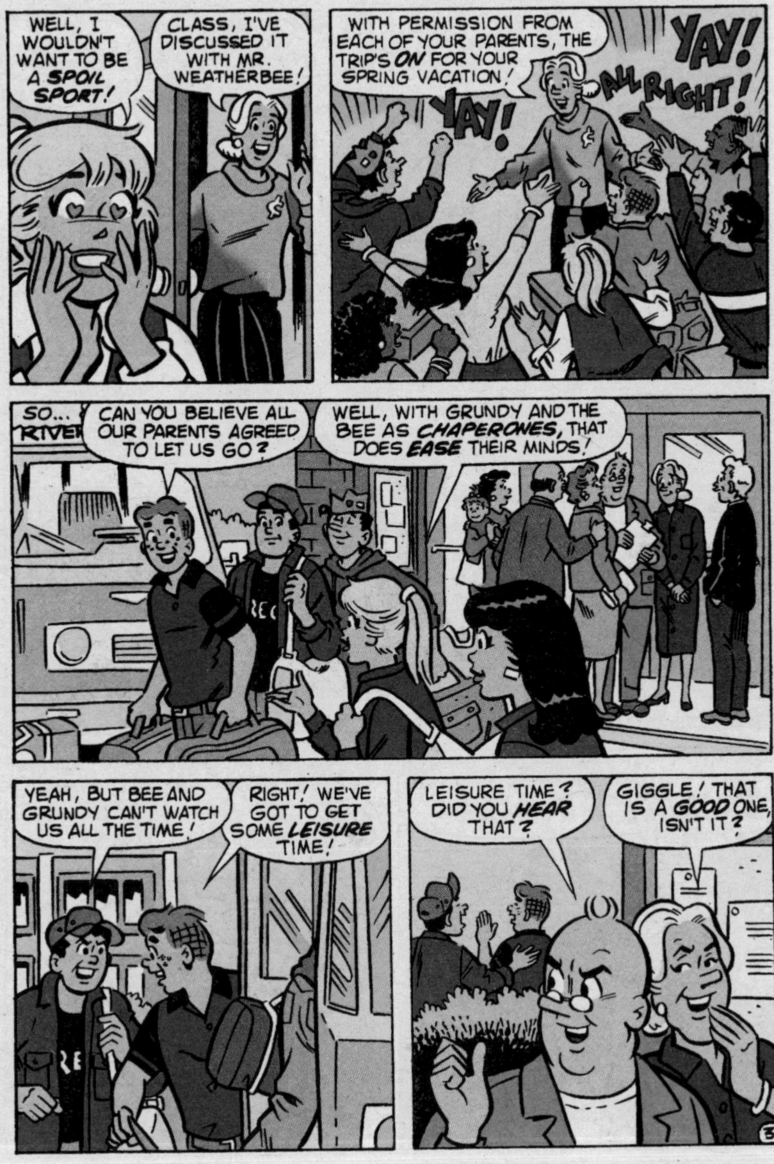
WELL, I WOULDN'T WANT TO BE A SPOIL SPORT!
CLASS, I'VE DISCUSSED IT WITH MR. WEATHERBEE!
WITH PERMISSION FROM EACH OF YOUR PARENTS, THE TRIP'S ON FOR YOUR SPRING VACATION!
YAY!
YAY!
ALL RIGHT!
SO... RIVER
CAN YOU BELIEVE ALL OUR PARENTS AGREED TO LET US GO?
WELL, WITH GRUNDY AND THE BEE AS CHAPERONES, THAT DOES EASE THEIR MINDS!
YEAH, BUT BEE AND GRUNDY CAN'T WATCH US ALL THE TIME!
RIGHT! WE'VE GOT TO GET SOME LEISURE TIME!
LEISURE TIME? DID YOU HEAR THAT?
GIGGLE! THAT IS A GOOD ONE, ISN'T IT?
3

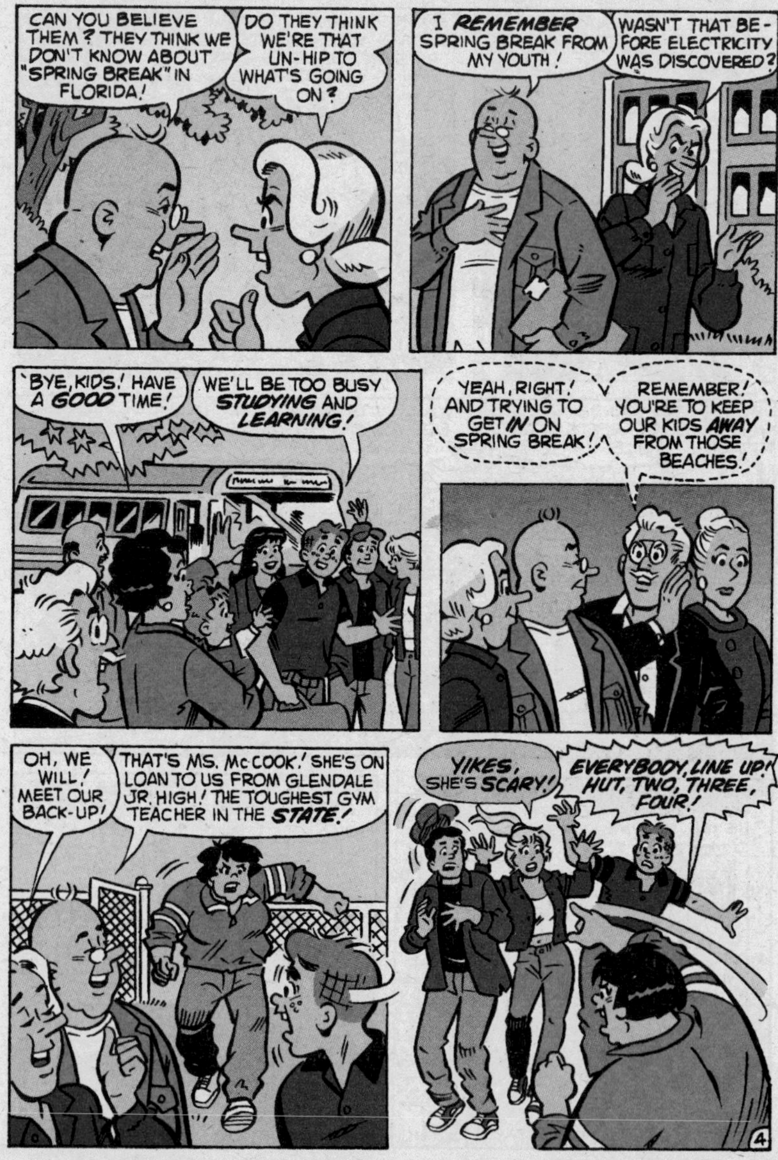
CAN YOU BELIEVE THEM? THEY THINK WE DON'T KNOW ABOUT "SPRING BREAK" IN FLORIDA!
DO THEY THINK WE'RE THAT UN-HIP TO WHAT'S GOING ON?
I REMEMBER SPRING BREAK FROM MY YOUTH!
WASN'T THAT BE-FORE ELECTRICITY WAS DISCOVERED?
'BYE, KIDS! HAVE A GOOD TIME!
WE'LL BE TOO BUSY STUDYING AND LEARNING!
YEAH, RIGHT! AND TRYING TO GET IN ON SPRING BREAK!
REMEMBER! YOU'RE TO KEEP OUR KIDS AWAY FROM THOSE BEACHES!
OH, WE WILL! MEET OUR BACK-UP!
THAT'S MS. McCOOK! SHE'S ON LOAN TO US FROM GLENDALE JR. HIGH! THE TOUGHEST GYM TEACHER IN THE STATE!
YIKES, SHE'S SCARY!
EVERYBODY, LINE UP! HUT, TWO, THREE, FOUR!
4

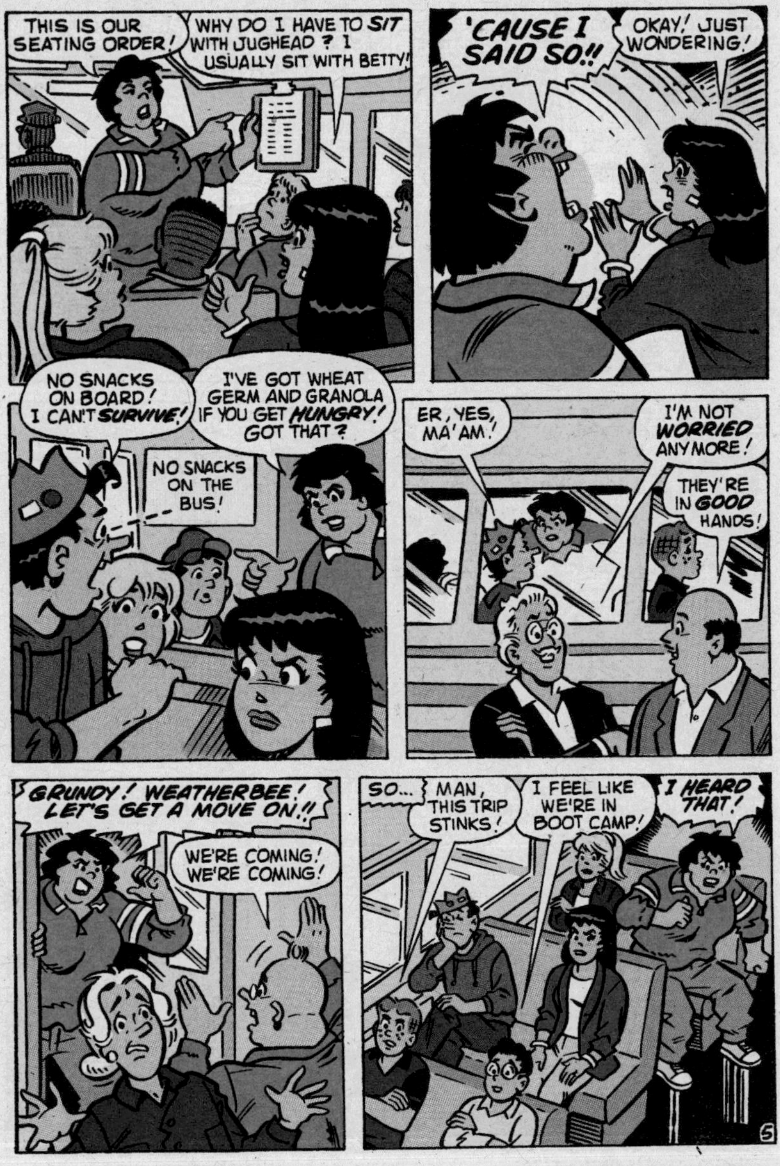
THIS IS OUR SEATING ORDER!
WHY DO I HAVE TO SIT WITH JUGHEAD? I USUALLY SIT WITH BETTY!
'CAUSE I SAID SO!!
OKAY! JUST WONDERING!
NO SNACKS ON BOARD! I CAN'T SURVIVE!
I'VE GOT WHEAT GERM AND GRANOLA IF YOU GET HUNGRY! GOT THAT?
NO SNACKS ON THE BUS!
ER, YES, MA'AM!
I'M NOT WORRIED ANYMORE!
THEY'RE IN GOOD HANDS!
GRUNDY! WEATHERBEE! LET'S GET A MOVE ON!!
WE'RE COMING! WE'RE COMING!
SO...
MAN, THIS TRIP STINKS!
I FEEL LIKE WE'RE IN BOOT CAMP!
I HEARD THAT!
5

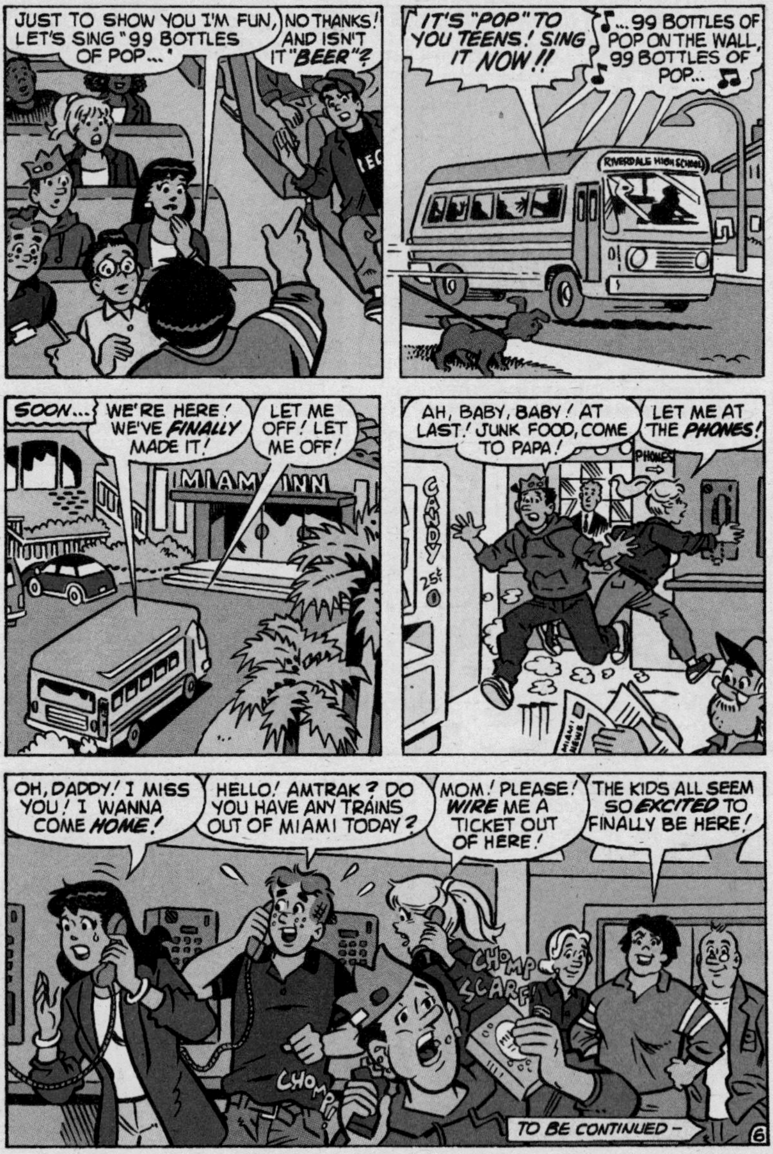
JUST TO SHOW YOU I'M FUN, LET'S SING "99 BOTTLES OF POP..."
NO THANKS! AND ISN'T IT "BEER"?
IT'S "POP" TO YOU TEENS! SING IT NOW!!
...99 BOTTLES OF POP ON THE WALL, 99 BOTTLES OF POP...
RIVERDALE HIGH SCHOOL
SOON...
WE'RE HERE! WE'VE FINALLY MADE IT!
LET ME OFF! LET ME OFF!
MIAMI INN
AH, BABY, BABY! AT LAST! JUNK FOOD, COME TO PAPA!
LET ME AT THE PHONES!
PHONES
CANDY
25¢
OH, DADDY! I MISS YOU! I WANNA COME HOME!
HELLO! AMTRAK? DO YOU HAVE ANY TRAINS OUT OF MIAMI TODAY?
MOM! PLEASE! WIRE ME A TICKET OUT OF HERE!
THE KIDS ALL SEEM SO EXCITED TO FINALLY BE HERE!
CHOMP
SCARF!
CHOMP!
TO BE CONTINUED -

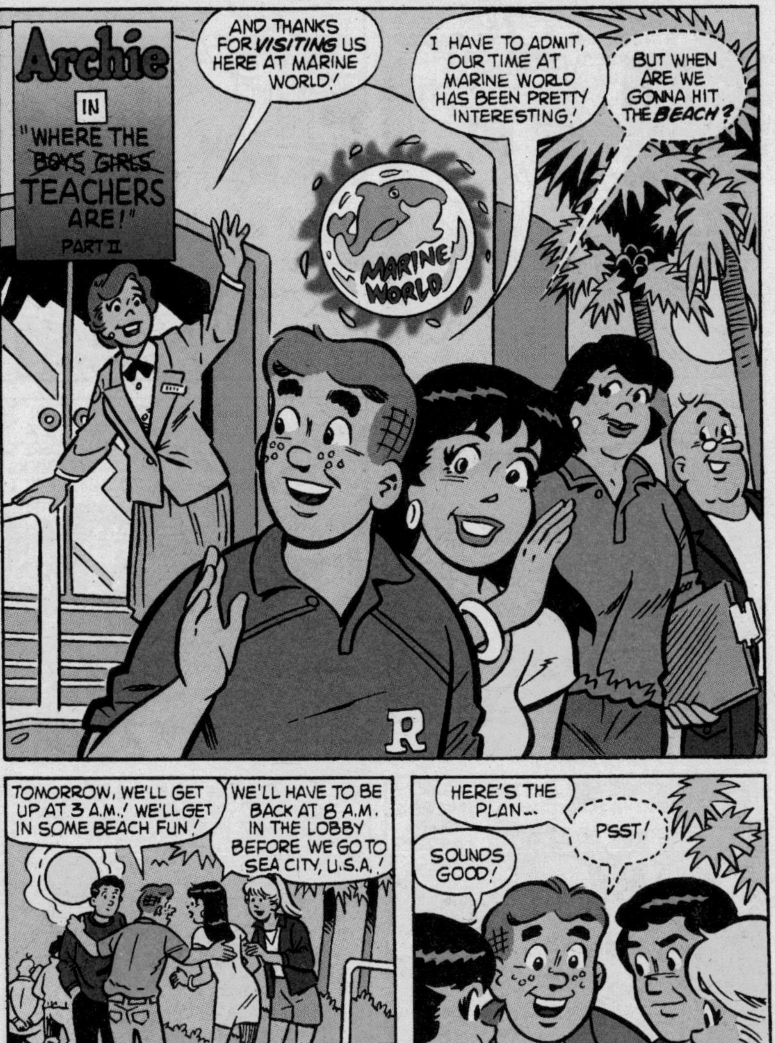
Archie
IN
"WHERE THE BOYS GIRLS TEACHERS ARE!"
PART II
AND THANKS FOR VISITING US HERE AT MARINE WORLD!
I HAVE TO ADMIT, OUR TIME AT MARINE WORLD HAS BEEN PRETTY INTERESTING!
BUT WHEN ARE WE GONNA HIT THE BEACH?
MARINE WORLD
R
TOMORROW, WE'LL GET UP AT 3 A.M.! WE'LL GET IN SOME BEACH FUN!
WE'LL HAVE TO BE BACK AT 8 A.M. IN THE LOBBY BEFORE WE GO TO SEA CITY, U.S.A.!
HERE'S THE PLAN...
PSST!
SOUNDS GOOD!
7

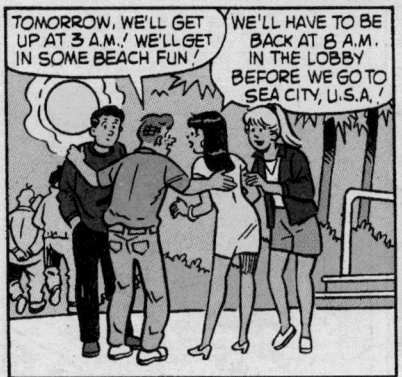

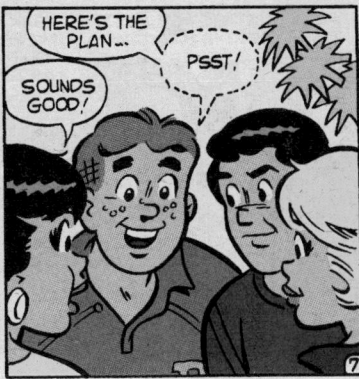

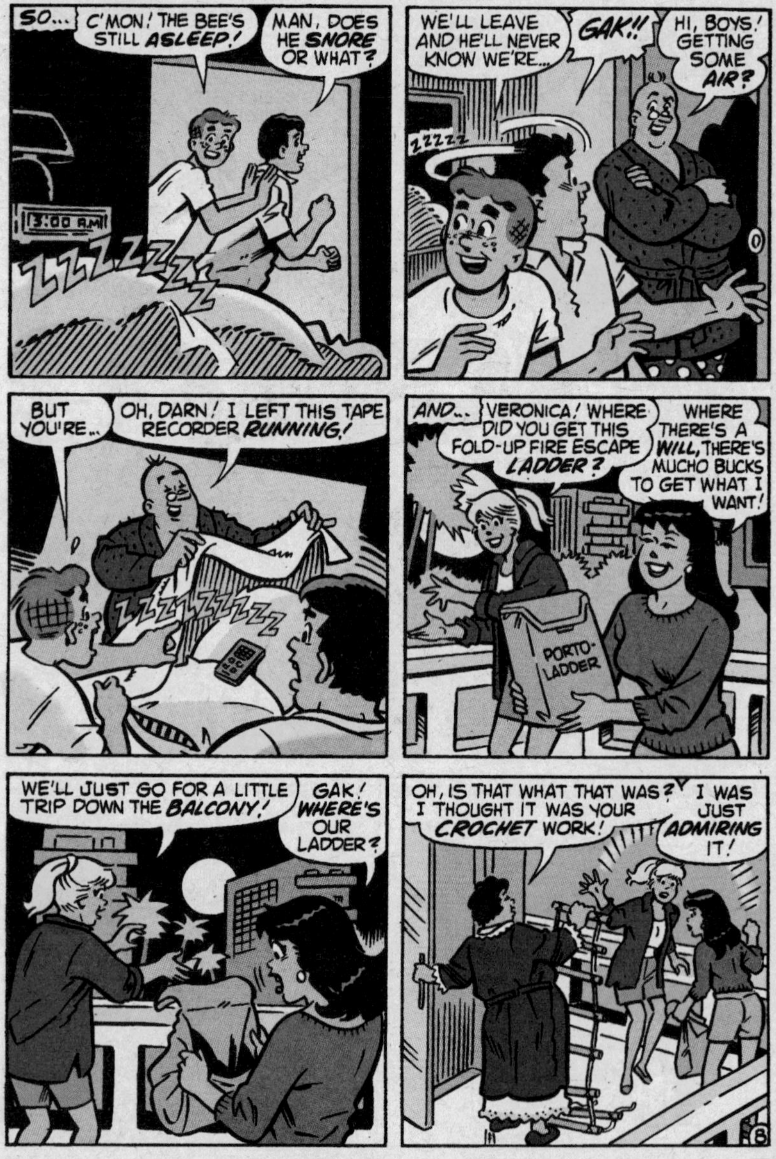
SO...
C'MON! THE BEE'S STILL ASLEEP!
MAN, DOES HE SNORE OR WHAT?
3:00 A.M.
WE'LL LEAVE AND HE'LL NEVER KNOW WE'RE...
GAK!!
HI, BOYS! GETTING SOME AIR?
BUT YOU'RE...
OH, DARN! I LEFT THIS TAPE RECORDER RUNNING!
AND...
VERONICA! WHERE DID YOU GET THIS FOLD-UP FIRE ESCAPE LADDER?
WHERE THERE'S A WILL, THERE'S MUCHO BUCKS TO GET WHAT I WANT!
PORTO-LADDER
WE'LL JUST GO FOR A LITTLE TRIP DOWN THE BALCONY!
GAK! WHERE'S OUR LADDER?
OH, IS THAT WHAT THAT WAS? I THOUGHT IT WAS YOUR CROCHET WORK!
I WAS JUST ADMIRING IT!
8

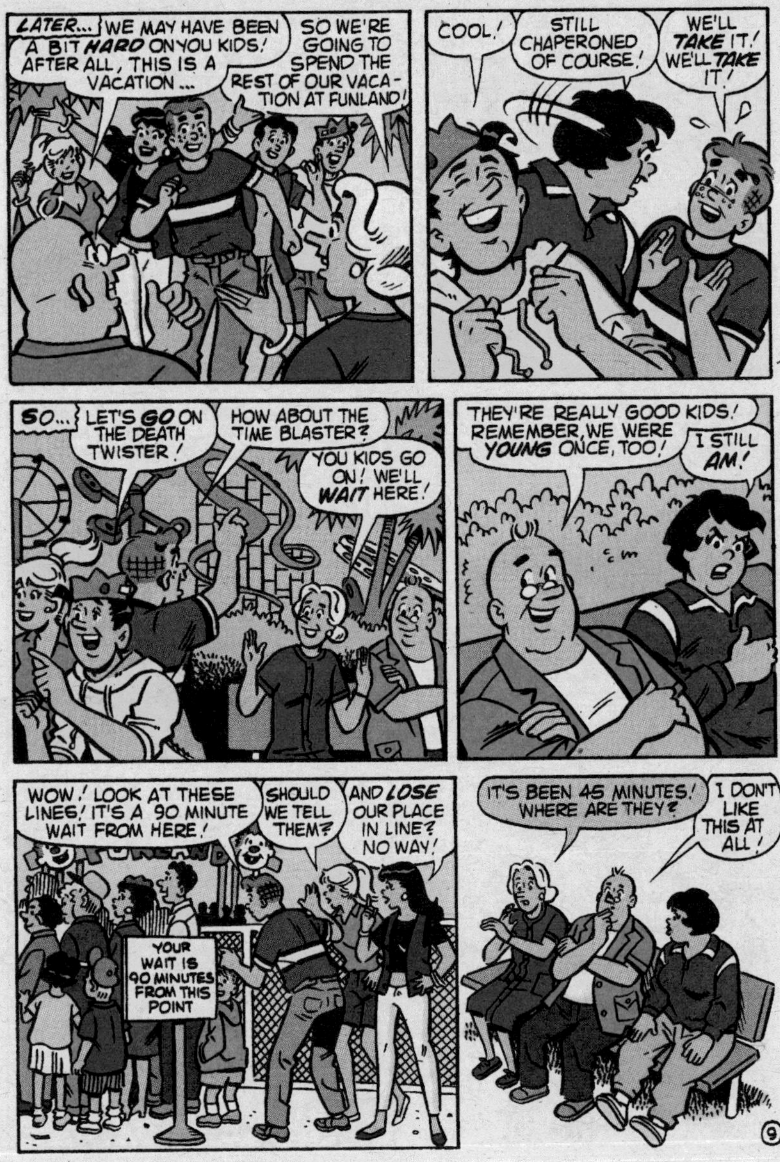
LATER...
WE MAY HAVE BEEN A BIT HARD ON YOU KIDS! AFTER ALL, THIS IS A VACATION ...
SO WE'RE GOING TO SPEND THE REST OF OUR VACATION AT FUNLAND!
COOL!
STILL CHAPERONED OF COURSE!
WE'LL TAKE IT! WE'LL TAKE IT!
SO...
LET'S GO ON THE DEATH TWISTER!
HOW ABOUT THE TIME BLASTER?
YOU KIDS GO ON! WE'LL WAIT HERE!
THEY'RE REALLY GOOD KIDS! REMEMBER, WE WERE YOUNG ONCE, TOO!
I STILL AM!
WOW! LOOK AT THESE LINES! IT'S A 90 MINUTE WAIT FROM HERE!
SHOULD WE TELL THEM?
AND LOSE OUR PLACE IN LINE? NO WAY!
YOUR WAIT IS 90 MINUTES FROM THIS POINT
IT'S BEEN 45 MINUTES! WHERE ARE THEY?
I DON'T LIKE THIS AT ALL!

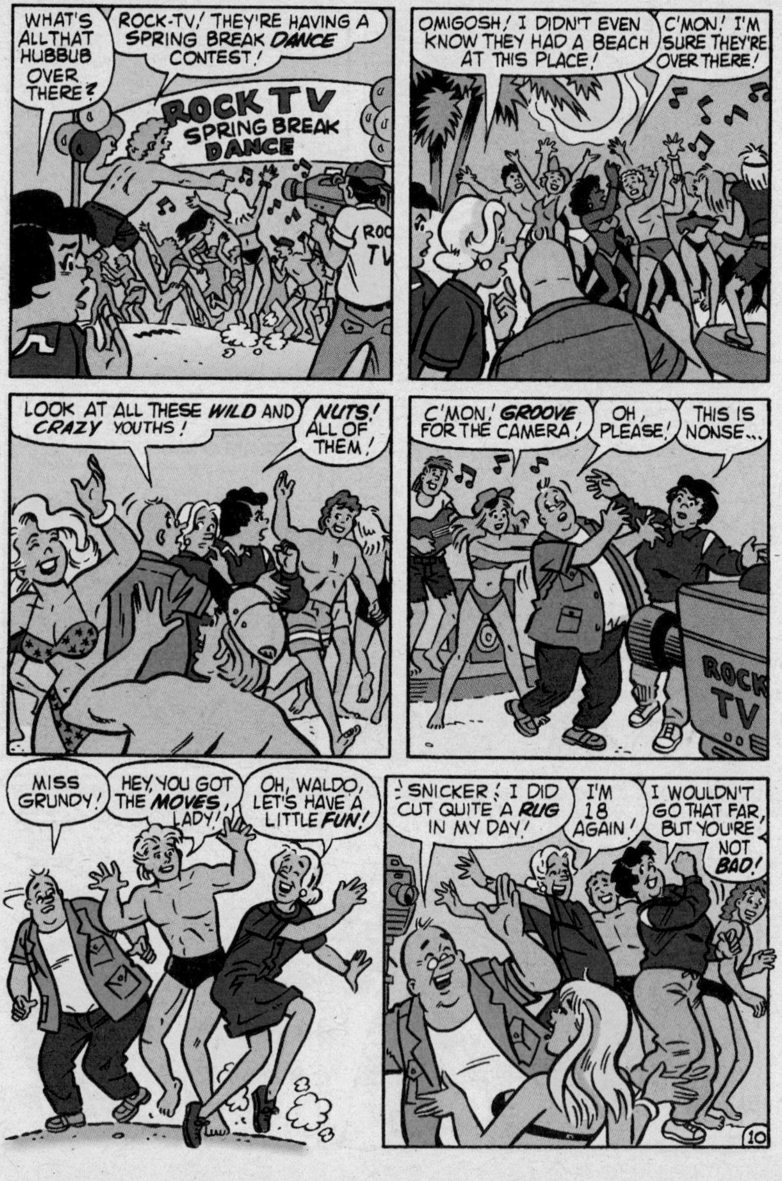
WHAT'S ALLTHAT HUBBUB OVER THERE?
ROCK-TV! THEY'RE HAVING A SPRING BREAK DANCE CONTEST!
ROCK TV SPRING BREAK DANCE
ROCK TV
OMIGOSH! I DIDN'T EVEN KNOW THEY HAD A BEACH AT THIS PLACE!
C'MON! I'M SURE THEY'RE OVER THERE!
LOOK AT ALL THESE WILD AND CRAZY YOUTHS!
NUTS! ALL OF THEM!
C'MON! GROOVE FOR THE CAMERA!
OH, PLEASE!
THIS IS NONSE...
ROCK TV
MISS GRUNDY!
HEY, YOU GOT THE MOVES, LADY!
OH, WALDO, LET'S HAVE A LITTLE FUN!
SNICKER! I DID CUT QUITE A RUG IN MY DAY!
I'M 18 AGAIN!
I WOULDN'T GO THAT FAR, BUT YOU'RE NOT BAD!

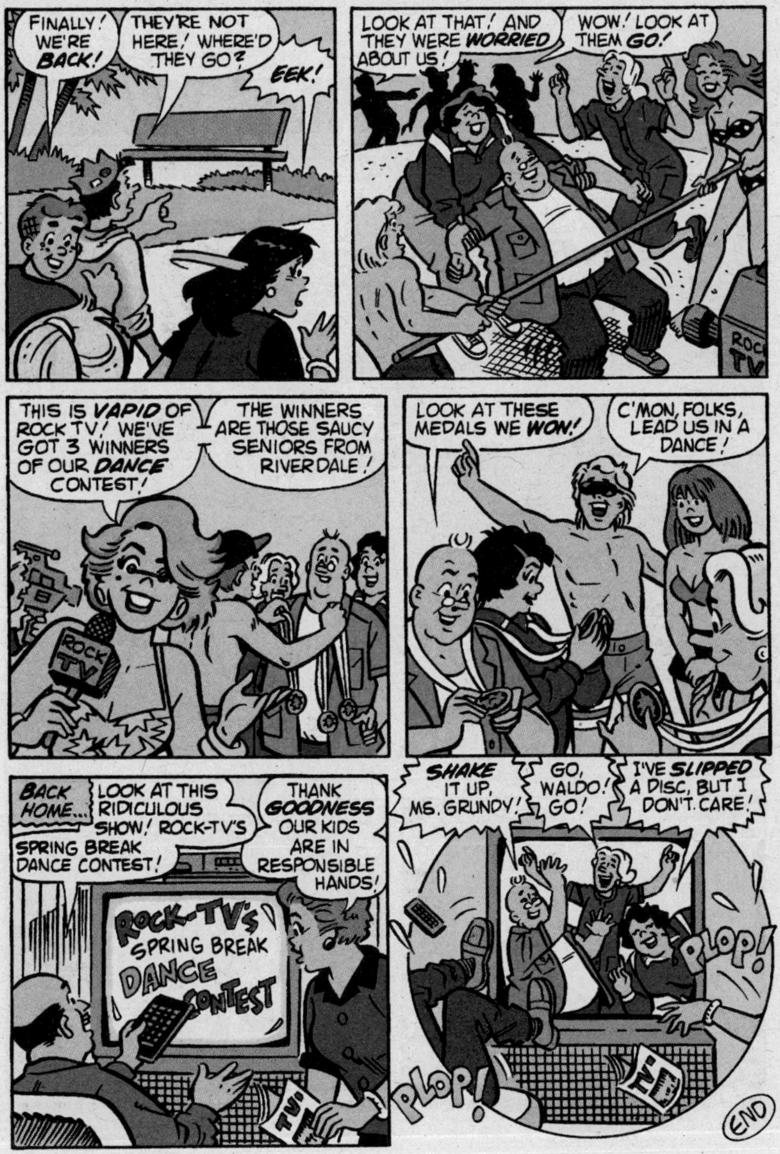
FINALLY! WE'RE BACK!
THEY'RE NOT HERE! WHERE'D THEY GO?
EEK!
LOOK AT THAT! AND THEY WERE WORRIED ABOUT US!
WOW! LOOK AT THEM GO!
ROCK TV
THIS IS VAPID OF ROCK TV! WE'VE GOT 3 WINNERS OF OUR DANCE CONTEST!
THE WINNERS ARE THOSE SAUCY SENIORS FROM RIVERDALE!
ROCK TV
LOOK AT THESE MEDALS WE WON!
C'MON, FOLKS, LEAD US IN A DANCE!
BACK HOME...
LOOK AT THIS RIDICULOUS SHOW! ROCK-TV'S SPRING BREAK DANCE CONTEST!
THANK GOODNESS OUR KIDS ARE IN RESPONSIBLE HANDS!
ROCK-TV'S SPRING BREAK DANCE CONTEST
SHAKE IT UP, MS. GRUNDY!
GO, WALDO! GO!
I'VE SLIPPED A DISC, BUT I DON'T CARE!
PLOP!
PLOP!
END

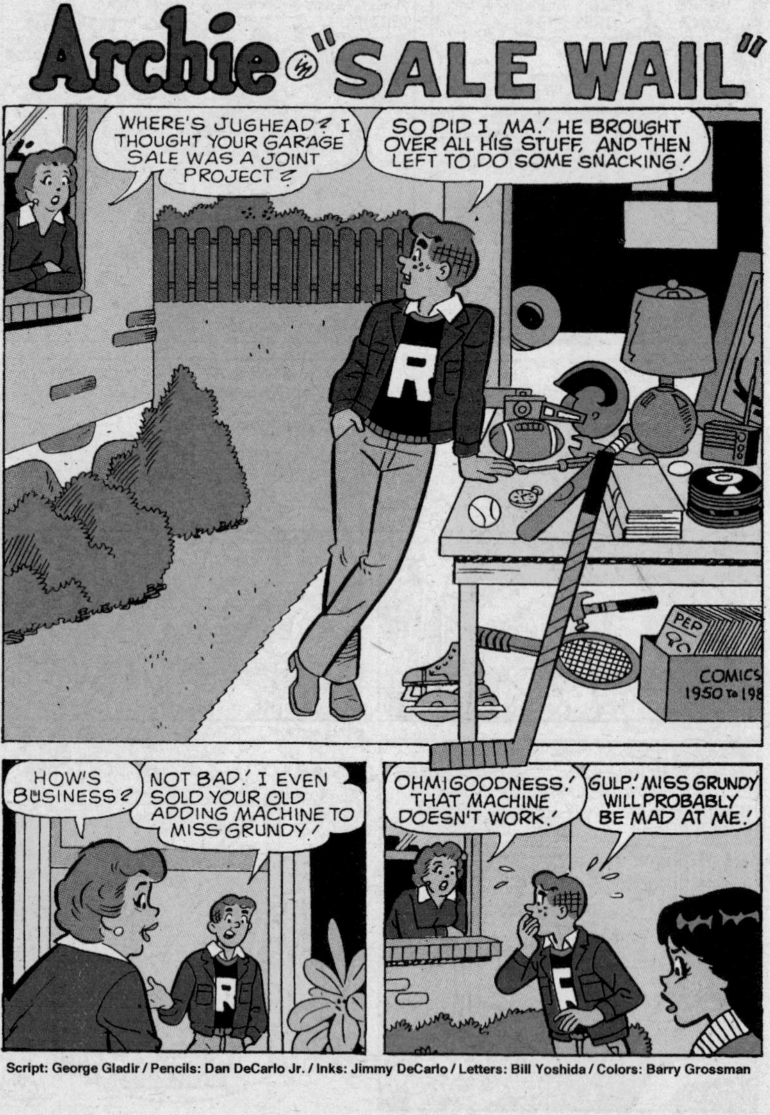
Archie in "SALE WAIL"
WHERE'S JUGHEAD? I THOUGHT YOUR GARAGE SALE WAS A JOINT PROJECT?
SO DID I, MA! HE BROUGHT OVER ALL HIS STUFF, AND THEN LEFT TO DO SOME SNACKING!
PEP
COMICS 1950 TO 198
HOW'S BUSINESS?
NOT BAD! I EVEN SOLD YOUR OLD ADDING MACHINE TO MISS GRUNDY!
OHMIGOODNESS! THAT MACHINE DOESN'T WORK!
GULP! MISS GRUNDY WILL PROBABLY BE MAD AT ME!

Script: George Gladir / Pencils: Dan DeCarlo Jr. / Inks: Jimmy DeCarlo / Letters: Bill Yoshida / Colors: Barry Grossman

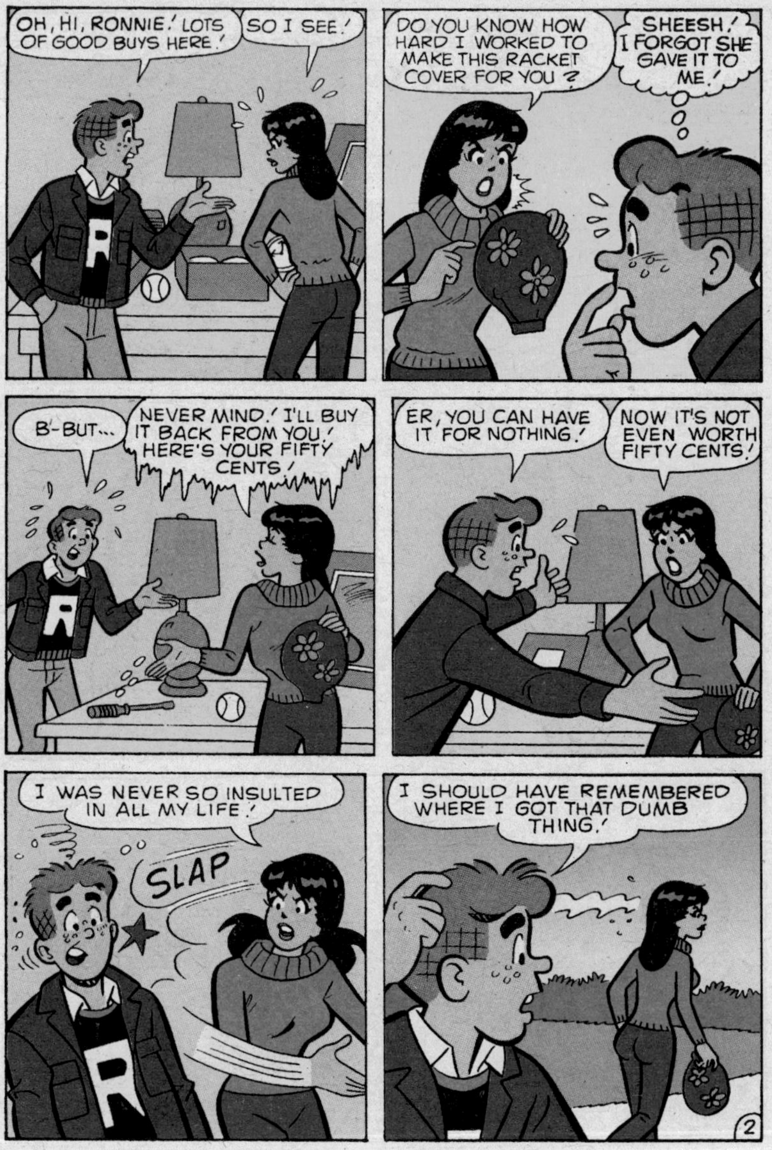
OH, HI, RONNIE! LOTS OF GOOD BUYS HERE!
SO I SEE!
DO YOU KNOW HOW HARD I WORKED TO MAKE THIS RACKET COVER FOR YOU?
SHEESH! I FORGOT SHE GAVE IT TO ME!
B-BUT...
NEVER MIND! I'LL BUY IT BACK FROM YOU! HERE'S YOUR FIFTY CENTS!
ER, YOU CAN HAVE IT FOR NOTHING!
NOW IT'S NOT EVEN WORTH FIFTY CENTS!
I WAS NEVER SO INSULTED IN ALL MY LIFE!
SLAP
I SHOULD HAVE REMEMBERED WHERE I GOT THAT DUMB THING!
2

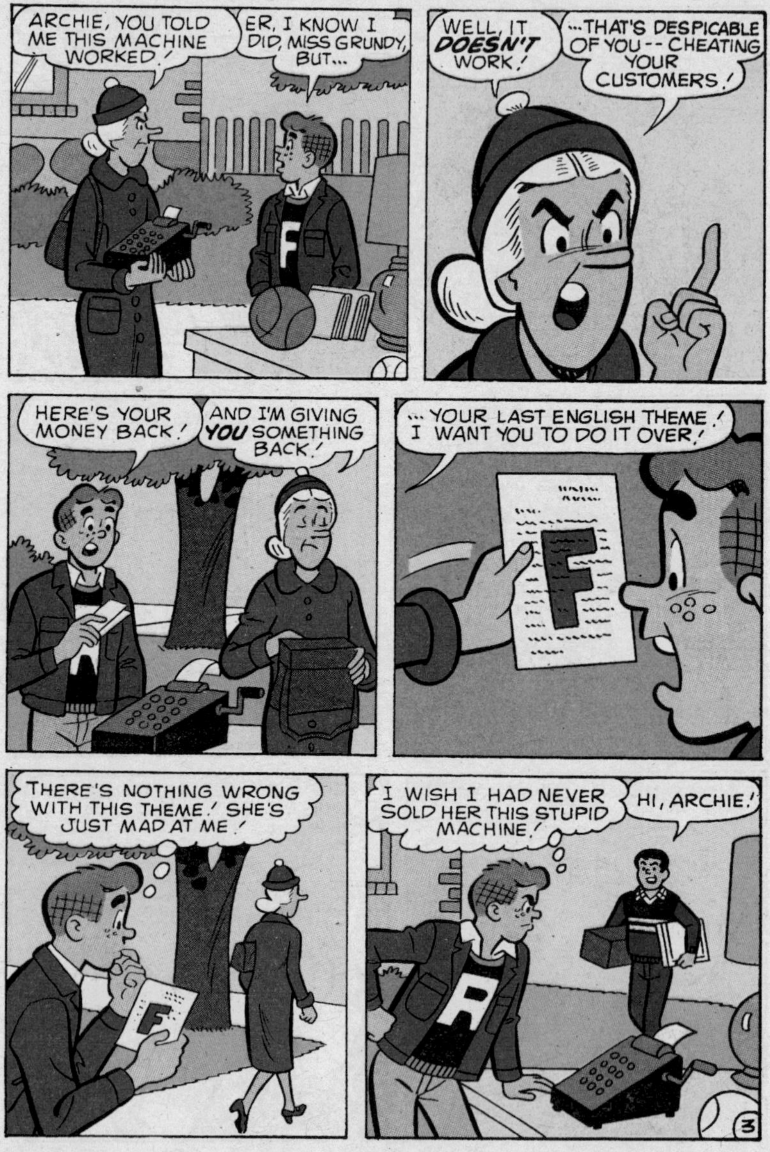
ARCHIE, YOU TOLD ME THIS MACHINE WORKED!
ER, I KNOW I DID, MISS GRUNDY, BUT...
WELL, IT DOESN'T WORK!
...THAT'S DESPICABLE OF YOU -- CHEATING YOUR CUSTOMERS!
HERE'S YOUR MONEY BACK!
AND I'M GIVING YOU SOMETHING BACK!
F
... YOUR LAST ENGLISH THEME! I WANT YOU TO DO IT OVER!
F
THERE'S NOTHING WRONG WITH THIS THEME! SHE'S JUST MAD AT ME!
F
I WISH I HAD NEVER SOLD HER THIS STUPID MACHINE!
HI, ARCHIE!
R
3

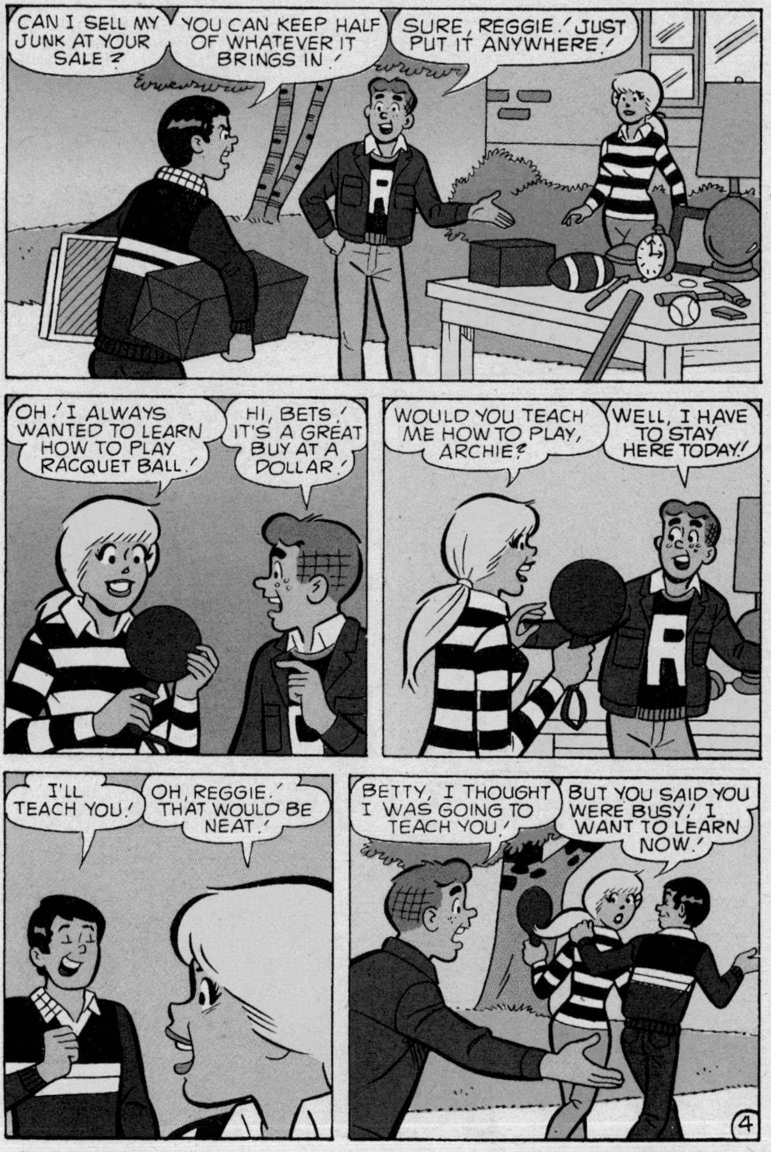
CAN I SELL MY JUNK AT YOUR SALE?
YOU CAN KEEP HALF OF WHATEVER IT BRINGS IN!
SURE, REGGIE! JUST PUT IT ANYWHERE!
OH! I ALWAYS WANTED TO LEARN HOW TO PLAY RACQUET BALL!
HI, BETS! IT'S A GREAT BUY AT A DOLLAR!
WOULD YOU TEACH ME HOW TO PLAY, ARCHIE?
WELL, I HAVE TO STAY HERE TODAY!
I'LL TEACH YOU!
OH, REGGIE! THAT WOULD BE NEAT!
BETTY, I THOUGHT I WAS GOING TO TEACH YOU!
BUT YOU SAID YOU WERE BUSY! I WANT TO LEARN NOW!
4

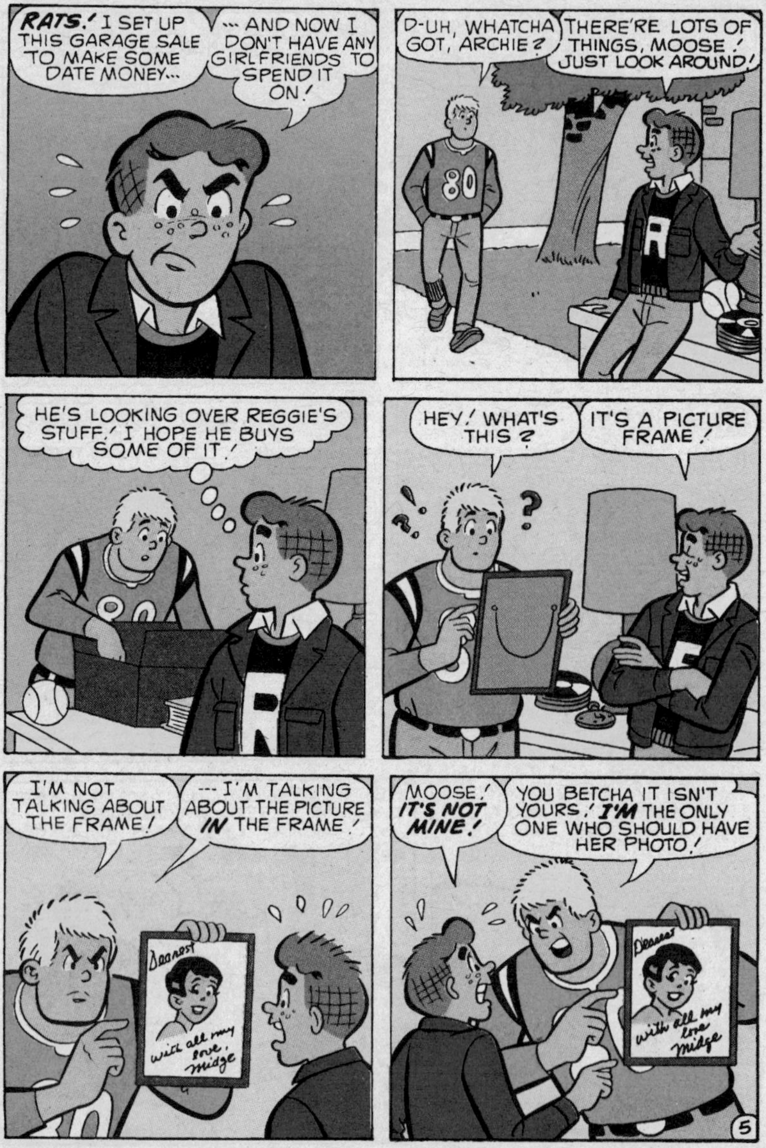
RATS! I SET UP THIS GARAGE SALE TO MAKE SOME DATE MONEY...
... AND NOW I DON'T HAVE ANY GIRLFRIENDS TO SPEND IT ON!
D-UH, WHATCHA GOT, ARCHIE?
THERE'RE LOTS OF THINGS, MOOSE! JUST LOOK AROUND!
HE'S LOOKING OVER REGGIE'S STUFF! I HOPE HE BUYS SOME OF IT!
HEY! WHAT'S THIS?
IT'S A PICTURE FRAME!
I'M NOT TALKING ABOUT THE FRAME!
--- I'M TALKING ABOUT THE PICTURE IN THE FRAME!
Dearest
with all my love, midge
MOOSE! IT'S NOT MINE!
YOU BETCHA IT ISN'T YOURS! I'M THE ONLY ONE WHO SHOULD HAVE HER PHOTO!
Dearest
with all my love midge
5

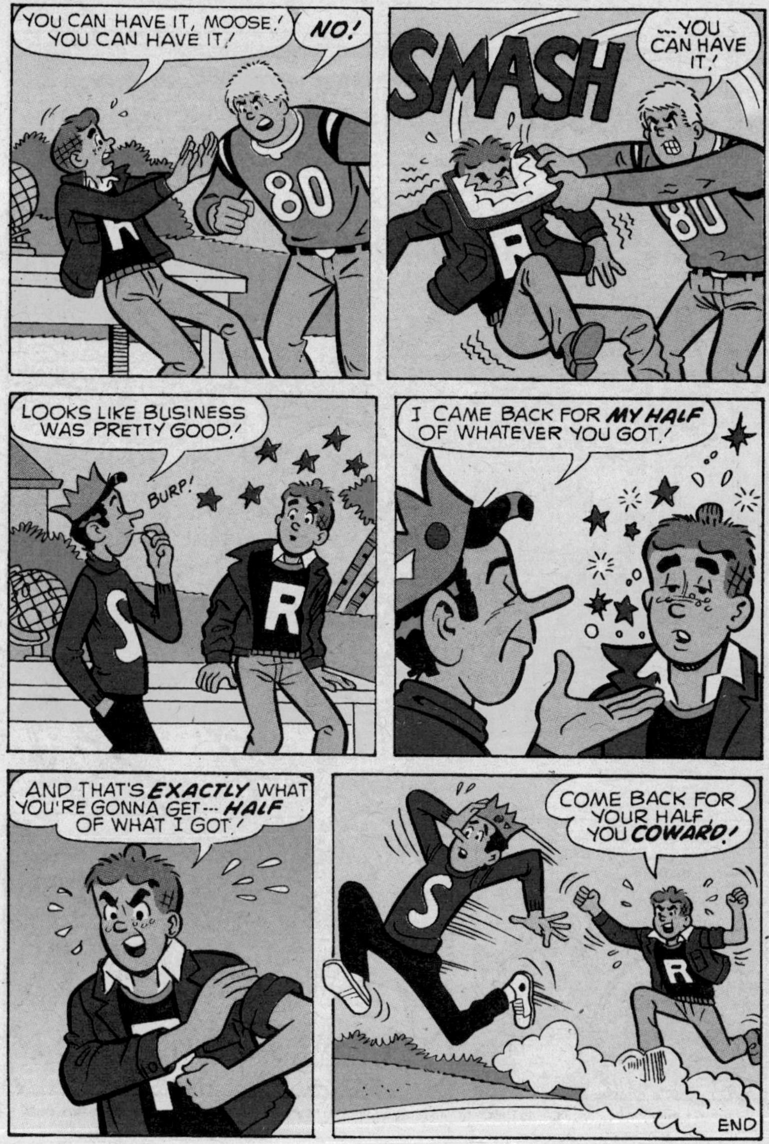
YOU CAN HAVE IT, MOOSE! YOU CAN HAVE IT!
NO!
SMASH
...YOU CAN HAVE IT!
LOOKS LIKE BUSINESS WAS PRETTY GOOD!
BURP!
I CAME BACK FOR MY HALF OF WHATEVER YOU GOT!
AND THAT'S EXACTLY WHAT YOU'RE GONNA GET--- HALF OF WHAT I GOT!
COME BACK FOR YOUR HALF, YOU COWARD!
END

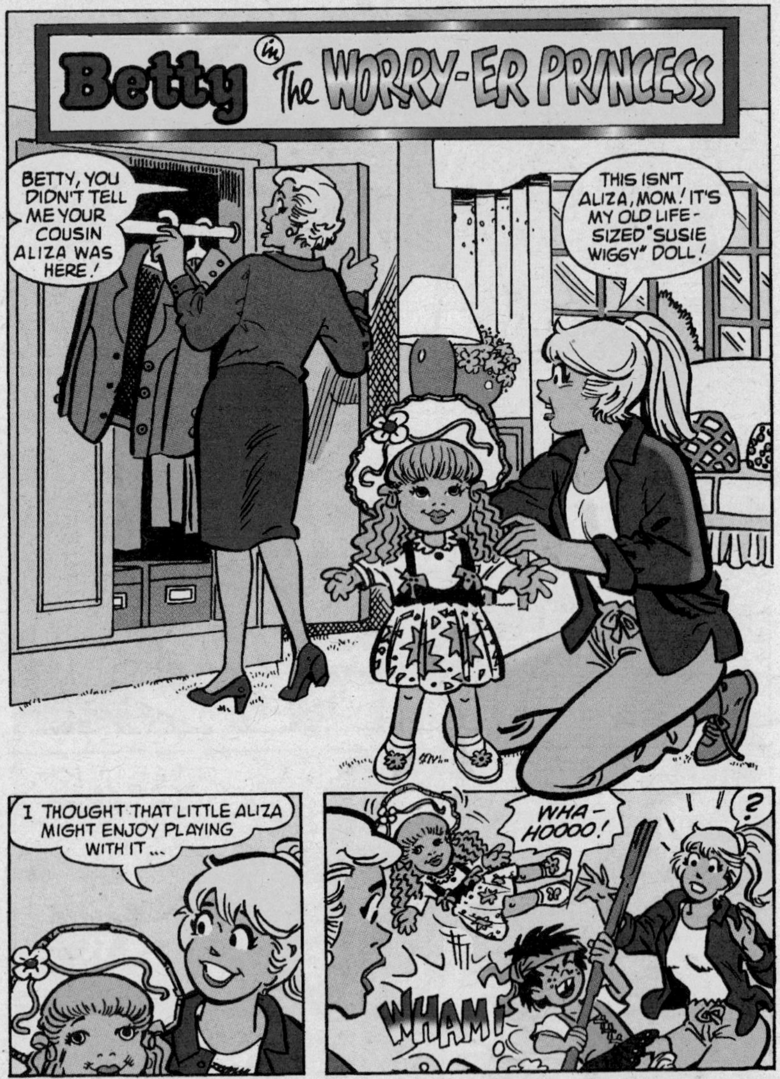
Betty in The WORRY-ER PRINCESS
BETTY, YOU DIDN'T TELL ME YOUR COUSIN ALIZA WAS HERE!
THIS ISN'T ALIZA, MOM! IT'S MY OLD LIFE-SIZED "SUSIE WIGGY" DOLL!
I THOUGHT THAT LITTLE ALIZA MIGHT ENJOY PLAYING WITH IT...
WHA-HOOOO!
?
WHAM!

Script: George Gladir / Pencils: Stan Goldberg / Inks: Mike Esposito / Letters: Bill Yoshida / Colors: Barry Grossman

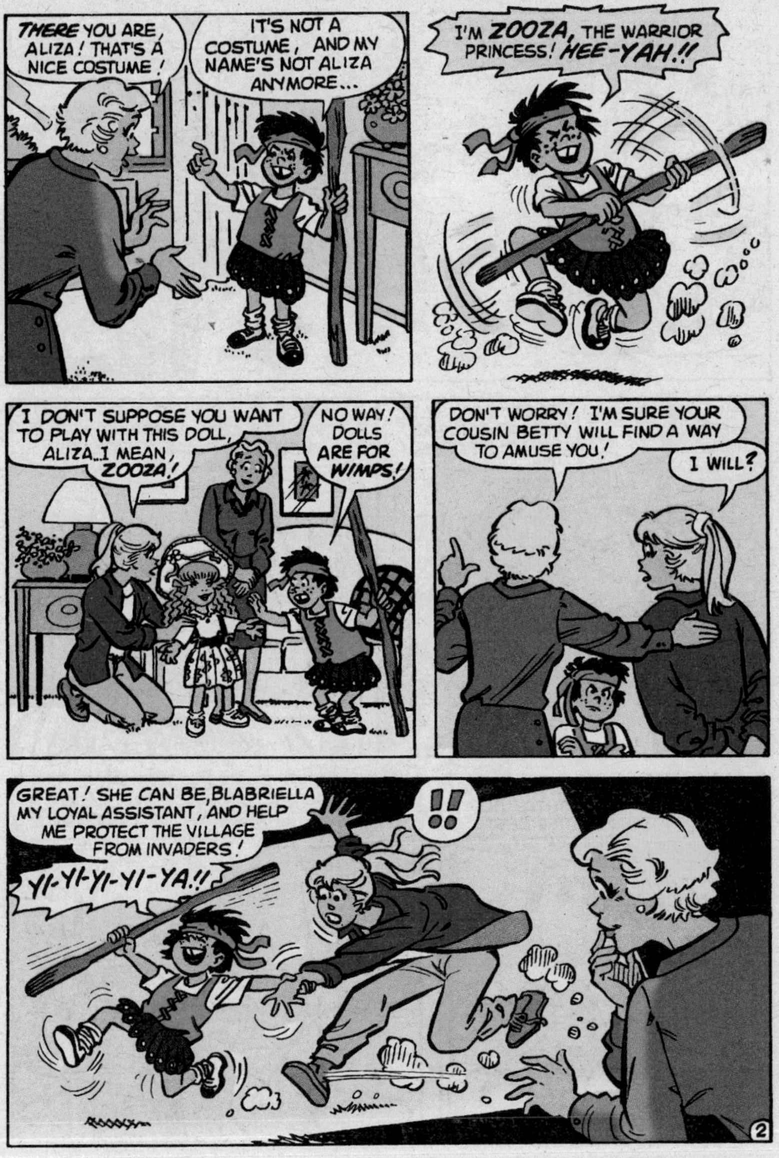
THERE YOU ARE, ALIZA! THAT'S A NICE COSTUME!
IT'S NOT A COSTUME, AND MY NAME'S NOT ALIZA ANYMORE...
I'M ZOOZA, THE WARRIOR PRINCESS! HEE-YAH!!
I DON'T SUPPOSE YOU WANT TO PLAY WITH THIS DOLL, ALIZA...I MEAN, ZOOZA!
NO WAY! DOLLS ARE FOR WIMPS!
DON'T WORRY! I'M SURE YOUR COUSIN BETTY WILL FIND A WAY TO AMUSE YOU!
I WILL?
GREAT! SHE CAN BE, BLABRIELLA MY LOYAL ASSISTANT, AND HELP ME PROTECT THE VILLAGE FROM INVADERS!
YI-YI-YI-YI-YA!!
!!
2

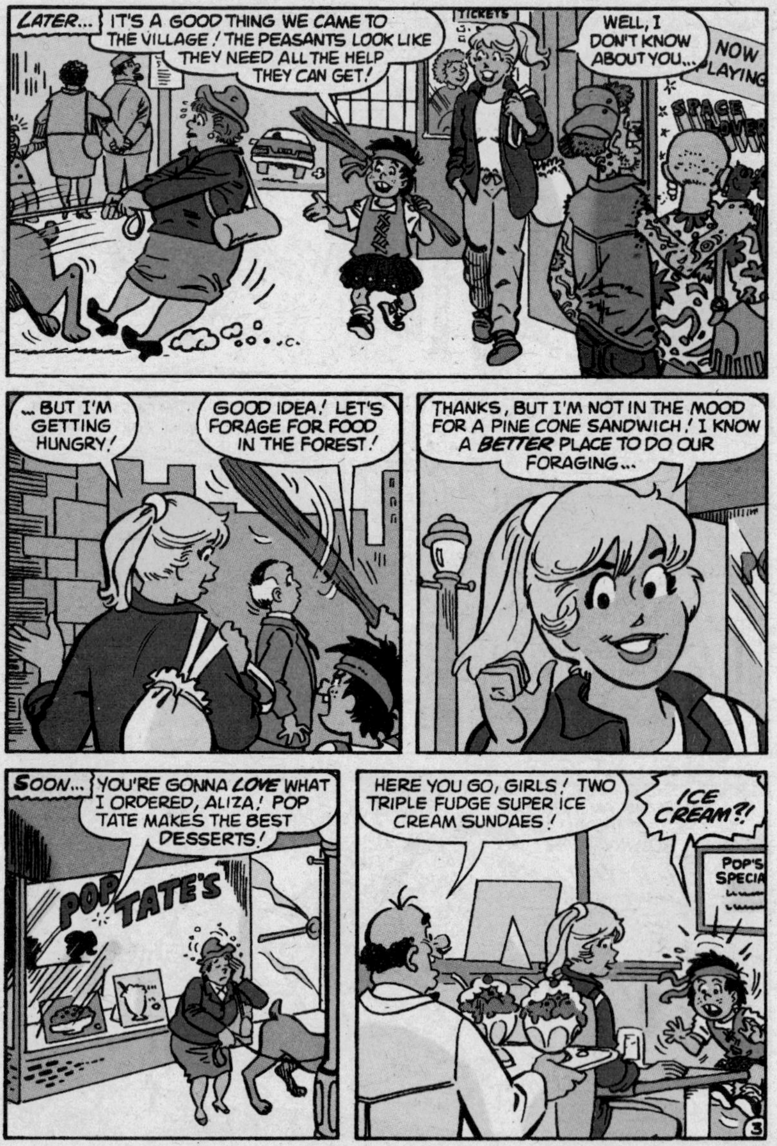
LATER...
IT'S A GOOD THING WE CAME TO THE VILLAGE! THE PEASANTS LOOK LIKE THEY NEED ALL THE HELP THEY CAN GET!
TICKETS
WELL, I DON'T KNOW ABOUT YOU...
NOW PLAYING
SPACE
...BUT I'M GETTING HUNGRY!
GOOD IDEA! LET'S FORAGE FOR FOOD IN THE FOREST!
THANKS, BUT I'M NOT IN THE MOOD FOR A PINE CONE SANDWICH! I KNOW A BETTER PLACE TO DO OUR FORAGING...
SOON...
YOU'RE GONNA LOVE WHAT I ORDERED, ALIZA! POP TATE MAKES THE BEST DESSERTS!
POP TATE'S
HERE YOU GO, GIRLS! TWO TRIPLE FUDGE SUPER ICE CREAM SUNDAES!
ICE CREAM?!
POP'S SPECIA
3

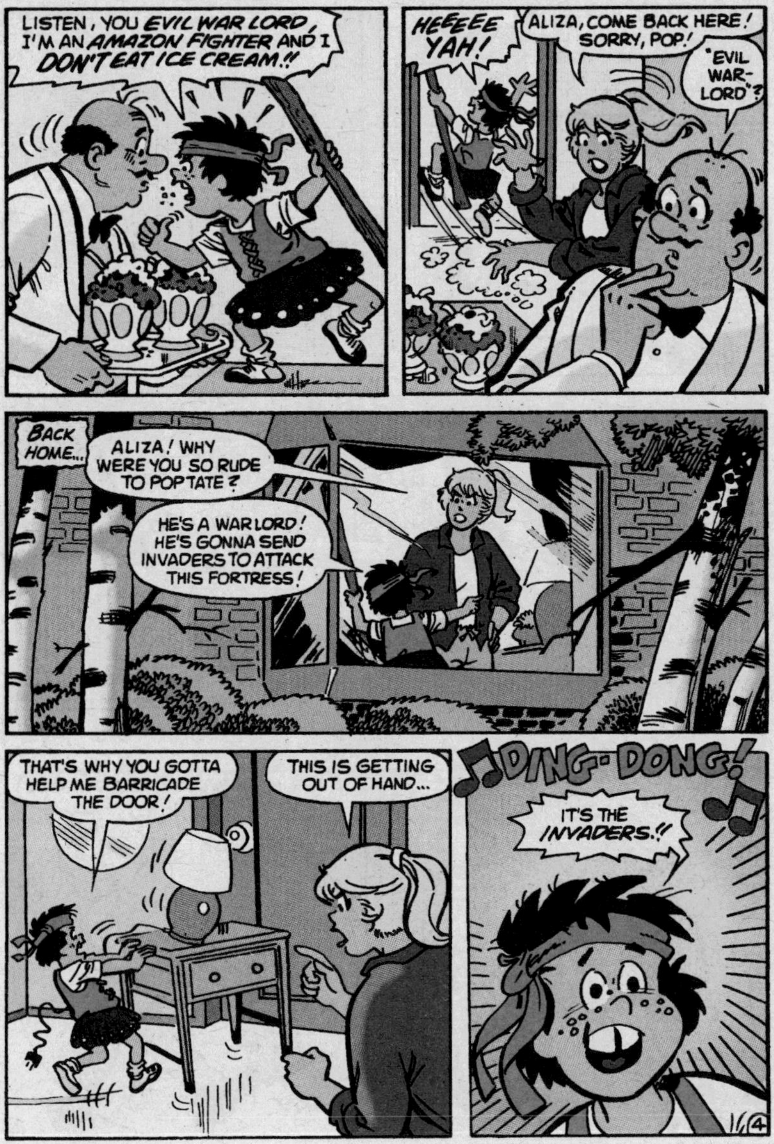
LISTEN, YOU EVIL WAR LORD, I'M AN AMAZON FIGHTER AND I DON'T EAT ICE CREAM!!
HEEEEEE YAH!
ALIZA, COME BACK HERE! SORRY, POP!
"EVIL WAR-LORD"?
BACK HOME...
ALIZA! WHY WERE YOU SO RUDE TO POP TATE?
HE'S A WAR LORD! HE'S GONNA SEND INVADERS TO ATTACK THIS FORTRESS!
THAT'S WHY YOU GOTTA HELP ME BARRICADE THE DOOR!
THIS IS GETTING OUT OF HAND...
DING-DONG!
IT'S THE INVADERS!!
4

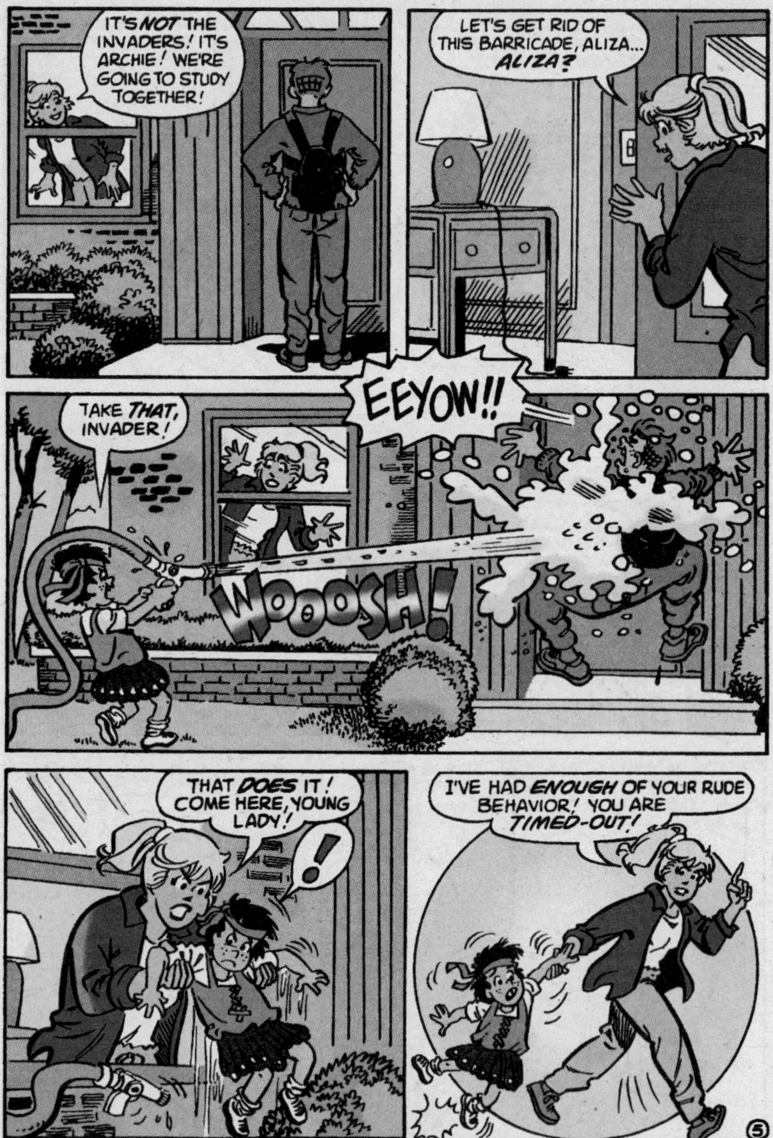
IT'S NOT THE INVADERS! IT'S ARCHIE! WE'RE GOING TO STUDY TOGETHER!
LET'S GET RID OF THIS BARRICADE, ALIZA... ALIZA?
TAKE THAT, INVADER!
EEYOW!!
WOOOSH!
THAT DOES IT! COME HERE, YOUNG LADY!
!
I'VE HAD ENOUGH OF YOUR RUDE BEHAVIOR! YOU ARE TIMED-OUT!
5

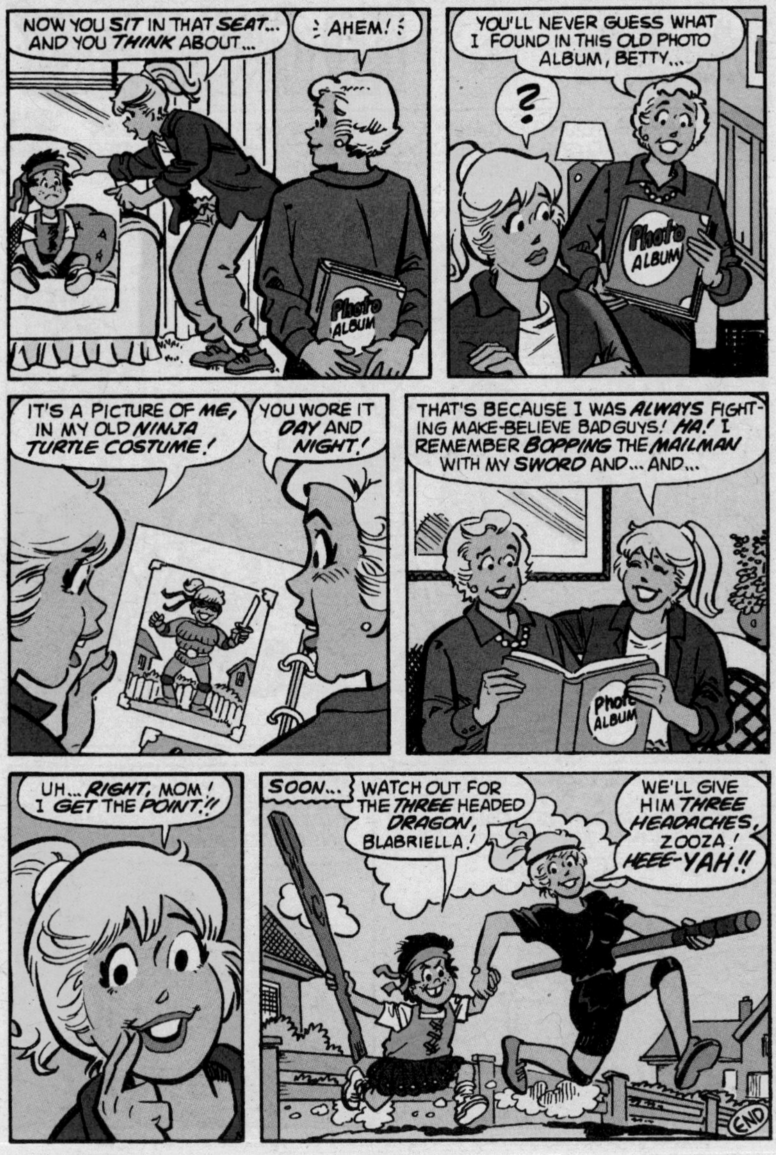
NOW YOU SIT IN THAT SEAT... AND YOU THINK ABOUT...
AHEM!
YOU'LL NEVER GUESS WHAT I FOUND IN THIS OLD PHOTO ALBUM, BETTY...
?
Photo ALBUM
IT'S A PICTURE OF ME, IN MY OLD NINJA TURTLE COSTUME!
YOU WORE IT DAY AND NIGHT!
THAT'S BECAUSE I WAS ALWAYS FIGHTING MAKE-BELIEVE BAD GUYS! HA! I REMEMBER BOPPING THE MAILMAN WITH MY SWORD AND... AND...
UH... RIGHT, MOM! I GET THE POINT!!
SOON...
WATCH OUT FOR THE THREE HEADED DRAGON, BLABRIELLA!
WE'LL GIVE HIM THREE HEADACHES, ZOOZA! HEEE-YAH!!
END

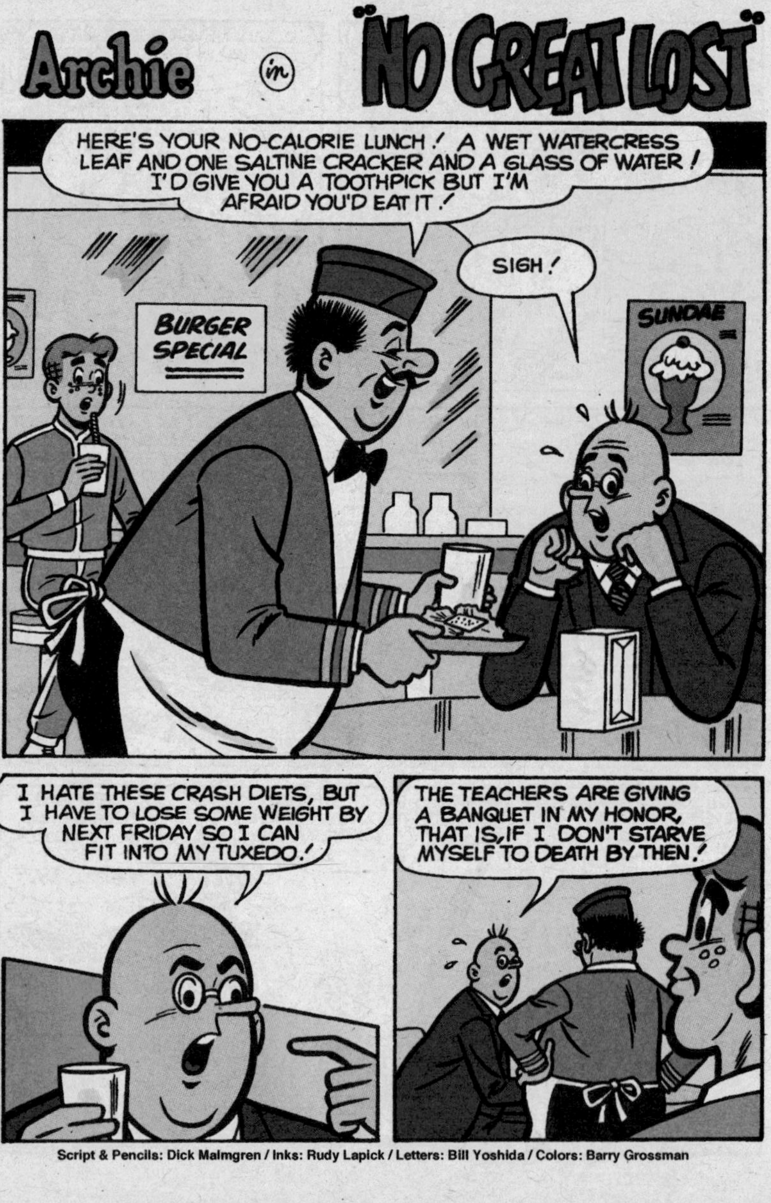
Archie in "NO GREAT LOST"
HERE'S YOUR NO-CALORIE LUNCH! A WET WATERCRESS LEAF AND ONE SALTINE CRACKER AND A GLASS OF WATER! I'D GIVE YOU A TOOTHPICK BUT I'M AFRAID YOU'D EAT IT!
SIGH!
BURGER SPECIAL
SUNDAE
I HATE THESE CRASH DIETS, BUT I HAVE TO LOSE SOME WEIGHT BY NEXT FRIDAY SO I CAN FIT INTO MY TUXEDO!
THE TEACHERS ARE GIVING A BANQUET IN MY HONOR, THAT IS, IF I DON'T STARVE MYSELF TO DEATH BY THEN!

Script & Pencils: Dick Malmgren / Inks: Rudy Lapick / Letters: Bill Yoshida / Colors: Barry Grossman

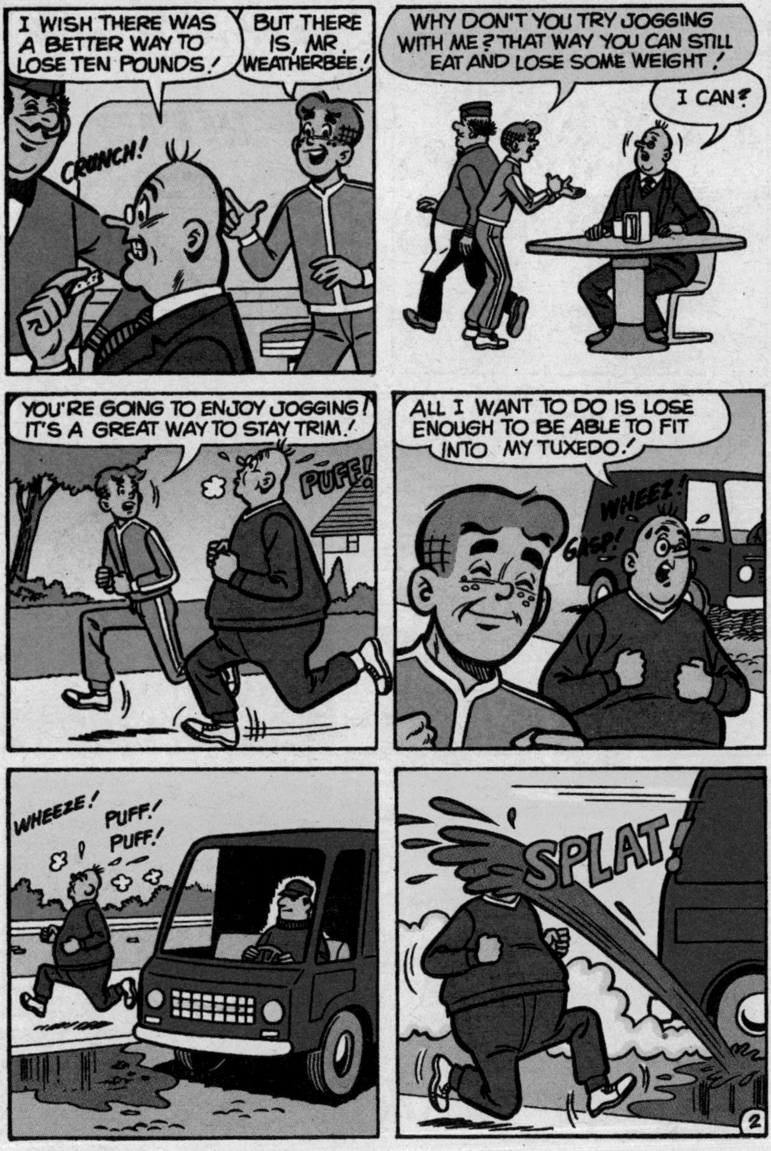
I WISH THERE WAS A BETTER WAY TO LOSE TEN POUNDS!
BUT THERE IS, MR. WEATHERBEE!
CRUNCH!
WHY DON'T YOU TRY JOGGING WITH ME? THAT WAY YOU CAN STILL EAT AND LOSE SOME WEIGHT!
I CAN?
YOU'RE GOING TO ENJOY JOGGING! IT'S A GREAT WAY TO STAY TRIM!
PUFF!
ALL I WANT TO DO IS LOSE ENOUGH TO BE ABLE TO FIT INTO MY TUXEDO!
WHEEZ!
GASP!
WHEEZE!
PUFF! PUFF!
SPLAT!
2

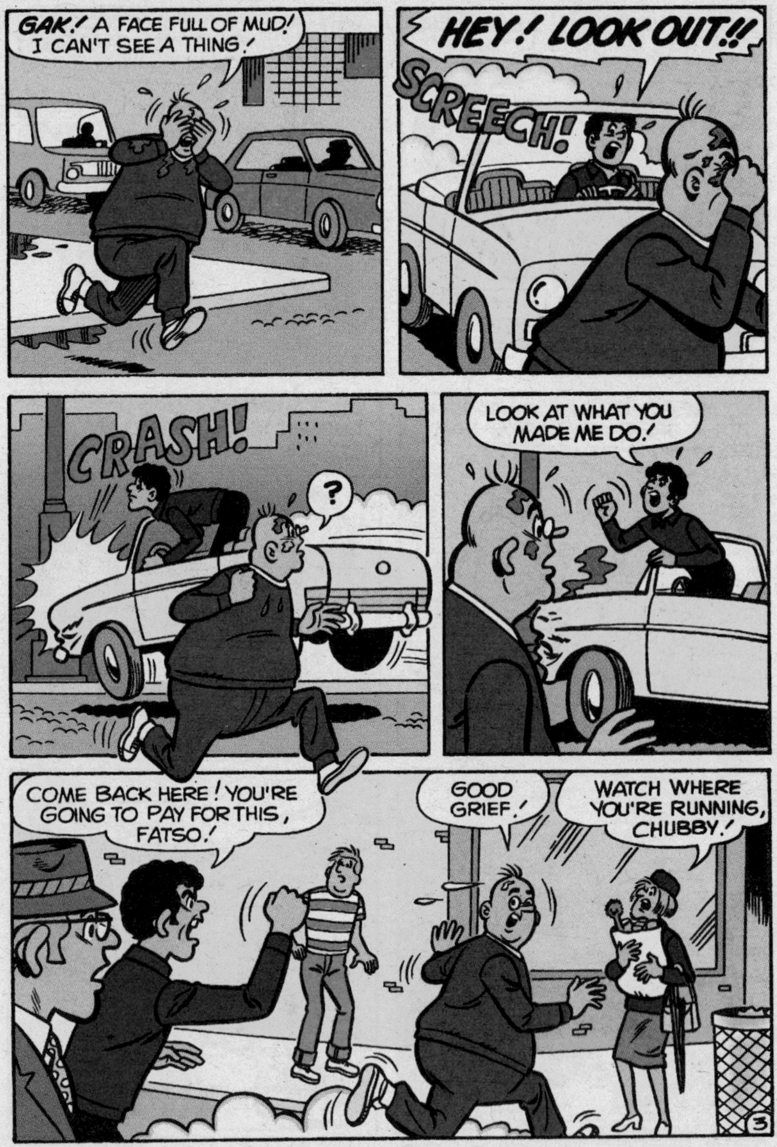
GAK! A FACE FULL OF MUD! I CAN'T SEE A THING!
HEY! LOOK OUT!!
SCREECH!
CRASH!
?
LOOK AT WHAT YOU MADE ME DO!
COME BACK HERE! YOU'RE GOING TO PAY FOR THIS, FATSO!
GOOD GRIEF!
WATCH WHERE YOU'RE RUNNING, CHUBBY!
3

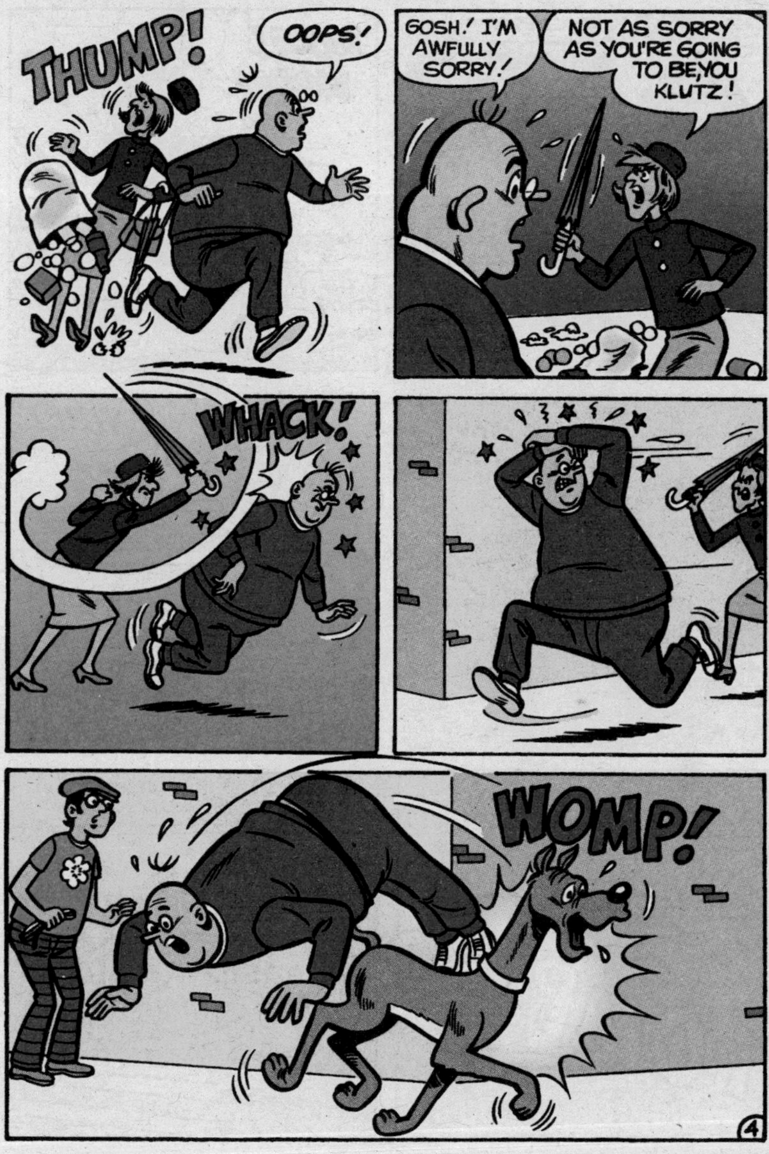
THUMP!
OOPS!
GOSH! I'M AWFULLY SORRY!
NOT AS SORRY AS YOU'RE GOING TO BE,YOU KLUTZ!
WHACK!
WOMP!
4

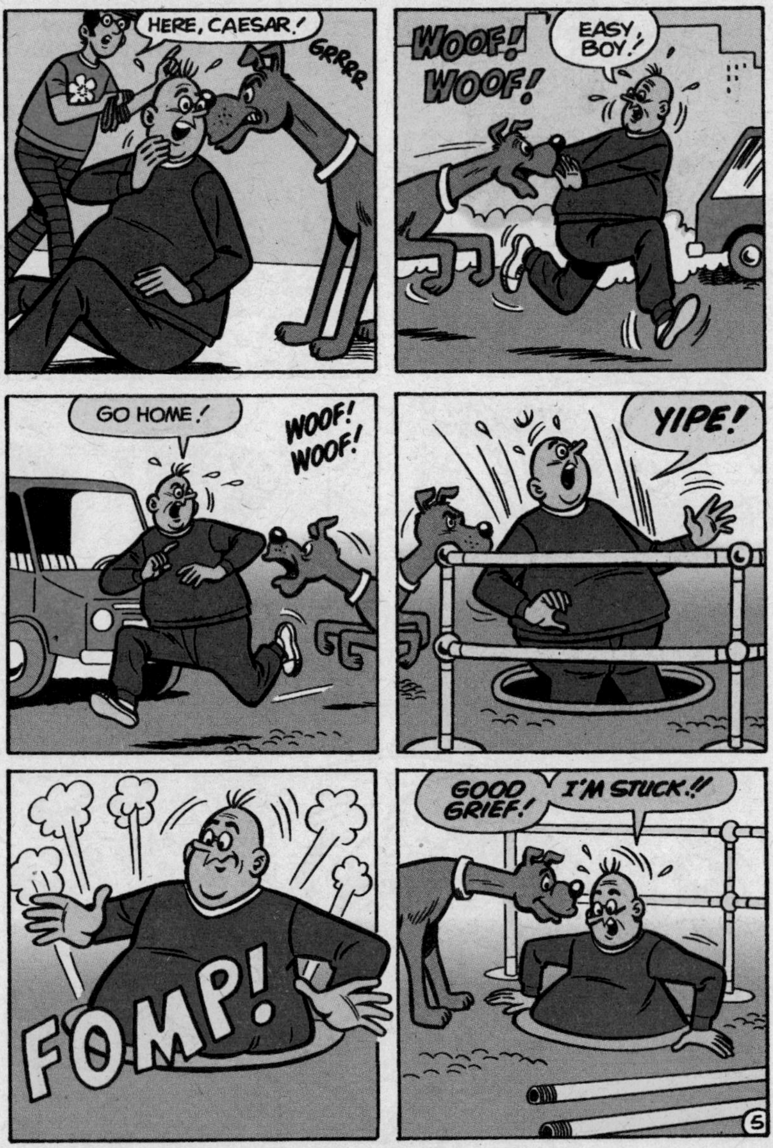
HERE, CAESAR!
GRRRR
WOOF! WOOF!
EASY, BOY!
GO HOME!
WOOF! WOOF!
YIPE!
FOMP!
GOOD GRIEF!
I'M STUCK!!
5

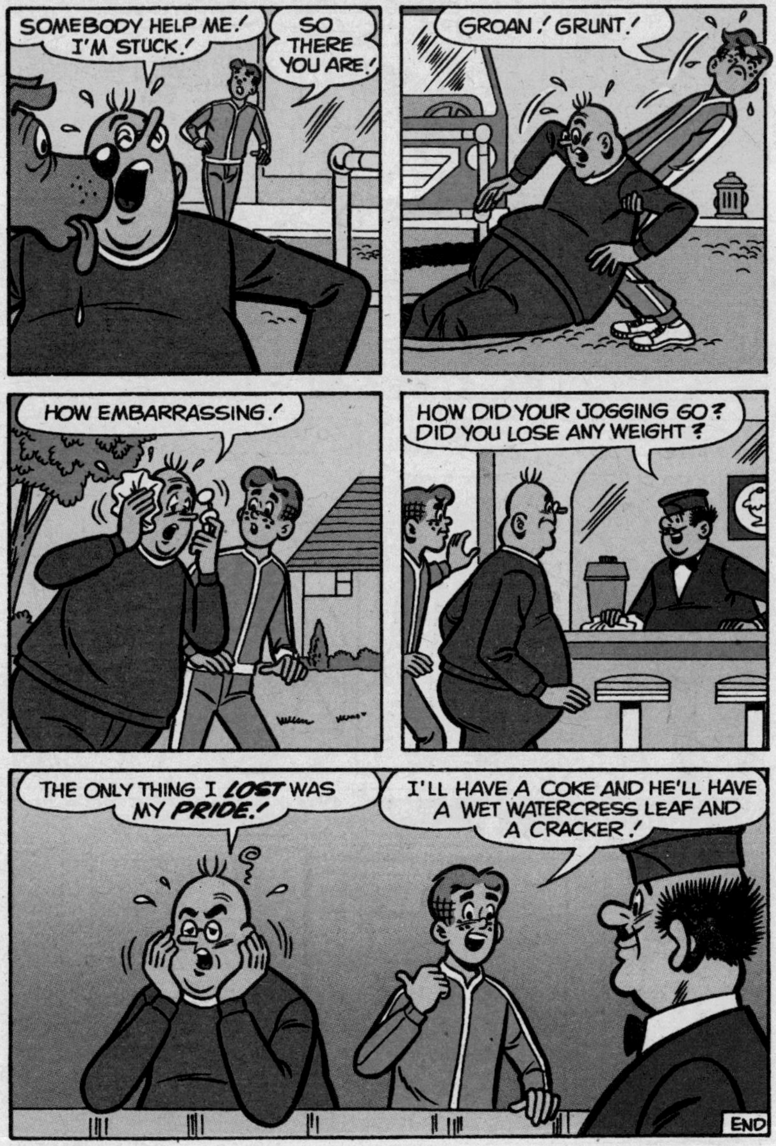
SOMEBODY HELP ME! I'M STUCK!
SO THERE YOU ARE!
GROAN! GRUNT!
HOW EMBARRASSING!
HOW DID YOUR JOGGING GO? DID YOU LOSE ANY WEIGHT?
THE ONLY THING I LOST WAS MY PRIDE!
I'LL HAVE A COKE AND HE'LL HAVE A WET WATERCRESS LEAF AND A CRACKER!
END

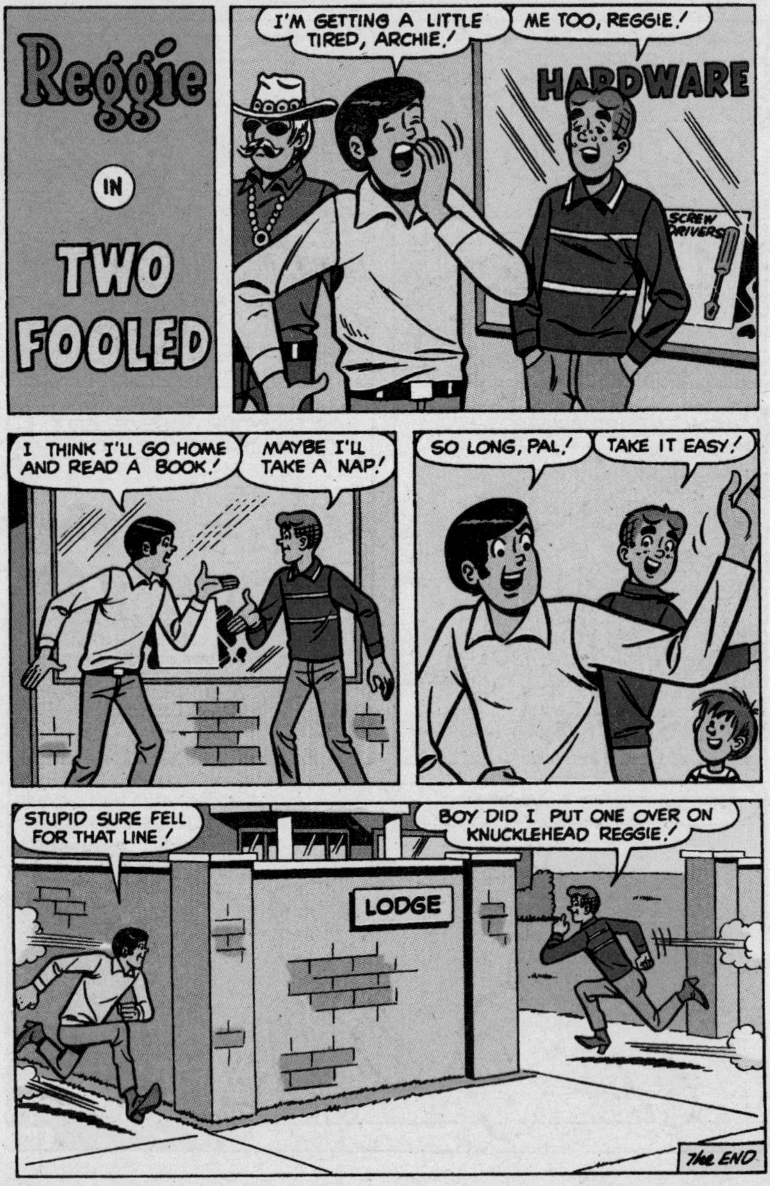
Reggie
IN
TWO FOOLED
I'M GETTING A LITTLE TIRED, ARCHIE!
ME TOO, REGGIE!
HARDWARE
SCREW DRIVERS
I THINK I'LL GO HOME AND READ A BOOK!
MAYBE I'LL TAKE A NAP!
SO LONG, PAL!
TAKE IT EASY!
STUPID SURE FELL FOR THAT LINE!
BOY DID I PUT ONE OVER ON KNUCKLEHEAD REGGIE!
LODGE
The END

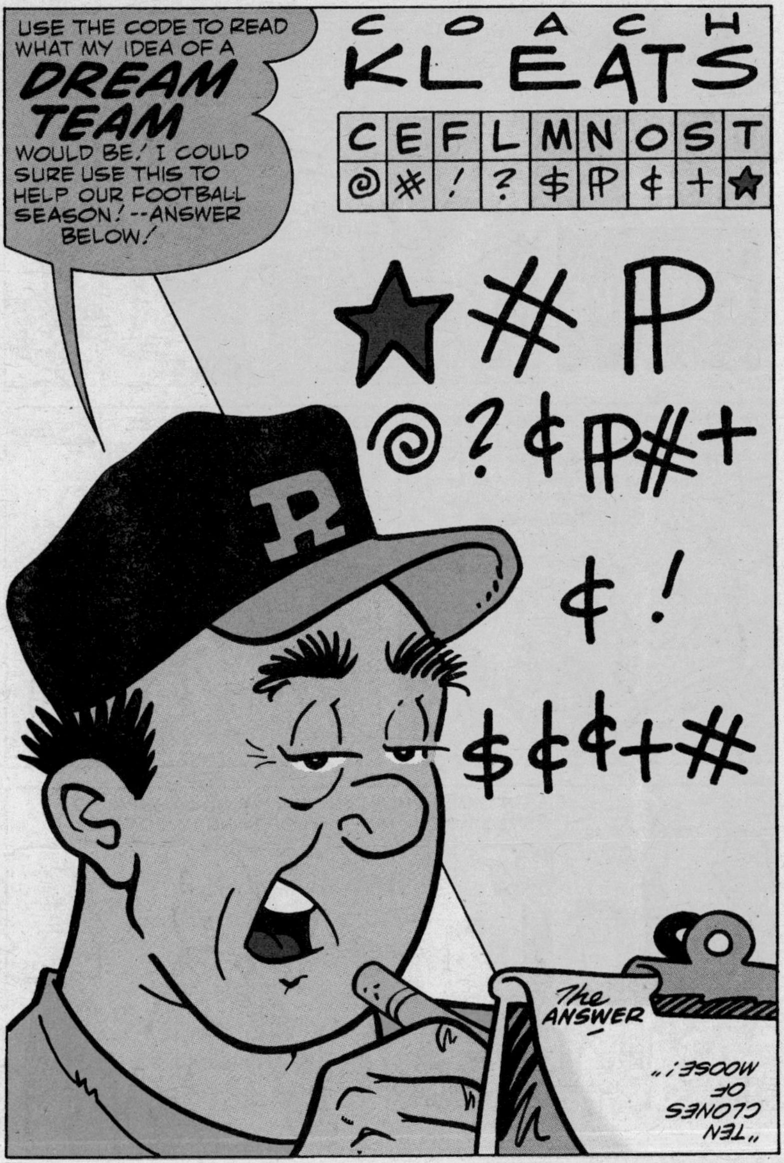
USE THE CODE TO READ WHAT MY IDEA OF A DREAM TEAM WOULD BE! I COULD SURE USE THIS TO HELP OUR FOOTBALL SEASON! --ANSWER BELOW!
COACH KLEATS
C E F L M N O S T
The ANSWER
"TEN CLONES OF MOOSE!"

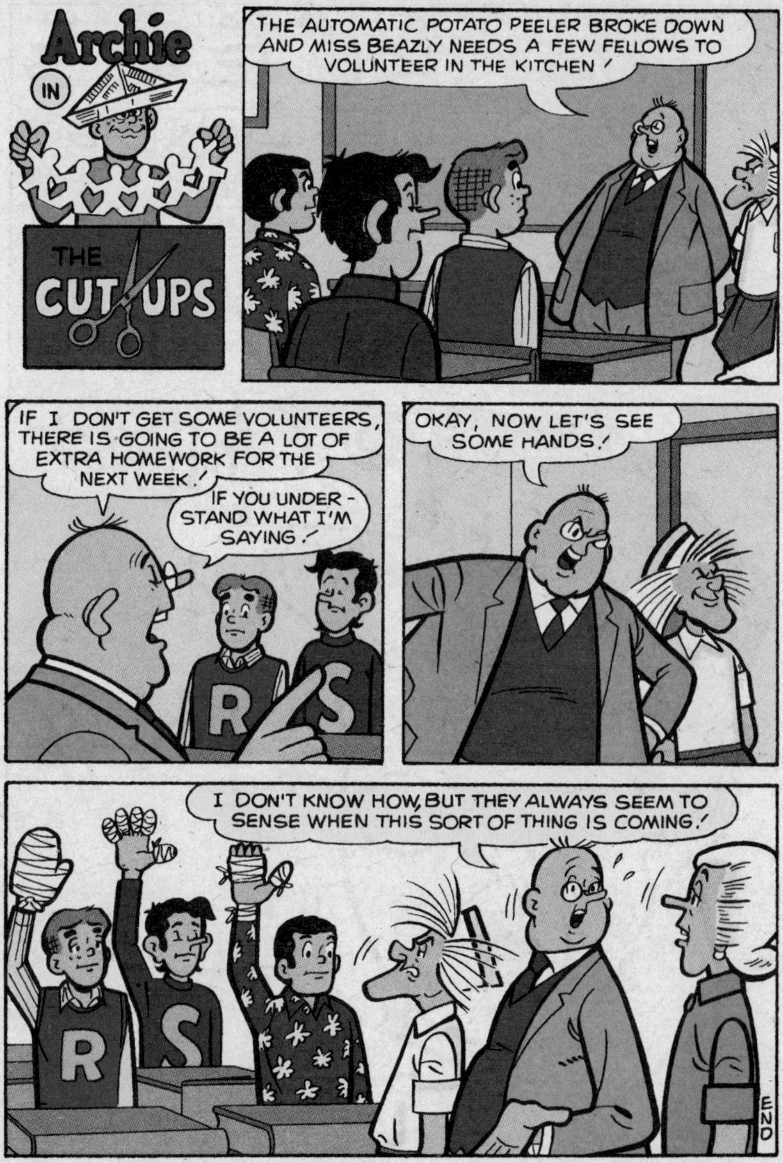
Archie
IN
THE CUT-UPS
THE AUTOMATIC POTATO PEELER BROKE DOWN AND MISS BEAZLY NEEDS A FEW FELLOWS TO VOLUNTEER IN THE KITCHEN!
IF I DON'T GET SOME VOLUNTEERS, THERE IS GOING TO BE A LOT OF EXTRA HOMEWORK FOR THE NEXT WEEK!
IF YOU UNDER-STAND WHAT I'M SAYING!
OKAY, NOW LET'S SEE SOME HANDS!
I DON'T KNOW HOW, BUT THEY ALWAYS SEEM TO SENSE WHEN THIS SORT OF THING IS COMING!
END

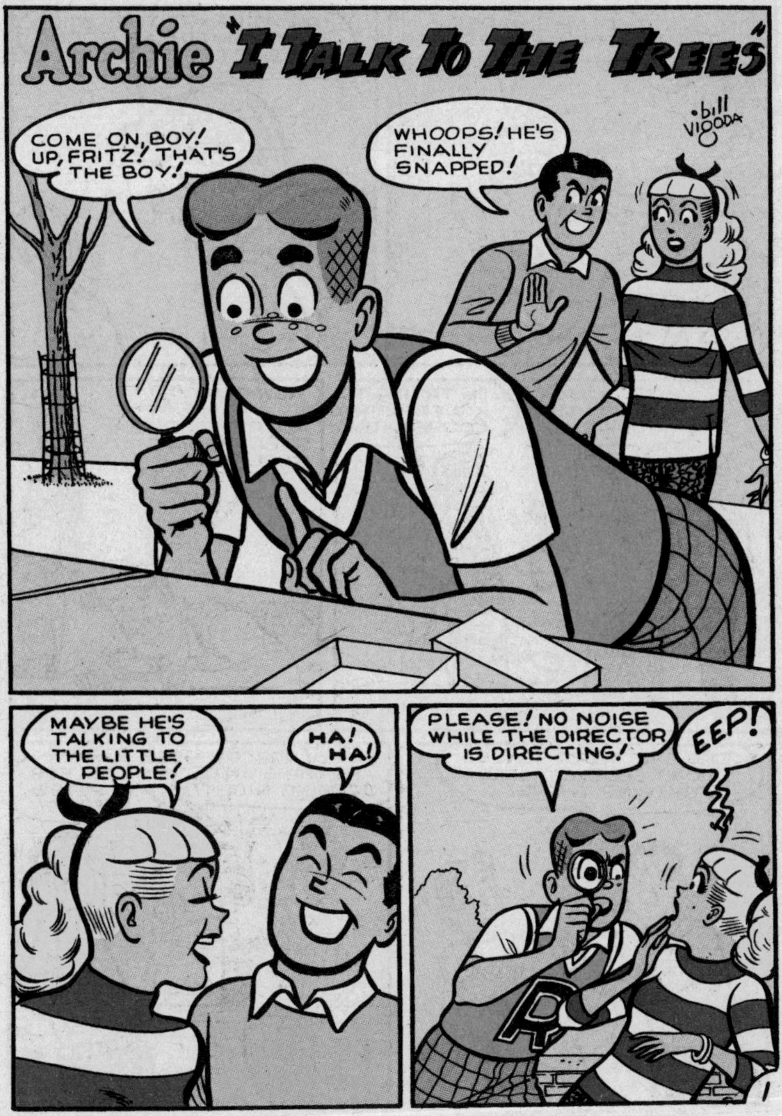
Archie "I Talk To The Trees"
bill vigoda
COME ON, BOY! UP, FRITZ! THAT'S THE BOY!
WHOOPS! HE'S FINALLY SNAPPED!
MAYBE HE'S TALKING TO THE LITTLE PEOPLE!
HA! HA!
PLEASE! NO NOISE WHILE THE DIRECTOR IS DIRECTING!
EEP!

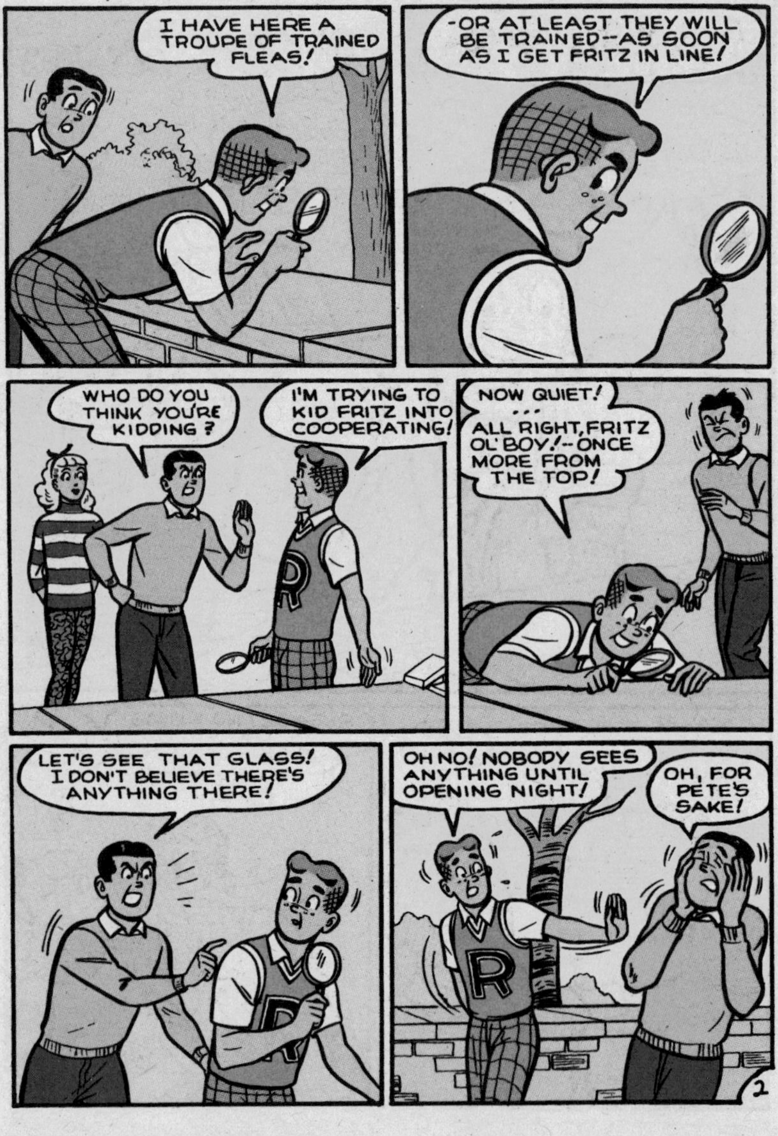
I HAVE HERE A TROUPE OF TRAINED FLEAS!
-OR AT LEAST THEY WILL BE TRAINED--AS SOON AS I GET FRITZ IN LINE!
WHO DO YOU THINK YOU'RE KIDDING?
I'M TRYING TO KID FRITZ INTO COOPERATING!
NOW QUIET! ... ALL RIGHT, FRITZ OL' BOY!--ONCE MORE FROM THE TOP!
LET'S SEE THAT GLASS! I DON'T BELIEVE THERE'S ANYTHING THERE!
OH NO! NOBODY SEES ANYTHING UNTIL OPENING NIGHT!
OH, FOR PETE'S SAKE!
2

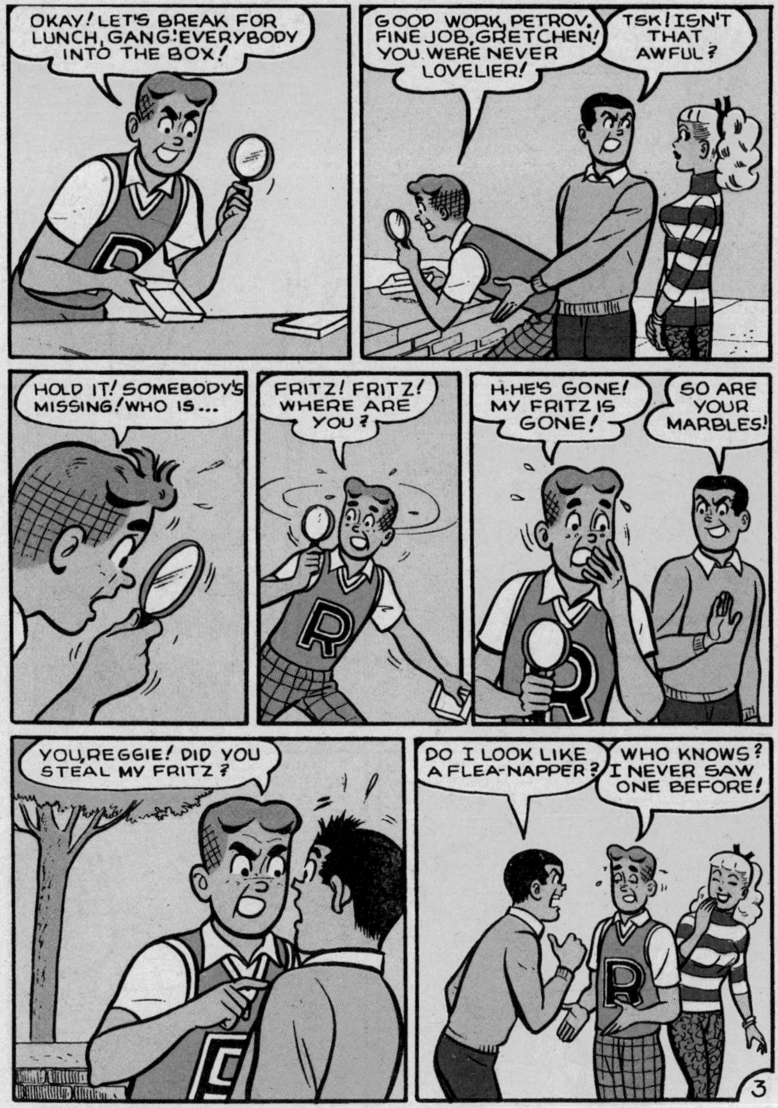
OKAY! LET'S BREAK FOR LUNCH, GANG! EVERYBODY INTO THE BOX!
GOOD WORK, PETROV. FINE JOB, GRETCHEN! YOU WERE NEVER LOVELIER!
TSK! ISN'T THAT AWFUL?
HOLD IT! SOMEBODY'S MISSING! WHO IS...
FRITZ! FRITZ! WHERE ARE YOU?
H-HE'S GONE! MY FRITZ IS GONE!
SO ARE YOUR MARBLES!
YOU, REGGIE! DID YOU STEAL MY FRITZ?
DO I LOOK LIKE A FLEA-NAPPER?
WHO KNOWS? I NEVER SAW ONE BEFORE!

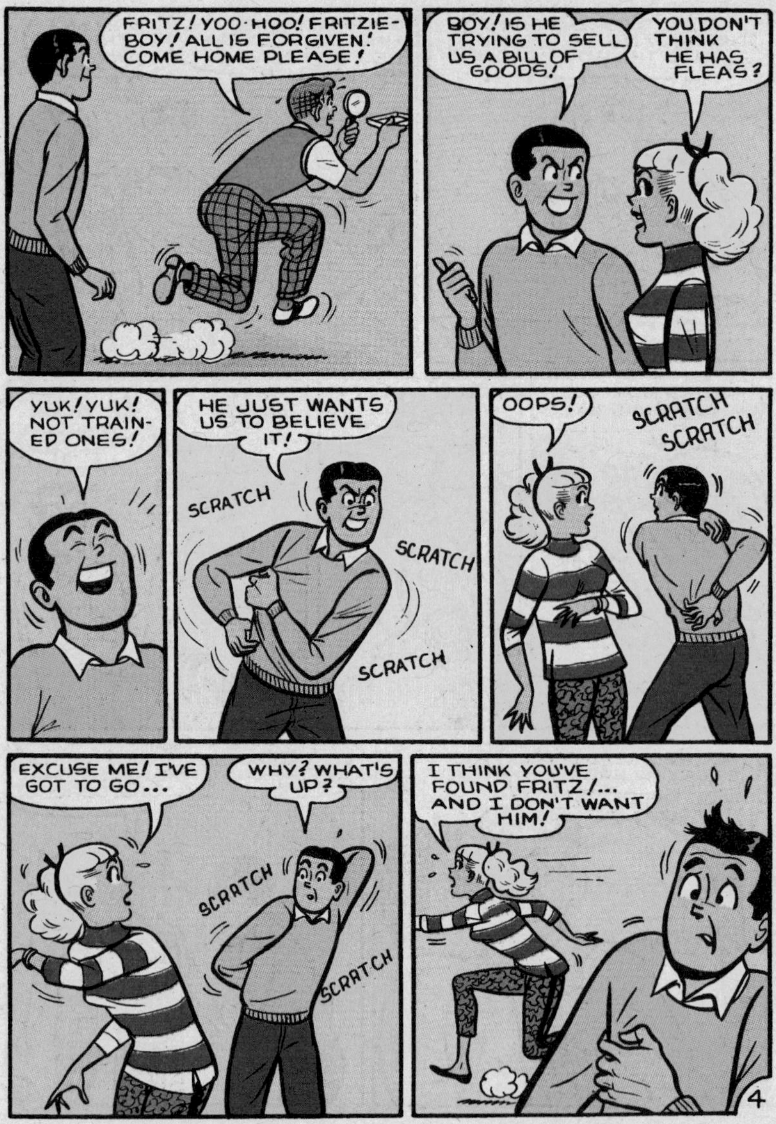
FRITZ! YOO-HOO! FRITZIE-BOY! ALL IS FORGIVEN! COME HOME PLEASE!
BOY! IS HE TRYING TO SELL US A BILL OF GOODS!
YOU DON'T THINK HE HAS FLEAS?
YUK! YUK! NOT TRAIN-ED ONES!
HE JUST WANTS US TO BELIEVE IT!
SCRATCH
SCRATCH
SCRATCH
OOPS!
SCRATCH
SCRATCH
EXCUSE ME! I'VE GOT TO GO...
WHY? WHAT'S UP?
SCRATCH
SCRATCH
I THINK YOU'VE FOUND FRITZ!... AND I DON'T WANT HIM!
4

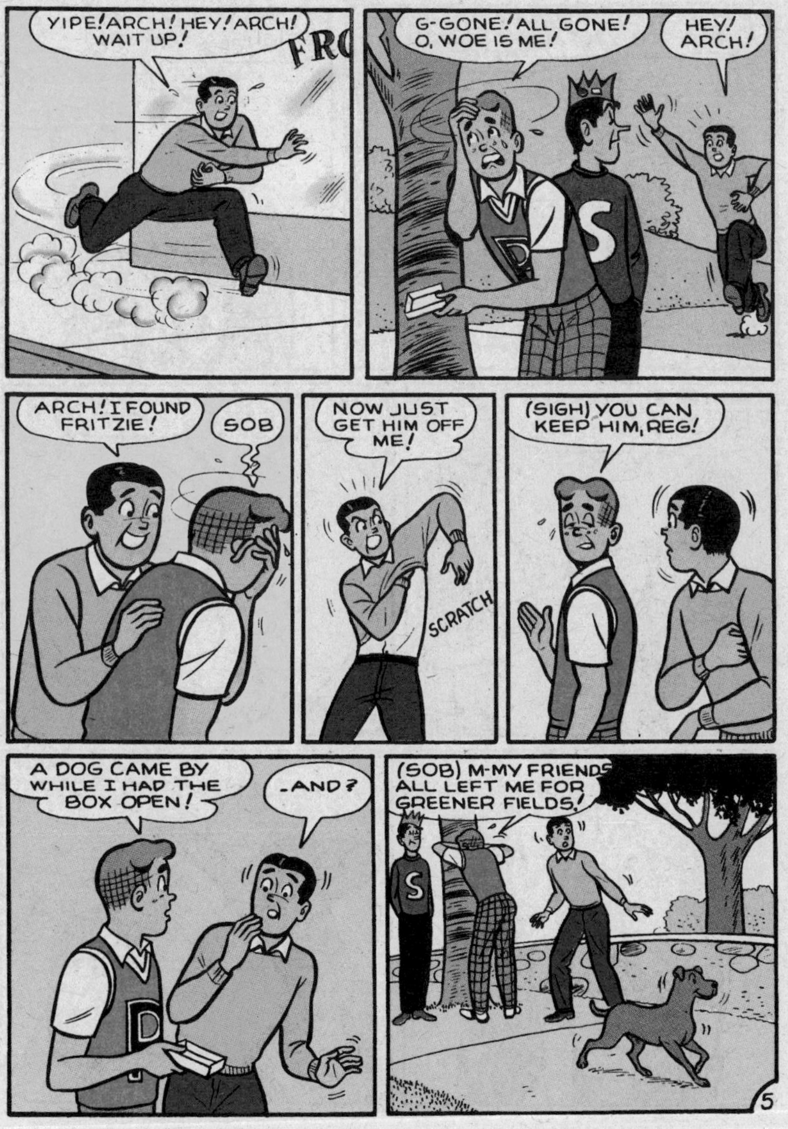
YIPE! ARCH! HEY! ARCH! WAIT UP!
FRO
G-GONE! ALL GONE! O, WOE IS ME!
HEY! ARCH!
ARCH! I FOUND FRITZIE!
SOB
NOW JUST GET HIM OFF ME!
SCRATCH
(SIGH) YOU CAN KEEP HIM, REG!
A DOG CAME BY WHILE I HAD THE BOX OPEN!
-AND?
(SOB) M-MY FRIENDS ALL LEFT ME FOR GREENER FIELDS!

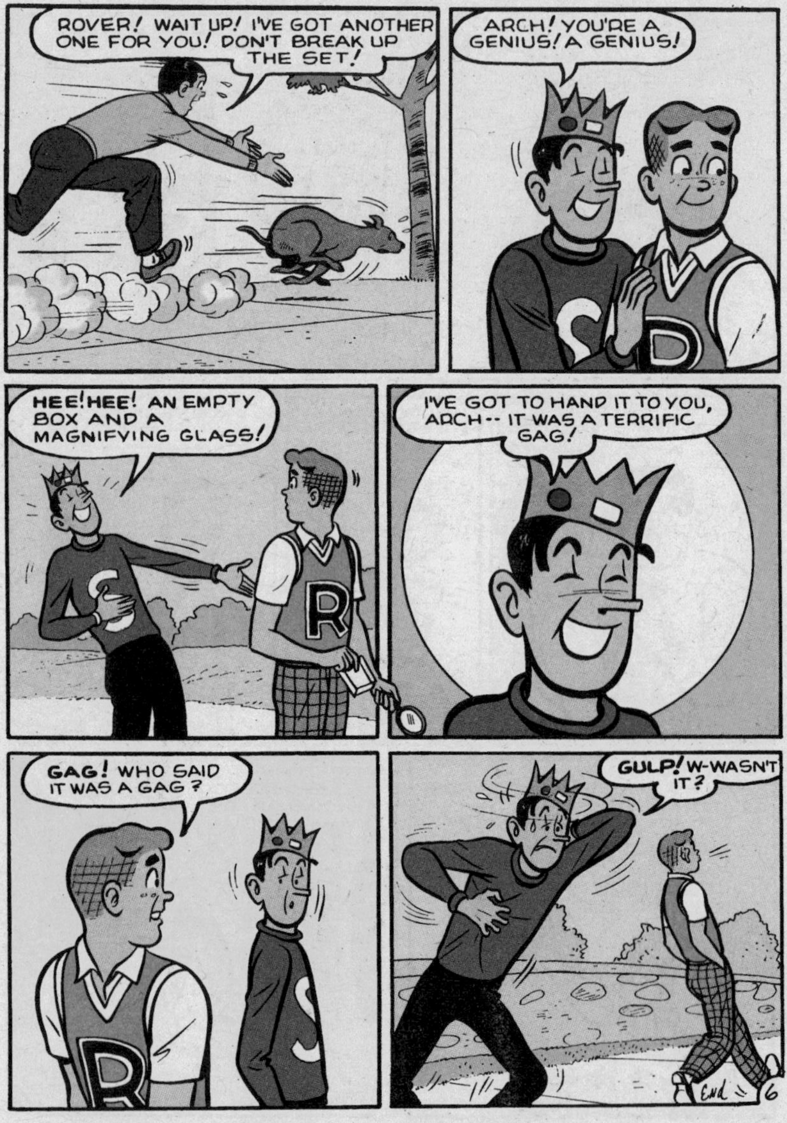
ROVER! WAIT UP! I'VE GOT ANOTHER ONE FOR YOU! DON'T BREAK UP THE SET!
ARCH! YOU'RE A GENIUS! A GENIUS!
HEE! HEE! AN EMPTY BOX AND A MAGNIFYING GLASS!
I'VE GOT TO HAND IT TO YOU, ARCH -- IT WAS A TERRIFIC GAG!
GAG! WHO SAID IT WAS A GAG?
GULP! W-WASN'T IT?
End
6

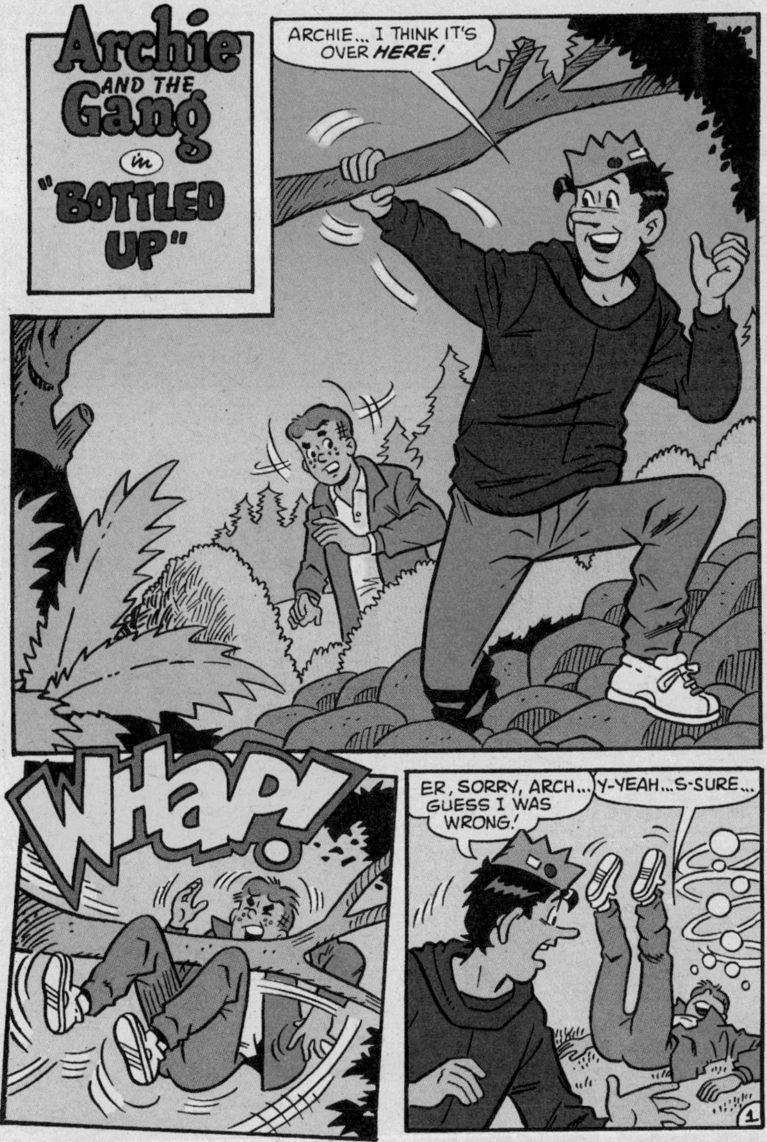
Archie AND THE Gang in "BOTTLED UP"
ARCHIE... I THINK IT'S OVER HERE!
WHAP!
ER, SORRY, ARCH... GUESS I WAS WRONG!
Y-YEAH...S-SURE...
1

Script: George Gladir / Pencils: Stan Goldberg / Inks: Rudy Lapick / Letters: Bill Yoshida / Colors: Barry Grossman

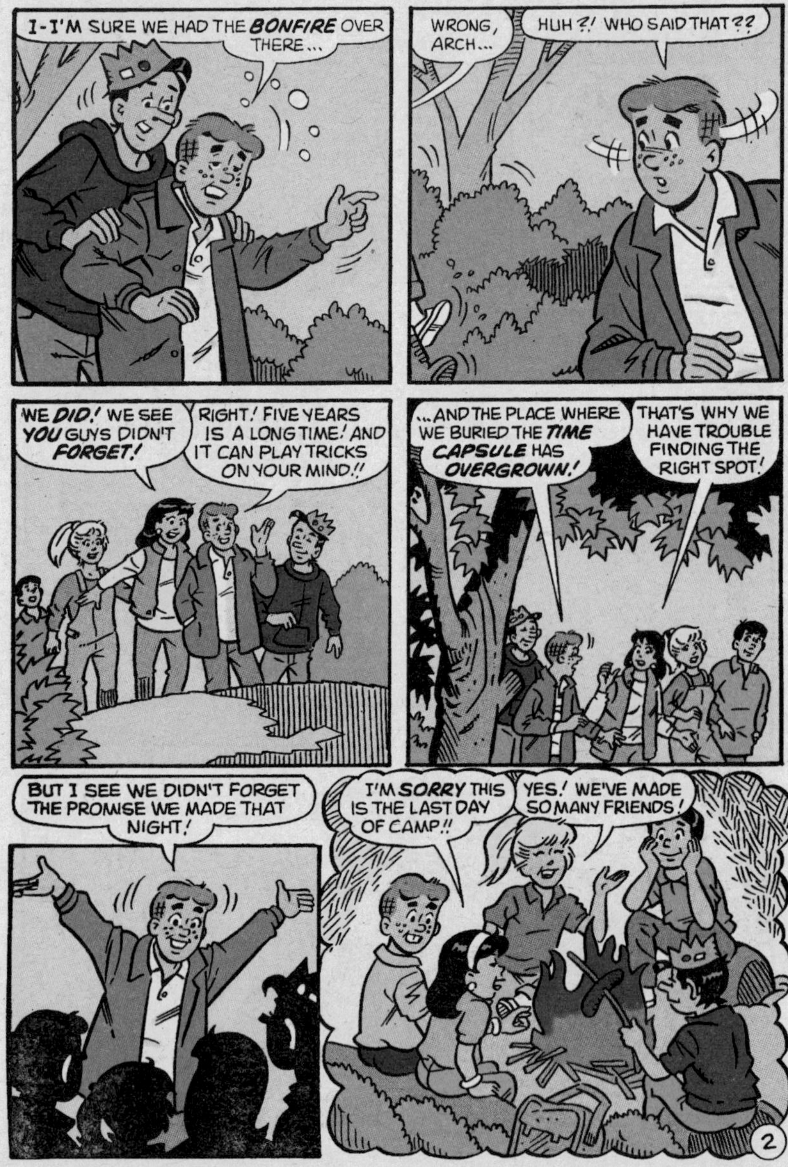
I-I'M SURE WE HAD THE BONFIRE OVER THERE...
WRONG, ARCH...
HUH ?! WHO SAID THAT ??
WE DID! WE SEE YOU GUYS DIDN'T FORGET!
RIGHT! FIVE YEARS IS A LONG TIME! AND IT CAN PLAY TRICKS ON YOUR MIND!!
...AND THE PLACE WHERE WE BURIED THE TIME CAPSULE HAS OVERGROWN!
THAT'S WHY WE HAVE TROUBLE FINDING THE RIGHT SPOT!
BUT I SEE WE DIDN'T FORGET THE PROMISE WE MADE THAT NIGHT!
I'M SORRY THIS IS THE LAST DAY OF CAMP!!
YES! WE'VE MADE SO MANY FRIENDS!
2

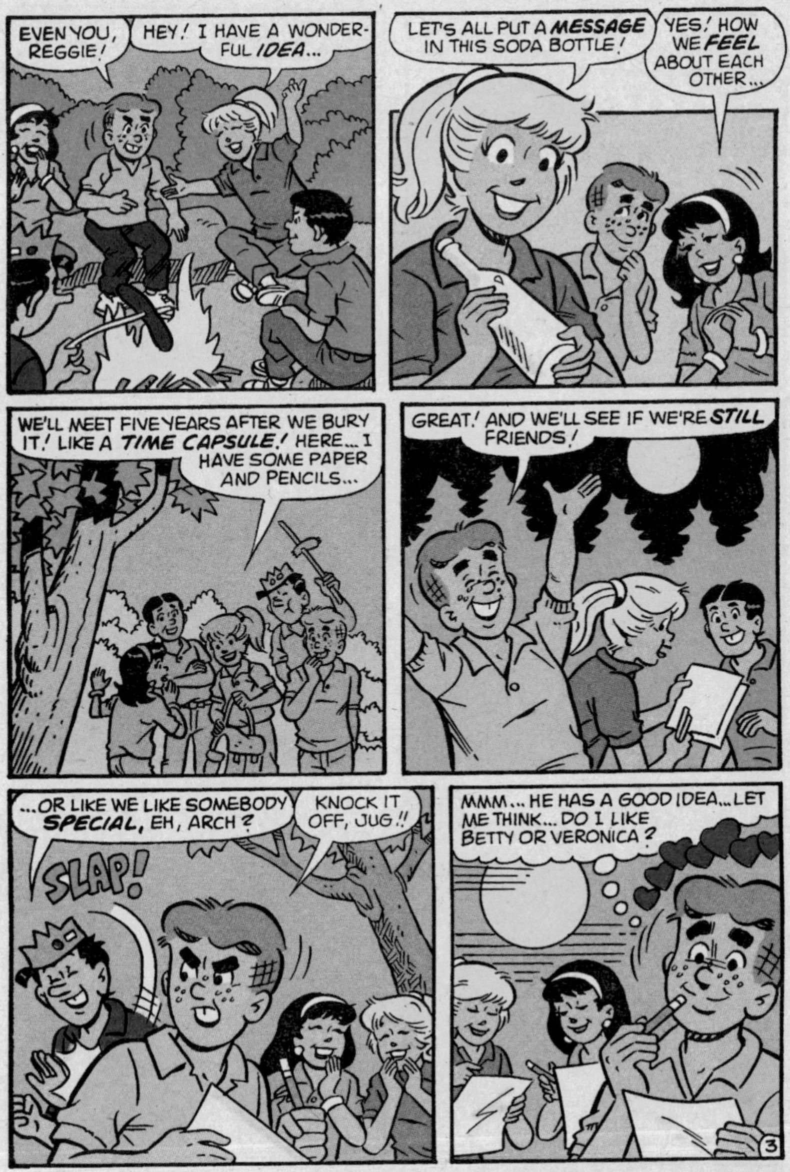
EVEN YOU, REGGIE!
HEY! I HAVE A WONDER-FUL *IDEA*...
LET'S ALL PUT A ***MESSAGE*** IN THIS SODA BOTTLE!
YES! HOW WE ***FEEL*** ABOUT EACH OTHER...
WE'LL MEET FIVE YEARS AFTER WE BURY IT! LIKE A ***TIME CAPSULE!*** HERE... I HAVE SOME PAPER AND PENCILS...
GREAT! AND WE'LL SEE IF WE'RE ***STILL*** FRIENDS!
...OR LIKE WE LIKE SOMEBODY ***SPECIAL***, EH, ARCH?
KNOCK IT OFF, JUG!!
SLAP!
MMM... HE HAS A GOOD IDEA... LET ME THINK... DO I LIKE BETTY OR VERONICA?
3

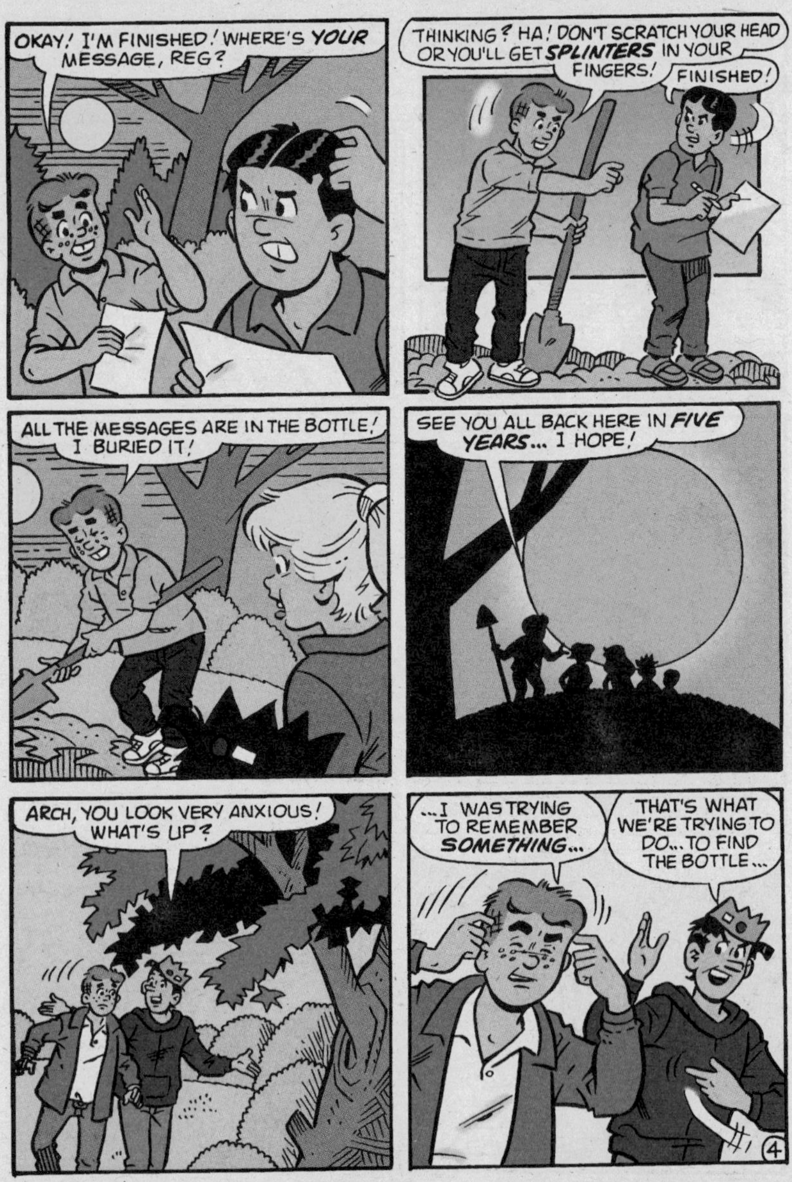
OKAY! I'M FINISHED! WHERE'S *YOUR* MESSAGE, REG?
THINKING? HA! DON'T SCRATCH YOUR HEAD OR YOU'LL GET *SPLINTERS* IN YOUR FINGERS!
FINISHED!
ALL THE MESSAGES ARE IN THE BOTTLE! I BURIED IT!
SEE YOU ALL BACK HERE IN *FIVE YEARS*... I HOPE!
ARCH, YOU LOOK VERY ANXIOUS! WHAT'S UP?
...I WAS TRYING TO REMEMBER *SOMETHING*...
THAT'S WHAT WE'RE TRYING TO DO... TO FIND THE BOTTLE...
4

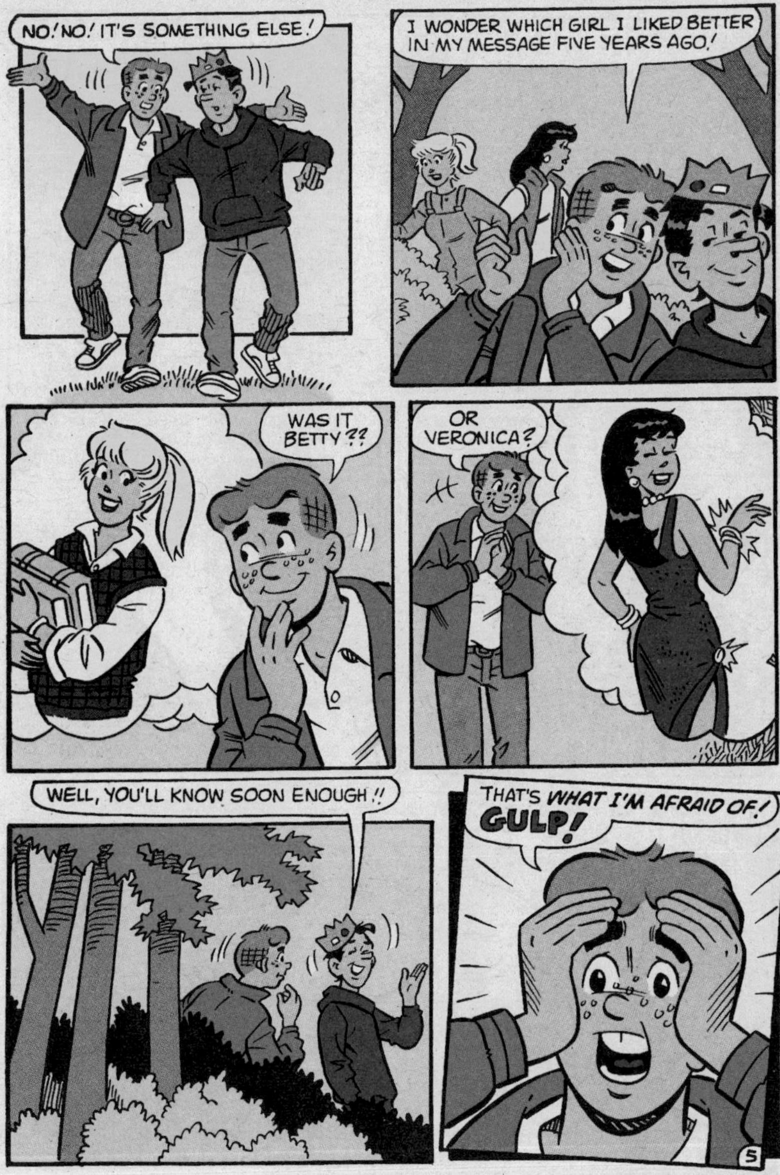
NO! NO! IT'S SOMETHING ELSE!
I WONDER WHICH GIRL I LIKED BETTER IN MY MESSAGE FIVE YEARS AGO!
WAS IT BETTY??
OR VERONICA?
WELL, YOU'LL KNOW SOON ENOUGH!!
THAT'S WHAT I'M AFRAID OF! GULP!
5

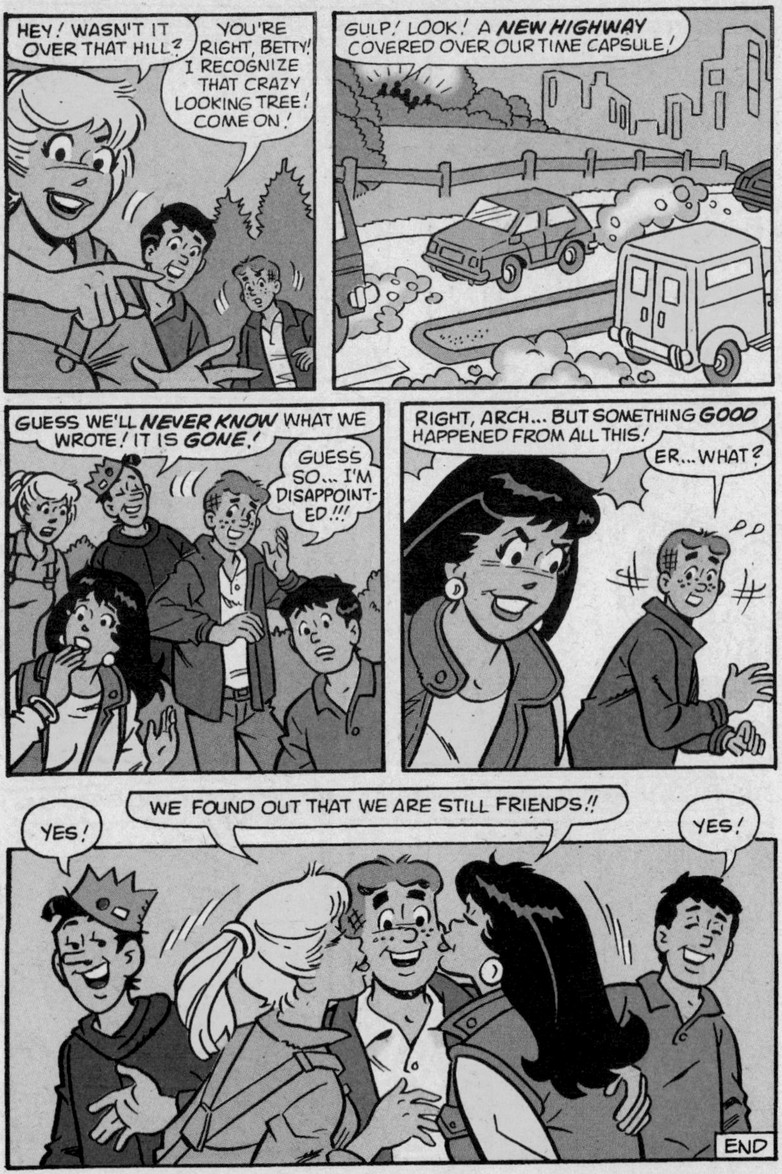
HEY! WASN'T IT OVER THAT HILL?
YOU'RE RIGHT, BETTY! I RECOGNIZE THAT CRAZY LOOKING TREE! COME ON!
GULP! LOOK! A NEW HIGHWAY COVERED OVER OUR TIME CAPSULE!
GUESS WE'LL NEVER KNOW WHAT WE WROTE! IT IS GONE!
GUESS SO... I'M DISAPPOINT-ED!!!
RIGHT, ARCH... BUT SOMETHING GOOD HAPPENED FROM ALL THIS!
ER...WHAT?
YES!
WE FOUND OUT THAT WE ARE STILL FRIENDS!!
YES!
END

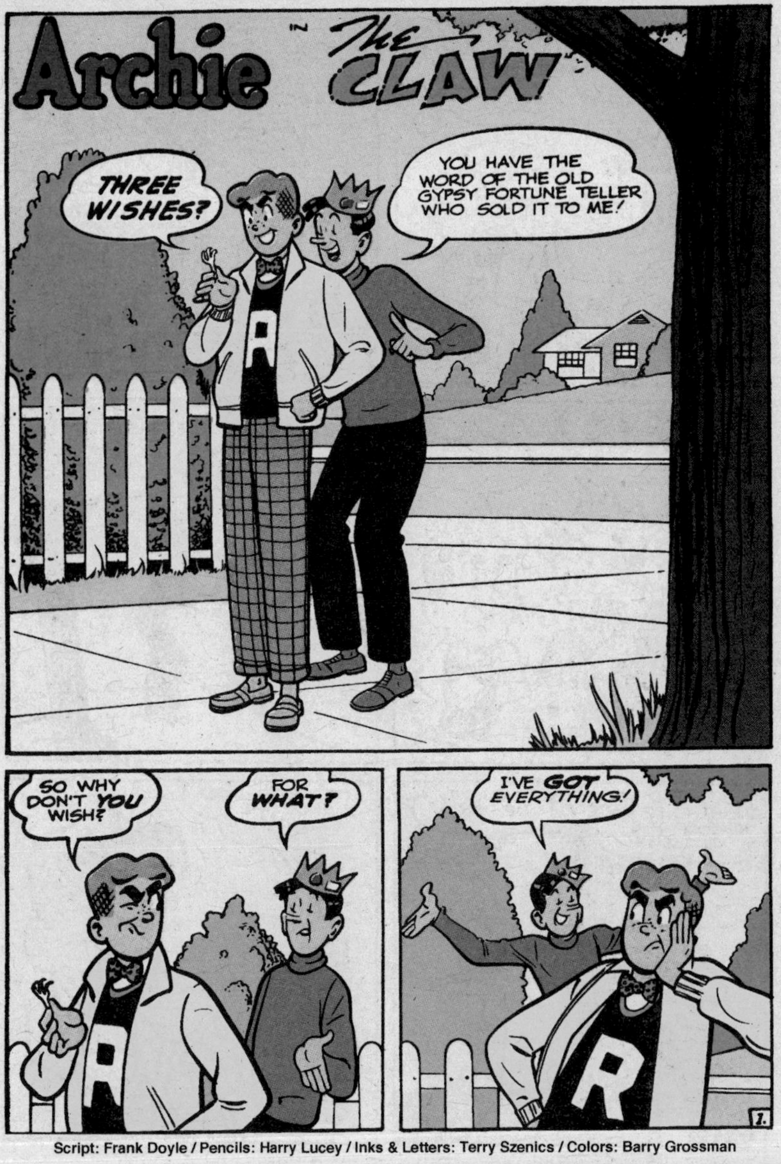
Archie
IN
The CLAW
THREE WISHES?
YOU HAVE THE WORD OF THE OLD GYPSY FORTUNE TELLER WHO SOLD IT TO ME!
SO WHY DON'T YOU WISH?
FOR WHAT?
I'VE GOT EVERYTHING!
1.

Script: Frank Doyle / Pencils: Harry Lucey / Inks & Letters: Terry Szenics / Colors: Barry Grossman

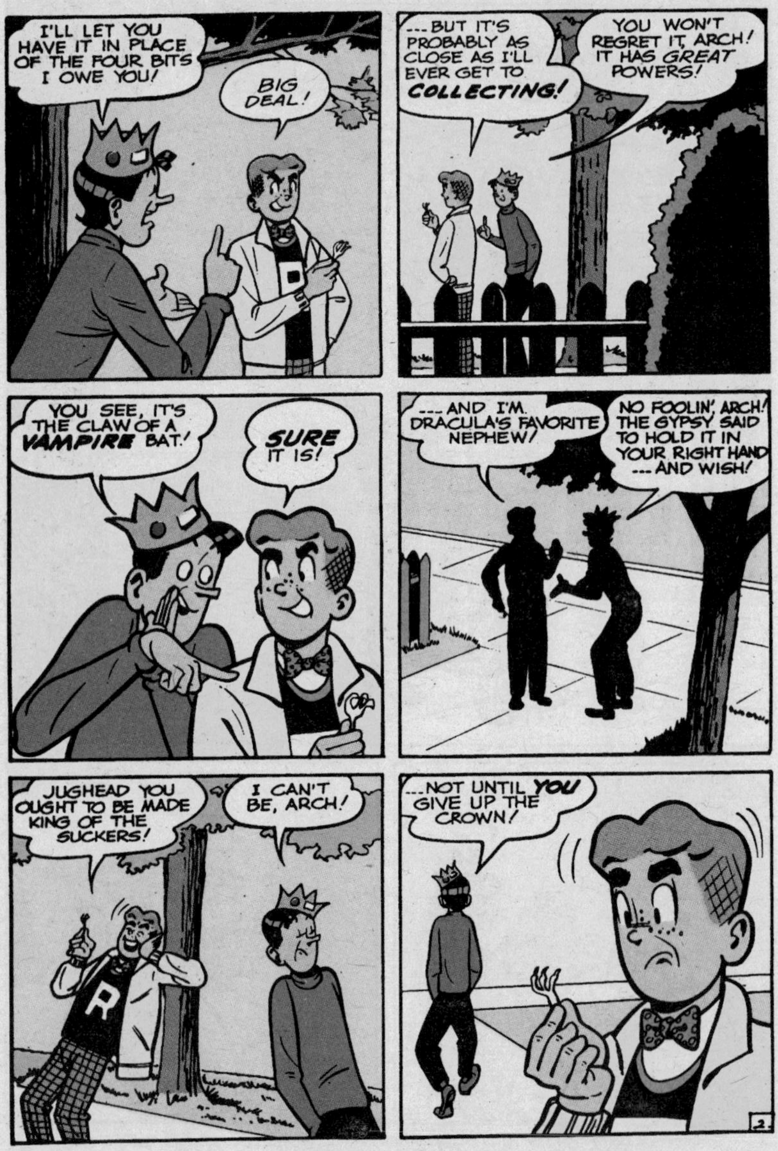
I'LL LET YOU HAVE IT IN PLACE OF THE FOUR BITS I OWE YOU!
BIG DEAL!
---BUT IT'S PROBABLY AS CLOSE AS I'LL EVER GET TO COLLECTING!
YOU WON'T REGRET IT, ARCH! IT HAS GREAT POWERS!
YOU SEE, IT'S THE CLAW OF A VAMPIRE BAT!
SURE IT IS!
---AND I'M DRACULA'S FAVORITE NEPHEW!
NO FOOLIN', ARCH! THE GYPSY SAID TO HOLD IT IN YOUR RIGHT HAND ---AND WISH!
JUGHEAD YOU OUGHT TO BE MADE KING OF THE SUCKERS!
I CAN'T BE, ARCH!
...NOT UNTIL YOU GIVE UP THE CROWN!
2

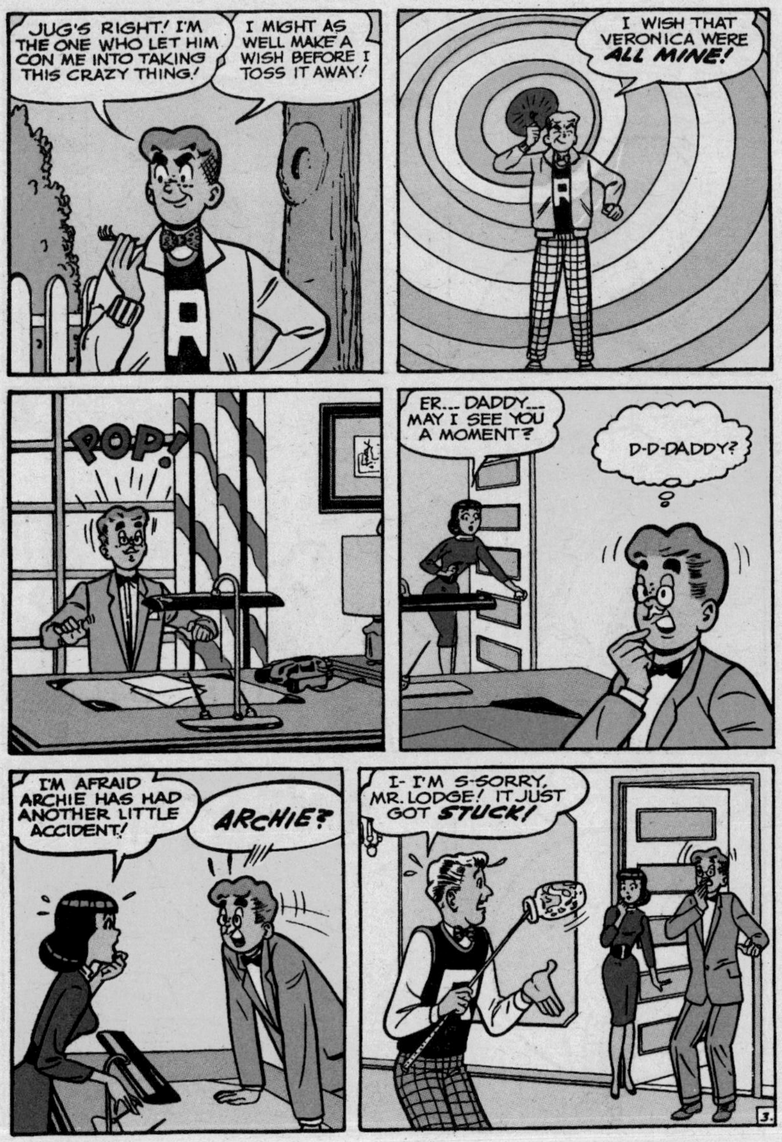
JUG'S RIGHT! I'M THE ONE WHO LET HIM CON ME INTO TAKING THIS CRAZY THING!
I MIGHT AS WELL MAKE A WISH BEFORE I TOSS IT AWAY!
I WISH THAT VERONICA WERE ALL MINE!
POP!
ER... DADDY... MAY I SEE YOU A MOMENT?
D-D-DADDY?
I'M AFRAID ARCHIE HAS HAD ANOTHER LITTLE ACCIDENT!
ARCHIE?
I- I'M S-SORRY, MR. LODGE! IT JUST GOT STUCK!
3.

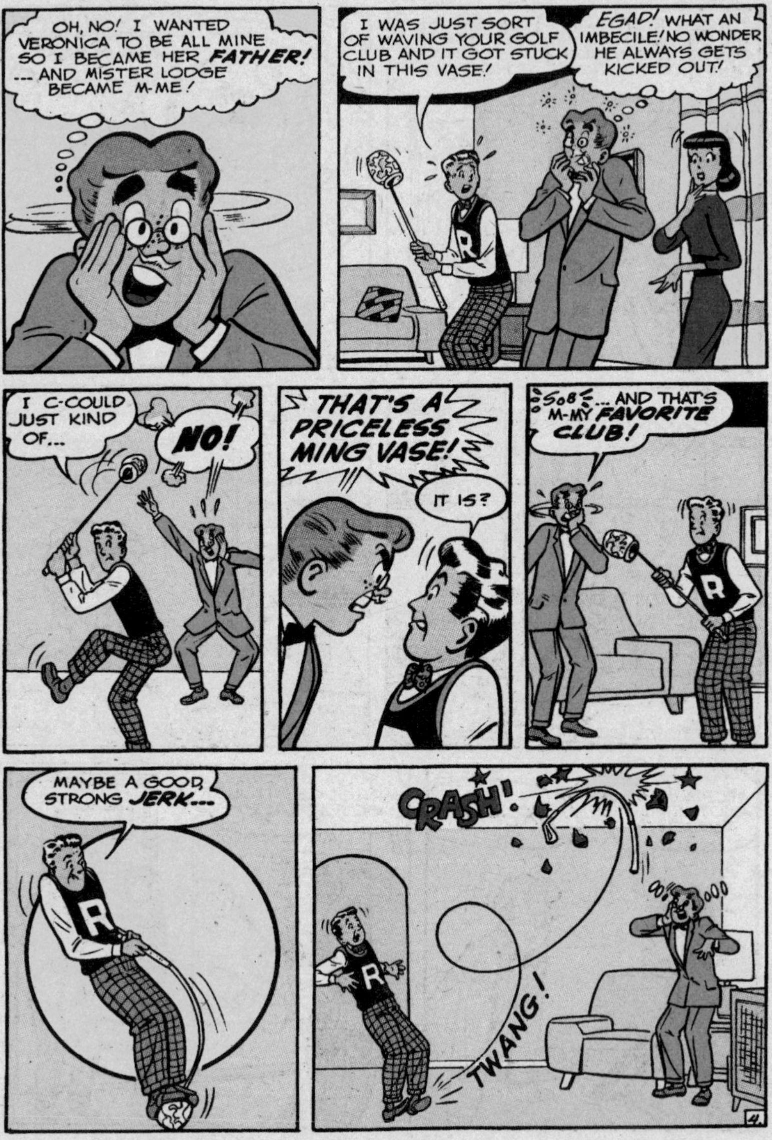
OH, NO! I WANTED VERONICA TO BE ALL MINE SO I BECAME HER FATHER! ... AND MISTER LODGE BECAME M-ME!
I WAS JUST SORT OF WAVING YOUR GOLF CLUB AND IT GOT STUCK IN THIS VASE!
EGAD! WHAT AN IMBECILE! NO WONDER HE ALWAYS GETS KICKED OUT!
I C-COULD JUST KIND OF...
NO!
THAT'S A PRICELESS MING VASE!
IT IS?
SOB ... AND THAT'S M-MY FAVORITE CLUB!
MAYBE A GOOD, STRONG JERK...
CRASH!
TWANG!
4

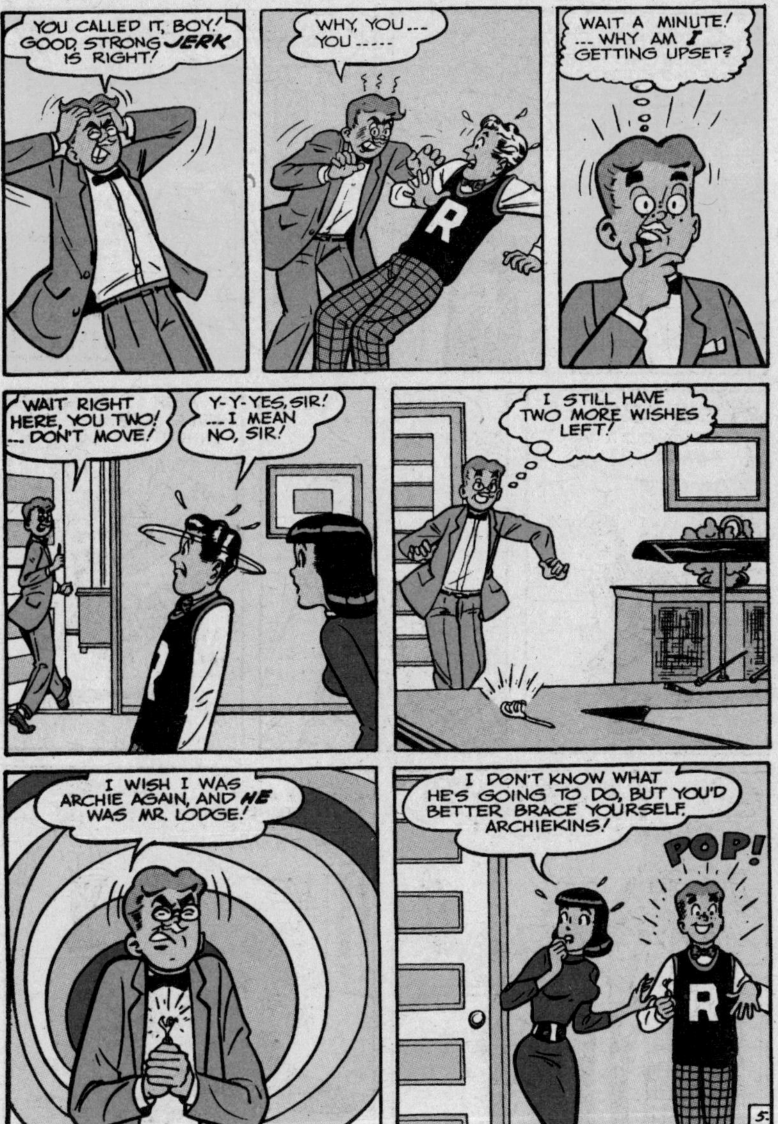
YOU CALLED IT, BOY! GOOD, STRONG JERK IS RIGHT!
WHY, YOU... YOU.....
WAIT A MINUTE! ...WHY AM I GETTING UPSET?
WAIT RIGHT HERE, YOU TWO! ...DON'T MOVE!
Y-Y-YES, SIR! ...I MEAN NO, SIR!
I STILL HAVE TWO MORE WISHES LEFT!
I WISH I WAS ARCHIE AGAIN, AND HE WAS MR. LODGE!
I DON'T KNOW WHAT HE'S GOING TO DO, BUT YOU'D BETTER BRACE YOURSELF, ARCHIEKINS!
POP!
5

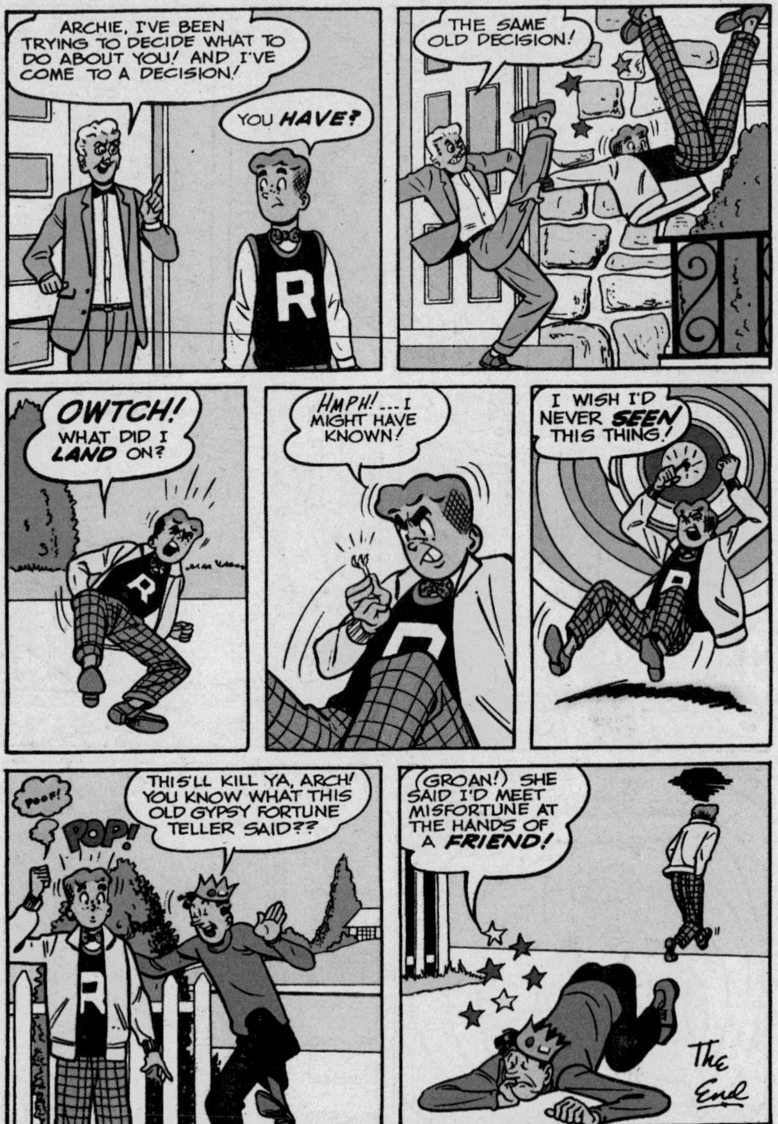

ARCHIE, I'VE BEEN TRYING TO DECIDE WHAT TO DO ABOUT YOU! AND I'VE COME TO A DECISION!
YOU HAVE?
THE SAME OLD DECISION!
OWTCH! WHAT DID I LAND ON?
HMPH! ... I MIGHT HAVE KNOWN!
I WISH I'D NEVER SEEN THIS THING!
POOF!
POP!
THIS'LL KILL YA, ARCH! YOU KNOW WHAT THIS OLD GYPSY FORTUNE TELLER SAID??
(GROAN!) SHE SAID I'D MEET MISFORTUNE AT THE HANDS OF A FRIEND!
The End

Archie in "WHEN THE RED, RED ROBIN COMES JOG, JOG, JOGGIN' ALONG"

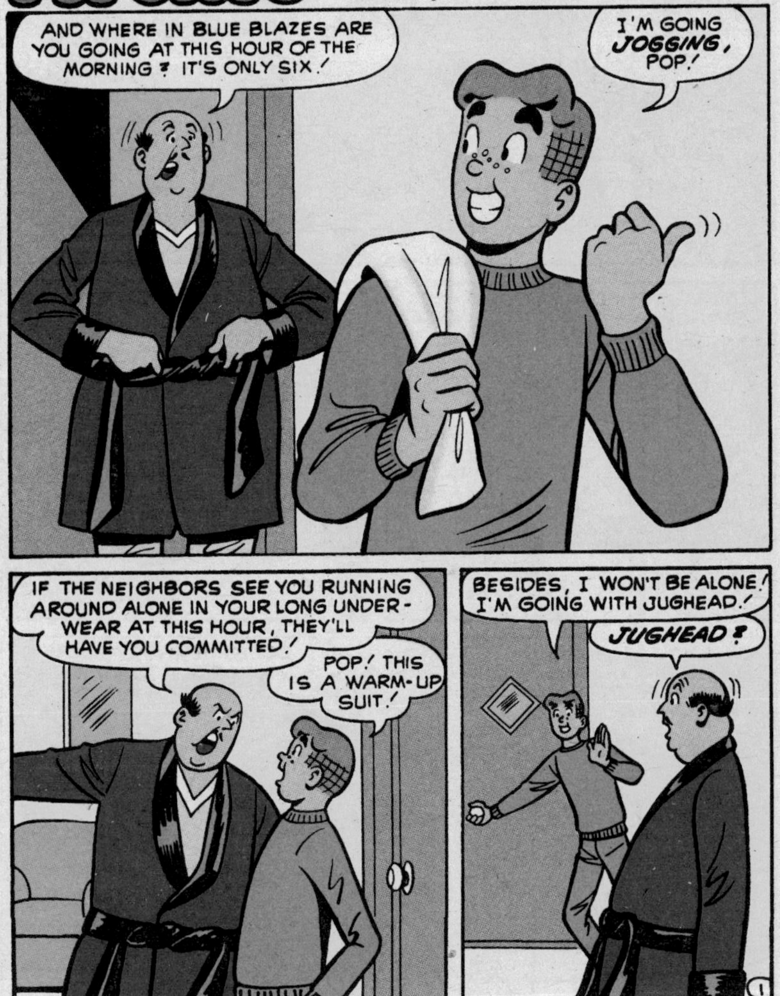
AND WHERE IN BLUE BLAZES ARE YOU GOING AT THIS HOUR OF THE MORNING? IT'S ONLY SIX!
I'M GOING *JOGGING*, POP!
IF THE NEIGHBORS SEE YOU RUNNING AROUND ALONE IN YOUR LONG UNDER-WEAR AT THIS HOUR, THEY'LL HAVE YOU COMMITTED!
POP! THIS IS A WARM-UP SUIT!
BESIDES, I WON'T BE ALONE! I'M GOING WITH JUGHEAD!
JUGHEAD?
1

Script: Frank Doyle / Pencils: Harry Lucey / Inks: Chic Stones / Letters: Bill Yoshida / Colors: Barry Grossman

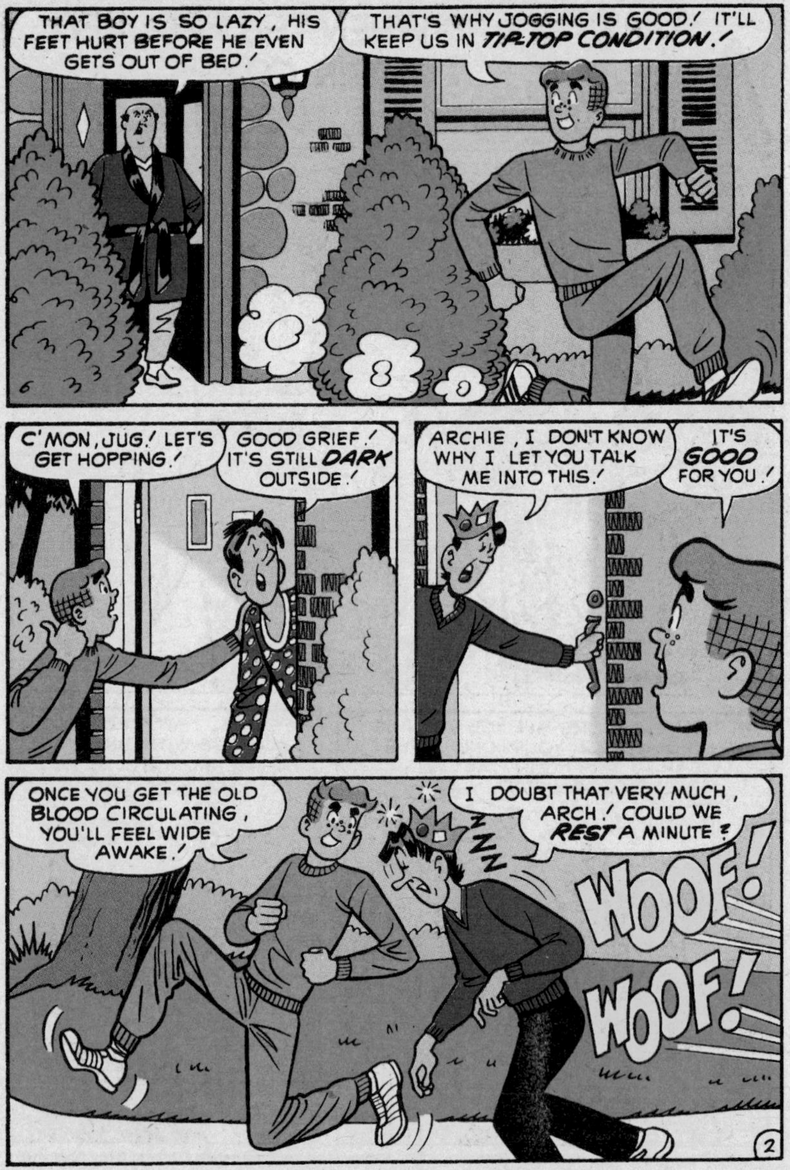
THAT BOY IS SO LAZY, HIS FEET HURT BEFORE HE EVEN GETS OUT OF BED!
THAT'S WHY JOGGING IS GOOD! IT'LL KEEP US IN TIP-TOP CONDITION!
C'MON, JUG! LET'S GET HOPPING!
GOOD GRIEF! IT'S STILL DARK OUTSIDE!
ARCHIE, I DON'T KNOW WHY I LET YOU TALK ME INTO THIS!
IT'S GOOD FOR YOU!
ONCE YOU GET THE OLD BLOOD CIRCULATING, YOU'LL FEEL WIDE AWAKE!
I DOUBT THAT VERY MUCH, ARCH! COULD WE REST A MINUTE?
ZZZ
WOOF!
WOOF!
2

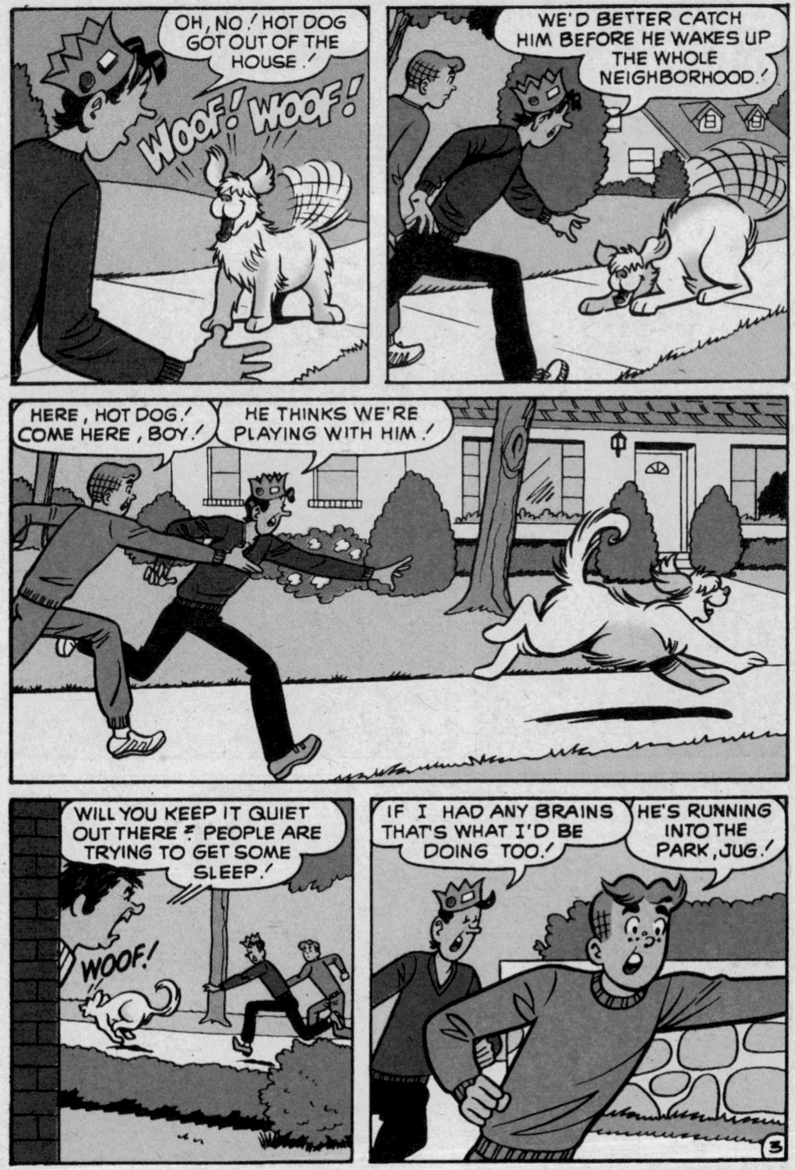
OH, NO! HOT DOG GOT OUT OF THE HOUSE!
WOOF! WOOF!
WE'D BETTER CATCH HIM BEFORE HE WAKES UP THE WHOLE NEIGHBORHOOD!
HERE, HOT DOG! COME HERE, BOY!
HE THINKS WE'RE PLAYING WITH HIM!
WILL YOU KEEP IT QUIET OUT THERE?! PEOPLE ARE TRYING TO GET SOME SLEEP!
WOOF!
IF I HAD ANY BRAINS THAT'S WHAT I'D BE DOING TOO!
HE'S RUNNING INTO THE PARK, JUG!
3

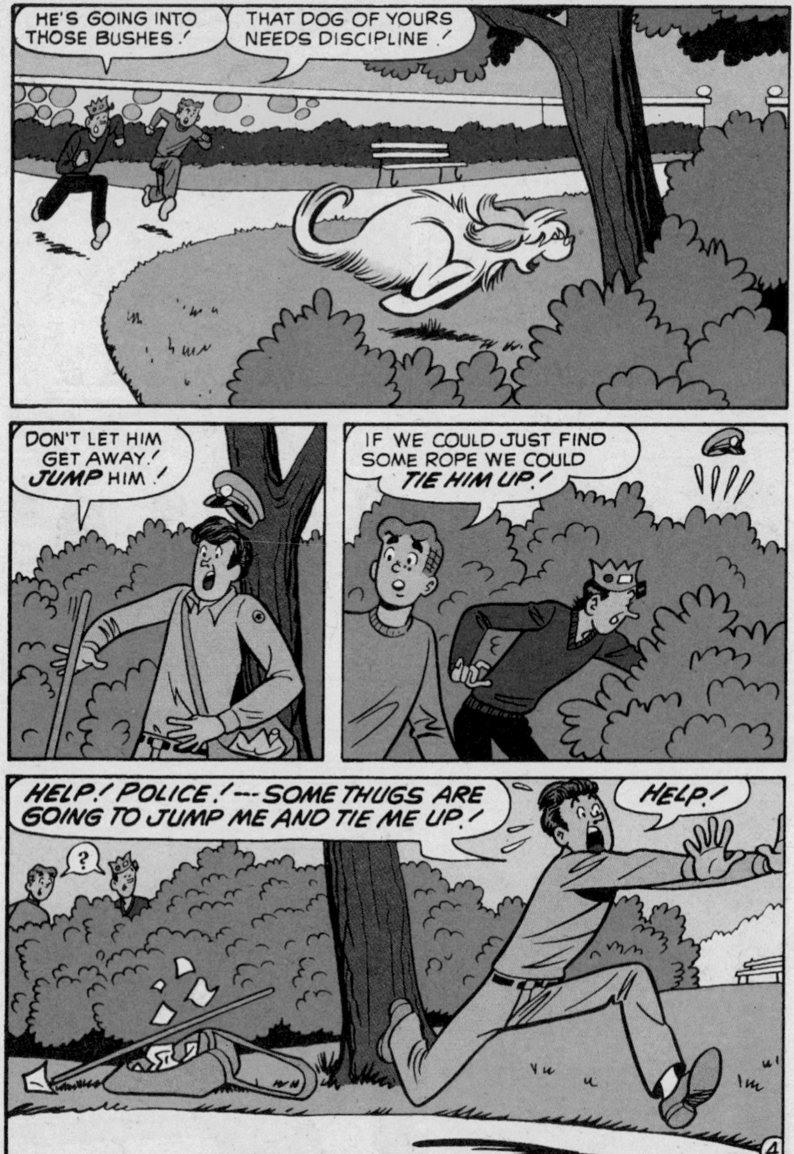
HE'S GOING INTO THOSE BUSHES!
THAT DOG OF YOURS NEEDS DISCIPLINE!
DON'T LET HIM GET AWAY! JUMP HIM!
IF WE COULD JUST FIND SOME ROPE WE COULD TIE HIM UP!
HELP! POLICE! --- SOME THUGS ARE GOING TO JUMP ME AND TIE ME UP!
HELP!
?
4

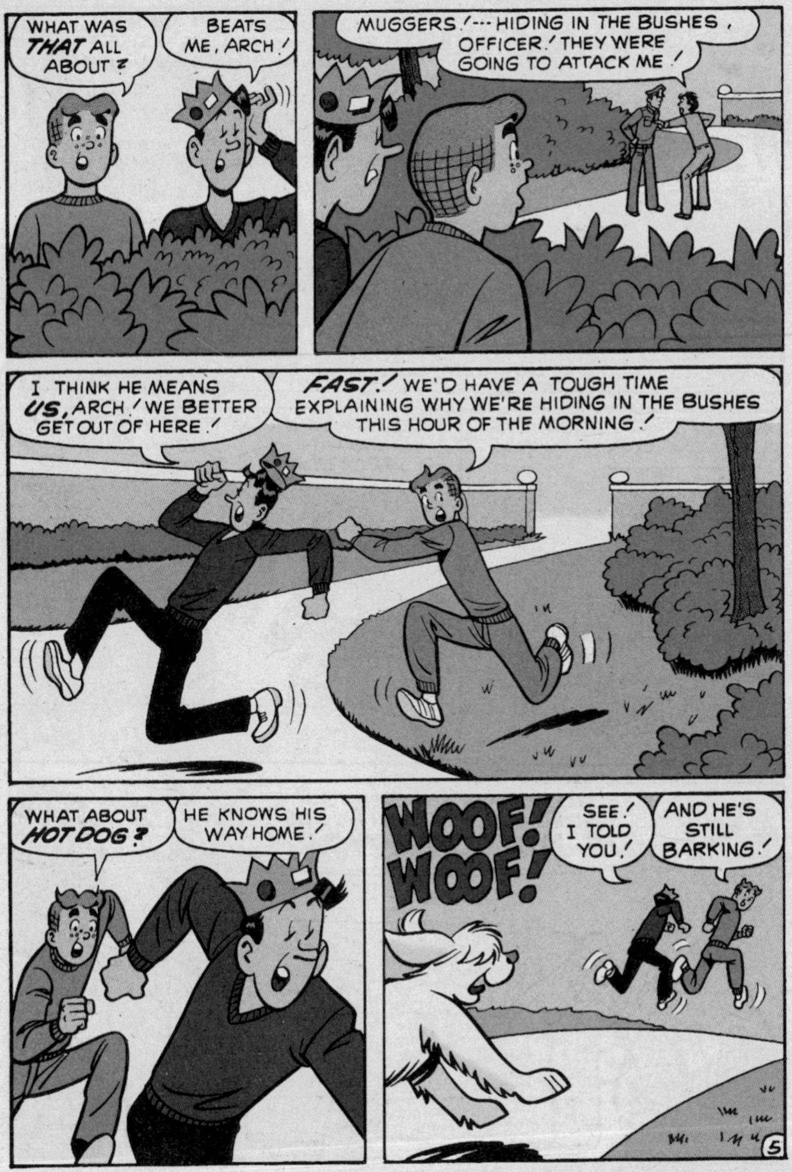
WHAT WAS THAT ALL ABOUT?
BEATS ME, ARCH!
MUGGERS!--- HIDING IN THE BUSHES, OFFICER! THEY WERE GOING TO ATTACK ME!
I THINK HE MEANS US, ARCH! WE BETTER GET OUT OF HERE!
FAST! WE'D HAVE A TOUGH TIME EXPLAINING WHY WE'RE HIDING IN THE BUSHES THIS HOUR OF THE MORNING!
WHAT ABOUT HOT DOG?
HE KNOWS HIS WAY HOME!
WOOF! WOOF!
SEE! I TOLD YOU!
AND HE'S STILL BARKING!
5

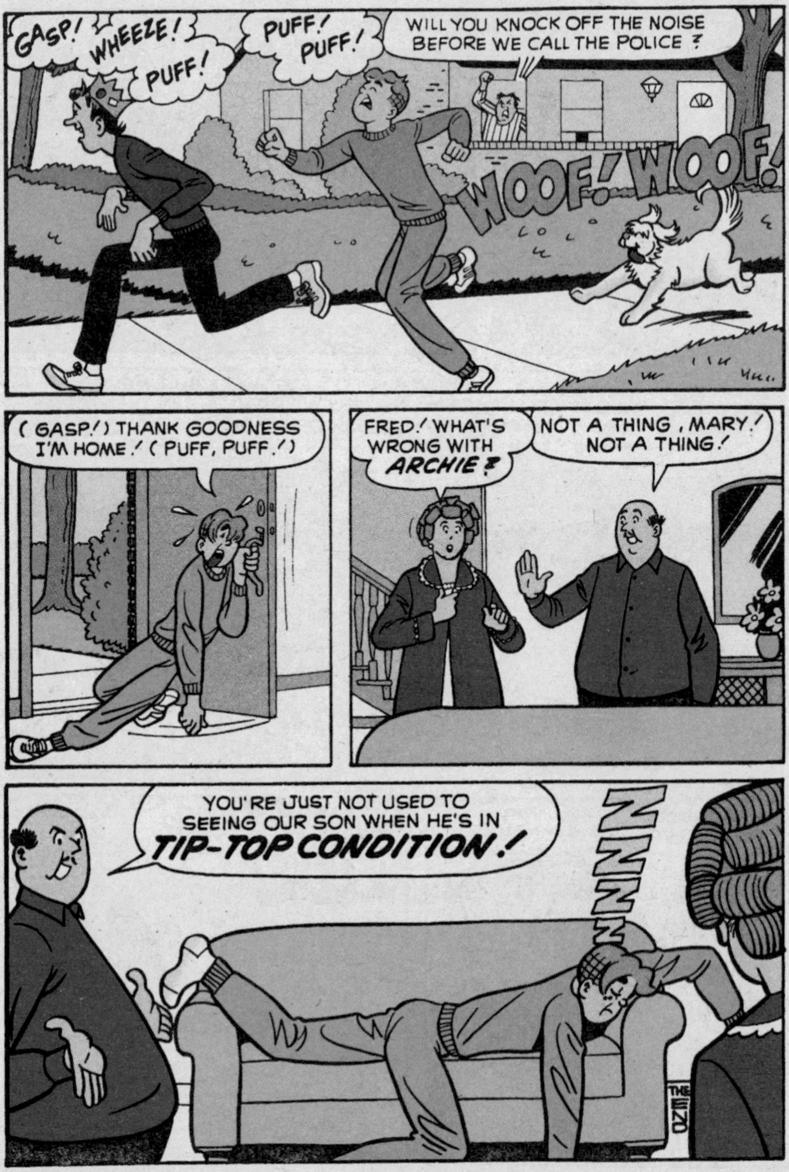
GASP!
WHEEZE!
PUFF!
PUFF! PUFF!
WILL YOU KNOCK OFF THE NOISE BEFORE WE CALL THE POLICE ?
WOOF! WOOF!
(GASP!) THANK GOODNESS I'M HOME! (PUFF, PUFF!)
FRED! WHAT'S WRONG WITH ARCHIE ?
NOT A THING, MARY! NOT A THING!
YOU'RE JUST NOT USED TO SEEING OUR SON WHEN HE'S IN TIP-TOP CONDITION!
ZZZZZ
THE END

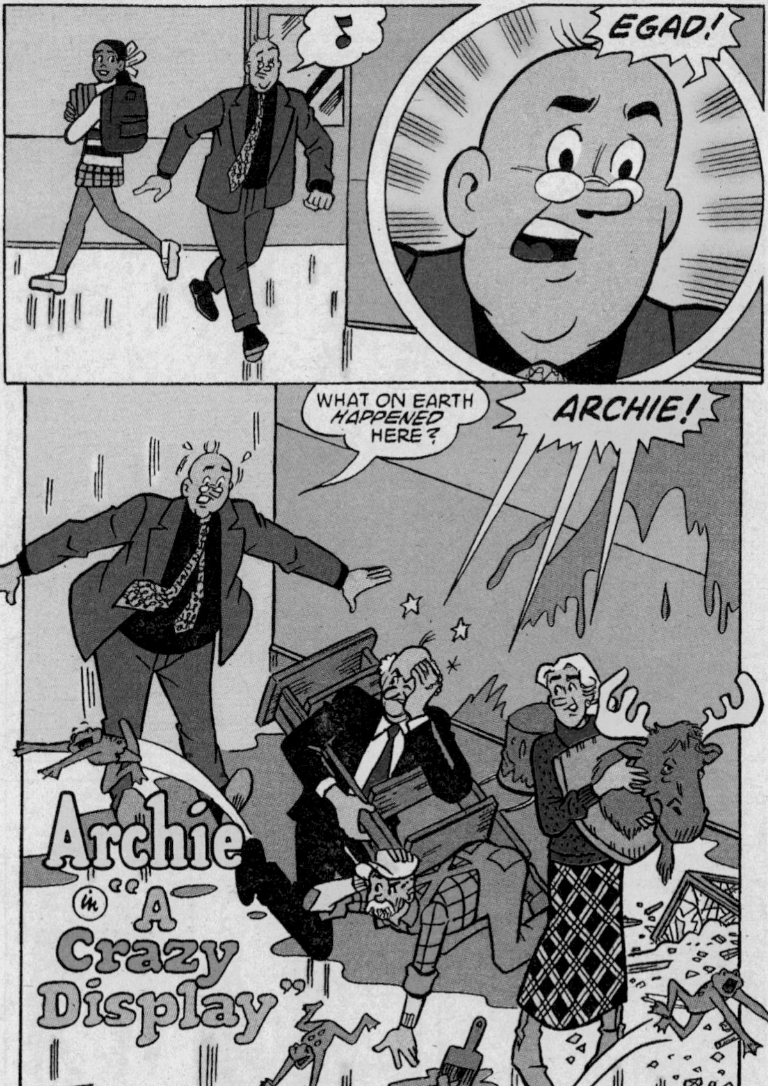
EGAD!
WHAT ON EARTH HAPPENED HERE?
ARCHIE!
Archie
in
"A Crazy Display"
Ruiz / Lapick / Yoshida / Grossman

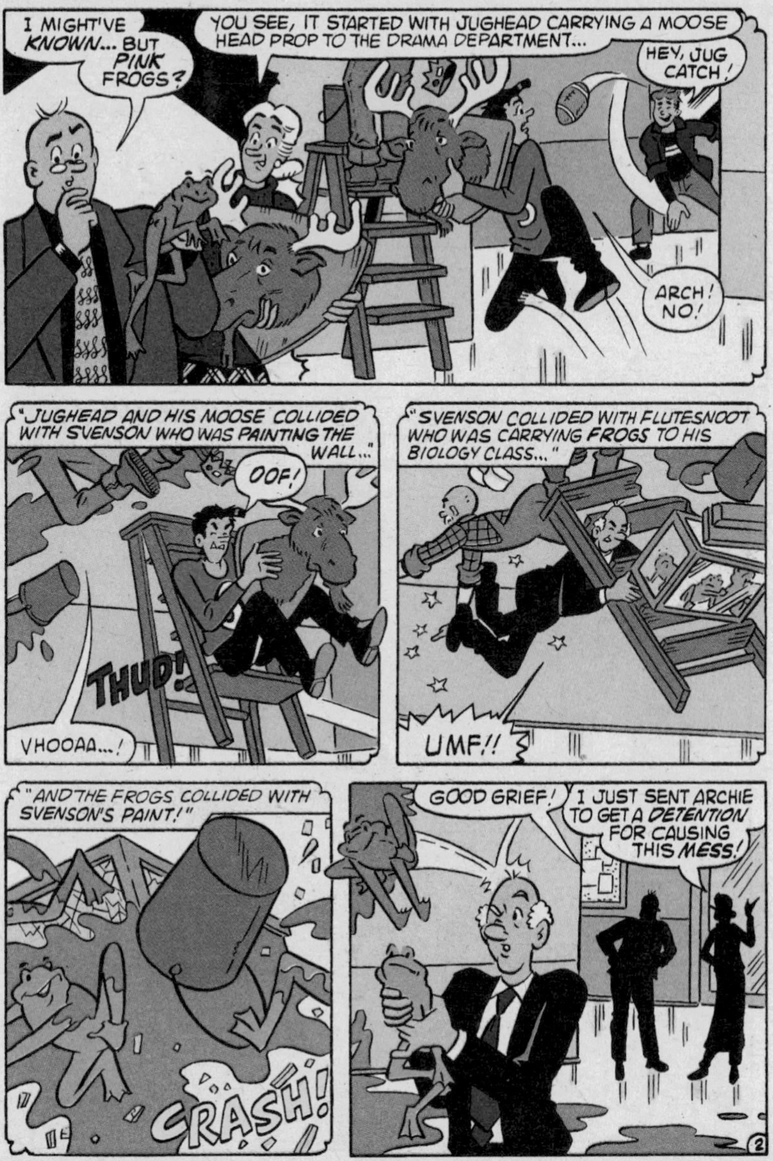
I MIGHT'VE KNOWN... BUT PINK FROGS?
YOU SEE, IT STARTED WITH JUGHEAD CARRYING A MOOSE HEAD PROP TO THE DRAMA DEPARTMENT...
HEY, JUG CATCH!
ARCH! NO!
"JUGHEAD AND HIS MOOSE COLLIDED WITH SVENSON WHO WAS PAINTING THE WALL..."
OOF!
THUD!
VHOOAA...!
"SVENSON COLLIDED WITH FLUTESNOOT WHO WAS CARRYING FROGS TO HIS BIOLOGY CLASS..."
UMF!!
"AND THE FROGS COLLIDED WITH SVENSON'S PAINT!"
CRASH!
GOOD GRIEF!
I JUST SENT ARCHIE TO GET A DETENTION FOR CAUSING THIS MESS!

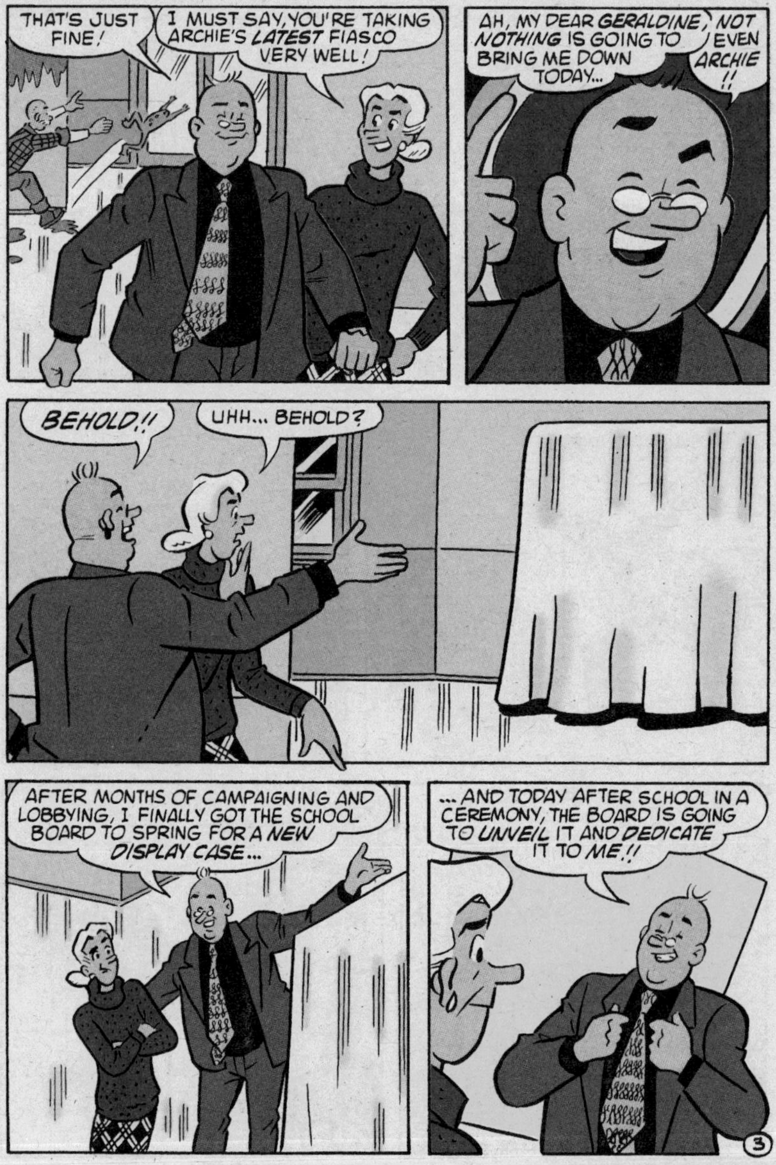
THAT'S JUST FINE!
I MUST SAY, YOU'RE TAKING ARCHIE'S *LATEST* FIASCO VERY WELL!
AH, MY DEAR *GERALDINE*, *NOTHING* IS GOING TO BRING ME DOWN TODAY...
NOT EVEN *ARCHIE*!!
BEHOLD!!
UHH... BEHOLD?
AFTER MONTHS OF CAMPAIGNING AND LOBBYING, I FINALLY GOT THE SCHOOL BOARD TO SPRING FOR A *NEW DISPLAY CASE*...
... AND TODAY AFTER SCHOOL IN A CEREMONY, THE BOARD IS GOING TO *UNVEIL* IT AND *DEDICATE* IT TO *ME*!!
3

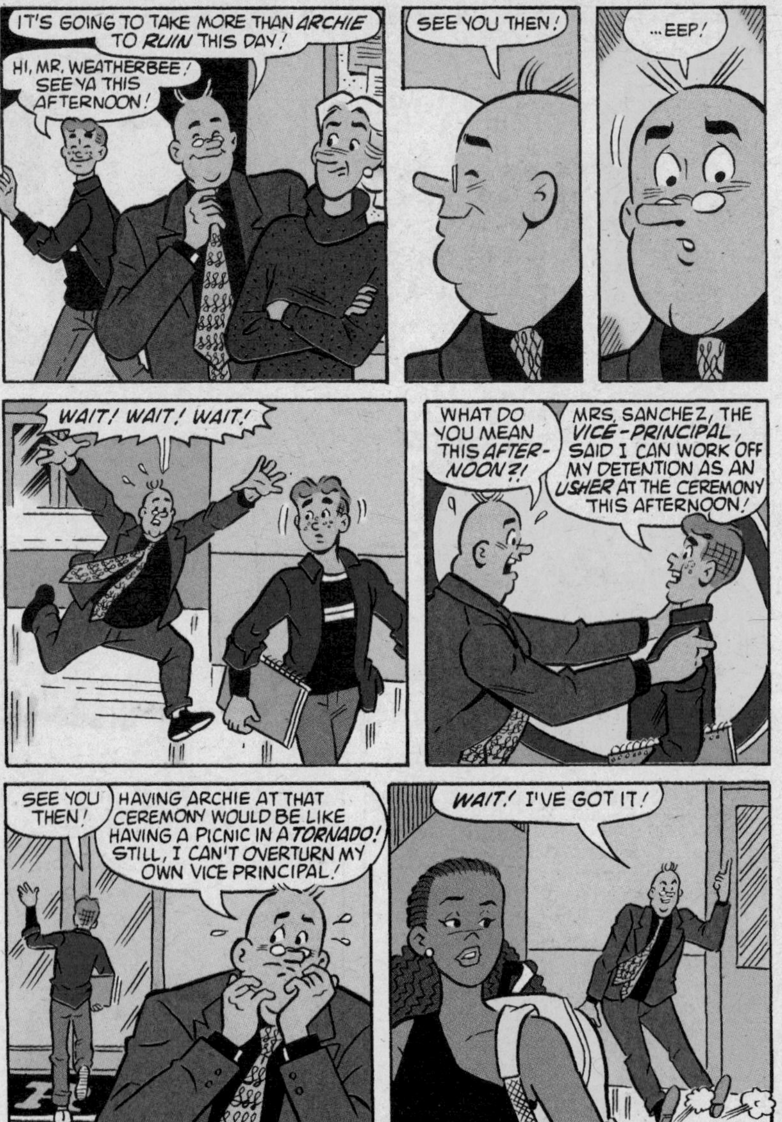
IT'S GOING TO TAKE MORE THAN ARCHIE TO RUIN THIS DAY!
HI, MR. WEATHERBEE! SEE YA THIS AFTERNOON!
SEE YOU THEN!
...EEP!
WAIT! WAIT! WAIT!
WHAT DO YOU MEAN THIS AFTERNOON?!
MRS. SANCHEZ, THE VICE-PRINCIPAL, SAID I CAN WORK OFF MY DETENTION AS AN USHER AT THE CEREMONY THIS AFTERNOON!
SEE YOU THEN!
HAVING ARCHIE AT THAT CEREMONY WOULD BE LIKE HAVING A PICNIC IN A TORNADO! STILL, I CAN'T OVERTURN MY OWN VICE PRINCIPAL!
WAIT! I'VE GOT IT!
4

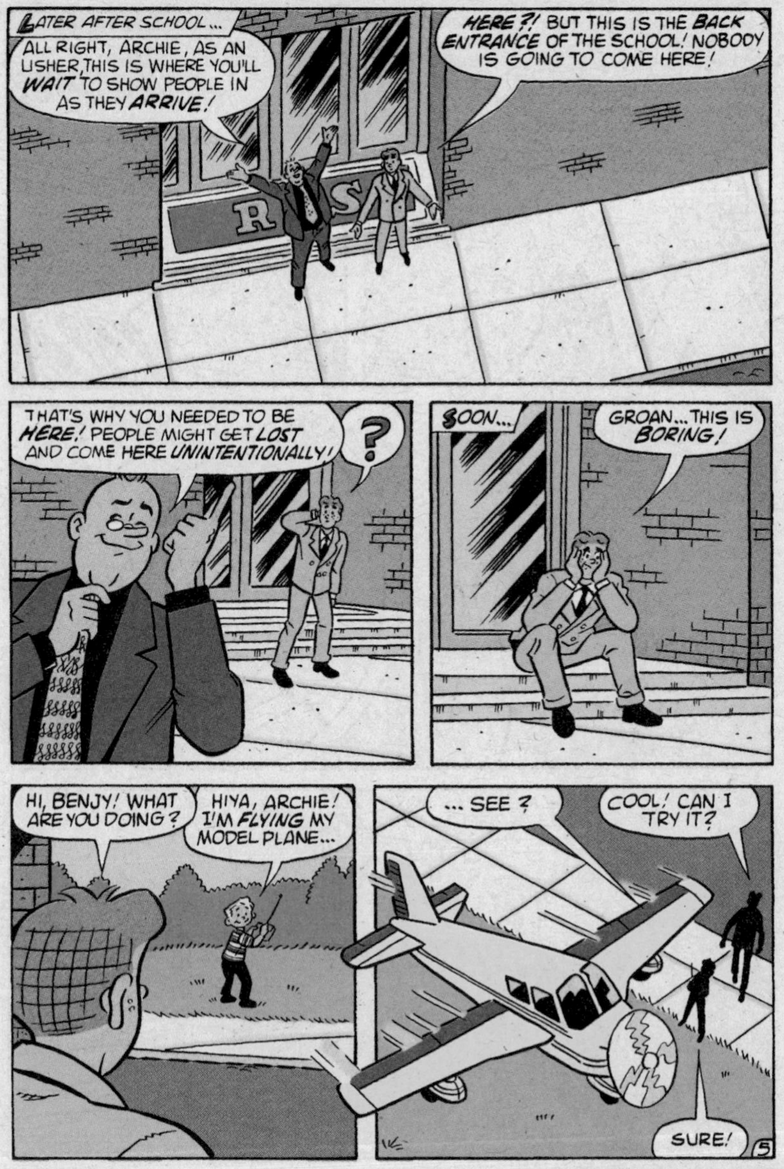
LATER AFTER SCHOOL...
ALL RIGHT, ARCHIE, AS AN USHER, THIS IS WHERE YOU'LL WAIT TO SHOW PEOPLE IN AS THEY ARRIVE!
HERE?! BUT THIS IS THE BACK ENTRANCE OF THE SCHOOL! NOBODY IS GOING TO COME HERE!
R S
THAT'S WHY YOU NEEDED TO BE HERE! PEOPLE MIGHT GET LOST AND COME HERE UNINTENTIONALLY!
?
SOON...
GROAN... THIS IS BORING!
HI, BENJY! WHAT ARE YOU DOING?
HIYA, ARCHIE! I'M FLYING MY MODEL PLANE...
... SEE?
COOL! CAN I TRY IT?
SURE!
5

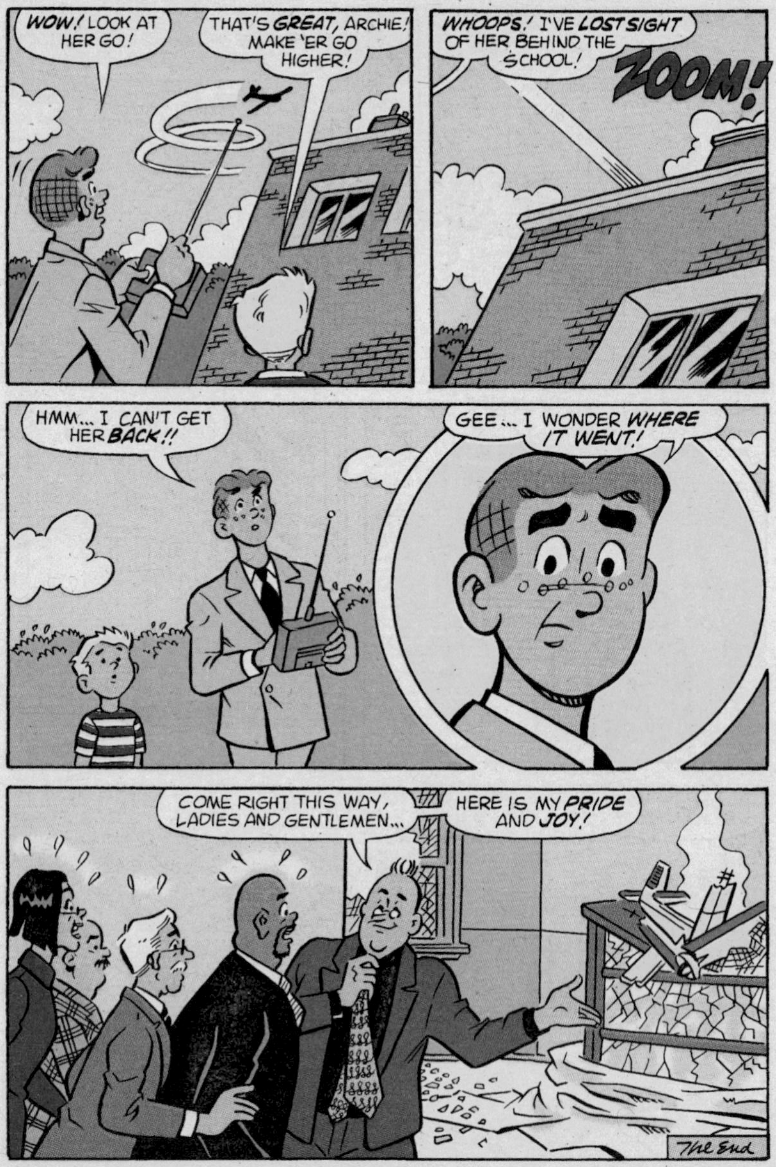
WOW! LOOK AT HER GO!
THAT'S GREAT, ARCHIE! MAKE 'ER GO HIGHER!
WHOOPS! I'VE LOST SIGHT OF HER BEHIND THE SCHOOL!
ZOOM!
HMM... I CAN'T GET HER BACK!!
GEE... I WONDER WHERE IT WENT!
COME RIGHT THIS WAY, LADIES AND GENTLEMEN...
HERE IS MY PRIDE AND JOY!
The End

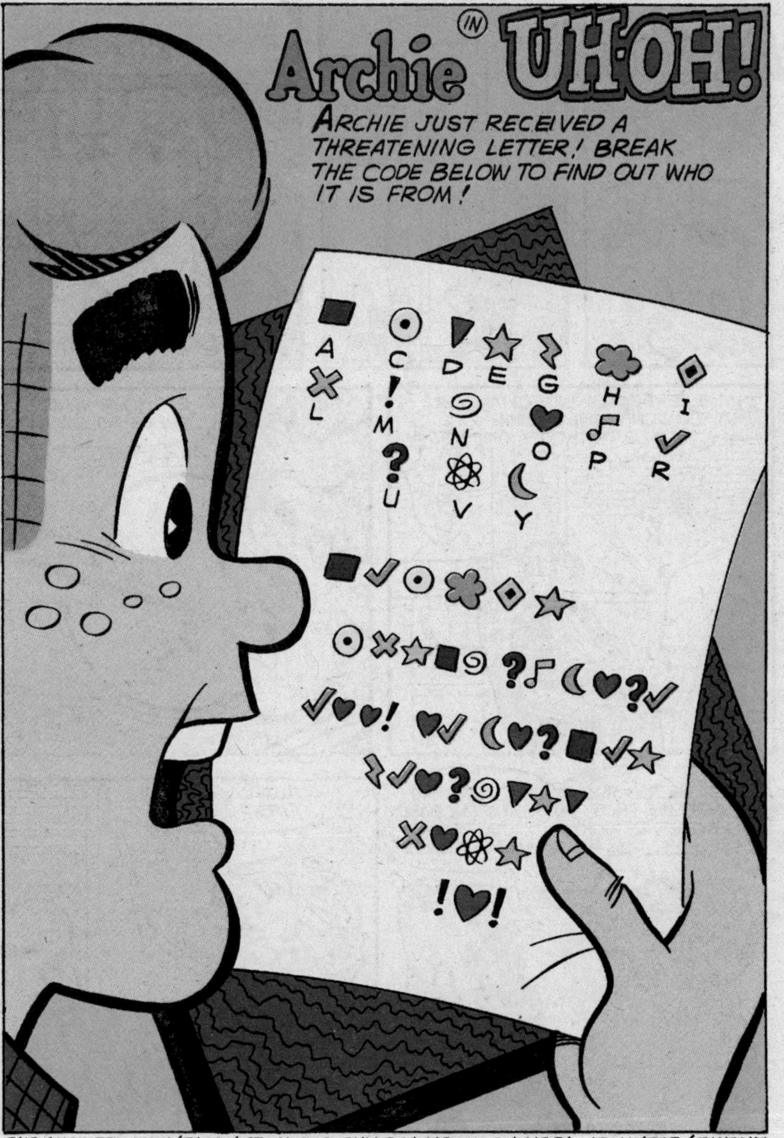
Archie IN UH-OH!
ARCHIE JUST RECEIVED A THREATENING LETTER! BREAK THE CODE BELOW TO FIND OUT WHO IT IS FROM!
A C D E G H I L M N O P R U V Y

THE ANSWER: ARCHIE, CLEAN UP YOUR ROOM OR YOU ARE GROUNDED! LOVE, MOM

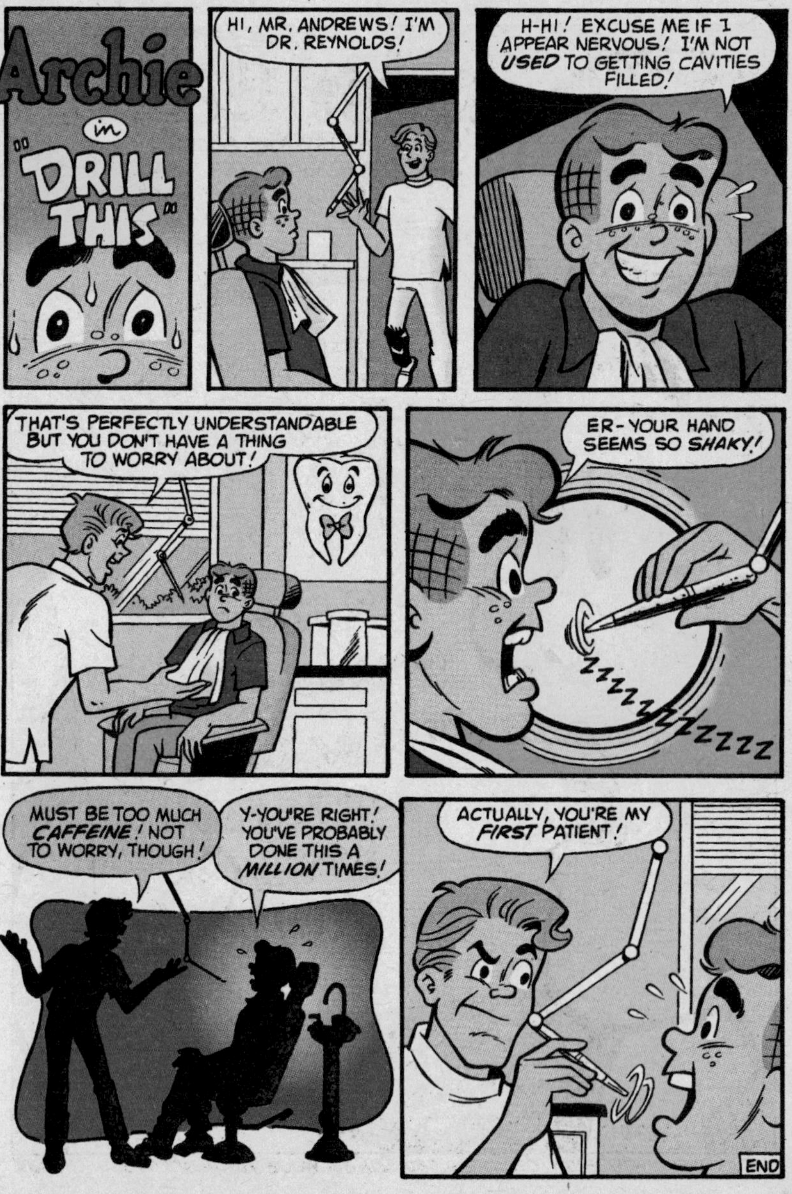
Archie
in
"DRILL THIS"
HI, MR. ANDREWS! I'M DR. REYNOLDS!
H-HI! EXCUSE ME IF I APPEAR NERVOUS! I'M NOT USED TO GETTING CAVITIES FILLED!
THAT'S PERFECTLY UNDERSTANDABLE BUT YOU DON'T HAVE A THING TO WORRY ABOUT!
ER- YOUR HAND SEEMS SO SHAKY!
ZZZZZZZZZZZ
MUST BE TOO MUCH CAFFEINE! NOT TO WORRY, THOUGH!
Y-YOU'RE RIGHT! YOU'VE PROBABLY DONE THIS A MILLION TIMES!
ACTUALLY, YOU'RE MY FIRST PATIENT!
END

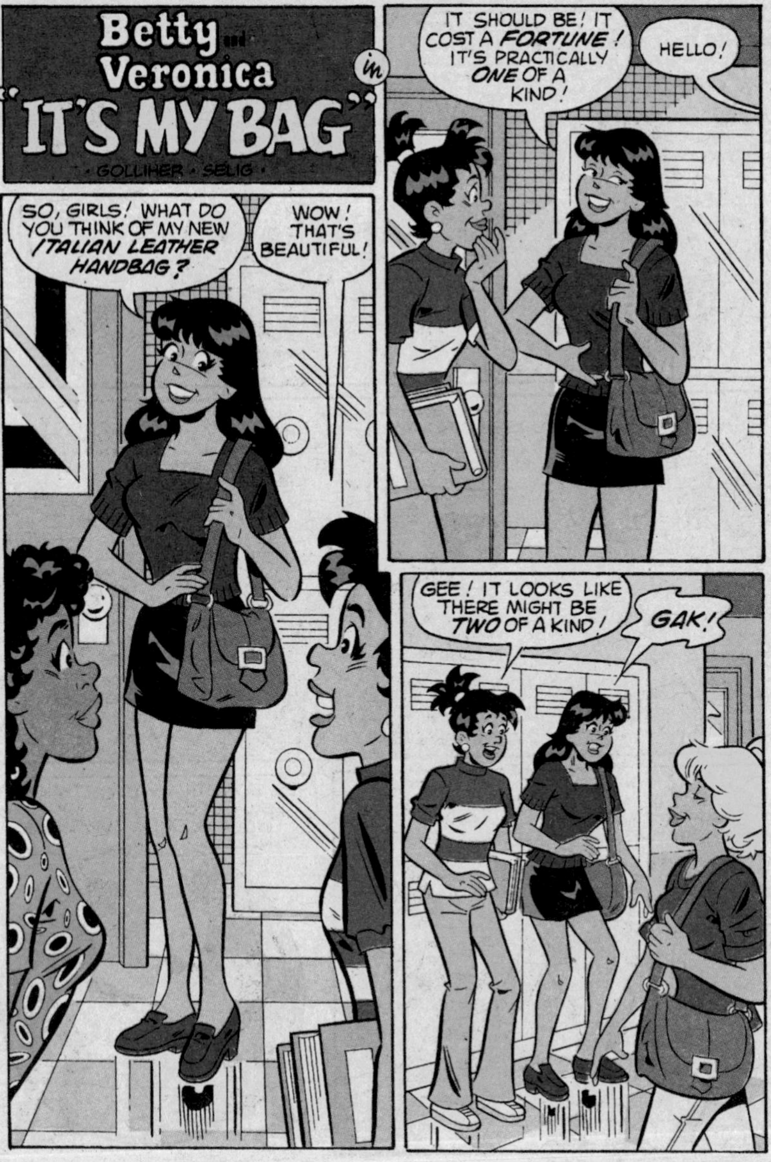
Betty and Veronica in
"IT'S MY BAG"
GOLLIHER • SELIG
SO, GIRLS! WHAT DO YOU THINK OF MY NEW ITALIAN LEATHER HANDBAG?
WOW! THAT'S BEAUTIFUL!
IT SHOULD BE! IT COST A FORTUNE! IT'S PRACTICALLY ONE OF A KIND!
HELLO!
GEE! IT LOOKS LIKE THERE MIGHT BE TWO OF A KIND!
GAK!

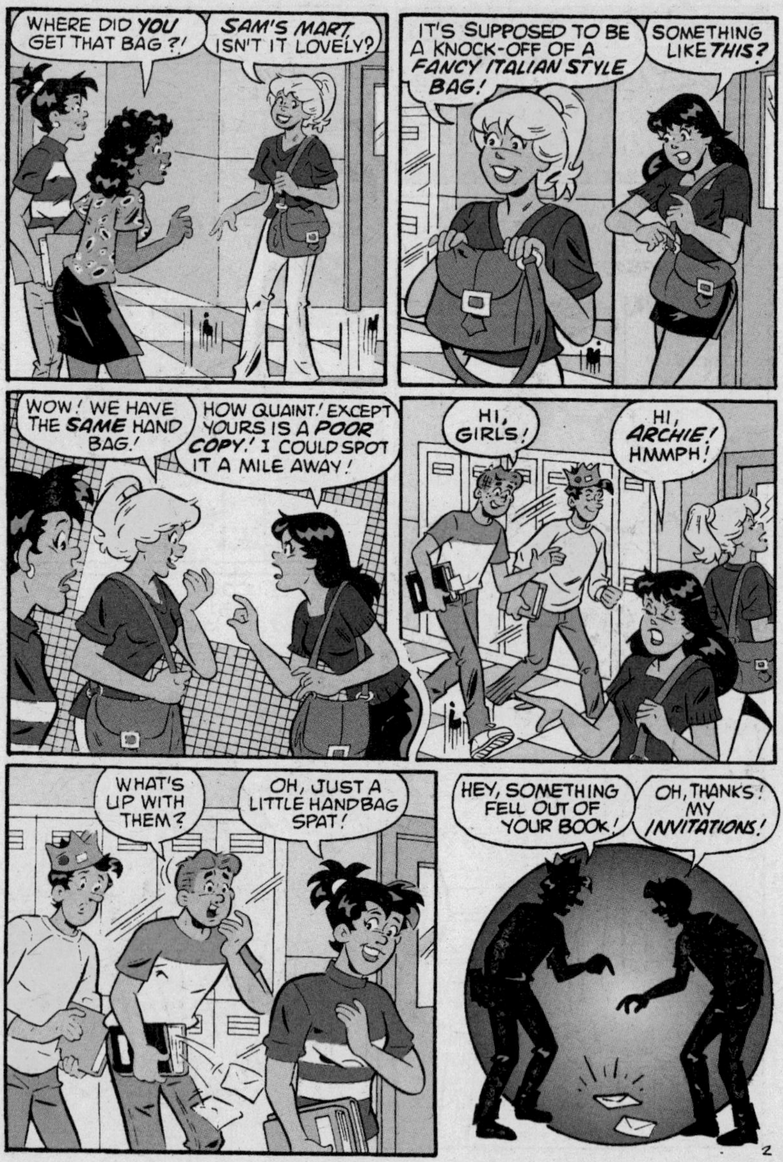
WHERE DID YOU GET THAT BAG ?!
SAM'S MART, ISN'T IT LOVELY?
IT'S SUPPOSED TO BE A KNOCK-OFF OF A FANCY ITALIAN STYLE BAG!
SOMETHING LIKE THIS?
WOW! WE HAVE THE SAME HAND BAG!
HOW QUAINT! EXCEPT YOURS IS A POOR COPY! I COULD SPOT IT A MILE AWAY!
HI, GIRLS!
HI, ARCHIE! HMMPH!
WHAT'S UP WITH THEM?
OH, JUST A LITTLE HANDBAG SPAT!
HEY, SOMETHING FELL OUT OF YOUR BOOK!
OH, THANKS! MY INVITATIONS!

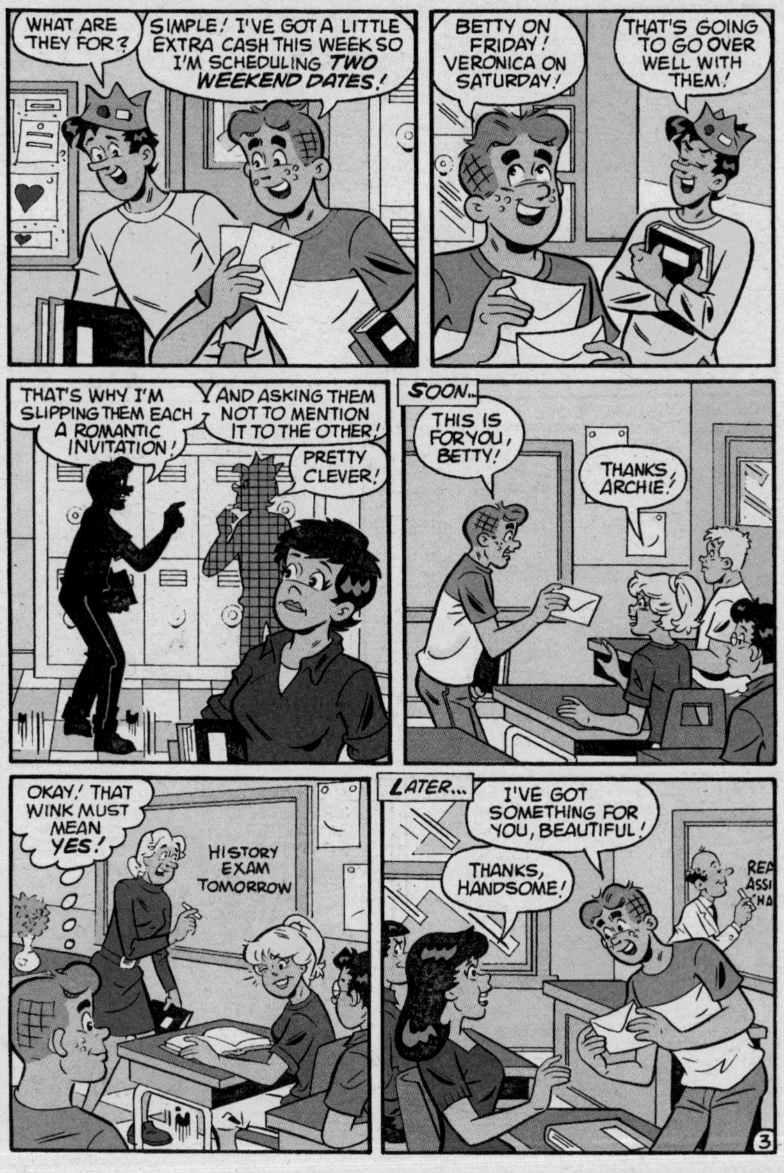
WHAT ARE THEY FOR?
SIMPLE! I'VE GOT A LITTLE EXTRA CASH THIS WEEK SO I'M SCHEDULING TWO WEEKEND DATES!
BETTY ON FRIDAY! VERONICA ON SATURDAY!
THAT'S GOING TO GO OVER WELL WITH THEM!
THAT'S WHY I'M SLIPPING THEM EACH A ROMANTIC INVITATION!
AND ASKING THEM NOT TO MENTION IT TO THE OTHER!
PRETTY CLEVER!
SOON...
THIS IS FOR YOU, BETTY!
THANKS, ARCHIE!
OKAY! THAT WINK MUST MEAN YES!
HISTORY EXAM TOMORROW
LATER...
I'VE GOT SOMETHING FOR YOU, BEAUTIFUL!
THANKS, HANDSOME!
3

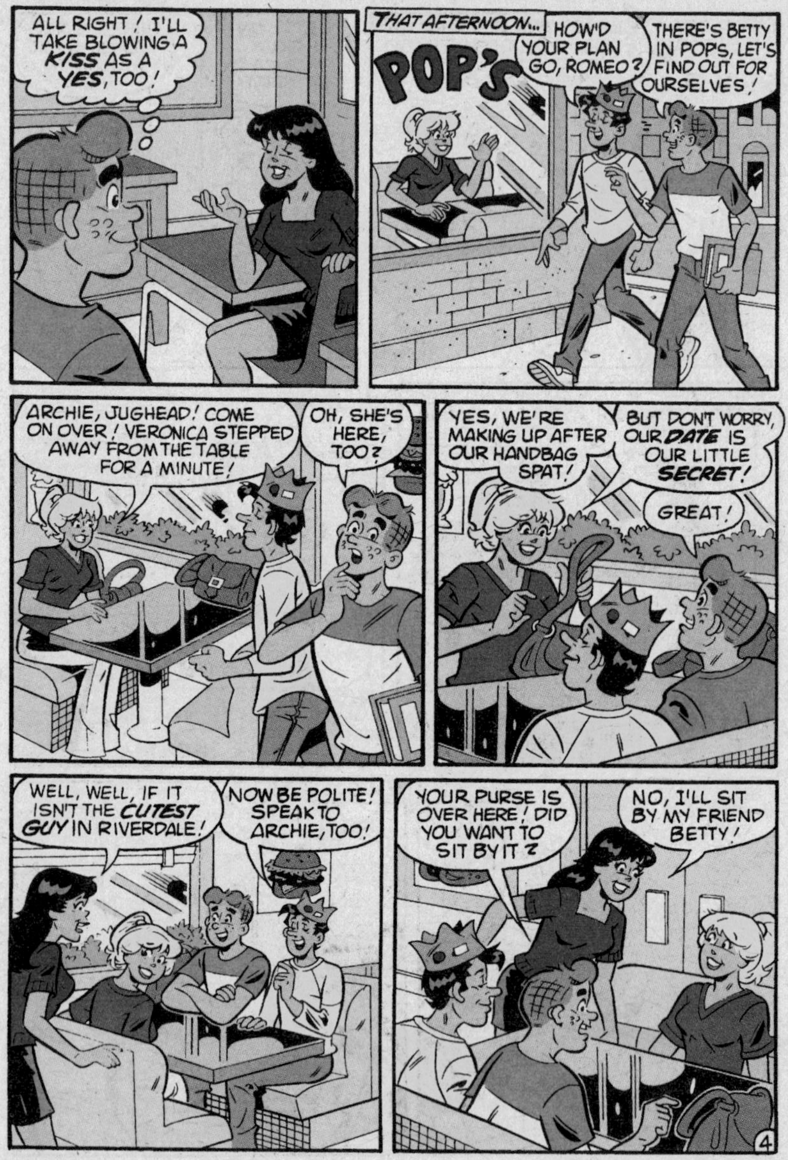
ALL RIGHT! I'LL TAKE BLOWING A KISS AS A YES, TOO!
THAT AFTERNOON...
POP'S
HOW'D YOUR PLAN GO, ROMEO?
THERE'S BETTY IN POP'S, LET'S FIND OUT FOR OURSELVES!
ARCHIE, JUGHEAD! COME ON OVER! VERONICA STEPPED AWAY FROM THE TABLE FOR A MINUTE!
OH, SHE'S HERE, TOO?
YES, WE'RE MAKING UP AFTER OUR HANDBAG SPAT!
BUT DON'T WORRY, OUR DATE IS OUR LITTLE SECRET!
GREAT!
WELL, WELL, IF IT ISN'T THE CUTEST GUY IN RIVERDALE!
NOW BE POLITE! SPEAK TO ARCHIE, TOO!
YOUR PURSE IS OVER HERE! DID YOU WANT TO SIT BY IT?
NO, I'LL SIT BY MY FRIEND BETTY!
4

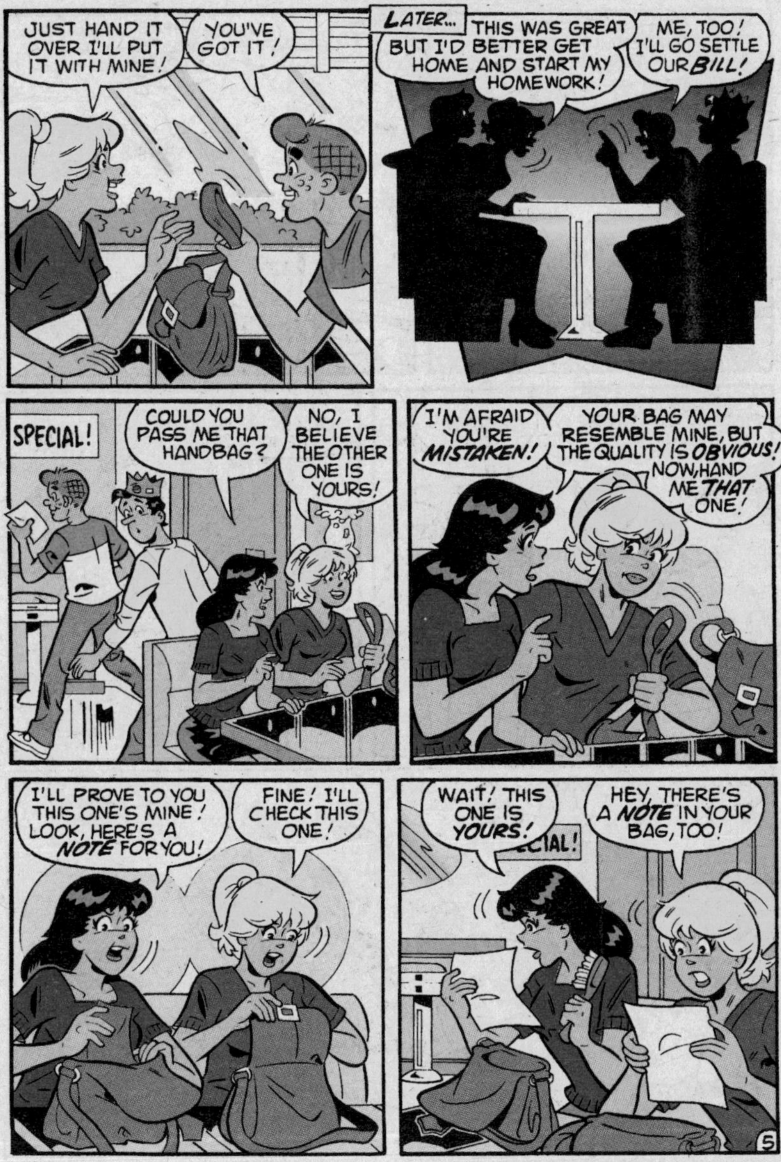
JUST HAND IT OVER I'LL PUT IT WITH MINE!
YOU'VE GOT IT!
LATER...
THIS WAS GREAT BUT I'D BETTER GET HOME AND START MY HOMEWORK!
ME, TOO! I'LL GO SETTLE OUR BILL!
SPECIAL!
COULD YOU PASS ME THAT HANDBAG?
NO, I BELIEVE THE OTHER ONE IS YOURS!
I'M AFRAID YOU'RE MISTAKEN!
YOUR BAG MAY RESEMBLE MINE, BUT THE QUALITY IS OBVIOUS! NOW, HAND ME THAT ONE!
I'LL PROVE TO YOU THIS ONE'S MINE! LOOK, HERE'S A NOTE FOR YOU!
FINE! I'LL CHECK THIS ONE!
WAIT! THIS ONE IS YOURS!
CIAL!
HEY, THERE'S A NOTE IN YOUR BAG, TOO!
5

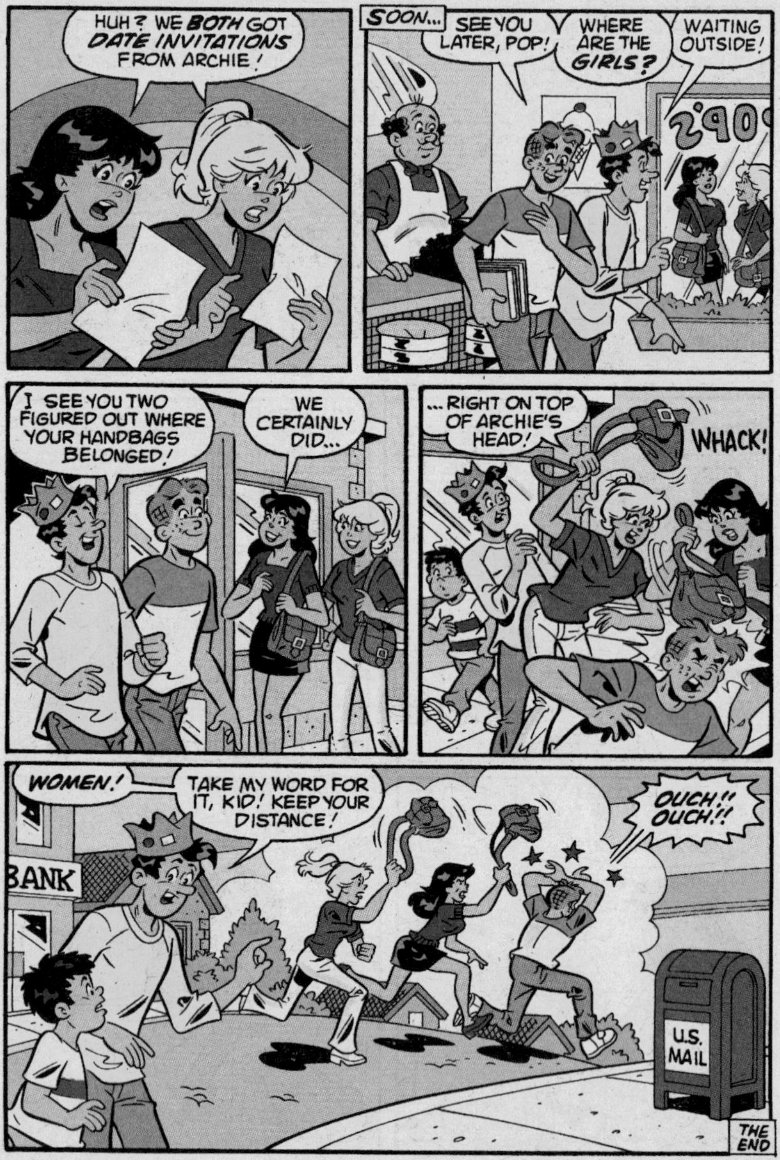
HUH? WE BOTH GOT DATE INVITATIONS FROM ARCHIE!
SOON...
SEE YOU LATER, POP!
WHERE ARE THE GIRLS?
WAITING OUTSIDE!
POP'S
I SEE YOU TWO FIGURED OUT WHERE YOUR HANDBAGS BELONGED!
WE CERTAINLY DID...
...RIGHT ON TOP OF ARCHIE'S HEAD!
WHACK!
WOMEN!
TAKE MY WORD FOR IT, KID! KEEP YOUR DISTANCE!
OUCH!! OUCH!!!
BANK
U.S. MAIL
THE END

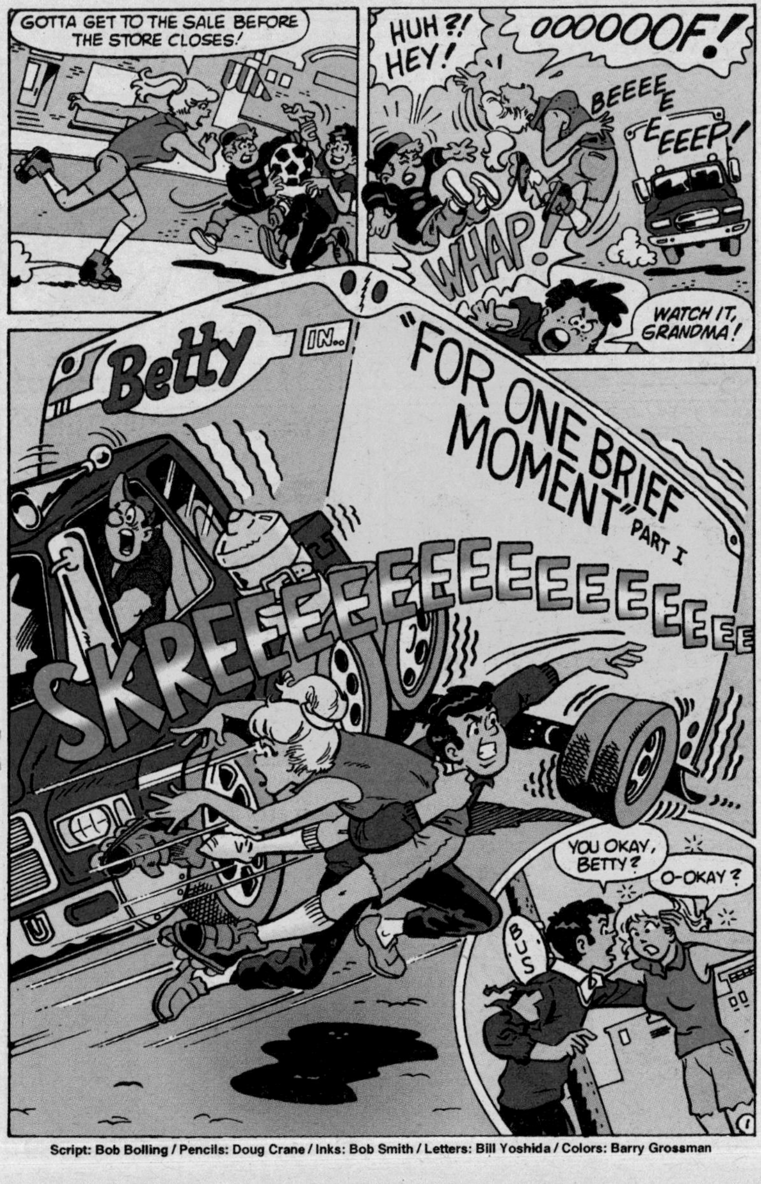
GOTTA GET TO THE SALE BEFORE THE STORE CLOSES!
HUH?! HEY!
OOOOOOF!
BEEEEEEEEEEP!
WHAP!
WATCH IT, GRANDMA!
Betty IN..
"FOR ONE BRIEF MOMENT" PART I
SKREEEEEEEEEEEEEEEEE
YOU OKAY, BETTY?
O-OKAY?
BUS
1

Script: Bob Bolling / Pencils: Doug Crane / Inks: Bob Smith / Letters: Bill Yoshida / Colors: Barry Grossman

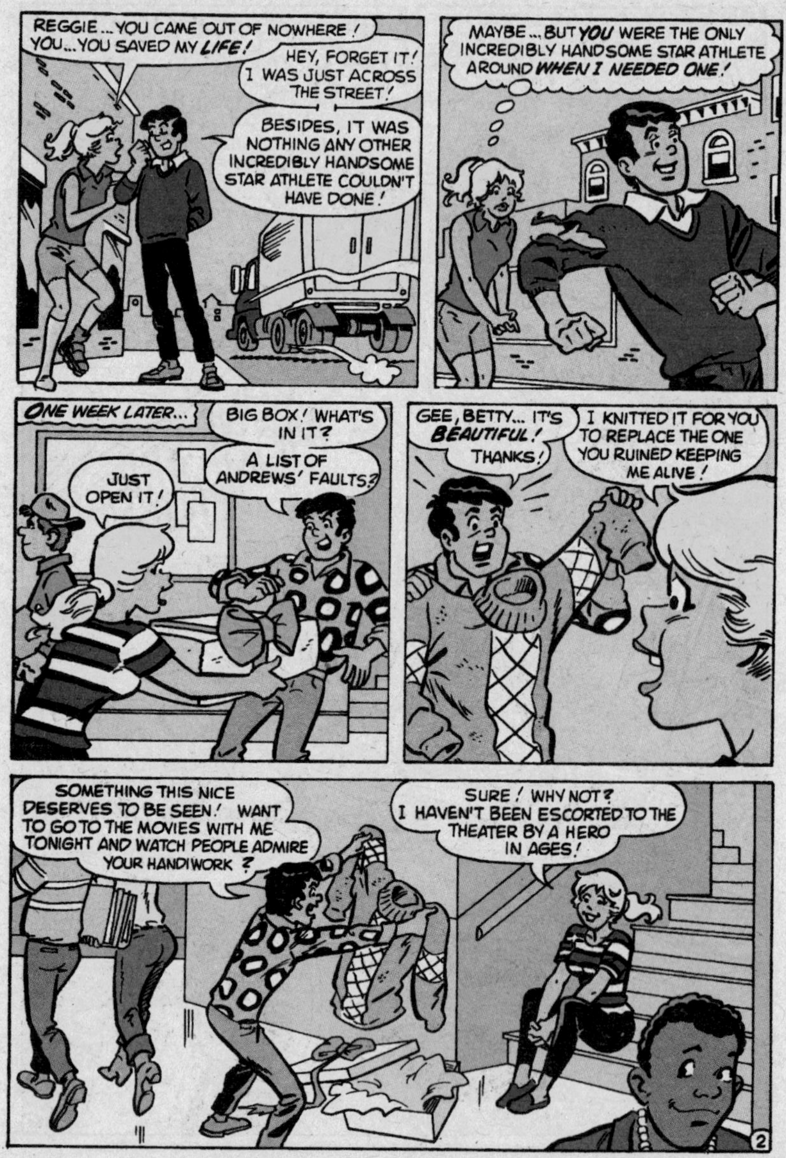
REGGIE... YOU CAME OUT OF NOWHERE! YOU... YOU SAVED MY LIFE!
HEY, FORGET IT! I WAS JUST ACROSS THE STREET!
BESIDES, IT WAS NOTHING ANY OTHER INCREDIBLY HANDSOME STAR ATHLETE COULDN'T HAVE DONE!
MAYBE... BUT YOU WERE THE ONLY INCREDIBLY HANDSOME STAR ATHLETE AROUND WHEN I NEEDED ONE!
ONE WEEK LATER...
BIG BOX! WHAT'S IN IT?
A LIST OF ANDREWS' FAULTS?
JUST OPEN IT!
GEE, BETTY... IT'S BEAUTIFUL! THANKS!
I KNITTED IT FOR YOU TO REPLACE THE ONE YOU RUINED KEEPING ME ALIVE!
SOMETHING THIS NICE DESERVES TO BE SEEN! WANT TO GO TO THE MOVIES WITH ME TONIGHT AND WATCH PEOPLE ADMIRE YOUR HANDIWORK?
SURE! WHY NOT? I HAVEN'T BEEN ESCORTED TO THE THEATER BY A HERO IN AGES!
2

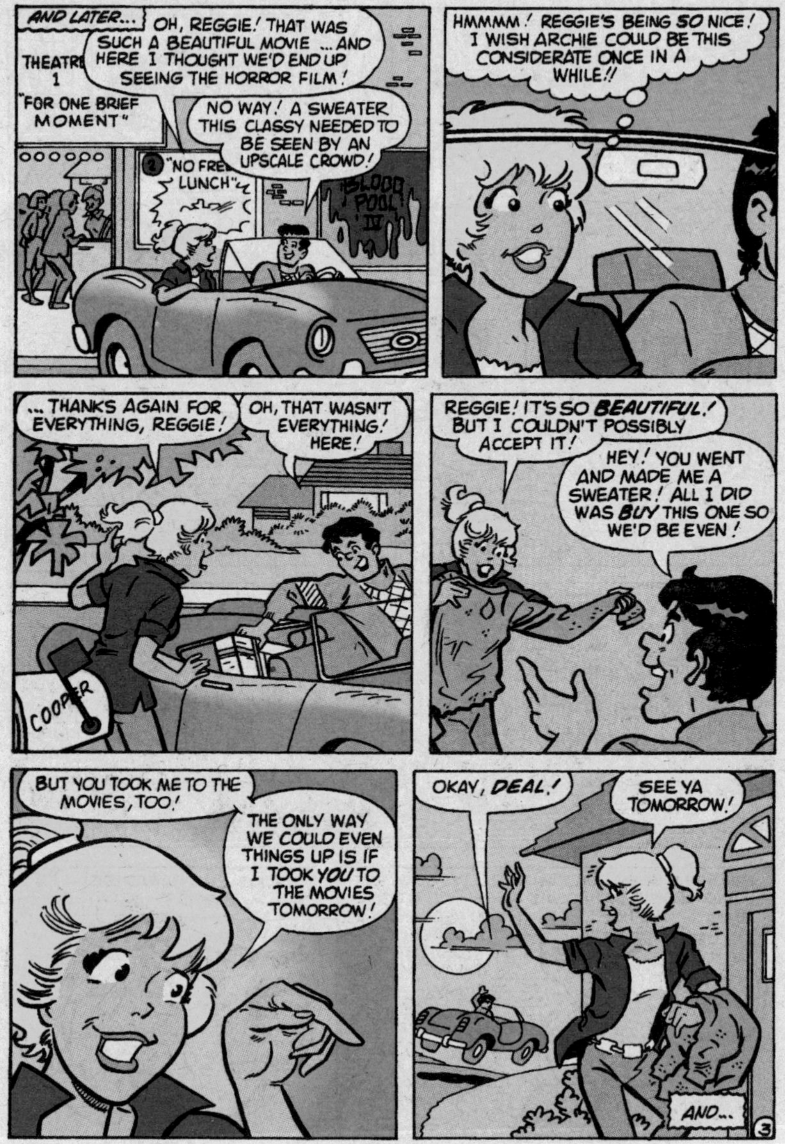
AND LATER...
OH, REGGIE! THAT WAS SUCH A BEAUTIFUL MOVIE ...AND HERE I THOUGHT WE'D END UP SEEING THE HORROR FILM!
THEATRE 1
"FOR ONE BRIEF MOMENT"
NO WAY! A SWEATER THIS CLASSY NEEDED TO BE SEEN BY AN UPSCALE CROWD!
2 "NO FRE LUNCH"
BLOOD POOL III
HMMMM! REGGIE'S BEING SO NICE! I WISH ARCHIE COULD BE THIS CONSIDERATE ONCE IN A WHILE!!
...THANKS AGAIN FOR EVERYTHING, REGGIE!
OH, THAT WASN'T EVERYTHING! HERE!
COOPER
REGGIE! IT'S SO BEAUTIFUL! BUT I COULDN'T POSSIBLY ACCEPT IT!
HEY! YOU WENT AND MADE ME A SWEATER! ALL I DID WAS BUY THIS ONE SO WE'D BE EVEN!
BUT YOU TOOK ME TO THE MOVIES, TOO!
THE ONLY WAY WE COULD EVEN THINGS UP IS IF I TOOK YOU TO THE MOVIES TOMORROW!
OKAY, DEAL!
SEE YA TOMORROW!
AND...
3

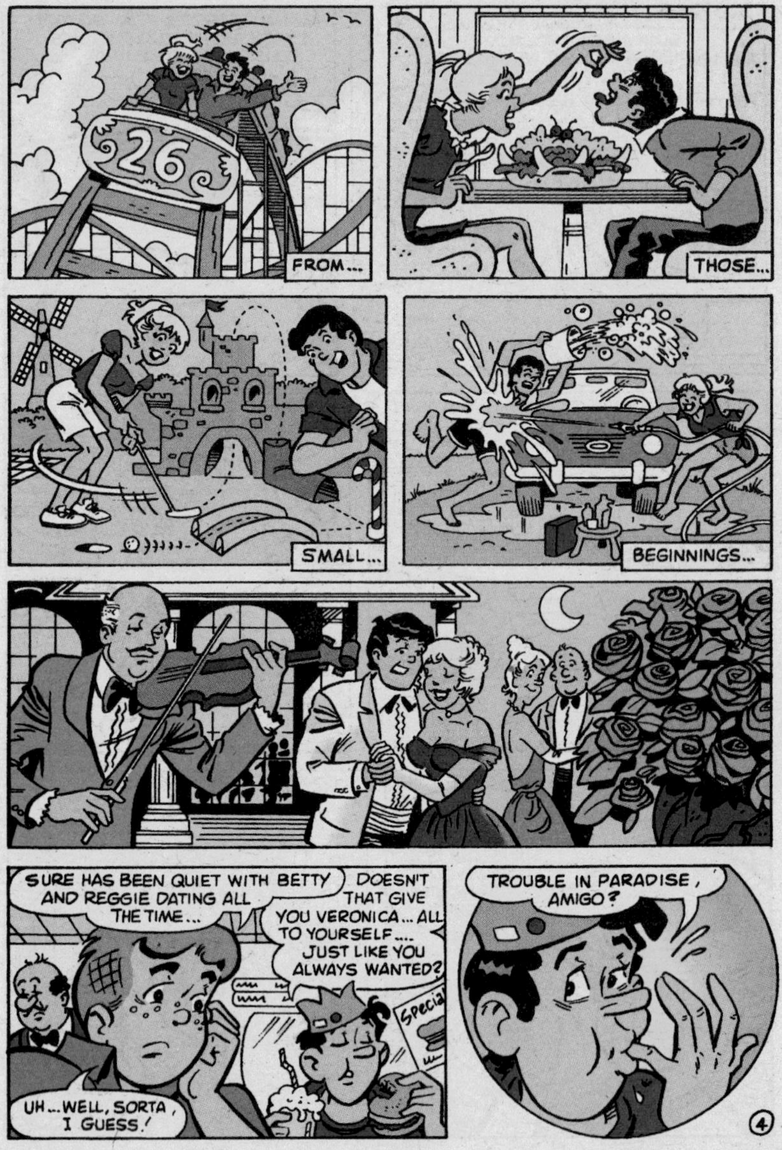

FROM...
THOSE...
SMALL...
BEGINNINGS...
SURE HAS BEEN QUIET WITH BETTY AND REGGIE DATING ALL THE TIME...
DOESN'T THAT GIVE YOU VERONICA... ALL TO YOURSELF.... JUST LIKE YOU ALWAYS WANTED?
UH... WELL, SORTA, I GUESS!
TROUBLE IN PARADISE, AMIGO?

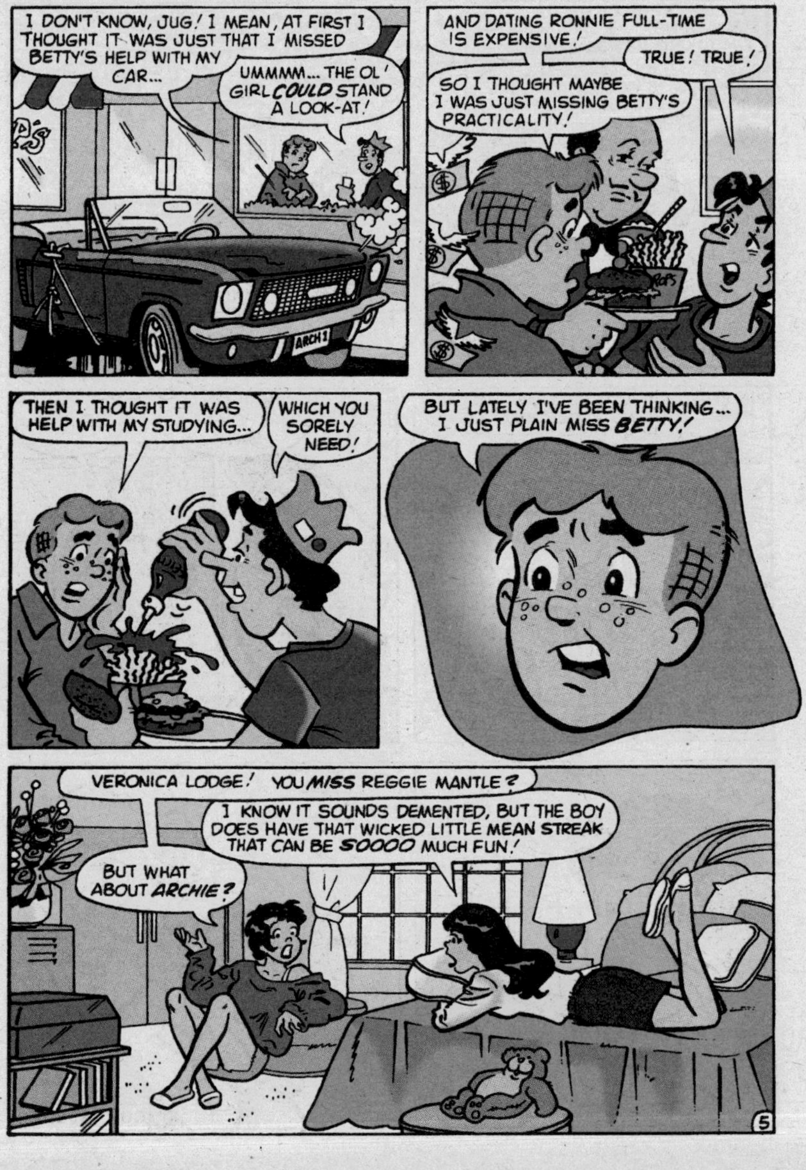
I DON'T KNOW, JUG! I MEAN, AT FIRST I THOUGHT IT WAS JUST THAT I MISSED BETTY'S HELP WITH MY CAR...
UMMMM... THE OL' GIRL COULD STAND A LOOK-AT!
ARCH 1
AND DATING RONNIE FULL-TIME IS EXPENSIVE!
TRUE! TRUE!
SO I THOUGHT MAYBE I WAS JUST MISSING BETTY'S PRACTICALITY!
THEN I THOUGHT IT WAS HELP WITH MY STUDYING...
WHICH YOU SORELY NEED!
BUT LATELY I'VE BEEN THINKING... I JUST PLAIN MISS BETTY!
VERONICA LODGE! YOU MISS REGGIE MANTLE?
I KNOW IT SOUNDS DEMENTED, BUT THE BOY DOES HAVE THAT WICKED LITTLE MEAN STREAK THAT CAN BE SOOOO MUCH FUN!
BUT WHAT ABOUT ARCHIE?
5

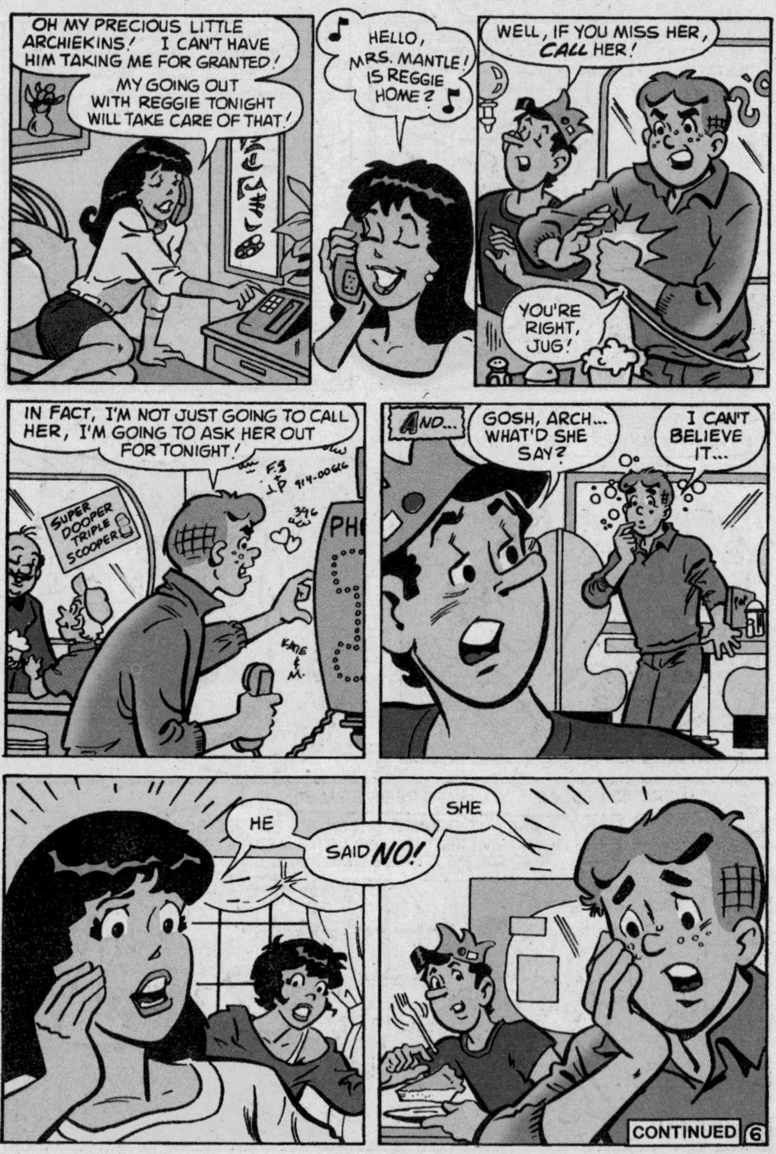
OH MY PRECIOUS LITTLE ARCHIEKINS! I CAN'T HAVE HIM TAKING ME FOR GRANTED!
MY GOING OUT WITH REGGIE TONIGHT WILL TAKE CARE OF THAT!
HELLO, MRS. MANTLE! IS REGGIE HOME?
WELL, IF YOU MISS HER, CALL HER!
YOU'RE RIGHT, JUG!
IN FACT, I'M NOT JUST GOING TO CALL HER, I'M GOING TO ASK HER OUT FOR TONIGHT!
SUPER DOOPER TRIPLE SCOOPER
AND...
GOSH, ARCH... WHAT'D SHE SAY?
I CAN'T BELIEVE IT...
HE
SHE
SAID NO!
CONTINUED
6

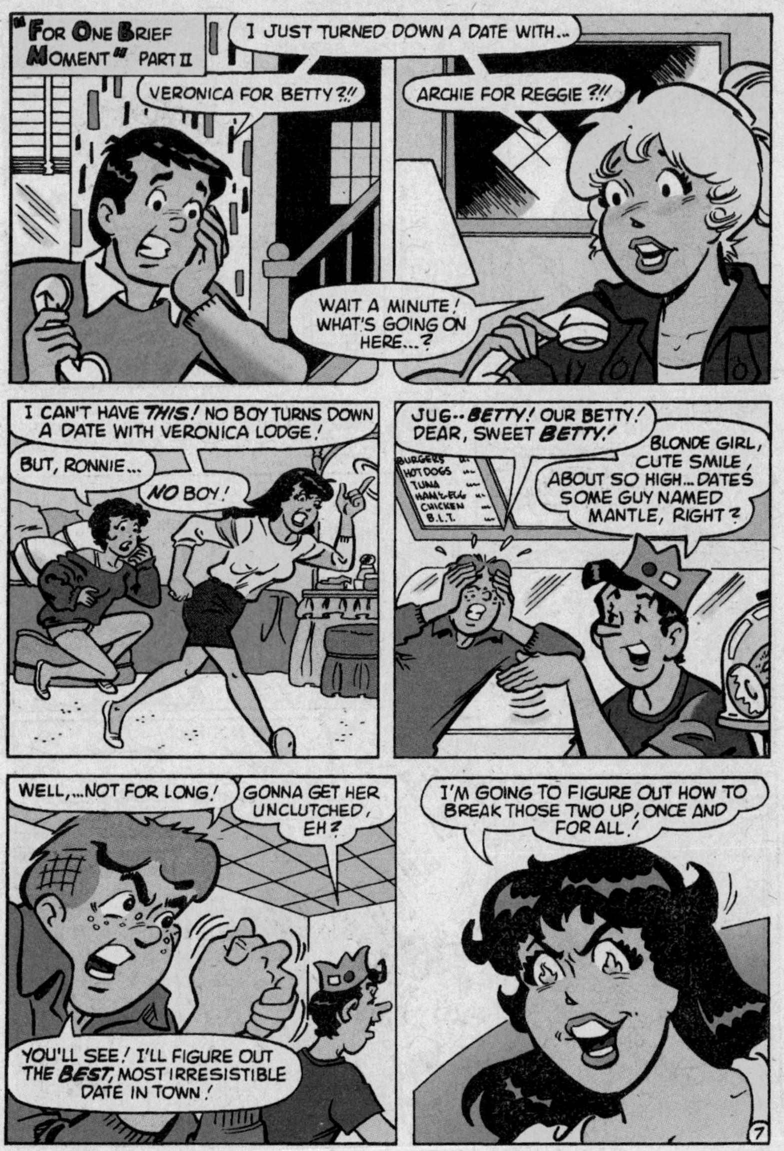
"FOR ONE BRIEF MOMENT" PART II
I JUST TURNED DOWN A DATE WITH...
VERONICA FOR BETTY ?!!
ARCHIE FOR REGGIE ?!!
WAIT A MINUTE! WHAT'S GOING ON HERE...?
I CAN'T HAVE THIS! NO BOY TURNS DOWN A DATE WITH VERONICA LODGE!
BUT, RONNIE...
NO BOY!
JUG-- BETTY! OUR BETTY! DEAR, SWEET BETTY!
BLONDE GIRL, CUTE SMILE, ABOUT SO HIGH... DATES SOME GUY NAMED MANTLE, RIGHT?
BURGERS
HOT DOGS
TUNA
HAM & EGG
CHICKEN
B.L.T.
WELL,...NOT FOR LONG!
GONNA GET HER UNCLUTCHED, EH?
YOU'LL SEE! I'LL FIGURE OUT THE BEST, MOST IRRESISTIBLE DATE IN TOWN!
I'M GOING TO FIGURE OUT HOW TO BREAK THOSE TWO UP, ONCE AND FOR ALL!
7

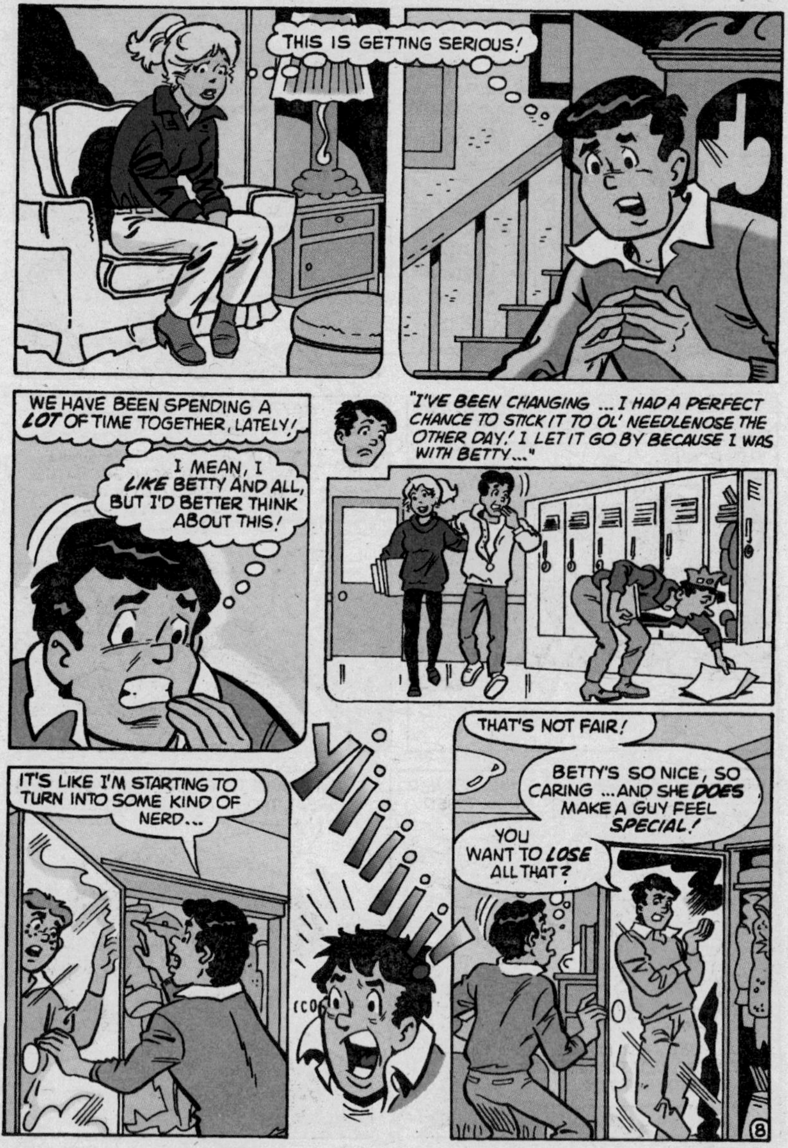
THIS IS GETTING SERIOUS!
WE HAVE BEEN SPENDING A LOT OF TIME TOGETHER, LATELY!
I MEAN, I LIKE BETTY AND ALL, BUT I'D BETTER THINK ABOUT THIS!
"I'VE BEEN CHANGING ... I HAD A PERFECT CHANCE TO STICK IT TO OL' NEEDLENOSE THE OTHER DAY! I LET IT GO BY BECAUSE I WAS WITH BETTY..."
IT'S LIKE I'M STARTING TO TURN INTO SOME KIND OF NERD...
YIIIII!
THAT'S NOT FAIR!
BETTY'S SO NICE, SO CARING ...AND SHE DOES MAKE A GUY FEEL SPECIAL!
YOU WANT TO LOSE ALL THAT?
8

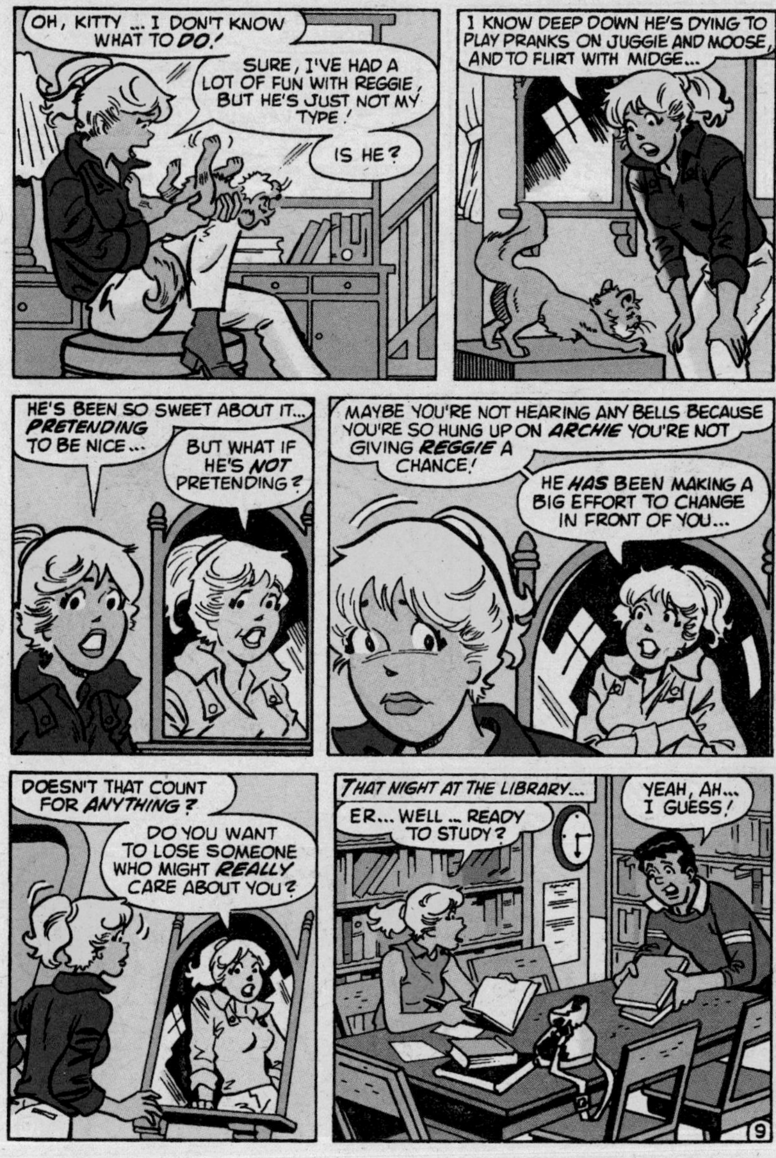
OH, KITTY ... I DON'T KNOW WHAT TO *DO!*
SURE, I'VE HAD A LOT OF FUN WITH REGGIE, BUT HE'S JUST NOT MY TYPE!
IS HE?
I KNOW DEEP DOWN HE'S DYING TO PLAY PRANKS ON JUGGIE AND MOOSE, AND TO FLIRT WITH MIDGE...
HE'S BEEN SO SWEET ABOUT IT... *PRETENDING* TO BE NICE...
BUT WHAT IF HE'S *NOT* PRETENDING?
MAYBE YOU'RE NOT HEARING ANY BELLS BECAUSE YOU'RE SO HUNG UP ON *ARCHIE* YOU'RE NOT GIVING *REGGIE* A CHANCE!
HE *HAS* BEEN MAKING A BIG EFFORT TO CHANGE IN FRONT OF YOU...
DOESN'T THAT COUNT FOR *ANYTHING?*
DO YOU WANT TO LOSE SOMEONE WHO MIGHT *REALLY* CARE ABOUT YOU?
THAT NIGHT AT THE LIBRARY...
ER... WELL ... READY TO STUDY?
YEAH, AH... I GUESS!
9

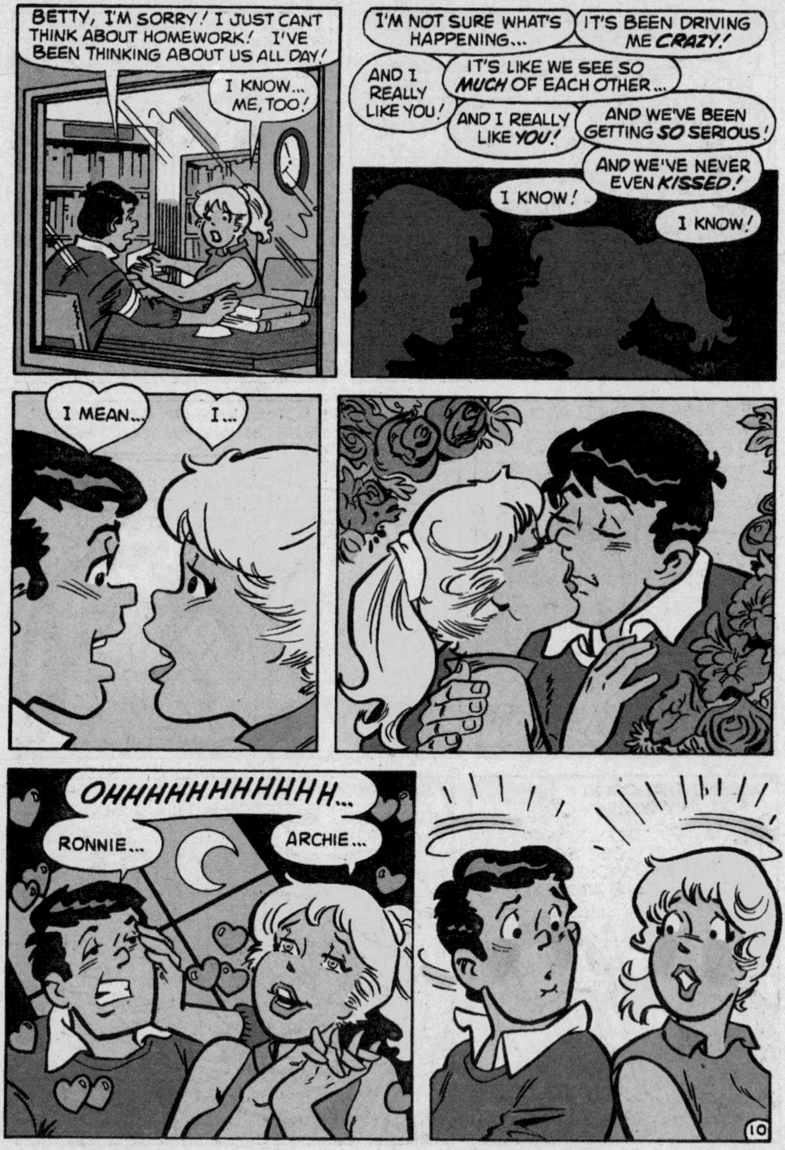

BETTY, I'M SORRY! I JUST CANT THINK ABOUT HOMEWORK! I'VE BEEN THINKING ABOUT US ALL DAY!
I KNOW... ME, TOO!
I'M NOT SURE WHAT'S HAPPENING...
IT'S BEEN DRIVING ME CRAZY!
AND I REALLY LIKE YOU!
IT'S LIKE WE SEE SO MUCH OF EACH OTHER...
AND I REALLY LIKE YOU!
AND WE'VE BEEN GETTING SO SERIOUS!
AND WE'VE NEVER EVEN KISSED!
I KNOW!
I KNOW!
I MEAN...
I...
OHHHHHHHHHHH...
RONNIE...
ARCHIE...

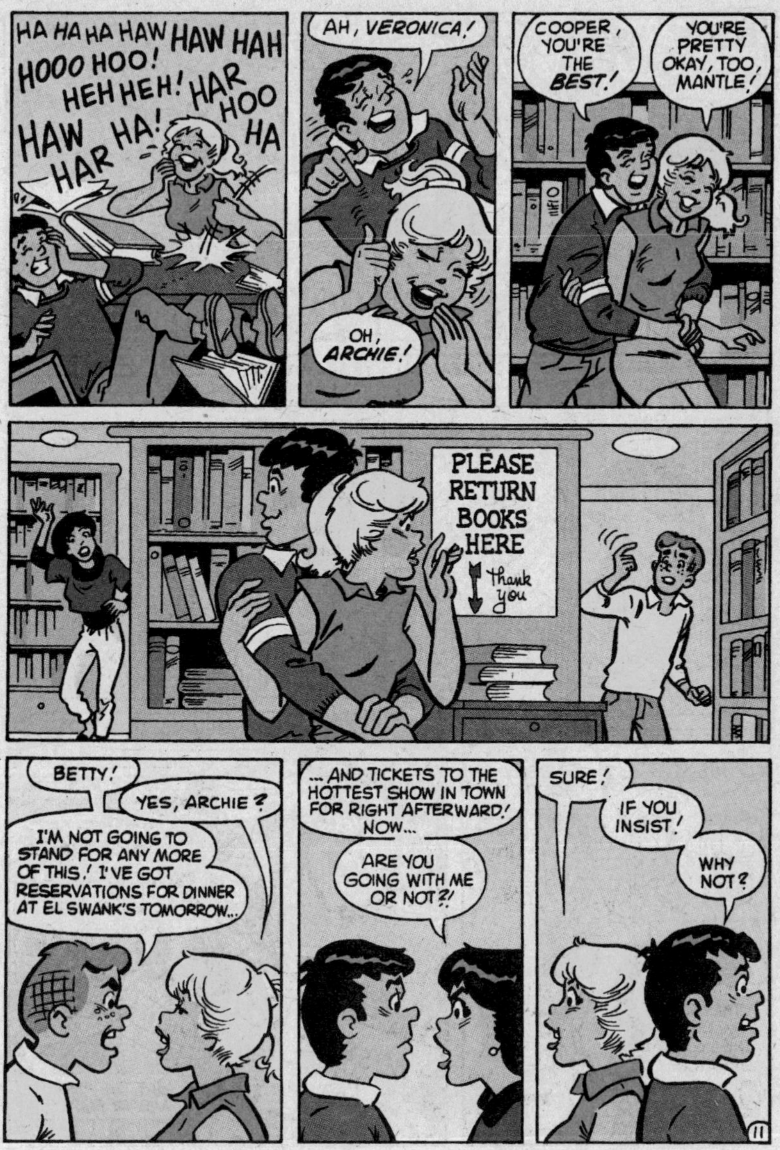
HA HA HA HAW HAW HAH
HOOO HOO!
HEH HEH!
HAR HOO
HAW
HA!
HA
HAR
AH, VERONICA!
OH, ARCHIE!
COOPER, YOU'RE THE BEST!
YOU'RE PRETTY OKAY, TOO, MANTLE!
PLEASE RETURN BOOKS HERE
Thank you
BETTY!
YES, ARCHIE?
I'M NOT GOING TO STAND FOR ANY MORE OF THIS! I'VE GOT RESERVATIONS FOR DINNER AT EL SWANK'S TOMORROW...
... AND TICKETS TO THE HOTTEST SHOW IN TOWN FOR RIGHT AFTERWARD! NOW...
ARE YOU GOING WITH ME OR NOT?!
SURE!
IF YOU INSIST!
WHY NOT?
11

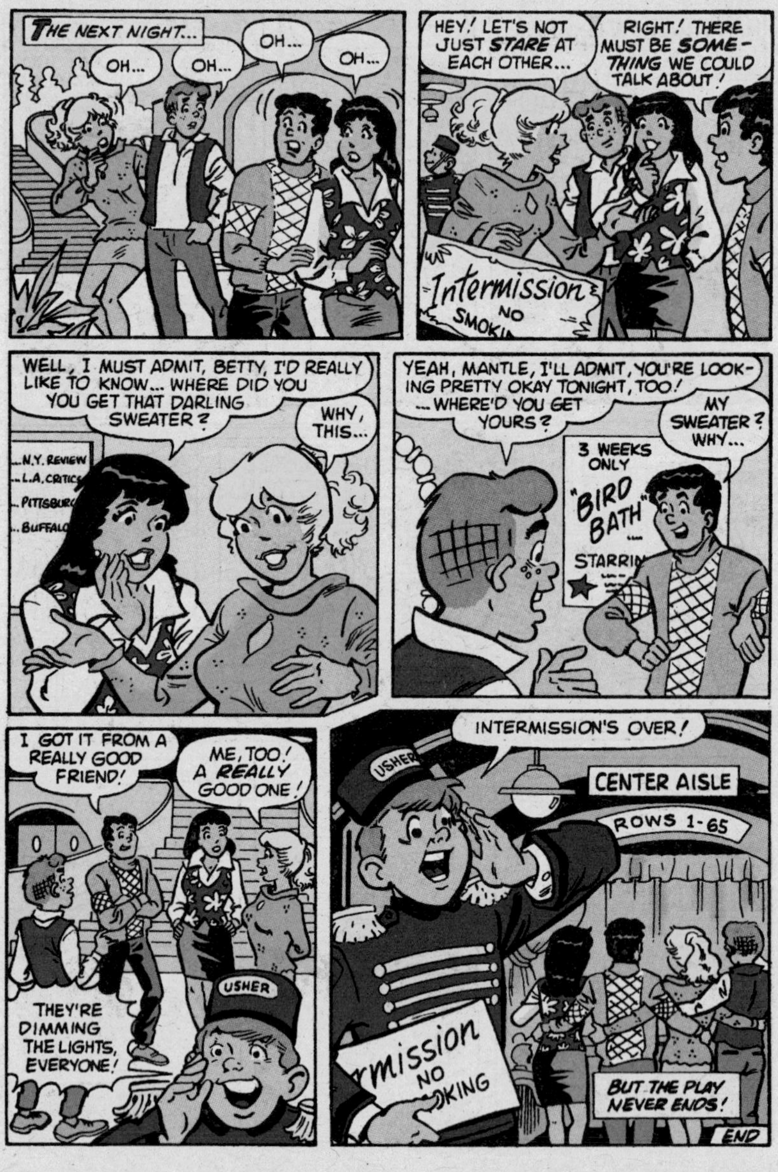
THE NEXT NIGHT...
OH...
OH...
OH...
OH...
HEY! LET'S NOT JUST STARE AT EACH OTHER...
RIGHT! THERE MUST BE SOME-THING WE COULD TALK ABOUT!
Intermission NO SMOKI
WELL, I MUST ADMIT, BETTY, I'D REALLY LIKE TO KNOW... WHERE DID YOU YOU GET THAT DARLING SWEATER?
WHY, THIS...
...N.Y. REVIEW
...L.A. CRITIC
...PITTSBURG
...BUFFALO
YEAH, MANTLE, I'LL ADMIT, YOU'RE LOOK-ING PRETTY OKAY TONIGHT, TOO! ...WHERE'D YOU GET YOURS?
MY SWEATER? WHY...
3 WEEKS ONLY
"BIRD BATH"
STARRIN
I GOT IT FROM A REALLY GOOD FRIEND!
ME, TOO! A REALLY GOOD ONE!
USHER
THEY'RE DIMMING THE LIGHTS, EVERYONE!
INTERMISSION'S OVER!
USHER
CENTER AISLE
ROWS 1-65
rmission NO OKING
BUT THE PLAY NEVER ENDS!
END

Betty and Veronica in "YOU NEVER KNOW..."

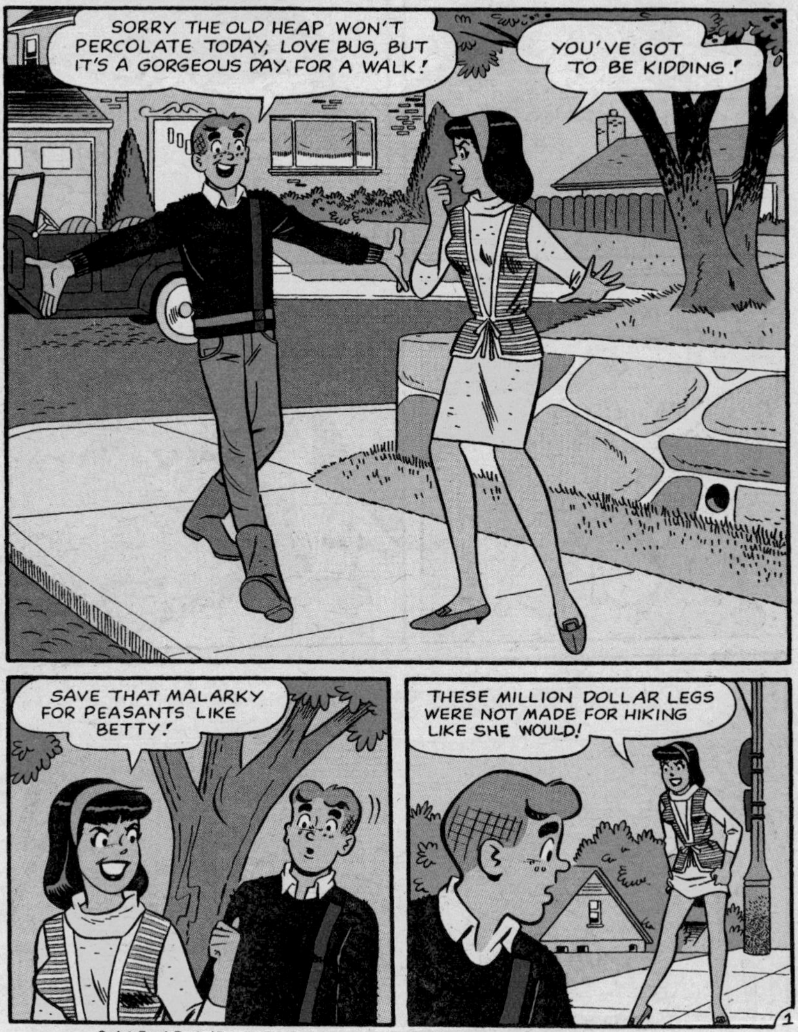
SORRY THE OLD HEAP WON'T PERCOLATE TODAY, LOVE BUG, BUT IT'S A GORGEOUS DAY FOR A WALK!
YOU'VE GOT TO BE KIDDING!
SAVE THAT MALARKY FOR PEASANTS LIKE BETTY!
THESE MILLION DOLLAR LEGS WERE NOT MADE FOR HIKING LIKE SHE WOULD!
1

Script: Frank Doyle / Pencils: Dan DeCarlo / Inks & Letters: Vince DeCarlo / Colors: Barry Grossman

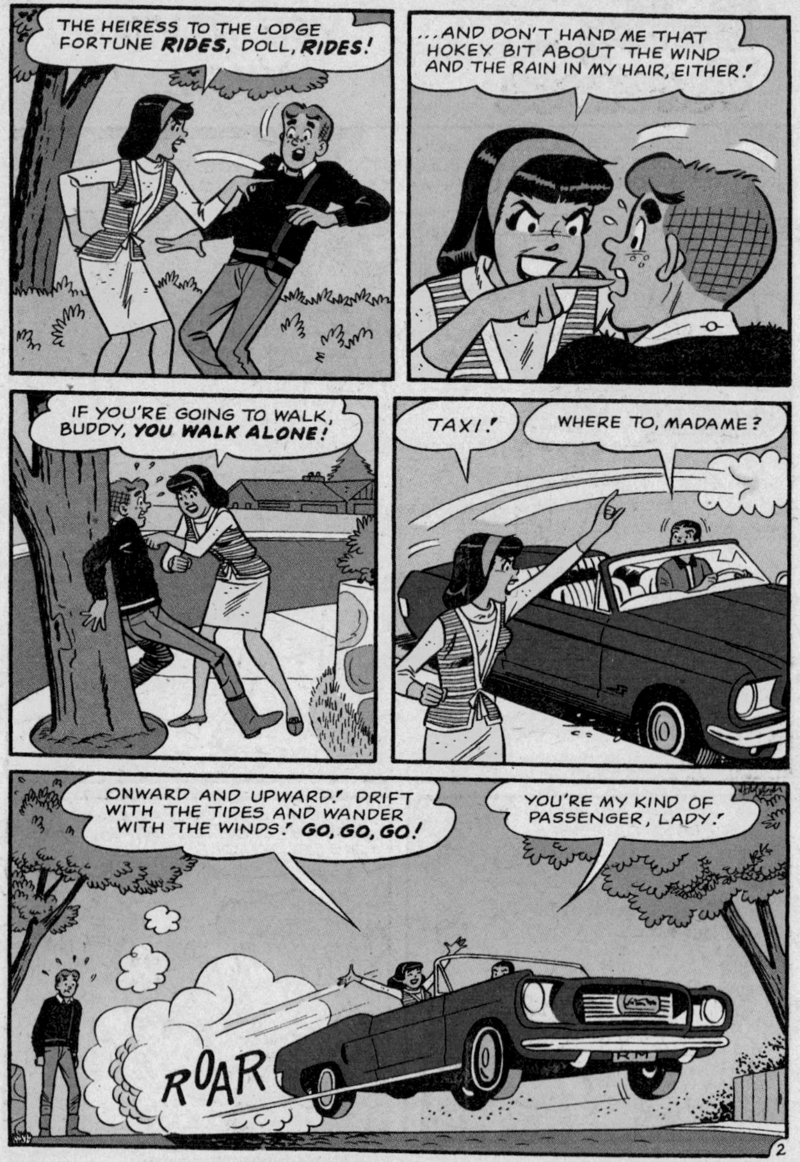
THE HEIRESS TO THE LODGE FORTUNE RIDES, DOLL, RIDES!
...AND DON'T HAND ME THAT HOKEY BIT ABOUT THE WIND AND THE RAIN IN MY HAIR, EITHER!
IF YOU'RE GOING TO WALK, BUDDY, YOU WALK ALONE!
TAXI!
WHERE TO, MADAME?
ONWARD AND UPWARD! DRIFT WITH THE TIDES AND WANDER WITH THE WINDS! GO, GO, GO!
YOU'RE MY KIND OF PASSENGER, LADY!
ROAR

BEAUTIFULLY DONE, AMIGO! JUST BEAUTIFUL!

IT WAS POSITIVELY ARTISTIC THE WAY YOU RID YOURSELF OF THAT PESKY FEMALE!

SMACK

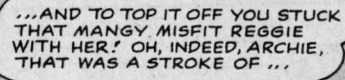

...AND TO TOP IT OFF YOU STUCK THAT MANGY, MISFIT REGGIE WITH HER! OH, INDEED, ARCHIE, THAT WAS A STROKE OF ...

SLAP!

WHY DON'T YOU SHUT UP?

(SIGH)—I WAS AFRAID OF THAT!

YOU NEVER SEE THE SILVER LINING ON THE DARK CLOUD OF DESPAIR!

3

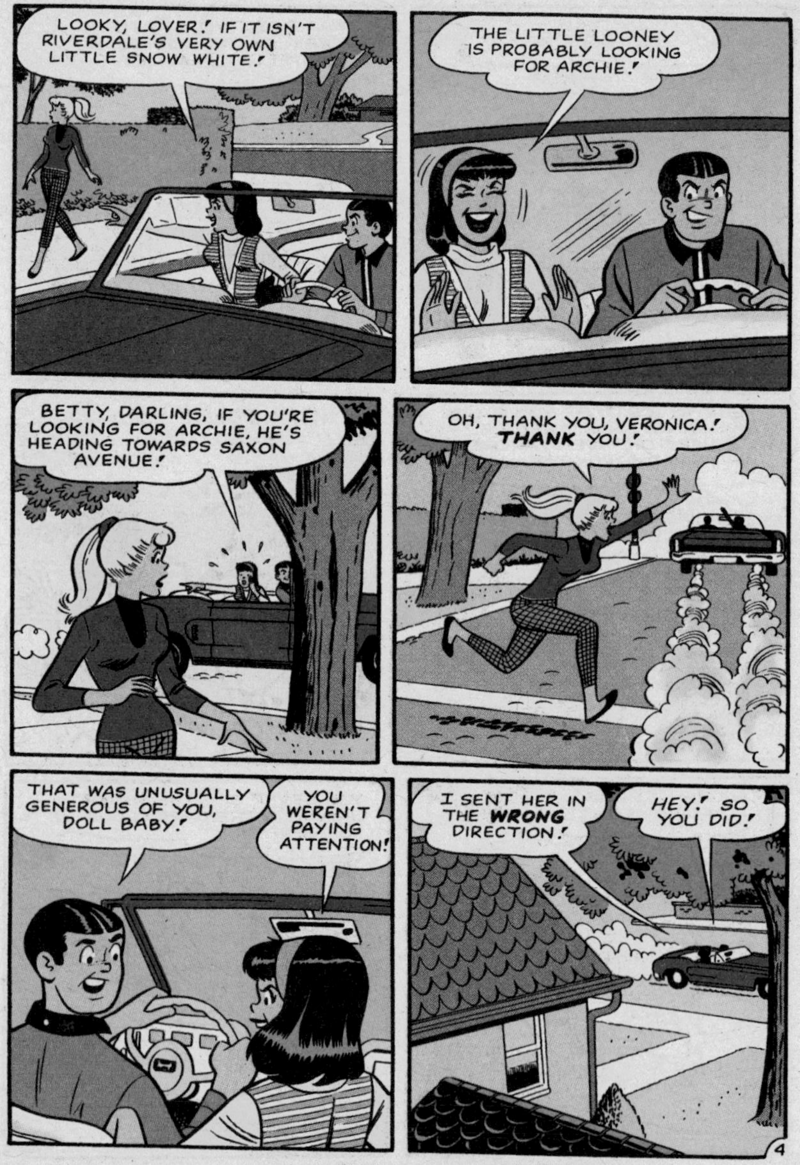
LOOKY, LOVER! IF IT ISN'T RIVERDALE'S VERY OWN LITTLE SNOW WHITE!
THE LITTLE LOONEY IS PROBABLY LOOKING FOR ARCHIE!
BETTY, DARLING, IF YOU'RE LOOKING FOR ARCHIE, HE'S HEADING TOWARDS SAXON AVENUE!
OH, THANK YOU, VERONICA! **THANK** YOU!
THAT WAS UNUSUALLY GENEROUS OF YOU, DOLL BABY!
YOU WEREN'T PAYING ATTENTION!
I SENT HER IN THE **WRONG** DIRECTION!
HEY! SO YOU DID!

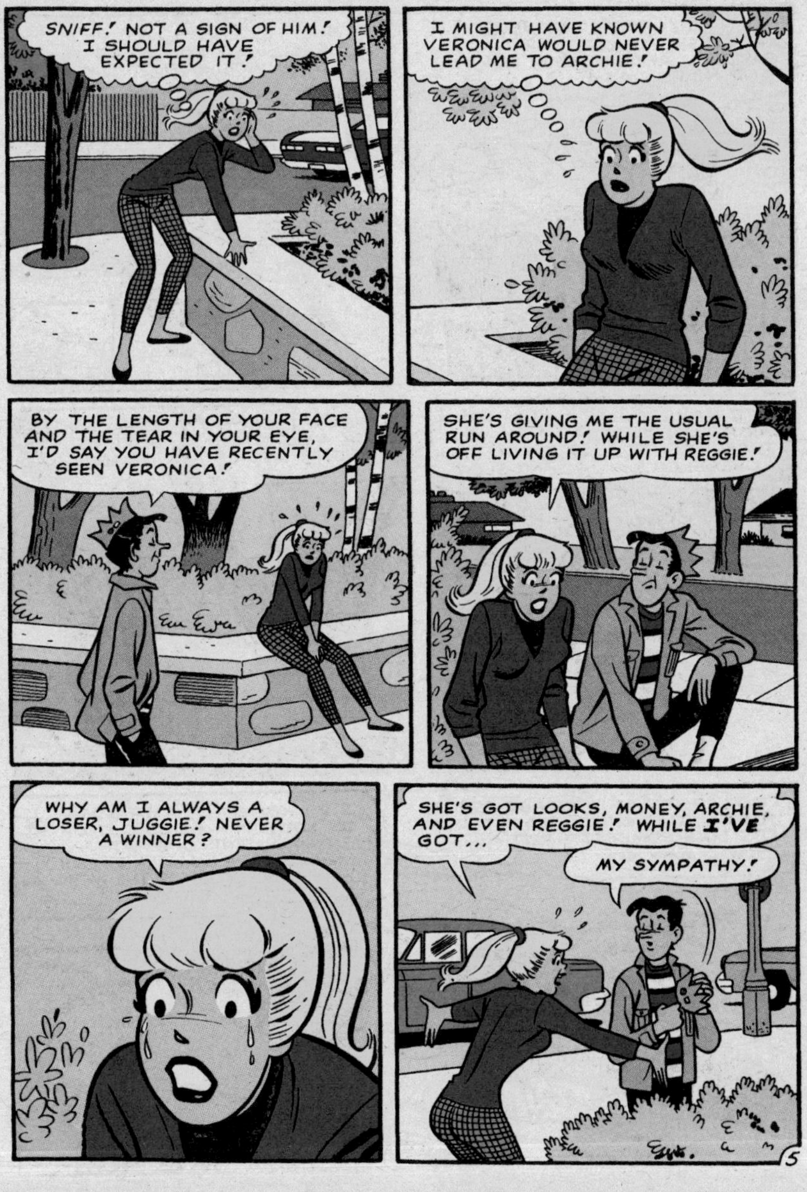
SNIFF! NOT A SIGN OF HIM! I SHOULD HAVE EXPECTED IT!
I MIGHT HAVE KNOWN VERONICA WOULD NEVER LEAD ME TO ARCHIE!
BY THE LENGTH OF YOUR FACE AND THE TEAR IN YOUR EYE, I'D SAY YOU HAVE RECENTLY SEEN VERONICA!
SHE'S GIVING ME THE USUAL RUN AROUND! WHILE SHE'S OFF LIVING IT UP WITH REGGIE!
WHY AM I ALWAYS A LOSER, JUGGIE! NEVER A WINNER?
SHE'S GOT LOOKS, MONEY, ARCHIE, AND EVEN REGGIE! WHILE **I'VE** GOT...
MY SYMPATHY!

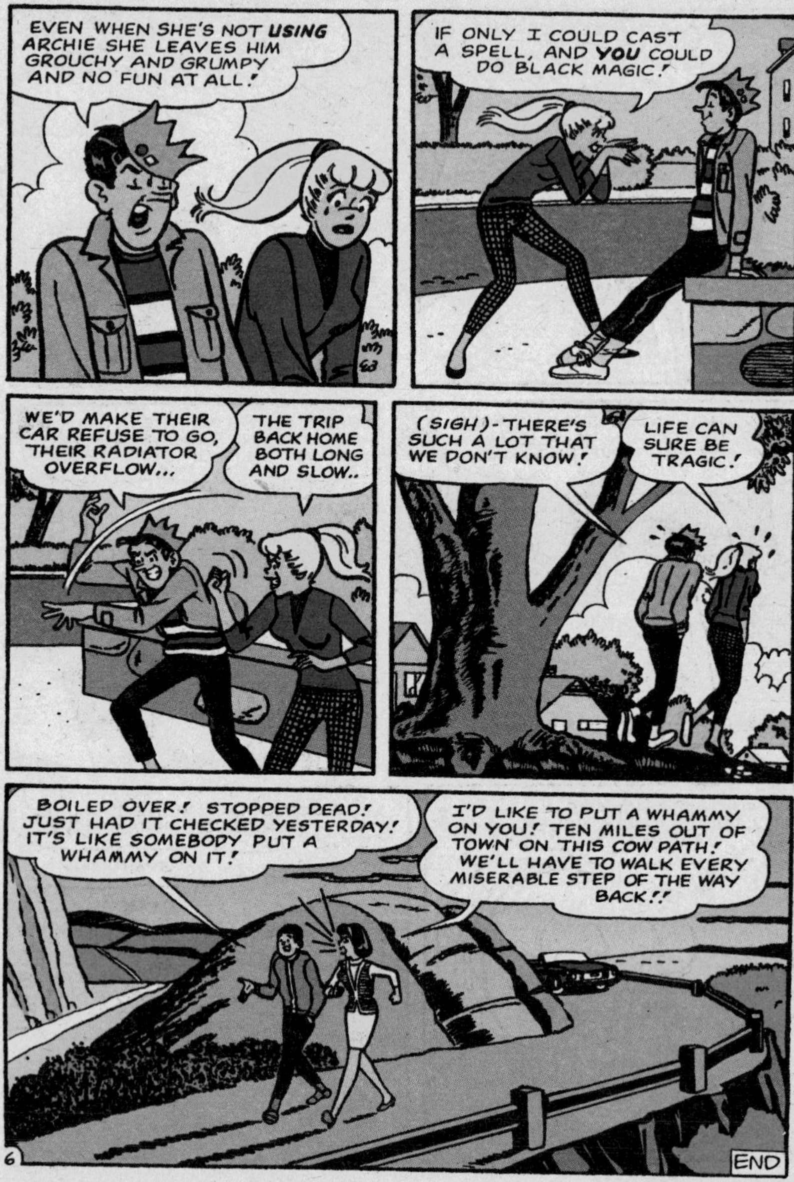
EVEN WHEN SHE'S NOT **USING** ARCHIE SHE LEAVES HIM GROUCHY AND GRUMPY AND NO FUN AT ALL!
IF ONLY I COULD CAST A SPELL, AND **YOU** COULD DO BLACK MAGIC!
WE'D MAKE THEIR CAR REFUSE TO GO, THEIR RADIATOR OVERFLOW...
THE TRIP BACK HOME BOTH LONG AND SLOW..
(SIGH)-THERE'S SUCH A LOT THAT WE DON'T KNOW!
LIFE CAN SURE BE TRAGIC!
BOILED OVER! STOPPED DEAD! JUST HAD IT CHECKED YESTERDAY! IT'S LIKE SOMEBODY PUT A WHAMMY ON IT!
I'D LIKE TO PUT A WHAMMY ON YOU! TEN MILES OUT OF TOWN ON THIS COW PATH! WE'LL HAVE TO WALK EVERY MISERABLE STEP OF THE WAY BACK!!
END

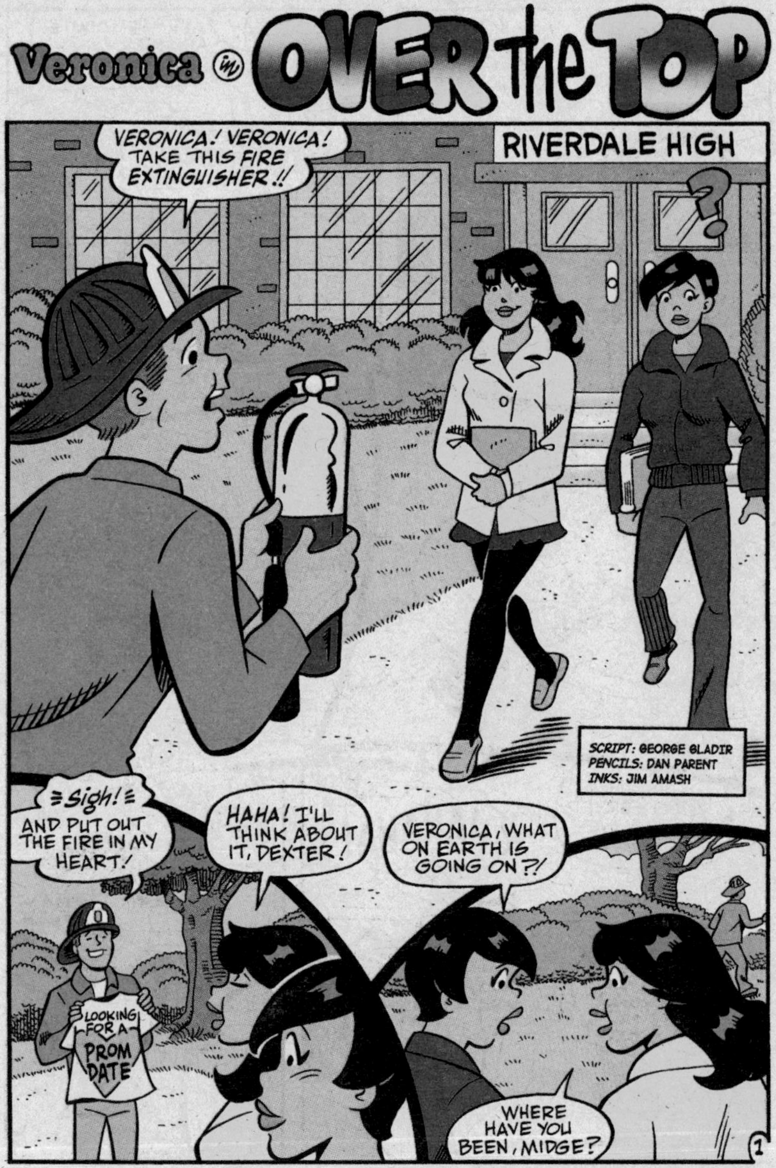

Veronica in OVER the TOP
VERONICA! VERONICA! TAKE THIS FIRE EXTINGUISHER!!
RIVERDALE HIGH
?
SCRIPT: GEORGE GLADIR
PENCILS: DAN PARENT
INKS: JIM AMASH
Sigh! AND PUT OUT THE FIRE IN MY HEART!
HAHA! I'LL THINK ABOUT IT, DEXTER!
VERONICA, WHAT ON EARTH IS GOING ON?!
LOOKING FOR A PROM DATE
WHERE HAVE YOU BEEN, MIDGE?
1

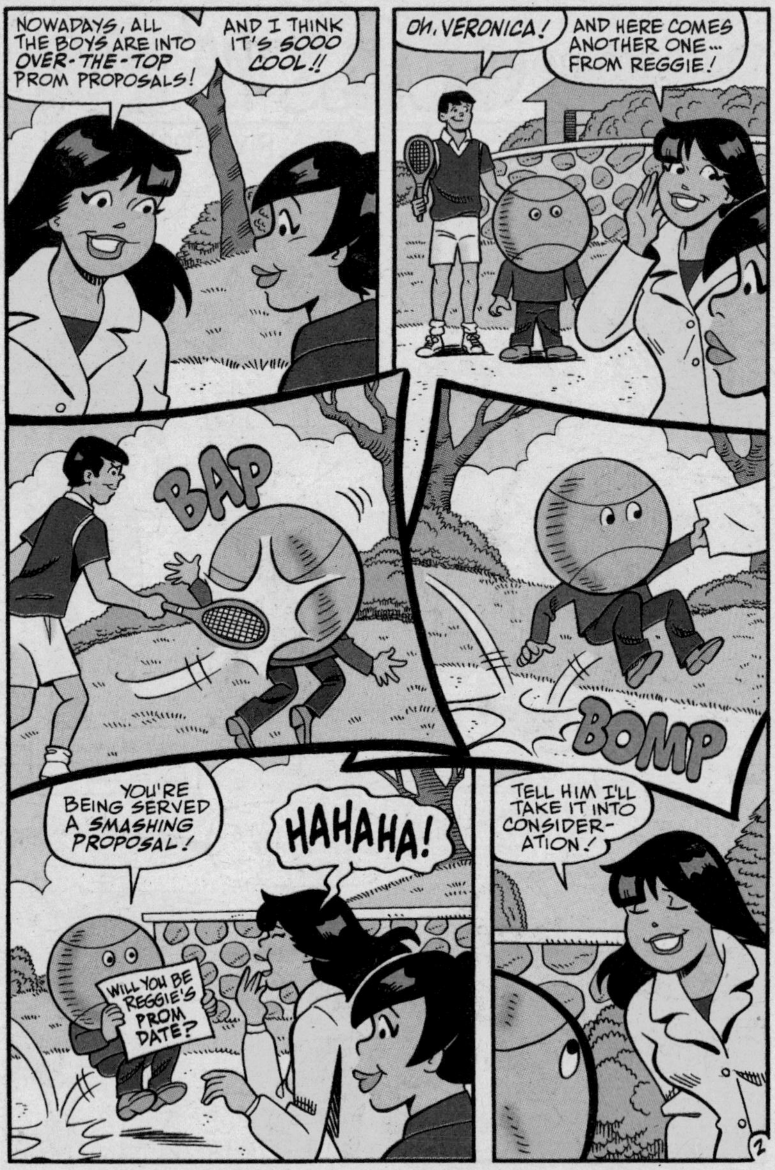
NOWADAYS, ALL THE BOYS ARE INTO OVER-THE-TOP PROM PROPOSALS!
AND I THINK IT'S SOOO COOL!!
Oh, VERONICA!
AND HERE COMES ANOTHER ONE... FROM REGGIE!
BAP
BOMP
YOU'RE BEING SERVED A SMASHING PROPOSAL!
HAHAHA!
WILL YOU BE REGGIE'S PROM DATE?
TELL HIM I'LL TAKE IT INTO CONSIDER-ATION!
2

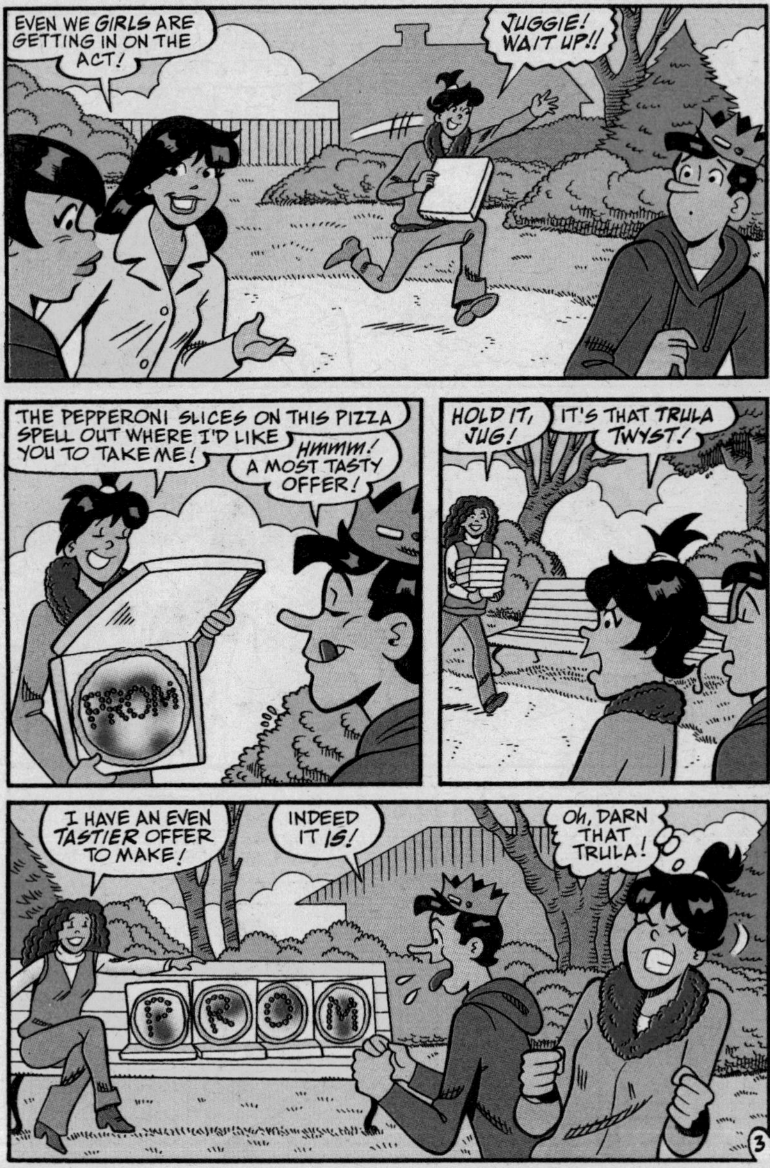
EVEN WE GIRLS ARE GETTING IN ON THE ACT!
JUGGIE! WAIT UP!!
THE PEPPERONI SLICES ON THIS PIZZA SPELL OUT WHERE I'D LIKE YOU TO TAKE ME!
HMMM! A MOST TASTY OFFER!
PROM
HOLD IT, JUG!
IT'S THAT TRULA TWYST!
I HAVE AN EVEN TASTIER OFFER TO MAKE!
INDEED IT IS!
OH, DARN THAT TRULA!
PROM

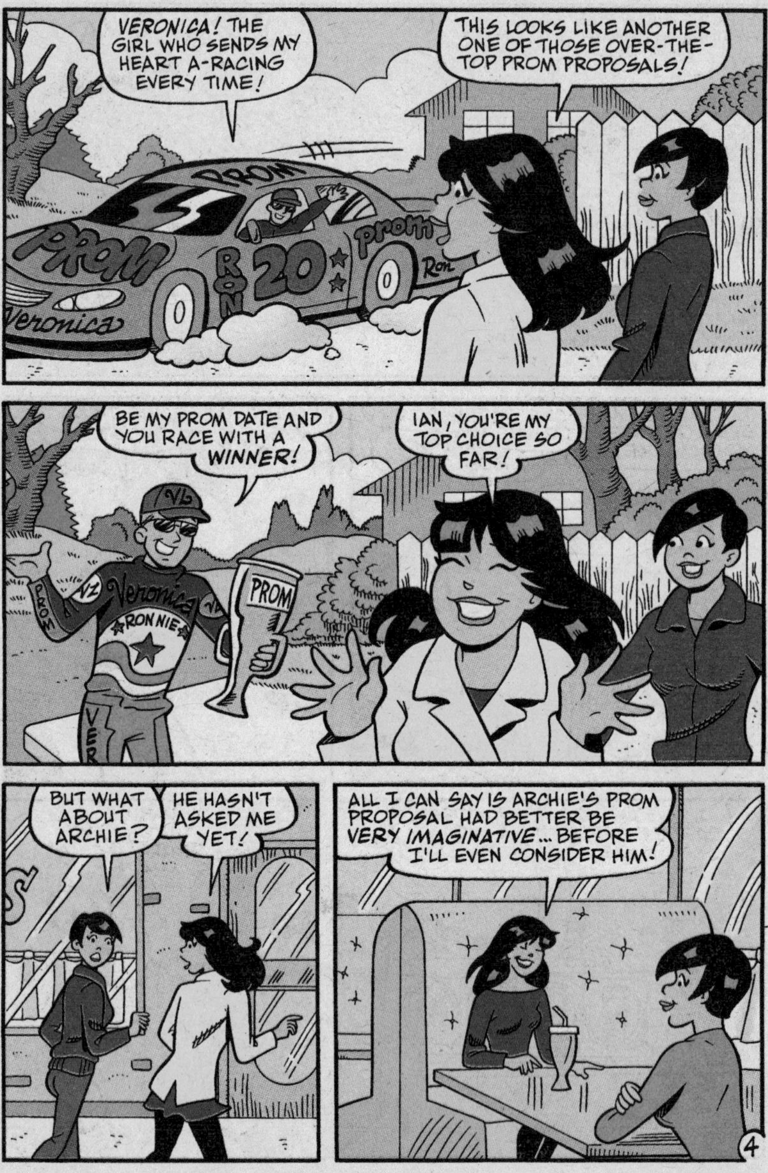
VERONICA! THE GIRL WHO SENDS MY HEART A-RACING EVERY TIME!
THIS LOOKS LIKE ANOTHER ONE OF THOSE OVER-THE-TOP PROM PROPOSALS!
PROM
PROM
prom
RON
20
Ron
Veronica
BE MY PROM DATE AND YOU RACE WITH A WINNER!
IAN, YOU'RE MY TOP CHOICE SO FAR!
PROM
Veronica
RONNIE
PROM
BUT WHAT ABOUT ARCHIE?
HE HASN'T ASKED ME YET!
ALL I CAN SAY IS ARCHIE'S PROM PROPOSAL HAD BETTER BE VERY IMAGINATIVE... BEFORE I'LL EVEN CONSIDER HIM!

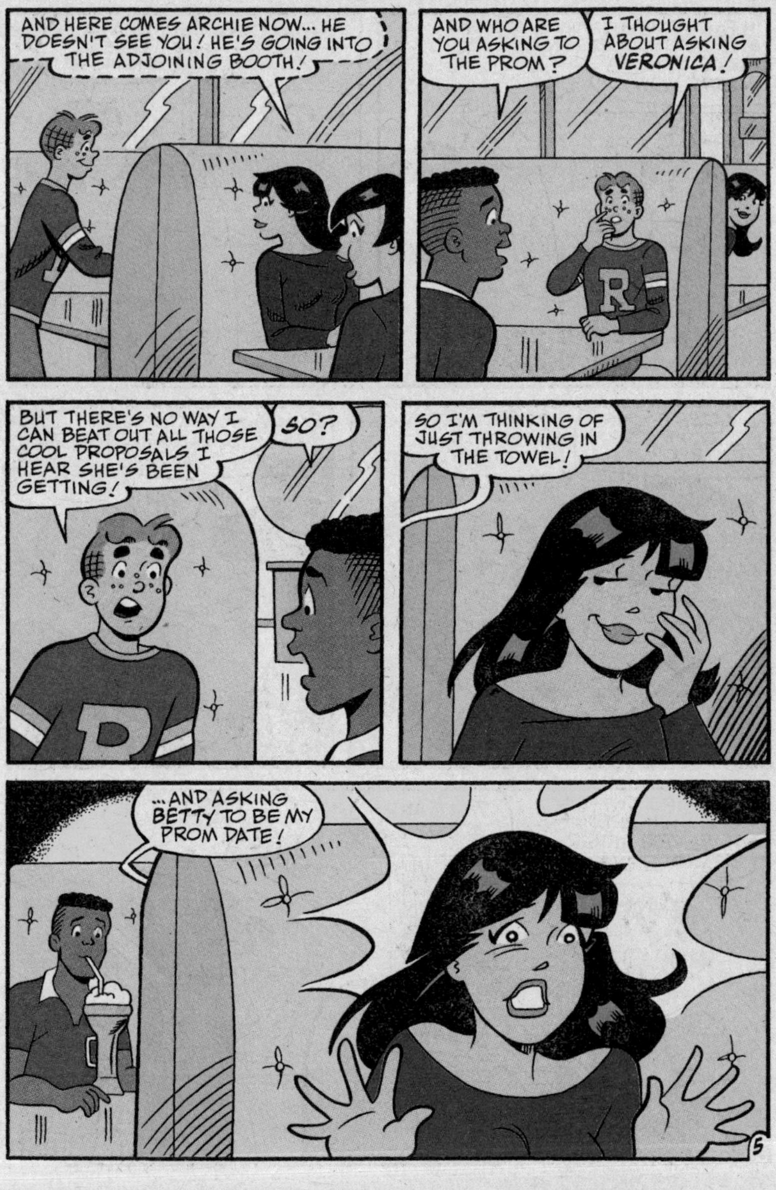
AND HERE COMES ARCHIE NOW... HE DOESN'T SEE YOU! HE'S GOING INTO THE ADJOINING BOOTH!
AND WHO ARE YOU ASKING TO THE PROM?
I THOUGHT ABOUT ASKING VERONICA!
BUT THERE'S NO WAY I CAN BEAT OUT ALL THOSE COOL PROPOSALS I HEAR SHE'S BEEN GETTING!
SO?
SO I'M THINKING OF JUST THROWING IN THE TOWEL!
...AND ASKING BETTY TO BE MY PROM DATE!
5

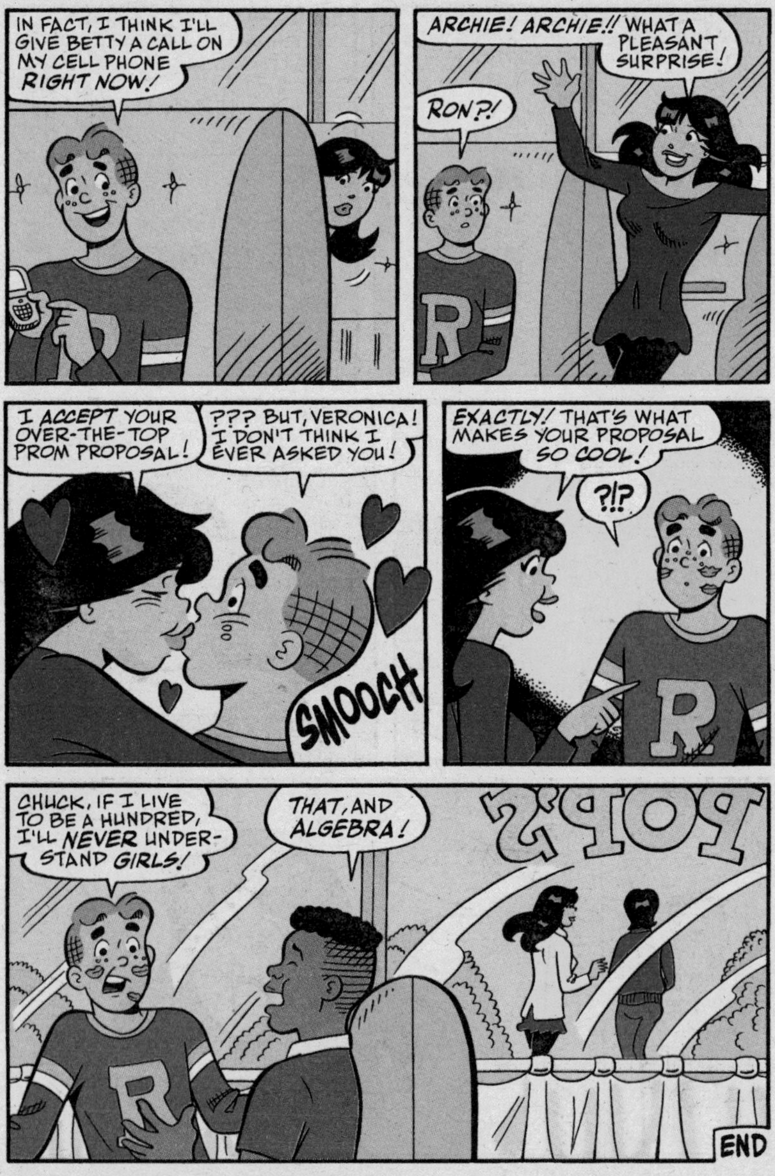
IN FACT, I THINK I'LL GIVE BETTY A CALL ON MY CELL PHONE RIGHT NOW!
ARCHIE! ARCHIE!! WHAT A PLEASANT SURPRISE!
RON?!
I ACCEPT YOUR OVER-THE-TOP PROM PROPOSAL!
??? BUT, VERONICA! I DON'T THINK I EVER ASKED YOU!
SMOOCH
EXACTLY! THAT'S WHAT MAKES YOUR PROPOSAL SO COOL!
?!?
POP'S
CHUCK, IF I LIVE TO BE A HUNDRED, I'LL NEVER UNDER-STAND GIRLS!
THAT, AND ALGEBRA!
END

Betty and Veronica PIN UP

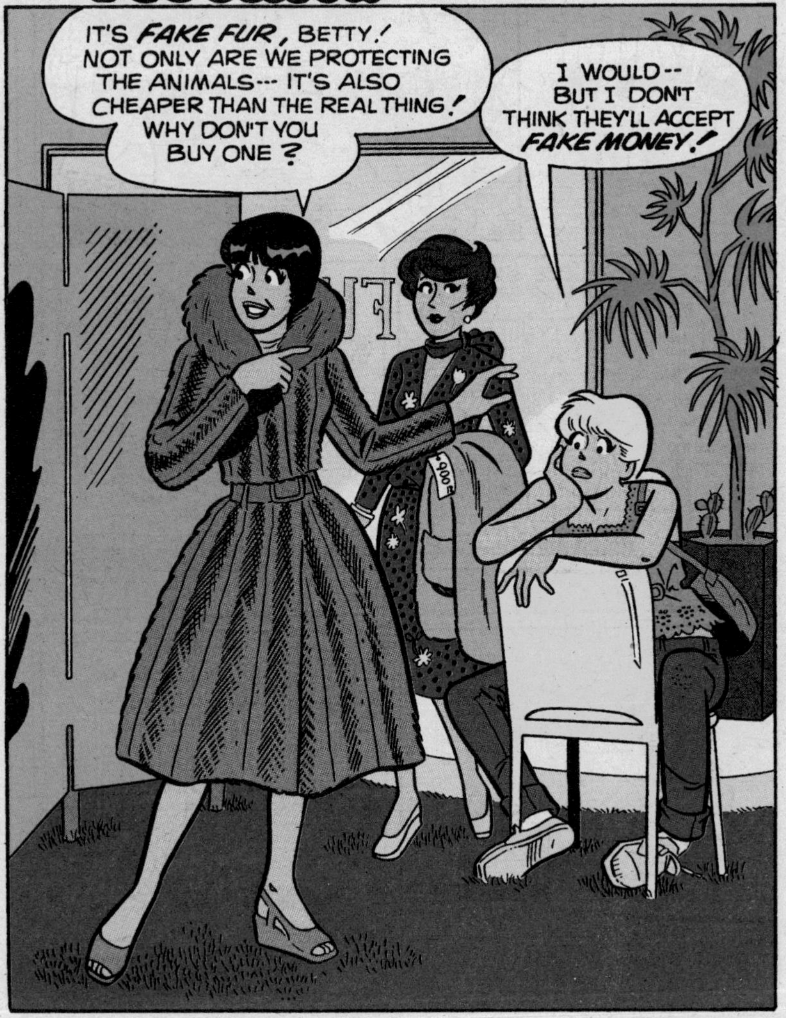
IT'S *FAKE FUR*, BETTY! NOT ONLY ARE WE PROTECTING THE ANIMALS--- IT'S ALSO CHEAPER THAN THE REAL THING! WHY DON'T YOU BUY ONE ?
I WOULD-- BUT I DON'T THINK THEY'LL ACCEPT *FAKE MONEY*!

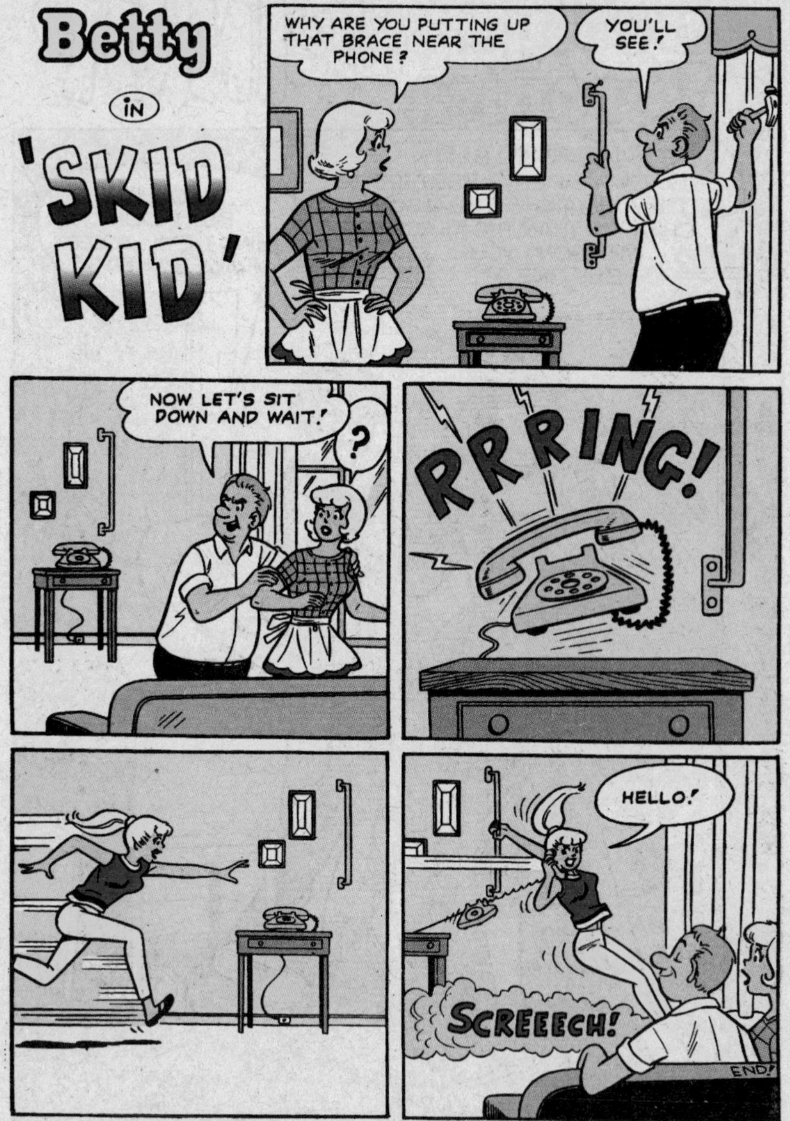
Betty
in
'SKID KID'
WHY ARE YOU PUTTING UP THAT BRACE NEAR THE PHONE?
YOU'LL SEE!
NOW LET'S SIT DOWN AND WAIT!
?
RRRING!
HELLO!
SCREEECH!
END!

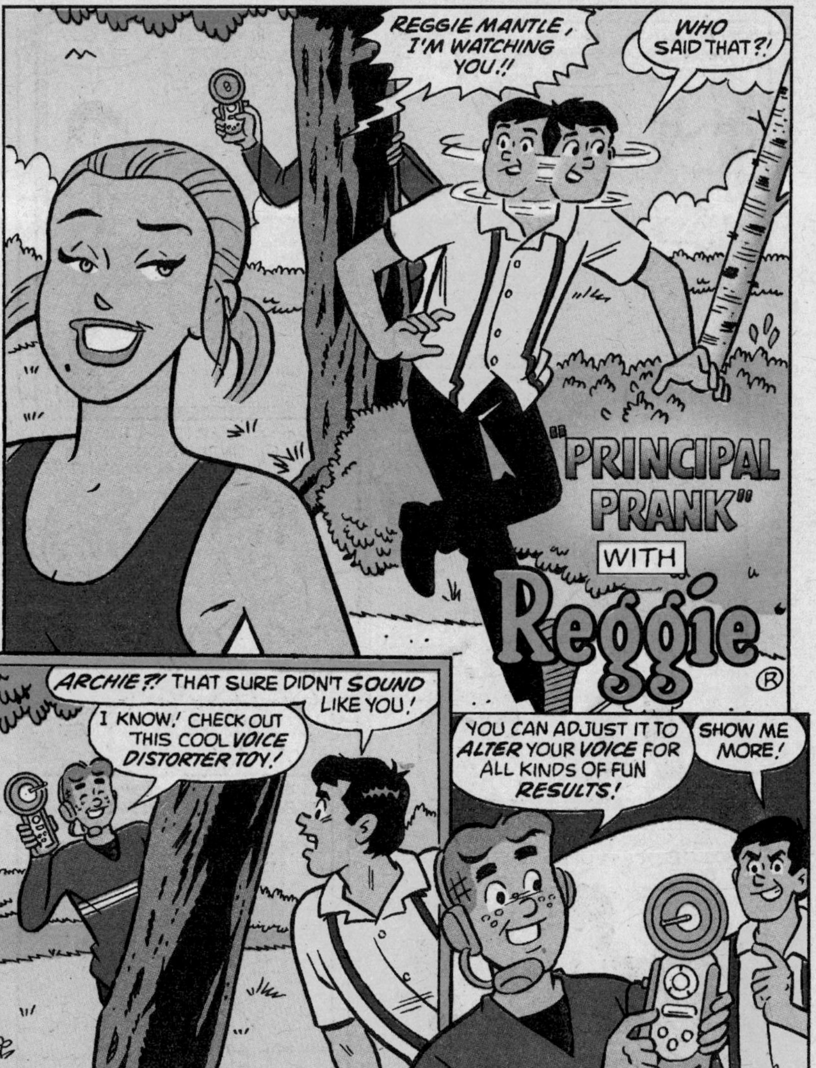
REGGIE MANTLE, I'M WATCHING YOU!!
WHO SAID THAT?!
"PRINCIPAL PRANK" WITH Reggie ®
ARCHIE?! THAT SURE DIDN'T SOUND LIKE YOU!
I KNOW! CHECK OUT THIS COOL VOICE DISTORTER TOY!
YOU CAN ADJUST IT TO ALTER YOUR VOICE FOR ALL KINDS OF FUN RESULTS!
SHOW ME MORE!

Script: **Bill Golliher** Pencils: **Fernando Ruiz** Inks: **Rudy Lapick**
Letters: **Bill Yoshida** Colors: **Barry Grossman**
Editor-In-Chief: **Victor Gorelick** President: **Mike Pellerito** Publisher: **Jon Goldwater**

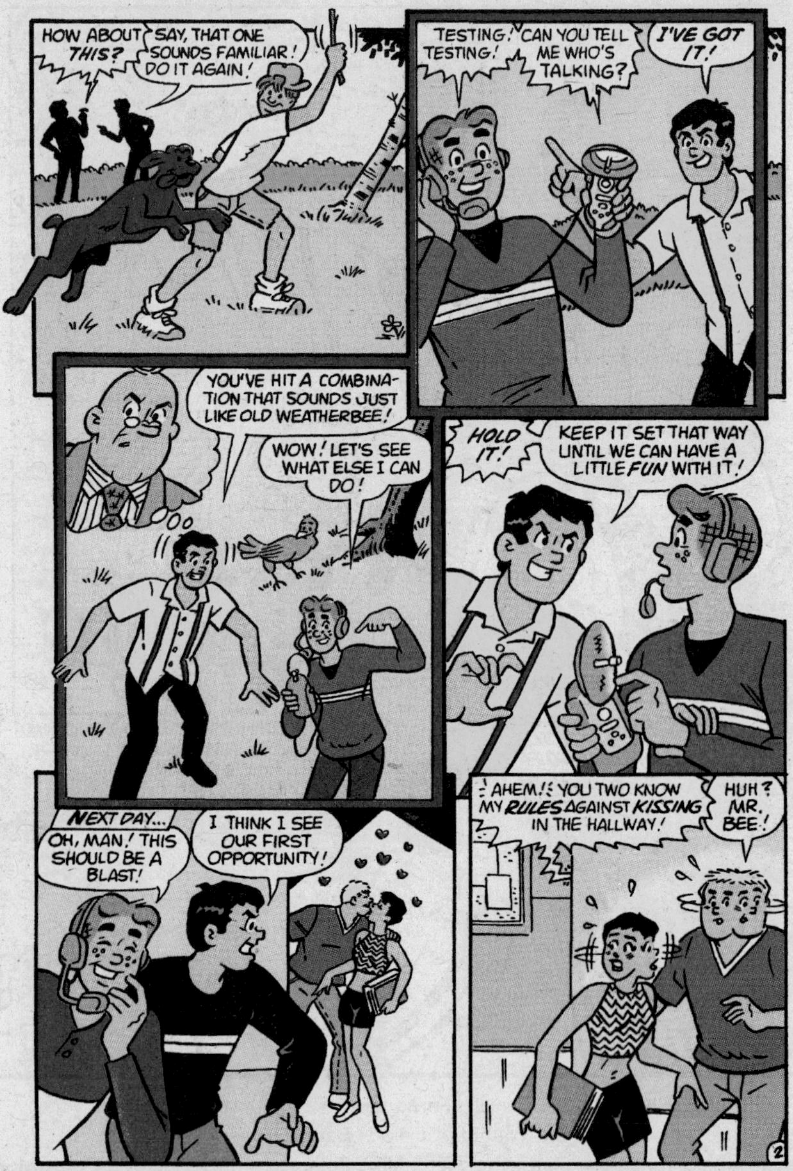
HOW ABOUT *THIS?*
SAY, THAT ONE SOUNDS FAMILIAR! DO IT AGAIN!
TESTING! TESTING!
CAN YOU TELL ME WHO'S TALKING?
I'VE GOT IT!
YOU'VE HIT A COMBINATION THAT SOUNDS JUST LIKE OLD WEATHERBEE!
WOW! LET'S SEE WHAT ELSE I CAN DO!
HOLD IT!
KEEP IT SET THAT WAY UNTIL WE CAN HAVE A LITTLE *FUN* WITH IT!
NEXT DAY...
OH, MAN! THIS SHOULD BE A BLAST!
I THINK I SEE OUR FIRST OPPORTUNITY!
AHEM! YOU TWO KNOW MY *RULES* AGAINST *KISSING* IN THE HALLWAY!
HUH? MR. BEE!
2

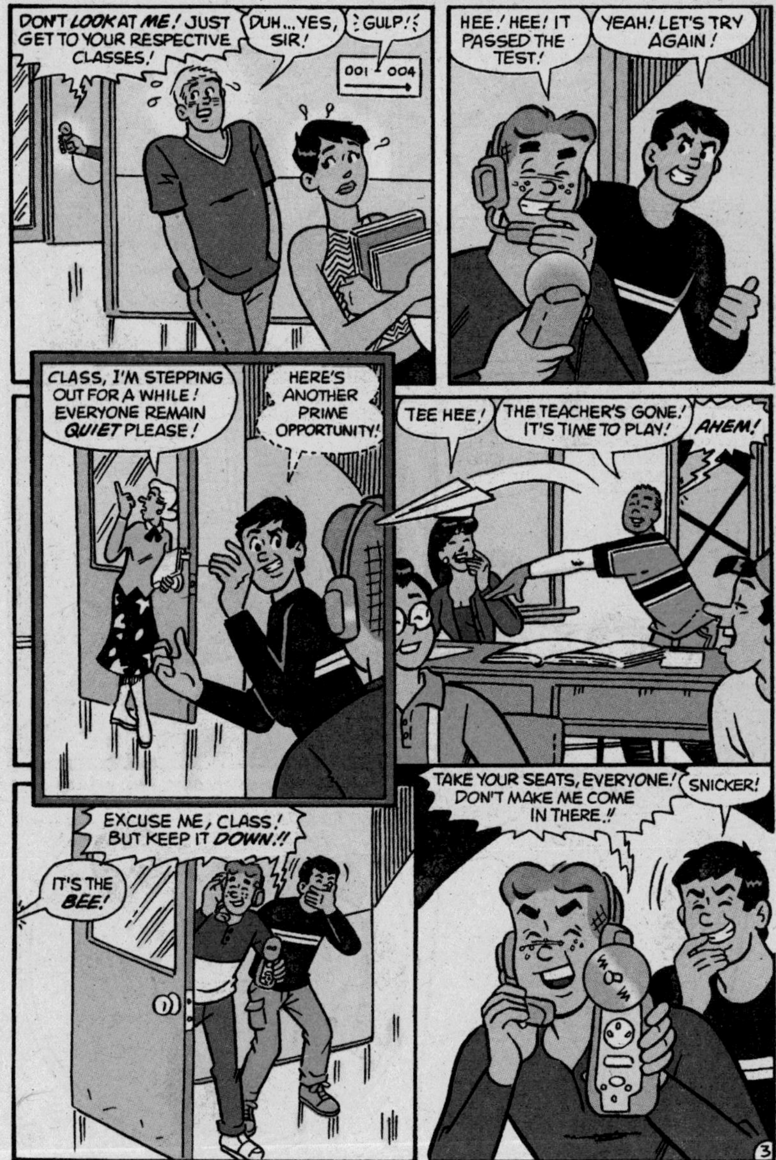
DON'T LOOK AT ME! JUST GET TO YOUR RESPECTIVE CLASSES!
DUH... YES, SIR!
GULP!
001 004
HEE! HEE! IT PASSED THE TEST!
YEAH! LET'S TRY AGAIN!
CLASS, I'M STEPPING OUT FOR A WHILE! EVERYONE REMAIN QUIET PLEASE!
HERE'S ANOTHER PRIME OPPORTUNITY!
TEE HEE!
THE TEACHER'S GONE! IT'S TIME TO PLAY!
AHEM!
EXCUSE ME, CLASS! BUT KEEP IT DOWN!!
IT'S THE BEE!
TAKE YOUR SEATS, EVERYONE! DON'T MAKE ME COME IN THERE!!
SNICKER!
3

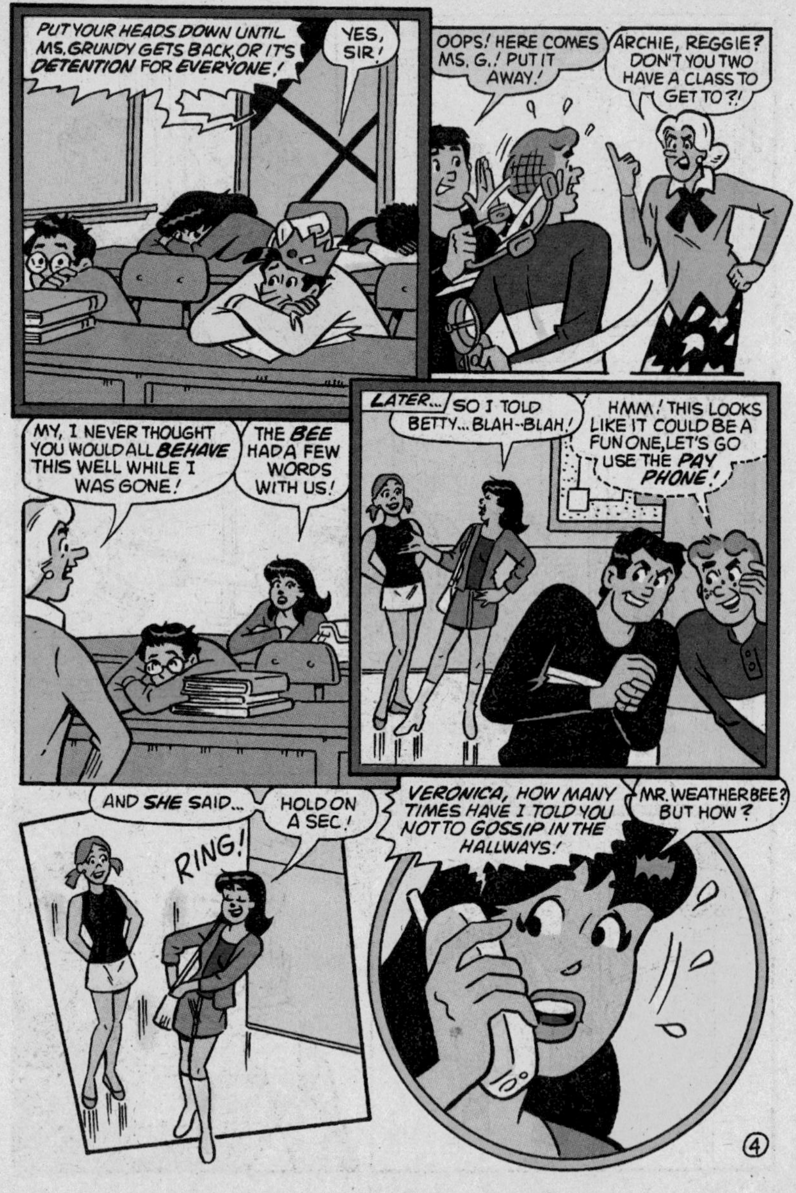

PUT YOUR HEADS DOWN UNTIL MS. GRUNDY GETS BACK, OR IT'S DETENTION FOR EVERYONE!
YES, SIR!
OOPS! HERE COMES MS. G.! PUT IT AWAY!
ARCHIE, REGGIE? DON'T YOU TWO HAVE A CLASS TO GET TO?!
MY, I NEVER THOUGHT YOU WOULD ALL BEHAVE THIS WELL WHILE I WAS GONE!
THE BEE HAD A FEW WORDS WITH US!
LATER...
SO I TOLD BETTY... BLAH--BLAH!
HMM! THIS LOOKS LIKE IT COULD BE A FUN ONE, LET'S GO USE THE PAY PHONE!
AND SHE SAID...
HOLD ON A SEC!
RING!
VERONICA, HOW MANY TIMES HAVE I TOLD YOU NOT TO GOSSIP IN THE HALLWAYS!
MR. WEATHERBEE? BUT HOW?

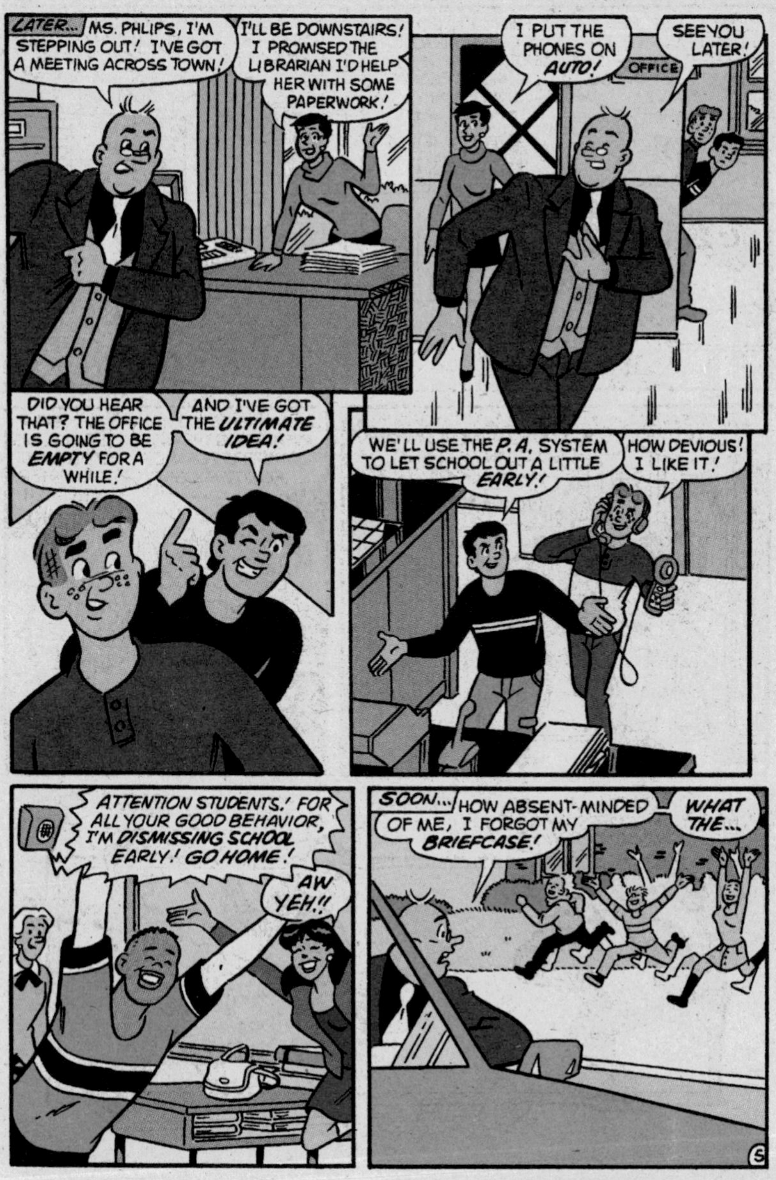
LATER...
MS. PHLIPS, I'M STEPPING OUT! I'VE GOT A MEETING ACROSS TOWN!
I'LL BE DOWNSTAIRS! I PROMISED THE LIBRARIAN I'D HELP HER WITH SOME PAPERWORK!
I PUT THE PHONES ON AUTO!
SEE YOU LATER!
OFFICE
DID YOU HEAR THAT? THE OFFICE IS GOING TO BE EMPTY FOR A WHILE!
AND I'VE GOT THE ULTIMATE IDEA!
WE'LL USE THE P.A. SYSTEM TO LET SCHOOL OUT A LITTLE EARLY!
HOW DEVIOUS! I LIKE IT!
ATTENTION STUDENTS! FOR ALL YOUR GOOD BEHAVIOR, I'M DISMISSING SCHOOL EARLY! GO HOME!
AW YEH!!
SOON...
HOW ABSENT-MINDED OF ME, I FORGOT MY BRIEFCASE!
WHAT THE...
5

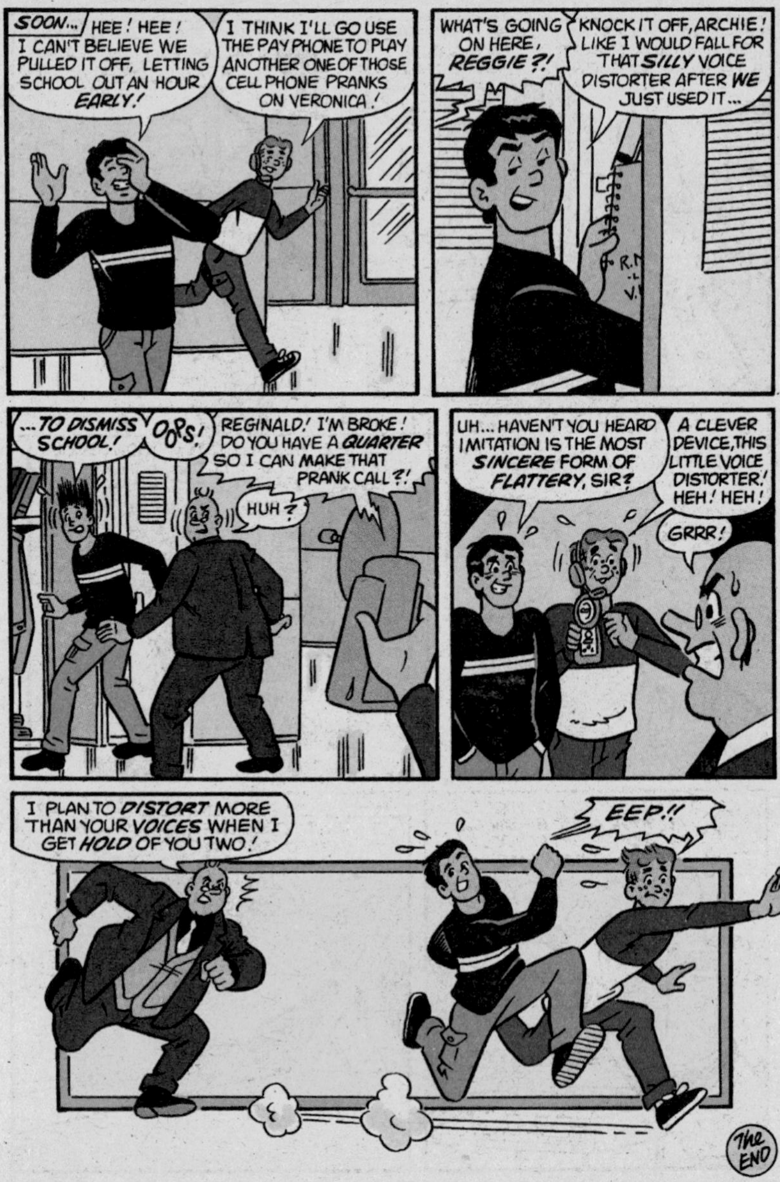
SOON...
HEE! HEE! I CAN'T BELIEVE WE PULLED IT OFF, LETTING SCHOOL OUT AN HOUR EARLY!
I THINK I'LL GO USE THE PAY PHONE TO PLAY ANOTHER ONE OF THOSE CELL PHONE PRANKS ON VERONICA!
WHAT'S GOING ON HERE, REGGIE?!
KNOCK IT OFF, ARCHIE! LIKE I WOULD FALL FOR THAT SILLY VOICE DISTORTER AFTER WE JUST USED IT...
...TO DISMISS SCHOOL!
OOPS!
REGINALD! I'M BROKE! DO YOU HAVE A QUARTER SO I CAN MAKE THAT PRANK CALL?!
HUH?
UH... HAVEN'T YOU HEARD IMITATION IS THE MOST SINCERE FORM OF FLATTERY, SIR?
A CLEVER DEVICE, THIS LITTLE VOICE DISTORTER! HEH! HEH!
GRRR!
I PLAN TO DISTORT MORE THAN YOUR VOICES WHEN I GET HOLD OF YOU TWO!
EEP!!
The END

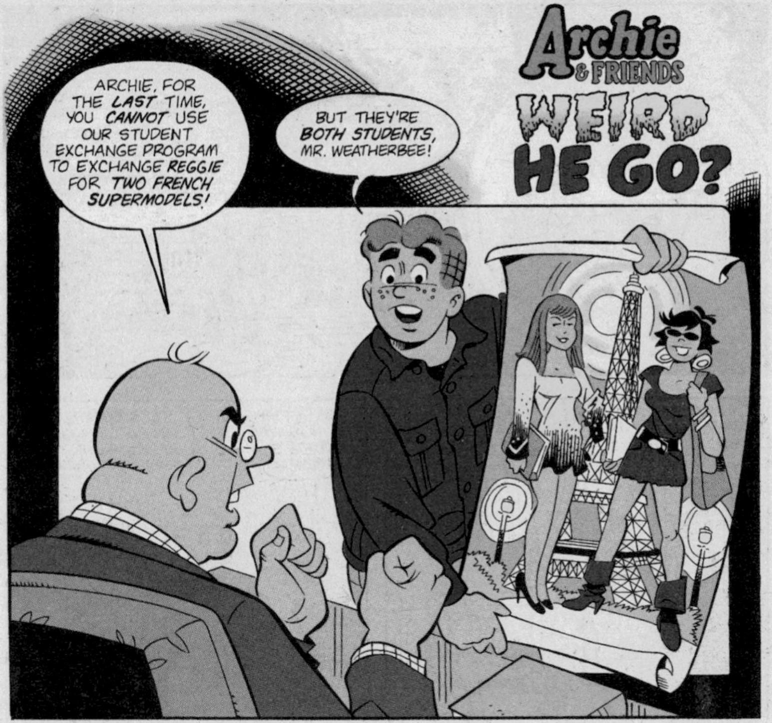
Archie & FRIENDS
WEIRD HE GO?
ARCHIE, FOR THE LAST TIME, YOU CANNOT USE OUR STUDENT EXCHANGE PROGRAM TO EXCHANGE REGGIE FOR TWO FRENCH SUPERMODELS!
BUT THEY'RE BOTH STUDENTS, MR. WEATHERBEE!

SCRIPT: ANGELO DECESARE PENCILS: STAN GOLDBERG INKING: JIM AMASH LETTERING: TERESA DAVIDSON COLORING: BARRY GROSSMAN

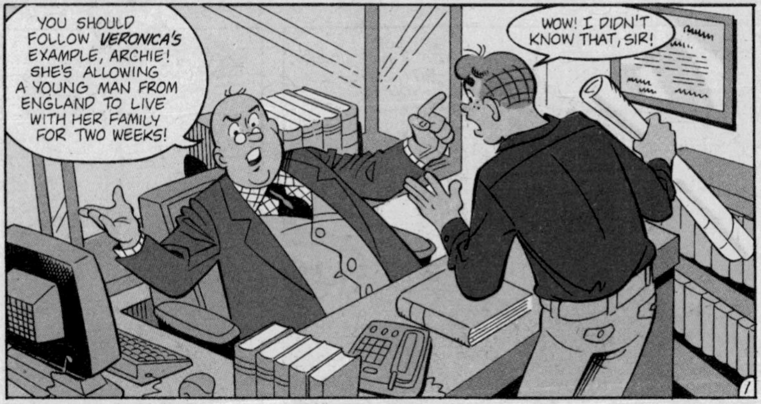
YOU SHOULD FOLLOW VERONICA'S EXAMPLE, ARCHIE! SHE'S ALLOWING A YOUNG MAN FROM ENGLAND TO LIVE WITH HER FAMILY FOR TWO WEEKS!
WOW! I DIDN'T KNOW THAT, SIR!

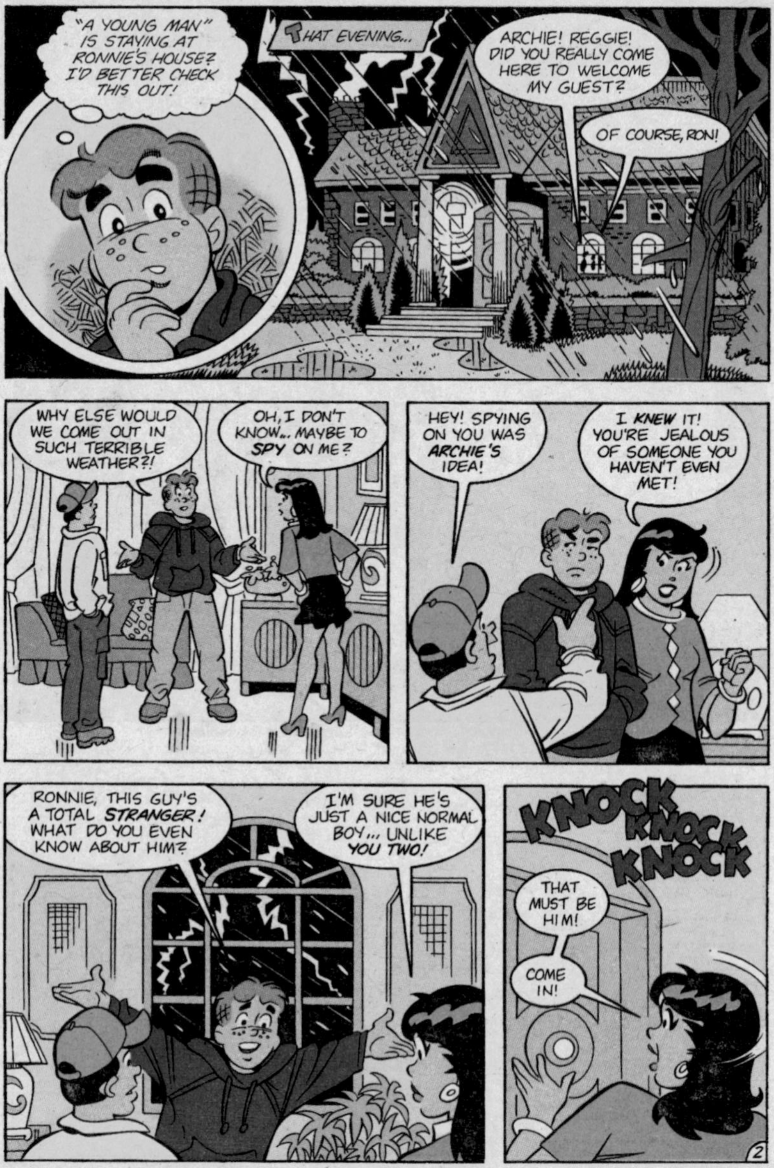
"A YOUNG MAN" IS STAYING AT RONNIE'S HOUSE? I'D BETTER CHECK THIS OUT!
THAT EVENING...
ARCHIE! REGGIE! DID YOU REALLY COME HERE TO WELCOME MY GUEST?
OF COURSE, RON!
WHY ELSE WOULD WE COME OUT IN SUCH TERRIBLE WEATHER?!
OH, I DON'T KNOW... MAYBE TO SPY ON ME?
HEY! SPYING ON YOU WAS ARCHIE'S IDEA!
I KNEW IT! YOU'RE JEALOUS OF SOMEONE YOU HAVEN'T EVEN MET!
RONNIE, THIS GUY'S A TOTAL STRANGER! WHAT DO YOU EVEN KNOW ABOUT HIM?
I'M SURE HE'S JUST A NICE NORMAL BOY... UNLIKE YOU TWO!
KNOCK KNOCK KNOCK
THAT MUST BE HIM!
COME IN!
2

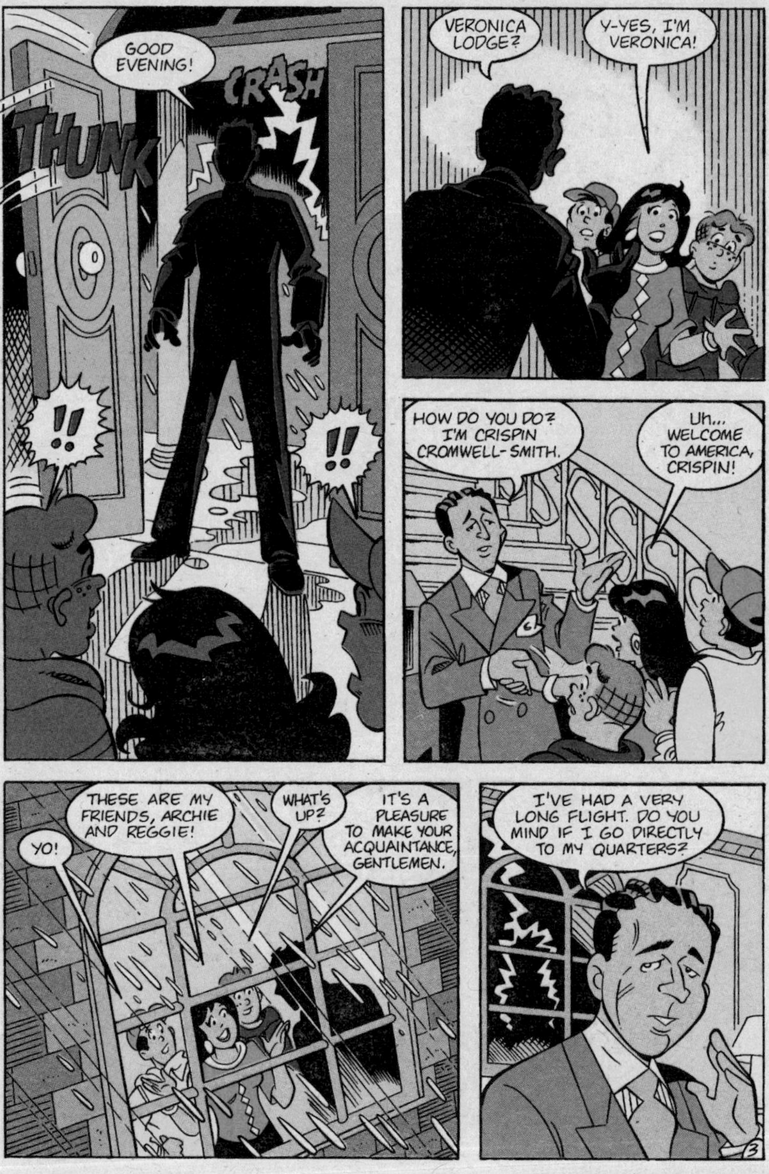
GOOD EVENING!
THUNK
CRASH
!!
!!
VERONICA LODGE?
Y-YES, I'M VERONICA!
HOW DO YOU DO? I'M CRISPIN CROMWELL-SMITH.
Uh... WELCOME TO AMERICA, CRISPIN!
YO!
THESE ARE MY FRIENDS, ARCHIE AND REGGIE!
WHAT'S UP?
IT'S A PLEASURE TO MAKE YOUR ACQUAINTANCE, GENTLEMEN.
I'VE HAD A VERY LONG FLIGHT. DO YOU MIND IF I GO DIRECTLY TO MY QUARTERS?
3

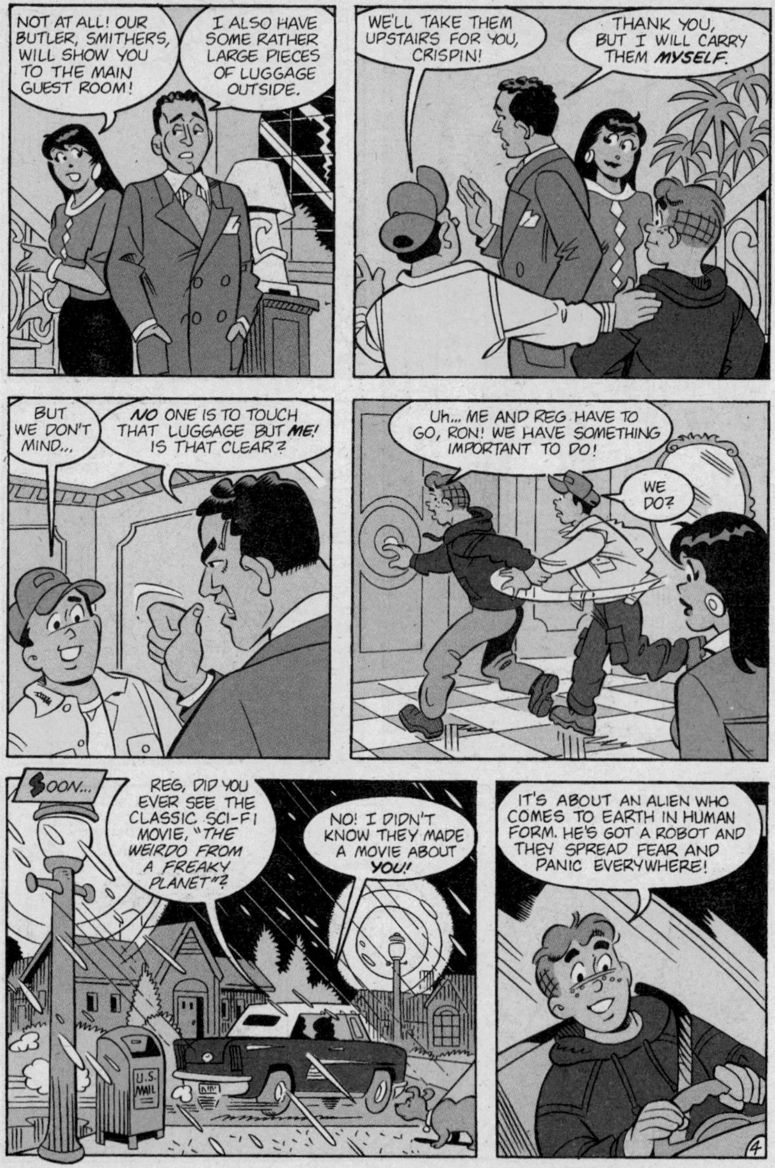
NOT AT ALL! OUR BUTLER, SMITHERS, WILL SHOW YOU TO THE MAIN GUEST ROOM!
I ALSO HAVE SOME RATHER LARGE PIECES OF LUGGAGE OUTSIDE.
WE'LL TAKE THEM UPSTAIRS FOR YOU, CRISPIN!
THANK YOU, BUT I WILL CARRY THEM *MYSELF*.
BUT WE DON'T MIND...
NO ONE IS TO TOUCH THAT LUGGAGE BUT *ME!* IS THAT CLEAR?
Uh... ME AND REG HAVE TO GO, RON! WE HAVE SOMETHING IMPORTANT TO DO!
WE DO?
SOON...
REG, DID YOU EVER SEE THE CLASSIC SCI-FI MOVIE, "*THE WEIRDO FROM A FREAKY PLANET*"?
NO! I DIDN'T KNOW THEY MADE A MOVIE ABOUT *YOU!*
U.S. MAIL
IT'S ABOUT AN ALIEN WHO COMES TO EARTH IN HUMAN FORM. HE'S GOT A ROBOT AND THEY SPREAD FEAR AND PANIC EVERYWHERE!
4

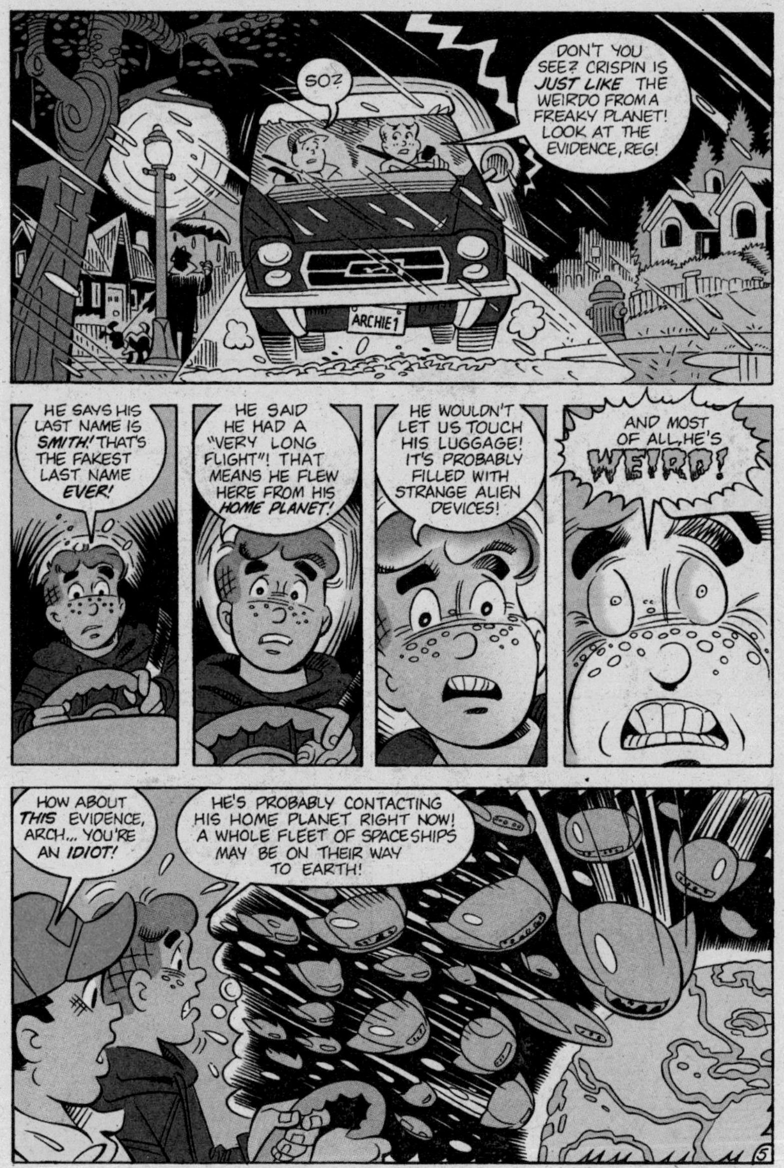
SO?
DON'T YOU SEE? CRISPIN IS JUST LIKE THE WEIRDO FROM A FREAKY PLANET! LOOK AT THE EVIDENCE, REG!
ARCHIE1
HE SAYS HIS LAST NAME IS SMITH! THAT'S THE FAKEST LAST NAME EVER!
HE SAID HE HAD A "VERY LONG FLIGHT"! THAT MEANS HE FLEW HERE FROM HIS HOME PLANET!
HE WOULDN'T LET US TOUCH HIS LUGGAGE! IT'S PROBABLY FILLED WITH STRANGE ALIEN DEVICES!
AND MOST OF ALL, HE'S WEIRD!
HOW ABOUT THIS EVIDENCE, ARCH... YOU'RE AN IDIOT!
HE'S PROBABLY CONTACTING HIS HOME PLANET RIGHT NOW! A WHOLE FLEET OF SPACESHIPS MAY BE ON THEIR WAY TO EARTH!

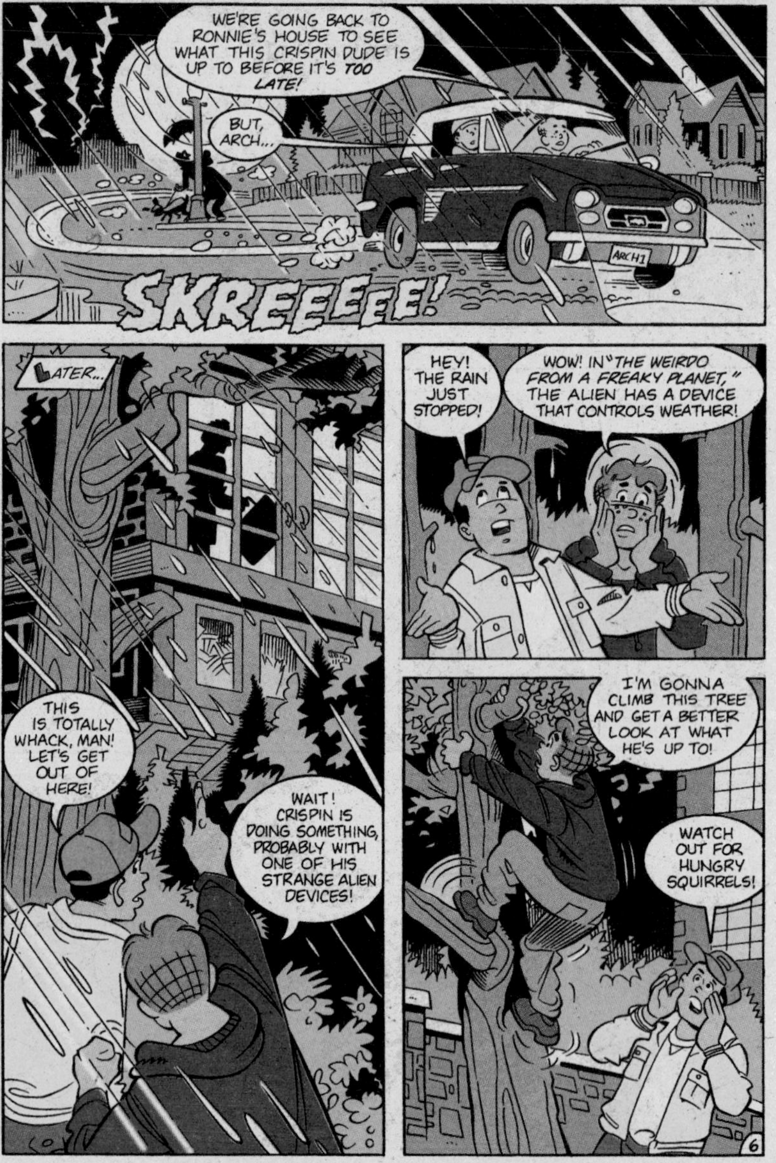
WE'RE GOING BACK TO RONNIE'S HOUSE TO SEE WHAT THIS CRISPIN DUDE IS UP TO BEFORE IT'S TOO LATE!
BUT, ARCH...
ARCH1
SKREEEEEE!
LATER...
THIS IS TOTALLY WHACK, MAN! LET'S GET OUT OF HERE!
WAIT! CRISPIN IS DOING SOMETHING, PROBABLY WITH ONE OF HIS STRANGE ALIEN DEVICES!
HEY! THE RAIN JUST STOPPED!
WOW! IN "THE WEIRDO FROM A FREAKY PLANET," THE ALIEN HAS A DEVICE THAT CONTROLS WEATHER!
I'M GONNA CLIMB THIS TREE AND GET A BETTER LOOK AT WHAT HE'S UP TO!
WATCH OUT FOR HUNGRY SQUIRRELS!
6

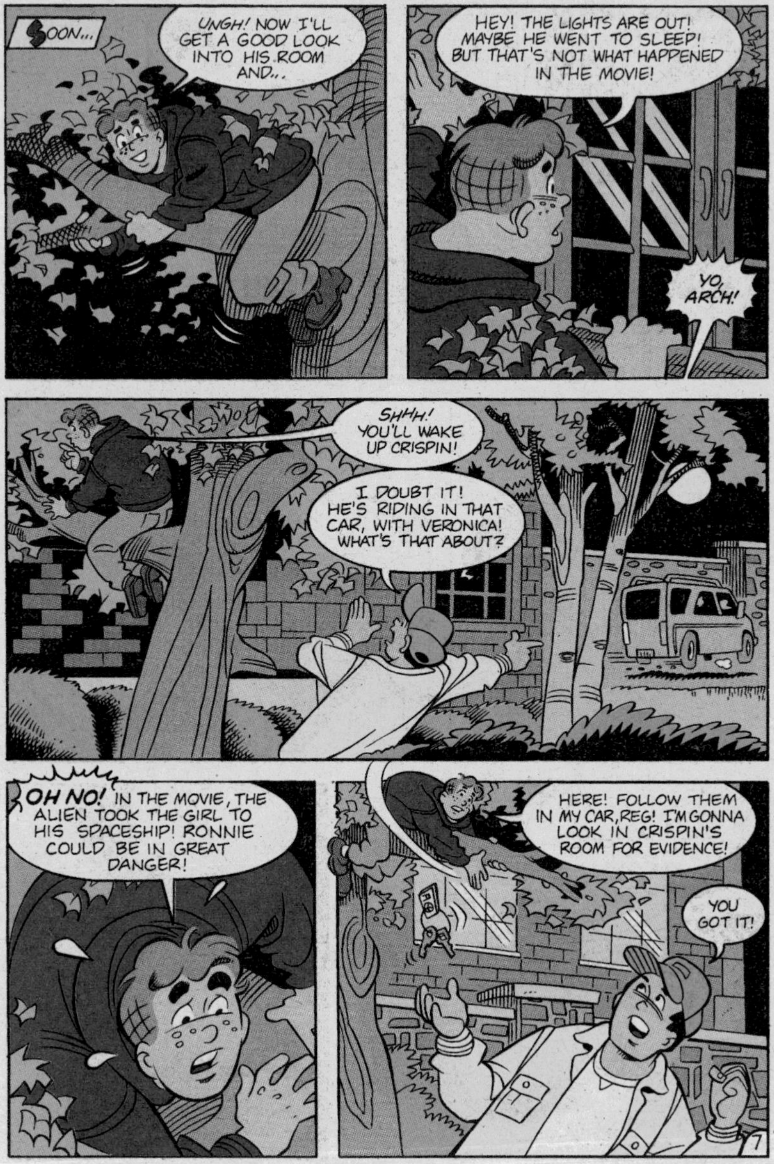
SOON...
UNGH! NOW I'LL GET A GOOD LOOK INTO HIS ROOM AND...
HEY! THE LIGHTS ARE OUT! MAYBE HE WENT TO SLEEP! BUT THAT'S NOT WHAT HAPPENED IN THE MOVIE!
YO, ARCH!
SHHH! YOU'LL WAKE UP CRISPIN!
I DOUBT IT! HE'S RIDING IN THAT CAR, WITH VERONICA! WHAT'S THAT ABOUT?
OH NO! IN THE MOVIE, THE ALIEN TOOK THE GIRL TO HIS SPACESHIP! RONNIE COULD BE IN GREAT DANGER!
HERE! FOLLOW THEM IN MY CAR, REG! I'M GONNA LOOK IN CRISPIN'S ROOM FOR EVIDENCE!
YOU GOT IT!

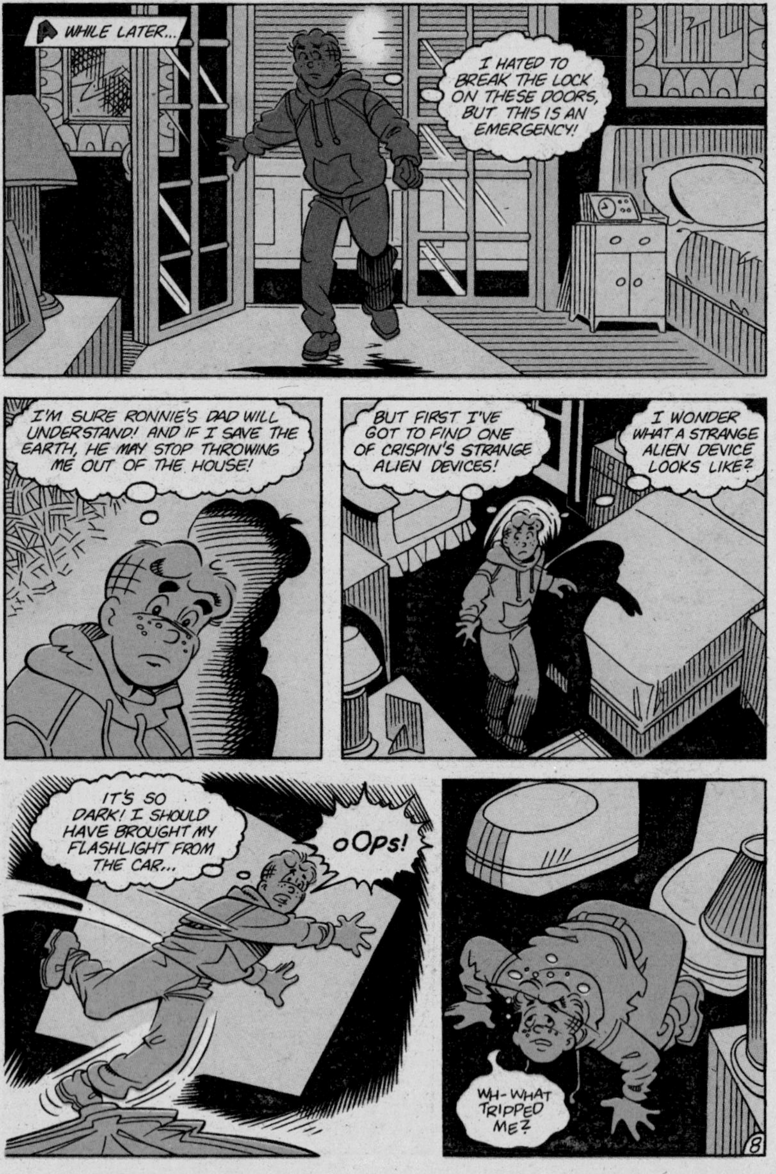
A WHILE LATER...
I HATED TO BREAK THE LOCK ON THESE DOORS, BUT THIS IS AN EMERGENCY!
I'M SURE RONNIE'S DAD WILL UNDERSTAND! AND IF I SAVE THE EARTH, HE MAY STOP THROWING ME OUT OF THE HOUSE!
BUT FIRST I'VE GOT TO FIND ONE OF CRISPIN'S STRANGE ALIEN DEVICES!
I WONDER WHAT A STRANGE ALIEN DEVICE LOOKS LIKE?
IT'S SO DARK! I SHOULD HAVE BROUGHT MY FLASHLIGHT FROM THE CAR...
oOps!
WH- WHAT TRIPPED ME?
8

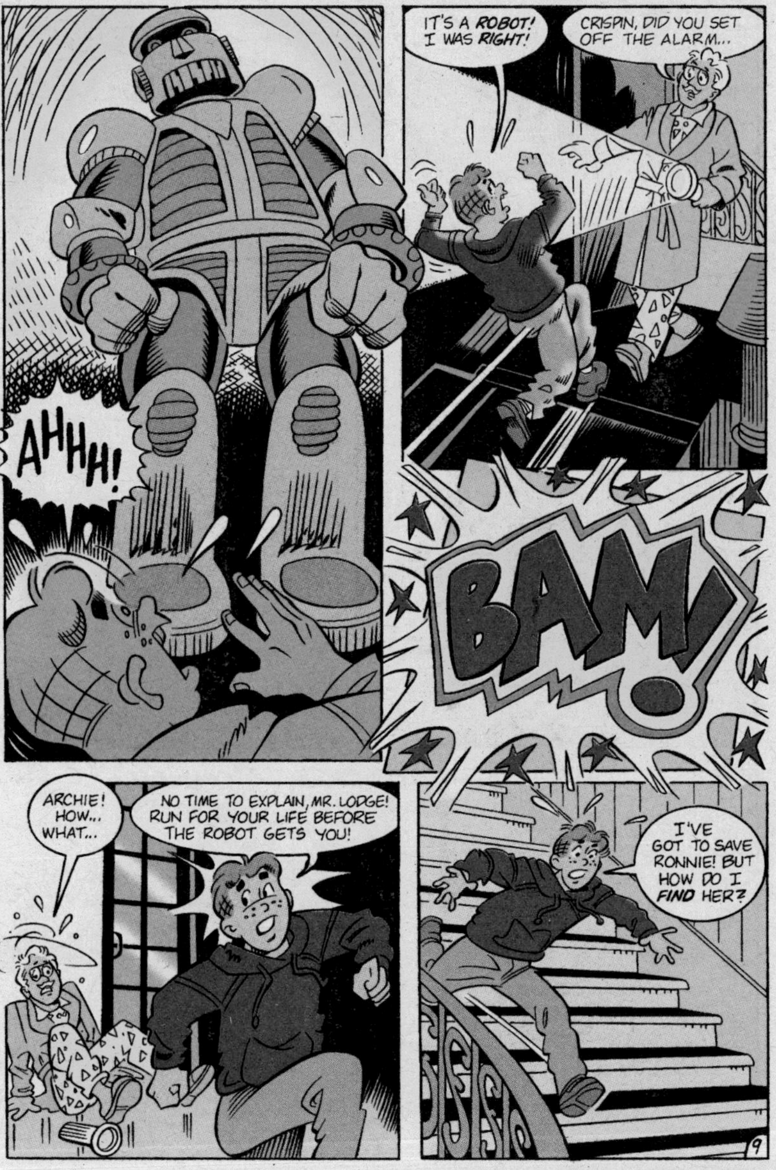
AHHHH!
IT'S A ROBOT! I WAS RIGHT!
CRISPIN, DID YOU SET OFF THE ALARM...
BAM!
ARCHIE! HOW... WHAT...
NO TIME TO EXPLAIN, MR. LODGE! RUN FOR YOUR LIFE BEFORE THE ROBOT GETS YOU!
I'VE GOT TO SAVE RONNIE! BUT HOW DO I FIND HER?

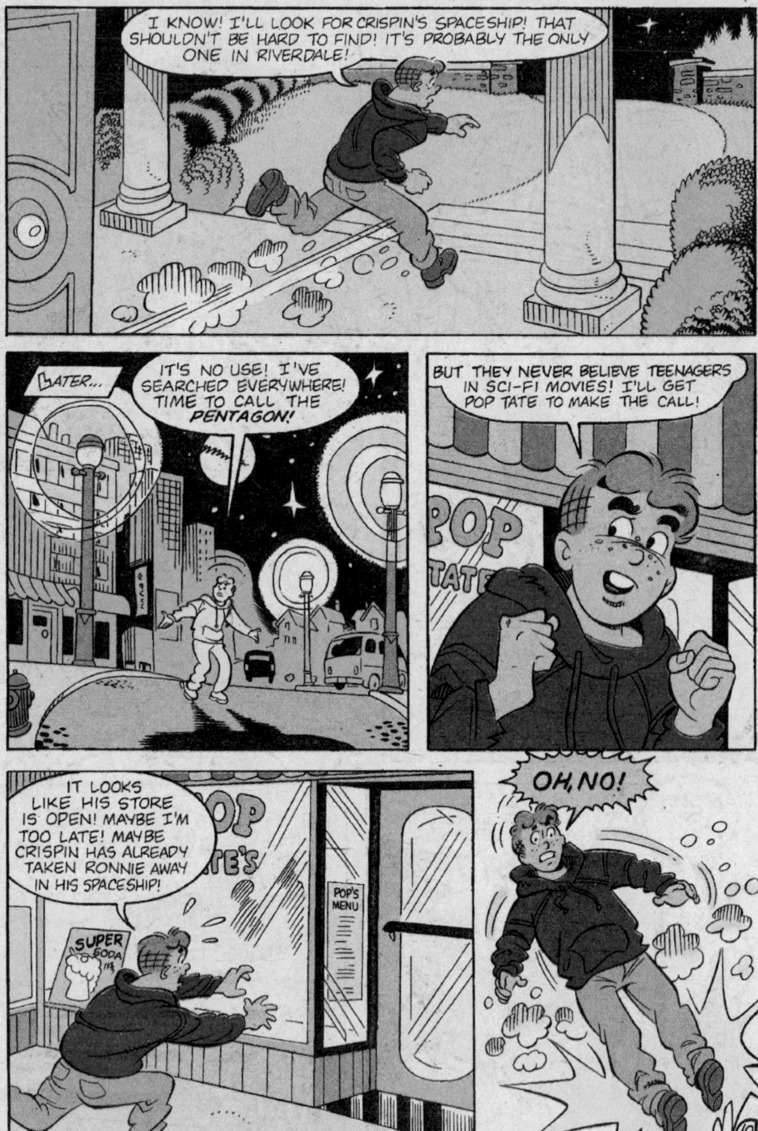
I KNOW! I'LL LOOK FOR CRISPIN'S SPACESHIP! THAT SHOULDN'T BE HARD TO FIND! IT'S PROBABLY THE ONLY ONE IN RIVERDALE!
LATER...
IT'S NO USE! I'VE SEARCHED EVERYWHERE! TIME TO CALL THE PENTAGON!
BUT THEY NEVER BELIEVE TEENAGERS IN SCI-FI MOVIES! I'LL GET POP TATE TO MAKE THE CALL!
POP TATE
IT LOOKS LIKE HIS STORE IS OPEN! MAYBE I'M TOO LATE! MAYBE CRISPIN HAS ALREADY TAKEN RONNIE AWAY IN HIS SPACESHIP!
SUPER SODA
POP'S MENU
OH, NO!
10

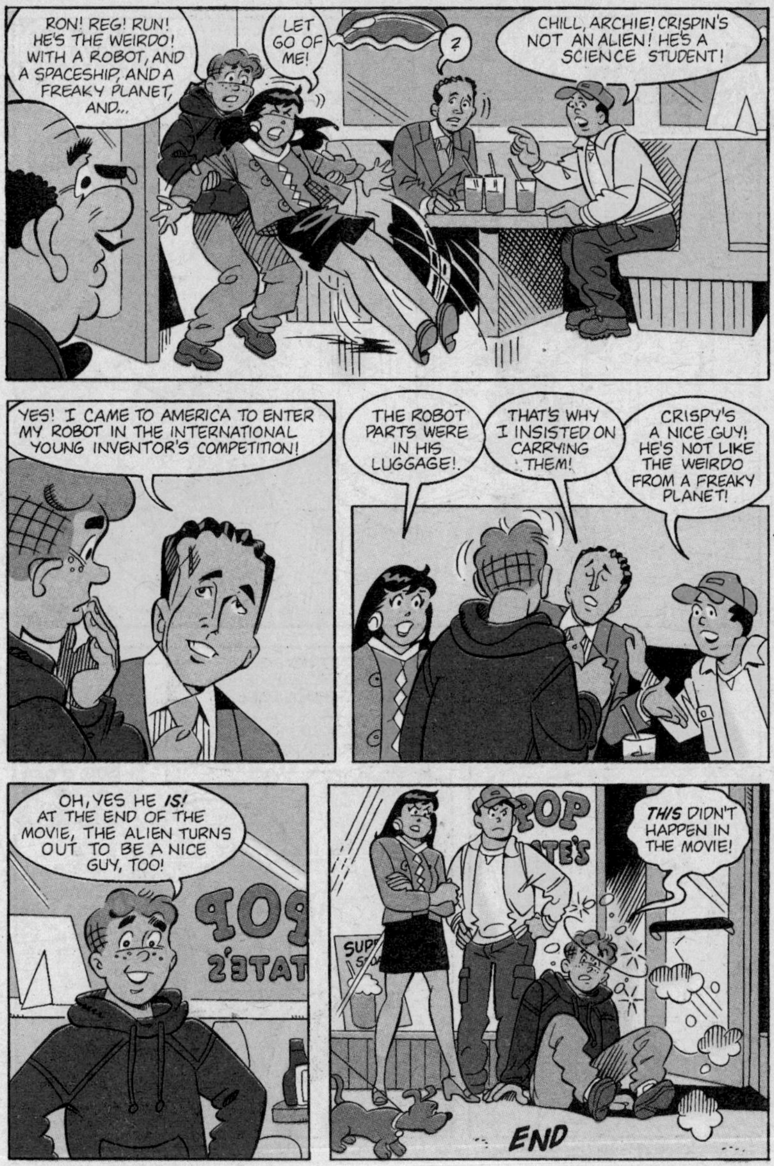
RON! REG! RUN! HE'S THE WEIRDO! WITH A ROBOT, AND A SPACESHIP, AND A FREAKY PLANET, AND...
LET GO OF ME!
?
CHILL, ARCHIE! CRISPIN'S NOT AN ALIEN! HE'S A SCIENCE STUDENT!
YES! I CAME TO AMERICA TO ENTER MY ROBOT IN THE INTERNATIONAL YOUNG INVENTOR'S COMPETITION!
THE ROBOT PARTS WERE IN HIS LUGGAGE!
THAT'S WHY I INSISTED ON CARRYING THEM!
CRISPY'S A NICE GUY! HE'S NOT LIKE THE WEIRDO FROM A FREAKY PLANET!
OH, YES HE *IS!* AT THE END OF THE MOVIE, THE ALIEN TURNS OUT TO BE A NICE GUY, TOO!
THIS DIDN'T HAPPEN IN THE MOVIE!
END

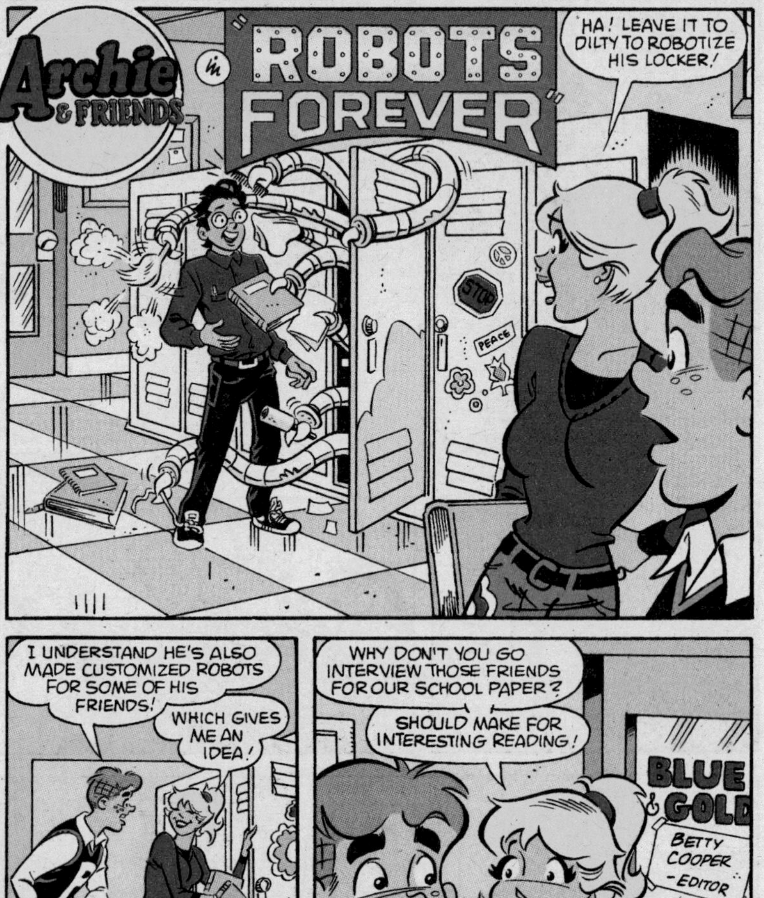
Archie & FRIENDS
in
"ROBOTS FOREVER"
HA! LEAVE IT TO DILTY TO ROBOTIZE HIS LOCKER!
STOP
PEACE
I UNDERSTAND HE'S ALSO MADE CUSTOMIZED ROBOTS FOR SOME OF HIS FRIENDS!
WHICH GIVES ME AN IDEA!
WHY DON'T YOU GO INTERVIEW THOSE FRIENDS FOR OUR SCHOOL PAPER?
SHOULD MAKE FOR INTERESTING READING!
BLUE & GOLD
BETTY COOPER - EDITOR

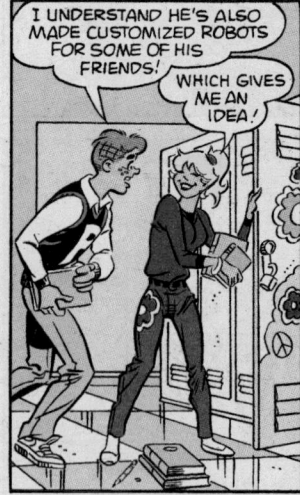

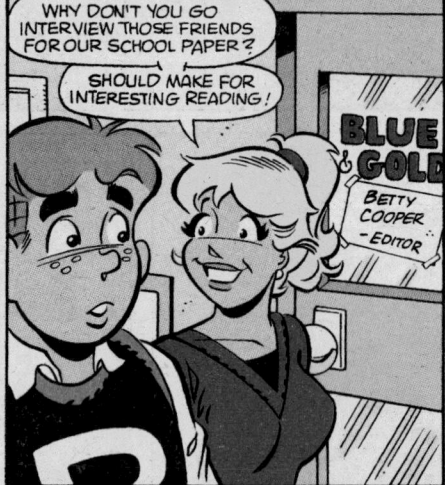

Script: George Gladir / Pencils: Al Bigley / Inks: Al Milgrom / Letters: Bill Yoshida / Colors: Barry Grossman

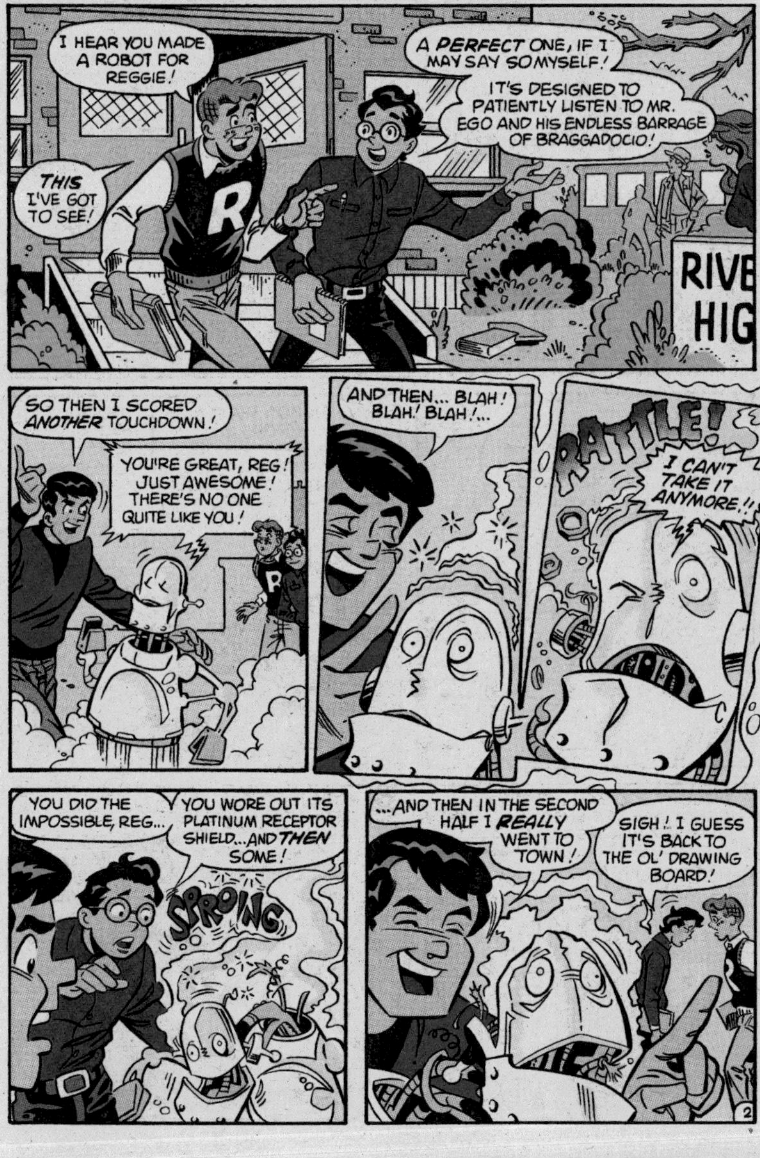
I HEAR YOU MADE A ROBOT FOR REGGIE!
THIS I'VE GOT TO SEE!
A PERFECT ONE, IF I MAY SAY SO MYSELF!
IT'S DESIGNED TO PATIENTLY LISTEN TO MR. EGO AND HIS ENDLESS BARRAGE OF BRAGGADOCIO!
RIVE
HIG
SO THEN I SCORED ANOTHER TOUCHDOWN!
YOU'RE GREAT, REG! JUST AWESOME! THERE'S NO ONE QUITE LIKE YOU!
AND THEN... BLAH! BLAH! BLAH!...
RATTLE!
I CAN'T TAKE IT ANYMORE!!
YOU DID THE IMPOSSIBLE, REG...
YOU WORE OUT ITS PLATINUM RECEPTOR SHIELD...AND THEN SOME!
SPROING
...AND THEN IN THE SECOND HALF I REALLY WENT TO TOWN!
SIGH! I GUESS IT'S BACK TO THE OL' DRAWING BOARD!
2

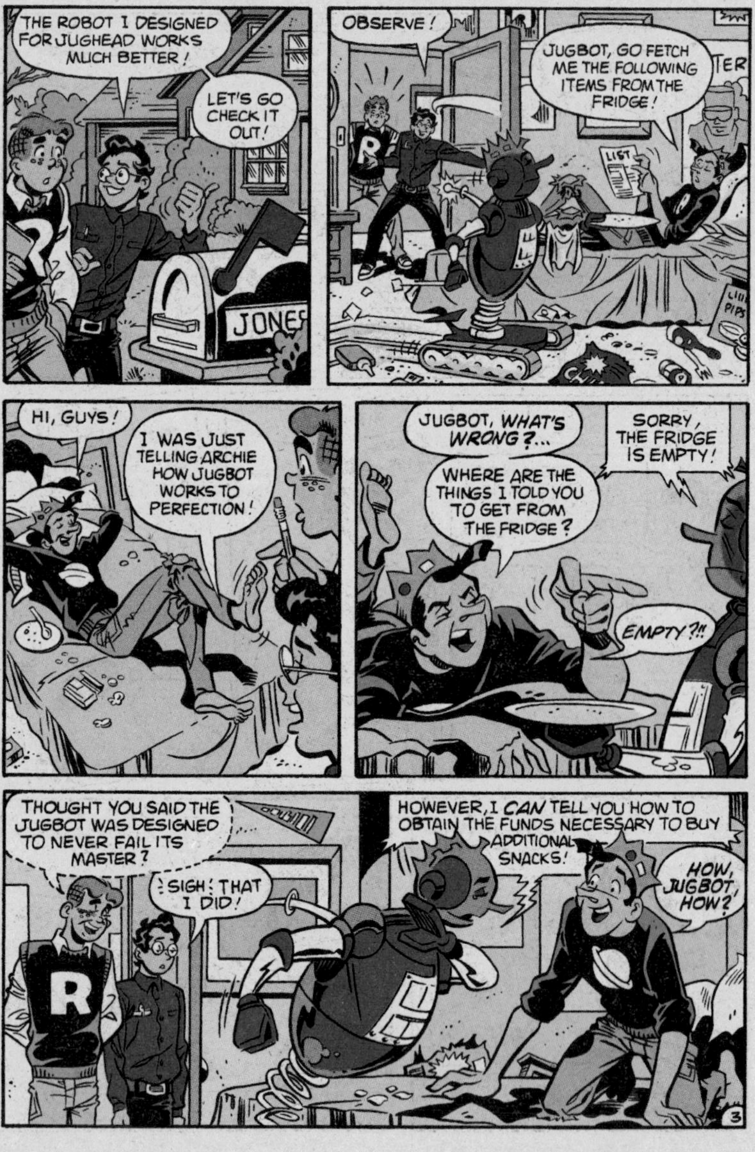
THE ROBOT I DESIGNED FOR JUGHEAD WORKS MUCH BETTER!
LET'S GO CHECK IT OUT!
JONES
OBSERVE!
JUGBOT, GO FETCH ME THE FOLLOWING ITEMS FROM THE FRIDGE!
LIST
HI, GUYS!
I WAS JUST TELLING ARCHIE HOW JUGBOT WORKS TO PERFECTION!
JUGBOT, WHAT'S WRONG?...
WHERE ARE THE THINGS I TOLD YOU TO GET FROM THE FRIDGE?
SORRY, THE FRIDGE IS EMPTY!
EMPTY?!!
THOUGHT YOU SAID THE JUGBOT WAS DESIGNED TO NEVER FAIL ITS MASTER?
SIGH! THAT I DID!
HOWEVER, I CAN TELL YOU HOW TO OBTAIN THE FUNDS NECESSARY TO BUY ADDITIONAL SNACKS!
HOW, JUGBOT, HOW?
3

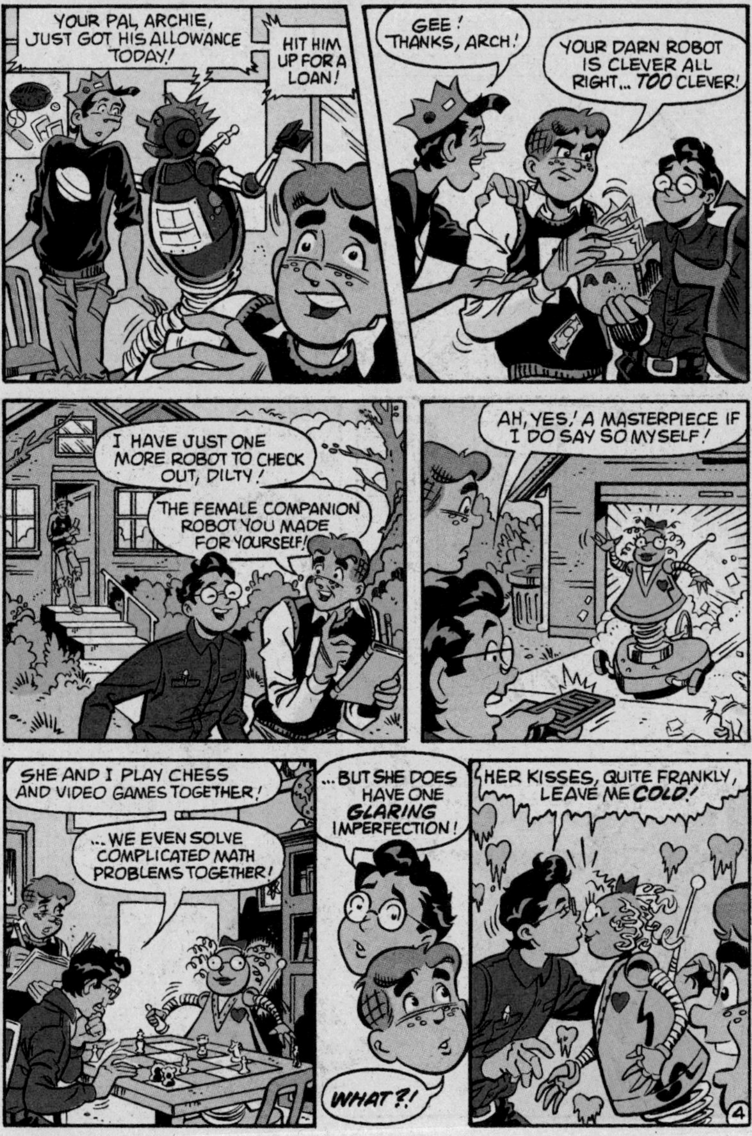
YOUR PAL, ARCHIE, JUST GOT HIS ALLOWANCE TODAY!
HIT HIM UP FOR A LOAN!
GEE! THANKS, ARCH!
YOUR DARN ROBOT IS CLEVER ALL RIGHT... TOO CLEVER!
I HAVE JUST ONE MORE ROBOT TO CHECK OUT, DILTY!
THE FEMALE COMPANION ROBOT YOU MADE FOR YOURSELF!
AH, YES! A MASTERPIECE IF I DO SAY SO MYSELF!
SHE AND I PLAY CHESS AND VIDEO GAMES TOGETHER!
...WE EVEN SOLVE COMPLICATED MATH PROBLEMS TOGETHER!
...BUT SHE DOES HAVE ONE GLARING IMPERFECTION!
WHAT?!
HER KISSES, QUITE FRANKLY, LEAVE ME COLD!
4

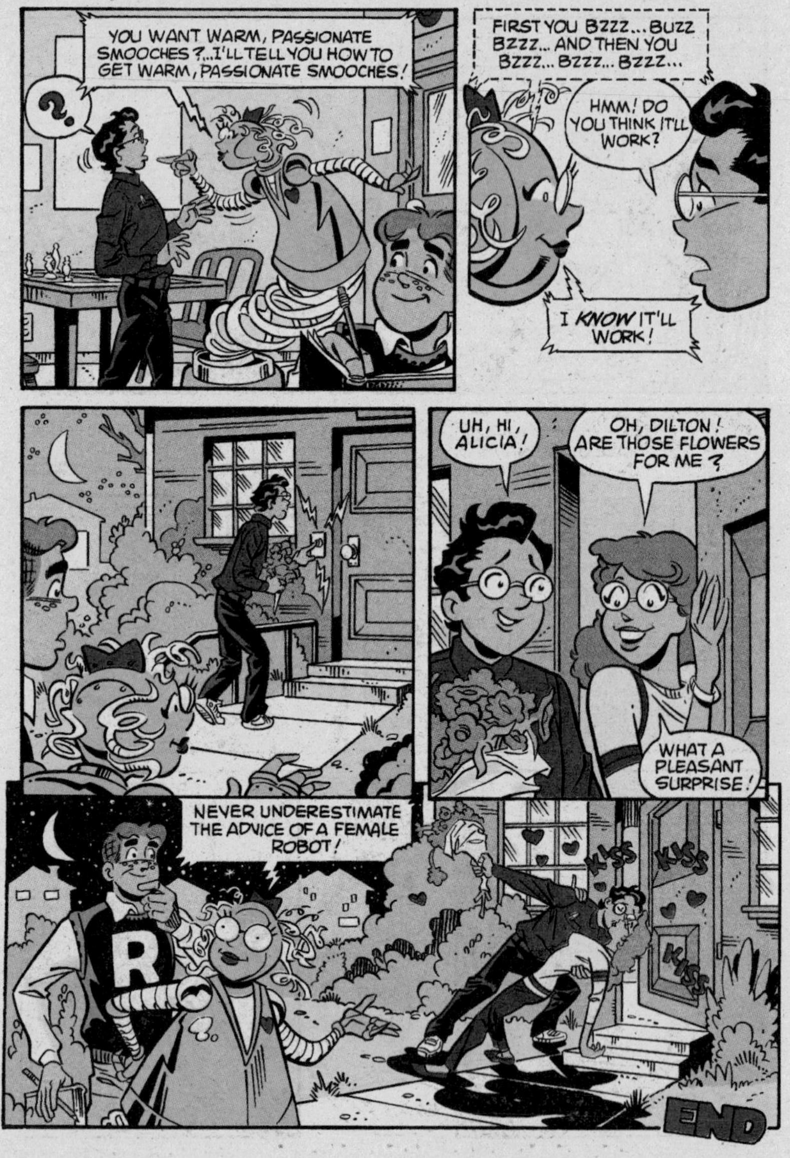

YOU WANT WARM, PASSIONATE SMOOCHES ?...I'LL TELL YOU HOW TO GET WARM, PASSIONATE SMOOCHES!
?
FIRST YOU BZZZ... BUZZ BZZZ... AND THEN YOU BZZZ... BZZZ... BZZZ...
HMM! DO YOU THINK IT'LL WORK?
I KNOW IT'LL WORK!
UH, HI, ALICIA!
OH, DILTON! ARE THOSE FLOWERS FOR ME?
WHAT A PLEASANT SURPRISE!
NEVER UNDERESTIMATE THE ADVICE OF A FEMALE ROBOT!
KISS
KISS
KISS
END

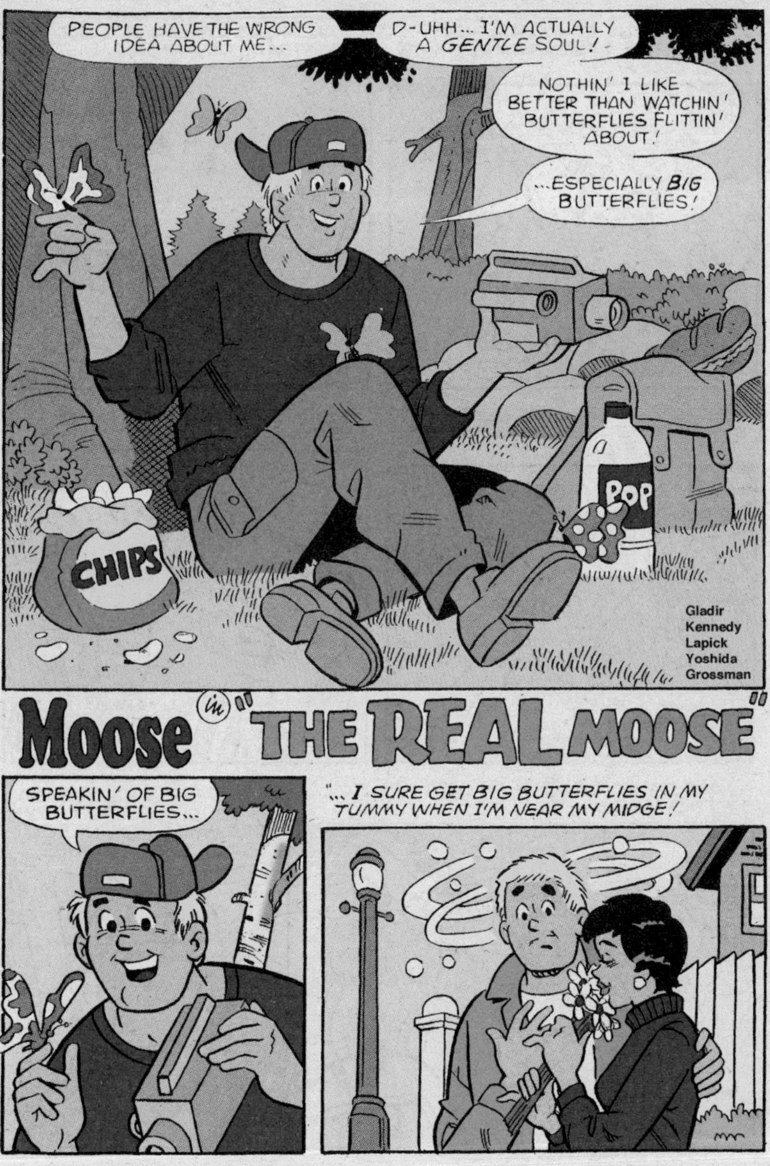
PEOPLE HAVE THE WRONG IDEA ABOUT ME...
D-UHH... I'M ACTUALLY A GENTLE SOUL!
NOTHIN' I LIKE BETTER THAN WATCHIN' BUTTERFLIES FLITTIN' ABOUT!
...ESPECIALLY BIG BUTTERFLIES!
CHIPS
POP
Gladir
Kennedy
Lapick
Yoshida
Grossman
Moose in "THE REAL MOOSE"
SPEAKIN' OF BIG BUTTERFLIES...
"... I SURE GET BIG BUTTERFLIES IN MY TUMMY WHEN I'M NEAR MY MIDGE!

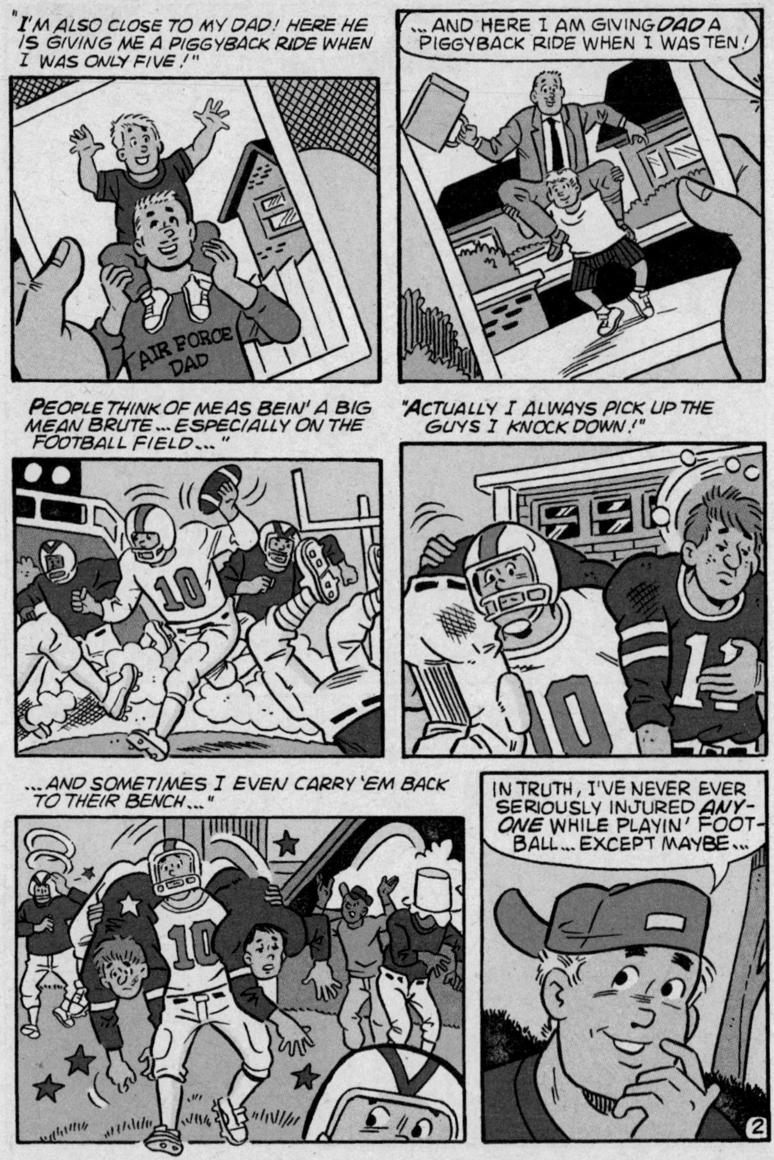
"I'M ALSO CLOSE TO MY DAD! HERE HE IS GIVING ME A PIGGYBACK RIDE WHEN I WAS ONLY FIVE!"
AIR FORCE DAD
...AND HERE I AM GIVING DAD A PIGGYBACK RIDE WHEN I WAS TEN!
PEOPLE THINK OF ME AS BEIN' A BIG MEAN BRUTE... ESPECIALLY ON THE FOOTBALL FIELD..."
10
"ACTUALLY I ALWAYS PICK UP THE GUYS I KNOCK DOWN!"
...AND SOMETIMES I EVEN CARRY 'EM BACK TO THEIR BENCH..."
10
IN TRUTH, I'VE NEVER EVER SERIOUSLY INJURED ANYONE WHILE PLAYIN' FOOTBALL... EXCEPT MAYBE...
2

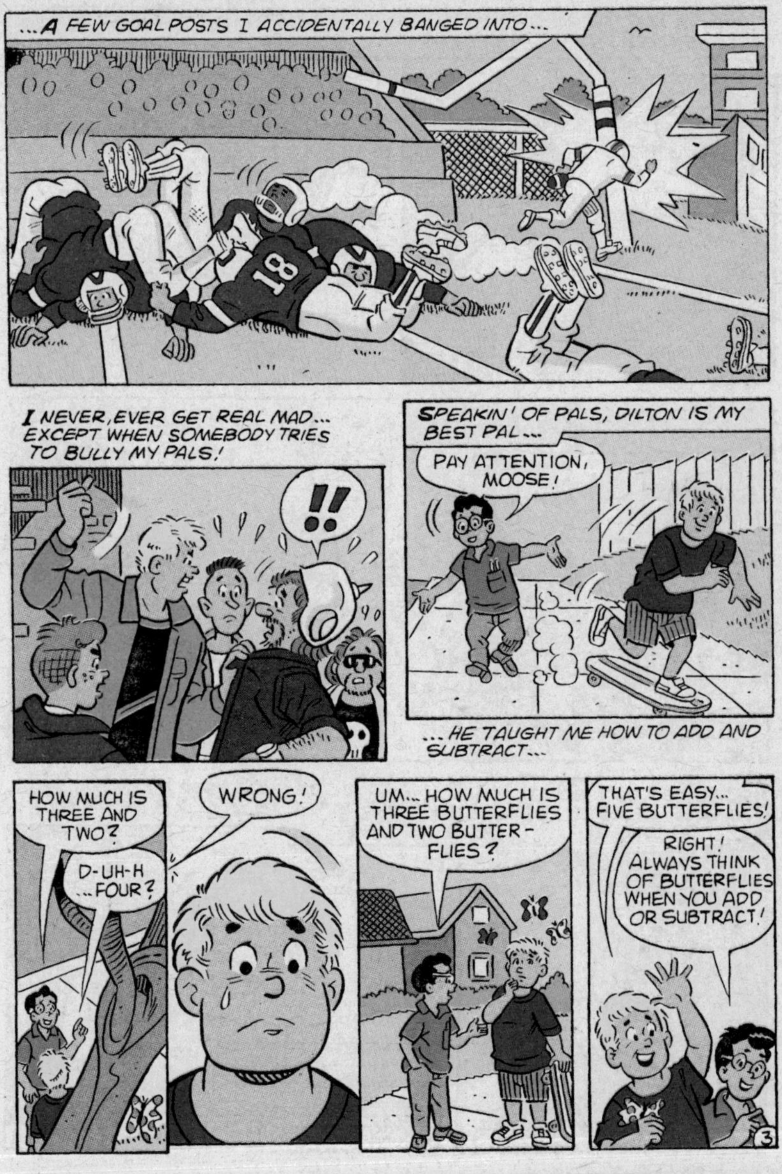
...A FEW GOAL POSTS I ACCIDENTALLY BANGED INTO...
18
I NEVER, EVER GET REAL MAD... EXCEPT WHEN SOMEBODY TRIES TO BULLY MY PALS!
!!
SPEAKIN' OF PALS, DILTON IS MY BEST PAL...
PAY ATTENTION, MOOSE!
...HE TAUGHT ME HOW TO ADD AND SUBTRACT...
HOW MUCH IS THREE AND TWO?
D-UH-H ...FOUR?
WRONG!
UM... HOW MUCH IS THREE BUTTERFLIES AND TWO BUTTER-FLIES?
THAT'S EASY... FIVE BUTTERFLIES!
RIGHT! ALWAYS THINK OF BUTTERFLIES WHEN YOU ADD OR SUBTRACT!
3

CHUCK IS ALSO MY PAL... ESPECIALLY SINCE HE LIKES DRAWIN' PITCHERS OF ME...!

UH, HOW'S THIS, MOOSE?

AWESOME!

D-UH, I GUESS DIS IS WHAT'S CALLED "ARTISTIC LICENSE"!

REPORT CARD
A
A
A

I'D CALL IT ARTISTIC FANTASY!

SOME PEOPLE TEND TO THINK OF ME AS NOT BEIN' TOO BRIGHT!

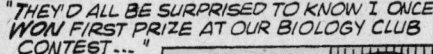

"THEY'D ALL BE SURPRISED TO KNOW I ONCE WON FIRST PRIZE AT OUR BIOLOGY CLUB CONTEST..."

YES, I DID!

4

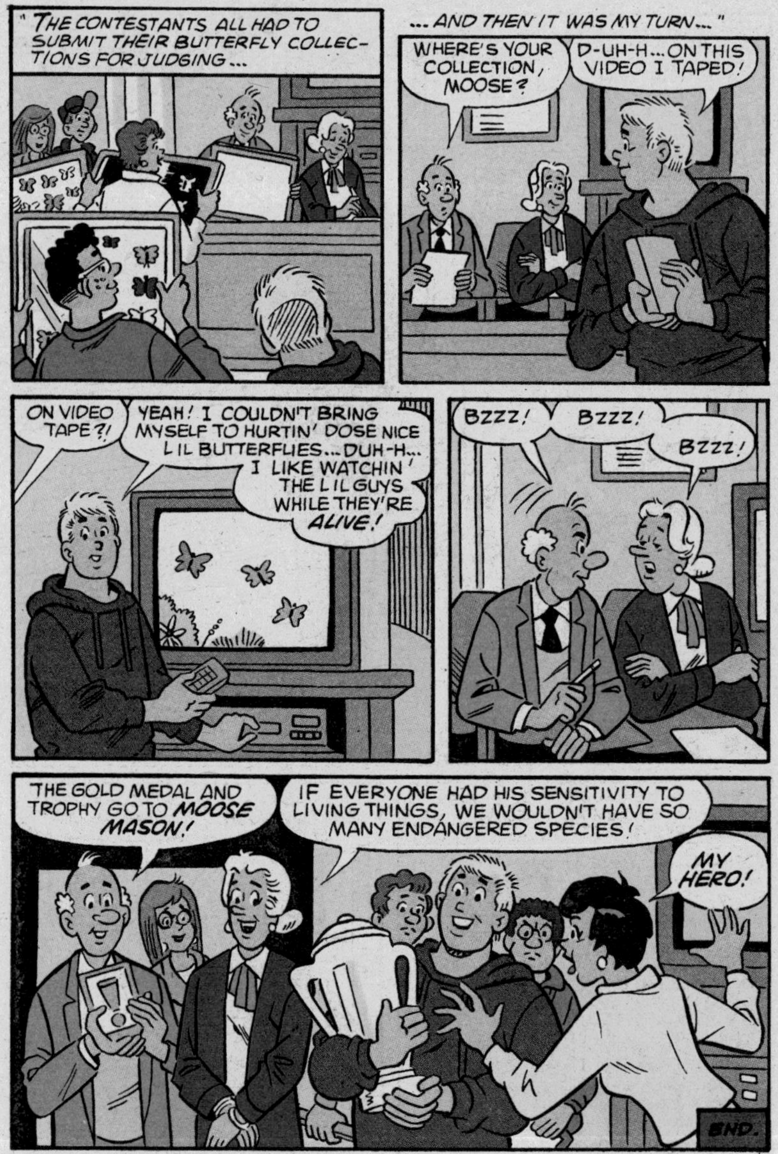
"THE CONTESTANTS ALL HAD TO SUBMIT THEIR BUTTERFLY COLLECTIONS FOR JUDGING...
... AND THEN IT WAS MY TURN..."
WHERE'S YOUR COLLECTION, MOOSE?
D-UH-H...ON THIS VIDEO I TAPED!
ON VIDEO TAPE?!
YEAH! I COULDN'T BRING MYSELF TO HURTIN' DOSE NICE LIL BUTTERFLIES...DUH-H... I LIKE WATCHIN' THE LIL GUYS WHILE THEY'RE ALIVE!
BZZZ!
BZZZ!
BZZZ!
THE GOLD MEDAL AND TROPHY GO TO MOOSE MASON!
IF EVERYONE HAD HIS SENSITIVITY TO LIVING THINGS, WE WOULDN'T HAVE SO MANY ENDANGERED SPECIES!
MY HERO!
END.

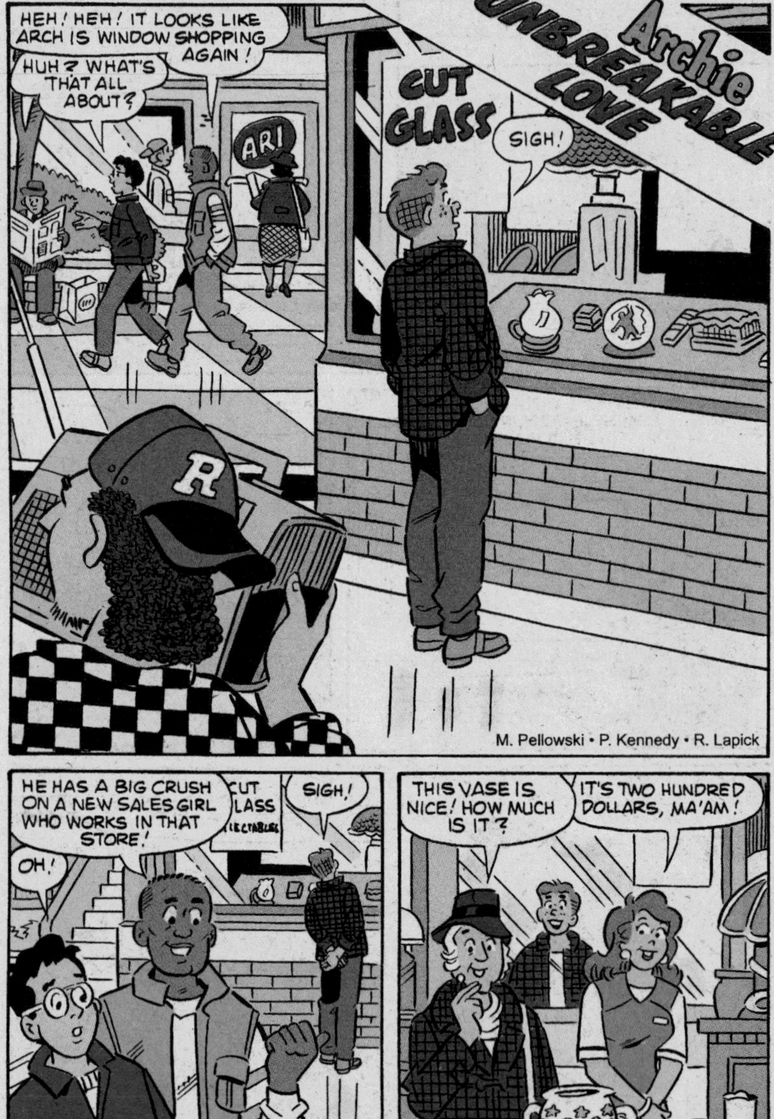
Archie
UNBREAKABLE LOVE
HEH! HEH! IT LOOKS LIKE ARCH IS WINDOW SHOPPING AGAIN!
HUH? WHAT'S THAT ALL ABOUT?
ARI
CUT GLASS
SIGH!
M. Pellowski • P. Kennedy • R. Lapick
HE HAS A BIG CRUSH ON A NEW SALES GIRL WHO WORKS IN THAT STORE!
OH!
SIGH!
THIS VASE IS NICE! HOW MUCH IS IT?
IT'S TWO HUNDRED DOLLARS, MA'AM!
1

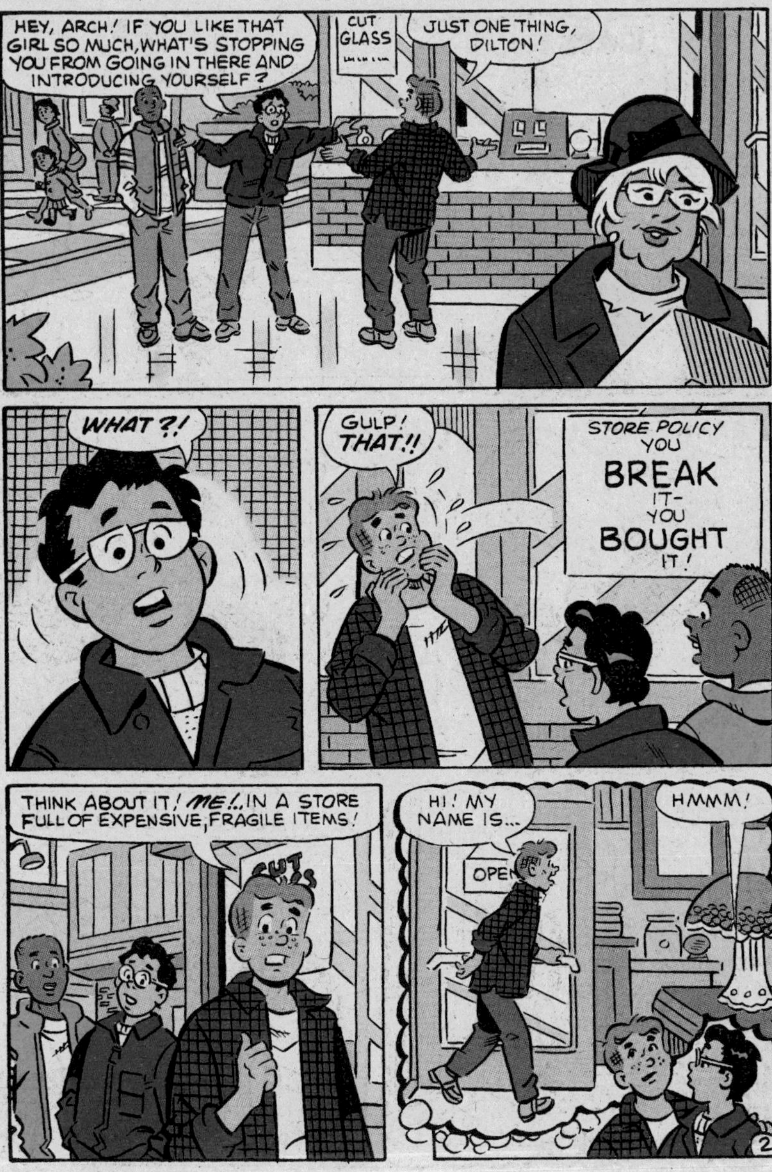

HEY, ARCH! IF YOU LIKE THAT GIRL SO MUCH, WHAT'S STOPPING YOU FROM GOING IN THERE AND INTRODUCING YOURSELF?
CUT GLASS
JUST ONE THING, DILTON!
WHAT?!
GULP! THAT!!
STORE POLICY YOU BREAK IT- YOU BOUGHT IT!
THINK ABOUT IT! ME!..IN A STORE FULL OF EXPENSIVE, FRAGILE ITEMS!
HI! MY NAME IS...
OPEN
HMMM!
2

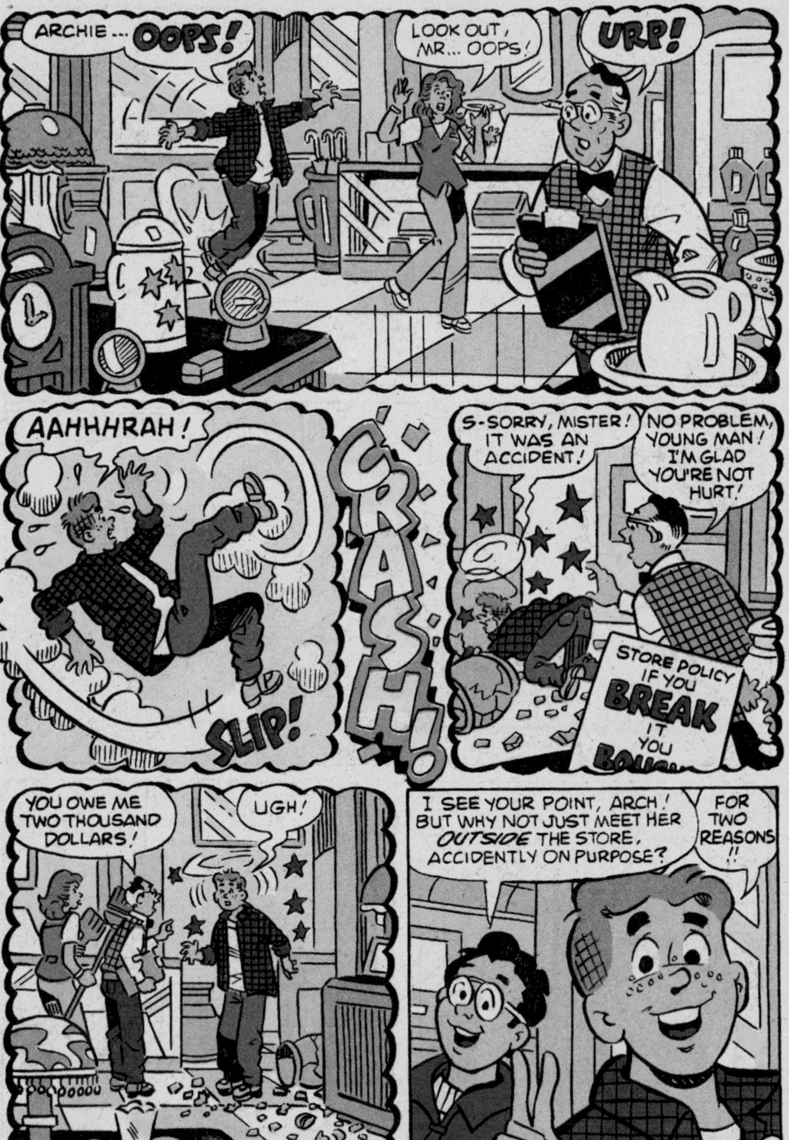

ARCHIE... OOPS!
LOOK OUT, MR... OOPS!
URP!
AAHHHRAH!
SLIP!
CRASH!
S-SORRY, MISTER! IT WAS AN ACCIDENT!
NO PROBLEM, YOUNG MAN! I'M GLAD YOU'RE NOT HURT!
STORE POLICY IF YOU BREAK IT YOU
YOU OWE ME TWO THOUSAND DOLLARS!
UGH!
I SEE YOUR POINT, ARCH! BUT WHY NOT JUST MEET HER *OUTSIDE* THE STORE, ACCIDENTLY ON PURPOSE?
FOR TWO REASONS!!
3

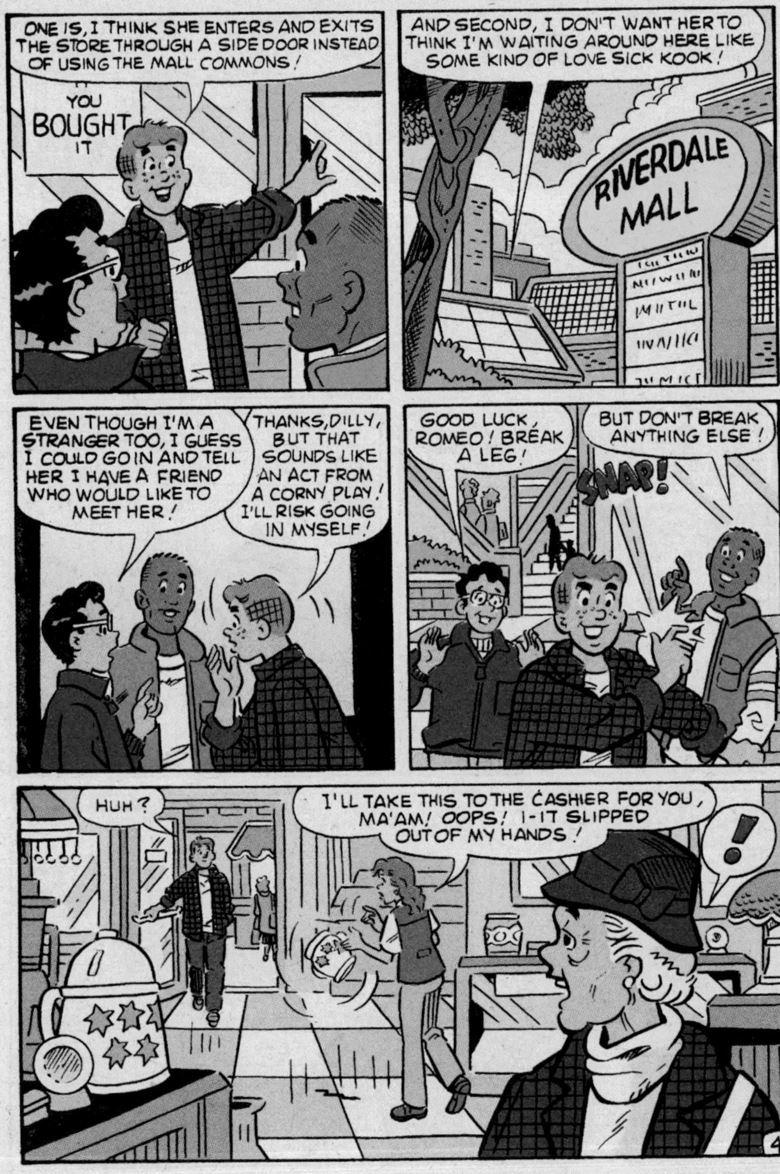
ONE IS, I THINK SHE ENTERS AND EXITS THE STORE THROUGH A SIDE DOOR INSTEAD OF USING THE MALL COMMONS!
YOU BOUGHT IT
AND SECOND, I DON'T WANT HER TO THINK I'M WAITING AROUND HERE LIKE SOME KIND OF LOVE SICK KOOK!
RIVERDALE MALL
EVEN THOUGH I'M A STRANGER TOO, I GUESS I COULD GO IN AND TELL HER I HAVE A FRIEND WHO WOULD LIKE TO MEET HER!
THANKS, DILLY, BUT THAT SOUNDS LIKE AN ACT FROM A CORNY PLAY! I'LL RISK GOING IN MYSELF!
GOOD LUCK, ROMEO! BREAK A LEG!
BUT DON'T BREAK ANYTHING ELSE!
SNAP!
HUH?
I'LL TAKE THIS TO THE CASHIER FOR YOU, MA'AM! OOPS! I-IT SLIPPED OUT OF MY HANDS!
!
4

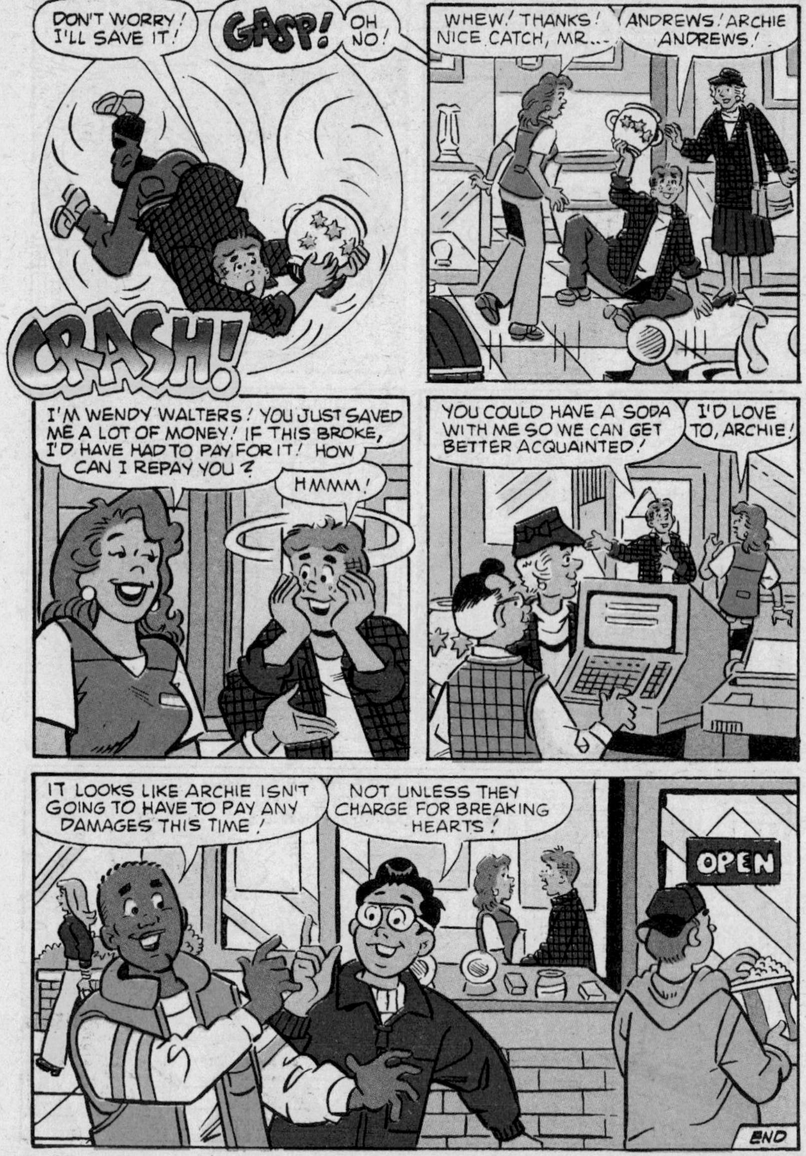
DON'T WORRY! I'LL SAVE IT!
GASP!
OH NO!
CRASH!
WHEW! THANKS! NICE CATCH, MR...
ANDREWS! ARCHIE ANDREWS!
I'M WENDY WALTERS! YOU JUST SAVED ME A LOT OF MONEY! IF THIS BROKE, I'D HAVE HAD TO PAY FOR IT! HOW CAN I REPAY YOU?
HMMM!
YOU COULD HAVE A SODA WITH ME SO WE CAN GET BETTER ACQUAINTED!
I'D LOVE TO, ARCHIE!
IT LOOKS LIKE ARCHIE ISN'T GOING TO HAVE TO PAY ANY DAMAGES THIS TIME!
NOT UNLESS THEY CHARGE FOR BREAKING HEARTS!
OPEN
END

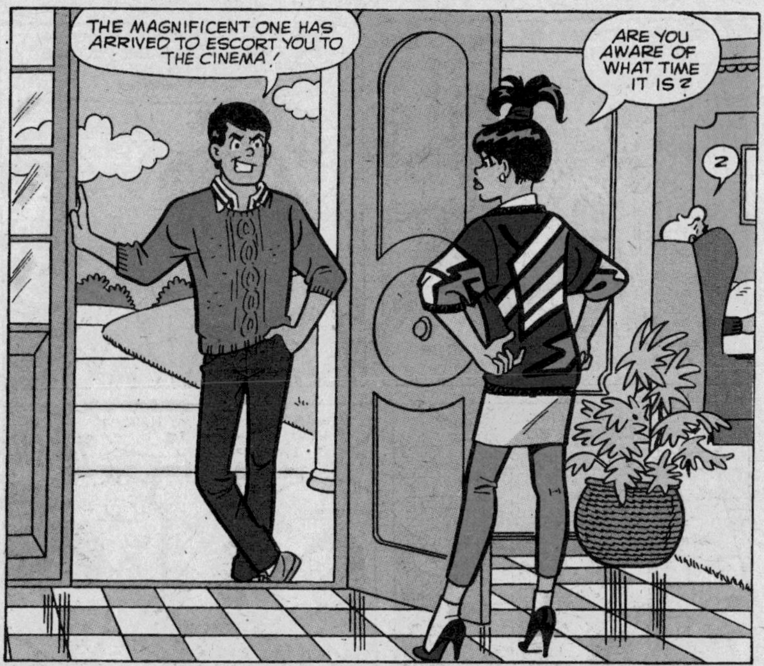
THE MAGNIFICENT ONE HAS ARRIVED TO ESCORT YOU TO THE CINEMA!
ARE YOU AWARE OF WHAT TIME IT IS?
Z

Veronica's "SURPRISE ENDING"

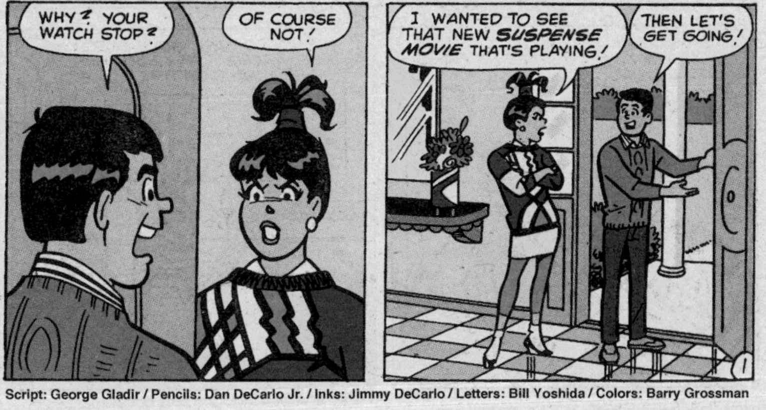
WHY? YOUR WATCH STOP?
OF COURSE NOT!
I WANTED TO SEE THAT NEW *SUSPENSE MOVIE* THAT'S PLAYING!
THEN LET'S GET GOING!
1

Script: George Gladir / Pencils: Dan DeCarlo Jr. / Inks: Jimmy DeCarlo / Letters: Bill Yoshida / Colors: Barry Grossman

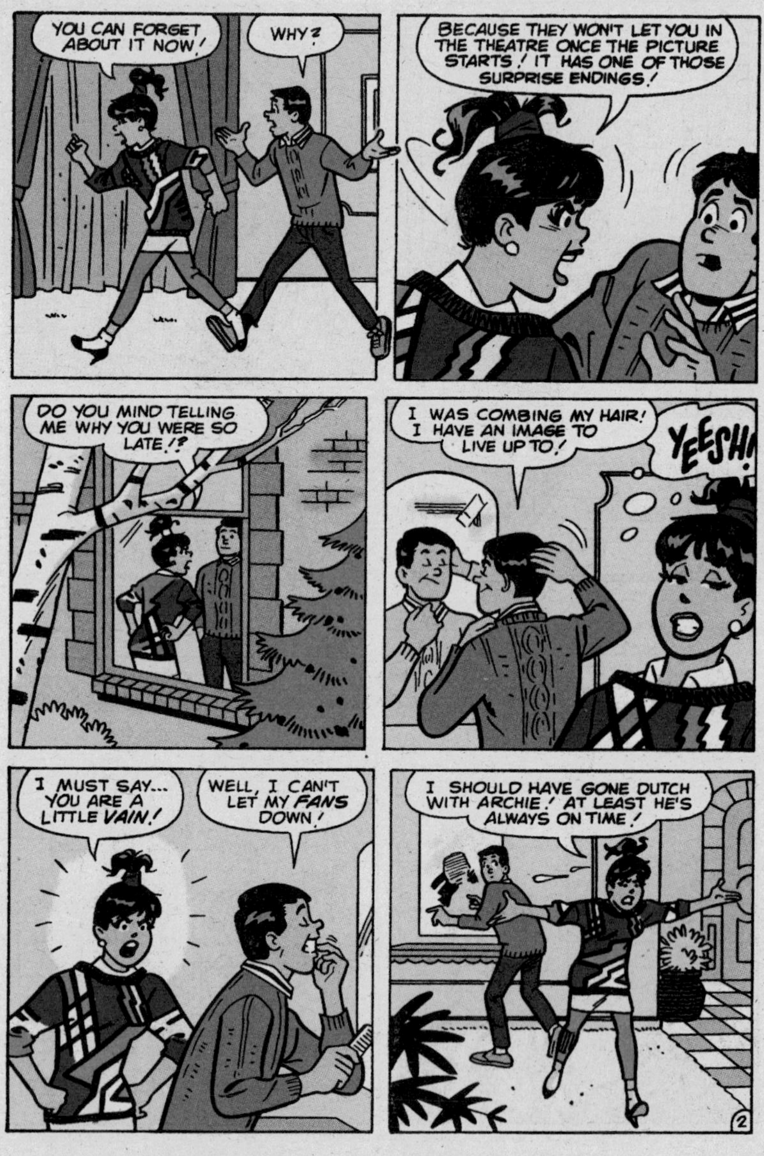
YOU CAN FORGET ABOUT IT NOW!
WHY?
BECAUSE THEY WON'T LET YOU IN THE THEATRE ONCE THE PICTURE STARTS! IT HAS ONE OF THOSE SURPRISE ENDINGS!
DO YOU MIND TELLING ME WHY YOU WERE SO LATE!?
I WAS COMBING MY HAIR! I HAVE AN IMAGE TO LIVE UP TO!
YEESH!
I MUST SAY... YOU ARE A LITTLE VAIN!
WELL, I CAN'T LET MY FANS DOWN!
I SHOULD HAVE GONE DUTCH WITH ARCHIE! AT LEAST HE'S ALWAYS ON TIME!
2

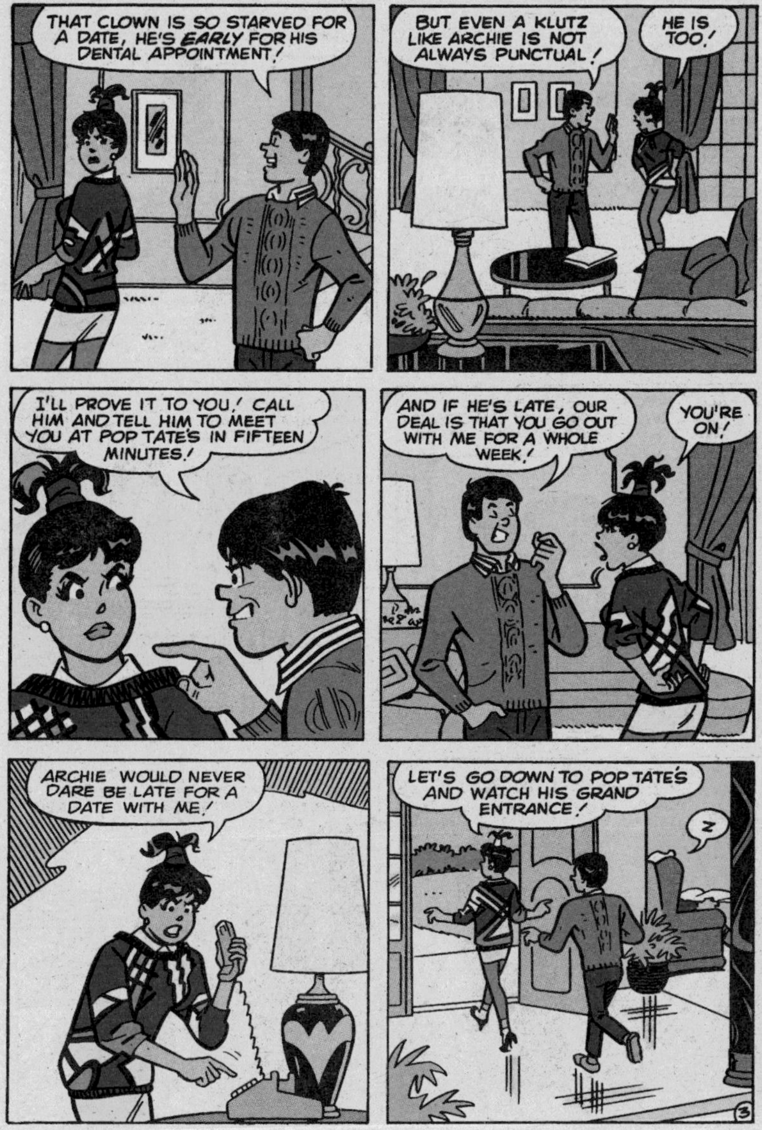
THAT CLOWN IS SO STARVED FOR A DATE, HE'S *EARLY* FOR HIS DENTAL APPOINTMENT!
BUT EVEN A KLUTZ LIKE ARCHIE IS NOT ALWAYS PUNCTUAL!
HE IS TOO!
I'LL PROVE IT TO YOU! CALL HIM AND TELL HIM TO MEET YOU AT POP TATE'S IN FIFTEEN MINUTES!
AND IF HE'S LATE, OUR DEAL IS THAT YOU GO OUT WITH ME FOR A WHOLE WEEK!
YOU'RE ON!
ARCHIE WOULD NEVER DARE BE LATE FOR A DATE WITH ME!
LET'S GO DOWN TO POP TATE'S AND WATCH HIS GRAND ENTRANCE!
Z
3

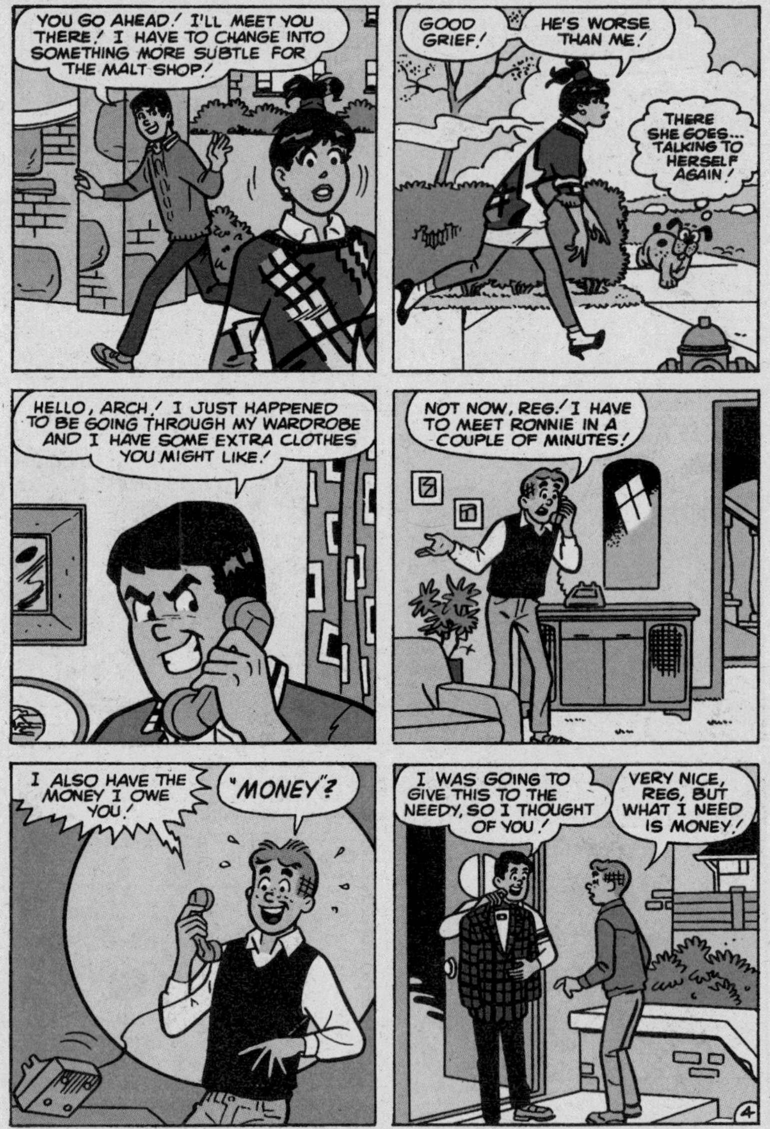
YOU GO AHEAD! I'LL MEET YOU THERE! I HAVE TO CHANGE INTO SOMETHING MORE SUBTLE FOR THE MALT SHOP!
GOOD GRIEF!
HE'S WORSE THAN ME!
THERE SHE GOES... TALKING TO HERSELF AGAIN!
HELLO, ARCH! I JUST HAPPENED TO BE GOING THROUGH MY WARDROBE AND I HAVE SOME EXTRA CLOTHES YOU MIGHT LIKE!
NOT NOW, REG! I HAVE TO MEET RONNIE IN A COUPLE OF MINUTES!
I ALSO HAVE THE MONEY I OWE YOU!
"MONEY"?
I WAS GOING TO GIVE THIS TO THE NEEDY, SO I THOUGHT OF YOU!
VERY NICE, REG, BUT WHAT I NEED IS MONEY!
4

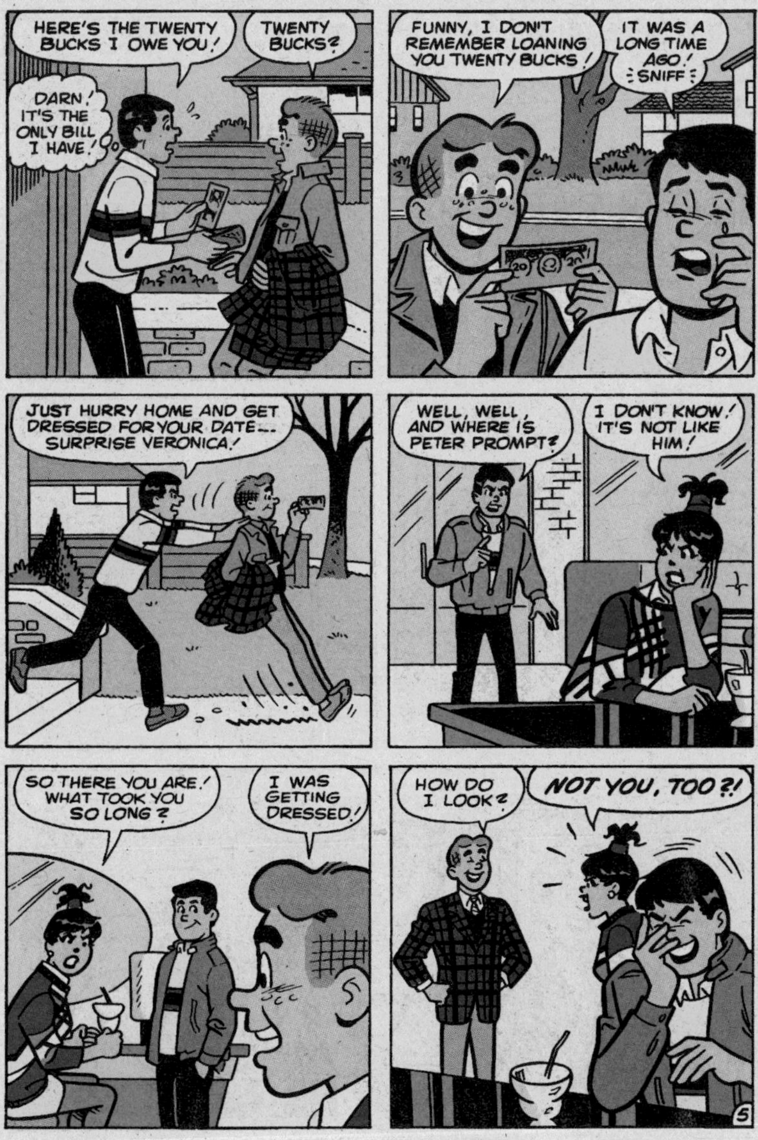
HERE'S THE TWENTY BUCKS I OWE YOU!
TWENTY BUCKS?
DARN! IT'S THE ONLY BILL I HAVE!
FUNNY, I DON'T REMEMBER LOANING YOU TWENTY BUCKS!
IT WAS A LONG TIME AGO! SNIFF
JUST HURRY HOME AND GET DRESSED FOR YOUR DATE... SURPRISE VERONICA!
WELL, WELL, AND WHERE IS PETER PROMPT?
I DON'T KNOW! IT'S NOT LIKE HIM!
SO THERE YOU ARE! WHAT TOOK YOU SO LONG?
I WAS GETTING DRESSED!
HOW DO I LOOK?
NOT YOU, TOO?!
5

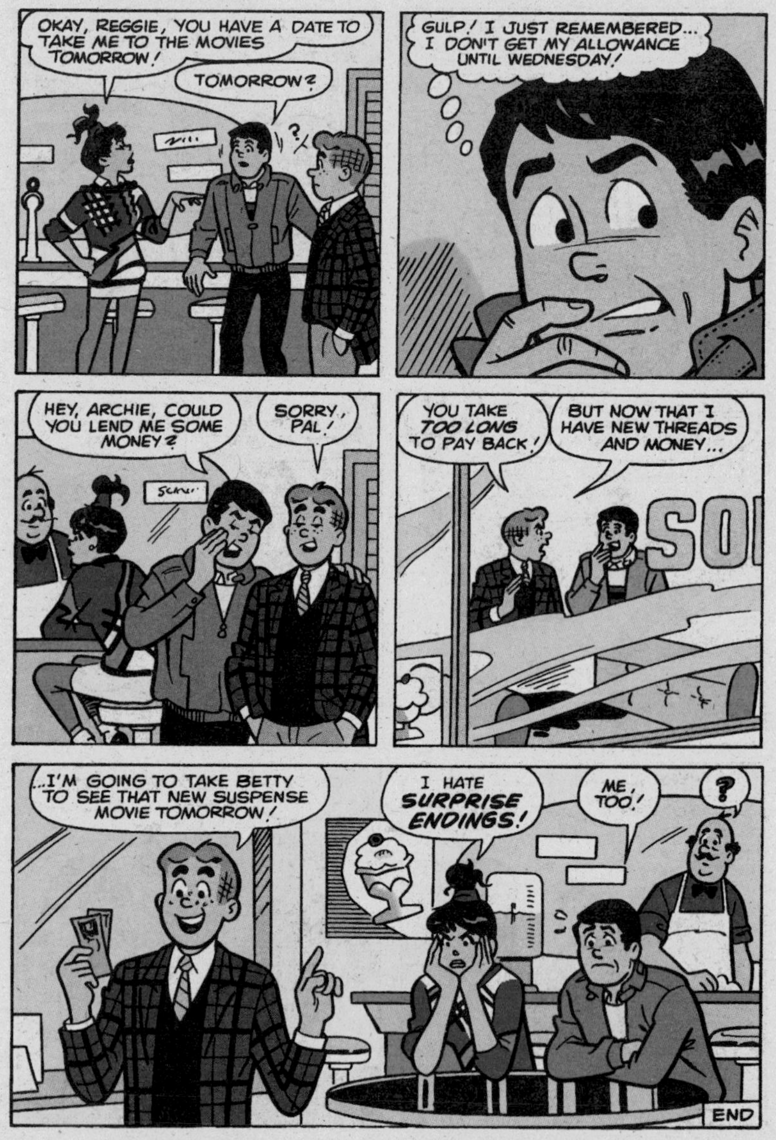
OKAY, REGGIE, YOU HAVE A DATE TO TAKE ME TO THE MOVIES TOMORROW!
TOMORROW?
GULP! I JUST REMEMBERED... I DON'T GET MY ALLOWANCE UNTIL WEDNESDAY!
HEY, ARCHIE, COULD YOU LEND ME SOME MONEY?
SORRY, PAL!
YOU TAKE TOO LONG TO PAY BACK!
BUT NOW THAT I HAVE NEW THREADS AND MONEY...
SO
...I'M GOING TO TAKE BETTY TO SEE THAT NEW SUSPENSE MOVIE TOMORROW!
I HATE SURPRISE ENDINGS!
ME, TOO!
?
END

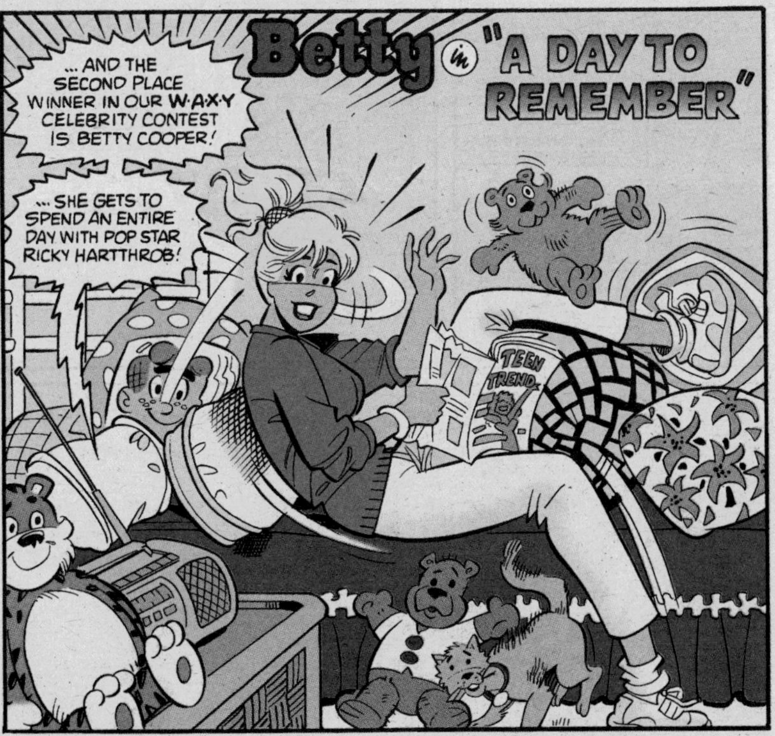
Betty in "A DAY TO REMEMBER"
... AND THE SECOND PLACE WINNER IN OUR W·A·X·Y CELEBRITY CONTEST IS BETTY COOPER!
... SHE GETS TO SPEND AN ENTIRE DAY WITH POP STAR RICKY HARTTHROB!
TEEN TREND

Script: Kathleen Webb / Pencils: Stan Goldberg / Inks: Jon Lowe / Letters: Bill Yoshida / Colors: Barry Grossman

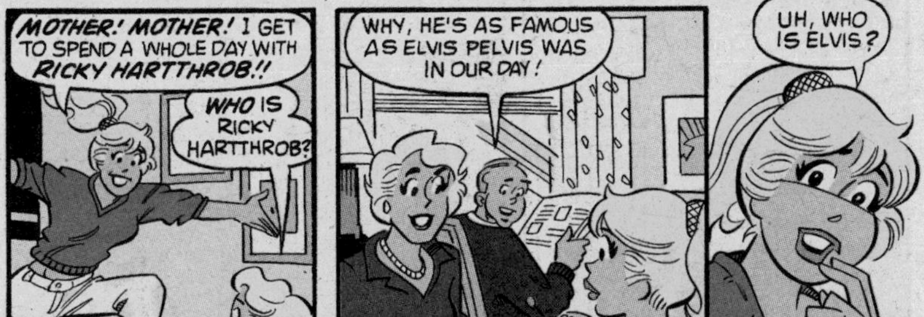
MOTHER! MOTHER! I GET TO SPEND A WHOLE DAY WITH RICKY HARTTHROB!!
WHO IS RICKY HARTTHROB?
WHY, HE'S AS FAMOUS AS ELVIS PELVIS WAS IN OUR DAY!
UH, WHO IS ELVIS?

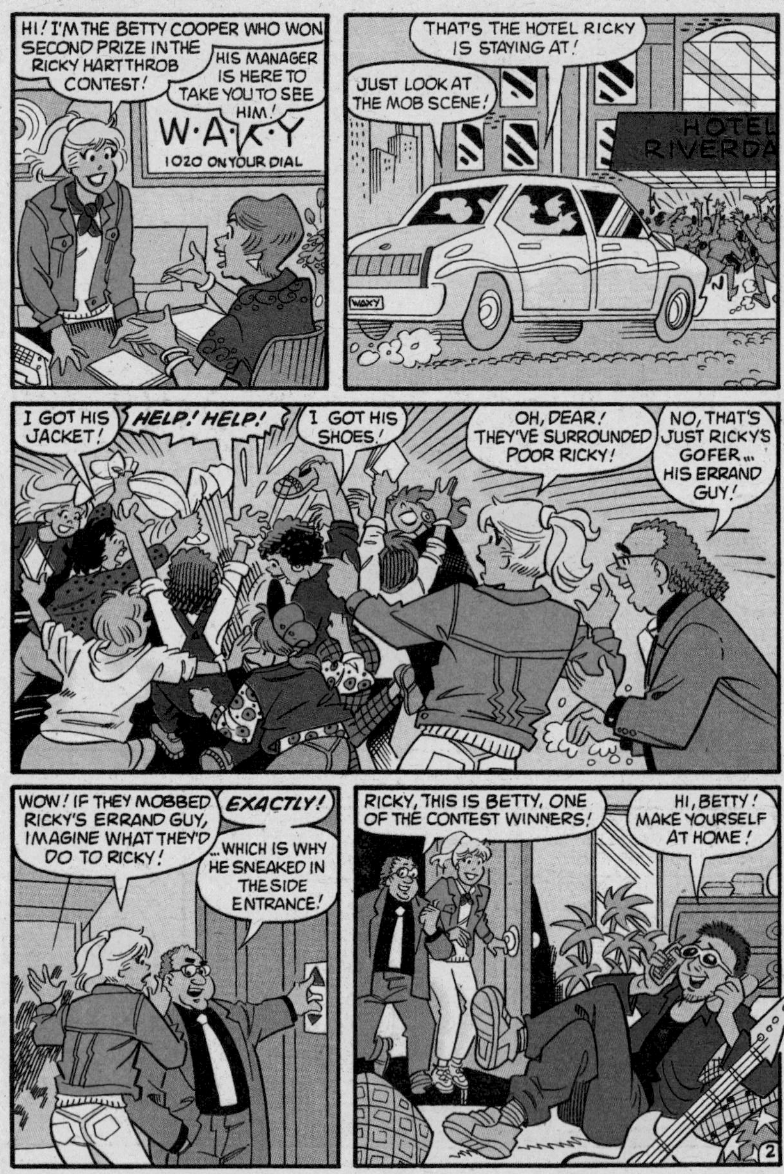
HI! I'M THE BETTY COOPER WHO WON SECOND PRIZE IN THE RICKY HARTTHROB CONTEST!
HIS MANAGER IS HERE TO TAKE YOU TO SEE HIM!
W·A·K·Y
1020 ON YOUR DIAL
THAT'S THE HOTEL RICKY IS STAYING AT!
JUST LOOK AT THE MOB SCENE!
HOTEL RIVERDA
WAKY
I GOT HIS JACKET!
HELP! HELP!
I GOT HIS SHOES!
OH, DEAR! THEY'VE SURROUNDED POOR RICKY!
NO, THAT'S JUST RICKY'S GOFER... HIS ERRAND GUY!
WOW! IF THEY MOBBED RICKY'S ERRAND GUY, IMAGINE WHAT THEY'D DO TO RICKY!
EXACTLY!
...WHICH IS WHY HE SNEAKED IN THE SIDE ENTRANCE!
RICKY, THIS IS BETTY, ONE OF THE CONTEST WINNERS!
HI, BETTY! MAKE YOURSELF AT HOME!
2

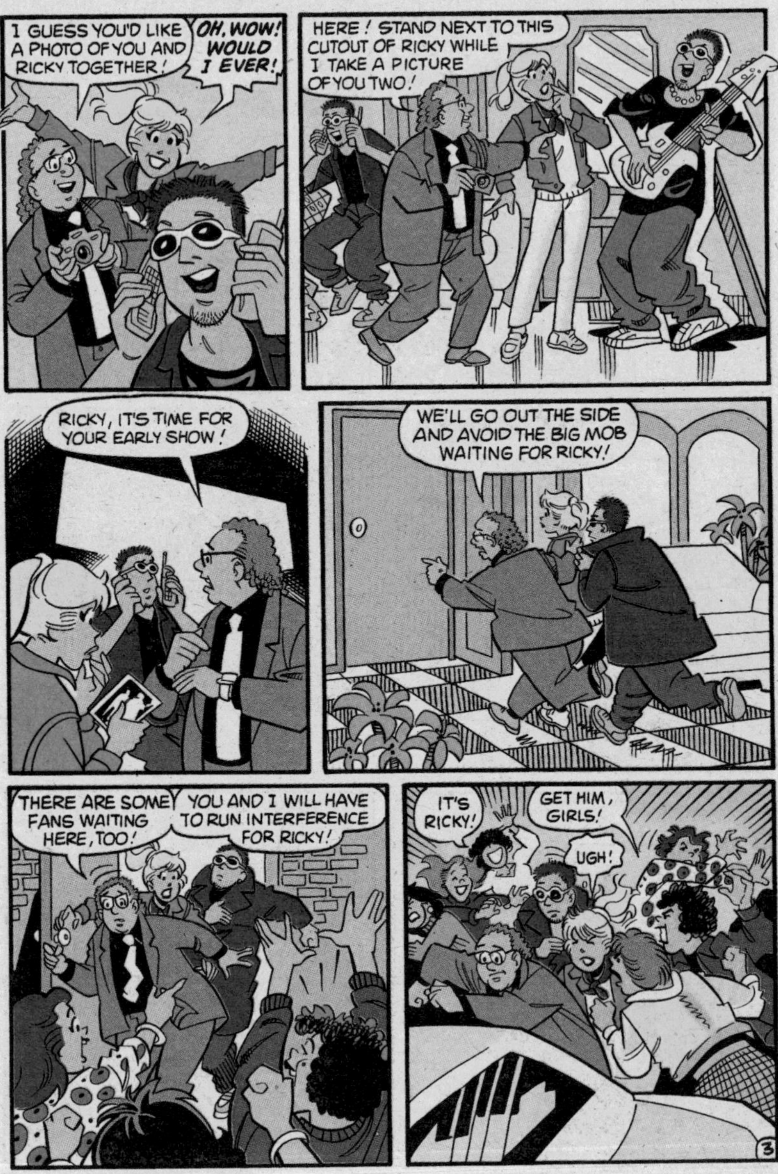
I GUESS YOU'D LIKE A PHOTO OF YOU AND RICKY TOGETHER!
OH, WOW! WOULD I EVER!
HERE! STAND NEXT TO THIS CUTOUT OF RICKY WHILE I TAKE A PICTURE OF YOU TWO!
RICKY, IT'S TIME FOR YOUR EARLY SHOW!
WE'LL GO OUT THE SIDE AND AVOID THE BIG MOB WAITING FOR RICKY!
THERE ARE SOME FANS WAITING HERE, TOO!
YOU AND I WILL HAVE TO RUN INTERFERENCE FOR RICKY!
IT'S RICKY!
GET HIM, GIRLS!
UGH!
3

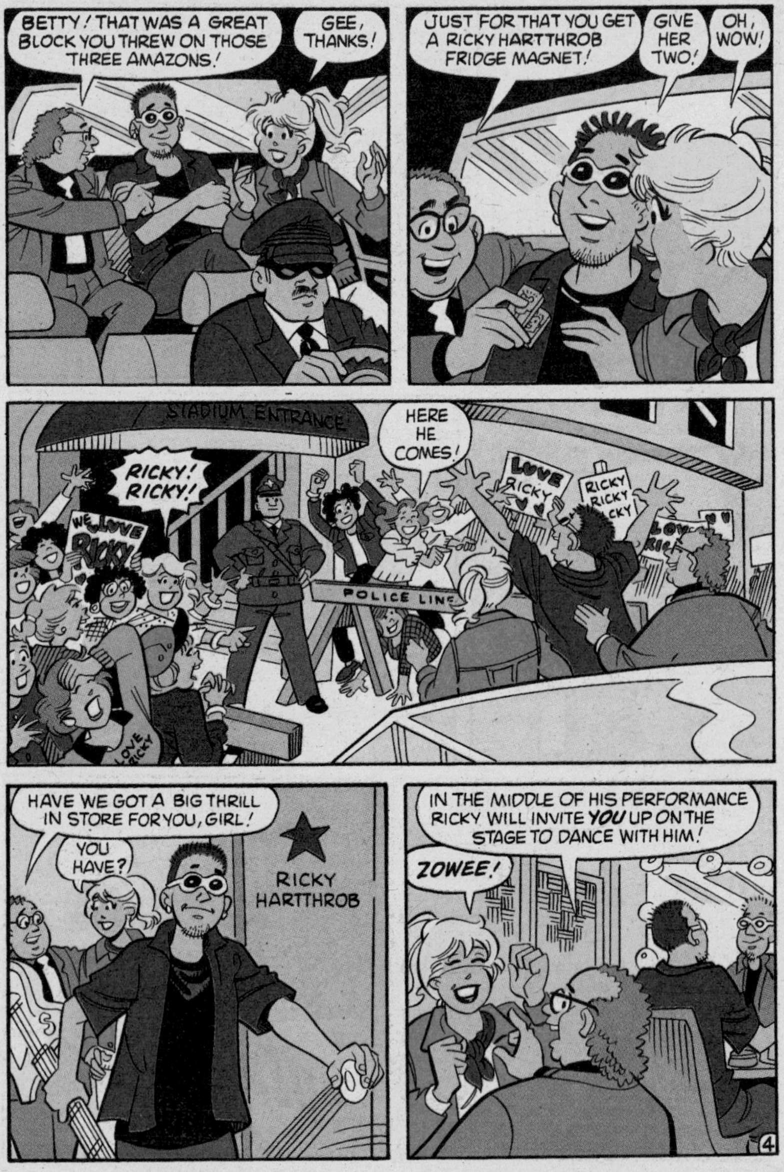
BETTY! THAT WAS A GREAT BLOCK YOU THREW ON THOSE THREE AMAZONS!
GEE, THANKS!
JUST FOR THAT YOU GET A RICKY HARTTHROB FRIDGE MAGNET!
GIVE HER TWO!
OH, WOW!
STADIUM ENTRANCE
RICKY! RICKY!
HERE HE COMES!
WE LOVE RICKY
LUVE RICKY
RICKY RICKY
POLICE LINE
HAVE WE GOT A BIG THRILL IN STORE FOR YOU, GIRL!
YOU HAVE?
RICKY HARTTHROB
IN THE MIDDLE OF HIS PERFORMANCE RICKY WILL INVITE *YOU* UP ON THE STAGE TO DANCE WITH HIM!
ZOWEE!
4

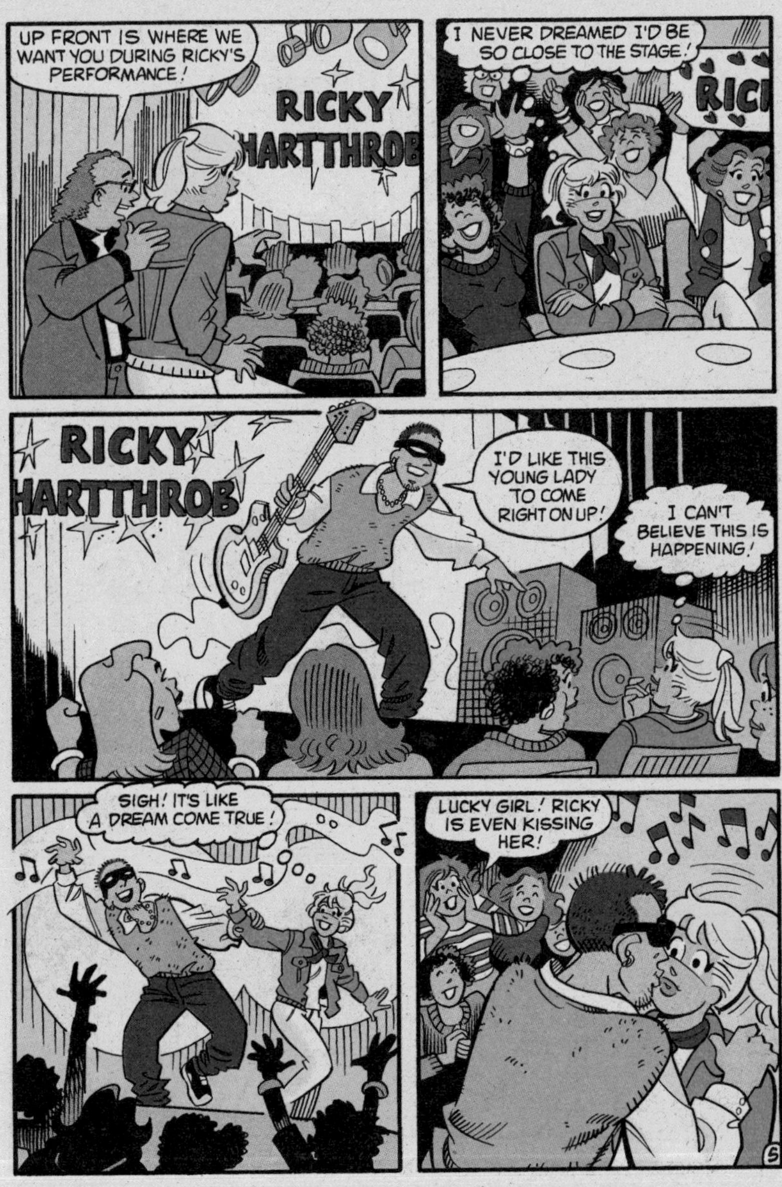
UP FRONT IS WHERE WE WANT YOU DURING RICKY'S PERFORMANCE!
RICKY HARTTHROB
I NEVER DREAMED I'D BE SO CLOSE TO THE STAGE!
RICKY HARTTHROB
I'D LIKE THIS YOUNG LADY TO COME RIGHT ON UP!
I CAN'T BELIEVE THIS IS HAPPENING!
SIGH! IT'S LIKE A DREAM COME TRUE!
LUCKY GIRL! RICKY IS EVEN KISSING HER!
5

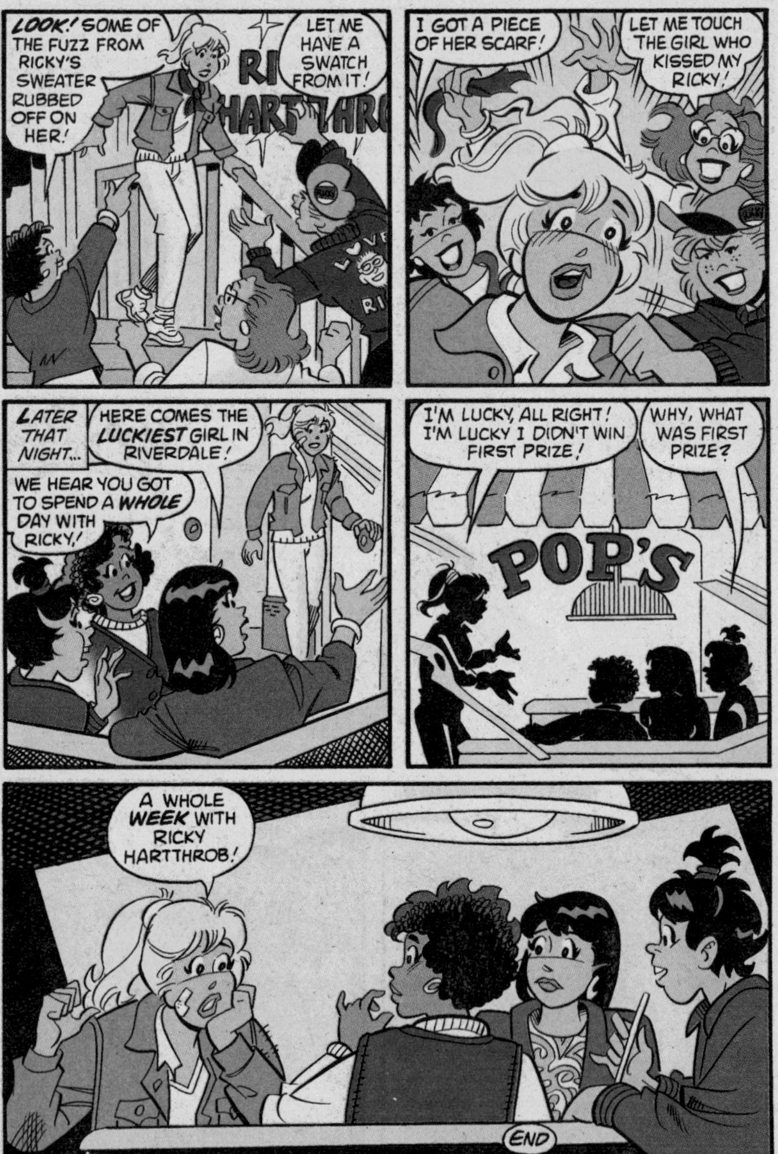
LOOK! SOME OF THE FUZZ FROM RICKY'S SWEATER RUBBED OFF ON HER!
LET ME HAVE A SWATCH FROM IT!
I GOT A PIECE OF HER SCARF!
LET ME TOUCH THE GIRL WHO KISSED MY RICKY!
LATER THAT NIGHT...
HERE COMES THE LUCKIEST GIRL IN RIVERDALE!
WE HEAR YOU GOT TO SPEND A WHOLE DAY WITH RICKY!
I'M LUCKY, ALL RIGHT! I'M LUCKY I DIDN'T WIN FIRST PRIZE!
WHY, WHAT WAS FIRST PRIZE?
POP'S
A WHOLE WEEK WITH RICKY HARTTHROB!
END

Betty and Veronica in "VERONICA'S KARMA"

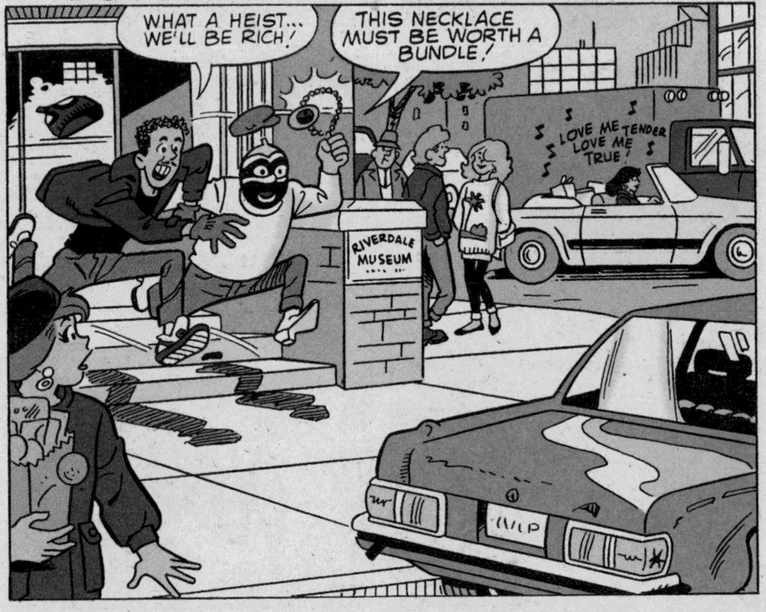
WHAT A HEIST... WE'LL BE RICH!
THIS NECKLACE MUST BE WORTH A BUNDLE!
LOVE ME TENDER LOVE ME TRUE!
RIVERDALE MUSEUM

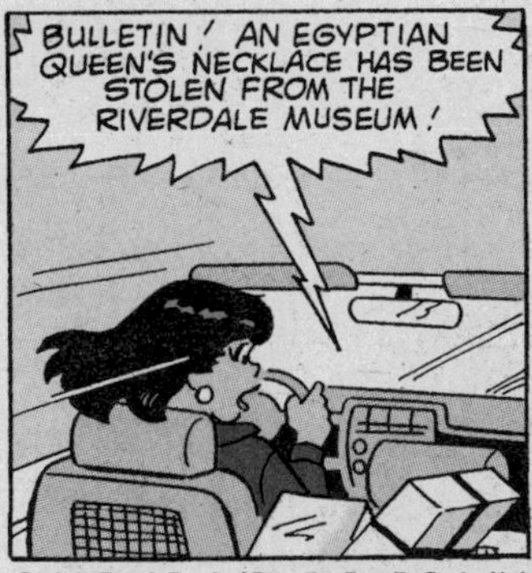
BULLETIN! AN EGYPTIAN QUEEN'S NECKLACE HAS BEEN STOLEN FROM THE RIVERDALE MUSEUM!

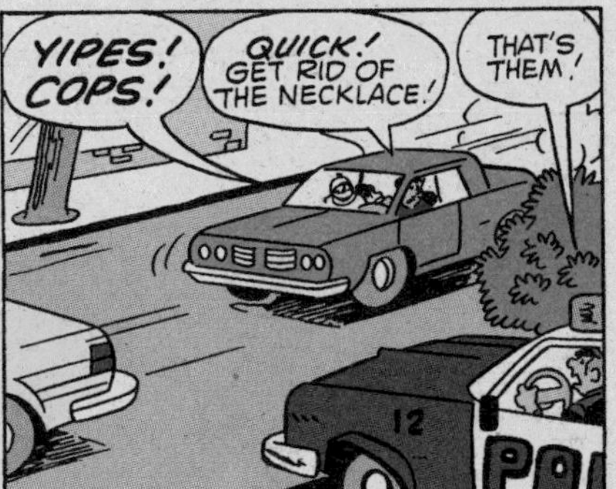
YIPES! COPS!
QUICK! GET RID OF THE NECKLACE!
THAT'S THEM!
12

Script: Frank Doyle / Pencils: Dan DeCarlo / Inks: Rudy Lapick / Letters: Bill Yoshida / Colors: Barry Grossman

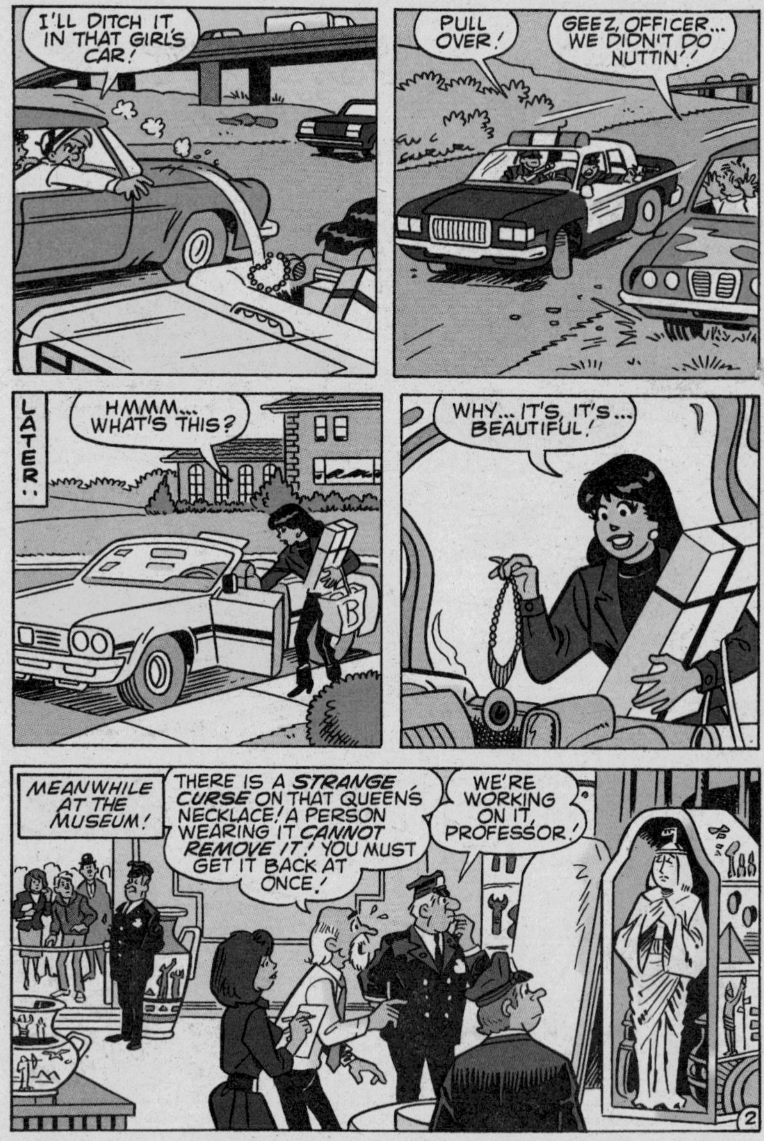
I'LL DITCH IT IN THAT GIRL'S CAR!
PULL OVER!
GEEZ, OFFICER... WE DIDN'T DO NUTTIN'!
LATER:
HMMM... WHAT'S THIS?
B
WHY... IT'S, IT'S... BEAUTIFUL!
MEANWHILE AT THE MUSEUM!
THERE IS A STRANGE CURSE ON THAT QUEEN'S NECKLACE! A PERSON WEARING IT CANNOT REMOVE IT! YOU MUST GET IT BACK AT ONCE!
WE'RE WORKING ON IT, PROFESSOR!
2

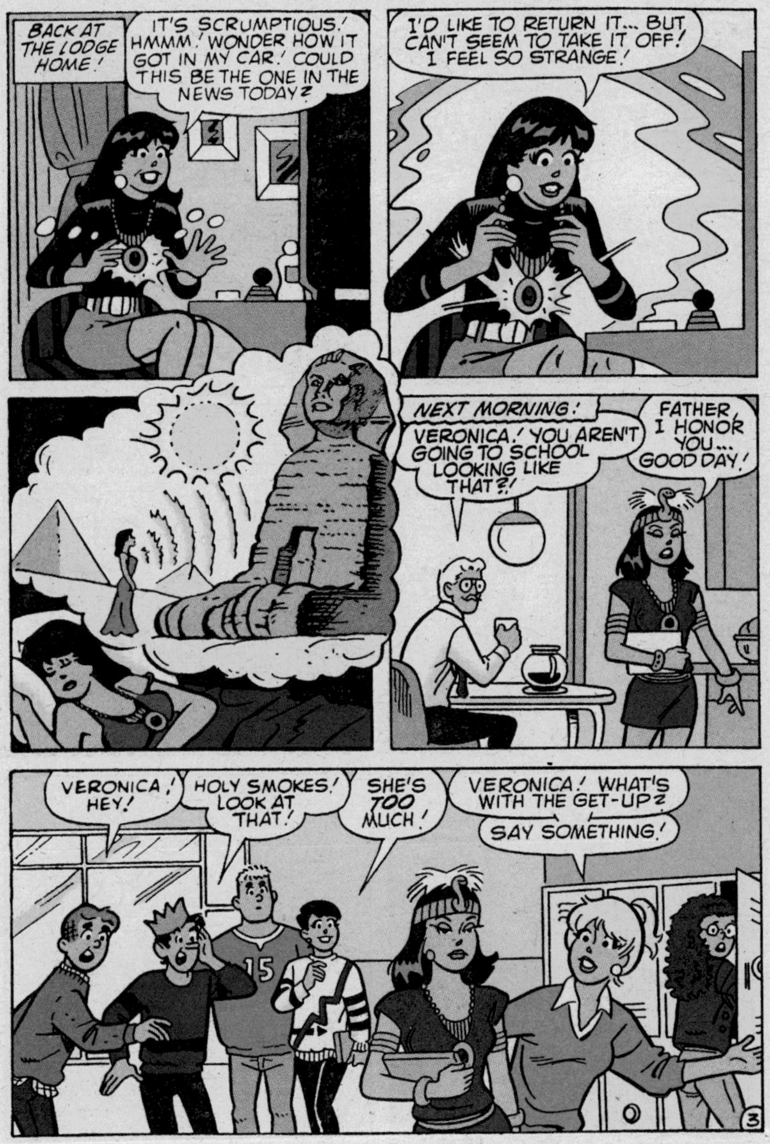
BACK AT THE LODGE HOME!
IT'S SCRUMPTIOUS! HMMM! WONDER HOW IT GOT IN MY CAR! COULD THIS BE THE ONE IN THE NEWS TODAY?
I'D LIKE TO RETURN IT... BUT CAN'T SEEM TO TAKE IT OFF! I FEEL SO STRANGE!
NEXT MORNING!
VERONICA! YOU AREN'T GOING TO SCHOOL LOOKING LIKE THAT?!
FATHER, I HONOR YOU... GOOD DAY!
VERONICA! HEY!
HOLY SMOKES! LOOK AT THAT!
SHE'S TOO MUCH!
VERONICA! WHAT'S WITH THE GET-UP?
SAY SOMETHING!
15
3

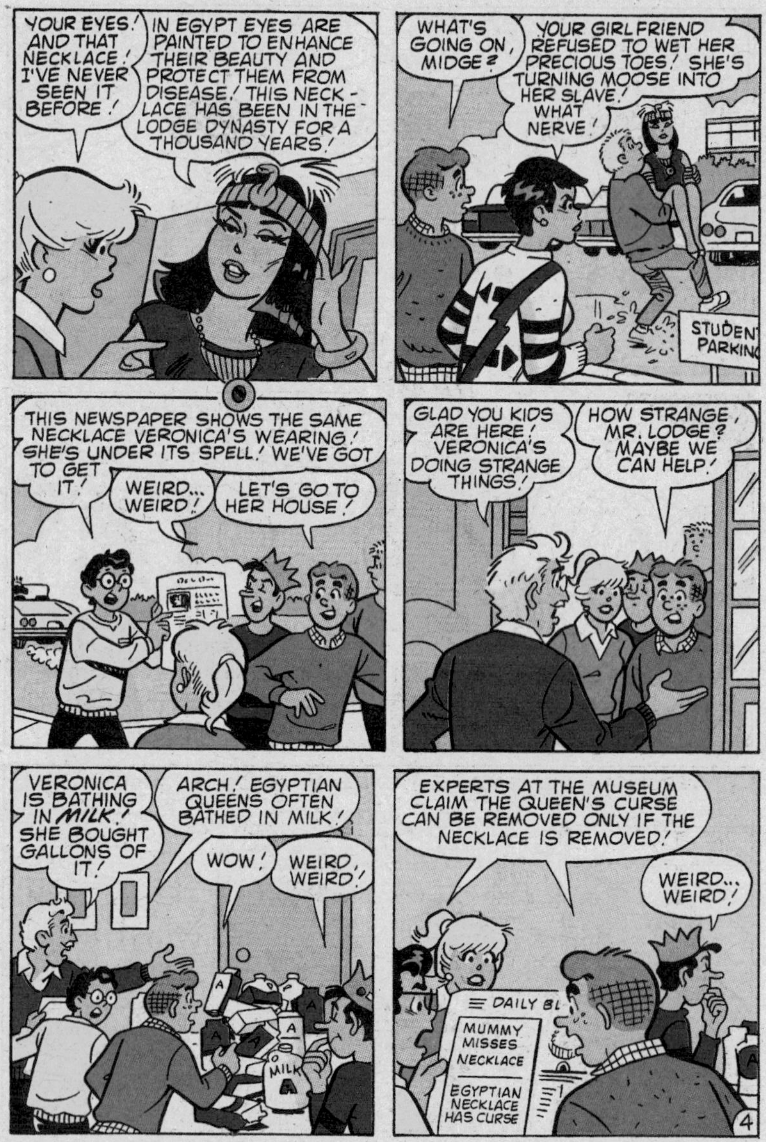
YOUR EYES! AND THAT NECKLACE! I'VE NEVER SEEN IT BEFORE!
IN EGYPT EYES ARE PAINTED TO ENHANCE THEIR BEAUTY AND PROTECT THEM FROM DISEASE! THIS NECKLACE HAS BEEN IN THE LODGE DYNASTY FOR A THOUSAND YEARS!
WHAT'S GOING ON, MIDGE?
YOUR GIRLFRIEND REFUSED TO WET HER PRECIOUS TOES! SHE'S TURNING MOOSE INTO HER SLAVE!
WHAT NERVE!
STUDENT PARKING
THIS NEWSPAPER SHOWS THE SAME NECKLACE VERONICA'S WEARING! SHE'S UNDER ITS SPELL! WE'VE GOT TO GET IT!
WEIRD... WEIRD!
LET'S GO TO HER HOUSE!
GLAD YOU KIDS ARE HERE! VERONICA'S DOING STRANGE THINGS!
HOW STRANGE, MR. LODGE? MAYBE WE CAN HELP!
VERONICA IS BATHING IN *MILK*! SHE BOUGHT GALLONS OF IT!
ARCH! EGYPTIAN QUEENS OFTEN BATHED IN MILK!
WOW!
WEIRD, WEIRD!
MILK
EXPERTS AT THE MUSEUM CLAIM THE QUEEN'S CURSE CAN BE REMOVED ONLY IF THE NECKLACE IS REMOVED!
WEIRD... WEIRD!
DAILY BL
MUMMY MISSES NECKLACE
EGYPTIAN NECKLACE HAS CURSE
4

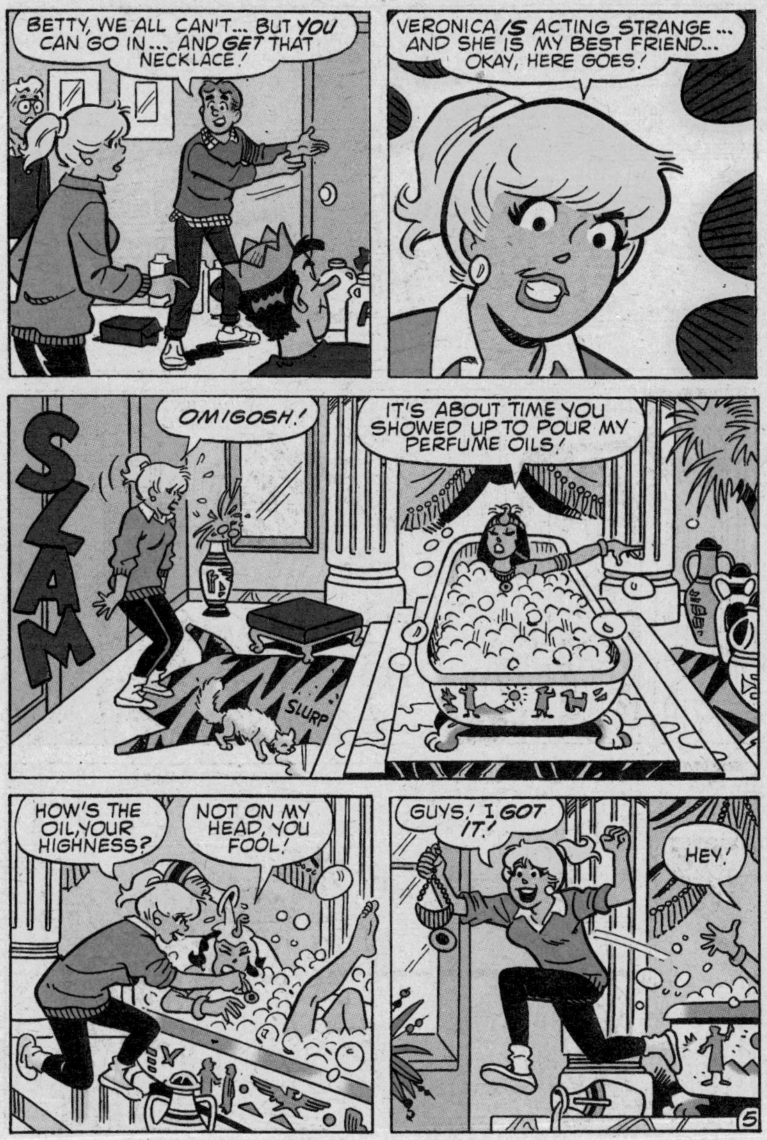
BETTY, WE ALL CAN'T... BUT YOU CAN GO IN... AND GET THAT NECKLACE!
VERONICA IS ACTING STRANGE... AND SHE IS MY BEST FRIEND... OKAY, HERE GOES!
SLAM
OMIGOSH!
SLURP
IT'S ABOUT TIME YOU SHOWED UP TO POUR MY PERFUME OILS!
HOW'S THE OIL, YOUR HIGHNESS?
NOT ON MY HEAD, YOU FOOL!
GUYS! I GOT IT!
HEY!
5

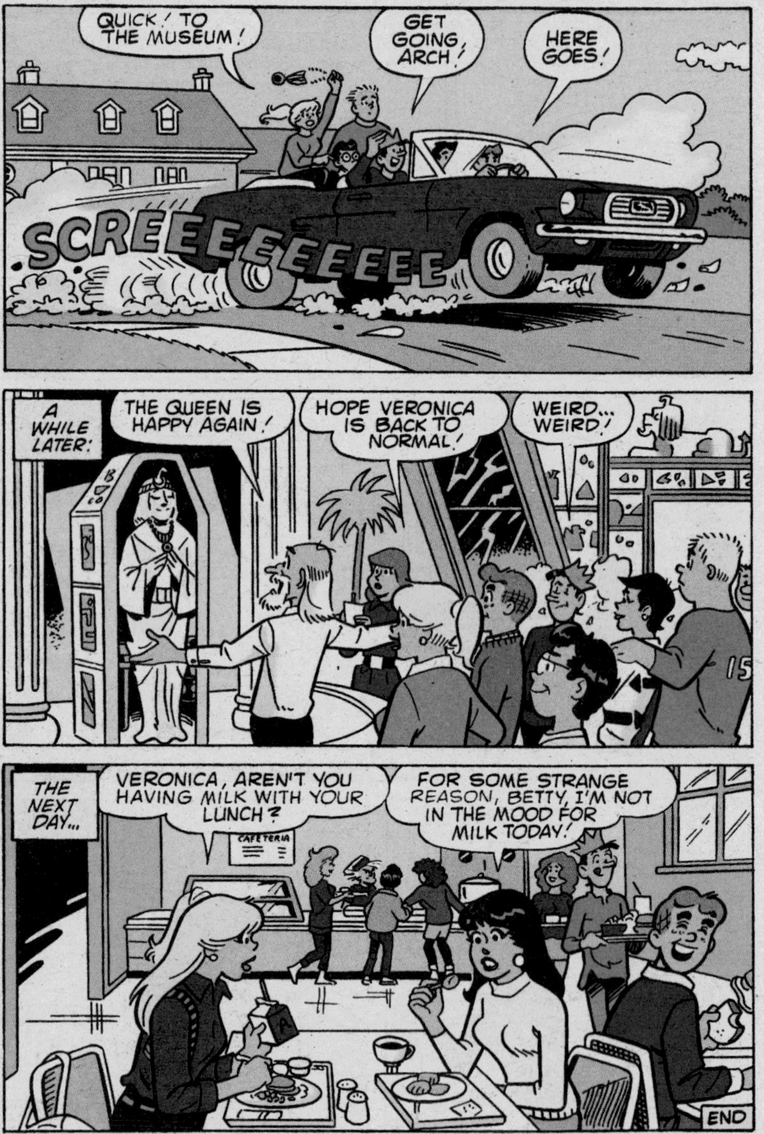
QUICK! TO THE MUSEUM!
GET GOING, ARCH!
HERE GOES!
SCREEEEEEEEEE
A WHILE LATER:
THE QUEEN IS HAPPY AGAIN!
HOPE VERONICA IS BACK TO NORMAL!
WEIRD... WEIRD!
THE NEXT DAY...
VERONICA, AREN'T YOU HAVING MILK WITH YOUR LUNCH?
FOR SOME STRANGE REASON, BETTY, I'M NOT IN THE MOOD FOR MILK TODAY!
CAFETERIA
END

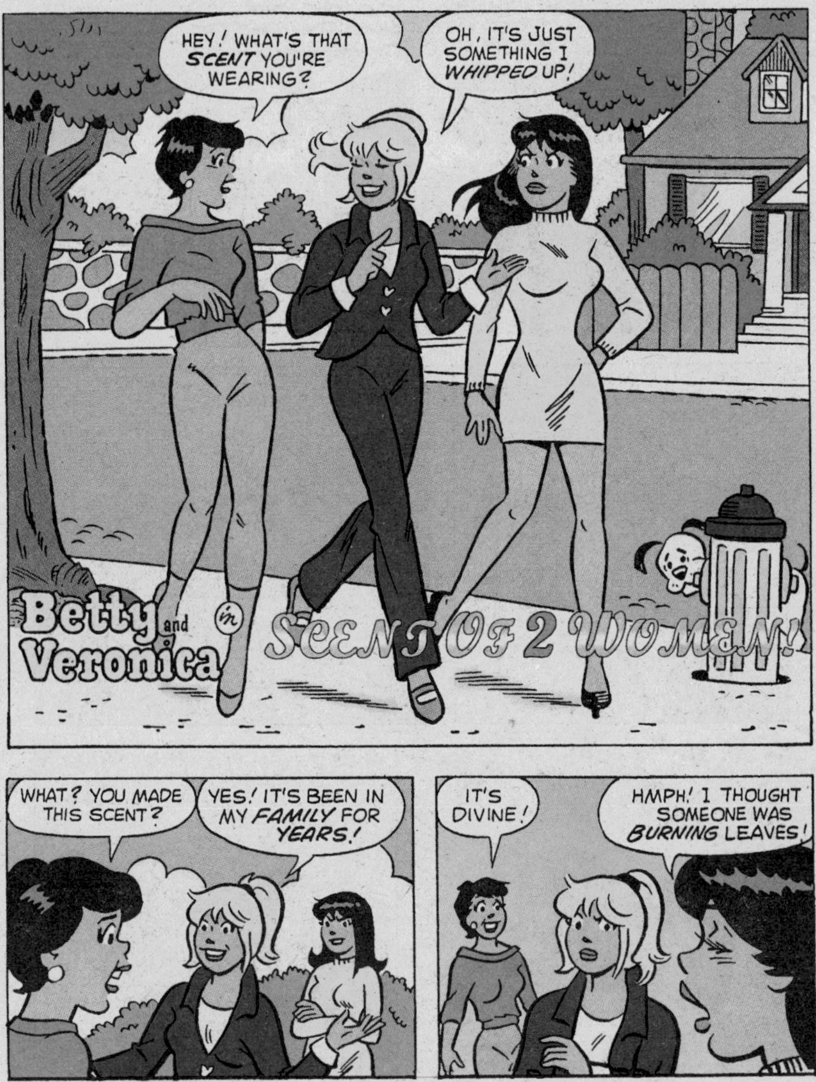
HEY! WHAT'S THAT SCENT YOU'RE WEARING?
OH, IT'S JUST SOMETHING I WHIPPED UP!
Betty and Veronica in SCENT OF 2 WOMEN!
WHAT? YOU MADE THIS SCENT?
YES! IT'S BEEN IN MY FAMILY FOR YEARS!
IT'S DIVINE!
HMPH! I THOUGHT SOMEONE WAS BURNING LEAVES!

Script & Pencils: Dan Parent / Inks: Al Nickerson / Letters: Bill Yoshida / Colors: Barry Grossman

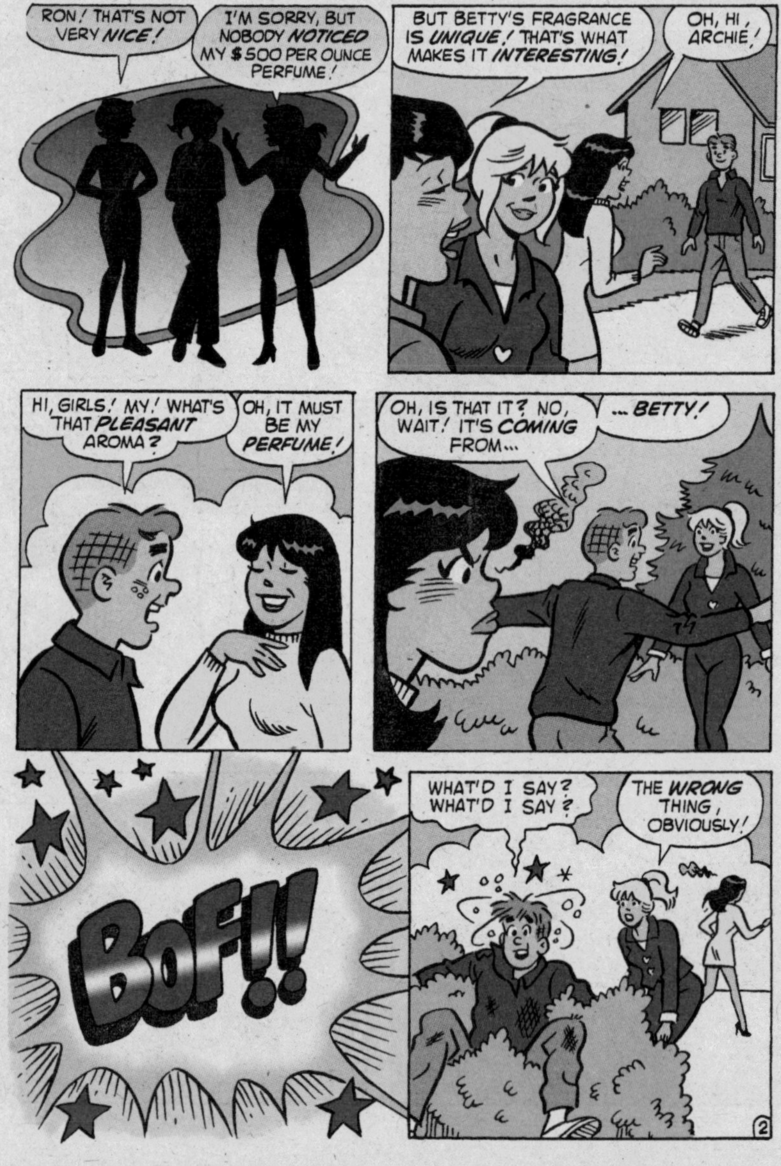
RON! THAT'S NOT VERY NICE!
I'M SORRY, BUT NOBODY NOTICED MY $500 PER OUNCE PERFUME!
BUT BETTY'S FRAGRANCE IS UNIQUE! THAT'S WHAT MAKES IT INTERESTING!
OH, HI, ARCHIE!
HI, GIRLS! MY! WHAT'S THAT PLEASANT AROMA?
OH, IT MUST BE MY PERFUME!
OH, IS THAT IT? NO, WAIT! IT'S COMING FROM...
...BETTY!
BOF!!
WHAT'D I SAY? WHAT'D I SAY?
THE WRONG THING, OBVIOUSLY!
2

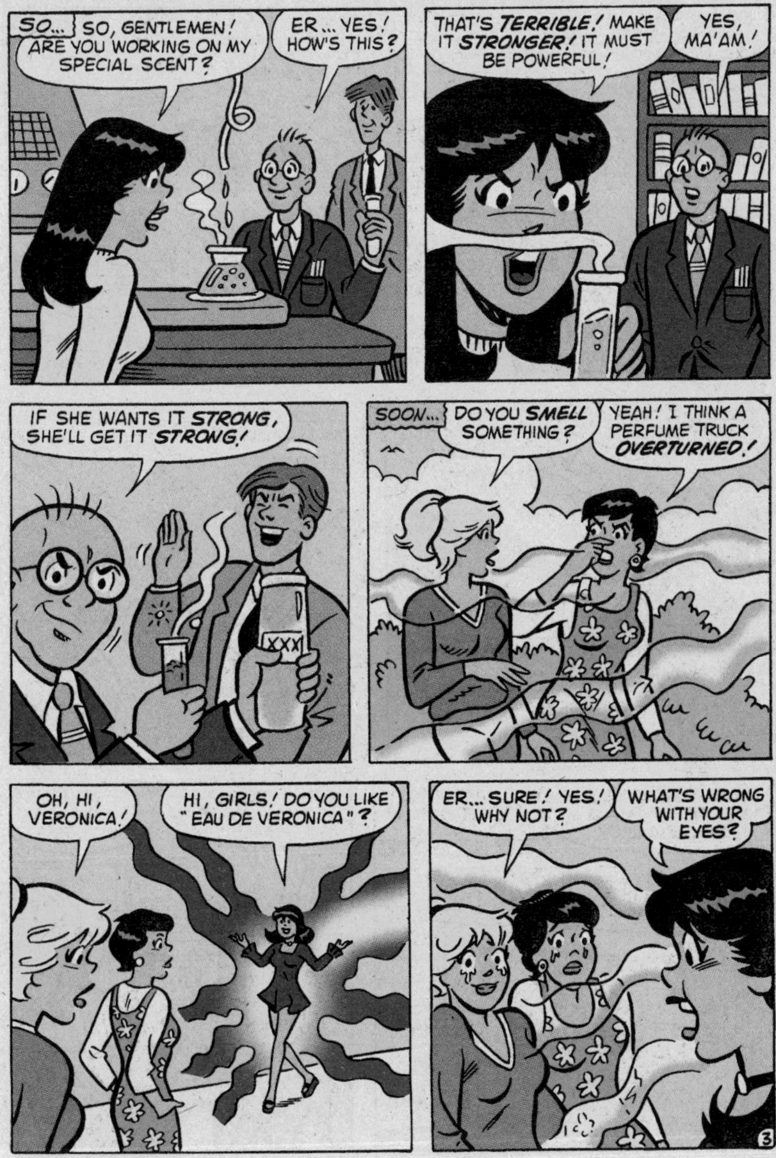
SO...
SO, GENTLEMEN! ARE YOU WORKING ON MY SPECIAL SCENT?
ER... YES! HOW'S THIS?
THAT'S TERRIBLE! MAKE IT STRONGER! IT MUST BE POWERFUL!
YES, MA'AM!
IF SHE WANTS IT STRONG, SHE'LL GET IT STRONG!
XXX
SOON...
DO YOU SMELL SOMETHING?
YEAH! I THINK A PERFUME TRUCK OVERTURNED!
OH, HI, VERONICA!
HI, GIRLS! DO YOU LIKE "EAU DE VERONICA"?
ER... SURE! YES! WHY NOT?
WHAT'S WRONG WITH YOUR EYES?
3

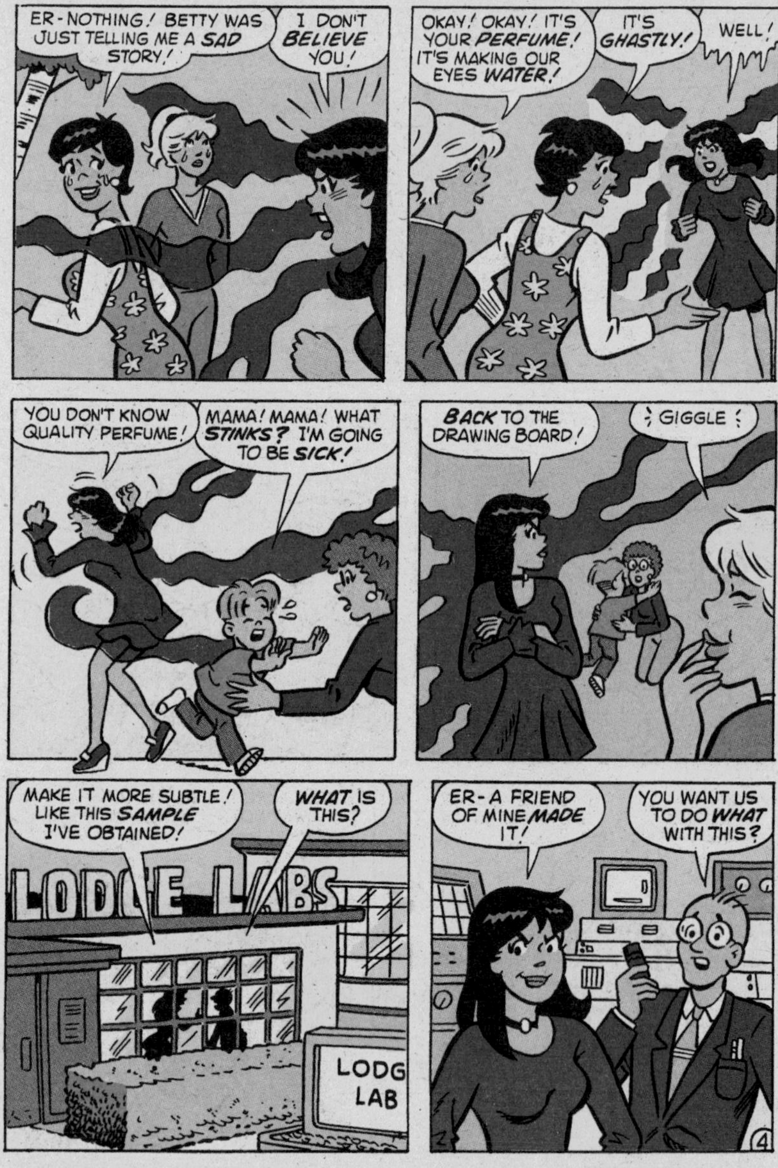
ER-NOTHING! BETTY WAS JUST TELLING ME A SAD STORY!
I DON'T BELIEVE YOU!
OKAY! OKAY! IT'S YOUR PERFUME! IT'S MAKING OUR EYES WATER!
IT'S GHASTLY!
WELL!
YOU DON'T KNOW QUALITY PERFUME!
MAMA! MAMA! WHAT STINKS? I'M GOING TO BE SICK!
BACK TO THE DRAWING BOARD!
GIGGLE
MAKE IT MORE SUBTLE! LIKE THIS SAMPLE I'VE OBTAINED!
WHAT IS THIS?
LODGE LABS
LODG LAB
ER-A FRIEND OF MINE MADE IT!
YOU WANT US TO DO WHAT WITH THIS?
4

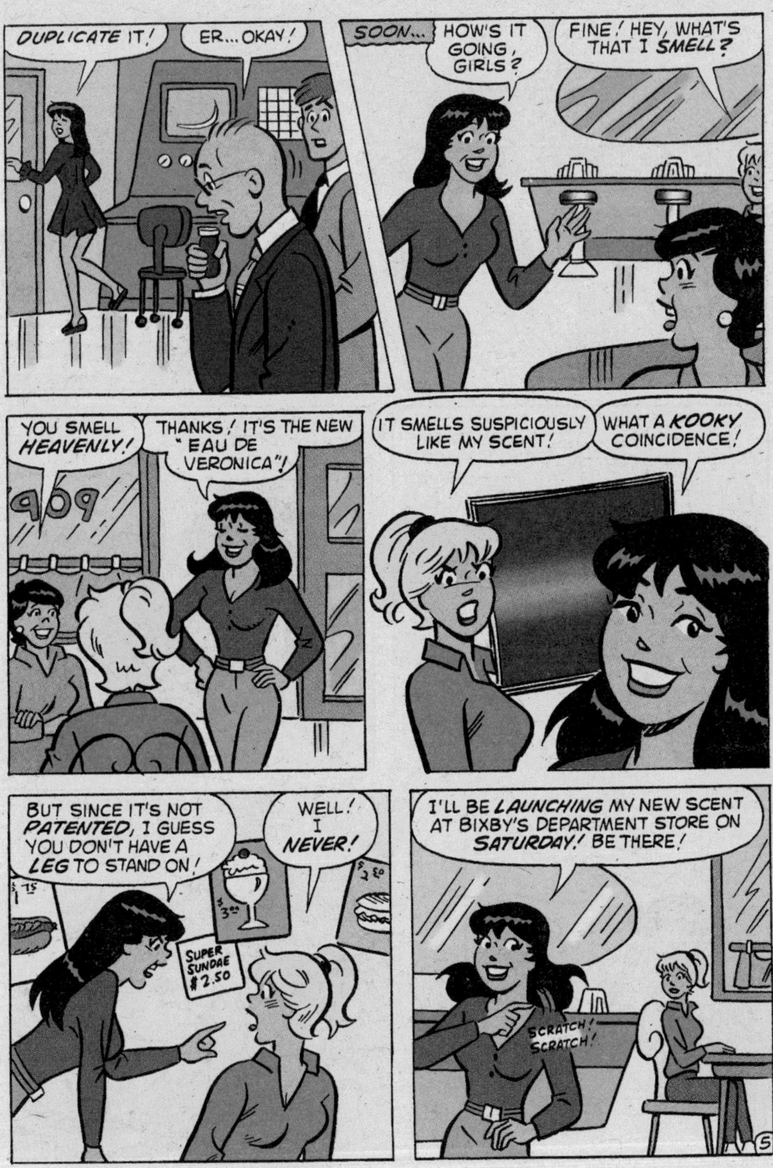
DUPLICATE IT!
ER... OKAY!
SOON...
HOW'S IT GOING, GIRLS?
FINE! HEY, WHAT'S THAT I SMELL?
YOU SMELL HEAVENLY!
THANKS! IT'S THE NEW "EAU DE VERONICA"!
POP
IT SMELLS SUSPICIOUSLY LIKE MY SCENT!
WHAT A KOOKY COINCIDENCE!
BUT SINCE IT'S NOT PATENTED, I GUESS YOU DON'T HAVE A LEG TO STAND ON!
WELL! I NEVER!
SUPER SUNDAE $2.50
I'LL BE LAUNCHING MY NEW SCENT AT BIXBY'S DEPARTMENT STORE ON SATURDAY! BE THERE!
SCRATCH! SCRATCH!
5

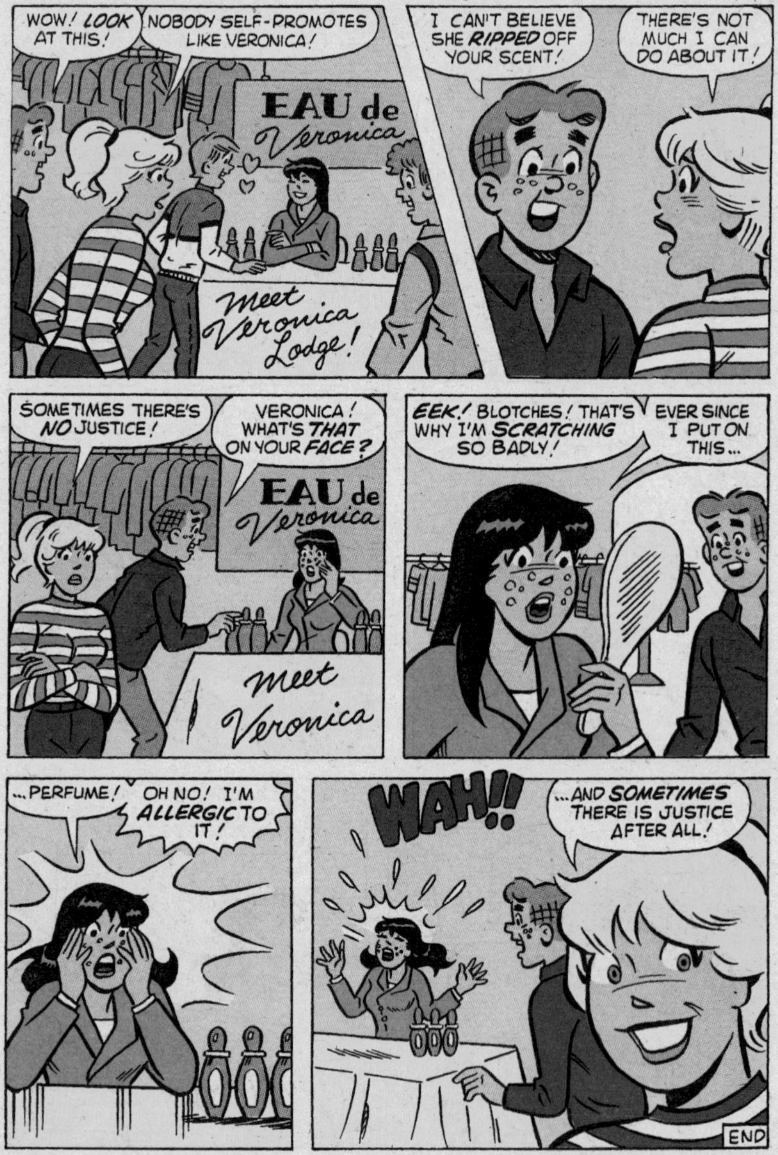
WOW! LOOK AT THIS!
NOBODY SELF-PROMOTES LIKE VERONICA!
EAU de Veronica
Meet Veronica Lodge!
I CAN'T BELIEVE SHE RIPPED OFF YOUR SCENT!
THERE'S NOT MUCH I CAN DO ABOUT IT!
SOMETIMES THERE'S NO JUSTICE!
VERONICA! WHAT'S THAT ON YOUR FACE?
EAU de Veronica
Meet Veronica
EEK! BLOTCHES! THAT'S WHY I'M SCRATCHING SO BADLY!
EVER SINCE I PUT ON THIS...
...PERFUME!
OH NO! I'M ALLERGIC TO IT!
WAH!!
...AND SOMETIMES THERE IS JUSTICE AFTER ALL!
END

Ethel in "A FLIP OF THE LIP"

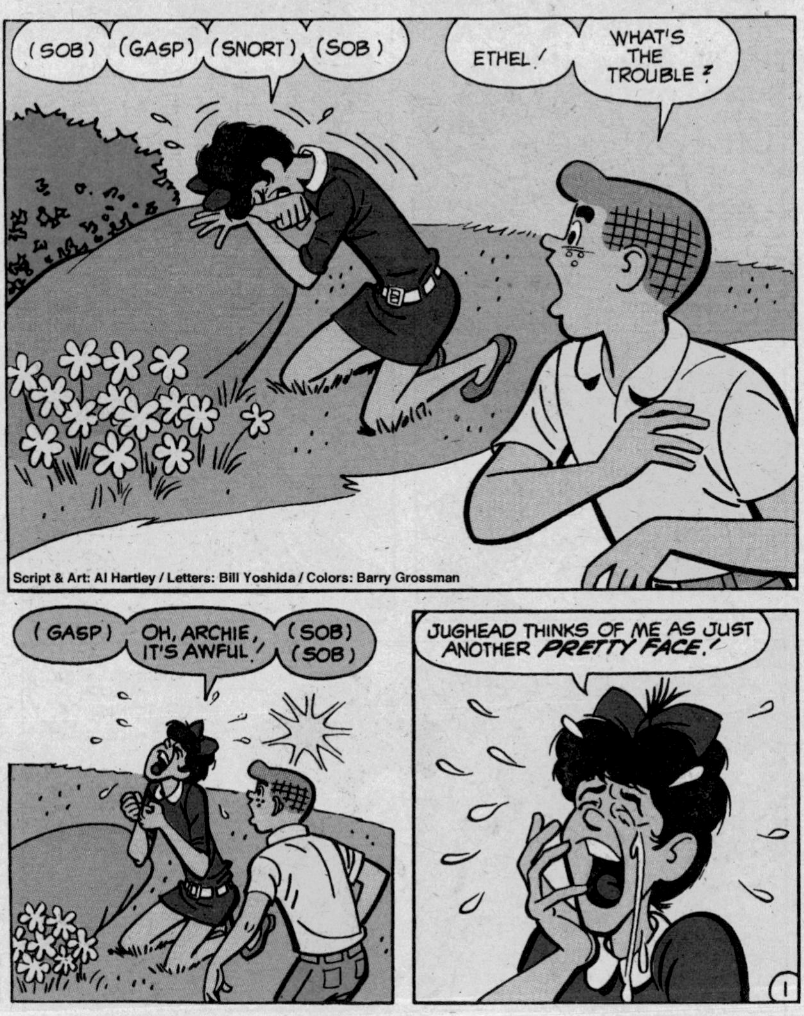
(SOB) (GASP) (SNORT) (SOB)
ETHEL!
WHAT'S THE TROUBLE?
Script & Art: Al Hartley / Letters: Bill Yoshida / Colors: Barry Grossman
(GASP)
OH, ARCHIE, IT'S AWFUL!
(SOB) (SOB)
JUGHEAD THINKS OF ME AS JUST ANOTHER *PRETTY FACE!*
1

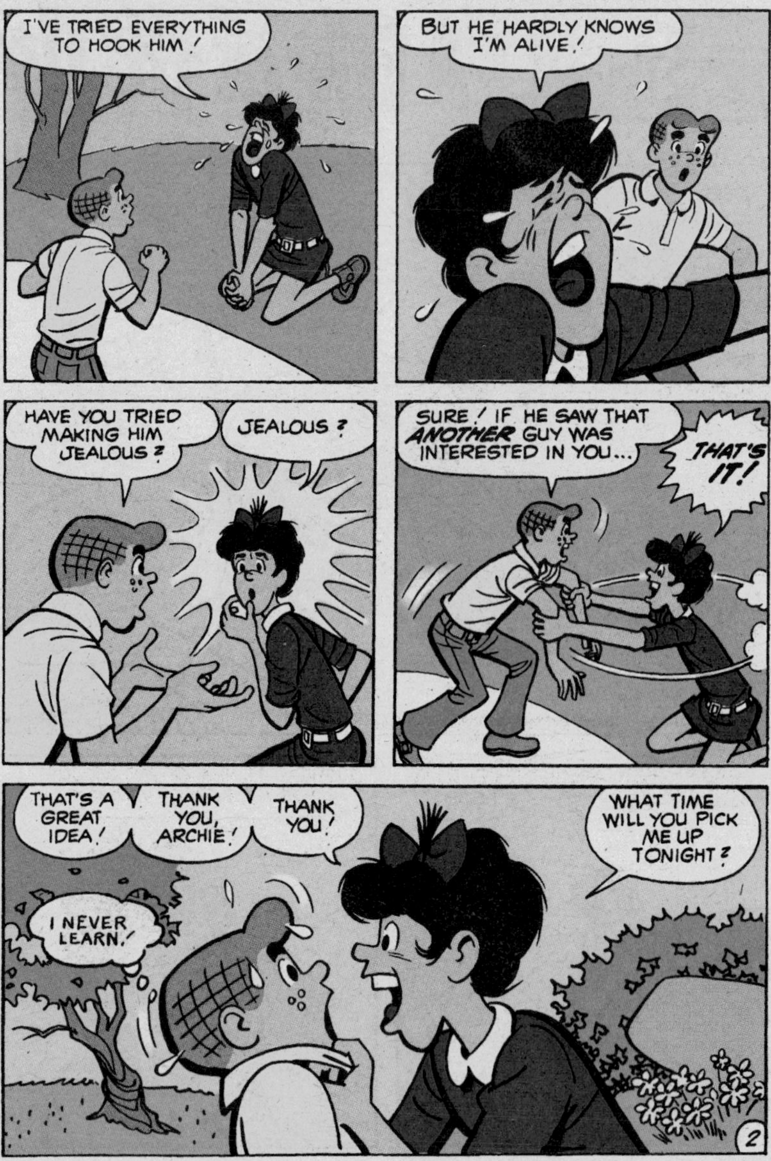

I'VE TRIED EVERYTHING TO HOOK HIM!
BUT HE HARDLY KNOWS I'M ALIVE!
HAVE YOU TRIED MAKING HIM JEALOUS?
JEALOUS?
SURE! IF HE SAW THAT ANOTHER GUY WAS INTERESTED IN YOU...
THAT'S IT!
THAT'S A GREAT IDEA!
THANK YOU, ARCHIE!
THANK YOU!
WHAT TIME WILL YOU PICK ME UP TONIGHT?
I NEVER LEARN!

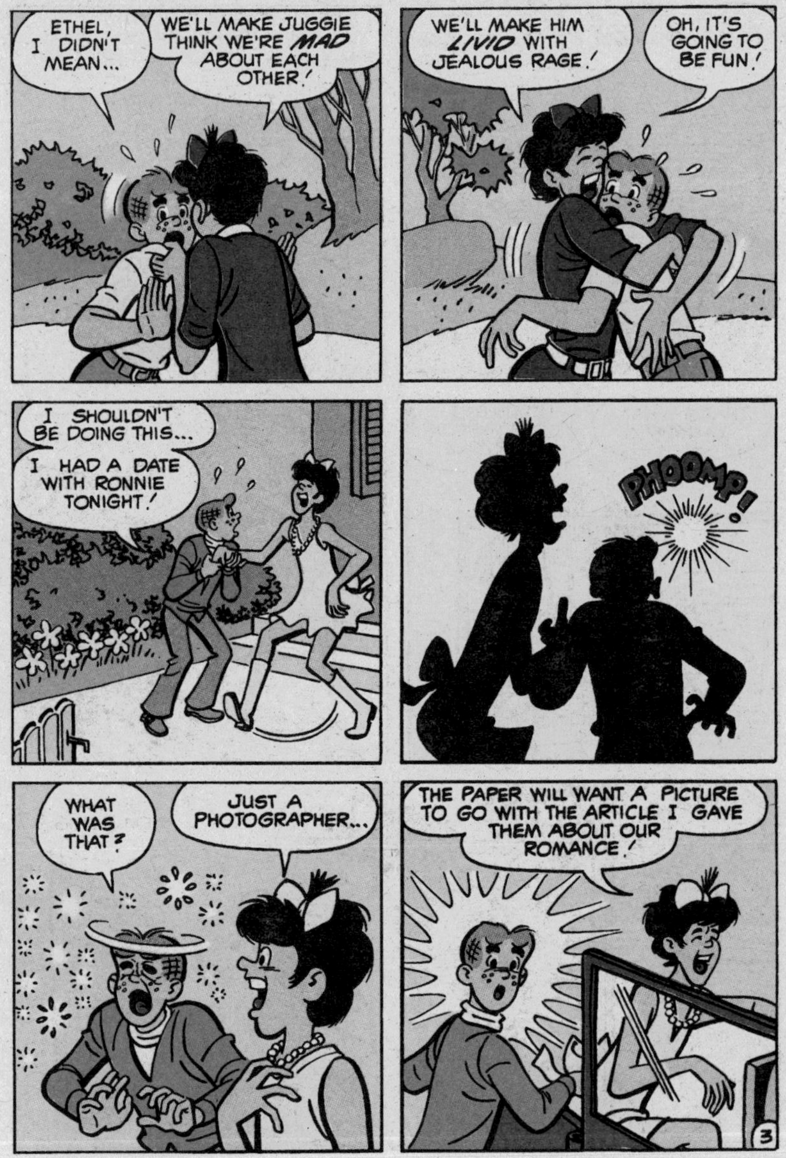
ETHEL, I DIDN'T MEAN...
WE'LL MAKE JUGGIE THINK WE'RE MAD ABOUT EACH OTHER!
WE'LL MAKE HIM LIVID WITH JEALOUS RAGE!
OH, IT'S GOING TO BE FUN!
I SHOULDN'T BE DOING THIS...
I HAD A DATE WITH RONNIE TONIGHT!
PHOOMP!
WHAT WAS THAT?
JUST A PHOTOGRAPHER...
THE PAPER WILL WANT A PICTURE TO GO WITH THE ARTICLE I GAVE THEM ABOUT OUR ROMANCE!
3

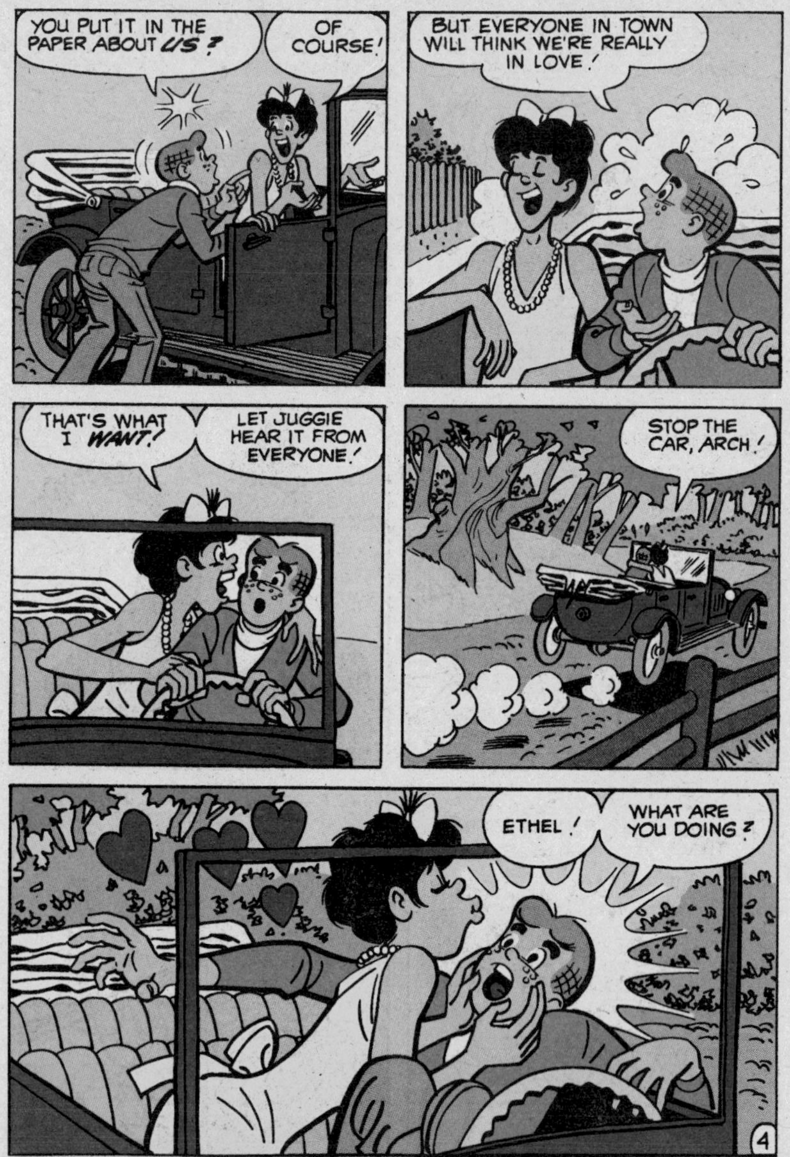
YOU PUT IT IN THE PAPER ABOUT US?
OF COURSE!
BUT EVERYONE IN TOWN WILL THINK WE'RE REALLY IN LOVE!
THAT'S WHAT I WANT!
LET JUGGIE HEAR IT FROM EVERYONE!
STOP THE CAR, ARCH!
ETHEL!
WHAT ARE YOU DOING?
4

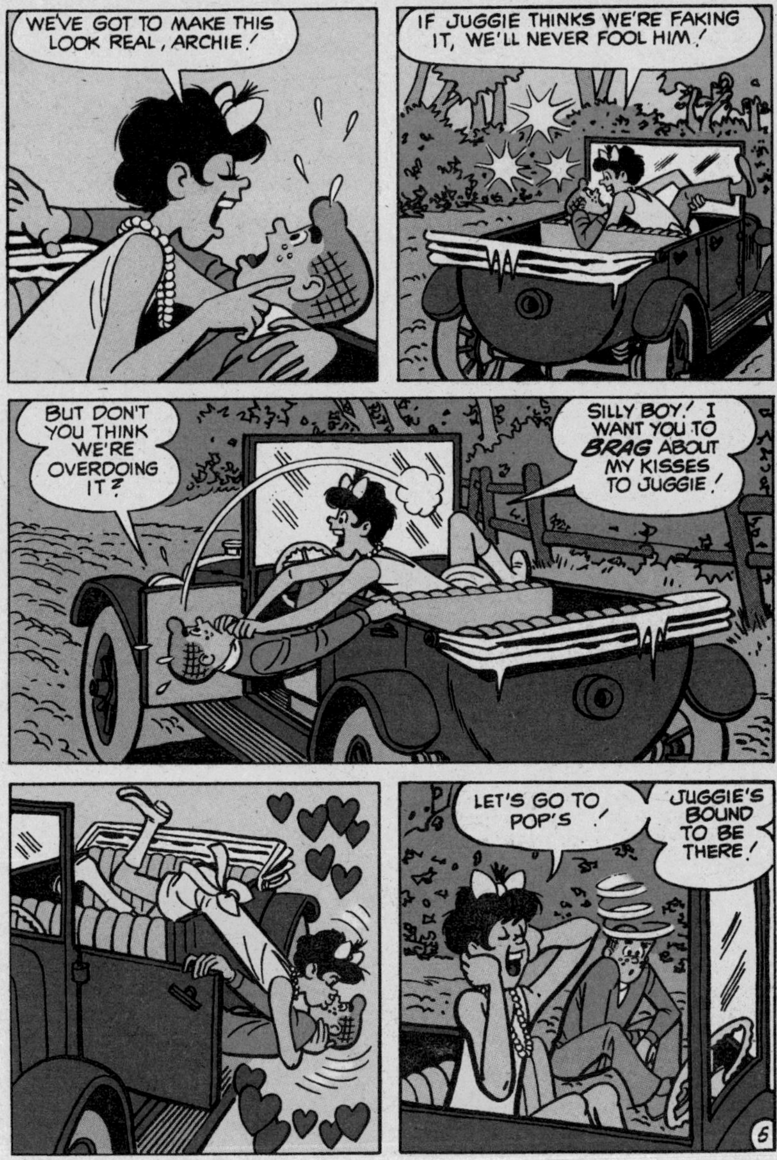
WE'VE GOT TO MAKE THIS LOOK REAL, ARCHIE!
IF JUGGIE THINKS WE'RE FAKING IT, WE'LL NEVER FOOL HIM!
BUT DON'T YOU THINK WE'RE OVERDOING IT?
SILLY BOY! I WANT YOU TO BRAG ABOUT MY KISSES TO JUGGIE!
LET'S GO TO POP'S!
JUGGIE'S BOUND TO BE THERE!
6

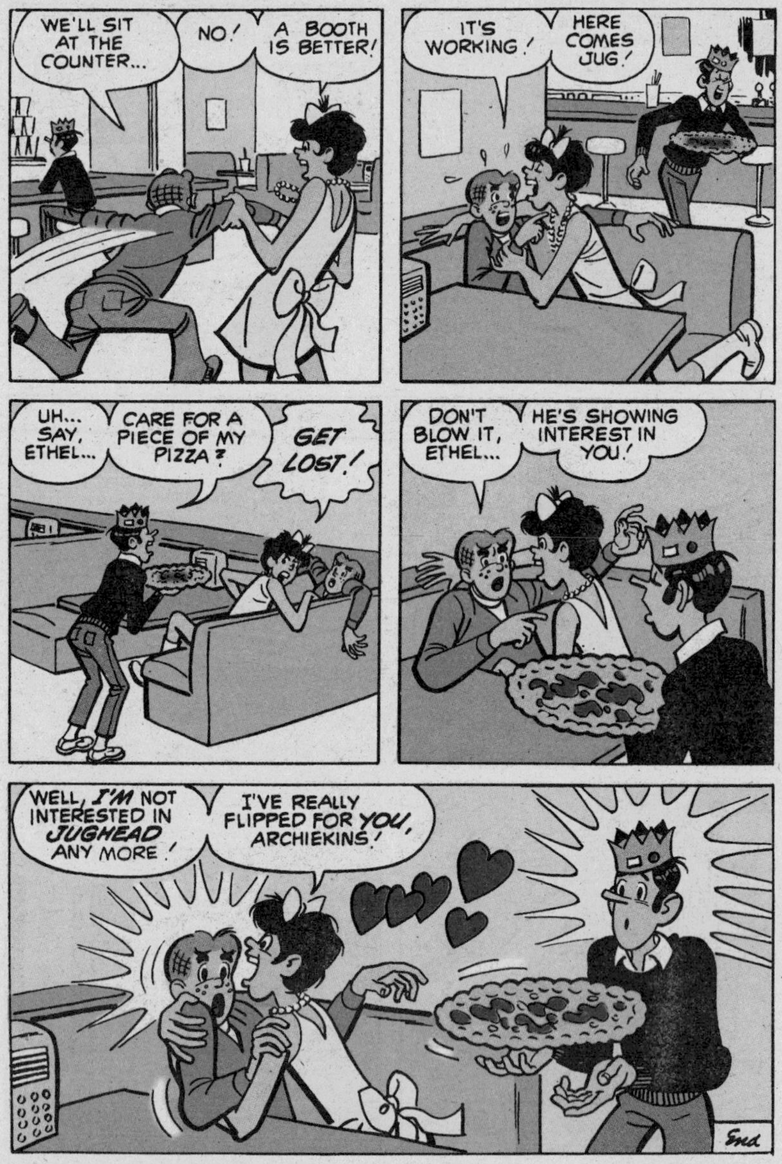
WE'LL SIT AT THE COUNTER...
NO!
A BOOTH IS BETTER!
IT'S WORKING!
HERE COMES JUG!
UH... SAY, ETHEL...
CARE FOR A PIECE OF MY PIZZA?
GET LOST!
DON'T BLOW IT, ETHEL...
HE'S SHOWING INTEREST IN YOU!
WELL, I'M NOT INTERESTED IN JUGHEAD ANY MORE!
I'VE REALLY FLIPPED FOR YOU, ARCHIEKINS!
End

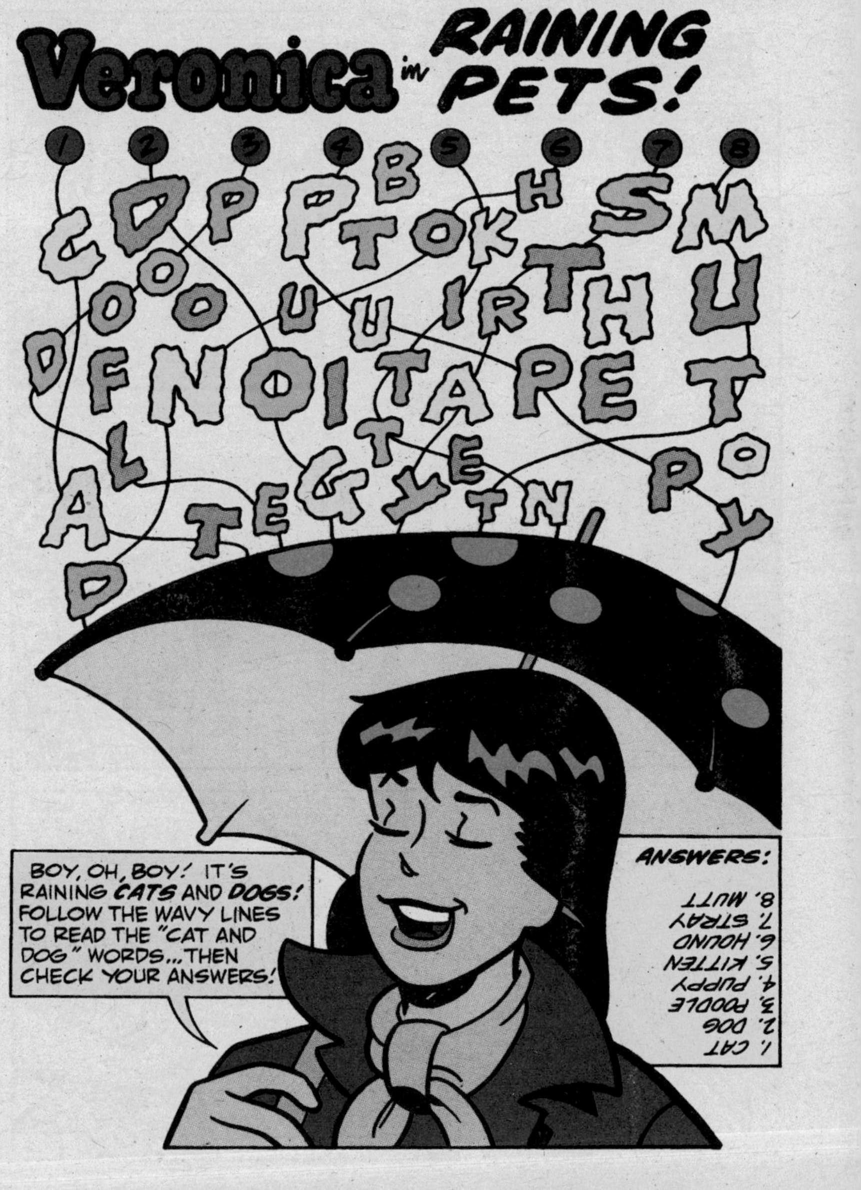
Veronica in RAINING PETS!
BOY, OH, BOY! IT'S RAINING CATS AND DOGS! FOLLOW THE WAVY LINES TO READ THE "CAT AND DOG" WORDS... THEN CHECK YOUR ANSWERS!
ANSWERS:
1. CAT
2. DOG
3. POODLE
4. PUPPY
5. KITTEN
6. HOUND
7. STRAY
8. MUTT

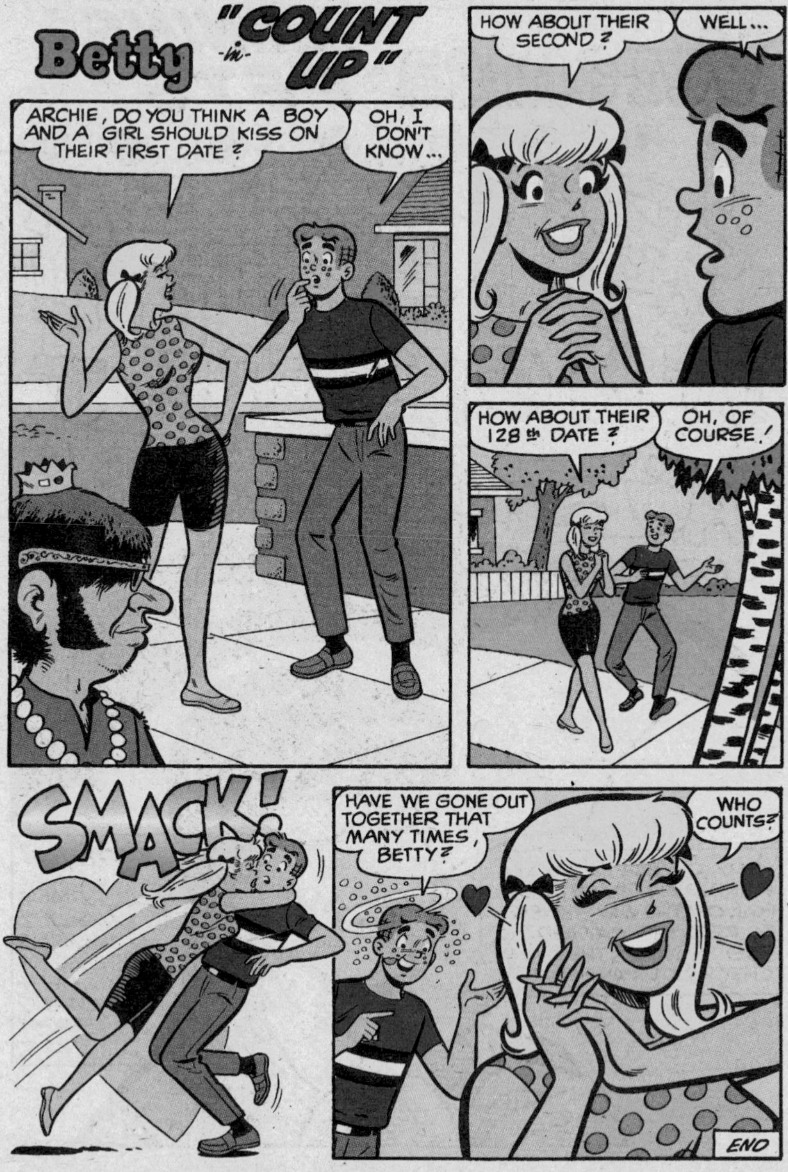

Betty -in- "COUNT UP"
ARCHIE, DO YOU THINK A BOY AND A GIRL SHOULD KISS ON THEIR FIRST DATE?
OH, I DON'T KNOW...
HOW ABOUT THEIR SECOND?
WELL...
HOW ABOUT THEIR 128th DATE?
OH, OF COURSE!
SMACK!
HAVE WE GONE OUT TOGETHER THAT MANY TIMES, BETTY?
WHO COUNTS?
END

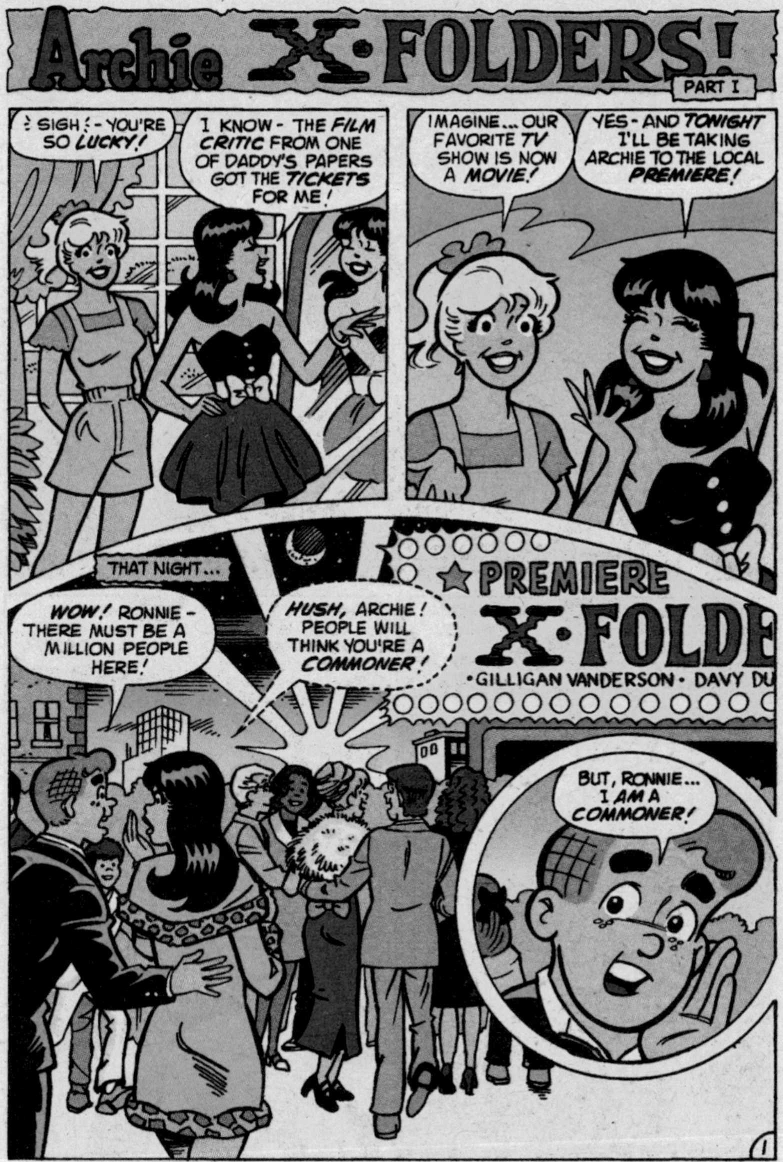
Archie X-FOLDERS!
PART I
⁝ SIGH ⁝ - YOU'RE SO LUCKY!
I KNOW - THE FILM CRITIC FROM ONE OF DADDY'S PAPERS GOT THE TICKETS FOR ME!
IMAGINE... OUR FAVORITE TV SHOW IS NOW A MOVIE!
YES - AND TONIGHT I'LL BE TAKING ARCHIE TO THE LOCAL PREMIERE!
THAT NIGHT...
WOW! RONNIE - THERE MUST BE A MILLION PEOPLE HERE!
HUSH, ARCHIE! PEOPLE WILL THINK YOU'RE A COMMONER!
PREMIERE
X-FOLDE
•GILLIGAN VANDERSON • DAVY DU
BUT, RONNIE... I AM A COMMONER!
1

Script: Bob Bolling / Art: Rex Lindsey / Letters: Bill Yoshida / Colors: Barry Grossman

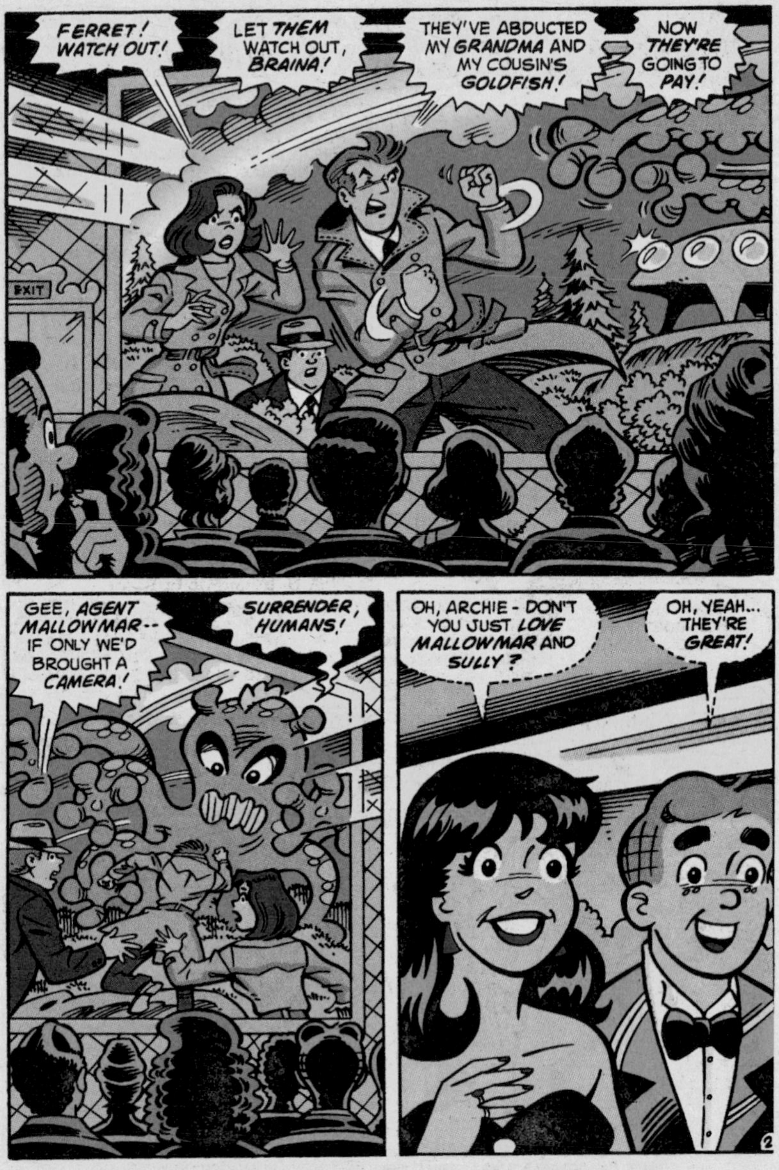
FERRET! WATCH OUT!
LET THEM WATCH OUT, BRAINA!
THEY'VE ABDUCTED MY GRANDMA AND MY COUSIN'S GOLDFISH!
NOW THEY'RE GOING TO PAY!
EXIT
GEE, AGENT MALLOWMAR-- IF ONLY WE'D BROUGHT A CAMERA!
SURRENDER, HUMANS!
OH, ARCHIE - DON'T YOU JUST LOVE MALLOWMAR AND SULLY?
OH, YEAH... THEY'RE GREAT!
2

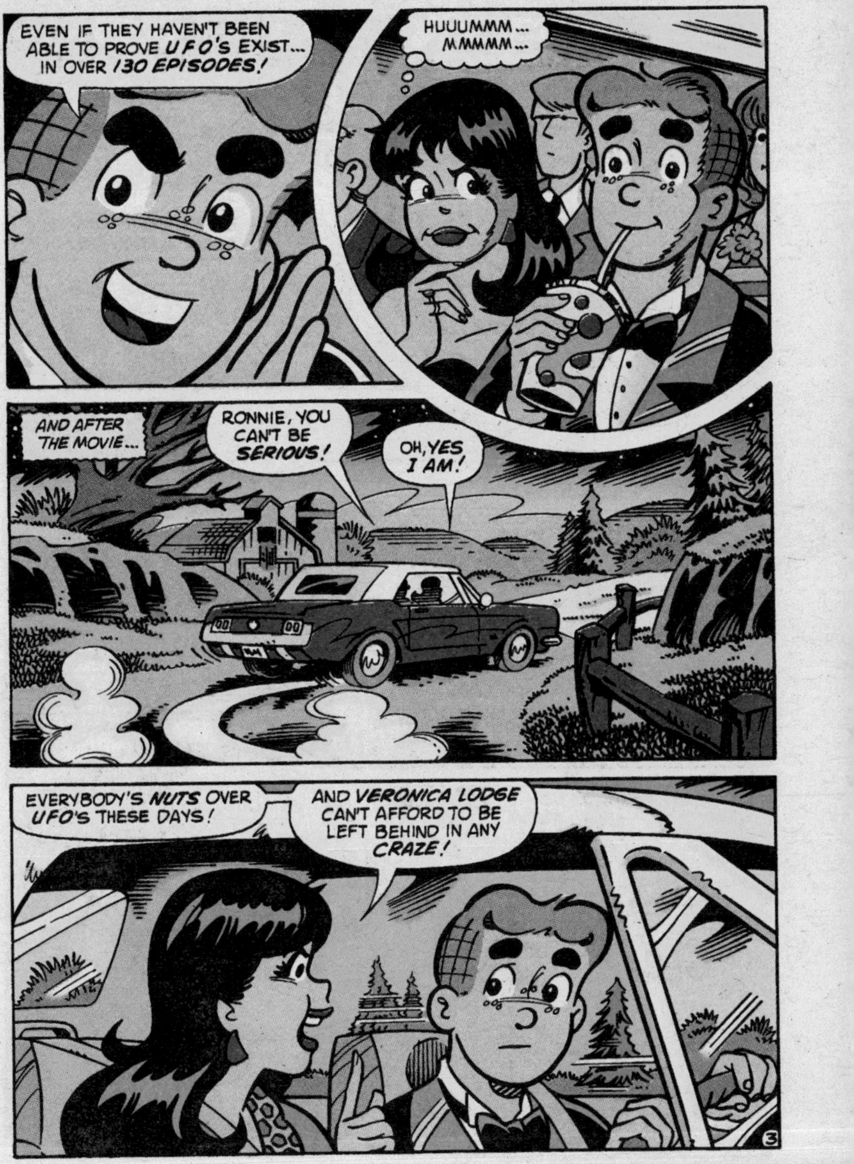
EVEN IF THEY HAVEN'T BEEN ABLE TO PROVE UFO's EXIST... IN OVER 130 EPISODES!
HUUUMMM... MMMMM...
AND AFTER THE MOVIE...
RONNIE, YOU CAN'T BE SERIOUS!
OH, YES I AM!
EVERYBODY'S NUTS OVER UFO'S THESE DAYS!
AND VERONICA LODGE CAN'T AFFORD TO BE LEFT BEHIND IN ANY CRAZE!
3

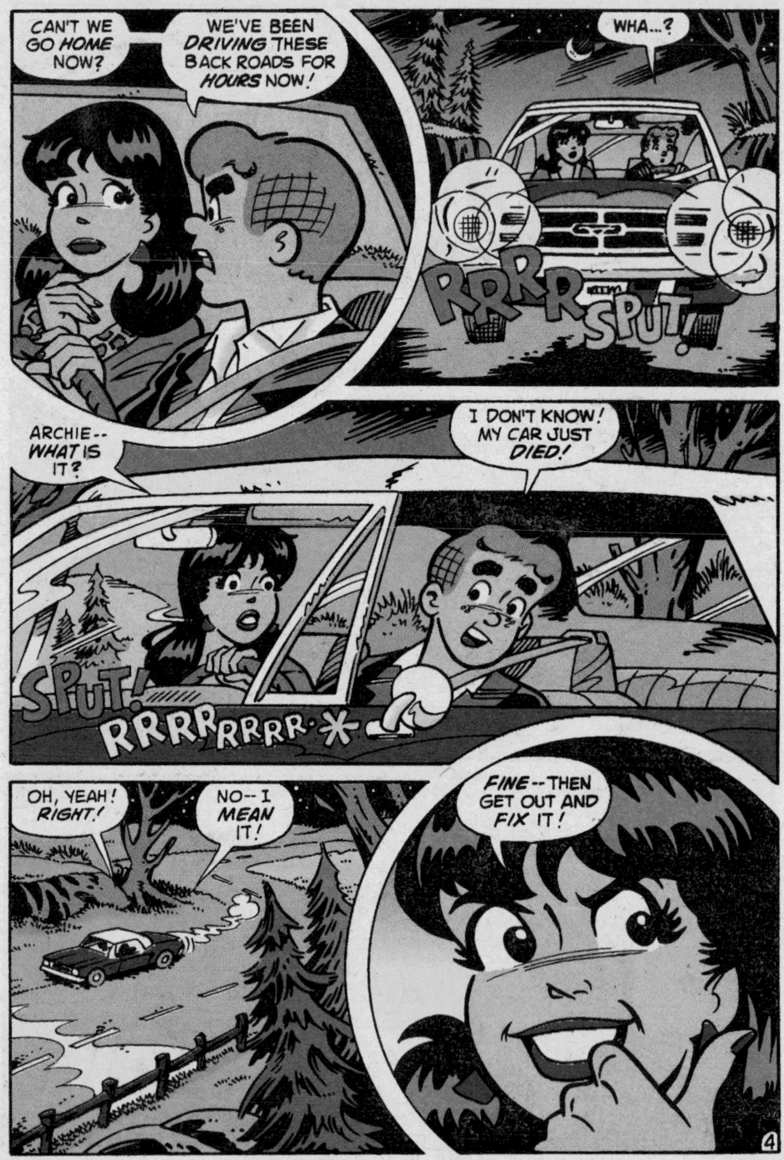
CAN'T WE GO HOME NOW?
WE'VE BEEN DRIVING THESE BACK ROADS FOR HOURS NOW!
WHA...?
RRRR SPUT!
ARCHIE-- WHAT IS IT?
I DON'T KNOW! MY CAR JUST DIED!
SPUT! RRRRRRRR*
OH, YEAH! RIGHT!
NO-- I MEAN IT!
FINE--THEN GET OUT AND FIX IT!
4

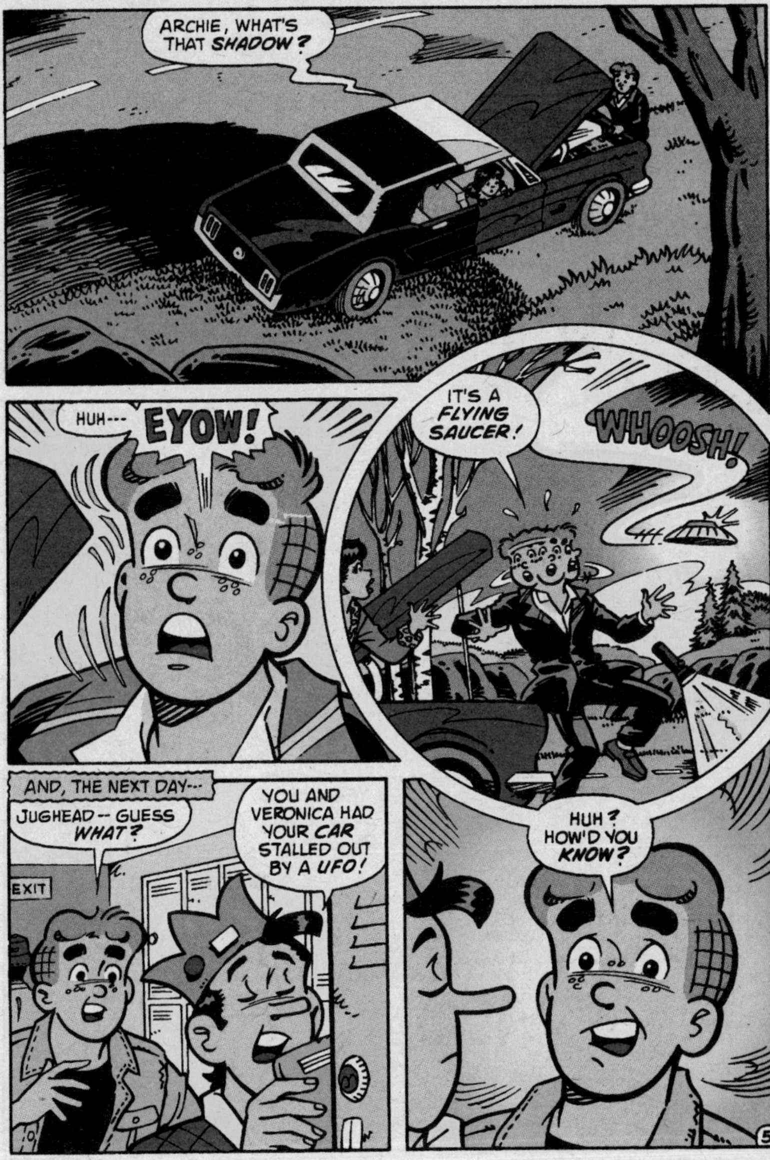

ARCHIE, WHAT'S THAT SHADOW?
HUH--- EYOW!
IT'S A FLYING SAUCER!
WHOOSH!
AND, THE NEXT DAY---
JUGHEAD -- GUESS WHAT?
YOU AND VERONICA HAD YOUR CAR STALLED OUT BY A UFO!
EXIT
HUH? HOW'D YOU KNOW?
5

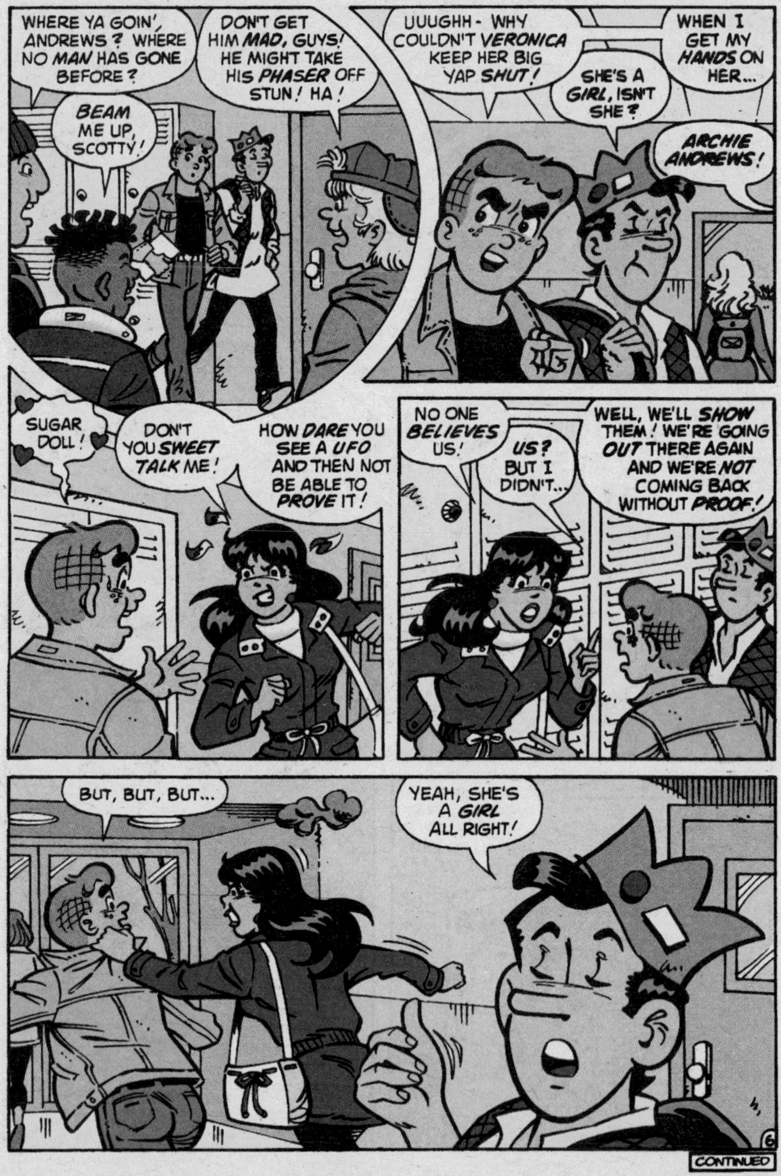
WHERE YA GOIN', ANDREWS? WHERE NO MAN HAS GONE BEFORE?
BEAM ME UP, SCOTTY!
DON'T GET HIM MAD, GUYS! HE MIGHT TAKE HIS PHASER OFF STUN! HA!
UUUGHH - WHY COULDN'T VERONICA KEEP HER BIG YAP SHUT!
SHE'S A GIRL, ISN'T SHE?
WHEN I GET MY HANDS ON HER...
ARCHIE ANDREWS!
SUGAR DOLL!
DON'T YOU SWEET TALK ME!
HOW DARE YOU SEE A UFO AND THEN NOT BE ABLE TO PROVE IT!
NO ONE BELIEVES US!
US? BUT I DIDN'T...
WELL, WE'LL SHOW THEM! WE'RE GOING OUT THERE AGAIN AND WE'RE NOT COMING BACK WITHOUT PROOF!
BUT, BUT, BUT...
YEAH, SHE'S A GIRL ALL RIGHT!
6
CONTINUED

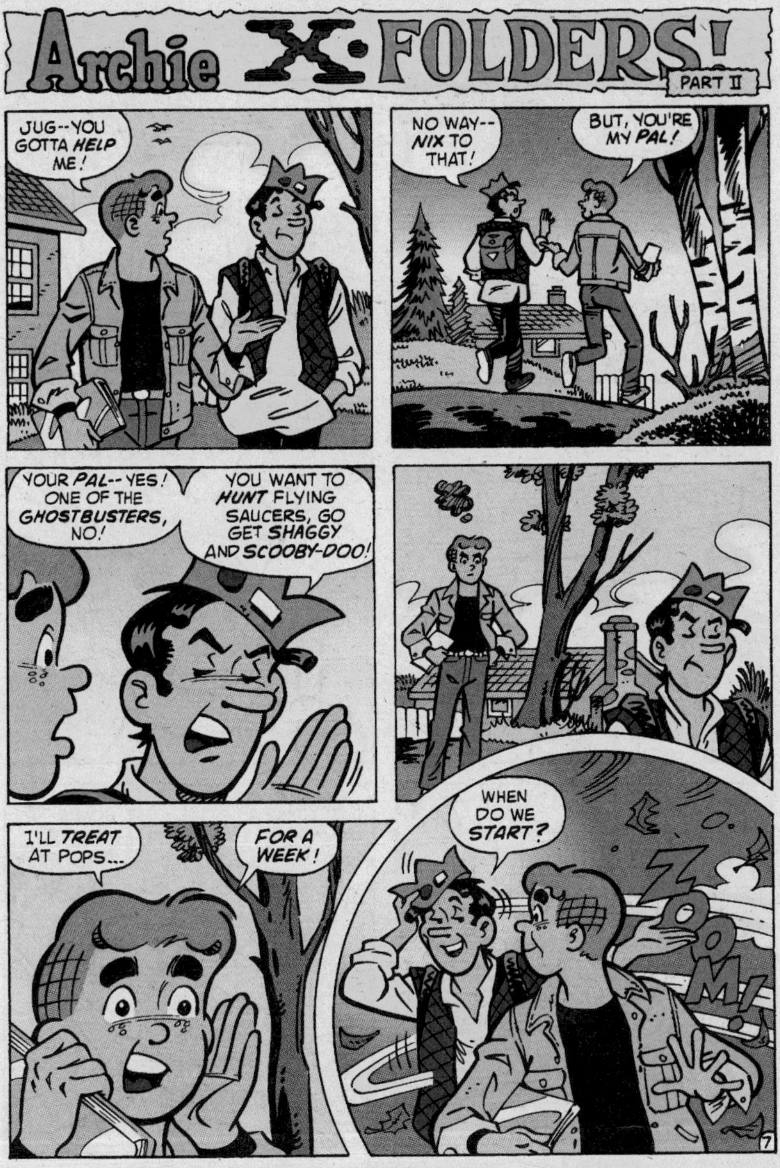
Archie X-FOLDERS!
PART II
JUG--YOU GOTTA HELP ME!
NO WAY-- NIX TO THAT!
BUT, YOU'RE MY PAL!
YOUR PAL-- YES! ONE OF THE GHOSTBUSTERS, NO!
YOU WANT TO HUNT FLYING SAUCERS, GO GET SHAGGY AND SCOOBY-DOO!
I'LL TREAT AT POPS...
FOR A WEEK!
WHEN DO WE START?
ZOOM!

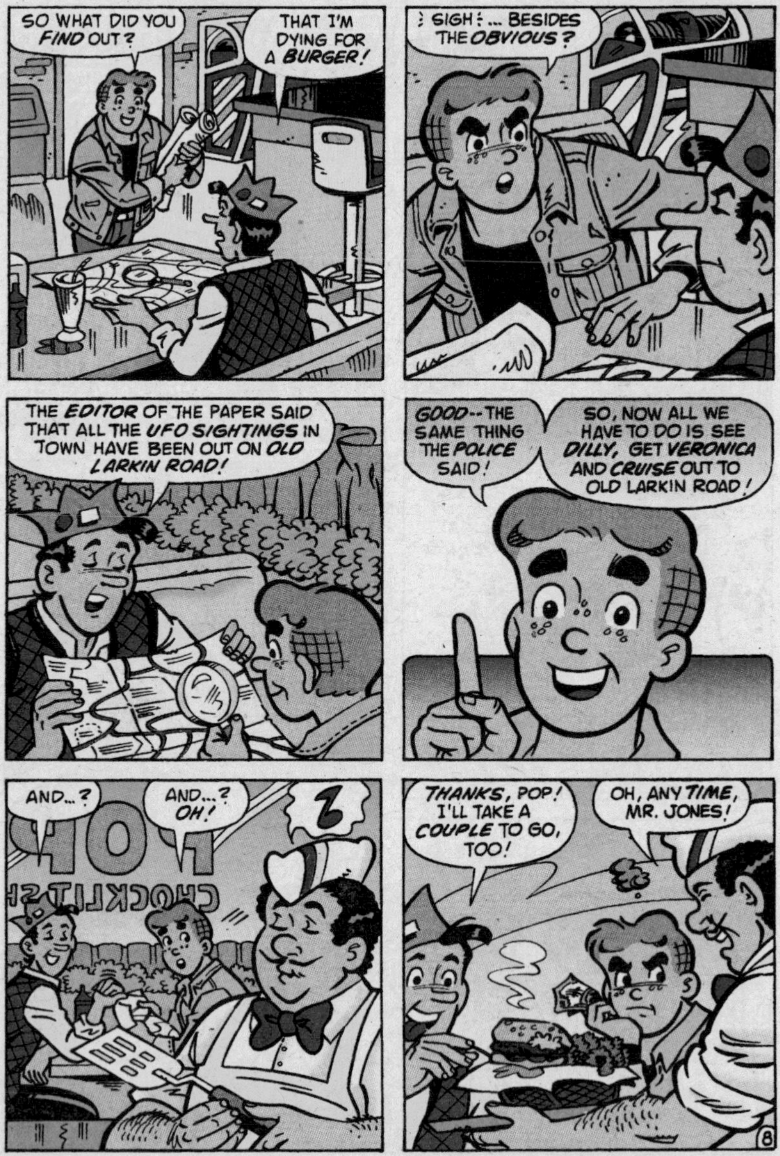
SO WHAT DID YOU FIND OUT?
THAT I'M DYING FOR A BURGER!
SIGH ... BESIDES THE OBVIOUS?
THE EDITOR OF THE PAPER SAID THAT ALL THE UFO SIGHTINGS IN TOWN HAVE BEEN OUT ON OLD LARKIN ROAD!
GOOD-- THE SAME THING THE POLICE SAID!
SO, NOW ALL WE HAVE TO DO IS SEE DILLY, GET VERONICA AND CRUISE OUT TO OLD LARKIN ROAD!
AND...?
AND...? OH!
POP
CHOCKLIT SH
THANKS, POP! I'LL TAKE A COUPLE TO GO, TOO!
OH, ANY TIME, MR. JONES!

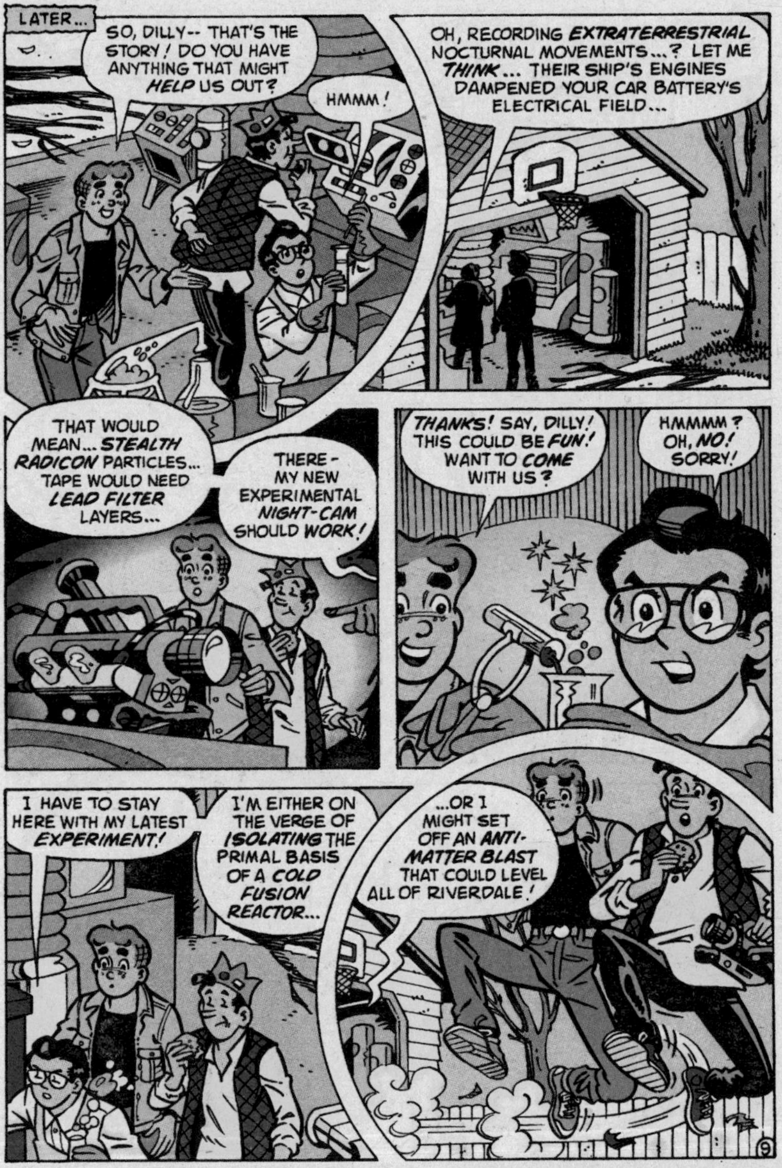
LATER...
SO, DILLY-- THAT'S THE STORY! DO YOU HAVE ANYTHING THAT MIGHT HELP US OUT?
HMMM!
OH, RECORDING EXTRATERRESTRIAL NOCTURNAL MOVEMENTS...? LET ME THINK... THEIR SHIP'S ENGINES DAMPENED YOUR CAR BATTERY'S ELECTRICAL FIELD...
THAT WOULD MEAN... STEALTH RADICON PARTICLES... TAPE WOULD NEED LEAD FILTER LAYERS...
THERE - MY NEW EXPERIMENTAL NIGHT-CAM SHOULD WORK!
THANKS! SAY, DILLY! THIS COULD BE FUN! WANT TO COME WITH US?
HMMMM? OH, NO! SORRY!
I HAVE TO STAY HERE WITH MY LATEST EXPERIMENT!
I'M EITHER ON THE VERGE OF ISOLATING THE PRIMAL BASIS OF A COLD FUSION REACTOR...
...OR I MIGHT SET OFF AN ANTI-MATTER BLAST THAT COULD LEVEL ALL OF RIVERDALE!
9

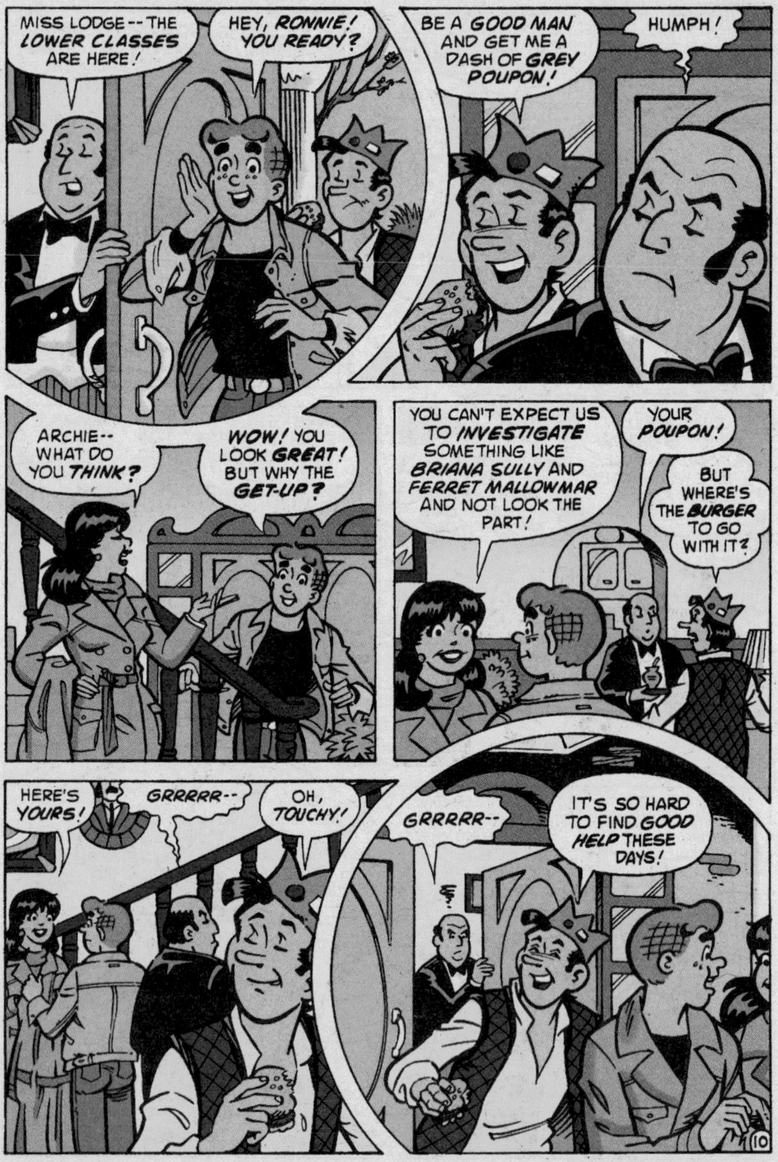
MISS LODGE -- THE LOWER CLASSES ARE HERE!
HEY, RONNIE! YOU READY?
BE A GOOD MAN AND GET ME A DASH OF GREY POUPON!
HUMPH!
ARCHIE -- WHAT DO YOU THINK?
WOW! YOU LOOK GREAT! BUT WHY THE GET-UP?
YOU CAN'T EXPECT US TO INVESTIGATE SOMETHING LIKE BRIANA SULLY AND FERRET MALLOWMAR AND NOT LOOK THE PART!
YOUR POUPON!
BUT WHERE'S THE BURGER TO GO WITH IT?
HERE'S YOURS!
GRRRRR --
OH, TOUCHY!
GRRRRR --
IT'S SO HARD TO FIND GOOD HELP THESE DAYS!
10

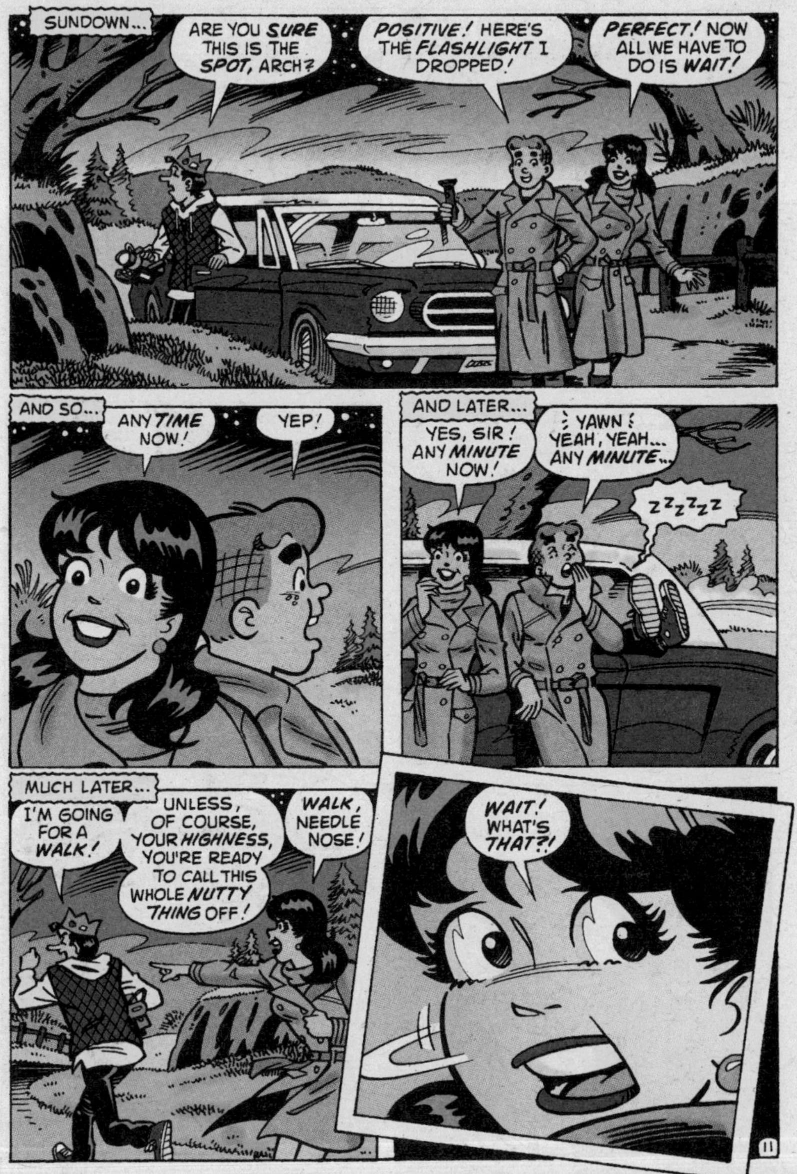
SUNDOWN...
ARE YOU SURE THIS IS THE SPOT, ARCH?
POSITIVE! HERE'S THE FLASHLIGHT I DROPPED!
PERFECT! NOW ALL WE HAVE TO DO IS WAIT!
AND SO...
ANY TIME NOW!
YEP!
AND LATER...
YES, SIR! ANY MINUTE NOW!
YAWN
YEAH, YEAH... ANY MINUTE...
ZZZZZZ
MUCH LATER...
I'M GOING FOR A WALK!
UNLESS, OF COURSE, YOUR HIGHNESS, YOU'RE READY TO CALL THIS WHOLE NUTTY THING OFF!
WALK, NEEDLE NOSE!
WAIT! WHAT'S THAT?!
11

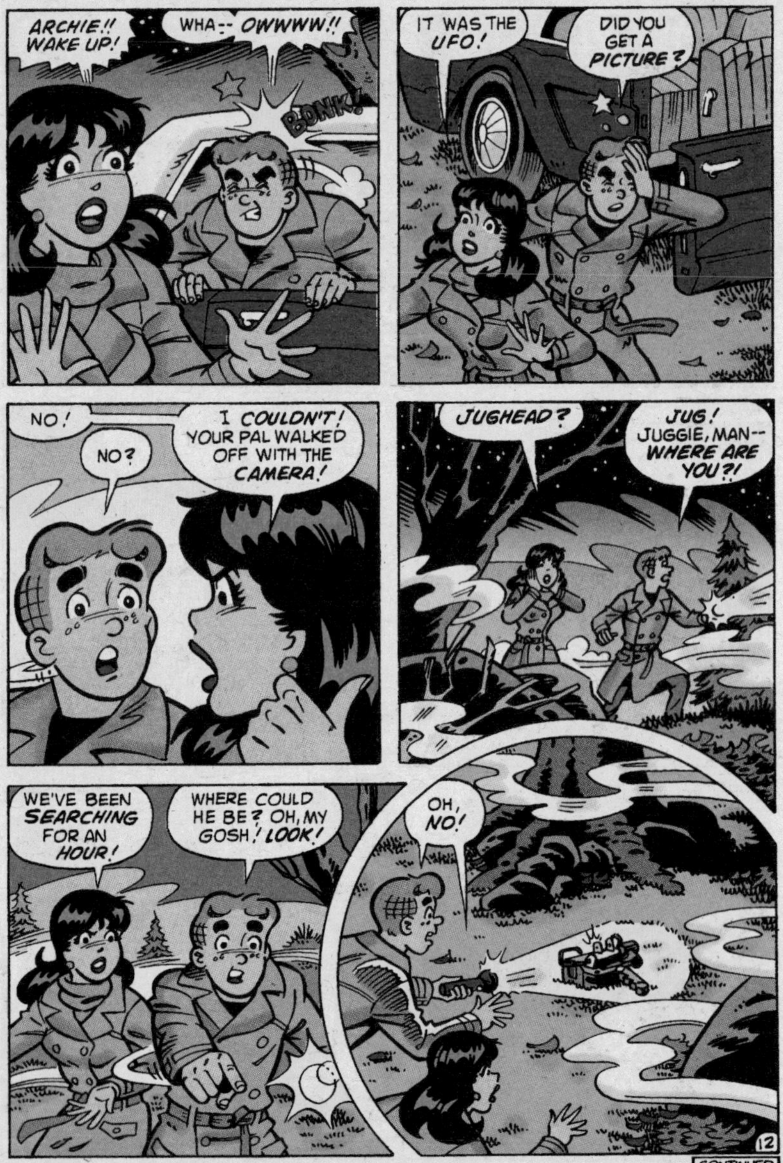
ARCHIE!! WAKE UP!
WHA-- OWWWW!!
BONK!
IT WAS THE UFO!
DID YOU GET A PICTURE?
NO!
NO?
I COULDN'T! YOUR PAL WALKED OFF WITH THE CAMERA!
JUGHEAD?
JUG! JUGGIE, MAN-- WHERE ARE YOU?!
WE'VE BEEN SEARCHING FOR AN HOUR!
WHERE COULD HE BE? OH, MY GOSH! LOOK!
OH, NO!
12
CONTINUED

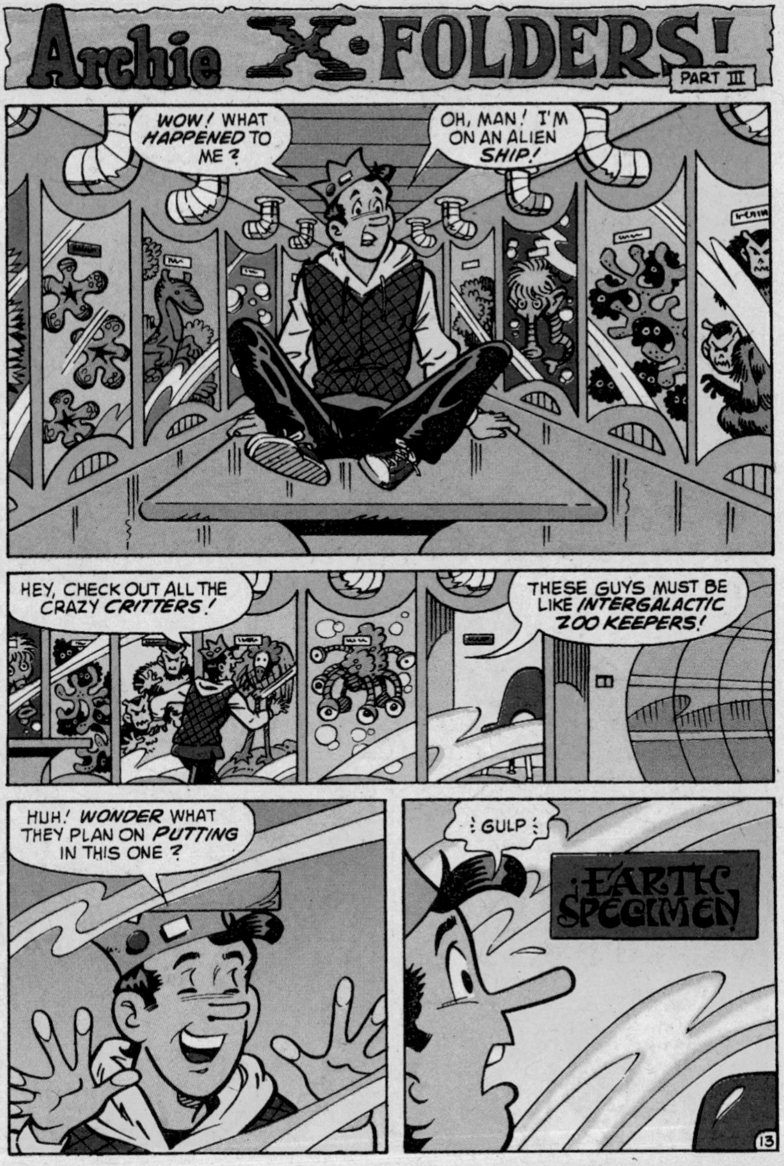
Archie X-FOLDERS!
PART III
WOW! WHAT HAPPENED TO ME?
OH, MAN! I'M ON AN ALIEN SHIP!
HEY, CHECK OUT ALL THE CRAZY CRITTERS!
THESE GUYS MUST BE LIKE INTERGALACTIC ZOO KEEPERS!
HUH! WONDER WHAT THEY PLAN ON PUTTING IN THIS ONE?
GULP
EARTH SPECIMEN
13

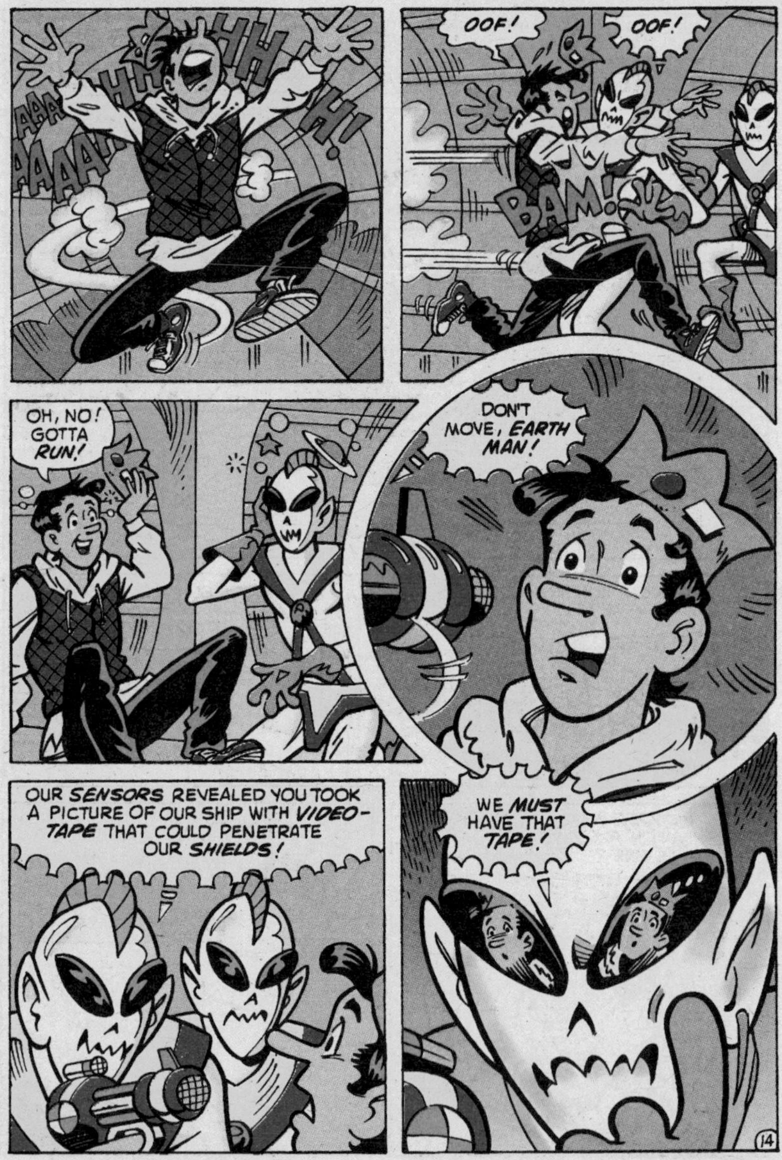
AAAAAAHHHHHHH!
OOF!
OOF!
BAM!
OH, NO! GOTTA RUN!
DON'T MOVE, EARTH MAN!
OUR SENSORS REVEALED YOU TOOK A PICTURE OF OUR SHIP WITH VIDEO-TAPE THAT COULD PENETRATE OUR SHIELDS!
WE MUST HAVE THAT TAPE!
14

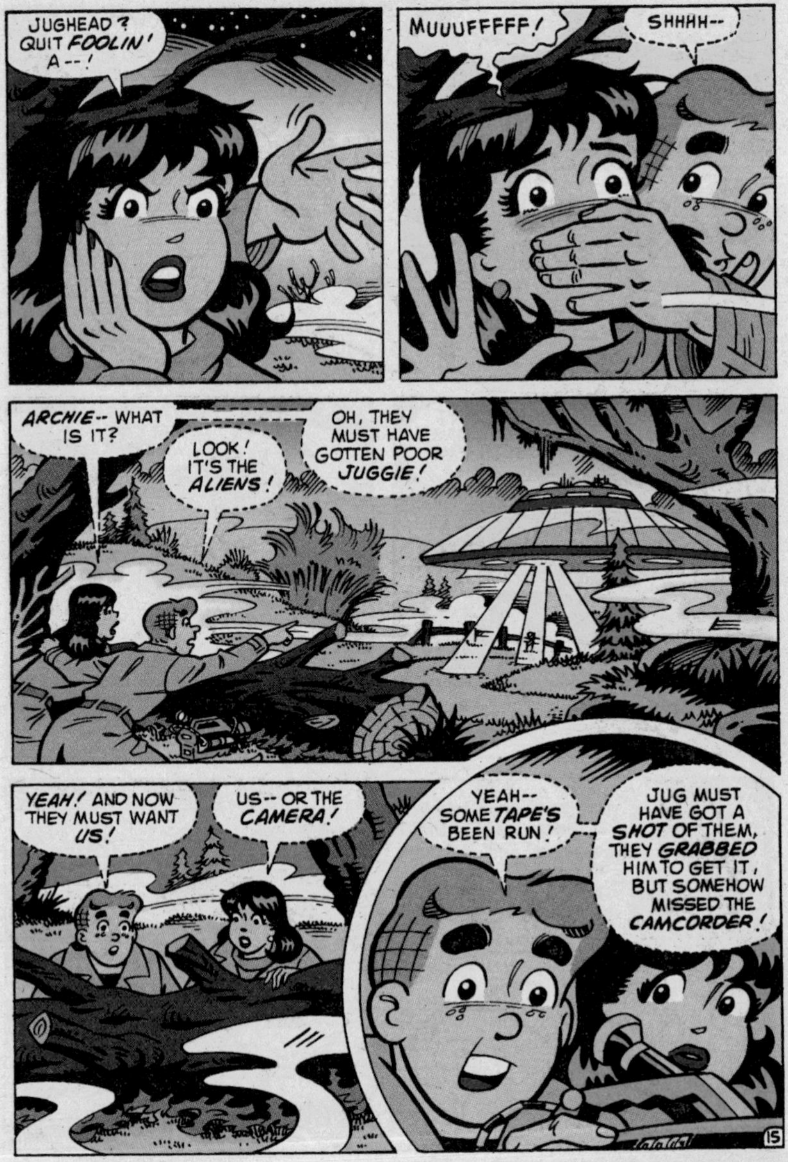
JUGHEAD? QUIT FOOLIN' A--!
MUUUFFFFF!
SHHHH--
ARCHIE-- WHAT IS IT?
LOOK! IT'S THE ALIENS!
OH, THEY MUST HAVE GOTTEN POOR JUGGIE!
YEAH! AND NOW THEY MUST WANT US!
US-- OR THE CAMERA!
YEAH-- SOME TAPE'S BEEN RUN!
JUG MUST HAVE GOT A SHOT OF THEM, THEY GRABBED HIM TO GET IT, BUT SOMEHOW MISSED THE CAMCORDER!

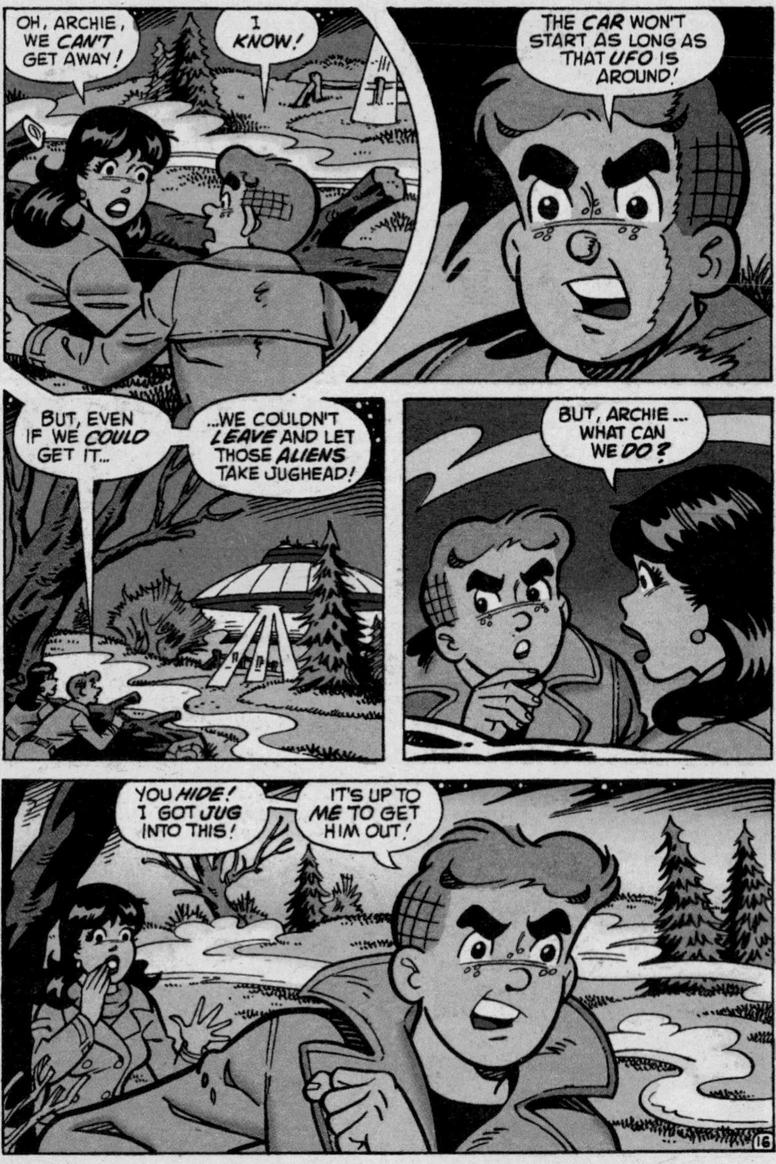
OH, ARCHIE, WE CAN'T GET AWAY!
I KNOW!
THE CAR WON'T START AS LONG AS THAT UFO IS AROUND!
BUT, EVEN IF WE COULD GET IT...
...WE COULDN'T LEAVE AND LET THOSE ALIENS TAKE JUGHEAD!
BUT, ARCHIE... WHAT CAN WE DO?
YOU HIDE! I GOT JUG INTO THIS!
IT'S UP TO ME TO GET HIM OUT!
16

HEY! YOU BEAMERS WANT THE PICTURES OF YOUR SHIP...
ULP! WELL, I'VE GOT THEM!
YOU CAN HAVE THEM ON ONE CONDITION!
YOU'VE GOT TO TRADE ME FOR MY FRIEND!
TAKE ME INSTEAD OF HIM!
VVVVVVVZZZZZZ
CONTINUED

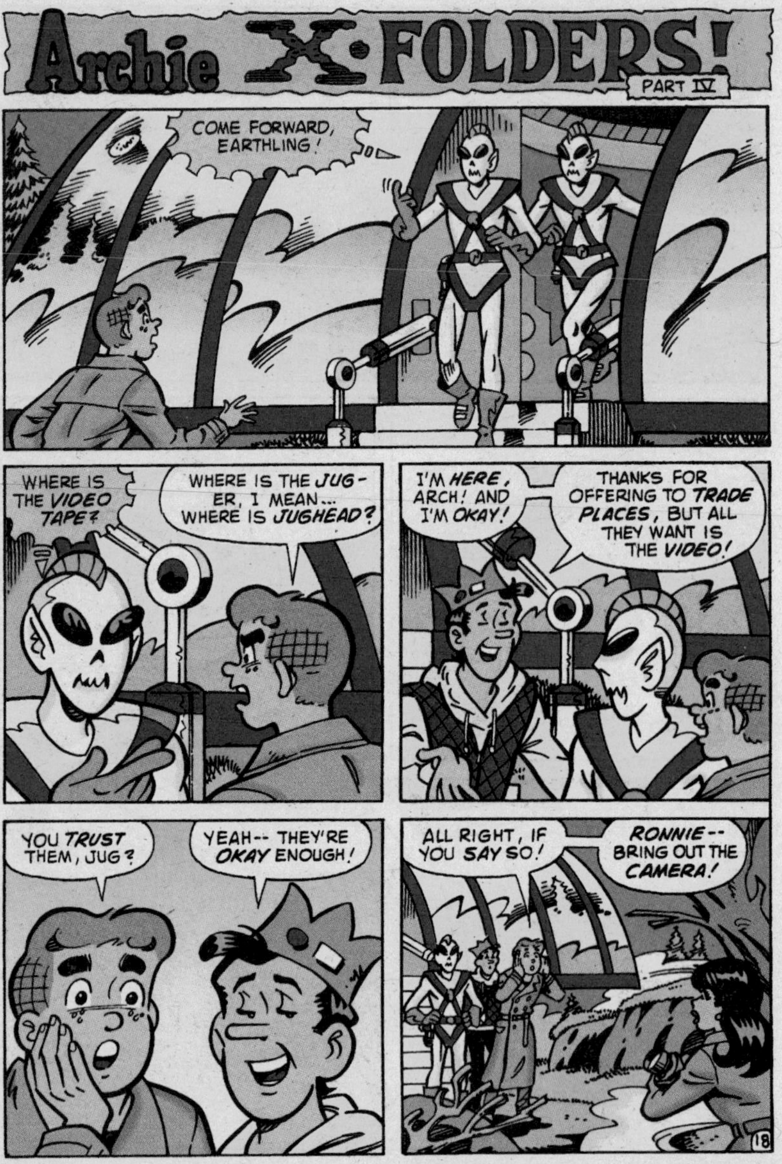

Archie X-FOLDERS!
PART IV
COME FORWARD, EARTHLING!
WHERE IS THE VIDEO TAPE?
WHERE IS THE JUG-ER, I MEAN... WHERE IS JUGHEAD?
I'M HERE, ARCH! AND I'M OKAY!
THANKS FOR OFFERING TO TRADE PLACES, BUT ALL THEY WANT IS THE VIDEO!
YOU TRUST THEM, JUG?
YEAH-- THEY'RE OKAY ENOUGH!
ALL RIGHT, IF YOU SAY SO!
RONNIE-- BRING OUT THE CAMERA!
18

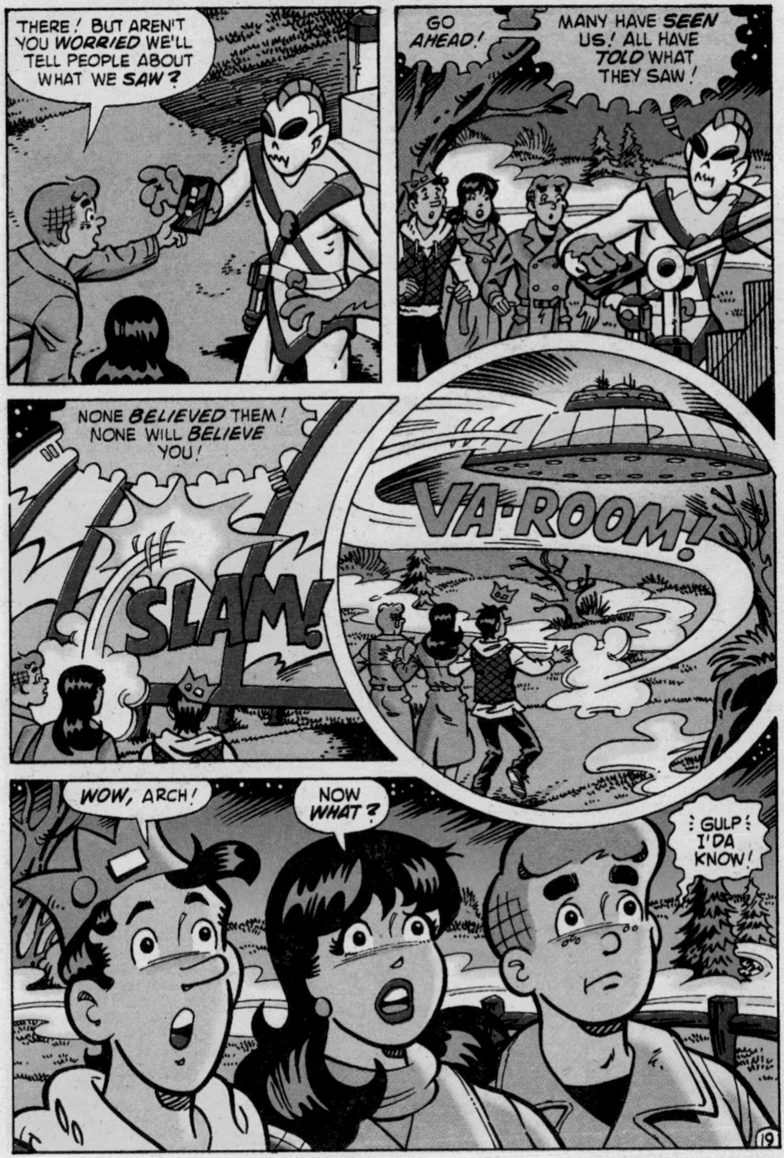
THERE! BUT AREN'T YOU WORRIED WE'LL TELL PEOPLE ABOUT WHAT WE SAW?
GO AHEAD!
MANY HAVE SEEN US! ALL HAVE TOLD WHAT THEY SAW!
NONE BELIEVED THEM! NONE WILL BELIEVE YOU!
SLAM!
VA-ROOM!
WOW, ARCH!
NOW WHAT?
GULP I'DA KNOW!

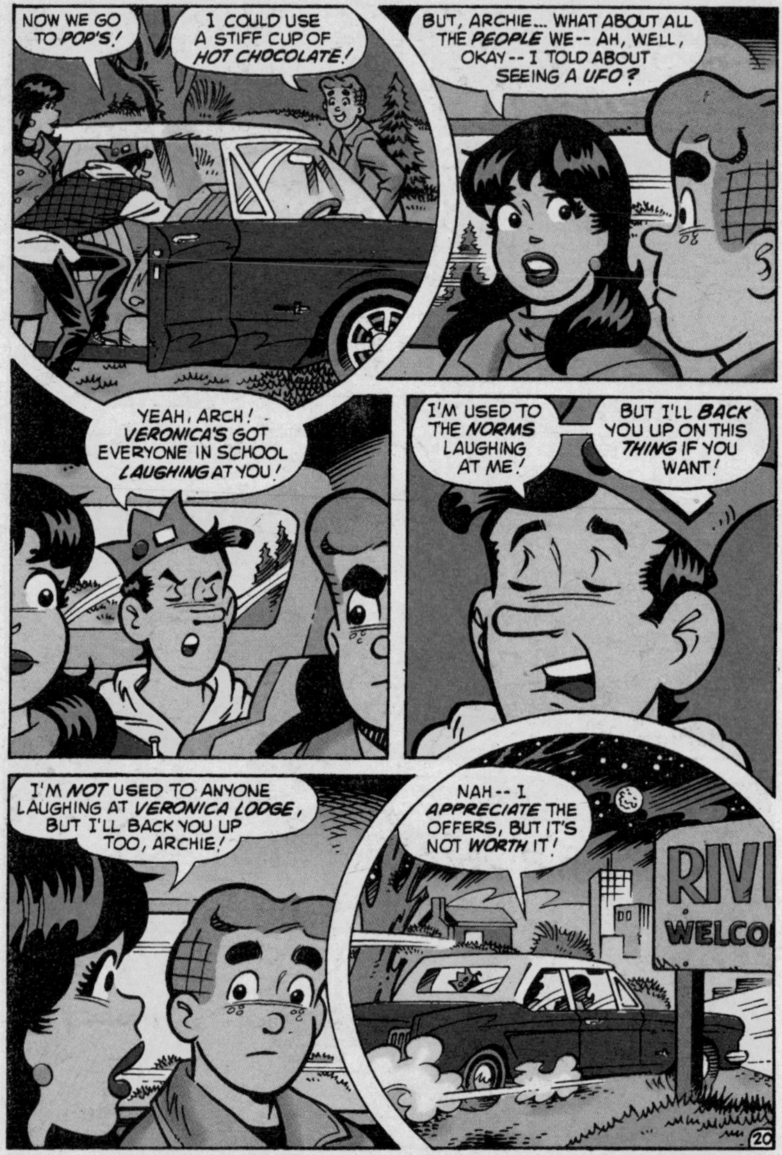
NOW WE GO TO POP'S!
I COULD USE A STIFF CUP OF HOT CHOCOLATE!
BUT, ARCHIE... WHAT ABOUT ALL THE PEOPLE WE-- AH, WELL, OKAY-- I TOLD ABOUT SEEING A UFO?
YEAH, ARCH! VERONICA'S GOT EVERYONE IN SCHOOL LAUGHING AT YOU!
I'M USED TO THE NORMS LAUGHING AT ME!
BUT I'LL BACK YOU UP ON THIS THING IF YOU WANT!
I'M NOT USED TO ANYONE LAUGHING AT VERONICA LODGE, BUT I'LL BACK YOU UP TOO, ARCHIE!
NAH-- I APPRECIATE THE OFFERS, BUT IT'S NOT WORTH IT!
RIV
WELCO

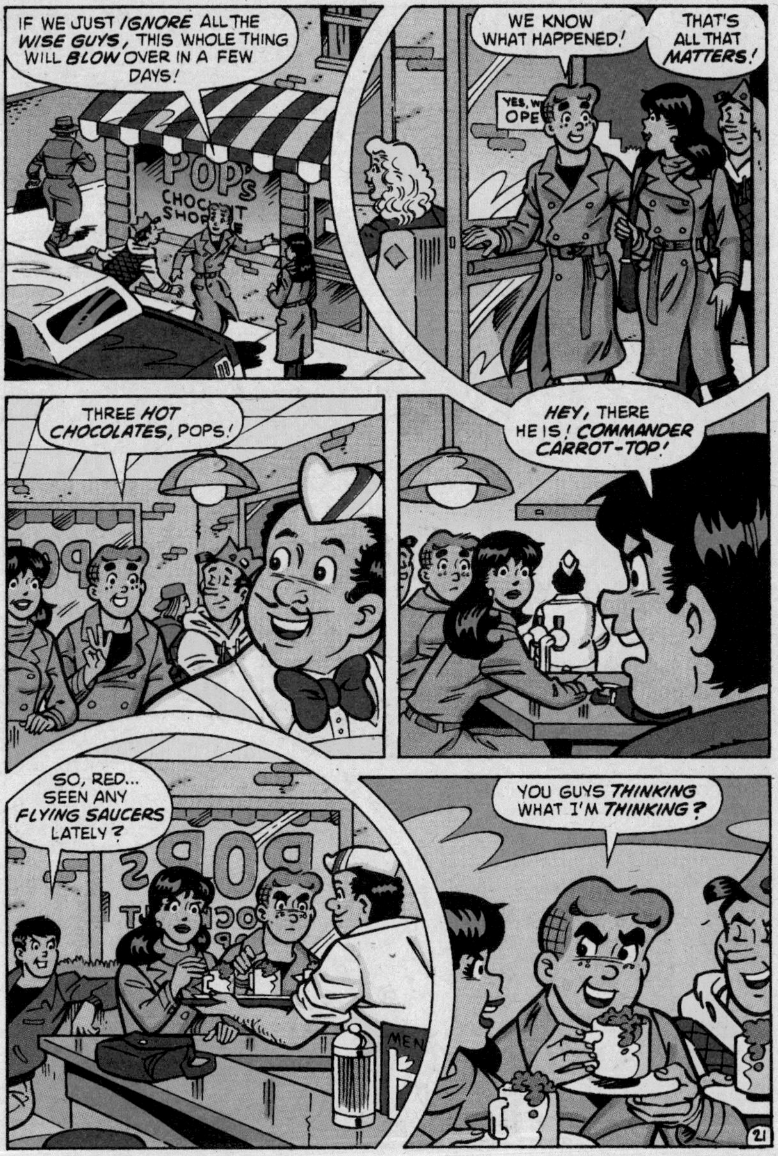
IF WE JUST IGNORE ALL THE WISE GUYS, THIS WHOLE THING WILL BLOW OVER IN A FEW DAYS!
POP'S
WE KNOW WHAT HAPPENED!
THAT'S ALL THAT MATTERS!
THREE HOT CHOCOLATES, POPS!
HEY, THERE HE IS! COMMANDER CARROT-TOP!
SO, RED... SEEN ANY FLYING SAUCERS LATELY?
YOU GUYS THINKING WHAT I'M THINKING?

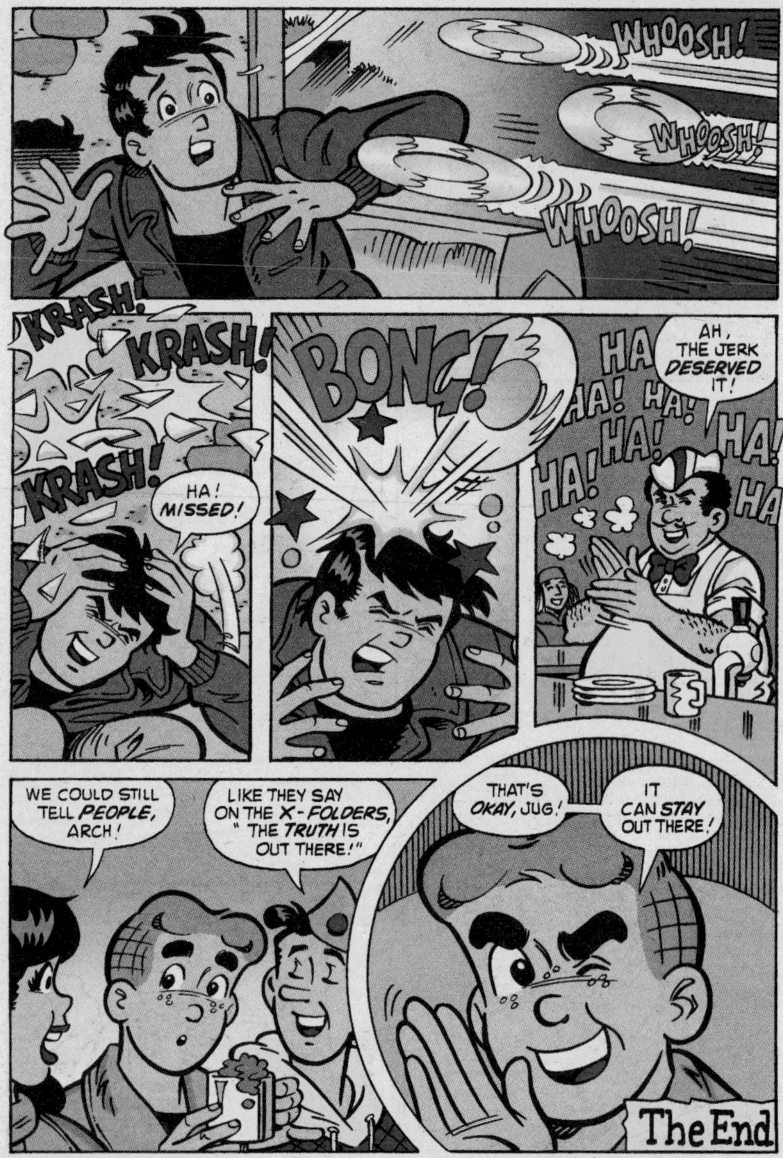
WHOOSH!
WHOOSH!
WHOOSH!
KRASH!
KRASH!
KRASH!
HA! MISSED!
BONG!
HA HA! HA! HA! HA! HA! HA! HA
AH, THE JERK DESERVED IT!
WE COULD STILL TELL PEOPLE, ARCH!
LIKE THEY SAY ON THE X-FOLDERS, " THE TRUTH IS OUT THERE!"
THAT'S OKAY, JUG!
IT CAN STAY OUT THERE!
The End

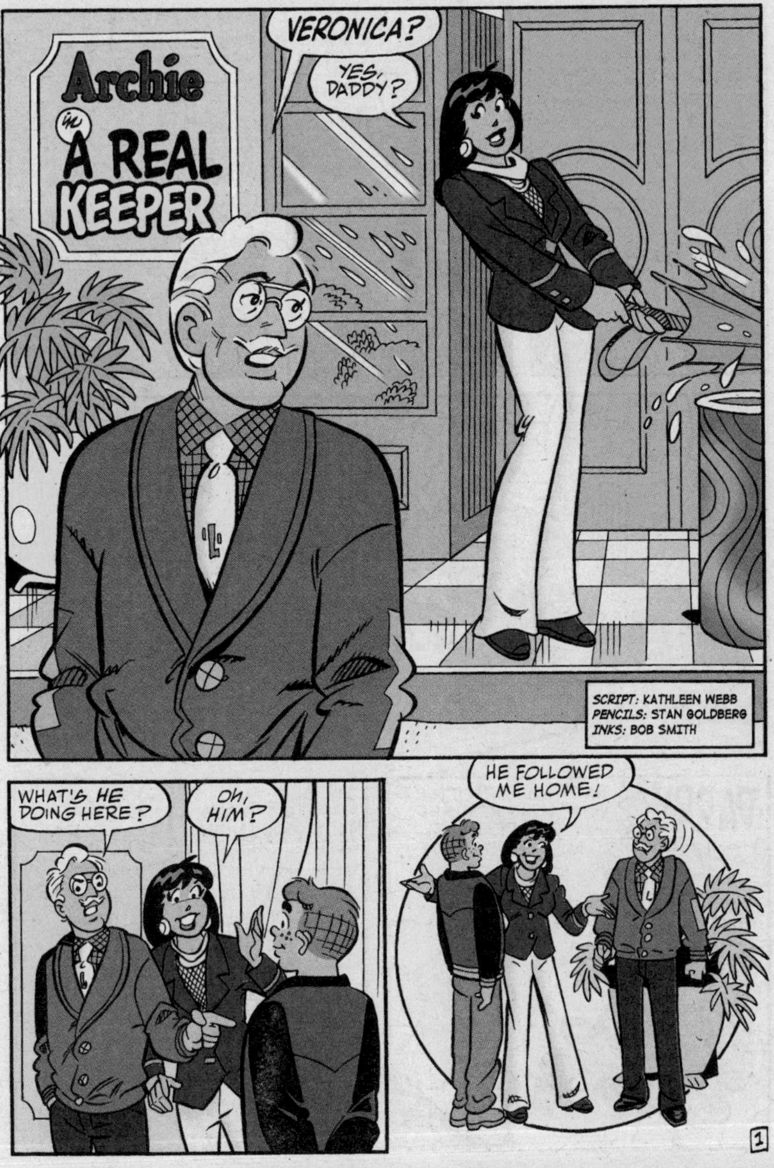

VERONICA?
YES, DADDY?
Archie in A REAL KEEPER
SCRIPT: KATHLEEN WEBB
PENCILS: STAN GOLDBERG
INKS: BOB SMITH
WHAT'S HE DOING HERE?
OH, HIM?
HE FOLLOWED ME HOME!

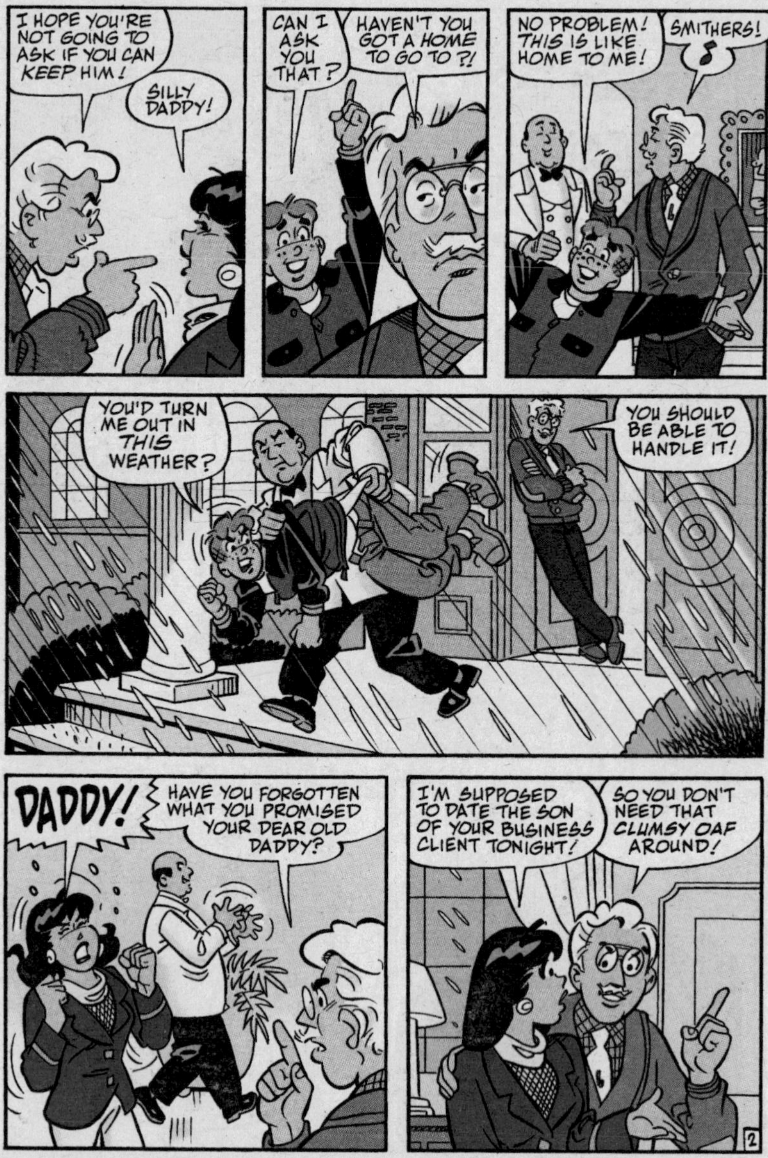
I HOPE YOU'RE NOT GOING TO ASK IF YOU CAN KEEP HIM!
SILLY DADDY!
CAN I ASK YOU THAT?
HAVEN'T YOU GOT A HOME TO GO TO?!
NO PROBLEM! THIS IS LIKE HOME TO ME!
SMITHERS! ♪
YOU'D TURN ME OUT IN THIS WEATHER?
YOU SHOULD BE ABLE TO HANDLE IT!
DADDY!
HAVE YOU FORGOTTEN WHAT YOU PROMISED YOUR DEAR OLD DADDY?
I'M SUPPOSED TO DATE THE SON OF YOUR BUSINESS CLIENT TONIGHT!
SO YOU DON'T NEED THAT CLUMSY OAF AROUND!
2

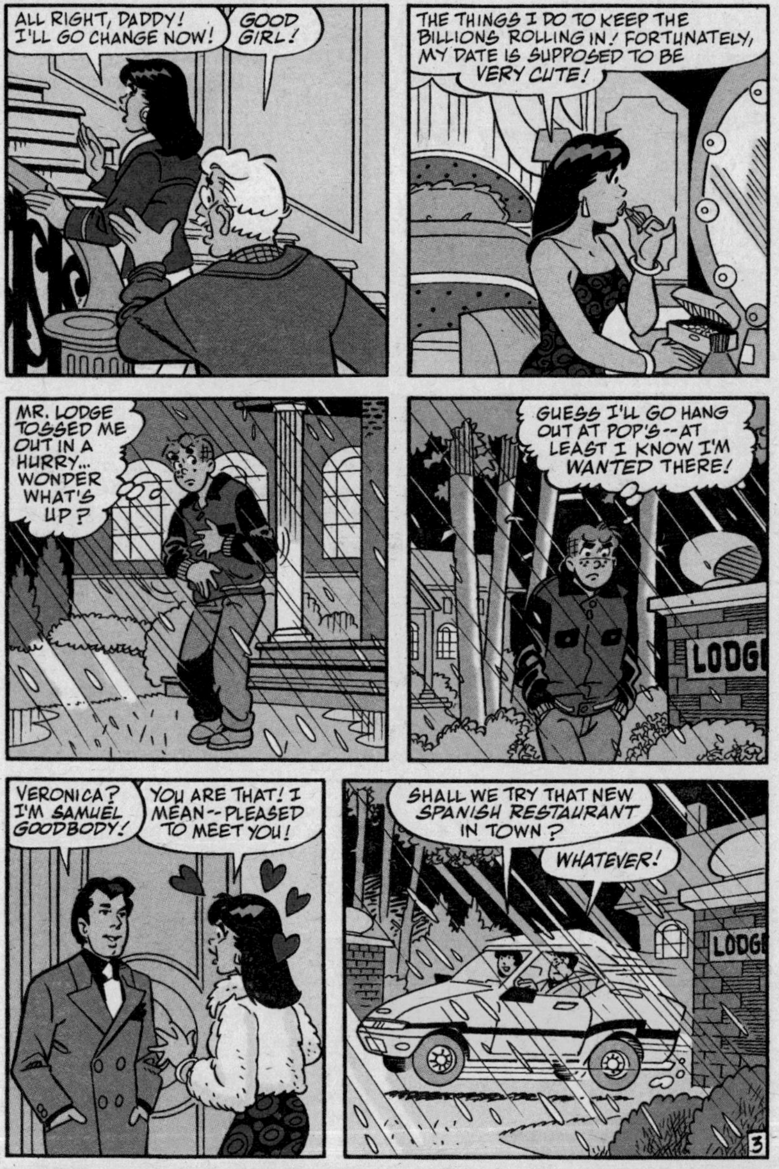
ALL RIGHT, DADDY! I'LL GO CHANGE NOW!
GOOD GIRL!
THE THINGS I DO TO KEEP THE BILLIONS ROLLING IN! FORTUNATELY, MY DATE IS SUPPOSED TO BE VERY CUTE!
MR. LODGE TOSSED ME OUT IN A HURRY... WONDER WHAT'S UP?
GUESS I'LL GO HANG OUT AT POP'S--AT LEAST I KNOW I'M WANTED THERE!
LODGE
VERONICA? I'M SAMUEL GOODBODY!
YOU ARE THAT! I MEAN--PLEASED TO MEET YOU!
SHALL WE TRY THAT NEW SPANISH RESTAURANT IN TOWN?
WHATEVER!
LODGE
3

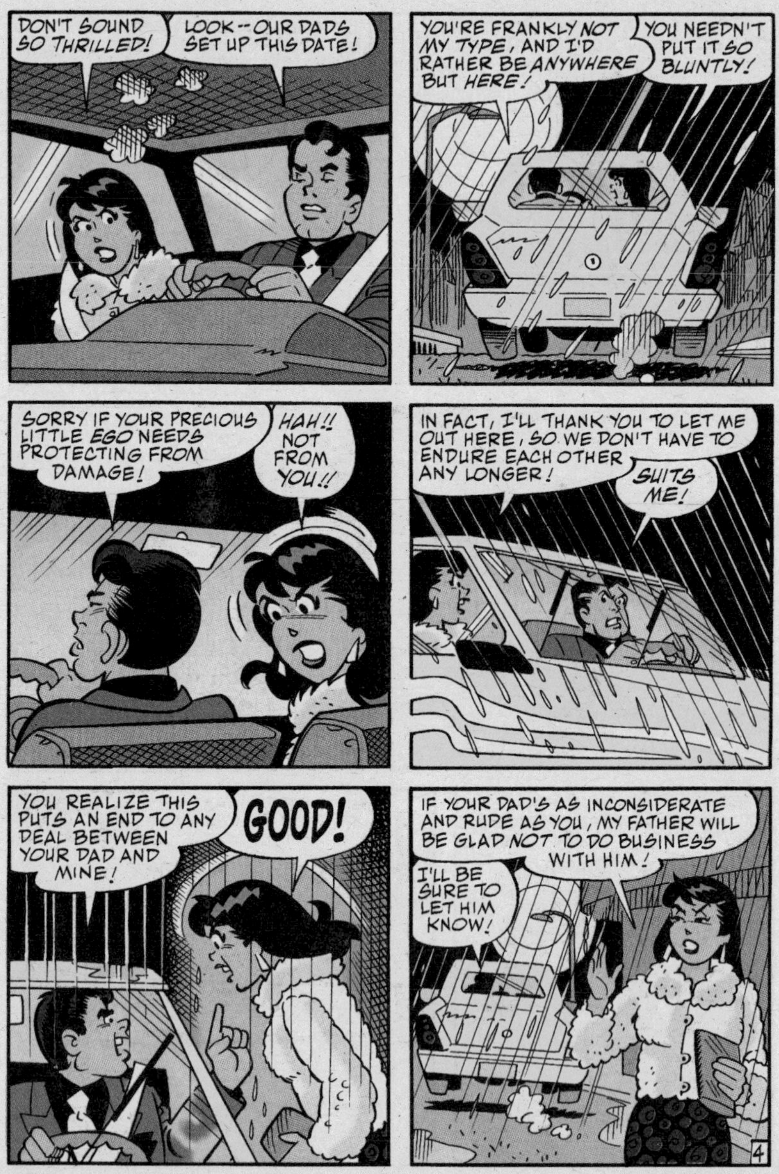

DON'T SOUND SO THRILLED!
LOOK--OUR DADS SET UP THIS DATE!
YOU'RE FRANKLY NOT MY TYPE, AND I'D RATHER BE ANYWHERE BUT HERE!
YOU NEEDN'T PUT IT SO BLUNTLY!
SORRY IF YOUR PRECIOUS LITTLE EGO NEEDS PROTECTING FROM DAMAGE!
HAH!! NOT FROM YOU!!
IN FACT, I'LL THANK YOU TO LET ME OUT HERE, SO WE DON'T HAVE TO ENDURE EACH OTHER ANY LONGER!
SUITS ME!
YOU REALIZE THIS PUTS AN END TO ANY DEAL BETWEEN YOUR DAD AND MINE!
GOOD!
IF YOUR DAD'S AS INCONSIDERATE AND RUDE AS YOU, MY FATHER WILL BE GLAD NOT TO DO BUSINESS WITH HIM!
I'LL BE SURE TO LET HIM KNOW!

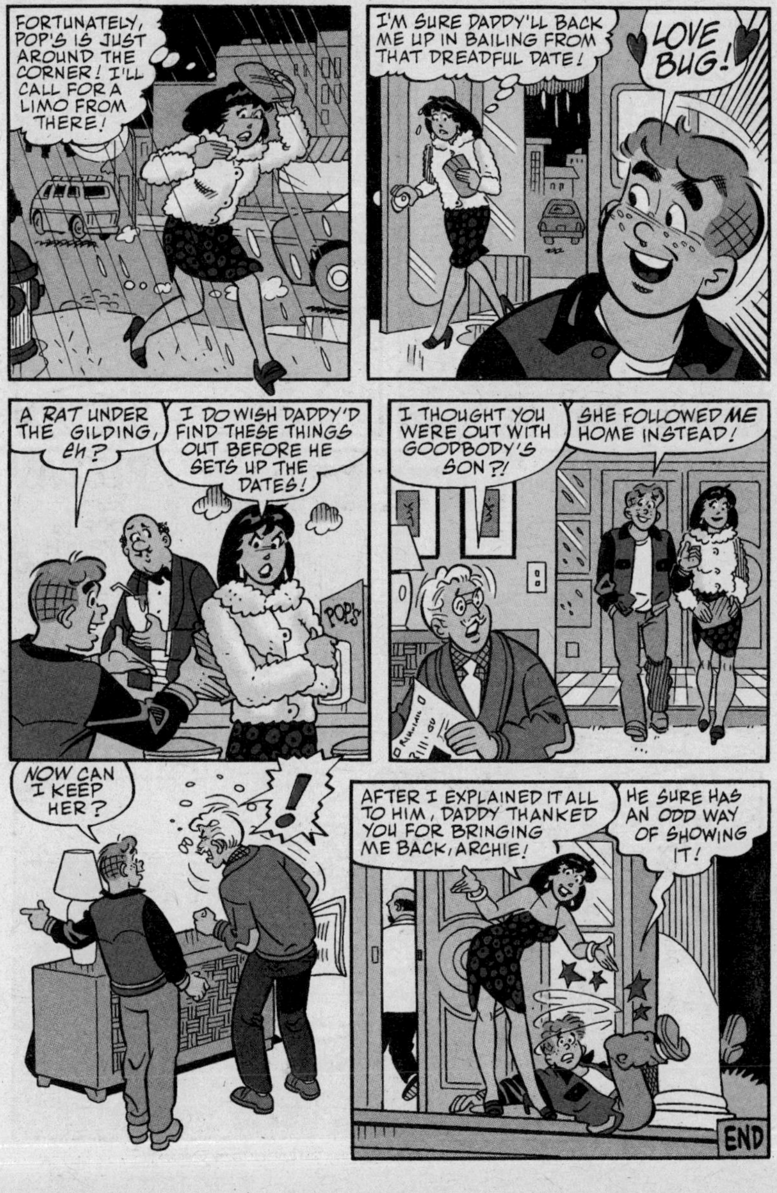

FORTUNATELY, POP'S IS JUST AROUND THE CORNER! I'LL CALL FOR A LIMO FROM THERE!
I'M SURE DADDY'LL BACK ME UP IN BAILING FROM THAT DREADFUL DATE!
LOVE BUG!
A RAT UNDER THE GILDING, eh?
I DO WISH DADDY'D FIND THESE THINGS OUT BEFORE HE SETS UP THE DATES!
POP'S
I THOUGHT YOU WERE OUT WITH GOODBODY'S SON?!
SHE FOLLOWED ME HOME INSTEAD!
NOW CAN I KEEP HER?
!
AFTER I EXPLAINED IT ALL TO HIM, DADDY THANKED YOU FOR BRINGING ME BACK, ARCHIE!
HE SURE HAS AN ODD WAY OF SHOWING IT!
END

BOY! I HOPE I GET THIS JOB!
WE'RE HIRING YOU TO DELIVER PIZZA, BUT ON A *TRIAL* BASIS!
IF YOU DON'T MAKE THE GRADE, WE'LL HAVE TO LET YOU GO!
I UNDERSTAND, SIR!
Archie IN "LATE STRAIT"
PIZZA PAL TOPS IN TOPPINGS
GULP! I HAVE TO MAKE EACH DELIVERY WITHIN A HALF-HOUR, OR THE CUSTOMER GETS THREE DOLLARS OFF THE PRICE!
BOY! THAT'S PRESSURE!
PIZZA PAL TOPS IN TOPPINGS
PIZZA PAL TOPS IN TOPPINGS

Script & Pencils: Bill Golliher / Letters: Bill Yoshida / Colors: Barry Grossman

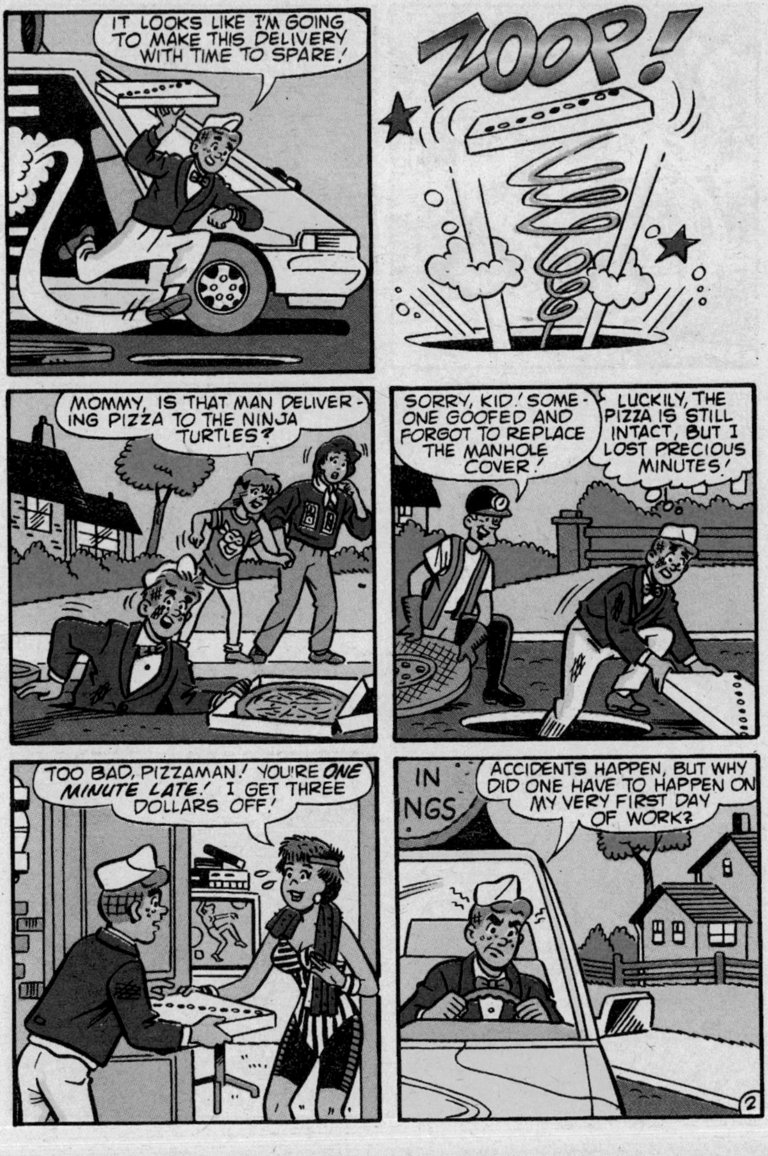
IT LOOKS LIKE I'M GOING TO MAKE THIS DELIVERY WITH TIME TO SPARE!
ZOOP!
MOMMY, IS THAT MAN DELIVERING PIZZA TO THE NINJA TURTLES?
SORRY, KID! SOMEONE GOOFED AND FORGOT TO REPLACE THE MANHOLE COVER!
LUCKILY, THE PIZZA IS STILL INTACT, BUT I LOST PRECIOUS MINUTES!
TOO BAD, PIZZAMAN! YOU'RE ONE MINUTE LATE! I GET THREE DOLLARS OFF!
IN
NGS
ACCIDENTS HAPPEN, BUT WHY DID ONE HAVE TO HAPPEN ON MY VERY FIRST DAY OF WORK?
2

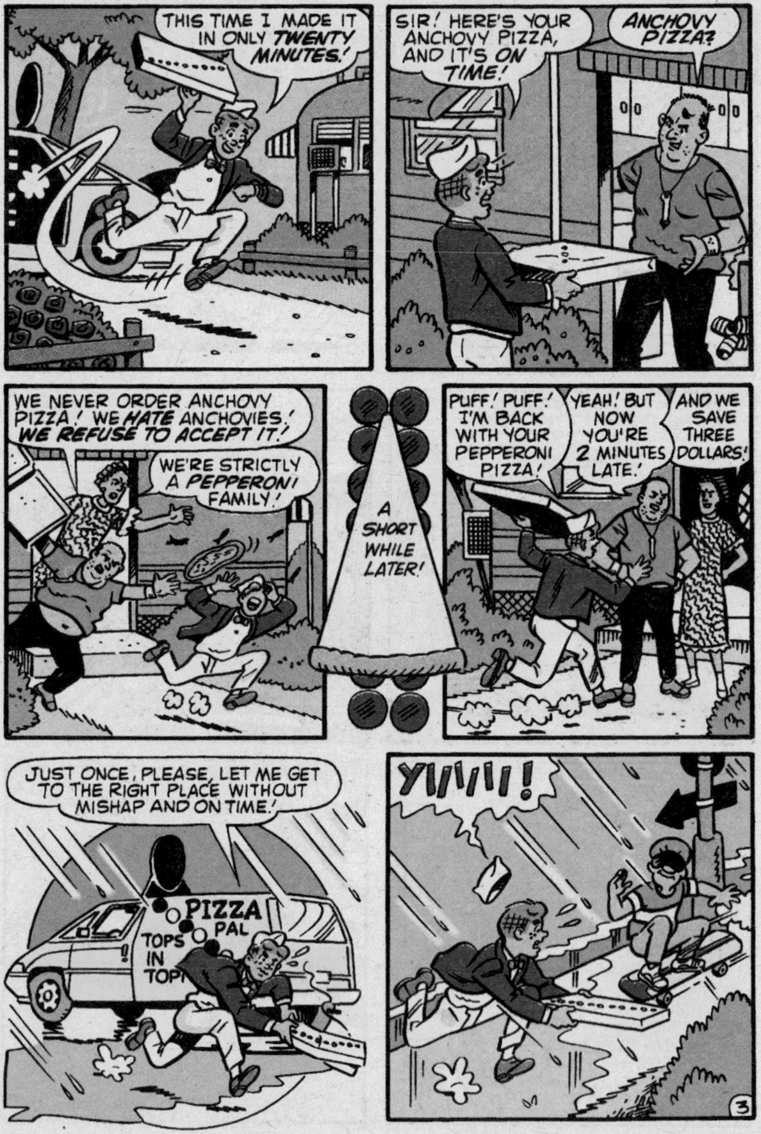
THIS TIME I MADE IT IN ONLY TWENTY MINUTES!
SIR! HERE'S YOUR ANCHOVY PIZZA, AND IT'S ON TIME!
ANCHOVY PIZZA?
WE NEVER ORDER ANCHOVY PIZZA! WE HATE ANCHOVIES! WE REFUSE TO ACCEPT IT!
WE'RE STRICTLY A PEPPERONI FAMILY!
A SHORT WHILE LATER!
PUFF! PUFF! I'M BACK WITH YOUR PEPPERONI PIZZA!
YEAH! BUT NOW YOU'RE 2 MINUTES LATE!
AND WE SAVE THREE DOLLARS!
JUST ONCE, PLEASE, LET ME GET TO THE RIGHT PLACE WITHOUT MISHAP AND ON TIME!
PIZZA PAL
TOPS IN TOP
YIIIIII!
3

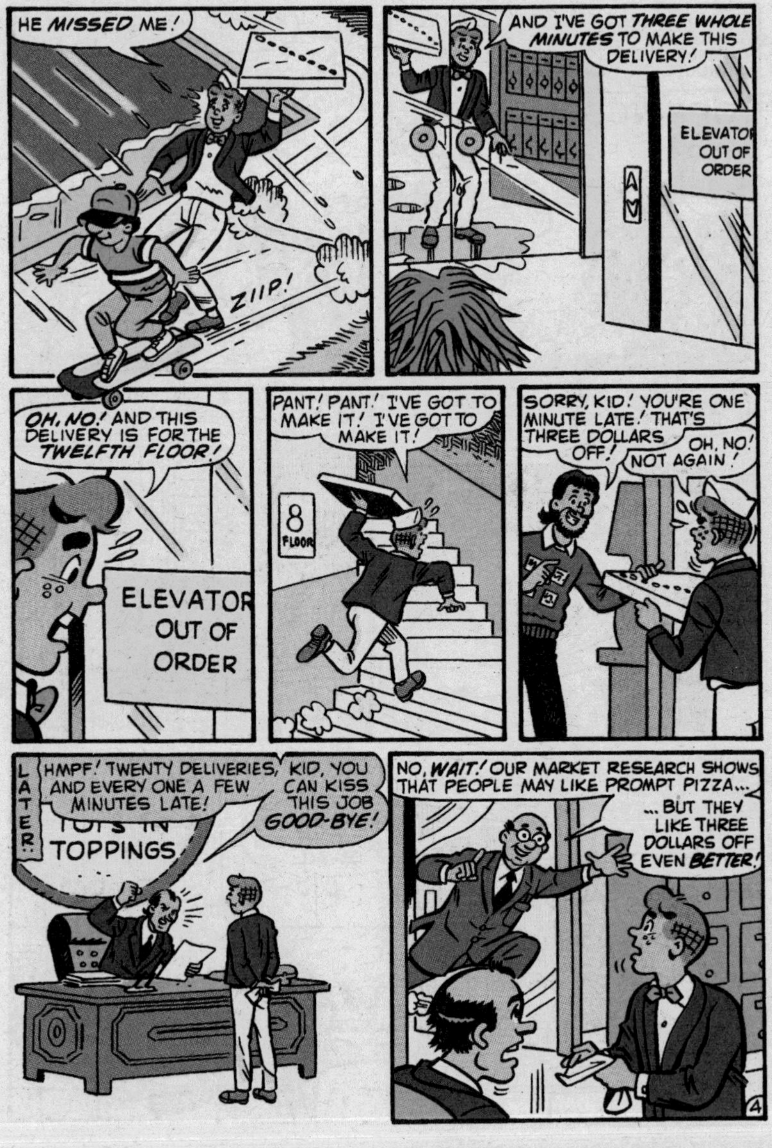
HE MISSED ME!
ZIIP!
AND I'VE GOT THREE WHOLE MINUTES TO MAKE THIS DELIVERY!
ELEVATOR OUT OF ORDER
OH, NO! AND THIS DELIVERY IS FOR THE TWELFTH FLOOR!
ELEVATOR OUT OF ORDER
PANT! PANT! I'VE GOT TO MAKE IT! I'VE GOT TO MAKE IT!
8 FLOOR
SORRY, KID! YOU'RE ONE MINUTE LATE! THAT'S THREE DOLLARS OFF!
OH, NO! NOT AGAIN!
LATER:
HMPF! TWENTY DELIVERIES, AND EVERY ONE A FEW MINUTES LATE!
KID, YOU CAN KISS THIS JOB GOOD-BYE!
TOPPINGS
NO, WAIT! OUR MARKET RESEARCH SHOWS THAT PEOPLE MAY LIKE PROMPT PIZZA...
... BUT THEY LIKE THREE DOLLARS OFF EVEN BETTER!
4

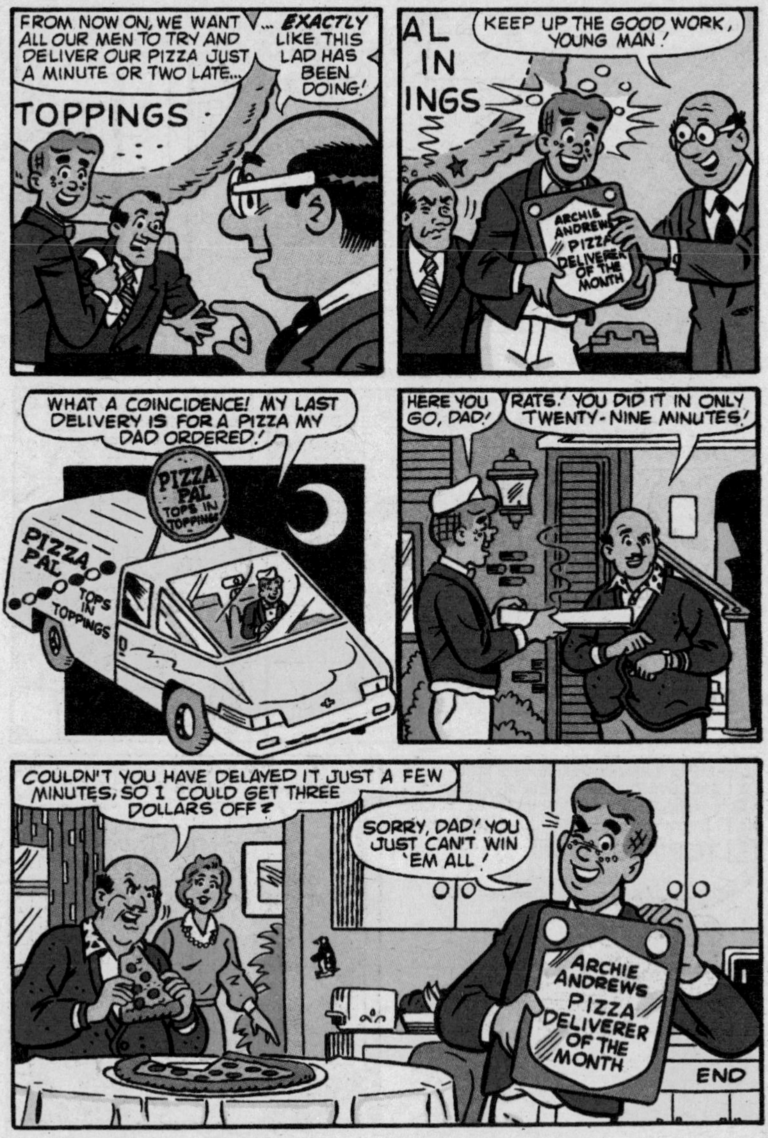
FROM NOW ON, WE WANT ALL OUR MEN TO TRY AND DELIVER OUR PIZZA JUST A MINUTE OR TWO LATE...
... EXACTLY LIKE THIS LAD HAS BEEN DOING!
TOPPINGS
AL IN INGS
KEEP UP THE GOOD WORK, YOUNG MAN!
ARCHIE ANDREWS PIZZA DELIVERER OF THE MONTH
WHAT A COINCIDENCE! MY LAST DELIVERY IS FOR A PIZZA MY DAD ORDERED!
PIZZA PAL TOPS IN TOPPINGS
PIZZA PAL TOPS IN TOPPINGS
HERE YOU GO, DAD!
RATS! YOU DID IT IN ONLY TWENTY-NINE MINUTES!
COULDN'T YOU HAVE DELAYED IT JUST A FEW MINUTES, SO I COULD GET THREE DOLLARS OFF?
SORRY, DAD! YOU JUST CAN'T WIN 'EM ALL!
ARCHIE ANDREWS PIZZA DELIVERER OF THE MONTH
END

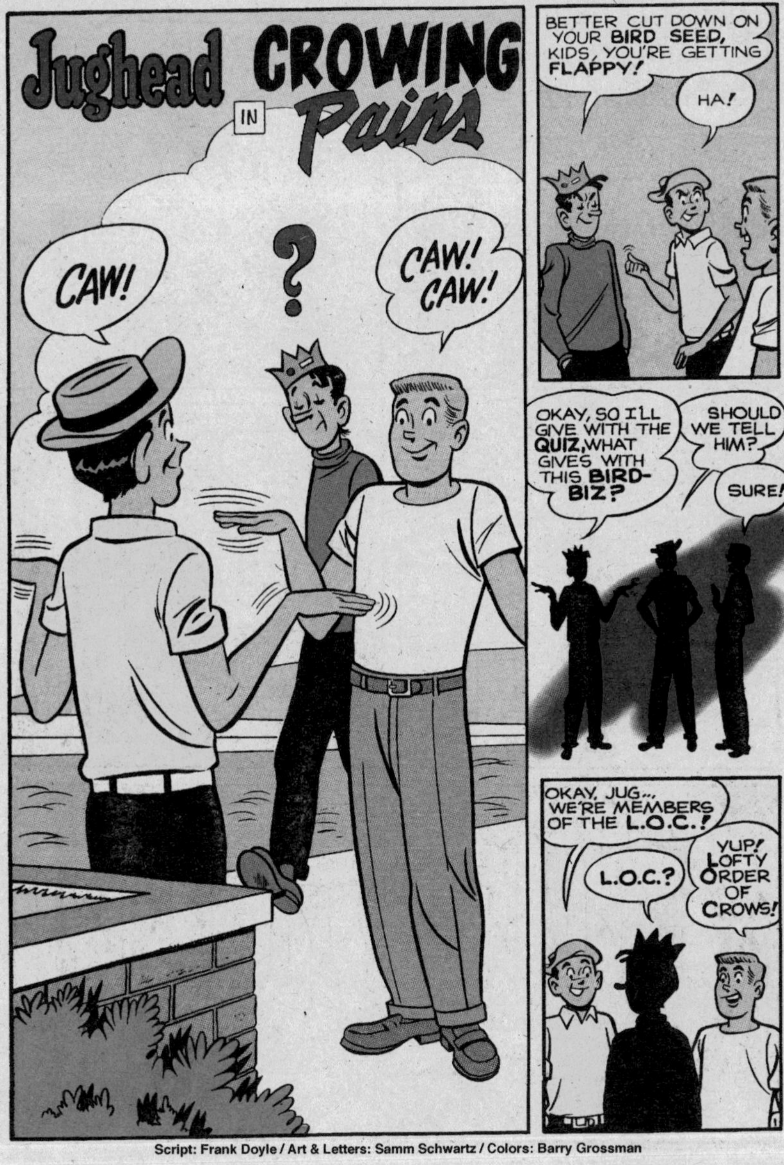
Jughead
IN
CROWING Pains
CAW!
?
CAW! CAW!
BETTER CUT DOWN ON YOUR BIRD SEED, KIDS, YOU'RE GETTING FLAPPY!
HA!
OKAY, SO I'LL GIVE WITH THE QUIZ, WHAT GIVES WITH THIS BIRD-BIZ?
SHOULD WE TELL HIM?
SURE!
OKAY, JUG.., WE'RE MEMBERS OF THE L.O.C.!
L.O.C.?
YUP! LOFTY ORDER OF CROWS!

Script: Frank Doyle / Art & Letters: Samm Schwartz / Colors: Barry Grossman

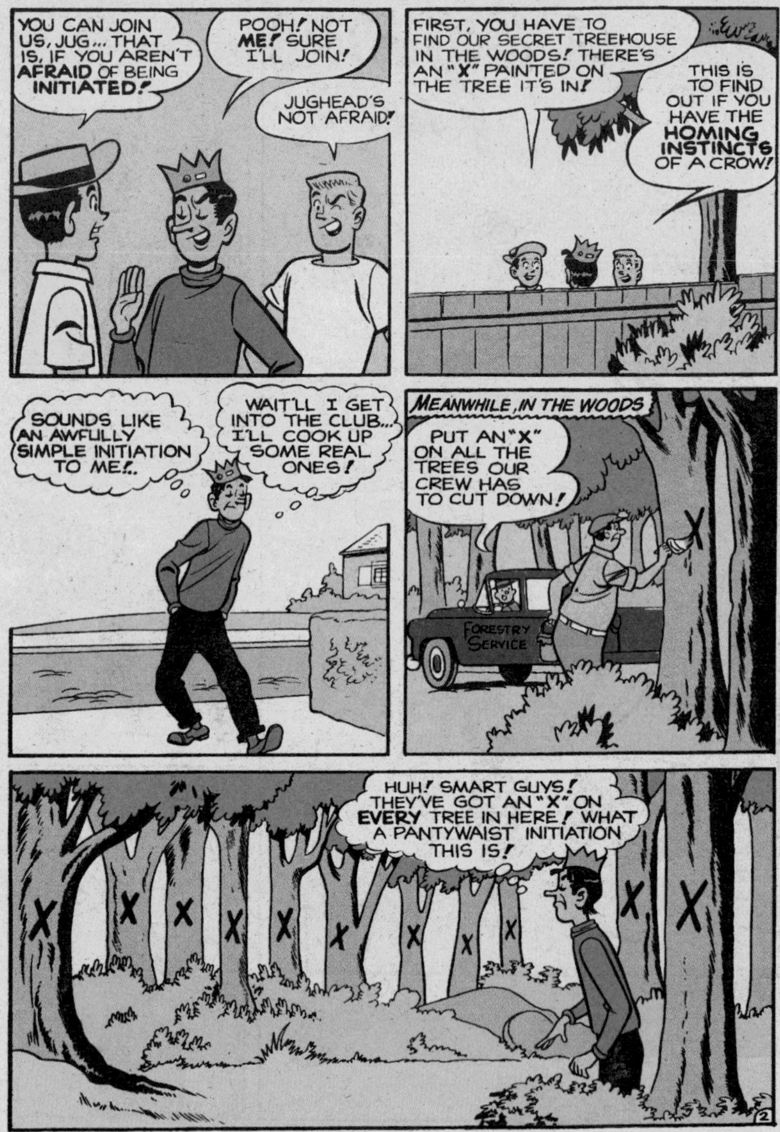
YOU CAN JOIN US, JUG... THAT IS, IF YOU AREN'T AFRAID OF BEING INITIATED!
POOH! NOT ME! SURE I'LL JOIN!
JUGHEAD'S NOT AFRAID!
FIRST, YOU HAVE TO FIND OUR SECRET TREEHOUSE IN THE WOODS! THERE'S AN "X" PAINTED ON THE TREE IT'S IN!
THIS IS TO FIND OUT IF YOU HAVE THE HOMING INSTINCTS OF A CROW!
SOUNDS LIKE AN AWFULLY SIMPLE INITIATION TO ME!..
WAIT'LL I GET INTO THE CLUB... I'LL COOK UP SOME REAL ONES!
MEANWHILE, IN THE WOODS
PUT AN "X" ON ALL THE TREES OUR CREW HAS TO CUT DOWN!
FORESTRY SERVICE
HUH! SMART GUYS! THEY'VE GOT AN "X" ON EVERY TREE IN HERE! WHAT A PANTYWAIST INITIATION THIS IS!
2

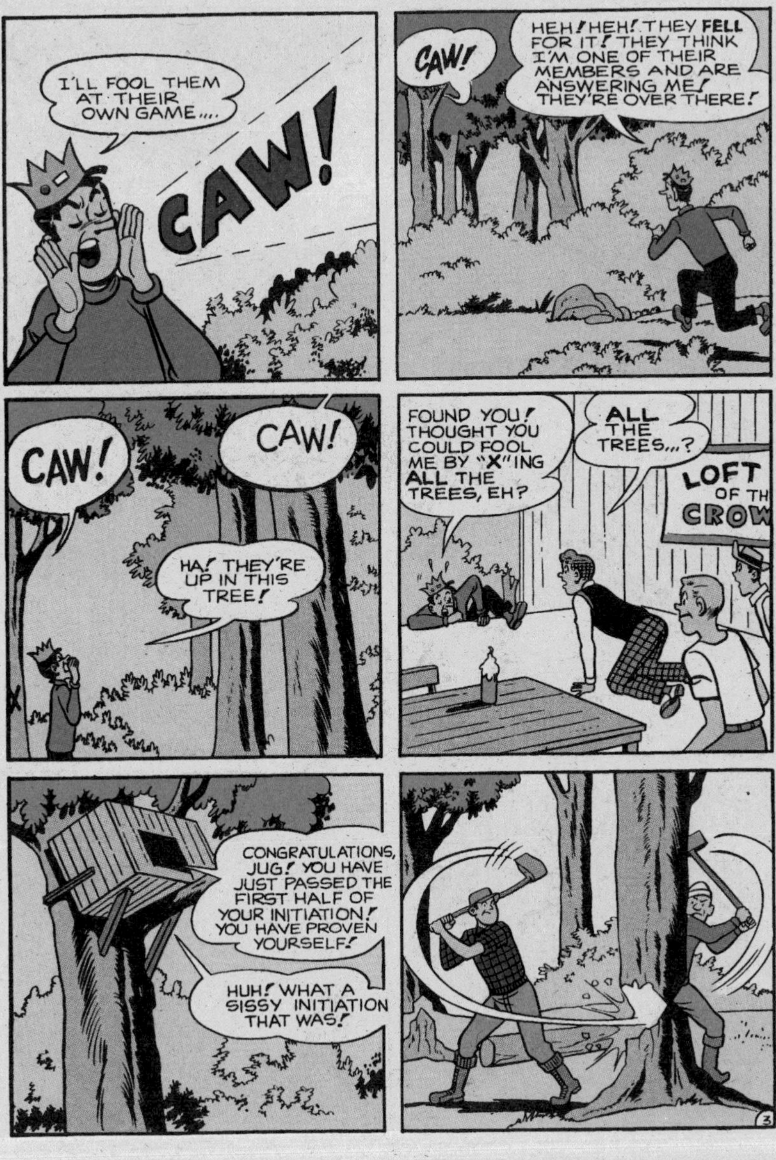
I'LL FOOL THEM AT THEIR OWN GAME....
CAW!
CAW!
HEH! HEH! THEY FELL FOR IT! THEY THINK I'M ONE OF THEIR MEMBERS AND ARE ANSWERING ME! THEY'RE OVER THERE!
CAW!
CAW!
HA! THEY'RE UP IN THIS TREE!
FOUND YOU! THOUGHT YOU COULD FOOL ME BY "X"ING ALL THE TREES, EH?
ALL THE TREES...?
LOFT OF TH
CROW
CONGRATULATIONS, JUG! YOU HAVE JUST PASSED THE FIRST HALF OF YOUR INITIATION! YOU HAVE PROVEN YOURSELF!
HUH! WHAT A SISSY INITIATION THAT WAS!
3

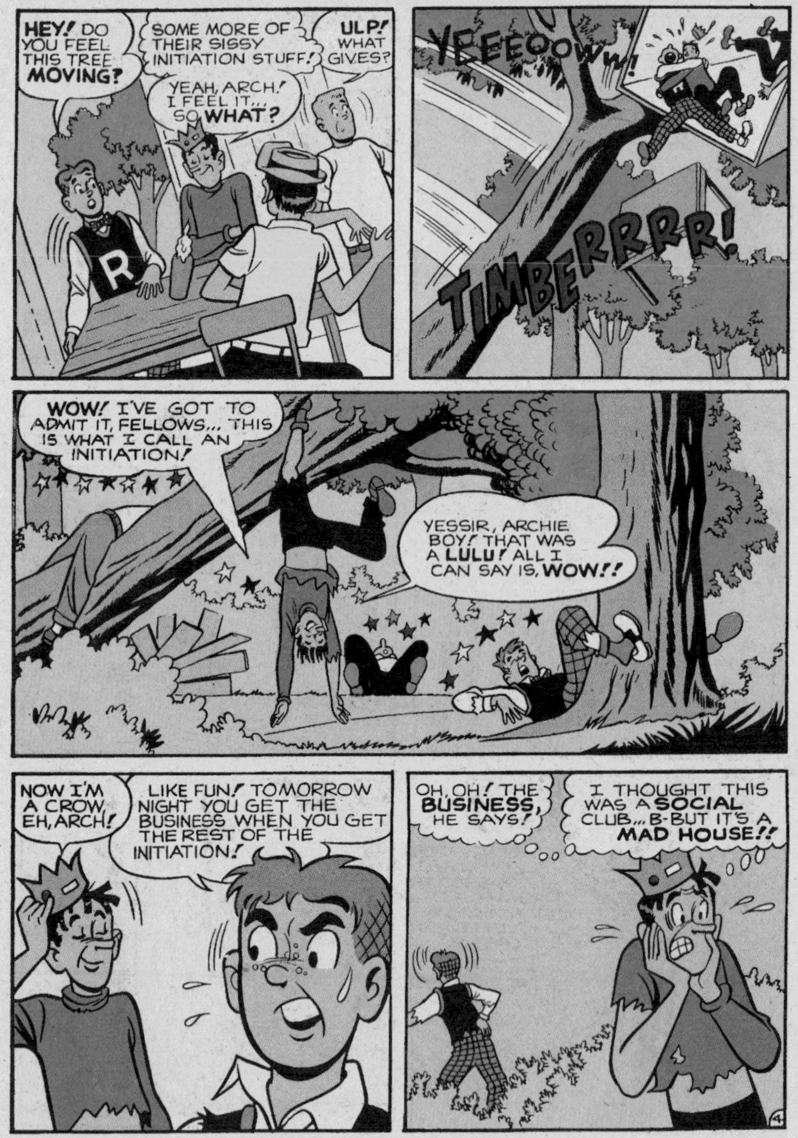
HEY! DO YOU FEEL THIS TREE MOVING?
SOME MORE OF THEIR SISSY INITIATION STUFF!
ULP! WHAT GIVES?
YEAH, ARCH! I FEEL IT... SO WHAT?
YEEEOOOWW!
TIMBERRRR!
WOW! I'VE GOT TO ADMIT IT, FELLOWS... THIS IS WHAT I CALL AN INITIATION!
YESSIR, ARCHIE BOY! THAT WAS A LULU! ALL I CAN SAY IS, WOW!!
NOW I'M A CROW, EH, ARCH!
LIKE FUN! TOMORROW NIGHT YOU GET THE BUSINESS WHEN YOU GET THE REST OF THE INITIATION!
OH, OH! THE BUSINESS, HE SAYS!
I THOUGHT THIS WAS A SOCIAL CLUB... B-BUT IT'S A MAD HOUSE!!
4

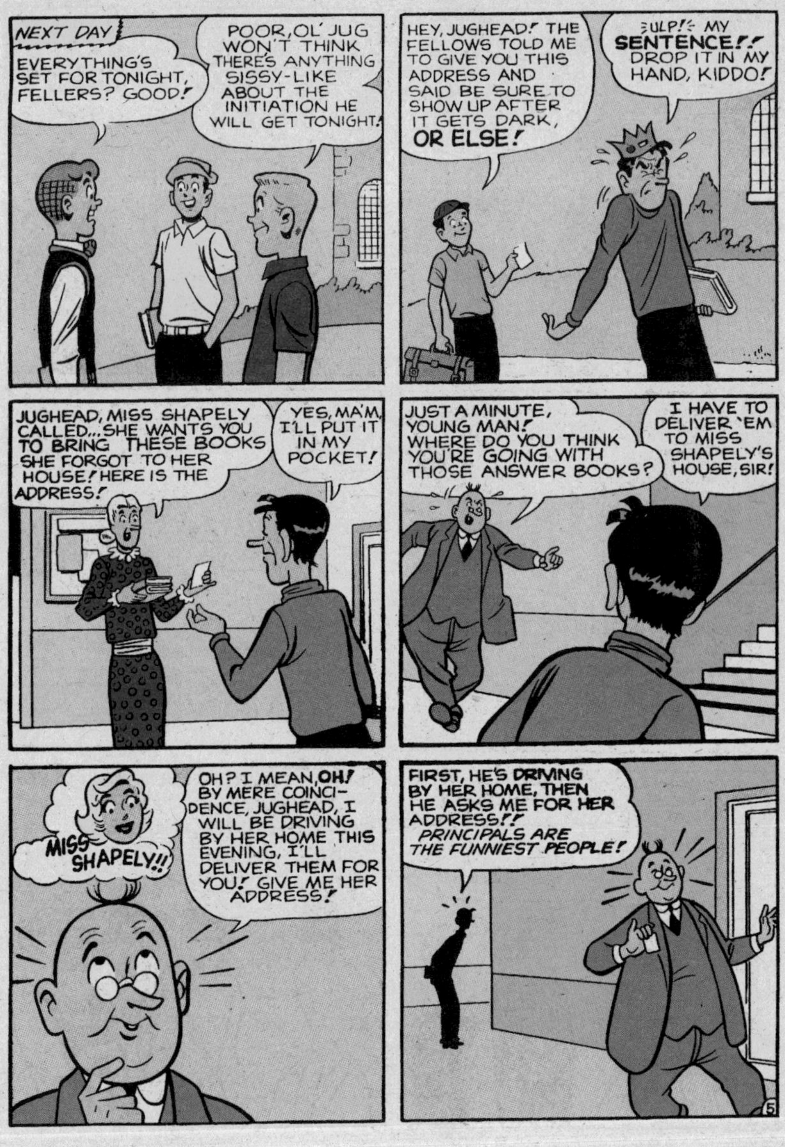
NEXT DAY
EVERYTHING'S SET FOR TONIGHT, FELLERS? GOOD!
POOR, OL' JUG WON'T THINK THERE'S ANYTHING SISSY-LIKE ABOUT THE INITIATION HE WILL GET TONIGHT!
HEY, JUGHEAD! THE FELLOWS TOLD ME TO GIVE YOU THIS ADDRESS AND SAID BE SURE TO SHOW UP AFTER IT GETS DARK, OR ELSE!
GULP! MY SENTENCE!! DROP IT IN MY HAND, KIDDO!
JUGHEAD, MISS SHAPELY CALLED... SHE WANTS YOU TO BRING THESE BOOKS SHE FORGOT TO HER HOUSE! HERE IS THE ADDRESS!
YES, MA'M, I'LL PUT IT IN MY POCKET!
JUST A MINUTE, YOUNG MAN! WHERE DO YOU THINK YOU'RE GOING WITH THOSE ANSWER BOOKS?
I HAVE TO DELIVER 'EM TO MISS SHAPELY'S HOUSE, SIR!
MISS SHAPELY!!
OH? I MEAN, OH! BY MERE COINCIDENCE, JUGHEAD, I WILL BE DRIVING BY HER HOME THIS EVENING, I'LL DELIVER THEM FOR YOU! GIVE ME HER ADDRESS!
FIRST, HE'S DRIVING BY HER HOME, THEN HE ASKS ME FOR HER ADDRESS!! PRINCIPALS ARE THE FUNNIEST PEOPLE!
5

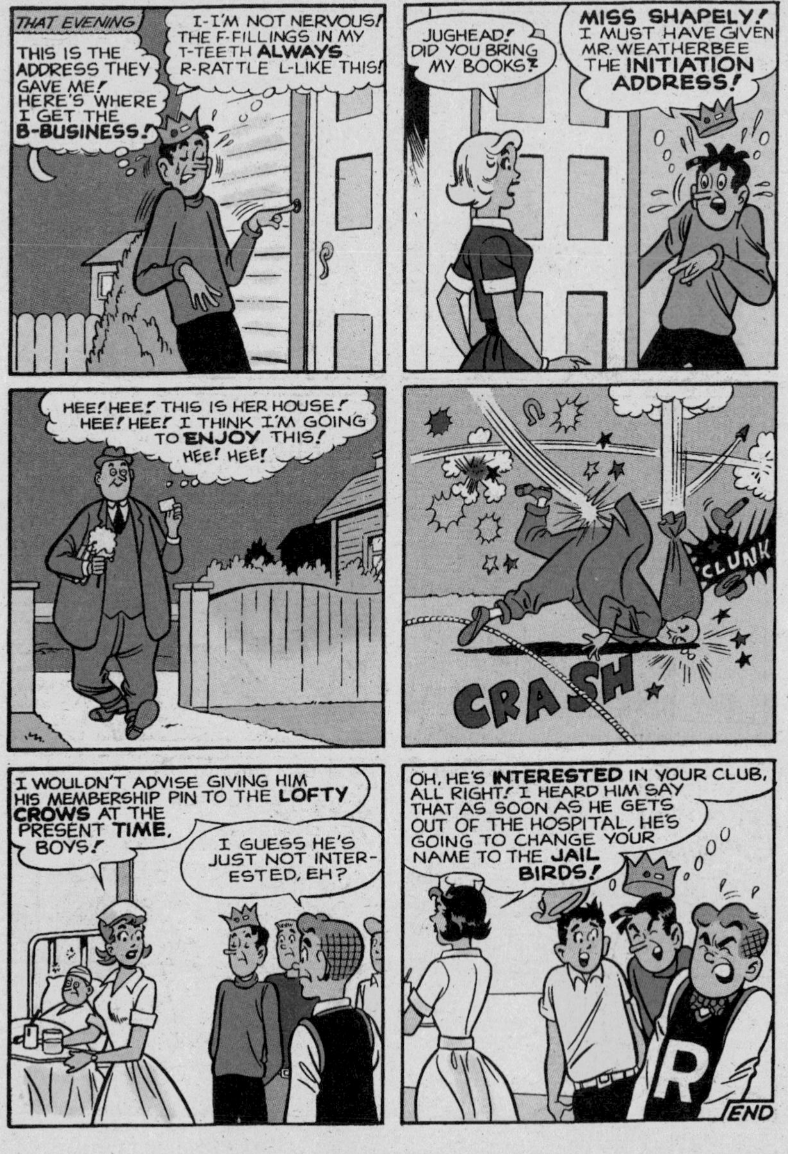
THAT EVENING
THIS IS THE ADDRESS THEY GAVE ME! HERE'S WHERE I GET THE B-BUSINESS!
I-I'M NOT NERVOUS! THE F-FILLINGS IN MY T-TEETH ALWAYS R-RATTLE L-LIKE THIS!
JUGHEAD! DID YOU BRING MY BOOKS?
MISS SHAPELY! I MUST HAVE GIVEN MR. WEATHERBEE THE INITIATION ADDRESS!
HEE! HEE! THIS IS HER HOUSE! HEE! HEE! I THINK I'M GOING TO ENJOY THIS! HEE! HEE!
CLUNK
CRASH
I WOULDN'T ADVISE GIVING HIM HIS MEMBERSHIP PIN TO THE LOFTY CROWS AT THE PRESENT TIME, BOYS!
I GUESS HE'S JUST NOT INTERESTED, EH?
OH, HE'S INTERESTED IN YOUR CLUB, ALL RIGHT! I HEARD HIM SAY THAT AS SOON AS HE GETS OUT OF THE HOSPITAL, HE'S GOING TO CHANGE YOUR NAME TO THE JAIL BIRDS!
R
END

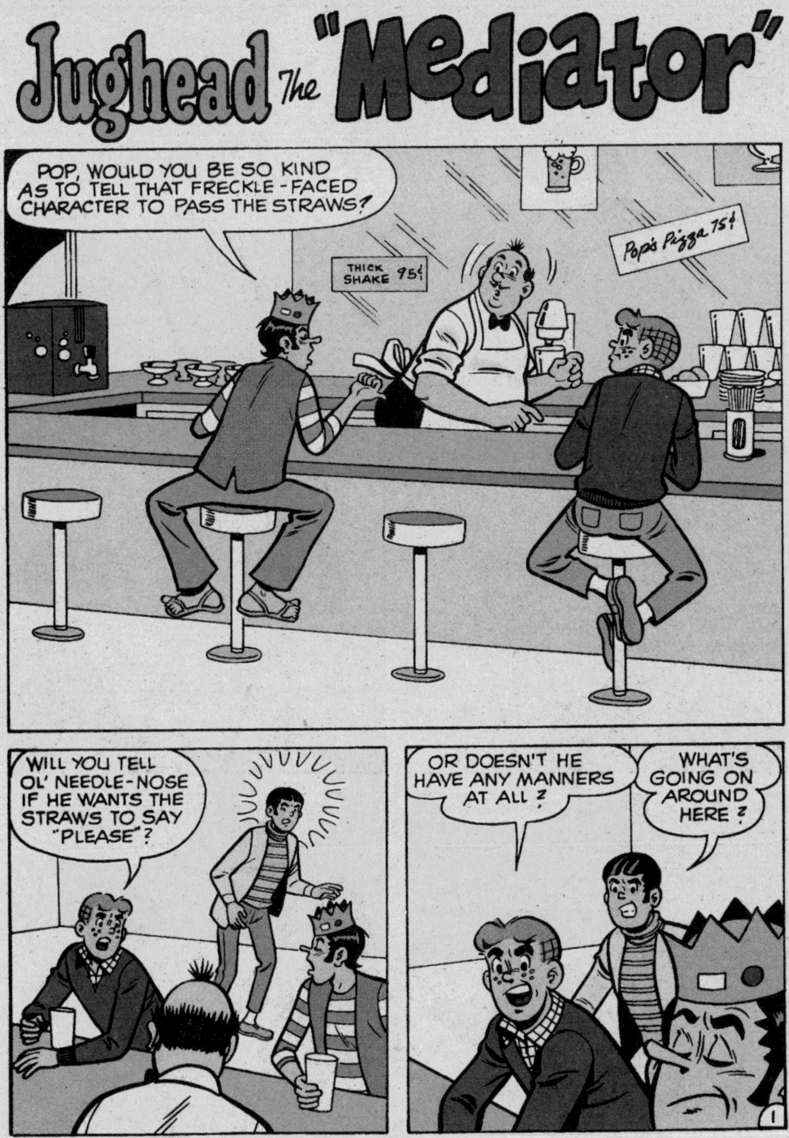
Jughead The "Mediator"
POP, WOULD YOU BE SO KIND AS TO TELL THAT FRECKLE-FACED CHARACTER TO PASS THE STRAWS?
THICK SHAKE 95¢
Pop's Pizza 75¢
WILL YOU TELL OL' NEEDLE-NOSE IF HE WANTS THE STRAWS TO SAY "PLEASE"?
OR DOESN'T HE HAVE ANY MANNERS AT ALL?
WHAT'S GOING ON AROUND HERE?
1

Script & Pencils: Al Hartley / Inks: Jon D'Agostino / Letters: Bill Yoshida / Colors: Barry Grossman

DON'T TELL ME YOU TWO LOYAL BOSOM BUDDIES ARE MAD AT EACH OTHER? I THOUGHT YOUR FRIENDSHIP WAS INSEPARABLE?

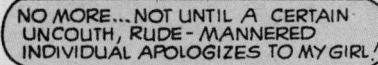

NO MORE...NOT UNTIL A CERTAIN UNCOUTH, RUDE-MANNERED INDIVIDUAL APOLOGIZES TO MY GIRL!

YOUR GIRL? SHE WANTS YOU FOR A BOYFRIEND LIKE SHE WANTS BRACES ON HER TEETH!

WHAT KIND OF REMARK WAS THAT? ...YOU TAKE THAT BACK, YOU WALKING GARBAGE CAN!

I WILL NOT! I'VE DONE YOU A GREAT, BIG FAVOR! YOU SHOULD THANK ME!

2

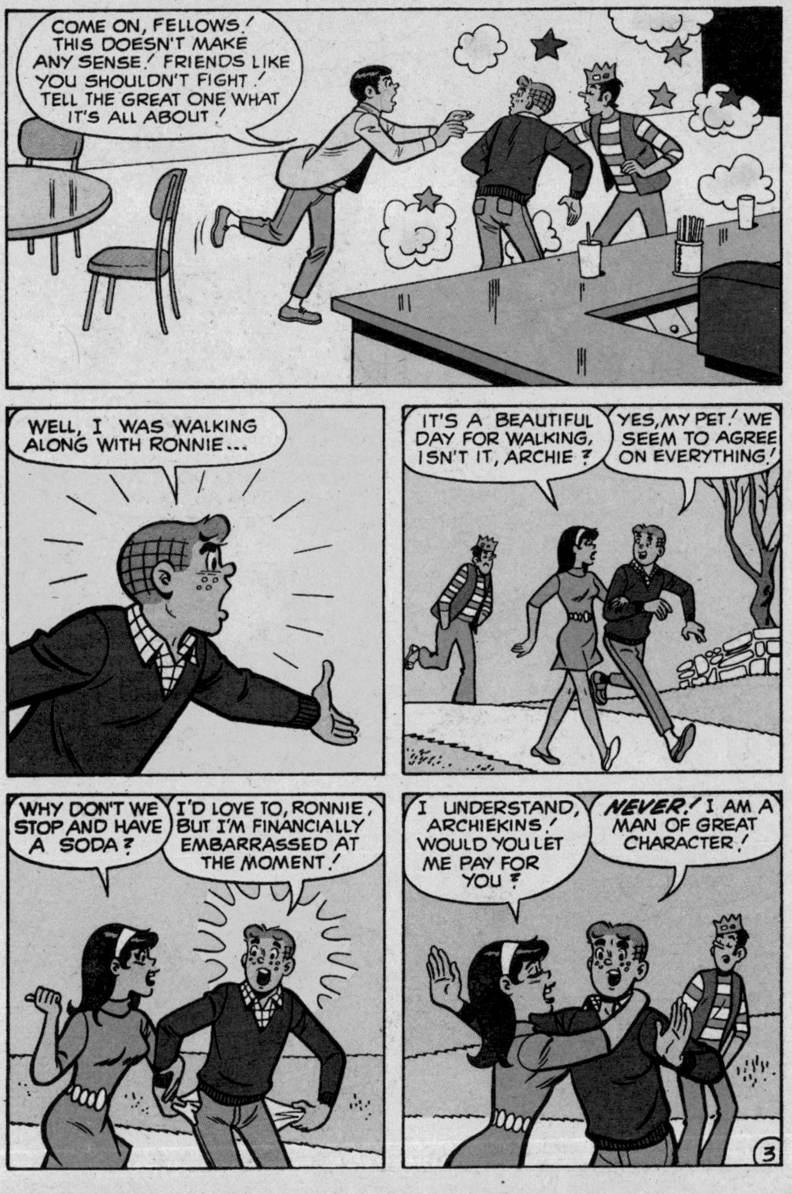
COME ON, FELLOWS! THIS DOESN'T MAKE ANY SENSE! FRIENDS LIKE YOU SHOULDN'T FIGHT! TELL THE GREAT ONE WHAT IT'S ALL ABOUT!
WELL, I WAS WALKING ALONG WITH RONNIE...
IT'S A BEAUTIFUL DAY FOR WALKING, ISN'T IT, ARCHIE?
YES, MY PET! WE SEEM TO AGREE ON EVERYTHING!
WHY DON'T WE STOP AND HAVE A SODA?
I'D LOVE TO, RONNIE, BUT I'M FINANCIALLY EMBARRASSED AT THE MOMENT!
I UNDERSTAND, ARCHIEKINS! WOULD YOU LET ME PAY FOR YOU?
NEVER! I AM A MAN OF GREAT CHARACTER!
3

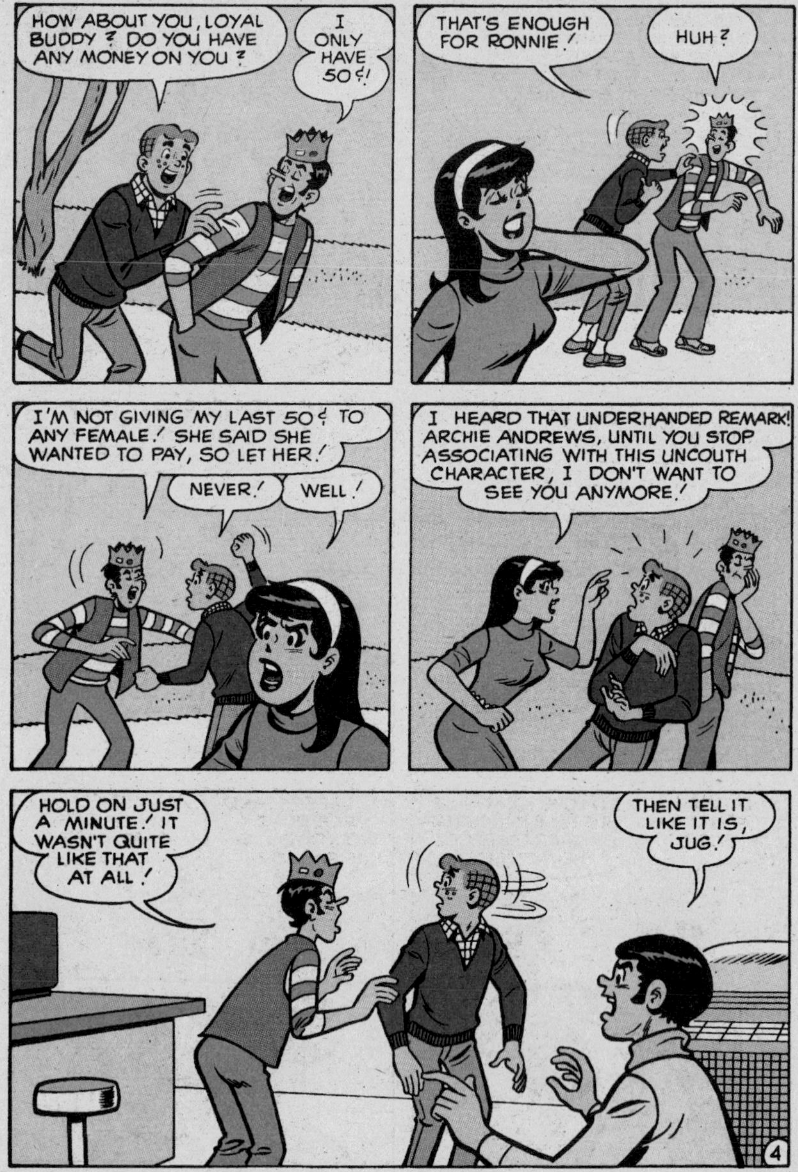
HOW ABOUT YOU, LOYAL BUDDY ? DO YOU HAVE ANY MONEY ON YOU ?
I ONLY HAVE 50¢!
THAT'S ENOUGH FOR RONNIE!
HUH ?
I'M NOT GIVING MY LAST 50¢ TO ANY FEMALE! SHE SAID SHE WANTED TO PAY, SO LET HER!
NEVER!
WELL!
I HEARD THAT UNDERHANDED REMARK! ARCHIE ANDREWS, UNTIL YOU STOP ASSOCIATING WITH THIS UNCOUTH CHARACTER, I DON'T WANT TO SEE YOU ANYMORE!
HOLD ON JUST A MINUTE! IT WASN'T QUITE LIKE THAT AT ALL!
THEN TELL IT LIKE IT IS, JUG!
4

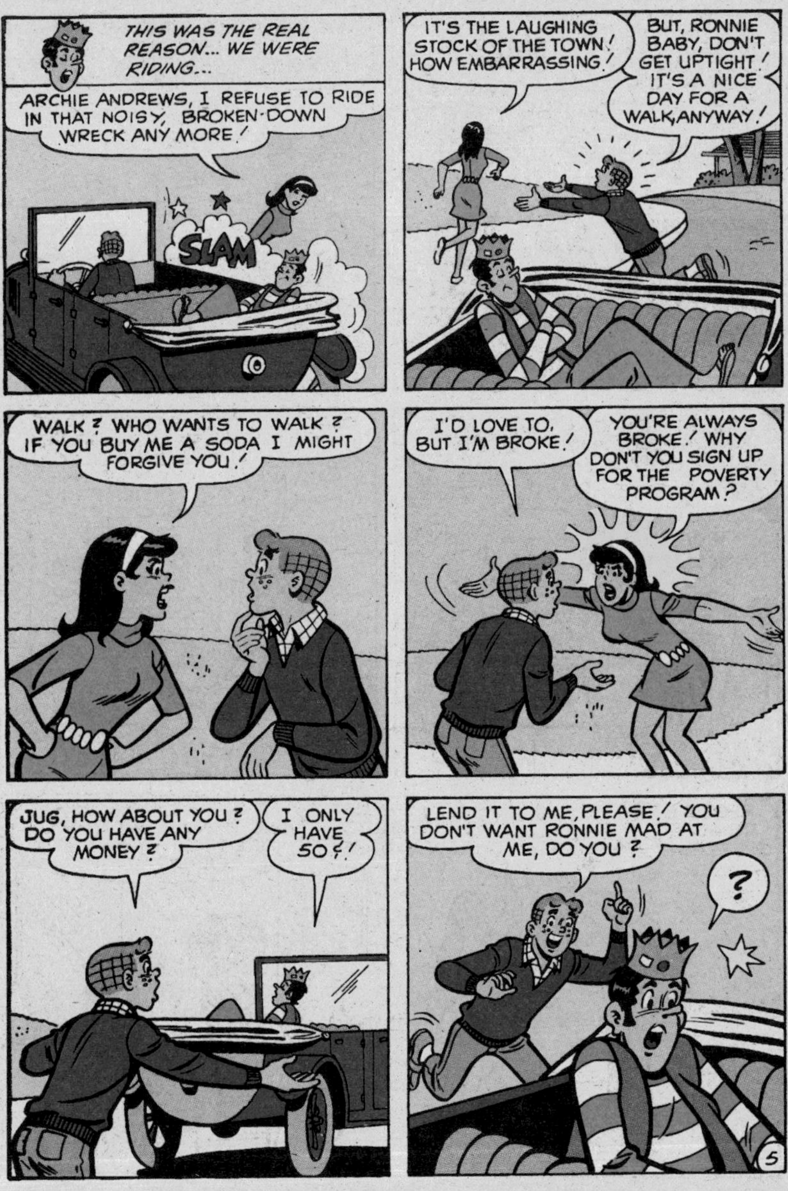
THIS WAS THE REAL REASON... WE WERE RIDING...
ARCHIE ANDREWS, I REFUSE TO RIDE IN THAT NOISY, BROKEN-DOWN WRECK ANY MORE!
SLAM
IT'S THE LAUGHING STOCK OF THE TOWN! HOW EMBARRASSING!
BUT, RONNIE BABY, DON'T GET UPTIGHT! IT'S A NICE DAY FOR A WALK, ANYWAY!
WALK? WHO WANTS TO WALK? IF YOU BUY ME A SODA I MIGHT FORGIVE YOU!
I'D LOVE TO, BUT I'M BROKE!
YOU'RE ALWAYS BROKE! WHY DON'T YOU SIGN UP FOR THE POVERTY PROGRAM?
JUG, HOW ABOUT YOU? DO YOU HAVE ANY MONEY?
I ONLY HAVE 50¢!
LEND IT TO ME, PLEASE! YOU DON'T WANT RONNIE MAD AT ME, DO YOU?
?
5

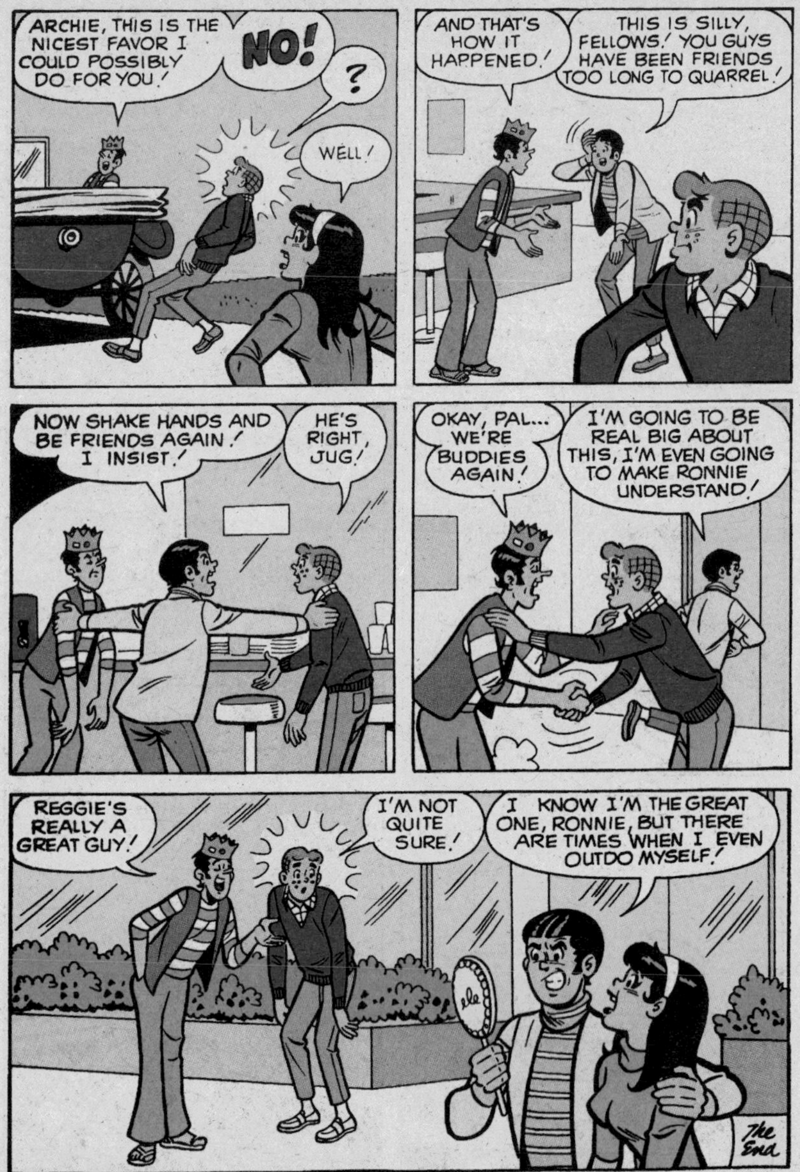
ARCHIE, THIS IS THE NICEST FAVOR I COULD POSSIBLY DO FOR YOU!
NO!
?
WELL!
AND THAT'S HOW IT HAPPENED!
THIS IS SILLY, FELLOWS! YOU GUYS HAVE BEEN FRIENDS TOO LONG TO QUARREL!
NOW SHAKE HANDS AND BE FRIENDS AGAIN! I INSIST!
HE'S RIGHT, JUG!
OKAY, PAL... WE'RE BUDDIES AGAIN!
I'M GOING TO BE REAL BIG ABOUT THIS, I'M EVEN GOING TO MAKE RONNIE UNDERSTAND!
REGGIE'S REALLY A GREAT GUY!
I'M NOT QUITE SURE!
I KNOW I'M THE GREAT ONE, RONNIE, BUT THERE ARE TIMES WHEN I EVEN OUTDO MYSELF!
The End

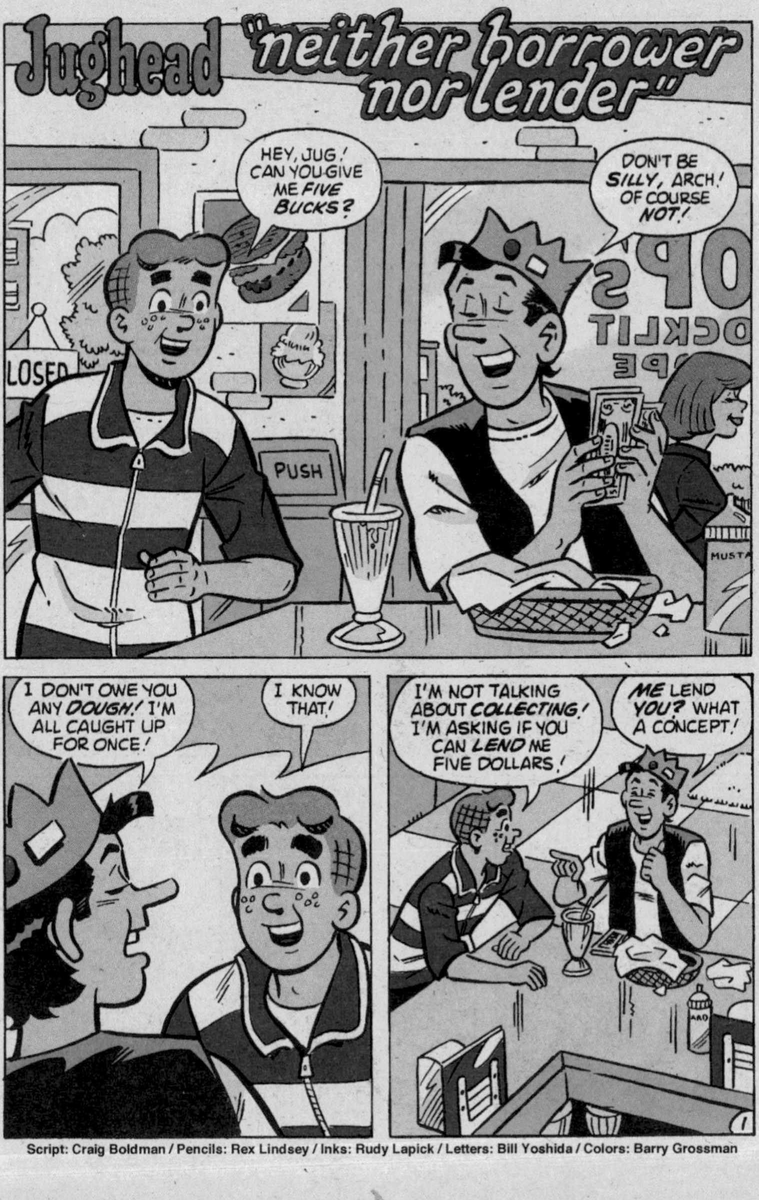
Jughead
"neither borrower nor lender"
HEY, JUG! CAN YOU GIVE ME FIVE BUCKS?
DON'T BE SILLY, ARCH! OF COURSE NOT!
LOSED
PUSH
MUSTA
I DON'T OWE YOU ANY DOUGH! I'M ALL CAUGHT UP FOR ONCE!
I KNOW THAT!
I'M NOT TALKING ABOUT COLLECTING! I'M ASKING IF YOU CAN LEND ME FIVE DOLLARS!
ME LEND YOU? WHAT A CONCEPT!
1

Script: Craig Boldman / Pencils: Rex Lindsey / Inks: Rudy Lapick / Letters: Bill Yoshida / Colors: Barry Grossman

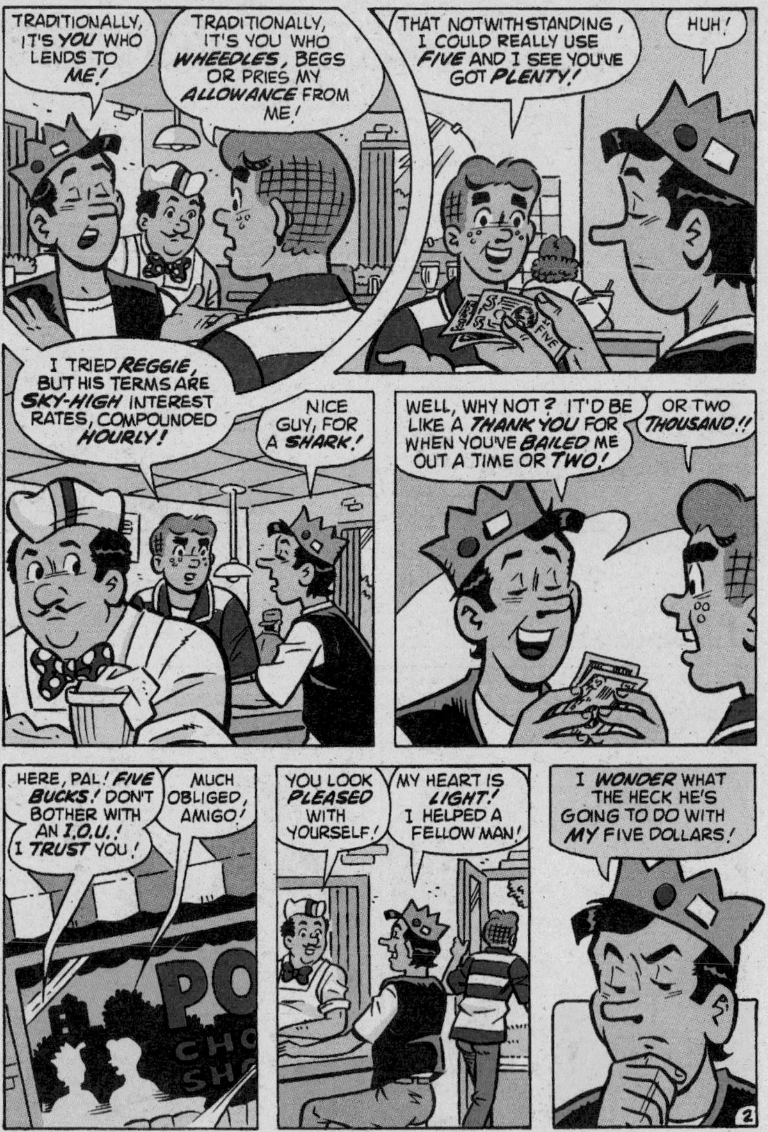
TRADITIONALLY, IT'S YOU WHO LENDS TO ME!
TRADITIONALLY, IT'S YOU WHO WHEEDLES, BEGS OR PRIES MY ALLOWANCE FROM ME!
THAT NOTWITHSTANDING, I COULD REALLY USE FIVE AND I SEE YOU'VE GOT PLENTY!
HUH!
I TRIED REGGIE, BUT HIS TERMS ARE SKY-HIGH INTEREST RATES, COMPOUNDED HOURLY!
NICE GUY, FOR A SHARK!
WELL, WHY NOT? IT'D BE LIKE A THANK YOU FOR WHEN YOU'VE BAILED ME OUT A TIME OR TWO!
OR TWO THOUSAND!!
HERE, PAL! FIVE BUCKS! DON'T BOTHER WITH AN I.O.U.! I TRUST YOU!
MUCH OBLIGED, AMIGO!
YOU LOOK PLEASED WITH YOURSELF!
MY HEART IS LIGHT! I HELPED A FELLOW MAN!
I WONDER WHAT THE HECK HE'S GOING TO DO WITH MY FIVE DOLLARS!
2

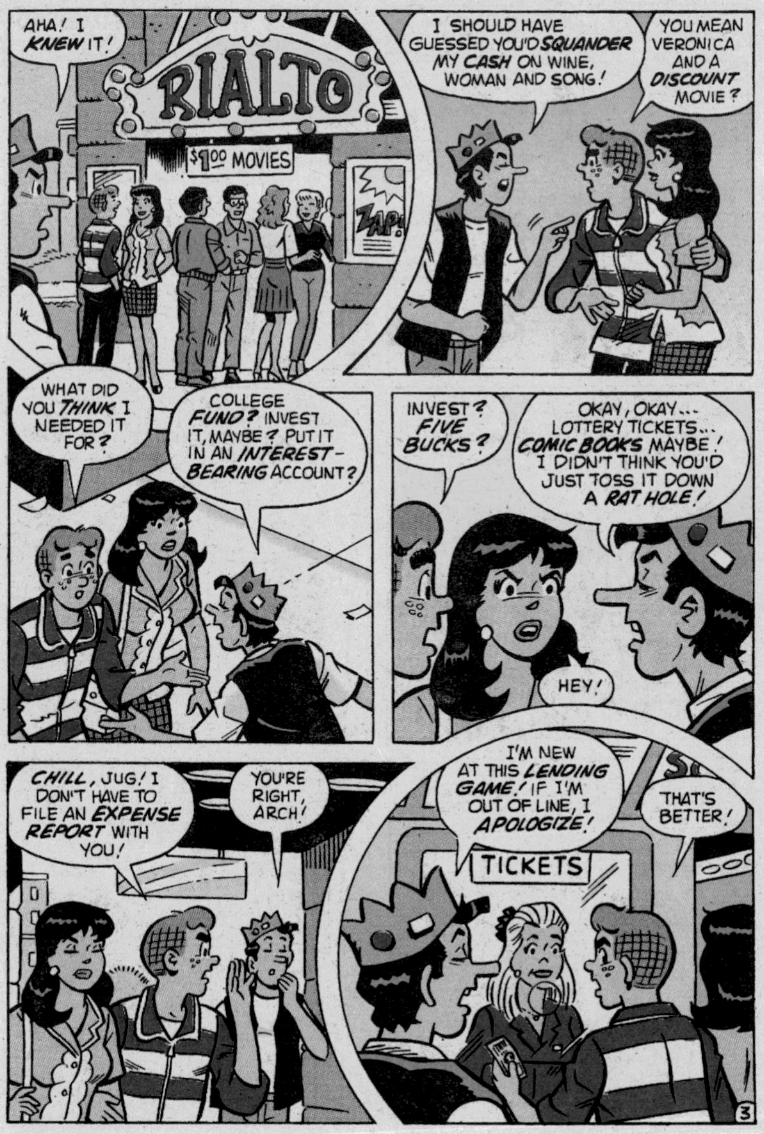

AHA! I KNEW IT!
RIALTO
$1.00 MOVIES
ZAP!
I SHOULD HAVE GUESSED YOU'D SQUANDER MY CASH ON WINE, WOMAN AND SONG!
YOU MEAN VERONICA AND A DISCOUNT MOVIE?
WHAT DID YOU THINK I NEEDED IT FOR?
COLLEGE FUND? INVEST IT, MAYBE? PUT IT IN AN INTEREST-BEARING ACCOUNT?
INVEST? FIVE BUCKS?
OKAY, OKAY... LOTTERY TICKETS... COMIC BOOKS MAYBE! I DIDN'T THINK YOU'D JUST TOSS IT DOWN A RAT HOLE!
HEY!
CHILL, JUG! I DON'T HAVE TO FILE AN EXPENSE REPORT WITH YOU!
YOU'RE RIGHT, ARCH!
I'M NEW AT THIS LENDING GAME! IF I'M OUT OF LINE, I APOLOGIZE!
TICKETS
THAT'S BETTER!
3

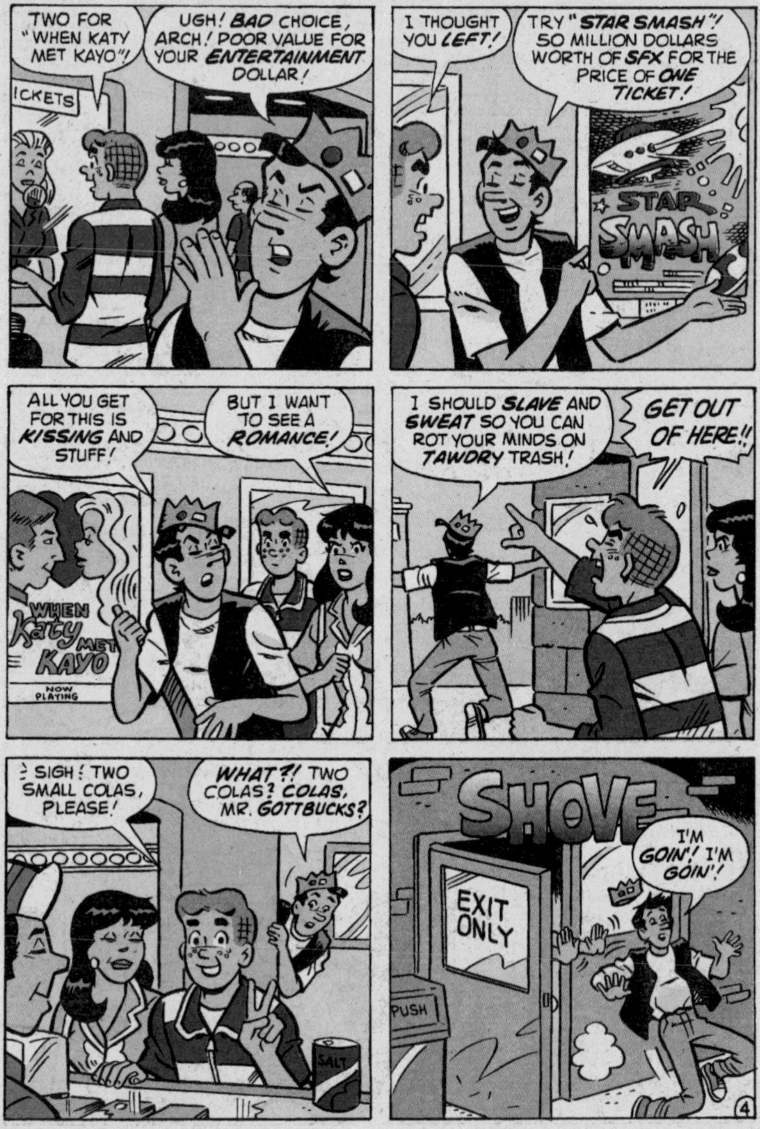
TWO FOR "WHEN KATY MET KAYO"!
UGH! BAD CHOICE, ARCH! POOR VALUE FOR YOUR ENTERTAINMENT DOLLAR!
!CKETS
I THOUGHT YOU LEFT!
TRY "STAR SMASH"! 50 MILLION DOLLARS WORTH OF SFX FOR THE PRICE OF ONE TICKET!
STAR SMASH
ALL YOU GET FOR THIS IS KISSING AND STUFF!
BUT I WANT TO SEE A ROMANCE!
WHEN Katy MET KAYO
NOW PLAYING
I SHOULD SLAVE AND SWEAT SO YOU CAN ROT YOUR MINDS ON TAWDRY TRASH!
GET OUT OF HERE!!
SIGH! TWO SMALL COLAS, PLEASE!
WHAT?! TWO COLAS? COLAS, MR. GOTTBUCKS?
SALT
SHOVE
EXIT ONLY
PUSH
I'M GOIN'! I'M GOIN'!
4

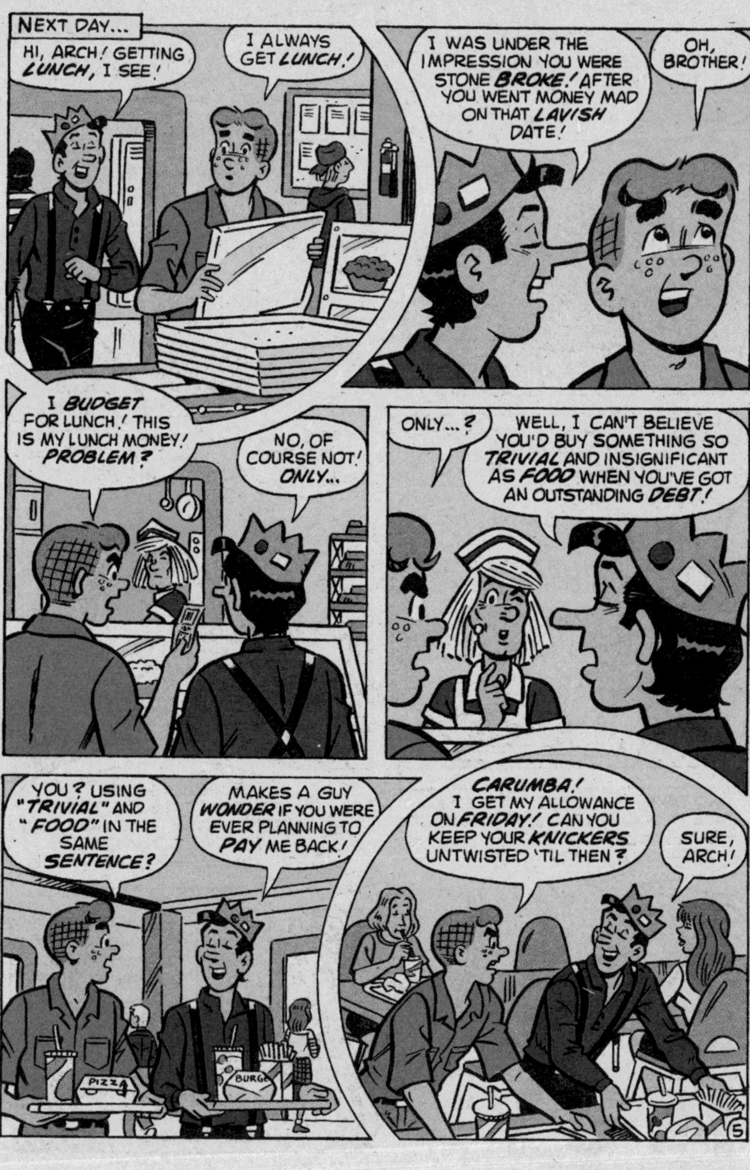
NEXT DAY...
HI, ARCH! GETTING LUNCH, I SEE!
I ALWAYS GET LUNCH!
I WAS UNDER THE IMPRESSION YOU WERE STONE BROKE! AFTER YOU WENT MONEY MAD ON THAT LAVISH DATE!
OH, BROTHER!
I BUDGET FOR LUNCH! THIS IS MY LUNCH MONEY! PROBLEM?
NO, OF COURSE NOT! ONLY...
ONLY...?
WELL, I CAN'T BELIEVE YOU'D BUY SOMETHING SO TRIVIAL AND INSIGNIFICANT AS FOOD WHEN YOU'VE GOT AN OUTSTANDING DEBT!
YOU? USING "TRIVIAL" AND "FOOD" IN THE SAME SENTENCE?
MAKES A GUY WONDER IF YOU WERE EVER PLANNING TO PAY ME BACK!
PIZZA
BURG
CARUMBA! I GET MY ALLOWANCE ON FRIDAY! CAN YOU KEEP YOUR KNICKERS UNTWISTED 'TIL THEN?
SURE, ARCH!
5

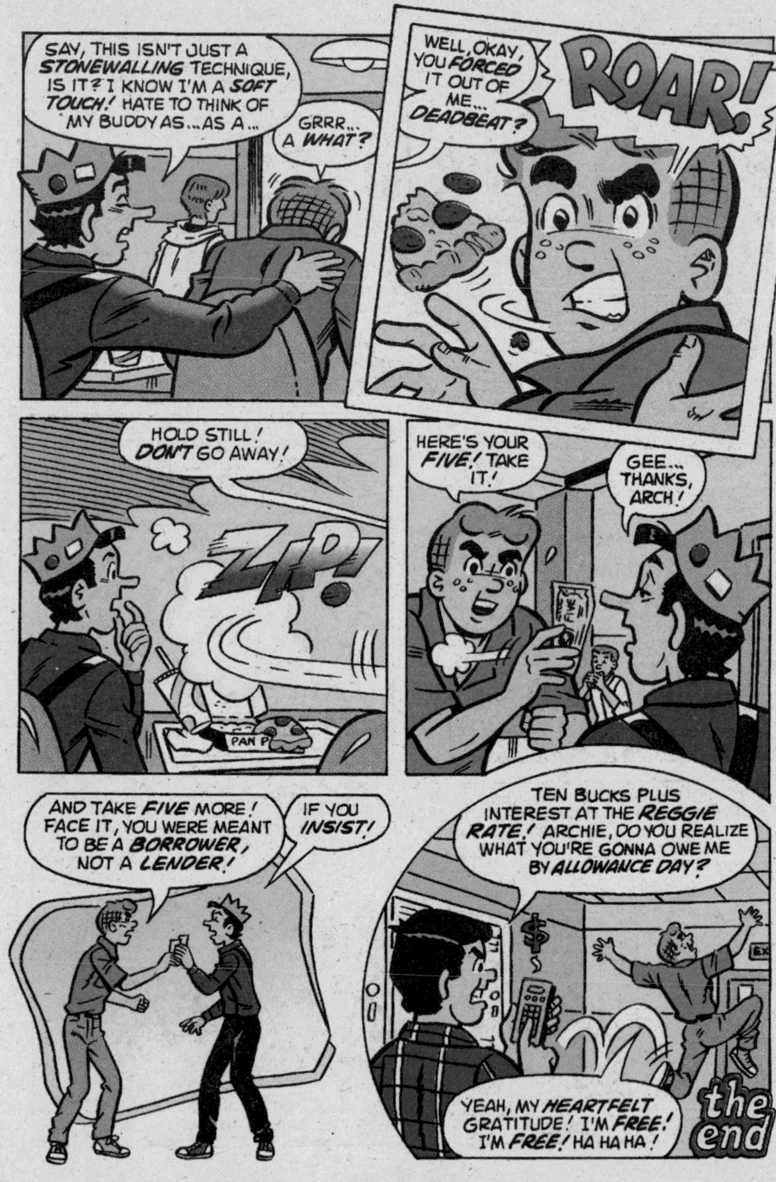
SAY, THIS ISN'T JUST A STONEWALLING TECHNIQUE, IS IT? I KNOW I'M A SOFT TOUCH! HATE TO THINK OF MY BUDDY AS...AS A...
GRRR... A WHAT?
WELL, OKAY, YOU FORCED IT OUT OF ME... DEADBEAT?
ROAR!
HOLD STILL! DON'T GO AWAY!
ZIP!
PAN P
HERE'S YOUR FIVE! TAKE IT!
GEE... THANKS, ARCH!
FIVE
AND TAKE FIVE MORE! FACE IT, YOU WERE MEANT TO BE A BORROWER, NOT A LENDER!
IF YOU INSIST!
TEN BUCKS PLUS INTEREST AT THE REGGIE RATE! ARCHIE, DO YOU REALIZE WHAT YOU'RE GONNA OWE ME BY ALLOWANCE DAY?
YEAH, MY HEARTFELT GRATITUDE! I'M FREE! I'M FREE! HA HA HA!
the end

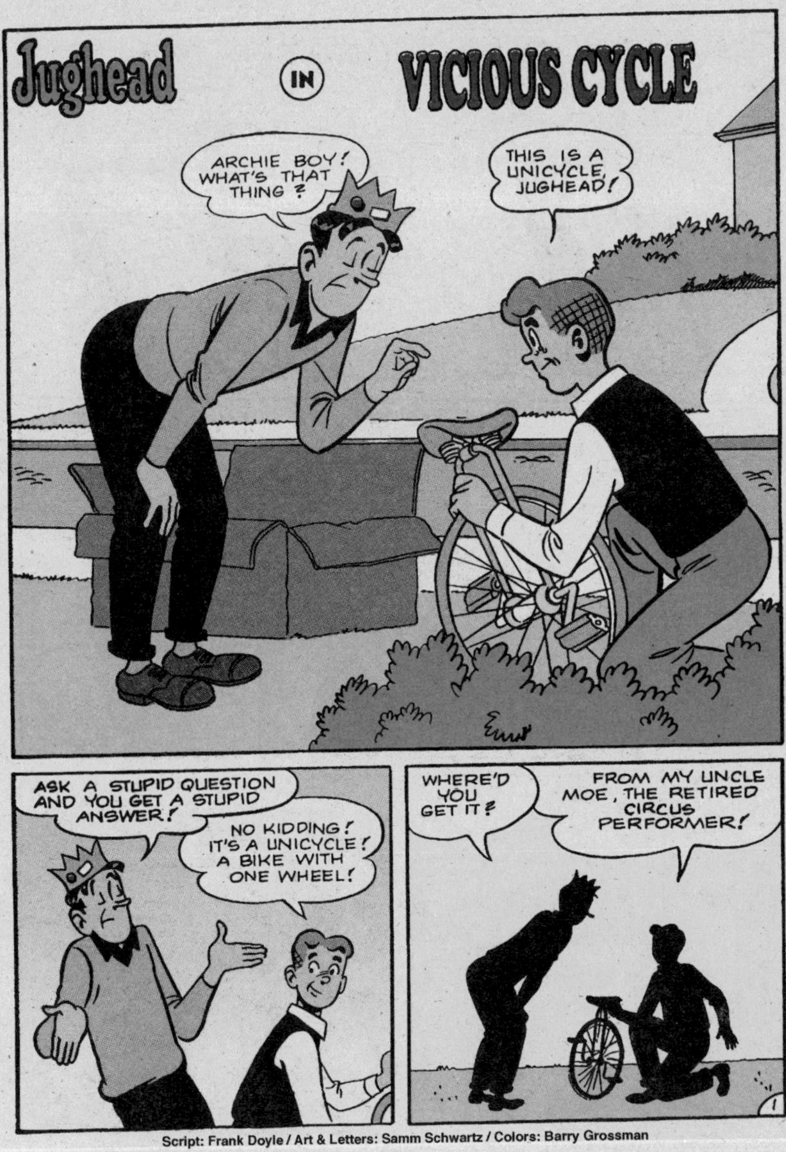
Jughead IN VICIOUS CYCLE
ARCHIE BOY! WHAT'S THAT THING?
THIS IS A UNICYCLE, JUGHEAD!
ASK A STUPID QUESTION AND YOU GET A STUPID ANSWER!
NO KIDDING! IT'S A UNICYCLE! A BIKE WITH ONE WHEEL!
WHERE'D YOU GET IT?
FROM MY UNCLE MOE, THE RETIRED CIRCUS PERFORMER!
1

Script: Frank Doyle / Art & Letters: Samm Schwartz / Colors: Barry Grossman

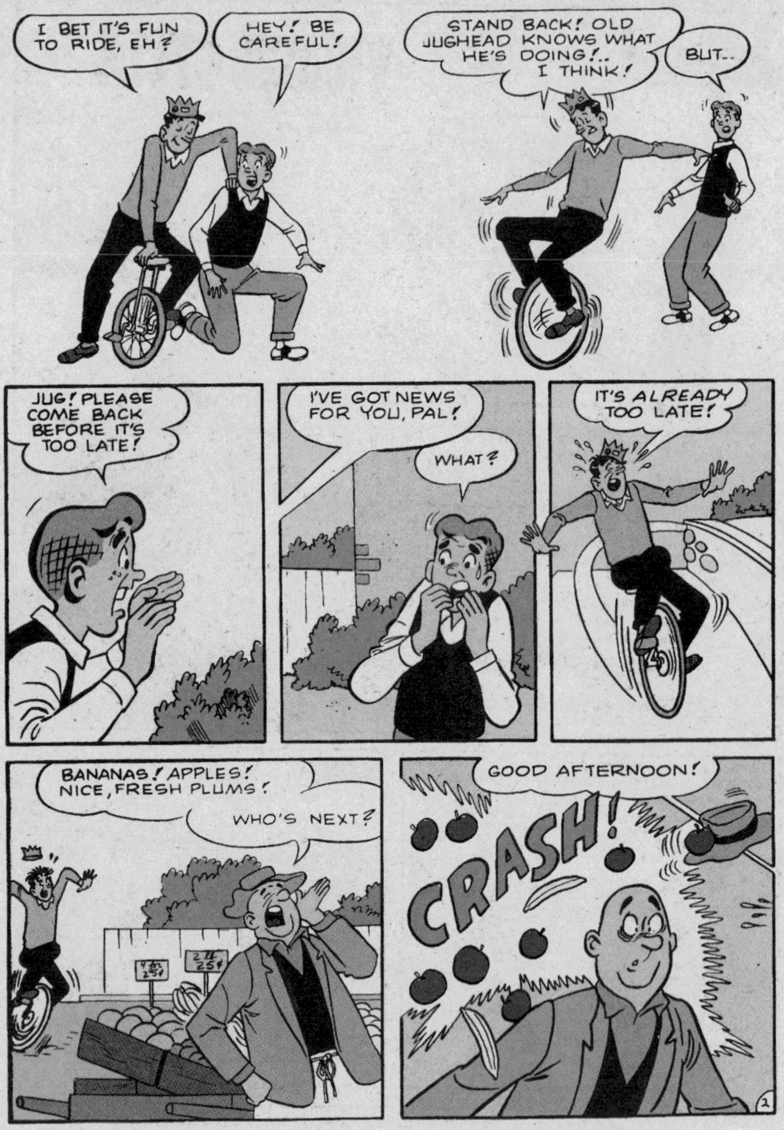
I BET IT'S FUN TO RIDE, EH?
HEY! BE CAREFUL!
STAND BACK! OLD JUGHEAD KNOWS WHAT HE'S DOING!.. I THINK!
BUT..
JUG! PLEASE COME BACK BEFORE IT'S TOO LATE!
I'VE GOT NEWS FOR YOU, PAL!
WHAT?
IT'S ALREADY TOO LATE!
BANANAS! APPLES! NICE, FRESH PLUMS!
WHO'S NEXT?
GOOD AFTERNOON!
CRASH!
2

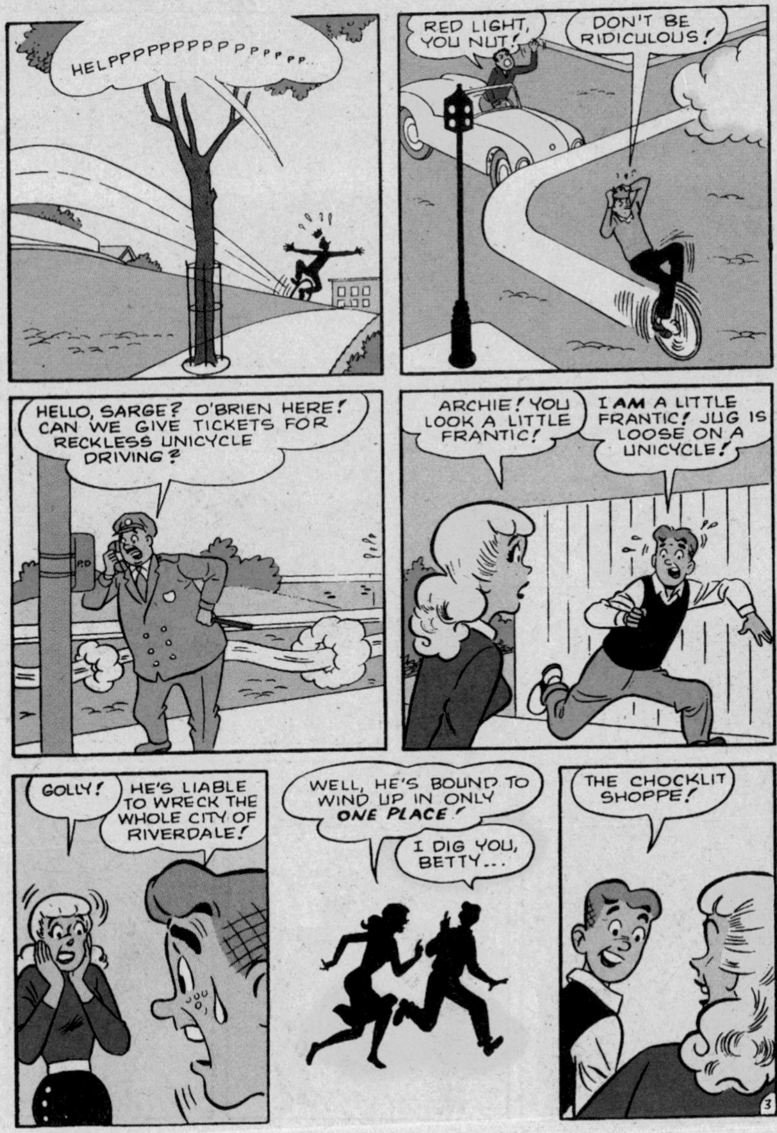
HELPPPPPPPPPPPPPPPP...
RED LIGHT, YOU NUT!
DON'T BE RIDICULOUS!
HELLO, SARGE? O'BRIEN HERE! CAN WE GIVE TICKETS FOR RECKLESS UNICYCLE DRIVING?
P.D
ARCHIE! YOU LOOK A LITTLE FRANTIC!
I AM A LITTLE FRANTIC! JUG IS LOOSE ON A UNICYCLE!
GOLLY!
HE'S LIABLE TO WRECK THE WHOLE CITY OF RIVERDALE!
WELL, HE'S BOUND TO WIND UP IN ONLY ONE PLACE!
I DIG YOU, BETTY...
THE CHOCKLIT SHOPPE!
3

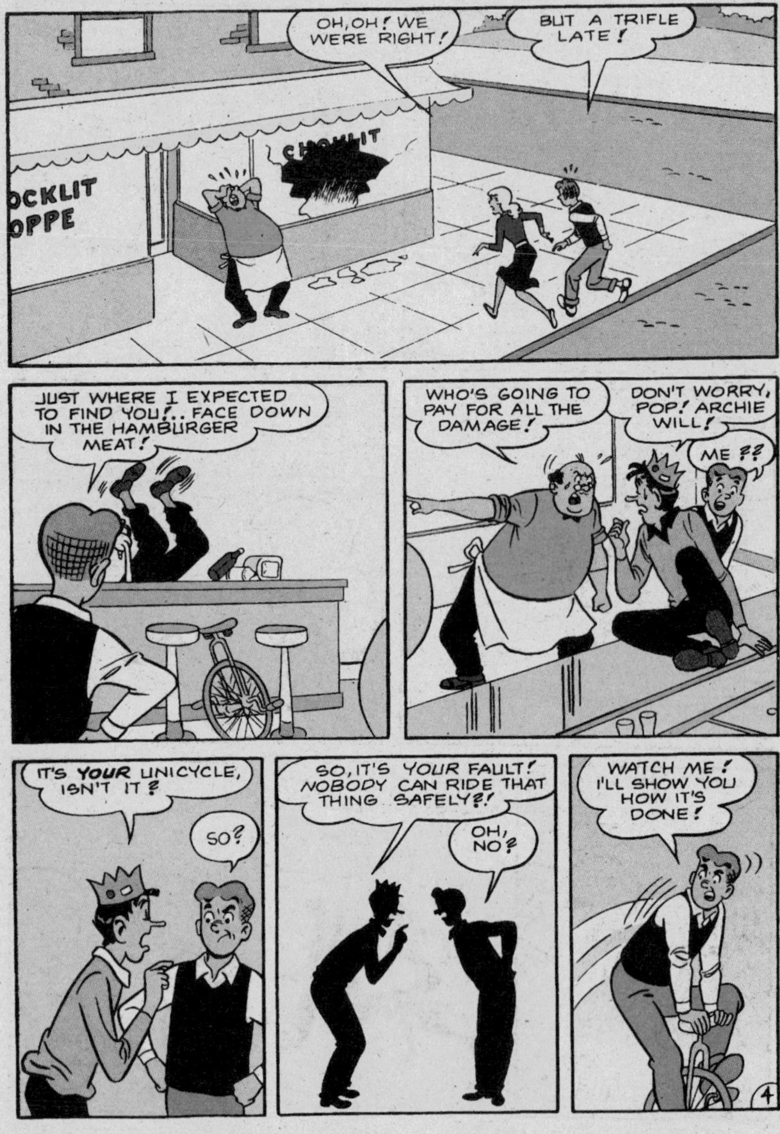
OH,OH! WE WERE RIGHT!
BUT A TRIFLE LATE!
CHOKLIT
OCKLIT OPPE
JUST WHERE I EXPECTED TO FIND YOU!.. FACE DOWN IN THE HAMBURGER MEAT!
WHO'S GOING TO PAY FOR ALL THE DAMAGE!
DON'T WORRY, POP! ARCHIE WILL!
ME ??
IT'S **YOUR** UNICYCLE, ISN'T IT?
SO?
SO, IT'S *YOUR* FAULT! *NOBODY* CAN RIDE THAT THING SAFELY?!
OH, NO?
WATCH ME! I'LL SHOW YOU HOW IT'S DONE!
4

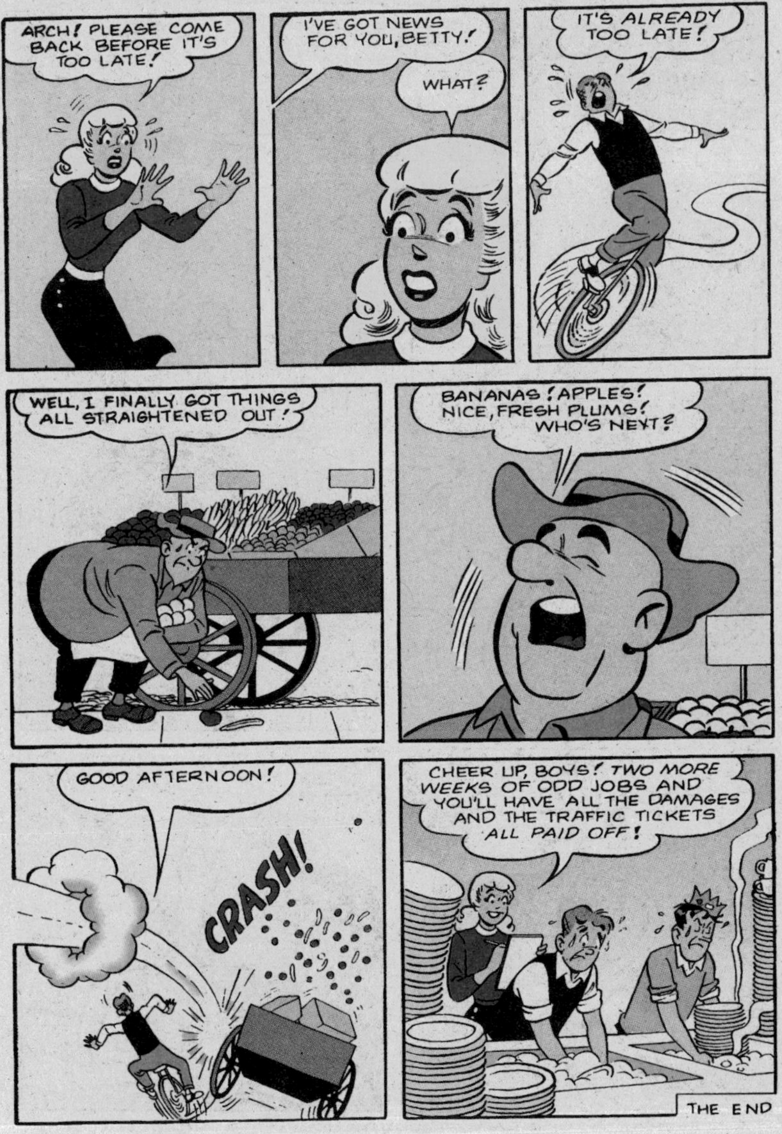
ARCH! PLEASE COME BACK BEFORE IT'S TOO LATE!
I'VE GOT NEWS FOR YOU, BETTY!
WHAT?
IT'S ALREADY TOO LATE!
WELL, I FINALLY GOT THINGS ALL STRAIGHTENED OUT!
BANANAS! APPLES! NICE, FRESH PLUMS! WHO'S NEXT?
GOOD AFTERNOON!
CRASH!
CHEER UP, BOYS! TWO MORE WEEKS OF ODD JOBS AND YOU'LL HAVE ALL THE DAMAGES AND THE TRAFFIC TICKETS ALL PAID OFF!
THE END

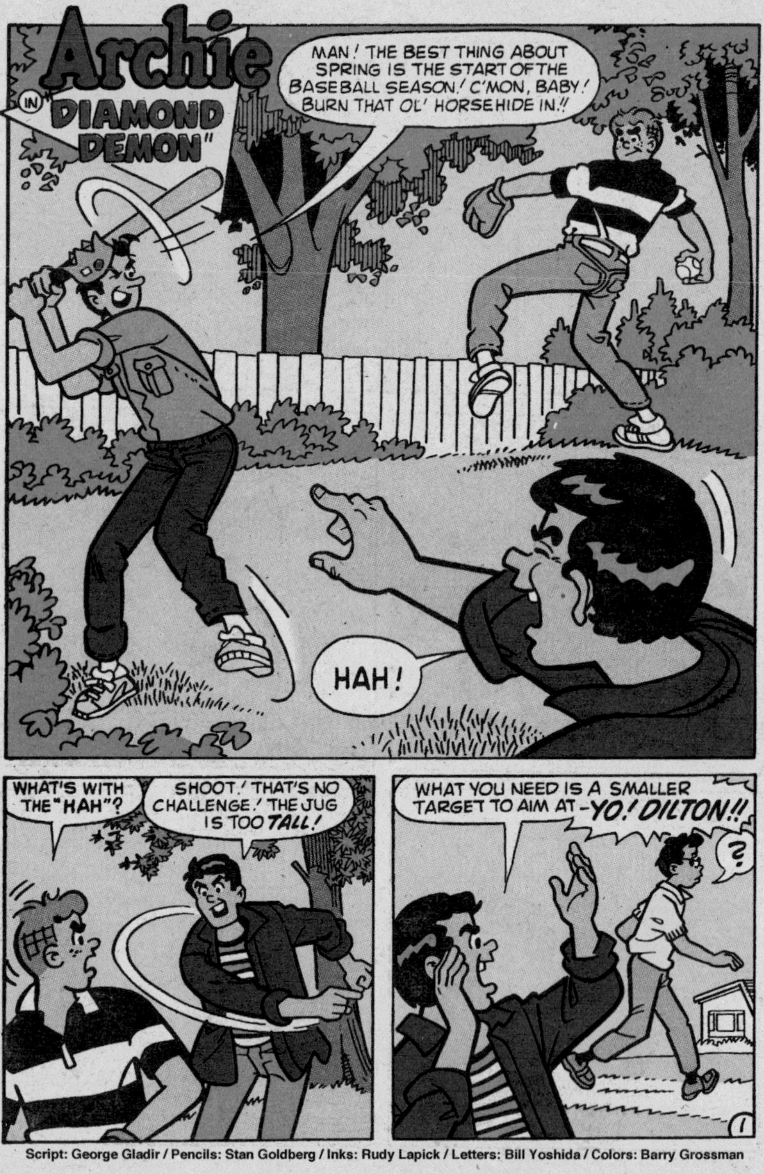
Archie
IN "DIAMOND DEMON"
MAN! THE BEST THING ABOUT SPRING IS THE START OF THE BASEBALL SEASON! C'MON, BABY! BURN THAT OL' HORSEHIDE IN!!
HAH!
WHAT'S WITH THE "HAH"?
SHOOT! THAT'S NO CHALLENGE! THE JUG IS TOO TALL!
WHAT YOU NEED IS A SMALLER TARGET TO AIM AT -YO! DILTON!!
?
1

Script: George Gladir / Pencils: Stan Goldberg / Inks: Rudy Lapick / Letters: Bill Yoshida / Colors: Barry Grossman

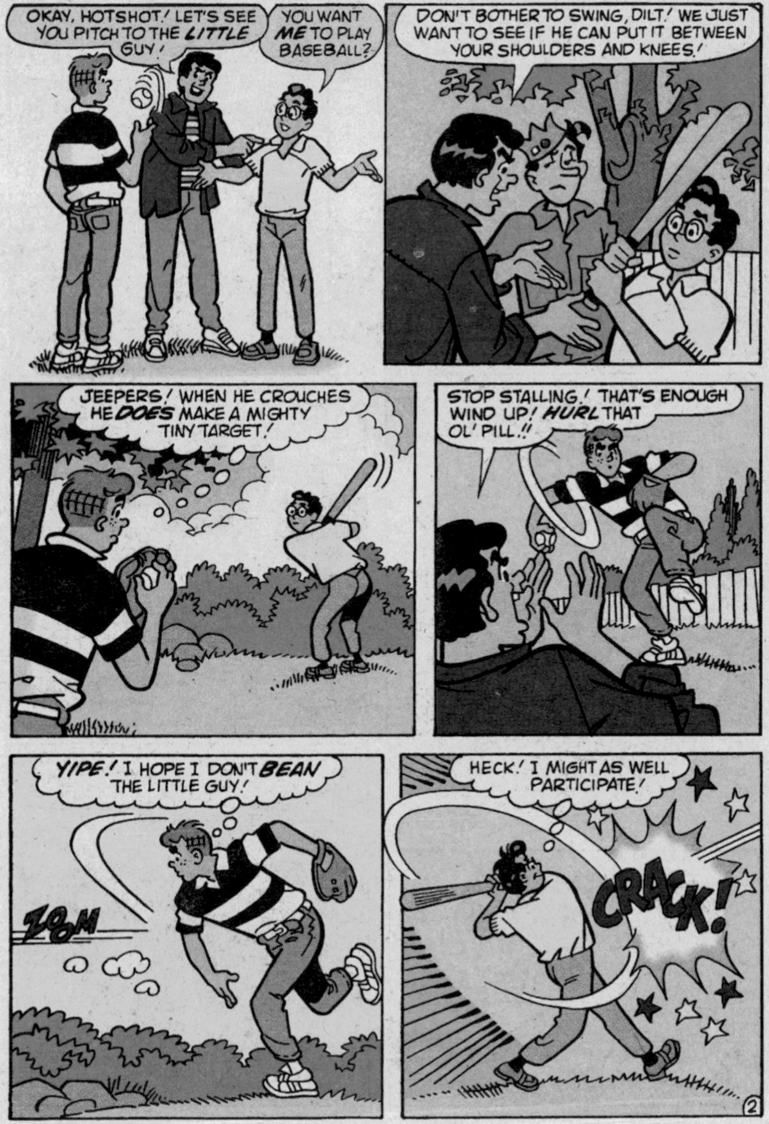
OKAY, HOTSHOT! LET'S SEE YOU PITCH TO THE LITTLE GUY!
YOU WANT ME TO PLAY BASEBALL?
DON'T BOTHER TO SWING, DILT! WE JUST WANT TO SEE IF HE CAN PUT IT BETWEEN YOUR SHOULDERS AND KNEES!
JEEPERS! WHEN HE CROUCHES HE DOES MAKE A MIGHTY TINY TARGET!
STOP STALLING! THAT'S ENOUGH WIND UP! HURL THAT OL' PILL!!
YIPE! I HOPE I DON'T BEAN THE LITTLE GUY!
ZOOM
HECK! I MIGHT AS WELL PARTICIPATE!
CRACK!
2

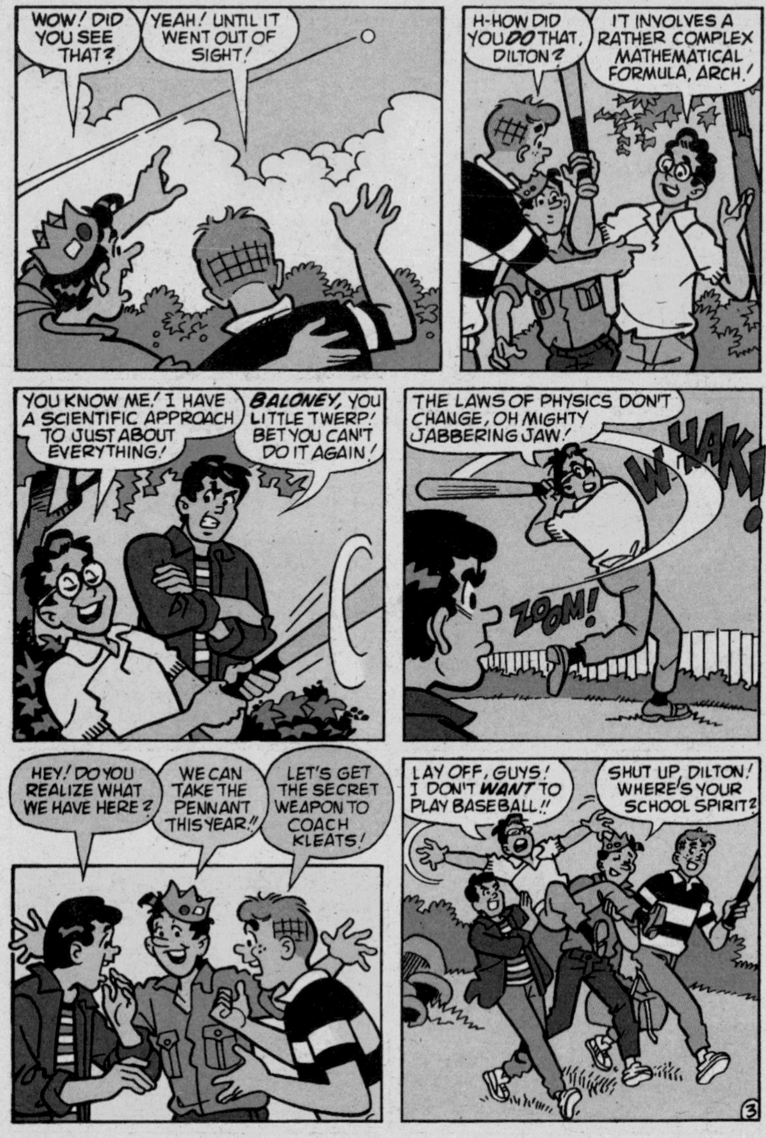
WOW! DID YOU SEE THAT?
YEAH! UNTIL IT WENT OUT OF SIGHT!
H-HOW DID YOU DO THAT, DILTON?
IT INVOLVES A RATHER COMPLEX MATHEMATICAL FORMULA, ARCH!
YOU KNOW ME! I HAVE A SCIENTIFIC APPROACH TO JUST ABOUT EVERYTHING!
BALONEY, YOU LITTLE TWERP! BET YOU CAN'T DO IT AGAIN!
THE LAWS OF PHYSICS DON'T CHANGE, OH MIGHTY JABBERING JAW!
WHAK!
ZOOM!
HEY! DO YOU REALIZE WHAT WE HAVE HERE?
WE CAN TAKE THE PENNANT THIS YEAR!!
LET'S GET THE SECRET WEAPON TO COACH KLEATS!
LAY OFF, GUYS! I DON'T WANT TO PLAY BASEBALL!!
SHUT UP, DILTON! WHERE'S YOUR SCHOOL SPIRIT?
3

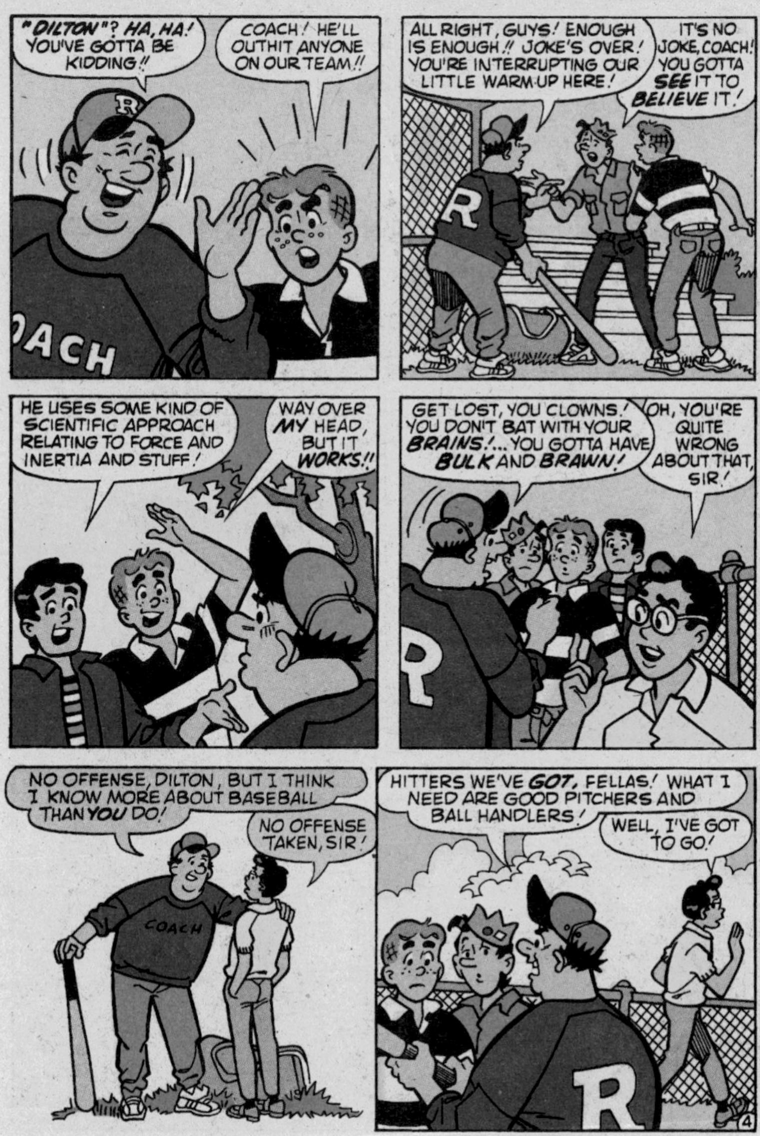
"DILTON"? HA, HA! YOU'VE GOTTA BE KIDDING!!
COACH! HE'LL OUTHIT ANYONE ON OUR TEAM!!
ALL RIGHT, GUYS! ENOUGH IS ENOUGH!! JOKE'S OVER! YOU'RE INTERRUPTING OUR LITTLE WARM-UP HERE!
IT'S NO JOKE, COACH! YOU GOTTA SEE IT TO BELIEVE IT!
HE USES SOME KIND OF SCIENTIFIC APPROACH RELATING TO FORCE AND INERTIA AND STUFF!
WAY OVER MY HEAD, BUT IT WORKS!!
GET LOST, YOU CLOWNS! YOU DON'T BAT WITH YOUR BRAINS!...YOU GOTTA HAVE BULK AND BRAWN!
OH, YOU'RE QUITE WRONG ABOUT THAT, SIR!
NO OFFENSE, DILTON, BUT I THINK I KNOW MORE ABOUT BASEBALL THAN YOU DO!
NO OFFENSE TAKEN, SIR!
HITTERS WE'VE GOT, FELLAS! WHAT I NEED ARE GOOD PITCHERS AND BALL HANDLERS!
WELL, I'VE GOT TO GO!
4

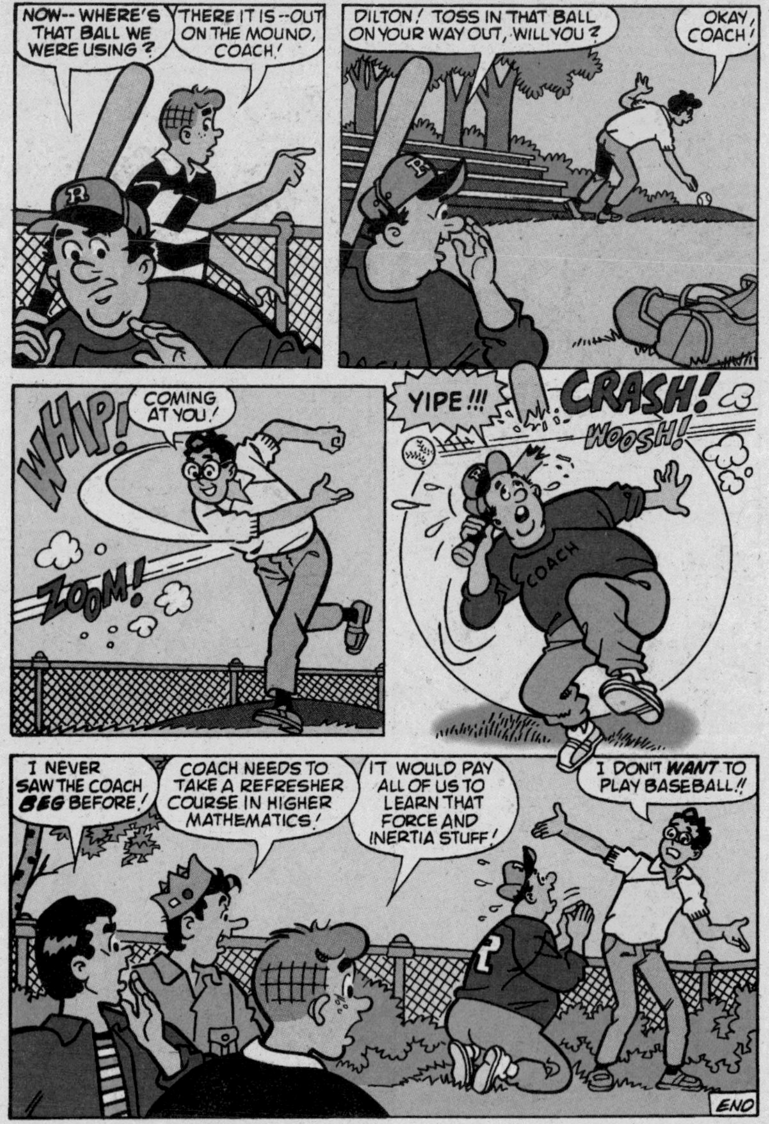
NOW-- WHERE'S THAT BALL WE WERE USING?
THERE IT IS --OUT ON THE MOUND, COACH!
DILTON! TOSS IN THAT BALL ON YOUR WAY OUT, WILL YOU?
OKAY, COACH!
WHIP!
COMING AT YOU!
ZOOM!
YIPE!!!
CRASH!
WOOSH!
COACH
I NEVER SAW THE COACH BEG BEFORE!
COACH NEEDS TO TAKE A REFRESHER COURSE IN HIGHER MATHEMATICS!
IT WOULD PAY ALL OF US TO LEARN THAT FORCE AND INERTIA STUFF!
I DON'T WANT TO PLAY BASEBALL!!
END

Jughead in True Romance!

IT'S BAD ENOUGH THAT ETHEL HAS TO COMPETE WITH GIRLS, NOW SHE HAS TO COMPETE WITH FOOD! UNSCRAMBLE THE FOLLOWING FOODS THAT STAND IN HER WAY!

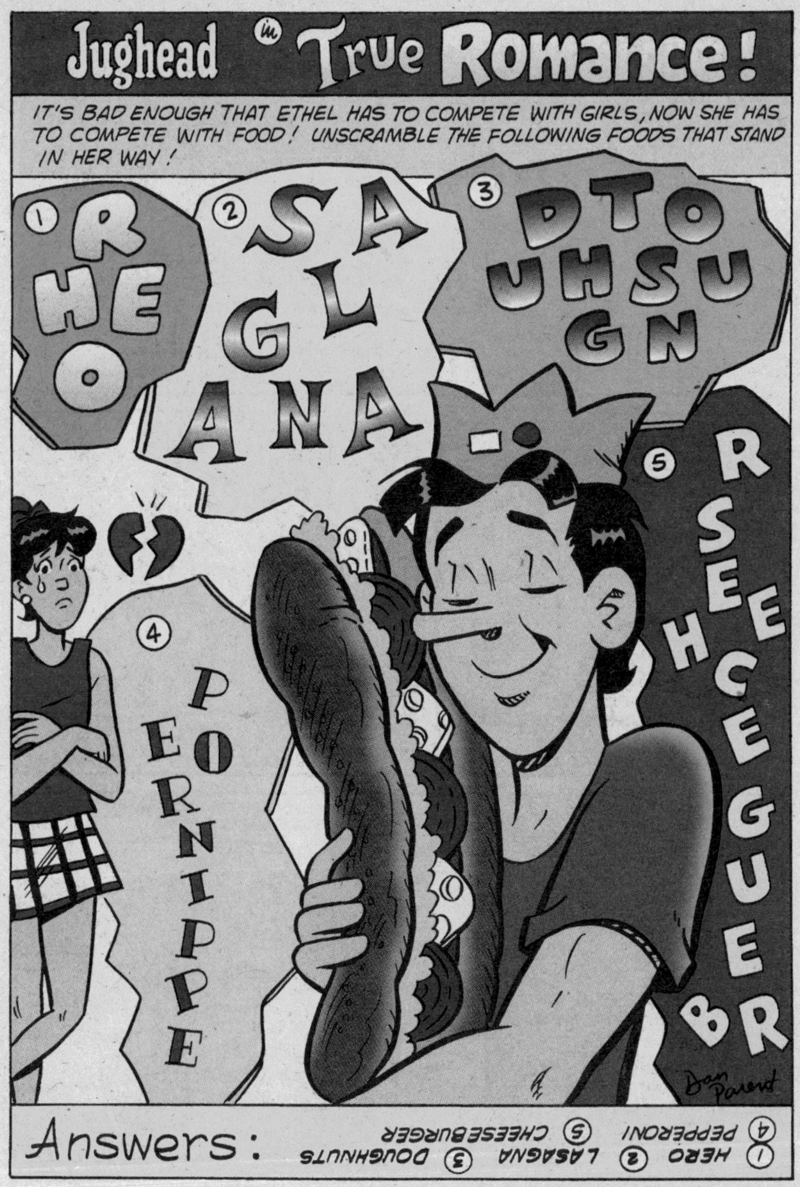

1 RHEO
2 SA GL ANA
3 DTO UHSU GN
4 PO ERNIPPE
5 RSEEHCEGUEBR
Dan Parent

Answers: 1 HERO 2 LASAGNA 3 DOUGHNUTS 4 PEPPERONI 5 CHEESEBURGER

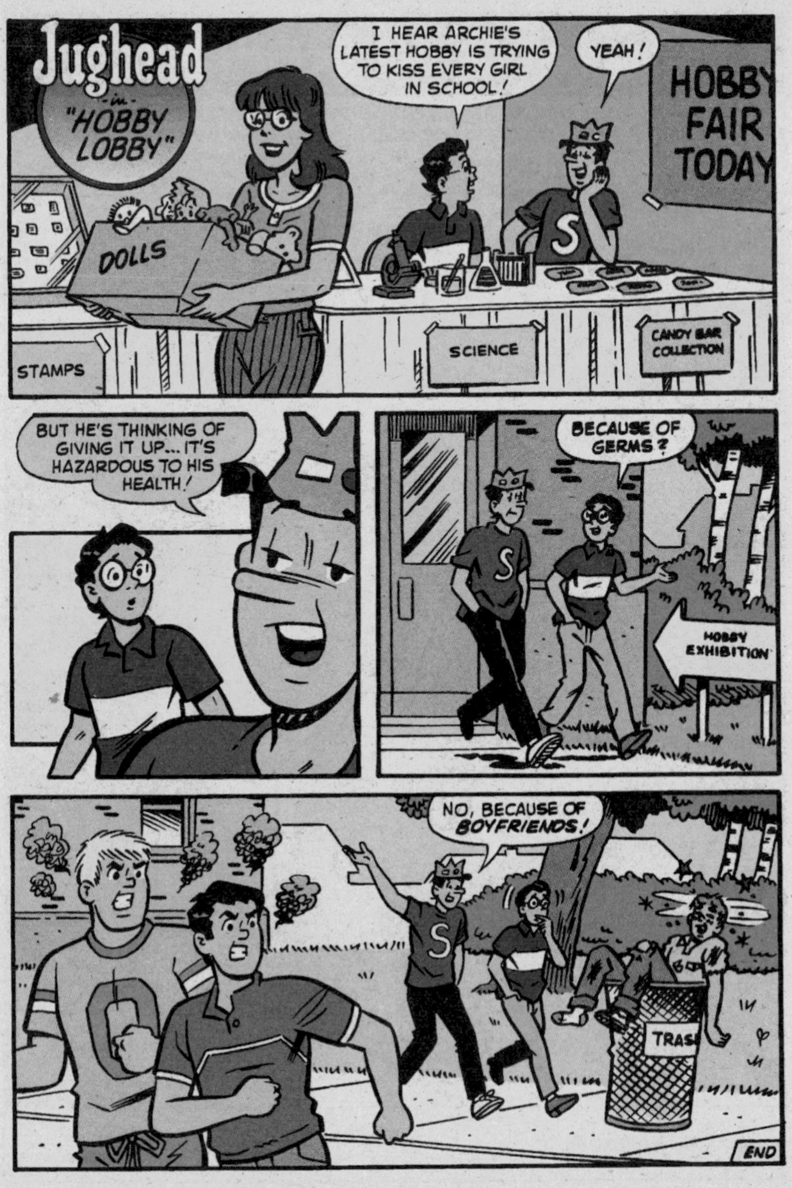
Jughead
-in-
"HOBBY LOBBY"
I HEAR ARCHIE'S LATEST HOBBY IS TRYING TO KISS EVERY GIRL IN SCHOOL!
YEAH!
HOBBY FAIR TODAY
DOLLS
STAMPS
SCIENCE
CANDY BAR COLLECTION
BUT HE'S THINKING OF GIVING IT UP... IT'S HAZARDOUS TO HIS HEALTH!
BECAUSE OF GERMS?
HOBBY EXHIBITION
NO, BECAUSE OF *BOYFRIENDS*!
TRAS
END

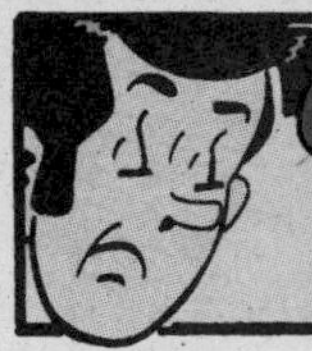

JUGHEAD'S LID QUIZ

CAN YOU PAIR THE HATS BELOW WITH THEIR CORRECT NAMES ? 12 RIGHT ANSWERS QUALIFIES YOU AS A LID EXPERT !

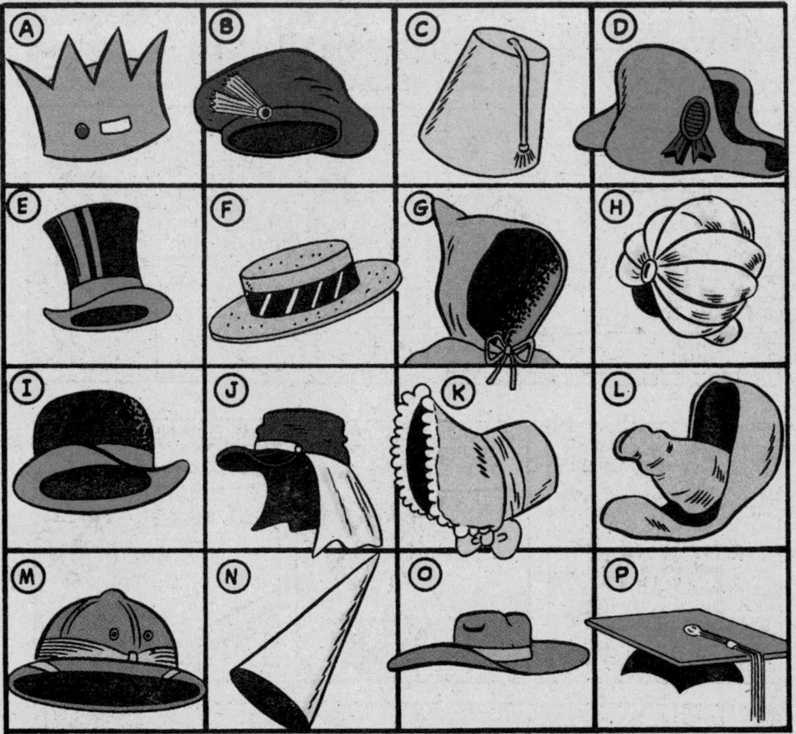

A
B
C
D
E
F
G
H
I
J
K
L
M
N
O
P

1. TOP HAT	5. CAPUCHIN	9. TAM-O'SHANTER	13. FEZ
2. KEPI	6. SUNBONNET	10 TOPEE	14. TURBAN
3. STRAW HAT	7. SOMBRERO	11. PANAMA	15. DERBY
4. DUNCE CAP	8. COCKED HAT	12. MORTARBOARD	16. JUGHEAD HAT

TURN PAGE UPSIDE DOWN FOR ANSWERS

A - 16	E - 1	I - 15	M - 10
B - 6	F - 3	J - 2	N - 4
C - 13	G - 5	K - 6	O - 11
D - 8	H - 14	L - 7	P - 12

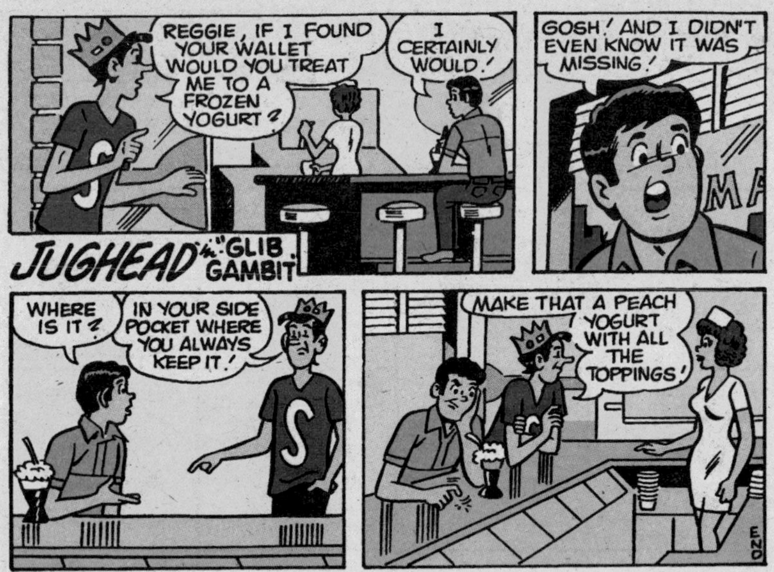
REGGIE, IF I FOUND YOUR WALLET WOULD YOU TREAT ME TO A FROZEN YOGURT?
I CERTAINLY WOULD!
JUGHEAD in "GLIB GAMBIT"
GOSH! AND I DIDN'T EVEN KNOW IT WAS MISSING!
WHERE IS IT?
IN YOUR SIDE POCKET WHERE YOU ALWAYS KEEP IT!
MAKE THAT A PEACH YOGURT WITH ALL THE TOPPINGS!
END

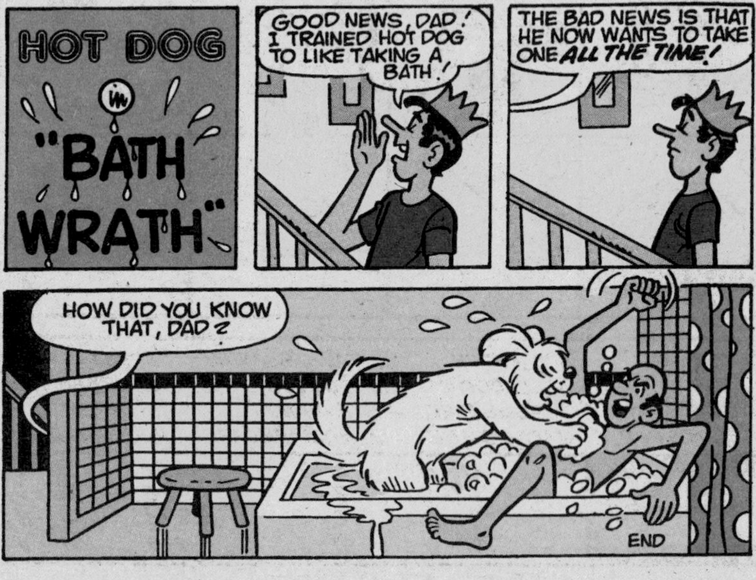
HOT DOG in "BATH WRATH"
GOOD NEWS, DAD! I TRAINED HOT DOG TO LIKE TAKING A BATH!
THE BAD NEWS IS THAT HE NOW WANTS TO TAKE ONE ALL THE TIME!
HOW DID YOU KNOW THAT, DAD?
END

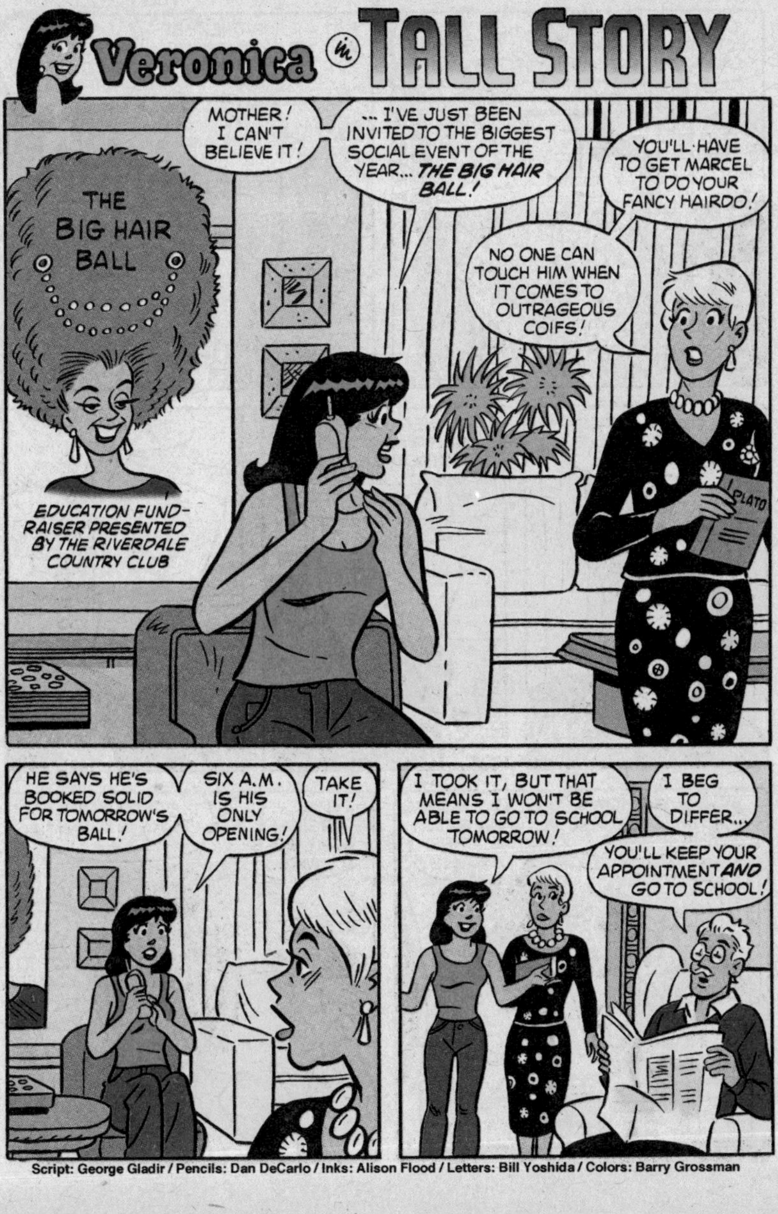
Veronica in TALL STORY
MOTHER! I CAN'T BELIEVE IT!
... I'VE JUST BEEN INVITED TO THE BIGGEST SOCIAL EVENT OF THE YEAR... THE BIG HAIR BALL!
THE BIG HAIR BALL
EDUCATION FUND-RAISER PRESENTED BY THE RIVERDALE COUNTRY CLUB
YOU'LL HAVE TO GET MARCEL TO DO YOUR FANCY HAIRDO!
NO ONE CAN TOUCH HIM WHEN IT COMES TO OUTRAGEOUS COIFS!
PLATO
HE SAYS HE'S BOOKED SOLID FOR TOMORROW'S BALL!
SIX A.M. IS HIS ONLY OPENING!
TAKE IT!
I TOOK IT, BUT THAT MEANS I WON'T BE ABLE TO GO TO SCHOOL TOMORROW!
I BEG TO DIFFER...
YOU'LL KEEP YOUR APPOINTMENT AND GO TO SCHOOL!

Script: George Gladir / Pencils: Dan DeCarlo / Inks: Alison Flood / Letters: Bill Yoshida / Colors: Barry Grossman

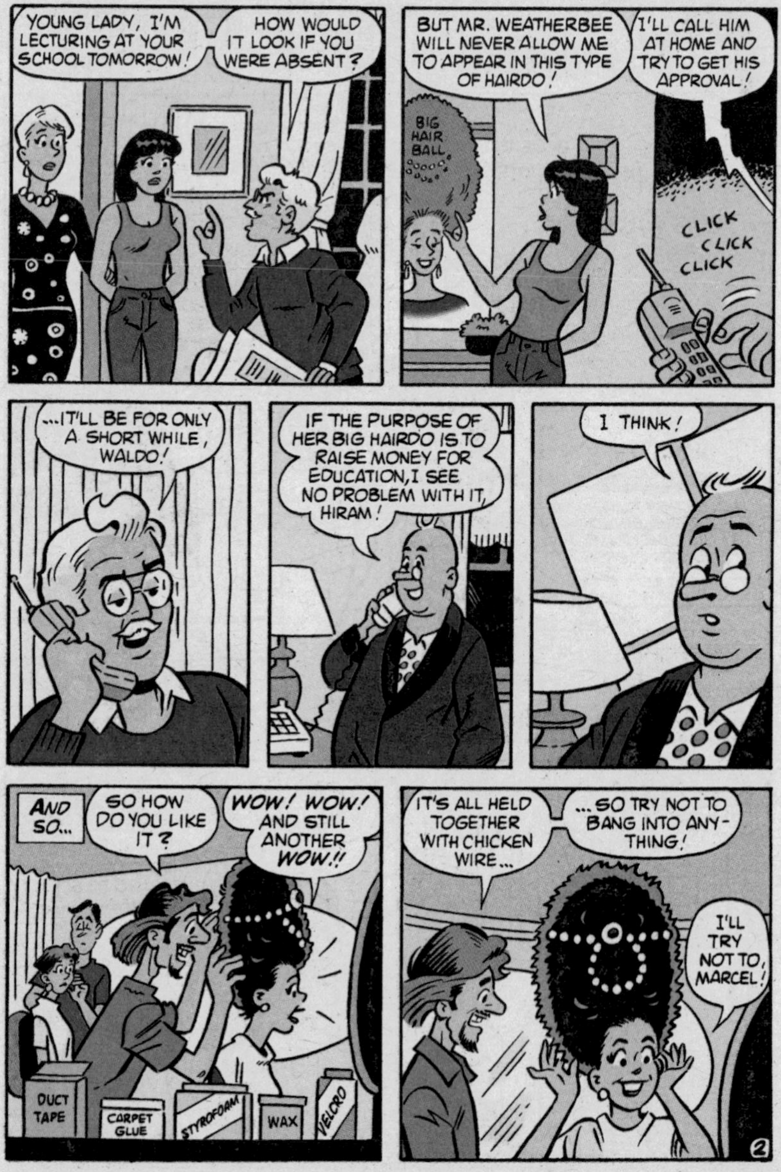
YOUNG LADY, I'M LECTURING AT YOUR SCHOOL TOMORROW!
HOW WOULD IT LOOK IF YOU WERE ABSENT?
BUT MR. WEATHERBEE WILL NEVER ALLOW ME TO APPEAR IN THIS TYPE OF HAIRDO!
BIG HAIR BALL
I'LL CALL HIM AT HOME AND TRY TO GET HIS APPROVAL!
CLICK CLICK CLICK
...IT'LL BE FOR ONLY A SHORT WHILE, WALDO!
IF THE PURPOSE OF HER BIG HAIRDO IS TO RAISE MONEY FOR EDUCATION, I SEE NO PROBLEM WITH IT, HIRAM!
I THINK!
AND SO...
SO HOW DO YOU LIKE IT?
WOW! WOW! AND STILL ANOTHER WOW!!
DUCT TAPE
CARPET GLUE
STYROFOAM
WAX
VELCRO
IT'S ALL HELD TOGETHER WITH CHICKEN WIRE...
...SO TRY NOT TO BANG INTO ANY-THING!
I'LL TRY NOT TO, MARCEL!
2

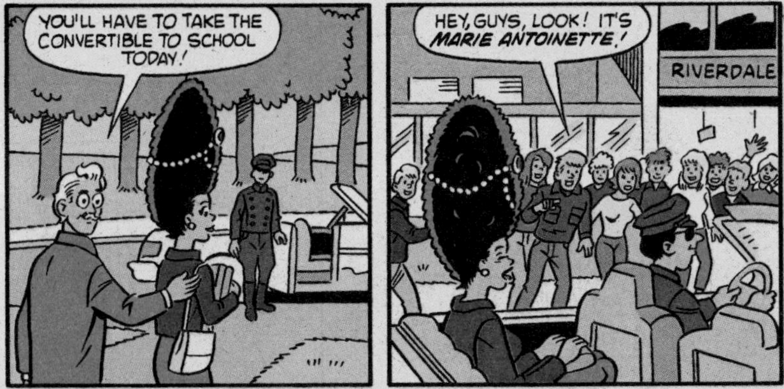

YOU'LL HAVE TO TAKE THE CONVERTIBLE TO SCHOOL TODAY!
HEY, GUYS, LOOK! IT'S *MARIE ANTOINETTE*!
RIVERDALE

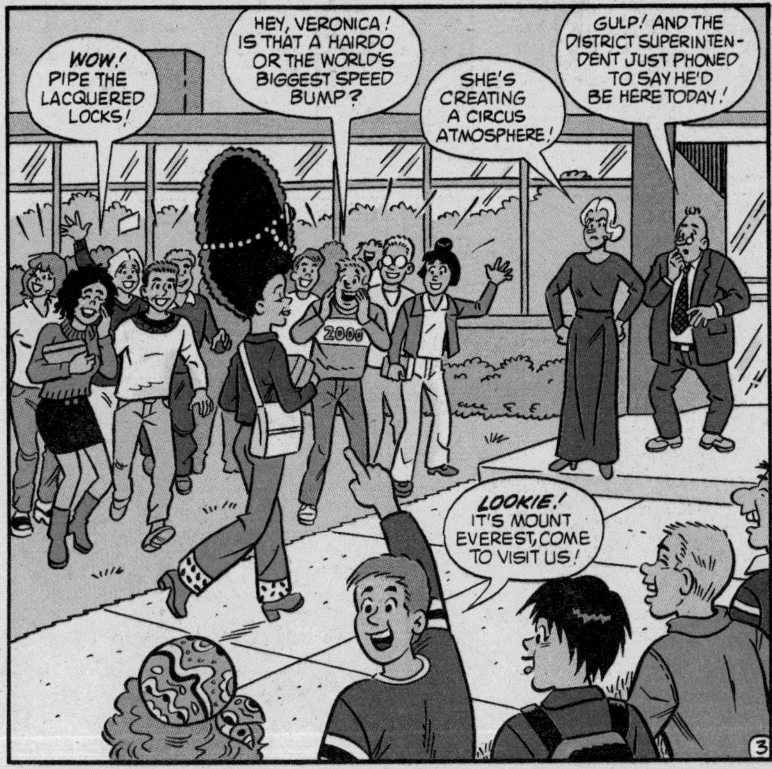

WOW! PIPE THE LACQUERED LOCKS!
HEY, VERONICA! IS THAT A HAIRDO OR THE WORLD'S BIGGEST SPEED BUMP?
SHE'S CREATING A CIRCUS ATMOSPHERE!
GULP! AND THE DISTRICT SUPERINTENDENT JUST PHONED TO SAY HE'D BE HERE TODAY!
2000
LOOKIE! IT'S MOUNT EVEREST, COME TO VISIT US!

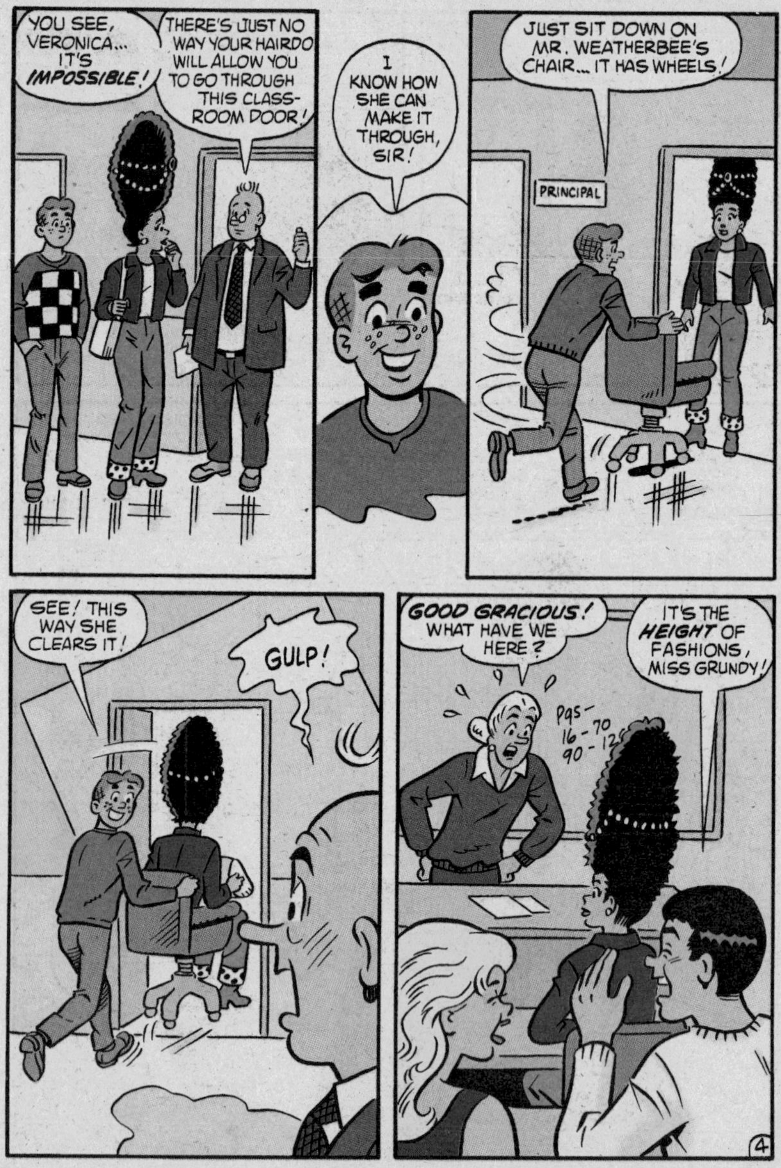
YOU SEE, VERONICA... IT'S IMPOSSIBLE!
THERE'S JUST NO WAY YOUR HAIRDO WILL ALLOW YOU TO GO THROUGH THIS CLASSROOM DOOR!
I KNOW HOW SHE CAN MAKE IT THROUGH, SIR!
JUST SIT DOWN ON MR. WEATHERBEE'S CHAIR... IT HAS WHEELS!
PRINCIPAL
SEE! THIS WAY SHE CLEARS IT!
GULP!
GOOD GRACIOUS! WHAT HAVE WE HERE?
IT'S THE HEIGHT OF FASHIONS, MISS GRUNDY!
4

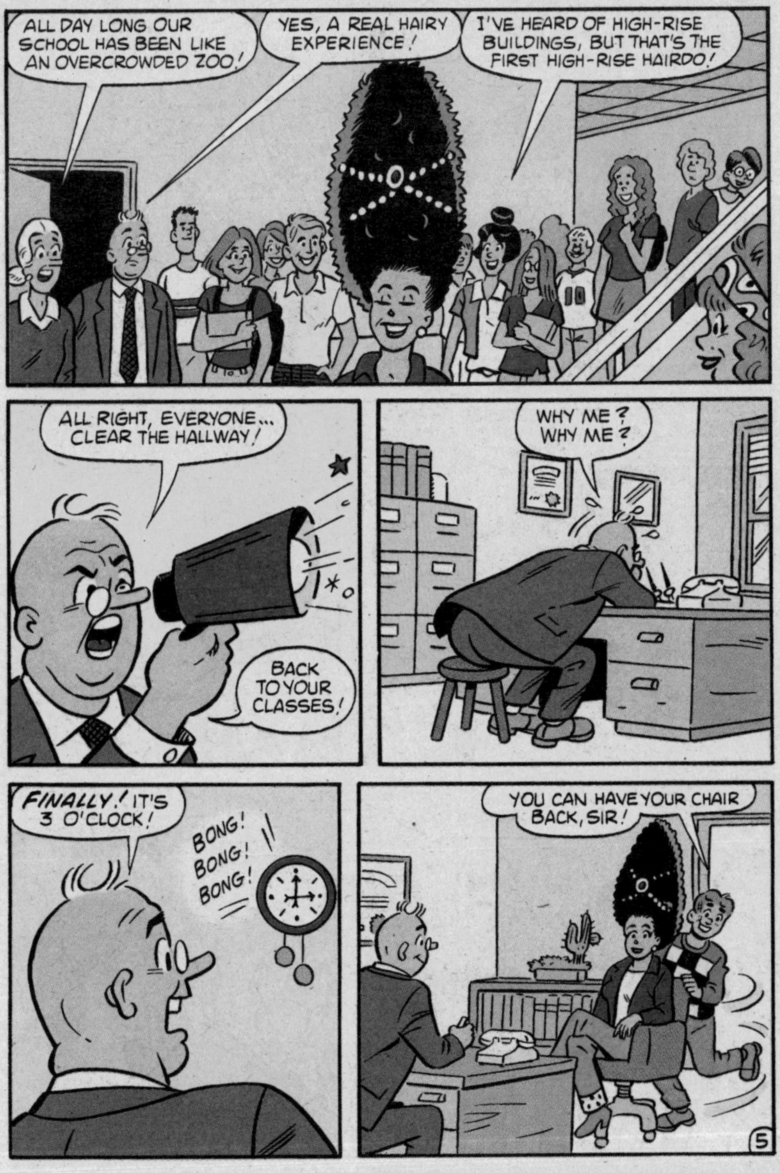
ALL DAY LONG OUR SCHOOL HAS BEEN LIKE AN OVERCROWDED ZOO!
YES, A REAL HAIRY EXPERIENCE!
I'VE HEARD OF HIGH-RISE BUILDINGS, BUT THAT'S THE FIRST HIGH-RISE HAIRDO!
ALL RIGHT, EVERYONE... CLEAR THE HALLWAY!
BACK TO YOUR CLASSES!
WHY ME? WHY ME?
FINALLY! IT'S 3 O'CLOCK!
BONG! BONG! BONG!
YOU CAN HAVE YOUR CHAIR BACK, SIR!
5

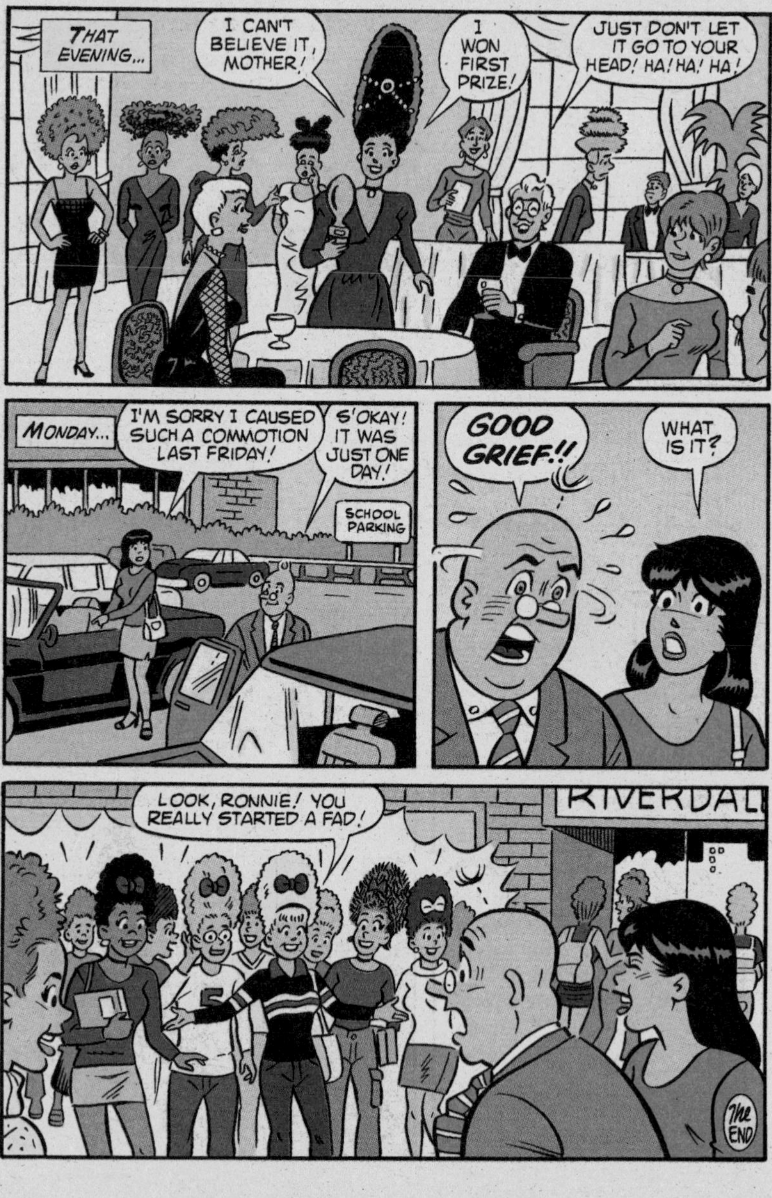
THAT EVENING...
I CAN'T BELIEVE IT, MOTHER!
I WON FIRST PRIZE!
JUST DON'T LET IT GO TO YOUR HEAD! HA! HA! HA!
MONDAY...
I'M SORRY I CAUSED SUCH A COMMOTION LAST FRIDAY!
S'OKAY! IT WAS JUST ONE DAY!
SCHOOL PARKING
GOOD GRIEF!!
WHAT IS IT?
LOOK, RONNIE! YOU REALLY STARTED A FAD!
RIVERDAL
The END

Betty and Veronica in "FAIR EXCHANGE"

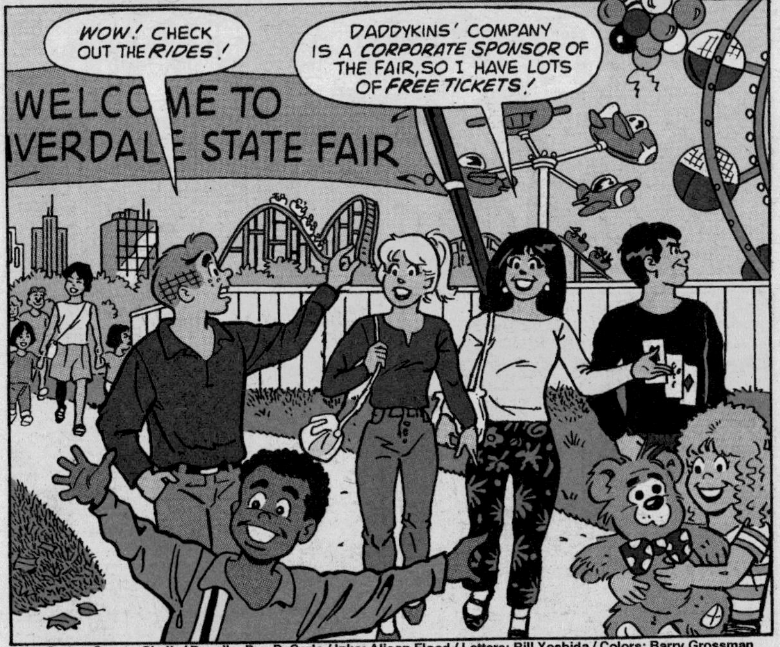

WOW! CHECK OUT THE RIDES!
DADDYKINS' COMPANY IS A CORPORATE SPONSOR OF THE FAIR, SO I HAVE LOTS OF FREE TICKETS!
WELCOME TO
VERDALE STATE FAIR

Script: George Gladir / Pencils: Dan DeCarlo / Inks: Alison Flood / Letters: Bill Yoshida / Colors: Barry Grossman

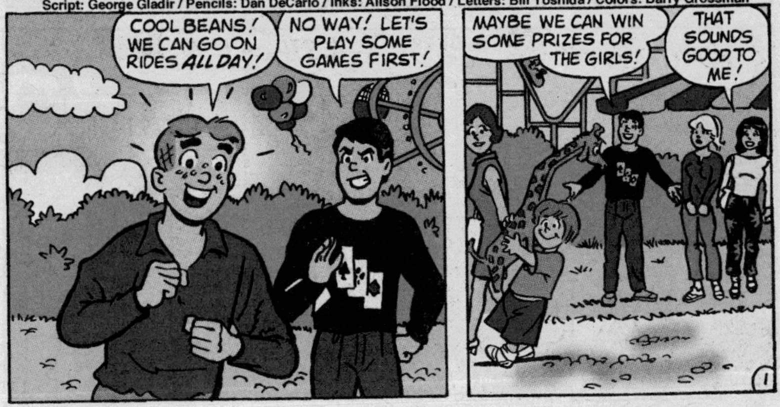

COOL BEANS! WE CAN GO ON RIDES ALL DAY!
NO WAY! LET'S PLAY SOME GAMES FIRST!
MAYBE WE CAN WIN SOME PRIZES FOR THE GIRLS!
THAT SOUNDS GOOD TO ME!
1

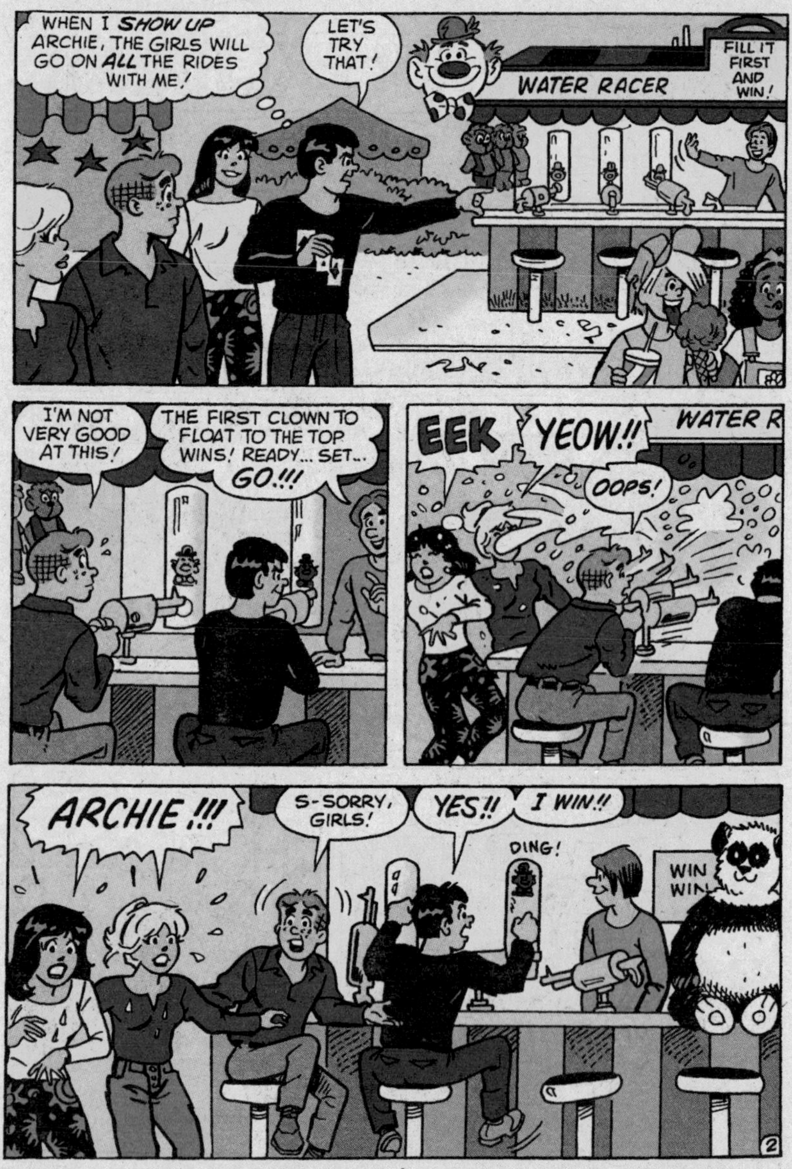
WHEN I SHOW UP ARCHIE, THE GIRLS WILL GO ON ALL THE RIDES WITH ME!
LET'S TRY THAT!
WATER RACER
FILL IT FIRST AND WIN!
I'M NOT VERY GOOD AT THIS!
THE FIRST CLOWN TO FLOAT TO THE TOP WINS! READY... SET... GO!!!
EEK
YEOW!!
WATER R
OOPS!
ARCHIE!!!
S-SORRY, GIRLS!
YES!!
I WIN!!
DING!
WIN
WIN
2

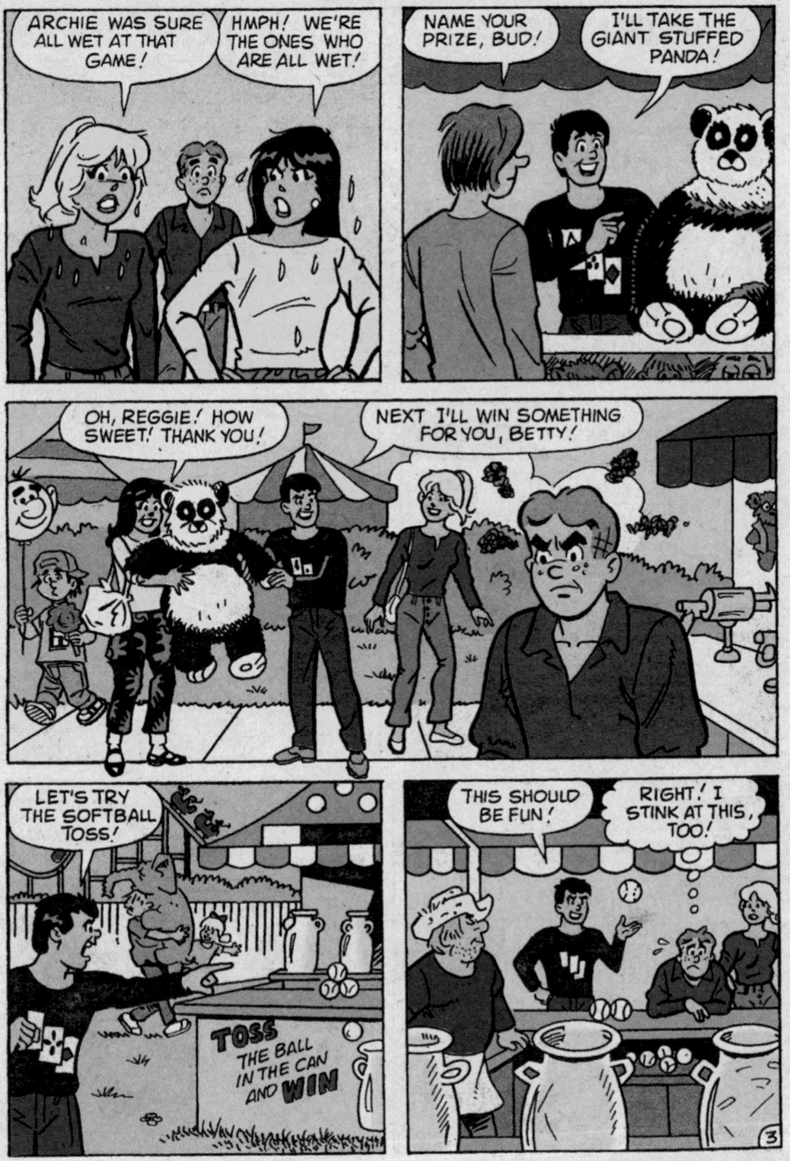

ARCHIE WAS SURE ALL WET AT THAT GAME!
HMPH! WE'RE THE ONES WHO ARE ALL WET!
NAME YOUR PRIZE, BUD!
I'LL TAKE THE GIANT STUFFED PANDA!
OH, REGGIE! HOW SWEET! THANK YOU!
NEXT I'LL WIN SOMETHING FOR YOU, BETTY!
LET'S TRY THE SOFTBALL TOSS!
TOSS THE BALL IN THE CAN AND WIN
THIS SHOULD BE FUN!
RIGHT! I STINK AT THIS, TOO!
3

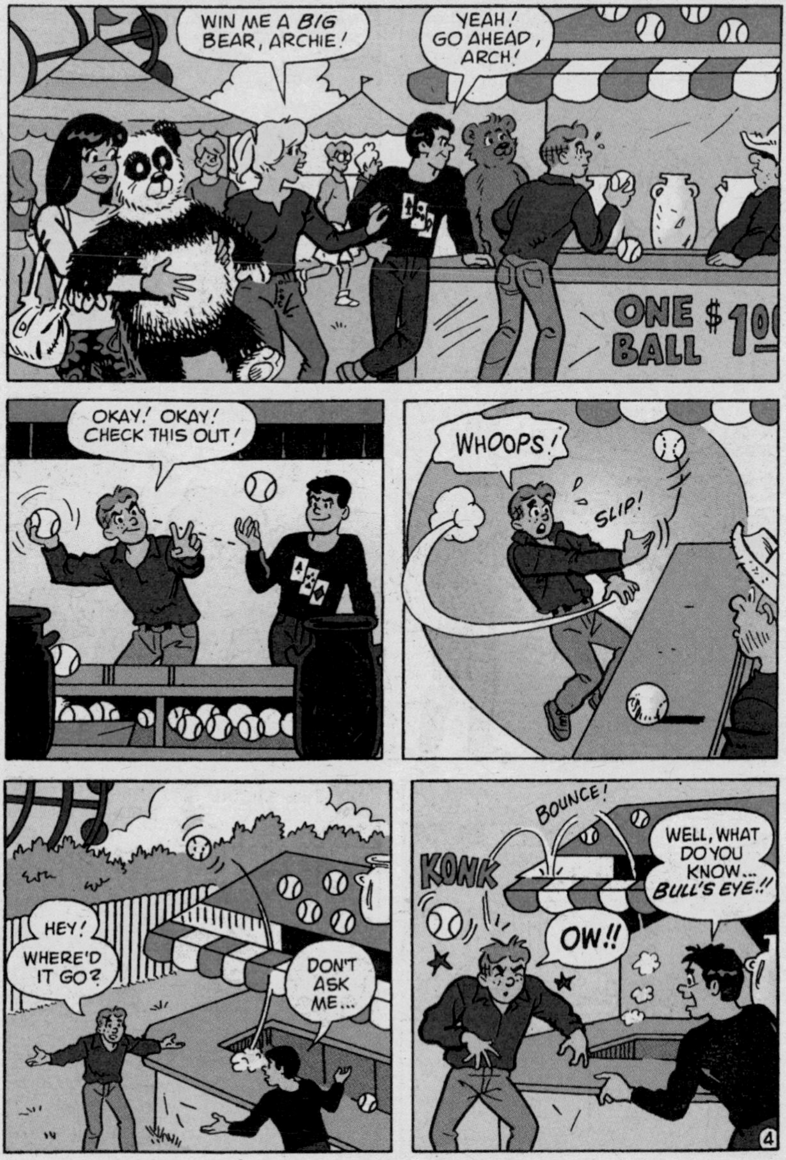
WIN ME A BIG BEAR, ARCHIE!
YEAH! GO AHEAD, ARCH!
ONE BALL $1.00
OKAY! OKAY! CHECK THIS OUT!
WHOOPS!
SLIP!
HEY! WHERE'D IT GO?
DON'T ASK ME...
BOUNCE!
KONK
WELL, WHAT DO YOU KNOW... BULL'S EYE!!
OW!!
4

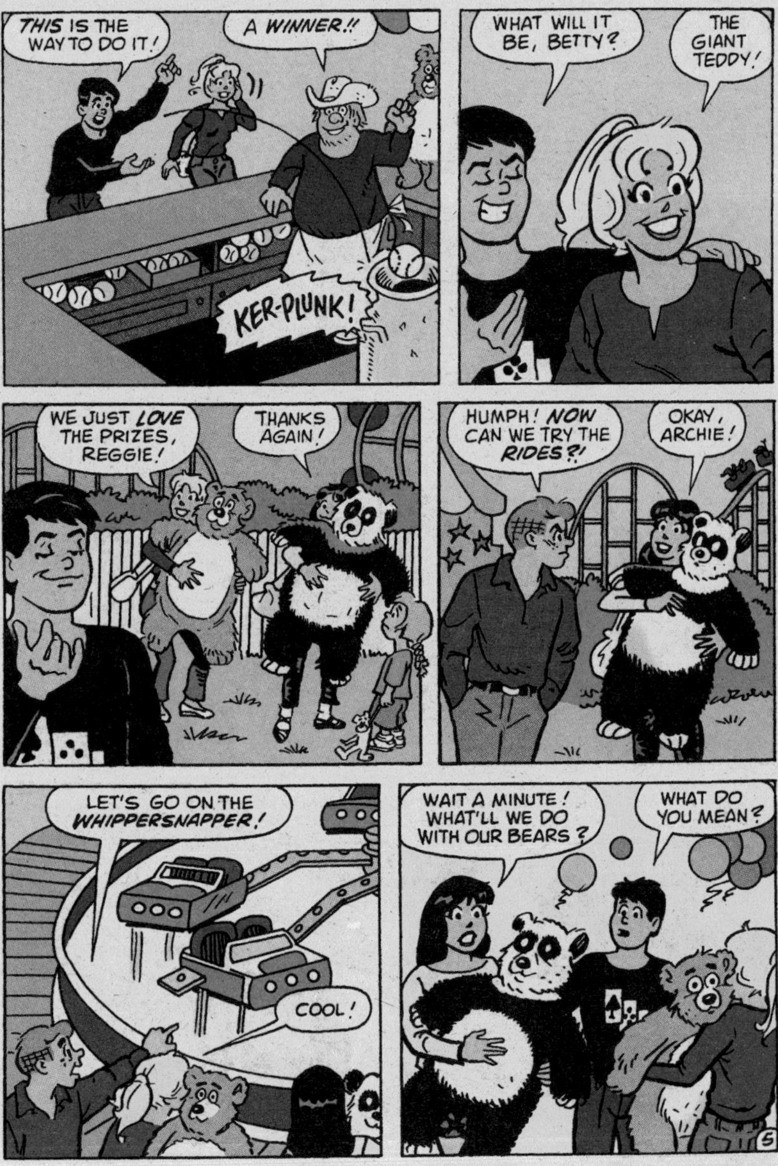
THIS IS THE WAY TO DO IT!
A WINNER!!
KER-PLUNK!
WHAT WILL IT BE, BETTY?
THE GIANT TEDDY!
WE JUST LOVE THE PRIZES, REGGIE!
THANKS AGAIN!
HUMPH! NOW CAN WE TRY THE RIDES?!
OKAY, ARCHIE!
LET'S GO ON THE WHIPPERSNAPPER!
COOL!
WAIT A MINUTE! WHAT'LL WE DO WITH OUR BEARS?
WHAT DO YOU MEAN?
5

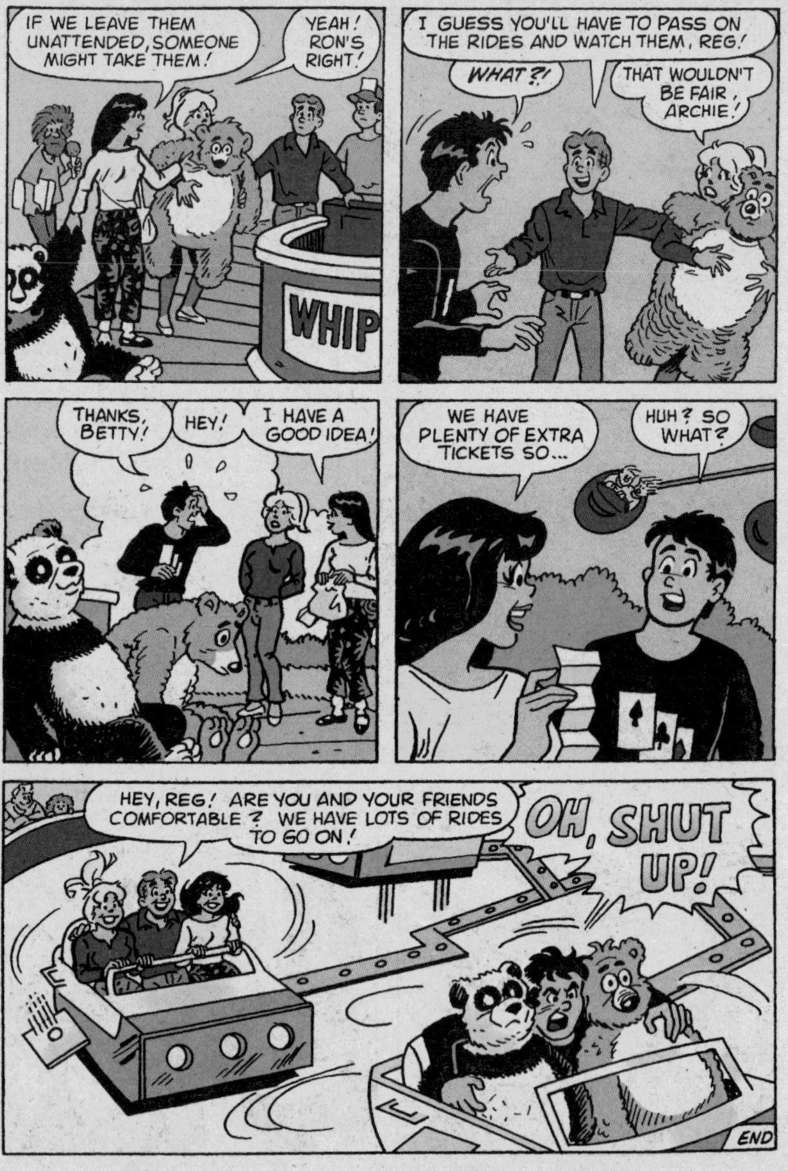
IF WE LEAVE THEM UNATTENDED, SOMEONE MIGHT TAKE THEM!
YEAH! RON'S RIGHT!
WHIP
I GUESS YOU'LL HAVE TO PASS ON THE RIDES AND WATCH THEM, REG!
WHAT?!
THAT WOULDN'T BE FAIR, ARCHIE!
THANKS, BETTY!
HEY!
I HAVE A GOOD IDEA!
WE HAVE PLENTY OF EXTRA TICKETS SO...
HUH? SO WHAT?
HEY, REG! ARE YOU AND YOUR FRIENDS COMFORTABLE? WE HAVE LOTS OF RIDES TO GO ON!
OH, SHUT UP!
END

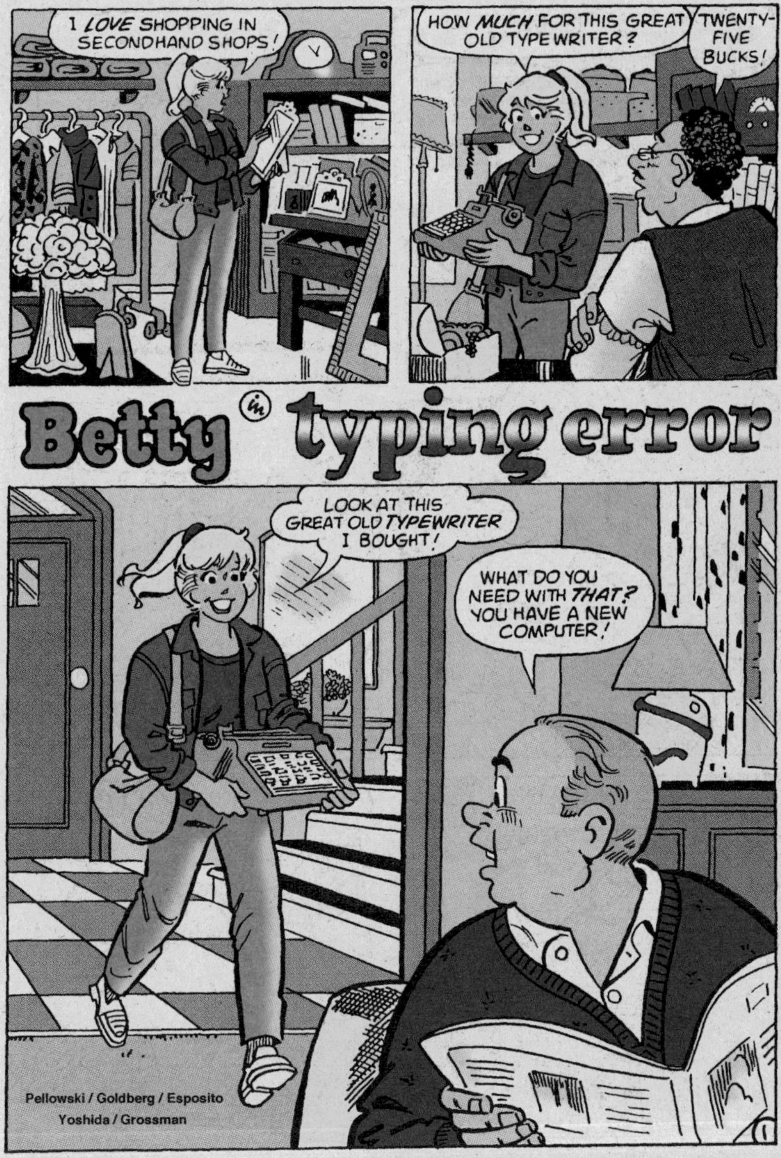

I LOVE SHOPPING IN SECONDHAND SHOPS!
HOW MUCH FOR THIS GREAT OLD TYPE WRITER?
TWENTY-FIVE BUCKS!
Betty in typing error
LOOK AT THIS GREAT OLD TYPEWRITER I BOUGHT!
WHAT DO YOU NEED WITH THAT? YOU HAVE A NEW COMPUTER!
Pellowski / Goldberg / Esposito
Yoshida / Grossman
1

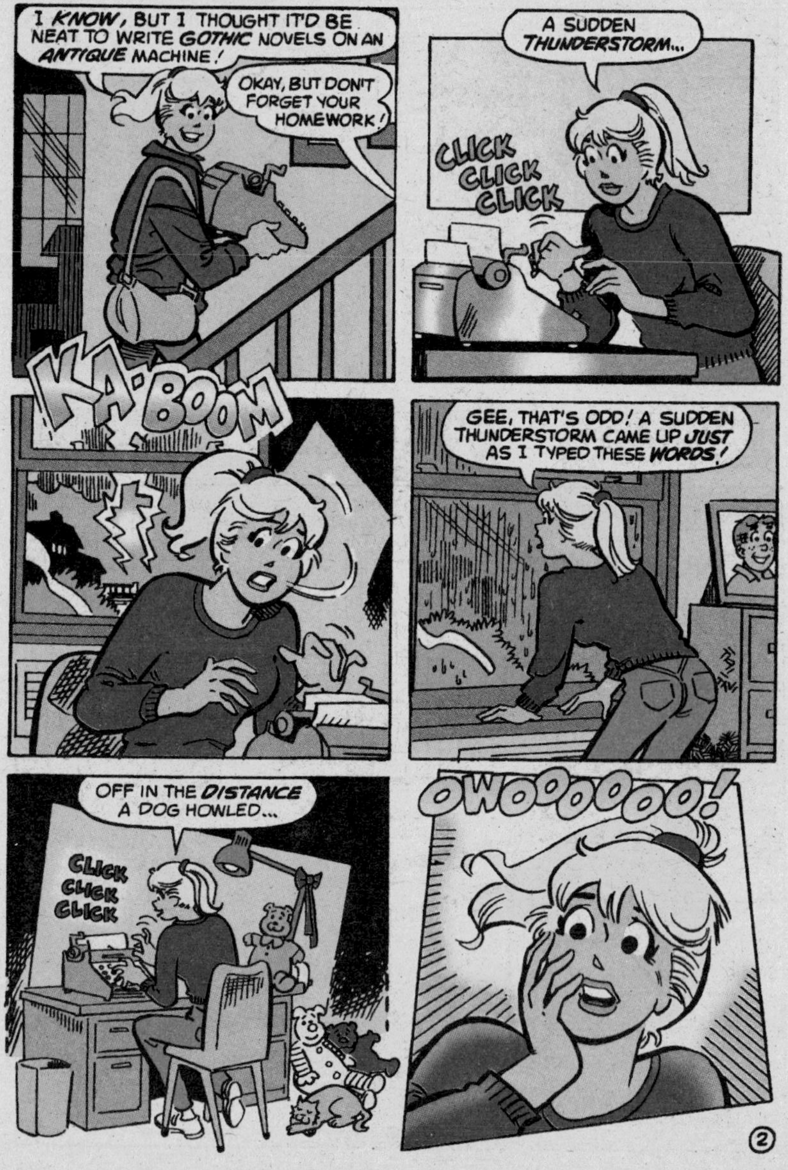
I KNOW, BUT I THOUGHT IT'D BE NEAT TO WRITE GOTHIC NOVELS ON AN ANTIQUE MACHINE!
OKAY, BUT DON'T FORGET YOUR HOMEWORK!
A SUDDEN THUNDERSTORM...
CLICK CLICK CLICK
KA-BOOM
GEE, THAT'S ODD! A SUDDEN THUNDERSTORM CAME UP JUST AS I TYPED THESE WORDS!
OFF IN THE DISTANCE A DOG HOWLED...
CLICK CLICK CLICK
OWOOOOOOO!

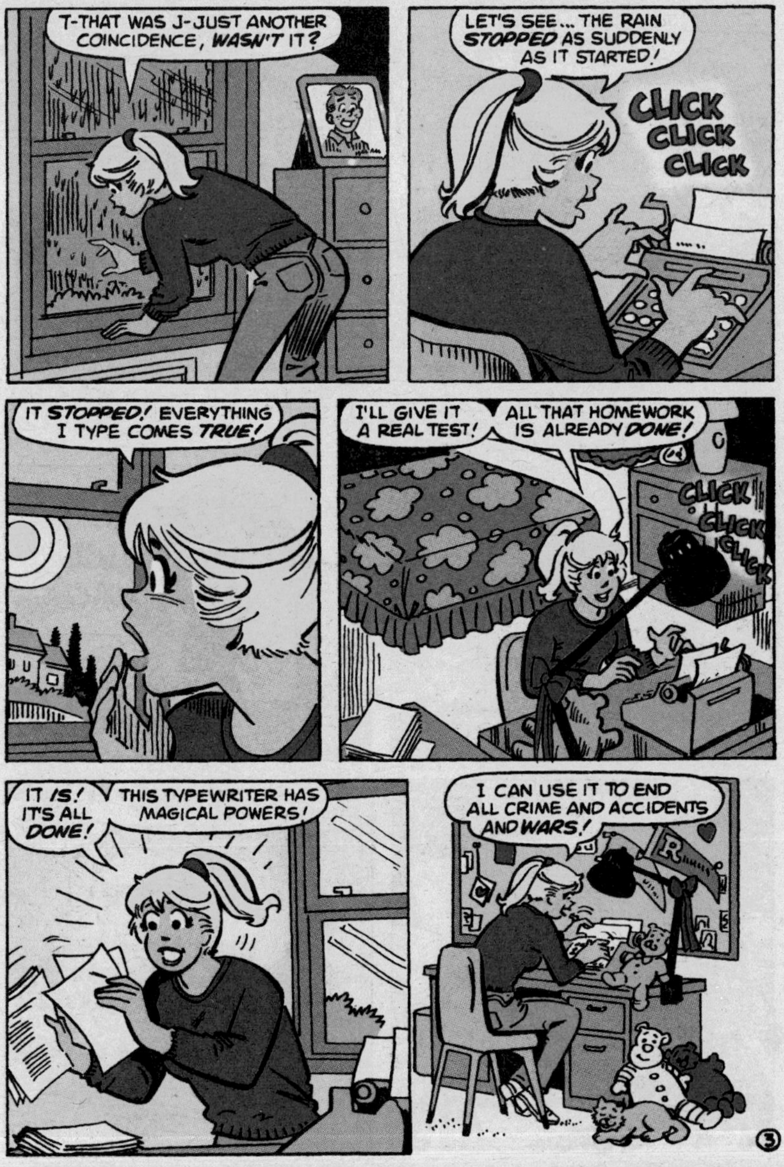
T-THAT WAS J-JUST ANOTHER COINCIDENCE, WASN'T IT?
LET'S SEE... THE RAIN STOPPED AS SUDDENLY AS IT STARTED!
CLICK CLICK CLICK
IT STOPPED! EVERYTHING I TYPE COMES TRUE!
I'LL GIVE IT A REAL TEST!
ALL THAT HOMEWORK IS ALREADY DONE!
CLICK CLICK CLICK
IT IS! IT'S ALL DONE!
THIS TYPEWRITER HAS MAGICAL POWERS!
I CAN USE IT TO END ALL CRIME AND ACCIDENTS AND WARS!

LATER | YOU'RE TELLING ME THAT *WHATEVER* YOU TYPE ON THAT MACHINE COMES *TRUE?*

YES!

I DON'T BELIEVE IT!

COME HOME WITH ME AND I'LL *PROVE* IT!

THE WALLS TURNED FROM BLUE TO ORANGE!

Oh, *WOW!* THEY *DID!* LET *ME* AT THAT MACHINE!

CLICK CLICK

VERONICA GOT THE NEW MOTORIZED SKATEBOARD THAT HER DAD WON'T LET HER HAVE!

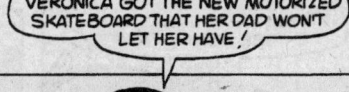

LOOK! IT'S *THERE!* IT'S *THERE!*

I'LL BE BACK LATER FOR *MORE* STUFF... *I'M* NOT ALLOWED TO HAVE!

SHE'S *SO* SHALLOW!

4

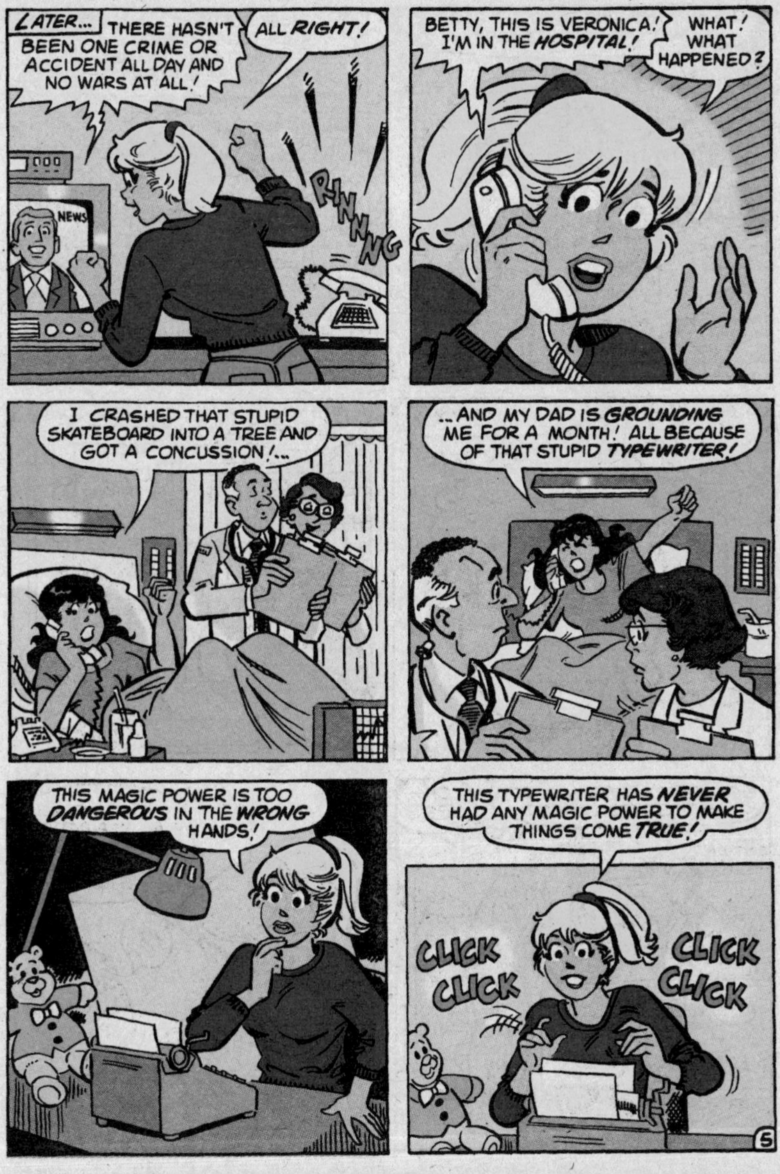
LATER...
THERE HASN'T BEEN ONE CRIME OR ACCIDENT ALL DAY AND NO WARS AT ALL!
ALL RIGHT!
NEWS
RINNNG
BETTY, THIS IS VERONICA! I'M IN THE HOSPITAL!
WHAT! WHAT HAPPENED?
I CRASHED THAT STUPID SKATEBOARD INTO A TREE AND GOT A CONCUSSION!...
...AND MY DAD IS GROUNDING ME FOR A MONTH! ALL BECAUSE OF THAT STUPID TYPEWRITER!
THIS MAGIC POWER IS TOO DANGEROUS IN THE WRONG HANDS!
THIS TYPEWRITER HAS NEVER HAD ANY MAGIC POWER TO MAKE THINGS COME TRUE!
CLICK CLICK
CLICK CLICK
5

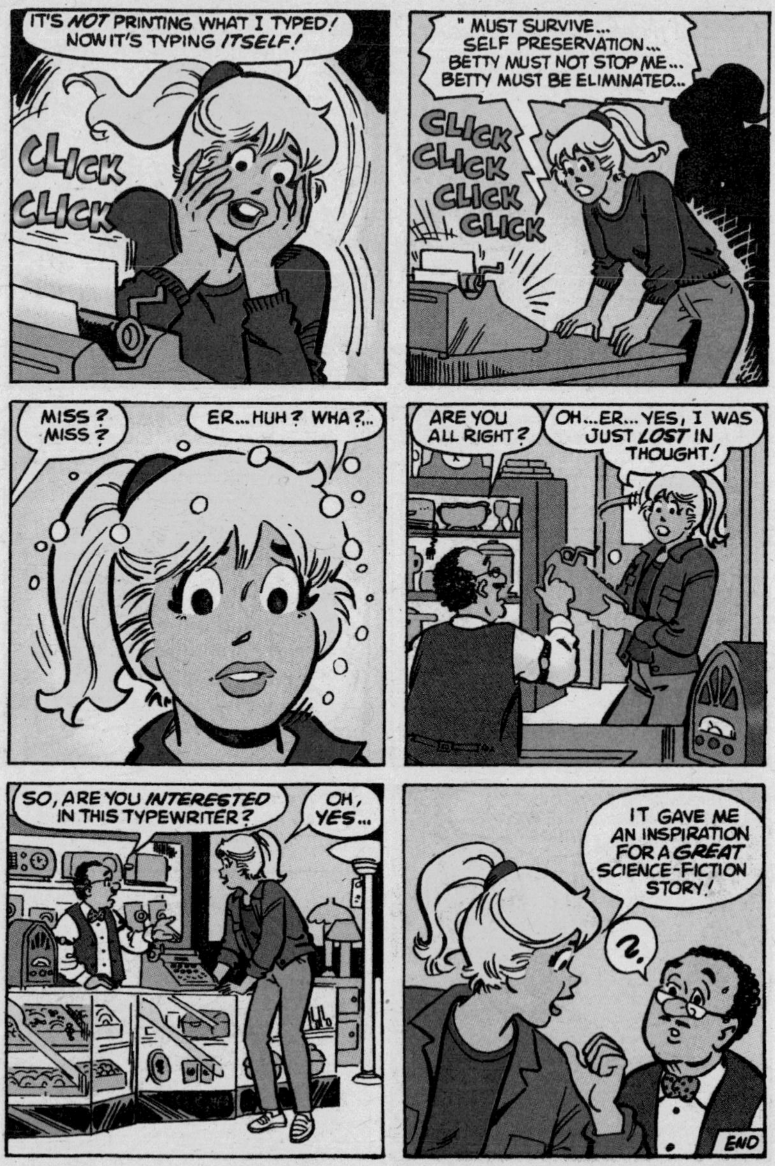
IT'S *NOT* PRINTING WHAT I TYPED! NOW IT'S TYPING *ITSELF*!
CLICK CLICK
" MUST SURVIVE... SELF PRESERVATION... BETTY MUST NOT STOP ME... BETTY MUST BE ELIMINATED...
CLICK CLICK CLICK CLICK
MISS? MISS?
ER...HUH? WHA?...
ARE YOU ALL RIGHT?
OH...ER...YES, I WAS JUST *LOST* IN THOUGHT!
SO, ARE YOU *INTERESTED* IN THIS TYPEWRITER?
OH, *YES*...
IT GAVE ME AN INSPIRATION FOR A *GREAT* SCIENCE-FICTION STORY!
?
END

Veronica in "GO WITH the CASH FLOW"

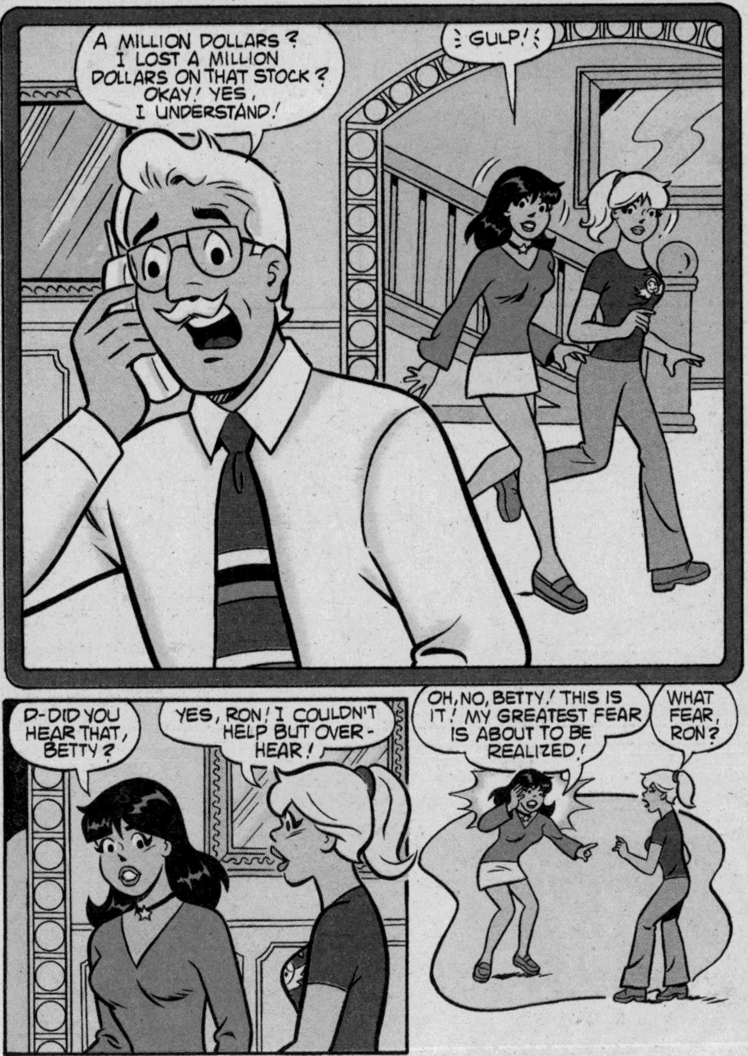

A MILLION DOLLARS? I LOST A MILLION DOLLARS ON THAT STOCK? OKAY! YES, I UNDERSTAND!
GULP!
D-DID YOU HEAR THAT, BETTY?
YES, RON! I COULDN'T HELP BUT OVER-HEAR!
OH, NO, BETTY! THIS IS IT! MY GREATEST FEAR IS ABOUT TO BE REALIZED!
WHAT FEAR, RON?

Script & Pencils: Dan Parent / Inks: Jon D'Agostino / Letters: Bill Yoshida / Colors: Barry Grossman

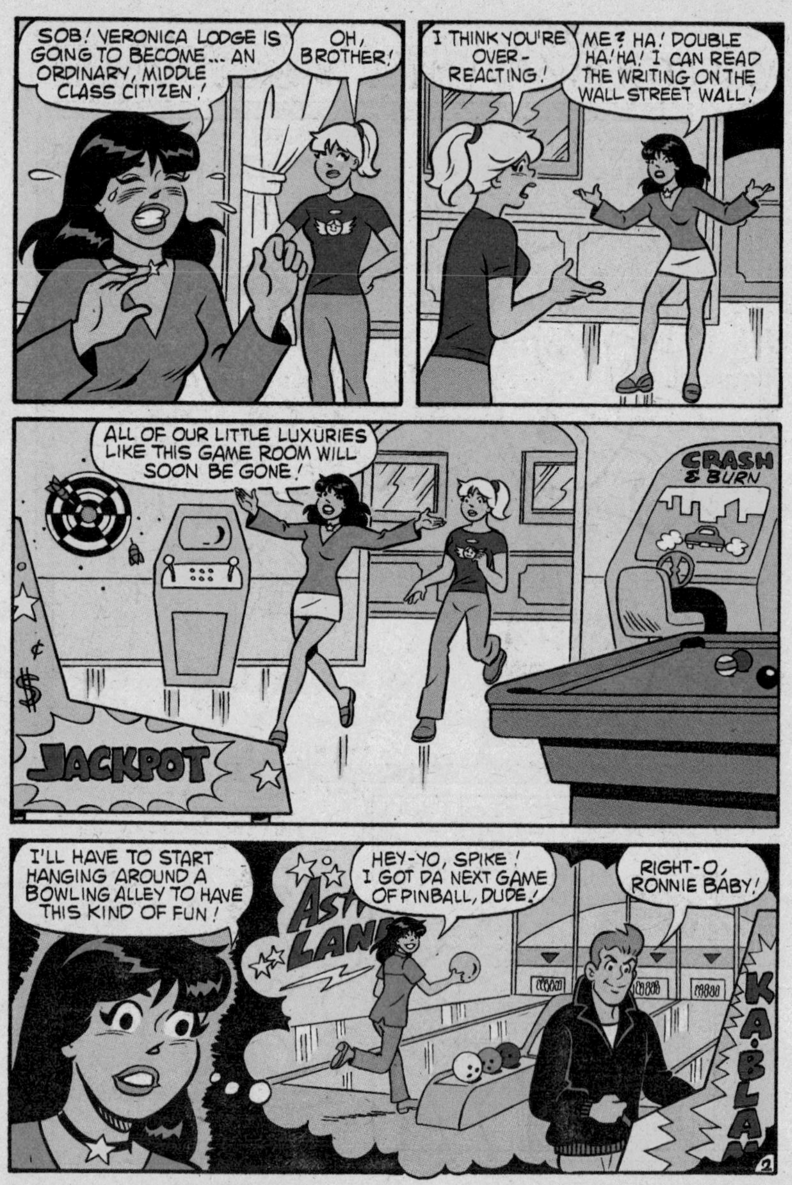

SOB! VERONICA LODGE IS GOING TO BECOME... AN ORDINARY, MIDDLE CLASS CITIZEN!
OH, BROTHER!
I THINK YOU'RE OVER-REACTING!
ME? HA! DOUBLE HA! HA! I CAN READ THE WRITING ON THE WALL STREET WALL!
ALL OF OUR LITTLE LUXURIES LIKE THIS GAME ROOM WILL SOON BE GONE!
CRASH & BURN
JACKPOT
I'LL HAVE TO START HANGING AROUND A BOWLING ALLEY TO HAVE THIS KIND OF FUN!
HEY-YO, SPIKE! I GOT DA NEXT GAME OF PINBALL, DUDE!
RIGHT-O, RONNIE BABY!
KA-BLAM
2

NO MORE PERFECT HAIR! NO MORE PERFECT NAILS! NO MORE PERFECT LIFE!

SHEESH!

I'LL HAVE TO MAKE SACRIFICES AND DO THINGS FOR MYSELF... LIKE STYLING MY OWN HAIR!

ARRUGH! WHAT HAPPENED?!

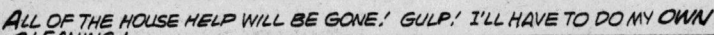

ALL OF THE HOUSE HELP WILL BE GONE! GULP! I'LL HAVE TO DO MY OWN CLEANING!

NO! NO! I REFUSE TO DO IT! I WENT FROM DIAMOND RINGS TO BATHTUB RINGS!

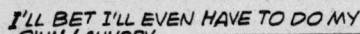

I'LL BET I'LL EVEN HAVE TO DO MY OWN LAUNDRY...

≥GASP!≤ HELP! HELP! HOW DO YOU WORK THIS THING?

B-BUT WORST OF ALL, I'LL PROBABLY HAVE TO... NO! I CAN'T SAY IT!

WHAT, RON? WHAT?

3

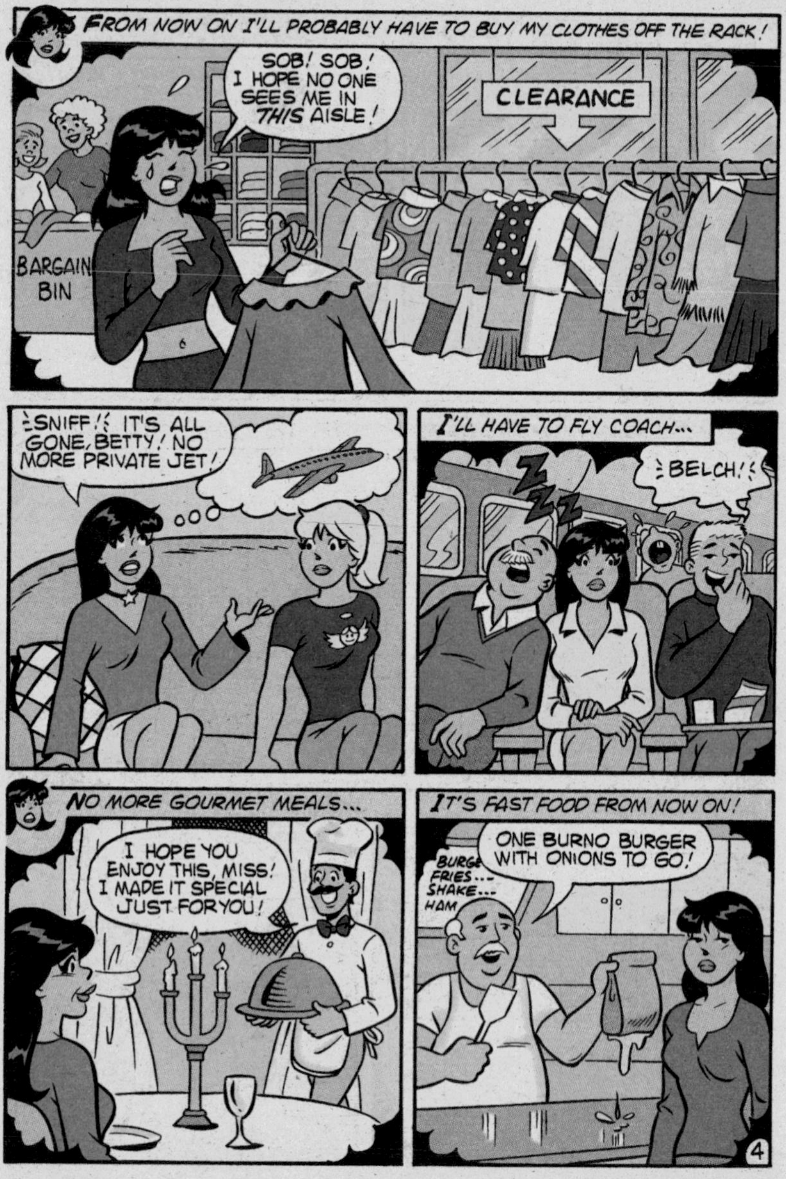
FROM NOW ON I'LL PROBABLY HAVE TO BUY MY CLOTHES OFF THE RACK!
SOB! SOB! I HOPE NO ONE SEES ME IN THIS AISLE!
CLEARANCE
BARGAIN BIN
SNIFF! IT'S ALL GONE, BETTY! NO MORE PRIVATE JET!
I'LL HAVE TO FLY COACH...
Z Z Z
BELCH!
NO MORE GOURMET MEALS...
I HOPE YOU ENJOY THIS, MISS! I MADE IT SPECIAL JUST FOR YOU!
IT'S FAST FOOD FROM NOW ON!
BURGE FRIES... SHAKE... HAM
ONE BURNO BURGER WITH ONIONS TO GO!
4

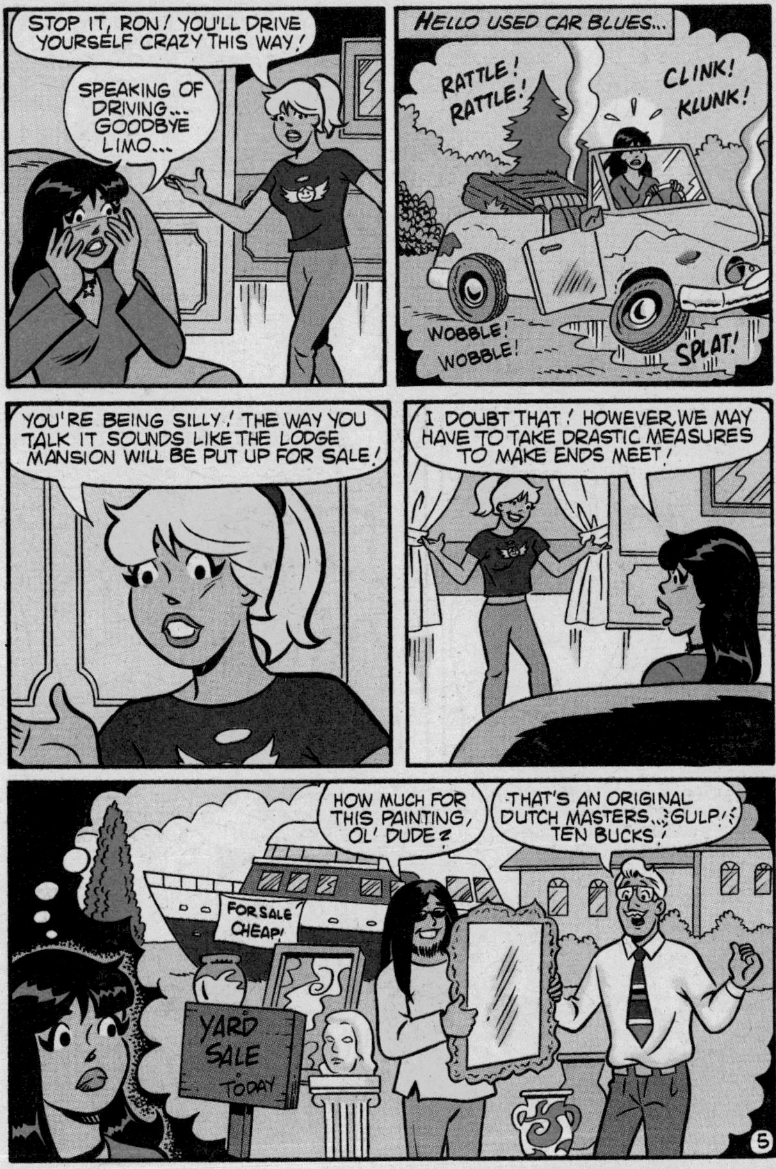
STOP IT, RON! YOU'LL DRIVE YOURSELF CRAZY THIS WAY!
SPEAKING OF DRIVING... GOODBYE LIMO...
HELLO USED CAR BLUES...
RATTLE! RATTLE!
CLINK! KLUNK!
WOBBLE! WOBBLE!
SPLAT!
YOU'RE BEING SILLY! THE WAY YOU TALK IT SOUNDS LIKE THE LODGE MANSION WILL BE PUT UP FOR SALE!
I DOUBT THAT! HOWEVER, WE MAY HAVE TO TAKE DRASTIC MEASURES TO MAKE ENDS MEET!
HOW MUCH FOR THIS PAINTING, OL' DUDE?
THAT'S AN ORIGINAL DUTCH MASTERS... GULP! TEN BUCKS!
FOR SALE CHEAP!
YARD SALE TODAY
5

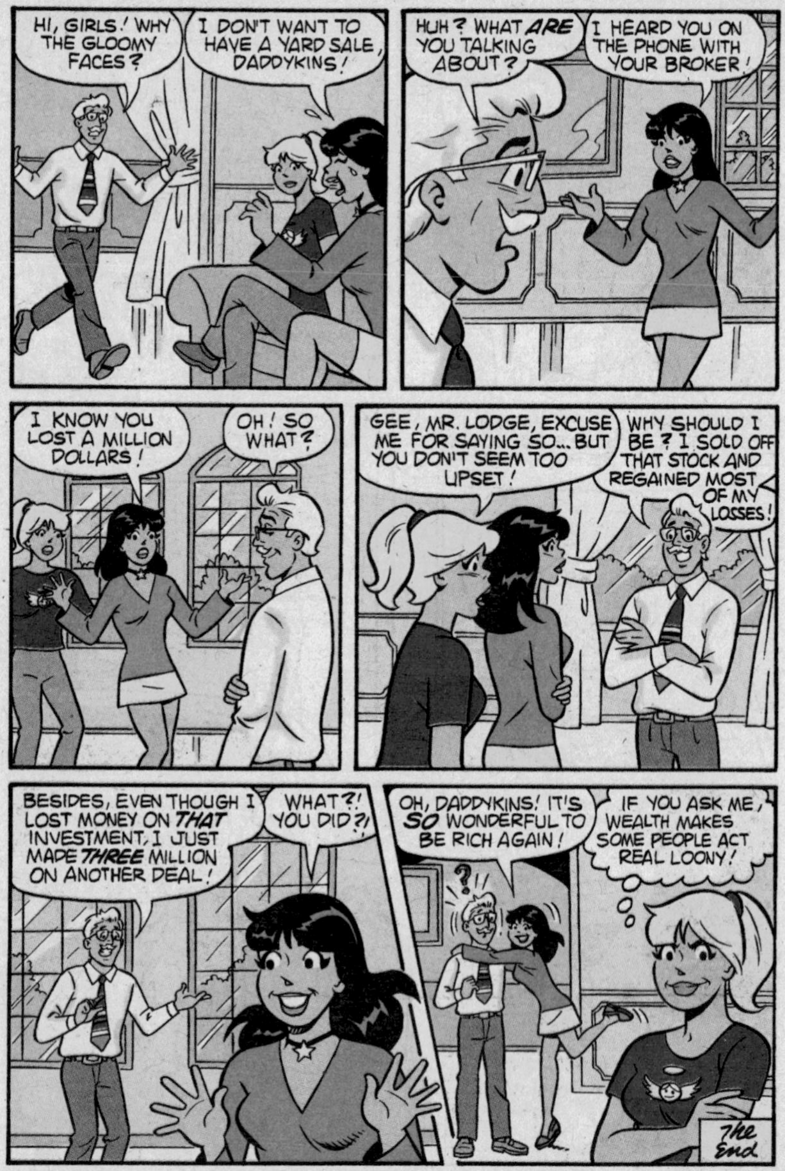
HI, GIRLS! WHY THE GLOOMY FACES?
I DON'T WANT TO HAVE A YARD SALE, DADDYKINS!
HUH? WHAT ARE YOU TALKING ABOUT?
I HEARD YOU ON THE PHONE WITH YOUR BROKER!
I KNOW YOU LOST A MILLION DOLLARS!
OH! SO WHAT?
GEE, MR. LODGE, EXCUSE ME FOR SAYING SO... BUT YOU DON'T SEEM TOO UPSET!
WHY SHOULD I BE? I SOLD OFF THAT STOCK AND REGAINED MOST OF MY LOSSES!
BESIDES, EVEN THOUGH I LOST MONEY ON THAT INVESTMENT, I JUST MADE THREE MILLION ON ANOTHER DEAL!
WHAT?! YOU DID?!
OH, DADDYKINS! IT'S SO WONDERFUL TO BE RICH AGAIN!
?!!
IF YOU ASK ME, WEALTH MAKES SOME PEOPLE ACT REAL LOONY!
The End

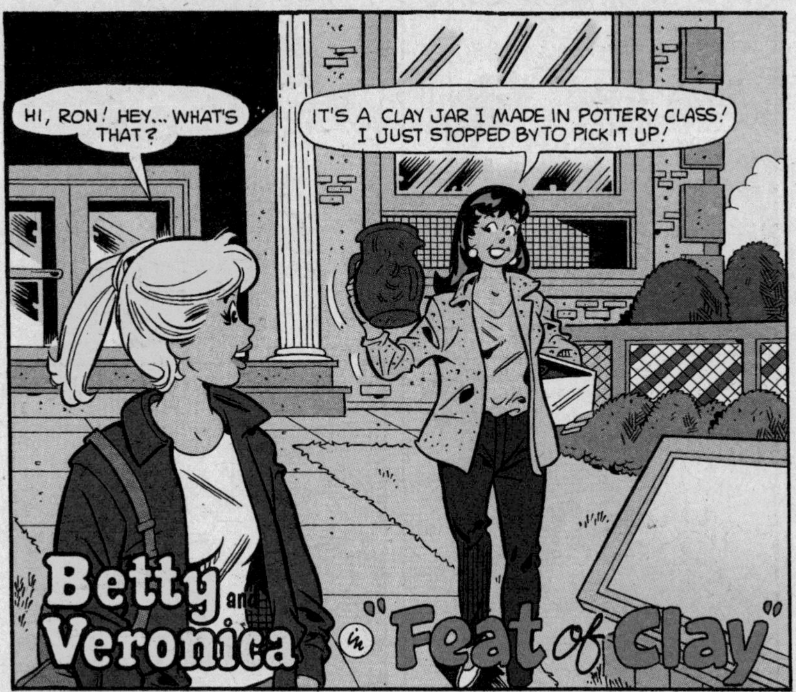
HI, RON! HEY... WHAT'S THAT?
IT'S A CLAY JAR I MADE IN POTTERY CLASS! I JUST STOPPED BY TO PICK IT UP!
Betty and Veronica
in "Feat of Clay"

Script: Mike Pellowski / Pencils: Tim Kennedy / Inks: Ken Selig / Letters: Bill Yoshida / Colors: Barry Grossman

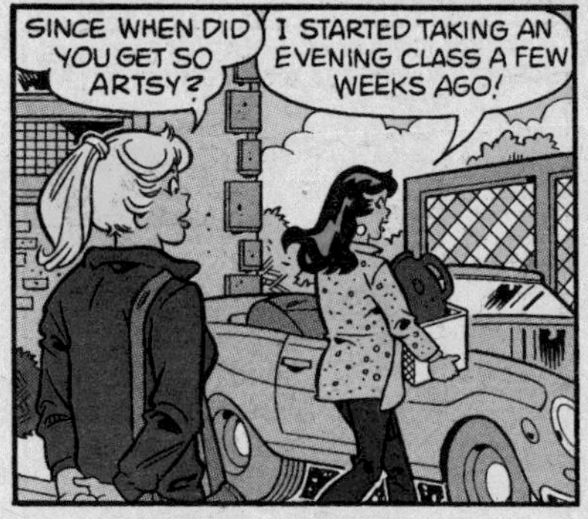
SINCE WHEN DID YOU GET SO ARTSY?
I STARTED TAKING AN EVENING CLASS A FEW WEEKS AGO!

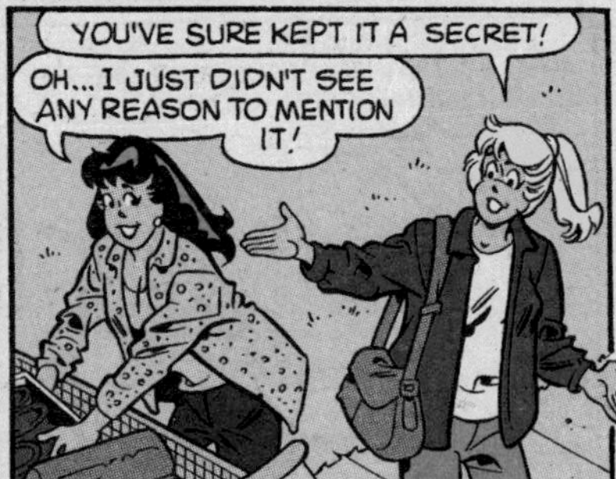
YOU'VE SURE KEPT IT A SECRET!
OH... I JUST DIDN'T SEE ANY REASON TO MENTION IT!

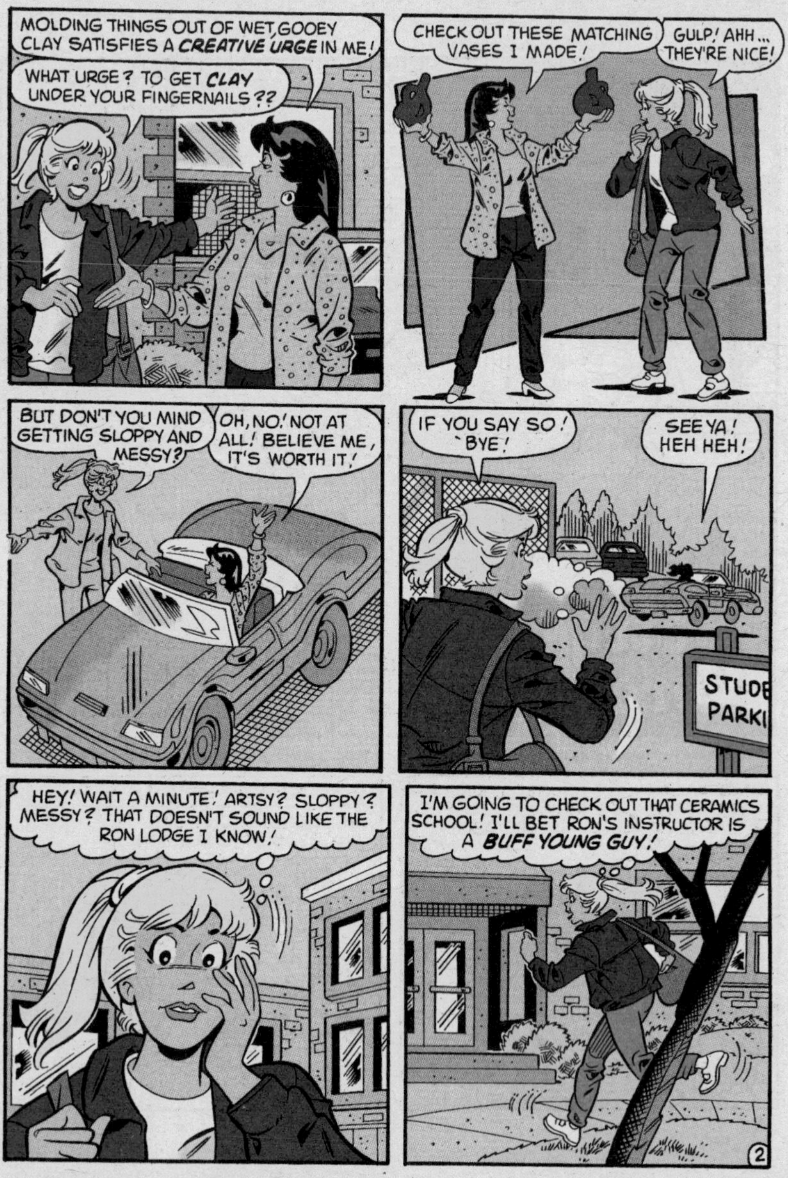
MOLDING THINGS OUT OF WET, GOOEY CLAY SATISFIES A *CREATIVE URGE* IN ME!
WHAT URGE? TO GET *CLAY* UNDER YOUR FINGERNAILS??
CHECK OUT THESE MATCHING VASES I MADE!
GULP! AHH... THEY'RE NICE!
BUT DON'T YOU MIND GETTING SLOPPY AND MESSY?
OH, NO! NOT AT ALL! BELIEVE ME, IT'S WORTH IT!
IF YOU SAY SO! 'BYE!
SEE YA! HEH HEH!
STUDE
PARKI
HEY! WAIT A MINUTE! ARTSY? SLOPPY? MESSY? THAT DOESN'T SOUND LIKE THE RON LODGE I KNOW!
I'M GOING TO CHECK OUT THAT CERAMICS SCHOOL! I'LL BET RON'S INSTRUCTOR IS A *BUFF YOUNG GUY*!
2

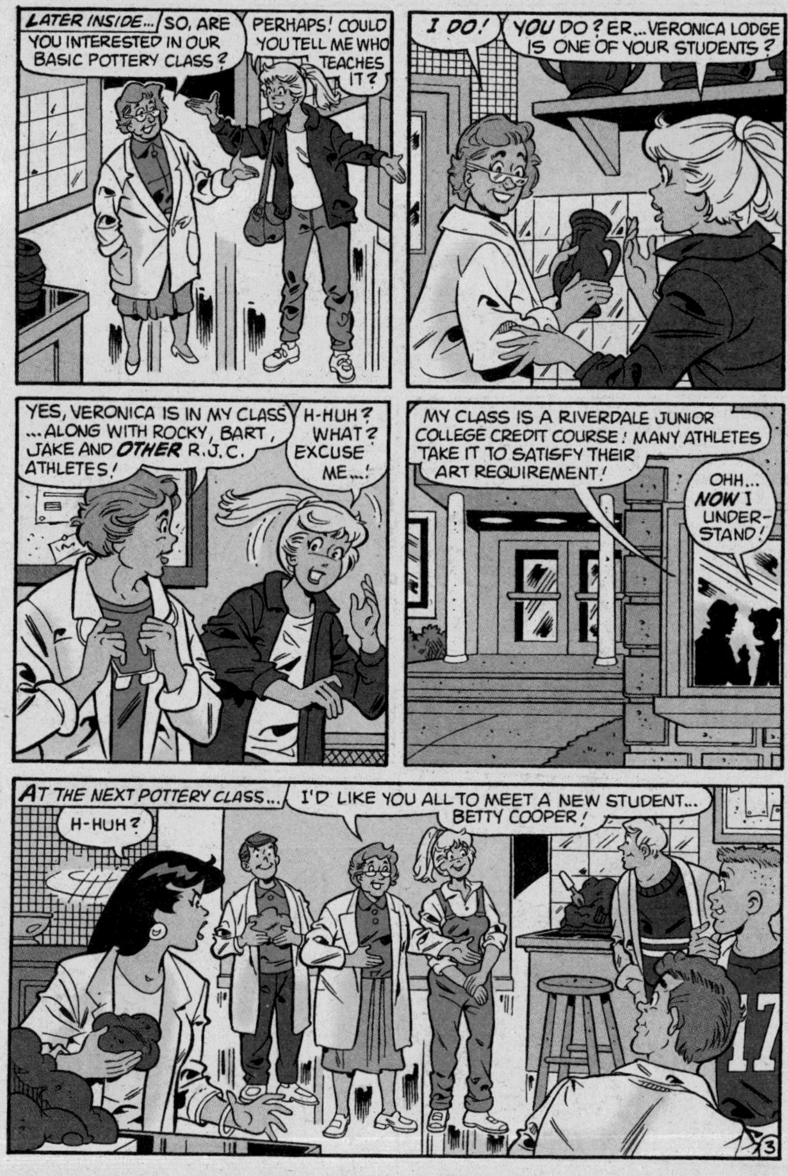

LATER INSIDE...
SO, ARE YOU INTERESTED IN OUR BASIC POTTERY CLASS?
PERHAPS! COULD YOU TELL ME WHO TEACHES IT?
I DO!
YOU DO? ER...VERONICA LODGE IS ONE OF YOUR STUDENTS?
YES, VERONICA IS IN MY CLASS ...ALONG WITH ROCKY, BART, JAKE AND OTHER R.J.C. ATHLETES!
H-HUH? WHAT? EXCUSE ME...!
MY CLASS IS A RIVERDALE JUNIOR COLLEGE CREDIT COURSE! MANY ATHLETES TAKE IT TO SATISFY THEIR ART REQUIREMENT!
OHH... NOW I UNDERSTAND!
AT THE NEXT POTTERY CLASS...
H-HUH?
I'D LIKE YOU ALL TO MEET A NEW STUDENT... BETTY COOPER!
17

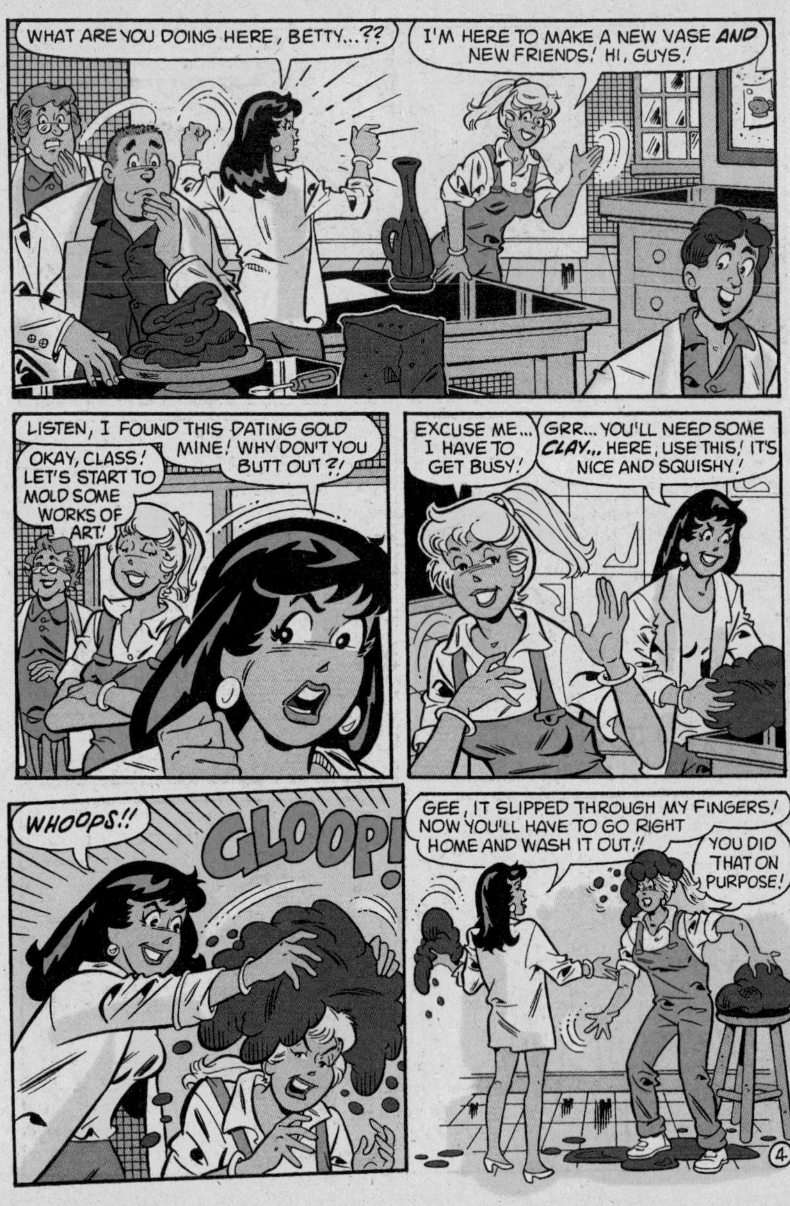
WHAT ARE YOU DOING HERE, BETTY...??
I'M HERE TO MAKE A NEW VASE AND NEW FRIENDS! HI, GUYS!
LISTEN, I FOUND THIS DATING GOLD MINE! WHY DON'T YOU BUTT OUT?!
OKAY, CLASS! LET'S START TO MOLD SOME WORKS OF ART!
EXCUSE ME... I HAVE TO GET BUSY!
GRR... YOU'LL NEED SOME CLAY... HERE, USE THIS! IT'S NICE AND SQUISHY!
WHOOPS!!
GLOOP!
GEE, IT SLIPPED THROUGH MY FINGERS! NOW YOU'LL HAVE TO GO RIGHT HOME AND WASH IT OUT!!
YOU DID THAT ON PURPOSE!
4

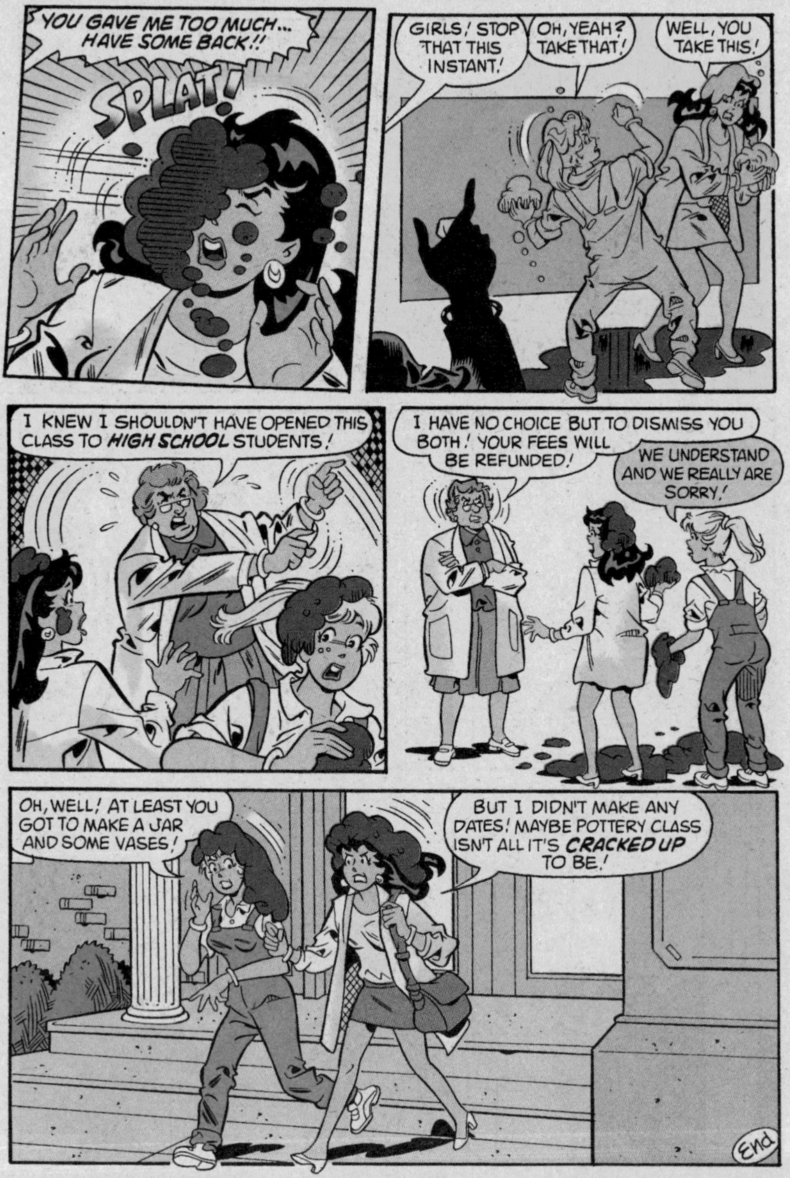
YOU GAVE ME TOO MUCH... HAVE SOME BACK!!
SPLAT!
GIRLS! STOP THAT THIS INSTANT!
OH, YEAH? TAKE THAT!
WELL, YOU TAKE THIS!
I KNEW I SHOULDN'T HAVE OPENED THIS CLASS TO HIGH SCHOOL STUDENTS!
I HAVE NO CHOICE BUT TO DISMISS YOU BOTH! YOUR FEES WILL BE REFUNDED!
WE UNDERSTAND AND WE REALLY ARE SORRY!
OH, WELL! AT LEAST YOU GOT TO MAKE A JAR AND SOME VASES!
BUT I DIDN'T MAKE ANY DATES! MAYBE POTTERY CLASS ISN'T ALL IT'S CRACKED UP TO BE!
End

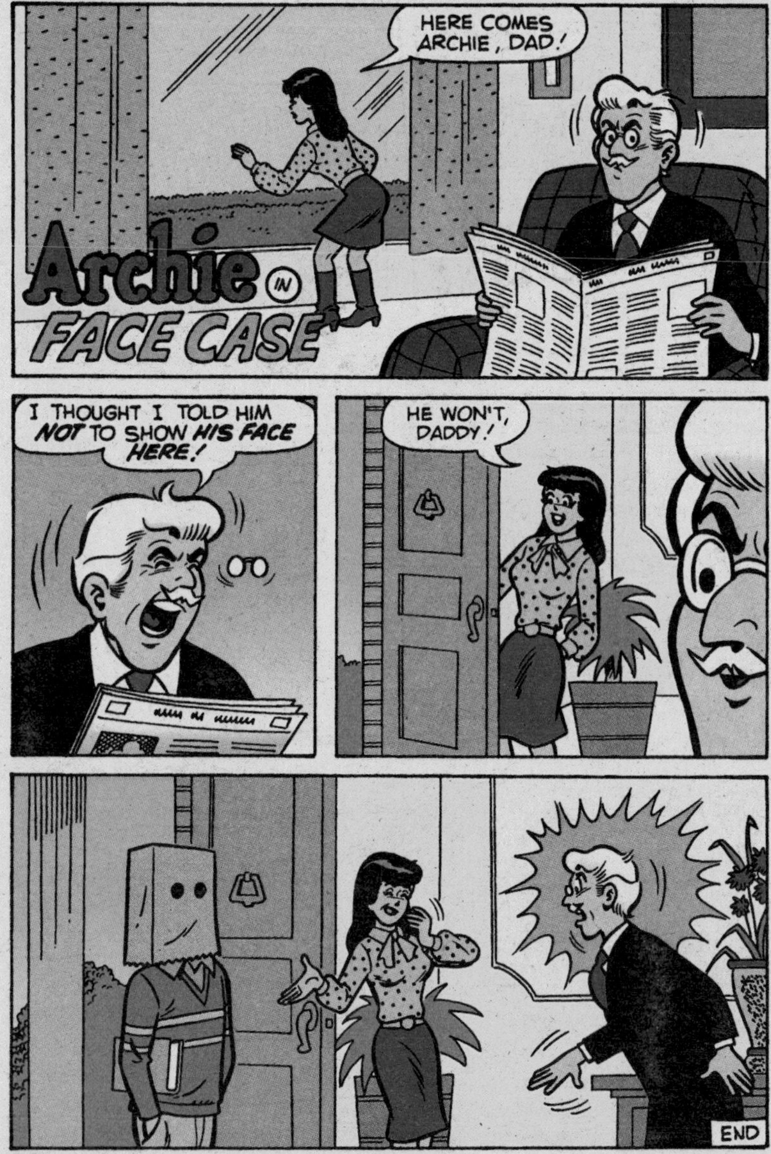
HERE COMES ARCHIE, DAD!
Archie IN
FACE CASE
I THOUGHT I TOLD HIM NOT TO SHOW HIS FACE HERE!
HE WON'T, DADDY!
END

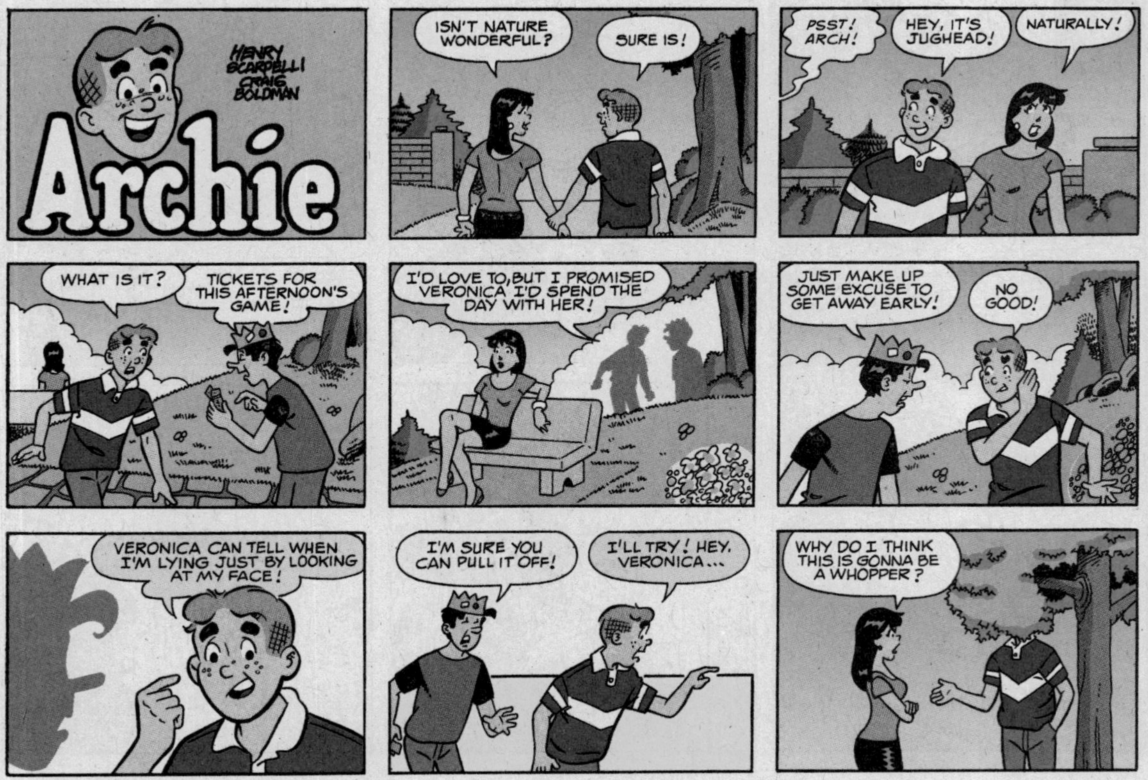
Archie
HENRY SCARPELLI
CRAIG BOLDMAN
ISN'T NATURE WONDERFUL?
SURE IS!
PSST! ARCH!
HEY, IT'S JUGHEAD!
NATURALLY!
WHAT IS IT?
TICKETS FOR THIS AFTERNOON'S GAME!
I'D LOVE TO, BUT I PROMISED VERONICA I'D SPEND THE DAY WITH HER!
JUST MAKE UP SOME EXCUSE TO GET AWAY EARLY!
NO GOOD!
VERONICA CAN TELL WHEN I'M LYING JUST BY LOOKING AT MY FACE!
I'M SURE YOU CAN PULL IT OFF!
I'LL TRY! HEY, VERONICA...
WHY DO I THINK THIS IS GONNA BE A WHOPPER?

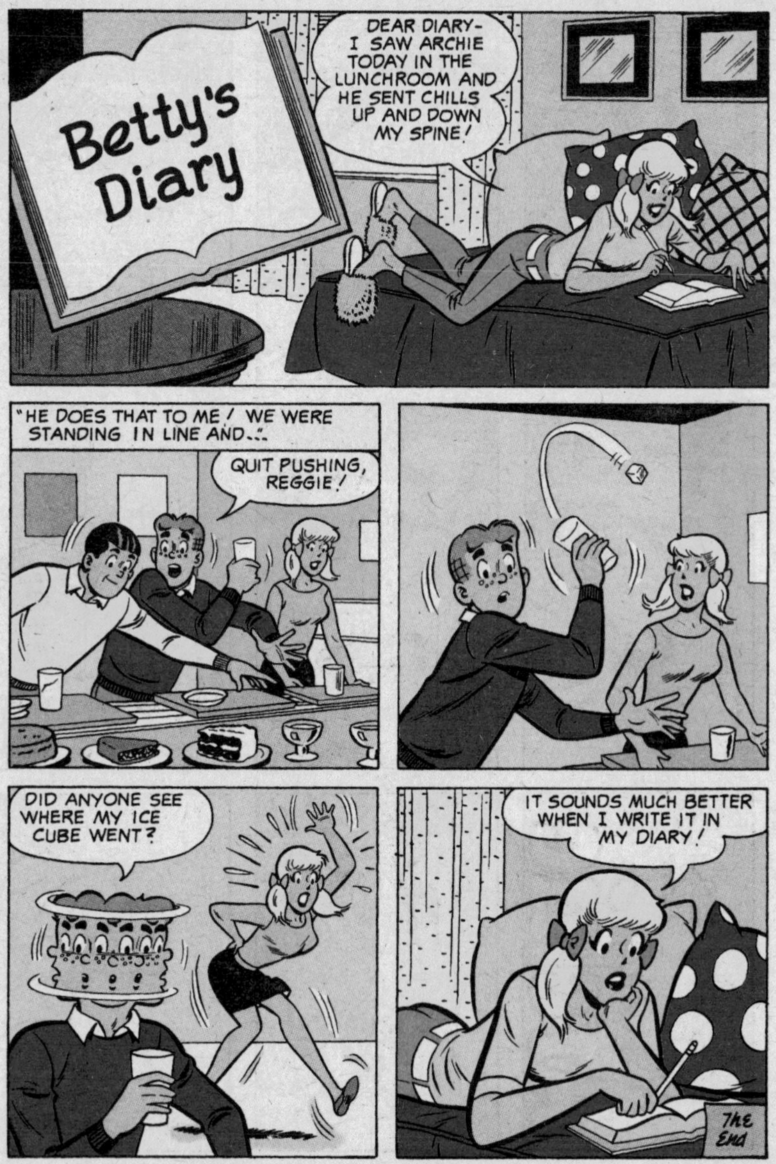
Betty's Diary
DEAR DIARY- I SAW ARCHIE TODAY IN THE LUNCHROOM AND HE SENT CHILLS UP AND DOWN MY SPINE!
"HE DOES THAT TO ME! WE WERE STANDING IN LINE AND..."
QUIT PUSHING, REGGIE!
DID ANYONE SEE WHERE MY ICE CUBE WENT?
IT SOUNDS MUCH BETTER WHEN I WRITE IT IN MY DIARY!
THE End

From the Vault of Archie comics

AN MLJ PUBLICATION

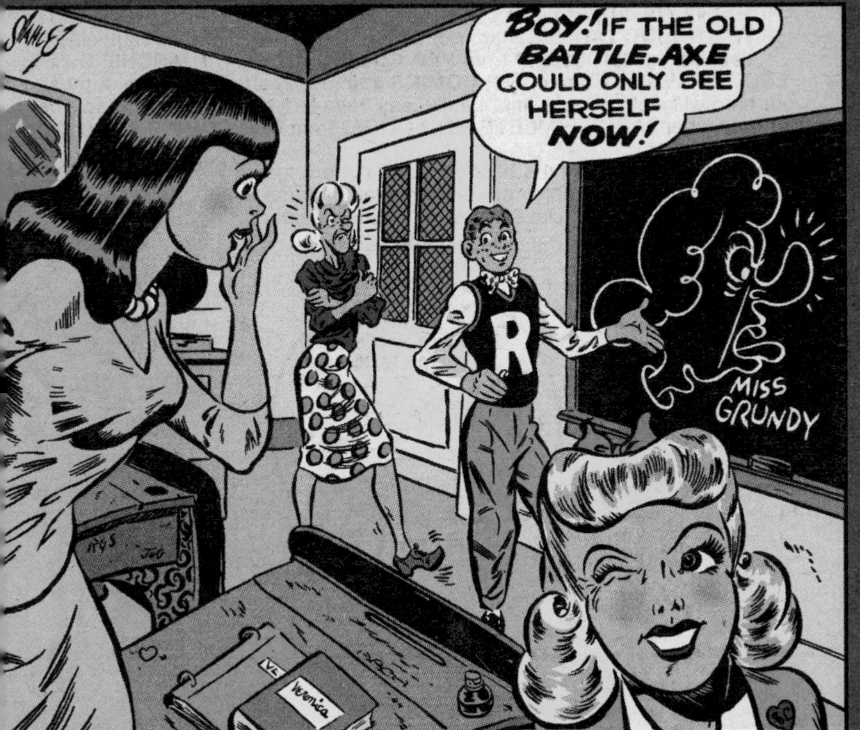
BOY! IF THE OLD BATTLE-AXE COULD ONLY SEE HERSELF NOW!
MISS GRUNDY
Veronica

From the Vault of Archie Comics!

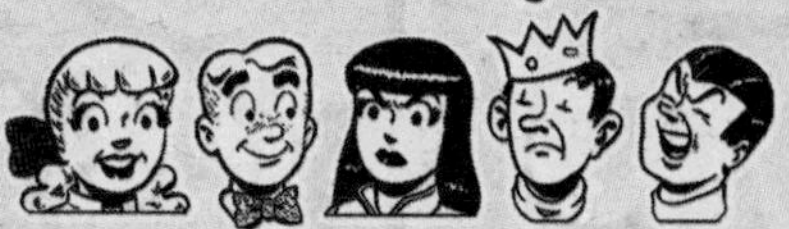

THE FABULOUS FORTIES

Welcome, pals and gals, to the dawn of ***ARCHIE COMICS***! In this section, you'll see the earliest versions of Archie and his friends! Witness **Archie Andrews** at his clumsiest, **Betty Cooper** being the sweetest girl ever, **Veronica Lodge** at her sultriest, **Jughead Jones** putting forth his *greatest* efforts towards doing nothing and **Reggie Mantle** being the cad that we all know and love!

This **ARCHIE VAULT** is especially amazing as we get *FOUR* crackerjack tales penned by one of the greatest of all Archie alumni, **Bob Montana! ARCHIE #2** ***(1943)*** **gives us a classic tale of knighthood in "SIR ARCHIBALD OF THE ROUND TABLE!" Then, get the skinny on the Riverdale High class elections in "TROUBLE!" from PEP COMICS #27** ***(1942)*****. "ARCHIE'S ESCORT SERVICE" from PEP COMICS #30** ***(1942)*** **showcases the depths our hero will sink to pay a fine! Lastly, say hello to a** ***pivotal character*** **for the** ***first time*** when "ARCHIE MEETS MR. LODGE" from **PEP COMICS #31** ***(1942)***!

Archie Comics are the best comics out there, gang! We hope you enjoy our presentation of these classic tales of Archie's past! Till next time, gang!

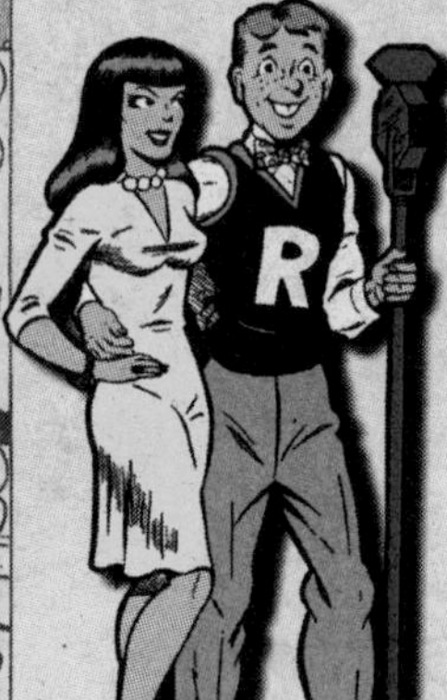

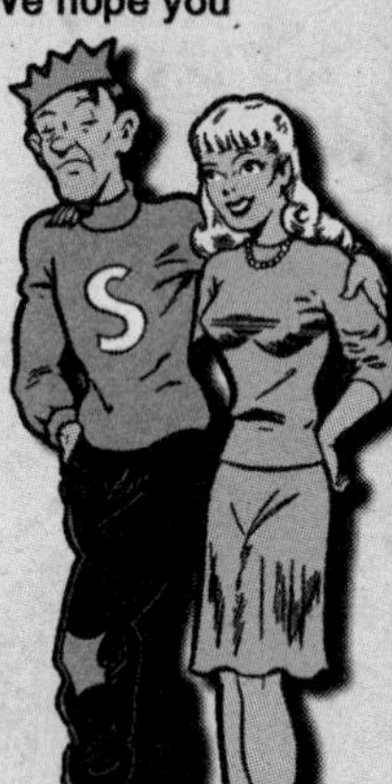

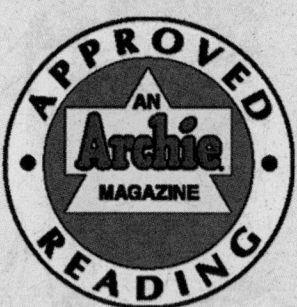

APPROVED
AN Archie MAGAZINE
READING

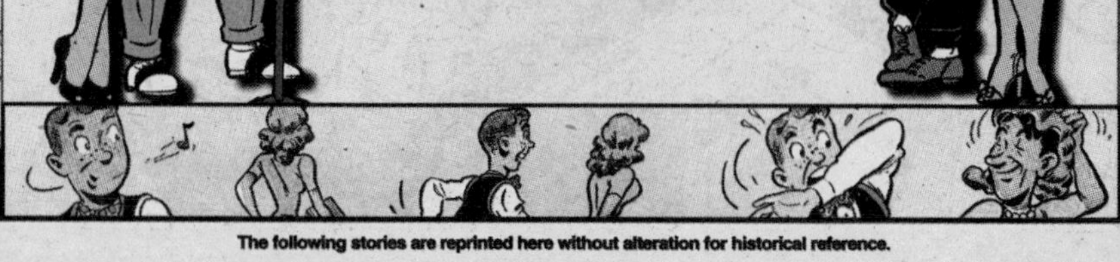

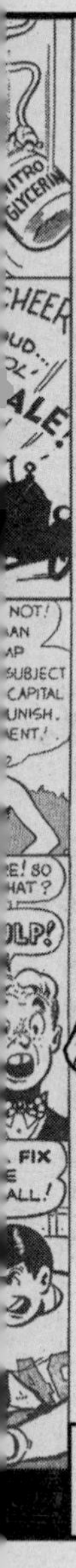
NOT!
SUBJECT
CAPITAL
FIX
ALL!

The following stories are reprinted here without alteration for historical reference.

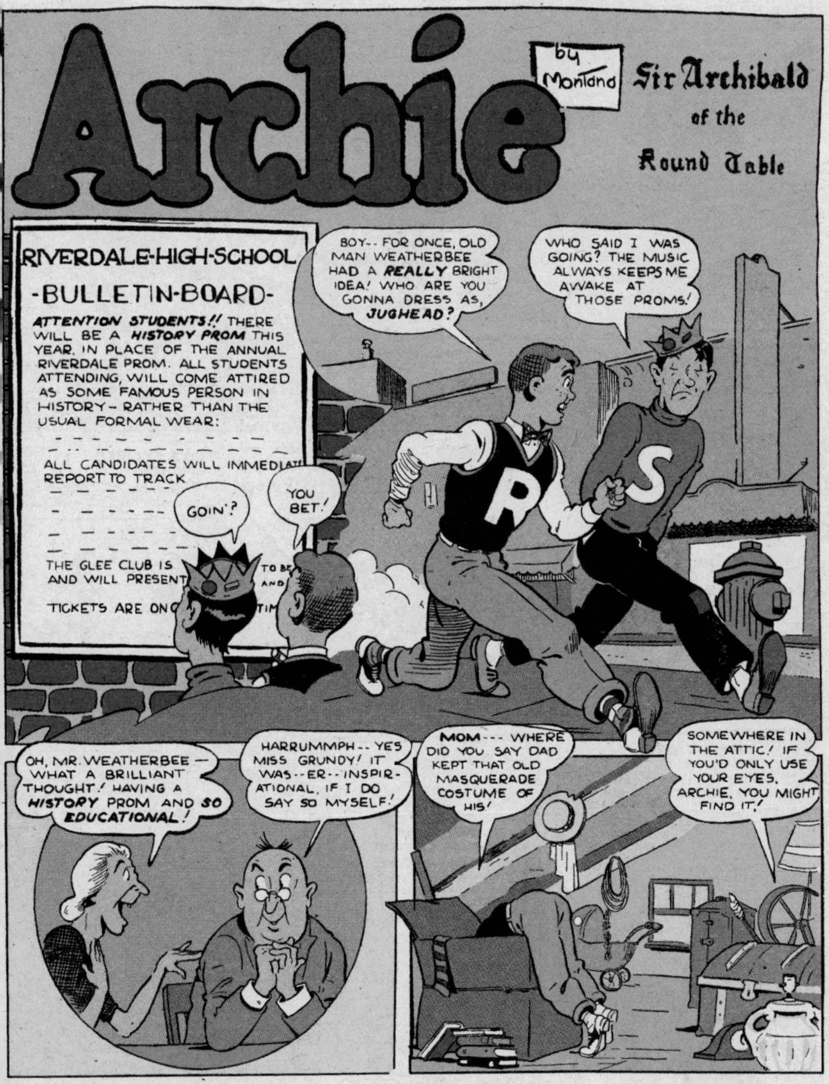
Archie
by Montana
Sir Archibald of the Round Table
RIVERDALE-HIGH-SCHOOL
-BULLETIN-BOARD-
ATTENTION STUDENTS!! THERE WILL BE A HISTORY PROM THIS YEAR, IN PLACE OF THE ANNUAL RIVERDALE PROM. ALL STUDENTS ATTENDING, WILL COME ATTIRED AS SOME FAMOUS PERSON IN HISTORY - RATHER THAN THE USUAL FORMAL WEAR:
ALL CANDIDATES WILL IMMEDIA
REPORT TO TRACK
THE GLEE CLUB IS
AND WILL PRESENT
TICKETS ARE ON
GOIN'?
YOU BET!
BOY-- FOR ONCE, OLD MAN WEATHERBEE HAD A REALLY BRIGHT IDEA! WHO ARE YOU GONNA DRESS AS, JUGHEAD?
WHO SAID I WAS GOING? THE MUSIC ALWAYS KEEPS ME AWAKE AT THOSE PROMS!
OH, MR. WEATHERBEE — WHAT A BRILLIANT THOUGHT! HAVING A HISTORY PROM AND SO EDUCATIONAL!
HARRUMMPH -- YES MISS GRUNDY! IT WAS--ER--INSPIR-ATIONAL, IF I DO SAY SO MYSELF!
MOM --- WHERE DID YOU SAY DAD KEPT THAT OLD MASQUERADE COSTUME OF HIS!
SOMEWHERE IN THE ATTIC! IF YOU'D ONLY USE YOUR EYES, ARCHIE, YOU MIGHT FIND IT!

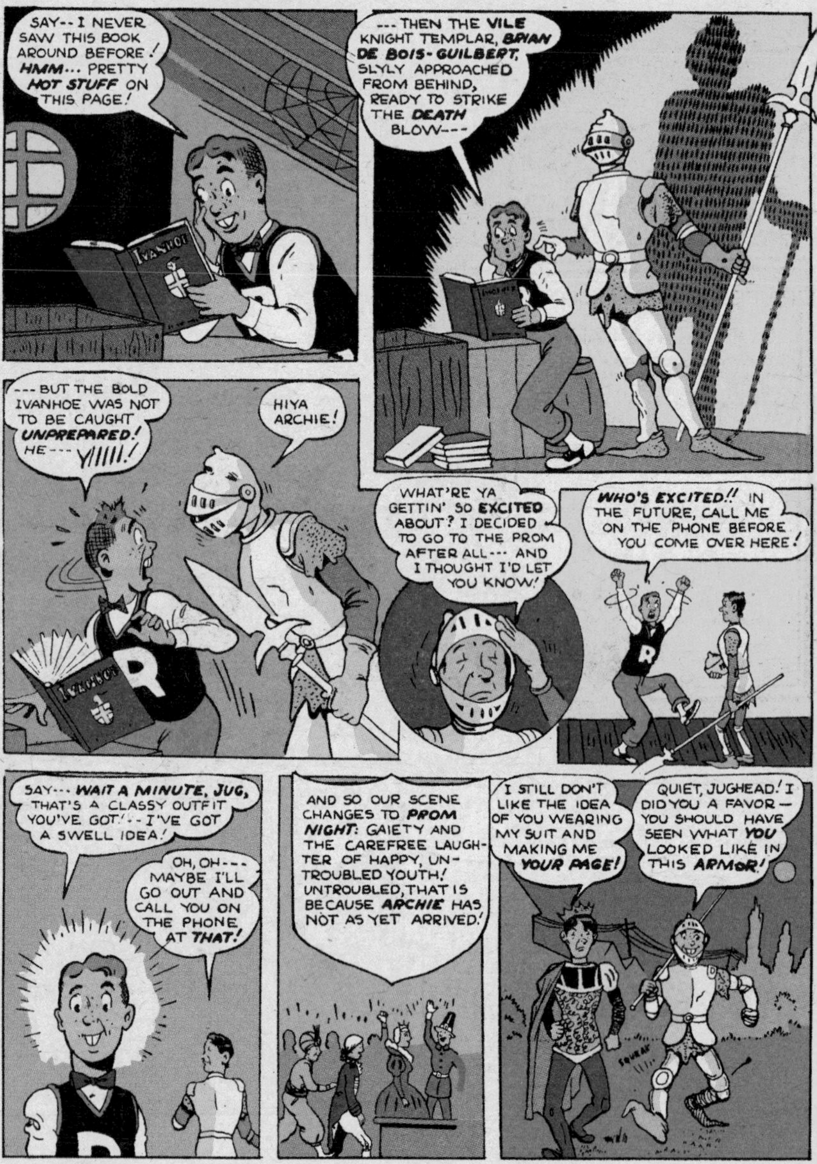
SAY-- I NEVER SAW THIS BOOK AROUND BEFORE! HMM... PRETTY HOT STUFF ON THIS PAGE!
IVANHOE
---THEN THE VILE KNIGHT TEMPLAR, BRIAN DE BOIS-GUILBERT, SLYLY APPROACHED FROM BEHIND, READY TO STRIKE THE DEATH BLOW---
---BUT THE BOLD IVANHOE WAS NOT TO BE CAUGHT UNPREPARED! HE--- YIIII!
HIYA ARCHIE!
IVANHOE
WHAT'RE YA GETTIN' SO EXCITED ABOUT? I DECIDED TO GO TO THE PROM AFTER ALL--- AND I THOUGHT I'D LET YOU KNOW!
WHO'S EXCITED!! IN THE FUTURE, CALL ME ON THE PHONE BEFORE YOU COME OVER HERE!
SAY--- WAIT A MINUTE, JUG, THAT'S A CLASSY OUTFIT YOU'VE GOT!--I'VE GOT A SWELL IDEA!
OH, OH--- MAYBE I'LL GO OUT AND CALL YOU ON THE PHONE AT THAT!
AND SO OUR SCENE CHANGES TO PROM NIGHT: GAIETY AND THE CAREFREE LAUGHTER OF HAPPY, UNTROUBLED YOUTH! UNTROUBLED, THAT IS BECAUSE ARCHIE HAS NOT AS YET ARRIVED!
I STILL DON'T LIKE THE IDEA OF YOU WEARING MY SUIT AND MAKING ME YOUR PAGE!
QUIET, JUGHEAD! I DID YOU A FAVOR — YOU SHOULD HAVE SEEN WHAT YOU LOOKED LIKE IN THIS ARMOR!
SQUEAK

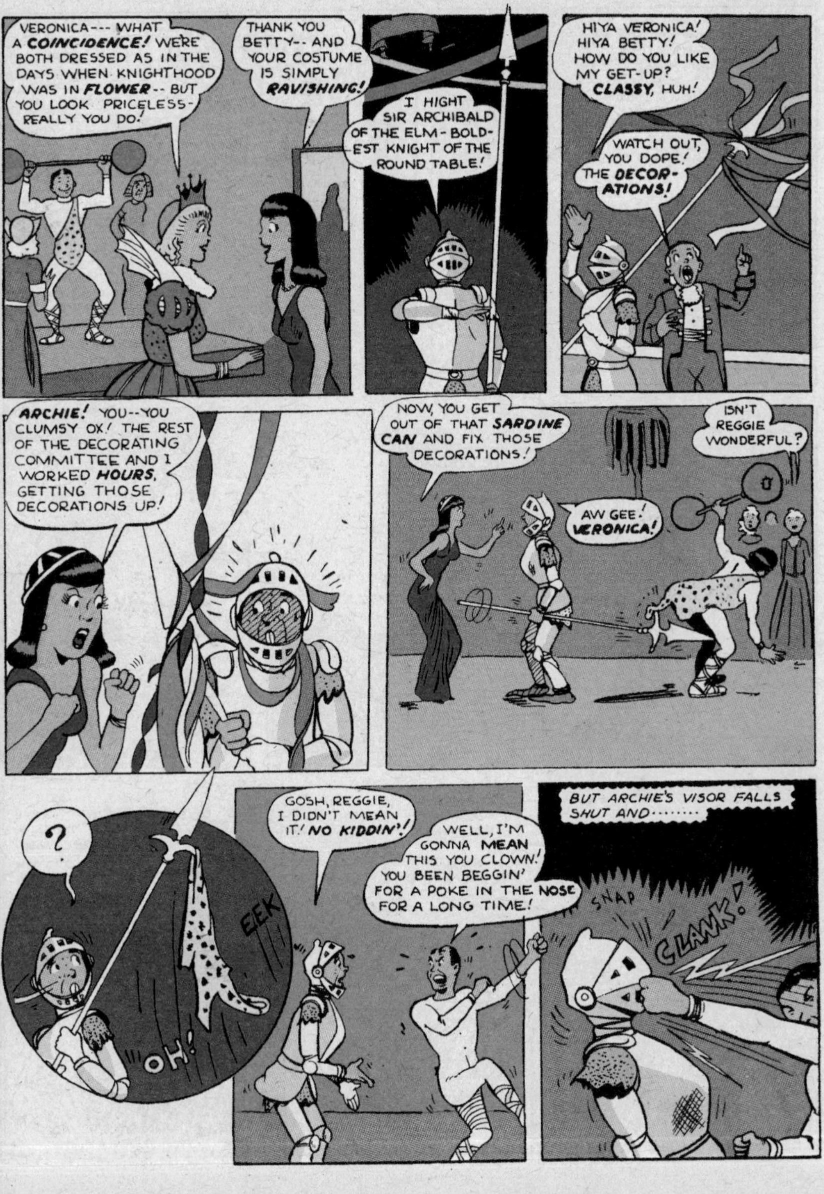
VERONICA--- WHAT A COINCIDENCE! WE'RE BOTH DRESSED AS IN THE DAYS WHEN KNIGHTHOOD WAS IN FLOWER-- BUT YOU LOOK PRICELESS-REALLY YOU DO!
THANK YOU BETTY-- AND YOUR COSTUME IS SIMPLY RAVISHING!
I HIGHT SIR ARCHIBALD OF THE ELM-BOLDEST KNIGHT OF THE ROUND TABLE!
HIYA VERONICA! HIYA BETTY! HOW DO YOU LIKE MY GET-UP? CLASSY, HUH!
WATCH OUT, YOU DOPE! THE DECORATIONS!
ARCHIE! YOU--YOU CLUMSY OX! THE REST OF THE DECORATING COMMITTEE AND I WORKED HOURS, GETTING THOSE DECORATIONS UP!
NOW, YOU GET OUT OF THAT SARDINE CAN AND FIX THOSE DECORATIONS!
AW GEE! VERONICA!
ISN'T REGGIE WONDERFUL?
?
EEK
OH!
GOSH, REGGIE, I DIDN'T MEAN IT! NO KIDDIN'!
WELL, I'M GONNA MEAN THIS YOU CLOWN! YOU BEEN BEGGIN' FOR A POKE IN THE NOSE FOR A LONG TIME!
BUT ARCHIE'S VISOR FALLS SHUT AND.........
SNAP
CLANK!

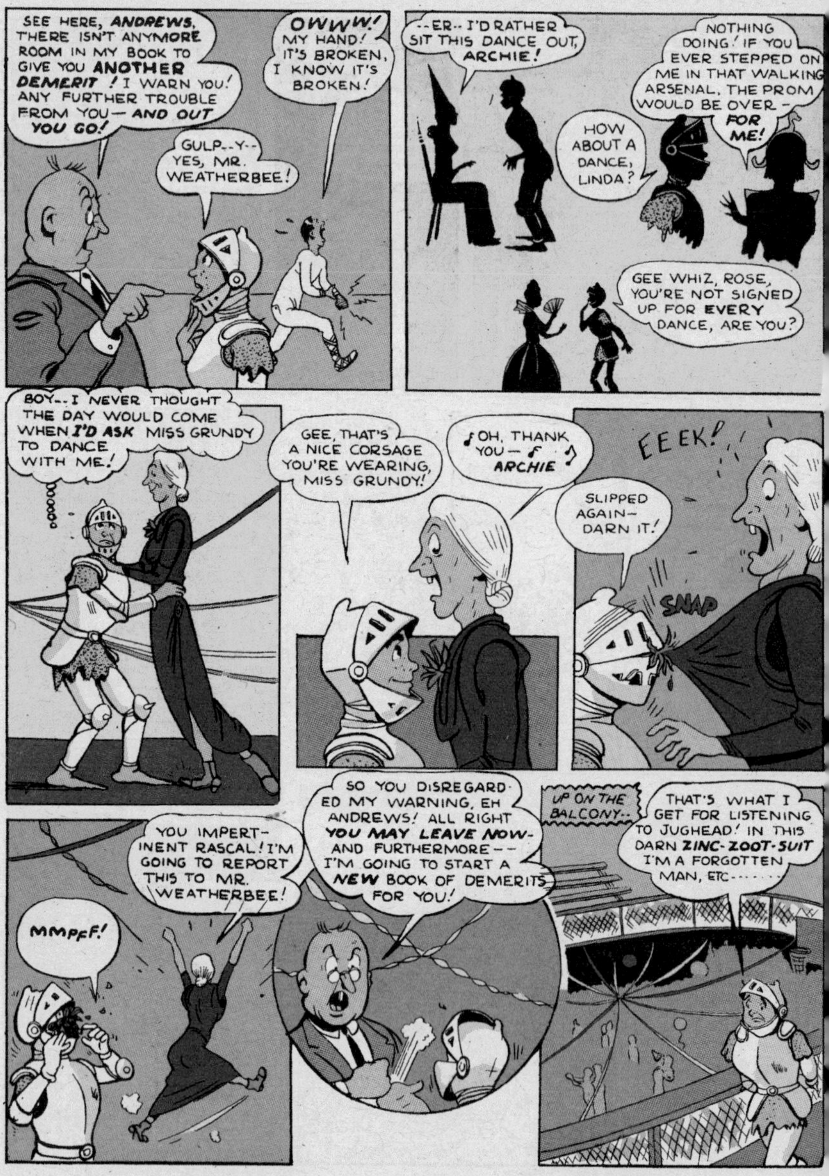

SEE HERE, ANDREWS, THERE ISN'T ANYMORE ROOM IN MY BOOK TO GIVE YOU ANOTHER DEMERIT! I WARN YOU! ANY FURTHER TROUBLE FROM YOU— AND OUT YOU GO!
GULP--Y-- YES, MR. WEATHERBEE!
OWWW! MY HAND! IT'S BROKEN, I KNOW IT'S BROKEN!
--ER-- I'D RATHER SIT THIS DANCE OUT, ARCHIE!
HOW ABOUT A DANCE, LINDA?
NOTHING DOING! IF YOU EVER STEPPED ON ME IN THAT WALKING ARSENAL, THE PROM WOULD BE OVER— FOR ME!
GEE WHIZ, ROSE, YOU'RE NOT SIGNED UP FOR EVERY DANCE, ARE YOU?
BOY--I NEVER THOUGHT THE DAY WOULD COME WHEN I'D ASK MISS GRUNDY TO DANCE WITH ME!
GEE, THAT'S A NICE CORSAGE YOU'RE WEARING, MISS GRUNDY!
OH, THANK YOU— ARCHIE
EEEK!
SLIPPED AGAIN— DARN IT!
SNAP
YOU IMPERTINENT RASCAL! I'M GOING TO REPORT THIS TO MR. WEATHERBEE!
MMPFF!
SO YOU DISREGARDED MY WARNING, EH ANDREWS! ALL RIGHT YOU MAY LEAVE NOW— AND FURTHERMORE-- I'M GOING TO START A NEW BOOK OF DEMERITS FOR YOU!
UP ON THE BALCONY..
THAT'S WHAT I GET FOR LISTENING TO JUGHEAD! IN THIS DARN ZINC-ZOOT-SUIT I'M A FORGOTTEN MAN, ETC-------

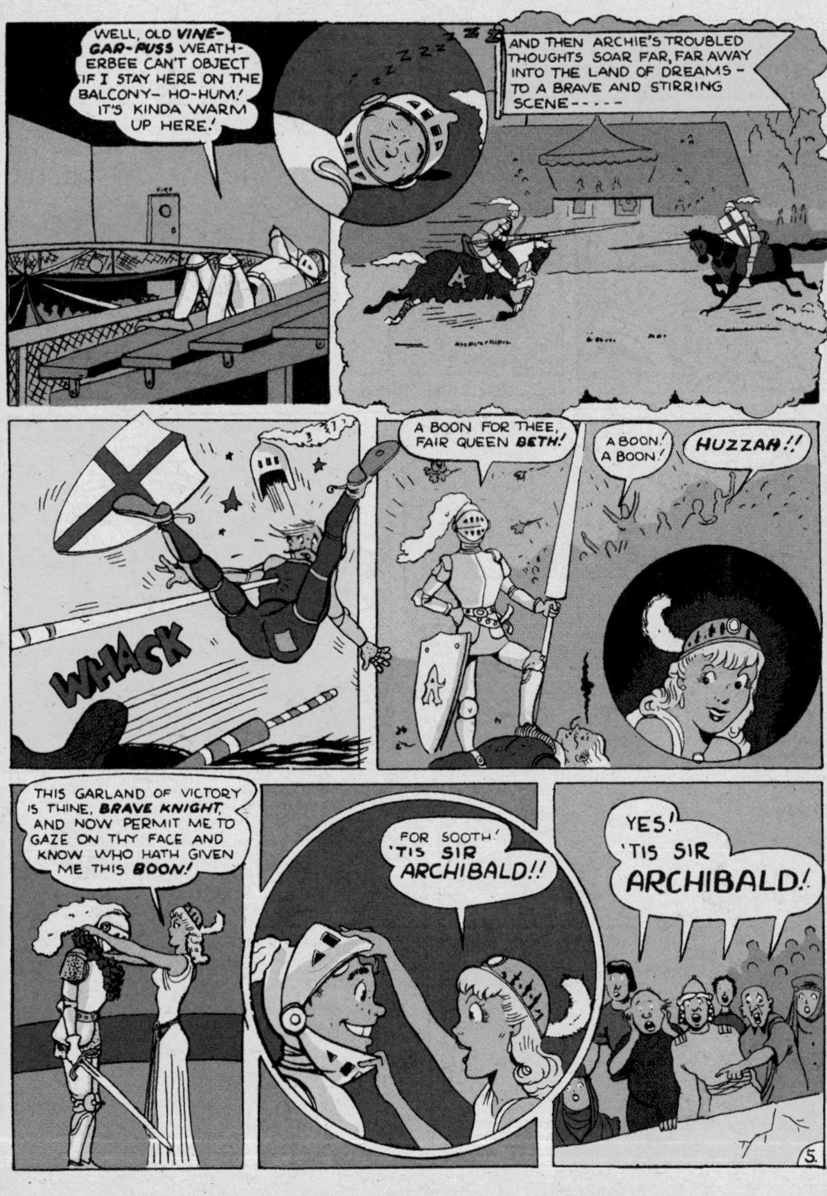

WELL, OLD VINEGAR-PUSS WEATHERBEE CAN'T OBJECT IF I STAY HERE ON THE BALCONY— HO-HUM! IT'S KINDA WARM UP HERE!
AND THEN ARCHIE'S TROUBLED THOUGHTS SOAR FAR, FAR AWAY INTO THE LAND OF DREAMS — TO A BRAVE AND STIRRING SCENE- - - -
WHACK
A BOON FOR THEE, FAIR QUEEN BETH!
A BOON! A BOON!
HUZZAH!!
THIS GARLAND OF VICTORY IS THINE, BRAVE KNIGHT, AND NOW PERMIT ME TO GAZE ON THY FACE AND KNOW WHO HATH GIVEN ME THIS BOON!
FOR SOOTH! 'TIS SIR ARCHIBALD!!
YES! 'TIS SIR ARCHIBALD!

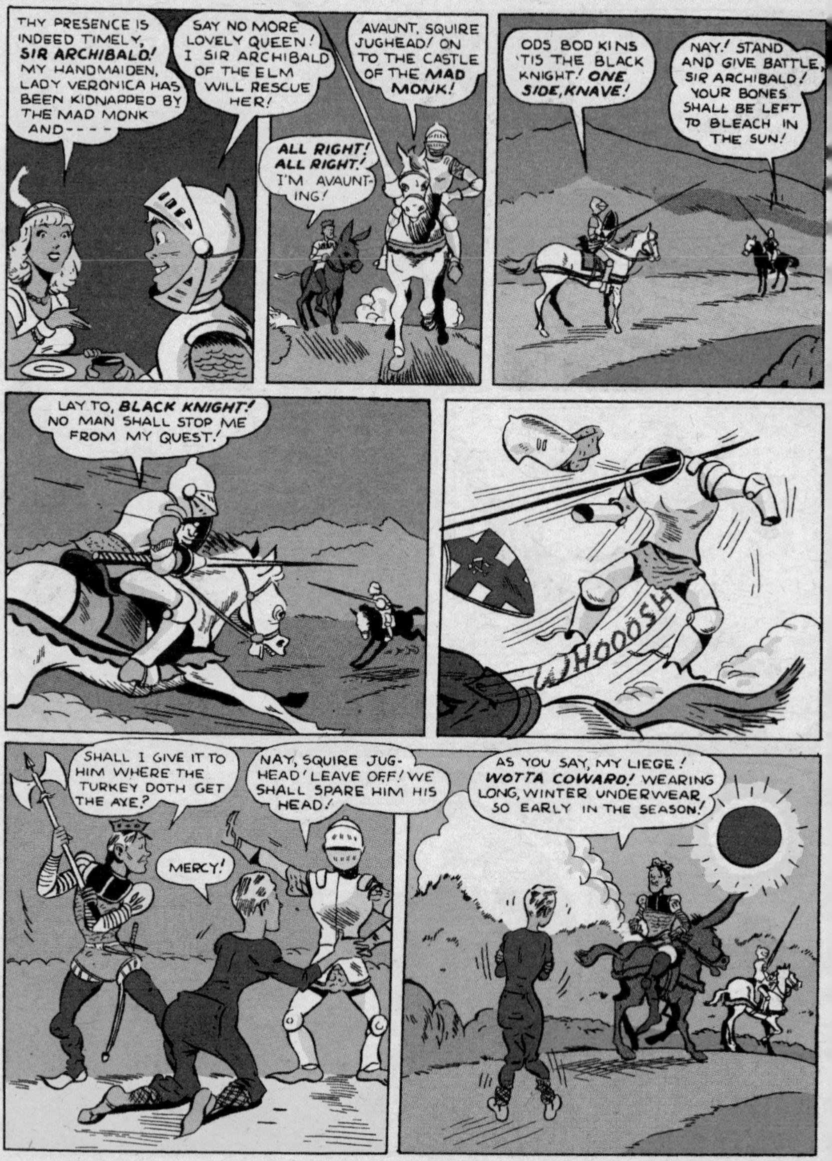
THY PRESENCE IS INDEED TIMELY, **SIR ARCHIBALD!** MY HANDMAIDEN, LADY VERONICA HAS BEEN KIDNAPPED BY THE MAD MONK AND----
SAY NO MORE LOVELY QUEEN! I SIR ARCHIBALD OF THE ELM WILL RESCUE HER!
AVAUNT, SQUIRE JUGHEAD! ON TO THE CASTLE OF THE **MAD MONK!**
ALL RIGHT! ALL RIGHT! I'M AVAUNTING!
ODS BODKINS 'TIS THE BLACK KNIGHT! **ONE SIDE, KNAVE!**
NAY! STAND AND GIVE BATTLE, SIR ARCHIBALD! YOUR BONES SHALL BE LEFT TO BLEACH IN THE SUN!
LAY TO, **BLACK KNIGHT!** NO MAN SHALL STOP ME FROM MY QUEST!
WHOOOSH
SHALL I GIVE IT TO HIM WHERE THE TURKEY DOTH GET THE AXE?
MERCY!
NAY, SQUIRE JUGHEAD! LEAVE OFF! WE SHALL SPARE HIM HIS HEAD!
AS YOU SAY, MY LIEGE! **WOTTA COWARD!** WEARING LONG, WINTER UNDERWEAR SO EARLY IN THE SEASON!

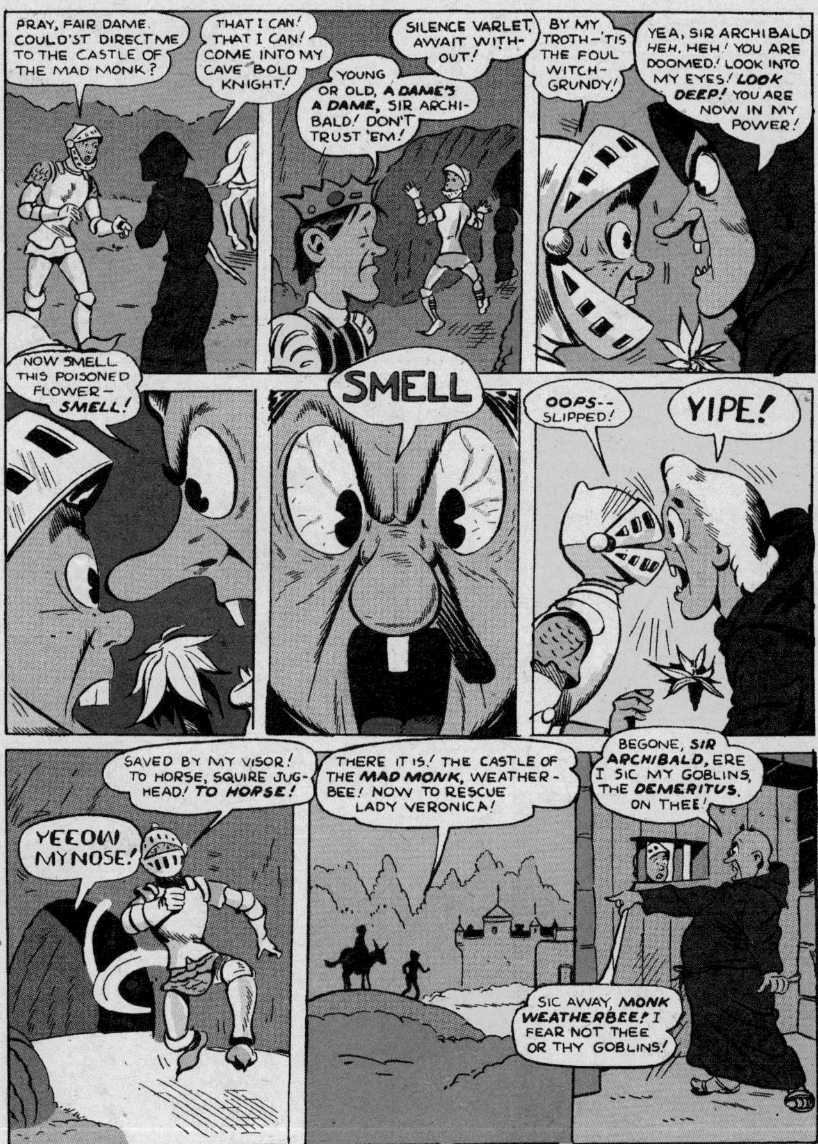
PRAY, FAIR DAME. COULD'ST DIRECT ME TO THE CASTLE OF THE MAD MONK?
THAT I CAN! THAT I CAN! COME INTO MY CAVE BOLD KNIGHT!
SILENCE VARLET, AWAIT WITHOUT!
YOUNG OR OLD, A DAME'S A DAME, SIR ARCHIBALD! DON'T TRUST 'EM!
BY MY TROTH—'TIS THE FOUL WITCH-GRUNDY!
YEA, SIR ARCHIBALD HEH, HEH! YOU ARE DOOMED! LOOK INTO MY EYES! LOOK DEEP! YOU ARE NOW IN MY POWER!
NOW SMELL THIS POISONED FLOWER—SMELL!
SMELL
OOPS--SLIPPED!
YIPE!
SAVED BY MY VISOR! TO HORSE, SQUIRE JUGHEAD! TO HORSE!
YEEOW MYNOSE!
THERE IT IS! THE CASTLE OF THE MAD MONK, WEATHERBEE! NOW TO RESCUE LADY VERONICA!
BEGONE, SIR ARCHIBALD, ERE I SIC MY GOBLINS, THE DEMERITUS, ON THEE!
SIC AWAY, MONK WEATHERBEE! I FEAR NOT THEE OR THY GOBLINS!

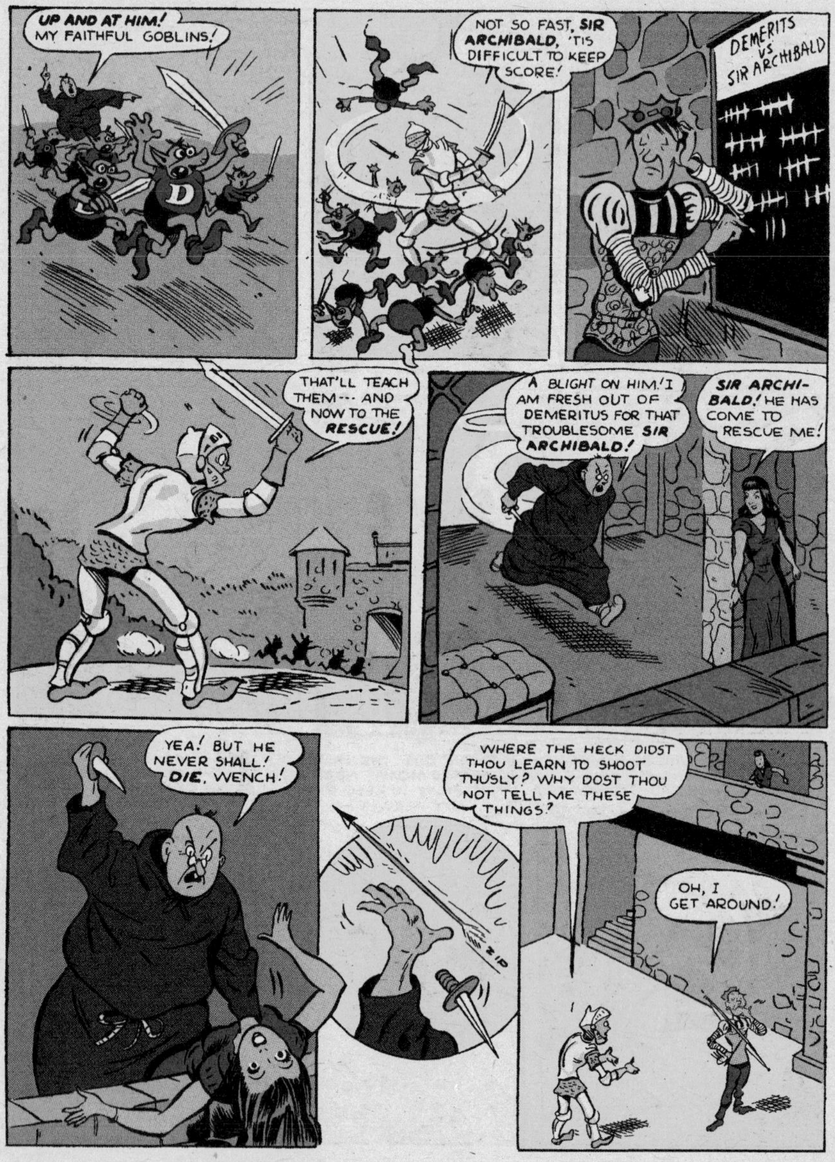
UP AND AT HIM! MY FAITHFUL GOBLINS!
D
D
NOT SO FAST, SIR ARCHIBALD, 'TIS DIFFICULT TO KEEP SCORE!
DEMERITS VS SIR ARCHIBALD
THAT'LL TEACH THEM--- AND NOW TO THE RESCUE!
A BLIGHT ON HIM! I AM FRESH OUT OF DEMERITUS FOR THAT TROUBLESOME SIR ARCHIBALD!
SIR ARCHIBALD! HE HAS COME TO RESCUE ME!
YEA! BUT HE NEVER SHALL! DIE, WENCH!
ZIP
WHERE THE HECK DIDST THOU LEARN TO SHOOT THUSLY? WHY DOST THOU NOT TELL ME THESE THINGS?
OH, I GET AROUND!

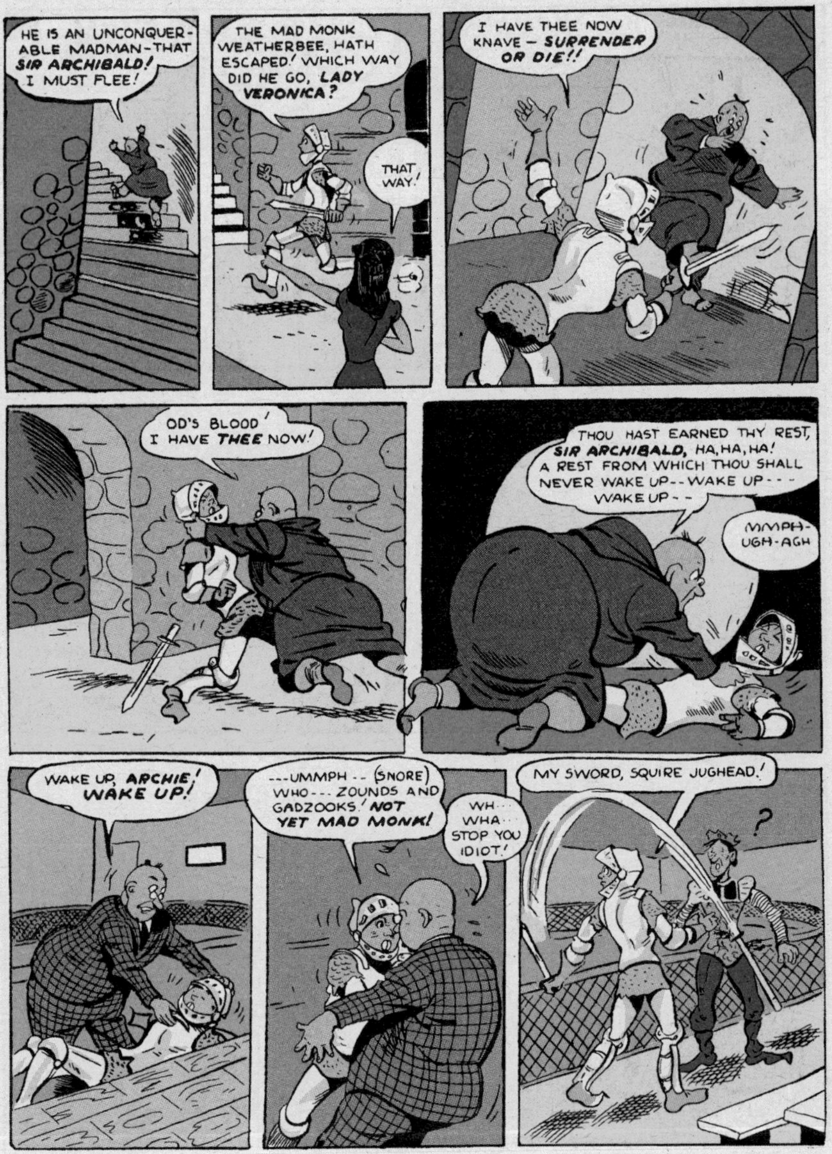
HE IS AN UNCONQUERABLE MADMAN-THAT SIR ARCHIBALD! I MUST FLEE!
THE MAD MONK WEATHERBEE, HATH ESCAPED! WHICH WAY DID HE GO, LADY VERONICA?
THAT WAY!
I HAVE THEE NOW KNAVE - SURRENDER OR DIE!!
OD'S BLOOD! I HAVE THEE NOW!
THOU HAST EARNED THY REST, SIR ARCHIBALD, HA, HA, HA! A REST FROM WHICH THOU SHALL NEVER WAKE UP-- WAKE UP--- WAKE UP--
MMPH-UGH-AGH
WAKE UP, ARCHIE! WAKE UP!
---UMMPH -- (SNORE) WHO--- ZOUNDS AND GADZOOKS! NOT YET MAD MONK!
WH.. WHA.. STOP YOU IDIOT!
MY SWORD, SQUIRE JUGHEAD!
?

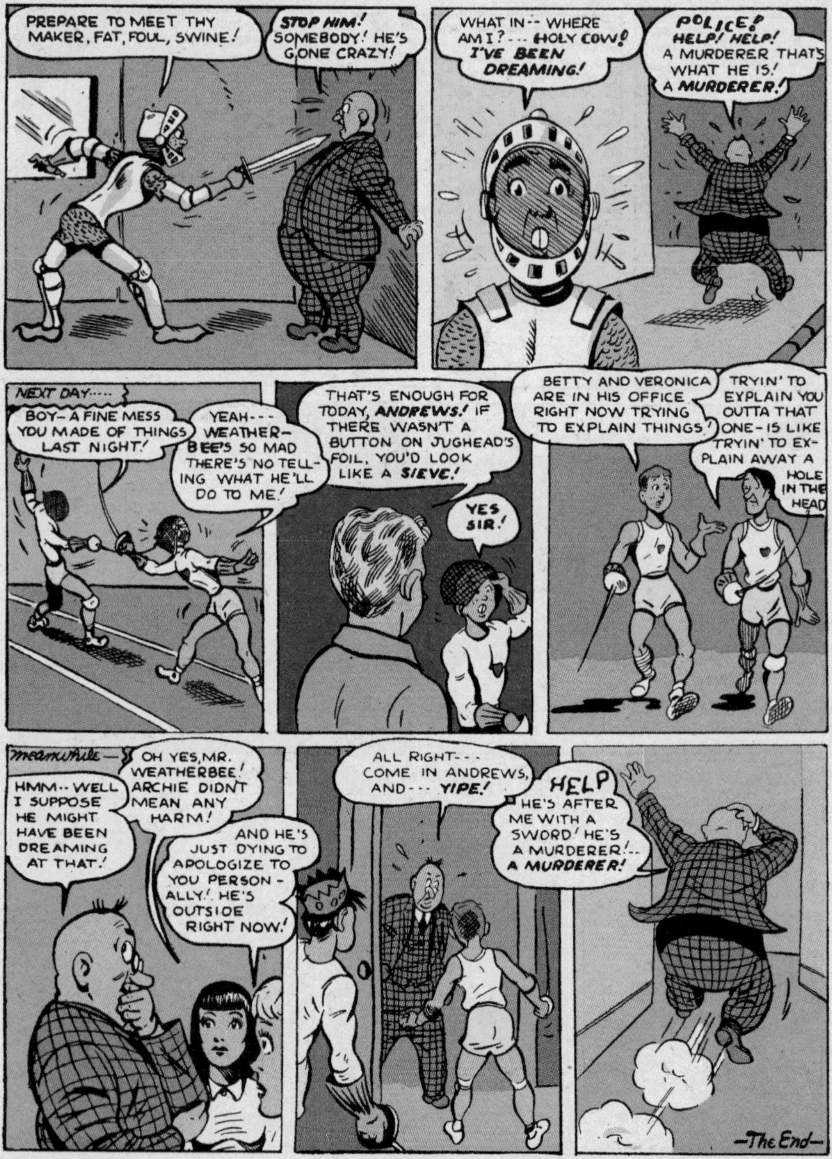
PREPARE TO MEET THY MAKER, FAT, FOUL, SWINE!
STOP HIM! SOMEBODY! HE'S GONE CRAZY!
WHAT IN -- WHERE AM I? --- HOLY COW! I'VE BEEN DREAMING!
POLICE! HELP! HELP! A MURDERER THAT'S WHAT HE IS! A MURDERER!
NEXT DAY.....
BOY- A FINE MESS YOU MADE OF THINGS LAST NIGHT!
YEAH--- WEATHERBEE'S SO MAD THERE'S NO TELLING WHAT HE'LL DO TO ME!
THAT'S ENOUGH FOR TODAY, ANDREWS! IF THERE WASN'T A BUTTON ON JUGHEAD'S FOIL, YOU'D LOOK LIKE A SIEVE!
YES SIR!
BETTY AND VERONICA ARE IN HIS OFFICE RIGHT NOW TRYING TO EXPLAIN THINGS.
TRYIN' TO EXPLAIN YOU OUTTA THAT ONE- IS LIKE TRYIN' TO EXPLAIN AWAY A HOLE IN THE HEAD
meanwhile—
OH YES, MR. WEATHERBEE! ARCHIE DIDN'T MEAN ANY HARM!
HMM-- WELL I SUPPOSE HE MIGHT HAVE BEEN DREAMING AT THAT!
AND HE'S JUST DYING TO APOLOGIZE TO YOU PERSONALLY! HE'S OUTSIDE RIGHT NOW!
ALL RIGHT--- COME IN ANDREWS, AND--- YIPE!
HELP HE'S AFTER ME WITH A SWORD! HE'S A MURDERER!-- A MURDERER!
—The End—

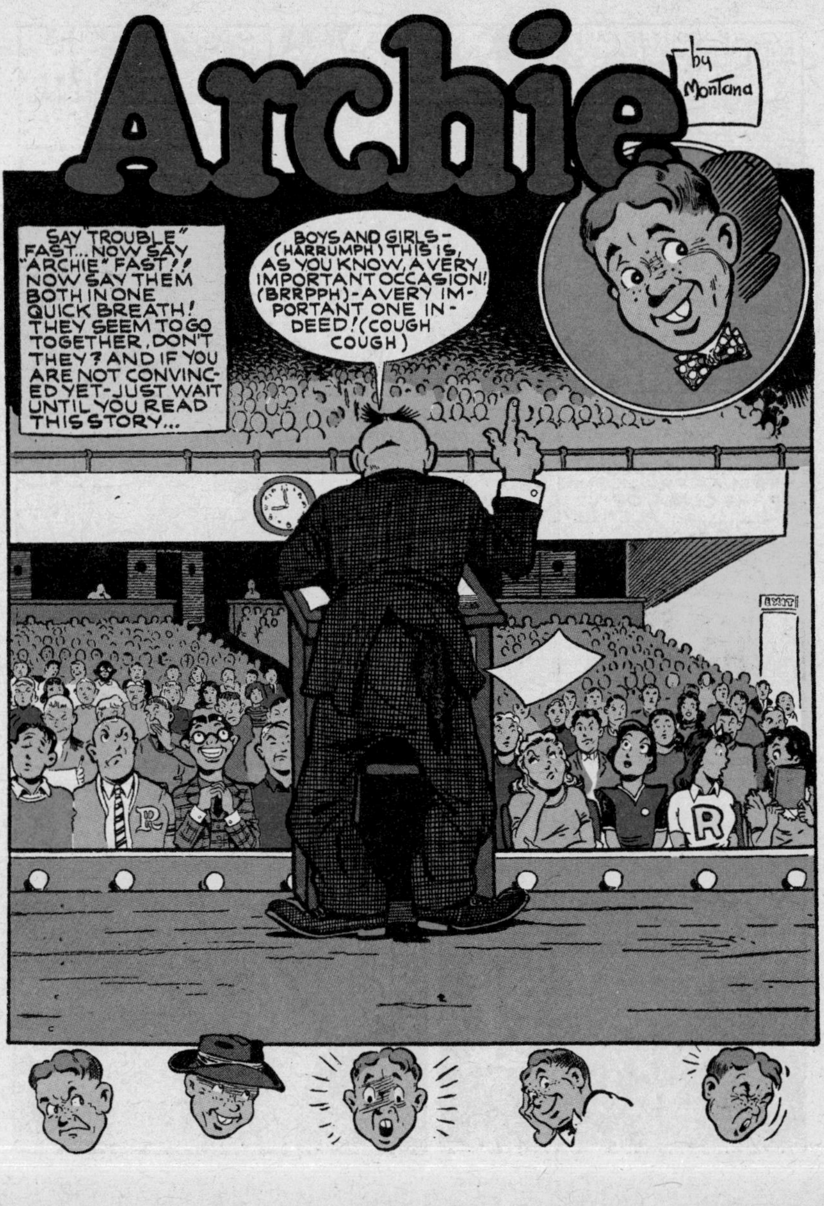
Archie
by Montana
SAY "TROUBLE" FAST... NOW SAY "ARCHIE" FAST!! NOW SAY THEM BOTH IN ONE QUICK BREATH! THEY SEEM TO GO TOGETHER, DON'T THEY? AND IF YOU ARE NOT CONVINCED YET-JUST WAIT UNTIL YOU READ THIS STORY...
BOYS AND GIRLS - (HARRUMPH) THIS IS, AS YOU KNOW, A VERY IMPORTANT OCCASION! (BRRPPH) - A VERY IMPORTANT ONE INDEED! (COUGH COUGH)
EXIT

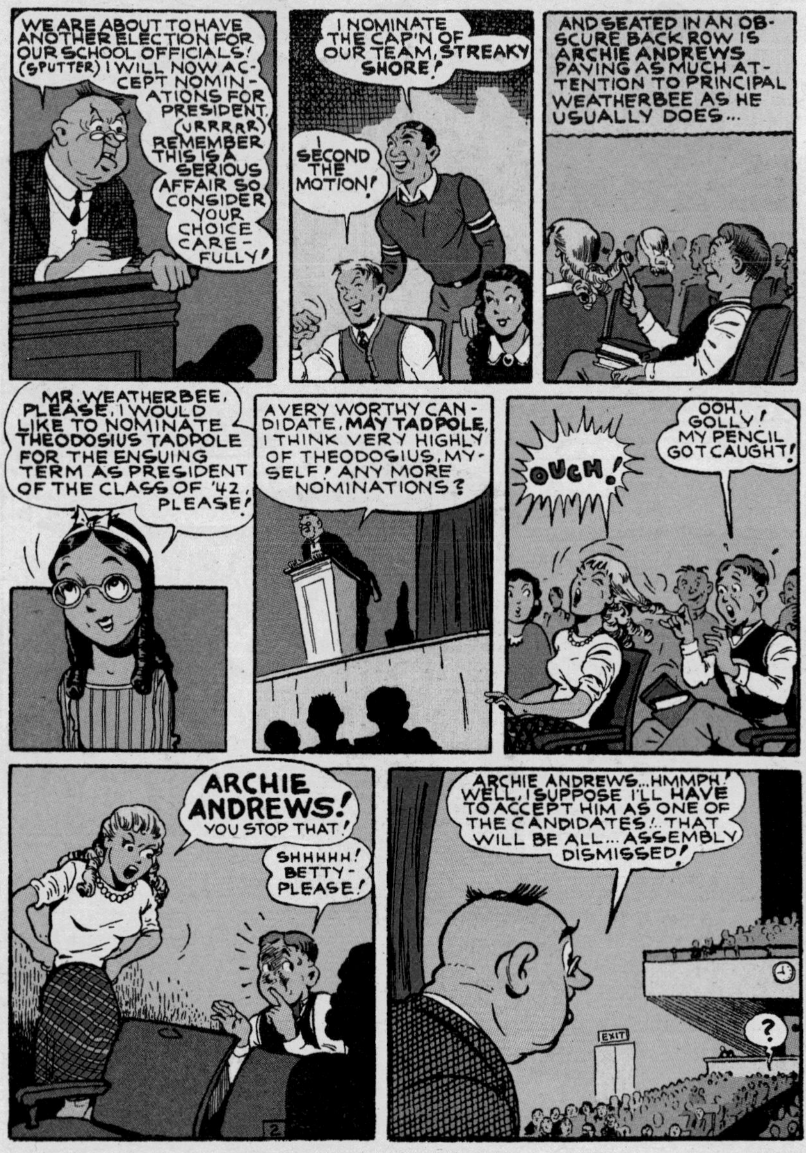
WE ARE ABOUT TO HAVE ANOTHER ELECTION FOR OUR SCHOOL OFFICIALS! (SPUTTER) I WILL NOW ACCEPT NOMINATIONS FOR PRESIDENT. (URRRRR) REMEMBER THIS IS A SERIOUS AFFAIR SO CONSIDER YOUR CHOICE CAREFULLY!
I NOMINATE THE CAP'N OF OUR TEAM, STREAKY SHORE!
I SECOND THE MOTION!
AND SEATED IN AN OBSCURE BACK ROW IS ARCHIE ANDREWS PAYING AS MUCH ATTENTION TO PRINCIPAL WEATHERBEE AS HE USUALLY DOES...
MR. WEATHERBEE, PLEASE, I WOULD LIKE TO NOMINATE THEODOSIUS TADPOLE FOR THE ENSUING TERM AS PRESIDENT OF THE CLASS OF '42, PLEASE!
A VERY WORTHY CANDIDATE, MAY TADPOLE, I THINK VERY HIGHLY OF THEODOSIUS, MYSELF! ANY MORE NOMINATIONS?
OUCH!
OOH, GOLLY! MY PENCIL GOT CAUGHT!
ARCHIE ANDREWS! YOU STOP THAT!
SHHHHH! BETTY - PLEASE!
2
ARCHIE ANDREWS... HMMPH! WELL, I SUPPOSE I'LL HAVE TO ACCEPT HIM AS ONE OF THE CANDIDATES!.. THAT WILL BE ALL... ASSEMBLY DISMISSED!
EXIT
?

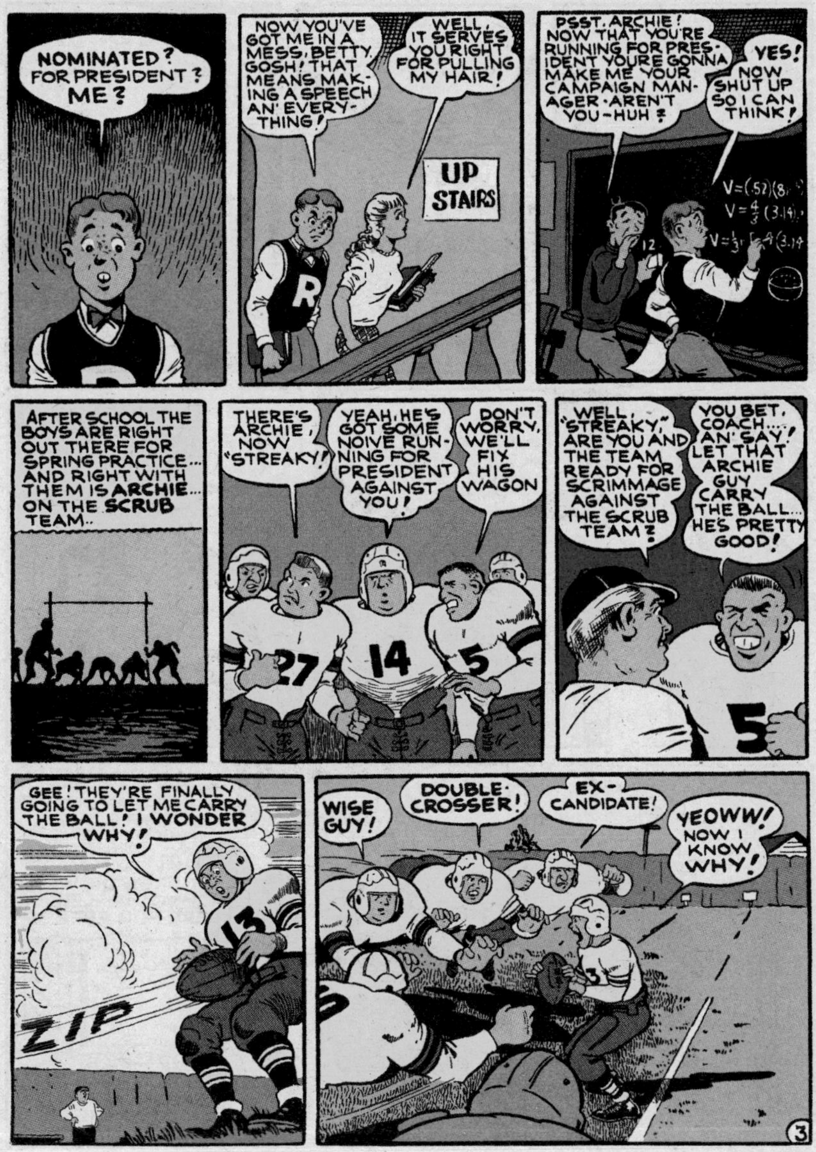
NOMINATED? FOR PRESIDENT? ME?
NOW YOU'VE GOT ME IN A MESS, BETTY. GOSH! THAT MEANS MAKING A SPEECH AN' EVERYTHING!
WELL, IT SERVES YOU RIGHT FOR PULLING MY HAIR!
UP STAIRS
PSST, ARCHIE! NOW THAT YOU'RE RUNNING FOR PRESIDENT YOU'RE GONNA MAKE ME YOUR CAMPAIGN MANAGER - AREN'T YOU - HUH?
YES! NOW SHUT UP SO I CAN THINK!
AFTER SCHOOL THE BOYS ARE RIGHT OUT THERE FOR SPRING PRACTICE... AND RIGHT WITH THEM IS ARCHIE... ON THE SCRUB TEAM..
THERE'S ARCHIE, NOW "STREAKY"!
YEAH, HE'S GOT SOME NOIVE RUNNING FOR PRESIDENT AGAINST YOU!
DON'T WORRY, WE'LL FIX HIS WAGON
WELL, "STREAKY," ARE YOU AND THE TEAM READY FOR SCRIMMAGE AGAINST THE SCRUB TEAM?
YOU BET, COACH.... AN' SAY! LET THAT ARCHIE GUY CARRY THE BALL... HE'S PRETTY GOOD!
GEE! THEY'RE FINALLY GOING TO LET ME CARRY THE BALL! I WONDER WHY!
ZIP
WISE GUY!
DOUBLE-CROSSER!
EX-CANDIDATE!
YEOWW! NOW I KNOW WHY!

AND THAT'S ONLY A SAMPLE OF WHAT YOU'LL GET IF YOU WIN THE ELECTION!

I'M CERTAINLY IN NO CONDITION TO DO MY HOMEWORK TO-NIGHT—I THINK I'LL GET THEODOSIUS AGAIN!

WELL?

HIYA, THEO! SAY, I'VE GOT A FEW MATH PROBLEMS DUE TOMORROW AND YOU'RE SO SMART—I THOUGHT..

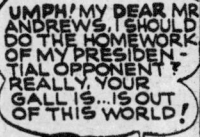

UMPH! MY DEAR MR. ANDREWS, I SHOULD DO THE HOMEWORK OF MY PRESIDENTIAL OPPONENT? REALLY, YOUR GALL IS...IS OUT OF THIS WORLD!

BOY, I'M GETTING IT FROM ALL SIDES! I'VE GOT TO MAKE SURE I DON'T GET ELECTED OR I'LL FLUNK MATH AND GET MY FACE PUSHED IN!

OH, VERONICA, HAVE YOU SEEN JUGHEAD?

HE'S IN THE GYM... SAY, I HOPE YOU WIN THE ELECTION, ARCHIE!

DON'T SAY THAT, VERONICA!

WELL, WHAT DO YOU THINK YOU'RE DOING?.....DOUBLING FOR THE HANGMAN?

THIS JUNIOR IS JUST A BETTER ACE ARCHIE

WHAT DO YOU THINK I'M DOING? I'M PUTTING AN AD UP FOR YOU WISE-GUY!

WELL, YOU CAN TAKE IT DOWN... RIGHT NOW!

WHADDAYA MEAN! I SPENT ALL NIGHT FIXING THAT DUMMY AND THAT'S THE THANKS I GET. GEE, THINK OF THE PUBLICITY...IN TWO MINUTES THE WHOLE SCHOOL WILL BE IN HERE FOR RECESS!

4

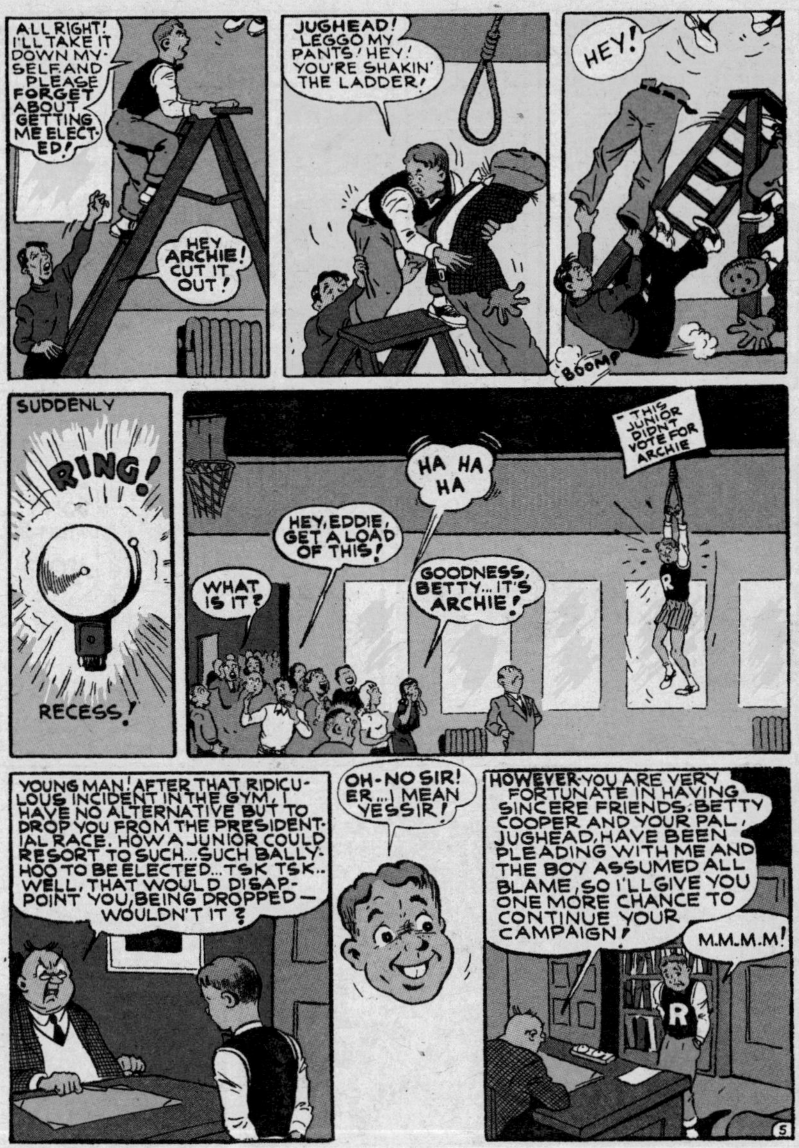

ALL RIGHT! I'LL TAKE IT DOWN MYSELF AND PLEASE FORGET ABOUT GETTING ME ELECTED!
HEY ARCHIE! CUT IT OUT!
JUGHEAD! LEGGO MY PANTS! HEY! YOU'RE SHAKIN' THE LADDER!
HEY!
BOOMP
SUDDENLY
RING!
RECESS!
THIS JUNIOR DIDN'T VOTE FOR ARCHIE
HA HA HA
WHAT IS IT?
HEY, EDDIE, GET A LOAD OF THIS!
GOODNESS, BETTY... IT'S ARCHIE!
YOUNG MAN! AFTER THAT RIDICULOUS INCIDENT IN THE GYM, I HAVE NO ALTERNATIVE BUT TO DROP YOU FROM THE PRESIDENTIAL RACE. HOW A JUNIOR COULD RESORT TO SUCH... SUCH BALLYHOO TO BE ELECTED... TSK TSK.. WELL, THAT WOULD DISAPPOINT YOU, BEING DROPPED — WOULDN'T IT?
OH-NO SIR! ER... I MEAN YESSIR!
HOWEVER-YOU ARE VERY FORTUNATE IN HAVING SINCERE FRIENDS. BETTY COOPER AND YOUR PAL, JUGHEAD, HAVE BEEN PLEADING WITH ME AND THE BOY ASSUMED ALL BLAME, SO I'LL GIVE YOU ONE MORE CHANCE TO CONTINUE YOUR CAMPAIGN!
M.M.M.M!
5

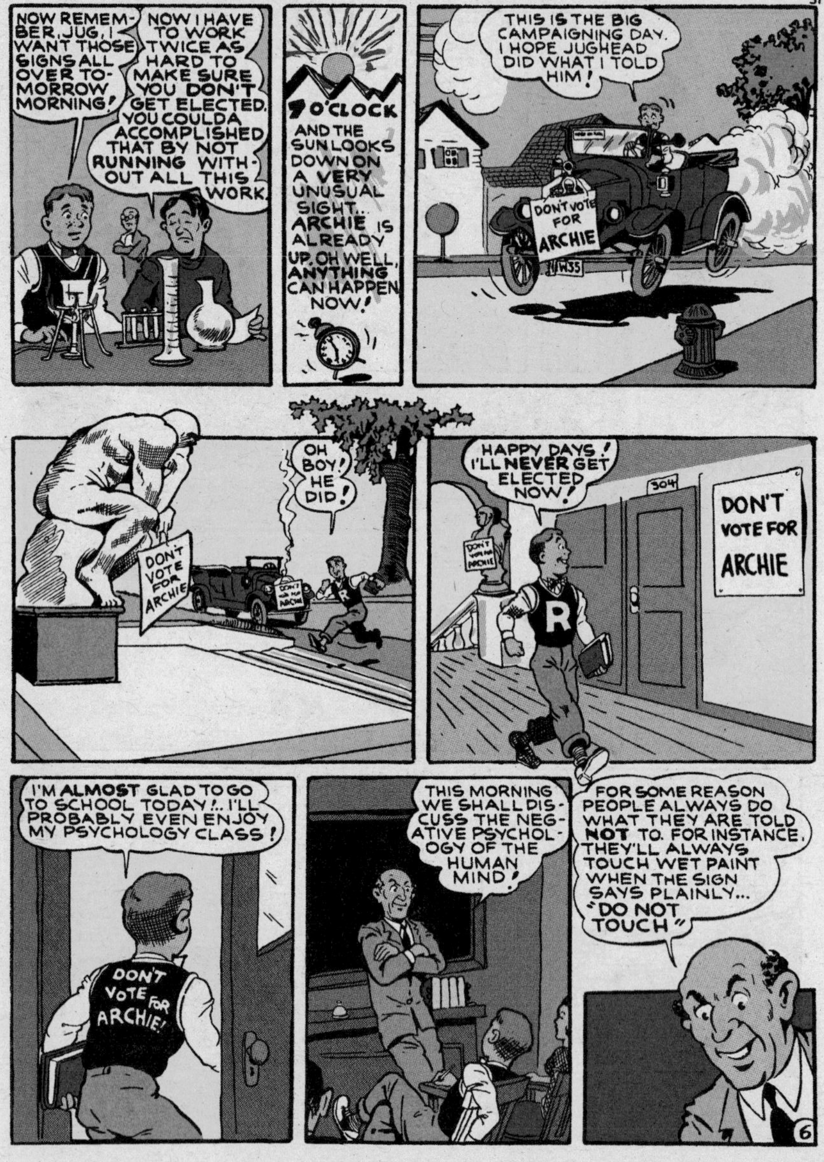
NOW REMEMBER, JUG, I WANT THOSE SIGNS ALL OVER TOMORROW MORNING!
NOW I HAVE TO WORK TWICE AS HARD TO MAKE SURE YOU DON'T GET ELECTED. YOU COULDA ACCOMPLISHED THAT BY NOT RUNNING WITHOUT ALL THIS WORK.
7 O'CLOCK
AND THE SUN LOOKS DOWN ON A VERY UNUSUAL SIGHT.. ARCHIE IS ALREADY UP. OH WELL, ANYTHING CAN HAPPEN NOW!
THIS IS THE BIG CAMPAIGNING DAY. I HOPE JUGHEAD DID WHAT I TOLD HIM!
DON'T VOTE FOR ARCHIE
OH BOY! HE DID!
DON'T VOTE FOR ARCHIE
HAPPY DAYS! I'LL NEVER GET ELECTED NOW!
304
DON'T VOTE FOR ARCHIE
I'M ALMOST GLAD TO GO TO SCHOOL TODAY!.. I'LL PROBABLY EVEN ENJOY MY PSYCHOLOGY CLASS!
DON'T VOTE FOR ARCHIE!
THIS MORNING WE SHALL DISCUSS THE NEGATIVE PSYCHOLOGY OF THE HUMAN MIND!
FOR SOME REASON PEOPLE ALWAYS DO WHAT THEY ARE TOLD NOT TO. FOR INSTANCE, THEY'LL ALWAYS TOUCH WET PAINT WHEN THE SIGN SAYS PLAINLY... "DO NOT TOUCH"
6

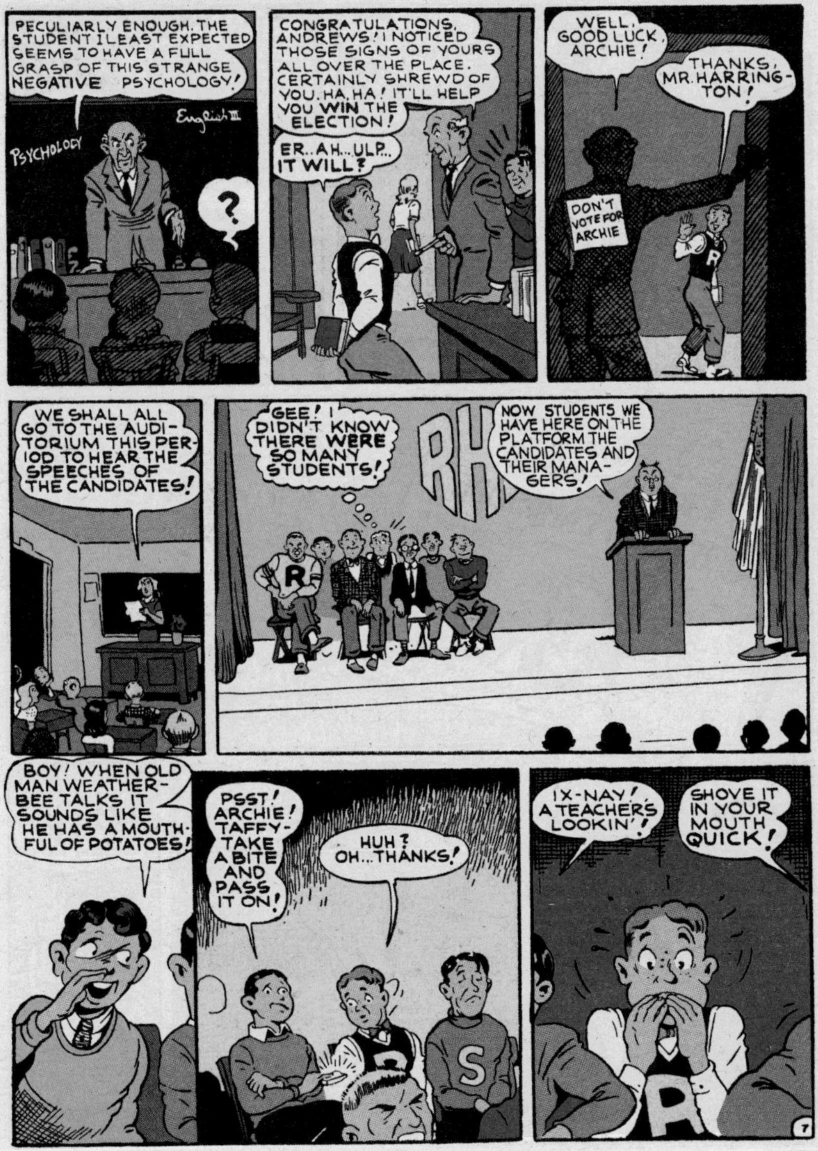
PECULIARLY ENOUGH, THE STUDENT I LEAST EXPECTED SEEMS TO HAVE A FULL GRASP OF THIS STRANGE NEGATIVE PSYCHOLOGY!
English III
PSYCHOLOGY
?
CONGRATULATIONS, ANDREWS! I NOTICED THOSE SIGNS OF YOURS ALL OVER THE PLACE. CERTAINLY SHREWD OF YOU. HA, HA! IT'LL HELP YOU WIN THE ELECTION!
ER..AH...ULP... IT WILL?
WELL, GOOD LUCK, ARCHIE!
THANKS, MR. HARRINGTON!
DON'T VOTE FOR ARCHIE
WE SHALL ALL GO TO THE AUDITORIUM THIS PERIOD TO HEAR THE SPEECHES OF THE CANDIDATES!
GEE! I DIDN'T KNOW THERE WERE SO MANY STUDENTS!
NOW STUDENTS WE HAVE HERE ON THE PLATFORM THE CANDIDATES AND THEIR MANAGERS!
BOY! WHEN OLD MAN WEATHERBEE TALKS IT SOUNDS LIKE HE HAS A MOUTHFUL OF POTATOES!
PSST! ARCHIE! TAFFY-TAKE A BITE AND PASS IT ON!
HUH? OH...THANKS!
IX-NAY! A TEACHER'S LOOKIN'!
SHOVE IT IN YOUR MOUTH QUICK!
7

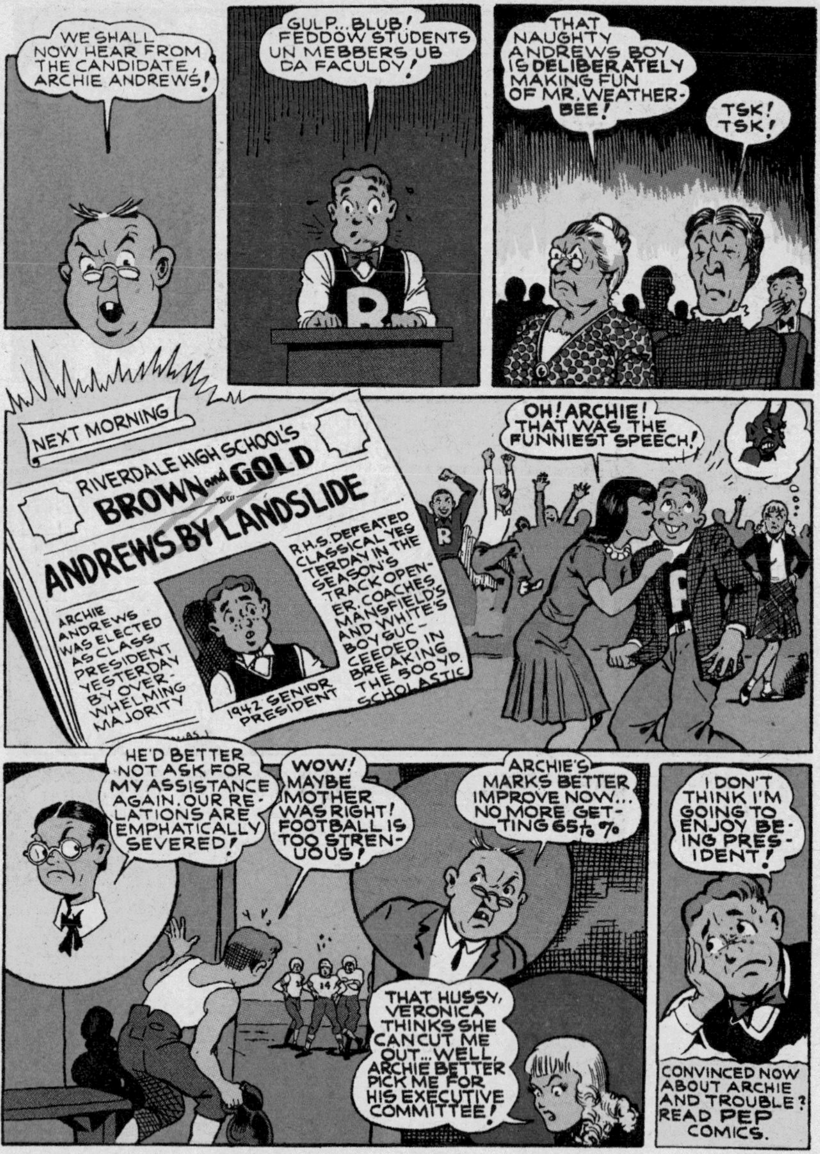
WE SHALL NOW HEAR FROM THE CANDIDATE, ARCHIE ANDREWS!
GULP... BLUB! FEDDOW STUDENTS UN MEBBERS UB DA FACULDY!
THAT NAUGHTY ANDREWS BOY IS DELIBERATELY MAKING FUN OF MR. WEATHER-BEE!
TSK! TSK!
NEXT MORNING
RIVERDALE HIGH SCHOOL'S
BROWN and GOLD
ANDREWS BY LANDSLIDE
ARCHIE ANDREWS WAS ELECTED AS CLASS PRESIDENT YESTERDAY BY OVER-WHELMING MAJORITY
1942 SENIOR PRESIDENT
R.H.S. DEFEATED CLASSICAL YES TERDAY IN THE SEASON'S TRACK OPEN-ER. COACHES MANSFIELD'S AND WHITE'S BOY SUC-CEEDED IN BREAKING THE 500 YD. SCHOLASTIC
OH! ARCHIE! THAT WAS THE FUNNIEST SPEECH!
HE'D BETTER NOT ASK FOR MY ASSISTANCE AGAIN. OUR RE-LATIONS ARE EMPHATICALLY SEVERED!
WOW! MAYBE MOTHER WAS RIGHT! FOOTBALL IS TOO STREN-UOUS!
ARCHIE'S MARKS BETTER IMPROVE NOW... NO MORE GET-TING 65 1/10 %
THAT HUSSY, VERONICA THINKS SHE CAN CUT ME OUT... WELL, ARCHIE BETTER PICK ME FOR HIS EXECUTIVE COMMITTEE!
I DON'T THINK I'M GOING TO ENJOY BE-ING PRES-IDENT!
CONVINCED NOW ABOUT ARCHIE AND TROUBLE? READ PEP COMICS.

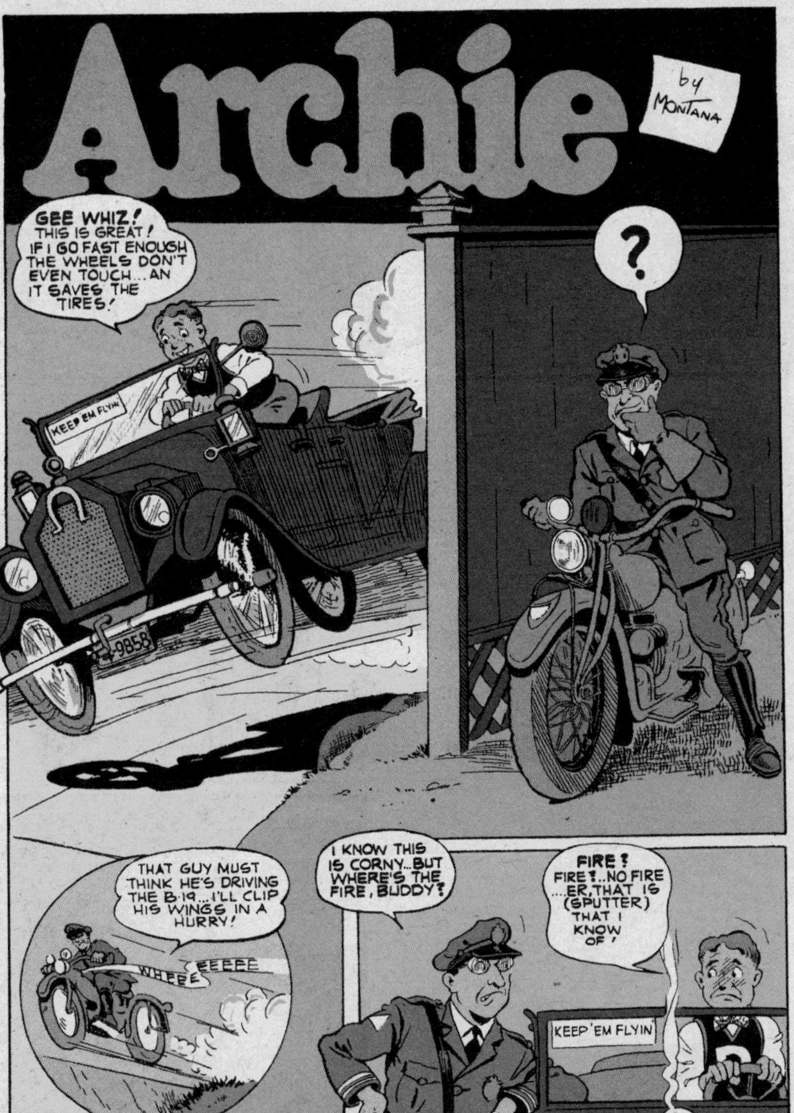
Archie
by MONTANA
GEE WHIZ! THIS IS GREAT! IF I GO FAST ENOUGH THE WHEELS DON'T EVEN TOUCH... AN IT SAVES THE TIRES!
KEEP 'EM FLYIN
?
THAT GUY MUST THINK HE'S DRIVING THE B-19... I'LL CLIP HIS WINGS IN A HURRY!
WHEEEEEEEE
I KNOW THIS IS CORNY... BUT WHERE'S THE FIRE, BUDDY?
FIRE? FIRE?.. NO FIRE ....ER, THAT IS (SPUTTER) THAT I KNOW OF!
KEEP 'EM FLYIN'

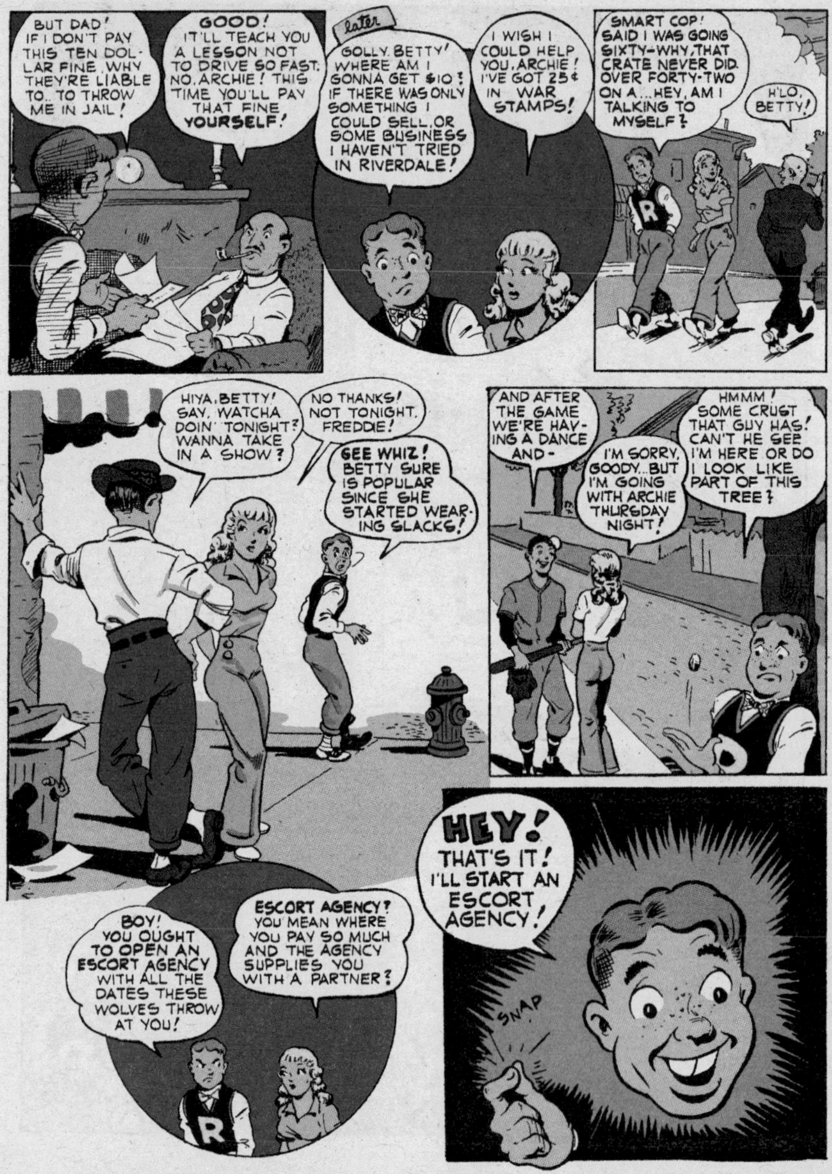
BUT DAD! IF I DON'T PAY THIS TEN DOLLAR FINE, WHY THEY'RE LIABLE TO.. TO THROW ME IN JAIL!
GOOD! IT'LL TEACH YOU A LESSON NOT TO DRIVE SO FAST. NO, ARCHIE! THIS TIME YOU'LL PAY THAT FINE YOURSELF!
later
GOLLY, BETTY! WHERE AM I GONNA GET $10? IF THERE WAS ONLY SOMETHING I COULD SELL, OR SOME BUSINESS I HAVEN'T TRIED IN RIVERDALE!
I WISH I COULD HELP YOU, ARCHIE! I'VE GOT 25¢ IN WAR STAMPS!
SMART COP! SAID I WAS GOING SIXTY-WHY, THAT CRATE NEVER DID OVER FORTY-TWO ON A...HEY, AM I TALKING TO MYSELF?
H'LO, BETTY!
HIYA, BETTY! SAY, WATCHA DOIN' TONIGHT? WANNA TAKE IN A SHOW?
NO THANKS! NOT TONIGHT, FREDDIE!
GEE WHIZ! BETTY SURE IS POPULAR SINCE SHE STARTED WEARING SLACKS!
AND AFTER THE GAME WE'RE HAVING A DANCE AND-
I'M SORRY, GOODY...BUT I'M GOING WITH ARCHIE THURSDAY NIGHT!
HMMM! SOME CRUST THAT GUY HAS! CAN'T HE SEE I'M HERE OR DO I LOOK LIKE PART OF THIS TREE?
BOY! YOU OUGHT TO OPEN AN ESCORT AGENCY WITH ALL THE DATES THESE WOLVES THROW AT YOU!
ESCORT AGENCY? YOU MEAN WHERE YOU PAY SO MUCH AND THE AGENCY SUPPLIES YOU WITH A PARTNER?
HEY! THAT'S IT! I'LL START AN ESCORT AGENCY!
SNAP

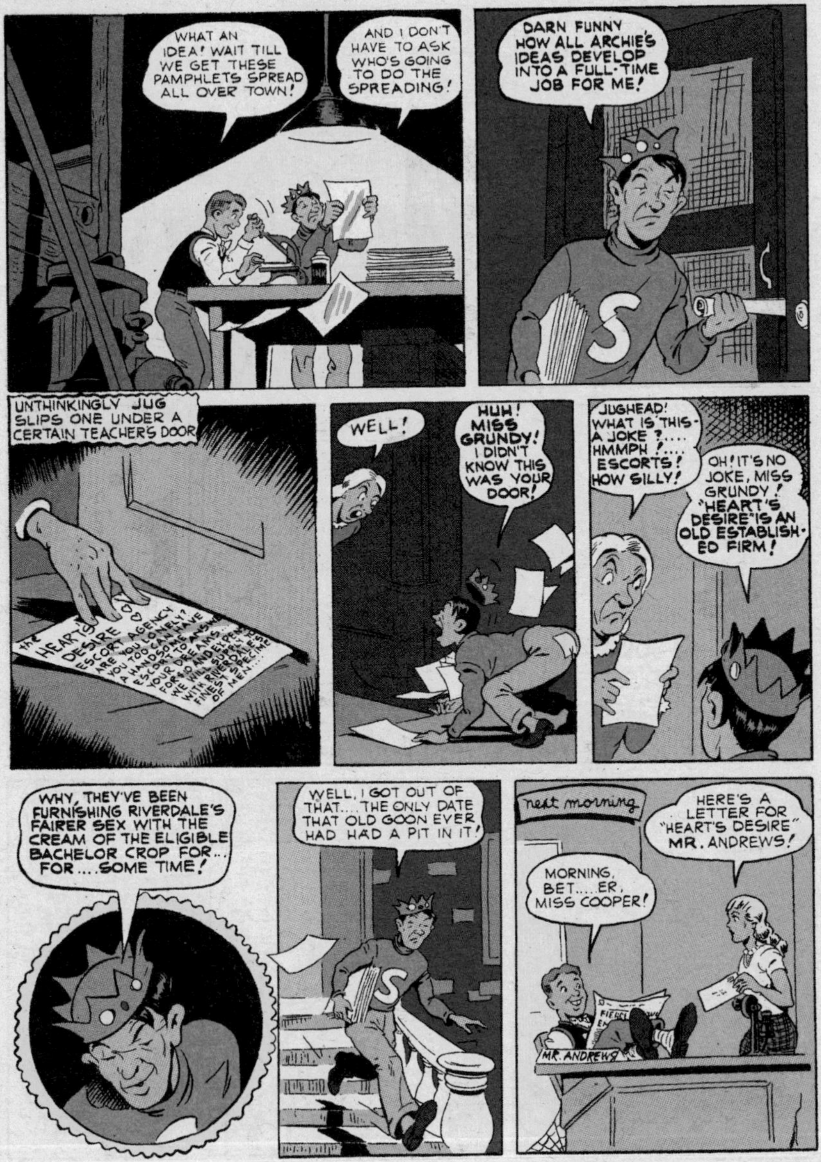
WHAT AN IDEA! WAIT TILL WE GET THESE PAMPHLETS SPREAD ALL OVER TOWN!
AND I DON'T HAVE TO ASK WHO'S GOING TO DO THE SPREADING!
INK
DARN FUNNY HOW ALL ARCHIE'S IDEAS DEVELOP INTO A FULL-TIME JOB FOR ME!
UNTHINKINGLY JUG SLIPS ONE UNDER A CERTAIN TEACHER'S DOOR
the HEART'S DESIRE ESCORT AGENCY ARE YOU LONELY? YOU TOO CAN HAVE A HANDSOME ESCORT TO ANSWER YOUR DREAMS... FOR $10 AND EXPENSES WE WILL SUPPLY YOU WITH RIVERDALE'S FINEST SPECIMENS OF MEN...
WELL!
HUH! MISS GRUNDY! I DIDN'T KNOW THIS WAS YOUR DOOR!
JUGHEAD! WHAT IS THIS - A JOKE ?.... HMMPH !.... ESCORTS! HOW SILLY!
OH! IT'S NO JOKE, MISS GRUNDY! "HEART'S DESIRE" IS AN OLD ESTABLISHED FIRM!
WHY, THEY'VE BEEN FURNISHING RIVERDALE'S FAIRER SEX WITH THE CREAM OF THE ELIGIBLE BACHELOR CROP FOR... FOR.... SOME TIME!
WELL, I GOT OUT OF THAT.... THE ONLY DATE THAT OLD GOON EVER HAD HAD A PIT IN IT!
next morning
MORNING, BET.....ER, MISS COOPER!
HERE'S A LETTER FOR "HEART'S DESIRE" MR. ANDREWS!
MR. ANDREWS

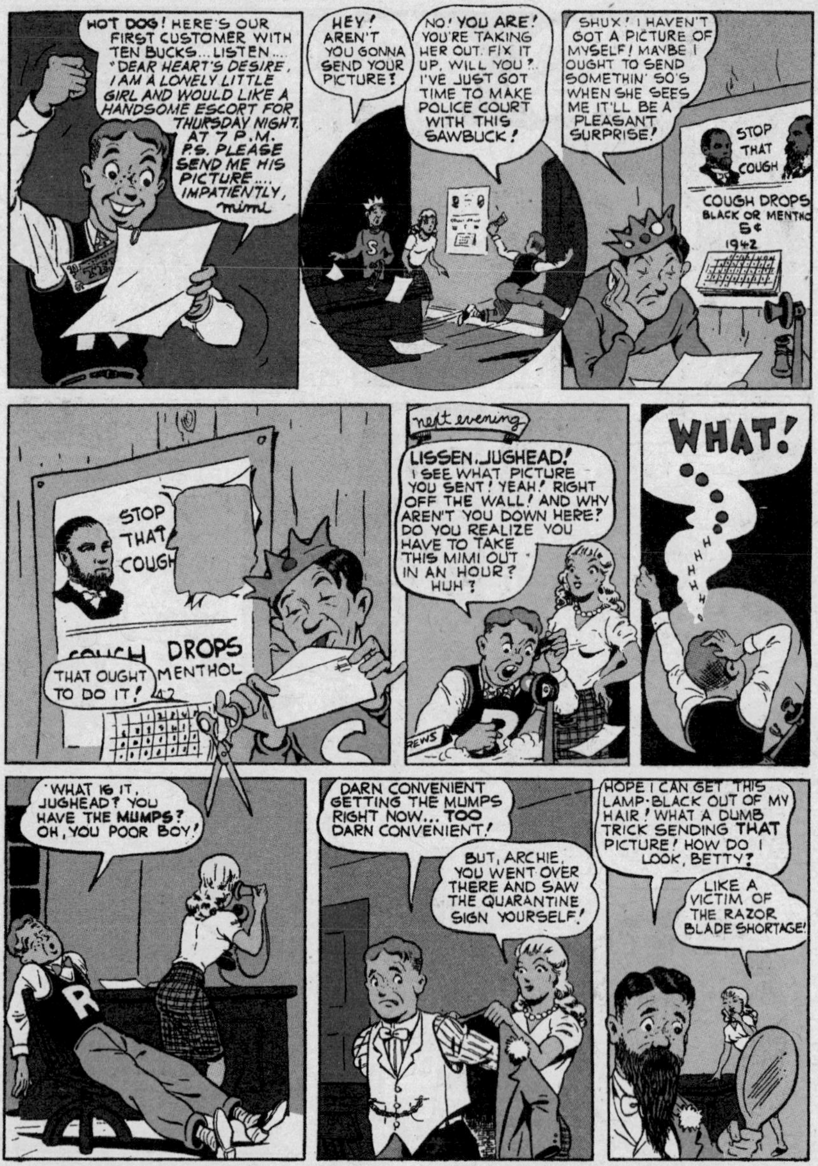
HOT DOG! HERE'S OUR FIRST CUSTOMER WITH TEN BUCKS... LISTEN.... "DEAR HEART'S DESIRE, I AM A LONELY LITTLE GIRL AND WOULD LIKE A HANDSOME ESCORT FOR THURSDAY NIGHT AT 7 P.M. P.S. PLEASE SEND ME HIS PICTURE.... IMPATIENTLY, mimi
HEY! AREN'T YOU GONNA SEND YOUR PICTURE?
NO! YOU ARE! YOU'RE TAKING HER OUT. FIX IT UP, WILL YOU? I'VE JUST GOT TIME TO MAKE POLICE COURT WITH THIS SAWBUCK!
SHUX! I HAVEN'T GOT A PICTURE OF MYSELF! MAYBE I OUGHT TO SEND SOMETHIN' SO'S WHEN SHE SEES ME IT'LL BE A PLEASANT SURPRISE!
STOP THAT COUGH
COUGH DROPS BLACK OR MENTHO 5¢
1942
STOP THAT COUGH
DROPS MENTHOL
THAT OUGHT TO DO IT!
next evening
LISSEN, JUGHEAD! I SEE WHAT PICTURE YOU SENT! YEAH! RIGHT OFF THE WALL! AND WHY AREN'T YOU DOWN HERE? DO YOU REALIZE YOU HAVE TO TAKE THIS MIMI OUT IN AN HOUR? HUH?
WHAT!
HHHHH
WHAT IS IT, JUGHEAD? YOU HAVE THE MUMPS? OH, YOU POOR BOY!
DARN CONVENIENT GETTING THE MUMPS RIGHT NOW... TOO DARN CONVENIENT!
BUT, ARCHIE, YOU WENT OVER THERE AND SAW THE QUARANTINE SIGN YOURSELF!
HOPE I CAN GET THIS LAMP-BLACK OUT OF MY HAIR! WHAT A DUMB TRICK SENDING THAT PICTURE! HOW DO I LOOK, BETTY?
LIKE A VICTIM OF THE RAZOR BLADE SHORTAGE!

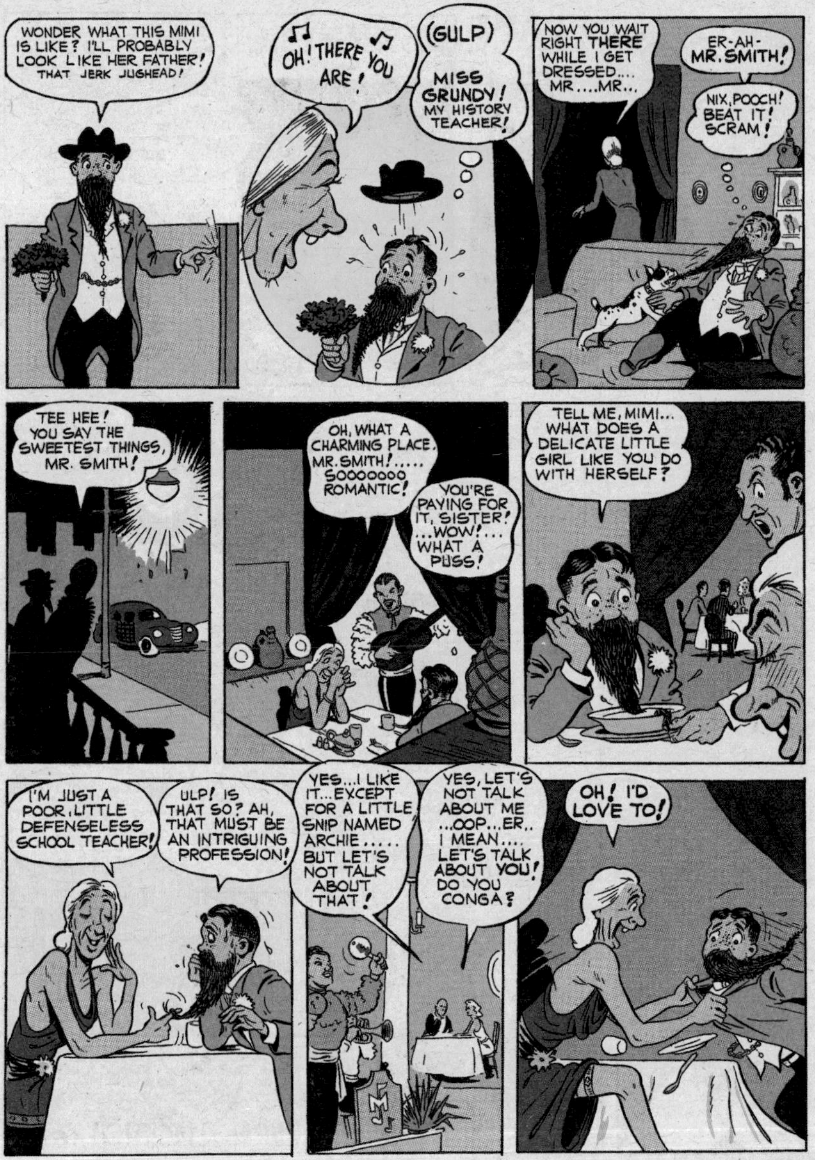
WONDER WHAT THIS MIMI IS LIKE? I'LL PROBABLY LOOK LIKE HER FATHER! THAT JERK JUGHEAD!
OH! THERE YOU ARE!
(GULP)
MISS GRUNDY! MY HISTORY TEACHER!
NOW YOU WAIT RIGHT THERE WHILE I GET DRESSED.... MR....MR...
ER-AH- MR. SMITH!
NIX, POOCH! BEAT IT! SCRAM!
TEE HEE! YOU SAY THE SWEETEST THINGS, MR. SMITH!
OH, WHAT A CHARMING PLACE, MR. SMITH!..... SOOOOOOO ROMANTIC!
YOU'RE PAYING FOR IT, SISTER! ...WOW!... WHAT A PUSS!
TELL ME, MIMI... WHAT DOES A DELICATE LITTLE GIRL LIKE YOU DO WITH HERSELF?
I'M JUST A POOR, LITTLE DEFENSELESS SCHOOL TEACHER!
ULP! IS THAT SO? AH, THAT MUST BE AN INTRIGUING PROFESSION!
YES...I LIKE IT...EXCEPT FOR A LITTLE SNIP NAMED ARCHIE..... BUT LET'S NOT TALK ABOUT THAT!
YES, LET'S NOT TALK ABOUT ME ...OOP...ER.. I MEAN.... LET'S TALK ABOUT YOU! DO YOU CONGA?
OH! I'D LOVE TO!

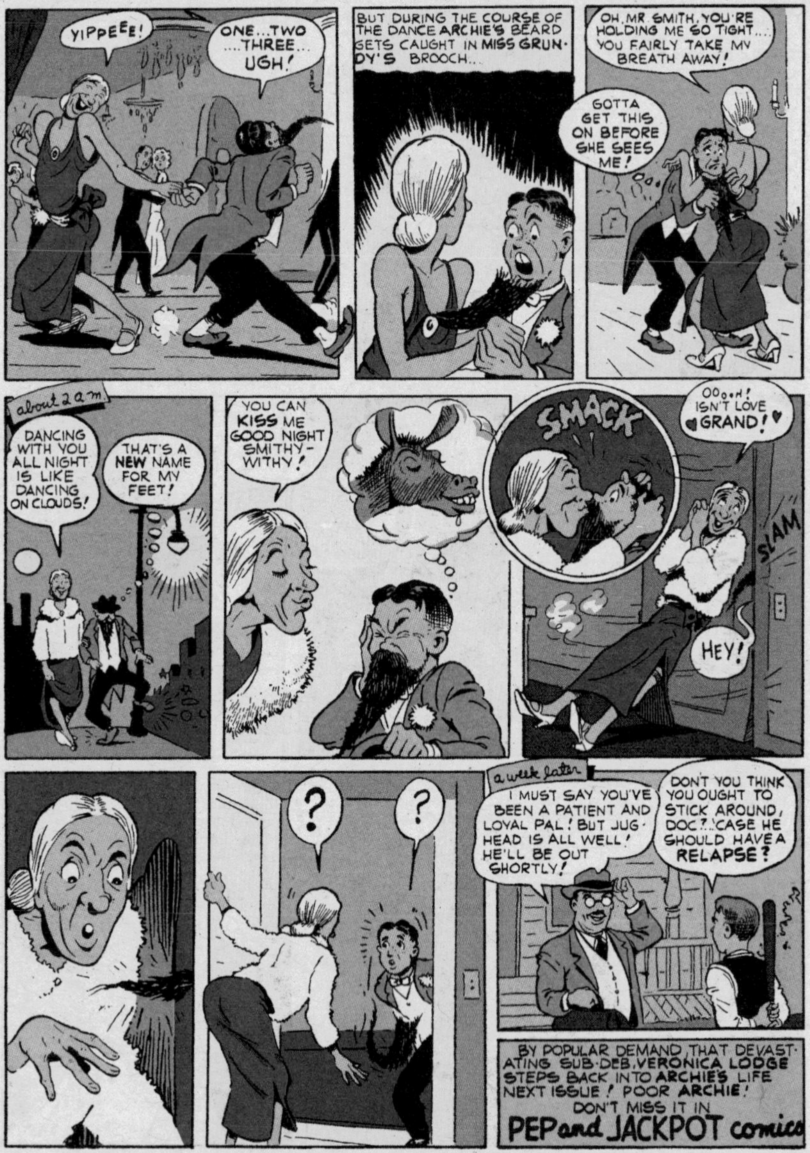
YIPPEEE!
ONE...TWO ....THREE... UGH!
BUT DURING THE COURSE OF THE DANCE ARCHIE'S BEARD GETS CAUGHT IN MISS GRUNDY'S BROOCH..
OH, MR. SMITH, YOU'RE HOLDING ME SO TIGHT... YOU FAIRLY TAKE MY BREATH AWAY!
GOTTA GET THIS ON BEFORE SHE SEES ME!
about 2 a.m.
DANCING WITH YOU ALL NIGHT IS LIKE DANCING ON CLOUDS!
THAT'S A NEW NAME FOR MY FEET!
YOU CAN KISS ME GOOD NIGHT SMITHY-WITHY!
SMACK
OOooH! ISN'T LOVE GRAND!
SLAM
HEY!
?
?
a week later
I MUST SAY YOU'VE BEEN A PATIENT AND LOYAL PAL! BUT JUGHEAD IS ALL WELL! HE'LL BE OUT SHORTLY!
DON'T YOU THINK YOU OUGHT TO STICK AROUND, DOC?...CASE HE SHOULD HAVE A RELAPSE?
BY POPULAR DEMAND, THAT DEVASTATING SUB-DEB, VERONICA LODGE STEPS BACK INTO ARCHIE'S LIFE NEXT ISSUE! POOR ARCHIE! DON'T MISS IT IN
PEP and JACKPOT comics

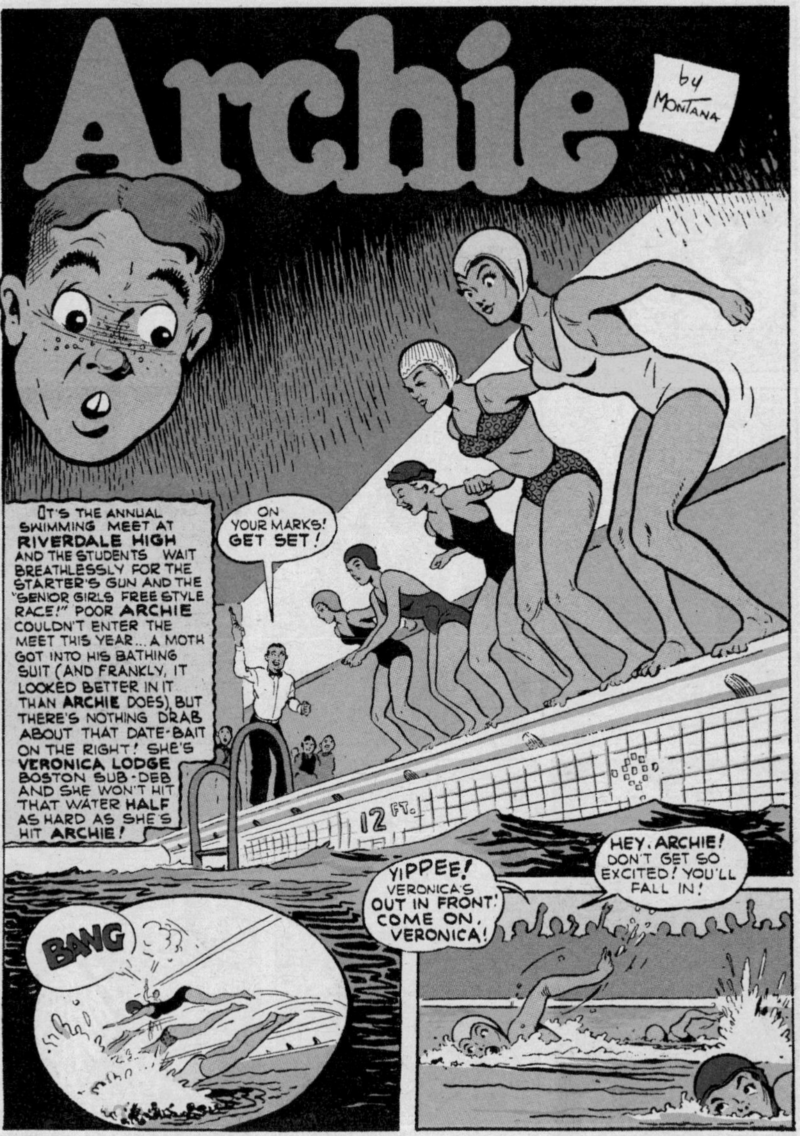
Archie
by MONTANA
IT'S THE ANNUAL SWIMMING MEET AT RIVERDALE HIGH AND THE STUDENTS WAIT BREATHLESSLY FOR THE STARTER'S GUN AND THE "SENIOR GIRLS FREE STYLE RACE!" POOR ARCHIE COULDN'T ENTER THE MEET THIS YEAR... A MOTH GOT INTO HIS BATHING SUIT (AND FRANKLY, IT LOOKED BETTER IN IT THAN ARCHIE DOES), BUT THERE'S NOTHING DRAB ABOUT THAT DATE-BAIT ON THE RIGHT! SHE'S VERONICA LODGE BOSTON SUB-DEB AND SHE WON'T HIT THAT WATER HALF AS HARD AS SHE'S HIT ARCHIE!
ON YOUR MARKS! GET SET!
12 FT.
BANG
YIPPEE! VERONICA'S OUT IN FRONT! COME ON, VERONICA!
HEY, ARCHIE! DON'T GET SO EXCITED! YOU'LL FALL IN!

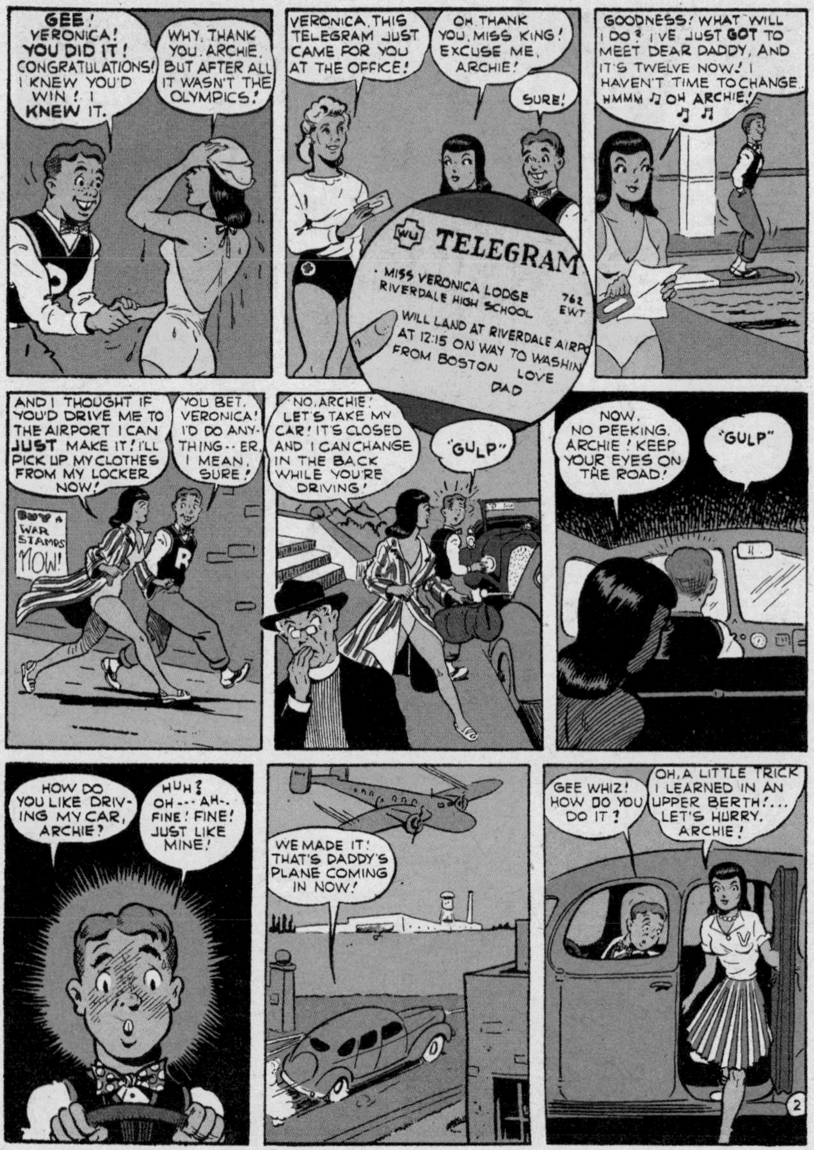
GEE! VERONICA! YOU DID IT! CONGRATULATIONS! I KNEW YOU'D WIN! I KNEW IT.
WHY, THANK YOU, ARCHIE. BUT AFTER ALL IT WASN'T THE OLYMPICS!
VERONICA, THIS TELEGRAM JUST CAME FOR YOU AT THE OFFICE!
OH, THANK YOU, MISS KING! EXCUSE ME, ARCHIE!
SURE!
WU TELEGRAM
MISS VERONICA LODGE RIVERDALE HIGH SCHOOL 762 EWT
WILL LAND AT RIVERDALE AIRP AT 12:15 ON WAY TO WASHIN FROM BOSTON LOVE DAD
GOODNESS! WHAT WILL I DO? I'VE JUST GOT TO MEET DEAR DADDY, AND IT'S TWELVE NOW! I HAVEN'T TIME TO CHANGE. HMMM ♫ OH ARCHIE! ♫ ♫
AND I THOUGHT IF YOU'D DRIVE ME TO THE AIRPORT I CAN JUST MAKE IT! I'LL PICK UP MY CLOTHES FROM MY LOCKER NOW!
YOU BET, VERONICA! I'D DO ANYTHING -- ER, I MEAN, SURE!
BUY A WAR STAMPS NOW!
NO, ARCHIE! LET'S TAKE MY CAR! IT'S CLOSED AND I CAN CHANGE IN THE BACK WHILE YOU'RE DRIVING!
"GULP"
NOW, NO PEEKING, ARCHIE! KEEP YOUR EYES ON THE ROAD!
"GULP"
HOW DO YOU LIKE DRIVING MY CAR, ARCHIE?
HUH? OH --- AH--. FINE! FINE! JUST LIKE MINE!
WE MADE IT! THAT'S DADDY'S PLANE COMING IN NOW!
GEE WHIZ! HOW DO YOU DO IT?
OH, A LITTLE TRICK I LEARNED IN AN UPPER BERTH!... LET'S HURRY, ARCHIE!
2

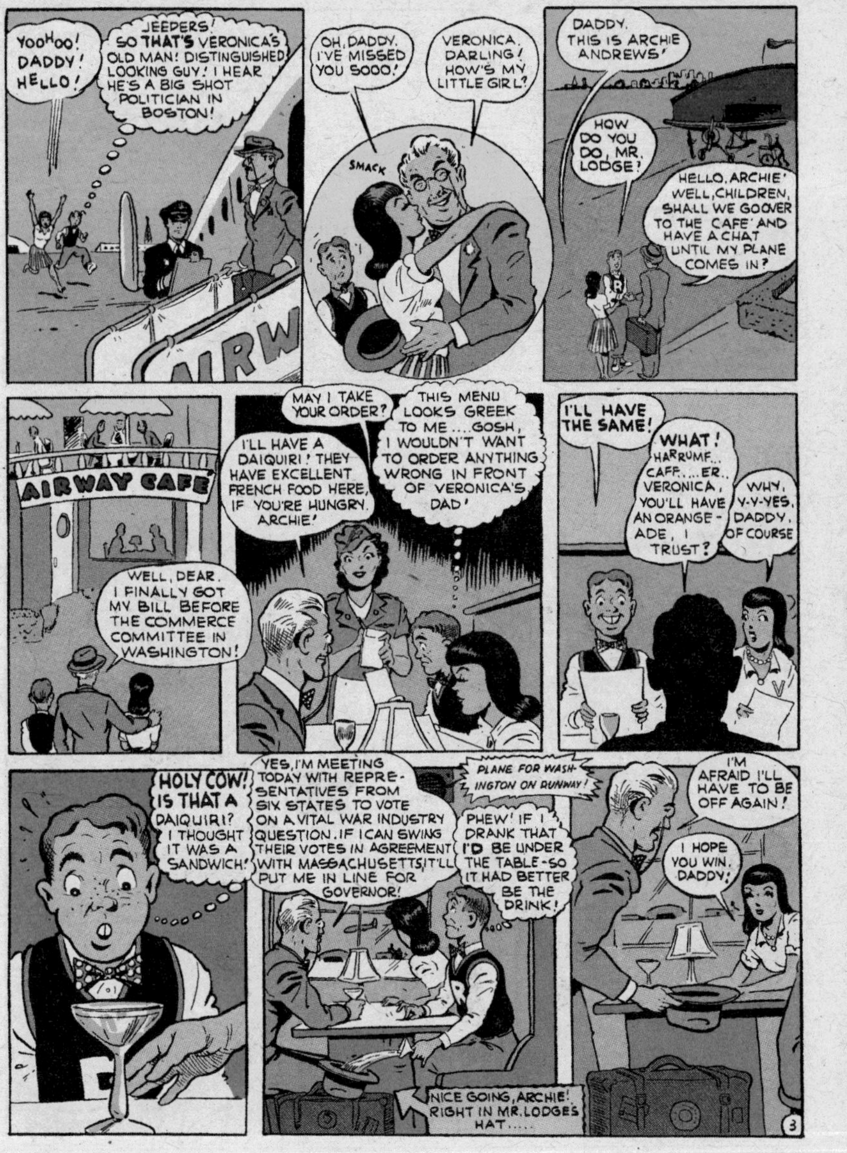
YOOHOO! DADDY! HELLO!
JEEPERS! SO THAT'S VERONICA'S OLD MAN! DISTINGUISHED LOOKING GUY! I HEAR HE'S A BIG SHOT POLITICIAN IN BOSTON!
AIRW
OH, DADDY. I'VE MISSED YOU SOOO!
VERONICA, DARLING! HOW'S MY LITTLE GIRL?
SMACK
DADDY, THIS IS ARCHIE ANDREWS'
HOW DO YOU DO, MR. LODGE!
HELLO, ARCHIE' WELL, CHILDREN, SHALL WE GO OVER TO THE CAFE' AND HAVE A CHAT UNTIL MY PLANE COMES IN?
AIRWAY CAFE
WELL, DEAR. I FINALLY GOT MY BILL BEFORE THE COMMERCE COMMITTEE IN WASHINGTON!
MAY I TAKE YOUR ORDER?
THIS MENU LOOKS GREEK TO ME....GOSH, I WOULDN'T WANT TO ORDER ANYTHING WRONG IN FRONT OF VERONICA'S DAD'
I'LL HAVE A DAIQUIRI! THEY HAVE EXCELLENT FRENCH FOOD HERE, IF YOU'RE HUNGRY, ARCHIE!
I'LL HAVE THE SAME!
WHAT! HARRUMF... CAFF....ER... VERONICA, YOU'LL HAVE AN ORANGE-ADE, I TRUST?
WHY, Y-Y-YES, DADDY, OF COURSE
HOLY COW! IS THAT A DAIQUIRI? I THOUGHT IT WAS A SANDWICH!
YES, I'M MEETING TODAY WITH REPRESENTATIVES FROM SIX STATES TO VOTE ON A VITAL WAR INDUSTRY QUESTION. IF I CAN SWING THEIR VOTES IN AGREEMENT WITH MASSACHUSETTS, IT'LL PUT ME IN LINE FOR GOVERNOR!
PLANE FOR WASHINGTON ON RUNWAY!
PHEW! IF I DRANK THAT I'D BE UNDER THE TABLE-SO IT HAD BETTER BE THE DRINK!
NICE GOING, ARCHIE! RIGHT IN MR. LODGE'S HAT....
I'M AFRAID I'LL HAVE TO BE OFF AGAIN!
I HOPE YOU WIN, DADDY!

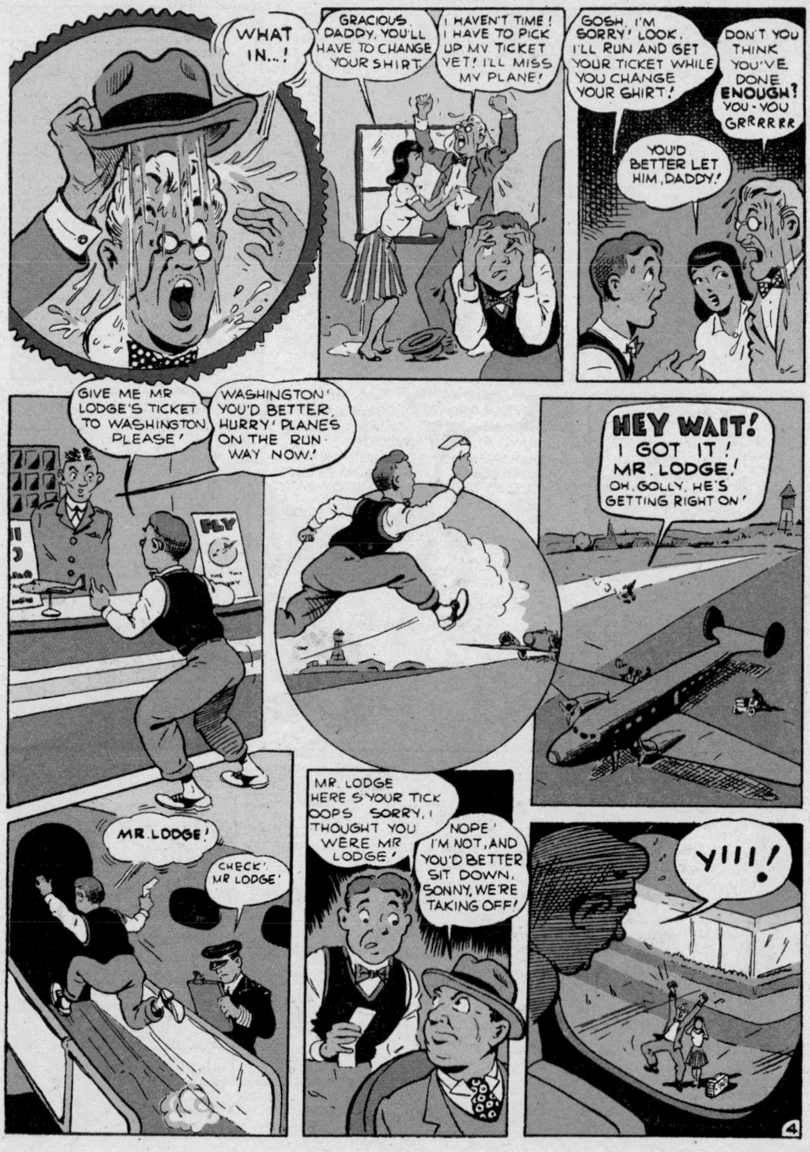

WHAT IN...!
GRACIOUS. DADDY, YOU'LL HAVE TO CHANGE YOUR SHIRT.
I HAVEN'T TIME! I HAVE TO PICK UP MY TICKET YET! I'LL MISS MY PLANE!
GOSH, I'M SORRY! LOOK, I'LL RUN AND GET YOUR TICKET WHILE YOU CHANGE YOUR SHIRT!
DON'T YOU THINK YOU'VE DONE ENOUGH? YOU-YOU GRRRRRR
YOU'D BETTER LET HIM, DADDY!
GIVE ME MR LODGE'S TICKET TO WASHINGTON PLEASE!
WASHINGTON! YOU'D BETTER HURRY! PLANES ON THE RUN WAY NOW!
FLY
HEY WAIT! I GOT IT! MR. LODGE! OH, GOLLY, HE'S GETTING RIGHT ON!
MR. LODGE!
CHECK! MR LODGE!
MR. LODGE HERE'S YOUR TICK OOPS SORRY, I THOUGHT YOU WERE MR LODGE!
NOPE! I'M NOT, AND YOU'D BETTER SIT DOWN, SONNY, WE'RE TAKING OFF!
YIII!
4

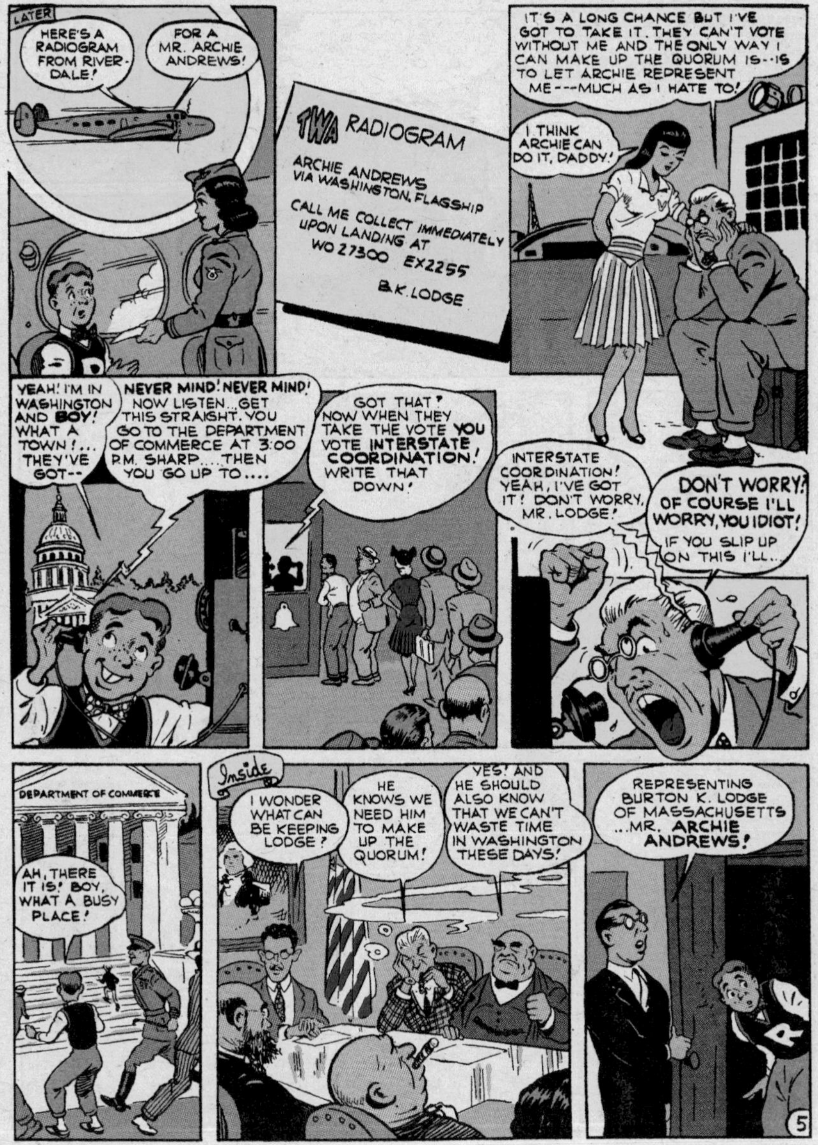

LATER
HERE'S A RADIOGRAM FROM RIVER-DALE!
FOR A MR. ARCHIE ANDREWS!
TWA RADIOGRAM
ARCHIE ANDREWS VIA WASHINGTON, FLAGSHIP
CALL ME COLLECT IMMEDIATELY UPON LANDING AT WO 27300 EX2255
B.K. LODGE
IT'S A LONG CHANCE BUT I'VE GOT TO TAKE IT. THEY CAN'T VOTE WITHOUT ME AND THE ONLY WAY I CAN MAKE UP THE QUORUM IS--IS TO LET ARCHIE REPRESENT ME---MUCH AS I HATE TO!
I THINK ARCHIE CAN DO IT, DADDY!
YEAH! I'M IN WASHINGTON AND BOY! WHAT A TOWN!... THEY'VE GOT--
NEVER MIND! NEVER MIND! NOW LISTEN...GET THIS STRAIGHT. YOU GO TO THE DEPARTMENT OF COMMERCE AT 3:00 P.M. SHARP.... THEN YOU GO UP TO....
GOT THAT? NOW WHEN THEY TAKE THE VOTE YOU VOTE INTERSTATE COORDINATION! WRITE THAT DOWN!
INTERSTATE COORDINATION! YEAH, I'VE GOT IT! DON'T WORRY, MR. LODGE!
DON'T WORRY? OF COURSE I'LL WORRY, YOU IDIOT! IF YOU SLIP UP ON THIS I'LL...
DEPARTMENT OF COMMERCE
AH, THERE IT IS! BOY, WHAT A BUSY PLACE!
Inside
I WONDER WHAT CAN BE KEEPING LODGE?
HE KNOWS WE NEED HIM TO MAKE UP THE QUORUM!
YES! AND HE SHOULD ALSO KNOW THAT WE CAN'T WASTE TIME IN WASHINGTON THESE DAYS!
REPRESENTING BURTON K. LODGE OF MASSACHUSETTS ...MR. ARCHIE ANDREWS!

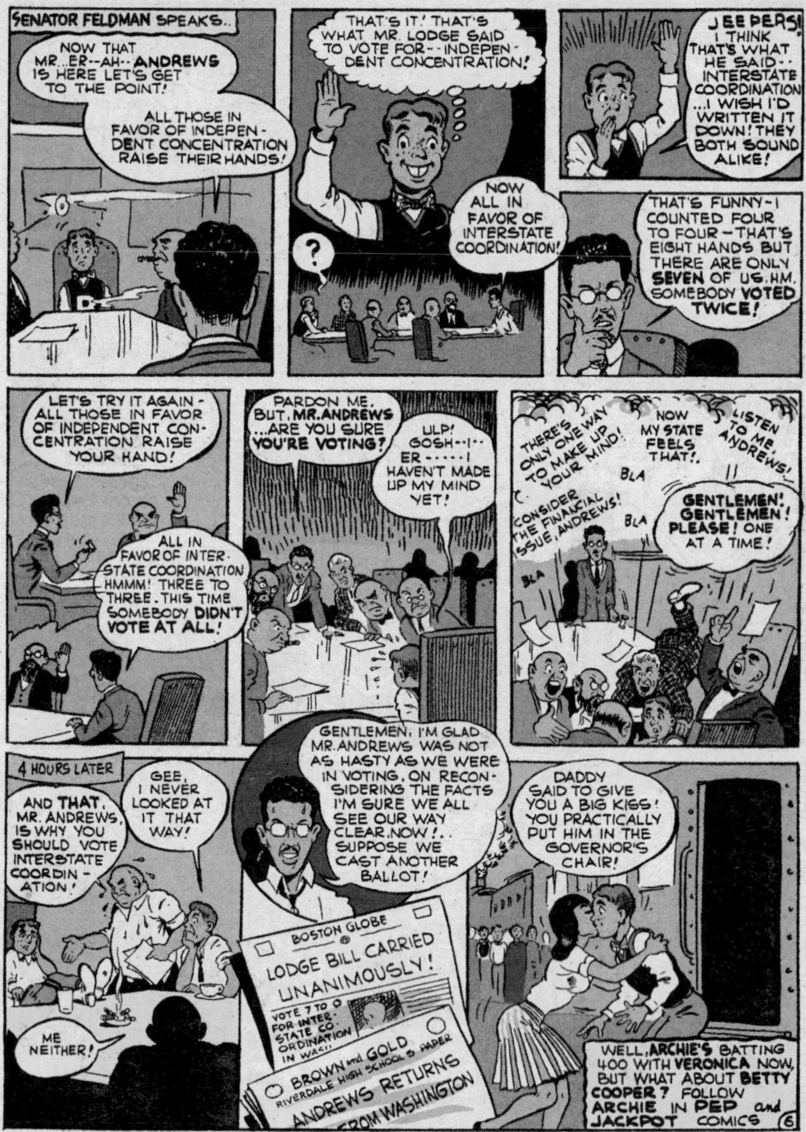
SENATOR FELDMAN SPEAKS..
NOW THAT MR...ER--AH--ANDREWS IS HERE LET'S GET TO THE POINT!
ALL THOSE IN FAVOR OF INDEPEN-DENT CONCENTRATION RAISE THEIR HANDS!
THAT'S IT! THAT'S WHAT MR. LODGE SAID TO VOTE FOR--INDEPEN-DENT CONCENTRATION!
?
NOW ALL IN FAVOR OF INTERSTATE COORDINATION!
JEEPERS! I THINK THAT'S WHAT HE SAID--INTERSTATE COORDINATION ...I WISH I'D WRITTEN IT DOWN! THEY BOTH SOUND ALIKE!
THAT'S FUNNY-I COUNTED FOUR TO FOUR-THAT'S EIGHT HANDS BUT THERE ARE ONLY SEVEN OF US. HM. SOMEBODY VOTED TWICE!
LET'S TRY IT AGAIN-ALL THOSE IN FAVOR OF INDEPENDENT CON-CENTRATION RAISE YOUR HAND!
ALL IN FAVOR OF INTER-STATE COORDINATION HMMM! THREE TO THREE. THIS TIME SOMEBODY DIDN'T VOTE AT ALL!
PARDON ME, BUT, MR. ANDREWS ...ARE YOU SURE YOU'RE VOTING?
ULP! GOSH--I--ER-----I HAVEN'T MADE UP MY MIND YET!
THERE'S ONLY ONE WAY TO MAKE UP YOUR MIND!
NOW MY STATE FEELS THAT!.
LISTEN TO ME, ANDREWS!
BLA
CONSIDER THE FINANCIAL ISSUE, ANDREWS!
BLA
GENTLEMEN! GENTLEMEN! PLEASE! ONE AT A TIME!
BLA
4 HOURS LATER
AND THAT, MR. ANDREWS, IS WHY YOU SHOULD VOTE INTERSTATE COORDIN-ATION!
GEE, I NEVER LOOKED AT IT THAT WAY!
ME NEITHER!
GENTLEMEN, I'M GLAD MR. ANDREWS WAS NOT AS HASTY AS WE WERE IN VOTING. ON RECON-SIDERING THE FACTS I'M SURE WE ALL SEE OUR WAY CLEAR NOW!.. SUPPOSE WE CAST ANOTHER BALLOT!
BOSTON GLOBE
LODGE BILL CARRIED UNANIMOUSLY!
VOTE 7 TO 0 FOR INTER-STATE CO-ORDINATION IN WASH
BROWN and GOLD
RIVERDALE HIGH SCHOOL'S PAPER
ANDREWS RETURNS FROM WASHINGTON
DADDY SAID TO GIVE YOU A BIG KISS! YOU PRACTICALLY PUT HIM IN THE GOVERNOR'S CHAIR!
WELL, ARCHIE'S BATTING 400 WITH VERONICA NOW, BUT WHAT ABOUT BETTY COOPER? FOLLOW ARCHIE IN PEP and JACKPOT COMICS
6

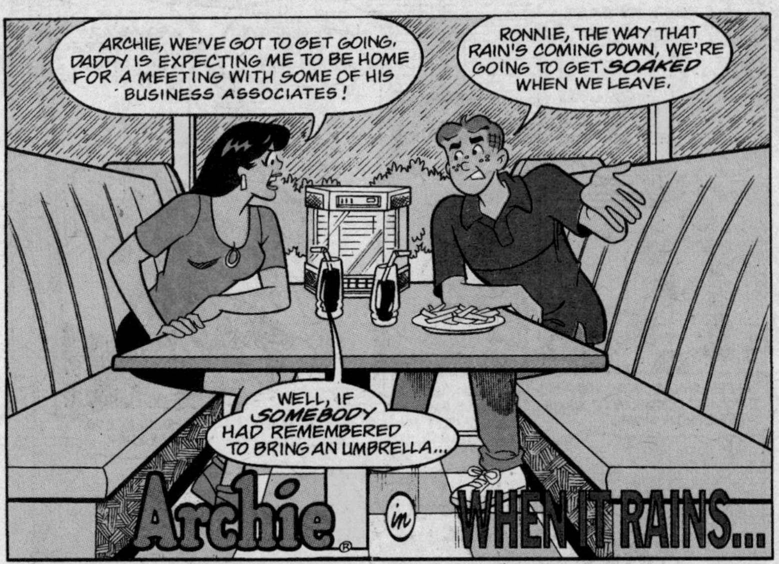
ARCHIE, WE'VE GOT TO GET GOING. DADDY IS EXPECTING ME TO BE HOME FOR A MEETING WITH SOME OF HIS BUSINESS ASSOCIATES!
RONNIE, THE WAY THAT RAIN'S COMING DOWN, WE'RE GOING TO GET SOAKED WHEN WE LEAVE.
WELL, IF SOMEBODY HAD REMEMBERED TO BRING AN UMBRELLA...
Archie in WHEN IT RAINS...

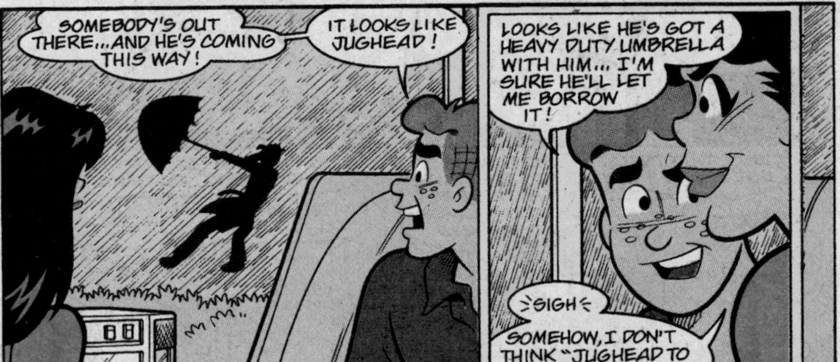
SOMEBODY'S OUT THERE...AND HE'S COMING THIS WAY!
IT LOOKS LIKE JUGHEAD!
LOOKS LIKE HE'S GOT A HEAVY DUTY UMBRELLA WITH HIM... I'M SURE HE'LL LET ME BORROW IT!
SIGH
SOMEHOW, I DON'T THINK "JUGHEAD TO THE RESCUE" IS THE ANSWER!

Script: **Bob Rozakis** Pencils: **Fernando Ruiz** Inks: **Rich Koslowski**
Letters: **Vickie Williams** Colors: **Barry Grossman**
Editor-In-Chief: **Victor Gorelick** President: **Mike Pellerito** Publisher: **Jon Goldwater**

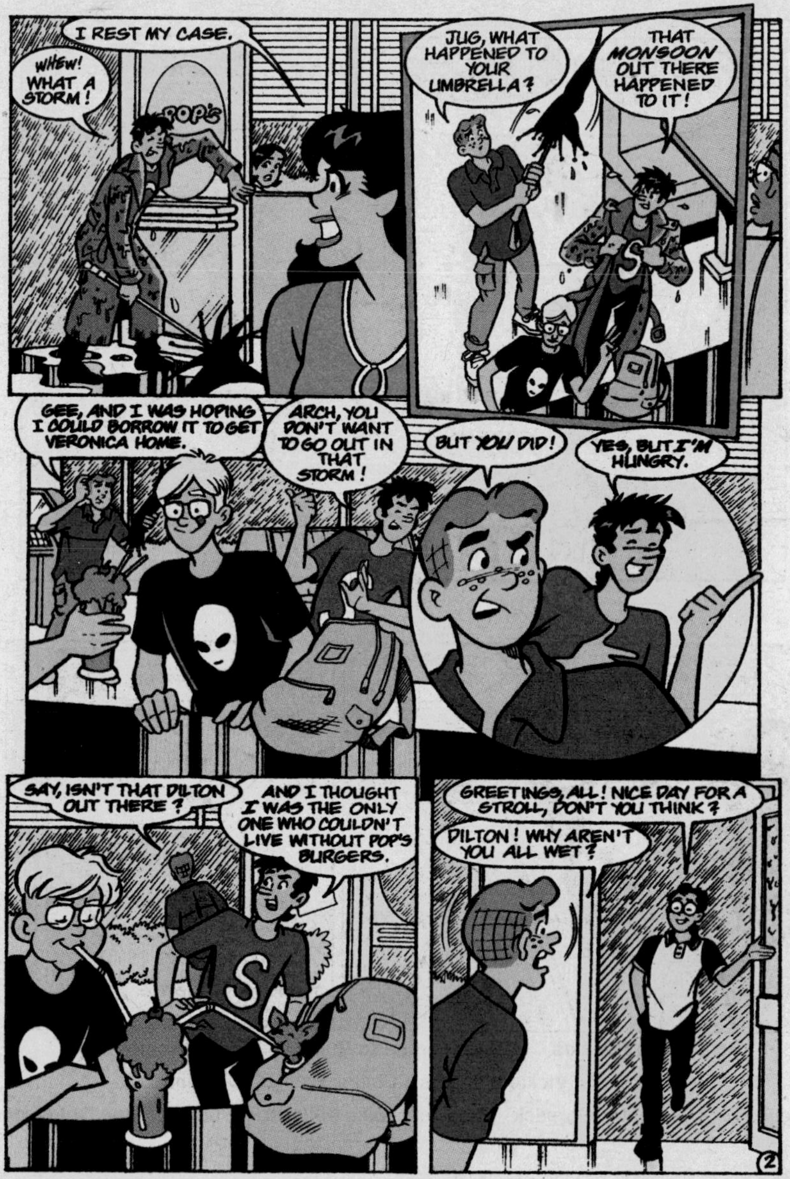

WHEW! WHAT A STORM!
I REST MY CASE.
POP'S
JUG, WHAT HAPPENED TO YOUR UMBRELLA?
THAT MONSOON OUT THERE HAPPENED TO IT!
GEE, AND I WAS HOPING I COULD BORROW IT TO GET VERONICA HOME.
ARCH, YOU DON'T WANT TO GO OUT IN THAT STORM!
BUT YOU DID!
YES, BUT I'M HUNGRY.
SAY, ISN'T THAT DILTON OUT THERE?
AND I THOUGHT I WAS THE ONLY ONE WHO COULDN'T LIVE WITHOUT POP'S BURGERS.
GREETINGS, ALL! NICE DAY FOR A STROLL, DON'T YOU THINK?
DILTON! WHY AREN'T YOU ALL WET?

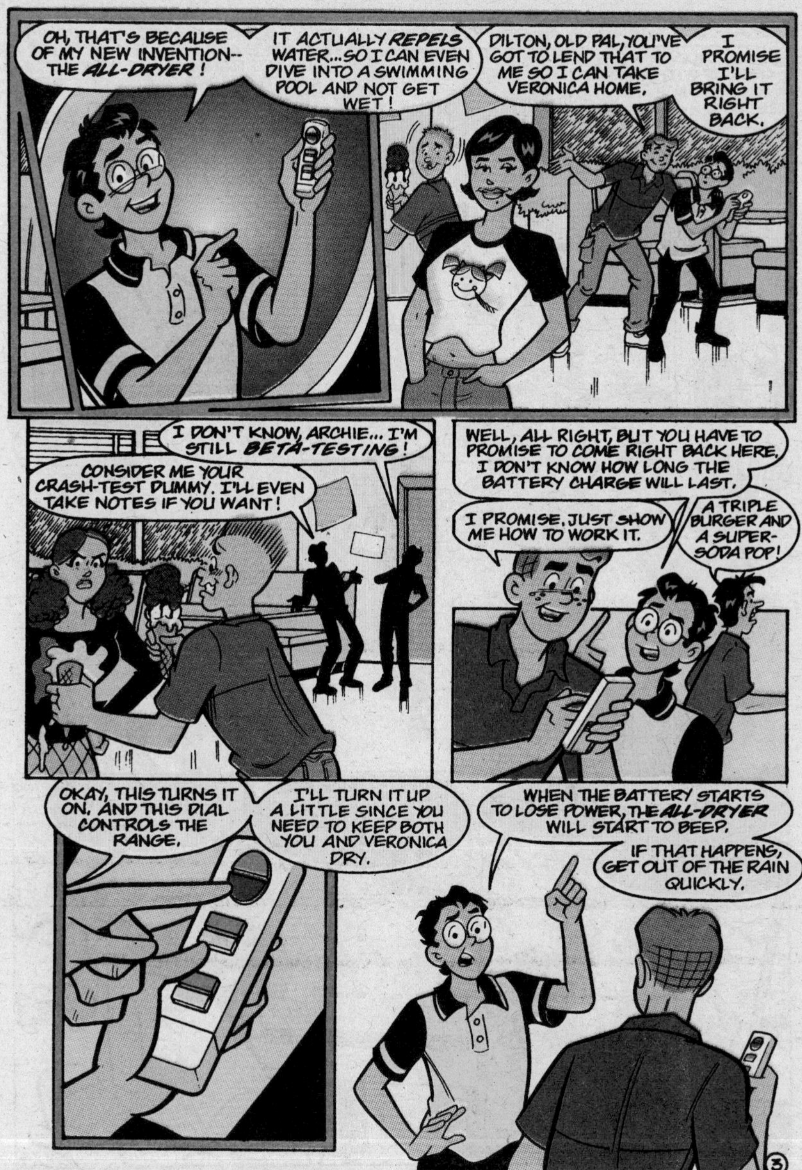

OH, THAT'S BECAUSE OF MY NEW INVENTION-- THE *ALL-DRYER* !
IT ACTUALLY *REPELS* WATER...SO I CAN EVEN DIVE INTO A SWIMMING POOL AND NOT GET WET!
DILTON, OLD PAL, YOU'VE GOT TO LEND THAT TO ME SO I CAN TAKE VERONICA HOME.
I PROMISE I'LL BRING IT RIGHT BACK.
I DON'T KNOW, ARCHIE... I'M STILL *BETA-TESTING*!
CONSIDER ME YOUR CRASH-TEST DUMMY. I'LL EVEN TAKE NOTES IF YOU WANT!
WELL, ALL RIGHT, BUT YOU HAVE TO PROMISE TO COME RIGHT BACK HERE. I DON'T KNOW HOW LONG THE BATTERY CHARGE WILL LAST.
I PROMISE. JUST SHOW ME HOW TO WORK IT.
A TRIPLE BURGER AND A SUPER-SODA POP!
OKAY, THIS TURNS IT ON, AND THIS DIAL CONTROLS THE RANGE.
I'LL TURN IT UP A LITTLE SINCE YOU NEED TO KEEP BOTH YOU AND VERONICA DRY.
WHEN THE BATTERY STARTS TO LOSE POWER, THE *ALL-DRYER* WILL START TO BEEP.
IF THAT HAPPENS, GET OUT OF THE RAIN QUICKLY.

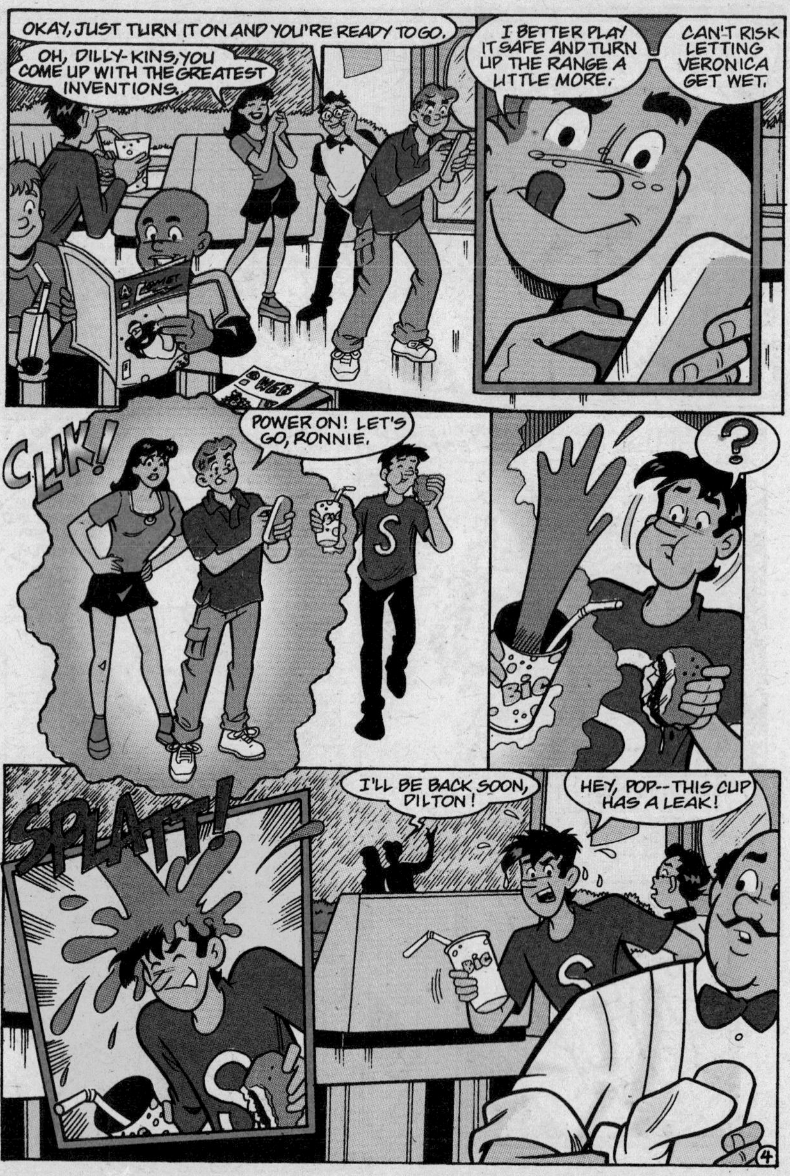
OKAY, JUST TURN IT ON AND YOU'RE READY TO GO.
OH, DILLY-KINS, YOU COME UP WITH THE GREATEST INVENTIONS.
I BETTER PLAY IT SAFE AND TURN UP THE RANGE A LITTLE MORE.
CAN'T RISK LETTING VERONICA GET WET.
CLIK!
POWER ON! LET'S GO, RONNIE.
?
SPLATT!
I'LL BE BACK SOON, DILTON!
HEY, POP--THIS CUP HAS A LEAK!

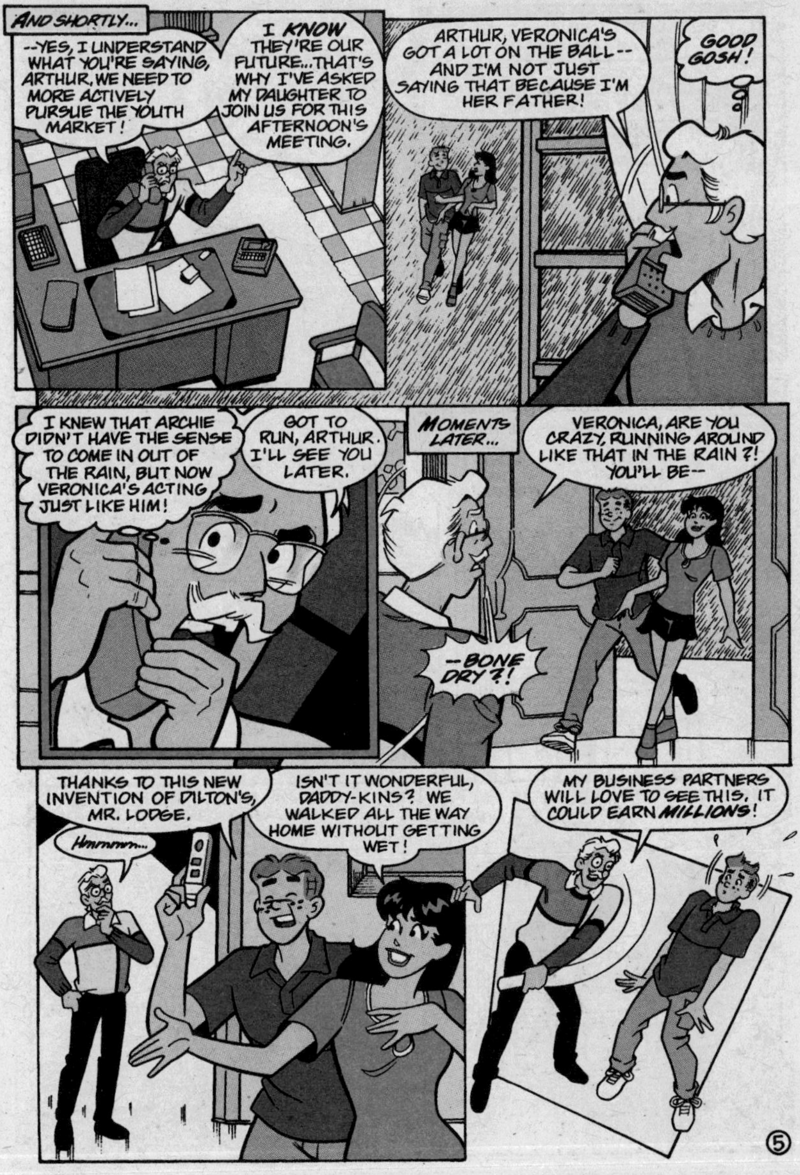
AND SHORTLY...
--YES, I UNDERSTAND WHAT YOU'RE SAYING, ARTHUR, WE NEED TO MORE ACTIVELY PURSUE THE YOUTH MARKET!
I KNOW THEY'RE OUR FUTURE...THAT'S WHY I'VE ASKED MY DAUGHTER TO JOIN US FOR THIS AFTERNOON'S MEETING.
ARTHUR, VERONICA'S GOT A LOT ON THE BALL-- AND I'M NOT JUST SAYING THAT BECAUSE I'M HER FATHER!
GOOD GOSH!
I KNEW THAT ARCHIE DIDN'T HAVE THE SENSE TO COME IN OUT OF THE RAIN, BUT NOW VERONICA'S ACTING JUST LIKE HIM!
GOT TO RUN, ARTHUR. I'LL SEE YOU LATER.
MOMENTS LATER...
VERONICA, ARE YOU CRAZY, RUNNING AROUND LIKE THAT IN THE RAIN?! YOU'LL BE--
--BONE DRY?!
THANKS TO THIS NEW INVENTION OF DILTON'S, MR. LODGE.
Hmmmm...
ISN'T IT WONDERFUL, DADDY-KINS? WE WALKED ALL THE WAY HOME WITHOUT GETTING WET!
MY BUSINESS PARTNERS WILL LOVE TO SEE THIS. IT COULD EARN MILLIONS!

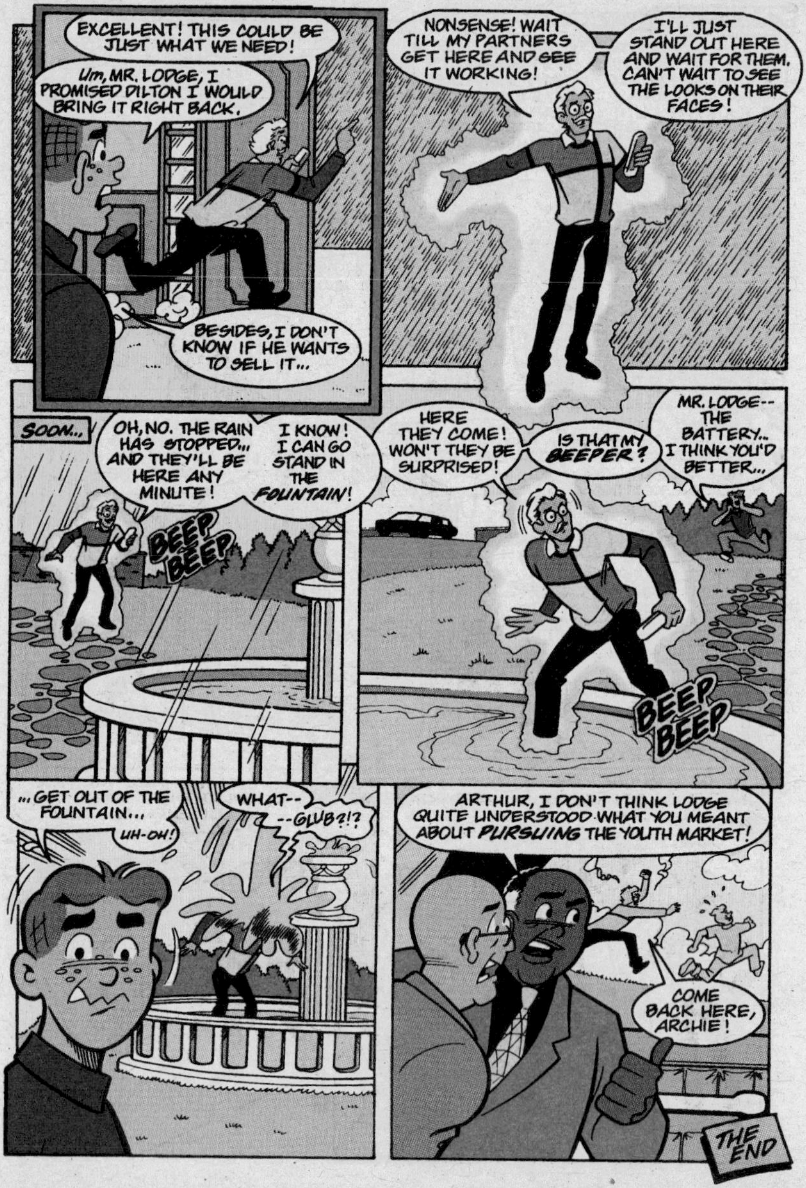
EXCELLENT! THIS COULD BE JUST WHAT WE NEED!
Um, MR. LODGE, I PROMISED DILTON I WOULD BRING IT RIGHT BACK.
BESIDES, I DON'T KNOW IF HE WANTS TO SELL IT...
NONSENSE! WAIT TILL MY PARTNERS GET HERE AND SEE IT WORKING!
I'LL JUST STAND OUT HERE AND WAIT FOR THEM. CAN'T WAIT TO SEE THE LOOKS ON THEIR FACES!
SOON...
OH, NO. THE RAIN HAS STOPPED... AND THEY'LL BE HERE ANY MINUTE!
I KNOW! I CAN GO STAND IN THE FOUNTAIN!
BEEP BEEP
HERE THEY COME! WON'T THEY BE SURPRISED!
IS THAT MY BEEPER?
MR. LODGE-- THE BATTERY... I THINK YOU'D BETTER...
BEEP BEEP
...GET OUT OF THE FOUNTAIN...
UH-OH!
WHAT--
--GLUB?!?
ARTHUR, I DON'T THINK LODGE QUITE UNDERSTOOD WHAT YOU MEANT ABOUT PURSUING THE YOUTH MARKET!
COME BACK HERE, ARCHIE!
THE END

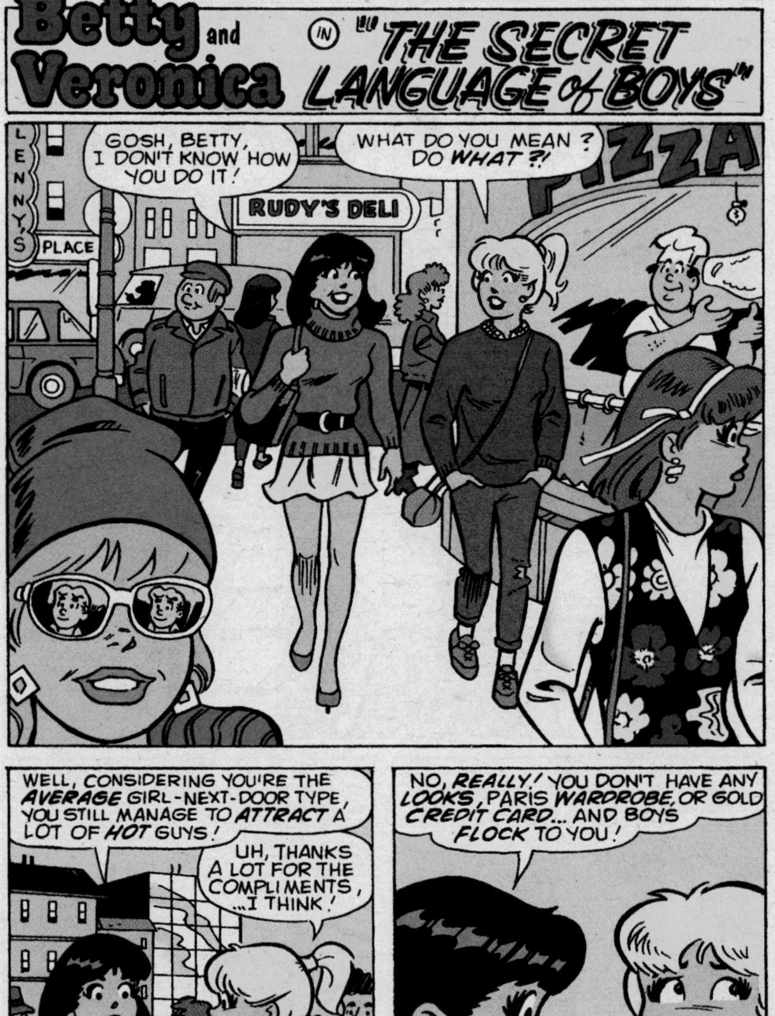
Betty and Veronica
IN "THE SECRET LANGUAGE of BOYS"
LENNY'S PLACE
RUDY'S DELI
PIZZA
GOSH, BETTY, I DON'T KNOW HOW YOU DO IT!
WHAT DO YOU MEAN? DO WHAT?!
WELL, CONSIDERING YOU'RE THE AVERAGE GIRL-NEXT-DOOR TYPE, YOU STILL MANAGE TO ATTRACT A LOT OF HOT GUYS!
UH, THANKS A LOT FOR THE COMPLIMENTS, ...I THINK!
NO, REALLY! YOU DON'T HAVE ANY LOOKS, PARIS WARDROBE, OR GOLD CREDIT CARD... AND BOYS FLOCK TO YOU!

Script: Kathleen Webb / Pencils: Dan DeCarlo / Inks: Rudy Lapick / Letters: Bill Yoshida / Colors: Barry Grossman

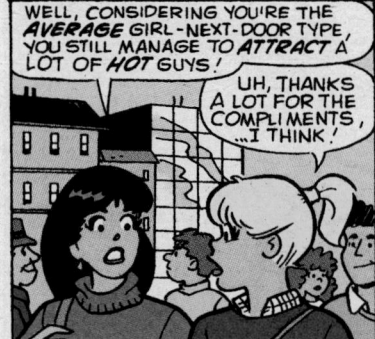

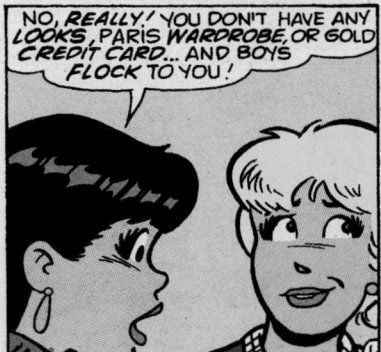

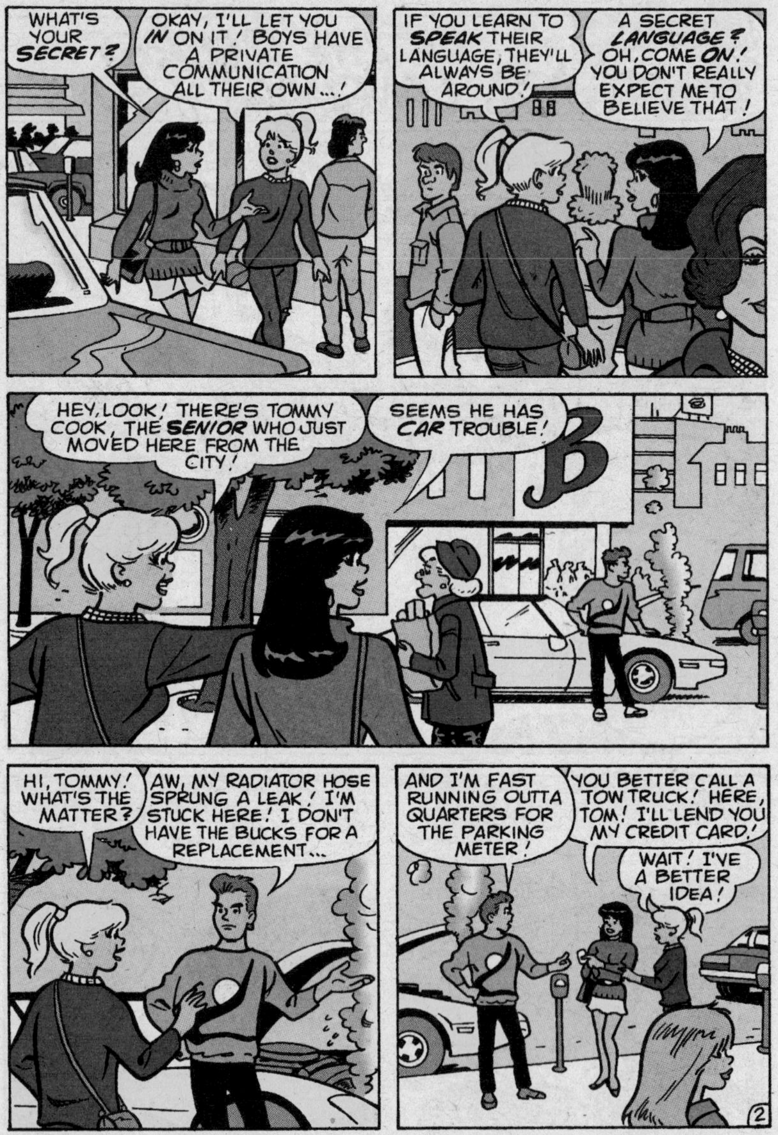
WHAT'S YOUR SECRET?
OKAY, I'LL LET YOU IN ON IT! BOYS HAVE A PRIVATE COMMUNICATION ALL THEIR OWN...!
IF YOU LEARN TO SPEAK THEIR LANGUAGE, THEY'LL ALWAYS BE AROUND!
A SECRET LANGUAGE? OH, COME ON! YOU DON'T REALLY EXPECT ME TO BELIEVE THAT!
HEY, LOOK! THERE'S TOMMY COOK, THE SENIOR WHO JUST MOVED HERE FROM THE CITY!
SEEMS HE HAS CAR TROUBLE!
HI, TOMMY! WHAT'S THE MATTER?
AW, MY RADIATOR HOSE SPRUNG A LEAK! I'M STUCK HERE! I DON'T HAVE THE BUCKS FOR A REPLACEMENT...
AND I'M FAST RUNNING OUTTA QUARTERS FOR THE PARKING METER!
YOU BETTER CALL A TOW TRUCK! HERE, TOM! I'LL LEND YOU MY CREDIT CARD!
WAIT! I'VE A BETTER IDEA!
2

GET SOME *DUCT TAPE* AND A SET OF *CLAMPS* FROM THE HARDWARE STORE! *BANDAGE* THE HOSE AND CLAMP IT DOWN ON EITHER *END*...!

LAZAAR HARDWARE

SAM'S CAFE

POP TATE'LL GIVE YOU A *BUCKET* OF WATER...BUT RUN YOUR *ENGINE* WHEN YOU POUR IN THE COLD WATER-- SO YOU DON'T CRACK THE *BLOCK*!

GEE, THANKS, BETS! YOU *SURE* KNOW A LOT ABOUT CARS!

POP'S SODA SHOP

HOW ABOUT A DATE THIS FRIDAY? YOU CAN *TEACH* ME SOME MORE!

A *DATE?* WONDERFUL, TOMMY! YOU'RE ON!

I'VE BEEN *AFTER* TOM TO ASK ME OUT FOR WEEKS, BETTY! YOU MADE THAT LOOK SO *EASY!*

LESSON NUMBER ONE! A BOY'S FAVORITE SUBJECT, NEXT TO GIRLS, THAT IS... IS *HIS* CAR!

HEY, BETTY!

ZOOM

THAT WAS *SOME* BASEBALL GAME LAST NIGHT! DID YOU SEE THE PLAY BY DARYL RASBERRY?

I KNOW! IT'S THE BOTTOM OF THE NINTH! THERE ARE TWO OUTS! HE'S GOT TWO STRIKES-- AND BUNTS HIS WAY ON BASE, WITH A DOUBLE STEAL ON!!

The RECORD SHOP

3

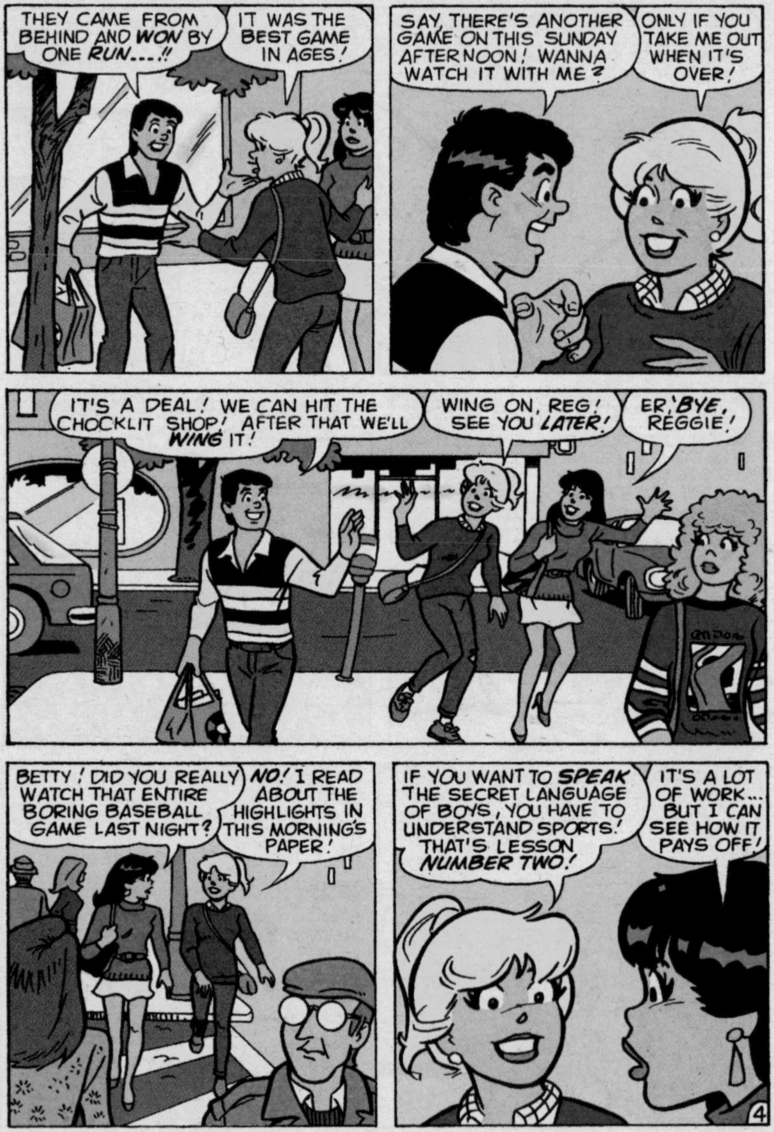
THEY CAME FROM BEHIND AND WON BY ONE RUN....!!
IT WAS THE BEST GAME IN AGES!
SAY, THERE'S ANOTHER GAME ON THIS SUNDAY AFTERNOON! WANNA WATCH IT WITH ME?
ONLY IF YOU TAKE ME OUT WHEN IT'S OVER!
IT'S A DEAL! WE CAN HIT THE CHOCKLIT SHOP! AFTER THAT WE'LL WING IT!
WING ON, REG! SEE YOU LATER!
ER, 'BYE, REGGIE!
BETTY! DID YOU REALLY WATCH THAT ENTIRE BORING BASEBALL GAME LAST NIGHT?
NO! I READ ABOUT THE HIGHLIGHTS IN THIS MORNING'S PAPER!
IF YOU WANT TO SPEAK THE SECRET LANGUAGE OF BOYS, YOU HAVE TO UNDERSTAND SPORTS! THAT'S LESSON NUMBER TWO!
IT'S A LOT OF WORK... BUT I CAN SEE HOW IT PAYS OFF!
4

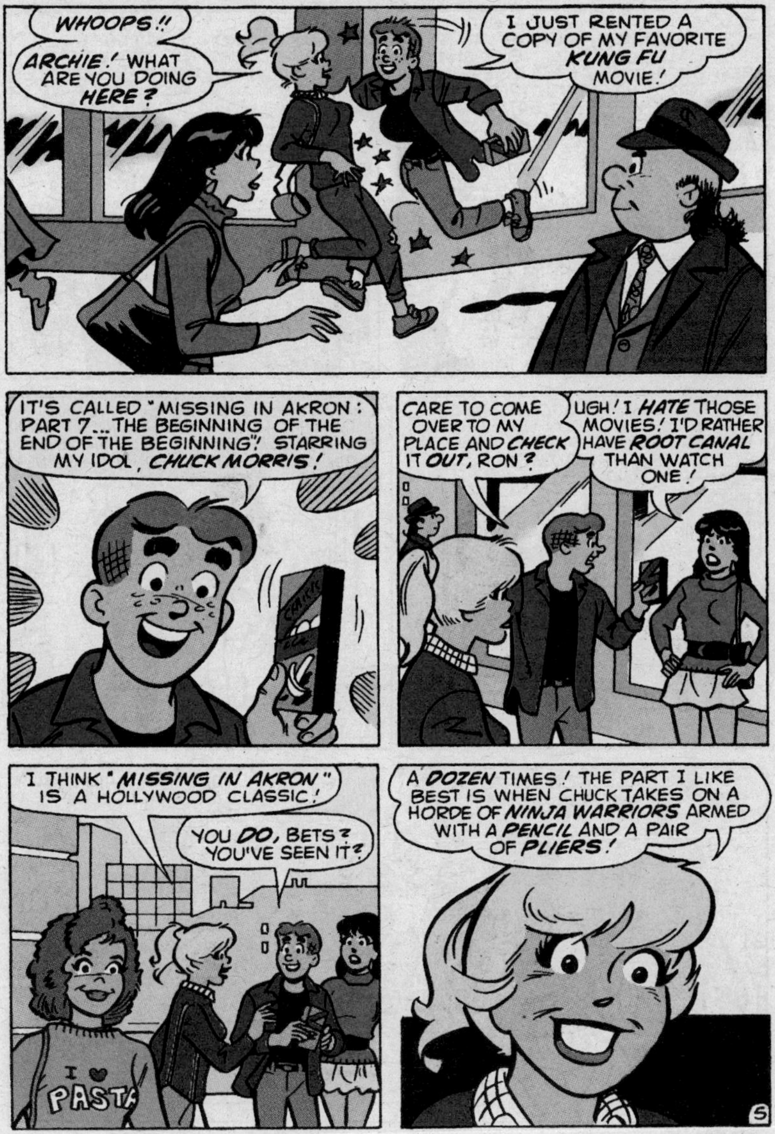
WHOOPS!!
ARCHIE! WHAT ARE YOU DOING HERE?
I JUST RENTED A COPY OF MY FAVORITE KUNG FU MOVIE!
IT'S CALLED "MISSING IN AKRON: PART 7... THE BEGINNING OF THE END OF THE BEGINNING"! STARRING MY IDOL, CHUCK MORRIS!
CARE TO COME OVER TO MY PLACE AND CHECK IT OUT, RON?
UGH! I HATE THOSE MOVIES! I'D RATHER HAVE ROOT CANAL THAN WATCH ONE!
I THINK "MISSING IN AKRON" IS A HOLLYWOOD CLASSIC!
YOU DO, BETS? YOU'VE SEEN IT?
I ♥ PASTA
A DOZEN TIMES! THE PART I LIKE BEST IS WHEN CHUCK TAKES ON A HORDE OF NINJA WARRIORS ARMED WITH A PENCIL AND A PAIR OF PLIERS!
5

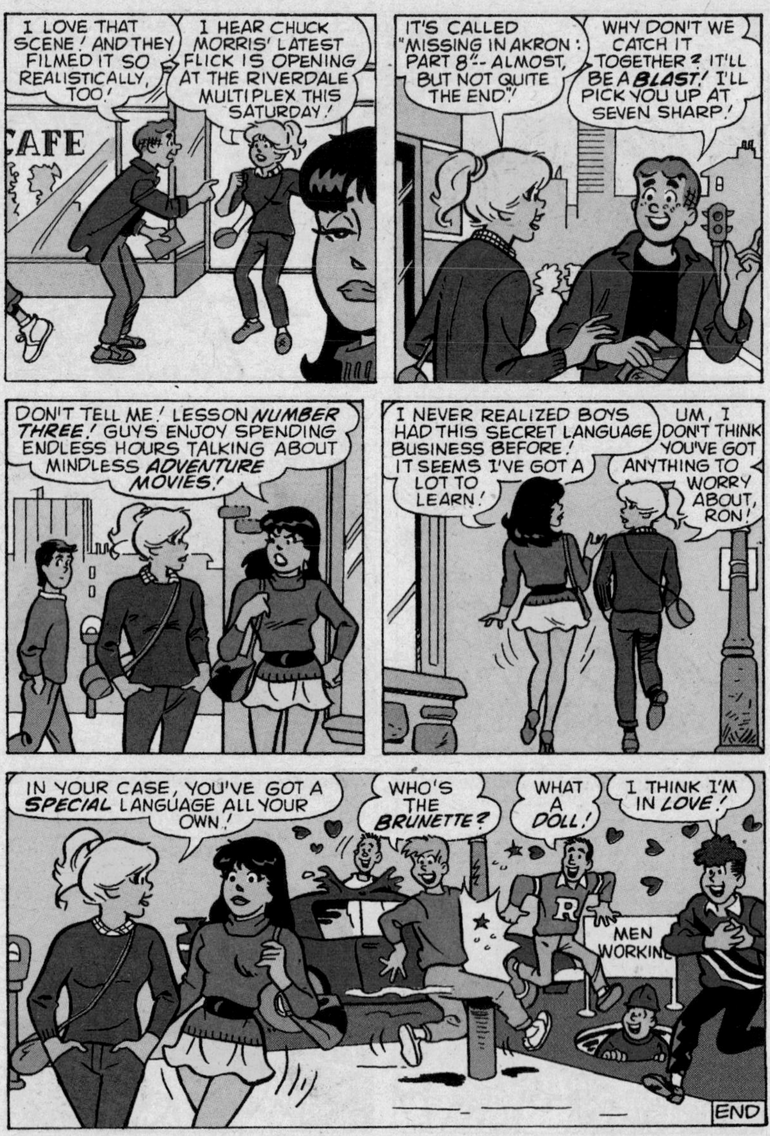
I LOVE THAT SCENE! AND THEY FILMED IT SO REALISTICALLY, TOO!
I HEAR CHUCK MORRIS' LATEST FLICK IS OPENING AT THE RIVERDALE MULTIPLEX THIS SATURDAY!
CAFE
IT'S CALLED "MISSING IN AKRON: PART 8"-- ALMOST, BUT NOT QUITE THE END"!
WHY DON'T WE CATCH IT TOGETHER? IT'LL BE A BLAST! I'LL PICK YOU UP AT SEVEN SHARP!
DON'T TELL ME! LESSON NUMBER THREE! GUYS ENJOY SPENDING ENDLESS HOURS TALKING ABOUT MINDLESS ADVENTURE MOVIES!
I NEVER REALIZED BOYS HAD THIS SECRET LANGUAGE BUSINESS BEFORE! IT SEEMS I'VE GOT A LOT TO LEARN!
UM, I DON'T THINK YOU'VE GOT ANYTHING TO WORRY ABOUT, RON!
IN YOUR CASE, YOU'VE GOT A SPECIAL LANGUAGE ALL YOUR OWN!
WHO'S THE BRUNETTE?
WHAT A DOLL!
I THINK I'M IN LOVE!
MEN WORKIN
END

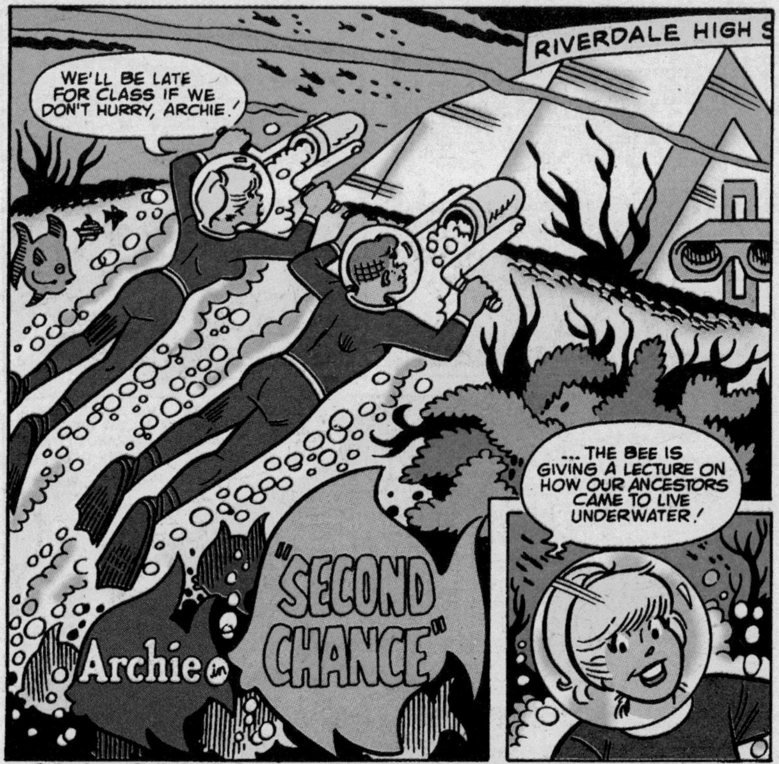
RIVERDALE HIGH
WE'LL BE LATE FOR CLASS IF WE DON'T HURRY, ARCHIE!
Archie in "SECOND CHANCE"
...THE BEE IS GIVING A LECTURE ON HOW OUR ANCESTORS CAME TO LIVE UNDERWATER!

Script: George Gladir / Pencils: Stan Goldberg / Inks: Rudy Lapick / Letters: Bill Yoshida / Colors: Barry Grossman

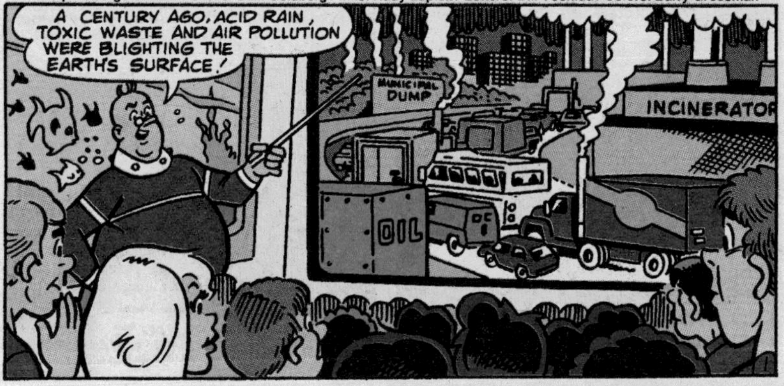
A CENTURY AGO, ACID RAIN, TOXIC WASTE AND AIR POLLUTION WERE BLIGHTING THE EARTH'S SURFACE!
MUNICIPAL DUMP
INCINERATOR
OIL

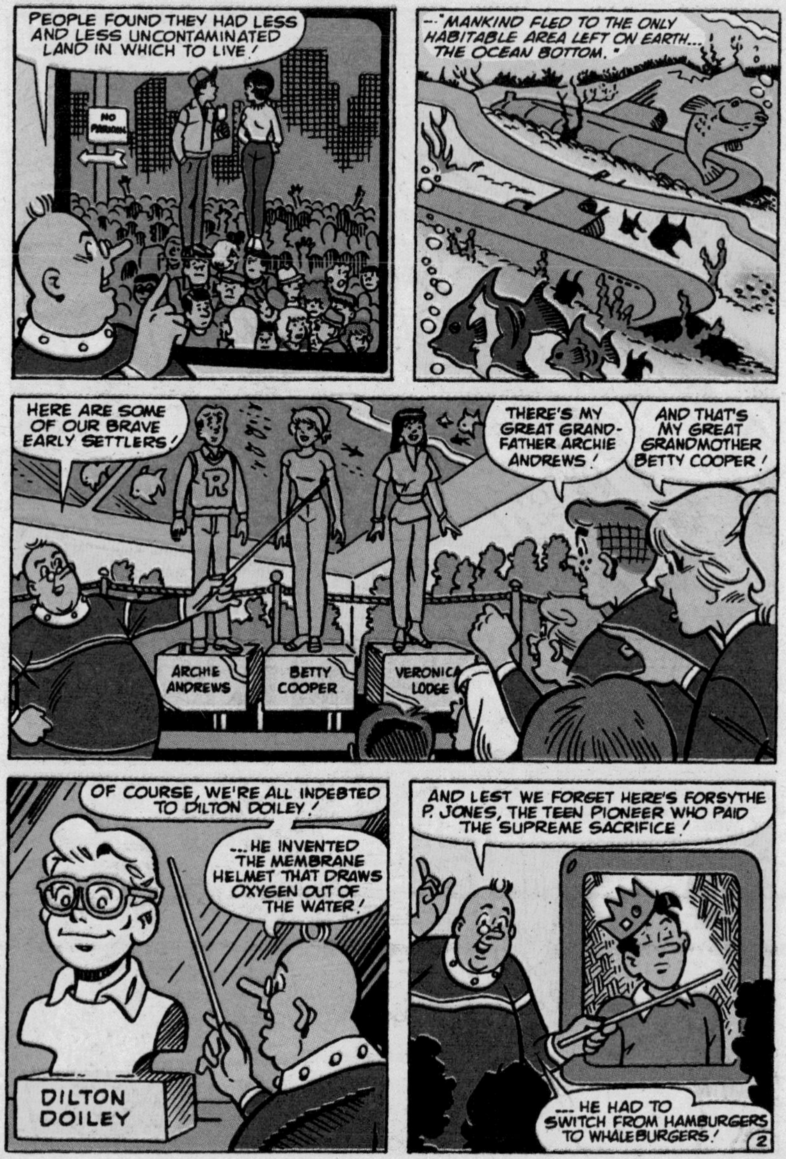
PEOPLE FOUND THEY HAD LESS AND LESS UNCONTAMINATED LAND IN WHICH TO LIVE!
NO PARKING
--"MANKIND FLED TO THE ONLY HABITABLE AREA LEFT ON EARTH... THE OCEAN BOTTOM."
HERE ARE SOME OF OUR BRAVE EARLY SETTLERS!
THERE'S MY GREAT GRAND-FATHER ARCHIE ANDREWS!
AND THAT'S MY GREAT GRANDMOTHER BETTY COOPER!
ARCHIE ANDREWS
BETTY COOPER
VERONICA LODGE
OF COURSE, WE'RE ALL INDEBTED TO DILTON DOILEY!
...HE INVENTED THE MEMBRANE HELMET THAT DRAWS OXYGEN OUT OF THE WATER!
DILTON DOILEY
AND LEST WE FORGET HERE'S FORSYTHE P. JONES, THE TEEN PIONEER WHO PAID THE SUPREME SACRIFICE!
...HE HAD TO SWITCH FROM HAMBURGERS TO WHALEBURGERS!
2

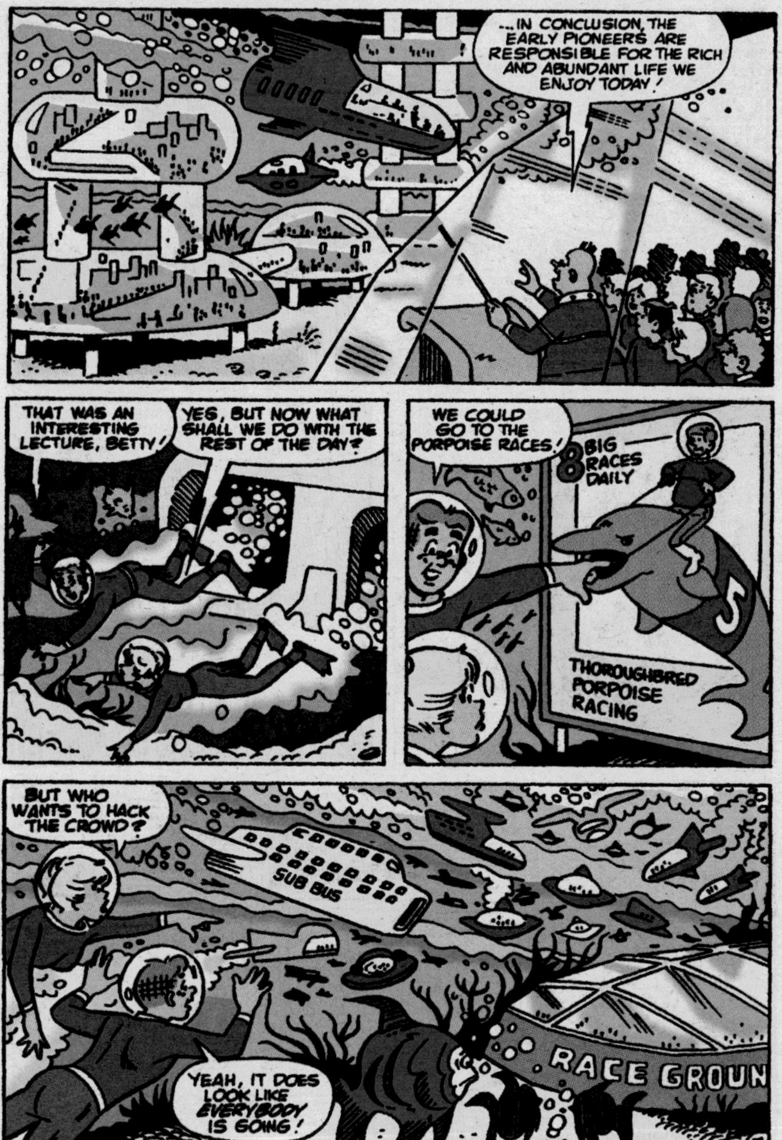
...IN CONCLUSION, THE EARLY PIONEERS ARE RESPONSIBLE FOR THE RICH AND ABUNDANT LIFE WE ENJOY TODAY!
THAT WAS AN INTERESTING LECTURE, BETTY!
YES, BUT NOW WHAT SHALL WE DO WITH THE REST OF THE DAY?
WE COULD GO TO THE PORPOISE RACES!
8 BIG RACES DAILY
5
THOROUGHBRED PORPOISE RACING
BUT WHO WANTS TO HACK THE CROWD?
SUB BUS
RACE GROUN
YEAH, IT DOES LOOK LIKE *EVERYBODY* IS GOING!

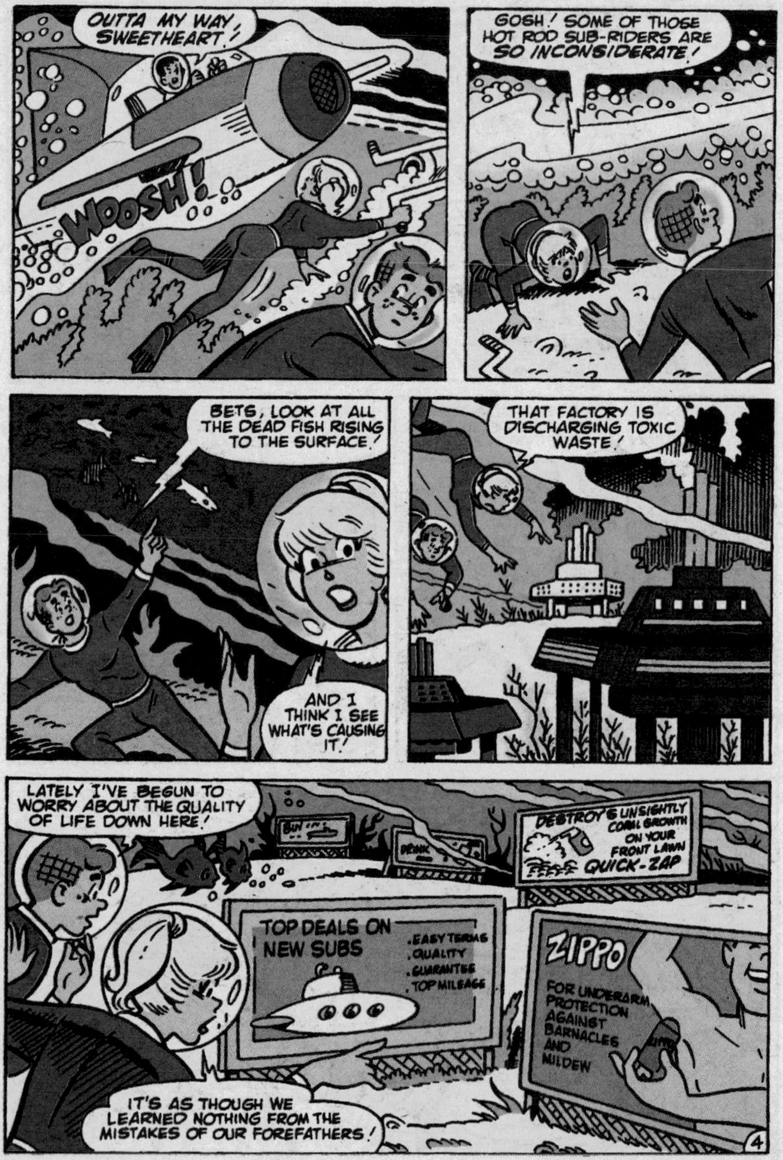

OUTTA MY WAY, SWEETHEART!
WOOSH!
GOSH! SOME OF THOSE HOT ROD SUB-RIDERS ARE SO INCONSIDERATE!
BETS, LOOK AT ALL THE DEAD FISH RISING TO THE SURFACE!
AND I THINK I SEE WHAT'S CAUSING IT!
THAT FACTORY IS DISCHARGING TOXIC WASTE!
LATELY I'VE BEGUN TO WORRY ABOUT THE QUALITY OF LIFE DOWN HERE!
DESTROY'S UNSIGHTLY CORAL GROWTH ON YOUR FRONT LAWN
QUICK-ZAP
TOP DEALS ON NEW SUBS
.EASY TERMS
.QUALITY
.GUARANTEE
.TOP MILEAGE
ZIPPO
FOR UNDERARM PROTECTION AGAINST BARNACLES AND MILDEW
IT'S AS THOUGH WE LEARNED NOTHING FROM THE MISTAKES OF OUR FOREFATHERS!
4

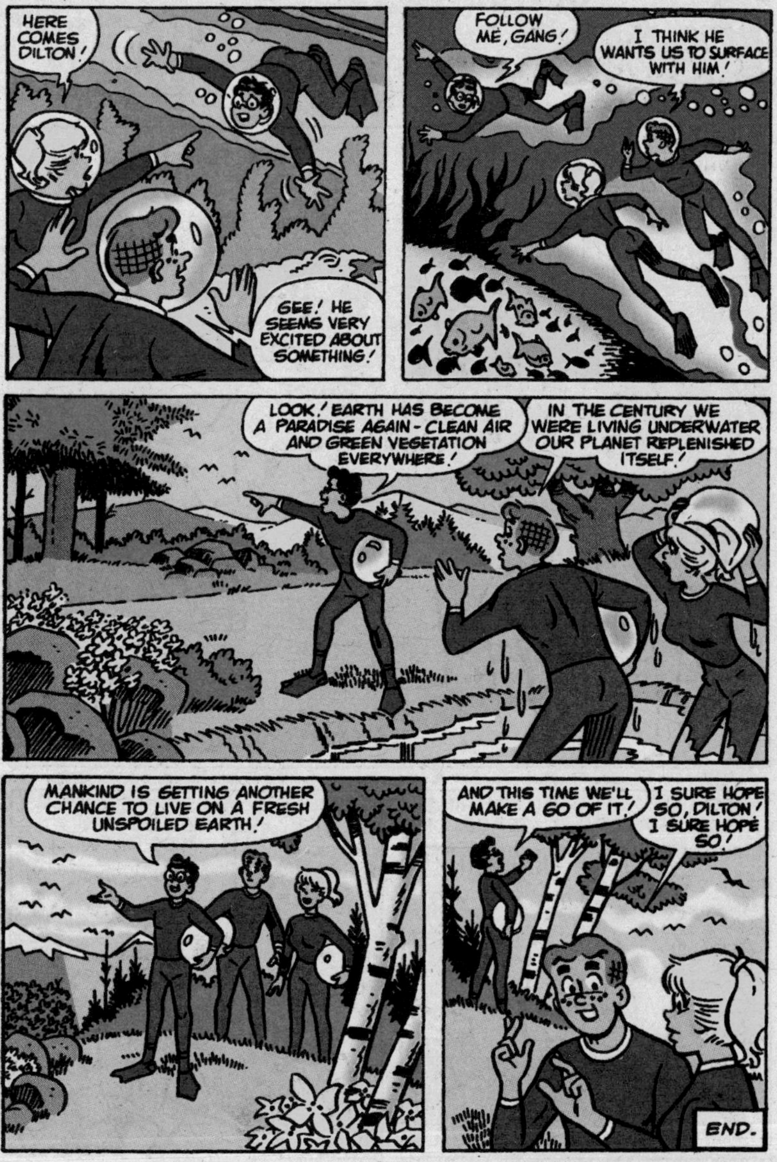
HERE COMES DILTON!
SEE! HE SEEMS VERY EXCITED ABOUT SOMETHING!
FOLLOW ME, GANG!
I THINK HE WANTS US TO SURFACE WITH HIM!
LOOK! EARTH HAS BECOME A PARADISE AGAIN - CLEAN AIR AND GREEN VEGETATION EVERYWHERE!
IN THE CENTURY WE WERE LIVING UNDERWATER OUR PLANET REPLENISHED ITSELF!
MANKIND IS GETTING ANOTHER CHANCE TO LIVE ON A FRESH UNSPOILED EARTH!
AND THIS TIME WE'LL MAKE A GO OF IT!
I SURE HOPE SO, DILTON! I SURE HOPE SO!
END.

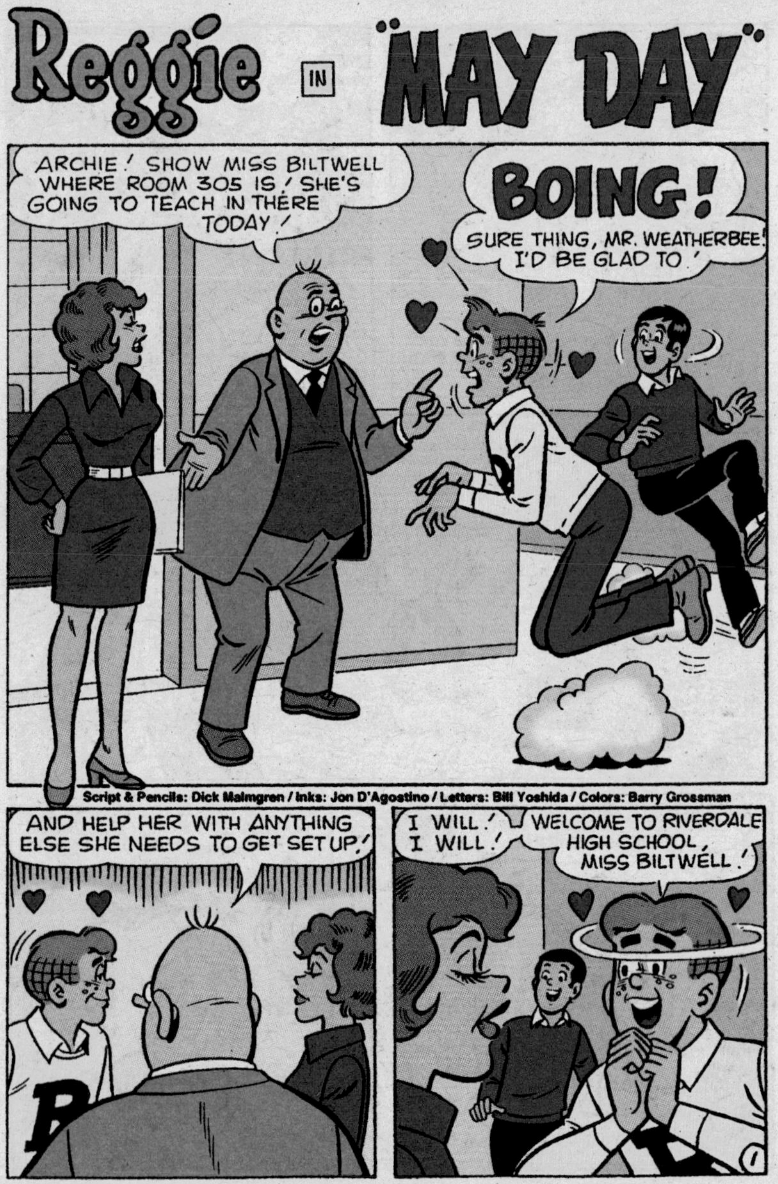
Reggie IN "MAY DAY"
ARCHIE! SHOW MISS BILTWELL WHERE ROOM 305 IS! SHE'S GOING TO TEACH IN THERE TODAY!
BOING!
SURE THING, MR. WEATHERBEE! I'D BE GLAD TO!
Script & Pencils: Dick Malmgren / Inks: Jon D'Agostino / Letters: Bill Yoshida / Colors: Barry Grossman
AND HELP HER WITH ANYTHING ELSE SHE NEEDS TO GET SET UP!
I WILL! I WILL!
WELCOME TO RIVERDALE HIGH SCHOOL, MISS BILTWELL!
1

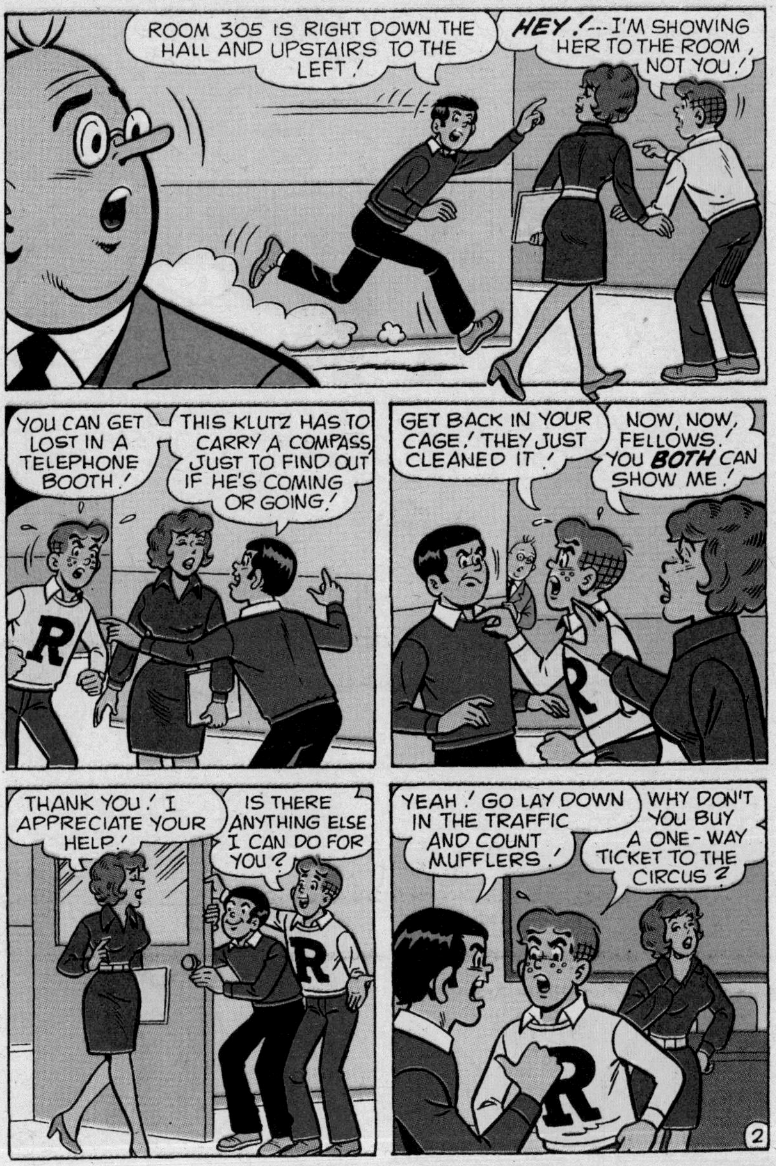
ROOM 305 IS RIGHT DOWN THE HALL AND UPSTAIRS TO THE LEFT!
HEY!--- I'M SHOWING HER TO THE ROOM, NOT YOU!
YOU CAN GET LOST IN A TELEPHONE BOOTH!
THIS KLUTZ HAS TO CARRY A COMPASS JUST TO FIND OUT IF HE'S COMING OR GOING!
GET BACK IN YOUR CAGE! THEY JUST CLEANED IT!
NOW, NOW, FELLOWS! YOU **BOTH** CAN SHOW ME!
THANK YOU! I APPRECIATE YOUR HELP!
IS THERE ANYTHING ELSE I CAN DO FOR YOU?
YEAH! GO LAY DOWN IN THE TRAFFIC AND COUNT MUFFLERS!
WHY DON'T YOU BUY A ONE-WAY TICKET TO THE CIRCUS?
2

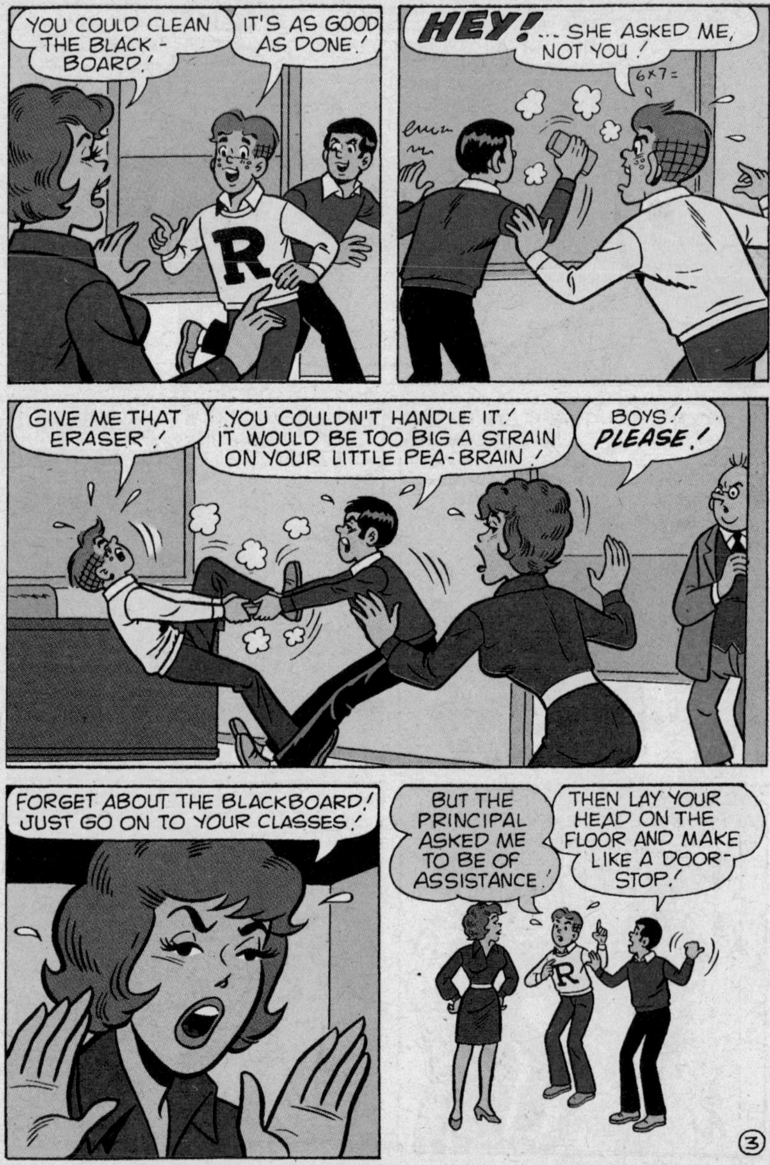
YOU COULD CLEAN THE BLACK-BOARD!
IT'S AS GOOD AS DONE!
HEY! ... SHE ASKED ME, NOT YOU!
6×7=
GIVE ME THAT ERASER!
YOU COULDN'T HANDLE IT! IT WOULD BE TOO BIG A STRAIN ON YOUR LITTLE PEA-BRAIN!
BOYS! PLEASE!
FORGET ABOUT THE BLACKBOARD! JUST GO ON TO YOUR CLASSES!
BUT THE PRINCIPAL ASKED ME TO BE OF ASSISTANCE!
THEN LAY YOUR HEAD ON THE FLOOR AND MAKE LIKE A DOOR-STOP!

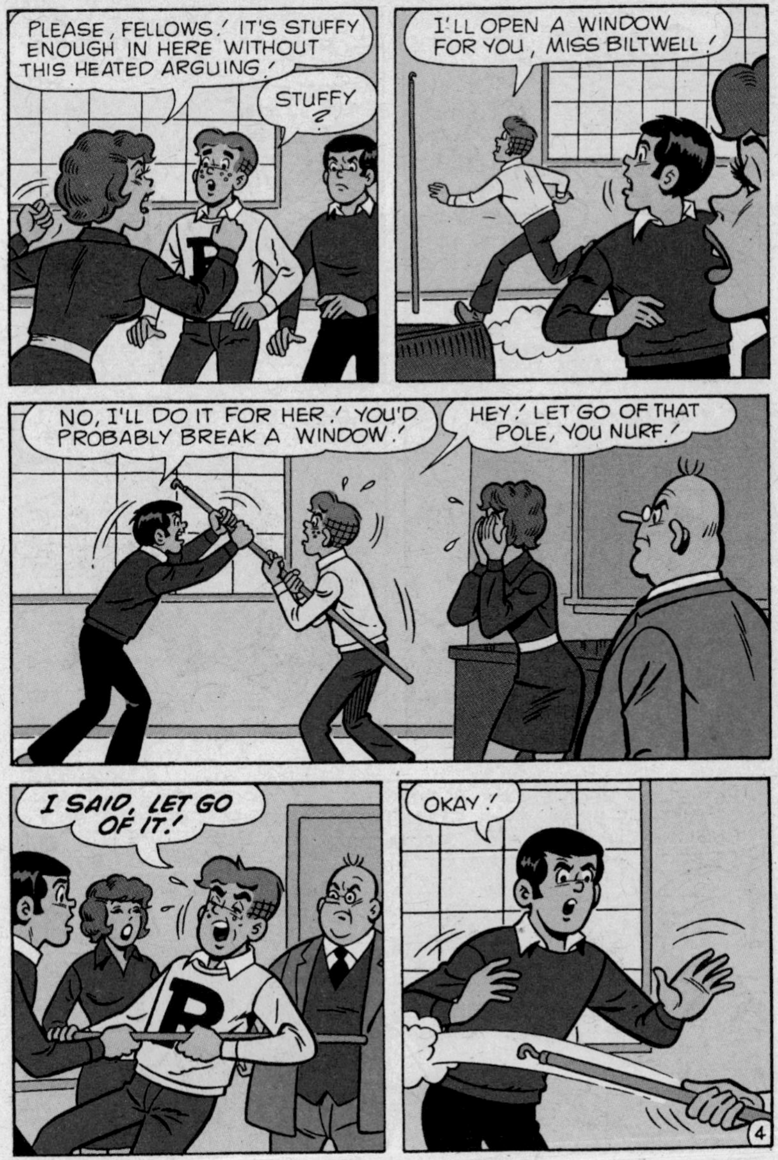
PLEASE, FELLOWS! IT'S STUFFY ENOUGH IN HERE WITHOUT THIS HEATED ARGUING!
STUFFY?
I'LL OPEN A WINDOW FOR YOU, MISS BILTWELL!
NO, I'LL DO IT FOR HER! YOU'D PROBABLY BREAK A WINDOW!
HEY! LET GO OF THAT POLE, YOU NURF!
I SAID, LET GO OF IT!
OKAY!
4

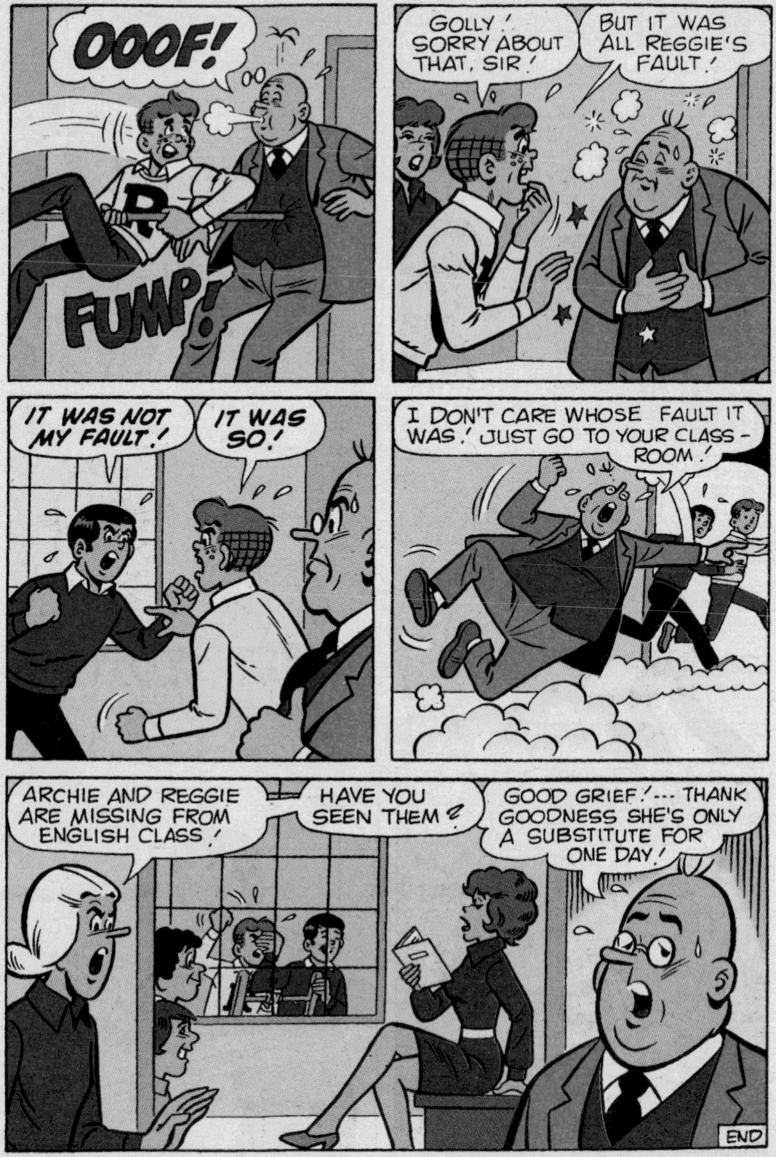
OOOF!
FUMP!
GOLLY! SORRY ABOUT THAT, SIR!
BUT IT WAS ALL REGGIE'S FAULT!
IT WAS NOT MY FAULT!
IT WAS SO!
I DON'T CARE WHOSE FAULT IT WAS! JUST GO TO YOUR CLASS-ROOM!
ARCHIE AND REGGIE ARE MISSING FROM ENGLISH CLASS!
HAVE YOU SEEN THEM?
GOOD GRIEF! --- THANK GOODNESS SHE'S ONLY A SUBSTITUTE FOR ONE DAY!
END

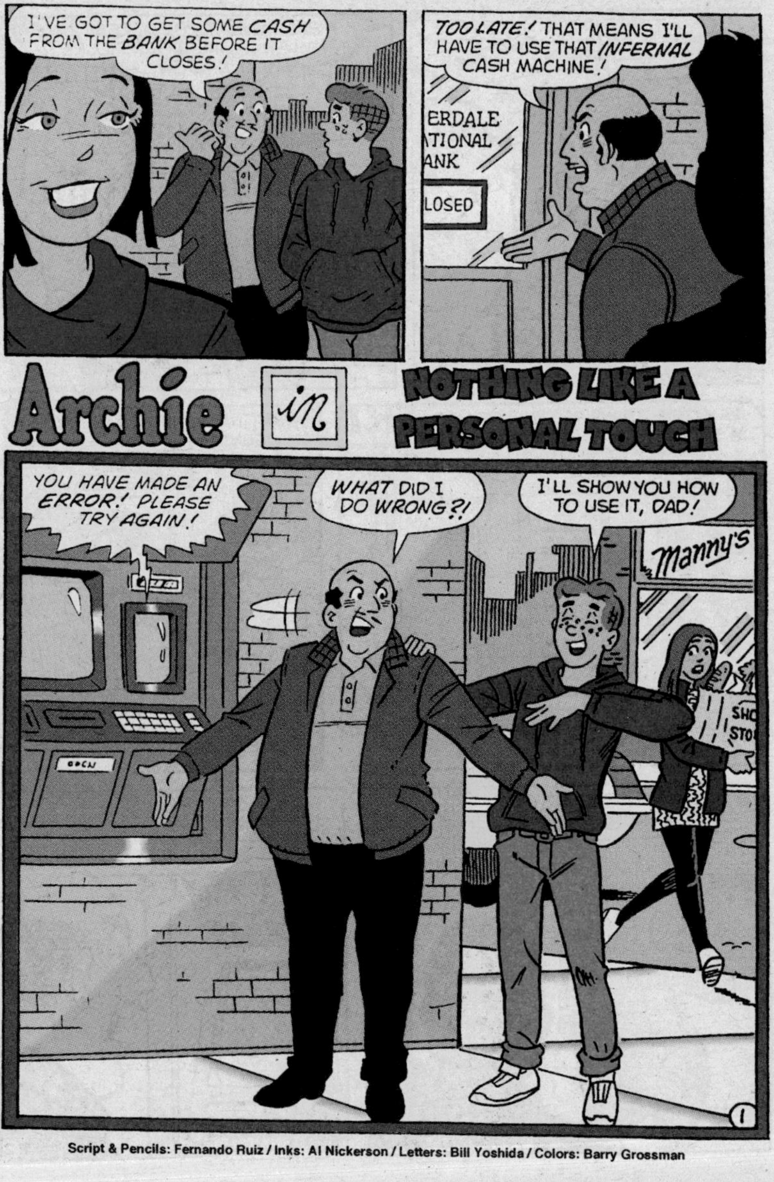
I'VE GOT TO GET SOME CASH FROM THE BANK BEFORE IT CLOSES!
TOO LATE! THAT MEANS I'LL HAVE TO USE THAT INFERNAL CASH MACHINE!
ERDALE
TIONAL
ANK
LOSED
Archie in NOTHING LIKE A PERSONAL TOUCH
YOU HAVE MADE AN ERROR! PLEASE TRY AGAIN!
WHAT DID I DO WRONG?!
I'LL SHOW YOU HOW TO USE IT, DAD!
Manny's
1

Script & Pencils: Fernando Ruiz / Inks: Al Nickerson / Letters: Bill Yoshida / Colors: Barry Grossman

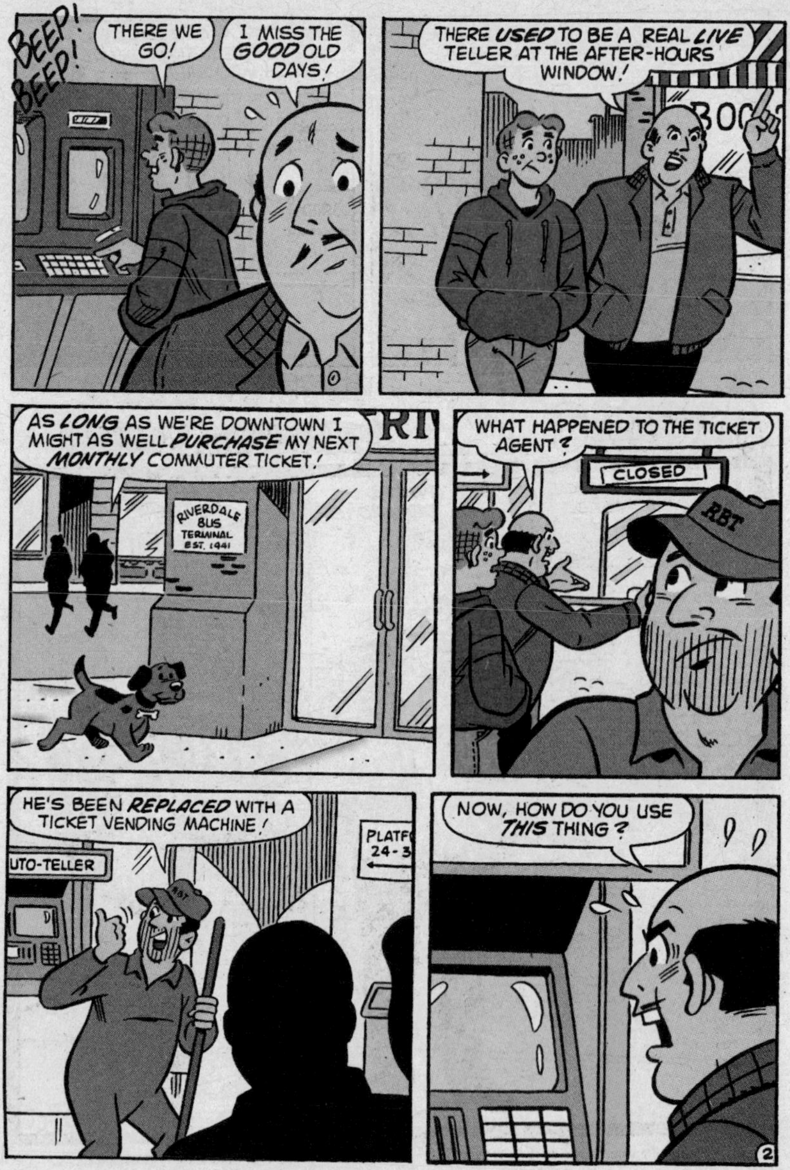
BEEP! BEEP!
THERE WE GO!
I MISS THE GOOD OLD DAYS!
THERE USED TO BE A REAL LIVE TELLER AT THE AFTER-HOURS WINDOW!
AS LONG AS WE'RE DOWNTOWN I MIGHT AS WELL PURCHASE MY NEXT MONTHLY COMMUTER TICKET!
RIVERDALE BUS TERMINAL EST. 1941
WHAT HAPPENED TO THE TICKET AGENT?
CLOSED
RBT
HE'S BEEN REPLACED WITH A TICKET VENDING MACHINE!
UTO-TELLER
PLATF 24-3
NOW, HOW DO YOU USE THIS THING?
2

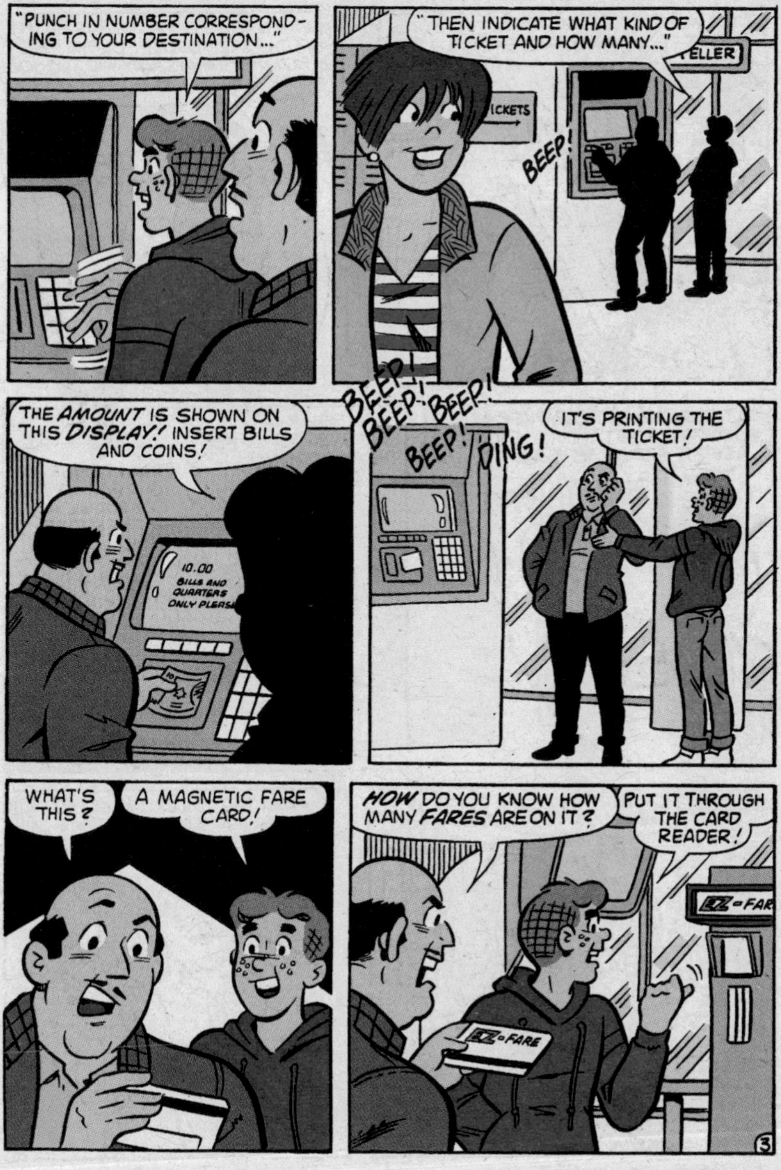
"PUNCH IN NUMBER CORRESPONDING TO YOUR DESTINATION..."
"THEN INDICATE WHAT KIND OF TICKET AND HOW MANY..."
TELLER
TICKETS
BEEP!
BEEP! BEEP! BEEP! BEEP!
THE AMOUNT IS SHOWN ON THIS DISPLAY! INSERT BILLS AND COINS!
10.00
BILLS AND QUARTERS ONLY PLEASE
DING!
IT'S PRINTING THE TICKET!
WHAT'S THIS?
A MAGNETIC FARE CARD!
HOW DO YOU KNOW HOW MANY FARES ARE ON IT?
PUT IT THROUGH THE CARD READER!
EZ-FARE
EZ-FARE

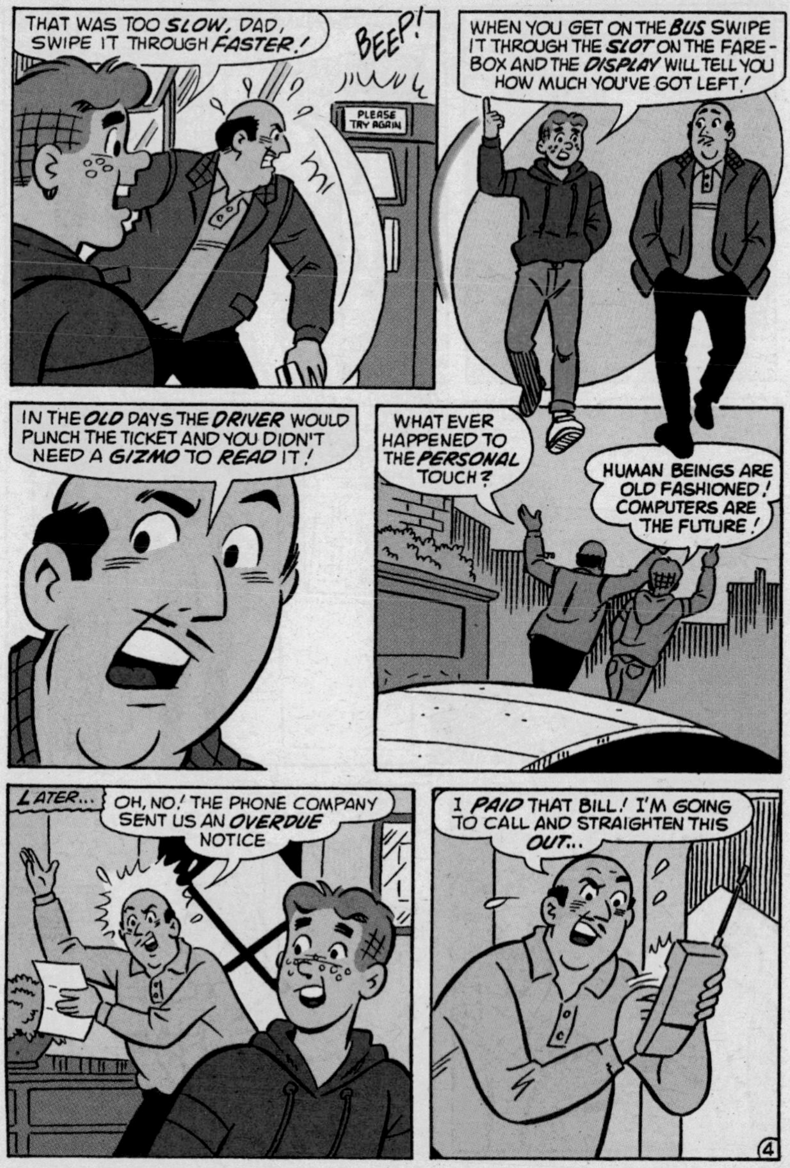
THAT WAS TOO SLOW, DAD, SWIPE IT THROUGH FASTER!
BEEP!
PLEASE TRY AGAIN
WHEN YOU GET ON THE BUS SWIPE IT THROUGH THE SLOT ON THE FARE-BOX AND THE DISPLAY WILL TELL YOU HOW MUCH YOU'VE GOT LEFT!
IN THE OLD DAYS THE DRIVER WOULD PUNCH THE TICKET AND YOU DIDN'T NEED A GIZMO TO READ IT!
WHAT EVER HAPPENED TO THE PERSONAL TOUCH?
HUMAN BEINGS ARE OLD FASHIONED! COMPUTERS ARE THE FUTURE!
LATER...
OH, NO! THE PHONE COMPANY SENT US AN OVERDUE NOTICE
I PAID THAT BILL! I'M GOING TO CALL AND STRAIGHTEN THIS OUT...
4

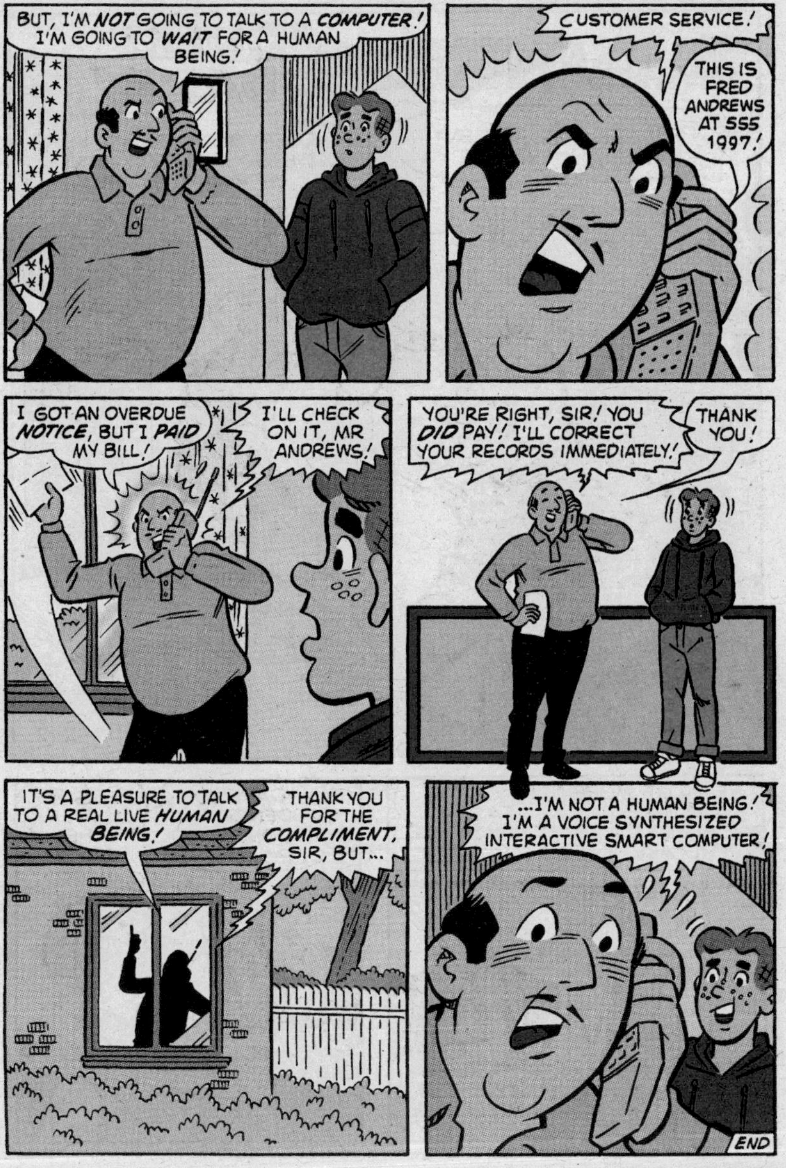
BUT, I'M NOT GOING TO TALK TO A COMPUTER! I'M GOING TO WAIT FOR A HUMAN BEING!
CUSTOMER SERVICE!
THIS IS FRED ANDREWS AT 555 1997!
I GOT AN OVERDUE NOTICE, BUT I PAID MY BILL!
I'LL CHECK ON IT, MR ANDREWS!
YOU'RE RIGHT, SIR! YOU DID PAY! I'LL CORRECT YOUR RECORDS IMMEDIATELY!
THANK YOU!
IT'S A PLEASURE TO TALK TO A REAL LIVE HUMAN BEING!
THANK YOU FOR THE COMPLIMENT, SIR, BUT...
...I'M NOT A HUMAN BEING! I'M A VOICE SYNTHESIZED INTERACTIVE SMART COMPUTER!
END

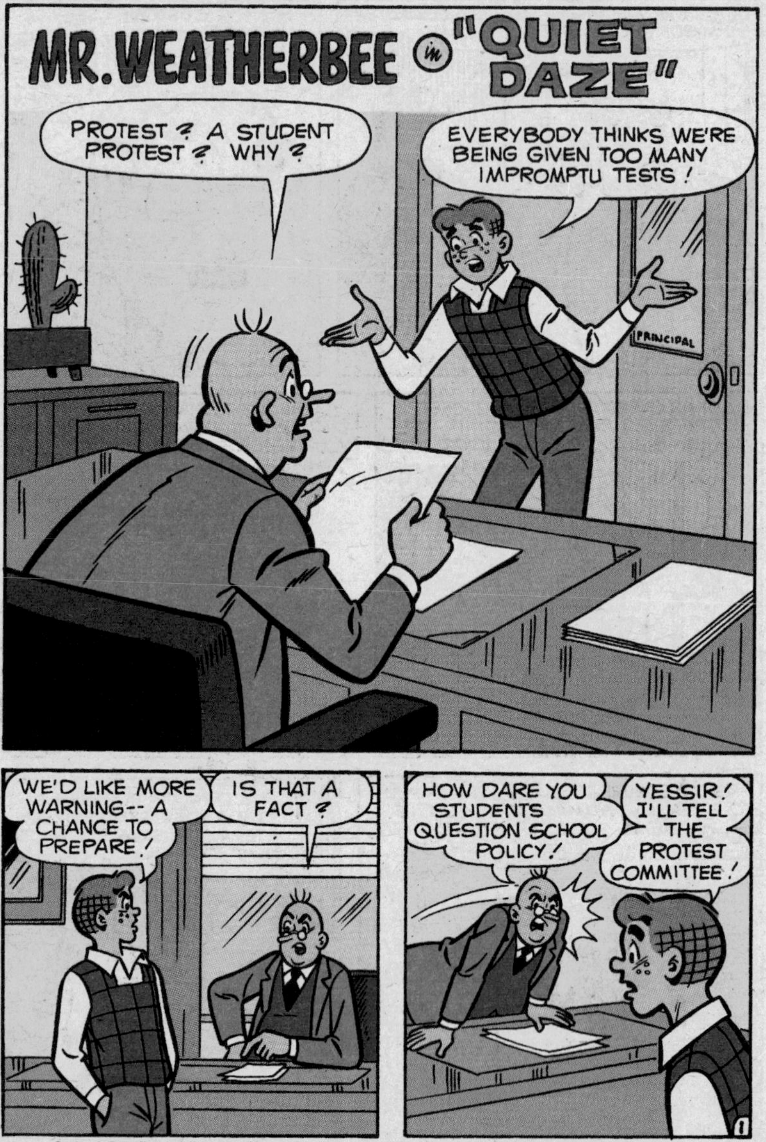
MR. WEATHERBEE in "QUIET DAZE"
PROTEST? A STUDENT PROTEST? WHY?
EVERYBODY THINKS WE'RE BEING GIVEN TOO MANY IMPROMPTU TESTS!
PRINCIPAL
WE'D LIKE MORE WARNING-- A CHANCE TO PREPARE!
IS THAT A FACT?
HOW DARE YOU STUDENTS QUESTION SCHOOL POLICY!
YESSIR! I'LL TELL THE PROTEST COMMITTEE!
1

Script & Pencils: Joe Edwards / Inks: Jon D'Agostino / Letters: Bill Yoshida / Colors: Barry Grossman

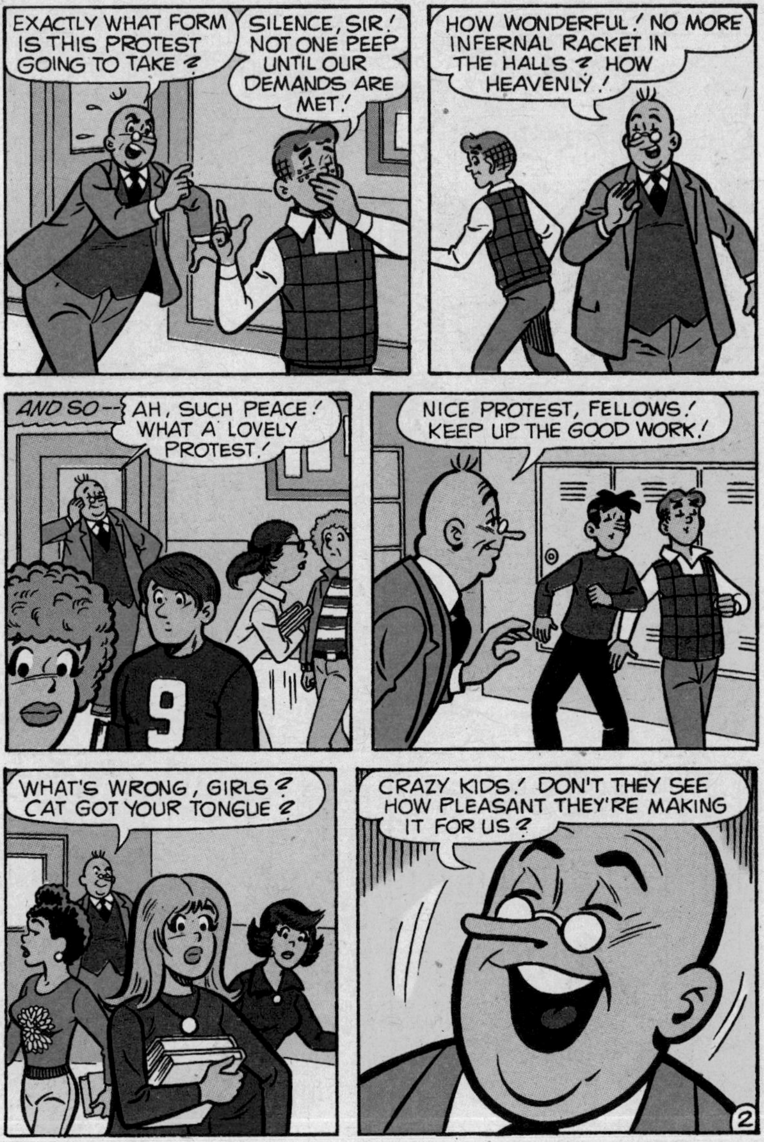
EXACTLY WHAT FORM IS THIS PROTEST GOING TO TAKE ?
SILENCE, SIR! NOT ONE PEEP UNTIL OUR DEMANDS ARE MET!
HOW WONDERFUL! NO MORE INFERNAL RACKET IN THE HALLS ? HOW HEAVENLY!
AND SO--
AH, SUCH PEACE! WHAT A LOVELY PROTEST!
NICE PROTEST, FELLOWS! KEEP UP THE GOOD WORK!
WHAT'S WRONG, GIRLS ? CAT GOT YOUR TONGUE ?
CRAZY KIDS! DON'T THEY SEE HOW PLEASANT THEY'RE MAKING IT FOR US ?
2

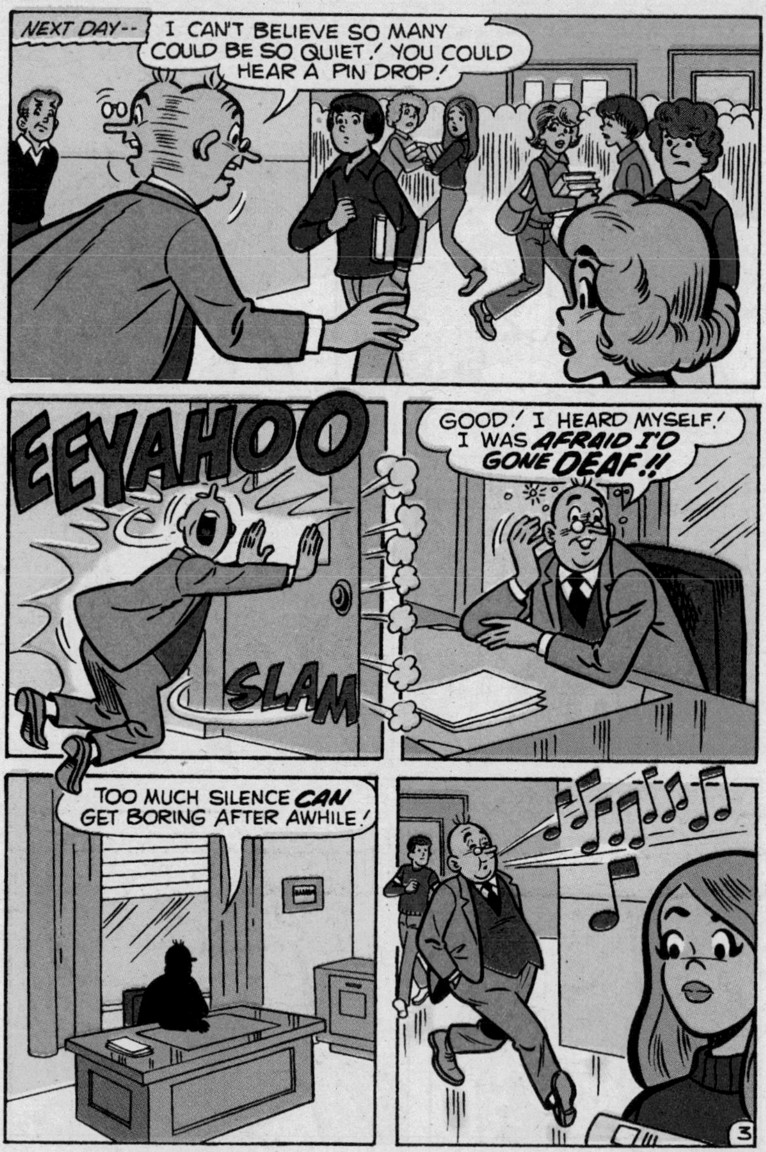
NEXT DAY--
I CAN'T BELIEVE SO MANY COULD BE SO QUIET! YOU COULD HEAR A PIN DROP!
EEYAHOO
SLAM
GOOD! I HEARD MYSELF! I WAS AFRAID I'D GONE DEAF!!
TOO MUCH SILENCE CAN GET BORING AFTER AWHILE!
3

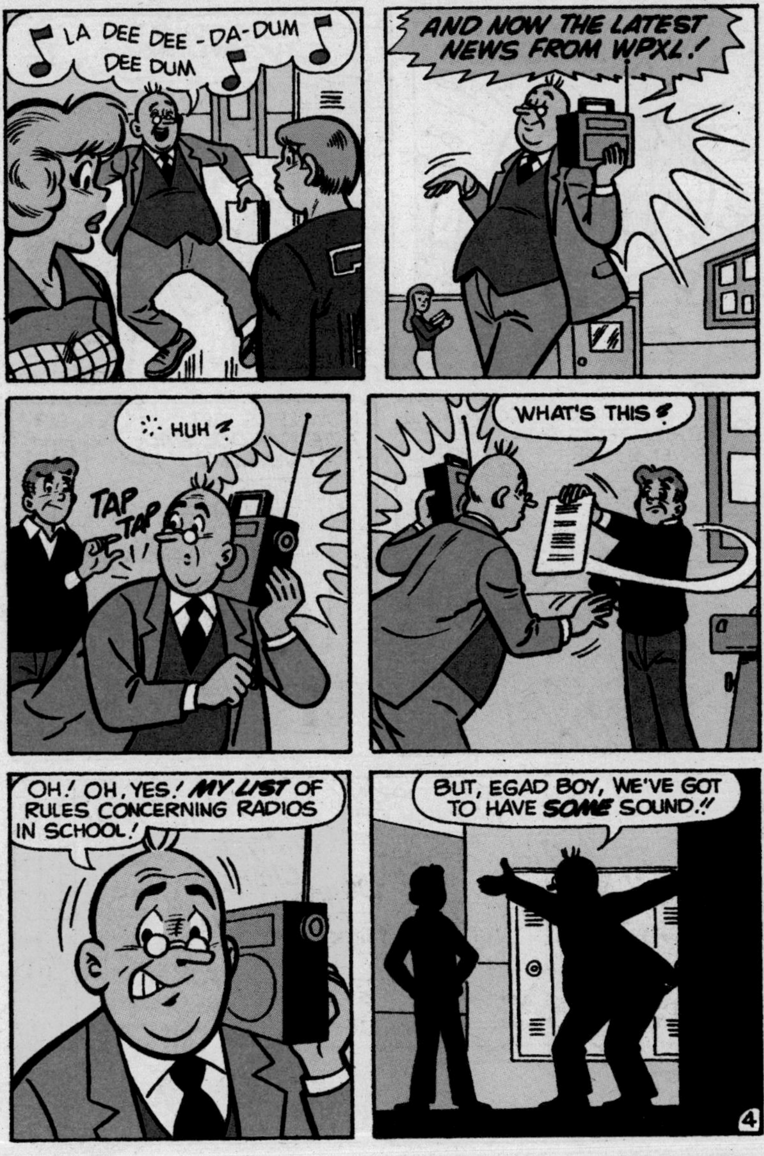
LA DEE DEE - DA - DUM DEE DUM
AND NOW THE LATEST NEWS FROM WPXL!
HUH?
TAP TAP
WHAT'S THIS?
OH! OH, YES! MY LIST OF RULES CONCERNING RADIOS IN SCHOOL!
BUT, EGAD BOY, WE'VE GOT TO HAVE SOME SOUND!!
4

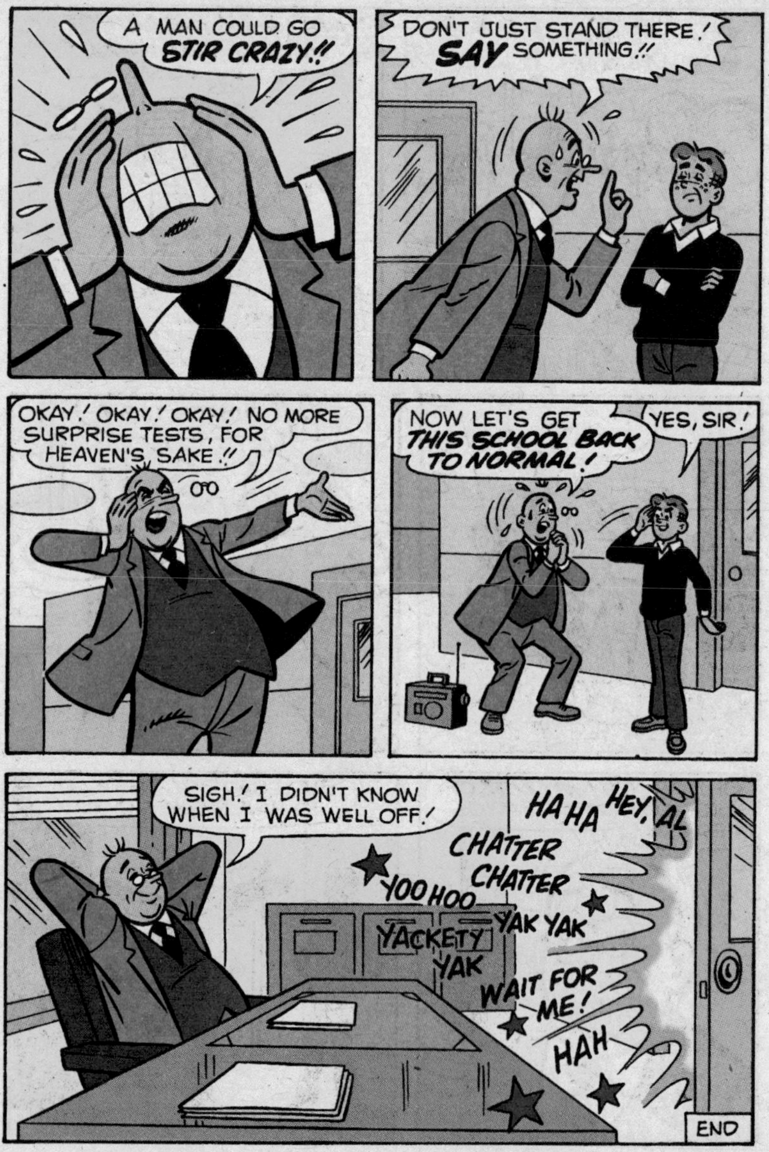
A MAN COULD GO STIR CRAZY!!
DON'T JUST STAND THERE! SAY SOMETHING!!
OKAY! OKAY! OKAY! NO MORE SURPRISE TESTS, FOR HEAVEN'S SAKE!!
NOW LET'S GET THIS SCHOOL BACK TO NORMAL!
YES, SIR!
SIGH! I DIDN'T KNOW WHEN I WAS WELL OFF!
HA HA
HEY, AL
CHATTER
CHATTER
YOO HOO
YAK YAK
YACKETY YAK
WAIT FOR ME!
HAH
END

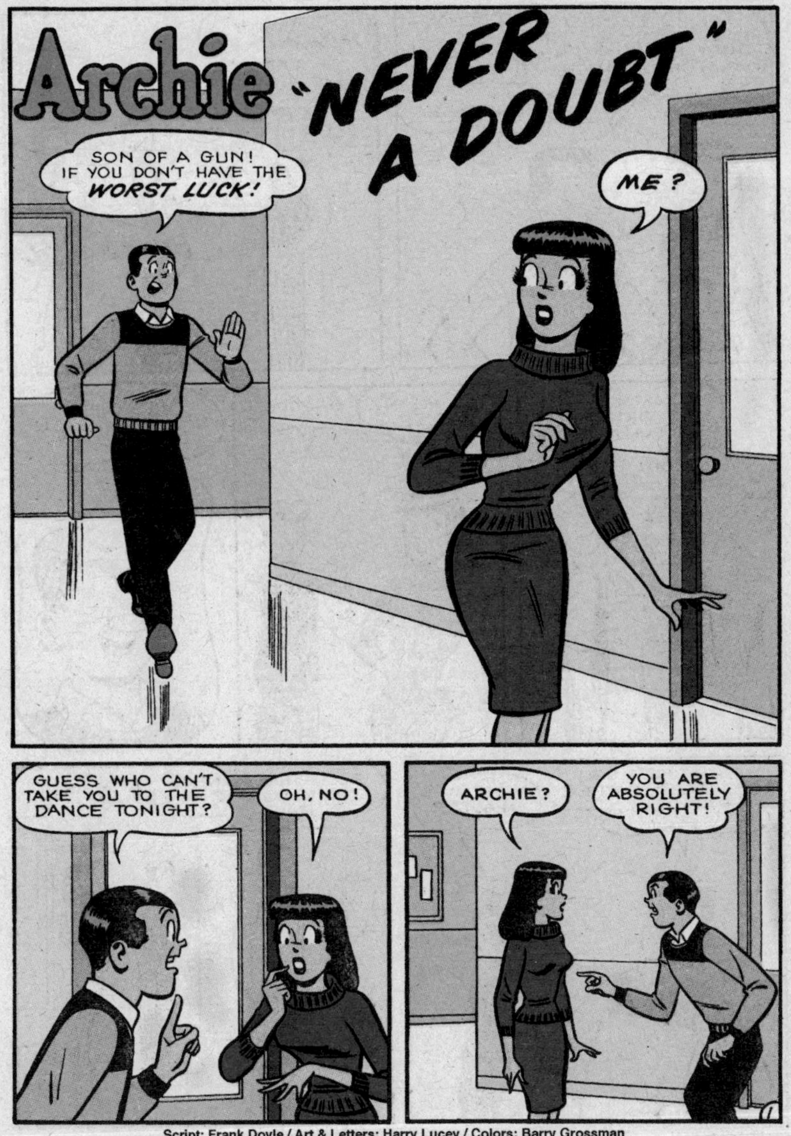
Archie
"NEVER A DOUBT"
SON OF A GUN! IF YOU DON'T HAVE THE WORST LUCK!
ME?
GUESS WHO CAN'T TAKE YOU TO THE DANCE TONIGHT?
OH, NO!
ARCHIE?
YOU ARE ABSOLUTELY RIGHT!

Script: Frank Doyle / Art & Letters: Harry Lucey / Colors: Barry Grossman

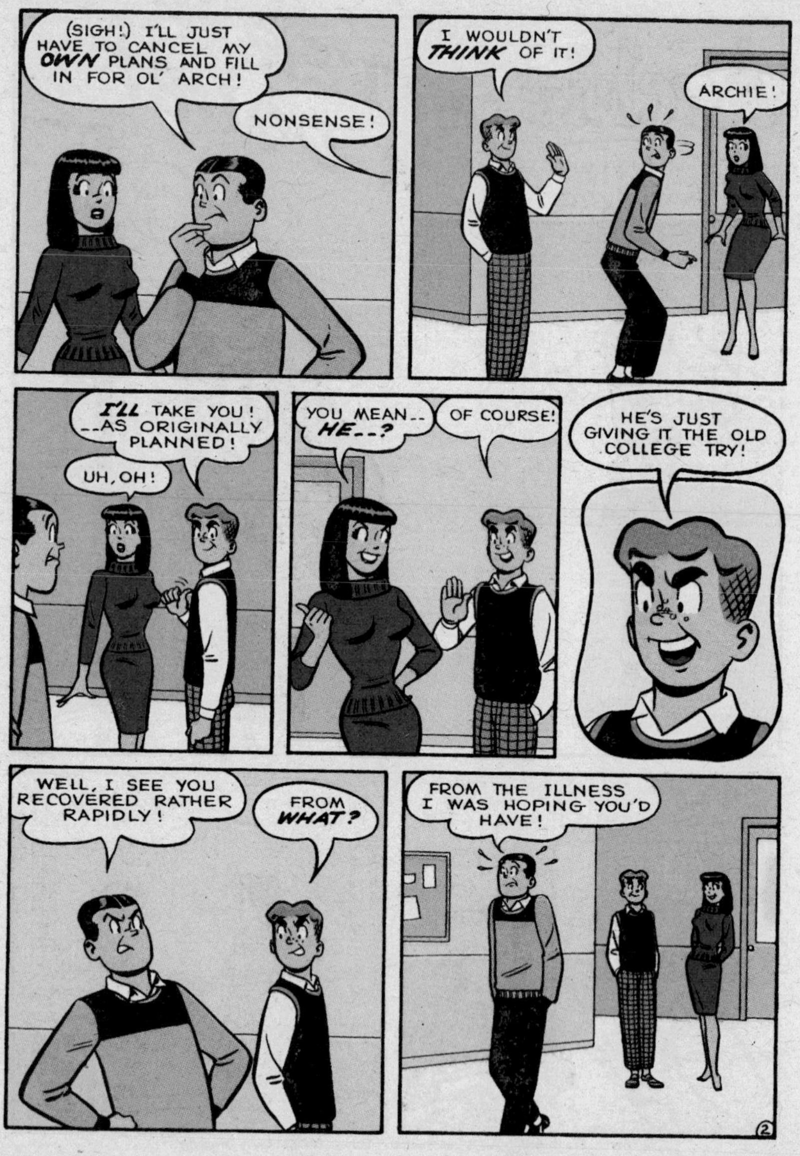
(SIGH!) I'LL JUST HAVE TO CANCEL MY **OWN** PLANS AND FILL IN FOR OL' ARCH!
NONSENSE!
I WOULDN'T **THINK** OF IT!
ARCHIE!
I'LL TAKE YOU! --AS ORIGINALLY PLANNED!
UH, OH!
YOU MEAN-- **HE--?**
OF COURSE!
HE'S JUST GIVING IT THE OLD COLLEGE TRY!
WELL, I SEE YOU RECOVERED RATHER RAPIDLY!
FROM **WHAT?**
FROM THE ILLNESS I WAS HOPING YOU'D HAVE!
2

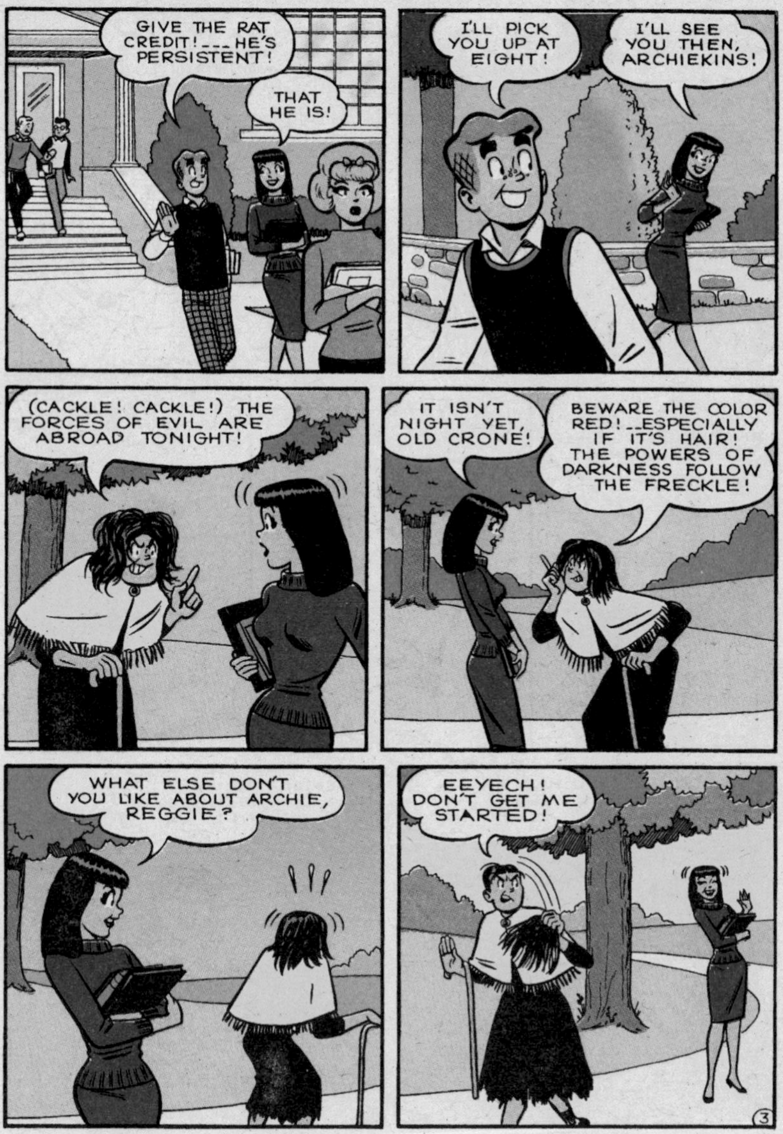
GIVE THE RAT CREDIT! --- HE'S PERSISTENT!
THAT HE IS!
I'LL PICK YOU UP AT EIGHT!
I'LL SEE YOU THEN, ARCHIEKINS!
(CACKLE! CACKLE!) THE FORCES OF EVIL ARE ABROAD TONIGHT!
IT ISN'T NIGHT YET, OLD CRONE!
BEWARE THE COLOR RED! --ESPECIALLY IF IT'S HAIR! THE POWERS OF DARKNESS FOLLOW THE FRECKLE!
WHAT ELSE DON'T YOU LIKE ABOUT ARCHIE, REGGIE?
EEYECH! DON'T GET ME STARTED!
3

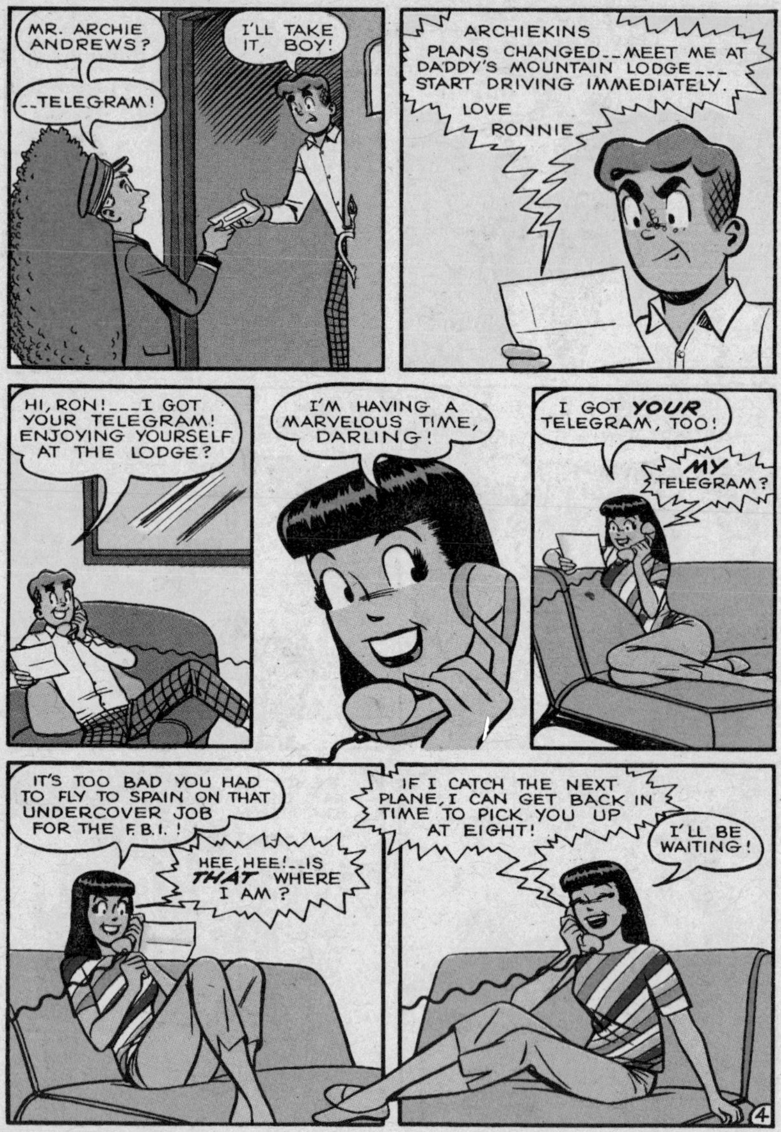
MR. ARCHIE ANDREWS?
--TELEGRAM!
I'LL TAKE IT, BOY!
ARCHIEKINS
PLANS CHANGED--MEET ME AT DADDY'S MOUNTAIN LODGE--- START DRIVING IMMEDIATELY.
LOVE
RONNIE
HI, RON!---I GOT YOUR TELEGRAM! ENJOYING YOURSELF AT THE LODGE?
I'M HAVING A MARVELOUS TIME, DARLING!
I GOT ***YOUR*** TELEGRAM, TOO!
MY TELEGRAM?
IT'S TOO BAD YOU HAD TO FLY TO SPAIN ON THAT UNDERCOVER JOB FOR THE F.B.I.!
HEE, HEE!--IS ***THAT*** WHERE I AM?
IF I CATCH THE NEXT PLANE, I CAN GET BACK IN TIME TO PICK YOU UP AT EIGHT!
I'LL BE WAITING!
4

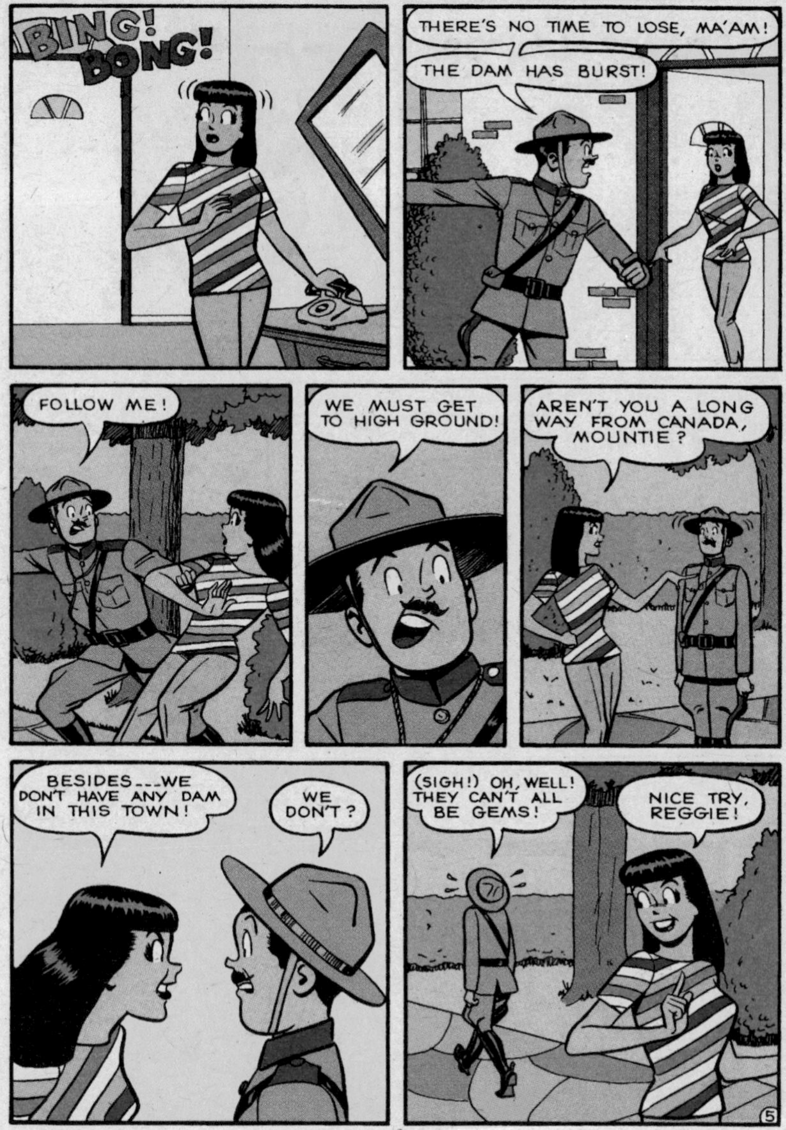
BING! BONG!
THERE'S NO TIME TO LOSE, MA'AM!
THE DAM HAS BURST!
FOLLOW ME!
WE MUST GET TO HIGH GROUND!
AREN'T YOU A LONG WAY FROM CANADA, MOUNTIE?
BESIDES---WE DON'T HAVE ANY DAM IN THIS TOWN!
WE DON'T?
(SIGH!) OH, WELL! THEY CAN'T ALL BE GEMS!
NICE TRY, REGGIE!
5

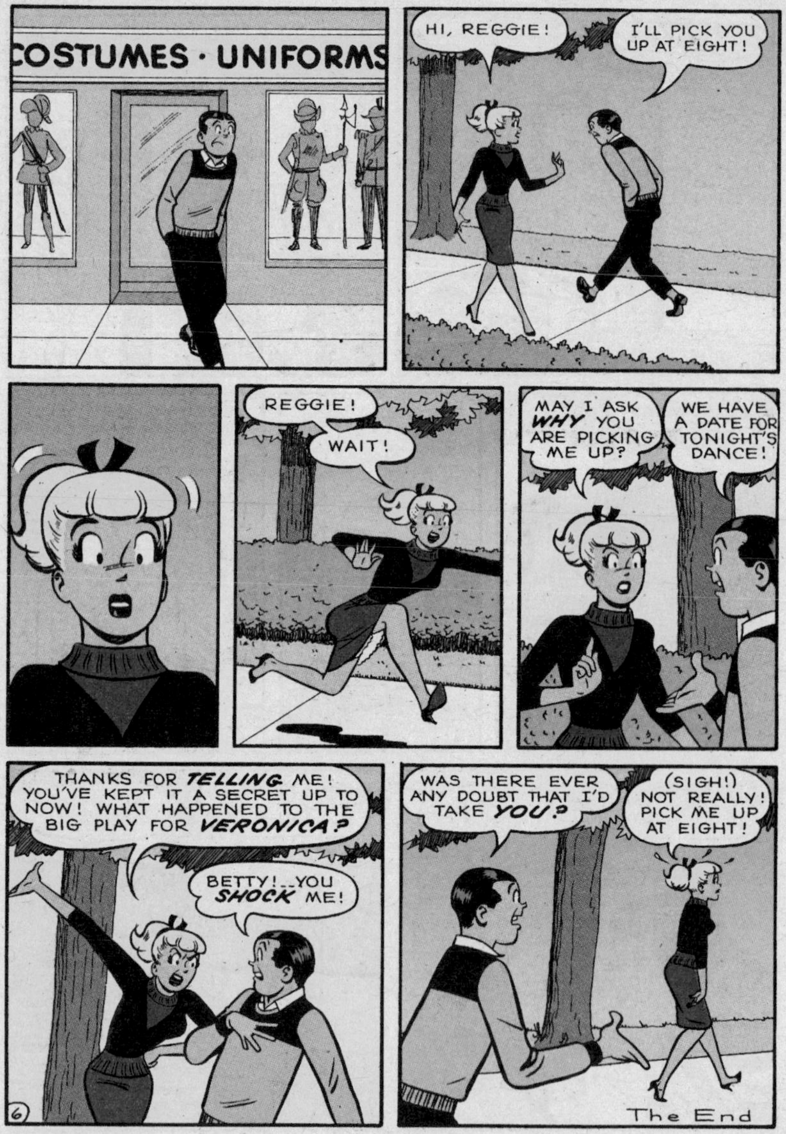
COSTUMES · UNIFORMS
HI, REGGIE!
I'LL PICK YOU UP AT EIGHT!
REGGIE!
WAIT!
MAY I ASK WHY YOU ARE PICKING ME UP?
WE HAVE A DATE FOR TONIGHT'S DANCE!
THANKS FOR TELLING ME! YOU'VE KEPT IT A SECRET UP TO NOW! WHAT HAPPENED TO THE BIG PLAY FOR VERONICA?
BETTY!..YOU SHOCK ME!
6
WAS THERE EVER ANY DOUBT THAT I'D TAKE YOU?
(SIGH!) NOT REALLY! PICK ME UP AT EIGHT!
The End

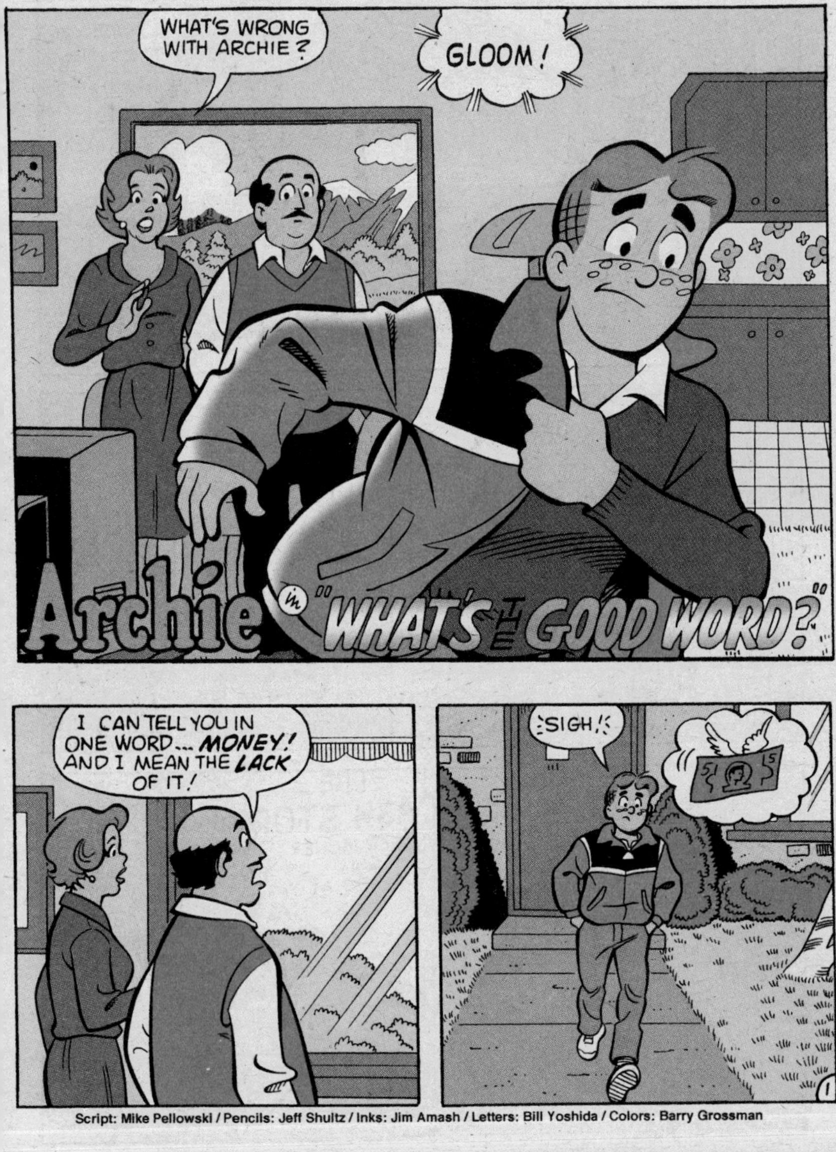
WHAT'S WRONG WITH ARCHIE?
GLOOM!
Archie in "WHAT'S THE GOOD WORD?"
I CAN TELL YOU IN ONE WORD... MONEY! AND I MEAN THE LACK OF IT!
SIGH!
1

Script: Mike Pellowski / Pencils: Jeff Shultz / Inks: Jim Amash / Letters: Bill Yoshida / Colors: Barry Grossman

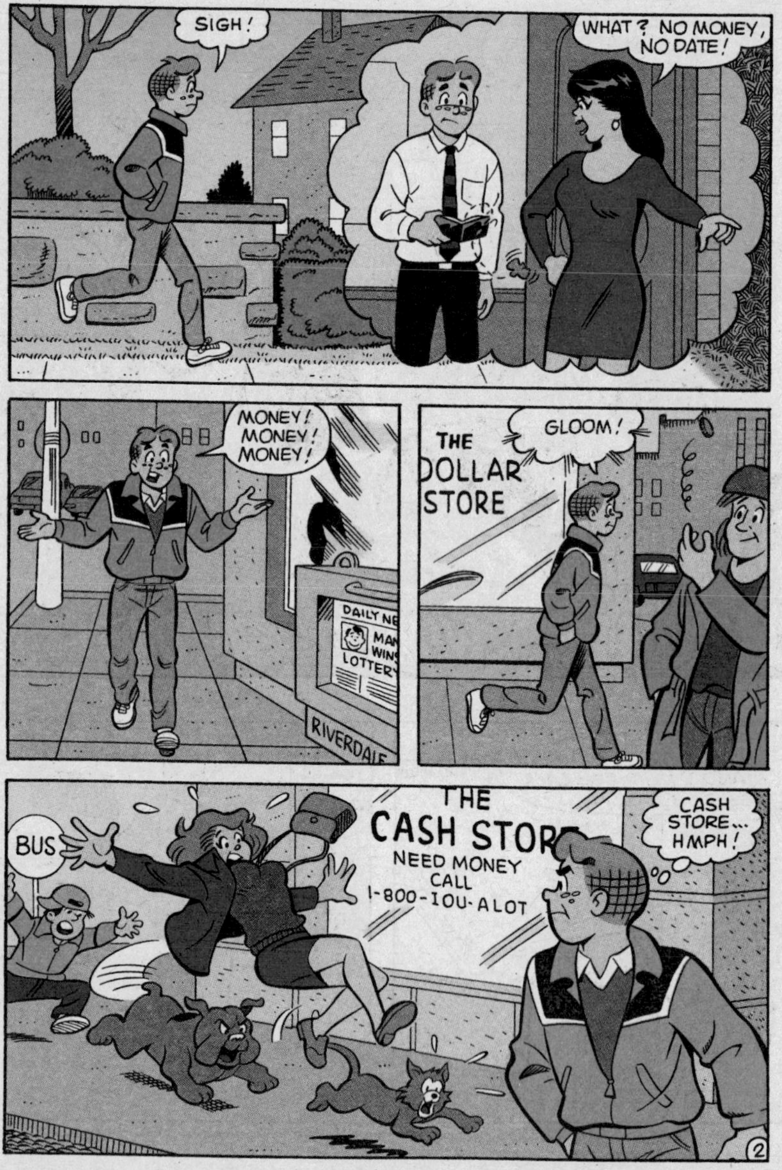
SIGH!
WHAT? NO MONEY, NO DATE!
MONEY! MONEY! MONEY!
DAILY NE
MAN WINS LOTTERY
RIVERDALE
THE DOLLAR STORE
GLOOM!
THE CASH STORE
NEED MONEY CALL 1-800-IOU-ALOT
BUS
CASH STORE... HMPH!
2

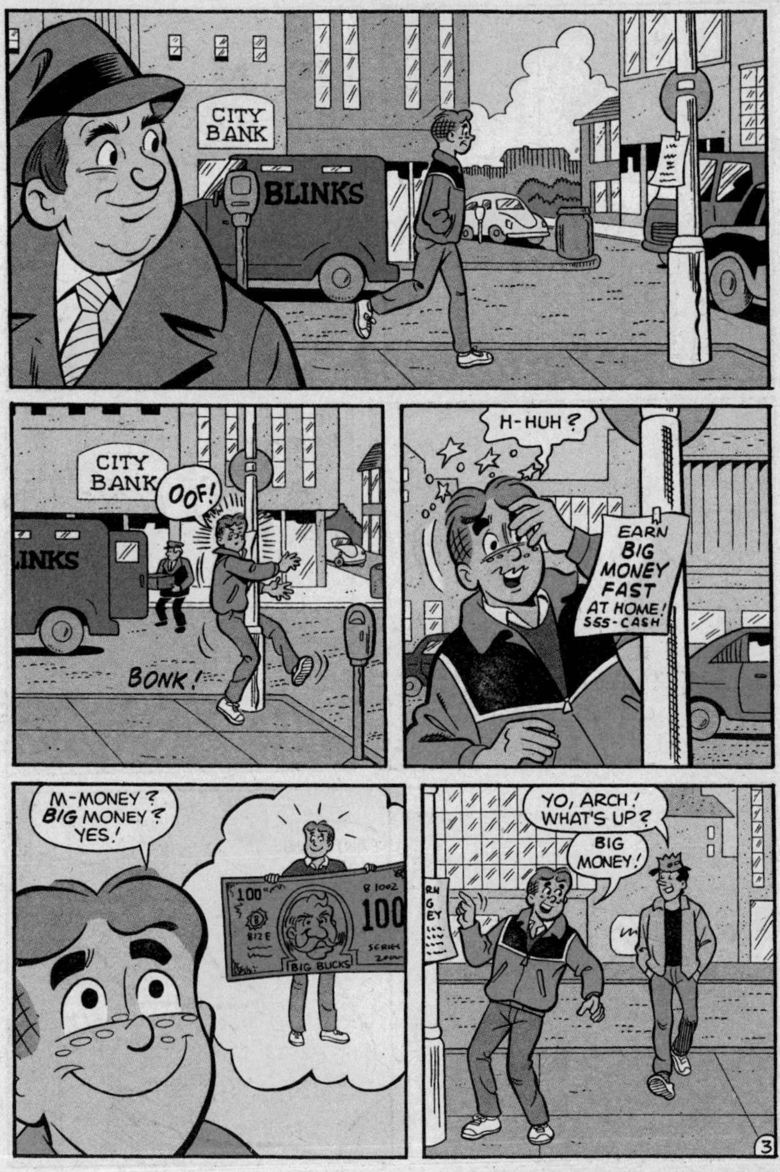
CITY BANK
BLINKS
CITY BANK
OOF!
LINKS
BONK!
H-HUH?
EARN BIG MONEY FAST AT HOME! 555-CASH
M-MONEY? BIG MONEY? YES!
100
BIG BUCKS
YO, ARCH! WHAT'S UP?
BIG MONEY!

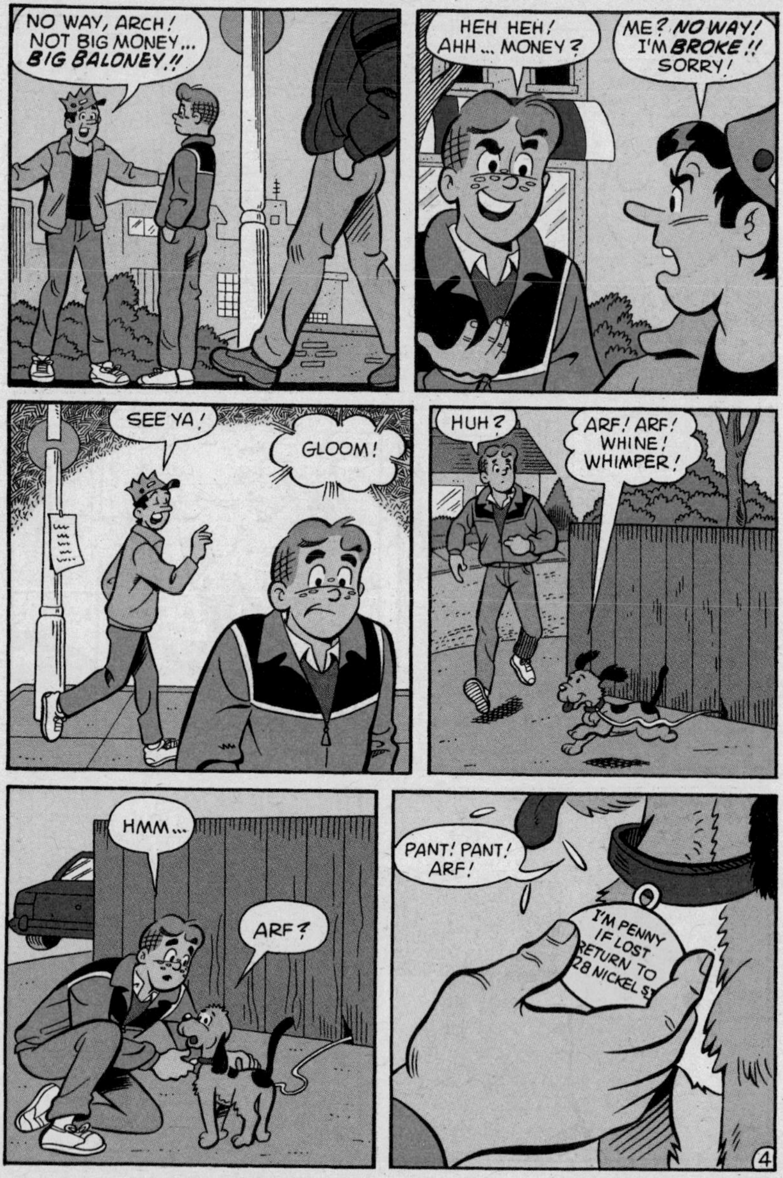
NO WAY, ARCH! NOT BIG MONEY... BIG BALONEY!!
HEH HEH! AHH ... MONEY?
ME? NO WAY! I'M BROKE!! SORRY!
SEE YA!
GLOOM!
HUH?
ARF! ARF! WHINE! WHIMPER!
HMM...
ARF?
PANT! PANT! ARF!
I'M PENNY IF LOST RETURN TO 28 NICKEL ST.
4

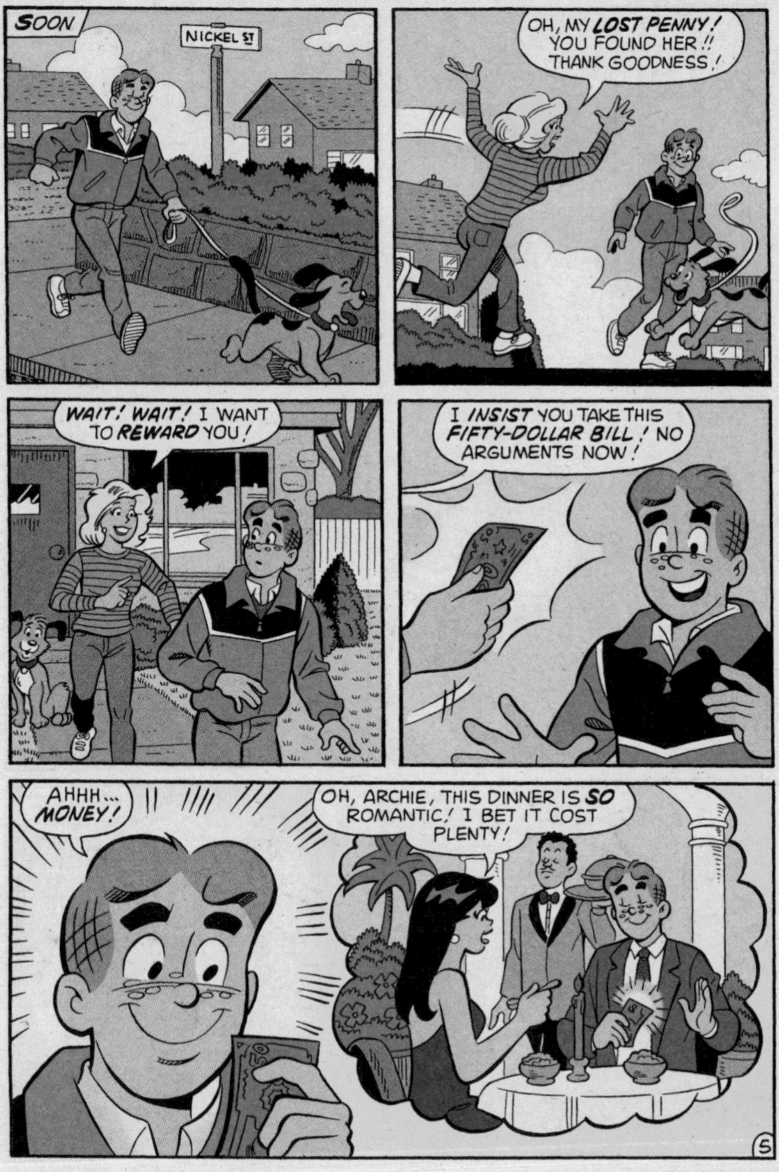
SOON
NICKEL ST
OH, MY LOST PENNY! YOU FOUND HER!! THANK GOODNESS!
WAIT! WAIT! I WANT TO REWARD YOU!
I INSIST YOU TAKE THIS FIFTY-DOLLAR BILL! NO ARGUMENTS NOW!
AHHH... MONEY!
OH, ARCHIE, THIS DINNER IS SO ROMANTIC! I BET IT COST PLENTY!
5

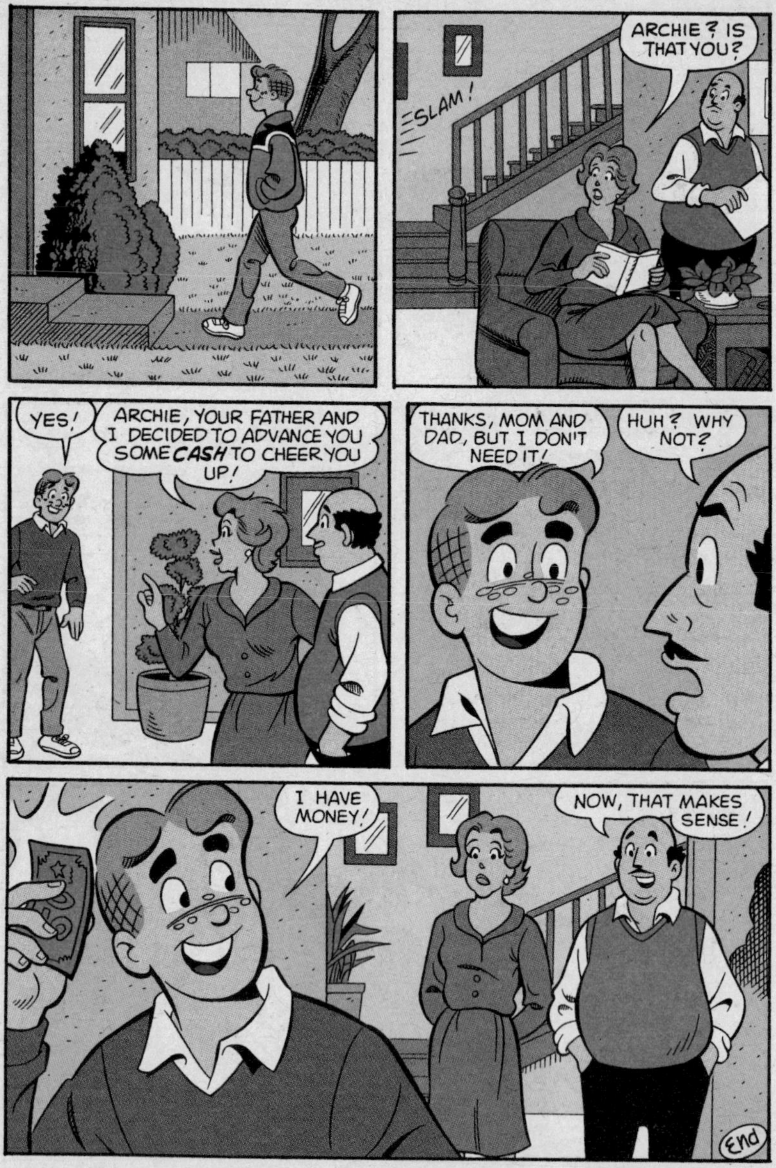

SLAM!
ARCHIE? IS THAT YOU?
YES!
ARCHIE, YOUR FATHER AND I DECIDED TO ADVANCE YOU SOME CASH TO CHEER YOU UP!
THANKS, MOM AND DAD, BUT I DON'T NEED IT!
HUH? WHY NOT?
I HAVE MONEY!
NOW, THAT MAKES SENSE!
End

Archie in "GOING BUGGY"

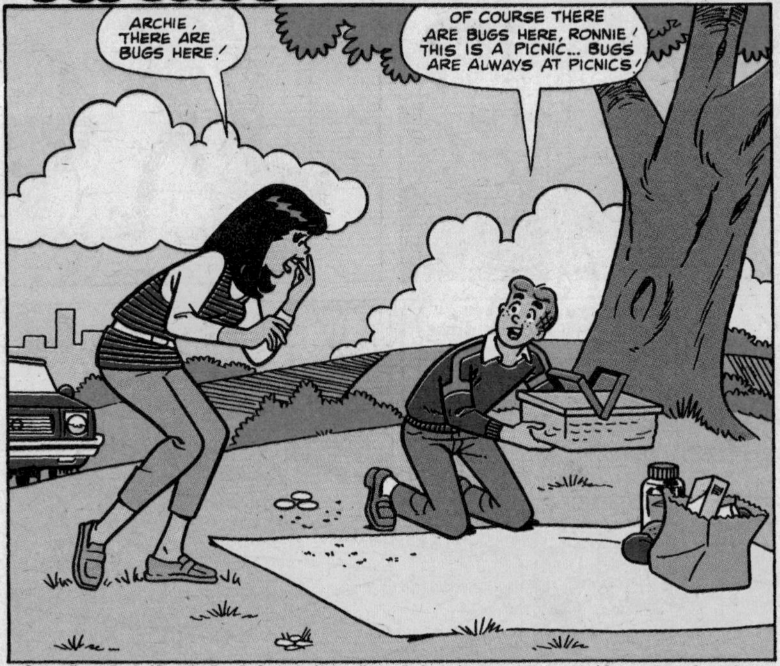

ARCHIE, THERE ARE BUGS HERE!
OF COURSE THERE ARE BUGS HERE, RONNIE! THIS IS A PICNIC... BUGS ARE ALWAYS AT PICNICS!

Script: Frank Doyle / Pencils: Dan DeCarlo Jr. / Inks: Jimmy DeCarlo / Letters: Bill Yoshida / Colors: Barry Grossman

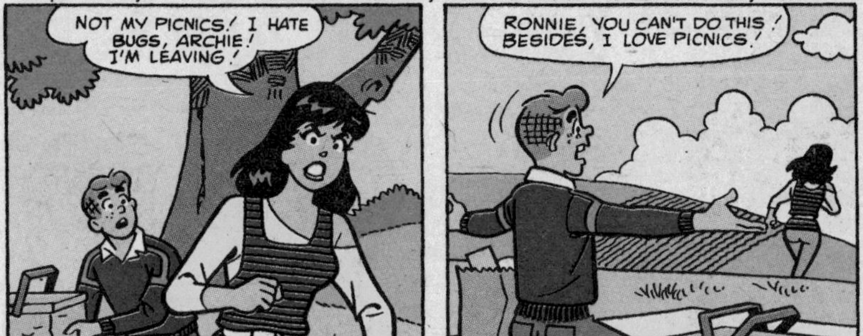

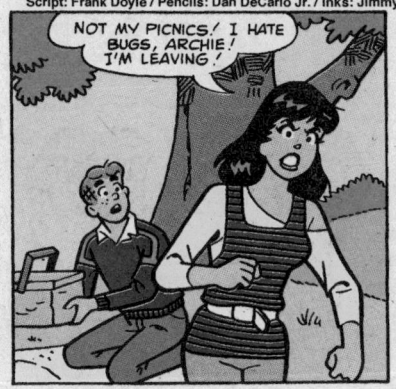

NOT MY PICNICS! I HATE BUGS, ARCHIE! I'M LEAVING!
RONNIE, YOU CAN'T DO THIS! BESIDES, I LOVE PICNICS!

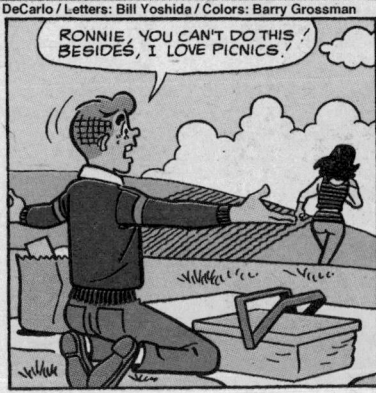

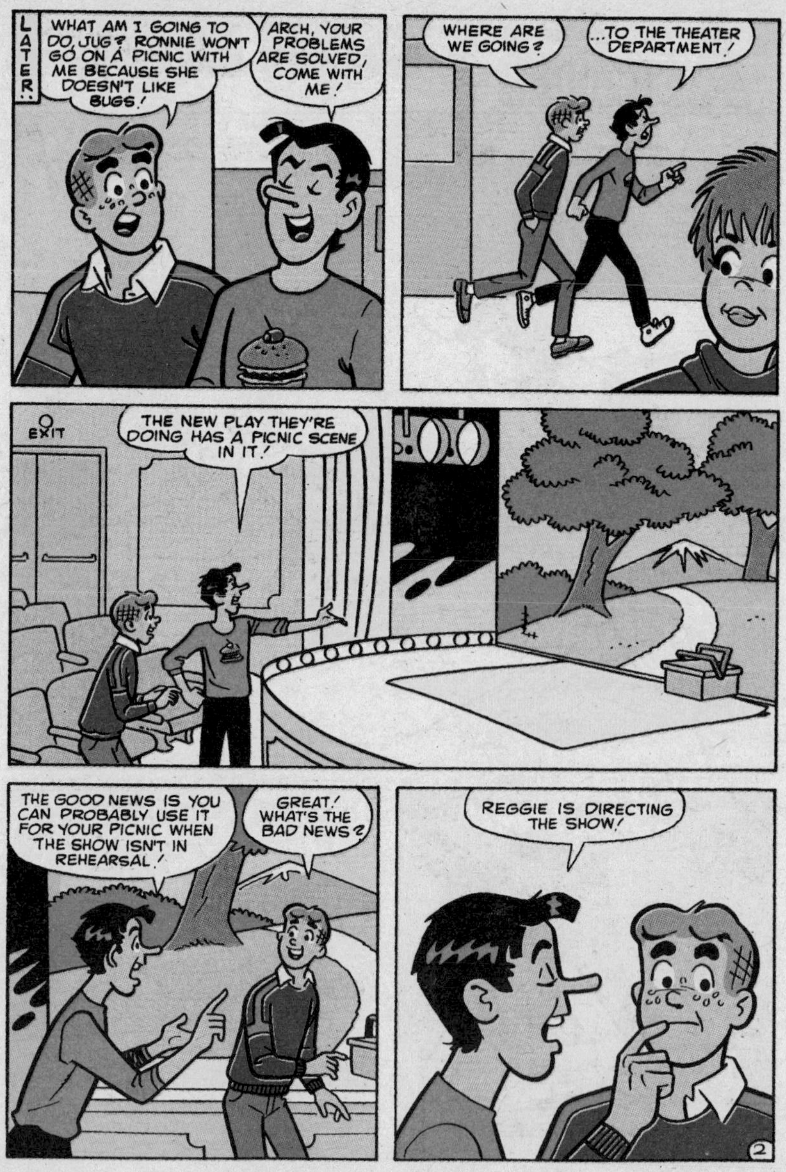
LATER:
WHAT AM I GOING TO DO, JUG? RONNIE WON'T GO ON A PICNIC WITH ME BECAUSE SHE DOESN'T LIKE BUGS!
ARCH, YOUR PROBLEMS ARE SOLVED, COME WITH ME!
WHERE ARE WE GOING?
...TO THE THEATER DEPARTMENT!
EXIT
THE NEW PLAY THEY'RE DOING HAS A PICNIC SCENE IN IT!
THE GOOD NEWS IS YOU CAN PROBABLY USE IT FOR YOUR PICNIC WHEN THE SHOW ISN'T IN REHEARSAL!
GREAT! WHAT'S THE BAD NEWS?
REGGIE IS DIRECTING THE SHOW!
2

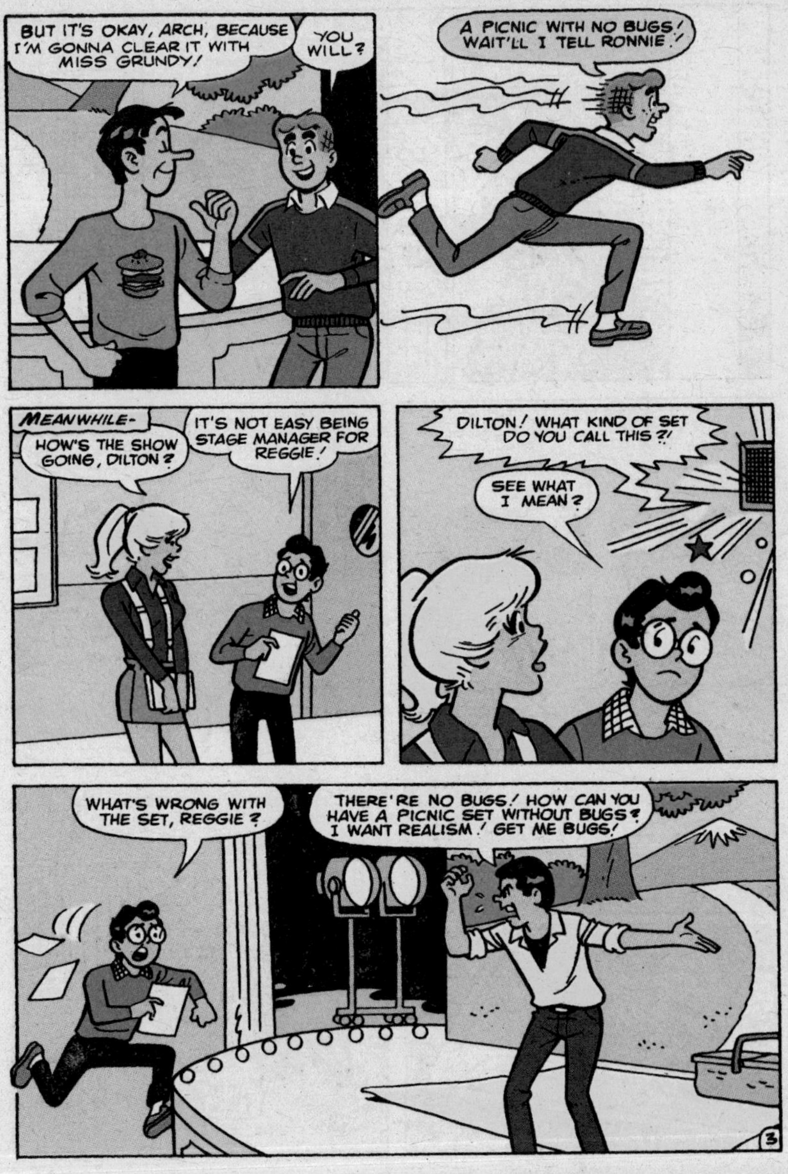
BUT IT'S OKAY, ARCH, BECAUSE I'M GONNA CLEAR IT WITH MISS GRUNDY!
YOU WILL?
A PICNIC WITH NO BUGS! WAIT'LL I TELL RONNIE!
MEANWHILE-
HOW'S THE SHOW GOING, DILTON?
IT'S NOT EASY BEING STAGE MANAGER FOR REGGIE!
DILTON! WHAT KIND OF SET DO YOU CALL THIS?!
SEE WHAT I MEAN?
WHAT'S WRONG WITH THE SET, REGGIE?
THERE'RE NO BUGS! HOW CAN YOU HAVE A PICNIC SET WITHOUT BUGS? I WANT REALISM! GET ME BUGS!
3

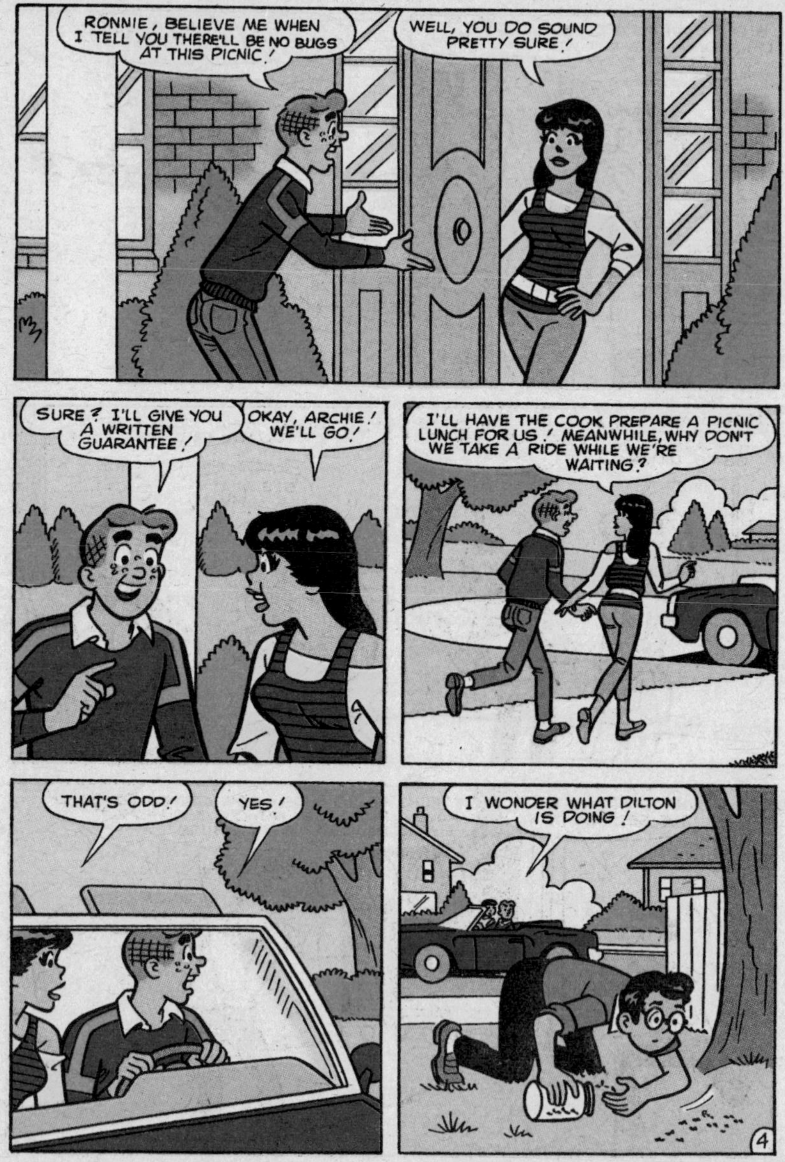
RONNIE, BELIEVE ME WHEN I TELL YOU THERE'LL BE NO BUGS AT THIS PICNIC!
WELL, YOU DO SOUND PRETTY SURE!
SURE? I'LL GIVE YOU A WRITTEN GUARANTEE!
OKAY, ARCHIE! WE'LL GO!
I'LL HAVE THE COOK PREPARE A PICNIC LUNCH FOR US! MEANWHILE, WHY DON'T WE TAKE A RIDE WHILE WE'RE WAITING?
THAT'S ODD!
YES!
I WONDER WHAT DILTON IS DOING!
4

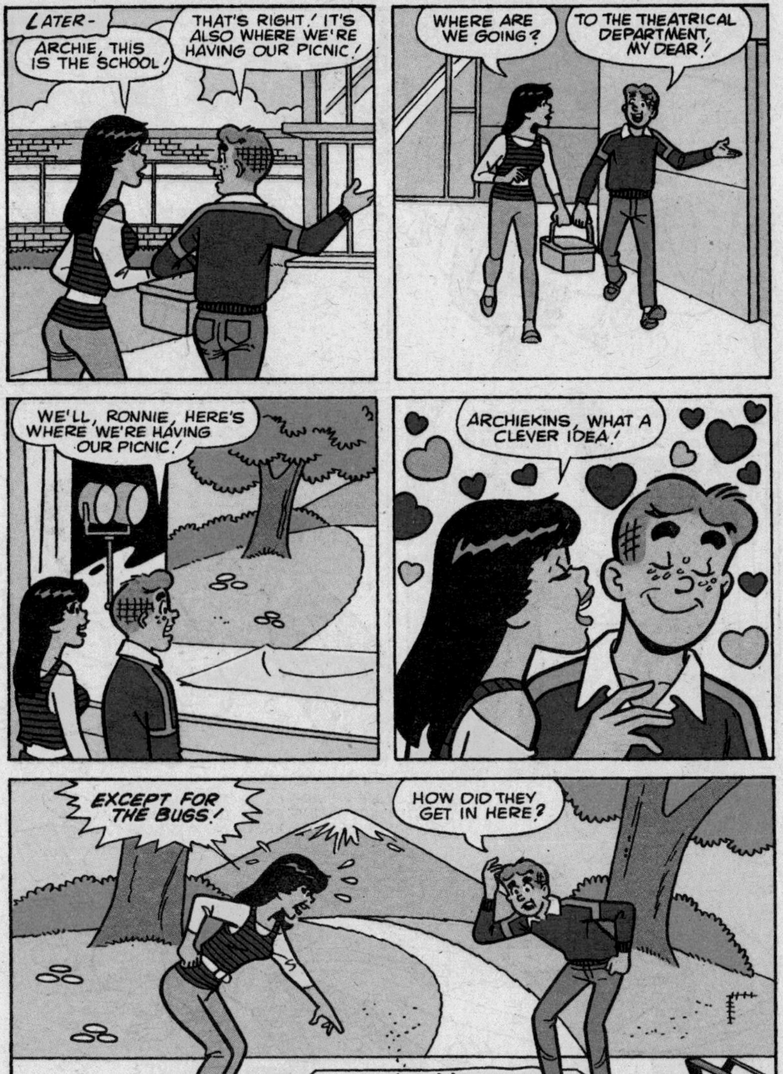
LATER-
ARCHIE, THIS IS THE SCHOOL!
THAT'S RIGHT! IT'S ALSO WHERE WE'RE HAVING OUR PICNIC!
WHERE ARE WE GOING?
TO THE THEATRICAL DEPARTMENT, MY DEAR!
WE'LL, RONNIE, HERE'S WHERE WE'RE HAVING OUR PICNIC!
ARCHIEKINS, WHAT A CLEVER IDEA!
EXCEPT FOR THE BUGS!
HOW DID THEY GET IN HERE?

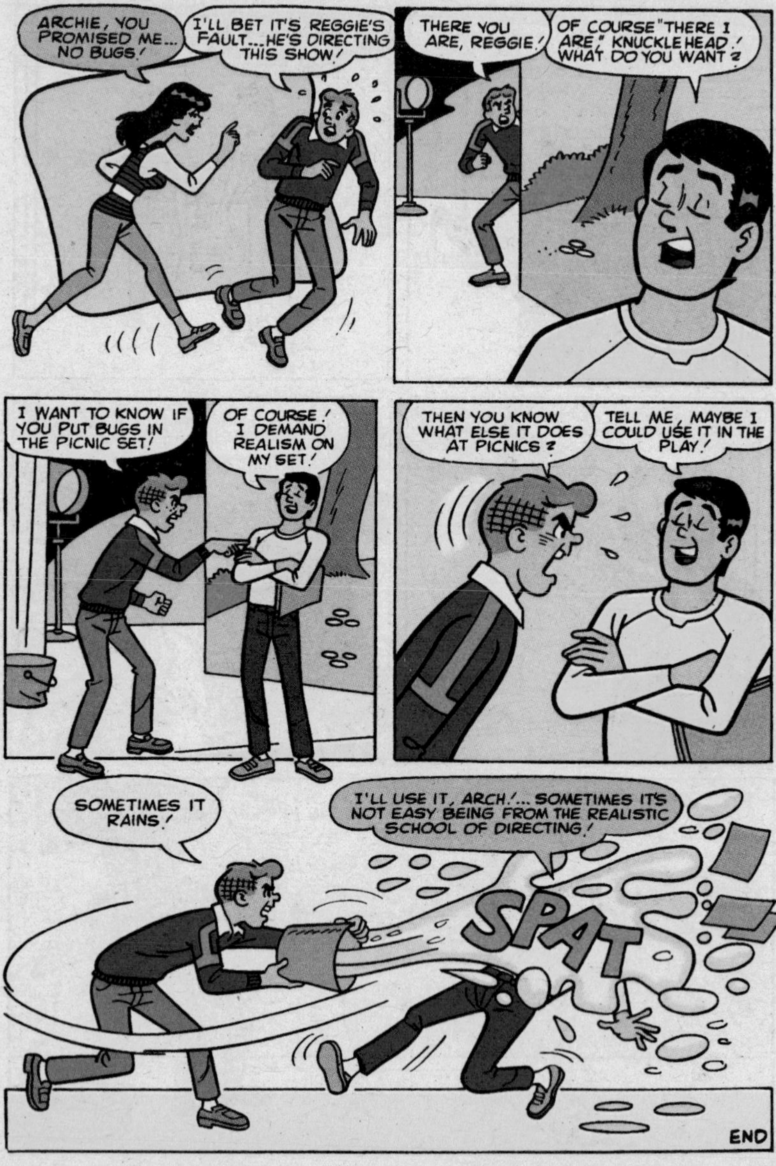

ARCHIE, YOU PROMISED ME... NO BUGS!
I'LL BET IT'S REGGIE'S FAULT...HE'S DIRECTING THIS SHOW!
THERE YOU ARE, REGGIE!
OF COURSE "THERE I ARE," KNUCKLEHEAD! WHAT DO YOU WANT?
I WANT TO KNOW IF YOU PUT BUGS IN THE PICNIC SET!
OF COURSE! I DEMAND REALISM ON MY SET!
THEN YOU KNOW WHAT ELSE IT DOES AT PICNICS?
TELL ME, MAYBE I COULD USE IT IN THE PLAY!
SOMETIMES IT RAINS!
I'LL USE IT, ARCH!... SOMETIMES IT'S NOT EASY BEING FROM THE REALISTIC SCHOOL OF DIRECTING!
SPAT
END

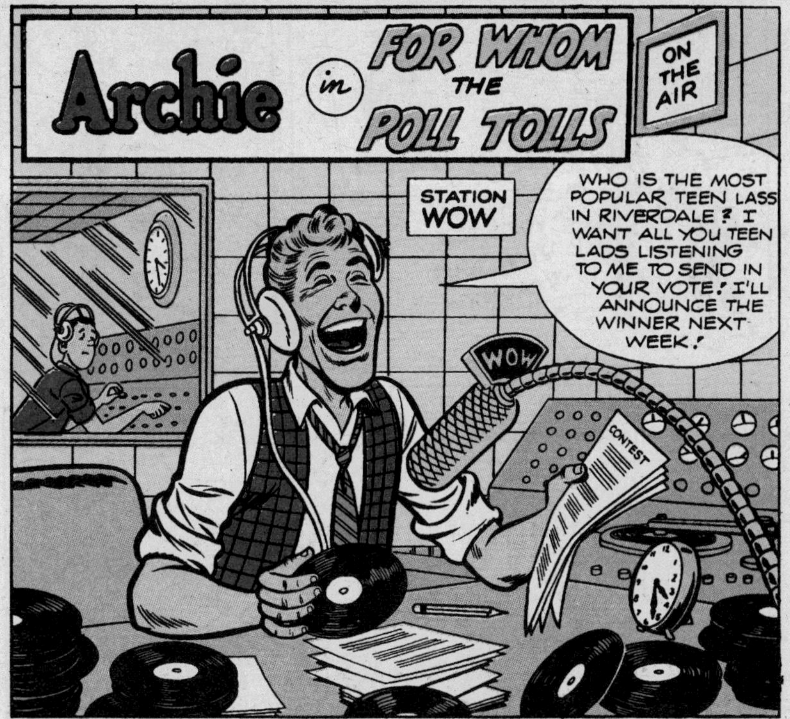
Archie in
FOR WHOM THE POLL TOLLS
ON THE AIR
STATION WOW
WHO IS THE MOST POPULAR TEEN LASS IN RIVERDALE? I WANT ALL YOU TEEN LADS LISTENING TO ME TO SEND IN YOUR VOTE! I'LL ANNOUNCE THE WINNER NEXT WEEK!
WOW
CONTEST

Script & Pencils: Al Hartley / Inks & Letters: Jon D'Agostino / Colors: Barry Grossman

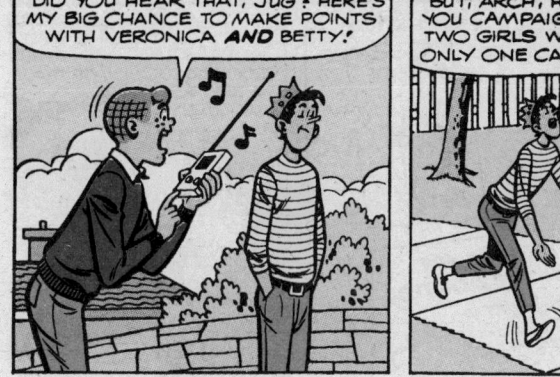

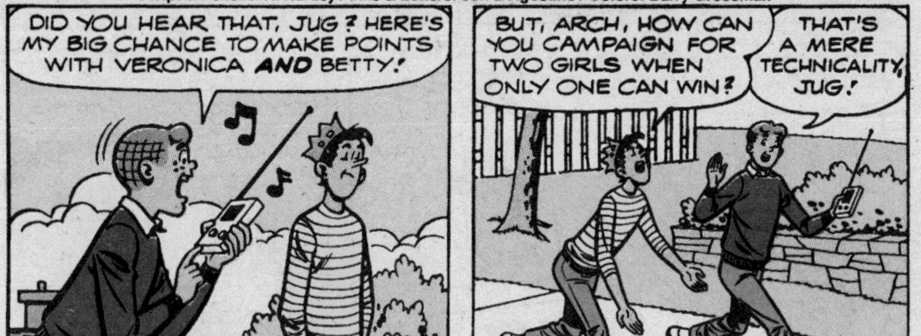
DID YOU HEAR THAT, JUG? HERE'S MY BIG CHANCE TO MAKE POINTS WITH VERONICA AND BETTY!
BUT, ARCH, HOW CAN YOU CAMPAIGN FOR TWO GIRLS WHEN ONLY ONE CAN WIN?
THAT'S A MERE TECHNICALITY, JUG!

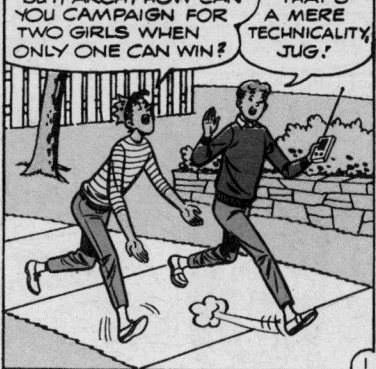

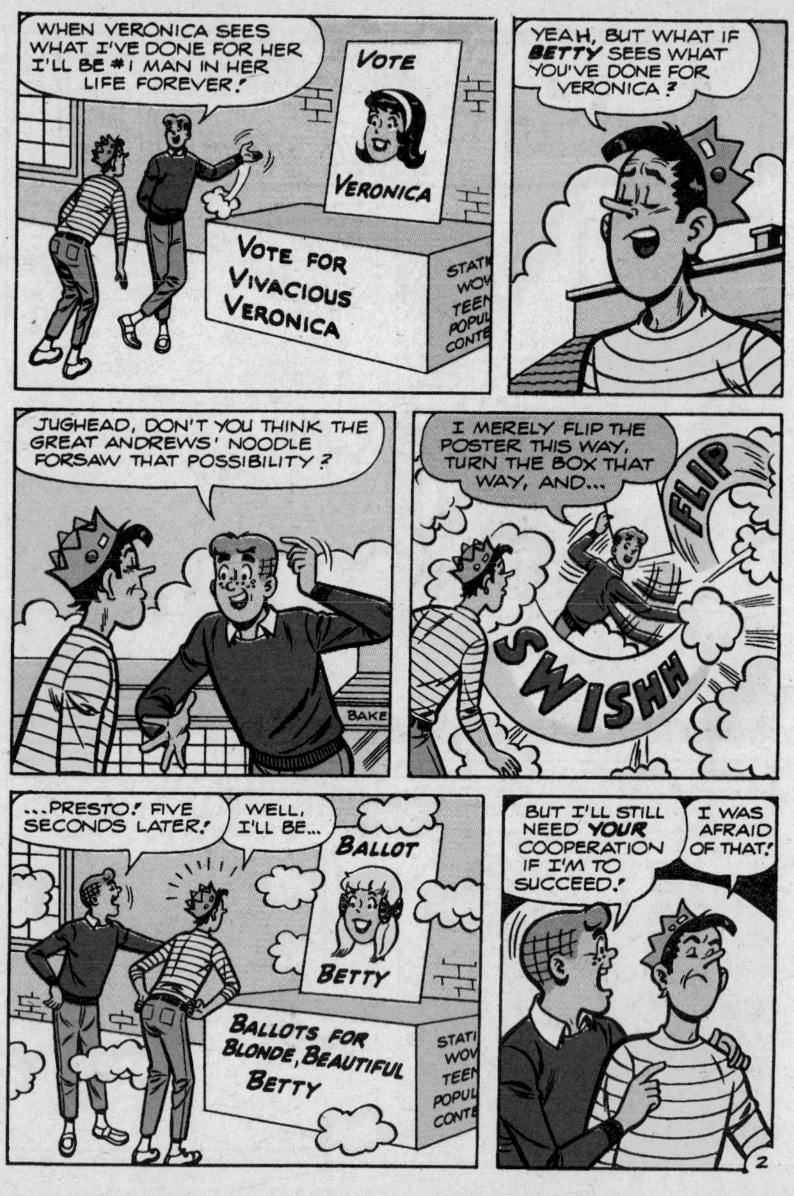
WHEN VERONICA SEES WHAT I'VE DONE FOR HER I'LL BE #1 MAN IN HER LIFE FOREVER!
VOTE
VERONICA
VOTE FOR VIVACIOUS VERONICA
YEAH, BUT WHAT IF BETTY SEES WHAT YOU'VE DONE FOR VERONICA?
JUGHEAD, DON'T YOU THINK THE GREAT ANDREWS' NOODLE FORSAW THAT POSSIBILITY?
BAKE
I MERELY FLIP THE POSTER THIS WAY, TURN THE BOX THAT WAY, AND...
FLIP
SWISHH
...PRESTO! FIVE SECONDS LATER!
WELL, I'LL BE...
BALLOT
BETTY
BALLOTS FOR BLONDE, BEAUTIFUL BETTY
BUT I'LL STILL NEED YOUR COOPERATION IF I'M TO SUCCEED!
I WAS AFRAID OF THAT!

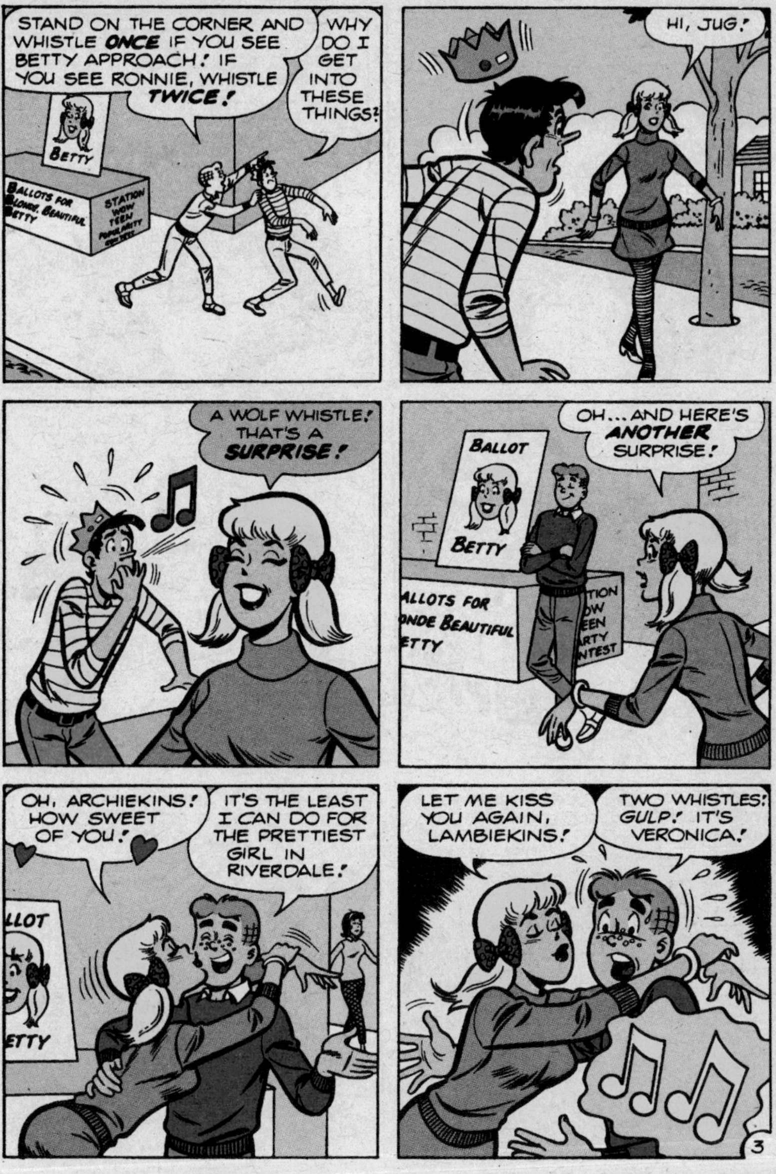

STAND ON THE CORNER AND WHISTLE **ONCE** IF YOU SEE BETTY APPROACH! IF YOU SEE RONNIE, WHISTLE **TWICE!**
WHY DO I GET INTO THESE THINGS?
BETTY
BALLOTS FOR BLONDE, BEAUTIFUL BETTY
STATION WOW TEEN POPULARITY CONTEST
HI, JUG!
A WOLF WHISTLE! THAT'S A **SURPRISE!**
OH... AND HERE'S **ANOTHER** SURPRISE!
BALLOT
BETTY
ALLOTS FOR ONDE BEAUTIFUL ETTY
OH, ARCHIEKINS! HOW SWEET OF YOU!
IT'S THE LEAST I CAN DO FOR THE PRETTIEST GIRL IN RIVERDALE!
LLOT
ETTY
LET ME KISS YOU AGAIN, LAMBIEKINS!
TWO WHISTLES! GULP! IT'S VERONICA!
3

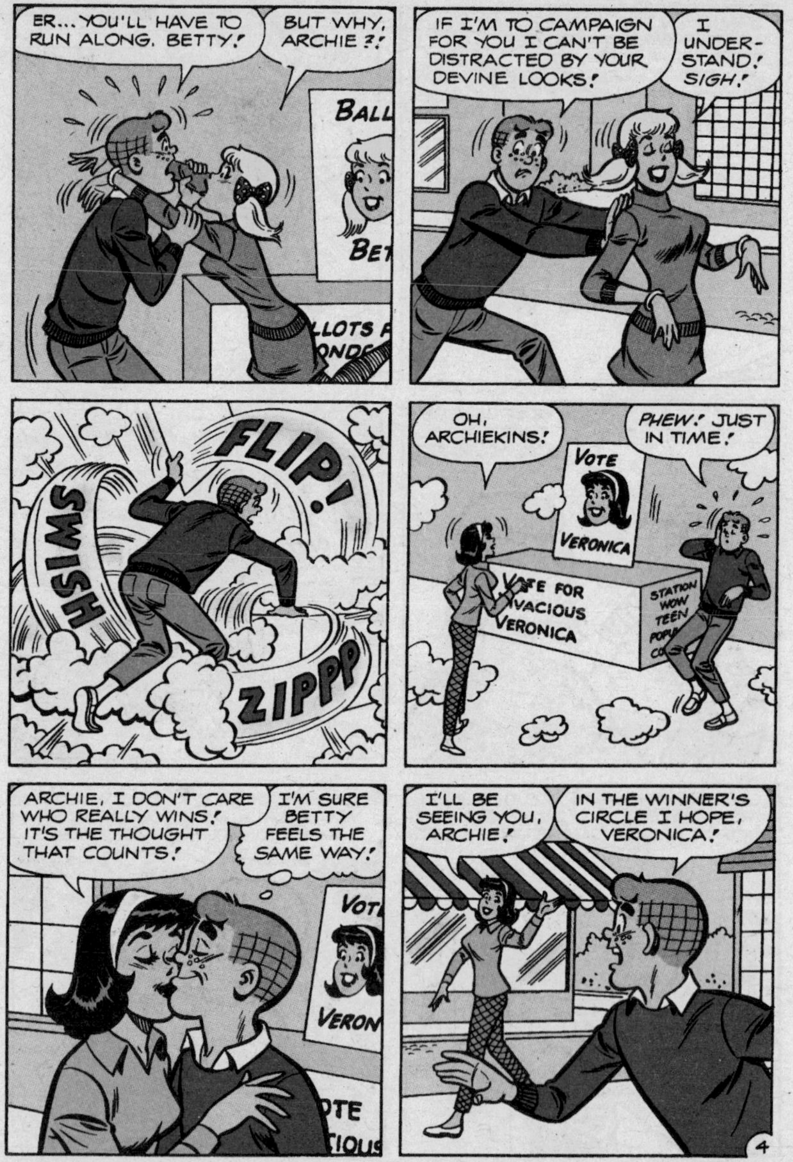
ER... YOU'LL HAVE TO RUN ALONG, BETTY!
BUT WHY, ARCHIE ?!
BALL
BET
LLOTS F
ONDC
IF I'M TO CAMPAIGN FOR YOU I CAN'T BE DISTRACTED BY YOUR DEVINE LOOKS!
I UNDER-STAND! SIGH!
FLIP!
SWISH
ZIPPP
OH, ARCHIEKINS!
PHEW! JUST IN TIME!
VOTE
VERONICA
VOTE FOR VIVACIOUS VERONICA
STATION WOW TEEN
ARCHIE, I DON'T CARE WHO REALLY WINS! IT'S THE THOUGHT THAT COUNTS!
I'M SURE BETTY FEELS THE SAME WAY!
VOTE
VERON
OTE
CIOUS
I'LL BE SEEING YOU, ARCHIE!
IN THE WINNER'S CIRCLE I HOPE, VERONICA!
4

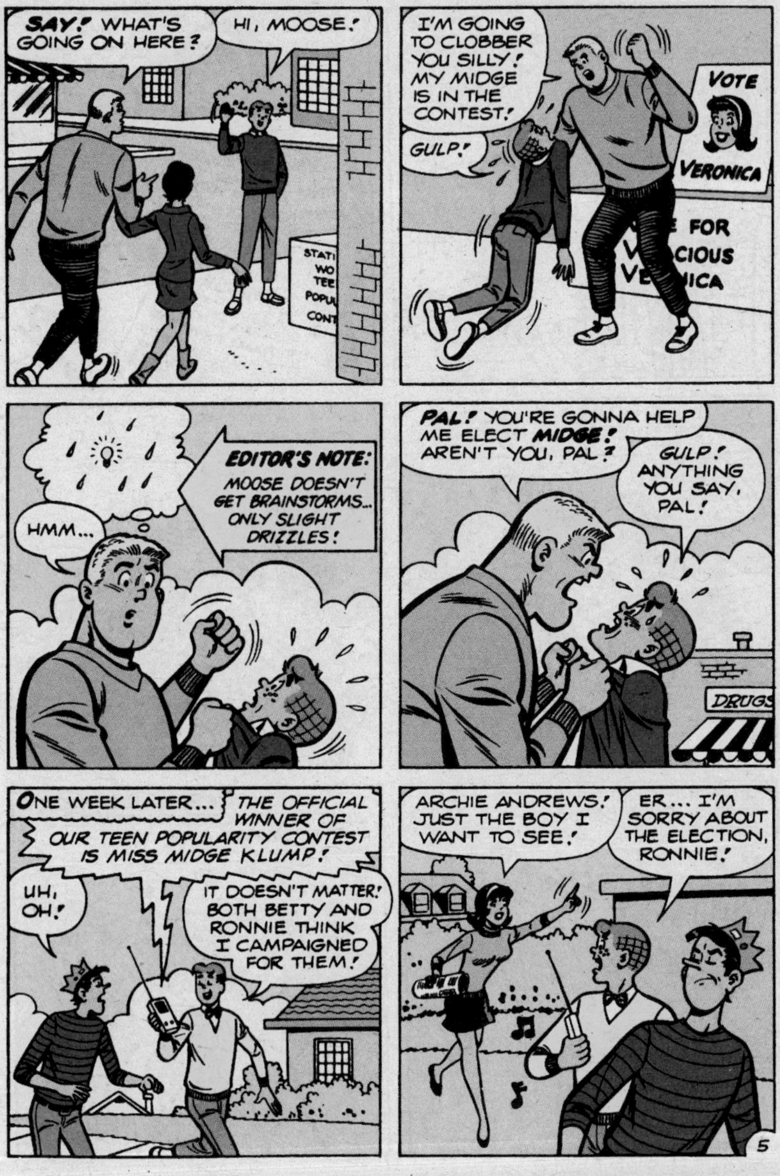

SAY! WHAT'S GOING ON HERE?
HI, MOOSE!
STATI WO TEE POPUL CONT
I'M GOING TO CLOBBER YOU SILLY! MY MIDGE IS IN THE CONTEST!
GULP!
VOTE VERONICA
FOR
HMM...
EDITOR'S NOTE: MOOSE DOESN'T GET BRAINSTORMS... ONLY SLIGHT DRIZZLES!
PAL! YOU'RE GONNA HELP ME ELECT MIDGE! AREN'T YOU, PAL?
GULP! ANYTHING YOU SAY, PAL!
DRUGS
ONE WEEK LATER...
THE OFFICIAL WINNER OF OUR TEEN POPULARITY CONTEST IS MISS MIDGE KLUMP!
UH, OH!
IT DOESN'T MATTER! BOTH BETTY AND RONNIE THINK I CAMPAIGNED FOR THEM!
ARCHIE ANDREWS! JUST THE BOY I WANT TO SEE!
ER... I'M SORRY ABOUT THE ELECTION, RONNIE!

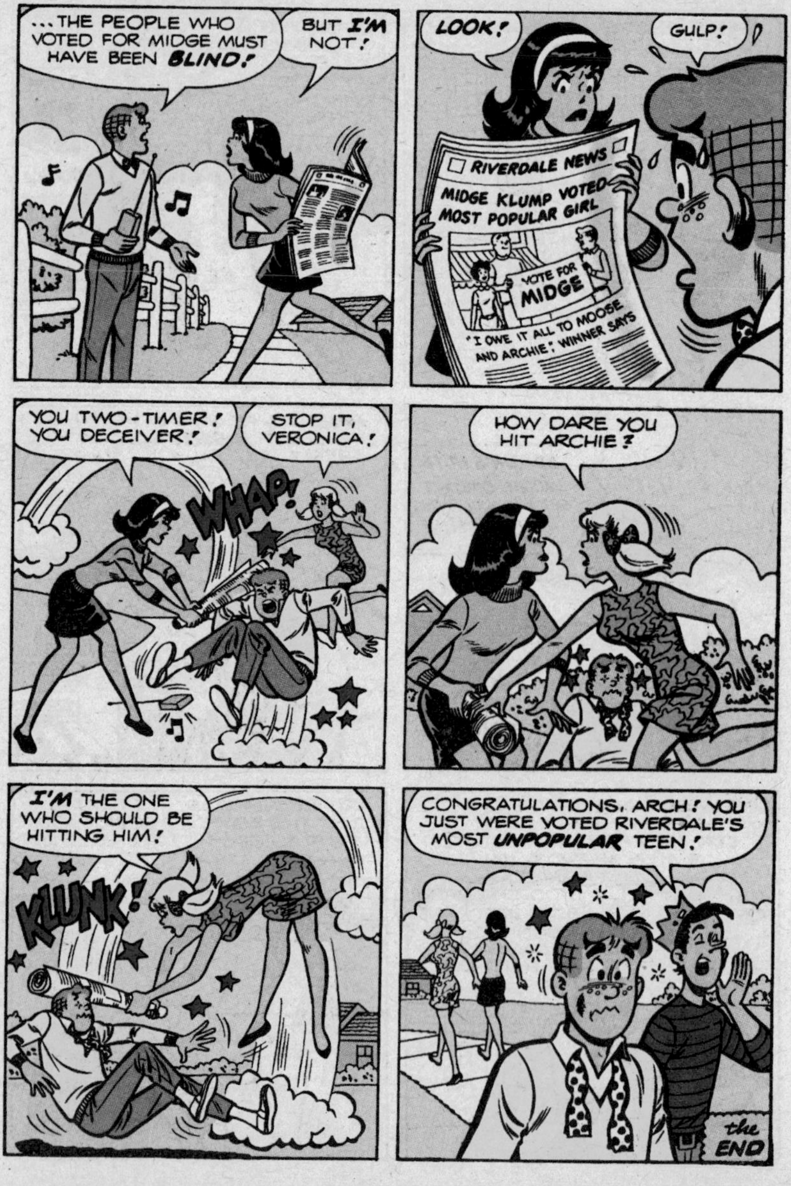
...THE PEOPLE WHO VOTED FOR MIDGE MUST HAVE BEEN BLIND!
BUT I'M NOT!
LOOK!
GULP!
RIVERDALE NEWS
MIDGE KLUMP VOTED MOST POPULAR GIRL
VOTE FOR MIDGE
"I OWE IT ALL TO MOOSE AND ARCHIE", WINNER SAYS
YOU TWO-TIMER! YOU DECEIVER!
STOP IT, VERONICA!
WHAP!
HOW DARE YOU HIT ARCHIE?
I'M THE ONE WHO SHOULD BE HITTING HIM!
KLUNK!
CONGRATULATIONS, ARCH! YOU JUST WERE VOTED RIVERDALE'S MOST UNPOPULAR TEEN!
the END

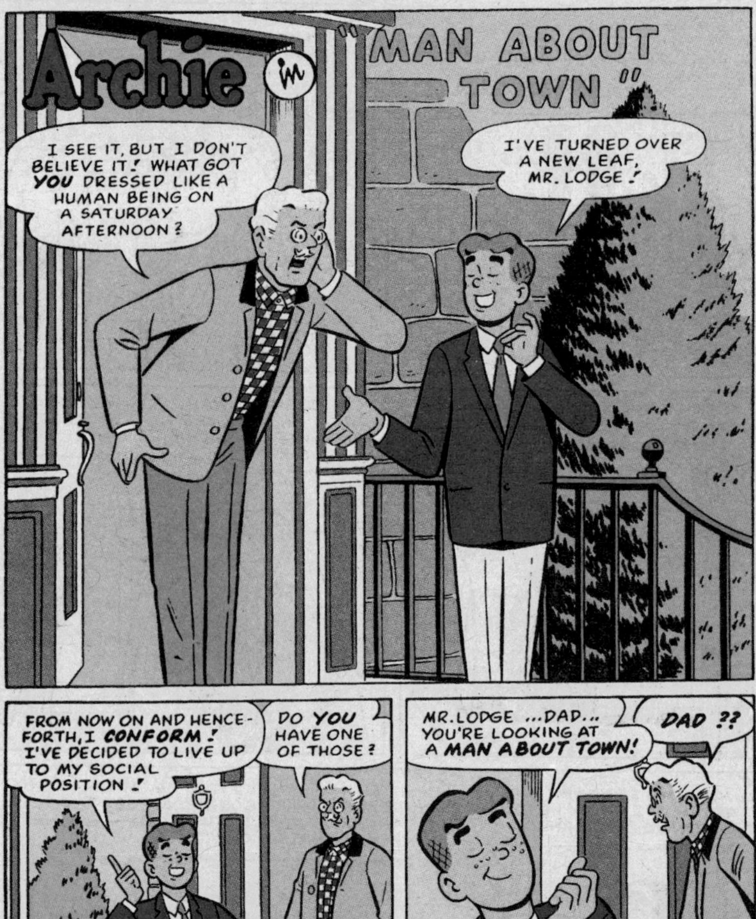
Archie in
"MAN ABOUT TOWN"
I SEE IT, BUT I DON'T BELIEVE IT! WHAT GOT YOU DRESSED LIKE A HUMAN BEING ON A SATURDAY AFTERNOON?
I'VE TURNED OVER A NEW LEAF, MR. LODGE!
FROM NOW ON AND HENCE-FORTH, I CONFORM! I'VE DECIDED TO LIVE UP TO MY SOCIAL POSITION!
DO YOU HAVE ONE OF THOSE?
MR. LODGE ...DAD... YOU'RE LOOKING AT A MAN ABOUT TOWN!
DAD ??

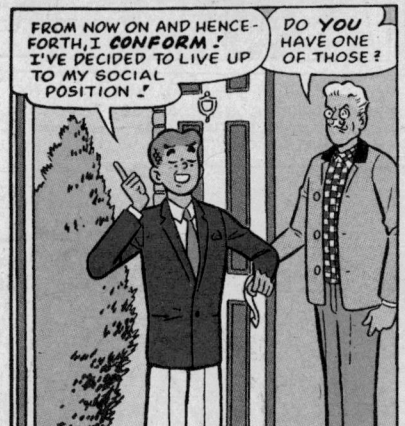

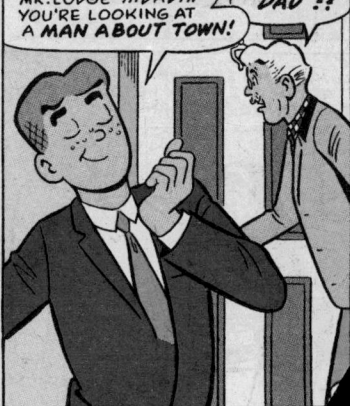

Script: Frank Doyle / Pencils: Harry Lucey / Inks & Letters: Vince DeCarlo / Colors: Barry Grossman

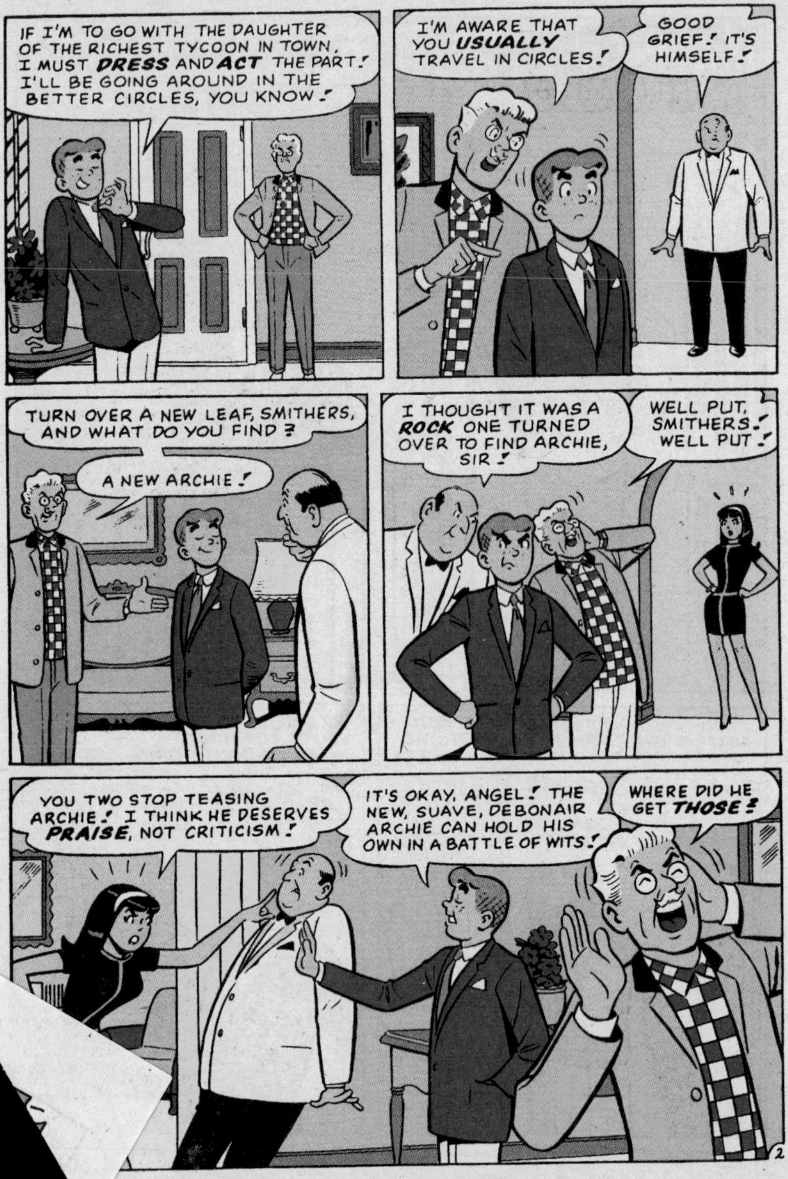
IF I'M TO GO WITH THE DAUGHTER OF THE RICHEST TYCOON IN TOWN, I MUST **DRESS** AND **ACT** THE PART! I'LL BE GOING AROUND IN THE BETTER CIRCLES, YOU KNOW!
I'M AWARE THAT YOU **USUALLY** TRAVEL IN CIRCLES!
GOOD GRIEF! IT'S HIMSELF!
TURN OVER A NEW LEAF, SMITHERS, AND WHAT DO YOU FIND?
A NEW ARCHIE!
I THOUGHT IT WAS A **ROCK** ONE TURNED OVER TO FIND ARCHIE, SIR!
WELL PUT, SMITHERS! WELL PUT!
YOU TWO STOP TEASING ARCHIE! I THINK HE DESERVES **PRAISE**, NOT CRITICISM!
IT'S OKAY, ANGEL! THE NEW, SUAVE, DEBONAIR ARCHIE CAN HOLD HIS OWN IN A BATTLE OF WITS!
WHERE DID HE GET **THOSE**?
2

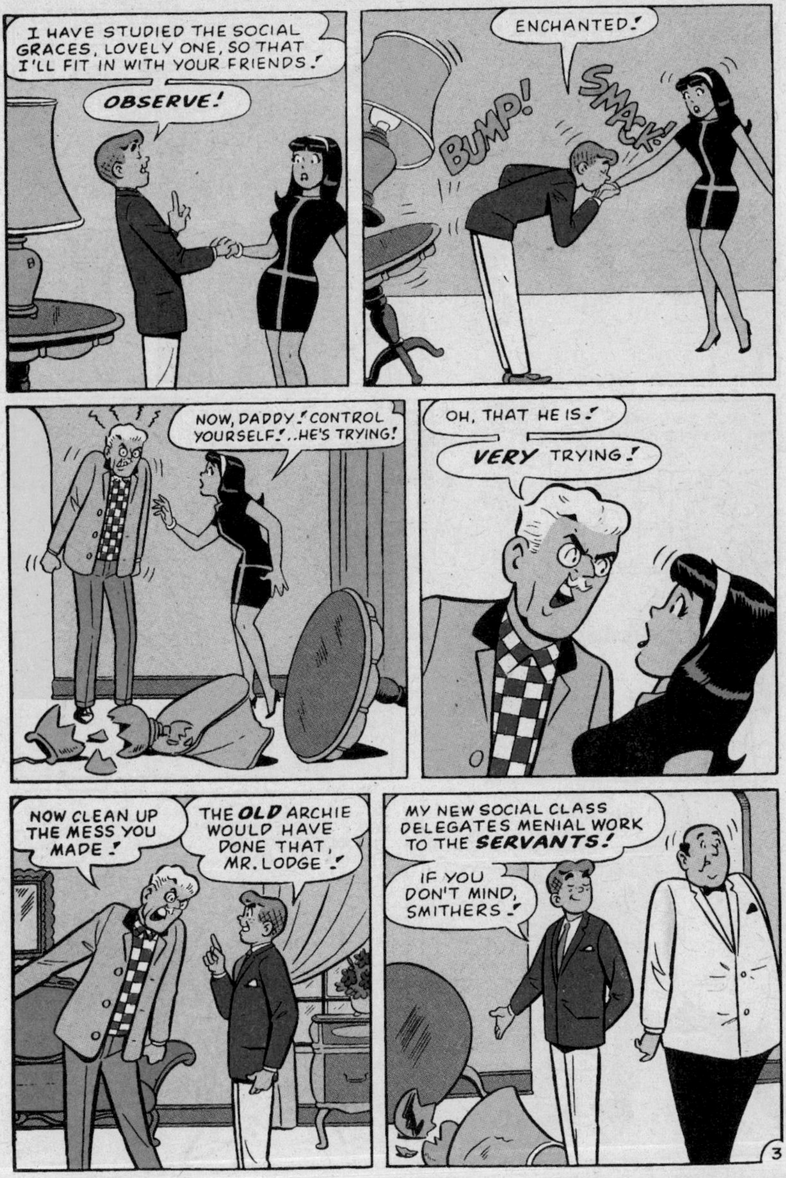
I HAVE STUDIED THE SOCIAL GRACES, LOVELY ONE, SO THAT I'LL FIT IN WITH YOUR FRIENDS!
OBSERVE!
ENCHANTED!
BUMP!
SMACK!
NOW, DADDY! CONTROL YOURSELF!..HE'S TRYING!
OH, THAT HE IS!
VERY TRYING!
NOW CLEAN UP THE MESS YOU MADE!
THE OLD ARCHIE WOULD HAVE DONE THAT, MR. LODGE!
MY NEW SOCIAL CLASS DELEGATES MENIAL WORK TO THE SERVANTS!
IF YOU DON'T MIND, SMITHERS!

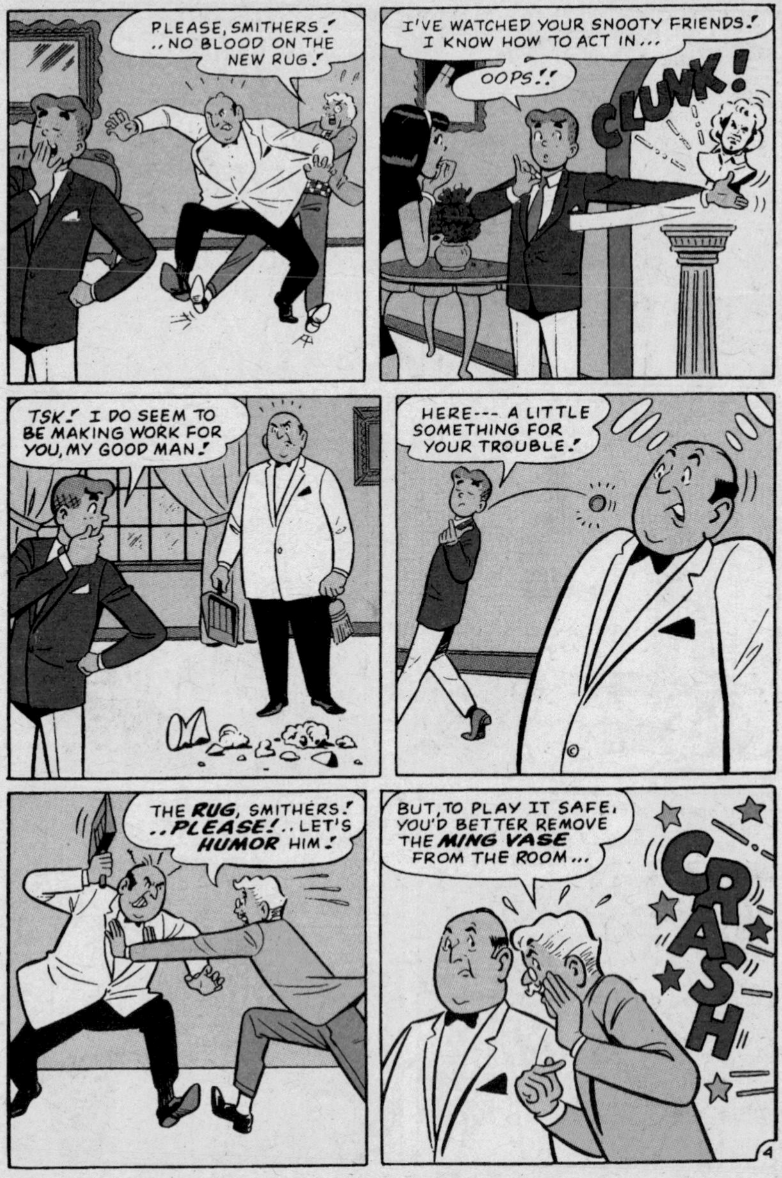
PLEASE, SMITHERS! .. NO BLOOD ON THE NEW RUG!
I'VE WATCHED YOUR SNOOTY FRIENDS! I KNOW HOW TO ACT IN...
OOPS!!
CLUNK!
TSK! I DO SEEM TO BE MAKING WORK FOR YOU, MY GOOD MAN!
HERE--- A LITTLE SOMETHING FOR YOUR TROUBLE!
THE RUG, SMITHERS! .. PLEASE! .. LET'S HUMOR HIM!
BUT, TO PLAY IT SAFE, YOU'D BETTER REMOVE THE MING VASE FROM THE ROOM...
CRASH
4

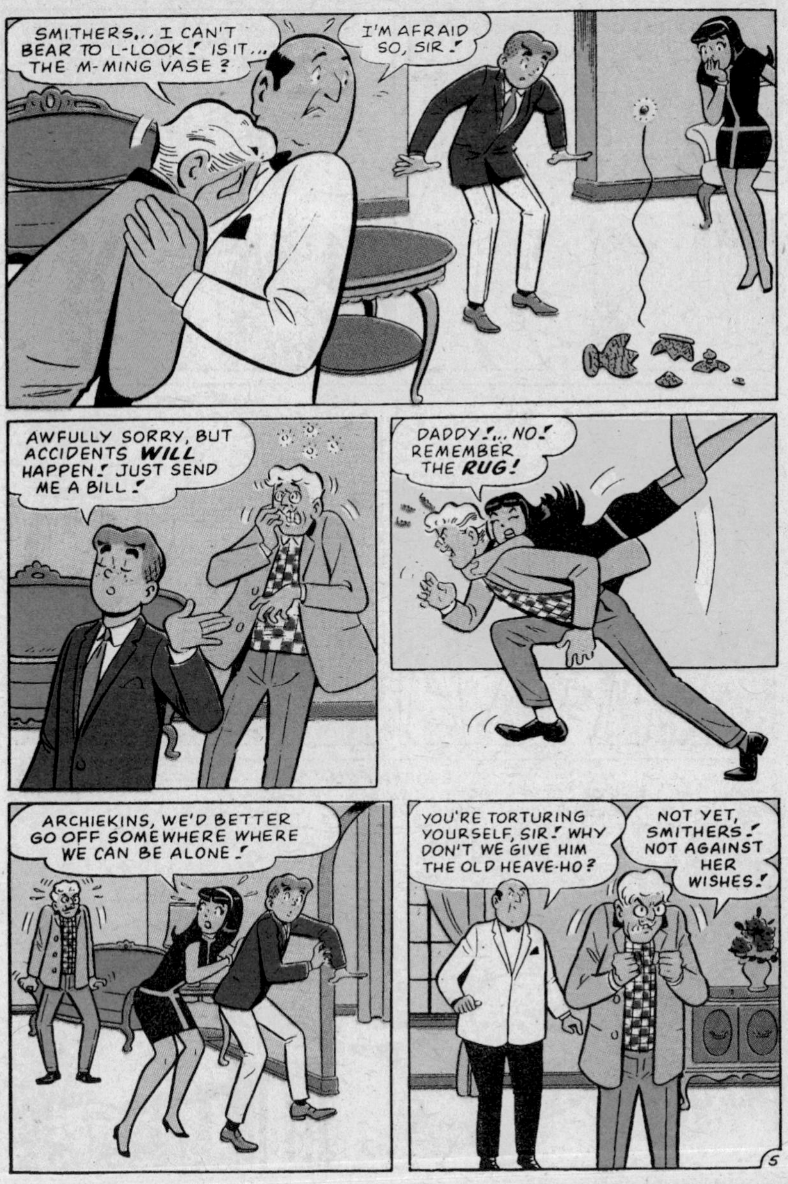
SMITHERS... I CAN'T BEAR TO L-LOOK! IS IT... THE M-MING VASE?
I'M AFRAID SO, SIR!
AWFULLY SORRY, BUT ACCIDENTS **WILL** HAPPEN! JUST SEND ME A BILL!
DADDY!... NO! REMEMBER THE **RUG!**
ARCHIEKINS, WE'D BETTER GO OFF SOMEWHERE WHERE WE CAN BE ALONE!
YOU'RE TORTURING YOURSELF, SIR! WHY DON'T WE GIVE HIM THE OLD HEAVE-HO?
NOT YET, SMITHERS! NOT AGAINST HER WISHES!

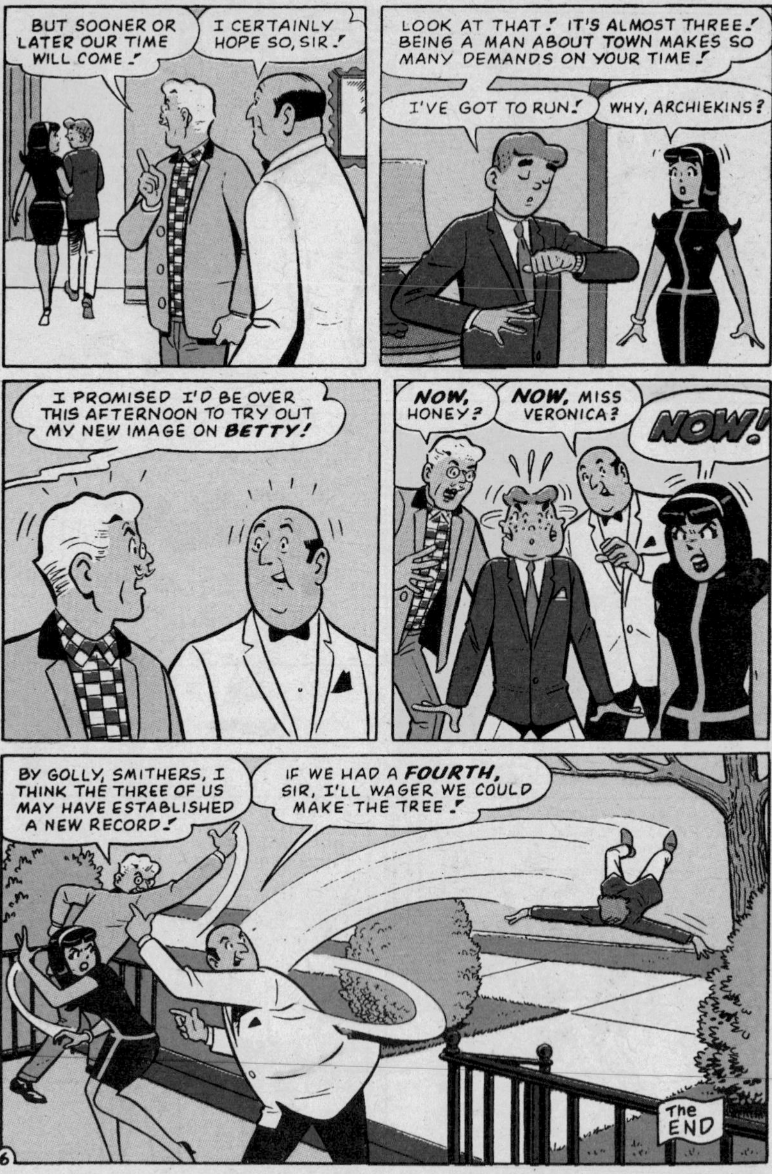
BUT SOONER OR LATER OUR TIME WILL COME!
I CERTAINLY HOPE SO, SIR!
LOOK AT THAT! IT'S ALMOST THREE! BEING A MAN ABOUT TOWN MAKES SO MANY DEMANDS ON YOUR TIME!
I'VE GOT TO RUN!
WHY, ARCHIEKINS?
I PROMISED I'D BE OVER THIS AFTERNOON TO TRY OUT MY NEW IMAGE ON BETTY!
NOW, HONEY?
NOW, MISS VERONICA?
NOW!
BY GOLLY, SMITHERS, I THINK THE THREE OF US MAY HAVE ESTABLISHED A NEW RECORD!
IF WE HAD A FOURTH, SIR, I'LL WAGER WE COULD MAKE THE TREE!
The END

Archie EXERCISE FIND!

CHECK OUT THE EXERCISE FIND FOR THE DIFFERENT EXERCISES ARCHIE DOES EVERY DAY! LOOK UP, DOWN, FORWARD, BACKWARD, AND DIAGONALLY! THEN--CROSS 'EM OFF ON THE WORD LIST BELOW!!

W	N	E	Y	U	O	D	A	N	Z	E	H	P	U	H	S	U	P	A
H	W	A	L	K	I	N	G	L	E	D	M	C	E	L	O	W	B	R
C	E	S	Q	H	O	S	O	M	U	J	C	Y	T	U	C	A	L	S
U	E	N	E	O	V	E	H	F	O	U	N	C	B	R	S	A	C	K
E	Y	L	S	I	T	U	P	G	L	E	D	L	A	N	D	I	L	I
N	D	I	H	I	D	D	G	L	E	O	F	I	T	H	E	J	G	I
E	E	N	T	E	M	I					N	N	S	M	E	U	N	P
D	G	E	O	O	N	F					I	G	U	L	R	M	I	J
E	N	E	N	G	T	E					G	H	M	I	K	P	T	U
S	I	D														R	F	T
P	M	N														O	I	S
I	M	G														P	L	F
M	I	U														E	T	R
O	W	V														I	H	E
E	S	A														N	G	D
S	E	R														S	I	D
L	W	L														K	E	R
O	S	T														E	W	D

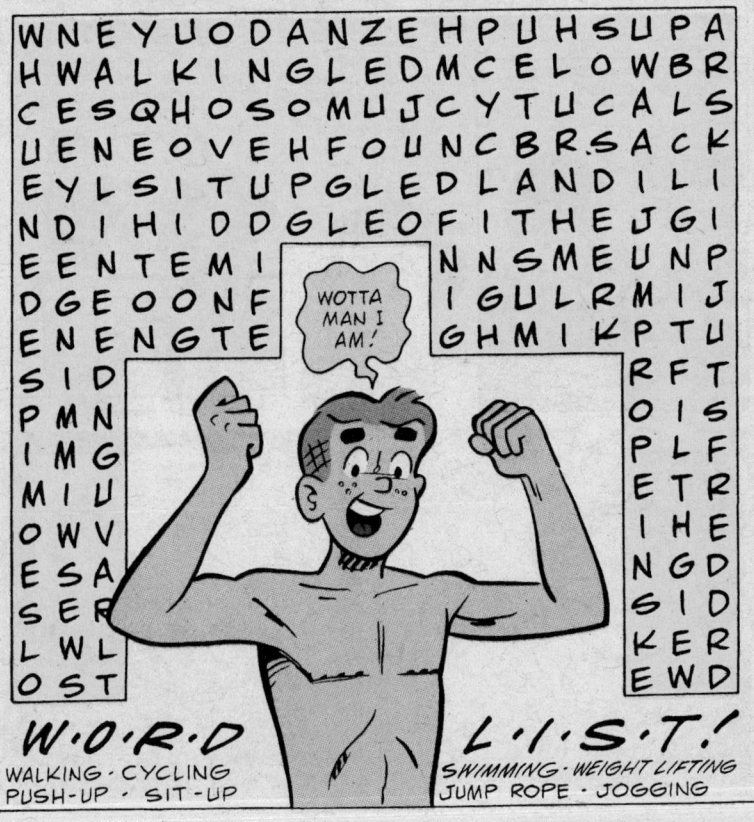

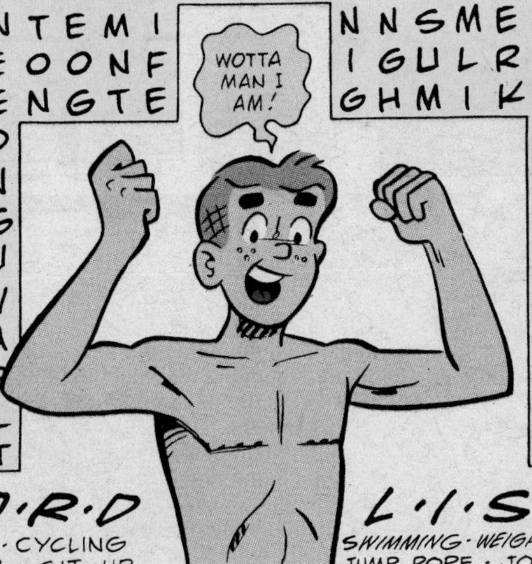
WOTTA MAN I AM!

W·O·R·D L·I·S·T!

WALKING · CYCLING · SWIMMING · WEIGHT LIFTING

PUSH-UP · SIT-UP · JUMP ROPE · JOGGING

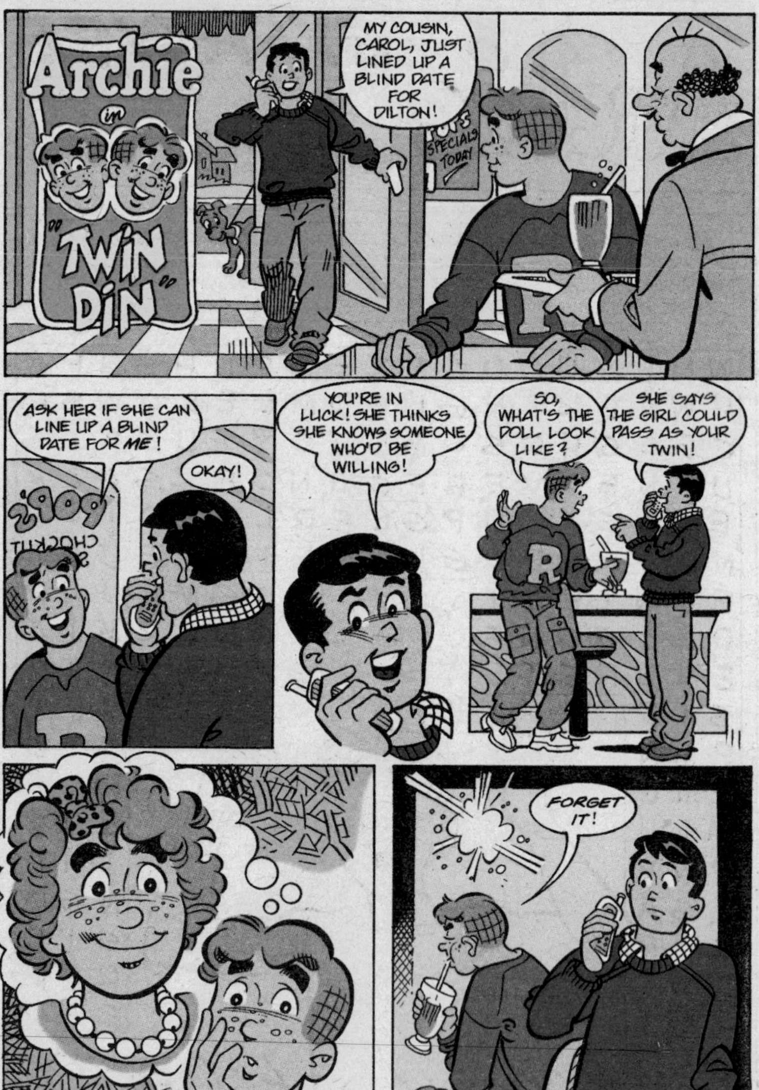
Archie in TWIN DIN
MY COUSIN, CAROL, JUST LINED UP A BLIND DATE FOR DILTON!
POP'S SPECIALS TODAY
ASK HER IF SHE CAN LINE UP A BLIND DATE FOR *ME*!
OKAY!
YOU'RE IN LUCK! SHE THINKS SHE KNOWS SOMEONE WHO'D BE WILLING!
SO, WHAT'S THE DOLL LOOK LIKE?
SHE SAYS THE GIRL COULD PASS AS YOUR TWIN!
FORGET IT!
END

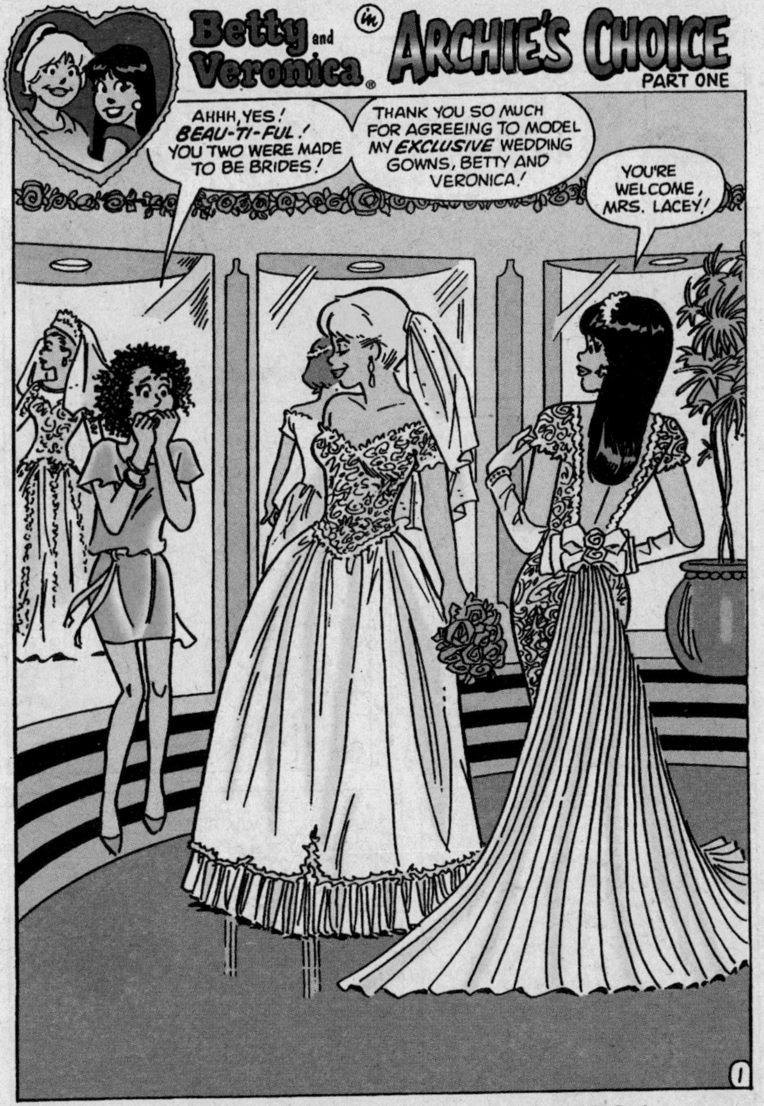
Betty and Veronica
in
ARCHIE'S CHOICE
PART ONE
AHHH, YES! BEAU-TI-FUL! YOU TWO WERE MADE TO BE BRIDES!
THANK YOU SO MUCH FOR AGREEING TO MODEL MY EXCLUSIVE WEDDING GOWNS, BETTY AND VERONICA!
YOU'RE WELCOME, MRS. LACEY!
1

Script: **Frank Doyle** Pencils: **Dan DeCarlo** Inks: **Jimmy DeCarlo**
Letters: **Bill Yoshida** Colors: **Barry Grossman**
Editor-In-Chief: **Victor Gorelick** President: **Mike Pellerito** Publisher: **Jon Goldwater**

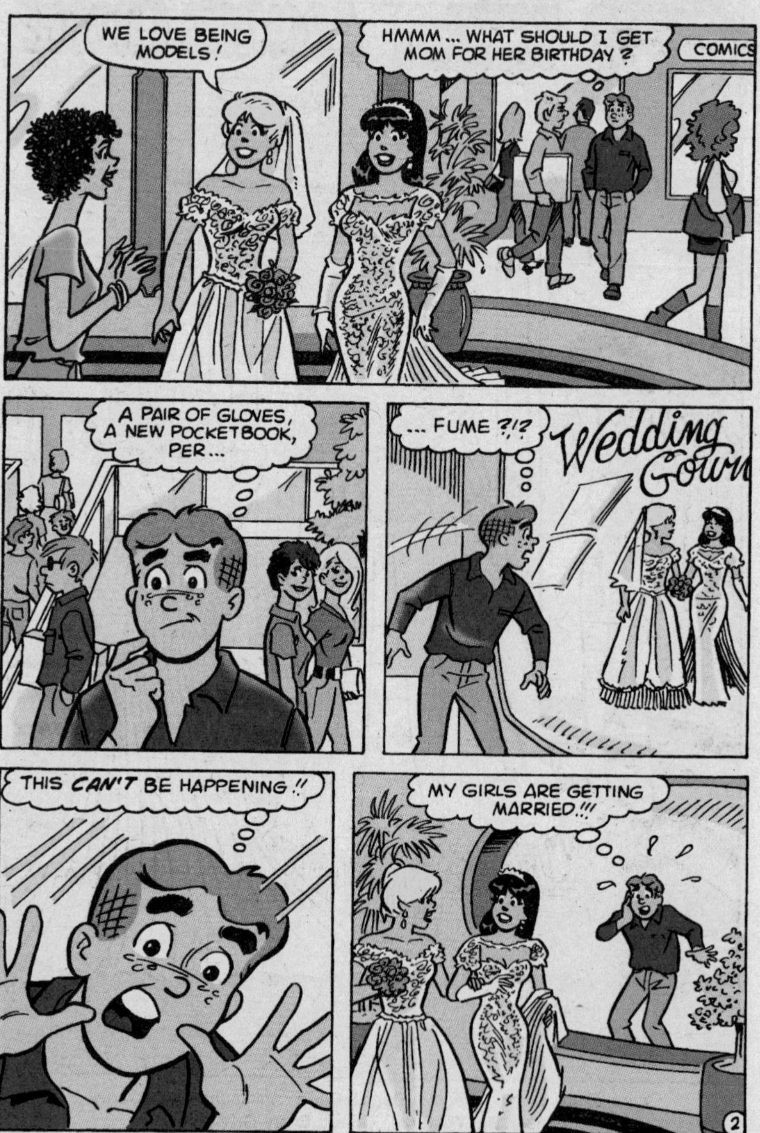
WE LOVE BEING MODELS!
HMMM ... WHAT SHOULD I GET MOM FOR HER BIRTHDAY ?
COMICS
A PAIR OF GLOVES, A NEW POCKETBOOK, PER...
... FUME ?!?
Wedding Gown
THIS CAN'T BE HAPPENING !!
MY GIRLS ARE GETTING MARRIED!!!
2

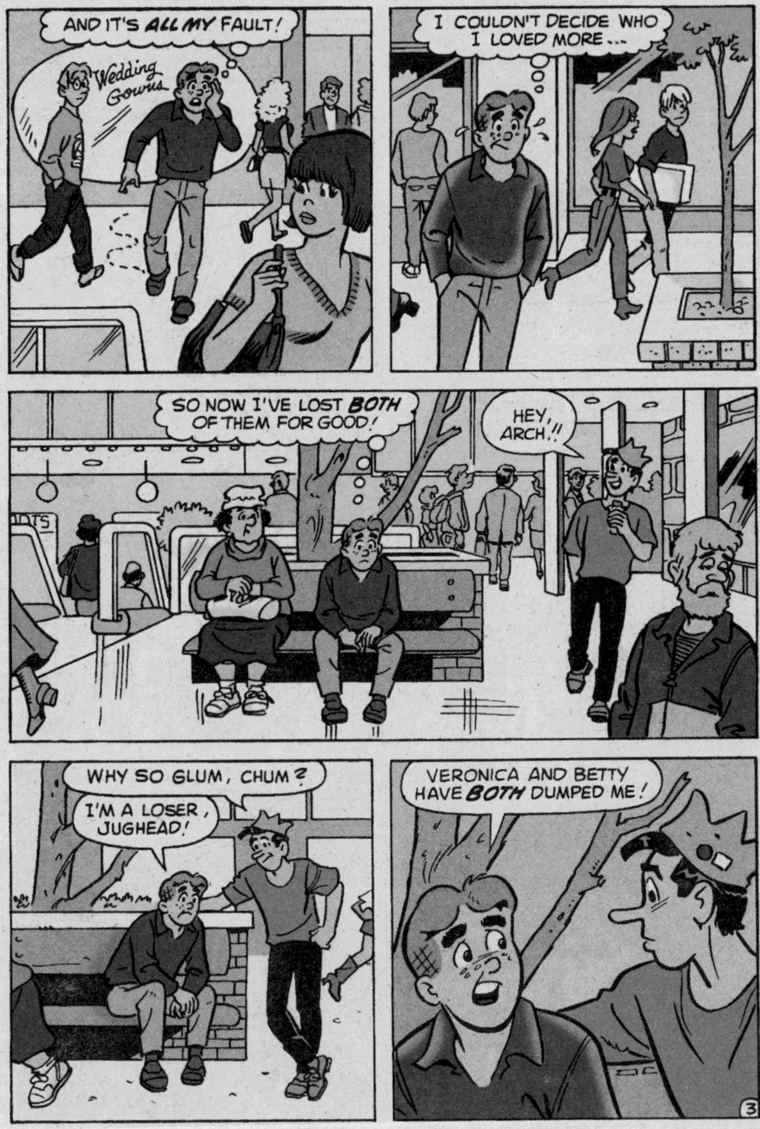
AND IT'S ALL MY FAULT!
Wedding Gowns
I COULDN'T DECIDE WHO I LOVED MORE...
SO NOW I'VE LOST BOTH OF THEM FOR GOOD!
HEY, ARCH.!!
WHY SO GLUM, CHUM?
I'M A LOSER, JUGHEAD!
VERONICA AND BETTY HAVE BOTH DUMPED ME!
3

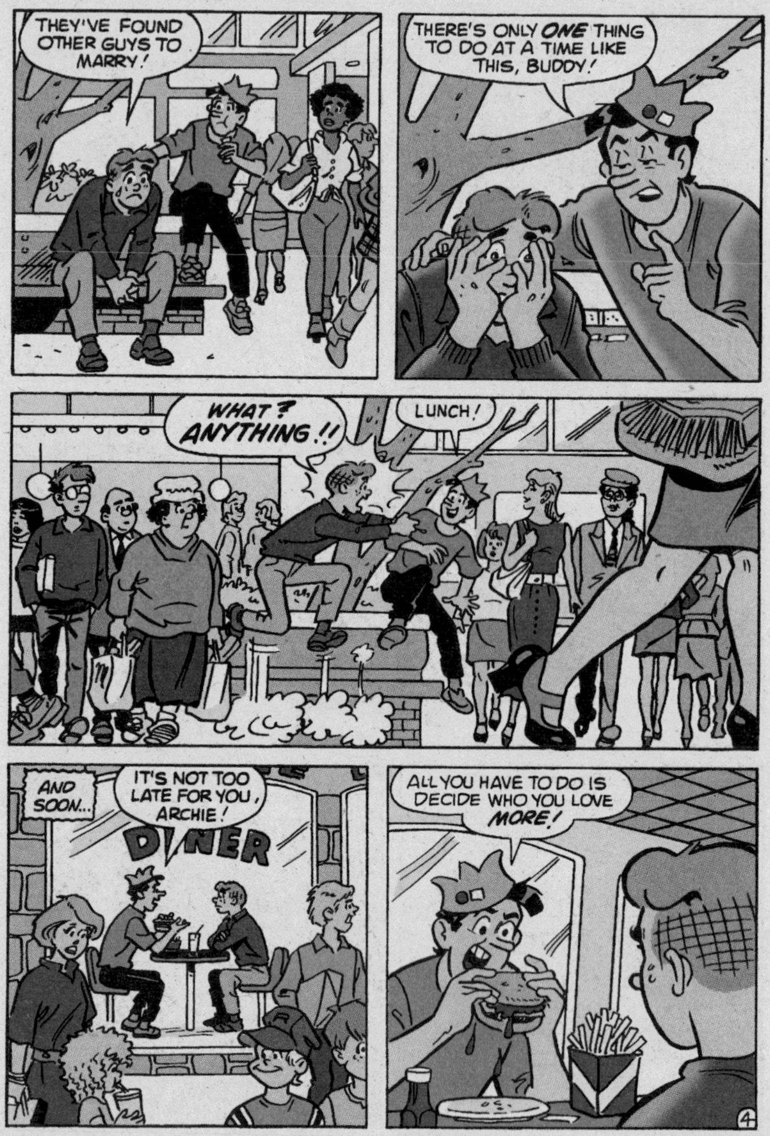
THEY'VE FOUND OTHER GUYS TO MARRY!
THERE'S ONLY ONE THING TO DO AT A TIME LIKE THIS, BUDDY!
WHAT? ANYTHING!!
LUNCH!
AND SOON...
IT'S NOT TOO LATE FOR YOU, ARCHIE!
DINER
ALL YOU HAVE TO DO IS DECIDE WHO YOU LOVE MORE!
4

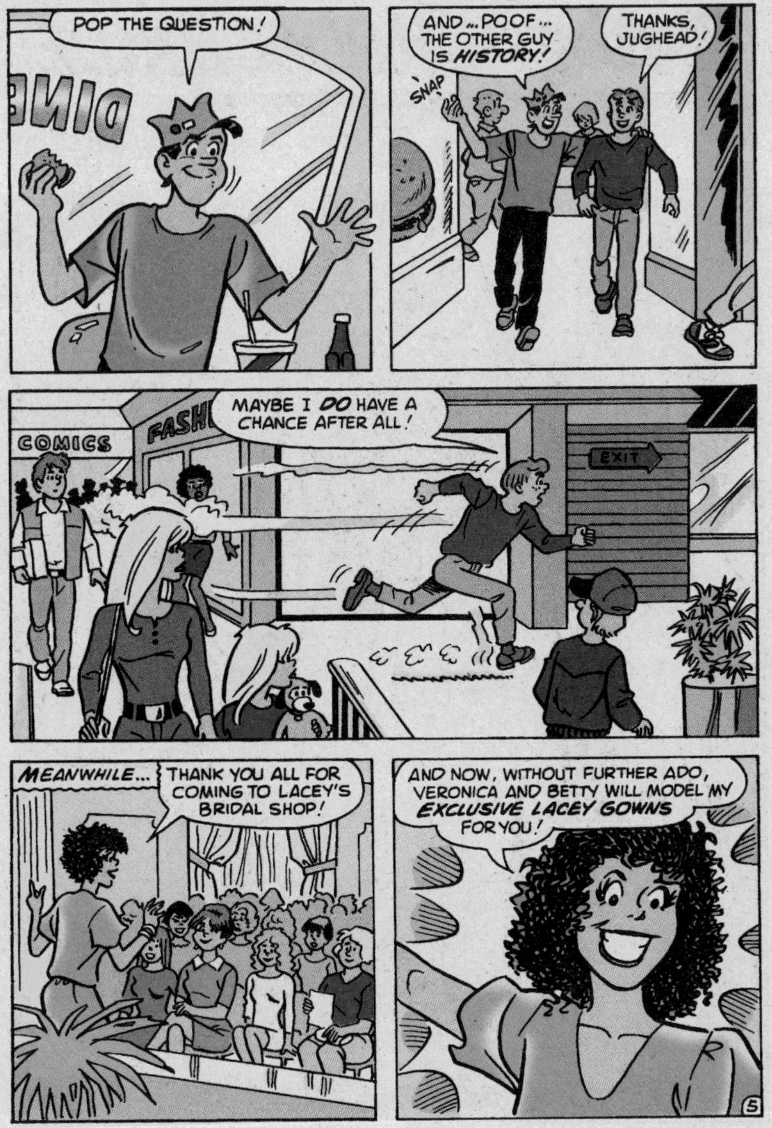
POP THE QUESTION!
DINE
AND ...POOF... THE OTHER GUY IS *HISTORY!*
THANKS, JUGHEAD!
SNAP
COMICS
FASH
MAYBE I *DO* HAVE A CHANCE AFTER ALL!
EXIT
MEANWHILE...
THANK YOU ALL FOR COMING TO LACEY'S BRIDAL SHOP!
AND NOW, WITHOUT FURTHER ADO, VERONICA AND BETTY WILL MODEL MY *EXCLUSIVE LACEY GOWNS* FOR YOU!
5

Betty the MODEL BRIDE

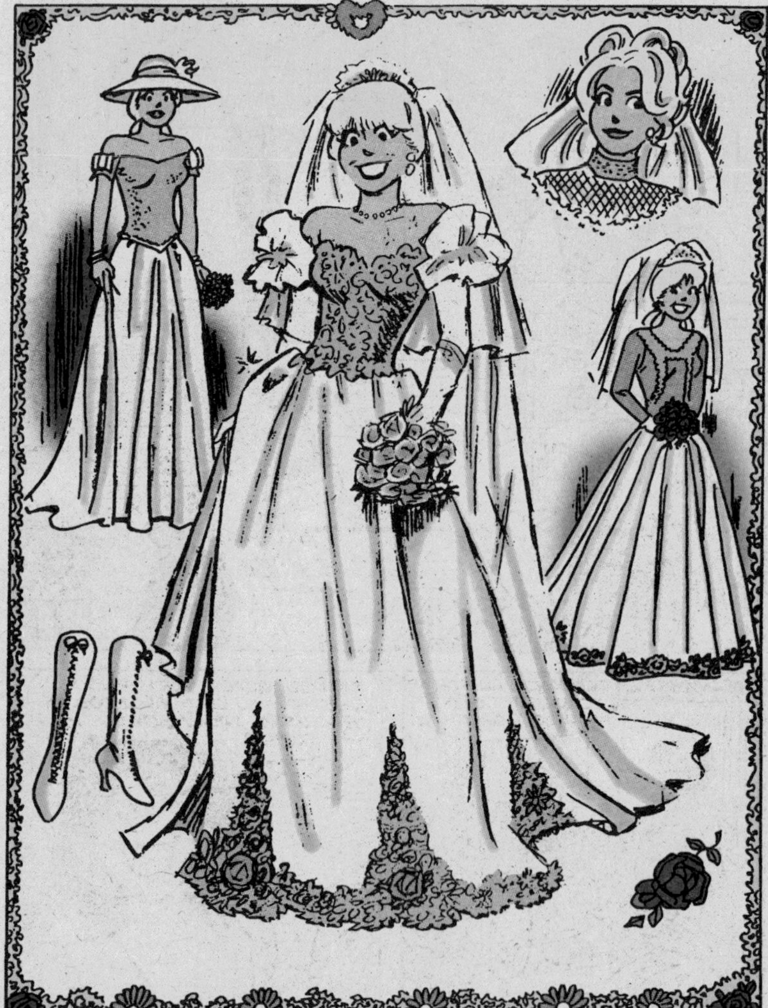

Veronica the MODEL BRIDE

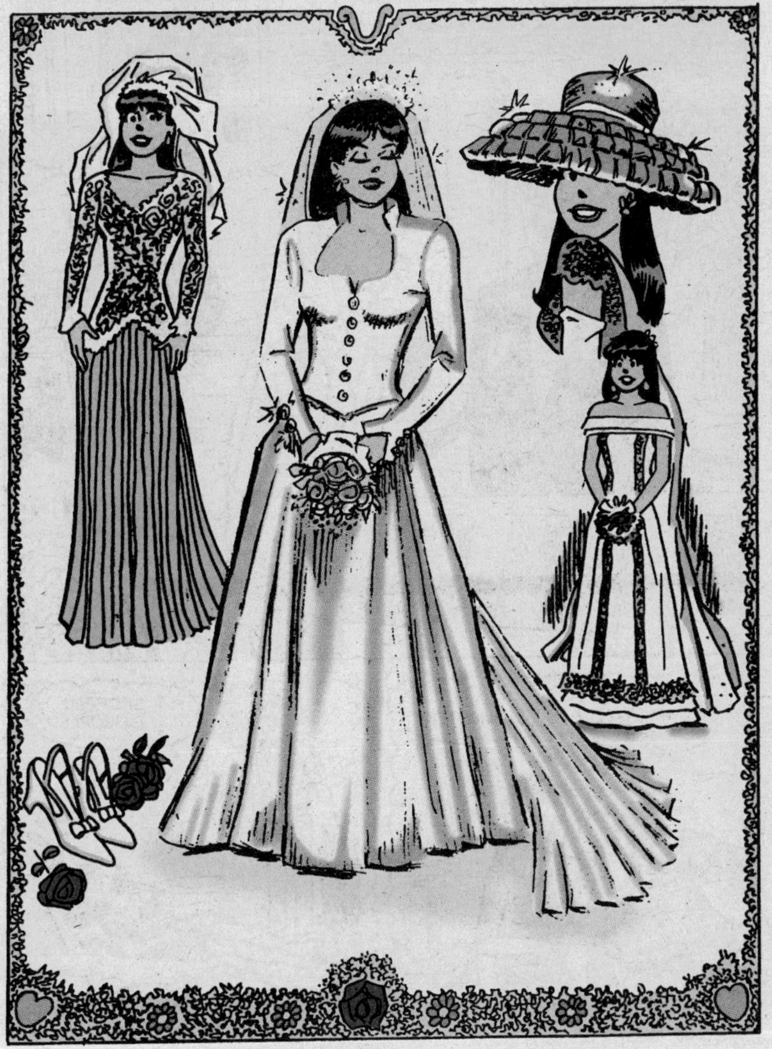

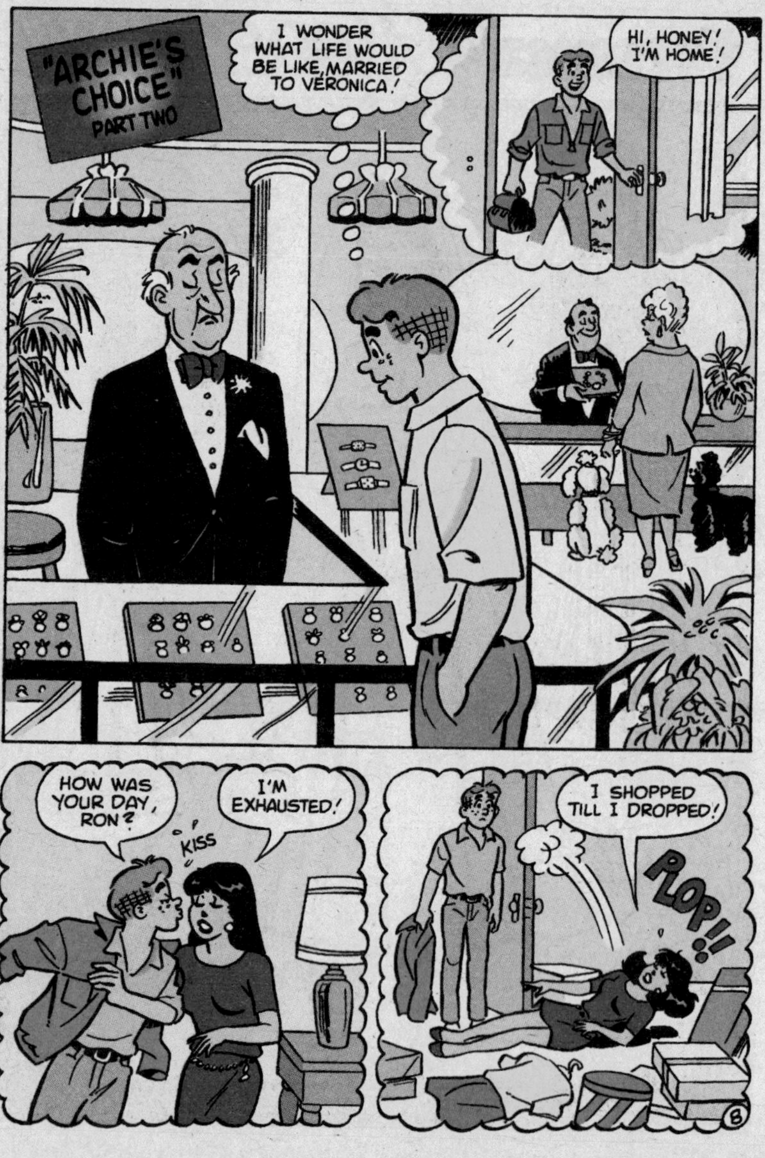
"ARCHIE'S CHOICE" PART TWO
I WONDER WHAT LIFE WOULD BE LIKE, MARRIED TO VERONICA!
HI, HONEY! I'M HOME!
HOW WAS YOUR DAY, RON?
KISS
I'M EXHAUSTED!
I SHOPPED TILL I DROPPED!
PLOP!!

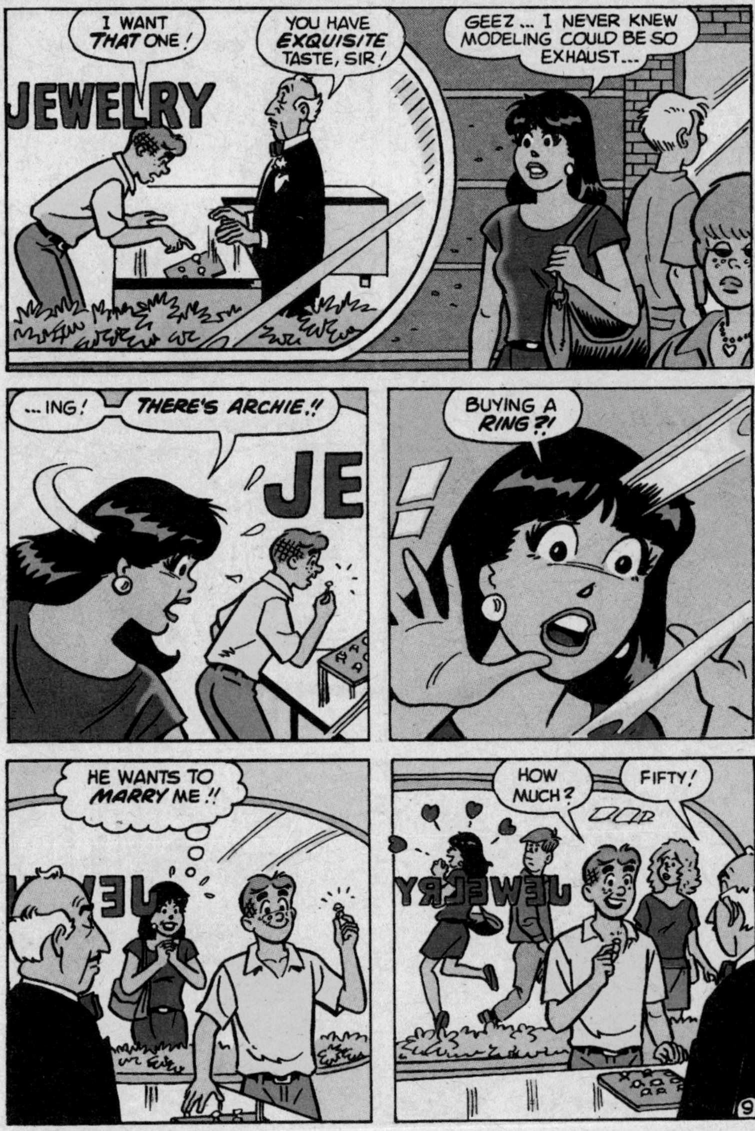
I WANT THAT ONE!
JEWELRY
YOU HAVE EXQUISITE TASTE, SIR!
GEEZ ... I NEVER KNEW MODELING COULD BE SO EXHAUST...
...ING!
THERE'S ARCHIE.!!
JE
BUYING A RING?!
HE WANTS TO MARRY ME!!
HOW MUCH?
FIFTY!
JEWELRY

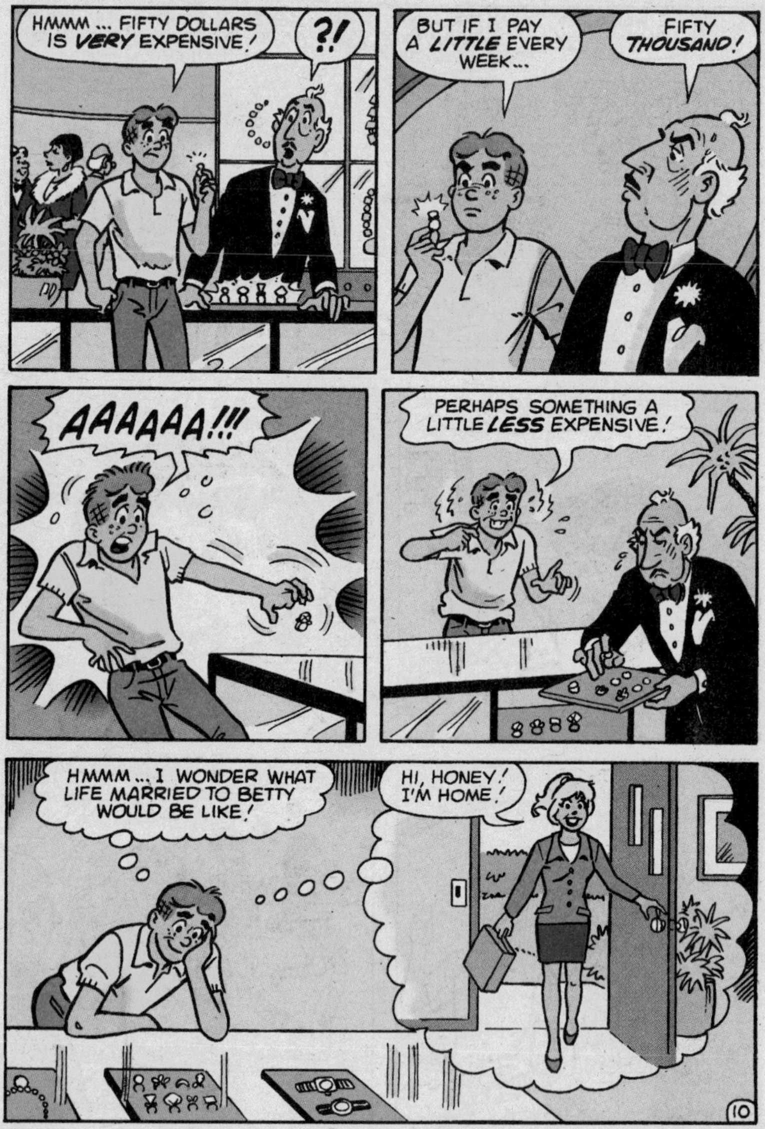
HMMM ... FIFTY DOLLARS IS *VERY* EXPENSIVE!
?!
BUT IF I PAY A *LITTLE* EVERY WEEK...
FIFTY *THOUSAND*!
AAAAAA!!!
PERHAPS SOMETHING A LITTLE *LESS* EXPENSIVE!
HMMM ... I WONDER WHAT LIFE MARRIED TO BETTY WOULD BE LIKE!
HI, HONEY! I'M HOME!
10

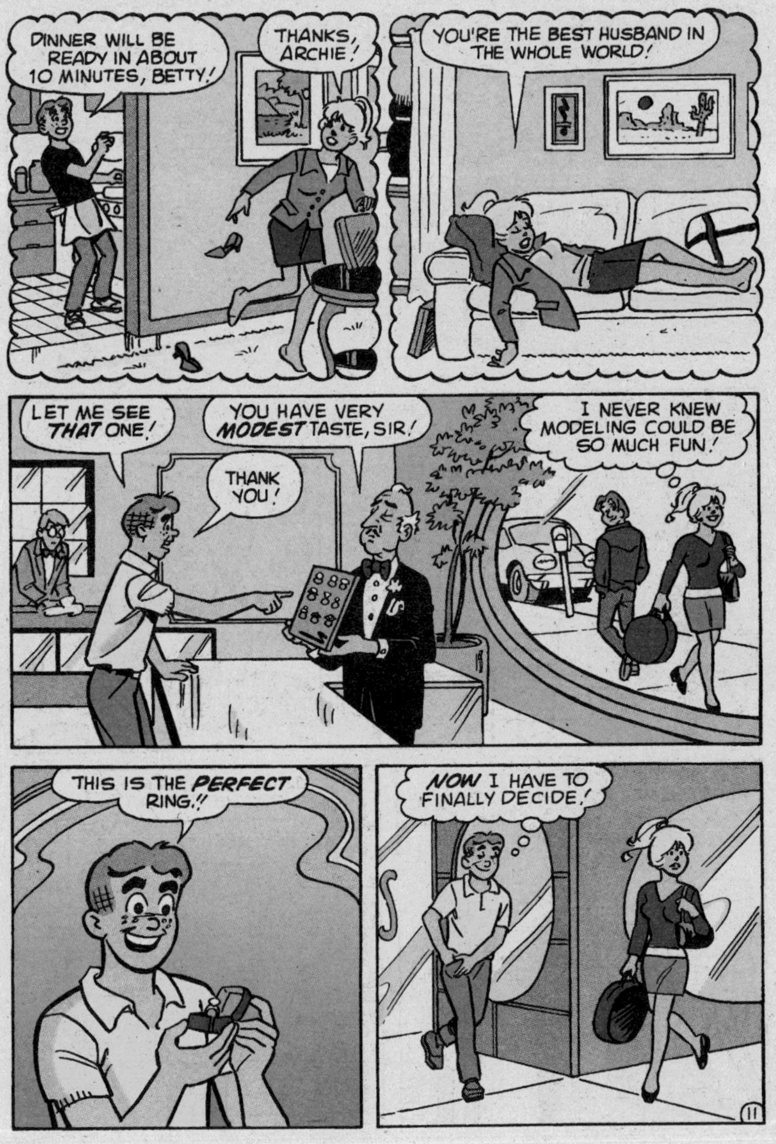
DINNER WILL BE READY IN ABOUT 10 MINUTES, BETTY!
THANKS, ARCHIE!
YOU'RE THE BEST HUSBAND IN THE WHOLE WORLD!
LET ME SEE *THAT* ONE!
THANK YOU!
YOU HAVE VERY *MODEST* TASTE, SIR!
I NEVER KNEW MODELING COULD BE SO MUCH FUN!
THIS IS THE *PERFECT* RING!!
NOW I HAVE TO FINALLY DECIDE!
11

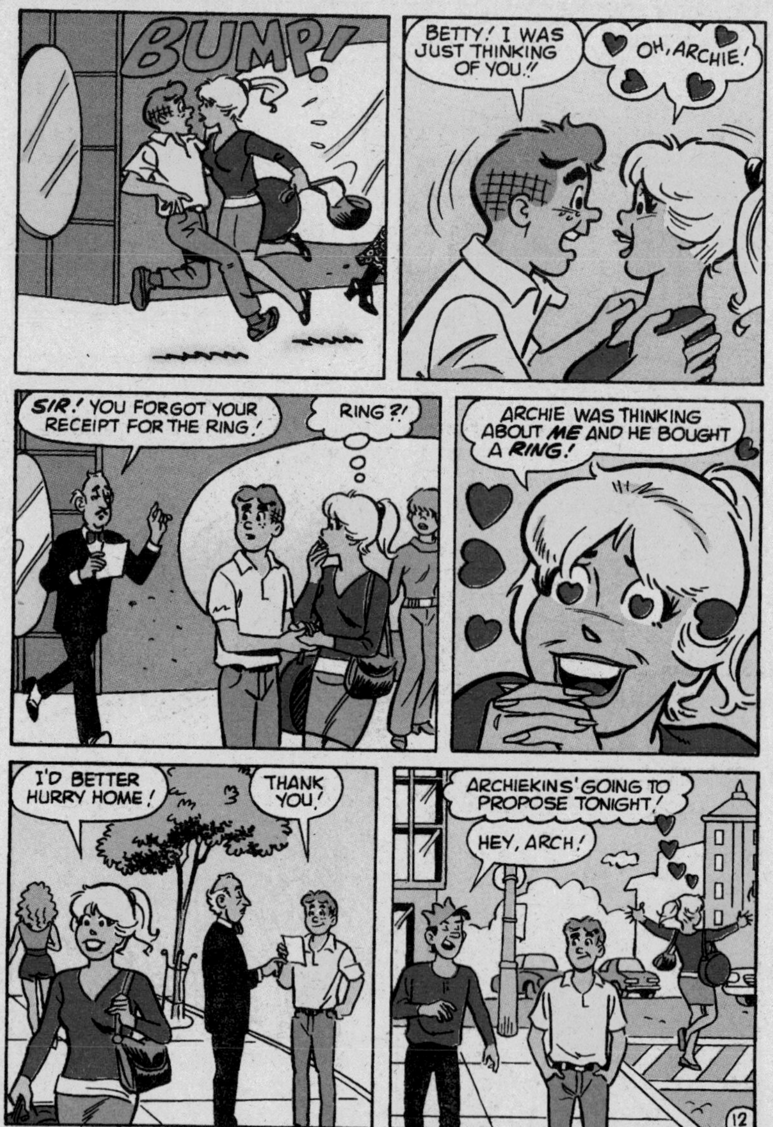
BUMP!
BETTY! I WAS JUST THINKING OF YOU!!
OH, ARCHIE!
SIR! YOU FORGOT YOUR RECEIPT FOR THE RING!
RING ?!
ARCHIE WAS THINKING ABOUT ME AND HE BOUGHT A RING!
I'D BETTER HURRY HOME!
THANK YOU!
ARCHIEKINS' GOING TO PROPOSE TONIGHT!
HEY, ARCH!
12

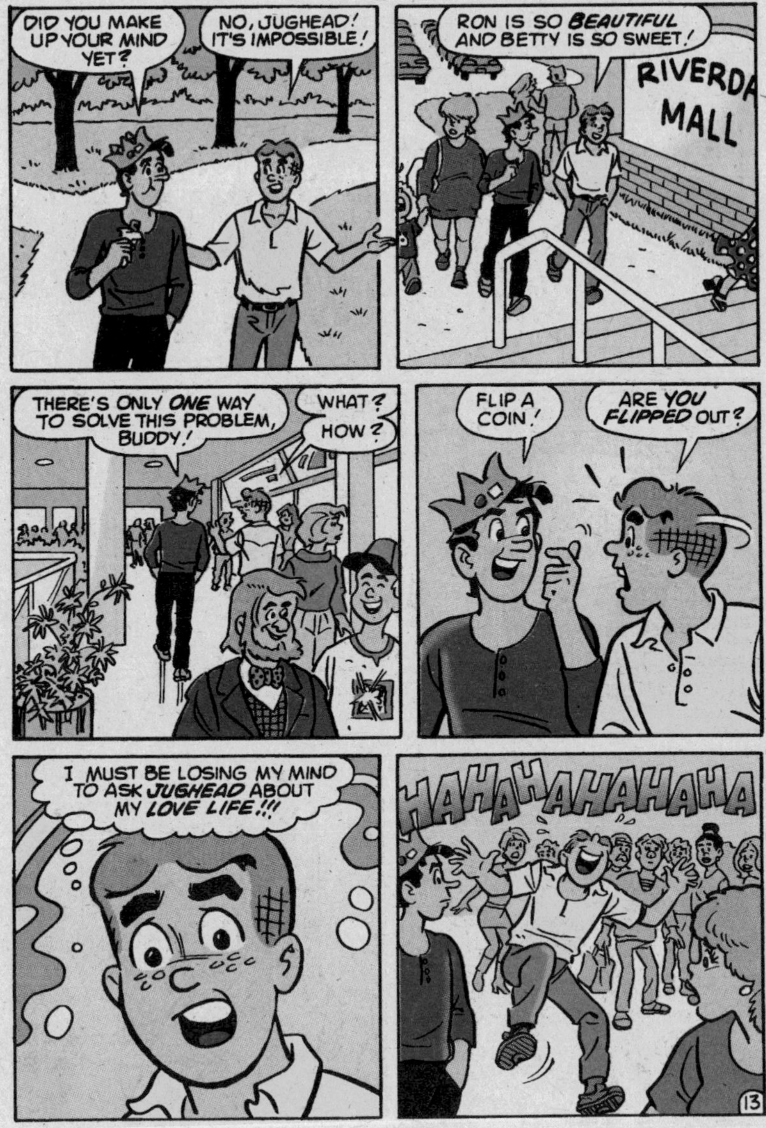
DID YOU MAKE UP YOUR MIND YET?
NO, JUGHEAD! IT'S IMPOSSIBLE!
RON IS SO BEAUTIFUL AND BETTY IS SO SWEET!
RIVERDA
MALL
THERE'S ONLY ONE WAY TO SOLVE THIS PROBLEM, BUDDY!
WHAT?
HOW?
FLIP A COIN!
ARE YOU FLIPPED OUT?
I MUST BE LOSING MY MIND TO ASK JUGHEAD ABOUT MY LOVE LIFE!!!
HAHAHAHAHAHAHAHA
13

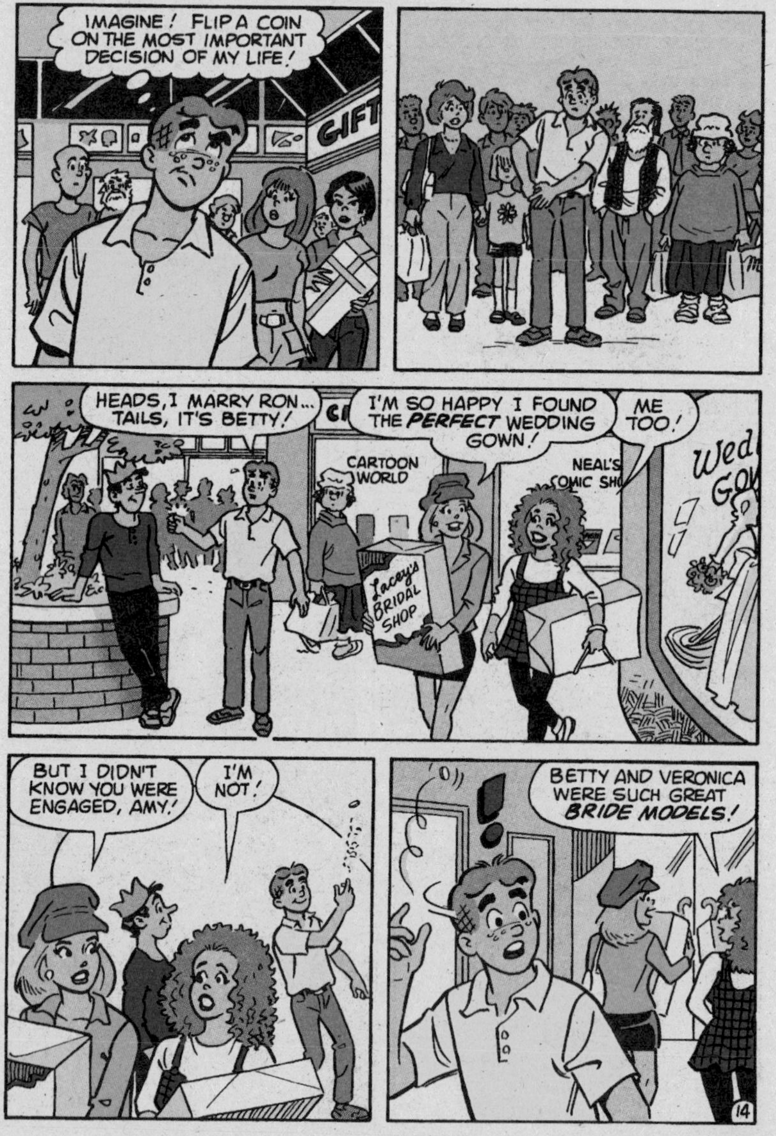
IMAGINE! FLIP A COIN ON THE MOST IMPORTANT DECISION OF MY LIFE!
GIFT
HEADS, I MARRY RON... TAILS, IT'S BETTY!
CARTOON WORLD
I'M SO HAPPY I FOUND THE *PERFECT* WEDDING GOWN!
NEAL'S COMIC SHO
ME TOO!
Lacey's BRIDAL SHOP
BUT I DIDN'T KNOW YOU WERE ENGAGED, AMY!
I'M NOT!
BETTY AND VERONICA WERE SUCH GREAT *BRIDE MODELS*!
14

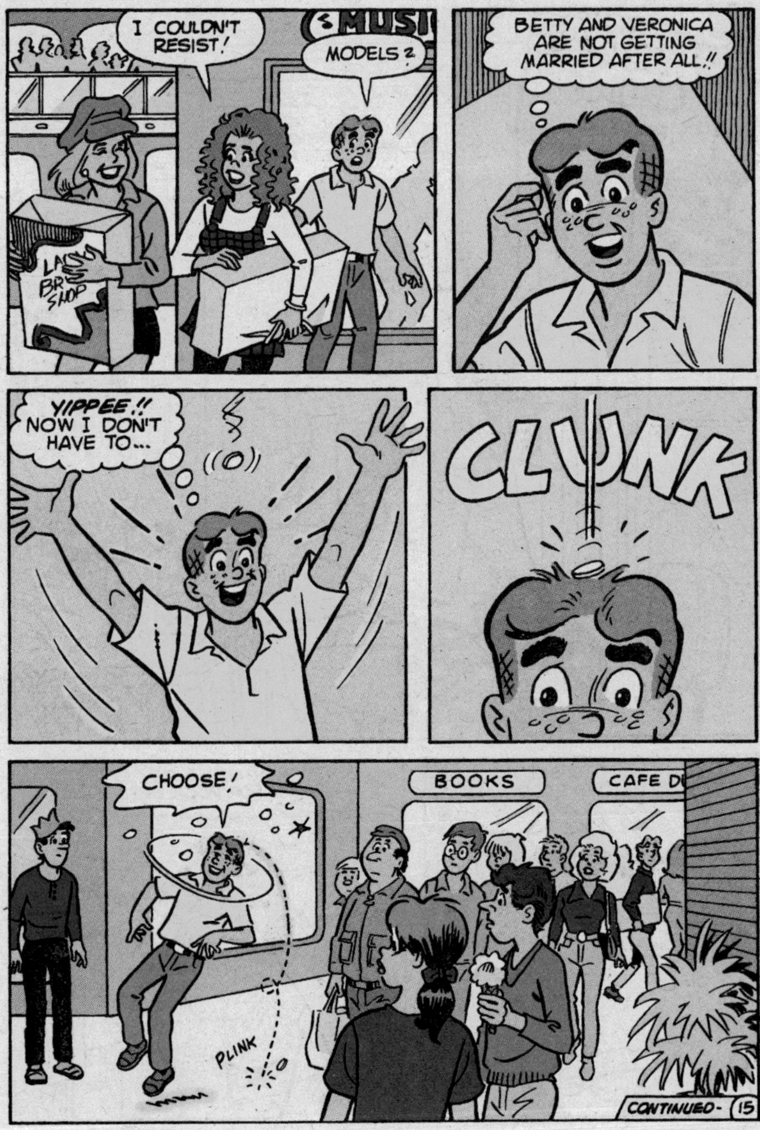
I COULDN'T RESIST!
MODELS?
BETTY AND VERONICA ARE NOT GETTING MARRIED AFTER ALL!!
YIPPEE!! NOW I DON'T HAVE TO...
CLUNK
CHOOSE!
BOOKS
PLINK
CONTINUED-
15

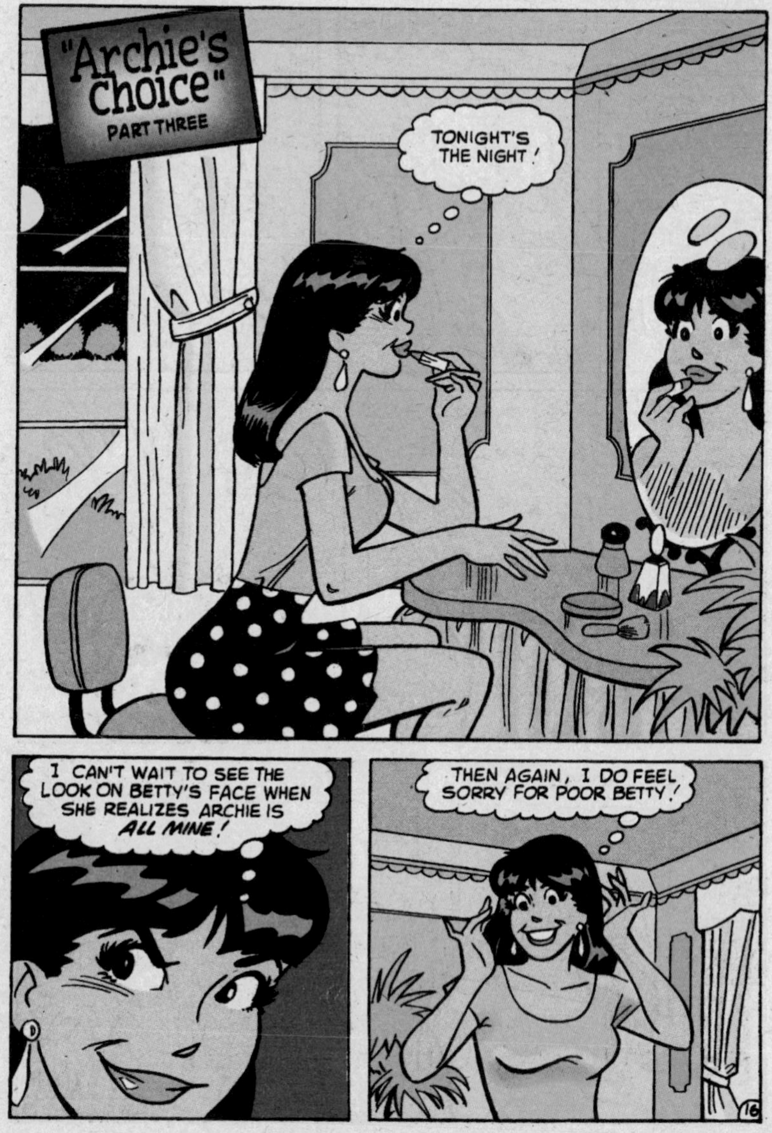
"Archie's Choice"
PART THREE
TONIGHT'S THE NIGHT!
I CAN'T WAIT TO SEE THE LOOK ON BETTY'S FACE WHEN SHE REALIZES ARCHIE IS ALL MINE!
THEN AGAIN, I DO FEEL SORRY FOR POOR BETTY!
16

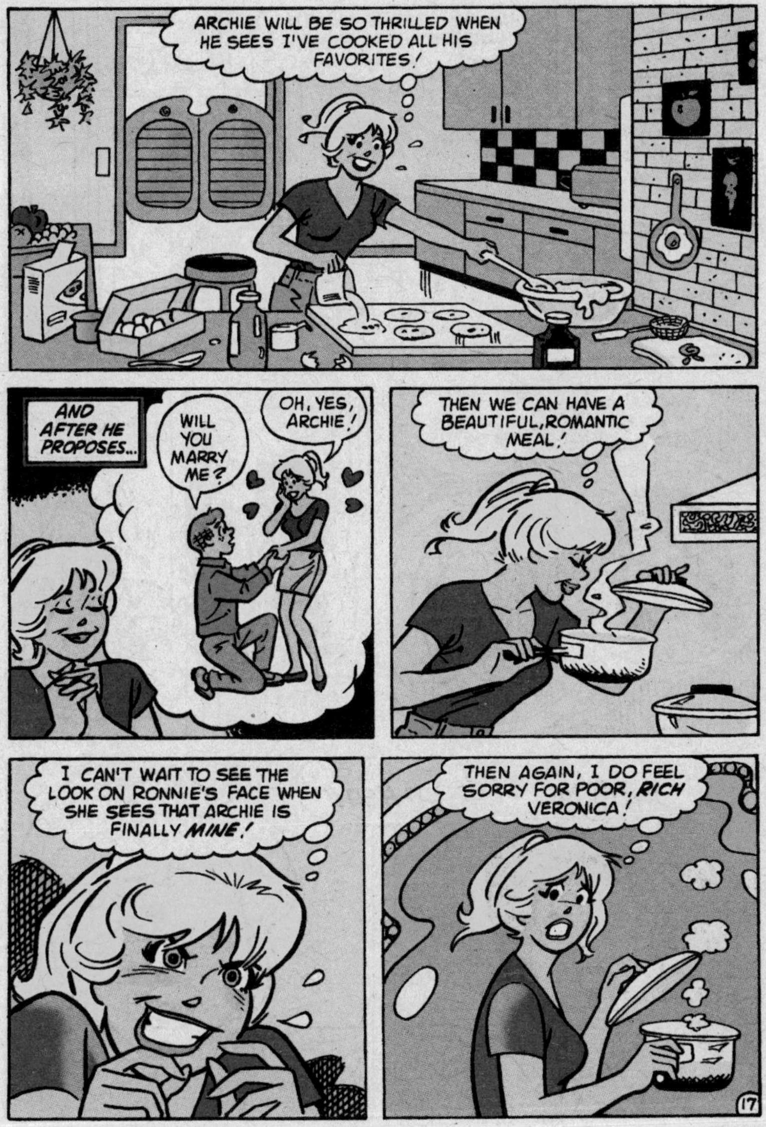
ARCHIE WILL BE SO THRILLED WHEN HE SEES I'VE COOKED ALL HIS FAVORITES!
AND AFTER HE PROPOSES...
WILL YOU MARRY ME?
OH, YES, ARCHIE!
THEN WE CAN HAVE A BEAUTIFUL, ROMANTIC MEAL!
I CAN'T WAIT TO SEE THE LOOK ON RONNIE'S FACE WHEN SHE SEES THAT ARCHIE IS FINALLY *MINE*!
THEN AGAIN, I DO FEEL SORRY FOR POOR, *RICH* VERONICA!

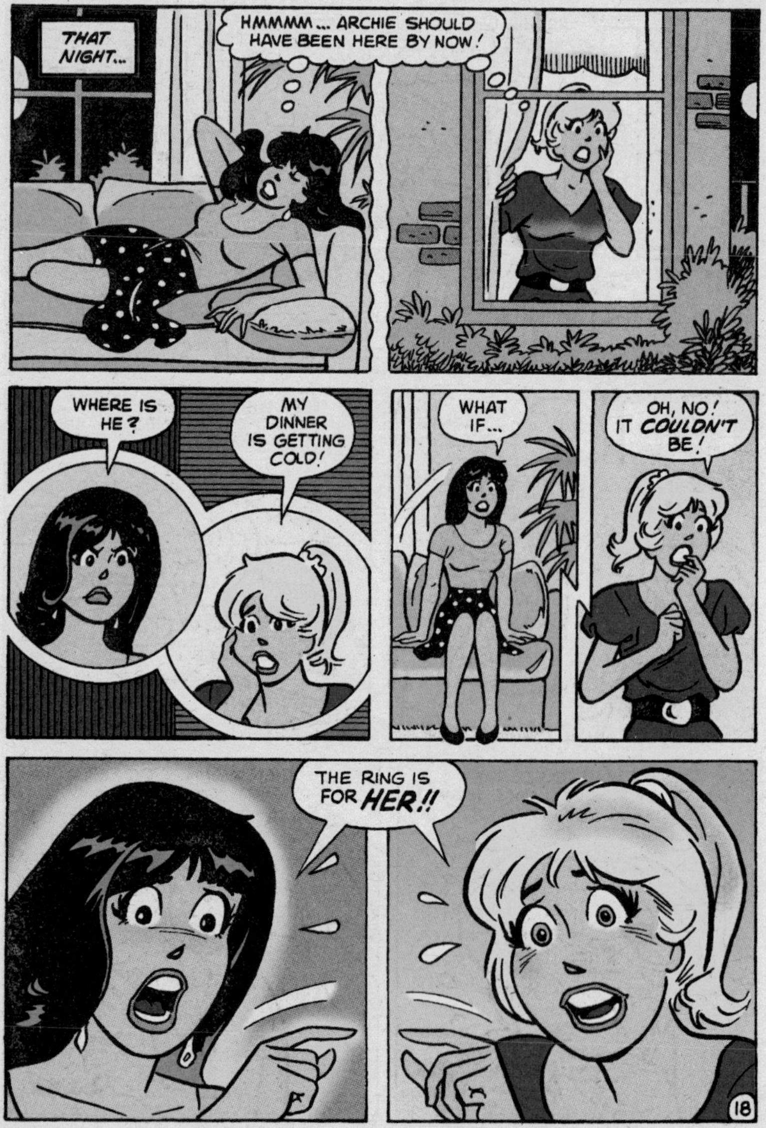
THAT NIGHT...
HMMMM... ARCHIE SHOULD HAVE BEEN HERE BY NOW!
WHERE IS HE?
MY DINNER IS GETTING COLD!
WHAT IF...
OH, NO! IT COULDN'T BE!
THE RING IS FOR HER!!
18

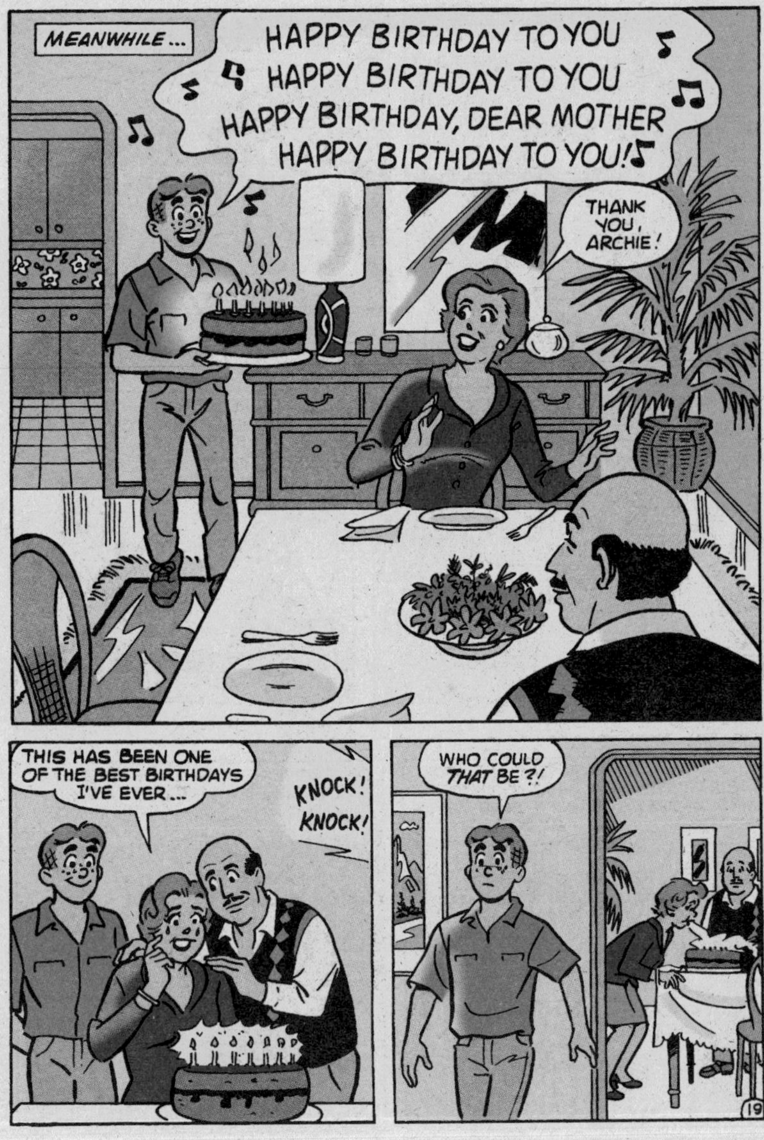
MEANWHILE...
HAPPY BIRTHDAY TO YOU
HAPPY BIRTHDAY TO YOU
HAPPY BIRTHDAY, DEAR MOTHER
HAPPY BIRTHDAY TO YOU!
THANK YOU, ARCHIE!
THIS HAS BEEN ONE OF THE BEST BIRTHDAYS I'VE EVER...
KNOCK! KNOCK!
WHO COULD *THAT* BE ?!
19

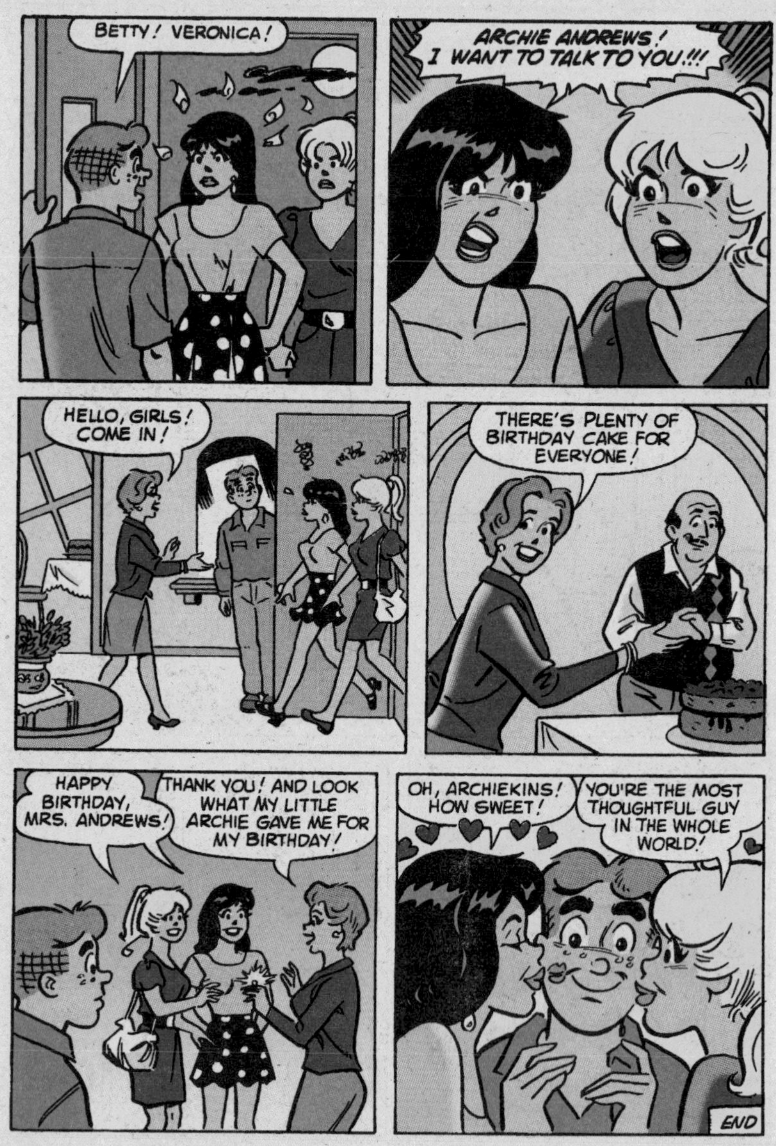
BETTY! VERONICA!
ARCHIE ANDREWS! I WANT TO TALK TO YOU!!!
HELLO, GIRLS! COME IN!
THERE'S PLENTY OF BIRTHDAY CAKE FOR EVERYONE!
HAPPY BIRTHDAY, MRS. ANDREWS!
THANK YOU! AND LOOK WHAT MY LITTLE ARCHIE GAVE ME FOR MY BIRTHDAY!
OH, ARCHIEKINS! HOW SWEET!
YOU'RE THE MOST THOUGHTFUL GUY IN THE WHOLE WORLD!
END

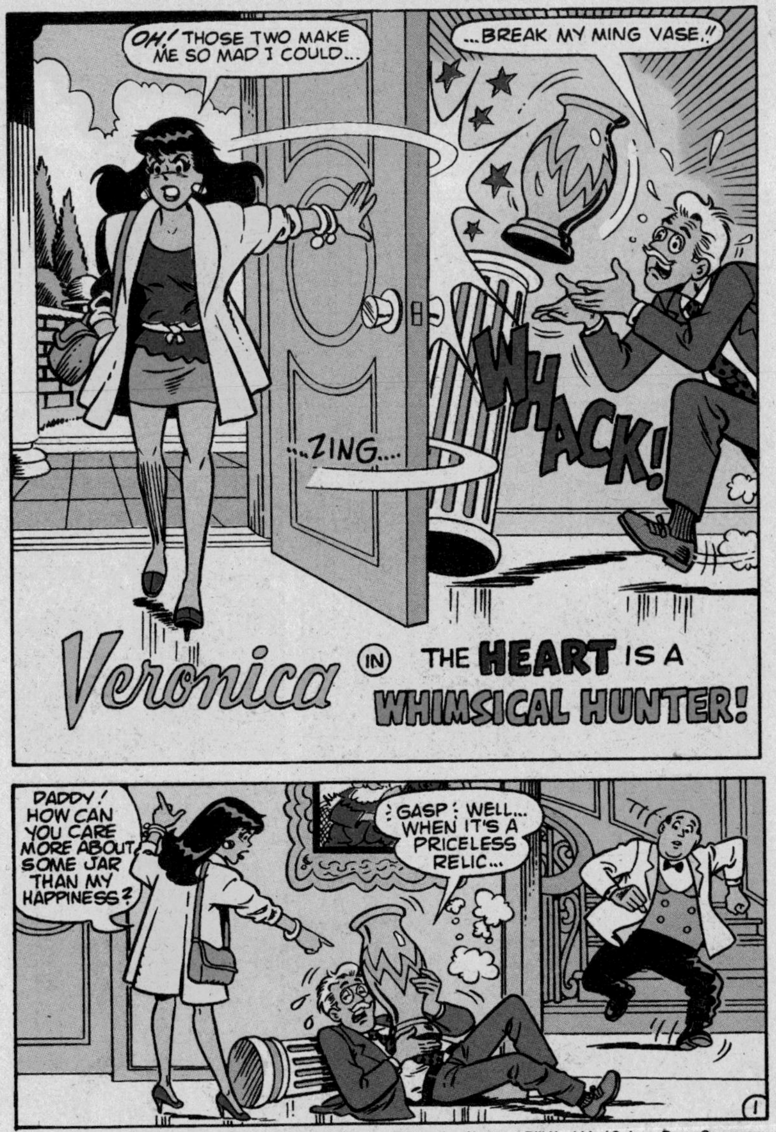
OH! THOSE TWO MAKE ME SO MAD I COULD...
...BREAK MY MING VASE!!
...ZING...
WHACK!
Veronica IN THE HEART IS A WHIMSICAL HUNTER!
DADDY! HOW CAN YOU CARE MORE ABOUT SOME JAR THAN MY HAPPINESS?
GASP! WELL... WHEN IT'S A PRICELESS RELIC...
1

Script: Kathleen Webb / Pencils: Stan Goldberg / Inks: Jon D'Agostino / Letters: Bill Yoshida / Colors: Barry Grossman

WELL, THAT'S ⸴SOB⸴ JUST FINE! M-MY OWN FATHER, ⸴SNIFF⸴ TURNING ON ME, TOO! BOO HOO HOOOOO!

OH, VERONICA...

I'M SORRY! YOU MEAN THE WORLD TO ME! LET'S TALK IN THE LIBRARY... WHAT'S BOTHERING YOU?

⸴HUCK⸴ ARCHIE AND B-BETTY!

SOON...

YOU'RE SURE THEY SAW YOU COMING?

YES! AND SHE RUSHED HIM INTO THE MALL WITH-OUT ME! SHE WANTS ARCHIE ALL TO HER-SELF! ⸴SOB⸴!

PERHAPS YOU NEED A LESSON FROM YOUR GREAT UNCLE LINCOLN LODGE...

THE BIG GAME HUNTER? I DON'T WANT ARCHIE'S HEAD ON A PLAQUE!

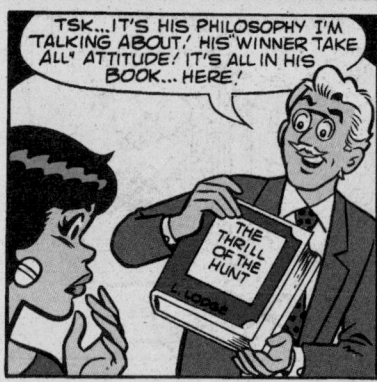

TSK... IT'S HIS PHILOSOPHY I'M TALKING ABOUT! HIS "WINNER TAKE ALL" ATTITUDE! IT'S ALL IN HIS BOOK... HERE!

THE THRILL OF THE HUNT

L. LODGE

NO THANKS, DADDY... I... HMM... THIS IS RATHER INTERESTING!

MM-HMM!

2

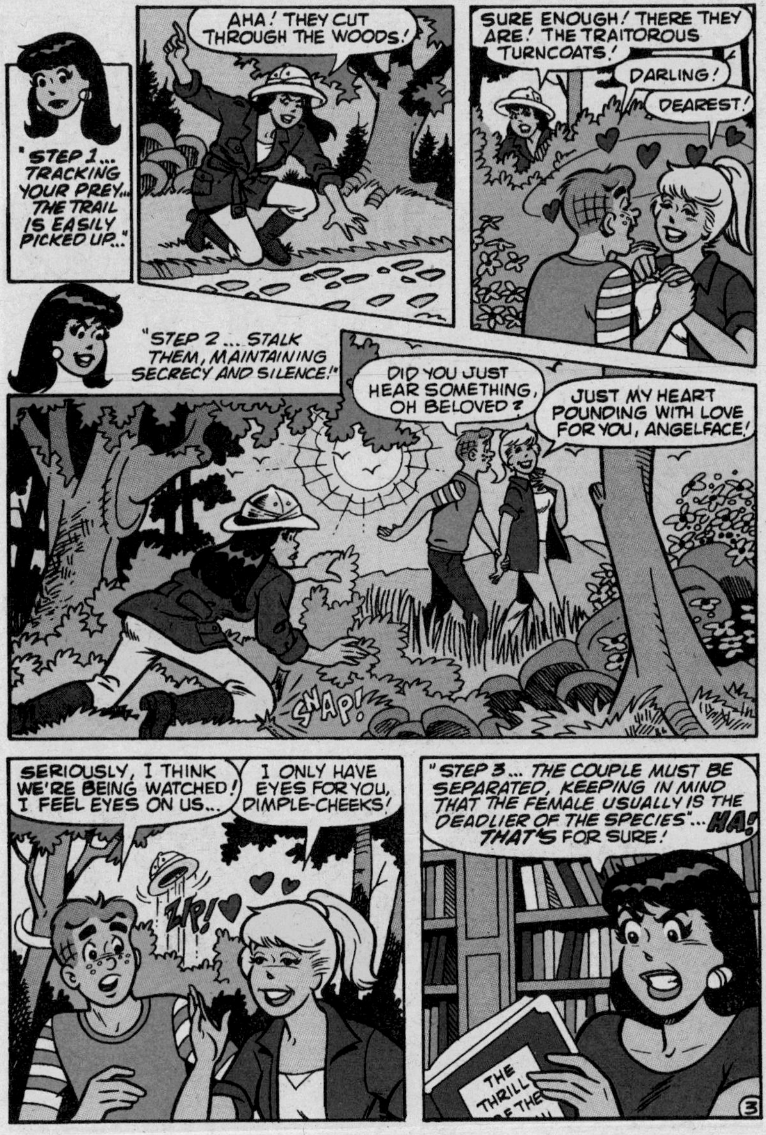
"STEP 1... TRACKING YOUR PREY... THE TRAIL IS EASILY PICKED UP..."
AHA! THEY CUT THROUGH THE WOODS!
SURE ENOUGH! THERE THEY ARE! THE TRAITOROUS TURNCOATS!
DARLING!
DEAREST!
"STEP 2 ... STALK THEM, MAINTAINING SECRECY AND SILENCE!"
DID YOU JUST HEAR SOMETHING, OH BELOVED?
JUST MY HEART POUNDING WITH LOVE FOR YOU, ANGELFACE!
SNAP!
SERIOUSLY, I THINK WE'RE BEING WATCHED! I FEEL EYES ON US...
I ONLY HAVE EYES FOR YOU, DIMPLE-CHEEKS!
ZIP!
"STEP 3... THE COUPLE MUST BE SEPARATED, KEEPING IN MIND THAT THE FEMALE USUALLY IS THE DEADLIER OF THE SPECIES"... HA! THAT'S FOR SURE!
THE THRILL OF THE
3

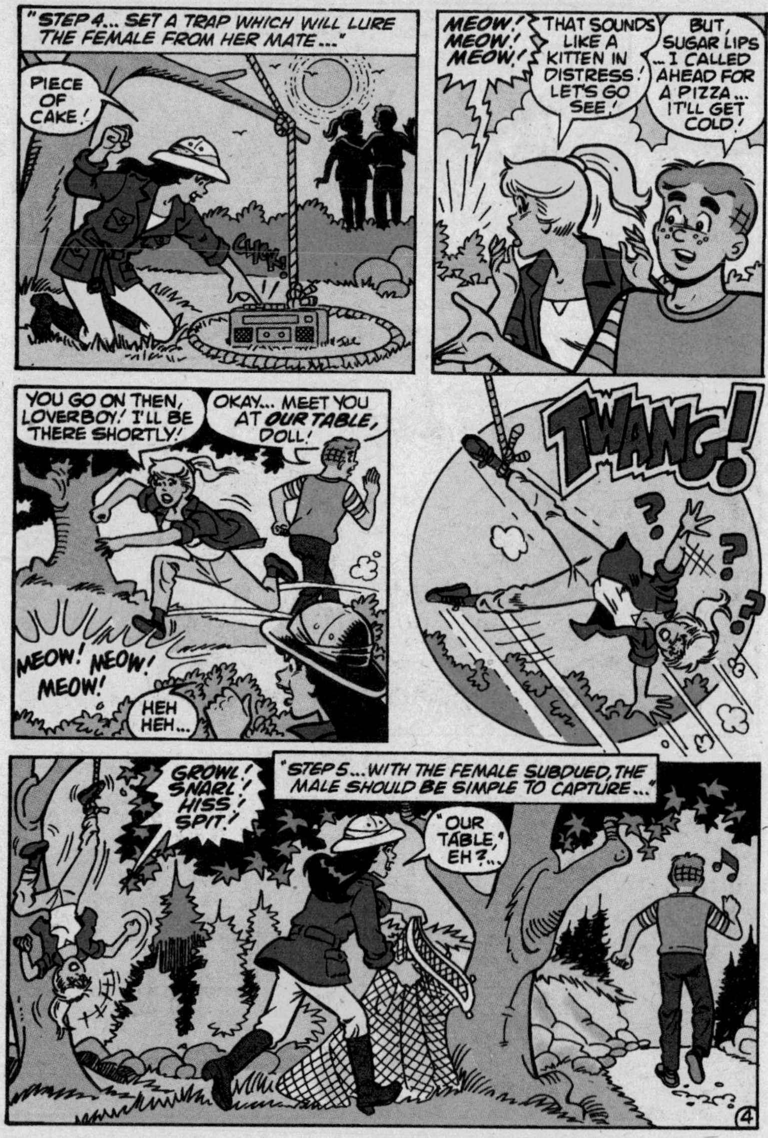
"STEP 4... SET A TRAP WHICH WILL LURE THE FEMALE FROM HER MATE..."
PIECE OF CAKE!
CHUK!
MEOW! MEOW! MEOW!
THAT SOUNDS LIKE A KITTEN IN DISTRESS! LET'S GO SEE!
BUT, SUGAR LIPS ...I CALLED AHEAD FOR A PIZZA... IT'LL GET COLD!
YOU GO ON THEN, LOVERBOY! I'LL BE THERE SHORTLY!
OKAY... MEET YOU AT OUR TABLE, DOLL!
MEOW! MEOW! MEOW!
HEH HEH...
TWANG!
GROWL! SNARL! HISS! SPIT!
"STEP 5...WITH THE FEMALE SUBDUED, THE MALE SHOULD BE SIMPLE TO CAPTURE..."
"OUR TABLE," EH?...
4

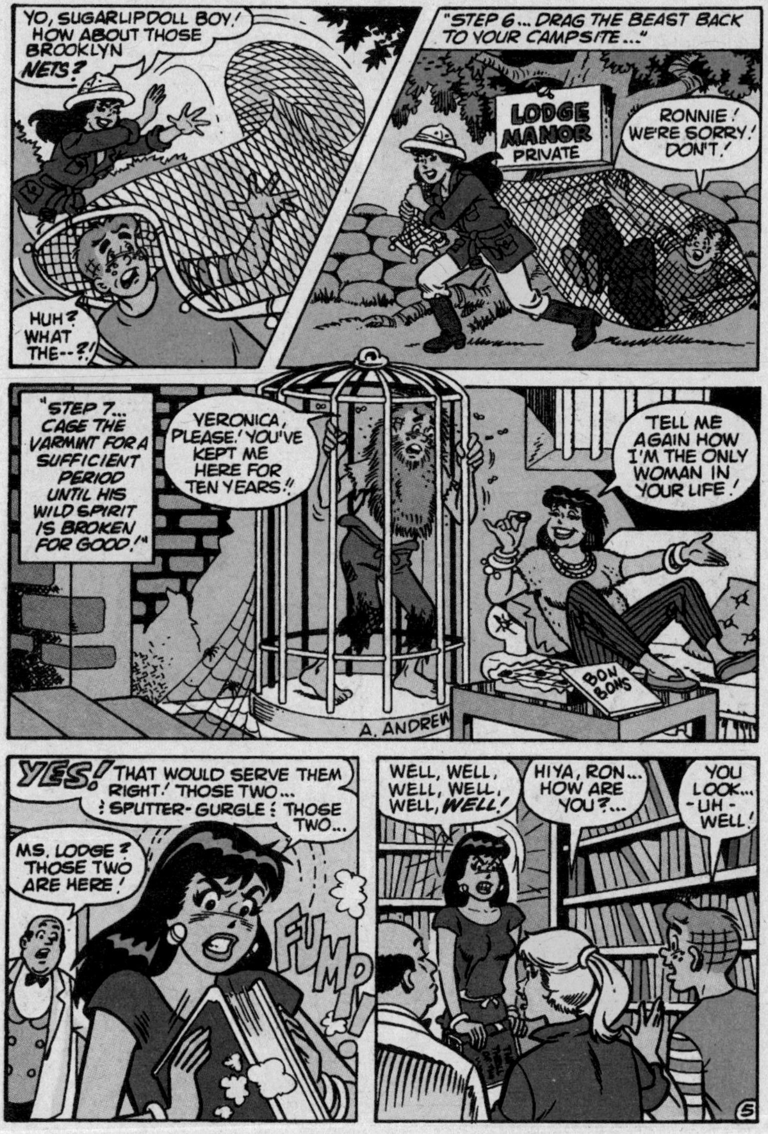
YO, SUGARLIPDOLL BOY! HOW ABOUT THOSE BROOKLYN NETS?
HUH? WHAT THE--?!
"STEP 6... DRAG THE BEAST BACK TO YOUR CAMPSITE..."
LODGE MANOR PRIVATE
RONNIE! WE'RE SORRY! DON'T!
"STEP 7... CAGE THE VARMINT FOR A SUFFICIENT PERIOD UNTIL HIS WILD SPIRIT IS BROKEN FOR GOOD!"
VERONICA, PLEASE! YOU'VE KEPT ME HERE FOR TEN YEARS!!
TELL ME AGAIN HOW I'M THE ONLY WOMAN IN YOUR LIFE!
BON BONS
A. ANDREW
YES! THAT WOULD SERVE THEM RIGHT! THOSE TWO... ⁝SPUTTER-GURGLE⁝ THOSE TWO...
MS. LODGE? THOSE TWO ARE HERE!
FUMP!
WELL, WELL, WELL, WELL, WELL, WELL!
HIYA, RON... HOW ARE YOU?...
YOU LOOK... -UH- WELL!

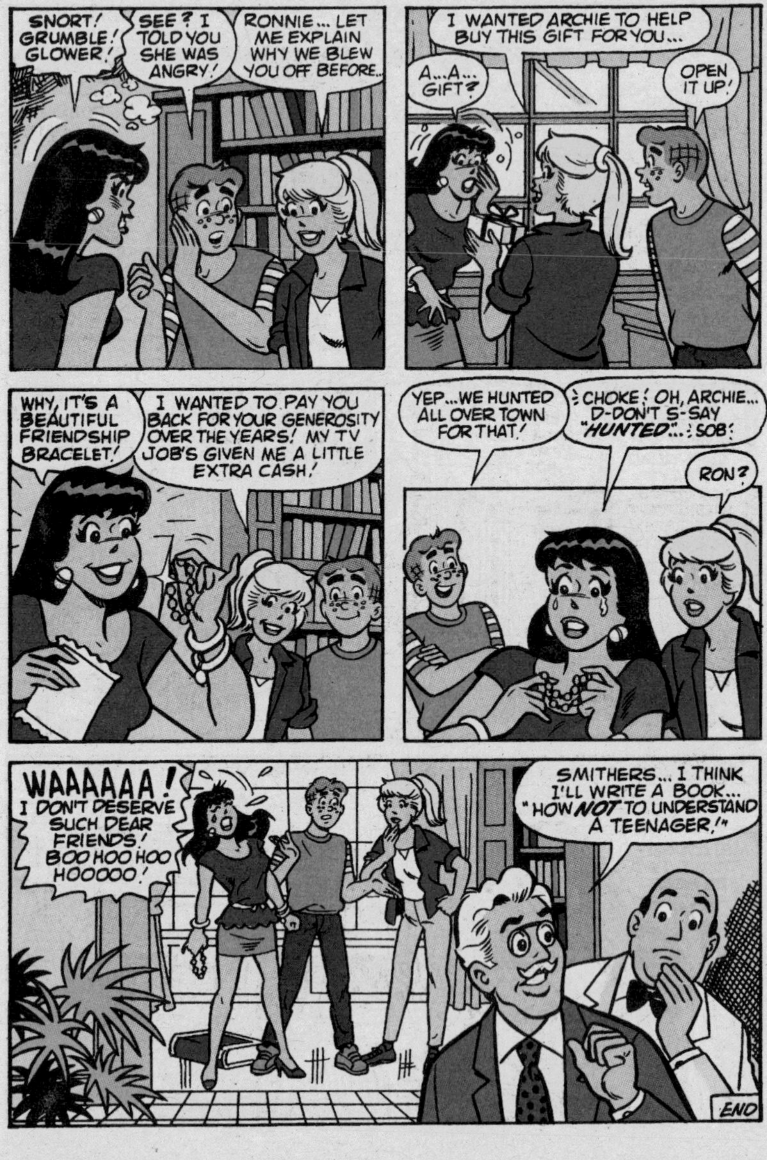
SNORT! GRUMBLE! GLOWER!
SEE? I TOLD YOU SHE WAS ANGRY!
RONNIE... LET ME EXPLAIN WHY WE BLEW YOU OFF BEFORE...
I WANTED ARCHIE TO HELP BUY THIS GIFT FOR YOU...
A...A... GIFT?
OPEN IT UP!
WHY, IT'S A BEAUTIFUL FRIENDSHIP BRACELET!
I WANTED TO PAY YOU BACK FOR YOUR GENEROSITY OVER THE YEARS! MY TV JOB'S GIVEN ME A LITTLE EXTRA CASH!
YEP...WE HUNTED ALL OVER TOWN FOR THAT!
:CHOKE: OH, ARCHIE... D-DON'T S-SAY "*HUNTED*"... :SOB:
RON?
WAAAAAA! I DON'T DESERVE SUCH DEAR FRIENDS! BOO HOO HOO HOOOOO!
SMITHERS... I THINK I'LL WRITE A BOOK... "HOW *NOT* TO UNDERSTAND A TEENAGER!"
END

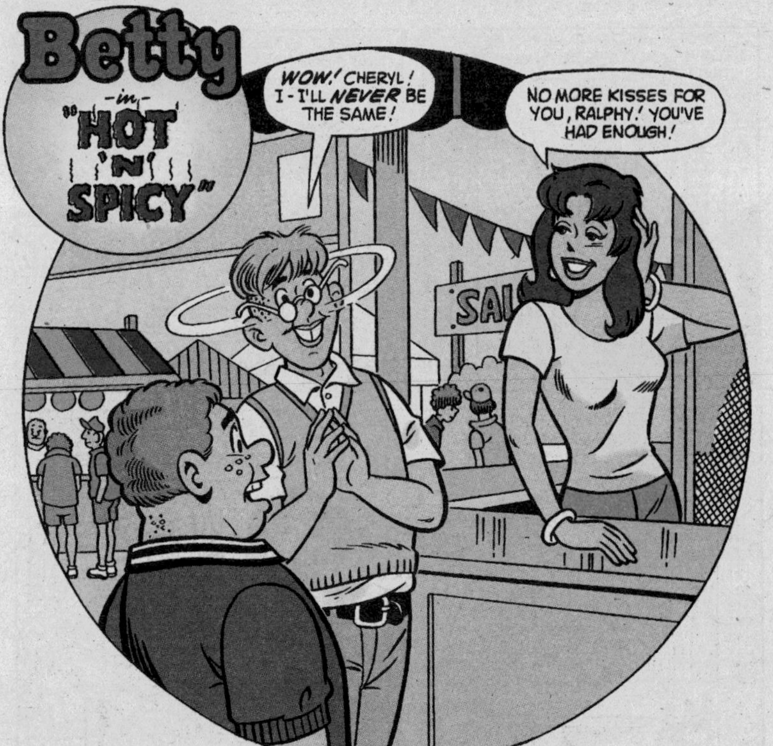
Betty
-in-
"HOT 'N' SPICY"
WOW! CHERYL! I-I'LL NEVER BE THE SAME!
NO MORE KISSES FOR YOU, RALPHY! YOU'VE HAD ENOUGH!
HEY, RALPH! FORGET CHERYL!
BETTY'S BOOTH IS WHERE THE ACTION IS!
...JUST LOOK AT THE MOB SCENE AT HER BOOTH!
ME NEXT, BETTY!
NO, ME!!
1

Script: George Gladir / Pencils: Tim Kennedy / Inks: Jon D'Agostino / Letters: Bill Yoshida / Colors: Barry Grossman

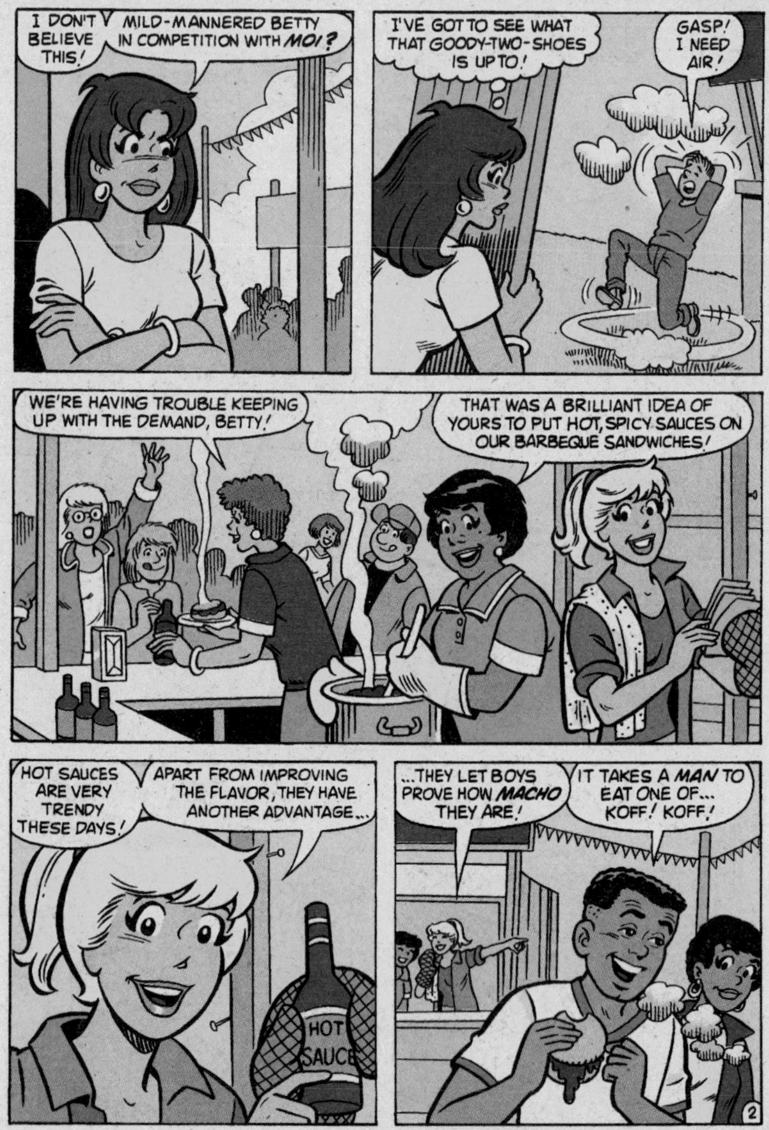
I DON'T BELIEVE THIS!
MILD-MANNERED BETTY IN COMPETITION WITH *MOI*?
I'VE GOT TO SEE WHAT THAT GOODY-TWO-SHOES IS UP TO!
GASP! I NEED AIR!
WE'RE HAVING TROUBLE KEEPING UP WITH THE DEMAND, BETTY!
THAT WAS A BRILLIANT IDEA OF YOURS TO PUT HOT, SPICY SAUCES ON OUR BARBEQUE SANDWICHES!
HOT SAUCES ARE VERY TRENDY THESE DAYS!
APART FROM IMPROVING THE FLAVOR, THEY HAVE ANOTHER ADVANTAGE...
HOT SAUCE
...THEY LET BOYS PROVE HOW *MACHO* THEY ARE!
IT TAKES A *MAN* TO EAT ONE OF... KOFF! KOFF!
2

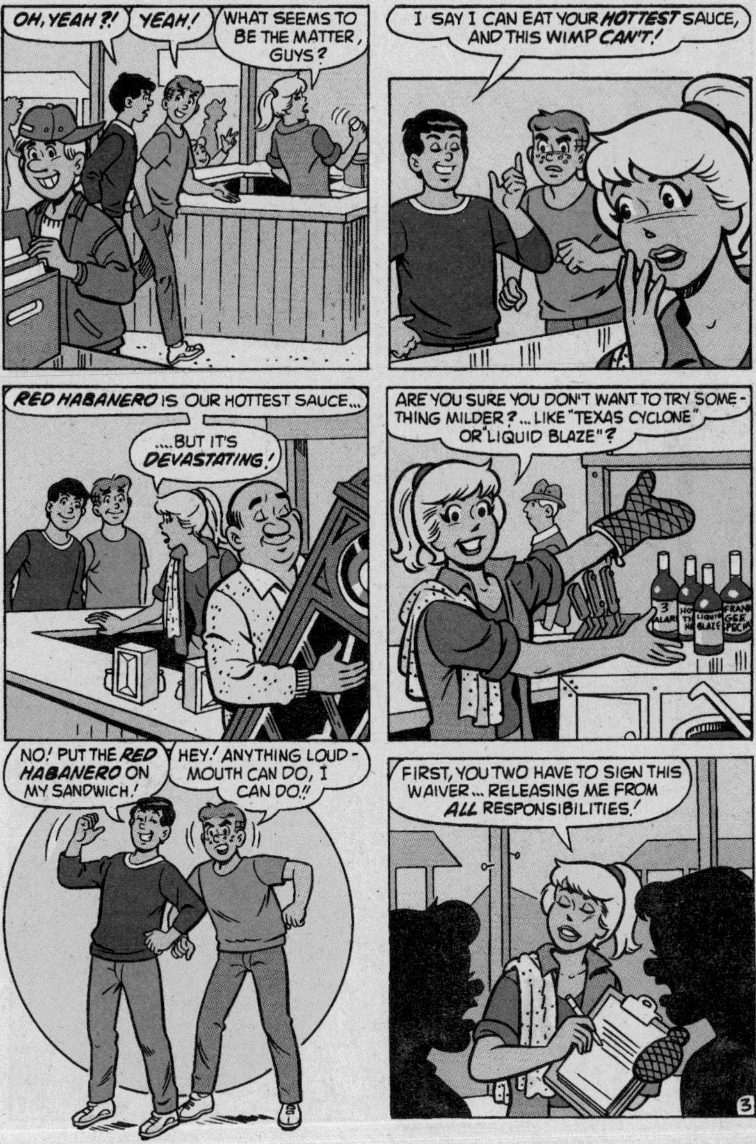
OH, YEAH ?!
YEAH!
WHAT SEEMS TO BE THE MATTER, GUYS?
I SAY I CAN EAT YOUR HOTTEST SAUCE, AND THIS WIMP CAN'T!
RED HABANERO IS OUR HOTTEST SAUCE...
....BUT IT'S DEVASTATING!
ARE YOU SURE YOU DON'T WANT TO TRY SOME-THING MILDER?... LIKE "TEXAS CYCLONE" OR "LIQUID BLAZE"?
LIQUID BLAZE
NO! PUT THE RED HABANERO ON MY SANDWICH!
HEY! ANYTHING LOUD-MOUTH CAN DO, I CAN DO!!
FIRST, YOU TWO HAVE TO SIGN THIS WAIVER... RELEASING ME FROM ALL RESPONSIBILITIES!
3

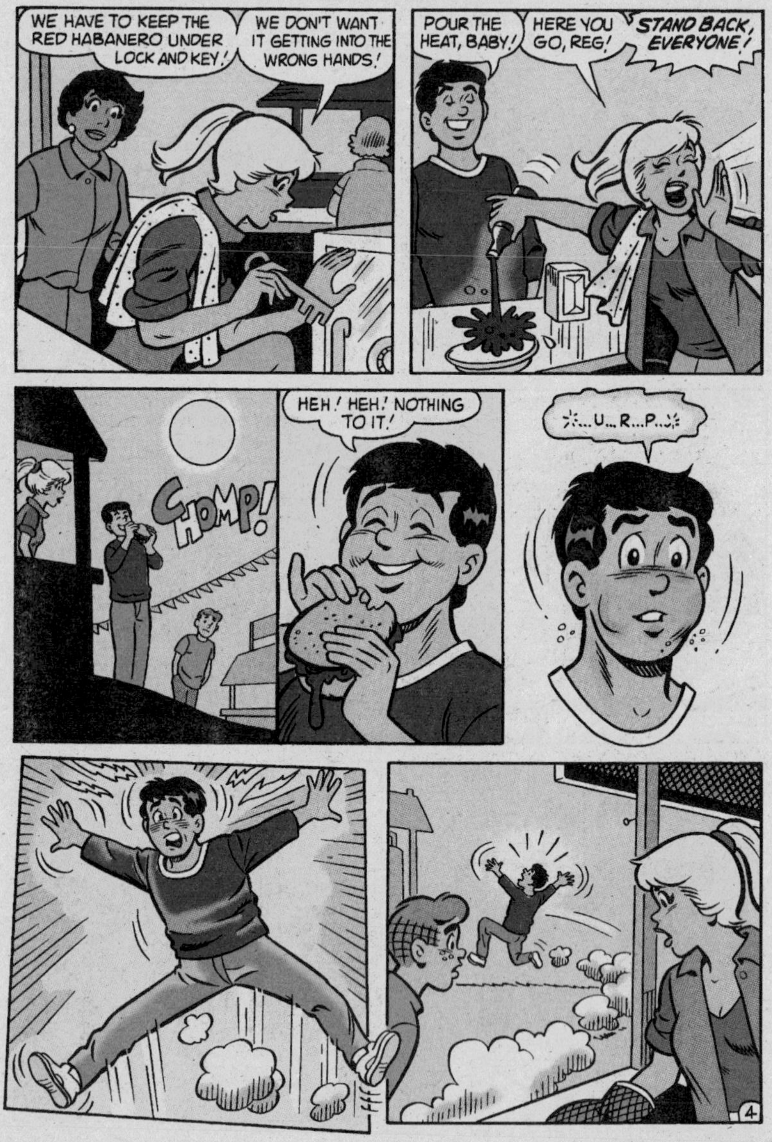
WE HAVE TO KEEP THE RED HABANERO UNDER LOCK AND KEY!
WE DON'T WANT IT GETTING INTO THE WRONG HANDS!
POUR THE HEAT, BABY!
HERE YOU GO, REG!
STAND BACK, EVERYONE!
CHOMP!
HEH! HEH! NOTHING TO IT!
...U...R...P...
4

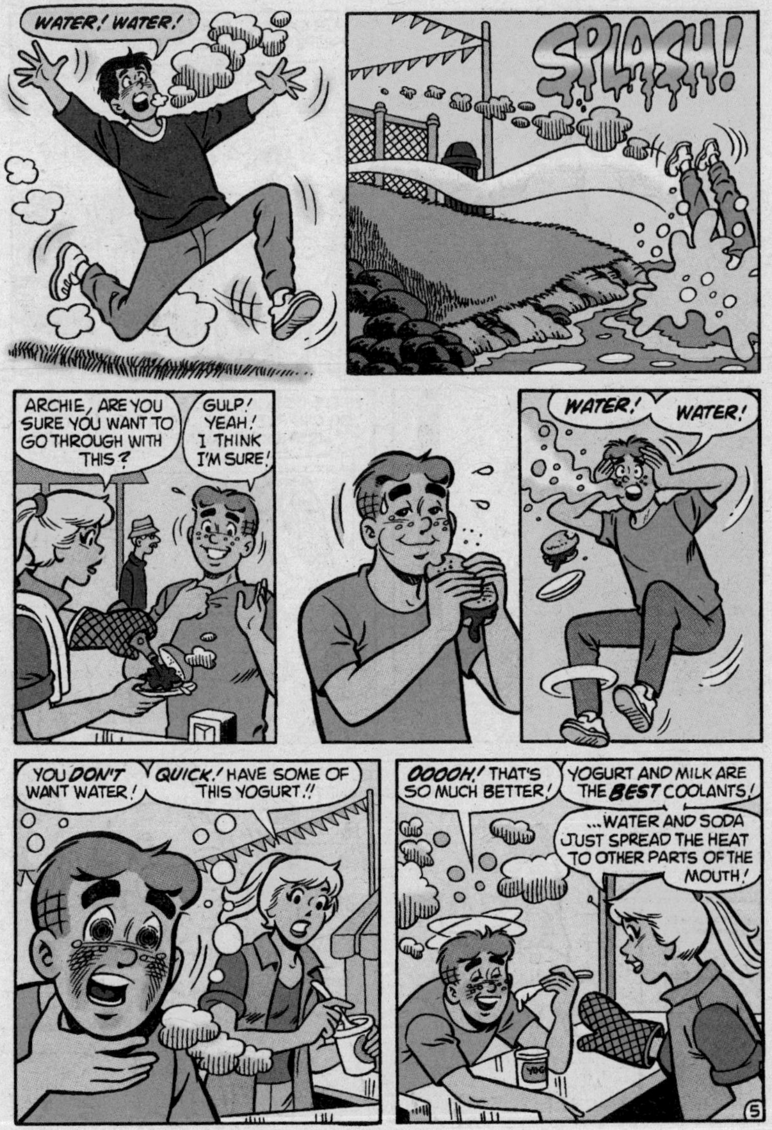

WATER! WATER!
SPLASH!
ARCHIE, ARE YOU SURE YOU WANT TO GO THROUGH WITH THIS?
GULP! YEAH! I THINK I'M SURE!
WATER!
WATER!
YOU DON'T WANT WATER!
QUICK! HAVE SOME OF THIS YOGURT!!
OOOOH! THAT'S SO MUCH BETTER!
YOGURT AND MILK ARE THE BEST COOLANTS!
...WATER AND SODA JUST SPREAD THE HEAT TO OTHER PARTS OF THE MOUTH!
5

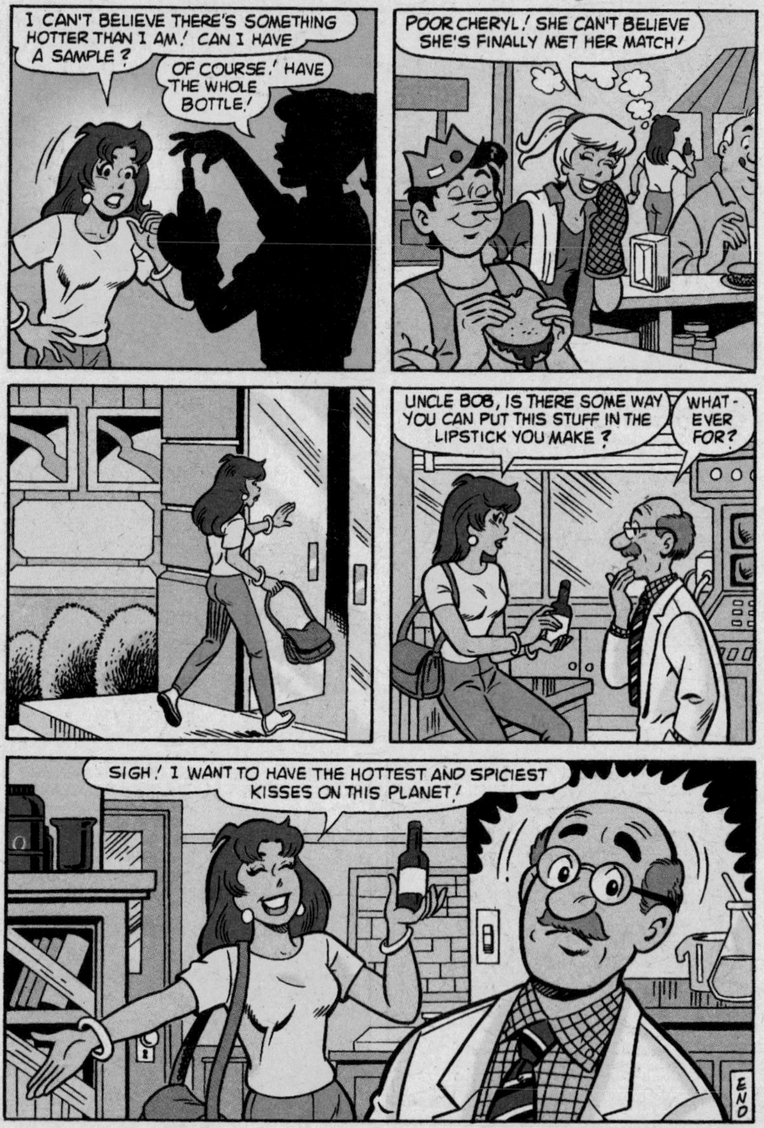
I CAN'T BELIEVE THERE'S SOMETHING HOTTER THAN I AM! CAN I HAVE A SAMPLE?
OF COURSE! HAVE THE WHOLE BOTTLE!
POOR CHERYL! SHE CAN'T BELIEVE SHE'S FINALLY MET HER MATCH!
UNCLE BOB, IS THERE SOME WAY YOU CAN PUT THIS STUFF IN THE LIPSTICK YOU MAKE?
WHAT-EVER FOR?
SIGH! I WANT TO HAVE THE HOTTEST AND SPICIEST KISSES ON THIS PLANET!
END

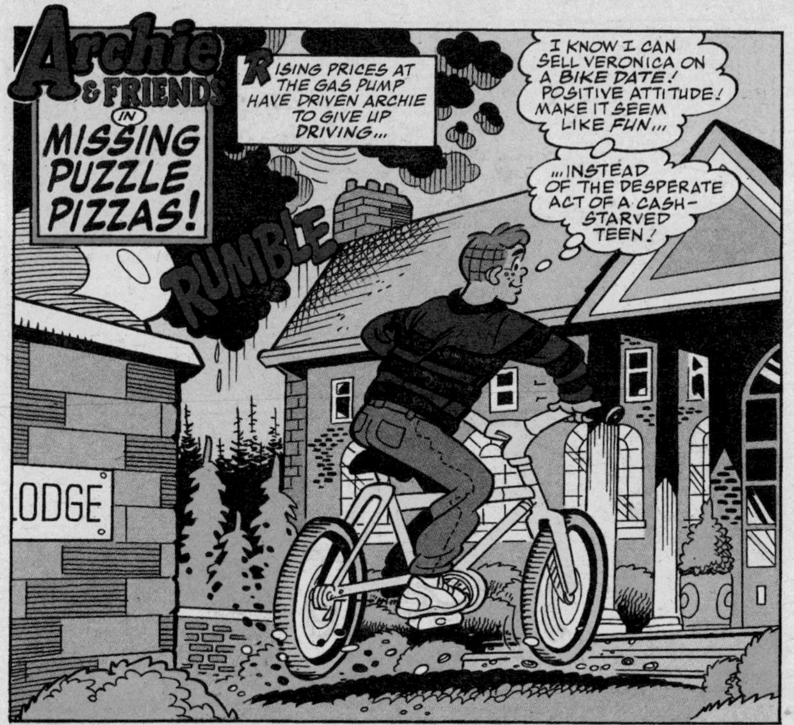
Archie & FRIENDS
IN
MISSING PUZZLE PIZZAS!
RISING PRICES AT THE GAS PUMP HAVE DRIVEN ARCHIE TO GIVE UP DRIVING...
I KNOW I CAN SELL VERONICA ON A BIKE DATE! POSITIVE ATTITUDE! MAKE IT SEEM LIKE FUN...
...INSTEAD OF THE DESPERATE ACT OF A CASH-STARVED TEEN!
RUMBLE
LODGE

SCRIPT: SCOTT CUNNINGHAM · PENCILS: STAN GOLDBERG · INKING: BOB SMITH · LETTERING: JACK MORELLI · COLORING: BARRY GROSSMAN

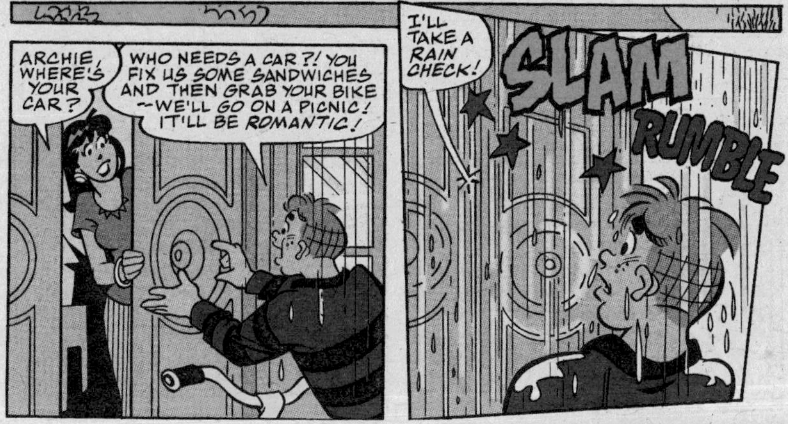
ARCHIE, WHERE'S YOUR CAR?
WHO NEEDS A CAR?! YOU FIX US SOME SANDWICHES AND THEN GRAB YOUR BIKE --WE'LL GO ON A PICNIC! IT'LL BE ROMANTIC!
I'LL TAKE A RAIN CHECK!
SLAM
RUMBLE

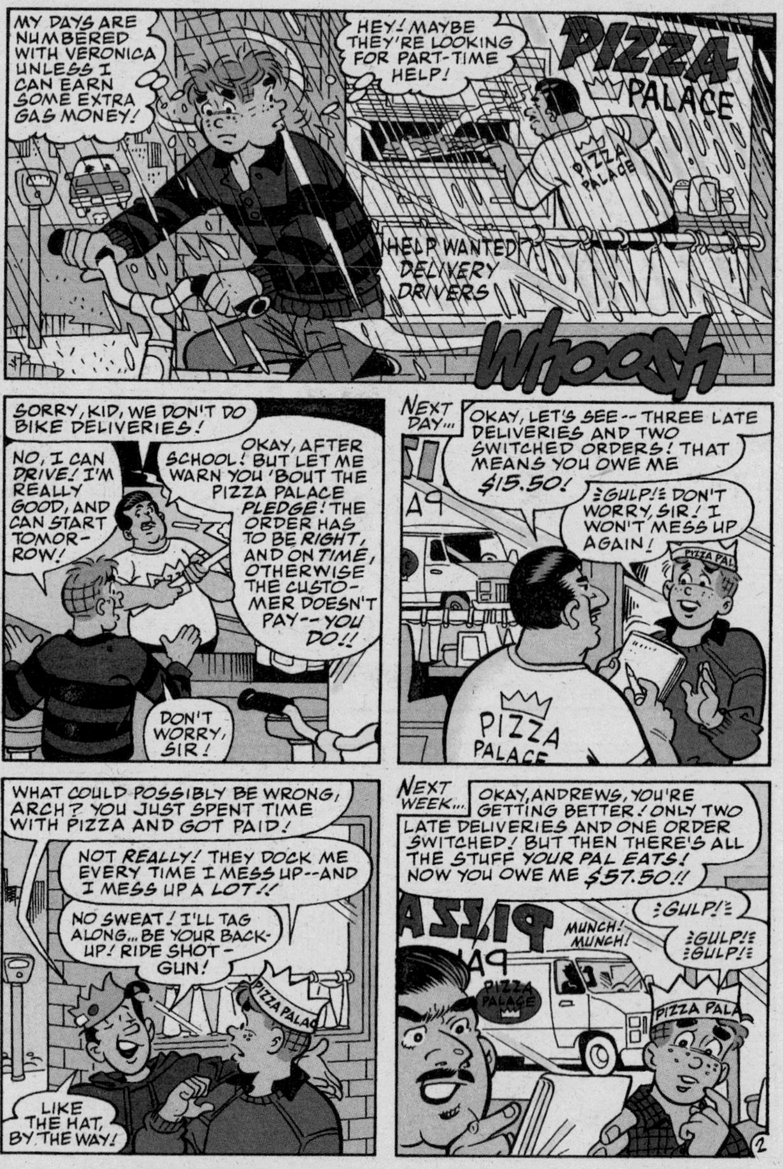
MY DAYS ARE NUMBERED WITH VERONICA UNLESS I CAN EARN SOME EXTRA GAS MONEY!
HEY! MAYBE THEY'RE LOOKING FOR PART-TIME HELP!
PIZZA PALACE
PIZZA PALACE
HELP WANTED DELIVERY DRIVERS
WHOOSH
SORRY, KID, WE DON'T DO BIKE DELIVERIES!
NO, I CAN DRIVE! I'M REALLY GOOD, AND CAN START TOMORROW!
OKAY, AFTER SCHOOL! BUT LET ME WARN YOU 'BOUT THE PIZZA PALACE PLEDGE! THE ORDER HAS TO BE RIGHT, AND ON TIME, OTHERWISE THE CUSTOMER DOESN'T PAY--YOU DO!!
DON'T WORRY, SIR!
NEXT DAY...
OKAY, LET'S SEE--THREE LATE DELIVERIES AND TWO SWITCHED ORDERS! THAT MEANS YOU OWE ME $15.50!
GULP! DON'T WORRY, SIR! I WON'T MESS UP AGAIN!
PIZZA PALACE
WHAT COULD POSSIBLY BE WRONG, ARCH? YOU JUST SPENT TIME WITH PIZZA AND GOT PAID!
NOT REALLY! THEY DOCK ME EVERY TIME I MESS UP--AND I MESS UP A LOT!!
NO SWEAT! I'LL TAG ALONG... BE YOUR BACK-UP! RIDE SHOT-GUN!
LIKE THE HAT, BY THE WAY!
NEXT WEEK...
OKAY, ANDREWS, YOU'RE GETTING BETTER! ONLY TWO LATE DELIVERIES AND ONE ORDER SWITCHED! BUT THEN THERE'S ALL THE STUFF YOUR PAL EATS! NOW YOU OWE ME $57.50!!
GULP!
MUNCH! MUNCH!
GULP! GULP!
PIZZA PALACE

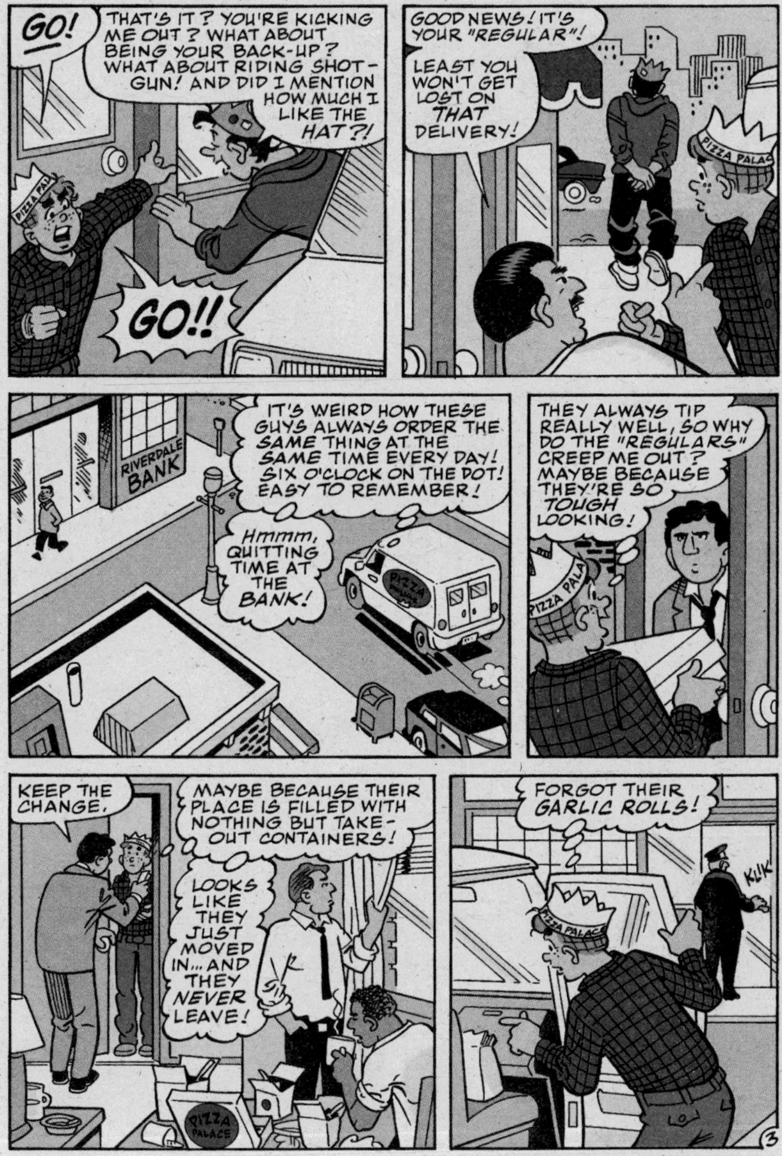
GO!
THAT'S IT? YOU'RE KICKING ME OUT? WHAT ABOUT BEING YOUR BACK-UP? WHAT ABOUT RIDING SHOT-GUN! AND DID I MENTION HOW MUCH I LIKE THE HAT?!
PIZZA PALA
GO!!
GOOD NEWS! IT'S YOUR "REGULAR"!
LEAST YOU WON'T GET LOST ON THAT DELIVERY!
PIZZA PALAC
RIVERDALE BANK
IT'S WEIRD HOW THESE GUYS ALWAYS ORDER THE SAME THING AT THE SAME TIME EVERY DAY! SIX O'CLOCK ON THE DOT! EASY TO REMEMBER!
Hmmm, QUITTING TIME AT THE BANK!
PIZZA
THEY ALWAYS TIP REALLY WELL, SO WHY DO THE "REGULARS" CREEP ME OUT? MAYBE BECAUSE THEY'RE SO TOUGH LOOKING!
PIZZA PALA
KEEP THE CHANGE.
MAYBE BECAUSE THEIR PLACE IS FILLED WITH NOTHING BUT TAKE-OUT CONTAINERS!
LOOKS LIKE THEY JUST MOVED IN... AND THEY NEVER LEAVE!
PIZZA PALACE
FORGOT THEIR GARLIC ROLLS!
KLIK
PIZZA PALACE
3

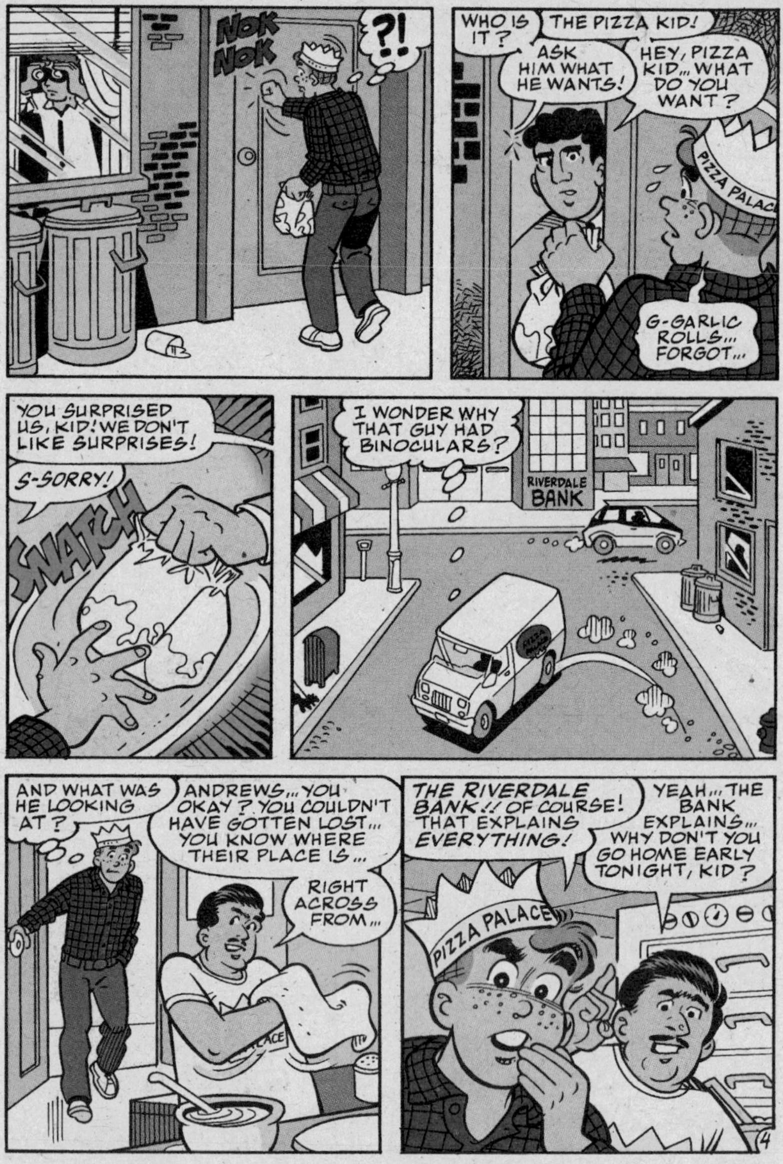
NOK NOK
?!
WHO IS IT?
THE PIZZA KID!
ASK HIM WHAT HE WANTS!
HEY, PIZZA KID... WHAT DO YOU WANT?
PIZZA PALACE
G-GARLIC ROLLS... FORGOT...
YOU SURPRISED US, KID! WE DON'T LIKE SURPRISES!
S-SORRY!
SNATCH
I WONDER WHY THAT GUY HAD BINOCULARS?
RIVERDALE BANK
AND WHAT WAS HE LOOKING AT?
ANDREWS... YOU OKAY? YOU COULDN'T HAVE GOTTEN LOST... YOU KNOW WHERE THEIR PLACE IS...
RIGHT ACROSS FROM...
THE RIVERDALE BANK!! OF COURSE! THAT EXPLAINS EVERYTHING!
YEAH... THE BANK EXPLAINS... WHY DON'T YOU GO HOME EARLY TONIGHT, KID?
PIZZA PALACE
4

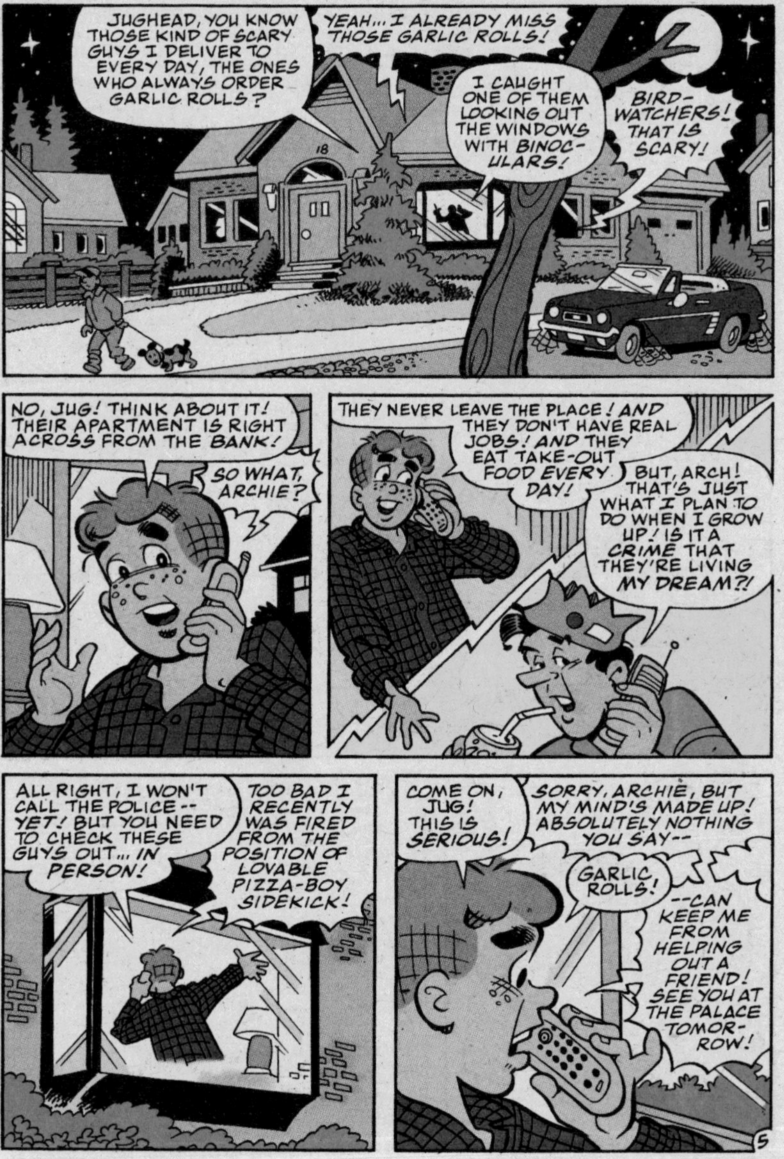
JUGHEAD, YOU KNOW THOSE KIND OF SCARY GUYS I DELIVER TO EVERY DAY, THE ONES WHO ALWAYS ORDER GARLIC ROLLS?
YEAH... I ALREADY MISS THOSE GARLIC ROLLS!
I CAUGHT ONE OF THEM LOOKING OUT THE WINDOWS WITH BINOC-ULARS!
BIRD-WATCHERS! THAT IS SCARY!
18
NO, JUG! THINK ABOUT IT! THEIR APARTMENT IS RIGHT ACROSS FROM THE BANK!
SO WHAT, ARCHIE?
THEY NEVER LEAVE THE PLACE! AND THEY DON'T HAVE REAL JOBS! AND THEY EAT TAKE-OUT FOOD EVERY DAY!
BUT, ARCH! THAT'S JUST WHAT I PLAN TO DO WHEN I GROW UP! IS IT A CRIME THAT THEY'RE LIVING MY DREAM?!
ALL RIGHT, I WON'T CALL THE POLICE -- YET! BUT YOU NEED TO CHECK THESE GUYS OUT... IN PERSON!
TOO BAD I RECENTLY WAS FIRED FROM THE POSITION OF LOVABLE PIZZA-BOY SIDEKICK!
COME ON, JUG! THIS IS SERIOUS!
SORRY, ARCHIE, BUT MY MIND'S MADE UP! ABSOLUTELY NOTHING YOU SAY--
GARLIC ROLLS!
--CAN KEEP ME FROM HELPING OUT A FRIEND! SEE YOU AT THE PALACE TOMOR-ROW!

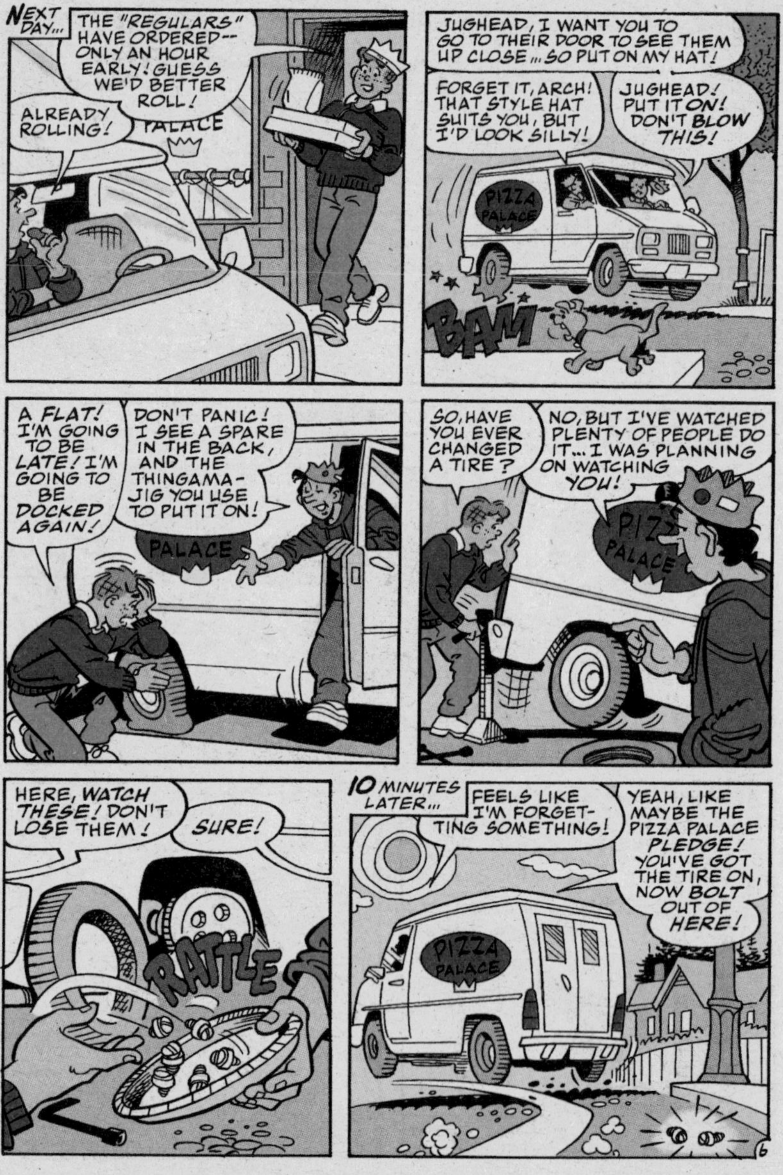
NEXT DAY...
THE "REGULARS" HAVE ORDERED-- ONLY AN HOUR EARLY! GUESS WE'D BETTER ROLL!
ALREADY ROLLING!
PALACE
JUGHEAD, I WANT YOU TO GO TO THEIR DOOR TO SEE THEM UP CLOSE... SO PUT ON MY HAT!
FORGET IT, ARCH! THAT STYLE HAT SUITS YOU, BUT I'D LOOK SILLY!
JUGHEAD! PUT IT ON! DON'T BLOW THIS!
PIZZA PALACE
BAM
A FLAT! I'M GOING TO BE LATE! I'M GOING TO BE DOCKED AGAIN!
DON'T PANIC! I SEE A SPARE IN THE BACK, AND THE THINGAMA-JIG YOU USE TO PUT IT ON!
PALACE
SO, HAVE YOU EVER CHANGED A TIRE?
NO, BUT I'VE WATCHED PLENTY OF PEOPLE DO IT... I WAS PLANNING ON WATCHING YOU!
PIZZA PALACE
HERE, WATCH THESE! DON'T LOSE THEM!
SURE!
RATTLE
10 MINUTES LATER...
FEELS LIKE I'M FORGET-TING SOMETHING!
YEAH, LIKE MAYBE THE PIZZA PALACE PLEDGE! YOU'VE GOT THE TIRE ON, NOW BOLT OUT OF HERE!
PIZZA PALACE

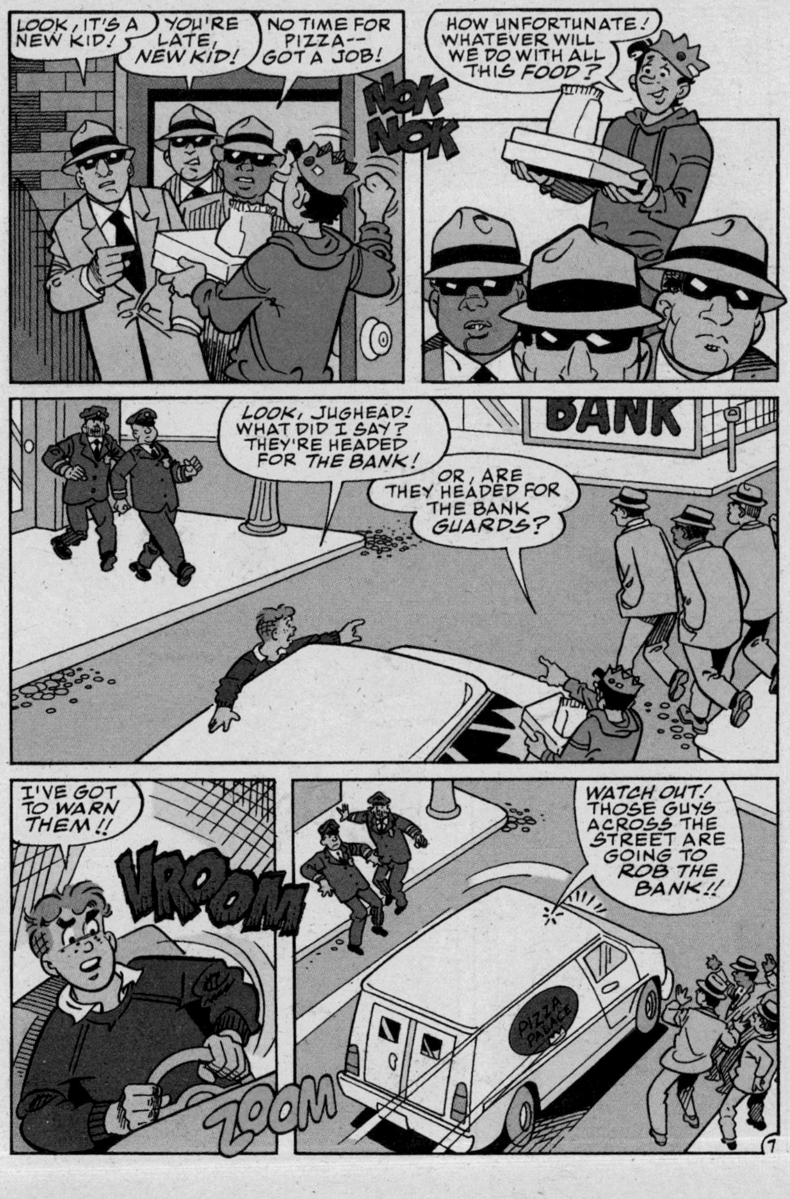
LOOK, IT'S A NEW KID!
YOU'RE LATE, NEW KID!
NO TIME FOR PIZZA-- GOT A JOB!
NOK NOK
HOW UNFORTUNATE! WHATEVER WILL WE DO WITH ALL THIS FOOD?
BANK
LOOK, JUGHEAD! WHAT DID I SAY? THEY'RE HEADED FOR THE BANK!
OR, ARE THEY HEADED FOR THE BANK GUARDS?
I'VE GOT TO WARN THEM!!
VROOM
ZOOM
WATCH OUT! THOSE GUYS ACROSS THE STREET ARE GOING TO ROB THE BANK!!
PIZZA PALACE
7

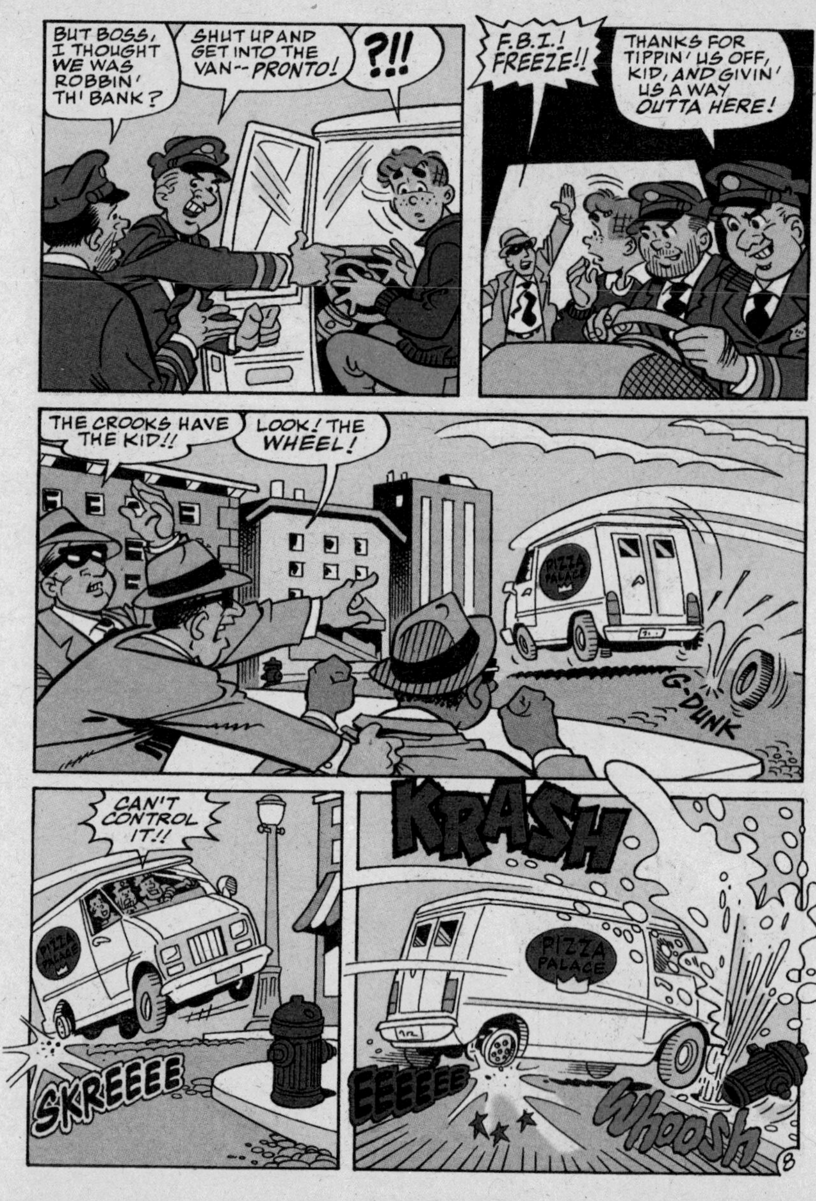
BUT BOSS, I THOUGHT WE WAS ROBBIN' TH' BANK?
SHUT UP AND GET INTO THE VAN-- PRONTO!
?!!
F.B.I.! FREEZE!!
THANKS FOR TIPPIN' US OFF, KID, AND GIVIN' US A WAY OUTTA HERE!
THE CROOKS HAVE THE KID!!
LOOK! THE WHEEL!
PIZZA PALACE
G-DUNK
CAN'T CONTROL IT!!
PIZZA PALACE
SKREEEEE
KRASH
PIZZA PALACE
EEEEEEE
WHOOSH

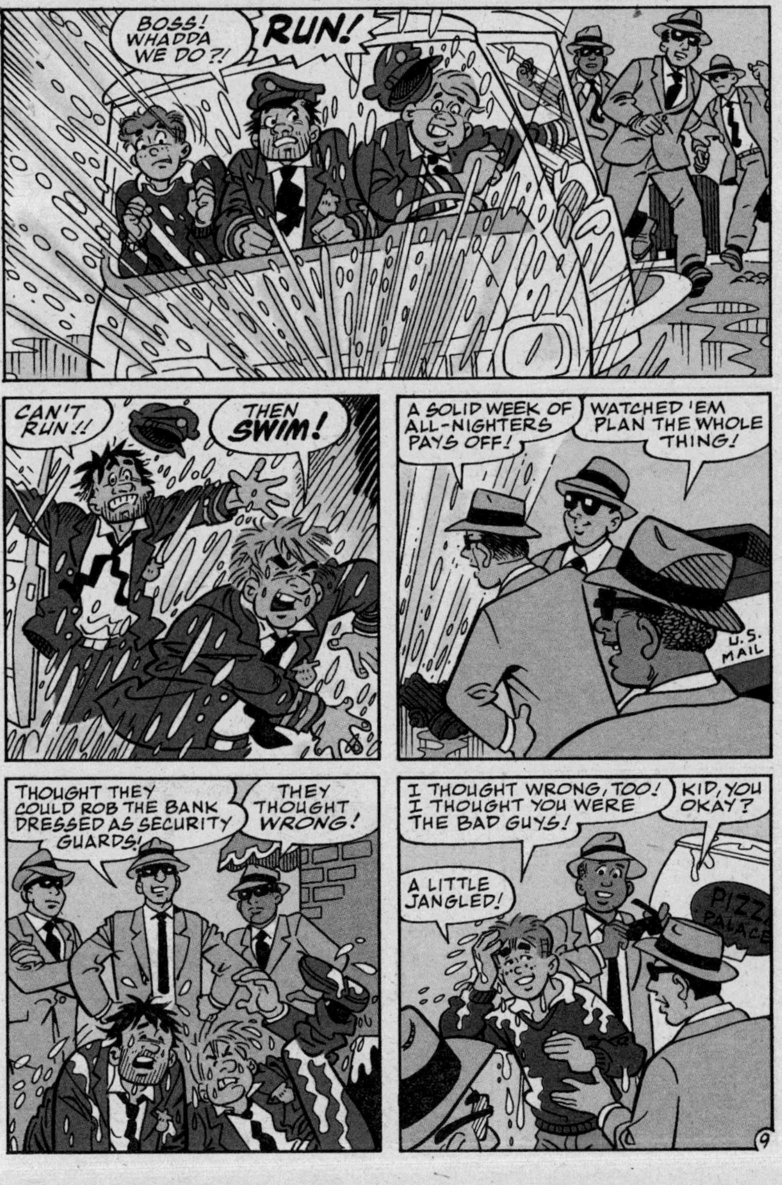
BOSS! WHADDA WE DO ?!
RUN!
CAN'T RUN !!
THEN SWIM!
A SOLID WEEK OF ALL-NIGHTERS PAYS OFF!
WATCHED 'EM PLAN THE WHOLE THING!
U.S. MAIL
THOUGHT THEY COULD ROB THE BANK DRESSED AS SECURITY GUARDS!
THEY THOUGHT WRONG!
I THOUGHT WRONG, TOO! I THOUGHT YOU WERE THE BAD GUYS!
KID, YOU OKAY?
A LITTLE JANGLED!
PIZZ PALACE

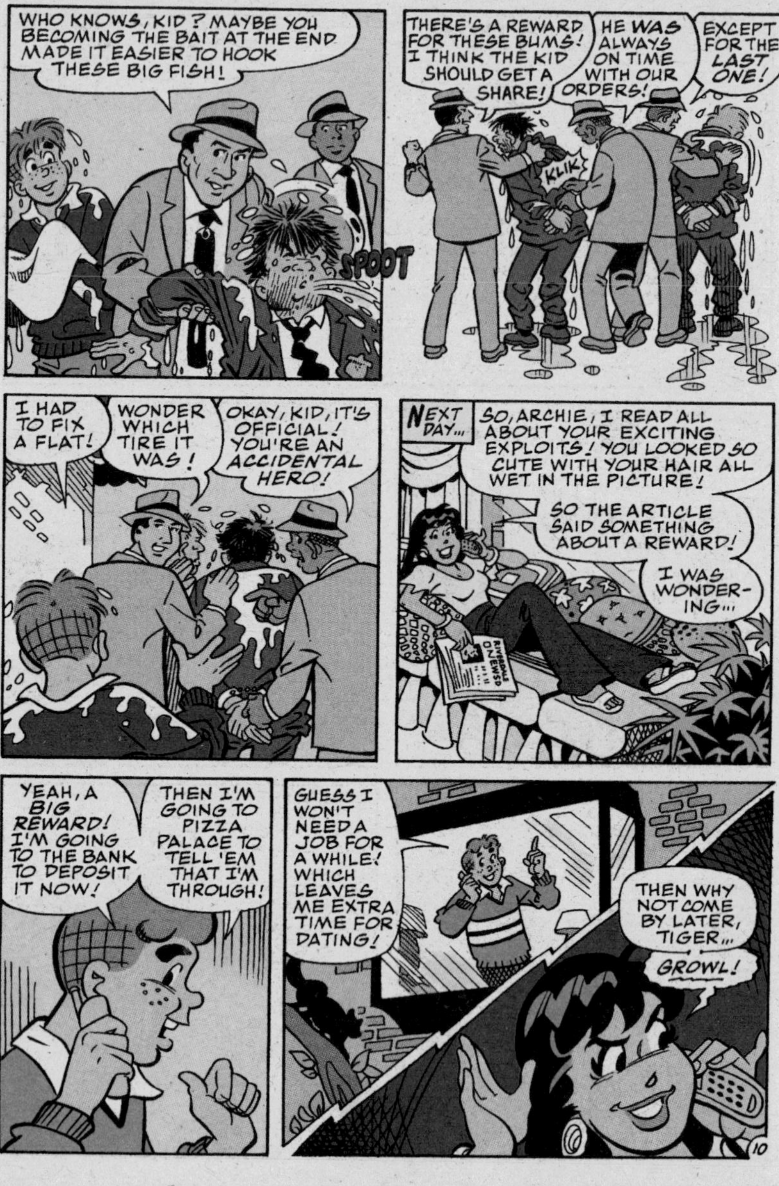
WHO KNOWS, KID? MAYBE YOU BECOMING THE BAIT AT THE END MADE IT EASIER TO HOOK THESE BIG FISH!
SPOOT
THERE'S A REWARD FOR THESE BUMS! I THINK THE KID SHOULD GET A SHARE!
HE WAS ALWAYS ON TIME WITH OUR ORDERS!
EXCEPT FOR THE LAST ONE!
KLIK
I HAD TO FIX A FLAT!
WONDER WHICH TIRE IT WAS!
OKAY, KID, IT'S OFFICIAL! YOU'RE AN ACCIDENTAL HERO!
NEXT DAY...
SO, ARCHIE, I READ ALL ABOUT YOUR EXCITING EXPLOITS! YOU LOOKED SO CUTE WITH YOUR HAIR ALL WET IN THE PICTURE!
SO THE ARTICLE SAID SOMETHING ABOUT A REWARD!
I WAS WONDERING...
RIVERDALE NEWS
YEAH, A BIG REWARD! I'M GOING TO THE BANK TO DEPOSIT IT NOW!
THEN I'M GOING TO PIZZA PALACE TO TELL 'EM THAT I'M THROUGH!
GUESS I WON'T NEED A JOB FOR A WHILE! WHICH LEAVES ME EXTRA TIME FOR DATING!
THEN WHY NOT COME BY LATER, TIGER...
GROWL!

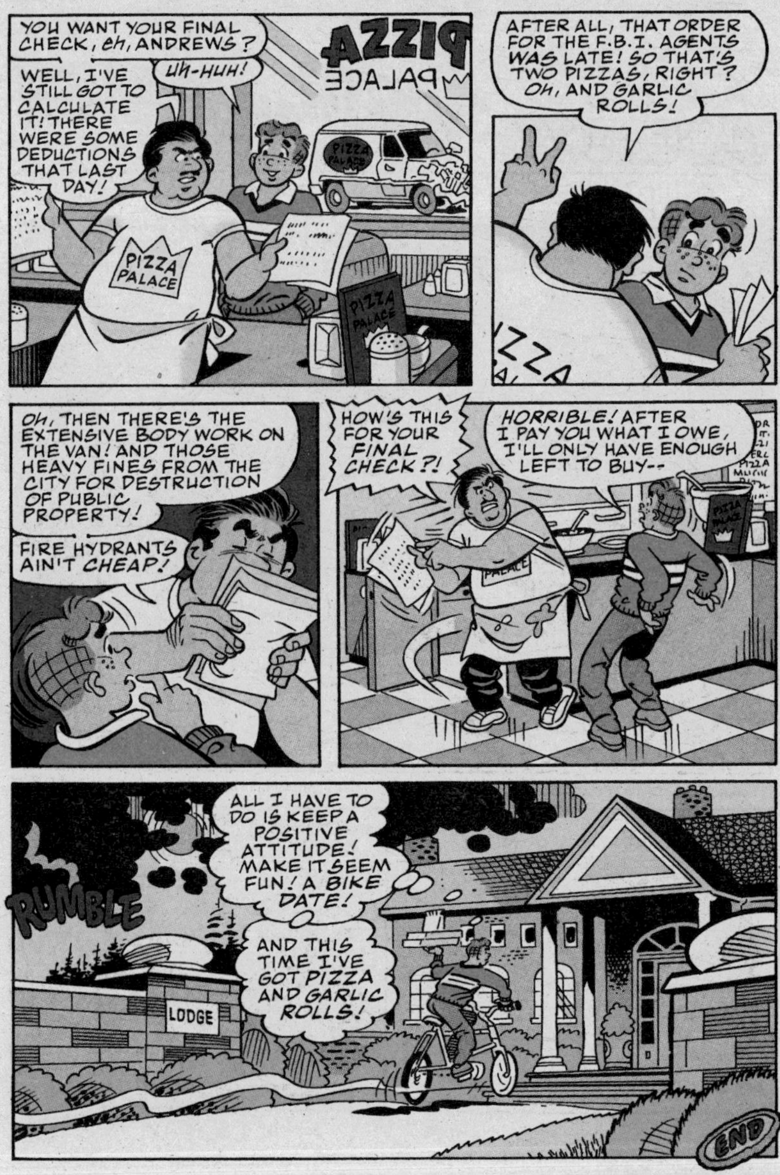
YOU WANT YOUR FINAL CHECK, eh, ANDREWS?
UH-HUH!
WELL, I'VE STILL GOT TO CALCULATE IT! THERE WERE SOME DEDUCTIONS THAT LAST DAY!
PIZZA PALACE
PIZZA PALACE
AFTER ALL, THAT ORDER FOR THE F.B.I. AGENTS WAS LATE! SO THAT'S TWO PIZZAS, RIGHT? Oh, AND GARLIC ROLLS!
Oh, THEN THERE'S THE EXTENSIVE BODY WORK ON THE VAN! AND THOSE HEAVY FINES FROM THE CITY FOR DESTRUCTION OF PUBLIC PROPERTY!
FIRE HYDRANTS AIN'T CHEAP!
HOW'S THIS FOR YOUR FINAL CHECK?!
HORRIBLE! AFTER I PAY YOU WHAT I OWE, I'LL ONLY HAVE ENOUGH LEFT TO BUY--
ALL I HAVE TO DO IS KEEP A POSITIVE ATTITUDE! MAKE IT SEEM FUN! A BIKE DATE!
AND THIS TIME I'VE GOT PIZZA AND GARLIC ROLLS!
RUMBLE
LODGE
END

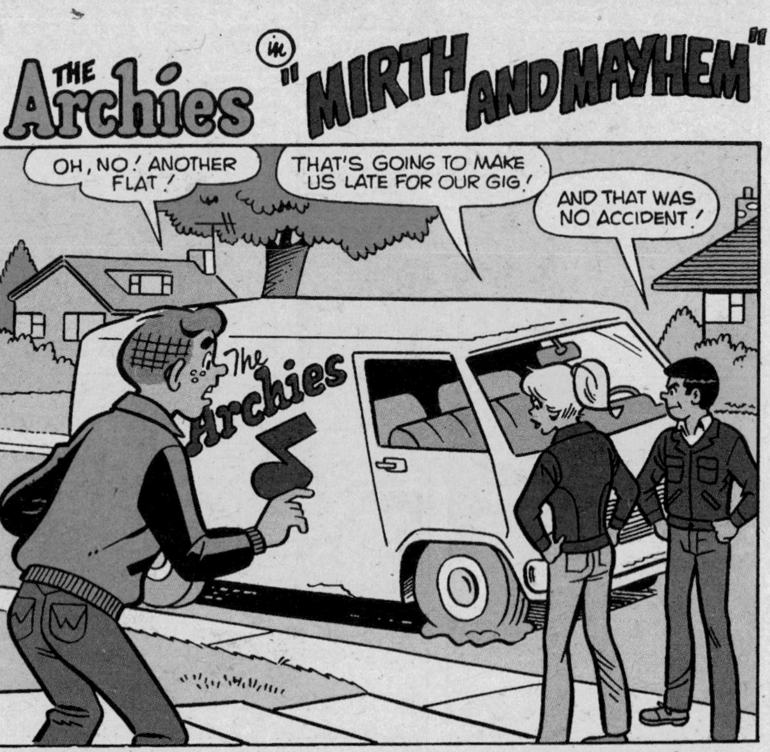
THE Archies in "MIRTH AND MAYHEM"
OH, NO! ANOTHER FLAT!
THAT'S GOING TO MAKE US LATE FOR OUR GIG!
AND THAT WAS NO ACCIDENT!
The Archies

Script: George Gladir / Pencils: Dan DeCarlo Jr. / inks: Rudy Lapick / Letters: Bill Yoshida / Colors: Barry Grossman

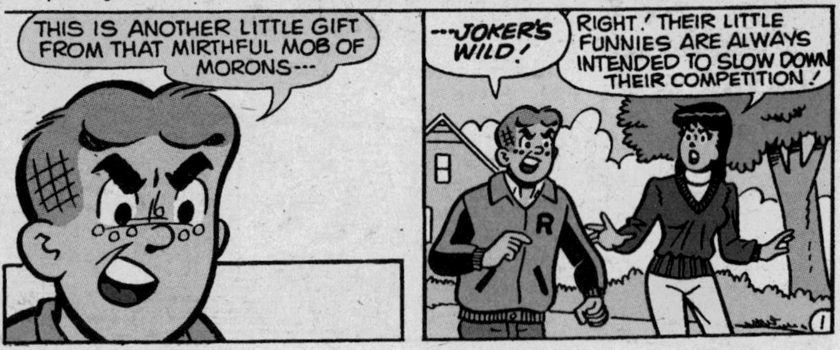
THIS IS ANOTHER LITTLE GIFT FROM THAT MIRTHFUL MOB OF MORONS---
---JOKER'S WILD!
RIGHT! THEIR LITTLE FUNNIES ARE ALWAYS INTENDED TO SLOW DOWN THEIR COMPETITION!
1

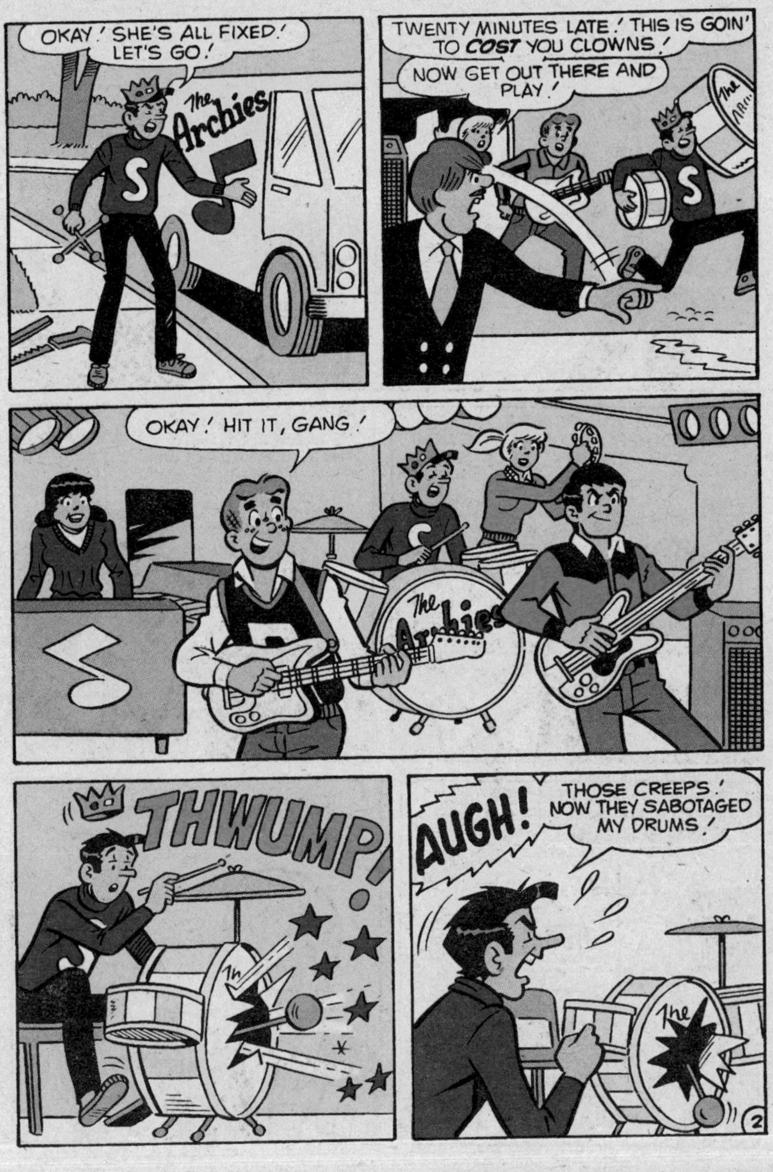
OKAY! SHE'S ALL FIXED! LET'S GO!
The Archies
TWENTY MINUTES LATE! THIS IS GOIN' TO COST YOU CLOWNS!
NOW GET OUT THERE AND PLAY!
OKAY! HIT IT, GANG!
The Archies
THWUMP!
AUGH!
THOSE CREEPS! NOW THEY SABOTAGED MY DRUMS!
2

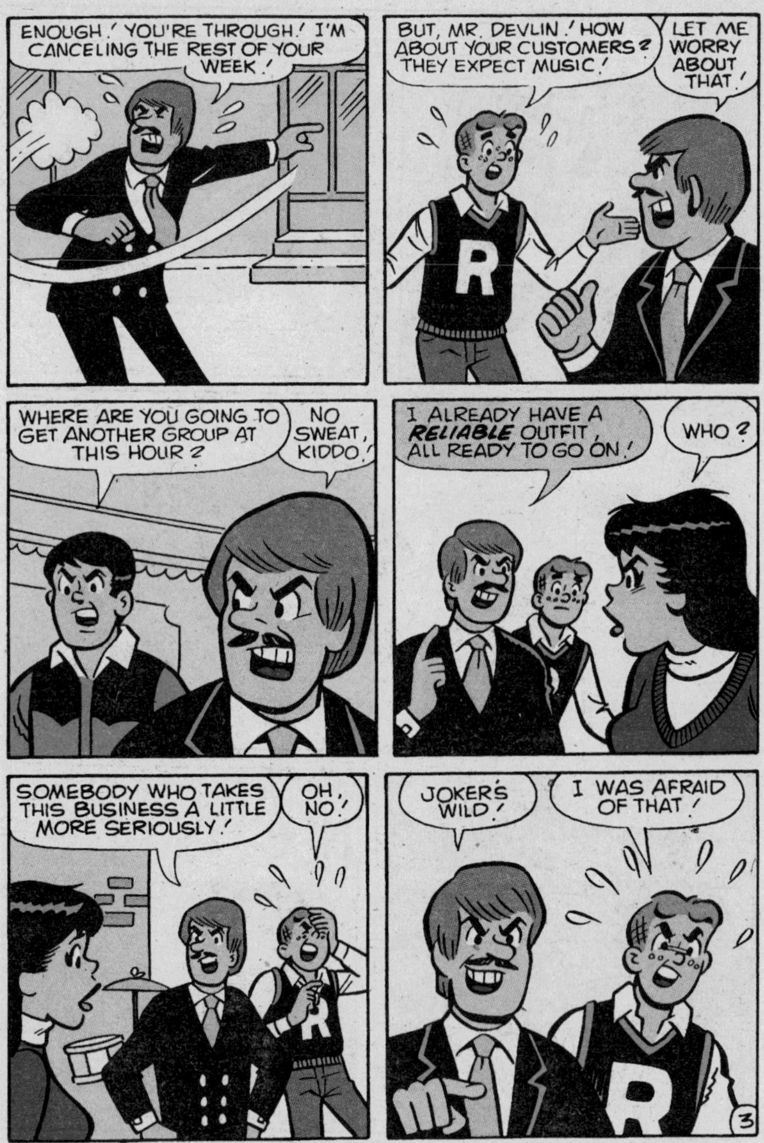
ENOUGH! YOU'RE THROUGH! I'M CANCELING THE REST OF YOUR WEEK!
BUT, MR. DEVLIN! HOW ABOUT YOUR CUSTOMERS? THEY EXPECT MUSIC!
LET ME WORRY ABOUT THAT!
WHERE ARE YOU GOING TO GET ANOTHER GROUP AT THIS HOUR?
NO SWEAT, KIDDO!
I ALREADY HAVE A RELIABLE OUTFIT, ALL READY TO GO ON!
WHO?
SOMEBODY WHO TAKES THIS BUSINESS A LITTLE MORE SERIOUSLY!
OH, NO!
JOKER'S WILD!
I WAS AFRAID OF THAT!
3

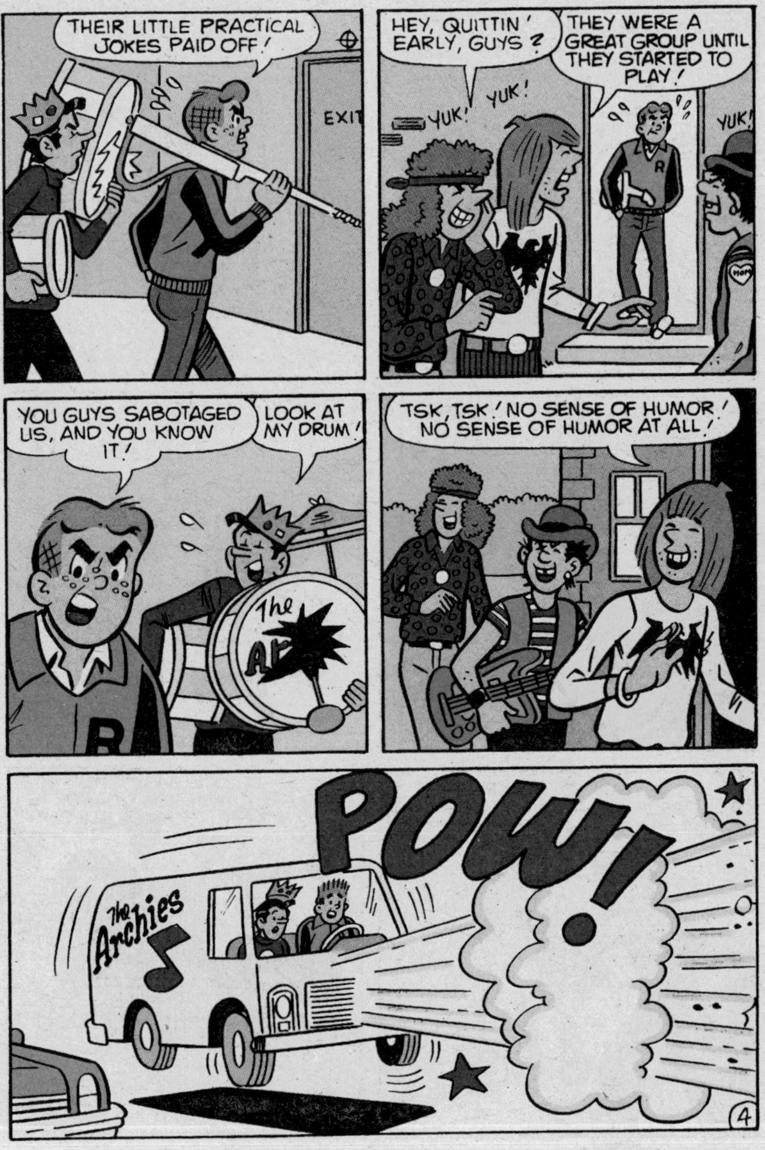
THEIR LITTLE PRACTICAL JOKES PAID OFF!
EXIT
HEY, QUITTIN' EARLY, GUYS?
THEY WERE A GREAT GROUP UNTIL THEY STARTED TO PLAY!
YUK!
YUK!
YUK!
YOU GUYS SABOTAGED US, AND YOU KNOW IT!
LOOK AT MY DRUM!
TSK, TSK! NO SENSE OF HUMOR! NO SENSE OF HUMOR AT ALL!
POW!
The Archies
4

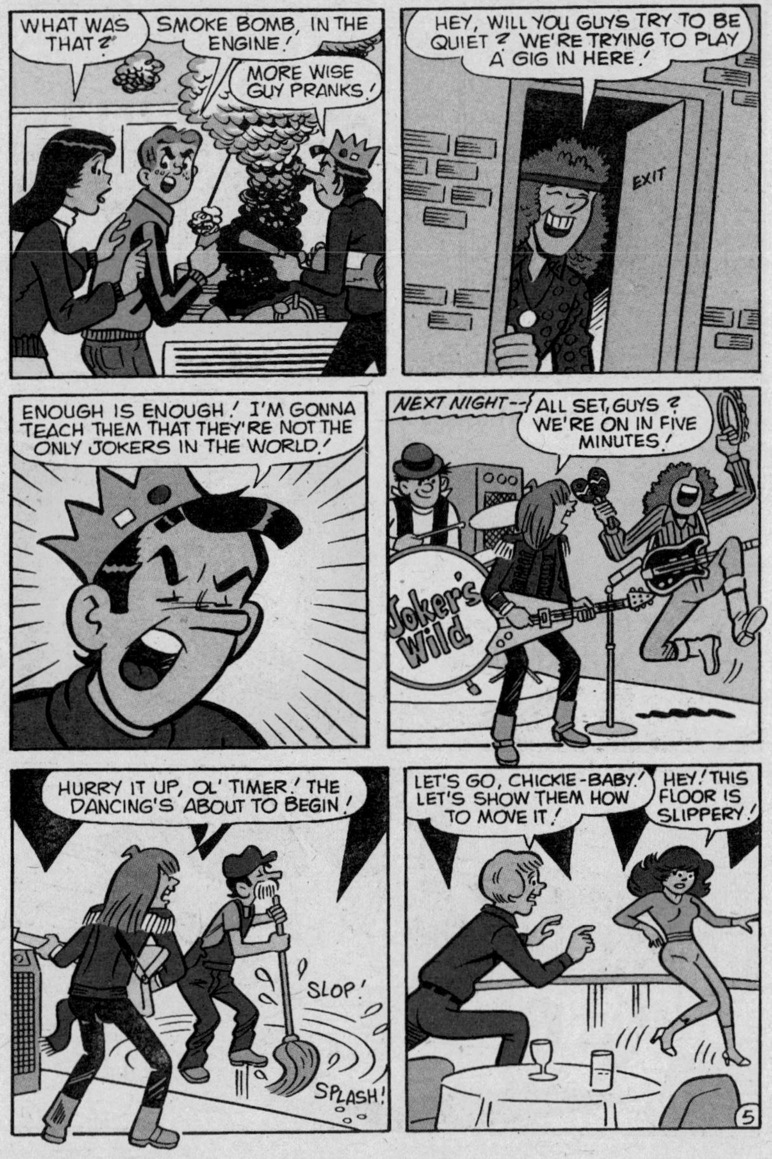
WHAT WAS THAT?
SMOKE BOMB, IN THE ENGINE!
MORE WISE GUY PRANKS!
HEY, WILL YOU GUYS TRY TO BE QUIET? WE'RE TRYING TO PLAY A GIG IN HERE!
EXIT
ENOUGH IS ENOUGH! I'M GONNA TEACH THEM THAT THEY'RE NOT THE ONLY JOKERS IN THE WORLD!
NEXT NIGHT--
ALL SET, GUYS? WE'RE ON IN FIVE MINUTES!
Joker's Wild
HURRY IT UP, OL' TIMER! THE DANCING'S ABOUT TO BEGIN!
SLOP!
SPLASH!
LET'S GO, CHICKIE-BABY! LET'S SHOW THEM HOW TO MOVE IT!
HEY! THIS FLOOR IS SLIPPERY!
5

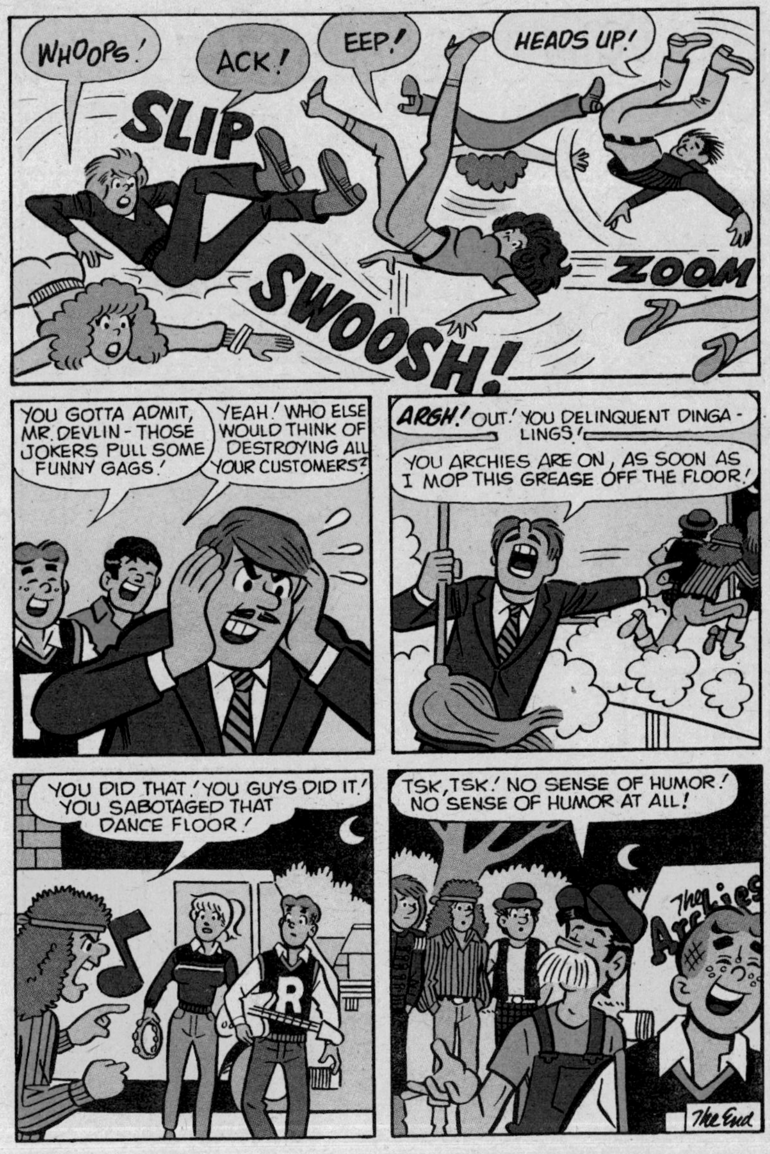
WHOOPS!
ACK!
EEP!
HEADS UP!
SLIP
SWOOSH!
ZOOM
YOU GOTTA ADMIT, MR. DEVLIN - THOSE JOKERS PULL SOME FUNNY GAGS!
YEAH! WHO ELSE WOULD THINK OF DESTROYING ALL YOUR CUSTOMERS?
ARGH! OUT! YOU DELINQUENT DINGA-LINGS!
YOU ARCHIES ARE ON, AS SOON AS I MOP THIS GREASE OFF THE FLOOR!
YOU DID THAT! YOU GUYS DID IT! YOU SABOTAGED THAT DANCE FLOOR!
TSK, TSK! NO SENSE OF HUMOR! NO SENSE OF HUMOR AT ALL!
The Archies
The End

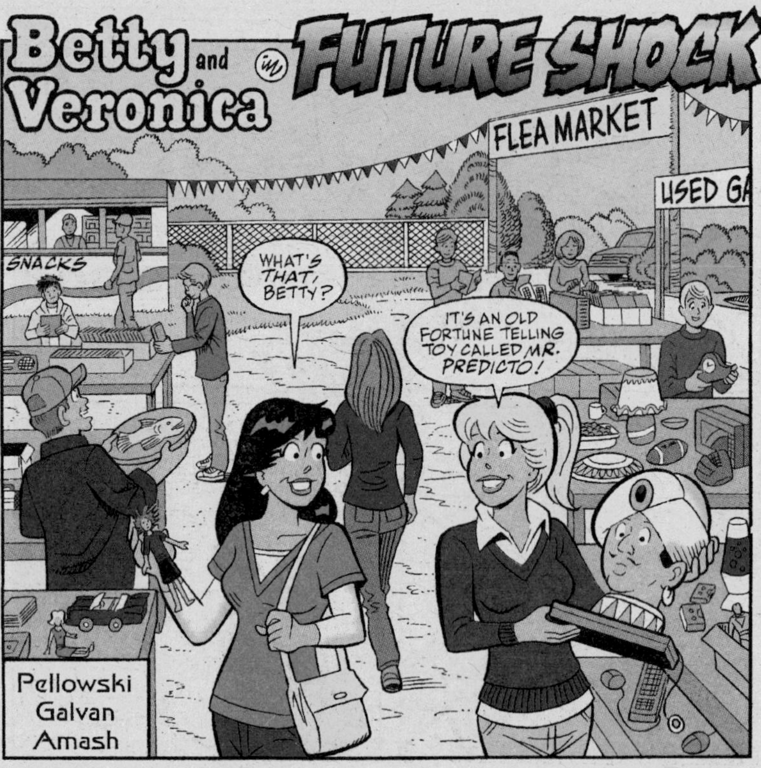
Betty and Veronica in FUTURE SHOCK
FLEA MARKET
USED GA
SNACKS
WHAT'S THAT, BETTY?
IT'S AN OLD FORTUNE TELLING TOY CALLED MR. PREDICTO!
Pellowski
Galvan
Amash

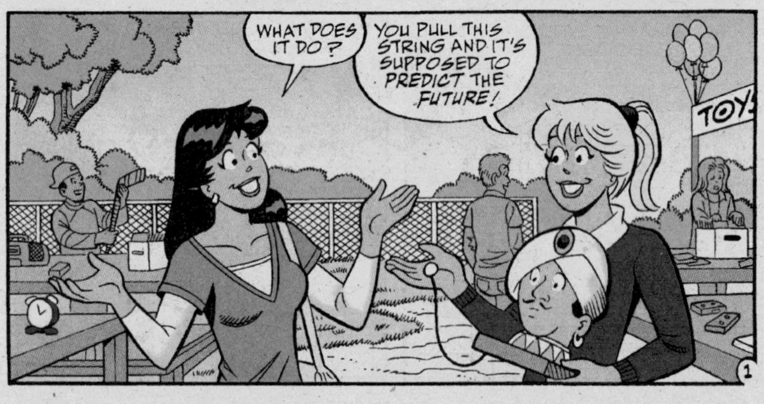
WHAT DOES IT DO?
YOU PULL THIS STRING AND IT'S SUPPOSED TO PREDICT THE FUTURE!
TOYS

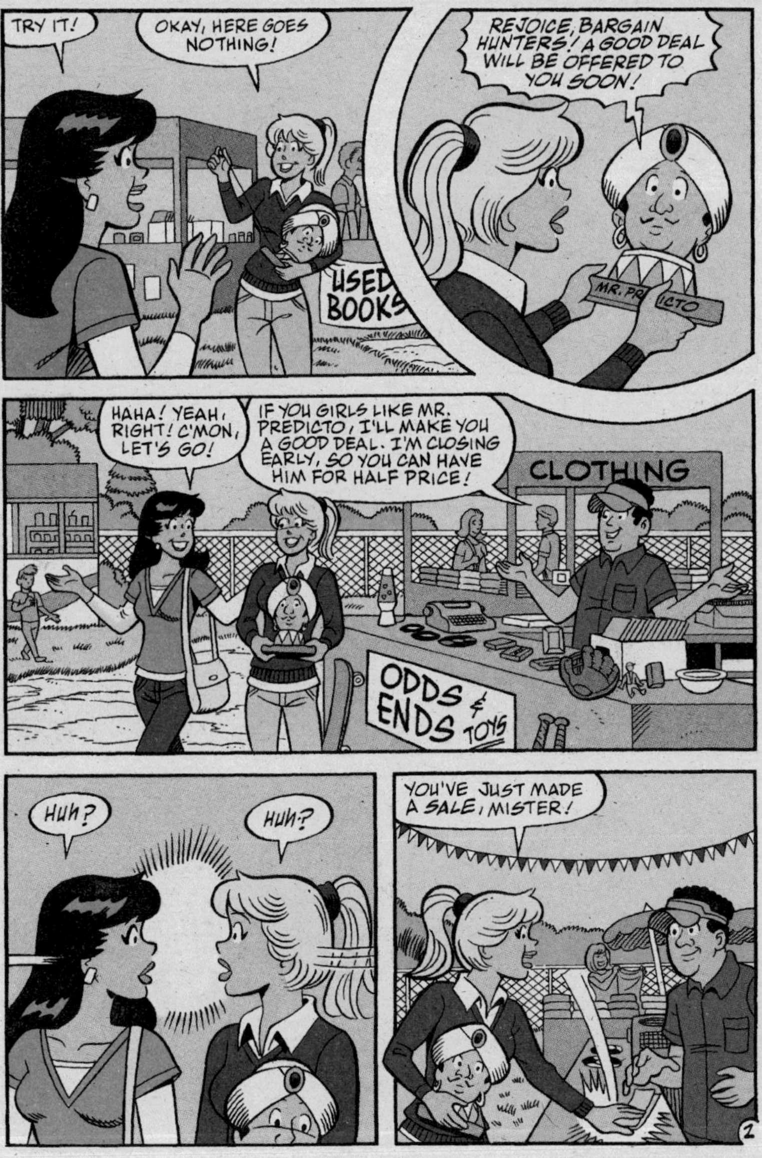
TRY IT!
OKAY, HERE GOES NOTHING!
USED BOOKS
REJOICE, BARGAIN HUNTERS! A GOOD DEAL WILL BE OFFERED TO YOU SOON!
MR. PREDICTO
HAHA! YEAH, RIGHT! C'MON, LET'S GO!
IF YOU GIRLS LIKE MR. PREDICTO, I'LL MAKE YOU A GOOD DEAL. I'M CLOSING EARLY, SO YOU CAN HAVE HIM FOR HALF PRICE!
CLOTHING
ODDS & ENDS TOYS
HUH?
HUH?
YOU'VE JUST MADE A SALE, MISTER!
2

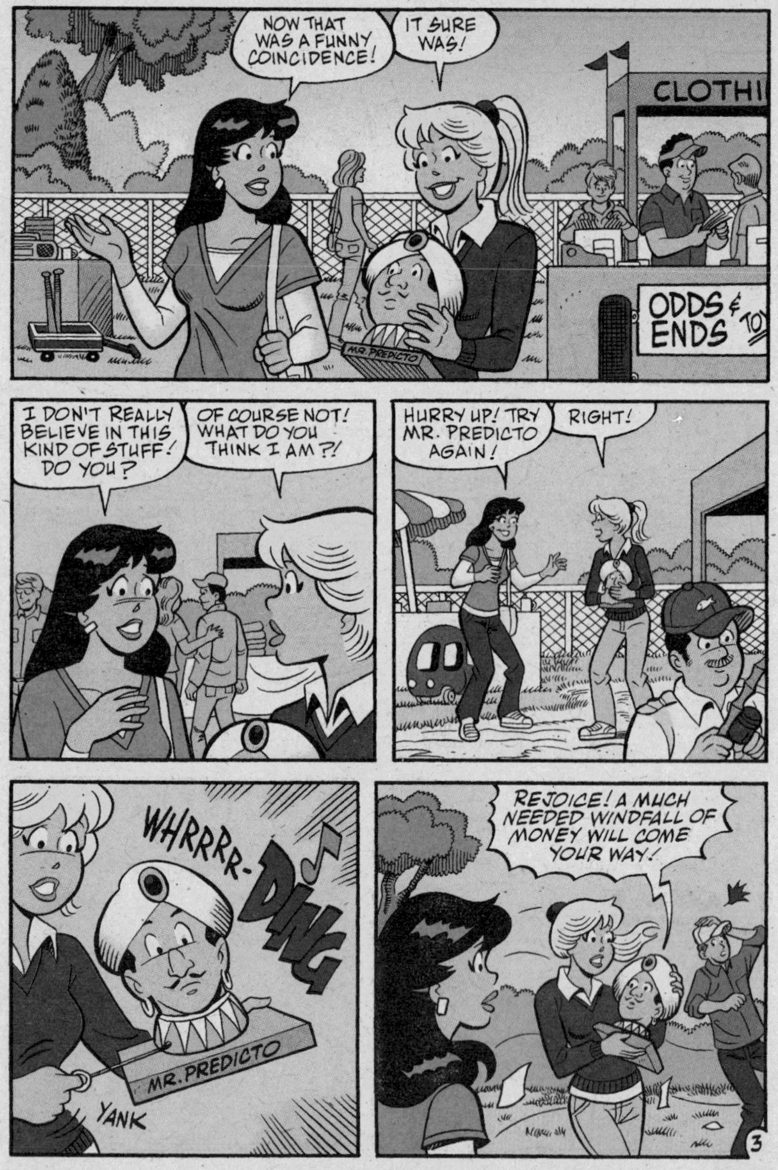
NOW THAT WAS A FUNNY COINCIDENCE!
IT SURE WAS!
CLOTHI
ODDS & ENDS
TOY
MR. PREDICTO
I DON'T REALLY BELIEVE IN THIS KIND OF STUFF! DO YOU?
OF COURSE NOT! WHAT DO YOU THINK I AM?!
HURRY UP! TRY MR. PREDICTO AGAIN!
RIGHT!
WHRRRR-DING
MR. PREDICTO
YANK
REJOICE! A MUCH NEEDED WINDFALL OF MONEY WILL COME YOUR WAY!

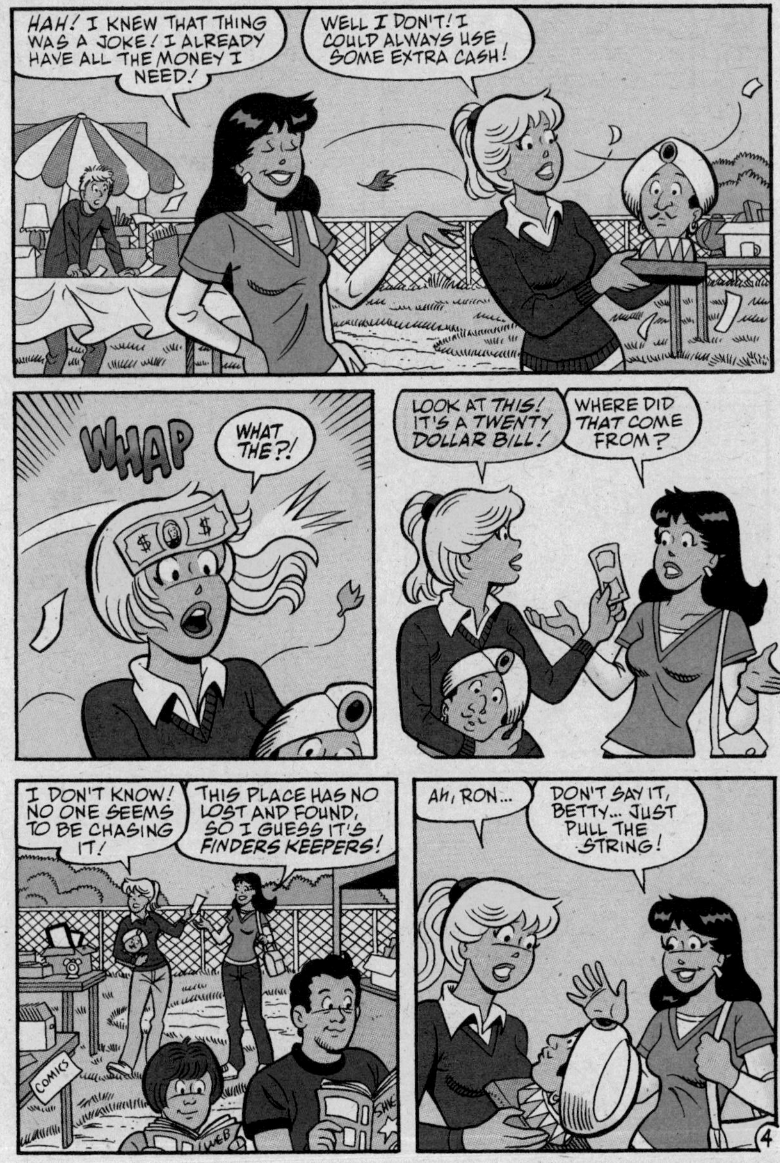
HAH! I KNEW THAT THING WAS A JOKE! I ALREADY HAVE ALL THE MONEY I NEED!
WELL I DON'T! I COULD ALWAYS USE SOME EXTRA CASH!
WHAP
WHAT THE?!
LOOK AT THIS! IT'S A TWENTY DOLLAR BILL!
WHERE DID THAT COME FROM?
I DON'T KNOW! NO ONE SEEMS TO BE CHASING IT!
THIS PLACE HAS NO LOST AND FOUND, SO I GUESS IT'S FINDERS KEEPERS!
COMICS
AH, RON...
DON'T SAY IT, BETTY... JUST PULL THE STRING!
4

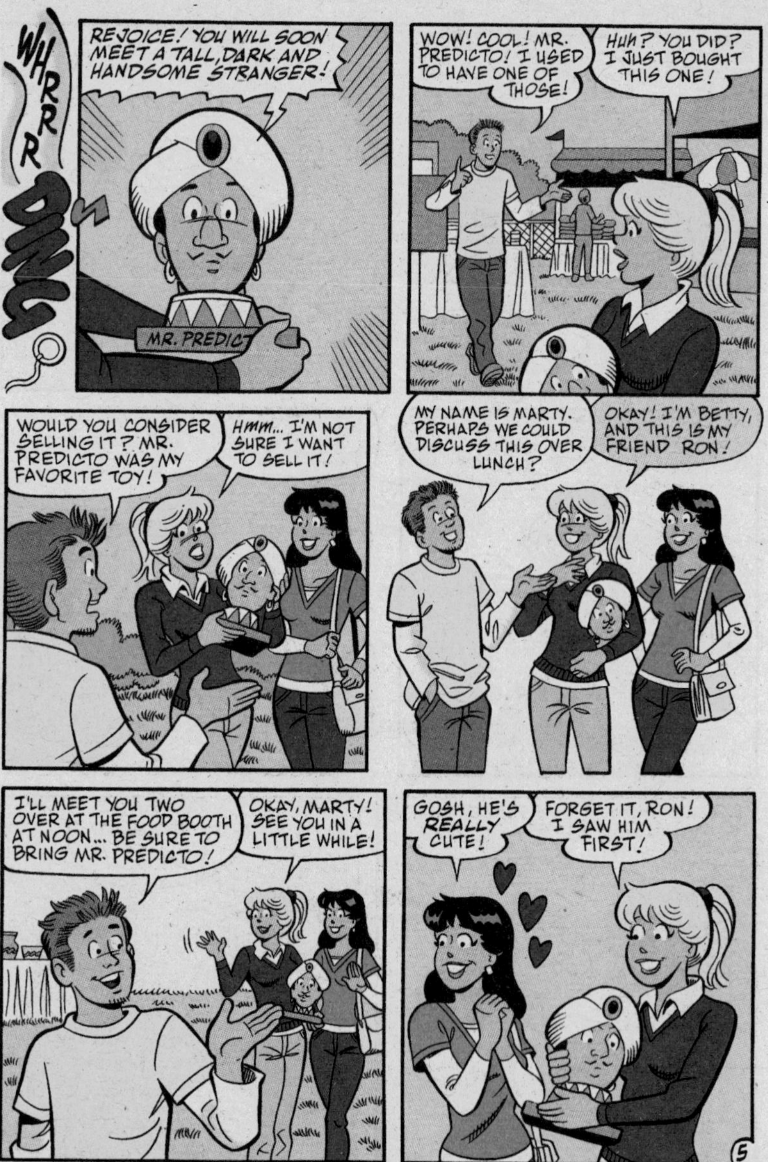
WHRRRR
DING
REJOICE! YOU WILL SOON MEET A TALL, DARK AND HANDSOME STRANGER!
MR. PREDICT
WOW! COOL! MR. PREDICTO! I USED TO HAVE ONE OF THOSE!
HUH? YOU DID? I JUST BOUGHT THIS ONE!
WOULD YOU CONSIDER SELLING IT? MR. PREDICTO WAS MY FAVORITE TOY!
HMM... I'M NOT SURE I WANT TO SELL IT!
MY NAME IS MARTY. PERHAPS WE COULD DISCUSS THIS OVER LUNCH?
OKAY! I'M BETTY, AND THIS IS MY FRIEND RON!
I'LL MEET YOU TWO OVER AT THE FOOD BOOTH AT NOON... BE SURE TO BRING MR. PREDICTO!
OKAY, MARTY! SEE YOU IN A LITTLE WHILE!
GOSH, HE'S REALLY CUTE!
FORGET IT, RON! I SAW HIM FIRST!

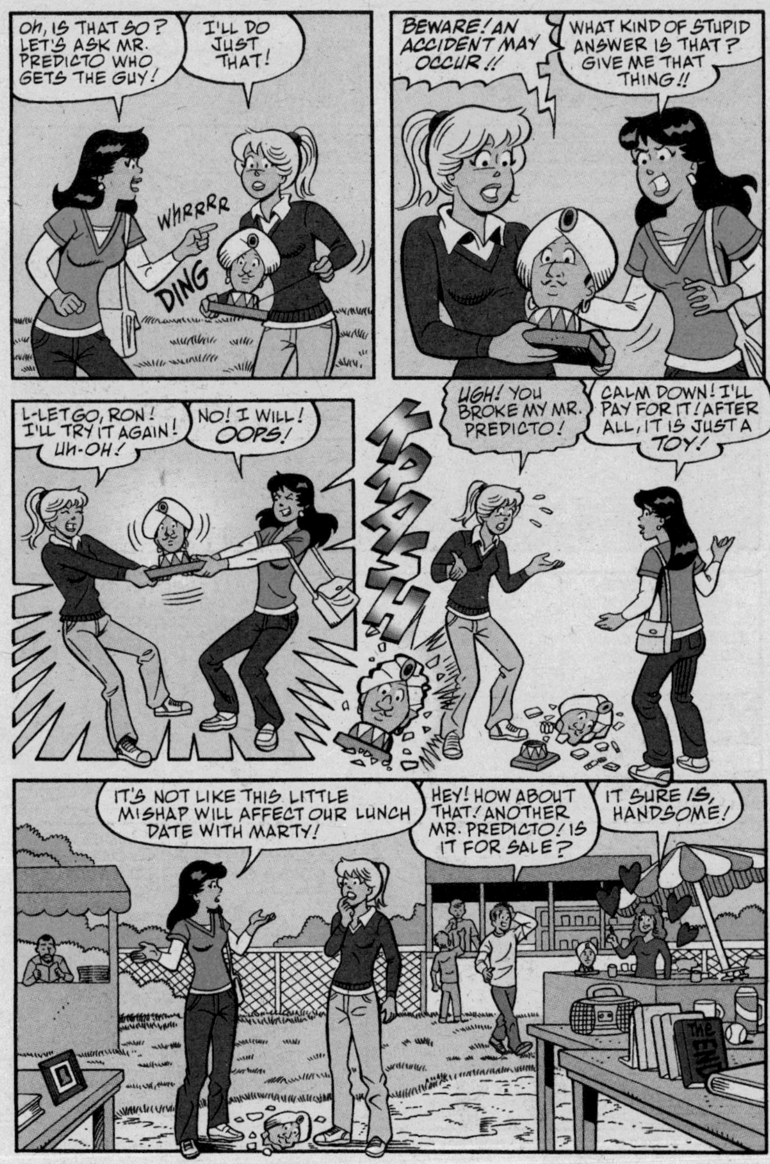
Oh, IS THAT SO? LET'S ASK MR. PREDICTO WHO GETS THE GUY!
I'LL DO JUST THAT!
WHRRRR
DING
BEWARE! AN ACCIDENT MAY OCCUR!!
WHAT KIND OF STUPID ANSWER IS THAT? GIVE ME THAT THING!!
L-LET GO, RON! I'LL TRY IT AGAIN! UH-OH!
NO! I WILL! OOPS!
KRASH
UGH! YOU BROKE MY MR. PREDICTO!
CALM DOWN! I'LL PAY FOR IT! AFTER ALL, IT IS JUST A TOY!
IT'S NOT LIKE THIS LITTLE MISHAP WILL AFFECT OUR LUNCH DATE WITH MARTY!
HEY! HOW ABOUT THAT! ANOTHER MR. PREDICTO! IS IT FOR SALE?
IT SURE IS, HANDSOME!
THE END

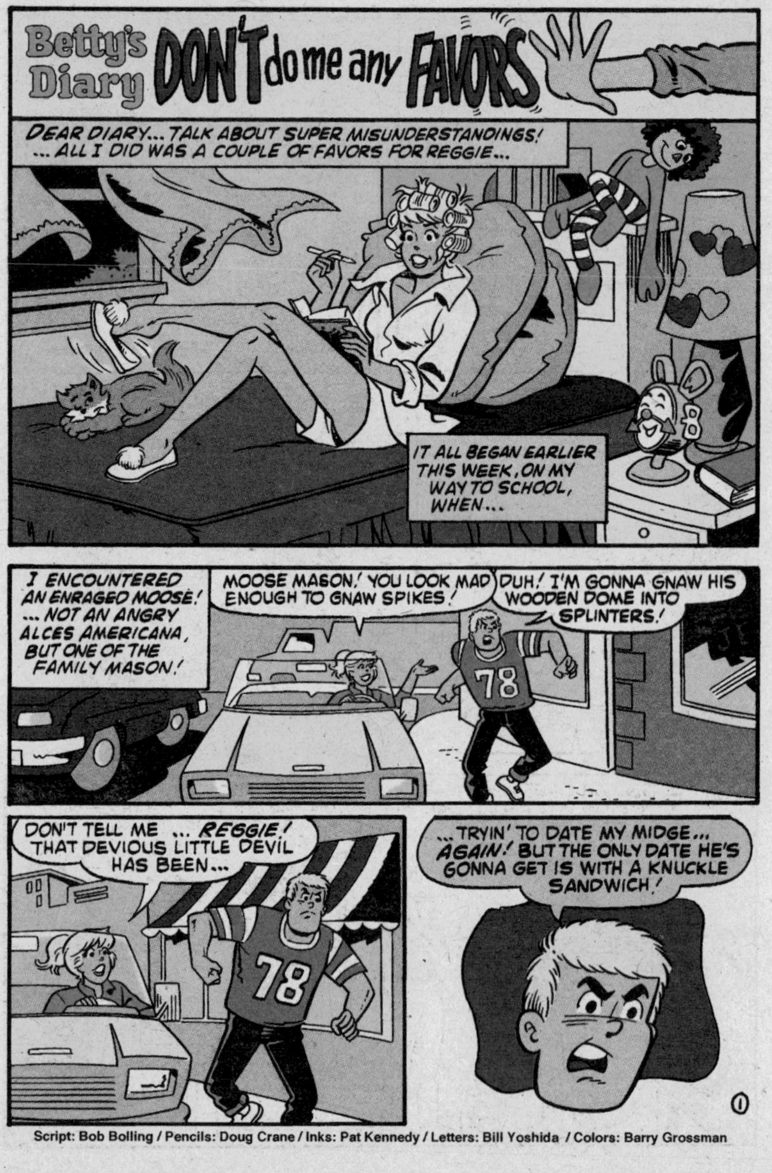
Betty's Diary
DON'T do me any FAVORS
DEAR DIARY... TALK ABOUT SUPER MISUNDERSTANDINGS! ... ALL I DID WAS A COUPLE OF FAVORS FOR REGGIE...
IT ALL BEGAN EARLIER THIS WEEK, ON MY WAY TO SCHOOL, WHEN...
I ENCOUNTERED AN ENRAGED MOOSE! ... NOT AN ANGRY ALCES AMERICANA, BUT ONE OF THE FAMILY MASON!
MOOSE MASON! YOU LOOK MAD ENOUGH TO GNAW SPIKES!
DUH! I'M GONNA GNAW HIS WOODEN DOME INTO SPLINTERS!
DON'T TELL ME ... REGGIE! THAT DEVIOUS LITTLE DEVIL HAS BEEN...
...TRYIN' TO DATE MY MIDGE... AGAIN! BUT THE ONLY DATE HE'S GONNA GET IS WITH A KNUCKLE SANDWICH!
78
1

Script: Bob Bolling / Pencils: Doug Crane / Inks: Pat Kennedy / Letters: Bill Yoshida / Colors: Barry Grossman

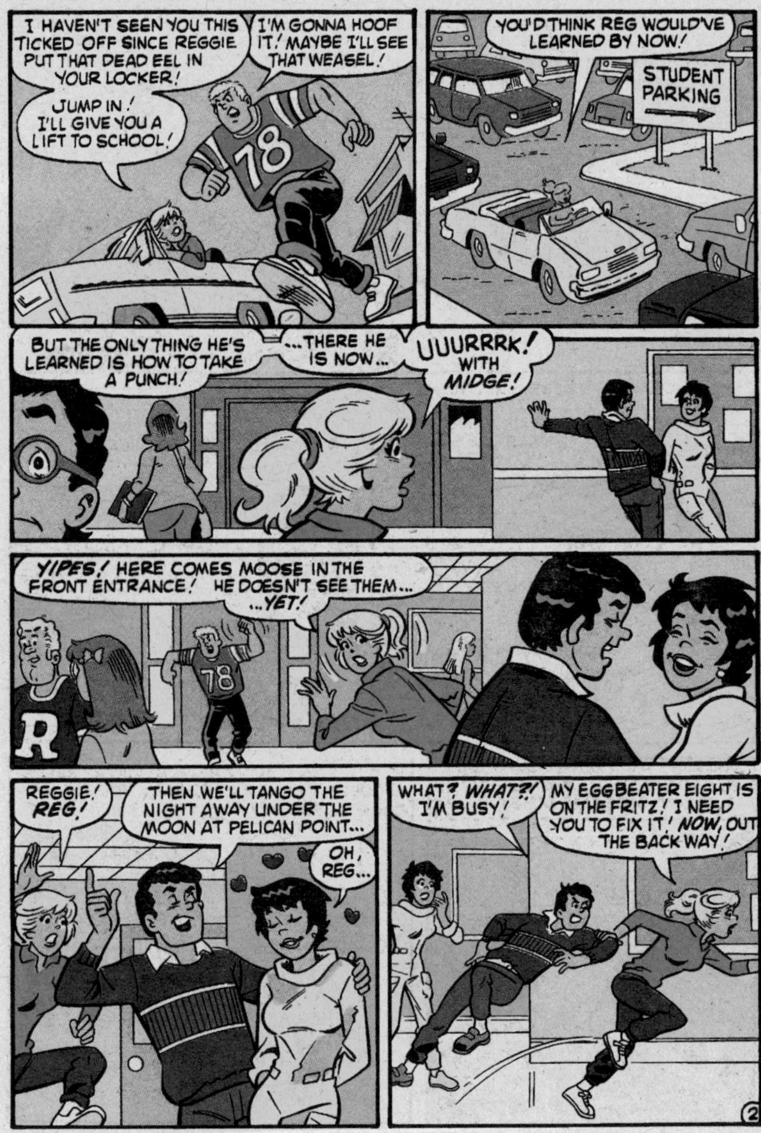
I HAVEN'T SEEN YOU THIS TICKED OFF SINCE REGGIE PUT THAT DEAD EEL IN YOUR LOCKER!
JUMP IN! I'LL GIVE YOU A LIFT TO SCHOOL!
I'M GONNA HOOF IT! MAYBE I'LL SEE THAT WEASEL!
78
YOU'D THINK REG WOULD'VE LEARNED BY NOW!
STUDENT PARKING
BUT THE ONLY THING HE'S LEARNED IS HOW TO TAKE A PUNCH!
...THERE HE IS NOW...
UUURRRK! WITH MIDGE!
YIPES! HERE COMES MOOSE IN THE FRONT ENTRANCE! HE DOESN'T SEE THEM... ...YET!
R
78
REGGIE! REG!
THEN WE'LL TANGO THE NIGHT AWAY UNDER THE MOON AT PELICAN POINT...
OH, REG...
WHAT? WHAT?! I'M BUSY!
MY EGGBEATER EIGHT IS ON THE FRITZ! I NEED YOU TO FIX IT! NOW, OUT THE BACK WAY!
2

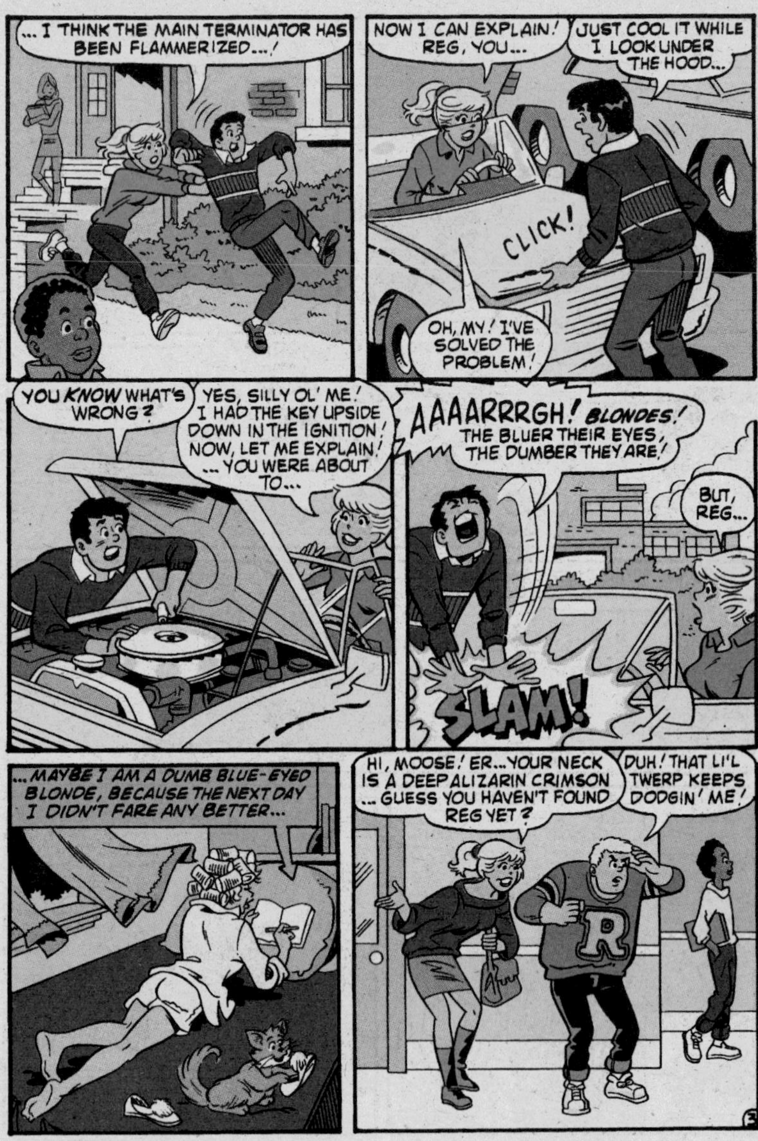
... I THINK THE MAIN TERMINATOR HAS BEEN FLAMMERIZED...!
NOW I CAN EXPLAIN! REG, YOU...
JUST COOL IT WHILE I LOOK UNDER THE HOOD...
CLICK!
OH, MY! I'VE SOLVED THE PROBLEM!
YOU KNOW WHAT'S WRONG?
YES, SILLY OL' ME! I HAD THE KEY UPSIDE DOWN IN THE IGNITION! NOW, LET ME EXPLAIN! ... YOU WERE ABOUT TO...
AAAARRRGH! BLONDES! THE BLUER THEIR EYES, THE DUMBER THEY ARE!
BUT, REG...
SLAM!
... MAYBE I AM A DUMB BLUE-EYED BLONDE, BECAUSE THE NEXT DAY I DIDN'T FARE ANY BETTER...
HI, MOOSE! ER... YOUR NECK IS A DEEP ALIZARIN CRIMSON ... GUESS YOU HAVEN'T FOUND REG YET?
DUH! THAT LI'L TWERP KEEPS DODGIN' ME!
3

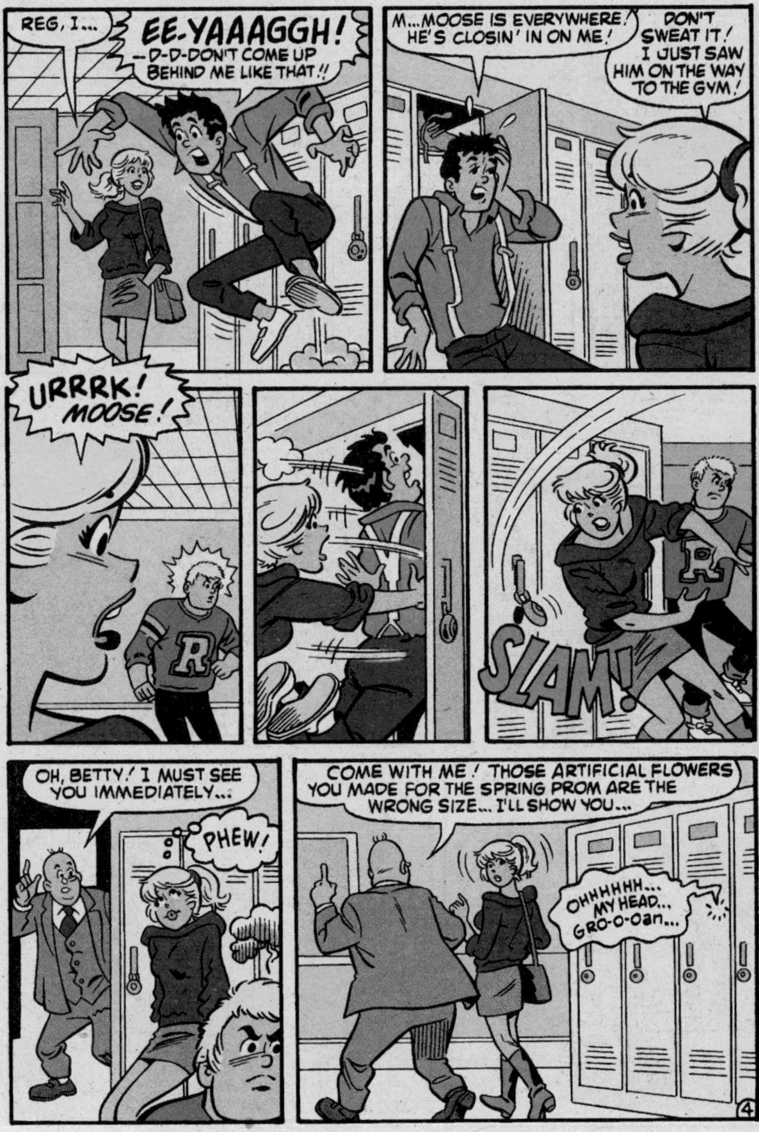
REG, I...
EE-YAAAGGH! --D-D-DON'T COME UP BEHIND ME LIKE THAT!!
M...MOOSE IS EVERYWHERE! HE'S CLOSIN' IN ON ME!
DON'T SWEAT IT! I JUST SAW HIM ON THE WAY TO THE GYM!
URRRK! MOOSE!
SLAM!
OH, BETTY! I MUST SEE YOU IMMEDIATELY...
PHEW!
COME WITH ME! THOSE ARTIFICIAL FLOWERS YOU MADE FOR THE SPRING PROM ARE THE WRONG SIZE... I'LL SHOW YOU...
OHHHHHH... MY HEAD... GRO-O-OAN...
4

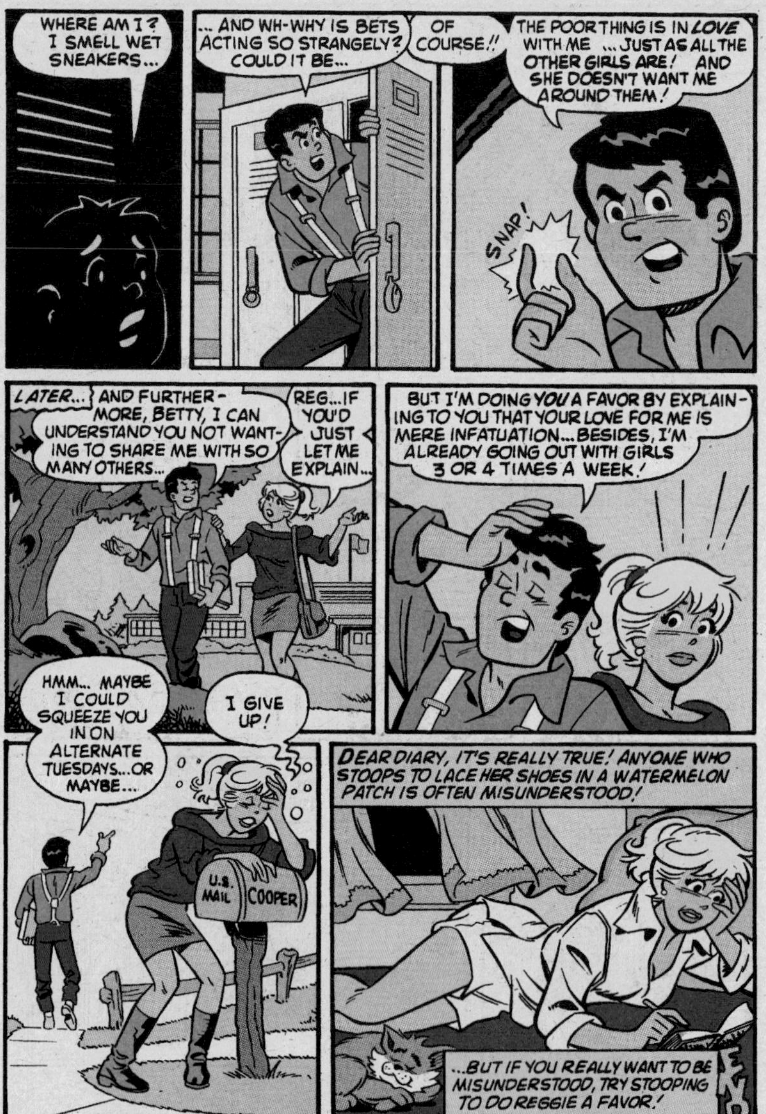
WHERE AM I? I SMELL WET SNEAKERS...
... AND WH-WHY IS BETS ACTING SO STRANGELY? COULD IT BE...
OF COURSE!!
THE POOR THING IS IN LOVE WITH ME ... JUST AS ALL THE OTHER GIRLS ARE! AND SHE DOESN'T WANT ME AROUND THEM!
SNAP!
LATER...
AND FURTHERMORE, BETTY, I CAN UNDERSTAND YOU NOT WANTING TO SHARE ME WITH SO MANY OTHERS...
REG...IF YOU'D JUST LET ME EXPLAIN...
HMM... MAYBE I COULD SQUEEZE YOU IN ON ALTERNATE TUESDAYS...OR MAYBE...
I GIVE UP!
BUT I'M DOING YOU A FAVOR BY EXPLAINING TO YOU THAT YOUR LOVE FOR ME IS MERE INFATUATION...BESIDES, I'M ALREADY GOING OUT WITH GIRLS 3 OR 4 TIMES A WEEK!
U.S. MAIL
COOPER
DEAR DIARY, IT'S REALLY TRUE! ANYONE WHO STOOPS TO LACE HER SHOES IN A WATERMELON PATCH IS OFTEN MISUNDERSTOOD!
...BUT IF YOU REALLY WANT TO BE MISUNDERSTOOD, TRY STOOPING TO DO REGGIE A FAVOR!

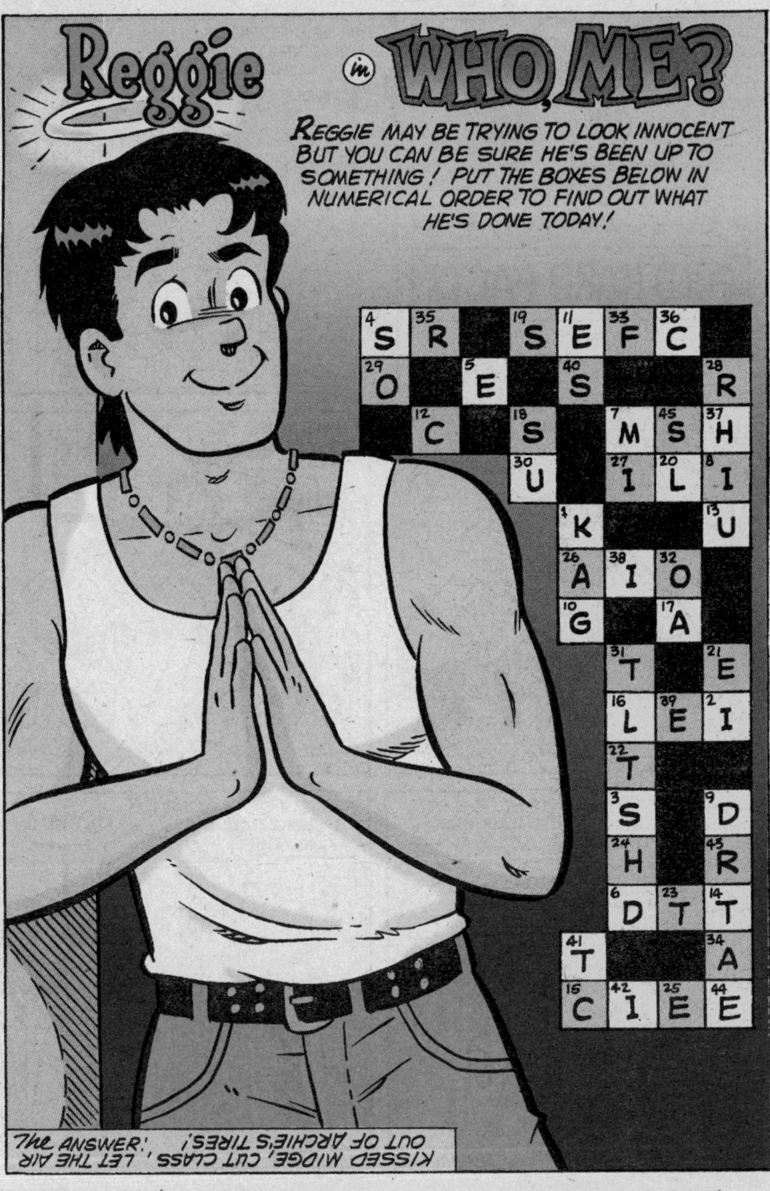
Reggie in WHO, ME?
REGGIE MAY BE TRYING TO LOOK INNOCENT BUT YOU CAN BE SURE HE'S BEEN UP TO SOMETHING! PUT THE BOXES BELOW IN NUMERICAL ORDER TO FIND OUT WHAT HE'S DONE TODAY!
4 S 35 R 19 S 11 E 33 F 36 C
29 O 5 E 40 S 28 R
12 C 18 S 7 M 45 S 37 H
30 U 27 I 20 L 8 I
1 K 13 U
26 A 38 I 32 O
10 G 17 A
31 T 21 E
16 L 39 E 2 I
22 T
3 S 9 D
24 H 43 R
6 D 23 T 14 T
41 T 34 A
15 C 42 I 25 E 44 E
The ANSWER: KISSED MIDGE, CUT CLASS, LET THE AIR OUT OF ARCHIE'S TIRES!

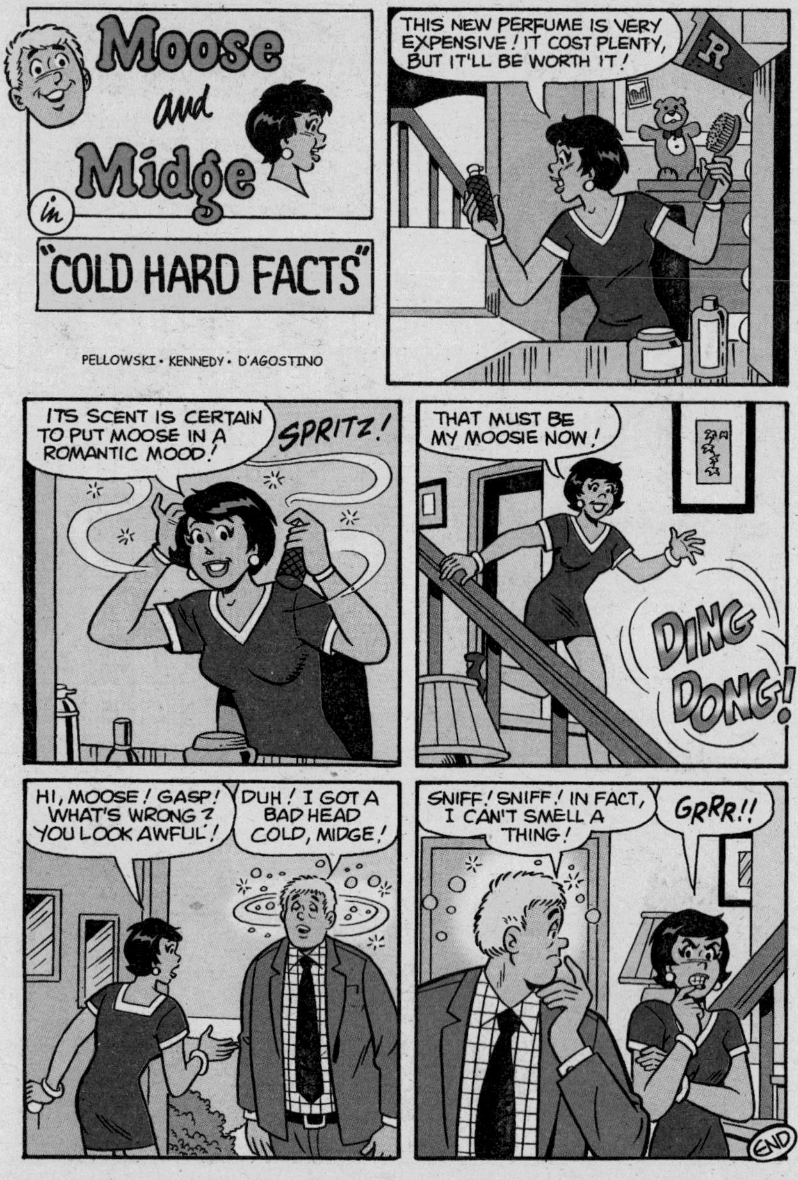
Moose and Midge in
"COLD HARD FACTS"
PELLOWSKI • KENNEDY • D'AGOSTINO
THIS NEW PERFUME IS VERY EXPENSIVE! IT COST PLENTY, BUT IT'LL BE WORTH IT!
R
ITS SCENT IS CERTAIN TO PUT MOOSE IN A ROMANTIC MOOD!
SPRITZ!
THAT MUST BE MY MOOSIE NOW!
DING DONG!
HI, MOOSE! GASP! WHAT'S WRONG? YOU LOOK AWFUL!
DUH! I GOT A BAD HEAD COLD, MIDGE!
SNIFF! SNIFF! IN FACT, I CAN'T SMELL A THING!
GRRR!!
END

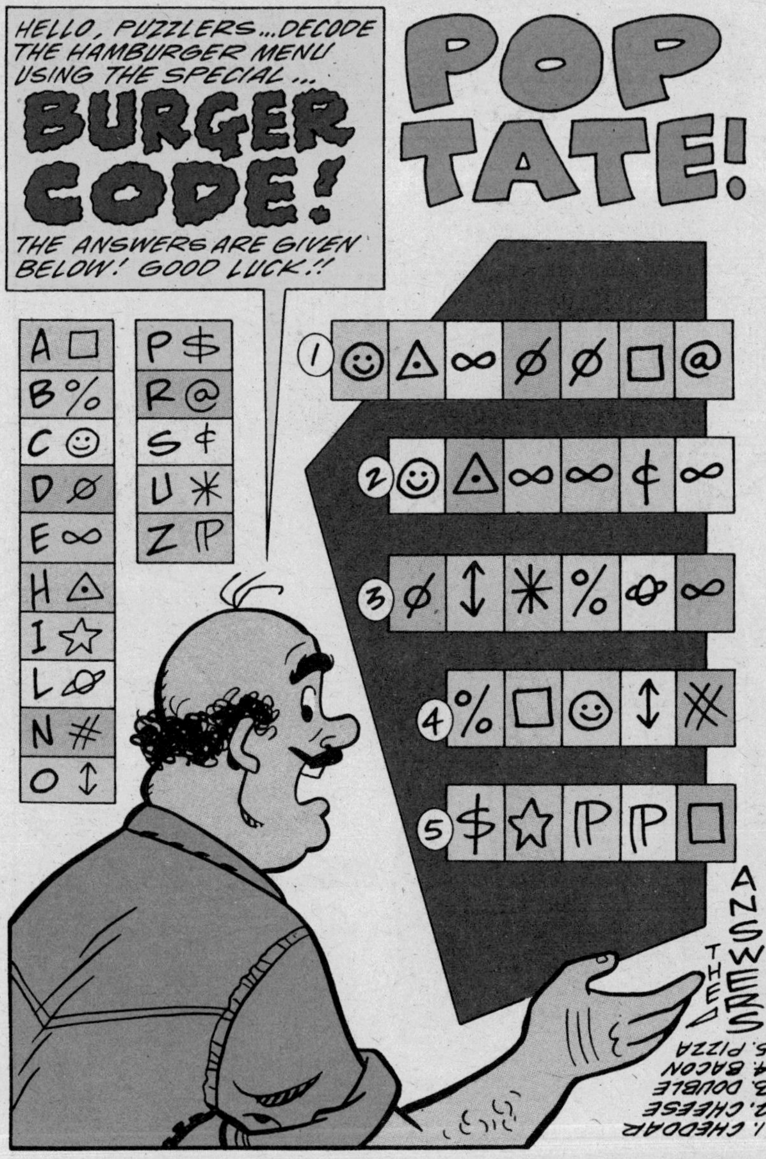

HELLO, PUZZLERS...DECODE THE HAMBURGER MENU USING THE SPECIAL ...
BURGER CODE!
THE ANSWERS ARE GIVEN BELOW! GOOD LUCK!!
POP TATE!
A B% C D E∞ H I L N# O
P$ R@ S¢ U Z
1
2
3
4
5
THE ANSWERS
1. CHEDDAR
2. CHEESE
3. DOUBLE
4. BACON
5. PIZZA

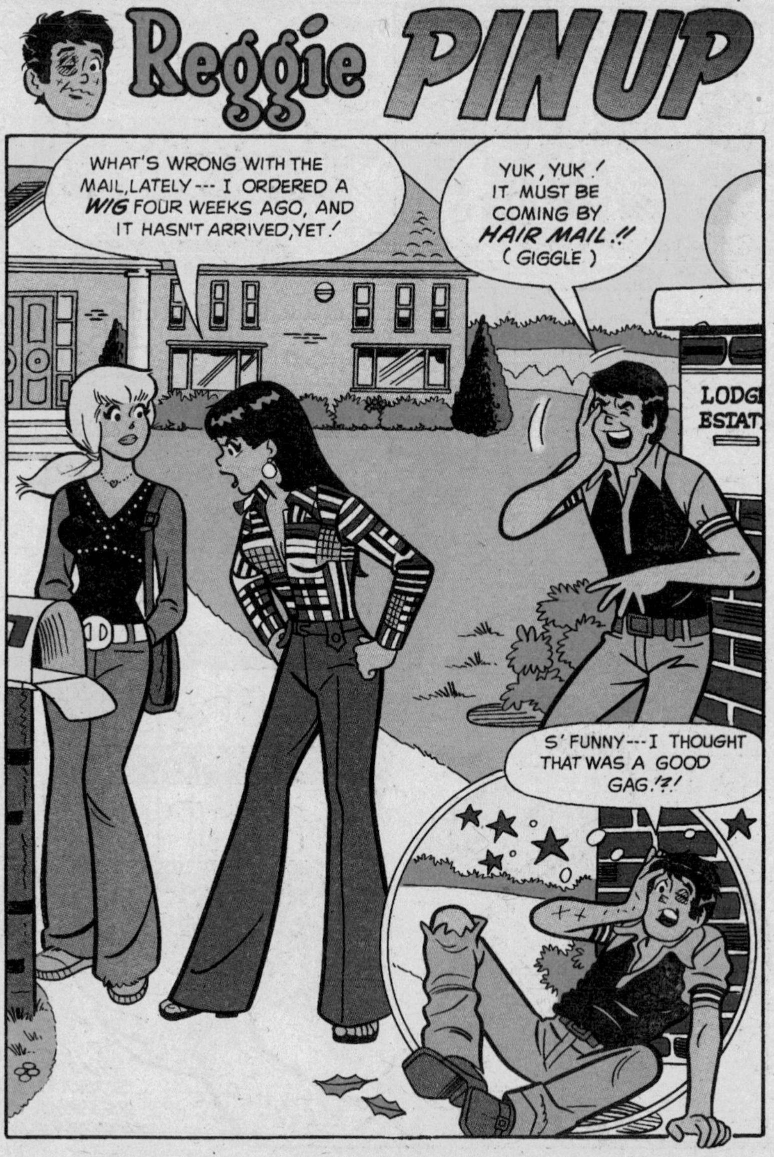
Reggie PINUP
WHAT'S WRONG WITH THE MAIL, LATELY --- I ORDERED A WIG FOUR WEEKS AGO, AND IT HASN'T ARRIVED, YET!
YUK, YUK! IT MUST BE COMING BY HAIR MAIL!! (GIGGLE)
LODGE ESTAT
S' FUNNY --- I THOUGHT THAT WAS A GOOD GAG!?!

From the Vault of Archie Comics!

Archie's Girls Betty and Veronica®

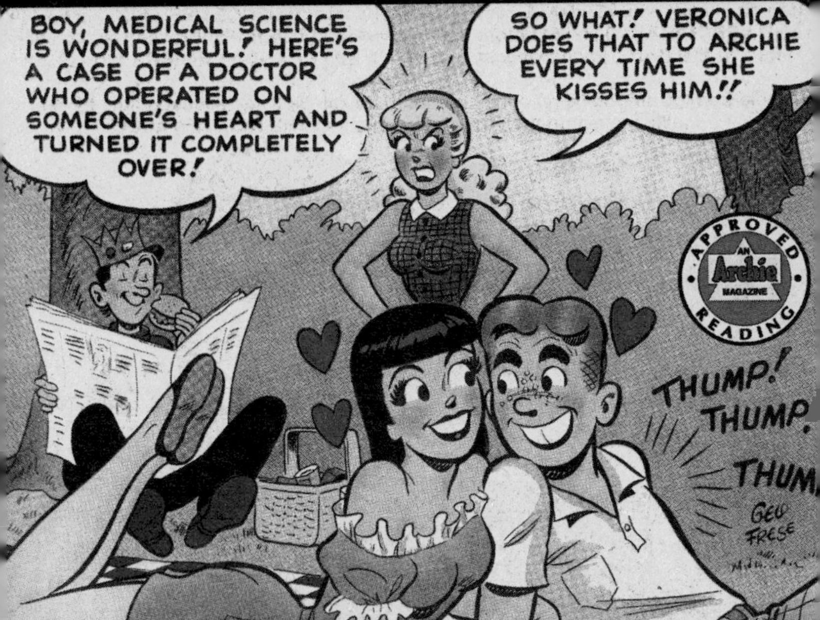

BOY, MEDICAL SCIENCE IS WONDERFUL! HERE'S A CASE OF A DOCTOR WHO OPERATED ON SOMEONE'S HEART AND TURNED IT COMPLETELY OVER!
SO WHAT! VERONICA DOES THAT TO ARCHIE EVERY TIME SHE KISSES HIM!!
APPROVED AN Archie MAGAZINE READING
THUMP! THUMP. THUM
GEO FRESE

From the Vault of Archie Comics!

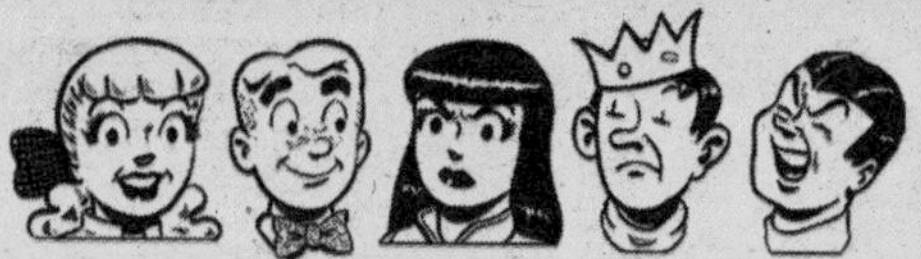

THE FABULOUS FIFTIES

Girls! *GIRLS!! GIRLS!!!* Welcome, pals and gals, to yet another riveting, jam-packed, lollapalooza laugh-fest that is the **ARCHIE VAULT**! Today we focus on that beautiful duo of bestest best friends (or best rivals if Archie is involved) -- ***Betty and Veronica***!

Today's tales from the house that Archie built are a series of specially crafted yarns tailor-made to tickle your funnybone! Leading the pack are "BELLS AND BELLES" and "PRESCRIPTION FOR LOVE" from **BETTY AND VERONICA #2** (1950). Meanwhile, in **BETTY AND VERONICA #18** (1955), Jughead helps Betty lay some "DATE BAIT" while Veronica pretends to be an "AN EARLY BIRD" and finagles Betty's help for some "INFERIOR DECORATING" before coming to terms with "JUGGY'S LAST STAND!" Both girls make a "LATE DATE" and encounter some "SCIENCE DEFIANCE" in **BETTY AND VERONICA #20** (1955) before hitting a "LANGUAGE BARRIER" and laying even more "DATE BAIT" (*didn't we just do that?*) in **BETTY AND VERONICA #21** (1955)!

Archie Comics are the best comics out there, folks! We'll see you next time for more sneak peeks into the best and brightest of THE ARCHIE VAULT!

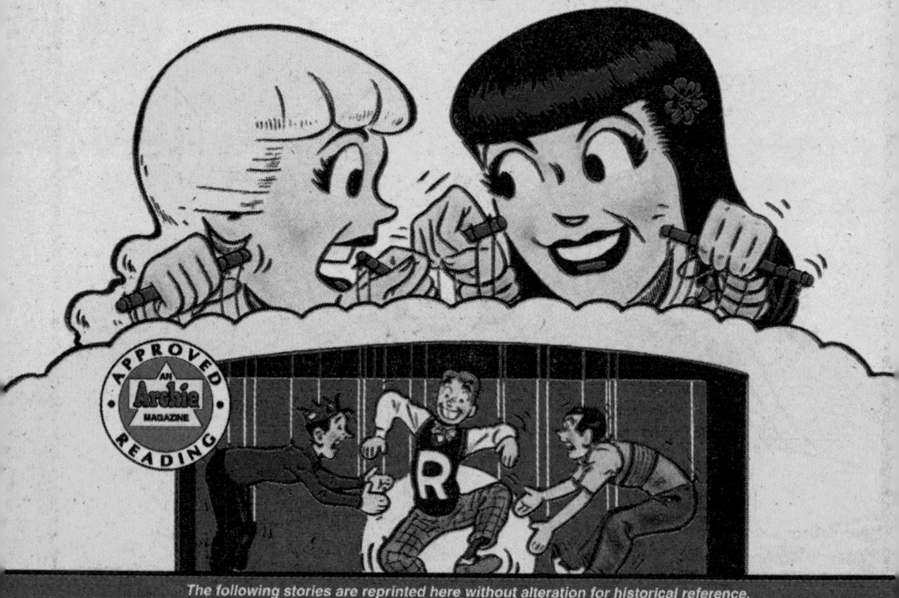
APPROVED
AN Archie MAGAZINE
READING

The following stories are reprinted here without alteration for historical reference.

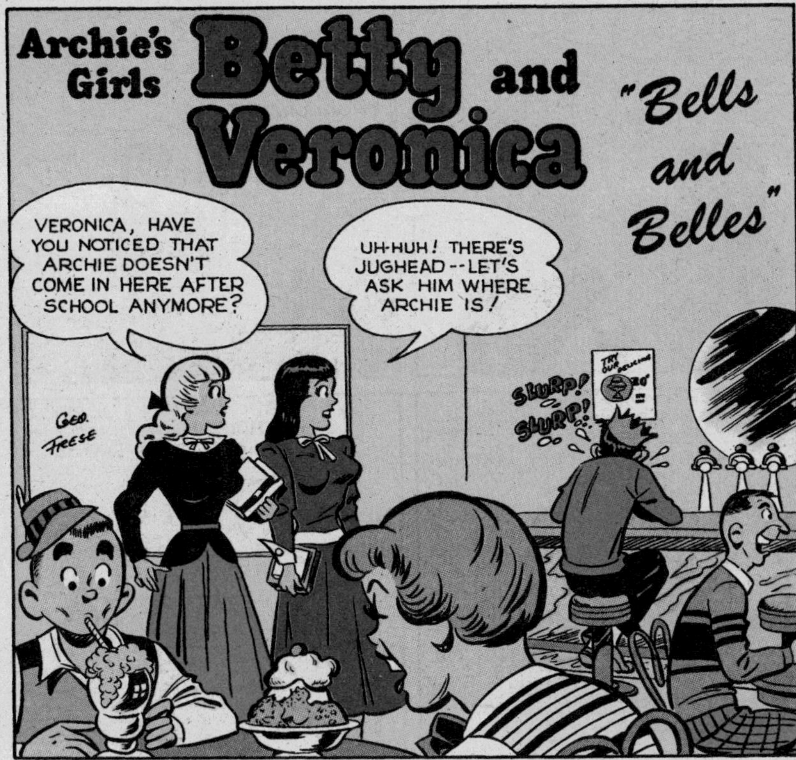
Archie's Girls Betty and Veronica
"Bells and Belles"
VERONICA, HAVE YOU NOTICED THAT ARCHIE DOESN'T COME IN HERE AFTER SCHOOL ANYMORE?
UH-HUH! THERE'S JUGHEAD--LET'S ASK HIM WHERE ARCHIE IS!
GEO. FREESE
SLURP! SLURP!

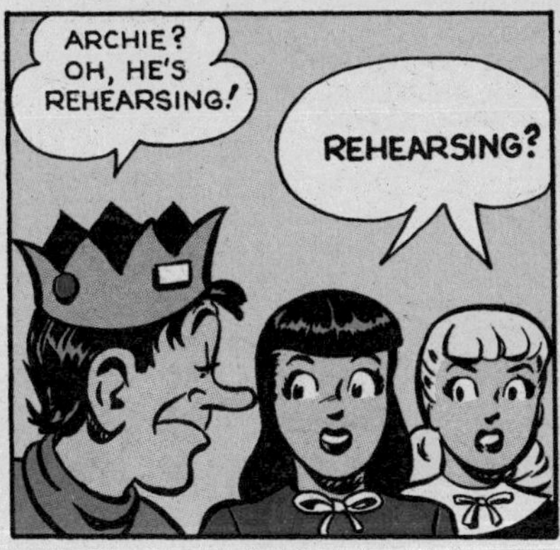
ARCHIE? OH, HE'S REHEARSING!
REHEARSING?

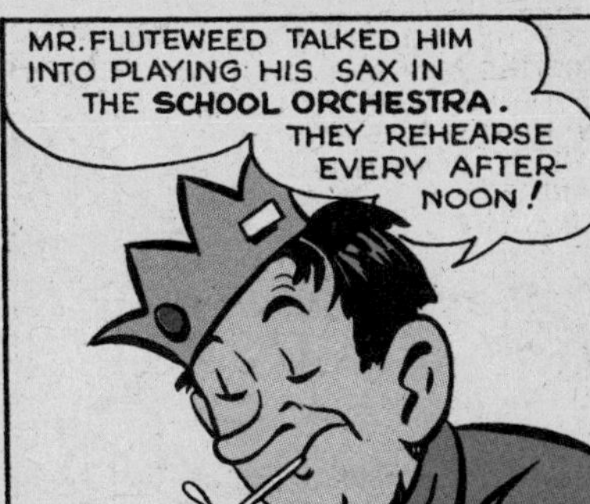
MR. FLUTEWEED TALKED HIM INTO PLAYING HIS SAX IN THE SCHOOL ORCHESTRA. THEY REHEARSE EVERY AFTER-NOON!

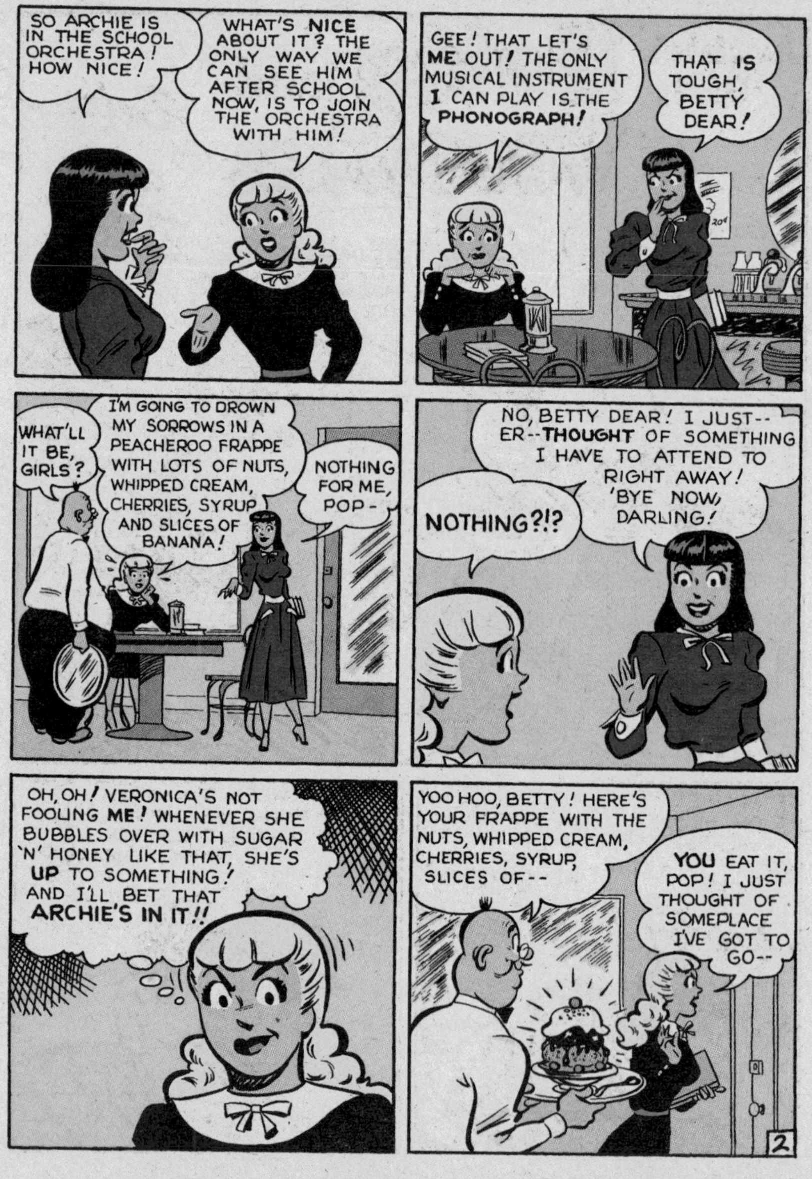
SO ARCHIE IS IN THE SCHOOL ORCHESTRA! HOW NICE!
WHAT'S **NICE** ABOUT IT? THE ONLY WAY WE CAN SEE HIM AFTER SCHOOL NOW, IS TO JOIN THE ORCHESTRA WITH HIM!
GEE! THAT LET'S **ME** OUT! THE ONLY MUSICAL INSTRUMENT **I** CAN PLAY IS THE **PHONOGRAPH!**
THAT **IS** TOUGH, BETTY DEAR!
WHAT'LL IT BE, GIRLS?
I'M GOING TO DROWN MY SORROWS IN A PEACHEROO FRAPPE WITH LOTS OF NUTS, WHIPPED CREAM, CHERRIES, SYRUP AND SLICES OF BANANA!
NOTHING FOR ME, POP-
NOTHING?!?
NO, BETTY DEAR! I JUST--ER--**THOUGHT** OF SOMETHING I HAVE TO ATTEND TO RIGHT AWAY! 'BYE NOW, DARLING!
OH, OH! VERONICA'S NOT FOOLING **ME**! WHENEVER SHE BUBBLES OVER WITH SUGAR 'N' HONEY LIKE THAT, SHE'S **UP** TO SOMETHING! AND I'LL BET THAT **ARCHIE'S IN IT!!**
YOO HOO, BETTY! HERE'S YOUR FRAPPE WITH THE NUTS, WHIPPED CREAM, CHERRIES, SYRUP, SLICES OF--
YOU EAT IT, POP! I JUST THOUGHT OF SOMEPLACE I'VE GOT TO GO--
2

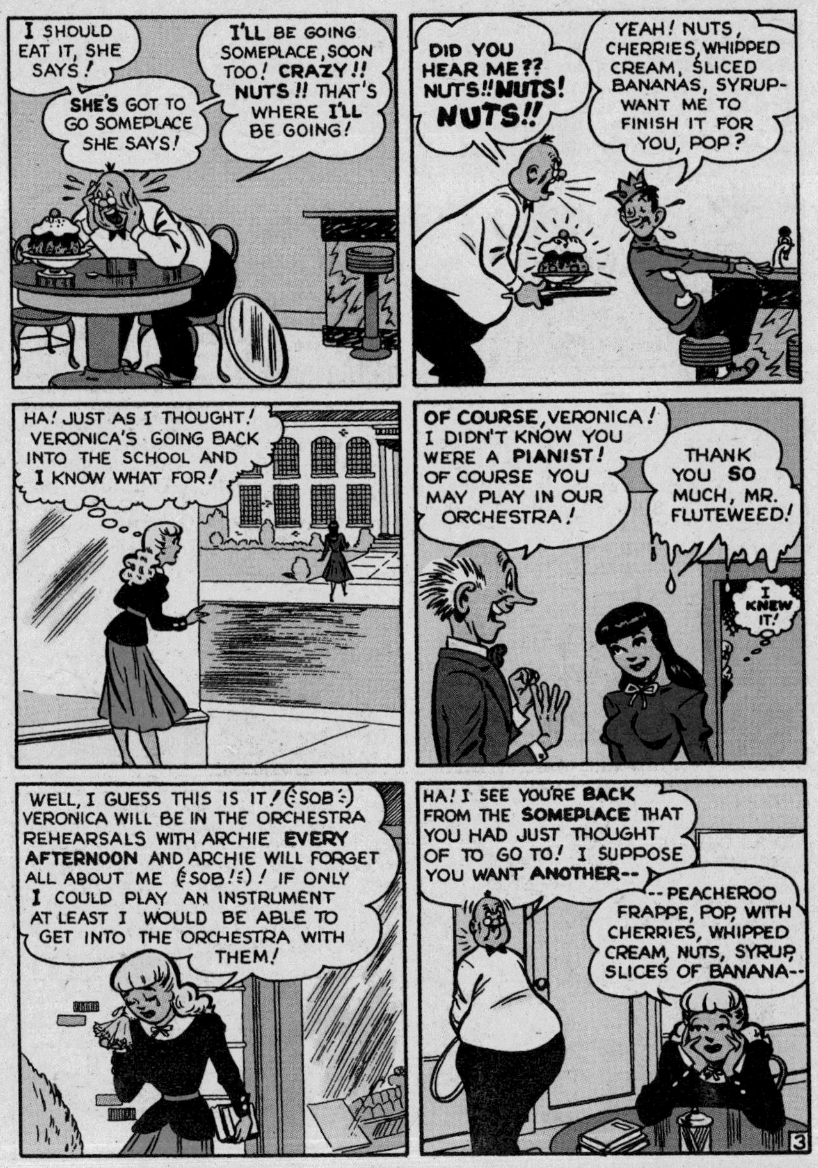

I SHOULD EAT IT, SHE SAYS!
SHE'S GOT TO GO SOMEPLACE SHE SAYS!
I'LL BE GOING SOMEPLACE, SOON TOO! CRAZY!! NUTS!! THAT'S WHERE I'LL BE GOING!
DID YOU HEAR ME?? NUTS!! NUTS! NUTS!!
YEAH! NUTS, CHERRIES, WHIPPED CREAM, SLICED BANANAS, SYRUP- WANT ME TO FINISH IT FOR YOU, POP?
HA! JUST AS I THOUGHT! VERONICA'S GOING BACK INTO THE SCHOOL AND I KNOW WHAT FOR!
OF COURSE, VERONICA! I DIDN'T KNOW YOU WERE A PIANIST! OF COURSE YOU MAY PLAY IN OUR ORCHESTRA!
THANK YOU SO MUCH, MR. FLUTEWEED!
I KNEW IT!
WELL, I GUESS THIS IS IT! (SOB) VERONICA WILL BE IN THE ORCHESTRA REHEARSALS WITH ARCHIE EVERY AFTERNOON AND ARCHIE WILL FORGET ALL ABOUT ME (SOB!)! IF ONLY I COULD PLAY AN INSTRUMENT AT LEAST I WOULD BE ABLE TO GET INTO THE ORCHESTRA WITH THEM!
HA! I SEE YOU'RE BACK FROM THE SOMEPLACE THAT YOU HAD JUST THOUGHT OF TO GO TO! I SUPPOSE YOU WANT ANOTHER--
--PEACHEROO FRAPPE, POP, WITH CHERRIES, WHIPPED CREAM, NUTS, SYRUP, SLICES OF BANANA--
3

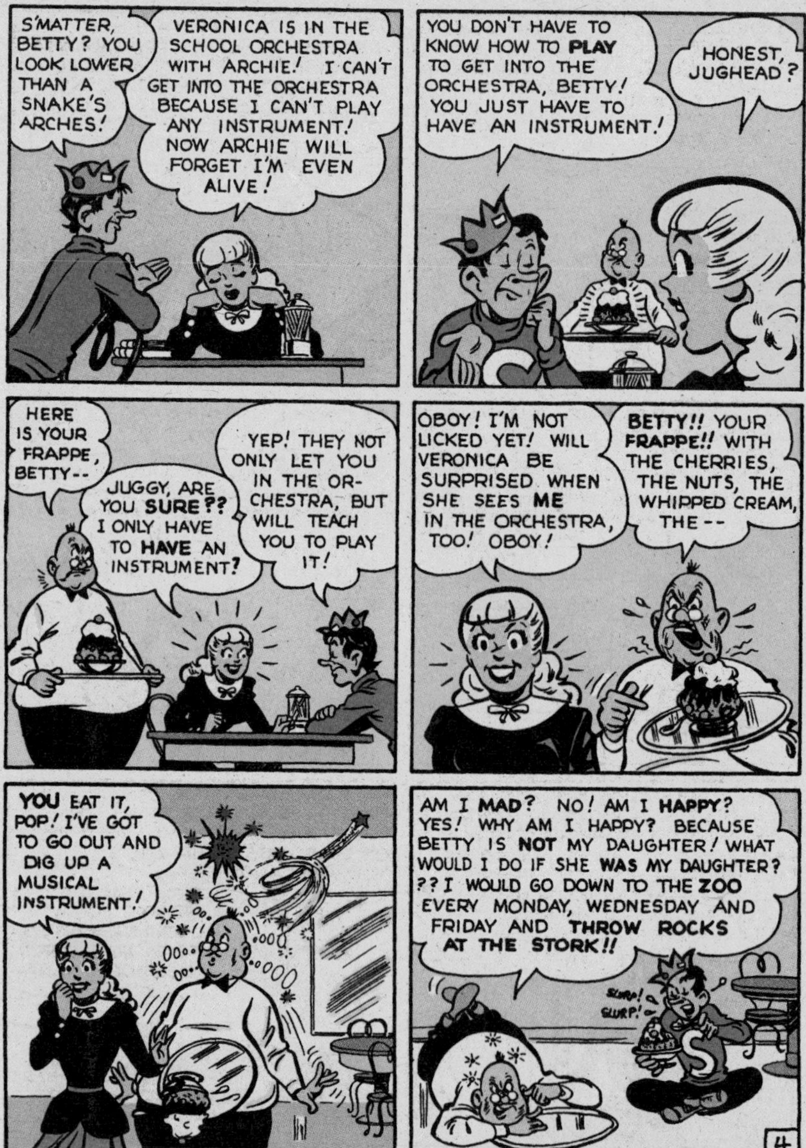
S'MATTER, BETTY? YOU LOOK LOWER THAN A SNAKE'S ARCHES!
VERONICA IS IN THE SCHOOL ORCHESTRA WITH ARCHIE! I CAN'T GET INTO THE ORCHESTRA BECAUSE I CAN'T PLAY ANY INSTRUMENT! NOW ARCHIE WILL FORGET I'M EVEN ALIVE!
YOU DON'T HAVE TO KNOW HOW TO **PLAY** TO GET INTO THE ORCHESTRA, BETTY! YOU JUST HAVE TO HAVE AN INSTRUMENT!
HONEST, JUGHEAD?
HERE IS YOUR FRAPPE, BETTY--
JUGGY, ARE YOU **SURE??** I ONLY HAVE TO **HAVE** AN INSTRUMENT?
YEP! THEY NOT ONLY LET YOU IN THE ORCHESTRA, BUT WILL TEACH YOU TO PLAY IT!
OBOY! I'M NOT LICKED YET! WILL VERONICA BE SURPRISED WHEN SHE SEES **ME** IN THE ORCHESTRA, TOO! OBOY!
BETTY!! YOUR **FRAPPE!!** WITH THE CHERRIES, THE NUTS, THE WHIPPED CREAM, THE--
YOU EAT IT, POP! I'VE GOT TO GO OUT AND DIG UP A MUSICAL INSTRUMENT!
AM I **MAD**? NO! AM I **HAPPY**? YES! WHY AM I HAPPY? BECAUSE BETTY IS **NOT** MY DAUGHTER! WHAT WOULD I DO IF SHE **WAS** MY DAUGHTER??? I WOULD GO DOWN TO THE **ZOO** EVERY MONDAY, WEDNESDAY AND FRIDAY AND **THROW ROCKS AT THE STORK!!**
SLURP! SLURP!
4

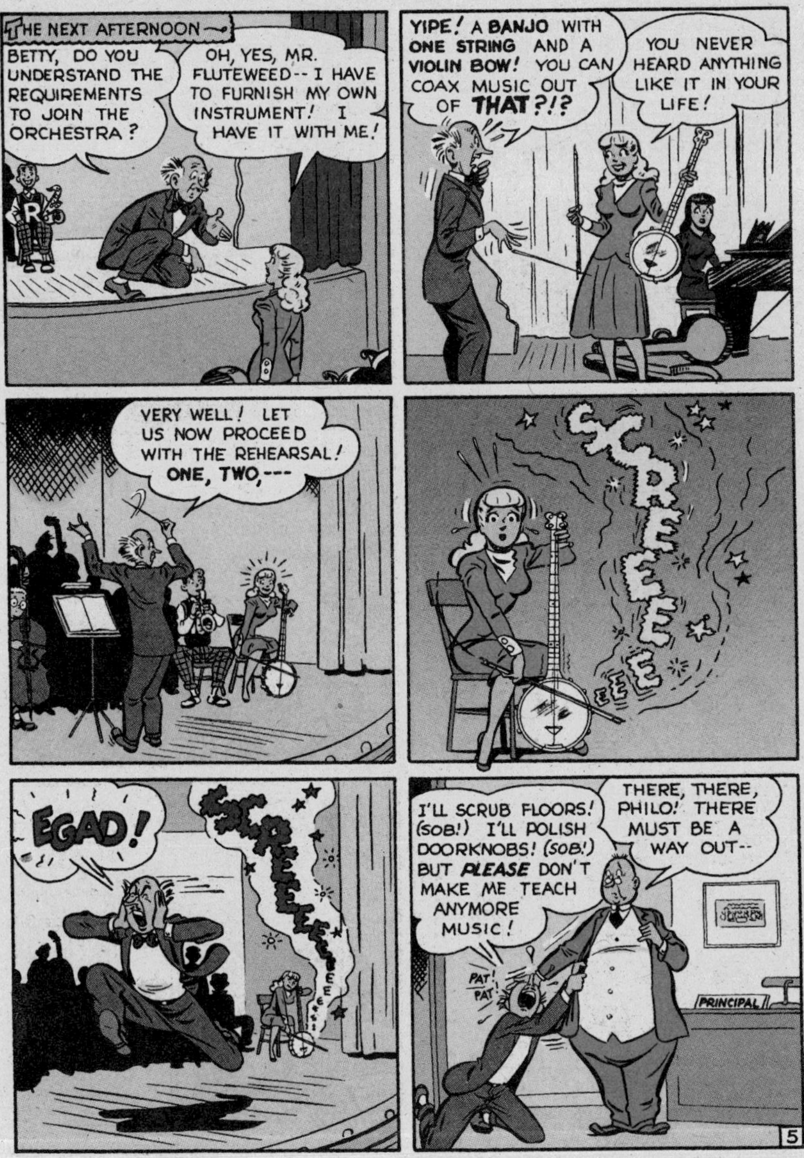
THE NEXT AFTERNOON
BETTY, DO YOU UNDERSTAND THE REQUIREMENTS TO JOIN THE ORCHESTRA?
OH, YES, MR. FLUTEWEED-- I HAVE TO FURNISH MY OWN INSTRUMENT! I HAVE IT WITH ME!
YIPE! A BANJO WITH ONE STRING AND A VIOLIN BOW! YOU CAN COAX MUSIC OUT OF THAT?!?
YOU NEVER HEARD ANYTHING LIKE IT IN YOUR LIFE!
VERY WELL! LET US NOW PROCEED WITH THE REHEARSAL! ONE, TWO,---
SKREEEEEE
EGAD!
SCREEEEEEEEE
I'LL SCRUB FLOORS! (SOB!) I'LL POLISH DOORKNOBS! (SOB!) BUT PLEASE DON'T MAKE ME TEACH ANYMORE MUSIC!
THERE, THERE, PHILO! THERE MUST BE A WAY OUT--
PAT! PAT!
PRINCIPAL
5

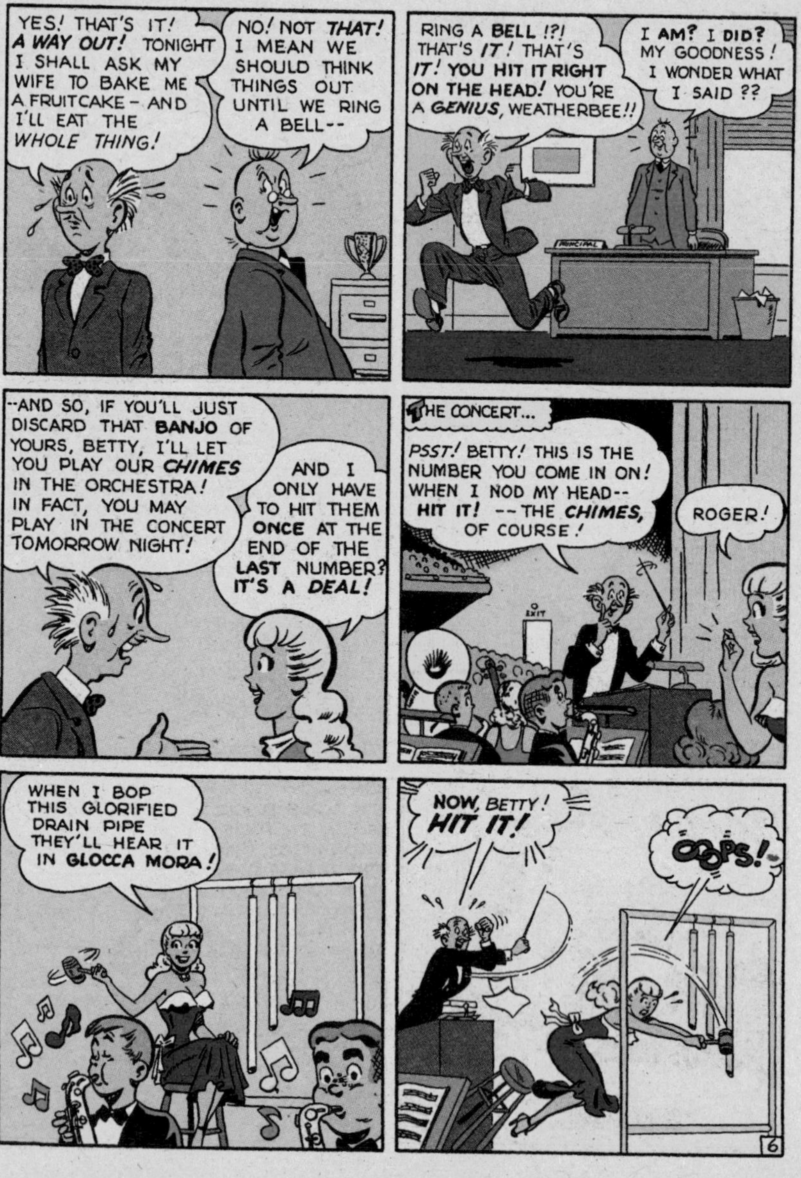

YES! THAT'S IT! A WAY OUT! TONIGHT I SHALL ASK MY WIFE TO BAKE ME A FRUITCAKE - AND I'LL EAT THE WHOLE THING!
NO! NOT THAT! I MEAN WE SHOULD THINK THINGS OUT UNTIL WE RING A BELL--
RING A BELL !?! THAT'S IT! THAT'S IT! YOU HIT IT RIGHT ON THE HEAD! YOU'RE A GENIUS, WEATHERBEE!!
I AM? I DID? MY GOODNESS! I WONDER WHAT I SAID ??
PRINCIPAL
--AND SO, IF YOU'LL JUST DISCARD THAT BANJO OF YOURS, BETTY, I'LL LET YOU PLAY OUR CHIMES IN THE ORCHESTRA! IN FACT, YOU MAY PLAY IN THE CONCERT TOMORROW NIGHT!
AND I ONLY HAVE TO HIT THEM ONCE AT THE END OF THE LAST NUMBER? IT'S A DEAL!
THE CONCERT...
PSST! BETTY! THIS IS THE NUMBER YOU COME IN ON! WHEN I NOD MY HEAD-- HIT IT! --THE CHIMES, OF COURSE!
ROGER!
EXIT
WHEN I BOP THIS GLORIFIED DRAIN PIPE THEY'LL HEAR IT IN GLOCCA MORA!
NOW, BETTY! HIT IT!
OOPS!
6

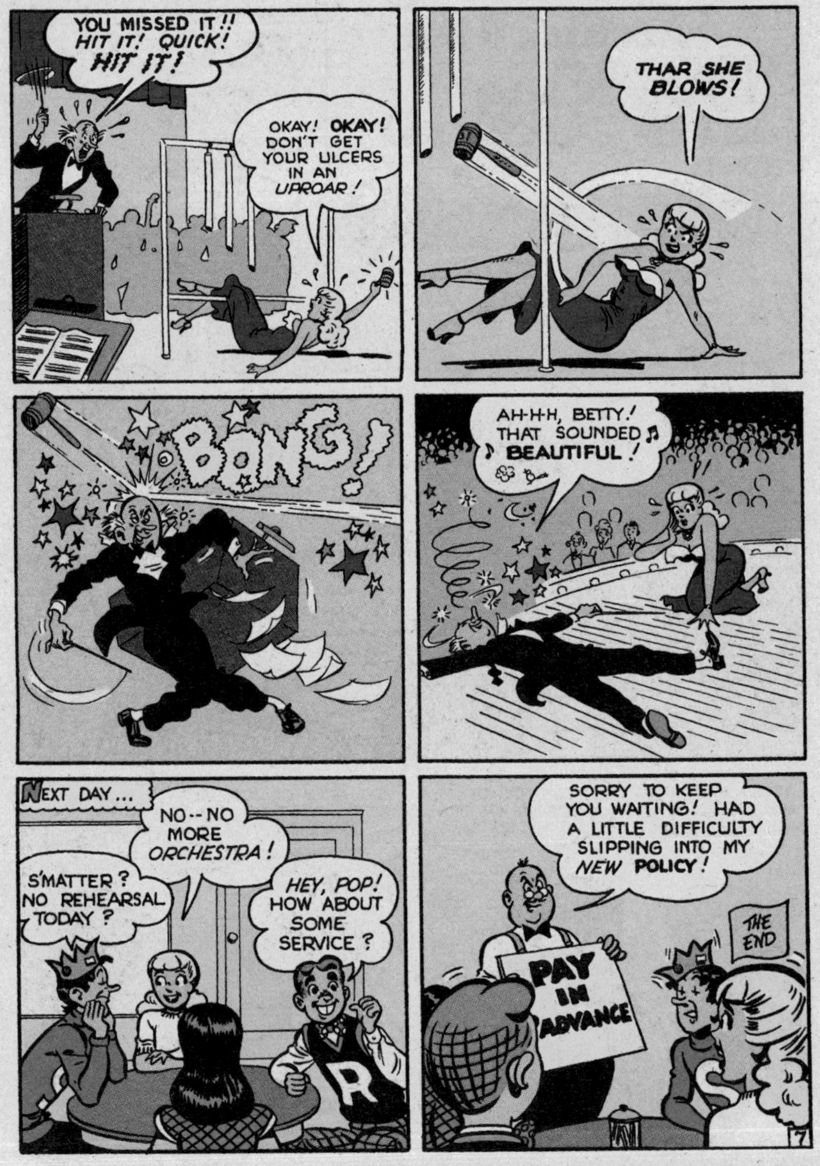
YOU MISSED IT!! HIT IT! QUICK! HIT IT!
OKAY! OKAY! DON'T GET YOUR ULCERS IN AN UPROAR!
THAR SHE BLOWS!
BONG!
AH-H-H, BETTY! THAT SOUNDED BEAUTIFUL!
NEXT DAY...
S'MATTER? NO REHEARSAL TODAY?
NO--NO MORE ORCHESTRA!
HEY, POP! HOW ABOUT SOME SERVICE?
SORRY TO KEEP YOU WAITING! HAD A LITTLE DIFFICULTY SLIPPING INTO MY NEW POLICY!
PAY IN ADVANCE
THE END
7

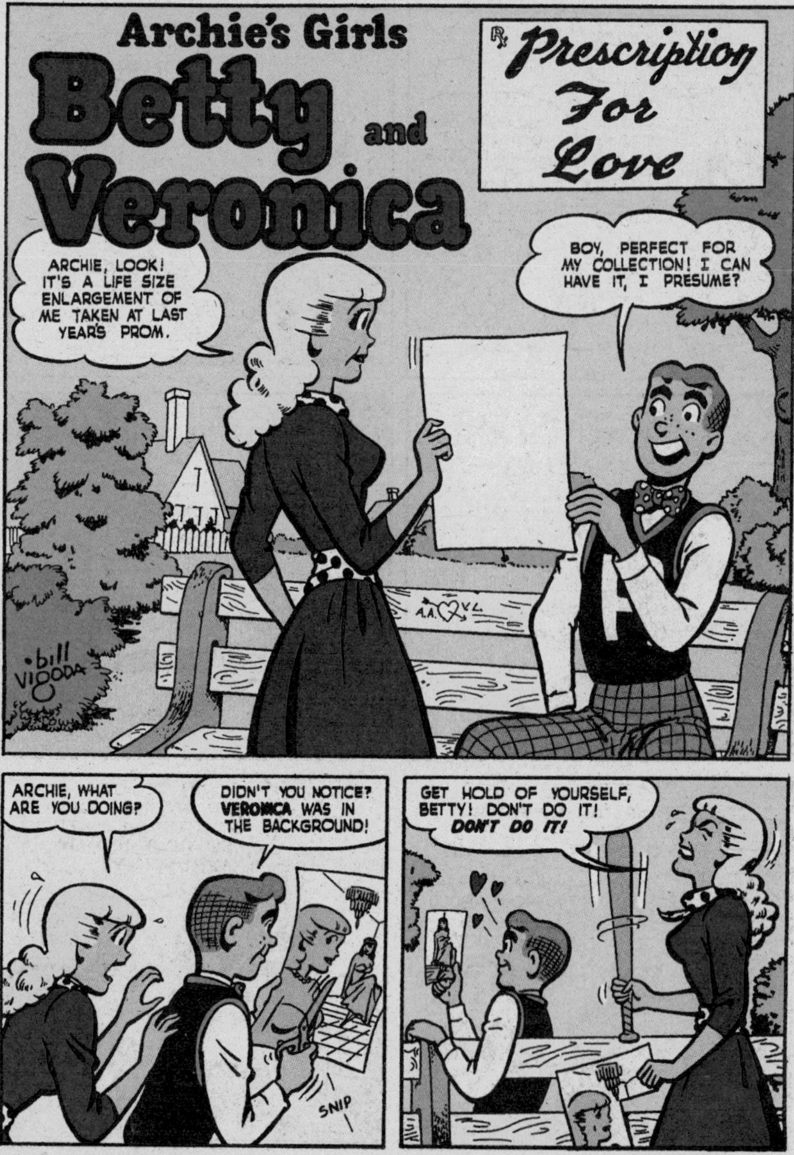
Archie's Girls
Betty and Veronica
Prescription For Love
ARCHIE, LOOK! IT'S A LIFE SIZE ENLARGEMENT OF ME TAKEN AT LAST YEAR'S PROM.
BOY, PERFECT FOR MY COLLECTION! I CAN HAVE IT, I PRESUME?
A.A. V.L.
bill VIGODA
ARCHIE, WHAT ARE YOU DOING?
DIDN'T YOU NOTICE? VERONICA WAS IN THE BACKGROUND!
SNIP
GET HOLD OF YOURSELF, BETTY! DON'T DO IT! DON'T DO IT!

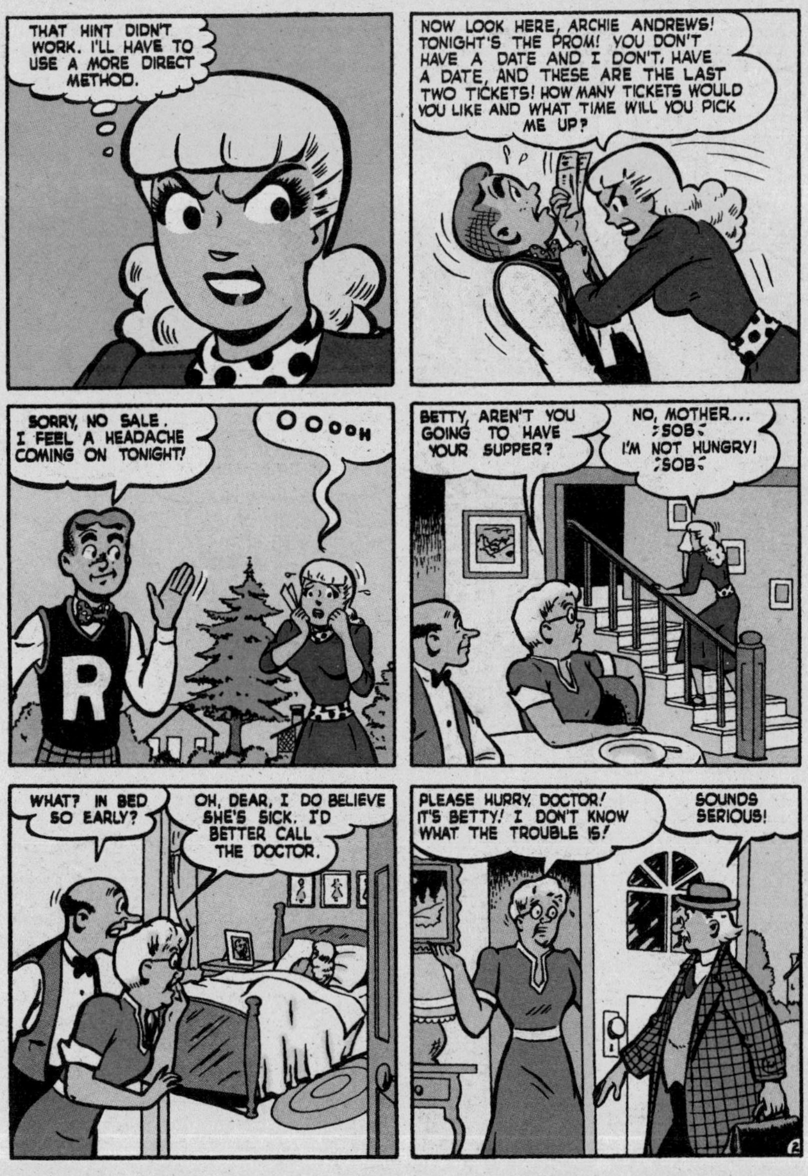
THAT HINT DIDN'T WORK. I'LL HAVE TO USE A MORE DIRECT METHOD.
NOW LOOK HERE, ARCHIE ANDREWS! TONIGHT'S THE PROM! YOU DON'T HAVE A DATE AND I DON'T HAVE A DATE, AND THESE ARE THE LAST TWO TICKETS! HOW MANY TICKETS WOULD YOU LIKE AND WHAT TIME WILL YOU PICK ME UP?
SORRY, NO SALE. I FEEL A HEADACHE COMING ON TONIGHT!
OOOOOH
R
BETTY, AREN'T YOU GOING TO HAVE YOUR SUPPER?
NO, MOTHER... SOB I'M NOT HUNGRY! SOB
WHAT? IN BED SO EARLY?
OH, DEAR, I DO BELIEVE SHE'S SICK. I'D BETTER CALL THE DOCTOR.
PLEASE HURRY, DOCTOR! IT'S BETTY! I DON'T KNOW WHAT THE TROUBLE IS!
SOUNDS SERIOUS!
2

DOCTOR, I JUST CAN'T EAT OR SLEEP!

HMMM! IT SEEMS TO ME YOU COME DOWN WITH THIS STRANGE MALADY EVERY YEAR AT THIS TIME!

BY THE WAY... HOW FAR OFF IS THE PROM?

TONIGHT! AND ARCHIE HASN'T ASKED ME AND HE KEEPS AVOIDING ME AND I NEVER WANT TO SEE HIM AGAIN!

IS IT SERIOUS, DOCTOR?

AT THAT AGE IT ALWAYS IS. BUT I THINK I KNOW HOW TO CURE IT!

WILL YOU PLEASE FILL THIS PRESCRIPTION OUT FOR BETTY COOPER IT'S AN EMERGENCY!

HUH! BETTY'S SICK?

ULP — WHAT'S WRONG WITH BETTY, DOC?

HEART TROUBLE ER... WOULD YOU DELIVER THIS PRESCRIPTION RIGHT AWAY, ARCHIE?

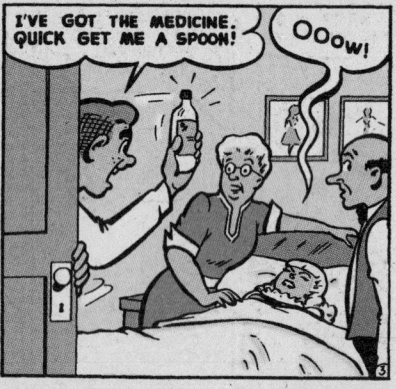

I'VE GOT THE MEDICINE. QUICK GET ME A SPOON!

OOOW!

3

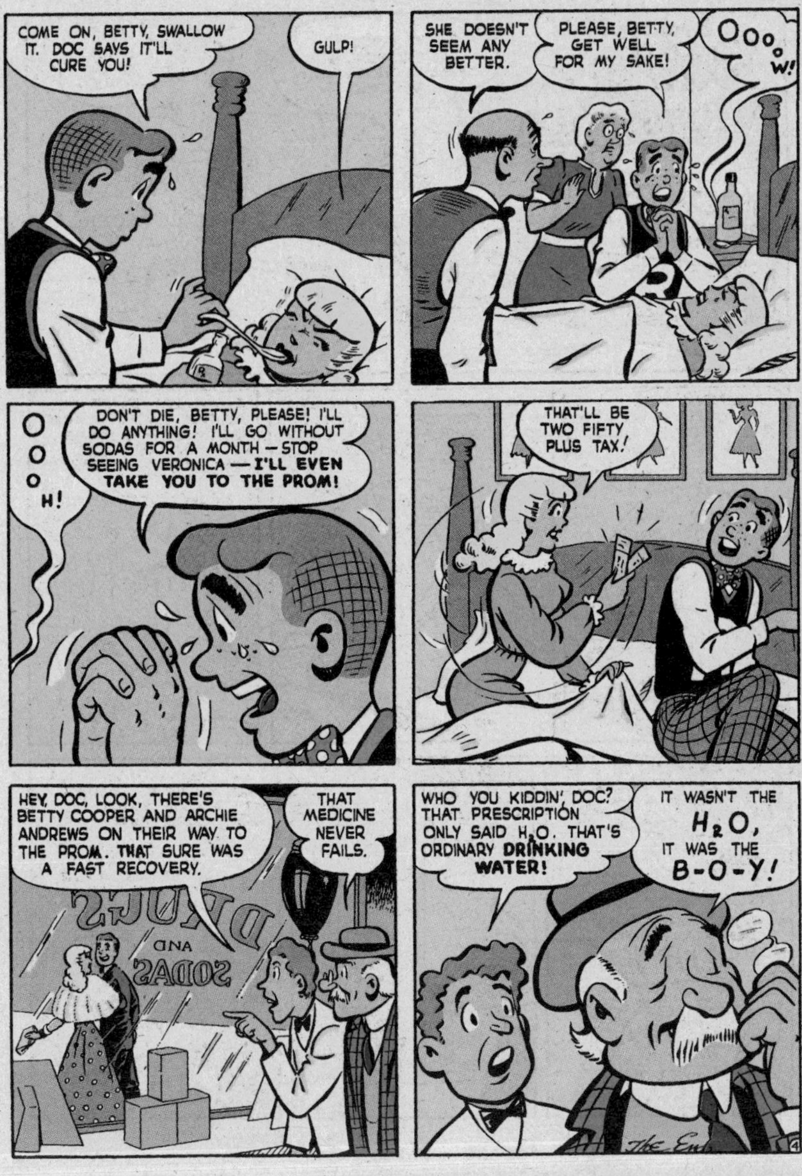
COME ON, BETTY, SWALLOW IT. DOC SAYS IT'LL CURE YOU!
GULP!
SHE DOESN'T SEEM ANY BETTER.
PLEASE, BETTY, GET WELL FOR MY SAKE!
Oooo W!
OOOH!
DON'T DIE, BETTY, PLEASE! I'LL DO ANYTHING! I'LL GO WITHOUT SODAS FOR A MONTH — STOP SEEING VERONICA — I'LL EVEN TAKE YOU TO THE PROM!
THAT'LL BE TWO FIFTY PLUS TAX!
HEY, DOC, LOOK, THERE'S BETTY COOPER AND ARCHIE ANDREWS ON THEIR WAY TO THE PROM. THAT SURE WAS A FAST RECOVERY.
THAT MEDICINE NEVER FAILS.
DRUGS AND SODAS
WHO YOU KIDDIN', DOC? THAT PRESCRIPTION ONLY SAID H2O. THAT'S ORDINARY DRINKING WATER!
IT WASN'T THE H2O, IT WAS THE B-O-Y!
THE END
4

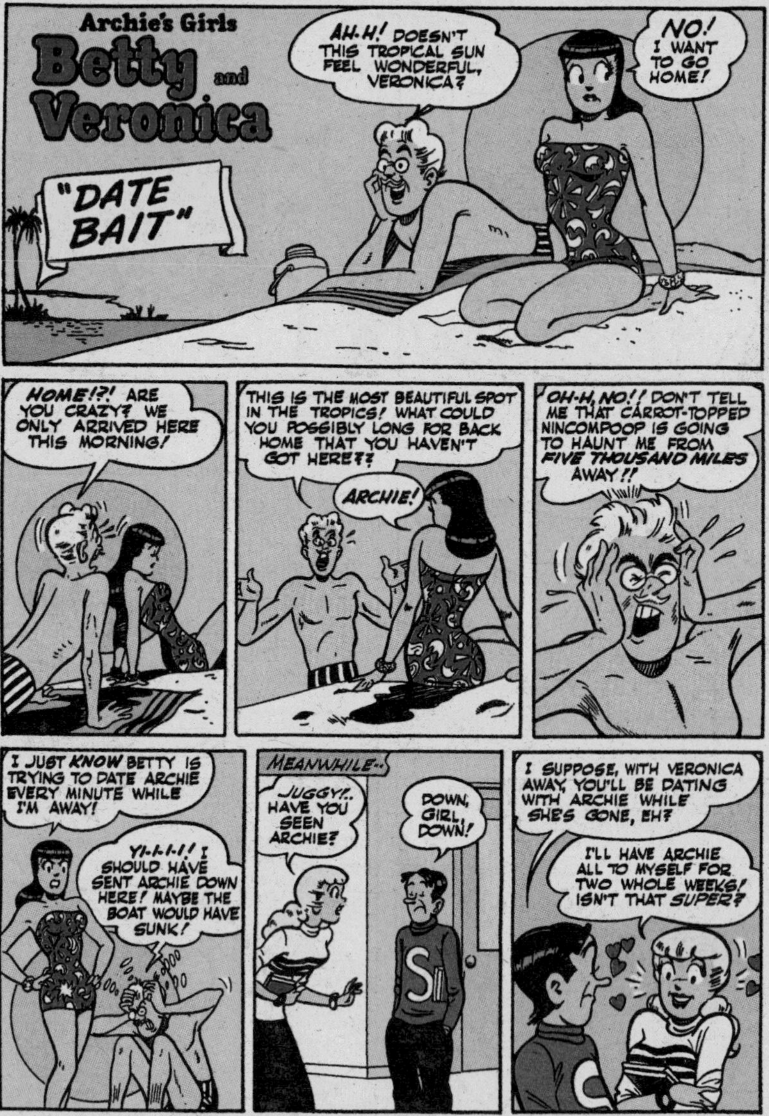
Archie's Girls Betty and Veronica
"DATE BAIT"
AH-H! DOESN'T THIS TROPICAL SUN FEEL WONDERFUL, VERONICA?
NO! I WANT TO GO HOME!
HOME!?! ARE YOU CRAZY? WE ONLY ARRIVED HERE THIS MORNING!
THIS IS THE MOST BEAUTIFUL SPOT IN THE TROPICS! WHAT COULD YOU POSSIBLY LONG FOR BACK HOME THAT YOU HAVEN'T GOT HERE??
ARCHIE!
OH-H, NO!! DON'T TELL ME THAT CARROT-TOPPED NINCOMPOOP IS GOING TO HAUNT ME FROM FIVE THOUSAND MILES AWAY!!
I JUST KNOW BETTY IS TRYING TO DATE ARCHIE EVERY MINUTE WHILE I'M AWAY!
YI-I-I-I!! I SHOULD HAVE SENT ARCHIE DOWN HERE! MAYBE THE BOAT WOULD HAVE SUNK!
MEANWHILE..
JUGGY!.. HAVE YOU SEEN ARCHIE?
DOWN, GIRL, DOWN!
I SUPPOSE, WITH VERONICA AWAY, YOU'LL BE DATING WITH ARCHIE WHILE SHE'S GONE, EH?
I'LL HAVE ARCHIE ALL TO MYSELF FOR TWO WHOLE WEEKS! ISN'T THAT SUPER?

PENCILS: GEORGE FRESE

INKS & LETTERS: TERRY SZENICS

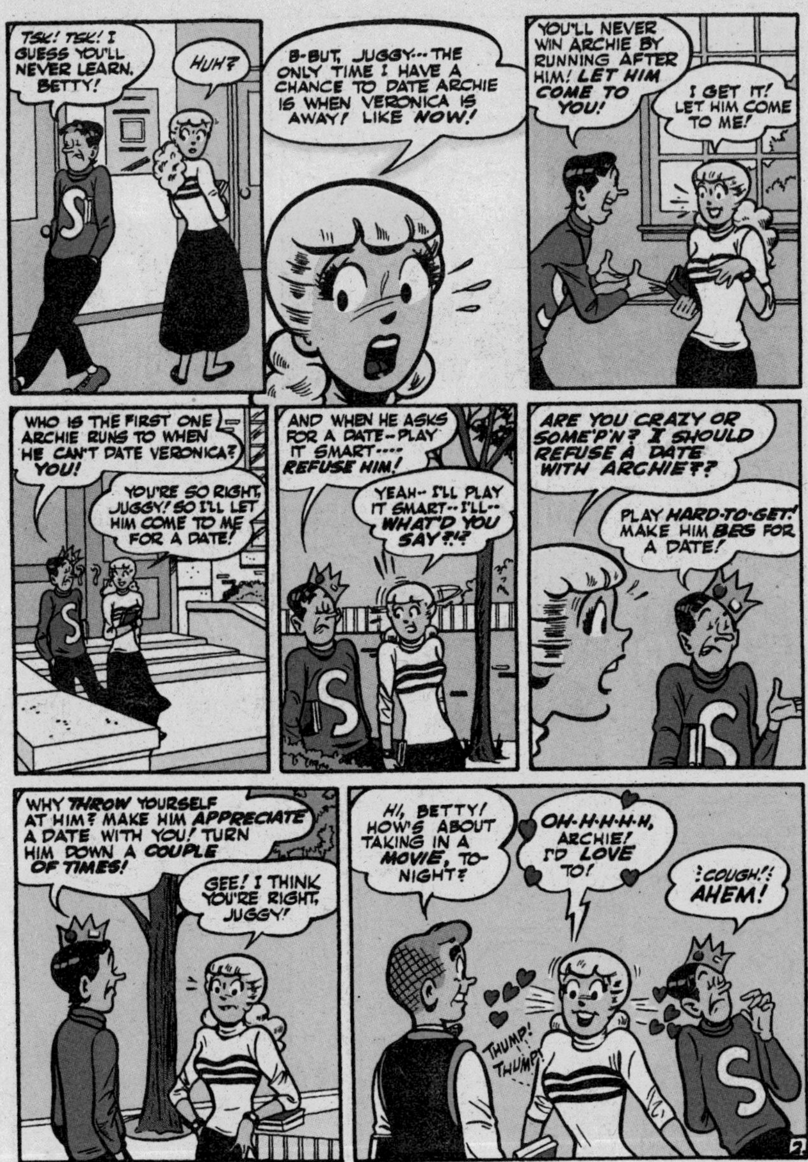

TSK! TSK! I GUESS YOU'LL NEVER LEARN, BETTY!
HUH?
B-BUT, JUGGY--- THE ONLY TIME I HAVE A CHANCE TO DATE ARCHIE IS WHEN VERONICA IS AWAY! LIKE NOW!
YOU'LL NEVER WIN ARCHIE BY RUNNING AFTER HIM! LET HIM COME TO YOU!
I GET IT! LET HIM COME TO ME!
WHO IS THE FIRST ONE ARCHIE RUNS TO WHEN HE CAN'T DATE VERONICA? YOU!
YOU'RE SO RIGHT, JUGGY! SO I'LL LET HIM COME TO ME FOR A DATE!
AND WHEN HE ASKS FOR A DATE-- PLAY IT SMART---- REFUSE HIM!
YEAH-- I'LL PLAY IT SMART-- I'LL-- WHAT'D YOU SAY?!?
ARE YOU CRAZY OR SOME'P'N? I SHOULD REFUSE A DATE WITH ARCHIE??
PLAY HARD-TO-GET! MAKE HIM BEG FOR A DATE!
WHY THROW YOURSELF AT HIM? MAKE HIM APPRECIATE A DATE WITH YOU! TURN HIM DOWN A COUPLE OF TIMES!
GEE! I THINK YOU'RE RIGHT, JUGGY!
HI, BETTY! HOW'S ABOUT TAKING IN A MOVIE, TO-NIGHT?
OH-H-H-H-H, ARCHIE! I'D LOVE TO!
THUMP! THUMP!
!COUGH!! AHEM!
2

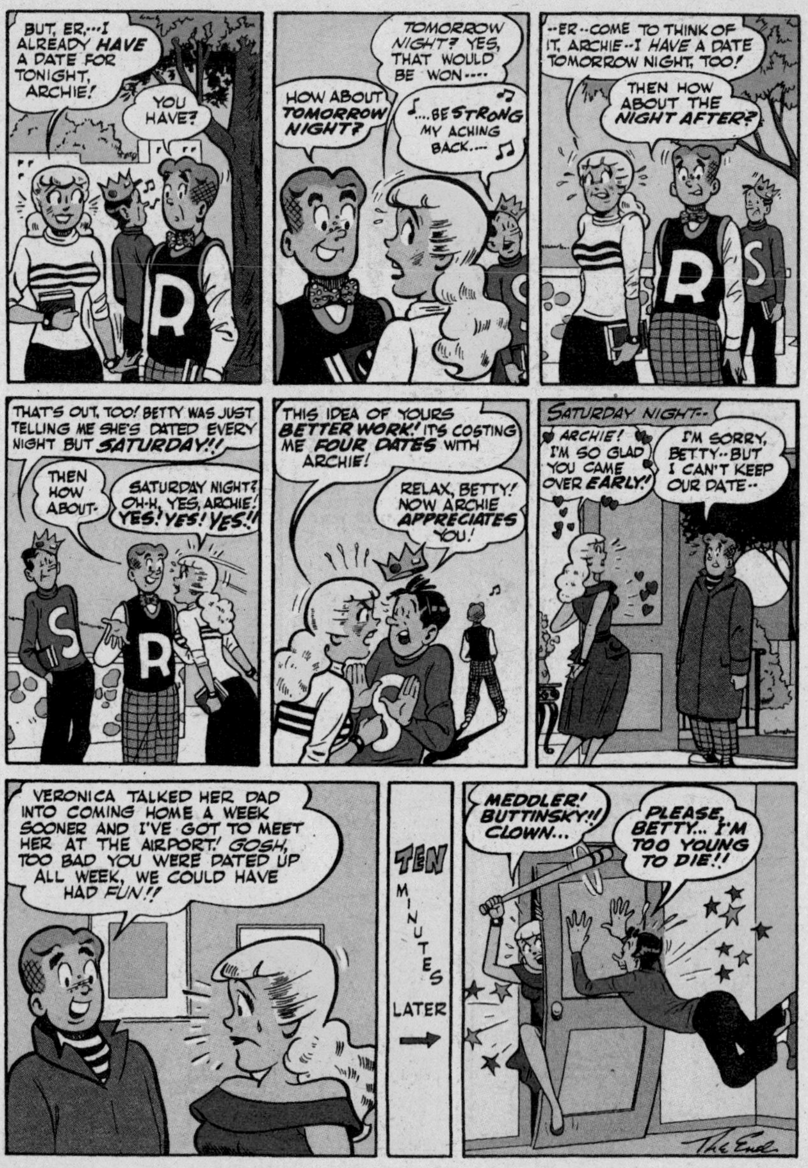
BUT, ER,--I ALREADY HAVE A DATE FOR TONIGHT, ARCHIE!
YOU HAVE?
HOW ABOUT TOMORROW NIGHT?
TOMORROW NIGHT? YES, THAT WOULD BE WON----
....BE STRONG MY ACHING BACK.---
--ER--COME TO THINK OF IT, ARCHIE--I HAVE A DATE TOMORROW NIGHT, TOO!
THEN HOW ABOUT THE NIGHT AFTER?
THAT'S OUT, TOO! BETTY WAS JUST TELLING ME SHE'S DATED EVERY NIGHT BUT SATURDAY!!
THEN HOW ABOUT-
SATURDAY NIGHT? OH-H, YES, ARCHIE! YES! YES! YES!!
THIS IDEA OF YOURS BETTER WORK! IT'S COSTING ME FOUR DATES WITH ARCHIE!
RELAX, BETTY! NOW ARCHIE APPRECIATES YOU!
SATURDAY NIGHT--
ARCHIE! I'M SO GLAD YOU CAME OVER EARLY!
I'M SORRY, BETTY--BUT I CAN'T KEEP OUR DATE--
VERONICA TALKED HER DAD INTO COMING HOME A WEEK SOONER AND I'VE GOT TO MEET HER AT THE AIRPORT! GOSH, TOO BAD YOU WERE DATED UP ALL WEEK, WE COULD HAVE HAD FUN!!
TEN MINUTES LATER
MEDDLER! BUTTINSKY!! CLOWN...
PLEASE, BETTY... I'M TOO YOUNG TO DIE!!
The End

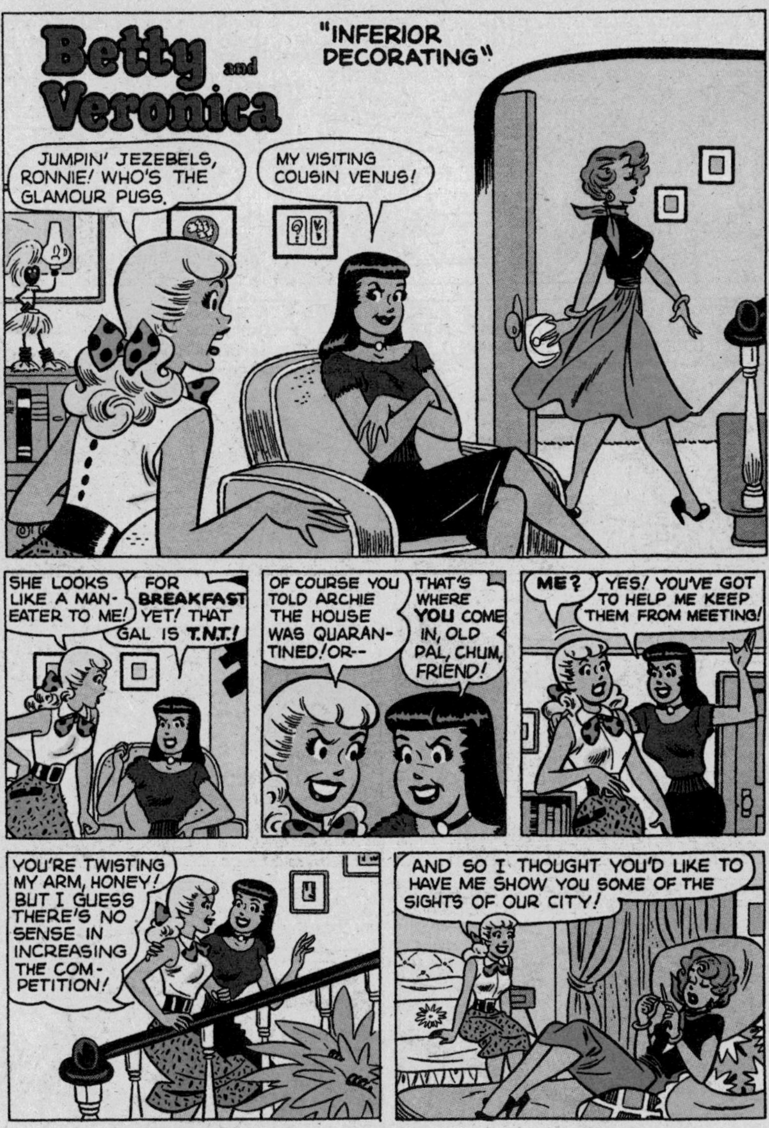
Betty and Veronica
"INFERIOR DECORATING"
JUMPIN' JEZEBELS, RONNIE! WHO'S THE GLAMOUR PUSS.
MY VISITING COUSIN VENUS!
SHE LOOKS LIKE A MAN-EATER TO ME!
FOR BREAKFAST YET! THAT GAL IS T.N.T.!
OF COURSE YOU TOLD ARCHIE THE HOUSE WAS QUARANTINED! OR--
THAT'S WHERE YOU COME IN, OLD PAL, CHUM, FRIEND!
ME?
YES! YOU'VE GOT TO HELP ME KEEP THEM FROM MEETING!
YOU'RE TWISTING MY ARM, HONEY! BUT I GUESS THERE'S NO SENSE IN INCREASING THE COMPETITION!
AND SO I THOUGHT YOU'D LIKE TO HAVE ME SHOW YOU SOME OF THE SIGHTS OF OUR CITY!

SCRIPT: *FRANK DOYLE*

PENCILS: *DAN DECARLO*

INKS: *RUDY LAPICK*

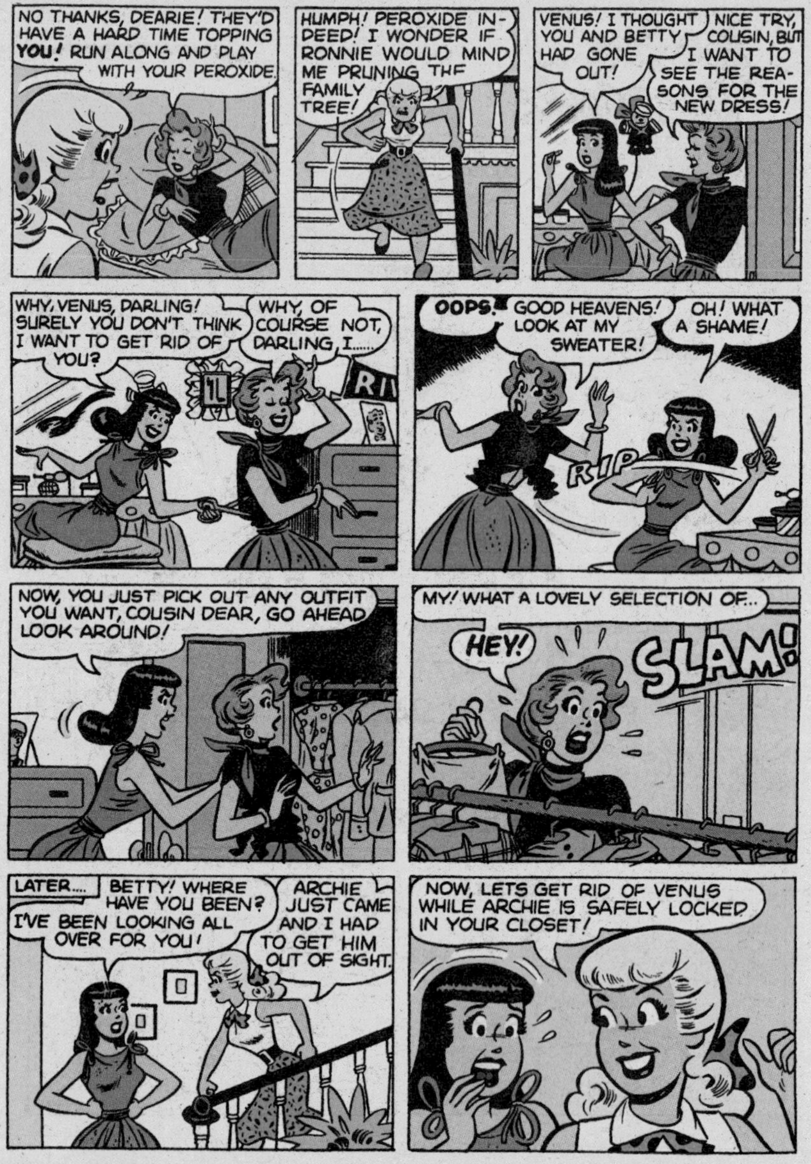
NO THANKS, DEARIE! THEY'D HAVE A HARD TIME TOPPING **YOU!** RUN ALONG AND PLAY WITH YOUR PEROXIDE.
HUMPH! PEROXIDE INDEED! I WONDER IF RONNIE WOULD MIND ME PRUNING THE FAMILY TREE!
VENUS! I THOUGHT YOU AND BETTY HAD GONE OUT!
NICE TRY, COUSIN, BUT I WANT TO SEE THE REASONS FOR THE NEW DRESS!
WHY, VENUS, DARLING! SURELY YOU DON'T THINK I WANT TO GET RID OF YOU?
WHY, OF COURSE NOT, DARLING, I......
OOPS.
GOOD HEAVENS! LOOK AT MY SWEATER!
OH! WHAT A SHAME!
RIP
NOW, YOU JUST PICK OUT ANY OUTFIT YOU WANT, COUSIN DEAR, GO AHEAD LOOK AROUND!
MY! WHAT A LOVELY SELECTION OF...
HEY!
SLAM!
LATER....
BETTY! WHERE HAVE YOU BEEN? I'VE BEEN LOOKING ALL OVER FOR YOU!
ARCHIE JUST CAME AND I HAD TO GET HIM OUT OF SIGHT.
NOW, LETS GET RID OF VENUS WHILE ARCHIE IS SAFELY LOCKED IN YOUR CLOSET!

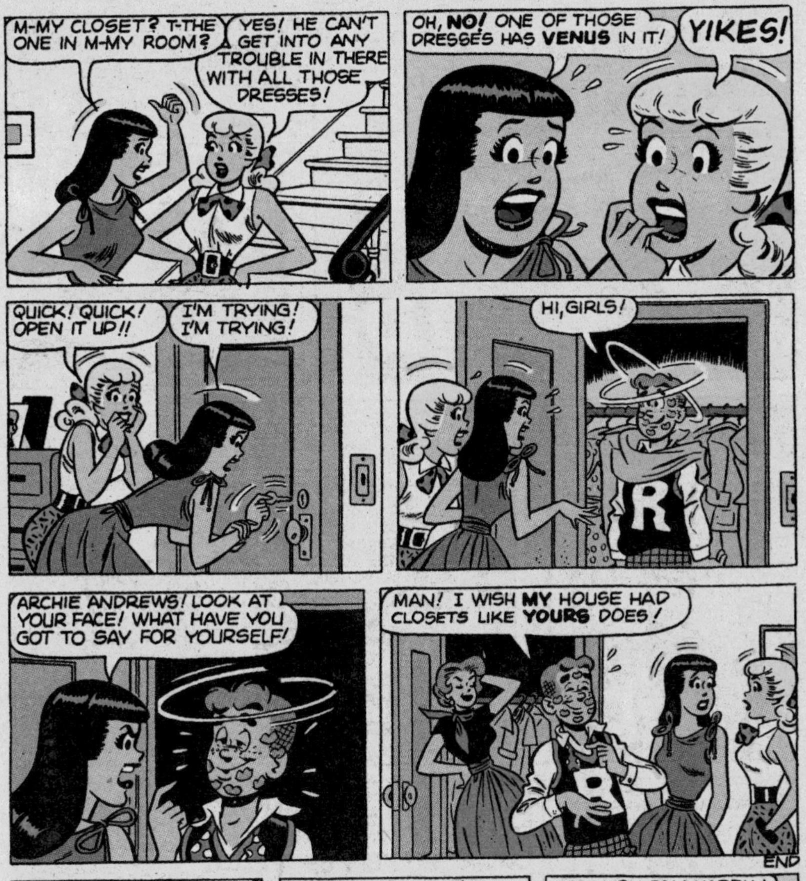
M-MY CLOSET? T-THE ONE IN M-MY ROOM?
YES! HE CAN'T GET INTO ANY TROUBLE IN THERE WITH ALL THOSE DRESSES!
OH, **NO!** ONE OF THOSE DRESSES HAS **VENUS** IN IT!
YIKES!
QUICK! QUICK! OPEN IT UP!!
I'M TRYING! I'M TRYING!
HI, GIRLS!
R
ARCHIE ANDREWS! LOOK AT YOUR FACE! WHAT HAVE YOU GOT TO SAY FOR YOURSELF!
MAN! I WISH **MY** HOUSE HAD CLOSETS LIKE **YOURS** DOES!
R
END

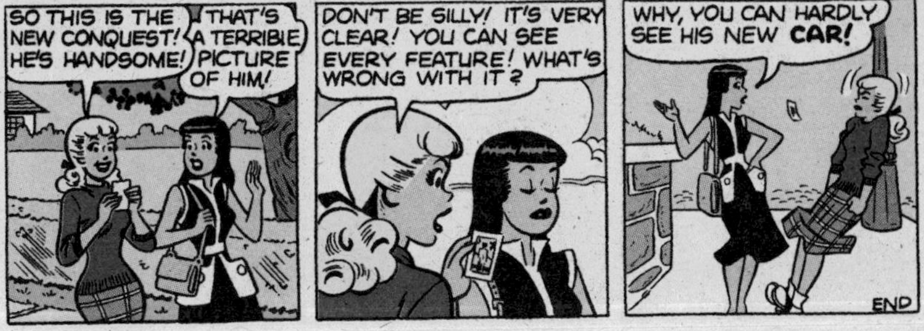
SO THIS IS THE NEW CONQUEST! HE'S HANDSOME!
THAT'S A TERRIBLE PICTURE OF HIM!
DON'T BE SILLY! IT'S VERY CLEAR! YOU CAN SEE EVERY FEATURE! WHAT'S WRONG WITH IT?
WHY, YOU CAN HARDLY SEE HIS NEW **CAR!**
END

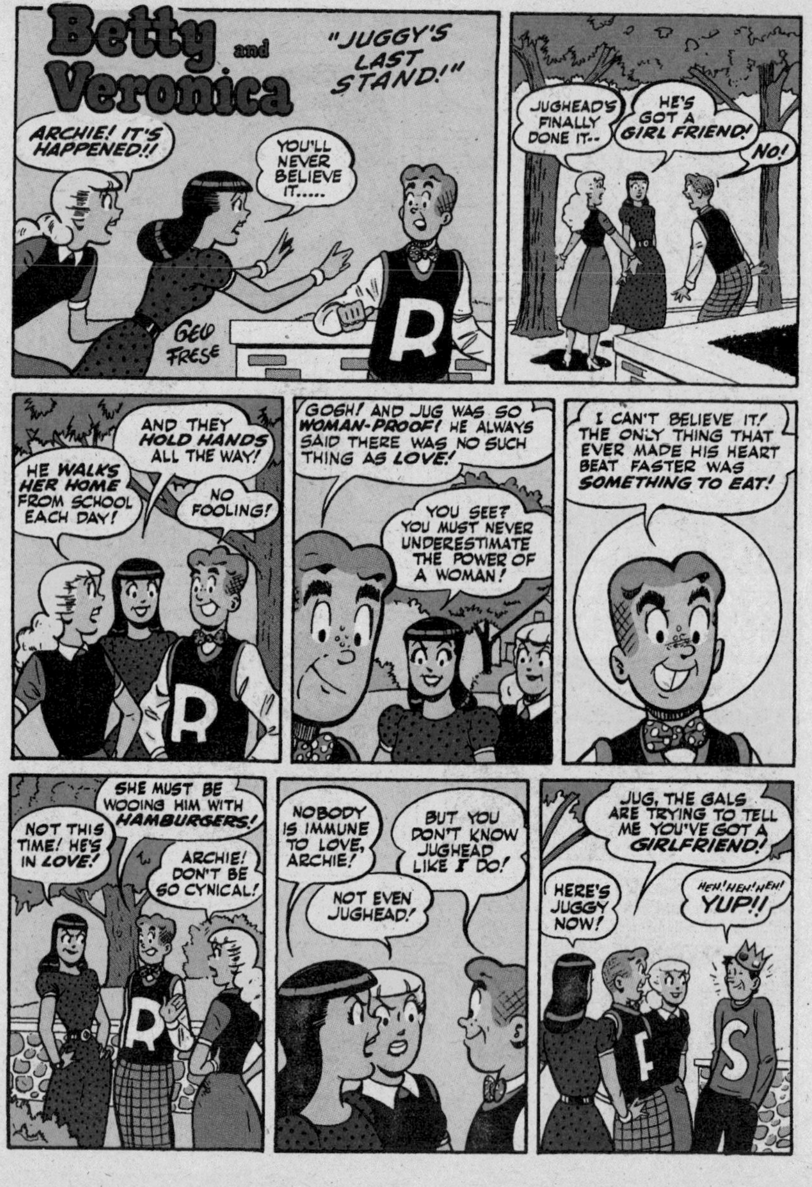
Betty and Veronica
"JUGGY'S LAST STAND!"
ARCHIE! IT'S HAPPENED!!
YOU'LL NEVER BELIEVE IT.....
GEO FRESE
JUGHEAD'S FINALLY DONE IT--
HE'S GOT A GIRL FRIEND!
NO!
HE WALKS HER HOME FROM SCHOOL EACH DAY!
AND THEY HOLD HANDS ALL THE WAY!
NO FOOLING!
GOSH! AND JUG WAS SO WOMAN-PROOF! HE ALWAYS SAID THERE WAS NO SUCH THING AS LOVE!
YOU SEE? YOU MUST NEVER UNDERESTIMATE THE POWER OF A WOMAN!
I CAN'T BELIEVE IT! THE ONLY THING THAT EVER MADE HIS HEART BEAT FASTER WAS SOMETHING TO EAT!
NOT THIS TIME! HE'S IN LOVE!
SHE MUST BE WOOING HIM WITH HAMBURGERS!
ARCHIE! DON'T BE SO CYNICAL!
NOBODY IS IMMUNE TO LOVE, ARCHIE!
NOT EVEN JUGHEAD!
BUT YOU DON'T KNOW JUGHEAD LIKE I DO!
JUG, THE GALS ARE TRYING TO TELL ME YOU'VE GOT A GIRLFRIEND!
HERE'S JUGGY NOW!
HEH! HEH! HEH!
YUP!!

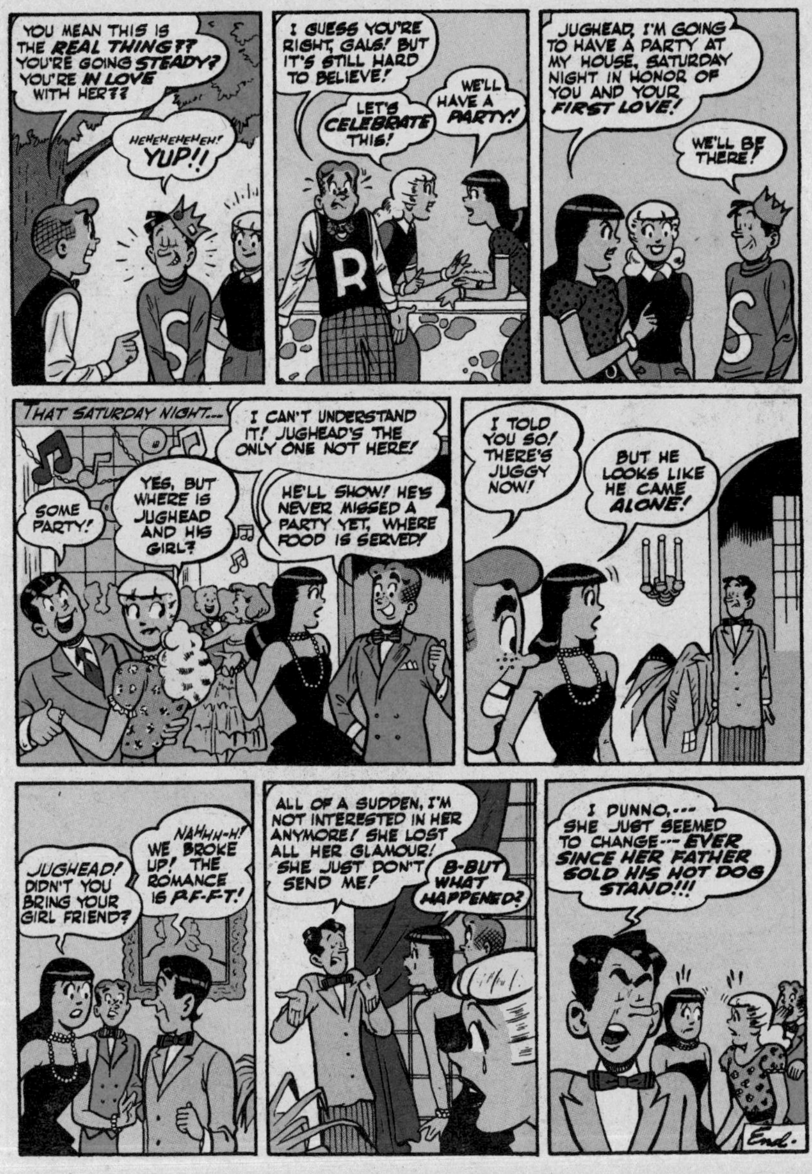
YOU MEAN THIS IS THE REAL THING?? YOU'RE GOING STEADY? YOU'RE IN LOVE WITH HER??
HEHEHEHEHEH! YUP!!
I GUESS YOU'RE RIGHT, GALS! BUT IT'S STILL HARD TO BELIEVE!
LET'S CELEBRATE THIS!
WE'LL HAVE A PARTY!
JUGHEAD, I'M GOING TO HAVE A PARTY AT MY HOUSE, SATURDAY NIGHT IN HONOR OF YOU AND YOUR FIRST LOVE!
WE'LL BE THERE!
THAT SATURDAY NIGHT...
I CAN'T UNDERSTAND IT! JUGHEAD'S THE ONLY ONE NOT HERE!
SOME PARTY!
YES, BUT WHERE IS JUGHEAD AND HIS GIRL?
HE'LL SHOW! HE'S NEVER MISSED A PARTY YET, WHERE FOOD IS SERVED!
I TOLD YOU SO! THERE'S JUGGY NOW!
BUT HE LOOKS LIKE HE CAME ALONE!
JUGHEAD! DIDN'T YOU BRING YOUR GIRL FRIEND?
NAHHH-H! WE BROKE UP! THE ROMANCE IS P-F-F-T!
ALL OF A SUDDEN, I'M NOT INTERESTED IN HER ANYMORE! SHE LOST ALL HER GLAMOUR! SHE JUST DON'T SEND ME!
B-BUT WHAT HAPPENED?
I DUNNO,... SHE JUST SEEMED TO CHANGE--- EVER SINCE HER FATHER SOLD HIS HOT DOG STAND!!!
End.

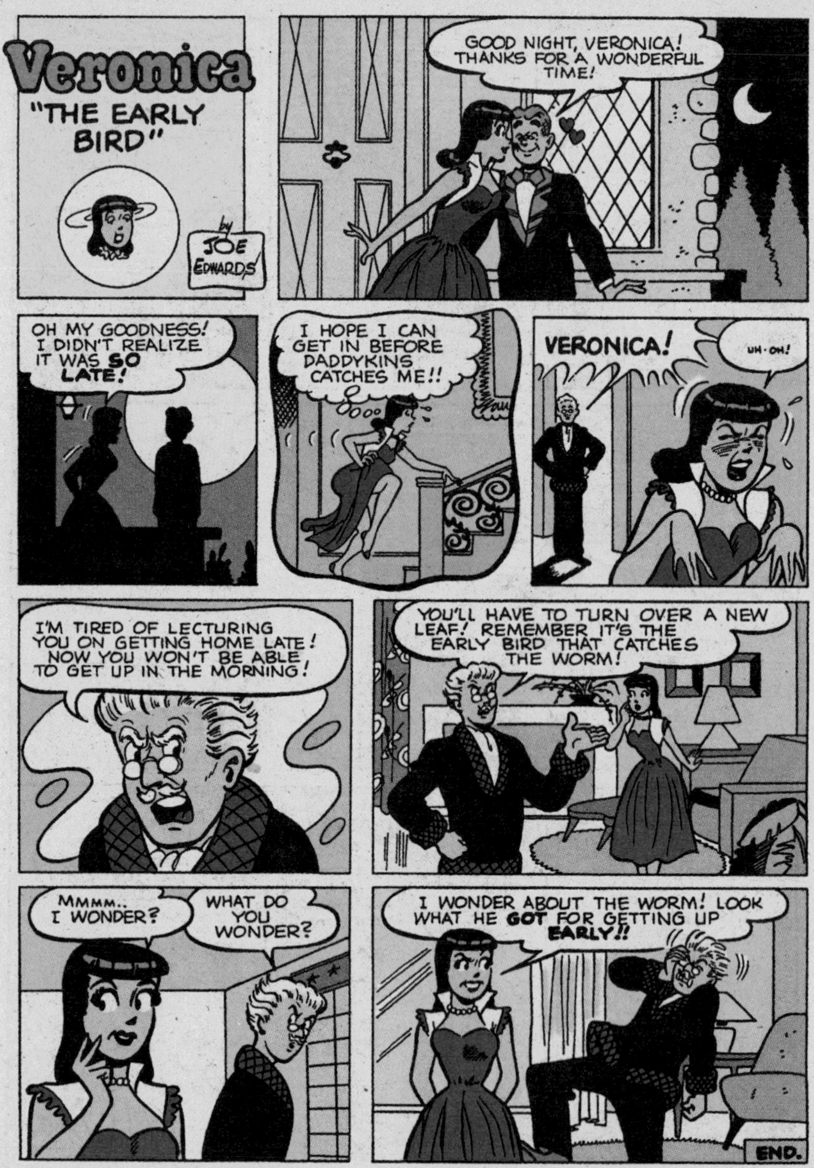
Veronica
"THE EARLY BIRD"
by JOE EDWARDS
GOOD NIGHT, VERONICA! THANKS FOR A WONDERFUL TIME!
OH MY GOODNESS! I DIDN'T REALIZE IT WAS SO LATE!
I HOPE I CAN GET IN BEFORE DADDYKINS CATCHES ME!!
VERONICA!
UH-OH!
I'M TIRED OF LECTURING YOU ON GETTING HOME LATE! NOW YOU WON'T BE ABLE TO GET UP IN THE MORNING!
YOU'LL HAVE TO TURN OVER A NEW LEAF! REMEMBER IT'S THE EARLY BIRD THAT CATCHES THE WORM!
MMMM.. I WONDER?
WHAT DO YOU WONDER?
I WONDER ABOUT THE WORM! LOOK WHAT HE GOT FOR GETTING UP EARLY!!
END.

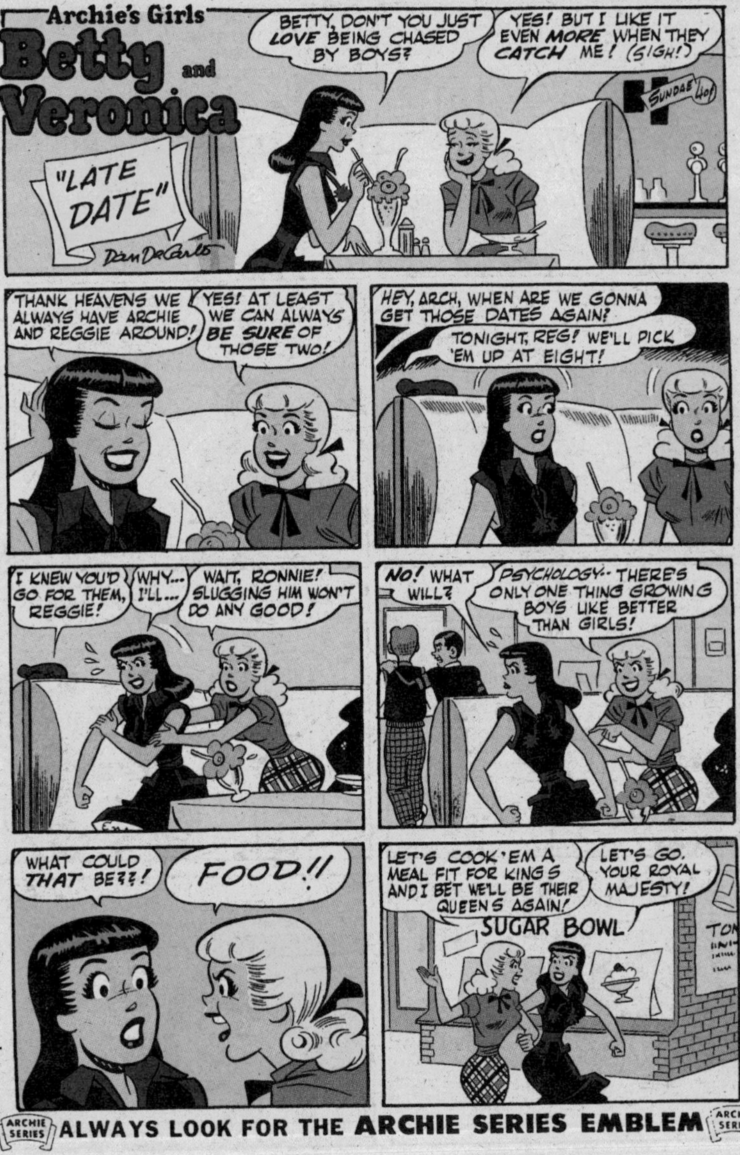

Archie's Girls Betty and Veronica
"LATE DATE"
Dan DeCarlo
BETTY, DON'T YOU JUST LOVE BEING CHASED BY BOYS?
YES! BUT I LIKE IT EVEN MORE WHEN THEY CATCH ME! (SIGH!)
SUNDAE 40¢
THANK HEAVENS WE ALWAYS HAVE ARCHIE AND REGGIE AROUND!
YES! AT LEAST WE CAN ALWAYS BE SURE OF THOSE TWO!
HEY, ARCH, WHEN ARE WE GONNA GET THOSE DATES AGAIN?
TONIGHT, REG! WE'LL PICK 'EM UP AT EIGHT!
I KNEW YOU'D GO FOR THEM, REGGIE!
WHY... I'LL...
WAIT, RONNIE! SLUGGING HIM WON'T DO ANY GOOD!
NO! WHAT WILL?
PSYCHOLOGY-- THERE'S ONLY ONE THING GROWING BOYS LIKE BETTER THAN GIRLS!
WHAT COULD THAT BE???!
FOOD!!
LET'S COOK 'EM A MEAL FIT FOR KINGS AND I BET WE'LL BE THEIR QUEENS AGAIN!
LET'S GO. YOUR ROYAL MAJESTY!
SUGAR BOWL

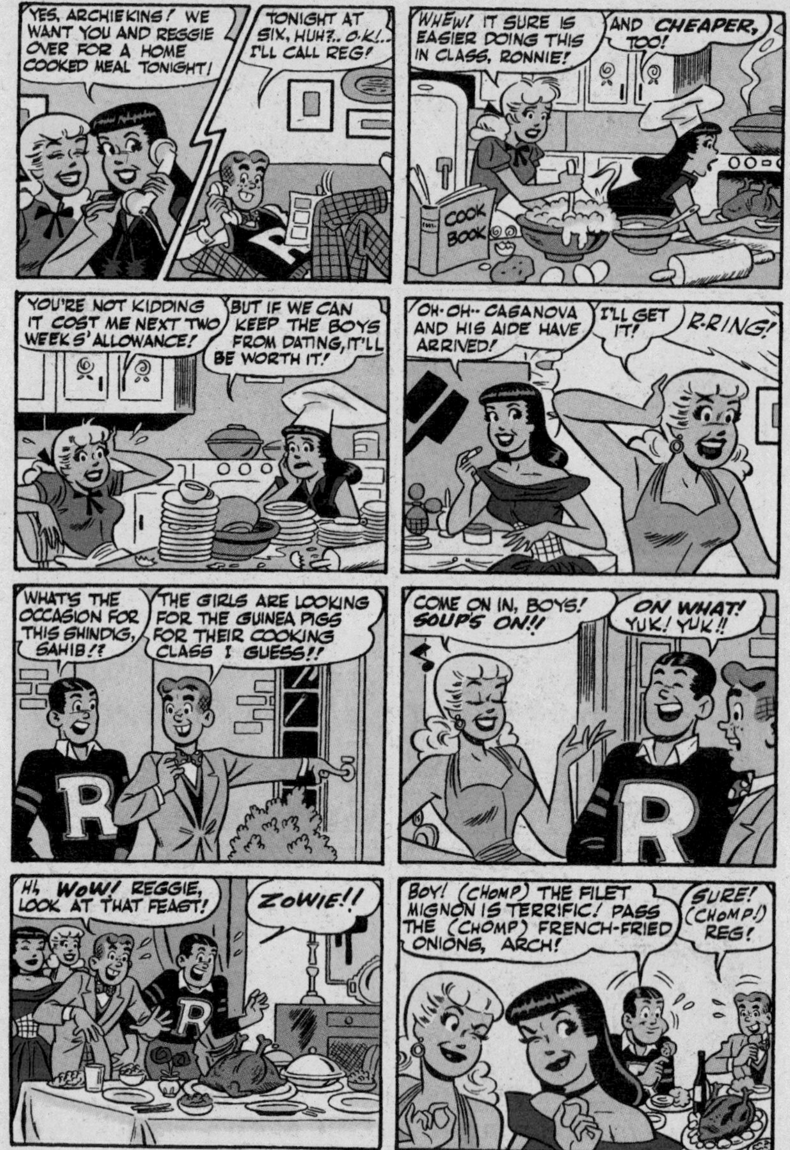
YES, ARCHIEKINS! WE WANT YOU AND REGGIE OVER FOR A HOME COOKED MEAL TONIGHT!
TONIGHT AT SIX, HUH?.. O.K!.. I'LL CALL REG!
WHEW! IT SURE IS EASIER DOING THIS IN CLASS, RONNIE!
AND CHEAPER, TOO!
COOK BOOK
YOU'RE NOT KIDDING IT COST ME NEXT TWO WEEKS' ALLOWANCE!
BUT IF WE CAN KEEP THE BOYS FROM DATING, IT'LL BE WORTH IT!
OH-OH-- CASANOVA AND HIS AIDE HAVE ARRIVED!
I'LL GET IT!
R-RING!
WHAT'S THE OCCASION FOR THIS SHINDIG, SAHIB!?
THE GIRLS ARE LOOKING FOR THE GUINEA PIGS FOR THEIR COOKING CLASS I GUESS!!
COME ON IN, BOYS! SOUP'S ON!!
ON WHAT! YUK! YUK!!
HI, WOW! REGGIE, LOOK AT THAT FEAST!
ZOWIE!!
BOY! (CHOMP) THE FILET MIGNON IS TERRIFIC! PASS THE (CHOMP) FRENCH-FRIED ONIONS, ARCH!
SURE! (CHOMP!) REG!

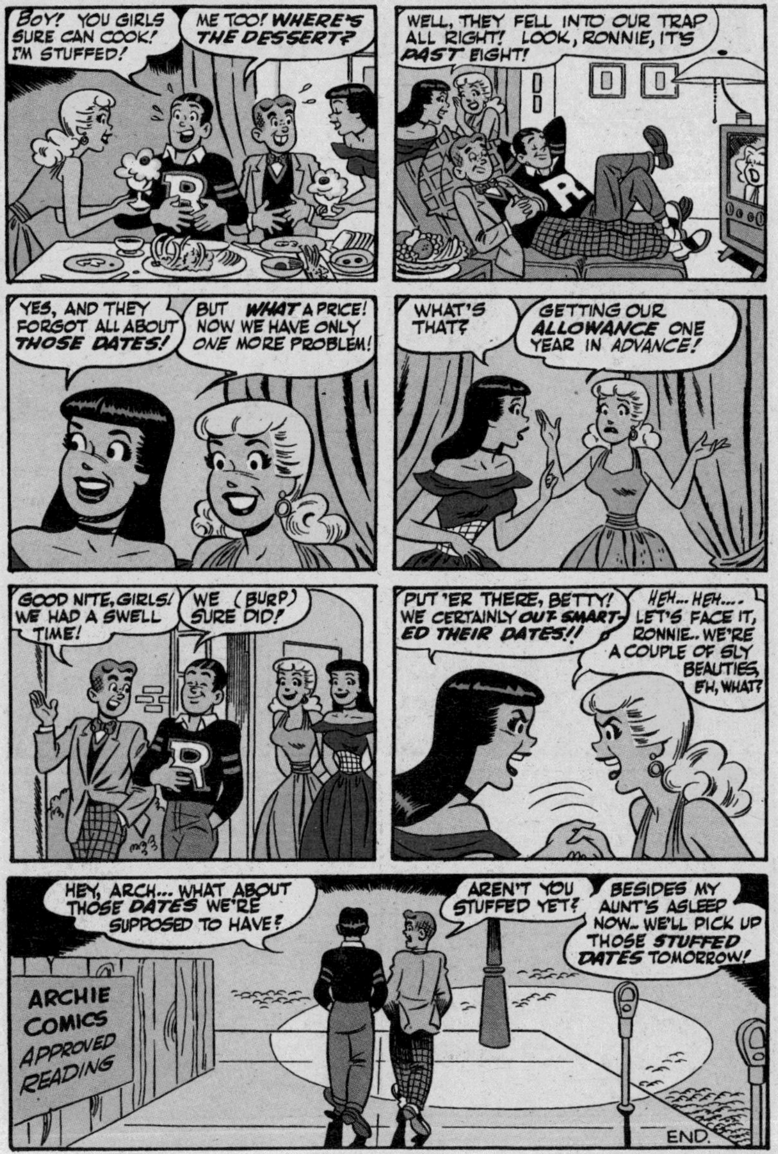

BOY! YOU GIRLS SURE CAN COOK! I'M STUFFED!
ME TOO! WHERE'S THE DESSERT?
WELL, THEY FELL INTO OUR TRAP ALL RIGHT! LOOK, RONNIE, IT'S PAST EIGHT!
YES, AND THEY FORGOT ALL ABOUT THOSE DATES!
BUT WHAT A PRICE! NOW WE HAVE ONLY ONE MORE PROBLEM!
WHAT'S THAT?
GETTING OUR ALLOWANCE ONE YEAR IN ADVANCE!
GOOD NITE, GIRLS! WE HAD A SWELL TIME!
WE (BURP) SURE DID!
PUT 'ER THERE, BETTY! WE CERTAINLY OUT-SMARTED THEIR DATES!!
HEH... HEH.... LET'S FACE IT, RONNIE.. WE'RE A COUPLE OF SLY BEAUTIES, EH, WHAT?
HEY, ARCH... WHAT ABOUT THOSE DATES WE'RE SUPPOSED TO HAVE?
AREN'T YOU STUFFED YET?
BESIDES MY AUNT'S ASLEEP NOW.. WE'LL PICK UP THOSE STUFFED DATES TOMORROW!
ARCHIE COMICS APPROVED READING
END.

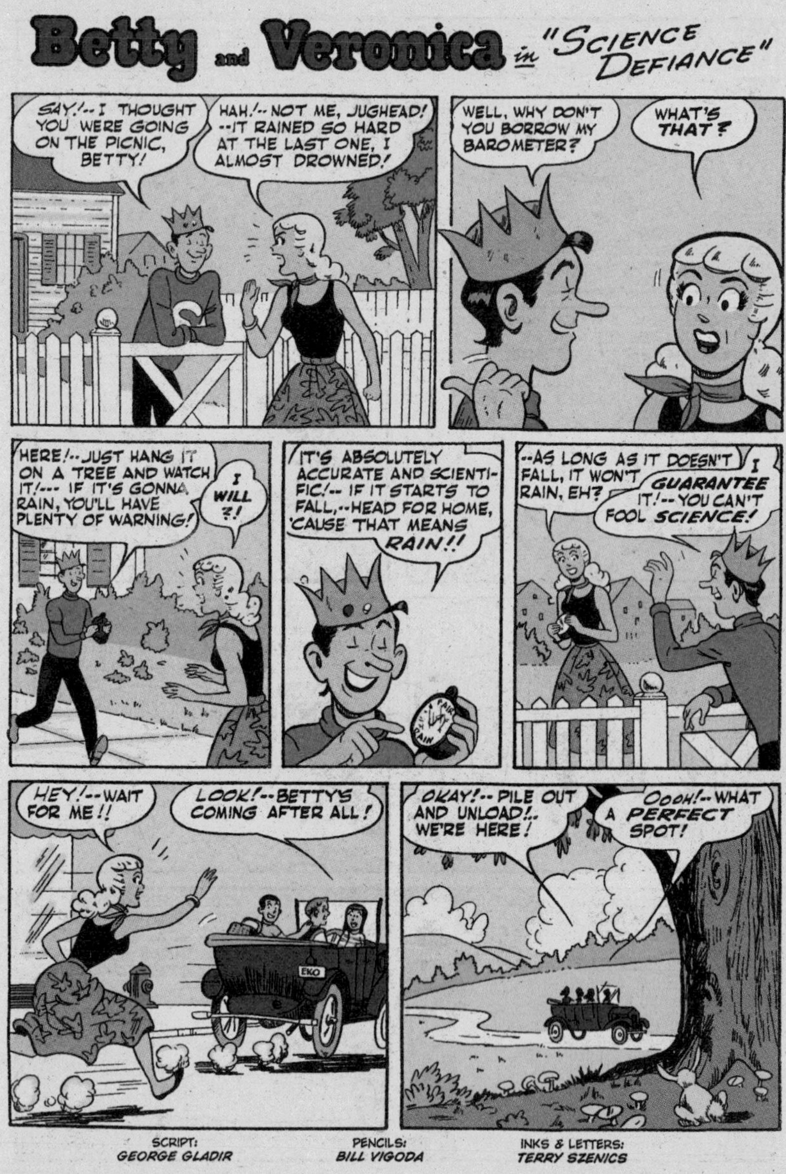
Betty and Veronica in "SCIENCE DEFIANCE"
SAY!--I THOUGHT YOU WERE GOING ON THE PICNIC, BETTY!
HAH!--NOT ME, JUGHEAD! --IT RAINED SO HARD AT THE LAST ONE, I ALMOST DROWNED!
WELL, WHY DON'T YOU BORROW MY BAROMETER?
WHAT'S THAT?
HERE!--JUST HANG IT ON A TREE AND WATCH IT!--- IF IT'S GONNA RAIN, YOU'LL HAVE PLENTY OF WARNING!
I WILL ?!
IT'S ABSOLUTELY ACCURATE AND SCIENTIFIC!-- IF IT STARTS TO FALL,--HEAD FOR HOME, 'CAUSE THAT MEANS RAIN!!
--AS LONG AS IT DOESN'T FALL, IT WON'T RAIN, EH?
I GUARANTEE IT!--YOU CAN'T FOOL SCIENCE!
HEY!--WAIT FOR ME!!
LOOK!--BETTY'S COMING AFTER ALL!
EKO
OKAY!--PILE OUT AND UNLOAD!.. WE'RE HERE!
Oooh!--WHAT A PERFECT SPOT!

SCRIPT: GEORGE GLADIR
PENCILS: BILL VIGODA
INKS & LETTERS: TERRY SZENICS

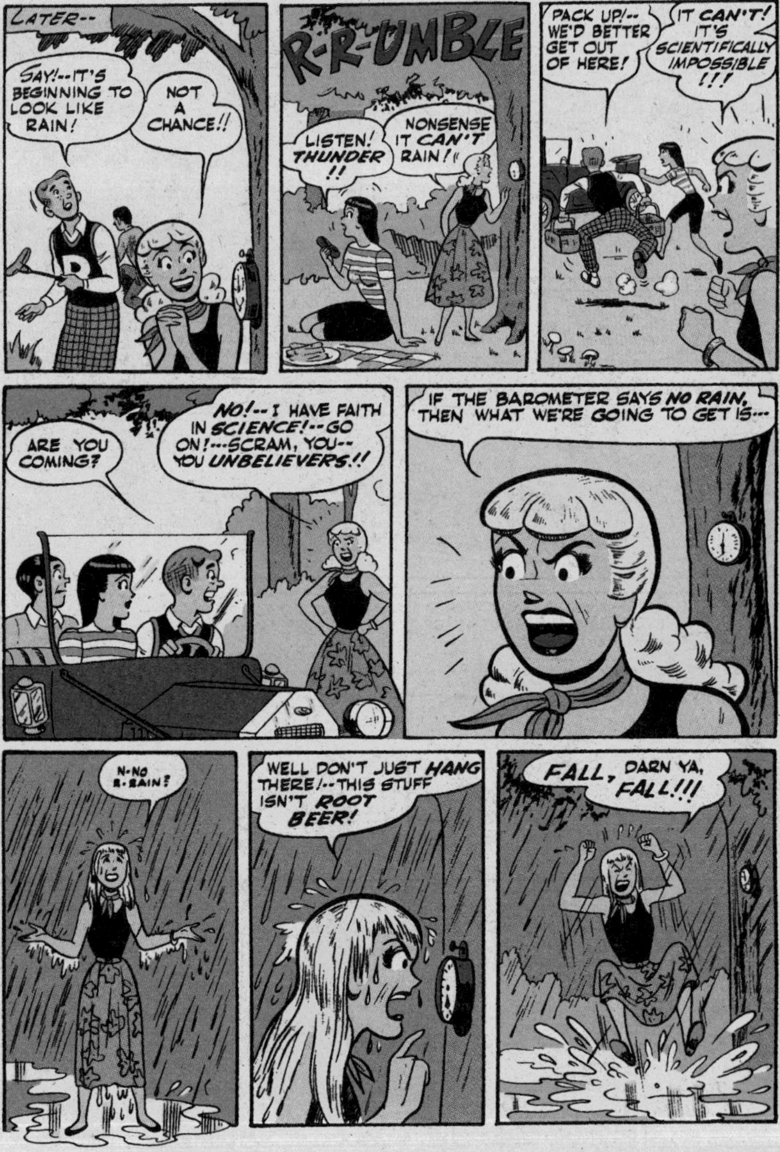
LATER--
SAY!--IT'S BEGINNING TO LOOK LIKE RAIN!
NOT A CHANCE!!
R-R-UMBLE
LISTEN! THUNDER!!
NONSENSE IT CAN'T RAIN!
PACK UP!-- WE'D BETTER GET OUT OF HERE!
IT CAN'T! IT'S SCIENTIFICALLY IMPOSSIBLE!!!
ARE YOU COMING?
NO!-- I HAVE FAITH IN SCIENCE!--GO ON!--SCRAM, YOU-- YOU UNBELIEVERS!!
IF THE BAROMETER SAYS NO RAIN, THEN WHAT WE'RE GOING TO GET IS---
N-NO R-RAIN?
WELL DON'T JUST HANG THERE!--THIS STUFF ISN'T ROOT BEER!
FALL, DARN YA, FALL!!!

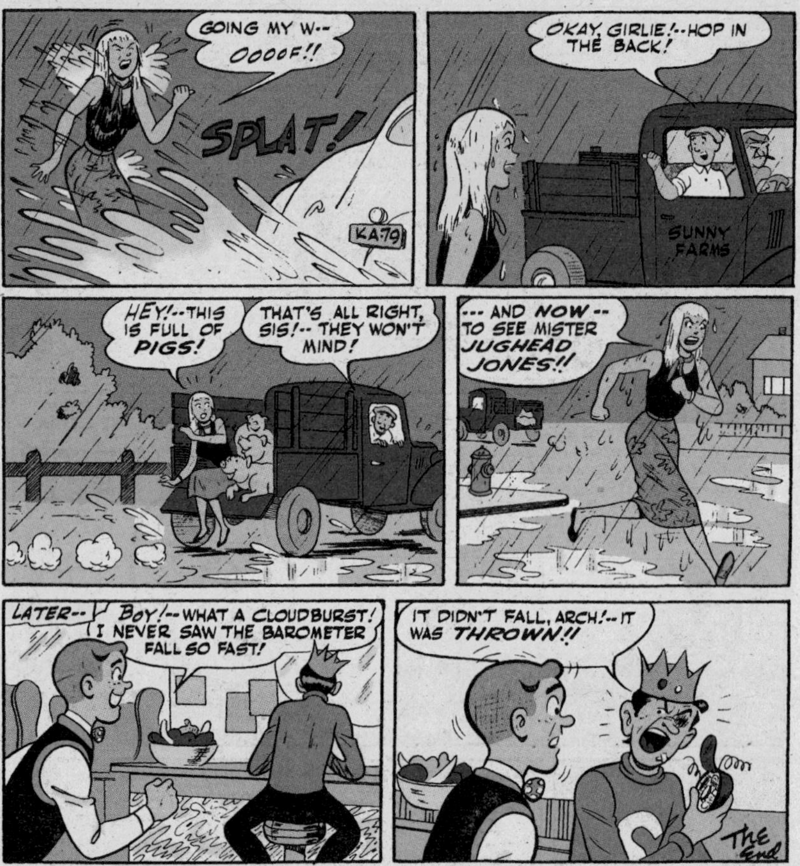
GOING MY W-- OOOOF!!
SPLAT!
KA-79
OKAY, GIRLIE!--HOP IN THE BACK!
SUNNY FARMS
HEY!--THIS IS FULL OF PIGS!
THAT'S ALL RIGHT, SIS!-- THEY WON'T MIND!
--- AND NOW -- TO SEE MISTER JUGHEAD JONES!!
LATER--
BOY!--WHAT A CLOUDBURST! I NEVER SAW THE BAROMETER FALL SO FAST!
IT DIDN'T FALL, ARCH!-- IT WAS THROWN!!
THE End

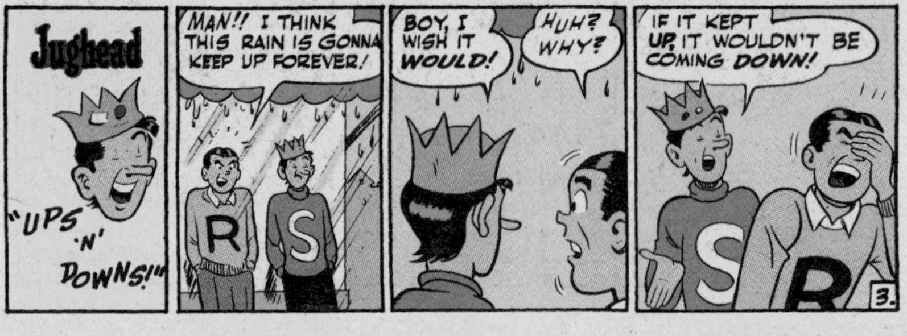
Jughead
"UPS 'N' DOWNS!"
MAN!! I THINK THIS RAIN IS GONNA KEEP UP FOREVER!
BOY, I WISH IT WOULD!
HUH? WHY?
IF IT KEPT UP, IT WOULDN'T BE COMING DOWN!
3.

Archie's Girls **Betty** and **Veronica** "LANGUAGE BARRIER"

BETTY! DID YOU HEAR? IT'S HAPPENING AGAIN!

YES! ISN'T IT TERRIBLE?

THE SAME OLD STORY! ARCHIE IS FAILING FRENCH AGAIN!

HMPH! THAT GUY COULDN'T PASS THE TIME OF DAY!

THE TROUBLE IS, THOSE GALS IN **ADVANCED** FRENCH WILL BE TRYING TO **TUTOR** HIM!

AND WHAT THEY'LL TUTOR, HE'S TOO **YOUNG** TO BE TAUGHTERED, -! I MEAN, TEACHED -ER- TO **LEARN**!!

I'LL SEE YOU LATER! I THINK I KNOW HOW ARCHIE CAN LEARN FRENCH - **SAFELY**!

HEE, HEE, NOW THAT **SHE'S** GONE, MAYBE I CAN PROTECT HIM FROM THOSE **OTHER** FEMMES!

WELL, THAT'S THAT! AND NOW TO STOP **BETTY** FROM TEACHING HIM ALL THE FRENCH THAT'S **NOT** IN THE BOOK!

SCRIPT:
GEORGE GLADIR

PENCILS, INKS & LETTERS:
SAMM SCHWARTZ

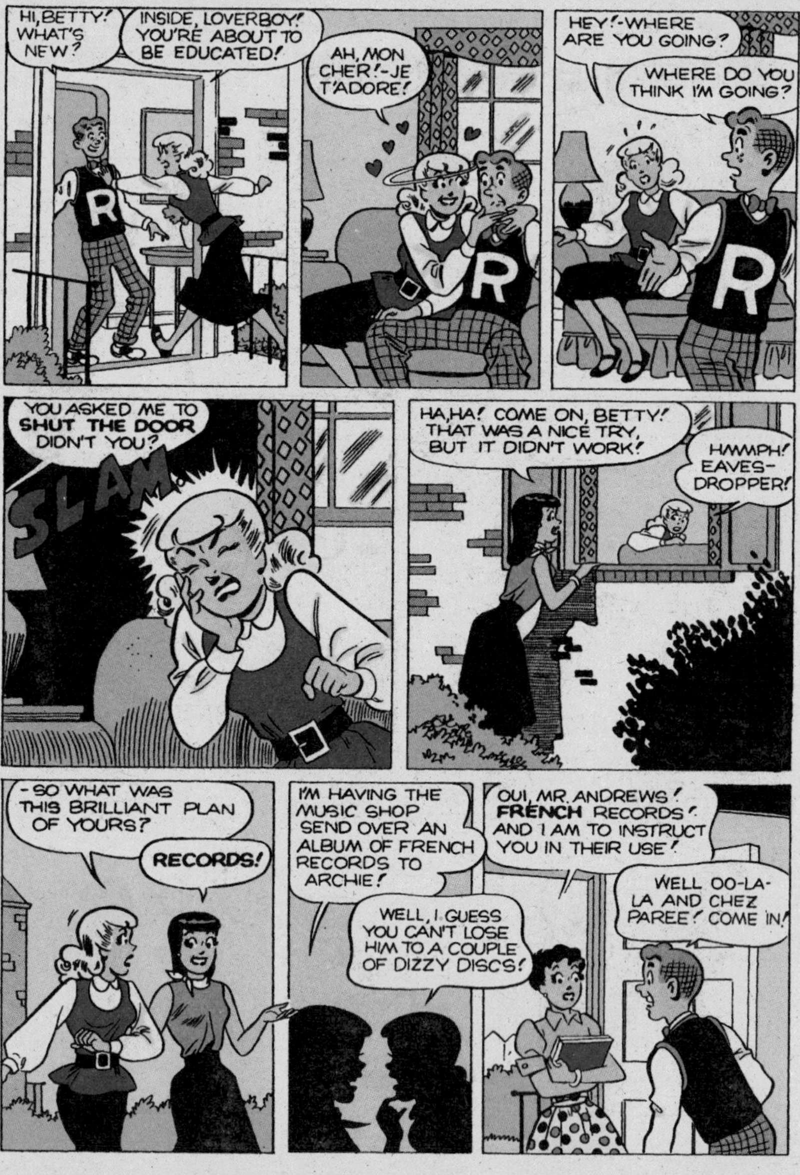
HI, BETTY! WHAT'S NEW?
INSIDE, LOVERBOY! YOU'RE ABOUT TO BE EDUCATED!
AH, MON CHER!-JE T'ADORE!
HEY!-WHERE ARE YOU GOING?
WHERE DO YOU THINK I'M GOING?
YOU ASKED ME TO SHUT THE DOOR DIDN'T YOU?
SLAM
HA,HA! COME ON, BETTY! THAT WAS A NICE TRY, BUT IT DIDN'T WORK!
HMMPH! EAVES-DROPPER!
-SO WHAT WAS THIS BRILLIANT PLAN OF YOURS?
RECORDS!
I'M HAVING THE MUSIC SHOP SEND OVER AN ALBUM OF FRENCH RECORDS TO ARCHIE!
WELL, I GUESS YOU CAN'T LOSE HIM TO A COUPLE OF DIZZY DISCS!
OUI, MR. ANDREWS! FRENCH RECORDS! AND I AM TO INSTRUCT YOU IN THEIR USE!
WELL OO-LA-LA AND CHEZ PAREE! COME IN!

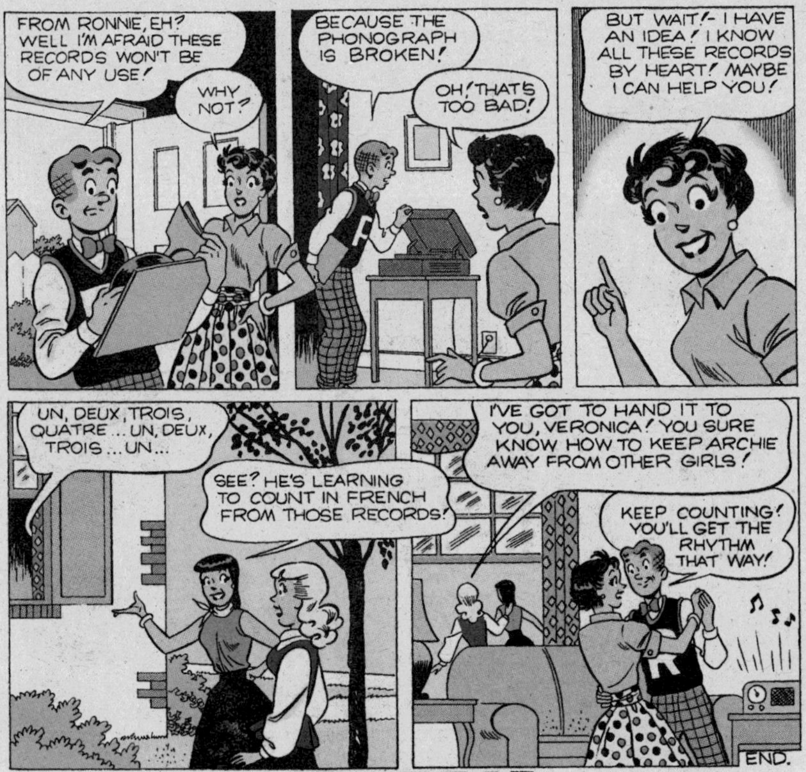
FROM RONNIE, EH? WELL I'M AFRAID THESE RECORDS WON'T BE OF ANY USE!
WHY NOT?
BECAUSE THE PHONOGRAPH IS BROKEN!
OH! THAT'S TOO BAD!
BUT WAIT!- I HAVE AN IDEA! I KNOW ALL THESE RECORDS BY HEART! MAYBE I CAN HELP YOU!
UN, DEUX, TROIS, QUATRE ... UN, DEUX, TROIS ... UN ...
SEE? HE'S LEARNING TO COUNT IN FRENCH FROM THOSE RECORDS!
I'VE GOT TO HAND IT TO YOU, VERONICA! YOU SURE KNOW HOW TO KEEP ARCHIE AWAY FROM OTHER GIRLS!
KEEP COUNTING! YOU'LL GET THE RHYTHM THAT WAY!
END.

REGGIE

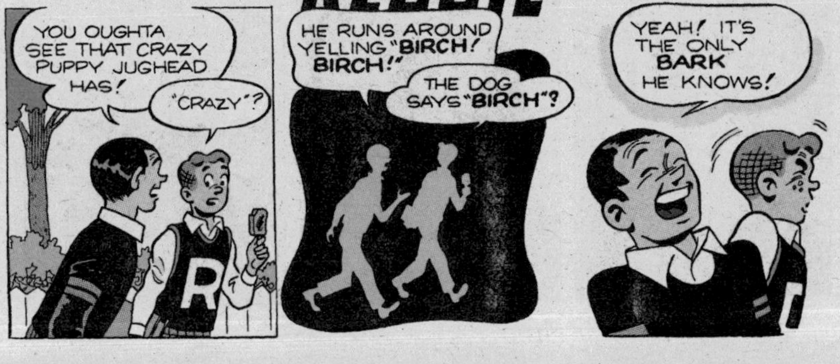
YOU OUGHTA SEE THAT CRAZY PUPPY JUGHEAD HAS!
"CRAZY"?
HE RUNS AROUND YELLING "BIRCH! BIRCH!"
THE DOG SAYS "BIRCH"?
YEAH! IT'S THE ONLY BARK HE KNOWS!

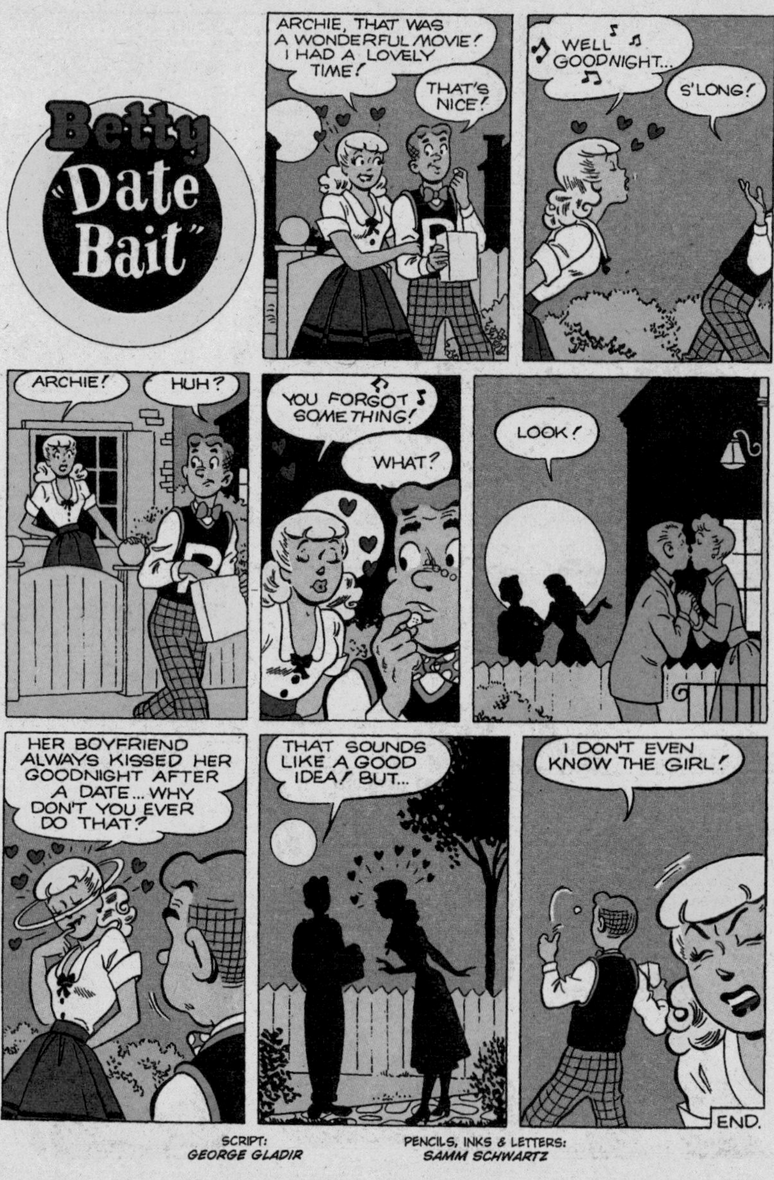
Betty
"Date Bait"
ARCHIE, THAT WAS A WONDERFUL MOVIE! I HAD A LOVELY TIME!
THAT'S NICE!
WELL GOODNIGHT...
S'LONG!
ARCHIE!
HUH?
YOU FORGOT SOMETHING!
WHAT?
LOOK!
HER BOYFRIEND ALWAYS KISSED HER GOODNIGHT AFTER A DATE... WHY DON'T YOU EVER DO THAT?
THAT SOUNDS LIKE A GOOD IDEA! BUT...
I DON'T EVEN KNOW THE GIRL!
END.

SCRIPT: GEORGE GLADIR

PENCILS, INKS & LETTERS: SAMM SCHWARTZ

Archie AND THE GANG in "SOUNDS CRAZY TO ME!"

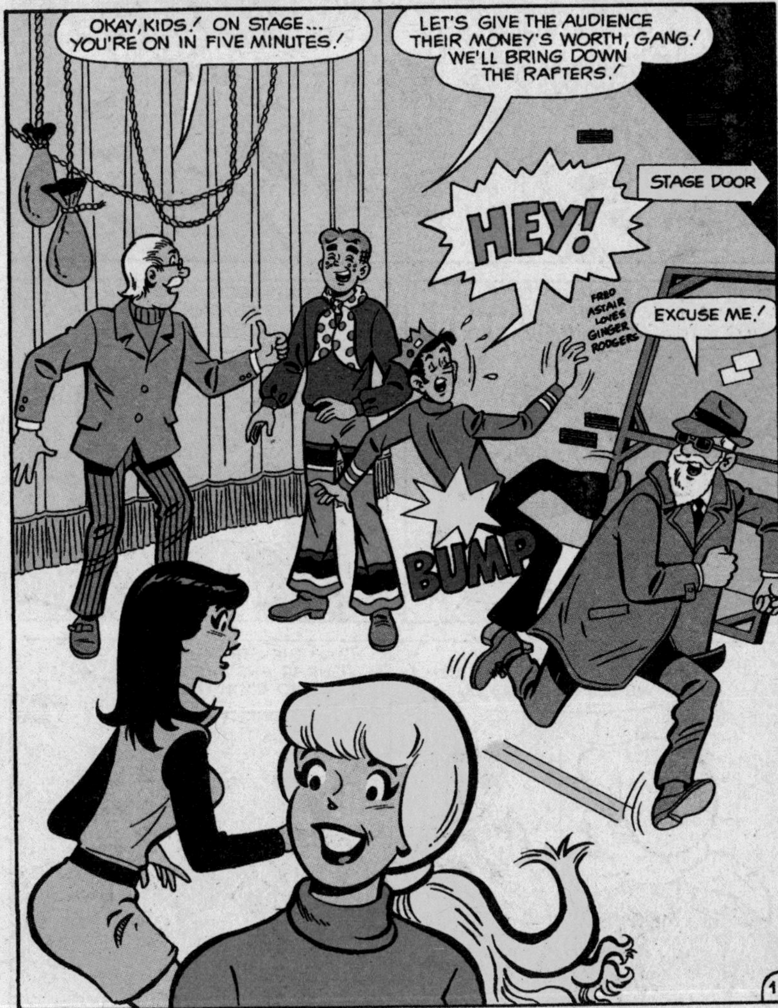
OKAY, KIDS! ON STAGE... YOU'RE ON IN FIVE MINUTES!
LET'S GIVE THE AUDIENCE THEIR MONEY'S WORTH, GANG! WE'LL BRING DOWN THE RAFTERS!
STAGE DOOR
HEY!
FRED ASTAIR LOVES GINGER RODGERS
EXCUSE ME!
BUMP
1

Script & Pencils: Gus LeMoine / Inks: Jon D'Agostino / Letters: Bill Yoshida / Colors: Barry Grossman

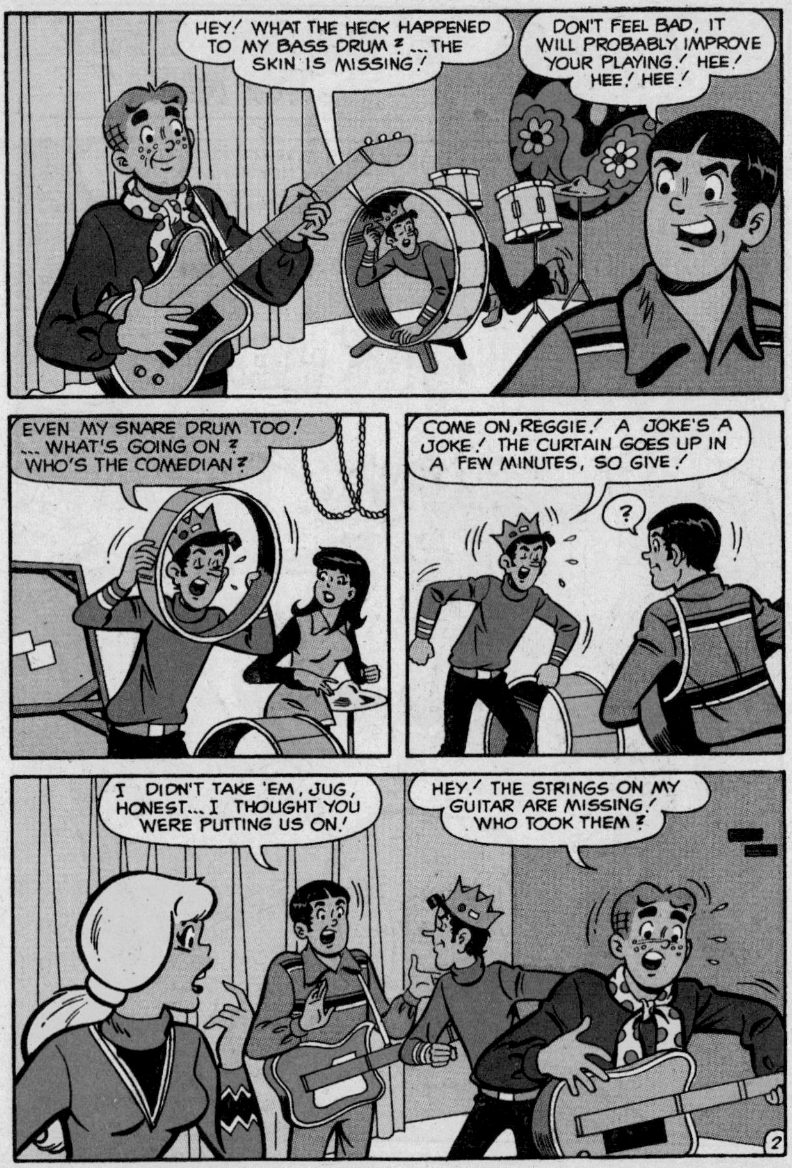
HEY! WHAT THE HECK HAPPENED TO MY BASS DRUM? ...THE SKIN IS MISSING!
DON'T FEEL BAD, IT WILL PROBABLY IMPROVE YOUR PLAYING! HEE! HEE! HEE!
EVEN MY SNARE DRUM TOO! ... WHAT'S GOING ON? WHO'S THE COMEDIAN?
COME ON, REGGIE! A JOKE'S A JOKE! THE CURTAIN GOES UP IN A FEW MINUTES, SO GIVE!
?
I DIDN'T TAKE 'EM, JUG, HONEST... I THOUGHT YOU WERE PUTTING US ON!
HEY! THE STRINGS ON MY GUITAR ARE MISSING! WHO TOOK THEM?
2

GASP! MINE TOO! SOMEBODY SWIPED MY STRINGS!

AND SOMEBODY HAS TAKEN THE REEDS OUT OF MY PIANO ORGAN!

THIS IS FLAKY!

FLAKY IS NOT THE WORD! LOOK AT MY TAMBOURINE! IT'S OUT OF SIGHT! THE ONLY THING LEFT IS THE FRAME!

WHAT GIVES?

I DON'T KNOW — BUT THE CROWD IS WAITING AND WE HAVE TO MAKE THE SCENE!

THERE'S ONLY ONE THING WE CAN DO IN A SITUATION LIKE THIS, REGGIE, GO TELL THE CROWD THERE WILL BE A SLIGHT DELAY!

WHAT ARE YOU GOING TO DO, ARCHIE?

CALL JOSIE AND THE PUSSYCATS!

3

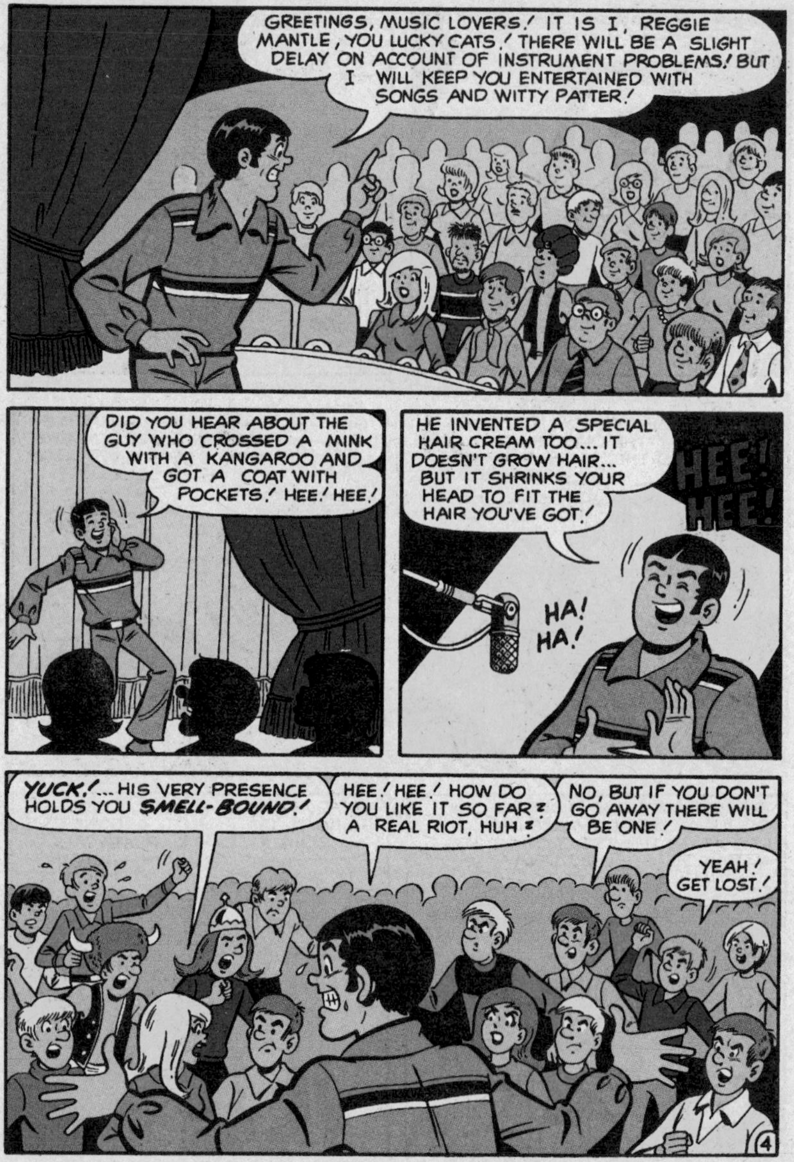
GREETINGS, MUSIC LOVERS! IT IS I, REGGIE MANTLE, YOU LUCKY CATS! THERE WILL BE A SLIGHT DELAY ON ACCOUNT OF INSTRUMENT PROBLEMS! BUT I WILL KEEP YOU ENTERTAINED WITH SONGS AND WITTY PATTER!
DID YOU HEAR ABOUT THE GUY WHO CROSSED A MINK WITH A KANGAROO AND GOT A COAT WITH POCKETS! HEE! HEE!
HE INVENTED A SPECIAL HAIR CREAM TOO... IT DOESN'T GROW HAIR... BUT IT SHRINKS YOUR HEAD TO FIT THE HAIR YOU'VE GOT!
HEE! HEE!
HA! HA!
YUCK!... HIS VERY PRESENCE HOLDS YOU SMELL-BOUND!
HEE! HEE! HOW DO YOU LIKE IT SO FAR? A REAL RIOT, HUH?
NO, BUT IF YOU DON'T GO AWAY THERE WILL BE ONE!
YEAH! GET LOST!
4

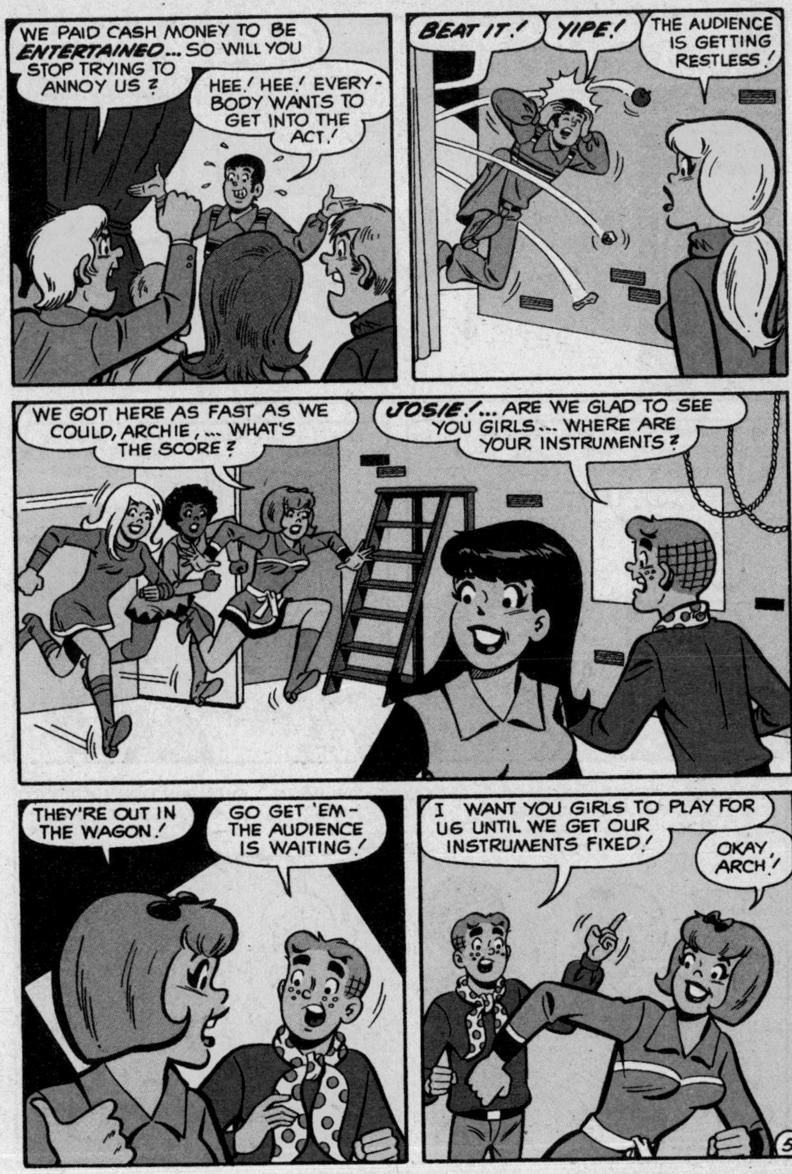
WE PAID CASH MONEY TO BE ENTERTAINED... SO WILL YOU STOP TRYING TO ANNOY US ?
HEE! HEE! EVERYBODY WANTS TO GET INTO THE ACT!
BEAT IT!
YIPE!
THE AUDIENCE IS GETTING RESTLESS!
WE GOT HERE AS FAST AS WE COULD, ARCHIE, ... WHAT'S THE SCORE ?
JOSIE!... ARE WE GLAD TO SEE YOU GIRLS... WHERE ARE YOUR INSTRUMENTS ?
THEY'RE OUT IN THE WAGON!
GO GET 'EM - THE AUDIENCE IS WAITING!
I WANT YOU GIRLS TO PLAY FOR US UNTIL WE GET OUR INSTRUMENTS FIXED!
OKAY ARCH!
5

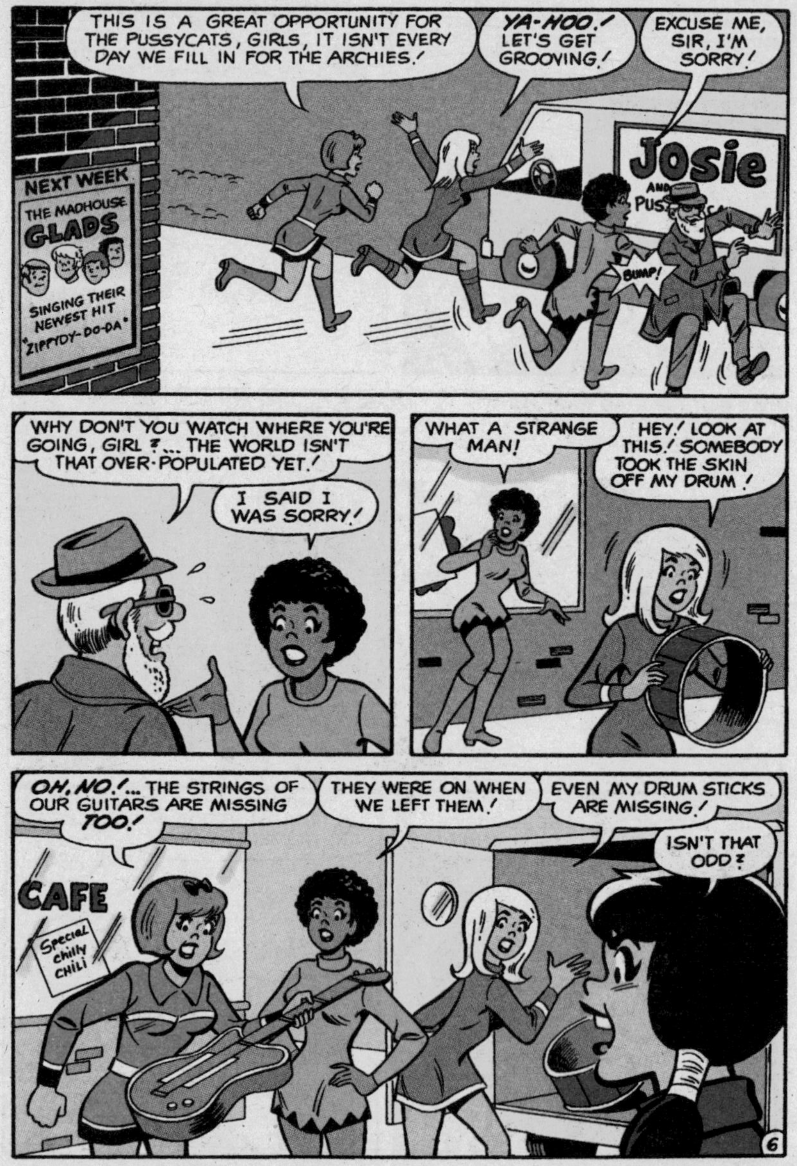
NEXT WEEK
THE MADHOUSE GLADS
SINGING THEIR NEWEST HIT "ZIPPYDY-DO-DA"
THIS IS A GREAT OPPORTUNITY FOR THE PUSSYCATS, GIRLS, IT ISN'T EVERY DAY WE FILL IN FOR THE ARCHIES.!
YA-HOO.! LET'S GET GROOVING.!
EXCUSE ME, SIR, I'M SORRY.!
Josie
BUMP!
WHY DON'T YOU WATCH WHERE YOU'RE GOING, GIRL?... THE WORLD ISN'T THAT OVER-POPULATED YET.!
I SAID I WAS SORRY.!
WHAT A STRANGE MAN!
HEY.! LOOK AT THIS.! SOMEBODY TOOK THE SKIN OFF MY DRUM.!
OH, NO.!... THE STRINGS OF OUR GUITARS ARE MISSING TOO!
CAFE
Special chilly CHILI
THEY WERE ON WHEN WE LEFT THEM.!
EVEN MY DRUM STICKS ARE MISSING.!
ISN'T THAT ODD?

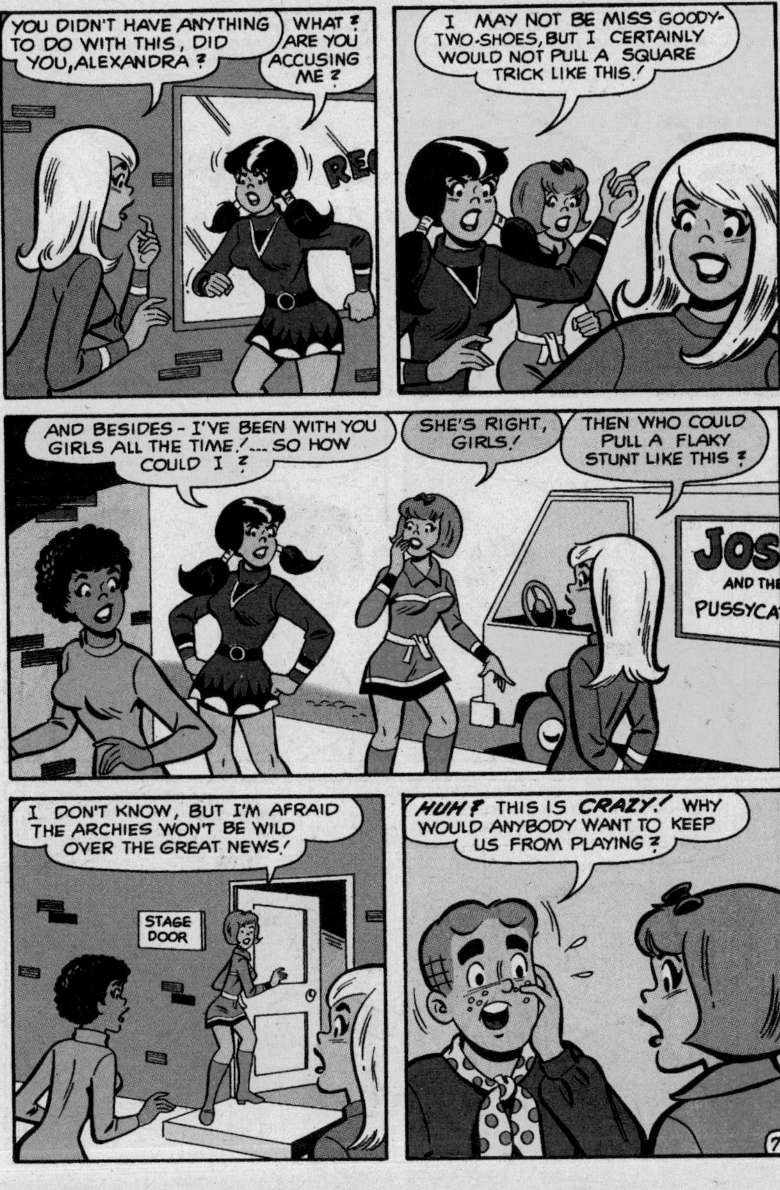
YOU DIDN'T HAVE ANYTHING TO DO WITH THIS, DID YOU, ALEXANDRA?
WHAT? ARE YOU ACCUSING ME?
I MAY NOT BE MISS GOODY-TWO-SHOES, BUT I CERTAINLY WOULD NOT PULL A SQUARE TRICK LIKE THIS!
AND BESIDES - I'VE BEEN WITH YOU GIRLS ALL THE TIME!... SO HOW COULD I?
SHE'S RIGHT, GIRLS!
THEN WHO COULD PULL A FLAKY STUNT LIKE THIS?
I DON'T KNOW, BUT I'M AFRAID THE ARCHIES WON'T BE WILD OVER THE GREAT NEWS!
STAGE DOOR
HUH? THIS IS CRAZY! WHY WOULD ANYBODY WANT TO KEEP US FROM PLAYING?
7

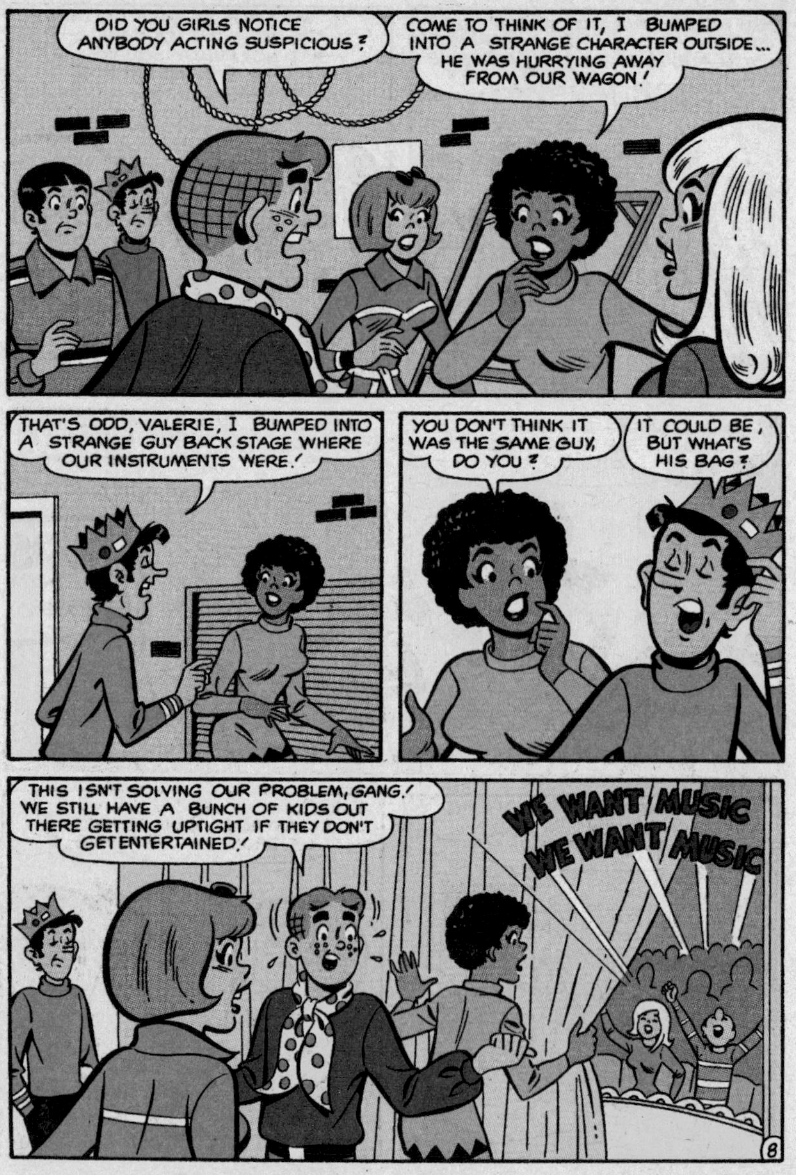
DID YOU GIRLS NOTICE ANYBODY ACTING SUSPICIOUS ?
COME TO THINK OF IT, I BUMPED INTO A STRANGE CHARACTER OUTSIDE... HE WAS HURRYING AWAY FROM OUR WAGON!
THAT'S ODD, VALERIE, I BUMPED INTO A STRANGE GUY BACK STAGE WHERE OUR INSTRUMENTS WERE!
YOU DON'T THINK IT WAS THE SAME GUY, DO YOU ?
IT COULD BE, BUT WHAT'S HIS BAG ?
THIS ISN'T SOLVING OUR PROBLEM, GANG! WE STILL HAVE A BUNCH OF KIDS OUT THERE GETTING UPTIGHT IF THEY DON'T GET ENTERTAINED!
WE WANT MUSIC
WE WANT MUSIC
8

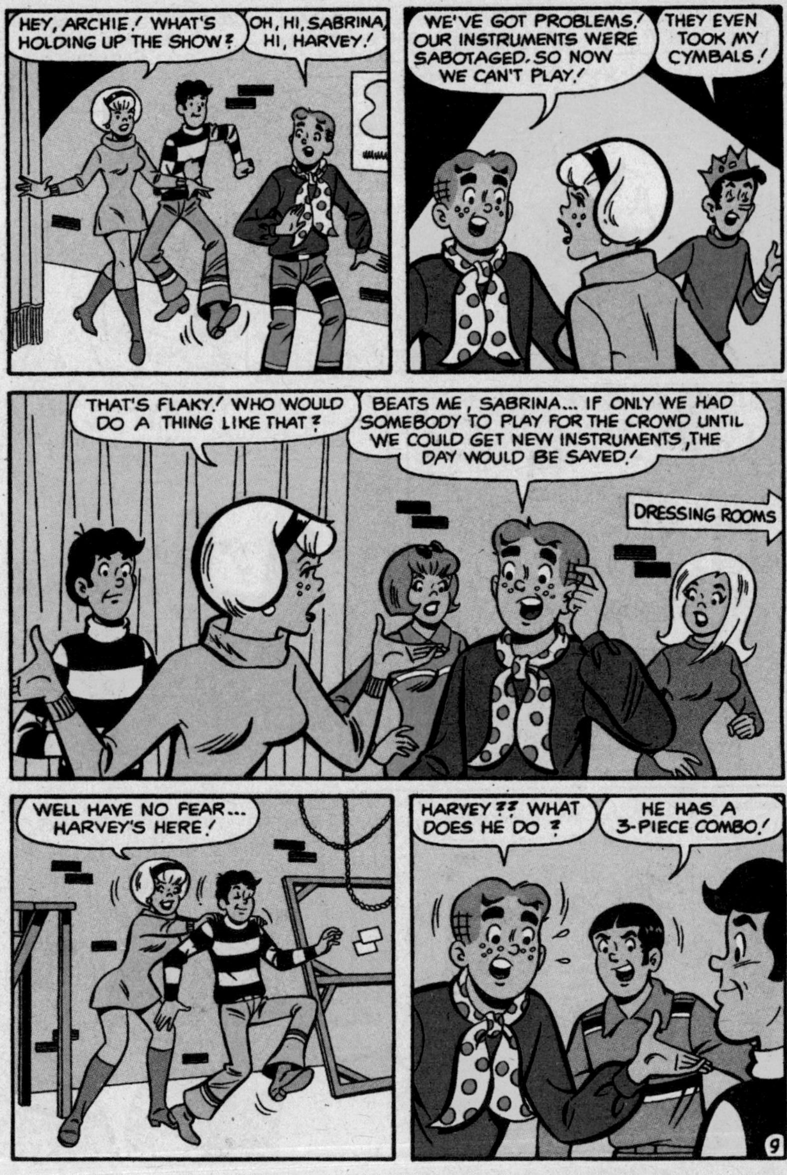
HEY, ARCHIE! WHAT'S HOLDING UP THE SHOW?
OH, HI, SABRINA, HI, HARVEY!
WE'VE GOT PROBLEMS! OUR INSTRUMENTS WERE SABOTAGED. SO NOW WE CAN'T PLAY!
THEY EVEN TOOK MY CYMBALS!
THAT'S FLAKY! WHO WOULD DO A THING LIKE THAT?
BEATS ME, SABRINA... IF ONLY WE HAD SOMEBODY TO PLAY FOR THE CROWD UNTIL WE COULD GET NEW INSTRUMENTS, THE DAY WOULD BE SAVED!
DRESSING ROOMS
WELL HAVE NO FEAR... HARVEY'S HERE!
HARVEY?? WHAT DOES HE DO?
HE HAS A 3-PIECE COMBO!
9

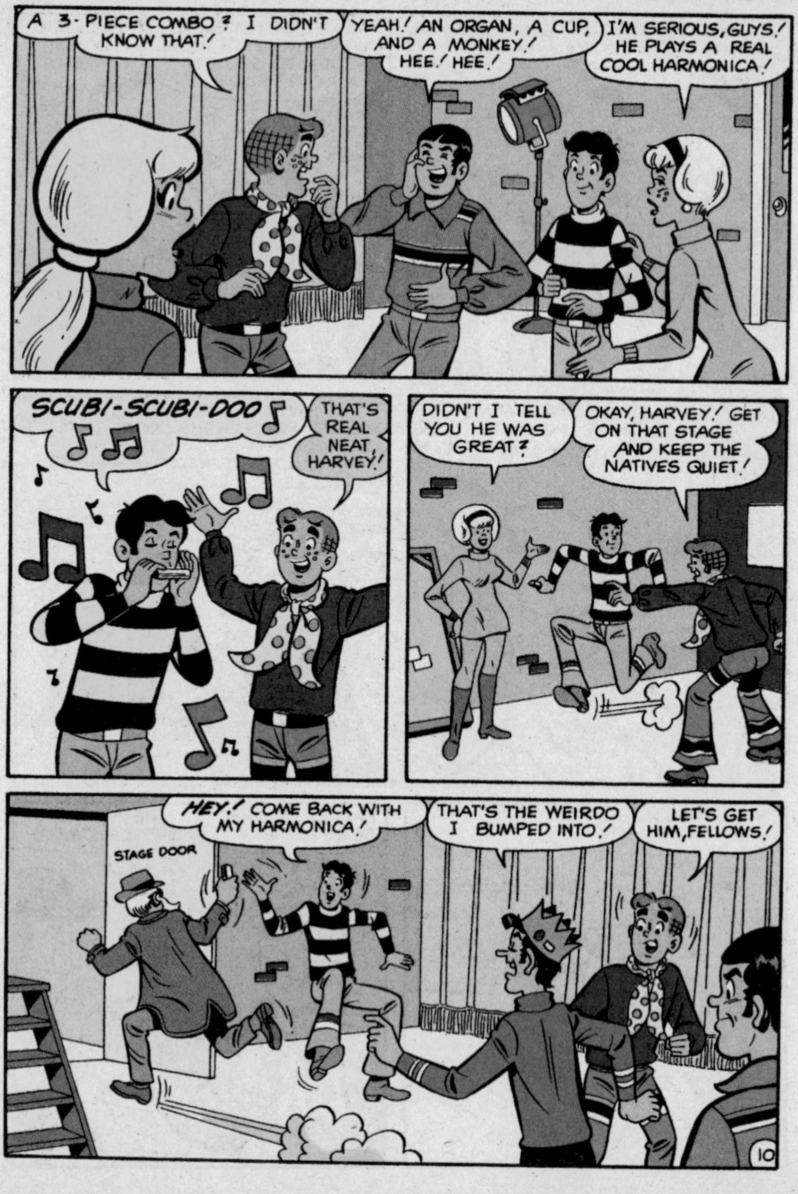
A 3-PIECE COMBO? I DIDN'T KNOW THAT!
YEAH! AN ORGAN, A CUP, AND A MONKEY! HEE! HEE!
I'M SERIOUS, GUYS! HE PLAYS A REAL COOL HARMONICA!
SCUBI-SCUBI-DOO
THAT'S REAL NEAT, HARVEY!
DIDN'T I TELL YOU HE WAS GREAT?
OKAY, HARVEY! GET ON THAT STAGE AND KEEP THE NATIVES QUIET!
STAGE DOOR
HEY! COME BACK WITH MY HARMONICA!
THAT'S THE WEIRDO I BUMPED INTO!
LET'S GET HIM, FELLOWS!
10

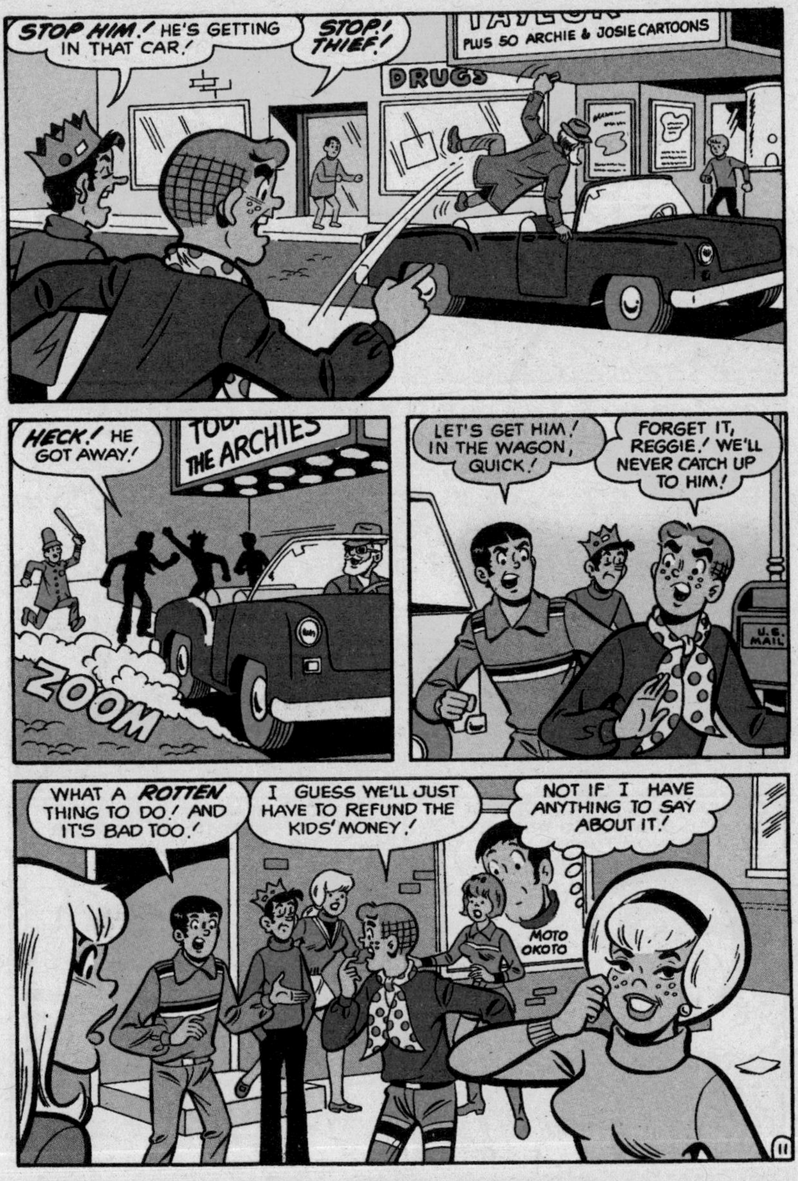

PLUS 50 ARCHIE & JOSIE CARTOONS
DRUGS
STOP HIM! HE'S GETTING IN THAT CAR!
STOP! THIEF!
THE ARCHIES
HECK! HE GOT AWAY!
ZOOM
LET'S GET HIM! IN THE WAGON, QUICK!
FORGET IT, REGGIE! WE'LL NEVER CATCH UP TO HIM!
U.S. MAIL
WHAT A ROTTEN THING TO DO! AND IT'S BAD TOO!
I GUESS WE'LL JUST HAVE TO REFUND THE KIDS' MONEY!
NOT IF I HAVE ANYTHING TO SAY ABOUT IT!
MOTO OKOTO

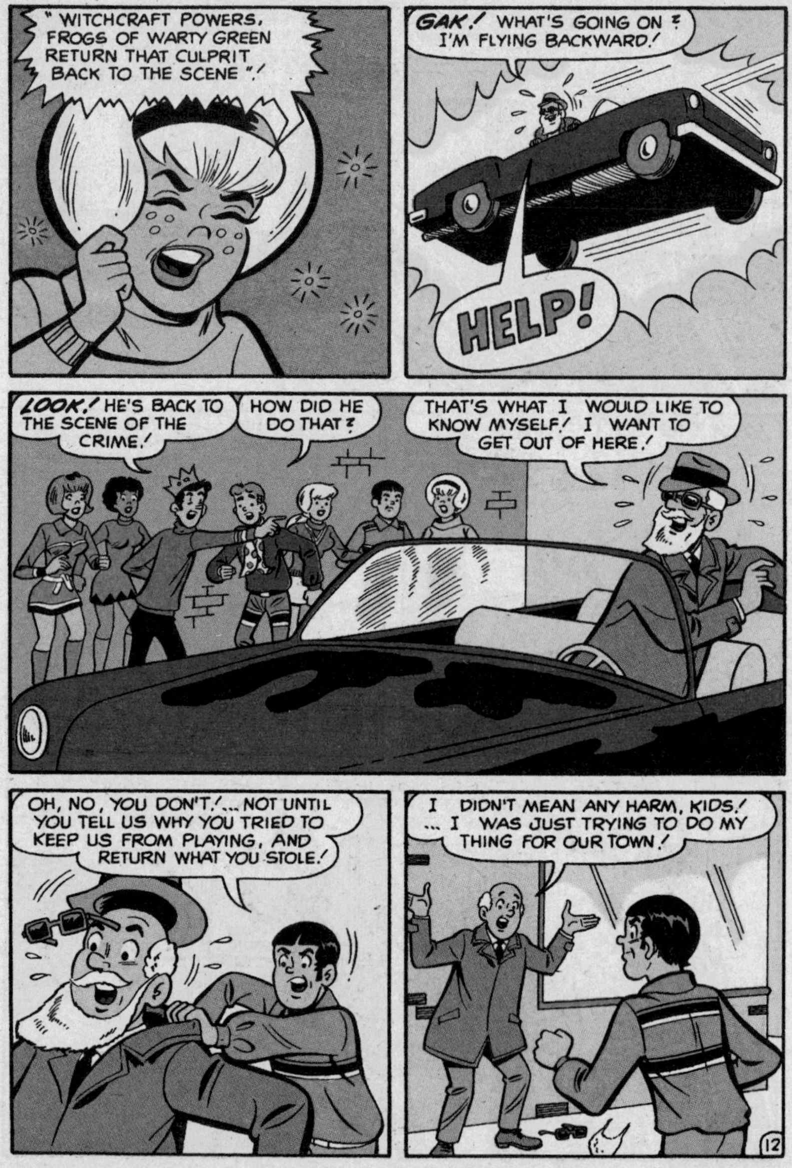
" WITCHCRAFT POWERS, FROGS OF WARTY GREEN RETURN THAT CULPRIT BACK TO THE SCENE "!
GAK! WHAT'S GOING ON ? I'M FLYING BACKWARD!
HELP!
LOOK! HE'S BACK TO THE SCENE OF THE CRIME!
HOW DID HE DO THAT ?
THAT'S WHAT I WOULD LIKE TO KNOW MYSELF! I WANT TO GET OUT OF HERE!
OH, NO, YOU DON'T!... NOT UNTIL YOU TELL US WHY YOU TRIED TO KEEP US FROM PLAYING, AND RETURN WHAT YOU STOLE!
I DIDN'T MEAN ANY HARM, KIDS! ... I WAS JUST TRYING TO DO MY THING FOR OUR TOWN!
12

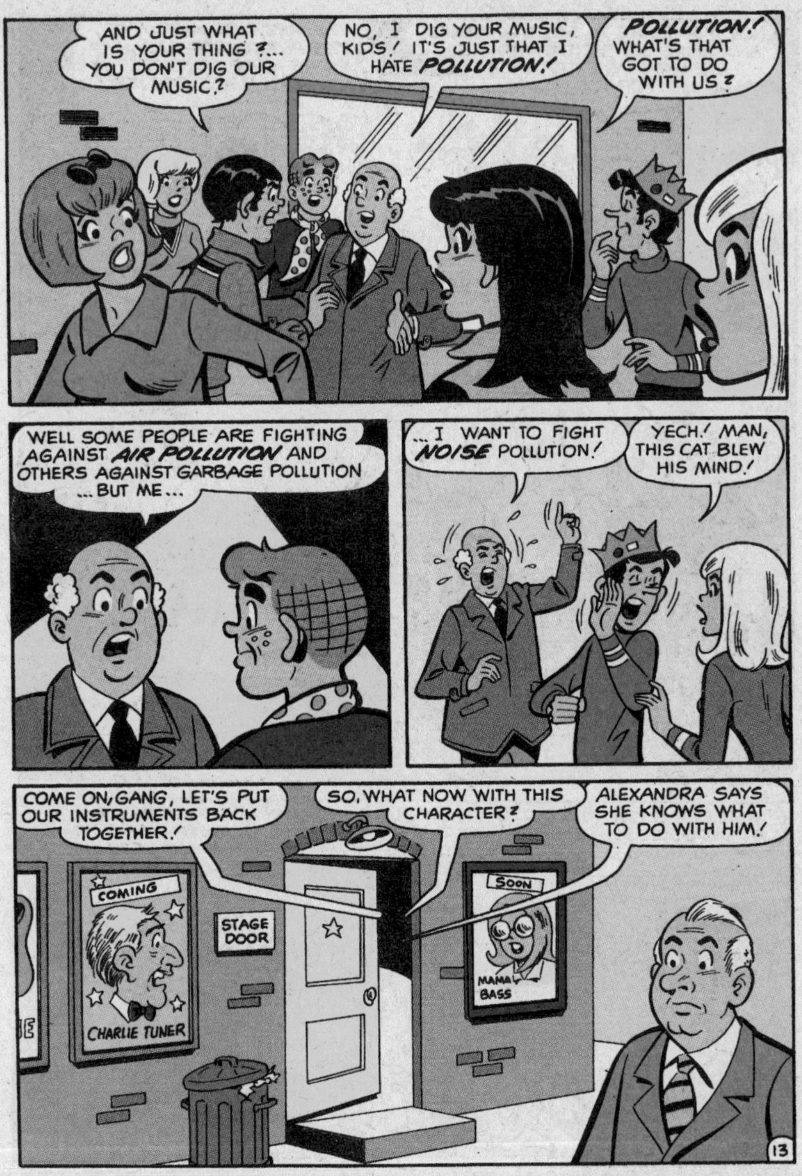
AND JUST WHAT IS YOUR THING ?... YOU DON'T DIG OUR MUSIC ?
NO, I DIG YOUR MUSIC, KIDS! IT'S JUST THAT I HATE POLLUTION!
POLLUTION! WHAT'S THAT GOT TO DO WITH US ?
WELL SOME PEOPLE ARE FIGHTING AGAINST AIR POLLUTION AND OTHERS AGAINST GARBAGE POLLUTION ... BUT ME...
... I WANT TO FIGHT NOISE POLLUTION!
YECH! MAN, THIS CAT BLEW HIS MIND!
COME ON, GANG, LET'S PUT OUR INSTRUMENTS BACK TOGETHER!
SO, WHAT NOW WITH THIS CHARACTER ?
ALEXANDRA SAYS SHE KNOWS WHAT TO DO WITH HIM!
COMING
CHARLIE TUNER
STAGE DOOR
SOON
MAMA BASS
13

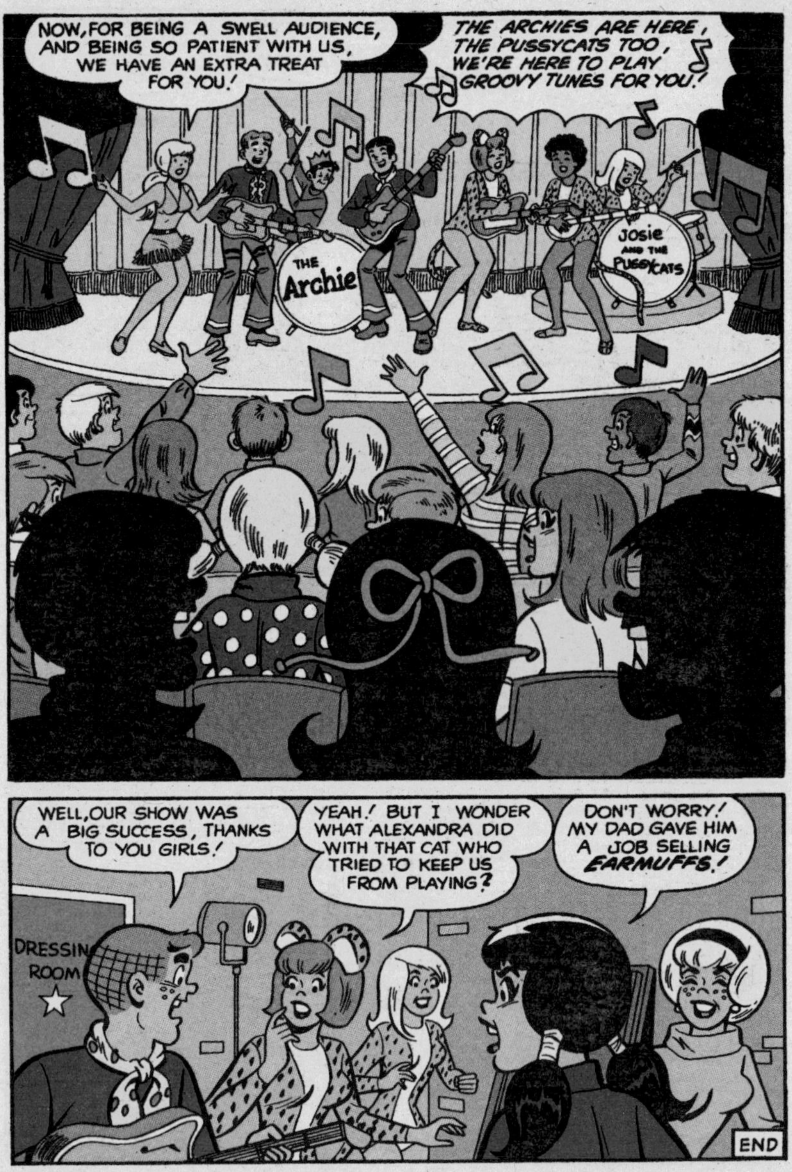
NOW, FOR BEING A SWELL AUDIENCE, AND BEING SO PATIENT WITH US, WE HAVE AN EXTRA TREAT FOR YOU!
THE ARCHIES ARE HERE, THE PUSSYCATS TOO, WE'RE HERE TO PLAY GROOVY TUNES FOR YOU!
THE Archie
JOSIE AND THE PUSSYCATS
WELL, OUR SHOW WAS A BIG SUCCESS, THANKS TO YOU GIRLS!
YEAH! BUT I WONDER WHAT ALEXANDRA DID WITH THAT CAT WHO TRIED TO KEEP US FROM PLAYING?
DON'T WORRY! MY DAD GAVE HIM A JOB SELLING EARMUFFS!
DRESSIN ROOM
END

Archie IN "PLANE FACTS"

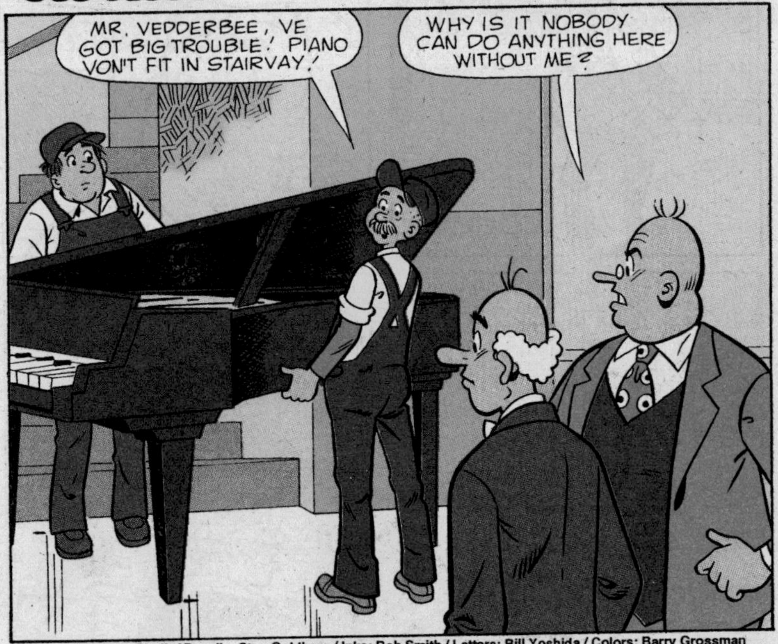
MR. VEDDERBEE, VE GOT BIG TROUBLE! PIANO VON'T FIT IN STAIRVAY!
WHY IS IT NOBODY CAN DO ANYTHING HERE WITHOUT ME?

Script: George Gladir / Pencils: Stan Goldberg / Inks: Bob Smith / Letters: Bill Yoshida / Colors: Barry Grossman

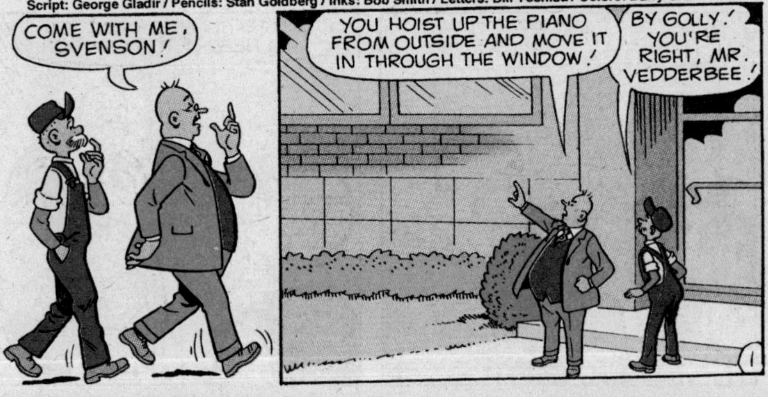
COME WITH ME, SVENSON!
YOU HOIST UP THE PIANO FROM OUTSIDE AND MOVE IT IN THROUGH THE WINDOW!
BY GOLLY! YOU'RE RIGHT, MR. VEDDERBEE!
1

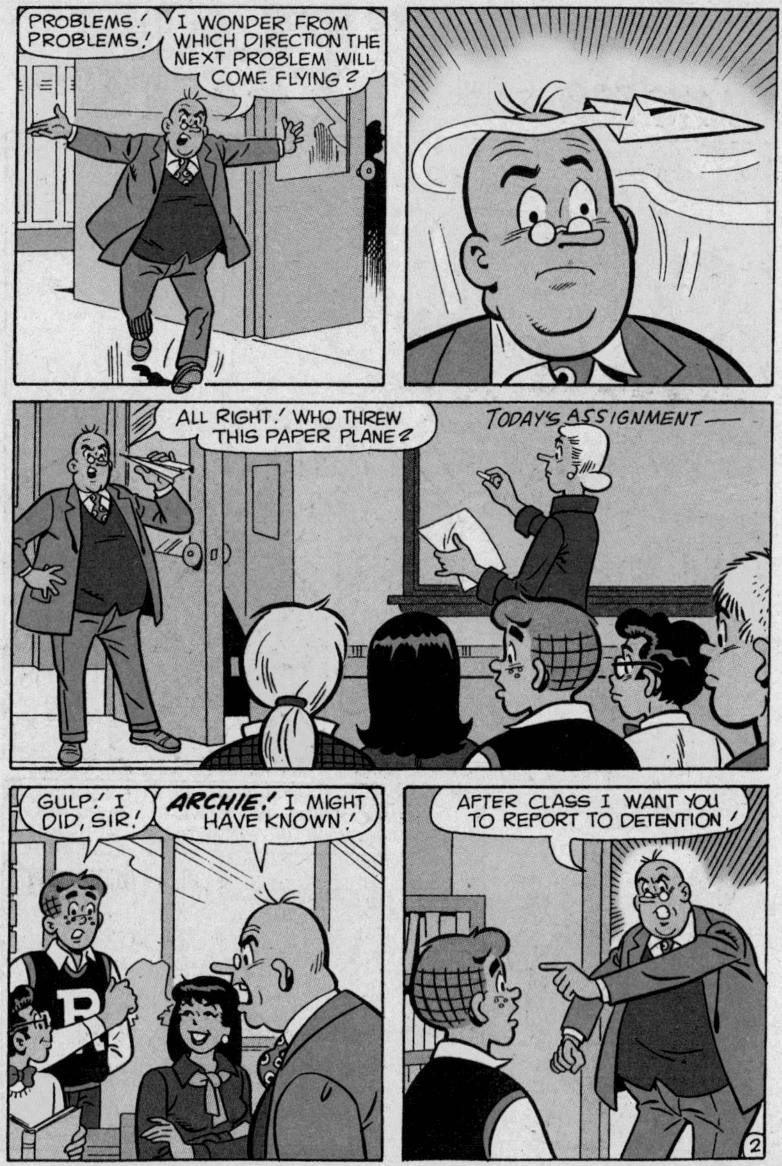
PROBLEMS! PROBLEMS!
I WONDER FROM WHICH DIRECTION THE NEXT PROBLEM WILL COME FLYING?
ALL RIGHT! WHO THREW THIS PAPER PLANE?
TODAY'S ASSIGNMENT —
GULP! I DID, SIR!
ARCHIE! I MIGHT HAVE KNOWN!
AFTER CLASS I WANT YOU TO REPORT TO DETENTION!
2

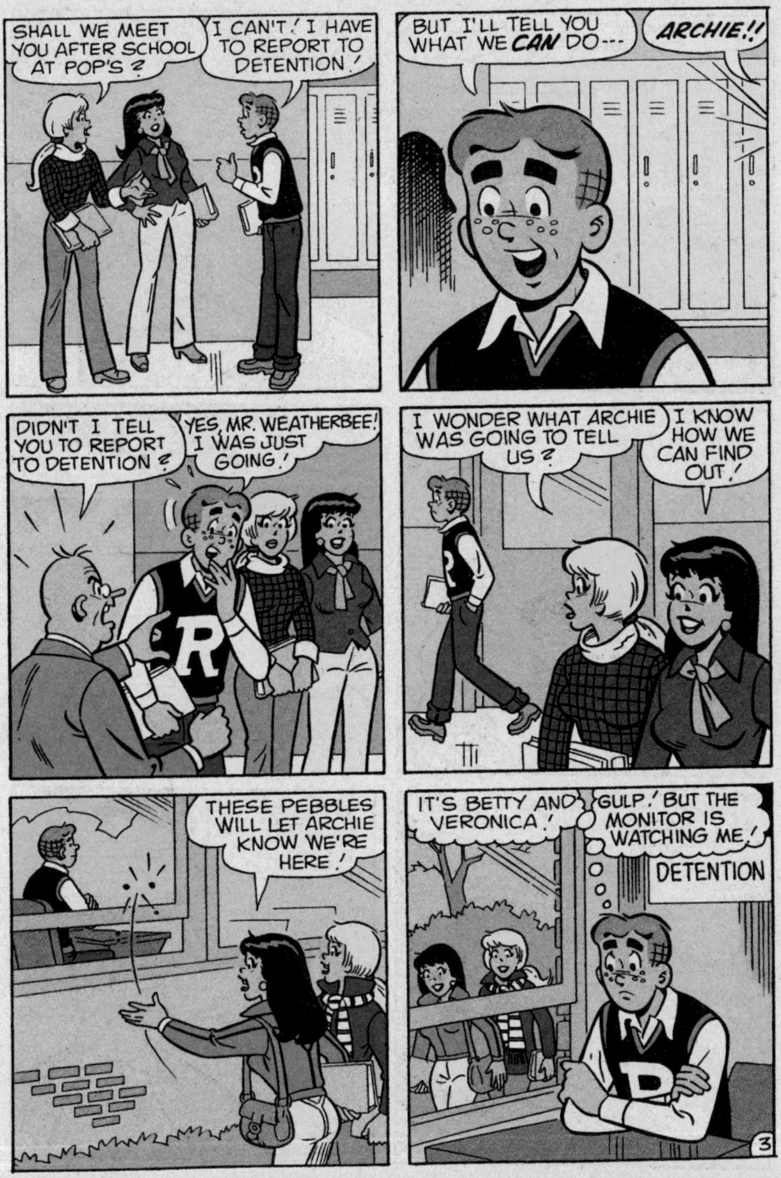
SHALL WE MEET YOU AFTER SCHOOL AT POP'S?
I CAN'T! I HAVE TO REPORT TO DETENTION!
BUT I'LL TELL YOU WHAT WE CAN DO---
ARCHIE!!
DIDN'T I TELL YOU TO REPORT TO DETENTION?
YES, MR. WEATHERBEE! I WAS JUST GOING!
I WONDER WHAT ARCHIE WAS GOING TO TELL US?
I KNOW HOW WE CAN FIND OUT!
THESE PEBBLES WILL LET ARCHIE KNOW WE'RE HERE!
IT'S BETTY AND VERONICA!
GULP! BUT THE MONITOR IS WATCHING ME!
DETENTION
3

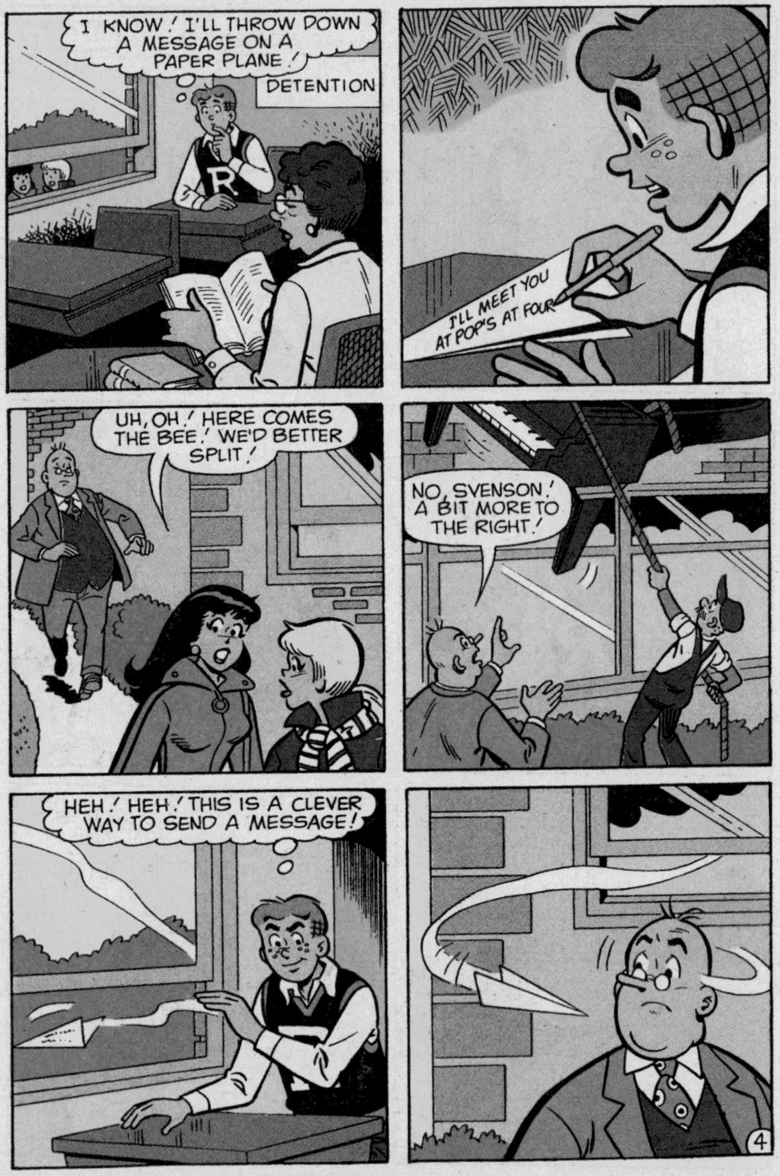
I KNOW! I'LL THROW DOWN A MESSAGE ON A PAPER PLANE!
DETENTION
I'LL MEET YOU AT POP'S AT FOUR
UH, OH! HERE COMES THE BEE! WE'D BETTER SPLIT!
NO, SVENSON! A BIT MORE TO THE RIGHT!
HEH! HEH! THIS IS A CLEVER WAY TO SEND A MESSAGE!
4

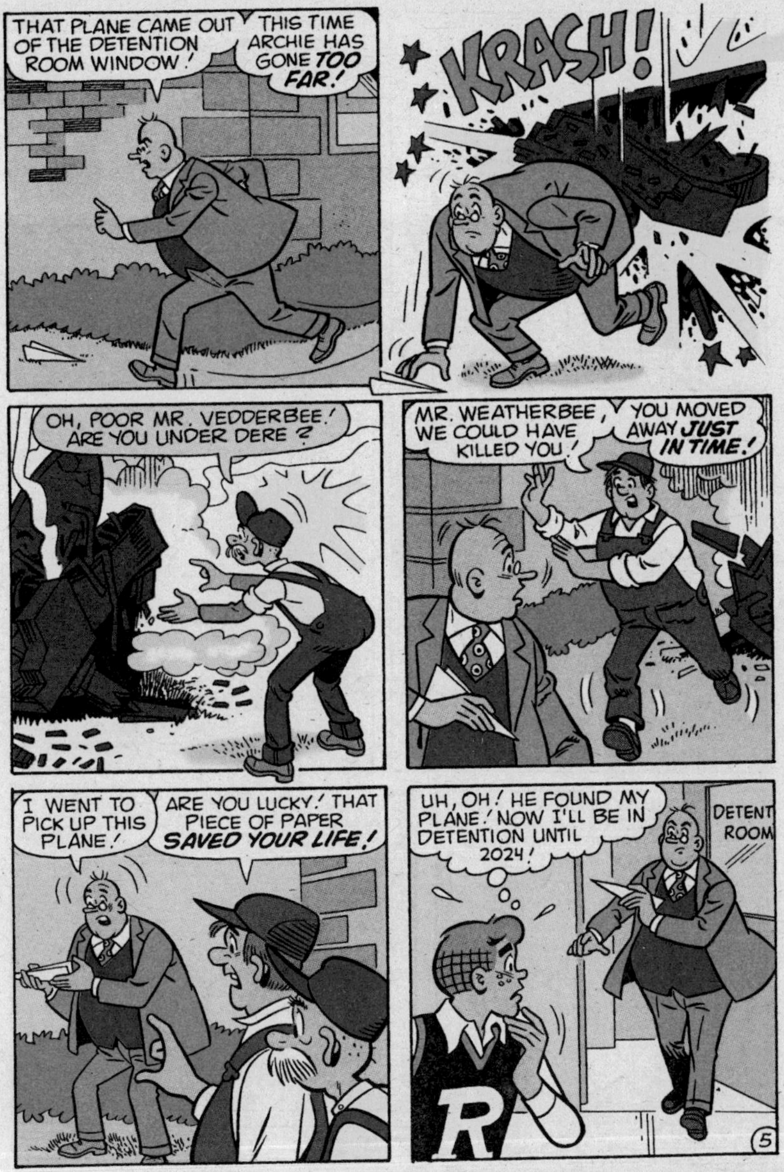
THAT PLANE CAME OUT OF THE DETENTION ROOM WINDOW!
THIS TIME ARCHIE HAS GONE TOO FAR!
KRASH!
OH, POOR MR. VEDDERBEE! ARE YOU UNDER DERE?
MR. WEATHERBEE, WE COULD HAVE KILLED YOU!
YOU MOVED AWAY JUST IN TIME!
I WENT TO PICK UP THIS PLANE!
ARE YOU LUCKY! THAT PIECE OF PAPER SAVED YOUR LIFE!
UH, OH! HE FOUND MY PLANE! NOW I'LL BE IN DETENTION UNTIL 2024!
DETENT ROOM
R
5

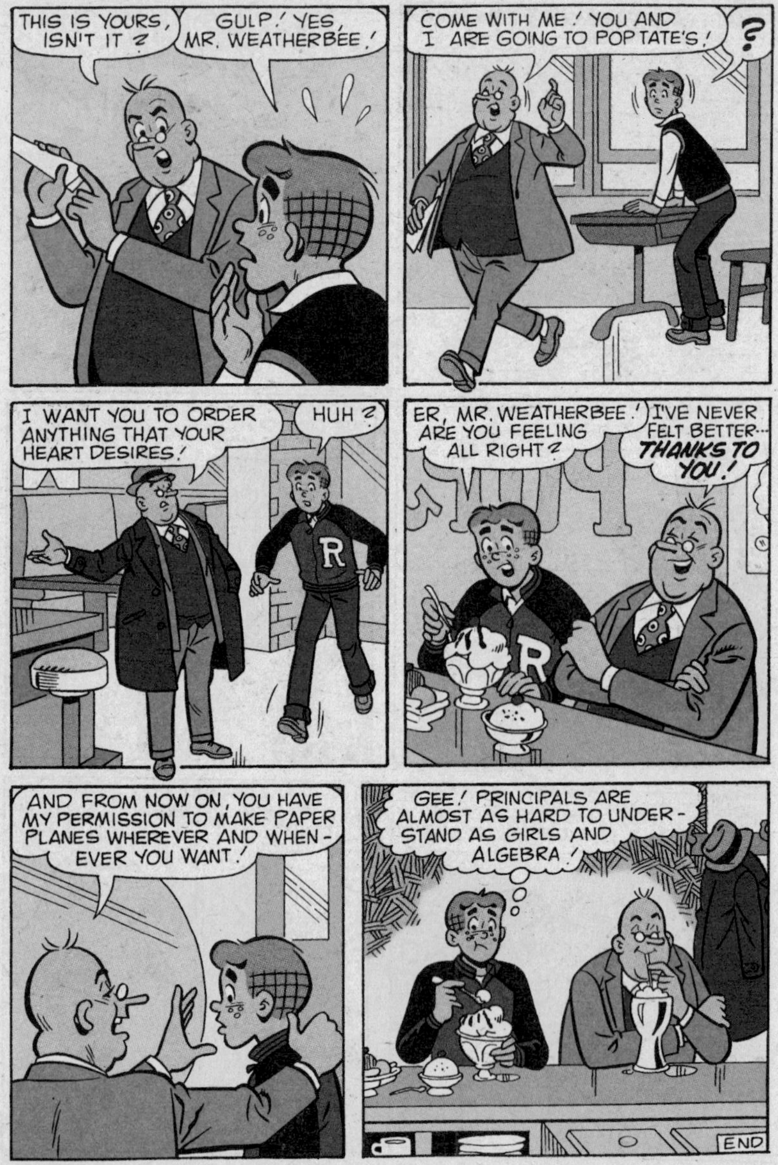
THIS IS YOURS, ISN'T IT ?
GULP! YES, MR. WEATHERBEE!
COME WITH ME! YOU AND I ARE GOING TO POP TATE'S!
?
I WANT YOU TO ORDER ANYTHING THAT YOUR HEART DESIRES!
HUH ?
ER, MR. WEATHERBEE! ARE YOU FEELING ALL RIGHT ?
I'VE NEVER FELT BETTER--- THANKS TO YOU!
AND FROM NOW ON, YOU HAVE MY PERMISSION TO MAKE PAPER PLANES WHEREVER AND WHEN-EVER YOU WANT!
GEE! PRINCIPALS ARE ALMOST AS HARD TO UNDER-STAND AS GIRLS AND ALGEBRA!
END

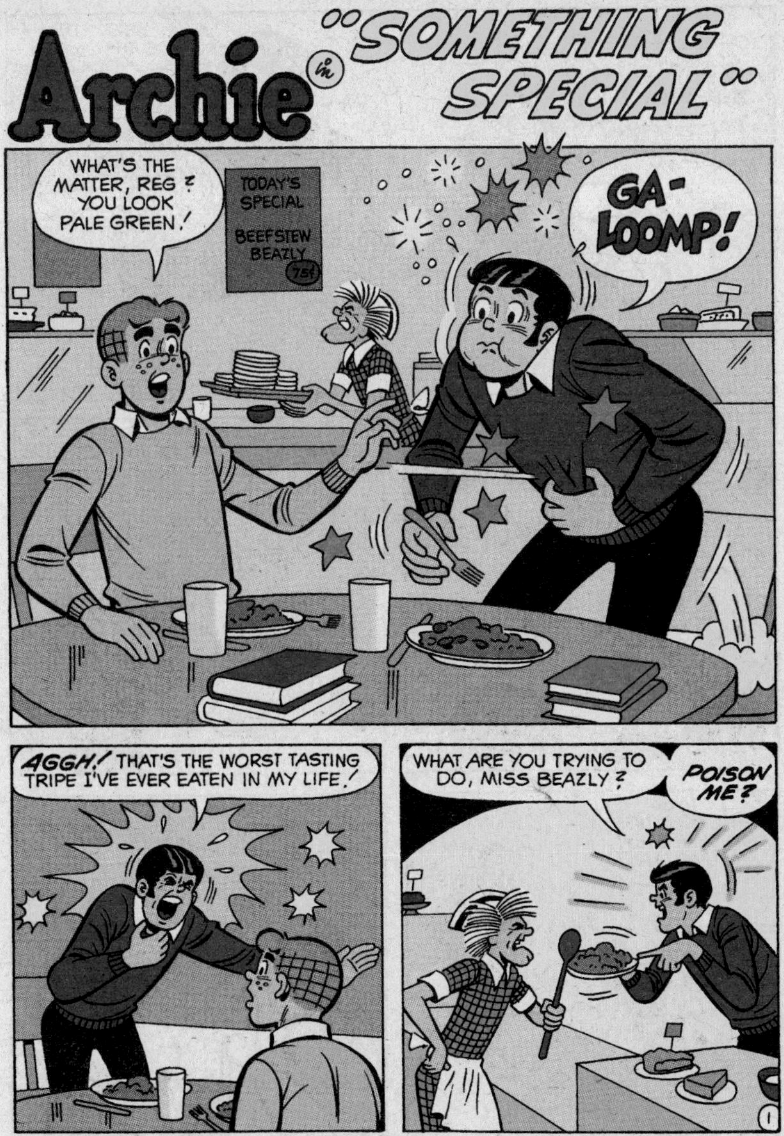
Archie in "SOMETHING SPECIAL"
WHAT'S THE MATTER, REG? YOU LOOK PALE GREEN!
TODAY'S SPECIAL BEEFSTEW BEAZLY 75¢
GA-LOOMP!
AGGH! THAT'S THE WORST TASTING TRIPE I'VE EVER EATEN IN MY LIFE!
WHAT ARE YOU TRYING TO DO, MISS BEAZLY?
POISON ME?
1

Script & Pencils: Al Hartley / Inks: Jon D'Agostino / Letters: Bill Yoshida / Colors: Barry Grossman

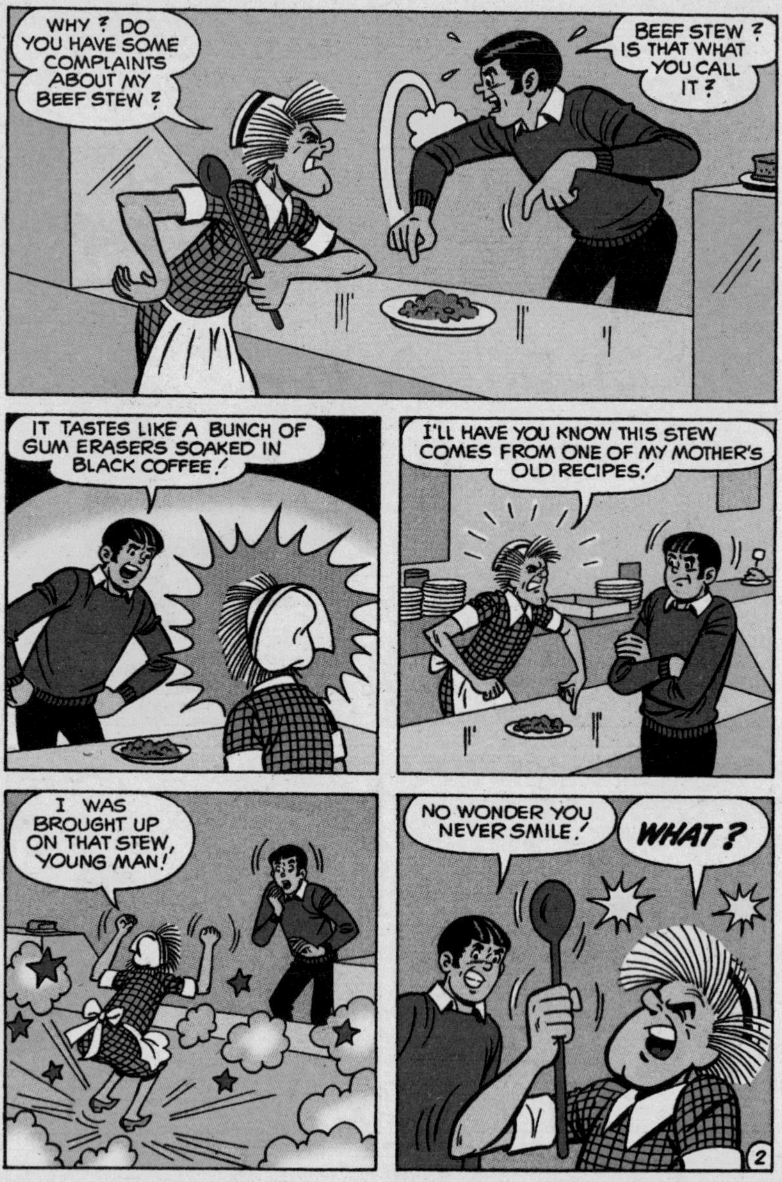
WHY ? DO YOU HAVE SOME COMPLAINTS ABOUT MY BEEF STEW ?
BEEF STEW ? IS THAT WHAT YOU CALL IT ?
IT TASTES LIKE A BUNCH OF GUM ERASERS SOAKED IN BLACK COFFEE!
I'LL HAVE YOU KNOW THIS STEW COMES FROM ONE OF MY MOTHER'S OLD RECIPES!
I WAS BROUGHT UP ON THAT STEW, YOUNG MAN!
NO WONDER YOU NEVER SMILE!
WHAT ?
2

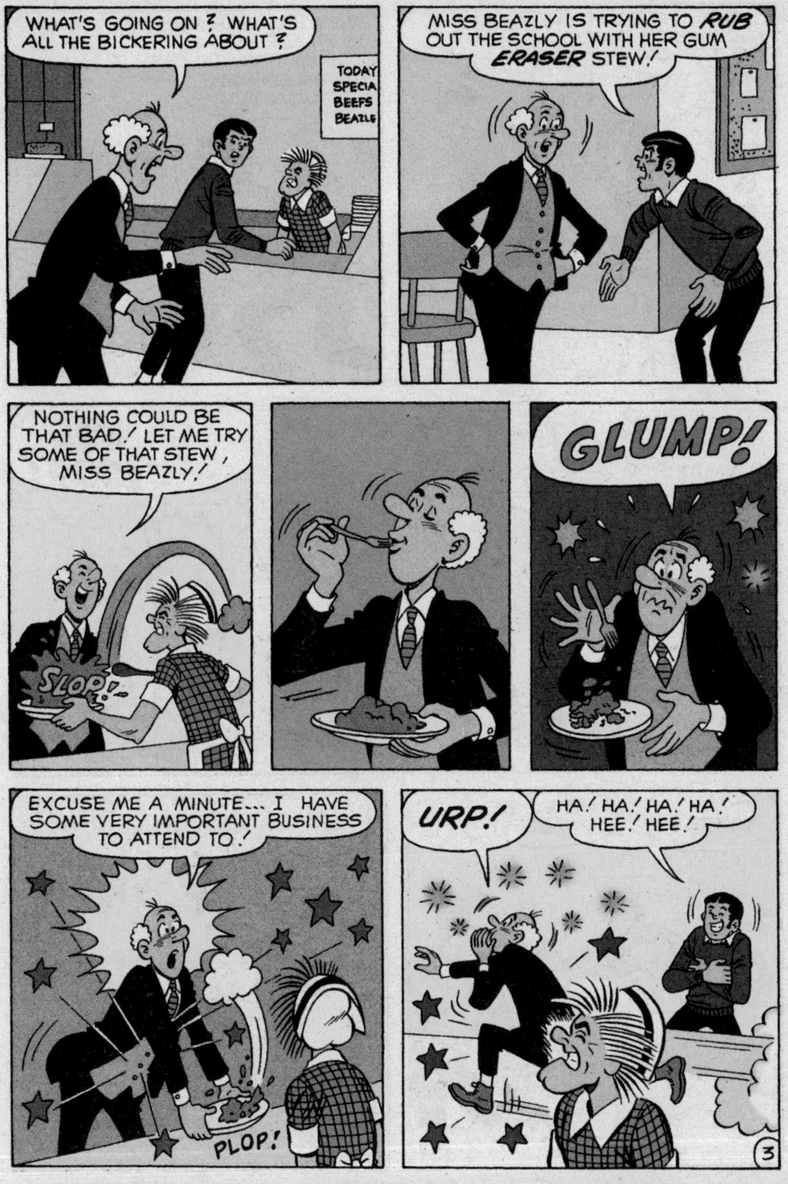
WHAT'S GOING ON ? WHAT'S ALL THE BICKERING ABOUT ?
TODAY SPECIA BEEFS BEAZLE
MISS BEAZLY IS TRYING TO RUB OUT THE SCHOOL WITH HER GUM ERASER STEW!
NOTHING COULD BE THAT BAD! LET ME TRY SOME OF THAT STEW, MISS BEAZLY!
SLOP!
GLUMP!
EXCUSE ME A MINUTE... I HAVE SOME VERY IMPORTANT BUSINESS TO ATTEND TO!
PLOP!
URP!
HA! HA! HA! HA! HEE! HEE!
3

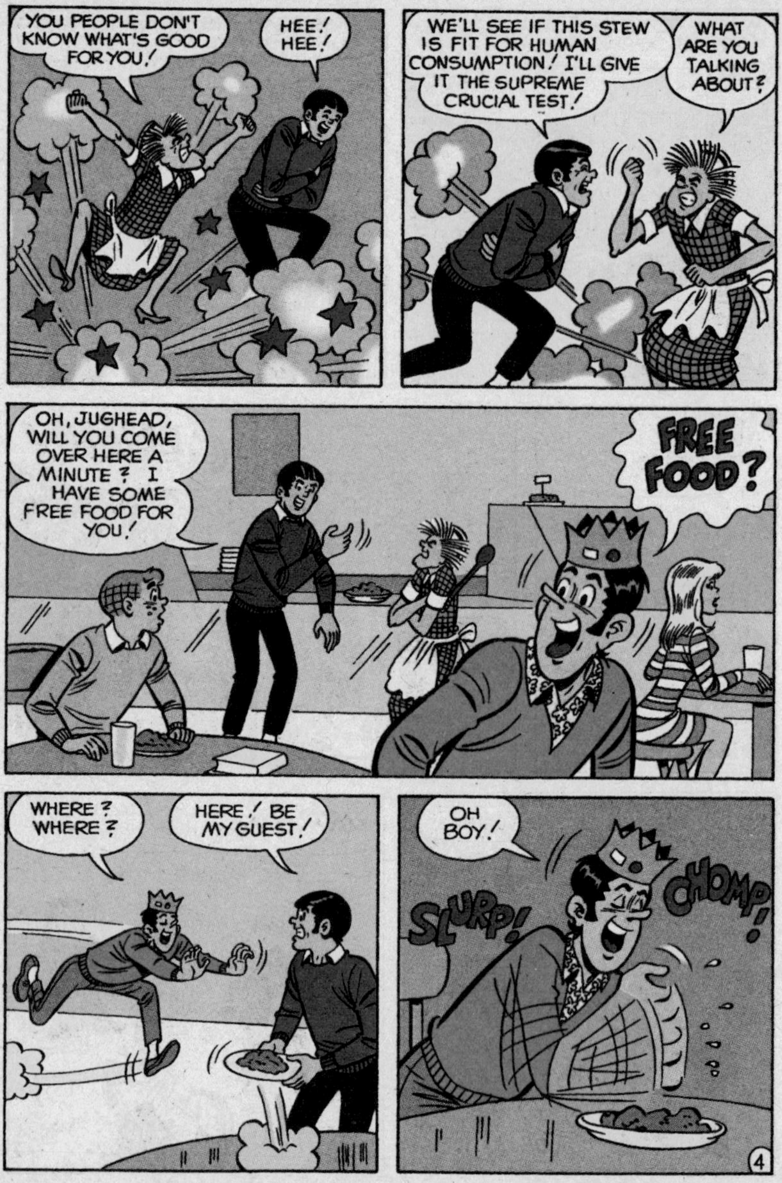

YOU PEOPLE DON'T KNOW WHAT'S GOOD FOR YOU!
HEE! HEE!
WE'LL SEE IF THIS STEW IS FIT FOR HUMAN CONSUMPTION! I'LL GIVE IT THE SUPREME CRUCIAL TEST!
WHAT ARE YOU TALKING ABOUT?
OH, JUGHEAD, WILL YOU COME OVER HERE A MINUTE? I HAVE SOME FREE FOOD FOR YOU!
FREE FOOD?
WHERE? WHERE?
HERE! BE MY GUEST!
OH BOY!
SLURP!
CHOMP!
4

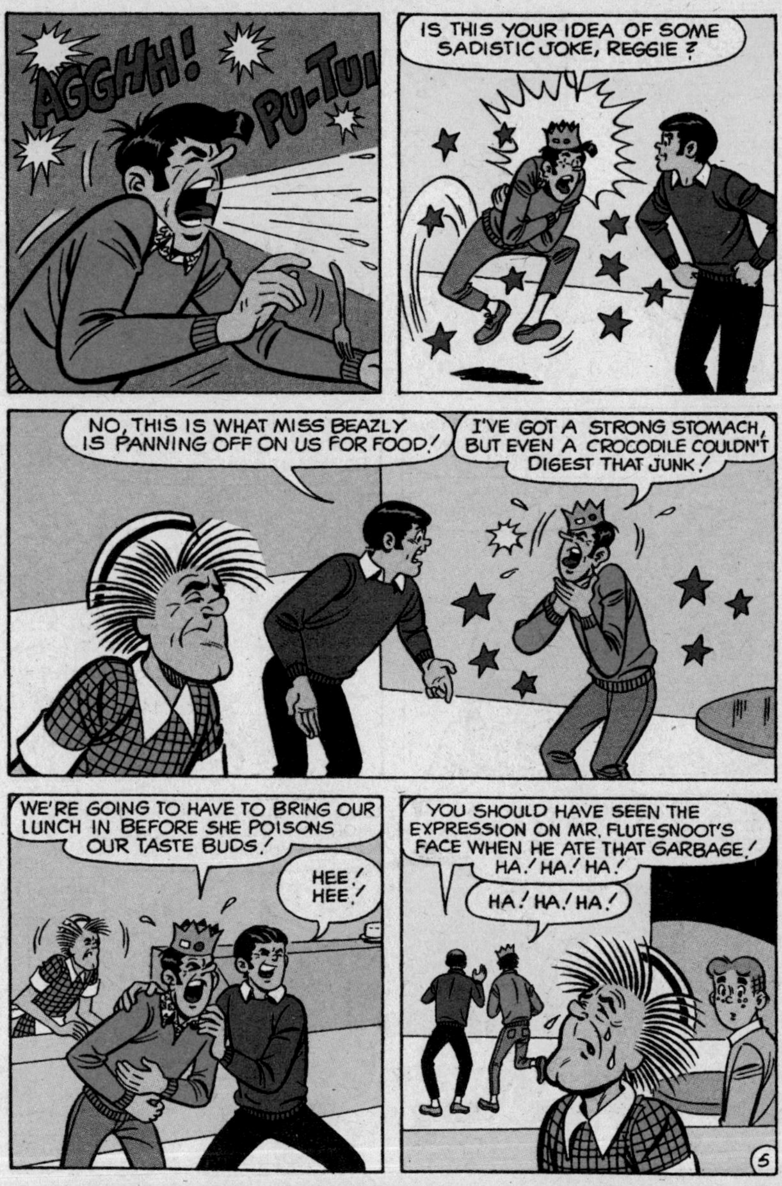
AGGHH!
PU-TUI
IS THIS YOUR IDEA OF SOME SADISTIC JOKE, REGGIE?
NO, THIS IS WHAT MISS BEAZLY IS PANNING OFF ON US FOR FOOD!
I'VE GOT A STRONG STOMACH, BUT EVEN A CROCODILE COULDN'T DIGEST THAT JUNK!
WE'RE GOING TO HAVE TO BRING OUR LUNCH IN BEFORE SHE POISONS OUR TASTE BUDS!
HEE! HEE!
YOU SHOULD HAVE SEEN THE EXPRESSION ON MR. FLUTESNOOT'S FACE WHEN HE ATE THAT GARBAGE! HA! HA! HA!
HA! HA! HA!
5

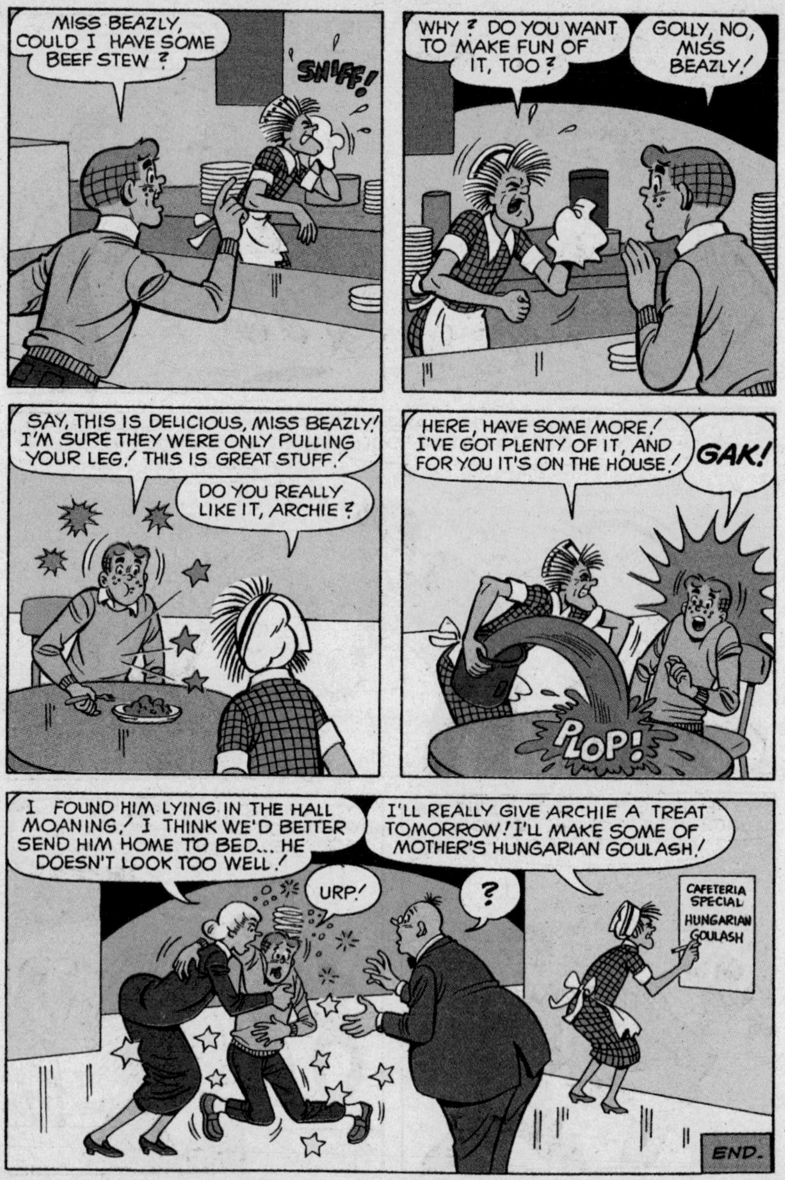
MISS BEAZLY, COULD I HAVE SOME BEEF STEW ?
SNIFF!
WHY ? DO YOU WANT TO MAKE FUN OF IT, TOO ?
GOLLY, NO, MISS BEAZLY!
SAY, THIS IS DELICIOUS, MISS BEAZLY! I'M SURE THEY WERE ONLY PULLING YOUR LEG! THIS IS GREAT STUFF!
DO YOU REALLY LIKE IT, ARCHIE ?
HERE, HAVE SOME MORE! I'VE GOT PLENTY OF IT, AND FOR YOU IT'S ON THE HOUSE!
GAK!
PLOP!
I FOUND HIM LYING IN THE HALL MOANING! I THINK WE'D BETTER SEND HIM HOME TO BED... HE DOESN'T LOOK TOO WELL!
URP!
?
I'LL REALLY GIVE ARCHIE A TREAT TOMORROW! I'LL MAKE SOME OF MOTHER'S HUNGARIAN GOULASH!
CAFETERIA SPECIAL
HUNGARIAN GOULASH
END.

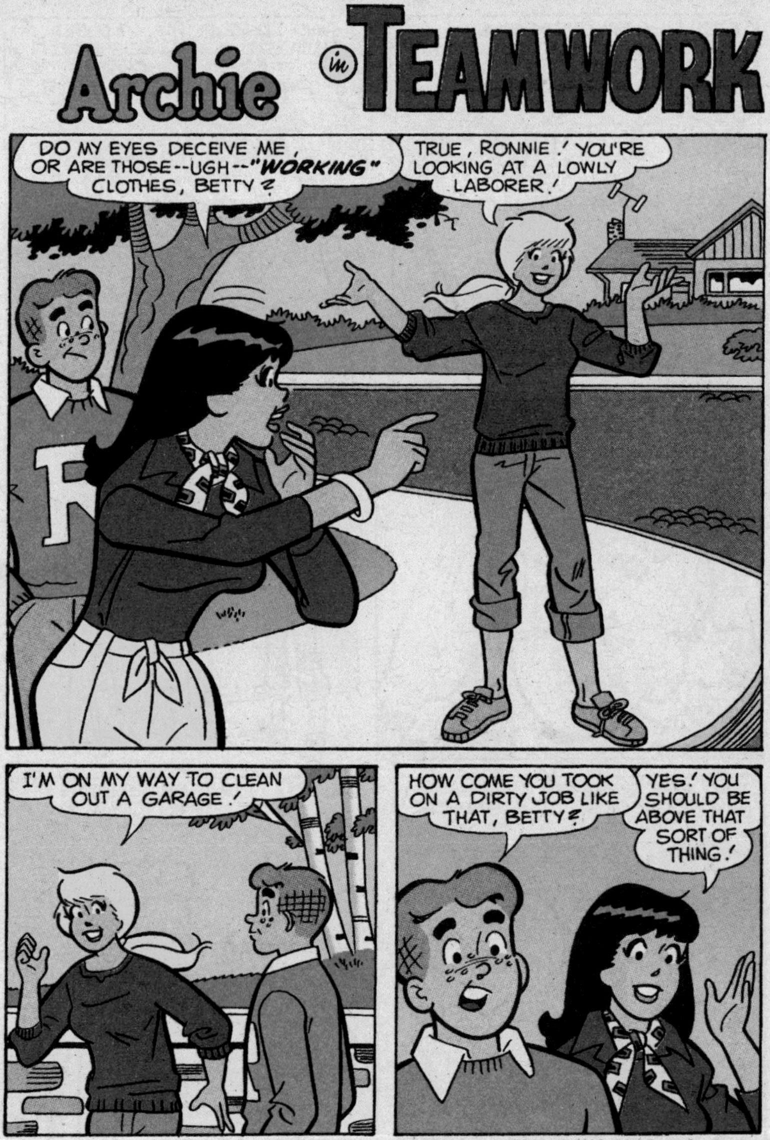
Archie in TEAMWORK
DO MY EYES DECEIVE ME, OR ARE THOSE--UGH--"WORKING" CLOTHES, BETTY?
TRUE, RONNIE! YOU'RE LOOKING AT A LOWLY LABORER!
I'M ON MY WAY TO CLEAN OUT A GARAGE!
HOW COME YOU TOOK ON A DIRTY JOB LIKE THAT, BETTY?
YES! YOU SHOULD BE ABOVE THAT SORT OF THING!

Script: Mike Pellowski / Pencils: Stan Goldberg / Inks: Mike Esposito / Letters: Bill Yoshida / Colors: Barry Grossman

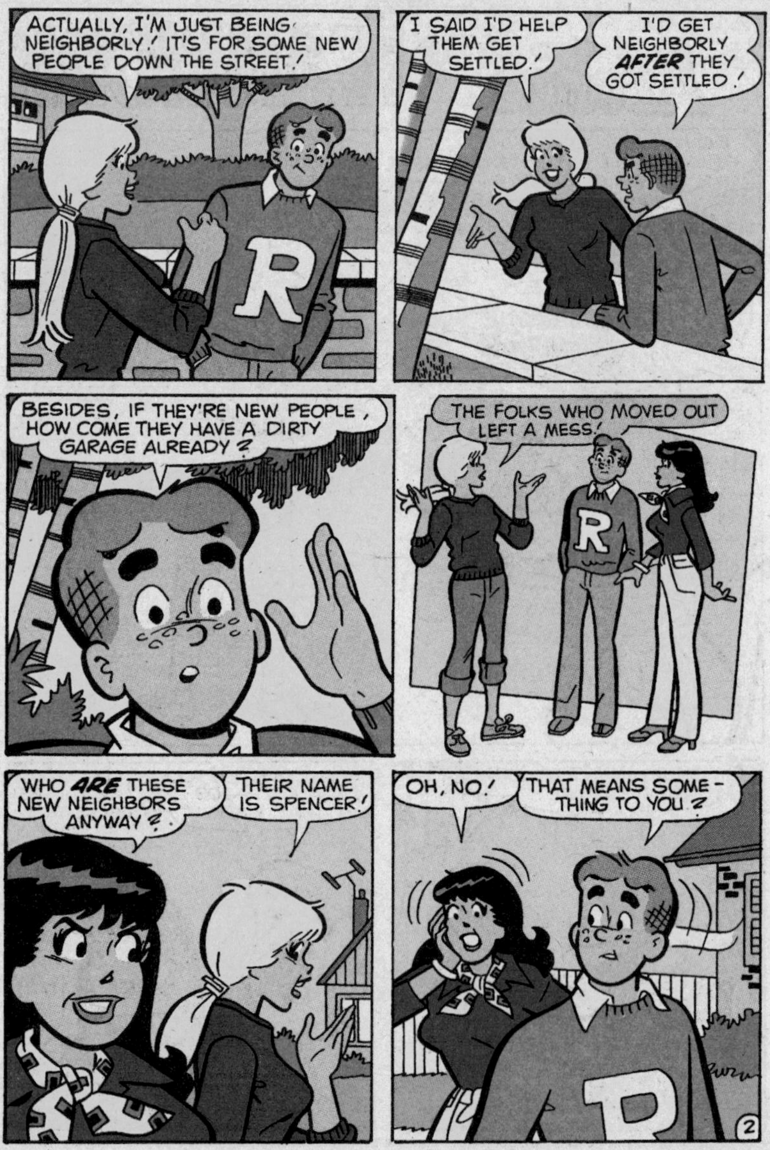
ACTUALLY, I'M JUST BEING NEIGHBORLY! IT'S FOR SOME NEW PEOPLE DOWN THE STREET!
I SAID I'D HELP THEM GET SETTLED!
I'D GET NEIGHBORLY AFTER THEY GOT SETTLED!
BESIDES, IF THEY'RE NEW PEOPLE, HOW COME THEY HAVE A DIRTY GARAGE ALREADY?
THE FOLKS WHO MOVED OUT LEFT A MESS!
WHO ARE THESE NEW NEIGHBORS ANYWAY?
THEIR NAME IS SPENCER!
OH, NO!
THAT MEANS SOME-THING TO YOU?
2

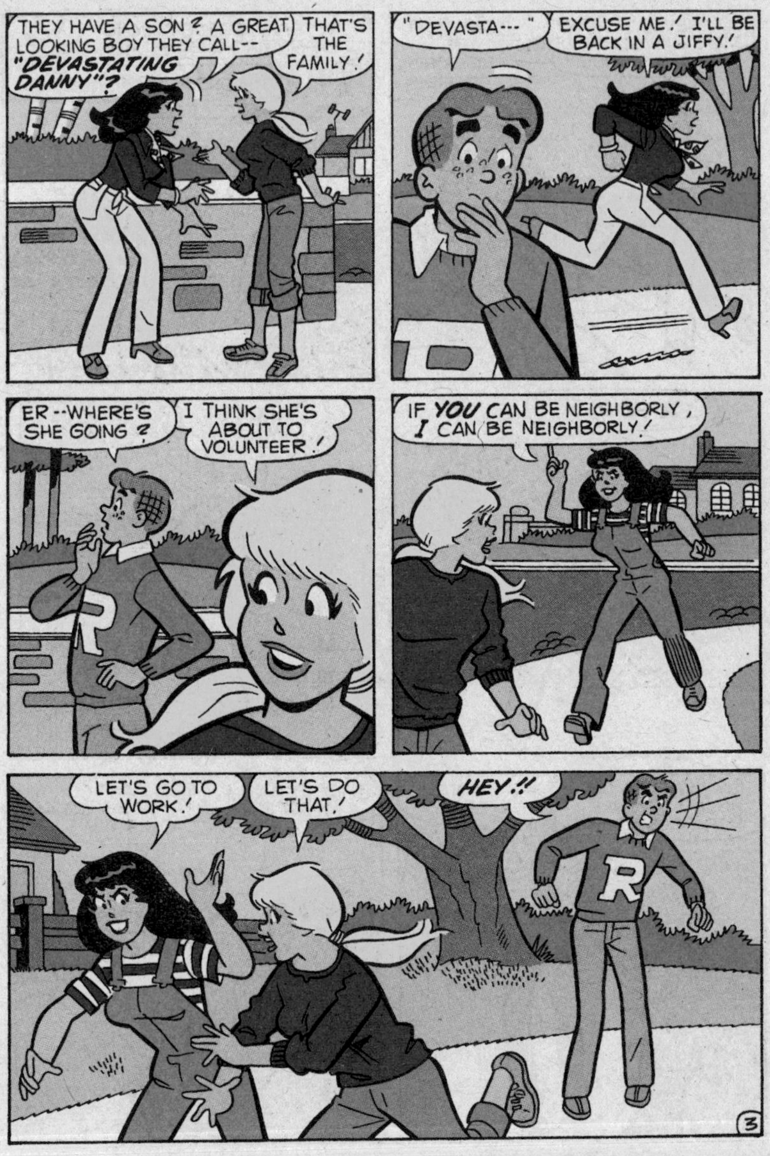

THEY HAVE A SON? A GREAT LOOKING BOY THEY CALL-- "DEVASTATING DANNY"?
THAT'S THE FAMILY!
"DEVASTA--- "
EXCUSE ME! I'LL BE BACK IN A JIFFY!
ER--WHERE'S SHE GOING?
I THINK SHE'S ABOUT TO VOLUNTEER!
IF YOU CAN BE NEIGHBORLY, I CAN BE NEIGHBORLY!
LET'S GO TO WORK!
LET'S DO THAT!
HEY!!
3

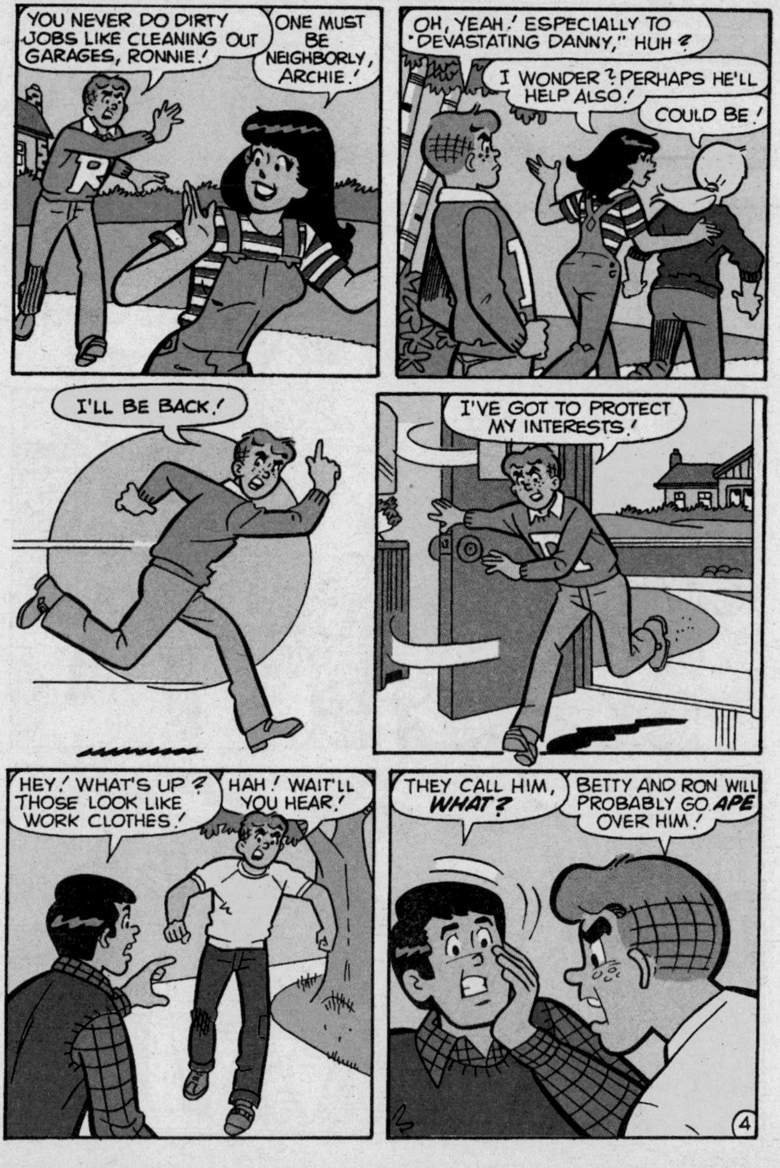
YOU NEVER DO DIRTY JOBS LIKE CLEANING OUT GARAGES, RONNIE!
ONE MUST BE NEIGHBORLY, ARCHIE!
OH, YEAH! ESPECIALLY TO "DEVASTATING DANNY," HUH?
I WONDER? PERHAPS HE'LL HELP ALSO!
COULD BE!
I'LL BE BACK!
I'VE GOT TO PROTECT MY INTERESTS!
HEY! WHAT'S UP? THOSE LOOK LIKE WORK CLOTHES!
HAH! WAIT'LL YOU HEAR!
THEY CALL HIM, WHAT?
BETTY AND RON WILL PROBABLY GO APE OVER HIM!
4

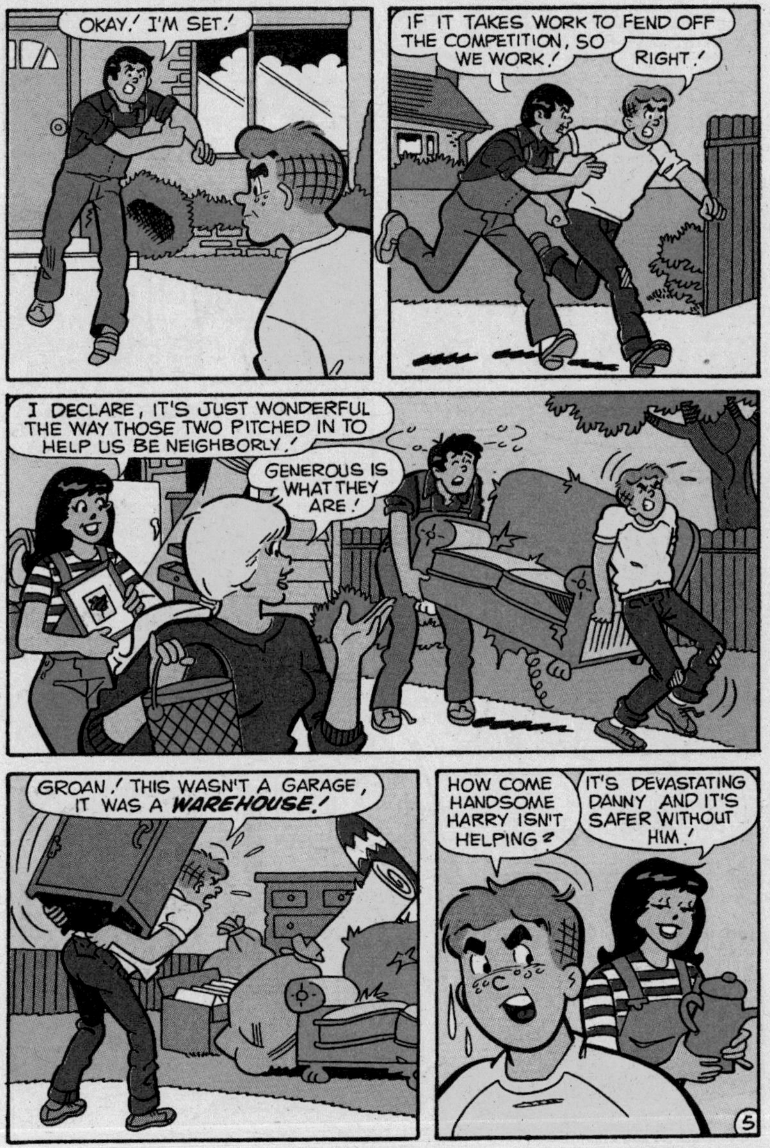
OKAY! I'M SET!
IF IT TAKES WORK TO FEND OFF THE COMPETITION, SO WE WORK!
RIGHT!
I DECLARE, IT'S JUST WONDERFUL THE WAY THOSE TWO PITCHED IN TO HELP US BE NEIGHBORLY!
GENEROUS IS WHAT THEY ARE!
GROAN! THIS WASN'T A GARAGE, IT WAS A WAREHOUSE!
HOW COME HANDSOME HARRY ISN'T HELPING?
IT'S DEVASTATING DANNY AND IT'S SAFER WITHOUT HIM!
5

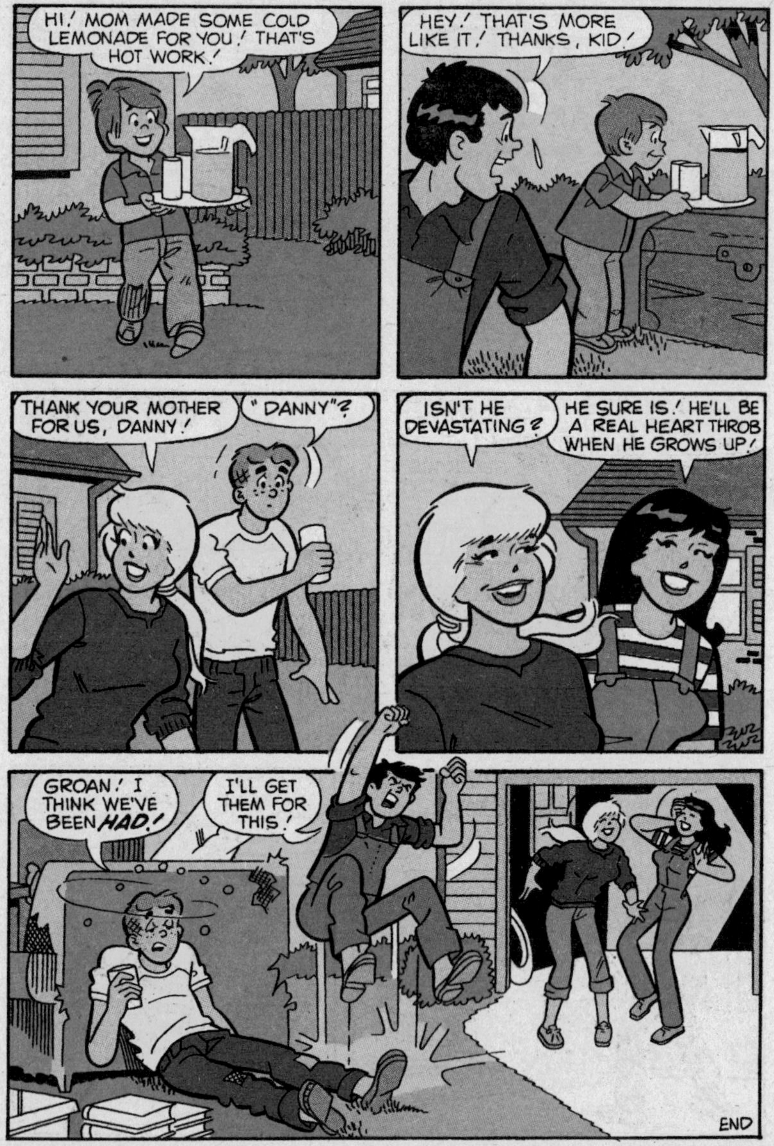
HI! MOM MADE SOME COLD LEMONADE FOR YOU! THAT'S HOT WORK!
HEY! THAT'S MORE LIKE IT! THANKS, KID!
THANK YOUR MOTHER FOR US, DANNY!
"DANNY"?
ISN'T HE DEVASTATING?
HE SURE IS! HE'LL BE A REAL HEART THROB WHEN HE GROWS UP!
GROAN! I THINK WE'VE BEEN *HAD*!
I'LL GET THEM FOR THIS!
END

Betty in "PARTING WAYS"

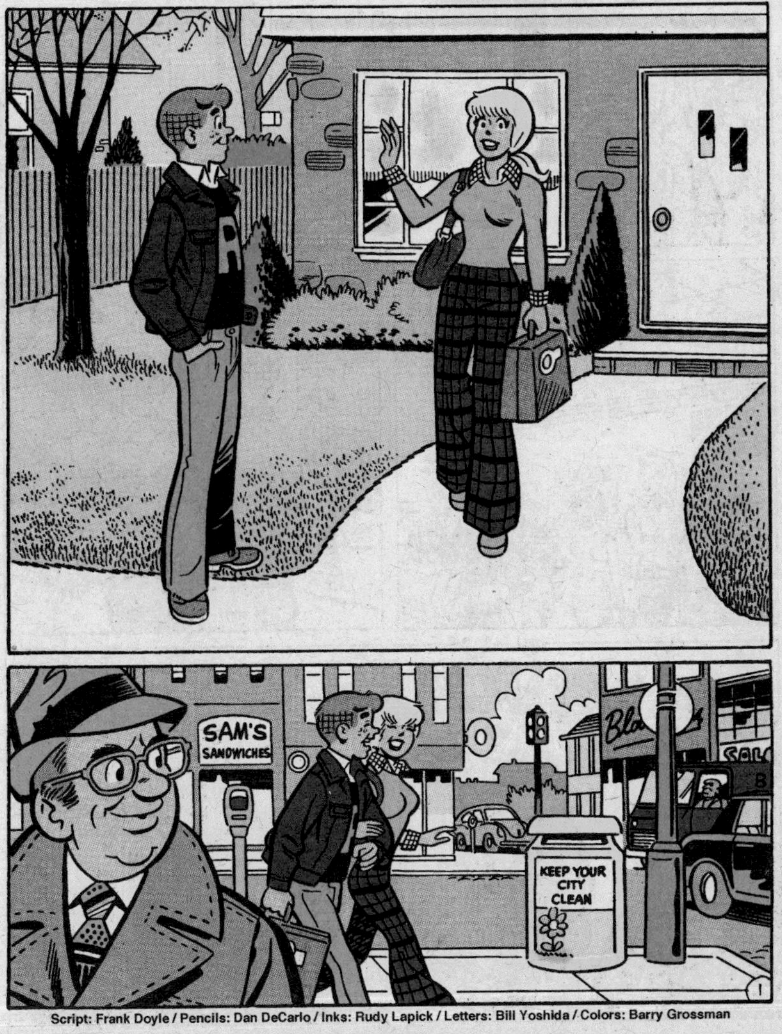
SAM'S
SANDWICHES
KEEP YOUR
CITY
CLEAN

Script: Frank Doyle / Pencils: Dan DeCarlo / Inks: Rudy Lapick / Letters: Bill Yoshida / Colors: Barry Grossman

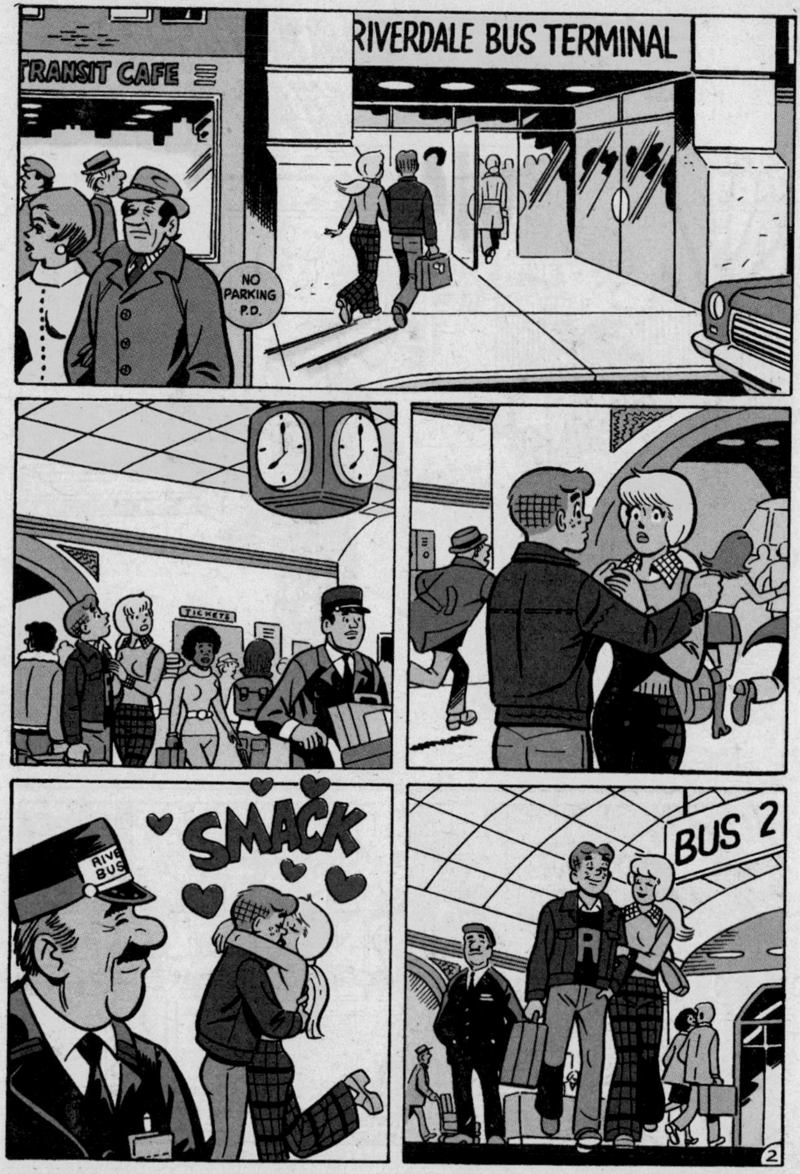
TRANSIT CAFE
RIVERDALE BUS TERMINAL
NO PARKING P.D.
TICKETS
SMACK
BUS 2
2

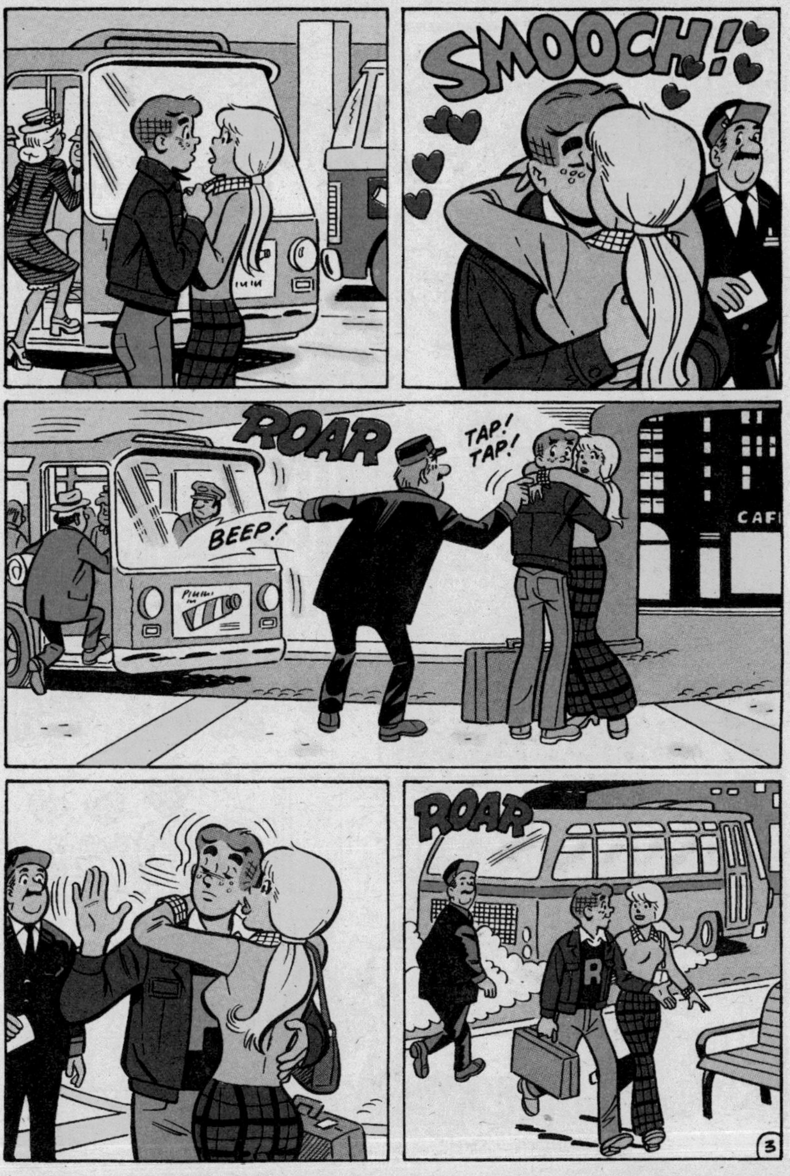
SMOOCH!
ROAR
TAP! TAP!
BEEP!
CAF
ROAR

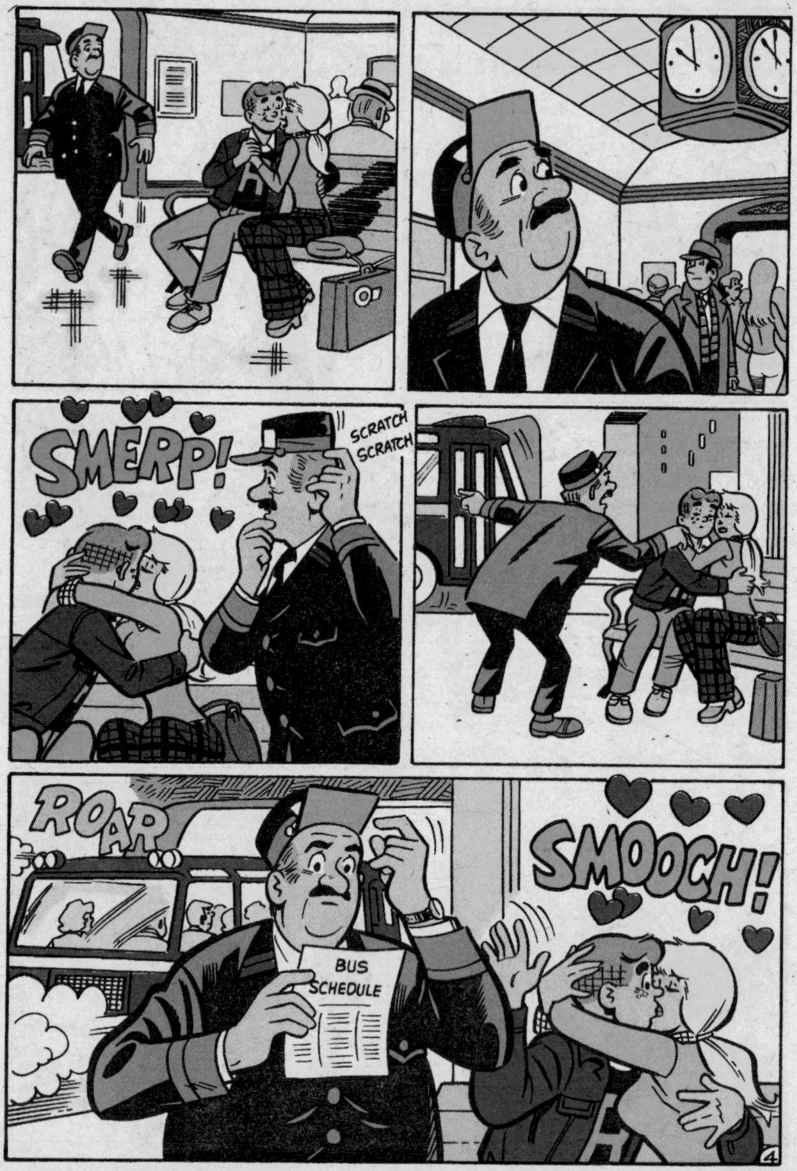
SMERP!
SCRATCH
SCRATCH
ROAR
BUS
SCHEDULE
SMOOCH!
4

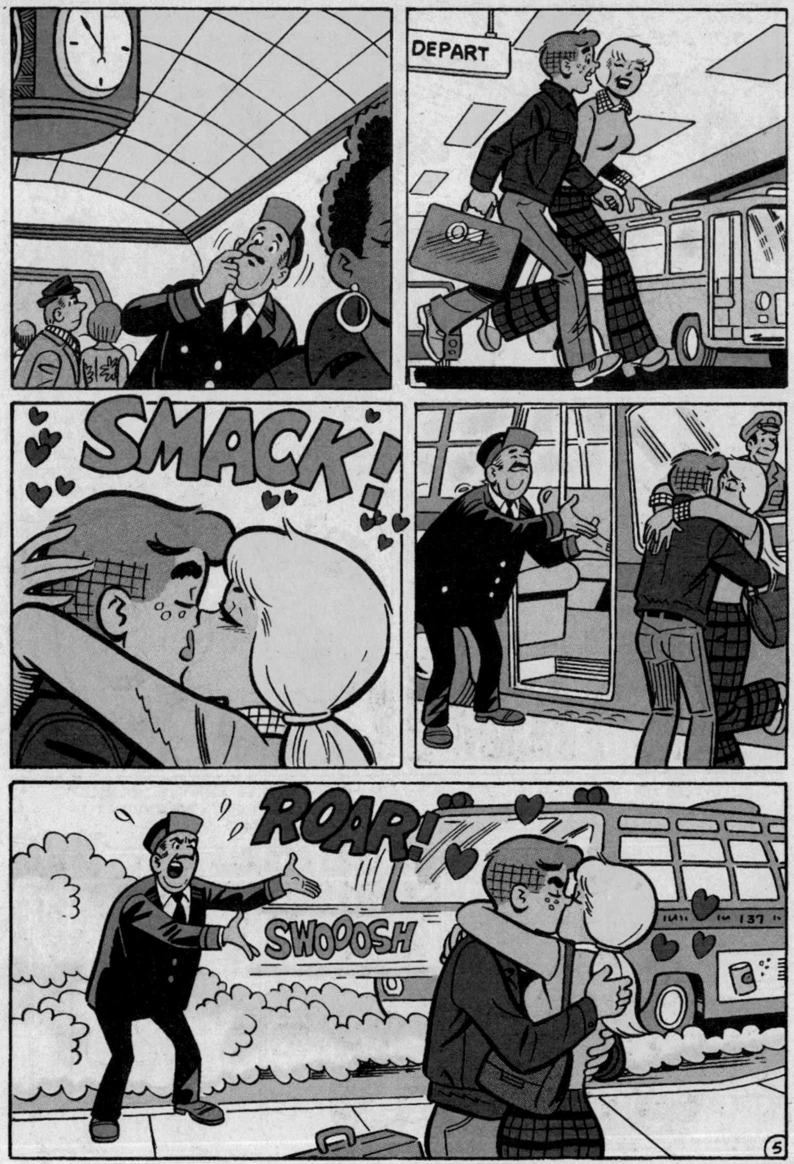
DEPART
SMACK!
ROAR!
SWOOOSH
137

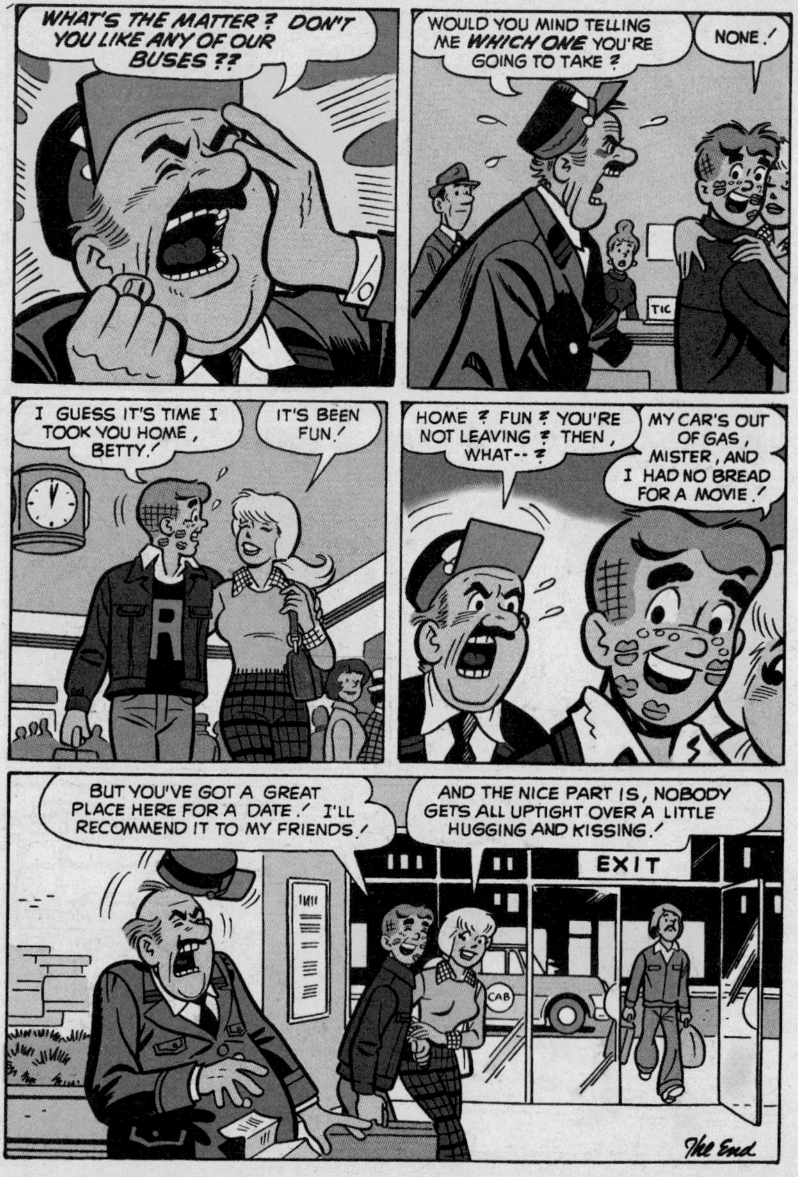
WHAT'S THE MATTER? DON'T YOU LIKE ANY OF OUR BUSES??
WOULD YOU MIND TELLING ME WHICH ONE YOU'RE GOING TO TAKE?
NONE!
TIC
I GUESS IT'S TIME I TOOK YOU HOME, BETTY!
IT'S BEEN FUN!
HOME? FUN? YOU'RE NOT LEAVING? THEN, WHAT--?
MY CAR'S OUT OF GAS, MISTER, AND I HAD NO BREAD FOR A MOVIE!
BUT YOU'VE GOT A GREAT PLACE HERE FOR A DATE! I'LL RECOMMEND IT TO MY FRIENDS!
AND THE NICE PART IS, NOBODY GETS ALL UPTIGHT OVER A LITTLE HUGGING AND KISSING!
EXIT
CAB
The End

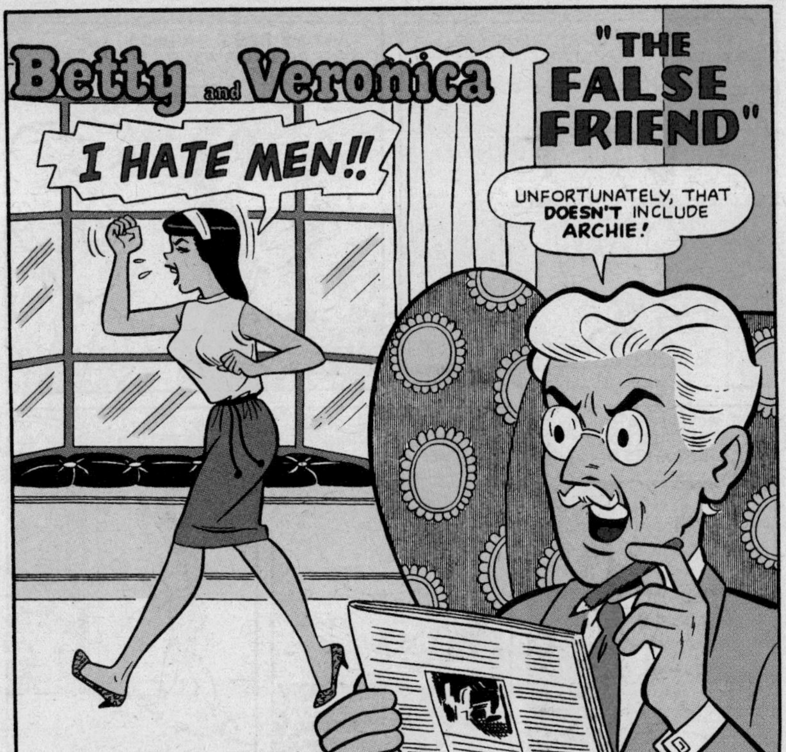
Betty and Veronica
"THE FALSE FRIEND"
I HATE MEN!!
UNFORTUNATELY, THAT DOESN'T INCLUDE ARCHIE!
HIM I HATE THE MOST!
SO DON'T SEE HIM TONIGHT!
I WON'T!
THAT'S WHY I HATE HIM!
HE HAS A DATE WITH BETTY FOR TONIGHT!

Script: Frank Doyle / Pencils: Dan DeCarlo / Inks: Rudy Lapick / Letters: Vince DeCarlo / Colors: Barry Grossman

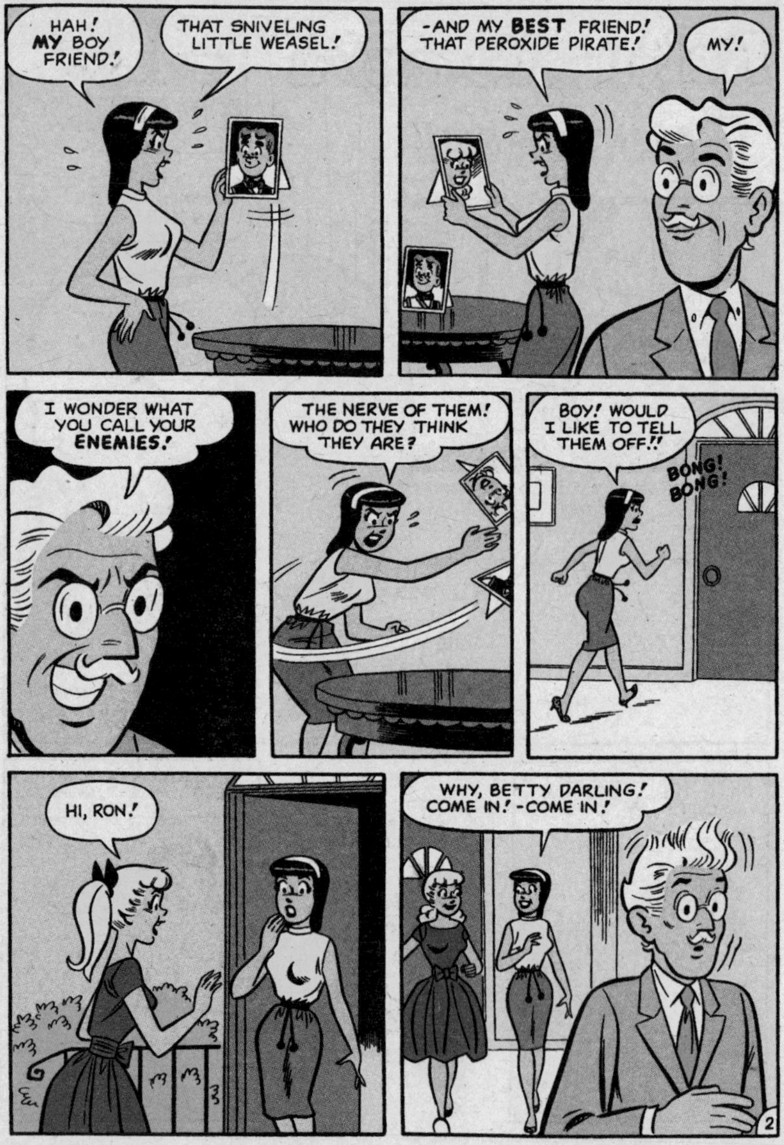
HAH! MY BOY FRIEND!
THAT SNIVELING LITTLE WEASEL!
-AND MY BEST FRIEND! THAT PEROXIDE PIRATE!
MY!
I WONDER WHAT YOU CALL YOUR ENEMIES!
THE NERVE OF THEM! WHO DO THEY THINK THEY ARE?
BOY! WOULD I LIKE TO TELL THEM OFF!!
BONG! BONG!
HI, RON!
WHY, BETTY DARLING! COME IN! -COME IN!
2

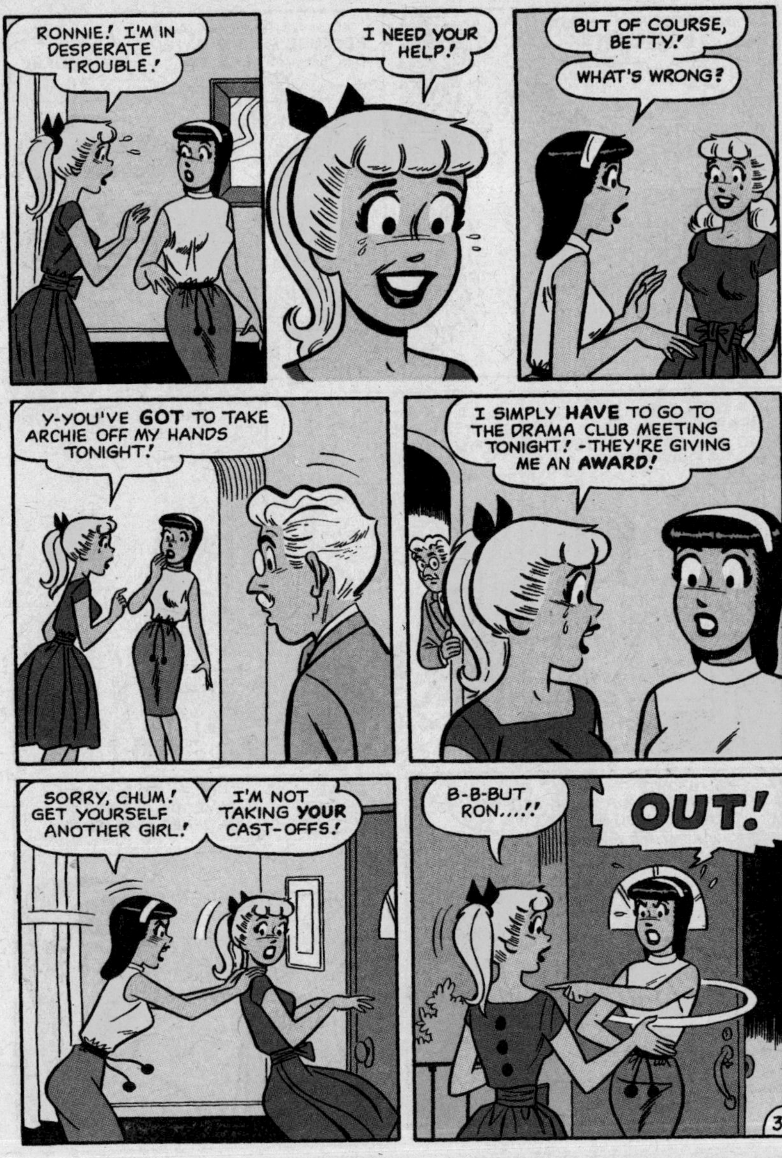
RONNIE! I'M IN DESPERATE TROUBLE!
I NEED YOUR HELP!
BUT OF COURSE, BETTY!
WHAT'S WRONG?
Y-YOU'VE **GOT** TO TAKE ARCHIE OFF MY HANDS TONIGHT!
I SIMPLY **HAVE** TO GO TO THE DRAMA CLUB MEETING TONIGHT! -THEY'RE GIVING ME AN **AWARD**!
SORRY, CHUM! GET YOURSELF ANOTHER GIRL!
I'M NOT TAKING **YOUR** CAST-OFFS!
B-B-BUT RON....!!
OUT!

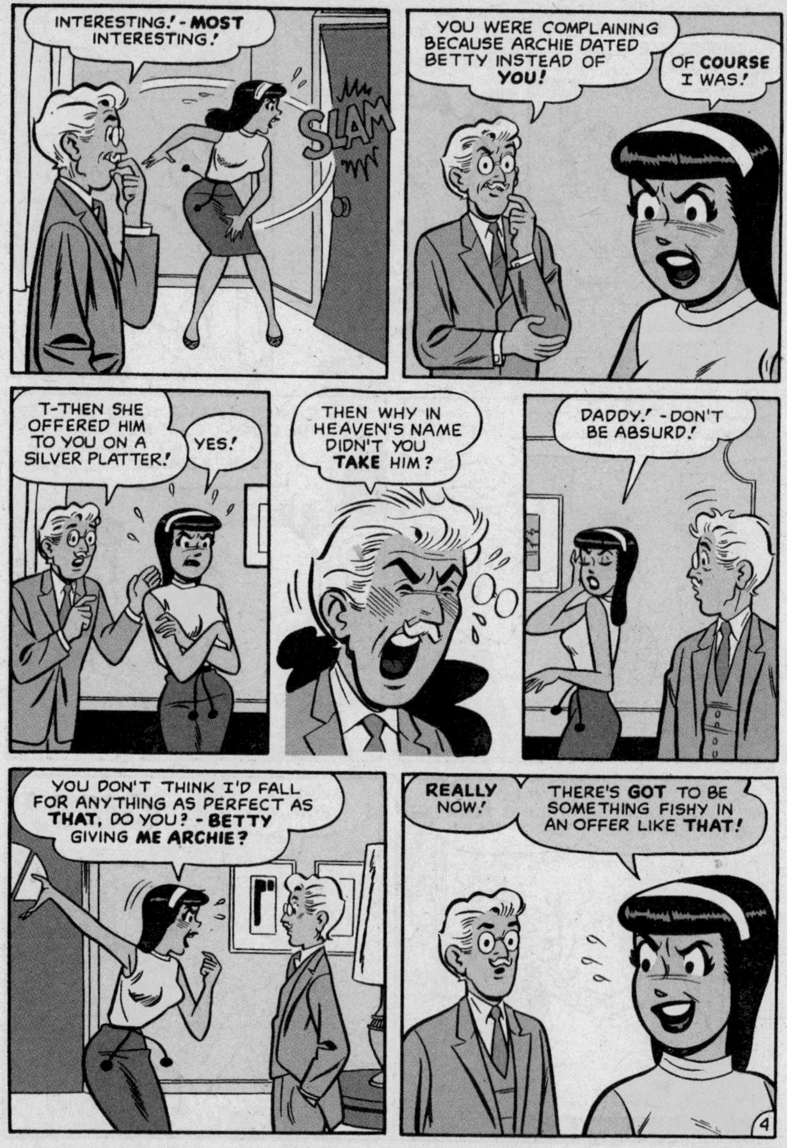

INTERESTING! - MOST INTERESTING!
SLAM
YOU WERE COMPLAINING BECAUSE ARCHIE DATED BETTY INSTEAD OF YOU!
OF COURSE I WAS!
T-THEN SHE OFFERED HIM TO YOU ON A SILVER PLATTER!
YES!
THEN WHY IN HEAVEN'S NAME DIDN'T YOU TAKE HIM?
DADDY! - DON'T BE ABSURD!
YOU DON'T THINK I'D FALL FOR ANYTHING AS PERFECT AS THAT, DO YOU? - BETTY GIVING ME ARCHIE?
REALLY NOW!
THERE'S GOT TO BE SOMETHING FISHY IN AN OFFER LIKE THAT!
4

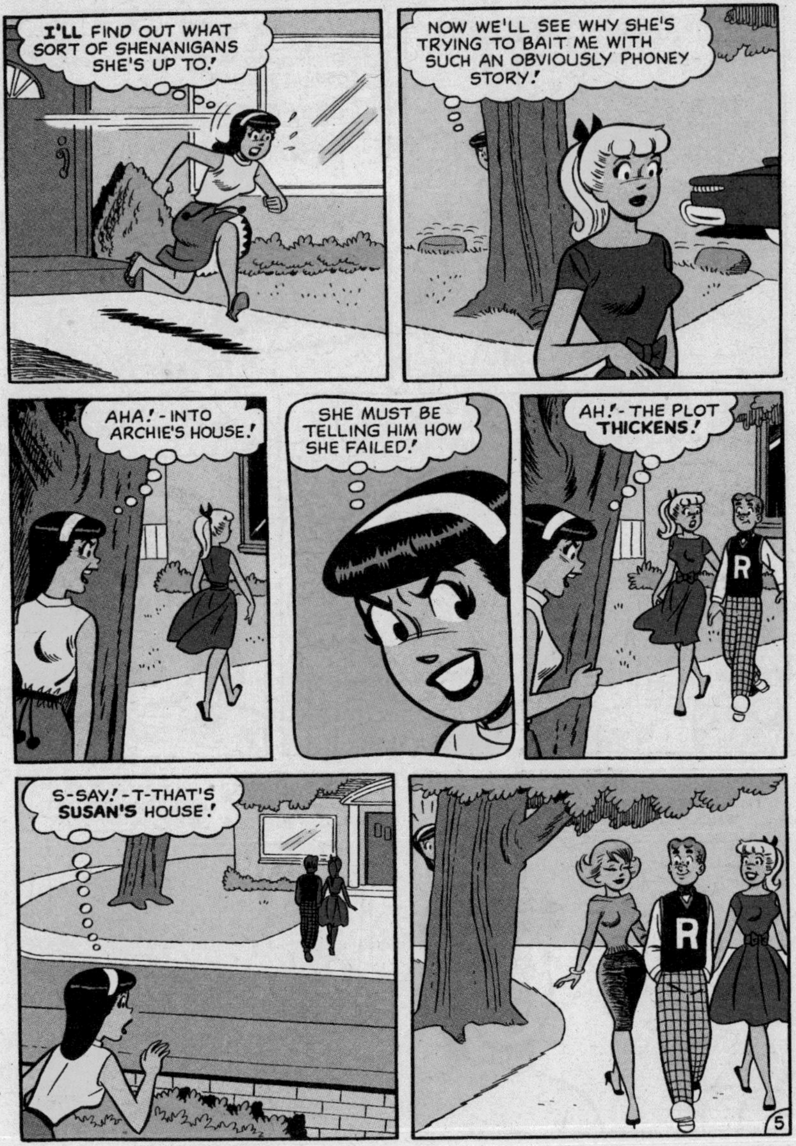
I'LL FIND OUT WHAT SORT OF SHENANIGANS SHE'S UP TO!
NOW WE'LL SEE WHY SHE'S TRYING TO BAIT ME WITH SUCH AN OBVIOUSLY PHONEY STORY!
AHA! - INTO ARCHIE'S HOUSE!
SHE MUST BE TELLING HIM HOW SHE FAILED!
AH! - THE PLOT THICKENS!
S-SAY! - T-THAT'S SUSAN'S HOUSE!
5

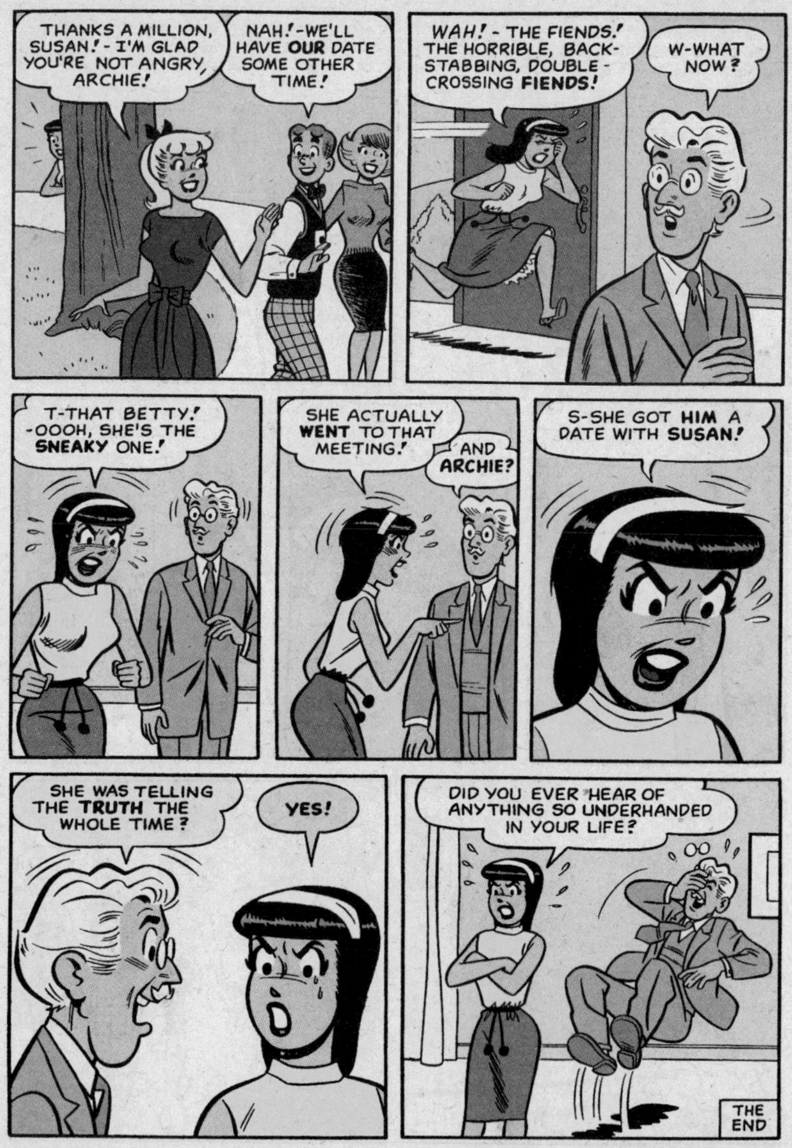
THANKS A MILLION, SUSAN! - I'M GLAD YOU'RE NOT ANGRY, ARCHIE!
NAH! -WE'LL HAVE **OUR** DATE SOME OTHER TIME!
WAH! - THE FIENDS! THE HORRIBLE, BACK-STABBING, DOUBLE-CROSSING **FIENDS!**
W-WHAT NOW?
T-THAT BETTY! -OOOH, SHE'S THE **SNEAKY** ONE!
SHE ACTUALLY **WENT** TO THAT MEETING!
AND **ARCHIE?**
S-SHE GOT **HIM** A DATE WITH **SUSAN!**
SHE WAS TELLING THE **TRUTH** THE WHOLE TIME?
YES!
DID YOU EVER HEAR OF ANYTHING SO UNDERHANDED IN YOUR LIFE?
THE END

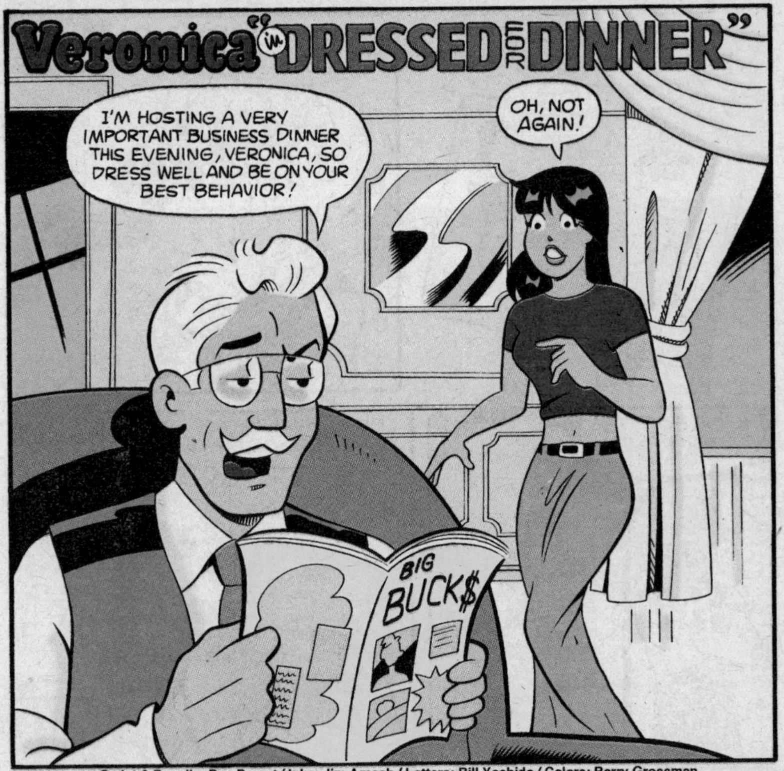
Veronica in "DRESSED FOR DINNER"
I'M HOSTING A VERY IMPORTANT BUSINESS DINNER THIS EVENING, VERONICA, SO DRESS WELL AND BE ON YOUR BEST BEHAVIOR!
OH, NOT AGAIN!
BIG BUCK$

Script & Pencils: Dan Parent / Inks: Jim Amash / Letters: Bill Yoshida / Colors: Barry Grossman

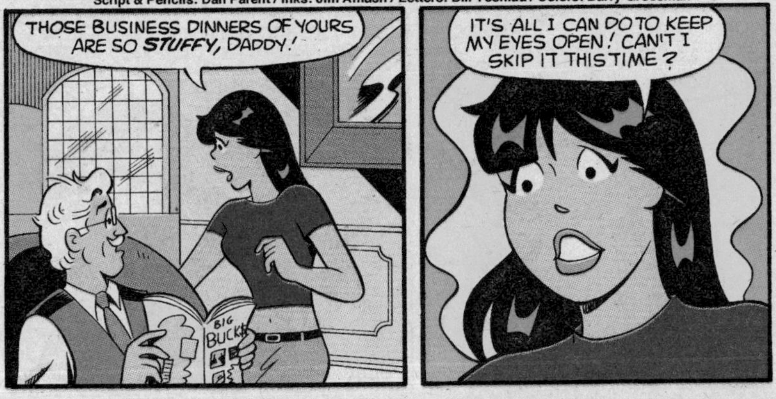
THOSE BUSINESS DINNERS OF YOURS ARE SO *STUFFY*, DADDY!
BIG BUCK$
IT'S ALL I CAN DO TO KEEP MY EYES OPEN! CAN'T I SKIP IT THIS TIME?

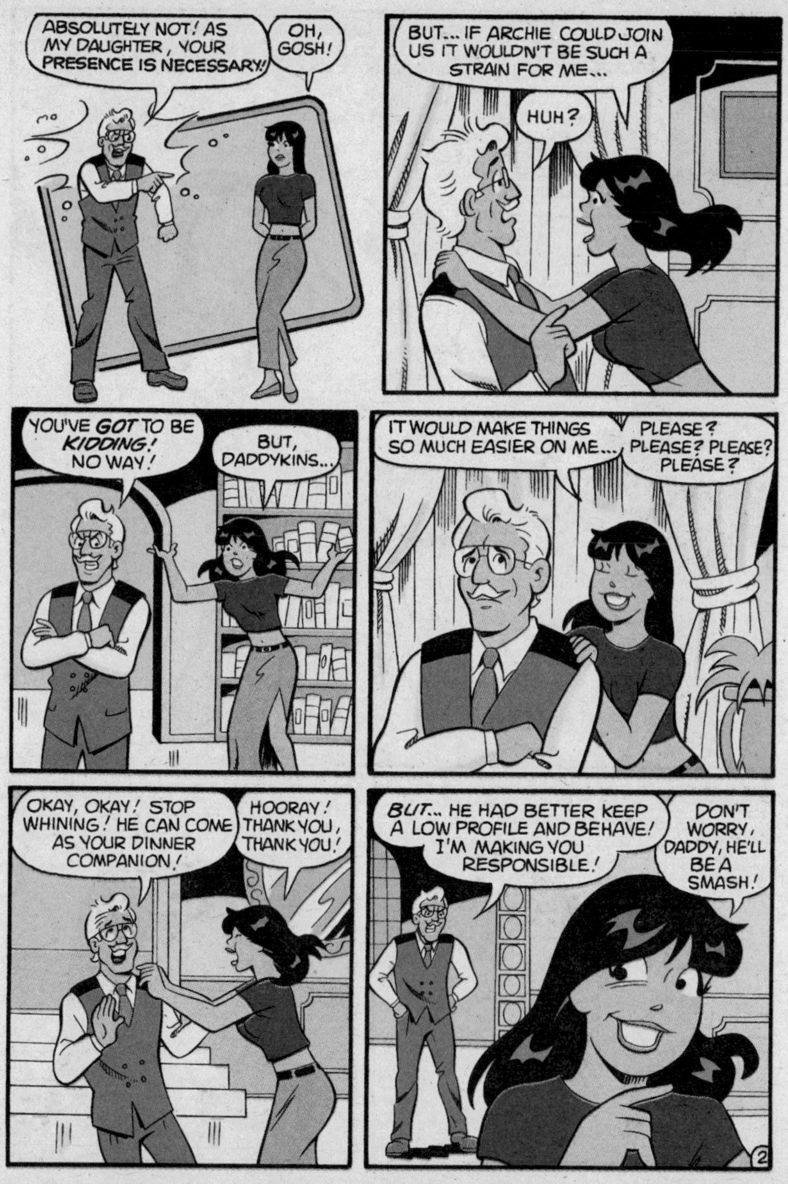
ABSOLUTELY NOT! AS MY DAUGHTER, YOUR PRESENCE IS NECESSARY!
OH, GOSH!
BUT... IF ARCHIE COULD JOIN US IT WOULDN'T BE SUCH A STRAIN FOR ME...
HUH?
YOU'VE GOT TO BE KIDDING! NO WAY!
BUT, DADDYKINS...
IT WOULD MAKE THINGS SO MUCH EASIER ON ME...
PLEASE? PLEASE? PLEASE? PLEASE?
OKAY, OKAY! STOP WHINING! HE CAN COME AS YOUR DINNER COMPANION!
HOORAY! THANK YOU, THANK YOU!
BUT... HE HAD BETTER KEEP A LOW PROFILE AND BEHAVE! I'M MAKING YOU RESPONSIBLE!
DON'T WORRY, DADDY, HE'LL BE A SMASH!

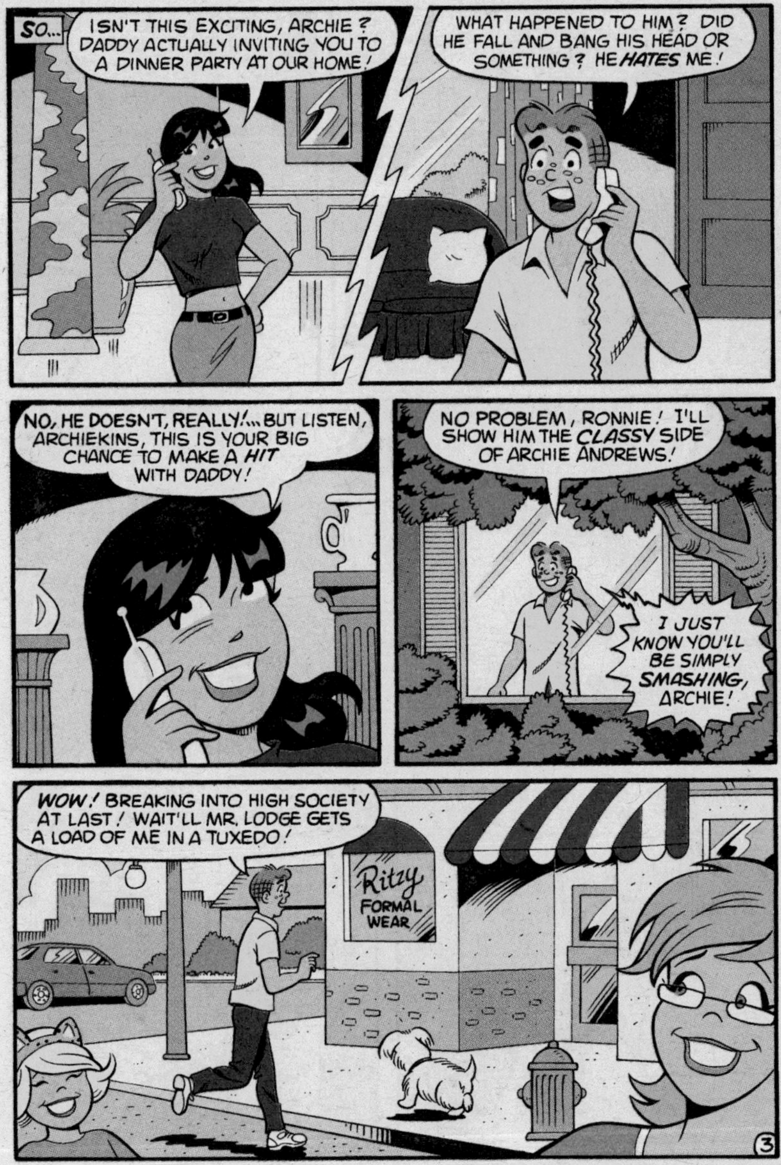
SO...
ISN'T THIS EXCITING, ARCHIE? DADDY ACTUALLY INVITING YOU TO A DINNER PARTY AT OUR HOME!
WHAT HAPPENED TO HIM? DID HE FALL AND BANG HIS HEAD OR SOMETHING? HE HATES ME!
NO, HE DOESN'T, REALLY!... BUT LISTEN, ARCHIEKINS, THIS IS YOUR BIG CHANCE TO MAKE A HIT WITH DADDY!
NO PROBLEM, RONNIE! I'LL SHOW HIM THE CLASSY SIDE OF ARCHIE ANDREWS!
I JUST KNOW YOU'LL BE SIMPLY SMASHING, ARCHIE!
WOW! BREAKING INTO HIGH SOCIETY AT LAST! WAIT'LL MR. LODGE GETS A LOAD OF ME IN A TUXEDO!
Ritzy FORMAL WEAR
3

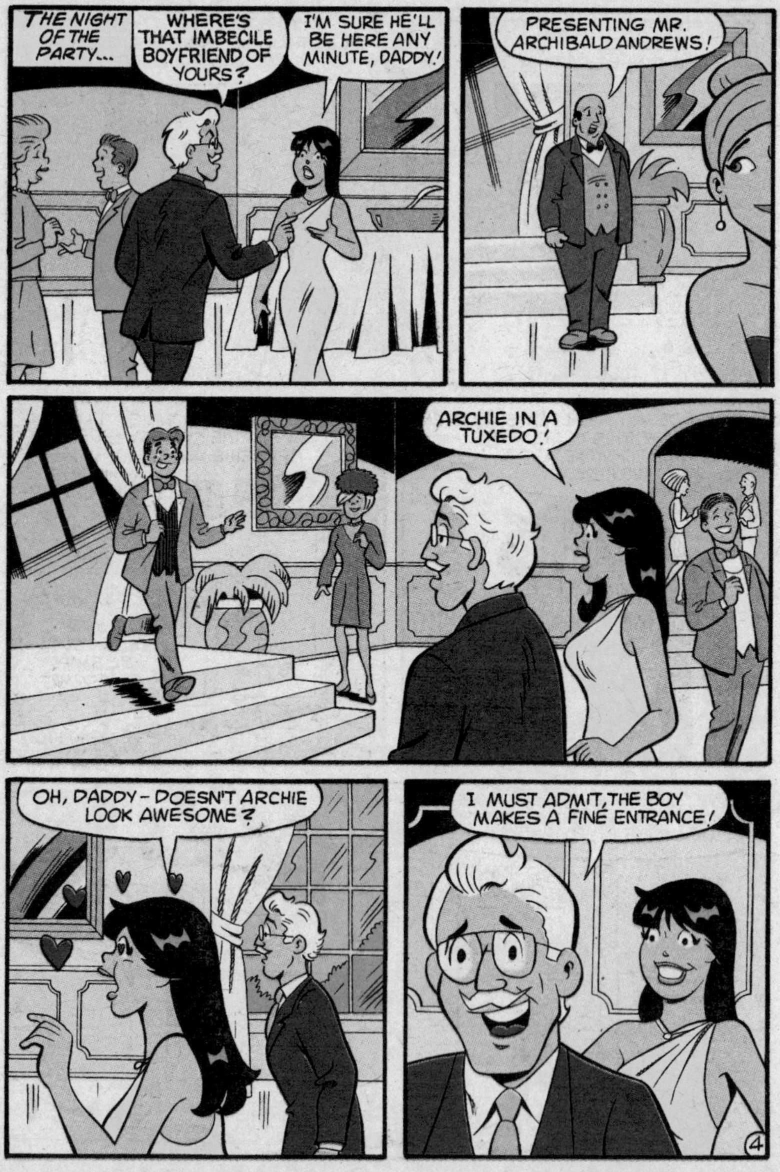
THE NIGHT OF THE PARTY...
WHERE'S THAT IMBECILE BOYFRIEND OF YOURS?
I'M SURE HE'LL BE HERE ANY MINUTE, DADDY!
PRESENTING MR. ARCHIBALD ANDREWS!
ARCHIE IN A TUXEDO!
OH, DADDY - DOESN'T ARCHIE LOOK AWESOME?
I MUST ADMIT, THE BOY MAKES A FINE ENTRANCE!
4

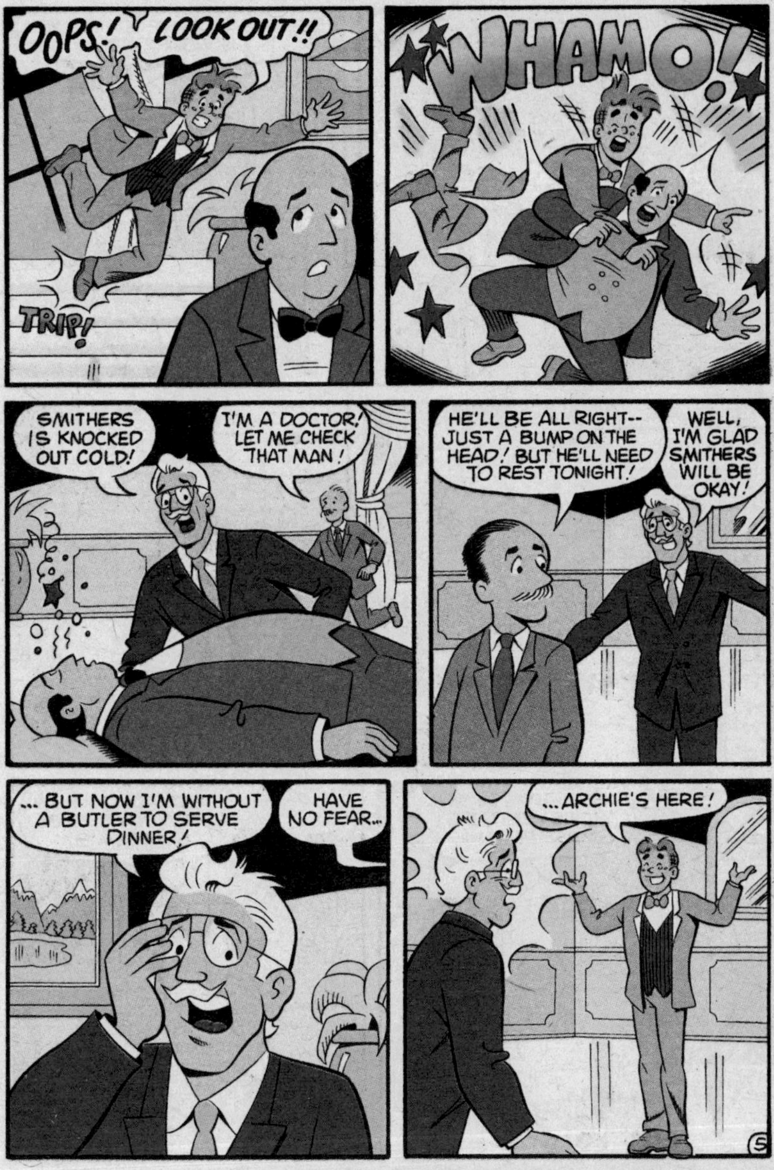
OOPS!
LOOK OUT!!
TRIP!
WHAMO!
SMITHERS IS KNOCKED OUT COLD!
I'M A DOCTOR! LET ME CHECK THAT MAN!
HE'LL BE ALL RIGHT-- JUST A BUMP ON THE HEAD! BUT HE'LL NEED TO REST TONIGHT!
WELL, I'M GLAD SMITHERS WILL BE OKAY!
... BUT NOW I'M WITHOUT A BUTLER TO SERVE DINNER!
HAVE NO FEAR...
... ARCHIE'S HERE!
5

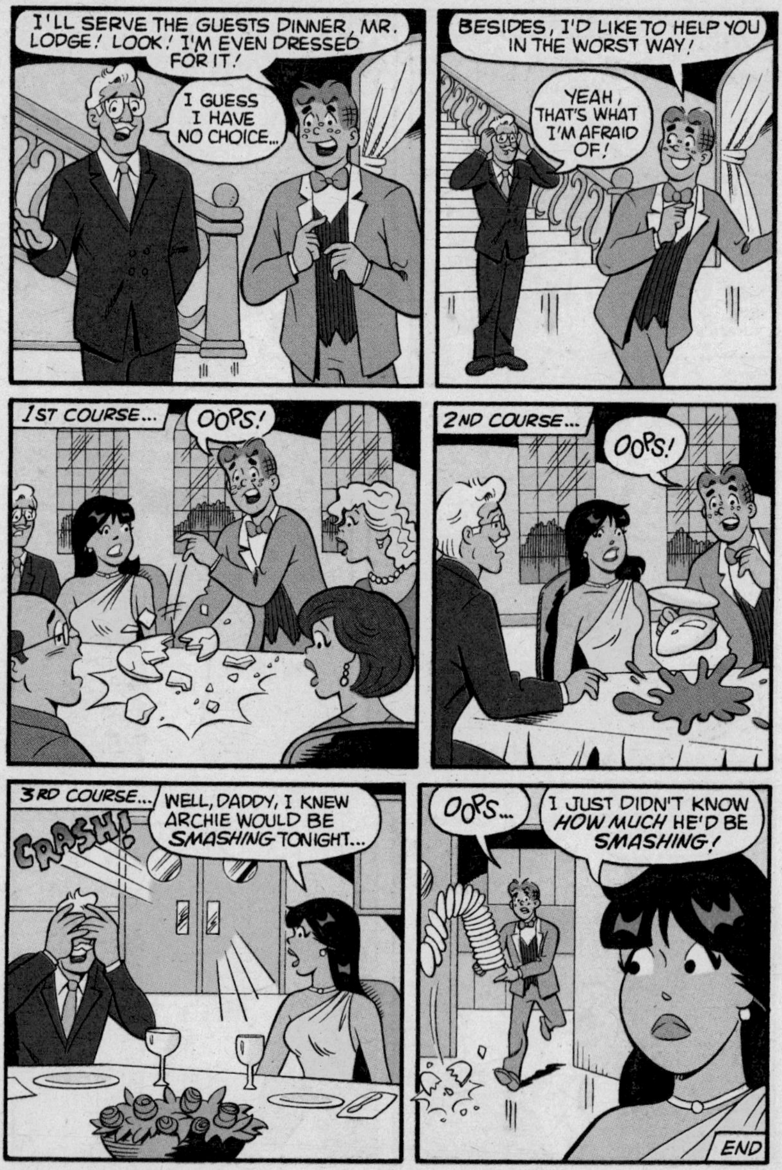
I'LL SERVE THE GUESTS DINNER, MR. LODGE! LOOK! I'M EVEN DRESSED FOR IT!
I GUESS I HAVE NO CHOICE...
BESIDES, I'D LIKE TO HELP YOU IN THE WORST WAY!
YEAH, THAT'S WHAT I'M AFRAID OF!
1ST COURSE...
OOPS!
2ND COURSE...
OOPS!
3RD COURSE...
CRASH!
WELL, DADDY, I KNEW ARCHIE WOULD BE *SMASHING* TONIGHT...
OOPS...
I JUST DIDN'T KNOW *HOW MUCH* HE'D BE *SMASHING*!
END

Betty and Veronica in BEAUTY and the BEAST

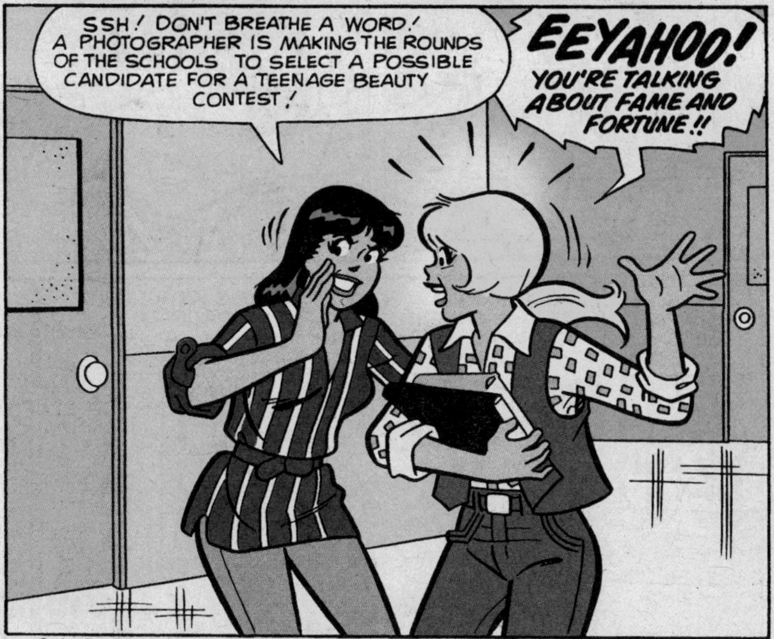
SSH! DON'T BREATHE A WORD! A PHOTOGRAPHER IS MAKING THE ROUNDS OF THE SCHOOLS TO SELECT A POSSIBLE CANDIDATE FOR A TEENAGE BEAUTY CONTEST!
EEYAHOO! YOU'RE TALKING ABOUT FAME AND FORTUNE!!

Script: Frank Doyle / Pencils: Dan DeCarlo / Inks: Rudy Lapick / Letters: Bill Yoshida / Colors: Barry Grossman

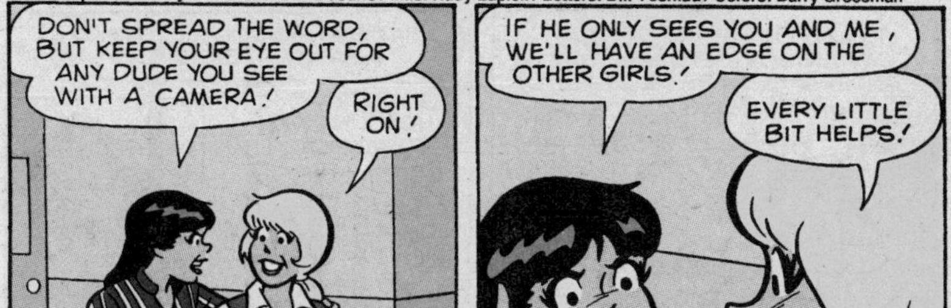
DON'T SPREAD THE WORD, BUT KEEP YOUR EYE OUT FOR ANY DUDE YOU SEE WITH A CAMERA!
RIGHT ON!
IF HE ONLY SEES YOU AND ME, WE'LL HAVE AN EDGE ON THE OTHER GIRLS!
EVERY LITTLE BIT HELPS!

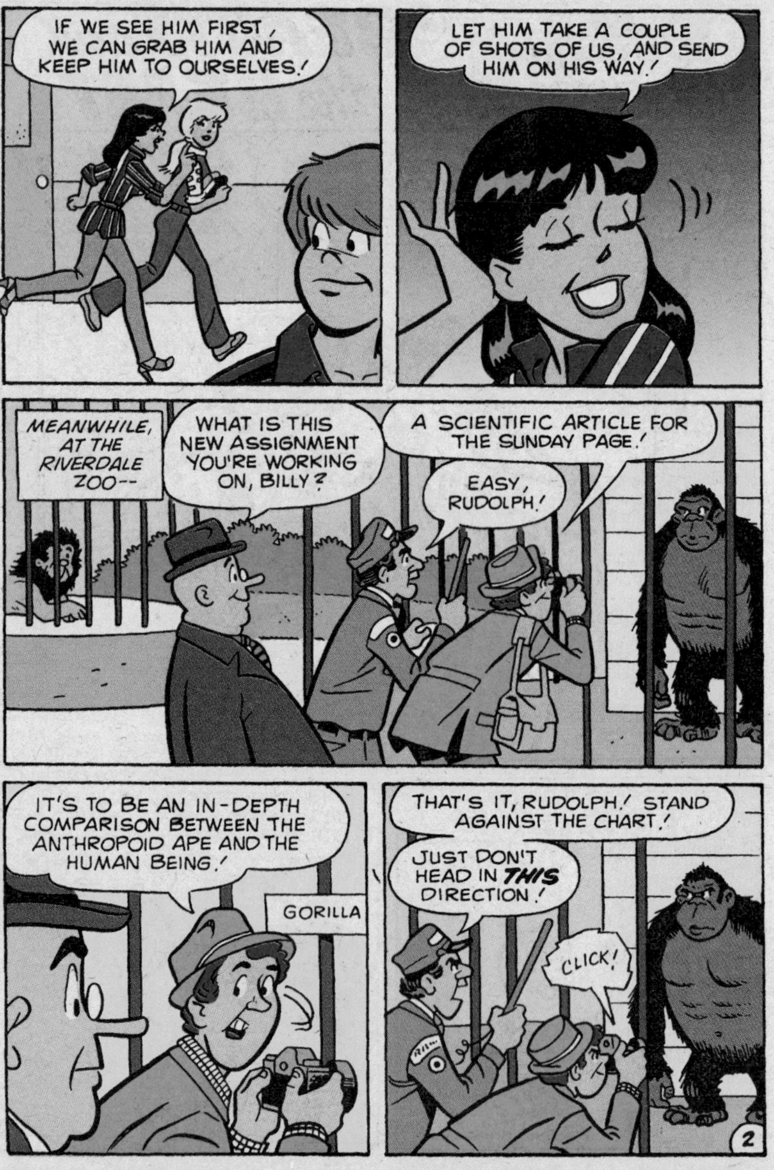
IF WE SEE HIM FIRST, WE CAN GRAB HIM AND KEEP HIM TO OURSELVES!
LET HIM TAKE A COUPLE OF SHOTS OF US, AND SEND HIM ON HIS WAY!
MEANWHILE, AT THE RIVERDALE ZOO--
WHAT IS THIS NEW ASSIGNMENT YOU'RE WORKING ON, BILLY?
A SCIENTIFIC ARTICLE FOR THE SUNDAY PAGE!
EASY, RUDOLPH!
IT'S TO BE AN IN-DEPTH COMPARISON BETWEEN THE ANTHROPOID APE AND THE HUMAN BEING!
GORILLA
THAT'S IT, RUDOLPH! STAND AGAINST THE CHART!
JUST DON'T HEAD IN ***THIS*** DIRECTION!
CLICK!
2

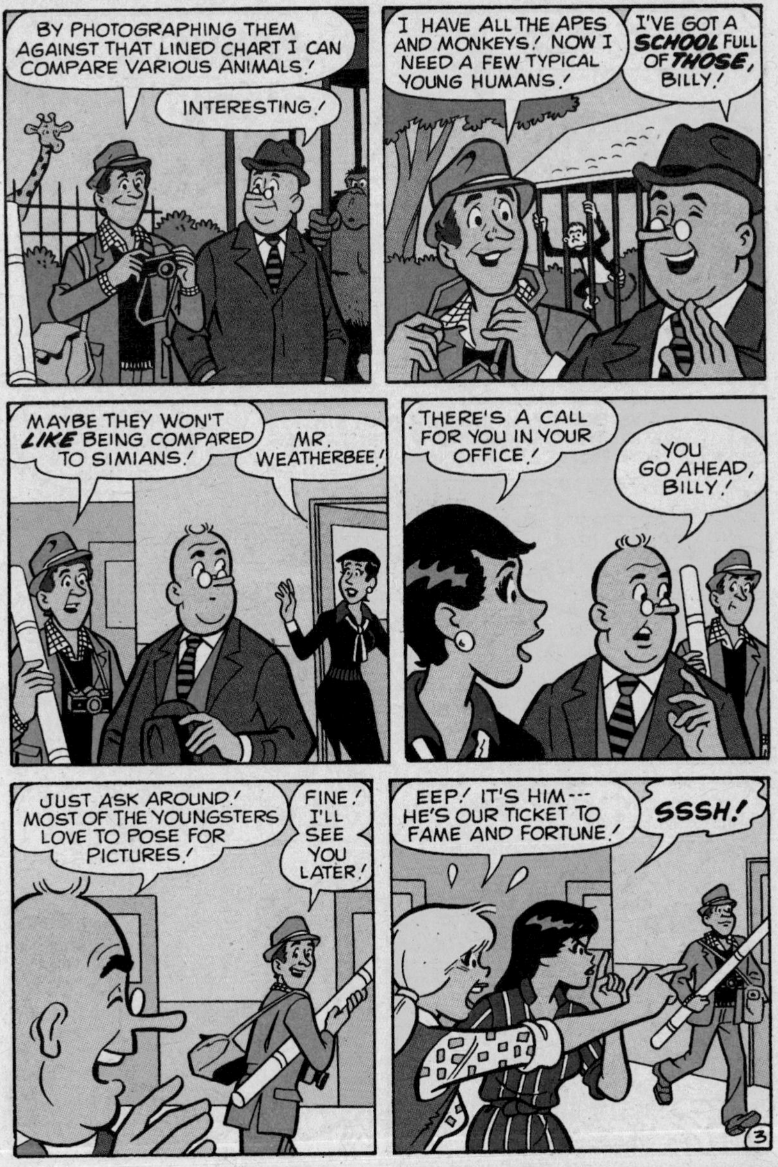
BY PHOTOGRAPHING THEM AGAINST THAT LINED CHART I CAN COMPARE VARIOUS ANIMALS!
INTERESTING!
I HAVE ALL THE APES AND MONKEYS! NOW I NEED A FEW TYPICAL YOUNG HUMANS!
I'VE GOT A SCHOOL FULL OF THOSE, BILLY!
MAYBE THEY WON'T LIKE BEING COMPARED TO SIMIANS!
MR. WEATHERBEE!
THERE'S A CALL FOR YOU IN YOUR OFFICE!
YOU GO AHEAD, BILLY!
JUST ASK AROUND! MOST OF THE YOUNGSTERS LOVE TO POSE FOR PICTURES!
FINE! I'LL SEE YOU LATER!
EEP! IT'S HIM--- HE'S OUR TICKET TO FAME AND FORTUNE!
SSSH!
3

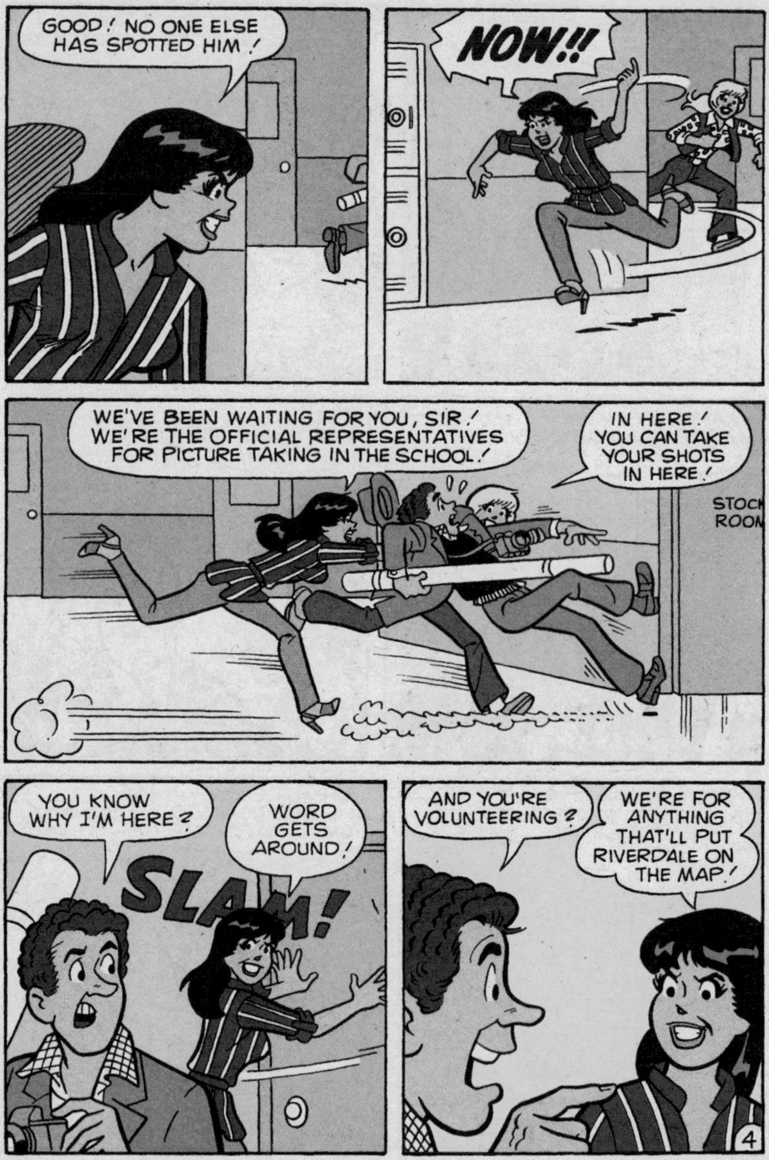
GOOD! NO ONE ELSE HAS SPOTTED HIM!
NOW!!
WE'VE BEEN WAITING FOR YOU, SIR! WE'RE THE OFFICIAL REPRESENTATIVES FOR PICTURE TAKING IN THE SCHOOL!
IN HERE! YOU CAN TAKE YOUR SHOTS IN HERE!
STOCK ROOM
YOU KNOW WHY I'M HERE?
WORD GETS AROUND!
SLAM!
AND YOU'RE VOLUNTEERING?
WE'RE FOR ANYTHING THAT'LL PUT RIVERDALE ON THE MAP!
4

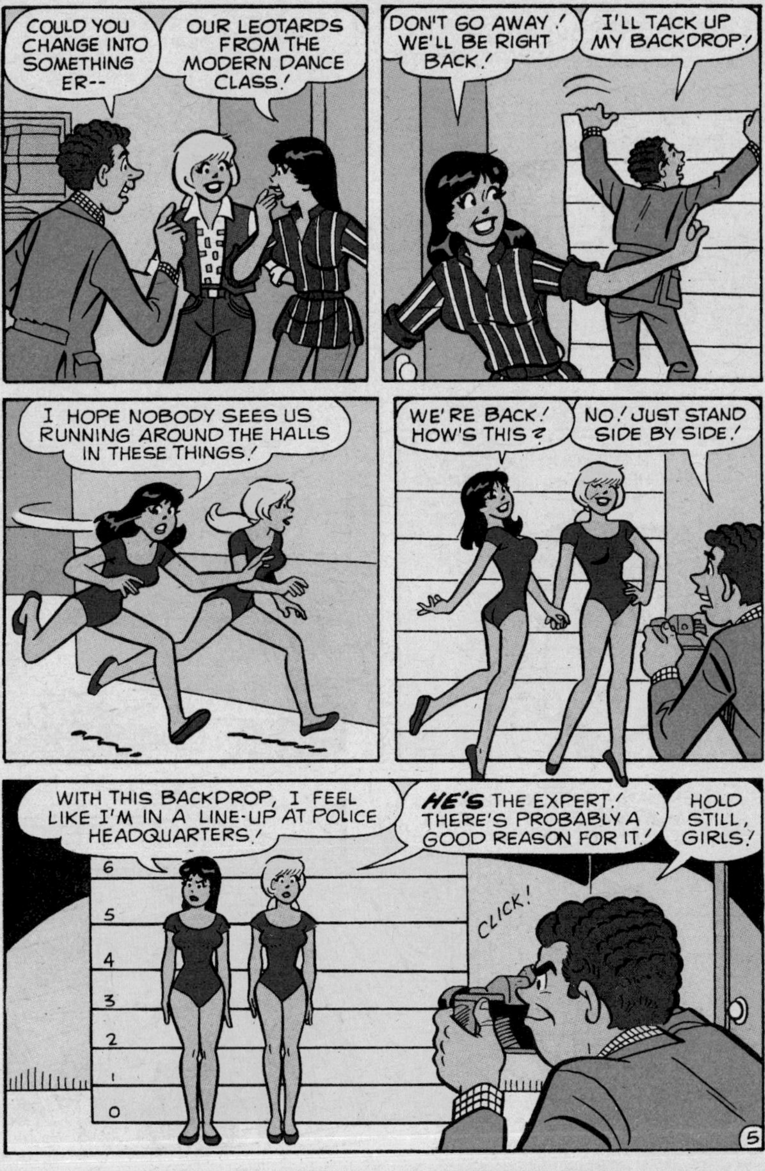

COULD YOU CHANGE INTO SOMETHING ER--
OUR LEOTARDS FROM THE MODERN DANCE CLASS!
DON'T GO AWAY! WE'LL BE RIGHT BACK!
I'LL TACK UP MY BACKDROP!
I HOPE NOBODY SEES US RUNNING AROUND THE HALLS IN THESE THINGS!
WE'RE BACK! HOW'S THIS?
NO! JUST STAND SIDE BY SIDE!
WITH THIS BACKDROP, I FEEL LIKE I'M IN A LINE-UP AT POLICE HEADQUARTERS!
HE'S THE EXPERT! THERE'S PROBABLY A GOOD REASON FOR IT!
HOLD STILL, GIRLS!
6
5
4
3
2
1
0
CLICK!
5

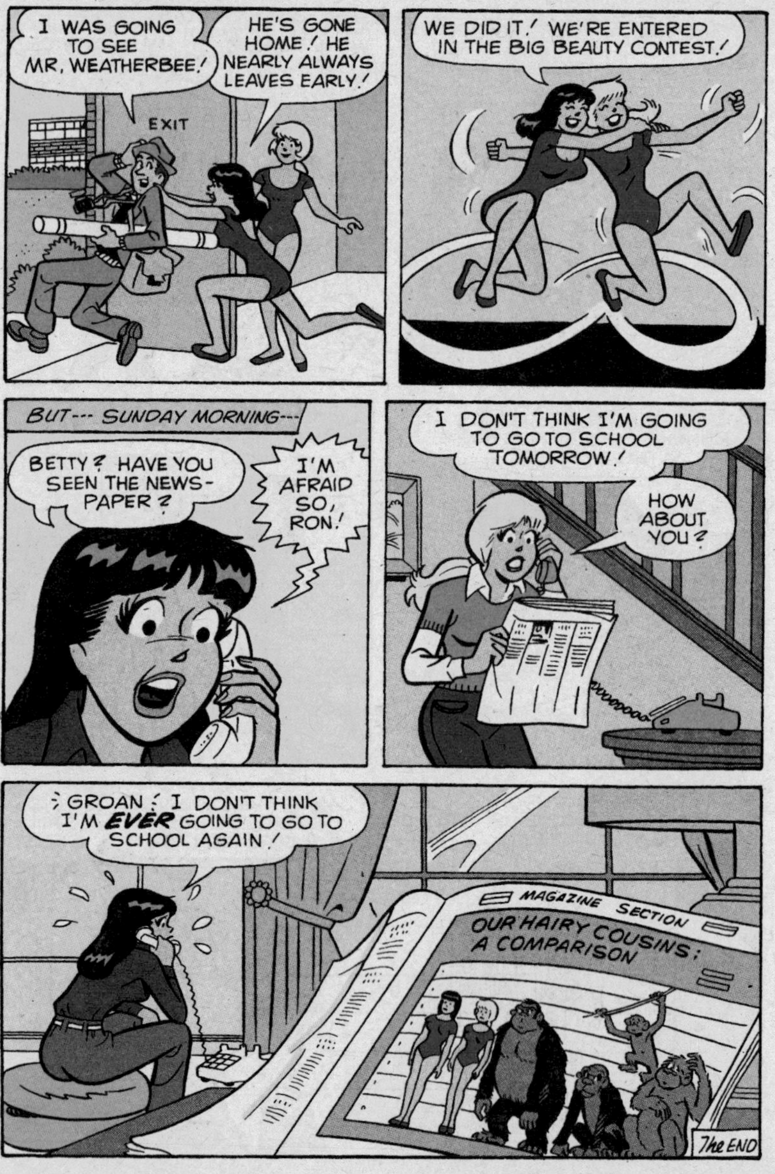
I WAS GOING TO SEE MR. WEATHERBEE!
HE'S GONE HOME! HE NEARLY ALWAYS LEAVES EARLY!
EXIT
WE DID IT! WE'RE ENTERED IN THE BIG BEAUTY CONTEST!
BUT--- SUNDAY MORNING---
BETTY? HAVE YOU SEEN THE NEWSPAPER?
I'M AFRAID SO, RON!
I DON'T THINK I'M GOING TO GO TO SCHOOL TOMORROW!
HOW ABOUT YOU?
GROAN! I DON'T THINK I'M EVER GOING TO GO TO SCHOOL AGAIN!
MAGAZINE SECTION
OUR HAIRY COUSINS; A COMPARISON
The END

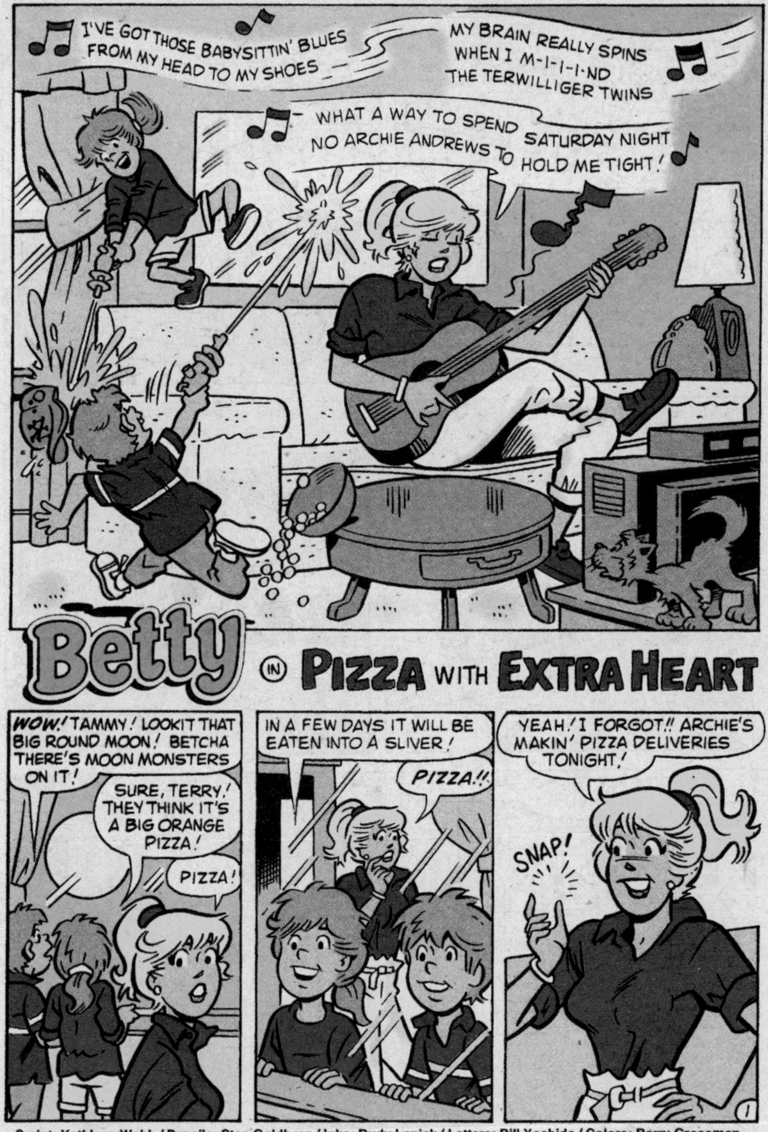
I'VE GOT THOSE BABYSITTIN' BLUES FROM MY HEAD TO MY SHOES
MY BRAIN REALLY SPINS WHEN I M-I-I-I-ND THE TERWILLIGER TWINS
WHAT A WAY TO SPEND SATURDAY NIGHT NO ARCHIE ANDREWS TO HOLD ME TIGHT!
Betty
IN PIZZA WITH EXTRA HEART
WOW! TAMMY! LOOKIT THAT BIG ROUND MOON! BETCHA THERE'S MOON MONSTERS ON IT!
SURE, TERRY! THEY THINK IT'S A BIG ORANGE PIZZA!
PIZZA!
IN A FEW DAYS IT WILL BE EATEN INTO A SLIVER!
PIZZA!!
YEAH! I FORGOT!! ARCHIE'S MAKIN' PIZZA DELIVERIES TONIGHT!
SNAP!
1

Script: Kathleen Webb / Pencils: Stan Goldberg / Inks: Rudy Lapick / Letters: Bill Yoshida / Colors: Barry Grossman

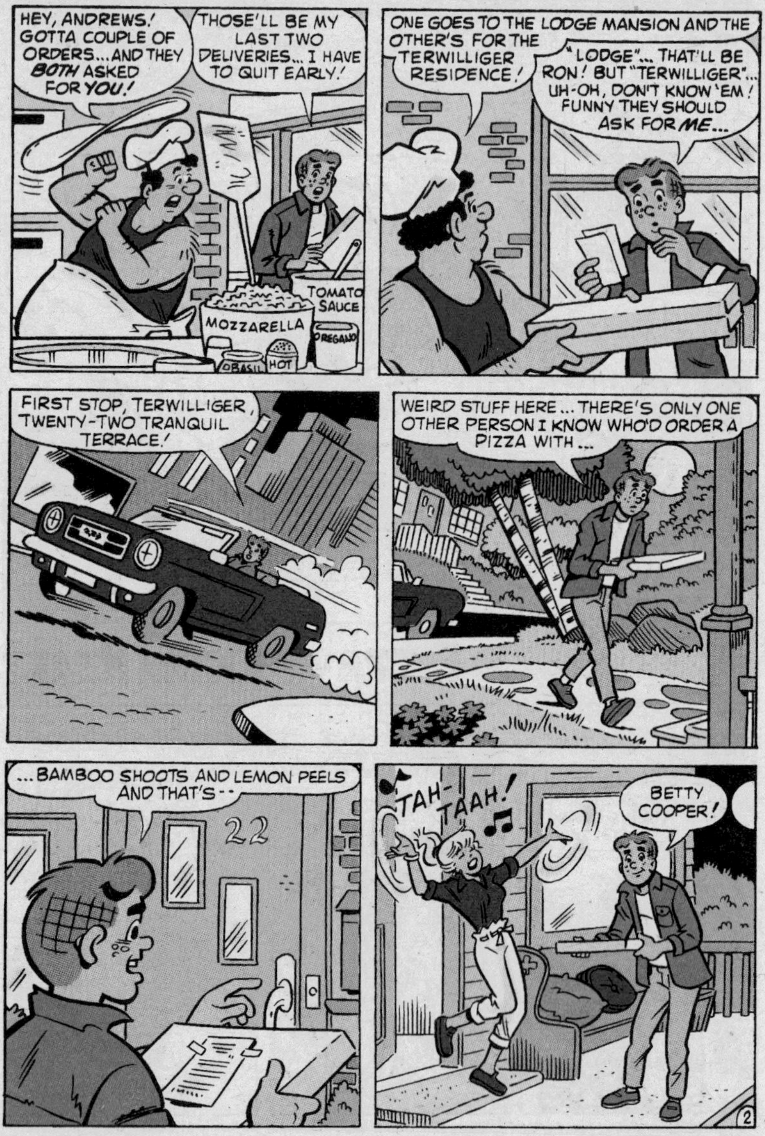
HEY, ANDREWS! GOTTA COUPLE OF ORDERS... AND THEY *BOTH* ASKED FOR *YOU*!
THOSE'LL BE MY LAST TWO DELIVERIES... I HAVE TO QUIT EARLY!
TOMATO SAUCE
MOZZARELLA
OREGANO
HOT
ONE GOES TO THE LODGE MANSION AND THE OTHER'S FOR THE TERWILLIGER RESIDENCE!
"LODGE"... THAT'LL BE RON! BUT "TERWILLIGER"... UH-OH, DON'T KNOW 'EM! FUNNY THEY SHOULD ASK FOR *ME*...
FIRST STOP, TERWILLIGER TWENTY-TWO TRANQUIL TERRACE!
WEIRD STUFF HERE... THERE'S ONLY ONE OTHER PERSON I KNOW WHO'D ORDER A PIZZA WITH...
... BAMBOO SHOOTS AND LEMON PEELS AND THAT'S--
22
TAH-TAAH!
BETTY COOPER!

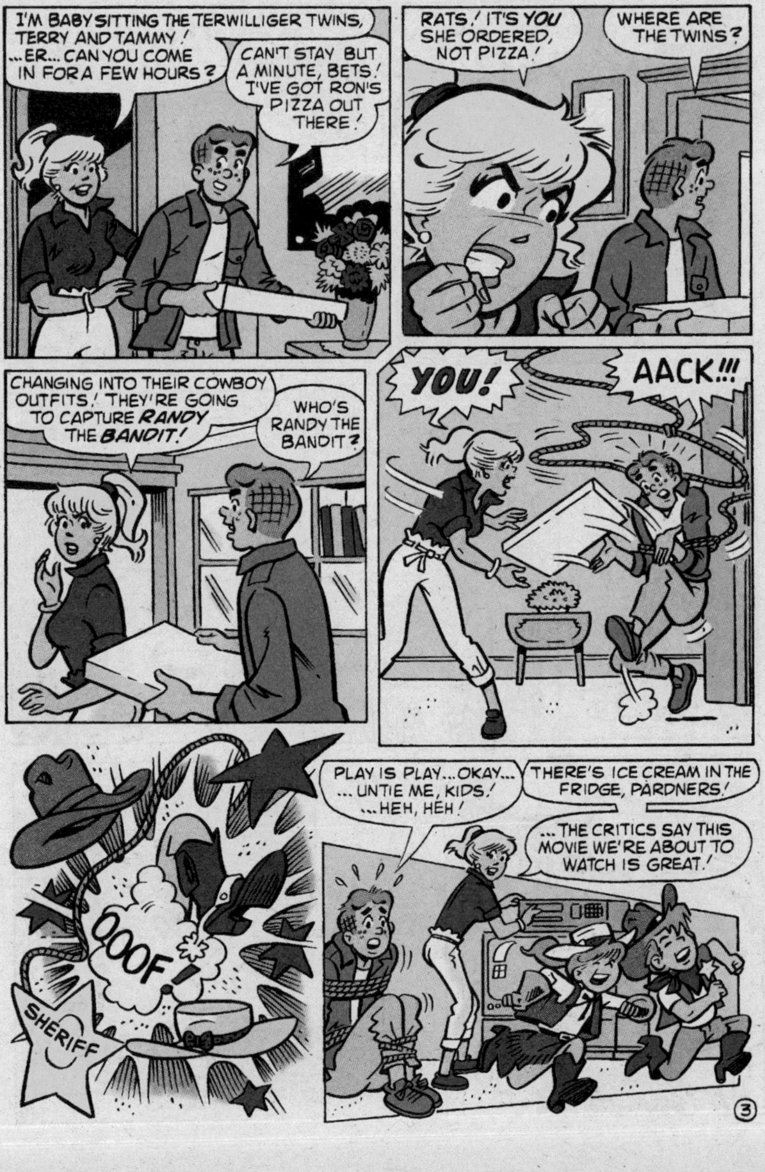
I'M BABYSITTING THE TERWILLIGER TWINS, TERRY AND TAMMY! ...ER... CAN YOU COME IN FOR A FEW HOURS?
CAN'T STAY BUT A MINUTE, BETS! I'VE GOT RON'S PIZZA OUT THERE!
RATS! IT'S *YOU* SHE ORDERED, NOT PIZZA!
WHERE ARE THE TWINS?
CHANGING INTO THEIR COWBOY OUTFITS! THEY'RE GOING TO CAPTURE ***RANDY*** THE ***BANDIT***!
WHO'S RANDY THE BANDIT?
YOU!
AACK!!!
OOOF!
SHERIFF
PLAY IS PLAY... OKAY... ... UNTIE ME, KIDS! ...HEH, HEH!
THERE'S ICE CREAM IN THE FRIDGE, PARDNERS!
...THE CRITICS SAY THIS MOVIE WE'RE ABOUT TO WATCH IS GREAT!

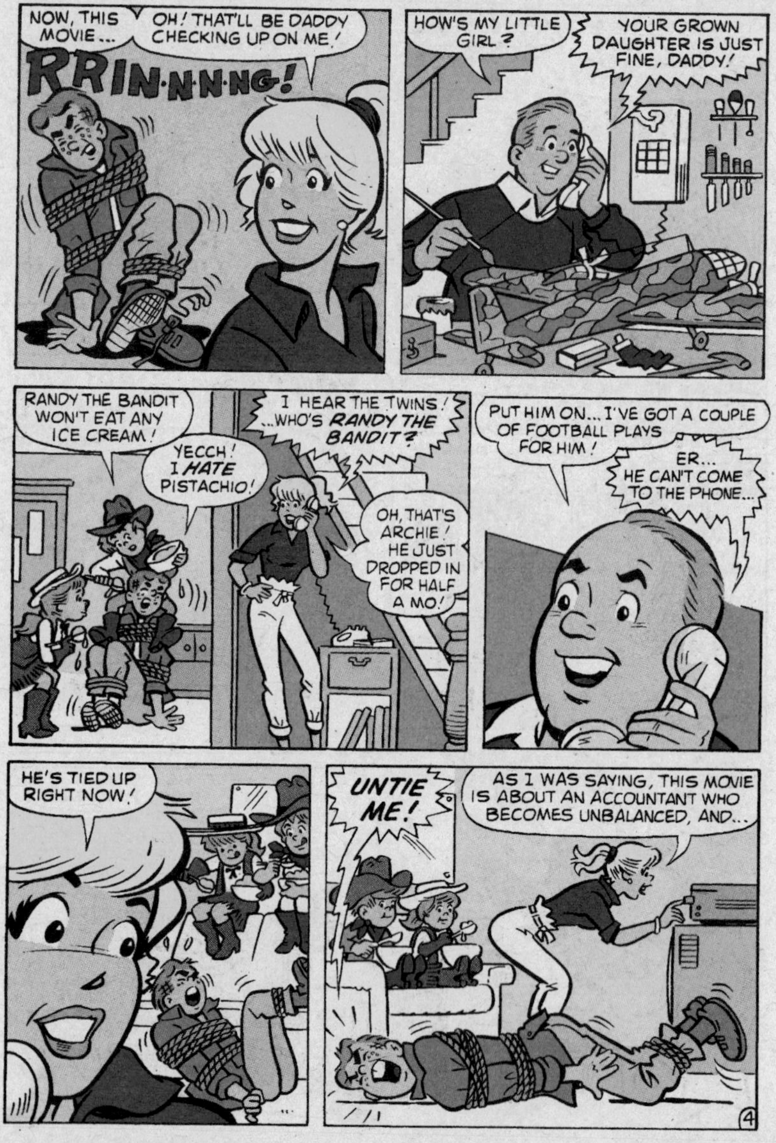
NOW, THIS MOVIE...
OH! THAT'LL BE DADDY CHECKING UP ON ME!
RRIN-N-N-NG!
HOW'S MY LITTLE GIRL?
YOUR GROWN DAUGHTER IS JUST FINE, DADDY!
RANDY THE BANDIT WON'T EAT ANY ICE CREAM!
YECCH! I HATE PISTACHIO!
I HEAR THE TWINS! ...WHO'S RANDY THE BANDIT?
OH, THAT'S ARCHIE! HE JUST DROPPED IN FOR HALF A MO!
PUT HIM ON... I'VE GOT A COUPLE OF FOOTBALL PLAYS FOR HIM!
ER... HE CAN'T COME TO THE PHONE...
HE'S TIED UP RIGHT NOW!
UNTIE ME!
AS I WAS SAYING, THIS MOVIE IS ABOUT AN ACCOUNTANT WHO BECOMES UNBALANCED, AND...
4

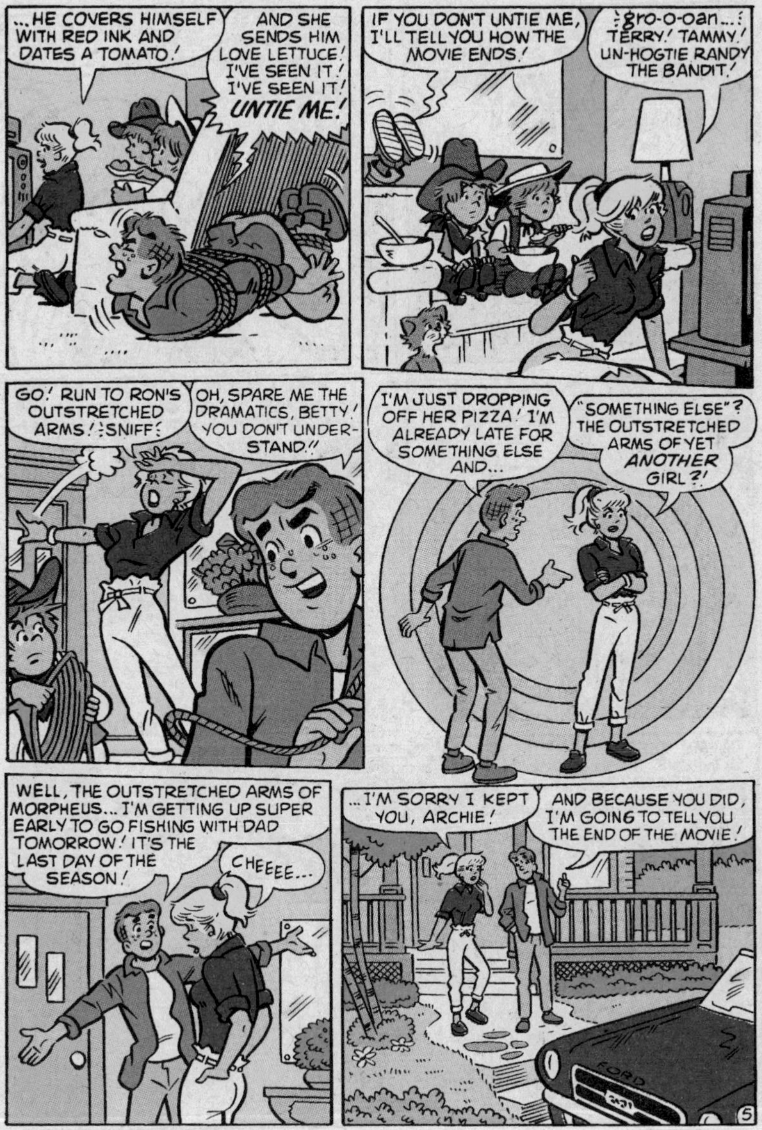
...HE COVERS HIMSELF WITH RED INK AND DATES A TOMATO!
AND SHE SENDS HIM LOVE LETTUCE! I'VE SEEN IT! I'VE SEEN IT! UNTIE ME!
IF YOU DON'T UNTIE ME, I'LL TELL YOU HOW THE MOVIE ENDS!
gro-o-oan... TERRY! TAMMY! UN-HOGTIE RANDY THE BANDIT!
GO! RUN TO RON'S OUTSTRETCHED ARMS! SNIFF
OH, SPARE ME THE DRAMATICS, BETTY! YOU DON'T UNDERSTAND!!
I'M JUST DROPPING OFF HER PIZZA! I'M ALREADY LATE FOR SOMETHING ELSE AND...
"SOMETHING ELSE"? THE OUTSTRETCHED ARMS OF YET ANOTHER GIRL?!
WELL, THE OUTSTRETCHED ARMS OF MORPHEUS... I'M GETTING UP SUPER EARLY TO GO FISHING WITH DAD TOMORROW! IT'S THE LAST DAY OF THE SEASON!
CHEEEE...
...I'M SORRY I KEPT YOU, ARCHIE!
AND BECAUSE YOU DID, I'M GOING TO TELL YOU THE END OF THE MOVIE!
FORD
5

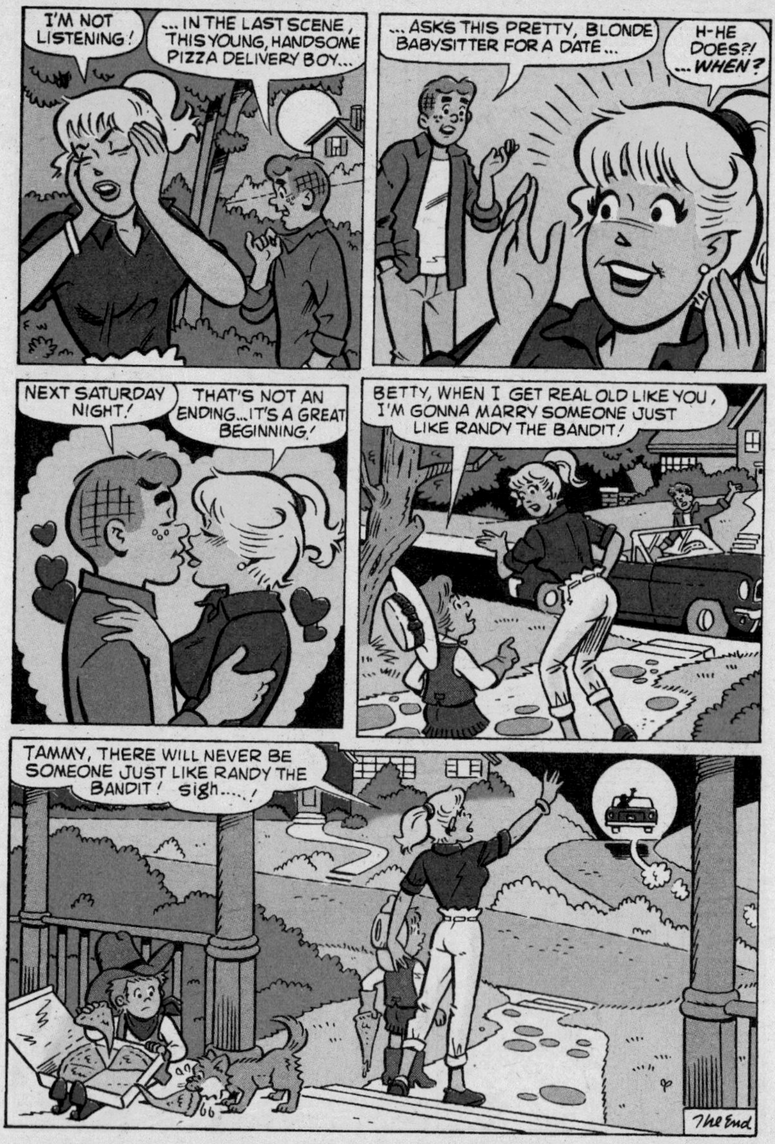

I'M NOT LISTENING!
...IN THE LAST SCENE, THIS YOUNG, HANDSOME PIZZA DELIVERY BOY...
...ASKS THIS PRETTY, BLONDE BABYSITTER FOR A DATE...
H-HE DOES?! ...WHEN?
NEXT SATURDAY NIGHT!
THAT'S NOT AN ENDING...IT'S A GREAT BEGINNING!
BETTY, WHEN I GET REAL OLD LIKE YOU, I'M GONNA MARRY SOMEONE JUST LIKE RANDY THE BANDIT!
TAMMY, THERE WILL NEVER BE SOMEONE JUST LIKE RANDY THE BANDIT! sigh....!
The End

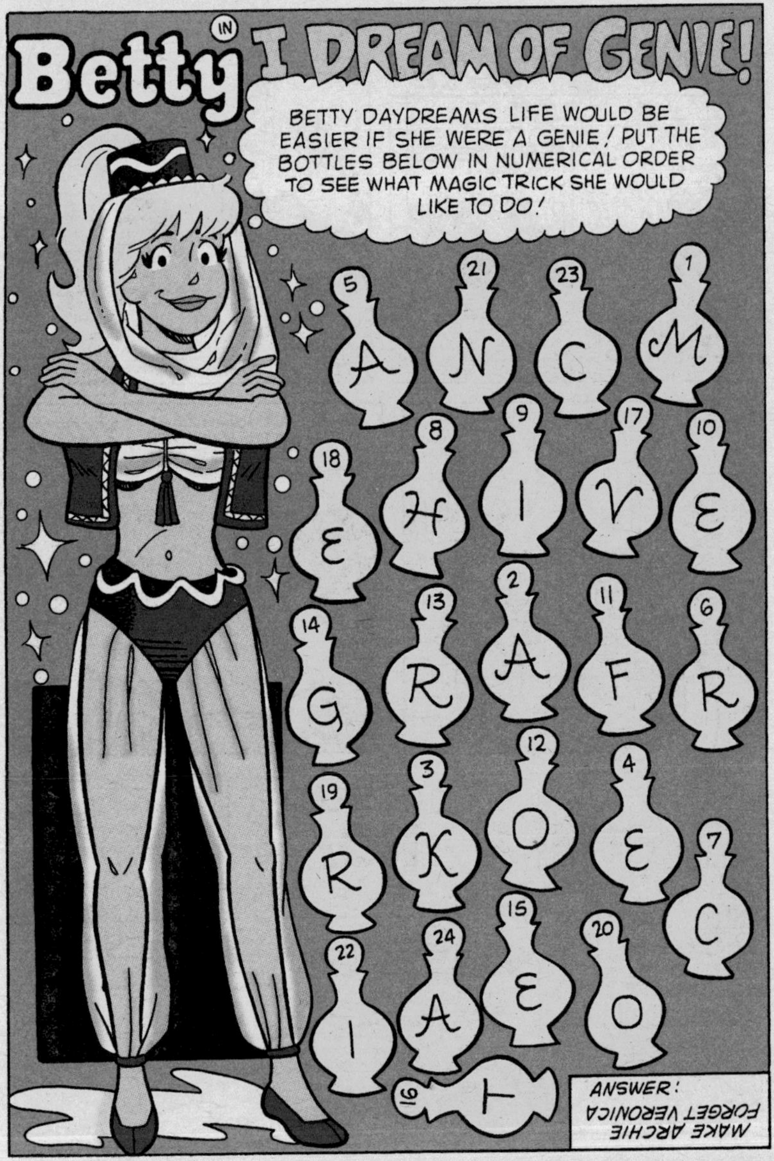
Betty IN I DREAM OF GENIE!
BETTY DAYDREAMS LIFE WOULD BE EASIER IF SHE WERE A GENIE! PUT THE BOTTLES BELOW IN NUMERICAL ORDER TO SEE WHAT MAGIC TRICK SHE WOULD LIKE TO DO!
5 A
21 N
23 C
1 M
18 E
8 H
9 I
17 V
10 E
14 G
13 R
2 A
11 F
6 R
19 R
3 K
12 O
4 E
7 C
22 I
24 A
15 E
20 O
16 T
ANSWER:
MAKE ARCHIE
FORGET VERONICA

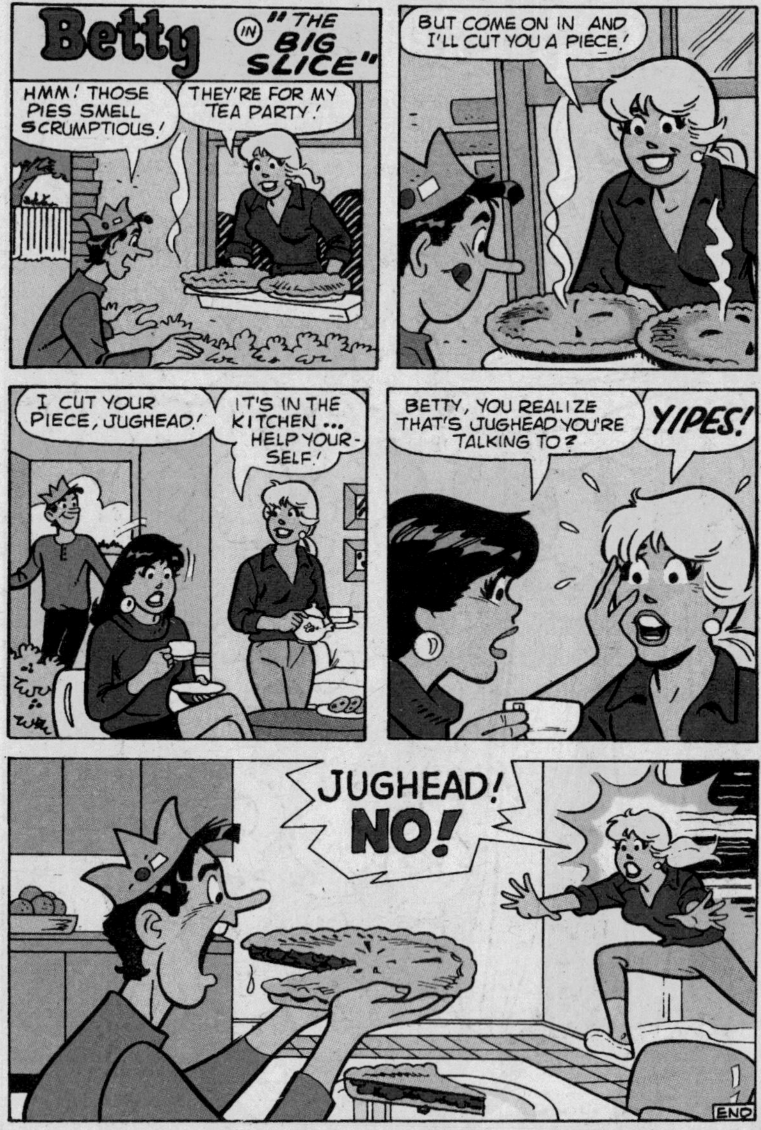

Betty IN "THE BIG SLICE"
HMM! THOSE PIES SMELL SCRUMPTIOUS!
THEY'RE FOR MY TEA PARTY!
BUT COME ON IN AND I'LL CUT YOU A PIECE!
I CUT YOUR PIECE, JUGHEAD!
IT'S IN THE KITCHEN ... HELP YOURSELF!
BETTY, YOU REALIZE THAT'S JUGHEAD YOU'RE TALKING TO?
YIPES!
JUGHEAD! NO!
END

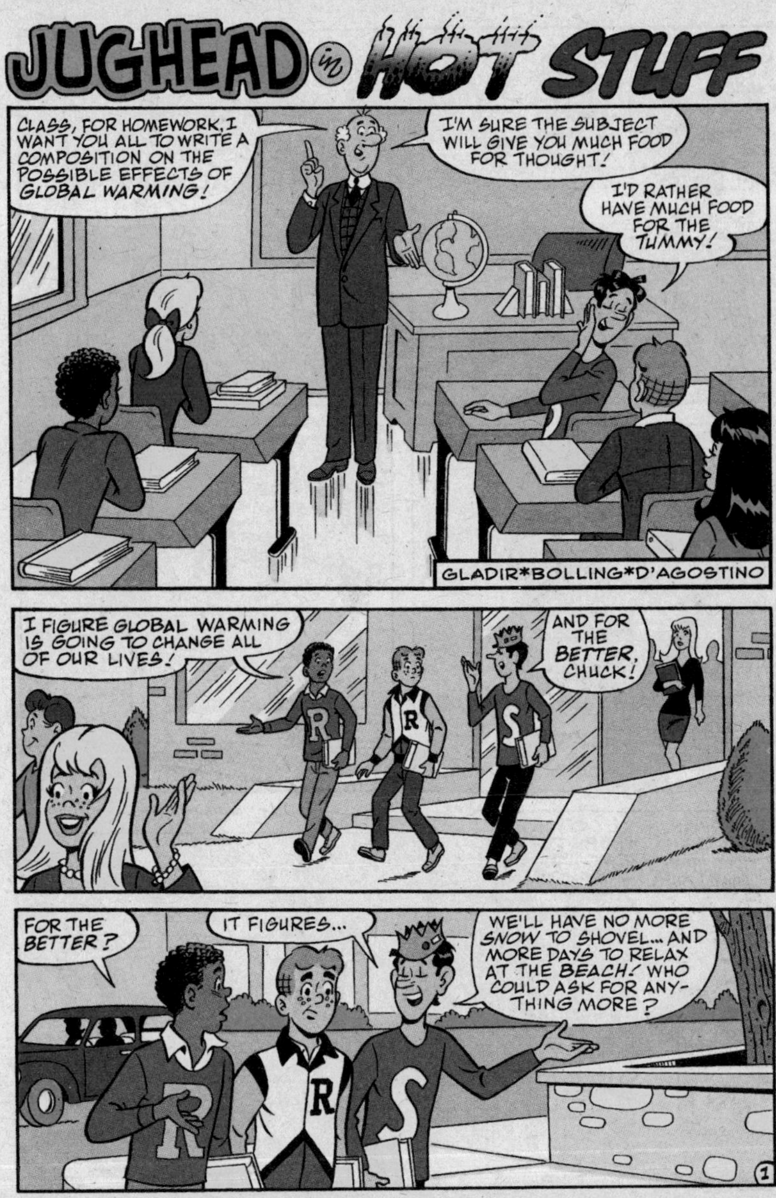
JUGHEAD in HOT STUFF
CLASS, FOR HOMEWORK, I WANT YOU ALL TO WRITE A COMPOSITION ON THE POSSIBLE EFFECTS OF GLOBAL WARMING!
I'M SURE THE SUBJECT WILL GIVE YOU MUCH FOOD FOR THOUGHT!
I'D RATHER HAVE MUCH FOOD FOR THE TUMMY!
GLADIR*BOLLING*D'AGOSTINO
I FIGURE GLOBAL WARMING IS GOING TO CHANGE ALL OF OUR LIVES!
AND FOR THE BETTER, CHUCK!
FOR THE BETTER?
IT FIGURES...
WE'LL HAVE NO MORE SNOW TO SHOVEL... AND MORE DAYS TO RELAX AT THE BEACH! WHO COULD ASK FOR ANYTHING MORE?
1

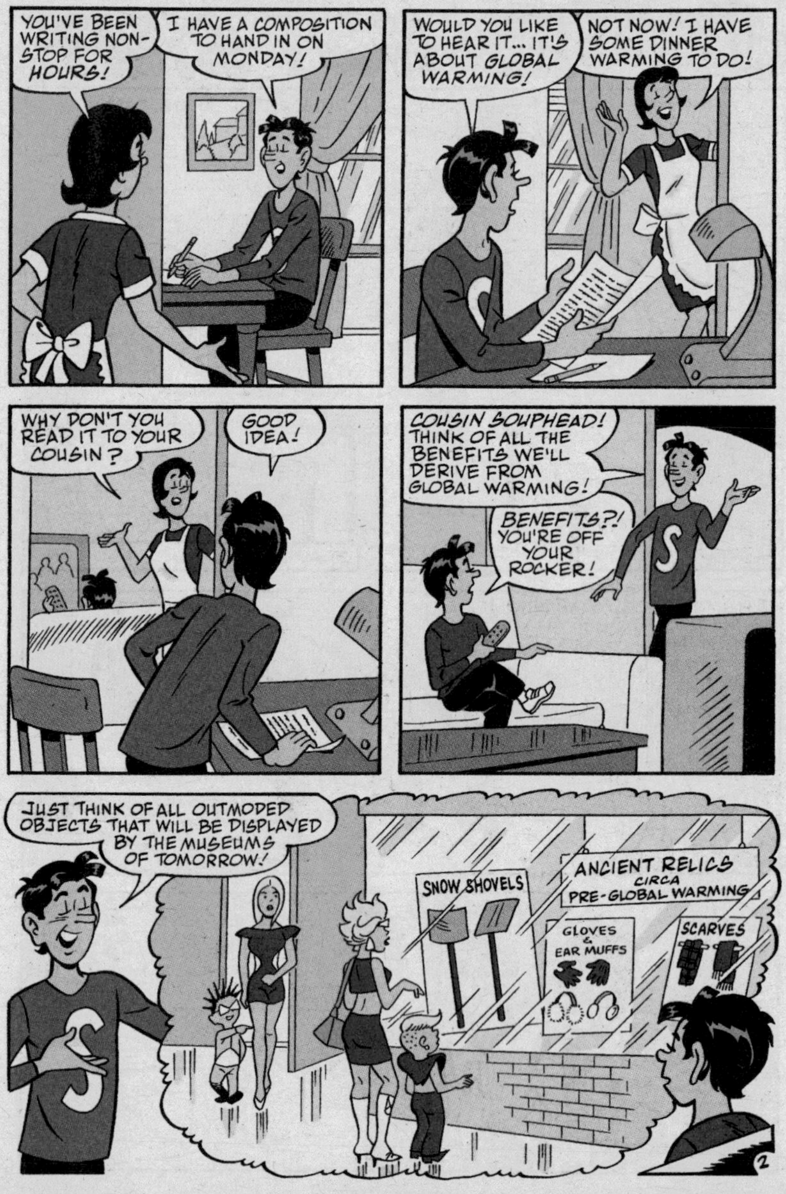
YOU'VE BEEN WRITING NON-STOP FOR HOURS!
I HAVE A COMPOSITION TO HAND IN ON MONDAY!
WOULD YOU LIKE TO HEAR IT... IT'S ABOUT GLOBAL WARMING!
NOT NOW! I HAVE SOME DINNER WARMING TO DO!
WHY DON'T YOU READ IT TO YOUR COUSIN?
GOOD IDEA!
COUSIN SOUPHEAD! THINK OF ALL THE BENEFITS WE'LL DERIVE FROM GLOBAL WARMING!
BENEFITS?! YOU'RE OFF YOUR ROCKER!
JUST THINK OF ALL OUTMODED OBJECTS THAT WILL BE DISPLAYED BY THE MUSEUMS OF TOMORROW!
SNOW SHOVELS
ANCIENT RELICS
CIRCA
PRE-GLOBAL WARMING
GLOVES & EAR MUFFS
SCARVES
2

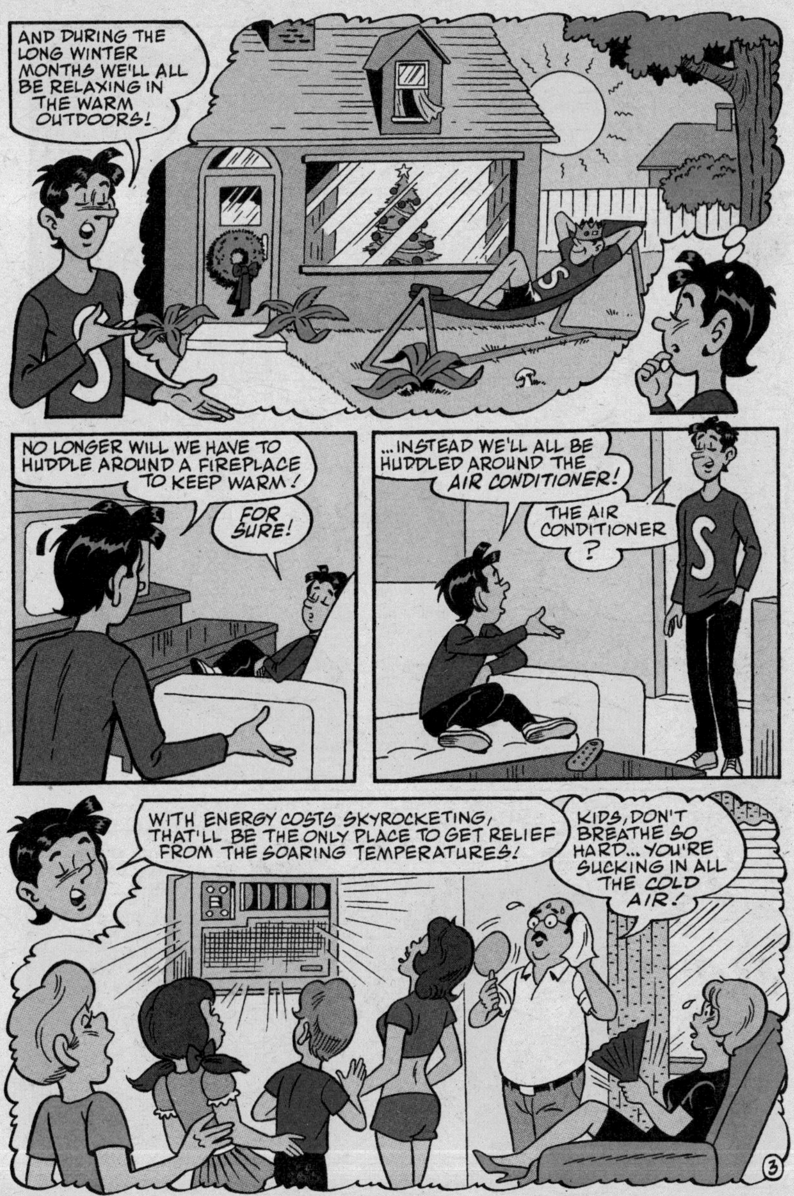
AND DURING THE LONG WINTER MONTHS WE'LL ALL BE RELAXING IN THE WARM OUTDOORS!
NO LONGER WILL WE HAVE TO HUDDLE AROUND A FIREPLACE TO KEEP WARM!
FOR SURE!
...INSTEAD WE'LL ALL BE HUDDLED AROUND THE AIR CONDITIONER!
THE AIR CONDITIONER ?
WITH ENERGY COSTS SKYROCKETING, THAT'LL BE THE ONLY PLACE TO GET RELIEF FROM THE SOARING TEMPERATURES!
KIDS, DON'T BREATHE SO HARD... YOU'RE SUCKING IN ALL THE COLD AIR!
3

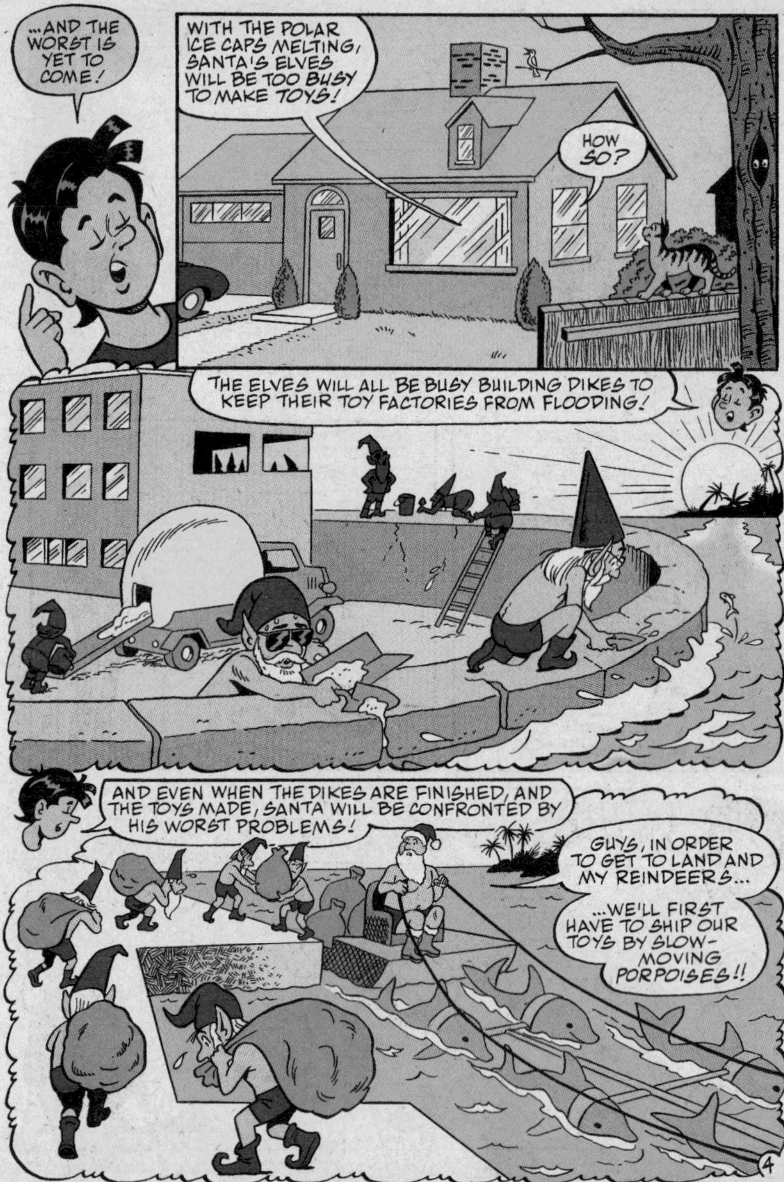
...AND THE WORST IS YET TO COME!
WITH THE POLAR ICE CAPS MELTING, SANTA'S ELVES WILL BE TOO BUSY TO MAKE TOYS!
HOW SO?
THE ELVES WILL ALL BE BUSY BUILDING DIKES TO KEEP THEIR TOY FACTORIES FROM FLOODING!
AND EVEN WHEN THE DIKES ARE FINISHED, AND THE TOYS MADE, SANTA WILL BE CONFRONTED BY HIS WORST PROBLEMS!
GUYS, IN ORDER TO GET TO LAND AND MY REINDEERS...
...WE'LL FIRST HAVE TO SHIP OUR TOYS BY SLOW-MOVING PORPOISES!!
4

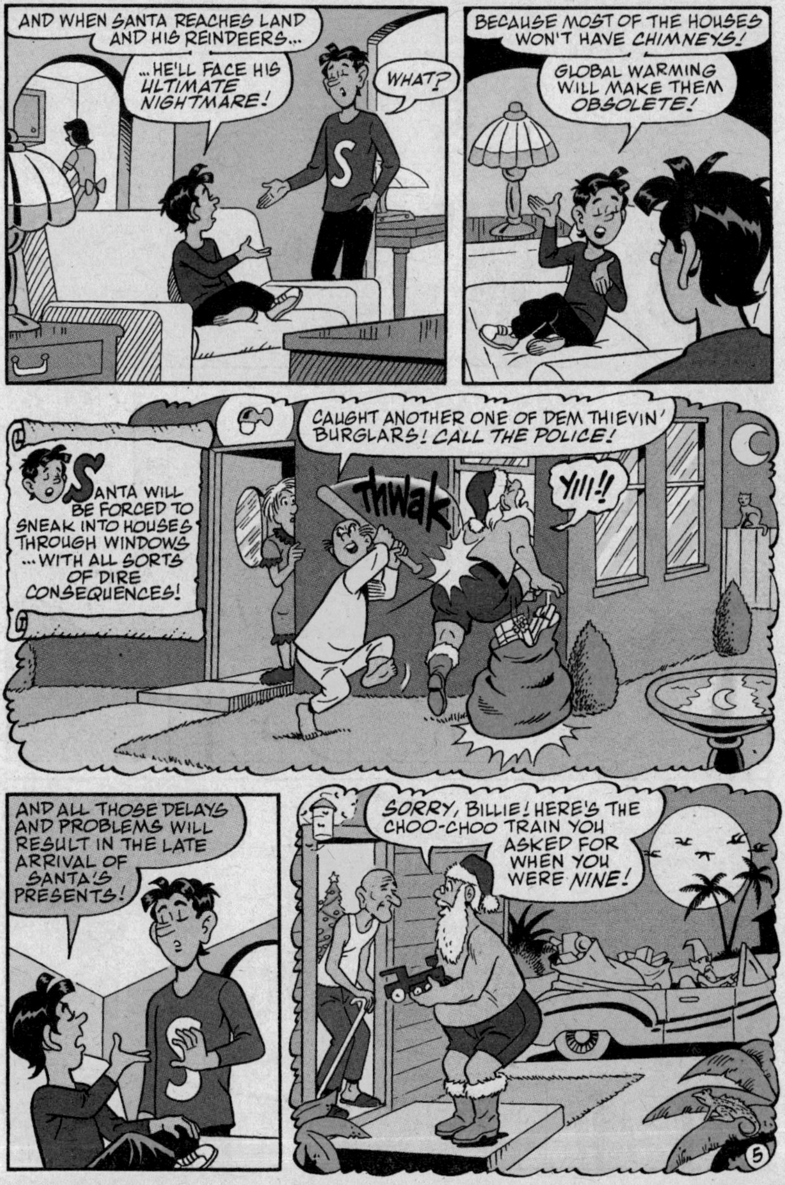
AND WHEN SANTA REACHES LAND AND HIS REINDEERS...
...HE'LL FACE HIS ULTIMATE NIGHTMARE!
WHAT?
BECAUSE MOST OF THE HOUSES WON'T HAVE CHIMNEYS!
GLOBAL WARMING WILL MAKE THEM OBSOLETE!
SANTA WILL BE FORCED TO SNEAK INTO HOUSES THROUGH WINDOWS ...WITH ALL SORTS OF DIRE CONSEQUENCES!
CAUGHT ANOTHER ONE OF DEM THIEVIN' BURGLARS! CALL THE POLICE!
THWAK
YIII!!
AND ALL THOSE DELAYS AND PROBLEMS WILL RESULT IN THE LATE ARRIVAL OF SANTA'S PRESENTS!
SORRY, BILLIE! HERE'S THE CHOO-CHOO TRAIN YOU ASKED FOR WHEN YOU WERE NINE!

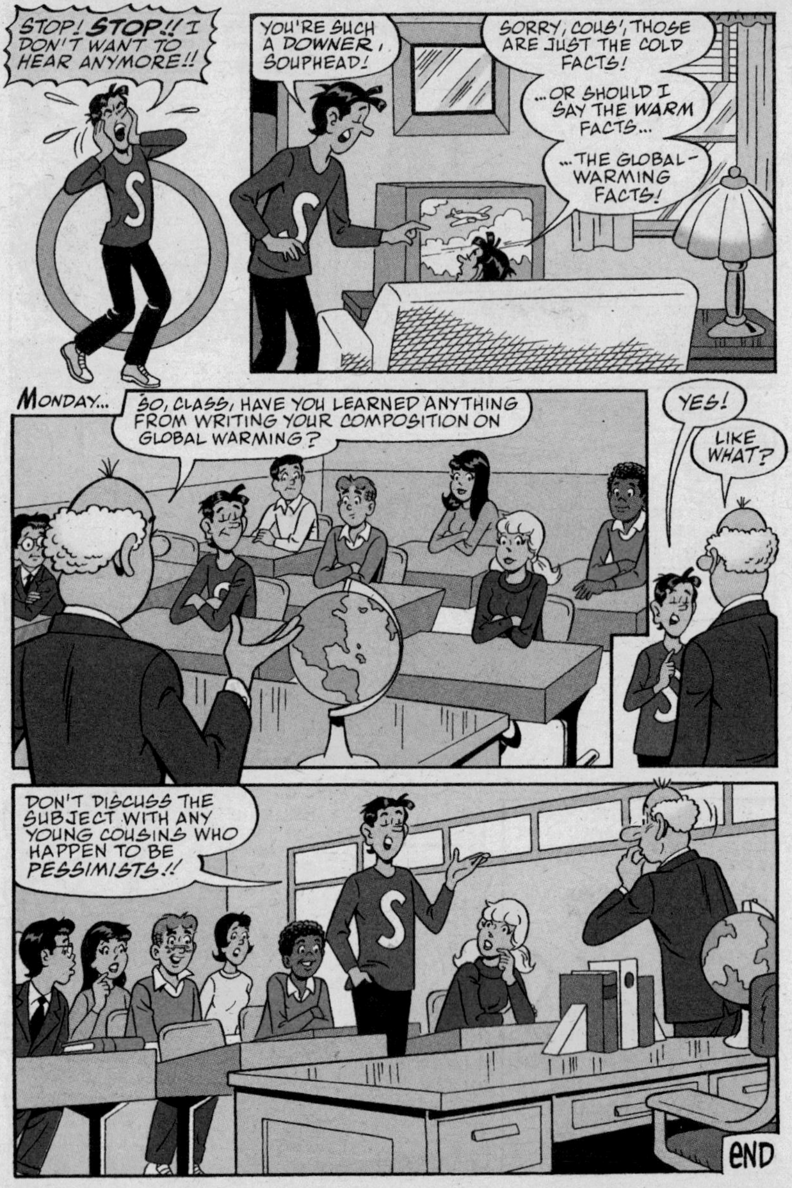
STOP! STOP!! I DON'T WANT TO HEAR ANYMORE!!
YOU'RE SUCH A DOWNER, SOUPHEAD!
SORRY, COUS', THOSE ARE JUST THE COLD FACTS!
...OR SHOULD I SAY THE WARM FACTS...
...THE GLOBAL-WARMING FACTS!
MONDAY...
SO, CLASS, HAVE YOU LEARNED ANYTHING FROM WRITING YOUR COMPOSITION ON GLOBAL WARMING?
YES!
LIKE WHAT?
DON'T DISCUSS THE SUBJECT WITH ANY YOUNG COUSINS WHO HAPPEN TO BE PESSIMISTS!!
END

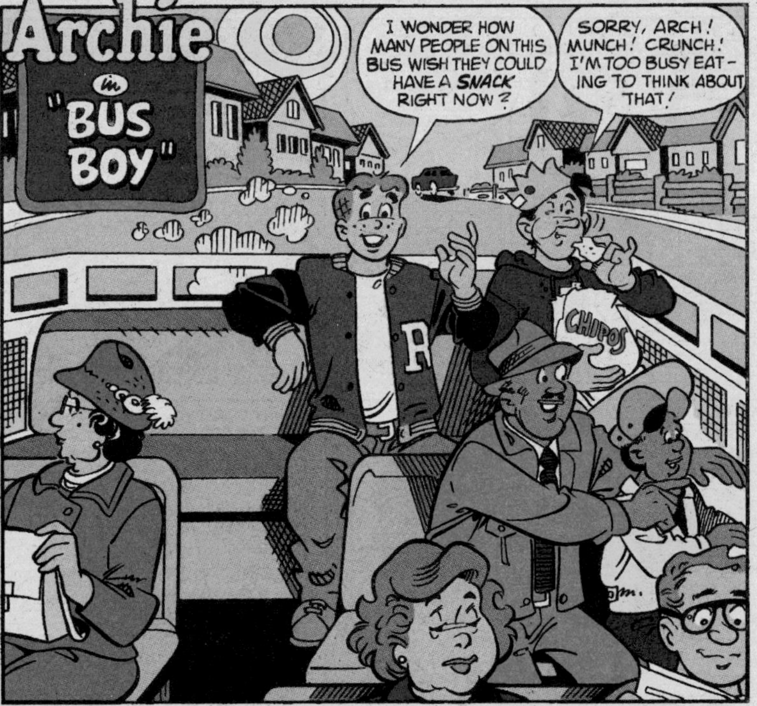
Archie in "BUS BOY"
I WONDER HOW MANY PEOPLE ON THIS BUS WISH THEY COULD HAVE A SNACK RIGHT NOW?
SORRY, ARCH! MUNCH! CRUNCH! I'M TOO BUSY EATING TO THINK ABOUT THAT!
CHIPOS

Script: George Gladir / Pencils: Stan Goldberg / Inks: Rudy Lapick / Letters: Bill Yoshida / Colors: Barry Grossman

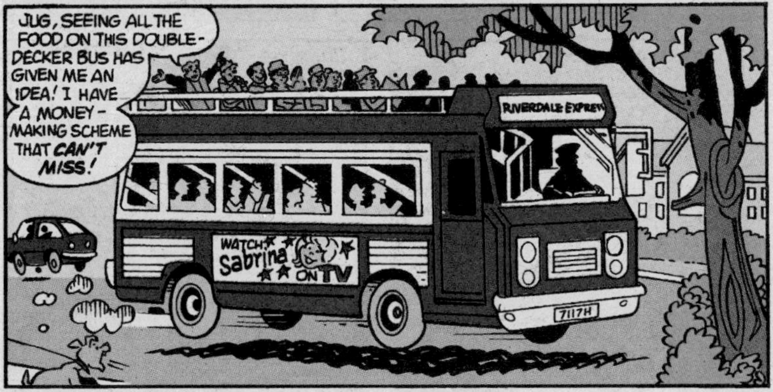
JUG, SEEING ALL THE FOOD ON THIS DOUBLE-DECKER BUS HAS GIVEN ME AN IDEA! I HAVE A MONEY-MAKING SCHEME THAT CAN'T MISS!
RIVERDALE EXPRESS
WATCH Sabrina ON TV
7117H

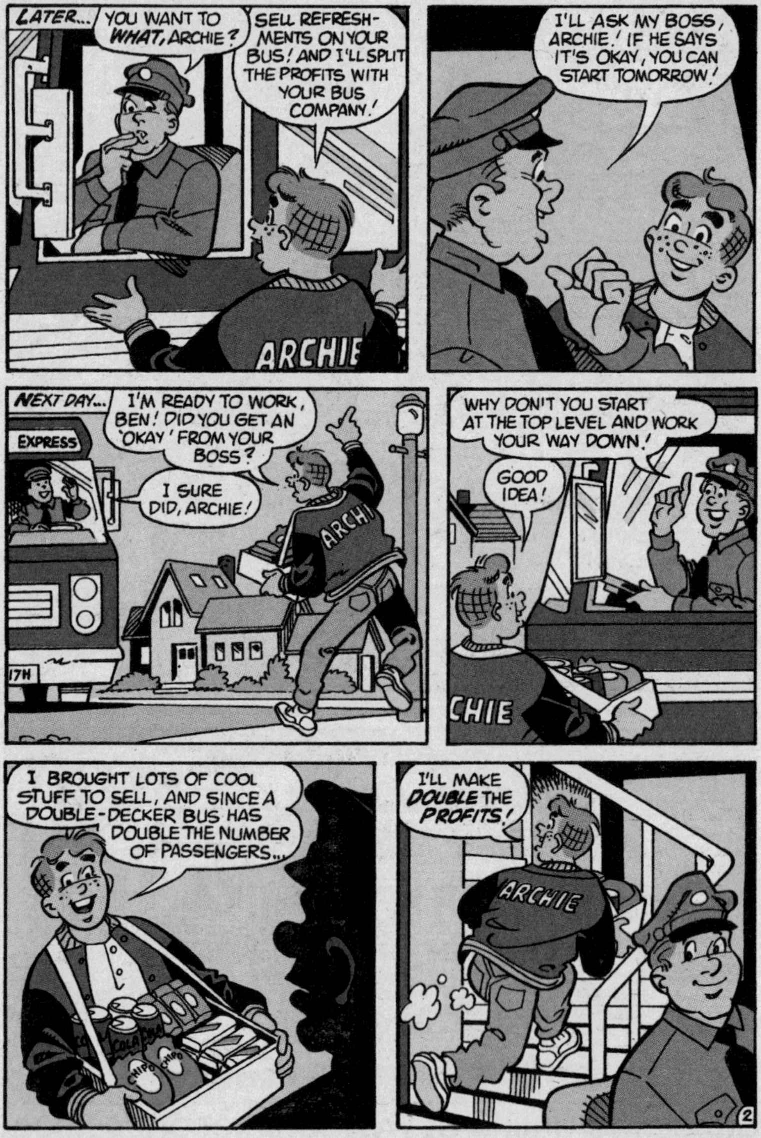
LATER...
YOU WANT TO WHAT, ARCHIE?
SELL REFRESHMENTS ON YOUR BUS! AND I'LL SPLIT THE PROFITS WITH YOUR BUS COMPANY!
ARCHIE
I'LL ASK MY BOSS, ARCHIE! IF HE SAYS IT'S OKAY, YOU CAN START TOMORROW!
NEXT DAY...
I'M READY TO WORK, BEN! DID YOU GET AN 'OKAY' FROM YOUR BOSS?
EXPRESS
I SURE DID, ARCHIE!
ARCHI
17H
WHY DON'T YOU START AT THE TOP LEVEL AND WORK YOUR WAY DOWN!
GOOD IDEA!
CHIE
I BROUGHT LOTS OF COOL STUFF TO SELL, AND SINCE A DOUBLE-DECKER BUS HAS DOUBLE THE NUMBER OF PASSENGERS...
COLA
CHIPS
I'LL MAKE DOUBLE THE PROFITS!
ARCHIE
2

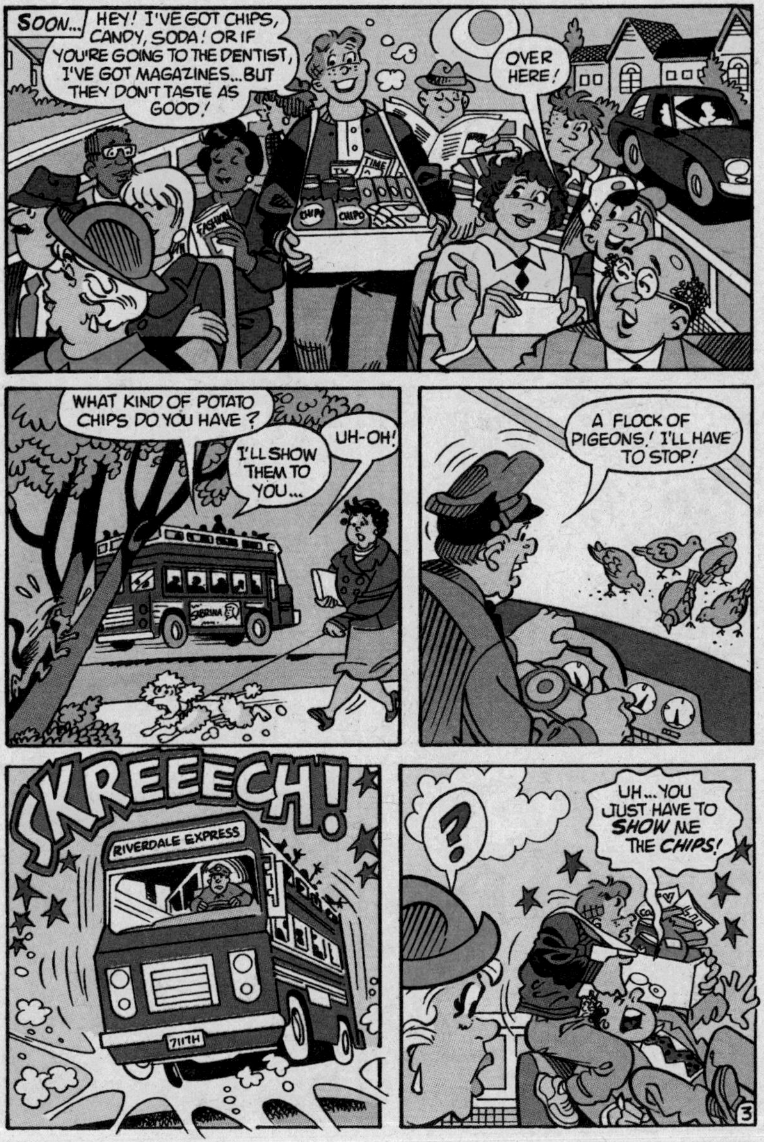
SOON...
HEY! I'VE GOT CHIPS, CANDY, SODA! OR IF YOU'RE GOING TO THE DENTIST, I'VE GOT MAGAZINES... BUT THEY DON'T TASTE AS GOOD!
OVER HERE!
CHIPO
CHIPO
FASHION
TIME
WHAT KIND OF POTATO CHIPS DO YOU HAVE?
I'LL SHOW THEM TO YOU...
UH-OH!
SABRINA
A FLOCK OF PIGEONS! I'LL HAVE TO STOP!
SKREEECH!
RIVERDALE EXPRESS
7117H
?
UH... YOU JUST HAVE TO SHOW ME THE CHIPS!
3

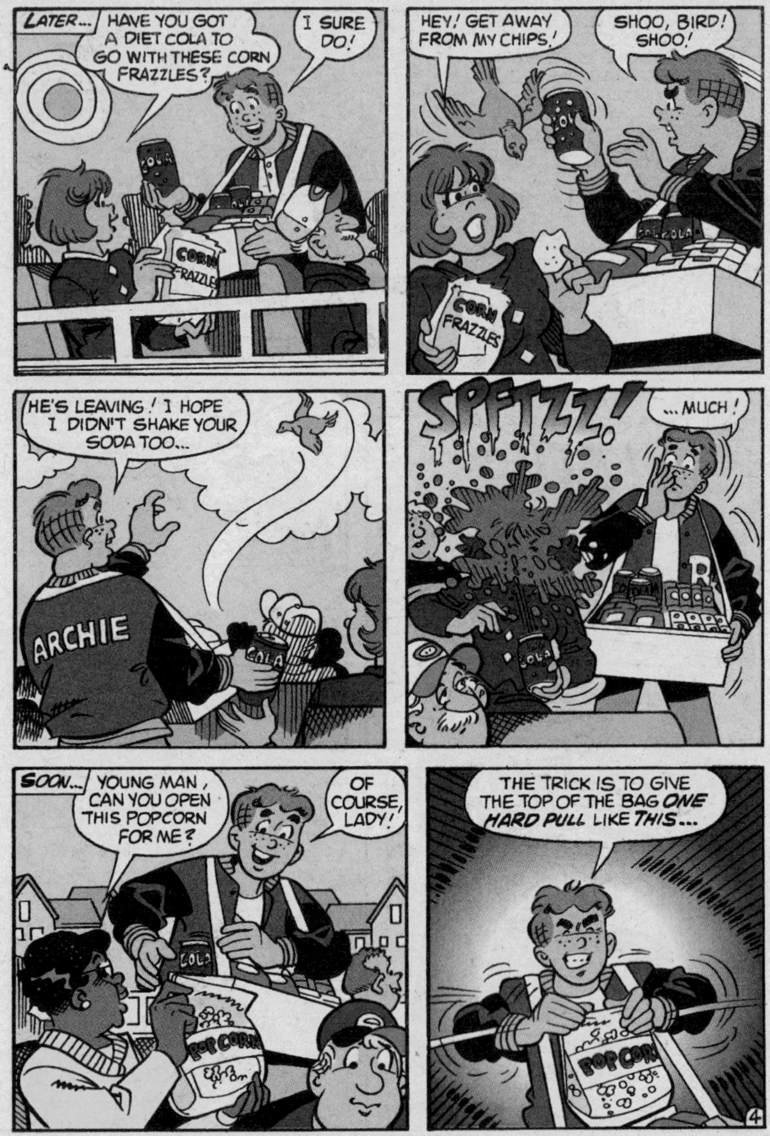
LATER...
HAVE YOU GOT A DIET COLA TO GO WITH THESE CORN FRAZZLES?
I SURE DO!
COLA
CORN FRAZZLES
HEY! GET AWAY FROM MY CHIPS!
SHOO, BIRD! SHOO!
CORN FRAZZLES
HE'S LEAVING! I HOPE I DIDN'T SHAKE YOUR SODA TOO...
ARCHIE
COLA
SPFTZZZ!
...MUCH!
COLA
SOON...
YOUNG MAN, CAN YOU OPEN THIS POPCORN FOR ME?
OF COURSE, LADY!
COLA
POPCORN
THE TRICK IS TO GIVE THE TOP OF THE BAG ONE HARD PULL LIKE THIS...
POPCORN
4

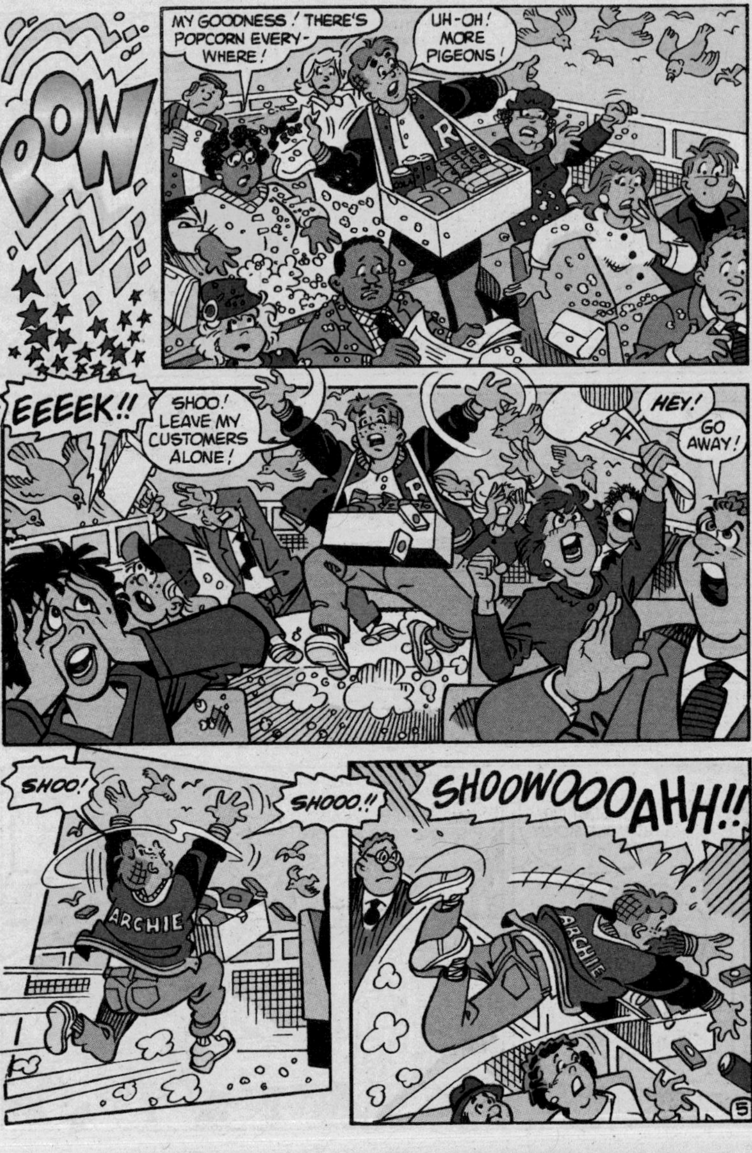
POW
MY GOODNESS! THERE'S POPCORN EVERY-WHERE!
UH-OH! MORE PIGEONS!
EEEEK!!
SHOO! LEAVE MY CUSTOMERS ALONE!
HEY!
GO AWAY!
SHOO!
SHOOO.!!
ARCHIE
SHOOWOOOAHH!!
ARCHIE

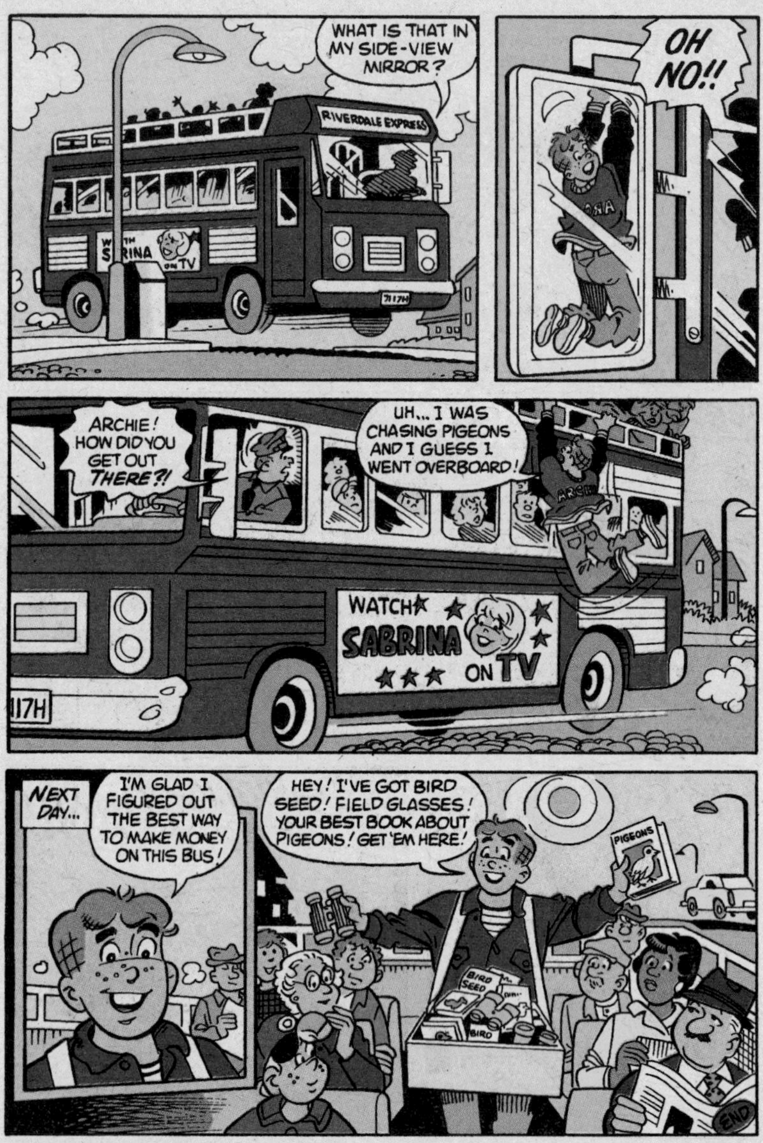
WHAT IS THAT IN MY SIDE-VIEW MIRROR?
RIVERDALE EXPRESS
WATCH SABRINA ON TV
OH NO!!
ARCHIE! HOW DID YOU GET OUT THERE?!
UH... I WAS CHASING PIGEONS AND I GUESS I WENT OVERBOARD!
WATCH SABRINA ON TV
NEXT DAY...
I'M GLAD I FIGURED OUT THE BEST WAY TO MAKE MONEY ON THIS BUS!
HEY! I'VE GOT BIRD SEED! FIELD GLASSES! YOUR BEST BOOK ABOUT PIGEONS! GET 'EM HERE!
PIGEONS
BIRD SEED
END

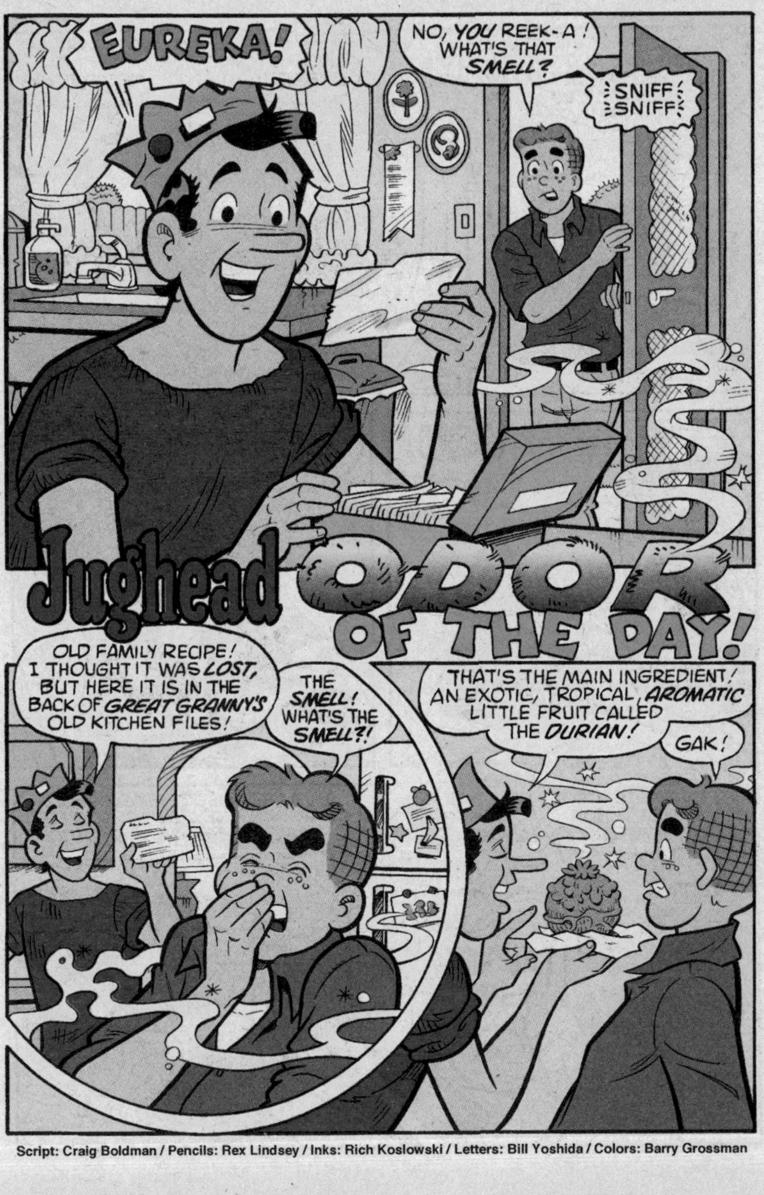
EUREKA!
NO, YOU REEK-A! WHAT'S THAT SMELL?
SNIFF SNIFF
Jughead
ODOR OF THE DAY!
OLD FAMILY RECIPE! I THOUGHT IT WAS LOST, BUT HERE IT IS IN THE BACK OF GREAT GRANNY'S OLD KITCHEN FILES!
THE SMELL! WHAT'S THE SMELL?!
THAT'S THE MAIN INGREDIENT! AN EXOTIC, TROPICAL, AROMATIC LITTLE FRUIT CALLED THE DURIAN!
GAK!

Script: Craig Boldman / Pencils: Rex Lindsey / Inks: Rich Koslowski / Letters: Bill Yoshida / Colors: Barry Grossman

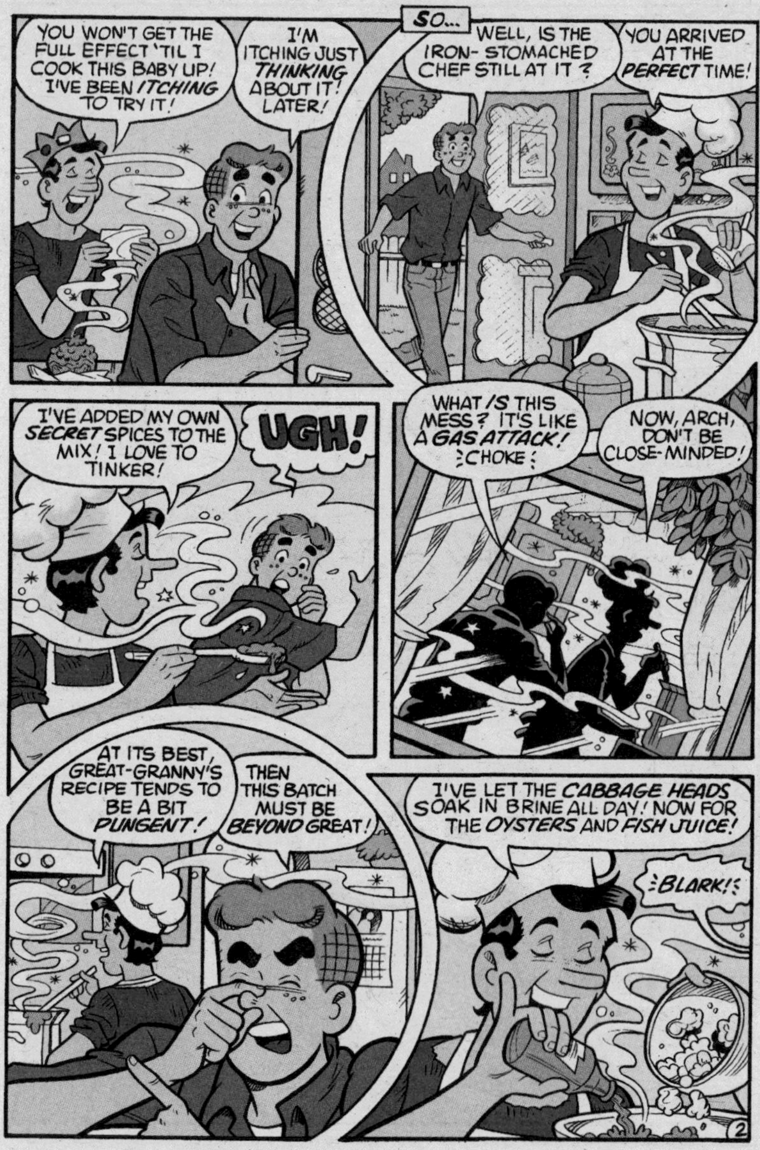
YOU WON'T GET THE FULL EFFECT 'TIL I COOK THIS BABY UP! I'VE BEEN ITCHING TO TRY IT!
I'M ITCHING JUST THINKING ABOUT IT! LATER!
SO...
WELL, IS THE IRON-STOMACHED CHEF STILL AT IT?
YOU ARRIVED AT THE PERFECT TIME!
I'VE ADDED MY OWN SECRET SPICES TO THE MIX! I LOVE TO TINKER!
UGH!
WHAT IS THIS MESS? IT'S LIKE A GAS ATTACK! CHOKE
NOW, ARCH, DON'T BE CLOSE-MINDED!
AT ITS BEST, GREAT-GRANNY'S RECIPE TENDS TO BE A BIT PUNGENT!
THEN THIS BATCH MUST BE BEYOND GREAT!
I'VE LET THE CABBAGE HEADS SOAK IN BRINE ALL DAY! NOW FOR THE OYSTERS AND FISH JUICE!
BLARK!
2

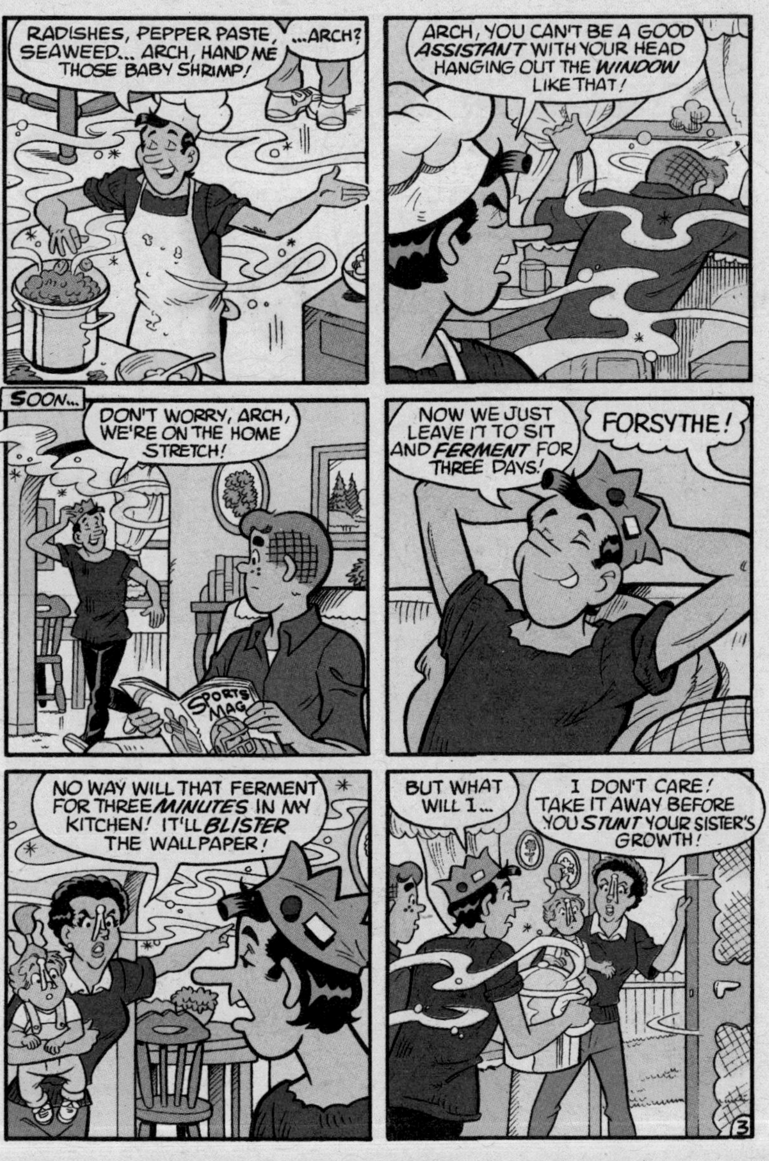
RADISHES, PEPPER PASTE, SEAWEED... ARCH, HAND ME THOSE BABY SHRIMP!
...ARCH?
ARCH, YOU CAN'T BE A GOOD ASSISTANT WITH YOUR HEAD HANGING OUT THE WINDOW LIKE THAT!
SOON...
DON'T WORRY, ARCH, WE'RE ON THE HOME STRETCH!
SPORTS MAG
NOW WE JUST LEAVE IT TO SIT AND FERMENT FOR THREE DAYS!
FORSYTHE!
NO WAY WILL THAT FERMENT FOR THREE MINUTES IN MY KITCHEN! IT'LL BLISTER THE WALLPAPER!
BUT WHAT WILL I...
I DON'T CARE! TAKE IT AWAY BEFORE YOU STUNT YOUR SISTER'S GROWTH!
3

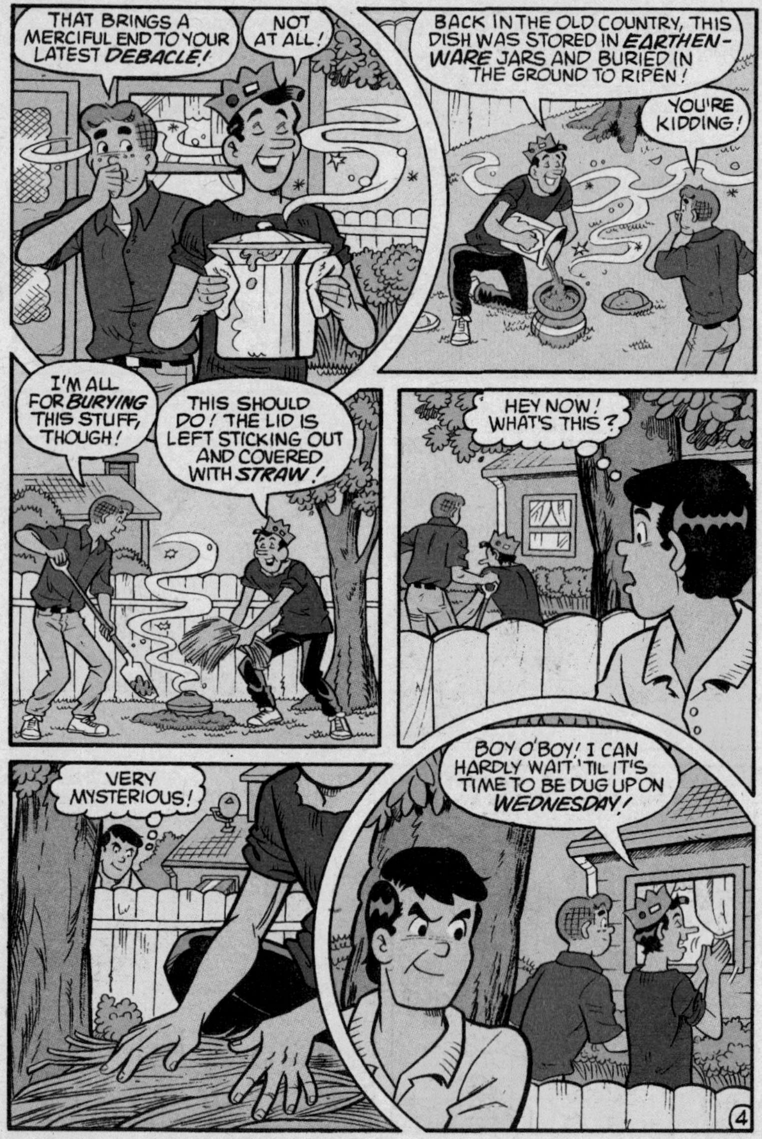
THAT BRINGS A MERCIFUL END TO YOUR LATEST DEBACLE!
NOT AT ALL!
BACK IN THE OLD COUNTRY, THIS DISH WAS STORED IN EARTHEN-WARE JARS AND BURIED IN THE GROUND TO RIPEN!
YOU'RE KIDDING!
I'M ALL FOR BURYING THIS STUFF, THOUGH!
THIS SHOULD DO! THE LID IS LEFT STICKING OUT AND COVERED WITH STRAW!
HEY NOW! WHAT'S THIS?
VERY MYSTERIOUS!
BOY O'BOY! I CAN HARDLY WAIT 'TIL IT'S TIME TO BE DUG UP ON WEDNESDAY!
4

HMM! WHAT KINDS OF THINGS DO PEOPLE BURY?

TREASURES! VALUABLES!

AND *WHY* DO THEY BURY THEM?

TO *HIDE* THEM FROM SOMEONE!

AND *WHO* WOULD THOSE TWO CHUCKLEHEADS BE HIDING SOMETHING OF *VALUE* FROM?

ME, OF COURSE!

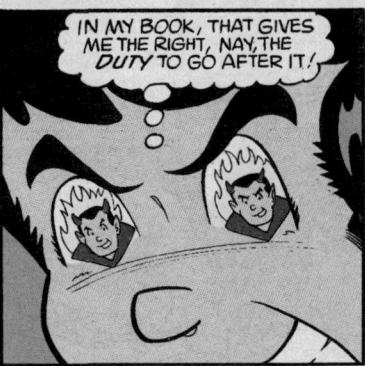

IN MY BOOK, THAT GIVES ME THE RIGHT, NAY, THE *DUTY* TO GO AFTER IT!

TUESDAY...

I'VE LAIN IN WAIT FOR TWO DAYS, GIVING THEM A FALSE SENSE OF SECURITY! TOMORROW THEY DIG IT UP!

SO TODAY... I *STRIKE!*

5

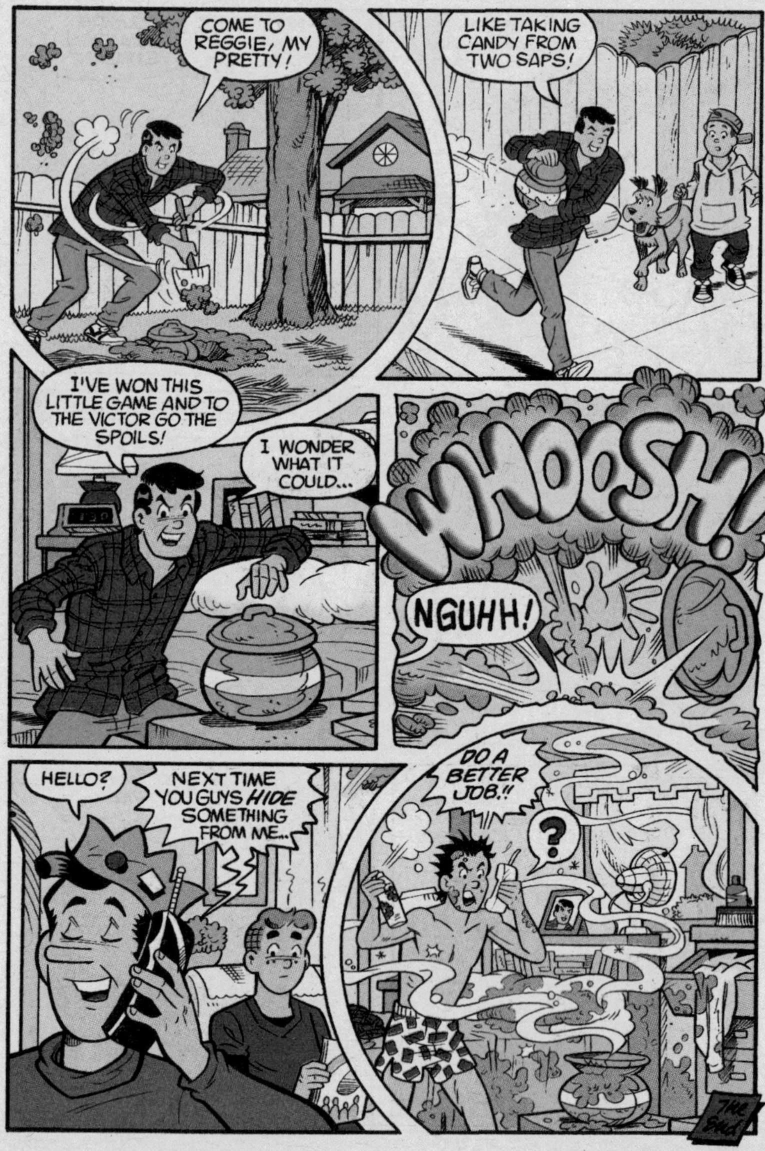
COME TO REGGIE, MY PRETTY!
LIKE TAKING CANDY FROM TWO SAPS!
I'VE WON THIS LITTLE GAME AND TO THE VICTOR GO THE SPOILS!
I WONDER WHAT IT COULD...
WHOOSH!!
NGUHH!
HELLO?
NEXT TIME YOU GUYS HIDE SOMETHING FROM ME...
DO A BETTER JOB!!
?
THE END

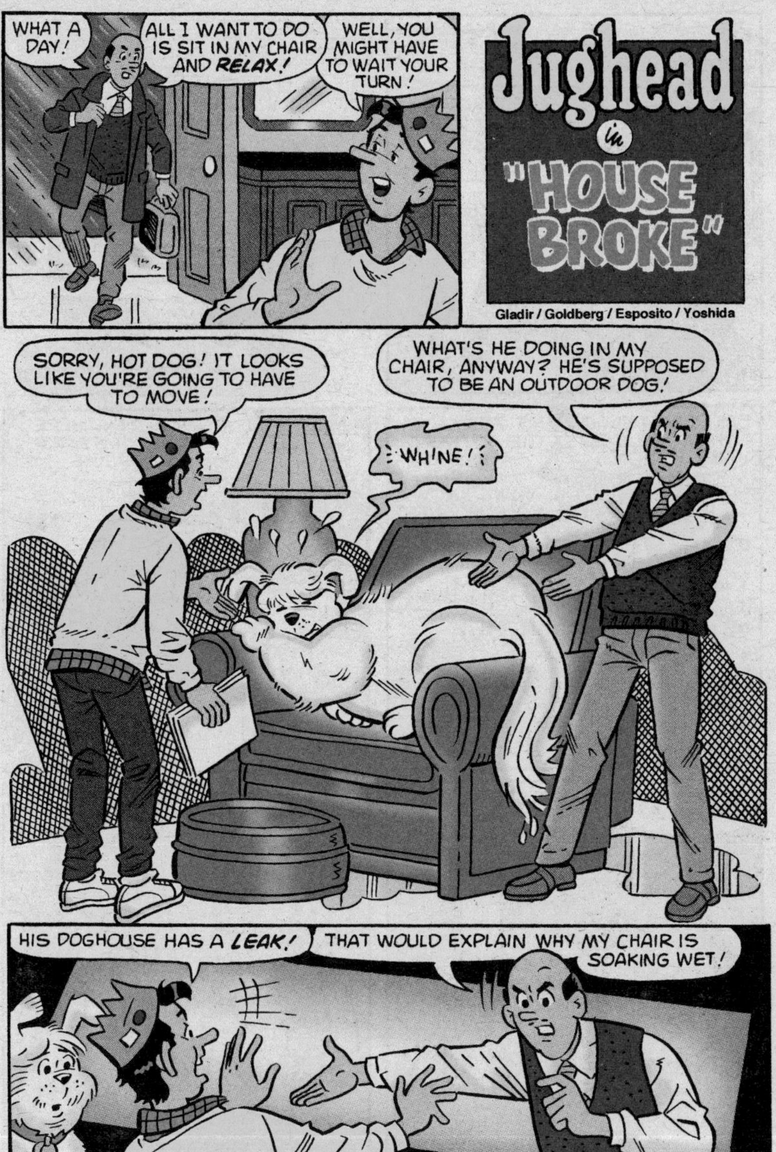
WHAT A DAY!
ALL I WANT TO DO IS SIT IN MY CHAIR AND RELAX!
WELL, YOU MIGHT HAVE TO WAIT YOUR TURN!
Jughead in "HOUSE BROKE"
Gladir / Goldberg / Esposito / Yoshida
SORRY, HOT DOG! IT LOOKS LIKE YOU'RE GOING TO HAVE TO MOVE!
WHAT'S HE DOING IN MY CHAIR, ANYWAY? HE'S SUPPOSED TO BE AN OUTDOOR DOG!
WHINE!
HIS DOGHOUSE HAS A LEAK!
THAT WOULD EXPLAIN WHY MY CHAIR IS SOAKING WET!

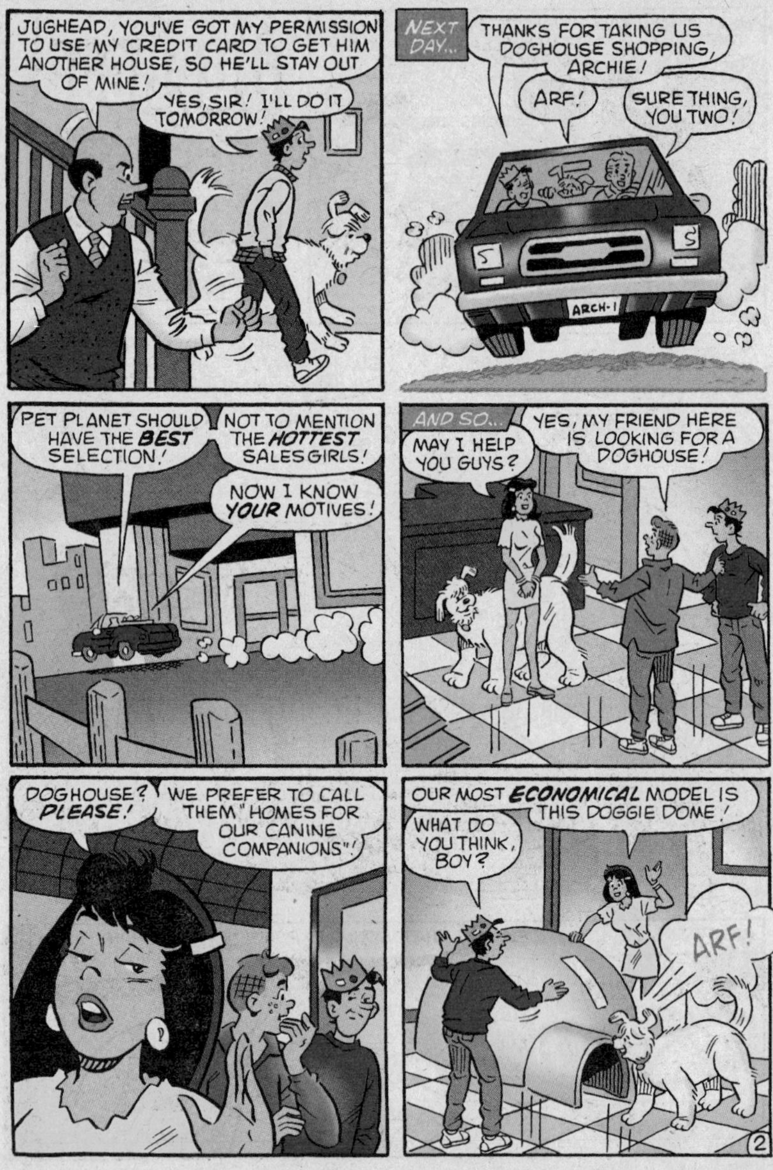
JUGHEAD, YOU'VE GOT MY PERMISSION TO USE MY CREDIT CARD TO GET HIM ANOTHER HOUSE, SO HE'LL STAY OUT OF MINE!
YES, SIR! I'LL DO IT TOMORROW!
NEXT DAY...
THANKS FOR TAKING US DOGHOUSE SHOPPING, ARCHIE!
ARF!
SURE THING, YOU TWO!
ARCH-1
PET PLANET SHOULD HAVE THE BEST SELECTION!
NOT TO MENTION THE HOTTEST SALES GIRLS!
NOW I KNOW YOUR MOTIVES!
AND SO...
MAY I HELP YOU GUYS?
YES, MY FRIEND HERE IS LOOKING FOR A DOGHOUSE!
DOGHOUSE? PLEASE!
WE PREFER TO CALL THEM "HOMES FOR OUR CANINE COMPANIONS"!
OUR MOST ECONOMICAL MODEL IS THIS DOGGIE DOME!
WHAT DO YOU THINK, BOY?
ARF!
2

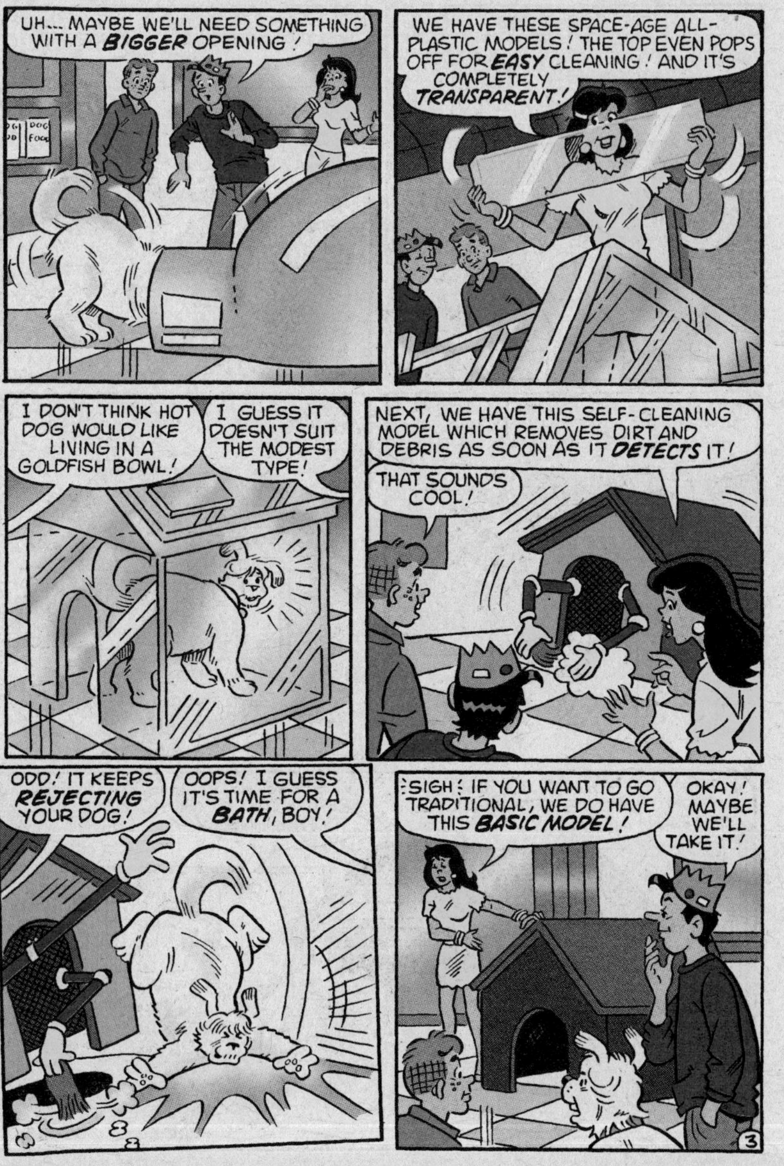
UH... MAYBE WE'LL NEED SOMETHING WITH A BIGGER OPENING!
DOG FOOD
WE HAVE THESE SPACE-AGE ALL-PLASTIC MODELS! THE TOP EVEN POPS OFF FOR EASY CLEANING! AND IT'S COMPLETELY TRANSPARENT!
I DON'T THINK HOT DOG WOULD LIKE LIVING IN A GOLDFISH BOWL!
I GUESS IT DOESN'T SUIT THE MODEST TYPE!
NEXT, WE HAVE THIS SELF-CLEANING MODEL WHICH REMOVES DIRT AND DEBRIS AS SOON AS IT DETECTS IT!
THAT SOUNDS COOL!
ODD! IT KEEPS REJECTING YOUR DOG!
OOPS! I GUESS IT'S TIME FOR A BATH, BOY!
:SIGH: IF YOU WANT TO GO TRADITIONAL, WE DO HAVE THIS BASIC MODEL!
OKAY! MAYBE WE'LL TAKE IT!
3

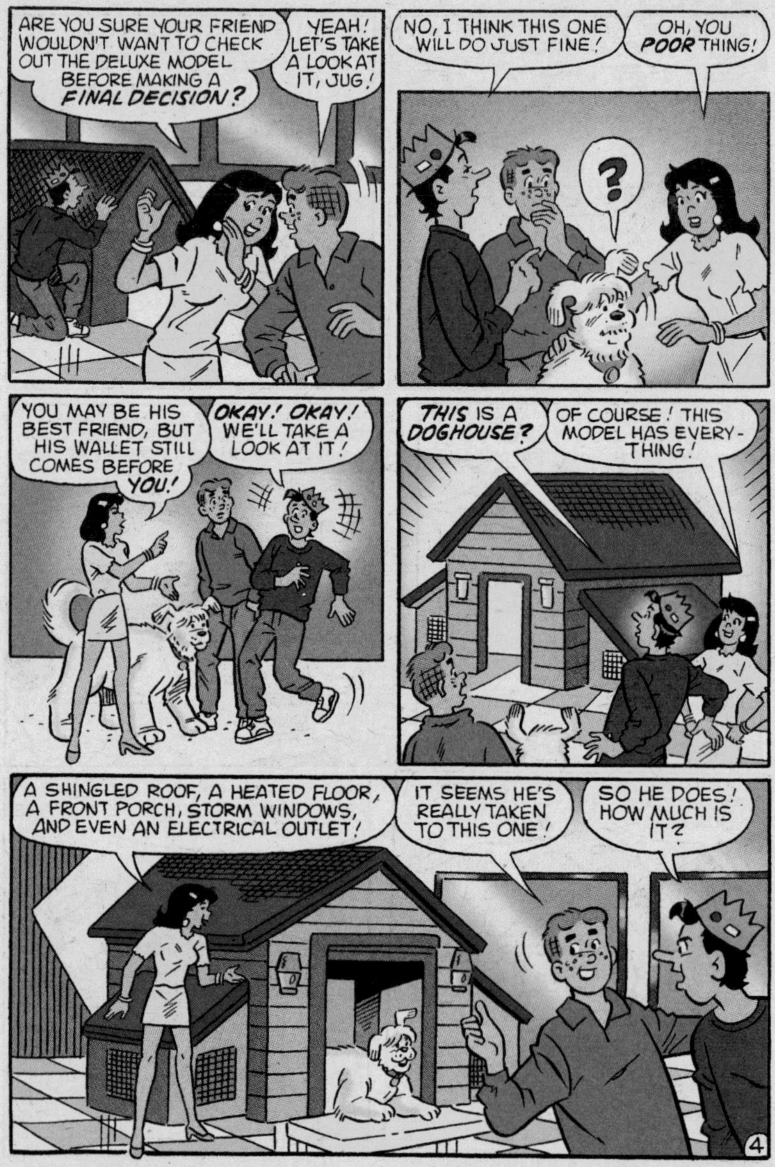

ARE YOU SURE YOUR FRIEND WOULDN'T WANT TO CHECK OUT THE DELUXE MODEL BEFORE MAKING A FINAL DECISION?
YEAH! LET'S TAKE A LOOK AT IT, JUG!
NO, I THINK THIS ONE WILL DO JUST FINE!
OH, YOU POOR THING!
?
YOU MAY BE HIS BEST FRIEND, BUT HIS WALLET STILL COMES BEFORE YOU!
OKAY! OKAY! WE'LL TAKE A LOOK AT IT!
THIS IS A DOGHOUSE?
OF COURSE! THIS MODEL HAS EVERY-THING!
A SHINGLED ROOF, A HEATED FLOOR, A FRONT PORCH, STORM WINDOWS, AND EVEN AN ELECTRICAL OUTLET!
IT SEEMS HE'S REALLY TAKEN TO THIS ONE!
SO HE DOES! HOW MUCH IS IT?
4

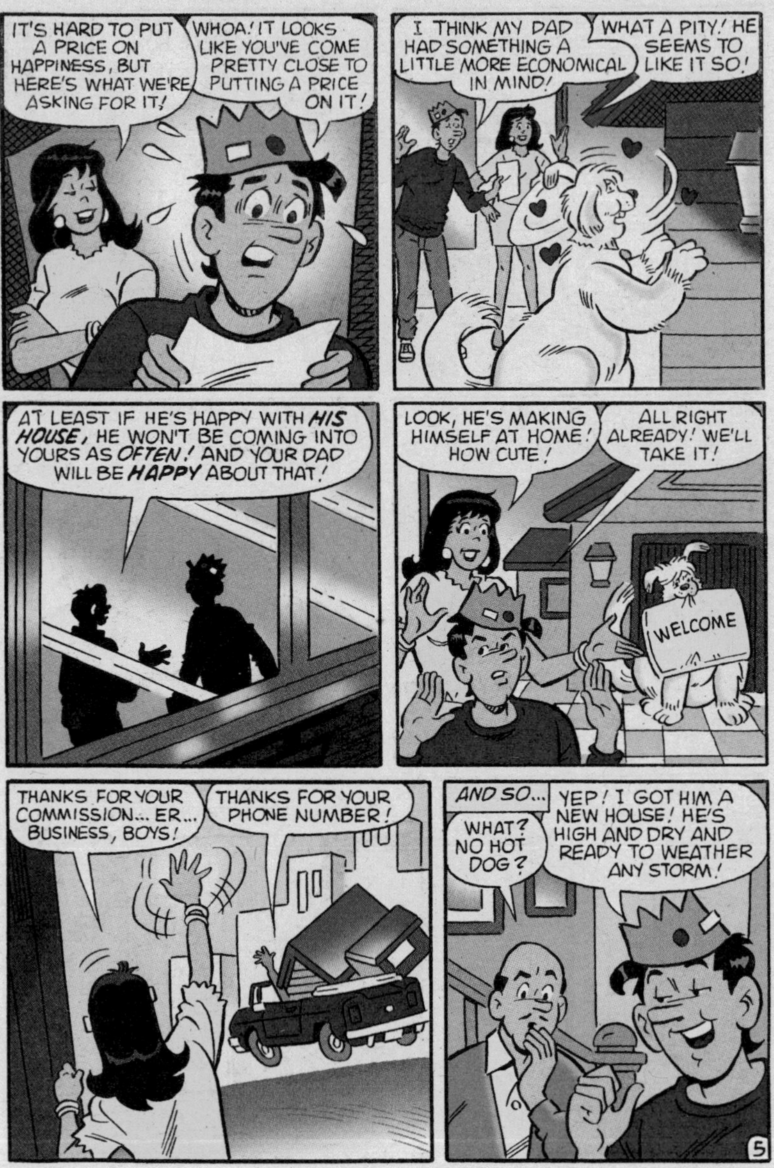
IT'S HARD TO PUT A PRICE ON HAPPINESS, BUT HERE'S WHAT WE'RE ASKING FOR IT!
WHOA! IT LOOKS LIKE YOU'VE COME PRETTY CLOSE TO PUTTING A PRICE ON IT!
I THINK MY DAD HAD SOMETHING A LITTLE MORE ECONOMICAL IN MIND!
WHAT A PITY! HE SEEMS TO LIKE IT SO!
AT LEAST IF HE'S HAPPY WITH HIS HOUSE, HE WON'T BE COMING INTO YOURS AS OFTEN! AND YOUR DAD WILL BE HAPPY ABOUT THAT!
LOOK, HE'S MAKING HIMSELF AT HOME! HOW CUTE!
ALL RIGHT ALREADY! WE'LL TAKE IT!
WELCOME
THANKS FOR YOUR COMMISSION... ER... BUSINESS, BOYS!
THANKS FOR YOUR PHONE NUMBER!
AND SO...
WHAT? NO HOT DOG?
YEP! I GOT HIM A NEW HOUSE! HE'S HIGH AND DRY AND READY TO WEATHER ANY STORM!
5

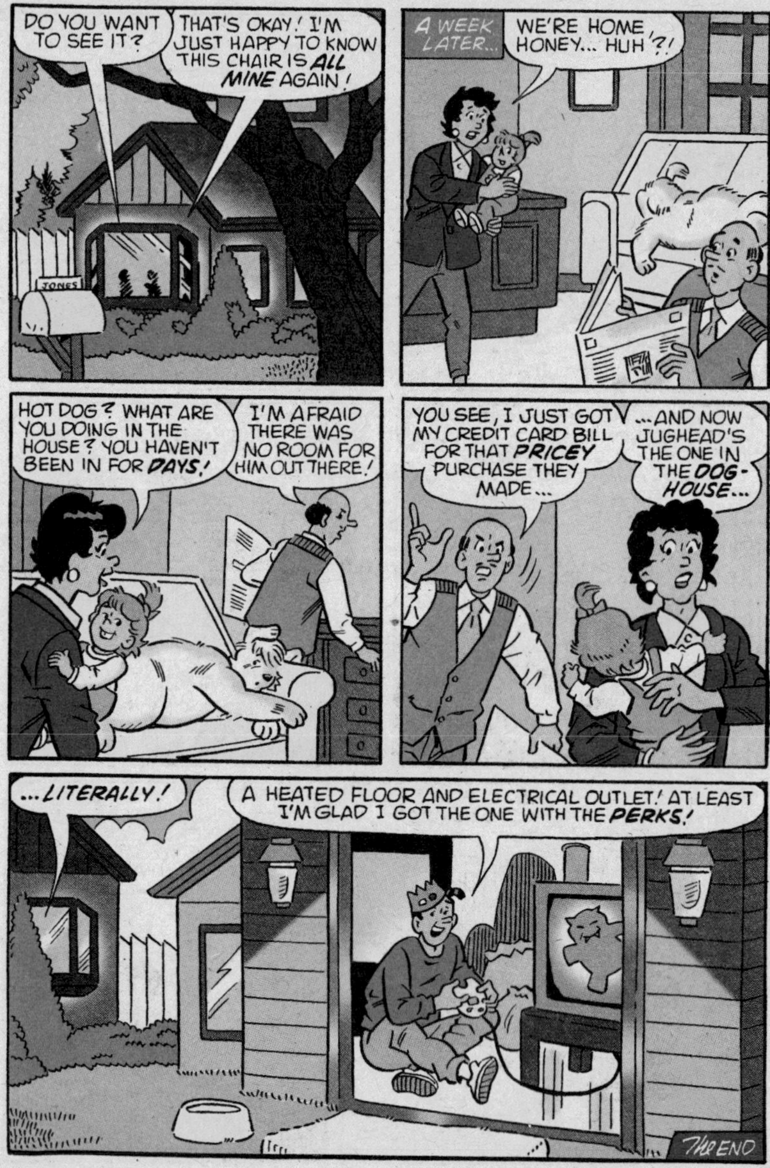
DO YOU WANT TO SEE IT?
THAT'S OKAY! I'M JUST HAPPY TO KNOW THIS CHAIR IS ALL MINE AGAIN!
JONES
A WEEK LATER...
WE'RE HOME, HONEY... HUH?!
HOT DOG? WHAT ARE YOU DOING IN THE HOUSE? YOU HAVEN'T BEEN IN FOR DAYS!
I'M AFRAID THERE WAS NO ROOM FOR HIM OUT THERE!
YOU SEE, I JUST GOT MY CREDIT CARD BILL FOR THAT PRICEY PURCHASE THEY MADE...
...AND NOW JUGHEAD'S THE ONE IN THE DOG-HOUSE...
...LITERALLY!
A HEATED FLOOR AND ELECTRICAL OUTLET! AT LEAST I'M GLAD I GOT THE ONE WITH THE PERKS!
THE END

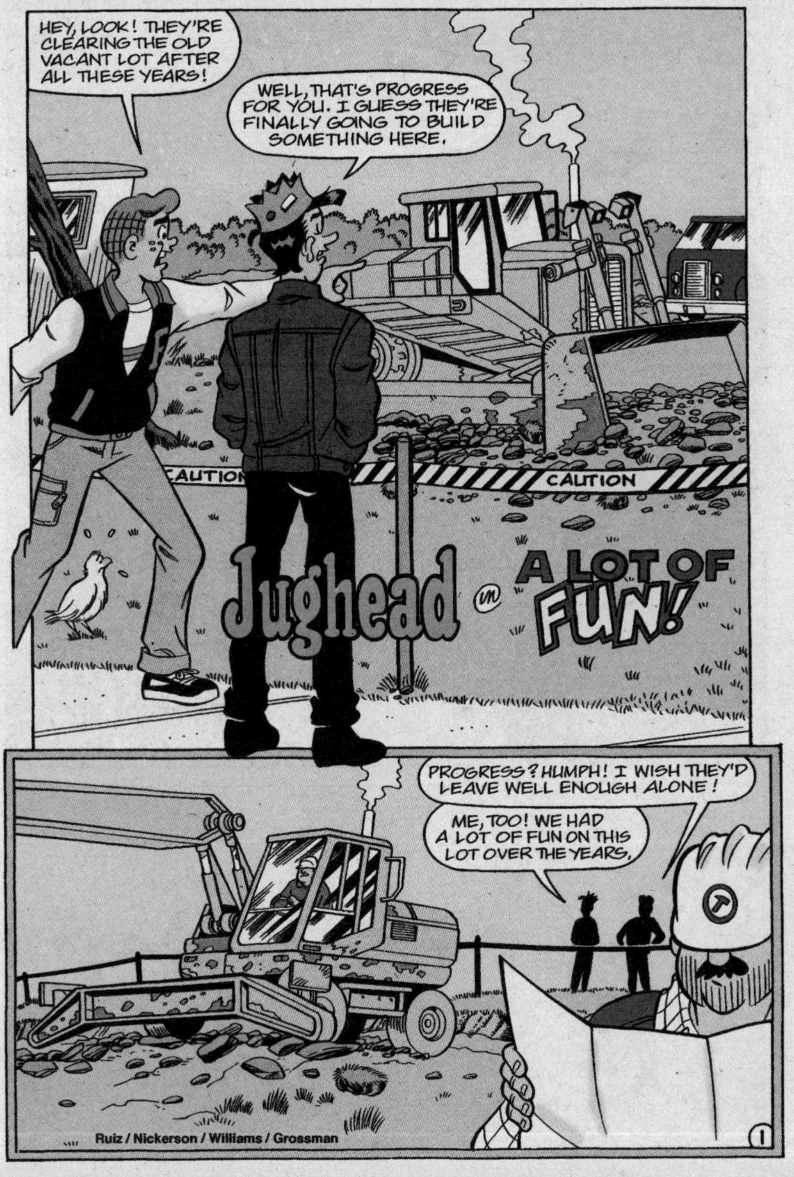
HEY, LOOK! THEY'RE CLEARING THE OLD VACANT LOT AFTER ALL THESE YEARS!
WELL, THAT'S PROGRESS FOR YOU. I GUESS THEY'RE FINALLY GOING TO BUILD SOMETHING HERE.
CAUTION
CAUTION
Jughead in A LOT OF FUN!
PROGRESS? HUMPH! I WISH THEY'D LEAVE WELL ENOUGH ALONE!
ME, TOO! WE HAD A LOT OF FUN ON THIS LOT OVER THE YEARS.
Ruiz / Nickerson / Williams / Grossman
1

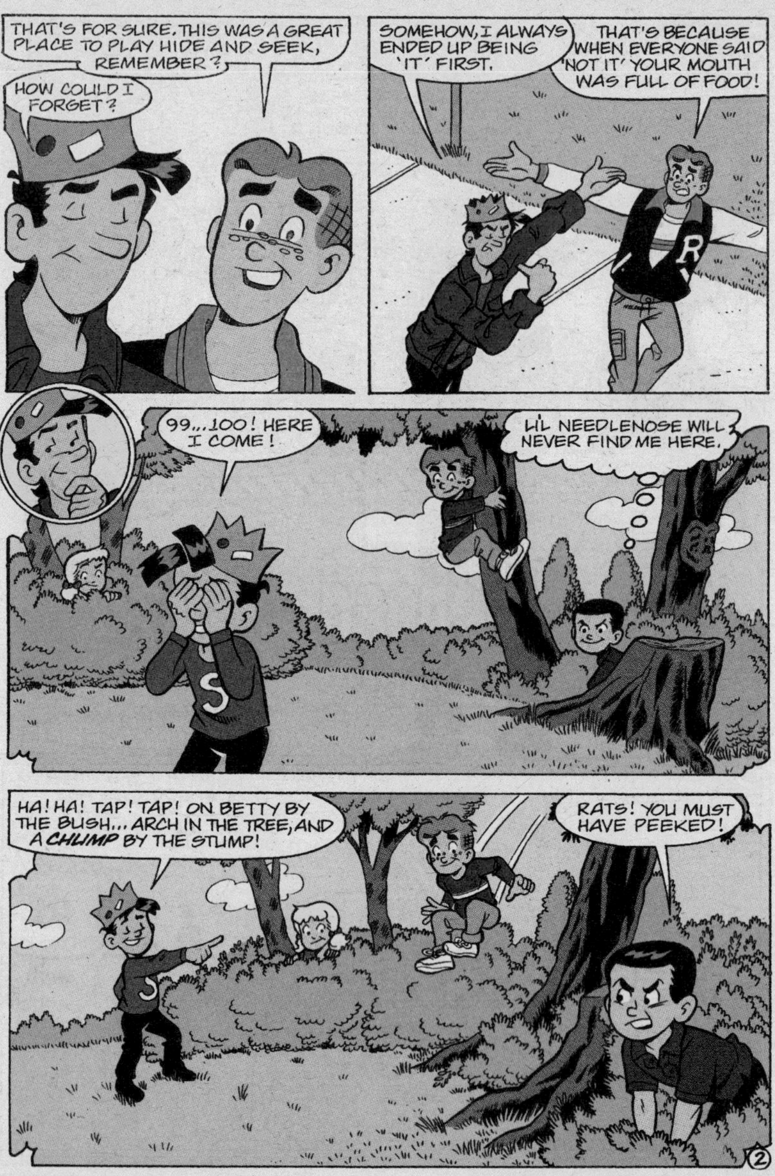
THAT'S FOR SURE. THIS WAS A GREAT PLACE TO PLAY HIDE AND SEEK, REMEMBER?
HOW COULD I FORGET?
SOMEHOW, I ALWAYS ENDED UP BEING 'IT' FIRST.
THAT'S BECAUSE WHEN EVERYONE SAID 'NOT IT' YOUR MOUTH WAS FULL OF FOOD!
99...100! HERE I COME!
LI'L NEEDLENOSE WILL NEVER FIND ME HERE.
HA! HA! TAP! TAP! ON BETTY BY THE BUSH... ARCH IN THE TREE, AND A *CHUMP* BY THE STUMP!
RATS! YOU MUST HAVE PEEKED!
2

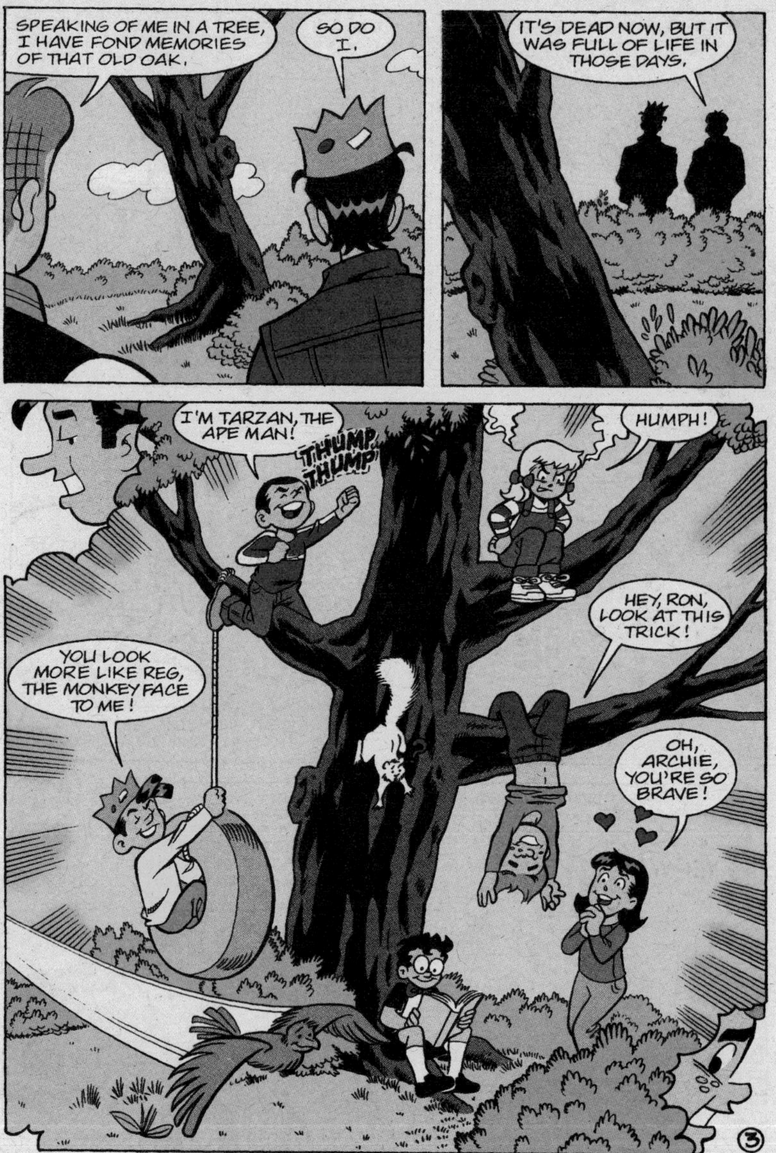

SPEAKING OF ME IN A TREE, I HAVE FOND MEMORIES OF THAT OLD OAK.
SO DO I.
IT'S DEAD NOW, BUT IT WAS FULL OF LIFE IN THOSE DAYS.
I'M TARZAN, THE APE MAN!
THUMP THUMP
HUMPH!
HEY, RON, LOOK AT THIS TRICK!
YOU LOOK MORE LIKE REG, THE MONKEY FACE TO ME!
OH, ARCHIE, YOU'RE SO BRAVE!
3

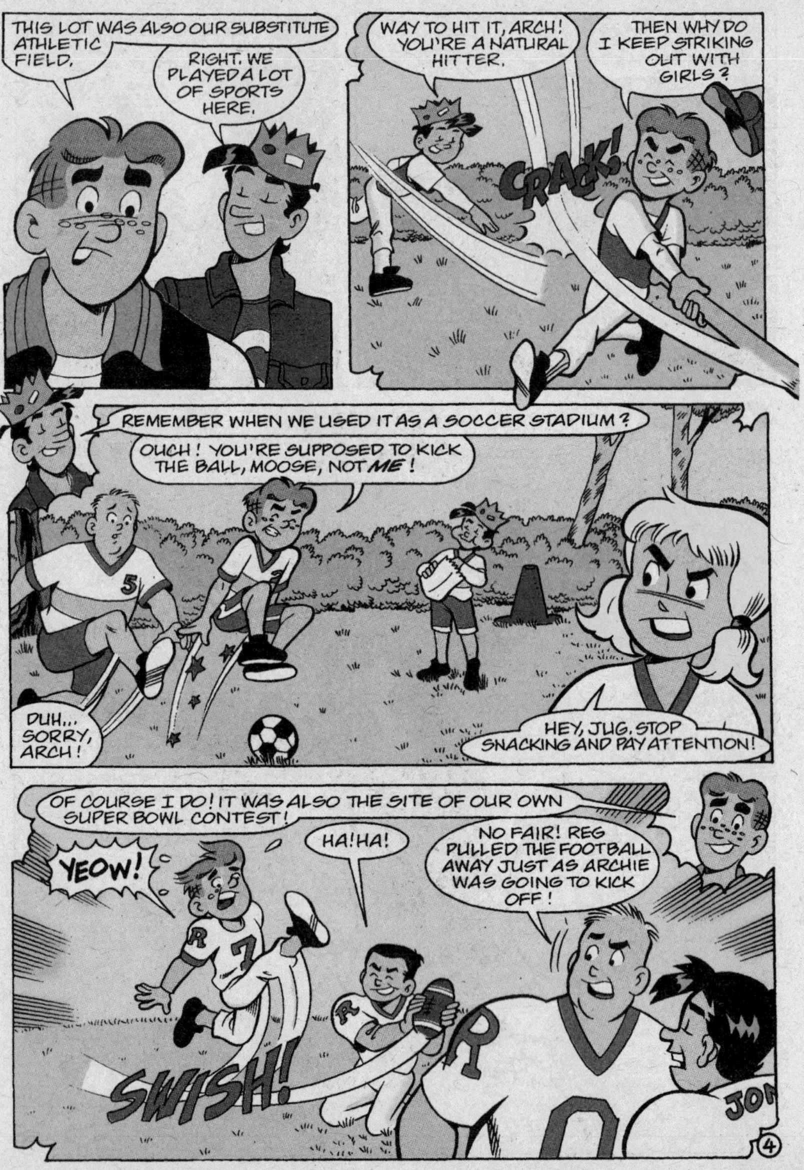
THIS LOT WAS ALSO OUR SUBSTITUTE ATHLETIC FIELD.
RIGHT. WE PLAYED A LOT OF SPORTS HERE.
WAY TO HIT IT, ARCH! YOU'RE A NATURAL HITTER.
THEN WHY DO I KEEP STRIKING OUT WITH GIRLS?
CRACK!
REMEMBER WHEN WE USED IT AS A SOCCER STADIUM?
OUCH! YOU'RE SUPPOSED TO KICK THE BALL, MOOSE, NOT ME!
DUH... SORRY, ARCH!
HEY, JUG. STOP SNACKING AND PAY ATTENTION!
OF COURSE I DO! IT WAS ALSO THE SITE OF OUR OWN SUPER BOWL CONTEST!
YEOW!
HA! HA!
NO FAIR! REG PULLED THE FOOTBALL AWAY JUST AS ARCHIE WAS GOING TO KICK OFF!
SWISH!
4

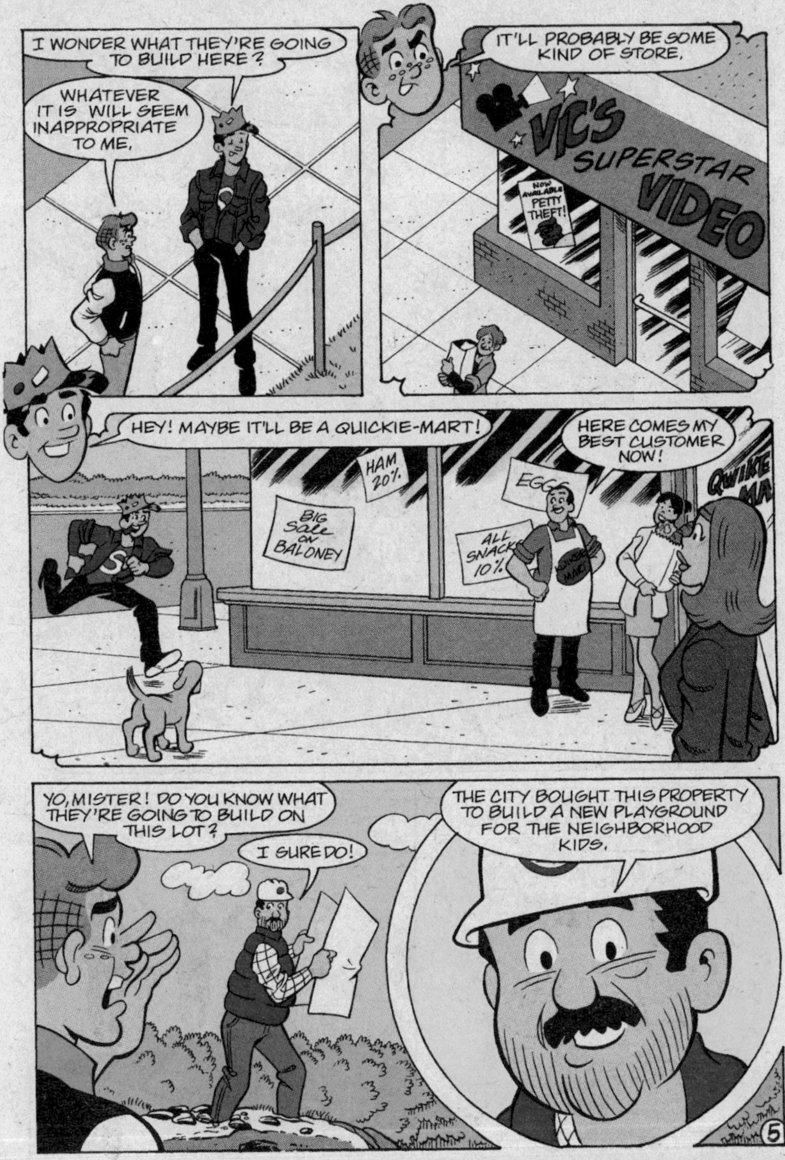
I WONDER WHAT THEY'RE GOING TO BUILD HERE?
WHATEVER IT IS WILL SEEM INAPPROPRIATE TO ME.
IT'LL PROBABLY BE SOME KIND OF STORE.
VIC'S SUPERSTAR VIDEO
NOW AVAILABLE PETTY THEFT!
HEY! MAYBE IT'LL BE A QUICKIE-MART!
HERE COMES MY BEST CUSTOMER NOW!
HAM 20%
BIG Sale ON BALONEY
EGGS
ALL SNACKS 10%
YO, MISTER! DO YOU KNOW WHAT THEY'RE GOING TO BUILD ON THIS LOT?
I SURE DO!
THE CITY BOUGHT THIS PROPERTY TO BUILD A NEW PLAYGROUND FOR THE NEIGHBORHOOD KIDS.

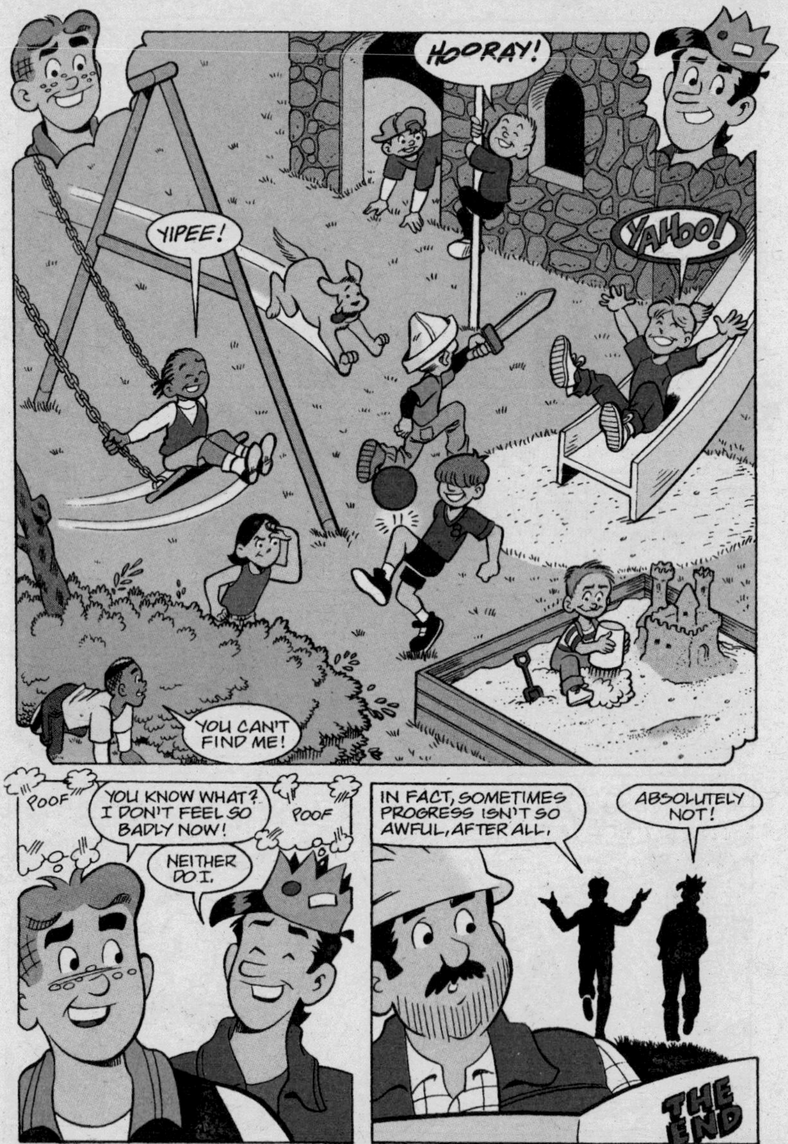
HOORAY!
YIPEE!
YAHOO!
YOU CAN'T FIND ME!
POOF
YOU KNOW WHAT? I DON'T FEEL SO BADLY NOW!
POOF
NEITHER DO I.
IN FACT, SOMETIMES PROGRESS ISN'T SO AWFUL, AFTER ALL.
ABSOLUTELY NOT!
THE END

Jughead Food Fest!

Jughead plans on hitting every type of eating establishment this weekend. Look at the word list and then look for that word in the following word search.

WORD List:

Drive-thru, Diner, Expensive, Pizza Parlor, Sushi Bar, Cajun, Italian, Pop's, French, Chinese

```
D R I V E   T H R U A B C
I D E   E F G H   S I J
N K L   X M P N U O C
E V     P C I J S K A
R M     E H Z C H P J
M I     N I Z Y I U U
I       S N A J B F N
T K     I E P T A Q T
A H     V S A D R F K
L L     P E E R O R R I
I S     Q W Y L Y E E I
A N     X Z P O P S N A
N O S   A E Q R I W C E
O U S V L J S D B U H P
```

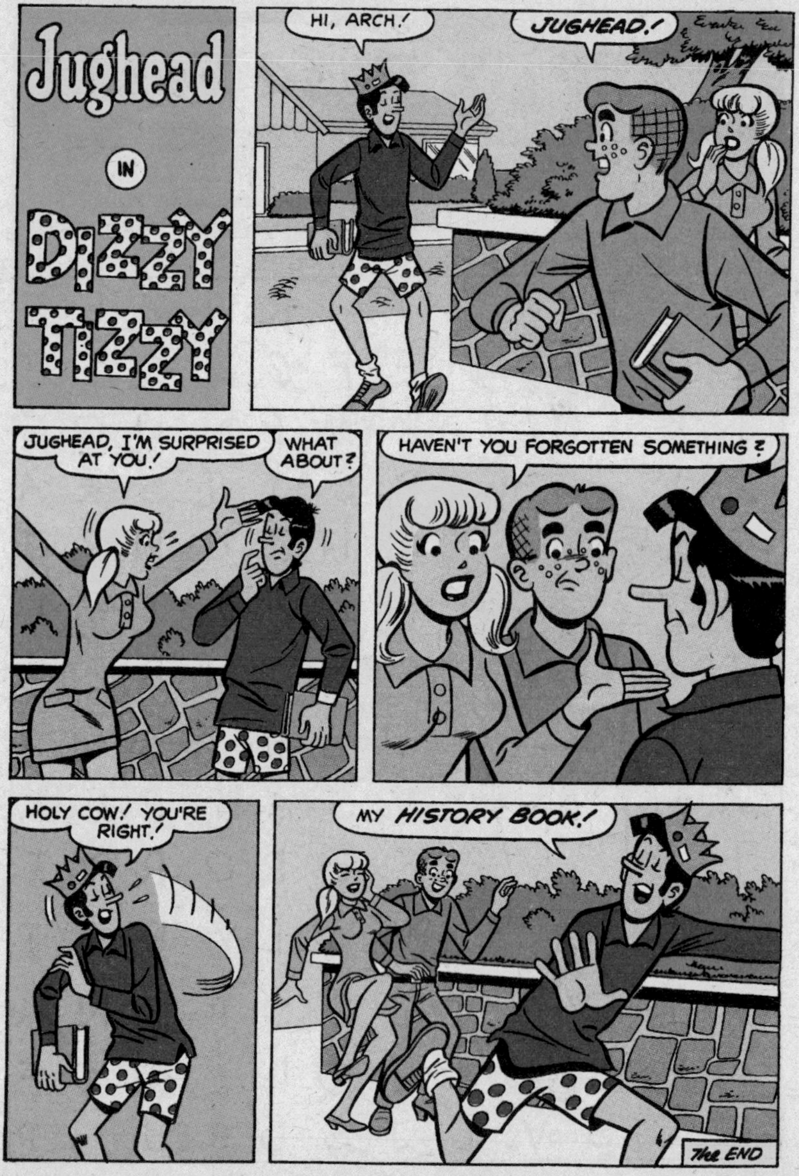
Jughead
IN
DIZZY TIZZY
HI, ARCH.!
JUGHEAD.!
JUGHEAD, I'M SURPRISED AT YOU.!
WHAT ABOUT?
HAVEN'T YOU FORGOTTEN SOMETHING?
HOLY COW.! YOU'RE RIGHT.!
MY HISTORY BOOK.!
The END

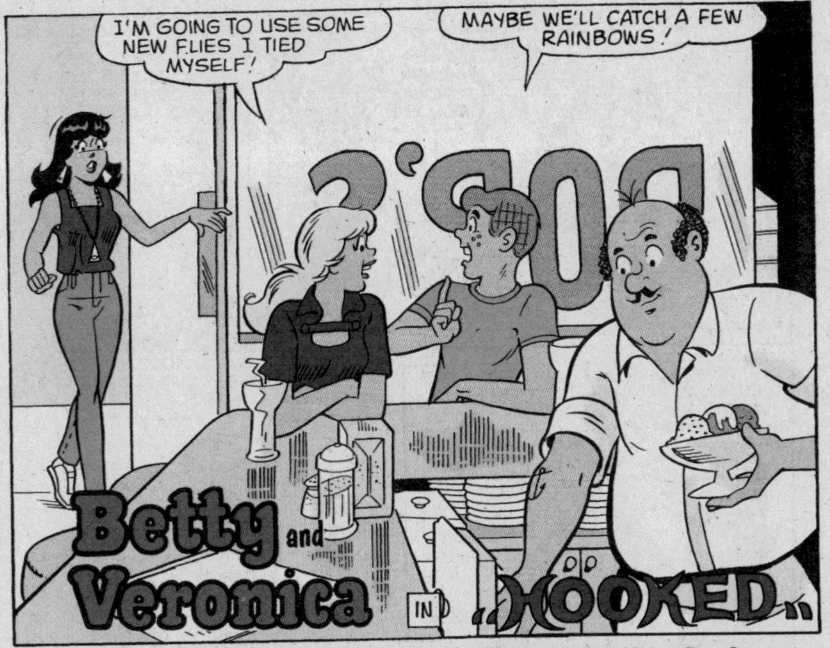
I'M GOING TO USE SOME NEW FLIES I TIED MYSELF!
MAYBE WE'LL CATCH A FEW RAINBOWS!
POP'S
Betty and Veronica IN "HOOKED"

Script: Mike Pellowski / Pencils: Bob Bolling / Inks: Jim Amash / Letters: Bill Yoshida / Colors: Barry Grossman

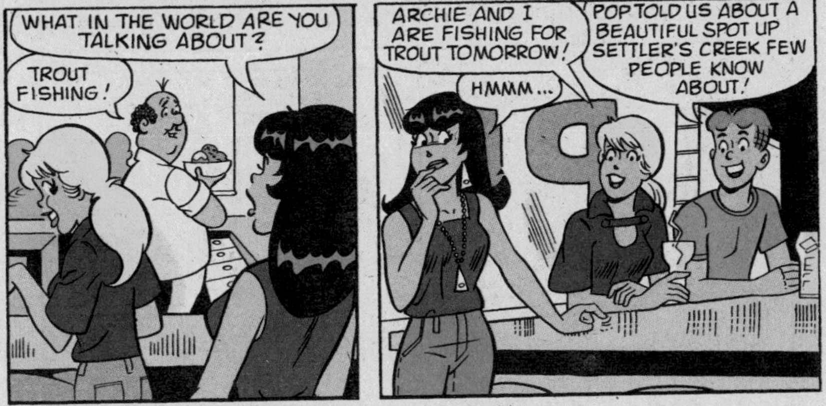
WHAT IN THE WORLD ARE YOU TALKING ABOUT?
TROUT FISHING!
ARCHIE AND I ARE FISHING FOR TROUT TOMORROW!
HMMM...
POP TOLD US ABOUT A BEAUTIFUL SPOT UP SETTLER'S CREEK FEW PEOPLE KNOW ABOUT!

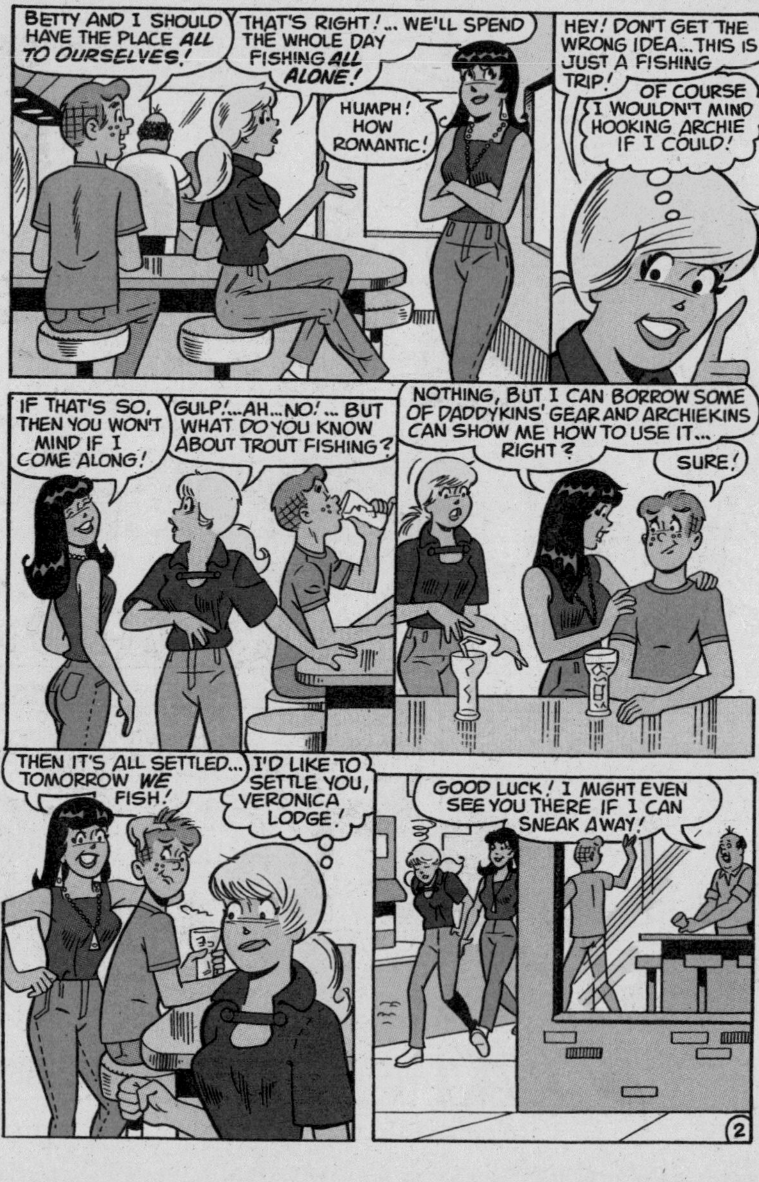
BETTY AND I SHOULD HAVE THE PLACE ALL TO OURSELVES!
THAT'S RIGHT! ... WE'LL SPEND THE WHOLE DAY FISHING ALL ALONE!
HUMPH! HOW ROMANTIC!
HEY! DON'T GET THE WRONG IDEA... THIS IS JUST A FISHING TRIP!
OF COURSE I WOULDN'T MIND HOOKING ARCHIE IF I COULD!
IF THAT'S SO, THEN YOU WON'T MIND IF I COME ALONG!
GULP!...AH...NO! ... BUT WHAT DO YOU KNOW ABOUT TROUT FISHING?
NOTHING, BUT I CAN BORROW SOME OF DADDYKINS' GEAR AND ARCHIEKINS CAN SHOW ME HOW TO USE IT... RIGHT?
SURE!
THEN IT'S ALL SETTLED... TOMORROW WE FISH!
I'D LIKE TO SETTLE YOU, VERONICA LODGE!
GOOD LUCK! I MIGHT EVEN SEE YOU THERE IF I CAN SNEAK AWAY!

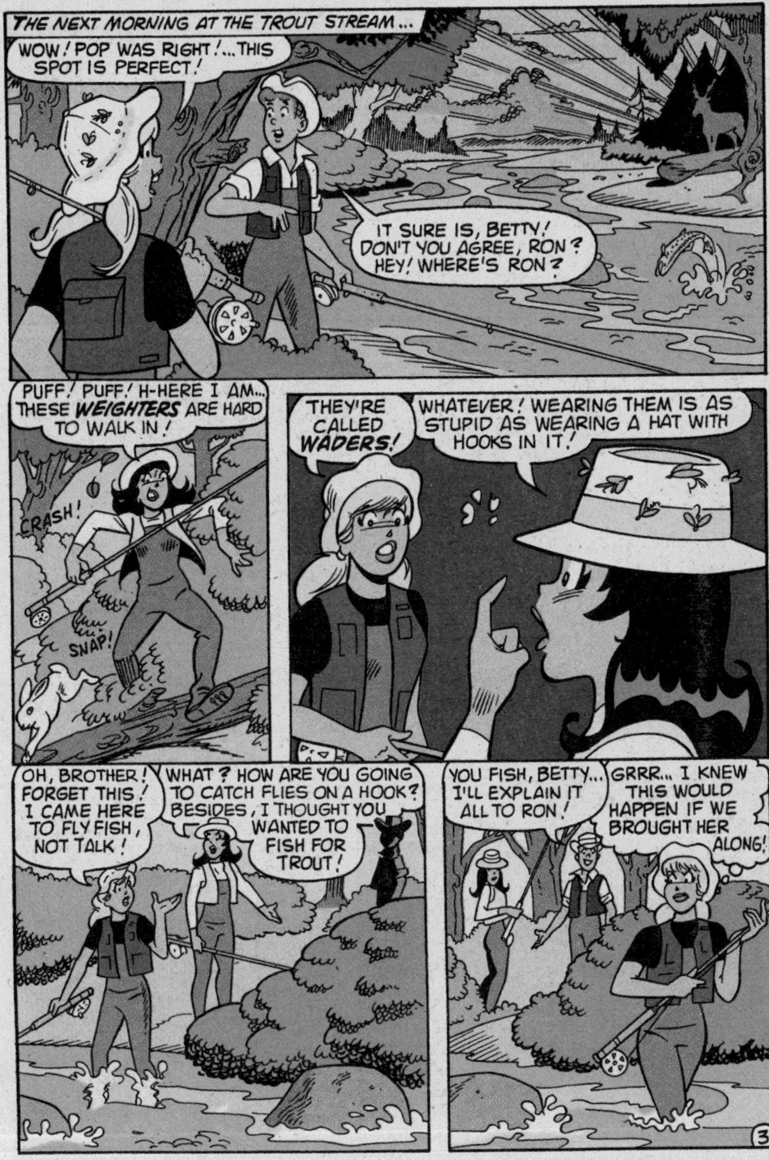
THE NEXT MORNING AT THE TROUT STREAM...
WOW! POP WAS RIGHT!...THIS SPOT IS PERFECT!
IT SURE IS, BETTY! DON'T YOU AGREE, RON? HEY! WHERE'S RON?
PUFF! PUFF! H-HERE I AM... THESE WEIGHTERS ARE HARD TO WALK IN!
CRASH!
SNAP!
THEY'RE CALLED WADERS!
WHATEVER! WEARING THEM IS AS STUPID AS WEARING A HAT WITH HOOKS IN IT!
OH, BROTHER! FORGET THIS! I CAME HERE TO FLY FISH, NOT TALK!
WHAT? HOW ARE YOU GOING TO CATCH FLIES ON A HOOK? BESIDES, I THOUGHT YOU WANTED TO FISH FOR TROUT!
YOU FISH, BETTY... I'LL EXPLAIN IT ALL TO RON!
GRRR... I KNEW THIS WOULD HAPPEN IF WE BROUGHT HER ALONG!
3

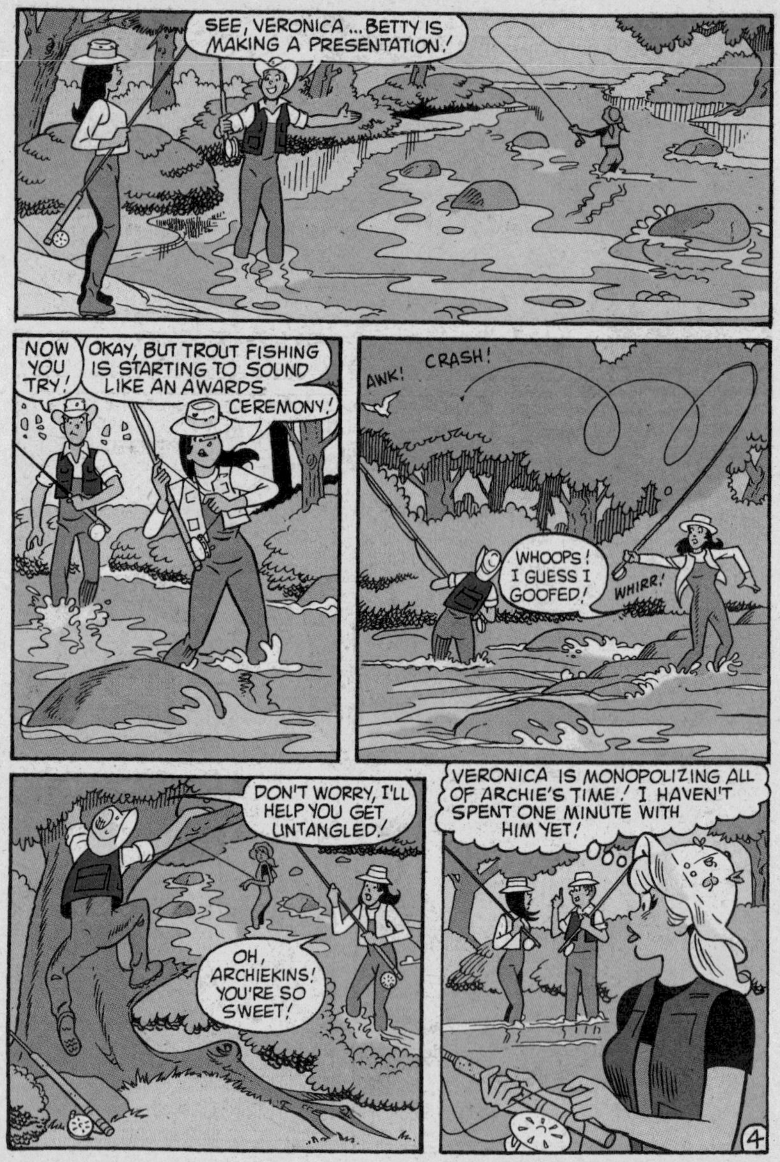
SEE, VERONICA ... BETTY IS MAKING A PRESENTATION!
NOW YOU TRY!
OKAY, BUT TROUT FISHING IS STARTING TO SOUND LIKE AN AWARDS CEREMONY!
AWK!
CRASH!
WHOOPS! I GUESS I GOOFED!
WHIRR!
DON'T WORRY, I'LL HELP YOU GET UNTANGLED!
OH, ARCHIEKINS! YOU'RE SO SWEET!
VERONICA IS MONOPOLIZING ALL OF ARCHIE'S TIME! I HAVEN'T SPENT ONE MINUTE WITH HIM YET!
4

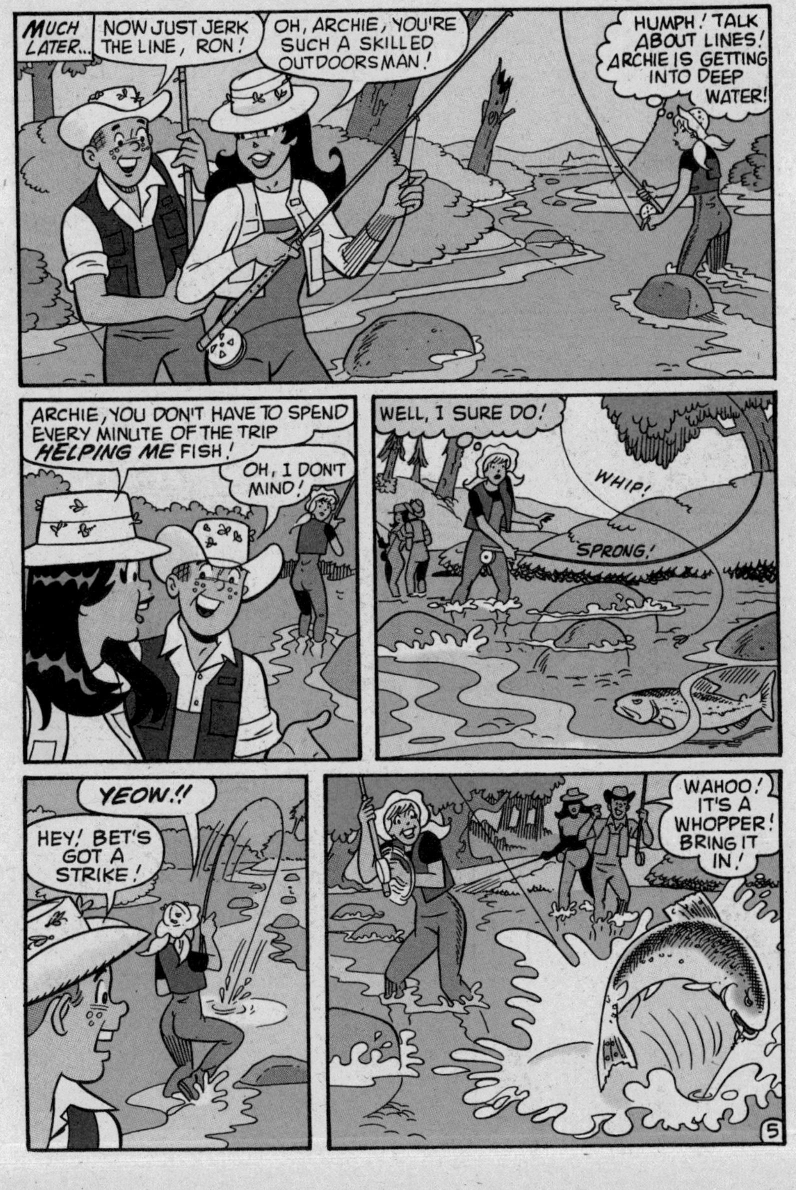
MUCH LATER...
NOW JUST JERK THE LINE, RON!
OH, ARCHIE, YOU'RE SUCH A SKILLED OUTDOORSMAN!
HUMPH! TALK ABOUT LINES! ARCHIE IS GETTING INTO DEEP WATER!
ARCHIE, YOU DON'T HAVE TO SPEND EVERY MINUTE OF THE TRIP HELPING ME FISH!
OH, I DON'T MIND!
WELL, I SURE DO!
WHIP!
SPRONG!
YEOW!!
HEY! BET'S GOT A STRIKE!
WAHOO! IT'S A WHOPPER! BRING IT IN!
5

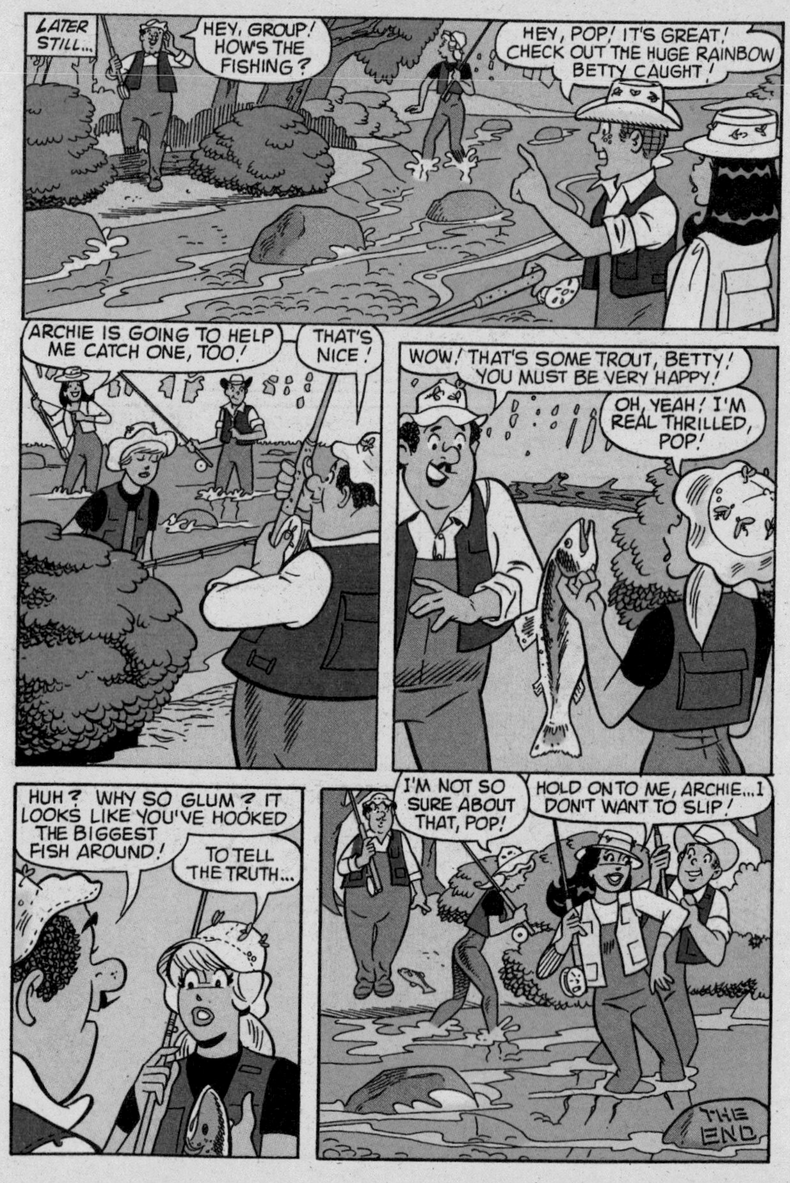
LATER STILL...
HEY, GROUP! HOW'S THE FISHING?
HEY, POP! IT'S GREAT! CHECK OUT THE HUGE RAINBOW BETTY CAUGHT!
ARCHIE IS GOING TO HELP ME CATCH ONE, TOO!
THAT'S NICE!
WOW! THAT'S SOME TROUT, BETTY! YOU MUST BE VERY HAPPY!
OH, YEAH! I'M REAL THRILLED, POP!
HUH? WHY SO GLUM? IT LOOKS LIKE YOU'VE HOOKED THE BIGGEST FISH AROUND!
TO TELL THE TRUTH...
I'M NOT SO SURE ABOUT THAT, POP!
HOLD ON TO ME, ARCHIE...I DON'T WANT TO SLIP!
THE END

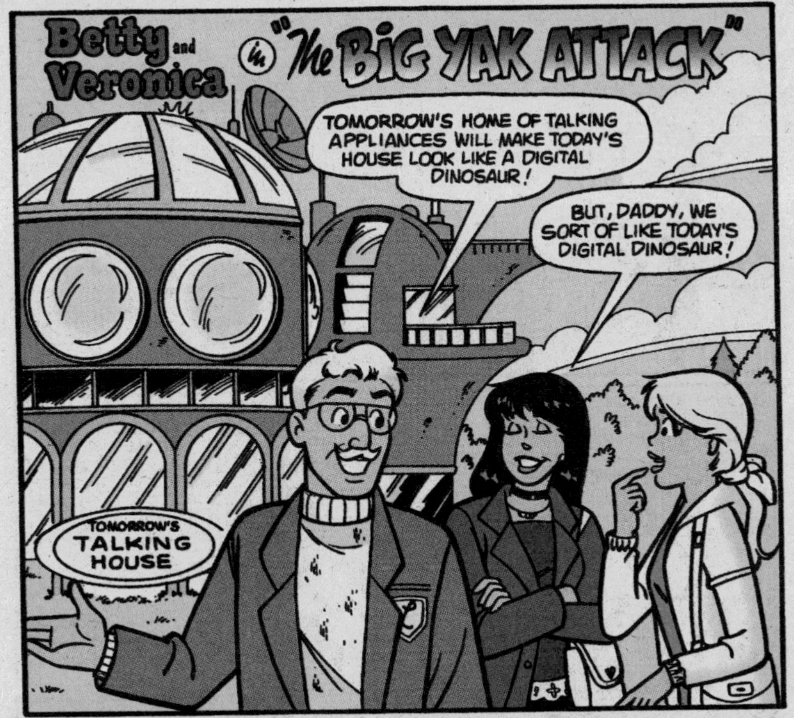
Betty and Veronica
in "The BIG YAK ATTACK"
TOMORROW'S HOME OF TALKING APPLIANCES WILL MAKE TODAY'S HOUSE LOOK LIKE A DIGITAL DINOSAUR!
BUT, DADDY, WE SORT OF LIKE TODAY'S DIGITAL DINOSAUR!
TOMORROW'S TALKING HOUSE

Script & Pencils: Holly G! / Inks: Jim Amash / Letters: Bill Yoshida / Colors: Barry Grossman

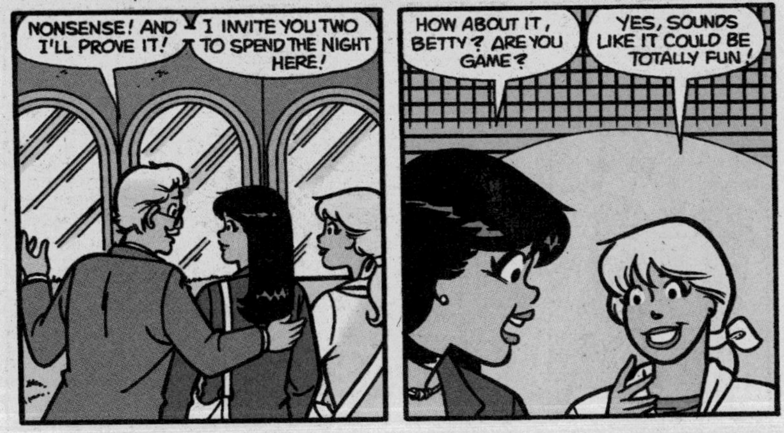
NONSENSE! AND I'LL PROVE IT!
I INVITE YOU TWO TO SPEND THE NIGHT HERE!
HOW ABOUT IT, BETTY? ARE YOU GAME?
YES, SOUNDS LIKE IT COULD BE TOTALLY FUN!

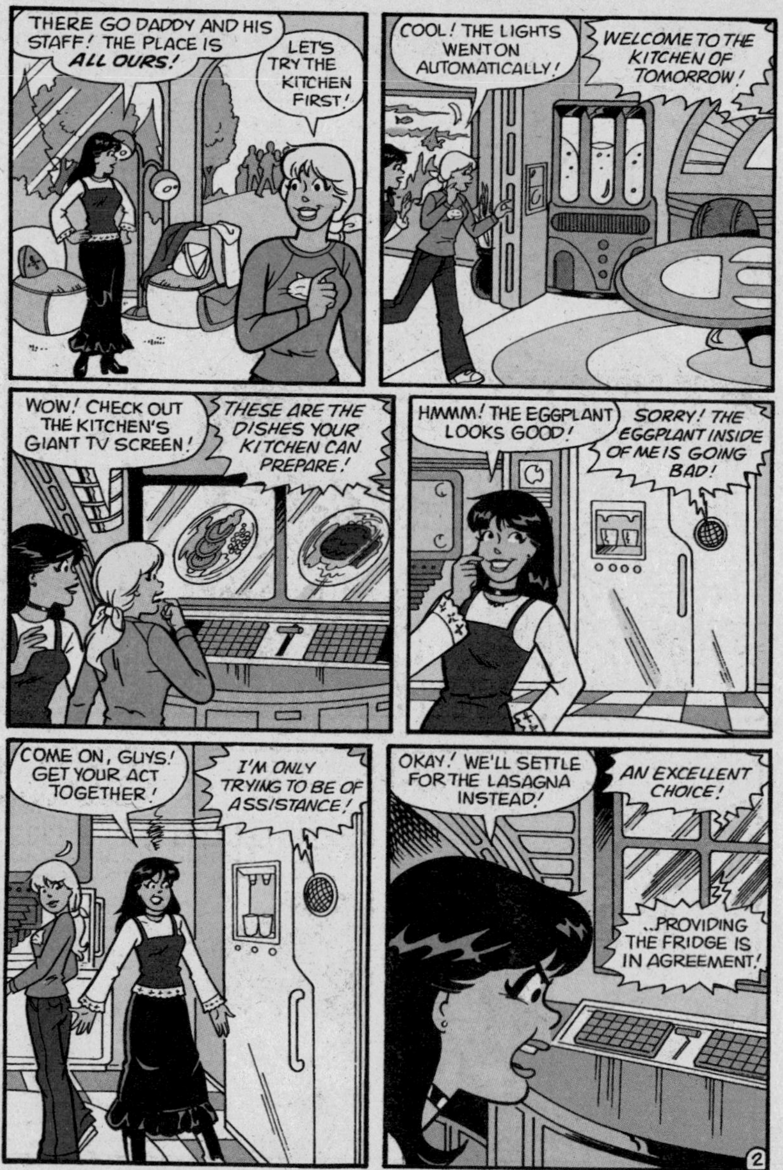
THERE GO DADDY AND HIS STAFF! THE PLACE IS **ALL OURS!**
LET'S TRY THE KITCHEN FIRST!
COOL! THE LIGHTS WENT ON AUTOMATICALLY!
WELCOME TO THE KITCHEN OF TOMORROW!
WOW! CHECK OUT THE KITCHEN'S GIANT TV SCREEN!
THESE ARE THE DISHES YOUR KITCHEN CAN PREPARE!
HMMM! THE EGGPLANT LOOKS GOOD!
SORRY! THE EGGPLANT INSIDE OF ME IS GOING BAD!
COME ON, GUYS! GET YOUR ACT TOGETHER!
I'M ONLY TRYING TO BE OF ASSISTANCE!
OKAY! WE'LL SETTLE FOR THE LASAGNA INSTEAD!
AN EXCELLENT CHOICE!
..PROVIDING THE FRIDGE IS IN AGREEMENT!
2

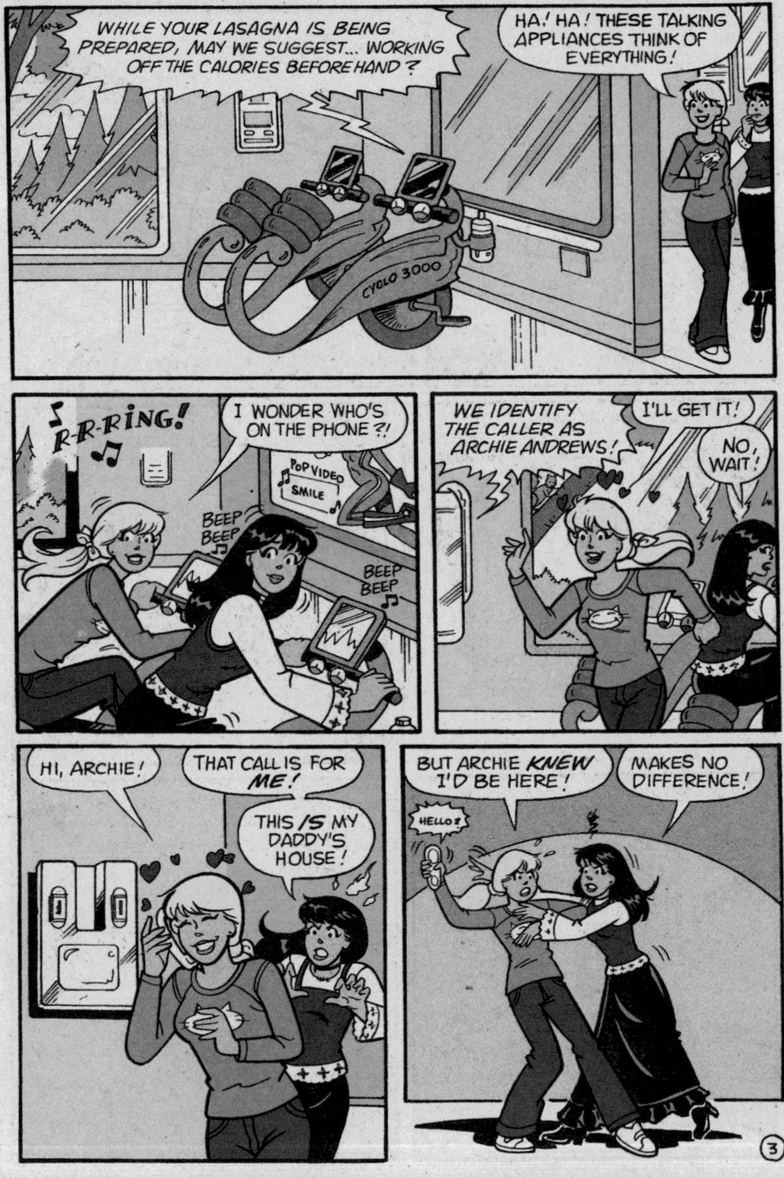
WHILE YOUR LASAGNA IS BEING PREPARED, MAY WE SUGGEST... WORKING OFF THE CALORIES BEFOREHAND ?
HA! HA! THESE TALKING APPLIANCES THINK OF EVERYTHING!
CYCLO 3000
R-R-RING!
I WONDER WHO'S ON THE PHONE ?!
POP VIDEO
SMILE
BEEP BEEP
BEEP BEEP
WE IDENTIFY THE CALLER AS ARCHIE ANDREWS!
I'LL GET IT!
NO, WAIT!
HI, ARCHIE!
THAT CALL IS FOR ME!
THIS IS MY DADDY'S HOUSE!
BUT ARCHIE KNEW I'D BE HERE!
MAKES NO DIFFERENCE!
HELLO?

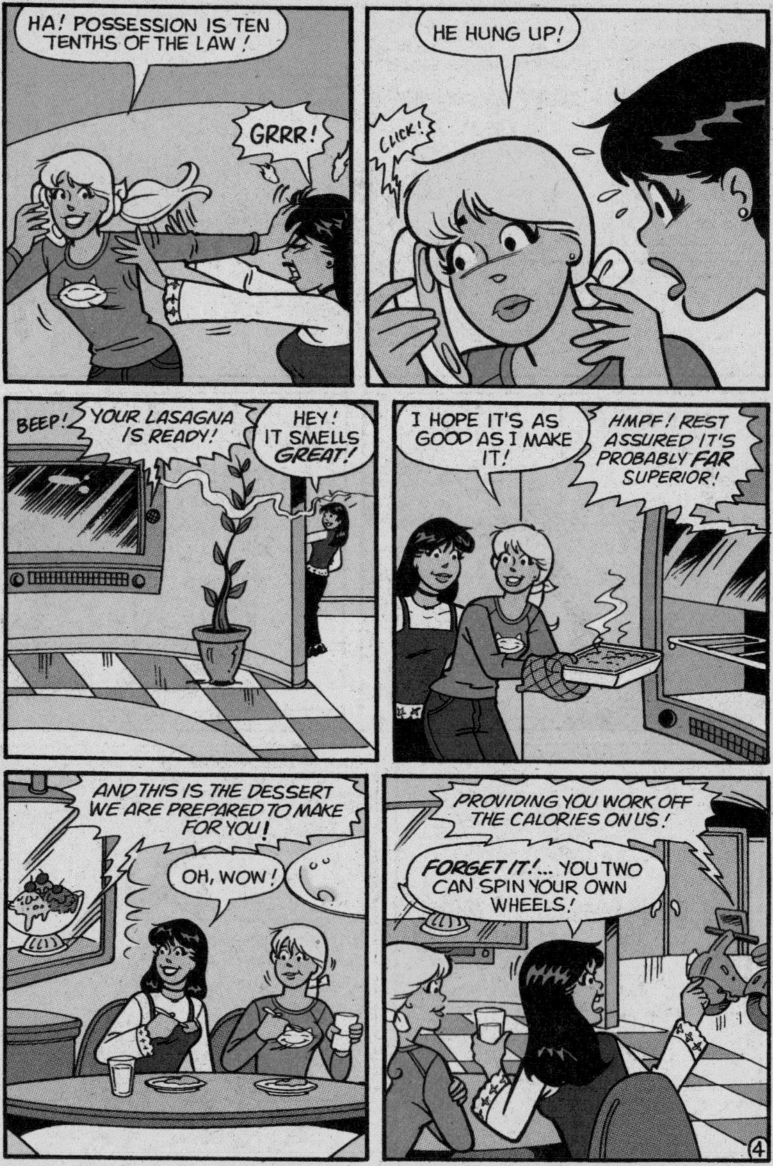
HA! POSSESSION IS TEN TENTHS OF THE LAW!
GRRR!
HE HUNG UP!
CLICK!
BEEP!
YOUR LASAGNA IS READY!
HEY! IT SMELLS *GREAT!*
I HOPE IT'S AS GOOD AS I MAKE IT!
HMPF! REST ASSURED IT'S PROBABLY *FAR* SUPERIOR!
AND THIS IS THE DESSERT WE ARE PREPARED TO MAKE FOR YOU!
OH, WOW!
PROVIDING YOU WORK OFF THE CALORIES ON US!
FORGET IT!... YOU TWO CAN SPIN YOUR OWN WHEELS!
4

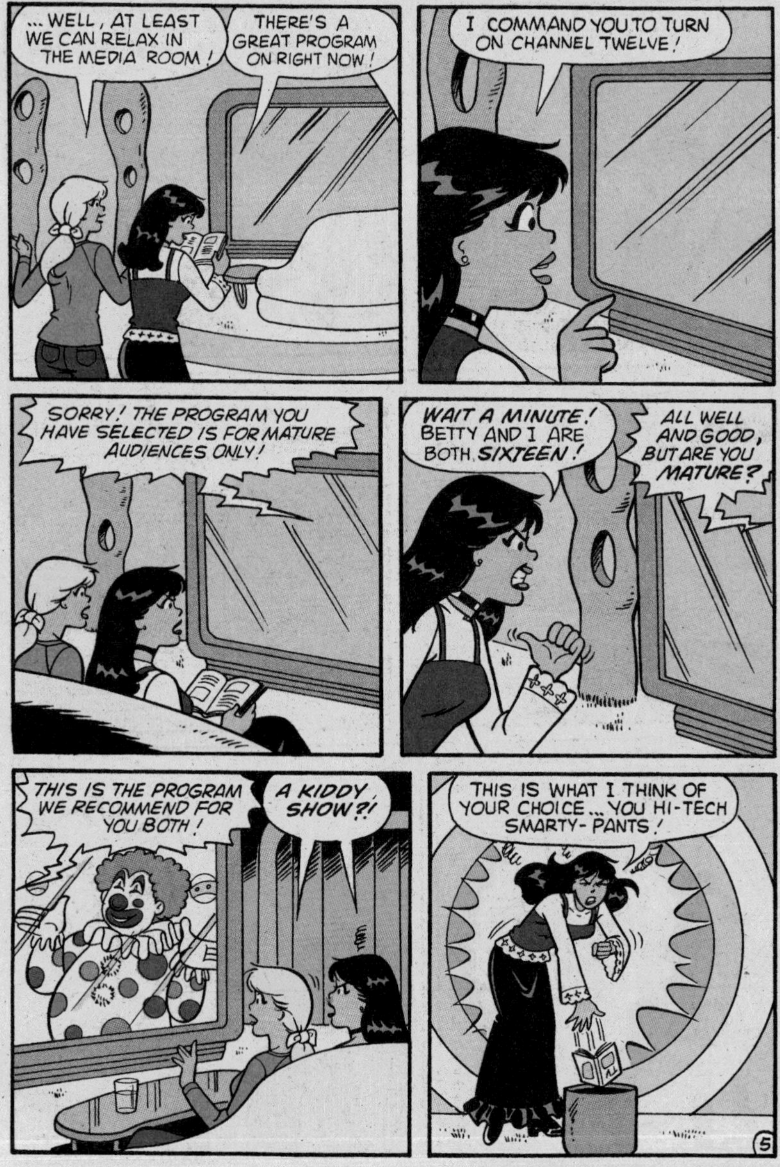

...WELL, AT LEAST WE CAN RELAX IN THE MEDIA ROOM!
THERE'S A GREAT PROGRAM ON RIGHT NOW!
I COMMAND YOU TO TURN ON CHANNEL TWELVE!
SORRY! THE PROGRAM YOU HAVE SELECTED IS FOR MATURE AUDIENCES ONLY!
WAIT A MINUTE! BETTY AND I ARE BOTH SIXTEEN!
ALL WELL AND GOOD, BUT ARE YOU MATURE?
THIS IS THE PROGRAM WE RECOMMEND FOR YOU BOTH!
A KIDDY SHOW?!
THIS IS WHAT I THINK OF YOUR CHOICE... YOU HI-TECH SMARTY-PANTS!
TV
5

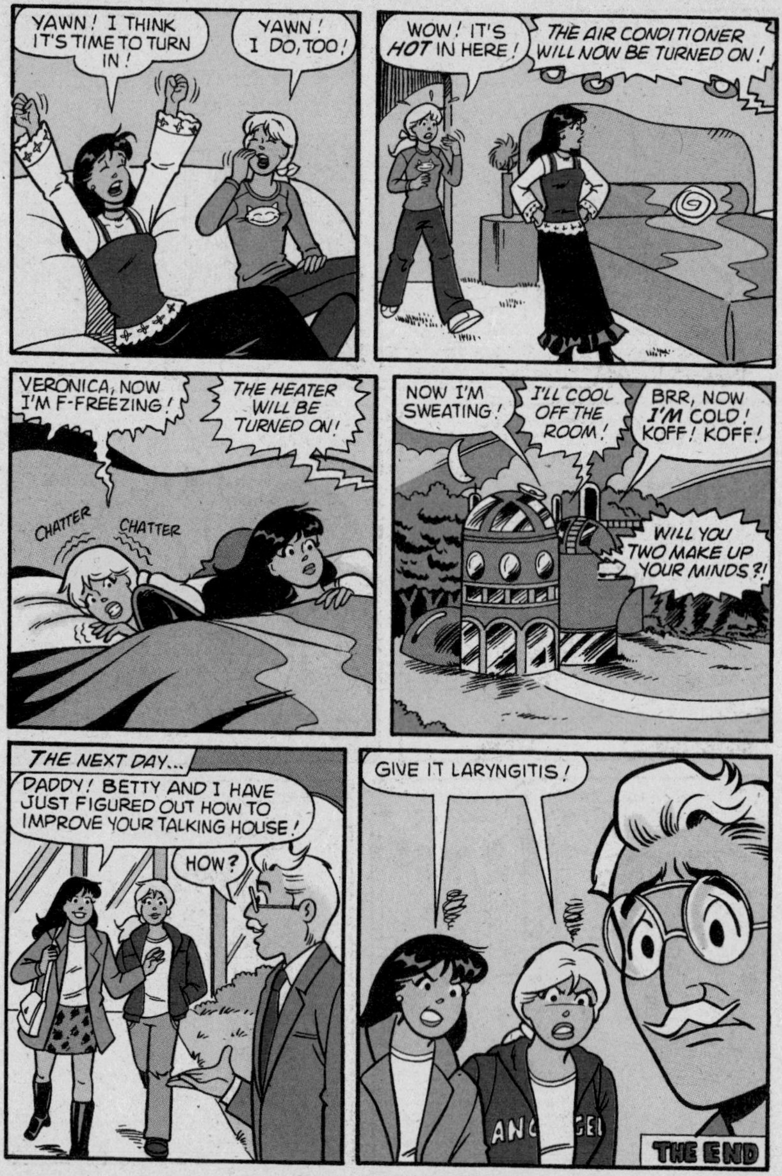
YAWN! I THINK IT'S TIME TO TURN IN!
YAWN! I DO, TOO!
WOW! IT'S HOT IN HERE!
THE AIR CONDITIONER WILL NOW BE TURNED ON!
VERONICA, NOW I'M F-FREEZING!
THE HEATER WILL BE TURNED ON!
CHATTER
CHATTER
NOW I'M SWEATING!
I'LL COOL OFF THE ROOM!
BRR, NOW I'M COLD! KOFF! KOFF!
WILL YOU TWO MAKE UP YOUR MINDS?!
THE NEXT DAY...
DADDY! BETTY AND I HAVE JUST FIGURED OUT HOW TO IMPROVE YOUR TALKING HOUSE!
HOW?
GIVE IT LARYNGITIS!
THE END

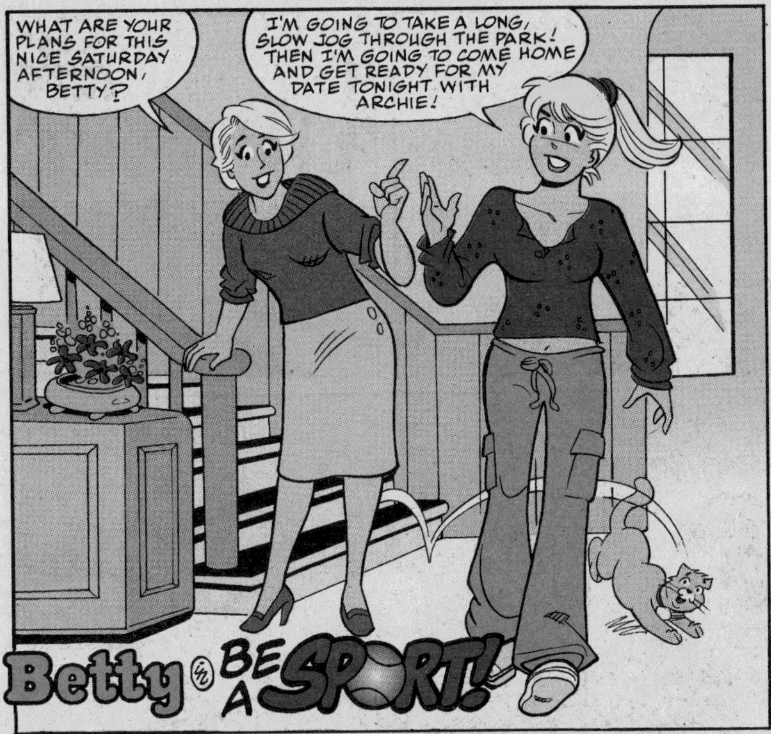
WHAT ARE YOUR PLANS FOR THIS NICE SATURDAY AFTERNOON, BETTY?
I'M GOING TO TAKE A LONG, SLOW JOG THROUGH THE PARK! THEN I'M GOING TO COME HOME AND GET READY FOR MY DATE TONIGHT WITH ARCHIE!
Betty
BE A SPORT!

SCRIPT: MIKE PELLOWSKI PENCILS: STAN GOLDBERG INKING: JOHN LOWE LETTERING: JACK MORELLI COLORING: BARRY GROSSMAN

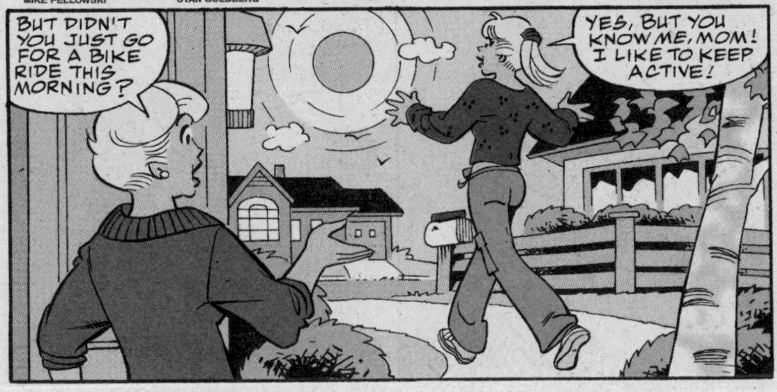
BUT DIDN'T YOU JUST GO FOR A BIKE RIDE THIS MORNING?
YES, BUT YOU KNOW ME, MOM! I LIKE TO KEEP ACTIVE!

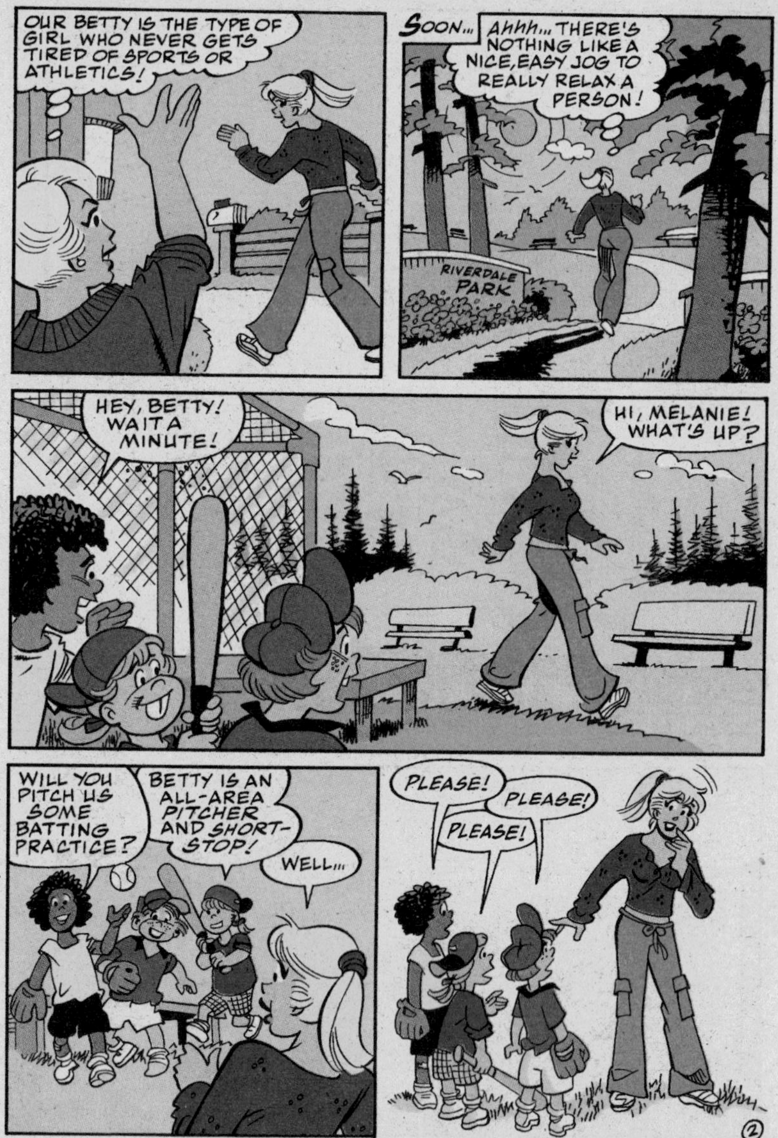
OUR BETTY IS THE TYPE OF GIRL WHO NEVER GETS TIRED OF SPORTS OR ATHLETICS!
SOON...
Ahhh... THERE'S NOTHING LIKE A NICE, EASY JOG TO REALLY RELAX A PERSON!
RIVERDALE PARK
HEY, BETTY! WAIT A MINUTE!
HI, MELANIE! WHAT'S UP?
WILL YOU PITCH US SOME BATTING PRACTICE?
BETTY IS AN ALL-AREA PITCHER AND SHORT-STOP!
WELL...
PLEASE!
PLEASE!
PLEASE!
2

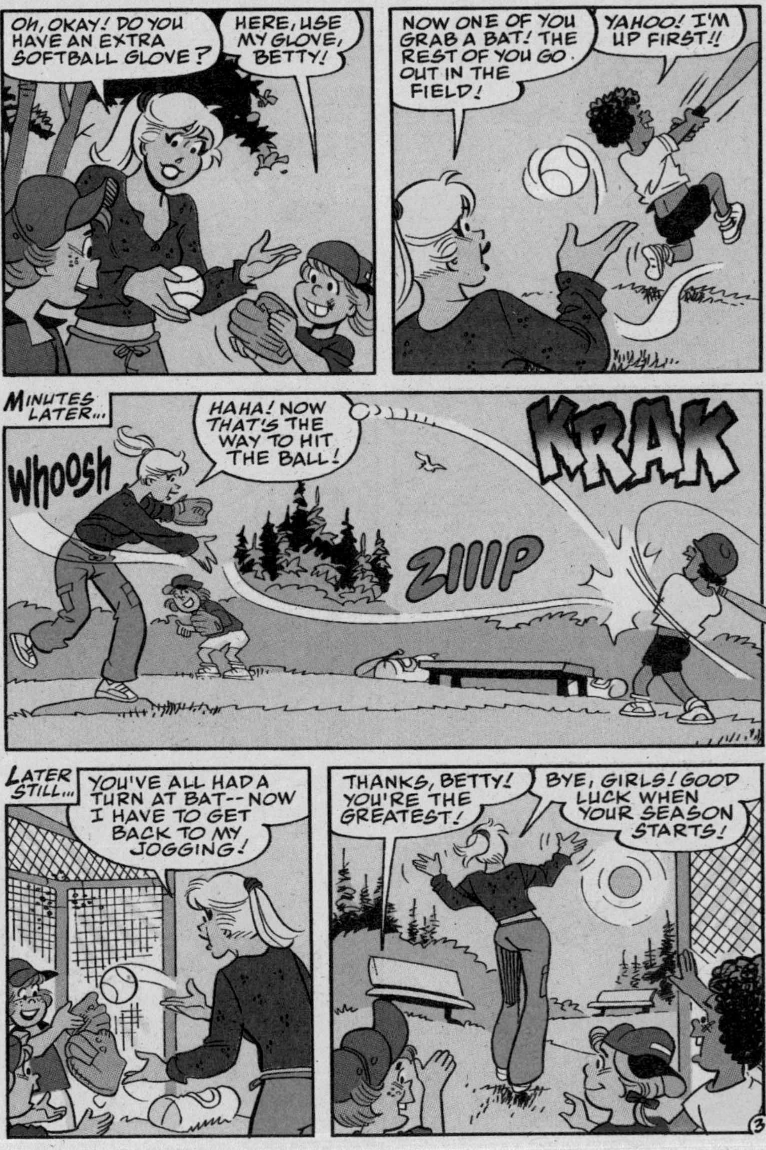
OH, OKAY! DO YOU HAVE AN EXTRA SOFTBALL GLOVE?
HERE, USE MY GLOVE, BETTY!
NOW ONE OF YOU GRAB A BAT! THE REST OF YOU GO OUT IN THE FIELD!
YAHOO! I'M UP FIRST!!
MINUTES LATER...
HAHA! NOW THAT'S THE WAY TO HIT THE BALL!
KRAK
WHOOSH
ZIIIP
LATER STILL...
YOU'VE ALL HAD A TURN AT BAT-- NOW I HAVE TO GET BACK TO MY JOGGING!
THANKS, BETTY! YOU'RE THE GREATEST!
BYE, GIRLS! GOOD LUCK WHEN YOUR SEASON STARTS!
3

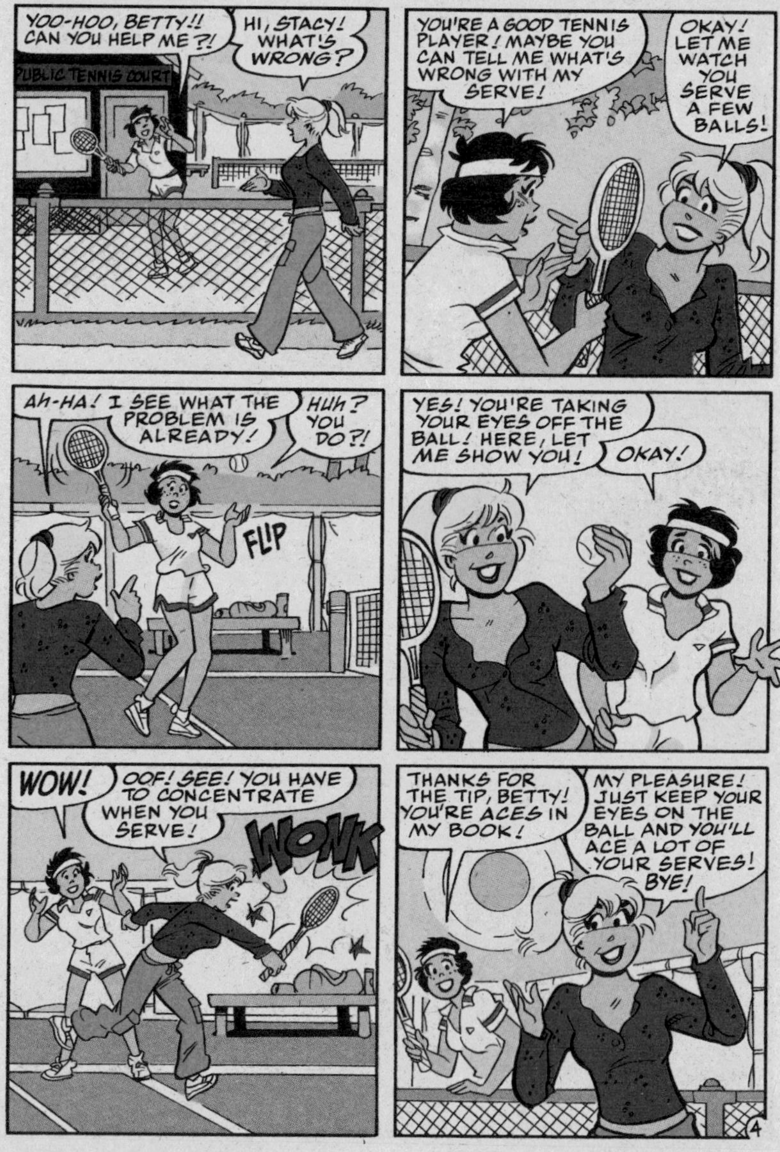

YOO-HOO, BETTY!! CAN YOU HELP ME ?!
HI, STACY! WHAT'S WRONG?
PUBLIC TENNIS COURT
YOU'RE A GOOD TENNIS PLAYER! MAYBE YOU CAN TELL ME WHAT'S WRONG WITH MY SERVE!
OKAY! LET ME WATCH YOU SERVE A FEW BALLS!
AH-HA! I SEE WHAT THE PROBLEM IS ALREADY!
HUH? YOU DO?!
FLIP
YES! YOU'RE TAKING YOUR EYES OFF THE BALL! HERE, LET ME SHOW YOU!
OKAY!
WOW!
OOF! SEE! YOU HAVE TO CONCENTRATE WHEN YOU SERVE!
WONK
THANKS FOR THE TIP, BETTY! YOU'RE ACES IN MY BOOK!
MY PLEASURE! JUST KEEP YOUR EYES ON THE BALL AND YOU'LL ACE A LOT OF YOUR SERVES! BYE!

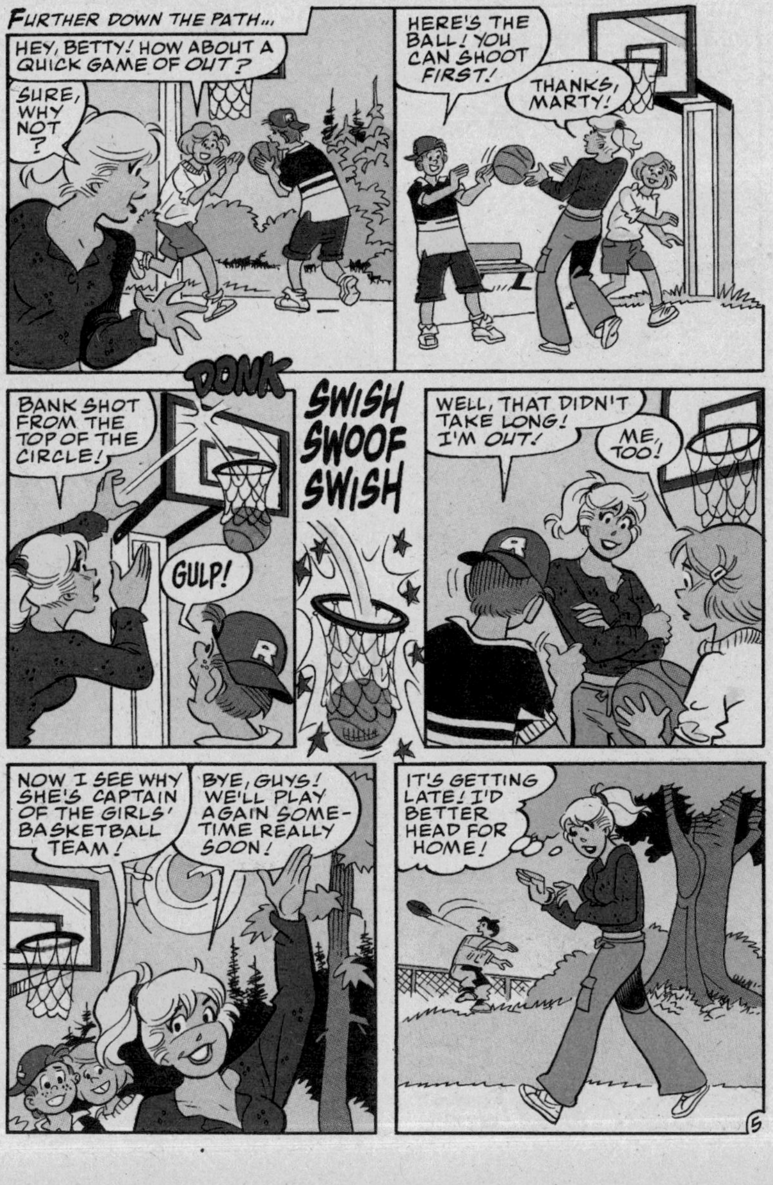
FURTHER DOWN THE PATH...
HEY, BETTY! HOW ABOUT A QUICK GAME OF OUT?
SURE, WHY NOT?
HERE'S THE BALL! YOU CAN SHOOT FIRST!
THANKS, MARTY!
DONK
BANK SHOT FROM THE TOP OF THE CIRCLE!
GULP!
SWISH SWOOF SWISH
WELL, THAT DIDN'T TAKE LONG! I'M OUT!
ME, TOO!
NOW I SEE WHY SHE'S CAPTAIN OF THE GIRLS' BASKETBALL TEAM!
BYE, GUYS! WE'LL PLAY AGAIN SOMETIME REALLY SOON!
IT'S GETTING LATE! I'D BETTER HEAD FOR HOME!

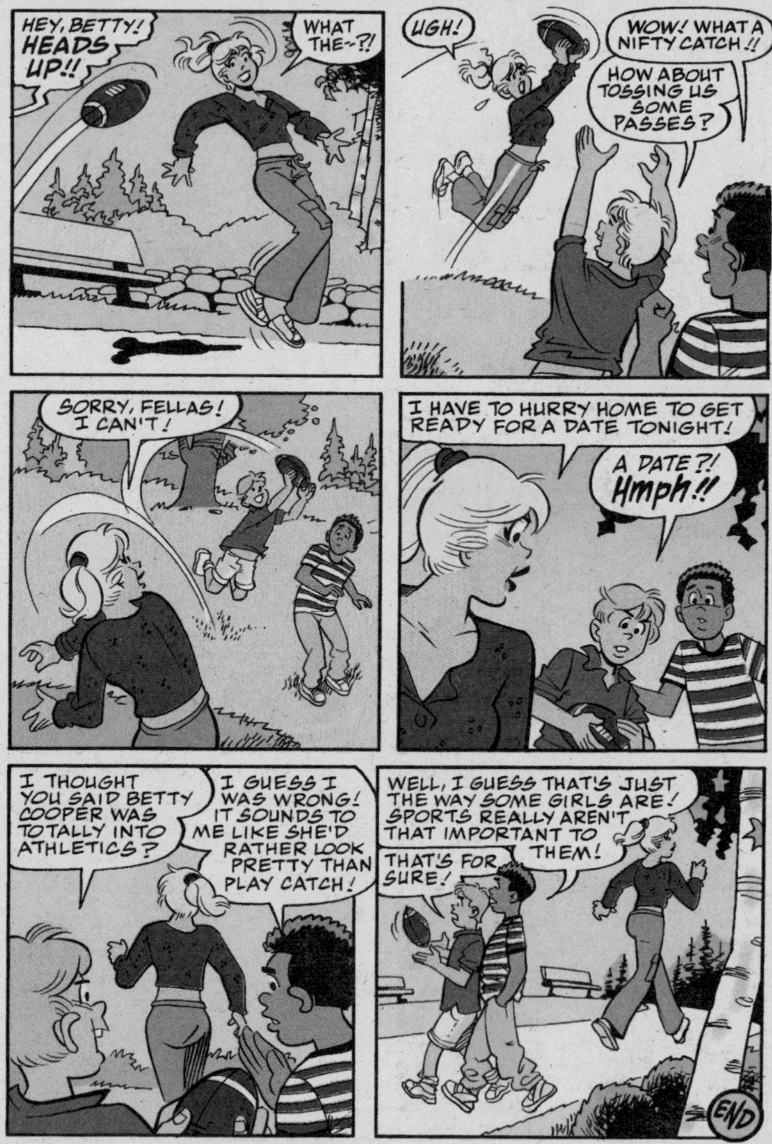
HEY, BETTY! HEADS UP!!
WHAT THE--?!
UGH!
WOW! WHAT A NIFTY CATCH!!
HOW ABOUT TOSSING US SOME PASSES?
SORRY, FELLAS! I CAN'T!
I HAVE TO HURRY HOME TO GET READY FOR A DATE TONIGHT!
A DATE?! Hmph!!
I THOUGHT YOU SAID BETTY COOPER WAS TOTALLY INTO ATHLETICS?
I GUESS I WAS WRONG! IT SOUNDS TO ME LIKE SHE'D RATHER LOOK PRETTY THAN PLAY CATCH!
WELL, I GUESS THAT'S JUST THE WAY SOME GIRLS ARE! SPORTS REALLY AREN'T THAT IMPORTANT TO THEM!
THAT'S FOR SURE!
END

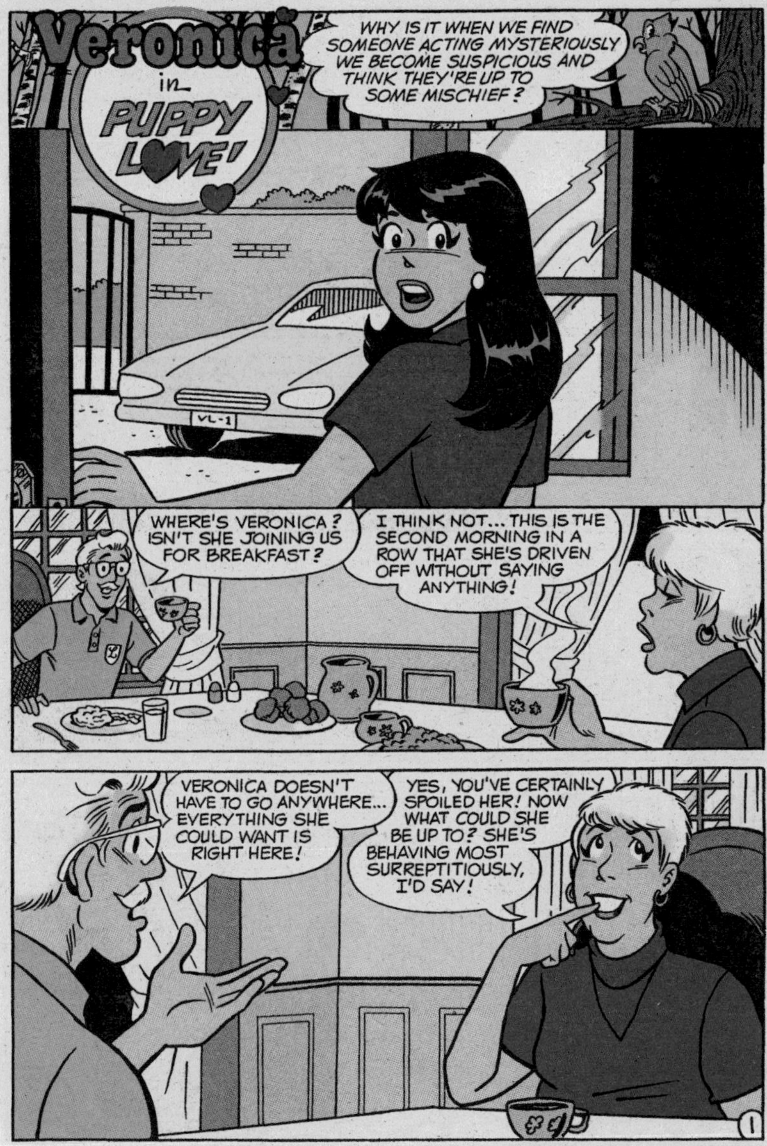
Veronica in PUPPY LOVE!
WHY IS IT WHEN WE FIND SOMEONE ACTING MYSTERIOUSLY WE BECOME SUSPICIOUS AND THINK THEY'RE UP TO SOME MISCHIEF?
VL-1
WHERE'S VERONICA? ISN'T SHE JOINING US FOR BREAKFAST?
I THINK NOT... THIS IS THE SECOND MORNING IN A ROW THAT SHE'S DRIVEN OFF WITHOUT SAYING ANYTHING!
VERONICA DOESN'T HAVE TO GO ANYWHERE... EVERYTHING SHE COULD WANT IS RIGHT HERE!
YES, YOU'VE CERTAINLY SPOILED HER! NOW WHAT COULD SHE BE UP TO? SHE'S BEHAVING MOST SURREPTITIOUSLY, I'D SAY!
1

Script: Kathleen Webb / Pencils: Bob Bolling / Inks: Jon D'Agostino / Letters: Bill Yoshida / Colors: Barry Grossman

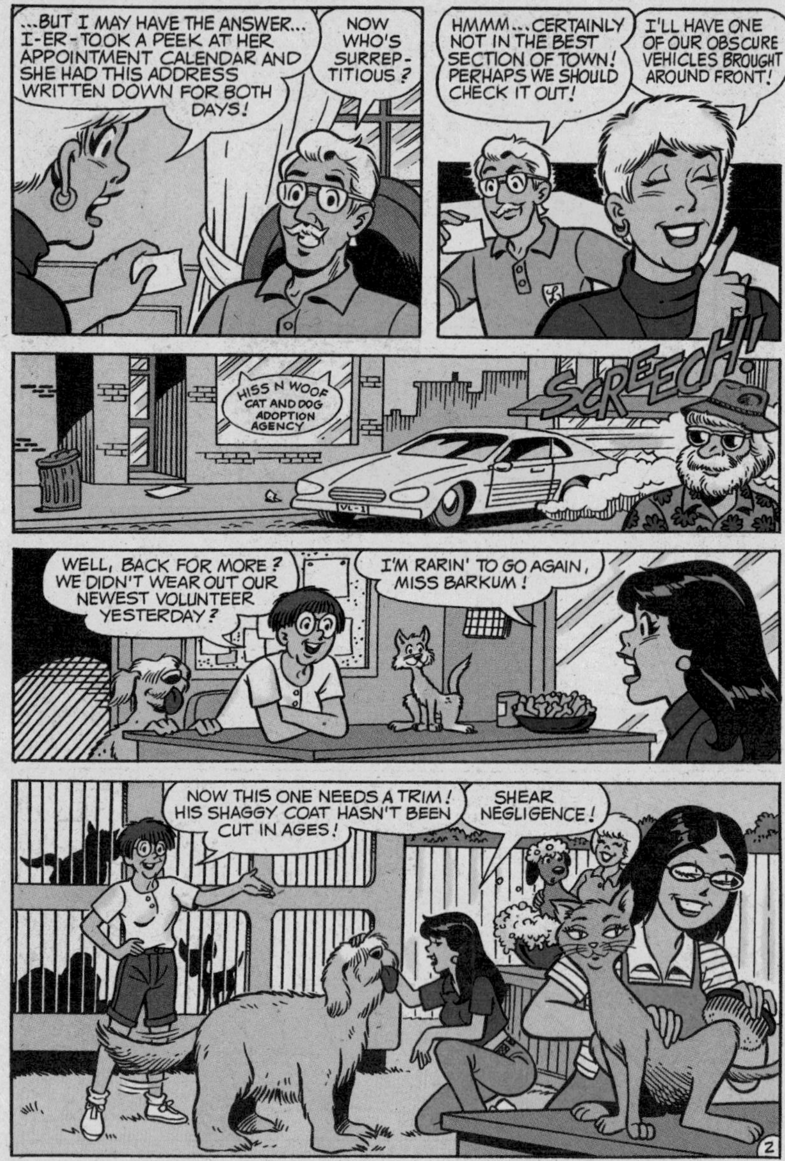
...BUT I MAY HAVE THE ANSWER... I-ER-TOOK A PEEK AT HER APPOINTMENT CALENDAR AND SHE HAD THIS ADDRESS WRITTEN DOWN FOR BOTH DAYS!
NOW WHO'S SURREP-TITIOUS?
HMMM...CERTAINLY NOT IN THE BEST SECTION OF TOWN! PERHAPS WE SHOULD CHECK IT OUT!
I'LL HAVE ONE OF OUR OBSCURE VEHICLES BROUGHT AROUND FRONT!
HISS N WOOF CAT AND DOG ADOPTION AGENCY
SCREECH!
VL-1
WELL, BACK FOR MORE? WE DIDN'T WEAR OUT OUR NEWEST VOLUNTEER YESTERDAY?
I'M RARIN' TO GO AGAIN, MISS BARKUM!
NOW THIS ONE NEEDS A TRIM! HIS SHAGGY COAT HASN'T BEEN CUT IN AGES!
SHEAR NEGLIGENCE!
2

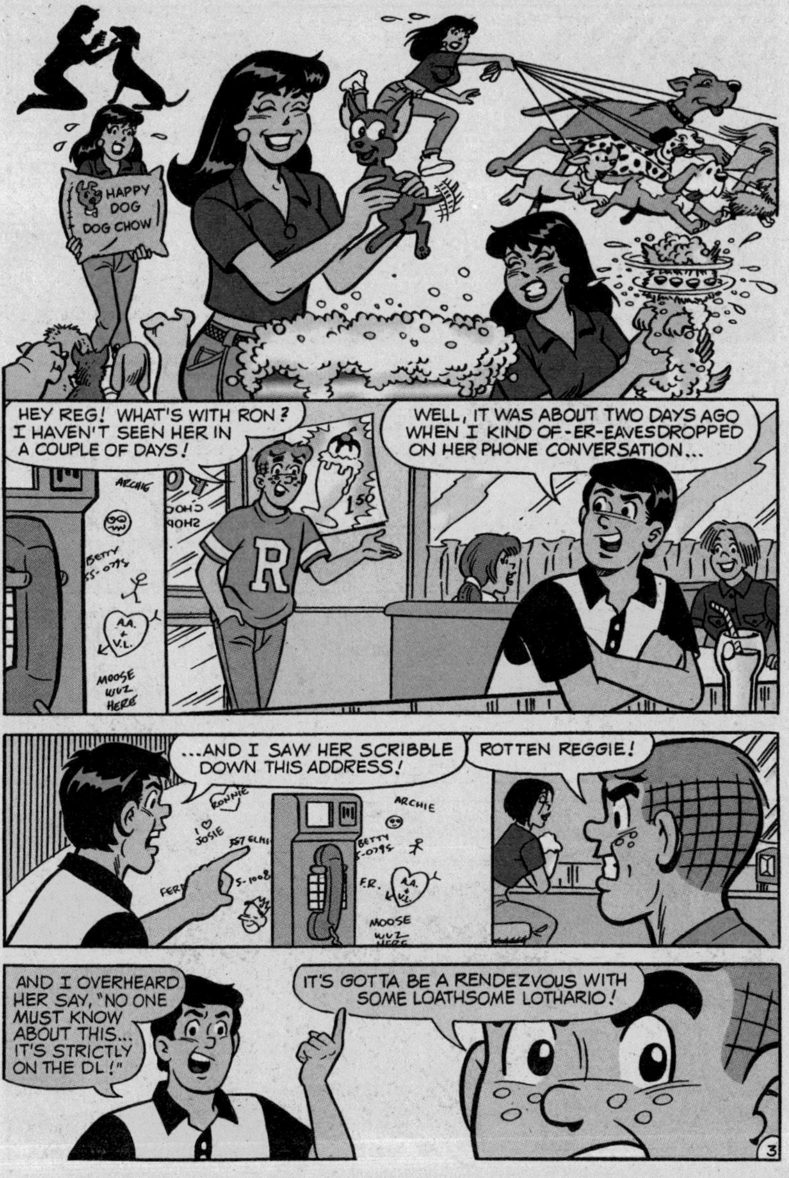
HAPPY DOG DOG CHOW
HEY REG! WHAT'S WITH RON? I HAVEN'T SEEN HER IN A COUPLE OF DAYS!
WELL, IT WAS ABOUT TWO DAYS AGO WHEN I KIND OF-ER-EAVESDROPPED ON HER PHONE CONVERSATION...
...AND I SAW HER SCRIBBLE DOWN THIS ADDRESS!
ROTTEN REGGIE!
AND I OVERHEARD HER SAY, "NO ONE MUST KNOW ABOUT THIS... IT'S STRICTLY ON THE DL!"
IT'S GOTTA BE A RENDEZVOUS WITH SOME LOATHSOME LOTHARIO!

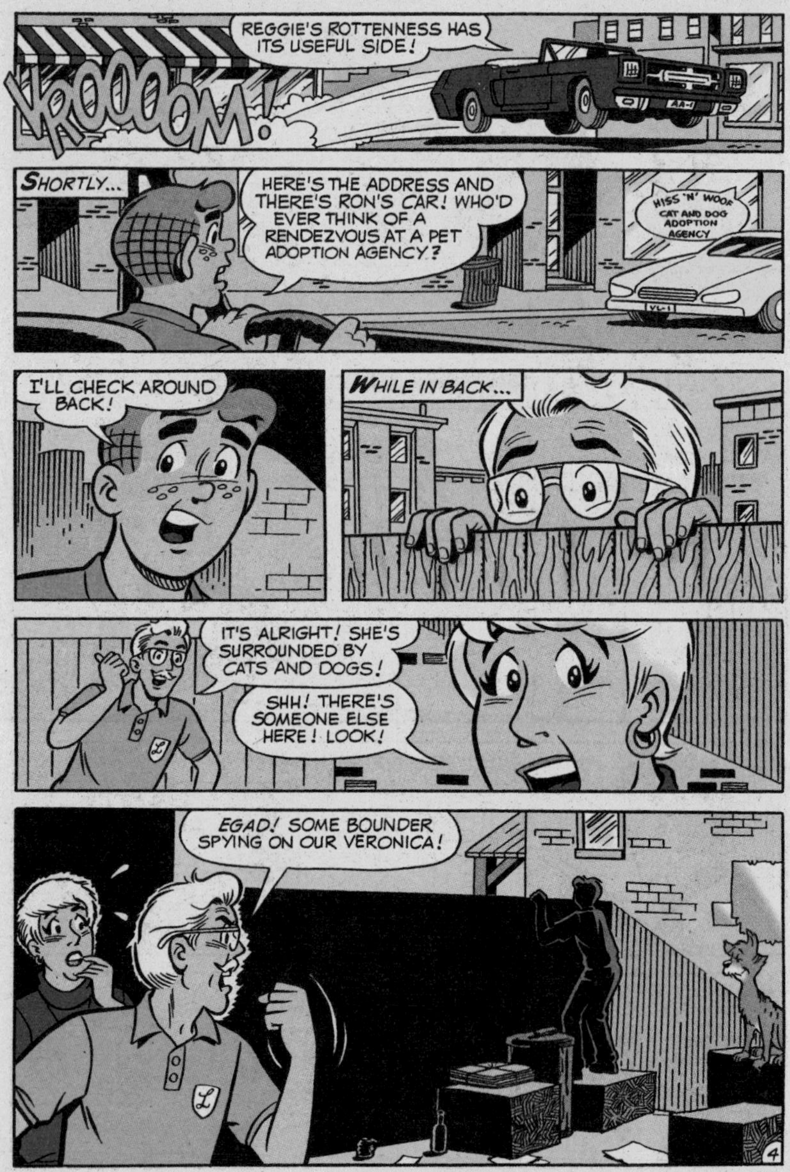
REGGIE'S ROTTENNESS HAS ITS USEFUL SIDE!
KROOOOM!
AA-1
SHORTLY...
HERE'S THE ADDRESS AND THERE'S RON'S CAR! WHO'D EVER THINK OF A RENDEZVOUS AT A PET ADOPTION AGENCY?
HISS 'N' WOOF CAT AND DOG ADOPTION AGENCY
VL-1
I'LL CHECK AROUND BACK!
WHILE IN BACK...
IT'S ALRIGHT! SHE'S SURROUNDED BY CATS AND DOGS!
SHH! THERE'S SOMEONE ELSE HERE! LOOK!
EGAD! SOME BOUNDER SPYING ON OUR VERONICA!
4

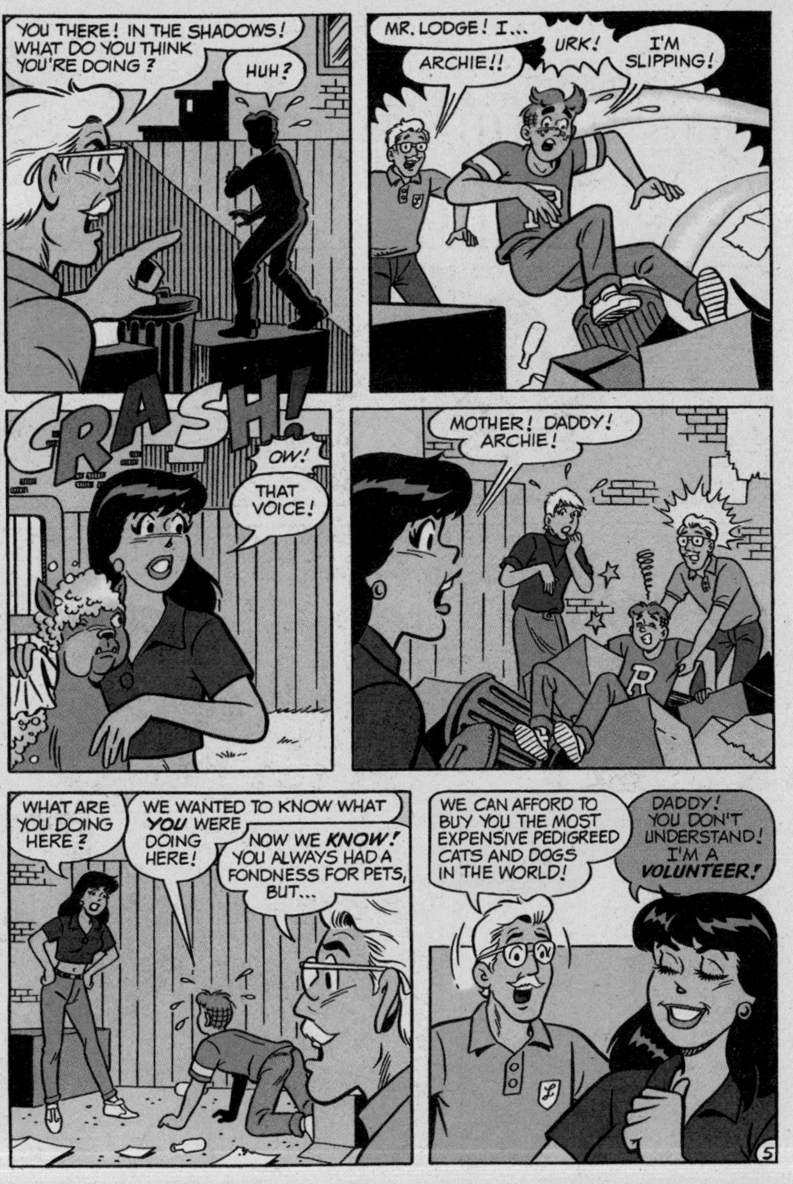
YOU THERE! IN THE SHADOWS! WHAT DO YOU THINK YOU'RE DOING?
HUH?
MR. LODGE! I...
ARCHIE!!
URK!
I'M SLIPPING!
CRASH!
OW!
THAT VOICE!
MOTHER! DADDY! ARCHIE!
WHAT ARE YOU DOING HERE?
WE WANTED TO KNOW WHAT *YOU* WERE DOING HERE!
NOW WE ***KNOW!*** YOU ALWAYS HAD A FONDNESS FOR PETS, BUT...
WE CAN AFFORD TO BUY YOU THE MOST EXPENSIVE PEDIGREED CATS AND DOGS IN THE WORLD!
DADDY! YOU DON'T UNDERSTAND! I'M A ***VOLUNTEER!***
5

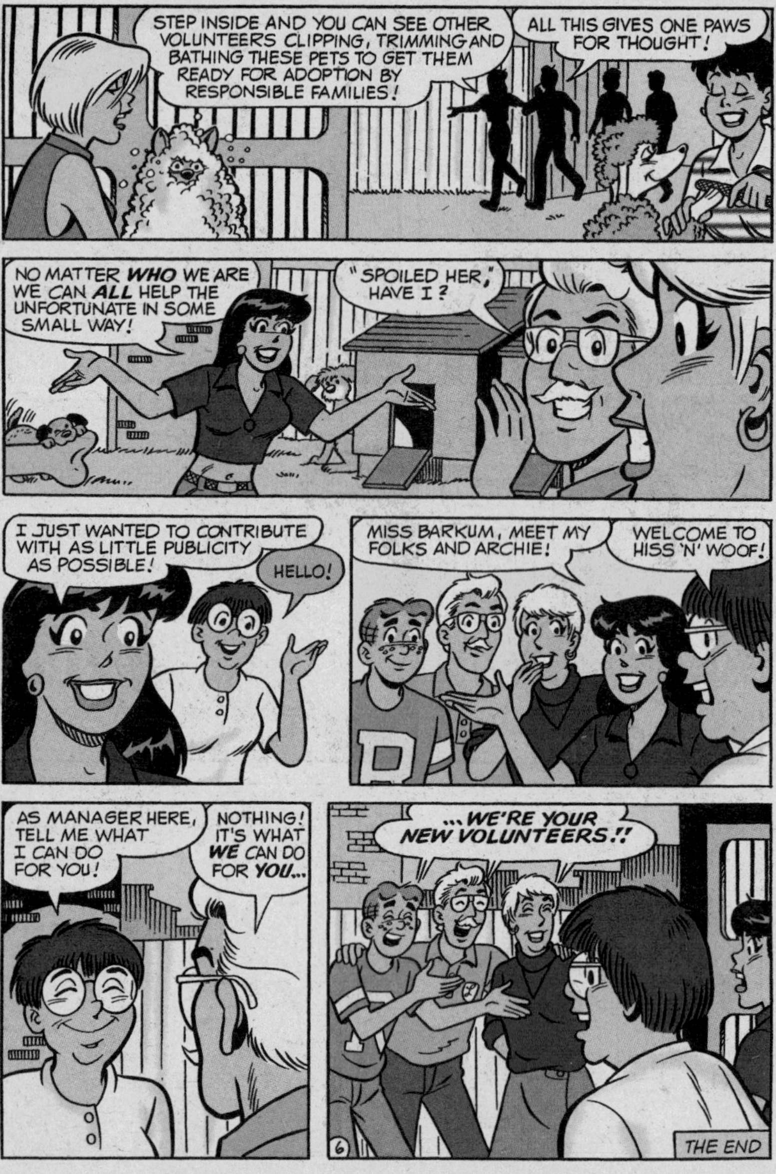
STEP INSIDE AND YOU CAN SEE OTHER VOLUNTEERS CLIPPING, TRIMMING AND BATHING THESE PETS TO GET THEM READY FOR ADOPTION BY RESPONSIBLE FAMILIES!
ALL THIS GIVES ONE PAWS FOR THOUGHT!
NO MATTER WHO WE ARE WE CAN ALL HELP THE UNFORTUNATE IN SOME SMALL WAY!
"SPOILED HER," HAVE I?
I JUST WANTED TO CONTRIBUTE WITH AS LITTLE PUBLICITY AS POSSIBLE!
HELLO!
MISS BARKUM, MEET MY FOLKS AND ARCHIE!
WELCOME TO HISS 'N' WOOF!
AS MANAGER HERE, TELL ME WHAT I CAN DO FOR YOU!
NOTHING! IT'S WHAT WE CAN DO FOR YOU...
...WE'RE YOUR NEW VOLUNTEERS!!
6
THE END

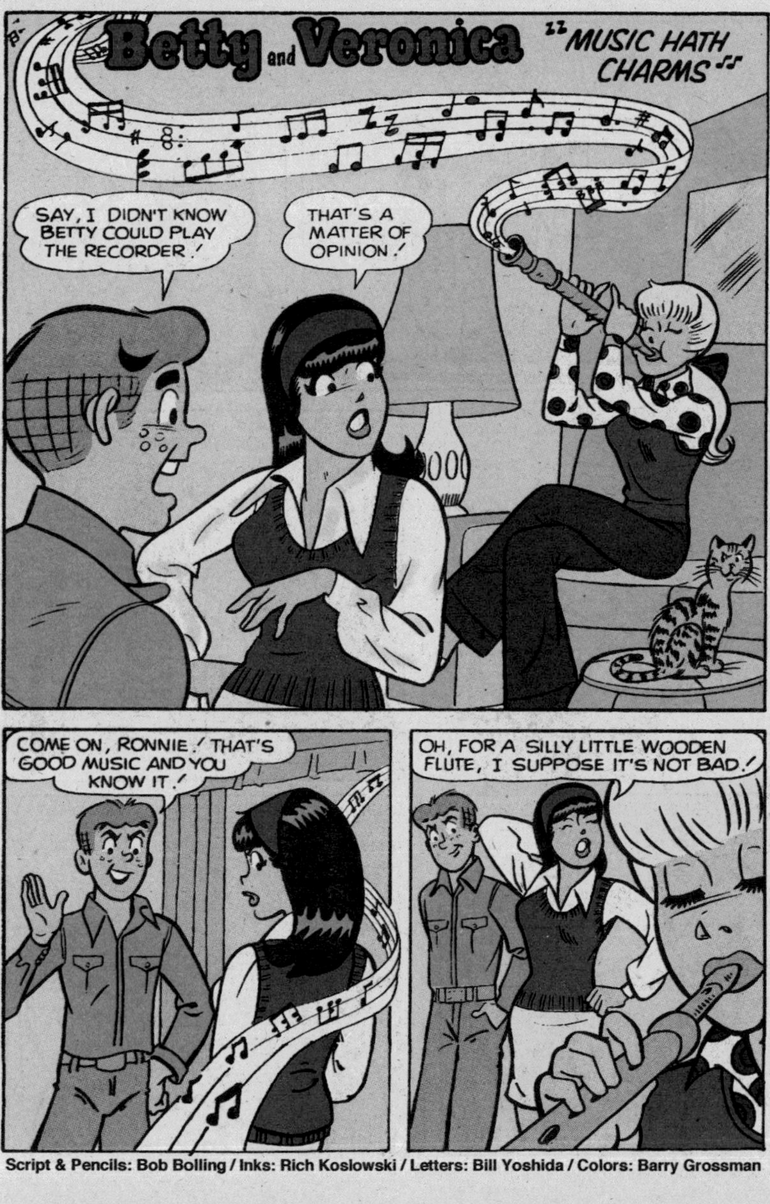
Betty and Veronica
"MUSIC HATH CHARMS"
SAY, I DIDN'T KNOW BETTY COULD PLAY THE RECORDER!
THAT'S A MATTER OF OPINION!
COME ON, RONNIE! THAT'S GOOD MUSIC AND YOU KNOW IT!
OH, FOR A SILLY LITTLE WOODEN FLUTE, I SUPPOSE IT'S NOT BAD!

Script & Pencils: Bob Bolling / Inks: Rich Koslowski / Letters: Bill Yoshida / Colors: Barry Grossman

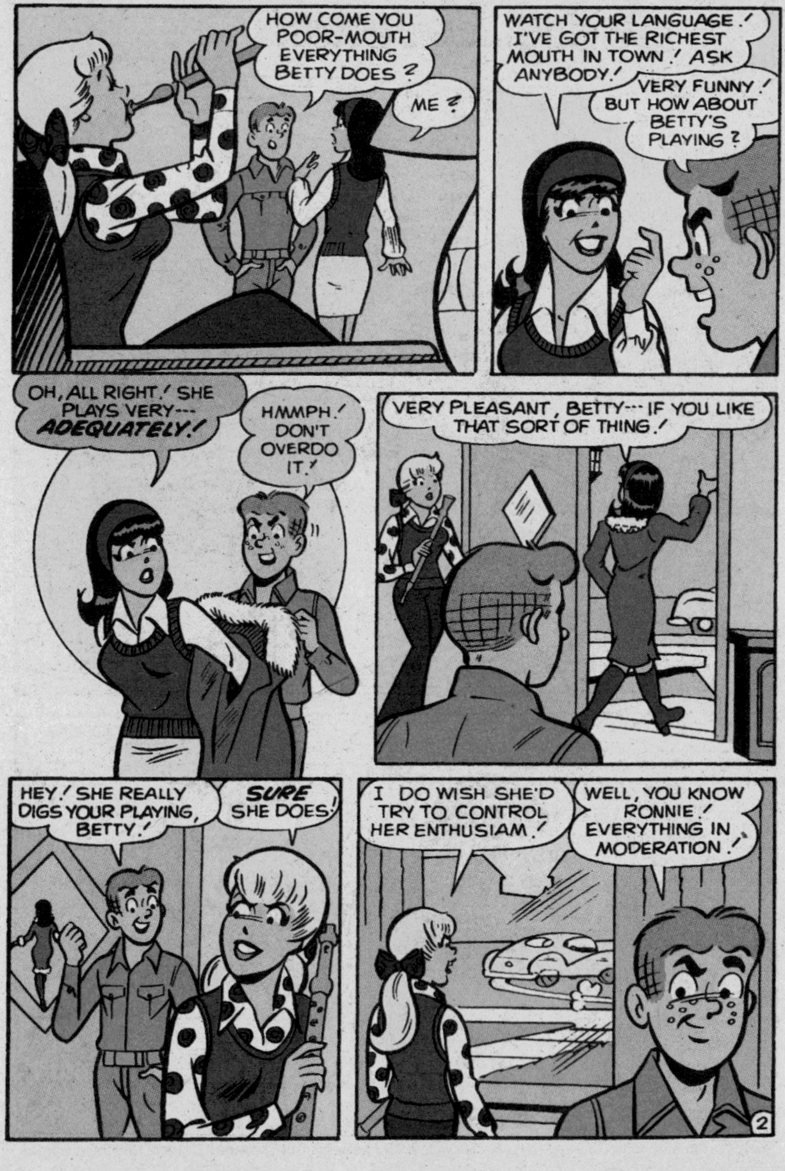
HOW COME YOU POOR-MOUTH EVERYTHING BETTY DOES?
ME?
WATCH YOUR LANGUAGE! I'VE GOT THE RICHEST MOUTH IN TOWN! ASK ANYBODY!
VERY FUNNY! BUT HOW ABOUT BETTY'S PLAYING?
OH, ALL RIGHT! SHE PLAYS VERY--- *ADEQUATELY!*
HMMPH! DON'T OVERDO IT!
VERY PLEASANT, BETTY--- IF YOU LIKE THAT SORT OF THING!
HEY! SHE REALLY DIGS YOUR PLAYING, BETTY!
SURE SHE DOES!
I DO WISH SHE'D TRY TO CONTROL HER ENTHUSIAM!
WELL, YOU KNOW RONNIE! EVERYTHING IN MODERATION!
2

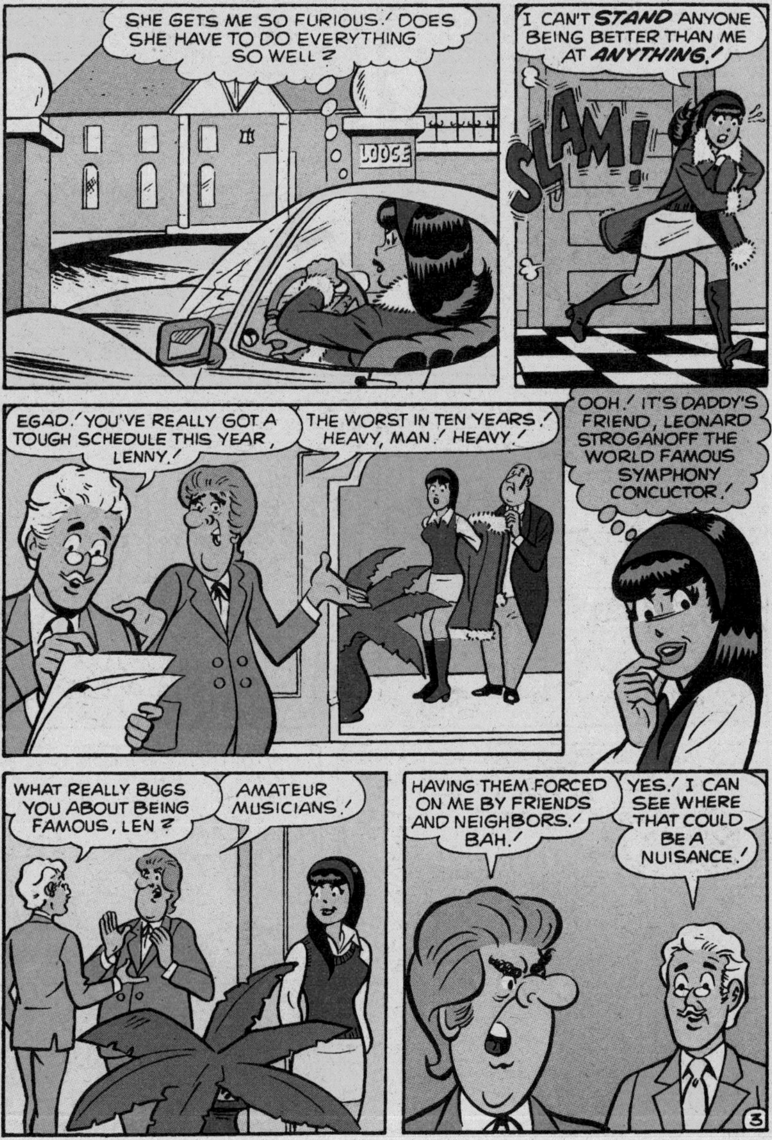
SHE GETS ME SO FURIOUS! DOES SHE HAVE TO DO EVERYTHING SO WELL?
LOOSE
I CAN'T STAND ANYONE BEING BETTER THAN ME AT ANYTHING!
SLAM!
EGAD! YOU'VE REALLY GOT A TOUGH SCHEDULE THIS YEAR, LENNY!
THE WORST IN TEN YEARS! HEAVY, MAN! HEAVY!
OOH! IT'S DADDY'S FRIEND, LEONARD STROGANOFF THE WORLD FAMOUS SYMPHONY CONCUCTOR!
WHAT REALLY BUGS YOU ABOUT BEING FAMOUS, LEN?
AMATEUR MUSICIANS!
HAVING THEM FORCED ON ME BY FRIENDS AND NEIGHBORS! BAH!
YES! I CAN SEE WHERE THAT COULD BE A NUISANCE!
3

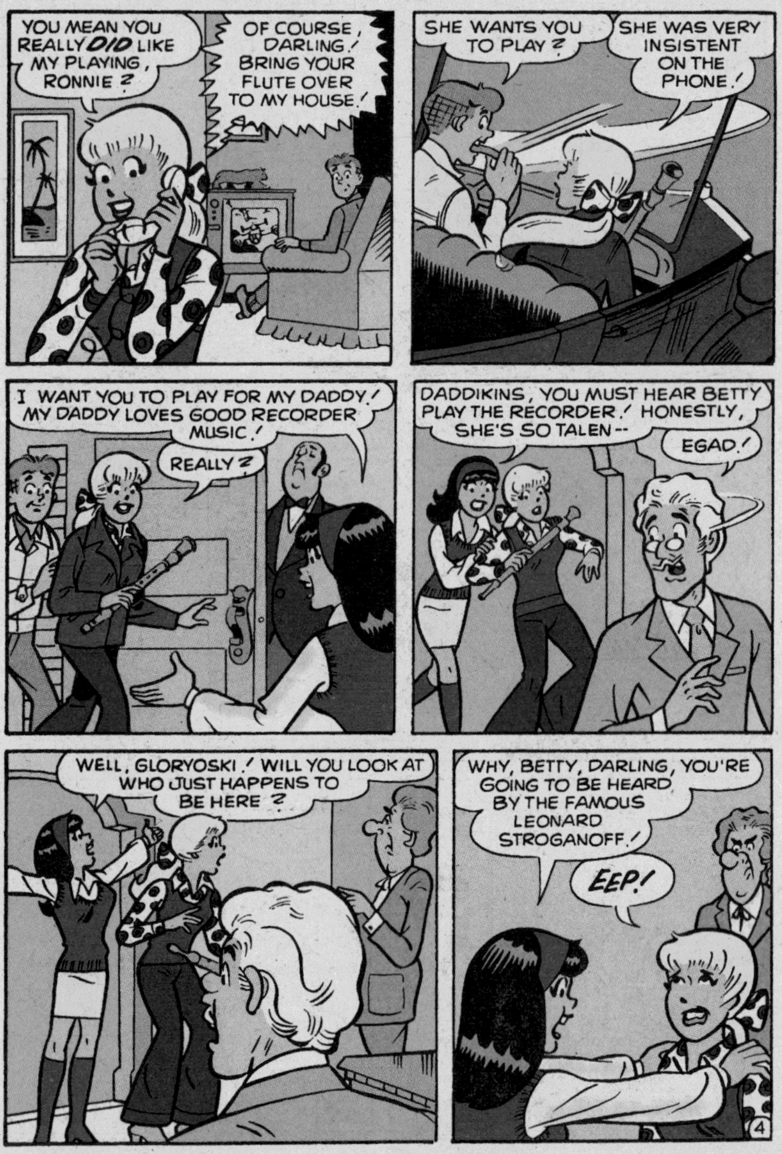
YOU MEAN YOU REALLY DID LIKE MY PLAYING, RONNIE?
OF COURSE, DARLING! BRING YOUR FLUTE OVER TO MY HOUSE!
SHE WANTS YOU TO PLAY?
SHE WAS VERY INSISTENT ON THE PHONE!
I WANT YOU TO PLAY FOR MY DADDY! MY DADDY LOVES GOOD RECORDER MUSIC!
REALLY?
DADDIKINS, YOU MUST HEAR BETTY PLAY THE RECORDER! HONESTLY, SHE'S SO TALEN--
EGAD!
WELL, GLORYOSKI! WILL YOU LOOK AT WHO JUST HAPPENS TO BE HERE?
WHY, BETTY, DARLING, YOU'RE GOING TO BE HEARD BY THE FAMOUS LEONARD STROGANOFF!
EEP!
4

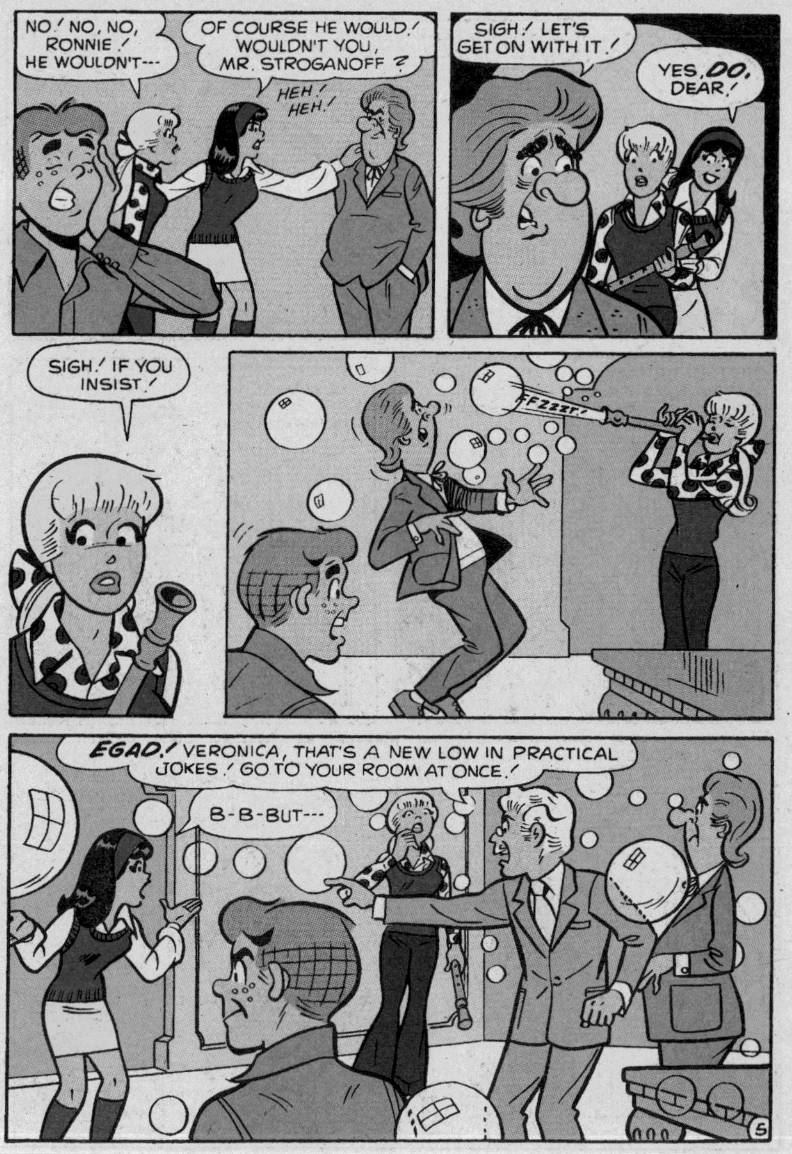
NO! NO, NO, RONNIE! HE WOULDN'T---
OF COURSE HE WOULD! WOULDN'T YOU, MR. STROGANOFF ?
HEH! HEH!
SIGH! LET'S GET ON WITH IT!
YES, DO, DEAR!
SIGH! IF YOU INSIST!
FFZzzzr!
EGAD! VERONICA, THAT'S A NEW LOW IN PRACTICAL JOKES! GO TO YOUR ROOM AT ONCE!
B-B-BUT---
5

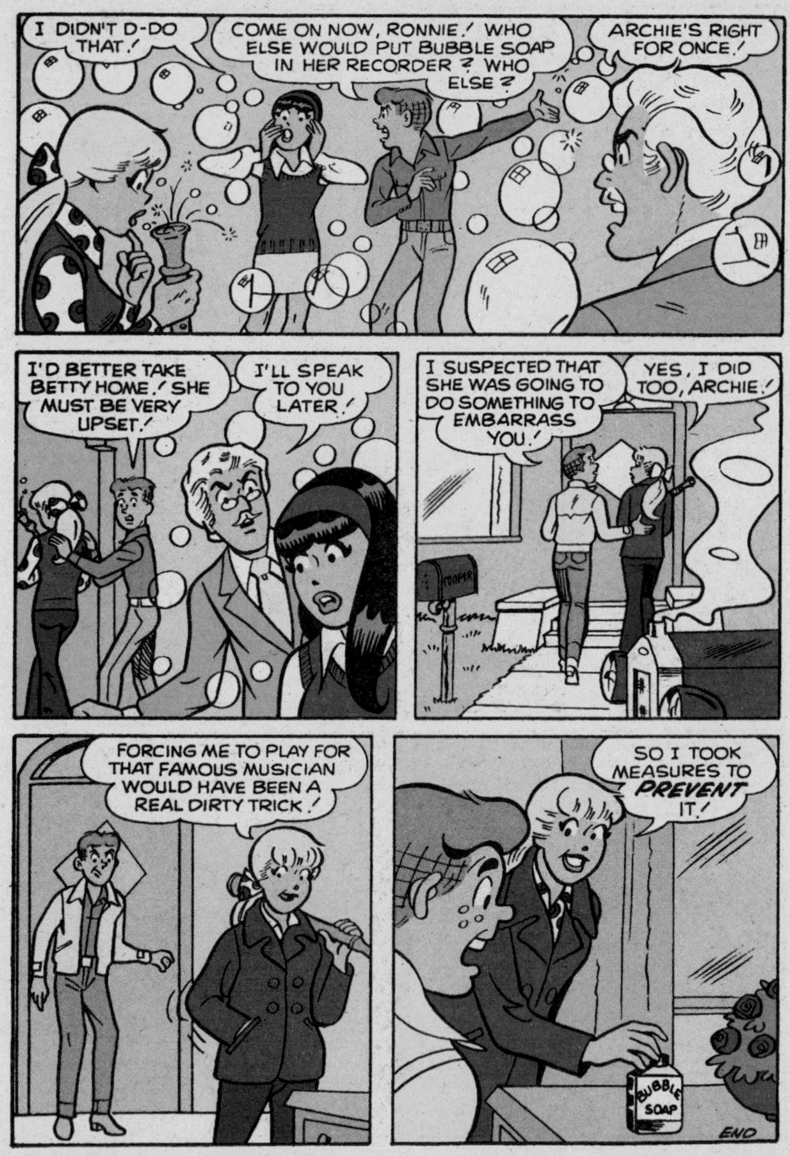
I DIDN'T D-DO THAT.!
COME ON NOW, RONNIE.! WHO ELSE WOULD PUT BUBBLE SOAP IN HER RECORDER ? WHO ELSE ?
ARCHIE'S RIGHT FOR ONCE.!
I'D BETTER TAKE BETTY HOME.! SHE MUST BE VERY UPSET.!
I'LL SPEAK TO YOU LATER.!
I SUSPECTED THAT SHE WAS GOING TO DO SOMETHING TO EMBARRASS YOU.!
YES, I DID TOO, ARCHIE.!
COOPER
FORCING ME TO PLAY FOR THAT FAMOUS MUSICIAN WOULD HAVE BEEN A REAL DIRTY TRICK.!
SO I TOOK MEASURES TO *PREVENT* IT.!
BUBBLE SOAP
END

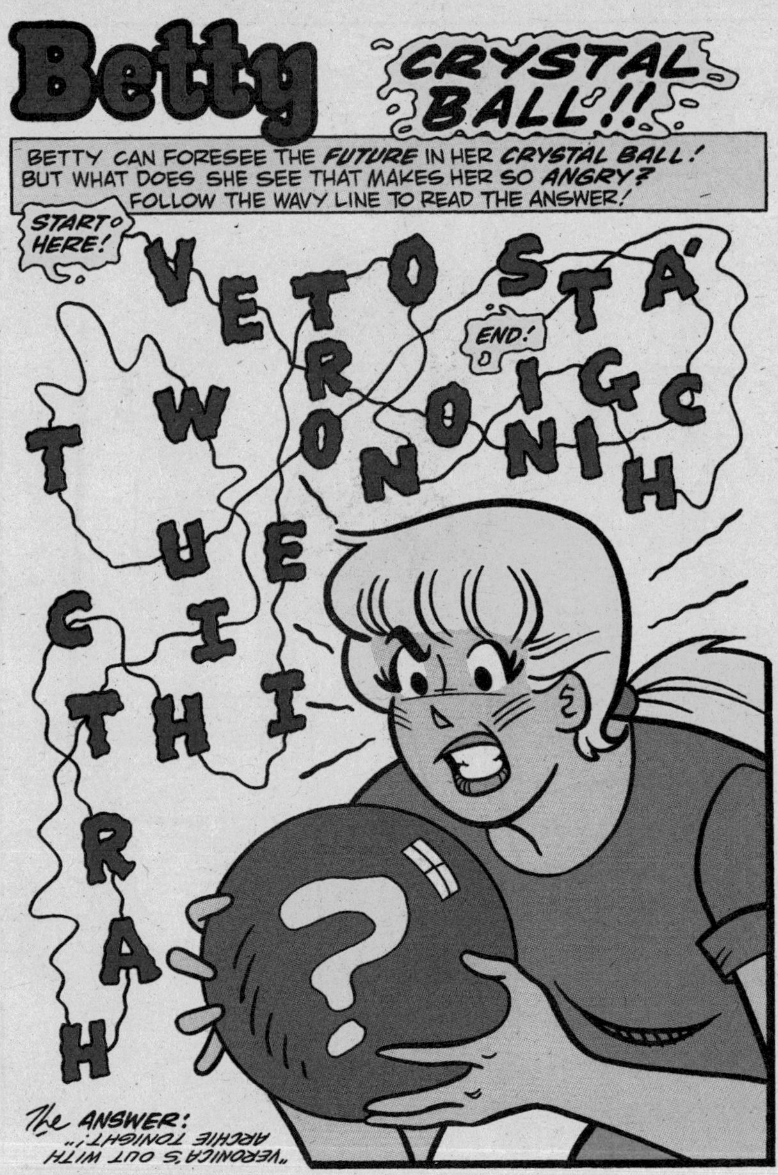

Betty
CRYSTAL BALL!!
BETTY CAN FORESEE THE FUTURE IN HER CRYSTAL BALL! BUT WHAT DOES SHE SEE THAT MAKES HER SO ANGRY? FOLLOW THE WAVY LINE TO READ THE ANSWER!
START HERE!
END!
The ANSWER:
"VERONICA'S OUT WITH ARCHIE TONIGHT!"

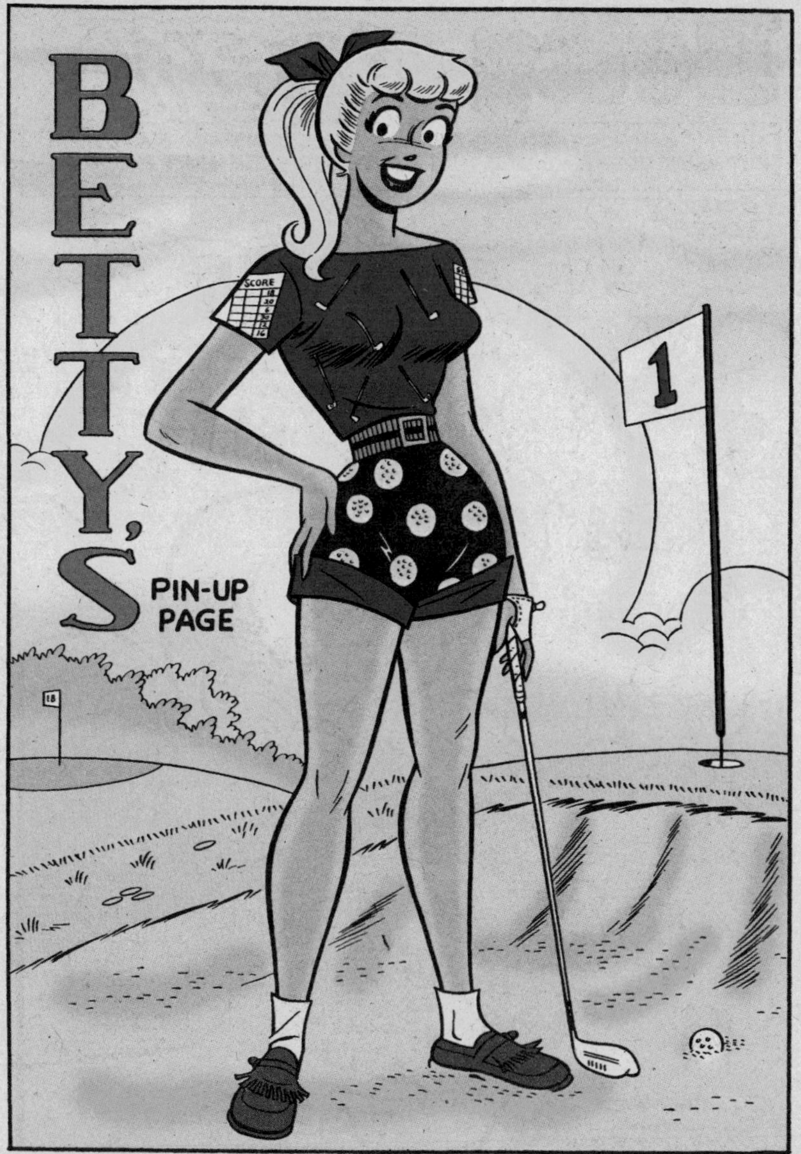
BETTY'S
PIN-UP PAGE
SCORE
18
30
6
30
12
16
1
18

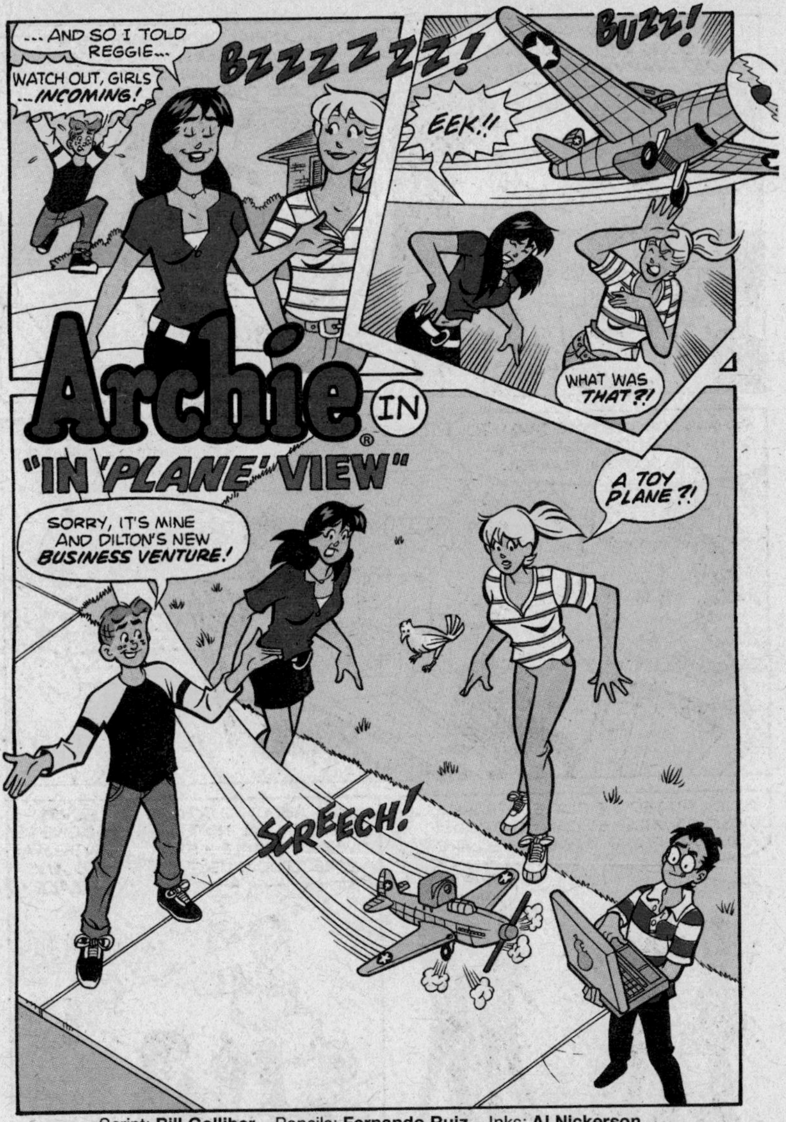
... AND SO I TOLD REGGIE...
WATCH OUT, GIRLS ...INCOMING!
BZZZZZZZ!
BUZZ!
EEK!!
WHAT WAS THAT?!
Archie IN
"IN 'PLANE' VIEW"
SORRY, IT'S MINE AND DILTON'S NEW BUSINESS VENTURE!
A TOY PLANE?!
SCREECH!

Script: **Bill Golliher** Pencils: **Fernando Ruiz** Inks: **Al Nickerson**
Letters: **Bill Yoshida** Colors: **Barry Grossman**
Editor-In-Chief: **Victor Gorelick** President: **Mike Pellerito** Publisher: **Jon Goldwater**

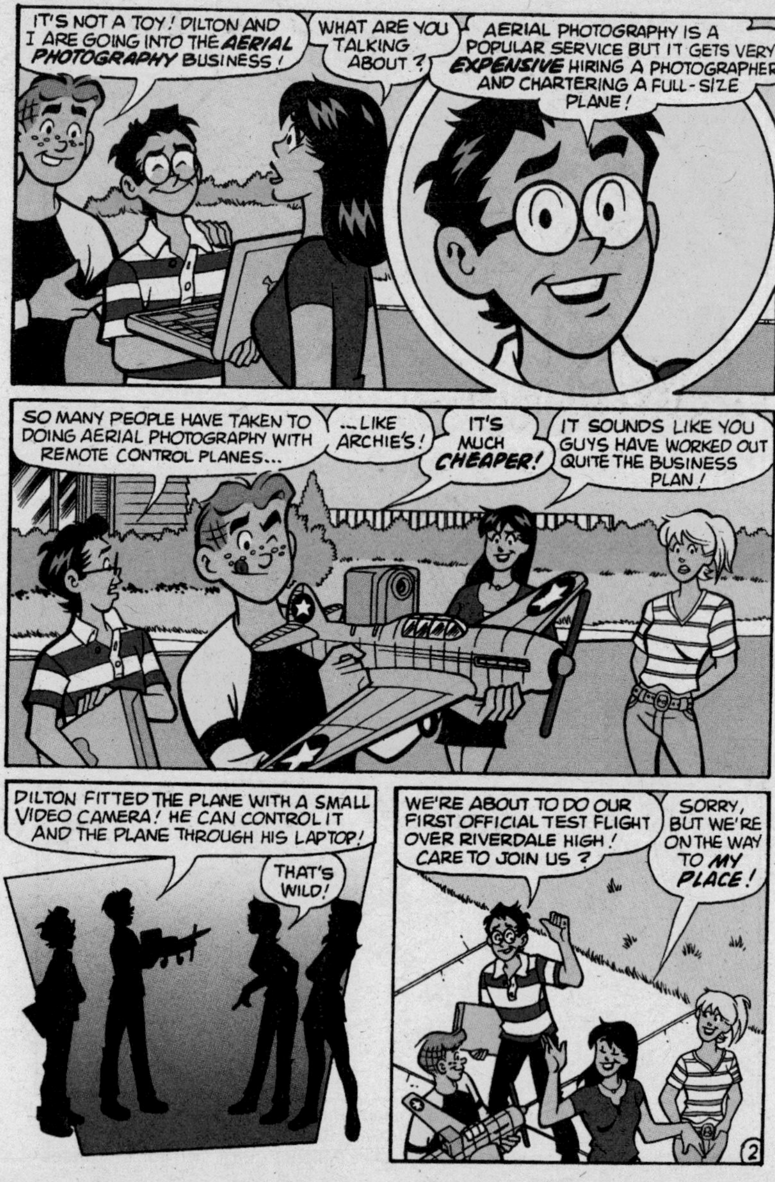
IT'S NOT A TOY! DILTON AND I ARE GOING INTO THE AERIAL PHOTOGRAPHY BUSINESS!
WHAT ARE YOU TALKING ABOUT?
AERIAL PHOTOGRAPHY IS A POPULAR SERVICE BUT IT GETS VERY EXPENSIVE HIRING A PHOTOGRAPHER AND CHARTERING A FULL-SIZE PLANE!
SO MANY PEOPLE HAVE TAKEN TO DOING AERIAL PHOTOGRAPHY WITH REMOTE CONTROL PLANES...
...LIKE ARCHIE'S!
IT'S MUCH CHEAPER!
IT SOUNDS LIKE YOU GUYS HAVE WORKED OUT QUITE THE BUSINESS PLAN!
DILTON FITTED THE PLANE WITH A SMALL VIDEO CAMERA! HE CAN CONTROL IT AND THE PLANE THROUGH HIS LAPTOP!
THAT'S WILD!
WE'RE ABOUT TO DO OUR FIRST OFFICIAL TEST FLIGHT OVER RIVERDALE HIGH! CARE TO JOIN US?
SORRY, BUT WE'RE ON THE WAY TO MY PLACE!
2

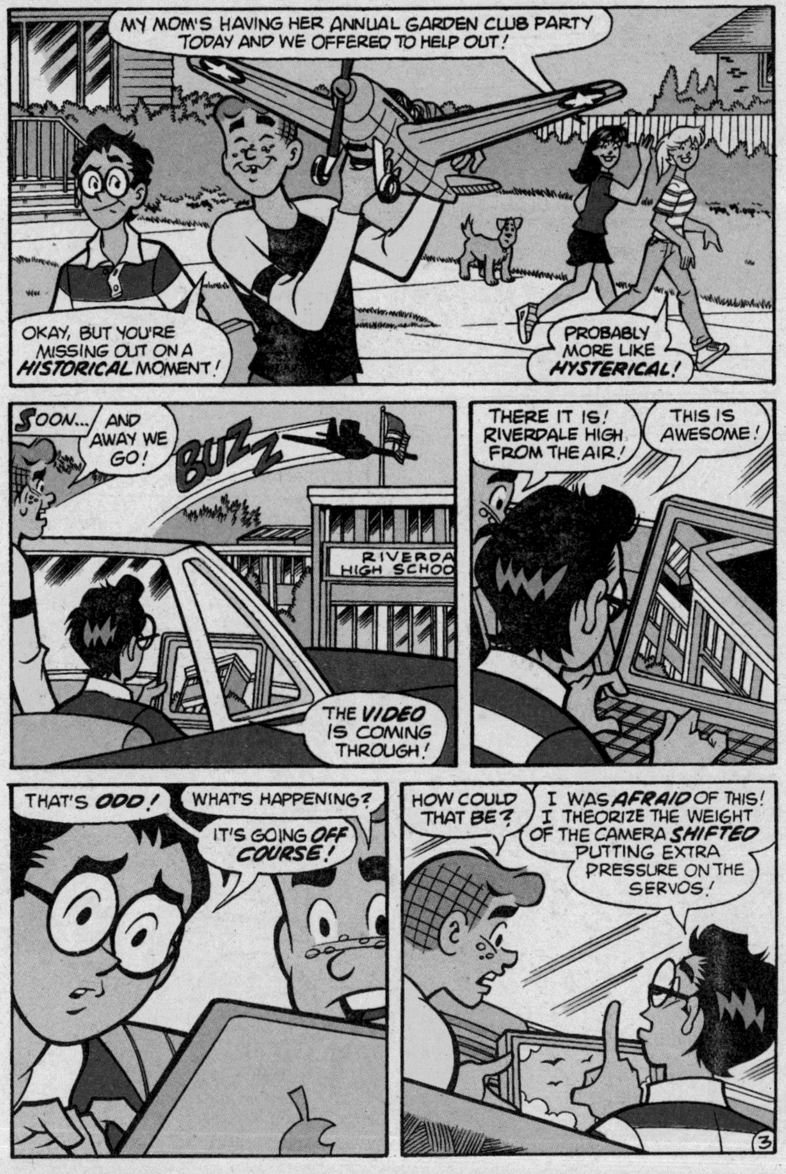
MY MOM'S HAVING HER ANNUAL GARDEN CLUB PARTY TODAY AND WE OFFERED TO HELP OUT!
OKAY, BUT YOU'RE MISSING OUT ON A HISTORICAL MOMENT!
PROBABLY MORE LIKE HYSTERICAL!
SOON...
AND AWAY WE GO!
BUZZ
RIVERDA HIGH SCHOO
THE VIDEO IS COMING THROUGH!
THERE IT IS! RIVERDALE HIGH FROM THE AIR!
THIS IS AWESOME!
THAT'S ODD!
WHAT'S HAPPENING?
IT'S GOING OFF COURSE!
HOW COULD THAT BE?
I WAS AFRAID OF THIS! I THEORIZE THE WEIGHT OF THE CAMERA SHIFTED PUTTING EXTRA PRESSURE ON THE SERVOS!
3

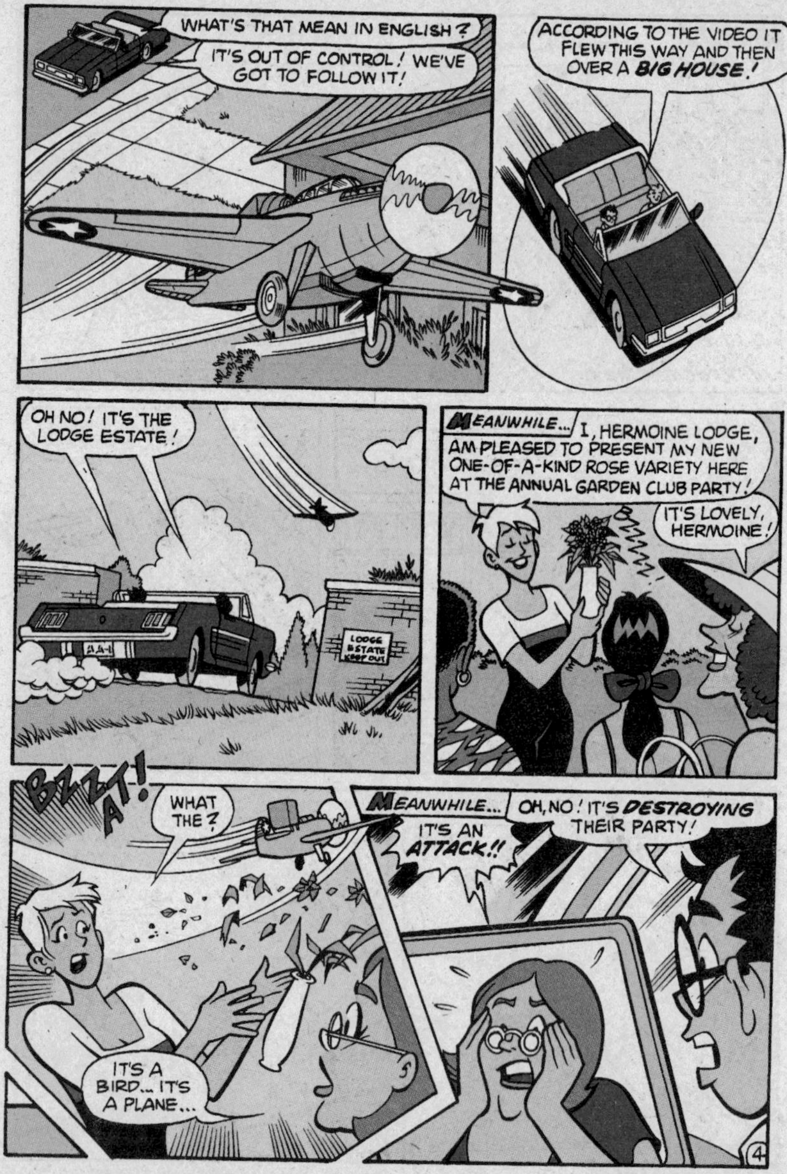
WHAT'S THAT MEAN IN ENGLISH?
IT'S OUT OF CONTROL! WE'VE GOT TO FOLLOW IT!
ACCORDING TO THE VIDEO IT FLEW THIS WAY AND THEN OVER A BIG HOUSE!
OH NO! IT'S THE LODGE ESTATE!
LODGE ESTATE KEEP OUT
MEANWHILE...
I, HERMOINE LODGE, AM PLEASED TO PRESENT MY NEW ONE-OF-A-KIND ROSE VARIETY HERE AT THE ANNUAL GARDEN CLUB PARTY!
IT'S LOVELY, HERMOINE!
BZZZAT!
WHAT THE?
IT'S A BIRD... IT'S A PLANE...
MEANWHILE...
IT'S AN ATTACK!!
OH, NO! IT'S DESTROYING THEIR PARTY!
4

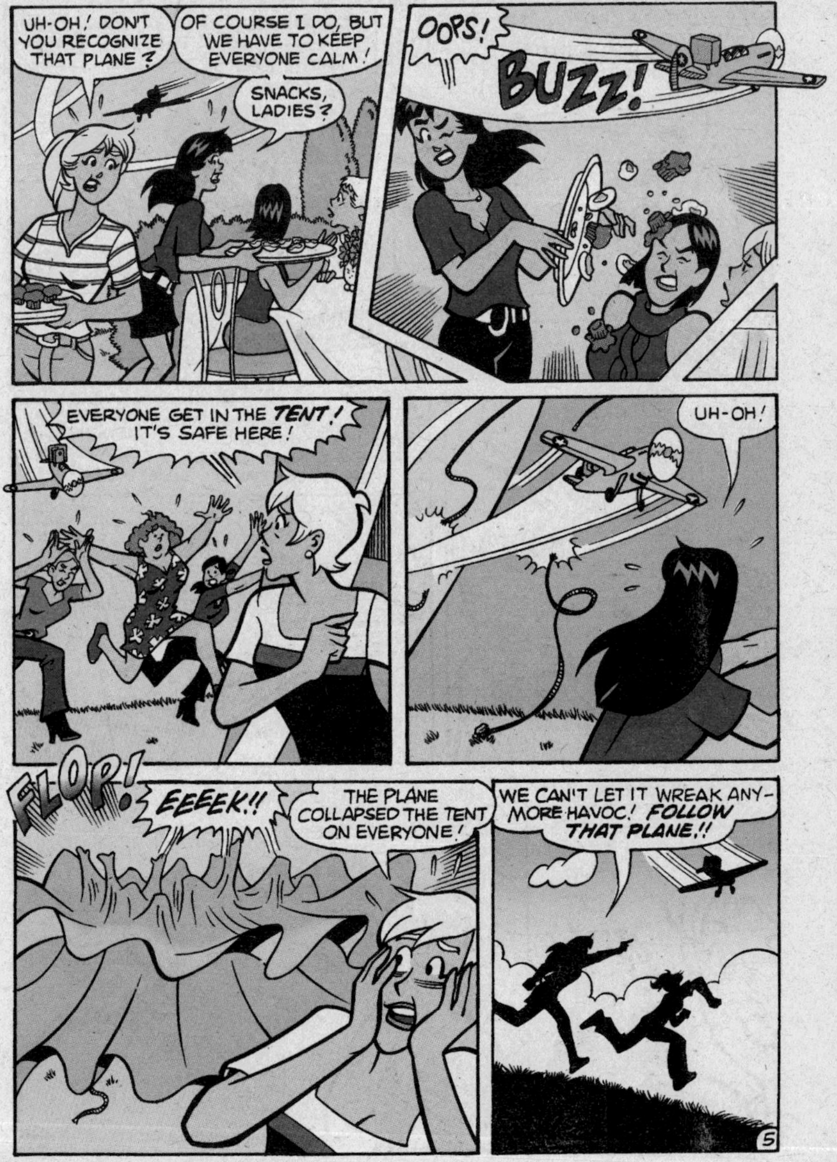
UH-OH! DON'T YOU RECOGNIZE THAT PLANE ?
OF COURSE I DO, BUT WE HAVE TO KEEP EVERYONE CALM!
SNACKS, LADIES ?
OOPS!
BUZZ!
EVERYONE GET IN THE TENT! IT'S SAFE HERE!
UH-OH!
FLOP!
EEEEK!!
THE PLANE COLLAPSED THE TENT ON EVERYONE!
WE CAN'T LET IT WREAK ANY-MORE HAVOC! FOLLOW THAT PLANE!!
5

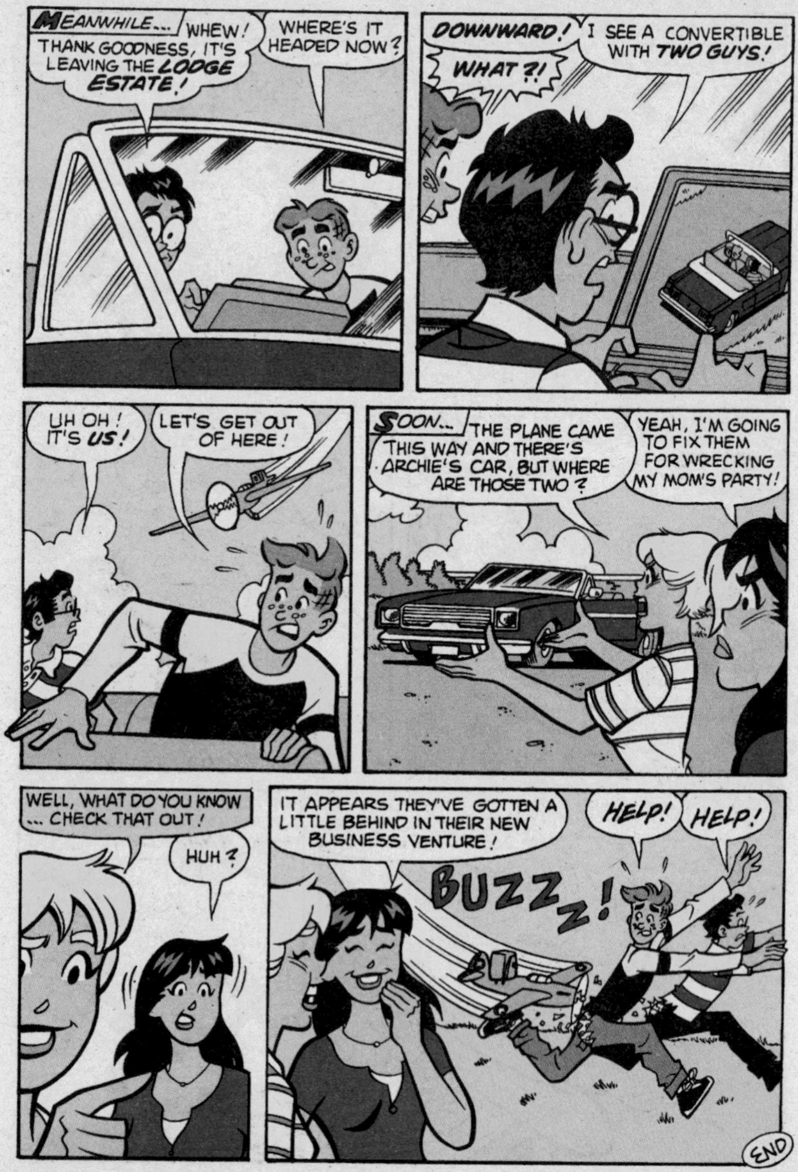
MEANWHILE...
WHEW! THANK GOODNESS, IT'S LEAVING THE LODGE ESTATE!
WHERE'S IT HEADED NOW?
DOWNWARD!
I SEE A CONVERTIBLE WITH TWO GUYS!
WHAT?!
UH OH! IT'S US!
LET'S GET OUT OF HERE!
SOON...
THE PLANE CAME THIS WAY AND THERE'S ARCHIE'S CAR, BUT WHERE ARE THOSE TWO?
YEAH, I'M GOING TO FIX THEM FOR WRECKING MY MOM'S PARTY!
WELL, WHAT DO YOU KNOW ... CHECK THAT OUT!
HUH?
IT APPEARS THEY'VE GOTTEN A LITTLE BEHIND IN THEIR NEW BUSINESS VENTURE!
HELP!
HELP!
BUZZZ!
END

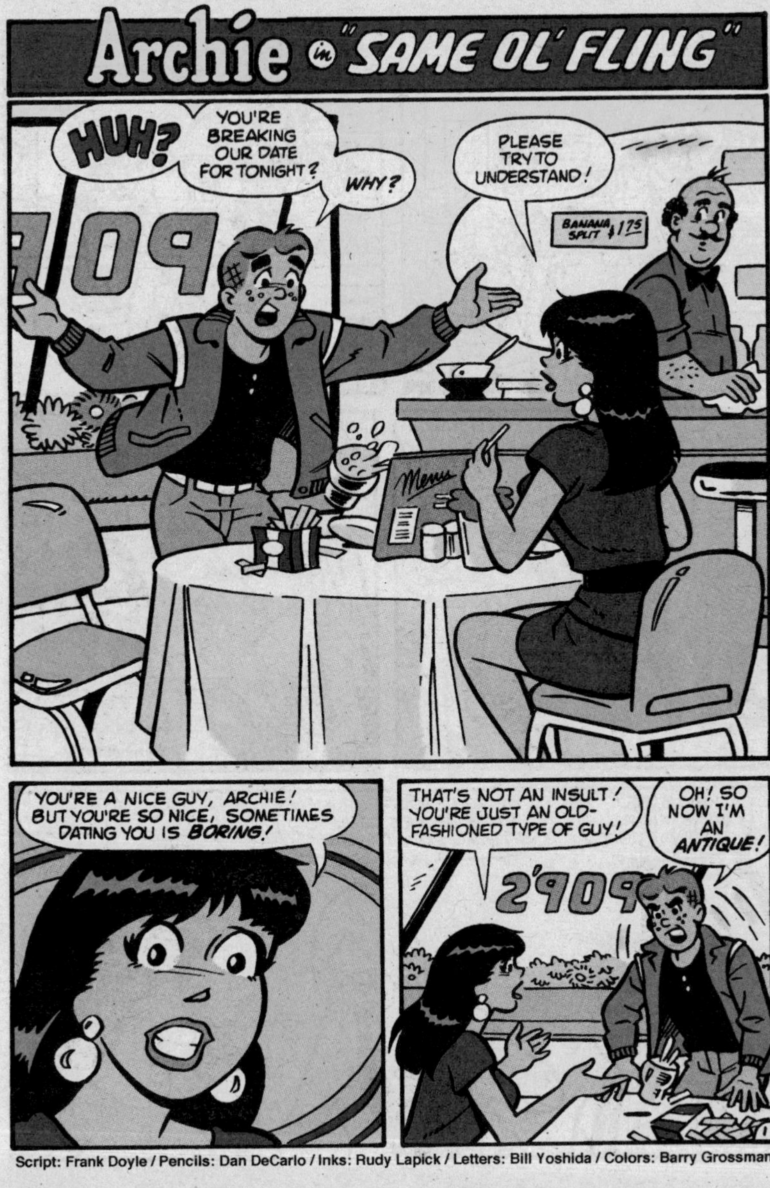
Archie in "SAME OL' FLING"
HUH?
YOU'RE BREAKING OUR DATE FOR TONIGHT? WHY?
PLEASE TRY TO UNDERSTAND!
BANANA SPLIT $1.75
POP
Menu
YOU'RE A NICE GUY, ARCHIE! BUT YOU'RE SO NICE, SOMETIMES DATING YOU IS BORING!
THAT'S NOT AN INSULT! YOU'RE JUST AN OLD-FASHIONED TYPE OF GUY!
OH! SO NOW I'M AN ANTIQUE!
POP'S
1

Script: Frank Doyle / Pencils: Dan DeCarlo / Inks: Rudy Lapick / Letters: Bill Yoshida / Colors: Barry Grossman

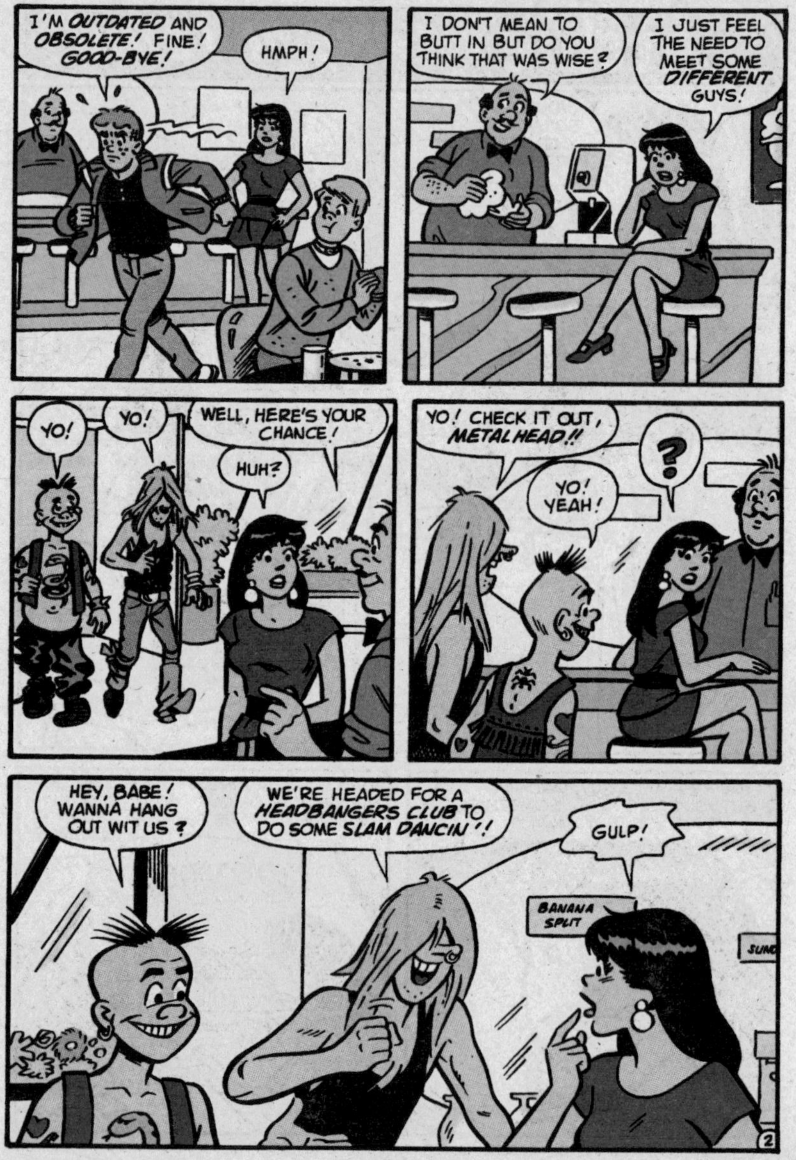
I'M OUTDATED AND OBSOLETE! FINE! GOOD-BYE!
HMPH!
I DON'T MEAN TO BUTT IN BUT DO YOU THINK THAT WAS WISE?
I JUST FEEL THE NEED TO MEET SOME DIFFERENT GUYS!
YO!
YO!
WELL, HERE'S YOUR CHANCE!
HUH?
YO! CHECK IT OUT, METALHEAD!!
YO! YEAH!
?
HEY, BABE! WANNA HANG OUT WIT US?
WE'RE HEADED FOR A HEADBANGERS CLUB TO DO SOME SLAM DANCIN'!
GULP!
BANANA SPLIT
2

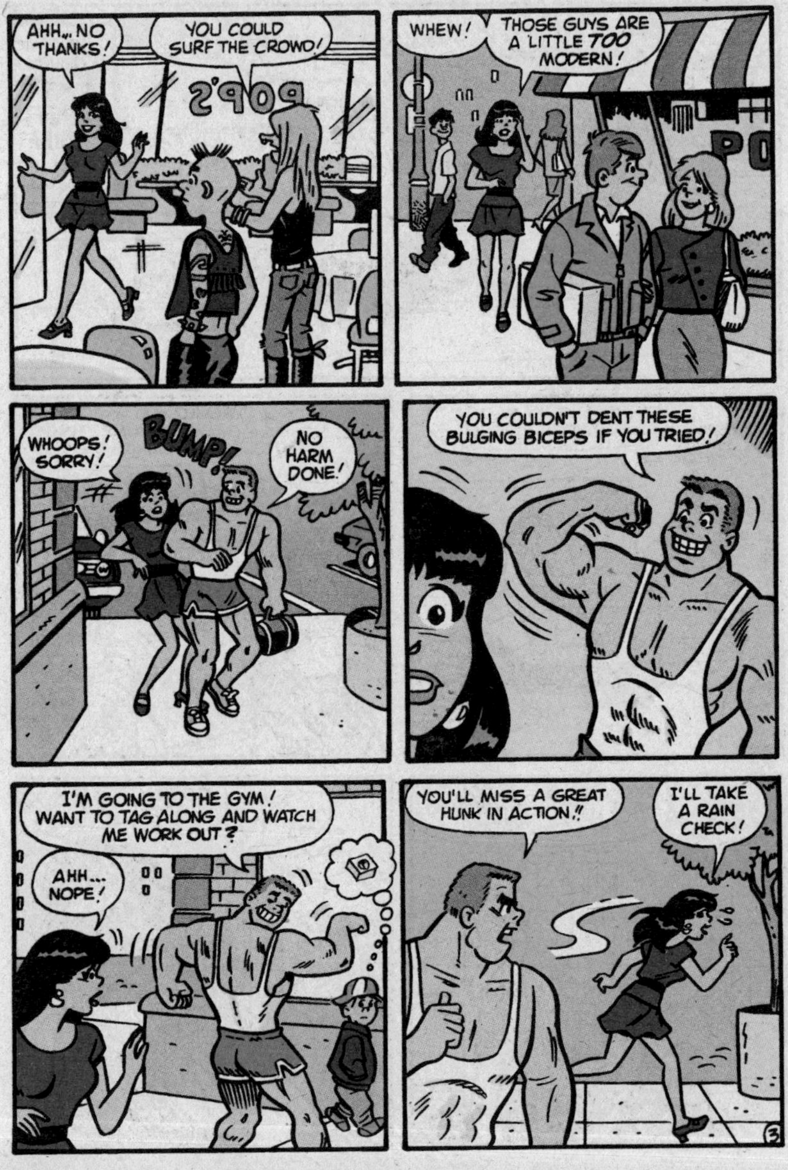

AHH... NO THANKS!
YOU COULD SURF THE CROWD!
POP'S
WHEW!
THOSE GUYS ARE A LITTLE TOO MODERN!
WHOOPS! SORRY!
BUMP!
NO HARM DONE!
YOU COULDN'T DENT THESE BULGING BICEPS IF YOU TRIED!
I'M GOING TO THE GYM! WANT TO TAG ALONG AND WATCH ME WORK OUT?
AHH... NOPE!
YOU'LL MISS A GREAT HUNK IN ACTION!!
I'LL TAKE A RAIN CHECK!
3

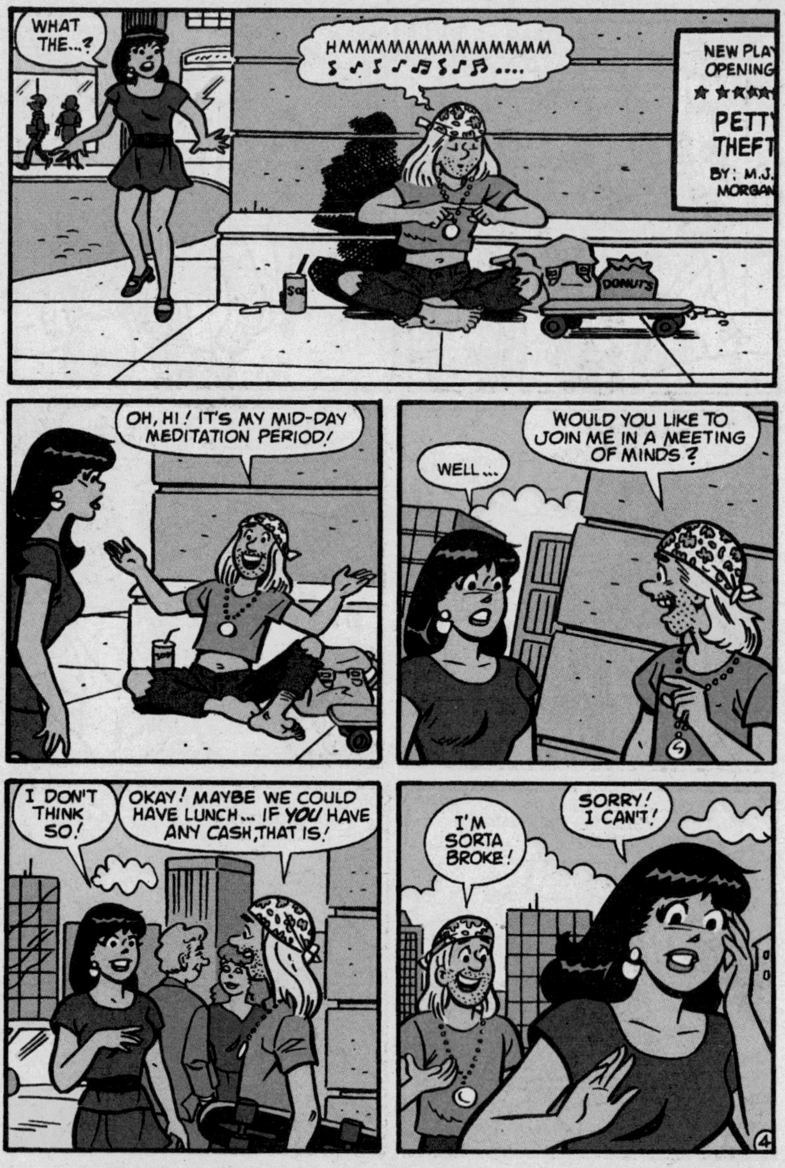
WHAT THE...?
HMMMMMMMM MMMMMMM ♪♪♪♪♫♪♪♫ ....
NEW PLAY OPENING
PETTY THEFT
BY: M.J. MORGAN
DONUTS
OH, HI! IT'S MY MID-DAY MEDITATION PERIOD!
WELL...
WOULD YOU LIKE TO JOIN ME IN A MEETING OF MINDS?
I DON'T THINK SO!
OKAY! MAYBE WE COULD HAVE LUNCH... IF *YOU* HAVE ANY CASH, THAT IS!
I'M SORTA BROKE!
SORRY! I CAN'T!
4

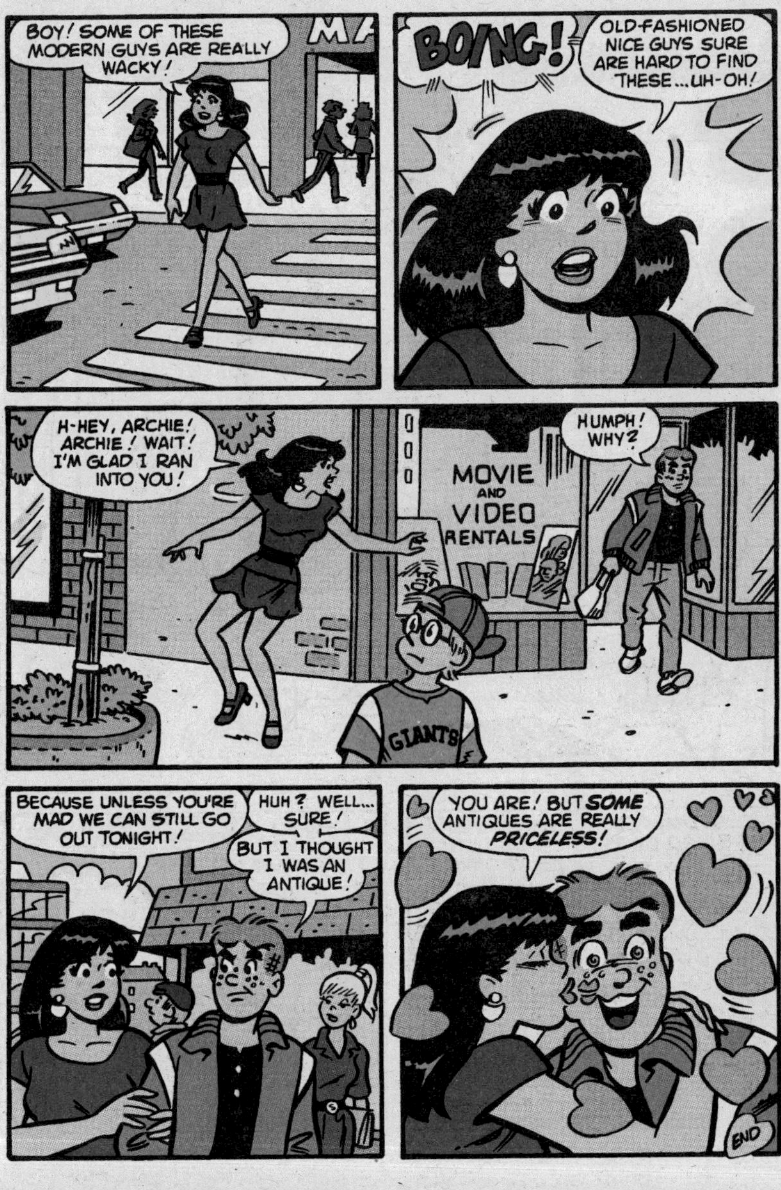
BOY! SOME OF THESE MODERN GUYS ARE REALLY WACKY!
MA
BOING!
OLD-FASHIONED NICE GUYS SURE ARE HARD TO FIND THESE... UH-OH!
H-HEY, ARCHIE! ARCHIE! WAIT! I'M GLAD I RAN INTO YOU!
MOVIE AND VIDEO RENTALS
HUMPH! WHY?
GIANTS
BECAUSE UNLESS YOU'RE MAD WE CAN STILL GO OUT TONIGHT!
HUH? WELL... SURE!
BUT I THOUGHT I WAS AN ANTIQUE!
YOU ARE! BUT SOME ANTIQUES ARE REALLY PRICELESS!
END

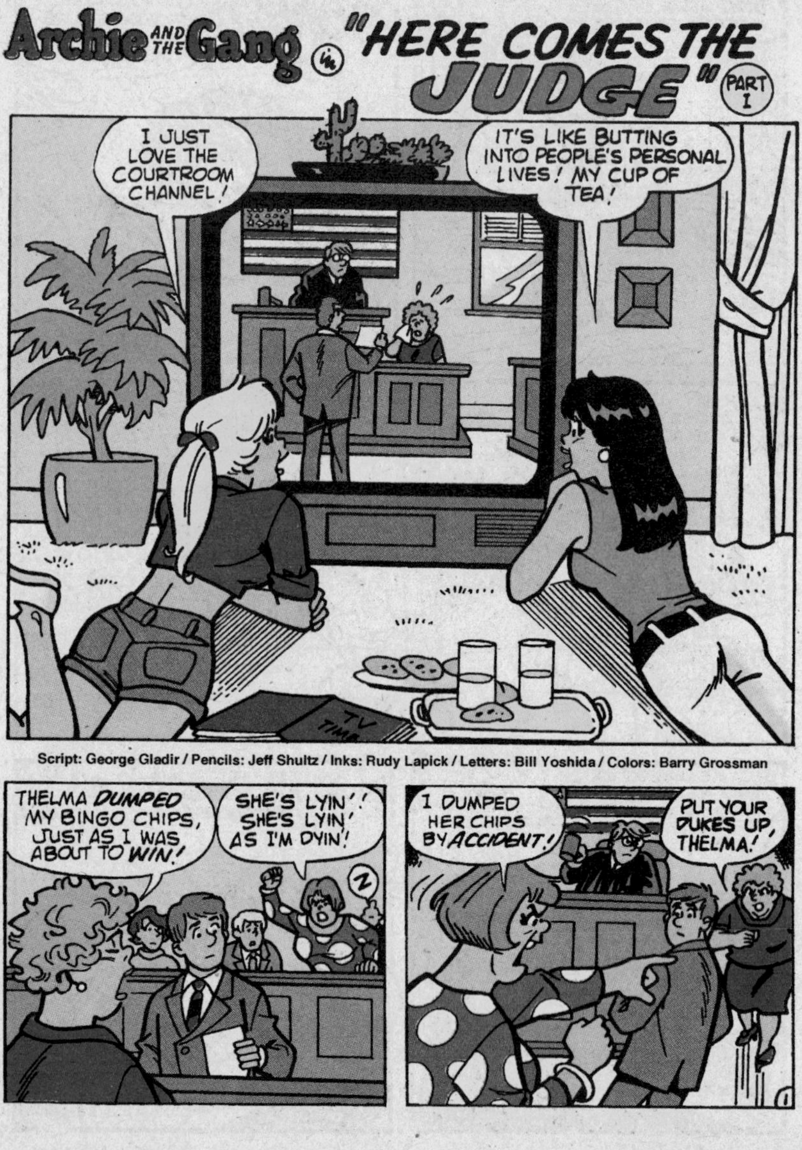

Archie AND THE Gang in "HERE COMES THE JUDGE" PART I
I JUST LOVE THE COURTROOM CHANNEL!
IT'S LIKE BUTTING INTO PEOPLE'S PERSONAL LIVES! MY CUP OF TEA!
TV TIME
Script: George Gladir / Pencils: Jeff Shultz / Inks: Rudy Lapick / Letters: Bill Yoshida / Colors: Barry Grossman
THELMA DUMPED MY BINGO CHIPS, JUST AS I WAS ABOUT TO WIN!
SHE'S LYIN'! SHE'S LYIN' AS I'M DYIN'!
Z
I DUMPED HER CHIPS BY ACCIDENT!
PUT YOUR DUKES UP, THELMA!
1

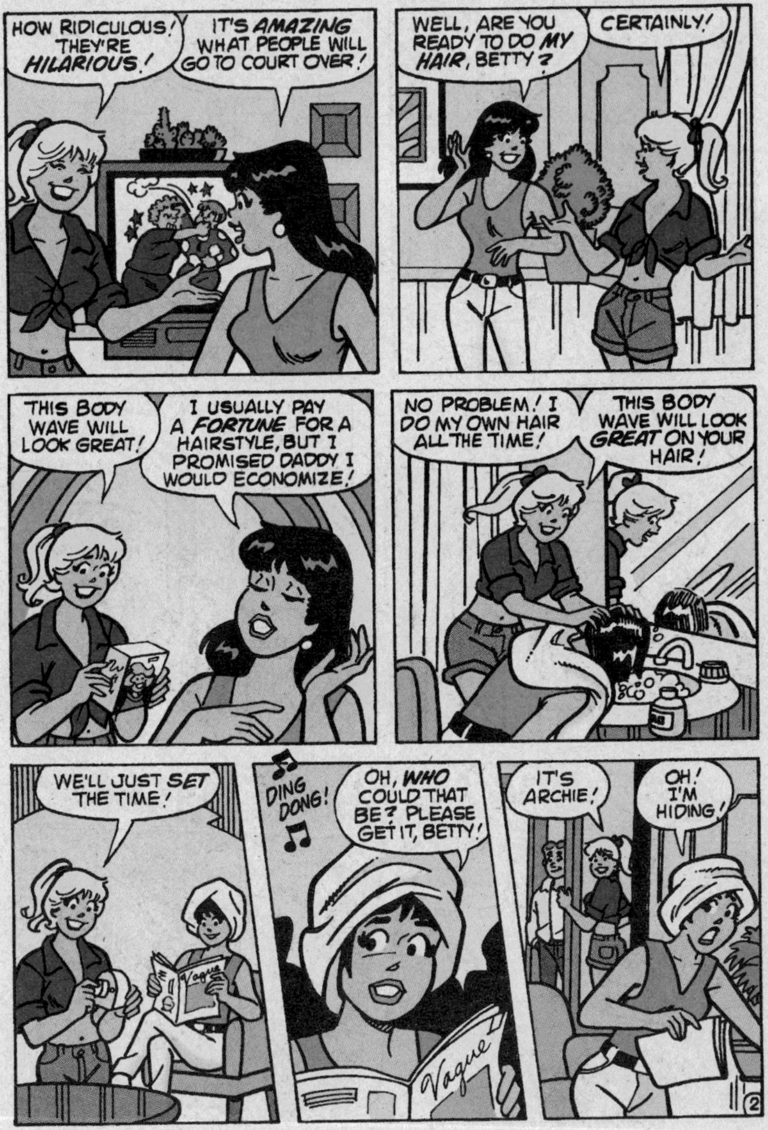

HOW RIDICULOUS! THEY'RE HILARIOUS!
IT'S AMAZING WHAT PEOPLE WILL GO TO COURT OVER!
WELL, ARE YOU READY TO DO MY HAIR, BETTY?
CERTAINLY!
THIS BODY WAVE WILL LOOK GREAT!
I USUALLY PAY A FORTUNE FOR A HAIRSTYLE, BUT I PROMISED DADDY I WOULD ECONOMIZE!
NO PROBLEM! I DO MY OWN HAIR ALL THE TIME!
THIS BODY WAVE WILL LOOK GREAT ON YOUR HAIR!
WE'LL JUST SET THE TIME!
DING DONG!
OH, WHO COULD THAT BE? PLEASE GET IT, BETTY!
Vogue
IT'S ARCHIE!
OH! I'M HIDING!
2

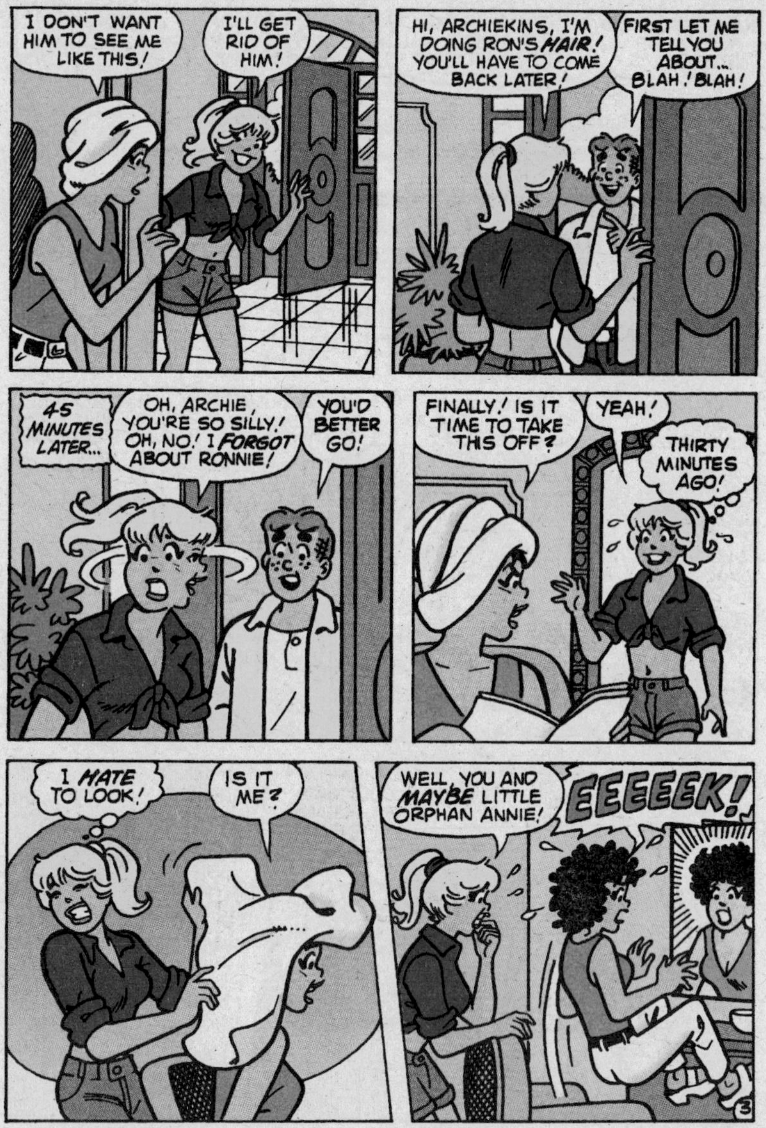

I DON'T WANT HIM TO SEE ME LIKE THIS!
I'LL GET RID OF HIM!
HI, ARCHIEKINS, I'M DOING RON'S HAIR! YOU'LL HAVE TO COME BACK LATER!
FIRST LET ME TELL YOU ABOUT... BLAH! BLAH!
45 MINUTES LATER...
OH, ARCHIE, YOU'RE SO SILLY! OH, NO! I FORGOT ABOUT RONNIE!
YOU'D BETTER GO!
FINALLY! IS IT TIME TO TAKE THIS OFF?
YEAH!
THIRTY MINUTES AGO!
I HATE TO LOOK!
IS IT ME?
WELL, YOU AND MAYBE LITTLE ORPHAN ANNIE!
EEEEEK!

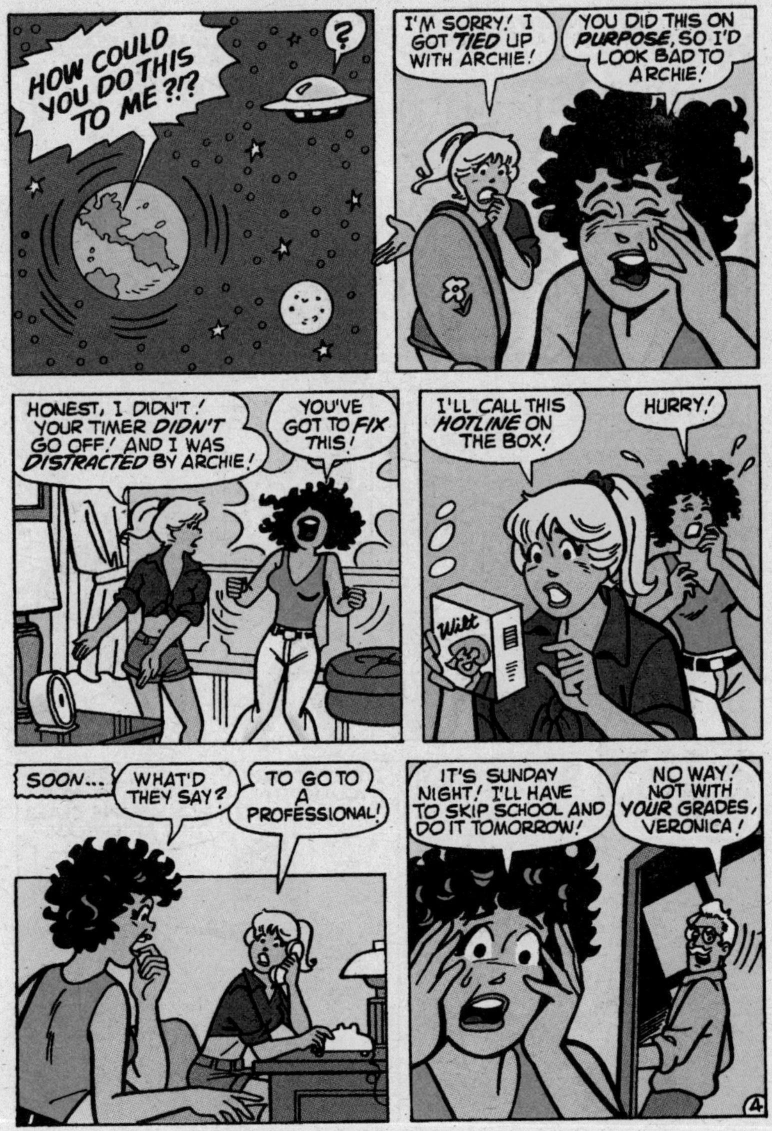

HOW COULD YOU DO THIS TO ME ?!?
?
I'M SORRY! I GOT TIED UP WITH ARCHIE!
YOU DID THIS ON PURPOSE, SO I'D LOOK BAD TO ARCHIE!
HONEST, I DIDN'T! YOUR TIMER DIDN'T GO OFF! AND I WAS DISTRACTED BY ARCHIE!
YOU'VE GOT TO FIX THIS!
I'LL CALL THIS HOTLINE ON THE BOX!
HURRY!
Wilt
SOON...
WHAT'D THEY SAY?
TO GO TO A PROFESSIONAL!
IT'S SUNDAY NIGHT! I'LL HAVE TO SKIP SCHOOL AND DO IT TOMORROW!
NO WAY! NOT WITH YOUR GRADES, VERONICA!
4

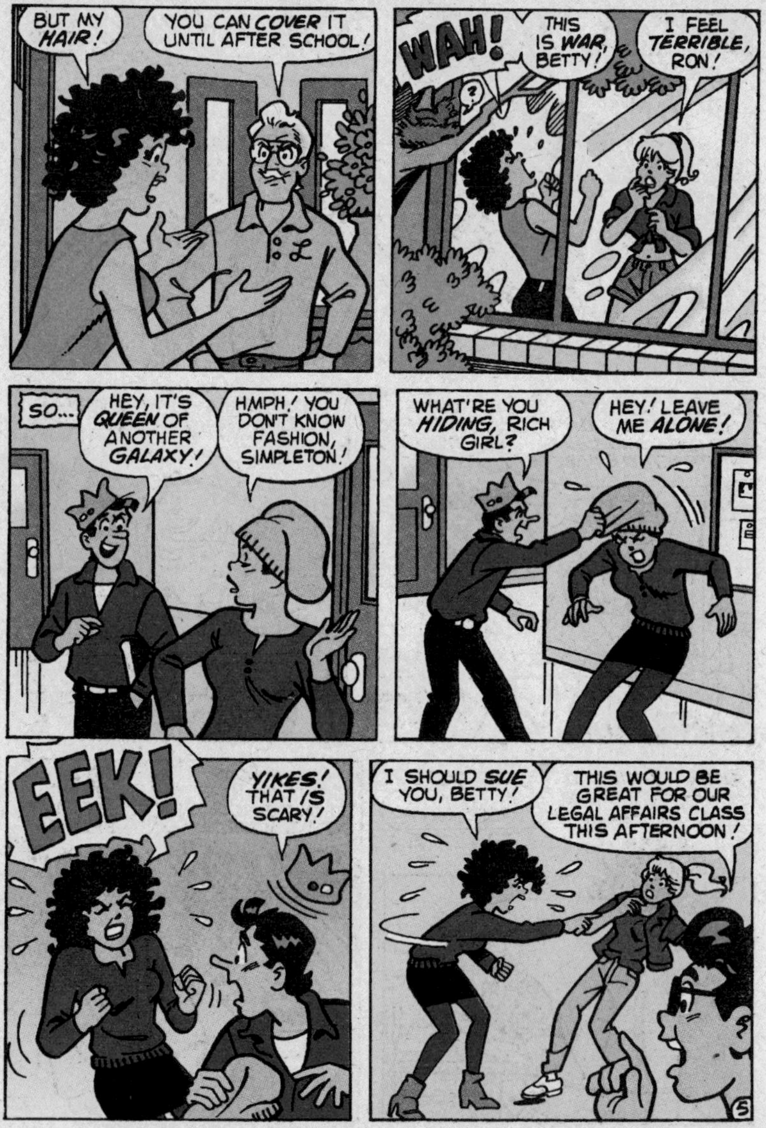
BUT MY HAIR!
YOU CAN COVER IT UNTIL AFTER SCHOOL!
WAH!
?
THIS IS WAR, BETTY!
I FEEL TERRIBLE, RON!
SO...
HEY, IT'S QUEEN OF ANOTHER GALAXY!
HMPH! YOU DON'T KNOW FASHION, SIMPLETON!
WHAT'RE YOU HIDING, RICH GIRL?
HEY! LEAVE ME ALONE!
EEK!
YIKES! THAT IS SCARY!
I SHOULD SUE YOU, BETTY!
THIS WOULD BE GREAT FOR OUR LEGAL AFFAIRS CLASS THIS AFTERNOON!
5

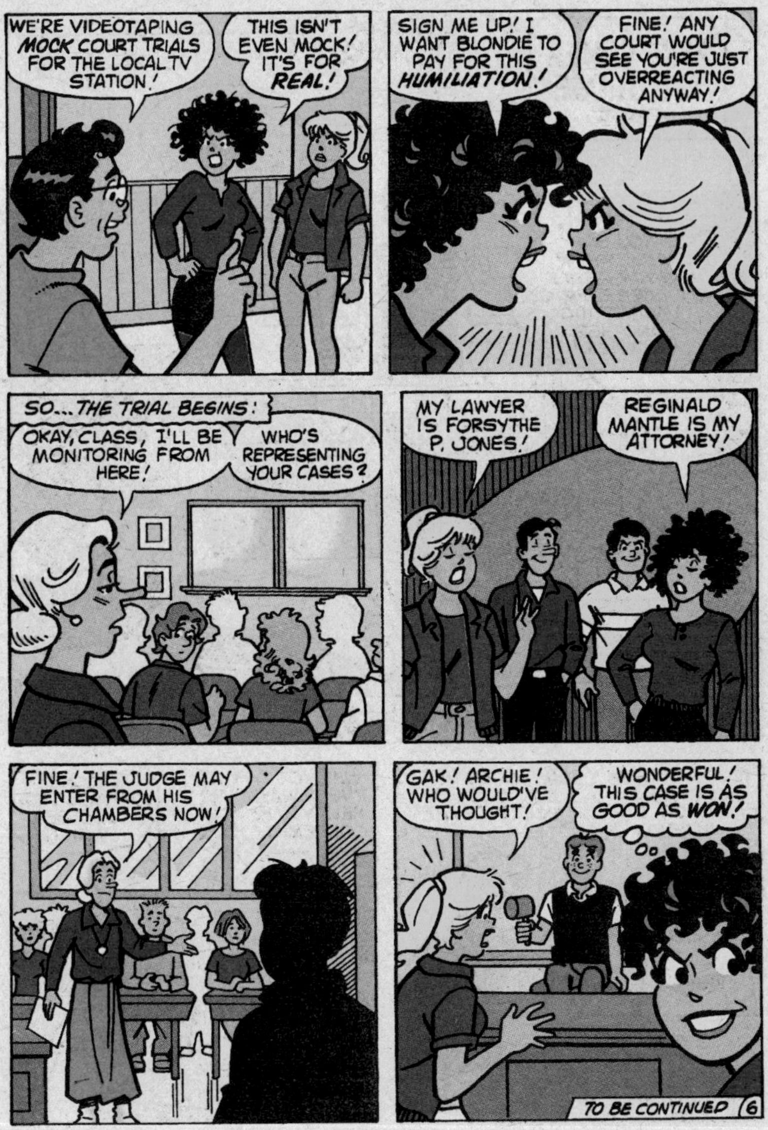
WE'RE VIDEOTAPING MOCK COURT TRIALS FOR THE LOCAL TV STATION!
THIS ISN'T EVEN MOCK! IT'S FOR REAL!
SIGN ME UP! I WANT BLONDIE TO PAY FOR THIS HUMILIATION!
FINE! ANY COURT WOULD SEE YOU'RE JUST OVERREACTING ANYWAY!
SO... THE TRIAL BEGINS:
OKAY, CLASS, I'LL BE MONITORING FROM HERE!
WHO'S REPRESENTING YOUR CASES?
MY LAWYER IS FORSYTHE P. JONES!
REGINALD MANTLE IS MY ATTORNEY!
FINE! THE JUDGE MAY ENTER FROM HIS CHAMBERS NOW!
GAK! ARCHIE! WHO WOULD'VE THOUGHT!
WONDERFUL! THIS CASE IS AS GOOD AS WON!
TO BE CONTINUED

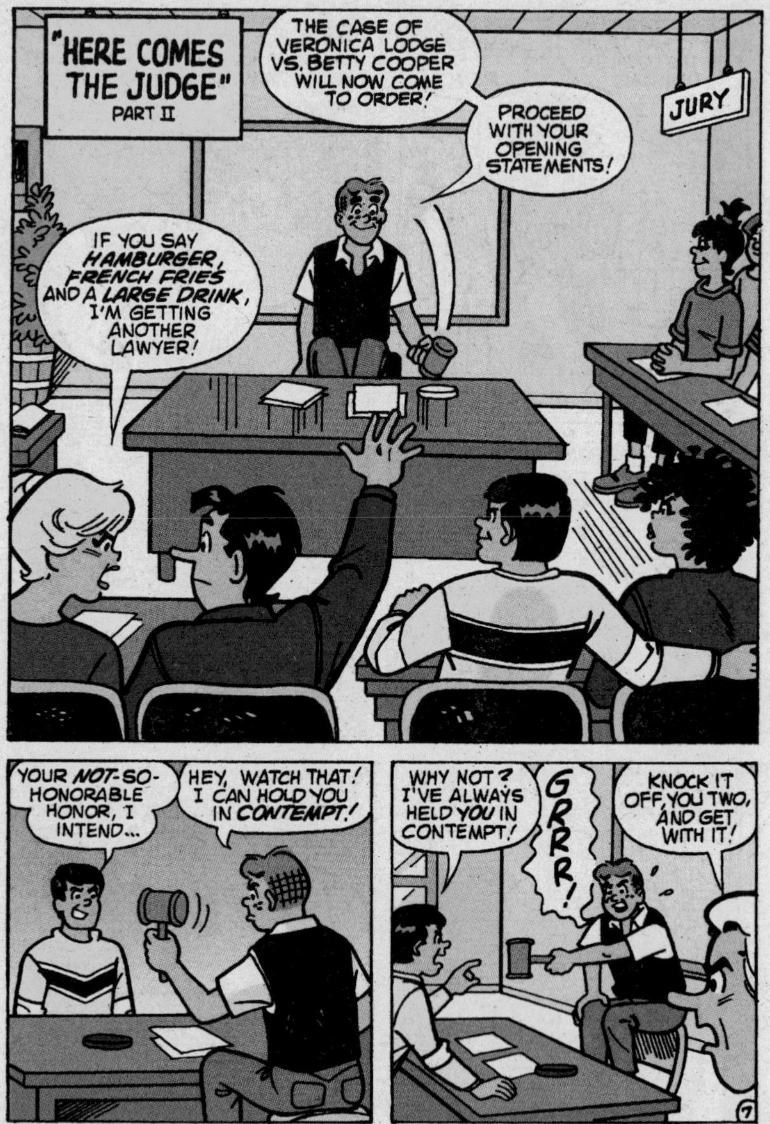
"HERE COMES THE JUDGE" PART II
THE CASE OF VERONICA LODGE VS. BETTY COOPER WILL NOW COME TO ORDER!
PROCEED WITH YOUR OPENING STATEMENTS!
JURY
IF YOU SAY HAMBURGER, FRENCH FRIES AND A LARGE DRINK, I'M GETTING ANOTHER LAWYER!
YOUR NOT-SO-HONORABLE HONOR, I INTEND...
HEY, WATCH THAT! I CAN HOLD YOU IN CONTEMPT!
WHY NOT? I'VE ALWAYS HELD YOU IN CONTEMPT!
GRRR!
KNOCK IT OFF, YOU TWO, AND GET WITH IT!
7

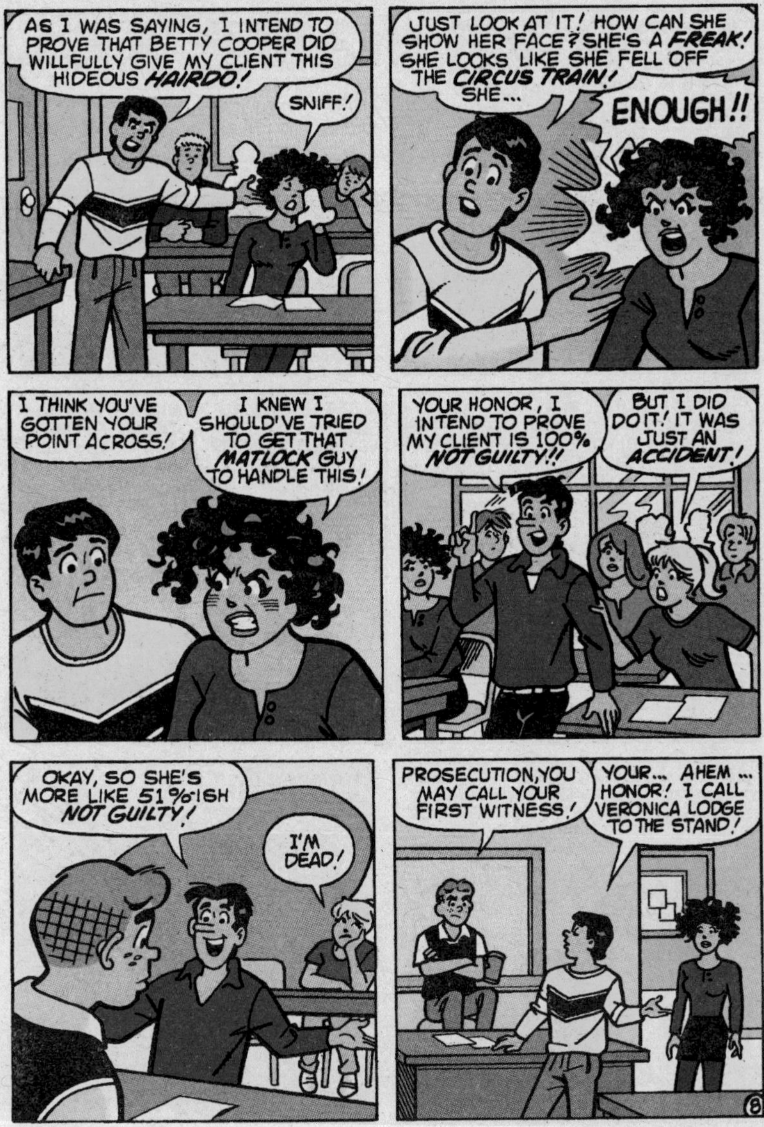
AS I WAS SAYING, I INTEND TO PROVE THAT BETTY COOPER DID WILLFULLY GIVE MY CLIENT THIS HIDEOUS HAIRDO!
SNIFF!
JUST LOOK AT IT! HOW CAN SHE SHOW HER FACE? SHE'S A FREAK! SHE LOOKS LIKE SHE FELL OFF THE CIRCUS TRAIN! SHE...
ENOUGH!!
I THINK YOU'VE GOTTEN YOUR POINT ACROSS!
I KNEW I SHOULD'VE TRIED TO GET THAT MATLOCK GUY TO HANDLE THIS!
YOUR HONOR, I INTEND TO PROVE MY CLIENT IS 100% NOT GUILTY!!
BUT I DID DO IT! IT WAS JUST AN ACCIDENT!
OKAY, SO SHE'S MORE LIKE 51%-ISH NOT GUILTY!
I'M DEAD!
PROSECUTION, YOU MAY CALL YOUR FIRST WITNESS!
YOUR... AHEM ... HONOR! I CALL VERONICA LODGE TO THE STAND!
8

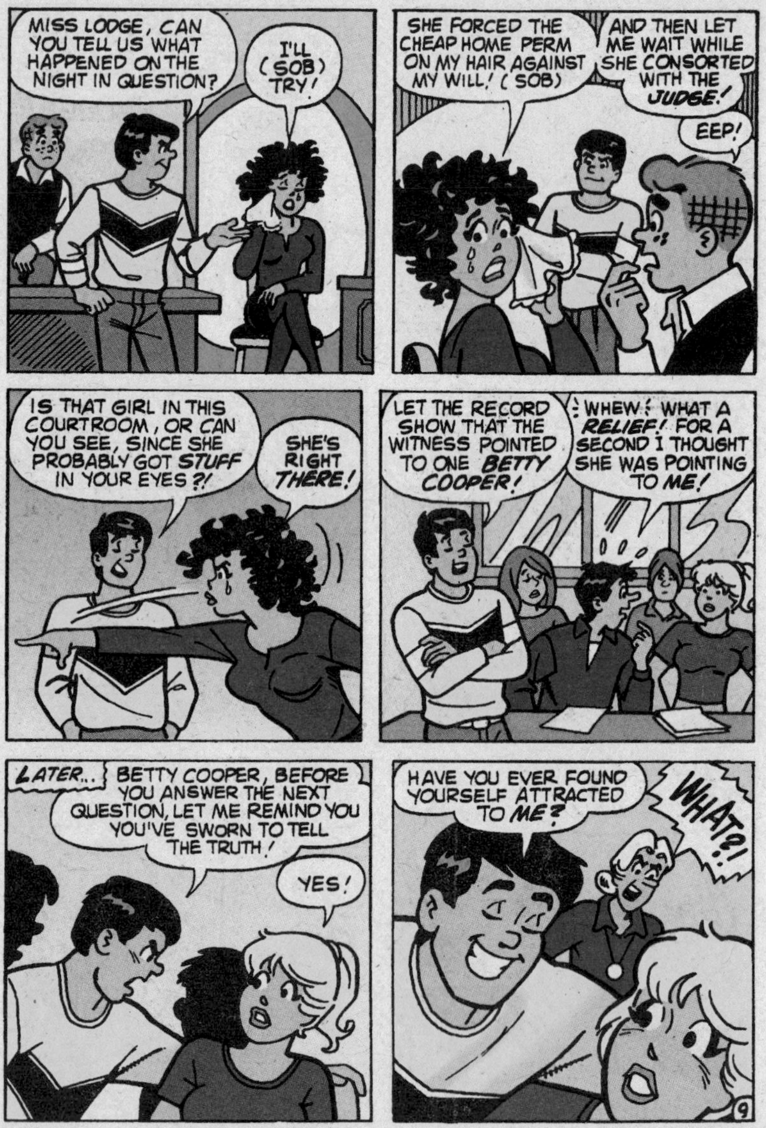

MISS LODGE, CAN YOU TELL US WHAT HAPPENED ON THE NIGHT IN QUESTION?
I'LL (SOB) TRY!
SHE FORCED THE CHEAP HOME PERM ON MY HAIR AGAINST MY WILL! (SOB)
AND THEN LET ME WAIT WHILE SHE CONSORTED WITH THE JUDGE!
EEP!
IS THAT GIRL IN THIS COURTROOM, OR CAN YOU SEE, SINCE SHE PROBABLY GOT STUFF IN YOUR EYES?!
SHE'S RIGHT THERE!
LET THE RECORD SHOW THAT THE WITNESS POINTED TO ONE BETTY COOPER!
WHEW! WHAT A RELIEF! FOR A SECOND I THOUGHT SHE WAS POINTING TO ME!
LATER...
BETTY COOPER, BEFORE YOU ANSWER THE NEXT QUESTION, LET ME REMIND YOU YOU'VE SWORN TO TELL THE TRUTH!
YES!
HAVE YOU EVER FOUND YOURSELF ATTRACTED TO ME?
WHAT?!
9

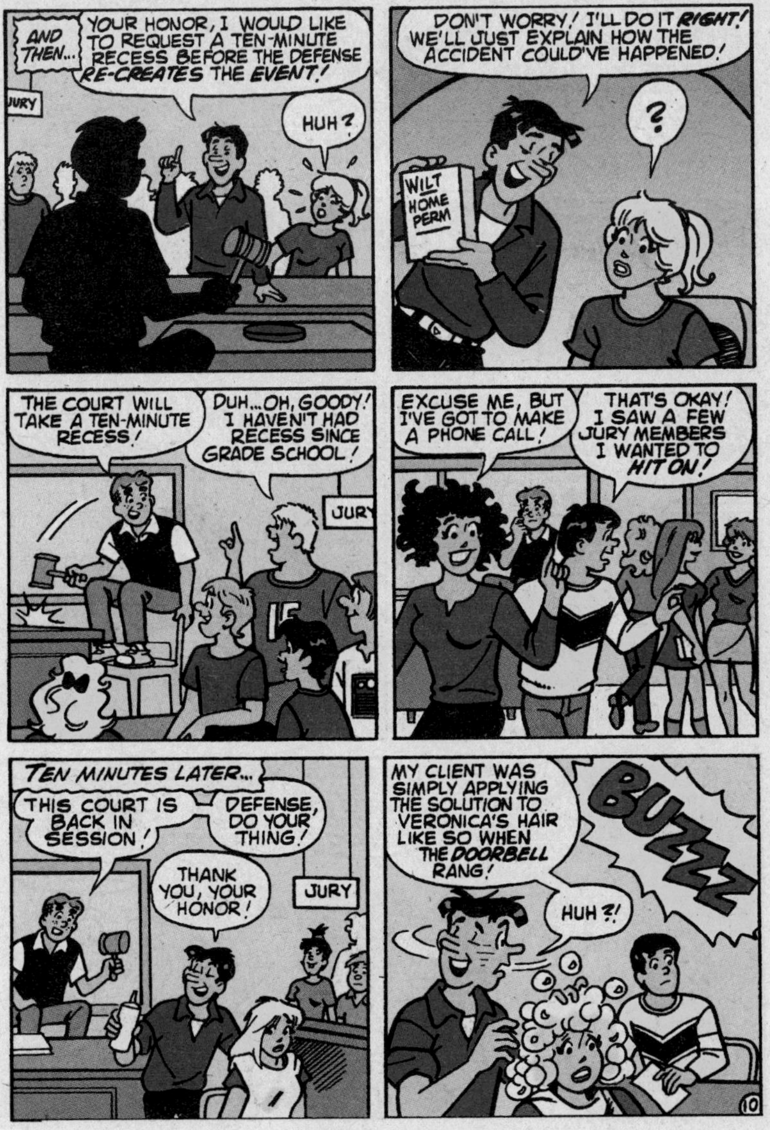
AND THEN...
YOUR HONOR, I WOULD LIKE TO REQUEST A TEN-MINUTE RECESS BEFORE THE DEFENSE RE-CREATES THE EVENT!
JURY
HUH?
DON'T WORRY! I'LL DO IT RIGHT! WE'LL JUST EXPLAIN HOW THE ACCIDENT COULD'VE HAPPENED!
?
WILT HOME PERM
THE COURT WILL TAKE A TEN-MINUTE RECESS!
DUH...OH, GOODY! I HAVEN'T HAD RECESS SINCE GRADE SCHOOL!
JURY
EXCUSE ME, BUT I'VE GOT TO MAKE A PHONE CALL!
THAT'S OKAY! I SAW A FEW JURY MEMBERS I WANTED TO HIT ON!
TEN MINUTES LATER...
THIS COURT IS BACK IN SESSION!
DEFENSE, DO YOUR THING!
THANK YOU, YOUR HONOR!
JURY
MY CLIENT WAS SIMPLY APPLYING THE SOLUTION TO VERONICA'S HAIR LIKE SO WHEN THE DOORBELL RANG!
BUZZZ
HUH?!
10

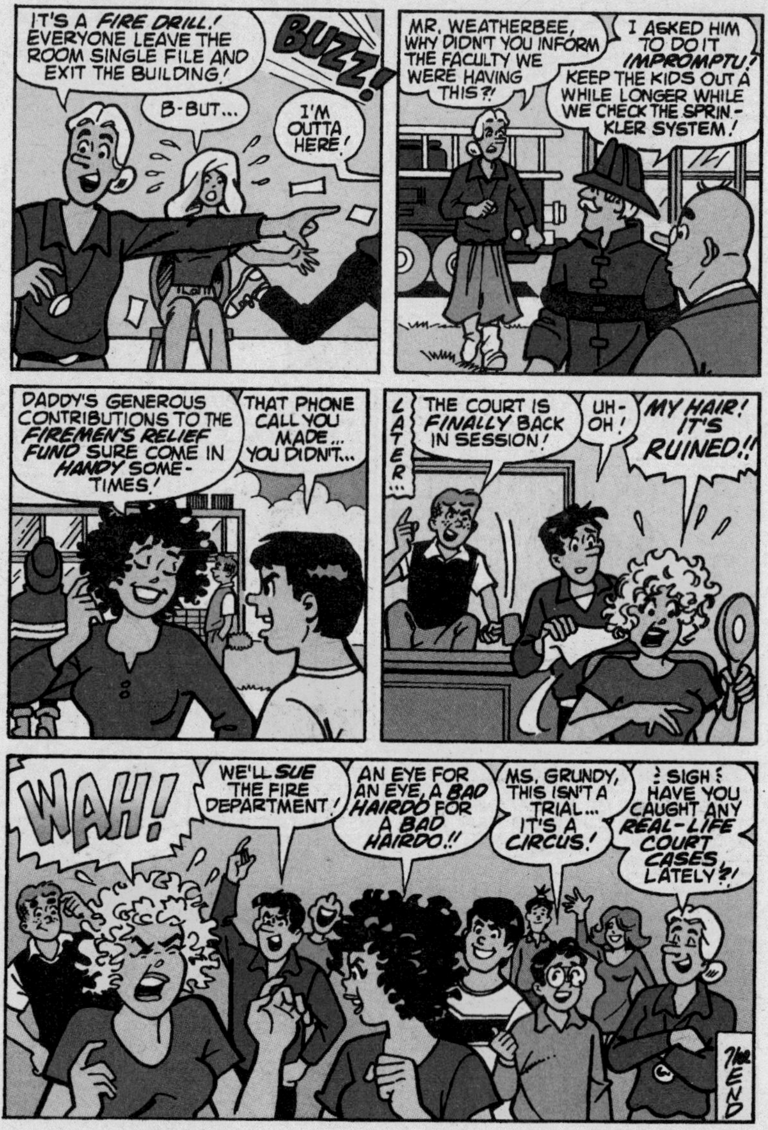
IT'S A FIRE DRILL! EVERYONE LEAVE THE ROOM SINGLE FILE AND EXIT THE BUILDING!
BUZZ!
B-BUT...
I'M OUTTA HERE!
MR. WEATHERBEE, WHY DIDN'T YOU INFORM THE FACULTY WE WERE HAVING THIS?!
I ASKED HIM TO DO IT IMPROMPTU! KEEP THE KIDS OUT A WHILE LONGER WHILE WE CHECK THE SPRIN-KLER SYSTEM!
DADDY'S GENEROUS CONTRIBUTIONS TO THE FIREMEN'S RELIEF FUND SURE COME IN HANDY SOME-TIMES!
THAT PHONE CALL YOU MADE... YOU DIDN'T...
LATER...
THE COURT IS FINALLY BACK IN SESSION!
UH-OH!
MY HAIR! IT'S RUINED!!
WAH!
WE'LL SUE THE FIRE DEPARTMENT!
AN EYE FOR AN EYE, A BAD HAIRDO FOR A BAD HAIRDO!!
MS. GRUNDY, THIS ISN'T A TRIAL... IT'S A CIRCUS!
SIGH HAVE YOU CAUGHT ANY REAL-LIFE COURT CASES, LATELY?!
THE END

Archie IN "The SCIENCE"

UH, OH.' ... IT'S ABOUT THAT TIME.'

WHAT TIME IS THAT?

Script & Pencils: Dick Malmgren / Inks: Jon D'Agostino / Letters: Bill Yoshida / Colors: Barry Grossman

WHEN ARCHIE CHANGES HIS CLASSES.'

OH?... WHAT DOES THAT MEAN?

IT MEANS I HAVE TO STAY OUT OF THE WAY.'

1

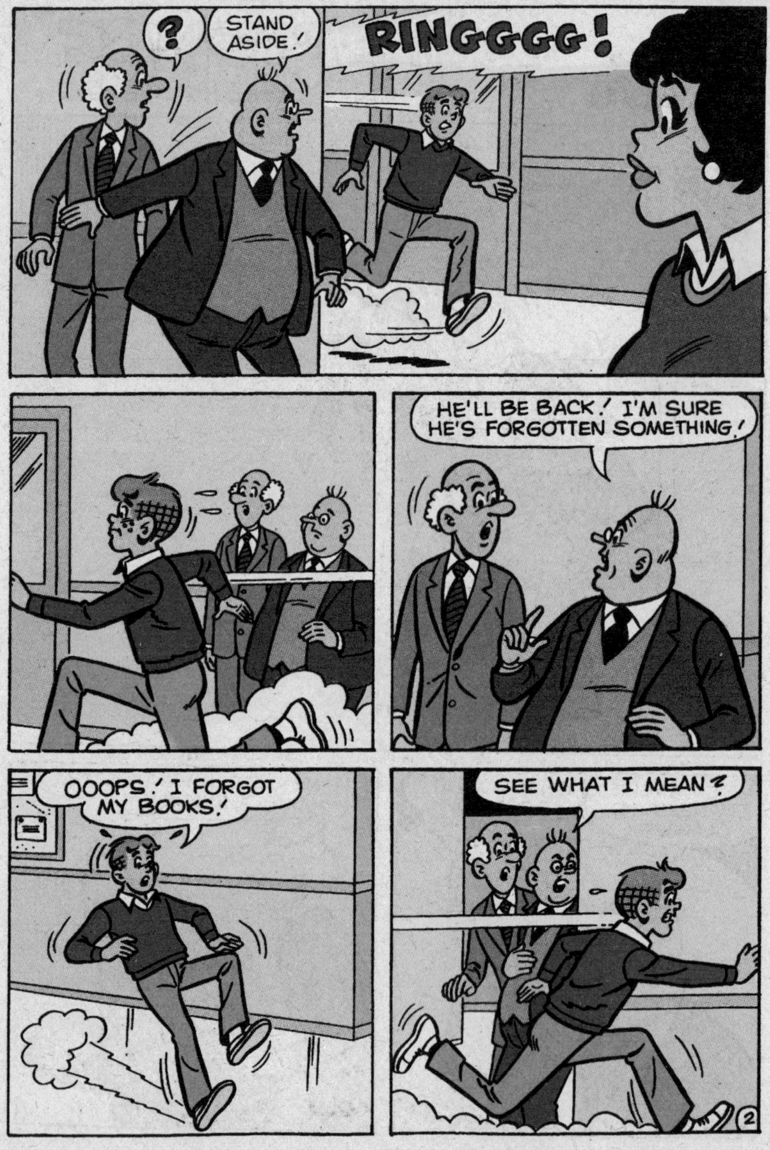
?
STAND ASIDE!
RINGGGG!
HE'LL BE BACK! I'M SURE HE'S FORGOTTEN SOMETHING!
OOOPS! I FORGOT MY BOOKS!
SEE WHAT I MEAN?
2

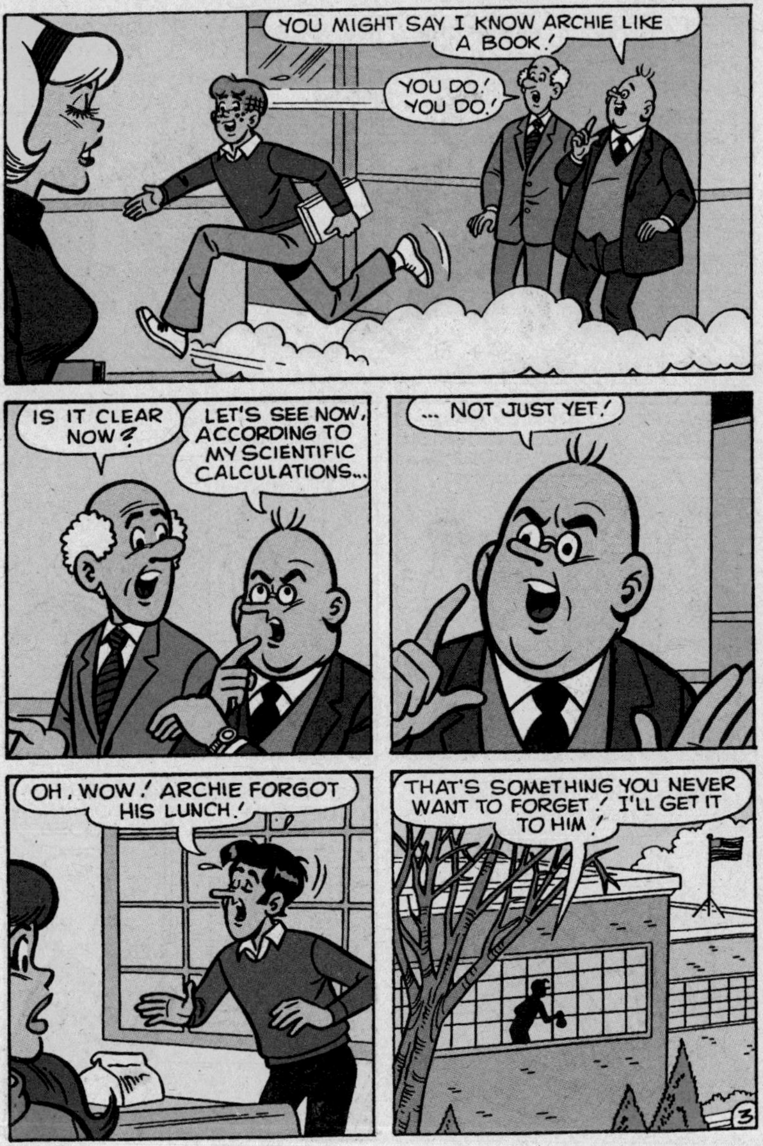
YOU MIGHT SAY I KNOW ARCHIE LIKE A BOOK!
YOU DO! YOU DO!
IS IT CLEAR NOW?
LET'S SEE NOW, ACCORDING TO MY SCIENTIFIC CALCULATIONS...
... NOT JUST YET!
OH, WOW! ARCHIE FORGOT HIS LUNCH!
THAT'S SOMETHING YOU NEVER WANT TO FORGET! I'LL GET IT TO HIM!
3

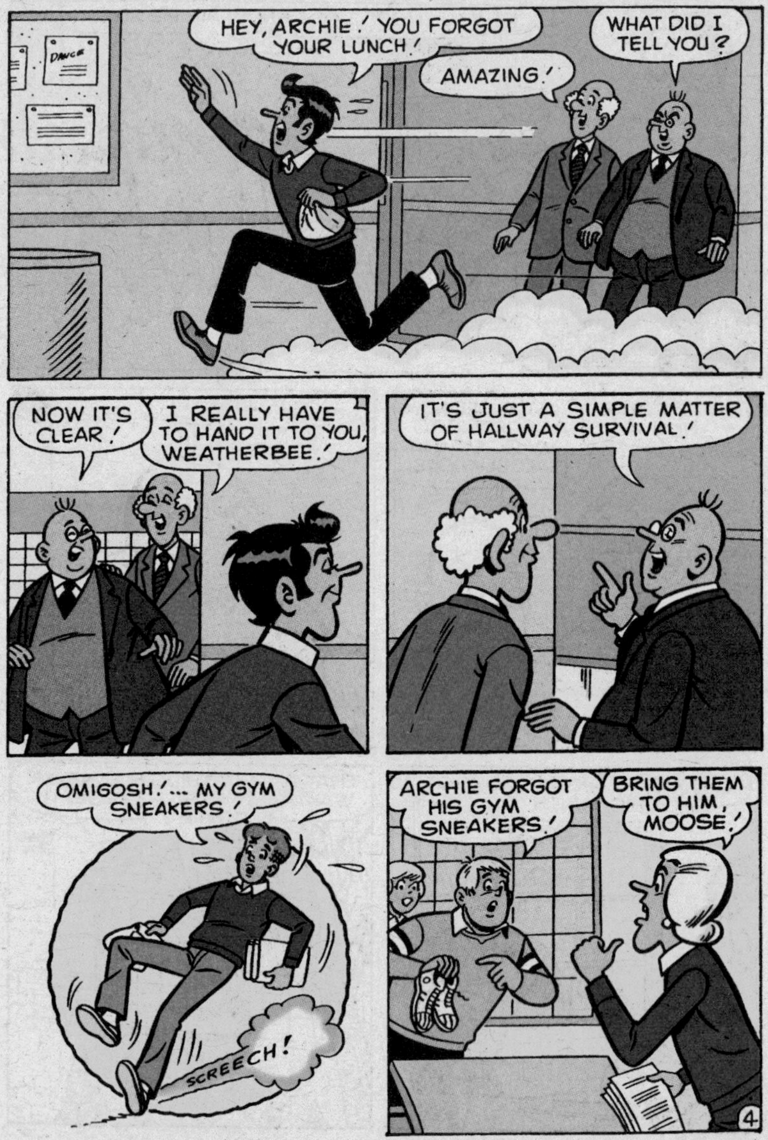
HEY, ARCHIE! YOU FORGOT YOUR LUNCH!
DANCE
AMAZING!
WHAT DID I TELL YOU?
NOW IT'S CLEAR!
I REALLY HAVE TO HAND IT TO YOU, WEATHERBEE!
IT'S JUST A SIMPLE MATTER OF HALLWAY SURVIVAL!
OMIGOSH!... MY GYM SNEAKERS!
SCREECH!
ARCHIE FORGOT HIS GYM SNEAKERS!
BRING THEM TO HIM, MOOSE!
4

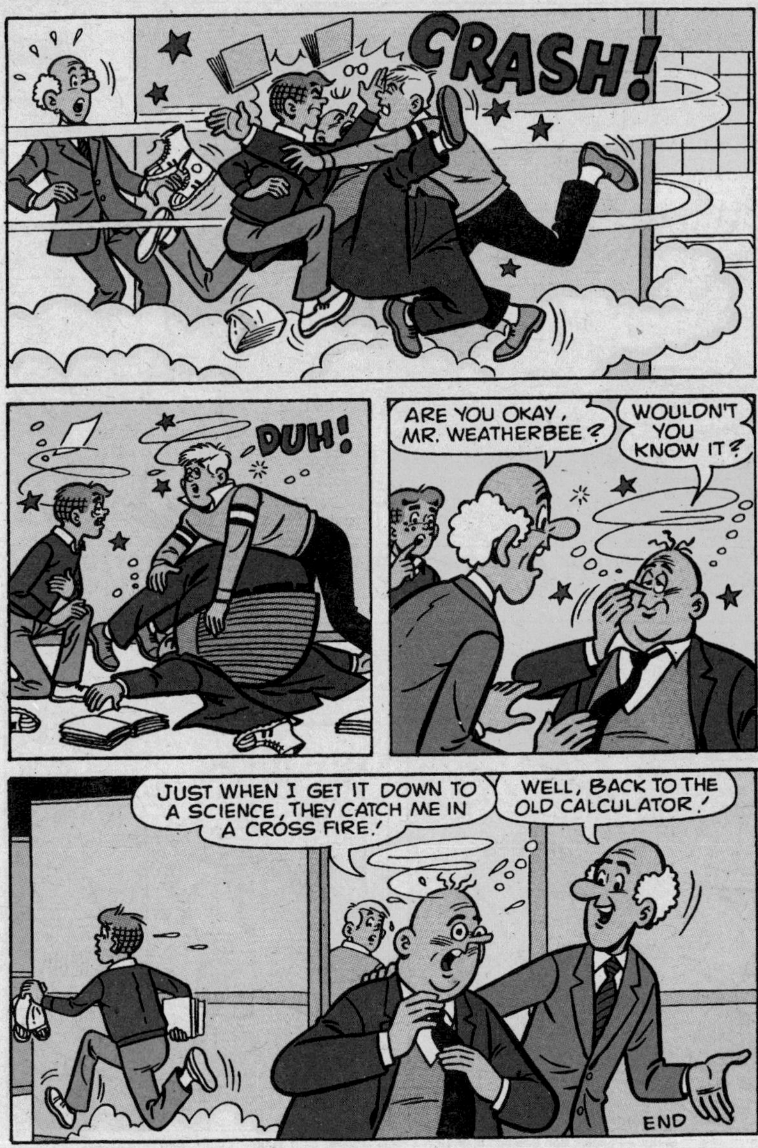

CRASH!
DUH!
ARE YOU OKAY, MR. WEATHERBEE?
WOULDN'T YOU KNOW IT?
JUST WHEN I GET IT DOWN TO A SCIENCE, THEY CATCH ME IN A CROSS FIRE!
WELL, BACK TO THE OLD CALCULATOR!
END

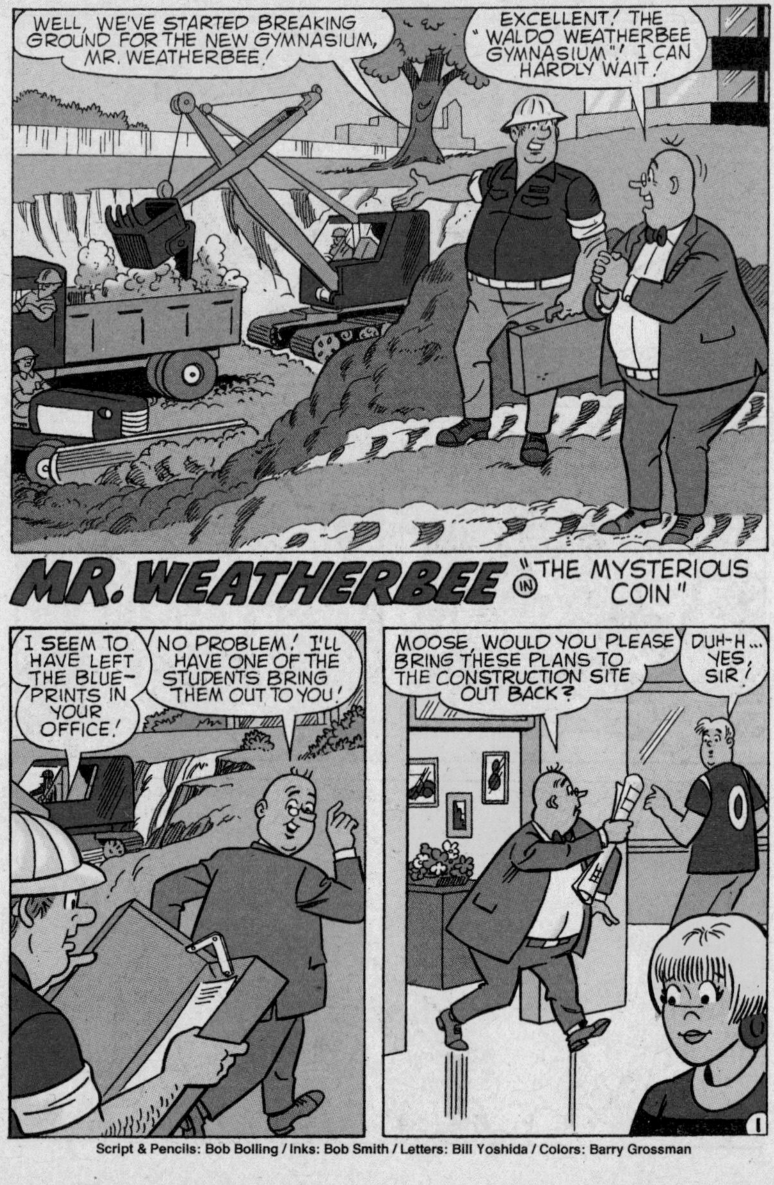
WELL, WE'VE STARTED BREAKING GROUND FOR THE NEW GYMNASIUM, MR. WEATHERBEE!
EXCELLENT! THE "WALDO WEATHERBEE GYMNASIUM"! I CAN HARDLY WAIT!
MR. WEATHERBEE IN "THE MYSTERIOUS COIN"
I SEEM TO HAVE LEFT THE BLUE-PRINTS IN YOUR OFFICE!
NO PROBLEM! I'LL HAVE ONE OF THE STUDENTS BRING THEM OUT TO YOU!
MOOSE, WOULD YOU PLEASE BRING THESE PLANS TO THE CONSTRUCTION SITE OUT BACK?
DUH-H... YES, SIR!
1

Script & Pencils: Bob Bolling / Inks: Bob Smith / Letters: Bill Yoshida / Colors: Barry Grossman

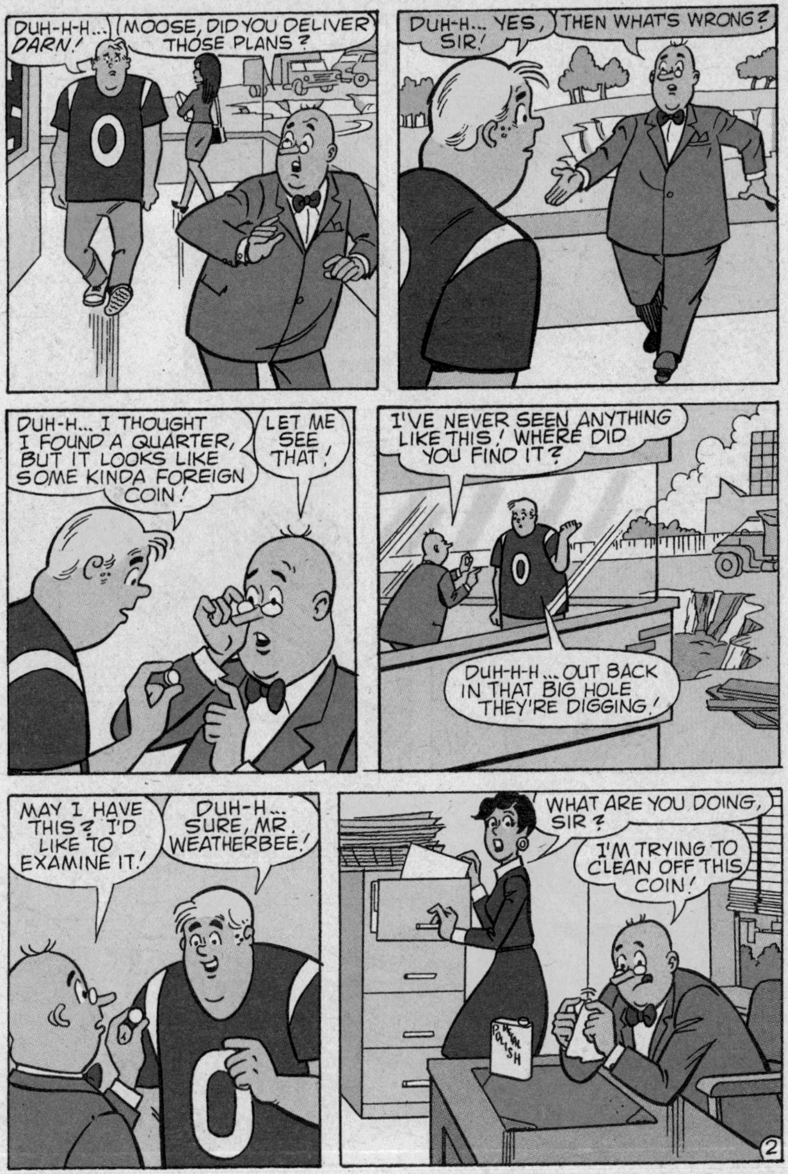
DUH-H-H... DARN!
MOOSE, DID YOU DELIVER THOSE PLANS?
DUH-H... YES, SIR!
THEN WHAT'S WRONG?
DUH-H... I THOUGHT I FOUND A QUARTER, BUT IT LOOKS LIKE SOME KINDA FOREIGN COIN!
LET ME SEE THAT!
I'VE NEVER SEEN ANYTHING LIKE THIS! WHERE DID YOU FIND IT?
DUH-H-H... OUT BACK IN THAT BIG HOLE THEY'RE DIGGING!
MAY I HAVE THIS? I'D LIKE TO EXAMINE IT!
DUH-H... SURE, MR. WEATHERBEE!
WHAT ARE YOU DOING, SIR?
I'M TRYING TO CLEAN OFF THIS COIN!
METAL POLISH
2

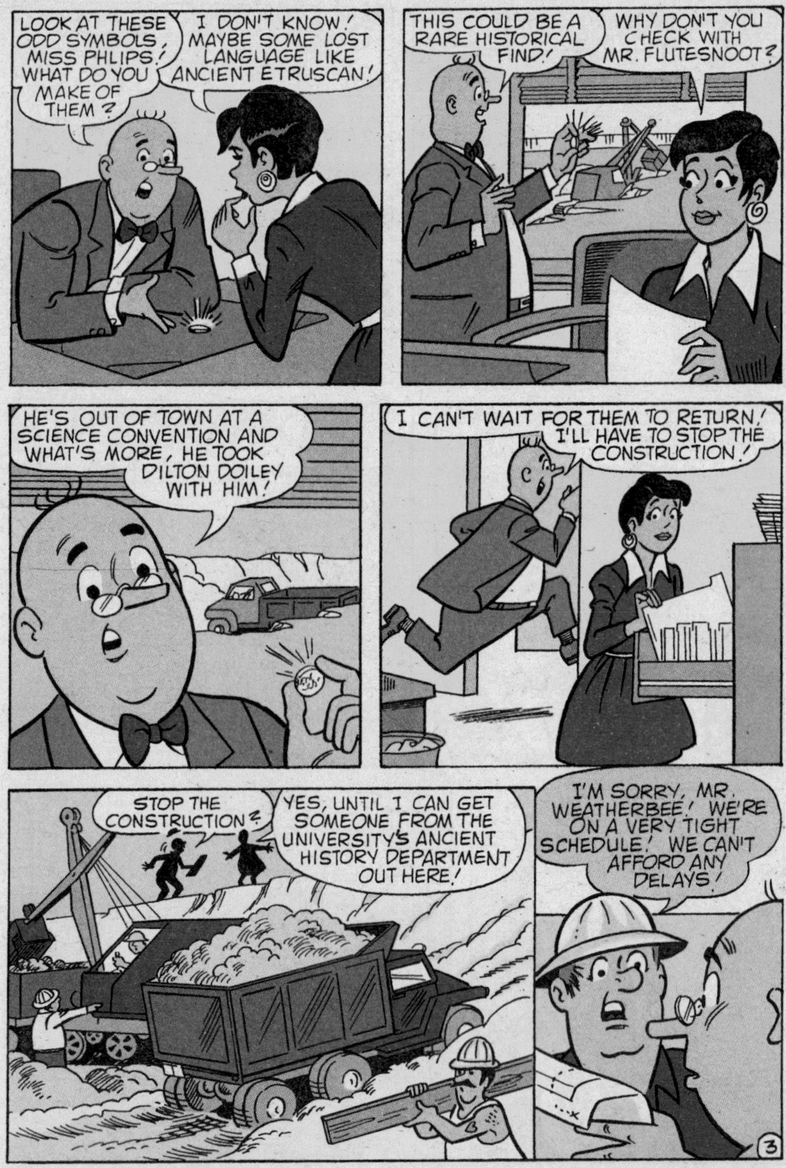
LOOK AT THESE ODD SYMBOLS, MISS PHLIPS! WHAT DO YOU MAKE OF THEM?
I DON'T KNOW! MAYBE SOME LOST LANGUAGE LIKE ANCIENT ETRUSCAN!
THIS COULD BE A RARE HISTORICAL FIND!
WHY DON'T YOU CHECK WITH MR. FLUTESNOOT?
HE'S OUT OF TOWN AT A SCIENCE CONVENTION AND WHAT'S MORE, HE TOOK DILTON DOILEY WITH HIM!
I CAN'T WAIT FOR THEM TO RETURN! I'LL HAVE TO STOP THE CONSTRUCTION!
STOP THE CONSTRUCTION?
YES, UNTIL I CAN GET SOMEONE FROM THE UNIVERSITY'S ANCIENT HISTORY DEPARTMENT OUT HERE!
I'M SORRY, MR. WEATHERBEE! WE'RE ON A VERY TIGHT SCHEDULE! WE CAN'T AFFORD ANY DELAYS!
3

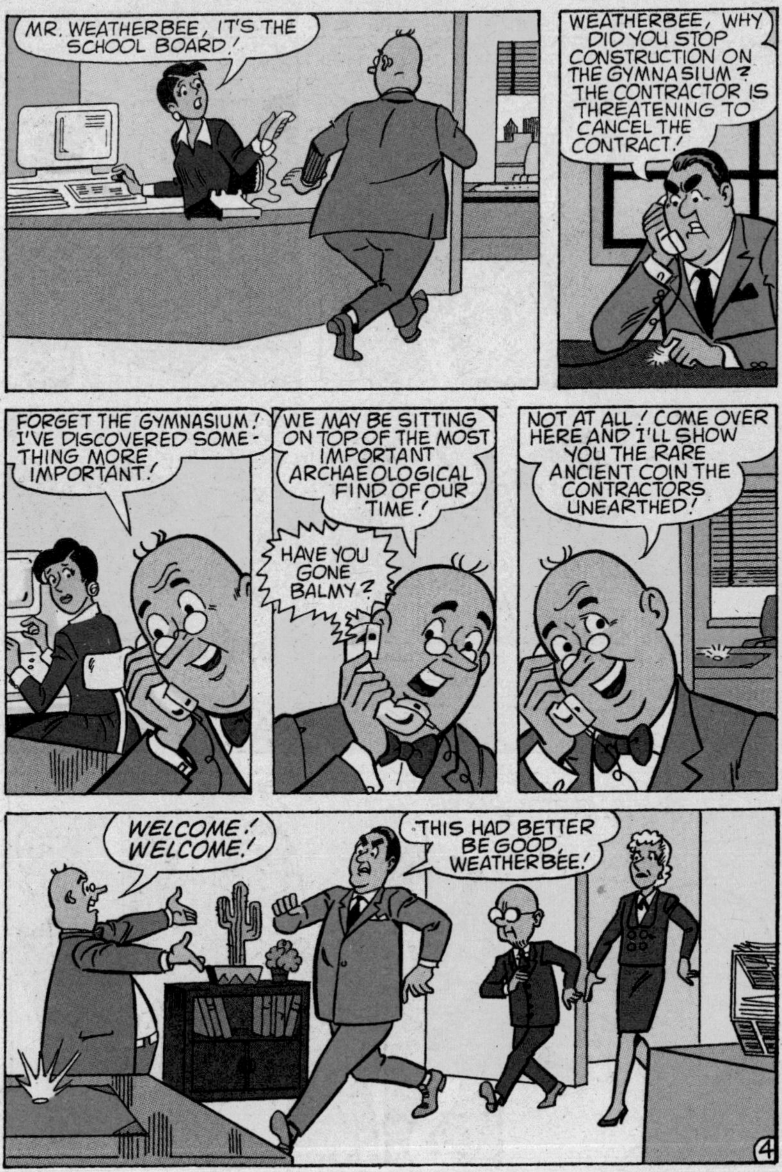
MR. WEATHERBEE, IT'S THE SCHOOL BOARD!
WEATHERBEE, WHY DID YOU STOP CONSTRUCTION ON THE GYMNASIUM? THE CONTRACTOR IS THREATENING TO CANCEL THE CONTRACT!
FORGET THE GYMNASIUM! I'VE DISCOVERED SOME-THING MORE IMPORTANT!
WE MAY BE SITTING ON TOP OF THE MOST IMPORTANT ARCHAEOLOGICAL FIND OF OUR TIME!
HAVE YOU GONE BALMY?
NOT AT ALL! COME OVER HERE AND I'LL SHOW YOU THE RARE ANCIENT COIN THE CONTRACTORS UNEARTHED!
WELCOME! WELCOME!
THIS HAD BETTER BE GOOD, WEATHERBEE!
4

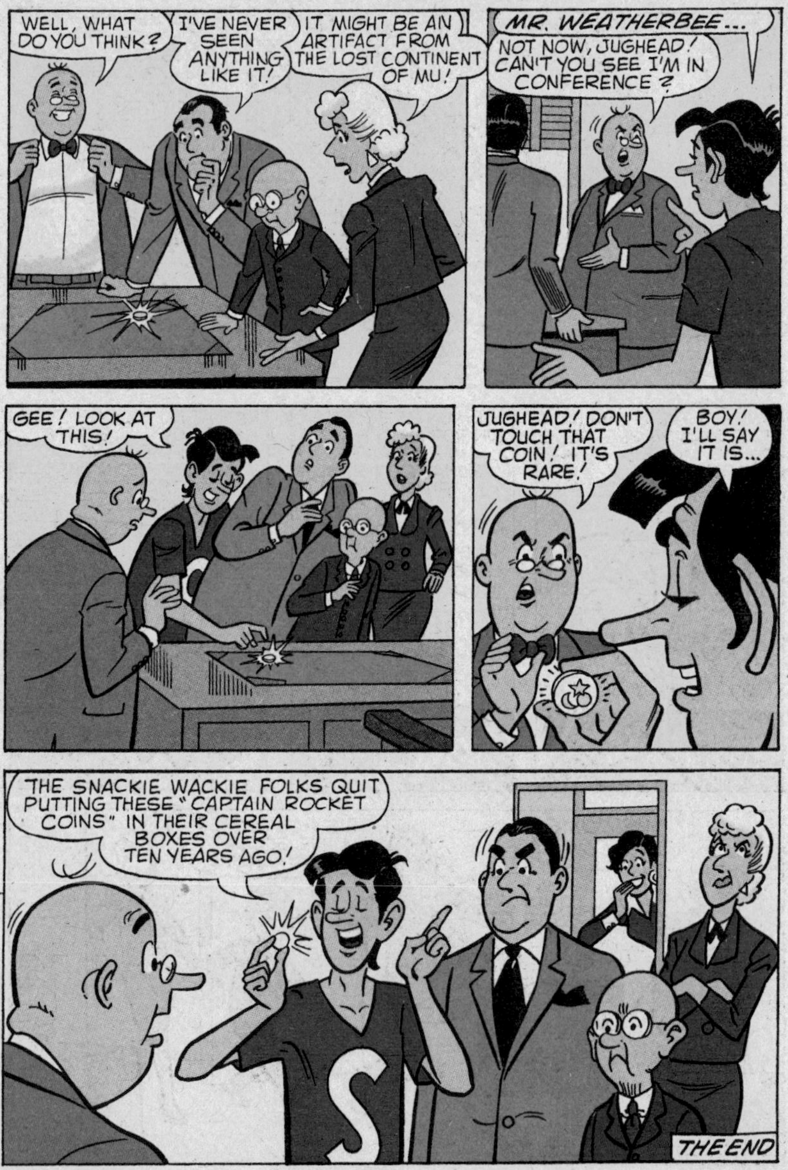
WELL, WHAT DO YOU THINK?
I'VE NEVER SEEN ANYTHING LIKE IT!
IT MIGHT BE AN ARTIFACT FROM THE LOST CONTINENT OF MU!
MR. WEATHERBEE...
NOT NOW, JUGHEAD! CAN'T YOU SEE I'M IN CONFERENCE?
GEE! LOOK AT THIS!
JUGHEAD! DON'T TOUCH THAT COIN! IT'S RARE!
BOY! I'LL SAY IT IS...
THE SNACKIE WACKIE FOLKS QUIT PUTTING THESE "CAPTAIN ROCKET COINS" IN THEIR CEREAL BOXES OVER TEN YEARS AGO!
THE END

Archie in "COLOR COMMENTARY"

GIRLS DON'T THINK THE SAME WAY AS GUYS!

OH, DON'T START AGAIN!

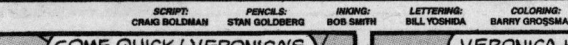

SCRIPT: CRAIG BOLDMAN PENCILS: STAN GOLDBERG INKING: BOB SMITH LETTERING: BILL YOSHIDA COLORING: BARRY GROSSMAN

COME QUICK! VERONICA'S GOT A *BRAND NEW COLOR* LIPSTICK!

VERONICA HAS THE *NEW COLOR!*

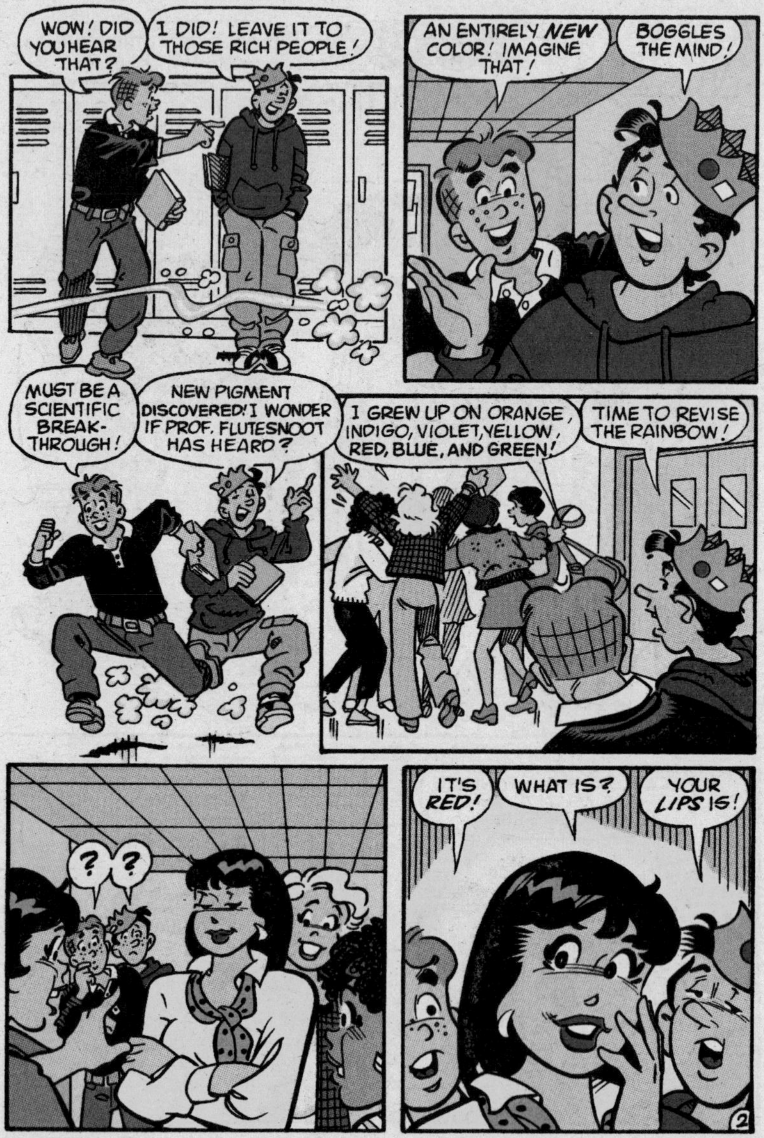
WOW! DID YOU HEAR THAT?
I DID! LEAVE IT TO THOSE RICH PEOPLE!
AN ENTIRELY NEW COLOR! IMAGINE THAT!
BOGGLES THE MIND!
MUST BE A SCIENTIFIC BREAK-THROUGH!
NEW PIGMENT DISCOVERED! I WONDER IF PROF. FLUTESNOOT HAS HEARD?
I GREW UP ON ORANGE, INDIGO, VIOLET, YELLOW, RED, BLUE, AND GREEN!
TIME TO REVISE THE RAINBOW!
? ?
IT'S RED!
WHAT IS?
YOUR LIPS IS!
2

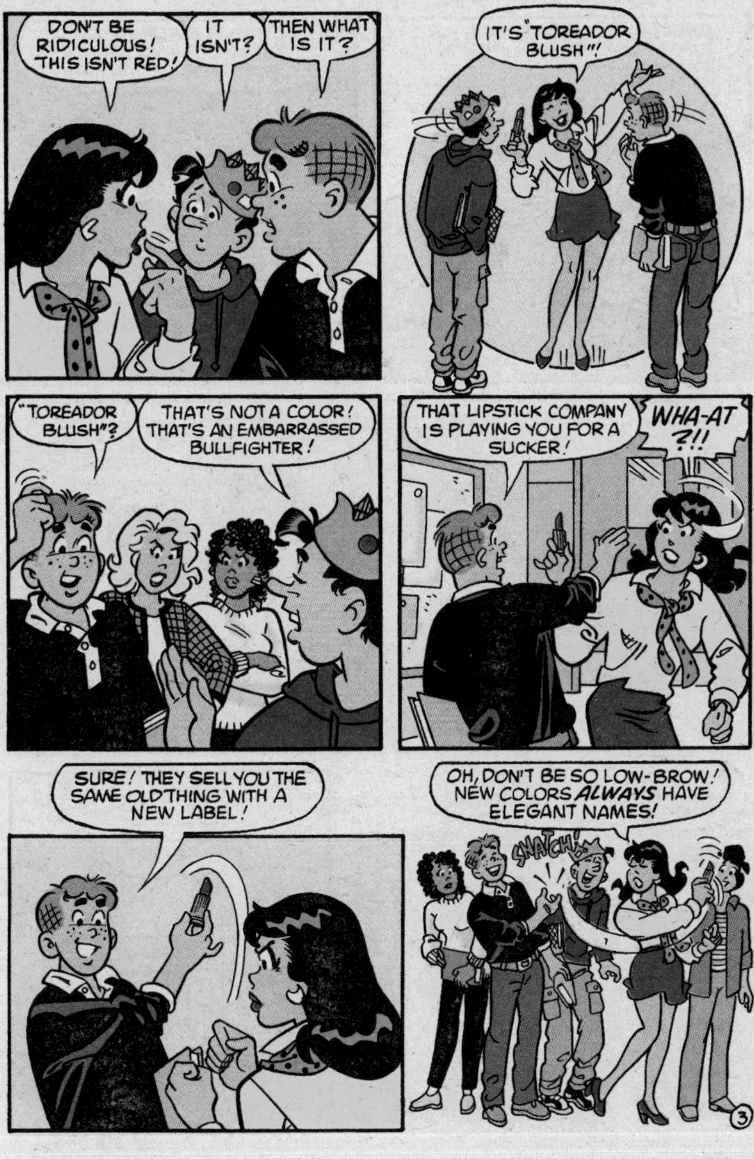

DON'T BE RIDICULOUS! THIS ISN'T RED!
IT ISN'T?
THEN WHAT IS IT?
IT'S "TOREADOR BLUSH"!
"TOREADOR BLUSH"?
THAT'S NOT A COLOR! THAT'S AN EMBARRASSED BULLFIGHTER!
THAT LIPSTICK COMPANY IS PLAYING YOU FOR A SUCKER!
WHA-AT ?!!
SURE! THEY SELL YOU THE SAME OLD THING WITH A NEW LABEL!
OH, DON'T BE SO LOW-BROW! NEW COLORS ALWAYS HAVE ELEGANT NAMES!
SNATCH!
3

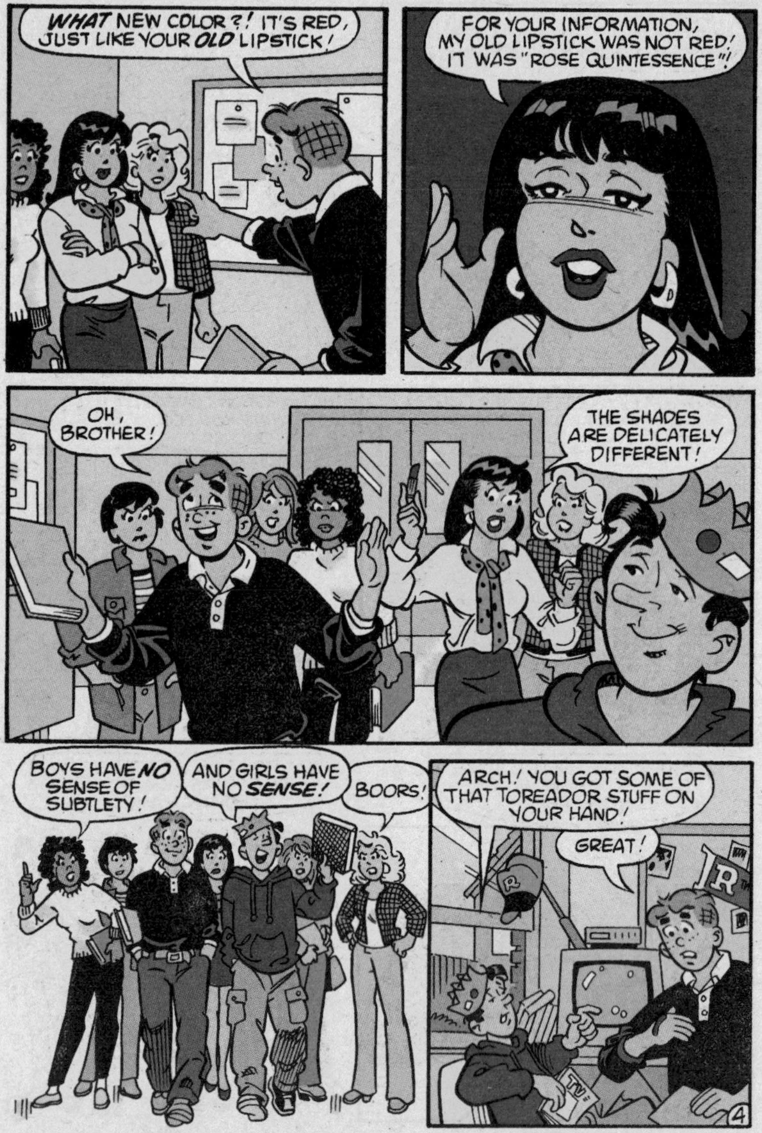
WHAT NEW COLOR?! IT'S RED, JUST LIKE YOUR OLD LIPSTICK!
FOR YOUR INFORMATION, MY OLD LIPSTICK WAS NOT RED! IT WAS "ROSE QUINTESSENCE"!
OH, BROTHER!
THE SHADES ARE DELICATELY DIFFERENT!
BOYS HAVE NO SENSE OF SUBTLETY!
AND GIRLS HAVE NO SENSE!
BOORS!
ARCH! YOU GOT SOME OF THAT TOREADOR STUFF ON YOUR HAND!
GREAT!
4

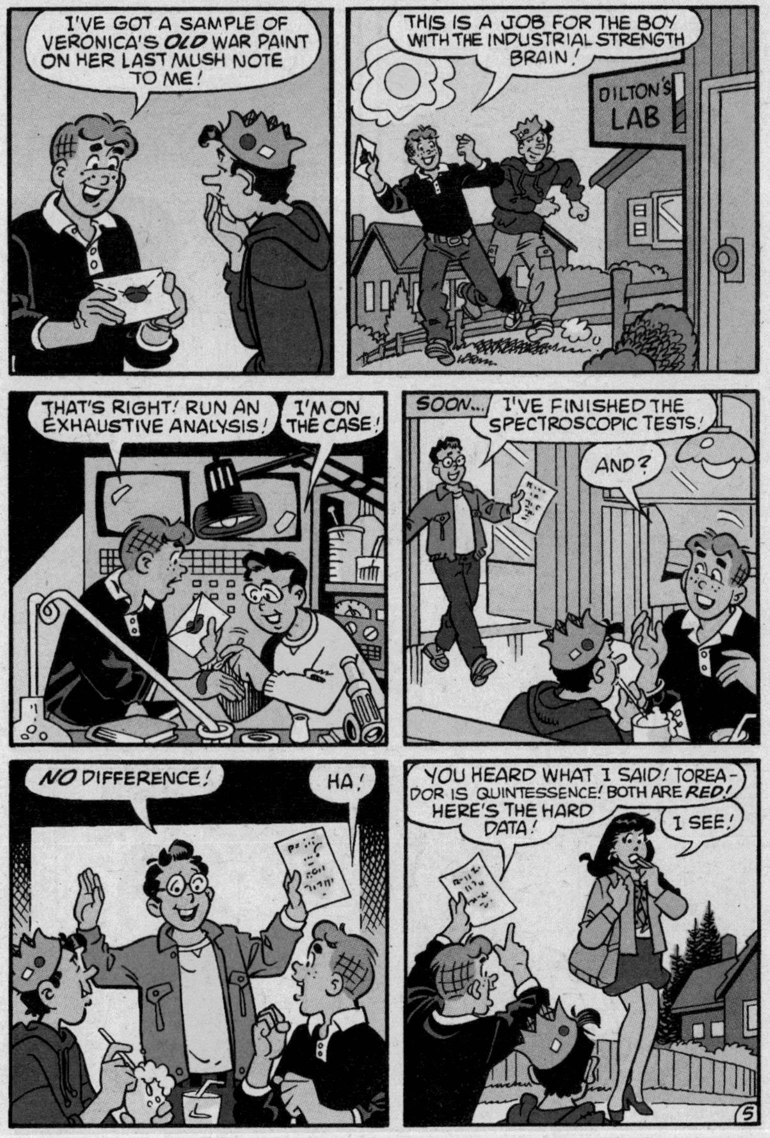
I'VE GOT A SAMPLE OF VERONICA'S OLD WAR PAINT ON HER LAST MUSH NOTE TO ME!
THIS IS A JOB FOR THE BOY WITH THE INDUSTRIAL STRENGTH BRAIN!
DILTON'S LAB
THAT'S RIGHT! RUN AN EXHAUSTIVE ANALYSIS!
I'M ON THE CASE!
SOON...
I'VE FINISHED THE SPECTROSCOPIC TESTS!
AND?
NO DIFFERENCE!
HA!
YOU HEARD WHAT I SAID! TOREADOR IS QUINTESSENCE! BOTH ARE RED! HERE'S THE HARD DATA!
I SEE!
5

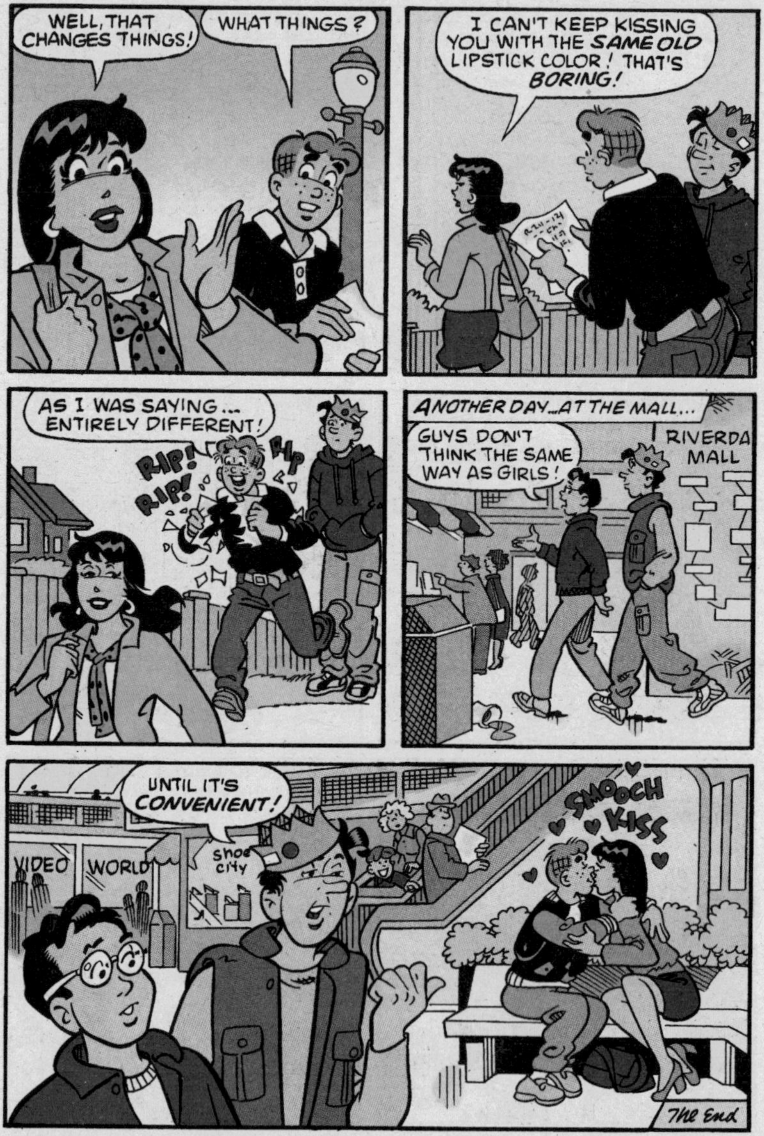
WELL, THAT CHANGES THINGS!
WHAT THINGS?
I CAN'T KEEP KISSING YOU WITH THE SAME OLD LIPSTICK COLOR! THAT'S BORING!
AS I WAS SAYING... ENTIRELY DIFFERENT!
RIP! RIP! RIP
ANOTHER DAY...AT THE MALL...
GUYS DON'T THINK THE SAME WAY AS GIRLS!
RIVERDA MALL
UNTIL IT'S CONVENIENT!
VIDEO WORLD
shoe city
SMOOCH KISS
The End

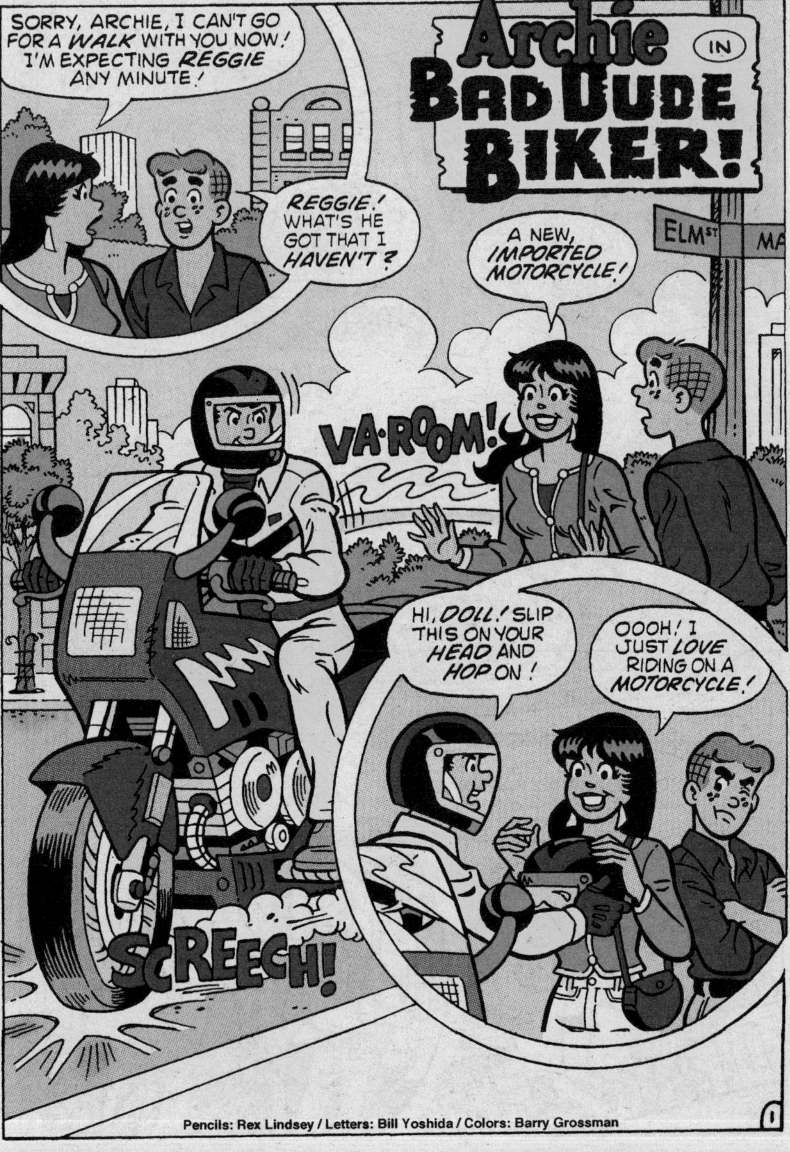
SORRY, ARCHIE, I CAN'T GO FOR A WALK WITH YOU NOW! I'M EXPECTING REGGIE ANY MINUTE!
Archie IN
BAD DUDE BIKER!
REGGIE! WHAT'S HE GOT THAT I HAVEN'T?
A NEW, IMPORTED MOTORCYCLE!
ELM ST
VA-ROOM!
HI, DOLL! SLIP THIS ON YOUR HEAD AND HOP ON!
OOOH! I JUST LOVE RIDING ON A MOTORCYCLE!
SCREECH!
1
Pencils: Rex Lindsey / Letters: Bill Yoshida / Colors: Barry Grossman

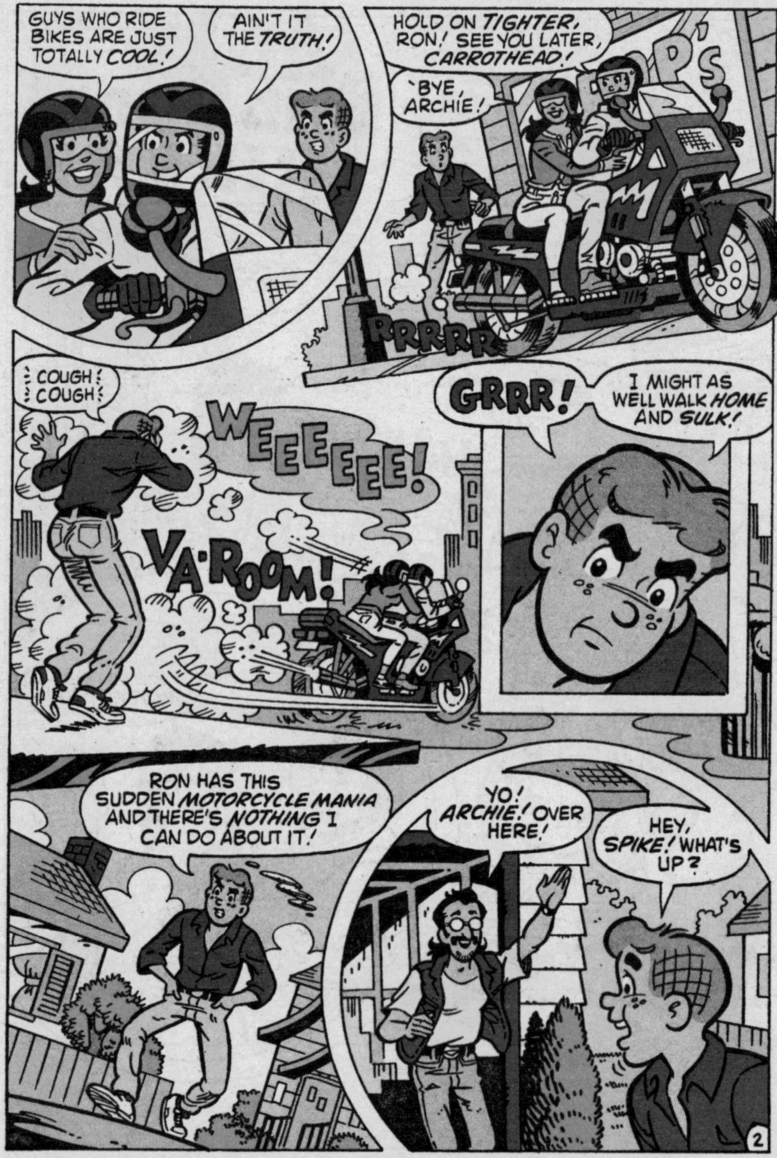
GUYS WHO RIDE BIKES ARE JUST TOTALLY COOL!
AIN'T IT THE TRUTH!
HOLD ON TIGHTER, RON! SEE YOU LATER, CARROTHEAD!
'BYE, ARCHIE!
RRRRRR
COUGH! COUGH!
WEEEEEE!
VA-ROOM!
GRRR!
I MIGHT AS WELL WALK HOME AND SULK!
RON HAS THIS SUDDEN MOTORCYCLE MANIA AND THERE'S NOTHING I CAN DO ABOUT IT!
YO! ARCHIE! OVER HERE!
HEY, SPIKE! WHAT'S UP?

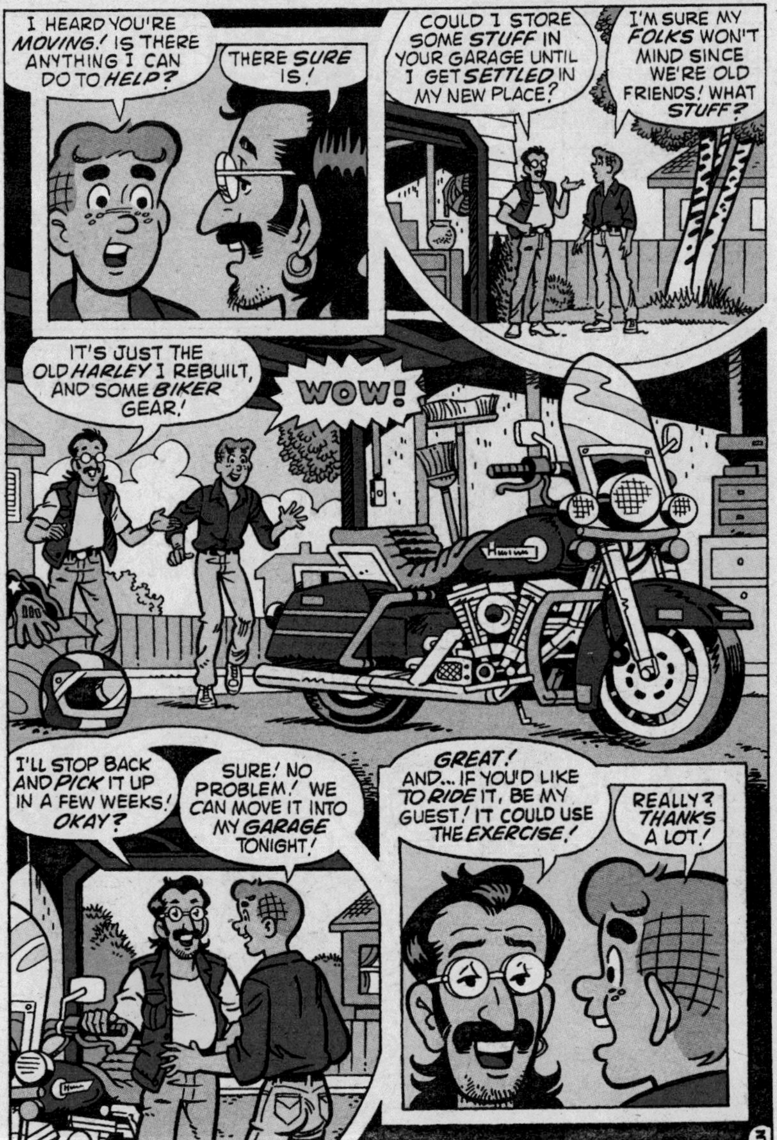
I HEARD YOU'RE MOVING! IS THERE ANYTHING I CAN DO TO HELP?
THERE SURE IS!
COULD I STORE SOME STUFF IN YOUR GARAGE UNTIL I GET SETTLED IN MY NEW PLACE?
I'M SURE MY FOLKS WON'T MIND SINCE WE'RE OLD FRIENDS! WHAT STUFF?
IT'S JUST THE OLD HARLEY I REBUILT, AND SOME BIKER GEAR!
WOW!
I'LL STOP BACK AND PICK IT UP IN A FEW WEEKS! OKAY?
SURE! NO PROBLEM! WE CAN MOVE IT INTO MY GARAGE TONIGHT!
GREAT! AND... IF YOU'D LIKE TO RIDE IT, BE MY GUEST! IT COULD USE THE EXERCISE!
REALLY? THANKS A LOT!
3

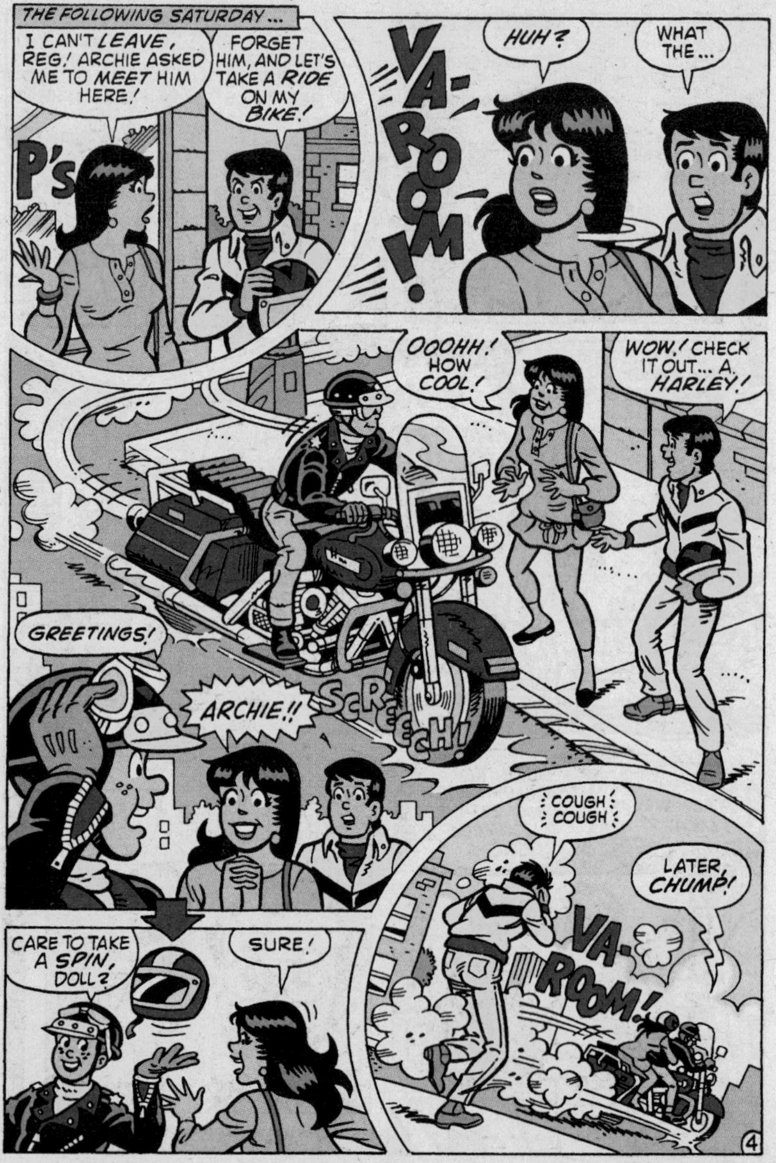
THE FOLLOWING SATURDAY ...
I CAN'T *LEAVE*, REG.! ARCHIE ASKED ME TO *MEET* HIM HERE!
FORGET HIM, AND LET'S TAKE A *RIDE* ON MY *BIKE*!
P's
VA-ROOM!
HUH?
WHAT THE...
OOOHH! HOW COOL!
WOW! CHECK IT OUT... A *HARLEY*!
SCREECH!
GREETINGS!
ARCHIE!!
CARE TO TAKE A *SPIN*, DOLL?
SURE!
COUGH COUGH
LATER, *CHUMP*!
VA-ROOM!
4

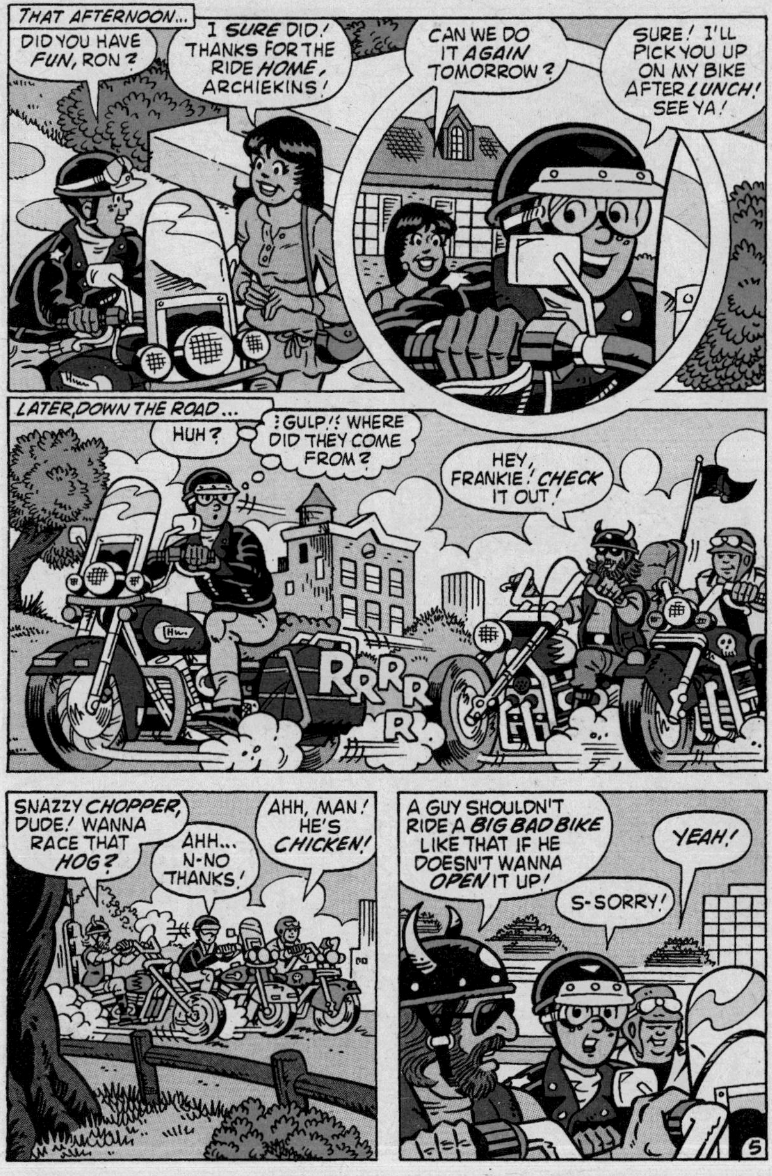
THAT AFTERNOON...
DID YOU HAVE FUN, RON?
I SURE DID! THANKS FOR THE RIDE HOME, ARCHIEKINS!
CAN WE DO IT AGAIN TOMORROW?
SURE! I'LL PICK YOU UP ON MY BIKE AFTER LUNCH! SEE YA!
LATER, DOWN THE ROAD...
HUH?
GULP! WHERE DID THEY COME FROM?
HEY, FRANKIE! CHECK IT OUT!
RRRRR
SNAZZY CHOPPER, DUDE! WANNA RACE THAT HOG?
AHH... N-NO THANKS!
AHH, MAN! HE'S CHICKEN!
A GUY SHOULDN'T RIDE A BIG BAD BIKE LIKE THAT IF HE DOESN'T WANNA OPEN IT UP!
YEAH!
S-SORRY!

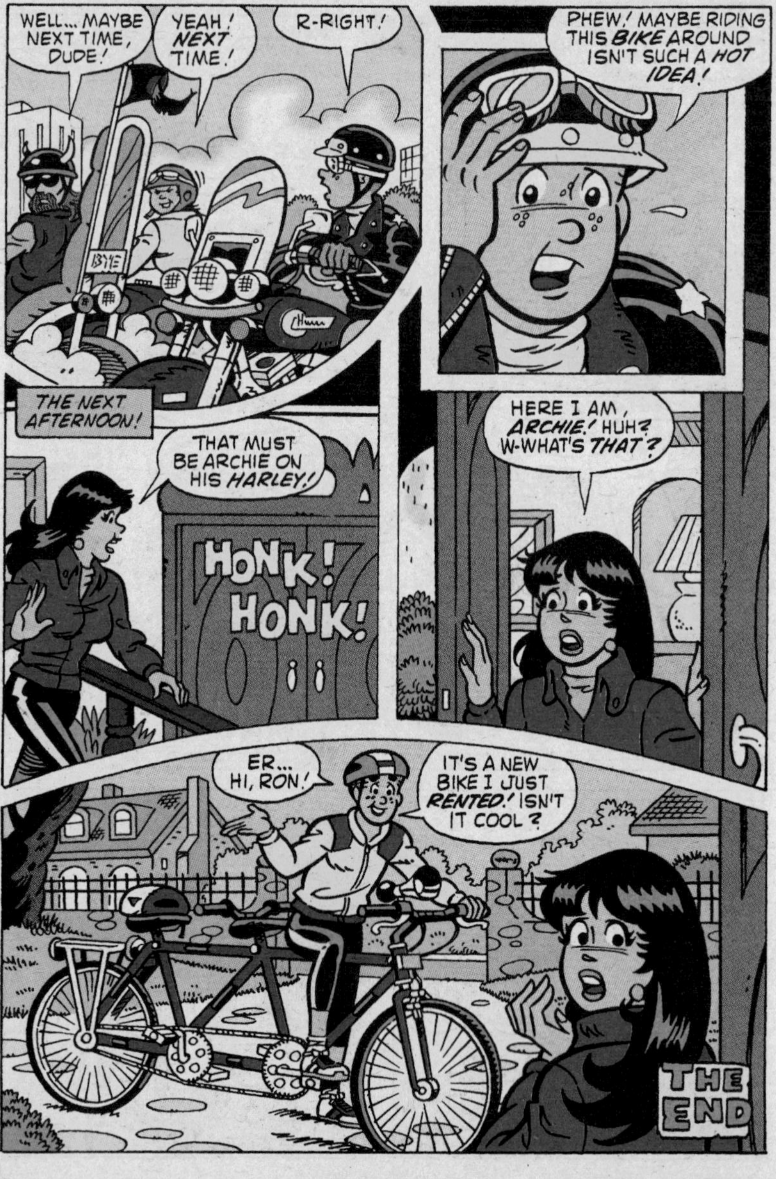
WELL... MAYBE NEXT TIME, DUDE!
YEAH! NEXT TIME!
R-RIGHT!
BYE
PHEW! MAYBE RIDING THIS BIKE AROUND ISN'T SUCH A HOT IDEA!
THE NEXT AFTERNOON!
THAT MUST BE ARCHIE ON HIS HARLEY!
HONK! HONK!
HERE I AM, ARCHIE! HUH? W-WHAT'S THAT?
ER... HI, RON!
IT'S A NEW BIKE I JUST RENTED! ISN'T IT COOL?
THE END

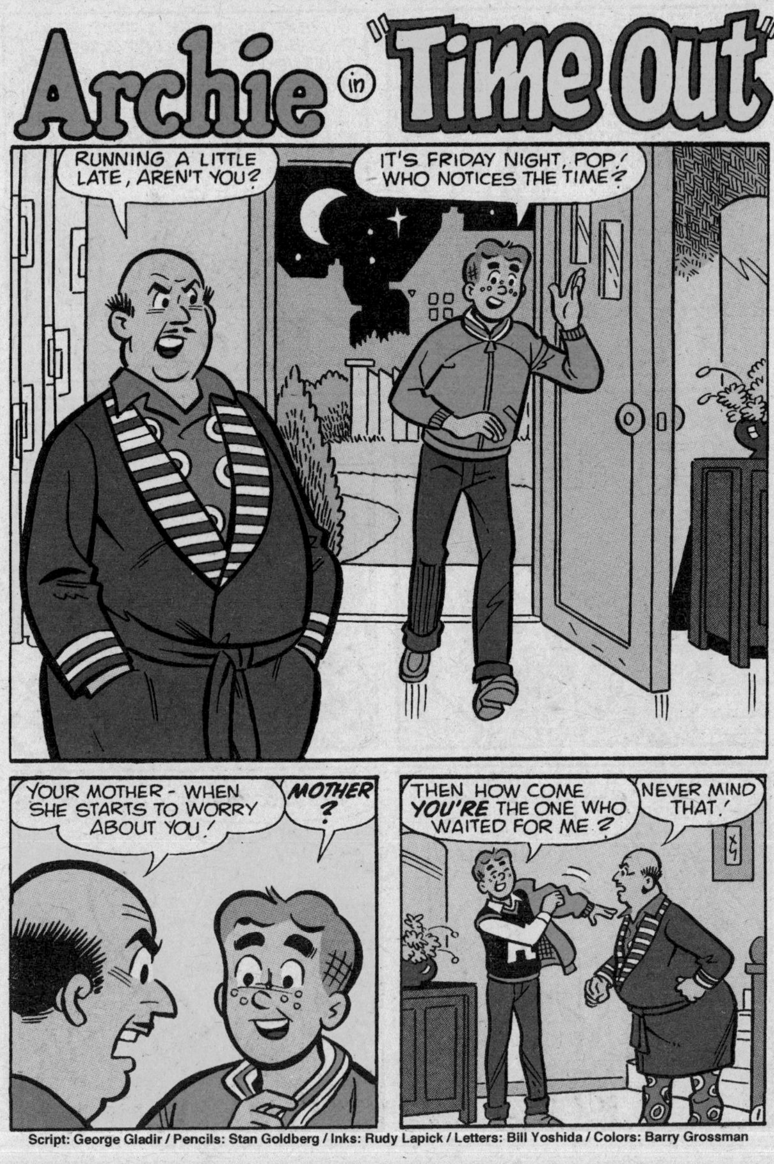
Archie in "Time Out"
RUNNING A LITTLE LATE, AREN'T YOU?
IT'S FRIDAY NIGHT, POP! WHO NOTICES THE TIME?
YOUR MOTHER - WHEN SHE STARTS TO WORRY ABOUT YOU!
MOTHER?
THEN HOW COME YOU'RE THE ONE WHO WAITED FOR ME?
NEVER MIND THAT!

Script: George Gladir / Pencils: Stan Goldberg / Inks: Rudy Lapick / Letters: Bill Yoshida / Colors: Barry Grossman

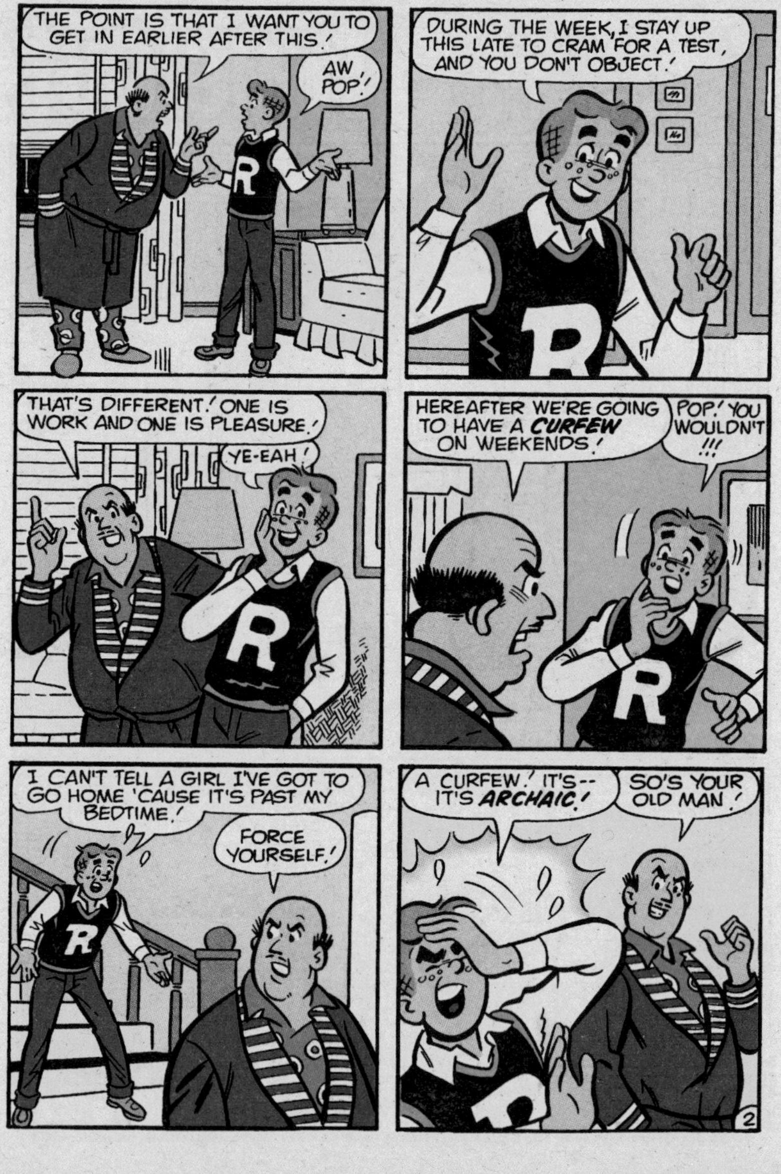
THE POINT IS THAT I WANT YOU TO GET IN EARLIER AFTER THIS!
AW, POP!
DURING THE WEEK, I STAY UP THIS LATE TO CRAM FOR A TEST, AND YOU DON'T OBJECT!
THAT'S DIFFERENT! ONE IS WORK AND ONE IS PLEASURE!
YE-EAH!
HEREAFTER WE'RE GOING TO HAVE A CURFEW ON WEEKENDS!
POP! YOU WOULDN'T !!!
I CAN'T TELL A GIRL I'VE GOT TO GO HOME 'CAUSE IT'S PAST MY BEDTIME!
FORCE YOURSELF!
A CURFEW! IT'S-- IT'S ARCHAIC!
SO'S YOUR OLD MAN!
2

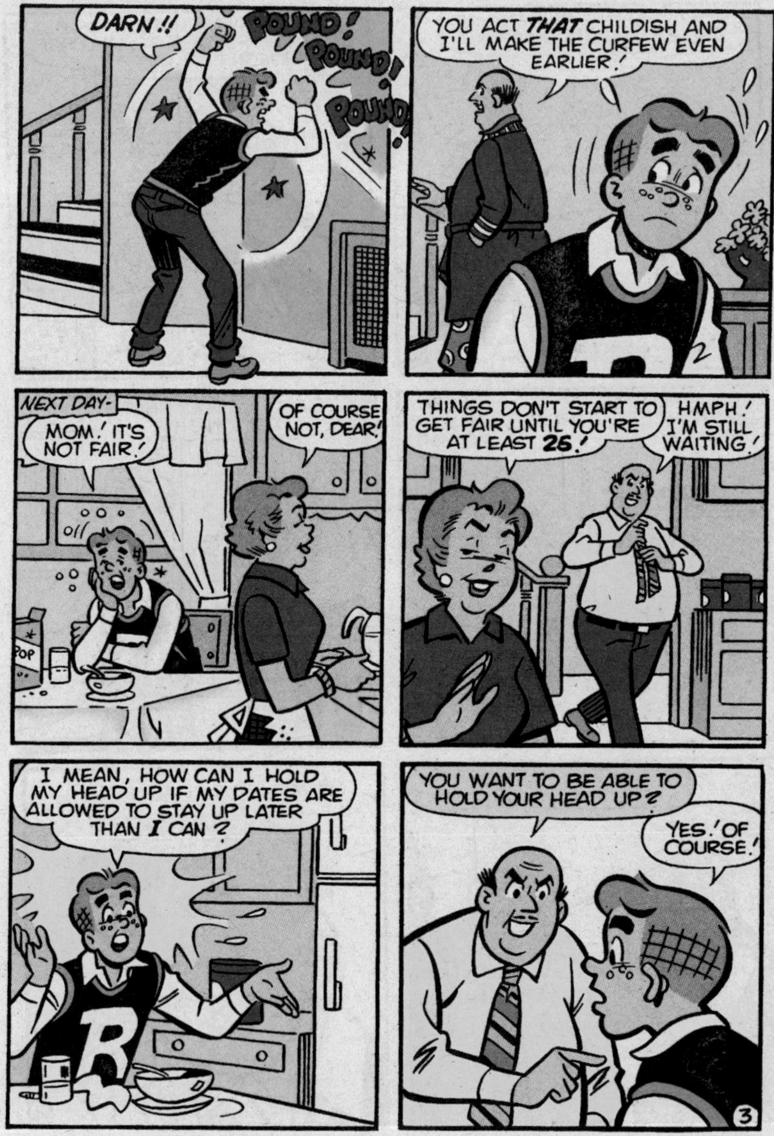
DARN!!
POUND! POUND! POUND!
YOU ACT THAT CHILDISH AND I'LL MAKE THE CURFEW EVEN EARLIER!
NEXT DAY-
MOM! IT'S NOT FAIR!
OF COURSE NOT, DEAR!
POP
THINGS DON'T START TO GET FAIR UNTIL YOU'RE AT LEAST 25!
HMPH! I'M STILL WAITING!
I MEAN, HOW CAN I HOLD MY HEAD UP IF MY DATES ARE ALLOWED TO STAY UP LATER THAN I CAN?
YOU WANT TO BE ABLE TO HOLD YOUR HEAD UP?
YES! OF COURSE!
3

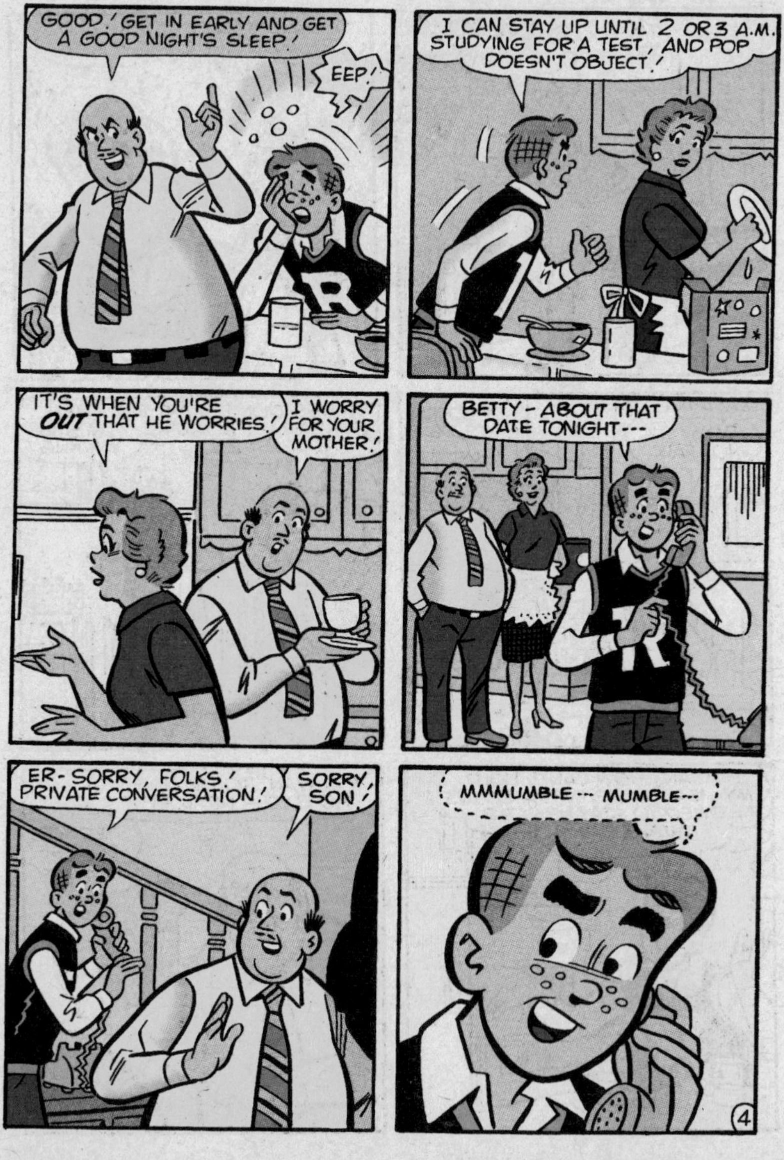
GOOD! GET IN EARLY AND GET A GOOD NIGHT'S SLEEP!
EEP!
I CAN STAY UP UNTIL 2 OR 3 A.M. STUDYING FOR A TEST, AND POP DOESN'T OBJECT!
IT'S WHEN YOU'RE OUT THAT HE WORRIES!
I WORRY FOR YOUR MOTHER!
BETTY - ABOUT THAT DATE TONIGHT---
ER- SORRY, FOLKS! PRIVATE CONVERSATION!
SORRY, SON!
MMMUMBLE --- MUMBLE---
4

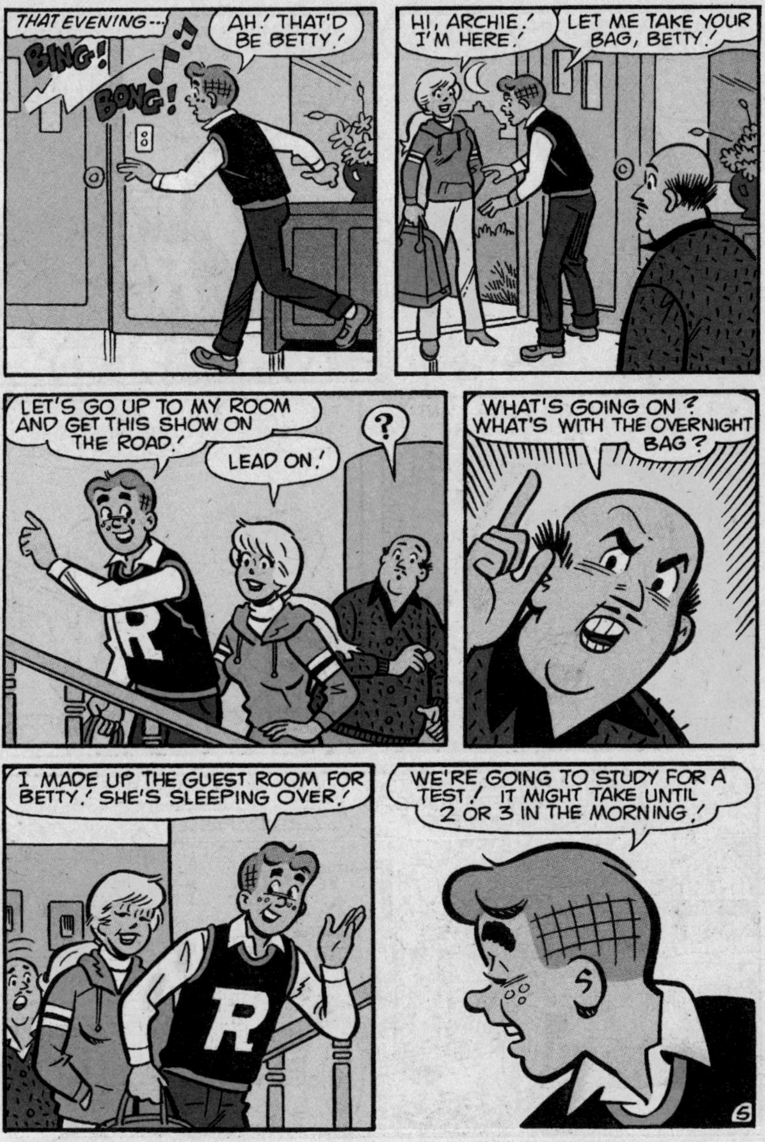
THAT EVENING---
BING!
BONG!
AH! THAT'D BE BETTY!
HI, ARCHIE! I'M HERE!
LET ME TAKE YOUR BAG, BETTY!
LET'S GO UP TO MY ROOM AND GET THIS SHOW ON THE ROAD!
LEAD ON!
?
WHAT'S GOING ON? WHAT'S WITH THE OVERNIGHT BAG?
I MADE UP THE GUEST ROOM FOR BETTY! SHE'S SLEEPING OVER!
WE'RE GOING TO STUDY FOR A TEST! IT MIGHT TAKE UNTIL 2 OR 3 IN THE MORNING!
5

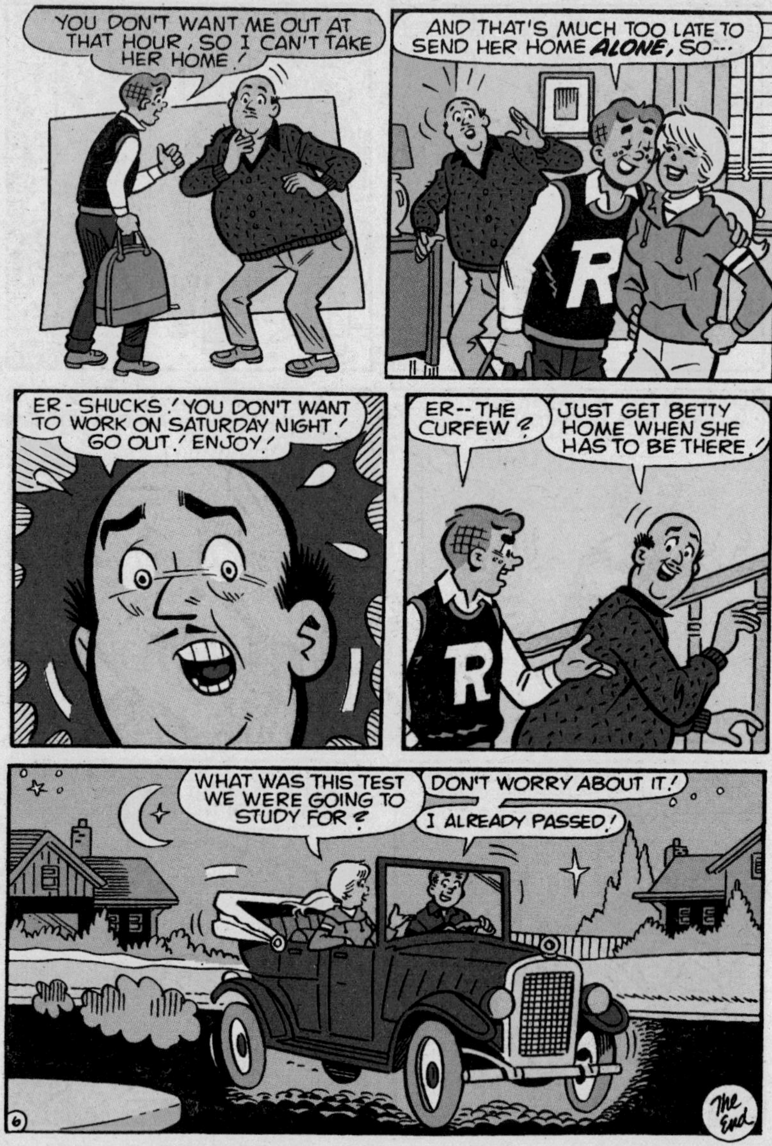
YOU DON'T WANT ME OUT AT THAT HOUR, SO I CAN'T TAKE HER HOME!
AND THAT'S MUCH TOO LATE TO SEND HER HOME ALONE, SO---
ER-SHUCKS! YOU DON'T WANT TO WORK ON SATURDAY NIGHT! GO OUT! ENJOY!
ER--THE CURFEW?
JUST GET BETTY HOME WHEN SHE HAS TO BE THERE!
WHAT WAS THIS TEST WE WERE GOING TO STUDY FOR?
DON'T WORRY ABOUT IT!
I ALREADY PASSED!
6
The End

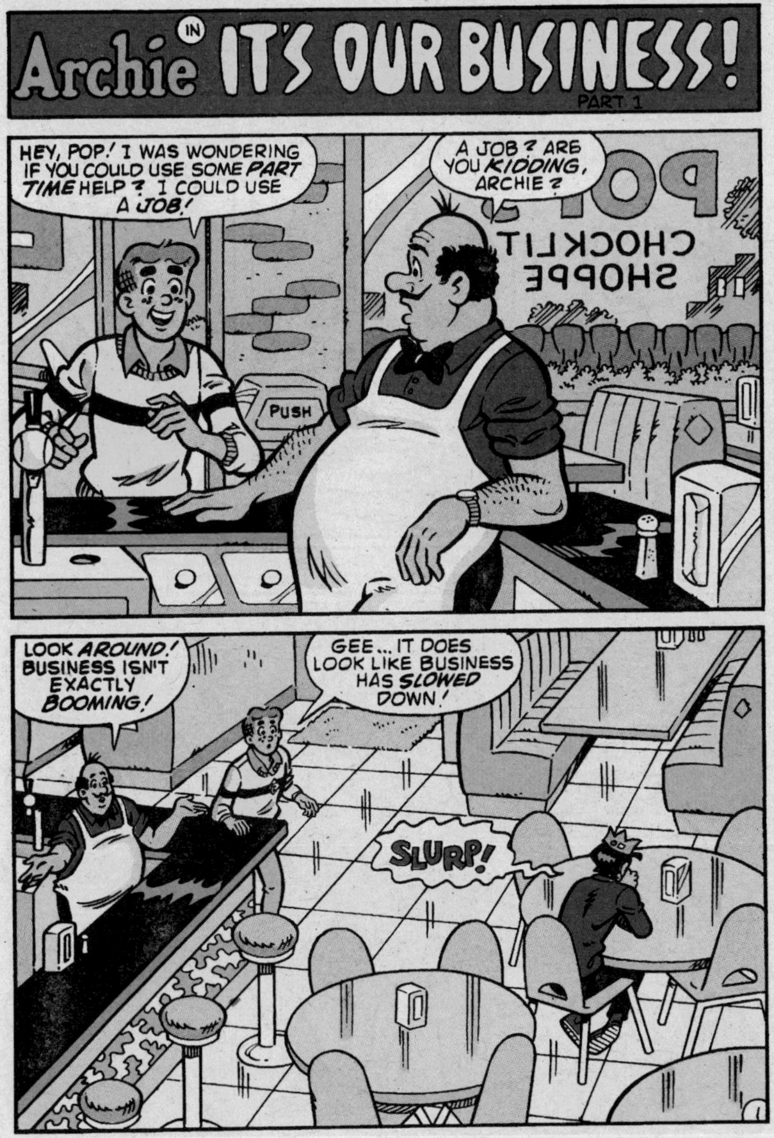
Archie IN IT'S OUR BUSINESS!
PART 1
HEY, POP! I WAS WONDERING IF YOU COULD USE SOME PART TIME HELP? I COULD USE A JOB!
A JOB? ARE YOU KIDDING, ARCHIE?
POP'S CHOCKLIT SHOPPE
PUSH
LOOK AROUND! BUSINESS ISN'T EXACTLY BOOMING!
GEE... IT DOES LOOK LIKE BUSINESS HAS SLOWED DOWN!
SLURP!

Script: George Gladir / Pencils: Rex Lindsey / Letters: Bill Yoshida / Colors: Barry Grossman

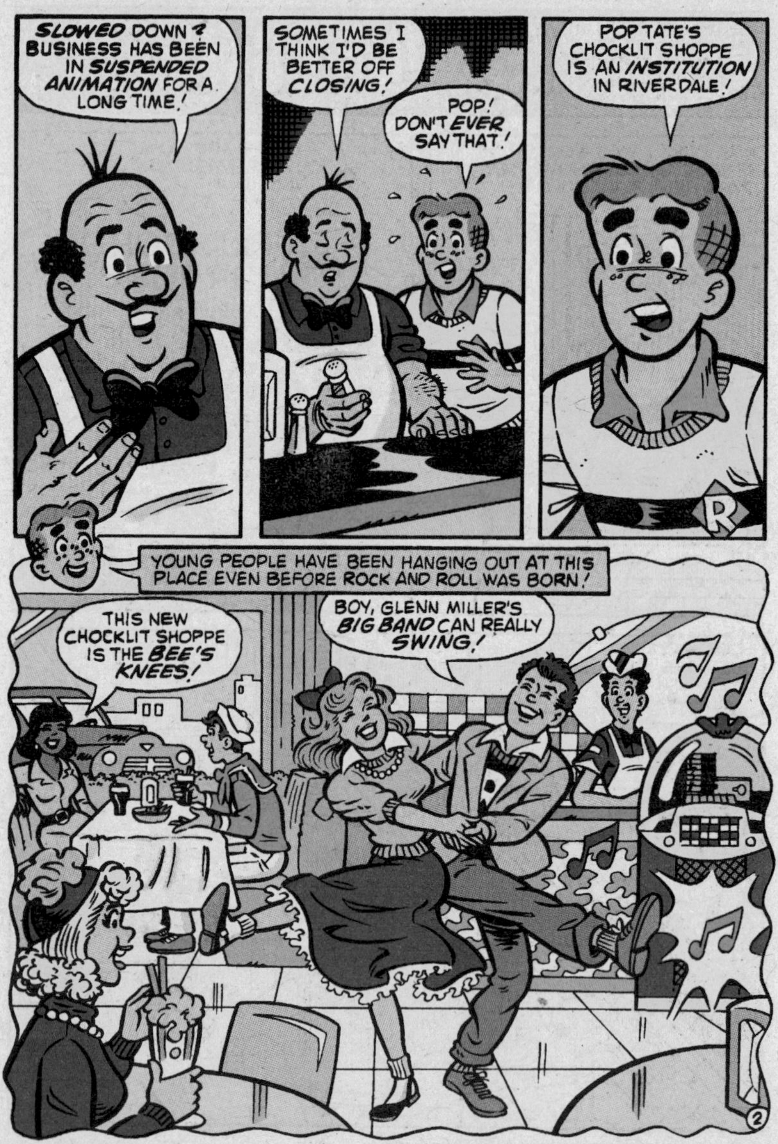
SLOWED DOWN? BUSINESS HAS BEEN IN SUSPENDED ANIMATION FOR A LONG TIME!
SOMETIMES I THINK I'D BE BETTER OFF CLOSING!
POP! DON'T EVER SAY THAT!
POP TATE'S CHOCKLIT SHOPPE IS AN INSTITUTION IN RIVERDALE!
YOUNG PEOPLE HAVE BEEN HANGING OUT AT THIS PLACE EVEN BEFORE ROCK AND ROLL WAS BORN!
THIS NEW CHOCKLIT SHOPPE IS THE BEE'S KNEES!
BOY, GLENN MILLER'S BIG BAND CAN REALLY SWING!
2

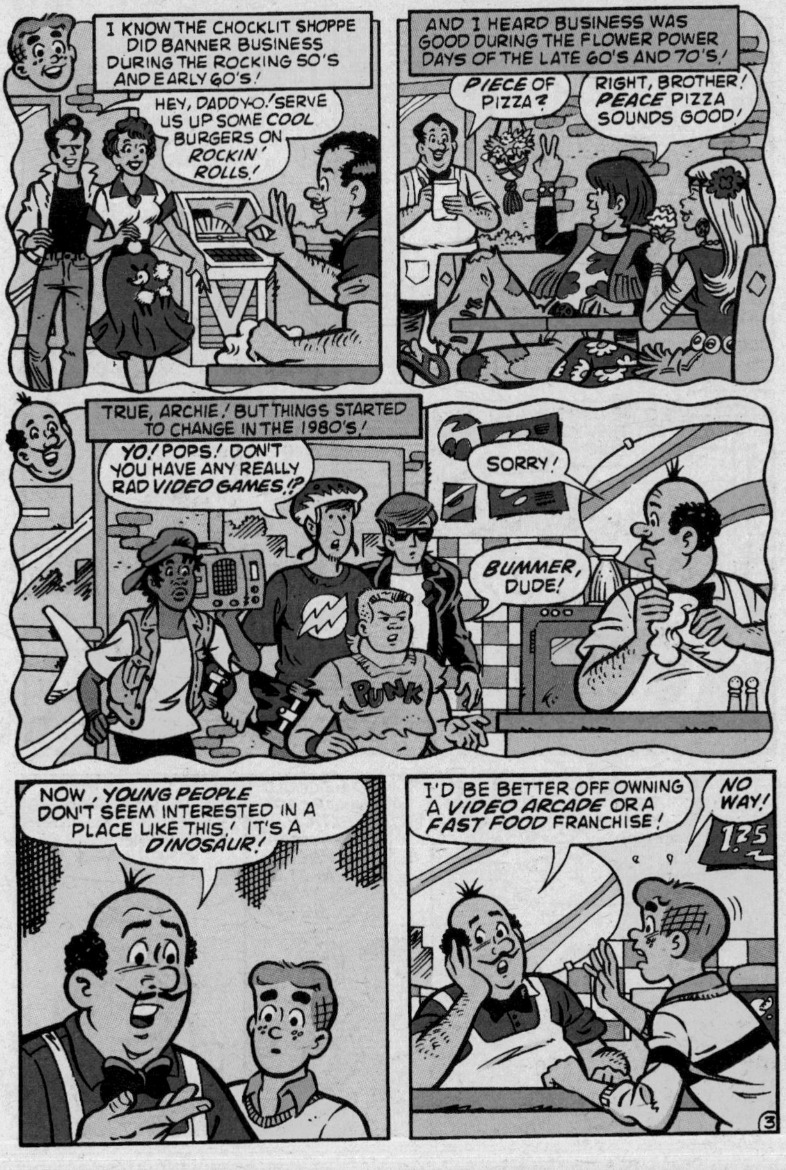

I KNOW THE CHOCKLIT SHOPPE DID BANNER BUSINESS DURING THE ROCKING 50'S AND EARLY 60'S!
HEY, DADDY-O! SERVE US UP SOME COOL BURGERS ON ROCKIN' ROLLS!
AND I HEARD BUSINESS WAS GOOD DURING THE FLOWER POWER DAYS OF THE LATE 60'S AND 70'S!
PIECE OF PIZZA?
RIGHT, BROTHER! PEACE PIZZA SOUNDS GOOD!
TRUE, ARCHIE! BUT THINGS STARTED TO CHANGE IN THE 1980'S!
YO! POPS! DON'T YOU HAVE ANY REALLY RAD VIDEO GAMES!?
PUNK
SORRY!
BUMMER, DUDE!
NOW, YOUNG PEOPLE DON'T SEEM INTERESTED IN A PLACE LIKE THIS! IT'S A DINOSAUR!
I'D BE BETTER OFF OWNING A VIDEO ARCADE OR A FAST FOOD FRANCHISE!
NO WAY!
1.25
3

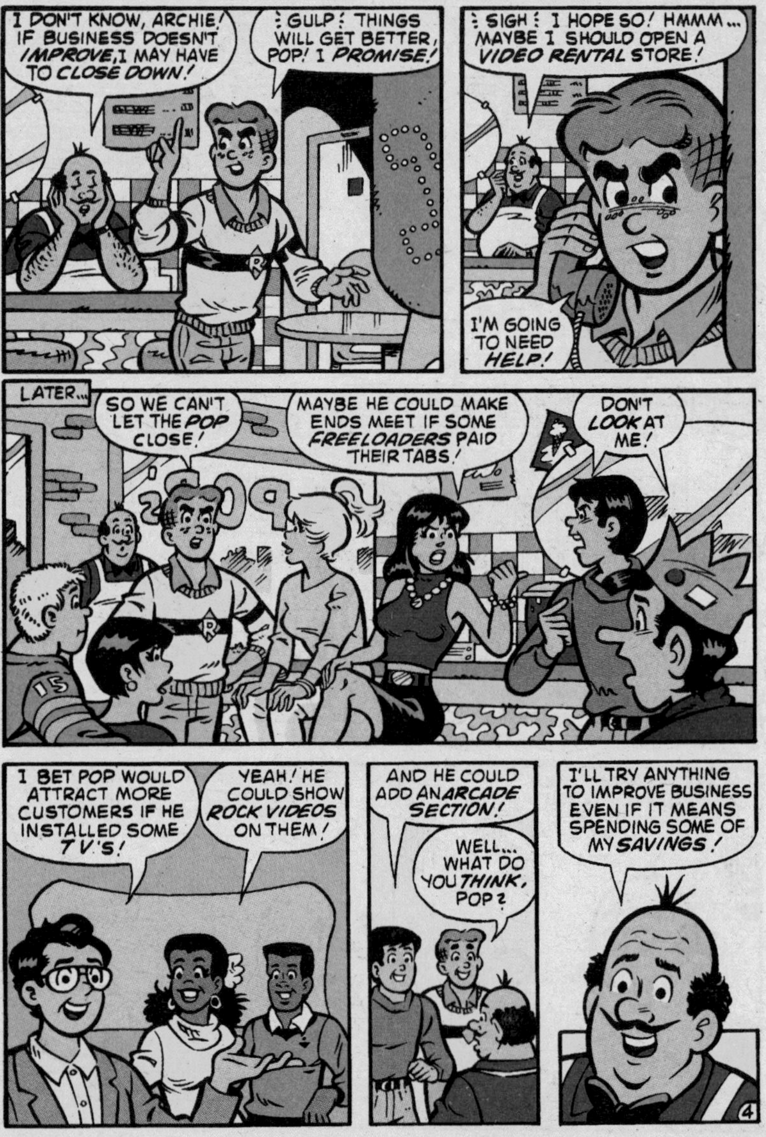
I DON'T KNOW, ARCHIE! IF BUSINESS DOESN'T IMPROVE, I MAY HAVE TO CLOSE DOWN!
GULP THINGS WILL GET BETTER, POP! I PROMISE!
SIGH I HOPE SO! HMMM... MAYBE I SHOULD OPEN A VIDEO RENTAL STORE!
I'M GOING TO NEED HELP!
LATER...
SO WE CAN'T LET THE POP CLOSE!
MAYBE HE COULD MAKE ENDS MEET IF SOME FREELOADERS PAID THEIR TABS!
DON'T LOOK AT ME!
I BET POP WOULD ATTRACT MORE CUSTOMERS IF HE INSTALLED SOME TV'S!
YEAH! HE COULD SHOW ROCK VIDEOS ON THEM!
AND HE COULD ADD AN ARCADE SECTION!
WELL... WHAT DO YOU THINK, POP?
I'LL TRY ANYTHING TO IMPROVE BUSINESS EVEN IF IT MEANS SPENDING SOME OF MY SAVINGS!
4

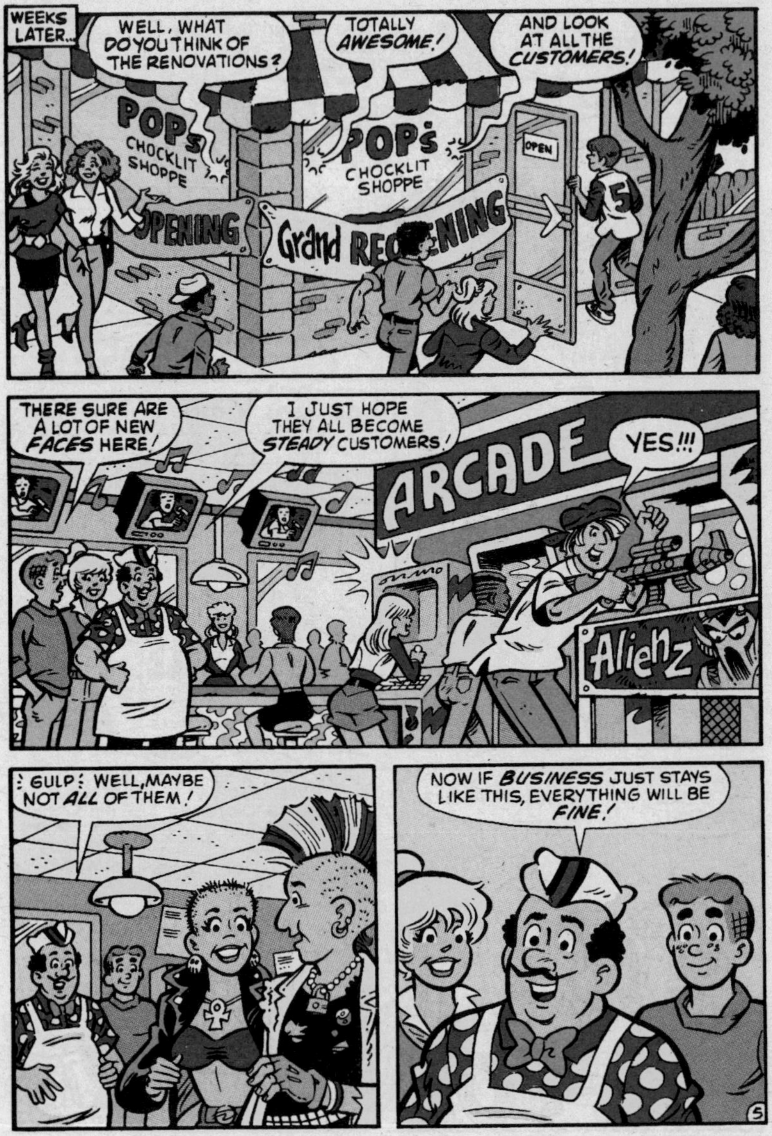
WEEKS LATER...
WELL, WHAT DO YOU THINK OF THE RENOVATIONS?
TOTALLY AWESOME!
AND LOOK AT ALL THE CUSTOMERS!
POP's CHOCKLIT SHOPPE
POP's CHOCKLIT SHOPPE
OPEN
OPENING
Grand REOPENING
THERE SURE ARE A LOT OF NEW FACES HERE!
I JUST HOPE THEY ALL BECOME STEADY CUSTOMERS!
ARCADE
YES!!!
Aliehz
GULP! WELL, MAYBE NOT ALL OF THEM!
NOW IF BUSINESS JUST STAYS LIKE THIS, EVERYTHING WILL BE FINE!
5

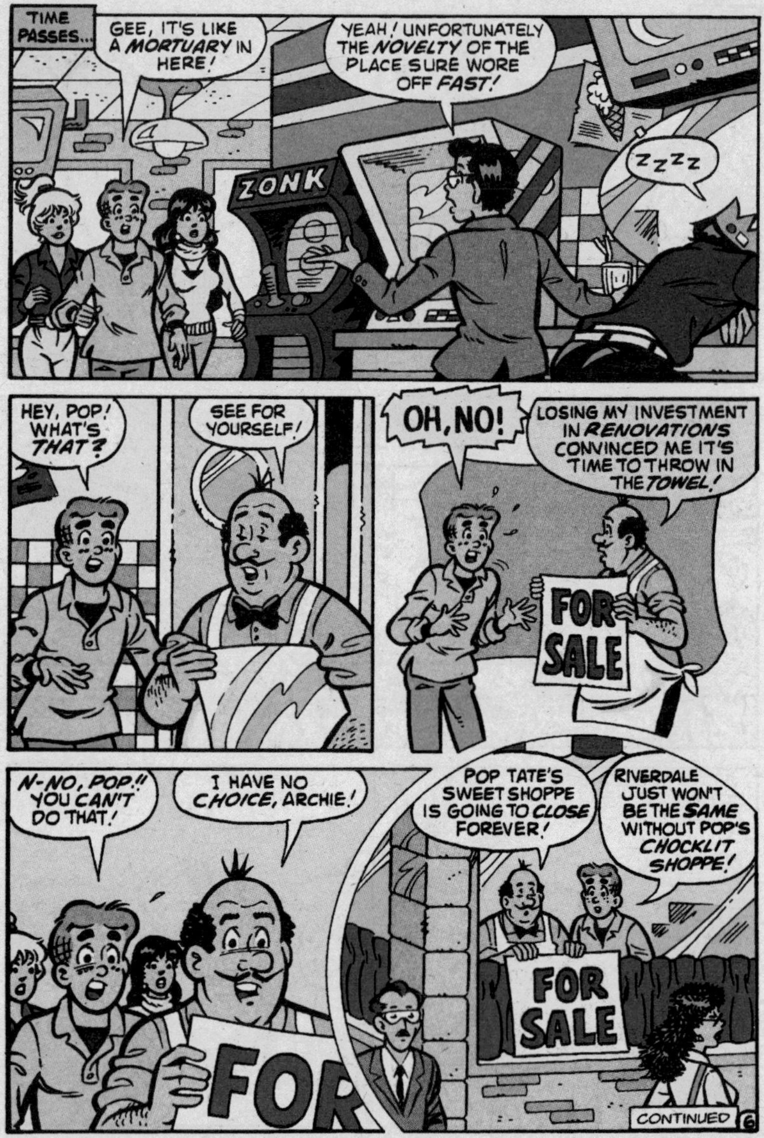
TIME PASSES...
GEE, IT'S LIKE A MORTUARY IN HERE!
YEAH! UNFORTUNATELY THE NOVELTY OF THE PLACE SURE WORE OFF FAST!
ZONK
ZZZZ
HEY, POP! WHAT'S THAT?
SEE FOR YOURSELF!
OH, NO!
LOSING MY INVESTMENT IN RENOVATIONS CONVINCED ME IT'S TIME TO THROW IN THE TOWEL!
FOR SALE
N-NO, POP!! YOU CAN'T DO THAT!
I HAVE NO CHOICE, ARCHIE!
FOR
POP TATE'S SWEET SHOPPE IS GOING TO CLOSE FOREVER!
RIVERDALE JUST WON'T BE THE SAME WITHOUT POP'S CHOCKLIT SHOPPE!
FOR SALE
CONTINUED
6

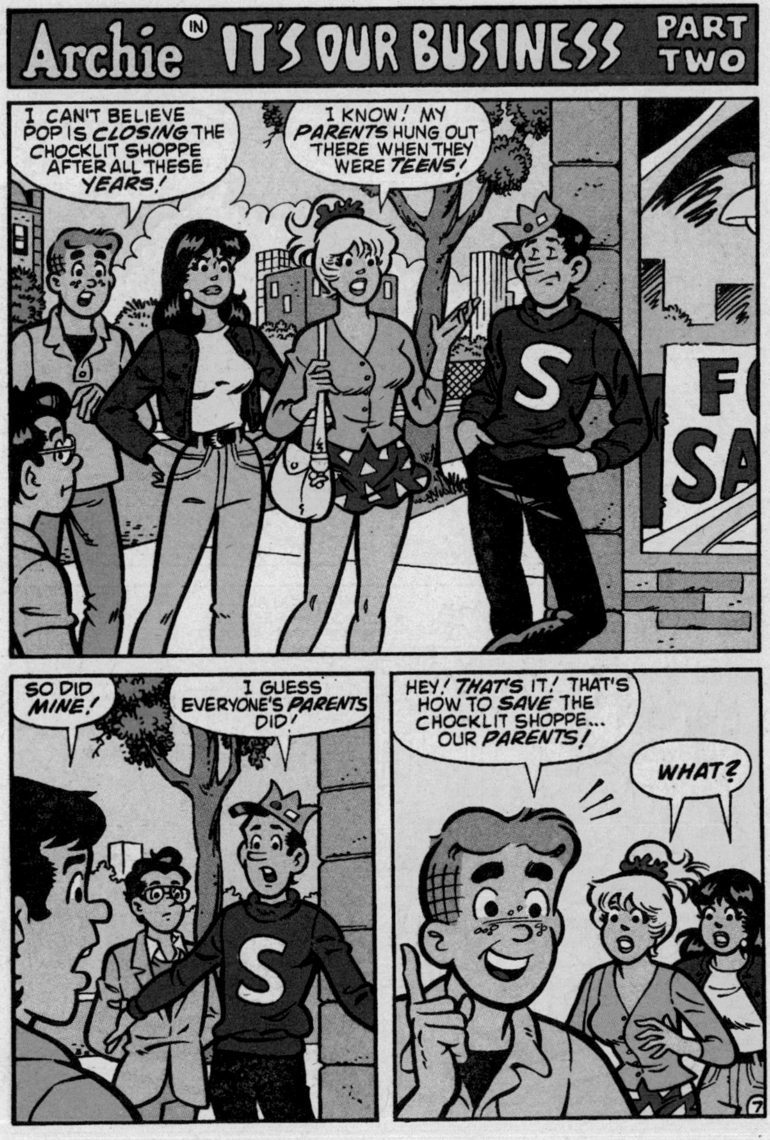
Archie IN IT'S OUR BUSINESS PART TWO
I CAN'T BELIEVE POP IS CLOSING THE CHOCKLIT SHOPPE AFTER ALL THESE YEARS!
I KNOW! MY PARENTS HUNG OUT THERE WHEN THEY WERE TEENS!
SO DID MINE!
I GUESS EVERYONE'S PARENTS DID!
HEY! THAT'S IT! THAT'S HOW TO SAVE THE CHOCKLIT SHOPPE... OUR PARENTS!
WHAT?
7

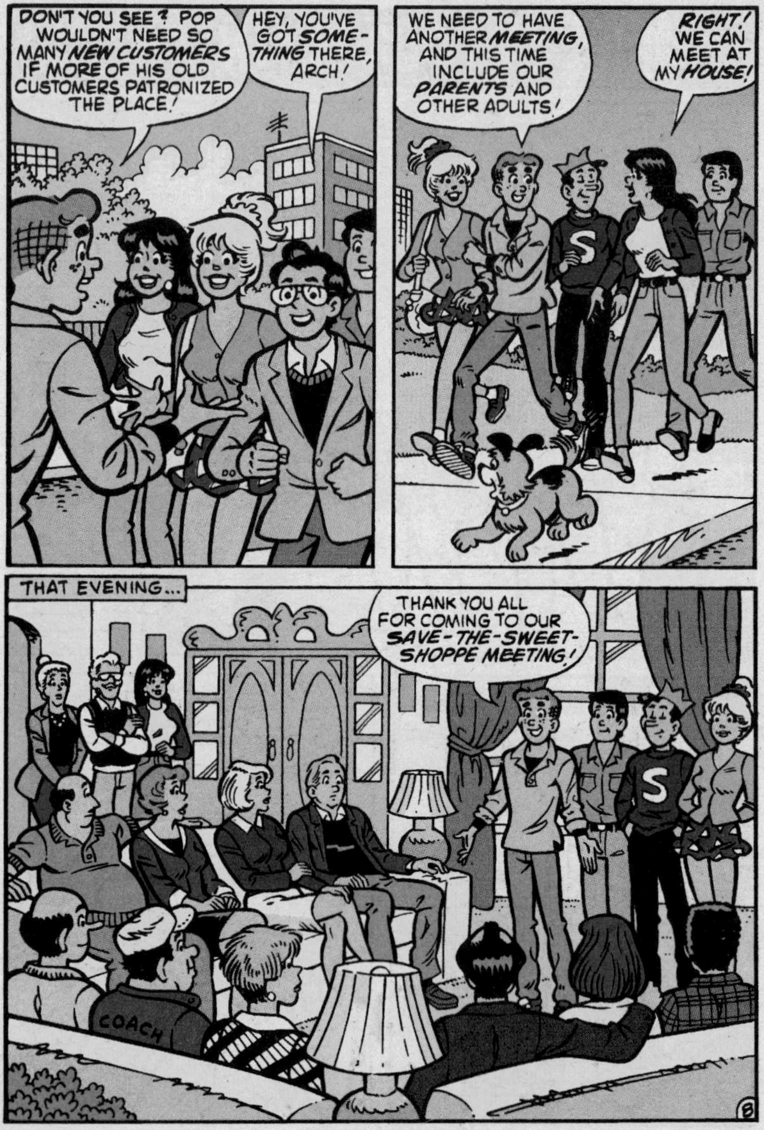

DON'T YOU SEE? POP WOULDN'T NEED SO MANY NEW CUSTOMERS IF MORE OF HIS OLD CUSTOMERS PATRONIZED THE PLACE!
HEY, YOU'VE GOT SOME-THING THERE, ARCH!
WE NEED TO HAVE ANOTHER MEETING, AND THIS TIME INCLUDE OUR PARENTS AND OTHER ADULTS!
RIGHT! WE CAN MEET AT MY HOUSE!
THAT EVENING...
THANK YOU ALL FOR COMING TO OUR SAVE-THE-SWEET-SHOPPE MEETING!
S
S
COACH
8

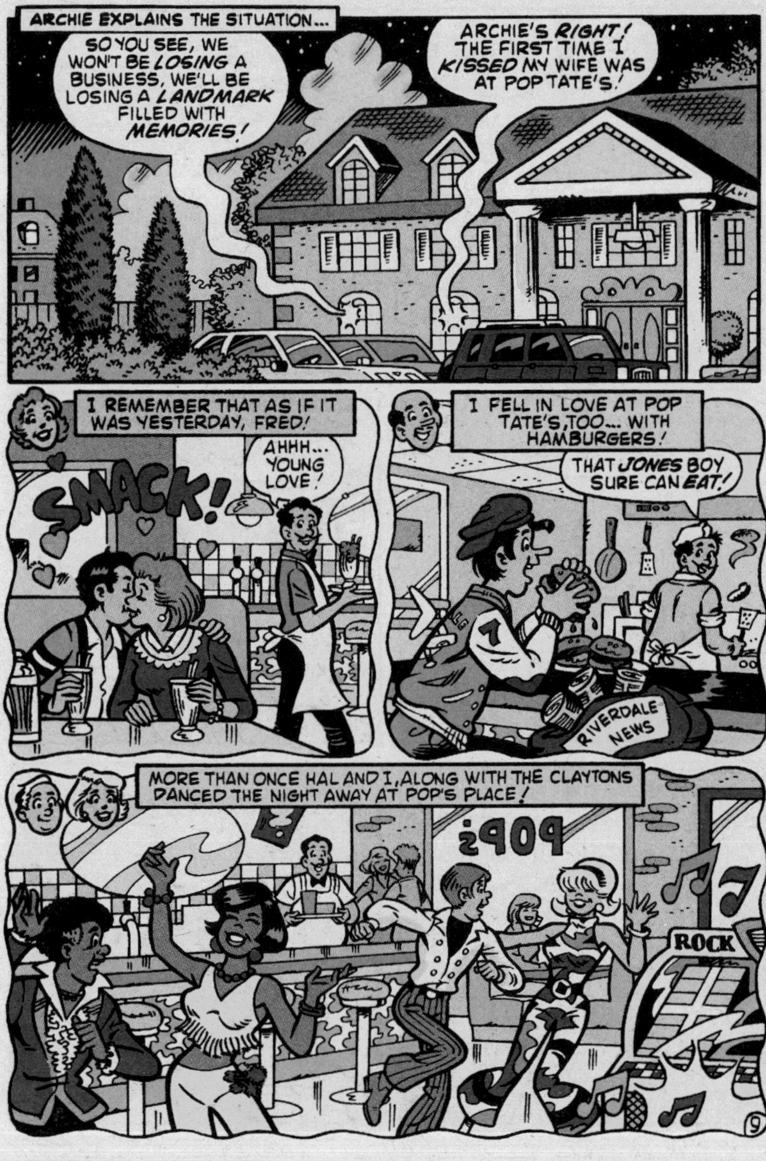

ARCHIE EXPLAINS THE SITUATION...
SO YOU SEE, WE WON'T BE *LOSING* A BUSINESS, WE'LL BE LOSING A *LANDMARK* FILLED WITH *MEMORIES*!
ARCHIE'S *RIGHT*! THE FIRST TIME I *KISSED* MY WIFE WAS AT POP TATE'S!
I REMEMBER THAT AS IF IT WAS YESTERDAY, FRED!
SMACK!
AHHH... YOUNG LOVE!
I FELL IN LOVE AT POP TATE'S, TOO... WITH HAMBURGERS!
THAT *JONES* BOY SURE CAN *EAT*!
RIVERDALE NEWS
MORE THAN ONCE HAL AND I, ALONG WITH THE CLAYTONS DANCED THE NIGHT AWAY AT POP'S PLACE!
POP'S
ROCK

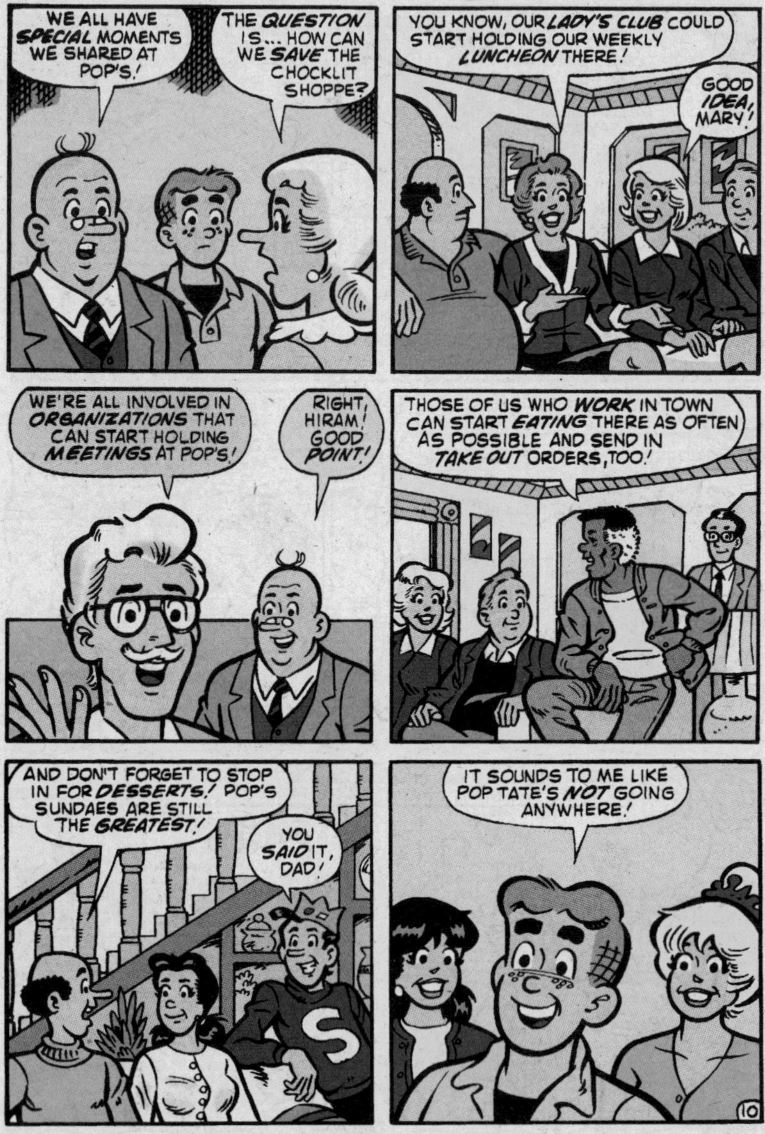
WE ALL HAVE SPECIAL MOMENTS WE SHARED AT POP'S!
THE QUESTION IS... HOW CAN WE SAVE THE CHOCKLIT SHOPPE?
YOU KNOW, OUR LADY'S CLUB COULD START HOLDING OUR WEEKLY LUNCHEON THERE!
GOOD IDEA, MARY!
WE'RE ALL INVOLVED IN ORGANIZATIONS THAT CAN START HOLDING MEETINGS AT POP'S!
RIGHT, HIRAM! GOOD POINT!
THOSE OF US WHO WORK IN TOWN CAN START EATING THERE AS OFTEN AS POSSIBLE AND SEND IN TAKE OUT ORDERS, TOO!
AND DON'T FORGET TO STOP IN FOR DESSERTS! POP'S SUNDAES ARE STILL THE GREATEST!
YOU SAID IT, DAD!
IT SOUNDS TO ME LIKE POP TATE'S NOT GOING ANYWHERE!
10

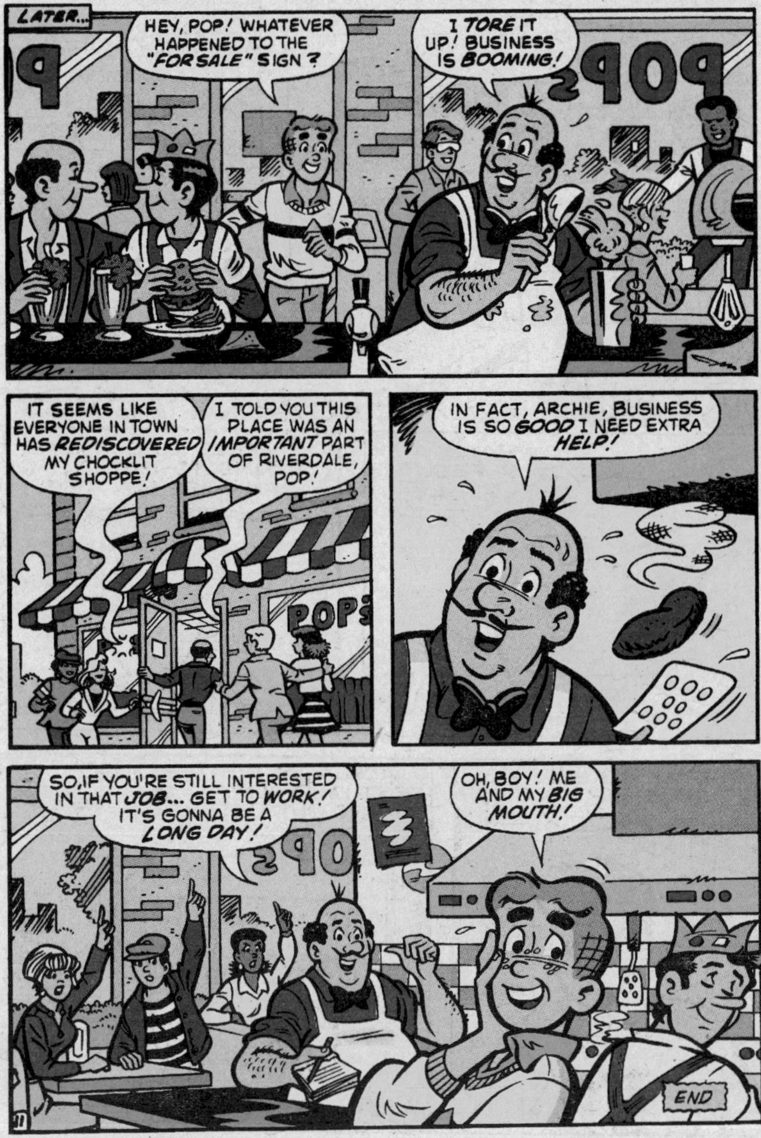
LATER...
HEY, POP! WHATEVER HAPPENED TO THE "FOR SALE" SIGN?
I TORE IT UP! BUSINESS IS BOOMING!
POP'S
IT SEEMS LIKE EVERYONE IN TOWN HAS REDISCOVERED MY CHOCKLIT SHOPPE!
I TOLD YOU THIS PLACE WAS AN IMPORTANT PART OF RIVERDALE, POP!
POP'S
IN FACT, ARCHIE, BUSINESS IS SO GOOD I NEED EXTRA HELP!
SO, IF YOU'RE STILL INTERESTED IN THAT JOB... GET TO WORK! IT'S GONNA BE A LONG DAY!
OH, BOY! ME AND MY BIG MOUTH!
END

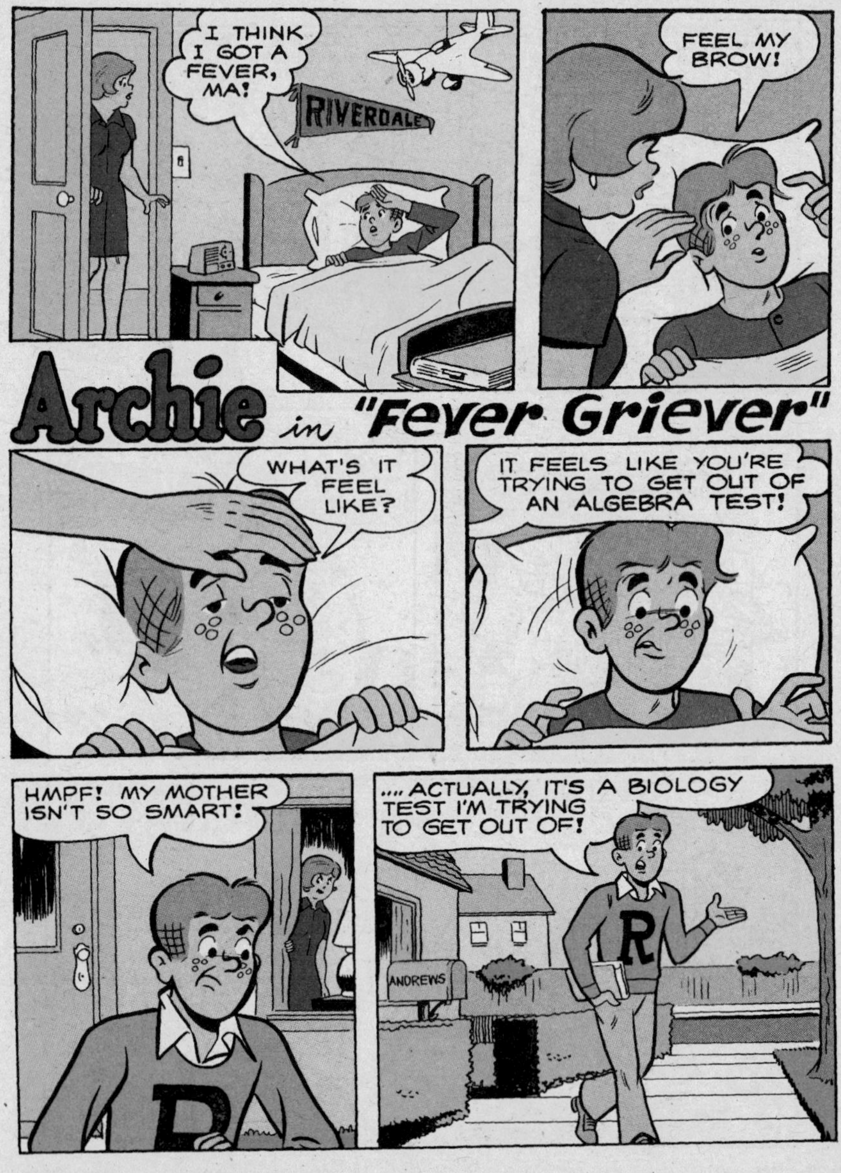
I THINK I GOT A FEVER, MA!
RIVERDALE
FEEL MY BROW!
Archie in "Fever Griever"
WHAT'S IT FEEL LIKE?
IT FEELS LIKE YOU'RE TRYING TO GET OUT OF AN ALGEBRA TEST!
HMPF! MY MOTHER ISN'T SO SMART!
....ACTUALLY, IT'S A BIOLOGY TEST I'M TRYING TO GET OUT OF!
ANDREWS

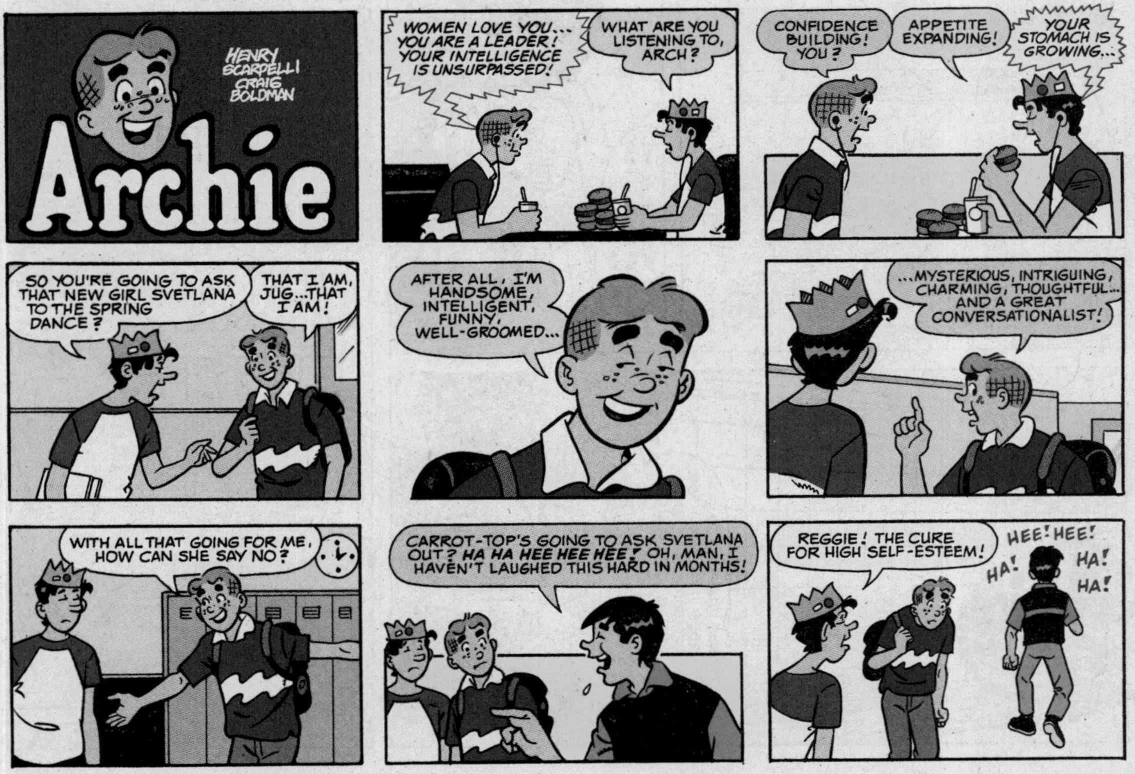
Archie
HENRY SCARPELLI CRAIG BOLDMAN
WOMEN LOVE YOU... YOU ARE A LEADER! YOUR INTELLIGENCE IS UNSURPASSED!
WHAT ARE YOU LISTENING TO, ARCH?
CONFIDENCE BUILDING! YOU?
APPETITE EXPANDING!
YOUR STOMACH IS GROWING...
SO YOU'RE GOING TO ASK THAT NEW GIRL SVETLANA TO THE SPRING DANCE?
THAT I AM, JUG...THAT I AM!
AFTER ALL, I'M HANDSOME, INTELLIGENT, FUNNY, WELL-GROOMED...
...MYSTERIOUS, INTRIGUING, CHARMING, THOUGHTFUL... AND A GREAT CONVERSATIONALIST!
WITH ALL THAT GOING FOR ME, HOW CAN SHE SAY NO?
CARROT-TOP'S GOING TO ASK SVETLANA OUT? HA HA HEE HEE HEE! OH, MAN, I HAVEN'T LAUGHED THIS HARD IN MONTHS!
REGGIE! THE CURE FOR HIGH SELF-ESTEEM!
HEE! HEE!
HA!
HA!
HA!

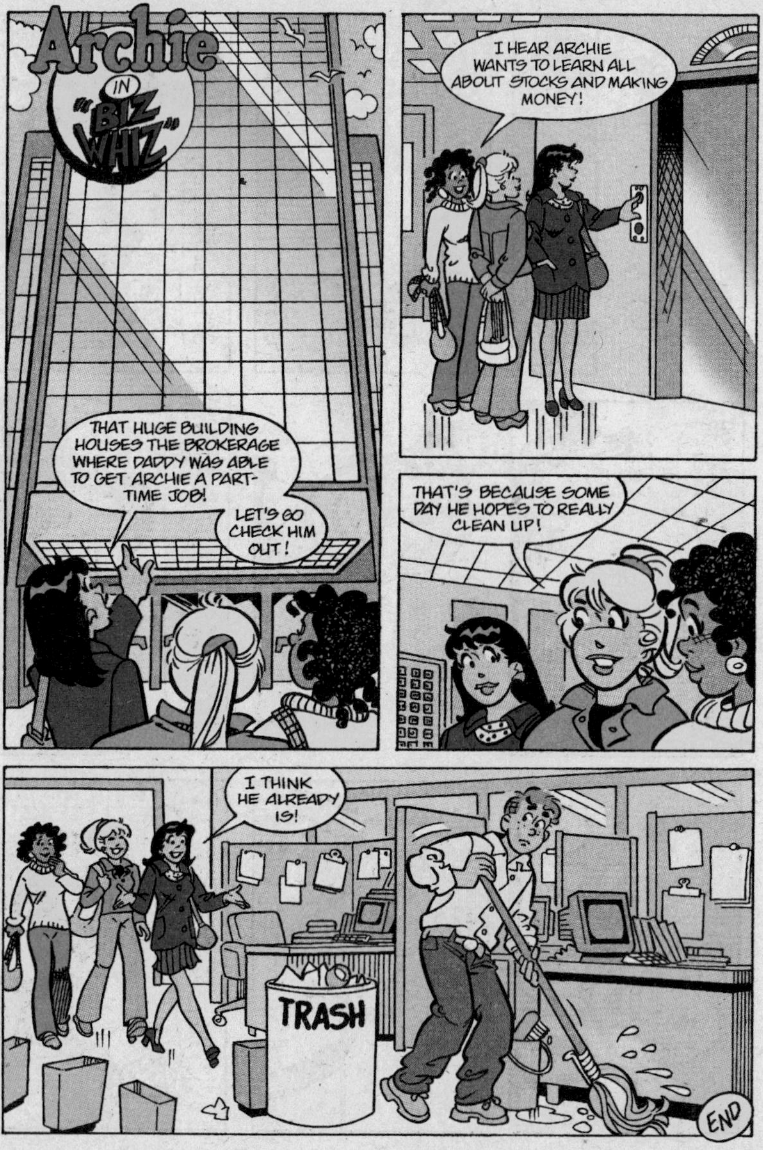
Archie
IN "BIZ WHIZ"
THAT HUGE BUILDING HOUSES THE BROKERAGE WHERE DADDY WAS ABLE TO GET ARCHIE A PART-TIME JOB!
LET'S GO CHECK HIM OUT!
I HEAR ARCHIE WANTS TO LEARN ALL ABOUT STOCKS AND MAKING MONEY!
THAT'S BECAUSE SOME DAY HE HOPES TO REALLY CLEAN UP!
I THINK HE ALREADY IS!
TRASH
END

Veronica in MONEY MATTERS... NOT!

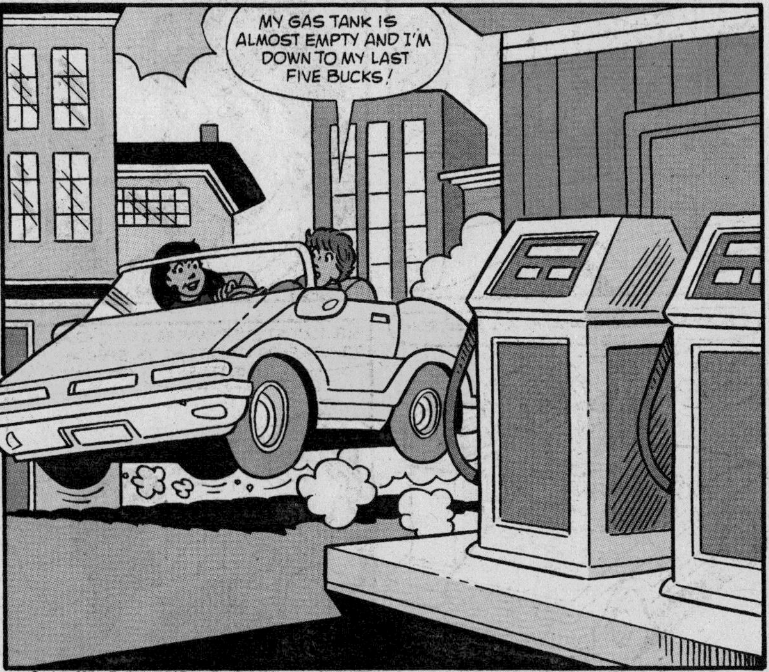
MY GAS TANK IS ALMOST EMPTY AND I'M DOWN TO MY LAST FIVE BUCKS!

Script: Mike Pellowski / Pencils: Pat Kennedy / Inks: Rudy Lapick / Letters: Bill Yoshida / Colors: Barry Grossman

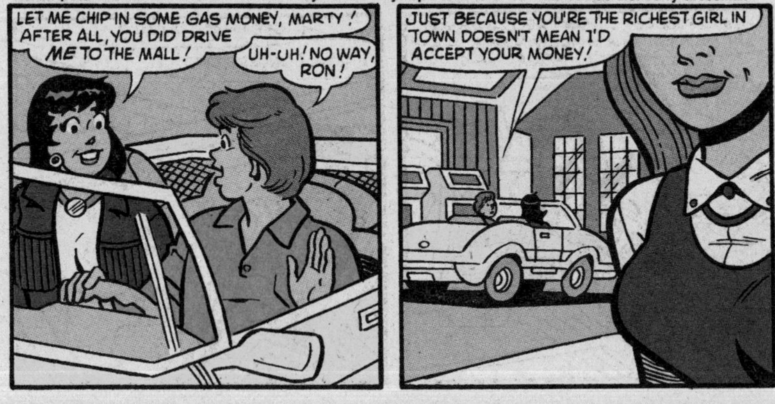
LET ME CHIP IN SOME GAS MONEY, MARTY! AFTER ALL, YOU DID DRIVE *ME* TO THE MALL!
UH-UH! NO WAY, RON!
JUST BECAUSE YOU'RE THE RICHEST GIRL IN TOWN DOESN'T MEAN I'D ACCEPT YOUR MONEY!

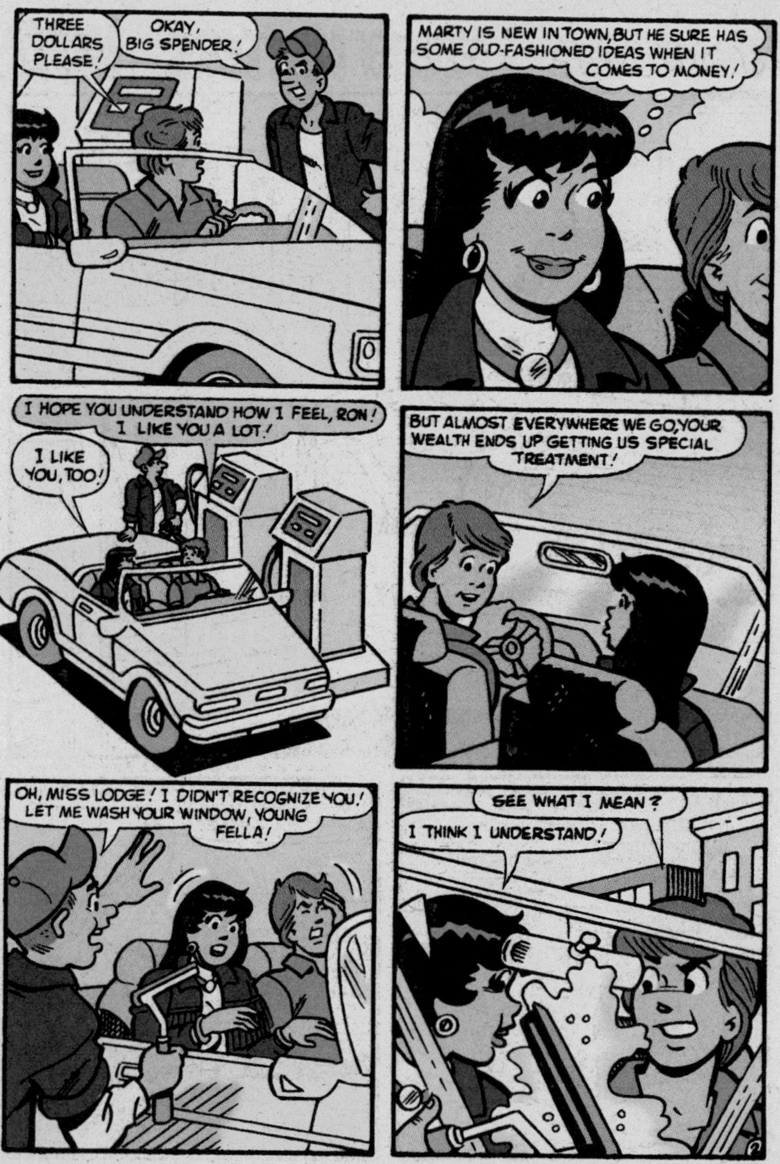
THREE DOLLARS PLEASE!
OKAY, BIG SPENDER!
MARTY IS NEW IN TOWN, BUT HE SURE HAS SOME OLD-FASHIONED IDEAS WHEN IT COMES TO MONEY!
I HOPE YOU UNDERSTAND HOW I FEEL, RON! I LIKE YOU A LOT!
I LIKE YOU, TOO!
BUT ALMOST EVERYWHERE WE GO, YOUR WEALTH ENDS UP GETTING US SPECIAL TREATMENT!
OH, MISS LODGE! I DIDN'T RECOGNIZE YOU! LET ME WASH YOUR WINDOW, YOUNG FELLA!
SEE WHAT I MEAN?
I THINK I UNDERSTAND!
2

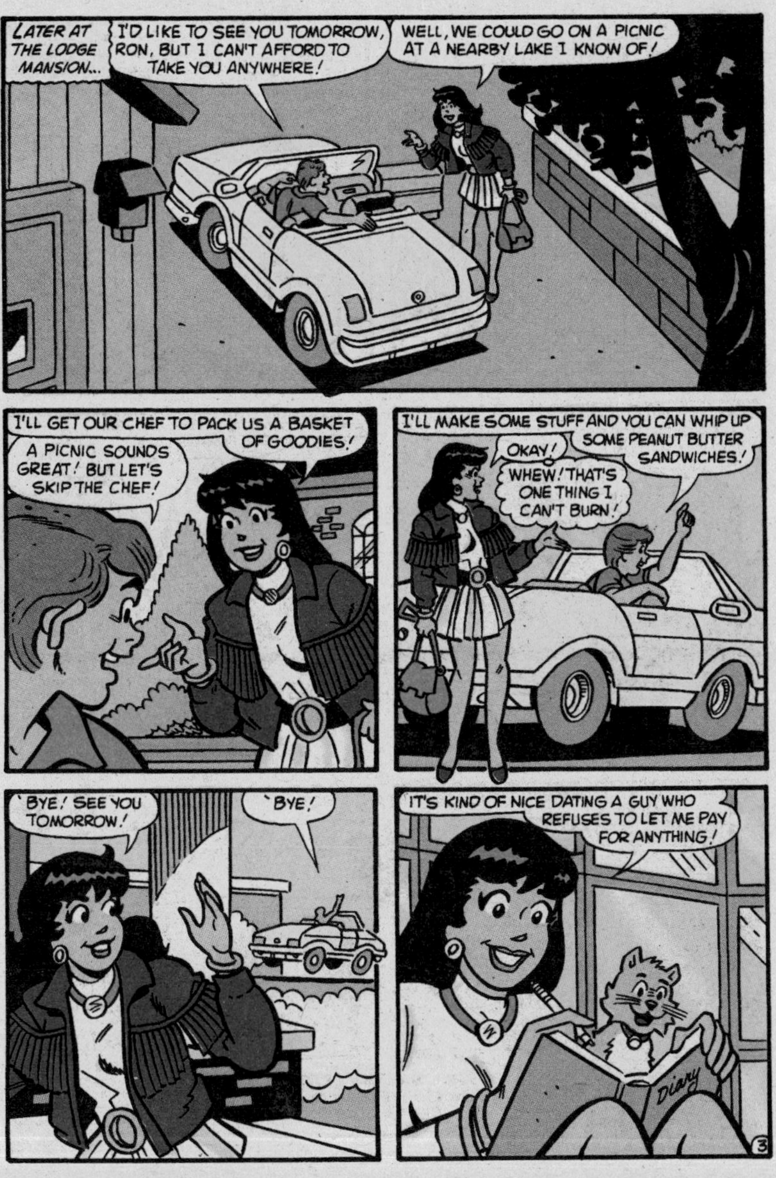
LATER AT THE LODGE MANSION...
I'D LIKE TO SEE YOU TOMORROW, RON, BUT I CAN'T AFFORD TO TAKE YOU ANYWHERE!
WELL, WE COULD GO ON A PICNIC AT A NEARBY LAKE I KNOW OF!
I'LL GET OUR CHEF TO PACK US A BASKET OF GOODIES!
A PICNIC SOUNDS GREAT! BUT LET'S SKIP THE CHEF!
I'LL MAKE SOME STUFF AND YOU CAN WHIP UP SOME PEANUT BUTTER SANDWICHES!
OKAY!
WHEW! THAT'S ONE THING I CAN'T BURN!
'BYE! SEE YOU TOMORROW!
'BYE!
IT'S KIND OF NICE DATING A GUY WHO REFUSES TO LET ME PAY FOR ANYTHING!
Diary
3

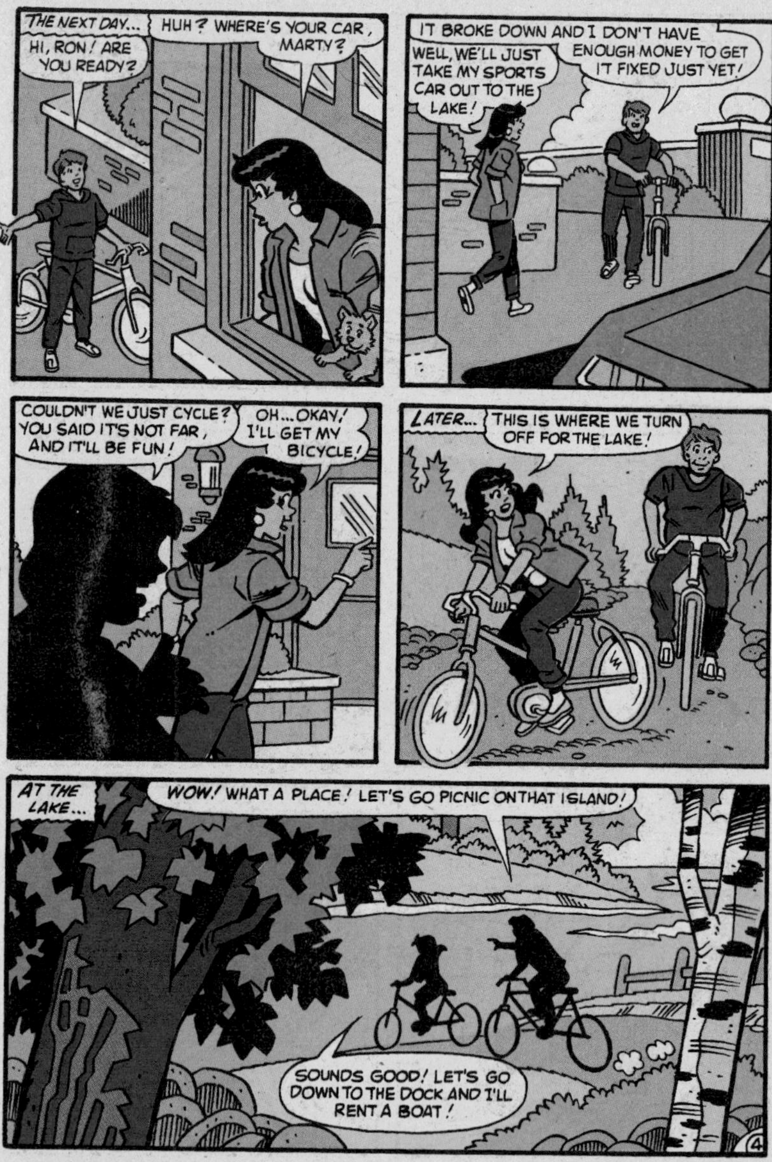
THE NEXT DAY...
HI, RON! ARE YOU READY?
HUH? WHERE'S YOUR CAR, MARTY?
IT BROKE DOWN AND I DON'T HAVE ENOUGH MONEY TO GET IT FIXED JUST YET!
WELL, WE'LL JUST TAKE MY SPORTS CAR OUT TO THE LAKE!
COULDN'T WE JUST CYCLE? YOU SAID IT'S NOT FAR, AND IT'LL BE FUN!
OH...OKAY! I'LL GET MY BICYCLE!
LATER...
THIS IS WHERE WE TURN OFF FOR THE LAKE!
AT THE LAKE...
WOW! WHAT A PLACE! LET'S GO PICNIC ON THAT ISLAND!
SOUNDS GOOD! LET'S GO DOWN TO THE DOCK AND I'LL RENT A BOAT!
4

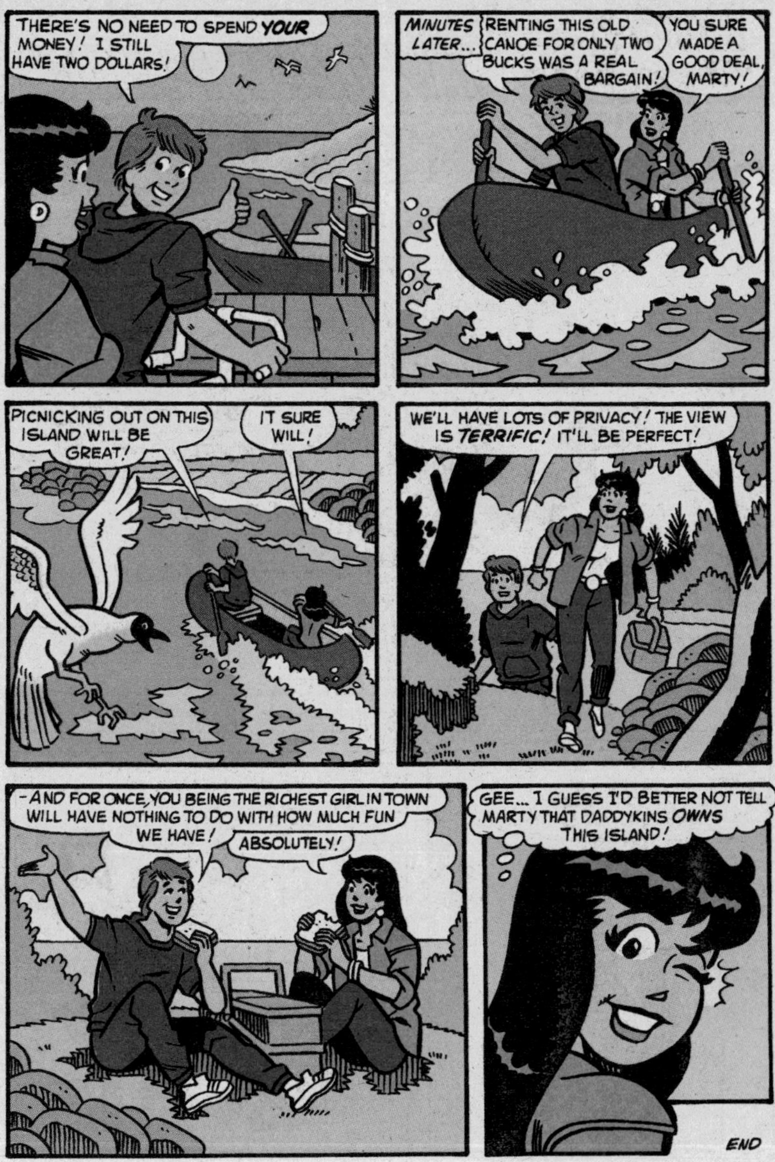
THERE'S NO NEED TO SPEND *YOUR* MONEY! I STILL HAVE TWO DOLLARS!
MINUTES LATER...
RENTING THIS OLD CANOE FOR ONLY TWO BUCKS WAS A REAL BARGAIN!
YOU SURE MADE A GOOD DEAL, MARTY!
PICNICKING OUT ON THIS ISLAND WILL BE GREAT!
IT SURE WILL!
WE'LL HAVE LOTS OF PRIVACY! THE VIEW IS *TERRIFIC!* IT'LL BE PERFECT!
-AND FOR ONCE, YOU BEING THE RICHEST GIRL IN TOWN WILL HAVE NOTHING TO DO WITH HOW MUCH FUN WE HAVE!
ABSOLUTELY!
GEE... I GUESS I'D BETTER NOT TELL MARTY THAT DADDYKINS *OWNS* THIS ISLAND!
END

Betty and Veronica in T.V. TEST PILOT

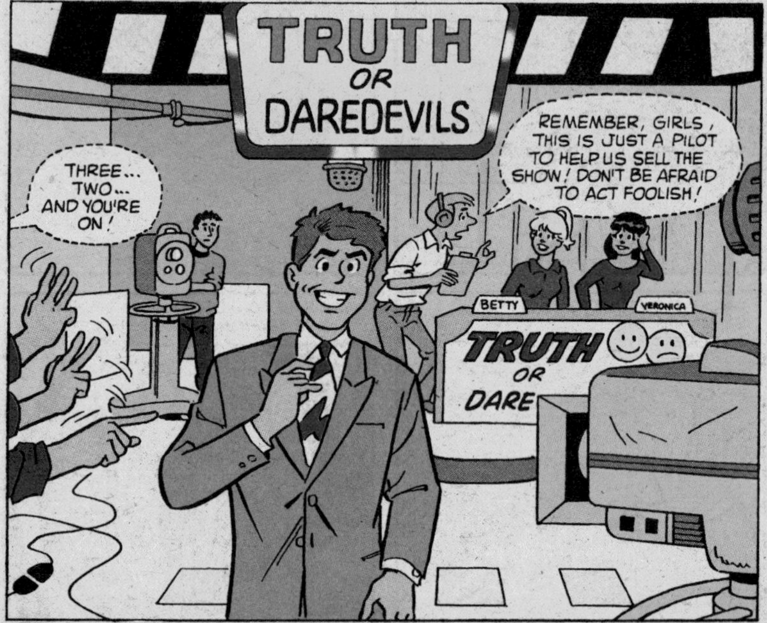
TRUTH OR DAREDEVILS
THREE... TWO... AND YOU'RE ON!
REMEMBER, GIRLS, THIS IS JUST A PILOT TO HELP US SELL THE SHOW! DON'T BE AFRAID TO ACT FOOLISH!
BETTY
VERONICA
TRUTH OR DARE

Script: George Gladir / Pencils: Dan DeCarlo / Inks: Jimmy DeCarlo / Letters: Bill Yoshida / Colors: Barry Grossman

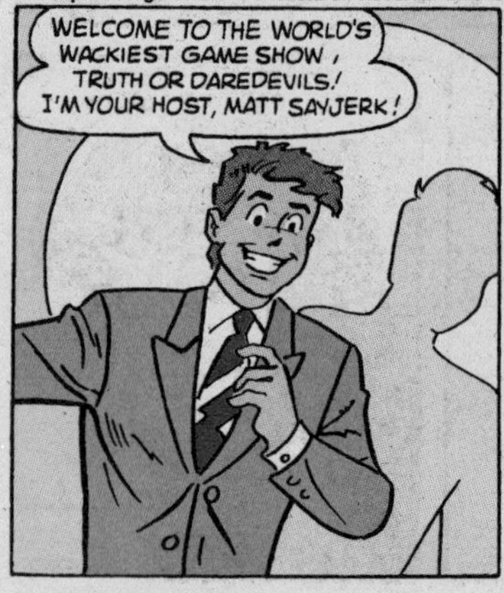
WELCOME TO THE WORLD'S WACKIEST GAME SHOW, TRUTH OR DAREDEVILS! I'M YOUR HOST, MATT SAYJERK!

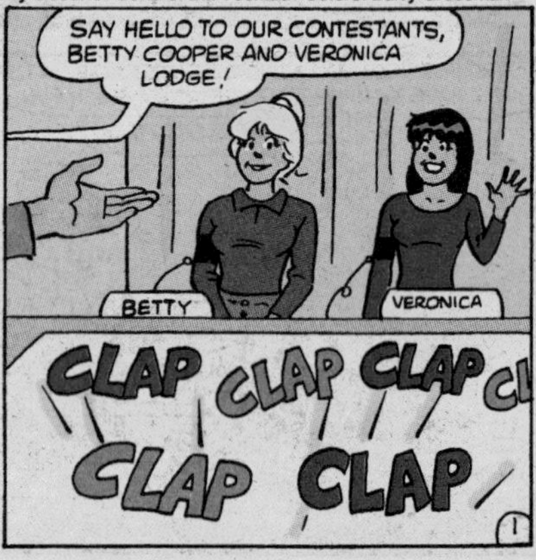
SAY HELLO TO OUR CONTESTANTS, BETTY COOPER AND VERONICA LODGE!
BETTY
VERONICA
CLAP CLAP CLAP
CLAP CLAP

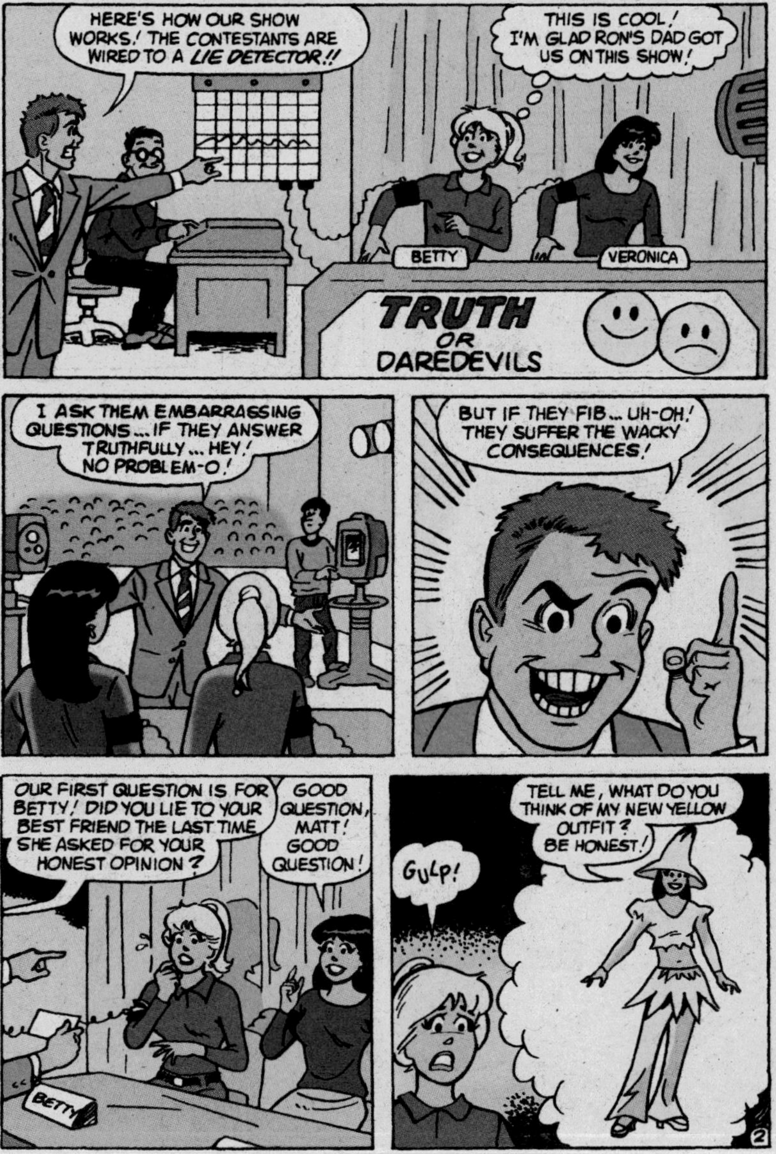
HERE'S HOW OUR SHOW WORKS! THE CONTESTANTS ARE WIRED TO A LIE DETECTOR!!
THIS IS COOL! I'M GLAD RON'S DAD GOT US ON THIS SHOW!
BETTY
VERONICA
TRUTH OR DAREDEVILS
I ASK THEM EMBARRASSING QUESTIONS... IF THEY ANSWER TRUTHFULLY... HEY! NO PROBLEM-O!
BUT IF THEY FIB... UH-OH! THEY SUFFER THE WACKY CONSEQUENCES!
OUR FIRST QUESTION IS FOR BETTY! DID YOU LIE TO YOUR BEST FRIEND THE LAST TIME SHE ASKED FOR YOUR HONEST OPINION?
GOOD QUESTION, MATT! GOOD QUESTION!
BETTY
GULP!
TELL ME, WHAT DO YOU THINK OF MY NEW YELLOW OUTFIT? BE HONEST!
2

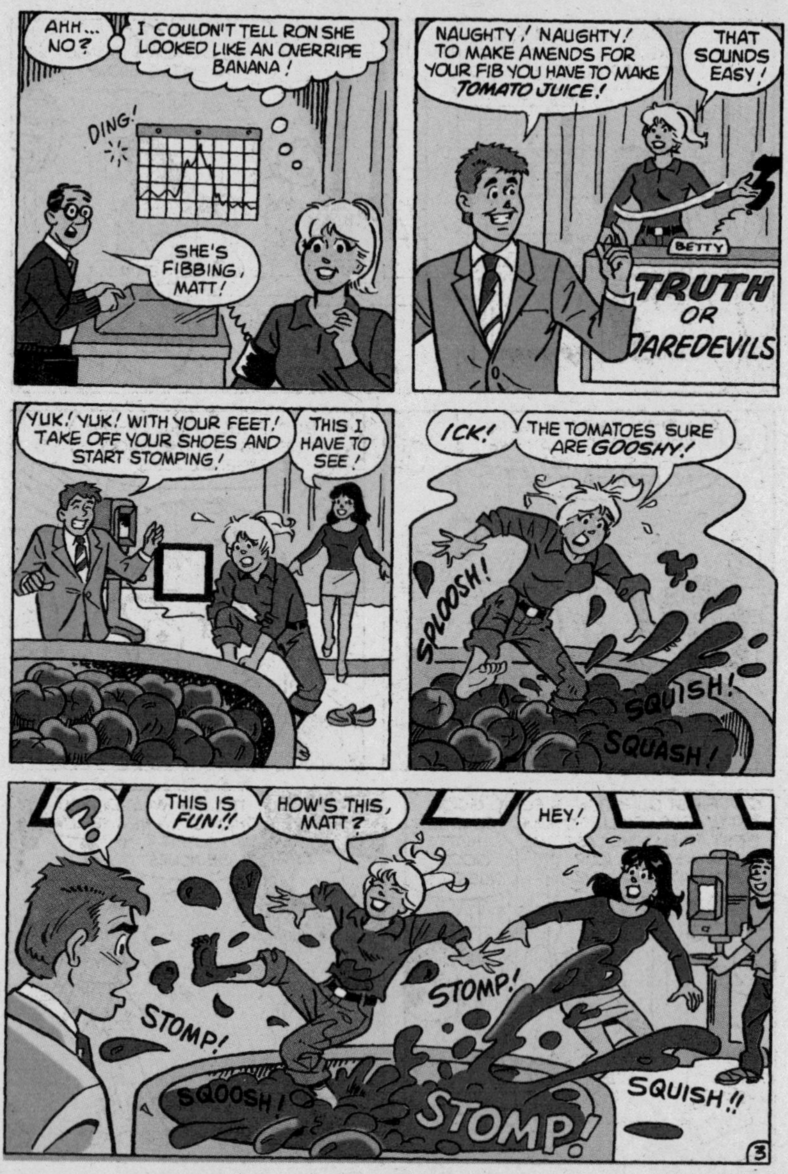
AHH... NO?
I COULDN'T TELL RON SHE LOOKED LIKE AN OVERRIPE BANANA!
DING!
SHE'S FIBBING, MATT!
NAUGHTY! NAUGHTY! TO MAKE AMENDS FOR YOUR FIB YOU HAVE TO MAKE TOMATO JUICE!
THAT SOUNDS EASY!
BETTY
TRUTH OR DAREDEVILS
YUK! YUK! WITH YOUR FEET! TAKE OFF YOUR SHOES AND START STOMPING!
THIS I HAVE TO SEE!
ICK!
THE TOMATOES SURE ARE GOOSHY!
SPLOOSH!
SQUISH!
SQUASH!
?
THIS IS FUN!!
HOW'S THIS, MATT?
HEY!
STOMP!
STOMP!
SQOOSH!
STOMP!
SQUISH!!
3

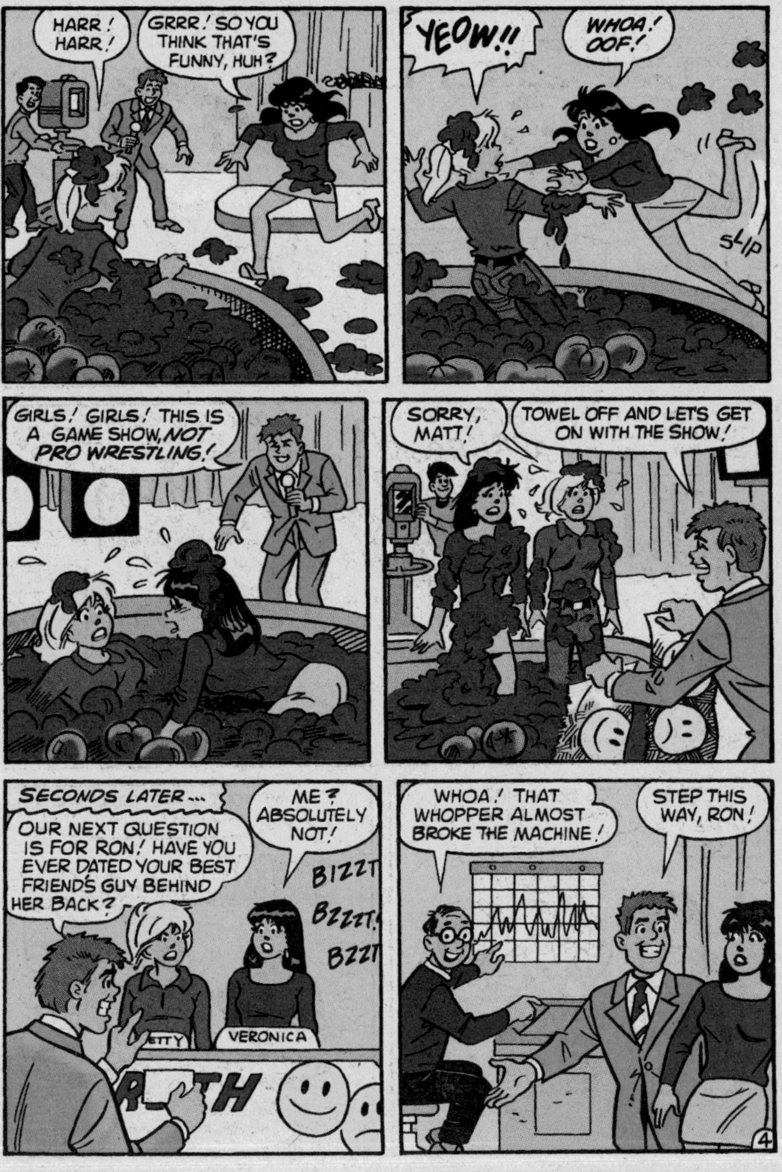
HARR! HARR!
GRRR! SO YOU THINK THAT'S FUNNY, HUH?
YEOW!!
WHOA! OOF!
SLIP
GIRLS! GIRLS! THIS IS A GAME SHOW, NOT PRO WRESTLING!
SORRY, MATT!
TOWEL OFF AND LET'S GET ON WITH THE SHOW!
SECONDS LATER...
OUR NEXT QUESTION IS FOR RON! HAVE YOU EVER DATED YOUR BEST FRIEND'S GUY BEHIND HER BACK?
ME? ABSOLUTELY NOT!
BIZZT
BZZZT!
BZZT
VERONICA
WHOA! THAT WHOPPER ALMOST BROKE THE MACHINE!
STEP THIS WAY, RON!
4

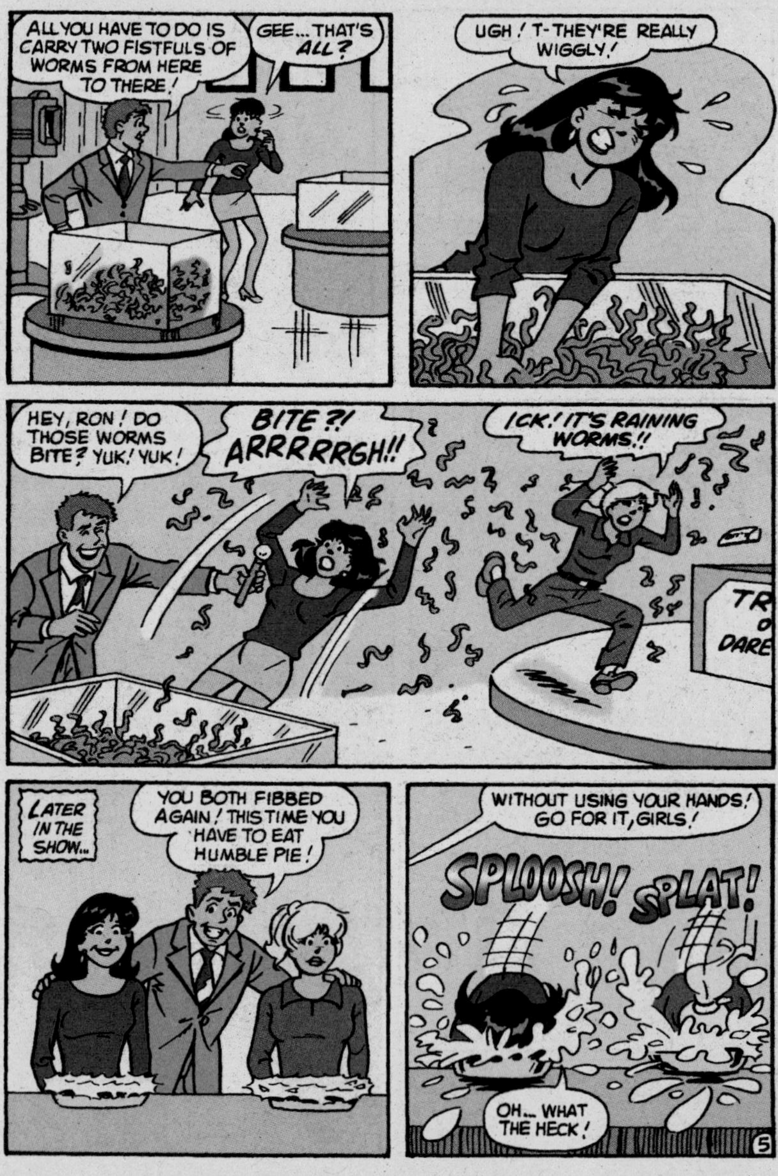
ALL YOU HAVE TO DO IS CARRY TWO FISTFULS OF WORMS FROM HERE TO THERE!
GEE... THAT'S ALL?
UGH! T-THEY'RE REALLY WIGGLY!
HEY, RON! DO THOSE WORMS BITE? YUK! YUK!
BITE?! ARRRRRGH!!
ICK! IT'S RAINING WORMS!!
TR
O
DARE
LATER IN THE SHOW...
YOU BOTH FIBBED AGAIN! THIS TIME YOU HAVE TO EAT HUMBLE PIE!
WITHOUT USING YOUR HANDS! GO FOR IT, GIRLS!
SPLOOSH! SPLAT!
OH... WHAT THE HECK!
5

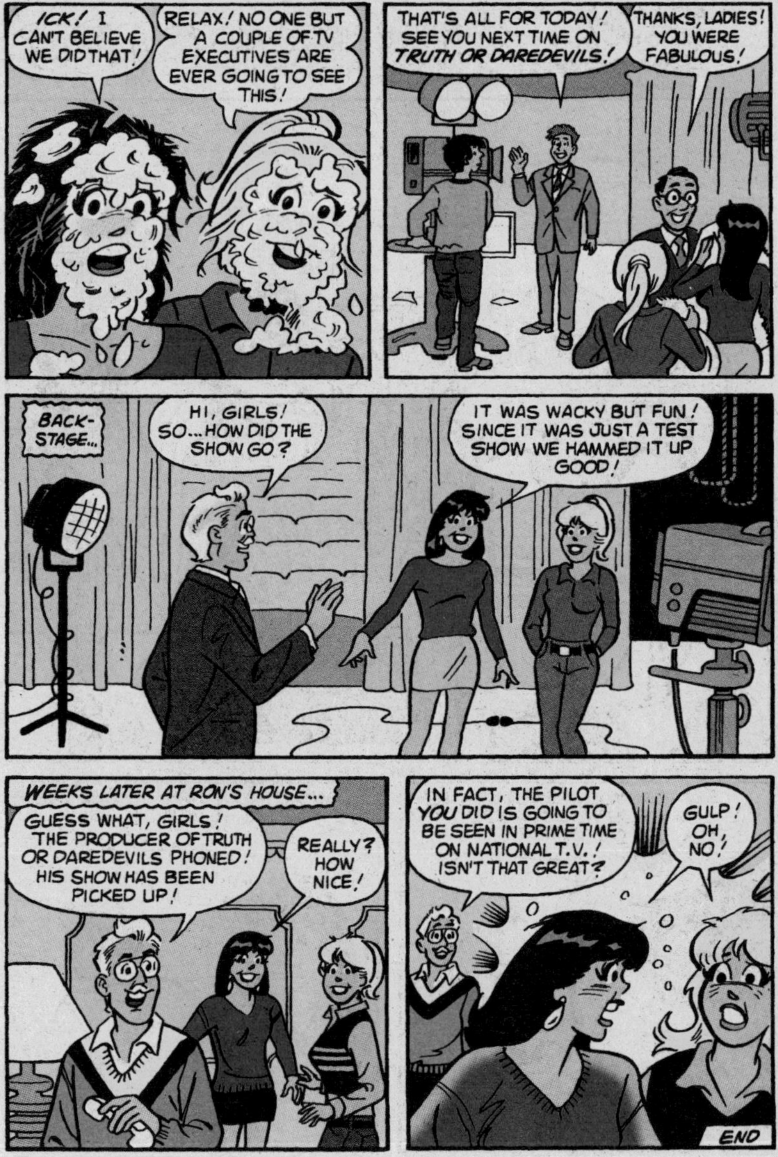
ICK! I CAN'T BELIEVE WE DID THAT!
RELAX! NO ONE BUT A COUPLE OF TV EXECUTIVES ARE EVER GOING TO SEE THIS!
THAT'S ALL FOR TODAY! SEE YOU NEXT TIME ON TRUTH OR DAREDEVILS!
THANKS, LADIES! YOU WERE FABULOUS!
BACK-STAGE...
HI, GIRLS! SO...HOW DID THE SHOW GO?
IT WAS WACKY BUT FUN! SINCE IT WAS JUST A TEST SHOW WE HAMMED IT UP GOOD!
WEEKS LATER AT RON'S HOUSE...
GUESS WHAT, GIRLS! THE PRODUCER OF TRUTH OR DAREDEVILS PHONED! HIS SHOW HAS BEEN PICKED UP!
REALLY? HOW NICE!
IN FACT, THE PILOT YOU DID IS GOING TO BE SEEN IN PRIME TIME ON NATIONAL T.V.! ISN'T THAT GREAT?
GULP! OH, NO!
END

Betty and Veronica in "THE INS AND OUTS"

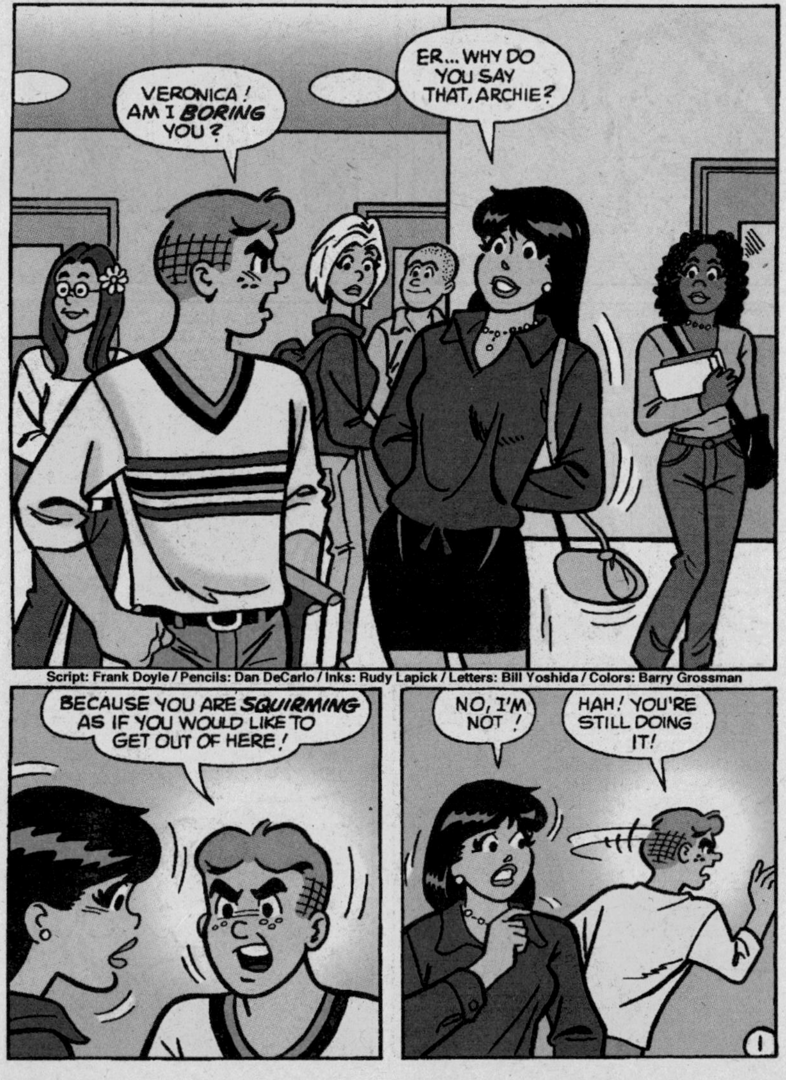
VERONICA! AM I BORING YOU?
ER... WHY DO YOU SAY THAT, ARCHIE?
Script: Frank Doyle / Pencils: Dan DeCarlo / Inks: Rudy Lapick / Letters: Bill Yoshida / Colors: Barry Grossman
BECAUSE YOU ARE SQUIRMING AS IF YOU WOULD LIKE TO GET OUT OF HERE!
NO, I'M NOT!
HAH! YOU'RE STILL DOING IT!
1

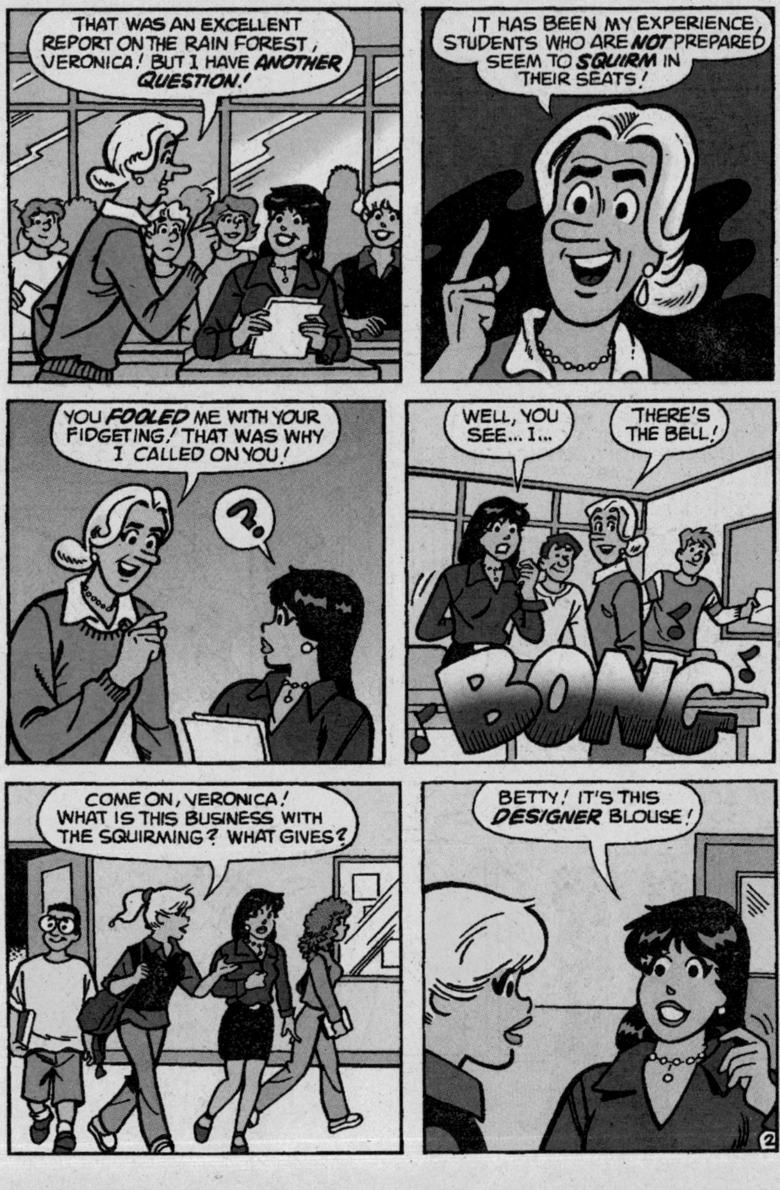
THAT WAS AN EXCELLENT REPORT ON THE RAIN FOREST, VERONICA! BUT I HAVE ANOTHER QUESTION!
IT HAS BEEN MY EXPERIENCE, STUDENTS WHO ARE NOT PREPARED SEEM TO SQUIRM IN THEIR SEATS!
YOU FOOLED ME WITH YOUR FIDGETING! THAT WAS WHY I CALLED ON YOU!
?
WELL, YOU SEE... I...
THERE'S THE BELL!
BONG
COME ON, VERONICA! WHAT IS THIS BUSINESS WITH THE SQUIRMING? WHAT GIVES?
BETTY! IT'S THIS DESIGNER BLOUSE!
2

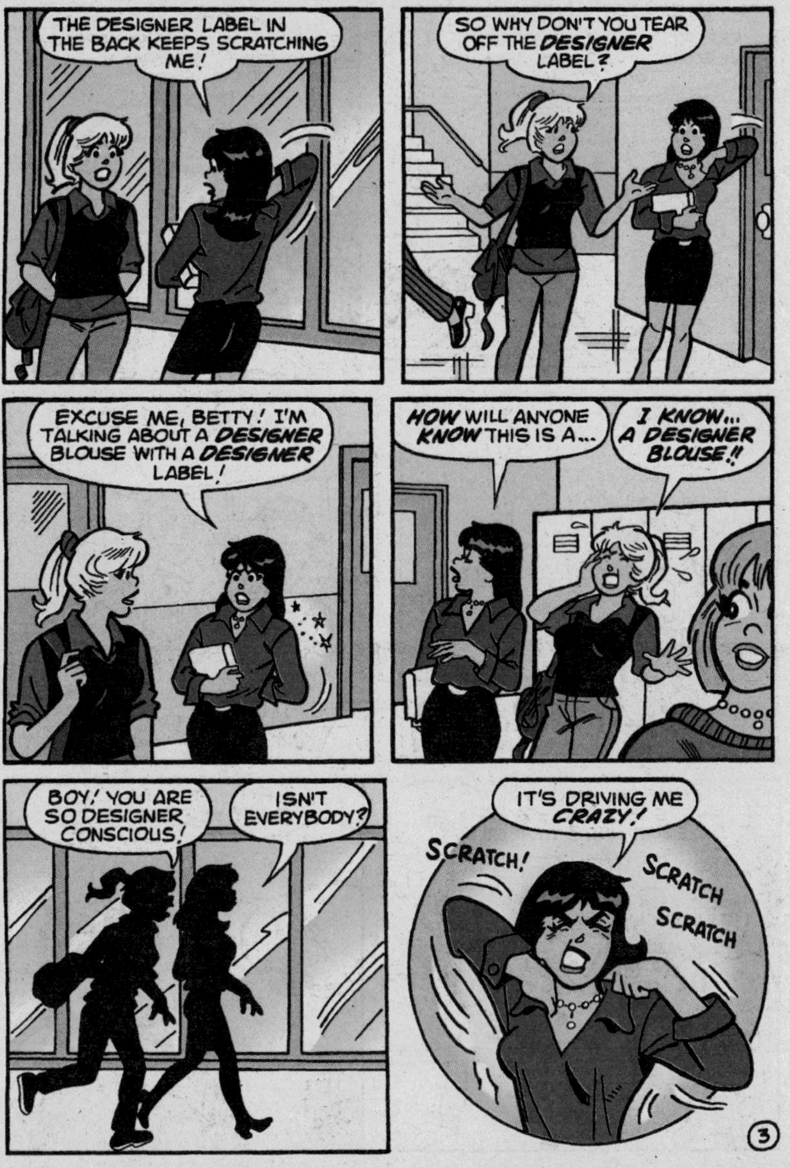
THE DESIGNER LABEL IN THE BACK KEEPS SCRATCHING ME!
SO WHY DON'T YOU TEAR OFF THE DESIGNER LABEL?
EXCUSE ME, BETTY! I'M TALKING ABOUT A DESIGNER BLOUSE WITH A DESIGNER LABEL!
HOW WILL ANYONE KNOW THIS IS A...
I KNOW... A DESIGNER BLOUSE!!
BOY! YOU ARE SO DESIGNER CONSCIOUS!
ISN'T EVERYBODY?
IT'S DRIVING ME CRAZY!
SCRATCH!
SCRATCH
SCRATCH
3

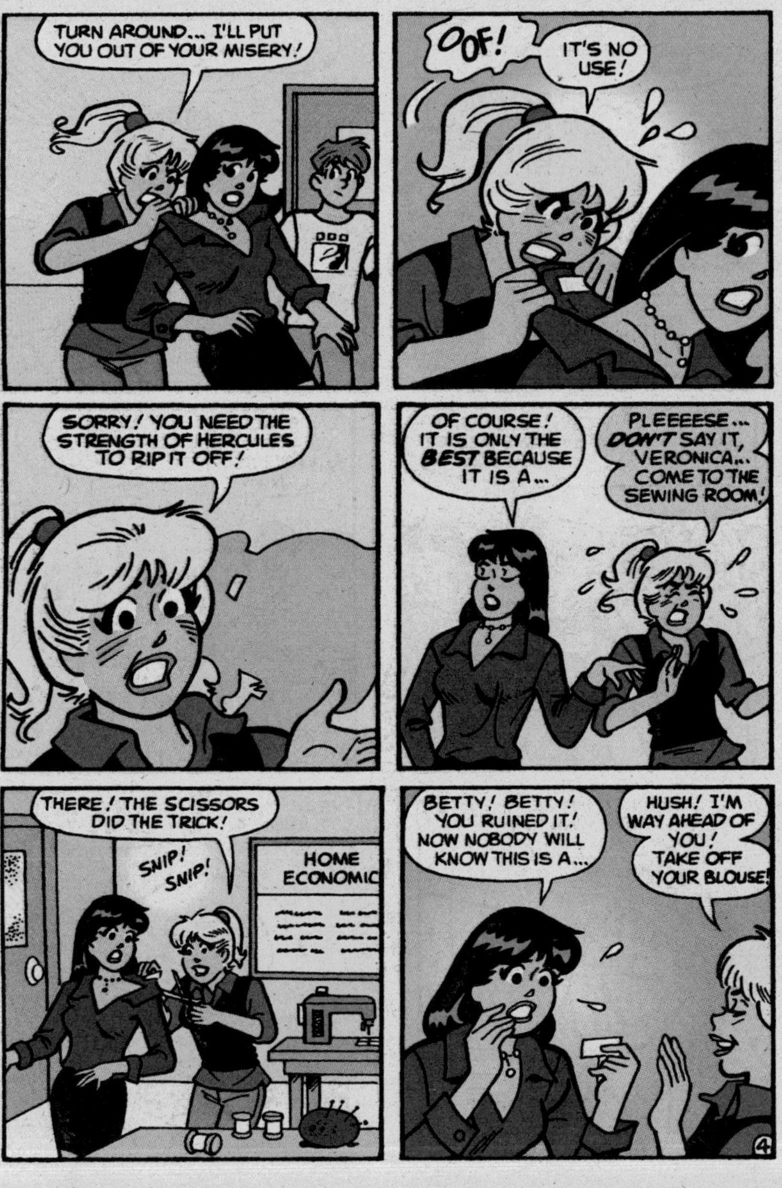
TURN AROUND... I'LL PUT YOU OUT OF YOUR MISERY!
OOF!
IT'S NO USE!
SORRY! YOU NEED THE STRENGTH OF HERCULES TO RIP IT OFF!
OF COURSE! IT IS ONLY THE BEST BECAUSE IT IS A...
PLEEEESE... DON'T SAY IT, VERONICA... COME TO THE SEWING ROOM!
THERE! THE SCISSORS DID THE TRICK!
SNIP! SNIP!
HOME ECONOMIC
BETTY! BETTY! YOU RUINED IT! NOW NOBODY WILL KNOW THIS IS A...
HUSH! I'M WAY AHEAD OF YOU! TAKE OFF YOUR BLOUSE!
4

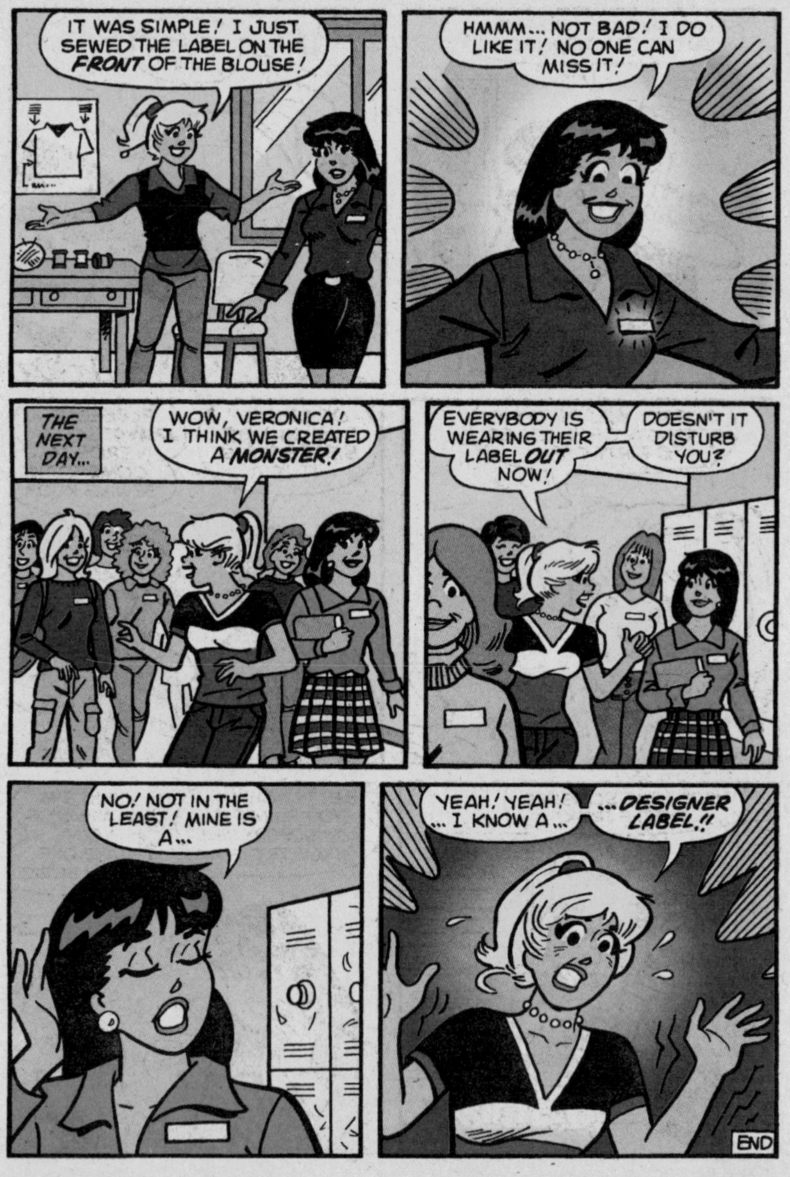
IT WAS SIMPLE! I JUST SEWED THE LABEL ON THE FRONT OF THE BLOUSE!
HMMM... NOT BAD! I DO LIKE IT! NO ONE CAN MISS IT!
THE NEXT DAY...
WOW, VERONICA! I THINK WE CREATED A MONSTER!
EVERYBODY IS WEARING THEIR LABEL OUT NOW!
DOESN'T IT DISTURB YOU?
NO! NOT IN THE LEAST! MINE IS A...
YEAH! YEAH! ... I KNOW A...
...DESIGNER LABEL!!
END

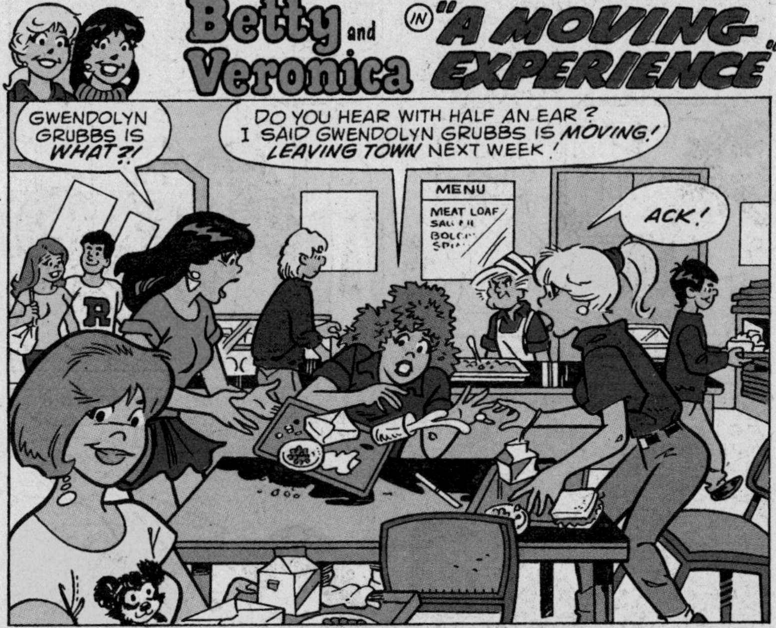
Betty and Veronica
IN "A MOVING-EXPERIENCE"
GWENDOLYN GRUBBS IS WHAT?!
DO YOU HEAR WITH HALF AN EAR? I SAID GWENDOLYN GRUBBS IS MOVING! LEAVING TOWN NEXT WEEK!
MENU
MEAT LOAF
ACK!
R

Script: Frank Doyle / Pencils: Dan DeCarlo / Inks: Rudy Lapick / Letters: Bill Yoshida / Colors: Barry Grossman

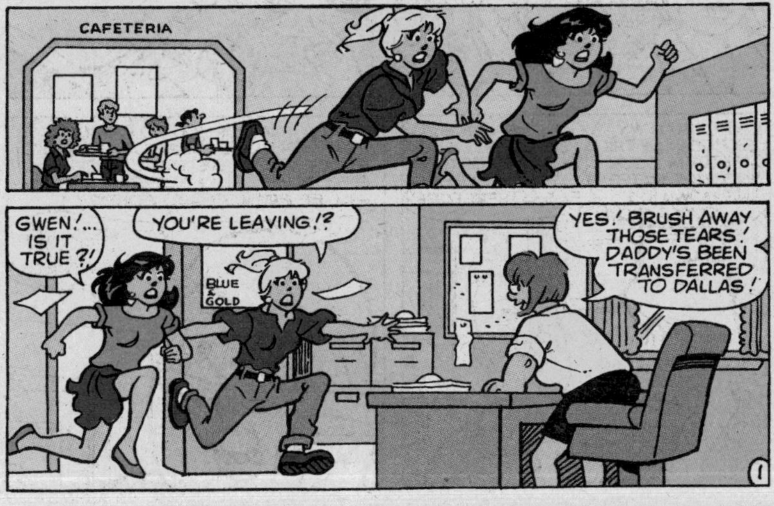
CAFETERIA
GWEN!... IS IT TRUE?!
YOU'RE LEAVING!?
BLUE & GOLD
YES! BRUSH AWAY THOSE TEARS! DADDY'S BEEN TRANSFERRED TO DALLAS!
1

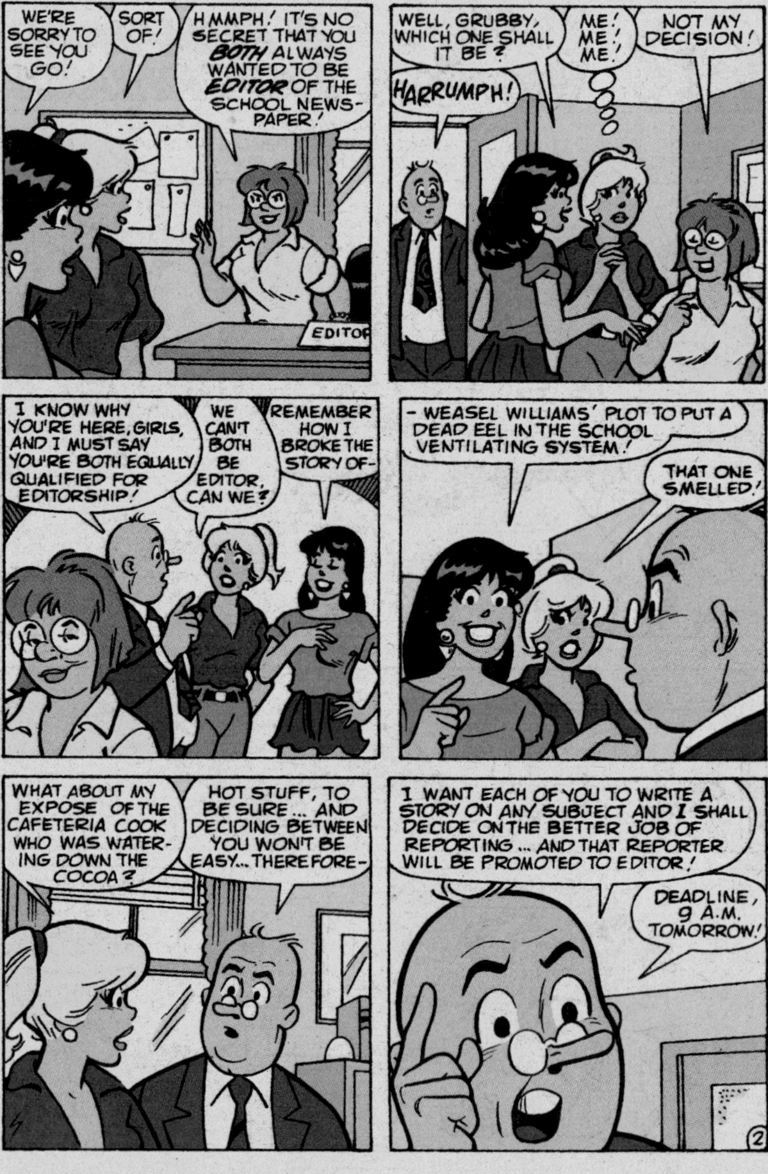
WE'RE SORRY TO SEE YOU GO!
SORT OF!
HMMPH! IT'S NO SECRET THAT YOU BOTH ALWAYS WANTED TO BE EDITOR OF THE SCHOOL NEWS-PAPER!
EDITOR
WELL, GRUBBY, WHICH ONE SHALL IT BE?
ME! ME! ME!
NOT MY DECISION!
HARRUMPH!
I KNOW WHY YOU'RE HERE, GIRLS, AND I MUST SAY YOU'RE BOTH EQUALLY QUALIFIED FOR EDITORSHIP!
WE CAN'T BOTH BE EDITOR, CAN WE?
REMEMBER HOW I BROKE THE STORY OF-
- WEASEL WILLIAMS' PLOT TO PUT A DEAD EEL IN THE SCHOOL VENTILATING SYSTEM!
THAT ONE SMELLED!
WHAT ABOUT MY EXPOSE OF THE CAFETERIA COOK WHO WAS WATER-ING DOWN THE COCOA?
HOT STUFF, TO BE SURE ... AND DECIDING BETWEEN YOU WON'T BE EASY... THEREFORE-
I WANT EACH OF YOU TO WRITE A STORY ON ANY SUBJECT AND I SHALL DECIDE ON THE BETTER JOB OF REPORTING ... AND THAT REPORTER WILL BE PROMOTED TO EDITOR!
DEADLINE, 9 A.M. TOMORROW!
2

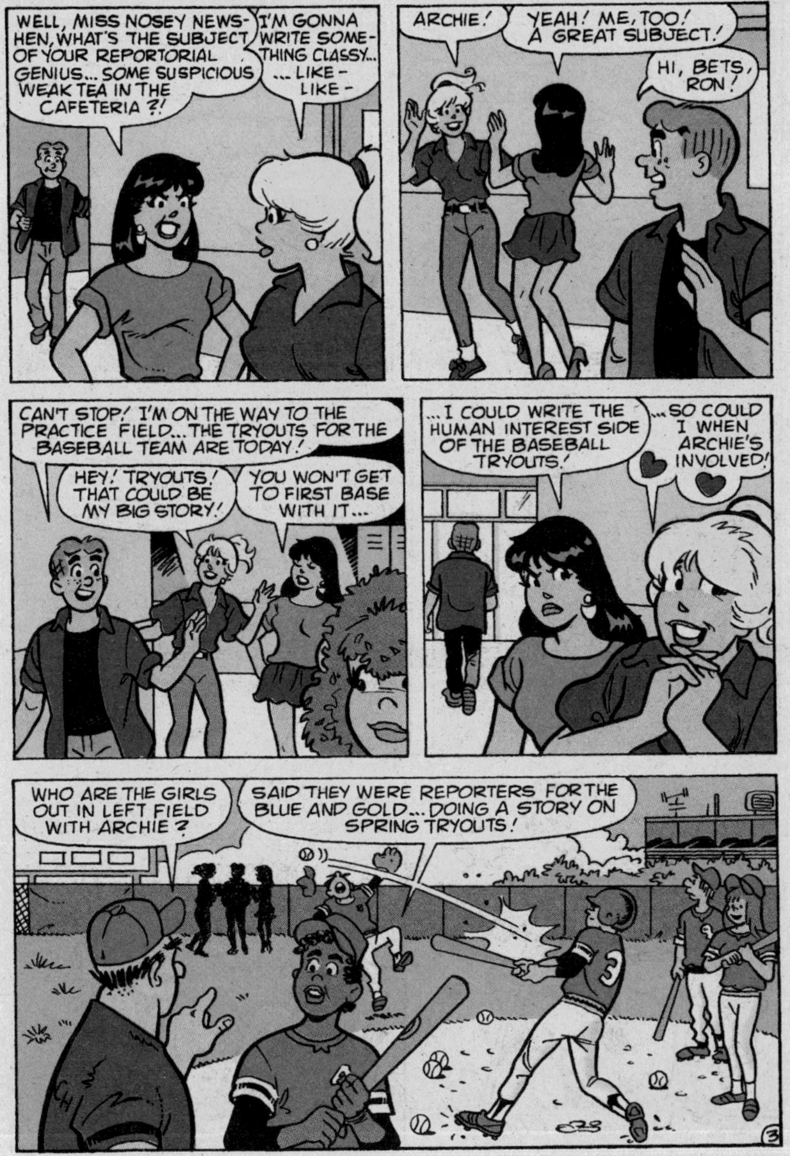
WELL, MISS NOSEY NEWS-HEN, WHAT'S THE SUBJECT OF YOUR REPORTORIAL GENIUS... SOME SUSPICIOUS WEAK TEA IN THE CAFETERIA ?!
I'M GONNA WRITE SOMETHING CLASSY... ...LIKE-LIKE-
ARCHIE!
YEAH! ME, TOO! A GREAT SUBJECT!
HI, BETS, RON!
CAN'T STOP! I'M ON THE WAY TO THE PRACTICE FIELD... THE TRYOUTS FOR THE BASEBALL TEAM ARE TODAY!
HEY! TRYOUTS! THAT COULD BE MY BIG STORY!
YOU WON'T GET TO FIRST BASE WITH IT...
...I COULD WRITE THE HUMAN INTEREST SIDE OF THE BASEBALL TRYOUTS!
...SO COULD I WHEN ARCHIE'S INVOLVED!
WHO ARE THE GIRLS OUT IN LEFT FIELD WITH ARCHIE?
SAID THEY WERE REPORTERS FOR THE BLUE AND GOLD... DOING A STORY ON SPRING TRYOUTS!
3

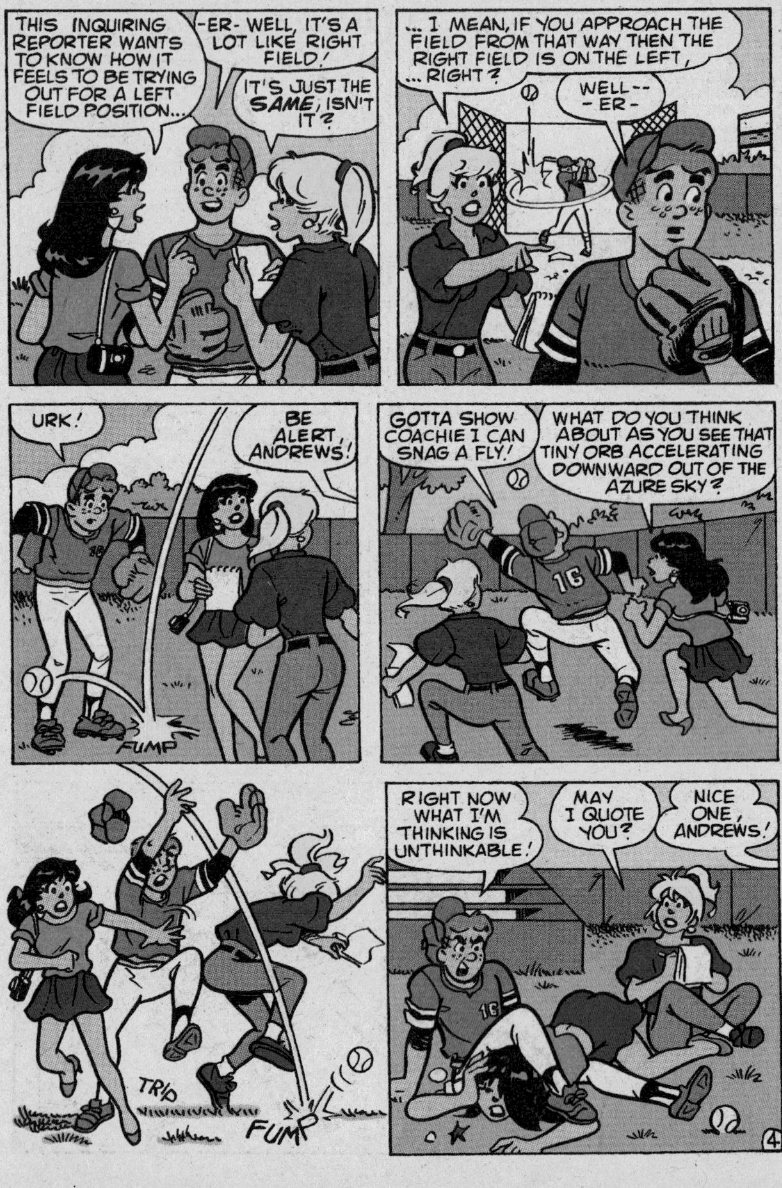
THIS INQUIRING REPORTER WANTS TO KNOW HOW IT FEELS TO BE TRYING OUT FOR A LEFT FIELD POSITION...
-ER- WELL, IT'S A LOT LIKE RIGHT FIELD!
IT'S JUST THE SAME, ISN'T IT?
... I MEAN, IF YOU APPROACH THE FIELD FROM THAT WAY THEN THE RIGHT FIELD IS ON THE LEFT, ... RIGHT?
WELL-- -ER-
URK!
BE ALERT, ANDREWS!
FUMP
GOTTA SHOW COACHIE I CAN SNAG A FLY!
WHAT DO YOU THINK ABOUT AS YOU SEE THAT TINY ORB ACCELERATING DOWNWARD OUT OF THE AZURE SKY?
TRIP
FUMP
RIGHT NOW WHAT I'M THINKING IS UNTHINKABLE!
MAY I QUOTE YOU?
NICE ONE, ANDREWS!
4

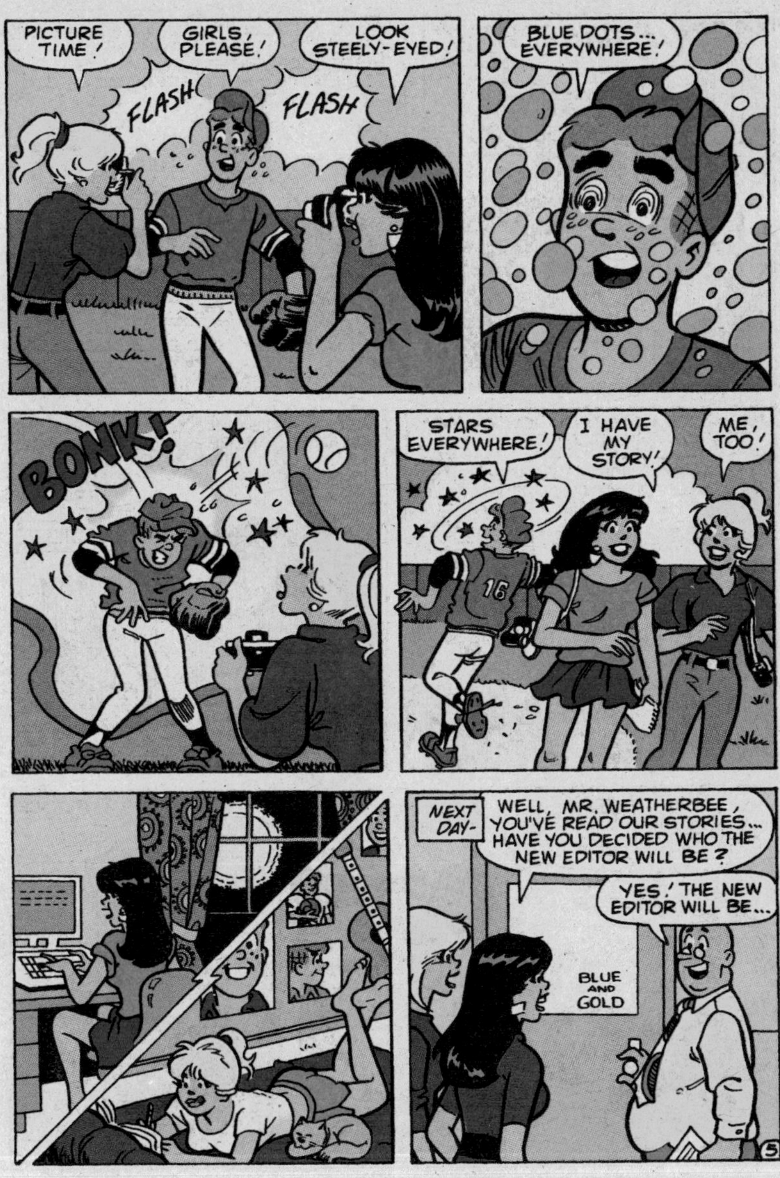
PICTURE TIME!
GIRLS, PLEASE!
LOOK STEELY-EYED!
FLASH
FLASH
BLUE DOTS... EVERYWHERE!
BONK!
STARS EVERYWHERE!
I HAVE MY STORY!
ME, TOO!
NEXT DAY-
WELL, MR. WEATHERBEE, YOU'VE READ OUR STORIES... HAVE YOU DECIDED WHO THE NEW EDITOR WILL BE?
YES! THE NEW EDITOR WILL BE...
BLUE AND GOLD
5

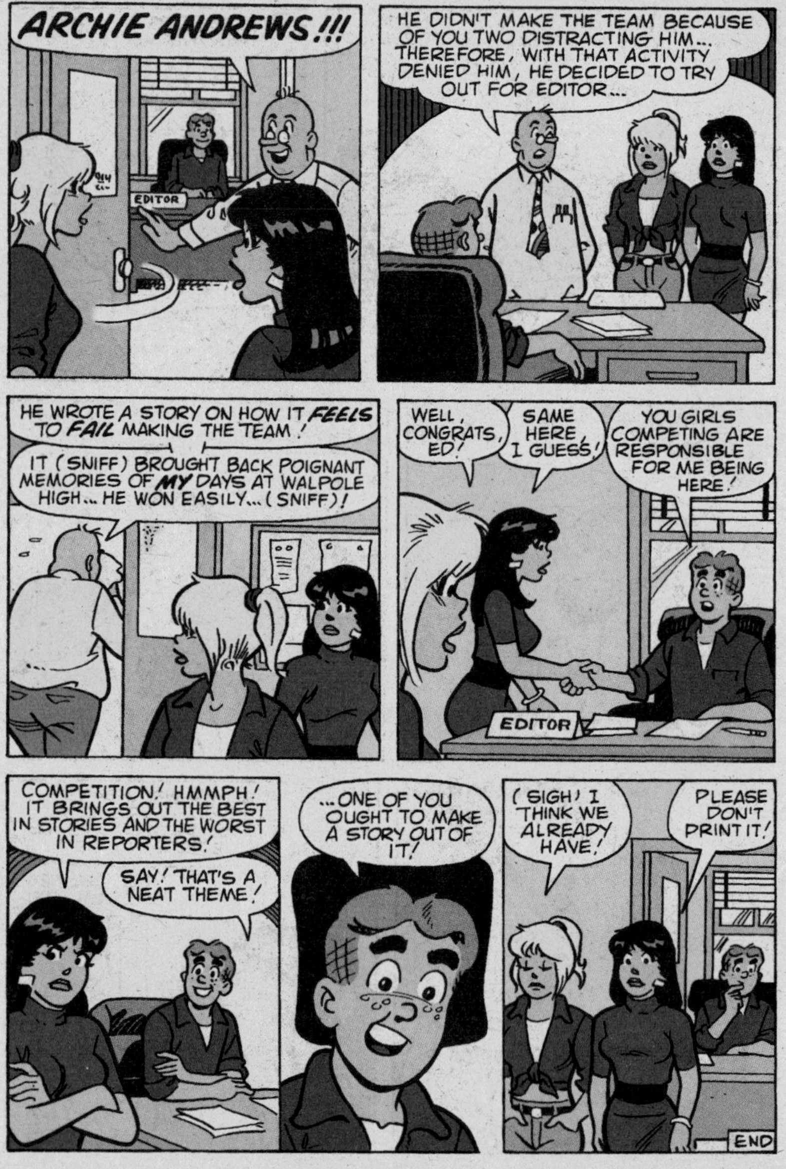
ARCHIE ANDREWS!!!
EDITOR
HE DIDN'T MAKE THE TEAM BECAUSE OF YOU TWO DISTRACTING HIM... THEREFORE, WITH THAT ACTIVITY DENIED HIM, HE DECIDED TO TRY OUT FOR EDITOR...
HE WROTE A STORY ON HOW IT FEELS TO FAIL MAKING THE TEAM!
IT (SNIFF) BROUGHT BACK POIGNANT MEMORIES OF MY DAYS AT WALPOLE HIGH... HE WON EASILY...(SNIFF)!
WELL, CONGRATS, ED!
SAME HERE, I GUESS!
YOU GIRLS COMPETING ARE RESPONSIBLE FOR ME BEING HERE!
EDITOR
COMPETITION! HMMPH! IT BRINGS OUT THE BEST IN STORIES AND THE WORST IN REPORTERS!
SAY! THAT'S A NEAT THEME!
...ONE OF YOU OUGHT TO MAKE A STORY OUT OF IT!
(SIGH) I THINK WE ALREADY HAVE!
PLEASE DON'T PRINT IT!
END

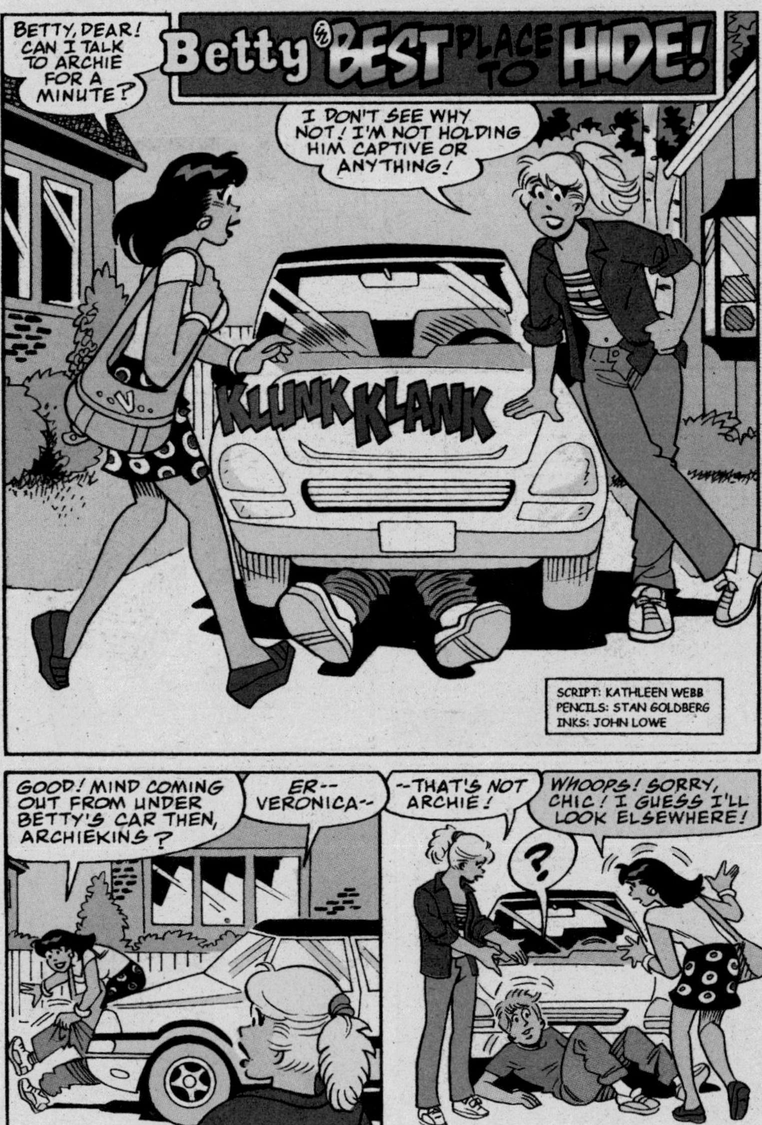

BETTY, DEAR! CAN I TALK TO ARCHIE FOR A MINUTE?
Betty's BEST PLACE TO HIDE!
I DON'T SEE WHY NOT! I'M NOT HOLDING HIM CAPTIVE OR ANYTHING!
KLUNK KLANK
SCRIPT: KATHLEEN WEBB
PENCILS: STAN GOLDBERG
INKS: JOHN LOWE
GOOD! MIND COMING OUT FROM UNDER BETTY'S CAR THEN, ARCHIEKINS?
ER-- VERONICA--
--THAT'S NOT ARCHIE!
?
WHOOPS! SORRY, CHIC! I GUESS I'LL LOOK ELSEWHERE!

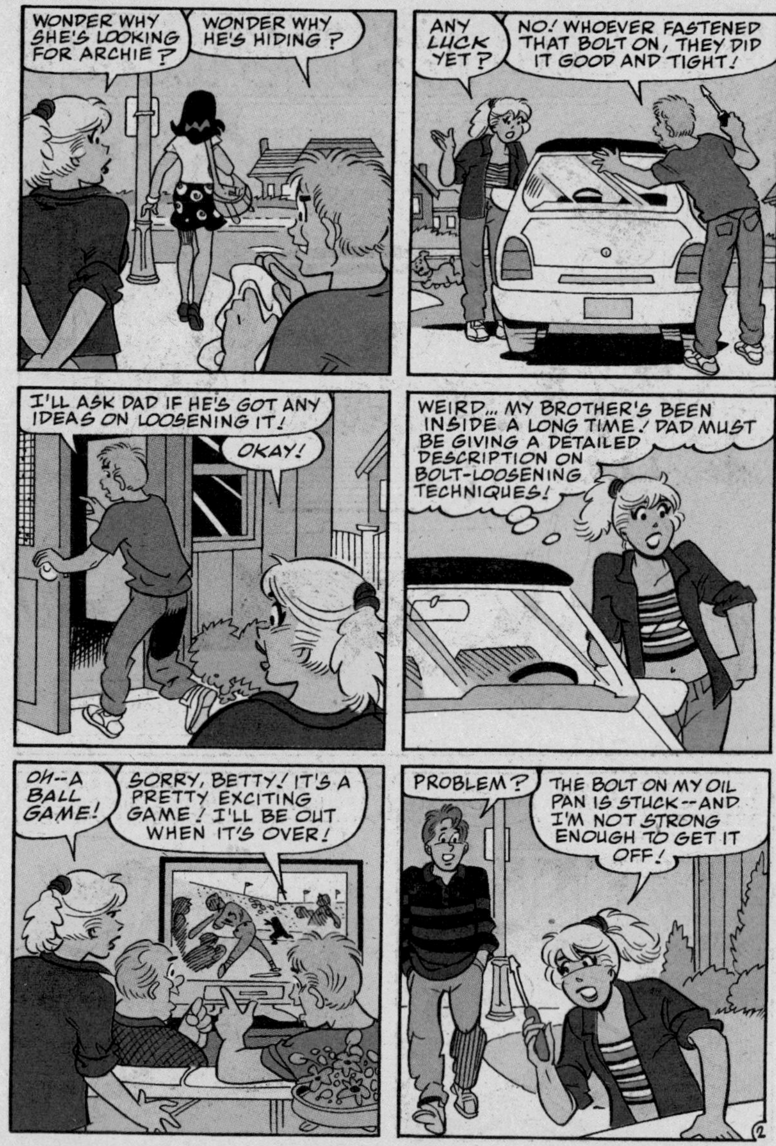
WONDER WHY SHE'S LOOKING FOR ARCHIE?
WONDER WHY HE'S HIDING?
ANY LUCK YET?
NO! WHOEVER FASTENED THAT BOLT ON, THEY DID IT GOOD AND TIGHT!
I'LL ASK DAD IF HE'S GOT ANY IDEAS ON LOOSENING IT!
OKAY!
WEIRD... MY BROTHER'S BEEN INSIDE A LONG TIME! DAD MUST BE GIVING A DETAILED DESCRIPTION ON BOLT-LOOSENING TECHNIQUES!
OH--A BALL GAME!
SORRY, BETTY! IT'S A PRETTY EXCITING GAME! I'LL BE OUT WHEN IT'S OVER!
PROBLEM?
THE BOLT ON MY OIL PAN IS STUCK--AND I'M NOT STRONG ENOUGH TO GET IT OFF!
2

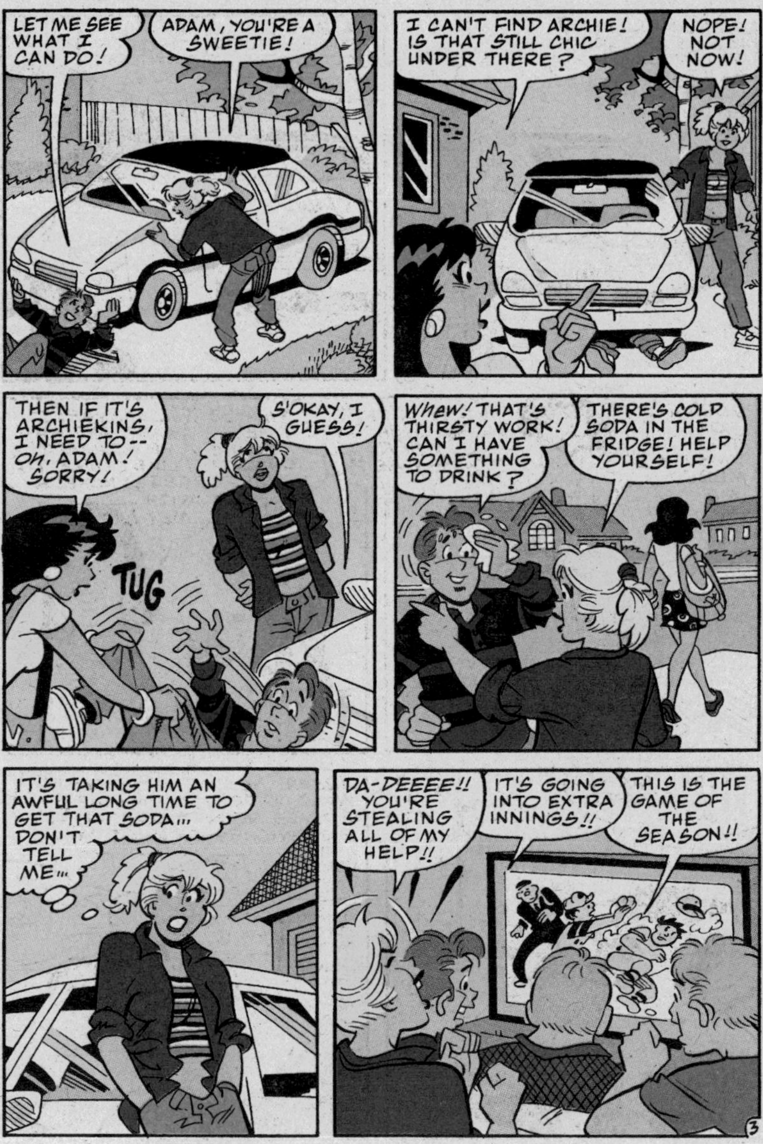
LET ME SEE WHAT I CAN DO!
ADAM, YOU'RE A SWEETIE!
I CAN'T FIND ARCHIE! IS THAT STILL CHIC UNDER THERE?
NOPE! NOT NOW!
THEN IF IT'S ARCHIEKINS, I NEED TO-- OH, ADAM! SORRY!
S'OKAY, I GUESS!
TUG
WHEW! THAT'S THIRSTY WORK! CAN I HAVE SOMETHING TO DRINK?
THERE'S COLD SODA IN THE FRIDGE! HELP YOURSELF!
IT'S TAKING HIM AN AWFUL LONG TIME TO GET THAT SODA... DON'T TELL ME...
DA-DEEEE!! YOU'RE STEALING ALL OF MY HELP!!
IT'S GOING INTO EXTRA INNINGS!!
THIS IS THE GAME OF THE SEASON!!
3

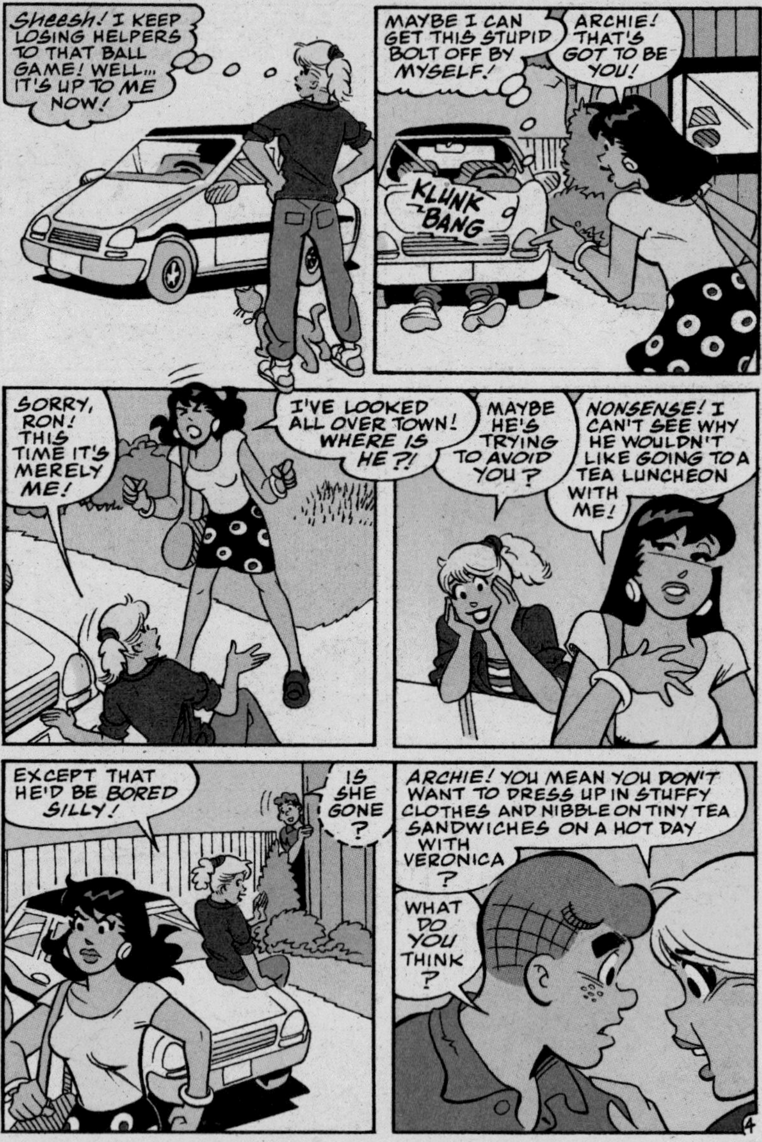
Sheesh! I KEEP LOSING HELPERS TO THAT BALL GAME! WELL... IT'S UP TO ME NOW!
MAYBE I CAN GET THIS STUPID BOLT OFF BY MYSELF!
ARCHIE! THAT'S GOT TO BE YOU!
KLUNK
BANG
SORRY, RON! THIS TIME IT'S MERELY ME!
I'VE LOOKED ALL OVER TOWN! WHERE IS HE?!
MAYBE HE'S TRYING TO AVOID YOU?
NONSENSE! I CAN'T SEE WHY HE WOULDN'T LIKE GOING TO A TEA LUNCHEON WITH ME!
EXCEPT THAT HE'D BE BORED SILLY!
IS SHE GONE?
ARCHIE! YOU MEAN YOU DON'T WANT TO DRESS UP IN STUFFY CLOTHES AND NIBBLE ON TINY TEA SANDWICHES ON A HOT DAY WITH VERONICA?
WHAT DO YOU THINK?
4

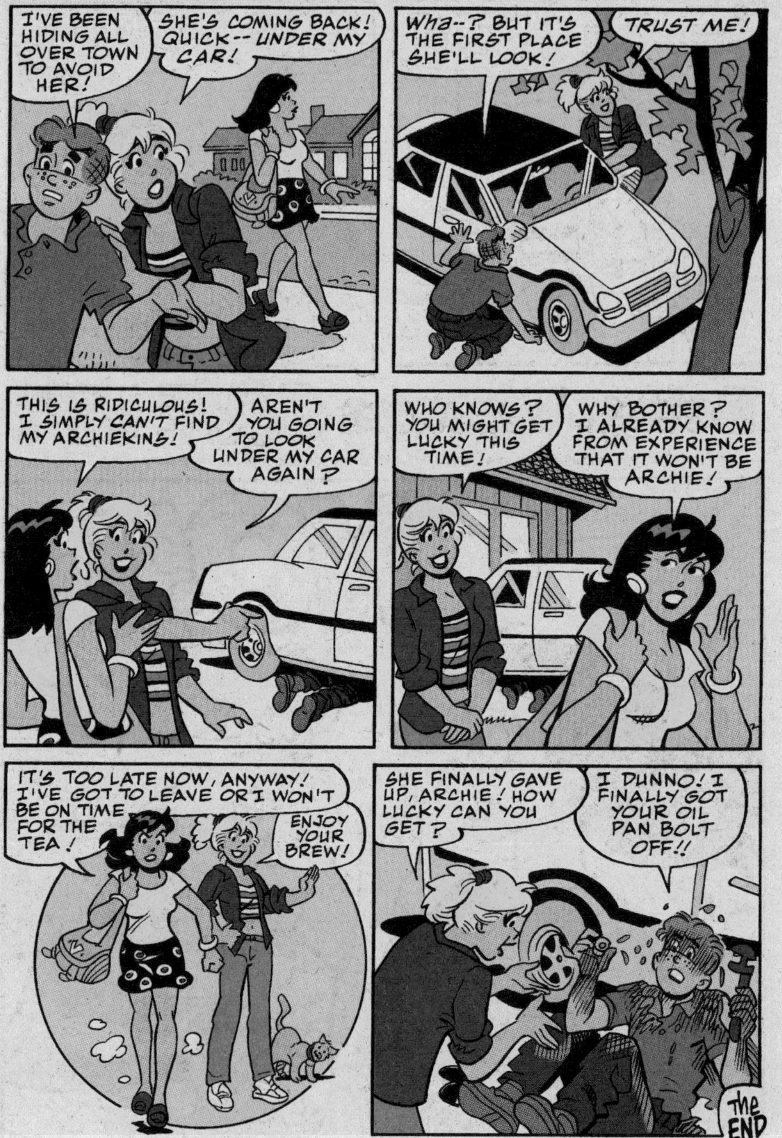
I'VE BEEN HIDING ALL OVER TOWN TO AVOID HER!
SHE'S COMING BACK! QUICK -- UNDER MY CAR!
Wha--? BUT IT'S THE FIRST PLACE SHE'LL LOOK!
TRUST ME!
THIS IS RIDICULOUS! I SIMPLY CAN'T FIND MY ARCHIEKINS!
AREN'T YOU GOING TO LOOK UNDER MY CAR AGAIN?
WHO KNOWS? YOU MIGHT GET LUCKY THIS TIME!
WHY BOTHER? I ALREADY KNOW FROM EXPERIENCE THAT IT WON'T BE ARCHIE!
IT'S TOO LATE NOW, ANYWAY! I'VE GOT TO LEAVE OR I WON'T BE ON TIME FOR THE TEA!
ENJOY YOUR BREW!
SHE FINALLY GAVE UP, ARCHIE! HOW LUCKY CAN YOU GET?
I DUNNO! I FINALLY GOT YOUR OIL PAN BOLT OFF!!
The END

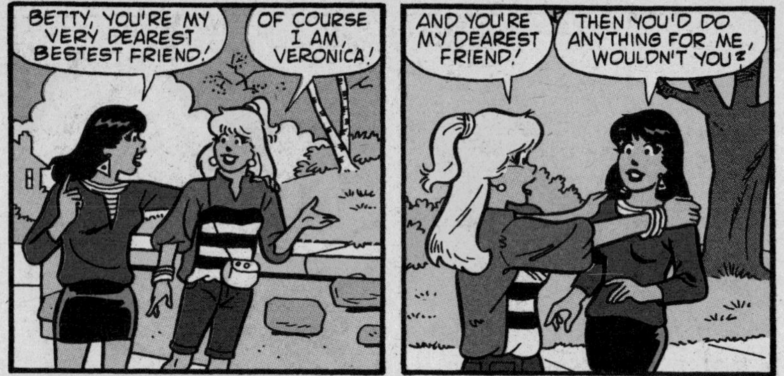
BETTY, YOU'RE MY VERY DEAREST BESTEST FRIEND!
OF COURSE I AM, VERONICA!
AND YOU'RE MY DEAREST FRIEND!
THEN YOU'D DO ANYTHING FOR ME, WOULDN'T YOU?

Betty and Veronica GIVE UP?

Pencils: Jeff Shultz / Inks: Al Milgrom / Letters: Bill Yoshida / Colors: Barry Grossman

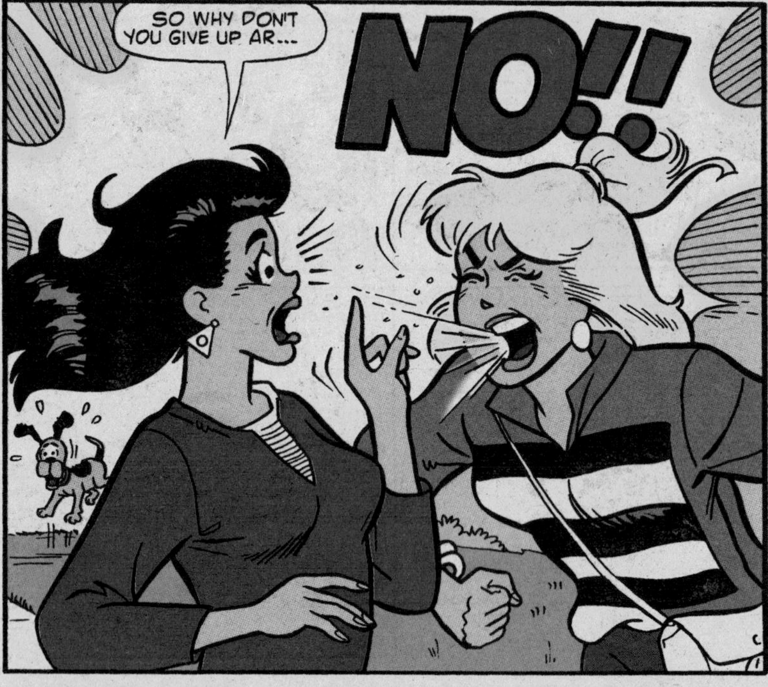
SO WHY DON'T YOU GIVE UP AR...
NO!!

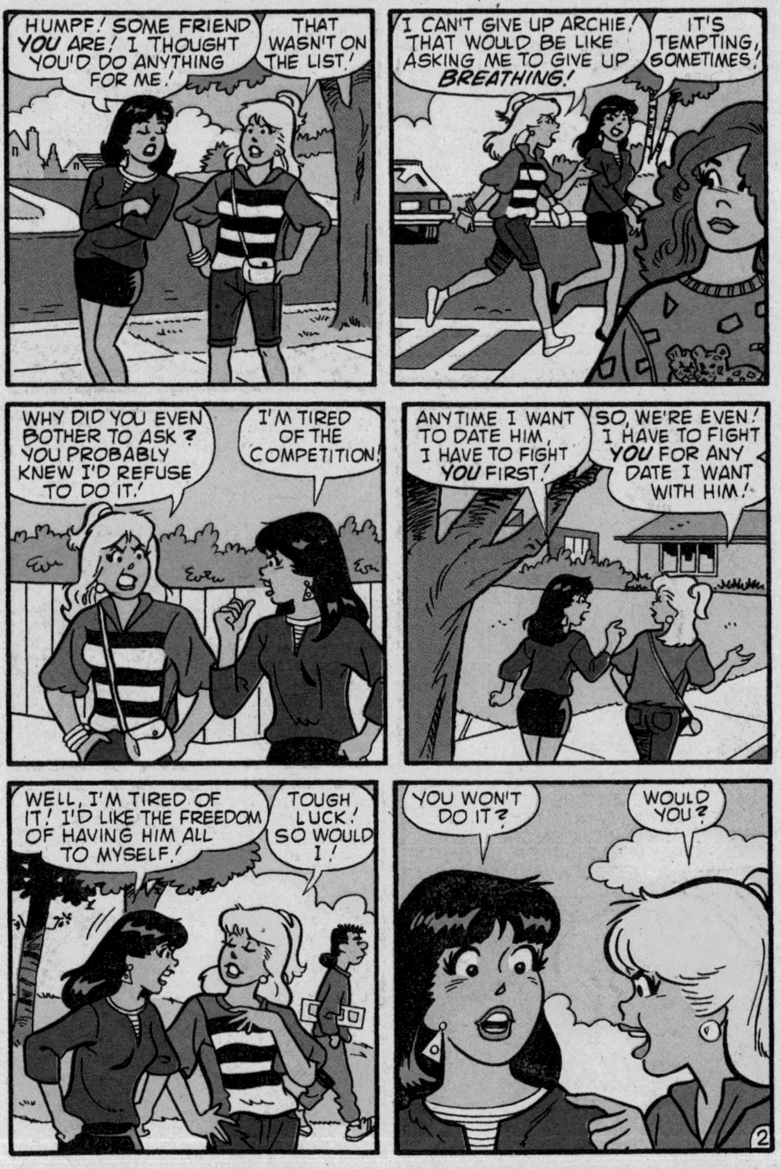

HUMPF! SOME FRIEND *YOU* ARE! I THOUGHT YOU'D DO ANYTHING FOR ME!
THAT WASN'T ON THE LIST!
I CAN'T GIVE UP ARCHIE! THAT WOULD BE LIKE ASKING ME TO GIVE UP *BREATHING!*
IT'S TEMPTING, SOMETIMES!
WHY DID YOU EVEN BOTHER TO ASK? YOU PROBABLY KNEW I'D REFUSE TO DO IT!
I'M TIRED OF THE COMPETITION!
ANYTIME I WANT TO DATE HIM, I HAVE TO FIGHT *YOU* FIRST!
SO, WE'RE EVEN! I HAVE TO FIGHT *YOU* FOR ANY DATE I WANT WITH HIM!
WELL, I'M TIRED OF IT! I'D LIKE THE FREEDOM OF HAVING HIM ALL TO MYSELF!
TOUGH LUCK! SO WOULD I!
YOU WON'T DO IT?
WOULD YOU?
2

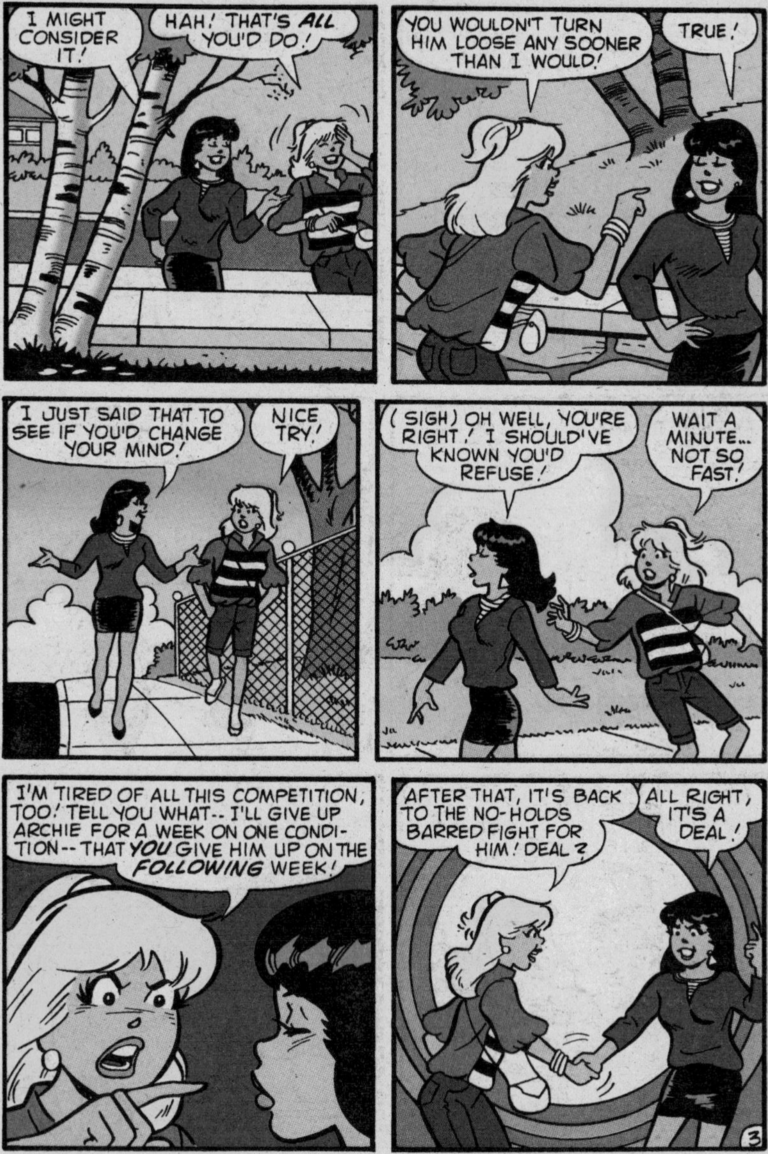
I MIGHT CONSIDER IT!
HAH! THAT'S ALL YOU'D DO!
YOU WOULDN'T TURN HIM LOOSE ANY SOONER THAN I WOULD!
TRUE!
I JUST SAID THAT TO SEE IF YOU'D CHANGE YOUR MIND!
NICE TRY!
(SIGH) OH WELL, YOU'RE RIGHT! I SHOULD'VE KNOWN YOU'D REFUSE!
WAIT A MINUTE... NOT SO FAST!
I'M TIRED OF ALL THIS COMPETITION, TOO! TELL YOU WHAT-- I'LL GIVE UP ARCHIE FOR A WEEK ON ONE CONDITION-- THAT YOU GIVE HIM UP ON THE FOLLOWING WEEK!
AFTER THAT, IT'S BACK TO THE NO-HOLDS BARRED FIGHT FOR HIM! DEAL?
ALL RIGHT, IT'S A DEAL!

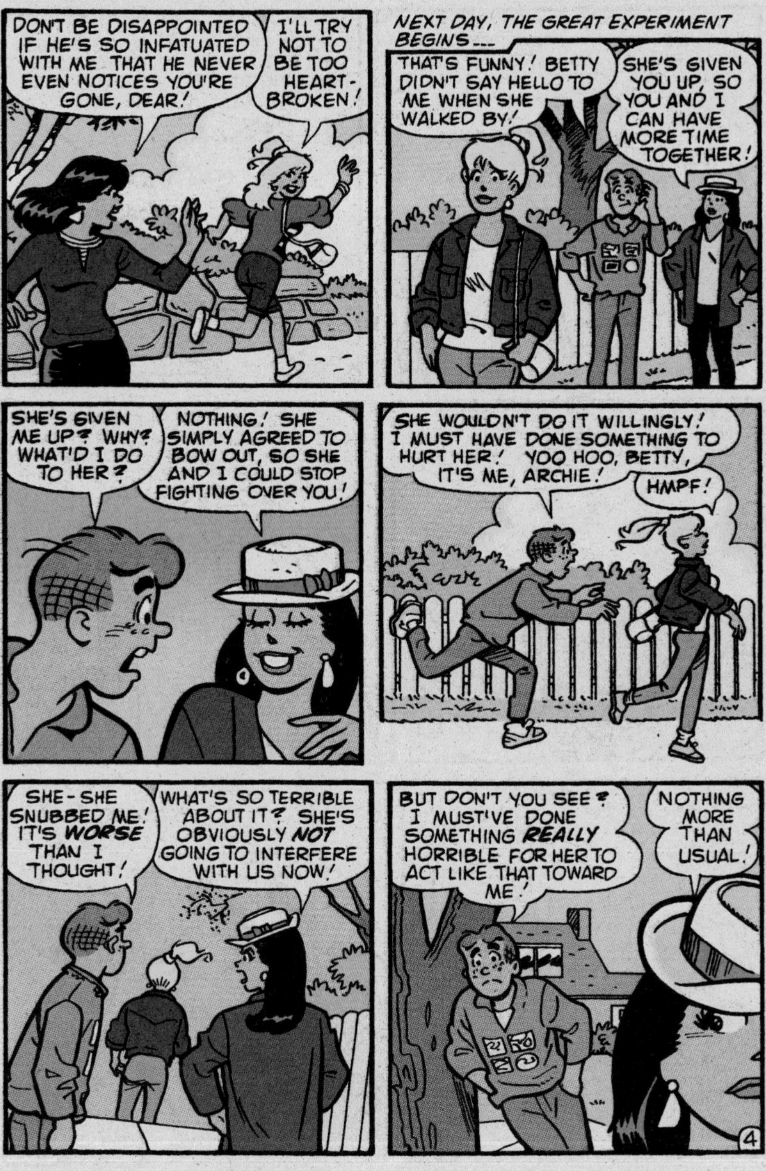
DON'T BE DISAPPOINTED IF HE'S SO INFATUATED WITH ME THAT HE NEVER EVEN NOTICES YOU'RE GONE, DEAR!
I'LL TRY NOT TO BE TOO HEART-BROKEN!
NEXT DAY, THE GREAT EXPERIMENT BEGINS...
THAT'S FUNNY! BETTY DIDN'T SAY HELLO TO ME WHEN SHE WALKED BY!
SHE'S GIVEN YOU UP, SO YOU AND I CAN HAVE MORE TIME TOGETHER!
SHE'S GIVEN ME UP? WHY? WHAT'D I DO TO HER?
NOTHING! SHE SIMPLY AGREED TO BOW OUT, SO SHE AND I COULD STOP FIGHTING OVER YOU!
SHE WOULDN'T DO IT WILLINGLY! I MUST HAVE DONE SOMETHING TO HURT HER! YOO HOO, BETTY, IT'S ME, ARCHIE!
HMPF!
SHE-SHE SNUBBED ME! IT'S WORSE THAN I THOUGHT!
WHAT'S SO TERRIBLE ABOUT IT? SHE'S OBVIOUSLY NOT GOING TO INTERFERE WITH US NOW!
BUT DON'T YOU SEE? I MUST'VE DONE SOMETHING REALLY HORRIBLE FOR HER TO ACT LIKE THAT TOWARD ME!
NOTHING MORE THAN USUAL!
4

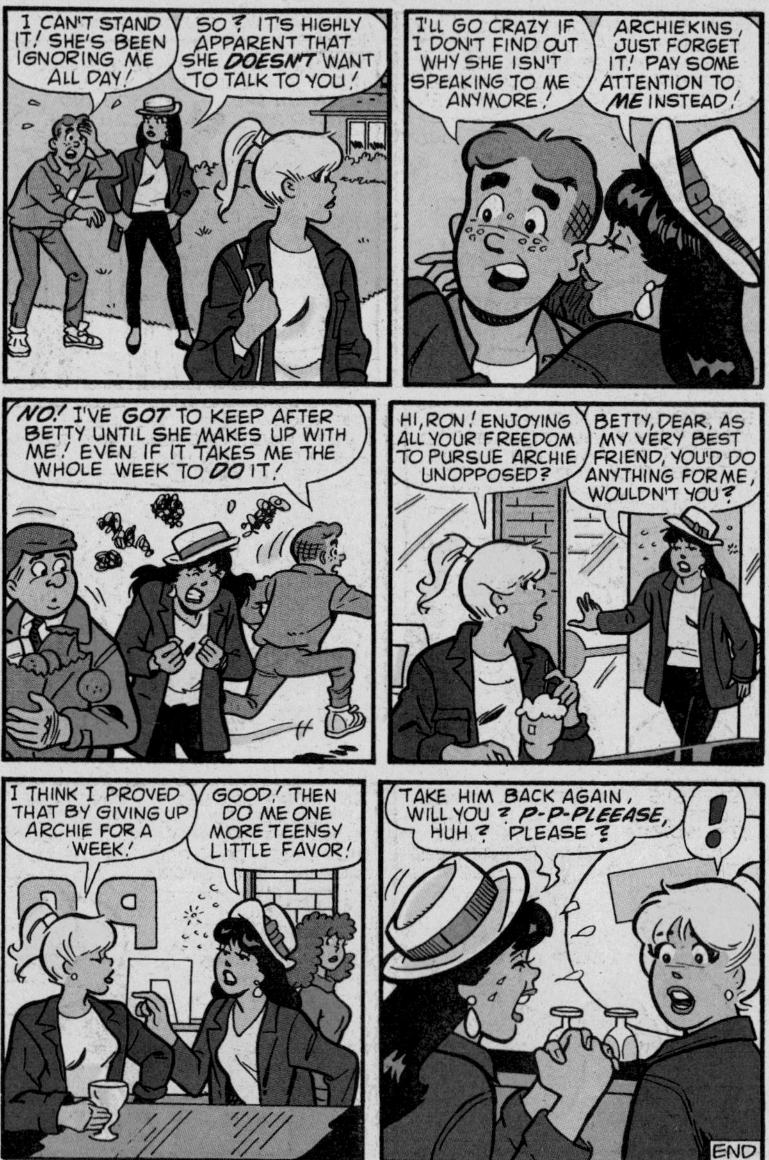
I CAN'T STAND IT! SHE'S BEEN IGNORING ME ALL DAY!
SO? IT'S HIGHLY APPARENT THAT SHE **DOESN'T** WANT TO TALK TO YOU!
I'LL GO CRAZY IF I DON'T FIND OUT WHY SHE ISN'T SPEAKING TO ME ANYMORE!
ARCHIEKINS, JUST FORGET IT! PAY SOME ATTENTION TO **ME** INSTEAD!
NO! I'VE **GOT** TO KEEP AFTER BETTY UNTIL SHE MAKES UP WITH ME! EVEN IF IT TAKES ME THE WHOLE WEEK TO **DO** IT!
HI, RON! ENJOYING ALL YOUR FREEDOM TO PURSUE ARCHIE UNOPPOSED?
BETTY, DEAR, AS MY VERY BEST FRIEND, YOU'D DO ANYTHING FOR ME, WOULDN'T YOU?
I THINK I PROVED THAT BY GIVING UP ARCHIE FOR A WEEK!
GOOD! THEN DO ME ONE MORE TEENSY LITTLE FAVOR!
TAKE HIM BACK AGAIN, WILL YOU? **P-P-PLEEASE,** HUH? PLEASE?
!
END

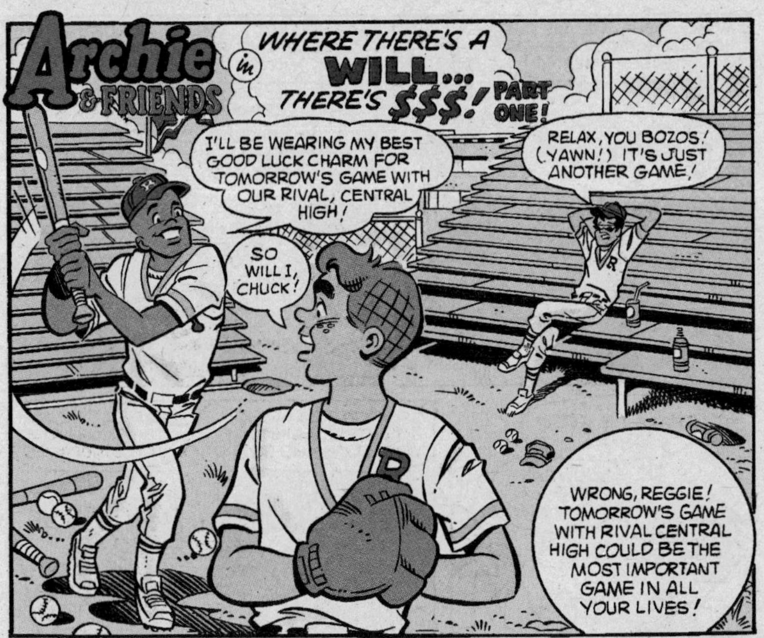
Archie & FRIENDS
in
WHERE THERE'S A WILL... THERE'S $$$! PART ONE!
I'LL BE WEARING MY BEST GOOD LUCK CHARM FOR TOMORROW'S GAME WITH OUR RIVAL, CENTRAL HIGH!
SO WILL I, CHUCK!
RELAX, YOU BOZOS! (YAWN!) IT'S JUST ANOTHER GAME!
WRONG, REGGIE! TOMORROW'S GAME WITH RIVAL CENTRAL HIGH COULD BE THE MOST IMPORTANT GAME IN ALL YOUR LIVES!

Script: George Gladir / Pencils: Al Bigley / Inks: Al Milgrom / Letters: Bill Yoshida / Colors: Barry Grossman

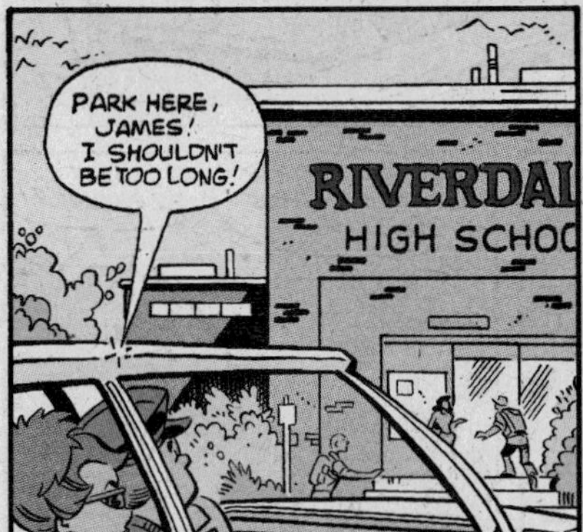
PARK HERE, JAMES! I SHOULDN'T BE TOO LONG!
RIVERDAL
HIGH SCHOO

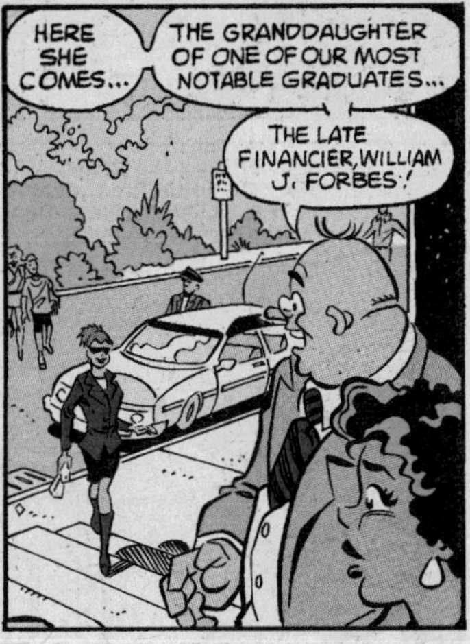
HERE SHE COMES...
THE GRANDDAUGHTER OF ONE OF OUR MOST NOTABLE GRADUATES...
THE LATE FINANCIER, WILLIAM J. FORBES!

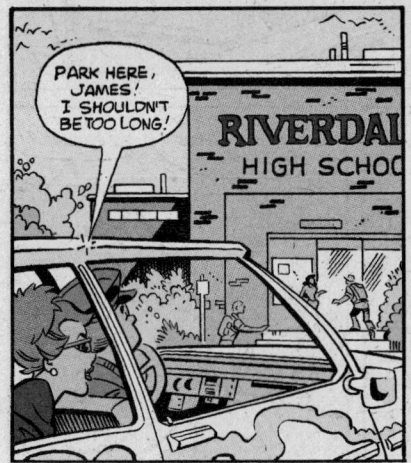

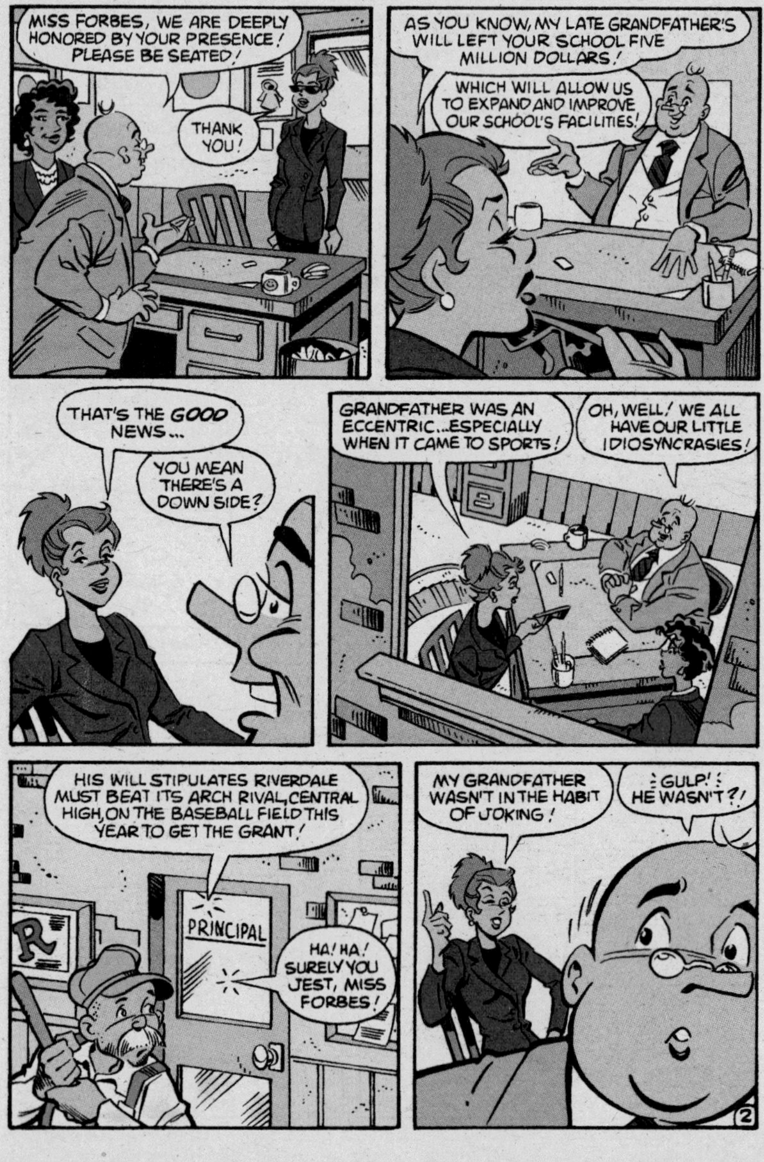
MISS FORBES, WE ARE DEEPLY HONORED BY YOUR PRESENCE! PLEASE BE SEATED!
THANK YOU!
AS YOU KNOW, MY LATE GRANDFATHER'S WILL LEFT YOUR SCHOOL FIVE MILLION DOLLARS!
WHICH WILL ALLOW US TO EXPAND AND IMPROVE OUR SCHOOL'S FACILITIES!
THAT'S THE GOOD NEWS...
YOU MEAN THERE'S A DOWN SIDE?
GRANDFATHER WAS AN ECCENTRIC...ESPECIALLY WHEN IT CAME TO SPORTS!
OH, WELL! WE ALL HAVE OUR LITTLE IDIOSYNCRASIES!
HIS WILL STIPULATES RIVERDALE MUST BEAT ITS ARCH RIVAL, CENTRAL HIGH, ON THE BASEBALL FIELD THIS YEAR TO GET THE GRANT!
PRINCIPAL
HA! HA! SURELY YOU JEST, MISS FORBES!
MY GRANDFATHER WASN'T IN THE HABIT OF JOKING!
GULP! HE WASN'T?!
2

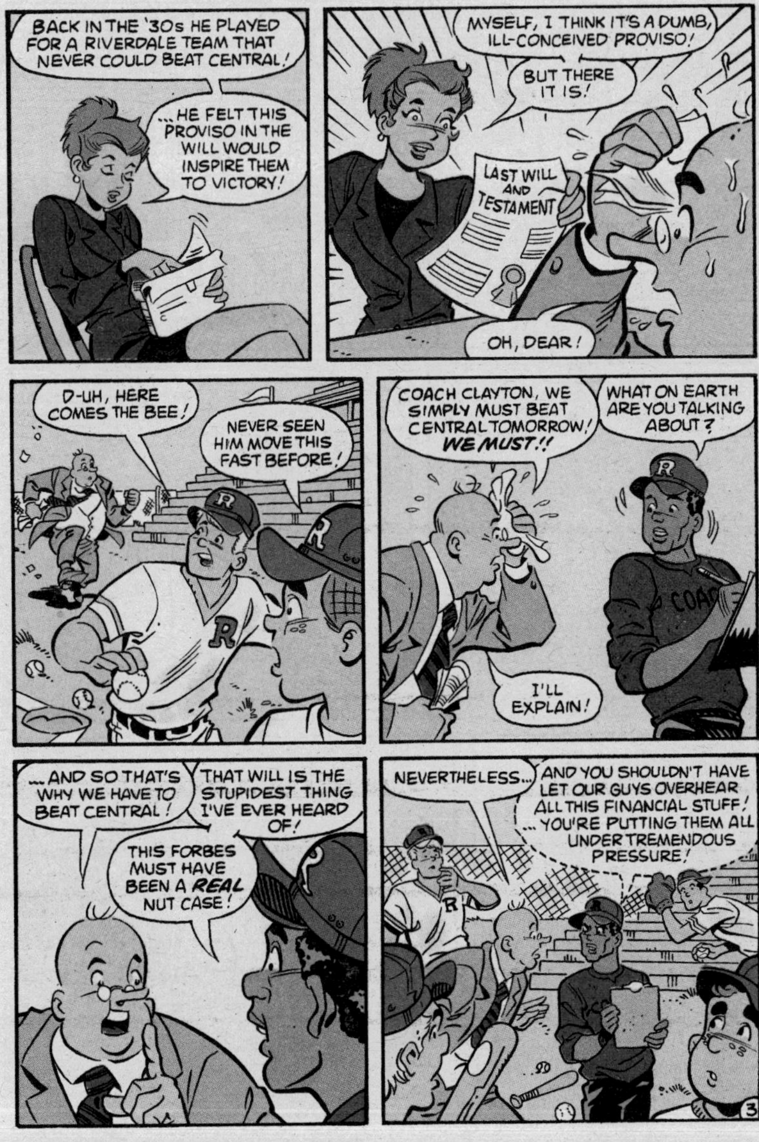
BACK IN THE '30s HE PLAYED FOR A RIVERDALE TEAM THAT NEVER COULD BEAT CENTRAL!
...HE FELT THIS PROVISO IN THE WILL WOULD INSPIRE THEM TO VICTORY!
MYSELF, I THINK IT'S A DUMB, ILL-CONCEIVED PROVISO!
BUT THERE IT IS!
LAST WILL AND TESTAMENT
OH, DEAR!
D-UH, HERE COMES THE BEE!
NEVER SEEN HIM MOVE THIS FAST BEFORE!
COACH CLAYTON, WE SIMPLY MUST BEAT CENTRAL TOMORROW! ***WE MUST!!***
WHAT ON EARTH ARE YOU TALKING ABOUT?
I'LL EXPLAIN!
...AND SO THAT'S WHY WE HAVE TO BEAT CENTRAL!
THAT WILL IS THE STUPIDEST THING I'VE EVER HEARD OF!
THIS FORBES MUST HAVE BEEN A ***REAL*** NUT CASE!
NEVERTHELESS...
AND YOU SHOULDN'T HAVE LET OUR GUYS OVERHEAR ALL THIS FINANCIAL STUFF! ...YOU'RE PUTTING THEM ALL UNDER TREMENDOUS PRESSURE!
3

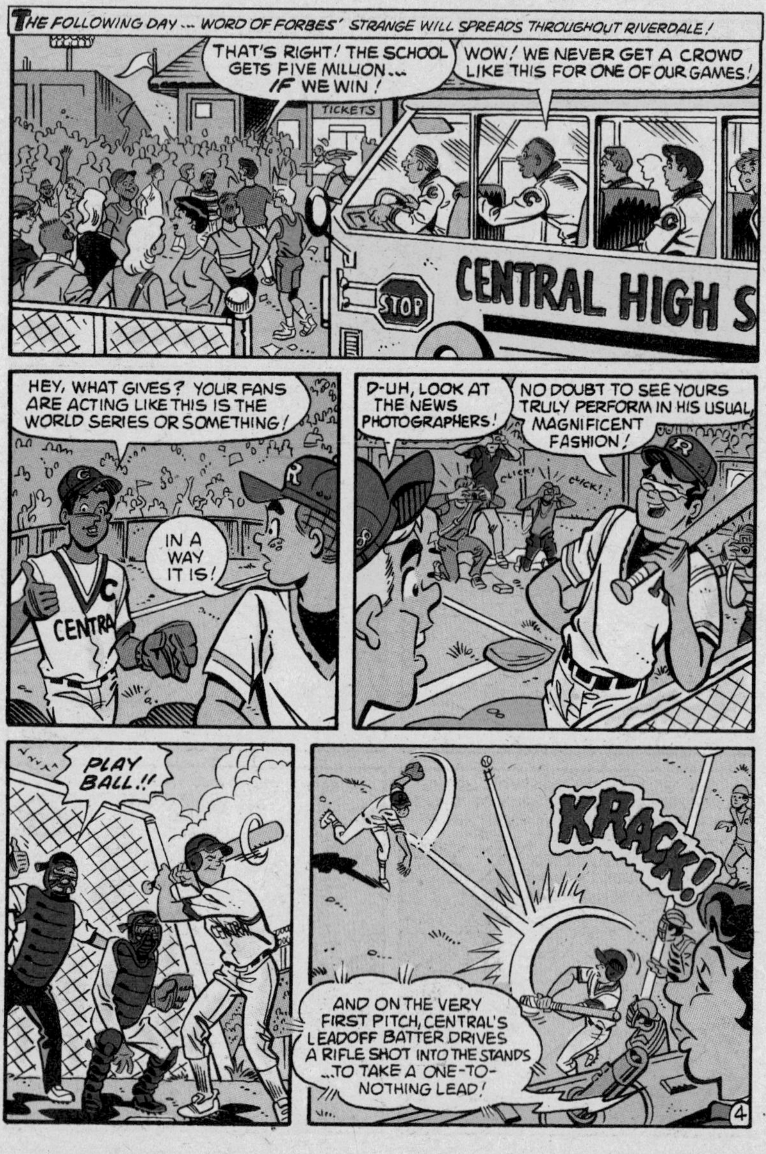
THE FOLLOWING DAY ... WORD OF FORBES' STRANGE WILL SPREADS THROUGHOUT RIVERDALE!
THAT'S RIGHT! THE SCHOOL GETS FIVE MILLION... IF WE WIN!
WOW! WE NEVER GET A CROWD LIKE THIS FOR ONE OF OUR GAMES!
TICKETS
STOP
CENTRAL HIGH S
HEY, WHAT GIVES? YOUR FANS ARE ACTING LIKE THIS IS THE WORLD SERIES OR SOMETHING!
IN A WAY IT IS!
CENTRA
D-UH, LOOK AT THE NEWS PHOTOGRAPHERS!
NO DOUBT TO SEE YOURS TRULY PERFORM IN HIS USUAL, MAGNIFICENT FASHION!
CLICK!
CLICK!
PLAY BALL!!
KRACK!
AND ON THE VERY FIRST PITCH, CENTRAL'S LEADOFF BATTER DRIVES A RIFLE SHOT INTO THE STANDS ...TO TAKE A ONE-TO-NOTHING LEAD!
4

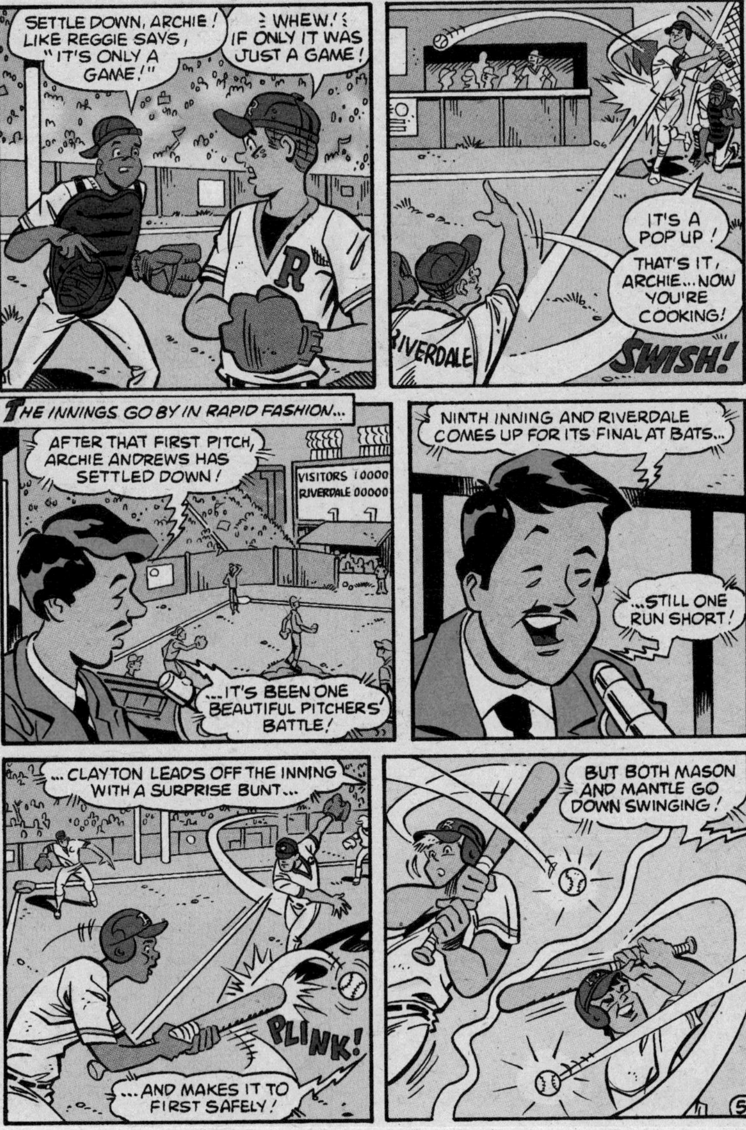
SETTLE DOWN, ARCHIE! LIKE REGGIE SAYS, "IT'S ONLY A GAME!"
WHEW! IF ONLY IT WAS JUST A GAME!
IT'S A POP UP!
THAT'S IT, ARCHIE... NOW YOU'RE COOKING!
RIVERDALE
SWISH!
THE INNINGS GO BY IN RAPID FASHION...
AFTER THAT FIRST PITCH, ARCHIE ANDREWS HAS SETTLED DOWN!
VISITORS 10000
RIVERDALE 00000
...IT'S BEEN ONE BEAUTIFUL PITCHERS' BATTLE!
NINTH INNING AND RIVERDALE COMES UP FOR ITS FINAL AT BATS...
...STILL ONE RUN SHORT!
...CLAYTON LEADS OFF THE INNING WITH A SURPRISE BUNT...
PLINK!
...AND MAKES IT TO FIRST SAFELY!
BUT BOTH MASON AND MANTLE GO DOWN SWINGING!
5

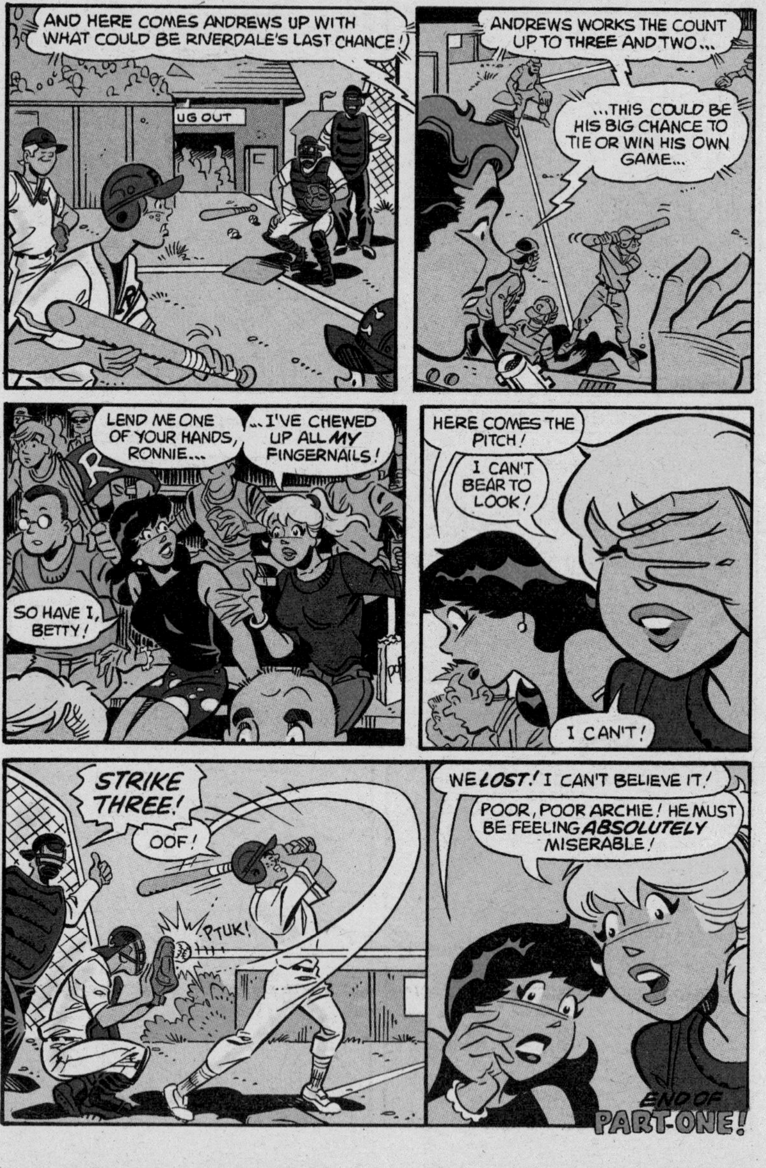
AND HERE COMES ANDREWS UP WITH WHAT COULD BE RIVERDALE'S LAST CHANCE!
UG OUT
ANDREWS WORKS THE COUNT UP TO THREE AND TWO...
...THIS COULD BE HIS BIG CHANCE TO TIE OR WIN HIS OWN GAME...
LEND ME ONE OF YOUR HANDS, RONNIE...
...I'VE CHEWED UP ALL *MY* FINGERNAILS!
SO HAVE I, BETTY!
HERE COMES THE PITCH!
I CAN'T BEAR TO LOOK!
I CAN'T!
STRIKE THREE!
OOF!
PTUK!
WE *LOST!* I CAN'T BELIEVE IT!
POOR, POOR ARCHIE! HE MUST BE FEELING *ABSOLUTELY* MISERABLE!
END OF PART ONE!

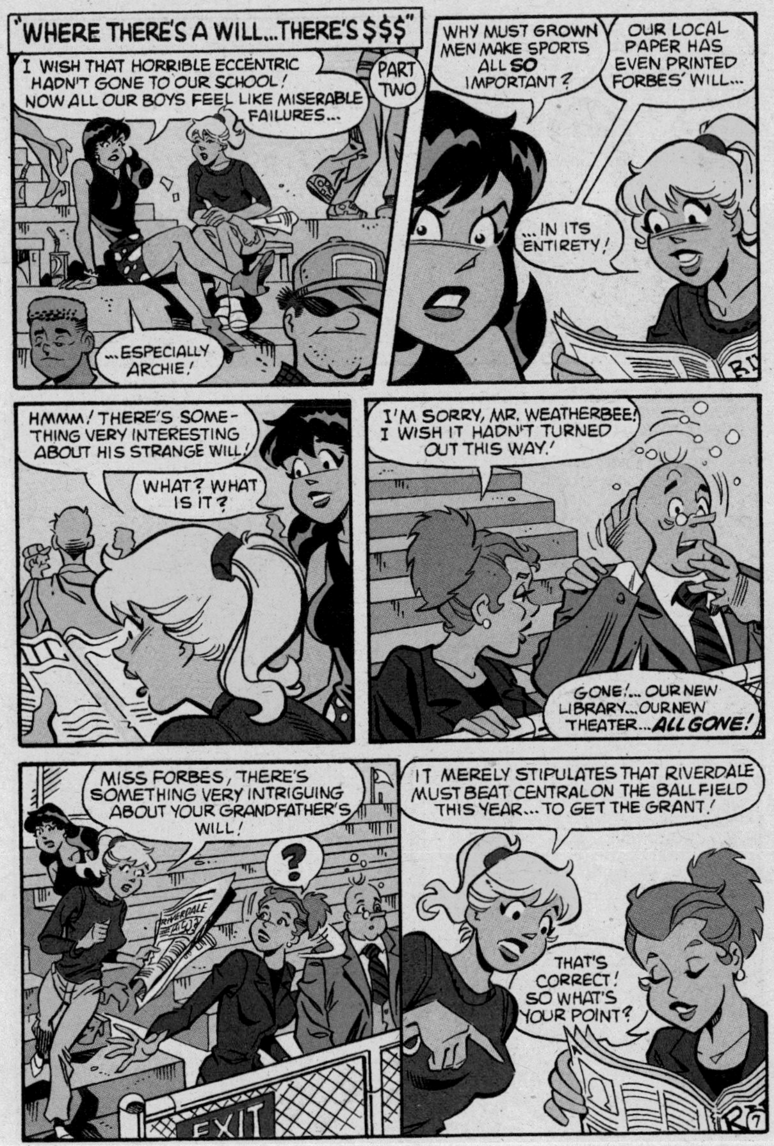
"WHERE THERE'S A WILL...THERE'S $$$"
PART TWO
I WISH THAT HORRIBLE ECCENTRIC HADN'T GONE TO OUR SCHOOL! NOW ALL OUR BOYS FEEL LIKE MISERABLE FAILURES...
...ESPECIALLY ARCHIE!
WHY MUST GROWN MEN MAKE SPORTS ALL SO IMPORTANT?
OUR LOCAL PAPER HAS EVEN PRINTED FORBES' WILL...
...IN ITS ENTIRETY!
HMMM! THERE'S SOMETHING VERY INTERESTING ABOUT HIS STRANGE WILL!
WHAT? WHAT IS IT?
I'M SORRY, MR. WEATHERBEE! I WISH IT HADN'T TURNED OUT THIS WAY!
GONE!... OUR NEW LIBRARY... OUR NEW THEATER... ALL GONE!
MISS FORBES, THERE'S SOMETHING VERY INTRIGUING ABOUT YOUR GRANDFATHER'S WILL!
?
RIVERDALE
EXIT
IT MERELY STIPULATES THAT RIVERDALE MUST BEAT CENTRAL ON THE BALLFIELD THIS YEAR... TO GET THE GRANT!
THAT'S CORRECT! SO WHAT'S YOUR POINT?
7

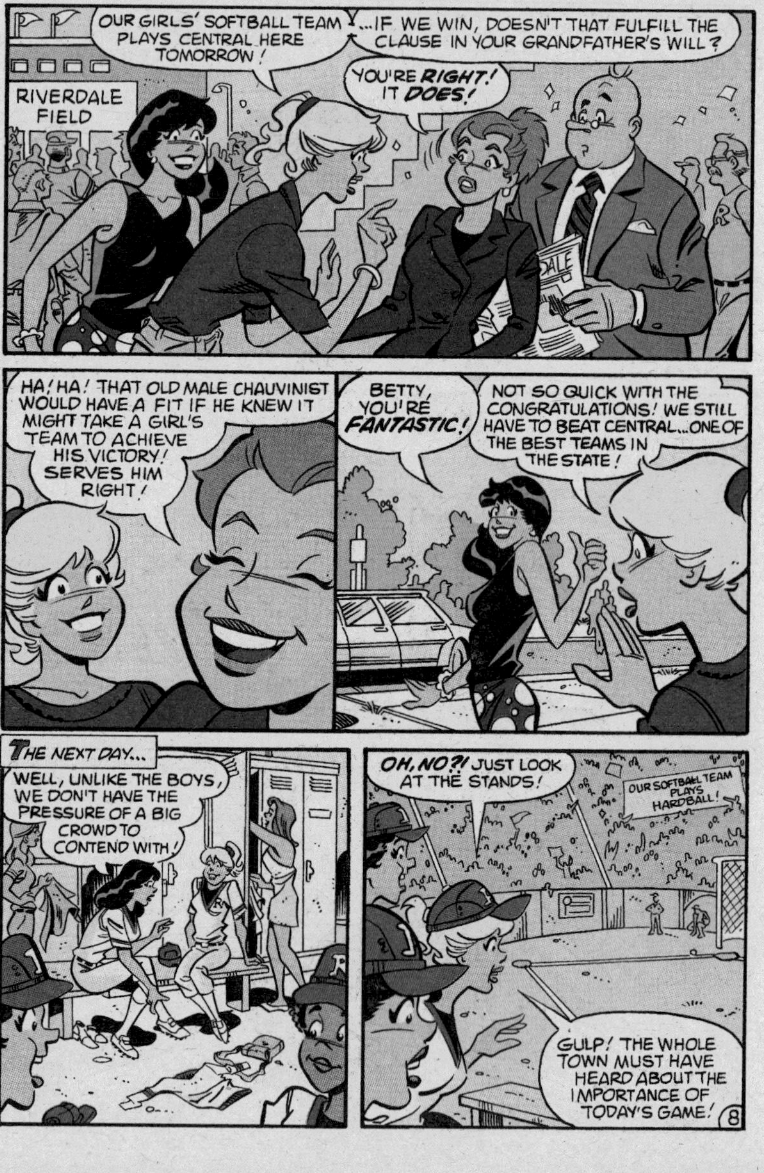

RIVERDALE FIELD
OUR GIRLS' SOFTBALL TEAM PLAYS CENTRAL HERE TOMORROW!
...IF WE WIN, DOESN'T THAT FULFILL THE CLAUSE IN YOUR GRANDFATHER'S WILL?
YOU'RE RIGHT! IT DOES!
HA! HA! THAT OLD MALE CHAUVINIST WOULD HAVE A FIT IF HE KNEW IT MIGHT TAKE A GIRL'S TEAM TO ACHIEVE HIS VICTORY! SERVES HIM RIGHT!
BETTY, YOU'RE FANTASTIC!
NOT SO QUICK WITH THE CONGRATULATIONS! WE STILL HAVE TO BEAT CENTRAL...ONE OF THE BEST TEAMS IN THE STATE!
THE NEXT DAY...
WELL, UNLIKE THE BOYS, WE DON'T HAVE THE PRESSURE OF A BIG CROWD TO CONTEND WITH!
OH, NO?! JUST LOOK AT THE STANDS!
OUR SOFTBALL TEAM PLAYS HARDBALL!
GULP! THE WHOLE TOWN MUST HAVE HEARD ABOUT THE IMPORTANCE OF TODAY'S GAME!

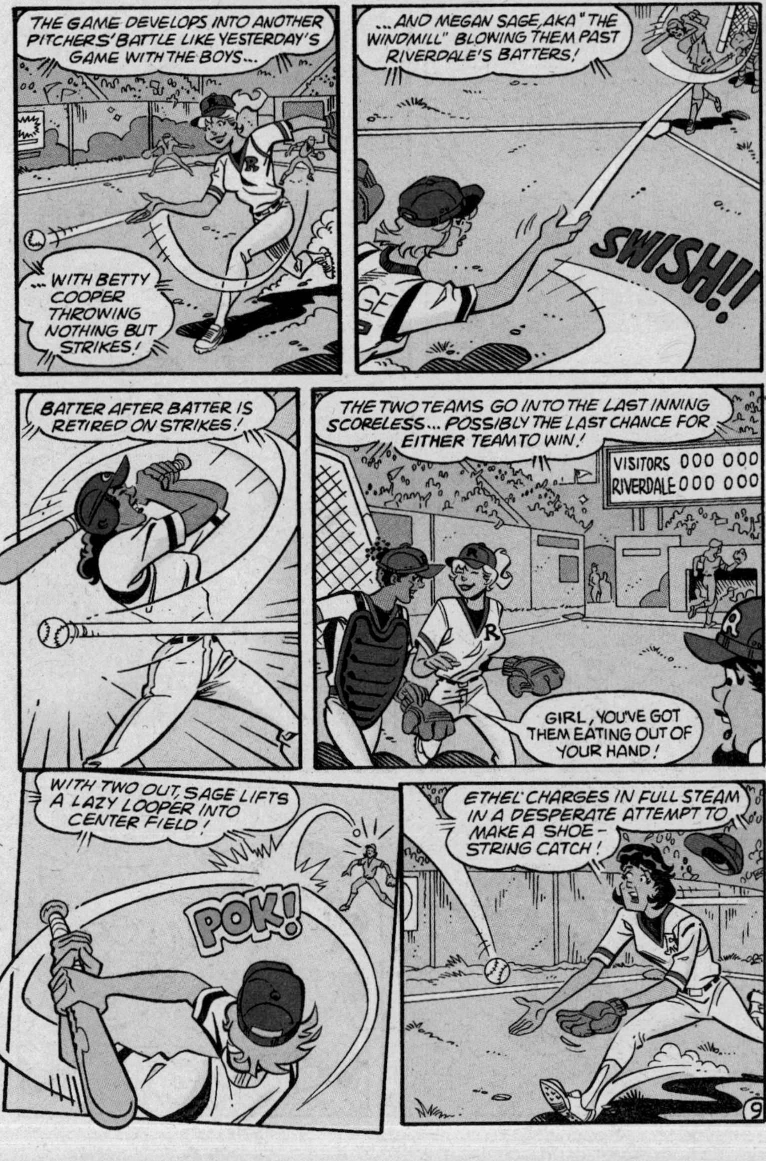
THE GAME DEVELOPS INTO ANOTHER PITCHERS' BATTLE LIKE YESTERDAY'S GAME WITH THE BOYS...
...WITH BETTY COOPER THROWING NOTHING BUT STRIKES!
...AND MEGAN SAGE, AKA "THE WINDMILL" BLOWING THEM PAST RIVERDALE'S BATTERS!
SWISH!!
GE
BATTER AFTER BATTER IS RETIRED ON STRIKES!
THE TWO TEAMS GO INTO THE LAST INNING SCORELESS... POSSIBLY THE LAST CHANCE FOR EITHER TEAM TO WIN!
VISITORS 000 000
RIVERDALE 000 000
GIRL, YOU'VE GOT THEM EATING OUT OF YOUR HAND!
WITH TWO OUT, SAGE LIFTS A LAZY LOOPER INTO CENTER FIELD!
POK!
ETHEL CHARGES IN FULL STEAM IN A DESPERATE ATTEMPT TO MAKE A SHOE-STRING CATCH!

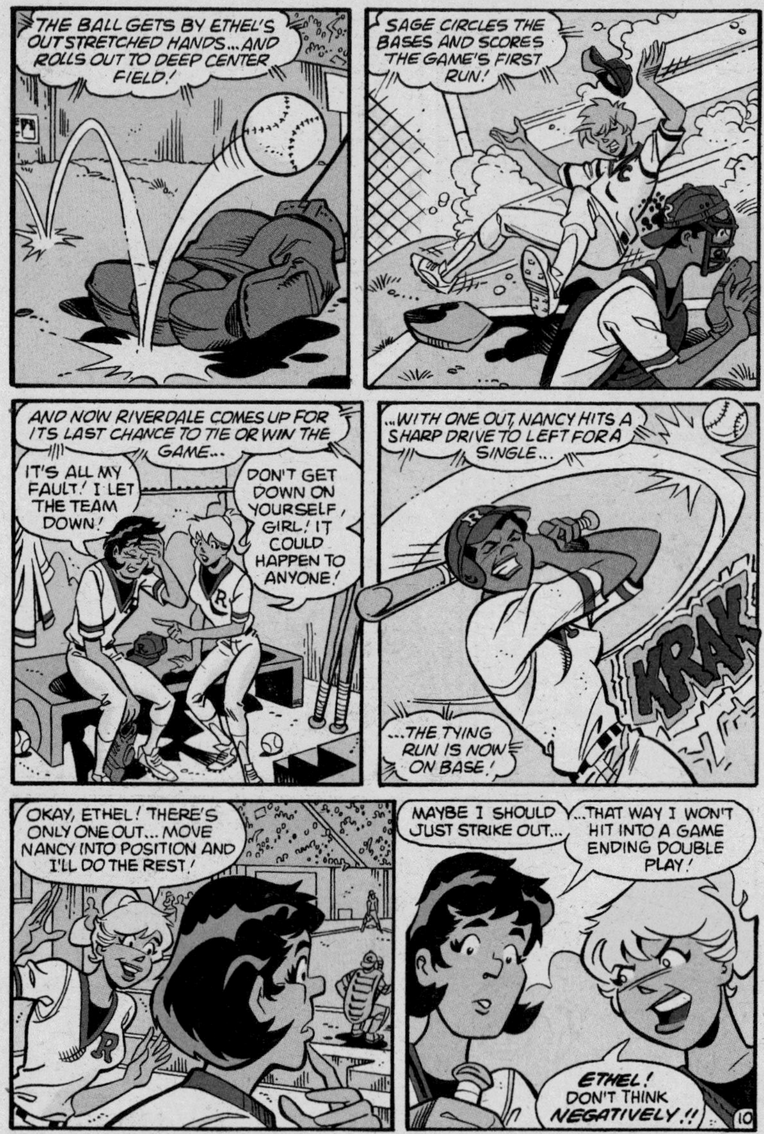
THE BALL GETS BY ETHEL'S OUTSTRETCHED HANDS... AND ROLLS OUT TO DEEP CENTER FIELD!
SAGE CIRCLES THE BASES AND SCORES THE GAME'S FIRST RUN!
AND NOW RIVERDALE COMES UP FOR ITS LAST CHANCE TO TIE OR WIN THE GAME...
IT'S ALL MY FAULT! I LET THE TEAM DOWN!
DON'T GET DOWN ON YOURSELF, GIRL! IT COULD HAPPEN TO ANYONE!
...WITH ONE OUT, NANCY HITS A SHARP DRIVE TO LEFT FOR A SINGLE...
KRAK
...THE TYING RUN IS NOW ON BASE!
OKAY, ETHEL! THERE'S ONLY ONE OUT... MOVE NANCY INTO POSITION AND I'LL DO THE REST!
MAYBE I SHOULD JUST STRIKE OUT...
...THAT WAY I WON'T HIT INTO A GAME ENDING DOUBLE PLAY!
ETHEL! DON'T THINK NEGATIVELY!!
10

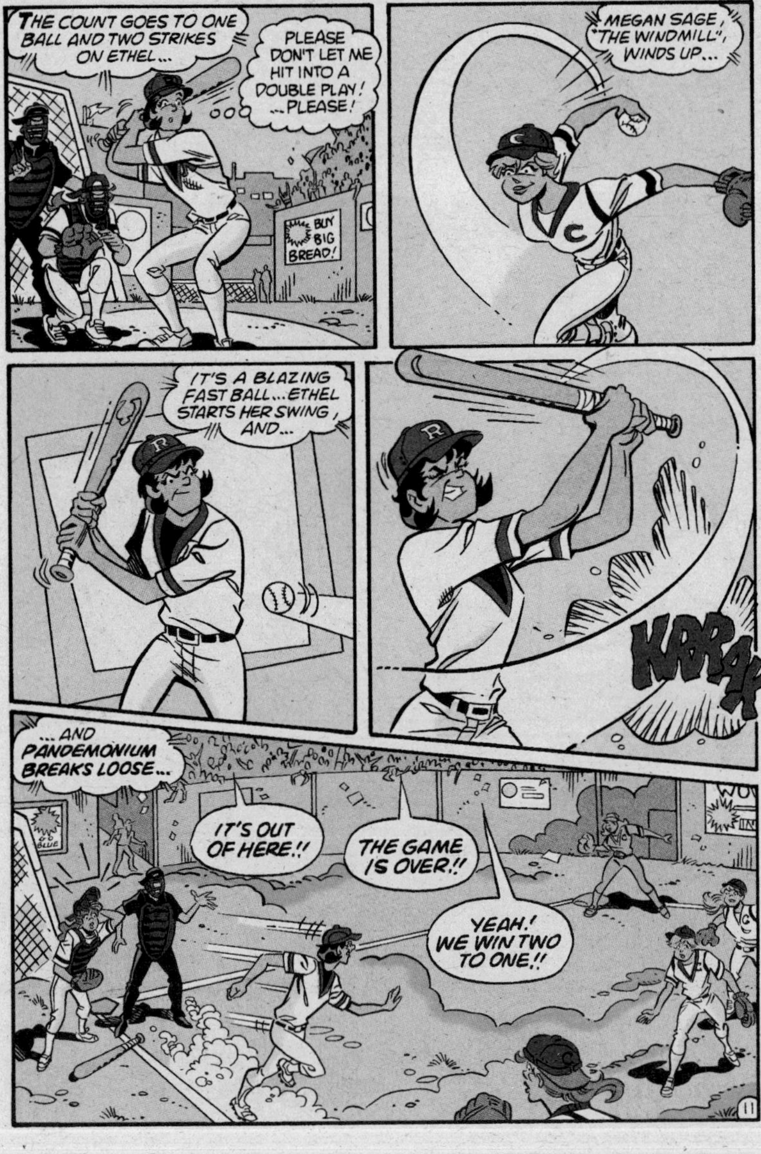
THE COUNT GOES TO ONE BALL AND TWO STRIKES ON ETHEL...
PLEASE DON'T LET ME HIT INTO A DOUBLE PLAY! ...PLEASE!
BUY BIG BREAD!
MEGAN SAGE, "THE WINDMILL", WINDS UP...
IT'S A BLAZING FAST BALL...ETHEL STARTS HER SWING, AND...
KRRAK
...AND PANDEMONIUM BREAKS LOOSE...
IT'S OUT OF HERE!!
THE GAME IS OVER!!
YEAH! WE WIN TWO TO ONE!!

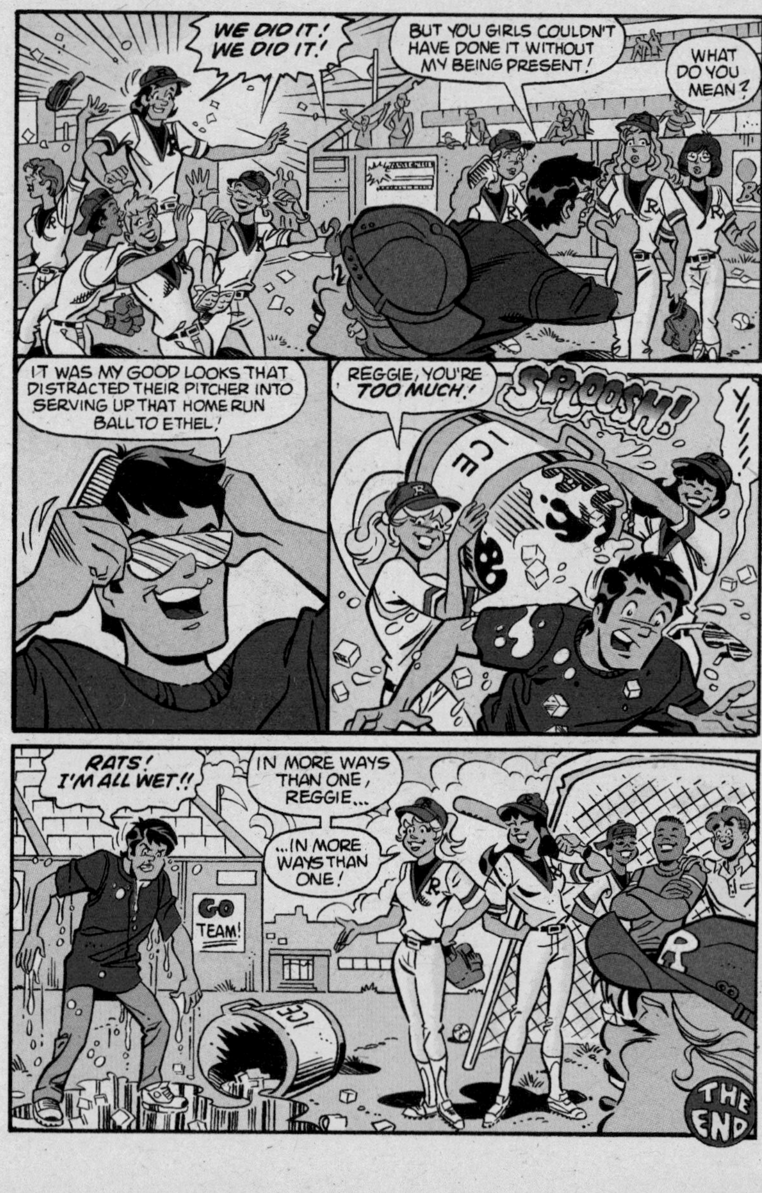
WE DID IT! WE DID IT!
BUT YOU GIRLS COULDN'T HAVE DONE IT WITHOUT MY BEING PRESENT!
WHAT DO YOU MEAN?
IT WAS MY GOOD LOOKS THAT DISTRACTED THEIR PITCHER INTO SERVING UP THAT HOME RUN BALL TO ETHEL!
REGGIE, YOU'RE TOO MUCH!
SPLOOSH!
ICE
Y-!
RATS! I'M ALL WET!!
IN MORE WAYS THAN ONE, REGGIE...
...IN MORE WAYS THAN ONE!
GO TEAM!
ICE
THE END

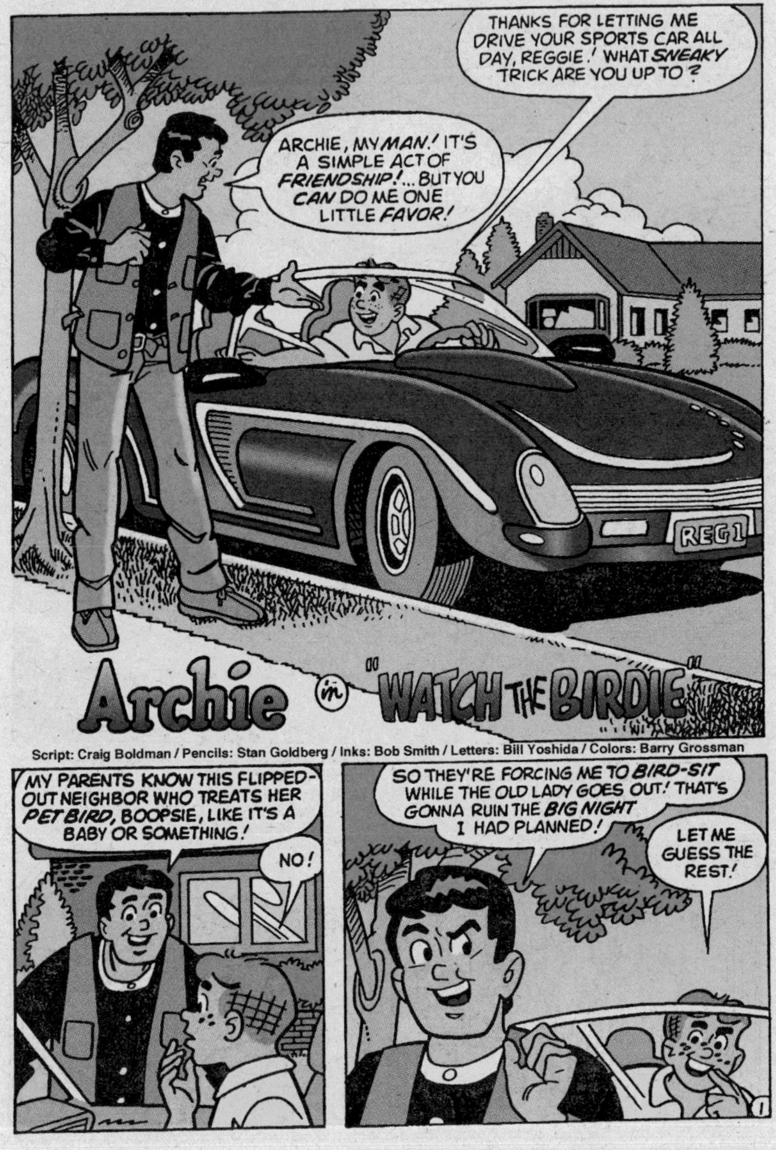
THANKS FOR LETTING ME DRIVE YOUR SPORTS CAR ALL DAY, REGGIE! WHAT SNEAKY TRICK ARE YOU UP TO?
ARCHIE, MY MAN! IT'S A SIMPLE ACT OF FRIENDSHIP!... BUT YOU CAN DO ME ONE LITTLE FAVOR!
REG 1
Archie in "WATCH THE BIRDIE"
Script: Craig Boldman / Pencils: Stan Goldberg / Inks: Bob Smith / Letters: Bill Yoshida / Colors: Barry Grossman
MY PARENTS KNOW THIS FLIPPED-OUT NEIGHBOR WHO TREATS HER PET BIRD, BOOPSIE, LIKE IT'S A BABY OR SOMETHING!
NO!
SO THEY'RE FORCING ME TO BIRD-SIT WHILE THE OLD LADY GOES OUT! THAT'S GONNA RUIN THE BIG NIGHT I HAD PLANNED!
LET ME GUESS THE REST!
1

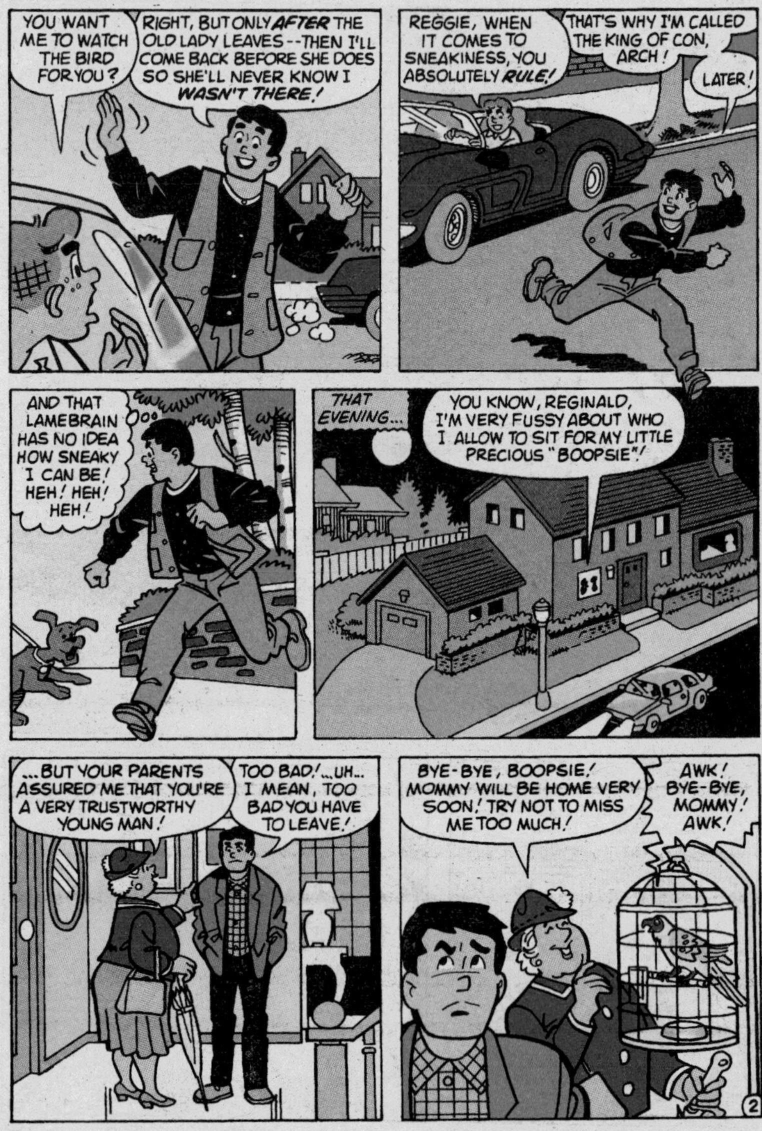
YOU WANT ME TO WATCH THE BIRD FOR YOU?
RIGHT, BUT ONLY AFTER THE OLD LADY LEAVES--THEN I'LL COME BACK BEFORE SHE DOES SO SHE'LL NEVER KNOW I WASN'T THERE!
REGGIE, WHEN IT COMES TO SNEAKINESS, YOU ABSOLUTELY RULE!
THAT'S WHY I'M CALLED THE KING OF CON, ARCH!
LATER!
AND THAT LAMEBRAIN HAS NO IDEA HOW SNEAKY I CAN BE! HEH! HEH! HEH!
THAT EVENING...
YOU KNOW, REGINALD, I'M VERY FUSSY ABOUT WHO I ALLOW TO SIT FOR MY LITTLE PRECIOUS "BOOPSIE"!
...BUT YOUR PARENTS ASSURED ME THAT YOU'RE A VERY TRUSTWORTHY YOUNG MAN!
TOO BAD! ...UH... I MEAN, TOO BAD YOU HAVE TO LEAVE!
BYE-BYE, BOOPSIE! MOMMY WILL BE HOME VERY SOON! TRY NOT TO MISS ME TOO MUCH!
AWK! BYE-BYE, MOMMY! AWK!
2

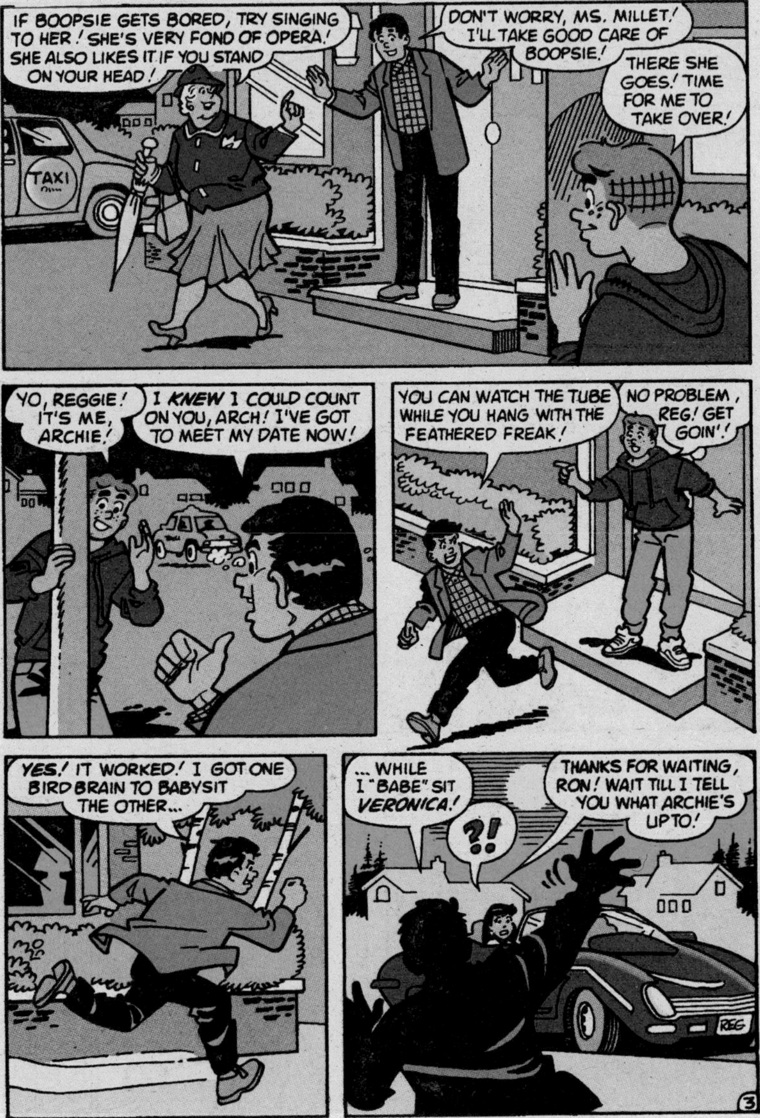
IF BOOPSIE GETS BORED, TRY SINGING TO HER! SHE'S VERY FOND OF OPERA! SHE ALSO LIKES IT IF YOU STAND ON YOUR HEAD!
DON'T WORRY, MS. MILLET! I'LL TAKE GOOD CARE OF BOOPSIE!
THERE SHE GOES! TIME FOR ME TO TAKE OVER!
TAXI
YO, REGGIE! IT'S ME, ARCHIE!
I *KNEW* I COULD COUNT ON YOU, ARCH! I'VE GOT TO MEET MY DATE NOW!
YOU CAN WATCH THE TUBE WHILE YOU HANG WITH THE FEATHERED FREAK!
NO PROBLEM, REG! GET GOIN'!
YES! IT WORKED! I GOT ONE BIRD BRAIN TO BABYSIT THE OTHER...
... WHILE I "BABE" SIT *VERONICA!*
?!
THANKS FOR WAITING, RON! WAIT TILL I TELL YOU WHAT ARCHIE'S UP TO!
REG
3

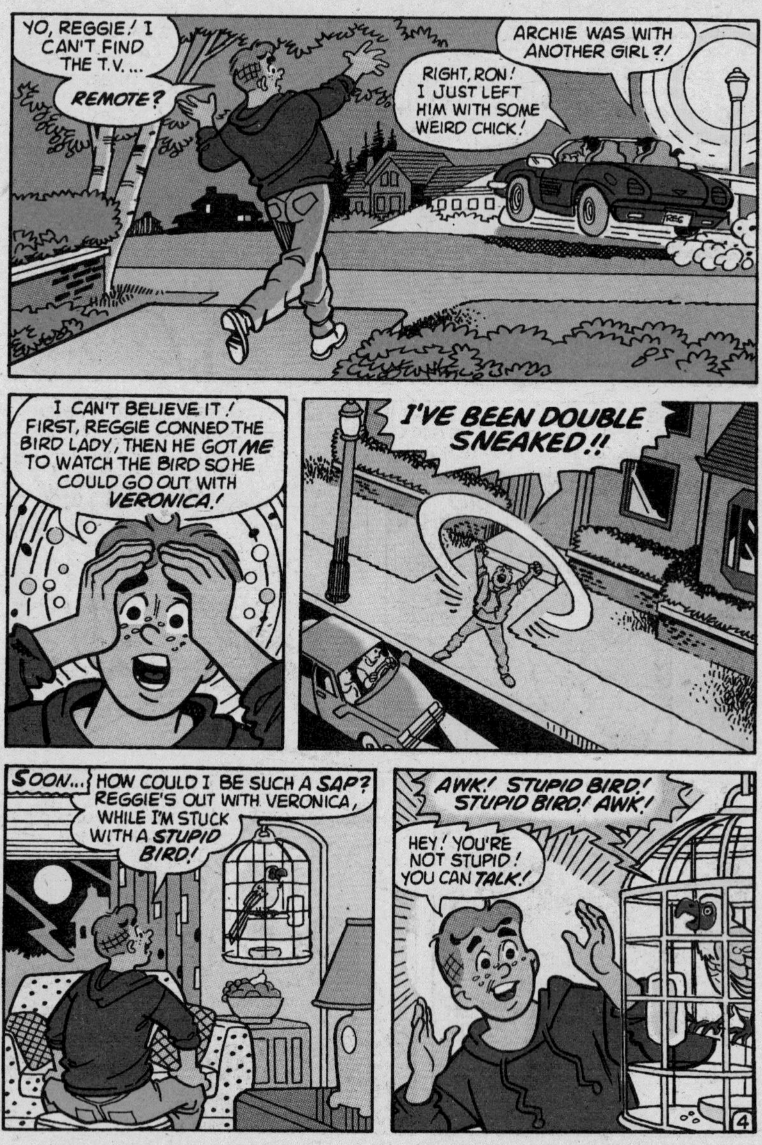
YO, REGGIE! I CAN'T FIND THE T.V. ...
REMOTE?
ARCHIE WAS WITH ANOTHER GIRL?!
RIGHT, RON! I JUST LEFT HIM WITH SOME WEIRD CHICK!
I CAN'T BELIEVE IT! FIRST, REGGIE CONNED THE BIRD LADY, THEN HE GOT ME TO WATCH THE BIRD SO HE COULD GO OUT WITH VERONICA!
I'VE BEEN DOUBLE SNEAKED!!
SOON...
HOW COULD I BE SUCH A SAP? REGGIE'S OUT WITH VERONICA, WHILE I'M STUCK WITH A STUPID BIRD!
AWK! STUPID BIRD! STUPID BIRD! AWK!
HEY! YOU'RE NOT STUPID! YOU CAN TALK!
4

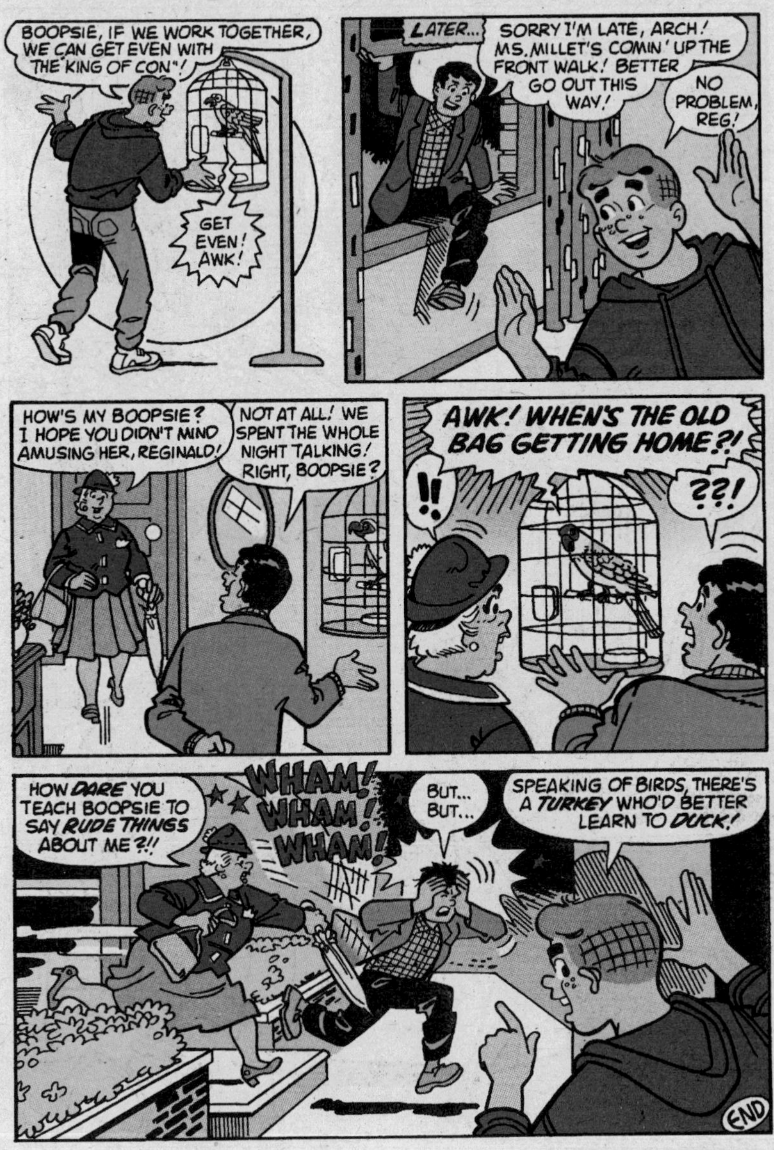
BOOPSIE, IF WE WORK TOGETHER, WE CAN GET EVEN WITH THE "KING OF CON"!
GET EVEN! AWK!
LATER...
SORRY I'M LATE, ARCH! MS. MILLET'S COMIN' UP THE FRONT WALK! BETTER GO OUT THIS WAY!
NO PROBLEM, REG!
HOW'S MY BOOPSIE? I HOPE YOU DIDN'T MIND AMUSING HER, REGINALD!
NOT AT ALL! WE SPENT THE WHOLE NIGHT TALKING! RIGHT, BOOPSIE?
AWK! WHEN'S THE OLD BAG GETTING HOME?!
!!
??!
HOW DARE YOU TEACH BOOPSIE TO SAY RUDE THINGS ABOUT ME?!!
WHAM! WHAM! WHAM!
BUT... BUT...
SPEAKING OF BIRDS, THERE'S A TURKEY WHO'D BETTER LEARN TO DUCK!
END

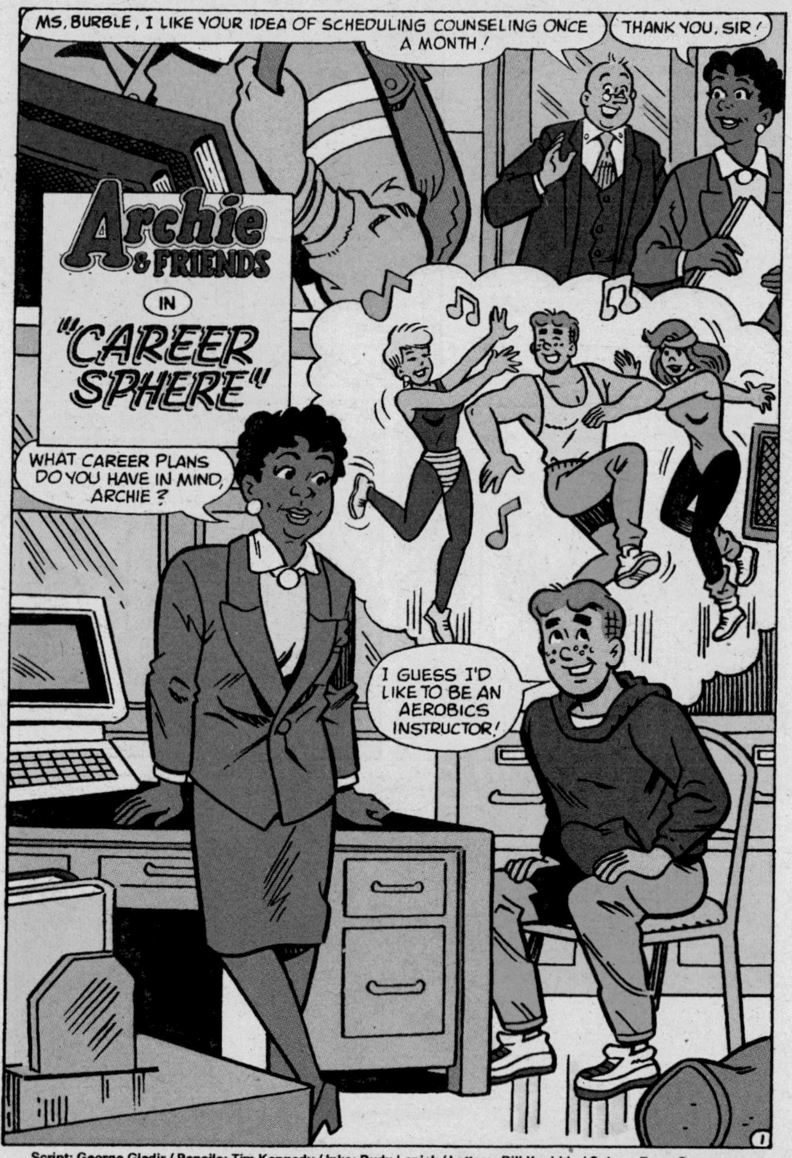
MS. BURBLE, I LIKE YOUR IDEA OF SCHEDULING COUNSELING ONCE A MONTH!
THANK YOU, SIR!
Archie & FRIENDS IN "CAREER SPHERE"
WHAT CAREER PLANS DO YOU HAVE IN MIND, ARCHIE?
I GUESS I'D LIKE TO BE AN AEROBICS INSTRUCTOR!
1

Script: George Gladir / Pencils: Tim Kennedy / Inks: Rudy Lapick / Letters: Bill Yoshida / Colors: Barry Grossman

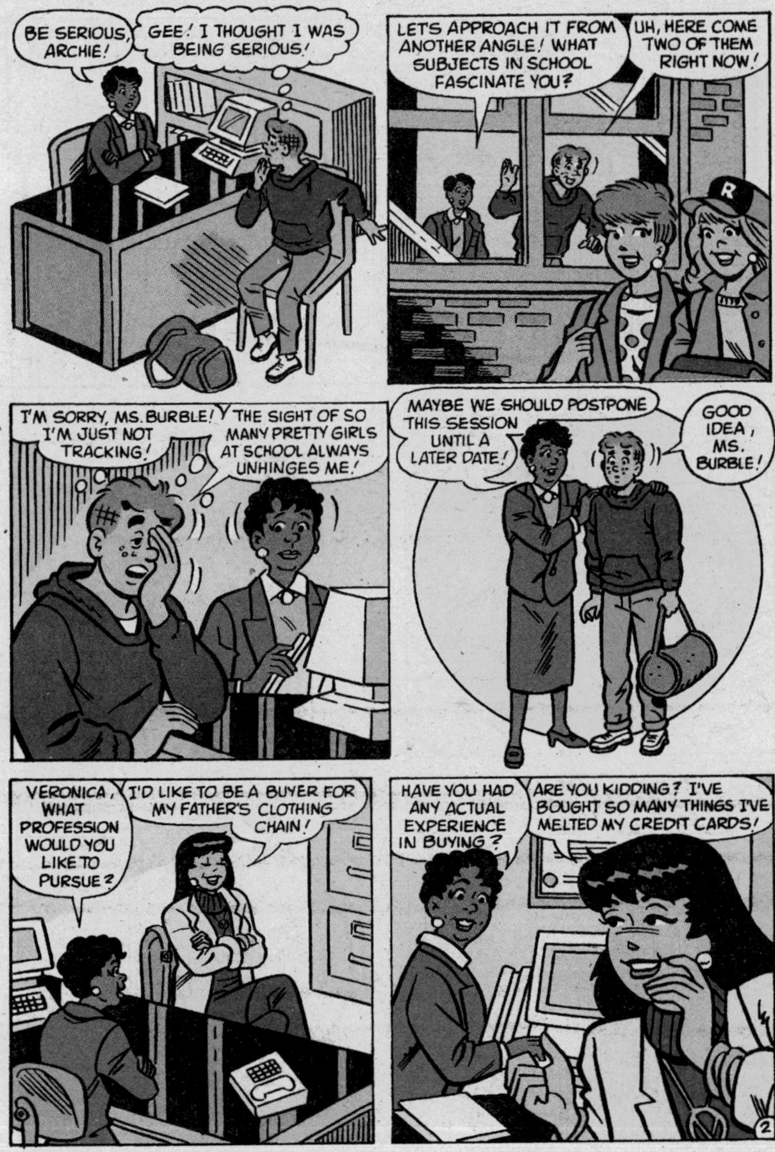
BE SERIOUS, ARCHIE!
GEE! I THOUGHT I WAS BEING SERIOUS!
LET'S APPROACH IT FROM ANOTHER ANGLE! WHAT SUBJECTS IN SCHOOL FASCINATE YOU?
UH, HERE COME TWO OF THEM RIGHT NOW!
R
I'M SORRY, MS. BURBLE! I'M JUST NOT TRACKING!
THE SIGHT OF SO MANY PRETTY GIRLS AT SCHOOL ALWAYS UNHINGES ME!
MAYBE WE SHOULD POSTPONE THIS SESSION UNTIL A LATER DATE!
GOOD IDEA, MS. BURBLE!
VERONICA, WHAT PROFESSION WOULD YOU LIKE TO PURSUE?
I'D LIKE TO BE A BUYER FOR MY FATHER'S CLOTHING CHAIN!
HAVE YOU HAD ANY ACTUAL EXPERIENCE IN BUYING?
ARE YOU KIDDING? I'VE BOUGHT SO MANY THINGS I'VE MELTED MY CREDIT CARDS!
2

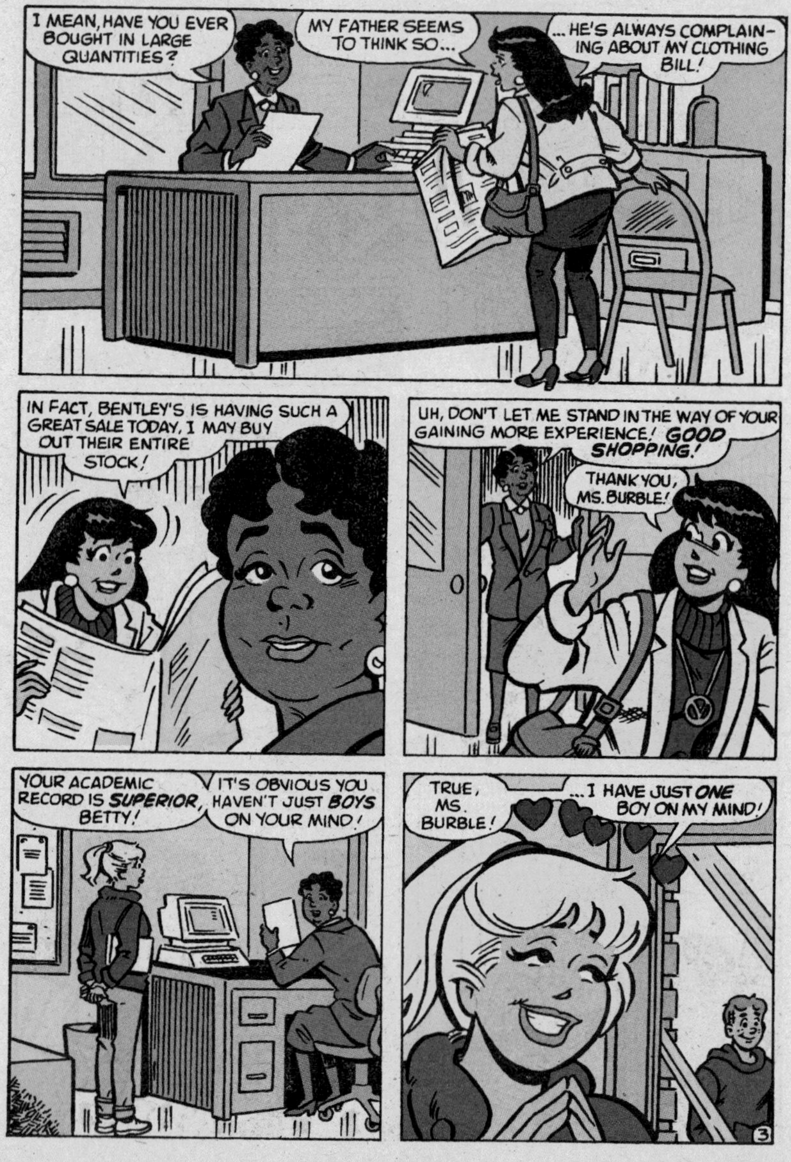
I MEAN, HAVE YOU EVER BOUGHT IN LARGE QUANTITIES?
MY FATHER SEEMS TO THINK SO...
... HE'S ALWAYS COMPLAINING ABOUT MY CLOTHING BILL!
IN FACT, BENTLEY'S IS HAVING SUCH A GREAT SALE TODAY, I MAY BUY OUT THEIR ENTIRE STOCK!
UH, DON'T LET ME STAND IN THE WAY OF YOUR GAINING MORE EXPERIENCE! GOOD SHOPPING!
THANK YOU, MS. BURBLE!
YOUR ACADEMIC RECORD IS SUPERIOR, BETTY!
IT'S OBVIOUS YOU HAVEN'T JUST BOYS ON YOUR MIND!
TRUE, MS. BURBLE!
... I HAVE JUST ONE BOY ON MY MIND!
3

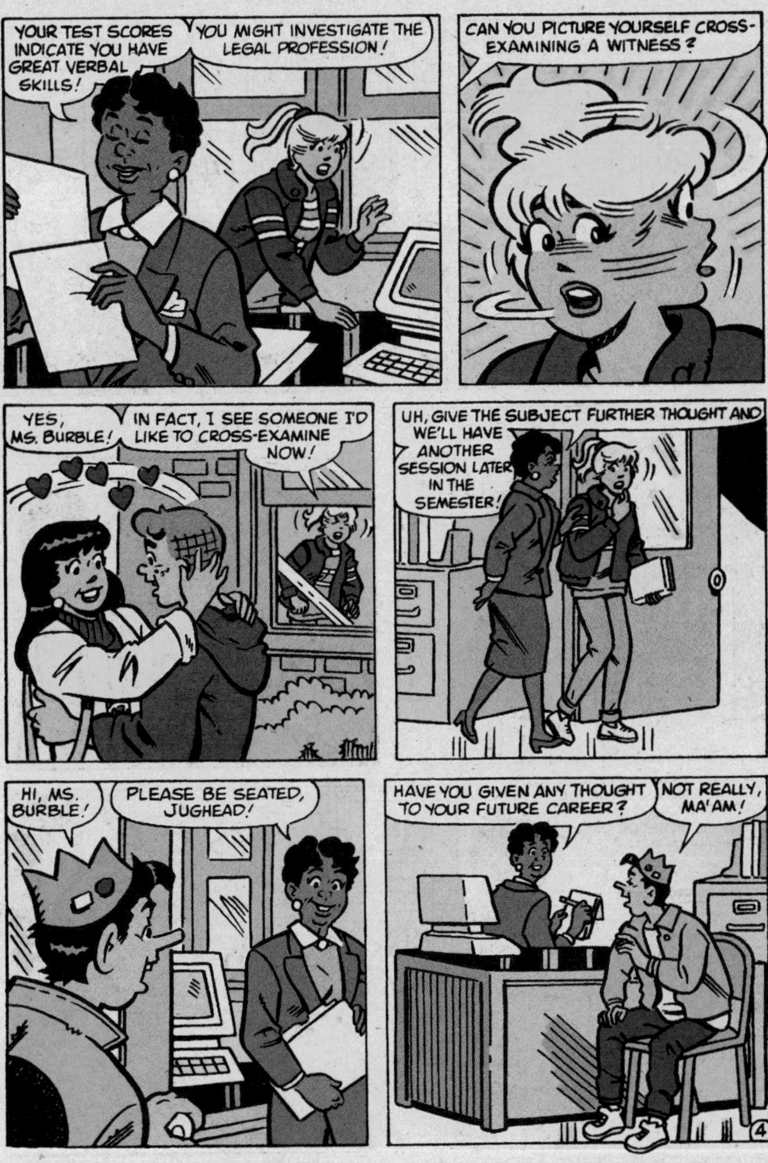
YOUR TEST SCORES INDICATE YOU HAVE GREAT VERBAL SKILLS!
YOU MIGHT INVESTIGATE THE LEGAL PROFESSION!
CAN YOU PICTURE YOURSELF CROSS-EXAMINING A WITNESS?
YES, MS. BURBLE!
IN FACT, I SEE SOMEONE I'D LIKE TO CROSS-EXAMINE NOW!
UH, GIVE THE SUBJECT FURTHER THOUGHT AND WE'LL HAVE ANOTHER SESSION LATER IN THE SEMESTER!
HI, MS. BURBLE!
PLEASE BE SEATED, JUGHEAD!
HAVE YOU GIVEN ANY THOUGHT TO YOUR FUTURE CAREER?
NOT REALLY, MA'AM!
4

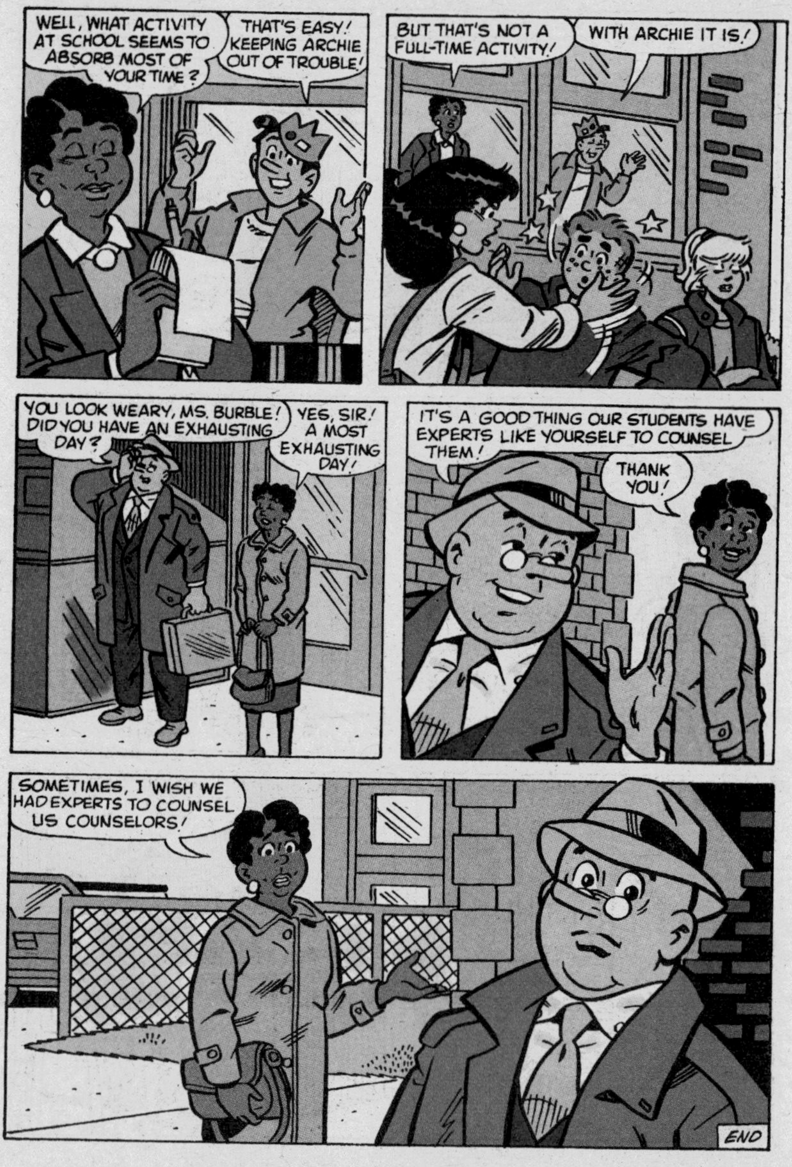
WELL, WHAT ACTIVITY AT SCHOOL SEEMS TO ABSORB MOST OF YOUR TIME?
THAT'S EASY! KEEPING ARCHIE OUT OF TROUBLE!
BUT THAT'S NOT A FULL-TIME ACTIVITY!
WITH ARCHIE IT IS!
YOU LOOK WEARY, MS. BURBLE! DID YOU HAVE AN EXHAUSTING DAY?
YES, SIR! A MOST EXHAUSTING DAY!
IT'S A GOOD THING OUR STUDENTS HAVE EXPERTS LIKE YOURSELF TO COUNSEL THEM!
THANK YOU!
SOMETIMES, I WISH WE HAD EXPERTS TO COUNSEL US COUNSELORS!
END

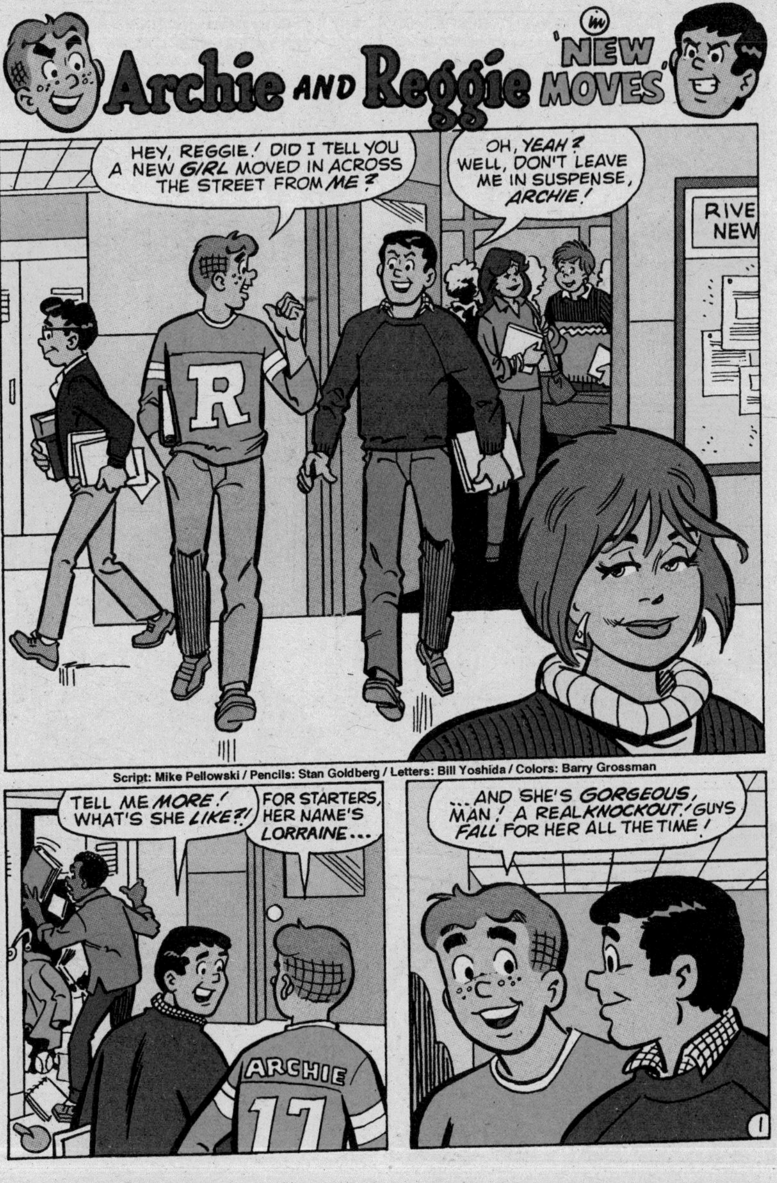
Archie AND Reggie in 'NEW MOVES'
HEY, REGGIE! DID I TELL YOU A NEW GIRL MOVED IN ACROSS THE STREET FROM ME?
OH, YEAH? WELL, DON'T LEAVE ME IN SUSPENSE, ARCHIE!
RIVE
NEW
Script: Mike Pellowski / Pencils: Stan Goldberg / Letters: Bill Yoshida / Colors: Barry Grossman
TELL ME MORE! WHAT'S SHE LIKE?!
FOR STARTERS, HER NAME'S LORRAINE...
ARCHIE
17
...AND SHE'S GORGEOUS, MAN! A REAL KNOCKOUT! GUYS FALL FOR HER ALL THE TIME!
1

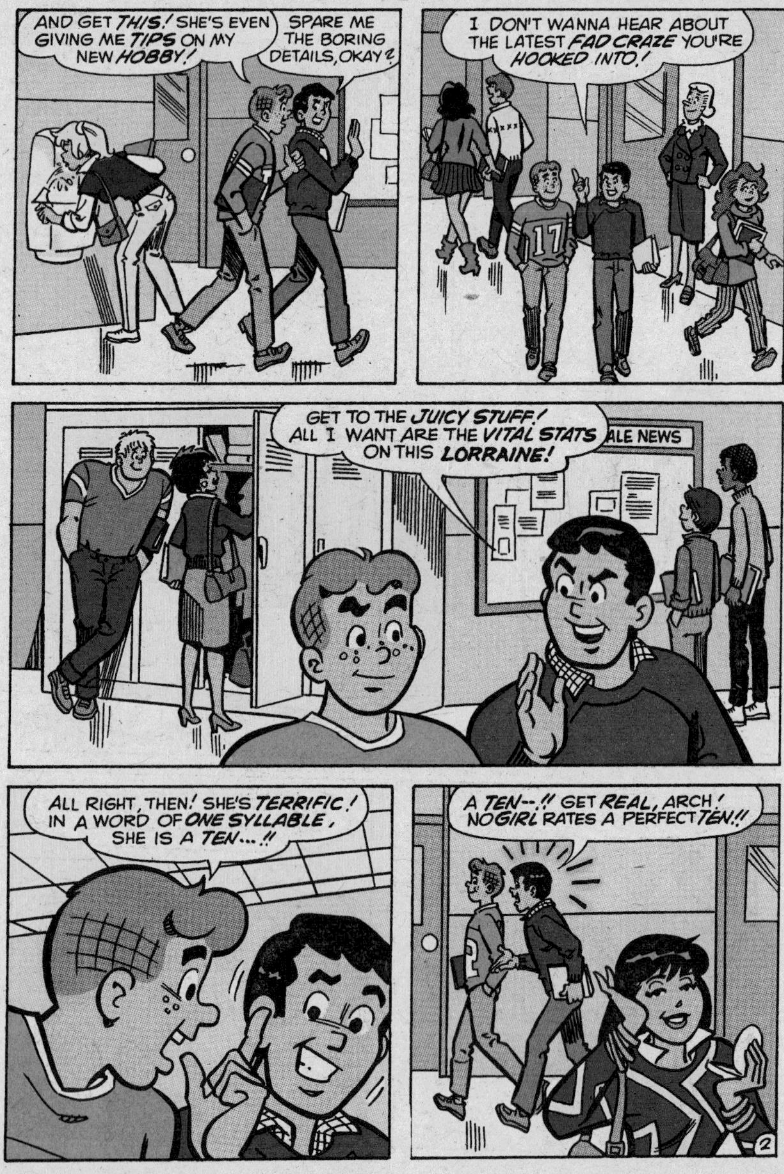
AND GET THIS! SHE'S EVEN GIVING ME TIPS ON MY NEW HOBBY!
SPARE ME THE BORING DETAILS, OKAY?
I DON'T WANNA HEAR ABOUT THE LATEST FAD CRAZE YOU'RE HOOKED INTO!
GET TO THE JUICY STUFF! ALL I WANT ARE THE VITAL STATS ON THIS LORRAINE!
ALE NEWS
ALL RIGHT, THEN! SHE'S TERRIFIC! IN A WORD OF ONE SYLLABLE, SHE IS A TEN...!!
A TEN--!! GET REAL, ARCH! NO GIRL RATES A PERFECT TEN!!
2

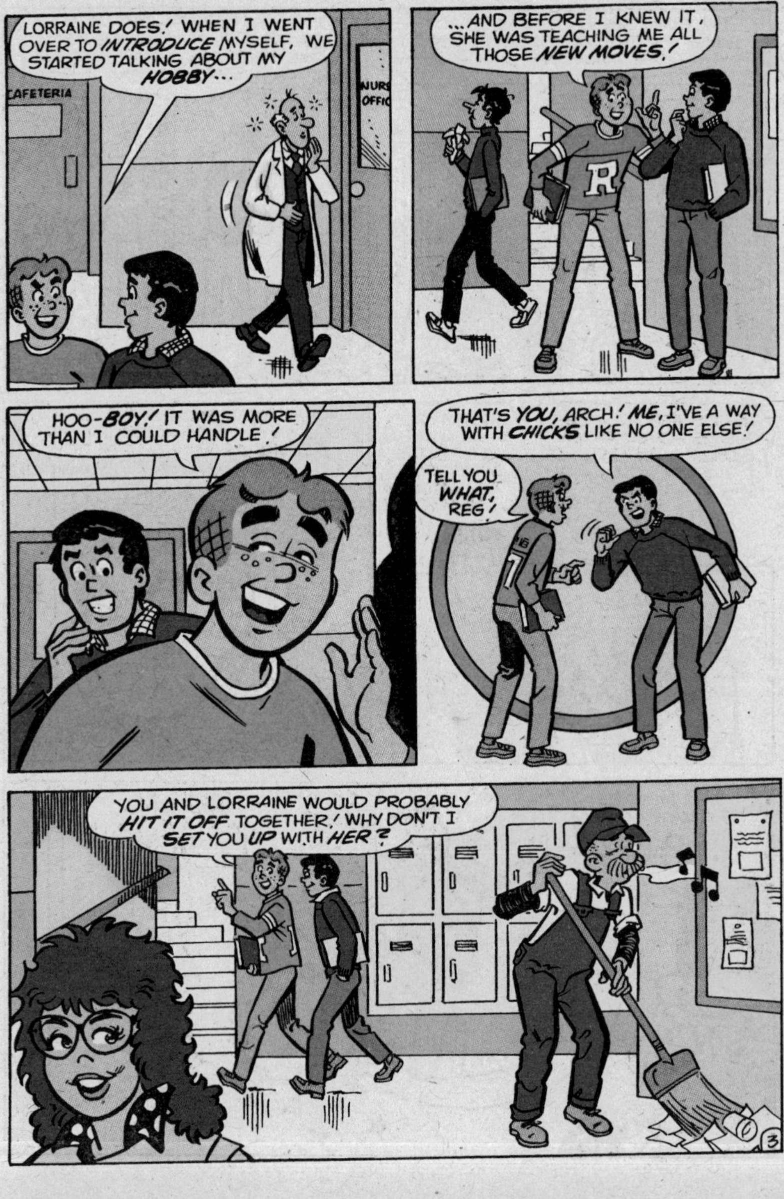
LORRAINE DOES! WHEN I WENT OVER TO INTRODUCE MYSELF, WE STARTED TALKING ABOUT MY HOBBY...
CAFETERIA
NURS OFFIC
...AND BEFORE I KNEW IT, SHE WAS TEACHING ME ALL THOSE NEW MOVES!
R
HOO-BOY! IT WAS MORE THAN I COULD HANDLE!
THAT'S YOU, ARCH! ME, I'VE A WAY WITH CHICKS LIKE NO ONE ELSE!
TELL YOU WHAT, REG!
YOU AND LORRAINE WOULD PROBABLY HIT IT OFF TOGETHER! WHY DON'T I SET YOU UP WITH HER?
3

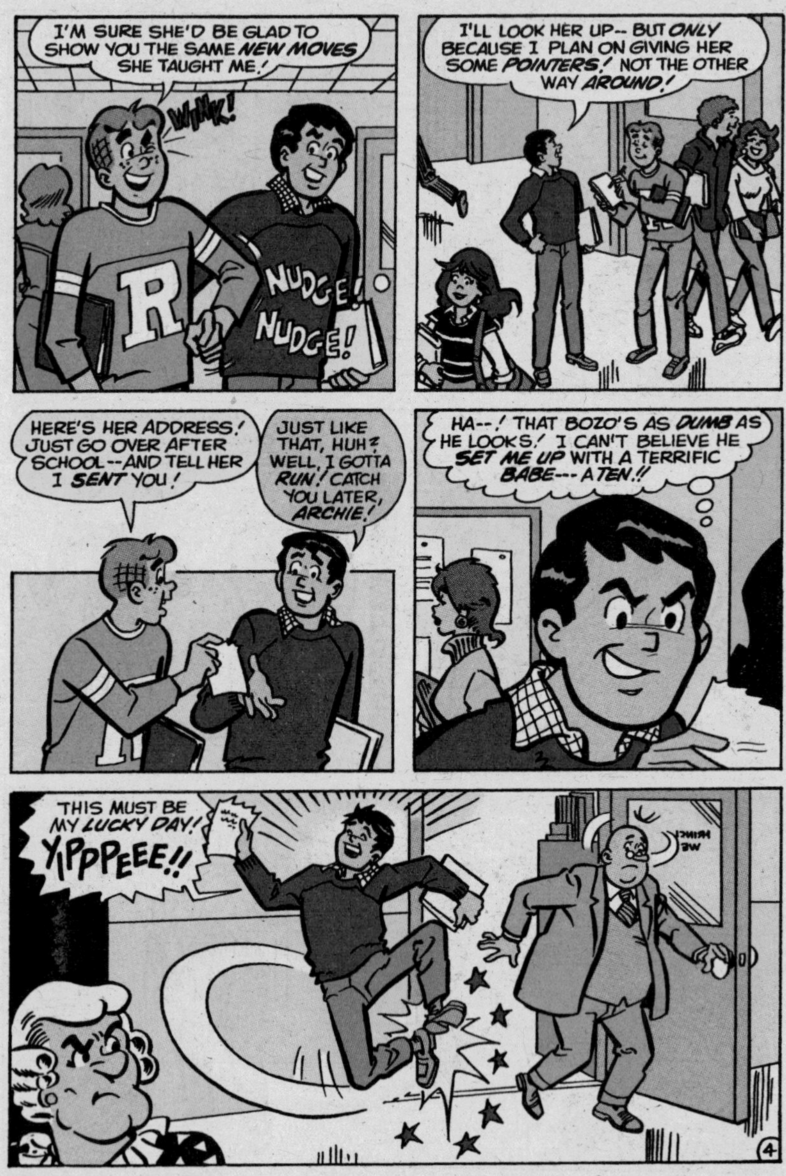
I'M SURE SHE'D BE GLAD TO SHOW YOU THE SAME NEW MOVES SHE TAUGHT ME!
WINK!
NUDGE! NUDGE!
I'LL LOOK HER UP-- BUT ONLY BECAUSE I PLAN ON GIVING HER SOME POINTERS! NOT THE OTHER WAY AROUND!
HERE'S HER ADDRESS! JUST GO OVER AFTER SCHOOL--AND TELL HER I SENT YOU!
JUST LIKE THAT, HUH? WELL, I GOTTA RUN! CATCH YOU LATER, ARCHIE!
HA--! THAT BOZO'S AS DUMB AS HE LOOKS! I CAN'T BELIEVE HE SET ME UP WITH A TERRIFIC BABE--- A TEN!!
THIS MUST BE MY LUCKY DAY!
YIPPPEEE!!
4

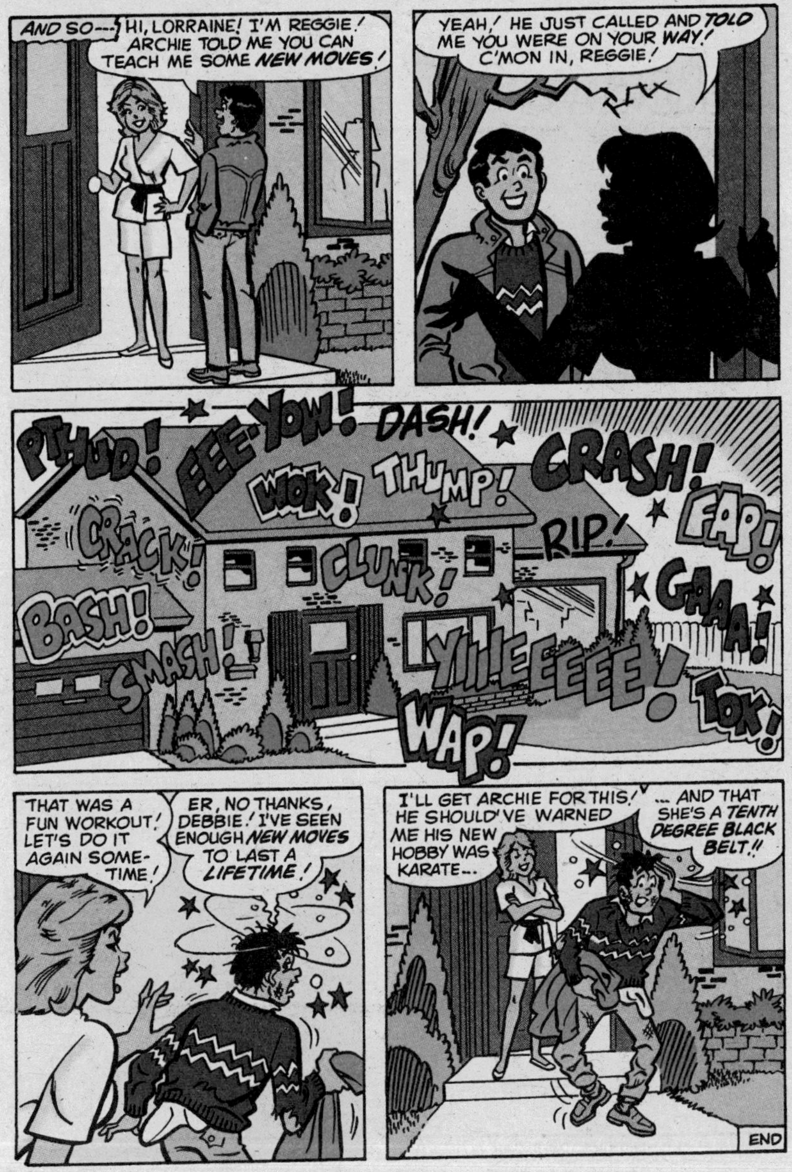
AND SO---
HI, LORRAINE! I'M REGGIE! ARCHIE TOLD ME YOU CAN TEACH ME SOME NEW MOVES!
YEAH! HE JUST CALLED AND TOLD ME YOU WERE ON YOUR WAY! C'MON IN, REGGIE!
PTHUD! EEE-YOW! DASH! WOK! THUMP! CRASH! FAP! CRACK! RIP! CLUNK! GAAAA! BASH! SMASH! YIIIEEEEEE! WAP! TOK!
THAT WAS A FUN WORKOUT! LET'S DO IT AGAIN SOMETIME!
ER, NO THANKS, DEBBIE! I'VE SEEN ENOUGH NEW MOVES TO LAST A LIFETIME!
I'LL GET ARCHIE FOR THIS! HE SHOULD'VE WARNED ME HIS NEW HOBBY WAS KARATE...
... AND THAT SHE'S A TENTH DEGREE BLACK BELT!!
END

Archie in SPEED DEMON

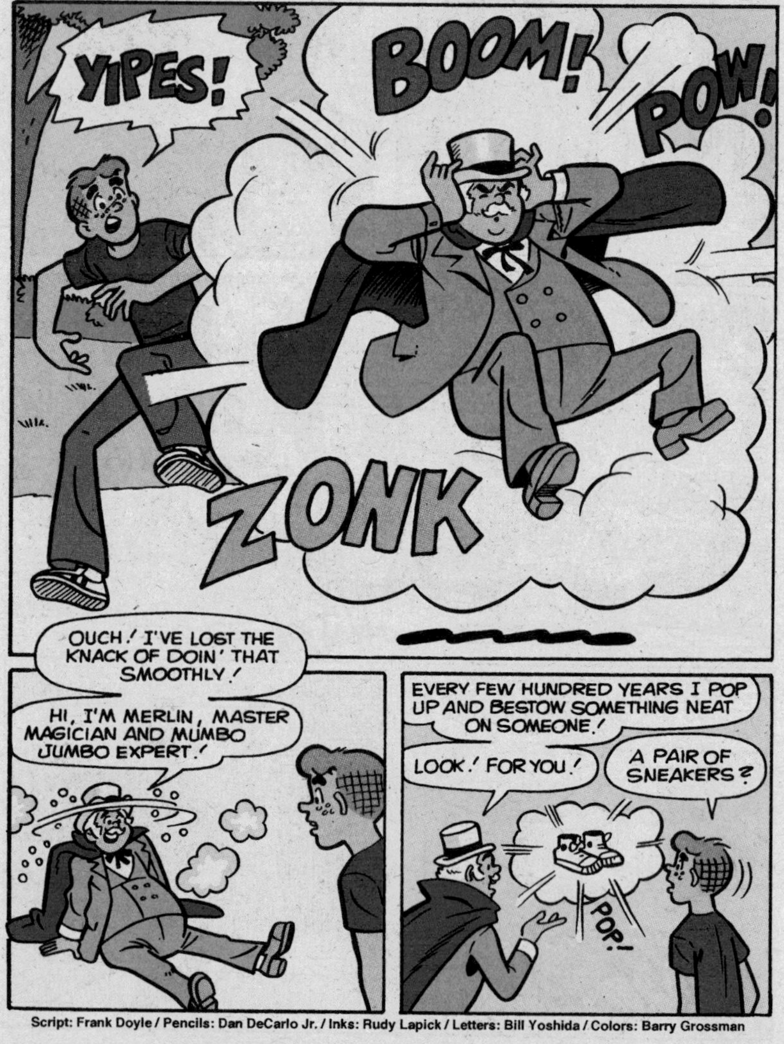
YIPES!
BOOM!
POW!
ZONK
OUCH! I'VE LOST THE KNACK OF DOIN' THAT SMOOTHLY!
HI, I'M MERLIN, MASTER MAGICIAN AND MUMBO JUMBO EXPERT!
EVERY FEW HUNDRED YEARS I POP UP AND BESTOW SOMETHING NEAT ON SOMEONE!
LOOK! FOR YOU!
A PAIR OF SNEAKERS?
POP!

Script: Frank Doyle / Pencils: Dan DeCarlo Jr. / Inks: Rudy Lapick / Letters: Bill Yoshida / Colors: Barry Grossman

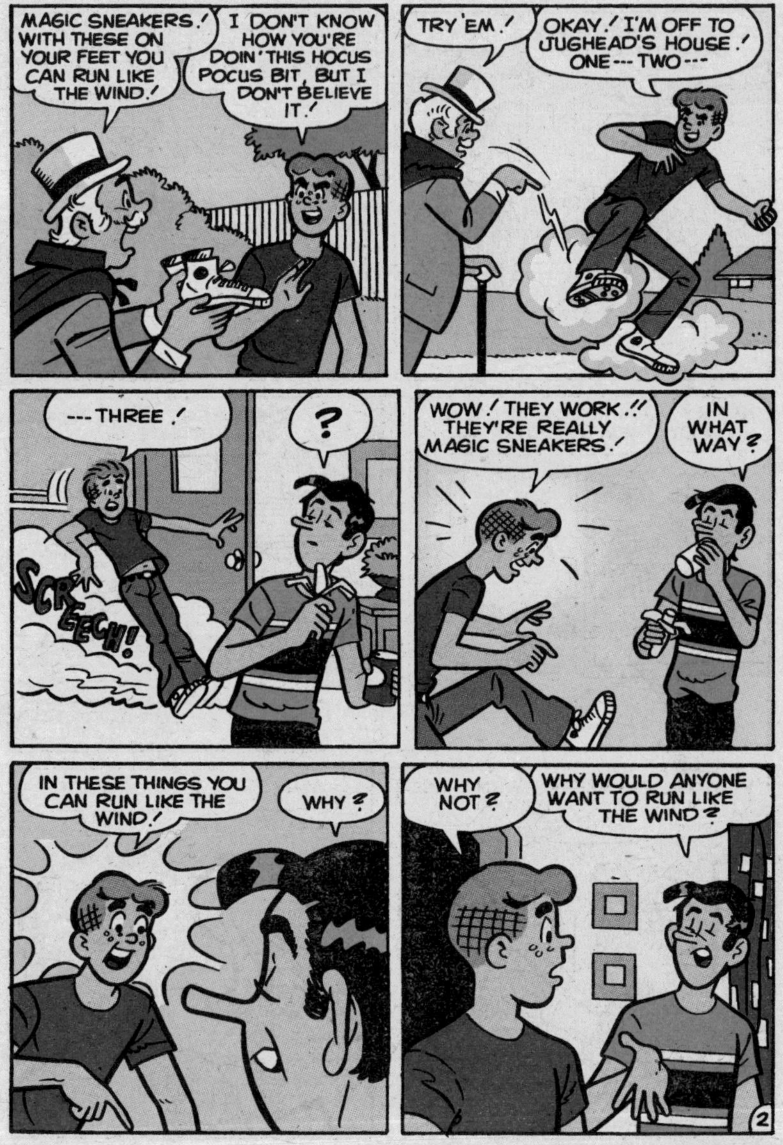
MAGIC SNEAKERS.! WITH THESE ON YOUR FEET YOU CAN RUN LIKE THE WIND.!
I DON'T KNOW HOW YOU'RE DOIN' THIS HOCUS POCUS BIT, BUT I DON'T BELIEVE IT.!
TRY 'EM.!
OKAY.! I'M OFF TO JUGHEAD'S HOUSE.! ONE --- TWO ---
--- THREE.!
?
SCREEECH!
WOW.! THEY WORK.!! THEY'RE REALLY MAGIC SNEAKERS.!
IN WHAT WAY?
IN THESE THINGS YOU CAN RUN LIKE THE WIND.!
WHY?
WHY NOT?
WHY WOULD ANYONE WANT TO RUN LIKE THE WIND?
2

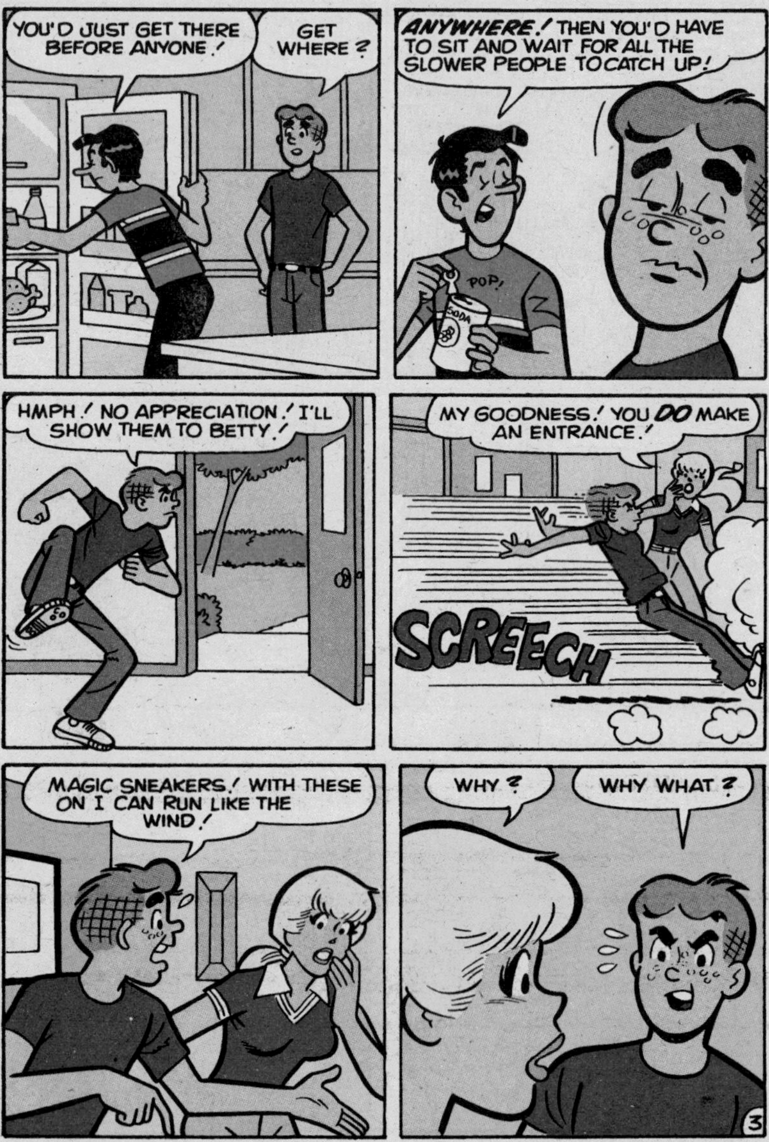
YOU'D JUST GET THERE BEFORE ANYONE!
GET WHERE?
ANYWHERE! THEN YOU'D HAVE TO SIT AND WAIT FOR ALL THE SLOWER PEOPLE TO CATCH UP!
POP!
SODA
HMPH! NO APPRECIATION! I'LL SHOW THEM TO BETTY!
MY GOODNESS! YOU DO MAKE AN ENTRANCE!
SCREECH
MAGIC SNEAKERS! WITH THESE ON I CAN RUN LIKE THE WIND!
WHY?
WHY WHAT?
3

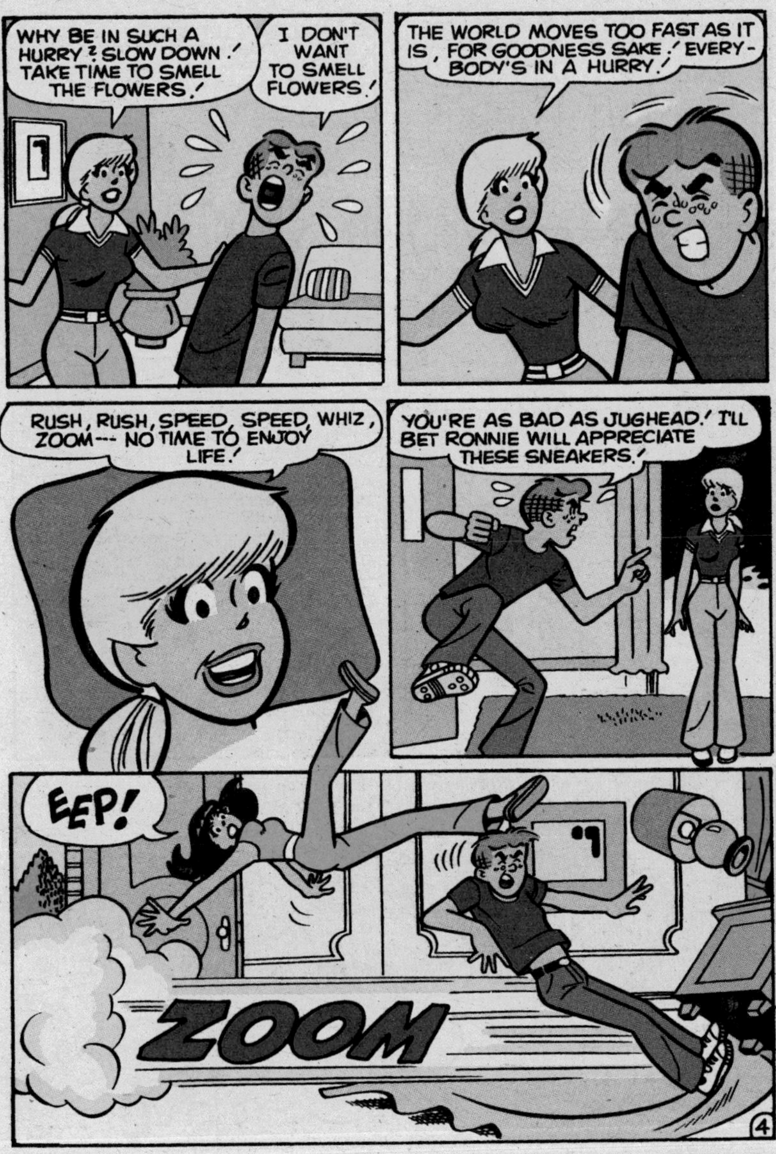
WHY BE IN SUCH A HURRY? SLOW DOWN! TAKE TIME TO SMELL THE FLOWERS!
I DON'T WANT TO SMELL FLOWERS!
THE WORLD MOVES TOO FAST AS IT IS, FOR GOODNESS SAKE! EVERYBODY'S IN A HURRY!
RUSH, RUSH, SPEED, SPEED, WHIZ, ZOOM--- NO TIME TO ENJOY LIFE!
YOU'RE AS BAD AS JUGHEAD! I'LL BET RONNIE WILL APPRECIATE THESE SNEAKERS!
EEP!
ZOOM
4

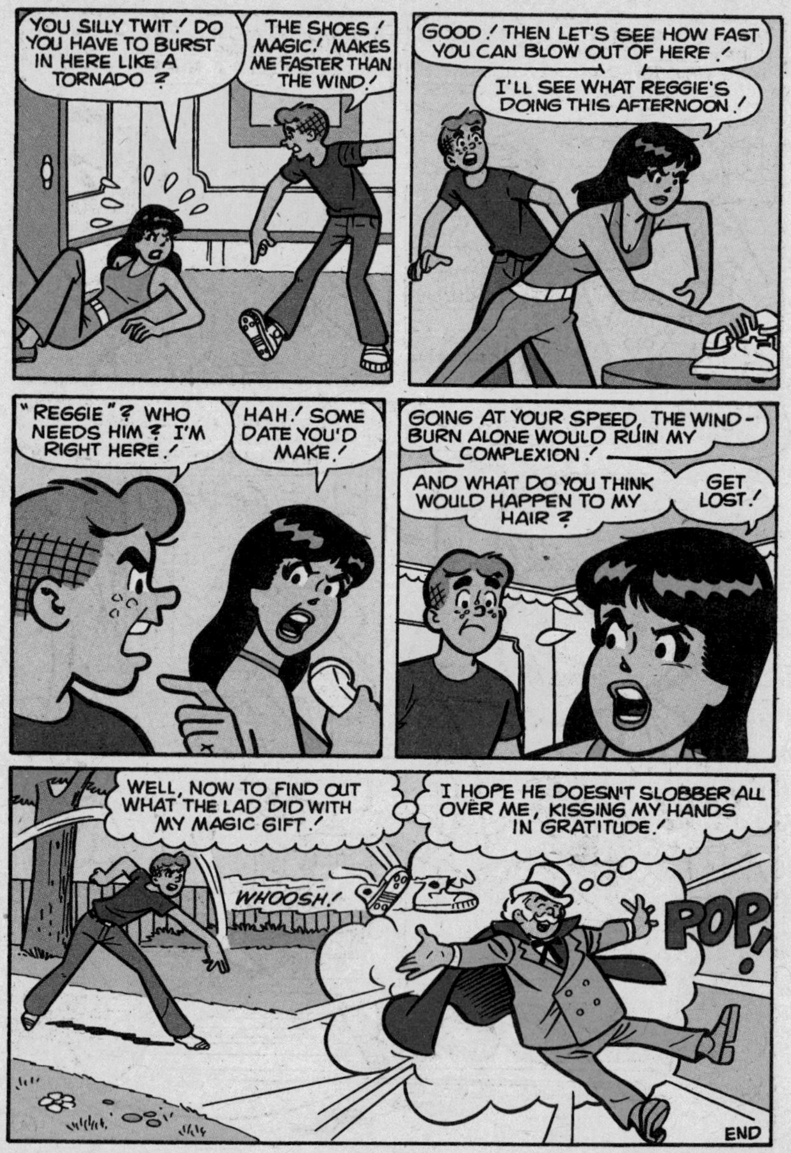
YOU SILLY TWIT! DO YOU HAVE TO BURST IN HERE LIKE A TORNADO?
THE SHOES! MAGIC! MAKES ME FASTER THAN THE WIND!
GOOD! THEN LET'S SEE HOW FAST YOU CAN BLOW OUT OF HERE!
I'LL SEE WHAT REGGIE'S DOING THIS AFTERNOON!
"REGGIE"? WHO NEEDS HIM? I'M RIGHT HERE!
HAH! SOME DATE YOU'D MAKE!
GOING AT YOUR SPEED, THE WIND-BURN ALONE WOULD RUIN MY COMPLEXION!
AND WHAT DO YOU THINK WOULD HAPPEN TO MY HAIR?
GET LOST!
WELL, NOW TO FIND OUT WHAT THE LAD DID WITH MY MAGIC GIFT!
I HOPE HE DOESN'T SLOBBER ALL OVER ME, KISSING MY HANDS IN GRATITUDE!
WHOOSH!
POP!
END

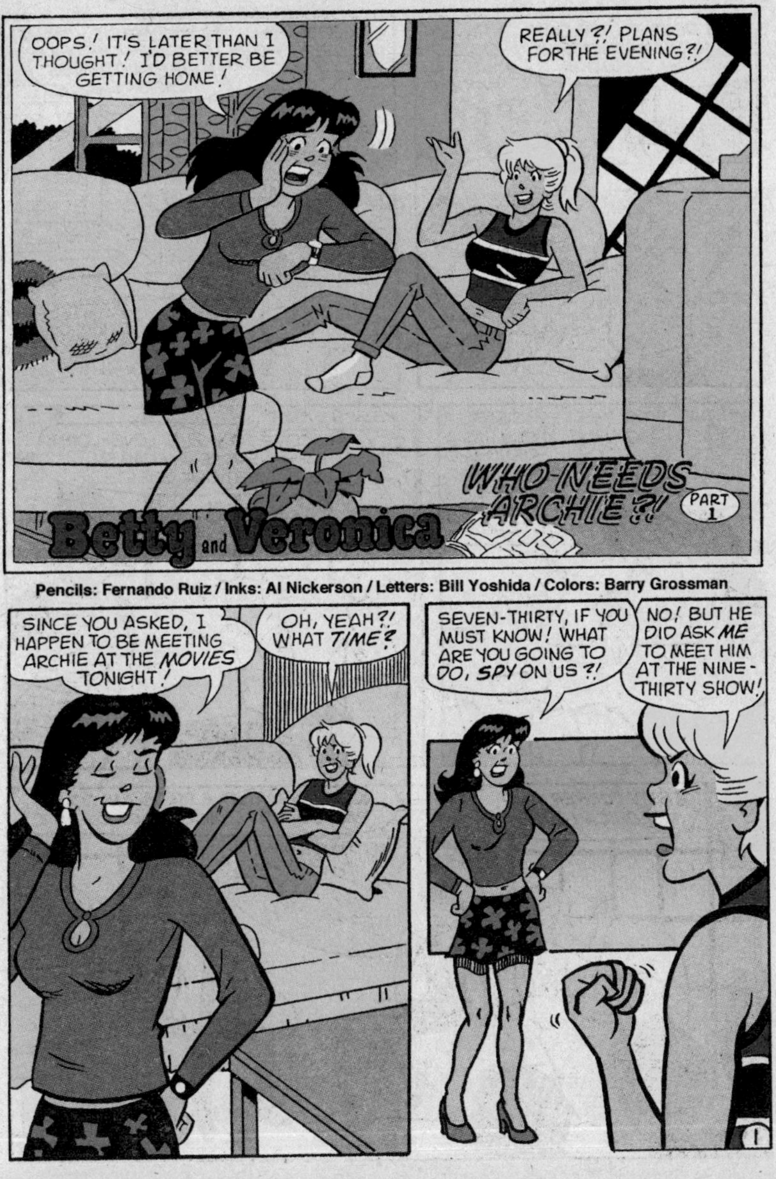
OOPS! IT'S LATER THAN I THOUGHT! I'D BETTER BE GETTING HOME!
REALLY?! PLANS FOR THE EVENING?!
WHO NEEDS ARCHIE?!
PART 1
Betty and Veronica
SINCE YOU ASKED, I HAPPEN TO BE MEETING ARCHIE AT THE MOVIES TONIGHT!
OH, YEAH?! WHAT TIME?
SEVEN-THIRTY, IF YOU MUST KNOW! WHAT ARE YOU GOING TO DO, SPY ON US?!
NO! BUT HE DID ASK ME TO MEET HIM AT THE NINE-THIRTY SHOW!

Pencils: Fernando Ruiz / Inks: Al Nickerson / Letters: Bill Yoshida / Colors: Barry Grossman

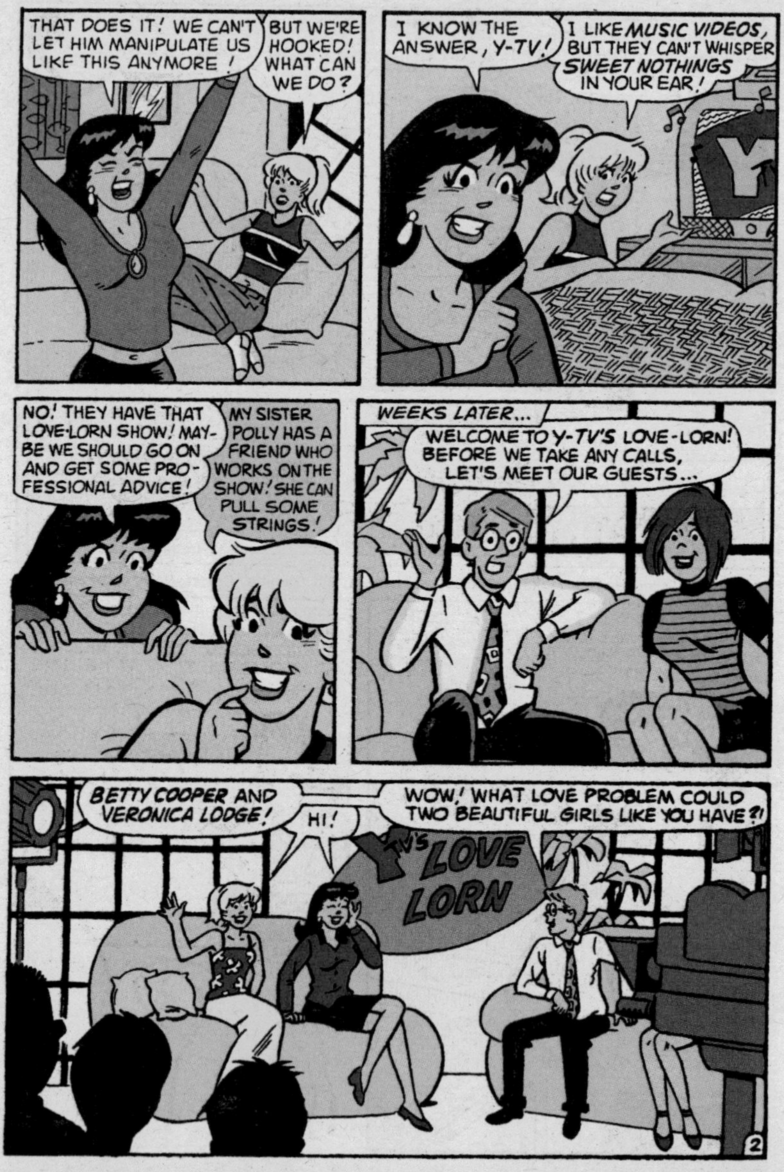
THAT DOES IT! WE CAN'T LET HIM MANIPULATE US LIKE THIS ANYMORE!
BUT WE'RE HOOKED! WHAT CAN WE DO?
I KNOW THE ANSWER, Y-TV!
I LIKE MUSIC VIDEOS, BUT THEY CAN'T WHISPER SWEET NOTHINGS IN YOUR EAR!
NO! THEY HAVE THAT LOVE-LORN SHOW! MAY-BE WE SHOULD GO ON AND GET SOME PRO-FESSIONAL ADVICE!
MY SISTER POLLY HAS A FRIEND WHO WORKS ON THE SHOW! SHE CAN PULL SOME STRINGS!
WEEKS LATER...
WELCOME TO Y-TV'S LOVE-LORN! BEFORE WE TAKE ANY CALLS, LET'S MEET OUR GUESTS...
BETTY COOPER AND VERONICA LODGE!
HI!
WOW! WHAT LOVE PROBLEM COULD TWO BEAUTIFUL GIRLS LIKE YOU HAVE?!
Y-TV'S LOVE LORN
2

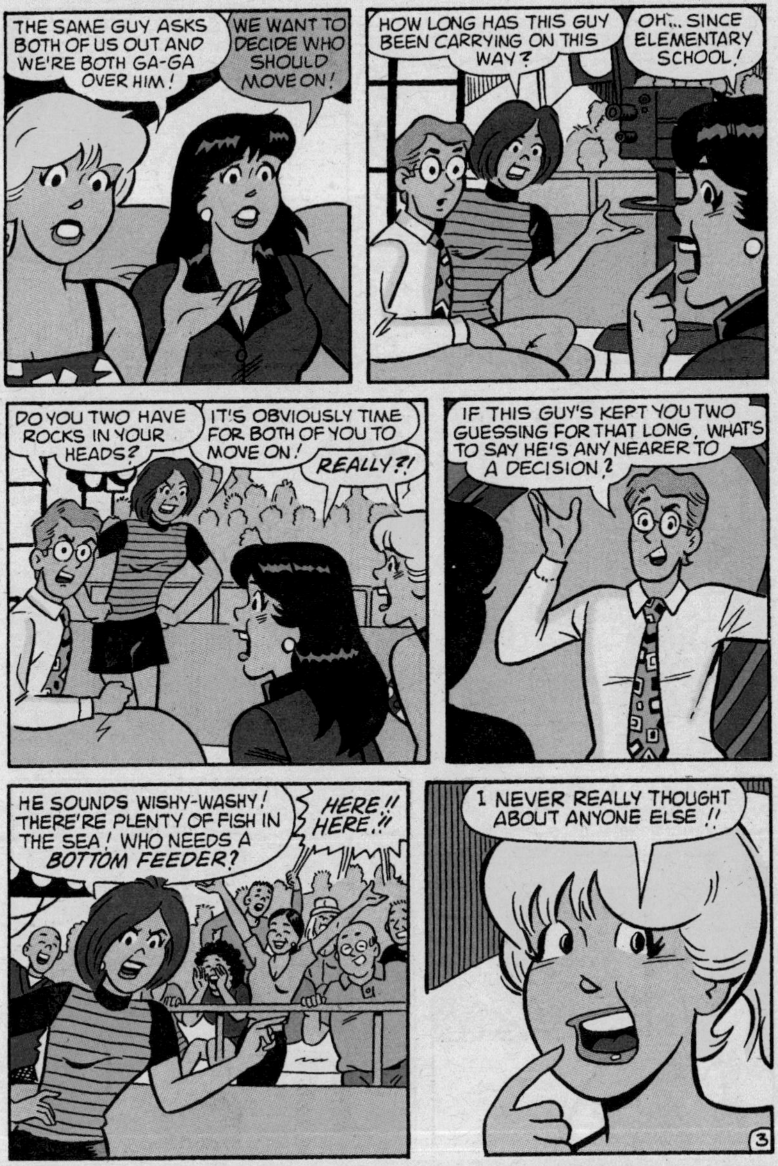
THE SAME GUY ASKS BOTH OF US OUT AND WE'RE BOTH GA-GA OVER HIM!
WE WANT TO DECIDE WHO SHOULD MOVE ON!
HOW LONG HAS THIS GUY BEEN CARRYING ON THIS WAY?
OH... SINCE ELEMENTARY SCHOOL!
DO YOU TWO HAVE ROCKS IN YOUR HEADS?
IT'S OBVIOUSLY TIME FOR BOTH OF YOU TO MOVE ON!
REALLY?!
IF THIS GUY'S KEPT YOU TWO GUESSING FOR THAT LONG, WHAT'S TO SAY HE'S ANY NEARER TO A DECISION?
HE SOUNDS WISHY-WASHY! THERE'RE PLENTY OF FISH IN THE SEA! WHO NEEDS A BOTTOM FEEDER?
HERE!! HERE!!
I NEVER REALLY THOUGHT ABOUT ANYONE ELSE!!
3

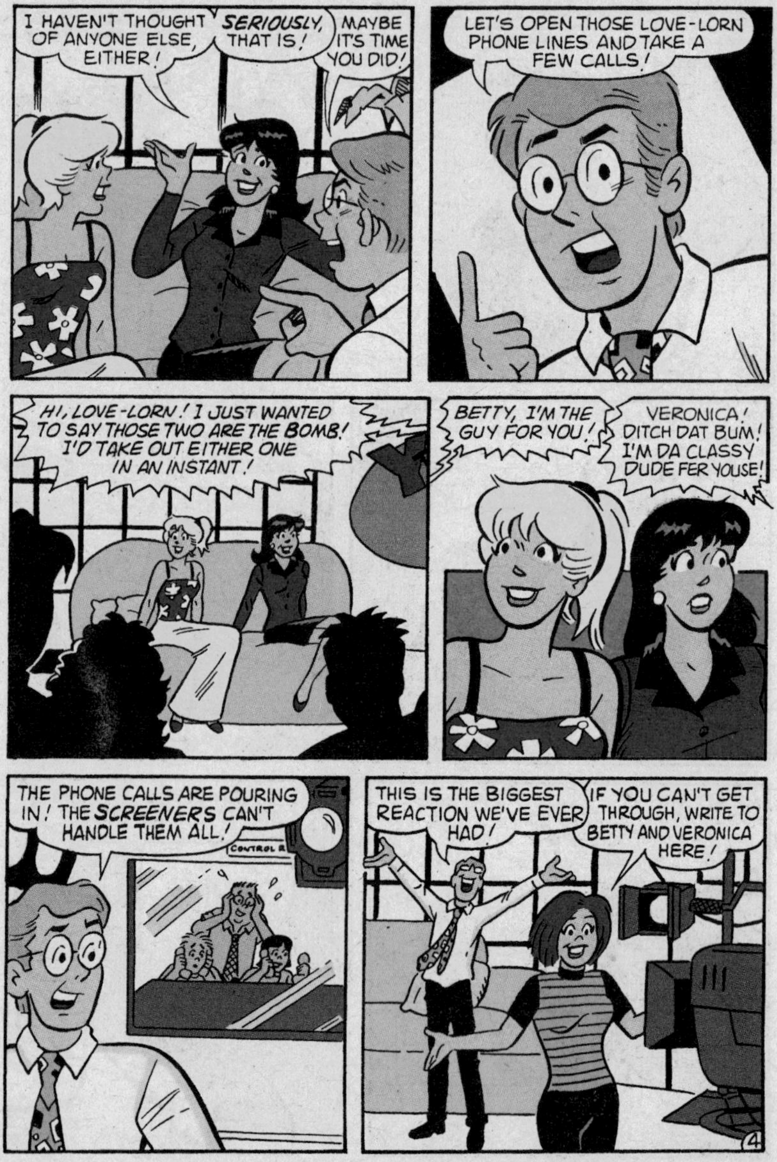
I HAVEN'T THOUGHT OF ANYONE ELSE, EITHER!
SERIOUSLY, THAT IS!
MAYBE IT'S TIME YOU DID!
LET'S OPEN THOSE LOVE-LORN PHONE LINES AND TAKE A FEW CALLS!
HI, LOVE-LORN! I JUST WANTED TO SAY THOSE TWO ARE THE BOMB! I'D TAKE OUT EITHER ONE IN AN INSTANT!
BETTY, I'M THE GUY FOR YOU!
VERONICA! DITCH DAT BUM! I'M DA CLASSY DUDE FER YOUSE!
THE PHONE CALLS ARE POURING IN! THE SCREENERS CAN'T HANDLE THEM ALL!
CONTROL R
THIS IS THE BIGGEST REACTION WE'VE EVER HAD!
IF YOU CAN'T GET THROUGH, WRITE TO BETTY AND VERONICA HERE!
4

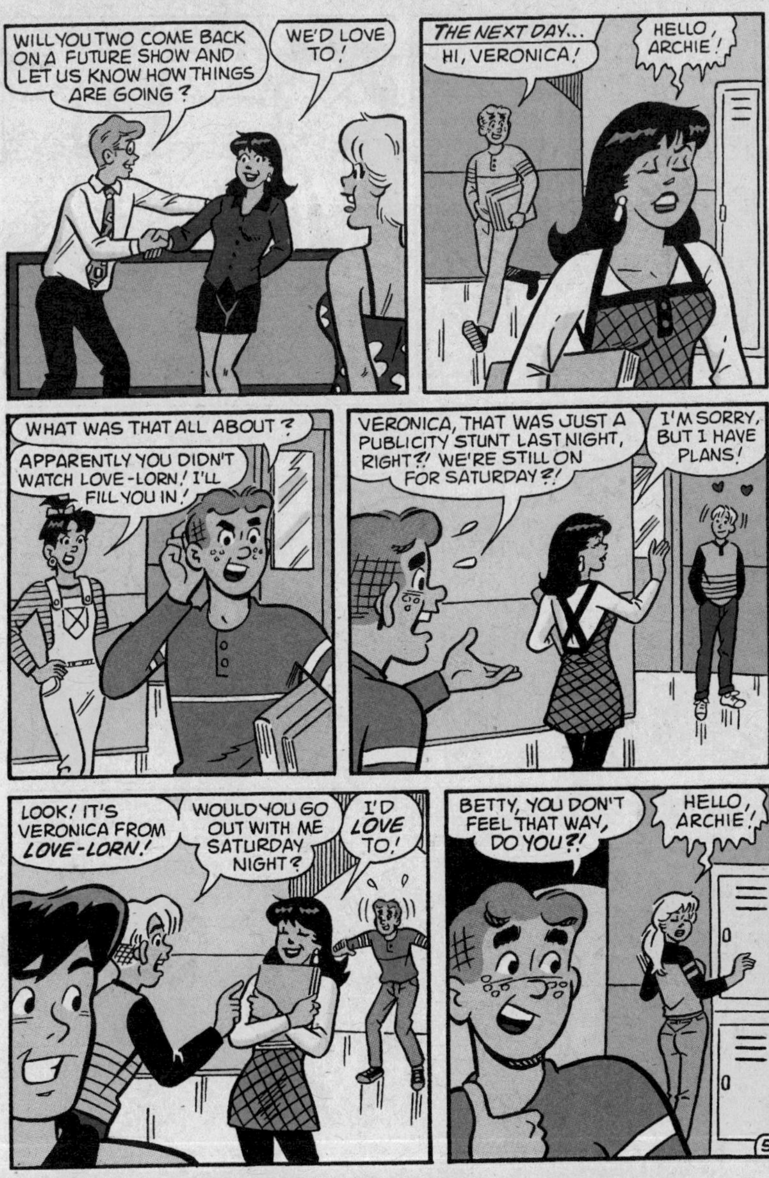
WILL YOU TWO COME BACK ON A FUTURE SHOW AND LET US KNOW HOW THINGS ARE GOING?
WE'D LOVE TO!
THE NEXT DAY...
HI, VERONICA!
HELLO, ARCHIE!
WHAT WAS THAT ALL ABOUT?
APPARENTLY YOU DIDN'T WATCH LOVE-LORN! I'LL FILL YOU IN!
VERONICA, THAT WAS JUST A PUBLICITY STUNT LAST NIGHT, RIGHT?! WE'RE STILL ON FOR SATURDAY?!
I'M SORRY, BUT I HAVE PLANS!
LOOK! IT'S VERONICA FROM LOVE-LORN!
WOULD YOU GO OUT WITH ME SATURDAY NIGHT?
I'D LOVE TO!
BETTY, YOU DON'T FEEL THAT WAY, DO YOU?!
HELLO, ARCHIE!
5

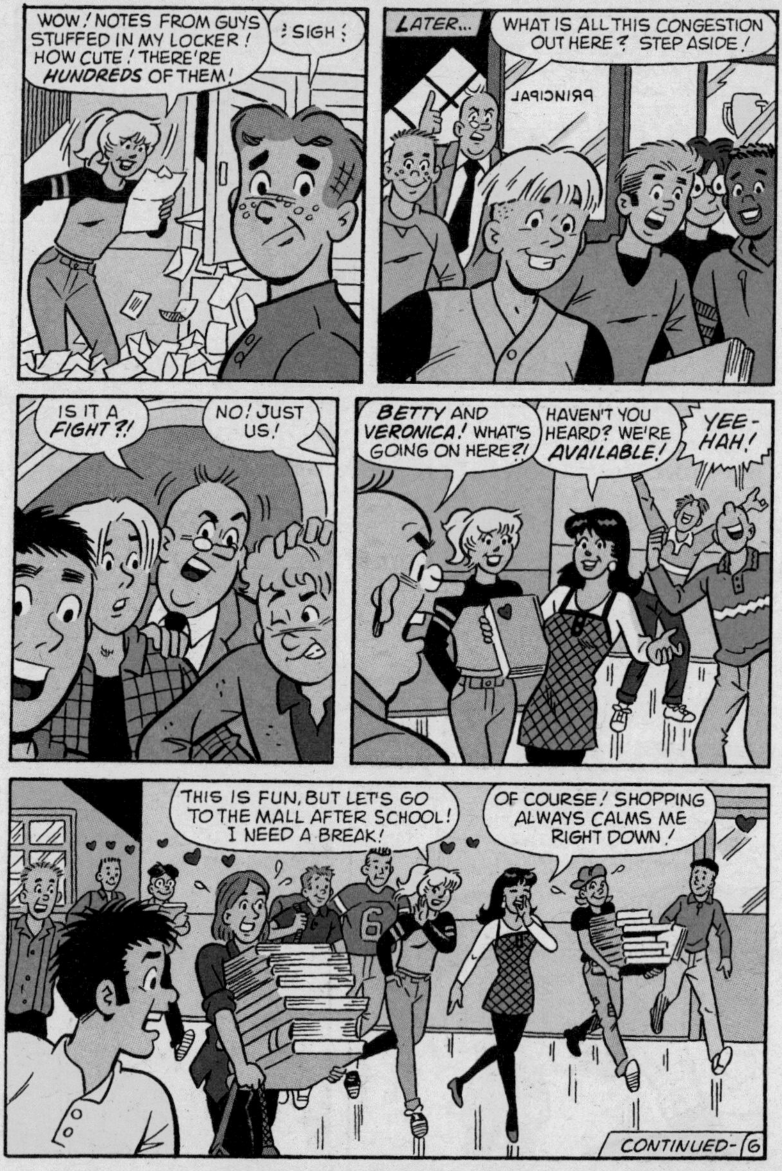
WOW! NOTES FROM GUYS STUFFED IN MY LOCKER! HOW CUTE! THERE'RE HUNDREDS OF THEM!
SIGH
LATER...
WHAT IS ALL THIS CONGESTION OUT HERE? STEP ASIDE!
PRINCIPAL
IS IT A FIGHT?!
NO! JUST US!
BETTY AND VERONICA! WHAT'S GOING ON HERE?!
HAVEN'T YOU HEARD? WE'RE AVAILABLE!
YEE-HAH!
THIS IS FUN, BUT LET'S GO TO THE MALL AFTER SCHOOL! I NEED A BREAK!
OF COURSE! SHOPPING ALWAYS CALMS ME RIGHT DOWN!
6
CONTINUED-

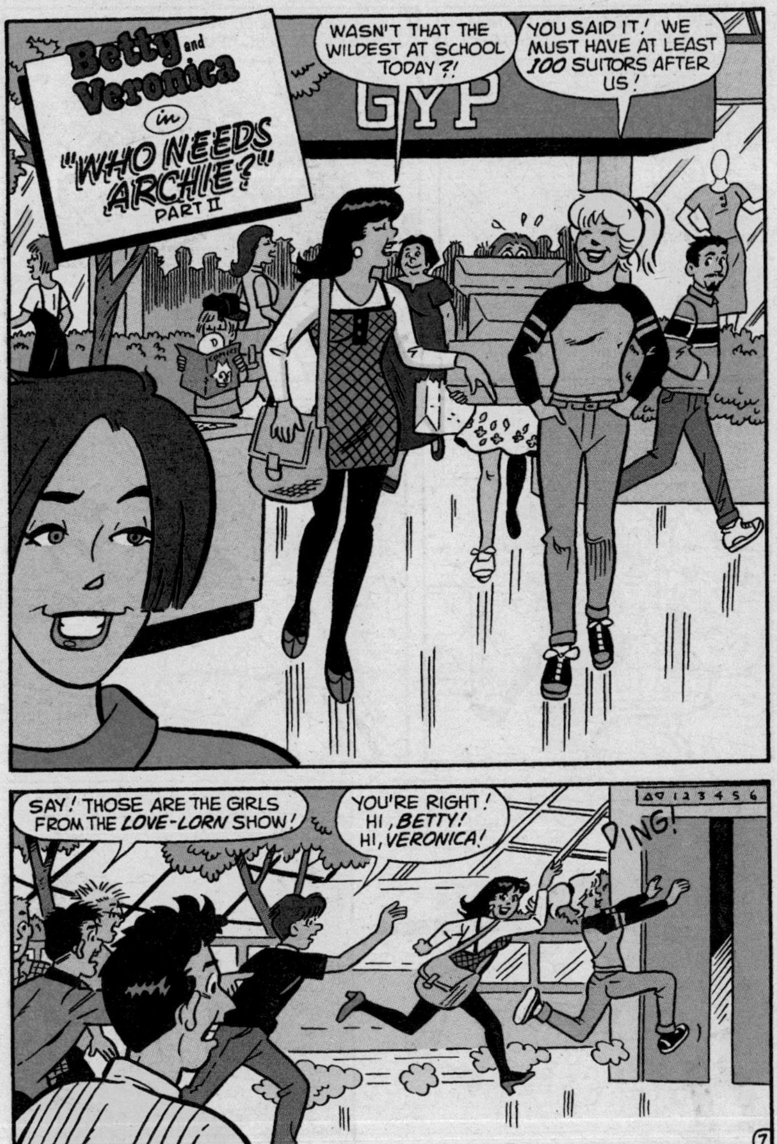
Betty and Veronica in
"WHO NEEDS ARCHIE?" PART II
GYP
WASN'T THAT THE WILDEST AT SCHOOL TODAY?!
YOU SAID IT! WE MUST HAVE AT LEAST 100 SUITORS AFTER US!
SAY! THOSE ARE THE GIRLS FROM THE LOVE-LORN SHOW!
YOU'RE RIGHT! HI, BETTY! HI, VERONICA!
1 2 3 4 5 6
DING!

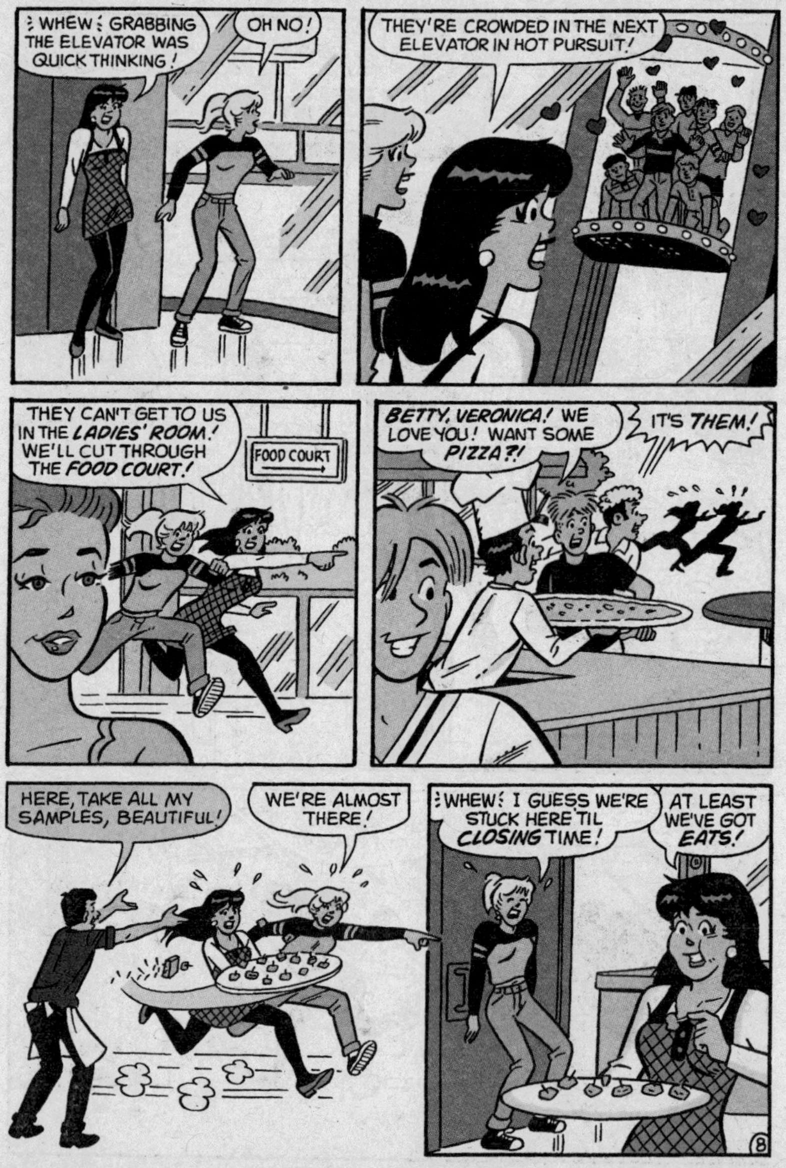
WHEW! GRABBING THE ELEVATOR WAS QUICK THINKING!
OH NO!
THEY'RE CROWDED IN THE NEXT ELEVATOR IN HOT PURSUIT!
THEY CAN'T GET TO US IN THE LADIES' ROOM! WE'LL CUT THROUGH THE FOOD COURT!
FOOD COURT
BETTY, VERONICA! WE LOVE YOU! WANT SOME PIZZA?!
IT'S THEM!
HERE, TAKE ALL MY SAMPLES, BEAUTIFUL!
WE'RE ALMOST THERE!
WHEW! I GUESS WE'RE STUCK HERE 'TIL CLOSING TIME!
AT LEAST WE'VE GOT EATS!

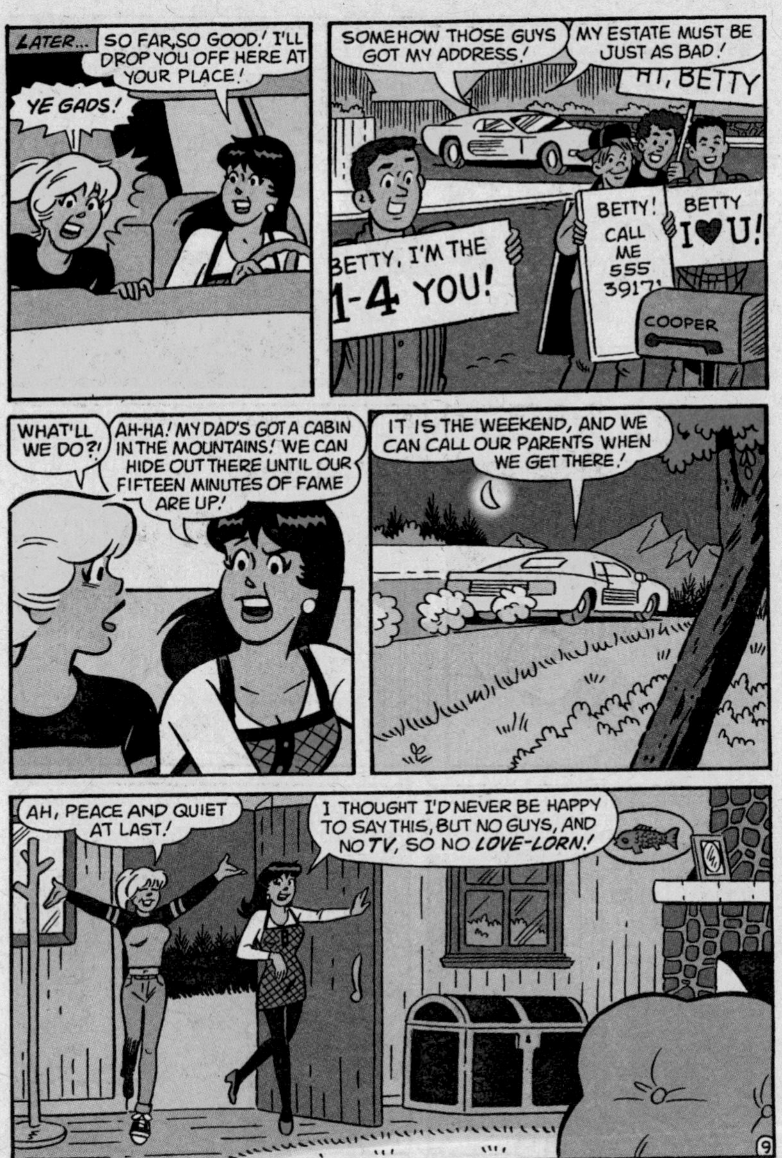
LATER...
SO FAR, SO GOOD! I'LL DROP YOU OFF HERE AT YOUR PLACE!
YE GADS!
SOMEHOW THOSE GUYS GOT MY ADDRESS!
MY ESTATE MUST BE JUST AS BAD!
HI, BETTY
BETTY, I'M THE 1-4 YOU!
BETTY! CALL ME 555 3917!
BETTY I ♥ U!
COOPER
WHAT'LL WE DO?!
AH-HA! MY DAD'S GOT A CABIN IN THE MOUNTAINS! WE CAN HIDE OUT THERE UNTIL OUR FIFTEEN MINUTES OF FAME ARE UP!
IT IS THE WEEKEND, AND WE CAN CALL OUR PARENTS WHEN WE GET THERE!
AH, PEACE AND QUIET AT LAST!
I THOUGHT I'D NEVER BE HAPPY TO SAY THIS, BUT NO GUYS, AND NO TV, SO NO LOVE-LORN!
9

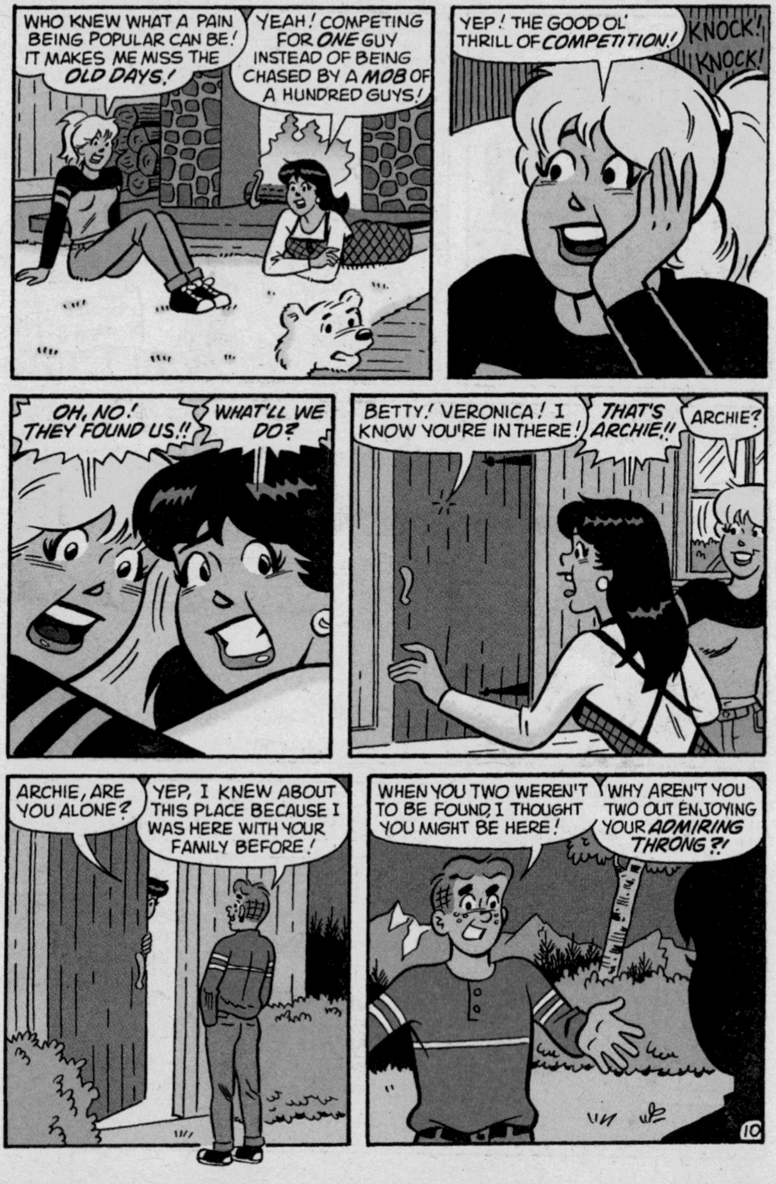
WHO KNEW WHAT A PAIN BEING POPULAR CAN BE! IT MAKES ME MISS THE OLD DAYS!
YEAH! COMPETING FOR ONE GUY INSTEAD OF BEING CHASED BY A MOB OF A HUNDRED GUYS!
YEP! THE GOOD OL' THRILL OF COMPETITION!
KNOCK! KNOCK!
OH, NO! THEY FOUND US!!
WHAT'LL WE DO?
BETTY! VERONICA! I KNOW YOU'RE IN THERE!
THAT'S ARCHIE!!
ARCHIE?
ARCHIE, ARE YOU ALONE?
YEP, I KNEW ABOUT THIS PLACE BECAUSE I WAS HERE WITH YOUR FAMILY BEFORE!
WHEN YOU TWO WEREN'T TO BE FOUND, I THOUGHT YOU MIGHT BE HERE!
WHY AREN'T YOU TWO OUT ENJOYING YOUR ADMIRING THRONG?!
10

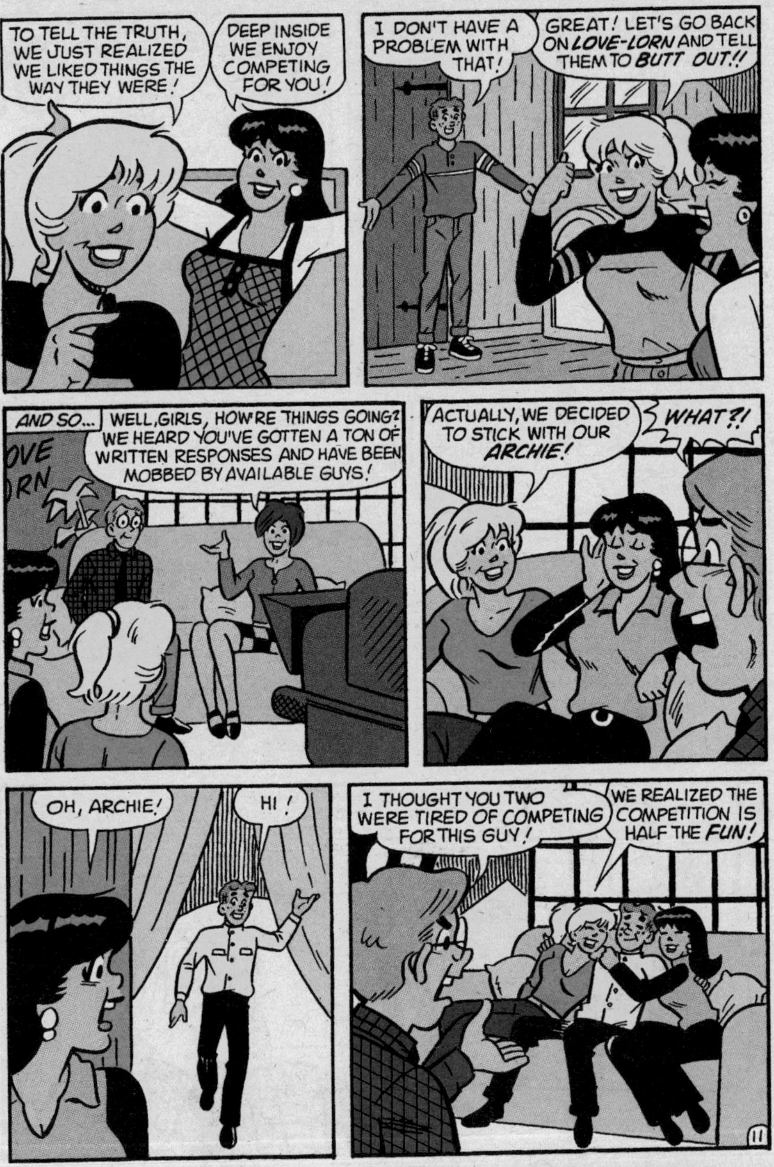
TO TELL THE TRUTH, WE JUST REALIZED WE LIKED THINGS THE WAY THEY WERE!
DEEP INSIDE WE ENJOY COMPETING FOR YOU!
I DON'T HAVE A PROBLEM WITH THAT!
GREAT! LET'S GO BACK ON LOVE-LORN AND TELL THEM TO BUTT OUT!!
AND SO...
WELL, GIRLS, HOW'RE THINGS GOING? WE HEARD YOU'VE GOTTEN A TON OF WRITTEN RESPONSES AND HAVE BEEN MOBBED BY AVAILABLE GUYS!
ACTUALLY, WE DECIDED TO STICK WITH OUR ARCHIE!
WHAT?!
OH, ARCHIE!
HI!
I THOUGHT YOU TWO WERE TIRED OF COMPETING FOR THIS GUY!
WE REALIZED THE COMPETITION IS HALF THE FUN!
11

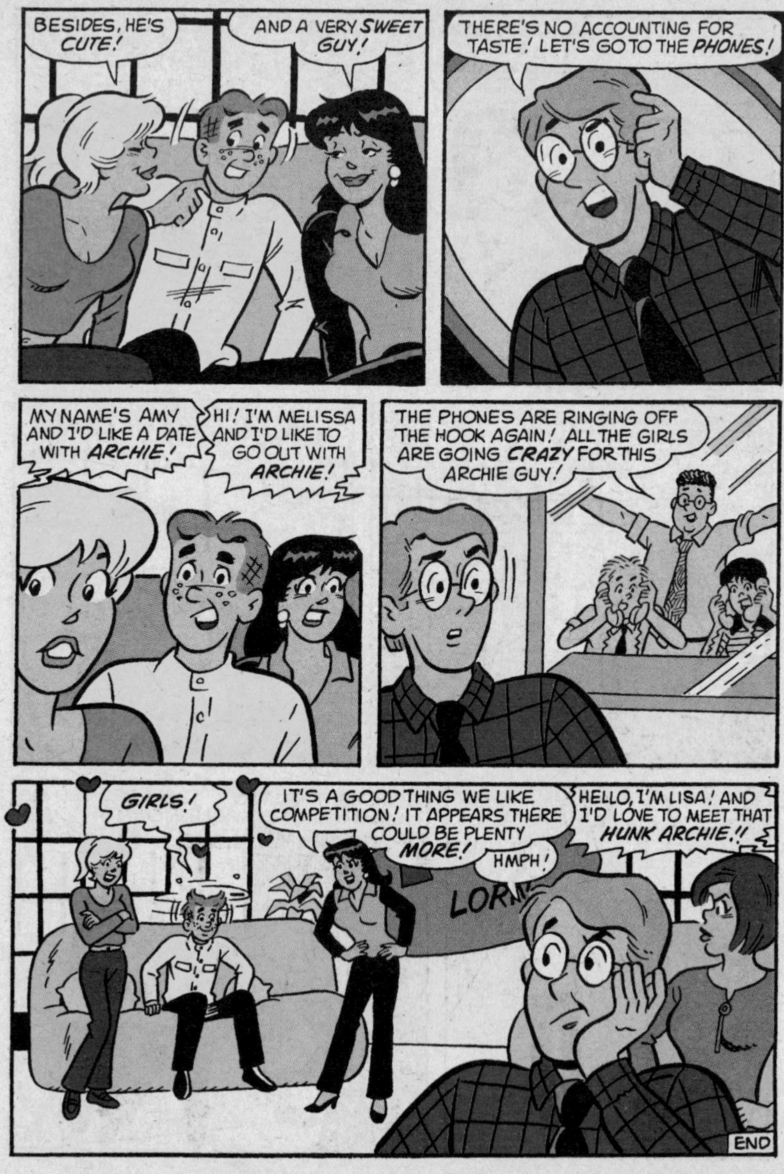
BESIDES, HE'S CUTE!
AND A VERY SWEET GUY!
THERE'S NO ACCOUNTING FOR TASTE! LET'S GO TO THE PHONES!
MY NAME'S AMY AND I'D LIKE A DATE WITH ARCHIE!
HI! I'M MELISSA AND I'D LIKE TO GO OUT WITH ARCHIE!
THE PHONES ARE RINGING OFF THE HOOK AGAIN! ALL THE GIRLS ARE GOING CRAZY FOR THIS ARCHIE GUY!
GIRLS!
IT'S A GOOD THING WE LIKE COMPETITION! IT APPEARS THERE COULD BE PLENTY MORE!
HMPH!
HELLO, I'M LISA! AND I'D LOVE TO MEET THAT HUNK ARCHIE!!
END

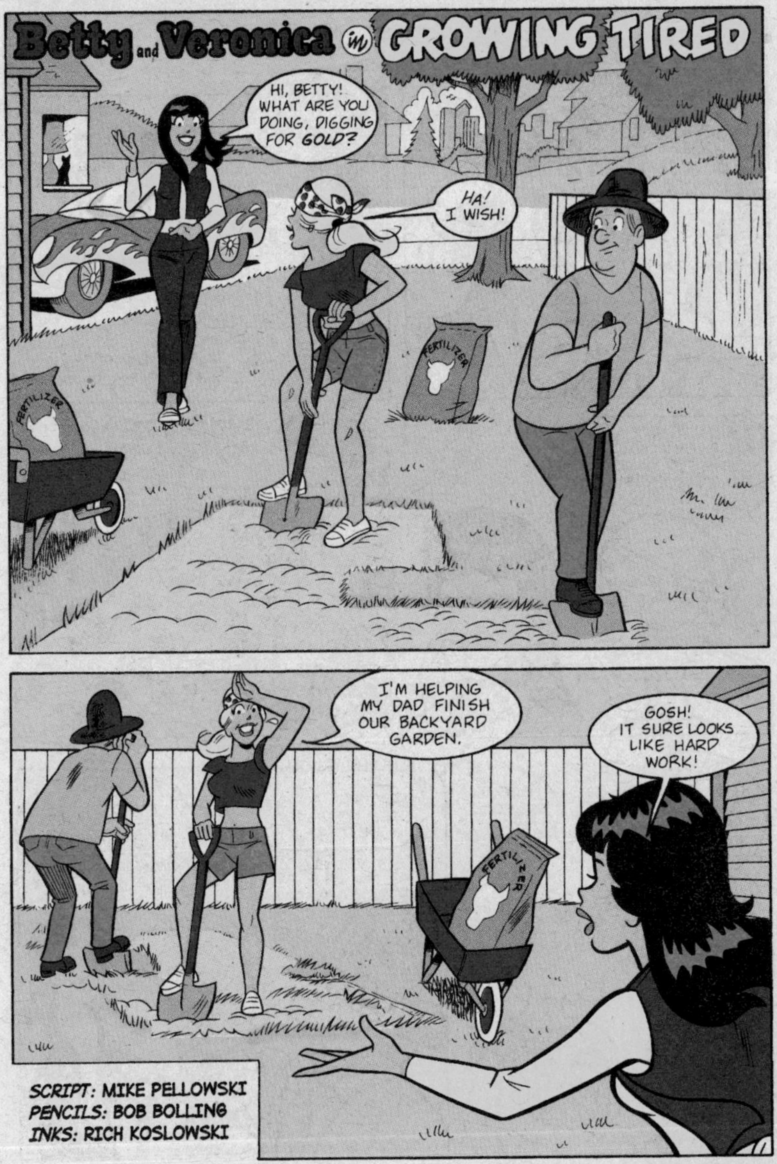
Betty and Veronica in GROWING TIRED
HI, BETTY! WHAT ARE YOU DOING, DIGGING FOR GOLD?
HA! I WISH!
FERTILIZER
FERTILIZER
I'M HELPING MY DAD FINISH OUR BACKYARD GARDEN.
GOSH! IT SURE LOOKS LIKE HARD WORK!
FERTILIZER
SCRIPT: MIKE PELLOWSKI
PENCILS: BOB BOLLING
INKS: RICH KOSLOWSKI

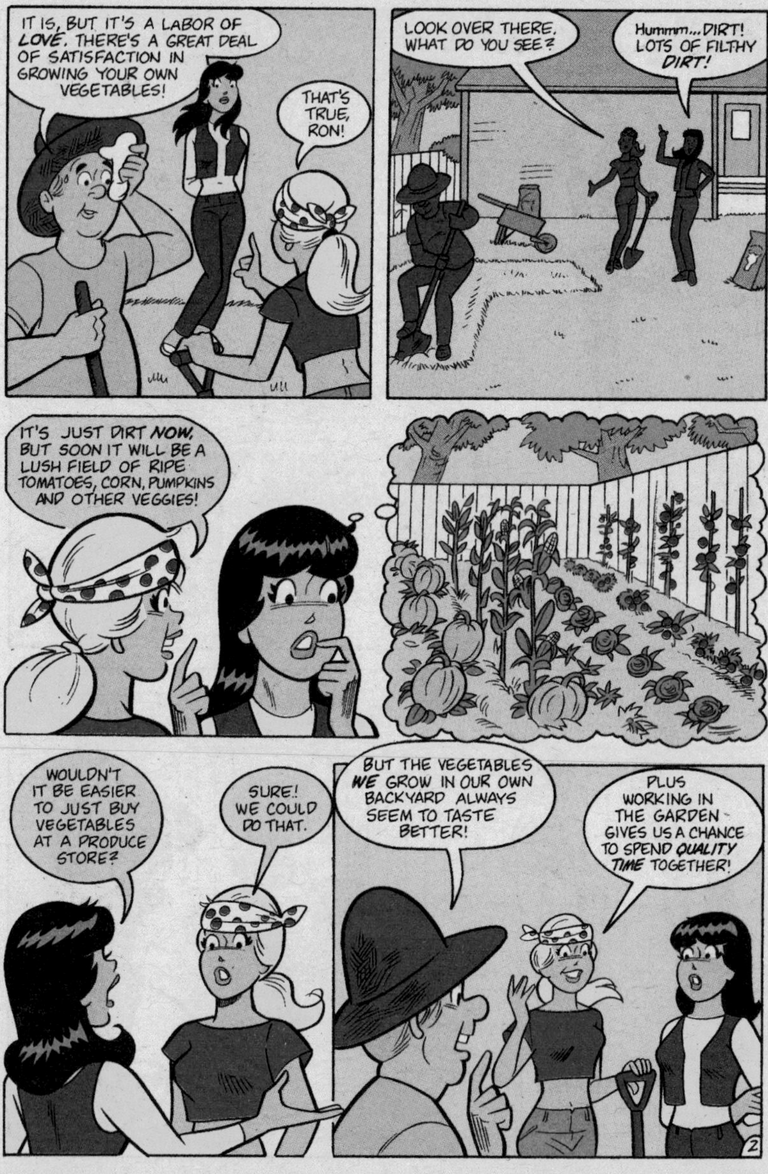
IT IS, BUT IT'S A LABOR OF LOVE. THERE'S A GREAT DEAL OF SATISFACTION IN GROWING YOUR OWN VEGETABLES!
THAT'S TRUE, RON!
LOOK OVER THERE. WHAT DO YOU SEE?
Hummm... DIRT! LOTS OF FILTHY DIRT!
IT'S JUST DIRT NOW, BUT SOON IT WILL BE A LUSH FIELD OF RIPE TOMATOES, CORN, PUMPKINS AND OTHER VEGGIES!
WOULDN'T IT BE EASIER TO JUST BUY VEGETABLES AT A PRODUCE STORE?
SURE! WE COULD DO THAT.
BUT THE VEGETABLES WE GROW IN OUR OWN BACKYARD ALWAYS SEEM TO TASTE BETTER!
PLUS WORKING IN THE GARDEN GIVES US A CHANCE TO SPEND QUALITY TIME TOGETHER!
2

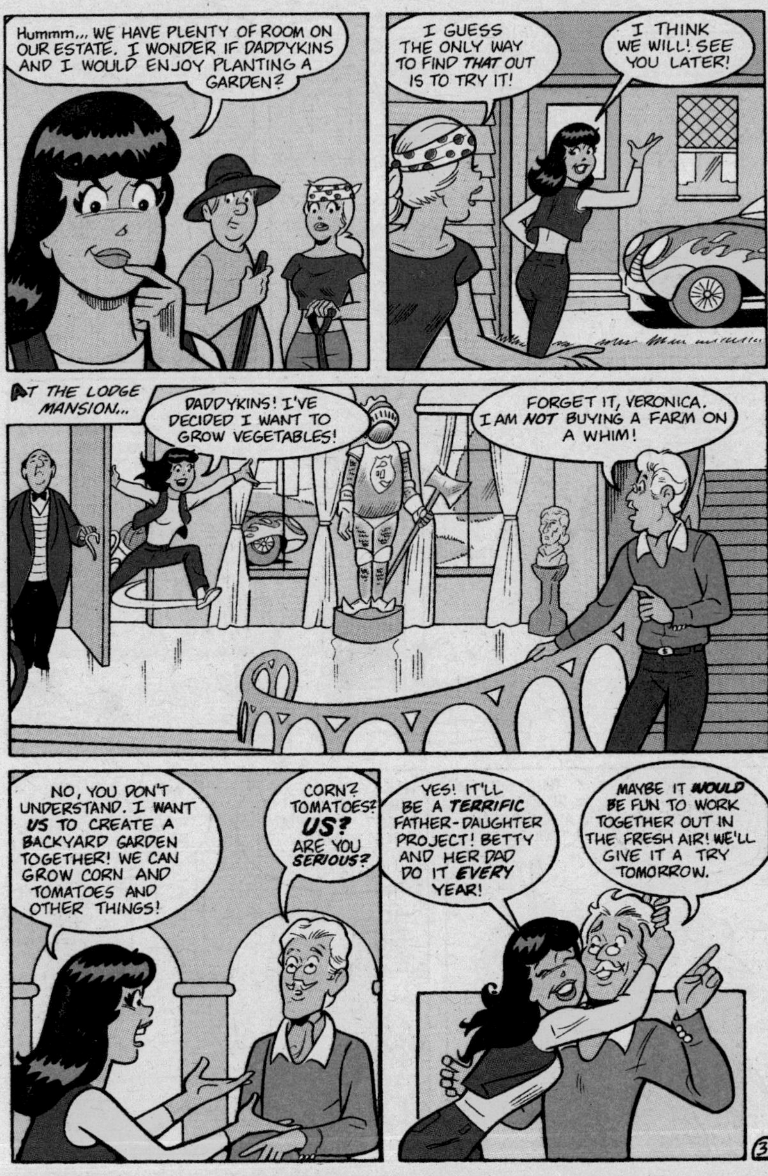
Hummm... WE HAVE PLENTY OF ROOM ON OUR ESTATE. I WONDER IF DADDYKINS AND I WOULD ENJOY PLANTING A GARDEN?
I GUESS THE ONLY WAY TO FIND THAT OUT IS TO TRY IT!
I THINK WE WILL! SEE YOU LATER!
AT THE LODGE MANSION...
DADDYKINS! I'VE DECIDED I WANT TO GROW VEGETABLES!
FORGET IT, VERONICA. I AM NOT BUYING A FARM ON A WHIM!
NO, YOU DON'T UNDERSTAND. I WANT US TO CREATE A BACKYARD GARDEN TOGETHER! WE CAN GROW CORN AND TOMATOES AND OTHER THINGS!
CORN? TOMATOES? US? ARE YOU SERIOUS?
YES! IT'LL BE A TERRIFIC FATHER-DAUGHTER PROJECT! BETTY AND HER DAD DO IT EVERY YEAR!
MAYBE IT WOULD BE FUN TO WORK TOGETHER OUT IN THE FRESH AIR! WE'LL GIVE IT A TRY TOMORROW.
3

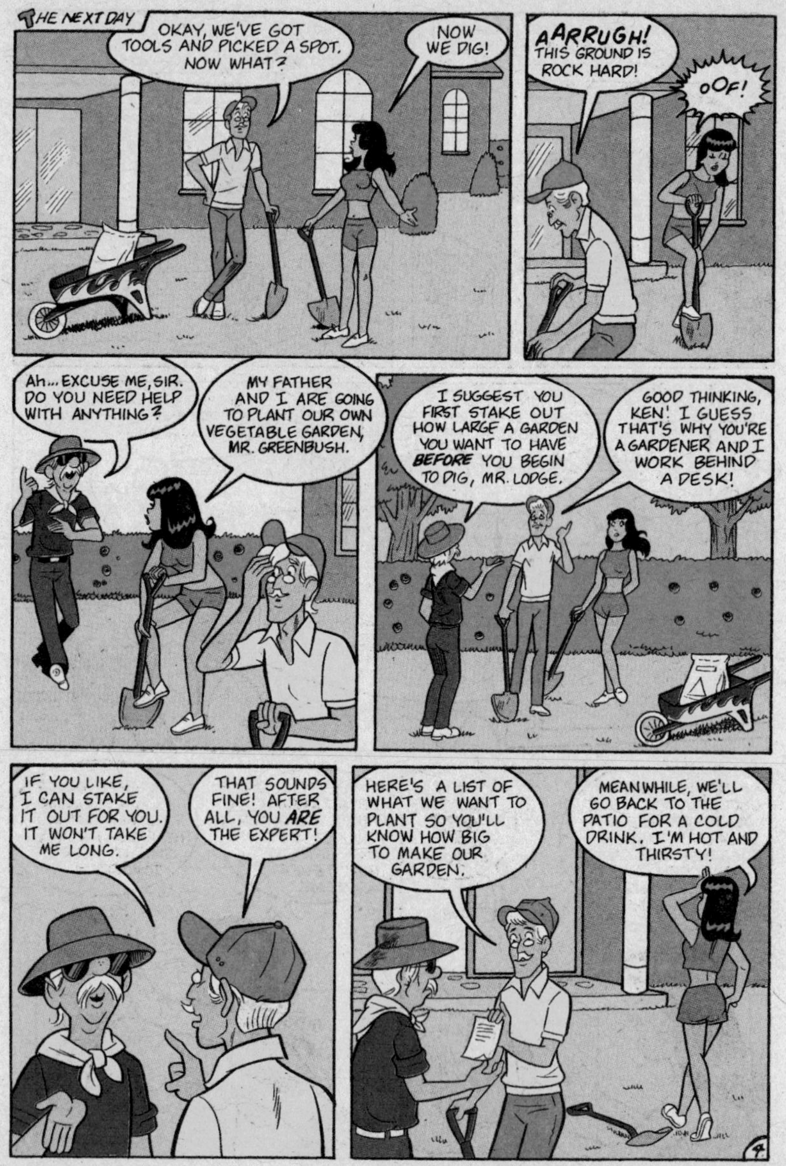
THE NEXT DAY
OKAY, WE'VE GOT TOOLS AND PICKED A SPOT. NOW WHAT?
NOW WE DIG!
AARRUGH! THIS GROUND IS ROCK HARD!
OOF!
Ah... EXCUSE ME, SIR. DO YOU NEED HELP WITH ANYTHING?
MY FATHER AND I ARE GOING TO PLANT OUR OWN VEGETABLE GARDEN, MR. GREENBUSH.
I SUGGEST YOU FIRST STAKE OUT HOW LARGE A GARDEN YOU WANT TO HAVE *BEFORE* YOU BEGIN TO DIG, MR. LODGE.
GOOD THINKING, KEN! I GUESS THAT'S WHY YOU'RE A GARDENER AND I WORK BEHIND A DESK!
IF YOU LIKE, I CAN STAKE IT OUT FOR YOU. IT WON'T TAKE ME LONG.
THAT SOUNDS FINE! AFTER ALL, YOU *ARE* THE EXPERT!
HERE'S A LIST OF WHAT WE WANT TO PLANT SO YOU'LL KNOW HOW BIG TO MAKE OUR GARDEN.
MEANWHILE, WE'LL GO BACK TO THE PATIO FOR A COLD DRINK. I'M HOT AND THIRSTY!
4

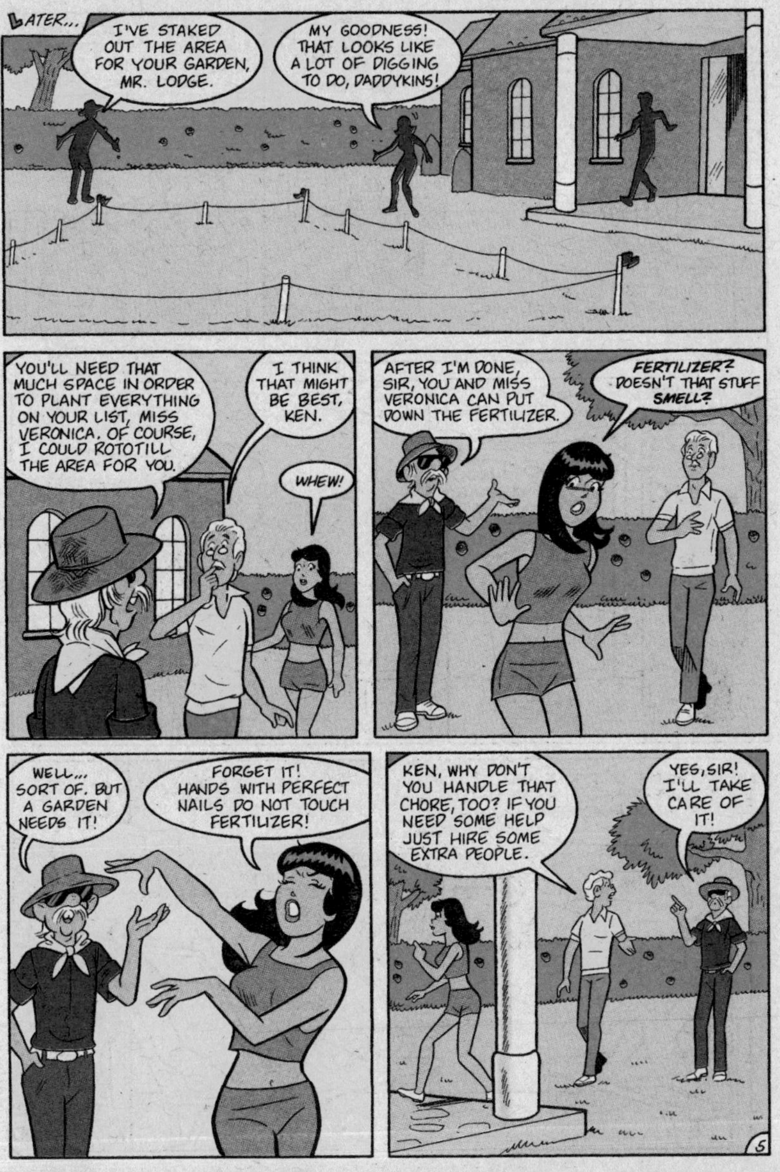
LATER...
I'VE STAKED OUT THE AREA FOR YOUR GARDEN, MR. LODGE.
MY GOODNESS! THAT LOOKS LIKE A LOT OF DIGGING TO DO, DADDYKINS!
YOU'LL NEED THAT MUCH SPACE IN ORDER TO PLANT EVERYTHING ON YOUR LIST, MISS VERONICA. OF COURSE, I COULD ROTOTILL THE AREA FOR YOU.
I THINK THAT MIGHT BE BEST, KEN.
WHEW!
AFTER I'M DONE, SIR, YOU AND MISS VERONICA CAN PUT DOWN THE FERTILIZER.
FERTILIZER? DOESN'T THAT STUFF SMELL?
WELL... SORT OF. BUT A GARDEN NEEDS IT!
FORGET IT! HANDS WITH PERFECT NAILS DO NOT TOUCH FERTILIZER!
KEN, WHY DON'T YOU HANDLE THAT CHORE, TOO? IF YOU NEED SOME HELP JUST HIRE SOME EXTRA PEOPLE.
YES, SIR! I'LL TAKE CARE OF IT!
5

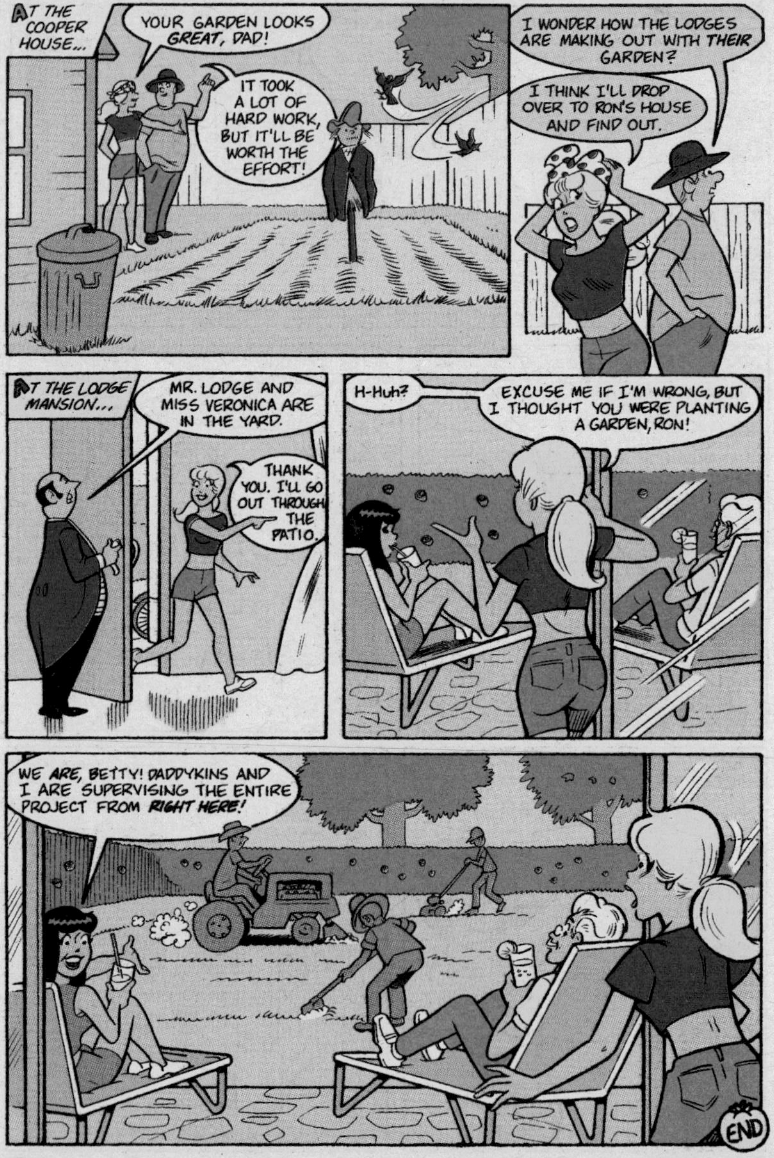
AT THE COOPER HOUSE...
YOUR GARDEN LOOKS GREAT, DAD!
IT TOOK A LOT OF HARD WORK, BUT IT'LL BE WORTH THE EFFORT!
I WONDER HOW THE LODGES ARE MAKING OUT WITH THEIR GARDEN?
I THINK I'LL DROP OVER TO RON'S HOUSE AND FIND OUT.
AT THE LODGE MANSION...
MR. LODGE AND MISS VERONICA ARE IN THE YARD.
THANK YOU. I'LL GO OUT THROUGH THE PATIO.
H-Huh?
EXCUSE ME IF I'M WRONG, BUT I THOUGHT YOU WERE PLANTING A GARDEN, RON!
WE ARE, BETTY! DADDYKINS AND I ARE SUPERVISING THE ENTIRE PROJECT FROM RIGHT HERE!
END

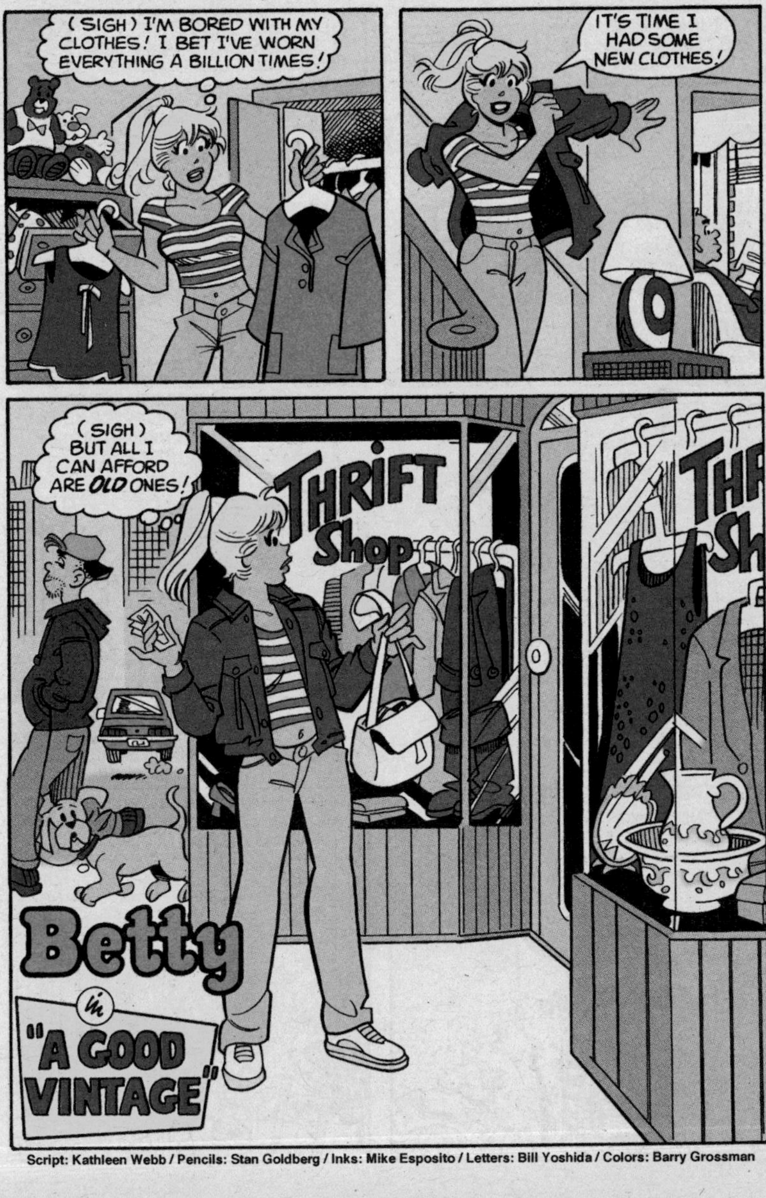
(SIGH) I'M BORED WITH MY CLOTHES! I BET I'VE WORN EVERYTHING A BILLION TIMES!
IT'S TIME I HAD SOME NEW CLOTHES!
(SIGH) BUT ALL I CAN AFFORD ARE OLD ONES!
THRIFT Shop
THR
Sh
Betty
in
"A GOOD VINTAGE"

Script: Kathleen Webb / Pencils: Stan Goldberg / Inks: Mike Esposito / Letters: Bill Yoshida / Colors: Barry Grossman

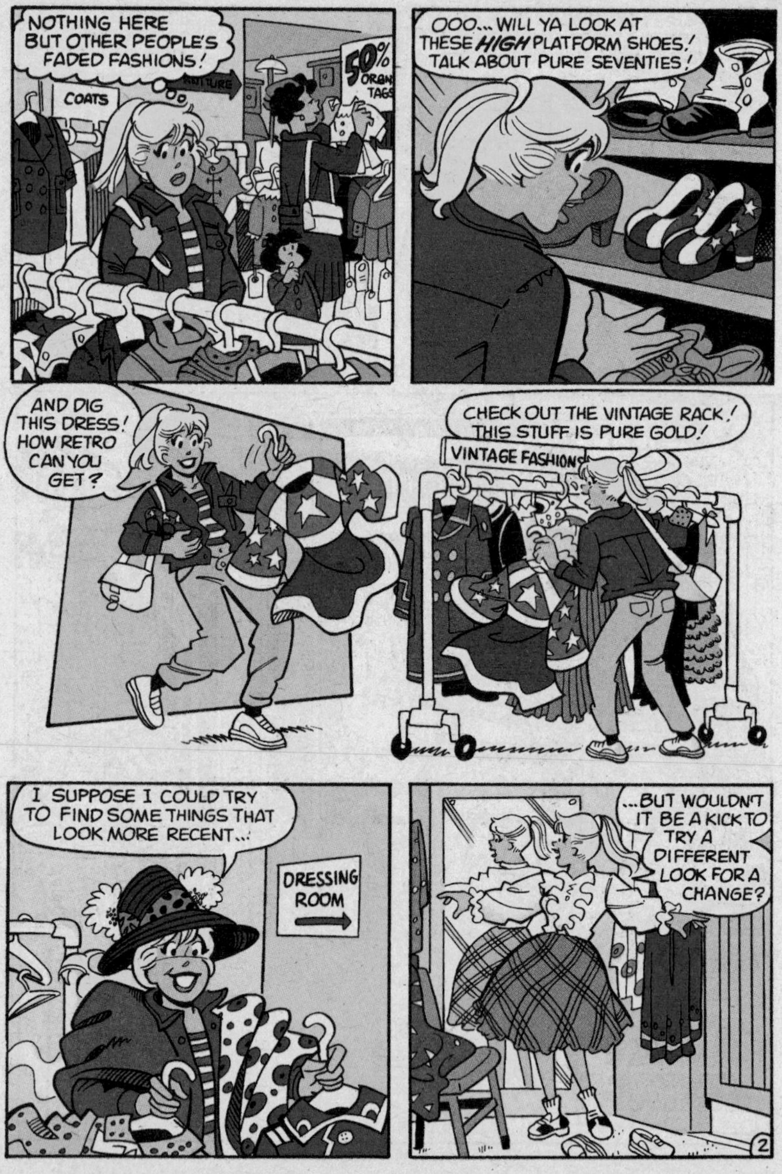
NOTHING HERE BUT OTHER PEOPLE'S FADED FASHIONS!
COATS
OOO... WILL YA LOOK AT THESE HIGH PLATFORM SHOES! TALK ABOUT PURE SEVENTIES!
AND DIG THIS DRESS! HOW RETRO CAN YOU GET?
CHECK OUT THE VINTAGE RACK! THIS STUFF IS PURE GOLD!
VINTAGE FASHIONS
I SUPPOSE I COULD TRY TO FIND SOME THINGS THAT LOOK MORE RECENT...
DRESSING ROOM
...BUT WOULDN'T IT BE A KICK TO TRY A DIFFERENT LOOK FOR A CHANGE?
2

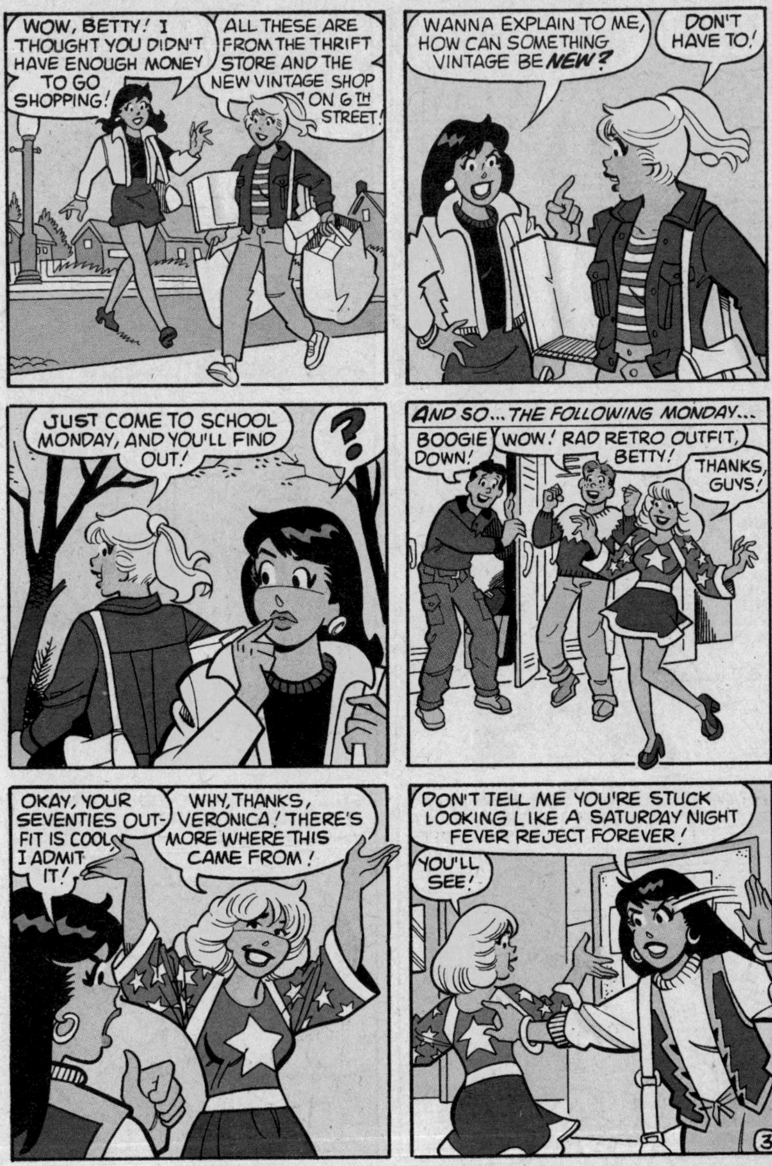
WOW, BETTY! I THOUGHT YOU DIDN'T HAVE ENOUGH MONEY TO GO SHOPPING!
ALL THESE ARE FROM THE THRIFT STORE AND THE NEW VINTAGE SHOP ON 6TH STREET!
WANNA EXPLAIN TO ME, HOW CAN SOMETHING VINTAGE BE NEW?
DON'T HAVE TO!
JUST COME TO SCHOOL MONDAY, AND YOU'LL FIND OUT!
?
AND SO... THE FOLLOWING MONDAY...
BOOGIE DOWN!
WOW! RAD RETRO OUTFIT, BETTY!
THANKS, GUYS!
OKAY, YOUR SEVENTIES OUT-FIT IS COOL, I ADMIT IT!
WHY, THANKS, VERONICA! THERE'S MORE WHERE THIS CAME FROM!
DON'T TELL ME YOU'RE STUCK LOOKING LIKE A SATURDAY NIGHT FEVER REJECT FOREVER!
YOU'LL SEE!
3

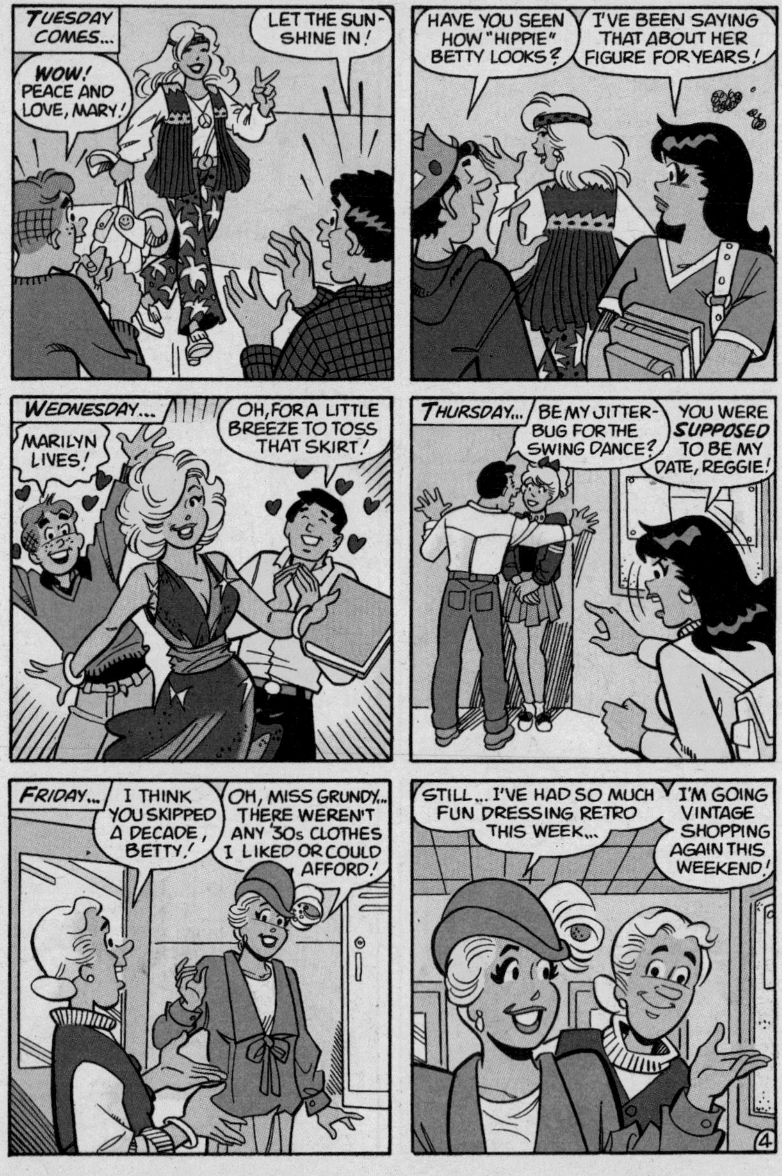
TUESDAY COMES...
WOW! PEACE AND LOVE, MARY!
LET THE SUN-SHINE IN!
HAVE YOU SEEN HOW "HIPPIE" BETTY LOOKS?
I'VE BEEN SAYING THAT ABOUT HER FIGURE FOR YEARS!
WEDNESDAY...
MARILYN LIVES!
OH, FOR A LITTLE BREEZE TO TOSS THAT SKIRT!
THURSDAY...
BE MY JITTER-BUG FOR THE SWING DANCE?
YOU WERE SUPPOSED TO BE MY DATE, REGGIE!
FRIDAY...
I THINK YOU SKIPPED A DECADE, BETTY!
OH, MISS GRUNDY... THERE WEREN'T ANY 30s CLOTHES I LIKED OR COULD AFFORD!
STILL... I'VE HAD SO MUCH FUN DRESSING RETRO THIS WEEK...
I'M GOING VINTAGE SHOPPING AGAIN THIS WEEKEND!
4

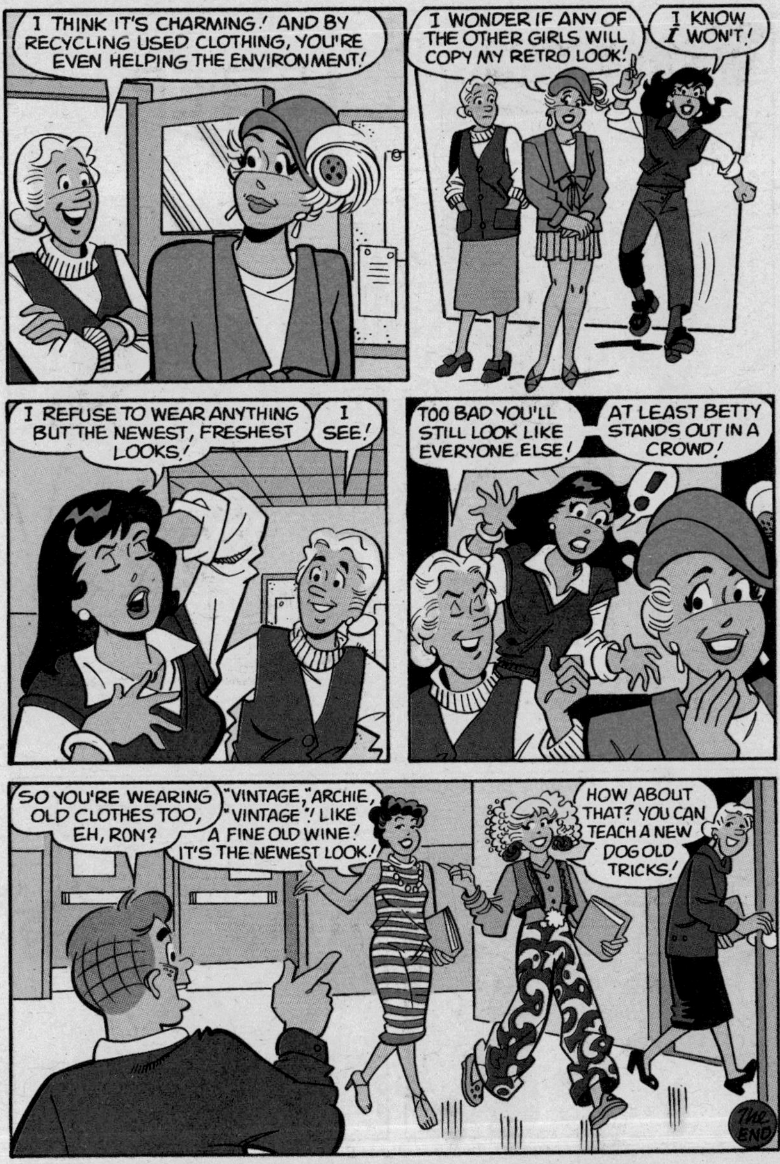
I THINK IT'S CHARMING! AND BY RECYCLING USED CLOTHING, YOU'RE EVEN HELPING THE ENVIRONMENT!
I WONDER IF ANY OF THE OTHER GIRLS WILL COPY MY RETRO LOOK!
I KNOW I WON'T!
I REFUSE TO WEAR ANYTHING BUT THE NEWEST, FRESHEST LOOKS!
I SEE!
TOO BAD YOU'LL STILL LOOK LIKE EVERYONE ELSE!
AT LEAST BETTY STANDS OUT IN A CROWD!
!
SO YOU'RE WEARING OLD CLOTHES TOO, EH, RON?
"VINTAGE," ARCHIE, "VINTAGE"! LIKE A FINE OLD WINE! IT'S THE NEWEST LOOK!
HOW ABOUT THAT? YOU CAN TEACH A NEW DOG OLD TRICKS!
THE END

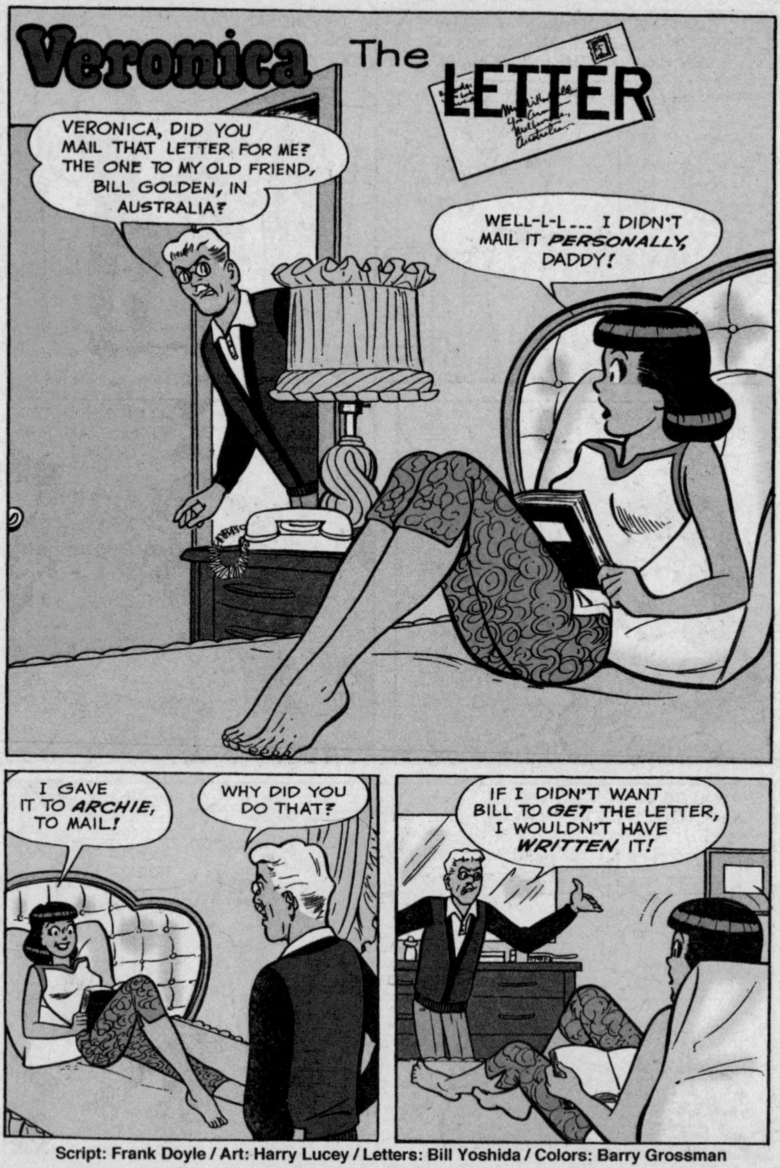

Veronica
The LETTER
VERONICA, DID YOU MAIL THAT LETTER FOR ME? THE ONE TO MY OLD FRIEND, BILL GOLDEN, IN AUSTRALIA?
WELL-L-L... I DIDN'T MAIL IT PERSONALLY, DADDY!
I GAVE IT TO ARCHIE, TO MAIL!
WHY DID YOU DO THAT?
IF I DIDN'T WANT BILL TO GET THE LETTER, I WOULDN'T HAVE WRITTEN IT!

Script: Frank Doyle / Art: Harry Lucey / Letters: Bill Yoshida / Colors: Barry Grossman

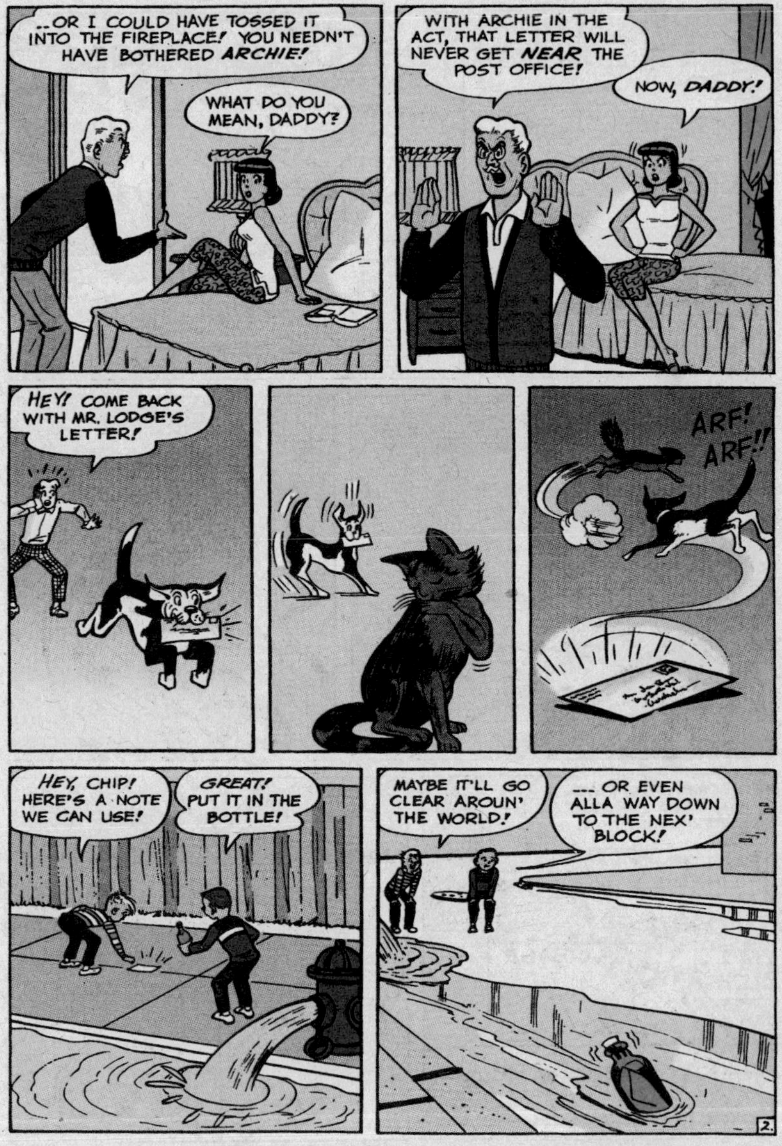

..OR I COULD HAVE TOSSED IT INTO THE FIREPLACE! YOU NEEDN'T HAVE BOTHERED ARCHIE!
WHAT DO YOU MEAN, DADDY?
WITH ARCHIE IN THE ACT, THAT LETTER WILL NEVER GET NEAR THE POST OFFICE!
NOW, DADDY!
HEY! COME BACK WITH MR. LODGE'S LETTER!
ARF! ARF!!
HEY, CHIP! HERE'S A NOTE WE CAN USE!
GREAT! PUT IT IN THE BOTTLE!
MAYBE IT'LL GO CLEAR AROUN' THE WORLD!
... OR EVEN ALLA WAY DOWN TO THE NEX' BLOCK!
2.

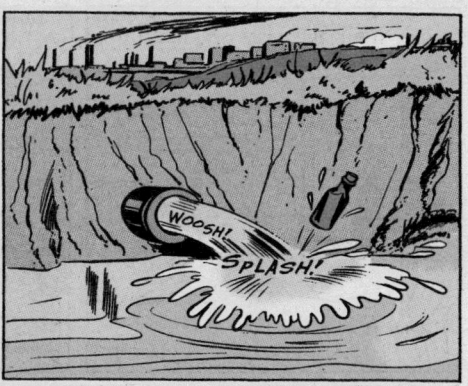

WOOSH!

SPLASH!

SOME CATCH! WE GOT MORE GARBAGE THAN FISH!

EAST END FISHERIES INC.

GARBAGE

EAST END FISH

TONY'S SANITATION

3.

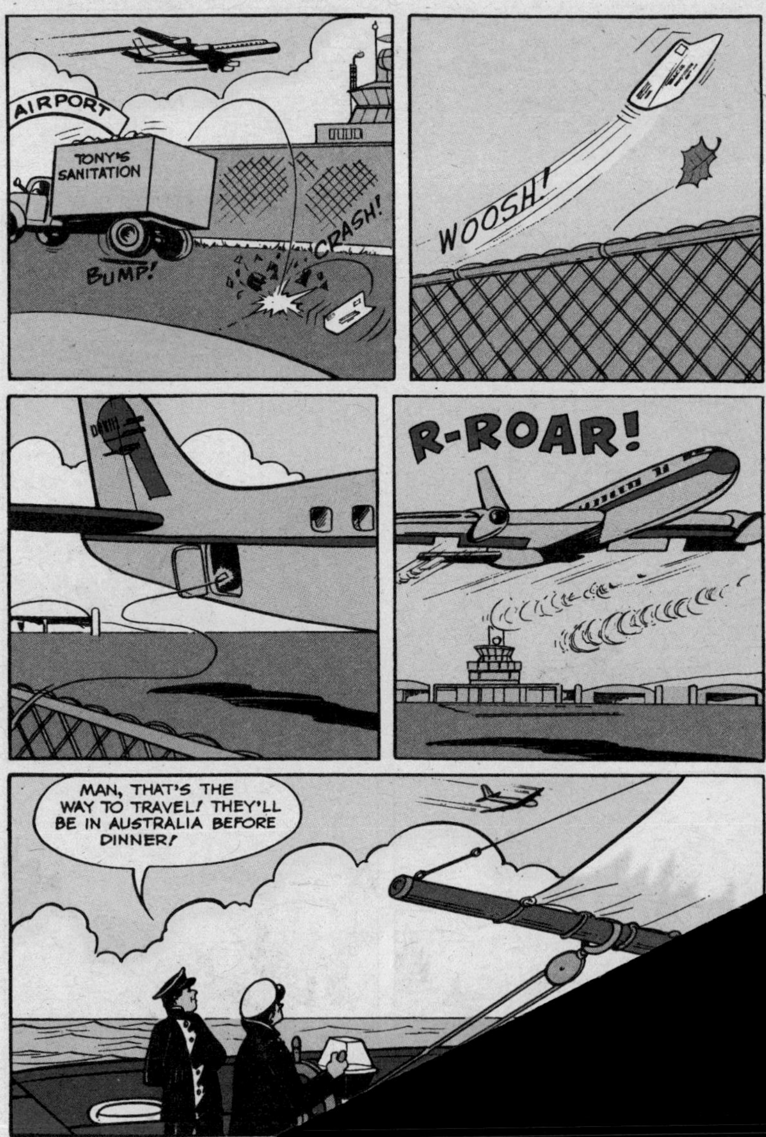
AIRPORT
TONY'S SANITATION
BUMP!
CRASH!
WOOSH!
R-ROAR!
MAN, THAT'S THE WAY TO TRAVEL! THEY'LL BE IN AUSTRALIA BEFORE DINNER!

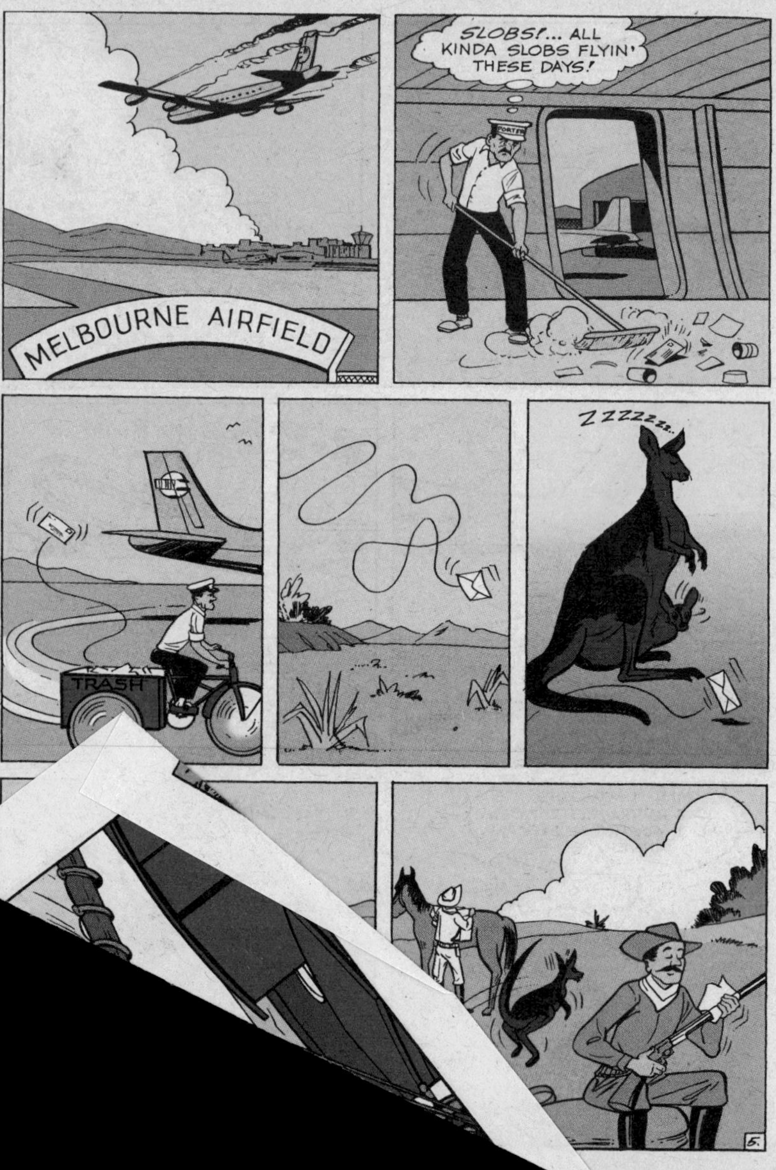
MELBOURNE AIRFIELD
SLOBS!... ALL KINDA SLOBS FLYIN' THESE DAYS!
TRASH
ZZZZZzz..

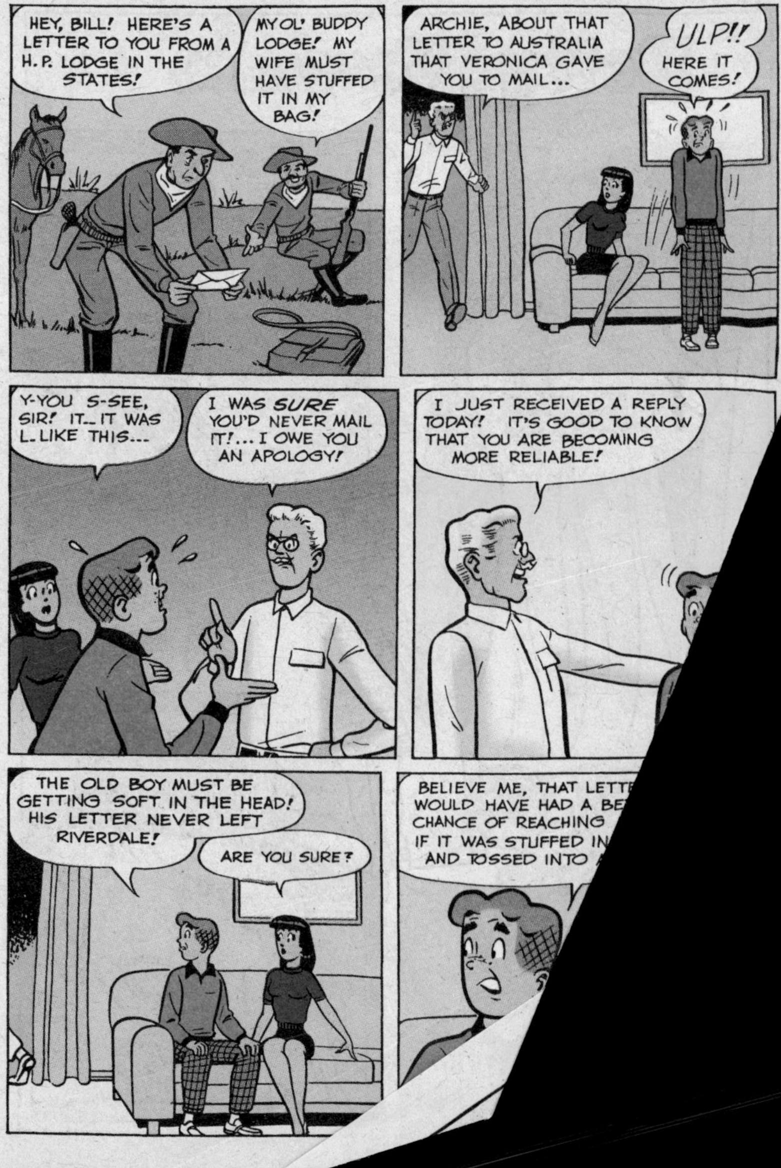
HEY, BILL! HERE'S A LETTER TO YOU FROM A H. P. LODGE IN THE STATES!
MY OL' BUDDY LODGE! MY WIFE MUST HAVE STUFFED IT IN MY BAG!
ARCHIE, ABOUT THAT LETTER TO AUSTRALIA THAT VERONICA GAVE YOU TO MAIL...
ULP!! HERE IT COMES!
Y-YOU S-SEE, SIR! IT_ IT WAS L_LIKE THIS...
I WAS SURE YOU'D NEVER MAIL IT!... I OWE YOU AN APOLOGY!
I JUST RECEIVED A REPLY TODAY! IT'S GOOD TO KNOW THAT YOU ARE BECOMING MORE RELIABLE!
THE OLD BOY MUST BE GETTING SOFT IN THE HEAD! HIS LETTER NEVER LEFT RIVERDALE!
ARE YOU SURE?
BELIEVE ME, THAT LETT
WOULD HAVE HAD A BE
CHANCE OF REACHING
IF IT WAS STUFFED IN
AND TOSSED INTO

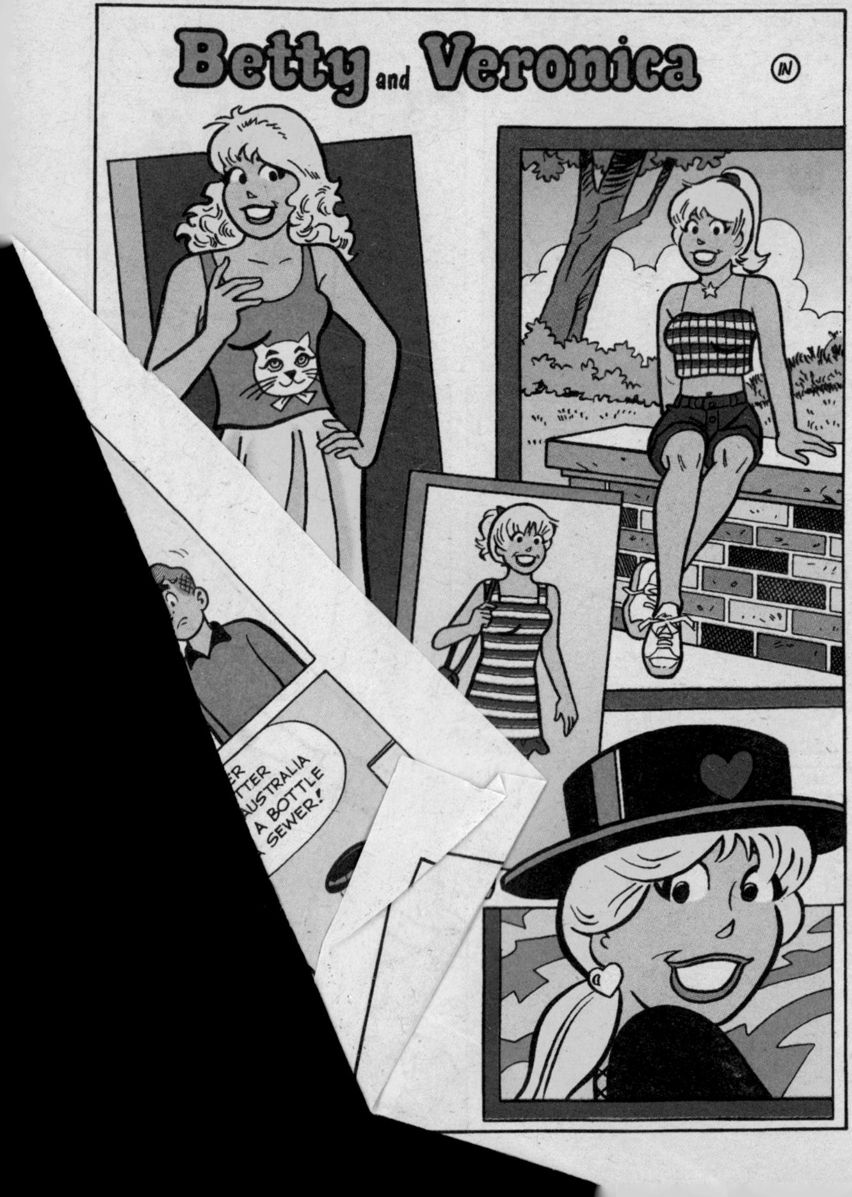
Betty and Veronica
IN
ER
TTER
AUSTRALIA
A BOTTLE
SEWER!

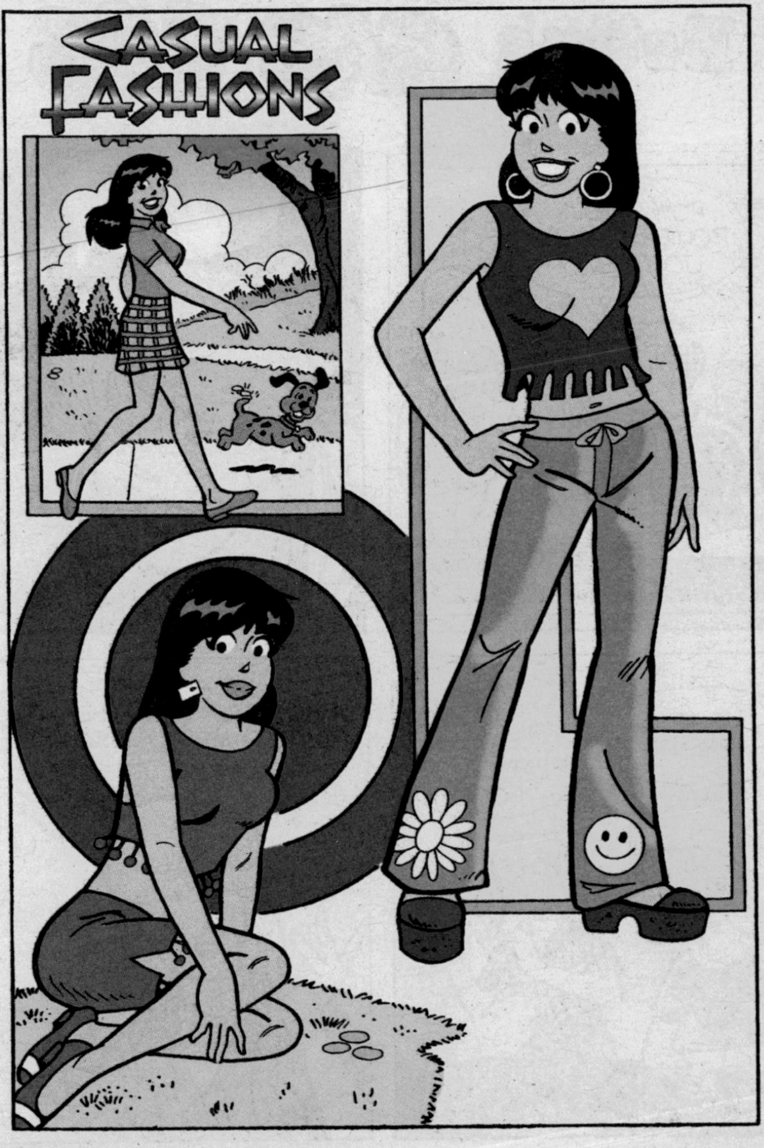
CASUAL FASHIONS

Betty's GAG BAG

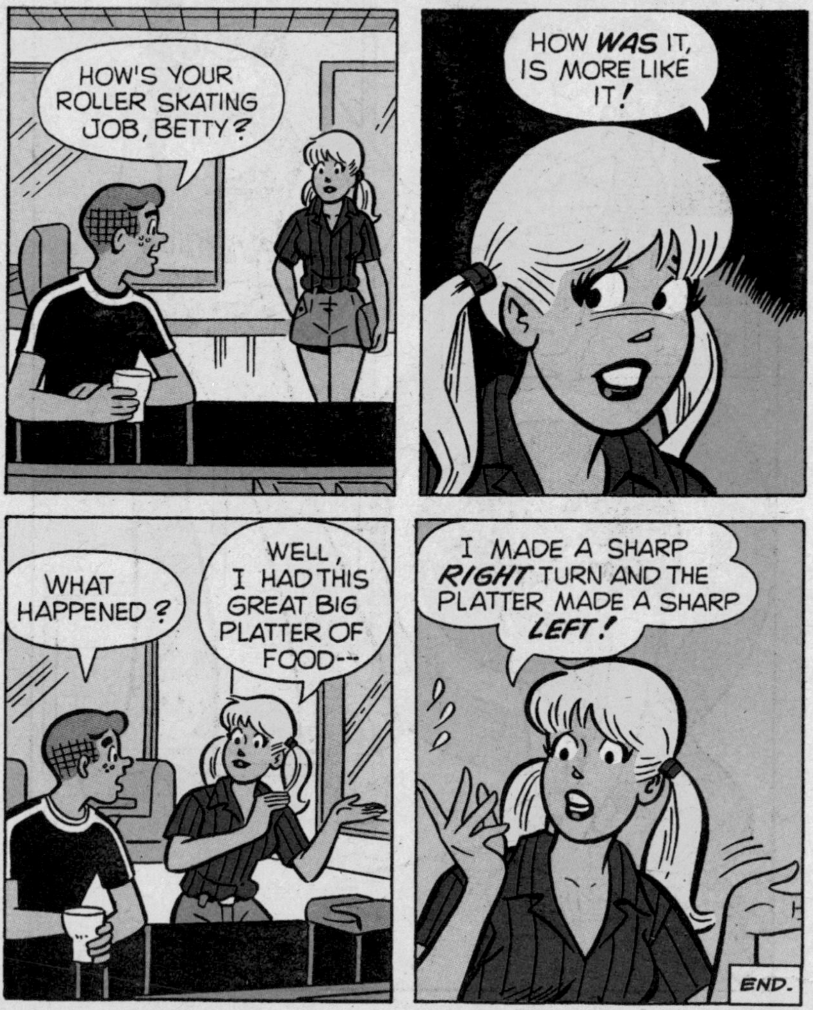
HOW'S YOUR ROLLER SKATING JOB, BETTY?
HOW *WAS* IT, IS MORE LIKE IT!
WHAT HAPPENED?
WELL, I HAD THIS GREAT BIG PLATTER OF FOOD---
I MADE A SHARP *RIGHT* TURN AND THE PLATTER MADE A SHARP *LEFT*!
END.

Archie in The "OBSERVER"

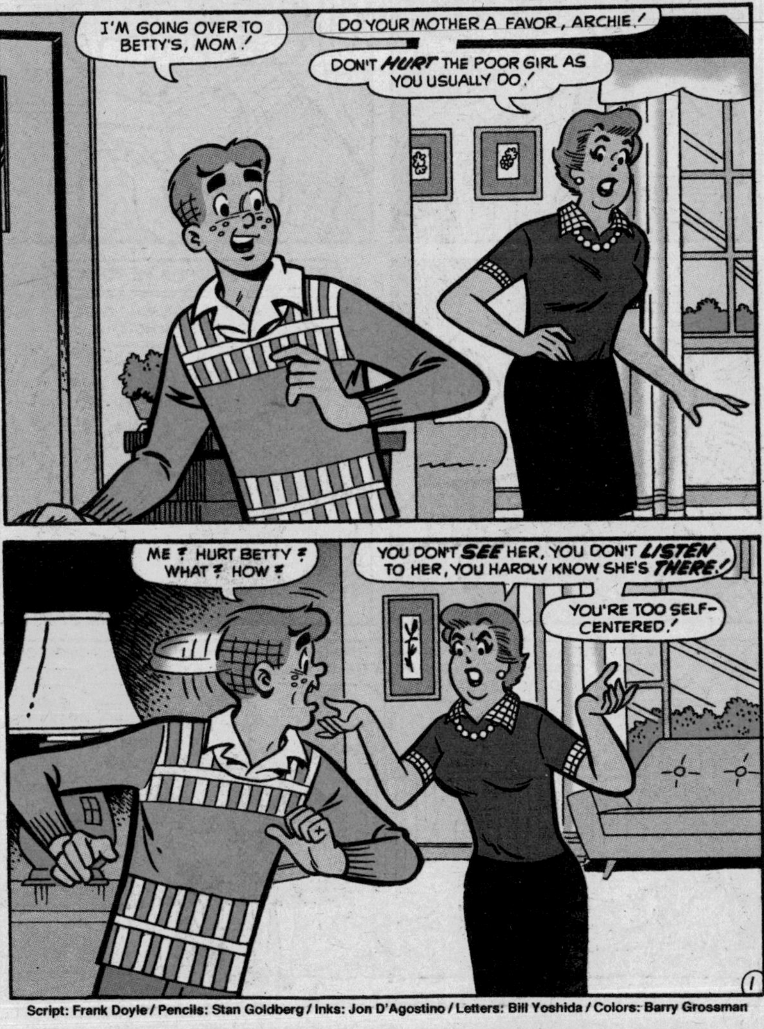
I'M GOING OVER TO BETTY'S, MOM!
DO YOUR MOTHER A FAVOR, ARCHIE!
DON'T HURT THE POOR GIRL AS YOU USUALLY DO!
ME? HURT BETTY? WHAT? HOW?
YOU DON'T SEE HER, YOU DON'T LISTEN TO HER, YOU HARDLY KNOW SHE'S THERE!
YOU'RE TOO SELF-CENTERED!
1

Script: Frank Doyle / Pencils: Stan Goldberg / Inks: Jon D'Agostino / Letters: Bill Yoshida / Colors: Barry Grossman

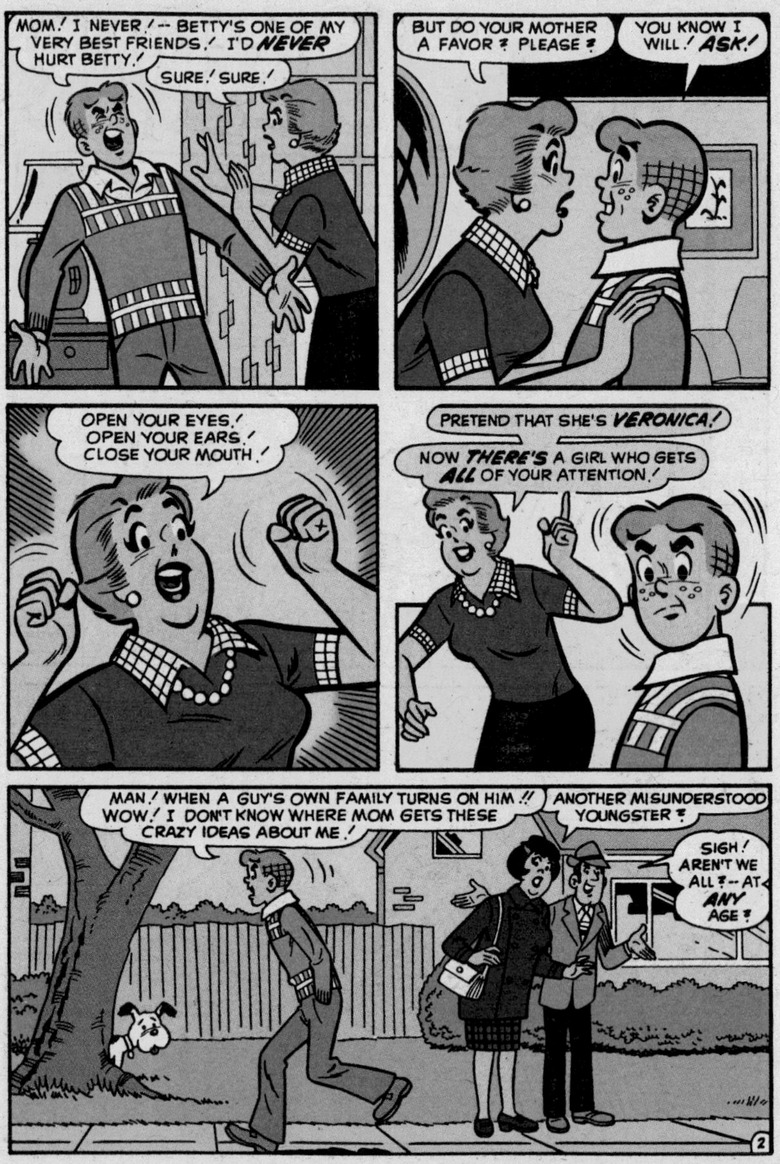
MOM! I NEVER! -- BETTY'S ONE OF MY VERY BEST FRIENDS! I'D NEVER HURT BETTY!
SURE! SURE!
BUT DO YOUR MOTHER A FAVOR? PLEASE?
YOU KNOW I WILL! ASK!
OPEN YOUR EYES! OPEN YOUR EARS! CLOSE YOUR MOUTH!
PRETEND THAT SHE'S VERONICA!
NOW THERE'S A GIRL WHO GETS ALL OF YOUR ATTENTION!
MAN! WHEN A GUY'S OWN FAMILY TURNS ON HIM!! WOW! I DON'T KNOW WHERE MOM GETS THESE CRAZY IDEAS ABOUT ME!
ANOTHER MISUNDERSTOOD YOUNGSTER?
SIGH! AREN'T WE ALL? -- AT ANY AGE?
2

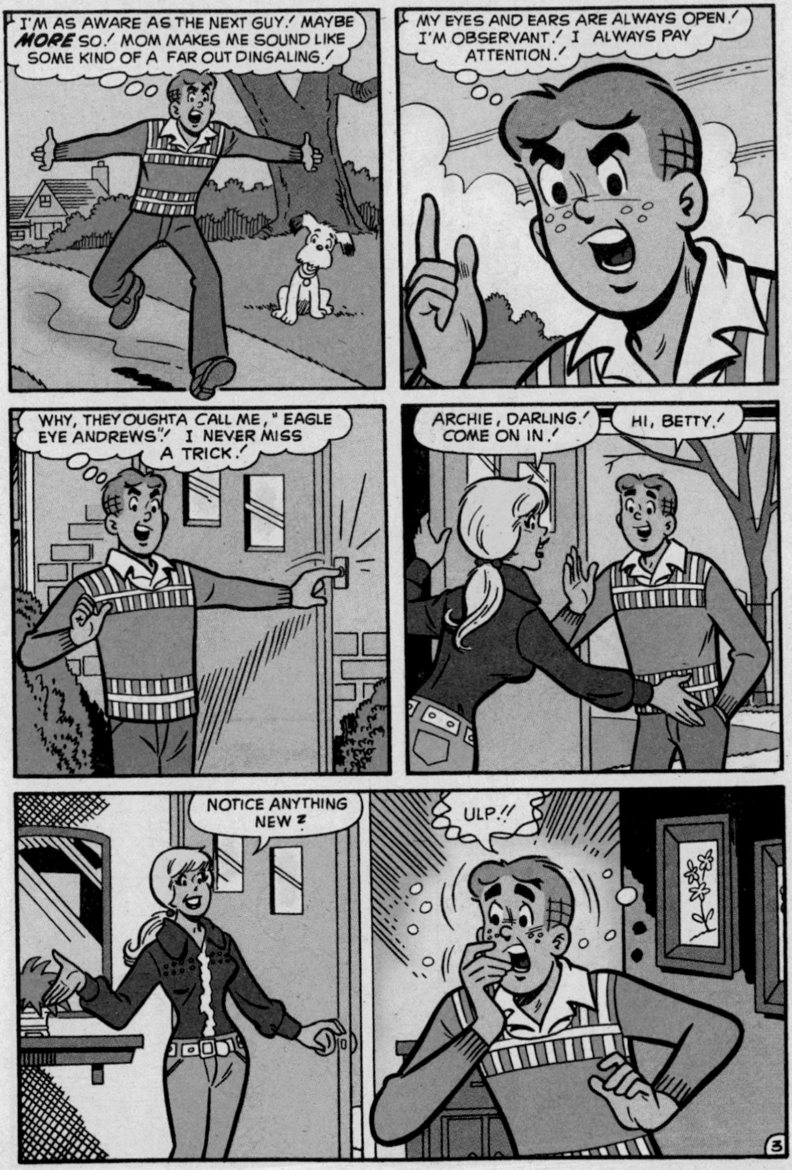
I'M AS AWARE AS THE NEXT GUY! MAYBE **MORE** SO! MOM MAKES ME SOUND LIKE SOME KIND OF A FAR OUT DINGALING!
MY EYES AND EARS ARE ALWAYS OPEN! I'M OBSERVANT! I ALWAYS PAY ATTENTION!
WHY, THEY OUGHTA CALL ME, "EAGLE EYE ANDREWS"! I NEVER MISS A TRICK!
ARCHIE, DARLING! COME ON IN!
HI, BETTY!
NOTICE ANYTHING NEW?
ULP!!
3

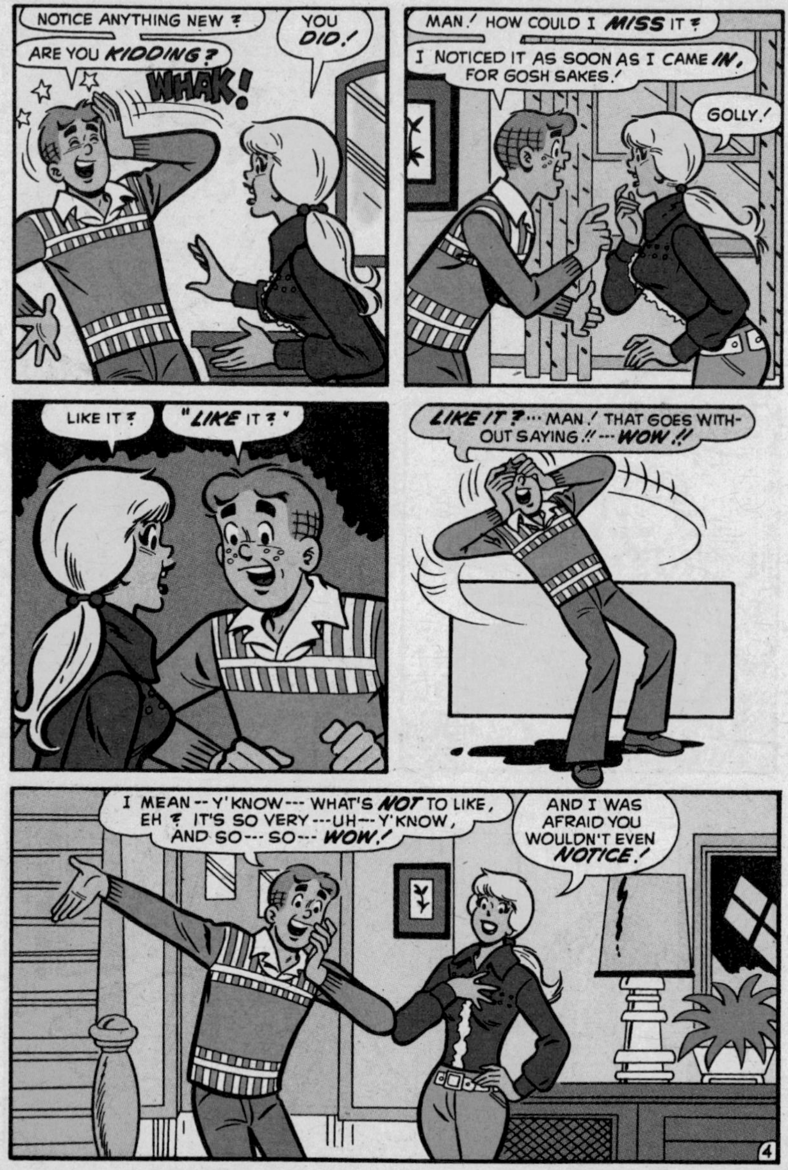
NOTICE ANYTHING NEW ?
ARE YOU KIDDING ?
WHAK!
YOU DID!
MAN! HOW COULD I MISS IT ?
I NOTICED IT AS SOON AS I CAME IN, FOR GOSH SAKES!
GOLLY!
LIKE IT ?
"LIKE IT ?"
LIKE IT ?... MAN! THAT GOES WITH-OUT SAYING!! --- WOW!!
I MEAN -- Y'KNOW --- WHAT'S NOT TO LIKE, EH ? IT'S SO VERY --- UH --- Y'KNOW, AND SO --- SO --- WOW!
AND I WAS AFRAID YOU WOULDN'T EVEN NOTICE!
4

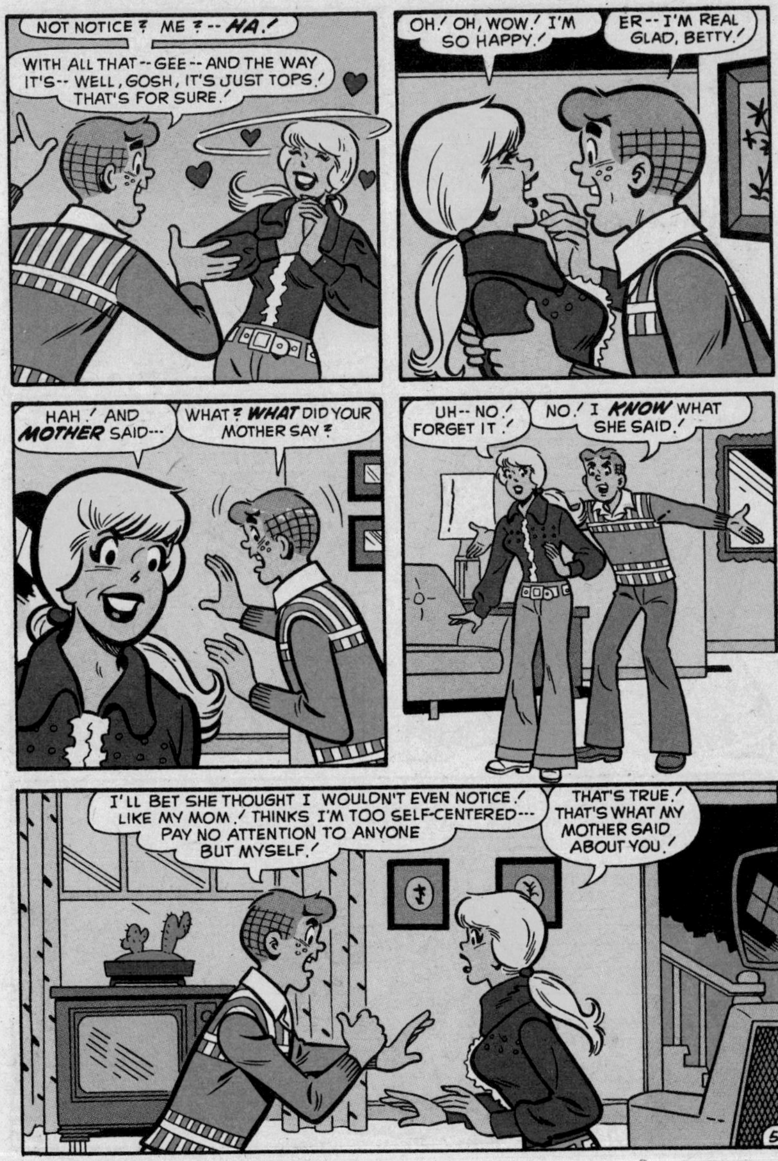
NOT NOTICE? ME? --HA!
WITH ALL THAT--GEE--AND THE WAY IT'S-- WELL, GOSH, IT'S JUST TOPS! THAT'S FOR SURE!
OH! OH, WOW! I'M SO HAPPY!
ER--I'M REAL GLAD, BETTY!
HAH! AND MOTHER SAID---
WHAT? WHAT DID YOUR MOTHER SAY?
UH--NO! FORGET IT!
NO! I KNOW WHAT SHE SAID!
I'LL BET SHE THOUGHT I WOULDN'T EVEN NOTICE! LIKE MY MOM! THINKS I'M TOO SELF-CENTERED--- PAY NO ATTENTION TO ANYONE BUT MYSELF!
THAT'S TRUE! THAT'S WHAT MY MOTHER SAID ABOUT YOU!

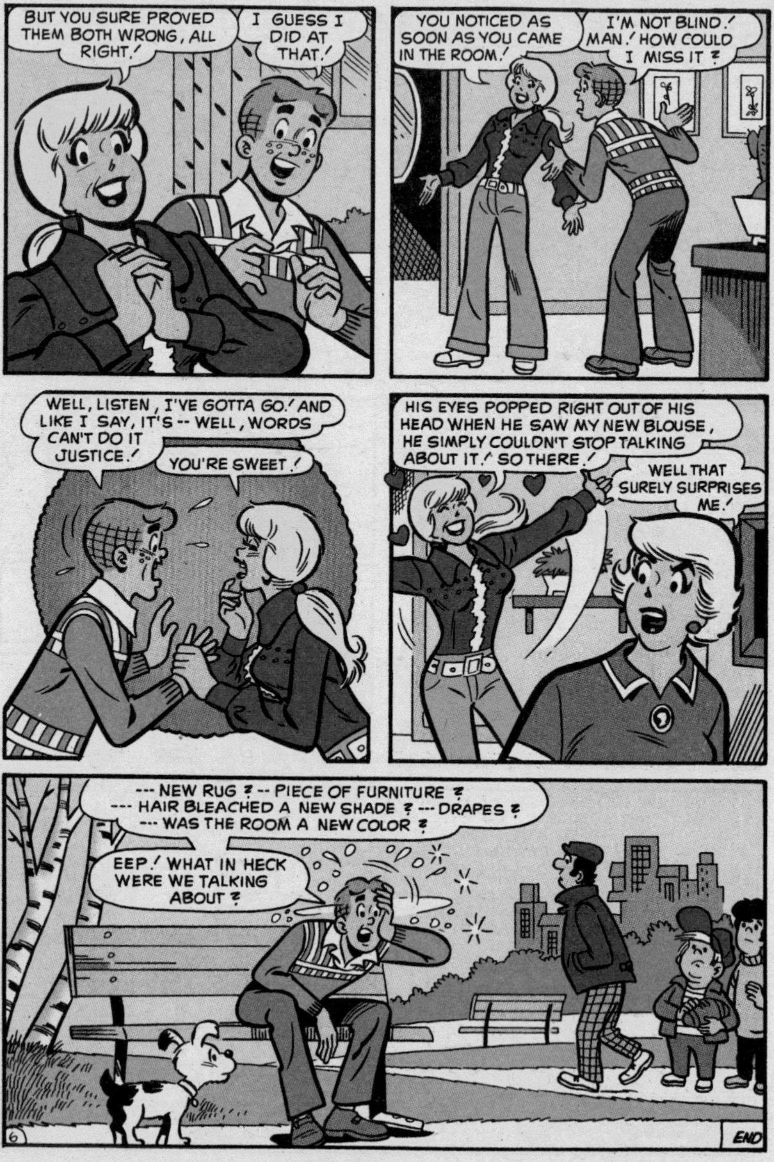
BUT YOU SURE PROVED THEM BOTH WRONG, ALL RIGHT!
I GUESS I DID AT THAT!
YOU NOTICED AS SOON AS YOU CAME IN THE ROOM!
I'M NOT BLIND! MAN! HOW COULD I MISS IT?
WELL, LISTEN, I'VE GOTTA GO! AND LIKE I SAY, IT'S -- WELL, WORDS CAN'T DO IT JUSTICE!
YOU'RE SWEET!
HIS EYES POPPED RIGHT OUT OF HIS HEAD WHEN HE SAW MY NEW BLOUSE, HE SIMPLY COULDN'T STOP TALKING ABOUT IT! SO THERE!
WELL THAT SURELY SURPRISES ME!
--- NEW RUG? -- PIECE OF FURNITURE? --- HAIR BLEACHED A NEW SHADE? --- DRAPES? --- WAS THE ROOM A NEW COLOR?
EEP! WHAT IN HECK WERE WE TALKING ABOUT?
6
END

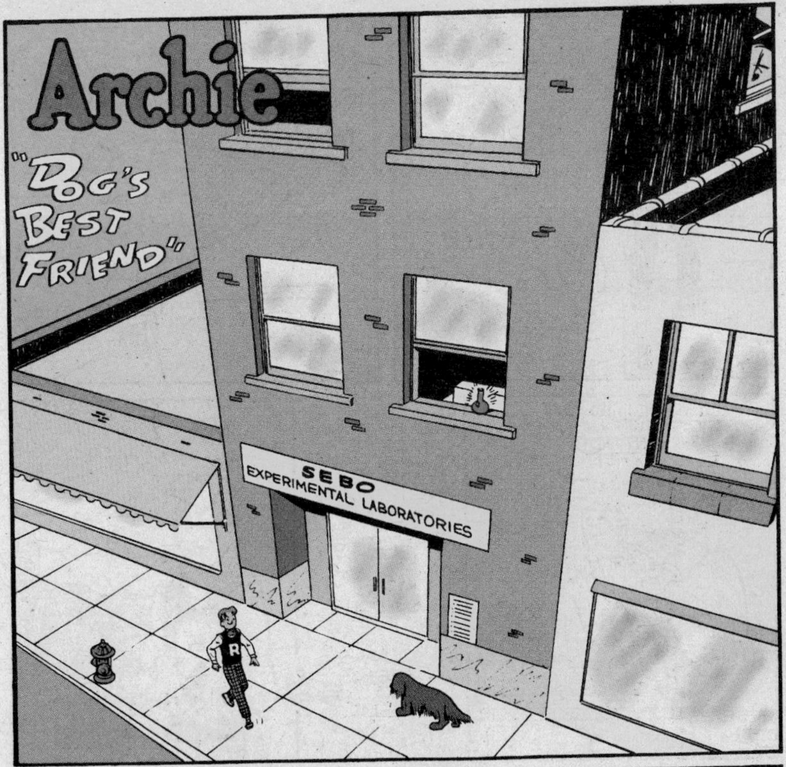
Archie
"DOG'S BEST FRIEND"
SEBO EXPERIMENTAL LABORATORIES
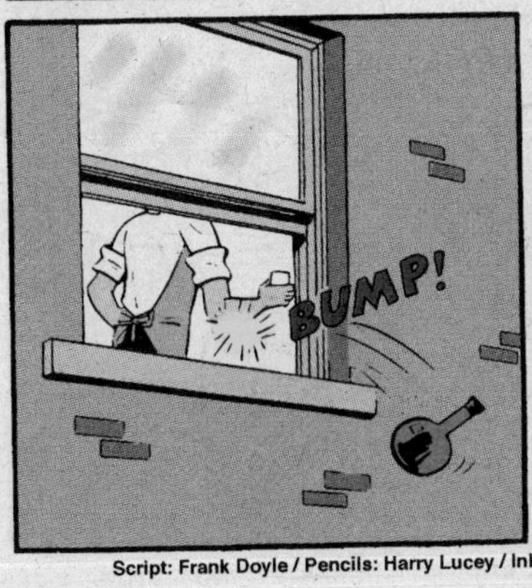
BUMP!
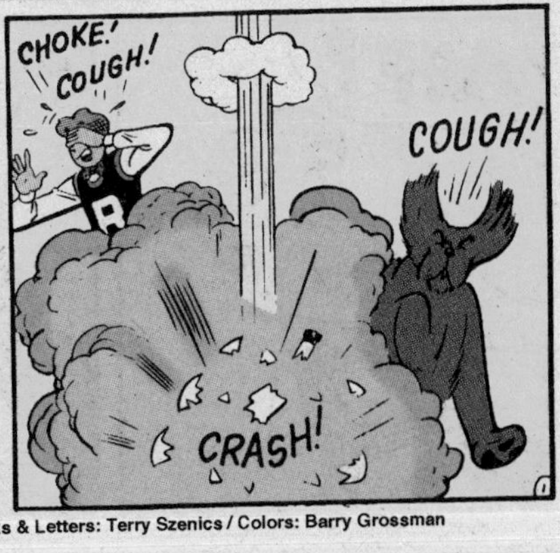
CHOKE! COUGH!
COUGH!
CRASH!
1

Script: Frank Doyle / Pencils: Harry Lucey / Inks & Letters: Terry Szenics / Colors: Barry Grossman

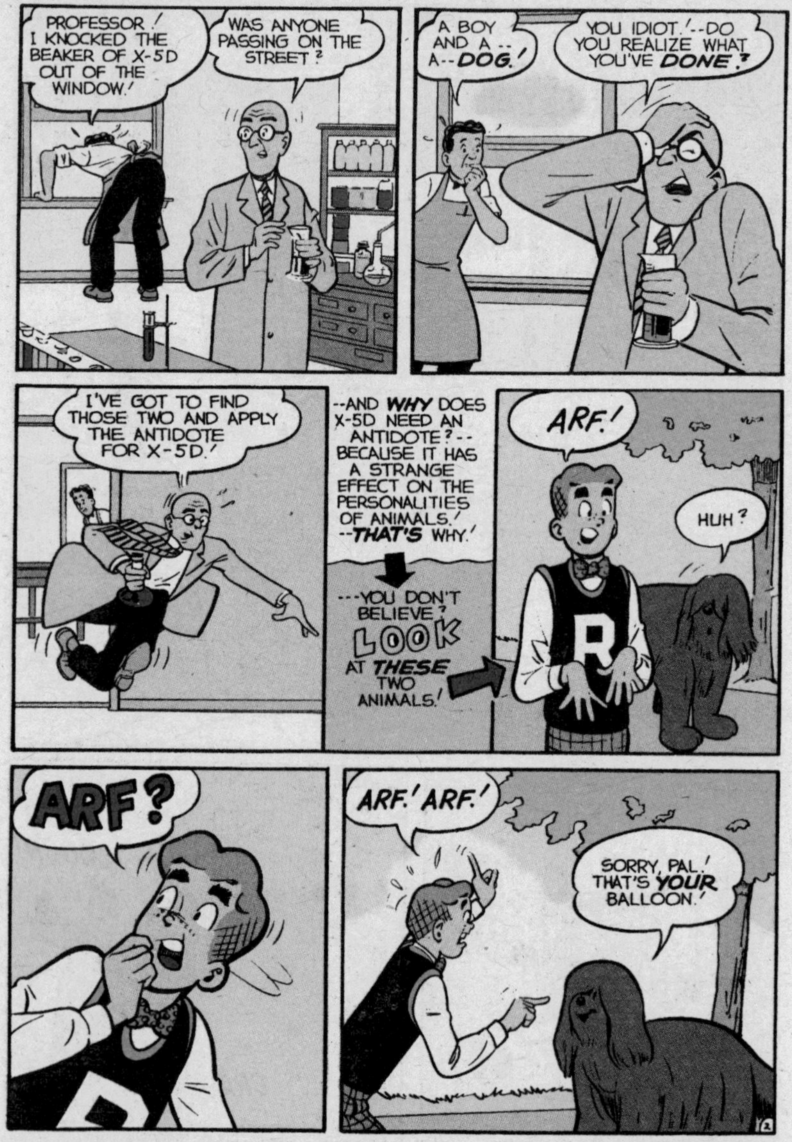
PROFESSOR! I KNOCKED THE BEAKER OF X-5D OUT OF THE WINDOW!
WAS ANYONE PASSING ON THE STREET?
A BOY AND A.. A--DOG!
YOU IDIOT!--DO YOU REALIZE WHAT YOU'VE DONE?
I'VE GOT TO FIND THOSE TWO AND APPLY THE ANTIDOTE FOR X-5D!
--AND WHY DOES X-5D NEED AN ANTIDOTE?--BECAUSE IT HAS A STRANGE EFFECT ON THE PERSONALITIES OF ANIMALS!--THAT'S WHY!
---YOU DON'T BELIEVE? LOOK AT THESE TWO ANIMALS!
ARF!
HUH?
ARF?
ARF! ARF!
SORRY, PAL! THAT'S YOUR BALLOON!
12

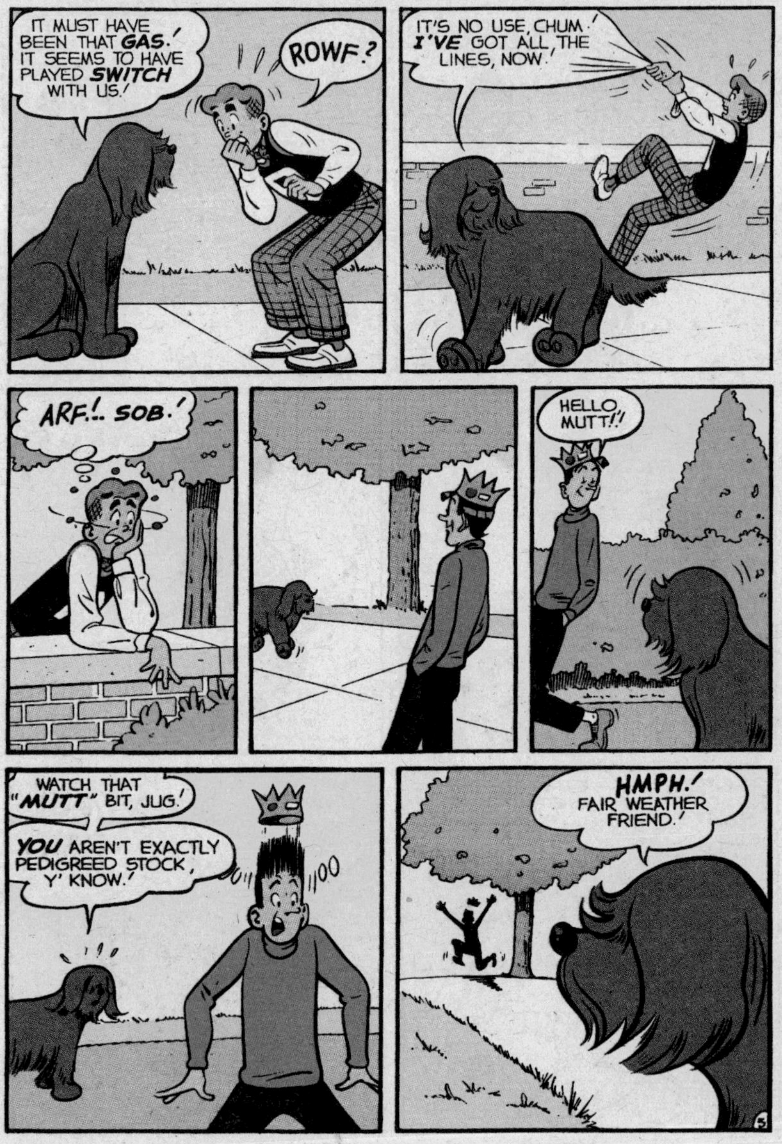

IT MUST HAVE BEEN THAT GAS! IT SEEMS TO HAVE PLAYED SWITCH WITH US!
ROWF?
IT'S NO USE, CHUM! I'VE GOT ALL THE LINES, NOW!
ARF!.. SOB.!
HELLO MUTT!!
WATCH THAT "MUTT" BIT, JUG!
YOU AREN'T EXACTLY PEDIGREED STOCK, Y' KNOW!
HMPH! FAIR WEATHER FRIEND!

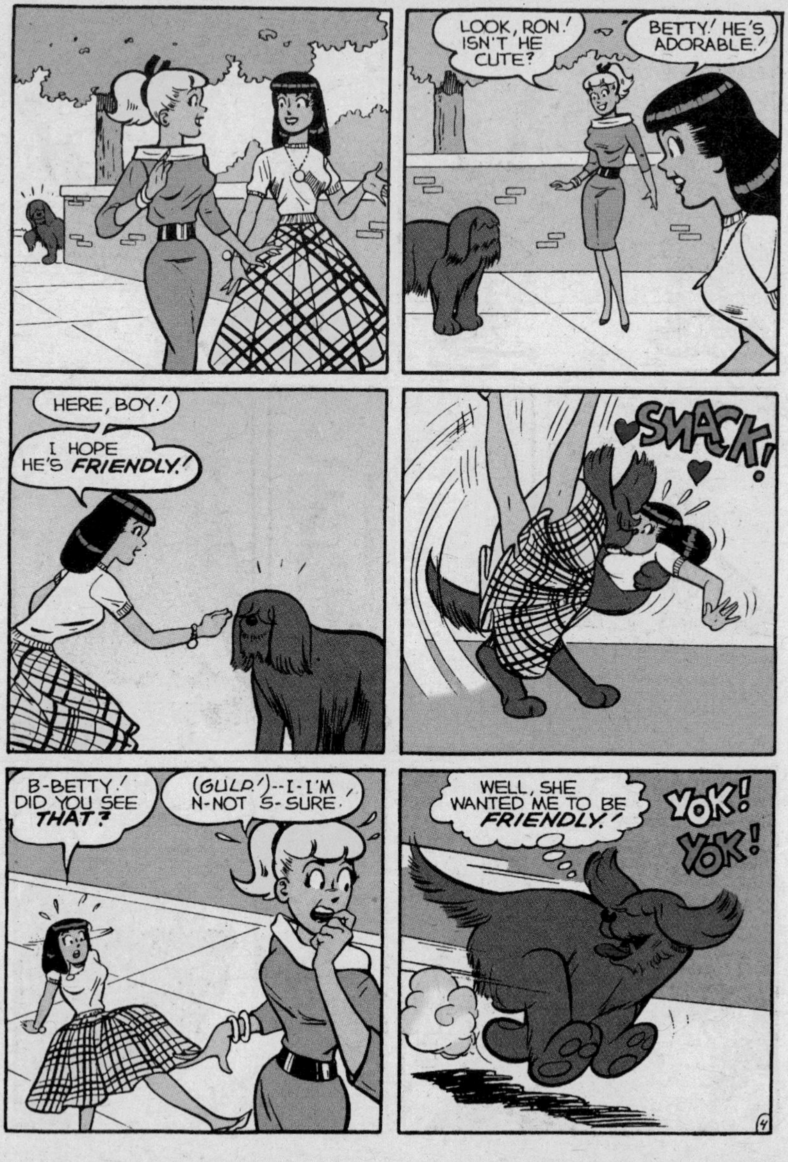
LOOK, RON! ISN'T HE CUTE?
BETTY! HE'S ADORABLE!
HERE, BOY!
I HOPE HE'S FRIENDLY!
SMACK!
B-BETTY! DID YOU SEE THAT?
(GULP!)--I-I'M N-NOT S-SURE!
WELL, SHE WANTED ME TO BE FRIENDLY!
YOK! YOK!
4

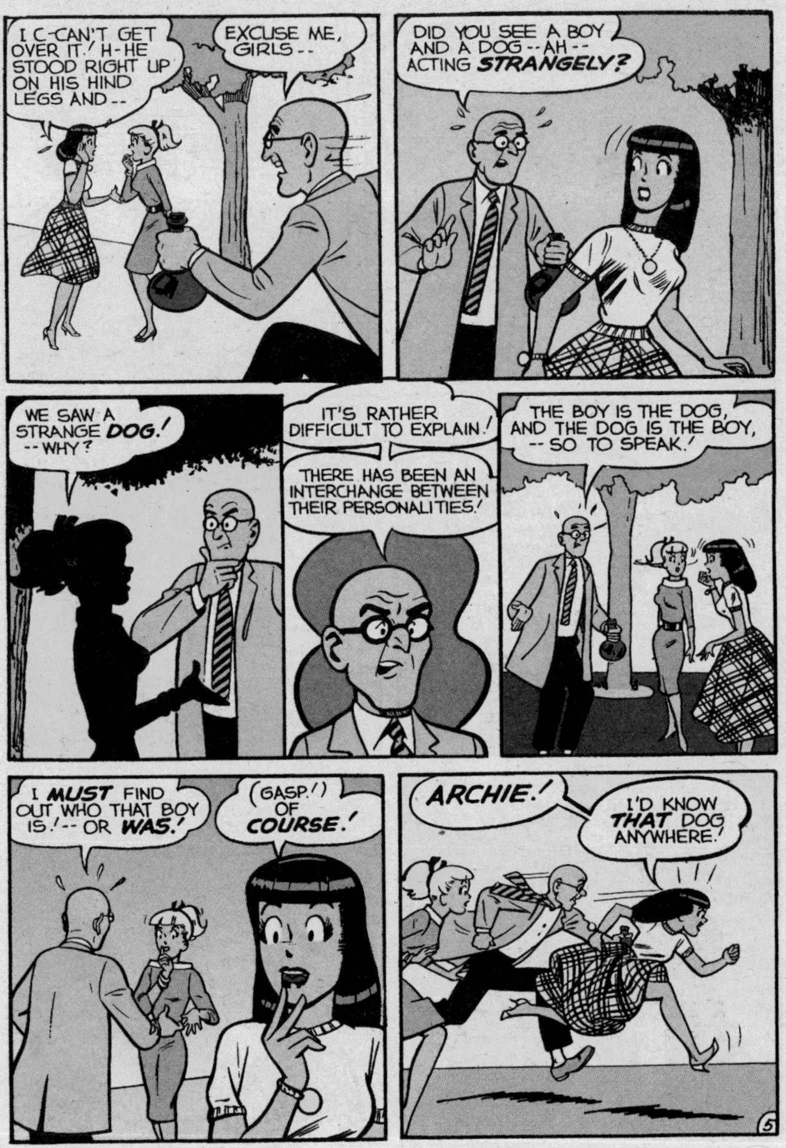
I C-CAN'T GET OVER IT! H-HE STOOD RIGHT UP ON HIS HIND LEGS AND --
EXCUSE ME, GIRLS --
DID YOU SEE A BOY AND A DOG -- AH -- ACTING STRANGELY?
WE SAW A STRANGE DOG! -- WHY?
IT'S RATHER DIFFICULT TO EXPLAIN!
THERE HAS BEEN AN INTERCHANGE BETWEEN THEIR PERSONALITIES!
THE BOY IS THE DOG, AND THE DOG IS THE BOY, -- SO TO SPEAK!
I MUST FIND OUT WHO THAT BOY IS! -- OR WAS!
(GASP!) OF COURSE!
ARCHIE!
I'D KNOW THAT DOG ANYWHERE!
5

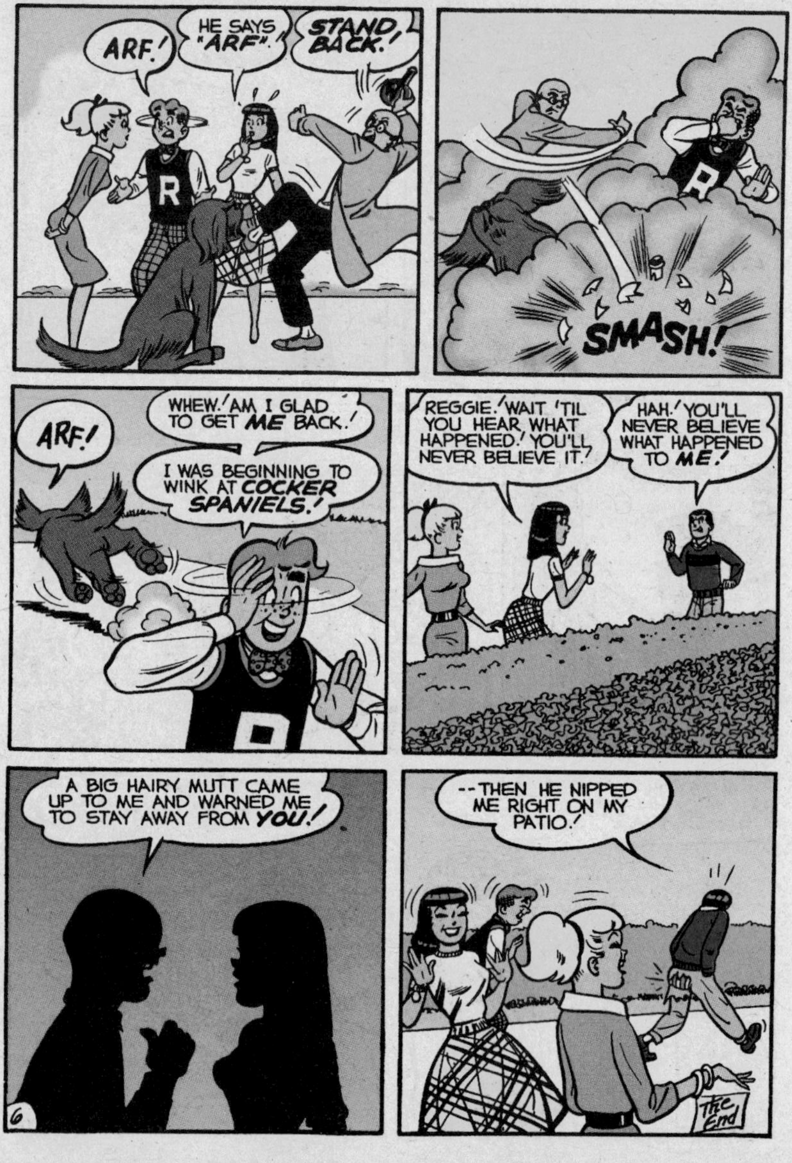
ARF!
HE SAYS "ARF"!
STAND BACK!
SMASH!
ARF!
WHEW! AM I GLAD TO GET ME BACK!
I WAS BEGINNING TO WINK AT COCKER SPANIELS!
REGGIE! WAIT 'TIL YOU HEAR WHAT HAPPENED! YOU'LL NEVER BELIEVE IT!
HAH! YOU'LL NEVER BELIEVE WHAT HAPPENED TO ME!
A BIG HAIRY MUTT CAME UP TO ME AND WARNED ME TO STAY AWAY FROM YOU!
6
--THEN HE NIPPED ME RIGHT ON MY PATIO!
The End

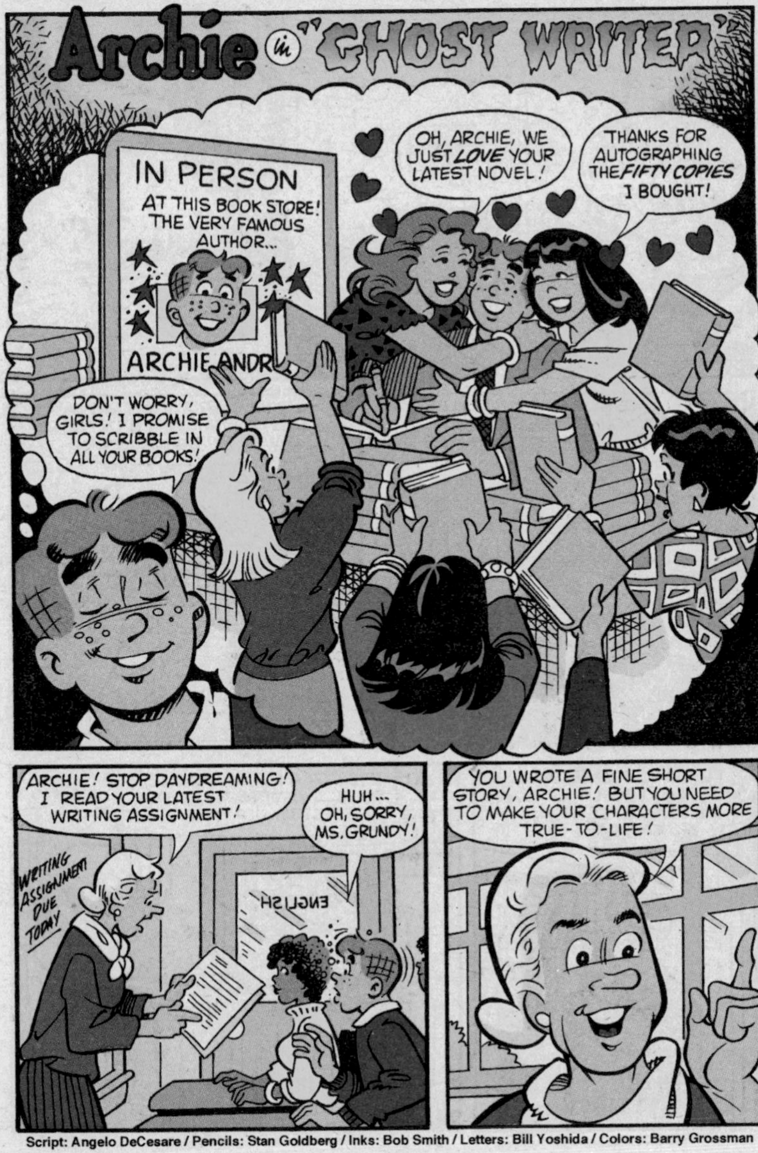
Archie in "GHOST WRITER"
IN PERSON AT THIS BOOK STORE! THE VERY FAMOUS AUTHOR...
ARCHIE ANDR
OH, ARCHIE, WE JUST LOVE YOUR LATEST NOVEL!
THANKS FOR AUTOGRAPHING THE FIFTY COPIES I BOUGHT!
DON'T WORRY, GIRLS! I PROMISE TO SCRIBBLE IN ALL YOUR BOOKS!
ARCHIE! STOP DAYDREAMING! I READ YOUR LATEST WRITING ASSIGNMENT!
WRITING ASSIGNMENT DUE TODAY
HUH... OH, SORRY, MS. GRUNDY!
YOU WROTE A FINE SHORT STORY, ARCHIE! BUT YOU NEED TO MAKE YOUR CHARACTERS MORE TRUE-TO-LIFE!

Script: Angelo DeCesare / Pencils: Stan Goldberg / Inks: Bob Smith / Letters: Bill Yoshida / Colors: Barry Grossman

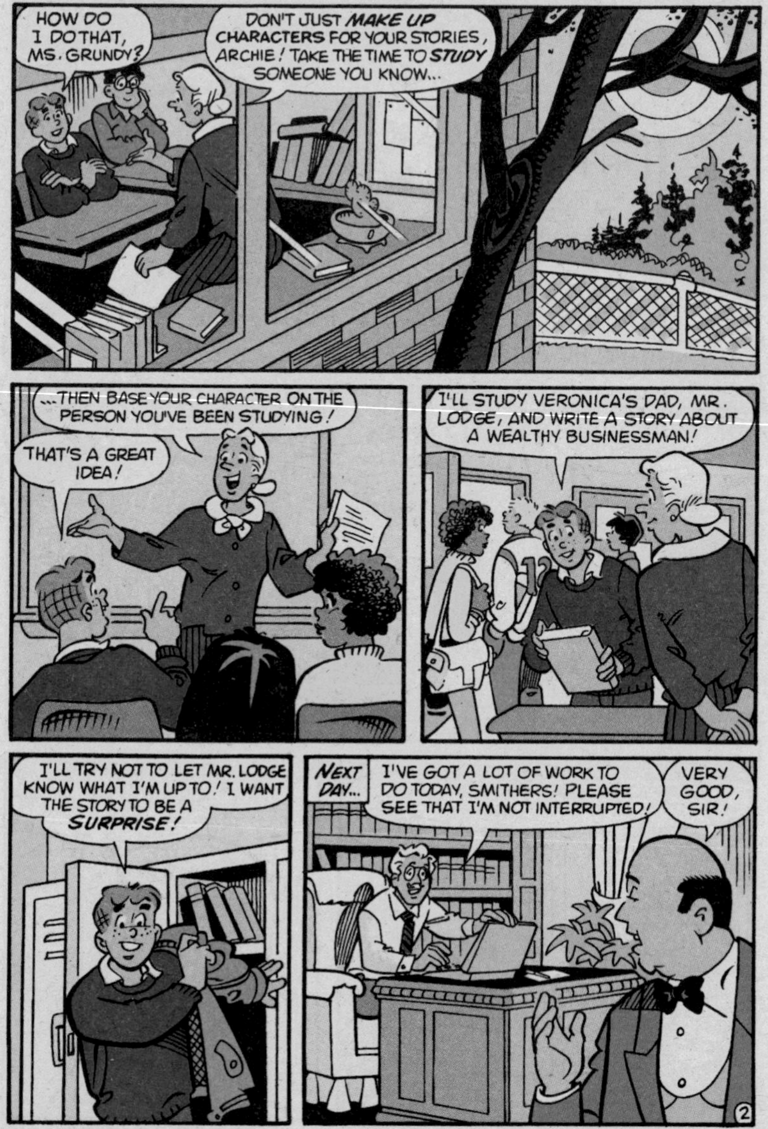
HOW DO I DO THAT, MS. GRUNDY?
DON'T JUST MAKE UP CHARACTERS FOR YOUR STORIES, ARCHIE! TAKE THE TIME TO STUDY SOMEONE YOU KNOW...
...THEN BASE YOUR CHARACTER ON THE PERSON YOU'VE BEEN STUDYING!
THAT'S A GREAT IDEA!
I'LL STUDY VERONICA'S DAD, MR. LODGE, AND WRITE A STORY ABOUT A WEALTHY BUSINESSMAN!
I'LL TRY NOT TO LET MR. LODGE KNOW WHAT I'M UP TO! I WANT THE STORY TO BE A SURPRISE!
NEXT DAY...
I'VE GOT A LOT OF WORK TO DO TODAY, SMITHERS! PLEASE SEE THAT I'M NOT INTERRUPTED!
VERY GOOD, SIR!
2

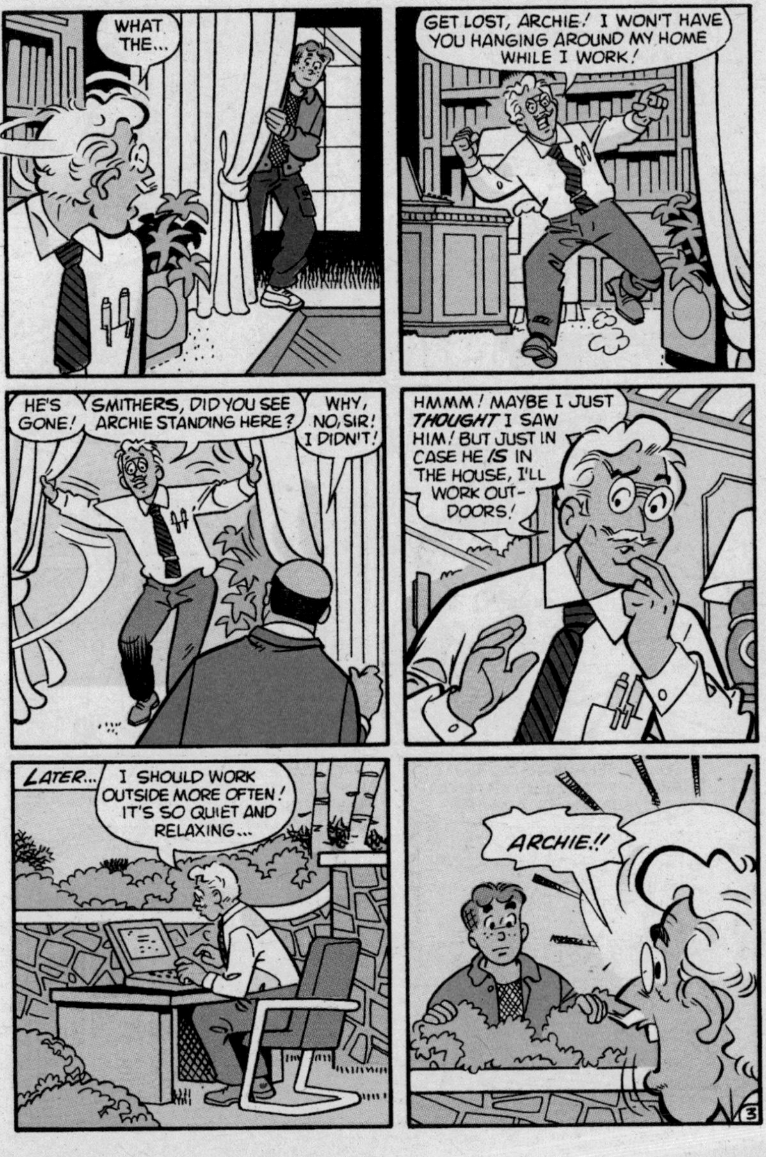
WHAT THE...
GET LOST, ARCHIE! I WON'T HAVE YOU HANGING AROUND MY HOME WHILE I WORK!
HE'S GONE!
SMITHERS, DID YOU SEE ARCHIE STANDING HERE?
WHY, NO, SIR! I DIDN'T!
HMMM! MAYBE I JUST THOUGHT I SAW HIM! BUT JUST IN CASE HE IS IN THE HOUSE, I'LL WORK OUT-DOORS!
LATER...
I SHOULD WORK OUTSIDE MORE OFTEN! IT'S SO QUIET AND RELAXING...
ARCHIE!!
3

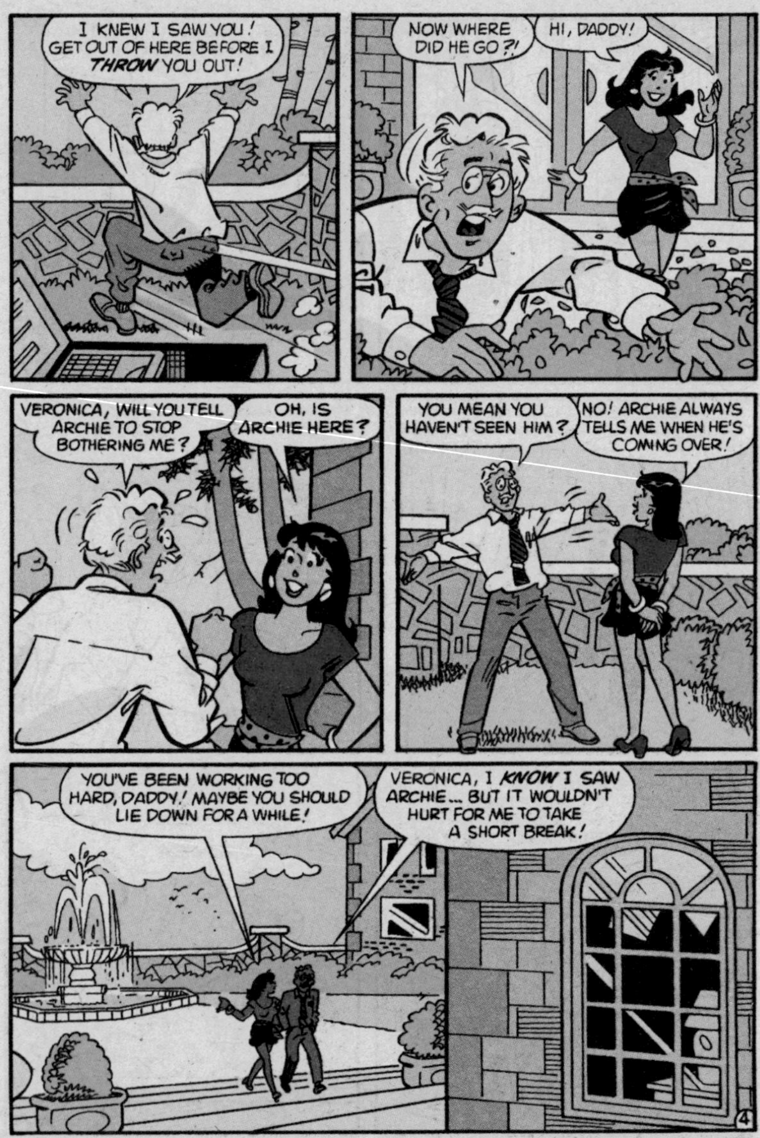

I KNEW I SAW YOU! GET OUT OF HERE BEFORE I *THROW* YOU OUT!
NOW WHERE DID HE GO?!
HI, DADDY!
VERONICA, WILL YOU TELL ARCHIE TO STOP BOTHERING ME?
OH, IS ARCHIE HERE?
YOU MEAN YOU HAVEN'T SEEN HIM?
NO! ARCHIE ALWAYS TELLS ME WHEN HE'S COMING OVER!
YOU'VE BEEN WORKING TOO HARD, DADDY! MAYBE YOU SHOULD LIE DOWN FOR A WHILE!
VERONICA, I *KNOW* I SAW ARCHIE... BUT IT WOULDN'T HURT FOR ME TO TAKE A SHORT BREAK!
4

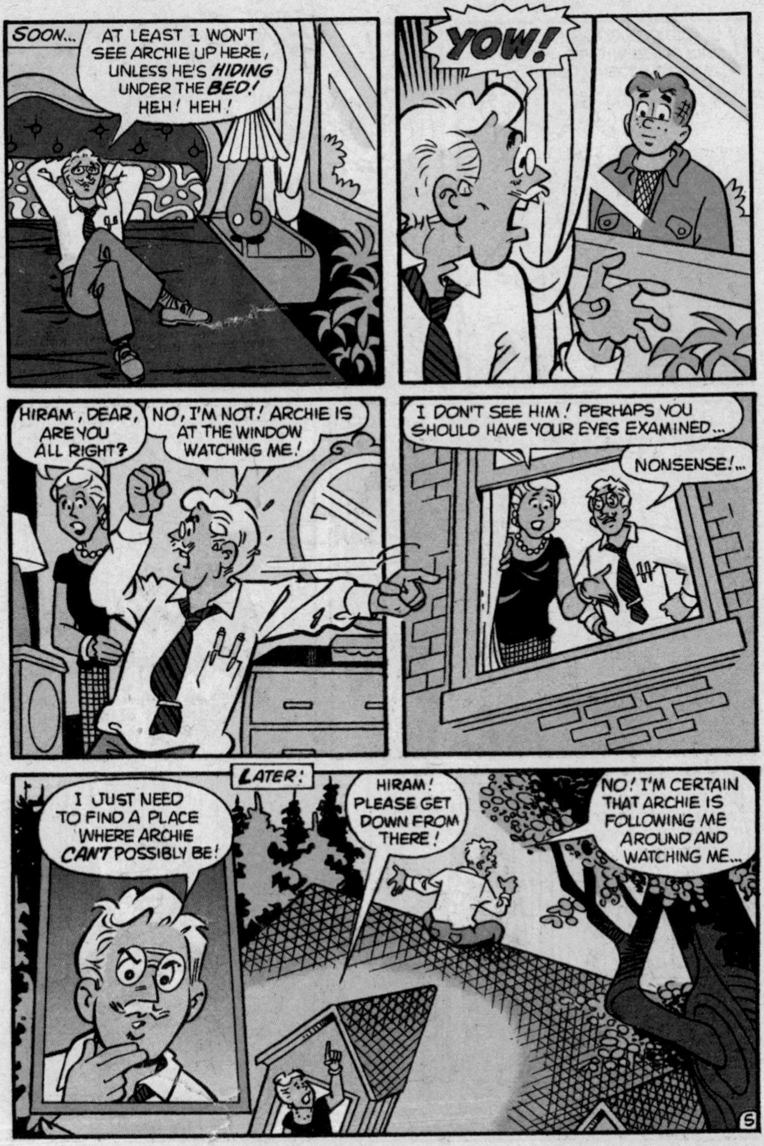
SOON...
AT LEAST I WON'T SEE ARCHIE UP HERE, UNLESS HE'S HIDING UNDER THE BED! HEH! HEH!
YOW!
HIRAM, DEAR, ARE YOU ALL RIGHT?
NO, I'M NOT! ARCHIE IS AT THE WINDOW WATCHING ME!
I DON'T SEE HIM! PERHAPS YOU SHOULD HAVE YOUR EYES EXAMINED...
NONSENSE!...
LATER:
I JUST NEED TO FIND A PLACE WHERE ARCHIE CAN'T POSSIBLY BE!
HIRAM! PLEASE GET DOWN FROM THERE!
NO! I'M CERTAIN THAT ARCHIE IS FOLLOWING ME AROUND AND WATCHING ME...
5

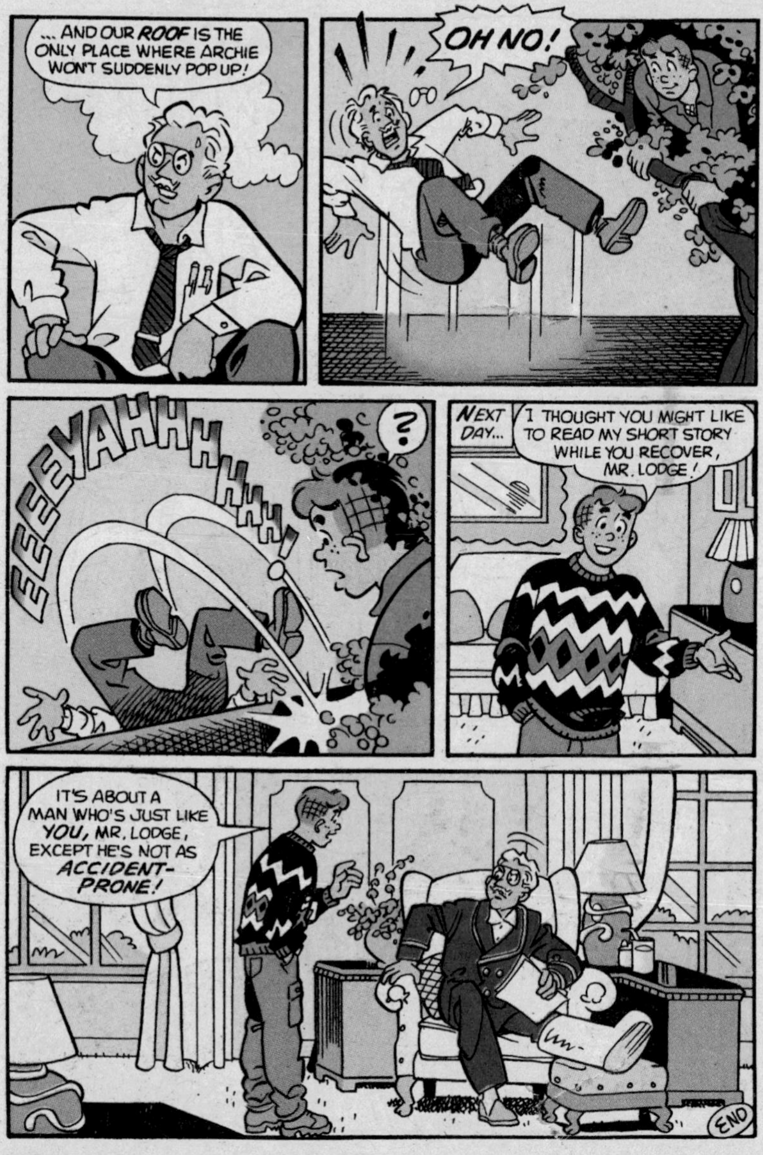
... AND OUR ROOF IS THE ONLY PLACE WHERE ARCHIE WON'T SUDDENLY POP UP!
OH NO!
EEEEYAHHHHHHH!
?
NEXT DAY...
I THOUGHT YOU MIGHT LIKE TO READ MY SHORT STORY WHILE YOU RECOVER, MR. LODGE!
IT'S ABOUT A MAN WHO'S JUST LIKE YOU, MR. LODGE, EXCEPT HE'S NOT AS ACCIDENT-PRONE!
END

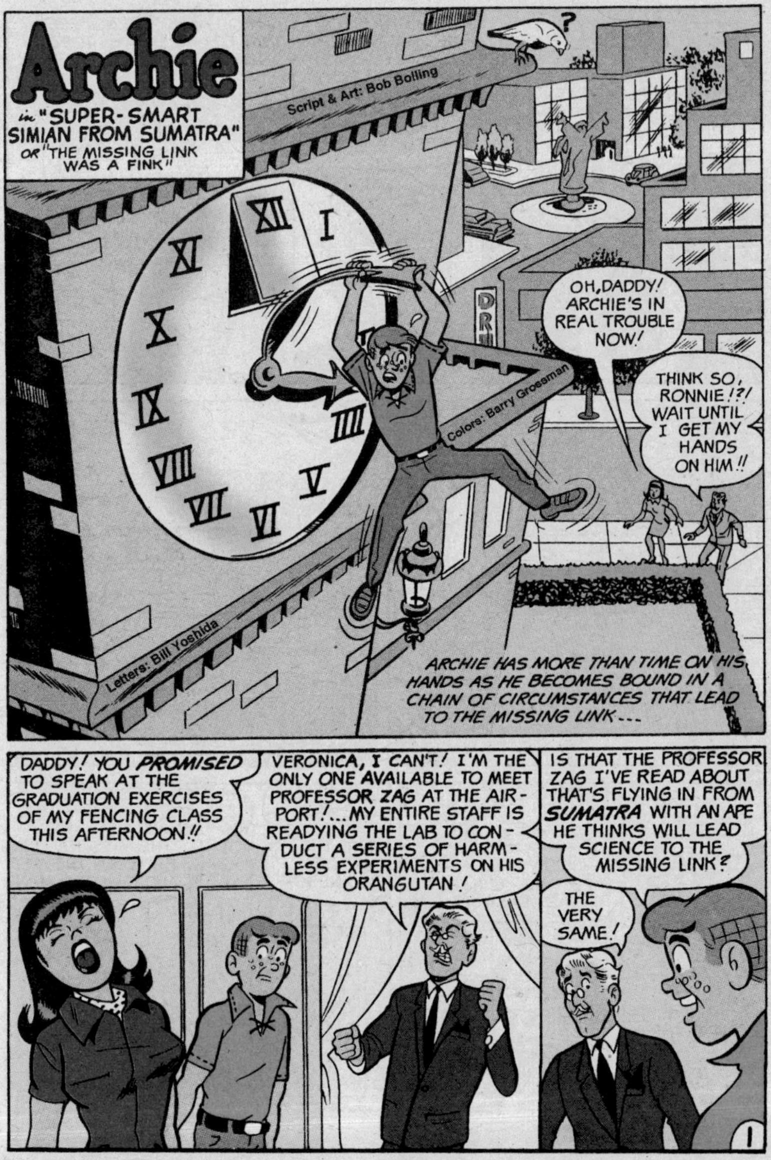
Archie
in "SUPER-SMART SIMIAN FROM SUMATRA"
or "THE MISSING LINK WAS A FINK"
Script & Art: Bob Bolling
DRU
OH, DADDY! ARCHIE'S IN REAL TROUBLE NOW!
THINK SO, RONNIE!?! WAIT UNTIL I GET MY HANDS ON HIM!!
Colors: Barry Grossman
Letters: Bill Yoshida
ARCHIE HAS MORE THAN TIME ON HIS HANDS AS HE BECOMES BOUND IN A CHAIN OF CIRCUMSTANCES THAT LEAD TO THE MISSING LINK...
DADDY! YOU PROMISED TO SPEAK AT THE GRADUATION EXERCISES OF MY FENCING CLASS THIS AFTERNOON!!
VERONICA, I CAN'T! I'M THE ONLY ONE AVAILABLE TO MEET PROFESSOR ZAG AT THE AIR-PORT!... MY ENTIRE STAFF IS READYING THE LAB TO CON-DUCT A SERIES OF HARM-LESS EXPERIMENTS ON HIS ORANGUTAN!
IS THAT THE PROFESSOR ZAG I'VE READ ABOUT THAT'S FLYING IN FROM SUMATRA WITH AN APE HE THINKS WILL LEAD SCIENCE TO THE MISSING LINK?
THE VERY SAME!
1

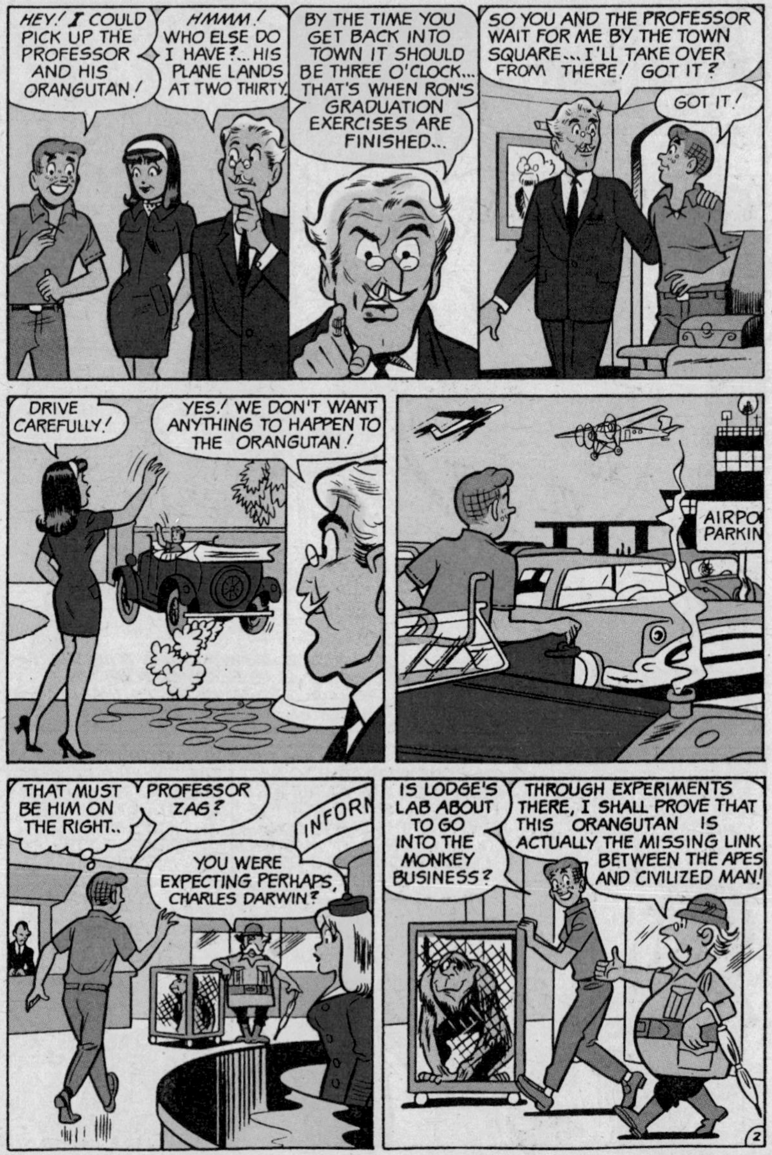

HEY! I COULD PICK UP THE PROFESSOR AND HIS ORANGUTAN!
HMMM! WHO ELSE DO I HAVE?... HIS PLANE LANDS AT TWO THIRTY.
BY THE TIME YOU GET BACK INTO TOWN IT SHOULD BE THREE O'CLOCK... THAT'S WHEN RON'S GRADUATION EXERCISES ARE FINISHED...
SO YOU AND THE PROFESSOR WAIT FOR ME BY THE TOWN SQUARE... I'LL TAKE OVER FROM THERE! GOT IT?
GOT IT!
DRIVE CAREFULLY!
YES! WE DON'T WANT ANYTHING TO HAPPEN TO THE ORANGUTAN!
AIRPO
PARKIN
THAT MUST BE HIM ON THE RIGHT..
PROFESSOR ZAG?
INFORM
YOU WERE EXPECTING PERHAPS, CHARLES DARWIN?
IS LODGE'S LAB ABOUT TO GO INTO THE MONKEY BUSINESS?
THROUGH EXPERIMENTS THERE, I SHALL PROVE THAT THIS ORANGUTAN IS ACTUALLY THE MISSING LINK BETWEEN THE APES AND CIVILIZED MAN!
2

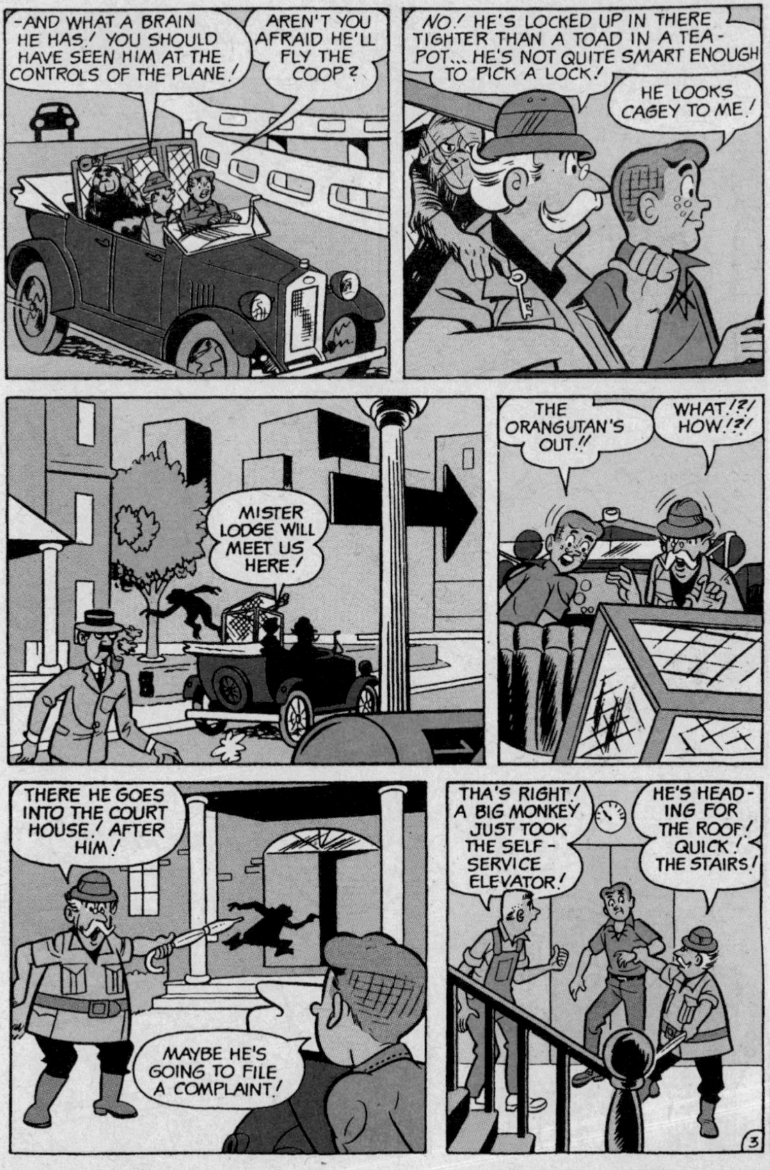
-AND WHAT A BRAIN HE HAS! YOU SHOULD HAVE SEEN HIM AT THE CONTROLS OF THE PLANE!
AREN'T YOU AFRAID HE'LL FLY THE COOP?
NO! HE'S LOCKED UP IN THERE TIGHTER THAN A TOAD IN A TEA-POT... HE'S NOT QUITE SMART ENOUGH TO PICK A LOCK!
HE LOOKS CAGEY TO ME!
MISTER LODGE WILL MEET US HERE!
THE ORANGUTAN'S OUT!!
WHAT!?! HOW!?!
THERE HE GOES INTO THE COURT HOUSE! AFTER HIM!
MAYBE HE'S GOING TO FILE A COMPLAINT!
THA'S RIGHT! A BIG MONKEY JUST TOOK THE SELF-SERVICE ELEVATOR!
HE'S HEAD-ING FOR THE ROOF! QUICK! THE STAIRS!
3

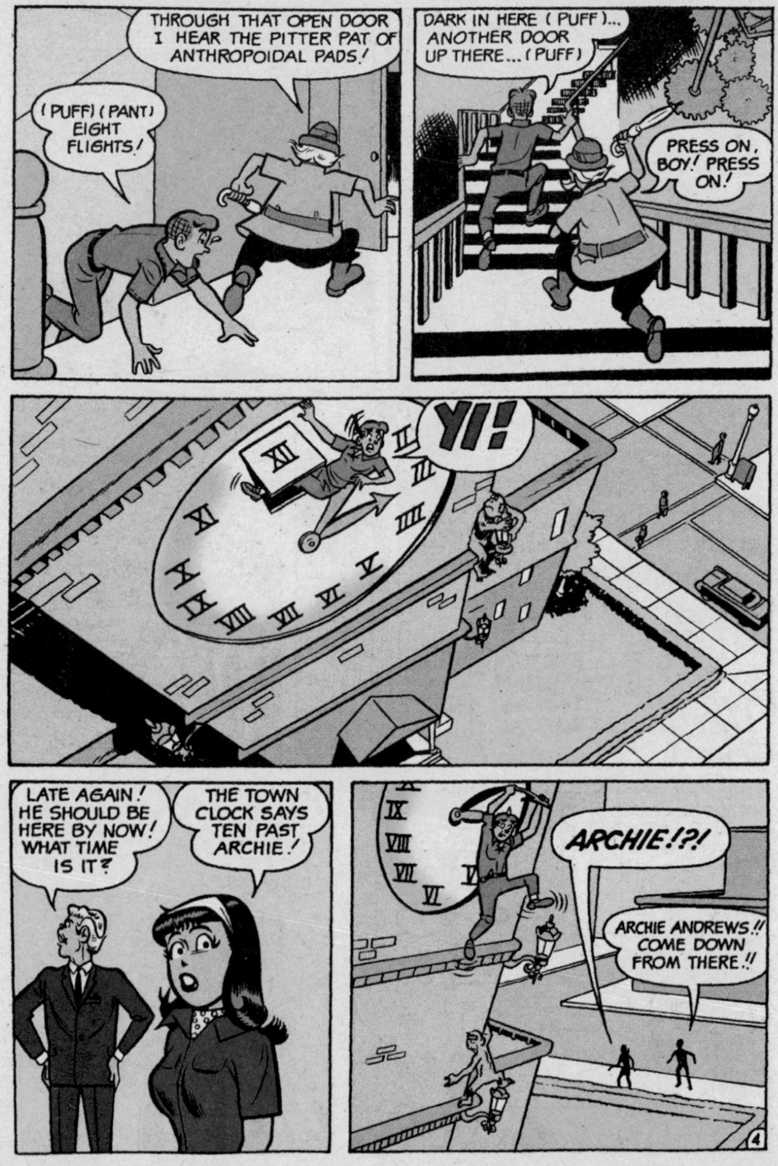
THROUGH THAT OPEN DOOR I HEAR THE PITTER PAT OF ANTHROPOIDAL PADS!
(PUFF) (PANT) EIGHT FLIGHTS!
DARK IN HERE (PUFF)... ANOTHER DOOR UP THERE... (PUFF)
PRESS ON, BOY! PRESS ON!
YI!
LATE AGAIN! HE SHOULD BE HERE BY NOW! WHAT TIME IS IT?
THE TOWN CLOCK SAYS TEN PAST ARCHIE!
ARCHIE!?!
ARCHIE ANDREWS!! COME DOWN FROM THERE!!
4

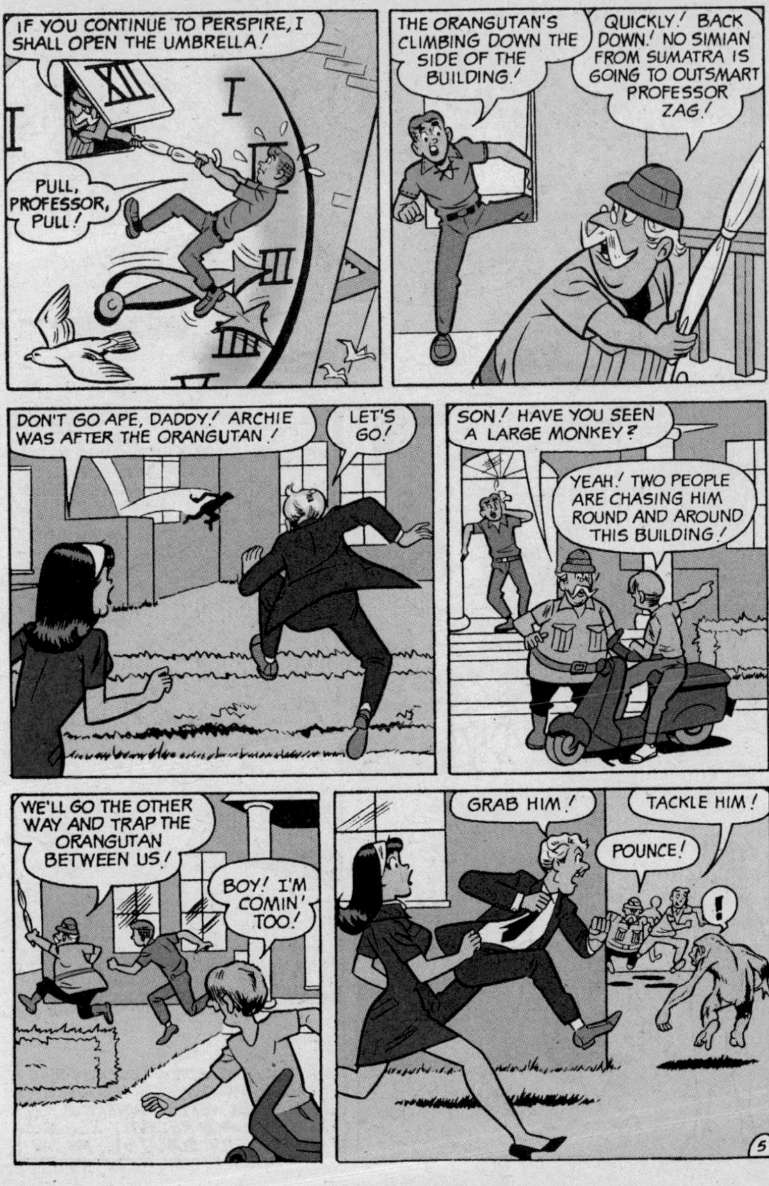
IF YOU CONTINUE TO PERSPIRE, I SHALL OPEN THE UMBRELLA!
PULL, PROFESSOR, PULL!
THE ORANGUTAN'S CLIMBING DOWN THE SIDE OF THE BUILDING!
QUICKLY! BACK DOWN! NO SIMIAN FROM SUMATRA IS GOING TO OUTSMART PROFESSOR ZAG!
DON'T GO APE, DADDY! ARCHIE WAS AFTER THE ORANGUTAN!
LET'S GO!
SON! HAVE YOU SEEN A LARGE MONKEY?
YEAH! TWO PEOPLE ARE CHASING HIM ROUND AND AROUND THIS BUILDING!
WE'LL GO THE OTHER WAY AND TRAP THE ORANGUTAN BETWEEN US!
BOY! I'M COMIN' TOO!
GRAB HIM!
TACKLE HIM!
POUNCE!
!
5

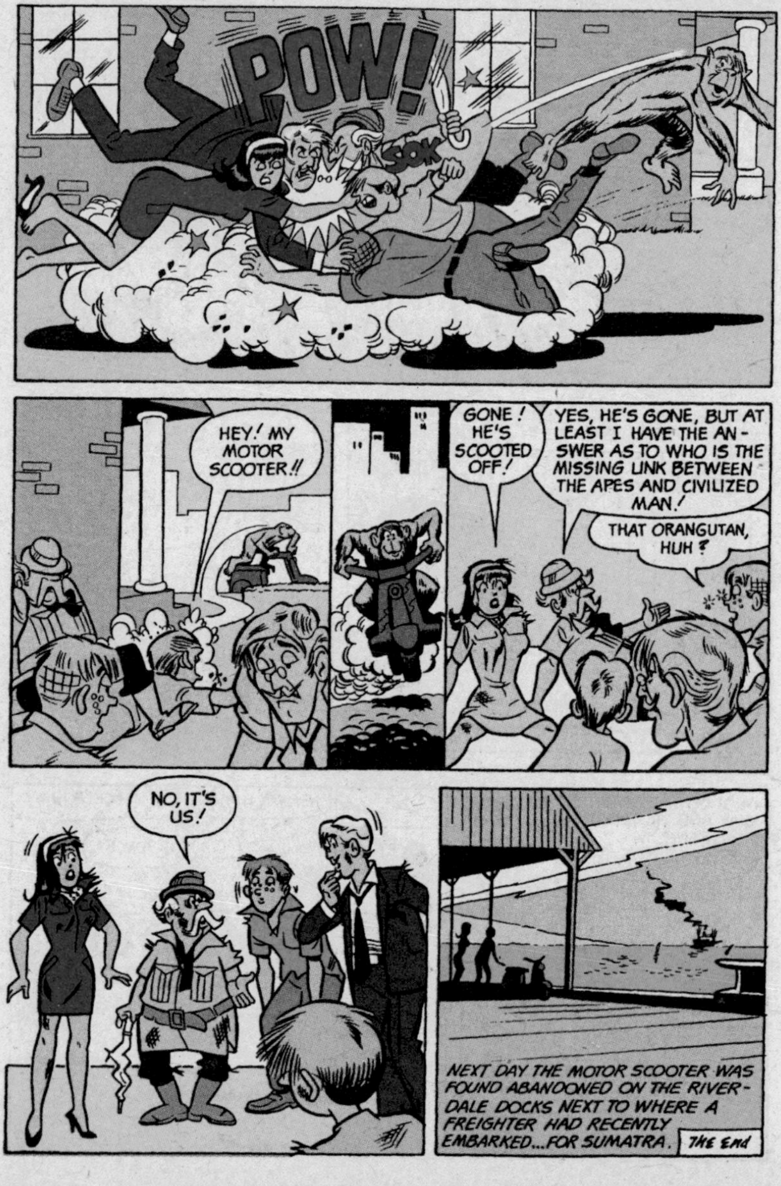
POW!
SOK
HEY! MY MOTOR SCOOTER!!
GONE! HE'S SCOOTED OFF!
YES, HE'S GONE, BUT AT LEAST I HAVE THE AN-SWER AS TO WHO IS THE MISSING LINK BETWEEN THE APES AND CIVILIZED MAN!
THAT ORANGUTAN, HUH?
NO, IT'S US!
NEXT DAY THE MOTOR SCOOTER WAS FOUND ABANDONED ON THE RIVER-DALE DOCKS NEXT TO WHERE A FREIGHTER HAD RECENTLY EMBARKED...FOR SUMATRA.
THE END

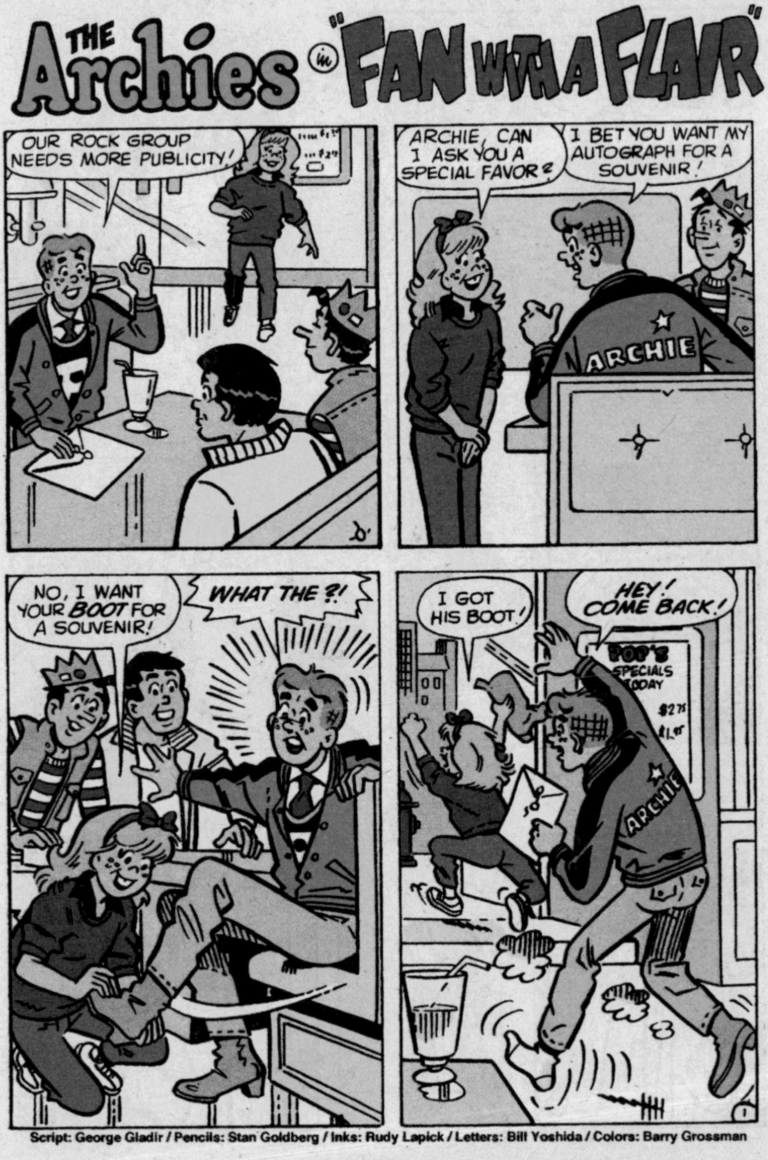
THE Archies in "FAN WITH A FLAIR"
OUR ROCK GROUP NEEDS MORE PUBLICITY!
ARCHIE, CAN I ASK YOU A SPECIAL FAVOR?
I BET YOU WANT MY AUTOGRAPH FOR A SOUVENIR!
ARCHIE
NO, I WANT YOUR BOOT FOR A SOUVENIR!
WHAT THE ?!
I GOT HIS BOOT!
HEY! COME BACK!
POP'S SPECIALS TODAY
ARCHIE
1

Script: George Gladir / Pencils: Stan Goldberg / Inks: Rudy Lapick / Letters: Bill Yoshida / Colors: Barry Grossman

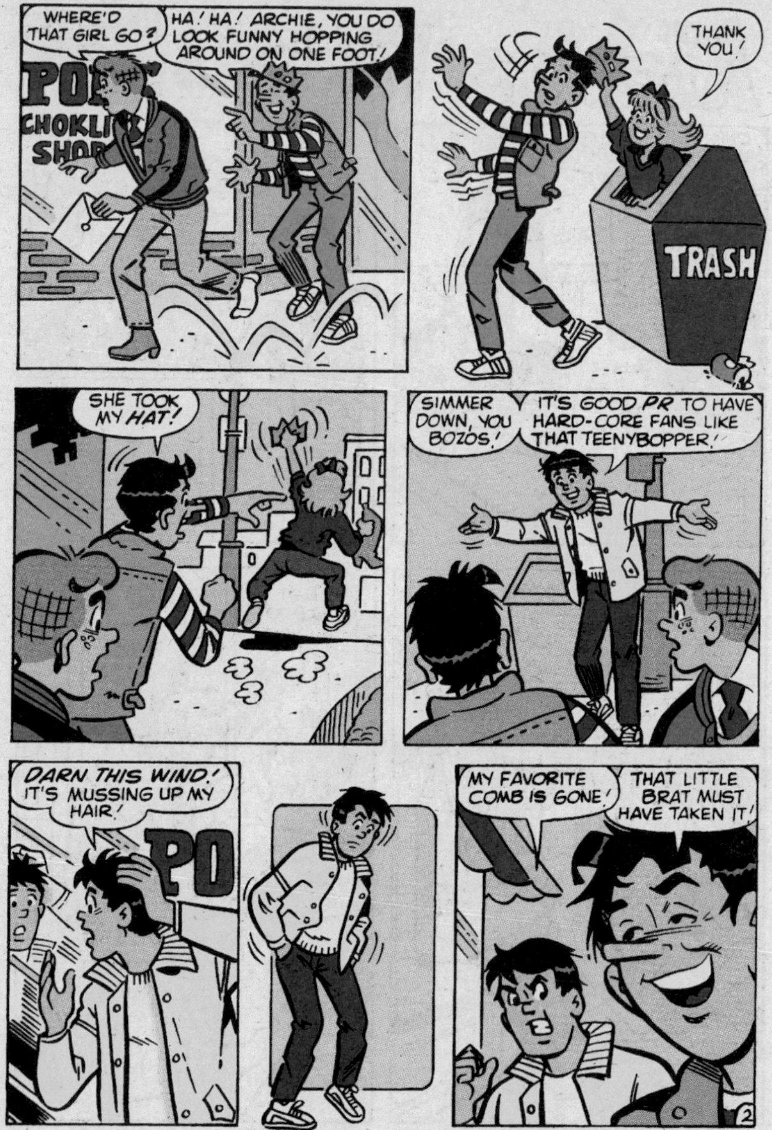
WHERE'D THAT GIRL GO?
HA! HA! ARCHIE, YOU DO LOOK FUNNY HOPPING AROUND ON ONE FOOT!
POP CHOKLIT SHOP
THANK YOU!
TRASH
SHE TOOK MY *HAT*!
SIMMER DOWN, YOU BOZOS!
IT'S GOOD *PR* TO HAVE HARD-CORE FANS LIKE THAT TEENYBOPPER!
DARN THIS WIND! IT'S MUSSING UP MY HAIR!
MY FAVORITE COMB IS GONE!
THAT LITTLE BRAT MUST HAVE TAKEN IT!
2

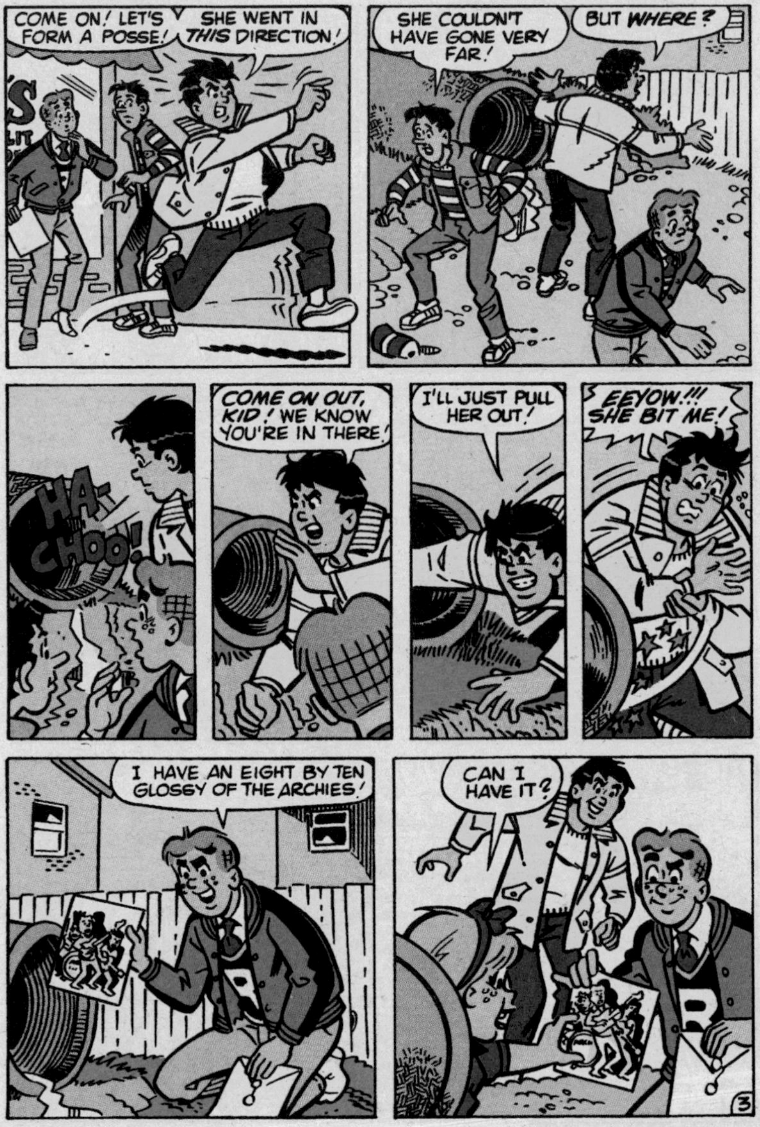
COME ON! LET'S FORM A POSSE!
SHE WENT IN *THIS* DIRECTION!
SHE COULDN'T HAVE GONE VERY FAR!
BUT *WHERE* ?
HA-CHOO!
COME ON OUT, KID! WE KNOW YOU'RE IN THERE!
I'LL JUST PULL HER OUT!
EEYOW!!! SHE BIT ME!
I HAVE AN EIGHT BY TEN GLOSSY OF THE ARCHIES!
CAN I HAVE IT?

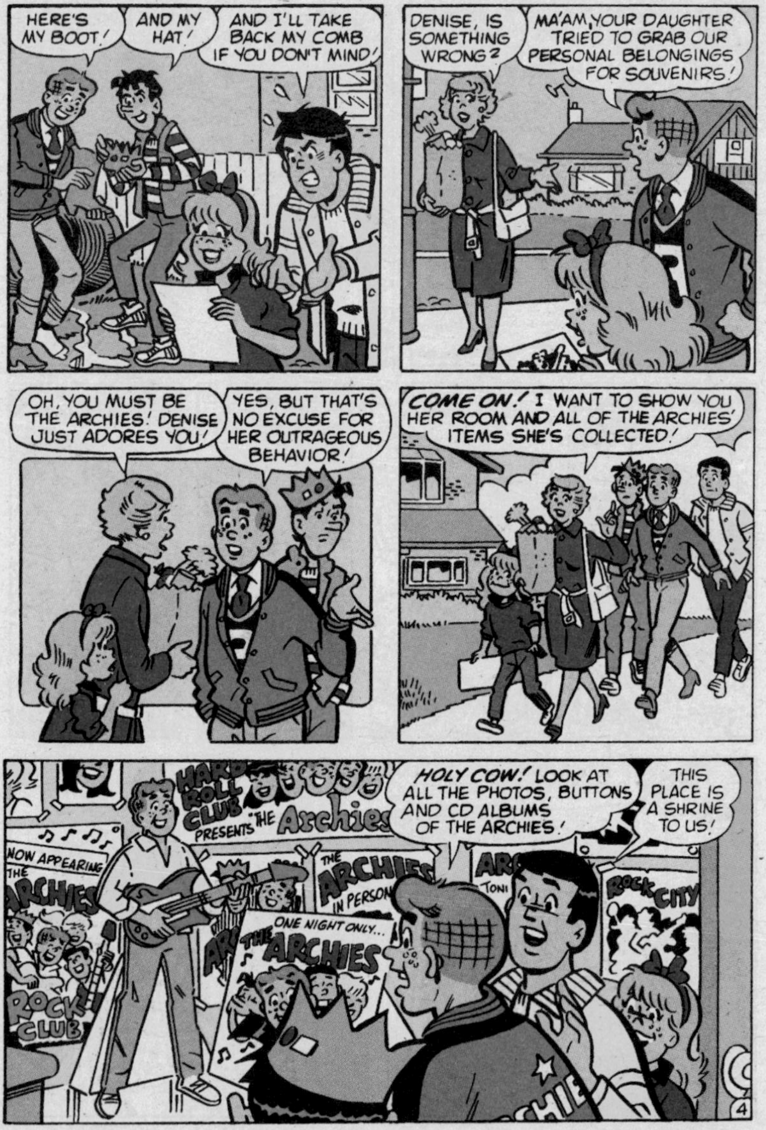
HERE'S MY BOOT!
AND MY HAT!
AND I'LL TAKE BACK MY COMB IF YOU DON'T MIND!
DENISE, IS SOMETHING WRONG?
MA'AM, YOUR DAUGHTER TRIED TO GRAB OUR PERSONAL BELONGINGS FOR SOUVENIRS!
OH, YOU MUST BE THE ARCHIES! DENISE JUST ADORES YOU!
YES, BUT THAT'S NO EXCUSE FOR HER OUTRAGEOUS BEHAVIOR!
COME ON! I WANT TO SHOW YOU HER ROOM AND ALL OF THE ARCHIES' ITEMS SHE'S COLLECTED!
HARD ROCK CLUB PRESENTS THE Archies
NOW APPEARING THE ARCHIES
THE ARCHIES IN PERSON
ONE NIGHT ONLY... THE ARCHIES
ROCK CITY
ROCK CLUB
HOLY COW! LOOK AT ALL THE PHOTOS, BUTTONS AND CD ALBUMS OF THE ARCHIES!
THIS PLACE IS A SHRINE TO US!
4

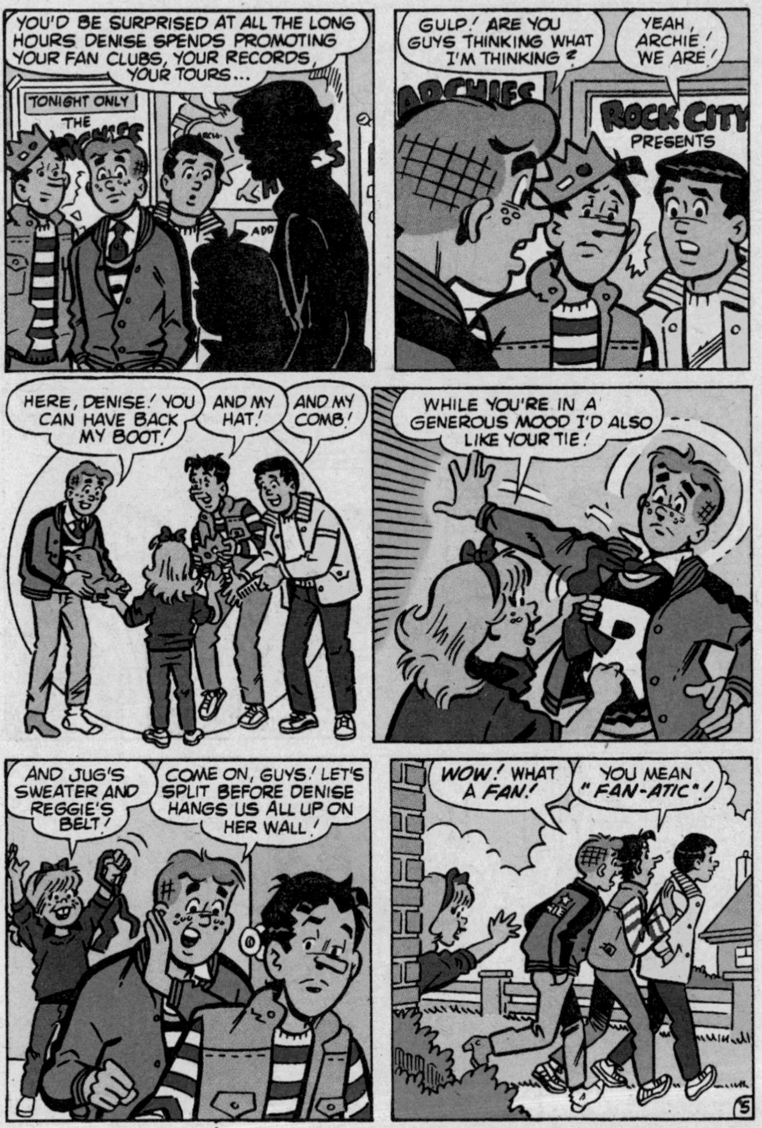
YOU'D BE SURPRISED AT ALL THE LONG HOURS DENISE SPENDS PROMOTING YOUR FAN CLUBS, YOUR RECORDS, YOUR TOURS...
TONIGHT ONLY
THE
GULP! ARE YOU GUYS THINKING WHAT I'M THINKING?
YEAH, ARCHIE! WE ARE!
ROCK CITY
PRESENTS
HERE, DENISE! YOU CAN HAVE BACK MY BOOT!
AND MY HAT!
AND MY COMB!
WHILE YOU'RE IN A GENEROUS MOOD I'D ALSO LIKE YOUR TIE!
AND JUG'S SWEATER AND REGGIE'S BELT!
COME ON, GUYS! LET'S SPLIT BEFORE DENISE HANGS US ALL UP ON HER WALL!
WOW! WHAT A FAN!
YOU MEAN "FAN-ATIC"!
5

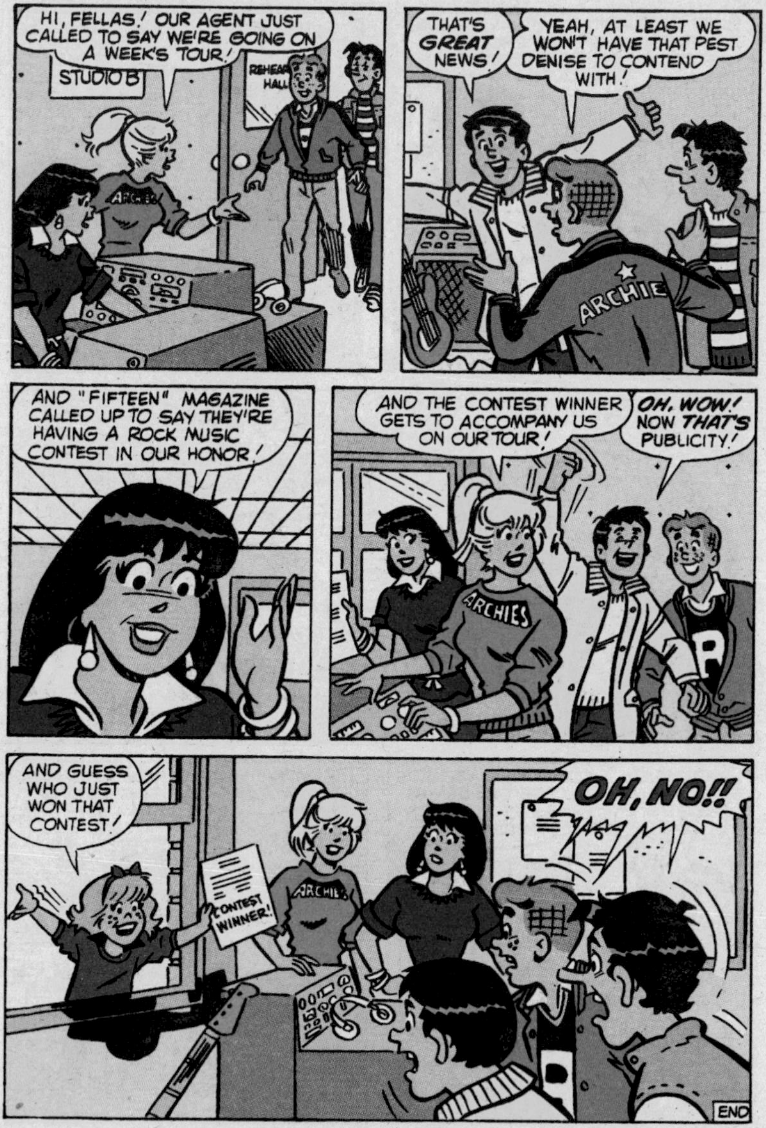
HI, FELLAS! OUR AGENT JUST CALLED TO SAY WE'RE GOING ON A WEEK'S TOUR!
STUDIO B
THAT'S **GREAT** NEWS!
YEAH, AT LEAST WE WON'T HAVE THAT PEST DENISE TO CONTEND WITH!
ARCHIE
AND "FIFTEEN" MAGAZINE CALLED UP TO SAY THEY'RE HAVING A ROCK MUSIC CONTEST IN OUR HONOR!
AND THE CONTEST WINNER GETS TO ACCOMPANY US ON OUR TOUR!
OH, WOW! NOW ***THAT'S*** PUBLICITY!
ARCHIES
AND GUESS WHO JUST WON THAT CONTEST!
CONTEST WINNER!
OH, NO!!
END

Archie FIND THE GIRLS!

YEP! FIND THE GIRLS IN THE NAME SEARCH BELOW! LOOK UP, DOWN, FORWARDS, BACKWARDS, AND DIAGONALLY! ...THEN, CHECK THE NAME LIST BELOW!!

```
G L G R S I I G E I B B E D G
I S I L G R L S S G S L L R I
R B R E N D A R L I R R S A G
            V G S L I D I R
            A I R L N S L V
            L G S I G I R E
            E S L I S A L R
            R L R I U G S O
            I G I G S I R N
            E L R S A L S I
            G I R L N S G C
            I B E T T Y I A
            R L G G S I R I
            G S I R L L S G
            D O N N A R L S
```

GIRLS' NAME LIST!

VALERIE · BETTY · VERONICA
DONNA · DEBBIE · BRENDA
LISA · SUSAN · LINDA

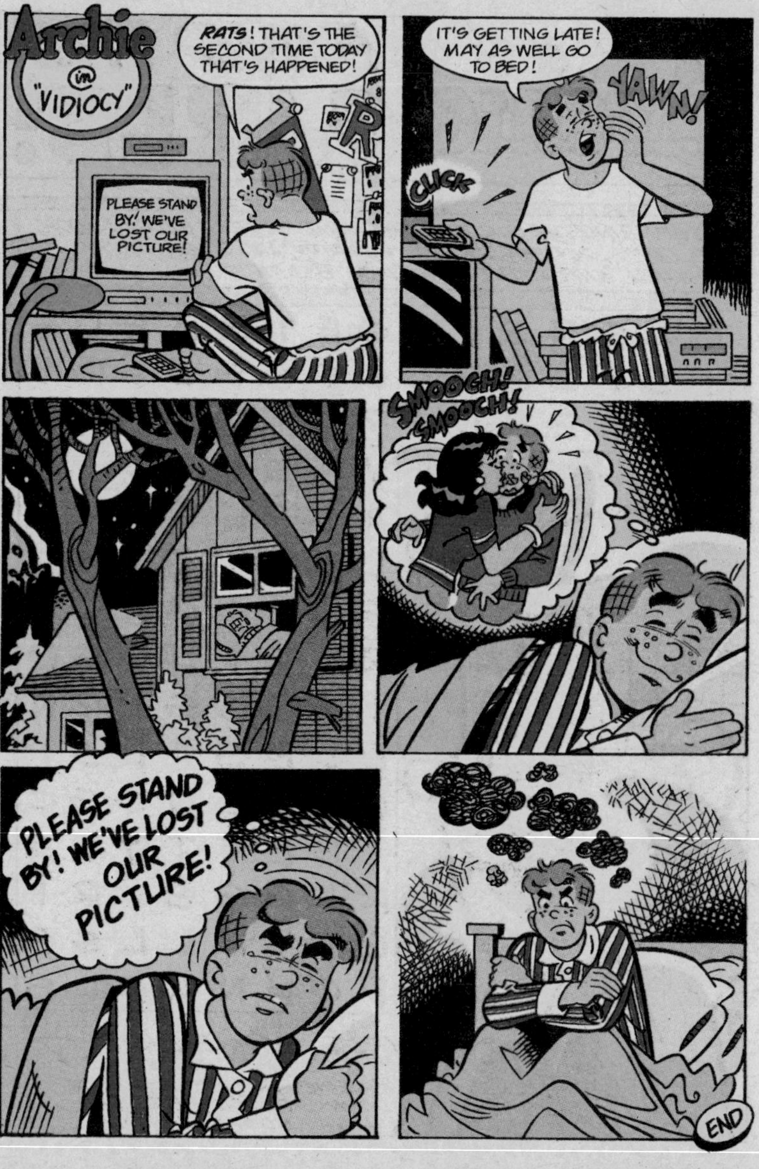

Archie in "VIDIOCY"
RATS! THAT'S THE SECOND TIME TODAY THAT'S HAPPENED!
PLEASE STAND BY! WE'VE LOST OUR PICTURE!
IT'S GETTING LATE! MAY AS WELL GO TO BED!
YAWN!
CLICK
SMOOCH! SMOOCH!
PLEASE STAND BY! WE'VE LOST OUR PICTURE!
END

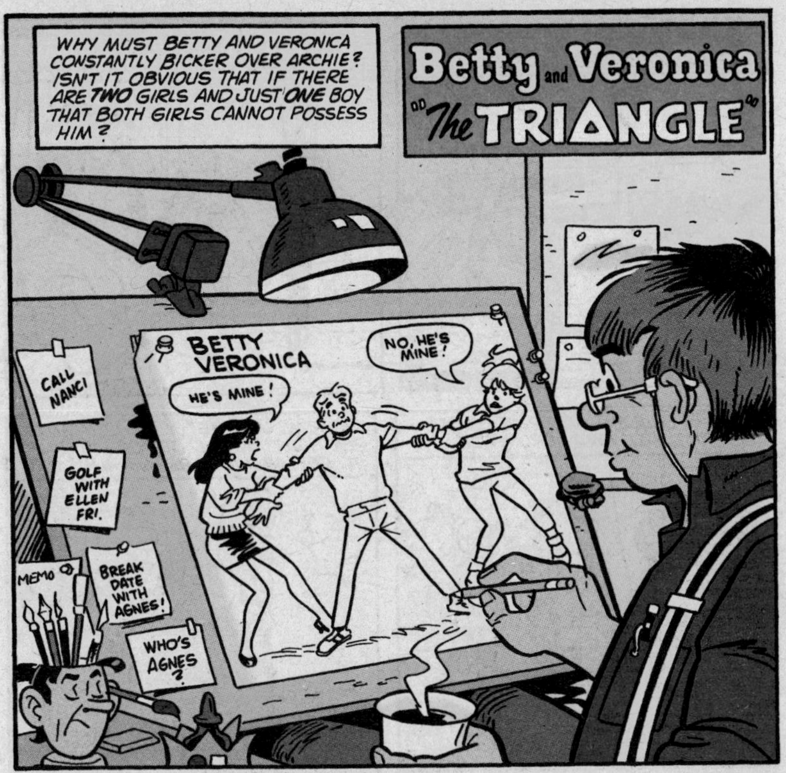
WHY MUST BETTY AND VERONICA CONSTANTLY BICKER OVER ARCHIE? ISN'T IT OBVIOUS THAT IF THERE ARE TWO GIRLS AND JUST ONE BOY THAT BOTH GIRLS CANNOT POSSESS HIM?
Betty and Veronica
"The TRIANGLE"
BETTY
VERONICA
HE'S MINE!
NO, HE'S MINE!
CALL NANCI
GOLF WITH ELLEN FRI.
MEMO
BREAK DATE WITH AGNES!
WHO'S AGNES?

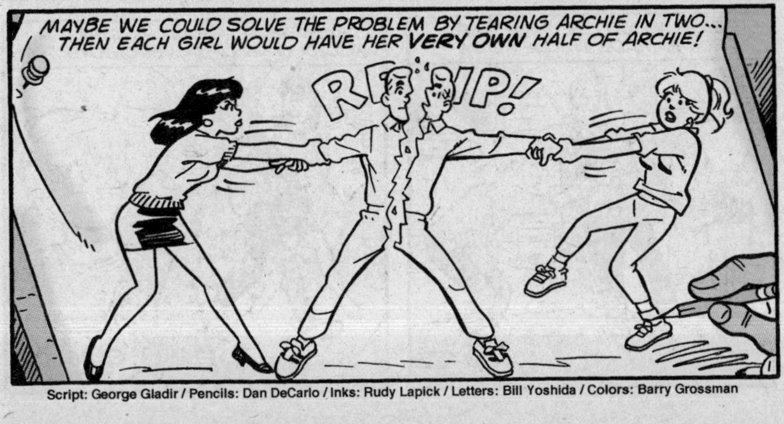
MAYBE WE COULD SOLVE THE PROBLEM BY TEARING ARCHIE IN TWO... THEN EACH GIRL WOULD HAVE HER VERY OWN HALF OF ARCHIE!
RRIP!

Script: George Gladir / Pencils: Dan DeCarlo / Inks: Rudy Lapick / Letters: Bill Yoshida / Colors: Barry Grossman

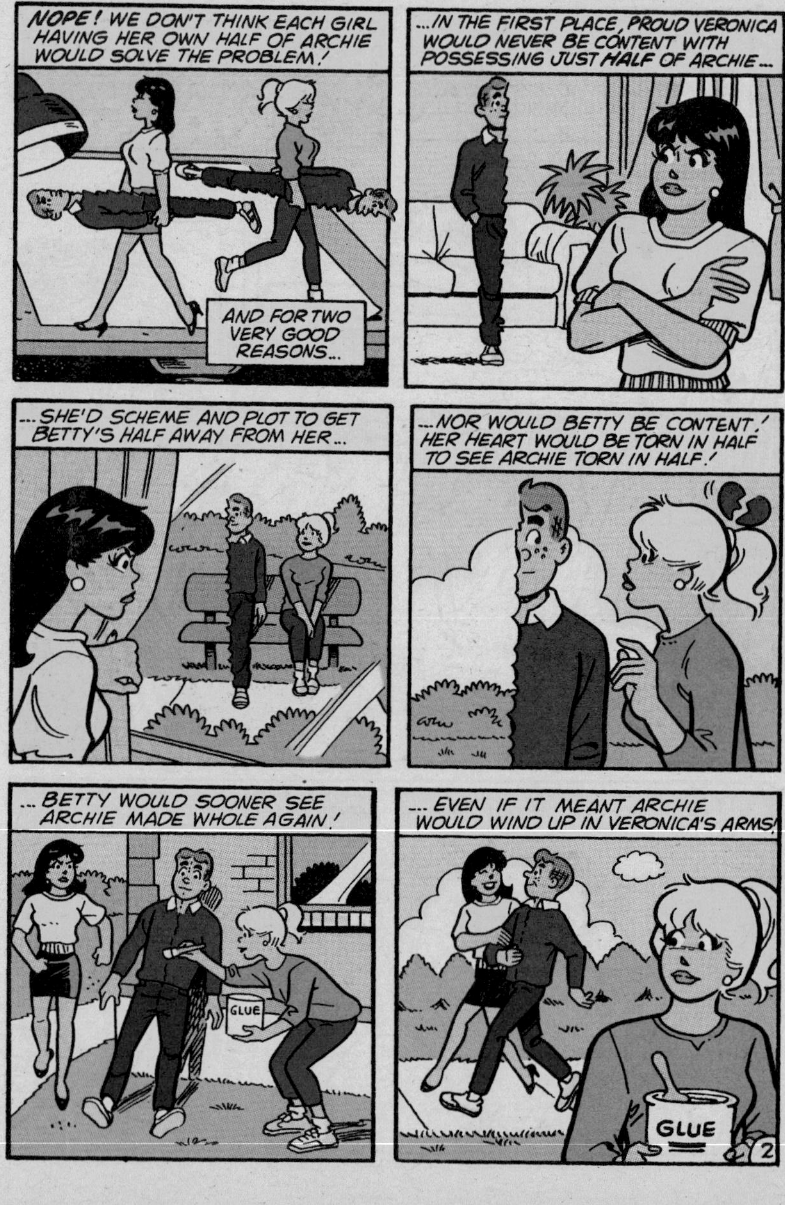
NOPE! WE DON'T THINK EACH GIRL HAVING HER OWN HALF OF ARCHIE WOULD SOLVE THE PROBLEM!
AND FOR TWO VERY GOOD REASONS...
...IN THE FIRST PLACE, PROUD VERONICA WOULD NEVER BE CONTENT WITH POSSESSING JUST HALF OF ARCHIE...
...SHE'D SCHEME AND PLOT TO GET BETTY'S HALF AWAY FROM HER...
...NOR WOULD BETTY BE CONTENT! HER HEART WOULD BE TORN IN HALF TO SEE ARCHIE TORN IN HALF!
... BETTY WOULD SOONER SEE ARCHIE MADE WHOLE AGAIN!
GLUE
... EVEN IF IT MEANT ARCHIE WOULD WIND UP IN VERONICA'S ARMS!
GLUE
2

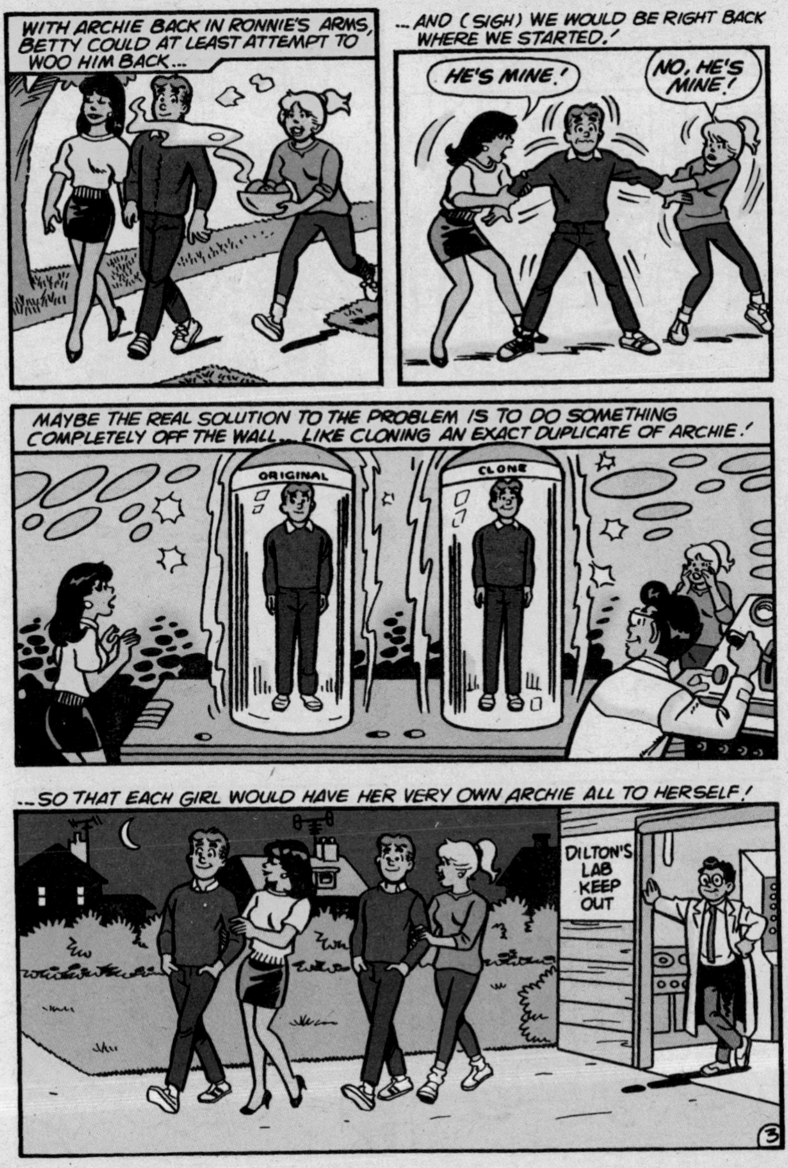
WITH ARCHIE BACK IN RONNIE'S ARMS, BETTY COULD AT LEAST ATTEMPT TO WOO HIM BACK...
...AND (SIGH) WE WOULD BE RIGHT BACK WHERE WE STARTED.'
HE'S MINE.'
NO, HE'S MINE!
MAYBE THE REAL SOLUTION TO THE PROBLEM IS TO DO SOMETHING COMPLETELY OFF THE WALL... LIKE CLONING AN EXACT DUPLICATE OF ARCHIE.'
ORIGINAL
CLONE
...SO THAT EACH GIRL WOULD HAVE HER VERY OWN ARCHIE ALL TO HERSELF!
DILTON'S LAB KEEP OUT
3

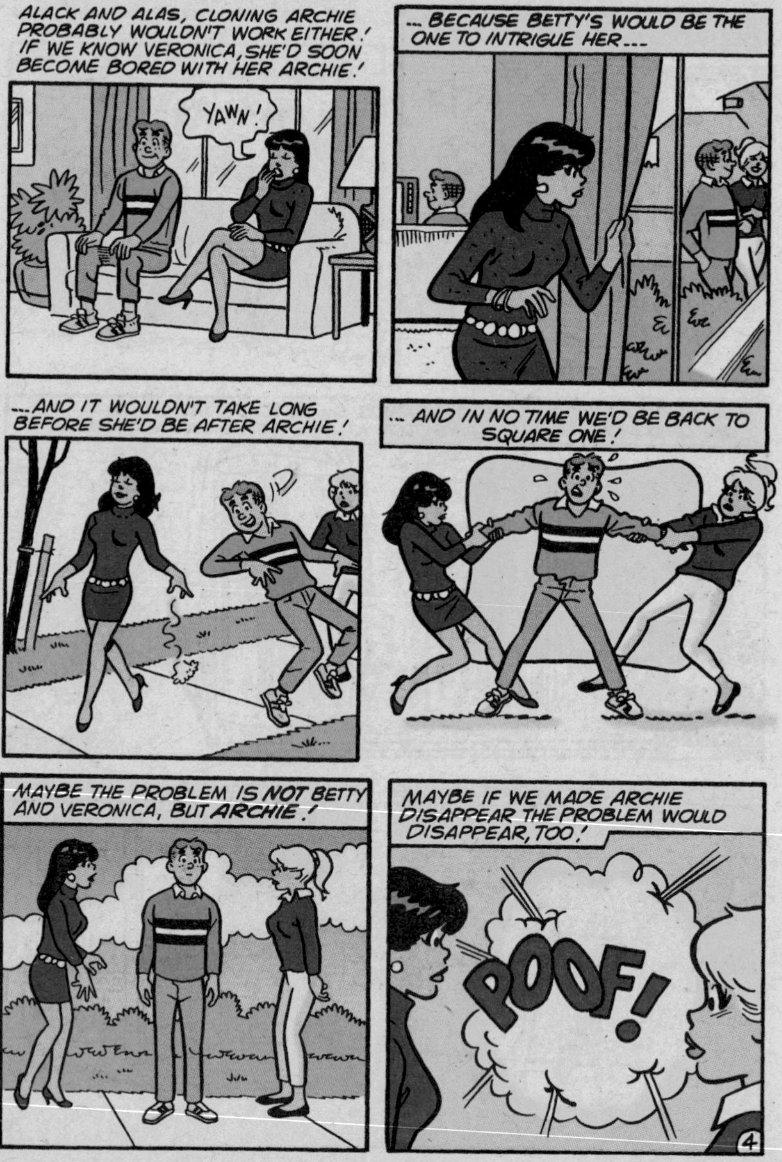
ALACK AND ALAS, CLONING ARCHIE PROBABLY WOULDN'T WORK EITHER! IF WE KNOW VERONICA, SHE'D SOON BECOME BORED WITH HER ARCHIE!
YAWN!
... BECAUSE BETTY'S WOULD BE THE ONE TO INTRIGUE HER...
...AND IT WOULDN'T TAKE LONG BEFORE SHE'D BE AFTER ARCHIE!
... AND IN NO TIME WE'D BE BACK TO SQUARE ONE!
MAYBE THE PROBLEM IS NOT BETTY AND VERONICA, BUT ARCHIE!
MAYBE IF WE MADE ARCHIE DISAPPEAR THE PROBLEM WOULD DISAPPEAR, TOO!
POOF!
4

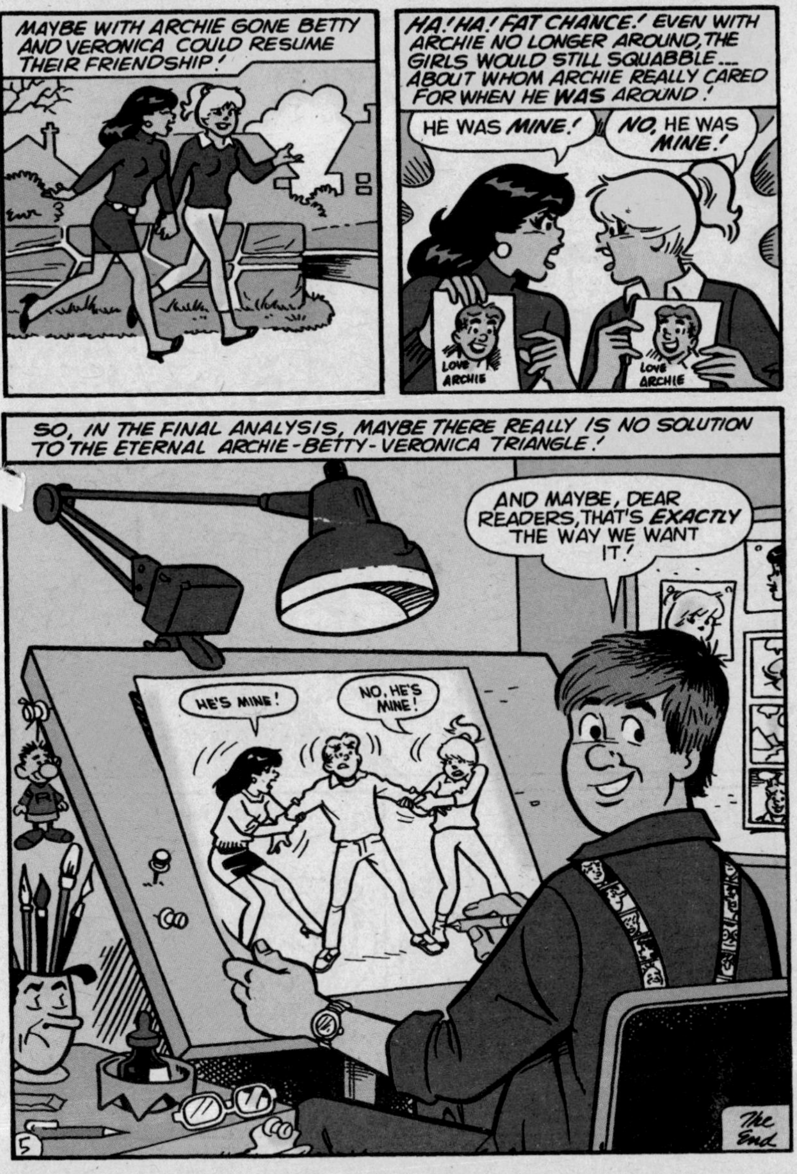
MAYBE WITH ARCHIE GONE BETTY AND VERONICA COULD RESUME THEIR FRIENDSHIP!
HA! HA! FAT CHANCE! EVEN WITH ARCHIE NO LONGER AROUND, THE GIRLS WOULD STILL SQUABBLE... ABOUT WHOM ARCHIE REALLY CARED FOR WHEN HE WAS AROUND!
HE WAS MINE!
NO, HE WAS MINE!
LOVE ARCHIE
LOVE ARCHIE
SO, IN THE FINAL ANALYSIS, MAYBE THERE REALLY IS NO SOLUTION TO THE ETERNAL ARCHIE-BETTY-VERONICA TRIANGLE!
AND MAYBE, DEAR READERS, THAT'S EXACTLY THE WAY WE WANT IT!
HE'S MINE!
NO, HE'S MINE!
The End
5

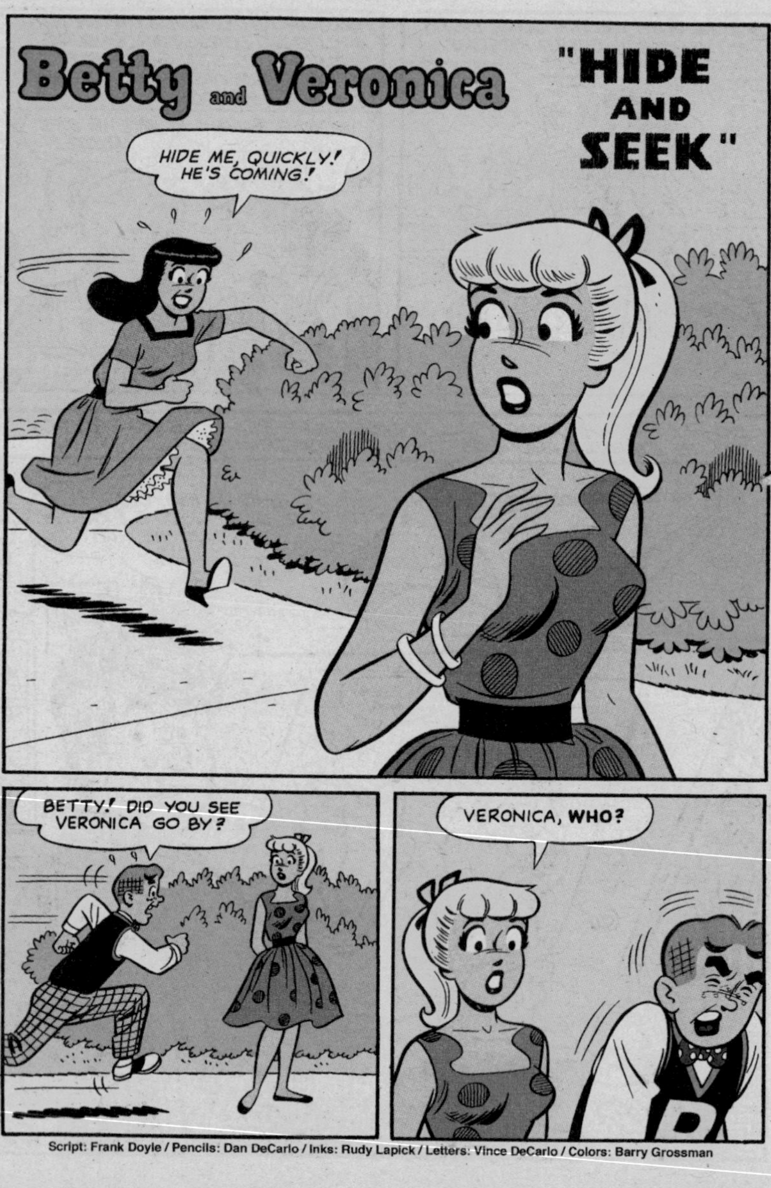
Betty and Veronica
"HIDE AND SEEK"
HIDE ME, QUICKLY! HE'S COMING!
BETTY! DID YOU SEE VERONICA GO BY?
VERONICA, **WHO?**

Script: Frank Doyle / Pencils: Dan DeCarlo / Inks: Rudy Lapick / Letters: Vince DeCarlo / Colors: Barry Grossman

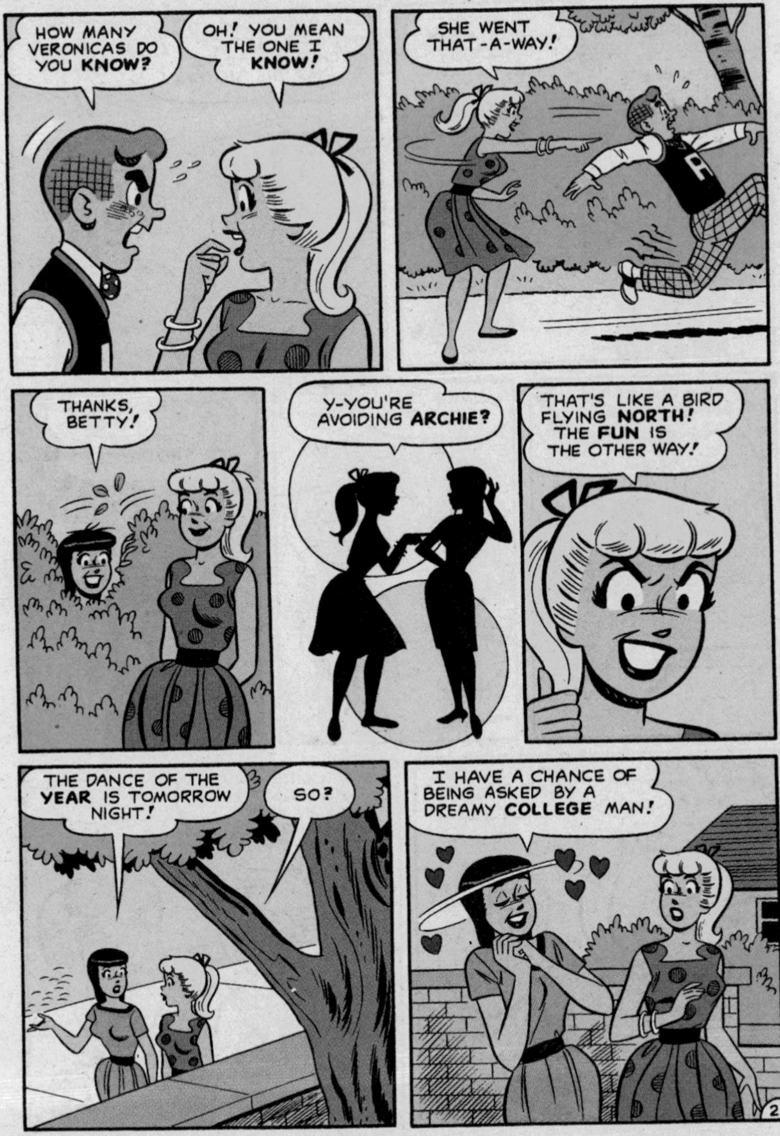
HOW MANY VERONICAS DO YOU **KNOW?**
OH! YOU MEAN THE ONE I **KNOW!**
SHE WENT THAT-A-WAY!
THANKS, BETTY!
Y-YOU'RE AVOIDING **ARCHIE?**
THAT'S LIKE A BIRD FLYING **NORTH!** THE **FUN** IS THE OTHER WAY!
THE DANCE OF THE **YEAR** IS TOMORROW NIGHT!
SO?
I HAVE A CHANCE OF BEING ASKED BY A DREAMY **COLLEGE** MAN!
2

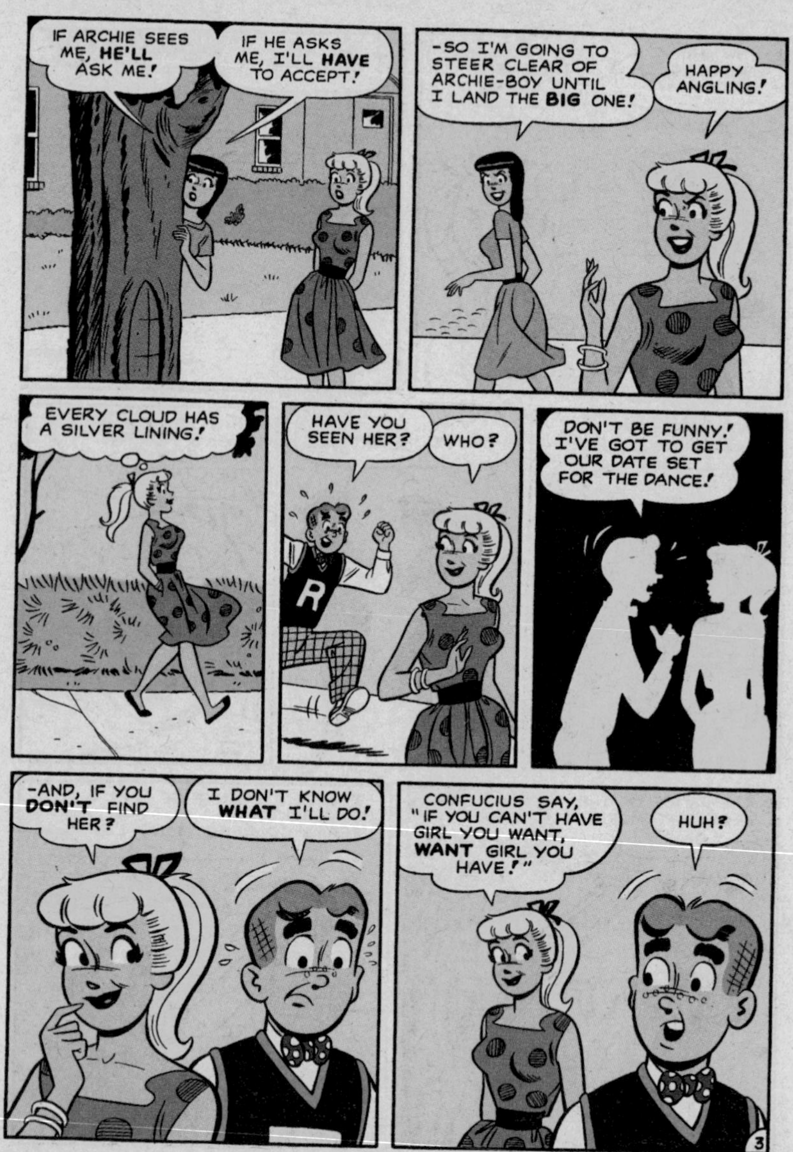
IF ARCHIE SEES ME, HE'LL ASK ME!
IF HE ASKS ME, I'LL HAVE TO ACCEPT!
-SO I'M GOING TO STEER CLEAR OF ARCHIE-BOY UNTIL I LAND THE BIG ONE!
HAPPY ANGLING!
EVERY CLOUD HAS A SILVER LINING!
HAVE YOU SEEN HER?
WHO?
DON'T BE FUNNY! I'VE GOT TO GET OUR DATE SET FOR THE DANCE!
-AND, IF YOU DON'T FIND HER?
I DON'T KNOW WHAT I'LL DO!
CONFUCIUS SAY, "IF YOU CAN'T HAVE GIRL YOU WANT, WANT GIRL YOU HAVE!"
HUH?
3

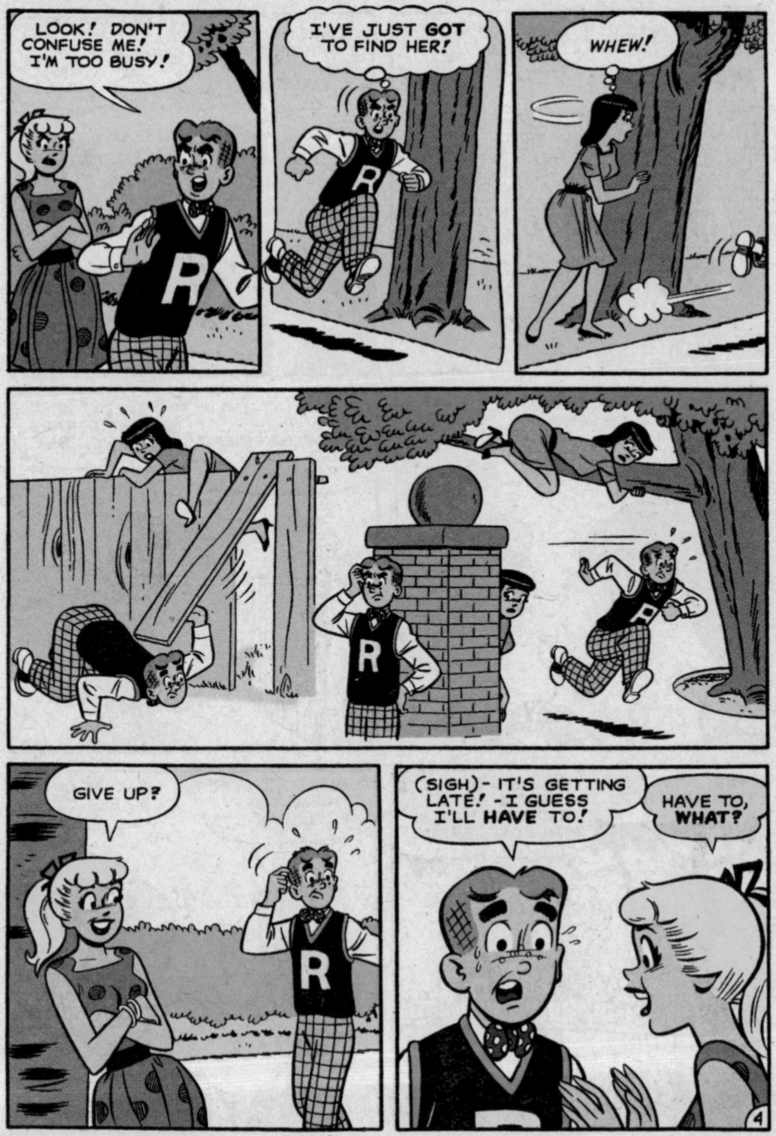
LOOK! DON'T CONFUSE ME! I'M TOO BUSY!
I'VE JUST GOT TO FIND HER!
WHEW!
GIVE UP?
(SIGH)- IT'S GETTING LATE! -I GUESS I'LL HAVE TO!
HAVE TO, WHAT?
4

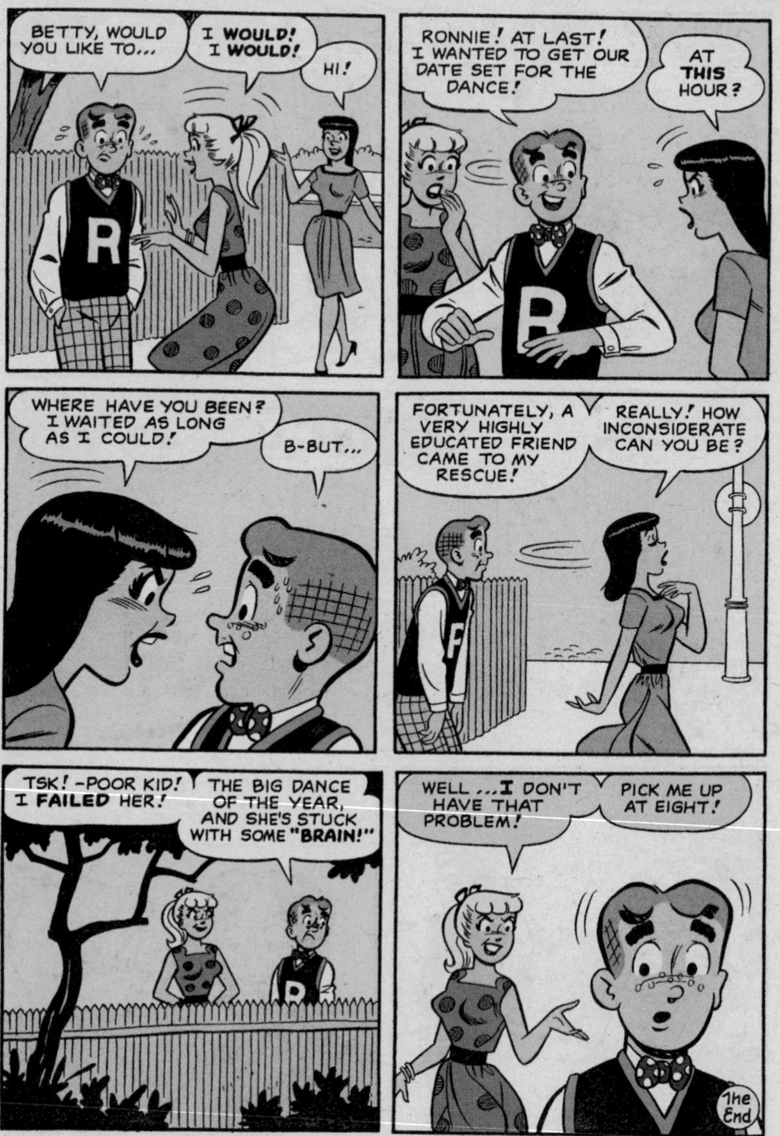
BETTY, WOULD YOU LIKE TO...
I WOULD! I WOULD!
HI!
RONNIE! AT LAST! I WANTED TO GET OUR DATE SET FOR THE DANCE!
AT THIS HOUR?
WHERE HAVE YOU BEEN? I WAITED AS LONG AS I COULD!
B-BUT...
FORTUNATELY, A VERY HIGHLY EDUCATED FRIEND CAME TO MY RESCUE!
REALLY! HOW INCONSIDERATE CAN YOU BE?
TSK! -POOR KID! I FAILED HER!
THE BIG DANCE OF THE YEAR, AND SHE'S STUCK WITH SOME "BRAIN!"
WELL ...I DON'T HAVE THAT PROBLEM!
PICK ME UP AT EIGHT!
The End

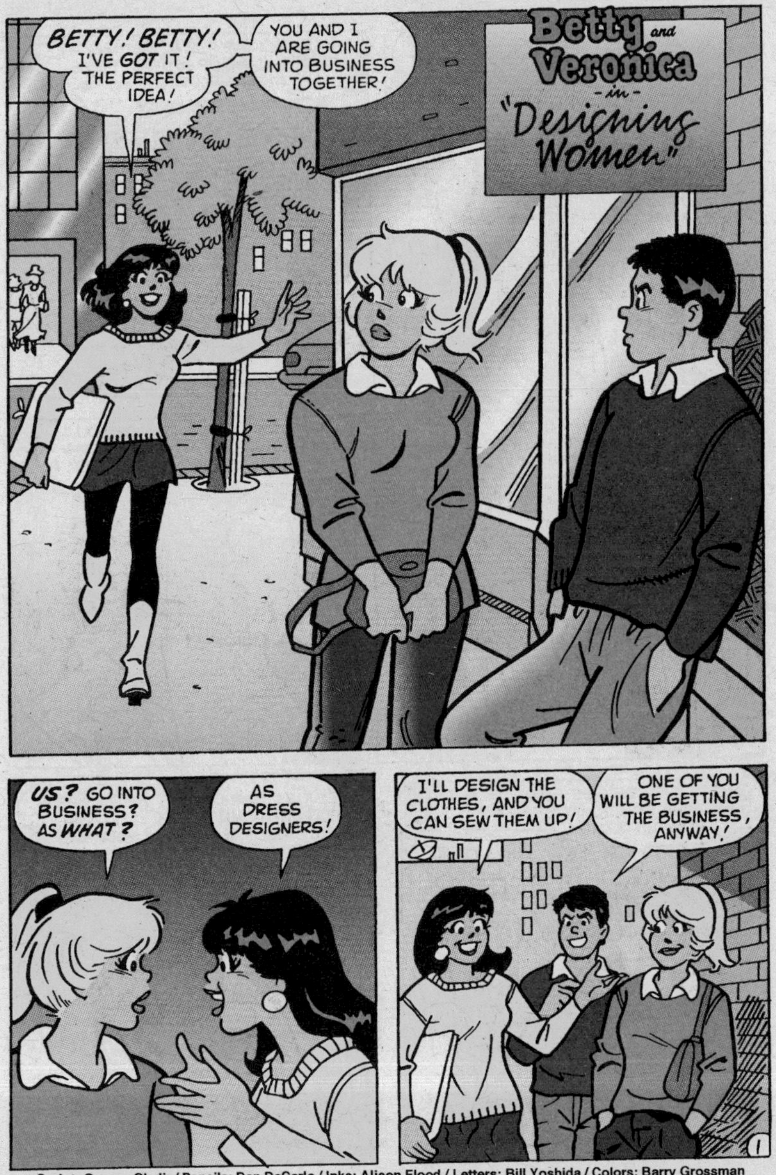
BETTY! BETTY! I'VE GOT IT! THE PERFECT IDEA!
YOU AND I ARE GOING INTO BUSINESS TOGETHER!
Betty and Veronica -in- "Designing Women"
US? GO INTO BUSINESS? AS WHAT?
AS DRESS DESIGNERS!
I'LL DESIGN THE CLOTHES, AND YOU CAN SEW THEM UP!
ONE OF YOU WILL BE GETTING THE BUSINESS, ANYWAY!
1

Script: George Gladir / Pencils: Dan DeCarlo / Inks: Alison Flood / Letters: Bill Yoshida / Colors: Barry Grossman

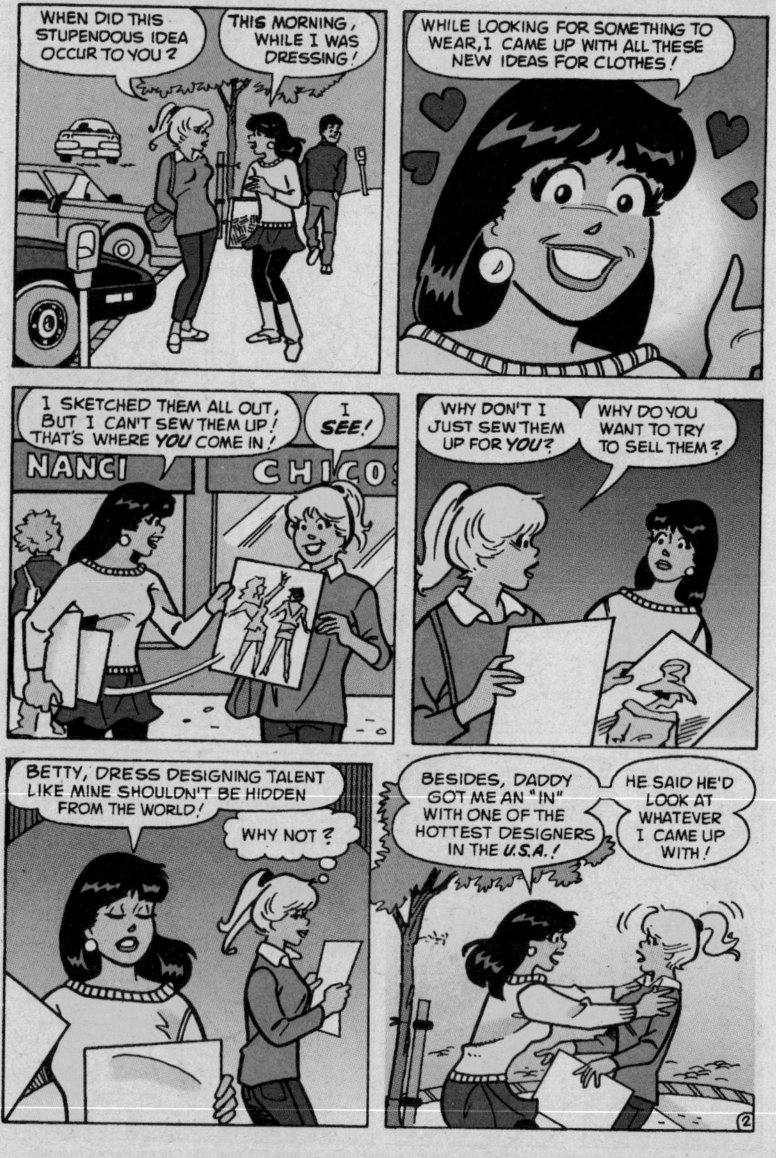
WHEN DID THIS STUPENDOUS IDEA OCCUR TO YOU?
THIS MORNING, WHILE I WAS DRESSING!
WHILE LOOKING FOR SOMETHING TO WEAR, I CAME UP WITH ALL THESE NEW IDEAS FOR CLOTHES!
I SKETCHED THEM ALL OUT, BUT I CAN'T SEW THEM UP! THAT'S WHERE YOU COME IN!
I SEE!
NANCI
CHICO
WHY DON'T I JUST SEW THEM UP FOR YOU?
WHY DO YOU WANT TO TRY TO SELL THEM?
BETTY, DRESS DESIGNING TALENT LIKE MINE SHOULDN'T BE HIDDEN FROM THE WORLD!
WHY NOT?
BESIDES, DADDY GOT ME AN "IN" WITH ONE OF THE HOTTEST DESIGNERS IN THE U.S.A.!
HE SAID HE'D LOOK AT WHATEVER I CAME UP WITH!
2

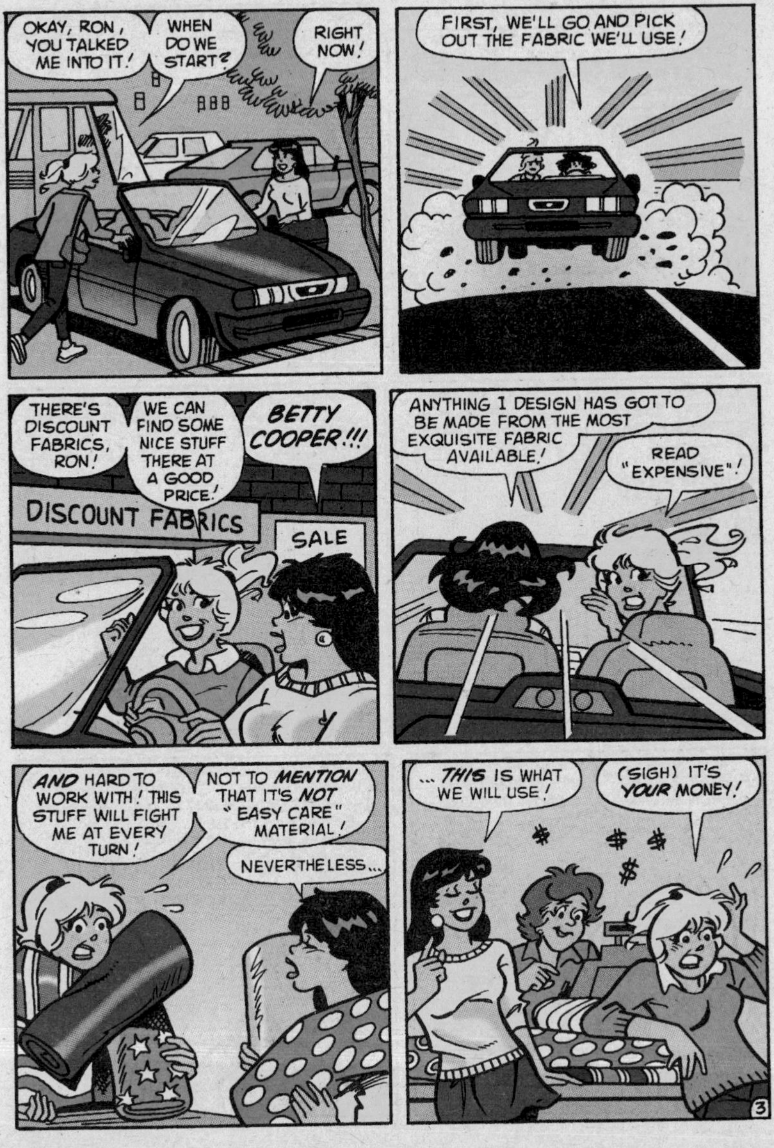
OKAY, RON, YOU TALKED ME INTO IT!
WHEN DO WE START?
RIGHT NOW!
FIRST, WE'LL GO AND PICK OUT THE FABRIC WE'LL USE!
THERE'S DISCOUNT FABRICS, RON!
WE CAN FIND SOME NICE STUFF THERE AT A GOOD PRICE!
BETTY COOPER!!!
DISCOUNT FABRICS
SALE
ANYTHING I DESIGN HAS GOT TO BE MADE FROM THE MOST EXQUISITE FABRIC AVAILABLE!
READ "EXPENSIVE"!
AND HARD TO WORK WITH! THIS STUFF WILL FIGHT ME AT EVERY TURN!
NOT TO MENTION THAT IT'S NOT "EASY CARE" MATERIAL!
NEVERTHELESS...
...THIS IS WHAT WE WILL USE!
(SIGH) IT'S YOUR MONEY!
3

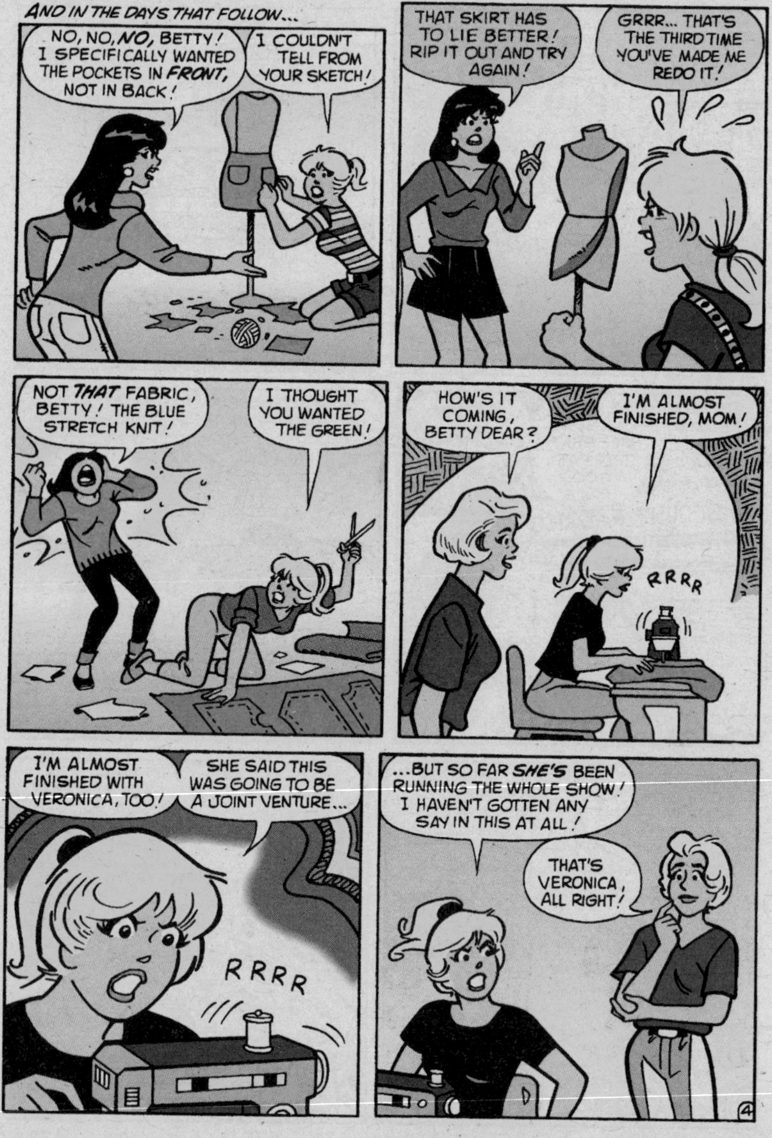
AND IN THE DAYS THAT FOLLOW...
NO, NO, NO, BETTY! I SPECIFICALLY WANTED THE POCKETS IN FRONT, NOT IN BACK!
I COULDN'T TELL FROM YOUR SKETCH!
THAT SKIRT HAS TO LIE BETTER! RIP IT OUT AND TRY AGAIN!
GRRR... THAT'S THE THIRD TIME YOU'VE MADE ME REDO IT!
NOT THAT FABRIC, BETTY! THE BLUE STRETCH KNIT!
I THOUGHT YOU WANTED THE GREEN!
HOW'S IT COMING, BETTY DEAR?
I'M ALMOST FINISHED, MOM!
RRRR
I'M ALMOST FINISHED WITH VERONICA, TOO!
SHE SAID THIS WAS GOING TO BE A JOINT VENTURE...
RRRR
...BUT SO FAR SHE'S BEEN RUNNING THE WHOLE SHOW! I HAVEN'T GOTTEN ANY SAY IN THIS AT ALL!
THAT'S VERONICA, ALL RIGHT!
4

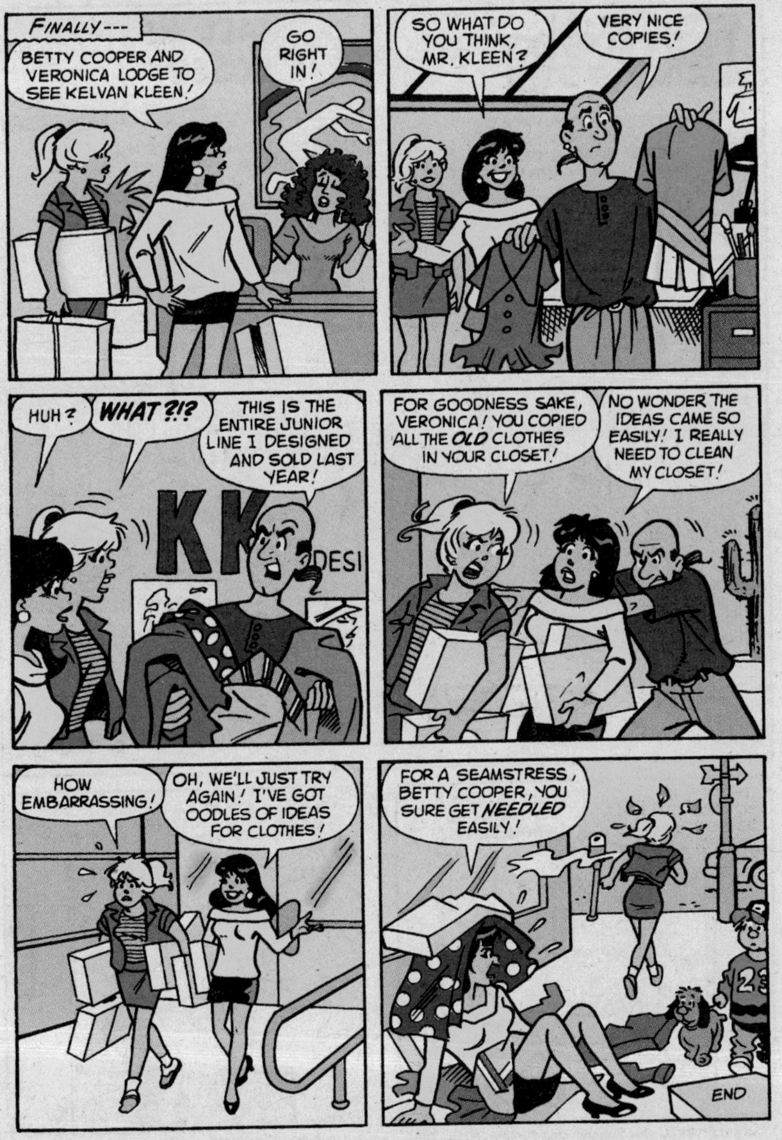
FINALLY---
BETTY COOPER AND VERONICA LODGE TO SEE KELVAN KLEEN!
GO RIGHT IN!
SO WHAT DO YOU THINK, MR. KLEEN?
VERY NICE COPIES!
HUH?
WHAT?!?
THIS IS THE ENTIRE JUNIOR LINE I DESIGNED AND SOLD LAST YEAR!
KK
DESI
FOR GOODNESS SAKE, VERONICA! YOU COPIED ALL THE OLD CLOTHES IN YOUR CLOSET!
NO WONDER THE IDEAS CAME SO EASILY! I REALLY NEED TO CLEAN MY CLOSET!
HOW EMBARRASSING!
OH, WE'LL JUST TRY AGAIN! I'VE GOT OODLES OF IDEAS FOR CLOTHES!
FOR A SEAMSTRESS, BETTY COOPER, YOU SURE GET NEEDLED EASILY!
END

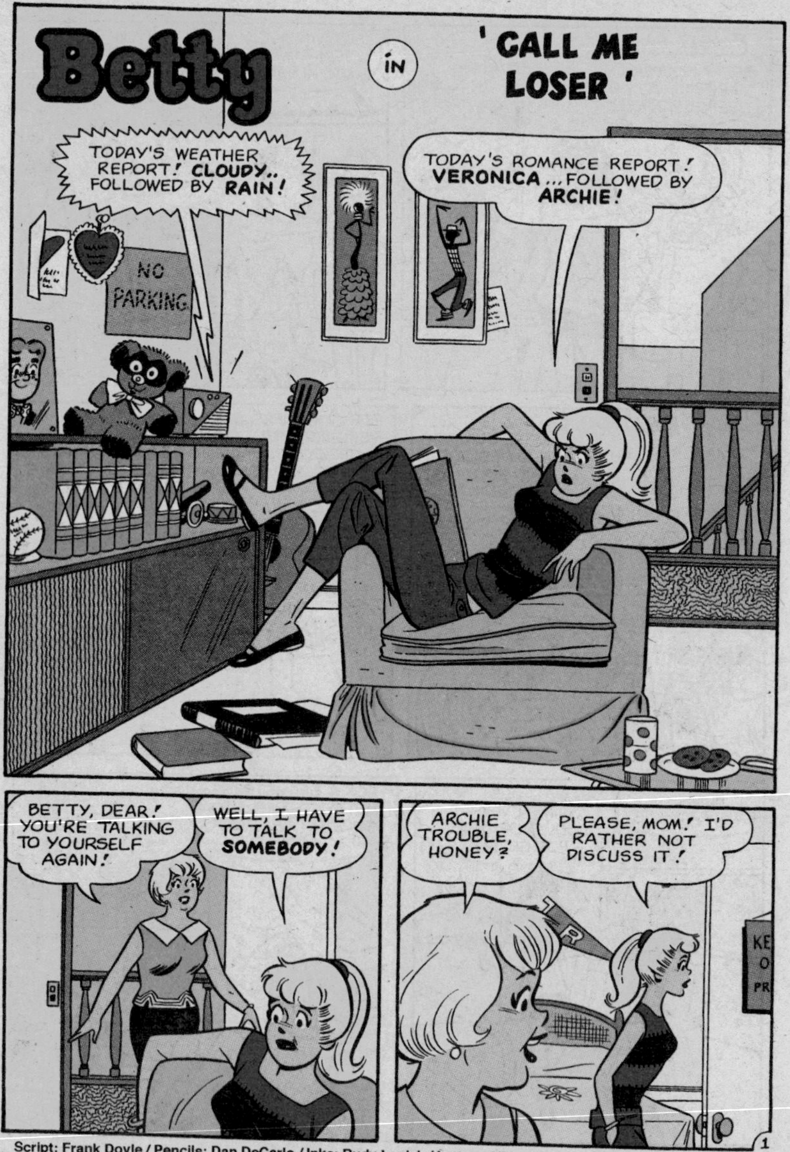
Betty
in
'CALL ME LOSER'
TODAY'S WEATHER REPORT! CLOUDY.. FOLLOWED BY RAIN!
TODAY'S ROMANCE REPORT! VERONICA ... FOLLOWED BY ARCHIE!
NO PARKING
BETTY, DEAR! YOU'RE TALKING TO YOURSELF AGAIN!
WELL, I HAVE TO TALK TO SOMEBODY!
ARCHIE TROUBLE, HONEY?
PLEASE, MOM! I'D RATHER NOT DISCUSS IT!

Script: Frank Doyle / Pencils: Dan DeCarlo / Inks: Rudy Lapick / Letters: Vince DeCarlo / Colors: Barry Grossman

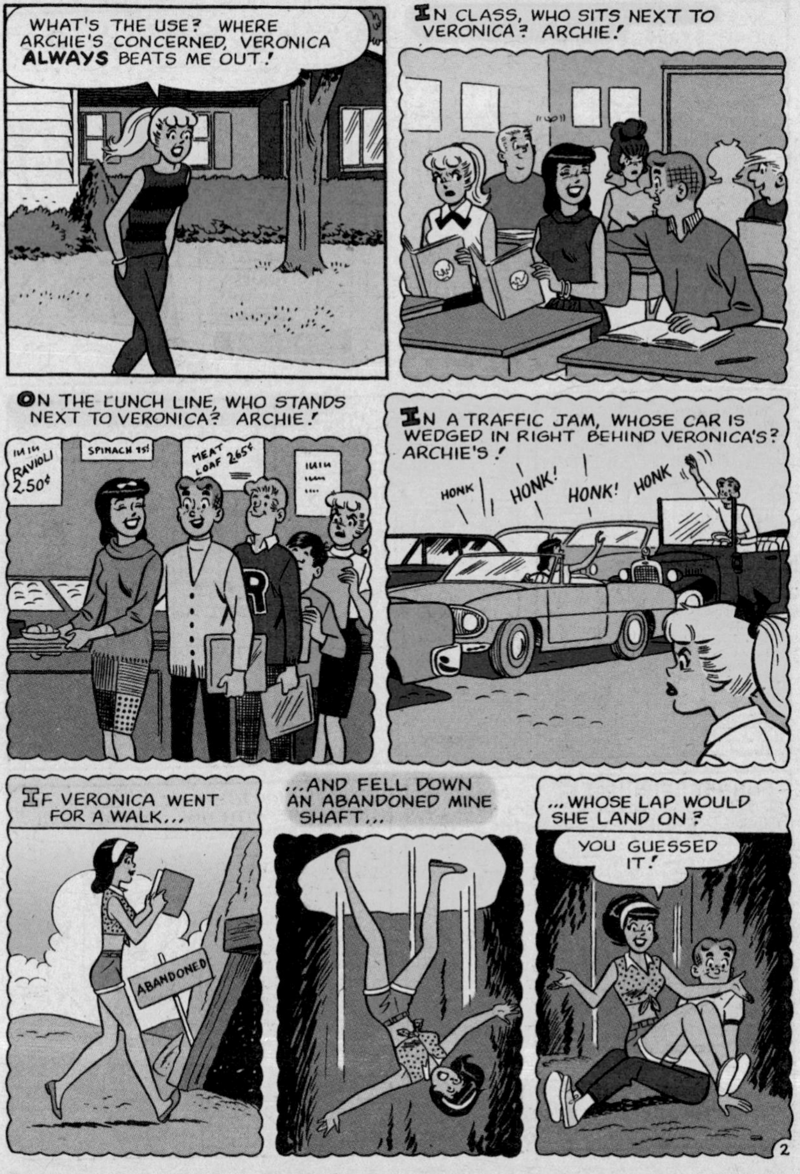

WHAT'S THE USE? WHERE ARCHIE'S CONCERNED, VERONICA **ALWAYS** BEATS ME OUT!
IN CLASS, WHO SITS NEXT TO VERONICA? ARCHIE!
ON THE LUNCH LINE, WHO STANDS NEXT TO VERONICA? ARCHIE!
RAVIOLI 2.50¢
SPINACH 15¢
MEAT LOAF 2.65¢
IN A TRAFFIC JAM, WHOSE CAR IS WEDGED IN RIGHT BEHIND VERONICA'S? ARCHIE'S!
HONK
HONK!
HONK!
HONK
IF VERONICA WENT FOR A WALK...
ABANDONED
...AND FELL DOWN AN ABANDONED MINE SHAFT...
...WHOSE LAP WOULD SHE LAND ON?
YOU GUESSED IT!

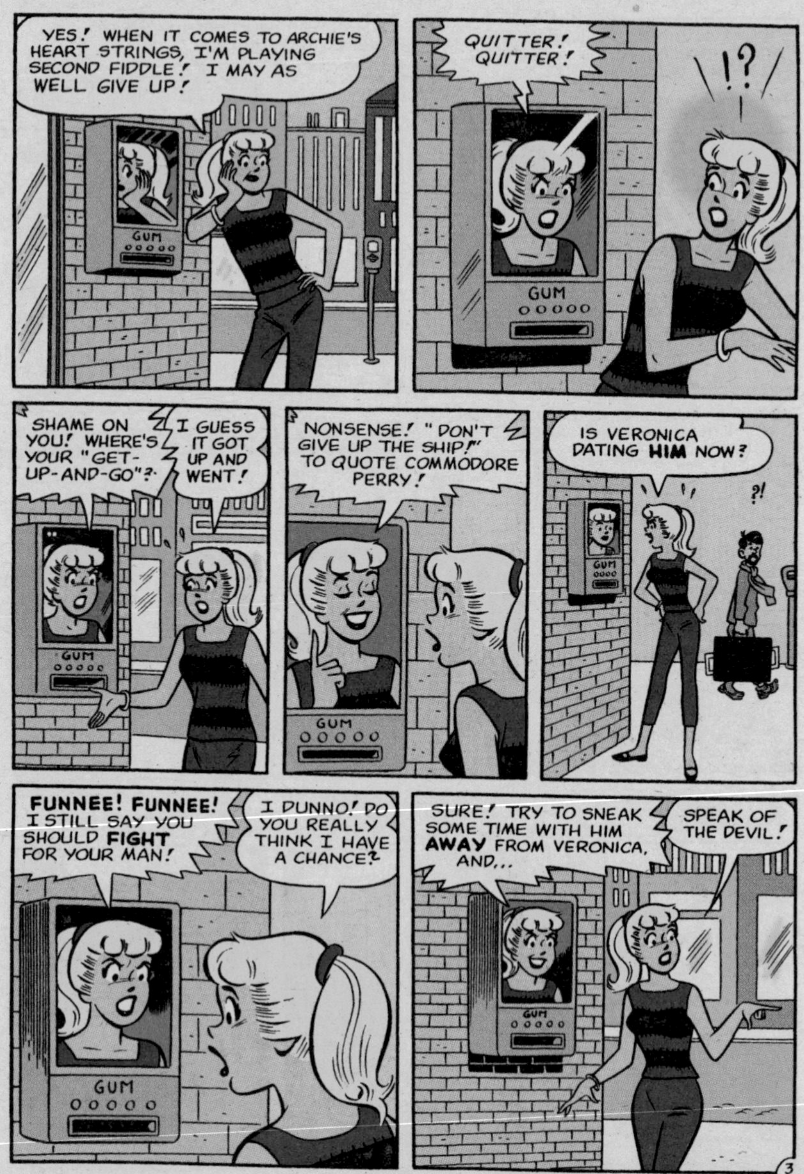
YES! WHEN IT COMES TO ARCHIE'S HEART STRINGS, I'M PLAYING SECOND FIDDLE! I MAY AS WELL GIVE UP!
QUITTER! QUITTER!
!?
GUM
SHAME ON YOU! WHERE'S YOUR "GET-UP-AND-GO"?
I GUESS IT GOT UP AND WENT!
NONSENSE! "DON'T GIVE UP THE SHIP!" TO QUOTE COMMODORE PERRY!
IS VERONICA DATING HIM NOW?
?!
FUNNEE! FUNNEE! I STILL SAY YOU SHOULD FIGHT FOR YOUR MAN!
I DUNNO! DO YOU REALLY THINK I HAVE A CHANCE?
SURE! TRY TO SNEAK SOME TIME WITH HIM AWAY FROM VERONICA, AND...
SPEAK OF THE DEVIL!

HI, BETTY!
OKAY..., WHERE IS HE?
WHERE'S WHO?
ARCHIE! ISN'T HE TAGGING ALONG BEHIND YOU, AS USUAL?
NOT TODAY, DEARIE! ARCHIE'S WORKING IN THE SCHOOL NEWSPAPER OFFICE...
...AND I'M ON MY WAY TO THE BEAUTY PARLOR! LUIGI IS GOING TO WASH AND SET MY RAVEN TRESSES!
SHE NEEDS TO BE BEAUTIFIED LIKE I NEED ROCKS IN MY HEAD!
WELL, DON'T STAND THERE, STUPID! FOR ONCE ARCHIE **WON'T** BE WITH VERONICA!
YOU'RE RIGHT!
GUM
WHAT A BREAK! I HOPE LUIGI KEEPS HER ALL DAY!
4

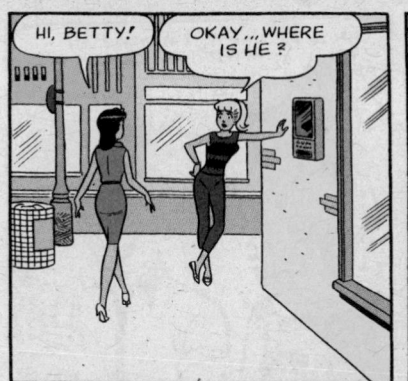

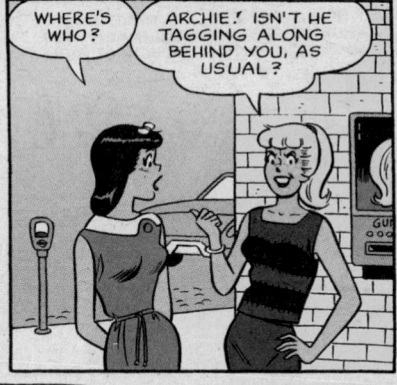

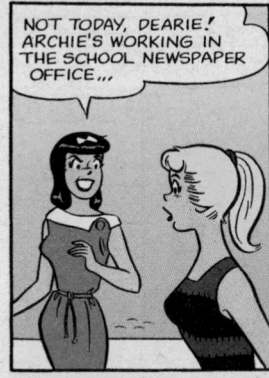

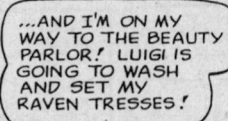

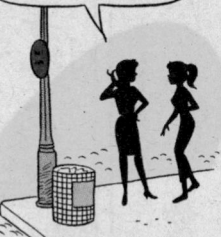

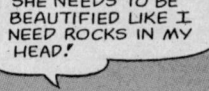

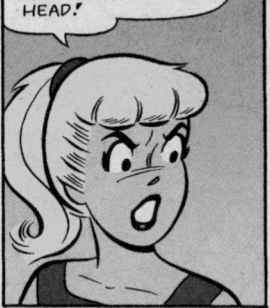

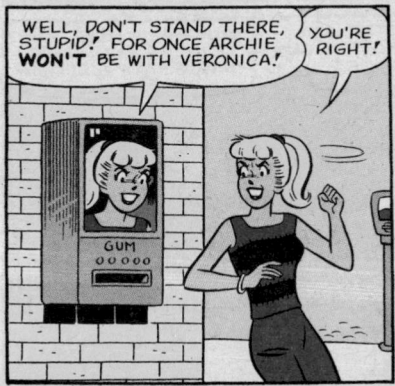

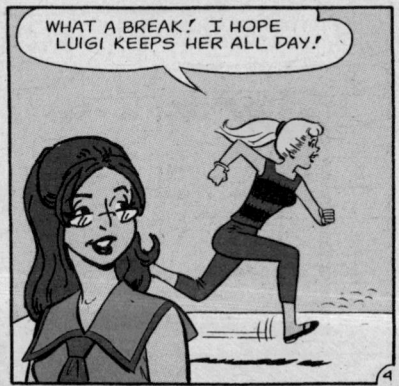

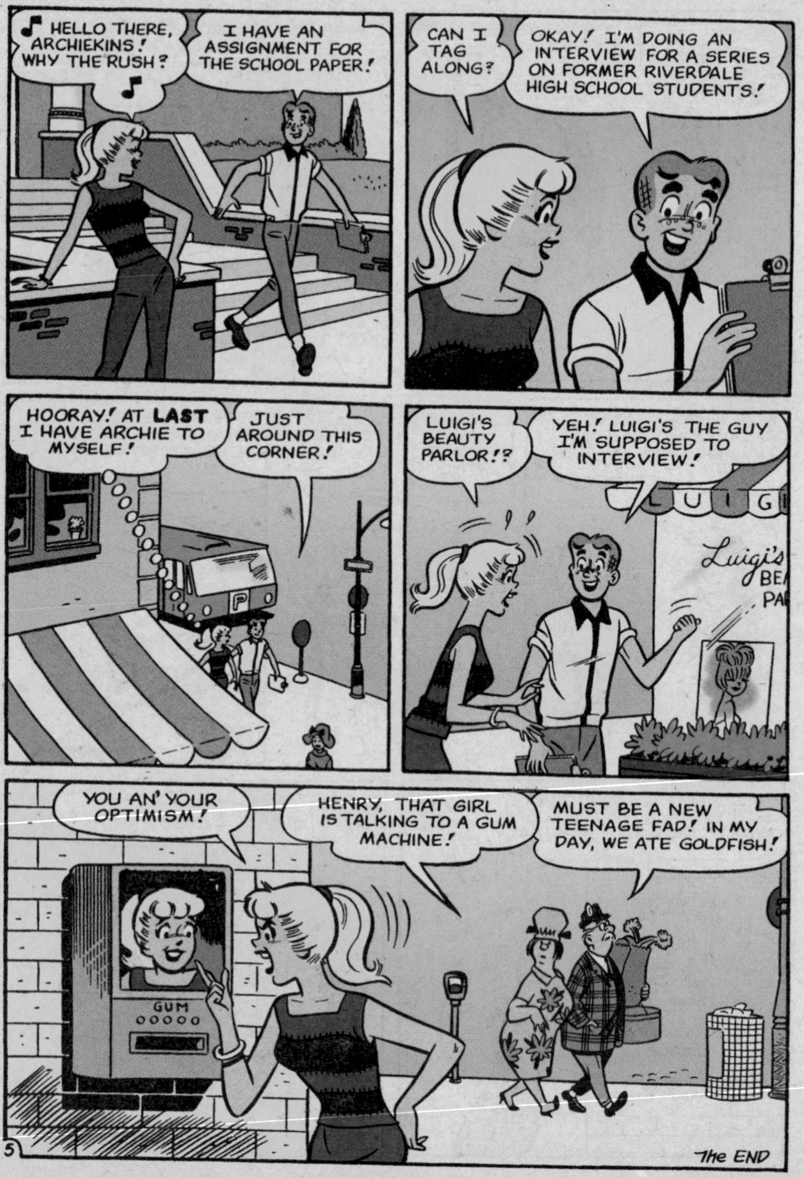
HELLO THERE, ARCHIEKINS! WHY THE RUSH?
I HAVE AN ASSIGNMENT FOR THE SCHOOL PAPER!
CAN I TAG ALONG?
OKAY! I'M DOING AN INTERVIEW FOR A SERIES ON FORMER RIVERDALE HIGH SCHOOL STUDENTS!
HOORAY! AT LAST I HAVE ARCHIE TO MYSELF!
JUST AROUND THIS CORNER!
P
LUIGI'S BEAUTY PARLOR!?
YEH! LUIGI'S THE GUY I'M SUPPOSED TO INTERVIEW!
LUIGI
Luigi's
YOU AN' YOUR OPTIMISM!
HENRY, THAT GIRL IS TALKING TO A GUM MACHINE!
MUST BE A NEW TEENAGE FAD! IN MY DAY, WE ATE GOLDFISH!
GUM
5
The END

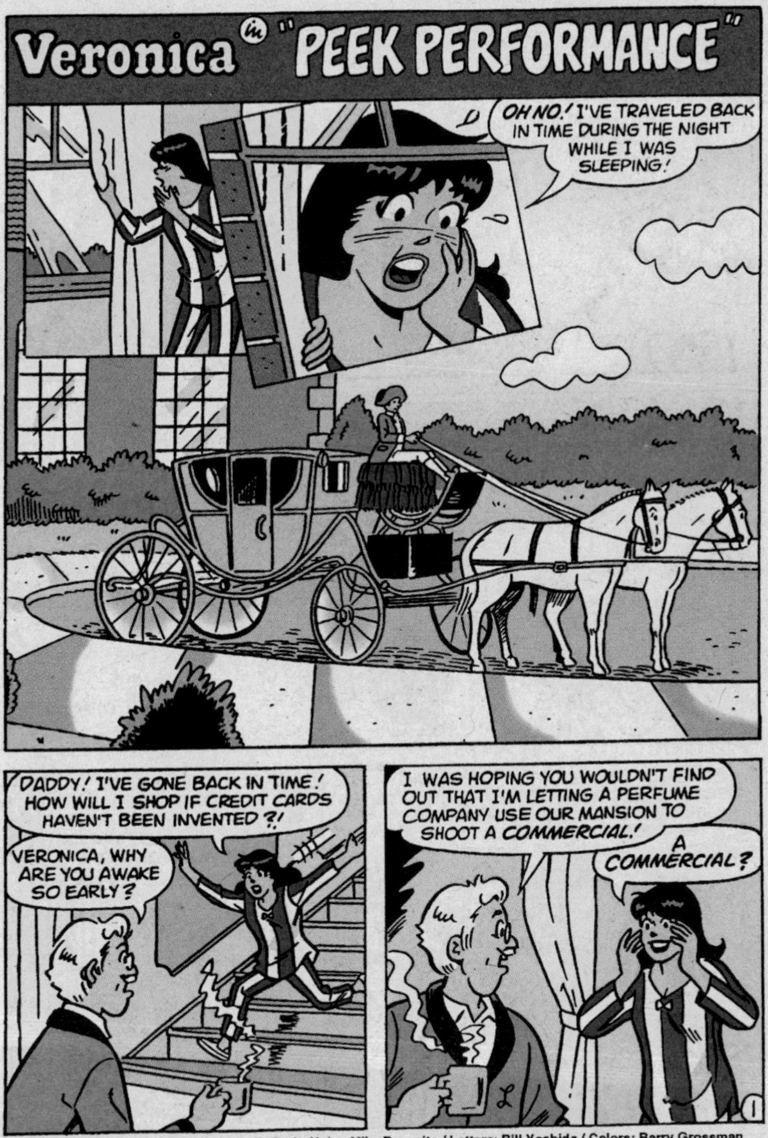
Veronica in "PEEK PERFORMANCE"
OH NO! I'VE TRAVELED BACK IN TIME DURING THE NIGHT WHILE I WAS SLEEPING!
DADDY! I'VE GONE BACK IN TIME! HOW WILL I SHOP IF CREDIT CARDS HAVEN'T BEEN INVENTED ?!
VERONICA, WHY ARE YOU AWAKE SO EARLY?
I WAS HOPING YOU WOULDN'T FIND OUT THAT I'M LETTING A PERFUME COMPANY USE OUR MANSION TO SHOOT A COMMERCIAL!
A COMMERCIAL?
1

Script: George Gladir / Pencils: Dan DeCarlo / Inks: Mike Esposito / Letters: Bill Yoshida / Colors: Barry Grossman

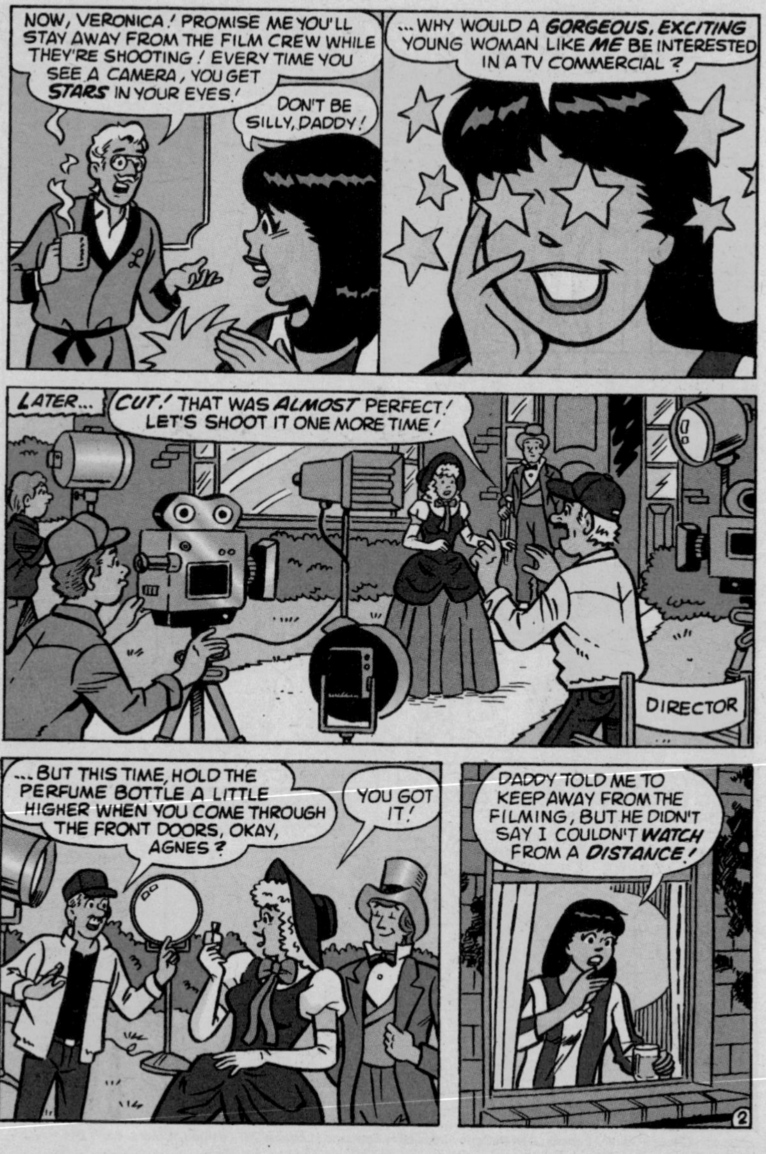
NOW, VERONICA! PROMISE ME YOU'LL STAY AWAY FROM THE FILM CREW WHILE THEY'RE SHOOTING! EVERY TIME YOU SEE A CAMERA, YOU GET STARS IN YOUR EYES!
DON'T BE SILLY, DADDY!
...WHY WOULD A GORGEOUS, EXCITING YOUNG WOMAN LIKE ME BE INTERESTED IN A TV COMMERCIAL?
LATER...
CUT! THAT WAS ALMOST PERFECT! LET'S SHOOT IT ONE MORE TIME!
DIRECTOR
...BUT THIS TIME, HOLD THE PERFUME BOTTLE A LITTLE HIGHER WHEN YOU COME THROUGH THE FRONT DOORS, OKAY, AGNES?
YOU GOT IT!
DADDY TOLD ME TO KEEP AWAY FROM THE FILMING, BUT HE DIDN'T SAY I COULDN'T WATCH FROM A DISTANCE!

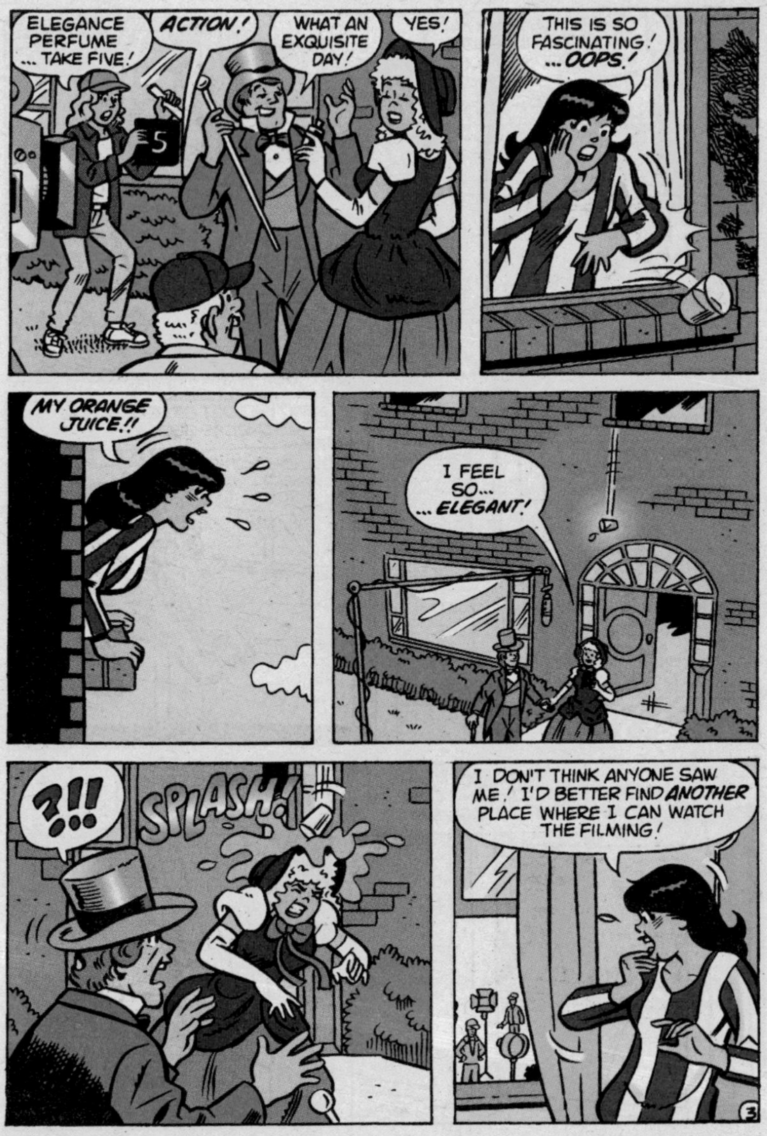
ELEGANCE PERFUME ... TAKE FIVE!
ACTION!
WHAT AN EXQUISITE DAY!
YES!
5
THIS IS SO FASCINATING! ... OOPS!
MY ORANGE JUICE!!
I FEEL SO... ... ELEGANT!
?!!
SPLASH!
I DON'T THINK ANYONE SAW ME! I'D BETTER FIND ANOTHER PLACE WHERE I CAN WATCH THE FILMING!
3

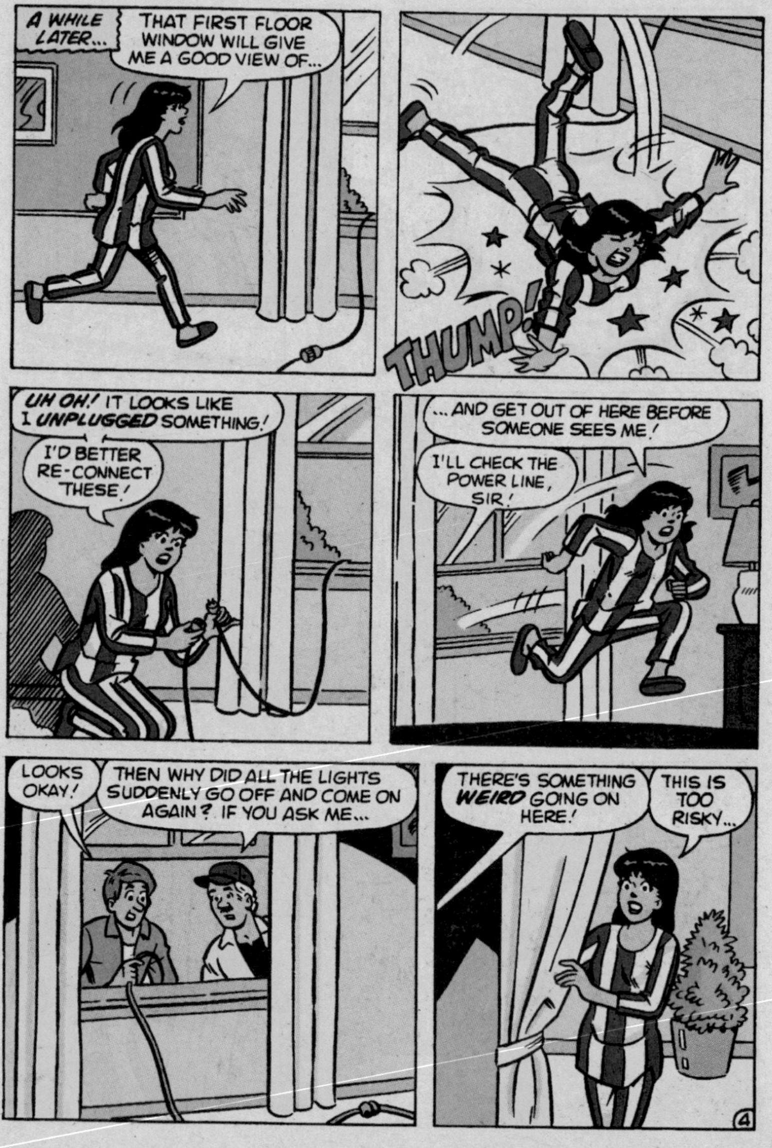
A WHILE LATER...
THAT FIRST FLOOR WINDOW WILL GIVE ME A GOOD VIEW OF...
THUMP!
UH OH! IT LOOKS LIKE I UNPLUGGED SOMETHING!
I'D BETTER RE-CONNECT THESE!
... AND GET OUT OF HERE BEFORE SOMEONE SEES ME!
I'LL CHECK THE POWER LINE, SIR!
LOOKS OKAY!
THEN WHY DID ALL THE LIGHTS SUDDENLY GO OFF AND COME ON AGAIN? IF YOU ASK ME...
THERE'S SOMETHING WEIRD GOING ON HERE!
THIS IS TOO RISKY...
4

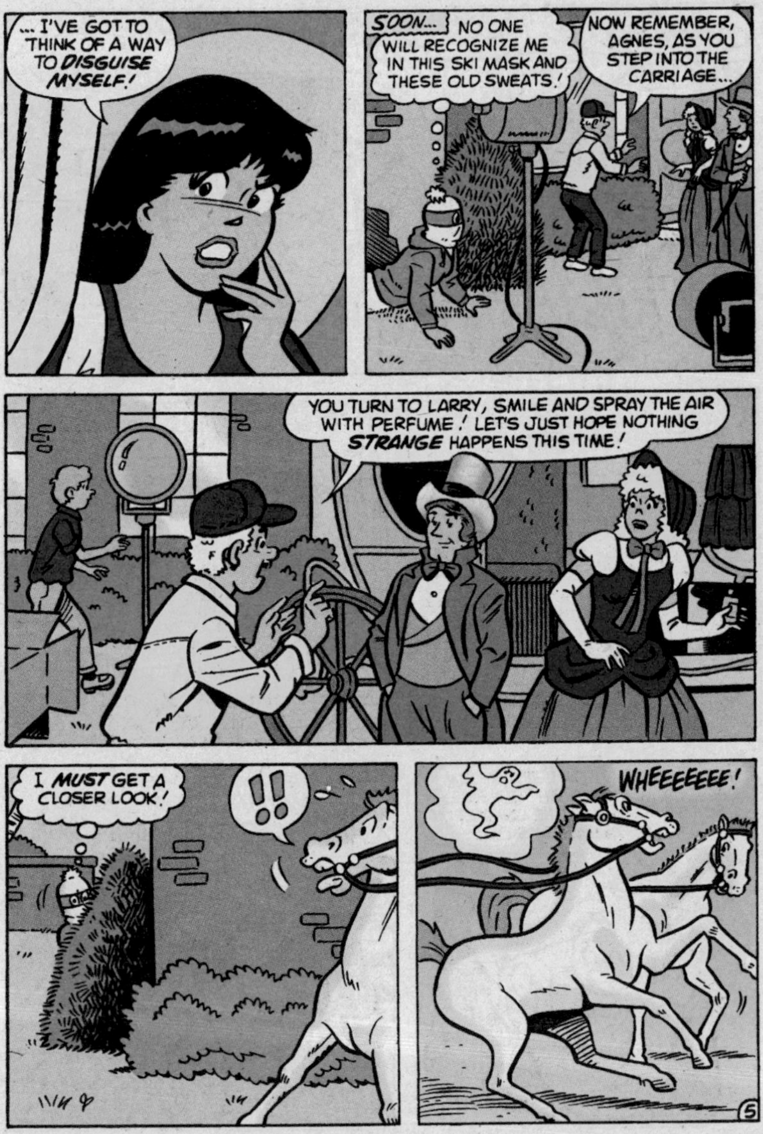
... I'VE GOT TO THINK OF A WAY TO DISGUISE MYSELF!
SOON...
NO ONE WILL RECOGNIZE ME IN THIS SKI MASK AND THESE OLD SWEATS!
NOW REMEMBER, AGNES, AS YOU STEP INTO THE CARRIAGE...
YOU TURN TO LARRY, SMILE AND SPRAY THE AIR WITH PERFUME! LET'S JUST HOPE NOTHING STRANGE HAPPENS THIS TIME!
I MUST GET A CLOSER LOOK!
!!
WHEEEEEEE!
5

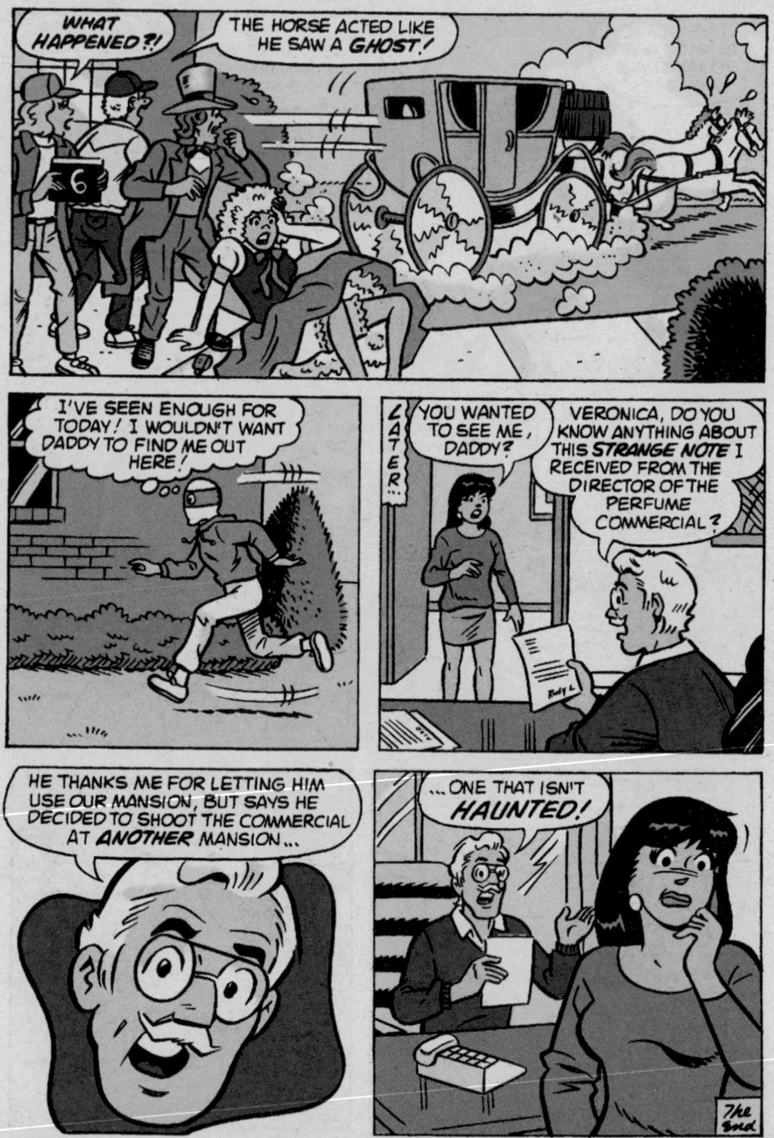
WHAT HAPPENED?!
THE HORSE ACTED LIKE HE SAW A GHOST!
6
I'VE SEEN ENOUGH FOR TODAY! I WOULDN'T WANT DADDY TO FIND ME OUT HERE!
LATER...
YOU WANTED TO SEE ME, DADDY?
VERONICA, DO YOU KNOW ANYTHING ABOUT THIS STRANGE NOTE I RECEIVED FROM THE DIRECTOR OF THE PERFUME COMMERCIAL?
HE THANKS ME FOR LETTING HIM USE OUR MANSION, BUT SAYS HE DECIDED TO SHOOT THE COMMERCIAL AT ANOTHER MANSION...
...ONE THAT ISN'T HAUNTED!
The End

Betty and Veronica in That's ART?

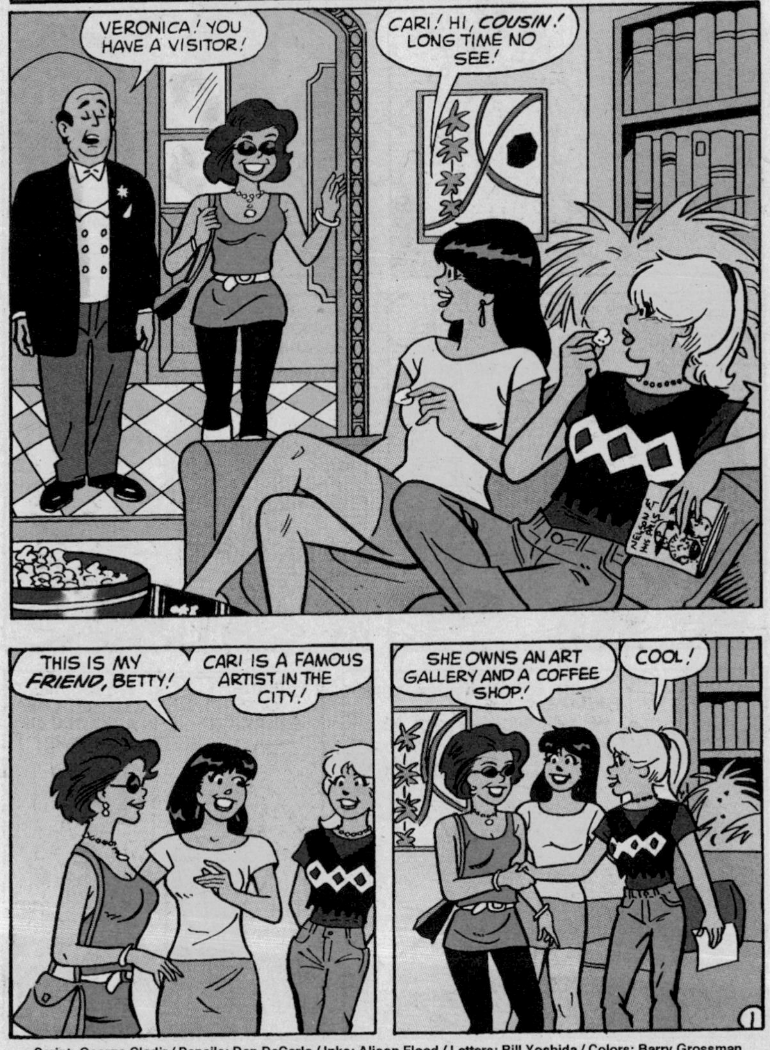
VERONICA! YOU HAVE A VISITOR!
CARI! HI, *COUSIN*! LONG TIME NO SEE!
THIS IS MY *FRIEND*, BETTY!
CARI IS A FAMOUS ARTIST IN THE CITY!
SHE OWNS AN ART GALLERY AND A COFFEE SHOP!
COOL!
1

Script: George Gladir / Pencils: Dan DeCarlo / Inks: Alison Flood / Letters: Bill Yoshida / Colors: Barry Grossman

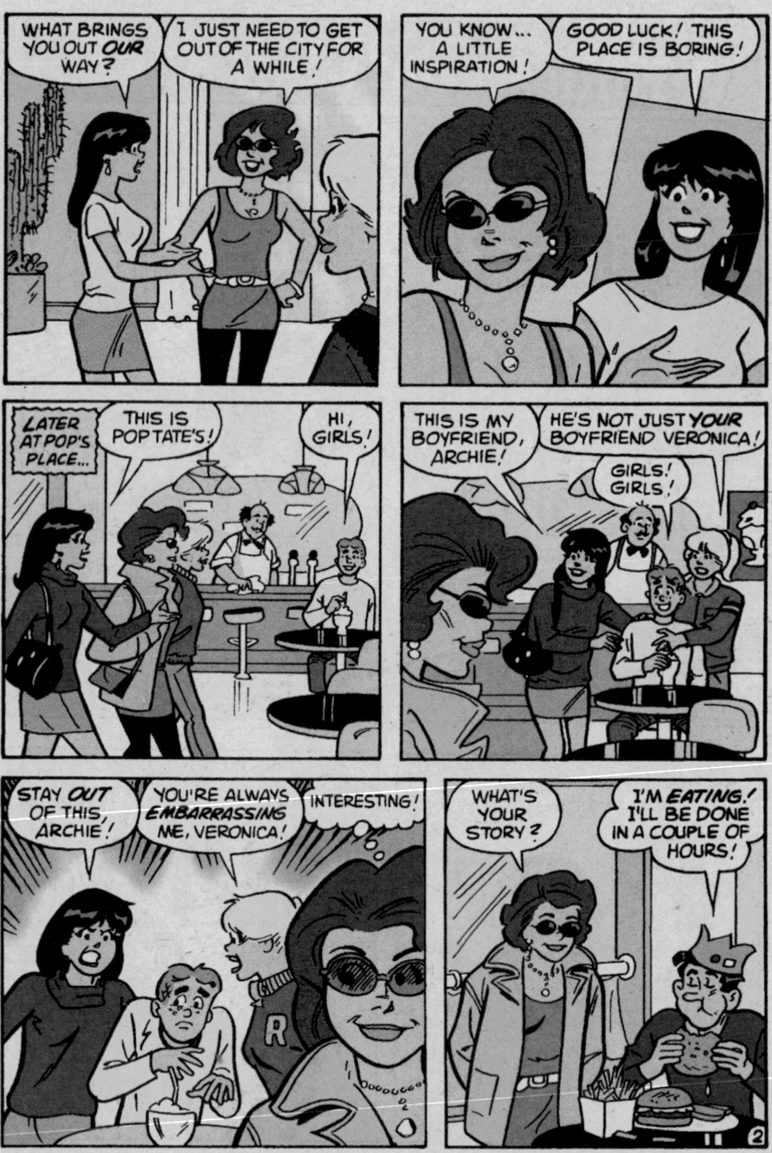
WHAT BRINGS YOU OUT OUR WAY?
I JUST NEED TO GET OUT OF THE CITY FOR A WHILE!
YOU KNOW... A LITTLE INSPIRATION!
GOOD LUCK! THIS PLACE IS BORING!
LATER AT POP'S PLACE...
THIS IS POP TATE'S!
HI, GIRLS!
THIS IS MY BOYFRIEND, ARCHIE!
HE'S NOT JUST YOUR BOYFRIEND VERONICA!
GIRLS! GIRLS!
STAY OUT OF THIS, ARCHIE!
YOU'RE ALWAYS EMBARRASSING ME, VERONICA!
INTERESTING!
WHAT'S YOUR STORY?
I'M EATING! I'LL BE DONE IN A COUPLE OF HOURS!
2

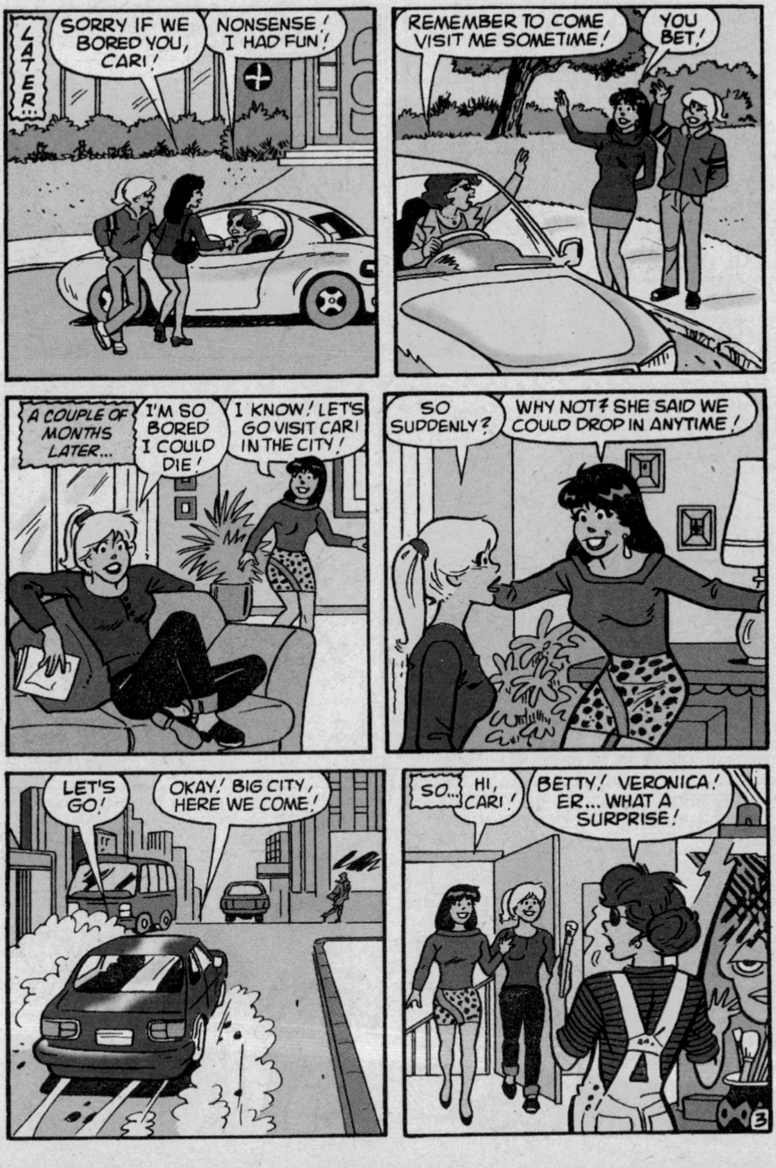
LATER...
SORRY IF WE BORED YOU, CARI!
NONSENSE! I HAD FUN!
REMEMBER TO COME VISIT ME SOMETIME!
YOU BET!
A COUPLE OF MONTHS LATER...
I'M SO BORED I COULD DIE!
I KNOW! LET'S GO VISIT CARI IN THE CITY!
SO SUDDENLY?
WHY NOT? SHE SAID WE COULD DROP IN ANYTIME!
LET'S GO!
OKAY! BIG CITY, HERE WE COME!
SO...
HI, CARI!
BETTY! VERONICA! ER... WHAT A SURPRISE!
3

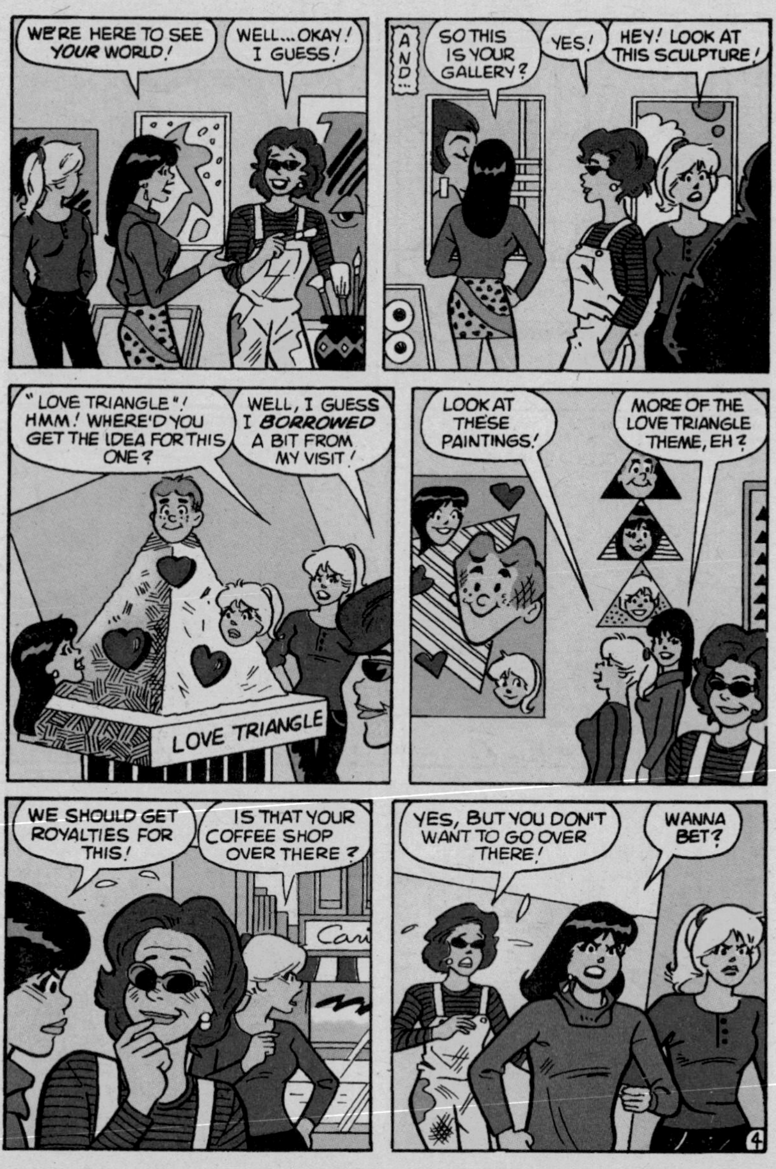
WE'RE HERE TO SEE YOUR WORLD!
WELL...OKAY! I GUESS!
AND...
SO THIS IS YOUR GALLERY?
YES!
HEY! LOOK AT THIS SCULPTURE!
"LOVE TRIANGLE"! HMM! WHERE'D YOU GET THE IDEA FOR THIS ONE?
WELL, I GUESS I BORROWED A BIT FROM MY VISIT!
LOVE TRIANGLE
LOOK AT THESE PAINTINGS!
MORE OF THE LOVE TRIANGLE THEME, EH?
WE SHOULD GET ROYALTIES FOR THIS!
IS THAT YOUR COFFEE SHOP OVER THERE?
YES, BUT YOU DON'T WANT TO GO OVER THERE!
WANNA BET?
4

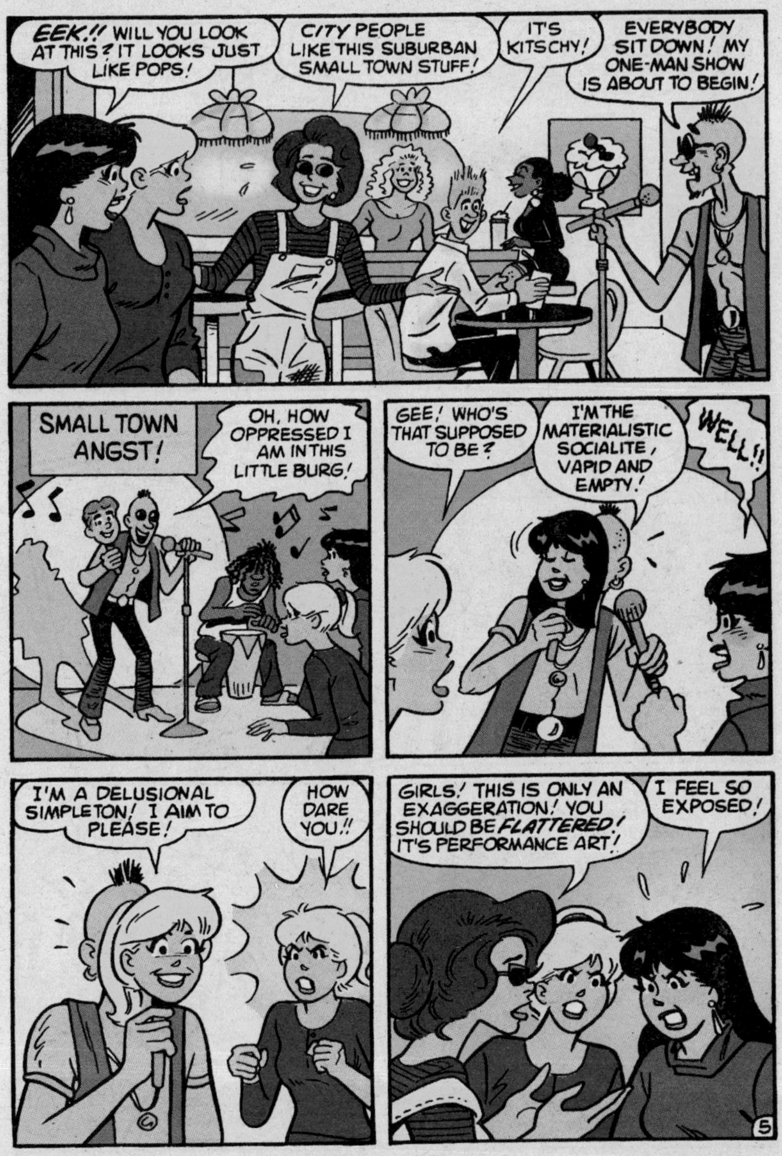
EEK!! WILL YOU LOOK AT THIS? IT LOOKS JUST LIKE POPS!
CITY PEOPLE LIKE THIS SUBURBAN SMALL TOWN STUFF!
IT'S KITSCHY!
EVERYBODY SIT DOWN! MY ONE-MAN SHOW IS ABOUT TO BEGIN!
SMALL TOWN ANGST!
OH, HOW OPPRESSED I AM IN THIS LITTLE BURG!
GEE! WHO'S THAT SUPPOSED TO BE?
I'M THE MATERIALISTIC SOCIALITE, VAPID AND EMPTY!
WELL!!
I'M A DELUSIONAL SIMPLETON! I AIM TO PLEASE!
HOW DARE YOU!!
GIRLS! THIS IS ONLY AN EXAGGERATION! YOU SHOULD BE FLATTERED! IT'S PERFORMANCE ART!
I FEEL SO EXPOSED!
5

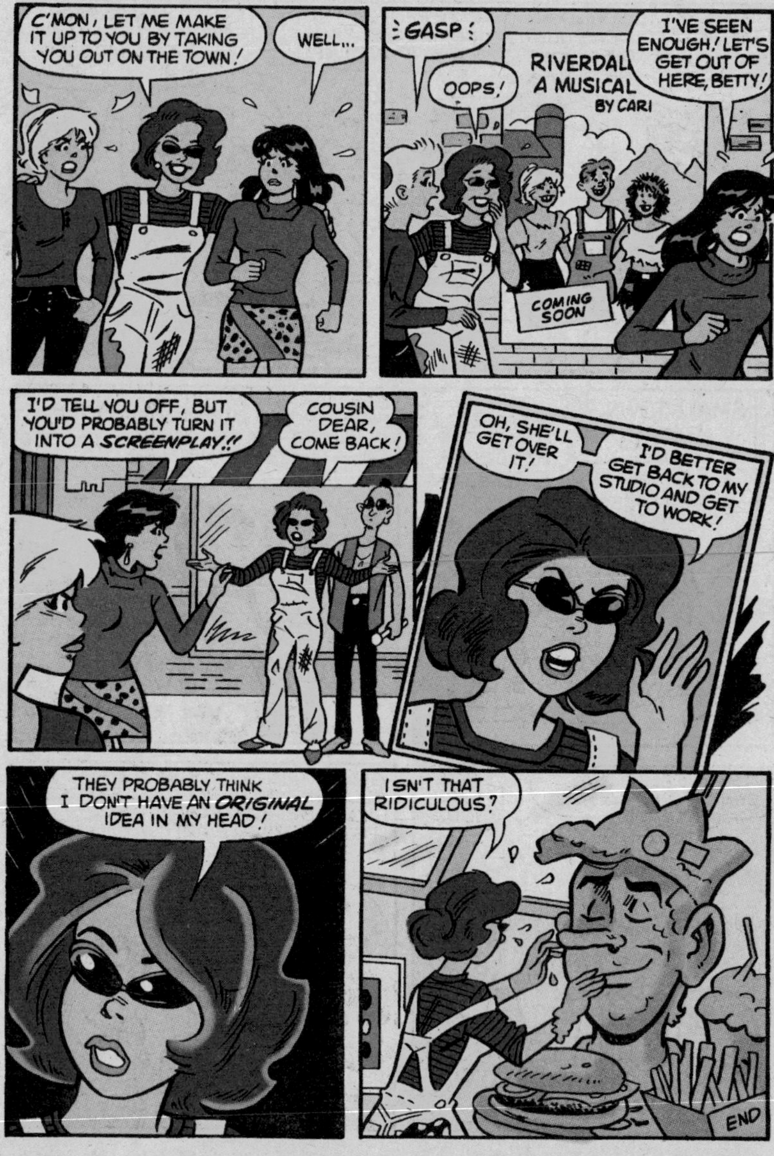
C'MON, LET ME MAKE IT UP TO YOU BY TAKING YOU OUT ON THE TOWN!
WELL...
GASP
OOPS!
RIVERDALE A MUSICAL BY CARI
I'VE SEEN ENOUGH! LET'S GET OUT OF HERE, BETTY!
COMING SOON
I'D TELL YOU OFF, BUT YOU'D PROBABLY TURN IT INTO A SCREENPLAY!!
COUSIN DEAR, COME BACK!
OH, SHE'LL GET OVER IT!
I'D BETTER GET BACK TO MY STUDIO AND GET TO WORK!
THEY PROBABLY THINK I DON'T HAVE AN ORIGINAL IDEA IN MY HEAD!
ISN'T THAT RIDICULOUS?
END

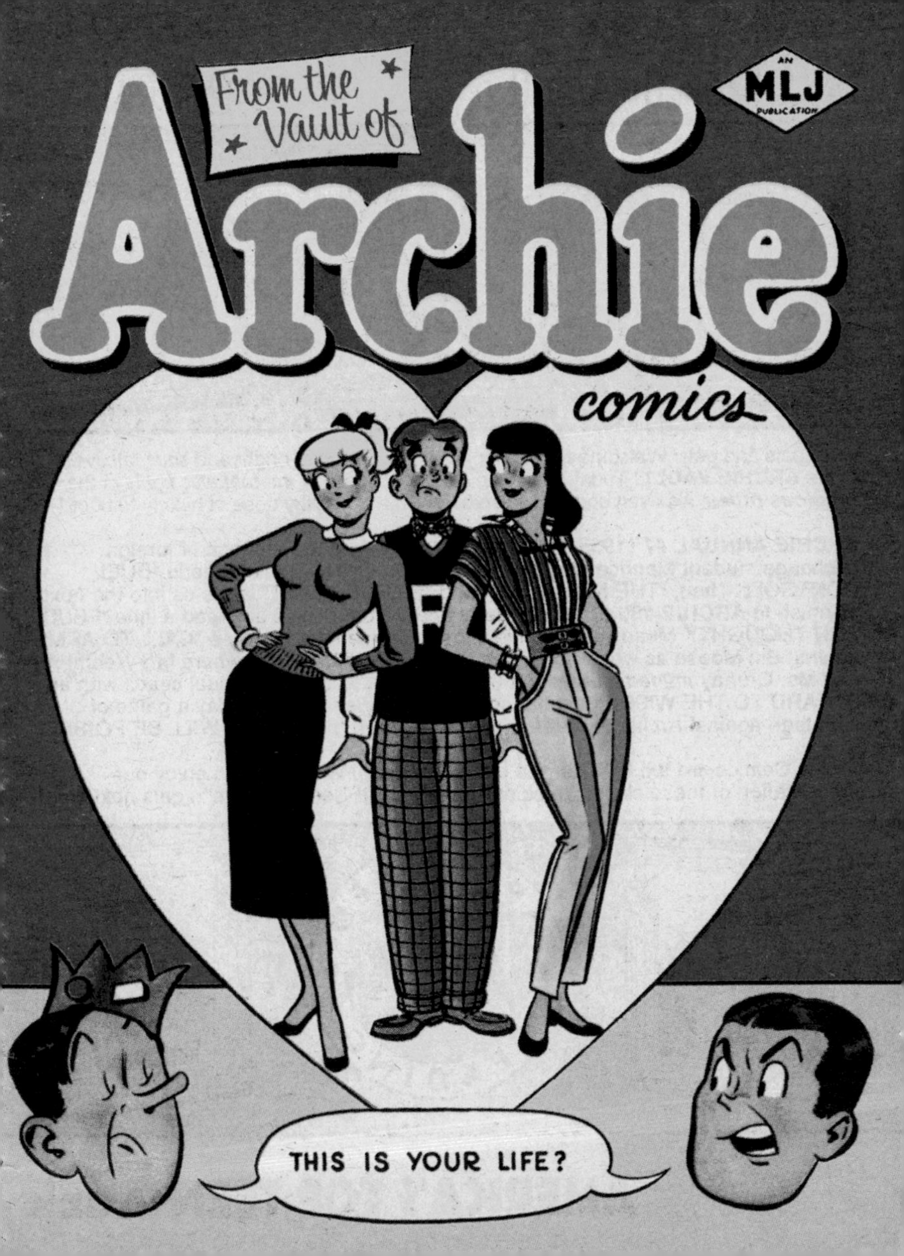
From the Vault of
Archie
AN MLJ PUBLICATION
comics
THIS IS YOUR LIFE?

From the Vault of Archie Comics!

VERONICA

ARCHIE

BETTY

Hiya, pals and gals! Welcome to another jovial jaunt into the bright and shiny alcoves of the **ARCHIE VAULT!** Today we'll take a peek at some of *the fantastic fights* of the *fabulous fifties!* It's everybody VS everybody (with a healthy dose of hilarity to boot)!

ARCHIE ANNUAL #7 (*1955-56*) pits our hero against the menace of foreign exchange student Maurice de Havré de Colisión Onzee Boulevarde in "DUEL CONTROL!" Then, "THE NEW LOOK" and "SILENT MIGHT" leads us into the next skirmish in **ARCHIE #86** (*1957*) as Betty and Veronica give Jughead a little "FEUD FOR THOUGHT!" Meanwhile, Archie shows Reggie how to rally a "CALL TO ARMS" against Big Moose as we switch gears to **ARCHIE #93** (*1958*) where Mr. Weatherbee and Ms. Grundy *immediately* regret their attempts to quell the usual chaos with an "AWARD TO THE WISE!" Last but not least, Betty and Reggie play a game of sabotage against Archie and Veronica only to learn that "POISE WILL BE POISE!"

Archie Comics are the best comics out there, gang! We hope you enjoy our presentation of these classic tales of Archie's past! See you guys 'n gals next time!

JUGHEAD

APPROVED
AN
Archie
MAGAZINE
· READING ·

REGGIE

The following stories are reprinted here without alteration for historical reference.

Archie - AMERICA'S TOP TEEN-AGER

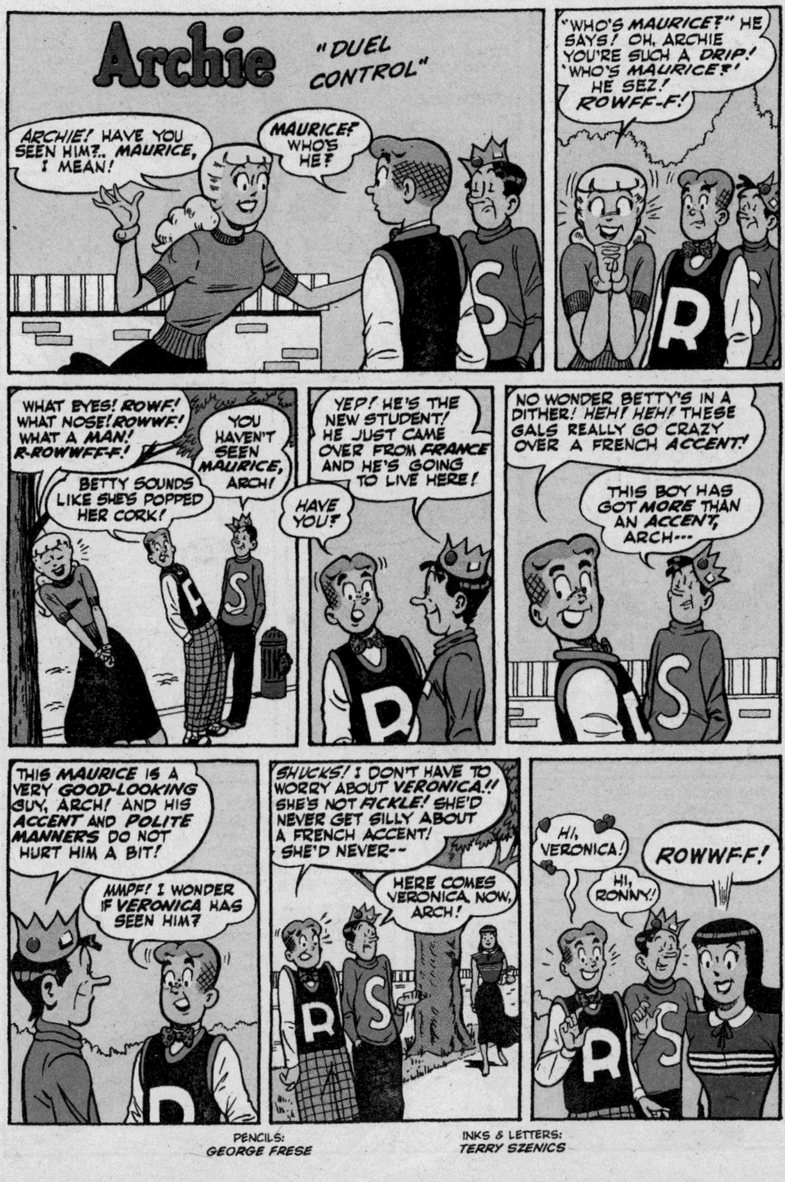
Archie
"DUEL CONTROL"
ARCHIE! HAVE YOU SEEN HIM?.. MAURICE, I MEAN!
MAURICE? WHO'S HE?
"WHO'S MAURICE?" HE SAYS! OH, ARCHIE YOU'RE SUCH A DRIP! 'WHO'S MAURICE?' HE SEZ! ROWFF-F!
WHAT EYES! ROWF! WHAT NOSE! ROWWF! WHAT A MAN! R-ROWWFF-F!
BETTY SOUNDS LIKE SHE'S POPPED HER CORK!
YOU HAVEN'T SEEN MAURICE, ARCH!
YEP! HE'S THE NEW STUDENT! HE JUST CAME OVER FROM FRANCE AND HE'S GOING TO LIVE HERE!
HAVE YOU?
NO WONDER BETTY'S IN A DITHER! HEH! HEH! THESE GALS REALLY GO CRAZY OVER A FRENCH ACCENT!
THIS BOY HAS GOT MORE THAN AN ACCENT, ARCH---
THIS MAURICE IS A VERY GOOD-LOOKING GUY, ARCH! AND HIS ACCENT AND POLITE MANNERS DO NOT HURT HIM A BIT!
MMPF! I WONDER IF VERONICA HAS SEEN HIM?
SHUCKS! I DON'T HAVE TO WORRY ABOUT VERONICA!! SHE'S NOT FICKLE! SHE'D NEVER GET SILLY ABOUT A FRENCH ACCENT! SHE'D NEVER--
HERE COMES VERONICA NOW, ARCH!
HI, VERONICA!
HI, RONNY!
ROWWF-F!
PENCILS: GEORGE FRESE
INKS & LETTERS: TERRY SZENICS

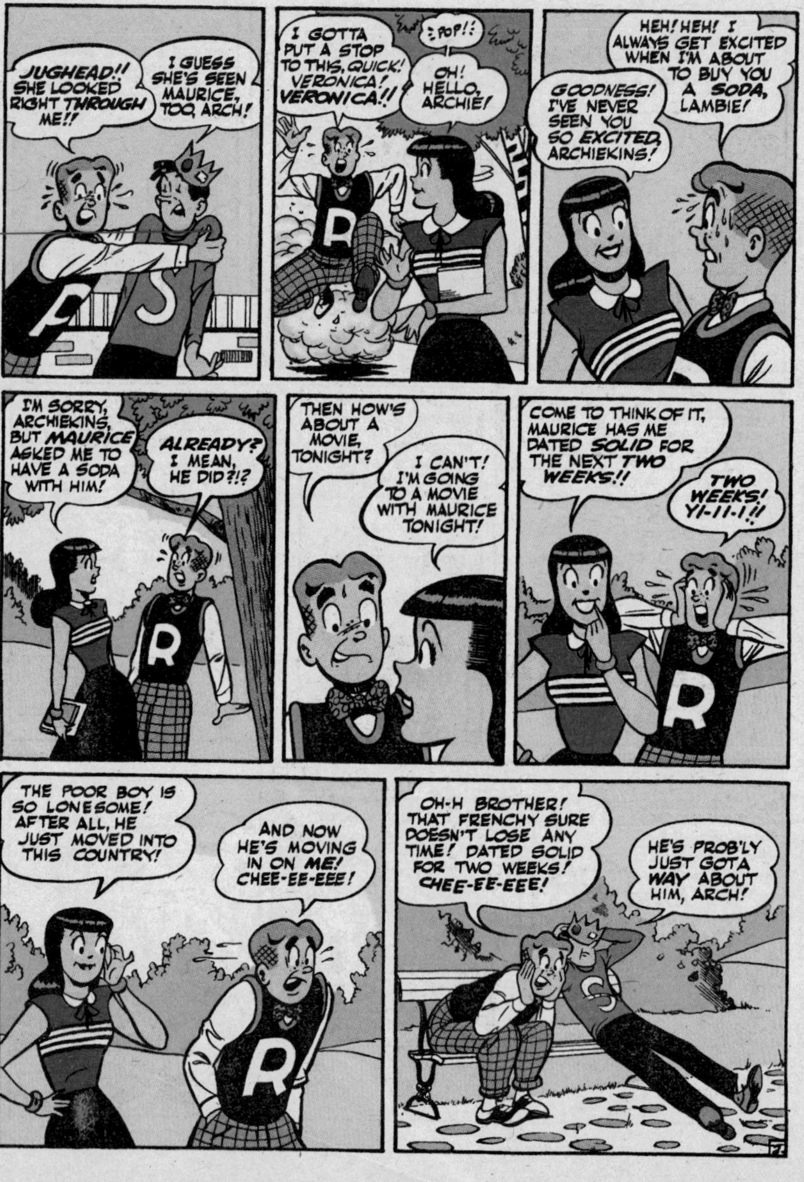
JUGHEAD!! SHE LOOKED RIGHT THROUGH ME!!
I GUESS SHE'S SEEN MAURICE, TOO, ARCH!
I GOTTA PUT A STOP TO THIS, QUICK! VERONICA! VERONICA!!
POP!!
OH! HELLO, ARCHIE!
GOODNESS! I'VE NEVER SEEN YOU SO EXCITED, ARCHIEKINS!
HEH! HEH! I ALWAYS GET EXCITED WHEN I'M ABOUT TO BUY YOU A SODA, LAMBIE!
I'M SORRY, ARCHIEKINS, BUT MAURICE ASKED ME TO HAVE A SODA WITH HIM!
ALREADY? I MEAN, HE DID?!?
THEN HOW'S ABOUT A MOVIE, TONIGHT?
I CAN'T! I'M GOING TO A MOVIE WITH MAURICE TONIGHT!
COME TO THINK OF IT, MAURICE HAS ME DATED SOLID FOR THE NEXT TWO WEEKS!!
TWO WEEKS! YI-II-I!!
THE POOR BOY IS SO LONESOME! AFTER ALL, HE JUST MOVED INTO THIS COUNTRY!
AND NOW HE'S MOVING IN ON ME! CHEE-EE-EEE!
OH-H BROTHER! THAT FRENCHY SURE DOESN'T LOSE ANY TIME! DATED SOLID FOR TWO WEEKS! CHEE-EE-EEE!
HE'S PROB'LY JUST GOT A WAY ABOUT HIM, ARCH!
7

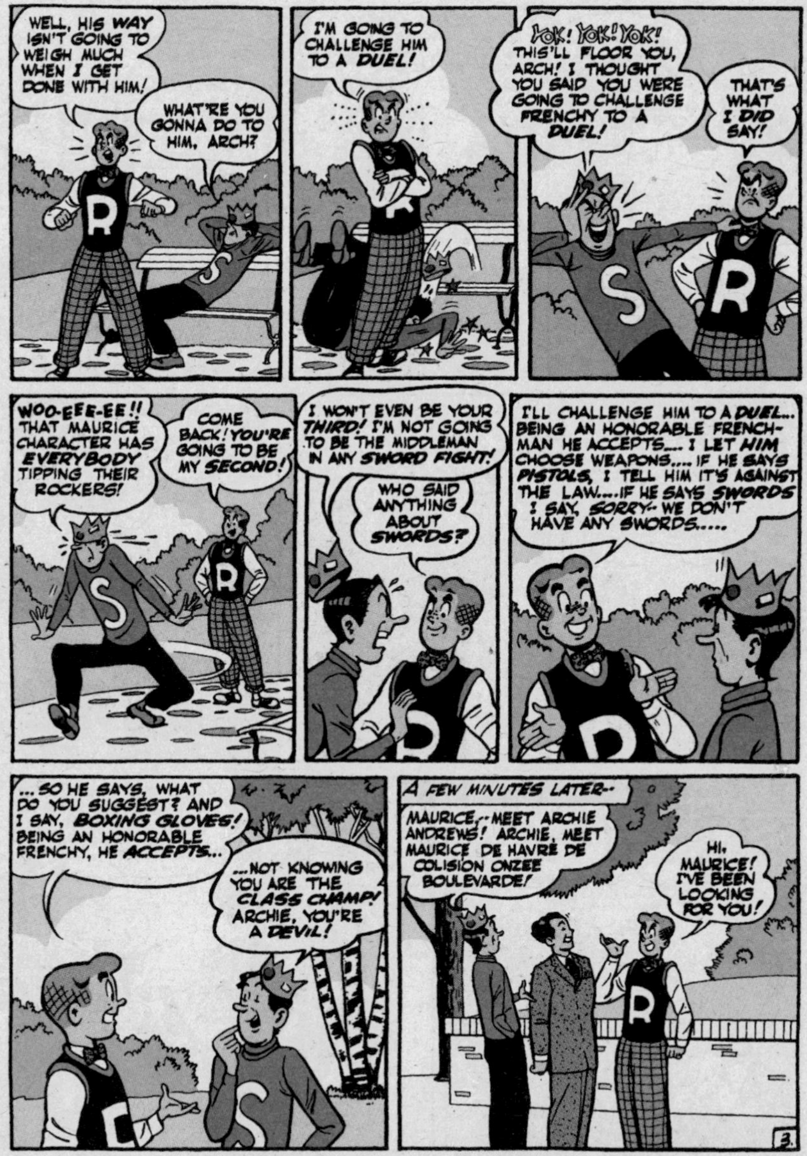
WELL, HIS WAY ISN'T GOING TO WEIGH MUCH WHEN I GET DONE WITH HIM!
WHAT'RE YOU GONNA DO TO HIM, ARCH?
I'M GOING TO CHALLENGE HIM TO A DUEL!
YOK! YOK! YOK! THIS'LL FLOOR YOU, ARCH! I THOUGHT YOU SAID YOU WERE GOING TO CHALLENGE FRENCHY TO A DUEL!
THAT'S WHAT I DID SAY!
WOO-EEE-EE!! THAT MAURICE CHARACTER HAS EVERYBODY TIPPING THEIR ROCKERS!
COME BACK! YOU'RE GOING TO BE MY SECOND!
I WON'T EVEN BE YOUR THIRD! I'M NOT GOING TO BE THE MIDDLEMAN IN ANY SWORD FIGHT!
WHO SAID ANYTHING ABOUT SWORDS?
I'LL CHALLENGE HIM TO A DUEL... BEING AN HONORABLE FRENCHMAN HE ACCEPTS.... I LET HIM CHOOSE WEAPONS.... IF HE SAYS PISTOLS, I TELL HIM IT'S AGAINST THE LAW....IF HE SAYS SWORDS I SAY, SORRY-- WE DON'T HAVE ANY SWORDS.....
... SO HE SAYS, WHAT DO YOU SUGGEST? AND I SAY, BOXING GLOVES! BEING AN HONORABLE FRENCHY, HE ACCEPTS...
...NOT KNOWING YOU ARE THE CLASS CHAMP! ARCHIE, YOU'RE A DEVIL!
A FEW MINUTES LATER--
MAURICE,--MEET ARCHIE ANDREWS! ARCHIE, MEET MAURICE DE HAVRÈ DE COLISION ONZEE BOULEVARDE!
HI, MAURICE! I'VE BEEN LOOKING FOR YOU!
3.

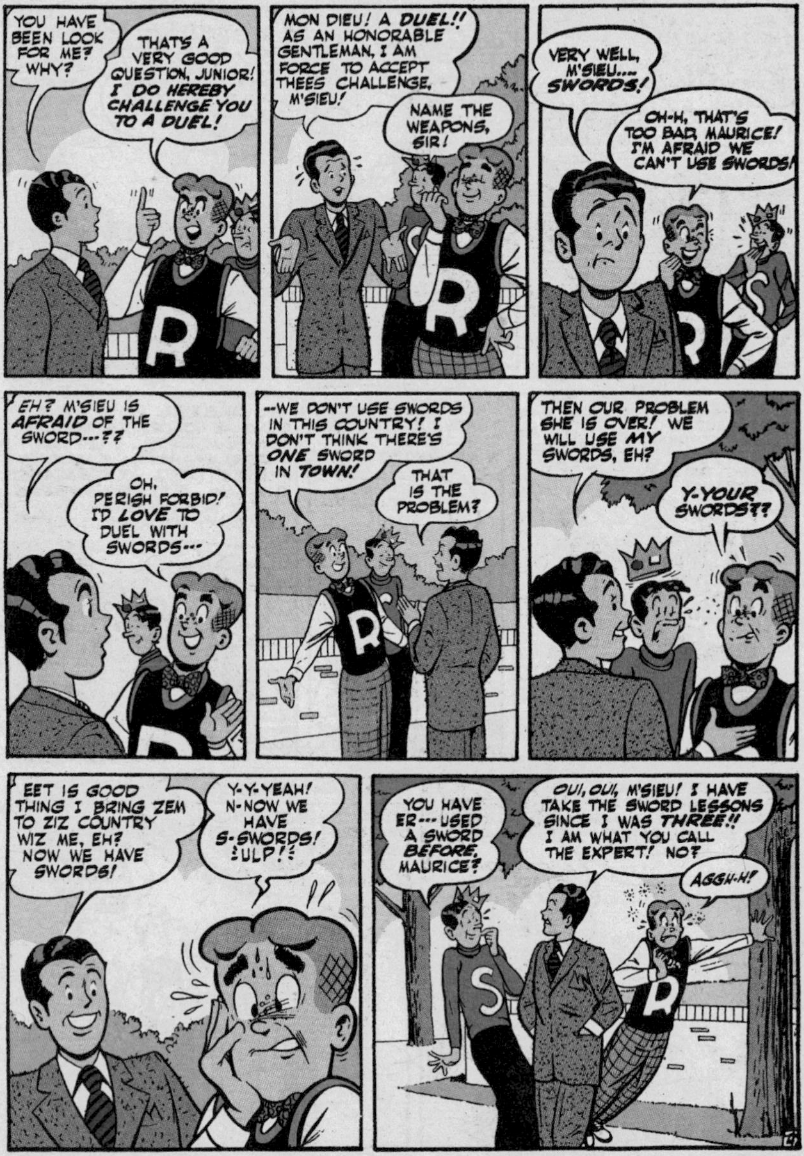
YOU HAVE BEEN LOOK FOR ME? WHY?
THAT'S A VERY GOOD QUESTION, JUNIOR! I DO HEREBY CHALLENGE YOU TO A DUEL!
MON DIEU! A DUEL!! AS AN HONORABLE GENTLEMAN, I AM FORCE TO ACCEPT THEES CHALLENGE, M'SIEU!
NAME THE WEAPONS, SIR!
VERY WELL, M'SIEU.... SWORDS!
OH-H, THAT'S TOO BAD, MAURICE! I'M AFRAID WE CAN'T USE SWORDS!
EH? M'SIEU IS AFRAID OF THE SWORD---??
OH, PERISH FORBID! I'D LOVE TO DUEL WITH SWORDS---
--WE DON'T USE SWORDS IN THIS COUNTRY! I DON'T THINK THERE'S ONE SWORD IN TOWN!
THAT IS THE PROBLEM?
THEN OUR PROBLEM SHE IS OVER! WE WILL USE MY SWORDS, EH?
Y-YOUR SWORDS??
EET IS GOOD THING I BRING ZEM TO ZIZ COUNTRY WIZ ME, EH? NOW WE HAVE SWORDS!
Y-Y-YEAH! N-NOW WE HAVE S-SWORDS! ULP!
YOU HAVE ER--- USED A SWORD BEFORE, MAURICE?
OUI, OUI, M'SIEU! I HAVE TAKE THE SWORD LESSONS SINCE I WAS THREE!! I AM WHAT YOU CALL THE EXPERT! NO?
AGGH-H!
4

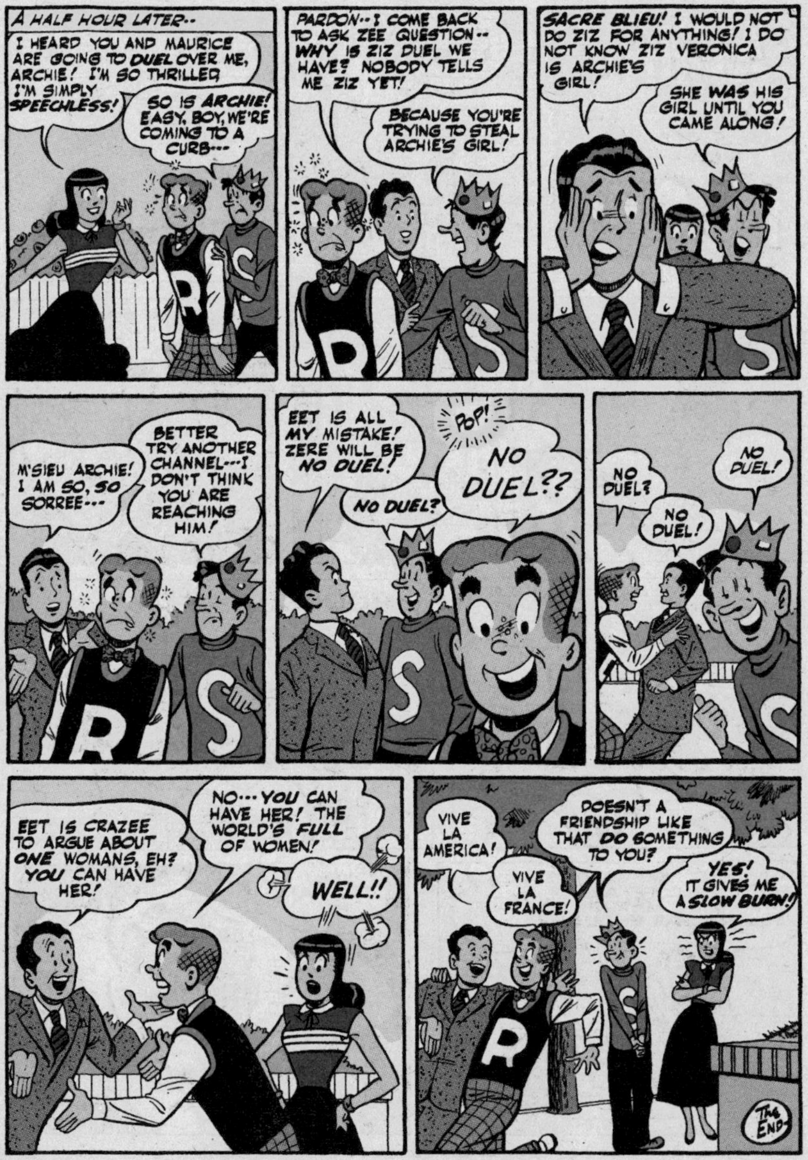

A HALF HOUR LATER--
I HEARD YOU AND MAURICE ARE GOING TO DUEL OVER ME, ARCHIE! I'M SO THRILLED I'M SIMPLY SPEECHLESS!
SO IS ARCHIE! EASY, BOY, WE'RE COMING TO A CURB---
PARDON-- I COME BACK TO ASK ZEE QUESTION-- WHY IS ZIZ DUEL WE HAVE? NOBODY TELLS ME ZIZ YET!
BECAUSE YOU'RE TRYING TO STEAL ARCHIE'S GIRL!
SACRE BLIEU! I WOULD NOT DO ZIZ FOR ANYTHING! I DO NOT KNOW ZIZ VERONICA IS ARCHIE'S GIRL!
SHE WAS HIS GIRL UNTIL YOU CAME ALONG!
M'SIEU ARCHIE! I AM SO, SO SORREE---
BETTER TRY ANOTHER CHANNEL---I DON'T THINK YOU ARE REACHING HIM!
EET IS ALL MY MISTAKE! ZERE WILL BE NO DUEL!
POP!
NO DUEL?
NO DUEL??
NO DUEL?
NO DUEL!
NO DUEL!
EET IS CRAZEE TO ARGUE ABOUT ONE WOMANS, EH? YOU CAN HAVE HER!
NO--- YOU CAN HAVE HER! THE WORLD'S FULL OF WOMEN!
WELL!!
VIVE LA AMERICA!
VIVE LA FRANCE!
DOESN'T A FRIENDSHIP LIKE THAT DO SOMETHING TO YOU?
YES! IT GIVES ME A SLOW BURN!
The End

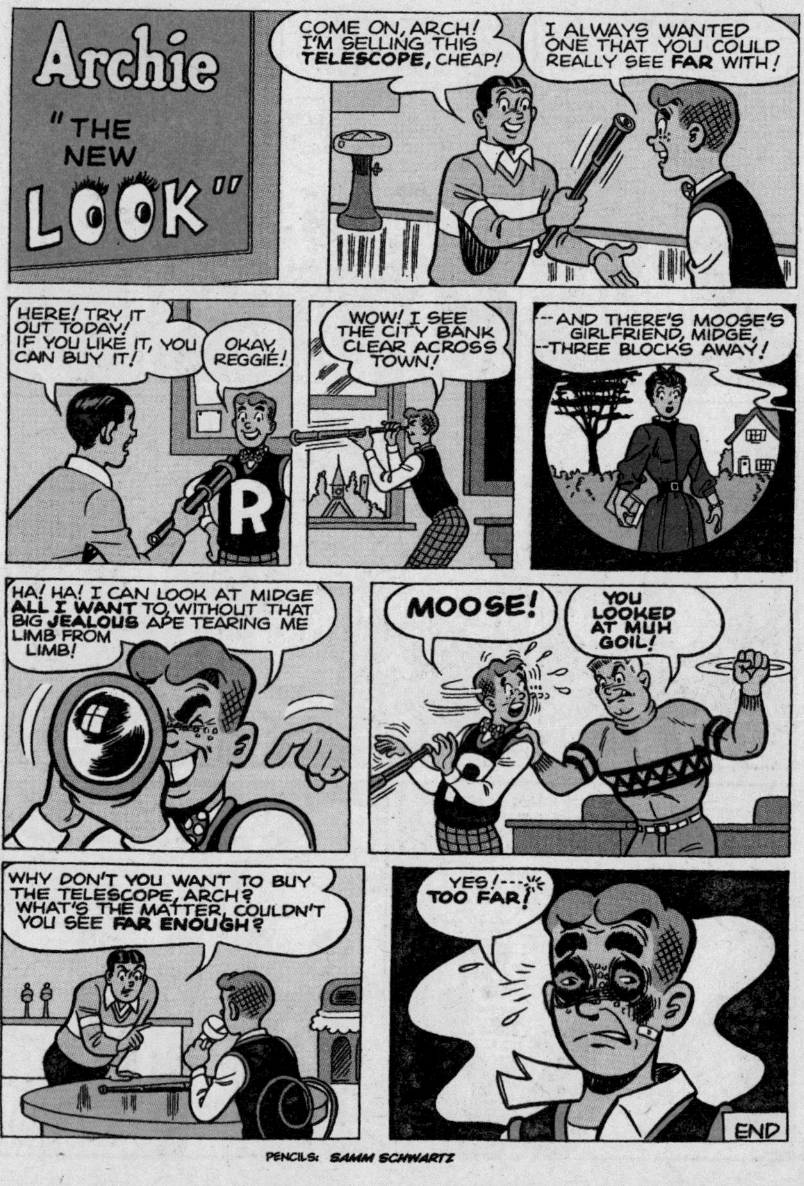
Archie
"THE NEW LOOK"
COME ON, ARCH! I'M SELLING THIS TELESCOPE, CHEAP!
I ALWAYS WANTED ONE THAT YOU COULD REALLY SEE FAR WITH!
HERE! TRY IT OUT TODAY! IF YOU LIKE IT, YOU CAN BUY IT!
OKAY, REGGIE!
WOW! I SEE THE CITY BANK CLEAR ACROSS TOWN!
--AND THERE'S MOOSE'S GIRLFRIEND, MIDGE, --THREE BLOCKS AWAY!
HA! HA! I CAN LOOK AT MIDGE ALL I WANT TO, WITHOUT THAT BIG JEALOUS APE TEARING ME LIMB FROM LIMB!
MOOSE!
YOU LOOKED AT MUH GOIL!
WHY DON'T YOU WANT TO BUY THE TELESCOPE, ARCH? WHAT'S THE MATTER, COULDN'T YOU SEE FAR ENOUGH?
YES!--- TOO FAR!
END

PENCILS: SAMM SCHWARTZ

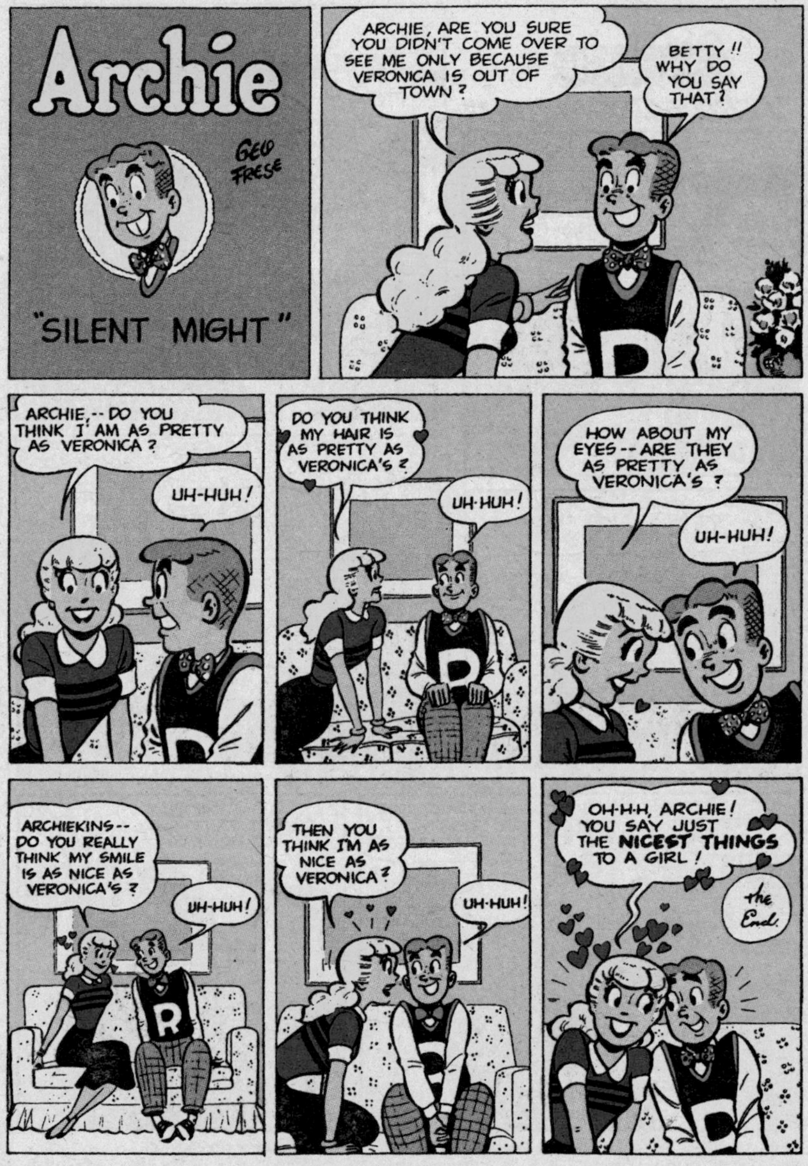
Archie
GEO FRESE
"SILENT MIGHT"
ARCHIE, ARE YOU SURE YOU DIDN'T COME OVER TO SEE ME ONLY BECAUSE VERONICA IS OUT OF TOWN?
BETTY!! WHY DO YOU SAY THAT?
ARCHIE,-- DO YOU THINK I'AM AS PRETTY AS VERONICA?
UH-HUH!
DO YOU THINK MY HAIR IS AS PRETTY AS VERONICA'S?
UH-HUH!
HOW ABOUT MY EYES--ARE THEY AS PRETTY AS VERONICA'S?
UH-HUH!
ARCHIEKINS-- DO YOU REALLY THINK MY SMILE IS AS NICE AS VERONICA'S?
UH-HUH!
THEN YOU THINK I'M AS NICE AS VERONICA?
UH-HUH!
OH-H-H, ARCHIE! YOU SAY JUST THE NICEST THINGS TO A GIRL!
the End.

Archie
"FEUD FOR THOUGHT"

HI, LAMB CHOP!

ARCHIEKINS! I'M GLAD YOU CAME OVER TONIGHT!

HOW!

HELLO JUGHEAD!

HEH! HEH! OL' JUG DIDN'T HAVE ANYTHING TO DO, SO I BROUGHT HIM ALONG!

SO I SEE! WHAT WOULD YOU BOYS LIKE TO DO?

I DUNNO! HOW ABOUT YOU, JUG?

WHAT'S TO EAT?

{SIGH!} THERE'S A GOOD LOVE STORY ON TV!

LOVE STORY? ...PHOOEY!

THERE'S A KEEN WESTERN ON CHANNEL FOUR!

GOOD! GOOD! ...TURN IT ON, JUG!

IT SO HAPPENS I PREFER THE LOVE STORY!

TUT! TUT! JUGHEAD IS YOUR GUEST! YOU DON'T WANT HIM TO FEEL HE'S NOT WANTED, DO YOU?

THAT'S EXACTLY HOW I WANT HIM TO FEEL!

PENCILS: HARRY LUCEY   INKS & LETTERS: TERRY SZENICS

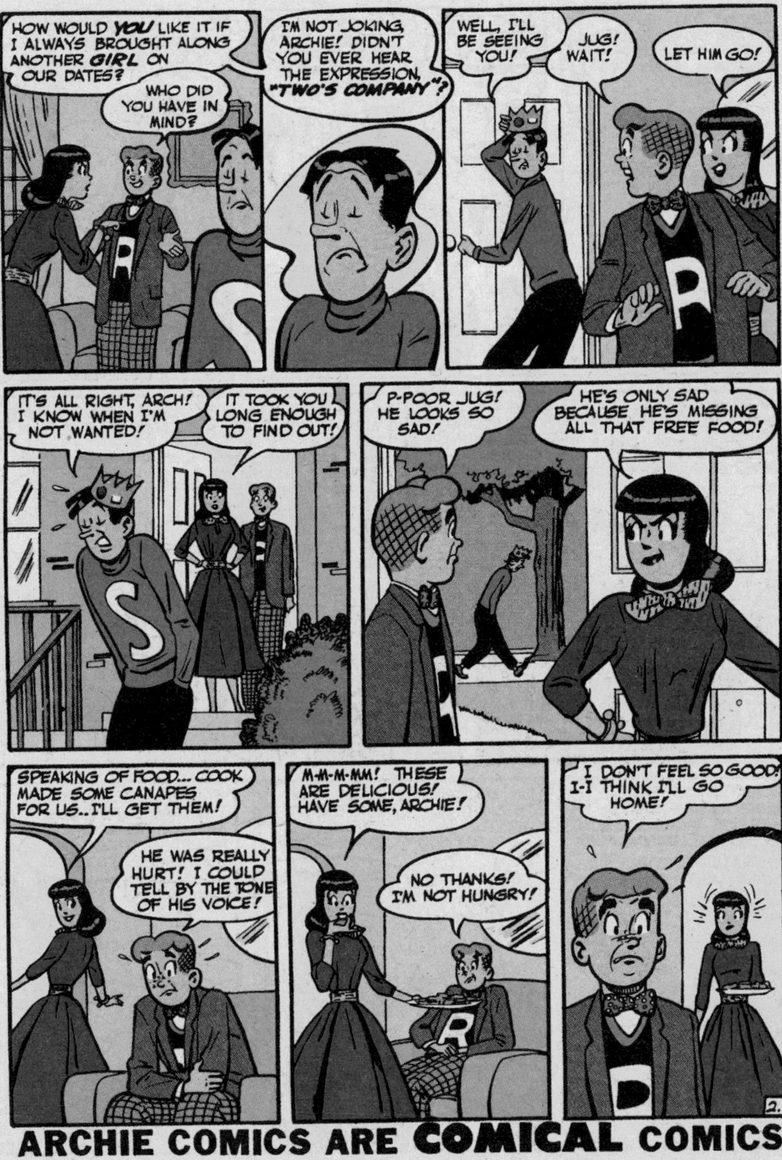
HOW WOULD YOU LIKE IT IF I ALWAYS BROUGHT ALONG ANOTHER GIRL ON OUR DATES?
WHO DID YOU HAVE IN MIND?
I'M NOT JOKING, ARCHIE! DIDN'T YOU EVER HEAR THE EXPRESSION, "TWO'S COMPANY"?
WELL, I'LL BE SEEING YOU!
JUG! WAIT!
LET HIM GO!
IT'S ALL RIGHT, ARCH! I KNOW WHEN I'M NOT WANTED!
IT TOOK YOU LONG ENOUGH TO FIND OUT!
P-POOR JUG! HE LOOKS SO SAD!
HE'S ONLY SAD BECAUSE HE'S MISSING ALL THAT FREE FOOD!
SPEAKING OF FOOD... COOK MADE SOME CANAPES FOR US..I'LL GET THEM!
HE WAS REALLY HURT! I COULD TELL BY THE TONE OF HIS VOICE!
M-M-M-MM! THESE ARE DELICIOUS! HAVE SOME, ARCHIE!
NO THANKS! I'M NOT HUNGRY!
I DON'T FEEL SO GOOD! I-I THINK I'LL GO HOME!
2.

ARCHIE COMICS ARE **COMICAL** COMICS

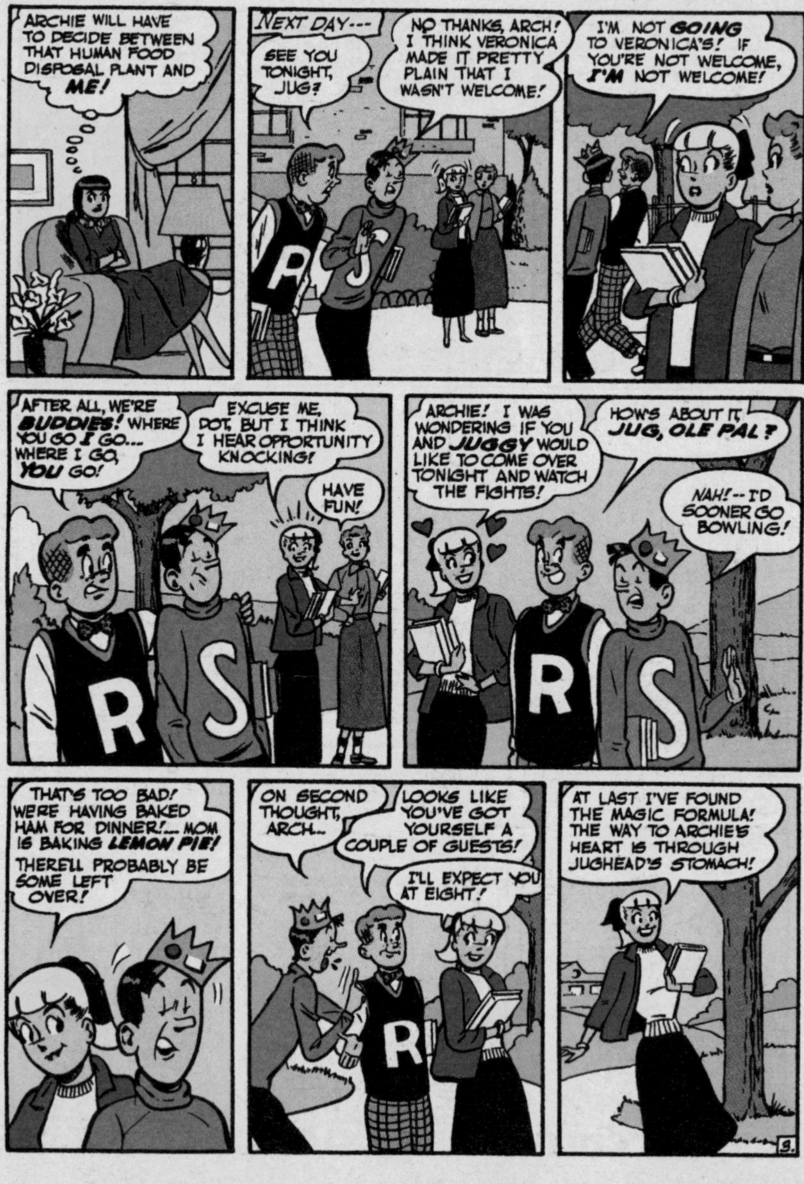

ARCHIE WILL HAVE TO DECIDE BETWEEN THAT HUMAN FOOD DISPOSAL PLANT AND ME!
NEXT DAY---
SEE YOU TONIGHT, JUG?
NO THANKS, ARCH! I THINK VERONICA MADE IT PRETTY PLAIN THAT I WASN'T WELCOME!
I'M NOT GOING TO VERONICA'S! IF YOU'RE NOT WELCOME, I'M NOT WELCOME!
AFTER ALL, WE'RE BUDDIES! WHERE YOU GO I GO... WHERE I GO, YOU GO!
EXCUSE ME, DOT, BUT I THINK I HEAR OPPORTUNITY KNOCKING!
HAVE FUN!
ARCHIE! I WAS WONDERING IF YOU AND JUGGY WOULD LIKE TO COME OVER TONIGHT AND WATCH THE FIGHTS!
HOW'S ABOUT IT, JUG, OLE PAL?
NAH! -- I'D SOONER GO BOWLING!
THAT'S TOO BAD! WE'RE HAVING BAKED HAM FOR DINNER!... MOM IS BAKING LEMON PIE!
THERE'LL PROBABLY BE SOME LEFT OVER!
ON SECOND THOUGHT, ARCH...
LOOKS LIKE YOU'VE GOT YOURSELF A COUPLE OF GUESTS!
I'LL EXPECT YOU AT EIGHT!
AT LAST I'VE FOUND THE MAGIC FORMULA! THE WAY TO ARCHIE'S HEART IS THROUGH JUGHEAD'S STOMACH!
9.

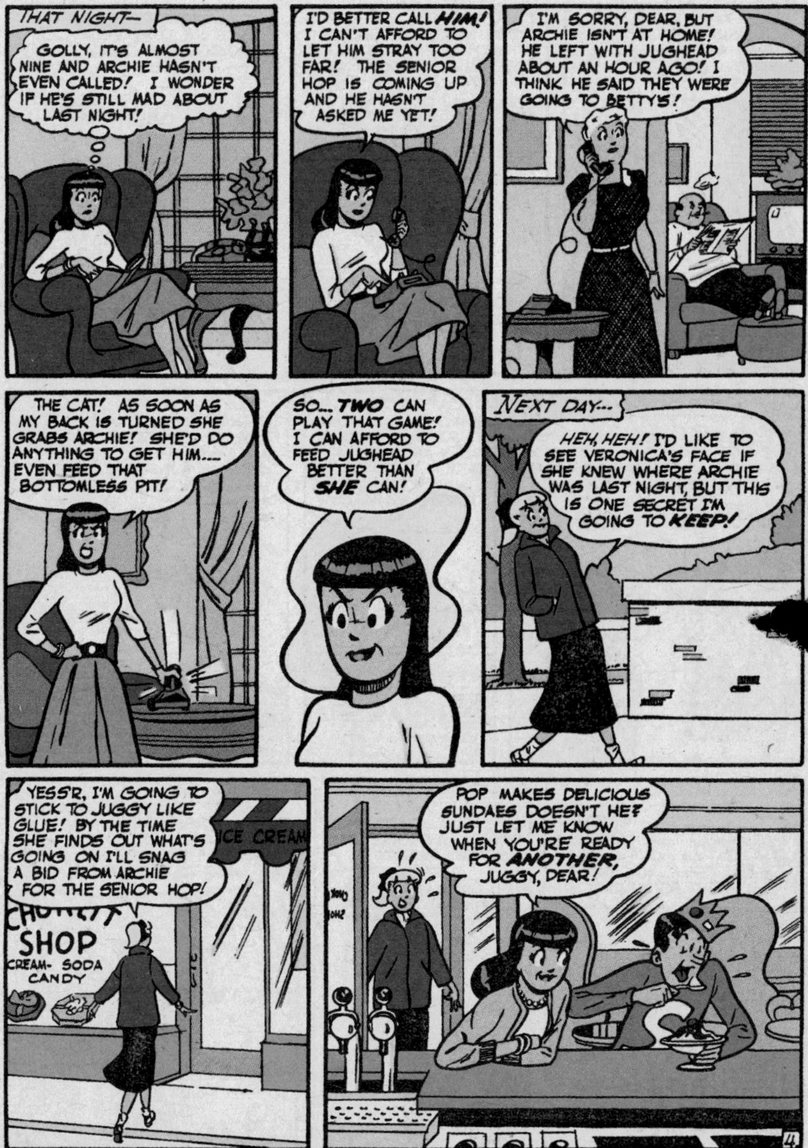
THAT NIGHT—
GOLLY, IT'S ALMOST NINE AND ARCHIE HASN'T EVEN CALLED! I WONDER IF HE'S STILL MAD ABOUT LAST NIGHT!
I'D BETTER CALL HIM! I CAN'T AFFORD TO LET HIM STRAY TOO FAR! THE SENIOR HOP IS COMING UP AND HE HASN'T ASKED ME YET!
I'M SORRY, DEAR, BUT ARCHIE ISN'T AT HOME! HE LEFT WITH JUGHEAD ABOUT AN HOUR AGO! I THINK HE SAID THEY WERE GOING TO BETTY'S!
THE CAT! AS SOON AS MY BACK IS TURNED SHE GRABS ARCHIE! SHE'D DO ANYTHING TO GET HIM.... EVEN FEED THAT BOTTOMLESS PIT!
SO... TWO CAN PLAY THAT GAME! I CAN AFFORD TO FEED JUGHEAD BETTER THAN SHE CAN!
NEXT DAY...
HEH, HEH! I'D LIKE TO SEE VERONICA'S FACE IF SHE KNEW WHERE ARCHIE WAS LAST NIGHT, BUT THIS IS ONE SECRET I'M GOING TO KEEP!
YESS'R, I'M GOING TO STICK TO JUGGY LIKE GLUE! BY THE TIME SHE FINDS OUT WHAT'S GOING ON I'LL SNAG A BID FROM ARCHIE FOR THE SENIOR HOP!
ICE CREAM
SHOP
CREAM- SODA
CANDY
POP MAKES DELICIOUS SUNDAES DOESN'T HE? JUST LET ME KNOW WHEN YOU'RE READY FOR ANOTHER, JUGGY, DEAR!
4

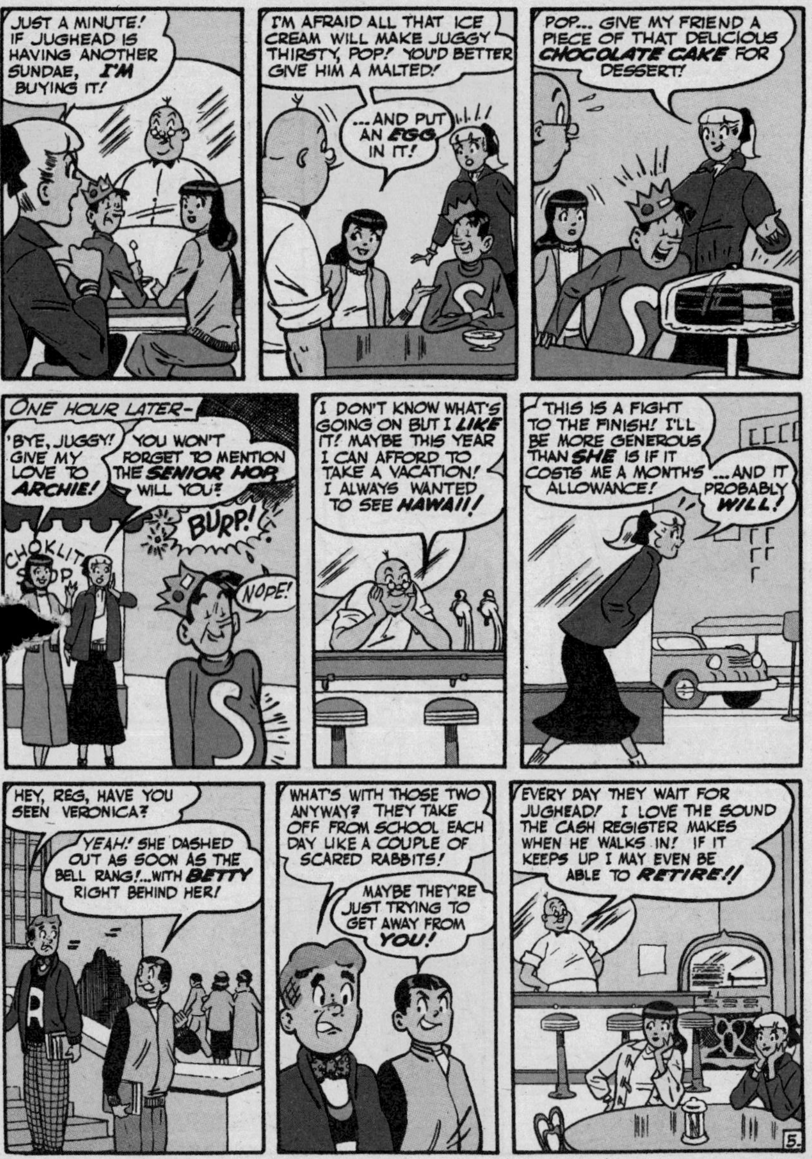

JUST A MINUTE! IF JUGHEAD IS HAVING ANOTHER SUNDAE, I'M BUYING IT!
I'M AFRAID ALL THAT ICE CREAM WILL MAKE JUGGY THIRSTY, POP! YOU'D BETTER GIVE HIM A MALTED!
...AND PUT AN EGG IN IT!
POP... GIVE MY FRIEND A PIECE OF THAT DELICIOUS CHOCOLATE CAKE FOR DESSERT!
ONE HOUR LATER-
'BYE, JUGGY! GIVE MY LOVE TO ARCHIE!
YOU WON'T FORGET TO MENTION THE SENIOR HOP, WILL YOU?
CHOKLIT SHOP
BURP!
NOPE!
I DON'T KNOW WHAT'S GOING ON BUT I LIKE IT! MAYBE THIS YEAR I CAN AFFORD TO TAKE A VACATION! I ALWAYS WANTED TO SEE HAWAII!
THIS IS A FIGHT TO THE FINISH! I'LL BE MORE GENEROUS THAN SHE IS IF IT COSTS ME A MONTH'S ALLOWANCE!
...AND IT PROBABLY WILL!
HEY, REG, HAVE YOU SEEN VERONICA?
YEAH! SHE DASHED OUT AS SOON AS THE BELL RANG!...WITH BETTY RIGHT BEHIND HER!
WHAT'S WITH THOSE TWO ANYWAY? THEY TAKE OFF FROM SCHOOL EACH DAY LIKE A COUPLE OF SCARED RABBITS!
MAYBE THEY'RE JUST TRYING TO GET AWAY FROM YOU!
EVERY DAY THEY WAIT FOR JUGHEAD! I LOVE THE SOUND THE CASH REGISTER MAKES WHEN HE WALKS IN! IF IT KEEPS UP I MAY EVEN BE ABLE TO RETIRE!!

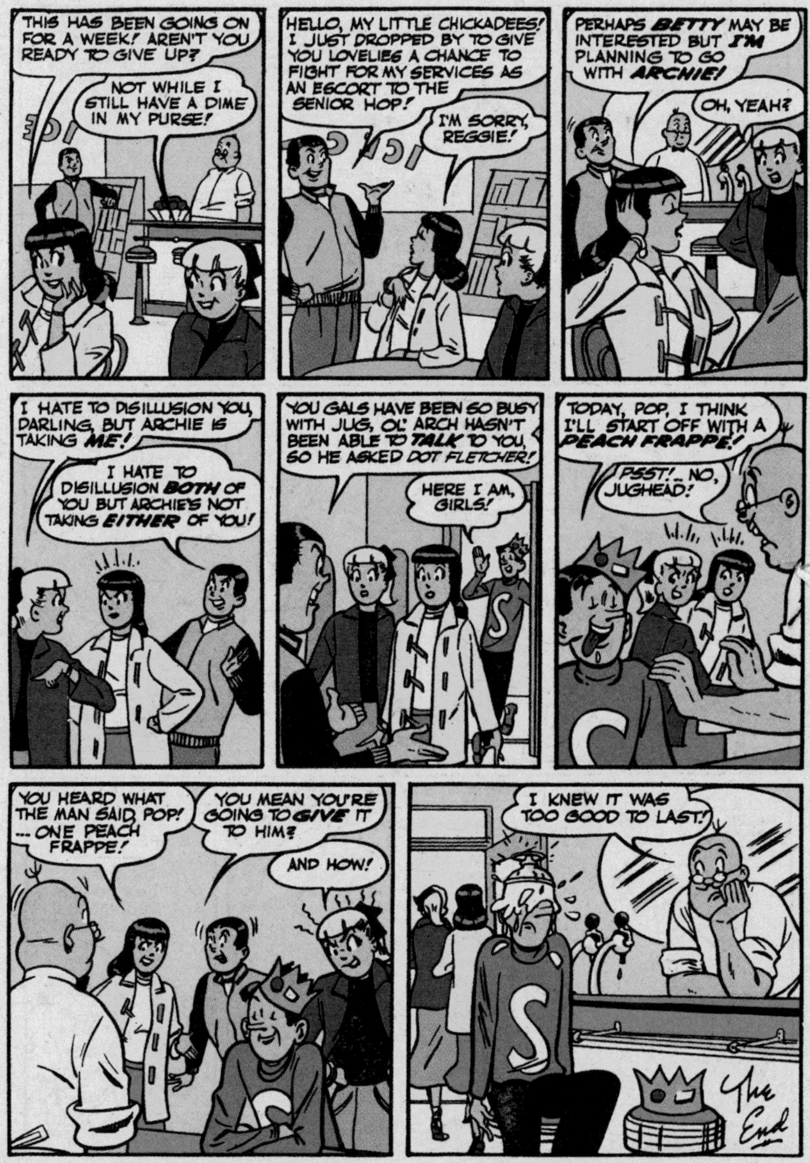
THIS HAS BEEN GOING ON FOR A WEEK! AREN'T YOU READY TO GIVE UP?
NOT WHILE I STILL HAVE A DIME IN MY PURSE!
HELLO, MY LITTLE CHICKADEES! I JUST DROPPED BY TO GIVE YOU LOVELIES A CHANCE TO FIGHT FOR MY SERVICES AS AN ESCORT TO THE SENIOR HOP!
I'M SORRY, REGGIE!
PERHAPS BETTY MAY BE INTERESTED BUT I'M PLANNING TO GO WITH ARCHIE!
OH, YEAH?
I HATE TO DISILLUSION YOU, DARLING, BUT ARCHIE IS TAKING ME!
I HATE TO DISILLUSION BOTH OF YOU BUT ARCHIE'S NOT TAKING EITHER OF YOU!
YOU GALS HAVE BEEN SO BUSY WITH JUG, OL' ARCH HASN'T BEEN ABLE TO TALK TO YOU, SO HE ASKED DOT FLETCHER!
HERE I AM, GIRLS!
TODAY, POP, I THINK I'LL START OFF WITH A PEACH FRAPPE!
PSST! _ NO, JUGHEAD!
YOU HEARD WHAT THE MAN SAID, POP! ... ONE PEACH FRAPPE!
YOU MEAN YOU'RE GOING TO GIVE IT TO HIM?
AND HOW!
I KNEW IT WAS TOO GOOD TO LAST!
The End

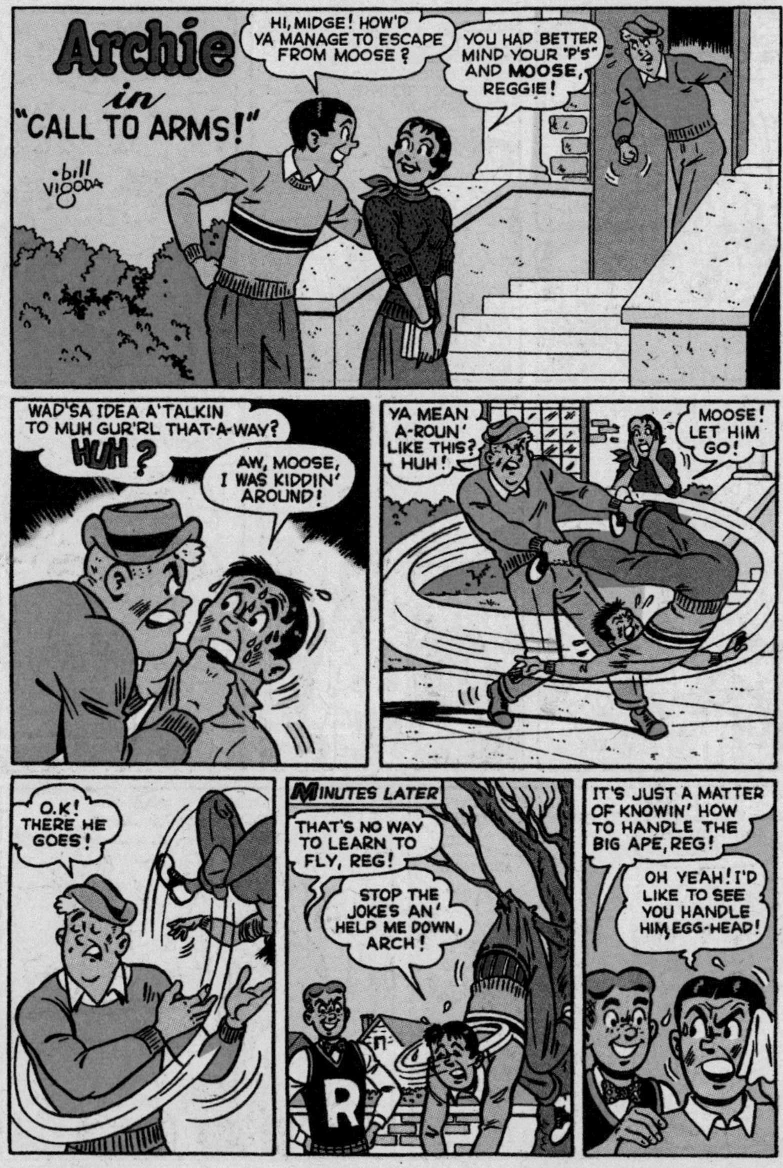
Archie
in
"CALL TO ARMS!"
bill VIGODA
HI, MIDGE! HOW'D YA MANAGE TO ESCAPE FROM MOOSE?
YOU HAD BETTER MIND YOUR "P'S" AND MOOSE, REGGIE!
WAD'SA IDEA A'TALKIN TO MUH GUR'RL THAT-A-WAY? HUH?
AW, MOOSE, I WAS KIDDIN' AROUND!
YA MEAN A-ROUN' LIKE THIS? HUH!
MOOSE! LET HIM GO!
O.K! THERE HE GOES!
MINUTES LATER
THAT'S NO WAY TO LEARN TO FLY, REG!
STOP THE JOKES AN' HELP ME DOWN, ARCH!
IT'S JUST A MATTER OF KNOWIN' HOW TO HANDLE THE BIG APE, REG!
OH YEAH! I'D LIKE TO SEE YOU HANDLE HIM, EGG-HEAD!

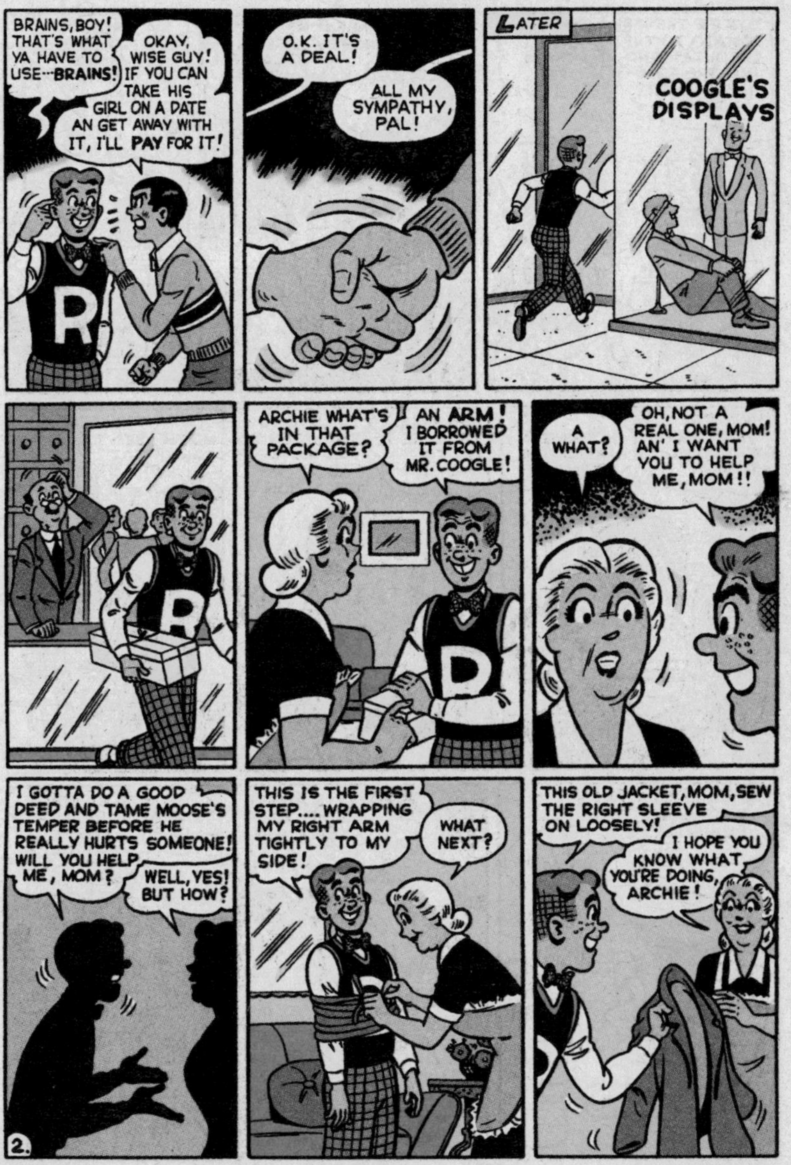
BRAINS, BOY! THAT'S WHAT YA HAVE TO USE···BRAINS!
OKAY, WISE GUY! IF YOU CAN TAKE HIS GIRL ON A DATE AN GET AWAY WITH IT, I'LL PAY FOR IT!
O.K. IT'S A DEAL!
ALL MY SYMPATHY, PAL!
LATER
COOGLE'S DISPLAYS
ARCHIE WHAT'S IN THAT PACKAGE?
AN ARM! I BORROWED IT FROM MR. COOGLE!
A WHAT?
OH, NOT A REAL ONE, MOM! AN' I WANT YOU TO HELP ME, MOM!!
I GOTTA DO A GOOD DEED AND TAME MOOSE'S TEMPER BEFORE HE REALLY HURTS SOMEONE! WILL YOU HELP ME, MOM?
WELL, YES! BUT HOW?
2.
THIS IS THE FIRST STEP.... WRAPPING MY RIGHT ARM TIGHTLY TO MY SIDE!
WHAT NEXT?
THIS OLD JACKET, MOM, SEW THE RIGHT SLEEVE ON LOOSELY!
I HOPE YOU KNOW WHAT YOU'RE DOING, ARCHIE!

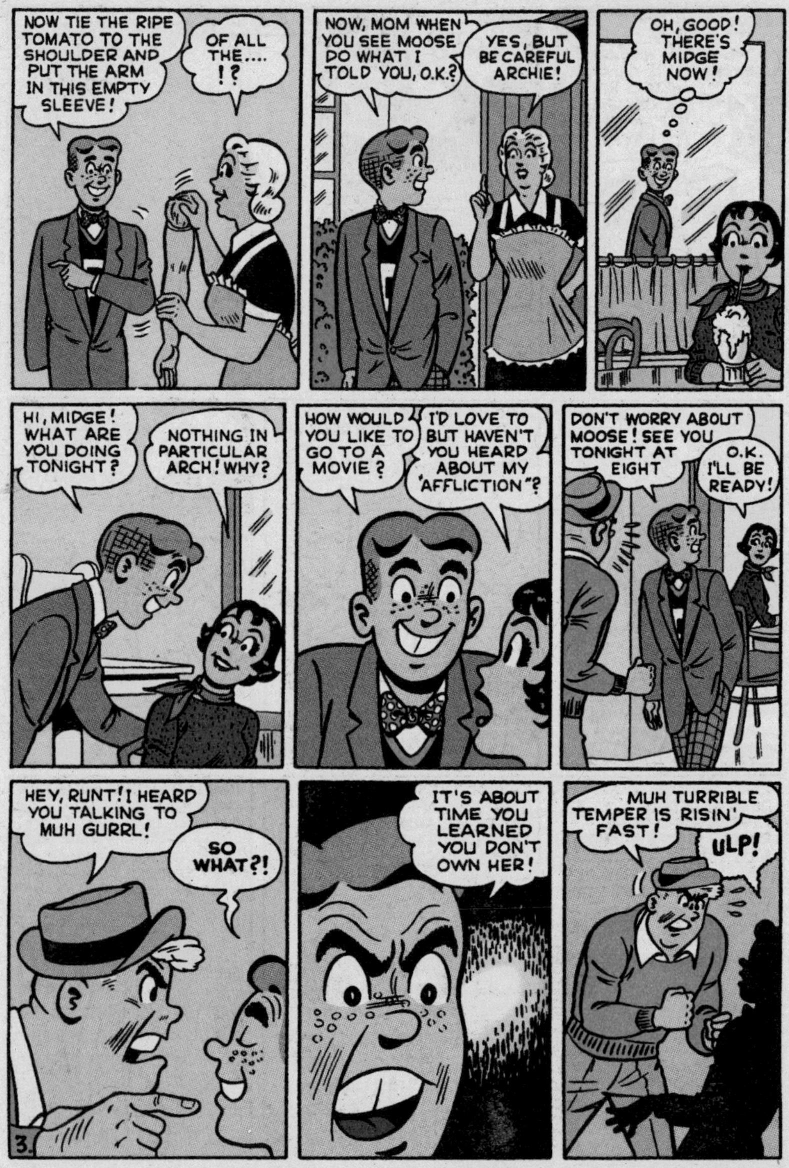
NOW TIE THE RIPE TOMATO TO THE SHOULDER AND PUT THE ARM IN THIS EMPTY SLEEVE!
OF ALL THE.... !?
NOW, MOM WHEN YOU SEE MOOSE DO WHAT I TOLD YOU, O.K.?
YES, BUT BE CAREFUL ARCHIE!
OH, GOOD! THERE'S MIDGE NOW!
HI, MIDGE! WHAT ARE YOU DOING TONIGHT?
NOTHING IN PARTICULAR ARCH! WHY?
HOW WOULD YOU LIKE TO GO TO A MOVIE?
I'D LOVE TO BUT HAVEN'T YOU HEARD ABOUT MY 'AFFLICTION"?
DON'T WORRY ABOUT MOOSE! SEE YOU TONIGHT AT EIGHT
O.K. I'LL BE READY!
HEY, RUNT! I HEARD YOU TALKING TO MUH GURRL!
SO WHAT?!
IT'S ABOUT TIME YOU LEARNED YOU DON'T OWN HER!
MUH TURRIBLE TEMPER IS RISIN' FAST!
ULP!
3.

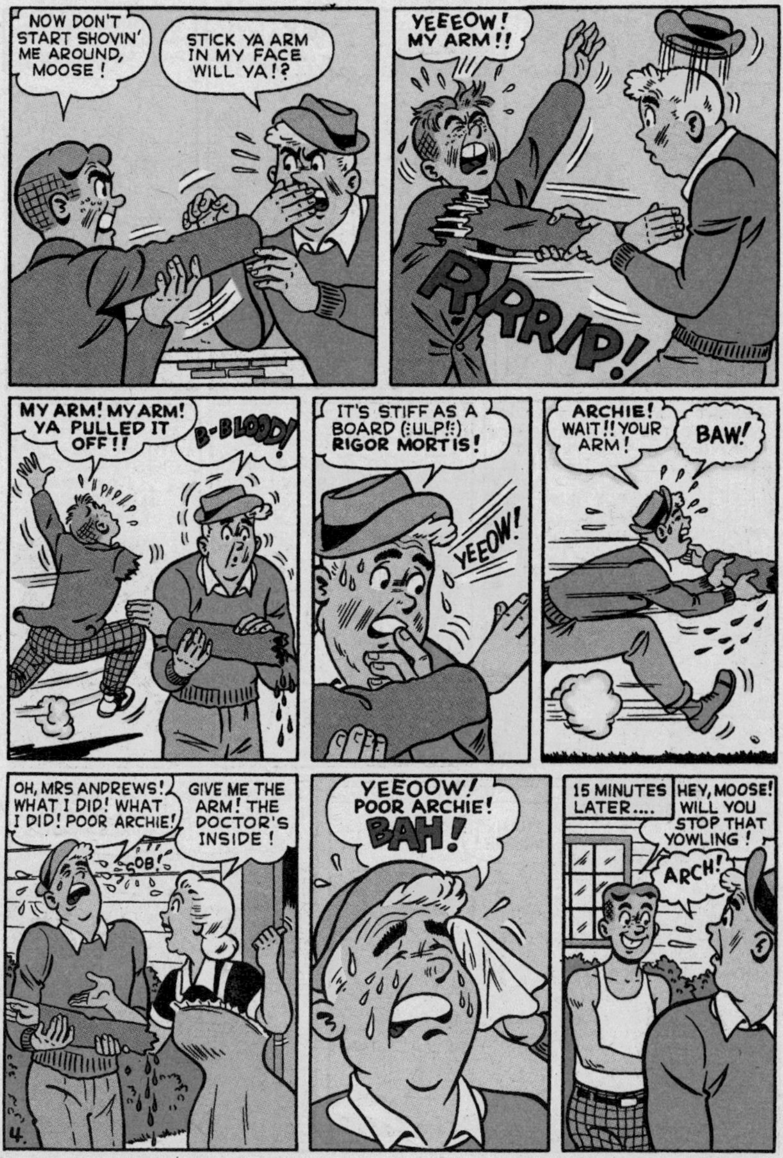
NOW DON'T START SHOVIN' ME AROUND, MOOSE!
STICK YA ARM IN MY FACE WILL YA!?
YEEEOW! MY ARM!!
RRRIP!
MY ARM! MY ARM! YA PULLED IT OFF!!
B-BLOOD!?
IT'S STIFF AS A BOARD (ULP!) RIGOR MORTIS!
YEEOW!
ARCHIE! WAIT!! YOUR ARM!
BAW!
OH, MRS ANDREWS! WHAT I DID! WHAT I DID! POOR ARCHIE!
SOB!
GIVE ME THE ARM! THE DOCTOR'S INSIDE!
YEEOOW! POOR ARCHIE! BAH!
15 MINUTES LATER....
HEY, MOOSE! WILL YOU STOP THAT YOWLING!
ARCH!
4.

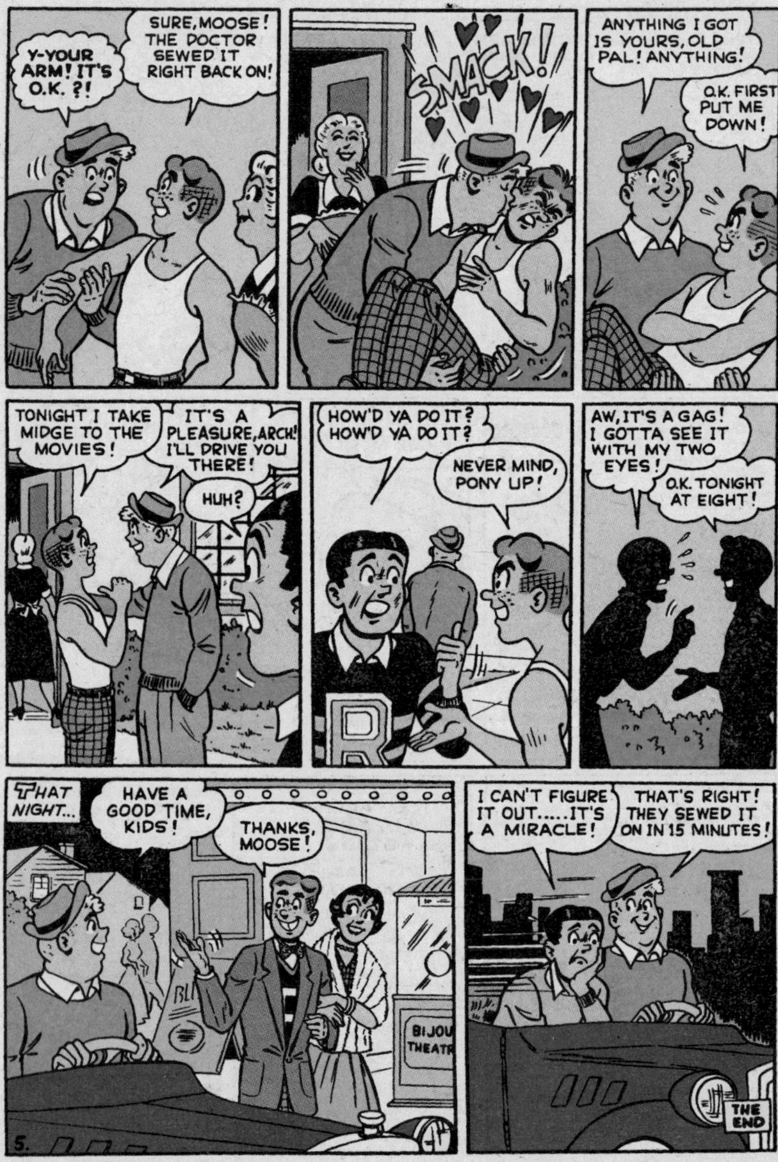

Y-YOUR ARM! IT'S O.K. ?!
SURE, MOOSE! THE DOCTOR SEWED IT RIGHT BACK ON!
SMACK!
ANYTHING I GOT IS YOURS, OLD PAL! ANYTHING!
O.K. FIRST PUT ME DOWN!
TONIGHT I TAKE MIDGE TO THE MOVIES!
IT'S A PLEASURE, ARCH! I'LL DRIVE YOU THERE!
HUH?
HOW'D YA DO IT? HOW'D YA DO IT?
NEVER MIND, PONY UP!
AW, IT'S A GAG! I GOTTA SEE IT WITH MY TWO EYES!
O.K. TONIGHT AT EIGHT!
THAT NIGHT...
HAVE A GOOD TIME, KIDS!
THANKS, MOOSE!
BIJOU THEATR
I CAN'T FIGURE IT OUT.....IT'S A MIRACLE!
THAT'S RIGHT! THEY SEWED IT ON IN 15 MINUTES!
THE END

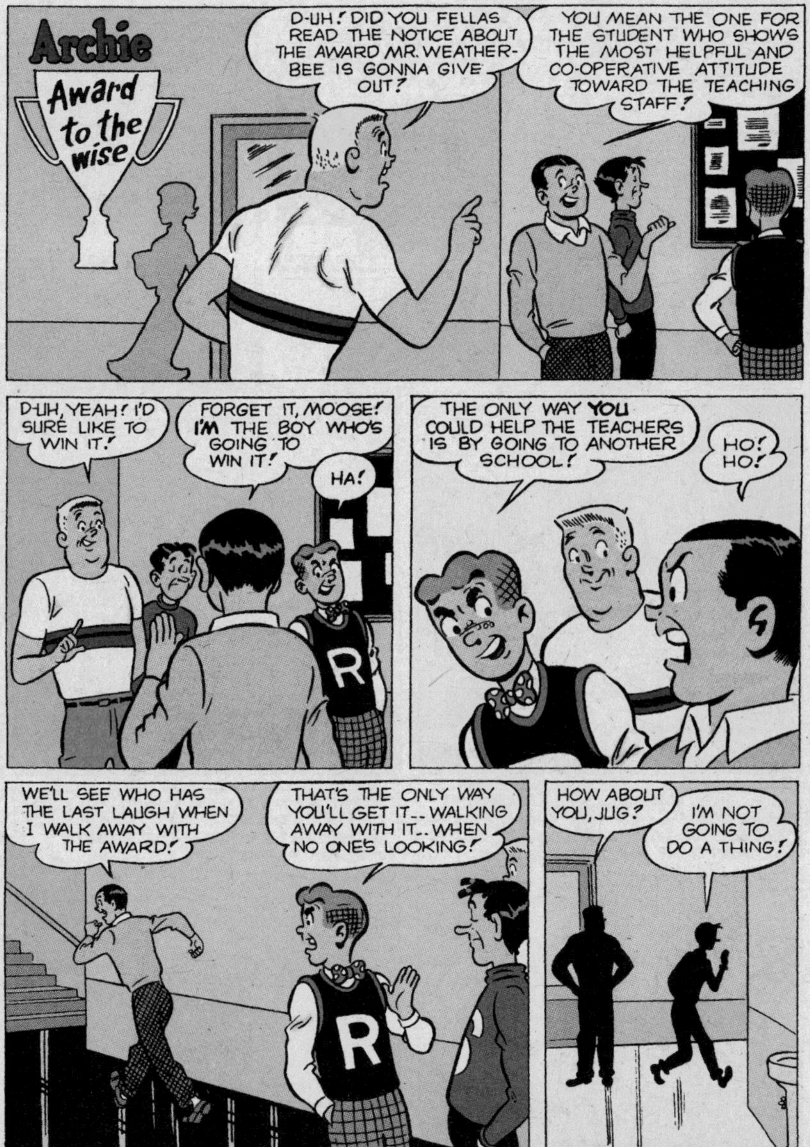
Archie
Award to the wise
D-UH! DID YOU FELLAS READ THE NOTICE ABOUT THE AWARD MR. WEATHERBEE IS GONNA GIVE OUT?
YOU MEAN THE ONE FOR THE STUDENT WHO SHOWS THE MOST HELPFUL AND CO-OPERATIVE ATTITUDE TOWARD THE TEACHING STAFF!
D-UH, YEAH! I'D SURE LIKE TO WIN IT!
FORGET IT, MOOSE! I'M THE BOY WHO'S GOING TO WIN IT!
HA!
THE ONLY WAY YOU COULD HELP THE TEACHERS IS BY GOING TO ANOTHER SCHOOL!
HO! HO!
WE'LL SEE WHO HAS THE LAST LAUGH WHEN I WALK AWAY WITH THE AWARD!
THAT'S THE ONLY WAY YOU'LL GET IT.. WALKING AWAY WITH IT.. WHEN NO ONE'S LOOKING!
HOW ABOUT YOU, JUG?
I'M NOT GOING TO DO A THING!

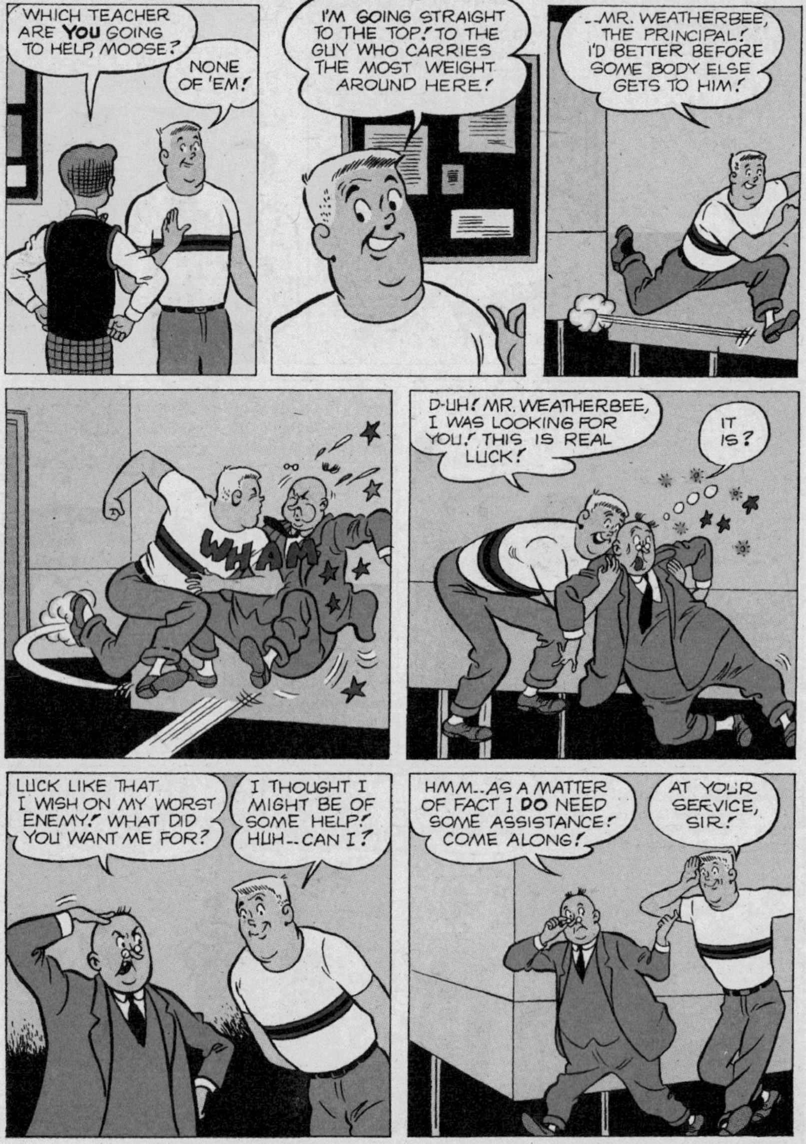
WHICH TEACHER ARE **YOU** GOING TO HELP, MOOSE?
NONE OF 'EM!
I'M GOING STRAIGHT TO THE TOP! TO THE GUY WHO CARRIES THE MOST WEIGHT AROUND HERE!
--MR. WEATHERBEE, THE PRINCIPAL! I'D BETTER BEFORE SOME BODY ELSE GETS TO HIM!
WHAM
D-UH! MR. WEATHERBEE, I WAS LOOKING FOR YOU! THIS IS REAL LUCK!
IT IS?
LUCK LIKE THAT I WISH ON MY WORST ENEMY! WHAT DID YOU WANT ME FOR?
I THOUGHT I MIGHT BE OF SOME HELP! HUH--CAN I?
HMM..AS A MATTER OF FACT I **DO** NEED SOME ASSISTANCE! COME ALONG!
AT YOUR SERVICE, SIR!

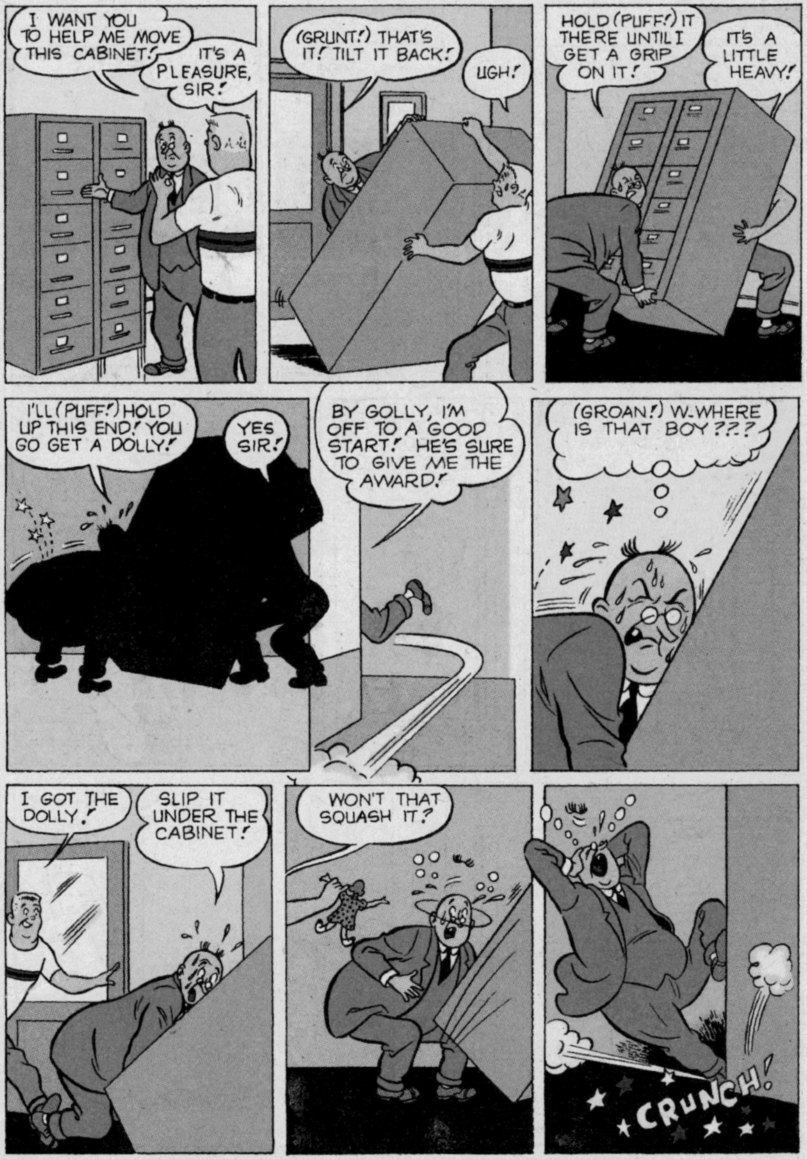
I WANT YOU TO HELP ME MOVE THIS CABINET!
IT'S A PLEASURE, SIR!
(GRUNT!) THAT'S IT! TILT IT BACK!
UGH!
HOLD (PUFF!) IT THERE UNTIL I GET A GRIP ON IT!
IT'S A LITTLE HEAVY!
I'LL (PUFF!) HOLD UP THIS END! YOU GO GET A DOLLY!
YES SIR!
BY GOLLY, I'M OFF TO A GOOD START! HE'S SURE TO GIVE ME THE AWARD!
(GROAN!) W-WHERE IS THAT BOY ???
I GOT THE DOLLY!
SLIP IT UNDER THE CABINET!
WON'T THAT SQUASH IT?
CRUNCH!

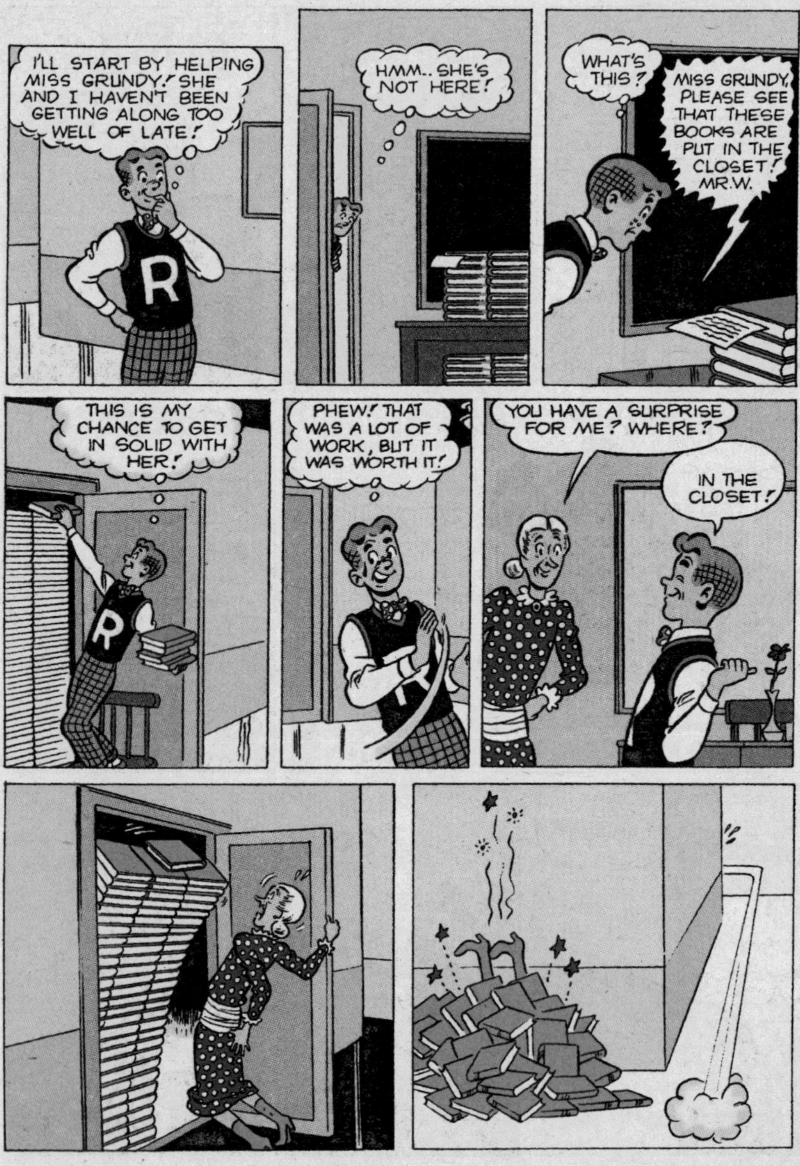
I'LL START BY HELPING MISS GRUNDY! SHE AND I HAVEN'T BEEN GETTING ALONG TOO WELL OF LATE!
HMM.. SHE'S NOT HERE!
WHAT'S THIS?
MISS GRUNDY, PLEASE SEE THAT THESE BOOKS ARE PUT IN THE CLOSET! MR.W.
THIS IS MY CHANCE TO GET IN SOLID WITH HER!
PHEW! THAT WAS A LOT OF WORK, BUT IT WAS WORTH IT!
YOU HAVE A SURPRISE FOR ME? WHERE?
IN THE CLOSET!

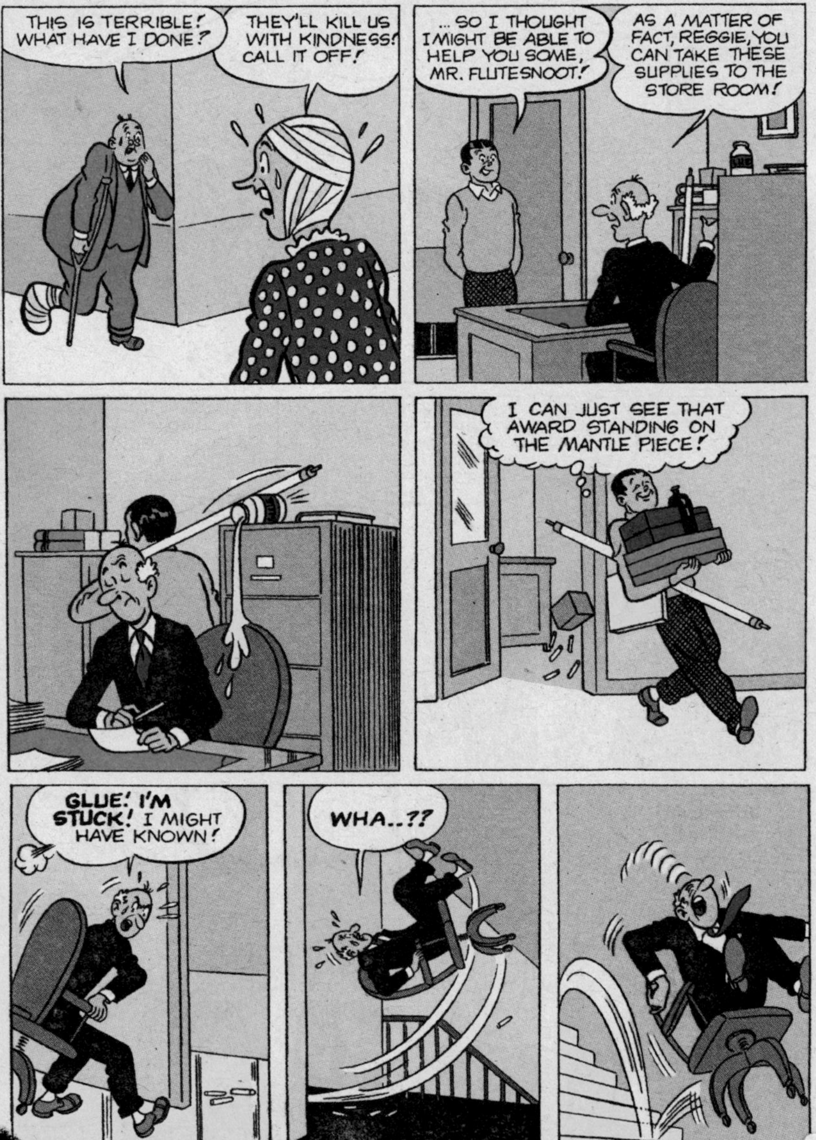
THIS IS TERRIBLE! WHAT HAVE I DONE?
THEY'LL KILL US WITH KINDNESS! CALL IT OFF!
... SO I THOUGHT I MIGHT BE ABLE TO HELP YOU SOME, MR. FLUTESNOOT!
AS A MATTER OF FACT, REGGIE, YOU CAN TAKE THESE SUPPLIES TO THE STORE ROOM!
I CAN JUST SEE THAT AWARD STANDING ON THE MANTLE PIECE!
GLUE! I'M STUCK! I MIGHT HAVE KNOWN!
WHA..??

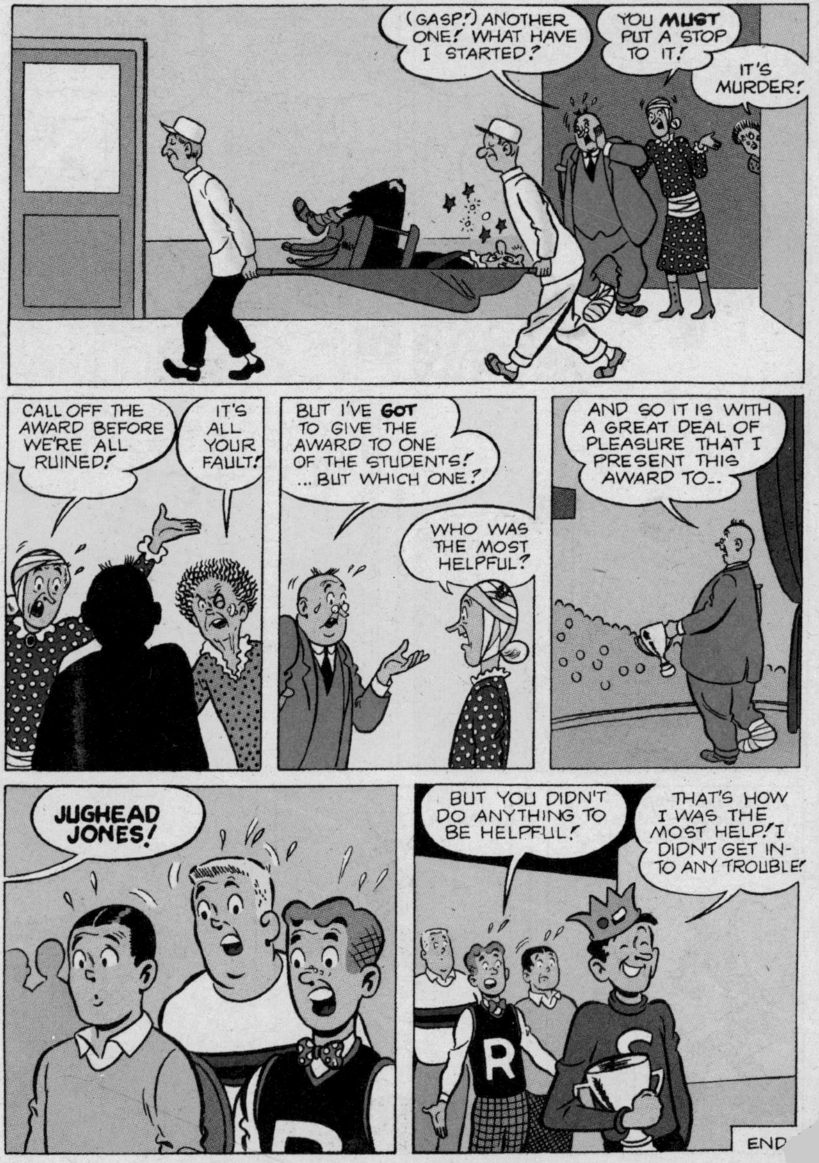
(GASP!) ANOTHER ONE! WHAT HAVE I STARTED?
YOU **MUST** PUT A STOP TO IT!
IT'S MURDER!
CALL OFF THE AWARD BEFORE WE'RE ALL RUINED!
IT'S ALL YOUR FAULT!
BUT I'VE **GOT** TO GIVE THE AWARD TO ONE OF THE STUDENTS! ... BUT WHICH ONE?
WHO WAS THE MOST HELPFUL?
AND SO IT IS WITH A GREAT DEAL OF PLEASURE THAT I PRESENT THIS AWARD TO..
JUGHEAD JONES!
BUT YOU DIDN'T DO ANYTHING TO BE HELPFUL!
THAT'S HOW I WAS THE MOST HELP! I DIDN'T GET INTO ANY TROUBLE!
END

Archie

"POISE WILL BE POISE"

R-ROWF! THAT NEW HISTORY TEACHER! HE'S SO *GRACEFUL*! SO *POISED*!

SO WHAT? *I'VE* GOT GRACE, AND POISE, TOO!

YUK, YUK! GRACE WHO? ANYONE WE KNOW?

(GROAN!) PLEASE, REGGIE! SPARE US YOUR HUMOR!

DON'T YOU AGREE, BETTY, THAT *POISE* IS IMPORTANT?

OH, ABSOLUTELY!

I'LL TAKE POISE EVERY TIME! ESPECIALLY *POISE* LIKE **ARCHIE**!

HEE, HEE, HA! *POISE* LIKE ARCHIE! YUK, YUK!

G-GET IT? *POISE*? BOYS?

I GOT POISE!

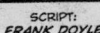

SCRIPT: FRANK DOYLE

PENCILS: DAN DECARLO

INKS: RUDY LAPICK

LETTERS: VINCE DECARLO

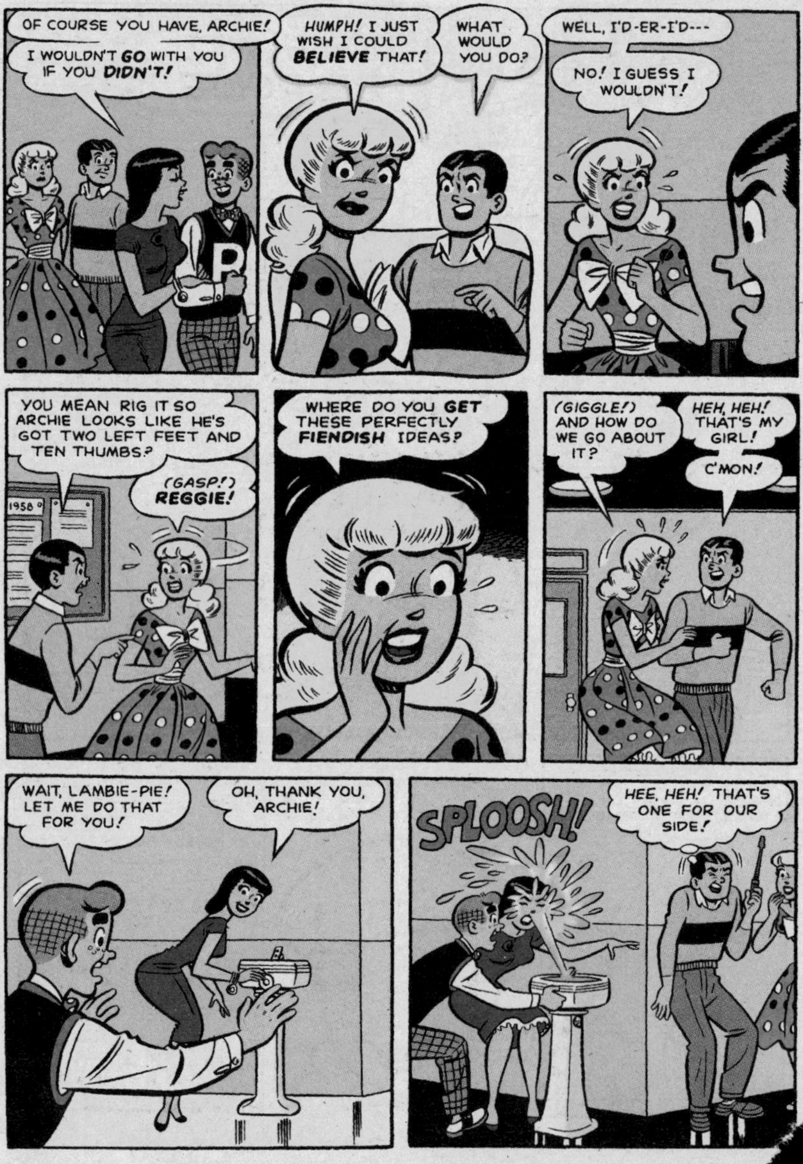
OF COURSE YOU HAVE, ARCHIE!
I WOULDN'T GO WITH YOU IF YOU DIDN'T!
HUMPH! I JUST WISH I COULD BELIEVE THAT!
WHAT WOULD YOU DO?
WELL, I'D-ER-I'D---
NO! I GUESS I WOULDN'T!
YOU MEAN RIG IT SO ARCHIE LOOKS LIKE HE'S GOT TWO LEFT FEET AND TEN THUMBS?
1958
(GASP!) REGGIE!
WHERE DO YOU GET THESE PERFECTLY FIENDISH IDEAS?
(GIGGLE!) AND HOW DO WE GO ABOUT IT?
HEH, HEH! THAT'S MY GIRL!
C'MON!
WAIT, LAMBIE-PIE! LET ME DO THAT FOR YOU!
OH, THANK YOU, ARCHIE!
SPLOOSH!
HEE, HEH! THAT'S ONE FOR OUR SIDE!

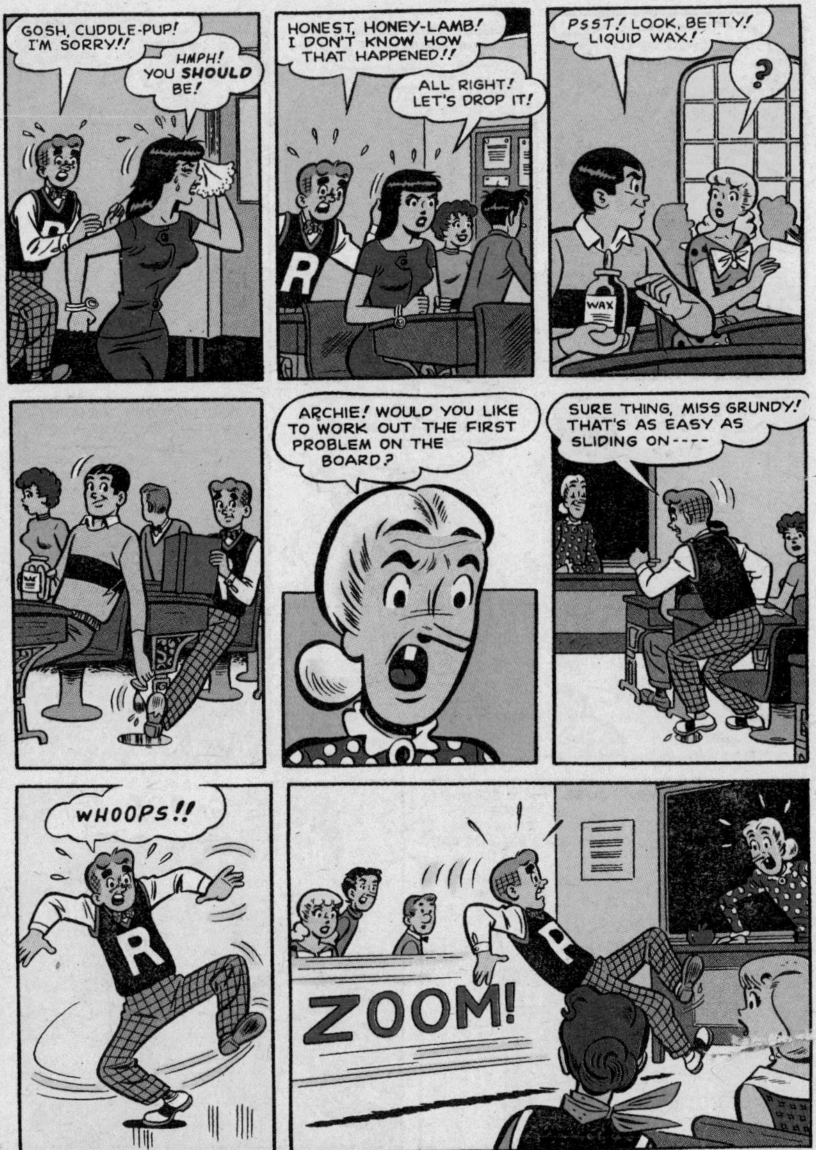
GOSH, CUDDLE-PUP! I'M SORRY!!
HMPH! YOU SHOULD BE!
HONEST, HONEY-LAMB! I DON'T KNOW HOW THAT HAPPENED!!
ALL RIGHT! LET'S DROP IT!
PSST! LOOK, BETTY! LIQUID WAX!
?
WAX
ARCHIE! WOULD YOU LIKE TO WORK OUT THE FIRST PROBLEM ON THE BOARD?
SURE THING, MISS GRUNDY! THAT'S AS EASY AS SLIDING ON----
WHOOPS!!
ZOOM!

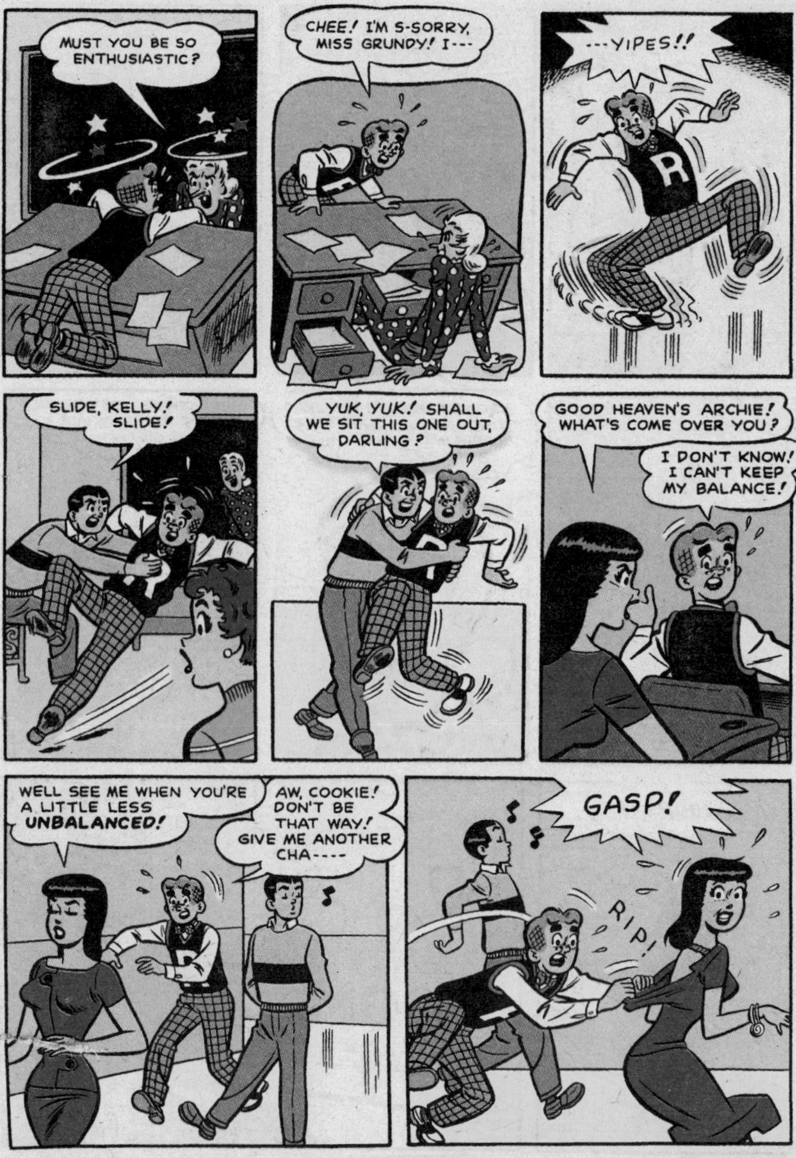
MUST YOU BE SO ENTHUSIASTIC?
CHEE! I'M S-SORRY, MISS GRUNDY! I---
---YIPES!!
SLIDE, KELLY! SLIDE!
YUK, YUK! SHALL WE SIT THIS ONE OUT, DARLING?
GOOD HEAVEN'S ARCHIE! WHAT'S COME OVER YOU?
I DON'T KNOW! I CAN'T KEEP MY BALANCE!
WELL SEE ME WHEN YOU'RE A LITTLE LESS **UNBALANCED!**
AW, COOKIE! DON'T BE THAT WAY! GIVE ME ANOTHER CHA----
GASP!
RIP!

HA, HA! REGGIE! IT WORKED! SHE'S DISGUSTED WITH HIM!

WAIT! THERE'S *MORE!*

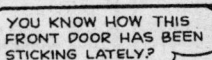
YOU KNOW HOW THIS FRONT DOOR HAS BEEN STICKING LATELY?

YES! IT'S ALMOST IMPOSSIBLE TO OPEN!

YUK, YUK! IT'S NOT *NOW!*

OIL

DUCK! HERE THEY COME!

RONNIE! PLEASE!! DON'T BE ANGRY!

I'VE GOT TO GO HOME AND CHANGE!

WAIT, HONEY! LET ME GET THAT DOOR! YOU'RE NOT STRONG ENOUGH!

JUST LET ME GET A GOOD GRIP ON IT, AND ---

CRASH!

TINKLE TINKLE

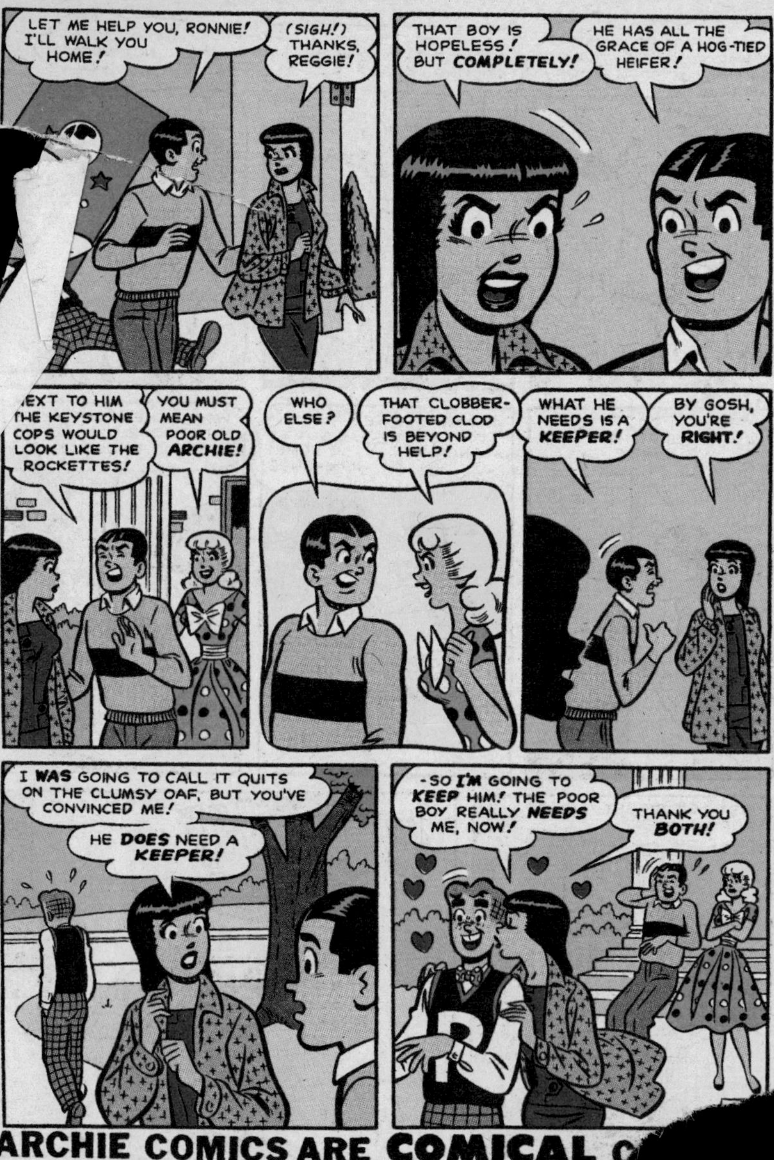
LET ME HELP YOU, RONNIE! I'LL WALK YOU HOME!
(SIGH!) THANKS, REGGIE!
THAT BOY IS HOPELESS! BUT COMPLETELY!
HE HAS ALL THE GRACE OF A HOG-TIED HEIFER!
NEXT TO HIM THE KEYSTONE COPS WOULD LOOK LIKE THE ROCKETTES!
YOU MUST MEAN POOR OLD ARCHIE!
WHO ELSE?
THAT CLOBBER-FOOTED CLOD IS BEYOND HELP!
WHAT HE NEEDS IS A KEEPER!
BY GOSH, YOU'RE RIGHT!
I WAS GOING TO CALL IT QUITS ON THE CLUMSY OAF, BUT YOU'VE CONVINCED ME!
HE DOES NEED A KEEPER!
-SO I'M GOING TO KEEP HIM! THE POOR BOY REALLY NEEDS ME, NOW!
THANK YOU BOTH!

ARCHIE COMICS ARE COMICAL C

MOSBY'S COMPREHENSIVE
REVIEW FOR THE

Canadian RN Exam

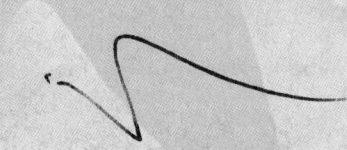

MOSBY'S COMPREHENSIVE REVIEW FOR THE

Canadian RN Exam

REVISED FIRST EDITION

Janice Marshall-Henty
RN, BScN, MEd
George Brown College, Toronto, ON

Cheryl Sams
RN, BScN, MSN
Seneca College, King City, ON

Jonathon Bradshaw
RN, MSN(c)
George Brown College, Toronto, ON

NOTICE

Knowledge and best practice in this field are constantly changing. As new research and expertise broaden our knowledge, changes in practice, treatment, and drug therapy may become necessary or appropriate. Readers are advised to check the most current information provided (i) on procedures featured or (ii) by the manufacturer of each product to be administered, to verify the recommended dose or formula, the method and duration of administration, and contraindications. It is the responsibility of the practitioners, relying on their own experience and knowledge of the client, to make diagnoses, to determine dosages and the best treatment for each individual client, and to take all appropriate safety precautions. To the fullest extent of the law, neither the Publisher nor the Authors assumes any liability for any injury and/or damage to persons or property arising out of or related to any use of the material contained in this book.

The Publisher

Library and Archives Canada Cataloguing in Publication

Marshall-Henty, Janice, 1948–

Mosby's comprehensive review for the Canadian RN exam / Janice Marshall-Henty, Cheryl Sams, Jonathon Bradshaw.
  – Rev. 1st ed.

Include bibliographical references and index.

ISBN 978-1-927406-29-8

   1. Canadian Registered Nurse Examination—Study guides.
2. Nursing—Canada—Examinations—Study guides. 3. Nurses— Canada—Examinations, questions, etc.
I. Sams, Cheryl   II. Bradshaw, Jonathon   III. Title.   IV. Title: Canadian RN exam.
V. Title: Comprehensive review for the Canadian RN exam.

RT55.M37 2013   610.73076   C2012-907836-0

Vice President, Publishing: Ann Millar
Managing Editor: Roberta A. Spinosa-Millman
Developmental Editor: Toni Chahley
Publishing Services Manager: Deborah L. Vogel
Project Manager: Pat Costigan
Proofreader: Jane A. Clark
Cover Design: Ashley Eberts
Interior Design: Brett J. Miller, BJM Graphic Design & Communications
Typesetting and Assembly: BJM Graphic Design & Communications

Elsevier Canada
905 King Street West, 4th Floor, Toronto, ON, Canada M6K 3G9
Phone: 1-866-896-3331
Ebook ISBN: 978-1-927406-27-4

2 3 4   16 15 14

JANICE MARSHALL-HENTY

To my children, their spouses, and my grandchildren: Jessica, Chris, Carys, Peter, Matthew, Jeremy, Sarah, and Benjamin. As always, to the moon and back.

CHERYL SAMS

To Stuart, my life-mate and constant source of support, and Alice and Ken Kester, my parents, who taught me that compassion is the essence of living.

CONTENTS

DETAILED CONTENTS

PREFACE

Mosby's Comprehensive Review for the Canadian RN Exam 2013 has been designed to provide a rapid reference with easily obtainable information for the student who is preparing for the Canadian Registered Nurse Examination (CRNE). It is uniquely Canadian, with content created specifically for the Canadian market. Expert contributors from across Canada have joined with editors to ensure that the text reflects current Canadian nursing practice and trends. The content, based on the blueprint for the CRNE, is a refresher of learned knowledge, with a focus on the role of the nurse, health promotion, professional practice, preventive and primary health care, teaching–learning, nursing judgement, and critical thinking. Gerontological considerations, evidence-informed practice, community focus, and nontraditional settings are included, as appropriate. Appendices include the CRNE Competencies, Medical Terminology, Abbreviations, Common Laboratory and Diagnostic Tests, and Mathematical Formulae. This revised edition includes updated 2010 competencies and identification of question taxonomies.

Beyond requiring a broad knowledge of nursing theory, students also need to feel confident tackling the particular types of questions found on the CRNE. For many, it is not a lack of nursing knowledge that affects their performance on the examination but difficulties in applying their knowledge in the exam situation. Chapters that introduce and describe the examination and that offer tips for mastering multiple-choice questions provide valuable guidelines. Each chapter in this comprehensive review includes practice questions representative of those found on the CRNE and authored within the framework of nursing practice in Canada. These questions provide the student with an opportunity to apply learned knowledge to the test situation, particularly at the critical thinking and application cognitive levels. In addition to these practice questions, two practice examinations are provided. Questions have been authored by nursing experts in the field of exam preparation and referenced to established resources.

ACKNOWLEDGEMENTS

We would like to acknowledge and thank the following individuals for their time, support, and expertise in the preparation of this text: Roberta Spinosa-Millman, Brenda Kirkconnell, Ann Millar, Martina van de Velde, and Pat Costigan of Elsevier.

Jennifer Cooke, RN, BScN, for her nursing and editorial expertise.

Eric McMullin, Penelope Vernon, Marjorie McColm.

Students, clients, and fellow colleagues, who have provided inadvertent inspiration for the case scenarios.

John Braham of Performance Assessment Group, the "guru" of item writing.

Friends and family: Scott, Jack, Patricia, Lesley, Sarah, Chris.

LIST OF CONTRIBUTORS

(in alphabetical order with chapter authored in parentheses)

Marion R. Alex, RN, BScN, MN, CNM
Associate Professor
School of Nursing, St. Francis Xavier University
Antigonish, NS
(Chapter 5: Health and Wellness)

Christine Barbetta, RN, BScN
George Brown College, Perinatal Intensive Care
Nursing Program
Toronto, ON
(Chapter 9: Maternal–Newborn Nursing)

Maureen A. Barry, RN, MScN
Lawrence S. Bloomberg Faculty of Nursing
University of Toronto
Toronto, ON
(Chapter 6: Nursing Fundamentals and Clinical Skills)

Leslie L. Brailsford, PhD, MS, MSc
George Brown College
Toronto, ON
(Chapter 7: Pharmacology and Nursing Practice)

Jennifer Cooke, RN, BScN
George Brown College
Toronto, ON
(Chapter 7: Pharmacology and Nursing Practice,
Appendix B: Medical Terminology,
Appendix D: Common Laboratory and
Diagnostic Tests,
Appendix E: Mathematical Formulae Related to the
Practice of Nursing)

Penny Davis, BScN, MEd
University of Manitoba
Winnipeg, MB
(Chapter 8: Medical–Surgical Nursing)

Karen Ellis-Scharfenberg, RN, BScN, MBA
Registered Nurses' Association of Ontario
Toronto, ON
(Chapter 3: Professional Practice and the Nurse–
Client Partnership)

Nancy Fletcher, RN, BScN, MEd
Director of Professional Practice
The Scarborough Hospital
Scarborough, ON
(Chapter 3: Professional Practice and the
Nurse–Client Partnership)

Patricia Hansen-Ketchum, RN, PhD(c)
Associate Professor
St. Francis Xavier University
Antigonish, NS
PhD Student, University of Alberta
Edmonton, AB
(Chapter 5: Health and Wellness)

Catherine Mayers, RN, MSN
Seneca College
Toronto, ON
(Chapter 4: Health Assessment Across the Lifespan)

Nancy McDonald, RN, BScN, MScN
Manager, Recruitment & Onboarding
Human Resources
The Hospital for Sick Children
Toronto, ON
(Chapter 10: Pediatric Nursing)

P. Jane Milliken, RN, BScN, MA, PhD
School of Nursing, University of Victoria
Victoria, BC
(Chapter 11: Mental Health Nursing)

Donna Pierrynowski Gallant, PhD, RN
Associate Professor
School of Nursing
St. Francis Xavier University
Antigonish, NS
(Chapter 5: Health and Wellness)

REVIEWERS

Elsa Arbuthnot, BScN, MN, RN
Associate Professor
School of Nursing
St. Francis Xavier University
Antigonish, NS

Virginia Birnie, RN, BSc(N), MSN
Nurse Educator
Department of Nursing
Camosun College
Victoria, BC

Mary Elliott, RN, BScN, MEd
Professor
UNB-Humber Collaborative Bachelor of Nursing
  Program
School of Health Sciences
Humber College Institute of Technology and
  Advanced Learning
Toronto, ON

Irene Koren, RN, BA(Hons), BScN, MScN
Assistant Professor
School of Nursing
Laurentian University
Sudbury, ON

Roxanne R. Laforge, RN, BSN, BA, MS
Lecturer and Clinical Instructor, College of Nursing
Coordinator, Perinatal Education Program
University of Saskatchewan
Saskatoon, SK

Anne Lamesse, RN, MScN, PHCNP, EdD(c)
Nursing Professor
Western-Fanshawe Collaborative Nursing Program
School of Nursing
Fanshawe College
London, ON

Manon Lemonde, RN, PhD
Associate Professor
Faculty of Health Sciences
University of Ontario Institute of Technology
Oshawa, ON

Catherine Linner, RNC, MScN
Professor
Collaborative Nursing
St. Clair College
Windsor, ON

Elizabeth O'Brien, BScN, MEd
Professor
PN Program
George Brown College
Toronto, ON

Donna Lynne Rosentreter, RN, CAE, BScN, MEd
Instructor
Baccalaureate Nursing Program
Langara College
Vancouver, BC

Margot Rykhoff, RN, BScN, MA(Ed)
Professor
School of Health Sciences
Humber Collaborative Bachelor of Nursing Program
School of Health Sciences
Humber College Institute of Technology and
Advanced Learning
Toronto, ON

Joy Shewchuk, RN, BSc, BSN, MSN
Professor and Program Coordinator
UNB-Humber Collaborative Bachelor of Nursing
  Program
School of Health Sciences
Humber College Institute of Technology and
  Advanced Learning
Toronto, ON

Bev Valkenier, RN, MSN
Lecturer
School of Nursing
University of British Columbia
Vancouver, BC

Wendy M. Wheeler, RN, BScN, MN
Instructor
Nursing Program
Red Deer College
Red Deer, AB

Introduction

Background to the Canadian
Registered Nurse Examination

BACKGROUND TO THE CANADIAN REGISTERED NURSE EXAMINATION

To practise as a nurse in Canada, you must be registered, or licensed. A component of the registration is successful completion of the Canadian Registered Nurse Examination (CRNE). With the exception of the province of Quebec, the examination is the same for all nursing applicants across Canada. The examination is developed and owned by the Canadian Nurses Association and administered by the individual provincial or territorial regulatory authorities. To write the exam, you must have completed an accredited nursing program or have foreign qualifications that have been assessed as being equivalent to a Canadian nursing education. In each jurisdiction, the candidates write the exam on the same day in a proctored environment. If you pass the exam in your home province or territory and meet all other requirements for registration, you qualify to apply for registration in all jurisdictions.

Questions on the CRNE are designed to evaluate the knowledge of a generalist nurse who has just finished his or her education. Nursing specialties are not tested. Testable material is applicable to all Canadian settings: large cities, small towns, the east coast or west coast, community clinics, acute care hospitals, as well as nontraditional settings. When writing the examination, you need to be able to answer based on the knowledge, skills, and behaviours of a model nurse, not just based on what you or your colleagues might have experienced in a particular setting.

The development of the examination begins with a specific blueprint, or framework. Individual questions are authored by a team of nursing experts from across Canada and are all referenced to at least two published or reliable online resources. Each test item is reviewed, validated, and then piloted on an existing examination prior to being placed in a test bank. It takes from one to one and a half years to complete this process. As a result, most questions you encounter on the CRNE will have been written at least a year ago and will contain information found only in reputable references.

For each examination, questions are randomly chosen from this test bank. No examination is the same, so candidates may write different exams in different locations, and the June exam will be different from the October or February exam. However, there are specific core questions on every examination. You may speak with others who describe past examinations as being focused, for example, on pediatric, mental health, or maternal–child nursing, but remember, all the exams are different.

In addition, each examination has a different pass mark. Some versions of the exam may be considered more difficult than other versions. A panel of experts determines the pass mark depending on the assessed difficulty of each exam. Those assessed as being at higher levels of difficulty will have lower pass marks than those exams that are considered to be easier.

A complex scoring system is used for marking, but essentially you receive a mark for all correct responses. Marks are not deducted for incorrect answers. The results of the examination are reported as "Pass" or "Fail." If, for example, the pass mark for a particular exam version is 500 and you score 500 or higher, you would pass. If, however, you score below 500, you would fail. No bell curve is applied to the examination results.

The CRNE differs from the nursing licensing examination in the United States in that the Canadian version includes fewer questions on pathology and physiology and more application and critical thinking questions. This is why it is preferable to use a Canadian study guide that is more closely linked to what you will experience on the CRNE.

Students who are about to write the examination often worry, "What happens if I fail?" With proper preparation, including management of "test stress," this should not happen. Approximately 90–95% of first-time candidates educated in Canada pass the examination. For those who received their education in other countries or who have English as a second language, the pass rates are somewhat lower. If you do not pass the first time you write the CRNE, you may rewrite the exam. All provinces and territories allow a candidate to write the exam a total of three times.

MOSBY'S COMPREHENSIVE REVIEW

Mosby's Comprehensive Review for the Canadian RN Exam is designed to provide a rapid reference with easily obtainable information for the student who is preparing for the CRNE. It is the only comprehensive review text that contains content specific to the Canadian examination. Each chapter, written by Canadian nursing experts, is a refresher of previously learned knowledge that provides need-to-know information focused on nursing judgement, actions, critical thinking, and the role of the nurse. Necessary medical terminology, relevant math formulae, and common laboratory and diagnostic tests are included as appendices at the end of the text.

Chapter 2 presents a description of the CRNE so that you may become familiar with the format of the test and the types of questions. Tips for studying and taking the multiple-choice examination are provided. Each subsequent chapter contains a review of a major clinical area, followed by questions that test the nurse's knowledge of principles and theories underlying nursing care in a range of different situations and settings. Rationales for correct answers for these practice questions are provided, as are 2010 competencies and identification of question taxonomies.

In addition, the text includes two practice examinations that are similar in format and content to the CRNE. These practice exams give you the opportunity to apply your knowledge to the particular types of questions you will experience in the CRNE. You can choose to write an entire exam to mimic true test conditions or to answer particular sections or questions.

When you have answered the questions, review the correct answers and rationales for each item. Analyze your mistakes. Were there knowledge gaps? Did you misread the question? Did you assume information that wasn't given in the question? Did you misunderstand what the question meant? Identify the frequency with which you made particular errors and use this information as a reference database for further study. Perhaps you need to review certain topics, practise your math skills, or increase your reading comprehension.

Do not attempt to memorize any of the information from the practice questions or to use any of the questions to study content. All test items on the CRNE are secure and have never been published; questions in this book will *not* be on the CRNE.

Remember, you are not expected to get a perfect score. If you correctly answer about 65% of the practice questions in this book, you are likely to succeed on the actual CRNE.

BIBLIOGRAPHY

Canadian Nurses Association. (2010). *Blueprint for the Canadian Registered Nurse Examination: June 2010–May 2015* (3rd ed.). Ottawa: Author.

Canadian Nurses Association. (2010). *The Canadian Registered Nurse Exam prep guide* (5th ed.). Ottawa: Author.

Canadian Nurses Association. (2012). *CRNE national report: Examination cycle 2011–2012*. Ottawa: Author.

Marshall-Henty, J., & Bradshaw, J. (2011). *Mosby's prep guide for the Canadian RN exam* (2nd ed.). Toronto: Mosby.

Chapter 2

Tips for Writing the CRNE

DESCRIPTION OF THE EXAMINATION AND TEST-TAKING TIPS

The Canadian Registered Nurse Exam (CRNE) consists of 180 to 200 operational questions, plus pilot questions, which are not counted toward your examination score. A pilot question is one that has not been statistically validated and is undergoing trial evaluation with exam candidates. You will not know which questions are the pilot questions, so answer all questions as though they count toward your grade. Writing time for the exam is 4 hours.

MULTIPLE-CHOICE QUESTIONS

The multiple-choice test items are written as either case-based or independent questions. Case-based questions present a health care situation along with approximately three to five questions related to the scenario. Independent, or stand-alone, items contain all the information necessary to answer the question.

Each multiple-choice question is made up of two components. The part of the item that asks the question or poses a problem is called the *stem*. The alternatives from which you are asked to select the best answer are called the *options*. There are four options; only one of the options is the correct answer. The other three options are called *distractors*. Distractors may seem to be reasonable answers but are, in fact, incorrect or incomplete.

Only one answer is correct. There are no combination options such as "1 and 2," "all of the above," or "none of the above." All questions are worth one mark. Marks are not deducted for wrong answers. Answers are coded on a scanning card, which counts the number of correct answers.

Sample Question

While receiving a blood transfusion, Mr. Ryan develops chills and a headache. What would be the nurse's initial action?

1. Notify the physician stat
2. Stop the transfusion immediately
3. Cover Mr. Ryan with a blanket and administer ordered acetaminophen (Tylenol®)
4. Slow the blood flow to keep the vein open

The correct answer is 2. Mr. Ryan is experiencing a transfusion reaction, thus the blood infusion must be stopped immediately.

EXAMINATION BLUEPRINT

The CRNE is written according to a blueprint that includes competencies, levels of cognitive ability

called taxonomies, age and gender, type of health care recipient, culture, health situation, and health care environment. It is not organized into sections on maternal–newborn nursing, medical-surgical nursing, pediatric nursing, mental health nursing, and so on.

Competencies

Competencies include knowledge, skills, behaviours, attitudes, and judgements that a nurse is expected to demonstrate in order to provide safe, professional care. In the exam, competencies are applied to various health situations and clients. For example, what are the safety hazards for the mental health client, the infant, or the older adult? How do you prevent the spread of infection in a hospital, a day care centre, or an immunocompromised client? Nurses learn these competencies in their education programs. There are 148 competencies in four categories. The exam asks approximately one question per competency. See Appendix A for a complete list of the CRNE competencies.

Competency Categories

Professional Practice
Professional practice means that the nurse is accountable for safe, competent, ethical nursing care. Professional practice includes legal responsibilities, scope of practice, and evidence-informed practice. Nearly one quarter of the questions on the exam (14 to 24%) will concern professional practice.

Sample Competency and Related Sample Question
- PP-5 – Maintains clear, concise, accurate, objective, and timely documentation

Question
Mrs. Leung was found by the nurse at 0100 hours lying on the floor beside her bed. What should the nurse document in the health record?

1. Mrs. Leung fell out of bed at 0100.
2. At 0100 hours, Mrs. Leung was found by the nurse on the floor beside her bed.
3. Mrs. Leung got out of bed at 0100 hours, slipped, and fell on the floor.
4. Mrs. Leung apparently fell out of bed at approximately 0100 hours.

The correct answer is 2. This notation provides factual and objective documentation about the nurse's observation.

Nurse–Client Partnership
About one or two questions in ten (9 to 19% of the exam) involve the therapeutic partnership between the nurse and the client, which includes interpersonal skills, teaching–learning principles, competent cultural care, and the maintenance of professional boundaries.

Sample Competency and Related Sample Question
- NCP-2 – Uses therapeutic verbal and nonverbal communication techniques with the client

Question
What is the most therapeutic response to Mr. Smith's question, "Am I going to die?"

1. "No, of course not."
2. "You have a very serious illness."
3. "Do you think you are going to die?"
4. "What have you been told about your illness and prognosis?"

The correct answer is 4. This response invites Mr. Smith to discuss his understanding of his illness and provides the nurse with baseline information for further dialogue.

Health and Wellness
About one quarter or more of the exam (21 to 31%) concerns health promotion, population health, illness and injury prevention, and primary health care.

Sample Competency and Related Sample Question
- HW-13 – Promotes healthy lifestyle practices

Question
Which of the following lunch menus would be most appropriate and nutritious for a healthy 2-year-old child?

1. Hamburger and french fries
2. Jelly sandwich and grape soda
3. Cheese sandwich and fruit slices
4. Macaroni and cheese and cookies

The correct answer is 3. This menu provides healthy nutrients and would appeal to a toddler.

Changes in Health
A maximum of half of the exam (40 to 50%) includes questions about clients who have health problems. Remember this when you are studying so that you do not focus all your time on care of the acutely ill client. Competencies in this category involve care for clients who require acute, chronic, rehabilitative, or palliative care. These competencies include calculating medication doses, applying appropriate sciences to nursing practice, prioritizing interventions, selecting appropriate interventions, identifying complications, and so on.

Sample Competency and Related Sample Question
- CH-58 – Inserts, maintains, and removes peripheral intravenous therapy

Question
The physician order reads, "IV TKVO." What does this mean?

1. Intravenous infusion rate of 10 mL per hour
2. Intravenous infusion rate of 15 mL per hour
3. Intravenous to keep volume output
4. Intravenous rate that will maintain the patency of the infusion

The correct answer is 4. TKVO means "to keep vein open."

Taxonomies of Questions

To test your thinking abilities, questions are written at different cognitive levels: knowledge/comprehension, application, and critical thinking. Knowing the percentage of questions on the exam pertaining to each cognitive level helps to guide your studying.

Knowledge and Comprehension
The knowledge–comprehension level requires recollection of facts. For these types of questions, you are required to define, identify, or select remembered information. Knowledge questions require basic memorization. A minimum of 10% of the questions on the CRNE are of the knowledge–comprehension type.

Sample Question
Which of the following is an adverse effect of digoxin?

1. Tachycardia
2. Bradycardia
3. Diarrhea
4. Urticaria

The answer is 2, bradycardia. To answer this question correctly, you need to have memorized the adverse effects of digoxin and the terms tachycardia and bradycardia.

Application
The application level of the intellectual process requires not only knowing and understanding information but also being able to apply it to a new situation. This level includes modifying, manipulating, or adapting information when providing client care. A minimum of 40% of the questions on the CRNE are application based.

Sample Question
Before taking Mr. Singh's vital signs, the nurse asks him if he is taking any medications. He answers, "Digoxin every morning and Tylenol® in the evening." Which of the following vital sign changes might the nurse anticipate?

1. Increased blood pressure to 140/85 mmHg
2. Decreased pulse to 53 beats per minute
3. Decreased respiratory rate to 10 breaths per minute
4. Increased temperature to 38.5°C

The answer is 2, decreased pulse. This question requires knowledge about several drugs, interpretation of vital signs, and application of this information to a particular client.

Critical Thinking

Critical-thinking questions require the most complex level of cognitive function. They ask you to analyze, evaluate, problem-solve, or interpret data from a variety of sources before you respond to them. This often involves prioritizing nursing actions. Many refer to critical-thinking questions as "tricky" or "unfair" because the options may all be correct but only one option is considered the most important or comprehensive response. A minimum of 40% of the questions on the CRNE are critical-thinking questions.

Sample Question

The nurse is about to give Mr. Singh his morning digoxin. The radial pulse in his left arm is 45 beats per minute. What should the nurse do first?

1. Check his apical rate
2. Check the pulse in his right arm
3. Notify the physician
4. Not give the digoxin until the pulse is 60 beats per minute

The answer is 1, check his apical rate. All the options could be correct, but checking the apical rate is the first thing the nurse should do. Consider the nursing process: validate your data.

Other Blueprint Variables

Type of Health Care Recipient

A client may be defined as an individual, family, population, or community.

Client Age and Gender

Questions reflect the statistical representation of Canadian populations for age and gender from birth to older adult. Questions also reflect health situations common to each of these age groups.

Males and females are represented equally in all of the age groupings except for the over-65-years group, in which females may outnumber males.

Culture

Because Canada comprises a variety of cultural backgrounds, the CRNE integrates sensitivity and respect for diverse beliefs and values. It does not specifically test knowledge of individual cultures, other than Canada's Aboriginal, Inuit, or First Nations peoples.

Health Situation

Demographic information concerning disease morbidity and mortality provides the basis for health situations

in test questions. Questions are designed to address client issues holistically, not just from a disease-based or pathology-based dimension.

Environment

The practice environment of the registered nurse (RN) includes a variety of settings. Thus, the competencies addressed in each question may be applied to any environment—clinics, hospitals, and communities—where nurses practise.

STUDY AND EXAMINATION TIPS

Although you may be academically well prepared to write the Canadian Registered Nurse Exam (CRNE), strategies for studying, stress management, and test-taking will increase your chances of success and help to alleviate test anxiety.

STUDY TIPS

It is easy to become overwhelmed as you prepare to study for the CRNE. Remember, though, that you know a lot more than you think you do. While studying is crucial, much learning is not a conscious activity. The first key to developing successful study strategies is to be realistic. Identify where you have incomplete knowledge or the need to refresh your learning.

Keep in mind that most of the questions on the exam do not merely test recalled facts, so you should try to understand the material that you read, rather than memorize it. The focus of your studies should be on principles of care and nursing interventions within a particular health situation, that is, what should the nurse do or say?

Because the exam will likely include approximately one or two questions per competency, make sure you do not get bogged down in one particular content area. For example, there may be only two competencies related to diagnostic tests, so you should not spend too much time studying a comprehensive list of diagnostics.

One of the best strategies for learning is to form a study group. Self-testing and peer testing have proven to be the most effective methods for consolidating material. Have each member of the group choose a topic to teach the other members. This way, you stimulate discussion and get different perspectives on the subjects, which will help you in understanding and remembering them. If you are unable to participate in a study group, try teaching yourself the information. Rephrase or reword the written information to aid in understanding rather than memorizing.

Repetition works well for many people. If you are having trouble remembering some knowledge material, it may help to record it so that you can play it aloud while performing other activities.

Schedule your studying. Start reviewing content several months prior to the exam so that you do not feel rushed or panicked at the volume of material you need to learn. Cramming or "all-nighters" may be useful for memorizing facts, but the CRNE is an exam that requires problem-solving based on a comprehensive knowledge base. It is better to think through and analyze the material, make judgements, and determine how the subject relates to nursing. By performing these analytical and reflective processes, you are more likely to commit the information to long-term memory, which is much more reliable than your short-term memory.

To remember the strategies for studying, you can use the initialism PQRS, which stands for planning, questions practice, repetition, and self- and peer testing.

While you study, remember to stay hydrated, eat sensibly, build in exercise breaks, and get plenty of sleep. It is also important to pursue other activities and not be involved solely in study. Research has shown that both sleep and "time out," in the form of exercise, social activities, or nutrition breaks, help to consolidate learned information.

MANAGING TEST STRESS

"If I take one more multiple-choice test, I think I may become physically ill. I won't be able to help myself. Can't they think of any other way of assessing how much we know?"

The student quoted above is setting himself up for failure because of his negativity toward the format of the test.

It is perfectly normal to feel nervous and anxious about the CRNE. You have worked hard to be successful in your nursing program, and now all that effort comes down to passing a 4-hour exam. As you prepare for the CRNE, empower yourself by developing a positive mental attitude. Henry Ford said, "Whether you think you can or think you can't. . .you're right."

Challenge your negative thoughts! Do not let them guide you.

Stress Management Tips

Become active and positive about your learning and your preparation. The more actively you plan and prepare, the more likely you will be successful. The following tips will help you manage stress:

- Try to avoid fellow students who feel overly anxious about the exam. Anxiety is like a communicable disease. You can catch it.
- Use the power of positive thinking. Build up your self-confidence by repeating to yourself, "I am well prepared. I will pass this exam."
- Practise yoga or other forms of exercise; they are great stress relievers.
- Try aromatherapy—lavender works well to promote relaxation. Sometimes just the smell will help you remember to relax and breathe.

- Eat a well-balanced diet, and get plenty of rest.

The Evening Before the Examination

"The night before a test, I can't sleep. Then I worry because I can't sleep. Then I can't sleep because I'm worrying that I'm worried that I can't sleep. By morning, I'm glad to get out of bed just to stop the terrible racket in my head."

The evening before the exam, organize your clothes and exam supplies (e.g., pens, pencils, ruler, erasers, identification, watch, and bottle of water). Make sure you know the location of the exam and have arranged your transport to the exam.

Then be nice to yourself. Do something you enjoy and get a good night's sleep. Information is processed during sleep, so sleep will help you retain what you have studied. Last-minute cramming may have aided you in past test situations but is helpful only for memorizing facts. It actually decreases your ability to problem-solve the application and critical-thinking types of questions that are on the CRNE.

The Day of the Examination

Eat a healthy breakfast of protein and complex carbohydrates. If you absolutely cannot eat, try drinking a sports electrolyte solution. Although you need to be adequately hydrated, do not drink too many fluids or cups of coffee. Dress in comfortable clothes, preferably in layers, so that you can add or take off articles depending on the temperature of the exam room. If possible, try to make time for light exercise, even if it is walking the last few blocks to the exam centre.

Plan to arrive at the test location at least 30 minutes ahead of the exam start time. This cushion will allow you time to relax, visit with friends, and prepare yourself mentally. However, avoid talking about the exam with your friends as conversations about it will only make you more anxious. Arriving early also gives you time for that last-minute washroom trip—stress is a potent diuretic. When you sit down in the exam room, make a conscious effort to relax and continue your positive thinking. You may want to consider chewing gum during the exam; recent research has shown that it improves test scores.

During the Examination

Remember to keep that positive focus during the exam. Repeat to yourself: "I know this information, and I can answer these questions. I will pass the exam." Reading and keeping focused is essential. It may become confusing about what information relates to the question. Take mini "brain breaks" by performing relaxation exercises in your seat, such as slow deep breaths, shoulder shrugs, neck rolls, and arm and leg rotations. It is wise to bring a bottle of water to ensure you are adequately hydrated. Use the water to splash on your face should you feel less than alert.

After the Examination

After the exam, you will likely feel a sense of relief that it is over, but you may also feel the need to review questions in your head and discuss answers with your peers. Try not to dwell on this activity for too long. These post-mortems can bring you down. Remember, you have probably done better than you think!

TIPS FOR WRITING MULTIPLE-CHOICE EXAMS

Listed below are some tips for completing the multiple choice questions particular to the CRNE:

A. Read and listen to the instructions carefully.

B. Plan your time and pace yourself. Place your watch on your desk so that you can keep track of time. You should answer approximately 25 to 30 questions in each half-hour.

C. Do not spend a lot of time on one question if you do not know the answer. Put a note in the margin and return to it later. Go on to a question that you find easy. The feeling of success will give you confidence.

D. Code responses on the scanning card as soon as you have selected your answer. Place a ruler under the corresponding question on the scanning card. Do not leave the transfer of answers to the card until the end of the exam—you may run out of time, and there is a greater chance of making a transcribing error. Only answers coded on the scanning card are counted.

E. Reading comprehension is crucial to success. Read the stem of each question carefully and make sure that you understand exactly what it asks. One of the most common test-taking errors is misreading the question. In the CRNE, important words are not highlighted, so you should identify and underline words such as *initial* or *most important* or *priority*. Take special note of any negatives such as *never* or *except*.

Sample Question

Ms. Chang is in the emergency room after being involved in a traffic accident. What would be an early sign of hemorrhagic shock?

1. Increased blood pressure
2. Pallor
3. Increased pulse
4. Shallow breathing

The key word is *early;* thus the correct answer is 3.

F. Because the majority of the questions are either at the application or critical-thinking cognitive levels, you must be prepared to problem-solve *every* question. There are no rules for answering questions. Each question must be approached with a view to solving the problem based on your nursing judgement in this particular situation.

G. Try to answer the question before looking at the multiple-choice options.

H. Read all the options before choosing one. Do not immediately assume a response is correct without looking at all the other options; another answer may be *more correct* than the one you choose first.

I. Read each option carefully, mentally crossing out the options you know are incorrect. Choose the best option out of the ones remaining.

J. Some questions that appear to be trick questions may, in reality, measure your ability to think critically. If you believe all the options are correct, choose the one that is most comprehensive, makes the most common sense, or is the most professional answer.

Sample Question

Which of the following is most important when performing a preoperative assessment?

1. Physical assessment
2. Cardiac assessment
3. Assessment of vital signs
4. Auscultation of breath sounds

All options are valid, but answer 1 is the most inclusive.

K. To choose the most important nursing action when all of the answers appear to be correct, use the following guidelines:

- Read the situation and question very carefully.
- In many cases, consider the mnemonic *ABC* (airway, breathing, circulation), or *CAB* (circulation, airway, breathing).
- Remember the "nursing process": collecting and validating information before acting.
- Consider safety—for the client and for yourself.
- Choose an action that can be completed quickly and safely, almost at the same time as other actions.
- Do not necessarily look for fancy answers.
- Choose simple, common-sense, safe actions.
- Choose the sickest, most unstable client as the priority.

L. A common error students make is choosing a response that might have been applicable in a specific client situation that they have experienced. Always answer according to "textbook," or standard, nursing principles.

M. Answer as you believe the perfect "textbook nurse" would answer.

N. Do not assume any information that is not given. Choose your answer based only on information in the question asked.

O. Do not panic if you have never heard of a particular disease or client situation. Apply general nursing principles to each question—the particular client health state may not matter. Candidates for the exam come from various academic backgrounds, and curricula are not identical in all universities. You are not expected to know all the answers, nor are you expected to write a perfect exam!

Sample Question
Ms. Townsend is suffering from Hick's asymmetrical dementia. Which of the following activities would be appropriate for her condition?

1. Vigorous exercise
2. Competitive games
3. Social stimulation in group activities
4. Solitary reading

Hick's asymmetrical dementia is a fictitious disorder. The care needs for a client with dementia are fundamental, so the correct response is answer 3. This is a "trick question" for the purpose of illustration. The CRNE, however, contains no trick questions.

P. Your first answer choice is usually correct. You may have learned some information subconsciously, and your first impression is often an automatic response to what you have learned. Do not second-guess yourself unless you are absolutely sure that you have misunderstood the question or provided a wrong answer. If you do decide to change an answer, ensure you completely erase the first answer from the scanning card.

Q. Select answers that are therapeutic, show respect, involve the client in care, and focus on nursing judgement rather than hospital rules or orders from other health team members.

Sample Question
Jessica tells the nurse, "I am tired of waiting for you to brush my hair. You're never here when I want you." Which of the following responses is the most appropriate for the nurse to give?

1. "I'm sorry you've had to wait. I'll get your hairbrush out for you and be back in 15 minutes to do your hair."
2. "That's not fair. I spent my lunch break with you yesterday."
3. "Jeremy down the hall is really sick, and he needs me more than you do right now."
4. "I'm doing my best, but I have a really busy assignment today."

Option 1 acknowledges the client's feelings, shows respect, and provides a clear, factual response.

Sample Question
Ms. Steele asks the nurse when she can start eating after surgery. What is the most appropriate response for the nurse to give?

1. "You'll have to ask the doctor."
2. "Tell me about your appetite."
3. "You'll likely start on clear fluids once bowel sounds can be heard."
4. "I'll have the dietitian consult with you about the most nutritious postsurgery menus."

Option 3 involves nursing judgement and directly answers the client's question.

R. Most questions will ask about actions that are based on nursing judgement rather than physician orders. However, some questions may test your knowledge of the scope of nursing practice and have as a correct response "contact the doctor." Examples of such situations include unclear or illegible orders, a specific request from a client, deteriorating client condition, and a client emergency.

S. In the case of communication questions, answers that demonstrate the nurse asking the client open-ended questions are most often correct.

Sample Question
Which of the following would elicit the best information from Mr. Loates about his pain?

1. "Do you have severe pain?"
2. "Do you have any pain?"
3. "Is your pain throbbing or stabbing?"
4. "Describe your pain to me."

Option 4 is open-ended—that is, it requires the client to give more than a one- or two-word answer. Phrasing questions in an open-ended fashion is a key component of therapeutic nursing communication.

T. Do not choose an answer because you have seen that question before and think you recall the answer. Questions on the exam may look similar to ones you have encountered during practice but will not be exactly the same. Therefore, the answer may also not be the same.

U. There is no pattern to the assigned answers. Do not change an answer because you have had too many answers in the same position.

V. If all else fails, guess. Never leave a question unanswered. You have at least a 25% chance of getting it correct.

Tips for Guessing

1. If two of the options are similar except for one or two words, choose one of those.

    Example
    Take the apical pulse
    Take the radial pulse

2. If two options have opposite meanings, choose one of those.

    Example
    Vasodilation
    Vasoconstriction

3. If two quantities or mathematical calculations are similar, choose one of those.

    Example
    0.14 mL
    0.014 mL

4. Choose the longest answer.

W. When you have finished the exam, be sure to check your scanning card against each of the questions to make sure that you have coded your answers correctly. Make sure the scanning card contains no marks other than those designating the options you have selected.

X. Answering 200 questions can be boring and tiring. You may find yourself becoming confused about what information relates to the question. Throughout the exam, take a mini-exercise break every 20 minutes; sip water, do neck rolls, and flex your arms and legs.

Y. Do not panic if someone leaves when you have completed only 20 questions. Most "early leavers" do not do better than exam writers who use the entire allotted time.

SUMMARY

Preparing for the examination well in advance, ensuring comprehensive content review, following the exam-taking tips, developing your reading comprehension, and maintaining a positive outlook will equip you with the necessary abilities to be successful in the CRNE.

BIBLIOGRAPHY

Canadian Nurses Association. (2010). *Blueprint for the Canadian Registered Nurse Examination: June 2010–May 2015* (3rd ed.). Ottawa: Author.

Canadian Nurses Association. (2010). *The Canadian Registered Nurse Exam prep guide* (5th ed.). Ottawa: Author.

Canadian Nurses Association. (2012). *CRNE national report: Examination cycle 2011–2012*. Ottawa: Author.

Canadian Nurses Association. (2008). *Nursing in Canada: Canadian Registered Nurse Examination*. Ottawa: Author. Retrieved January 16, 2013, from http://www.cna-aiic.ca/CNA/nursing/rnexam/default_e.aspx

Canadian Nurses Association. (n.d.). *LeaRN CNRE readiness test*. Ottawa: Author. Retrieved January 16, 2013, from http://readiness.cna-aiic.ca/

Dickson, K. (2008). *Mastering exam anxiety*. Athabasca, AB: Student and Academic Services for Counselling Services. Retrieved January 16, 2013, from http://www.athabascau.ca/counselling/exam_anxiety.php

Eyles, M. (2005). *Mosby's comprehensive review of practical nursing for the NCLEX-PN examination* (14th ed.). St. Louis: Mosby.

Hanoski, T. (n.d.). *Test anxiety: What it is and how to cope with it*. Edmonton: Student Counselling Services. Retrieved January 16, 2013, from http://www.ualberta.ca/~uscs/managing_test_anxiety.htm

Marshall-Henty, J., & Bradshaw, J. (2011). *Mosby's prep guide for the Canadian RN exam* (2nd ed.). Toronto: Mosby.

Nugent, P. M., & Vitale, B. A. (2004). *Fundamentals success: A course review applying critical thinking to test taking*. Philadelphia: F.A. Davis.

Saxton, D., Nugent, P., & Pelikan, P. (2006). *Mosby's comprehensive review of nursing for the NCLEX-RN examination* (18th ed.). St. Louis: Mosby.

Student Development Services. (2005). *Managing test anxiety*. London, ON: Author. Retrieved January 16, 2013, from http://www.sdc.uwo.ca/learning/index.html?mcanx

Student Development Services. (2005). *Writing multiple choice tests*. London, ON: Author. Retrieved January 16, 2013, from http://www.sdc.uwo.ca/learning/index.html?mcwrit

WEB SITES

Association for Applied Psychophysiology and Biofeedback (http://www.aapb.org): This site contains information and resources concerning biofeedback and its benefits.

How Successful Students Prepare for Tests (http://www.mtsu.edu/~studskl/sucstu.html): This is a site from Middle Tennessee State University that provides useful tips about how to learn material and prepare for examinations.

Medical Mnemonics (http://www.medicalmnemonics.com): This site lists mnemonics that can help students to memorize information related to specific topics in anatomy and pathology.

Test Anxiety (http://ub-counseling.buffalo.edu/stresstestanxiety.shtml): This site was developed at the University of Buffalo to help with test anxiety.

Professional Practice and the Nurse–Client Partnership

Karen Ellis-Scharfenberg, RN, BScN, MBA

Nancy Fletcher, RN, BScN, MEd

The registered nurse in Canada is a major contributor to and an essential part of the health care system. There have been significant changes in the focus of nursing roles over the past several years. Traditionally, nurses were focused on providing care and comfort as they performed their nursing roles. Today the role of the Canadian nurse has expanded and evolved into an interrelated, complex set of responsibilities in a variety of settings. Our constantly changing health care environment requires that nurses work in roles and settings that reflect the rapid advances being made in health-related knowledge, technology, and skills. As an autonomous and collaborative practitioner, the nurse provides health promotion, advises on illness prevention, and cares for the sick at all ages and stages of illness (Canadian Nurses Association [CNA], 2007). In 2011, the International Council of Nurses (ICN) identified other key nursing roles, including health education, advocacy, research, policy, and education (ICN, 2011). The nurse provides care to the individual, family, group, community, and larger populations.

REGULATION AND LICENSING OF NURSING IN CANADA

In Canada, nursing is a profession that is self-regulating and consists of several different groups of nurses. These groups are as follows (Canadian Institute for Health Information [CIHI], 2008):

- Registered nurses (RNs)
- Registered practical nurses (RPNs) in Ontario or licensed practical nurses (LPNs) in the rest of Canada
- Registered psychiatric nurses (RPNs) who practise only in British Columbia, Alberta, Saskatchewan, and Manitoba
- Nurse practitioners (NPs)

The regulatory nursing organizations are responsible for the licensing and registration of all the nursing groups in the provinces and territories. As a regulatory body, these nursing organizations are responsible for setting the scope of practice, standards of practice, and codes of ethics that nurses must meet and are accountable for. Self-regulation also means that the regulator or licensing organization is responsible for disciplining nurses who do not meet the established standards of practice.

The CNA is the national voice of RNs. This association represents to the federal government and other national organizations nurses' concerns on items such as poverty, the determinants of health, and the public's access to health care services (Potter, Perry, Ross-Kerr, & Wood, 2010).

NURSING PRACTICE ACTS

Nursing practice acts or health professions acts regulate the registration or licensing of nurses, describe continuing competency requirements and any restricted or controlled acts, and explain discipline procedures for the profession. Nursing practice acts have been revised throughout the country to reflect the growing autonomy and expanding roles of the nurse. The legislative acts are principally put in place to protect the public in terms of health, safety, and welfare. Most provinces and territories provide a registration certificate, while others provide a licence. Legislation also provides title protection for nurses. Using the titles RN, LPN, RPN, and, in some provinces and territories, NP is limited to only those nurses who are authorized to do so by their legislative and regulatory bodies.

NURSING SCOPE OF PRACTICE

In Canada, the RN scope of practice is determined by legislation and is accompanied by the standards, guidelines, and policies of the provincial and territorial regulatory bodies (CIHI, 2006). Standards of Nursing Practice define the expectation for nurses in various practice settings and situations and generally guide nursing practice.

Nurses must be able to practise entry-level competencies using knowledge, skill, and judgement. The nurse is determined to be competent by successfully completing an approved Canadian nursing educational program or an equivalent non-Canadian nursing program and by passing a national Canadian Registered Nurse Examination (CRNE) (CNA, 2007). The only exception is Quebec, which sets its own regulatory body examinations.

Non-Canadians must meet specific criteria of language fluency in English or French and must have landed immigrant status or Canadian citizenship, provide good character references, establish proof of providing recent competent nursing practice, have not been involved in criminal activity, and have completed a CNA-approved nursing program. In addition, nurses must meet the eligibility of their specific jurisdiction in order to be approved to write the CNA or Quebec registration examinations instead of the CRNE and then must successfully pass the examination.

Reciprocity between provinces and territories may allow nurses to practise in different provinces and territories. This reciprocity occurs once the RN has completed the registration process.

The Jurisdictional Competency Project (JCP) (2006) identified examples of common national RN entry-level competency statements, which are as follows:

- Professional responsibility and accountability
- Specialized body of knowledge
- Competent application of knowledge
- Ethical practice
- Service to the public
- Self-regulation

EDUCATION

For the RN, the entry-level educational requirement is a four-year baccalaureate degree in nursing, with the exception of Quebec, which accepts a three-year college diploma. Many nurses go further in their education and study for a master's or doctoral degree in nursing or in other disciplines.

The common nursing education abbreviations include the following:

- Bachelor of nursing (BN)
- Bachelor of science in nursing (BScN)
- Master's in nursing (MN)
- Master's of science in nursing (MScN)
- Doctor of philosophy (PhD)
- Registered nurse (RN)

RNs can use their designation and other educational degrees when signing documents if they maintain their registration or licence (CNA, 2007).

RNs are educated to be generalists when they graduate. Experience and further education play a role in developing the novice nurse into an expert such as a clinical nurse specialist (CNS).

It is important that nurses continually update their knowledge and skills. In today's rapidly changing health care workplace, there are frequent advances in research, technology, and practice. It is essential for nurses to be lifelong learners and to expand their knowledge base as well as keep current with practice standards.

PRACTICE ENVIRONMENTS

RNs work in a multitude of practice environments in Canada and around the world. The practice settings are in every part of Canada and range from acute-care hospitals in the south to isolated outposts in the north. The variety of practice settings is matched by the diversity of RN roles available in direct care, education, administration, research, and policy (CNA, 2007). These roles are continually expanding and new roles are being formed to meet the ever-changing health needs of the population.

Nurses also bring their breadth of education and critical thinking abilities to roles outside of nursing. Many different career pathways are open to nurses that benefit a variety of employers in the public and private sectors. The majority of RNs work in acute care, rehabilitation, long-term care, and community health.

ACUTE-CARE FACILITIES

Acute-care or tertiary institutions are the most common employer of RNs in Canada, constituting 62.2% of the nursing workforce in 2006 according to the CIHI (2006). Acute-care settings have clients with complex, multisystem conditions who have many health care needs. RNs in these settings must possess a wide variety of technical skills and meet the physical and the psychological needs of these acutely ill clients and their families.

EXTENDED-CARE AND REHABILITATION FACILITIES

Rehabilitation centres are focused on helping clients to be as independent as possible in order to take care of their own needs. The percentage of RNs working in this setting is about 13% of the total number of RNs working. They work as part of an extensive health care team that plans clients' rehabilitation and their return to the community. These clients may have had a chronic or an acute episodic illness.

Extended- or long-term care facilities are mostly residential and provide the level of nursing care that is required for individuals who have chronic illnesses and cannot be cared for in their homes. Many of these residents are permanently placed in these facilities. The facilities also provide respite care.

COMMUNITY

Community nursing employs approximately 12% of Canadian RNs. Many community nurses are involved in such important roles as performing assessments for the community as a whole or providing direct care to clients or groups such as families that need parenting skills. The scope of community nursing practice includes population-focused health promotion, protection, maintenance, and restoration. The term "community nursing" is broad, encompassing public health nursing, community health nursing, and community-based nursing.

In recent years, clients are being sent home earlier from acute-care facilities. This trend has increased the need for community-based RNs. The nursing services that are required are of a more complex nature as the level of care needed in these community populations is increasingly acute. This acuity is in part due to the earlier discharges from hospitals, but in addition, more clients are being cared for at home rather than being admitted to long-term care facilities. For example, nurses now require the skills to provide home care for clients with ventilators, tracheostomies, central venous lines, chemotherapy, and home dialysis.

Public health nurses (PHNs) are critical to keeping communities, as well as individuals, healthy and vital. Assessments are an important task for PHNs. The practice of the PHN is centred on health promotion and illness prevention. The Canadian PHN assesses the health needs of individuals, families, groups, and communities. For example, the information PHNs have provided on smoking cessation and establishing smoke-free public buildings has helped to create a healthier environment in many Canadian cities.

NURSING ROLES

A wide range of nursing roles are available in Canada. RNs provide either direct or indirect care to all sectors of the health care system. RNs are caregivers, client and family advocates, clinical educators, administrators, professors, and researchers, as well as fulfilling many other roles. Most RNs, however, continue to focus on the practice of direct client care (CNA, 2007).

Contemporary nursing requires that the nurse possess knowledge and skills for a variety of professional roles and responsibilities. As health care agencies and the health care system incorporate advancing technology and knowledge, the positions in which nurses work are evolving. The categories of nursing roles are summarized in Table 3.1. Examples of career roles include the following:

ADVANCED PRACTICE ROLES

Some roles in nursing require further education. These roles include advanced nursing practice (ANP) nurses. ANP nurses are described by the CNA through the national framework for ANP (CNA, 2007). The role is described as an advanced level of nursing practice that maximizes the use of in-depth nursing knowledge and skill in meeting the health needs of individuals, families, communities, and populations, and extends the boundaries of nursing scope of practice. ANPs contribute to nursing knowledge as well as to the development and advancement of the profession. The minimal level of education is a master's degree in nursing. The two ANP roles are NPs and CNSs.

NPs have a higher level of education and have met specific registration requirements to obtain the title and authority of NP. This role requires additional education in health assessment, diagnosis, and management of illnesses and injuries, including ordering and interpreting tests and prescribing drugs. All provinces and territories have legislation for

Table 3.1 Categories of Nursing Roles

Nurse Clinician	A nurse who provides direct care.
Advanced Practice Nurse	A clinical nurse with graduate preparation in nursing who provides primary care, usually in partnership with a physician or group of physicians. The advanced practice nurse has authority to prescribe medications (with the exception of narcotics) and treat health problems within the scope of nursing practice.
Clinical Nurse Specialist	An advanced practice nurse with preparation in a specialized area of nursing practice, e.g., in a specific disease, such as cancer or AIDS, or in a specific field, such as pediatrics or gerontology.
Nurse Practitioner	A nurse with advanced preparation in nursing who usually works in an outpatient, ambulatory, or community-based setting. Provides care for clients with complex problems using a holistic approach.
Nurse Educator	A nurse with graduate preparation who works primarily in schools of nursing, staff development departments of health care agencies, and client education departments. Educators in schools of nursing teach students to become professional nurses. Educators in staff development departments provide programs for nurses within their institutions, such as safety training and instruction about new equipment or procedures. Educators in client education departments teach ill or disabled clients and their families how to provide care in the home.
Nursing Administrator	A nurse prepared at the graduate level who manages client care and the delivery of specific nursing services in a health care agency. Needs to understand all aspects of nursing and client care as well as to be skilled in business and management. Functions may include budgeting, staffing, strategic planning of programs and services, employee evaluation, and employee development.
Nursing Researcher	A nurse prepared at the doctoral level who investigates problems in order to improve nursing care or to further define and expand the scope of nursing practice. May be employed in an academic setting, hospital, or independent professional or community service agency.

Source: Potter, P. A., Perry, A. G., Ross-Kerr, J. C., & Wood, M. (Eds.). (2010). *Canadian fundamentals of nursing* (Rev. 4th ed., p. 35). Toronto: Elsevier.

NPs; however, the scope of practice varies according to the province and territory, and the title of "nurse practitioner" is not protected in all provinces. In Ontario, for example, the registered nurse with extended class (EC) supports an NP role with additional controlled acts, including communicating a diagnosis, prescribing drugs, and ordering the application of energy, such as ultrasounds. The scope of the EC role has been gradually increasing.

NPs in the 12 jurisdictions can diagnose a disease, disorder, or condition; order and interpret diagnostic and screening tests; and prescribe medication (CIHI, 2006). NPs work in acute-care settings, clinics, and community health care centres.

CNSs have in-depth knowledge and skills and are specialized in specific practice fields. Their scope of practice varies depending on the organization that they work for. CNSs provide problem solving and solutions for complex health problems. CNS responsibilities may include procedures that are physician directed (CNA, 2006).

MIDWIVES

Midwives come from a variety of backgrounds, including nurse-midwifery, lay midwifery, and direct entry midwifery. Midwifery education and practice standards still vary among individual provinces and territories. Midwives focus on caring for clients during pregnancy, labour, and birth, as well as the postpartum period. They may function independently when no complications are present or in conjunction with a physician or obstetrician when necessary.

In some Canadian provinces and territories where midwifery is regulated, colleges regulate requirements and competency standards of practice in their own jurisdictions (British Columbia, Saskatchewan, Manitoba, Ontario, Quebec, and Nova Scotia). (Canadian Association of Midwives/Association canadienne des sages-femmes, 2012).

CERTIFIED NURSING SPECIALTIES

Nursing specialization refers to a focus on a specific field of nursing practice or health care (CNA, 2007). There is an increasing trend for nurses to authenticate their competency for their chosen specialty by certification. The CNA offers a voluntary certification program for various specialties that provides a credential that is evidence that nurses meet the national certification requirements for knowledge and skill. CNA's certification program has helped nurses and other health professionals to recognize the specialized knowledge and skills necessary in many areas of practice.

As of 2011, the CNA offers the following 19 specialty certifications for nurses (CNA, 2011):

- Cardiovascular
- Community Health
- Critical Care
- Critical Care, Pediatrics
- Emergency
- Gastroenterology
- Gerontology
- Hospice Palliative Care
- Nephrology
- Neurosciences
- Occupational Health
- Oncology
- Orthopedics
- Perinatal
- Perioperative
- Psychiatric/Mental Health
- Rehabilitation

THE ROLE OF THE PRACTICAL NURSE

LPNs and RPNs in Ontario are synonymous nursing roles that have a different scope of practice from that of the RN.

The practical nurse role in Canada is titled a registered practical nurse in Ontario, and a licensed practical nurse in the rest of the provinces and territories. The educational requirements for LPNs vary, but in Ontario. RPNs graduate from a two-year community college program and must achieve a diploma.

LPNs and Ontario's RPNs need to comply with related legislation within their own jurisdictions. In Ontario, for example, RPNs must write a registration exam and meet the knowledge, skill, and judgement requirements of the province's professional regulatory body (Registered Nurses' Association of Ontario [RNAO], 2008). RPNs are overseen by RNs in several provinces but not all. Some provinces allow the LPN (RPN in Ontario) to practise autonomously.

The differences in the RN and LPN/RPN role are related to level of education and scope of practice. The RN education is more comprehensive, and RNs have a more in-depth knowledge base in areas such as clinical practice, critical thinking, and research utilization. The LPN/RPN has a more focused education, and clinical skills are emphasized. The RN is trained to care for a client who may have complex needs or whose condition may be unpredictable or unstable, whereas an RPN is more suited to caring for a client with fewer complex requirements (RNAO, 2011).

THE ROLE OF THE UNREGULATED HEALTH CARE WORKER

Unregulated health care workers (UCWs) may also be referred to as unlicensed assistive personnel (UAP) or unlicensed care personnel or providers (UCPs). These individuals are not licensed under law in a jurisdiction. There are many other titles for this role, such as ward aide, personal support worker, or orderly. These workers are usually employees of a facility or agency and are bound to perform in their role as per the terms of their employment agreement. Registered staff working with these individuals must be aware of the role expectations set by the employer for this category of worker and of the level of competence of the individual worker. Registered staff are not accountable for the care provided by the UCW (Potter et al., 2010).

NURSING PRACTICE AND THE LAW

It is important for nurses to know the legal parameters that they work within in order to protect their clients' rights as well as their own. Nurses also need to know the specific laws of the jurisdiction in which they practise and the federal law under the *Canada Health Act* (1984) that applies across Canada relating to nursing practice. Legislatures of the provinces and territories create statute laws that apply only to the jurisdiction in which they were passed. Nursing practice acts describe the boundaries of nursing practice within a jurisdiction. These statute laws also give authority to the nursing regulatory bodies (Potter et al., 2010).

The nursing regulatory bodies are responsible to the public. Their mandate is to ensure that the nursing care that is delivered is safe and competent and meets the standards of care and code of ethics that are set by that regulatory body. In addition, the regulatory bodies set the examinations and grant registration or licensure.

These regulatory bodies also can revoke or suspend a nurse's licence if a nurse violates the parameters of the registration statute. An investigation of public complaints or misconduct is carried out by the regulatory body, and a hearing may be held. The nurse must be informed of the charges. Further legal action may occur if the nurse's registration is revoked or removed from the jurisdiction's register and there are criminal or civil wrongdoings (Potter et al., 2010).

Most health care organizations are accredited by Accreditation Canada. The accreditation requires that these organizations have clear, written nursing policies and procedures that meet the standards of care and guide a nurse's practice. If a charge of negligence is brought against an individual nurse that results in a lawsuit, the nurse's actions and practice are compared to the organization's standards of care and the provincial or territorial nursing standards of practice. If an organizational policy violates the jurisdictional standards of practice, then the organizational policy is overridden by law. It is the nurse's responsibility to know the jurisdictional law and standards of practice (Potter et al., 2010).

LEGAL LIABILITY

A tort is civil wrong, intentional or unintentional, made against a person or property (Potter et al., 2010) and not involving a contract (Duhaime, n.d.). A tort is not a criminal act, but if it is serious enough, a nurse may be charged with a criminal offence. There are two classifications of torts, intentional and unintentional. Most lawsuits involving nurses are for negligence or malpractice, which comes under the unintentional classification. The terms "negligence" and "malpractice" are sometimes used interchangeably (Sneiderman, Irvine, & Osborne, 2003).

Intentional Torts

Intentional torts are deliberate actions that violate another's rights and include assault, battery, invasion of privacy, and false imprisonment (Duhaime, n.d.). They include the following:

- Assault is a physical or verbal threat that creates apprehension or a fear of being harmed. No contact is necessary. For example, if a nurse threatens to start an intravenous line without a client's consent, then the nurse could be sued for assault. Consent would negate the possibility of a lawsuit (Fridman, 2003; Sneiderman et al., 2003).
- Battery is an intentional physical contact with an individual without that person's consent. The contact may not necessarily be harmful but may be offensive (Fridman, 2003; Osborne, 2003; Potter et al., 2010). If the nurse started the intravenous line without consent, the nurse could be sued for battery.
- Invasion of privacy protects the client's rights to be free from intrusion into his or her private affairs. For example, a nurse would be liable if the nurse released confidential information about a client to an unauthorized individual without the client's consent.
- False imprisonment is intended to protect an individual's freedom and basic rights. For example, a nurse may be liable if the nurse prevents a client from leaving a health care agency voluntarily. Also, a nurse who uses restraints (chemical or physical) inappropriately may be considered liable (Potter et al., 2010).

Unintentional Torts

Negligence can be considered a liable act if it causes injury even if there was no intent. It is a failure to take the care that a reasonable nurse in similar circumstances would have taken (Canadian Nurses Protective Society [CNPS], 2004). Nurses are negligent if they do not meet the standards of practice that are set by their regulatory body and cause injury to the client because of a lack of nursing care or prevention of injury (Potter et al., 2010). Usually, the courts consider negligence to be the failure to use that degree of skill or learning ordinarily used under the same or similar circumstances by other nursing professionals (Potter et al., 2010). In order for a nurse to be found negligent, the court must have evidence that the nurse:

- Did not meet the duty of care, a term meaning that the client relies on the nurse's professional skill and knowledge and the nurse has a legal duty to take reasonable care.
- Breached the standard of care, meaning that the court will determine what constituted reasonable nursing care in the circumstances.
- Caused foreseeable harm through a breach in the standard of care, meaning that the client was actually harmed. It must be proven that the nurses' negligent acts caused the harm (Osborne, 2003).

Nurses are accountable for their own actions. An agency may also be found jointly liable with the nurse if the agency does not ensure that Standards of Nursing Practice are being met in its facility. Common negligent acts are listed in Box 3.1.

Box 3.1 Common Negligent Acts

- Medication errors that result in injury to clients
- Intravenous therapy errors resulting in infiltrations or phlebitis
- Burns to clients caused by equipment, bathing, or spills of hot liquids and foods
- Falls resulting in injury to clients
- Failure to use aseptic technique where required
- Errors in sponge, instrument, or needle counts in surgical cases
- Failure to give a report, or giving an incomplete report, to an oncoming shift
- Failure to adequately monitor a client's condition
- Failure to notify a physician of a significant change in a client's status

Source: Potter, P. A., Perry, A. G., Ross-Kerr, J. C., & Wood, M. (Eds.). (2010). *Canadian fundamentals of nursing* (Rev. 4th ed., p. 106, Box 9-2). Toronto: Elsevier.

CRIMINAL PROSECUTION

Nurses may be reported to the police if involvement in criminal activity is suspected. The police may investigate, and charges will be laid under the Criminal Code of Canada, if there is sufficient evidence. Nurses are interviewed by the investigators, and a formal statement will be requested. Any information given by the nurse can be used as evidence in the trial proceedings. Therefore, it is important for a nurse to consult with a criminal lawyer before giving any statement or answering questions (CNPS, 2005).

Some examples of criminal activities that nurses could be charged with include the following:

- Theft of narcotics
- Theft of client or agency property

- Assisted suicide
- Criminal negligence
- Battery by threatening or inflicting bodily harm
- Sexual assault

NURSING PROFESSIONAL PRACTICE

NURSING ACCOUNTABILITY

Nursing accountability is one of the cornerstones of ethical practice in the standards of nursing care in Canada. The CNA's definition of accountability is that "nurses are accountable for their actions and answerable for their practice" (CNA, 2008a, p. 18). Accountability is one of seven ethical values in the ethical practice of standards of the CNA. The CNA description of the meaning of accountability to professional nursing in Canada is adapted from the *Code of Ethics for Registered Nurses*, 2008, pages 18–19, and is as follows (CNA, 2008a):

- Nurses practise according to the values and responsibilities in the *Code of Ethics for Registered Nurses* and in keeping with the professional standards, laws, and regulations supporting ethical practice.
- Nurses are honest and practise with integrity in all of their interactions.
- Nurses practise within the limit of their competence. When aspects of care are beyond their level of competence, they seek additional information or knowledge, seek help from their supervisor or a competent practitioner, and/or request a different work assignment. Nurses remain with the person receiving care until another nurse is available.
- Nurses maintain their fitness to practise. If they are aware that they do not have the necessary physical, mental, or emotional capacity to practise safely and competently, they withdraw from the provision of care until someone else can attend to their client's health care needs. Nurses then take the necessary steps to regain their fitness to practise.
- Nurses are attentive to signs that a colleague is unable to perform his or her duties. If so, nurses will take the necessary steps to protect the safety of persons receiving care.
- Nurses clearly and accurately represent themselves with respect to their name, title, and role.
- If nursing care is requested that is in conflict with the nurse's moral beliefs and values but in keeping with professional practice, the nurse provides safe, compassionate, competent, and ethical care until alternative care arrangements are in place to meet the person's needs or desires. If nurses anticipate such a conflict, they have an obligation to notify their employer so that alternative arrangements can be made.
- Nurses identify and address conflicts of interest. They disclose actual or potential conflicts of interest that arise in their professional roles and relationships and resolve them in the interest of persons receiving care.

- Nurses share their knowledge and provide feedback, mentorship, and guidance for the professional development of nursing students, novice nurses, and other health care team members.

ETHICAL NURSING PRACTICE

Ethical values are the foundation of nursing practice in Canada and are written into the CNA *Code of Ethics*. The *Code* guides nursing practice, educates nurses about their ethical responsibilities, and informs them about moral commitments.

Many experiential factors influence a nurse's value system. It is critical that nurses examine their own personal values and beliefs and integrate

---

Box 3.2 Canadian Nurses Association *Code of Ethics*

The following is the CNA's statement of the seven values that must be upheld in nursing practice. The complete code of ethics also includes responsibility statements outlining how nurses can incorporate these values into their practice; it can be found on the CNA Web site (see the recommended Web sites at the end of this chapter).

Values

Providing Safe, Compassionate, Competent, and Ethical Care
Nurses provide safe, compassionate, competent, and ethical care.

Promoting Health and Well-Being
Nurses work with people to enable them to attain their highest level of health and well-being.

Promoting and Respecting Informed Decision-Making
Nurses recognize, respect, and promote a person's right to be informed and make decisions.

Preserving Dignity
Nurses recognize and respect the intrinsic worth of each person.

Maintaining Privacy and Confidentiality
Nurses recognize the importance of privacy and confidentiality and safeguard personal, family, and community information obtained in the context of a professional relationship.

Promoting Justice
Nurses uphold principles of justice by safeguarding human rights, equity, and fairness, and by promoting the public good.

Being Accountable
Nurses are accountable for their actions and answerable for their practice.

Source: Canadian Nurses Association. (2008a). *Code of ethics for registered nurses.* Ottawa, ON: Author. © Canadian Nurses Association. Reprinted with permission. Further reproduction prohibited.

---

their professional ethical value system into their nursing practice. The CNA nursing code of ethics in Canada is structured around seven primary values that are central to ethical nursing practice (CNA, 2008a). The CNA *Code of Ethics* is outlined in Box 3.2.

NURSING PROFESSIONAL RELATIONSHIPS AND COMMUNICATION

THE THERAPEUTIC NURSE–CLIENT RELATIONSHIP

The nurse–client relationship is central to nursing. A professional relationship is created through the nurse's application of knowledge, communication theory, understanding of human behaviour, and a commitment to ethical behaviour. Helping relationships are at the foundation of clinical nursing practice. The nurse is considered the helper and interacts with the client in consideration of the client's unique health needs, human responses, and patterns of living (Potter et al., 2010). The key points in this relationship are as follows:

- The relationship is based on trust, respect, empathy, and professional intimacy and requires the appropriate use of power.
- The purpose of the relationship is to meet the needs of the client.
- Nurses establish, maintain, re-establish, and terminate relationships with clients.
- Nurses use a client-centred care approach to ensure that all professional behaviours and actions meet the therapeutic needs of the client.
- Nurses are responsible for effectively establishing and maintaining the boundaries in the relationship.
- Nurses protect the client from harm by ensuring that abuse is prevented or stopped and reported (Potter et al., 2010).

The nurse–client relationship goes through a series of developmental steps. The four steps, outlined below, are identified as pre-interaction, orientation, working, and termination:

- Pre-interaction begins before the nurse meets the client and may involve accessing information about the client, a diagnosis, or a procedure. It includes identifying a suitable setting and anticipation of the client's needs, issues, or concerns.
- The orientation phase involves the meeting of the nurse and the client. This stage begins with a social exchange and expands to include decision making regarding the client's goals, the role of both the client and the nurse in facilitating fulfillment of the goals, and the expected length of the relationship.
- The working stage consists of the nurse and the client working together to facilitate the accomplishment of

the client's goals. It is important for the nurse to use therapeutic communication skills to encourage the client to self-explore and take action to meet his or her goals.

- The final stage is termination. It is a time to evaluate the achievement of goals and for the nurse and the client to separate and make the transition whereby the client or another caregiver assumes responsibility for the care (Potter et al., 2010).

Communication

It is critical that nurses develop and use effective communication skills in order to facilitate optimum relationship building. Communication is an ongoing, dynamic, and multidimensional process that consists of a variety of interactions between a sender and a receiver. The sender encodes a message, the content of the communication, and sends it to a receiver, who decodes the message. The message may be influenced by many factors, including the environment in which the communication occurs and interpersonal variables, such as the educational, developmental, or cultural background that each individual brings to the communication. Feedback is the message returned by the receiver.

For effective communication, both the sender and the receiver need to be sensitive and open to each other's message. In the nurse–client relationship, the nurse needs to take primary responsibility for ensuring that communication is open, purposeful, and therapeutic. Figure 3.1 illustrates the concepts of active communication.

Interpersonal variables
Channel
Referent
Referent
Message
Sender
Receiver
Feedback
Environment

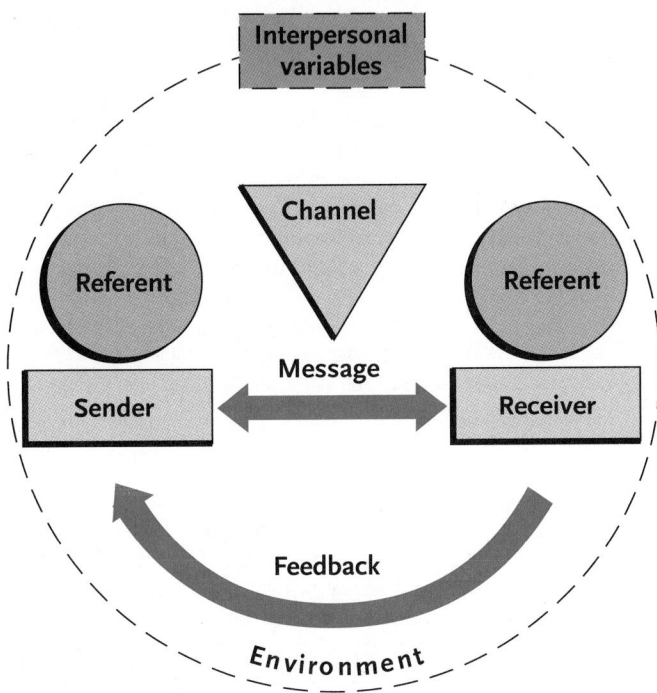

FIGURE 3.1
Communication is an active process between a sender and a receiver

Source: Potter, P. A., Perry, A. G., Ross-Kerr, J. C., & Wood, M. (Eds.). (2010). *Canadian fundamentals of nursing* (Rev. 4th ed., p. 248, Figure 18-1). Toronto: Elsevier.

Nurses use a wide range of effective communication strategies and interpersonal skills to guide their interactions with clients and with all members of the interprofessional team. Nurses must have an awareness of cultural factors that influence communication. Nurses plan and provide care by recognizing and respecting the diversity of different cultures. Positive interpersonal communication is vital for creating a positive therapeutic environment and includes the following:

- The use of warmth and genuineness as the nurse ensures confidentiality, connects with clients, and demonstrates respect for spiritual, psychological, and physical aspects of care;
- Being respectful with clients and other members of the interprofessional team;
- Being empathetic to the client experience; and
- Using self-disclosure appropriately.

Communication involves the use of verbal and nonverbal means:

- Verbal communication includes the spoken word, and nonverbal communication includes factors such as tone, rate, and volume of the voice, as well as facial expression, mannerisms, and appearance.
- When delivering or receiving communication, it is important to consider both verbal and nonverbal aspects of the message.
- A key factor associated with communication is the use of effective listening skills.
- Listening is an active process that involves paying attention to both the spoken word and the nonverbal cues and is required by the nurse when interacting with clients, other nurses, and members of the interprofessional team.

Conflict Resolution

The health care team is composed of many different people. Each team member brings a different background, professional knowledge and expertise, values, beliefs, and goals into the workplace, and these differences can lead to conflict and disagreements.

Conflict occurs at four levels:

- Intrapersonal conflict that occurs within the individual
- Interpersonal conflict that occurs between two or more individuals
- Intragroup conflict that occurs within a group
- Intergroup conflict that occurs between two or more groups, departments, or organizations

Many factors contribute to conflict, such as unclear roles and responsibilities, limited resources, unresolved prior conflicts, and ineffective communication. It is important to resolve conflicts when they occur.

Table 3.2 Legal Guidelines for Recording

Guidelines	Rationale	Correct Action
Do not erase, apply correction fluid, or scratch out errors made while recording.	Charting becomes illegible; it may appear as if you are attempting to hide information or deface the record.	Draw a single line through the error, write the word "error" above it, and sign your name or initials and date. Then record the note correctly.
Do not write retaliatory or critical comments about client or care by other health care professionals.	Statements can be used as evidence for nonprofessional behaviour or poor quality of care.	Enter only objective descriptions of client's behaviour; client comments should be quoted.
Correct all errors promptly.	Errors in recording can lead to errors in treatment.	Avoid rushing to complete charting; be sure information is accurate.
Record all facts.	The record must be accurate and reliable.	Be certain the entry is factual; do not speculate or guess.
Do not leave blank spaces in nurse's notes.	Another person can add incorrect information in space.	Chart consecutively, line by line; if space is left, draw a line horizontally through it and sign your name at the end.

Source: Extracted from Potter, P. A., Perry, A. G., Ross-Kerr, J. C., & Wood, M. (Eds.). (2010). *Canadian fundamentals of nursing* (Rev. 4th ed., p. 211, Table 16-1). Toronto: Elsevier.

Table 3.3 Comparison of Do's and Don'ts of the Change-of-Shift Report

Do's	Don'ts
Provide only essential background information about client (i.e., name, sex, age, physician's diagnosis, and medical history).	Don't review all routine care procedures or tasks (e.g., bathing, scheduled changes).
Identify client's nursing diagnosis or health care problems and their related causes.	Don't review all biographical information already available in written form.
Describe objective measurements of observations about client's condition and response to health problem; emphasize recent changes.	Don't use critical comments about client's behaviour, such as "Mrs. Wills is so demanding."
Share significant information about family members as it relates to client's problems.	Don't make assumptions about relationships between family members.
Continuously review ongoing discharge plan (e.g., need for resources, client's level of preparation to go home).	Don't engage in idle gossip.
Relay to staff significant changes in the way therapies are given (e.g., different position for pain relief, new medication).	Don't describe basic steps of a procedure.
Describe instructions given in teaching plan and client's response.	Don't explain detailed content unless staff members ask for clarification.
Evaluate results of nursing or medical care measure (e.g., effect of back rub or analgesic administration).	Don't simply describe results as "good" or "poor." Be specific.
Be clear about priorities for staff at shift changes.	Don't force oncoming staff to guess what to do first.

Source: Potter, P. A., Perry, A. G., Ross-Kerr, J. C., & Wood, M. (Eds.). (2010). *Canadian fundamentals of nursing* (Rev. 4th ed., p. 230, Table 16-4). Toronto: Elsevier.

Effective conflict resolution begins with an acknowledgement that there is a conflict and that it needs to be positively addressed. Collaboration is the best approach to conflict resolution. It satisfies the interests of most parties because they are required to work together to resolve the conflict. Collaboration involves the use of active listening and the setting of a clear agreement as the conflict is resolved.

PRACTICE STANDARD DOCUMENTATION

Accurate documentation by nurses is an important standard of care from a legal as well as an ethical perspective. Nurses document important details of client care on the client health record. Accurate and detailed documentation improves client outcomes because the health care team can better plan care, improve assessment, and evaluate the effectiveness of care interventions. Verbal documentation such as verbal physician's orders should be avoided except in specific—usually emergency—situations because of the increased risk of error or misinterpretation. People who have the authority to write orders, including physicians and NPs, need to sign any verbal order they made as soon as possible after the event. Individual health care facilities have telephone communication policies in place to facilitate this process. Nurses should refer to agency policy for issues relating to late entries, correcting errors, or completing an omission. Late entries are often documented by writing the current date and time in the next available space and writing "late entry for (date and shift)" (Potter et al., 2010).

Documentation is important in all other aspects of nursing practice as well. Documentation formats have changed; electronic records and fax transmissions are replacing paper records. Electronic and fax records must also be kept confidential. Confidentiality of health records is integral to the documentation and accountability and ethical standards for nurses.

From a legal and ethical perspective, nurses must keep all client information confidential and can only release the information with the written consent of the client or authorized designate such as a guardian or power of attorney/power of care. Clients or other authorized designates and other members of the specific client's health care team can access and read the client health record. Individual health care facilities all have a system in place and specific policies to ensure that client confidentiality is maintained. Accreditation Canada has developed six criteria for providing good documentation. The documentation includes information that is factual, accurate, complete, and current and complies with the standards of Accreditation Canada (Potter et al., 2010), as outlined below:

- Documentation should include factual records that contain descriptive and objective information.

- It should be accurate, with exact measurements, the agency's approved abbreviations, correct spelling, date and time, and the recorder's name and role, such as Cheryl Sams, RN, which confirms that the nursing care has been delivered.
- Current records need to be recorded with timed entries on a regular basis and always as soon as possible in the following instances:

  - When vital signs are monitored
  - Preparation for tests or surgeries
  - Change in client status and who was notified of the change
  - Admission, transfer, discharge, or death of a client
  - Treatment for a sudden change in status

- It should be organized, with the information presented in a logical order.
- It must comply with standards set by the Accreditation Canada as well as jurisdictional legislation and regulatory bodies.

Each health care facility also has its own policies that need to be followed to ensure consistency and complete information recording. Some examples include the following:

- Subjective-Objective-Assessment-Plan (SOAP)
- Problem-Intervention-Evaluation (PIE), which can be added to the SOAP format
- Narrative notes that describe the nursing care delivered and the client's response
- Focus charting, which includes Data (subjective and objective), Action, or nursing interventions, and Response from the the client (DAR)
- Charting by exception (CBE) systems, in which the nurse only records abnormal findings and trends in clinical care (Potter et al., 2010)

Table 3.2 describes the legal guidelines for recordings.

The change-of-shift report is very important in settings where one nurse takes over care responsibilities from another nurse. The communication about the client's condition is only a small part of the report. The shift-change report needs to be concise but comprehensive so that the nurse starting the new shift will be able to provide a level of continuity of care. However, the change-of-shift report is not a part of the legal permanent client health record. Table 3.3 provides a comparison of do's and don'ts of the change-of-shift report.

CONSENT

ETHICAL IMPLICATIONS

Consent to treatment is a very important aspect of ethical care. It is critical that clients are fully informed and fully understand the implications of the treatment before authorizing the care, whether via a signed consent or verbal consent. In their advocacy role, nurses encourage clients to participate in their health care by helping them to obtain the needed information so that they can make a fully informed decision (CNA, 2008a).

The CNA *Code of Ethics* (2008a) provides guidance to nurses within the "promotion and respecting informed decision making" value. This value affects informed consent, as listed below:

- Nurses need to provide persons with the information that is necessary to make informed decisions as regards their health and well-being. The health information needs to be delivered in an open, accurate, and transparent manner.
- Nurses need to respect the desires of capable persons to decline to receive information on their health status.
- Nurses need to recognize that capable persons may defer from self to family or community values in decision making.
- Nurses must make certain that nursing care is provided with the person's informed consent and recognize and support that the person has the right to refuse care or withdraw consent for care or treatment at any time in the care process.
- Nurses must respect and accept the health care choices when a capable person is fully informed (CNA, 2008).
- If a person who requires care is clearly incapable of consent, the nurse respects the law on capacity assessment and substitute decision making according to his or her jurisdiction.

LEGAL IMPLICATIONS

There are also legal implications in relation to informed consent. Clients must fully understand the implications of the consent and receive full disclosure on all the risks, benefits, alternatives, and consequences of refusal of treatment or care (Black, 1999). The legal obligation falls to the physician or health care provider to disclose the information in such a way that the client can understand all the information that is being delivered. The consent needs to have the specific details of the procedure written on it. For example, the client needs to know the names of the personnel who are performing the procedure. The person who is performing the procedure should be the one who obtains the consent. It is essential to remember that except in emergency situations, failure to obtain consent for treatment (whether written or verbal) could result in a lawsuit with charges of battery.

Nurses cannot obtain informed consent for surgeries because they do not perform the surgery. This applies to other procedures that require a consent that will not be performed by the nurse. It is the physician's responsibility to obtain consent for the procedure if he or she will be performing the procedure. Nurses may sign as witnesses to the client's written consent, proving that the client appears to be mentally competent and

confirming the identity of the signature and that the client signed voluntarily, although some agency policies may not support this practice. The nurse should ask if the client understands the procedure before the consent is witnessed. If there is a suspicion that the client does not understand, the physician needs to inform the client further. In case of refusal of the consent, the nurse needs to explore and determine the reason for refusal and discuss it with the health care team.

At this time, nurses who are performing specific procedures rarely require a written consent from a client; however, the nurse must obtain a verbal consent before starting the procedure. This ensures that the client understands the care goals and reduces the risk that a battery lawsuit could occur toward the nurse (CNA, 2008a).

Consent can be verbal, written, or implicit. For example, if a client lifts up a leg for the nurse to provide wound care, then it is implicit that the client is giving consent.

In an emergency situation, if the client or other legally authorized Substitute Decision Maker cannot give consent, then the treatment can be delivered without fear of a battery lawsuit. Parents of pediatric clients can sign the consent if they are the legal guardians or have legal custody of the child (CNA, 2008a). If a parent refuses treatment for a child and the physician deems it necessary, then the hospital can go to court and get legal authorization making the child a temporary ward of the court while the child receives the treatment.

The age at which children can give informed consent varies depending on the jurisdiction. Nurses need to know the legislation around consent for their jurisdiction.

If the client is unable to understand the nature of the consent, then a Substitute Decision Maker with the appropriate authority will need to provide consent for care, which may involve signing a consent form. The Substitute Decision Maker may receive the authority by proxy or power of attorney/power of care or may be appointed through court guardianship. Clients with mental health issues or older adults may still have the ability to provide informed consent and to refuse treatment unless the court has ruled that they are legally incompetent to make personal health care decisions (CNA, 2008a).

RESTRAINTS

Restraints are physical, chemical, or a restricted environment. There has been much controversy over the past few years concerning the risks and benefits of restraints. The ethical question of consent for restraints has also arisen, as well as the possible liability issues of lack of consent. The ideal situation is not to use restraints, but it may be necessary for clients, particularly those with mental illness, who are at risk of harming themselves or others. Statistics clearly indicate that personal injuries are higher when a client is restrained (Potter et al., 2010).

Clients have been asphyxiated by physical restraints. Other complications from the use of restraints include pressure ulcers, constipation, pneumonia, urinary and fecal incontinence, and urinary retention. There is also the issue of the anxiety and fear experienced by clients under restraint, as well as the impact on the client's self-esteem (Potter et al., 2010). A policy of least restraint is the usual agency approach, which ensures that all care alternatives have been attempted prior to restraint. It is important for nurses to know the restraint policies of their agencies and the legal implications of these.

If restraints are used, nurses need to check the restraints and the client's condition frequently to make sure that the client's circulation is not impaired and that no other injuries or potential risks are present. It is always recommended that nurses try alternative methods of intervention to address difficult behaviour, such as frequent toileting to reduce agitation and utilizing a "sitter."

END-OF-LIFE DECISIONS AND RESUSCITATION GUIDELINES

ADVANCE DIRECTIVES AND END-OF-LIFE NURSING PRACTICE

One of the most important roles that nurses have is to work with and support clients and families as they make difficult end-of-life decisions. This is a complex issue that presents many legal and ethical dilemmas as well as nursing practice implications. The CNA defines the nursing responsibilities that ensure that client autonomy is promoted and that the individual who is considering end-of-life directives is fully informed and up to date on care options. This client, or the Substitute Decision Maker, should express his or her health care needs and personal values of health before making end-of-life directives (CNA, 2008b).

In 2008, the CNA put forward a position statement on end-of-life issues (CNA, 2008b) that states that the CNA believes in an individual's right to self-determination and to make fully informed decisions about his or her own health care. This self-determinism is particularly true when making end-of-life decisions and using advance directives (CNPS, 2006). Clients do have the right to refuse life-sustaining measures.

In Canada, living wills and advance directives are not considered legal documents at this time. Two types of advance directives are available for Canadians. Instructional advance directives give individuals the option to give directions on levels of health interventions that should be provided if they were to become incapacitated and unable to make health care decisions. Some examples of directives are whether the client wants to have cardiopulmonary resuscitation (CPR) administered, to be admitted to an intensive care unit, to be transferred to another agency, to receive tube feeding, or to receive blood transfusions (CNA, 2008b). The second advance directive is a form that names a Substitute Decision Maker in the event that the individual becomes incapacitated. Clients with directives can revise their directives at any time. Advance directives are still evolving in terms of their legal status, and there are some differences throughout the provinces and territories. Nurses need to know the legalities and regulations of living wills and directives as well as the nursing role responsibilities for their individual jurisdictions (CNA, 2008).

CARDIOPULMONARY RESUSCITATION

CPR is the standard treatment for respiratory or cardiac arrest in many health care facilities. CPR is commonly performed as it has the potential to revive clients. Because CPR is considered a treatment, client consent may be required before initiating the resuscitation, although emergency situations are unique (CNPS, 2006).

When a capable client does not want to have CPR performed, the refusal must be documented in the client health record. This refusal is often documented by the physician. Some provincial or territorial legislation allows nurses to accept the refusal for CPR and document the refusal in the client's health record as Do Not Resuscitate (DNR). If the client is legally capable of making decisions, then the family cannot overrule the client's treatment or care wishes.

Health care facilities should have DNR policies in place that guide the health care team in the decision-making process surrounding the DNR issue. Jurisdictions and agencies have different sets of resuscitation protocols from legal and regulatory bodies. DNR orders are necessary in some areas, and in others, CPR requires consent. It is essential that nurses know the protocols in their jurisdictions.

It is the responsibility of the health care team to discuss the potential care requirements with the client and his or her family, including providing CPR, and together to devise a comprehensive plan of treatment. This plan needs to be documented in the client health record. Health professionals do not have to provide CPR if it will not benefit the client. CPR may, in fact, be harmful in some situations by increasing pain and suffering and prolonging the dying process. The plan of care must include the client's current condition and the expectation for the future condition. The plan must be based on current best practices and treatment goals. The client must consent to the treatment plan. If the client requests CPR and the health care team does not think that CPR will benefit the client, then the health care team must discuss this decision with the client and his or her family. Variations of the DNR can allow for partial resuscitation in accordance with the client's request. The DNR can be suspended at any time and then reinstated when the client would like it reordered (CNPS, 2006).

The regulatory body of the nurse's jurisdiction provides standards of care for resuscitation. For example, the CNO practice standard of resuscitation is based on ethical values of nursing, including the following (CNO, 2009):

- Respect for the client's well-being
- Client choice
- Privacy and confidentiality
- Respect for life
- Maintaining commitments
- Truthfulness and fairness

Nurses play an important role in making certain that the client's wishes are identified and communicated clearly to the health care team. In addition, nurses must encourage the client to be the decision maker in the treatment plan, document communication about end-of-life and resuscitation concerns in the health record, review the resuscitation wishes, advocate on behalf of the client, and implement the client's wishes (CNA, 2008b). It is critical that nurses discuss the presence of living wills or advance directives and meet the legislation requirements of their jurisdiction. It is important that nurses follow the capable client's wishes whether or not there is a written order on the client's health record.

Nurses are expected to be competent in providing CPR if required for their role. Some health care facilities require a formal credential such as Basic Cardio Life Saving (BCLS) or Advanced Cardio Life Saving (ACLS).

Euthanasia and Assisted Suicide

Nurses play an important role in palliative care. Nurses provide much of the care for this type of client. The CNA has identified palliative care as providing active, compassionate, and supportive care of the dying (CNA, 2008b). In October 1994, the CNA produced a brief to the Special Senate Committee on Euthanasia and Assisted Suicide. This brief outlined the public understanding of end-of-life issues, advance directives, palliative care, palliative care at home, and withholding or withdrawing treatment. The CNA (2000) made the following recommendations for governments and health professionals:

- Lead extensive discussion on end-of-life issues with the Canadian public before making any legislative decisions on euthanasia and assisted suicide.
- Encourage increased public awareness of and support for advance directives, including legislation where needed.
- Promote increased accessibility to palliative care for Canadians, educate health care professionals in palliative care, and support increased research into palliative care.
- Support, advance, and finance a continuum of services including palliative care at home.

- Promote a change in parliamentary law that would eliminate ambiguity in the Canadian Criminal Code regarding health care providers withholding or withdrawing futile or unwanted treatments with the client's consent (CNA, 2000).

Caring for the palliative population requires palliative education to provide quality of care and adequate pain control. Nurses help to decrease suffering and support a dignified and peaceful death.

Palliative care is not euthanasia, and only rarely do interventions shorten life (CNA, 2008b). Active euthanasia is a deliberate act that causes the death of another, and assisted suicide is helping an individual commit suicide. Both are illegal in Canada. Passive euthanasia is withdrawal of life-sustaining treatment and is legal in Canada.

MEDICATION ADMINISTRATION

Medication administration is an important role for nurses in Canada. Medication is used for a variety of purposes, including diagnosis, treatment, cure, relief, or prevention of health problems. Nurses give medications in many practice settings with many nursing responsibilities. Nurses are responsible for delivering the medication accurately and safely to their client, teaching the client about the medication, and evaluating the effect of the medication on the client (Potter et al., 2010).

Implications for Administering Medications

The scope of practice of nurses is determined by legislative acts at the federal and provincial/territorial levels. Nurses must know their own jurisdictional laws that affect drug administration. There are differences in these laws. For example, advanced practice nurses can now prescribe medication in some provinces and territories (Potter et al., 2010). In addition, nurses must be aware of their own practice agencies' drug policies before they administer medications. They must have the knowledge, skill, and judgement before they give drugs. This knowledge is particularly necessary in the case of controlled substances that are regulated by law. Misuse of narcotics, for example, can lead to a loss of nursing licence and registration (Potter et al., 2010).

Medication Actions

There are many variables in how medications act and their types of actions. There are factors other than the characteristics of the drug that affect the medication actions. For example, individuals react very differently to drugs and may not react the same way to successive doses. It is very important for nurses to understand all the effects of the medications on individuals so that drug impact can be evaluated. Types of medication effects are listed below:

- Therapeutic effect is the expected or predicted physiological response from the medication and is the desired outcome.
- Side effects are unintended, secondary effects that a medication predictably will cause. The side effects can be harmless or can harm the individual.
- Toxic effects can develop after taking a drug for a long time or when the level of a medication increases in the blood because of impaired metabolism and drug clearance. Toxic effects can be lethal depending on the drug action.
- Adverse effects are generally severe, negative responses to medication that were unexpected and not seen during drug testing. These effects should be reported to the Health Protection Branch of the federal government. Reporting is voluntary.
- Idiosyncratic reactions are unpredictable and occur when an individual overreacts to a medication or has a different reaction from the norm.
- Allergic reactions are unpredictable responses to a medication after repeated doses. The drug is perceived by the body as an allergen, causing a release of antibodies. The reaction can be mild or severe and cause an anaphylactic reaction leading to airway obstruction from swelling of the larynx and pharynx, severe wheezing, and shortness of breath. Urticaria, angioedema, and the delayed action of a rash and fever are other possible symptoms. This event can be life-threatening, particularly when the individual becomes hypotensive from vasodilation.
- Medication interactions can occur when one medication potentiates (increases) or decreases the action of another. This commonly occurs when several medications are taken. Two drugs can have a synergistic effect, and the drugs together cause more of a drug effect than if they had been given separately (Potter et al., 2010).

Medication Dose Responses

After a medication is taken, it breaks down in the body and is absorbed, distributed, metabolized, and excreted. The individual's metabolism, weight, gender, and body size affect the drug response. Many drugs take some time to be absorbed, with the exception of intravenous medications, which are absorbed directly into the bloodstream. It is important that the drug is kept at a constant level in the blood—one within the therapeutic range between the peak high (the highest serum concentration) and a trough low. The therapeutic level prevents toxicity and resultant damage to the body. In order to keep the medication at a therapeutic level, the nurse needs to administer the drug at regular times throughout the day. With intravenous infusions, the peak concentration occurs quickly, but the serum

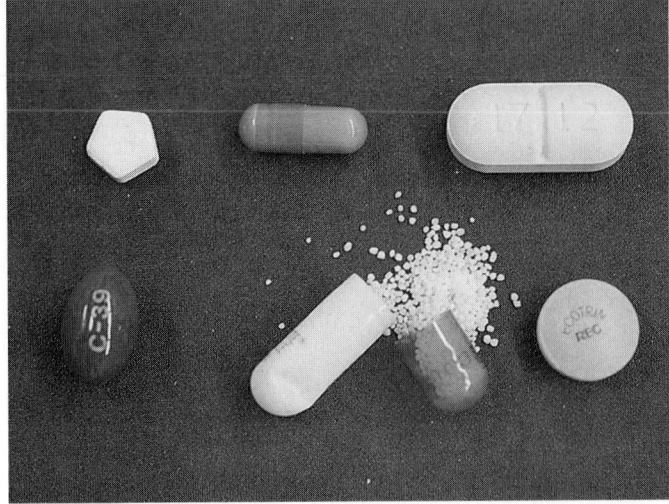

Figure 3.2
Forms of oral medications. *Top row:* **Uniquely shaped tablet, capsule, scored tablet.** *Bottom row:* **Gelatin-coated liquid, extended-release capsule, enteric-coated tablet.**

Source: Potter, P. A., Perry, A. G., Ross-Kerr, J. C., & Wood, M. (Eds.). (2010). *Canadian fundamentals of nursing* (Rev. 4th ed., p. 676, Figure 30-1). Toronto: Elsevier.

level also begins to fall immediately. It is important for the nurse to teach the client to take the drugs on the prescribed schedule to maximize their effect. Refer to Figure 3.2 to see a picture of the different forms of oral medication.

Nursing Roles in Medication Administration

Nurses must have the knowledge necessary to administer and evaluate medications effectively. This knowledge comes from the life sciences and includes an understanding of pharmacokinetics (the study of drug concentrations), human growth and development, human anatomy, nutrition, and mathematics. In addition to the knowledge, nurses and employers need to assess nurses' ability to carry out their roles relating to medications competently and safely in each situation. Nurses need the knowledge, skill, and judgement to independently meet the medication standard of practice. Nurses must also hold the competencies and resources to provide interventions during an adverse reaction. Nurses must be provided with enough opportunities to give the medications in clinical practice settings in order to maintain competency (CNO, 2005). The nurse needs a working knowledge of the medication action.

A critical role for nursing in medication administration is client teaching. The nurse needs to assess the client's ability to safely administer his or her own medication. The situations can be complex, and the nurse needs to be able to assess for client attitude, knowledge, physical and mental status, and responses.

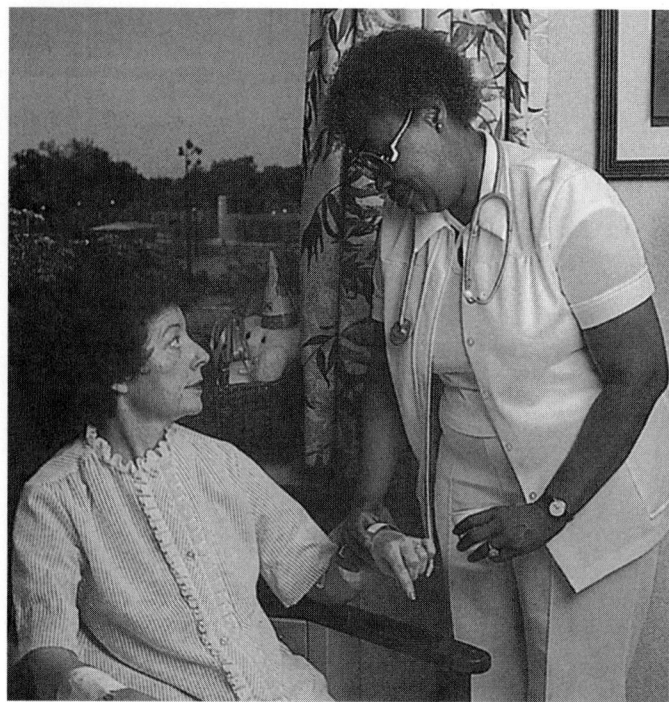

FIGURE 3.3
Before administering any medication, the nurse checks the client's identification bracelet.

Source: deWit, S. (2005). *Fundamental concepts and skills for nursing* (2nd ed.). Philadelphia: W. B. Saunders.

In order to accurately and safely administer medications, nurses must learn to use the "7 rights" to ensure accuracy. These rights are as follows:

- Right medication
- Right dose
- Right client (see Figure 3.3)
- Right route
- Right time
- Right documentation
- Right reason

A nurse meets the medication standard of practice by doing the following:

- Verifying that the prescription is complete and accurate or following up with the prescriber to get a complete prescription
- Assessing the appropriateness of the drug as prescribed for the client in the particular situation
- Not implementing or giving a medication order that is incomplete, illegible, or misinterpreted and following up with the prescriber
- Considering the medication when scheduling dosing times if not specified
- Knowing the trade and generic medication names
- Knowing the accepted abbreviations for their agency
- Processing the prescription as written and not substituting generic or therapeutic interchanges
- Making any necessary changes to the medication administration record (MAR) to record the medication name
- Requesting written orders when the prescriber is present and avoiding the use of verbal orders except in emergencies
- Repeating verbal or telephone orders in their entirety for accuracy and documenting them in the health record
- Assessing if the medication is ordered appropriately for that particular situation
- Retaining faxed and printed e-mail orders and refusing unsecured e-mail orders
- Consulting with colleagues and presenting a clear, evidence-informed rationale explaining their concerns is a must if nurses disagree with a medication order. The nurses then present their concerns to the prescriber, discuss the situation with their immediate nursing authority if the concern is unresolved, and contact the prescriber for more discussion. If the concern is still unresolved, then they must contact a higher nursing authority and inform the prescriber. Next, nurses document their concerns in the health record and fill out an unusual occurrence form or incident report.

ROUTES OF MEDICATION ADMINISTRATION

The route of the medication is prescribed according to the medication properties and desired effect on the client's condition. The nurse collaborates with the prescriber to decide on the best route. The medication administration routes are as follows:

- Oral medications are given by mouth. This is the most common and easiest route and has the slowest and most prolonged effect.
- Sublingual medications are placed under the tongue and absorbed. This medication should not be swallowed.
- Buccal route medications are placed against the mucous membrane of the cheek until the solid medication dissolves. They shouldn't be swallowed or chewed.
- Parenteral medications are injected into body tissues. The four main sites are intradermal, subcutaneous (only for volumes of 0.5–2 mL), intramuscular (for volumes of up to 3 mL), and intravenous. Other sites for injections into body cavities include epidural, intrathecal, intraosseous, intraperitoneal, intrapleural, and intra-arterial. Additional education may be needed to administer medications at these extra sites.
- Topical medications are applied by spreading them on the skin, applying moist dressings, soaking body parts in a solution, flushing the affected part, or giving medicated baths. The effects can be systemic if the client's skin is thin or broken down, if the concentration is too high, or if contact with the skin is prolonged. Transdermal discs or patches can also be used. Instilling drops or ointment to the mucous membranes can also be done.

- The inhalation route can be used to administer medications through nasal passages, orally, by endotracheal tube, or via a tracheostomy.
- Using the intraocular route involves inserting a medication directly into the client's eye.
- Ear installation involves placing a solution into the ear canal for product dissolving and absorption.
- Intravaginal or intra-anal medications (suppositories) are inserted into the anal or vaginal cavities and melt when they reach body temperature, releasing the medication for absorption (Potter et al., 2010).

NURSING ISSUES AND TRENDS

The Nursing Process

A nurse uses the nursing process to guide, plan, organize, provide, and evaluate nursing care. A nurse must use the nursing process in combination with an ability to think critically and the ability to synthesize relevant knowledge, clinical experiences, and standards of practice. Figure 3.4 outlines critical thinking and the nursing assessment process.

Assessment

Assessment is a collection of personal, sociocultural, physiological, and psychological health status data, as well as general information. It is a determination of current health status from the physical assessment.

Analysis

Analysis is a classification of data: screening, organizing, and grouping significant, related information. It is also a definition of a client's problem: determining an appropriate nursing diagnosis that is a definitive statement of the client's actual or potential difficulties, concerns, or deficits that can be altered through nursing interventions.

Planning

Planning involves the client, family or significant others, and nurse, who collaborates with the appropriate health team members to formulate the plan. Planning also establishes client outcomes. Outcomes are expected changes in the client's behaviour, activity, or physical state. Outcomes must be objective, realistic, and measurable and include a realistic period for accomplishment.

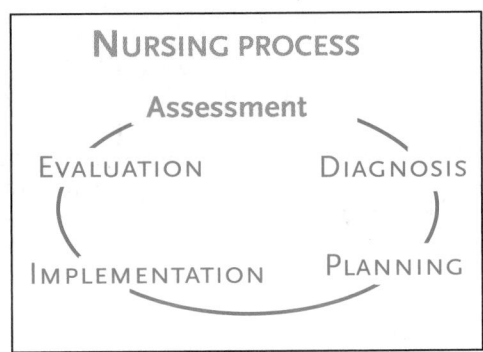

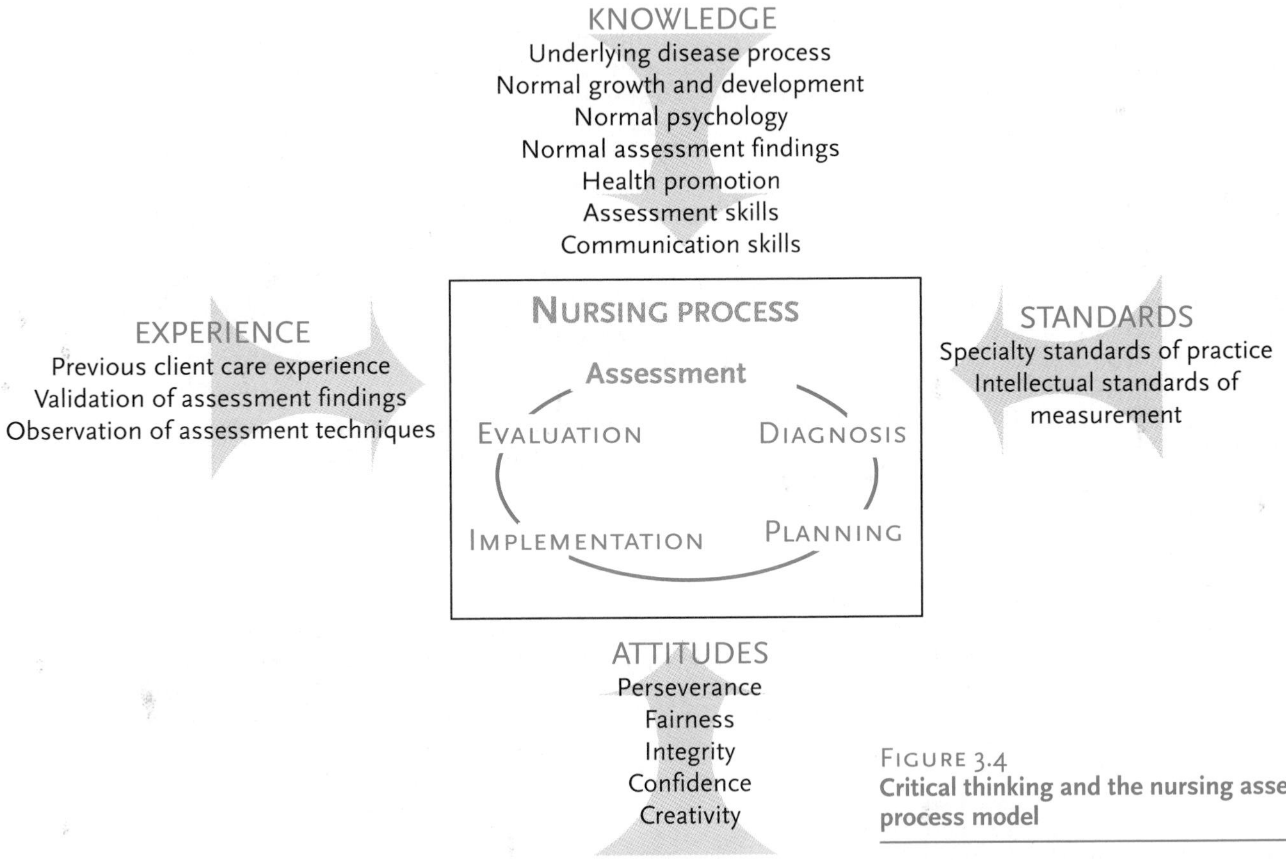

KNOWLEDGE
Underlying disease process
Normal growth and development
Normal psychology
Normal assessment findings
Health promotion
Assessment skills
Communication skills

EXPERIENCE
Previous client care experience
Validation of assessment findings
Observation of assessment techniques

NURSING PROCESS

Assessment

EVALUATION   DIAGNOSIS

IMPLEMENTATION   PLANNING

STANDARDS
Specialty standards of practice
Intellectual standards of measurement

ATTITUDES
Perseverance
Fairness
Integrity
Confidence
Creativity

FIGURE 3.4
Critical thinking and the nursing assessment process model

Source: Potter, P. A., Perry, A. G., Ross-Kerr, J. C., & Wood, M. (Eds.). (2010). *Canadian fundamentals of nursing* (Rev. 4th ed., p. 191, Figure 14-5). Toronto: Elsevier.

Implementation

Implementation is the actual administration of the planned care.

Evaluation, Outcome, and Revision of Care

If an outcome is not reached in the specified time, the client is reassessed. Reordering of priorities may be necessary because the process of evaluation is ongoing.

EVIDENCE-INFORMED PRACTICE AND BEST PRACTICE GUIDELINES

Evidence-informed practice is the systematic application of the best available evidence to decision making in relation to clinical management and policy setting. Nurses are using evidence-informed practice as they manage the need for efficiency and improved client outcomes along with increasing demands for accountability.

Best Practice Guidelines (BPGs) are evidence-informed tools that when implemented improve client, nurse, and organizational outcomes. These guidelines are systematically developed statements, based on the best available evidence, that assist nurses to make decisions about appropriate care. Goals for using Best Practice Guidelines include the following:

- Improved client care
- Reduction in the variation in care
- Transfer of research evidence into practice
- Assistance with clinical decision making
- Reduction of cost

ADVOCACY

All nurses are expected to take on advocacy roles within the Canadian health care system.

They are expected to advocate for the best health interest for their clients and families and to advocate for the client's wishes and expectations, especially when clients are unable to express their needs clearly.

Nurses advocate for organizational or system changes that will improve quality care for clients. When nurses advocate, they give their clients a voice. When done correctly, advocacy leads to empowered clients. Empowered clients ask questions to gain a better understanding of all the options available within their plan of care. Nurses are expected to be client advocates within all practice areas and within the health care team.

POLITICAL ACTIVISM

Nurses may become politically active within their profession and communities. Political activism is usually seen as nurses advocating for the Canadian public in general or involving themselves in current health care issues that clients are experiencing (e.g., access to services).

Political activities can include lobbying all levels of government to introduce policies, laws, and regulations that benefit the health of Canadians, such as increased funding for community care or cancer treatment centres. Nurses also lobby for broad-based issues such as reducing poverty rates or bans on pesticide use.

In addition to lobbying governments or businesses, nurses may also be elected by community members to represent constituents in a formal political venue. Nurses are able to hold office within municipal councils or provincial and federal governments and present their concerns about health care within the system.

A nurse's involvement in nursing organizations is based on the province or territory in which the nurse is employed as well as individual choice. In all cases, if the individual is employed as a nurse, he or she must be a member of the appropriate nursing regulatory body (for example, the CNO). In addition, in some provinces or territories, the nurse must also join the professional nursing association. In those situations, the regulatory organization and professional association are one entity (such as the College of Registered Nurses of Manitoba). The regulatory function, whether part of the professional association or not, involves registering or licensing individuals to the profession, setting standards of practice, and disciplining nurses who do not meet the standards (Potter et al., 2010). When the regulatory body is separate from the nursing professional association, the individual nurse has the choice to join or not join the professional nursing association (such as the RNAO). The regulatory body registers the nurse and has a mandate of public protection. The professional association represents the nursing profession and promotes the role and use of nurses in the health care system.

Labour organizations (often termed unions) are separate from both the professional association and the regulatory organization. The Canadian Confederation of Nurses' Unions was established in 2004 to represent the interests of nurses in both watchdog and lobbying activities. This organization arose with the decline of the National Federation of Nurses' Unions (Potter et al., 2010). Unions assist nurses with workplace issues, including the application and interpretation of labour laws and health and safety issues. When a nurse is employed by an organization that has an established union contract, the nurse must then pay associated fees to the union. Membership in the union is voluntary, but payment of union fees becomes mandatory.

REFERENCES

Black, H. C. (1999). *Black's law dictionary* (7th ed.). St. Paul, MN: West Publishing.

Canadian Association of Midwives/Association canadienne des sages-femmes. (2012). *Midwifery practice—standards & guidelines.* Montreal: Author. Retrieved January 16, 2013, from http://www.canadianmidwives.org/standards-guidelines.html

Canadian Institute for Health Information. (2006). *The regulation and supply of nurse practitioners in Canada.* Ottawa: Author. Retrieved January 16, 2013, from http://secure.CIHIweb/products/ TheNursePractitioner_workforce_in_Canada_2006_update_FINAL.pdf

Canadian Institute for Health Information. (2008). *Regulated nurses: Trends, 2003 to 2007.* Ottawa: Author. Retrieved January 16, 2013, from http://secure.cihi.ca/cihiweb/products/nursing_report_2003_to_2007_e.pdf

Canadian Midwifery Regulators Consortium. (2012). *What is a Canadian Registered Midwife?* Winnipeg: Author. Retrieved January 16, 2013, from http://www.cmrc-ccosf.ca/node/19

Canadian Nurses Association. (2000). *A question of respect: Nurses and end-of-life treatment dilemmas.* Author: Ottawa. Retrieved January 16, 2013, from http://www.cna-aiic.ca/en/improve-your-workplace/nursing-ethics/other-resources/

Canadian Nurses Association. (2006). *Report of 2005 dialogue on advanced nursing practice.* Ottawa: Author.

Canadian Nurses Association. (2007). *Framework for the practice of the registered nurse in Canada.* Ottawa: Author.

Canadian Nurses Association. (2008a). *Code of ethics for registered nurses.* Ottawa: Author.

Canadian Nurses Association. (2008b). *Position statement: Providing nursing care at the end of life.* Ottawa: Author. Retrieved January 16, 2013, from http://www2.cna-aiic.ca/CNA/documents/pdf/publications/PS96_End_of_Life_e.pdf

Canadian Nurses Association. (2011). *Certification.* Retrieved January 16, 2013, from http:www.nurseone.ca/Default.aspx?portlet=StaticHtmlViewerPortlet&plang=1&ptdi=153

Canadian Nurses Protective Society. (2004). Negligence: When would a nurse face an allegation of negligence? *InfoLAW, 3*(1). Ottawa: Author.

Canadian Nurses Protective Society. (2005). Legal risks in nursing. *InfoLAW, 8*(1). Ottawa: Author.

Canadian Nurses Protective Society. (2006). Consent for CPR. *InfoLAW, 15*(2). Ottawa: Author.

College of Nurses of Ontario. (2005). *Practice standard: Medication.* Toronto: Author.

College of Nurses of Ontario. (2009). *Guiding decisions about end of life.* Toronto: Author. Retrieved January 16, 2013, from http://www.cno.org/en/search/?q=cardiopulmonary+resuscitation&p=1

deWit, S. (2005). *Fundamental concepts and skills for nursing* (2nd ed.). Philadelphia: W. B. Saunders.

Duhaime, L. (n.d.). Tort. *Duhaime's legal dictionary.* Retrieved January 16, 2013, from http://www.duhaime.org/LegalDictionary/T/Tort.aspx

Fridman, G. (2003). *Introduction to the Canadian law of torts* (2nd ed.). Markham, ON: LexisNexis Canada.

International Council of Nurses. (2011). *ICN networks.* Geneva: Author. Retrieved January 16, 2013, from http://www.icn.ch/networks/icn-networks/

Jurisdictional Competency Project. (2006). *Competencies in the context of entry-level registered nurse practice.* Vancouver: Author.

Osborne, P. H. (2003). *Essentials of Canadian law: The law of torts* (2nd ed.). Toronto: Irwin Law.

Potter, P. A., Perry, A. G., Ross-Kerr, J. C., & Wood, M. (2010). *Canadian fundamentals of nursing* (Rev. 4th ed.). Toronto: Elsevier.

Registered Nurses' Association of Ontario. (2011). *Types of nursing.* Retrieved January 16, 2013, from http://careersinnursing.ca.why-nursing/career-options/types-nursing

Sneiderman, B., Irvine, J., & Osborne, P. (2003). *Canadian medical law* (3rd ed.). Scarborough, ON: Thomson Canada.

BIBLIOGRAPHY

Balzer Riley, J. (2004). *Communication in nursing* (5th ed.). Philadelphia, Mosby.

Canadian Nurses Association. (2005). *Canadian nurse practitioner core competency framework.* Ottawa: Author.

College & Association of Registered Nurses of Alberta. (2005). *Professional boundaries: A discussion guide and teaching tool.* Edmonton, AB: Author. Retrieved January 16, 2013, from http://www.nurses.ab.ca/Carna-Admin/Uploads/Professional%20Boundaries%20Discussion%20Guide.pdf

College of Nurses of Ontario. (2005). Mastering communication. *The Standard, 30*(3). Toronto: Author. Retrieved January 16, 2013, from http://www.cno.org/pubs/mag/2005/09Sept/feat_comm.htm

College of Nurses of Ontario. (2005). *Practice guideline: Culturally sensitive care.* Toronto: Author. Retrieved January 16, 2013, from http://www.cno.org/docs/prac/41040_CulturallySens.pdf

College of Nurses of Ontario. (2006). *Practice standard: Therapeutic nurse–client relationship.* Toronto: Author. Retrieved January 16, 2013, from http://www.cno.org/docs/prac/41033_Therapeutic.pdf

DeVito, J. A., Shimoni, R., & Clarke, D. (2001). *Messages: Building interpersonal communication skills* (Canadian ed.). Toronto: Pearson.

Registered Nurses' Association of Ontario. (2006). *E-Learning: Establishing therapeutic relationships.* Toronto: Author. Retrieved January 16, 2013, from http://www.rnao.org/TR_e-learning/index.html

Stein-Parbury, J. (2005). *Patient & person: Interpersonal skills in nursing* (3rd ed.). Marrickville, AU: Elsevier.

WEB SITES

Canadian Nurses Association: CNA Code of Ethics for Registered Nurses (http://www.cna-nurses.ca/cna/documents/pdf/publications/Code_of_Ethics_2008_e.pdf): This document serves as a foundation for nurses' ethical practice.

College & Association of Registered Nurses of Alberta: Nursing Practice Standards (https://www.nurses.ab.ca/Carna-Admin/Uploads/new_nps_with_ethics.pdf): This document details the practice standards of the College & Association of Registered Nurses of Alberta.

College of Nurses of Ontario (http://www.cno.org): This site contains links to information related to all aspects of being a registered nursing professional in Ontario.

College of Nurses of Ontario: Registration Information (http://www.cno.org/reg/index.htm): This site contains information about how to become a registered nurse in Ontario.

College of Registered Nurses of British Columbia (http://www.rnabc.bc.ca): This site contains links to information related to all aspects of being a registered nursing professional in British Columbia.

College of Registered Nurses of Manitoba (http://www.crnm.mb.ca/reg.php): This site contains information about how to become a registered nurse in Manitoba.

CHAPTER 3

Practice Questions

Case 1

A nurse educator has revised the hospital's orientation program in anticipation of the hospital orientating many new graduate nurses within the next three months. The nurse educator decides to use sample client health records to highlight areas of professional practice. He conducts his first education session with the new graduates.

Questions 1–5 refer to this case.

1. During the documentation session, one of the new nurses asks what abbreviations can be used within the client's health record. What abbreviations should the nurse use?

    1. Abbreviations learned in nursing school
    2. Abbreviations that have been approved by the Canadian Nurses Association
    3. Abbreviations that have been approved by the hospital
    4. Abbreviations that are in common use on specific units within the hospital

2. Which of the following statements is the most accurate information with regard to client consent?

    1. Nurses are responsible for ensuring that clients sign all consent forms on the health record
    2. The health care professional proposing the procedure requiring written consent is the person who must ensure that written client consent is obtained
    3. Verbal consent for an operative procedure is acceptable, and signed consents are not always necessary
    4. When a client is admitted to the hospital, the client signs a written consent that covers all treatments

3. In the sample client's health record, the new graduate nurses discover that a nurse has written "Verbal Order, acetaminophen (Tylenol®), 325 mg, PO, prn, for pain." There is no evidence that this was an emergency situation. Which of the following describes accepted practice in relation to verbal medication orders?

    1. Verbal orders are to be avoided, except in an emergency situation.
    2. Nurses should follow the same practice for verbal orders as for telephone orders
    3. Verbal orders should never be accepted, including in emergency situations
    4. Only RNs may receive verbal orders for medications from a physician

4. The new graduate nurses find a medication order in the sample health record that states:

"Acetaminophen one to two tablets q3–4h for pain." What would be the correct medication order?

    1. Acetaminophen 325 mg PO for pain
    2. Acetaminophen 325–650 mg PO for pain q3–4h prn
    3. Acetaminophen 325–650 mg PO for pain as needed
    4. Acetaminophen 325 or 650 mg q3–4h prn

5. During the orientation, the nurse educator explains that the hospital uses evidence-informed practice to guide clinical decision making. Which of the following statements best describes evidence-informed practice?

    1. An opportunity to obtain funding from the government
    2. An opportunity to transfer research findings into practice
    3. A chance for professionals to trial untested research findings
    4. A way to promote enhanced assessment skills

Case 2

A manager of home care nurses has noticed over the past three months a lack of clarity about the roles of the team members, poor team morale, increasing negative communication, and team conflict. The manager decides to support her staff by providing an education session.

Questions 6–9 refer to this case.

6. One of the new team members is a clinical nurse specialist (CNS). How should the manager describe the level of education for the CNS?

    1. A nurse who has specialty certification from the Canadian Nurses Association
    2. A nurse who has taken a special interest course in a unique field
    3. A nurse who has an undergraduate degree in a discipline other than nursing
    4. A nurse educated at the master's level with a specialization in a particular practice area

7. The manager is preparing the education session for her staff group. Which of the following is true in relation to the teaching and learning process?

    1. It is important to use the same approach with all types of learners
    2. It is better to introduce all new knowledge instead of connecting it to previously learned knowledge
    3. Learning occurs best when the individual has an identified need to learn
    4. It is always best to deliver education quickly and at the same time of day

8. The manager explains that effective interpersonal communication with clients and team members includes which of the following?

   1. The use of "you" statements when interacting with clients and colleagues
   2. The use of warmth and genuineness in interactions
   3. The use of questions that illicit single-word responses in order to promote efficient communication
   4. The use of frequent self-disclosure to ensure that others will share your point of view

9. In situations in which a team conflict has arisen, what would be the best statement by the manager to her staff?

   1. "We should put aside our differences and work together as a team"
   2. "I think we should employ a conflict resolution specialist to help us"
   3. "Let's have a discussion about what we can agree is expected team behaviour"
   4. "These are the guidelines for team behaviour in this agency"

Case 3

A nurse works in a long-term care facility where many of the residents experience acute agitation.

Questions 10–13 refer to this case.

10. The facility follows a "least-restraint policy." What is the most important consideration with a "least-restraint policy"?

    1. That a family conference is organized prior to the implementation of a restraint
    2. That all possible alternative interventions have been exhausted before a restraint is implemented
    3. That the client has no manifestations of delirium or dementia
    4. That the client has signed consent for the application of restraints

11. The nurse charts the behaviour of a client. Which of the following statements would be the most appropriate documentation?

    1. "The client was agitated today."
    2. "The client was confused this morning."
    3. "The client was shaking his fist at the nurse at 1100 hrs."
    4. "The client was behaving inappropriately during the evening shift."

12. On occasion, the nurse finds she has difficult ethical decisions to make as she plans care for her clients. Which of the following primary values from the

Code of Ethics would influence the nurse's decision making concerning the application of restraints?

   1. Confidentiality
   2. Justice
   3. Safe, competent, and ethical care
   4. Quality practice environment

13. The nurse consults the provincial or territorial Standards of Nursing Practice as she further contemplates the use of restraints. What is the most important purpose for using Standards of Nursing Practice?

   1. Standards will help the nurse to make decisions about ongoing learning needs
   2. Standards will act as a guide to the nurse's clinical decision making
   3. Standards will help the nurse in malpractice situations
   4. Standards will guide the nurse to be aware of protecting her own health, safety, and welfare

Case 4

A nurse has immigrated to Canada from Poland. She received her nursing education in Poland and is now studying for the Canadian Registered Nurse Examination. She has discovered many differences in terms and meaning between nursing practice in Canada and nursing practice in Poland.

Questions 14–16 refer to this case.

14. The nurse knows she must be able to articulate the differences and similarities between various nursing organizations. The mandate of nursing regulatory organizations is which of the following?

   1. Protection of the public
   2. Protection of nurses
   3. Protection of nursing employers
   4. Protection of all regulated health professionals

15. The nurse is trying to distinguish the difference between Standards of Nursing Practice and the nursing Best Practice Guidelines. What are the Best Practice Guidelines?

   1. Classifications that assist in the analysis and grouping of data
   2. Advance directives that clearly indicate the client's wishes and needs
   3. Tools based on proven criteria that improve client, nurse, and organizational outcomes
   4. Policies that guide compassionate care and ethical nursing decisions

16. The nurse has noticed the term DNR in one of the sample questions in the exam preparatory book. What does DNR mean?

1. Do not perform cardiopulmonary resuscitation
2. Do not administer cardiac compressions
3. Do not perform any life-saving actions
4. Do not perform any form of resuscitation that has not been agreed upon by the client or Substitute Decision Maker

INDEPENDENT QUESTIONS

Questions 17–30 do not refer to a particular case.

17. Meaghan, age 17 years, attends a community eating disorder support group. Meaghan was hospitalized last year for anorexia nervosa, and she continues to restrict her diet to 700 calories per day. Meaghan stated at today's meeting that she is three months pregnant. The public health nurse, who facilitates the support group, is concerned about Meaghan and the fetus. Which of the following actions should the nurse take?

    1. Call the family physician and notify him of the pregnancy
    2. Call Meaghan's parents and notify them of the pregnancy
    3. Obtain Meaghan's consent to contact the physician
    4. Contact Children's Aid Society after the baby is born and explain the situation

18. A nurse is temporarily employed in a family physician's office while the regular nurse is on vacation. The physician has left a note for the temporary nurse to complete a referral to a gynecologist for a client requesting a therapeutic abortion. The nurse has strong religious values against abortion, and she was unaware that working with clients requesting abortions would be part of her role in the office. What is the best action for the nurse?

    1. Leave a note for the physician indicating she refuses to make the referral for an abortion
    2. Complete the referral to the gynecologist as part of her obligation to provide care for the client in the absence of the regular office nurse
    3. Notify the physician that she will not be working in the office after today's shift
    4. Tell the client that the usual RN will make the referral when she returns from vacation next week

19. A nurse working her first evening shift as the "in charge" nurse in a long-term care facility hears an unregulated care provider (UCP) tell a client: "If you don't stay quiet in your bed while I help this other resident, I won't feed you your supper." What would be the priority action for the nurse?

    1. Ask the resident to repeat what the UCP stated
    2. Make sure that the UCP is not assigned to that resident

when future resident assignments are developed
    3. Remove the UCP from the client situation and report the incident to the nurse manager the next morning
    4. Determine if the UCP needs help with the residents

20. A resident in a long-term care facility tells the nurse that his leg hurts from the fall he had an hour ago. The nurse was unaware of the fall and obtains details about the fall from the unregulated care provider (UCP) who cared for the resident at the time of the fall. Which statement related to accountability is correct?

    1. The nurse is accountable in all situations for the actions of the UCP
    2. The nurse is not accountable for the actions of the UCP because she was on her lunch break at the time of the fall
    3. The nurse is accountable for the resident's fall because the nurse was the only registered/licensed staff on duty at the time of the fall
    4. The nurse is not accountable for the care or actions of the UCP

21. A nurse has been asked by his manager to work an extra four hours after his 12-hour shift because three nurses have called in sick. The nurse has worked four 12-hour shifts consecutively. He admits he is tired and not sure whether he is too fatigued to work the extra four hours. Which of the following is the most appropriate?

    1. The nurse cannot refuse to work the additional four hours as his manager has made the request and there are no other replacements
    2. The nurse has no obligation to work the additional four hours, and he should report his decision to his union representative
    3. The nurse must be offered time and a half for the extra four additional hours
    4. The nurse's first priority in deciding to work the extra four hours is whether he is competent to provide safe care

22. Brandon, age 6, has arrived at the emergency unit after a car accident. Brandon is spending the weekend with family friends. Brandon's next of kin cannot be located. Brandon has been diagnosed with multiple fractures and requires immediate treatment. Which of the following is true with regard to consent?

    1. Brandon is unable to provide consent for the treatment of the fractures because he is not 21 years old
    2. Treatment must be delayed because Brandon's parents cannot be reached
    3. The family friends may act as Substitute Decision Makers (SDMs) for Brandon
    4. Since this is an emergency situation, parental consent for treatment is not required

23. A second-year nursing student obtains an apical heart rate of 140 bpm on Cara, a 6-year-old child. The student nurse assumes she has made an error in counting the beats. She did not take any action in relation to her findings, and she did not report the elevated heart rate to anyone. Who is responsible for this error in care?

1. The student nurse because she did not report the heart rate or take any action
2. The staff nurse working with the student nurse because she should have asked about the heart rate
3. The student nurse's clinical instructor because she knows the student nurse's strengths and weaknesses
4. The clinical instructor, student nurse, and staff nurse are all equally responsible

24. A client is ordered 325 mg of acetylsalicylic acid (ASA) prn for headache. The nurse is aware that this client is also receiving warfarin (Coumadin). Which of the following is the most appropriate action to be taken by the nurse?

1. Contact the doctor for clarification of the orders
2. Ask the client if he has taken aspirin before while also taking Coumadin
3. Contact the pharmacist about the potential drug interaction
4. Consult with nursing colleagues about whether to give the ASA to the client

25. A third-year nursing student has asked his preceptor about the use of restraints. Which of the following is not considered a restraint category?

1. Chemical
2. Physical
3. Hazardous
4. Environmental

26. A nurse who works for a community nursing agency is a strong advocate of increasing funding to community agencies. She is running for election to her municipal council to bring this issue forward. The nurse should be aware of which of the following?

1. She would be unable to be elected into municipal council as that is considered unprofessional conduct
2. She can only be a candidate for municipal council if she resigns her employment
3. There are too many risks and conflicts in the environment to be an effective municipal councillor
4. She can be a candidate for municipal council and accept the role if elected

27. A student nurse has forgotten her computer password. She asks a staff nurse to share her password in order to access a client's chart. What should the staff nurse do?

1. Share the password since the student provided direct client care
2. Ask the student to write the care on a piece of paper, and the staff nurse will enter it later
3. Do not share the password and direct the student to the policy on retrieving forgotten passwords
4. Explain the situation to the charge nurse, who will locate a password

28. A client is ordered venlafaxine (Effexor®) for depression. The client refuses to take the medication, stating that it causes headaches. What should the nurse do?

1. Do not give the medication because the client has withdrawn her consent
2. Tell the charge nurse the situation to see if she can convince the client to take the medication
3. Administer the medication because the client has been diagnosed with depression
4. Insist the client take the medication but tell her she will give her Tylenol® for the headache

29. In a hospital setting, what is the priority practice by a nurse to ensure administration of the correct medication to the correct client?

1. Check each client's identification bracelet
2. Address each client by his or her last name prior to administering the medication
3. Check each client's health card or hospital identification card
4. Check the names that are posted above the client's bed or attached to the bottom of the bed

30. The nurse is not able to read the obstetrician's handwriting for postpartum orders for a client. The obstetrician has returned to her office outside the hospital. What should the nurse do?

1. Ask the client what her obstetrician ordered for postpartum pain relief
2. Contact the obstetrician for clarification of the orders
3. Ask the unit clerk for clarification of the obstetrician's handwriting
4. Consult other postpartum charts for this obstetrician to compare similar orders

Answers and Rationales for Practice Questions

1.   C: Professional Practice   T: Application

1. Abbreviations must be approved by the organization or agency.
2. The Canadian Nurses Association does not approve abbreviations for documentation.
3. Abbreviations must be approved by the organization or agency.
4. Abbreviations must be approved by the organization or agency, not the individual unit.

2.   C: Professional Practice   T: Critical Thinking

1. The person most involved in the procedure must obtain client consent. Nurses do not obtain consent for procedures performed by others.
2. The person most involved in the procedure and the one who can explain the procedure fully should obtain client consent.
3. Verbal consent is acceptable for some procedures, but surgery usually requires written consent.
4. Consent can be withdrawn at any time during investigation or treatment, even if a signed consent had previously been obtained.

3.   C: Professional Practice   T: Application

1. Verbal orders are not telephone orders and should not be utilized unless in an emergency situation.
2. Verbal orders are not equivalent to telephone orders.
3. Verbal orders may need to be accepted in emergency situations.
4. There are no regulations that define which kind of nurse can accept verbal orders.

4.   C: Professional Practice   T: Application

1. The dose is not correct, and the frequency is not identified.
2. The dose is accurate, the route is identified, the frequency is identified, and the qualifier is identified.
3. The dose is not correct, and the frequency is not identified.
4. The dose is not correct, and the route is not identified.

5.   C: Professional Practice   T: Knowledge

1. Evidence-informed care does not relate to government funding.
2. Evidence-informed care is founded in the transfer of current research into practice.
3. Evidence-informed care is described after research has been completed.
4. Not all evidence-informed care focuses on assessment skills.

6.   C: Professional Practice   T: Knowledge

1. The Canadian Nurses Association does not grant CNS certificates.
2. This is not correct.
3. This is not correct.
4. A clinical nurse specialist is usually educated at the master's level.

7.   C: Nurse–Client Partnership   T: Application

1. Different learning styles require different teaching approaches.
2. Learning is easier when the material is connected to what the learner already knows.
3. Learning occurs best when the learner identifies a learning need.
4. It is best to offer a variety of options to learners because some individuals learn best in the morning, whereas others learn best in the afternoon or evening.

8.   C: Nurse–Client Partnership   T: Application

1. "I" statements should be utilized with clients and colleagues.
2. When genuineness and warmth are utilized, the communication is more effective.
3. Communication is better facilitated by open-ended questions.
4. Self-disclosure should be utilized minimally and only to build a therapeutic nurse–client relationship, not to share the nurse's point of view.

9.   C: Nurse–Client Partnership   T: Critical Thinking

1. Differences may contribute to conflict, but the conflict must then be acknowledged and resolved rather than the differences suppressed.
2. Team collaboration is the most effective method of conflict resolution, even more effective than introducing a third party.
3. Team collaboration is the most effective method of conflict resolution. The team is required to work together to resolve the conflict.
4. At times there must be imposed guidelines, but team collaboration is most effective.

10.   C: Professional Practice   T: Critical Thinking

1. This may not be practical or applicable in every client situation.
2. This is the primary consideration prior to the decision to apply restraints.
3. This is not a consideration.
4. Consent may be required, but it may be verbal, or it may be from a Substitute Decision Maker. It does not necessarily have to be a signed consent.

11.   C: Professional Practice   T: Application

1. This is an assumption rather than factual documentation and does not note the exact time.
2. As in choice 1.
3. This is factual documentation.
4. As in choice 1.

12.   C: Professional Practice   T: Critical Thinking

1. Confidentiality involves nurses safeguarding client information and ensuring that the information stays within the health care team.
2. Justice involves the upholding of the principles of equity and fairness.
3. Nurses value the ability to provide safe, competent, and ethical care that allows them to fulfill their ethical and professional obligations to the public.
4. Quality practice environments mean that nurses value and advocate for practice environments that have structures and resources that ensure safety and respect.

13.   C: Professional Practice   T: Critical Thinking

1. Standards may help the nurse identify learning gaps, but this is not the most important purpose.
2. Standards of Nursing Practice define the expectation for nurses in various practice settings and situations and generally guide nursing practice.
3. While Standards of Nursing Practice focus on defining expectations for acceptable practice, they do not focus on malpractice.
4. The primary purpose of nursing practice and health professions acts, and thereby Standards of Nursing Practice, is to protect the public's (not the nurse's) health, safety, and welfare.

14.   C: Professional Practice   T: Knowledge

1. The primary mandate of a health regulatory organization is protection of the public.
2. Labour organizations have the mandate of protecting nurses.
3. The employer has a responsibility to serve the clients to whom they provide service.
4. The nursing regulatory body protects the public from unsafe, unethical nursing care—it cannot be generalized to any other regulated profession.

15.   C: Professional Practice   T: Application

1. Analysis and grouping of data is part of the nursing process, not the Best Practice Guidelines.

2. Advance directives are individualized to specific clients; they cannot be generalized as best practice for whole groups.
3. Evidence-informed guidelines are tools that improve client, nurse, and organizational outcomes. They involve care that is based on actual observed and proven outcomes, not tradition-based care.
4. A code of ethics provides guidelines for compassionate care, educates about ethical responsibilities, and informs about moral commitments.

16.   C: Professional Practice   T: Critical Thinking

1. This is a generally accepted interpretation but is not the most correct answer as the health care team has the responsibility to determine the client's exact wishes.
2. DNR may be open to interpretation and not involve only cardiac compressions.
3. This is too vague an interpretation.
4. The client or Substitute Decision Maker must decide what, if any, resuscitation is desired. The nurse has the responsibility to comply with the stated wishes of the capable client, whether they are written as a DNR or not.

17.   C: Nurse–Client Partnership   T: Application

1. The nurse does not have Meaghan's consent to call her physician.
2. The nurse does not have consent from Meaghan to call her parents.
3. The nurse requires consent from Meaghan to contact the physician or parents.
4. If the nurse suspects potential abuse or neglect, she must involve the Children's Aid Society immediately rather than wait until after the birth.

18.   C: Nurse–Client Partnership   T: Application

1. This does not ensure that client care is provided. The nurse has an ethical obligation to provide the required client care or find a substitute to provide the care.
2. The nurse has an ethical obligation to provide client care since no one else is available to provide the care.
3. The nurse must first provide the care (the referral to the gynecologist) or find a substitute to provide the care.
4. The client's care cannot be deferred until next week. The nurse has an ethical obligation to provide the required care.

19.   C: Professional Practice   T: Critical Thinking

1. The resident may not accurately recall what was said or may be afraid to discuss the event for fear of reprisal from the UCP.
2. This action does not deal with the issue of verbal abuse. Situations of abuse must be addressed as close to the time of the incident as possible.
3. It is the professional responsibility of the nurse to stop the abuse immediately and notify the manager in order to ensure resident safety.
4. This action does not deal with the issue of verbal abuse.

20.   C: Professional Practice   T: Application

1. The nurse is not accountable for the actions of the UCP; the UCP is accountable for her own actions.
2. The nurse is not accountable for the actions of the UCP despite being on her lunch break.
3. The nurse is not accountable for the actions of the UCP despite being the only registered/licensed staff on duty at the time of the fall.
4. UCPs are accountable for their care, including any actions or inactions taken that relate to the resident falling.

21.   C: Professional Practice   T: Application

1. The nurse's decision to work the additional hours is his choice.
2. The nurse's involvement of the labour union is separate from the nurse's accountability to provide safe and effective care.
3. Payment of overtime is not the primary concern for the nurse; he must be competent to provide care.
4. The nurse's first priority is to provide high-quality client care. He must determine if he is too tired to provide competent care.

22.   C: Professional Practice   T: Application

1. Age is not a consideration in consent when it is an emergency situation.
2. Treatment in an emergency situation can be provided.
3. The friends would require a written letter from Brendan's parents designating them as SDMs.
4. In an emergency, if the client is not capable of making a treatment decision, a SDM is located. If this is not possible, treatment may be performed if the client is experiencing severe suffering or is at risk of serious bodily harm. In this case, because there is no legal SDM, he will be treated under general consent due to the urgency of the situation and the risk of bodily harm without treatment.

23.   C: Professional Practice   T: Critical Thinking

1. The student nurse is responsible for her knowledge and actions.
2. The staff nurse working with the student is not responsible for the student's actions.
3. The student nurse is accountable for her knowledge and actions, not the clinical instructor.
4. The student nurse is responsible for her knowledge and actions.

24.   C: Professional Practice   T: Critical Thinking

1. ASA is contraindicated for clients who are receiving Coumadin. The nurse must clarify the order with the physician.
2. The client may not have accurate knowledge of his medications.
3. The pharmacist cannot change the prescribed drug order.
4. The nurse does not need to consult with colleagues.

25.   C: Professional Practice   T: Knowledge

1. Chemical restraints include medications.
2. Physical restraints include side rails, Posey vests, etc.
3. "Hazardous" is not a restraint category.
4. Environmental restraints include a locked ward or room.

26.   C: Professional Practice   T: Application

1. It is not unprofessional nursing conduct to be elected to municipal, provincial, federal, or territorial positions.
2. The nurse does not need to resign from employment.
3. The nurse would manage any risks or conflicts following political processes.
4. It is within the professional role of the nurse to run for and hold political office.

27.   C: Professional Practice   T: Application

1. Passwords should never be shared even if client care is provided.
2. The student nurse who provided the care should document the care.
3. Passwords should not be shared. Anyone who will be documenting client care should be provided with a password.
4. The student nurse should take responsibility for retrieving a forgotten password.

CHAPTER 3

28.   **C: Professional Practice   T: Application**

1. The client has withdrawn consent; the nurse cannot force treatment.
2. The client has expressed her wishes. This does not require intervention from the charge nurse.
3. The diagnosis of depression does not mean the client is unable to provide informed consent for treatments.
4. It is not ethical nor therapeutic for the nurse to insist the client take the medication.

29.   **C: Professional Practice   T: Critical Thinking**

1. Checking the client's identification bracelet is the safest method to ensure the "right client."
2. Clients may have similar names.

3. Some clients may not have access to their health card or hospital identification card.
4. Clients may not be in the correct bed.

30.   **C: Professional Practice   T: Application**

1. The client may not have accurate knowledge of the obstetrician's orders for postpartum pain relief.
2. Nurses must have the original prescriber clarify the order.
3. Clarification must be obtained from the prescriber, not other health care providers.
4. As in choice 2.

Health Assessment Across the Lifespan

Catherine Mayers, RN, MSN

Health assessment is the collection of information about an individual's well-being. The information can come from a variety of sources; there is verbal information from the person or the person's family; there is physical information that the nurse obtains through inspection, percussion, palpation, and auscultation; and there is laboratory testing. All these and any other sources of information are gathered to assist the practitioner to obtain a complete picture of the individual's well-being.

For the purpose of easy access, this chapter is divided into site-specific sections. Normally, the nurse must consider the person as a whole rather than as the sum of many individual parts. However, this chapter focuses on one system or area at a time. One of the arts of nursing is to paint the whole picture once all the parts are known. Imagine an artist's palette; the areas of information are the colours on the palette, and the care for the client will be determined once the picture has been painted.

As a member of the health care team, it is imperative that the nurse assess the client and that the assessment be recorded. The nurse must believe what she or he hears and report it, especially if it is abnormal. The nurse, especially the novice nurse, must not second-guess and ignore the findings due to feelings of doubt. If you are in doubt, report the findings and ask a more experienced member of the team to verify them.

The most important aspect of health assessment is the history. Not only is *what* is said important, but *how* it is said is also key. The role of the nurse is to get the whole story by asking pertinent questions and steering the conversation in a way that is productive and time-efficient. The physical examination will confirm or refute the story and assist the nurse in obtaining the information needed to help make the diagnosis. Whether the result is a nursing diagnosis or a medical diagnosis, the story is a vital component.

INTERVIEWING SKILLS AND HISTORY-TAKING

COMMUNICATION TECHNIQUES

To take a history, or to listen to a history, the nurse must use a variety of question types, as summarized in Table 4.1.

How the nurse responds to the answers can be as important as the questions themselves. Table 4.2 provides a number of responses, descriptors, and examples.

It is not just the spoken word of an interview that can give you the complete story. It is important to observe the client's posture, eye contact, facial expressions, voice, language, the use of touch, and any gestures. All these enhance the depth and meaning of

Table 4.1 Communication Techniques

Type of Question	Description of Question	Examples
Open-Ended Questions	• Good at the beginning of the interview • Can lead to a lot of information • Unbiased • The nurse must be an active and interested listener and encourage the story; e.g., use "Tell me more" to promote more information • Person can go off on many tangents	"How are you feeling today?" "Tell me about your health concerns." "Why have you come to the clinic today?"
Closed or Direct Questions	• Good for specific details • Use to fill in the gaps from the open-ended response • Can be used to expedite the interview • Ask one question at a time only • Use culturally appropriate language • Answers are quite often "yes" or "no"	"Do you have any drug allergies?" "Do you get short of breath climbing a flight of stairs?" "When was the last time you ate anything?"

Table 4.2 Examples of Responses and Descriptors

Response	Description of Response	Examples
Facilitation	• Encourages further information • Shows an interest in the information being shared, which will promote storytelling	"Yes" Nodding your head Good eye contact "Mm-hmm" or "Uh-huh" "Go on, I'm listening."
Silence	• Good after open-ended questions • Maintain good eye contact • Try not to interrupt • Watch person for nonverbal clues	
Reflection	• Repeat part of what the person said to allow him or her to expand on it • Expand on an important concept • Specifically focus on an emotional aspect of what the person has said	Client: "I don't understand how to do it. I feel so scared." Nurse: "You feel scared?" Client: "I suffered from this last year and now it's back." Nurse: "You had this last year?"
Empathy	• Gives the person a sense of feeling understood • Can promote the therapeutic relationship • Gives the green light to the person to talk about his or her thoughts and feelings	"This is probably very scary for you to go through." "I can imagine that if that happened to me I would also be scared, frightened, upset . . . " etc. "I can understand how frustrating this must be for you."
Clarification	• Use when you do not understand what the person is saying or when you think that what he or she is saying can be interpreted in more than one way • Use as a point of clarification. Are you on the right track?	Client: "My job is very heavy." Nurse: "You do a lot of heavy lifting in your job?" Nurse "Let me get this straight: the pain occurs only in the morning, you get relief when you drink three cups of coffee, and the pain does not return until the following morning. Is that correct?" Client: "Yes, that's right."
Confrontation Interpretation Explanation Summary	• Leave these responses to the end and use as a wrap-up of the interview • If you do not agree with something that the client has said, question him or her on it • Helps the person identify with an emotion or explanation as to why something has happened • Use explanation to literally explain the why and what of some notion Using summarizing can clarify the issues, put them into sequence, restate your client's perceptions and your own, and validate the information with the client.	"You say that you are okay with being in the hospital, but you seem to be so sad and worried." "Do you realize that every time you come to the emergency department with abdominal pain, your mother-in-law is visiting from out of town?" "You must drink the CT dye so that the X-ray will be clear for the doctor to interpret."

the spoken word. Table 4.3 gives examples of positive and negative nonverbal behaviours of the interviewer.

A complete history can take up to an hour or even longer to obtain, which is not always practical even at the best of times. The nurse must therefore decide what information is a priority in a shortened amount of time. Over the course of caring for the client, the nurse can continue to ask questions and listen to the whole story. Another reason to do a complete history is to find out any areas of concern in which health teaching and health promotion would be beneficial.

It is not always possible for the history to come from the client. For an infant or young child, the

Table 4.3 Nonverbal Behaviours of the Interviewer

Positive	Negative
Appropriate professional appearance	Appearance objectionable to client
Equal-status seating	Standing
Close proximity to client	Sitting behind desk, far away, turned away
Relaxed open posture	Tense posture
Leaning slightly toward person	Slouched back
Occasional facilitating gestures	Critical or distracting gestures: pointing finger, clenched fist, finger-tapping, foot-swinging, looking at watch
Facial animation, interest	Bland expression, yawning, tight mouth
Appropriate smiling	Frowning, lip-biting
Appropriate eye contact	Shifty, avoiding eye contact, focusing on notes
Moderate tone of voice	Strident, high-pitched tone
Moderate rate of speech	Rate too slow or too fast
Appropriate touch	Too frequent or inappropriate touch

Source: Jarvis, C., Browne, A. J., MacDonald-Jenkins, J., & Luctkar-Flude, M. (2009). *Physical examination & health assessment* (1st Canadian ed., p. 59, Table 4-2). Toronto: Saunders.

history will come from the child's caregiver (parent, grandparent, or guardian). In the case of an adult who is comatose or too ill to engage in conversation, the information may come from a spouse, a child, or a friend. Understand that information gathered in these circumstances is modified by the person relaying it. Watch the child closely for nonverbal communication. Be inclusive and call the person by name. Now you must build up a therapeutic relationship not just with the client but also with the provider of information.

Interviewing adolescents can present its challenges. Teens want to be considered as adults but can revert to wanting a parent close by, especially when they are in a stressful situation. Certain information will not be shared unless a good trusting relationship has been built, which may happen only if the parent is not present. Not all adolescents are the same. Levels of maturity, understanding, and the ability to express oneself can range widely. Starting with the easiest questions can be helpful, and when there is a greater sense of trust, the more sensitive questions can be broached.

Interviewing the older adult can be a much slower process. Giving the client more time to answer will decrease the potential for frustration and stress. Open-ended questions might take longer to answer because they may cover a lengthy life history. If the client has a deficit in short-term memory, the nurse will need to rely on the family members to fill in the gaps.

If a client has a hearing deficit, sit directly in front of the client. Speak clearly and loudly enough for the client to hear and understand what you are saying. If the deficit is significant, make sure that the person is wearing hearing aids if appropriate or that a sign-language interpreter is available.

If there is a language barrier, if possible, use an interpreter who is not a family member. The family member might not translate all the information, thinking that he or she is protecting the client from difficult information.

If the client starts to cry during the interview process, let the person cry. Crying is an important expression of grief and release. Do not move on to another topic to avoid the painful issue. Offer a tissue and perhaps a hand on the shoulder, if this is culturally acceptable.

Be careful if you sense a threat of violence. Nurses can be very vulnerable in the workplace to clients who are under the influence of drugs and alcohol or who are very angry. Recognizing these factors and positioning yourself accordingly can prevent possible physical abuse that might be directed at you. Do not stay in a closed room alone with such a client. Always make sure that other members of the health care team can see you.

If you suspect there is a potential for violence, protect yourself, do not take any risks, and think of safety first. Talk calmly and quietly; do not raise your voice and argue with the client. Verbal abuse from clients or toward clients is also not acceptable. Nurses must make it known that they are health professionals and must be treated accordingly.

Cross-cultural issues in client care can be a learning experience for both parties but can also be a deterrent to complete care. Be careful to try to understand cultural differences. What are the codes of behaviour? Who can be touched or not, and who can be in a room without a chaperone? If there is a language barrier, such differences might be more difficult to interpret. What are the client's perceptions of health care workers, the system, and the treatments? In order to build a trusting therapeutic relationship with clients from some cultures, you may have to divulge some information about yourself, too. It is best to start the interview process formally. Stand to greet the client, let him or her know how you would like to be referred to, and elicit the same from them. Keep a good distance apart; 1.5–3 metres is acceptable. Be tolerant of different cultural beliefs and adjust your questions and responses accordingly.

THE COMPLETE HEALTH HISTORY

A complete history includes many aspects. Keep in mind who is providing the information, which may be the client, a parent, the spouse, a friend, or someone else. If the client is very ill or if it is an emergency situation, stress will be an added factor in the presentation of the story. The following is a list of the different areas of information to be collected:

- Biographical data
- Reason for seeking care
- Present health or history of the present illness
- Past history
- Family history
- Review of all systems
- Functional assessment or activities of daily living

If there is pain, further information is needed. Use the mnemonic "PQRSTU" (Jarvis, 2008) to explore all areas:

P: Provocative: What starts the pain? What makes it worse? What makes it better?

Q: Quality of the pain: Neuropathic or nociceptive? How does it feel?

R: Region or Radiation: Where is the pain? Does it spread?

S: Severity scale: On a scale of 0–10, where 0 is no pain and 10 is the most severe pain that you can imagine, where is your pain?

T: Timing: When did the pain start? How often does the pain occur, and how long does it last?

U: Understanding client's perception of the problem. What do you think that it means?

Keep in mind any cultural differences. If the client is not native to Canada, determine when he or she arrived, the country or region of origin, and the conditions in that location. Are there any religious considerations that would affect blood-product transfusions, dietary options, the need for clergy, or perhaps the necessity of a chaperone during an examination?

If the client is an infant, include details of pre- and postnatal health and labour and delivery. Also ask about the developmental history. It is challenging at times to get a complete history from adolescents. Keep in mind that it is important to include a psychological assessment as adolescents can be very vulnerable to depression and suicide.

THE MENTAL STATUS EXAMINATION

A person's mental status is defined as his or her emotional and cognitive function assessed through behaviour. By assessing mental status first, the nurse can establish a baseline, and reassessment can monitor any changes, especially in response to the stress of illness and feeling of being unwell. Serious health problems such as alcoholism, renal failure, diabetes, liver disease, or brain disease might alter the mental assessment. Various medications can also alter the assessment, as will lower educational levels.

It is difficult to assess mental status in a child, but the older the child, the easier it is as the cerebral cortex matures and the attention span increases with age. Assessing the older adult client often takes longer because the client may need more time to answer the questions, and there may also be recent memory loss. As well as memory loss, sensory losses of sight and hearing can cause frustration, social isolation, and apathy. The older adult client might also have experienced a number of losses, such as loved ones, friends, job, income, or health, giving rise to an added risk of depression and despair.

The behaviour assessment should include the following factors:

- Consciousness
- Language
- Mood affect
- Orientation
- Attention
- Memory
- Abstract reasoning
- Thought process
- Thought content
- Perceptions

For the average client, the mental assessment can be incorporated into the rest of the health history. The four main headings are appearance, behaviour, cognition, and thought process (ABCT) (Jarvis, 2008). The Mini-Mental State Examination (MMSE) can be performed if a more thorough assessment is needed (Folstein, Folstein, & McHugh, 1975).

ASSESSMENT TECHNIQUES

The nurse uses the following techniques when objectively assessing the client:

- Inspection
- Palpation
- Percussion
- Auscultation

The techniques are performed in order with the exception of the examination of the abdomen, when auscultation is done immediately after inspection.

The Technique of Inspection

Inspection is the most powerful of all the technical skills. It yields the most data because the nurse's physical examination is guided by the observation of any abnormalities. The inspection starts as soon as the practitioner sees the person and continues throughout the whole encounter. Nurses must learn to be astute in the art of looking. It is very difficult at first not to touch the client. So just stand back and observe. Perform a general body scan. Watch for behaviour, as well as generalized symmetry. Then move on to more specific observations. The tools for inspection may include good lighting, an otoscope, an ophthalmoscope, a nasal or vaginal speculum, and a penlight.

The Technique of Percussion

Percussion involves tapping the client's skin. There is direct percussion and indirect percussion. Direct percussion is tapping the skin directly. Indirect percussion involves laying the nondominant middle finger, hyperextended, laterally on the client's skin over the area to be percussed and tapping it with the dominant middle finger of the other hand. Tap quickly with a floppy, relaxed wrist movement. Tap twice with the tip of the finger, not the pad of the finger. It is important to alternate from one side of the body to the other to compare the symmetry of the sound. Percussion is used to map out the size and location of a superficial organ, to detect the presence of a superficial mass no more than 5 cm below the skin, and for eliciting a painful area.

Different sounds are perceived by using the percussion technique, which are listed in Table 4.4.

Table 4.4 Sounds of Percussion

Sound	Body Structure
Resonant	Over normal lung tissue
Hyper-resonant	Normal over infant and young child's lung tissue
	Abnormal over adult lung with increased amount of air-trapping, as in emphysema
Dull	Over dense organs
Flat	Over normal bone, thigh muscle, or tumour
Tympanic	Over air-filled visceral organs, such as the stomach and intestines

The Technique of Palpation

Palpation is the art of touching the body to assess the skin and the underlying organs, as well as any abnormalities. The sense of touch can be used to feel texture; temperature; moisture; vibration; pulsation; swelling; rigidity; spasticity; organ location; crepitations; the presence of any lumps, bumps, or lesions; or the presence of any pain or tenderness.

Generally, the pads of the fingertips are used. Make sure that your hands are warm. Be careful not to poke the skin but to gently rub the fingertips in a circular motion. Palpation should feel good to the client and should be soothing and relaxed. If there is a painful area, palpate it last. If the client is very ticklish, place the client's hand on the skin first, put your hand on next, ask the client to start palpating, and then gently slide the client's hand out. Start with light palpation and progress to deep palpation where appropriate.

The dorsa of the hands are used for assessing temperature and moisture. The skin on the back of the hand is thinner and more sensitive. The base of the fingers or the ulnar edge of the hand is used to detect vibrations. Bimanual palpation is the use of both hands at the same time.

The Technique of Auscultation

Auscultation is listening to body sounds through a stethoscope. The earpieces should be comfortable and directed toward the nose. As you bend your head to listen, the earpieces should make a perfect seal with the natural curvature of the ear canal. There are two parts to the stethoscope, the diaphragm and the bell. The diaphragm is used to listen to high-pitched sounds, such as bowel, respiratory, or heart sounds, whereas the bell is useful for hearing low-pitched sounds, such as heart murmurs or bruits. The bell must be placed on the skin very lightly, and the diaphragm should be pressed firmly down on the skin. Clean the stethoscope with an alcohol wipe between uses as it can become a vector for cross-contamination. The neck of the stethoscope should be 30–35 cm in length. The noise in the surrounding areas should be minimal. If the client's chest is particularly hairy, wet the hair to avoid mistaking it for "crackles" in the lungs. The sounds are more accurate if listened to over bare skin and not over clothes.

THE GENERAL SURVEY

At your first encounter with the client, start your general survey. Establish that the airway is clear, that the client is breathing, and that there is circulation (CAB or ABC for newborns). Throughout the general survey, establish that appearance, behaviour, cognition, and thought processes are all intact (ABCT).

Physical Appearance: Does the client look his or her stated age? Is the client oriented to time, place, and person? Is the sexual development appropriate for the client's age and gender? Do a general scan of the colour and condition of the skin. Are there any signs of acute distress?

Body Structure: Check height and weight. Are these the expected values? Look at body symmetry and posture. How comfortable is the client sitting or lying down? Is the body proportionate?

Mobility: Assess gait if possible. Note the range of motion of the limbs and joints.

Vital Signs: Take the pulse, respiratory rate, blood pressure, temperature, and oxygen saturation and assess for pain.

For infants, measure the circumference of the head and the length of the body.

HEAD AND NECK WITH REGIONAL LYMPHATICS ASSESSMENT

THE ANATOMY AND LANDMARKS OF THE HEAD AND NECK

Keep in mind that there are two halves to the body, the left and the right. Remember to examine both sides of the body and always assess for symmetry. The symmetry is not perfect, but, for the most part, it is very close.

The skull is composed of cranial bones; sutures separate the frontal, temporal, parietal, and occipital bones. At birth, the sutures have not approximated completely to allow room for the brain to grow. The areas where they have not joined together are called fontanelles. The posterior fontanelle closes within the first two months of birth, and the frontal fontanelle closes sometime between nine months and two years.

There are 14 facial bones, and the head sits upon the vertebrae of the cervical spine. The first vertebra, C1, is located at the base of the spine and is called the atlas; the second, C2, is called the axis. The cervical vertebrae continue down to C7, which is called the vertebra prominens. The prominens is highly palpable when the neck is flexed forward as it has a long spinous process.

Many muscles control the face and facial expressions. The motor component to cranial nerve VII, or the facial nerve, innervates most of the muscles. Cranial nerve V, the trigeminal nerve, controls the movement of the masseter muscles—which assist in talking and chewing—from the mandible and the temporomandibular joint. The sensory component of the trigeminal nerve is responsible for feeling light touch along the areas controlled by the three sections of the nerve: the forehead, the cheek, and the chin. The sensory component of the facial nerve is taste on the anterior two-thirds of the tongue.

The pulsation of the temporal artery can be felt anterior to the ear. This artery supplies blood and nutrients to the face and head.

Salivary glands protect the teeth and mucosa by rinsing them and aid digestion by containing enzymes to start the digestive process and providing lubrication for the food bolus. The parotid gland is located anterior to and slightly below the tragus of the ear on either side of the face. The submandibular gland is located at the angle of the jaw and below the mandible. The sublingual glands are under the tongue at the front of the mouth. None of the glands are normally palpable.

The muscles of the neck are the sternomastoid, the trapezius, and the omohyoid. They are innervated by cranial nerve XI, the spinal accessory nerve. These muscles are responsible for holding the head up and providing the range of motion of the head. At the base of the neck is the clavicle. Down along the neck there are a variety of structures: the hyoid bone, the thyroid cartilage, the cricoid cartilage, the trachea, and the manubrium at the bottom.

The thyroid gland is an endocrine gland that synthesizes and secretes thyroxine (T_4) and triiodothyronine (T_3), hormones that regulate cellular metabolism and growth. The thyroid gland is also responsible for calcitonin, which regulates the amount of calcium in the bloodstream and stimulates growth. The gland has two lobes and should be smooth, without lumps or bumps. The cricoid cartilage is just above the thyroid.

THE ANATOMY AND LANDMARKS OF THE REGIONAL LYMPHATIC SYSTEM

The lymphatic system plays a vital role in the body. It is responsible for cleaning the blood, returning fluid to the blood from the tissues, and fighting infection. The lymph nodes that are situated along the pathways of the lymphatic system filter bacteria and foreign particles from the lymph fluid. If there is an infection, the lymph nodes become swollen and sore. If they become cancerous, they are fixed, nontender, and firm. There are many lymph nodes in the head and neck region, named as follows: the preauricular, postauricular, occipital, jugulodigastric, submandibular,

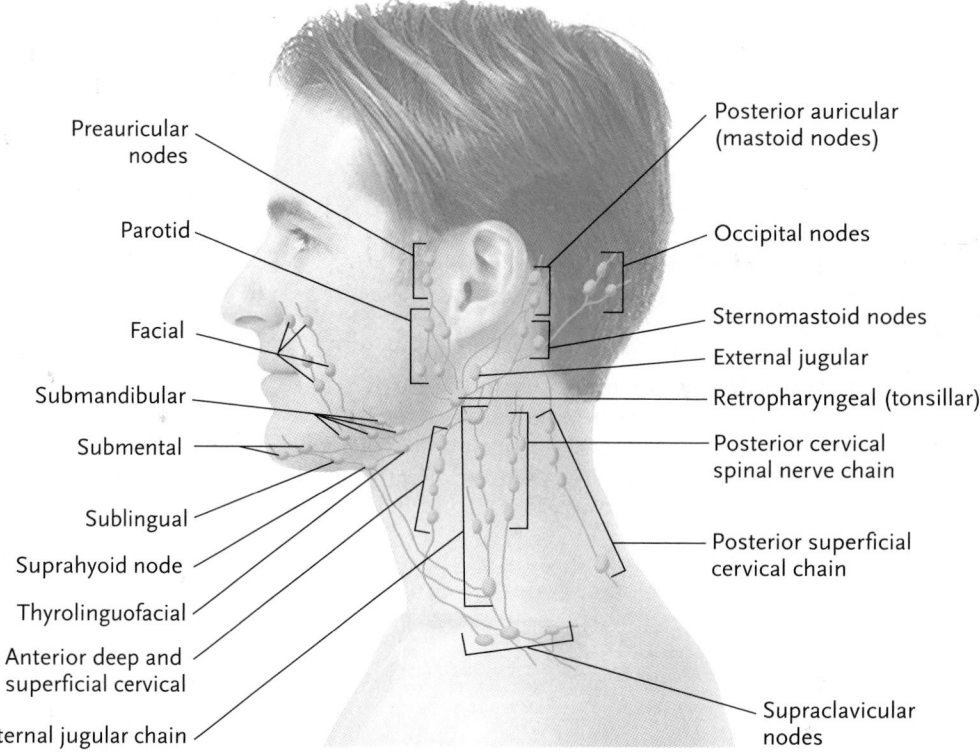

Preauricular nodes
Parotid
Facial
Submandibular
Submental
Sublingual
Suprahyoid node
Thyrolinguofacial
Anterior deep and superficial cervical
Internal jugular chain
Posterior auricular (mastoid nodes)
Occipital nodes
Sternomastoid nodes
External jugular
Retropharyngeal (tonsillar)
Posterior cervical spinal nerve chain
Posterior superficial cervical chain
Supraclavicular nodes

FIGURE 4.1
The Lymphatic Drainage System of the Head and Neck
If a group of nodes is commonly referred to by another name, the second name appears in parentheses.

Source: Seidel, H. M., Ball, J. W., Dains, J. E., & Benedict, G. W. (2006). *Mosby's guide to physical examination* (6th ed., p. 236, Figure 9-10). St. Louis: Mosby.

submental, superficial cervical chain, deep cervical chain, posterior cervical, and supraclavicular. Refer to Figure 4.1, which illustrates the head and neck lymph node locations.

Subjective Data Specific to the Head and Neck

*Questions specific to the older adult

- Are you experiencing any headaches?
- If yes, describe the headache.
- What types of stress do you have in your life?
- What coping strategies have you been using?
- Are you taking any medications?
- Do you have any allergies?
- Have you had a recent head injury?
- Did you lose consciousness?
- * Do you have any illnesses now, such as diabetes or lung or heart disease?
- * Are you experiencing vertigo or dizziness? If yes, does it interfere with your daily routine?
- Do you have any neck pain?
- * Have you noticed any decrease in the range of motion of your neck? If yes, does it restrict your ability to do your daily activities or work?
- Have you had any trouble breathing?
- Have you had any trouble swallowing?
- Do you smoke? If so, how many cigarettes per day and for how many years?
- How often do you drink alcohol?
- Have you noticed any lumps or bumps in your neck?
- Have you had a cold recently?
- Have you ever had surgery to the head or neck region?
- If the client is an infant: Were there any difficulties with the pregnancy, labour, or delivery? Has your baby been following a normal growth pattern?

Objective Data Specific to the Head and Neck

- Inspect and palpate the head and hair. Look at and feel the head for redness, swelling, lumps, bumps, and lesions. Check the hair for texture and the presence of lice. The eggs are white ovals that stick to the hair strands and will not brush off easily. They come off individually when they are pulled off with fingernails, as opposed to dandruff, which will flake off or blow off the hair quite easily. The nits are black and can jump around the head. They tend to migrate to the base of the hair at the back of the neck and around the posterior of the ears. They can be very irritating to the skin.
- Palpating the head should be relaxing to the client. At every opportunity, make the examination process a relaxing and calm one for the client and for you.
- For an infant, measure the circumference of the head. Assess for any tenderness over any of the cranial bones.
- Palpate the temporal artery pulse.
- Palpate the temporomandibular joint (TMJ), assessing for tenderness, cracking, or crepitus. Test for range of movement, as well as smooth movement when the mouth is opened.

- Test the movement of the mandible against resistance for strength.
- Inspect the face, looking at the skin condition, facial expressions, and symmetry. Note any tics or fasciculation.
- Inspect and palpate the neck. Assess for symmetry and that the trachea is midline.
- Look for the client's ability to perform voluntary head movements. Perform a series of range of motion exercises with the neck and assess for strength using movement against resistance. With an infant, assess the head posture and control. By 4 months, an infant should have head control.
- Using the fingertips and creeping down the skin, not poking it, feel for all the lymph nodes in the neck. If there is a palpable node, note its size and consistency and feel for tenderness. Check both sides simultaneously for symmetry.
- Assess the thyroid from behind the client or from the anterior position. Let the client know what you are going to do so he or she is not frightened of your hands around the neck. With your hands gently around the neck, ask the client to swallow. Feel for the movement of the cricoid cartilage and then use it as a landmark for the thyroid, which is just distal to it. Displace the gland to one side and palpate it for any lumps, bumps, or tenderness. Repeat on the other side. The thyroid should be smooth. If the gland is enlarged, assess for the presence of a bruit or turbulent blood flow through it. Using the bell of the stethoscope, assess for a low whooshing sound.

EYE ASSESSMENT

LANDMARKS OF THE EYE

- Palpebral fissures are the space between the upper and lower eyelids. When the eye is closed, the eyelids approximate with no distance between them. When

open, the eye is partially covered to the upper part of the iris by the upper eyelid.

- The limbus is where the sclera and cornea come together.
- The canthus can be found where the eyelids meet in the corners of the eye. The lateral (outer) canthus is toward the ear, and the medial (inner) canthus is toward the nose. At the inner canthus is the caruncle, a fleshy area that contains sebaceous glands.
- The upper lids contain Meibomian glands within the tarsal plate. The tarsal plates contain connective tissue that gives the eyelid its shape. In the older adult, the connective tissue loses elasticity, thus not maintaining the eyelid's shape. The Meibomian glands secrete an oily substance that lubricates the eye, prevents the tears from overflowing, and maintains a good seal when the eyes are closed.
- The palpebral conjunctiva is a thin mucous membrane. It lines the inside of the eyelids and is clear with many blood vessels. The bulbar conjunctiva covers the eyeball, overlying the sclera. The bulbar conjunctiva merges with the cornea at the limbus, where the cornea covers and protects the iris and pupil.
- The lacrimal apparatus provides protection to the eye by providing an irrigation system to keep the cornea and the conjunctiva moist and lubricated. Tears form in the lacrimal gland and wash over the eyes. The tears drain out of the eye through the puncta at the inner canthus into the lacrimal sac and down the lacrimal duct into the inferior meatus and turbinates of the nose.
- Eye movement is controlled by six extraocular muscles attached to the eye and the orbit. The muscles provide straight and rotary movement. The muscles of the eyes are coordinated so that the eyes move in a parallel fashion (called conjugate movement). This movement is important as the brain can only perceive one image at a time. Cranial nerves III, IV, and VI (oculomotor, trochlear, and abducens) innervate the muscles of the eye to produce various movements. The direction of eye movement is illustrated in Figure 4.2.

FIGURE 4.2
Direction of Eye Movement

Source: Seidel, H. M., Ball, J. W., Dains, J. E., & Benedict, G. W. (2006). *Mosby's guide to physical examination* (6th ed., p. 293, Figure 11-20). St. Louis: Mosby.

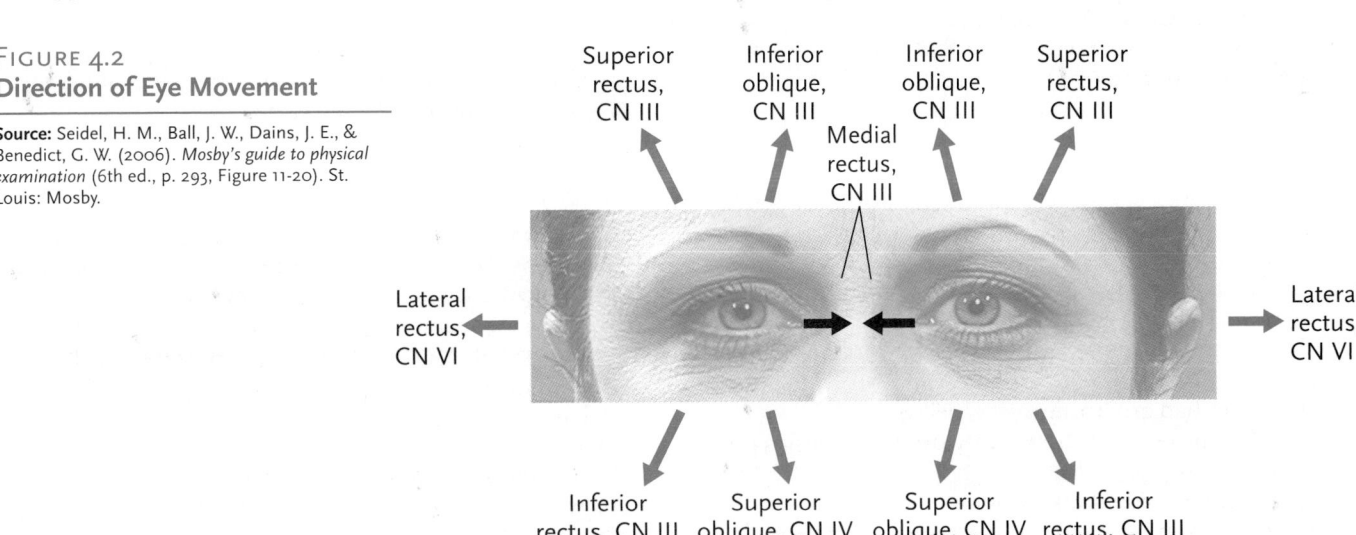

Superior rectus, CN III

Inferior oblique, CN III

Medial rectus, CN III

Inferior oblique, CN III

Superior rectus, CN III

Lateral rectus, CN VI

Lateral rectus, CN VI

Inferior rectus, CN III   Superior oblique, CN IV   Superior oblique, CN IV   Inferior rectus, CN III

THE INTERNAL ANATOMY OF THE EYE

The outer layer of the eye is called the sclera. It is made up of a white fibrous tissue and should have a smooth consistency. It serves as a protective shield and is continuous with the transparent cornea that protects the iris and pupil.

The cornea bends (refracts) the incoming light rays, which are then directed back to the retina. The cornea is very sensitive to touch. The corneal reflex is tested by touching the cornea with a wisp of cotton. If the reflex is normal, the fifth cranial nerve (the trigeminal nerve) sends a message to the brain and cranial nerve VII sends a message to the eye to blink.

The eye's middle layer consists of the choroid, iris, pupil, lens, and anterior and posterior chambers. The choroid protects the retina by supplying blood to it and by decreasing the amount of light that reflects internally. Anteriorly, it is continuous with the muscle of the ciliary body, which controls the thickness of the lens. The muscle fibres in the iris contract, or dilate, the pupil to vary the amount of light admitted into the eye. This is called the papillary reflex. A direct reflex occurs when the light is shone into the eye; a consensual light reflex is the constriction of the contralateral pupil—in other words, when the light is shone into one eye, the pupil of the other eye also constricts. Accommodation occurs when the pupils constrict to help the eye to focus on close objects. The lens lies posterior to the pupil. It flattens to see distant objects and bulges to see close objects. After the age of 40 years, a person's lens starts to lose elasticity and the ability to see close objects diminishes; this is called presbyopia. By 70 years of age, the lens begins to thicken due to a clumping of proteins and yellow deposits called nuclear stenosis or senile cataract.

The posterior chamber contains the aqueous humour. It provides nutrients and removes waste products to the surrounding tissues. The anterior chamber, which sits between the cornea and the lens and iris, allows the outflow of the aqueous humour. Intraocular pressure measures the balance between the amount of aqueous humour produced and the resistance to its outflow. Increased intraocular pressure, or glaucoma, increases with age and is three to six times more likely to occur in people of African descent.

The inner retinal layer is responsible for changing the waves of light into nerve impulses. When you are looking through an ophthalmoscope, the optic disc, where the optic nerve lies, is located toward the nose. The disc is yellow-orange to pink, is oval to round in shape, and is where fibres from the retina converge to form the optic nerve. The physiological cup inside the optic disc is a brighter yellow than the disc and is the location of the entrance and exit of the retinal blood vessels. The blood vessels drain through the cup. The macula is grey in colour and is responsible for central vision. Through an ophthalmoscope, it can be located by looking toward the ear. It is at the macula that

the sharpest vision can be seen. Age can decrease the effectiveness of the macula, decreasing central vision. The retinal vessels converge into the optic disc. The arteries are redder and smaller than the veins. The background of the fundus depends on the person's skin colour. Generally, it has a reddish-orange hue.

SUBJECTIVE DATA SPECIFIC TO THE EYE

- Do you have any difficulty with your vision?
- Have you noticed any difficulty reading or seeing close objects?
- Do you have any difficulty with night vision?
- Do you have any pain in your eyes?
- Do you see double?
- Have you ever had "crossed eyes"?
- Do you have any redness or swelling in your eyes?
- Do you have any discharge or watering in your eyes?
- Do your eyes feel dry or burning?
- Do you have any past history of eye problems?
- Do you have any past history of glaucoma?
- When was the last time you were checked for glaucoma?
- Do you have any family history of glaucoma?
- Do you use glasses or contacts?
- Do they work well for you?
- When was your last eye examination?
- Were you given a prescription for glasses?
- Have you ever had any surgery on your eyes?
- Do you take any medications or drops for your eyes?

OBJECTIVE DATA SPECIFIC TO THE EYE

- Test for vision. Test the function of cranial nerve II, the optic nerve.
- Use a Snellen eye chart. The person should stand 20 feet away from a 20 foot chart or 10 feet from a 10-foot chart, cover one eye with a shield, and read the letters aloud, starting from left to right, top to bottom. Ask the person not to use a hand to cover the eye as this can compress the eyeball and distort its vision. The client should read the lowest line that he or she can without making more than two mistakes. Switch to the other eye, this time asking the person to read from right to left. Reading glasses must be removed, but glasses with corrective lenses for distance should stay on. Normal vision is 20/20; in other words, the person can read at 20 feet what a person with normal vision can read at 20 feet. The numerator is the distance from the client to the chart, and the denominator is the distance from which a person with normal vision can read the same line.
- For children who do not know the alphabet or for those who cannot read English letters, use a picture chart or an E chart.
- Newborn infants can be tested for visual acuity using light perception. The infant should blink when you shine a light into the eyes.

- To test for presbyopia, use the Jaegar chart. The person should hold the card 35 cm away from the eye and be able to read it. Test each eye separately.
- Test visual fields for peripheral vision loss. The confrontation test is a broad or gross examination of peripheral vision. Stand two feet from the client and at his or her level. Cover your right eye and the client's left eye with opaque cards. Tell the client to look straight at your uncovered eye. Wiggle your finger and move it slowly from the periphery into the centre between you and the client. Assuming that your own peripheral vision is good, the client should see the finger at the same time you do. Then switch to the other eye.
- Test cranial nerves III, IV, and VI (oculomotor, trochlear, and abducens).
- Test the corneal light reflex (Hirschberg test). Shine a light from a distance of 12 inches into the client's eyes and ask him or her to look straight ahead. There should be a symmetrical reflection of the light in both eyes. If not, then perform the cover test.
- The cover test: Ask the person to look forward and stare at your nose. Cover one eye while the person is staring; the other eye should maintain the stare and not jump around to fixate again. Repeat the test with the other eye.
- Diagnostic position test (the six fields of gaze): Direct the client to follow the movement of your outstretched finger with his or her eyes and without moving the head. Move your finger to the left superior oblique, left lateral, left inferior oblique, right superior oblique, right lateral, and right inferior oblique, returning to the centre each time. The eyes should move in a parallel fashion. Watch for any shaking of the eyeball (nystagmus). It is not abnormal to see it at the far lateral point.

Inspect the External Eye

- Eyebrows, eyelashes: Observe for hair distribution and the presence of scaling or lice.
- Eyelids: Observe for lid lag. The upper eyelid should cover the upper area of the iris. The lashes should approximate when closed. The skin should be without lumps, bumps, redness, or lesions.
- Eyeballs: The eyeballs should not be sunken in or protruding.
- Conjunctiva and sclera: Ask the client to look up; pull the lower lids down and inspect the conjunctiva for colour (very red may be infection, pallor may be anemia), lumps, bumps, or lesions. The sclera should be china white without lesions. In people of African descent, you may find brown macules and yellow fat deposits.
- Lacrimal apparatus: Note that the eyes are glossy and well lubricated without excess tearing. Press with your thumbs on the lacrimal gland and sac and assess for tenderness, redness, blocked ducts, and swelling.
- Cornea and lens: Shine a light on the cornea from the side and assess for any scratches or opacities.
- Iris and pupil: Note the size, shape, and equality of the pupils. Anisocoria (two different pupil sizes) occurs in 5% of the population. Test for direct and consensual pupillary light reflex. In a darkened area, shine a light into one eye and note the constriction of the pupil of that eye and the consensual constriction of that of the other eye. Repeat the test with the other eye.
- Accommodation: Ask the client to look at a distant object. The pupils will dilate. Then quickly get them to focus on a close object. The pupils will constrict, and the eyeballs will converge. Record the findings as PERRLA: Pupils Equal, Round, React to Light, and Accommodation.

Inspect the Ocular Fundus

Use your right eye to look into the client's right eye (to avoid mouth-to-mouth contact) with an ophthalmoscope. Shine the light into the eye from the side. Look beyond the red reflex, focus on the back of the eye, and examine the retina. Note the appearance of the retina and the size of the blood vessels and any bulging or lesions. Then follow the blood vessels toward the nose to assess the optic disc and physiological cup. If you follow the blood vessels the other way to the ear, you can inspect the macula, which should be a darker grey in colour.

Superior nasal arteries and veins
Superior temporal arteries and veins
Optic disc
Fovea centralis
Inferior nasal arteries and veins
Inferior temporal arteries and veins

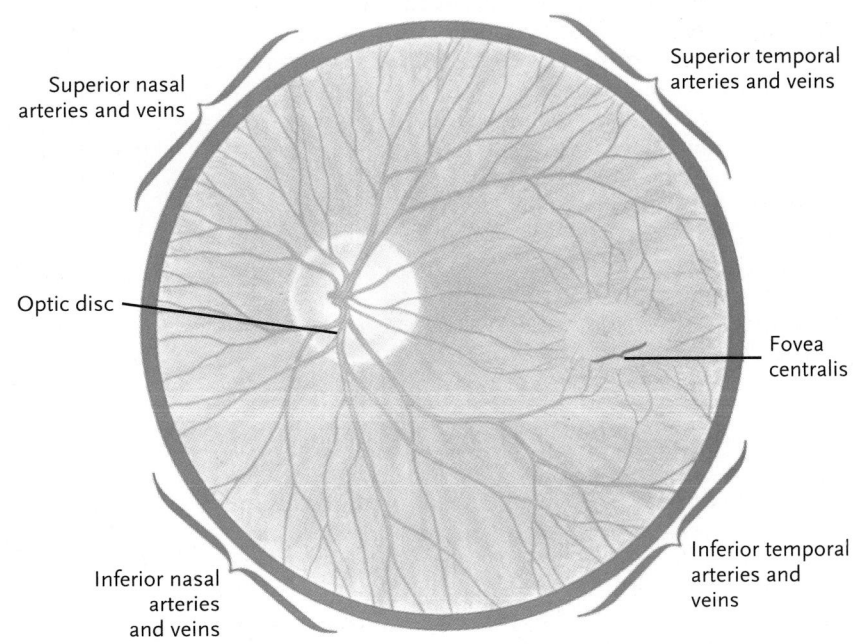

FIGURE 4.3 **Normal Ocular Fundus**

Source: Seidel, H. M., Ball, J. W., Dains, J. E., & Benedict, G. W. (2006). *Mosby's guide to physical examination* (6th ed., p. 296, Figure 11-24). St. Louis: Mosby.

In older adults, the fundus can lose some of its shine, the blood vessels can appear paler, and there can be benign degenerative hyaline deposits, which look like little yellow spots, on the retinal surface. Figure 4.3 shows a normal ocular fundus.

EAR ASSESSMENT

The ear is a sensory organ responsible for hearing and equilibrium. Cranial nerve VIII, the acoustic nerve, is responsible for the sense of hearing. There are three parts to the ear: the outer or external, middle, and inner ear. Behind the ear is a bony prominence called the mastoid process. In Figure 4.4, the three parts of the ear are illustrated.

The Anatomy and Landmarks of the Ear

The External or Outer Ear

The outer ear consists of the auricle, the external auditory canal, and the tympanic membrane. The auricle, or pinna, consists of cartilage and skin. The tragus is the projection of skin-covered cartilage that is proximal to the opening (meatus) to the external canal. Sound waves enter the ear through the meatus and travel through the external canal. In the adult ear, the canal has a slight S-shape.

Cerumen (wax) is produced by small glands that line the canal. The cerumen is necessary to lubricate the canal and to protect it from foreign material. It is yellow and sticky. The wax is naturally excreted from the ear through the mechanisms of chewing and talking. Some people make more cerumen than the average person. The use of cotton swabs to clean out the cerumen is poor practice as the swab can impact, or compress, the cerumen, causing a build-up and blockage in the canal. It is better to dissolve excessive cerumen with a few drops of olive oil in the ear at night, sealed with a small cotton ball at the meatus.

At the end of the external canal is the tympanic membrane. Commonly known as the eardrum, the tympanic membrane is the dividing line between the external and middle ear. It is translucent and pearly grey in colour. It is possible to see parts of the malleus bone (umbo, manubrium, and short process) through the membrane of the middle ear. The tympanic membrane will bulge out into the external canal if there is an excess of fluid or exudate in the middle ear. If there is an infection in the middle ear, the membrane will be a red colour. A blockage of the tympanic membrane with either fluid or exudate will impair hearing. For the young child, when language

Malleus
Incus
Semicircular canals
Facial nerve
Auricle
Auditory nerve (cochlear and vestibular branch)
Cochlea
Oval window
External auditory canal
Round window
Eustachian tube
Tympanic membrane
Stapes and footplate

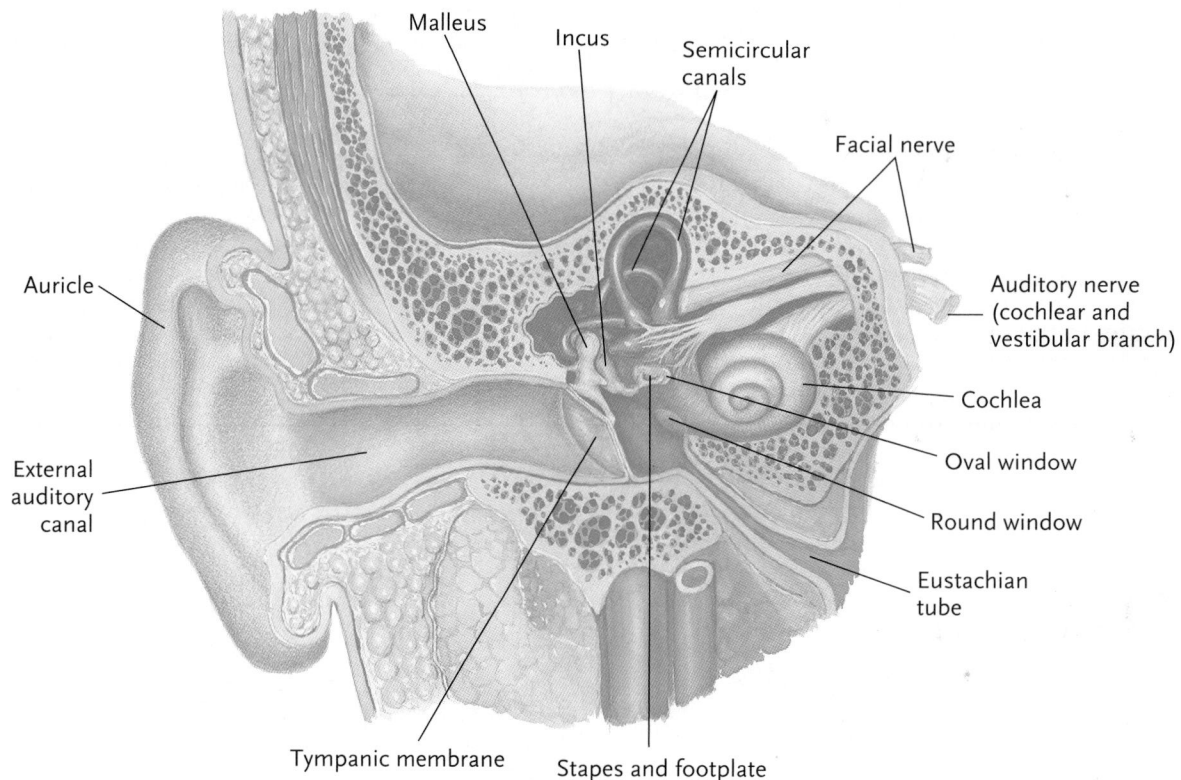

FIGURE 4.4 **Anatomy of the Ear**

Source: Seidel, H. M., Ball, J. W., Dains, J. E., Flynn, J. A., Solomon, B. S., & Stewart, R. W. (2011). *Mosby's guide to physical examination* (7th ed., p. 298, Figure 12-2). St. Louis: Mosby.

development is so important, a decrease in hearing can be very detrimental.

The Middle Ear

The middle ear consists of the small ear bones and is a small cavity filled with air. The middle ear has three functions: protection of the inner ear from loud sound by reducing the amplitude; conducting sound waves through the vibration of the three little bones (malleus, incus, and stapes) to the inner ear through the oval window; and maintaining equalization of pressure on either side of the membrane using the eustachian tube. The eustachian tube connects the middle ear to the nasopharynx. The eustachian tube is shorter and straighter in infants and small children, giving rise to an increased risk of middle-ear infections in that population.

The Inner Ear

The inner ear consists of the bony labyrinth that contains the vestibule and the semicircular canals. The cochlea, which is the central hearing apparatus, is also present in the inner ear. The sensory organs for hearing and equilibrium are within the inner ear.

Sound vibrations continue from the middle ear into the inner ear and into the cochlea. Basilar membranes vibrate depending on the frequency of the sound. Along the basilar membrane are receptor hair cells of the organ of Corti. As the hairs bend, the vibration is transformed into electrical impulses that cranial nerve VIII (the acoustic nerve) can transmit to the brainstem. In the cortex, the sound is interpreted.

Hearing can be divided into two types: conductive hearing, through both air and bone, and sensorineural hearing. Conductive hearing loss is a mechanical dysfunction in the outer or middle ear. It might be a blockage in the canal or, in the adult, a hardening of the footplate of the stapes so that it becomes fixed and cannot vibrate. In the older adult, the cilia lining the ear canal can become coarse and stiff, decreasing the conduction of sound waves through the canal.

Sensorineural hearing loss occurs when there is gradual nerve degeneration of the acoustic nerve. This starts at approximately 50 years of age and gets progressively worse. At 70 years of age, the transmission time for the sound to travel to the brain slows, which decreases the reaction time for older adults.

There can also be a mixed hearing loss. This loss is a combination of conductive and sensorineural hearing loss.

SUBJECTIVE DATA SPECIFIC TO THE EAR

- Do you have any pain in your ear?
- Do you have a history of ear infections, recent or as a child?

- Have you noticed that your child is having any difficulty hearing or is talking unusually loudly?
- Have you ever had surgery on your ear?
- Do you have any discharge coming out of your ear? If so, what colour is it? Does it have an odour?
- Do you have any trouble hearing? If so, is this new for you?
- Do you experience any excess noise at home, at work, or during leisure activities?
- Do you notice any ringing in your ear?
- Have you ever taken a drug called cisplatin?
- Are you taking any medication?
- Do you have any allergies?
- Are you experiencing any vertigo or dizziness?
- Do you feel as if the room is spinning around or that you are spinning around?
- When was your last hearing test?
- Do you wear any hearing aids?

OBJECTIVE DATA SPECIFIC TO THE EAR

Inspect and Palpate the Outer Ear

- Assess the size, shape, and position of the ears. They should be symmetrical and positioned in line with the eye from the top of the ear. Inspect and palpate the skin for colour, lumps, bumps, or lesions. Note the edge of the helix for basal cell carcinoma.
- Assess the ear for tenderness: Press on the tragus to test for possible otitis media and wiggle the auricle for possible otitis externa. Palpate the mastoid process for any tenderness.
- Using the otoscope, inspect the canal for the presence of cerumen, lesions, discharge, and redness. For the adult, lift the pinna up and back, but for the infant and young child, pull the pinna down in order to straighten out the canal. Be careful not to touch the bony area of the canal, which can be very sensitive. Inspect the tympanic membrane, being very careful not to perforate it. Check for a light reflex, a cone of light, in the anterior–inferior quadrant of the tympanic membrane. Look at the colour and determine whether or not there is any bulging or retraction of the tympanic membrane or there are any perforations. You should be able to see the bone attachment in the middle ear shining through the translucent membrane (see Figure 4.5). Inspect for scarring, which looks like white spots.

Tests for Hearing Acuity

There are three tests for hearing acuity: the whisper test, Weber test, and Rinne test. These are all crude tests, and if positive, the client will have to be seen for more thorough tests.

- The whispered voice test: Ask the client to repeat after you two-syllable words that you whisper 30 to 60 cm from one ear while the other ear is occluded. Repeat

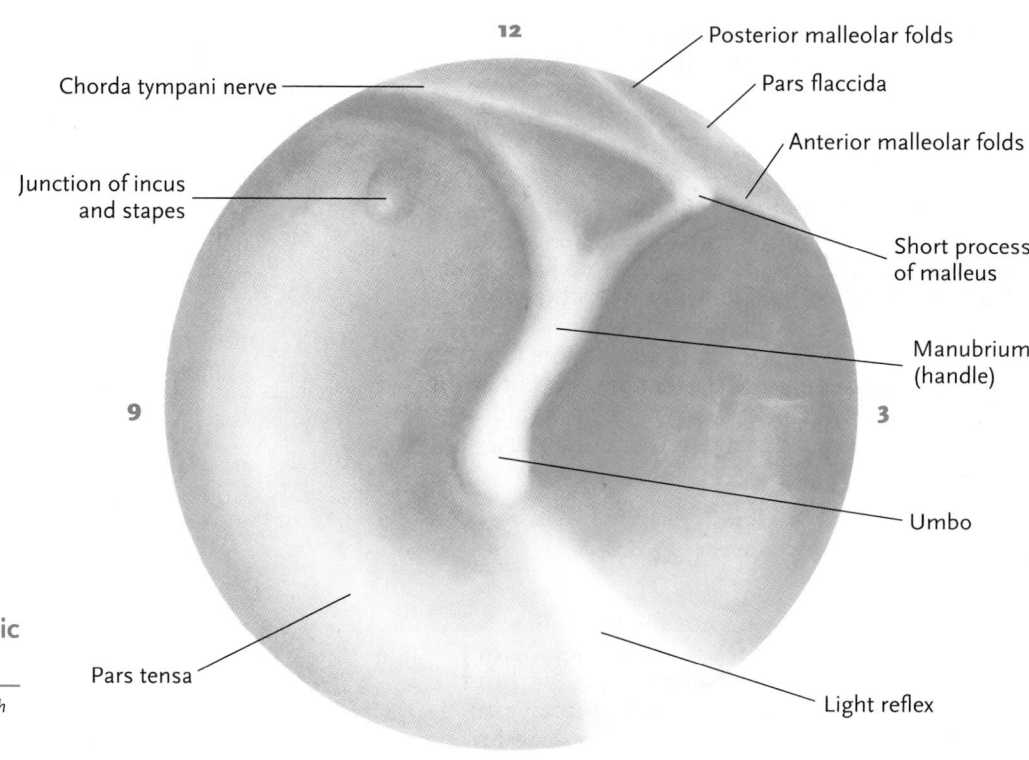

12
Posterior malleolar folds
Chorda tympani nerve
Pars flaccida
Anterior malleolar folds
Junction of incus and stapes
Short process of malleus
Manubrium (handle)
9
3
Umbo
Pars tensa
Light reflex
6

FIGURE 4.5
Landmarks of the Tympanic Membrane

Source: Barkauskas, V. H. (1998). *Health and physical assessment* (2nd ed.) St. Louis: Mosby.

with the other ear. A whisper is a high-pitched sound. The inability to hear it shows some high-tone loss.

- Weber test: Hit the tuning fork, taking care to hold it at the base of the handle, and place it in the middle of the head. If that is not possible, place it anywhere down the midline on a bone, such as on the forehead or chin. The sound should be heard by the client equilaterally in both ears. If there is lateralization of the sound, then the ear that hears the sound more loudly may have conductive or sensorineural loss.
- Rinne test: This test compares bone conduction with air conduction. Air conduction should take twice as long as bone conduction. To test bone conduction, hit the tuning fork, place the base onto the client's mastoid process, and say, "Can you hear this? (Yes!) Tell me when you cannot hear it anymore," and then start counting. When the client cannot hear it, place the tip of the tuning fork to the opening of the ear canal to test air conduction. Do this quickly and avoid touching the hair or skin of the client. Repeat the same question and count again. The air conduction count should be twice as long as the bone conduction count.

Testing for Balance

The Romberg test is to assess for altered equilibrium.

- Ask the client to stand with arms at his or her sides and close his or her eyes for 20 seconds. Stand close to the client in case he or she loses balance. The Romberg test also assesses the function of the cerebellum.

NOSE, MOUTH, AND THROAT ASSESSMENT

Anatomy and Landmarks of the Nose

The nose is the beginning of the airway. It has several functions apart from being a distinguishing feature on a person's face. The nose is rich in blood supply so that it can warm up the outside air before the air travels into the lungs. The hairs in the nose trap and filter large airborne particles, and the mucosal lining traps fine airborne particles before they travel into the lungs. With age, the nasal hairs can become coarse and stiff and not filter as well.

The nasal cavity is split down the centre by the nasal septum. Kiesselbach's plexus is in the anterior of the septum. It is very rich in blood supply and is the most common area for nosebleeds. The septum can be misaligned in some people, making it difficult to breathe from one nare or the other. Along the walls of each nasal cavity lie the turbinates. The sinuses and nasolacrimal duct drain into the turbinates.

The olfactory receptors are spread across the upper area of the cavity and along the upper third of the septum. The receptors merge into cranial nerve I, the olfactory nerve, which is responsible for smell. Without the sense of smell, it is difficult to taste. Over time, the number of receptors can decrease, reducing the sense of smell.

Paranasal sinuses are located in the cranium. They are air-filled spaces that aerate the head, keeping it light. When they get filled with mucus, the head feels heavy. The sinus ducts are in the nose and can get blocked, increasing the chance of sinusitis.

There are four sets of sinuses. The ethmoid sinuses are behind the orbits, and the sphenoid sinuses are deep within the sphenoid bone. These are not possible to examine without medical imaging. The maxillary sinuses, which are behind the upper cheeks under the orbits, and the frontal sinuses, which are above the medial aspect of the eyebrow, are easier to access. The frontal and maxillary sinuses are not present at birth but grow from the age of 6–8 years. The sphenoid sinus, although present at birth, does not grow until after puberty.

ANATOMY AND LANDMARKS OF THE MOUTH

The mouth is also an opening for the respiratory system, but more importantly, it is the opening to and the beginning of the digestive system. Within the mouth are the tongue, gums (gingiva), buccal and lingual mucosa, teeth, and salivary glands. The lips frame the opening of the mouth.

The roof of the mouth is divided into the hard palate (anterior) and the soft palate. The uvula hangs from the soft palate at the back of the mouth. In the infant, the lip or palate might not have approximated, leaving a cleft, a condition more common in people of Asian and Aboriginal descent, up to 50% of whom have a bony ridge, called the torsus palatinus, that runs along the hard palate.

The tongue is a mass of muscle tissue that has the ability to move and change shape. It helps in speech, chewing, swallowing, and cleaning the teeth. The taste buds are embedded into the tongue. The frenulum is a midline fold of tissue that joins the bottom of the tongue to the floor of the mouth. When children start to talk, it is noticeable if the frenulum is too short. This tongue-tied situation usually corrects itself, or the frenulum may need to be clipped to loosen it.

Over a lifetime, humans develop two sets of teeth. The first set contains 20 teeth that start to erupt between 6 months and 2½ years and fall out between 6 and 12 years. They are replaced by 32 permanent teeth. With age, teeth or gums that are not well cared for may develop tooth decay or gingivitis, which can lead to tooth loss. Bone resorption may also occur. Without teeth, the older adult may experience changes in nutrition because of an inability to chew properly.

The salivary glands provide lubrication to the mouth, which is very important in speech, cleaning the teeth, and digestion. There are three sets of salivary glands. The largest are the parotid glands. The parotid glands can be found in the cheeks, anterior to and slightly below the tragus of the ears. The duct of this gland, the Stensen's duct, can be found on the upper outer area of the buccal mucosa. The submandibular gland can be found where the

mandible and upper jaw meet. The opening, the Wharton's duct, is on either side of the frenulum. The sublingual gland is on the anterior floor of the mouth and has many openings beside it.

ANATOMY AND LANDMARKS OF THE THROAT

Behind the mouth and the nose is the pharynx, or the throat. It is divided into the nasopharynx behind the nose, where the eustachian tubes drain and the adenoids are located, and the oropharynx, which is continuous with the mouth and contains the tonsils.

SUBJECTIVE DATA SPECIFIC TO THE NOSE, MOUTH, AND THROAT

- Are you experiencing any discharge from the nose?
- Do you get colds often? Are you experiencing any pain in the sinus area?
- Do you get nosebleeds often?
- Do you have any allergies?
- Are you taking any medications?
- Have you ever had any trauma to the nose, mouth, or throat?
- Have you ever had any surgery to the nose, mouth, or throat?
- Have you had any change in smell or taste?
- Do you have any sores in your mouth?
- Do you have a sore throat? If yes, do you have any cold symptoms?
- Do your gums bleed?
- Has there been any change to your voice?
- Do you have any difficulty swallowing?
- Is your mouth unusually dry? Do you smoke or drink alcohol? When was your last visit to the dentist?
- How often do you brush your teeth?
- Do you have any dentures or removable teeth?
- Do you grind your teeth?

OBJECTIVE DATA SPECIFIC TO THE NOSE, MOUTH, AND THROAT

Inspect and Palpate the Nose

- Inspect the nose for symmetry and to see if it is without deviation. Inspect the skin for any lumps, bumps, or lesions. Check patency by getting the client to close one nostril and breathe through the other. Repeat with the other nostril.
- Test cranial nerve I: Ask the client to close one nostril again and to close the eyes while you introduce something for the client to smell. Ask the client to identify the scent. Repeat with the other nostril and another scent.
- Inspect the nasal cavity with a speculum and a light source. Look at the turbinates. If the client has a cold,

the turbinates will be reddened, and if the client has allergies, the turbinates will have a grey-lavender hue. In some clients, the turbinates will look corroded, particularly if the client has been using cocaine. Other causes of corrosion include the overuse of decongestants, foreign objects in the nose, or nasal trauma. Note any deviation or holes in the septum, foreign bodies, polyps, swelling, or discharge.

Inspect and Palpate the Sinuses, Mouth, and Throat

- Palpate or gently tap over the sinus areas and assess for pain.
- Inspect the lips inside and out. Note any cracking, swelling, or lesions. In infants, it is normal to see a sucking tubercle caused by the friction of sucking on the breast or bottle.
- Inspect the teeth for any large caries; check for signs of bone resorption, gingivitis, or missing teeth and observe the gum line and buccal and lingual mucosa. In small children, assess for "baby bottle syndrome," in which the front teeth have been destroyed by the baby sucking on sugary fluid such as juice or sugar water. With a glove on, palpate the mucosa for lumps, bumps, and lesions. Assess the salivary ducts.
- Check cranial nerves IX and X, the glossopharyngeal and vagus nerves. Using a tongue depressor and light source, ask the client to say "Ahhhh" and watch for the soft palate and the uvula to move up and back in the mouth. Then move the tongue depressor back quickly to illicit a gag response.
- Inspect the tonsils for closeness to each other and for exudate. Rate the tonsils 1+ = visible, 2+ = halfway between the tonsillar pillars and the uvula, 3+ = touching the uvula, or 4+ = touching each other.
- Test cranial nerve XII, the hypoglossal nerve. Ask the client to say "light," "tight," and "dynamite" to assess for the client's lingual speech. Instruct the client to push the tongue into the cheek against the resistance of your hand outside on the face to check tongue strength. Repeat on the other side. Ask the client to stick out the tongue and inspect it for fissures, colour, and symmetry.

RESPIRATORY ASSESSMENT

ANATOMY AND LANDMARKS OF THE THORAX AND LUNGS

The function of the respiratory system is to provide a gas exchange that supplies oxygen to the body for energy production and that removes carbon dioxide. It also maintains an acid–base equilibrium of the arterial blood. In addition, respiration helps to regulate the heat of the body, although less so in humans than in animals.

The thoracic cage is composed of the clavicle, sternum, ribs, scapulae, and vertebrae. The floor of the thoracic cage is the diaphragm. The function of the thoracic cage is to give shape to the body and to protect the organs found within, such as the lungs, heart, and liver. The chest is larger in people of European and African descent than in people of Asian and Aboriginal descent.

The anterior landmarks include the clavicle on either side at the top. Between the clavicles is the top of the sternum, the manubrium. Just below the manubrium, where the sternum joins, is the manubriosternal notch, or angle of Louis. The notch protrudes slightly and is the landmark for the second rib and where the trachea bifurcates. The sternum, or breast bone, is connected to the first seven of the 12 pairs of ribs. The costal angle should be 90°. This is the angle between the costal margins; the xiphoid process is in the middle.

The posterior landmarks include the seven cervical vertebrae, the vertebra prominens, the scapulae—where the inferior border is at the level of the eighth rib—and the thoracic vertebrae. The spinous processes stick out, making it easier to count them. The twelfth, or floating, rib is not present on the anterior side. See Figure 4.6 for illustrations of the anterior cage and the posterior thoracic cage.

It is important to imagine and understand the landmark lines on the thoracic cage. They are as follows:

- Midsternal line – the line along the sternum
- Midclavicular line – a vertical line down from the middle of the clavicle
- Anterior axillary line – a vertical line down from the anterior axillary fold
- Posterior axillary line – a vertical line down from the posterior axillary fold
- Midaxillary line – a vertical line from the apex of the axilla

The Lung Borders: Looking from the anterior, the apex of each lung is 3 cm above the clavicle. From an anterior perspective, the upper right lobe extends down to the fourth rib at the sternum and the fifth rib at the anterior axillary line. The right middle lobe extends from the fourth rib at the sternum and the fifth rib at the anterior axillary line down to the sixth rib at the midclavicular line. The right lower lobe extends from the fifth rib at the anterior axillary line down to the sixth rib at the midclavicular line and to the seventh rib at the anterior axillary line.

From a posterior perspective, the right and left upper lobes start at the level of cervical spine 7 and down to thoracic spine 10 (T10) on inspiration and T12 on expiration.

The Pleurae: There is a thin slippery layer lining the chest wall and diaphragm called the parietal pleura and one lining the outside of the lungs called the visceral pleura. Between these linings is a very small amount of lubricating fluid to help the lungs move smoothly and noiselessly with the movement of respiration. There is normally vacuum pressure between these two layers. Any additional fluid or air between these pleural layers will compromise the expansion of the lungs and hence air exchange.

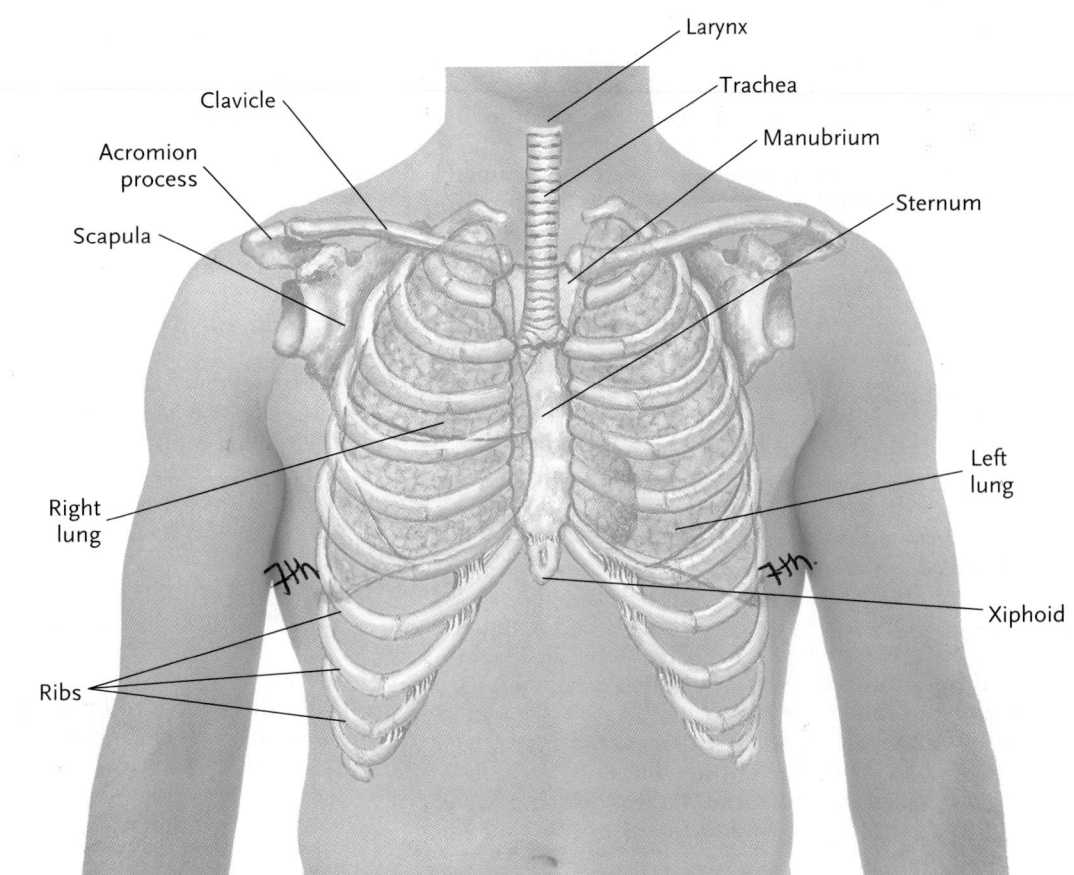

A
Larynx
Trachea
Clavicle
Manubrium
Acromion process
Sternum
Scapula
Right lung
Left lung
Xiphoid
Ribs
B
Thoracic vertebrae
Clavicle
Acromion process
Scapula
Right lung
Left lung
Ribs

FIGURE 4.6
A. Anterior Thoracic Cage
B. Posterior Thoracic Cage

Source: Thompson, J. M., & Wilson, S. F. (1996). *Health assessment for nursing practice.* St. Louis: Mosby.

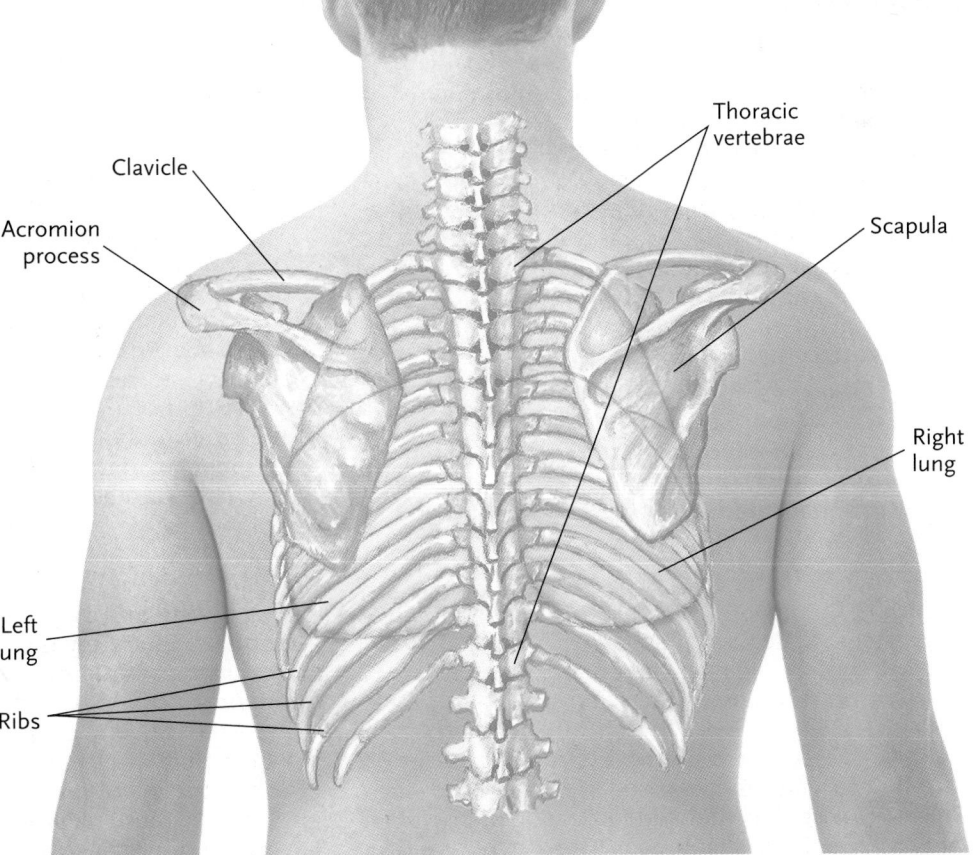

Air enters the mouth or nose and travels down the trachea, which bifurcates just below the sternal angle, and into the bronchioles, the alveolar ducts and sacs, and, finally, the alveoli. Gas exchange occurs in the alveoli. These are protected from debris by the bronchi, which have goblet cells that secrete mucus to trap debris and cilia that move the debris upward, where it can then be swallowed or coughed out of the mouth.

The control of respiration occurs in the respiratory centre in the brainstem, specifically in the pons and medulla. The need for respirations is guided by an increase in carbon dioxide in the blood and less so by a decrease in oxygen.

With each inspiration, the diaphragm moves down, causing a slight negative pressure relative to the atmosphere outside the body, which results in air rushing in to fill the vacuum. Expiration is more passive.

In infants, the rib cage is more elastic; this increases the work of breathing when the chest is recoiling and re-expanding during episodes of respiratory distress.

In the older adult, there can be calcification of the costal cartilage and a loss of elasticity of the lung tissue, decreasing its ability to recoil. There is also a decrease in the number of alveoli, causing an equivalent decrease in gas exchange. This leaves the older adult at a higher risk for infection, a weakened cough reflex, increased secretions, and dyspnea on exertion.

SUBJECTIVE DATA SPECIFIC TO THE THORAX AND LUNGS

- Do you have a cough?
- If so, does a change in position change the cough?
- If so, is the cough productive?
- If so, what colour is the sputum?
- Are you experiencing any shortness of breath? Can you walk up a flight of stairs without having to stop in the middle? Do you have any chest wall pain?
- Do you have any pain on breathing?
- Have you had problems with your respiratory system in the past? Was it chronic or acute?
- Do you smoke? What do you smoke? How many per day and for how many years?
- Are there any environmental irritants at work or home that can affect your breathing?
- When was your last chest X-ray, tuberculosis test, and influenza or pneumonia vaccine?

OBJECTIVE DATA SPECIFIC TO THE THORAX AND LUNGS

Inspection of the Anterior Chest

- Assess the level of consciousness.
- Note the size and configuration of the chest. The anterior–posterior measurement should be half the length of the transverse.

- Note the musculature of the neck and chest. Is the client using the accessory muscles or the muscles of the intercostal spaces to assist in breathing? Examine the skin for colour, texture, temperature, moisture, lumps, bumps, or lesions; observe the facial expression and the use of pursed lips to breathe. Inspect the downward slope of the ribs and the presence of a 45° costal margin angle from the ribs to the xiphoid process. Check the respiratory rate, depth, and ease.

Palpation of the Anterior Chest

- Palpate the anterior chest wall for skin temperature, moisture, texture, turgor, lumps, bumps, tenderness, or pain.
- Symmetrical chest expansion: With your hands shaped like a butterfly, rest them on the chest along the costal margins, capture a bit of skin and fat in the middle of the chest at the xiphoid process with your thumbs, and ask the client to breathe. The chest wall should move symmetrically, your thumbs should move an equal distance apart, and the fold of fat and skin should flatten.
- Assess for tactile fremitus, which is a palpable vibration, by asking the client to say "99" every time you move your hand. You can use either the ulnar edge of the hand or the bottom of the fingers on the palm to assess for vibration. Place your hands symmetrically at the area just above the clavicle and move down the chest at 5-cm intervals. You should feel vibration at the top, and it should diminish quickly as you test further down the chest wall.

Percussion of the Anterior Chest

- Percuss the anterior chest and listen to the dominant note over the lung fields. Start at the apex of the lung, about 3 cm above the clavicles. Move across and then down and repeat in 5-cm intervals down along the chest wall. In females, avoid the breast tissue.
- Resonance is the usual sound over the lung tissue. Infants and those with emphysema may have hyper-resonance. Over the bone, the sound is flat. Over the liver and heart, the sound is dull.

Auscultation of the Anterior Chest

- Auscultate the lungs. Say to the client, "Every time that I move my stethoscope, I would like you to take a breath." This will give you control over the examination, and you will be able to hear the complete breath sound. Follow the same pattern as that for percussion.
- Listen to the complete breath sound—a complete inspiration and expiration—as a wheeze might only be audible at the end of the expiration. There should be tracheal breath sounds over the trachea, bronchovesicular sounds over the bronchi, and vesicular sounds over the rest of the chest.
- Listen for abnormal or adventitious sounds, including wheezing, stridor, crackles, and pleural friction.

- If the breath sounds are abnormal, then assess voice sounds. Bronchophony, egophony, and whispered pectoriloquy are examples of voice sounds.

Inspection of the Posterior Chest

- Inspect the posterior chest.
- Assess the curvature of the spine. Ask the client to bend over at the waist and look at the scapulae. Are the scapulae symmetrical?
- Is the client using the accessory muscles or the muscles of the intercostal spaces to assist in breathing?
- Examine the skin for colour, texture, temperature, moisture, lumps, bumps, or lesions. Carefully inspect the skin for the presence of moles. The client might not be aware of these, and they should be monitored for any change in size, shape, and appearance.

Palpation of the Posterior Chest

- Palpate the posterior chest wall for skin temperature, moisture, texture, turgor, lumps, bumps, tenderness, or pain.
- Palpate for symmetrical chest expansion: With your hands shaped like a butterfly, rest your hands on the chest along the costal margins at the level of T10, capture a bit of skin and fat in the middle of the back with your thumbs, and ask the client to breathe. The chest wall should move symmetrically, your thumbs should move apart an equal distance, and the fold of fat and skin should flatten.
- Assess for tactile fremitus by asking the client to say "99" every time you move your hand. You can use either the ulnar edge of the hand or the bottom of the fingers on the palm to assess for vibration. Place your hands symmetrically at the area of the vertebral prominens, C7, and move down the chest in 5-cm intervals. You should feel vibration at the top, and it should diminish quickly as you test further down the back. Increased vibration can mean a density of some kind, such as a tumour.

Percussion of the Posterior Chest

- Percuss the back. Avoid the spine and the scapulae as you will only get a flat sound.
- Assess the depth of the respirations by performing diaphragmatic excursion. Ask the client to inhale, then to exhale all the way, and then to hold his or her breath. Percuss down to find the lower border of the lung on one side. Ask the client to breathe. Note the point of dullness. Then ask the client to take a big breath and hold it. Percuss down from the previous mark at which the resonance became dull; it should now sound like resonance. Percuss down until the sound changes to dull. Note this mark. The difference between these two marks is the depth of respiration. Assess the other side. The two sides should be equal in length, 3–5 cm.

Auscultation of the Posterior Chest

- Auscultate the lung tissue on the back. There should be bronchovesicular sounds from C7 to T5 in the centre of the back. The sounds over the rest of the lungs should be vesicular sounds. Listen for any abnormal or adventitious sounds.

ANATOMY AND LANDMARKS OF THE BREASTS AND REGIONAL LYMPHATICS

The breasts, or mammary glands, can be found anterior to the pectoralis major muscles and the serratus muscles in both males and females. They lie between the second and the sixth ribs, the sternum medially, and the tail of Spence and midaxillary line laterally.

For females, the breasts serve as part of the reproductive system. Their function is to produce milk for the newborn. The nipple is just below the centre of the breast and around it is the areola, a darker pigmented area. Within the areola are Montgomery's glands, which lubricate the areola during lactation.

Internally, the breasts are composed of glandular tissue, fibrous tissue, and adipose tissue. The glandular tissue produces the milk in lobules, and it is excreted through a series of ducts. The fibrous tissue, including Cooper's ligaments, supports the breast tissue and attaches it to the chest wall. Cooper's ligaments contract with the presence of cancer, causing a dimpling effect on the skin. With age, the elasticity of these ligaments decreases and with it the support of the breast. An illustration of the anatomy of the breast is shown in Figure 4.7.

There is an extensive network of lymph nodes and vessels around the breast area. There are four groups of nodes: the central axillary nodes, the pectoral nodes, the subscapular nodes, and the lateral nodes.

Breast cancer is the second cause of cancer death in women. Early detection and treatment can decrease the mortality rate. The risk factors for breast cancer are as follows: increase in age, nulliparous, not breastfeeding, increased fat in the diet, postmenopausal hormone therapy, family history of breast cancer, a positive *BRCA1* or *BRCA2* blood test, and a first child born after age 30.

SUBJECTIVE DATA SPECIFIC TO THE BREASTS AND REGIONAL LYMPHATICS

*Specific questions for the older woman
^Specific questions for the adolescent girl

- Do you have any pain in the breast area?
- Have you noticed any discharge from your nipple?
- Have you noticed any lumps in your breast or under your arm?

Clavicle
Intercostal muscle
Pectoralis major muscle
Alveolus
Ductule
Duct
Lactiferous duct
Lactiferous sinus
Nipple pore
Suspensory ligaments of Cooper

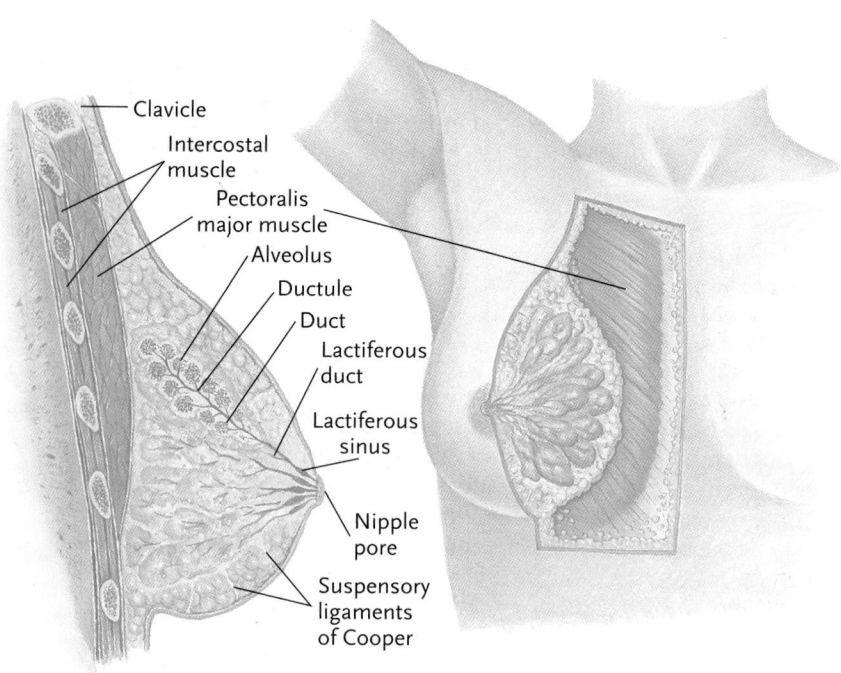

FIGURE 4.7 **Anatomy of the Breast**

Source: Seidel, H. M., Ball, J. W., Dains, J. E., Flynn, J. A., Solomon, B. S., & Stewart, R. W. (2011). *Mosby's guide to physical examination* (7th ed., p. 457, Figure 16-1). St. Louis: Mosby.

- Have you noticed any swelling in one or both of your breasts?
- Have you noticed any skin changes to your breast, such as a rash or an "orange-skin" appearance?
- Has there been any recent trauma to either of your breasts?
- Do you have any history of breast disease?
- When did you experience menarche?

* When did you start menopause?
* Have you taken hormone replacement therapy?

- How many pregnancies or live births have you had?
- Did you breastfeed your children? If yes, for how long?
- Do you have any family history of breast disease?
- Did you ever have surgery to your breast or underarm?
- Do you perform breast self-examination? If yes, how often?

* When was your last mammogram?
^ Have you noticed any change in your breasts?
^ Is there anyone you can talk to about the changes in your body?

Objective Data Specific to the Breasts and Regional Lymphatics

Inspection of the Breast and Lymphatics

- Note the general appearance of the breasts.
- Inspect for symmetry and symmetrical movement. Ask the client to raise her arms sideways, in front, and above her head. Ask the client to place her hands together and squeeze the chest muscles. Assess for any pulling or dimpling of the skin. Inspect the skin for the look of peau d'orange ("orange-peel" skin).
- Inspect the skin for areas of redness, lumps, bumps, or lesions.
- Inspect the nipple for colour, discharge, and the presence of a supernumerary nipple (extra nipple).

Palpation of the Breast and Lymphatics

- Palpate the axilla for lymph nodes. Rest the client's right forearm on your right forearm and hold the elbow with your right hand. You now have full manoeuvrability of the right arm. Move it up, down, and side to side while palpating the right axilla with your left hand. Repeat the examination on the other side. You do not want the muscles to be taut as a tight muscle will prevent the subtle palpation of the underlying lymph nodes. Imagine dividing the breast tissue into a pattern such as the spokes of a wheel. With the pads of your fingertips and in a circular motion, palpate throughout the entire breast. Do not poke at the tissue; a breast lump might be very difficult to feel, and poking it will only push it deeper.
- Repeat the palpation with the woman lying down. Raise her arm over her head and assess the axilla again. If you find a lump, assess the size, texture, shape, position, and whether or not it is tender.
- Gently squeeze the nipple and look for any discharge.

For the male client, inspect and palpate the breast and assess for signs of gynecomastia.

HEART AND NECK VESSEL ASSESSMENT

Anatomy and Landmarks of the Heart

The heart is a mechanical pump that pumps blood through two different circulations, the pulmonary circulation and the systemic circulation. The pulmonary circulation brings blood to the lungs via the pulmonary arteries. Here gas exchange occurs, oxygenating the blood and ridding the body of carbon dioxide. The pulmonary circulation then returns the oxygen-rich blood to the heart via the pulmonary veins. At this point, the systemic circulation takes the oxygen-rich blood and pumps it around the body via the systemic arteries. The blood leaves the heart via the aorta and returns to the heart via the systemic veins, entering the inferior and superior vena cava and re-entering the pulmonary circulation. The cycle is continuous.

The heart is upside down, with the apex at the bottom. It can be found at the fifth intercostal space, 7–9 cm from the midsternal border. The base of the heart, which is wider than the apex, can be found at the top of the heart by the second intercostal space. The heart is rotated slightly so that the right side is more anterior and the left side is more posterior. In an infant, the heart is more midline and assumes the adult position when the child is six years old.

The heart wall comprises three layers. The pericardium is the outermost and is divided into two layers with a small amount of pericardial fluid in between so that there is smooth movement of the heart muscle. The pericardium is a tough, fibrous, protective layer. The myocardium is the muscle of the heart. The endocardium is the inner lining of the heart chambers (ventricles and atria) and the valves. There are four chambers in the heart, two ventricles and two atria. Valves divide the chambers so that there is no backflow of the blood. The right atrioventricular (AV) valve is the tricuspid valve and the left is the mitral valve. The AV valves open during the diastole so the ventricles can

fill. The systole occurs when the pulmonic and aortic valves (semilunar valves) open to allow the blood to be pumped out of the heart. An illustration of the heart anatomy is shown in Figure 4.8.

The first heart sound, S_1, occurs with the closure of the AV valves. This sound can be heard loudest using the diaphragm of the stethoscope over the apex of the heart. The second sound, S_2, occurs at the end of systole, when the semilunar valves close, and can be heard best at the base of the heart. The S_3 sound is an abnormal sound that occurs with vibration at ventricular filling and can be heard immediately after S_2. S_4 occurs just before S_1 when there is resistance to the ventricles accepting the blood from the atrium.

A murmur is the sound of turbulent blood flow through the valves of the heart. This can happen from increased speed of the blood through the heart from, for example, exercise, a decrease in blood viscosity, structural defects in the valves, or structural defects on the wall of the chambers.

The heart has its own conduction system. The pacemaker is the sinoatrial node that is located near the superior vena cava and starts the conduction. It is then passed on over the atria to the AV node that is low in the atrial septum. After waiting for the atria to contract, the electrical current then moves on to the bundle of histidene (His) and then over the ventricles.

FIGURE 4.8 **Anatomy of the Heart**

Source: Seidel, H. M., Ball, J. W., Dains, J. E., Flynn, J. A., Solomon, B. S., & Stewart, R. W. (2011). *Mosby's guide to physical examination* (7th ed., p. 386, Figure 14-10). St. Louis: Mosby.

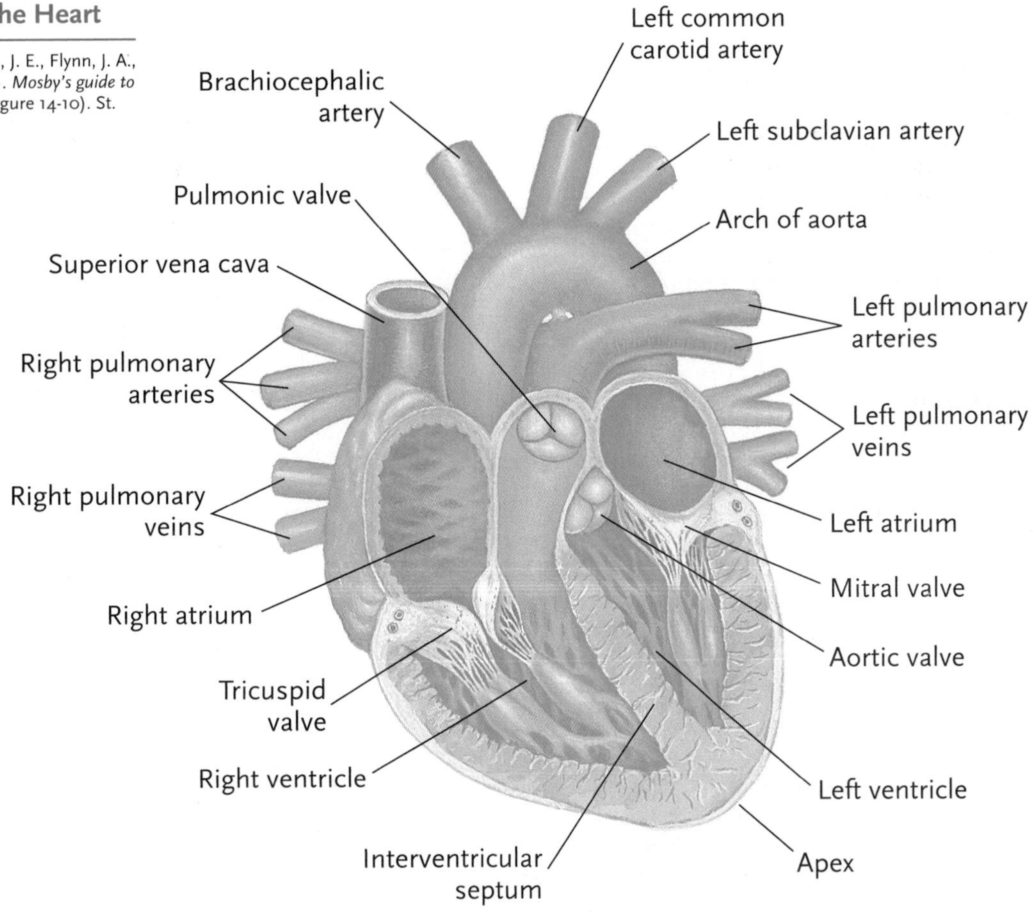

ANATOMY AND LANDMARKS OF THE NECK VESSELS

The neck vessels include the two carotid arteries that supply the brain with blood. They are considered central arteries as they are the closest to the heart. The pulsation of the carotid artery can be found at the space between the sternomastoid muscle and the trachea. Each side should be palpated separately as you do not want to cut off all blood supply to the brain.

The jugular veins bring unoxygenated blood to the heart via the superior vena cava. If they flutter or oscillate, the jugular vein pulsations may indicate a problem with the pumping efficiency of the right side of the heart. The right external jugular vein can be seen lateral to the sternomastoid muscle, just above the clavicle, and is the easiest of the jugular veins to see.

Risk factors for heart disease and stroke are smoking, high blood pressure, obesity, sedentary lifestyle, diabetes, high serum cholesterol, and stress. Adults of African descent have a higher risk of heart disease and stroke than any other group.

SUBJECTIVE DATA SPECIFIC TO THE HEART AND NECK VESSELS

*Specific questions for the older woman
^Specific questions for the adolescent girl

- Do you experience any chest pain?
- Do you take nitroglycerine pills?
- Do you have any shortness of breath?
- How many pillows do you use at night to sleep?
- Do you have a cough?
- Is the cough worse at night?
- Do you get tired easily?
- Have you or your family noticed any change in your skin colour?
- Have you noticed any puffiness around your eyes or in your feet and ankles?
- How many times do you wake up in the middle of the night to urinate?
- Do you or any family members have a history of heart disease?
- ^ Were the pregnancy, labour, and delivery normal?
- ^ Does the baby turn blue when feeding?
- ^ Have you noticed any growth or mobility problems?
- ^ Is the child able to participate in regular activities and sports at school?
- ^ Does the child have frequent nosebleeds?
- ^ Has the child complained of unexplained joint or bone pain?
- ^ Does the child have an increased number of colds or streptococcal infections?
- * Do you have any lung disease?
- * Do you have to climb stairs at home? Can you manage climbing them?
- Cardiac risk factors:

- Please describe your normal daily diet.
- Do you smoke? What, how many, and for how long?
- Do you drink alcohol? How much, how often, and for how long?
- Do you exercise? How often, what type of exercise, and for how long?
- Do you take any cardiac drugs or birth control pills? Which ones, for how long, and how much do you take?

OBJECTIVE DATA SPECIFIC TO THE HEART AND NECK VESSELS

Explain to the client that you are going to listen to the heart and neck in many places and that they should not become alarmed if you are listening for a long time. Take the client's blood pressure. If you suspect orthostatic hypotension, take the blood pressure when the client is lying down and again quickly when the client sits up. Note any fall in pressure between the two positions.

Inspection, Palpation, and Auscultation of the Neck Vessels

- Palpate the carotid arteries; assess the amplitude, strength, and contour of the pulse.
- With the bell of the stethoscope, listen for bruits in the carotid arteries at the angle of the jaw, lateral to the thyroid, and at the base of the neck.
- Inspect the jugular venous pressure. Place the client flat without a pillow on a bed and raise the head of the bed 30°. Place a ruler vertically on the angle of Louis (second rib at the sternal line), place another ruler at the top of the flutter of the external jugular vein horizontally, and measure how high the flutter goes up on the vertical ruler. The measurement should be less than 2 cm.
- A venous hum is a turbulent sound in the jugular vein that is normal in a child.

Inspection of the Precordium

- Inspect the anterior chest. Look for any heaves or bulges.
- Find the apical pulse at the fifth intercostal space, midclavicular line. If you cannot see the apical pulse, palpate it. If that is difficult, ask the client to lie on his or her left side or to sit up and lean forward so that the heart moves closer to the chest wall and palpate again.
- With the ulnar edge of the hand, palpate over the aortic, pulmonic, mitral, and tricuspid valves and Erb's point, that is, on the left sternal border at the fourth intercostal space, for vibrations (thrills).
- Palpate the skin for lumps, bumps, lesions, and tenderness or pain.

Percussion of the Precordium

- Use percussion to assess for the borders of the heart to check for cardiac enlargement.
- Percussion of the heart is rarely done now because other types of cardiac testing are more accurate.

Auscultation of the Precordium

- With the diaphragm of the stethoscope, auscultate the aortic valve at the second right intercostal space, the pulmonic valve at the second left intercostal space, the tricuspid valve at the left lower sternal border, the mitral valve at the fifth intercostal space midclavicular line, and Erb's point, located at the fourth intercostal space.
- Listen to the normal heart sounds, S_1 at the tricuspid and mitral valve region and S_2 at the aortic and pulmonic valves, and for the abnormal sounds S_3 and S_4.
- Listen to the apical pulse for one minute.
- Feel the carotid pulse while listening to the S_1 sounds. They should match in rhythm and rate.
- Turn the stethoscope to the bell and listen again to all points for the presence of murmurs.
- Turn the client over on one side and listen for murmurs, S_3 or S_4 sounds, again.
- Murmurs can be categorized into six grades depending on the loudness of the murmur. The louder it is, the higher the number. It is common for children to have functional or innocent murmurs. These are best heard at the left lower sternal border. A clinical portrait of a client with a heart murmur is shown in Table 4.5.

Table 4.5 Common Sources of Heart Murmurs

Type and Detection	Findings on Examination	Description
MITRAL STENOSIS Heard with bell at apex, patient in left lateral decubitus position	Low-frequency diastolic rumble, more intense in early and late diastole, does not radiate; systole usually quiet; palpable thrill at apex in late diastole common; S_1 increased and often palpable at left sternal border; S_2 split often with accented P_2, opening snap follows P_2 closely Visible lift in right parasternal area if right ventricle hypertrophied Arterial pulse amplitude decreased	Narrowed valve restricts forward flow; forceful ejection into ventricle Often occurs with mitral regurgitation Caused by rheumatic fever or cardiac infection
AORTIC STENOSIS Heard over aortic area; ejection sound at second right intercostal border	Midsystolic (ejection) murmur, medium pitch, coarse, diamond-shaped,* crescendo-decrescendo; radiates along left sternal border (sometimes to apex) and to carotid with palpable thrill; S_1 often heard best at apex, disappearing when stenosis is severe, often followed by ejection click; S_2 soft or absent and may not be split; S_4 palpable; ejection sound muted in calcified valves; the more severe the stenosis, the later the peak of the murmur in systole Apical thrust shifts down and left and is prolonged if left ventricular hypertrophy is also present	Calcification of valve cusps restricts forward flow; forceful ejection from ventricle into systemic circulation Caused by congenital bicuspid (rather than the usual tricuspid) valve, rheumatic heart disease, atherosclerosis May be the cause of sudden death, particularly in children and adolescents, either at rest or during exercise; risk apparently related to degree of stenosis

Mitral valve
Mitral valve stenosis

Aortic valve
Aortic valve stenosis

Continued on next page

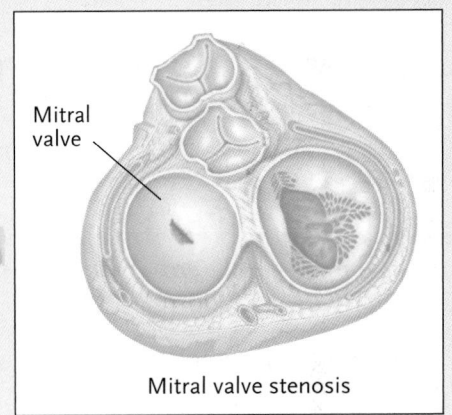

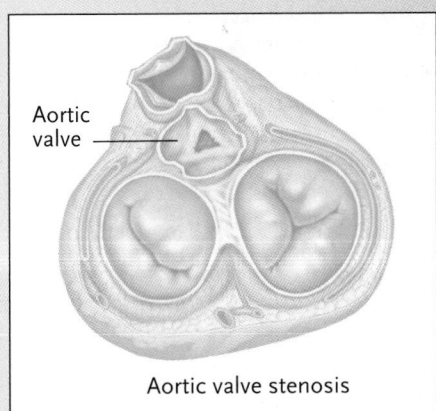

Table 4.5 Common Sources of Heart Murmurs (cont'd)

Type and Detection	Findings on Examination	Description	
SUBAORTIC STENOSIS Heard at apex and along left sternal border	Murmur fills systole, diamond-shaped medium pitch, coarse; thrill often palpable during systole at apex and right sternal border; multiple waves in apical impulses; S_2 usually split; S_3 and S_4 often present Arterial pulse brisk, double wave in carotid common; jugular venous pulse prominent	Fibrous ring, usually 1–4 mm below aortic valve; most pronounced on ventricular septal side; may become progressively severe with time; difficult to distinguish from aortic stenosis on clinical grounds alone	Subaortic fibrous ringSubaortic stenosis
PULMONIC STENOSIS Heard over pulmonic area radiating to left and into the neck; thrill in second and third left intercostal space	Systolic (ejection) murmur, diamond-shaped, medium pitch, coarse; usually with thrill; S_1 often followed quickly by ejection click; S_2 often diminished, usually wide split; P_2 soft or absent; S_4 common in right ventricular hypertrophy; murmur may be prolonged and confused with that of a ventricular septal defect	Valve restricts forward flow; forceful ejection from ventricle into pulmonary circulation Cause is almost always congenital	Pulmonic valvePulmonic valve stenosis
TRICUSPID STENOSIS Heard with bell over tricuspid area	Diastolic rumble accentuated early and late in diastole, resembling mitral stenosis but louder on inspiration; diastolic thrill palpable over right ventricle; S_2 may be split during inspiration Arterial pulse amplitude decreased; jugular venous pulse prominent, especially a wave; slow fall of v wave	Calcification of valve cusps restricts forward flow; forceful ejection into ventricles Usually seen with mitral stenosis, rarely occurs alone Caused by rheumatic heart disease, congenital defect, endocardial fibroelastosis, right atrial myxoma	Tricuspid valveTricuspid valve stenosis

Continued on next page

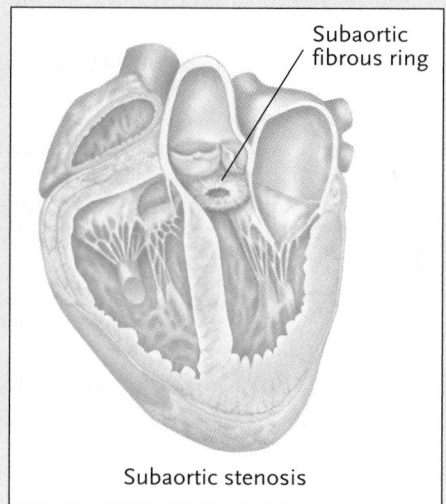

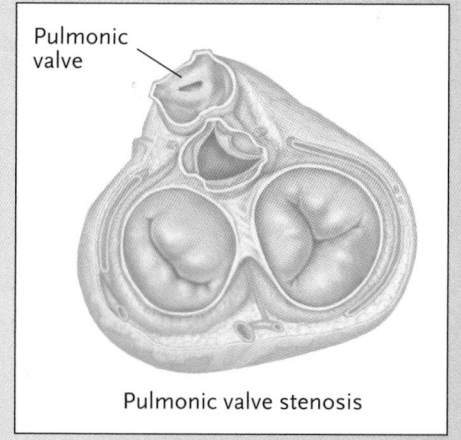

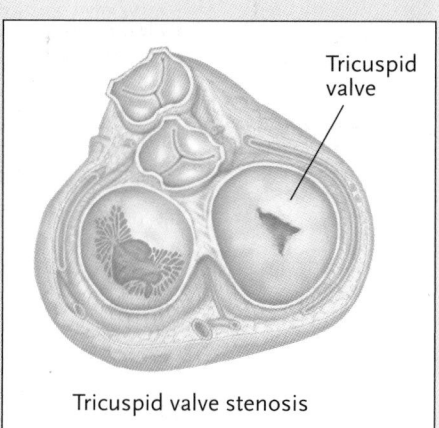

Table 4.5   Common Sources of Heart Murmurs (cont'd)

Type and Detection	Findings on Examination	Description	
MITRAL REGURGITATION Heard best at apex; loudest there, transmitted into left axilla	Holosystolic, plateau-shaped intensity, high pitch, hard blowing quality, often quite loud and may obliterate S_2; radiates from apex to base or to left axilla; thrill may be palpable at apex during systole: S_1 intensity diminished; S_2 more intense with P_2 often accented; S_3 often present; S_3–S_4 gallop common in late disease If mild, late systolic murmur crescendos; if severe, early systolic intensity decrescendos; apical thrust more to left and down in ventricular hypertrophy	Valve incompetence allows backflow from ventricle to atrium Caused by rheumatic fever, myocardial infarction, myxoma, rupture of chordae	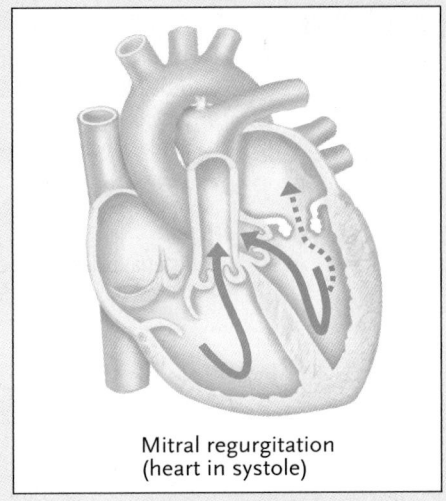 Mitral regurgitation (heart in systole)
MITRAL VALVE PROLAPSE Heard at apex and left lower sternal border; easily missed in supine position; also listen with patient upright	Typically late systolic murmur preceded by midsystolic clicks, but both murmur and clicks highly variable in intensity and timing	Valve is competent early in systole but prolapses into atrium later in systole; may become progressively severe, resulting in a holosystolic murmur; often concurrent with pectus excavatum	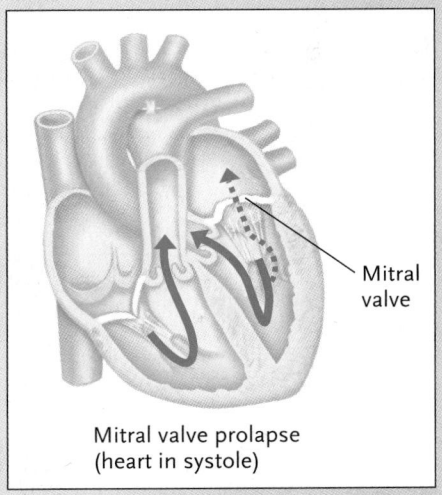 Mitral valve Mitral valve prolapse (heart in systole)
AORTIC REGURGITATION Heard with diaphragm, patient sitting and leaning forward; Austin–Flint murmur heard with bell; ejection click heard in second intercostal space	Early diastolic, high pitch, blowing, often with diamond-shaped* midsystolic murmur, sounds often not prominent; duration varies with blood pressure; low-pitched, rumbling murmur at apex common (Austin–Flint); early ejection click sometimes present; S_1 soft; S_2 split may have a tambour-like quality; M_1 and A_2 often intensified, S_3–S_4 gallop common In left ventricular hypertrophy, prominent prolonged apical impulse down and to left Pulse pressure wide; water-hammer or bisferiens pulse common in carotid, brachial, and femoral arteries	Valve incompetence allows backflow from aorta to ventricle Caused by rheumatic heart disease, endocarditis, aortic diseases (Marfan syndrome, medial necrosis), syphilis, ankylosing spondylitis, dissection, cardiac trauma	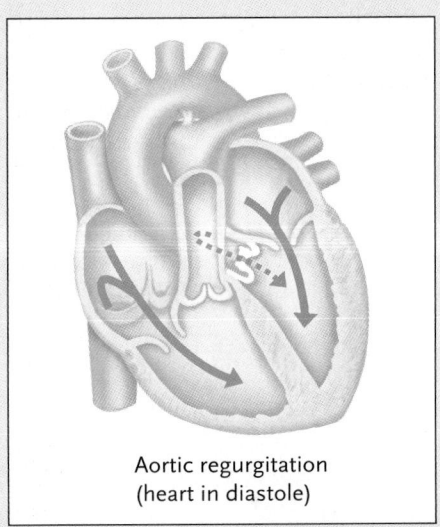 Aortic regurgitation (heart in diastole)

Continued on next page

Table 4.5 Common Sources of Heart Murmurs (cont'd)

Type and Detection	Findings on Examination	Description	
PULMONIC REGURGITATION	Difficult to distinguish from aortic regurgitation on physical examination	Valve incompetence allows backflow from pulmonary artery to ventricle Secondary to pulmonary hypertension or bacterial endocarditis	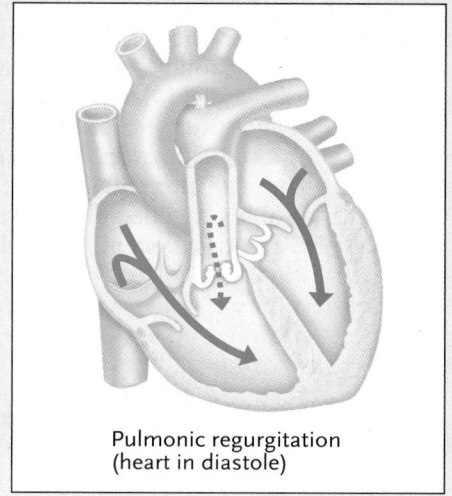 Pulmonic regurgitation (heart in diastole)
TRICUSPID REGURGITATION Heard at left lower sternum, occasionally radiating a few centimetres to left	Holosystolic murmur over right ventricle, blowing, increased on inspiration; S₃ and thrill over tricuspid area common In pulmonary hypertension, pulmonary artery impulse palpable over second left intercostal space and P₂ accented; in right ventricular hypertrophy, visible lift to right of sternum Jugular venous pulse has large v waves	Valve incompetence allows backflow from ventricle to atrium Caused by congenital defects, bacterial endocarditis (especially in intravenous drug users), pulmonary hypertension, cardiac trauma	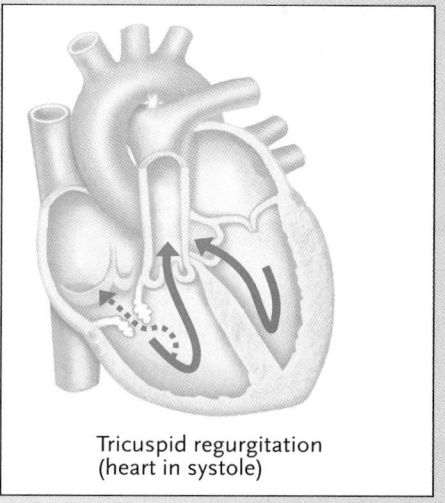 Tricuspid regurgitation (heart in systole)

*A diamond-shaped murmur is named for its recorded shape on a phonocardiogram (a crescendo-decrescendo sound).

Source: Seidel, H. M., Ball, J. W., Dains, J. E., & Benedict, G. W. (2006). *Mosby's guide to physical examination* (6th ed., pp. 446–449, Table 14-5). St. Louis: Mosby.

PERIPHERAL VASCULAR AND LYMPHATIC SYSTEMS ASSESSMENT

ANATOMY AND LANDMARKS OF THE PERIPHERAL VASCULAR AND LYMPHATIC SYSTEMS

The peripheral vascular system is made up of the blood vessels that travel away from and toward the heart. The lymphatic system runs parallel to the circulatory system. The arteries in the blood provide the tissues with oxygen and nutrients, and the veins act as a transport for the unoxygenated blood to go back to the heart and lungs to start the cycle again.

The arteries will have a pulse as the blood flows in a wave-like pattern with the recoil and expansion of the vessel. The pulse areas are brachial, ulnar, radial, femoral, popliteal, posterior tibialis, and dorsalis pedis.

Ischemia is the lack of blood flow to the tissues. It is usually caused by a blockage in the artery. When the client exercises and the tissues need a greater supply of oxygen and nutrients, more pain will occur from the ischemia. If the blockage is complete, the distal cells will die.

There are two sets of veins: the deep veins and the superficial veins. In addition, the perforators are small veins that join these two types together. As long as the deep veins are working well, the superficial, saphenous, veins can be removed safely.

The skeletal muscles assist in pushing the blood back to the heart by contracting and relaxing. There are also valves that prevent the backflow of the blood.

In the older adult, the veins and arteries may occlude partially or fully due to atherosclerosis or arteriosclerosis. Prolonged bed rest, long airplane flights or sitting, cancer, and the birth control pill increase the risk of a deep vein thrombosis, which, if it breaks off, can lead to a myocardial infarction or a stroke.

The lymphatic system runs alongside the blood system. It is responsible for returning the excess fluid and proteins from the interstitial tissues to the blood. It is also responsible for collecting waste products, supporting the immune system, and collecting lipids from the intestinal tract.

The easiest lymph nodes to feel are the cervical, axillary, epitrochlear, and inguinal. The nodes should not be enlarged. If they are, assess for mobility, firmness, tenderness, and matting. Check proximally for signs of infection. Cancerous nodes are usually firm, nontender, and fixed, and if advanced, they can be matted. The spleen, tonsils, and thymus are also part of the lymphatic immune system. It is not unusual for children to have small, shoddy nodes that are not pathological.

SUBJECTIVE DATA SPECIFIC TO THE PERIPHERAL VASCULAR AND LYMPHATIC SYSTEMS

- Have you noticed any pain in your legs, especially the calves? If yes, does it become worse when you walk?
- Has there been any swelling in your legs or arms or puffiness around your eyes? If so, is the swelling worse in the evening?
- Do you have any skin sores that have not healed in a reasonable amount of time?
- Has there been any change in the temperature or hair distribution on one of your extremities?
- Have you felt any swollen glands?
- Do you have a history of cardiac disease, diabetes, high blood pressure, or pregnancy?
- Do you smoke? If so, how much and how often?
- Are you on any medication?

OBJECTIVE DATA SPECIFIC TO THE PERIPHERAL VASCULAR AND LYMPHATIC SYSTEMS

Inspection and Palpation of the Peripheral Vascular and Lymphatic Systems

- Inspect and palpate the arms for skin colour, texture, condition, temperature, and symmetry.
- Take vital signs, including brachial, radial, and ulnar pulses.
- Assess pulses for rate, symmetry, rhythm, and amplitude.
- Inspect nails for profile sign to assess for clubbing and

measure the capillary refill. It should be less than three seconds.
- Do the modified Allen test to assess for collateral circulation from the radial and ulnar arteries.
- Inspect and palpate the legs for skin colour, texture, condition, and temperature, as well as for symmetry.
- Palpate the femoral, popliteal, posterior tibial, and dorsalis pedis pulses.
- Measure the calf circumference for symmetry, and if the measurement is off by more than 1 cm, refer the client for deep vein thrombosis assessment.
- Palpate the skin for edema starting from the ankle and moving your way up the leg. If edema is present, measure the distance of the edema from the knee. Inspect the backs of the legs for varicosities, especially in pregnant women or women who have had multiple pregnancies. Inspect the skin for hair distribution. In the older adult, there may be a decrease in hair growth and peripheral pulses, and the skin can become shiny and thin. These are normal signs of aging caused by a decrease in arterial circulation.

ABDOMINAL ASSESSMENT

ANATOMY AND LANDMARKS OF THE ABDOMEN

The abdomen is a large cavity that extends from the diaphragm at the top to the pelvis at the bottom, to the vertebra and paravertebral muscles in the back, and to the lower ribs and abdominal muscles in the front.

There are four abdominal muscles, including the rectus abdominis, which is joined along the midline by the linea alba. The umbilicus is the midpoint in the abdomen. It should be slightly inverted and uniform in colour with the rest of the skin. With abdominal bleeding, the blood can be seen around the umbilicus; it will have a blue circle around it called Cullen's sign. In the newborn, the umbilicus is very pronounced. The clamp and the extra tissue will turn black and fall off a few days after birth.

The contour of the abdomen varies. There are flat, round, protuberant, and scaphoid shapes. The first two are normal; the scaphoid shape can be a sign of malnutrition, and the protuberant shape can be a sign of obesity or ascites.

Within the abdominal cavity are many viscera. The solid viscera include the liver, which can be found in the upper right quadrant above the costal margin; the spleen, which should normally be posterior to the left midaxillary line parallel to the tenth rib; the pancreas, which is behind the stomach; the kidneys, which are retroperitoneal along the eleventh and twelfth ribs for the left one and slightly lower for the right; the adrenal glands, which are on top of the kidneys; the aorta, which is just left of the midline at the upper part of the abdomen and extends down to 2 cm above the umbilicus, where it bifurcates into the iliac arteries; and the ovaries and uterus, which are in the lower abdomen and pelvis. The liver decreases

A

External oblique
External oblique aponeurosis
Transversus abdominis
Rectus sheath
White line (linea alba)
Rectus abdominis
Internal oblique

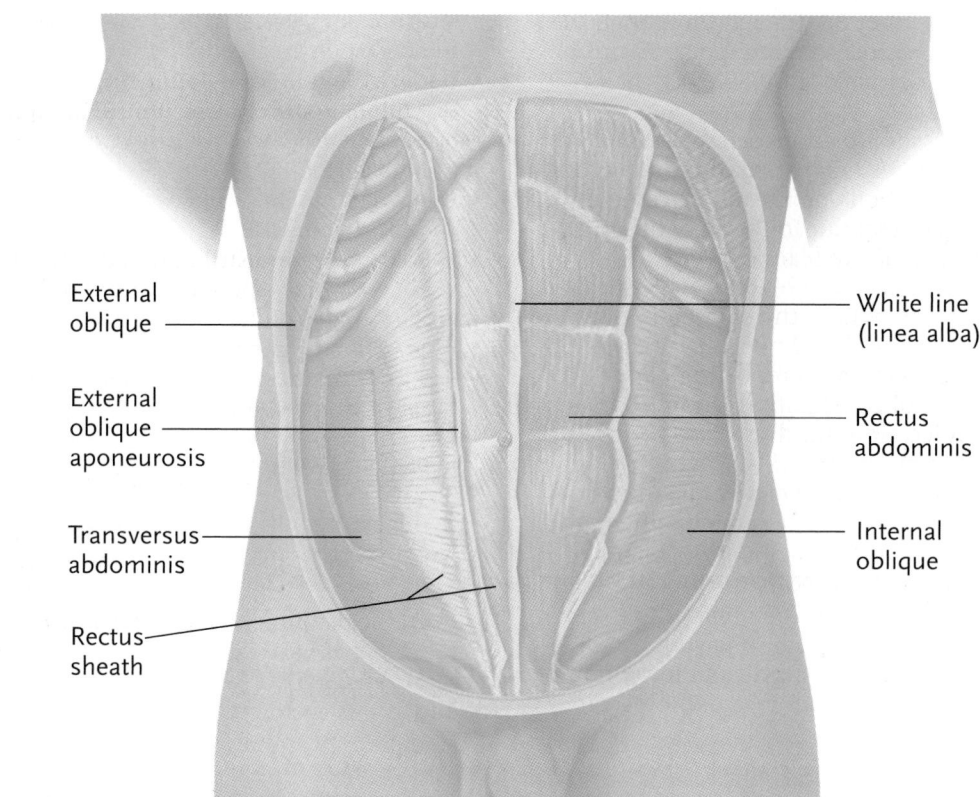

FIGURE 4.9A & B
Anatomic Structures of the Abdominal Cavity

Source: Seidel, H. M., Ball, J. W., Dains, J. E., Flynn, J. A., Solomon, B. S., & Stewart, R. W. (2011). *Mosby's guide to physical examination* (7th ed., p. 485, Figure 17-1). St. Louis: Mosby.

B

Liver
Gallbladder
Ascending colon
Small intestine
Cecum
Appendix
Spleen
Stomach
Transverse colon
Descending colon
Sigmoid colon
Bladder

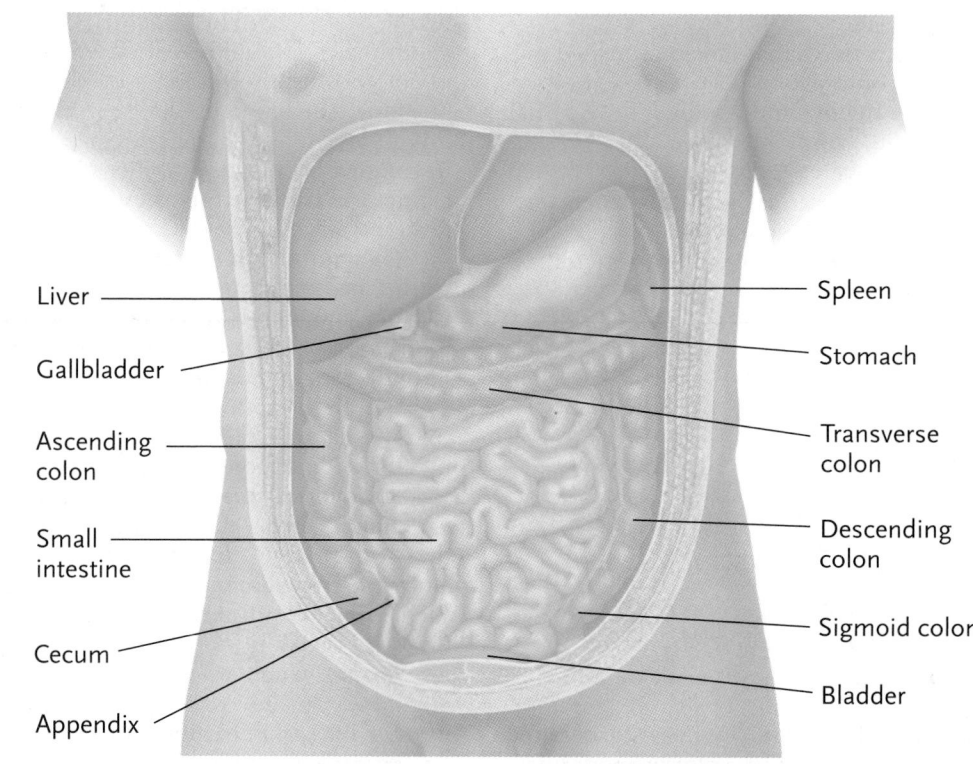

in size with age, especially after 80 years, even though the function remains normal, except for drug metabolism. In the newborn, the liver is normally felt 0.5–2.5 cm below the costal margin.

The hollow viscera include the stomach, which is below the diaphragm midline; the small intestine, which is in all quadrants; the large intestine (colon); the gallbladder, which is posterior to the liver at the right midclavicular line; and the bladder, which is at the top of the pelvis. In the infant, the bladder is positioned higher. The ileocecal valve, where the small intestine and the colon meet, is in the right lower quadrant.

With age, there is an increased reporting of constipation. The causes of constipation (more than three days between defecation, hard stool, straining, and the feeling of incomplete emptying) include a decrease in mobility; not enough water intake; low-residue foods; adverse effects of medication; difficulty getting to a bathroom or commode; hypothyroidism; irritable bowel syndrome; and bowel obstruction. Figure 4.9 illustrates the abdominal organs.

SUBJECTIVE DATA SPECIFIC TO THE ABDOMEN

*Specific questions for the older adult
^Specific questions concerning the infant

- Has there been any change to your appetite?
- What have you eaten in the last 24 hours?
- * Who prepares your food or buys the groceries?
- * Do you eat alone?
- ^ Does the child breastfeed?
- ^ Have you introduced any new foods into the diet?
- Have you gained or lost weight recently?
- Do you have any difficulty swallowing?
- Are there any foods that you cannot eat?
- Are you allergic to any foods?
- Are you experiencing any abdominal pain?
- Do you have any nausea or vomiting?
- What are you vomiting?
- How often do you have a bowel movement?
- Has there been a recent change to your bowel movements?
- Has there been any change to the consistency of the stool?
- Do you have a history of any problems with your gastrointestinal system?
- Do you take any medications?
- Do you exercise at all? If so, what do you do and for how long?

OBJECTIVE DATA SPECIFIC TO THE ABDOMEN

Inspection of the Abdomen

- Inspect the abdominal shape or contour. Stand at the foot of the bed and assess the shape of the abdomen.

To check for symmetry and masses, shine a light across the abdomen and see if any shadows fall on the skin.

- Inspect the skin for colour, temperature, moisture, condition, texture, scars, lumps, bumps, or lesions.
- Check the umbilicus for any sign of hernia, Cullen's sign, or infection.
- Check for any pulsation and peristalsis. It is quite common to see the pulsation of the aorta.
- What is the hair distribution like? Normally, a male will have a diamond hair pattern on the abdomen and a female will have a triangle pattern. Assess the position of the client.
- Does the client look comfortable? What is the breathing pattern like?

Auscultation of the Abdomen

Auscultate next so that the bowel sounds are accurate. Palpation and percussion will increase the sounds.

- With the diaphragm of the stethoscope, listen for up to five minutes in each quadrant for the tinkling sound of gas, fluid, and stool passing through the bowels. As soon as you hear and assess the bowel sound in one quadrant, move on to the next quadrant.
- Start auscultation in the lower right quadrant, the location of the ileocecal valve, as more sounds will be there.
- Auscultate next with the bell of the stethoscope for bruits in the arteries. Start at the aorta to the left of the central line below the xiphoid process. The renal arteries can be found above the level of the umbilicus and to the right and left of it. The iliac arteries are below the umbilicus and to the right and left of it, and the femoral arteries are in the groin. Normally, there are no sounds in these locations.

Percussion of the Abdomen

- Percuss the abdomen next. Using indirect percussion, listen for the sound of tympany throughout the abdomen.
- To assess the span of the liver, percuss from above the nipple line at the right midclavicular line to hear resonance. Percuss down until the sound changes to dull (the top border of the liver), note the spot, and then go below the costal margin and listen for the tympanic sound. Move up until the sound changes to dull (the lower border of the liver). Measure the distance between the two points. The liver should normally be above the costal margin. Exceptions include infants and clients with emphysema as the liver has been displaced by the overinflated lungs. The normal liver span is 6–12 cm.
- Percuss for splenic dullness. Start percussing at the eleventh intercostal space on the left and percuss toward the axilla line. The spleen should not be anterior to the midaxilla line. The tympanic sound

should be present until posterior to the midaxilla line. Then percuss up to the ninth space along the line or so, until you hear the resonance of the lung.

- Next, percuss to assess pain in the kidneys. With the client sitting up facing away from you, place your left hand on the costovertebral angle at the twelfth rib on the back, and with your right hand make a fist and bang your left hand with the ulnar part of the fist. Assess for pain or tenderness. Repeat on the other side.
- If you are questioning the presence of ascites, you can percuss for shifting dullness. Percuss from the midline across to the left side until you hear the sound change from tympany to dullness. Ask the client to roll onto the right side and percuss to assess if the fluid (dullness) has now shifted to the front of the abdomen.

Palpation of the Abdomen

- Lightly palpate the abdomen and assess for pain or tenderness, temperature, moisture, lumps, or bumps. Palpate any tender areas last to decrease the amount of guarding.
- If the client is ticklish, place your hand on top of the client's, start palpating, and then gently slide the client's hand out from under yours.
- Follow with deep palpation, assessing for organs, masses, and tenderness. Use bimanual palpation to feel for the kidneys, liver, and spleen.
- Use your opposing thumb and fingers to assess the size of the aorta. It should be 2.5–4 cm wide.
- To check for peritonitis and appendicitis, test for Blumberg's sign or rebound tenderness. In the area away from the pain, insert your hand straight down and remove it quickly. Look for signs of pain when you remove your hand. You can also do the iliopsoas muscle test. Lift the right leg up, and while you provide resistance, ask the client to put it down. If this causes pain, this muscle is inflamed. The obturator test will assess for a perforated appendix. Bend the client's leg at the knee. Move and rotate the ankle and knee externally and internally. It should not normally elicit any pain.
- For Murphy's sign, push your hand, fingers pointing down, into the abdomen under the liver area. Ask the client to take a deep breath; if there is a lot of pain, it is highly suggestive of gallbladder irritation.

MUSCULOSKELETAL SYSTEM ASSESSMENT

ANATOMY AND LANDMARKS OF THE MUSCULOSKELETAL SYSTEM

The musculoskeletal system comprises the bones, muscles, and joints. The system protects the inside core of the body and keeps the body erect. Bone marrow is produced in the bone, giving rise to the blood cells. The bones also store calcium and phosphorus. Another component to this system is movement. Most of the assessment will focus on movement.

There are many joints in the body, of which there are two types: synovial and nonsynovial joints. The nonsynovial joints are fixed, while the synovial ones are movable. In the synovial joint, there is a layer of cartilage over the opposing bones, and the joint is encased with synovial fluid lubricating it. Ligaments are attached from one bone to another, adding strength to the joint. A bursa is a small synovia-filled sac that adds protection to the bone.

Muscles make up 40–50% of the body's weight. There are three types of muscles: skeletal, smooth, and cardiac. The skeletal muscles are involved with the assessable movement of the body. The muscles are attached to the bone with tendons. When the muscles contract, they create movement. There are many different types of movement: flexion, extension, adduction, abduction, pronation, supination, circumduction, inversion, eversion, rotation, protraction, retraction, elevation, and depression.

SUBJECTIVE DATA SPECIFIC TO THE MUSCULOSKELETAL SYSTEM

*Specific questions for the older adult
^Specific questions concerning the infant

- Are you experiencing any joint pain or stiffness?
- Have you noticed any swelling or redness around your joints?
- Do you get any cramping in your muscles?
- Do you have cramping in your calf muscles when you walk?
- Have you noticed any weakness in your muscles?
- * Has there been any change in the weakness recently?
- * Do you use any aids to help you walk, such as a cane or walker?
- Do you have any bone pain?
- Have you ever broken a bone?
- Do you have any numbness or tingling sensations?
- Have you noticed any deformities in the bone?
- ^ Has the infant progressed in a normal growth pattern?
- * Have you noticed that you have stumbled or fallen more over the last few months?
- Are you involved in any exercise program?
- Are you involved in any sports?
- Do you have any difficulty getting around or maintaining your activities of daily living?
- Have you ever had surgery on your muscles, bones, or joints?
- Do you take any medication?

OBJECTIVE DATA SPECIFIC TO THE MUSCULOSKELETAL SYSTEM

Inspection and Palpation of the Musculoskeletal System

- Perform a general inspection of the body. Can the client walk and support the body?
- Is there a general symmetry? Is the client protecting a limb?
- Inspect each joint for redness, size and contour, and deformity.
- Inspect the muscles for symmetry, size, and tone. Inspect for curvature of the spine by asking the client to bend over. The scapulae should be even, as should the buttocks, and the spine should follow a straight line down.
- Palpate each joint for temperature, pain or tenderness, swelling, and smoothness in movement.
- Perform a range of motion examination for all the muscles, both upper body and lower body. Watch closely for symmetry. Note any restrictions in the movement. Measure the flexion and extension with a goniometer if you think that there is a problem. Check the muscle strength using movement against resistance.

NEUROLOGICAL SYSTEM ASSESSMENT

ANATOMY AND LANDMARKS OF THE NEUROLOGICAL SYSTEM

The Central Nervous System

The neurological system can be divided into the central system, which includes the brain and the spinal cord, and the peripheral system, which includes the 12 pairs of cranial nerves and the 31 pairs of spinal nerves.

The central nervous system is complex. The brain has two hemispheres; the right side governs the left side of the body, and the left side governs the right side of the body. It is very important to always assess both sides of the body. The four lobes that make up the brain are the frontal lobe, needed for personality, intellect, emotions, and voluntary movement; the parietal lobe, responsible for sensation; the occipital lobe, which has the visual receptors; and the temporal lobe, which is the centre for hearing. Within the temporal lobe is Wernicke's area, responsible for language comprehension. In the frontal lobe, there is Broca's area, which is responsible for motor speech.

In the aging adult, there is a progressive loss of brain functioning due to a loss of neurons. Also, the speed at which information travels along the neurons decreases with age. There may also be a decrease in the amount of blood reaching the brain, as well as an increased risk of stroke, both hemorrhagic and thrombotic. The infant's nervous system is not fully developed at birth. As myelinization occurs, the nervous response increases.

The neural pathways are split between the sensory and motor pathways. The sensory ones include the spinothalamic tract, where sensations of soft touch, hot and cold, and pain are carried to the thalamus and on to the sensory cortex for interpretation. The posterior column is responsible for the sense of position, vibration, and finely localized touch.

The motor pathways are responsible for the movement and coordination of the muscles. They include the pyramidal and extrapyramidal tracts, the cerebellum, and the upper and lower motor neurons. The cerebellum is more responsible for fine motor coordination and balance.

The Peripheral Nervous System

The peripheral nervous system includes the cranial nerves, the reflexes, and the spinal nerves. There are four types of reflexes: deep tendon (biceps: C5–C6, triceps: C7–C9, brachioradialis: C5–C6, quadriceps: L2–L4, and Achilles: L5–S2); superficial (abdominal: T8–T10 and T10–T12, cremasteric: L1–L2, and plantar: L4–S2); visceral (pupillary response to light and accommodation); and pathologic (abnormal). The reflexes are all involuntary movements.

There are 12 cranial nerves that enter and exit the brain. Nerves I and II extend from the cerebrum, while III–VII extend from the brainstem and diencephalons. These are both sensory and motor nerves, some of which are responsible for both.

There are 31 pairs of spinal nerves. They enter and exit from the spinal column. There are eight cervical (arms, neck and side of the head, and top of the chest), 12 thoracic (chest and abdomen), five lumbar (legs), five sacral (inner thigh, ankle, and groin), and one coccygeal nerve. Figure 4.10 shows the spinal nerves and dermatomes.

SUBJECTIVE DATA SPECIFIC TO THE NEUROLOGICAL SYSTEM

*Specific questions for the older adult
^Specific questions concerning the infant

- Have you been experiencing frequent headaches recently?
- Did you recently have any head injury? If yes, what part of your head was hit?
- Have you been experiencing either vertigo (a spinning sensation) or dizziness (feeling faint)?
- Have you had any seizures? If so, describe them.
- Do you have any tremors? If so, are they worse with stress?
- Have you noticed any signs of tingling or numbness (pins and needles)?
- Have you noticed any weakness?
- Do you have any problems with coordination?

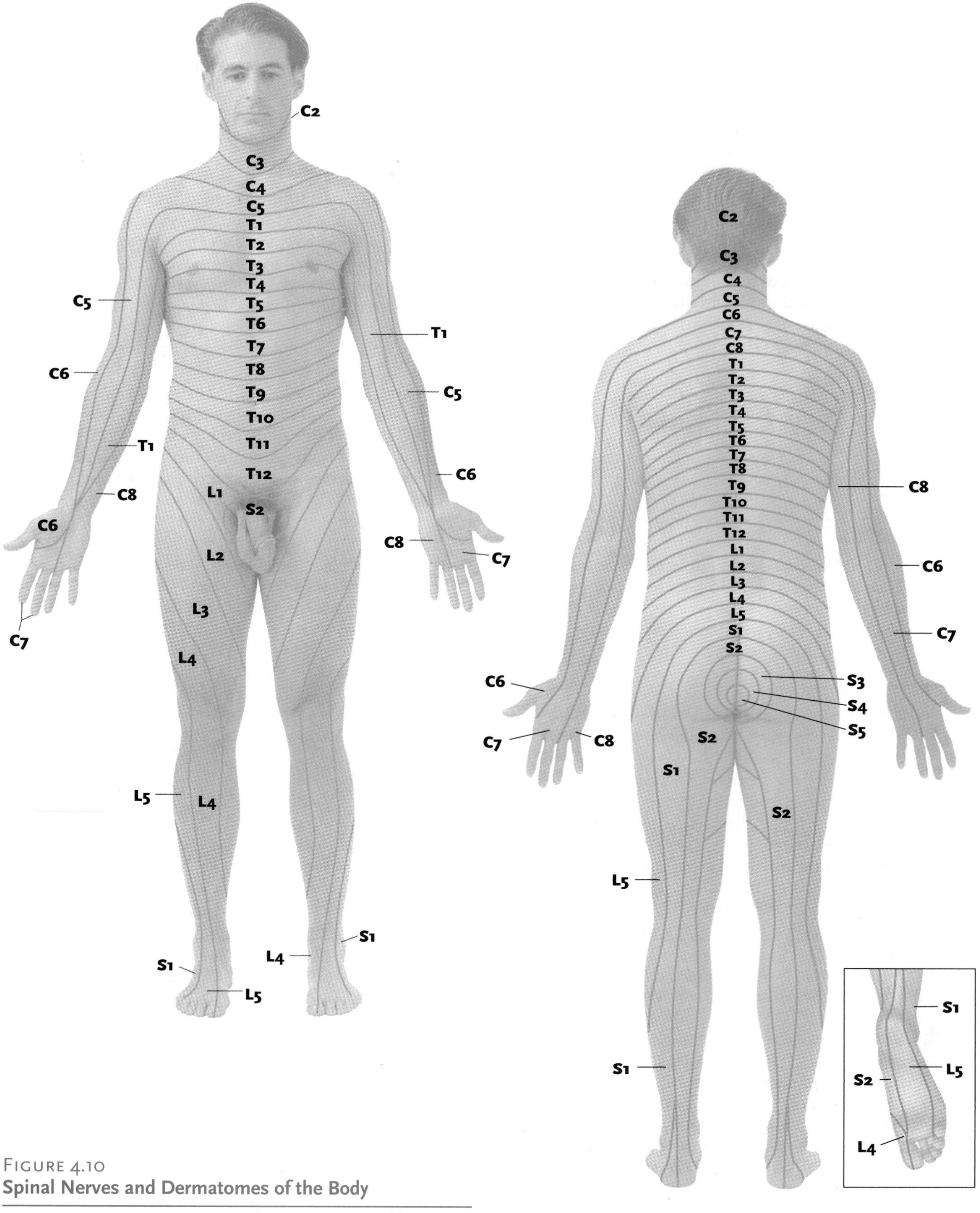
C2
C3
C4
C5
T1
T2
T3
T4
T5
T6
T7
T8
T9
T10
T11
T12
L1
S2
L2
L3
L4
L5
L4
S1
L5
L4
S1
C5
C6
T1
C8
C6
C7
T1
C5
C6
C8
C7
C2
C3
C4
C5
C6
C7
C8
T1
T2
T3
T4
T5
T6
T7
T8
T9
T10
T11
T12
L1
L2
L3
L4
L5
S1
S2
S3
S4
S5
C8
C6
C7
C6
C7
C8
S2
S1
S2
L5
S1
S1
L5
S2
L4

FIGURE 4.10
Spinal Nerves and Dermatomes of the Body

Source: Seidel, H. M., Ball, J. W., Dains, J. E., Flynn, J. A., Solomon, B. S., & Stewart, R. W. (2011). *Mosby's guide to physical examination* (7th ed., p. 708, Figure 22-6). St. Louis: Mosby.

- Have you noticed any difficulty with speech?
- Have you noticed any difficulty with swallowing?
- Are you taking any medication?
- Do you have any allergies?
- Are there any environmental hazards at work or home?
- * Have you or your family noticed any change in your mental function?
- ^ Was the labour and delivery without difficulty?

OBJECTIVE DATA SPECIFIC TO THE NEUROLOGICAL SYSTEM

It is important to perform a general mental survey in the neurological examination. Include an assessment of the client's appearance, behaviour, cognition, and thought process (ABCT).

Cranial Nerve Testing

- Olfactory (I): Sensory nerve. Check for nasal patency and introduce a scent for each nostril while the client closes the eyes and smells.
- Optic (II): Sensory nerve. Use the Snellen chart and Jaeger test chart for eye acuity and the confrontation test for peripheral vision and examine the ocular fundus and optic disc with an ophthalmoscope.
- Oculomotor (III), trochlear (IV), and abducens (VI): Motor nerves. Perform the six fields of gaze test, watching for nystagmus (normal in the far lateral gaze), and check for PERRLA with direct and consensual light reaction.
- Trigeminal (V): Sensory and motor nerve. Assess for fine touch at the areas of the three branches of the nerve: the forehead, cheek, and chin on both sides. For the motor component, test the movement of the mandible (jaw) and also its movement against resistance.
- Facial (VII): Sensory and motor nerve. Test the anterior two-thirds of the tongue for taste. For the motor component, test the movement of the face by asking the client to smile, frown, puff out the cheeks, and squeeze the eyes shut. Watch for symmetry. The corneal reflex is used to test the sensory V and motor VII; omit doing this test unless there are abnormalities in the other tests.
- Acoustic (VIII): Sensory nerve. Assess the client's hearing using the whisper test, the Weber test, and the Rinne test.
- Glossopharyngeal (IX) and vagus (X): Both sensory and motor nerves. It is not possible to test the sensory component of the glossopharyngeal nerve as it governs taste in the posterior one-third of the tongue. For the motor component, ask the client to say "Ahhh" and look in the mouth to see if the soft palate and uvula move up and back in the back of the mouth. Check the gag reflex.
- Spinal accessory (XI): Motor nerve. Check for range of motion and movement against resistance of the neck and shoulders.
- Hypoglossal (XII): Motor nerve. Check the range of motion and movement against resistance in the tongue. Ask the client to stick out the tongue and assess for any tremors and have the client repeat after you, "Light, tight, dynamite."

Motor, Sensory, Cerebellum, and Reflex Nerve Testing

- To test the cerebellum, ask the client to walk normally and then with a heel-to-toe tandem walk, knee bends, and Romberg test (ask the client to stand for 30 seconds with the feet together and the hands close to the sides and to close the eyes). For these tests, assess for coordination and balance. In addition, assess for fine motor coordination using rapid alternating movements. If the client cannot get out of bed, ask the client to run an ankle up and down the opposite shin.
- To assess the spinothalamic tract, use a cotton ball for soft touch and a broken tongue depressor with a sharp and dull side or, alternatively, two test tubes, one with cold water and one with hot water. For each of the tests, assess for symmetry and sensation. For soft touch, say to the client, "Every time you feel me touching you, say 'now.'" For the sensation of pain, don't follow any pattern but apply both the sharp and dull sides of the stick and say, "Let me know if you feel sharpness or dullness when I touch you." For hot and cold, let the client feel the difference and ask the client to tell you if he or she feels hot or cold. Follow the dermatomes around the body making sure to test the most distal areas.
- The posterior tract can be tested for vibration by striking a tuning fork and asking the client if he or she can feel the vibration as you place it on a bone of the big toes and thumbs. If not, work your way up the bony prominences until a sensation can be felt. It is normal for the older adult not to feel the vibration at the outer periphery.
- For position sensation, show the client that "up" is when you lift the finger or toe upward and "down" is when you move the finger downward. Ask the client to close his or her eyes and say "up" or "down" with the movement. Hold the finger or toe on the outside edges rather than on the top and bottom.
- For fine touch, use stereognosis: with the client's eyes closed, place a small object in the hand and ask the client to tell you what it is. Don't forget to repeat it with the other hand. Test for graphesthesia as well: with the client's eyes closed, draw a number or a letter on the hand and ask the client to identify it. Two-point discrimination involves using two points on the skin and asking the client to tell you if one or two points can be felt. Move the points together slowly and see at what distance the client can only feel one point.
- Check for symmetry on the other side. Extinction is the test to assess if the client can identify whether or not he was touched with one or two points. With point location, you are testing to see if the client can

point to where you just touched him or her. These are all testing the sensory cortex. With the older adult, these sensations likely will be reduced and delayed.

- Reflexes are best tested when the client is in a relaxed state. Strike the tendon with a reflex hammer directly, except for the bicep, where it is best to strike your finger placed over the tendon. Use your wrist action to make sure that the strike is hard enough. Check for symmetry and grade the reflex out of a possible 4:
    - 4+ Very brisk with clonus (rapid contractions of the muscle)
    - 3+ More brisk than normal
    - 2+ Average, normal
    - 1+ Reduced response or no response
- Check the biceps, triceps, brachioradialis, quadriceps, and Achilles deep tendon reflexes. Then check the abdominal, plantar, and, if male, cremasteric superficial reflexes.
- In an infant, check the rooting, grasping, Moro, sucking, stepping, and tonic neck reflexes. There should normally be a Babinski reflex up until the infant is 2 to 2½ years of age.
- Motor nerves should be checked simultaneously whenever possible so that you can check for symmetry. Assess the muscles for tone, size, range of motion, and strength using movement against resistance. Watch for any involuntary movements.

MALE GENITOURINARY SYSTEM ASSESSMENT

Anatomy and Landmarks of the Male Genitourinary System

The male genitourinary system is composed of the bladder, penis, testicles, scrotum, prostate, and inguinal area. Figure 4.11 illustrates these structures. The bladder is the storage area for urine. The urine leaves the bladder via the urethra, passing through the penis and out of the body.

FIGURE 4.11
The Male Pelvic Organs

Source: Seidel, H. M., Ball, J. W., Dains, J. E., Flynn, J. A., Solomon, B. S., & Stewart, R. W. (2011). *Mosby's guide to physical examination* (7th ed., p. 602, Figure 19-1). St. Louis: Mosby.

Urinary bladder
Rectum
Seminal vesicle
Symphysis pubis
Levator ani muscle
Prostate gland
Ejaculatory duct
Corpus cavernosum
Corpus spongiosum
Penis
Anus
Urethra
Glans
Bulbocavernosus muscle
Epididymis
Testis

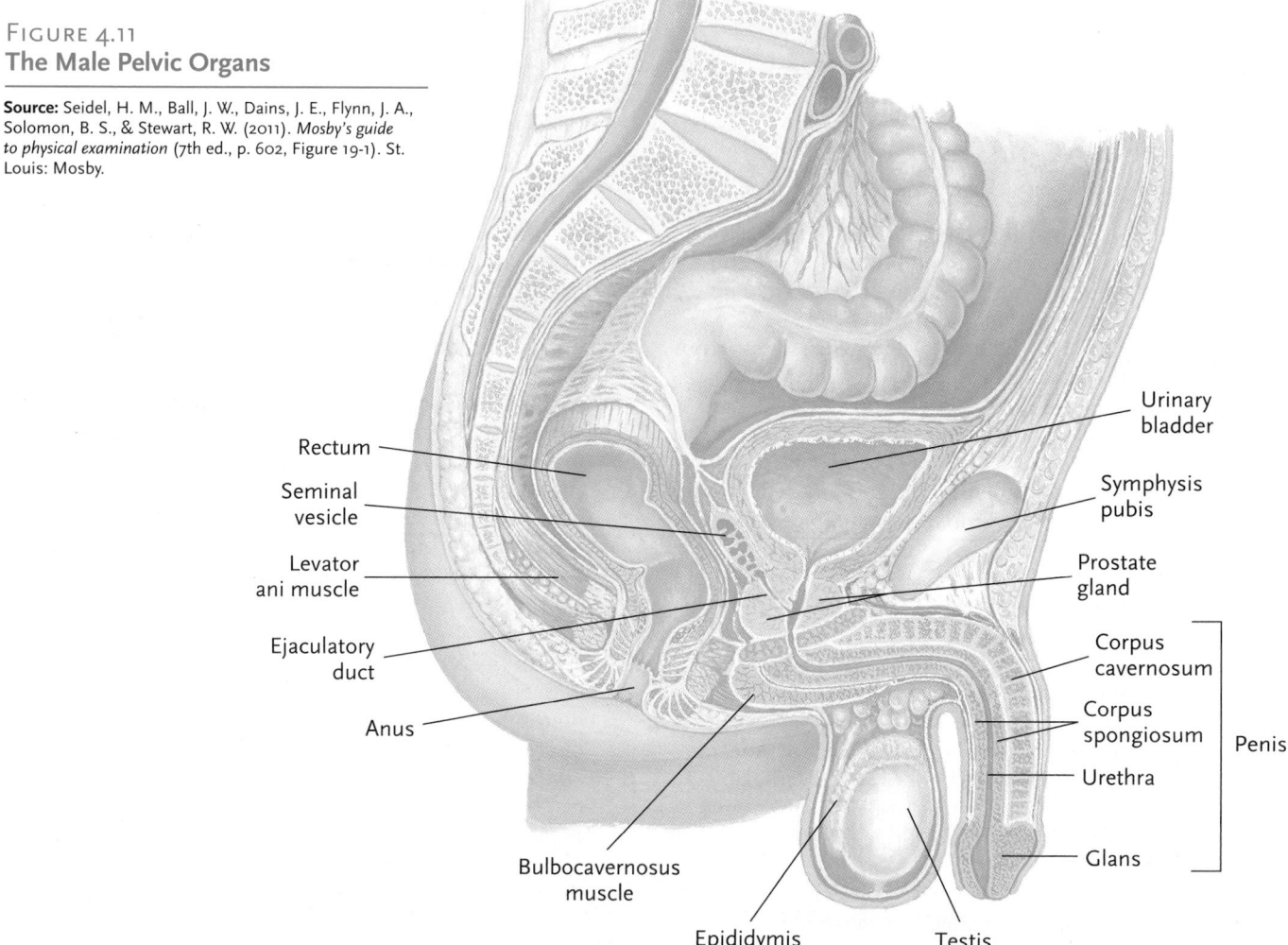

The penis is a sexual organ as well as a functional organ. Sexually, it provides the transportation of the male sperm to the woman's vaginal vault. A milky alkaline fluid that protects the sperm's viability is produced in the prostate. Prostate cancer is one of the leading cancers in men. The incidence is higher in men of African descent. Signs of benign prostatic hypertrophy (enlarged prostate) or cancer of the prostate are nocturia, frequency, decreased flow, urgency, and the feeling of not emptying the bladder.

The scrotum is a protective sac for the testicles. The testicles produce the sperm needed for reproduction. The cremaster muscle controls the elasticity of the scrotum. The muscle will permit the scrotum to shrink in cold conditions, drawing the testicles closer to the body, and to allow the testicles to descend in warm conditions to prevent them from overheating. It is important to check that the male infant's testicles are descended. Cancer of the testes is more likely to occur in men 17–25 years of age.

Within the inguinal area are the inguinal lymph nodes, the inguinal canal, and the femoral arteries and veins.

SUBJECTIVE DATA SPECIFIC TO THE MALE GENITOURINARY SYSTEM

*Specific questions for the older adult
^Specific questions concerning the infant or child

- Do you have any burning or pain when you urinate or ejaculate?
- Do you have any trouble starting to urinate?
- What colour is your urine?
- Do you have any lumps, bumps, or lesions on your penis?
- Is there any discharge coming from your penis?
- Are there any lumps or bumps that you have noticed on your testicles?
- Are you experiencing any pain in the scrotum?
- Do you do testicular self-examination?
- Are you sexually active?
- Are you having difficulty maintaining an erection?
- Do you use condoms?
- How many sexual partners have you had in the last six months?
- Have you been exposed to any sexually transmitted infections?
- ^ Is the child toilet-trained?
- ^ Is the child holding on to his genitals and crying when he urinates?
- ^ Does the child have both testicles?
- ^ Is the child urinating a lot or constantly thirsty?
- * Do you have trouble with urine leaking?
- * How many times do you get up at night to urinate?
- * Do you have trouble with urgency?
- * How many times do you urinate during the day?

OBJECTIVE DATA SPECIFIC TO THE MALE GENITOURINARY SYSTEM

Inspection and Palpation of the Male Genitourinary System

Inspect and palpate the penis. It should be smooth and without lesions. The foreskin should retract easily. The urethral meatus should be central in the glans. The distribution, colour, and density of the pubic hair should be normal for the client's age group and should be lice-free.

Inspect and palpate the scrotum. The scrotum skin should be free of lesions. Be careful to examine the underside of the scrotum. Gently feel the testicles for any lumps.

Inspect and palpate the inguinal area. Assess the femoral pulse and inguinal nodes and feel for the inguinal canal. Ask the client to cough while holding your fingers on the canal and assess for loops of bowel coming through the canal.

FEMALE GENITOURINARY SYSTEM ASSESSMENT

ANATOMY AND LANDMARKS OF THE FEMALE GENITOURINARY SYSTEM

The female genitourinary system is made up of the external (vulva) and internal genitalia, the bladder, the urethra, and the urethral meatus. The vulva comprises the labia majora and labia minora. These are folds of skin from the mons pubis. The clitoris is at the top of the labia majora and is highly sensitive to tactile stimulation. The urethral opening is close to the vaginal opening and not far from the anus, so it is very possible for bacteria to enter this opening, giving rise to a bladder infection.

The internal genitalia include the vaginal vault and the cervix, which is the opening to the uterus. The fallopian tubes and the ovaries extend from the uterus.

The labia of the infant at birth are quite engorged due to the presence of the mother's estrogen. The first signs of puberty usually occur between 8½ and 13 years of age.

In the aging adult, the hormone level drops, giving rise to menopause, shrinkage and drooping of the uterus, shortening of the vagina, and decreased vaginal secretions. The internal female genitalia are illustrated in Figure 4.12.

It is important to note that a vaccine is now available to eradicate most human papilloma viruses (HPV), which are the major risk factor for cervical cancer.

Ampulla of uterine tube
Isthmus of uterine tube
Infundibulopelvic ligament
Ovarian ligament
Fundus of uterus
Infundibulum of uterine tube
Body of uterus
Uterine body cavity
Endometrium
Myometrium
Fimbriae
Ovary
Internal os of cervix
Broad ligament
Uterine artery and vein
Cervix of uterus
Cervical canal
Reflection of peritoneum
External os of vaginal cervix
Vagina
Fornix of vagina

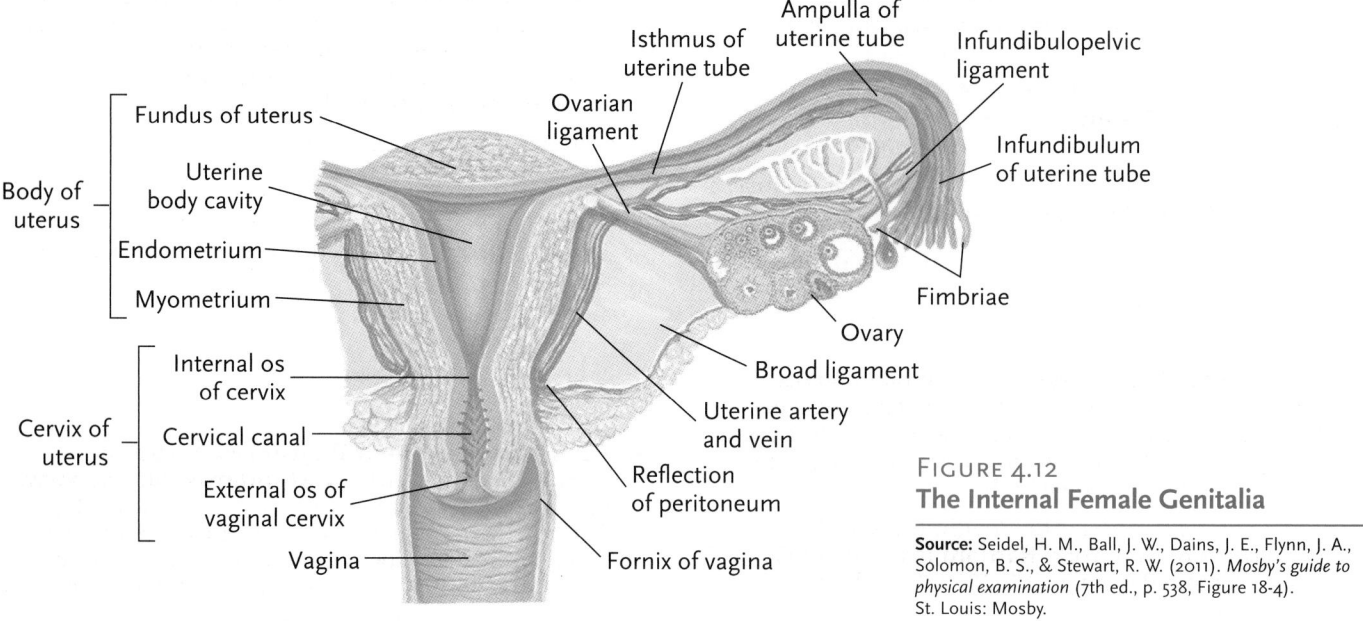

FIGURE 4.12
The Internal Female Genitalia

Source: Seidel, H. M., Ball, J. W., Dains, J. E., Flynn, J. A., Solomon, B. S., & Stewart, R. W. (2011). *Mosby's guide to physical examination* (7th ed., p. 538, Figure 18-4). St. Louis: Mosby.

SUBJECTIVE DATA SPECIFIC TO THE FEMALE GENITOURINARY SYSTEM

*Specific questions for the older adult
^Specific questions concerning the infant or child

- Do you have any burning or pain when you urinate?
- Do you have any trouble starting to urinate?
- What colour is your urine?
- Are there any lumps or bumps that you have noticed on the perineum?
- ^ Is the child toilet-trained?
- ^ Does she cry when she urinates?
- ^ Is the child urinating a lot or constantly thirsty?
- * Do you have trouble with urine leaking?
- * How many times do you get up at night to urinate?
- * Do you have trouble with urgency?
- * How many times do you urinate during the day?
- Do you or your sexual partners use condoms?
- How many sexual partners have you had in the last six months?
- Have you been exposed to any sexually transmitted infections?
- How old were you at menarche?
- How many times have you been pregnant?
- How old were you at the first pregnancy?
- How many live births have you had?
- How many abortions have you had?
- What was the date of your last menstrual period?
- * When did you start menopause?
- * Do you experience any pain or bleeding during or after intercourse?
- Do you experience any bleeding between your periods?
- * Does sneezing or laughing cause you to urinate?

OBJECTIVE DATA SPECIFIC TO THE FEMALE GENITOURINARY SYSTEM

- Place the client in the lithotomy position and examine the external genitalia.
- Inspect the pubic hair for distribution and lice; the skin for colour and the presence of any lumps, bumps, or lesions; the urethral meatus for position and condition; and the vaginal opening and the anus for discharge.
- Palpate the vagina for pain, lumps, or bumps and for musculature. Ask the woman to strain down and feel if there is any bulging of the vaginal wall or any incontinence.
- Assess the Bartholin's glands.
- For the internal examination, use a vaginal speculum and inspect the vaginal vault, the cervix, and perform a Papanicolaou smear (PAP). Remove the speculum and insert two lubricated fingers into the vagina. With the other hand on the abdomen, palpate for the uterus and ovaries. Then carefully slip one finger into the anus and do a rectal examination.

REFERENCES

Barkauskas, V. H., et al. (1998). *Health and physical assessment* (2nd ed.). St. Louis: Mosby.

Folstein, M. F., Folstein, S. E., & McHugh, P. R. (1975). Mini-mental state: A practical method for grading the cognitive state of clients for the clinician. *Journal of Psychiatry Research, 12*(3), 189–198.

Jarvis, C., Browne, A. J., MacDonald-Jenkins, J., Luctkar-Flude, M. (2009). *Physical examination & health assessment* (1st Canadian ed.). Toronto: Saunders.

Seidel, H. M., Ball, J. W., Dains, J. E., & Benedict, G. W. (2006). *Mosby's guide to physical examination* (6th ed.). St. Louis: Mosby.

Seidel, H. M., Ball, J. W., Dains, J. E., Flynn, J. A., Solomon, B. S., & Stewart, R. W. (2011). *Mosby's guide to physical examination* (7th ed.). St. Louis: Mosby.

Thompson, J. M. & Wilson, S. F. (1996). *Health assessment for nursing practice*. St. Louis: Mosby.

BIBLIOGRAPHY

Flaherty, E. (2007). Pain assessment for older adults. *Try this: Best practices in nursing care to older adults, 7.* New York: Hartford Institute for Geriatric Health. Retrieved January 17, 2013, from http://www.hartfordign.org/publications/trythis/issue07.pdf

Hartford Institute for Geriatric Health. (2008). *Resources: Assessment tools.* New York: Hartford Institute for Geriatric Health. Retrieved January 17, 2013, from http://www.consultgerirn.org/resources

Kurlowicz, L., & Wallace, M. (1999). The Mini Mental State Examination (MMSE). *Try this: Best practices in nursing care to older adults, 3.* New York: Hartford Institute for Geriatric Health. Retrieved January 17, 2013, from http://www.getnhp.com/PDFs/ProviderPDF/Provider_Manual/023%20APPENDIX/Appendix%202012/Tab%2013%20Mini%20Mental%20State.pdf

Registered Nurses' Association of Ontario. (2003). *Nursing best practice guideline: Screening for delirium, dementia and depression in older adults: Summary of recommendations.* Toronto: Author. Retrieved January 17, 2013, from http://rnao.ca/bpg/guidelines/screening-delirium-dementia-and-depression-older-adult

Registered Nurses' Association of Ontario. (2012). *Nursing best practice guideline: Assessment and management of foot ulcers for people with diabetes.* Toronto: Author. Retrieved January 17, 2013, from http://rnao.ca/bpg/guidelines/assessment-and-management-foot-ulcers-people-diabetes

Registered Nurses' Association of Ontario. (2012). *Nursing best practice guideline: Assessment and management of pain.* Toronto: Author. Retrieved January 17, 2013, from http://rnao.ca/bpg/guidelines/assessment-and-management-pain

Registered Nurses' Association of Ontario. (2012). *Nursing best practice guideline: Assessment and management of venous leg ulcers.* Toronto: Author. Retrieved January 17, 2013, from http://rnao.ca/bpg/guidelines/assessment-and-management-venous-leg-ulcers

Registered Nurses' Association of Ontario. (2008). *Nursing best practice guideline: Oral health: Nursing assessment and interventions: Summary of recommendations.* Toronto: Author. Retrieved January 17, 2013, from http://rnao.ca/bpg/guidelines/oral-health-nursing-assessment-and-intervention

WEB SITES

College & Association of Registered Nurses of Alberta: Nursing Practice Standards (https://www.nurses.ab.ca/Carna/index.aspx/new_nps_with_ethics.pdf): This site outlines the requirements to become a registered nurse in Alberta. There are many resources, policy issues, position statements, and practice standards.

College of Nurses of Ontario (http://www.cno.org): This site contains links to information related to all aspects of being a registered nursing professional in Ontario.

College of Nurses of Ontario: Registration Information (http://www.cno.org/en/become-a-nurse): This site contains information about how to become a registered nurse in Ontario.

College of Registered Nurses of British Columbia (http://www.crnbc.ca/pages/default.aspx): This site contains links to information related to all aspects of being a registered nursing professional in British Columbia.

College of Registered Nurses of Manitoba (http://www.crnm.mb.ca/applicants-becominganrn.php): This site contains information about how to become a registered nurse in Manitoba.

Nursing Statistics (http://www.cna-nurses.ca/CNA/nursing/statistics/2002highlights/default_e.aspx): This site provides links to statistics related to nursing in Canada, including information about the number of nurses working in different specialties and for different types of facilities and organizations.

CHAPTER 4

Practice Questions

Case 1

A registered nurse is newly employed in a retirement residence. Her duties include performing annual health assessments for the residents. Mrs. Clara Sloane, 86, arrives for her health assessment with the nurse.

Questions 1–7 refer to this case.

1. What is the most appropriate approach for the nurse to use during the interview stage of the health assessment with Mrs. Sloane?

   1. Address her as Clara rather than Mrs. Sloane as older adults respond better to use of their first name
   2. Be sure to speak loudly to Mrs. Sloane if she is hard of hearing
   3. Adjust the pace of the interview to provide extra time for Mrs. Sloane to answer questions
   4. Be careful not to touch Mrs. Sloane as she may be uncomfortable with this familiarity

2. The nurse measures Mrs. Sloane and finds her to be 110 cm. Mrs. Sloane states that she used to be 114 cm and asks why she is now shorter. What is the primary reason older adults lose height as they age?

   1. Decreased muscle mass
   2. Thinning of the vertebral discs
   3. Many older adults develop osteoporosis
   4. Most older adults have some degree of kyphosis

3. The nurse takes Mrs. Sloane's blood pressure. Which of the following is true concerning blood pressure in older adults?

   1. Both systolic and diastolic pressures are decreased
   2. Diastolic pressure increases, while systolic pressure remains the same
   3. Blood pressure readings become variable and unstable
   4. There is a widening pulse pressure

4. The nurse performs a skin survey with Mrs. Sloane. Which of the following would be a normal finding?

   1. Acrochordons (skin tags) on her eyelids and neck
   2. Edema in her lower limbs
   3. Decreased hair on her upper lip and chin
   4. Thicker skin on the dorsa of her hands and forearms

5. The nurse examines Mrs. Sloane's eyes and finds a grey-white arc around the cornea. What would the nurse say to Mrs. Sloane about this finding?

   1. "You have the beginnings of cataracts and should see an eye surgeon."
   2. "These are a normal finding in your age group and will not affect vision."

   3. "This is caused by thickening of your cornea and is probably causing some blurring of your vision."
   4. "The discoloration in your eyes is called xanthelasma and is caused by high levels of cholesterol."

6. The nurse performs an otoscopic examination of Mrs. Sloane's ears and finds impacted cerumen. What initial intervention should the nurse perform?

   1. Ear canal irrigation
   2. Removal of coarse ear hairs
   3. Referral to an ear, nose, and throat (ENT) physician
   4. Evacuation of the cerumen using a cotton-tipped swab

7. The nurse is aware that in the older age group, neurological assessment is important. Which of the following results of Mrs. Sloane's neurological assessments would be of most concern to the nurse?

   1. Mrs. Sloane is not sure which day of the week it is today
   2. Mrs. Sloane's Mini-Mental State Examination has declined from 27 last year to 25 today
   3. Mrs. Sloane states that she often misplaces her hearing aid
   4. Mrs. Sloane believes she presently lives in her former home, which she left two years ago

Case 2

A community nurse is employed to visit families the day after they have given birth. Ms. Perlstein delivered a healthy 3200-g boy yesterday. The nurse schedules an appointment to perform a health assessment with Ms. Perlstein and the baby.

Questions 8–13 refer to this case.

8. When the nurse arrives, baby Perlstein is asleep. What assessment should the nurse first perform?

   1. Respirations
   2. Apical heart rate
   3. Temperature
   4. General appearance

9. Which of the following should the nurse be aware of when examining baby Perlstein?

   1. The baby should be completely naked for the entire examination
   2. The parents should not be present as they may be distressed by the examination
   3. She should use a soft, crooning voice
   4. The examination is best done just before feeding

10. Which of the following would be part of a normal respiratory assessment for neonate Perlstein?

1. Observation of abdominal breathing
2. Obtaining a respiratory rate of 70 per minute
3. Noting a breathing pattern that is regular, with an even rate
4. Assessing that he is primarily mouth-breathing rather than nose-breathing

11. The nurse measures the head circumference of baby Perlstein. Why is this a component of a neonatal examination?

1. The circumference indicates the degree of moulding resulting from the birth process
2. It is part of the Apgar score
3. Variations from normal may indicate a genetic abnormality or increased intracranial pressure
4. Abnormalities in fontanelles are more accurately assessed

12. How would the nurse best confirm a patent rectum and anus in baby Perlstein?

1. The passage of meconium within 24–48 hours after birth
2. Stroke the anus and note a quick contraction of the sphincter
3. Introduce a rectal thermometer or cotton-tipped swab into the anus
4. Gently insert a gloved well-lubricated fifth finger into the rectum

13. How would the nurse elicit the Moro reflex from baby Perlstein?

1. Stroke the bottom of his feet
2. Hold him on his back and allow his head and trunk to drop back a short distance
3. Perform a sharp handclap beside his ear
4. Hold him vertically, allowing one foot to touch a surface

Case 3

A registered nurse working in the community provides health care to students at a secondary school as part of his job.

Questions 14–20 refer to this case.

14. How should the nurse approach health assessments and teaching with adolescents?

1. Involve the parents as they will be able to reinforce health teaching with their teenagers
2. Maintain a professional and strict attitude as adolescents will respond positively to authority
3. Provide factual information about how students can manage specific problems they identify
4. Provide information related to future health problems, such as risk for heart disease and osteoporosis

15. A thin 16-year-old girl, Hilary, is worried that she has not yet begun to menstruate. What question might the nurse ask Hilary?

1. "Tell me about your alcohol intake."
2. "Have any women in your family had ovarian cancer?"
3. "What kinds and amounts of food do you eat?"
4. "How much sleep do you get each night?"

16. Bradley, age 14, states that his friends make fun of him because he is short and still looks "like a kid." Which response by the nurse is the most appropriate?

1. "It is normal to be teased by your friends; don't let it worry you."
2. "You are very short for your age, so perhaps the doctor should examine you."
3. "I will show you some exercises that will help you to develop your muscles."
4. "All boys begin puberty at different ages, so you will probably grow and become more muscular when this happens."

17. Genevieve, age 13, tells the nurse that her parents want her assessed for scoliosis. How would the nurse assess if Genevieve has scoliosis?

1. Have her bend at the waist to inspect for asymmetry of the scapulae
2. Ask her to stand sideways to him so he may measure any degree of kyphosis
3. Tell Genevieve to rotate sideways and observe for uneven shoulder height
4. Observe Genevieve from the back as she climbs a flight of stairs

18. Sheldon, age 16, says he is very pleased that he was chosen to play for the school football team. What safety-related assessment question is important for the nurse to ask Sheldon?

1. "Do your parents come to watch you play?"
2. "Are you able to manage attending your games and completing your school work?"
3. "Are you planning to play professional football one day?"
4. "Do you use special protective equipment?"

19. Some teachers are concerned about Warren, age 18, because he has been exhibiting labile, unusual behaviours they describe as "paranoic." They wonder if he is abusing street drugs or has a mental health disorder such as schizophrenia. The nurse performs a mental health examination. What might he say to Warren to best determine his thought processes and perceptions?

1. "What are your grades like in school?"
2. "How do you feel today?"

3. "I am going to ask you to remember four words, and in a few minutes, I will ask you to recall them."

4. "Do other people talk about you?"

20. The nurse teaches a group of students about skin care. What is the most common skin problem in adolescence?

1. Contact dermatitis
2. Acne
3. Eczema
4. Rosacea

INDEPENDENT QUESTIONS

Questions 21–30 do not refer to a particular case.

21. Ms. Edwards is a new client in the health clinic. The nurse auscultates her chest and hears a heart murmur. What should be the initial action by the nurse?

1. Ask Ms. Edwards about her past cardiac history and present symptoms
2. Consult with the clinic physician
3. Recognize that most murmurs are benign but document this finding
4. Check her carotid pulses

22. Which of the following correctly outlines the sequence of events the nurse should follow when examining the abdomen?

1. Inspection, auscultation, percussion, palpation
2. Percussion, palpation, inspection, auscultation
3. Light palpation, inspection, auscultation, percussion
4. Inspection, palpation, auscultation, percussion

23. Which pulse would be of most concern to the nurse?

1. Two-month-old infant: 110 bpm at rest
2. Ten-year-old boy: 104 bpm after exercise
3. Seventeen-year-old athlete: 50 bpm at rest
4. Five-day-old infant: 70 bpm after crying

24. Which of the following would be of most concern to the nurse if noted in an 8-year-old child after he fell from his bike and hit his head?

1. Nausea
2. Memory loss for familiar surroundings and objects
3. Swelling and aching pain at the site of injury
4. Blood pressure changing from 100/60 to 110/70 mm Hg

25. Mrs. Sandoz tells the nurse her stools are a light grey to a very light brown colour. Which of the following conditions might the nurse suspect as the cause?

1. Renal failure
2. Intestinal polyps
3. Gallbladder disease
4. Celiac disease

26. The nurse is assessing Mr. Robin for possible discharge from a psychiatric facility. He must assess Mr. Robin's ability to make sound judgements and decisions. Which of the following assessment questions would best evaluate this ability?

1. Ask Mr. Robin to explain a proverb such as "a stitch in time saves nine"
2. Ask Mr. Robin to spell moose backwards
3. Ask Mr. Robin what action he would take if his house caught fire
4 Ask Mr. Robin how a train and an airplane are similar

27. Ms. Leigh is examined in the emergency department by a nurse who notes on the chart "PERRLA." Which organ does this notation pertain to?

1. Eyes
2. Ears
3. Mouth
4. Lungs

28. Where would the nurse place his or her hands to assess a client for the possible presence of a goitre?

1. Over the scapulae
2. Over the maxillary sinuses
3. Over the anterior portion of the neck
4. Over the angle of Louis

29. A nurse is employed in an Inuit community. Many adolescent men live on the reserve. What would be the most important assessment to be aware of in this population?

1. Risk for suicide
2. Risk for type 2 diabetes
3. Risk for cardiovascular disease
4. Risk for tuberculosis

30. Ms. Martin is a pregnant woman who comes to the clinic for her first prenatal appointment. Protocol in the clinic is that every woman is screened for intimate-partner violence. How would the nurse best introduce the topic to Ms. Martin?

1. "Since you have been pregnant, has your partner every physically hurt you?"
2. "Have you ever been the victim of domestic abuse?"
3. "It is clinic policy to ask if you are in an abusive relationship."
4. "Because domestic violence is so prevalent in our society, we ask all women about any experience with abuse."

Answers and Rationales for Practice Questions

1.   **C: Nurse–Client Partnership   T: Application**

1. Nurses should always address the person by the last name as some older adults may resent being called by their first names by younger persons.
2. If Mrs. Sloane was hard of hearing, it is best for the nurse to face her directly so that her mouth and face are visible. Speaking loudly or shouting may distort speech.
3. It is important to adjust the pace of the interview to allow older adults sufficient time to report background historical information. Also, it may take the older adult a greater amount of response time to interpret the question and process the answer.
4. Touch is a nonverbal skill that is very important to older people. Touch communicates empathy and understanding of their problems.

2.   **C: Changes in Health   T: Critical Thinking**

1. Older adults do lose muscle mass as they age, but this is not the cause of shortened stature.
2. With age, the intervertebral discs become thinner, thus shortening the spinal column and leading to shortened stature.
3. Many older adults develop osteoporosis leading to decreased height, but this is not the prime reason.
4. Kyphosis mostly occurs as a result of osteoporosis.

3.   **C: Changes in Health   T: Knowledge**

1. Systolic, but not diastolic, pressures tend to increase.
2. As in choice 1.
3. Blood pressure does not become variable due to age.
4. As the heart pumps against a stiffer aorta, the systolic pressure increases, leading to a widened pulse pressure.

4.   **C: Changes in Health   T: Knowledge**

1. Skin tags are overgrowths of normal skin that form a stalk and are polyplike. They occur frequently on the eyelids, cheeks, neck, axillae, and trunk of the older adult.
2. Edema is an abnormal finding and may indicate a circulatory or cardiac problem.
3. There is often increased hair on the chin, upper lip, and eyebrows of older females due to unopposed androgens.
4. Older adults have thinner skin on the backs of their hands, forearms, lower legs, and dorsa of feet and over bony prominences.

5.   **C: Changes in Health   T: Application**

1. This greyish-white arc is called arcus senilis. It is not related to cataracts.
2. Arcus senilis is commonly seen around the cornea and is due to deposition of lipid material. Although the cornea may appear thickened and raised, it does not affect vision.
3. Although arcus senilis may cause the cornea to look thickened, it does not affect vision.
4. Xanthelasma are soft raised yellow plaques occurring on the lids at the inner canthus and are more frequent in women. They are found with both high and normal blood levels of cholesterol.

6.   **C: Changes in Health   T: Application**

1. Impacted cerumen ("ear wax") is a common but reversible cause of hearing loss in older people. Ear canal irrigation can remove the impacted cerumen and is the appropriate initial intervention.
2. Although coarse ear hairs may increase the accumulation of cerumen, removal of the wax is the initial action.
3. This is not necessary unless the cerumen cannot be removed by irrigation.
4. It is likely that use of a cotton swab will push the cerumen farther into the ear canal and could cause damage to the canal and eardrum.

7.   **C: Changes in Health   T: Critical Thinking**

1. It is normal for many older adults to temporarily forget the day of the week, especially due to the lack of structure or routine of not going out to a job. While a person may not provide the precise date, Mrs. Sloane would be considered oriented if she knew generally the present period of time and place.
2. Scores of 24–27 indicate no cognitive impairment. A slight decline to 25 may be a normal variable.
3. Most people temporarily misplace articles. It would be of concern if Mrs. Sloane were placing her belongings in inappropriate places, such as putting her hearing aid in the refrigerator.
4. This indicates confusion, loss of orientation, and impairment of short-term memory and is an indication of dementia.

8.   **C: Changes in Health   T: Critical Thinking**

1. This would be the second assessment.
2. This would be done early in the assessment provided that the infant was not crying.
3. This would disturb the infant and should be left until after the general assessment, heart rate, and respirations.

4. Prior to the nurse disturbing the infant, she should develop an overall impression: body symmetry, spontaneous position, flexion of limbs, spontaneous movement, and any obvious facial abnormalities.

9.   C: Changes in Health   T: Application

1. Although the baby needs to be examined while naked, there may be concerns about heat regulation if the environment is not warm. In addition, particularly for male babies, the diaper should be left on until the genitalia and anus are examined.
2. The parents should be present so they may be reassured by the examination, so they may learn about the normal growth and development of their infant, and so the infant is calmed by their presence.
3. The baby responds to a soft, soothing tone of voice.
4. The exam should be scheduled 1–2 hours after feeding, when he is not hungry or drowsy.

10.   C: Changes in Health   T: Application

1. An infant's respirations are primarily diaphragmatic rather than thoracic; thus, the abdomen is watched to count and evaluate respirations.
2. The normal respiratory rate for a newborn is 30–60. A rate of 70 is tachypnea.
3. Infants display a respiratory pattern that is irregular, from rapid breaths to short periods of apnea.
4. Young infants are obligatory nose-breathers up to the age of 3 months, at which point they become nose- and mouth-breathers, so mouth-breathing would be an abnormal finding.

11.   C: Changes in Health   T: Application

1. This may be visually assessed and is rarely clinically important.
2. Head circumference is not part of the Apgar score.
3. The newborn's head measures about 32–38 cm and is about 2 cm larger than the chest. The measurement is plotted on a standard growth chart. An enlarged head circumference may be an indication of increased intracranial pressure, such as in hydrocephalus. A smaller than normal head circumference is an indication of microcephaly resulting from genetic or congenital problems.
4. Fontanelles are assessed visually and by palpation.

12.   C: Changes in Health   T: Critical Thinking

1. This is the most reliable and least invasive determination of a patent rectum and anus. It guarantees that the intestine is sufficiently patent to allow the passage of stool.
2. This is the anal reflex and is used to check sphincter tone.
3. This is not a recommended practice as there is danger of harming the rectal mucosa.
4. This should not be necessary, and even the fifth finger may be too large for the size of the newborn rectum.

13.   C: Changes in Health   T: Knowledge

1. This elicits the Babinski reflex.
2. This will elicit the Moro reflex, as will placing the infant on a flat surface and hitting the surface sharply.
3. This will elicit the startle reflex.
4. This will elicit the stepping reflex.

14.   C: Nurse–Client Partnership   T: Application

1. Depending on the age of the teenager, it may not be appropriate to involve the parents. Most adolescents need to feel in control of their bodies and their lives and may not want parents involved unless a serious problem is identified.
2. Adolescents may not respond positively to authority, particularly in a health assessment situation. It is more important for the nurse to obtain their trust.
3. With this approach, the nurse will be able to gain the trust of the adolescent.
4. Future health problems will not be of interest or concern to the adolescent.

15.   C: Changes in Health   T: Application

1. Alcohol has no effect on menstruation.
2. Family history of ovarian cancer has no relation to the onset of menstruation.
3. Because Hilary is thin, she may have anorexia and be malnourished. Onset of menstruation is affected by nutritional status.
4. Sleep has no effect on menstruation.

16.   C: Nurse–Client Partnership   T: Critical Thinking

1. This does nothing to reassure Bradley and may sound patronizing.
2. It is normal for boys of Bradley's age to be short prior to a growth spurt at puberty. Evaluation by a physician is necessary only if Bradley is extremely short.
3. While some exercises may help to increase muscle size, they will not affect Bradley's height. It is more important to reassure him that this will occur at puberty.

4. This is a factual answer that will reassure Bradley that he is normal and that he will grow and be more like his friends when he reaches puberty.

17.   C: Changes in Health   T: Application

1. This is called the forward bend test. The spine should appear vertical. If there is unequal height of scapulae, shoulders, or iliac crests, scoliosis is suspected.
2. Kyphosis is common during adolescence because of chronic poor posture. This is not a test for scoliosis.
3. This will not identify scoliosis.
4. This will not help to identify a curvature of the spine seen in scoliosis.

18.   C: Health and Wellness   T: Application

1. This question may solicit information about the parent–child relationship but is not the most important safety-related question.
2. This question is directed at finding information concerning Sheldon's ability to manage the stress of balancing sports and school demands, but it is not the most important safety-related question.
3. This question may lead to an assessment of Sheldon's goals and aspirations for his future but is not the most important safety-related question at this time.
4. Adolescents playing football are at particular risk of injury. The nurse needs to obtain information regarding protective equipment.

19.   C: Changes in Health   T: Critical Thinking

1. This obtains information about his cognitive function and compliance with academic expectations, not thought processes.
2. This is a question that may obtain information about mood and affect.
3. This is a test of a person's ability to remember new learning. It is more useful in assessing for dementia.
4. Paranoia and auditory and visual hallucinations occur with psychiatric and organic brain disease and with psychedelic drugs.

20.   C: Changes in Health   T: Knowledge

1. This is a common inflammatory condition of the skin but is not the most common skin condition in adolescence.
2. All teens have some form of acne, although with some, it is in the milder form of open comedones (blackheads).
3. Eczema is a type of dermatitis with various forms. It is not specific to the adolescent.
4. Rosacea is a type of acne found primarily in adults.

21.   C: Changes in Health   T: Critical Thinking

1. Many murmurs are "functional" and not of concern. Because Ms. Edwards is a new client, the nurse does not know if this is a new finding or if she is aware of a previous history of heart murmur. The nurse needs to obtain this information prior to referral to the physician.
2. The nurse should consult with the physician after obtaining the relevant cardiac history.
3. Most murmurs are benign, but as the nurse does not know what type of murmur Ms. Edwards has, she must obtain further data.
4. Although part of a cardiac assessment, this will be of limited use at this stage of examination.

22.   C: Changes in Health   T: Application

1. This is the correct sequence as auscultation must precede percussion and palpation in order not to increase peristalsis.
2. Percussion and palpation may increase peristalsis and yield incorrect information.
3. Light palpation may increase peristalsis.
4. Auscultation must precede palpation to obtain accurate data.

23.   C: Changes in Health   T: Application

1. This is a normal heart rate for a 2-month-old infant.
2. This is a normal heart rate for a child this age after exercise.
3. Although lower than the textbook normal heart rate, 50 is not abnormal in a young, well-conditioned athlete.
4. This is bradycardia in a 5-day-old infant. Although there are wide variations published as normal neonatal heart rates that range from approximately 100–160, this rate, especially after crying, is below normal.

24.   C: Changes in Health   T: Critical Thinking

1. This is a common but not ominous sign in a client who has had a head injury.
2. This is of concern as it implies that there has been some injury to the brain with loss of memory and cognitive function.
3. This is a normal finding postinjury and implies superficial rather than brain injury.
4. The blood pressure presently remains within normal limits. It may become elevated due to pain, or there may be later deviations indicative of shock or brain swelling.

25. **C: Changes in Health** **T: Knowledge**

1. Renal failure has no effect on the colour of stool.
2. Intestinal polyps do not alter the colour of stool.
3. Gallbladder disease causing limited bile to be released may cause the stools to lighten in colour.
4. Celiac disease is a condition of gluten intolerance. While stools may change in consistency, there are no colour changes as indicated by Mrs. Sandoz.

26. **C: Changes in Health** **T: Application**

1. This tests abstract reasoning, not judgement and decision making.
2. This is a test of cognitive function and does not evaluate judgement.
3. This requires Mr. Robin to apply judgement and decision-making abilities to develop a wise course of action.
4. This tests abstract reasoning.

27. **C: Changes in Health** **T: Knowledge**

1. PERRLA is the acronym for Pupils Equal Round React to Light and Accommodation. It is an evaluation of function of the pupil in the eyes.
2. PERRLA does not relate to ears.
3. As in choice 2.
4. As in choice 2.

28. **C: Changes in Health** **T: Knowledge**

1. A goitre is an enlarged thyroid. The thyroid is located in the neck area, not the scapulae.
2. The thyroid is not located in the face.

3. This is the correct position for assessing the thyroid, which can be palpated to assess for enlargement or goitre.
4. This is located in the sternum, not the neck.

29. **C: Changes in Health** **T: Critical Thinking**

1. The suicide rates in Aboriginal communities are three to five times greater than the national rates. Suicide is a particular risk in the young male population.
2. The prevalence of type 2 diabetes in this population is three to five times greater than the national rate. Although it occurs at a younger age, it is still not common in adolescence.
3. There are higher rates of cardiac disease with this population but not specifically in this age group.
4. People of Aboriginal descent have a rate of tuberculosis almost seven times higher than that of the rest of Canada. However, the numbers still do not compare to the number of suicides in the adolescent age group.

30. **C: Nurse–Client Partnership** **T: Critical Thinking**

1. This is a question that would be asked as part of an abuse assessment screening but is not an appropriate introduction to the topic.
2. As in choice 1.
3. This introduction implies that the nurse is asking about abuse only because of clinic policy.
4. This introduction alerts the woman that questions will be asked about domestic violence and ensures that she is aware that she is not being singled out.

Health and Wellness

Donna Pierrynowski Gallant, PhD, RN

Patricia Hansen-Ketchum, RN, PhD (c)

Marion R. Alex, RN, BScN, MN, CNM

According to every theory of nursing, and every nursing practice act in Canada, health promotion is considered an essential role for nurses. However, how we define health, and what we consider to be priorities for health promotion, has varied across time, cultures, and geography. In Canada today, there is growing recognition that health promotion involves promoting health for individuals or families (changing the person) as well as promoting changes in the community and population that result in healthier environments (changing the world). This chapter provides an overview of the meaning and determinants of health, of the strategies toward health promotion involving individual or family action, and of population health initiatives with the goal of fostering healthy environments in Canada.

GUIDING PHILOSOPHIES FOR HEALTH AND WELLNESS

A DEFINITION OF HEALTH

The definition of health and wellness has a unique meaning to each individual and family. This uniqueness in defining health is true of larger groups of people, communities, and populations. A very important goal of nursing is to help individuals and groups to achieve their optimum level of health and wellness. Numerous definitions of health continue to influence how nurses attain this goal within the Canadian health system. Some common conceptualizations of health that currently inform nursing practice are as follows:

- An individual's perception of health is multidimensional and is based on a myriad of interacting parts of the human experience. The interconnected parts include physical, mental, social, and spiritual health (Pender, Murdaugh, & Parsons, 2006).
- The World Health Organization (WHO) defines health as "a state of complete physical, mental, and social well-being, not merely the absence of disease or infirmity" (WHO, 1986).
- Health is a balance of "biopsychological, spiritual, cultural and environmental dimensions" (Pender et al., 2006, p. 30).
- Health is also a "product of reciprocal interactions between individuals and their environments" (McMurray, 2007, p. 7).

DETERMINANTS OF HEALTH

Informed by studies on the factors influencing health, Health Canada has delineated 12 key determinants of health (PHAC, 2011; see Table 5.1). Each determinant interacts with and has an impact on the others. Our understanding of these determinants continues to evolve, and so, too, does our work in addressing and

influencing them (Health Canada, 2002; Potter, Perry, Ross-Kerr, & Wood, 2010).

APPROACHES TO HEALTH

In the west, there are currently three main approaches to health that influence the structure of our health services (Laverack, 2004).

Medical Approach

The medical approach has historically been the most prevalent in our health system and remains the most common. In terms of health and wellness, the medical approach encourages health care professionals to focus on disease prevention among high-risk groups. This approach is commonly considered "top down" and is directed by what some consider "expert" knowledge of the risks for disease.

The Behavioural, or Lifestyle, Approach

The behavioural, or lifestyle, approach includes health teaching and awareness campaigns that help to change individual health behaviours and lifestyles. This approach became popular in the 1970s with the help of the 1974 LaLonde report (LaLonde, 1974), a Canadian government report that recognized the health and economic limitations to the medical model and hospital-based care.

The Socioenvironmental Approach

The socioenvironmental approach became popular in the 1980s when a new concept of health emerged that accounted for the structural influences on health behaviours, influences such as poverty and appropriate housing (Laverack, 2004). It was then that we began to understand and articulate the broad determinants of health and the interrelationships among them. More recently, nurses have begun to build on this approach

Table 5.1   Determinants of Health

Health Determinants	Description
Income and Social Status	Greatest influence on health status, behaviours, and the use of health care services. Lower-income Canadians have poorer health with more chronic illness and earlier death than higher-income Canadians, regardless of age, gender, culture, race, or residence.
Social Support Networks	Social contacts and support networks are linked with better health by providing emotional support, caregiving, and improved management of adversity.
Education and Literacy	Higher education improves a person's state of health. Education increases opportunities for earning higher incomes and improves problem-solving capacity and access to health information.
Employment/Working Conditions	Unemployment or employment that is stressful or unsafe is linked to poorer health. Income, social contacts, and emotional health are all affected by the workplace.
Social Environments	Community, region, province, and country provide resource sharing and social networks, which create safety nets and improve overall health for their community members.
Physical Environments	Environmental contaminants in the air, soil, water, and food can cause poor health, such as respiratory conditions or other serious illnesses. Environments in the built community can impact on health in many ways, such as poor air quality and unsafe building codes.
Personal Health Practices and Coping Skills	This segment refers to those measures that individuals can do themselves to promote their own health and manage challenges. Self-sufficiency and making healthy choices will optimize their level of health.
Healthy Child Development	What happens to a child during the growing years will impact on the child's long-term health and the development of chronic illnesses; e.g., low-birth-weight infants have almost twice the incidence of lifelong diseases.
Biology and Genetic Endowment	Genetics play an important role in individuals' health status. Genetic predisposition to certain conditions, as well as environmental interrelationships, puts certain individuals at risk for specific diseases.
Health Services	Available health services have a direct impact on individuals', families', groups', and communities' ability to prevent disease and adequately treat secondary conditions. There are still inequities in terms of accessibility to these essential services; e.g., urban populations with increased access to health services have better morbidity and mortality rates than rural populations with less access.
Gender	Gender refers to differences in biologics, roles in society, personalities, attitudes, values, and socioeconomic position. These differences have a direct bearing on health. A gender-specific predisposition for certain disease states and treatment programs exists as well.
Culture	There are health risks related to cultural and ethnic backgrounds that affect an individual and family. Culturally specific lifestyles may influence health choices. Socioeconomic status has a major influence on health. For example, access and health care may be difficult for new immigrants who don't know the language and how to enter and manoeuvre the health care system. It is essential that culturally appropriate care be available.

Source: Adapted from Public Health Agency of Canada. (2011). *What determines health? Determinants of health: What makes Canadians healthy or unhealthy?* Retrieved January 17, 2013, from http://www.phac-aspc.gc.ca/ph-sp/determinants/index-eng.php#determinants. [Reproduced with the permission of the Minister of Health, 2012.

by using a socioecological model to guide their work. A socioecological model of health offers a critical framework for understanding the system of interrelated sociocultural, political, and physical environmental influences on health (Best et al., 2003; Green, Richard, & Potvin, 1996; Richard, Potvin, Kishchuk, Prlic, & Green, 1996; Sallis & Owen, 1997).

DEFINING HEALTH PROMOTION AND DISEASE AND INJURY PREVENTION

Health promotion and disease and injury prevention in nursing build on our conceptualizations of and approaches to health. Health promotion is most often defined and advanced in the following ways:

- Health promotion is "the process of enabling people to increase control over, and to improve, their health" (WHO, 1986). It involves helping people optimize their sense of well-being and health potential (Pender et al., 2006).
- Health promotion is based on " . . . a positive and inclusive concept of health as a determinant of the quality of life . . . encompassing mental and spiritual well-being" (WHO, 2005, p. 1).
- Health promotion, then, "emphasizes the importance of interventions to prevent disease and promote well-being rather than relying upon remedial action to treat damaging effects" (Laverack, 2004).
- From a socioecological perspective, health promotion is more effective if the individual as well as the organizational, community, and policy levels are targeted (Edwards, Mill, & Kothari, 2004; Krieger, 2001; McLeroy, Bibeau, Steckler, & Glantz, 1988; Pender et al., 2006; Stokols, 1996).
- The 1986 Ottawa Charter for Health Promotion (WHO, 1986) highlights the significance of health promotion activities that extend beyond the individual level to address the context and the resources needed to promote the health of community members. The charter outlines five main strategies for health promotion (see Figure 5.1).
- Building healthy public policy through intersectoral collaborations. This strategy recognizes that collaboration among multiple sectors, such as education, industry, justice, health, and recreation, is critical to developing policies that influence health.
- Creating supportive environments through physical and social resources. This involves engaging people in creating healthy physical and social environments in their homes, organizations, and communities.
- Strengthening community action. This means that community citizens should be involved in sharing health-related information and capitalizing on each other's strengths and resources to foster health within their communities.
- Developing personal skills through community-based education. This involves creating opportunities for the development of the knowledge and skills necessary for citizens to promote their own health as well as the health of their families and communities.
- Reorienting health services. This strategy means that health services should reflect the health promotion needs of the community and should be designed and operationalized with the involvement of citizens, practitioners, and decision makers from multiple sectors.

Stanhope and Lancaster (2006) offer a visual depiction that provides an example of how the Ottawa Charter can inform interventions for the prevention of the human papilloma virus for an aggregate population of females (see Figure 5.2).

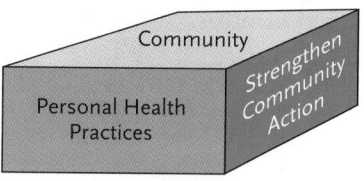

STRENGTHEN COMMUNITY ACTION
ENABLE
MEDIATE
ADVOCATE
DEVELOP
PERSONAL
SKILLS
CREATE SUPPORTIVE ENVIRONMENT
REORIENT HEALTH SERVICES
BUILD HEALTHY PUBLIC POLICY

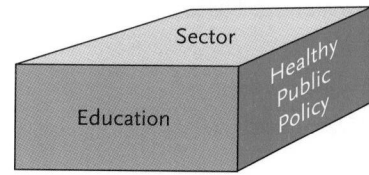

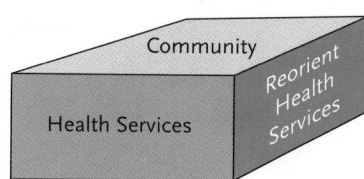

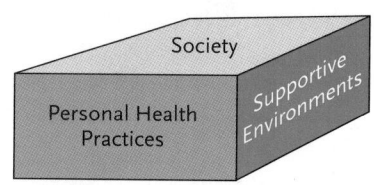

FIGURE 5.1 **The Ottawa Charter for Health Promotion**

Source: WHO, 1986. *The Ottawa Charter for Health Promotion: Health Promotion Emblem.* Retrieved February 13, 2013, from http://www.who.int/healthpromotion/conferences/previous/ottawa/en/index4.html.

Community
Personal Health Practices
Strengthen Community Action
e.g.: Support community action to obtain available human papilloma virus (HPV) vaccine and establish an HPV program.
Sector
Education
Healthy Public Policy
e.g.: Boards of Education can ensure that HPV vaccine information is included in the school curriculum.
Community
Health Services
Reorient Health Services
e.g.: Communities can provide opportunities for HPV testing, HPV counselling, and administration of the HPV vaccine and ensure that all opportunities are available and accessible.
Society
Personal Health Practices
Supportive Environments
e.g.: Social marketing campaigns can heighten public awareness of the importance and availability of the HPV vaccine.

FIGURE 5.2 **The Population Health Promotion Model Applied to a Female Aggregate**

Source: Adapted from Health Canada. (2001). *Population health promotion: An integrated model of population health and health promotion.* Retrieved from http://www.phac-aspc.gc.ca/ph-sp/php-psp/php3-eng.php. Reproduced with the permission of the Minister of Health, 2012.

Table 5.2 Comparing the Theoretical Differences Between Health Promotion and Disease and Injury Prevention

Health Promotion	Disease and Injury Prevention
Wellness focused	Disease and illness focused
Aims to enhance the potential for health	Aims to avoid threats to health
Approach oriented; interventions encourage and enable engagement in healthy activities	Interventions foster avoidance of risks

Disease and Injury Prevention

Disease prevention is also commonly referred to as health protection. It involves helping people reduce their risks for disease, detect it early, or maintain optimal functioning while living with disease (Pender et al., 2006; Potter et al., 2010). Examples include screening for disease (such as breast self-examination and mammography), health education for behaviour change (such as self-care activities for clients with diabetes), and environmental intervention (for example, the availability of fecal occult blood tests through local pharmacies for the early detection of bowel cancer). Pender et al. (2006) identify three main distinctions between health promotion and disease and injury prevention, which are outlined in Table 5.2.

There are three main levels of prevention that help to further distinguish between nursing initiatives aiming to optimize health and well-being, to prevent disease and injury, to screen for disease, and to improve or maintain health while living with disease and injury (McMurray, 2007). These are as follows:

Primary Prevention: Activities that promote health and reduce risks for disease and injury. Example: Promoting healthy nutrition, rest, and physical activity by educating community members at a local health fair.

Secondary Prevention: Early detection of disease or steps taken to recover from disease and injury. Example: Screening for skin cancer during regular client assessments.

Tertiary Prevention: Maintaining an optimal level of health while living with disease and injury. Examples: Creating cancer support groups and exercise programs for women with osteoarthritis.

Upstream, midstream, and downstream interventions are terms that are sometimes used to describe primary, secondary, and tertiary prevention (refer to Figure 5.3).

Figure 5.4 depicts how these levels of prevention fit

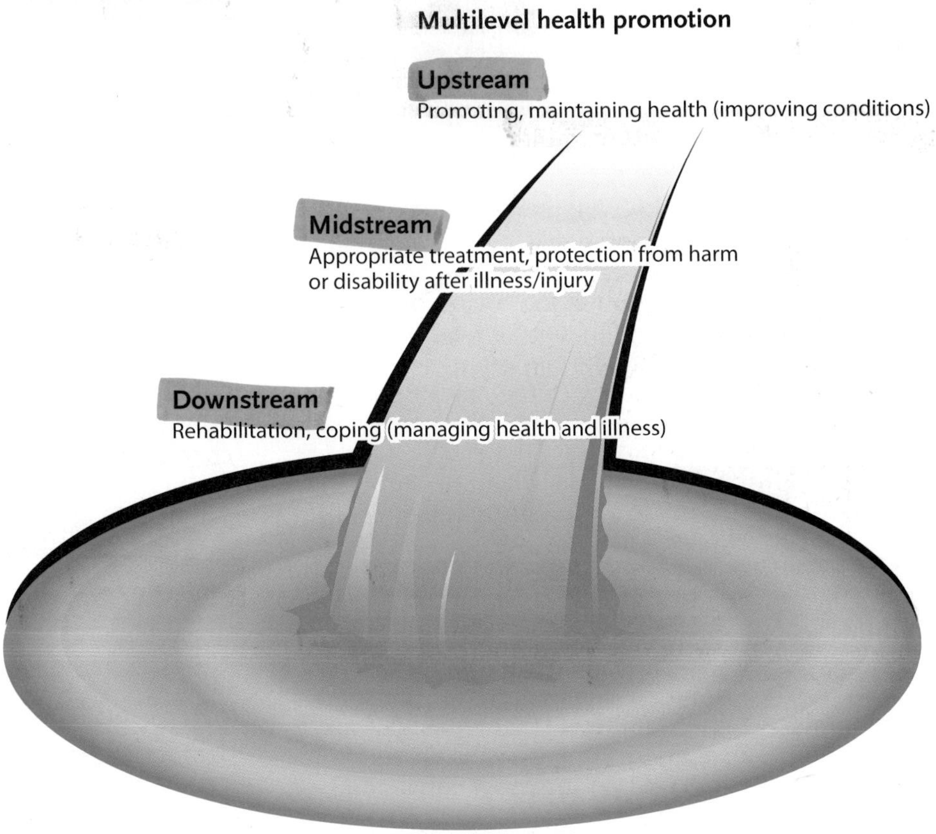
Multilevel health promotion
Upstream
Promoting, maintaining health (improving conditions)
Midstream
Appropriate treatment, protection from harm or disability after illness/injury
Downstream
Rehabilitation, coping (managing health and illness)

FIGURE 5.3 **Primary, Secondary, and Tertiary Prevention: Upstream, Midstream, and Downstream Interventions**

Source: McMurray, A. (2007). *Community health and wellness: A socio-ecological approach* (3rd ed). © 2007, Sydney: Elsevier (p. 29, Fig. 2-1).

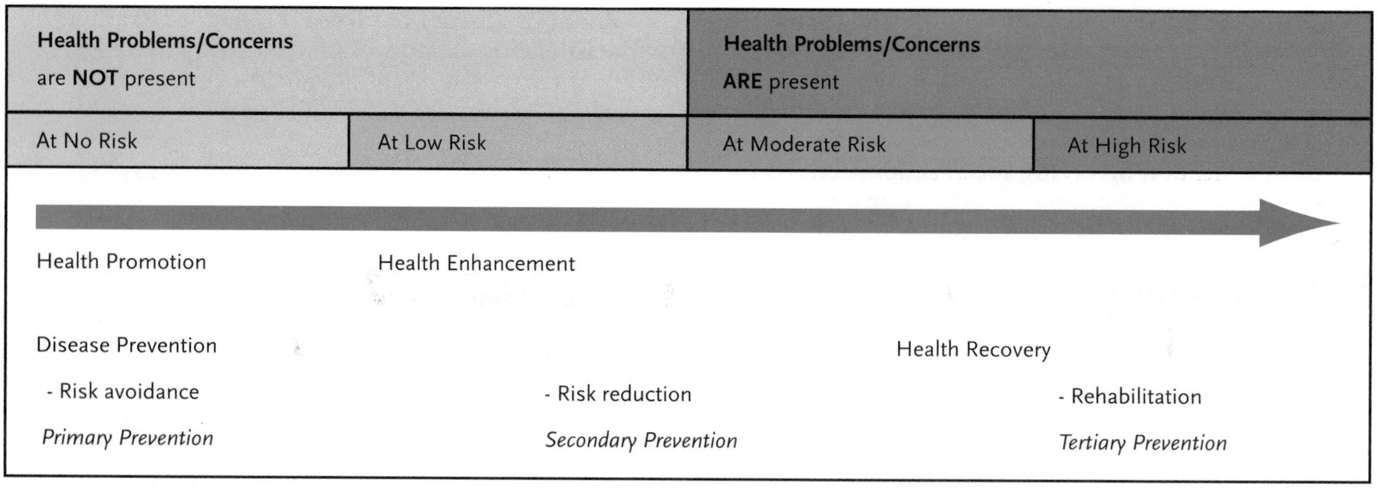
Health Problems/Concerns are NOT present
Health Problems/Concerns ARE present
At No Risk
At Low Risk
At Moderate Risk
At High Risk
Health Promotion
Health Enhancement
Disease Prevention
Health Recovery
- Risk avoidance
- Risk reduction
- Rehabilitation
Primary Prevention
Secondary Prevention
Tertiary Prevention

FIGURE 5.4 **Health Promotion, Disease Prevention, and the Risk Continuum**

Source: Adapted from Prevention Source B.C. (n.d.). *The workbook on prevention concepts: Prevention strategies.* Retrieved November 19, 2006, from http://preventionsource.org/guides/workbook/sec6.html; and Skinner, W. (2006). *Mapping a model system of services and supports for addictions.* Retrieved January 17, 2013, from http://www.ccsa.ca/2006%20CCSA%20Documents/ccsa-summinst-Skinner-2006-e.pdf

within the constructs of health promotion and disease prevention. For instance, health promotion and disease prevention overlap in the area of primary prevention. In primary prevention, upstream interventions are aimed at preventing the development of health problems before there are risks to health. In secondary prevention, midstream interventions focus on enhancing health by minimizing (low to moderate) risks to health. Tertiary prevention entails working downstream where health problems and concerns are evident.

Socioecological System

Health promotion and disease and injury prevention occur at multiple levels within the socioecological system and require a combination of health education, advocacy, and community development, as well as political activity and policy change in the social, workplace, and community environments (McMurray, 2007).

Health Education: Example: Client teaching and learning about healthy eating, healthy relationships, and physical activity (individual level)

Advocacy and Community Development: Examples: Collaborating with colleagues from multiple sectors to advocate for changes in hospital discharge teaching practice or collaborating with community health boards to advocate for the development of safe walking trails to enable "walk-to-school" programs that encourage accessible outdoor physical activity for children (organizational and community levels)

Political Activity and Policy Change in the Social, Workplace and Community Environments: Examples: Involvement in hospital committees to change the organization's smoking regulations or reformulating protocols for preoperative teaching (policy level)

Facilitating Learning Is Integral to Nursing

Health promotion inevitably involves facilitating learning. All nursing practice acts in Canada call upon nurses to be health teachers and client educators. Understanding how to teach needs to be guided by an understanding of how people learn.

Teaching in professional nursing involves knowledge of content (information shared by a nurse is current, comprehensive, and evidence informed) and process (communicating in ways that clients can understand and be enabled to learn).

"Patient education is the process of influencing behaviour, producing changes in knowledge, attitudes, and skills required to maintain or improve health. The process may begin with imparting of information, but it also includes interpretation and integration of information to bring about attitudinal or behavioural changes that benefit a person's health status" (Rankin & Duffy Stallings, 2001, p. 78).

Rankin and Duffy Stallings (2001) contend that the orientation of quality health education is toward cooperation (working together with the client) rather than compliance (simply having the client follow our suggestions).

Teaching and Learning Theories Relevant to Nursing

Paolo Freire's Theory of Community Empowerment, 1970

Education is never neutral, and in participatory community education, community members must be involved in naming their own problems and proposing their own solutions (Freire, 1970). This involves helping people to work together, listen to each other, compare and contrast central issues in their lives, and construct new strategies for change together (Rankin & Duffy Stallings, 2001). Freire's theory can be applied to health education involving social action—efforts to change a whole community rather than one person at a time. Community empowerment philosophy also seeks to give voice to those affected by forces of oppression that include poverty, racism, and violence, influences that have such devastating health effects.

Prochaska and DiClemente's Model of Planned Behaviour Change, 1998

Prochaska and DiClemente developed a transtheoretical model of behaviour change (DiClemente & Prochaska, 1998). This model describes behaviour change and involves the following stages:

- Precontemplation: There is little conscious intent to change, as well as resistance or defensiveness.
- Contemplation: The person experiences ambivalence but is more serious about changing a behaviour.
- Preparation: There are preliminary healthy behaviour attempts and conscious planning for change.
- Action: The person lives the plan.
- Maintenance: The individual employs relapse prevention strategies.

This model has been used to explain the process of changing behaviours that are most resistant to change, such as addictions, diet and weight control, sexual behaviour related to HIV control (DiClemente & Prochaska, 1998), or women's process of leaving relationships involving intimate-partner violence (Khaw & Hardesty, 2007).

Alfred Bandura's Social Cognitive Theory, 1977

Human health is a social matter, not just an individual one. This theory proposes that self-efficacy beliefs operate together with goals, outcome expectations, and perceived environmental facilitators and impediments in regulating human motivation, behaviour, and well-being (Bandura, 2004). The theory holds that people with high self-efficacy (the belief that "I can do it") can accomplish what they set out to learn or to do. Nurses can help clients to develop the following sources of self-efficacy (Rankin & Duffy Stallings, 2001):

- Personal mastery: Developing awareness of past successes in similar situations
- Vicarious experiences: Observing role models, recognizing what has worked for others
- Verbal persuasion: Encouragement, receiving information, having questions answered
- Physiological feedback: Evidence of positive bodily changes

Bandura's theory has been utilized, for example, in breastfeeding support (Rankin & Duffy Stallings, 2001) and in promoting fitness in older adults with osteoarthritis (Hughes et al., 2006).

Nola Pender's Health Promotion Model, 2006

Nola Pender's health promotion model integrates knowledge from nursing with the behavioural sciences to explore motivations for health-promoting behaviours and how health care professionals can promote such behaviours in the persons they serve. Her model (Pender et al., 2006) includes the following ideas:

- Persons have the capacity for reflective self-awareness, including assessment of their own abilities.
- Persons commit to engaging in behaviours from which they anticipate deriving personally valued benefits.
- Perceived barriers can constrain commitment to health-promoting actions.
- Greater perceived self-efficacy results in fewer perceived barriers to a health behaviour.
- Persons can modify thoughts and emotions and their environment to create incentives for health actions.
- Families, peers, and health care providers are important sources of influence that can increase or decrease commitment to and engagement in health-promoting behaviour.

Pender's model is based on the concept of the human capacity for reflection, change, and action.

HEALTH CARE IN CANADA: POLITICAL, SOCIAL, AND ECONOMIC CONSIDERATIONS

FUNDING HEALTH CARE

Publicly Funded Care: Universal coverage for Canadians that includes all medically necessary hospital and physician services that are funded by Medicare, a national health insurance system, and governed by the *Canada Health Act*. The principles of the *Canada Health Act* are universality, accessibility, portability, comprehensiveness, and public administration (Health Canada, 2012).

Privately Funded Care: Supplemental health services that are usually purchased from a for-profit organization as extended health coverage, either through an employer or through a policy (such as private hospital rooms, workplace drug and dental plans, and private MRI clinics).

Voluntary Services: Not-for-profit organizations provide financial support and services for the prevention and detection of illness and for specific health problems (for example, the Canadian Heart and Stroke Foundation, Canadian Diabetes Association, and Canadian Red Cross).

THE ORGANIZATION OF THE HEALTH CARE SYSTEM

It is the responsibility of the provinces and territories to manage, organize, and deliver health care services. Health Canada described Medicare as a set of 13 interlocking provincial and territorial health insurance plans, all of which have commonalities and basic standards of coverage (Health Canada, 2010). The federal government also plays a role in health care administration.

LEVELS OF CARE

There are five levels of health care: promotive, preventive, curative (diagnosis and treatment), rehabilitative, and supportive.

- Health promotion services and activities are designed to enable people to increase their control over, and improve, their health (for example, the promotion of self-esteem in children and adolescents, advocacy for healthy public policy) (WHO, 1986).
- Disease and injury prevention services are designed to reduce risk factors for disease and injury (including screening, immunization, and support groups).
- Diagnosis and treatment services provide diagnosis and treatment of an existing health care problem. Care provided at this level can be labelled as primary, secondary, or tertiary and is described below (Potter et al., 2010):

  - Primary care is the first contact a person makes with the health care system, which leads to diagnosis and management of the person's actual or potential health problem.
  - Secondary care involves the provision of a specialized medical service by a medical specialist in his or her office, clinic, or hospital. The client has developed recognizable signs and symptoms that have been diagnosed or require a further diagnostic workup.
  - Tertiary care is specialized consultative care, usually on referral from primary or secondary medical care providers, provided by specialists working in a setting that has personnel and facilities for diagnosing and treating complicated health problems.

- Rehabilitation helps clients attain their maximum level of physical, mental, social, and vocational functioning (Clemen-Stone, McGuire, & Eigsti, 2002). Rehabilitation generally occurs after a physical or mental illness, injury, or chemical addiction and

focuses on improving quality of life while promoting independence and self-care (Potter et al., 2010).

- Supportive care services are provided over prolonged periods of time to clients who are disabled, who are not functioning independently, or who have a terminal illness (Potter et al., 2010). Types of supportive care include palliative and respite care.

SETTINGS FOR HEALTH CARE DELIVERY

Institutional Sector

- "Institutional sector" refers to hospitals, long-term care facilities, psychiatric facilities, and rehabilitation centres, which provide services to inpatients as well as outpatients (Potter et al., 2010).
- Hospitals generally specialize in providing care over a short period of time for the purpose of diagnosis and treatment of health care problems (acute care). Examples of services within a hospital include emergency and diagnostic services, general inpatient services, intensive care units, outpatient services, surgical intervention, and rehabilitation facilities.
- Long-term care facilities provide accommodations for clients who require the delivery of 24-hour, on-site, supervised care, including professional health services, personal care, and services such as meals, laundry, and housekeeping (Health Canada, 2010).
- Psychiatric facilities are located in hospitals, independent outpatient clinics, or mental health clinics and provide inpatient and outpatient care for clients with mental disorders and or those who are experiencing emotional crisis (Potter et al., 2010; Varcarolis, Carson, & Shoemaker, 2006).
- Rehabilitation centres provide on-site therapy and training to clients with the purpose of minimizing the client's dependence on care (Potter et al., 2010).

Community Sector

- There has been a shift from institution-based care to community-based care, *although community-based care is not guaranteed public funding as hospital-based care has been.*
- With a focus on primary and secondary care, this sector provides services for clients that are available where clients live, work, and learn (Potter et al., 2010).
- The sector provides surveillance and monitoring of the environment and the health of the community through the public sector.
- The sector provides specialized services that meet specific client needs (such as food banks or meals on wheels).
- Focus is generally on health promotion and illness prevention as well as palliative and restorative care (Potter et al., 2010).

- Common community settings include public health departments, physicians' offices, community health centres, assisted living facilities, home care, adult day care centres, community and voluntary agencies, palliative and respite care services, and parish nursing.

CHALLENGES TO THE HEALTH CARE SYSTEM

Two of the main challenges to the Canadian health care system are the increasing cost of care and problems with providing equal and accessible care for all Canadians (Potter et al., 2010).

Cost of Health Services

Many factors have caused an increase in health expenditures, including new and improved technology, new pharmaceuticals, an increase in chronic and age-related diseases, an aging population, women becoming pregnant later in life, and expectations of the health care consumer (Canadian Institute for Health Information [CIHI], 2004), as well as salary increases for health care providers.

Equality and Access

There continue to be issues with accessibility to health care services, including the following (Potter et al., 2010):

- Low-income Canadians experience unequal access to those factors that determine health, such as nutritious food and safe shelter, and therefore commonly have poorer health. Also, while hospital and physician services are available to all under the terms of the *Canada Health Act*, services such as pharmacy, dental, and vision care often involve private-pay or private-insurance systems and hence are available only to those with the means to pay for them.
- Many experts believe that Medicare can only be saved by privatizing certain services within the health care system.
- A shortage of nurses and physicians is compromising accessibility of health care services.

CANADA AS A DIVERSE SOCIETY

Approximately 19% of Canada's population has been born outside the country (Statistics Canada, 2010a). Increasingly, immigrants to Canada are from Asian countries, including the Middle East. In 1961, only 3% of immigrants to Canada were Asian and 90% were European; by 2006, 60% of immigrants were Asian (Statistics Canada, 2010b), and only 19% were European. Immigration has now outpaced the natural birth rate, accounting for an estimated 58% of all population growth (Potter et al., 2010; Statistics Canada, 2011).

Culture and Health

Culture has a direct impact on health and health behaviours. These behaviours include the following (Potter et al., 2010):

- Specific health problems
- Biological response to treatments
- Birth rites
- Death rites
- Dietary beliefs and practices
- Time orientation
- Attitude toward older adults
- Personal space
- Gender roles
- Social roles
- Attitude toward the health care system
- Beliefs about illness and treatments

Providing Culturally Competent Care

According to the Canadian Nurses Association's (CNA) position statement, cultural competence is the application by the nurse of knowledge, skill, attitudes, and personal attributes in order to provide care and services appropriate to clients' cultural characteristics. Clients include individuals, families, groups, or populations. Nurses need to value diversity, to know about the cultural mores and traditions of the population, and to be sensitive to these when they are caring for the individual (CNA, 2005). In order to provide culturally sensitive care, it is important for nurses to do the following:

- Identify their own cultural beliefs and values and assess how they may differ from the client's beliefs and how they may influence nursing care
- Research information about the client's cultural background
- Assess the client's health behaviours and methods of communication
- Avoid stereotyping, generalizations, and assumptions
- Work with the individual client to develop the most culturally appropriate health interventions (Potter et al., 2010).

REFORMS IN THE CANADIAN HEALTH CARE SYSTEM

Two national reports, the Kirby Report, *The Health of Canadians* (Kirby, 2002), and the Romanow Report, *The Future of Health Care in Canada* (Romanow, 2002), have provided recommendations for reforming health care in Canada. One important recommendation includes improving and expanding primary health care (PHC).

Primary Health Care

PHC is described as the key to health care reform and sustainability. It is a philosophy and model for

Table 5.3　Examples of Community Health Nursing Practice Areas

Community Health Nurses	Definition	Practice Settings	Client Group	Educational Preparation	Examples of Roles and Activities	Funding
Public Health Nurse (PHN)	Public health nurses use knowledge of nursing, social sciences, and public health sciences for the promotion and protection of health and for the prevention of disease among populations	• Community groups • Community health centres • Workplaces • Street clinics • Schools • Outpost settings • Homes	• Population • Aggregates and groups • Community • Family • Individual	Baccalaureate degree in nursing	• Health promotion • Disease prevention • Client advocacy • Education • Direct care in clinics	Provincial and municipal governments
Home Health Nurse (HHN)	Home health nurses use their knowledge and skills to provide direct care and treatment for individuals to maintain and restore health or palliation during illness	• Client's home • Schools • Clinics • Workplaces	• Individual • Family • Caregivers	Registered nurse (RN) Registered practical nurse (RPN)*	• Direct client care • Disease prevention • Health promotion with individual clients	Public or private funding
Occupational Health Nurse (OHN)	An RN who specializes in workplace health and safety, health promotion, disease prevention, and rehabilitation for workers	• Workplaces	• Employees	RN with certificate in Occupational Health	• Direct care • Assessment of the workplace • Education of employees on health and safety issues	Employer
Parish Nurse	An RN who serves the health and wellness needs of faith community members	• Client's home • Places of worship • Hospitals	• Individual • Family • Group	RN	• Health promotion • Health counsellor • Liaison • Health advocate • Integrator of faith and health	Place of worship
Primary Health Care Nurse Practitioner (PHC-NP)	An RN with advanced-practice education, which allows for an expanded role, such as diagnosing episodic illnesses, prescribing medication, and ordering diagnostic tests	• Community health centres • Clinics • Physicians' offices • Emergency room (ER) in hospitals • Nursing stations • Long-term care facilities	• Individual • Family • Group • Community	Baccalaureate degree in nursing, minimum of postbaccalaureate diploma with licensing in Extended Class (EC)	• Direct care: i.e., health assessment, diagnosis, and treatment of episodic illness • Health promotion • Disease prevention • Community development and planning	Public or private funding

	Description	Setting		Clients	Functions	Funding
Outpost Nurse	An RN who works in an outpost or rural setting that is often geographically separated from face-to-face physician contact	• Nursing stations • Client's home • Community settings	RN	• Individual • Family • Group • Rural community	• Direct care • Health promotion • Liaison with other health professionals • Referral	Provincial or federal funding
Forensic Nurse	A registered nurse who has completed continuing education programs in the area of forensic science	• Sexual assault treatment settings, often in hospital ER departments	RN	• Adults and children who are victims of acute sexual assault or survivors of intimate-partner violence	• Direct care for collection of physical evidence • Providing crisis response, such as counselling and referral	Provincial funding
Telenurse	A registered nurse who possesses strong assessment skills, communication skills, and a knowledge base to provide nursing service over the telephone	• Community agencies	RN	• Individual • Family • Caregivers	• Telephone advice using protocols and direction to the most appropriate source of care via telephone assessment and through telehealth network (live video links for nurse-led telehealth clinics)	Provincial funding provided to private companies

*Some Canadian provinces and territories designate licensed practical nurses (LPNs) or registered practical nurses (RPNs) to work in some settings, such as home health nursing and public health nursing.
Source: Stanhope, M., Lancaster, J., Jessup-Falcioni, H., & Viverais-Dresler, G. A. (2008). *Community health nursing in Canada* (pp. 4–5, Table 1–1). Toronto: Elsevier.

improving health that focuses on preventing illness and promoting health (CNA, 2005). PHC is based on a social justice approach (equal access for all) and addresses the factors in a person's social, economic, and physical environment that make them ill. Building community capacity for sustainable health is the main goal of PHC (McMurray, 2007). The five principles of PHS include accessibility, public participation, health promotion, appropriate skills and technology, and intersectoral cooperation (WHO, 1978).

Accessibility: Health services are available to all Canadians regardless of location and economic status.

Public participation: Clients participate in making decisions about their own health and identify health needs in the community as well as strategies to address those needs.

Health promotion: A process is put in place that enables people to increase control over and improve their health.

Appropriate skills and technology: Includes methods of care, service delivery, procedures, and equipment that are socially acceptable and affordable.

Intersectoral cooperation: All sectors, including government, community, and health, are committed to meeting the needs of Canadians.

COMMUNITY HEALTH NURSING

Changes in the health care system (including increased health spending, technology and medical advances, and client involvement in health care) have created a situation whereby clients are receiving care in their homes and communities.

- Goals for community health nursing include keeping individuals healthy, providing in-home care to those who are sick and disabled, encouraging participation in care, and cost containment (Potter et al., 2010).
- Community health nursing is a specialty nursing practice that may be carried out in a variety of settings. Examples of community health practice areas include public health nursing, home health nursing, occupational health nursing, parish nursing, and outpost nursing. Refer to Table 5.3.
- Community health nurses (CHNs) promote and protect the health of individuals, families, groups, communities, and populations. CHNs coordinate care and are involved in the planning of services, programs, and policies while collaborating with others (Potter et al., 2010).
- CHNs must complete community assessments in order to promote client (individual, family, group, community) health and identify needs for health policy, program development, and services (Potter et al., 2010). The three components of a community that should be assessed by the CHN include structure or locale, the people, and the social systems (Potter et al., 2010).

HEALTH PROMOTION AND DISEASE AND INJURY PREVENTION: PRACTICE FOCUS

NUTRITION AND HEALTHY EATING

Categories of Nutrients

Six nutrients are necessary for body processes and function. These nutrients are water, carbohydrates, proteins, fats, vitamins, and minerals and are described below (Johnson, Greaves, & Repta, 2007):

Water

- Water makes up 60–70% of body weight.
- Water acts as a solvent for metabolic processes.
- Daily losses are through urine, feces, respiration, and perspiration; losses increase with exercise, hot weather, and fever.
- Adult intake should be approximately 3–4 L per day, including fluid and solid food sources.

Carbohydrates

- The diet should provide approximately 55% of energy in the form of carbohydrates, the major source of energy for the body.
- Sources are primarily plants and include simple forms (sugars) and complex forms (starches).
- Complex carbohydrates are the preferred energy source.
- Fibre is an indigestible form of complex carbohydrate and is thought to be an important dietary factor in the prevention of some diseases.

Proteins

- Approximately 20% of the diet should come from proteins.
- Proteins are necessary for tissue growth, maintenance, and repair; synthesis of hormones and enzymes; composition of DNA; acid–base balance; blood clotting; and other metabolic processes.
- Complete proteins contain all the essential amino acids and come primarily from animals and seafood.
- Incomplete proteins are found in lentils, nuts, grains, soya, and peas.
- Vegetarians must ensure that they include appropriate ratios and combinations of plant proteins in order to obtain all necessary amino acids.

Fats

- The diet should include no more than 25–30% fat and no more than 10% as saturated fat.

- Fats or lipids are necessary as an energy source; for insulation, hormone production, vitamin absorption, nerve conduction; as a component of cell walls; and for padding and insulation of organs and the body.
- Saturated fats, found primarily in animal products, have been implicated in cardiovascular disease, cancers, and obesity.
- Unsaturated fats from plant sources (such as olive oil and flaxseed oil) are considered healthier.
- Omega-3 fatty acids from oily fish sources are believed to decrease levels of low-density lipoproteins and are recommended as part of the weekly diet.
- Plant-based unsaturated fats that have been hydrogenated to a solid form are called trans fats; these fats, found in solid margarines, baked goods, and table spreads, have health risks similar to those of saturated fats.

Vitamins

- Vitamins are elements obtained through dietary intake that are necessary for normal metabolism.
- Vitamins found in fresh foods are preferable to synthetic supplements.
- Vitamins are classified as water soluble (B complex and C) and fat soluble (A, D, E, K); fat-soluble vitamins can be stored by the body and are not easily destroyed in cooking or storage; water-soluble vitamins are not stored in the body and are easily lost in cooking.
- Vitamins A, C, and E and beta-carotene may act as antioxidants, neutralizing free radicals that cause oxidative damage to cells.

Minerals

- Minerals are inorganic elements essential to the body as catalysts in biochemical reactions.

Healthy eating is fundamental to good health, assists in healthy development, and is important in the prevention and control of chronic diseases such as obesity, diabetes, cancer, and cardiovascular disease (Johnson et al., 2007). There is a complex set of interactions among the determinants of healthy eating, which are both individual and collective in nature. Examples of these determinants include physiological influences; food preferences; nutritional knowledge; perceptions of healthy eating; influence of family and friends; and physical, social, and economic impacts, as well as policy influences (Raine, 2005).

Determinants of Healthy Eating

Physiological Influences: Physiological development or deterioration at both ends of the lifespan (childhood and older adult) affects eating behaviour.

Food Preferences: Food preference may be individual in nature or affected by social and cultural norms.

Nutritional Knowledge: Amount of nutritional knowledge affects healthy eating choices in adults but has not been demonstrated in children and adolescents.

Perceptions of Healthy Eating: Perceptions of healthy eating are influenced by current dietary guidelines and cultural influences.

Psychological Factors: Psychological factors shown to affect food choices include self-esteem, body image, chronic dieting, mood, and focus of attention.

Interpersonal Influences: Family, peers, and feelings of social isolation affect patterns of healthy eating.

Physical Environment: This determines the availability of food and access to that food, such as the proximity of supermarkets.

Economic Environment: Eating behaviours are influenced by corporate-driven economic interests.

Social Environment: Social status and culture often influence food choice; for example, Canadian society devalues preparation of food in the home and favours take-out and quick meals from the freezer.

Healthy Public Policy: Policies define what is considered relevant and influence our food choices, such as through the subsidization of low-energy, nutrient-dense foods.

Eating Well With Canada's Food Guide

The purpose of *Eating Well With Canada's Food Guide* (Figure 5.5) is to assist people in making food choices that promote health and prevent nutrition-related disease. It does not prescribe a particular dietary pattern but promotes desirable ways of eating (Katamay et al., 2007). The food guide provides special recommendations for children, women of childbearing age, and adults over the age of 50 (Johnson et al., 2007). Canada's Food Guide for First Nations, Inuit, and Métis is also available to assist Aboriginal Canadians in incorporating traditional food choices into their diet (Health Canada, 2007). Canada's Food Guide is also available in 10 languages, including Arabic, Chinese, Farsi (Persian), Korean, Punjabi, Russian, Spanish, Tagalog, Tamil, and Urdu.

- Children: Children should be provided with small meals and snacks throughout the day; foods that contain fat should not be restricted as fat provides a source of calories required for growth; children learn eating behaviours from adults, who serve as important role models.
- Women of childbearing age: A multivitamin containing 400 mcg of folic acid should be taken at least three months before becoming pregnant and during pregnancy and lactation.
- Extra calories are required during pregnancy and lactation; an extra 2–3 food guide servings are recommended each day.
- Adults over the age of 50: Vitamin D requirements increase at age 50 (to 400 IU) and then again at age 70 (to 600 IU). Vitamin D intake is associated with health benefits that include improved muscle strength, higher bone mineral density, reduced fracture rates, reduced rates of falling, and improved mobility.

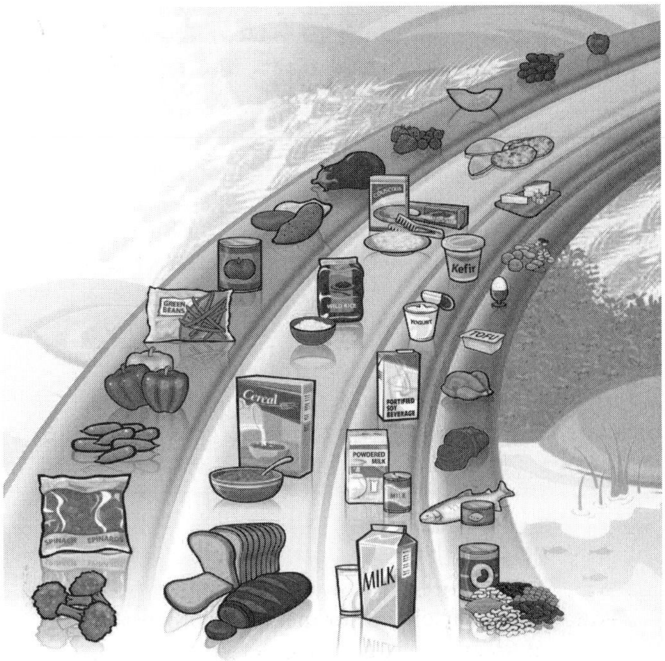
GREEN BEANS
Cereal
Kefir
TOFU
FORTIFIED SOY BEVERAGE
POWDERED MILK
MILK
SPINACH

FIGURE 5.5 **Eating Well With Canada's Food Guide**

Source: Extracted from Health Canada. (2007). *Eating well with Canada's food guide* (Cat. No. H164-38/I-2007E). Retrieved January 30, 2009, from http://www.hc-sc.gc.ca/fn-an/alt_formats/hpfb-dgpsa/pdf/food-guide-aliment/view_eatwell_vue_bienmang-eng.pdf. Reproduced with permission of the Minister of Public Works and Government Services Canada, 2008.

Physical Activity

The importance of regular exercise is becoming increasingly clear as more research studies are done. The impact of physical activity on health is listed below.

- Regular physical exercise promotes health and well-being from a physical perspective as well as a psychological one.
- Exercise increases respiratory capacity, improves digestion and fat metabolism, strengthens bones and improves joint flexibility, improves circulation, improves mood and reduces psychological symptoms, reduces the risk of heart disease, lowers body fat and reduces weight, and increases muscle strength and tone (Hales & Lauzon, 2007).
- An estimated two million people around the world die annually because they are not physically active (Health Canada, 2011).
- The health risks of inactivity include premature death, heart disease, obesity, high blood pressure, adult-onset diabetes, osteoporosis, stroke, depression, and colon cancer (Health Canada, 2011).
- Clients should be assessed by a physician before starting an exercise program.
- The amount of physical activity required on a daily basis is directly correlated to the intensity of the workout (Health Canada, 2011).
- The three types of activities required to keep the body healthy are endurance exercises, flexibility activities, and strength activities (Health Canada, 2011).

- Adults should engage in 30 minutes of moderate-intensity exercises four days per week (Health Canada, 2011).
- Over half of Canadian children are not active enough for optimal growth and development. Lack of exercise among children is a major contributor to weight gain and obesity (Johnson et al., 2007).
- Benefits of regular physical activity for older adults include continued independent living, reduced risk of falls, improved quality of life, improved balance and posture, and prevention of bone loss (Health Canada, 2011).

REST AND SLEEP

Rest and sleep are as important to health as proper nutrition and exercise (Johnson et al., 2007).

- Sleep promotes tissue repair and recovery of body systems and is essential for cognitive and emotional function.
- Sleep is governed by an individual's sleep–wake cycles, or circadian rhythms; circadian rhythms are influential in controlling the pattern of major biological functions such as body temperature, heart rate, blood pressure, hormone and electrolyte secretions, and sensory acuity.
- Circadian rhythms are affected by light, temperature, and social factors (such as shift work).
- All people have individual sleep–wake cycles; hospital routines rarely take these into consideration.
- Although individual needs vary, most people require approximately 7–9 hours of sleep per night.
- Any disruption in the sleep–wake cycle may lead to suppressed immunity, decreased tissue repair, impaired judgement, irritability, decreased appetite, and weight loss; some accidents are believed to result from sleep deprivation, which leads to distortion of sensory perceptions.
- Sleep cycles are categorized as non–rapid eye movement (REM) and REM; non-REM stage 4 is the deepest level of sleep and is believed to be important for physical restoration; heart rate and respirations are decreased in stage 4.
- REM sleep is important for psychological restoration; dreaming occurs most often in this stage; heart rate and respirations increase in REM sleep.

Sleep Disturbances

- Changes in sleep habits and rituals may alter the ability to sleep (including shift workers and hospital clients).
- Stress or anxiety may cause loss of sleep and less time spent in REM sleep.
- Large or spicy meals before bedtime, as well as caffeine and alcohol, may cause difficulty in sleeping.
- Excessive environmental stimulation and noise will interfere with sleep (as in intensive care unit [ICU] psychosis).

- Discomfort and illness may cause difficulties in falling or staying asleep (such as pain, respiratory difficulty, restless leg syndrome).
- Enuresis (bedwetting) and nocturia (urination during the night) disrupt the sleep cycle.
- Side effects from medications, both prescription and over-the-counter (OTC), may lead to insomnia and disturbances in the sleep cycle; overuse of sedatives may lead to insomnia and sleep-cycle disturbances.

Sleep Abnormalities

- Insomnia is difficulty falling asleep or staying asleep; it may be temporary or chronic.
- Hypersomnia is too much sleep and may be caused by a physical illness or depression.
- Narcolepsy is brief, uncontrollable episodes of sleep that last from a few seconds to 30 minutes.
- Somnambulism (sleepwalking) is most common in children.
- Sleep apnea—pauses in breathing lasting over 10 seconds—is most commonly caused by upper-airway obstruction due to relaxed muscles in the oral cavity; it occurs most often in overweight, middle-aged men and postmenopausal women; loud snoring and excessive daytime sleepiness are manifestations of sleep apnea.

A HEALTHY ENVIRONMENT

The socioecological model of health described in the first section provides the theoretical basis for nurses to address individual needs as well as the social and physical environment in an effort to create conditions that support and facilitate healthy behaviours and lifestyles. More and more research is suggesting that our economic and social environment has a greater effect on our health than do advances in medicine (McMurray, 2007).

Nurses strive to promote and restore the health of individuals with an understanding that the health of these individuals is inescapably tied to the health of their families, communities, and societies (Pender et al., 2006). The social environment must be taken into account in health promotion and disease and injury prevention and be addressed in combination with health education. "Enduring, large-scale behaviour change is best achieved by changing standards of acceptable behaviour in communities rather than by attempting to change the behaviour of individuals against overwhelming social odds" (McMurray, 2007). The social environment is a critical determinant of health (see Table 5.1), and researchers contend that it is as influential as healthy eating or physical activity (PHAC, 2011). To effect changes in the social environment, nurses can do the following:

- Involve families in their own care
- Connect clients and families to appropriate resources in the community (support groups, family resource centres, community kitchens)
- Help strengthen the social environment

Social Environment

A healthy social environment is created through regulations and policies that foster cohesive, safe communities with supportive social networks and resources. To be effective and sustainable, these regulations and policies must be developed, enacted, and evaluated jointly by multiple sectors (for example, education, housing, environment, health, justice) and community members themselves.

- Example 1: In targeting smoking behaviours, nurses raise awareness of the effects of smoking and strategies for cessation, and address the social environment by advocating for no-smoking regulations in public places and for controls on media advertisements and the accessibility of tobacco.
- Example 2: In a community faced with high levels of crime, nurses educate youths and their families on minimizing risky behaviours. Nurses work with other sectors to identify high-risk areas within the community and to improve policing and supervision of those areas. Safe and accessible recreational opportunities for youth are also developed.

Physical Environment

The physical environment is an important determinant of health (PHAC, 2011). Factors such as contaminants in the indoor and outdoor environment influence health. These contaminants, whether transmitted through air, water, food, or soil, can cause cancer, birth defects, or respiratory illness (CNA, 2005; PHAC, 2011). Research indicates that 5–10% of cancers are linked to environmental contaminants (Canadian Cancer Society, 2012). Children are particularly at risk for adverse effects due to the immaturity of their metabolism and limited physiological ability to detoxify and excrete chemicals. They inhale more air in proportion to their body weight, are closer to the ground where toxins may exist, and are more apt to put things in their mouths (CNA, 2005; Endleman & Mandle, 2002). Those living in poverty are also disproportionately affected by environmental contaminants (Kuo, 2001) because "(t)heir burden of physical, chemical and biological exposure is greater (for example, living close to factories or expressways, and in older buildings that may have lead paint or asbestos insulation); and . . . they have less access to resources that help mitigate the negative effects of this exposure (for example, nutritious food and high quality medical care)" (CNA, 2005, p. 4).

Nurses have a responsibility to address environmental health problems through their care for clients, families, and communities. Box 5.1 highlights recommendations from the CNA in 2005 (CNA, 2005).

The CNA has fundamental position statements on environmental health:

Box 5.1 Nurses' Roles and Responsibilities in Environmental Health

1. Nurses in all settings should be well prepared to identify and assess potential environmental health issues related to workplaces, neighbourhoods, houses, and schools.

2. Given that environmental health is a rapidly evolving field, nurses should know where to go to find current and credible scientific information.

3. Nurses are considered to be trusted sources of information regarding environmental health risks. As such, they are often in a position to translate information from other experts in fields such as toxicology and epidemiology, making it comprehensible to their clients.

4. Nurses are often in a position to identify environmental health issues because they may recognize patterns of symptoms in people who live or work in the same areas. Nurses should be prepared to investigate and act when they see such patterns.

Source: Canadian Nurses Association. (2005). *CNA Backgrounder: The ecosystem, the natural environment, and health and nursing: A summary of the issues* (p. 5). Retrieved January 17, 2013, from http://www.cna-aiic.ca/CNA/documents/pdf/publications/BG4_The_Ecosystem_e.pdf

---

- The environment is a determinant of health, and the Canadian Nurses Association and the Canadian Medical Association jointly developed a position statement on environmentally responsible activity in the health sector. The position statement is titled *The Ecosystem, the Natural Environment, and Health and Nursing* (CNA, 2005).

Through a combination of health education and awareness campaigns, as well as ongoing changes to regulations and policy, nurses need to help reduce harmful exposure to environmental contaminants such as air pollutants (indoor and outdoor), pesticides, polluted water, lead, and radon. Some examples of how this might be accomplished include the following:

- Example 1: Providing health education to clients, families, schools, and communities on issues such as avoiding harmful exposure to pesticides and chemicals
- Example 2: Working with community health boards or groups to change pesticide by-laws or working with hospital-based teams to improve air quality and hospital recycling programs

In conjunction with interventions aimed at limiting contaminant exposure, nurses need to use the ample (yet often underutilized) evidence that suggests that interacting with natural environments (in the form of gardens, plants, and animals) can have many

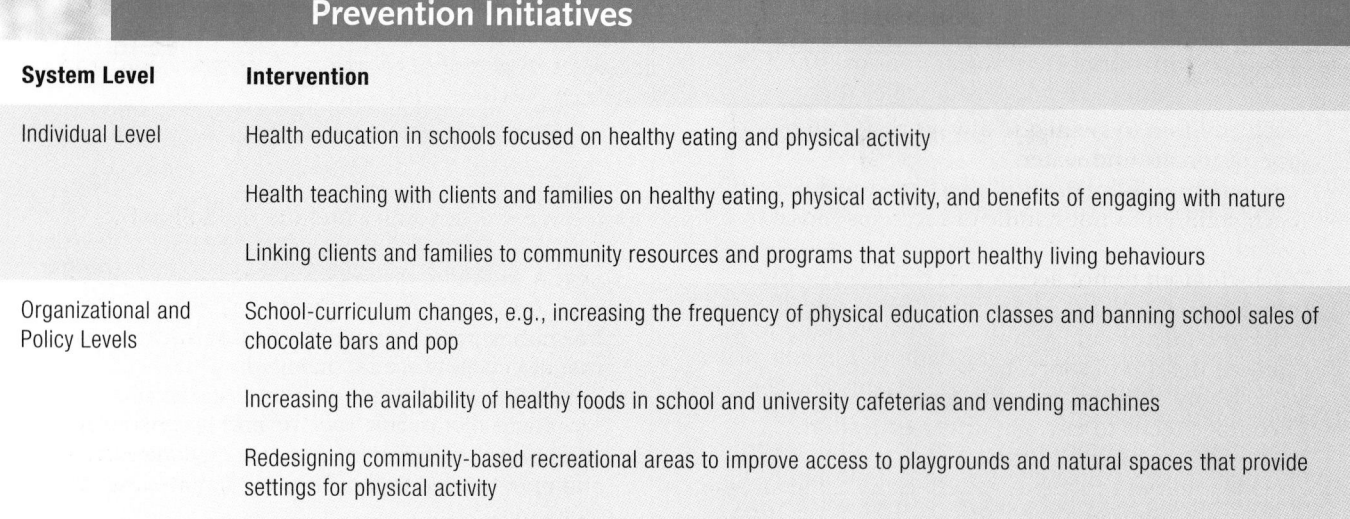

Table 5.4   Examples of Multilevel Health Promotion and Disease Prevention Initiatives

System Level	Intervention
Individual Level	Health education in schools focused on healthy eating and physical activity
	Health teaching with clients and families on healthy eating, physical activity, and benefits of engaging with nature
	Linking clients and families to community resources and programs that support healthy living behaviours
Organizational and Policy Levels	School-curriculum changes, e.g., increasing the frequency of physical education classes and banning school sales of chocolate bars and pop
	Increasing the availability of healthy foods in school and university cafeterias and vending machines
	Redesigning community-based recreational areas to improve access to playgrounds and natural spaces that provide settings for physical activity
	Creating community and nature-based walking trails that enable walk-to-school programs

positive spiritual, physical, and mental effects (Kahn, 1999; Kaplan, 2001; Kuo, 2001; St. Leger, 2003) and can influence behaviours that then help to protect and sustain the health of the planet (Bixler, Floyd, & Hammitt, 2002; Corcoran, 1999). Two examples follow; see Table 5.4 for additional examples:

- Example 1: Providing health education to clients and families about the health benefits of interacting with nature as well as ways to engage with the natural environment to promote their health, such as encouraging outdoor physical activity in green spaces
- Example 2: Working with hospital "green teams" to redesign hospital spaces that incorporate more green plants, gardens, and window access to natural spaces. Green teams strive to create environmentally responsive health care settings and sectors (Johnson et al., 2007).

PROMOTING CLIENT SAFETY

The Concept of Safety Promotion and Injury Prevention

Injuries, a leading cause of disability and death, are usually preventable. Nurses can integrate discussions of safety promotion and injury prevention into all health care encounters, particularly with more vulnerable populations, such as children, youth, and older adults. Injury prevention requires both client education and collective action to build safer environments.

PROMOTING INFANT SAFETY

Most infant injuries happen in the home and are attributed to lapses in caregiver attention, the presence of household hazards, and enhanced mobility of older infants as they develop. Accidental falls are the leading cause of infant injury in Canada. Other common infant injuries include lacerations, burns, poisonings, and choking (Pickett, Streight, Simpson, & Brison, 2003).

Approaches to reduce the risk of injury in infants include the following:

- Install smoke alarms and check them every month.
- Ensure that baby equipment, including second-hand equipment, meets Canadian safety standards, such as rear facing infant car seats. Please see specific car seat safety regulations in Chapter 10.
- Keep small objects such as buttons or coins out of babies' reach. Do not feed candy, nuts, popcorn, grapes, or hotdogs to a baby as these can cause choking.
- Avoid ribbons and ties on baby clothes and toys.
- Keep one hand on the baby at all times during care such as diaper changes. Babies can easily roll off beds and change tables.
- Do not use baby walkers with wheels.
- Microwaved food can be very hot on the inside while the outside is cool and can burn a baby. Stir and check the temperature before feeding.
- Hot bath water can burn a baby. Always test the water first.
- Put the baby on his or her back to sleep.
- Keep medicines, cleaning products, alcohol, tobacco products, and cosmetics out of reach. The most common form of poisoning involves unintentional ingestion of medicines (Endleman & Mandle, 2002).

Safety Promotion with Children and Youth

Injuries are the leading cause of death and disability among children and adolescents (Canadian Institute of Child Health [CICH], 2001). Leading forms of injuries include motor vehicle occupant and pedestrian accidents, drowning, and residential fires (Deal, Gomby, Zippiroli, & Behman, 2000). Approaches to reduce the risk of injury in childhood include the following:

- Teach children to swim and always maintain supervision around water.
- Teach children how to cross streets and parking lots.
- Teach children to not handle or eat items found in the street or grass.
- Teach children to not accept gifts from or go with strangers.
- Teach the safe use of equipment for play and work. Promote the use of sports helmets.
- Never allow children access to firearms.
- Encourage teens to enrol in driver education.
- Teach safe use of the Internet.
- Provide information about the effects of using alcohol and drugs (Potter et al., 2010).
- Install speed bumps on residential streets and route heavy traffic around residential areas.
- Change the design of products such as toys and sports equipment used by children.
- Ensure that there are padded dashboards and shatterproof windows in automobiles.
- Subsidize the costs of safety equipment such as bicycle helmets so that these items are affordable (Deal et al., 2000).

For more information on pediatric safety, refer to Chapter 10.

Safety Promotion with Older Adults

Falls are a leading cause of injuries among older adults (Potter et al., 2010). Approaches to reduce the risk of falls include the following:

- Ensure that stairs are of uniform size, treaded, and well lit.
- Install grab rails near the toilet and tub.
- Secure all mats and carpets so they do not skid.
- Promote the wearing of skid-free footwear.
- Remove clutter.
- Provide close supervision of confused clients.
- Lock beds and wheelchairs when transferring clients.
- Use alternatives to restraints (relaxation techniques, scheduled toileting, instituting scheduled walking and ambulation routines). Restraints do not prevent falls and injury and may actually increase the severity of injury (Potter et al., 2010).

UNDERSTANDING THE CONCEPT OF SEXUAL HEALTH

Sexual health is evidenced in the free and responsible expressions of sexual capabilities that foster harmonious personal and social wellness, enriching individual and social life. It is not merely the absence of dysfunction, disease, or infirmity (Pan American Health Organization [PAHO] & WHO, 1978). Sexual health requires a positive and respectful approach to sexuality and sexual relations, one free of coercion, discrimination, and violence (Taylor & Davis, 2007).

Components of Sexuality

Components of sexuality include the following:

- Sex: A multidimensional biological construct that encompasses anatomy, physiology, genes, and hormones, which together create a human "package" that affects how we are labelled.
- Gender: A social construct that is culturally based and historically specific and is constantly changing. Gender refers to the socially prescribed and experienced dimensions of "femaleness" and "maleness."
- Gender roles: The behavioural norms applied to males and females in societies, which influence individuals' everyday actions, expectations, and experiences. In some cultures, these are sharply defined; in other cultures, the lines between male and female gender roles may be more blurred.
- Gender identity: Our gender identity describes how we see ourselves as male or female (or as third gender or "two-spirited") (Johnson et al., 2007).

Sexual Behaviours

Sexually healthy behaviours include the appreciation of one's own body; interacting with both genders in respectful ways; expressing love and intimacy in appropriate ways; avoiding exploitative or manipulative relationships; identifying and living according to one's values; effective communication with family, peers, and partners; making informed choices about family options and lifestyles; seeking prenatal and reproductive health care; avoiding contracting or transmitting a sexually transmitted infection; and preventing sexual abuse (Sexuality Information and Education Council of the United States, 2008).

The Nurse's Role in Sexual Health Promotion

- Promoting positive sexual health is essential for all health professionals, including nurses. Sexuality impacts all areas of life and human development. Growing concerns about epidemics of sexually transmitted infections, the impact of sexual violence on health, and sexual dysfunction also require that nurses understand the prevention of disease.
- Sensitivity is essential as nurses strive to explore and better understand clients' experiences of sexuality in health and illness. There many different sexual cultural norms, and these norms influence attitudes toward sexual practices. The PLISSIT model may serve

nurses to assess and intervene sensitively in matters related to sexual health and well-being (Taylor & Davis, 2007).

- **P**ermission-giving: allowing the client to share concerns, experiences, and ask questions
- **L**imited **I**nformation
- **S**pecific **S**uggestions
- **I**ntensive **T**herapy

All nurses should be able to encourage clients to discuss matters related to sexual health and to give limited information and specific suggestions as entry-level competencies, depending on their own scope of knowledge. It is important for nurses to examine their own attitudes toward sexuality and be comfortable with different types of sexuality so that they can approach clients in an ethical, professional, and nonjudgemental way.

Alterations in sexual health include infertility; sexual dysfunction (including dyspareunia, lack of libido, erectile dysfunction); sexually transmitted infections; lack of comfort with sexual orientation, gender identity, or gender role; body image disturbance; sexual deviation; and sexual abuse (Johnson et al., 2007).

PROMOTING MENTAL WELLNESS AND STRESS MANAGEMENT

Emotions and Health

- Negative emotions, such as depression, anxiety, and anger or hostility, trigger neuroendocrine and immune responses, which, in turn, promote the development of a range of chronic health problems, such as cardiovascular disease, certain cancers, osteoporosis, type 2 diabetes, prolonged infection, and decreased wound healing (Kiecolt-Glaser, McGuire, Robles, & Glaser, 2002).
- The "fight or flight" response to stress has been described in the literature for over 60 years. The response is a general arousal of the sympathetic nervous system, which causes increasing heart and respiratory rates, decreased intestinal perfusion, increased alertness, increased blood pressure, and increased blood sugar levels.
- More recently, there was an investigation of the "tend and befriend" response, which claims that the hormone involved in the biobehaviour of nurturance and affiliation, oxytocin, causes some women experiencing stress to nurture one another rather than to run or fight and that this response is more common among women (Taylor et al., 2000).

Coping

Coping is defined as a person's effort to manage psychological stress. Coping involves some combination of problem-focused and emotion-focused

strategies (Lazarus, 1999). For example, gathering information about a stressor focuses on the problem and what to do about it; resisting learning about a condition is a way of regulating unpleasant emotions. Coping approaches vary among individuals and in different situations and times.

Emotional Intelligence

Emotional intelligence allows an individual to have self-awareness and to give and receive love. Goleman (1997) describes emotional intelligence as involving the following components:

- Self-awareness
- Altruism
- Personal motivation
- Empathy
- The ability to love and be loved

Approaches to Stress Management

Approaches to stress management include intrapersonal, interpersonal, and spiritual approaches, including the following (Hales, 2005):

- Connecting with others, developing support systems
- Regular exercise
- Obtaining sufficient sleep
- Learning time-management techniques
- Using guided imagery and visualization
- Practising progressive muscle relaxation
- Obtaining assertiveness training
- Journal-writing
- Maintaining a clear separation between work and home life
- Maintaining humour, laughter
- Learning to accept, respect, and love oneself; letting intuition be a guide
- Stretching oneself—learning something new in order to grow
- Helping others
- Practising prayer, meditation, experiences in nature
- Seeking treatment in crisis and in mental illness

COMPLEMENTARY AND ALTERNATIVE THERAPIES

Canadian Context

Interest and involvement in complementary and alternative medicine (CAM) is a fast-growing trend in Canada. A nation of immigrants, we represent the world's cultures coming together, and the WHO estimates that 80% of the world's population and more than 70% of Canadians uses medicines that would be considered alternatives to conventional North American medicines (PHAC, 2008; WHO, 2008). Growing awareness of the limits of conventional medicine and requests for holistic care—care that involves connectedness, integration, consciousness, entrainment, synchrony, nature, and ecology—also fuel the movement toward the increased use of CAM (CNA, 1999a).

Definitions

- Complementary therapies are those therapies used in addition to conventional treatment. An example would be the use of aromatherapy to lessen postsurgical anxiety.
- Alternative therapies, while they may include similar methods, are primarily intended to replace conventional therapies. An example would be the use of a special diet to treat cancer rather than the chemotherapy recommended by a doctor trained in conventional medicine (National Center for Complementary and Alternative Medicine [NCCAM], 2007).
- Integrative therapies involve building bridges between complementary and mainstream medicine and developing clinical approaches that encourage mainstream and complementary practitioners to work together in the client's best interest (CNA, 1999a).

Categories of CAM

- Alternative medical systems, such as homeopathy, naturopathy, Ayurvedic medicine from India, and traditional Chinese medicine
- Mind–body interventions, such as meditation, prayer, and art, music, or dance therapy
- Biologically based therapies, such as the use of herbs, foods, and vitamins
- Manipulative and body-based therapies, such as massage and chiropractic
- Energy therapies, which include biofield therapies such as Qigong, Reiki, and Therapeutic Touch and bioelectromagnetic-based therapies, such as use of pulsating magnetic fields (NCCAM, 2007)

BENEFITS, RISKS, CONTROVERSIES, AND NURSING RESPONSIBILITIES

CAM holds much promise. Considerable research has found great efficacy in some CAM therapies, particularly in promoting relaxation and in pain relief, thereby strengthening the immune response in health and illness. More and more complementary therapies have become integrated into "traditional" approaches; for example, registered nurses certified in Therapeutic Touch are applying this practice with ventilated clients in ICUs. Oncology nurses practise imagery in talking children through cancer procedures. Clients are asking nurses for massage and aromatherapy and about herbal remedies not found in any Canadian textbooks.

Many complementary therapies would seem to fall naturally into the practice of nursing (NCCAM, 2007) as nurses are called upon to promote holistic health, prevent disease, and provide care in episodic or chronic illness.

CAM also involves controversy. Some methods are unsupported by research, and some may involve harm and risk (NCCAM, 2007). For example, herbal remedies are not standardized, and some may be toxic or interact with other medicines a person may be using. Many practitioners of CAM remain unlicensed and unregulated. Without regulation, one can call oneself a practitioner or therapist with substandard or insufficient educational preparation or supervision. Without adherence to a professional code of ethics, practitioners may exploit frightened or uninformed people for personal or financial gain. Efforts to regulate practitioners of some CAM are in progress in Canada (CNA, 1999a).

Professional guidelines for nurses' involvement in CAM are evolving. In 2005, for example, the College of Registered Nurses of Nova Scotia (CRNNS) cautioned nurses to be careful in designating a particular therapy as "nursing" and associating it with RN work (CRNNS, 2006). For example, the use of Therapeutic Touch, imagery, hypnotherapy, meditation, prayer, and art therapy by nurses can fall within conventional nursing practice if nurses are adequately prepared in their practice, "Angel therapy," a form of spiritual healing involving working with a person's angels and archangels, can currently not be considered to fall within conventional RN practice (CRNNS, 2006).

With any therapy—conventional or otherwise—nurses are called upon to provide ethical care, promoting genuine and voluntary consent free of duress, fraud, or misrepresentation and to ensure that sufficient information is given about the nature and expected benefits of a treatment, its side effects, consequences of refusal, and possible alternatives (Lorenzo, 2003).

IMMUNIZATION

The goal of immunization is to eliminate vaccine-preventable diseases (National Advisory Committee on Immunization [NACI], 2006). Immunization enables the immune system to build up resistance to disease. Vaccines contain small amounts of viruses or bacteria that are dead (inactivated), weakened (live attenuated), or purified (subunit) components (NACI, 2006). Vaccines prompt the immune system to produce antibodies that will attack the virus or bacteria to prevent disease. The immune system stores the information about how to produce those antibodies and responds if there is exposure to that same virus or bacteria in the future (Hales & Lauzon, 2007). The *Canadian Immunization Guide* (2006) provides up-to-date information on the use of vaccines in Canada. It includes specific

Table 5.5 Adult Immunization Schedule—Routinely for All

Vaccine	Dosing Schedule (no record or unclear history of immunization)	Booster Schedule (primary series completed)
Tetanus and diphtheria given as Td and pertussis given as Tdap	Doses 1 and 2 4–8 weeks apart and dose 3 at 6–12 months later; one of the doses should be given as Tdap for pertussis protection	Td every 10 years; 1 dose should be given as Tdap if not previously given in adulthood
Measles, mumps, and rubella given as MMR	1 dose for adults born in or after 1970 without a history of measles or those individuals without evidence of immunity to rubella or mumps; second dose for selected groups	Not routinely required
Varicella	Doses 1 and 2 at least 4 weeks apart for susceptible adults (no history of natural disease or seronegativity)	Not currently recommended

* It is important to check schedules frequently for updates.

Source: Public Health Agency of Canada, (2006). *Canadian Immunization Guide, Seventh Edition*. This information is also available at http://www.phac-aspc.gc.ca/im/is-cv/index-eng.php (Table 5). Reproduced with permission from the Minister of Health, 2012.

recommendations for certain population groups, including children and adults (NACI, 2006). Table 5.5 details the schedule for adults (over 18). Recommended schedules for children and adolescents are provided in Chapter 10.

Vaccination and Risk Communication

Nurses must be knowledgeable not only in the principles and practices of immunization but also in risk communication as public concerns about safety continue to mount. The NACI has described five risk communication strategies that health professionals can use in their daily practice (NACI, 2006, pp. 29–30):

- Communicate current knowledge: Have a wide variety of information formats that are tailored to different languages and levels of education. Take into account what the client knows and the information requested.
- Respect differences of opinion about immunization: Understand the underlying reasons for a client's refusal of a vaccine and the strength of his or her position.
- Represent the risks and benefits of vaccines fairly and openly: Compare the known risks associated with the vaccine with the risks associated with the vaccine-preventable infection.
- Adopt a client-centred approach: All clients have input into their decision to vaccinate and retain responsibility of their own health or the health of their children.
- Make the most of each opportunity to present clear, evidence-informed messages regarding vaccines and immunizations: Clarify commonly held misconceptions, encourage the client to ask questions, and provide appropriate resources based on evidence.

WORKPLACE SAFETY FOR NURSES

Infection Control

- Nurses provide intimate bodily care to others, including those with infectious diseases.
- Hand hygiene before and after any client contact is essential to reducing transmission. Universal precautions apply to blood, semen, and vaginal secretions; cerebrospinal, synovial, pleural, peritoneal, pericardial, and amniotic fluids; and any items or surfaces (such as laundry, dressings, floors, and tabletops) in contact with them. Protective barriers such as gloves, gowns, masks, and protective eyewear can reduce the risk of exposure.
- Take caution with the use and disposal of needles, scalpel blades, and other sharps. Never recap a used needle. Use special puncture-resistant containers for sharps.
- Adhere to public health recommendations for the immunization of health care workers.
- Additional isolation precautions may be necessary for airborne infections or those involving droplets, such as the use of gowns, masks, and reverse airflow engineering systems (Division of Healthcare Quality Promotion, 2005; Potter et al., 2010).

For further information about infection control related to specific diseases, refer to Chapter 6, p. 128.

Safe Client Handling

Health care workers experience musculoskeletal disorders at a rate exceeding the rate of workers in construction, mining, and manufacturing (Nelson, Fragala, & Menzel, 2003). These disorders are associated with excessive back and shoulder loading due to lifting heavy loads during manual client handling or the required use of awkward postures during client care (Waters, Collins, Galinsky, & Caruso, 2006).

Training in good body mechanics has been shown to be insufficient in reducing back injuries among nurses. Evidence supports the use of mechanical lifts and transfer devices to reduce musculoskeletal injuries among health care workers (Waters et al., 2006).

Preventing Workplace Violence

- The Canadian Centre for Occupational Health and Safety (CCOHS) defines workplace violence as "any act in which a person is abused, threatened, intimidated, or assaulted in his or her employment" (CCOHS, 2005).
- Nurses work with the public, including unstable or volatile clients. Nurses have access to narcotics. Most nurses are women. Concern is growing about violent incidents in the health care workplace, including concern about the tolerance of violence as "part of the job" (Gilmour, 2006; International Council of Nurses [ICN], 2007).
- The ICN condemns all forms of violence and abuse against nursing personnel (ICN, 2007). Furthermore, if quality client care is to be provided, nurses must be ensured a safe work environment and respectful treatment.
- The ICN (2007) recommends the following:

  - Promoting comfort and reducing client frustration in health care settings
  - Instituting programs such as the Nonviolent Crisis Prevention program, which is available to help nurses learn respectful, noninvasive methods for de-escalating anger and safely managing disruptive and assaultive behaviour through behaviour management while still protecting the therapeutic relationship with those in their care (Crisis Prevention Institute [CPI], 2012)
  - Ensuring that staff are not alone in emergency and other high-risk settings
  - Installing and maintaining alarm systems
  - Liaising with local police and reporting all incidents of violence

REDUCING THE RISK OF HEART DISEASE AND CANCER

Leading Causes of Morbidity and Mortality in Canada

The leading causes of morbidity and mortality among adults in Canada are cardiovascular disease and cancer. As with other diseases, the incidence is higher among low-income Canadians (Health Canada, 2002). This group is a vulnerable population that is more likely than middle-income Canadians to have poor nutrition and to experience higher levels of stress. Nurses can contribute toward building healthier communities and to educating clients about modifying controllable risk factors.

Forms of cardiovascular disease include coronary artery disease, myocardial infarction (heart attack), and cerebral vascular accidents (CVAs, or stroke). Common forms of cancer include lung cancer in both men and women and breast cancer in women.

Risk Factors for Cardiovascular Disease

The risk factors for developing cardiovascular disease are as follows:

- A sedentary lifestyle
- Tobacco use
- Obesity
- High levels of blood fats (cholesterol, high-density lipoproteins, triglycerides)
- Diabetes mellitus
- Negative emotions, such as anxiety, depression, and anger
- Illegal drug use (cocaine, amphetamines, hallucinogens, heroin)
- Heredity
- African descent
- Male gender if under age 45
- Older age

Prevention

- Primary prevention of cardiovascular disease involves modification of any of the above risk factors that are within one's control: eating a balanced diet, avoiding illicit drugs and tobacco products, and maintaining a normal body weight.
- Secondary prevention of cardiovascular disease includes screening for hypertension, elevated blood glucose levels, and blood fat levels. With medical advice, certain medications, such as statins and aspirin, may also limit the progression of cardiovascular disease (Hales, 2005).

Reducing Risk Factors for Cancer

- Minimize exposure to carcinogens in the environment.
- Cigarette smoke is a leading cause of lung cancer. Efforts to reduce or eliminate tobacco use involve smoking prevention and cessation programs.
- Promote cancer-smart nutrition: diets high in antioxidant-rich fruits and vegetables; reducing dietary fats; avoiding smoked, cured, and barbecued meats; and maintaining a healthy body weight (Hales, 2005).
- Risk factors for breast cancer include female gender; advancing age; menarche prior to age 12; combined estrogen–progesterone hormone replacement therapy; and heavy use of alcohol (Hales, 2005). However, 70% of women diagnosed with breast cancer have no known risks other than being female (Canadian Cancer Society, 2011). Having a first child in one's teens or twenties

(Hales, 2005) and breastfeeding at any age do provide some protection from breast cancer.

- Skin cancers are malignancies that most often develop due to chronic or sporadic but intense overexposure to both natural and artificial sources of ultraviolet (UV) light. Most are preventable (Maguire-Eisen, Rothman, & Demierre, 2005). Fair skin colouring, freckling tendency, high nevi count, a family history of skin cancer, and childhood sun-exposure history influence an individual's risk of skin cancer (Maguire-Eisen et al., 2005). As the incidence of skin cancer rises, concerns have been mounting about damage to the ozone layer, which acts as planetary "sunscreen," reflecting and absorbing UV radiation, *in addition to* a trend to lifestyles that promote sun exposure (Maguire-Eisen et al., 2005). Artificial tanning is a billion-dollar industry frequented by increasing numbers of teenaged girls and young women—and contributing to rising rates of skin cancer. Commercial advertising promotes sunscreens as effective for "safe tanning." However, while sunscreens are useful as an adjunct to protective clothing and help to prevent sunburn and squamous cell carcinomas, they do not show preventive activity against basal cell carcinomas and melanoma (Boniol, Autier, & Dore, 2007).
- Best-practice sun protection involves precautions that correspond to UV indexes. With low UV indexes of 1–2, sunglasses are sufficient. With moderate UV indexes of 3–5, sunglasses and sunscreen are recommended. With high UV indexes of 6–7, sunglasses, sunscreen, and protective clothing are recommended. With very high UV indexes of 8+, staying out of direct sunlight is recommended (Maguire-Eisen et al., 2005).

In their role as health educators, nurses have a responsibility to disseminate knowledge about cancer prevention, to help enable people to choose positive health behaviours, and to contribute to reducing our "ecological footprint" in our own workplaces. Ecological changes that reduce the emission of carcinogens (such as toxic wastes and pesticides) into the air, water, and soil we share involve collective action in our communities and nations and commitment to planetary health.

Program Evaluation

Evaluation processes are critical entry-level competencies required of registered nurses. In health promotion practice, evaluation is essential to assessing, improving, and sustaining effective behavioural and environmental interventions that help to promote the health of individuals, families, and communities (Pender et al., 2006). Evaluation data, such as findings from a research study, can be used to advocate for policy change and to acquire funding to support the continuation and development of health promotion initiatives. Evaluation should be ongoing throughout the design and implementation of health promotion interventions and programs. Process and outcome evaluations are two types of evaluations aimed at understanding the effectiveness of the content, approach, and results of the health promotion interventions. Process evaluations most often target health teaching content and delivery and are therefore helpful in improving the design and implementation of the interventions. On the other hand, outcome evaluations help us to understand the effects of our interventions on health. Outcome evaluations help to pinpoint what health-related changes have occurred as a result of the health promotion intervention (Pender et al., 2006).

For example, process evaluation might entail effectively evaluating health promotion teaching interventions with a group of clients recovering from a myocardial infarction may involve having these same people evaluate the content of what was covered, the teaching style, and the usability of the pamphlets provided. Outcome evaluations of these same interventions could be delineated by tracking the rates of readmission for cardiac-related problems.

REFERENCES

Bandura, A. (2004). Health promotion by social cognitive means. *Health Education and Behavior, 31*(2), 143.

Best, A., Stokols, D., Green, L. W., Leischow, S., Holmes, B., & Buchholz, K. (2003). An integrative framework for community partnering to translate theory into effective health promotion strategy. *American Journal of Health Promotion, 18*(2), 168–176.

Bixler, R. D., Floyd, M. F., & Hammitt, W. E. (2002). Environmental socialization: Quantitative tests of the childhood play hypothesis. *Environment and Behavior, 34*(6), 795–818.

Boniol, M., Autier, P., & Dore, F. (2007). Photoprotection. *The Lancet, 370,* 1481–1483.

Canadian Cancer Society. (2011). *Causes of breast cancer.* Retrieved January 17, 2013, from http://www.cancer.ca/Canada-wide/About%20cancer/Types%20of%20cancer/Causes%20of%20breast%20cancer.aspx?sc_lang=en

Canadian Cancer Society. (2012). *Harmful substances and environmental risks.* Toronto: Author. Retrieved January 17, 2013, from http://www.cancer.ca/Canada-wide/Prevention/Harmful%20substances%20and%20environmental%20risks.aspx?sc_lang=en

Canadian Centre for Occupational Health and Safety. (2005). *Violence in the workplace: Canada's national occupational health & safety resource.* Hamilton, ON: Author.

Canadian Institute for Health Information. (2004). *Health spending in Canada, 1993–2000.* Ottawa: Author.

Canadian Institute of Child Health. (2001). *The health of Canada's children: A CICH profile: Pocket guide.* Ottawa: Author. Retrieved January 17, 2013, from http://www.cich.ca/PDFFiles/ProfilePocketGuide.pdf

Canadian Institute of Child Health, Safe Kids Canada, & Safe Start. (2001). *Fact sheets: Keep your kids safe.* Ottawa: Canadian Institute of Child Health. Retrieved January 17, 2013, from http://www.cich.ca/Publications_safeenvironment.html

Canadian Nurses Association. (1999). Complementary therapies—Finding the right balance. *Nursing Now: Issues and trends in Canadian nursing, 6.* Ottawa: Author.

Canadian Nurses Association. (2004). *Position Statement: Promoting culturally competent care.* Ottawa: Author. Retrieved January 17, 2013, from http://www2.cna-aiic.ca/CNA/documents/pdf/publications/PS73_Promoting_Culturally_Competent_Care_March_2004_e.pdf

Canadian Nurses Association. (2005). *Primary health care: A summary of the issues.* Retrieved September 3, 2012, from http://www2.cna-aiic.ca/CNA/documents/pdf/publications/BG7_Primary_Health_Care_e.pdf

Canadian Nurses Association. (2005). *CNA Backgrounder: The ecosystem, the natural environment, and health and nursing: A summary of the issues* (p. 5). Retrieved January 17, 2013, from http://www.cna-aiic.ca/CNA/documents/pdf/publications/BG4_The_Ecosystem_e.pdf

Canadian Recommended Immunization Schedule, *Canadian Immunization Guide, Seventh Edition.* (2006). Ottawa: Author. Retrieved January 17, 2013, from http://www.phac-aspc.gc.ca/im/is-cv/index.html#a(Table 4). Reproduced with the permission of The Ministry of Public Works and Government Services Canada, 2008.

Clemen-Stone, S., McGuire, S. L., & Eigsti, D. G. (2002). *Comprehensive community health nursing: Family, aggregate and community practice* (6th ed.). St. Louis: Mosby.

College of Registered Nurses of Nova Scotia. (2006). *Complementary and alternative therapies: A guide for registered nurses.* Halifax: Author.

Corcoran, P. B. (1999). Formative influences in the lives of environmental educators in the United States. *Environmental Education Research, 5*(2), 207–220.

Crisis Prevention Institute. (2012). *About CPI.* Brookfield, WI: Author. Retrieved January 17, 2013, from http://www.crisisprevention.com/about/history.html

Deal, L. W., Gomby, D. S., Zippiroli, L., & Behman, R. E. (2000). Unintentional injuries in childhood: Analysis and recommendations. *The Future of Children, 10*(1), 4–23.

DiClemente, C. C., & Prochaska, J. O. (1998). Toward a comprehensive, transtheoretical model of change: Stages of change and addictive behaviors. In W. R. Miller & N. Heather (Eds.), *Treating addictive behaviours* (2nd ed., pp. 3–24). New York: Plenum.

Division of Healthcare Quality Promotion. (2005). *Fact sheet: Universal precautions for prevention and transmission of HIV and other blood borne infections.* Atlanta: Centers for Disease Control and Prevention. Retrieved January 17, 2013, from http://www.nbcht.org/Resources/CDC%20doc%20%20Universal%20Precautions%20for%20Prevention%20of%20Transmission%20of%20HIV.pdf

Edwards, N., Mill, J., & Kothari, A. (2004). Multiple intervention research programs in community health. *Canadian Journal of Nursing Research, 36*(1), 40–55.

Endleman, C., & Mandle, C. (2002). *Health promotion throughout the lifespan* (5th ed.). St. Louis: Mosby.

Freire, P. (1970). *Pedagogy of the oppressed.* New York: Continuum.

Gilmour, J. (2006). Violence in the workplace. *Nephrology Nursing Journal, 33*(3), 254–255.

Goleman, D. (1997). *Emotional intelligence.* New York: Bantam Books.

Green, L. W., Richard, L., & Potvin, L. (1996). Ecological foundations of health promotion. *American Journal of Health Promotion, 10*(4), 270–281.

Hales, D. (2005). *An invitation to health.* Belmont, CA: Thomson Wadsworth.

Hales, D., & Lauzon, L. (2007). *An invitation to health* (Canadian ed.). Toronto: Thomson.

Health Canada. (2001). *Population health promotion: An integrated model of population health and wealth promotion.* Retrieved January 17, 2013, from http://www.phac-aspc.gc.ca/ph-sp/php-psp/php3-eng.php

Health Canada. (2007). Eating well with *Canada's food guide* (H164-38/1-2007E). Ottawa: Author. Retrieved January 17, 2013, from http://www.hc-sc.gc.ca/fn-an/food-guide-aliment/index_e.html

Health Canada. (2008). *Complementary and alternative health.* Retrieved from January 17, 2013, http://www.phac-aspc.gc.ca/chn-rcs/cah-acps-eng.php

Health Canada (2008). Canada Health Act annual report 2006-2007: Introduction (H1-4/2007E-PDF). Ottawa: Author. Retrieved January 17, 2013 from http://www.hc-sc.gc.ca/hcs-sss/pubs/cha-lcs/2006-cha-lcs-ar-ra/index-eng.php

Health Canada. (2010). *Canada Health Act: Overview.* Ottawa: Author. Retrieved January 17, 2013, from http://www.hc-sc.gc.ca/hcs-sss/medi-assur/index-eng.php

Health Canada. (2011). *Why physical activity is important for you* (H39-429/1998-1E). Ottawa: Author. Retrieved January 17, 2013, from http://www.phac-aspc.gc.ca/pau-uap/paguide/why.html

Hughes, S. L., Seymour, R. B., Campbell, R. T., Huber, G., Pollak, N., Sharma, L., et al. (2006). Long-term impact of Fit and Strong! on older adults with osteoarthritis. *Gerontologist, 46,* 801–814.

International Council of Nurses. (2007). *Guidelines on coping with violence in the workplace.* Geneva: Author. Retrieved January 17, 2013, from http://www.icn.ch/images/stories/documents/publications/guidelines/guideline_violence.pdf

Johnson, J., Greaves, L., & Repta, R. (2007). *Better science with sex and gender: A primer for health research.* Vancouver: Women's Health Research Network.

Kahn, P. (1999). *The human relationship with nature: Development and culture.* Cambridge, MA: MIT Press.

Kaplan, R. (2001). The nature of the view from home—Psychological benefits. *Environment and Behavior, 33*(4), 507–542.

Katamay, S., Esslinger, K., Vigneault, M., Johnson, J., Junkins, B., Robbins, L., et al. (2007). Eating well with Canada's food guide: Development of the food intake pattern. *Nutrition Reviews, 65*(4), 155–166.

Khaw, L., & Hardesty, J. L. (2007). Theorizing the process of leaving: Turning points and trajectories in the stages of change. *Family Relations, 56*(4), 413–426.

Kiecolt-Glaser, J. K., McGuire, L., Robles, T., & Glaser, R. (2002). Emotions, morbidity, and mortality: New perspectives from psychoneuroimmunology. *Annual Review of Psychology, 53,* 83–107.

Kirby, M. (2002). *Vol. 6: Recommendations for reform. The health of Canadians–The federal role.* Ottawa: The Standing Senate Committee on Social Affairs, Science and Technology.

Krieger, N. (2001). Theories for social epidemiology in the 21st century: An ecosocial perspective. *International Journal of Epidemiology, 30,* 668–677.

Kuo, F. E. (2001). Coping with poverty: Impacts of environment and attention in the inner city. *Environment & Behavior, 33*(1), 5–34.

LaLonde, M. (1974). *A new perspective on the health of Canadians. A working document.* Ottawa: Government of Canada. Retrieved January 17, 2013, from http://www.hc-sc.gc.ca/hcs-sss/alt_formats/hpb-dgps/pdf/pubs/1974-lalonde/lalonde-eng.pdf

Laverack, G. (2004). *Health promotion practice: Power and empowerment.* London, UK: Sage.

Lazarus, R. (1999). *Stress and emotion: A new synthesis.* New York: Springer.

Lorenzo, P. (2003). Complementary therapies–They're not without risk. *RN, 66*(1), 65–68.

Maguire-Eisen, M., Rothman, K., & Demierre, M. F. (2005). The ABCs of sun protection for children. *Dermatology Nursing, 17*(6), 419–433.

McLeroy, K., Bibeau, D., Steckler, A., & Glantz, K. (1988). An ecological perspective on health promotion programs. *Health Education Quarterly, 15,* 351–377.

McMurray, A. (2007). *Community health and wellness: A socio-ecological approach* (3rd ed.). Sydney: Elsevier.

National Advisory Committee on Immunization. (2006). *Canadian immunization guide* (7th ed.) (HP40-3/2006E). Ottawa: Public Health Agency of Canada.

National Center for Complementary and Alternative Medicine. (2007). *What is CAM?* Bethesda, MD: Author. Retrieved January 17, 2013, from http://nccam.nih.gov/health/whatiscam/

Nelson, A., Fragala, G., & Menzel, N. (2003). Myths and facts about back injuries in nursing. *American Journal of Nursing, 103*(2), 32–40.

Pan American Health Organization & World Health Organization. (2000). *Promotion of sexual health: Recommendations for action.* Geneva: World Health Organization.

Pender, N., Murdaugh, C., & Parsons, M. (2006). *Health promotion in nursing practice* (5th ed.). Upper Saddle River, NJ: Pearson Prentice Hall.

Prevention Source B.C. (n.d.). *The workbook on prevention concepts: Prevention strategies.* Retrieved January 17, 2013, from http://preventionsource.org/guides/workbook/sac6.html

Pickett, W., Streight, S., Simpson, K., & Brison, R. J. (2003). Injuries experienced by infant children: A population-based epidemiological analysis. *Pediatrics, 111*(4), 365–370.

Potter, P. A., & Perry, A. G. (2006). *Canadian fundamentals of nursing* (3rd Canadian ed.). Toronto: Mosby.

Potter, P., Perry, A., Ross-Kerr, J. C., & Wood, M. (2010). *Canadian fundamentals of nursing* (4th revised ed.). Toronto: Mosby

Public Health Agency of Canada. (2006). Canadian Required Immunization Schedule. *Canadian Immunization Guide, Seventh Edition, 2006.* Available at http://www.phac-aspc.gc.ca/im/is-cv/index-eng.php

Public Health Agency of Canada (2011). *What determines health? Determinants of health; What makes Canadians healthy or unhealthy?* Retrieved January 17, 2013, from http://www.phac-aspc.gc.ca/ph-sp/determinants/index-eng.php#determinants

Raine, K. (2005). Determinants of healthy eating: An overview and synthesis. *Canadian Journal of Public Health, 96*(Suppl. 3), S8–S14.

Rankin, S. H., & Duffy Stallings, K. (2001). *Patient education: Principles and practice.* Philadelphia: Lippincott.

Richard, L., Potvin, L., Kishchuk, N., Prlic, H., & Green, L. (1996). Assessment of the integration of the ecological approach in health promotion programs. *American Journal of Health Promotion, 10*(4), 318–328.

Romanow, R. J. (2002). *Building on values: The future of health care in Canada—Final report* (CP32-85/2002E-IN). Ottawa: Commission on the Future of Health Care in Canada.

Sallis, F., & Owen, N. (1997). *Ecological models.* In K. Glanz, L. Lewis, & R. K. Rimer (Eds.), *Health behaviour and health education: Theory, research and practice* (2nd ed., pp. 403–424). San Francisco: Jossey-Bass Inc.

Sexuality Information and Education of the United States. (2008). *Human development.* Washington, DC: Author. Retrieved January 17, 2013, from http://www.sexedlibrary.org/index.cffm?pageId=723

Skinner, W. (2006). *Mapping a model of services and supports for addictions.* Retrieved January 17, 2013, from http://www.ccsa.ca/2006%20CCSA%20documents/ccsa-summinst-Skinner-2006-e.pdf

St. Leger, L. (2003). Health and nature: New challenges for health promotion. *Health Promotion International, 18*(3), 173–175.

Stanhope, M., & Lancaster, J. (2006). *Foundations of community health nursing: Community-oriented practice* (2nd ed.). St. Louis: Mosby.

Stanhope, M., Lancaster, J., Jessup-Falcioni, H., & Viverais-Dresler, G. A. (2008) *Community health nursing in Canada* (1st Canadian ed.). Toronto: Elsevier.

Statistics Canada. (2010a). *Selected trend data for Canada, 1996, 2001 and 2006 censuses.* Retrieved January 17, 2013, from: http://www12.statcan.gc.ca/census-recensement/2006/dp-pd/92-596/P1-2.cfm?Lang=eng&T=PR&PRCODE=01&GEOCODE=01&GEOLVL=PR&TID=0

Statistics Canada. (2010b). *Ethnic diversity and immigration.* Retrieved January 17, 2013, from: http://www41.statcan.gc.ca/2009/30000/cybac30000_000-eng.htm

Statistics Canada. (2011). *Components and factors of demographic growth.* Retrieved January 17, 2013, from http://www.statcan.gc.ca/daily-quotidien/110928/t110928a1-eng.htm

Stokols, D. (1996). Translating social ecological theory into guidelines for community health promotion. *American Journal of Health Promotion, 10*(4), 282–298.

Taylor, B., & Davis, S. (2007). The extended PLISSIT model for addressing the sexual wellbeing of individuals with an acquired disability or chronic illness. *Sexuality and Disability, 25(3)*, 135–139.

Taylor, S. E., Klein, L. C., Lewis, B. P., Gruenewald, T. L., Gurung, R. A. R., & Updegraff, J. A. (2000). Biobehavioral responses to stress in females: Tend-and-befriend, not fight-or-flight. *Psychological Review, 107(3)*, 411–429.

Varcarolis, E., Carson, V., & Shoemaker, N. (2006). *Foundations of psychiatric mental health nursing: A clinical approach.* Philadelphia: Saunders.

Waters, T., Collins, J., Galinsky, T., & Caruso, C. (2006). NIOSH research efforts to prevent musculoskeletal disorders in the healthcare industry. *Orthopaedic Nursing, 25(6)*, 380–389.

World Health Organization. (1978). *Alma-Ata declaration: Health for all by the year 2000.* Geneva: Author.

World Health Organization. (1986). *Ottawa charter for health promotion.* Geneva: Author.

World Health Organization. (2002). WHO unmasks another killer: Inactivity. *Bulletin of the World Health Organization, 80(5)*, 425. Geneva: Author.

World Health Organization. (2003). *Fact sheet 134: Traditional medicine.* Geneva: Author. Retrieved January 17, 2013, from http://www.who.int/mediacentre/factsheets/fs134/en/

World Health Organization. (2005). *The Bangkok charter for health promotion in a globalized world.* Geneva: Author.

World Health Organization. (2008). *Fact sheet 134: Traditional medicine.* Geneva: Author. Retrieved January 17, 2013, from http://www.who.int/mediacentre/factsheets/fs134/en/

BIBLIOGRAPHY

Bandura, A. (1977). *Social learning theory.* Englewood Cliffs, NJ: Prentice Hall.

Breast Cancer Society of Canada. (2007). *Facts on breast cancer.* Sarnia, ON: Author. Retrieved January 17, 2013, from http://www.bcsc.ca./breasthealth.htm# Facts_on_Breast_Cancer_

Canadian Institute of Child Health, Safe Kids Canada, & Safe Start. (2001). *Fact sheets: Keep your kids safe.* Ottawa: Canadian Institute of Child Health. Retrieved January 17, 2013, from http://www.cich.ca/PDFFiles/InjuryPreventionFactSheets/English/

Canadian Nurses Association. (2000). *The environment is a determinant of health.* Ottawa: Author.

Canadian Nurses Association. (2000). *Position statement: The environment is a determinant of health.* Ottawa: Author. Retrieved January 17, 2013, from http://www.cna-aiic.ca/CNA/documents/pdf/publications/PS45_env_determinant_health_June_2000_e.pdf

DiClemente, C. C. (2007). The transtheoretical model of intentional behaviour change. *Drugs and Alcohol Today, 7(1)*, 29–33.

Edwards, N. (1999). Population health: Determinants and interventions. *Canadian Journal of Public Health, 90(1)*, 10–11.

Health Canada. (2005). *What is long-term facilities-based care?* Retrieved January 17, 2013, from http://www.hc-sc.gc.ca/hcs-sss/home-domicile/longdur/index_e.html

International Council of Nurses. (2001). *Nurses, always there for you: United against violence: Anti-violence tool kit.* Geneva, CH: Author. Retrieved January 17, 2013, from http://www.icn.ch/indkit2001_01.pdf

Shantakumar, S., Terry, M. B., Teitelbaum, S. L., & Britton, J. A. (2007). Reproductive factors and breast cancer risk among older women. *Breast Cancer Research and Treatment, 102(3)*, 365–375.

World Health Organization. (n.d.). *Sexual health.* Retrieved January 17, 2013, from http://www.who.int/reproductive-health/gender/sexualhealth.htm

WEB SITES

Dietary Reference Intakes Tables (http://www.hc-sc.gc.ca/fn-an/nutrition/reference/table/index_e.html#rvm): This Health Canada site contains information about daily requirements for different nutrients.

Eating Well with Canada's Food Guide (http://www.hc-sc.gc.ca/fn-an/food-guide-aliment/index_e.html): This site links to an up-to-date version of the Food Guide, which is available in many languages, and a wealth of other links pertaining to nutrition in Canada.

Joint CNA/CMA Position Statement on Environmentally Responsible Activity in the Health Sector (http://www2.cna-aiic.ca/CNA/documents/pdf/publications/JPS99_Environmental_e.pdf _Joint_Stat_Envir_Resp_Activity_Health_Sector_Feb_2006_e.pdf): This is a statement by the Canadian Nurses Association and Canadian Medical Association advocating for environmental awareness and environmentally sound conduct on the part of health professionals.

Natural Health Products (http://www.hc-sc.gc.ca/dhp-mps/prodnatur/index-eng.php): Health Canada describes different aspects of consuming natural health products and the ways in which the industry is regulated.

Prevention and Control of Occupational Infections in Health Care (http://www.phac-aspc.gc.ca/publicat/ccdr-rmtc/02pdf/28s1e.pdf): These are governmental guidelines for health care workers to stop the spread of infections in hospitals and other health care facilities.

CHAPTER 5

Practice Questions

Case 1

The Canadian Nurses Association has recommended that nurses be involved in efforts to promote more environmentally responsible health care. An RN is involved in her hospital's "green team." The green team's goals are to improve the hospital's recycling practices, reduce energy use, and promote more environmentally preferable health care products.

Questions 1–3 refer to this case.

1. The nurse understands that both the energy used and the waste produced by the health sector significantly contribute to which of the following?

   1. Global climate change and emissions of dioxins
   2. Landfill run-off
   3. Contamination of indoor air
   4. The development of wind energy alternatives

2. The green team understands that the support of all hospital staff, health care consumers, and community administrators is critical to designing and implementing effective, sustainable disease and injury prevention initiatives. This process is best referred to as which of the following?

   1. Conflict resolution
   2. Advocacy and community building
   3. Focus-group planning
   4. Community promotion

3. How would the RN and the green team best increase environmentally responsible behaviours within their agency?

   1. Meet with administrators to outline required policy changes
   2. Assess all clients for exposure to environmental contaminants
   3. Develop and implement educational sessions on environmentally responsible health care
   4. Sell environmentally friendly products in the hospital gift store to increase visibility of the issues

Case 2

An RN is a nurse at a shelter for the homeless in a large Canadian city. Many clients have substance abuse problems and malnutrition. All fall into the low-income bracket.

Questions 4–7 refer to this case.

4. The nurse approaches the local food bank to ask for donations. What types of foods would be most appropriate for his clients?

   1. Calorie-rich
   2. Nutrient-rich
   3. Inexpensive
   4. Canned

5. The nurse is committed to improving the health of the clients in the shelter. What strategy has the greatest chance of sustaining improved health for the homeless?

   1. Treatment of addictions
   2. Stable housing
   3. Treatment of chronic illnesses
   4. Improved nutrition

6. There is an outbreak of tuberculosis at the shelter. What is the best action by the nurse to ensure that the affected clients comply with their medication regimen?

   1. Arrange for the affected individuals to be admitted to hospital
   2. Provide directly observed therapy (DOT)
   3. Administer the drugs in a sustained-release formula
   4. Select drugs that have the lowest incidence of side effects

7. Many of the nurse's clients have chronic open and infected wounds. What is the most likely reason for these lesions to be chronic?

   1. Injuries are sustained while on the streets, which are not clean
   2. Inadequate clothes and footwear to protect the skin
   3. Close association with others who have infected sores
   4. Protein–calorie malnutrition leads to poor wound healing

Case 3

A registered nurse at City Hospital is a certified Reiki therapist. A client, Olga, has asked the nurse to practise Reiki on her as she recovers from breast cancer. The nurse is well informed and experienced with Reiki in her native Germany.

Questions 8 and 9 refer to this case.

8. What is the nurse's responsibility in this situation?

   1. Therapies such as Reiki are controversial, and the nurse must not practise Reiki in an accredited hospital
   2. The nurse may practise Reiki within her role as an RN as she is fully competent, and Olga has made an informed and legitimate request

3. The nurse may practise Reiki at City Hospital but only after her assigned shift and not as part of her RN duties
4. The nurse may practise Reiki but only after Olga is discharged from hospital

9. Reiki is considered to be a complementary therapy. What is the definition of complementary therapy?

1. A therapy that is used in conjunction with traditional Western medicine
2. A therapy that is used instead of traditional Western medicine
3. A therapy that is considered to be homeopathic
4. A therapy that uses only natural methods for treatment

Case 4

Mrs. Broadfoot, age 42, is admitted to a large hospital from her remote northern community. She is experiencing complications from her type 2 diabetes, including kidney failure and peripheral vascular disease. Mrs. Broadfoot is of Aboriginal descent.

Questions 10–13 refer to this case.

10. How should the nurse develop a plan of care to recognize Mrs. Broadfoot's cultural beliefs and practices?

1. Based on recognized Aboriginal cultural factors
2. According to Mrs. Broadfoot's individually expressed wishes
3. After interviewing the family for culturally specific guidelines
4. No differently from other clients on the unit

11. During morning care, the nurse begins a dialogue with Mrs. Broadfoot about her illness. Mrs. Broadfoot is quiet and often silent during this interaction. What is the most likely reason for Mrs. Broadfoot's silence?

1. She does not understand English
2. She is too tired and weak to speak
3. She is in denial about her health and does not wish to speak about it
4. This is a culturally common form of communication within Mrs. Broadfoot's community

12. The nurse reviews the laboratory results and discovers that Mrs. Broadfoot has a hemoglobin (Hg) of 6.0 mmol/L. Which of the following foods would be best to include in Mrs. Broadfoot's diet in response to this Hg level?

1. Beef liver
2. Tofu

3. Spinach
4. Fortified cereals

13. Mrs. Broadfoot has a sudden and unexpected myocardial infarction. Her family is notified but is not able to arrive by plane before she dies. What should the nurse do prior to performing end-of-life care for Mrs. Broadfoot?

1. Leave Mrs. Broadfoot in her bed so the family may view the body
2. Ensure that there is consent for autopsy
3. Avoid touching the body until the traditional shaman has provided permission
4. Identify cultural death rites that should be respected

INDEPENDENT QUESTIONS

Questions 14–31 do not refer to a particular case.

14. Ms. Nguyen is ready for discharge home after giving birth to a healthy baby girl. Which of the following safety instructions should be given to all families with infants?

1. Infants should be positioned on their backs to sleep
2. Infants should be positioned on their bellies to sleep
3. Infants should be prohibited from co-sleeping with their mothers
4. Infants should be bundled up in hats and booties when they sleep

15. Which of the following is an example of primary prevention?

1. Annual Papanicolaou (PAP) smears
2. Megavitamin therapy as a complementary therapy while receiving chemotherapy
3. Removal of an inflamed appendix before it ruptures
4. Remaining out of direct sunlight when working outdoors in summertime

16. What is the leading cause of preventable child mortality and morbidity in Canada?

1. Cancer
2. Asthma
3. Injuries
4. Congenital anomalies

17. Various types of pediatric disease are the result of exposure to contaminants in the indoor and outdoor environment. These health problems include which of the following?

1. Respiratory diseases
2. Type 1 diabetes
3. Juvenile arthritis
4. Irritable bowel syndrome

18. Mr. Jones, age 60, is admitted to the hospital following a stroke. Mr. Jones weighs 132 kg and has limited mobility. The RN plans to assist Mr. Jones to move from his bed to sit in a special chair. What is the safest way for the nurse to move Mr. Jones?

1. Practise good body mechanics
2. Wait until Mr. Jones has recovered more before moving him
3. Use a mechanical lift
4. Obtain the assistance of a male nurse to do the heavy lifting

19. At the antenatal clinic, an RN interviews Ms. Capelas, who is nine weeks pregnant. Ms. Capelas tells the nurse she has been experiencing a lot of nausea but finds that chewing on crystallized ginger root alleviates the nausea. The nurse should do which of the following?

1. Tell Ms. Capelas to take only medications prescribed by a medical doctor
2. Inform Ms. Capelas that there is no scientific basis for this and she is likely experiencing a placebo effect
3. Review current research about ginger as an antiemetic and share this information with Ms. Capelas
4. Caution Ms. Capelas that no drugs or home remedies are safe in the first trimester of pregnancy while the baby's organs are forming

20. Mr. Drosinsky has had nerve-sparing surgery for prostate cancer. The RN includes sexuality in his postoperative health teaching. Which of the following sentences would best introduce the topic?

1. "I know that you are concerned about achieving an erection after prostate surgery."
2. "Are you in a sexual relationship now?"
3. "Many men feel concerned about their sexuality after prostate surgery."
4. "You are lucky that with nerve-sparing surgery you will not experience sexual difficulties."

21. Carmen, age 6, has been determined to be obese for her age and height. Of the following, which is the most likely to have been the major factor leading to her obesity?

1. She does not participate in school sports
2. She eats a lot of fast foods
3. She watches a lot of TV
4. Her parents are obese

22. What is the most effective diet to achieve sustained weight loss?

1. A low-fat diet
2. A low-carbohydrate diet
3. A low-calorie diet
4. A Canada Food Guide diet with reduced portions

23. Ms. Blanche has been advised by a nutritionist to increase her intake of vitamin D to 1000 international units (IU). How would Ms. Blanche best achieve this?

1. Increase the amount of time she spends in the sunshine to at least one hour each day
2. Increase her intake of milk
3. Take a vitamin D supplement
4. Eat a fortified ready-to-eat cereal each morning

24. The parents of children at Humber Valley Public School are concerned that sexuality is to be included in the Grade 5 health curriculum. The school nurse makes a presentation about the sexual health component of the curriculum at a parent–teacher meeting. She explains which of the following concerning children and sexuality?

1. All people, regardless of age, are sexual beings
2. It is best for children to learn the correct facts about sexuality at school rather than from family or friends
3. A discussion about sexuality will prepare them for sexual intercourse
4. In Canadian culture, society values children learning about sexuality at an early age

25. Brendan, age 17, talks to the nurse at the student health centre at the university he attends. He tells the nurse that he frequently feels too tired to attend classes. What would be the first question the nurse would ask Brendan?

1. "How many hours of sleep do you get each night?"
2. "What time do you go to bed every night?"
3. "What time do you get up in the morning?"
4. "Do you have any health problems that would interfere with sleeping?"

26. The RN visits Mr. and Mrs. Wales, a retired couple in their 80s. The Waleses are fairly active but feel they are not as strong as they used to be, and both experience occasional moments of unsteadiness. The RN performs an environmental assessment of their home. Of the following, what would be the most important assistive device to arrange for Mr. and Mrs. Wales?

1. Walkers
2. Grab bars in the bathtub
3. Blocks under the chair and sofa
4. A hand-held shower attachment

27. Which of the following would be the best heart-healthy lunch menu?
1. Chicken soup, bagel
2. Delicatessen luncheon meat sandwich, Caesar salad
3. Purchased bran muffin, cheddar cheese slices
4. Grilled chicken, lettuce, and tomato sandwich on whole-grain bread.

28. The Collins family regularly visits their mother, age 95, who is in a long-term care facility. What is the most important advice for the nurse to provide the family when they visit in order to protect their mother from a communicable disease?

1. Do not visit if they feel sick
2. Use the alcohol gel hand wash located outside her room before entering
3. Do not bring children younger than 5 years to visit
4. If they have to cough or sneeze while visiting, use a disposable tissue

29. Ms. Price is a single mother who works part-time at a fast-food outlet. She has three children. Her youngest child, Kyle, has just been prescribed three different medications by the doctor for his asthma, in addition to an over-the-counter antihistamine for his allergies. What would be important for the nurse to say to Ms. Price related to Kyle's treatment?

1. "These medications are expensive. If you are not sure you can afford them, I can help you obtain financial assistance."
2. "Kyle really needs these medications. You must be sure you buy them and give them to him as directed."
3. "If you can't afford all these medications, don't give Kyle the antihistamine."

4. "There are generic forms of these medications. I will change the prescription to the less expensive forms of the drugs."

30. The mother of a five-year-old child asks the nurse how best to teach her child to cross a street safely. What would the nurse respond?

1. Buy him a computer game about road safety for children
2. Reward the child every time he crosses the street in an approved manner
3. Talk to him daily about the rules of crossing the road
4. Provide role modelling and practise street safety

31. A nurse works in a street clinic. Many of the clients at the clinic are intravenous drug users. On a visit to the clinic washroom one day, the nurse finds several used syringes and needles. What initial action should the nurse take?

1. Contact the police and municipal authorities
2. Place a puncture-proof sharps container in the bathroom
3. Wear protective clothing and dispose of needles in a puncture-proof container
4. Ask the client whom the nurse suspects left the needles and syringes to dispose of them

Answers and Rationales for Practice Questions

1.   C: Health and Wellness   T: Application

1. The health sector uses a significant amount of electrical energy by burning nonrenewable fossil fuels. This process produces greenhouse gases and significantly contributes to global climate change. Hospital waste and incineration practices contribute emissions of dioxins, mercury, and other heavy metals, which are toxic to human health.
2. Although hospital practices often lead to waste that could otherwise be recycled or avoided, any landfill run-off is not directly associated with hospital practices.
3. The energy used and the waste produced affect the quality of the outdoor environment—the air, food, soil, and water.
4. Although wind energy may be an alternative source of energy, it is not the result of the energy used and the waste produced by the health sector.

2.   C: Health and Wellness   T: Application

1. This assumes there is a conflict, which may not be true.
2. For effective and sustainable change, it is critical to build a community of people within the organization who understand and are motivated to work on the issues.
3. Focus groups may be used to facilitate discussion and input on the issues but are only mechanisms for the advocacy process and community building.
4. Community promotion is not an actual process.

3.   C: Health and Wellness   T: Critical Thinking

1. Administrators are not likely to support policy changes without first understanding the rationale for and significance of the problem.
2. Assessing clients for exposure to environmental contaminants would not increase awareness of environmentally responsible behaviours within the organization.
3. Developing and implementing educational sessions on environmentally responsible health care would help to increase awareness of the issues among staff and administrators.
4. Selling environmentally friendly products in the hospital gift store would not be the most effective strategy for increasing awareness of environmentally responsible behaviours in the health sector.

4.   C: Health and Wellness   T: Critical Thinking

1. Calorie-rich foods provide energy but often lack other essential nutrients.
2. Nutrient-rich foods are best to correct and prevent malnutrition-related diseases.
3. Inexpensive foods may not necessarily provide the nutrients required for a population that is malnourished.
4. Some canned foods are nutrient-rich, but canned foods are not the only source of nutrient-rich foods.

5.   C: Health and Wellness   T: Critical Thinking

1. This improves health but is a long-term goal that may not be achieved.
2. Studies have shown that stable housing is the most important determinant for homeless clients to improve their socioeconomic status and health.
3. This is a long-term goal but is unlikely to be achieved if there is no stable housing.
4. This will improve general health, but stable housing has a greater influence.

6.   C: Health and Wellness   T: Critical Thinking

1. Most cases of tuberculosis may be treated in the community. Unless the person is a danger to others due to the communicability of the tuberculosis, the client cannot be forced into hospital.
2. Directly observed therapy is recommended for clients, such as those at a shelter for the homeless, known to be at risk for noncompliance.
3. The medications do not come in sustained-release formulations.
4. This may improve compliance but is not the best method to ensure treatment. Drugs that have the fewest side effects may not be the most effective for the particular strain of tuberculosis.

7.   C: Health and Wellness   T: Critical Thinking

1. While it is true that homeless people are more likely to be injured on the streets, if they are adequately nourished, the injuries would not likely become chronic.
2. This may cause skin breakdown and injuries; however, with adequate nutrition, the lesions would not necessarily be chronic.
3. Communicability of pathogens is possible; however, improved nutrition would strengthen the immune system to fight the pathogens.
4. Major complications of protein–calorie malnutrition are delayed wound healing and increased susceptibility to infection from a compromised immune system.

8.   C: Health and Wellness   T: Application

1. Complementary therapies may be controversial, but fully informed clients may request them, and nurses can become trained and certified.

2. Reiki is a complementary therapy. Such therapies may be integrated into the scope of professional practice provided that the practitioners have the requisite knowledge, skill, and competency; the client has made an informed decision; and it is sanctioned by agency policies and procedures.
3. The nurse does not need to schedule Reiki treatments outside of her scheduled shift.
4. Olga is asking for Reiki treatment now, not after discharge.

9.   C: Health and Wellness   T: Knowledge

1. Complementary therapies are those therapies used in addition to and in conjunction with conventional, or traditional, Western medicine.
2. Therapies that are used instead of traditional or conventional medicine are called alternative therapies. Many of the same interventions can be complementary and alternative therapies.
3. Homeopathic remedies are a type of alternative or complementary therapy.
4. Most complementary therapies are considered to be natural; however, this is not the definition.

10.   C: Health and Wellness   T: Application

1. Mrs. Broadfoot has not stated that this is how she wishes to be treated. This is not individualized care.
2. This is client-centred, individualized care.
3. Mrs. Broadfoot should be providing information about her plan of care, not the family.
4. Clients should not all be treated the same. They should be treated as individuals.

11.   C: Nurse–Client Partnership   T: Application

1. While there are many Aboriginal dialects, most people of Aboriginal descent speak and understand English.
2. There is no indication from her admission diagnosis that she would be too weak to talk.
3. There is no indication that she is in denial.
4. Use of silence is a common communication phenomenon among members of Aboriginal communities.

12.   C: Health and Wellness   T: Application

1. Red meats have high iron content that is well absorbed by the body. There is no indication that Mrs. Broadfoot is vegetarian and will not eat a meat-containing diet.
2. Plant sources of iron are not as well absorbed as those in meat.
3. As in choice 2.
4. As in choice 2.

13.   C: Health and Wellness   T: Critical Thinking

1. This may be neither practical nor possible as it is not known how long it will take the family to arrive. And it is not known if they wish to view the body.
2. There will likely be an autopsy as this is an unexpected death, but the consent is not required.
3. There is no indication that this is necessary. If it were, it would be included in specific cultural death rites.
4. This is the most inclusive answer. The nurse should obtain information by telephone from the family or consult other cultural resources.

14.   C: Health and Wellness   T: Application

1. The Canadian Paediatric Society recommends that babies be positioned "back to sleep" to reduce the risk of sudden infant death syndrome (SIDS).
2. Research has found associations between SIDS and the prone position for sleep.
3. There is controversy regarding co-sleeping. While some studies do suggest it is a factor in SIDS, it is not as important as positioning infants on their backs.
4. Hats and booties are required only when babies are exposed to cold.

15.   C: Health and Wellness   T: Application

1. Early detection is secondary prevention.
2. Megavitamin therapy is controversial and in this situation "postdiagnosis" of disease.
3. Surgical treatment (appendectomy) is tertiary-level prevention.
4. Research has shown that remaining out of direct sunlight contributes to primary risk reduction of skin cancers.

16.   C: Health and Wellness   T: Knowledge

1. Although cancer remains a serious life-threatening illness, the overall incidence of cancer in children is low, and survival rates among children with cancer have improved significantly in recent decades. It is not possible at this time to prevent most cancers.
2. Asthma is common but not a common cause of death. Some asthma attacks can be prevented but not the disease.
3. Injuries are by far the most common preventable cause of child death in Canada.
4. Although some children have congenital anomalies that are incompatible with life, most are not preventable.

17.   C: Health and Wellness   T: Application

1. Research indicates that respiratory disease can be directly linked to contaminants in the environment.
2. The development of type 1 diabetes is not associated with exposure to environmental contaminants.
3. Juvenile arthritis is not directly associated with exposure to environmental contaminants.
4. Irritable bowel is not directly associated with exposure to environmental contaminants.

18.   C: Health and Wellness   T: Application

1. Research has shown that good body mechanics alone are insufficient to prevent back injuries among nurses.
2. Prolonged bed rest has significant health risks for the client.
3. Use of a mechanical lift is the only safe way to accomplish this transfer.
4. The gender of the nurse is irrelevant here; both men and women can sustain injuries.

19.   C: Health and Wellness   T: Application

1. Some herbal remedies are safe, but pregnant women need full information.
2. Ginger is known to have many medicinal properties.
3. Although knowledge about herbal remedies is incomplete, research about the pharmacology of ginger is available and can be shared with clients to enable their informed decision making.
4. The first trimester is a time of organogenesis; however, women need to be able to differentiate between benign, helpful, and harmful exposures.

20.   C: Nurse–Client Partnership   T: Critical Thinking

1. This statement assumes that the nurse knows what Mr. Drosinsky is feeling and may elicit an answer based on bravado.
2. Initially, Mr. Drosinsky may not want to reveal information about his sexual relationships.
3. This sentence assures Mr. Drosinsky that he is not unique in his possible concerns and opens up the discussion about sexuality.
4. While nerve-sparing surgery is effective, this is not a conclusion that can be definite.

21.   C: Health and Wellness   T: Critical Thinking

1. This is a factor in childhood obesity, but it is not the major factor.
2. As in choice 1.

3. As in choice 1.
4. Childhood obesity is a multifactorial problem that is likely a combination of genetics and environment. She may have inherited a tendency to be overweight, combined with the role-modelling of her parents that led to their obesity.

22.   C: Health and Wellness   T: Critical Thinking

1. Reducing fat alone does not cause weight loss unless total calories are restricted. It is difficult to sustain a low-fat diet because many people feel unsatisfied and hungry. It is better to replace bad fats with good fats.
2. Complex carbohydrates are essential to good health. Restricting sources of fibre and phytochemicals has the potential to adversely impact health.
3. Low-calorie diets are most appropriate for clients who need to lose weight quickly. Very-low-calorie diets may be deficient in some nutrients. Choice is restricted and boredom is common, so the diet is difficult to sustain.
4. By observing serving size from each food group, nutritional intake is balanced and calories are relatively controlled. This appears to be the optimal approach to achieving sustained weight loss.

23.   C: Health and Wellness   T: Critical Thinking

1. Because of Canada's geographical location, Ms. Blanche is not likely to obtain adequate vitamin D all year round. There is also the danger of skin cancer as a result of being exposed to direct sunlight.
2. Milk is a source of vitamin D, but it is not likely that Ms. Blanche will be able to drink enough to achieve 1000 IU per day.
3. Although in most cases it is best to achieve optimum nutrition through the diet, in the case of vitamin D, an intake of 1000 IU can best be achieved by taking a supplement.
4. Fortified cereals contain vitamin D, but it is not likely that Ms. Blanche will be able to eat sufficient to achieve 1000 IU per day.

24.   C: Health and Wellness   T: Application

1. All people, regardless of age, handicap, or life choices, are sexual beings. Sexuality involves one's inner sense of being male or female, gender role, and biological identity.
2. Many parents would disagree with this statement, preferring that their children learn about sexuality in the home.
3. The purpose of teaching children about sexuality is not to prepare them for sexual intercourse. This may be what the parents are concerned about.

4. This is not necessarily a Canadian value. All cultures must be respected with discussions about sexuality.

25.   C: Health and Wellness   T: Critical Thinking

1. The nurse needs to first find out the total hours of sleep to determine if there is a sleep deficit. Adolescents and young adults frequently do not have sufficient sleep due to daytime responsibilities and extracurricular activities that do not fit with their circadian rhythms.
2. This is important information, but the total number of hours of sleep is more pertinent.
3. As in choice 2.
4. This may be an underlying reason for Brendan's tiredness, but first the total number of hours of sleep must be determined.

26.   C: Health and Wellness   T: Application

1. There is no indication that the Waleses need assistance with walking.
2. Older adults are at risk for falls in the bathtub and shower, where the water causes the surfaces to be slippery. Grab bars assist people to safely get in and out of the bath.
3. These raise the height of the furniture to enable less difficulty rising from a sitting position. There is no indication that this is a problem for the Waleses.
4. This enables people to sit in the shower while holding the attachment to wash themselves. There is no indication that the Waleses are not able to stand in the shower.

27.   C: Health and Wellness   T: Application

1. Prepared chicken soup often has high levels of sodium, and most bagels are high in calories and have trans fats.
2. Delicatessen meat sandwiches have high levels of sodium. Caesar salad dressing is high in fat content.
3. Purchased bakery bran muffins often have high levels of trans fats. Cheddar cheese contains fat and is high in sodium.
4. This menu provides low-calorie protein, vegetables, and fibre and is low in sodium.

28.   C: Health and Wellness   T: Critical Thinking

1. This is good advice, but people are not always symptomatic at the beginning of a communicable disease. It is not as important as hand washing.
2. Hand hygiene is the single most effective action to stop the spread of communicable diseases.
3. Young children are at increased risk of having and transmitting communicable diseases, but this is not

the most important action.
4. It is now recommended that people cough or sneeze into their upper arm to redirect aerosol particles away from others. If a tissue is used, it must be disposed of appropriately, and the hands must be washed immediately afterward.

29.   C: Health and Wellness   T: Application

1. One way in which poverty adversely affects health is the inability to purchase needed medications. The nurse needs to determine that Ms. Price is able to buy Kyle's drugs. If not, the nurse may be able to access alternate means of obtaining the necessary medications.
2. This is not a therapeutic approach, particularly if Ms. Price does not have the financial resources to purchase the medications.
3. It is not within the scope of nursing practice or ethical to tell a client which drugs are not important for Kyle.
4. It is not within the scope of nursing practice or legal to change a physician's prescription.

30.   C: Health and Wellness   T: Critical Thinking

1. The most effective teaching and learning is experiential. A computer game, while it may be a good supplement, is not as effective as actual practice.
2. Rewards may work to reinforce learned behaviours but are not as effective as role-modelling as a teaching tool.
3. Role-modelling and actual practice are more effective.
4. Children learn best from role-modelling and practice.

31.   C: Professional Practice   T: Application

1. This is not a practical solution, and it is unlikely that this is a police responsibility.
2. This does not solve the initial problem of the contaminated needles and syringes and may encourage future use of the washroom as a place for the clients to inject.
3. The needles and syringes must be disposed of so they are not a hazard to others. The nurse, as an RN, has the knowledge to safely dispose of these articles.
4. This is not an ethical choice, particularly if the client was not the person who used the needles and syringes. The nurse may take the opportunity to later discuss the incident with this client.

Nursing Fundamentals and Clinical Skills

Maureen A. Barry, RN, MScN

Nurses need a strong knowledge base that is rooted in the best evidence in order to provide high-quality and safe care to clients in the hospital and in the community. This chapter is a review of the fundamental knowledge that underlies all nursing care and the clinical skills that are needed to enact this care.

VITAL SIGNS

BODY TEMPERATURE

Body temperature represents the balance between heat produced and heat lost by the body. Acceptable body temperatures range from 36–38°C, but there is not one temperature that is normal for all people. The average oral or tympanic temperature is 37°C for a healthy adult and 36°C for an older adult. Rectal temperatures are 0.5°C higher (37.5°C) and axillary temperatures are 0.5°C lower (36.5°C) than oral temperatures (Potter, Perry, Ross-Kerr, & Wood, 2010).

Core and Surface Temperatures

- Core temperatures (temperatures of the deep tissues) are relatively constant. Examples include rectal, tympanic, esophageal, pulmonary artery, and urinary bladder temperatures.
- Surface temperatures fluctuate depending on blood flow to the skin and environmental conditions. Examples include skin, axillary, and oral temperatures.

Temperature Measurement Sites

The temperature measurement sites used routinely are the mouth, rectum, axilla, and tympanic membrane. It is the nurse's responsibility to choose the safest and most accurate site for a particular client. Listed below are some advantages and disadvantages of the commonly used sites (Potter et al., 2010).

Oral Temperature

Oral temperatures reflect rapid fluctuations in the core temperature. They cannot be used in infants, small children, or confused, uncooperative, or unconscious clients. It is also necessary to wait 20–30 minutes before taking an oral temperature if the client has smoked or ingested hot or cold liquids or foods.

Rectal Temperature

Rectal temperatures are the preferred method of measurement in young children who cannot use oral thermometers but should not be used for newborns due to the risk of anal perforation. Some disadvantages are that rectal temperatures may lag behind a core temperature during rapid temperature changes, and they require privacy and the use of a lubricant.

Axillary Temperature

Axillary temperature is the safest site to measure temperatures in newborns. Disadvantages include a longer measurement time and a lag behind core temperature during rapid temperature changes.

Tympanic Membrane Temperature

The tympanic membrane is an easily accessible site that provides a core temperature quickly; however, it has greater variability in results than other core temperature methods due to user variability. Inconsistencies regarding the accuracy of tympanic membrane temperature (TMT) measurements in determining fever in infants and small children have been reported in the literature (Lanham, Walker, Klocke, & Jennings, 1999).

PULSE

Pulse is the palpable bounding of blood flow noted at various points on the body (Potter et al., 2010). Any artery can be used for checking the pulse, but the radial and carotid arteries are most commonly used as they are easily palpable. The carotid pulse is commonly used in emergency situations.

Common Pulse Rate Assessment Sites

The radial and apical locations are the most common sites for pulse rate assessment in adults.

Radial Pulse

Assessment of the radial pulse includes measurement of the rate (60–100 beats per minute in adults), rhythm (regular or irregular), strength or force (bounding, strong, weak, or thready), and equality (assessing radial pulses in both arms). If the pulse is regular, the nurse counts the pulse rate for 30 seconds and multiplies by 2. If the pulse is irregular, the nurse counts the pulse rate for a full minute.

Apical Pulse

The apical pulse is measured with a stethoscope. It is located at the fifth intercostal space at the left midclavicular line. The apical rate is used to count the heart rate in infants and young children where the heart rates are very rapid and difficult to palpate and count accurately at a peripheral site. The apical site is also used to auscultate heart sounds when an abnormal peripheral pulse is palpated.

Key Terms Related to Pulse

- **Bradycardia** is a heart rate below 60 beats per minute in an adult.
- **Tachycardia** is a heart rate above 100 beats per minute in an adult.
- **Dysrhythmia** is an irregular or abnormal rhythm.
- **Sinus arrhythmia** is a normal increase in heart rate associated with inspiration. It is more common in children but often found in adults.
- **Pulse deficit** is the difference between the apical and radial pulse rates. It is frequently associated with an abnormal rhythm and is a result of ineffective heart contractions where the pulse wave is not transmitted to the periphery (Potter et al., 2010). Apical and radial rates are assessed at the same time by two nurses to determine the presence of a pulse deficit.

RESPIRATIONS

Respiration is the means by which the body exchanges gases between the atmosphere and the blood, and the blood and the cells (Potter et al., 2010).

Assessment of Respirations

Accurate measurement of respirations requires observation and palpation of chest wall movement. A complete assessment includes assessment of respiratory rate (12–20 breaths per minute in adults), depth (deep, normal, or shallow), and rhythm (regular or irregular). The nurse counts respirations for 30 seconds if respirations are normal and for one full minute if abnormalities are suspected.

Key Terms Related to Alterations in Adult Breathing Patterns

- **Bradypnea** is regular but slow breathing at a rate of less than 12 breaths per minute (Potter et al., 2010).
- **Tachypnea** is regular but rapid breathing at a rate of greater than 24 breaths per minute (Potter et al., 2010).
- **Hyperpnea** is laboured, deep respirations at a rate of greater than 20 breaths per minute. It occurs normally with exercise (Potter et al., 2010).
- **Apnea** is the temporary cessation of breathing (Venes, 2002).
- **Dyspnea** is shortness of breath resulting in laboured or difficult breathing (Venes, 2002).
- **Orthopnea** is breathing that is laboured when the client is lying down but relieved if he or she sits up (Venes, 2002).

Pulse Oximetry

Pulse oximetry is the indirect measure of arterial oxygen saturation. The pulse oximeter measures pulse saturation (SpO$_2$), which is a reliable estimate of SaO$_2$ (the percentage of hemoglobin that is bound with oxygen in the arteries or the percentage of saturation of hemoglobin) (Potter et al., 2010). It is usually between 95–100%. Pulse oximetry is less accurate at saturations less than 70%. Some factors that affect accurate readings include peripheral vascular disease, hypothermia, hypotension, peripheral edema, jaundice, and the presence of nail polish (Potter et al., 2010).

BLOOD PRESSURE

Blood pressure (BP) is the force of the blood under pressure pushing on the walls of an artery (Jarvis, 2009). BP depends on the cardiac output (CO) and peripheral vascular resistance (R). BP is a good indicator of cardiovascular health.

Measurement of BP

- BP is recorded in millimetres of mercury (mm Hg) as the systolic over the diastolic reading (for example, 120/80). Optimal BP is less than 120/80.
- Systolic BP is the peak of maximum pressure when the left ventricle contracts and ejects blood under high pressure into the aorta.
- Diastolic pressure is the minimum pressure (resting pressure) exerted on the arterial walls when the ventricles relax.
- Pulse pressure is the difference between the systolic and diastolic pressures. For a BP of 130/90, the pulse pressure is 40 mm Hg.

Korotkoff Sounds

Korotkoff sounds are the sounds auscultated during BP measurement. There are five sounds; the first sound (onset of clear rhythmic tapping) and the last sound (disappearance of sound) are used for the systolic and diastolic BP readings in adolescents and adults (Jarvis, 2009).

Auscultatory Gap

The auscultatory gap is the temporary disappearance of Korotkoff sounds during auscultation of BP. It typically occurs between the first and second Korotkoff sounds and may range from 10–40 mm Hg. It is more common in clients with hypertension or older adults. It can cause underestimation of systolic BP or overestimation of diastolic BP (Jarvis, 2009; Potter et al., 2010).

Nursing Considerations Related to Measurement of BP

- Verify BP in both arms initially to compare and collect baseline data.
- Lower extremities (for example, the popliteal artery behind the knee) can be used if the arms are not accessible.
- Choose a cuff with a bladder size matched to the size of the arm. For BP measurements by auscultation, the bladder width should be close to 40% of arm circumference and bladder length should cover 80–100% of arm circumference (Canadian Hypertension Education Program, 2007b).
- Avoid applying the BP cuff to an arm with intravenous (IV) therapy, an arteriovenous shunt or fistula, breast or axillary surgery, a cast, or a bulky bandage.

Hypertension

Hypertension is persistently elevated BP and is often asymptomatic. It is the result of thickening and loss of elasticity of arterial walls. Hypertension is present when diastolic readings are greater than 90 mm Hg and systolic readings are greater than 140 mm Hg. The diagnosis of high normal BP is a diastolic reading between 85–89 mm Hg and systolic BP between 130–139 mm Hg. The diagnosis of high normal BP or hypertension is made on the basis of two or more BP readings on consecutive visits (Canadian Hypertension Education Program, 2007a).

Hypotension

Hypotension occurs when the systolic BP falls to 90 mm Hg or below (Potter et al., 2010). This can be a normal BP for some adults, but it is often associated with illness. Possible causes of low BP include pregnancy, medications (particularly drugs used to treat high BP), heart or endocrine problems, dehydration, severe blood loss, severe infection (septicemia), allergic reaction (anaphylaxis), or nutritional deficiencies.

Orthostatic Hypotension

Orthostatic hypotension or postural hypotension occurs when a person with BP within the normal range develops symptoms as well as low BP when moving to an upright position. Symptoms include fainting, weakness, or lightheadedness, as well as a drop in BP and a rise in pulse rate. Clients at risk for orthostatic hypotension include clients with dehydration, anemia, recent blood loss, prolonged immobility, or new medications, such as antihypertensives. To assess for orthostatic hypotension, the nurse records BP and pulse (P) with the client supine, sitting, and standing (Potter et al., 2010).

INFECTION PREVENTION AND CONTROL

INFECTIOUS PROCESS

Infection is the invasion of the body by pathogens (disease-producing organisms) and the reaction of the tissues to their presence and to the toxins generated by them. Signs and symptoms of infection may be local or systemic.

- Areas of localized infection may exhibit redness, swelling, and warmth or heat due to inflammation. Other symptoms may include discharge or exudate and pain or tenderness at the site.
- Systemic infections cause more generalized symptoms, such as fever, fatigue, and malaise. Other symptoms include enlargement of lymph nodes in the involved area, loss of appetite, nausea, or vomiting.
- Infections in older adults may not present typically as they tend to have lower body temperatures, decreased pain sensation, and a reduced immune response to infection. They may have advanced infection before it is identified.

Chain of Infection

The development of an infection occurs in a cycle that depends on the presence of all of the six elements described below: infectious agent, reservoir, portal of exit, mode of transmission, portal of entry, and susceptible host (Potter et al., 2010). Health care workers follow infection prevention and control practices to break the links in this chain so that infections will not develop.

1. Infectious agent (pathogen): An invading organism (such as a bacterium, virus, fungus, or protozoan)
2. Reservoir: An environment in which a pathogen can survive and may or may not multiply. The human body is the most common reservoir.
3. Portal of exit: A mode of escape from the reservoir (for example, the mouth, nose, or respiratory or gastrointestinal tract)
4. Mode of transmission: The method by which a pathogen is transmitted to a new host (direct or indirect contact, airborne, food, and so on)
5. Portal of entry: The means by which the pathogen enters a new host (such as via the respiratory tract or through broken skin or mucous membranes)
6. Susceptible host: Susceptibility depends on the individual degree of resistance to a pathogen.

NOSOCOMIAL OR HEALTH CARE–ASSOCIATED INFECTIONS (HAIs)

HAIs are infections acquired after admission to a hospital or another health care agency that were not present or incubating at the time of admission. Clients most susceptible are children and older adults and individuals with severe underlying illness, a weak immune system, poor nutritional status, or loss of skin integrity. Clients in intensive care settings are most susceptible due to the necessity for many invasive lines (including vascular access devices and urinary catheters) and the heavy use of antibiotics.

MEDICAL AND SURGICAL ASEPSIS

Medical Asepsis

Medical asepsis (clean technique) refers to procedures used to reduce and prevent the spread of microorganisms. Common examples include hand hygiene, using clean disposable gloves to prevent direct contact with blood or body fluids, and cleaning the environment and equipment routinely (Potter et al., 2010).

Surgical Asepsis

Surgical asepsis (sterile technique) includes all procedures used to eliminate all microorganisms, including pathogens and spores, from an object or area. Examples of surgical asepsis include (a) procedures in which the client's skin is punctured (such as IV insertion or injections); (b) nonintact skin due to injury or surgery; and (c) insertion of catheters or surgical instruments into sterile body cavities (urinary catheterization, peritoneal dialysis catheters, and so on) (Potter et al., 2010).

Key Principles of Surgical Asepsis

- A sterile object remains sterile only when touched by another sterile object.
- Only sterile objects may be placed on a sterile field.
- A sterile object or field out of the range of vision or an object held below a person's waist is considered contaminated.
- A sterile object or field becomes contaminated by prolonged exposure to airborne microorganisms.
- When a sterile surface comes in contact with a wet, contaminated surface, the sterile object or field becomes contaminated by microorganisms drawn from above or below by capillary action.
- Fluid flows in the direction of gravity.
- The edges of a sterile field or container are considered to be unsterile.
- Qualities such as conscientiousness or an "infection control conscience," vigilance, and honesty are very important in maintaining surgical asepsis (Kozier et al., 2004; Potter et al., 2010).

INFECTION PREVENTION AND CONTROL GUIDELINES

The risk of transmitting infection in the hospital is high, so health care workers must follow strict infection control guidelines to prevent and control the spread of infection. Guidelines consist of two tiers: one tier of precautions to be followed for the care of all clients, called Routine Practices, and a second tier called Additional Precautions to be used to contain or isolate pathogens in one area.

Routine Practices

Routine Practices (called Standard Precautions by the US Centers for Disease Control and Prevention [CDC]) are infection control precautions designed for the care of "all clients in any setting regardless of their diagnosis or presumed infectiousness" (Potter et al., 2010). Routine Practices "apply when a health care worker is or potentially may be exposed to (a) blood; (b) all body fluids, secretions, and excretions except sweat; (c) non-intact skin; or (d) mucous membranes" (Potter et al., 2010). Routine Practices include hand hygiene; use of personal protective equipment (PPE) such as gloves, masks, eye protection, face shields, or gowns; proper disposal of sharps; routine cleaning of client equipment; waste disposal; care of laundry; and routine environmental cleaning. A key element of Routine Practices is "to assess the risk of transmission of microorganisms before any interaction with patients/clients/residents" and then to decide on risk reduction strategies (Canadian Committee on Antibiotic Resistance [CCAR], 2007, p. 12).

Additional Precautions

Additional Precautions (called transmission-based precautions by the CDC) are designed to contain pathogens in one area, usually the client's room, so they are also called isolation precautions. These precautions are in addition to Routine Practices. There are three categories of precautions (airborne, droplet, and contact), and the category that is used depends on how a particular pathogen is spread.

Airborne Precautions

Airborne precautions are used for known or suspected infections caused by microbes transmitted by airborne droplets, such as measles, chickenpox (varicella), disseminated varicella zoster, and tuberculosis (TB). Barrier protection used with airborne precautions includes (a) a private negative-pressure room (door closed) and (b) a respiratory device (such as an N-95 respirator mask if the client has TB or when the client has the other conditions mentioned and the health care worker is not immune). A mask is also placed on the client if it is necessary for the client to leave the room (Potter et al., 2010; Silvestri, 2011).

Droplet Precautions

Droplet precautions are used for known or suspected infections caused by microbes transmitted by droplets produced by coughing, sneezing, or talking. Examples include diphtheria, rubella, influenza, pertussis, mumps, mycoplasmal or meningococcal pneumonia, scarlet fever, and sepsis. Barrier protection with droplet precautions includes (a) using a private room or cohorting clients (room door must be closed) and (b) using a mask (Potter et al., 2010; Silvestri, 2011).

Contact Precautions

Contact precautions are used for known or suspected infections caused by direct or indirect contact, such as colonization or infection with antibiotic-resistant organisms (AROs); major wound infections; respiratory infections such as respiratory syncytial virus (RSV); enteric infections such as *Clostridium difficile*; skin infections such as herpes simplex, impetigo, pediculosis, and scabies; and eye infections such as conjunctivitis. Barrier protection with contact precautions includes (a) using a private room or cohorting clients (the door can be open) and (b) using gloves and a mask when in contact with the client (Potter et al., 2010; Silvestri, 2011).

Hand Hygiene

Hand hygiene is the practice of removing or killing pathogens on the hands and maintaining good skin integrity (Ontario Ministry of Health and Long-Term Care, 2007a, 2007b, 2007c). Hand hygiene consists of the use of alcohol-based hand rubs or hand washing and is the most important method of preventing HAIs.

Alcohol-Based Hand Rubs

Alcohol-based hand rubs or alcohol hand antiseptics are the gold standard for hand hygiene. They are quicker, easier, and more effective than hand washing if used correctly.

Hand Washing

Hand washing must be performed when hands are visibly soiled. The mechanical action of washing, rinsing, and drying hands removes pathogens (Ontario Ministry of Health and Long-Term Care, 2007a, 2007b, 2007c). Hands need to be washed for 15 seconds, with special attention to areas that are frequently missed, such as around the nails, the thumb area, and between the fingers.

Personal Protective Equipment

PPE refers to clothing or equipment worn by health care providers for their protection. The use of PPE is part of Routine Practices when the nurse is likely to be in contact with blood, body fluids, mucous membranes, nonintact skin, body tissues, or contaminated equipment or surfaces (Ontario Ministry of Health and Long-Term Care, 2007a, 2007b, 2007c). PPE includes the use of any or all of the following: masks, gloves, gowns, face protection, or eye

protection. The choice of PPE is also dependent on the situation, procedure, or type of Additional Precautions required.

Multidrug-Resistant Organisms

Multidrug-resistant organisms (MDROs), also known as AROs or "superbugs," are "microorganisms, predominantly bacteria, that are resistant to one or more classes of antimicrobial agents" (Healthcare Infection Control Practices Advisory Committee [HICPAC], 2006, p. 5). The two most common are MRSA (methicillin-resistant *Staphylococcus aureus*) and VRE (vancomycin-resistant *Enterococcus*). During the last few decades, MDROs in hospitals have been increasing at alarming rates. Options for treating clients with these infections are extremely limited. Increased lengths of stay in hospital, costs, and mortality are associated with MDROs (HICPAC, 2006). There is strong evidence to suggest that MDROs are carried from client to client via the hands of health care providers (Duckro, Blom, Lyle, Weinstein, & Hayden, 2005).

Community-Associated MRSA

MRSA infections that are acquired by persons who have not been hospitalized within the last year or undergone a medical procedure such as dialysis or surgery are known as community-associated MRSA infections. "Staph" or MRSA infections in the community are on the rise and usually manifest as skin infections (pimples and boils) in otherwise healthy people (CDC, 2005).

MEDICATION ADMINISTRATION

The administration of medications is one of the primary responsibilities of nurses. It is important for nurses to have knowledge about the actions and effects of the medications that they give to clients. To safely and accurately administer medications, nurses also need knowledge about pharmacological concepts, human anatomy, growth and development, nutrition, and mathematics (Potter et al., 2010).

PHARMACOLOGICAL CONCEPTS

Drug Names

A drug has several different names, including a chemical, a generic, and a trade name:

1. The chemical name is a description of the medication's composition and molecular structure. This name is rarely used in clinical practice. An example of a chemical name is acetylsalicylic acid (Potter et al., 2010).
2. The generic or nonproprietary name is the first manufacturer's name for the drug, and this name is

protected by law. It is the official name that is listed in the *Compendium of Pharmaceuticals and Specialties (CPS)* and *Canadian Formulary (CF)*. An example of a generic name is aspirin (Potter et al., 2010).

3. The trade name, brand name, or proprietary name denotes the marketing name that the manufacturer uses to sell a medication. The trade name has a ™ symbol beside it (as in Bufferin™ or Aspergum™) indicating that the name is trademarked (Potter et al., 2010).

Classification

Each drug can be categorized in one or more subcategories called classifications. Drugs that affect the body in similar ways are in the same classification. Drug classification indicates "the effect of the medication on a body system, the symptoms the medication relieves, or the medication's desired effects" (Potter et al., 2010). Drugs can be in more than one classification if they have several different types of therapeutic effects, such as aspirin, which is an analgesic, an antipyretic, and an anti-inflammatory. Other examples of drug classifications include antibiotics and antihypertensives.

SYSTEMS OF MEDICATION ADMINISTRATION

Metric System

The metric system involves decimals and uses divisions and multiples of 10. The basic units are metre (length), litre (volume), and gram (weight). Most countries, including Canada, use metric as their standard of measurement.

- Common metric abbreviations for volume include L (litre) and mm (millimetre).
- Common metric abbreviations for weight include kg (kilogram); g (gram); mg (milligram); and mcg (microgram).

Household Measurements

Prescriptions to be self-administered at home are often written in household measures. Examples include cups, teaspoons, or pints for volume and ounces and pounds for weight.

Conversions and Calculations

Conversion Between Metric Units

To convert larger to smaller, multiply by 1000 or move the decimal point three places to the right. For example, to convert 1 g to milligrams, multiply by 1000 (1 × 1000 = 1000 mg). To convert smaller to larger, divide by 1000 or move the decimal point three places to the left. For example, to convert 500 mL to litres, divide by

1000 or move the decimal point three places to the left (500 ÷ 1000 = 0.5 L).

Conversions Between Systems

The nurse may find it necessary to convert weights or volumes from one system to another. Metric units may need to be converted to household measurements for home administration. The nurse must know or refer to an equivalence table in this case. For example, if the client is to take 10 mL of Dimetapp elixir at home, the nurse must know that 1 teaspoon (tsp) equals 5 mL and that 10 mL = 2 tsp. Common conversions include the following:

2.2 lb = 1 kg; 1 tbsp = 15 mL; and 1 tsp = 5 mL.

Dose Calculations

There are several methods of calculating medication doses. The following formula is useful for either solid or liquid doses:

$$\frac{\text{Dose Desired (DD)} \times \text{Amount on Hand (Q)}}{\text{Dose on Hand (DH)}} = \text{Amount to Administer (X)}$$

Example using the formula:
The doctor has ordered 4 mg of morphine to be given subcutaneously. The morphine is available in 10 mg/mL ampoules. Using the formula, the amount to administer would be 0.4 mL (4 mg ÷ 10 mg × 1 mL = 0.4 mL).

ROUTES OF MEDICATION ADMINISTRATION

Oral Route

The oral route is convenient and easy, but it has a slower onset of action. This route is avoided when the client has gastrointestinal alterations such as vomiting or reduced intestinal motility or has had gastrointestinal surgery.

- Sublingual tablets are designed for rapid absorption when placed under the tongue.
- Buccal administration involves placing the solid medication in the mouth and against the mucous membranes of the cheek until the medication dissolves.
- Enteric-coated tablets and sustained-released capsules delay absorption until the medication reaches the small intestine, so these medications cannot be crushed.
- Liquid medications in quantities of less than 5 mL should be measured in an oral syringe for accuracy.
- If possible, tablets and capsules should be swallowed with 60–100 mL of fluid.

Parenteral Route

Parenteral administration is injecting a medication into body tissues. There are four routes: intradermal (ID), subcutaneous, intramuscular (IM), and IV.

Intradermal Route

ID injection is an injection into the dermis just under the epidermis. It is used for the tuberculin skin test or allergy testing. The most common site is the inner forearm. The bevel of the needle is pointing up during the injection so that medication is less likely to be deposited into tissues below the dermis. It is given at a 5–15° angle. A small bleb (resembling a mosquito bite) appears. The area should not be massaged.

Subcutaneous Route

Subcutaneous (subcut) injections involve injecting medication into the loose connective tissue under the dermis at a 45–90° angle. Absorption of medication is slower via this route than via IM sites because adipose tissue is not very vascular. The most common sites are the outer posterior aspects of the upper arms, the abdomen, and the anterior aspects of the thighs. Only 0.5–1 mL should be given subcutaneously as subcutaneous injections can be painful. Injecting into a blood vessel during subcutaneous injections is very rare, so aspiration is not necessary. Pinch the skin before injection to elevate the skin and subcutaneous tissue above the muscle.

Subcutaneous Medications Requiring Special Consideration

- Insulin injection sites for diabetes should be rotated, with no one site being used again for one month to avoid the development of hard lumps and fat deposits.
- Injections of heparin and its derivative, low-molecular-weight heparin (LMWH), are best given in the abdomen. To prevent bruising, these injection sites should not be massaged.

IM Route

IM injections are given directly into the muscle at a 90° angle. This route provides fast absorption due to the greater vascularity of muscle. The muscle can also tolerate more viscous or irritating substances. From 1–3 mL can be given intramuscularly, depending on the site. The skin is pulled taut at the site to ensure that the medication is injected into the muscle. IM injections are associated with more risks, and it is important that bony landmarks are used for landmarking all IM sites. The common IM injection sites are the ventrogluteal, dorsogluteal, vastus lateralis, and deltoid muscles.

Ventrogluteal Site

The ventrogluteal muscle is the safest site and the preferred site for adults and children over 7–12 months of age. It is free of major nerves and blood vessels and has easily palpable bony landmarks. The bony landmarks are the anterior superior iliac spine (ASIS) and the trochanter. The heel of the hand is placed over the greater trochanter with the thumb toward the groin and the fingers toward the client's head. The index finger (on the ASIS), the middle finger (on the iliac crest in the direction of the buttock), and the iliac crest form the injection site triangle. See Figure 6.1.

Anterosuperior iliac spine
Site of injection
X

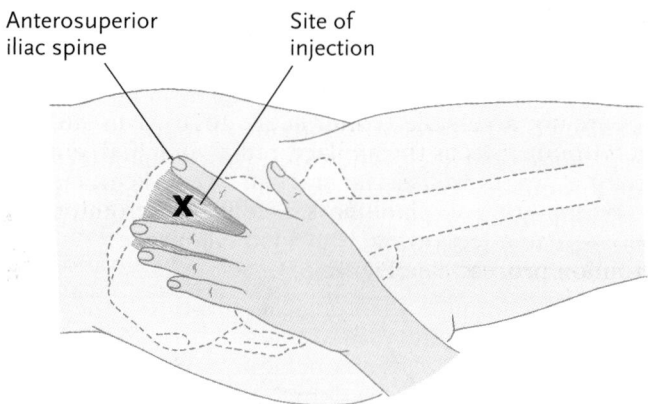

FIGURE 6.1 **Landmarks for the Ventrogluteal Site**

Source: Potter, P. A., & Perry, A. G. (2009). *Fundamentals of nursing* (7th ed., p. 752, Figure 35-24A). St. Louis: Mosby.

Dorsogluteal Site

The dorsogluteal muscle was the traditional site for IM injections but is no longer recommended. Bony landmarks are the greater trochanter and the posterior superior iliac crest (PSIC). There is risk of damage to the sciatic nerve as well as risk of injecting into the thicker subcutaneous tissue rather than the muscle in the area.

Vastus Lateralis Site

The vastus lateralis muscle is a site commonly used with infants and young children but may be used with adults as well. It is the preferred site for infants under 12

Femoral artery
Greater trochanter
Vastus lateralis
Knee
X
Rectus femoris

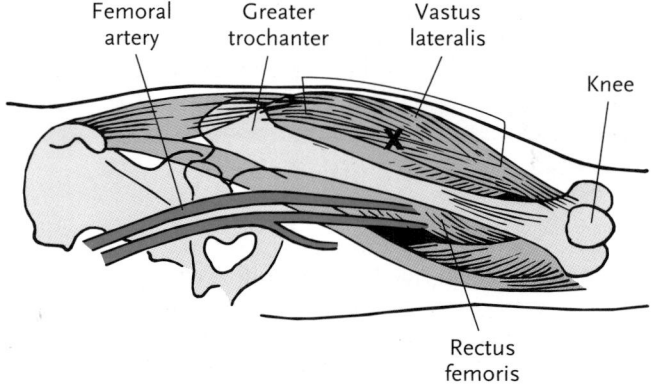

FIGURE 6.2 **Landmarks for the Vastus Lateralis Site**

Source: Potter, P. A., & Perry, A. G. (2009). *Fundamentals of nursing* (7th ed., p. 752, Figure 35-25A). St. Louis: Mosby.

months receiving immunizations (Potter et al., 2010). The muscle is located on the anterior–lateral aspect of the thigh. Bony landmarks are the trochanter and the knee. The site for injection is the middle third of the muscle, a handbreadth below the trochanter and a handbreadth above the knee. See Figure 6.2.

Deltoid Site

The deltoid muscle is an easily accessible site but is not well developed in all clients. This site should be used only for small medication volumes (less than 1 mL), when giving immunizations, or when other sites are not accessible (Potter et al., 2010). This site is not without risks as the axillary, radial, brachial, and ulnar nerves, as well as the brachial artery, lie in close proximity. The bony landmark used is the acromion process. The injection site is 3–5 cm below the acromion process. See Figure 6.3.

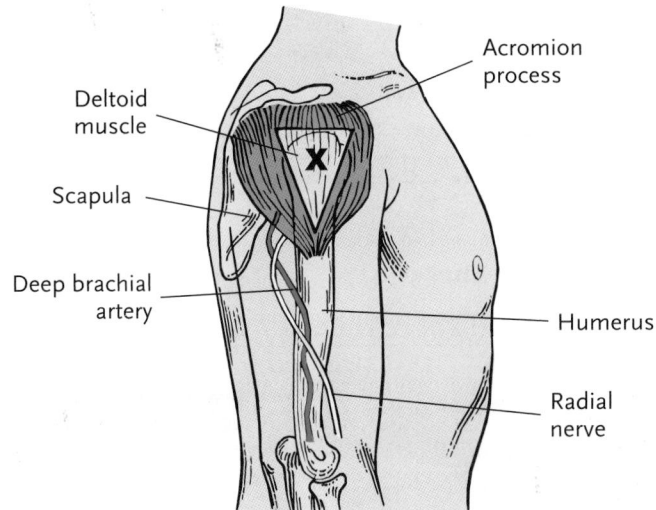

Acromion process
Deltoid muscle
Scapula
Deep brachial artery
Humerus
Radial nerve

FIGURE 6.3 **Landmarks for the Deltoid Site**

Source: Potter, P. A., & Perry, A. G. (2009). *Fundamentals of nursing* (7th ed., p. 753, Figure 35-26A). St. Louis: Mosby.

IV Route

IV injections are given directly into a vein. Medications are rapidly absorbed, and adverse reactions can happen immediately.

General Principles for Preparing Parenteral Injections

- When using a vial, inject air equal to the amount of medication that needs to be withdrawn into the vial to prevent negative pressure and to help with aspiration.
- When using an ampoule, tap the neck to force medication into the ampoule. Protect your fingers with an unopened alcohol wipe or a small gauze pad when snapping off the top of the ampoule.
- Change the needle after drawing up medication from an ampoule or vial.

- Use the appropriate-length needle to make sure the medication is deposited where it is intended to go.
- Aspirate for blood when administering IM injections. If blood is present, discard the syringe and medication and repeat the entire procedure.
- Inject medication slowly at a rate of 1 mL per 10 seconds to decrease pain and allow time for dispersion.
- The Z-track method is recommended for highly irritating substances given by IM injection, and there is some evidence that all injections should be given this way. Z-track injections seal medications into muscle tissue and minimize local skin irritation. The skin and overlying subcutaneous tissues are pulled laterally prior to the injection, the needle is left in place for 10 seconds, and the skin is released after the injection. This leaves a zigzag path that seals the needle path and locks the medication in the muscle.
- Never recap needles. Use a one-handed scoop technique if it is absolutely necessary to recap.
- Use safety-engineered needles or needleless systems to eliminate the risk of needle-stick injuries. Several provinces in Canada have mandatory regulations for safety-engineered devices under their occupational health and safety acts.

Table 6.1 Common Medication Administration Abbreviations

Abbreviation	Meaning
AC or ac	Before meals
ad lib	As desired
At bedtime	At bedtime (do not use abbreviation)
bid, BID	Twice a day
Daily or every day	Daily (do not use abbreviation)
gtt	Drops
PC or pc	After meals
po or PO	By mouth
prn	Whenever there is a need
q	Every
Qam	Every morning
q1h	Every hour
q2h	Every 2 hr
qid, QID	Four times a day
STAT	Give immediately
Tid, TID	Three times a day

Skin Route

Topical Medications

Topical medications are applied to the skin by painting them, spreading them over an area, applying a moist dressing, soaking body parts in a solution, or giving medicated baths. These medications generally have local effects.

Transdermal Medications

Transdermal medications have a systemic effect because they are applied topically via a transdermal disc or patch (such as nitroglycerine or estrogen) that secures the medication to the skin and stays in place for 1–7 days (Potter et al., 2010). The old transdermal patch must be removed before applying the new patch, and it is important to use gloves for application of the new patch to prevent accidental absorption of the medication through the nurse's skin.

Mucous Membrane Medications

Eyes: Medications for eyes are available in the form of eye drops or eye ointments. Have the client look up before administering ophthalmic medications. Expose the lower conjunctiva. If using drops, place them in the lower conjunctiva near the outer canthus. If using ointment, squeeze a ribbon of ointment into the lower conjunctiva, moving from the inner to the outer canthus. Do not touch the eye with the bottle or tube. Have the client blink a few times to disperse the medication.

Ears: Otic medications are available in the form of ear drops or irrigations. If the client is supine, ask him or her to turn onto the unaffected side to aid gravitational flow. If he or she is sitting, tilt the client's head toward the unaffected side. Straighten the ear canal by pulling the pinna up and back for adults or down and back for infants and children under 3 years. Have the client remain on his or her side for 2–3 minutes to allow the medication to reach the inner ear canal.

Nose: Nasal medications are available in atomizers or in drops. Clients should blow their noses first to clear any mucus. The client should be positioned with the head tilted back to aid in gravitational flow. The atomizer is squeezed quickly and firmly, or the correct number of drops is instilled in each nostril.

Vagina: Vaginal medications are available as liquid douches, creams, suppositories, or tablets. The client should void prior to receiving vaginal medication. The client should be in the dorsal recumbent position with hips and knees flexed if possible. The applicator or suppository may need to be lubricated with a water-soluble lubricant. The labia are separated, and the applicator is inserted approximately 5–7.5 cm (angled downward and back).

Rectum: Rectal medications are available in the form of suppositories. The client is positioned in a left Sims' position. The suppository is lubricated with a water-soluble lubricant and inserted approximately 10 cm (past the internal anal sphincter) toward the wall of the rectum in the direction of the umbilicus. The client is encouraged to hold the suppository as long as possible for the medication to be effective.

Inhalation: Inhalants are available primarily in the form of metered-dose inhalers (MDIs) or dry powder inhalers (DPIs). They are designed to produce local effects such as bronchodilation. An MDI delivers a premeasured amount of medication with each push of the canister. A spacer may be used with an MDI for the client who is having difficulty coordinating all the steps involved in self-administration. DPIs hold dry powdered medication and create an aerosol when the client inhales.

ABBREVIATIONS

Error-Prone Abbreviations, Symbols, and Dose Designations

The nurse should avoid unusual abbreviations and symbols and should always be familiar with the agency-approved abbreviation policy in the place of employment. Many terms are frequently misinterpreted and have been involved in harmful medication errors; these terms should not be used in communicating medical information (see Table 6.2).

NURSING STANDARDS FOR ADMINISTRATION OF MEDICATION: THE "7 RIGHTS"

To administer medications safely and effectively in all practice settings, the nurse needs to be aware of provincial legislation and regulation as well as practice standards. Administering a medication requires knowledge, skill, and judgement. To ensure safe medication administration, the nurse needs to be aware of the following "7 rights" of medication administration.

Right Medication (Drug)

- Administer only the drugs that you prepare. Do not leave medications unattended. The nurse who administers the drug is responsible if there is an error.
- Perform three checks to compare the label on the medication package to the medication administration record (MAR). The three checks occur before removing the medication from the drawer or shelf, as the medication ordered is removed from the container or drawer, and before returning the container to the storage area (or before opening at the client's bedside for unit-dose medications).
- Compare any inconsistencies with the original doctor's orders.
- Listen to the client's concerns if the client states that the medication is different.
- Know both the generic and the trade name for the medication. Consult the pharmacist if you are unsure of a medication.

Table 6.2 List of Error-Prone Abbreviations, Symbols, and Dose Designations

Term	Intended Meaning	Misinterpretation	Correction
μg	microgram	Mistaken as "mg"	Use "mcg"
U or u	Unit	Mistaken as number 0 or 4 (e.g., 4U seen as "40" or 4U seen as "44")	Use "unit"
OD or od	Once daily	Mistaken as "right eye" (OD: oculus dexter)	Use "daily"
q.d. or QD	Every day	Mistaken as q.i.d.	Use "daily"
SC, SQ, sub q	Subcutaneous	SC mistaken as SL (sublingual); SQ mistaken as "5 every"	Use "subcut" or "subcutaneously"
Trailing zero after decimal point (e.g., 1.0 mg)	1 mg	Mistaken as 10 mg if decimal point not seen	Do not use trailing zeros
"Naked" decimal point (e.g., .5 mg)	0.5 mg	Mistaken as 5 mg if decimal point not seen	Use zero before a decimal point when the dose is less than a whole unit

Source: Adapted from Institute for Safe Medication Practices. (2006). *List of error-prone abbreviations, symbols, and dose designations.* Retrieved January 17, 2013, from http://www.ismp.org/tools/errorproneabbreviations.pdf

Right Dose

- Know the customary dose and appropriateness for different ages and sizes. Consult a reference book or pharmacist if uncertain.
- All calculated doses or "high-alert medications" should be checked by another registered nurse. Make sure that double-checking is truly independent. High-alert drugs are drugs that have a high incidence of medication errors associated with their administration. Some examples of high-alert drugs are insulin, morphine, hydromorphone (Dilaudid), and heparin (Institute for Safe Medicine Practices Canada [ISMP], 2006).
- Pill cutters should be used to split pills, and crushing devices should be used to crush pills. Enteric-coated pills or sustained-release capsules cannot be crushed or split.

Right Client

- Use two unique client identifiers to identify your client. For example, check the MAR against the client's identification bracelet and ask the client to state his or her full name.
- Acquire a new ID bracelet for the client if one is missing, illegible, or incorrect.

Right Route

- Contact the prescriber if the route is not specified.
- Prepare injections from preparations designated "for injectable use only."

- Use special oral syringes (not compatible with IV tubing) for oral medications.

Right Time

- Give medications within 30 minutes of the time ordered unless agency policy specifies differently.
- Understand why a medication is ordered for certain times of the day and whether the times can be altered. For example, a medication is ordered every 8 hours around the clock to maintain a therapeutic blood level in comparison with a medication ordered TID and meant to be given only during the hours the client is awake.
- Exercise clinical judgement in determining the proper time for administration of certain medications, such as prn medications.

Right Documentation

- Chart the time administered as well as the site for injections with your signature.
- Sign the MAR at the bedside after seeing the client take the medication.
- Chart preadministration data such as BP, pulse, or blood glucose level.
- Chart the effectiveness of certain medications, such as prn medications (such as analgesics or antiemetics).

Right Reason

- Understand why the client is getting the medication and if it makes sense.

MEDICATION ADMINISTRATION FOR OLDER ADULTS

- Allow extra time for administration of medications to older adults.
- Assess functional status to see if a client will need help in taking the medications.
- Have older clients drink a little fluid before taking oral medications to ease swallowing and encourage them to drink 150–180 mL after medications to prevent the medication from lodging in the esophagus.
- Have clients sit up straight in bed and tuck in their chins to decrease the risk of aspiration when taking medications.
- Request liquid medications from the prescriber if the client has trouble swallowing large pills or capsules.

MEDICATION ERRORS

Medication errors are preventable events associated with the prescribing, transcribing, dispensing, or administering of medications. Many medication errors are not reported. Unreported errors mean that no one can correct their cause or reduce their incidence. Errors are rarely the fault of individual health care professionals but instead stem from failures of a complicated health care system. The best approach is a nonpunitive, multidisciplinary approach in which the process is targeted rather than the practitioner. This approach focuses on why an error occurred rather than blaming the person or people involved. When an error occurs, it should be acknowledged immediately and reported to the appropriate hospital personnel. Measures to counteract the effects of the error may also be necessary. Client safety is the first concern of the nurse. The nurse is also responsible for completing an incident report for the agency about the details of the incident. The nurse follows agency policy about disclosure to the client and client's family. See Chapter 7: Pharmacology and Nursing Practice for a more detailed discussion of medications.

ACTIVITY AND EXERCISE

BODY MECHANICS

Body mechanics are "the coordinated efforts of the musculoskeletal and nervous systems to maintain balance, posture, and body alignment during lifting, bending, moving, and performing activities of daily living (ADLs)" (Potter et al., 2010, p. 775). Proper use of body mechanics will conserve energy, reduce stress and strain on body structures, increase safety for the caregiver and the client, and reduce the possibility of personal injury. Repeated lifting and forceful movements associated with care of clients can lead to

work-related injury or illness, such as musculoskeletal disorders (MSDs). The activities of lifting, transferring, and repositioning clients place health care workers at risk for MSDs, especially back injuries. Body mechanics training has proven ineffective in preventing job-related injuries (American Nurses Association [ANA], 2006). Research has shown, however, that sound ergonomics programs in health care facilities can lead to reductions in injuries (ANA, 2006). The use of technology such as lifting devices and the use of special algorithms for each client who needs help to move are crucial to the success of ergonomics programs. Box 6.1 lists ways in which health care workers can prevent back injuries.

EXERCISE

Exercise is physical activity for the purpose of toning the body, improving health, and maintaining fitness. It can also be used therapeutically to correct a deformity or restore the client's body to a maximal state of health. Activity tolerance (the kind and amount of exercise or activity that a client is able to perform) must be assessed

---

Box 6.1 Using Proper Body Mechanics

- Arrange for adequate assistance when moving or transferring a client.

- Use algorithms to determine the safest equipment and client-handling technique to use for each activity or movement to be completed.

- When possible, use mechanical aids such as lifts, transfer chairs or boards, or pivot devices for lifts and transfers.

- Instruct clients about moving safely and encourage them to assist as much as possible to minimize the workload for the nurse.

- Keep the spine, neck, pelvis, and feet aligned. Avoid twisting.

- Flex the knees; keep the feet wide apart to broaden the base of support.

- Position yourself close to the client (or object being lifted) to minimize the load.

- Use the stronger, larger muscles of the arms and legs rather than those of the back.

- Slide the client toward you using a pull sheet rather than pulling or lifting.

- Tighten your abdominal and gluteal muscles in preparation for a move.

Source: Adapted from Potter, P. A., Perry, A. G., Ross-Kerr, J. C., & Wood, M. (Eds.). (2006). *Canadian fundamentals of nursing* (3rd ed., p. 957, Table 31-1). Toronto: Elsevier.

prior to planning physical activity for clients with health problems. Some of the factors that influence activity tolerance include pain, lack of sleep, prior exercise pattern, anxiety, age, and muscular or skeletal impairments (Potter et al., 2010). See Chapter 5: Health and Wellness for a more detailed discussion of exercise.

CLIENT SAFETY

RESTRAINTS

Types of Restraints

- Physical restraints are any manual method or any physical or mechanical device, material, or piece of equipment that reduces the ability of the client to move freely. Examples include locked geriatric chairs, restrictive side rails, belts, hand mitts, sheet ties, and chest restraints.
- Chemical restraints are medications given to restrict or manage a client's behaviour or to restrict a client's movement that are not a standard therapy or dose for the client's condition.
- Environmental restraints control a client's mobility. Examples include a locked room, as in the case of clients placed in seclusion.

Use of Least Restraint

Least restraint means that all other possible interventions have been attempted before the decision is made to use a restraint. Restraints are a temporary or short-term intervention, and the least restrictive method for the shortest duration possible is chosen. The optimal goal is a restraint-free environment. Research indicates that restraints do not actually prevent falls and injury and may even increase the severity of injury. They require a physician's order and are part of the client's individualized plan of care. Regularly reviewing the continued use of restraints is essential. It is important that the client and client's family or Substitute Decision Maker are informed and involved in the plan of care as well.

Assessment of Restraints

Routine assessment of a client in restraints is essential to prevent client injury. The restraint must be removed and the client checked and repositioned at regular intervals. Restraints should be tied with a quick-release tie rather than a knot. Proper placement of the restraint, skin integrity, pulses, and colour and sensation of the restrained part should be assessed every hour or according to agency policy. It is important to document this information.

Alternatives to Restraints

Alternatives to restraints include low-height beds, bedside mats and hip guards, bed sensors or monitoring devices, and the presence of a family member or paid companion to stay with the client at risk.

SEIZURE DISORDER PRECAUTIONS

Seizures are sudden, transient alterations in brain function that result from excessive levels of electrical activity in the brain and lead to a sudden, violent, involuntary series of contractions of a group of muscles (Potter et al., 2010). Seizures can vary in severity, and the client may or may not lose consciousness.

Nursing Interventions

- Protect clients from traumatic injury. If they are standing or sitting, lay them on the floor, bed, or other flat surface. If they are in hospital, make sure the bed is flat and the side rails are elevated and padded. Place a pillow or folded blanket under the head. Loosen restrictive clothing. Do not attempt to restrain clients but clear the area of hazards and articles that might harm them.
- Position clients for adequate ventilation and drainage of oral secretions. Clients need to be on a flat surface. Nothing should be inserted into the mouth except in the case of status epilepticus (a medical emergency in which there are continual seizures), and then an oral airway is necessary. If possible, turn clients on their side.
- Provide privacy and support following the procedure. Stay with clients, observing and timing the seizure. Immediately following the seizure, place clients in the recovery position to prevent aspiration and remain with them until they have recovered fully. Explain what happened and answer client questions. Some clients may experience postseizure confusion and may need to have explanations repeated.

HYGIENE

BATHING

During hygienic care, the nurse incorporates other activities, such as communication, physical assessment, skin and wound care, health teaching, assessment of self-care abilities, and range-of-motion (ROM) exercises. The nurse provides hygienic care according to the client's needs and preferences, taking into consideration cultural and developmental factors.

- A complete bed bath is a bath for clients who are completely dependent and require all their care to be provided by another person.
- A partial bed bath involves bathing only certain parts of the body (such as the face, hands, underarms, and perineal area) to refresh clients and because certain areas may be more prone to skin breakdown or odour if not bathed.

Guidelines for Bathing

- Provide privacy by exposing only the areas being bathed.
- Maintain safety by keeping side rails up and providing a call bell when you are away from the bedside.
- Maintain warmth by exposing only the areas being bathed and keeping bath water warm.
- Unless contraindicated, bathe limbs from distal to proximal areas (fingers to axilla) with long, firm strokes to promote circulation and venous return.
- Promote independence by encouraging the client to participate as much as possible.
- Anticipate needs by having all your equipment at hand.

Perineal Care

Special attention to perineal care is needed for clients with in-dwelling catheters, recent rectal or gynecological surgery, recent childbirth, morbid obesity, or urinary or fecal incontinence as these clients are the most at risk for infection. In these cases, the nurse performs perineal care even if the client is able to do so so that the nurse may assess the perineal area for skin breakdown or infection and is able to clean the area thoroughly.

NAIL AND FOOT CARE

Clients with diabetes mellitus or peripheral vascular disease require special nail and foot care as they are at risk of complications such as infection due to poor circulation, especially in their feet. Diabetics also have reduced sensation to the feet. The nurse should not trim the nails of a client with impaired lower extremity circulation before checking agency policy to see if a physician's order is necessary.

Foot Care Guidelines for High-Risk Clients

- Inspect feet daily and do not walk barefoot.
- People with diabetes should see a qualified health professional, such as a podiatrist, for a thorough yearly foot exam.
- Wash feet daily with lukewarm water but do not soak them as that can cause maceration. Dry well and do not put cream between toes.
- Do not cut corns or calluses or use commercial removers. Consult a podiatrist.
- File the toenails straight across and square and do not use clippers or scissors. Get help to cut nails if necessary.
- Avoid crossing the legs or wearing elastic stockings and knee-high hose that can impair circulation to the lower extremities.
- Wear clean socks and stockings daily that remain dry and free of holes.
- Wear properly fitting, nonslip shoes that fully cover the feet.
- Exercise regularly to promote lower extremity circulation.

- Do not use heating pads or hot water bottles on extremities.
- Wash all cuts immediately, dry thoroughly, and treat with a mild antiseptic (Potter et al., 2006; Registered Nurses' Association of Ontario [RNAO], 2007b).

ORAL HYGIENE

Oral hygiene includes the brushing and flossing of teeth as well as care of the mouth, gums, and lips. Oral hygiene is an important practice that maintains the health of the mouth, teeth, gums, and lips; enhances comfort; and stimulates appetite.

Mouth Care for Unconscious Clients

Unconscious clients are more susceptible to drying of the mouth because they are not eating or drinking, cannot swallow oral secretions, and frequently breathe through their mouths. Oxygen therapy can also be very drying to the mouth. Proper oral hygiene reduces the incidence of pneumonia, which can be caused by gram-negative bacteria aspirated from the mouth and into the lung (Potter et al., 2010). When giving oral hygiene, it is important to prevent the client from choking and aspiration. The client should be positioned on the side with the head turned toward the dependent side. Suction machine equipment should also be close at hand. If possible, a padded tongue blade can be used behind the back molars to separate upper and lower teeth. The mouth can be cleansed with a toothbrush or toothette moistened with water or hydrogen peroxide. A bulb syringe can be used to rinse the oral cavity; it should then be suctioned to make sure that no fluid is left in the mouth.

Stomatitis

Stomatitis is inflammation of the mouth that is caused by a variety of conditions, including viral infections, chemical irritation, radiation therapy, and chemotherapy. Gentle brushing and flossing is important. Clients with this condition should not use commercial mouthwash, drink alcohol, or smoke. Normal saline mouthwashes can be given every two hours if necessary, and a mild analgesic might be necessary for pain.

CARDIOPULMONARY FUNCTIONING AND OXYGENATION

SUCTIONING

Suctioning is the aspiration of secretions from the trachea and bronchial tree by application of negative-pressure suction (Saxton, Marshall-Henty, & Vernon,

2003). It is used to maintain a patent airway, collect sputum specimens, or stimulate a cough (Saxton et al., 2003). Clients should be encouraged to cough and suctioned only when necessary as it is uncomfortable and traumatic to the airway. Signs that the client needs to be suctioned may include one or more of the following: gurgling respirations, respiratory distress, low oxygen saturation levels, and coarse crackles on auscultation.

Types of Suctioning

- Oropharyngeal and nasopharyngeal suctioning is used when the client is able to cough effectively but is unable to clear secretions by coughing or swallowing.
- Orotracheal or nasotracheal suctioning utilizes a catheter that is passed through the nose or mouth to the trachea. This route is used when the client is not able to cough and manage his or her own secretions. It is a sterile procedure.
- Tracheal suctioning is done through an artificial airway, such as an endotracheal or tracheostomy tube. Surgical asepsis is maintained for new tracheostomies and endotracheal suctioning.

Principles of Suctioning

- Suctioning should not be performed routinely but should follow a comprehensive respiratory assessment that includes chest auscultation (Day, Farnell, & Wilson-Barnett, 2002).
- Lubricate the catheter with sterile normal saline, except for nasopharyngeal or nasotracheal suctioning, which requires the use of a water-soluble lubricant.
- Insert the catheter until resistance is met or the client coughs and then pull back 1 cm for tracheal suctioning (Day et al., 2002); insert 16 cm in adults for nasopharyngeal suctioning and 16–20 cm in adults for nasotracheal suctioning.
- Do not apply suction while inserting the catheter.
- While removing the catheter, apply suction intermittently and rotate the catheter to prevent injury to the mucosa. Do not suction longer than 10–15 seconds as this can increase the risk of mucosal damage and hypoxemia (Day et al., 2002).
- Wait 1–2 minutes between passes to allow the client to rest.
- It may be necessary to hyperoxygenate the client before and after suctioning by using a manual resuscitation bag, increasing the oxygen flow rate, or having the client take deep breaths, especially if the client has had signs of cardiopulmonary compromise in the past.
- Evaluate the client's response postprocedure. Suctioning can cause hypoxemia, hypotension, arrhythmias, and possible trauma to the mucosa of the lung.

TRACHEOSTOMY CARE

Tracheostomy care is the removal of copious, thick, tenacious, or dried secretions from the tracheostomy tube in order to maintain a patent airway, prevent infection, and prevent irritation.

Guidelines for Tracheostomy Care

- Provide tracheostomy care every eight hours.
- Suction to remove secretions from the lumen of the tube when necessary.
- If an inner cannula is present,
  - Remove the disposable inner cannula and replace it with a new one.
  - Care for a nondisposable inner cannula involves (a) removing and placing the cannula in hydrogen peroxide; (b) removing secretions from the cannula with a sterile brush; (c) rinsing the cannula with normal saline; (d) draining excess saline before inserting the cannula; and (e) locking the inner cannula in place.
- Clean around the stoma with saline; use hydrogen peroxide on a cotton-tipped swab to cleanse if necessary but rinse off well afterward.
- Change the tracheostomy tape or ties if necessary, being careful not to dislodge the cannula and to secure the tracheostomy tube by holding the cannula in place by lightly pressing with one finger and using a double square knot. The knot should be located on the side rather than at the back of the neck, where it would cause pressure.
- Insert a sterile tracheostomy dressing under the ties and faceplate to absorb drainage and to prevent pressure on the clavicle (Saxton et al., 2003).

CHEST TUBES

A chest tube is a catheter inserted through the thorax to remove abnormal accumulations of air, fluid, or blood from the pleural space or mediastinum. The chest tube drainage system returns negative pressure to the intrapleural space.

Commercial Drainage Systems

- The collection chamber collects drainage from the chest tube in a series of calibrated columns.
- The water seal chamber prevents atmospheric air from entering the pleural space. The fluid level will fluctuate with respirations until the lung is fully expanded. Continuous bubbling may indicate a leak in the chest tube system.
- If gravity drainage is insufficient, the suction control chamber is used to provide suction between 10–20 cm of water and will drain air and fluid from the chest cavity. Gentle bubbling in this section indicates that there is suction. (See Figure 6.4 for an example of a Pleur-Evac drainage system.)

Nursing Care of the Client With a Chest Tube

- Monitor drainage; notify the physician if drainage is greater than 100 mL per hour or if drainage becomes bright red or increases suddenly.

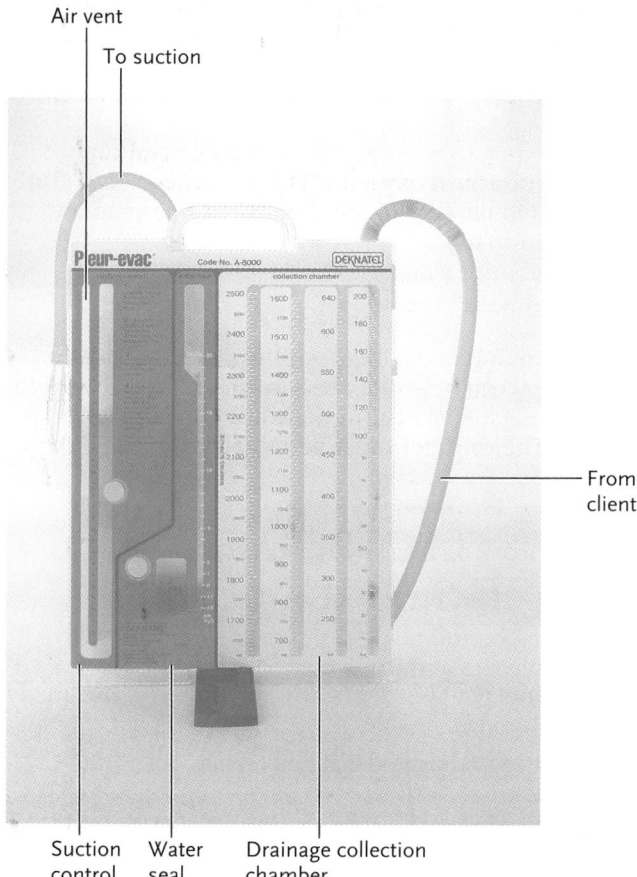

Air vent

To suction

Suction control

Water seal

Drainage collection chamber

FIGURE 6.4 **The Pleur-Evac® Drainage System, a Commercial Three-Bottle Chest Drainage Device**

Source: Ignatavicius, D., & Workman, M. (2010). *Medical-surgical nursing: Patient-centered collaborative care* (6th ed., p. 647, Figure 32-15). Philadelphia: Saunders.

From client

- Mark the chest tube drainage in the collection chamber at 1–4 hr intervals, according to hospital policy to monitor output.
- Ensure that the tubing is not kinked, all connections are secure, and there are no dependent loops.
- Maintain the drainage system below the level of the chest to prevent reflux and decrease the risk of infection.
- Maintain a sterile occlusive dressing at the insertion site to prevent an air leak.
- Turn the client frequently to promote drainage and ventilation.
- Observe for fluctuation of fluid in the water seal chamber; the level will rise on inhalation and fall on exhalation; if there are no fluctuations, either the lung has re-expanded or the chest tube is clogged (Saxton et al., 2003).
- The suction control chamber should be monitored to make sure there is gentle bubbling in the suction control chamber. Vigorous bubbling indicates an air leak, and the physician should be notified (Saxton et al., 2003).

- Encourage coughing and deep breathing every two hours with splinting of the chest area if necessary.
- Determine agency policy regarding clamping of chest tubes. Chest tubes are rarely clamped, and a chest tube should never be clamped without a written order from a physician. Clamping can cause a tension pneumothorax where air pressure builds up in the pleural space, collapsing the lung and creating a life-threatening emergency (Saxton et al., 2003).
- If the drainage system cracks or breaks, insert the chest tube temporarily into a bottle of sterile water to maintain a water seal and then replace the drainage system.
- If the chest tube is pulled out of the chest accidentally, pinch the skin together, apply an occlusive dressing, and call the physician immediately.
- Keep a clamp, a bottle of sterile water, and a sterile occlusive dressing at the bedside at all times. Clamps are kept at the bedside for special procedures such as changing the chest drainage system.

OXYGEN THERAPY

Oxygen is a drug and as such can have serious side effects, such as absorption atelectasis or oxygen toxicity. The goal of oxygen therapy is to relieve or prevent hypoxia (reduced tissue oxygenation despite adequate perfusion). Signs of worsening hypoxia include increasing tachypnea and dyspnea, skin colour changes (pale at first, then cyanotic), increasing tachycardia, hypertension, restlessness, and disorientation (Lewis, Heitkemper, Dirksen, O'Brien, & Bucher, 2010; Potter et al., 2010).

Methods of Oxygen Delivery

Low-Flow Devices

Low-flow devices provide oxygen in concentrations that vary with the person's respiratory effort (Lewis et al., 2010; Pruitt & Jacobs, 2003). When the total ventilation exceeds the capacity of the oxygen reservoir, room air is entrained. The final concentration of oxygen delivered depends on the ventilatory demands of the client, the size of the oxygen reservoir, and the rate at which the reservoir is filled. Most methods of oxygen delivery are low-flow systems. Examples of low-flow devices are nasal cannulas, the simple face mask, and reservoir masks.

Nasal Cannula

The nasal cannula (nasal prongs) is a low-flow device used at rates of 1–6 L/min, providing oxygen concentrations of 24% (at 1 L/min) and 44% (at 6 L/min) (Silvestri, 2005, p. 730). Flow rates above 4 L/min can be very drying for the nasal mucosa and cause irritation. The nurse also needs to be alert for skin breakdown over the ears and in the nares from nasal prongs that are too tight.

Oxygen Masks

Oxygen masks are devices used to administer oxygen, humidity, or both. Different types of face masks are described below:

- The simple face mask delivers 30–60% oxygen concentrations. It is used for short-term oxygen therapy or for the delivery of oxygen in an emergency (Silvestri, 2005). This mask is contraindicated for clients with CO_2 retention.
- The partial rebreather mask combines a mask and a reservoir bag. It provides an oxygen concentration of 70–90% with a flow rate of 6–15 L/min (Silvestri, 2005, p. 730).
- The nonrebreather mask provides the highest oxygen concentration of the low-flow systems. It has a mask and a reservoir bag and can deliver an oxygen concentration of 60–100%, depending on the client's ventilatory efforts (Silvestri, 2005, p. 730). It is commonly used for the client with deteriorating respiratory status who might need to be intubated. The flow rate is 10–15 L/min to maintain the reservoir bag two-thirds full.

High-Flow Devices

High-flow devices deliver oxygen at rates above the normal inspiratory flow and maintain a fixed F_iO_2 (fraction of inspired oxygen) independent of the client's respiratory pattern (Lewis et al., 2010; Pruitt & Jacobs, 2003). The most common example is the Venturi mask, which entrains room air to achieve a consistent, precise oxygen concentration. Other examples include aerosol devices such as the face tent and the tracheostomy collar or mask.

Venturi Masks

The Venturi mask, or air-entrainment mask, delivers oxygen concentrations of 24–55%, with flow rates between 2–14 L/min (Silvestri, 2005, p. 731). The Venturi mask is useful for delivering low, precise oxygen concentrations to clients with chronic obstructive pulmonary disease (COPD) (Lewis et al., 2010).

Oxygen Therapy for Clients with COPD

A client who has hypoxemia (low oxygen levels in the blood) and is a chronic CO_2 retainer may require low levels of oxygen delivery at 1–2 L/min. COPD clients can lose the stimulus to breathe if given too much oxygen as their stimulus to breathe—rather than a high CO_2 level in the average person—is a low arterial oxygen level. Careful, ongoing assessment when administering oxygen therapy to COPD clients is very important (Lewis et al., 2010).

Home Oxygen Therapy

- Indications for home oxygen therapy include a PaO_2 of 55 mm Hg or less via arterial blood gas analysis or an SpO_2 of 88% or less via pulse oximetry on room air at rest, on exertion, or with exercise (Potter et al., 2010). This therapy improves clients' exercise tolerance and fatigue levels and may assist with the management of dyspnea.
- Home oxygen is usually delivered by nasal cannula or transtracheal oxygen (TTO); a tracheostomy collar is used in the case of the client with a permanent tracheostomy.

Transtracheal Oxygen

A TTO system is a small catheter inserted surgically into the trachea between the second and third tracheal cartilage rings. It is a common home oxygen delivery method. The catheter must be replaced every 90 days (Pruitt & Jacobs, 2003).

FLUID, ELECTROLYTE, AND ACID–BASE BALANCES

FLUID AND ELECTROLYTE BALANCE

- Body fluids are distributed in two compartments: one containing intracellular fluids (intracerebral fluid, or all the fluid within body cells, comprising 40% of body weight) and the other extracellular fluids (ECF) (extracerebral fluid, or all the fluid outside body cells, comprising 20% of body weight) (Potter et al., 2006).
- Body fluids are regulated by (a) fluid intake and the thirst mechanism; (b) hormonal controls such as ADH, aldosterone, and renin; and (c) fluid output through the kidneys, the skin, the lungs, and the gastrointestinal system, with the kidneys being the most important in regulating fluid balance. This physiological balance is called homeostasis (Potter et al., 2010).
- Clients who are very young or very old as well as clients with chronic or serious illnesses are at greater risk for fluid, electrolyte, and acid–base imbalances.
- Assessment of fluid, electrolyte, and acid–base alterations includes collating data from the nursing health history and physical and behavioural assessments, as well as measuring intake and output, weighing the clients daily, and analyzing specific laboratory data, such as electrolyte results (Potter et al., 2010). See Chapter 8: Medical–Surgical Nursing for a more detailed discussion of electrolyte balance and homeostasis.

VENOUS ACCESS DEVICES

Venous access devices (VADs) are devices inserted into a vein for the purpose of delivering medication or fluids directly into the bloodstream. To determine the most appropriate type of VAD, the nurse needs to consider the following factors: prescribed therapy, duration of therapy, physical assessment, client health history, support system and resources, device availability, and client preference (RNAO, 2004).

Types of VADs

Peripheral Venous Access Devices

Peripheral venous access devices (PVADs) are designed for short-term use. There are two common types: short peripheral and midline. Short peripheral IVs are most commonly placed in the arm and are described in more detail under PVAD infusion therapy, in the section below. Midline catheters range in length from 7.5–25 cm and lie deep in the cephalic or basilic vein with the tip not extending past the axilla. They can stay in place for up to four weeks (Cook, 2007).

Central Venous Access Devices

Central venous access devices (CVADs) or central venous catheters (CVCs) are used for administering medications and solutions irritating to veins, for delivery of long-term therapy, and for rapid infusion of medications or large amounts of fluid. Some examples of CVADs are nontunnelled CVCs (Figure 6.5), peripheral inserted central catheters (PICCs), tunnelled CVCs (Figure 6.6), and implanted infusion ports (Figure 6.7). With the exception of the PICC device, these catheters are inserted in the central part of the body by way of the internal jugular, subclavian, or femoral vein. All central-line devices terminate in the vena cava immediately above the right atrium, where blood flow is very rapid at 2 L/min. The following is a discussion of the four types of CVADs (Cook, 2007):

Central catheter site
Right subclavian vein
Cephalic vein
Internal jugular veins
Clavicle
PICC site
Basilic vein
Superior vena cava

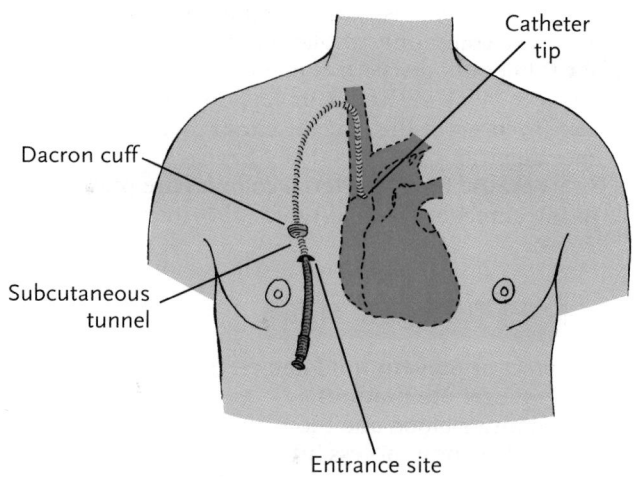

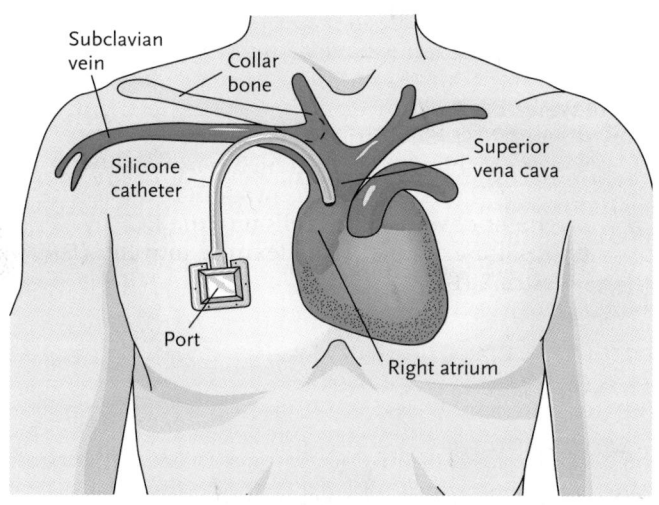

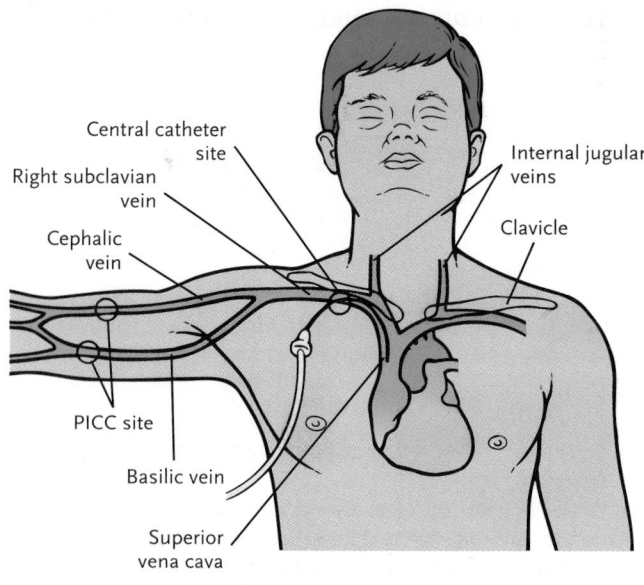

FIGURE 6.5 **Central Venous Catheter at Subclavian Site and Diagram of Peripheral Inserted Central Catheter (PICC) Insertion Sites (Basilic or Cephalic Vein)**

Source: Lewis, S. L., Heitkemper, M. M., Dirksen, S. R., O'Brien, P. G., & Bucher, L. (2007). *Medical-surgical nursing: Assessment and management of clinical problems* (7th ed., p. 966, Figure 40-7). St. Louis: Mosby. (Redrawn from Mahan, L. K., & Arlin, M. (1992). *Krause's food, nutrition, and diet therapy* (8th ed.). Philadelphia: Saunders.)

Catheter tip
Dacron cuff
Subcutaneous tunnel
Entrance site

FIGURE 6.6 **Tunnelled Central Venous Catheter Threaded into Superior Vena Cava**

Source: Perry, A. G., & Potter, P. A. (2009). *Clinical nursing skills and techniques* (7th ed., p. 771, Figure 28-6). St. Louis: Mosby.

Subclavian vein
Collar bone
Superior vena cava
Silicone catheter
Port
Right atrium

FIGURE 6.7 **Implanted Infusion Port and Central Venous Catheter**

Source: Perry, A. G., & Potter, P. A. (2009). *Clinical nursing skills and techniques* (7th ed., p. 772, Figure 28-8C). St. Louis: Mosby.

1. Nontunnelled catheters are inserted by a physician, and clients with these catheters must remain in the acute care setting. There is a high rate of infection with nontunnelled catheters because they are inserted percutaneously in areas that are warm and moist, such as the neck and groin. For this reason, they are not left in place for as long as other CVADs.
2. Tunnelled catheters, such as Hickman catheters, are inserted in the operating room under a local anaesthetic and can be left in for years. They are hard to disguise and require daily care but can be cared for in the home setting.
3. Implanted ports (for example, Port-A-Caths) require insertion in the operating room with local

anaesthesia and also can be left in place for years. They are commonly implanted in the chest.

4. PICC lines are placed most commonly in peripheral veins, such as the basilic or cephalic veins. They are easy to insert at the bedside either by doctors or specially trained nurses. They have a low infection rate because fewer bacterial colonies are present in the antecubital fossa (Cook, 2007; Lewis et al., 2010).

Purpose of Infusion Therapy

- To correct or prevent fluid and electrolyte imbalances
- To administer medications
- To administer blood and blood products
- To provide venous access in emergency situations
- To correct or prevent nutritional imbalances

Types of Solutions

1. Isotonic solutions have the same osmolality as body fluids. They are used most commonly for ECF replacement, for example, 0.9%, or normal, saline (NS) or 5% dextrose in water (D_5W) (Silvestri, 2011).
2. Hypotonic solutions have a lower osmolality than body fluids. These solutions cause the movement of water into cells by osmosis, for example, 0.45% saline (½ NS) (Silvestri, 2011).
3. Hypertonic solutions have a higher osmolality than body fluids. They concentrate ECF and cause movement of water from cells into the ECF by osmosis, for example, 10% dextrose in water ($D_{10}W$) (Silvestri, 2011).

Nursing Care of Clients with PVAD Infusion Therapy

Initiation of Infusion Therapy

- Common IV sites are the veins in the hand, forearm, and antecubital fossa.
- The IV infusion is started by venipuncture through the use of a butterfly (metal) needle or an over-the-needle plastic catheter.
- The IV infusion is started distally to provide the option of proceeding up the extremity if necessary later.
- The nurse needs to check the IV solution against the prescriber's orders for the type, amount, and percentage of solution and the rate of flow.

Regulation of Infusion Flow Rate

- The nurse must regulate the rate of infusion according to the prescriber's orders.
- The nurse calculates the infusion rate to prevent too slow or too rapid administration of IV fluids. Fluids that run by gravity are adjusted by means of a regulator or roller clamp. An electronic infusion pump can also regulate the rate that is preset by the nurse.
- For IV infusions running by gravity, the nurse calculates the minute flow rate or drop rate based on

the drop factor of the infusion, set using this formula: Total Volume × Drop Factor ÷ Infusion Time in Minutes = Drop Rate

For example, the minute flow rate or drop rate for an IV running at 100 mL/hr with a drop factor of 15 gtt/mL would be:

$$\frac{100 \text{ mL} \times 15 \text{ gtt}}{60 \text{ min}} = 25 \text{ gtt/min}$$

Maintenance of Infusion Therapy

- The venipuncture site should be changed every 48–72 hr, the IV dressing every 72 hr, and the IV tubing every 24–72 hr (depending on agency policy).
- Incompatibilities between certain solutions and medications can occur.
- Assess the "rights" for administration of medications.
- Assess the IV site and equipment regularly for complications.

INTERMITTENT INFUSION SETS OR SALINE LOCKS

Saline locks are used when intravascular access is desired for intermittent administration of medications by IV bolus (push) or IV piggyback (secondary administration of medications). It allows the client to be free from an IV line except when medication must be given, and it allows emergency IV access if necessary. Patency is maintained by periodic flushing with 1–3 mL of normal saline (depending on agency policy).

Complications of Infusion Therapy

Common complications of infusion therapy are infiltration, phlebitis (inflammation of the vein), infection, fluid (circulatory) overload, and bleeding or bruising at the site.

BLOOD TRANSFUSIONS

Purpose of Blood Transfusions

- To restore blood volume after hemorrhage, surgery, or trauma
- To restore the oxygen-carrying capacity of the blood and to increase hemoglobin levels in severe anemias
- To replace specific blood components, such as clotting factors, platelets, or albumin

Nursing Care of Clients Receiving a Blood Transfusion

- Check that the blood or blood components have been typed and cross-matched, indicating that the blood of the donor and the recipient are compatible.

- Blood should never be administered straight from the refrigerator and should be returned to the blood bank fridge if not used immediately.
- Baseline vital signs (including temperature) should be taken preadministration and frequently throughout administration (check agency policy).
- An IV with NS infusing through a blood administration set with a special filter is used to start the infusion.
- Maintain Routine Practices (Standard Precautions) when handling blood and IV equipment.
- The client needs to sign a blood administration consent form in many agencies.
- Before beginning the infusion, two nurses verify the blood type, Rh factor, client and blood numbers, and expiration date of the blood.
- Invert the container gently to suspend the red blood cells (RBCs) within the plasma.
- Stay with the client for the first 15 minutes as that is when a reaction most often occurs.
- Observe for signs of a hemolytic reaction, which generally occur early in the transfusion (within the first 5–15 min). Signs include shivering, headache, lower back pain, increased pulse and respiratory rate, hemoglobinuria, oliguria, and hypotension (Saxton et al., 2003).
- Observe for signs of a febrile reaction (usually within 30 minutes). Signs include shaking, headache, elevated temperature, back pain, confusion, and hematemesis (Saxton et al., 2003).
- Observe for signs of an allergic reaction, such as hives, wheezing, pruritis, and joint pain (Saxton et al., 2003).
- If any reaction occurs, stop the infusion immediately and maintain patency of the IV with normal saline; monitor vital signs; notify the physician; stay with the client; and prepare to administer emergency drugs and to perform cardiopulmonary resuscitation if necessary. A urine sample may be needed to determine the presence of hemoglobin as a result of RBC hemolysis.

PAIN AND COMFORT

Pain is an "unpleasant sensory and emotional experience associated with actual or potential tissue damage, or described in terms of such damage" (Subcommittee on Taxonomy, 1986). Pain is subjective, and the client's self-report about pain is key to effective management. The process between an injury and perceiving pain involves four steps: transduction, transmission, modulation, and perception.

TYPES OF PAIN

Nociceptive and Neuropathic Pain

Pain is categorized as nociceptive, neuropathic, or both, according to underlying pathology. Nociceptive pain is caused by damage to somatic or visceral tissue.

Examples include pain from a surgical incision, a broken leg, arthritis, or angina (Lewis et al., 2010). Neuropathic pain is caused by damage to nerve cells or changes in spinal cord processing and is described as burning, shooting, or stabbing. This type can be difficult to treat. Examples include phantom limb pain and diabetic neuropathies (Lewis et al., 2010).

Acute and Chronic or Persistent Pain

Acute pain usually has a sudden onset and diminishes over time as healing occurs. Examples include postoperative pain, labour pain, or angina. Chronic pain persists beyond the normal time for healing. It can be disabling and is often accompanied by depression and anxiety.

PAIN SCALES

Descriptive scales are an objective means of measuring pain intensity. Various scales can be used for adults and children to rate pain before and after interventions. The most common one used with adults is the numeric rating scale, with which clients rate their pain on a scale of 0 to 10 (0 being no pain; 10 being the most severe pain ever experienced). Pain should be rated before and after administration of analgesics.

BEST PRACTICES FOR PAIN CONTROL

- Practice guidelines are available that recommend systematic ways of using analgesics. One example is the analgesic ladder developed by the World Health Organization (WHO). This plan uses a three-step ladder approach, depending on the severity of the pain (WHO, 1996).
- Using a regular schedule of analgesic administration ("around the clock") according to the duration of action of the drug is more effective than a prn schedule in controlling pain (RNAO, 2007a).
- Patient- or client-controlled analgesia (PCA) is an infusion pump that is programmed for dose and time intervals, allowing clients to control analgesic administration without overdose. The PCA pump can be IV, subcutaneous, or epidural and is a good short-term option for postoperative pain. Research has shown that PCA clients are more satisfied with their postoperative pain control, have fewer pulmonary problems, ambulate earlier, and have shorter hospital stays (D'Arcy, 2008).

Nonpharmacological Methods of Pain Relief

These methods can be used alone or in combination with pharmacological methods. Examples include progressive relaxation, guided imagery, biofeedback, transcutaneous electrical nerve stimulation (TENS), music therapy, acupressure, massage, and the application of heat or cold.

NUTRITION

Nutrients are the elements necessary for body processes and functions. A balanced diet with carbohydrates, fats, proteins, vitamins, and minerals provides the essential nutrients to carry out the body's normal physiological functioning.

- Carbohydrates are the main source of energy in the diet.
- Proteins are made from amino acids and are essential for the growth, maintenance, and repair of body tissue.
- Fats (lipids) are the most calorie-dense nutrient and are composed of triglycerides and fatty acids. They provide a concentrated source and stored form of energy.
- Vitamins facilitate metabolism of proteins, fats, and carbohydrates and are essential for normal metabolism. Vitamin content is usually highest in fresh foods that are used quickly and exposed minimally to cooking, storage, preparation, and processing.
- Fat-soluble vitamins A, D, E, and K can be stored in the body and are not easily destroyed by cooking or storage.
- Water-soluble vitamins (B complex and C) are not stored in the body, are easily destroyed by cooking, and can be excreted in the urine.
- Vitamin K is important in the production of prothrombin (necessary for the coagulation of blood).
- Vitamin C functions in the production of collagen, which is important in wound healing.
- Vitamin A is important in the maintenance of eyesight and epithelial linings.
- Minerals are essential to the body as catalysts in biochemical reactions. Examples include calcium, chloride, magnesium, phosphorus, potassium, sodium, iron, and zinc (Potter et al., 2010).

EATING WELL WITH CANADA'S FOOD GUIDE

Eating Well With Canada's Food Guide helps clients to make appropriate nutritional choices from the four basic food groups: vegetables and fruit; grain products; milk and alternatives; and meat and alternatives. The different sizes of the arcs in the rainbow represent the proportion of each of the four food groups that is recommended for healthy eating. The vegetables and fruit food group is the most prominent arc, emphasizing the important role these foods play. The recommendations are based on age and gender. Guidelines for dietary change advocate reducing the intake of fats, saturated fats, sodium, refined sugar,

and cholesterol and increasing the intake of complex carbohydrates and fibre. See Chapter 5 for the Canada Food Guide, Figure 5.5 on p. 101, and more detailed nutritional information.

THERAPEUTIC DIETS

A therapeutic diet is a diet intended to treat disease or help to manage a medical condition. See Table 6.3 for types of therapeutic diets, indications for use of these diets, and foods permitted on the diets.

ENTERAL NUTRITION

Enteral nutrition (EN) delivers liquid nutrients into the gastrointestinal tract via a tube. EN is used when the client cannot ingest food but can still digest and absorb nutrients.

Types of Feeding Tubes

- Nasogastric (NG) tubes are inserted through the nose to the stomach (see the section on bowel elimination, pp. 149–150, for more details).
- Nasoenteral, or small-bore, feeding tubes (such as the Keofeed and Dobbhoff tubes) are placed through the nose into the stomach and then moved into the duodenum. Placement is checked by radiography prior to commencing tube feedings.

Surgically Placed Feeding Tubes

- A gastrostomy tube (G-tube) is placed directly into the stomach through the abdominal wall and sutured in place.
- A jejunostomy tube (J-tube) is inserted directly into the jejunum for clients with pathological conditions of the upper gastrointestinal tract.

Feeding Tubes Inserted by Endoscopy

In this procedure, the stomach or the jejunum is punctured during a laporotomy or an endoscopy procedure that does not require a general anaesthetic. The two types are PEG (percutaneous endoscopic gastrostomy) and PEJ (percutaneous endoscopic jejunostomy).

Nursing Care of Clients with EN

- The head of the bed should be elevated 30° at all times to prevent regurgitation of feedings and aspiration into the lungs.
- Monitor the client for abdominal distension and check the residual contents of the stomach regularly to see if the client is tolerating the feeds. Aspirate all stomach contents (residual), measure the amount, and return the contents to the stomach if the residual is less than 100–150 mL (depending on agency policy). If the residual

Table 6.3 Therapeutic Diets

Type of Diet	Uses of Diet	Foods Permitted
Clear Fluids	Often a postoperative diet, also used for diarrhea or initial feeding after complete bowel rest	Broth, coffee, tea, carbonated beverages, clear fruit juices, Popsicles, Jell-O
Thickened Fluids	Used for clients who have dysphagia (difficulty swallowing) and are at risk for aspiration	Any liquid can be thickened with thickening agents
Full Fluids	Can be used after clear fluids following surgery. Also for clients who are unable to chew or swallow.	Clear fluids, plus smooth-textured dairy products, puddings and custards, refined cooked cereals, ice cream, and all fruit juices
Puréed	Can be used for client with dental problems or problems swallowing or chewing	All of the above, with the addition of scrambled eggs, puréed meats, vegetables, fruits, mashed potatoes and gravy
Mechanical Soft	Can be used for client with dental problems, problems swallowing or chewing, and mouth ulcerations	All of the above, with the addition of foods such as ground or finely diced meats, flaked fish, cheese, rice, potatoes, cooked vegetables, bananas, soups, etc.
High Fibre	Can be used for clients with constipation or to prevent constipation	Addition of fresh uncooked fruits, steamed vegetables, bran, oatmeal, and dried fruits
Low Sodium	For control of hypertension (no added salt [NAS]) and to reduce edema in clients with heart failure	Can vary from NAS to severe sodium restrictions
Low Cholesterol	Used for clients with high cholesterol levels	Restrictions on foods high in cholesterol, such as eggs, regular cheese and ice cream, organ meats, fried food, various fast foods, etc.
Diabetic	Used for diabetic clients	Clients with diabetes follow a healthy diet recommended for the general population as outlined in *Eating Well With Canada's Food Guide*. In hospitals, the meals are often labelled "diabetic" or "no added sugar" to indicate that the meal plan follows the Canadian Diabetes Association's current nutritional guidelines for diabetics.
Regular		No restrictions

Source: Adapted from Potter, P. A., Perry, A. G., Ross-Kerr, J. C., & Wood, M. (Eds.). (2010). *Canadian fundamentals of nursing* (Rev. 4th ed., p. 1070, Box 43-8). Toronto: Elsevier.

volume is more than 150 mL, it indicates delayed gastric emptying, which places the client at a higher risk of aspiration, and the feeds should be withheld.

- Check placement of the tube by (1) aspirating the gastric contents; (2) checking the pH with litmus paper; or (3) injecting 5–10 mL of air and listening for gurgling or a "whoosh" over the stomach region (see the detailed procedure under Nasogastric Tubes in the Bowel Elimination section, p. 150).
- Assess bowel sounds; if absent, withhold feeds and notify the physician.
- Feeding pumps may be used for continuous feeds.
- For bolus feeds (300–400 mL of formula every 3–6 hr), leave the client in the high Fowler's position for 30 minutes after feeding.
- Change the feeding container and tubing every 24 hours to prevent bacterial growth.
- Do not hang more than four hours' worth of formula to prevent bacterial growth.
- Flush with 30–60 mL of water (according to agency policy) with an irrigation syringe after feeding.

Complications of EN

Complications of EN include aspiration, diarrhea, vomiting, abdominal distension, and clogging of the feeding tube.

PARENTERAL NUTRITION

Parenteral nutrition (PN) is a form of specialized nutrition support in which nutrients are provided intravenously to provide a positive nitrogen balance. PN can be administered in the home as well as the hospital.

Types of PN

- Peripheral parenteral nutrition (PPN) is the administration of isotonic lipid and amino acid solutions through a peripheral vein.
- Total parenteral nutrition (TPN) is administration of carbohydrates in the form of dextrose, fats in special emulsified form, proteins in the form of amino acids, vitamins, minerals, and water. High-osmolality solutions (25% dextrose) are administered in conjunction with 5–10% amino acids, electrolytes, minerals, and vitamins. TPN is administered via a central line (usually the superior vena cava) (Potter et al., 2006; Saxton et al., 2003).
- Intralipid therapy is an infusion of 10–20% fat emulsion that provides essential fatty acids. It is usually administered at the same time as PPN or TPN (Saxton et al., 2003).
- Total nutrient admixture (TNA) is a combination of dextrose, amino acids, and lipids in one container. TNA is administered over 24 hours through a central line (Saxton et al., 2003).

Indications for PN

Indications for initiation of PN include a nonfunctional gastrointestinal tract (for example, following bowel surgery; trauma to the head, neck, or abdomen; intestinal obstruction; chemotherapy; or radiation therapy); extended bowel rest (for example, due to inflammatory bowel disease, severe diarrhea, or pancreatitis); or preoperative TPN (such as in the case of severe malnutrition or preoperative bowel rest).

Nursing Care of Clients with PN

- Infuse TPN through a large vein, such as the subclavian, due to the high osmolarity of the solution.
- Ensure proper placement of the line after insertion and prior to starting TPN. Placement should be confirmed by X-ray as accidental pneumothorax can occur during insertion.
- Regulate flow carefully using an infusion pump. Rapid infusion can cause movement of fluid into the intravascular compartment, causing dehydration, circulatory overload, and hyperglycemia (Saxton et al., 2003). Slow infusion can result in hypoglycemia as the body adapts to the high osmolarity by secreting more insulin; for this reason, therapy is never terminated abruptly (Saxton et al., 2003).
- Use aseptic technique when handling the infusion and IV tubing or when changing dressings. Check agency policy regarding the frequency of tubing change (usually every 24 hours) and dressing change (usually every 48 hours).
- Use an in-line filter to remove crystals from the TPN solution.
- Record daily weights and monitor blood glucose levels frequently.

- Check laboratory reports daily (glucose, creatinine, blood urea nitrogen, and electrolytes); also check serum lipids and liver function if lipids are administered (Saxton et al., 2003).
- Monitor temperature every four hours as infection is the most common TPN complication; obtain cultures of blood, urine, and sputum (according to agency policy) to rule out other sources of infection if the client develops a fever (Saxton et al., 2003).

URINARY ELIMINATION

KEY TERMS RELATED TO URINARY ELIMINATION

- **Anuria** is the absence of urine formation.
- **Diuresis** is the passage of large amounts of urine.
- **Dysuria** is painful or difficult urination.
- **Frequency** is voiding at frequent intervals (less than two-hour intervals) (Potter et al., 2006).
- **Hematuria** is the presence of blood in the urine.
- **Nocturia** is excessive or frequent urination after going to bed.
- **Oliguria** is urine output of less than 400 mL/day (Venes, 2002).
- **Polyuria** is voiding large amounts of urine.

ALTERED URINARY ELIMINATION

Urinary Retention

Urinary retention is the marked accumulation of urine in the bladder as a result of the inability of the bladder to empty. Retention can occur in the postoperative period due to the effect of the anaesthetic. Prolonged retention can lead to stasis of urine in the bladder and increased risk of a urinary tract infection (UTI). Signs and symptoms of retention include any of the following: frequent voiding of small amounts, absence of urine output with palpable tender bladder, dull sound on percussion, sensation of bladder fullness, abdominal discomfort, restlessness, diaphoresis, and dribbling.

Urinary Tract Infection

UTI is the most common HAI due to the frequency of urinary catheterizations. If left untreated, UTIs can spread to the kidneys, causing kidney infection and eventually kidney damage. Signs and symptoms include any of the following: dysuria, fever, chills, frequency, urgency, hematuria, and concentrated, cloudy (possibly foul-smelling) urine (Potter et al., 2010).

Urinary Incontinence

Urinary incontinence is the loss of control over micturition. It may present as any of the following types (RNAO, 2005):

Transient: Loss of urine outside of or affecting the urinary system that resolves when the underlying cause(s), such as acute confusion or UTI, are treated

Urge: Involuntary passage of urine after a strong sense of urgency to void, for example, with alcohol or caffeine ingestion or a UTI

Stress: Leakage of small volumes of urine caused by a sudden increase in intra-abdominal pressure, such as during coughing or sneezing

Mixed: Having features of both stress and urge incontinence

Functional: Involuntary, unpredictable passage of urine in a client with an intact urinary and nervous system, as in the case when an older adult with bladder control is unable to reach the toilet

Overflow: Voluntary or involuntary loss of a small amount of urine (20–30 mL) from an overdistended bladder (as in the case of diabetics or spinal cord injury clients)

Reflex: Involuntary loss of urine occurring at somewhat predictable intervals

Total: Continuous and unpredictable loss of urine

Urinary Diversions

Urinary diversions divert the flow of urine from the kidneys directly to the abdominal surface via a urinary stoma. The diversion can be permanent or temporary and either continent or incontinent.

MAINTAINING NORMAL URINARY ELIMINATION

- Promote fluid intake of 1500–2000 mL daily for the average adult and an increased intake for clients at risk of UTI and renal calculi, as well as clients with catheters.
- Maintain normal voiding habits. Void every three to four hours to maintain a normal bladder capacity (400–500 mL) and to avoid urinary stasis.

MEASURING INTAKE AND OUTPUT

- Fluid intake should equal output. Intake is considered all dietary items that are fluid at room temperature as well as IV fluids, including blood. Output is urine, vomitus, suction drainage, bleeding, and insensible loss, such as sweating.
- Normal urine output is 60 mL/hr or 1500 mL/day. Urine outputs below 30 mL/hr (0.5 mL/kg/hr) for more than two hours in an adult should be reported.
- Daily weights are the single most important indicator of fluid status. Clients should be weighed daily on the same weigh scale at the same time after voiding.

URINE TESTING AND SPECIMEN COLLECTION

Urine samples can be random (routine urinalysis), clean-catch or midstream (culture and sensitivity), or sterile (culture and sensitivity). For midstream urine specimens, the client cleans the perineum with an antiseptic solution, initiates urination to cleanse the meatus, and then urinates into a sterile specimen container. Some tests require 24-hour collection of urine, such as the creatinine clearance test. The urine is collected in a special collection container that may have a preservative added.

CATHETERIZATION AND CATHETER CARE

Intermittent Catheterization

A straight single-lumen catheter is introduced to empty the bladder and removed after the bladder is drained. Indications for use include relief of bladder distension and obtaining a sterile urine specimen.

In-Dwelling Catheterization (Retention or Foley Catheterization)

A catheter with an inflatable balloon is inserted into the bladder on a short- or long-term basis. Indications for use include prostate enlargement, measuring urine output in critically ill clients, or ulcers or wounds irritated by contact with urine.

Catheterization for Residual Urine

Catheterization for residual urine involves inserting a catheter after a client voids to check for the amount of urine remaining in the bladder. The bladder normally holds less than 50 mL after voiding. If the volume of urine (residual volume) is greater than 100 mL, the catheter may be left in situ.

Catheter Care

- Keep the urinary drainage bag below the level of the bladder to prevent reflux, which can lead to UTIs.
- Tape the catheter to the client's inner thigh or abdomen to reduce the pressure on the urethra and the possibility of tissue injury.
- Keep the drainage tubing coiled on the bed to aid gravity drainage.
- Do not open a closed system unless absolutely necessary, to lessen the chance of UTIs.
- Perform catheter care twice daily with soap and water to cleanse the urinary meatus and encrustations on the catheter in order to reduce infections.
- Empty the drainage bag every eight hours and record the amount, colour, odour, and consistency of urinary drainage.

- Change the urinary catheter bag and catheter regularly according to agency policy.
- Remove the catheter as soon as clinically possible to prevent UTIs.

BLADDER IRRIGATION

Closed and open catheter or bladder irrigations are irrigations or flushes used to maintain the patency of in-dwelling catheters or to wash out the bladder and treat local infections.

BOWEL ELIMINATION

COMMON BOWEL ELIMINATION CHALLENGES

- Constipation usually involves infrequent bowel movements, difficult defecation, inability to defecate at will, and hard feces (Potter et al., 2010). It can also involve abdominal distension and pain and pressure in the rectum.
- Fecal impaction is a condition in which a collection of hardened feces cannot be expelled from the rectum. The common sign is inability to pass stool for several days. Impaction should be suspected if there is a continuous oozing of diarrhea (liquid feces from higher in the bowel is seeping around the impaction).
- Diarrhea is the passage of liquid feces and an increase in the number of stools. The greatest danger from diarrhea is fluid and electrolyte imbalance.
- Fecal incontinence is the inability to control the passage of feces and gas. Skin breakdown can occur after repeated contact with liquid stool.
- Flatulence is excessive gas in the stomach and intestine. Reduction in gastrointestinal motility, resulting from opiates, general anaesthetics, abdominal surgery, or immobilization, can cause abdominal distension due to flatulence.
- Hemorrhoids (internal and external) are dilated, engorged veins in the rectal area (either external or internal). They can make defecation painful.

BOWEL DIVERSIONS

Bowel diversions divert the feces from the bowel directly to the abdominal surface. Surgical openings can be created in the ileum (ileostomy) or colon (colostomy) to create an artificial opening called a stoma. The location of the ostomy determines the consistency of the stool, with the ileostomy having more frequent liquid stools and the colostomy resulting in more solid formed stool. Proper selection and maintenance of an ostomy pouching system is important to prevent damage to the skin around the stoma.

PROMOTING REGULAR OR NORMAL DEFECATION

- Foods high in fibre and an increased fluid intake keep feces soft.
- Provide clients with as much privacy as possible. Lack of privacy may cause the client to ignore the urge to defecate.
- Provide clients with a position as close to normal as possible for defecation (such as on a commode chair) and give them enough time.
- Be aware of the client's normal routine and when defecation is most likely to occur, for example, one hour after a meal. Establishing a specific time for defecation may help to prevent constipation.
- Regular exercise within the client's physical ability is important in stimulating peristalsis and a regular bowel routine.
- Warm fluids and certain juices (prune) can stimulate bowel motility.

ENEMAS

Enemas are an instillation of a solution into the rectum and sigmoid colon. They stimulate peristalsis and initiate defecation. They are commonly used for relief of constipation but can also deliver medications that have a local effect on the rectal mucosa. The most common types of enemas are cleansing and oil retention. Enemas may also be used in preparing for diagnostic tests or for performing diagnostic tests of the bowel or rectum, such as barium enemas.

Types of Enemas

- Cleansing enemas include tap water, normal saline, low-volume hypertonic (Fleet), and soap suds.
- Oil retention enemas lubricate the rectum and colon. The feces become softer and easier to pass. The client is advised to hold the enema for 30 minutes to three hours.

Nursing Care of Clients Receiving an Enema

- Explain the procedure to the client and ensure privacy. Explain how long the client must retain the enema.
- The client is positioned in a left Sims' position.
- The rectal tube attached to the enema bag is lubricated and inserted 10–15 cm into the rectum.
- Ensure that the client has access to a bathroom, commode, or bedpan.
- Observe and record the amount and consistency of the return from the enema.

DIGITAL REMOVAL OF STOOL

Digital removal of stool is used when the client has a fecal impaction. The nurse breaks up the fecal mass with a finger and removes it in sections. This procedure can be painful, can damage the rectal mucosa, and can cause vagal stimulation (resulting in reflex slowing of the heart rate). In some agencies, a physician's order is necessary to remove a fecal impaction. Vital signs should be checked before and after the procedure.

NASOGASTRIC TUBES

NG tubes are pliable tubes inserted through the nasopharynx and into the stomach. Commonly used types are Levin or Salem sump NG tubes.

Purposes of NG Tubes

Decompression: Removal of secretions from the gastrointestinal tract for the prevention and relief of abdominal distension

Feeding or Gavage: Instillation of liquid nutritional supplements into the stomach for clients unable to swallow

Compression: Internal application of pressure by means of an inflated balloon to prevent internal esophageal or gastrointestinal hemorrhage

Lavage: Irrigation of the stomach for active bleeding or poisoning

Insertion of an NG Tube

- Place the client in the high Fowler's position.
- Measure from the tip of the nose to the earlobe to the xiphoid process to determine the length of insertion.
- Lubricate 7.5 cm with water-soluble lubricant.
- Instruct the client to bend the head forward to close the epiglottis.
- Insert the tube into the patent nostril and advance it backward into the nasopharynx.
- Have the client dry swallow or sip on water (if allowed) and advance the tube as the client swallows to the predetermined length.
- If the client experiences respiratory distress (coughing or choking), remove the tube and resume the procedure when the client has recovered.
- Tape the tube in place and confirm placement of the tube.

Assessment of Tube Placement

- The most reliable method to check placement is by radiography.
- Assess tube placement every four hours and before administering medications or feedings.
- The most reliable method to assess tube placement at the bedside is to aspirate gastric contents and test the gastric pH. Gastric pH should be less than 4. Intestinal aspirates are greater than 4, and respiratory aspirates are greater than 5.5.
- Another method of testing tube placement is to insert 5–10 mL of air into the NG tube and listen with a stethoscope for the "whoosh" of air over the stomach. This method is a less reliable method of checking placement.

- Irrigation of a NG tube is gentle instillation of 30–50 mL of water or normal saline (check agency policy) to check and maintain patency of the NG tube. Check placement of the tube prior to irrigating. A doctor's order may be required to irrigate the NG tube of gastric surgery clients.

Medication Administration via a NG Tube

- Crush medications or open capsules (if allowed) or use liquid forms.
- Dissolve medication in 10–30 mL of warm water and draw up into a 60-mL syringe.
- Check placement of the NG tube as well as residual volume in the stomach.
- Flush the NG tube with 30 mL of water (check agency policy).
- Instill medication into the tube.
- Flush the NG tube with 30–60 mL of water (check agency policy).
- Clamp the tube for 30–60 min if the client is on intermittent suction (check agency policy).

Considerations Relating to the Older Adult

- Constipation can be a common complaint in older adults due to a combination of impaired general health, use of medication, decreased motility, and physical activity.

MOBILITY AND IMMOBILITY

Mobility refers to the ability to move easily and independently. Certain illnesses, surgery, pain, and aging can impair mobility temporarily or permanently. It is important to know the hazards of immobility and how to prevent them as well as how to care for clients who are immobile.

SYSTEMIC EFFECTS OF IMMOBILITY

When there is an alteration in mobility, each body system is at risk for impairment. Some of the changes that can happen— the "hazards of immobility"—are discussed below:

- Metabolic changes include a lowered metabolic rate, a negative nitrogen balance, anorexia (loss of appetite), and a negative calcium balance (calcium is lost from bones).
- Respiratory changes include shallow respirations and decreased vital capacity, pooling of respiratory secretions, atelectasis (collapse of alveoli), and hypostatic pneumonia (inflammation of the lung from stasis or pooling of secretions).
- Cardiovascular changes include diminished cardiac reserve, increased use of the Valsalva manoeuvre

(such as when the client holds his or her breath to change position in bed), orthostatic hypotension, and venous dilation and stasis, which can cause edema and deep vein thrombosis (DVT).

- Musculoskeletal changes include disuse osteoporosis, disuse atrophy, contractures, foot drop (foot permanently fixed in plantar flexion), and external hip rotation.
- Urinary elimination changes include urinary stasis, urinary calculi, urinary retention, and urinary infection.
- Gastrointestinal system changes include constipation and decreased peristalsis.
- Integumentary changes include less skin turgor (elasticity) and possible skin breakdown, as well as the formation of pressure sores or ulcers (Kozier et al., 2004; Potter et al., 2010).

POSITIONING AND BODY ALIGNMENT

- Immobile clients need to be repositioned at least every two hours or more frequently if there are reddened skin areas. The 30° lateral position is best as it does not put direct pressure on the trochanter.
- Clients should be placed in a variety of positions to prevent pressure areas. Different bed positions used include Fowler's; supine (dorsal) recumbent; prone (face down); side-lying (lateral); and Sims' (semi-prone).
- Limbs need to be anatomically aligned in a slightly flexed position. Bony surfaces should not touch; for example, a pillow is often placed between knees. Trochanter rolls can be used to prevent external hip rotation, footboards to prevent foot drop, and hand–wrist or foot–ankle splints to keep the joints anatomically aligned.

RANGE-OF-MOTION (ROM) EXERCISES

- ROM exercises can be active (the client is able to move all joints through their ROM unassisted) or passive (the client is unable to move some or all of the joints independently, and the nurse assists certain or all joints through their ROM).
- Exercises should begin as soon as possible as joints begin to stiffen within 24 hours of loss of movement in an extremity or joint (Potter et al., 2010). It is best to schedule them at specific times, such as during the bath.
- Each joint movement is repeated five times during each session. No force is exerted.

MOVING AND TRANSFERRING CLIENTS SAFELY

A thorough assessment must be made prior to moving or positioning a client. The client needs to be assessed for the degree of exertion permitted, capabilities such as mobility and strength, comprehension, pain level, weight, and presence of orthostatic hypotension. The nurse must also assess his or her own strength and ability to move the client and how much assistance is available from other care providers or if mechanical lifts are available. Finally, the nurse must assess the environment to make sure the transfer can be done safely.

- Consider the client's abilities and disabilities when deciding appropriate transfer technique and the need for assistive devices; for example, for hemiplegia, place the wheelchair on the side opposite the affected extremities; for paraplegia, the client may use a trapeze, slide board, or wheelchair with a removable arm).
- Use the principles of good body mechanics (described earlier in Activity and Exercise, p. 136).

WOUND CARE

TYPES OF WOUNDS

- Acute wounds, such as surgical wounds, follow the normal healing process in a predictable and timely fashion.
- Chronic wounds, such as pressure ulcers, do not heal easily, and the normal reparative process is interrupted.

TYPES OF WOUND HEALING

Primary Intention

Wounds that heal by primary intention have little or no tissue loss, have well-approximated wound margins, and heal quickly. Two examples are a clean surgical wound or a paper cut.

Secondary Intention

Wounds that heal by secondary intention have loss of tissue, such as second- or third-degree burns, or pressure ulcers, and there is no approximation of the wound edges. Healing and granulation take place from the edges inward and from the base of the wound to the top. The wound is left open and takes longer to heal (Potter et al., 2010).

COMPLICATIONS OF WOUND HEALING

- Hemorrhage or bleeding from the wound may occur externally or internally.
- Wound infection is the second most common HAI. Signs of wound infection may include any of the following: pain and tenderness at the site, erythema, edema, inflammation of wound edges, purulent

drainage, warmth of tissues at the site, fever or chills, elevated white blood cell (WBC) count, and delayed healing (Potter et al., 2010).

- Dehiscence is the partial or total separation of the wound layers (Potter et al., 2010). It usually occurs at 3–11 days postinjury or surgery. It most commonly involves surgical wounds of the abdomen and can occur after a vigorous bout of coughing or straining.
- Evisceration is protrusion of the abdominal organs through the wound opening. This is a medical emergency and requires surgical intervention. The nurse should cover the organs with sterile saline-soaked towels, keep the client NPO, and monitor for signs and symptoms of shock.
- A fistula is an "abnormal passage between two organs or between an organ and the outside of the body" (Potter et al., 2010). It is the result of infection or poor wound healing or as a complication of diseases such as Crohn's disease.

TYPES OF WOUND DRAINAGE

Wound drainage can be serous (clear and watery), purulent (thick green, yellow, or brown and containing pus cells), serosanguineous (thin, watery, and blood-tinged), or sanguineous (bloody).

WOUND ASSESSMENT

Wound assessment includes observing wound appearance (size, location, stage of healing, approximation, and condition of skin around the wound); the character and amount of drainage; the presence and amount of drainage from drains such as the Penrose, Hemovac, or Jackson-Pratt; and the presence of sutures, staples, or packing. Wound assessment may also involve palpating the wound for warmth, tenderness, hardness, or pain and may require collection of a wound culture if the wound appears infected.

PRESSURE ULCERS

A pressure ulcer is a localized injury to the skin or underlying tissue or both, usually over a bony prominence, as a result of pressure or pressure in combination with shear and friction (National Pressure Ulcer Advisory Panel [NPUAP], 2007). Pressure is the main cause of pressure ulcers and often occurs over a bony prominence when tissue is compressed between the bone and a hard surface such as a bed or chair. The following are other factors that work with pressure to cause skin damage and necrosis:

- Friction is when two surfaces are rubbed against each other. For example, dragging a client across the sheets can cause an abrasion.
- Shear is the parallel force that happens when the skin and underlying subcutaneous tissue are pulled taut, obstructing capillary blood flow and causing tissue necrosis in the deep tissue layers. Shear occurs when the client is moved incorrectly, for example, when he or she is dragged instead of lifted clear of the mattress, or when the head of the bed is elevated above 30° for long periods of time, causing the client to slide down in bed.
- Moisture caused by wound discharge, excess diaphoresis, or incontinence can be a factor leading to skin breakdown.

Risk Assessment for Pressure Ulcers

Identify at-risk clients early by using a validated risk assessment tool such as the Braden Scale. The Braden Scale measures sensory perception, moisture, activity, mobility, nutrition, and friction and shear. The scale needs to be used preventively (on admission) and consistently (daily in high-risk clients). As soon as a client is identified to be at risk for developing pressure ulcers, prevention strategies should be started.

Staging System for Pressure Ulcers

Suspected Deep Tissue Injury: A purple or maroon localized area of discoloured intact skin or blood-filled blister, caused by damage to the underlying soft tissue from pressure or shear, or both

Stage I Pressure Ulcer: Intact skin with nonblanchable redness of a localized area, usually over a bony prominence. Darkly pigmented skin may not have visible blanching; its colour may differ from that of the surrounding skin.

Stage II Pressure Ulcer: Partial-thickness loss of dermis presenting as a shallow open ulcer with a red-pink wound bed, without slough

Stage III Pressure Ulcer: Full-thickness tissue loss. Subcutaneous fat may be visible, but bone, tendon, or muscle is not exposed. Slough may be present.

Stage IV Pressure Ulcer: Full-thickness tissue loss with exposed bone, tendon, or muscle

Unstageable Pressure Ulcer: Full-thickness tissue loss in which the base of the ulcer is covered in slough, eschar, or both. Slough is a viscous yellow layer that often covers the wound, and eschar is thick, dry, black, necrotic tissue covering a wound (NPUAP, 2007).

Prevention of Pressure Ulcers

- Reposition clients every two hours or more if they are high risk.
- Inspect the condition of the client's skin at least daily and examine bony prominences carefully. Nonblanchable erythema or discoloration of the skin may indicate early signs of tissue injury.
- Keep linens dry to prevent maceration of skin and wrinkle-free to prevent pressure.
- Position the client in a 30° lateral position to either side to avoid pressure on the trochanter.
- Do not massage over bony prominences or reddened areas.

- Avoid elevating the head of the bed to more than 30° as that increases the shearing force.
- Use pressure redistribution devices, such as pressure-reducing and pressure-relieving mattresses, for at-risk clients. A pressure-reducing mattress reduces the interface pressure (the pressure between the body and the support surface) but not below the capillary-closing pressure (Potter et al., 2010). A pressure-relieving mattress relieves the interface pressure below the capillary-closing pressure, which is 32 mm Hg (Potter et al., 2010).
- Promote a diet that is high in protein and calories and ensure adequate hydration.
- Keep skin clean and well hydrated.

Treatment of Pressure Ulcers

- Perform a comprehensive assessment of the pressure ulcer, including staging, measurement of size (depth, width, and length), character and amount of exudate, wound bed characteristics, pain, condition of surrounding skin, and evidence of tunnelling or undermining (NPUAP, 2001).
- Determine the need for local wound care by assessing the wound bed for debris, infection, and moisture balance. If slough is present, the wound may need to be irrigated, debrided, or both.
- Wound debridement removes necrotic material that interferes with healing. There are different methods of debridement, such as surgical or sharp, autolytic, enzymatic, or mechanical. Mechanical debridement (also called a wet-to-dry dressing) is no longer recommended as it is not selective and can damage new granulating tissue (Keast, Parslow, Houghton, Norton, & Fraser, 2007).
- Moist interactive wound healing involves keeping the wound bed moist and warm and not disturbing it too much by changing the dressing. A moist, interactive wound healing environment results in faster healing, better tissue quality, and reduced pain (Keast et al., 2007).
- Vacuum-assisted closure (VAC) is "a device that assists in wound closure by applying localized negative pressure to draw the edges of a wound together" (Potter et al., 2006, p. 1547). It can be used with both acute and chronic wounds. It removes fluid from the area surrounding the wound and can accelerate healing.

APPLYING DRY DRESSINGS

- The purpose of dressings is to protect the wound from contamination, aid hemostasis, absorb drainage, and promote a moist healing environment.
- Wounds are commonly cleansed with normal saline, which is not toxic to cells.
- The wound or incision should be cleansed from the least contaminated area (the wound or incision) to the most contaminated (the surrounding skin).
- Acute wounds are usually changed using sterile aseptic technique, while chronic wounds may require

only clean technique.
- Observe the character, colour, amount, and odour of drainage on the dressing and the appearance of the wound, as well as the skin around the wound.

Applying an Elastic Bandage

- An elastic bandage is used to create pressure over a body part, to immobilize a body part, to support a wound, to reduce or minimize edema, to secure a splint, or to secure dressings.
- The bandage is applied from distal to proximal to promote venous return.
- Assess distal circulation when the bandage is first applied and every four hours afterward. Check limb distally for colour, warmth, sensation, and movement. Palpate and compare pulses bilaterally and check capillary refill.

SENSORY ALTERATIONS

Sensory deficits are losses in the normal function of sensory reception and perception, such as vision or hearing impairments. Aging most commonly results in a gradual decline of acuity in all senses. Clients who are immobilized or isolated are at risk for sensory alterations.

SENSORY DEPRIVATION

Sensory deprivation is the result of inadequate sensory stimuli (either in quality or quantity). Sensory deprivation can be the result of (a) reduced sensory input, as in the case of vision or hearing impairment; (b) the elimination of order or meaning from input, for example, exposure to strange environments; or (c) restriction in the environment, as when a client is confined to bed rest or receives reduced cues or no variation in cues from the environment (Potter et al., 2010).

SENSORY OVERLOAD

Sensory overload occurs when clients receive multiple sensory stimuli and cannot disregard or filter out some stimuli. Their tolerance to sensory overload may vary depending on many factors, such as level of fatigue, attitude, or state of well-being (physical, mental, and emotional) (Potter et al., 2010).

CARE OF SURGICAL CLIENTS

PREOPERATIVE SURGICAL PHASE

Informed Consent

The surgeon is responsible for obtaining the client's informed consent for surgery before sedation is given.

Minors require a parent or guardian to sign the consent.

Nutrition

When the client is going to have general anaesthesia, solid foods and liquids are usually withheld after midnight the night before surgery to avoid the possibility of vomiting and subsequent aspiration during surgery. An IV line may be initiated prior to surgery or in the operating room.

Elimination

An enema or laxative may be ordered for clients having intestinal or abdominal surgery. The client should void immediately before surgery, or the insertion of a Foley catheter may be ordered.

Care of Surgical Site

The surgical site may be scrubbed with an antiseptic soap the night before surgery, or the client may be required to take a chlorhexidine shower and scrub the night before and the morning of the surgery. Shaving the skin is no longer recommended because it causes microscopic cuts. Hair is removed only if it interferes with surgery, and clippers instead of razors are used for hair removal.

Preoperative Teaching

The client needs to be informed before surgery about what to expect postoperatively. Teaching involves topics such as pain relief and use of the PCA (patient- or client-controlled analgesia) pump, postoperative breathing exercises and the use of the incentive spirometer, foot and leg exercises, and instructions about invasive lines or devices to be expected after surgery (such as chest tubes, Foley catheter, drains, NG tubes, etc.).

Psychological Preparation

Monitor the client's anxiety level and provide support as needed. Answer any of the client's questions or concerns or those of the client's family.

Preoperative Medication

Most clients will be told to take their routine cardiac, antihypertensive, and asthma medications on the day of surgery, but there is no routine protocol. If the medications are oral, they are taken with a minimal amount of water. Eye drops are often ordered preoperatively for clients undergoing cataract or other eye surgery. IV antibiotics are often given as prophylaxis against infection for orthopedic, cardiac, and gastrointestinal surgery clients. Sedatives are occasionally ordered, and it is important that the consent is signed before the client receives sedatives or narcotics.

Preoperative Checklist

The preoperative checklist needs to be reviewed thoroughly before the client is transferred to surgery. The client needs to be wearing an identification bracelet. The nurse needs to check the chart for recorded allergies, signed consent forms for surgery and blood transfusions, or both; a complete history and physical examination; routine blood work results (including urinalysis, electrolytes, and complete blood count); electrocardiogram and chest X-ray results; and blood cross and type results, if ordered. All jewellery, makeup, nail polish, dentures, and prostheses need to be removed. All valuables should be given to family members or locked away for safekeeping. The nurse needs to document when the client last ate or drank, when the client last voided, if the client was given preoperative medication, and a current set of baseline vital signs.

INTRAOPERATIVE SURGICAL PHASE

The operating room nurse verifies the client's identification bracelet with the chart and the client's verbal response. The nurse reviews the chart for completeness and confirms the operative procedure and operative site. The primary focus of the intraoperative phase is to prevent injury and complications related to anaesthesia, surgery, positioning, and equipment used. Operating room nurses act as client advocates during the intraoperative phase. The scrub nurse maintains a sterile field during the procedure, hands the surgeon sterile instruments and supplies, and counts sponges, needles, and instruments during and after the surgery. The circulating nurse positions the client on the operating room table, drapes the client, assists the anaesthetist to intubate, assists the surgeon and scrub nurse to don sterile attire, and maintains complete and accurate written records.

POSTOPERATIVE SURGICAL PHASE

Immediate Postoperative Stage

The immediate postoperative stage is the period 1–4 hr after surgery (Silvestri, 2011).

Respiratory Status

The respiratory status may be depressed as a result of anaesthesia. Maintain a patent airway until the gag reflex returns. Position the client on his or her side to prevent aspiration and the accumulation of secretions. Monitor heart rate and rhythm, symmetry of chest movement, breath sounds, pulse oximeter readings, and colour. Administer oxygen as ordered and suction as needed to remove secretions.

Circulatory Status

The circulatory status may be compromised by anaesthesia and immobility during surgery. Monitor the heart rate and rhythm as well as BP at least every 15 minutes while in the postanaesthesia care unit. Monitor peripheral circulation by noting the colour, temperature, capillary refill, and presence of pulses. Monitor for hemorrhage by watching for hypotension and observing and measuring wound drainage.

Neurological Status

The client's neurological status may be affected by preoperative and anaesthetic agents that depress the central nervous system. Monitor the client's level of consciousness and responses to stimuli. Monitor blink and gag reflexes. Monitor for loss or return of sensation or movement when specific areas have been surgically treated. Reorient the client to time, place, and situation and call the client by name. Answer questions simply and reassure the client.

Wound Care

Note the location of the wound and the colour, odour, amount, and consistency of drainage. Circle drainage on the dressing to assess the extent of bleeding over time. Reinforce postoperative dressings as the first dressing change is often done by the surgeon.

Care of Drains and Tubes

Maintain the patency of all tubing. Attach to suction when ordered. Monitor drain output to assess for hemorrhage.

Fluid and Electrolyte Needs

Maintain IV therapy as ordered. Record intake and output accurately.

Comfort Needs

Assess the client's level of pain on the 0–10 scale. Medicate as ordered to reduce pain and increase postoperative compliance with coughing, deep breathing, and activity. Splinting at the surgical site may decrease discomfort when coughing. Instruct the client in the use of PCA.

Care of Clients with Regional Anaesthesia

Regional anaesthesia causes the loss of sensation to an area of the body. No loss of consciousness occurs, but the client may receive sedation. Examples include nerve blocks and spinal or epidural anaesthesia. For both spinal and epidural anaesthesia, the client must be observed closely for signs of autonomic nervous system blockade, signalled by hypotension, bradycardia, nausea, and vomiting (Lewis et al., 2010). If the block or level of anaesthesia rises (in other words, if spinal anaesthesia migrates up the spinal cord), breathing may be affected (Lewis et al., 2010). Burns and other trauma can also occur on the parts of the body affected by the anaesthesia without the client feeling it, so it is important to monitor the position of the extremities and the condition of the skin (Potter et al., 2010).

Intermediate Postoperative Stage

The intermediate postoperative stage is the period from 4–24 hr after surgery (Silvestri, 2011).

Respiratory Status

Continue to monitor vital signs every 2–4 hr according to agency policy using the same assessments from the immediate postoperative stage. Encourage coughing and deep breathing and incentive spirometer every 1–2 hr.

Circulatory Status

Continue to monitor circulatory status as described above every 2–4 hr, according to agency policy. Use antiembolism or elastic stockings, if prescribed, to promote venous return.

Musculoskeletal Status

Encourage progressive ambulation, starting with leg-dangling at the bedside as soon as possible and following doctors' orders. If the client is unable to ambulate, reposition him or her in bed every two hours.

Gastrointestinal Status

Monitor intake and output. Administer frequent mouth care. Assess for bowel sounds in all four quadrants. When oral fluids are permitted, start with ice chips and water. The client advances from clear fluids to a full diet when bowel sounds are heard. Monitor the client for flatus and encourage ambulation.

Renal Status

Monitor urine output, which should be greater than 30 mL/hr (0.5 mL/kg/hr). Clients without Foley catheters should void at least 200 mL within 6–8 hr postoperatively.

Wound Care

Assess surgical site and drains and maintain an intact, dry dressing. Monitor the amount of drainage from drains and the incision. Reinforce dressing as needed.

Extended Postoperative Stage

The extended postoperative stage is the period 1–4 days postoperatively (Silvestri, 2011).

The assessments from the intermediate stage continue in this stage but less frequently. Continue to encourage ambulation to promote peristalsis and the passage of flatus. Continue to increase ambulation to regain muscle strength. Change the dressing as needed using aseptic technique and assess the incision and drainage. Monitor for signs and symptoms of infection by checking for pain, redness, and swelling at the incision site, fever, or an elevated WBC.

Postoperative Complications

Respiratory complications such as pneumonia and atelectasis are the most common. Other postoperative complications include hypoxia, pulmonary embolism, hemorrhage, shock, thrombophlebitis (inflammation of a vein accompanied by clot formation), urinary retention, constipation, and paralytic ileus (loss of the forward flow of intestinal contents as a result of anaesthetic medications or manipulation of the bowel during surgery, wound infection, wound dehiscence, or wound evisceration).

POSTOPERATIVE EXERCISES

Respiratory Exercises

Deep Breathing

The client is instructed to take 10 slow deep breaths every hour during the postoperative period until mobile. Diaphragmatic and pursed-lip breathing are examples of different methods of deep breathing.

Use of Incentive Spirometer

Incentive spirometry (IS) is a way to encourage deep breathing in clients by providing visual feedback about their inspiratory volume. It is used to prevent or treat atelectasis in the postoperative client and should be used hourly while awake. IS is used in many practice settings, but research does not support its benefit over other methods, such as coughing, deep breathing, and ambulation (Potter et al., 2010).

Controlled Coughing

The client is in the upright position and takes two slow, deep breaths, inhaling through the nose and out through the mouth. On the third intake of breath, the client holds to a count of three and gives two to three consecutive coughs without inhaling between coughs.

Leg Exercises

Leg exercises should be performed at least every two hours for five successive times while awake. They include foot circles, alternating dorsiflexion and plantar flexion of both feet, quadriceps (thigh) setting, and hip and knee movements.

PALLIATIVE CARE

Palliative care is supportive care or treatment that relieves or reduces the severity of symptoms rather than providing a cure. Palliative care is designed for individuals and family members who are living with a life-threatening illness, often at an advanced stage (Health Canada, 2004). It is a philosophy of total care with the aim of relieving suffering, emphasizing dignity, and improving the quality of living and dying, from diagnosis to the end of life and bereavement. Care is provided by a multidisciplinary team that consists of many health professionals, such as nurses, physicians, social workers, chaplains, volunteers, pharmacists, physiotherapists, occupational therapists, and alternative therapists, such as massage therapists. Palliative care occurs in many settings, including hospitals, long-term care facilities, hospices, and clients' homes. Client and family needs are the focus of any interventions.

REFERENCES

American Nurses Association. (2006). *Preventing back injuries: Safe patient handling and movement.* Silver Spring, MD: Author. Retrieved January 17, 2013, from http://www.nursingworld.org/MainMenuCategories/ WorkplaceSafety/SafePatient/PreventingBackInjuries.pdf

Canadian Committee on Antibiotic Resistance. (2007). *Infection prevention and control best practices for long term care, home and community care including health care offices and ambulatory clinics.* Vancouver: Author. Retrieved January 17, 2013, from http://www.ccar-ccra.com/ english/pdfs/IPC-BestPractices-June2007.pdf

Centers for Disease Control and Prevention. (2011). *MRSA statistics. information for the public.* Atlanta: Author. Retrieved January 17, 2013, from http://www.cdc.gov/ mrsa/statistics/

Cook, L. S. (2007). Choosing the right intravenous catheter. *Home Healthcare Nurse, 25*(8), 523–531.

D'Arcy, Y. (2008). Keep your patient safe during PCA. *Nursing, 38*(1), 50–55.

Day, T., Farnell, S., & Wilson-Barnett, J. (2002). Suctioning: A review of current research recommendations. *Intensive and Critical Care Nursing, 18*(2), 79–89.

Duckro, A. N., Blom, D. W., Lyle, E. A., Weinstein, R. A., & Hayden, M. K. (2005). Transfer of vancomycin-resistant *enterococci* via health care worker hands. *Archives of Internal Medicine, 165*(3), 302–307.

Health Canada. (2009). *Palliative and end-of-life care.* Ottawa: Author. Retrieved January 17, 2013, from http://www.hc-sc.gc.ca/hcs-sss/palliat/sect/index_e.html

Healthcare Infection Control Practices Advisory Committee. (2006). *Management of multidrug-resistant organisms in healthcare settings.* Atlanta: Centers for Disease Control and Prevention. Retrieved January 17, 2013, from www.cdc.gov/hicpac/mdro/mdro_0.html

Hypertension Canada. (2012a). *The 2012 Canadian Hypertension Education Program Recommendations.* Markham, ON: Author. Retrieved January 17,

2013, from http://www.hypertension.ca/chep-recommendations

Hypertension Canada. (2012b). *Measuring blood pressure.* Markham, ON: Author. Retrieved January 17, 2013, from http://www.hypertension.ca/measuring-blood-pressure

Ignatavicius, D., & Workman, M. (2010). *Medical-surgical nursing: Patient-Centered collaborative care* (6th ed.). Philadelphia: Saunders.

Institute for Safe Medication Practices. (2006). *List of error-prone abbreviations, symbols, and dose designations.* Retrieved January 17, 2013, from http://www.ismp.org/tools/errorproneabbreviations.pdf

Institute for Safe Medicine Practices Canada. (2006). Top 10 drugs reported as causing harm through medication error. *Canada Safety Bulletin, 6*(1), 1–2. Toronto: Author.

Jarvis, C., Browne, A. J., MacDonald-Jenkins, J., Luctkar-Flude, M. (2009). *Physical examination and health assessment* (1st Canadian ed.). Toronto: Saunders.

Keast, D., Parslow, N., Houghton, P. E., Norton, L., & Fraser, C. (2007). Best practice recommendations for the prevention and treatment of pressure ulcers: Update 2006. *Advances in Skin and Wound Care, 20*(8), 447–460.

Kozier, B., Erb, G., Berman, A., Burke, K., Bouchal, D., & Hirst, S. (2004). *Fundamentals of nursing: The nature of nursing practice in Canada.* Toronto: Prentice Hall.

Lanham, D. M., Walker, B., Klocke, E., & Jennings, M. (1999). Accuracy of tympanic temperature readings in children under 6 years of age. *Pediatric Nursing, 25*(1), 39–42.

Lewis, S. M., Heitkemper, M. M., Dirksen, S. R., O'Brien, P., Giddens, J. F., Bucher, L., et al. (2006). *Medical-surgical nursing in Canada: Assessment and management of clinical problems.* (1st Canadian ed.). Toronto: Elsevier.

Lewis, S. M., Heitkemper, M. M., Dirksen, S. R., O'Brien, P., Bucher, L., Barry, M. A., et al. (2010). *Medical-surgical nursing in Canada: Assessment and management of clinical problems.* (2nd Canadian ed.). Toronto: Elsevier.

Mahan, L. K., & Arlin, M. (1992). *Krause's food, nutrition, and diet therapy* (8th ed.). Philadelphia: Saunders.

National Pressure Ulcer Advisory Panel. (2010). *Pressure ulcer treatment: A competency-based curriculum.* Reston, VA: Author. Retrieved January 17, 2013, from http://www.npuap.org/resources/educational-and-clinical-resources/nursing-curriculum/

National Pressure Ulcer Advisory Panel. (2007). *Pressure ulcer stages revised by NPUAP.* Reston, VA: Author. Retrieved January 17, 2013, from http://www.npuap.org/resources/educational-and-clinical-resources/npuap-pressure-ulcer-stagescategories/

Perry, A. G., & Potter, P. A. (2009). *Clinical nursing skills and techniques. (7th ed.).* St. Louis: Mosby.

Potter, A. G., & Potter, P. A. (2010). *Clinical nursing skills and techniques* (7th ed.). St. Louis: Mosby.

Potter, P. A., Perry, A. G., Ross-Kerr, J. C., & Wood, M. (Eds.). (2006). *Canadian fundamentals of nursing* (3rd ed.). Toronto: Elsevier.

Potter, P. A., Perry, A. G., Ross-Kerr, J. C., & Wood, M. (Eds.). (2010). *Canadian fundamentals of nursing* (Rev. 4th ed.). Toronto: Elsevier.

Pruitt, W., & Jacobs, M. (2003). Breathing lessons: Basics of oxygen therapy. *Nursing, 33*(10), 43–45.

Registered Nurses' Association of Ontario. (2004). *Summary of recommendations.* In *Nursing best practice guideline: Assessment and device selection for vascular access.* Toronto: Author. Retrieved January 17, 2013, from http://rnao.ca/bpg/guidelines/assessment-and-device-selection-vascular-access

Registered Nurses' Association of Ontario. (2005). *Nursing best practice guideline: Promoting continence using prompted voiding.* Toronto: Author. Retrieved January 17, 2013, from http://rnao.ca/bpg/guidelines/promoting-continence-using-prompted-voiding

Registered Nurses' Association of Ontario. (2007a). *Nursing best practice guideline: Assessment and management of pain.* Toronto: Author. Retrieved January 17, 2013, from http://rnao.ca/bpg/guidelines/promoting-continence-using-prompted-voiding

Registered Nurses' Association of Ontario. (2007b). *Nursing best practice guideline: Reducing foot complications for people with diabetes.* Toronto: Author. Retrieved January 17, 2013, from http://rnao.ca/bpg/guidelines/reducing-foot-complications-people-diabetes

Saxton, D., Marshall-Henty, J., & Vernon, P. (2003). *Mosby's Canadian comprehensive review of nursing* (2nd Canadian ed.). Toronto: Mosby.

Silvestri, L. A. (2005). *Comprehensive review for the NCLEX-RN examination* (3rd ed.) Philadelphia: Elsevier.

Silvestri, L. A. (2010). *Comprehensive review for NCLEX-RN examination* (5th ed.). Philadelphia: Elsevier.

Subcommittee on Taxonomy. (1986). Classification of chronic pain syndromes and definitions of pain terms. *Pain, 3*(Suppl. 3), S1–S226.

Venes, D. (Ed.). (2002). *Taber's cyclopedic medical dictionary* (19th ed.). Philadelphia: F.A. Davis.

World Health Organization. (1996). *Cancer pain relief* (2nd ed.). Geneva: Author.

BIBLIOGRAPHY

Annersten, A., & Willman, A. (2005). Performing subcutaneous injections: A literature review. *Worldviews on Evidence-based Nursing, 2*(3), 122–130.

Capriotti, T. (2007). Resistant "superbugs" create need for novel antibiotics. *Dermatology Nursing, 19*(1), 65–70.

College of Nurses of Ontario. (2005). *Practice standard: Medication.* Toronto: Author. Retrieved January 17, 2013, from http://www.cno.org/docs/prac/41007_ Medication.pdf

College of Nurses of Ontario; (Revised 2008). *Medication (#41007).* Retrieved January 17, 2013, from http://www.cno.org/Global/docs/prac/41007_Medication.pdf

Dew, P. L. (2006). Is tympanic membrane thermometry the best method for recording temperature in children? *Journal of Child Health Care, 10*(2), 96–110.

Health and Welfare Canada. (2007). *Eating well with Canada's food guide.* Ottawa: Author. Retrieved January 17, 2013, from http://hc-sc.gc.ca/fn-an/food-guide-aliment/index-eng.php

Healthcare Infection Control Practices Advisory Committee. (2007). *Guideline for isolation precautions: Preventing transmission of infectious agents in healthcare settings.* Atlanta: Centers for Disease Control and Prevention. Retrieved January 17, 2013, from http://www.cdc.gov/ncidod/dhqp/pdf/guidelines/Isolation2007.pdf

Ignatavicius, D., & Workman, M. (2010). *Medical-surgical nursing: Patient-centered collaborative care* (6th ed.). Philadelphia: Saunders.

Institute for Safe Medication Practices. (2006). *List of error-prone abbreviations, symbols and dose designations.* Retrieved January 17, 2013, from http://www.ismp.org/tools/errorproneabbreviations.pdf

National Pressure Ulcer Advisory Panel. (2007). *Pressure ulcer prevention points.* Reston, VA: Author. Retrieved January 17, 2013, from http://www.npuap.org/PU_Prev_Points.pdf

Park, M., & Tang, J. (2007). Evidence-based guideline: Changing the practice of physical restraint use in acute care. *Journal of Gerontological Nursing, 33*(2), 9–16.

Perry, A. G., & Potter, P. A. (2006). *Clinical nursing skills & techniques* (6th ed.). St. Louis: Mosby.

Public Health Agency of Canada. (1999). Routine practices and additional precautions for preventing the transmission of infection in health care [electronic version]. *Canadian Communicable Disease Report, 25*(Suppl. 4), S1–S142. Ottawa: Author.

Registered Nurses' Association of Ontario. (Revised 2005). *Nursing best practice guideline: Risk assessment and prevention of pressure ulcers.* Retrieved January 17, 2013, from http://www.rnao.org/Page.asp?PageID=924&ContentID=816

Registered Nurses' Association of Ontario. (Revised 2006). *Nursing best practice guideline: Prevention of constipation in the older adult population.* Retrieved January 17, 2013, from http://rnao.ca/bpg/guidelines/prevention-constipation-older-adult-population

Registered Nurses' Association of Ontario. (2006). *Nursing best practice guideline*: *Care and maintenance to reduce vascular access complications: Summary of recommendations.* Toronto: Author. Retrieved January 17, 2013, from http://www.rnao.org/Storage/11/571_BPG_Reduce_Vascular_Access_Complications_summary.pdf

Registered Nurses' Association of Ontario. (Revised 2007) *Nursing best practice guidelines: Assessment and management of stage I to IV pressure ulcers: Practice recommendations.* Retrieved January 17, 2013, from http://rnao.ca/bpg/guidelines/assessment-and-management-stage-i-iv-pressure-ulcers

WEB SITES

Canadian Association of Nurses in Oncology (http://www.cano-acio.org/): This site provides information about oncological nursing in Canada, including standards of care and practice guidelines.

Infection Prevention and Control Best Practices (http://nurses.ab.ca/carna/index.aspx?webstructureID=2770): These are best practice guidelines for infection control from the College & Association of Registered Nurses of Alberta (CARNA). This document describes modes of pathogen transmission, the correct use of personal protection equipment, routine practices, and other aspects of infection control. The appendices contain posters for health care providers and the public that can be printed for use in health care settings.

Infection Prevention and Control Core Competency Education (http://www.health.gov.on.ca/english/providers/program/infectious/infect_prevent/ipccce_mn.html): This is the Ontario Ministry of Health and Long-Term Care's site on infection control for health professionals. It contains online educational modules and fact sheets about various aspects of infection control.

The Institute for Safe Medication Practices Canada (http://www.ismp-canada.org/index.htm): The Institute for Safe Medication Practices Canada site provides information and research about common medication errors, factors that can potentially lead to medication errors, and methods by which to mitigate these factors.

Just Clean Your Hands (http://www.justcleanyourhands.ca): This is the Ontario Ministry of Health and Long-Term Care's site on hand hygiene. It reviews clinical situations in which hand hygiene is important and links to other educational resources on this subject.

Medication Administration: Guidelines for Registered Nurses (http://www.nurses.ab.ca/Carna-Admin/Uploads/Medication_Administration_Guidelines_for_RNs.pdf): These are practice guidelines from the College & Association of Registered Nurses of Alberta (CARNA) for safe medication administration. The guidelines include information about using different administration systems and medication administration in different health care settings. Policy development relevant to creating safe practice environments is also examined.

Practice Questions

Case 1

A new graduate nurse is working a 12-hour day shift on a complex medicine unit. She has four clients assigned to her care.

Questions 1–6 refer to this case.

1. The nurse knows that it is important to take accurate blood pressure measurements because many of her clients are on antihypertensive medications. Which of the following statements is correct about measurement of blood pressure?

   1. All older adults have an auscultatory gap
   2. Normal pulse pressure, or the difference between systolic and diastolic pressures, is 50–60 mm Hg
   3. Orthostatic hypotension is measured by recording blood pressure and pulse with the client sitting
   4. An auscultatory gap can cause underestimation of systolic blood pressure or overestimation of diastolic blood pressure

2. Mrs. Lucas, 88 years old, has been febrile for several days due to a severe kidney infection. The physician asks the nurse to check a core temperature for the next set of vital signs. Which of the following temperature sites can the nurse use to check a core temperature?

   1. Rectal
   2. Oral
   3. Axillary
   4. Skin

3. Mr. Hamas, age 55, requires an intramuscular injection of iron dextran (Imferon). In the drug handbook, the nurse reads that it can stain the skin and should be given by the Z-track method. What does the nurse need to remember when giving a Z-track injection?

   1. Give the injection over 10 seconds so that it has time to disperse into the muscle
   2. Massage the injection site gently after the injection
   3. Displace some subcutaneous tissue with her hand prior to injection to provide a discontinuous path between the skin and the muscle
   4. Use the dorsogluteal site for injection in case staining occurs accidentally

4. The nurse accidentally sustains a needle-stick injury after giving Mr. Hamas his injection. What could have prevented this injury?

   1. Giving the injection by the regular method rather than the Z-track method
   2. Using safety-engineered needles to reduce the risk of needle-stick injuries

   3. Advocating for oral rather than parenteral administration of medications
   4. Wearing gloves when giving the injection

5. Mr. Aboud, 24 years old, has an intravenous (IV) order for 1000 mL of normal saline to run over eight hours. The IV is started at 1100 hours, and 600 mL is left in the bag at 1500 hours. What adjustment in the flow rate must the nurse make to ensure that the solution is infused no earlier or later than 1900 hours as ordered?

   1. Regulate the IV flow rate to 75 mL/hr
   2. Regulate the IV flow rate to 100 mL/hr
   3. Regulate the IV flow rate to 125 mL/hr
   4. Regulate the IV flow rate to 150 mL/hr

6. Mrs. Roman, 77, has heart failure and a history of angina. The nurse must apply a transdermal patch of nitroglycerine at 0800 hours. Which of the following statements about transdermal medications is correct?

   1. They may be applied to any area of the body regardless of hair distribution as this does not interfere with absorption
   2. Transdermal medications are applied to the skin by patch or disc and stay in place for seven days
   3. Removal of the old patch or disc prior to applying the new medication is recommended but not mandatory as all the medication has been absorbed from the old patch
   4. Transdermal medications can be absorbed through the skin of the nurse's hands in the process of applying the medication to Mrs. Roman

Case 2

Mrs. Gupta, age 55, has had a total hysterectomy. She has an intravenous drip of normal saline infusing at 100 mL/hr.

Questions 7–12 refer to this case.

7. Mrs. Gupta has just returned from surgery. Her vital signs are blood pressure 88/60, pulse 74, respiratory rate 16, and oxygen saturation 95%. What is the first priority for the nurse after taking these vital signs?

   1. Ask Mrs. Gupta how she is feeling and review the health record for baseline vital signs
   2. Call the doctor to report the vital signs
   3. Increase the intravenous rate to 125 mL/hr as Mrs. Gupta is probably dehydrated
   4. Position Mrs. Gupta in a modified Trendelenburg position

8. After surgery, Mrs. Gupta is started on a clear fluid diet until bowel sounds return. Which of the following foods are permitted on a clear fluid diet?

1. Porridge, broth, apple juice
2. Cream soup, ice cream, orange juice
3. Broth, Popsicles, orange juice
4. Tea, Jell-O, apple juice

9. Postoperatively, Mrs. Gupta develops a paralytic ileus. What is the most likely reason for this postoperative complication?

1. She did not ambulate soon enough after surgery
2. She should have eaten a full diet after surgery to stimulate peristalsis
3. She is experiencing the effects of the anaesthetic and the manipulation of the bowel
4. She did not receive a rectal suppository to stimulate peristalsis on the first day after her surgery

10. The nurse helps Mrs. Gupta wash her legs. She removes the elastic (TED) stockings and notices that one calf is larger than the other. What should the nurse do next?

1. Examine the calf carefully and ask Mrs. Gupta if she has any pain
2. Put the TED stocking back on her leg and elevate her leg
3. Measure the calf with a tape measure and call the doctor immediately
4. Wash her leg and ask her to exercise that leg a bit more to reduce the swelling

11. Mrs. Gupta vomits 600 mL of bile-coloured fluid. After consulting with the physician, the nurse inserts a nasogastric tube to decompress the stomach. Which of the following is correct with regard to insertion of a nasogastric tube?

1. Measure from the tip of the nose to the xiphoid process prior to inserting the tube
2. Have the client swallow as much water as possible during the insertion to close the epiglottis
3. The placement of the nasogastric tube must be confirmed by radiography
4. A reliable method of testing the correct placement of the tube is aspirating gastric contents and testing pH

12. In addition to her primary IV, an intravenous infusion of normal saline with 20 mEq KCl is ordered to replace Mrs. Gupta's nasogastric losses. What is the drop rate for her replacement IV if 640 mL must infuse over the next 8 hours and the drop factor is 15?

1. 80 mL/hr
2. 100 mL/hr
3. 20 gtts/min
4. 25 gtts/min

Case 3

Ms. Abbey, a 20-year-old malnourished woman, requires surgery for her Crohn's disease. The health care team decides to start her on total parenteral nutrition (TPN) prior to surgery. This is the nurse's first time caring for a client with TPN.

Questions 13–16 refer to this case.

13. What important nursing consideration does the nurse need to know when managing Ms. Abbey's TPN?

1. All intravascular delivery system components up to the hub are changed weekly to prevent infection
2. Serum glucose levels and weights are checked weekly
3. Some elevation of liver enzymes is expected in the first few days of treatment
4. Speeding up or slowing the infusion rate is contraindicated

14. Which of the following statements is true about parenteral nutrition (PN)?

1. Peripheral parenteral nutrition (PPN) involves the administration of hypertonic lipid and amino acid solutions through a peripheral vein
2. TPN requires daily temperatures as infection is the most common complication of TPN
3. Stopping TPN abruptly can cause hypoglycemia as the body has adapted to the high osmolarity of the solution by secreting more insulin
4. Central TPN solutions are hypotonic, with high glucose contents from 20–50%

15. Ms. Abbey has a fever of 39°C. The nurse gives her an antipyretic and notifies the physician. What orders might the nurse anticipate?

1. Isolate the client for possible septicemia
2. Collect blood, urine, and sputum cultures to isolate the cause of infection
3. Hold the TPN until blood cultures are clear of pathogens
4. Run dextrose 10% via the central line until the cause of the infection is discovered

16. Ms. Abbey's dressing for her subclavian central line is changed using strict aseptic technique to prevent infection. Which of the following actions by the nurse would compromise the principles of surgical asepsis during this dressing change?

1. The normal saline cap drops onto the floor after the nurse pours the saline onto her tray
2. The nurse discards the disposable gloves used to remove the old dressing prior to opening her sterile tray

3. The nurse uses a hand sanitizer for 15 seconds prior to starting the dressing change
4. The normal saline was opened previously, and there is no date and time on it

Case 4

Mr. Roustas, 42 years old, has a spinal cord injury. He is isolated for a methicillin-resistant *Staphylococcus aureus* (MRSA) infection of a decubitus ulcer on his coccyx. He had the pressure ulcer on admission to the hospital but acquired the infection postadmission. He is in a private room. The sign on his door says Isolation Precautions.

Questions 17–21 refer to this case.

17. Mr. Roustas has a health care–associated infection (HAI, or nosocomial infection). Which of the following would be the most significant factor in his susceptibility to HAI?

1. Administration of antibiotics
2. Diagnosis of spinal cord injury
3. Age
4. Skin breakdown

18. The nurse wears a mask, a gown, and gloves when caring for Mr. Roustas. What is the principal mode of transmission of an antibiotic-resistant organism such as MRSA?

1. A colonized or infected health care worker
2. Transfer from client to client on the hands of hospital personnel
3. Environmental contamination
4. Droplet transmission

19. Mr. Roustas is receiving vancomycin (Vancocin) intravenously for his wound infection. The nurse observes redness around the IV site, and Mr. Roustas is complaining that the site is painful. What corrective action should the nurse take?

1. Slow the rate of infusion
2. Change the site of the infusion
3. Notify the physician
4. Stop the infusion for at least 24 hr

20. Mr. Roustas will be receiving long-term vancomycin (Vancocin) therapy. The health care team discusses whether to use a peripherally inserted central line (PICC) or a tunnelled central line. What is an advantage of a PICC device when compared with a tunnelled central line?

1. Less susceptibility to infection
2. Can be left in situ for a longer period of time
3. More convenient for the client
4. Ease of placement

21. Mr. Roustas has his pressure ulcer debrided by the skin care nurse. His dressing is changed daily after debridement. The nurse irrigates the wound with normal saline and packs it with saline-soaked gauze to promote moist, interactive wound healing. What is the benefit of moist, interactive wound healing?

1. It can be used with iodine, which is an effective antimicrobial agent
2. It promotes faster healing and better tissue quality
3. It requires fewer supplies and equipment
4. There is less incidence of bacterial invasion of the wound

INDEPENDENT QUESTIONS

Questions 22–40 do not refer to a particular case.

22. What is the most effective method for the nurse to validate the effectiveness of pain relief with most clients?

1. Ask clients to rate their pain verbally from mild to severe
2. Monitor their facial expressions before and after administration of analgesics
3. Monitor their vital signs in response to analgesics given
4. Ask clients to rate pain using a numeric rating scale before and after analgesics

23. A community nurse is training a family member to care for her 92-year-old mother who has diabetes. What should the nurse teach the family member about foot care for her mother?

1. Soak both feet daily for less than 15 minutes
2. File the mother's toenails straight across and square
3. Inspect the mother's feet at least twice a month for problems
4. Keep the mother's feet warm with heavy socks and a hot water bottle

24. How does the nurse know when to suction a client with a tracheostomy tube?

1. The client is coughing up copious amounts of sputum from the tracheostomy
2. The client tells the nurse when suctioning is necessary
3. The doctor specifies how often to suction in the orders
4. The nurse bases her decision on assessment data heard on lung auscultation

25. Mrs. DeLuca, 34 years old, gave birth to her third child six hours ago and would like to be discharged. She has not urinated since the birth. On palpation, the nurse determines a full bladder, and the bladder scanner indicates 1000 mL of urine in her bladder. What should the nurse do?

1. Have her sit in a warm bath to see if she can void in the bathtub
2. Insert an intermittent catheter and drain the bladder
3. Let her go home as Mrs. DeLuca feels she will be able to void in the privacy of her own home
4. Insert an in-dwelling catheter for 24 hr so that her bladder will remain empty and her uterus will involute normally

26. A nursing instructor is teaching her first-year nursing students the difference between medical and surgical asepsis. Which of the following would the teacher use as an example of medical asepsis?

1. Inserting a urinary catheter for postoperative urinary retention
2. Changing an abdominal dressing for the first time after surgery
3. Cleaning the hospital environment and equipment routinely
4. Giving an intramuscular injection in the ventrogluteal region

27. An emergency room nurse admits a client who is bleeding profusely from an injury to the femoral artery. Why does the nurse put on personal protective equipment (PPE)?

1. To reduce his exposure to blood borne microorganisms
2. To prevent the client from acquiring a health care–associated infection
3. To protect himself from potentially infectious substances
4. To protect both himself and his client

28. Omotayo, 1 month old, is receiving ampicillin (Ampicin) every six hours. The hospital formulary indicates that a safe dose is 200–400 mg/kg/day. What is the recommended dosage range for Omotayo, who weighs 11 pounds?

1. 11,000–44,000 mg/day
2. 1100–4400 mg/day
3. 1000–2000 mg/day
4. 1000–2000 mg/dose

29. Which of the following is correct regarding subcutaneous injections?

1. Hold the skin taut at the site of the injection to compress the subcutaneous tissue
2. All subcutaneous injection sites can be massaged, with the exception of those for insulin
3. Best practice is not to aspirate for all subcutaneous injections, except for heparin
4. Aspiration is not necessary as it is rare to inject into a blood vessel

30. Mr. Valencia, 83 years old, is confused after his hip-replacement surgery and has been trying to get out of bed when the family is not present. His family wants him to be restrained so he does not injure himself. What should the nurse explain to the family?

1. "Restraining your father will only make him more agitated."
2. "We do not restrain clients anymore as it is against the law."
3. "Would it be possible to have a family member stay with him until he is less confused?"
4. "Would you like me to call the doctor to get an order for restraints for your father?"

31. Mrs. Parsons has stomatitis as a result of recent chemotherapy. The nurse knows that Mrs. Parsons understands the oral hygiene instructions given by the nurse when she makes which of the following comments?

1. "I don't brush my teeth everyday, but when I do, I use my ordinary toothbrush."
2. "I use diluted Listerine mouthwash every four hours. It stings, so I know it is working."
3. "Rinsing my mouth with normal saline every two hours has helped me tremendously."
4. "I never need analgesics. If my mouth is too painful, I just do not brush or rinse for a day or two and the pain passes."

32. Mr. Pelletier returns from surgery with chest tubes in place. What should the nurse say to Mr. Pelletier concerning his chest tubes?

1. "You have chest tubes to remove abnormal accumulations of fluid from inside your lungs."
2. "You need to turn in bed frequently to promote drainage from the pleural space and improve lung expansion."
3. "Your chest tubes will be clamped every time you get out of bed to prevent a leak from developing in the drainage system."
4. "The chest tube drainage system should remain at the level of the chest at all times."

33. Mr. Singh requires a blood transfusion. Which of the following statements is correct about blood administration?

1. The nurse stays with the client for the first five minutes as this is when reactions are most likely to occur
2. Two nurses are required to check the client's blood bag, chart, and ID band prior to administration of the blood product
3. Vital signs must be checked before and after blood administration and during administration if there are any untoward reactions

4. Signs of a febrile reaction are hives, wheezing, pruritus, and joint pain

34. A nurse works in a long-term care facility. In a rush to complete the 1000 hour medications, the nurse gives Mr. Smith the wrong medication. What is the nurse's first responsibility?

1. Disclose the incident to Mr. Smith and his family
2. Inform the unit manager and prescriber of the medication error
3. Complete an incident report for the agency about the details of the incident
4. Assess Mr. Smith to ensure that he is not in immediate danger

35. What are the responsibilities of a nurse who is caring for a client in wrist restraints?

1. Remove the restraints and arrange for a paid sitter as soon as possible
2. Make sure that the restraints are tied tightly and secured with a knot
3. Check skin integrity, pulses, colour, and sensation of the restrained part as often as every 1–2 hr
4. Ensure that the physician reorders the wrist restraints on a weekly basis

36. A nurse working in a community clinic sees many older clients. Which of the following facts does the nurse need to be aware of when treating older clients?

1. Normal temperature for an older adult is 36.5°C orally
2. The older adult might have an advanced infection before it is identified
3. The older adult has increased sensitivity to pain sensation
4. The constipation common in older clients is primarily due to polypharmacy

37. Mr. and Mrs. McNamara ask the nurse for advice about caring for their 24-year-old son, who has been newly diagnosed with a seizure disorder. What will the nurse teach them about care of their son during a seizure?

1. Restrain him gently until the seizure passes
2. Use a padded tongue blade to prevent damage to his tongue during the seizure

3. Put him in a side-lying position as soon as the seizure starts
4. Loosen restrictive clothing and clear the area of hazards and articles that might harm him

38. Mrs. Hathaway, age 98 years, is admitted to an acute care hospital from a long-term care facility. The nurse documents the Braden Scale score on her chart shortly after she arrives on the unit. What is the main purpose of the Braden Scale?

1. To identify clients at risk for pressure ulcers early
2. To identify interventions that can be implemented to treat pressure ulcers
3. To measure friction- and shear-related skin problems on admission to the hospital
4. To identify preventive measures to reduce the incidence of pressure ulcers

39. Mr. Ciavallo, age 57 years, has been diagnosed with lung cancer and is scheduled for resection of his right lung tomorrow. What will the nurse teach him about what to expect with his postoperative care?

1. "You will have incentive spirometry at least four times daily to prevent atelectasis."
2. "Leg exercises will be carried out every two hours while you are awake."
3. "Vigorous coughing will be necessary to expectorate excess sputum."
4. "There will be a right-sided chest tube, and you will be on bed rest until it is removed."

40. Mrs. Lin, age 45 years, has end-stage breast cancer with metastases to her lungs and brain. Her family and the palliative care team are caring for her at home. Which of the following best describes palliative care for Mrs. Lin?

1. Mrs. Lin will be kept comfortable and free from pain
2. Enteral feeds will be started to prevent starvation and malnutrition
3. Interventions will be focused only on the needs of Mrs. Lin
4. Services by the team terminate at the death of Mrs. Lin

Answers and Rationales for Practice Questions

1.   C: Changes in Health   T: Knowledge

1. An auscultatory gap is more common in older clients or clients with hypertension, but it does not always occur in these populations.
2. Normal pulse pressure is 40 mm Hg.
3. Orthostatic hypertension is measured by recording blood pressure (BP) and pulse with the client in three positions: supine, sitting, and standing.
4. This statement is correct. The nurse might make the mistake of recording the last sound at the beginning of the auscultatory gap as diastolic BP or the last sound at the end of the auscultatory gap as systolic BP.

2.   C: Changes in Health   T: Knowledge

1. Rectal is the correct site for core temperatures.
2. Oral is only a surface temperature.
3. Axillary is a surface temperature.
4. Skin is only a surface temperature.

3.   C: Changes in Health   T: Application

1. It is not stated how much Imferon will be given. The rate of injection is 1 mL per 10 seconds for every intramuscular injection.
2. The injection site should not be massaged as this could cause the iron preparation to leak onto the skin and stain the area. Injections by Z-track method should never be massaged.
3. Z-track injections seal medications into muscle tissue. The skin and overlying subcutaneous tissues are pulled laterally prior to the injection, the injection is given, the needle is left in place for 10 seconds, and the skin and overlying subcutaneous tissue are released after the injection. This leaves a zigzag path that seals the needle path and locks the medication in the muscle.
4. The dorsogluteal site was the traditional site for intramuscular injections but is no longer recommended as there is risk of damage to the sciatic nerve and risk of injection into the thick subcutaneous layer rather than the muscle in the area.

4.   C: Professional Practice   T: Application

1. The Imferon injection must be given by the Z-track method to prevent staining of the skin, so this is not an option.
2. Safety-engineered needles retract after the injection is given and reduce the risk of needle-stick injuries.
3. This is not appropriate in this case.
4. Wearing gloves prevents the nurse from coming in contact with any blood that oozes from the injection site. It does not prevent needle-stick injuries. It might prevent the needle from entering the nurse's skin as deeply or decrease the amount of blood entering the nurse's skin from the needle tip.

5.   C: Changes in Health   T: Application

1. It is not correct to slow down the IV line if the nurse needs it to finish within the 8-hr time limit.
2. It is not correct to slow down the IV line if the nurse needs it to finish within the 8-hr time limit.
3. The IV line would normally be running at 125 mL/hr, but that rate must be increased slightly as there is 100 mL extra in the IV bag at 1500 hours.
4. The IV line is 100 mL behind schedule, and there is 600 mL to be infused over the next four hours. To calculate the new rate, divide the volume remaining over the time remaining: 600 mL ÷ 4 hr = 150 mL/hr. Although agency policies should be consulted, it is acceptable to increase the IV rate (25 mL/hr over the ordered rate) in this situation as the client is not an older adult, has no apparent cardiac history, is not at risk for fluid overload, and does require the fluid volume as ordered.

6.   C: Changes in Health   T: Application

1. Transdermal patches or discs should not be applied to hairy areas. They do not stick well to hairy areas, and that could affect the amount of medication absorbed.
2. Transdermal medications can stay in place from one to seven days depending on what drug is being used.
3. All old patches and discs of the same medication must be removed prior to applying a new transdermal medication or an overdose could occur.
4. The nurse should wear gloves when applying transdermal medications as they can be absorbed through the skin during application.

7.   C: Changes in Health   T: Critical Thinking

1. Mrs. Gupta may have a baseline blood pressure of 90/60. The nurse needs to check the health record for previous baseline vital signs. If Mrs. Gupta is feeling faint or lightheaded, she could be symptomatic from the hypotension and needs treatment. The other vital signs are all within the normal range.
2. The nurse needs more information before calling the doctor. The doctor will want to know the baseline vital signs, and the nurse will want to recheck the client's blood pressure prior to calling the doctor.
3. Dehydration or decreased circulating blood volume can cause the blood pressure to be lower, but that

cannot be assumed before checking the urine output, asking the client how she feels, and looking at the baseline vital signs.
4. Modified Trendelenburg is a position in which the legs are elevated to promote venous return to the heart and thus increase cardiac output and blood pressure. That is not necessary unless Mrs. Gupta is going into shock, which her vital signs do not indicate.

8.   C: Changes in Health   T: Application

1. Porridge is only allowed on a full fluid diet. Broth and apple juice would be permitted on a clear fluid diet.
2. None of these foods are part of a clear fluid diet but can be eaten with a full fluid diet.
3. Broth and Popsicles are part of a clear fluid diet, but orange juice would only be permitted on a full fluid diet.
4. All these foods would be allowed on a clear fluid diet.

9.   C: Changes in Health   T: Application

1. Limited mobility and exercise can be contributing factors, but they are not the cause of paralytic ileus in this situation.
2. Eating too much too soon after surgery is much more likely to contribute to paralytic ileus. In a postoperative client, it is advised to wait until bowel sounds return after surgery before advancing to the postoperative diet.
3. Paralytic ileus in a postoperative client is most often caused by the action of narcotics and anaesthetics, delayed gastric emptying, slowed peristalsis resulting from the handling of the bowel during surgery, and resumption of the oral intake too soon after surgery.
4. Mrs. Gupta might need a rectal suppository (often on postoperative day 2 or later) to stimulate peristalsis and expulsion of the flatus; however, not giving it on postoperative day 1 would not have caused a paralytic ileus.

10.   C: Changes in Health   T: Critical Thinking

1. The nurse's first priority is to do a further assessment, which should include looking for redness or swelling in the calf area, measuring calf circumference in both legs, asking Mrs. Gupta if she has any pain in that area, and possibly gently palpating the area.
2. It is possible that Mrs. Gupta has a clot in her leg (thrombophlebitis), so it is best not to put the TED stocking back on until the medical team does a further assessment. It is appropriate to place the leg on a pillow to promote venous return to the heart.

3. The calf circumference should be measured, but both legs should be measured to compare results. This is done after the area is assessed for redness and pain and the client is asked about the history of the present swelling. The doctor would be notified after the nurse has done her assessment.
4. The nurse should not wash the client's leg or encourage her to exercise the leg until she is sure that there is no clot in her leg. Clots from the leg can travel to the lungs and cause a pulmonary embolism.

11.   C: Changes in Health   T: Application

1. Measuring from the tip of the nose to the earlobe to the xiphoid process is the correct measurement to determine length of insertion.
2. The client should not have too much water as this may cause aspiration. The client can dry swallow or sip on water (if allowed) while the nurse advances the tube. The client swallows to the predetermined length.
3. Radiography is the most reliable way to check placement of nasogastric tubes. Many health care settings only insist on radiography to check the placement of small-bore feeding tubes prior to the start of enteral feeds. Some agencies may require X-ray confirmation of the placement of all nasogastric tubes prior to enteral feeds. In this scenario, a placement X-ray is not necessary as the tube is being used for decompression.
4. As the nasogastric tube is to be used for decompression, assessing tube placement by aspirating gastric contents and testing pH is reliable. Gastric pH should be less than 4.

12.   C: Changes in Health   T: Application

1. This is the hourly flow rate for the replacement IV (640 mL ÷ 8 hr = 80 mL/hr).
2. This is the hourly flow rate for the main IV.
3. This rate is correct, using the following formula:

$$\frac{80 \text{ mL} \times 15 \text{ gtts/mL}}{60 \text{ min}} = 20 \text{ gtts/minn}$$

4. This is using an hourly flow rate of 100 mL/hr for the calculations rather than 80 mL.

13.   C: Changes in Health   T: Application

1. All intravascular delivery system components up to the hub are changed every 24–72 hr, according to agency policy, to prevent infection.
2. When TPN infusions are started, serum glucose levels are checked frequently at the bedside as some elevation of blood glucose is expected. Weights are taken daily to monitor the client's hydration status and weight gain with therapy.

3. Liver enzymes should remain normal. Some elevation of serum glucose levels can be expected in the first few days after TPN is started.
4. Speeding up the rate can cause hyperglycemia and slowing the rate can cause hypoglycemia. TPN is almost always managed with an infusion pump.

14.   C: Changes in Health   T: Application

1. PPN involves the administration of isotonic lipid and amino acid solutions through a peripheral vein.
2. TPN requires that the client's temperature be checked every four hours due to the high risk of infection.
3. TPN is never terminated abruptly due to the risk of hypoglycemia. The body adapts to the high osmolarity by secreting more insulin.
4. Central TPN solutions are hypertonic rather than hypotonic.

15.   C: Changes in Health   T: Critical Thinking

1. It is not necessary to isolate a client for a catheter-related infection and septicemia.
2. A blood culture will determine if the infection is from the TPN site. Other common sources of infection are the bladder or lung, thus the urine and sputum tests.
3. The TPN is not held. If the blood cultures are positive, the central line might be removed and a new one started elsewhere. Antibiotics would be prescribed, but TPN would not be stopped abruptly.
4. There is no reason to stop the TPN and run dextrose 10%. The central line might need to be relocated, however, if it is thought to be the cause of the infection.

16.   C: Changes in Health   T: Application

1. This does not interfere with sterile technique as the saline has already been poured.
2. This is correct procedure and does not compromise sterile technique.
3. This is medical asepsis and correct procedure prior to doing a dressing change.
4. This compromises sterile technique. If the normal saline was already open and not labelled, the nurse cannot assume that it is still sterile. It is considered sterile for only 24 hours after opening.

17.   C: Changes in Health   T: Critical Thinking

1. Overuse of antibiotics predisposes clients to HAIs such as MRSA, although this is not likely to be the most significant factor with Mr. Roustas.
2. Spinal cord injury could lead to skin breakdown and the decubitus ulcer, but the actual skin breakdown is the most significant factor.

3. Mr. Roustas is only 42, which is generally not an age that predisposes him to decreased immunity, poorer nutrition, inadequate circulation, or skin breakdown.
4. With skin breakdown, pathogens are able to enter the body, making this the most significant factor in the development of his HAI.

18.   C: Changes in Health   T: Critical Thinking

1. A colonized or infected health care worker may disseminate the organism, but this is not the principal mode of transmission. The most frequently colonized site is the anterior nares.
2. The principal mode of transmission is transfer from client to client on the hands of hospital personnel.
3. Environmental contamination is uncommon.
4. Droplet transmission may occur during the care of a client with MRSA pneumonia, but this is not common.

19.   C: Changes in Health   T: Application

1. Slowing the rate will not help to correct the tissue irritation.
2. These are signs that the vancomycin is irritating the IV site and it needs to be changed.
3. It is not necessary to notify the physician.
4. The infusion will be stopped briefly while the IV site is changed.

20.   C: Changes in Health   T: Application

1. No studies to date indicate fewer infections with PICC lines when compared with tunnelled catheters.
2. A PICC line may be left in situ for up to one year, while a tunnelled central line may, theoretically, be left in situ indefinitely.
3. A tunnelled central line may be more convenient for the client. Location of the PICC in an arm is uncomfortable for some clients and may restrict certain activities in that arm.
4. The PICC line is more easily inserted into a peripheral vein, often the basilic or cephalic. This can be done at the bedside in many hospitals, sometimes by a certified nurse. A tunnelled central line is surgically placed under local anaesthesia by a physician. It requires the creation of a subcutaneous tunnel on the chest wall and a venotomy to access the internal jugular vein, the preferred insertion site.

21.   C: Changes in Health   T: Knowledge

1. Iodine should not be used on a wound bed as this solution is toxic to cells involved in wound healing.

2. Moist, interactive wound healing promotes faster healing, better tissue quality, and less pain than other methods. Other methods, such as wet-to-dry dressings for pressure ulcers, are no longer recommended as they cause mechanical debridement that is not selective and can damage healthy tissue.
3. Moist dressings often require more supplies than simple dry dressings.
4. There is no current research to indicate increased bacteria in a moist dressing.

22.   C: Changes in Health   T: Critical Thinking

1. To validate pain relief, the nurse needs to ask the client to rate the pain before and after administration of analgesics. The words "mild" and "severe" may not be specific enough.
2. Facial expressions do not always reflect the amount of pain that a client is experiencing.
3. Vital signs may or may not change when clients are in pain or after they receive analgesics. It is important to ask clients to rate their pain before and after analgesics as pain is subjective. Only the client knows the level of pain and pain relief.
4. An effective way to rate pain relief in most adults is to use a numeric rating scale from 0–10 (0 being no pain; 10 being the most severe pain) before and after the administration of analgesics. For clients unable to respond to other pain intensity scales (such as children and older adults), a series of faces ranging from "smiling" to "crying" can be used. The rating scale has been shown to be ineffective in some studies, but it remains the most effective tool at present.

23.   C: Changes in Health   T: Application

1. People with diabetes should not soak their feet as the skin can become macerated and more susceptible to injury and infection.
2. Nails should be filed straight across. Clippers or scissors should not be used on the toenails of diabetic clients.
3. The feet of diabetic clients should be inspected daily as they have poor circulation in their feet.
4. Hot water bottles or heating pads should not be used with people with diabetes as they sometimes have loss of sensation in their lower limbs. They might suffer a burn without being aware of it.

24.   C: Changes in Health   T: Application

1. If the client is coughing up the sputum, it is not necessary to suction. Suctioning is traumatic and should be used only when there are indications that the client cannot cough up the secretions without assistance.

2. Sometimes the client is able to tell the nurse when to suction but not always. Clients with a new tracheostomy or clients who are unconscious might not be able to communicate the need for suctioning.
3. Suctioning is not a medical order. The nurse uses her clinical judgement in deciding when to suction a particular client.
4. The nurse uses clinical judgement to decide whether the client needs to be suctioned. Signs that the client needs to be suctioned may include one or more of the following: gurgling respirations, respiratory distress, low oxygen-saturation levels, and coarse crackles on auscultation.

25.   C: Changes in Health   T: Application

1. The client should not sit in a bathtub of warm water as she has just given birth and infection is a possibility.
2. The bladder needs to be emptied via catheterization. An intermittent catheterization carries less risk of infection.
3. The client should not go home until her bladder has been emptied. The full bladder would interfere with uterine contractions that are necessary to expel blood and any remaining uterine contents.
4. An in-dwelling catheter is not necessary. It might be a source of a health care–associated infection (nosocomial infection).

26.   C: Changes in Health   T: Application

1. Urinary catheterization is an example of surgical asepsis or sterile technique. This includes all procedures used to eliminate all microorganisms from an area.
2. Surgical asepsis or sterile technique is used to change a dressing on nonintact skin immediately postoperatively.
3. Cleaning the hospital environment and equipment routinely with approved solutions is used to reduce and prevent the spread of microorganisms. This is called medical asepsis or clean technique.
4. An intramuscular injection is given using surgical asepsis. A sterile needle is used to perforate the client's skin.

27.   C: Changes in Health   T: Application

1. This is true, but it is not the complete rationale for PPE.
2. PPE will not necessarily prevent a health care–associated infection (HAI).
3. It is true that it will protect the nurse from possible infection, but this is not the most correct answer.

4. The nurse assesses the risk for exposure and puts on the appropriate PPE to protect himself and his client. The nurse is using "Routine Practices," which are infection control practices designed for the care of all clients all the time regardless of their diagnosis or presumed infectiveness.

28.   C: Changes in Health   T: Application

1. Incorrect calculation.
2. Incorrect calculation.
3. This is the correct calculation. The child's weight must first be converted from pounds to kilograms (1 kg = 2.2 pounds). Omotayo weighs 11 pounds, which is 11 lbs ÷ 2.2 lbs = 5 kg. The lowest dosage is 200 mg × 5 kg = 1000 mg/day. The highest dosage is 400 mg × 5 kg = 2000 mg/day.
4. This is not correct as it is for one dose only rather than the range for the day.

29.   C: Changes in Health   T: Application

1. This is the method for giving an intramuscular injection. For a subcutaneous injection, the skin should be pinched before injection to elevate the skin and subcutaneous tissue above the muscle and ensure that the injection is given subcutaneously rather than intramuscularly.
2. The site of a heparin injection should not be massaged as this can cause bruising.
3. It is not necessary to aspirate for subcutaneous injections as adipose tissue is not very vascular and injection into a blood vessel is rare. It is particularly important not to aspirate heparin because it can cause bruising.
4. Aspiration for subcutaneous injections is not necessary as adipose tissue is not very vascular and injection into a blood vessel is rare.

30.   C: Professional Practice   T: Critical Thinking

1. Restraints might possibly make him more agitated, but this is not the most appropriate explanation.
2. Most health care facilities are either restraint-free or advocate minimum restraints. This statement makes the nurse appear to be basing action on rules rather than professional judgement.
3. Restraints should be a last resort. The presence of a family member may prevent him from trying to get out of bed. If a family member could be present around the clock, it might be a good short-term solution until Mr. Valencia's confusion clears.
4. It is true that the doctor must order restraints, but this is not the best answer. It is better to use restraints as a last resort.

31.   C: Changes in Health   T: Application

1. With stomatitis, it is important to continue gentle flossing and brushing with a soft toothbrush or toothette to keep the mouth, teeth, and gums clean and prevent infection.
2. Commercial mouthwashes contain alcohol, which stings and dries mucous membranes. Commercial mouthwashes such as Listerine are not recommended.
3. Normal saline mouthwashes are recommended as often as every two hours if necessary for clients with stomatitis.
4. Regular oral hygiene is important for clients with stomatitis to prevent infections. It is recommended that the client use a mild analgesic if necessary for pain so that mouth care can be done.

32.   C: Changes in Health   T: Application

1. Chest tubes can remove air and fluid from the pleural space, not the lungs.
2. Turning in bed or ambulating can shift the position of the chest tube in the pleural space slightly and promote drainage. Lying on the side of the unaffected lung can expand the affected lung more fully as well.
3. Chest tubes are not commonly clamped as clamping can cause a tension pneumothorax. Air pressure builds up in the pleural space, collapsing the lung and creating a life-threatening emergency. Clamping chest tubes requires an order from the physician.
4. The chest tube drainage system should remain below the chest to aid gravity by drainage and to prevent reflux of drainage back into the chest cavity.

33.   C: Changes in Health   T: Application

1. Reactions most commonly occur during the first 15 minutes.
2. Before beginning the infusion, two nurses verify the blood type, Rh factor, client and blood numbers, and expiration date on the blood bag and the chart.
3. This is not frequent enough. The nurse needs pre- and postadministration vital signs but also continues to monitor the client throughout and obtains vital signs periodically during the transfusion as directed by agency policy.
4. These are signs of an allergic reaction. Signs of a febrile reaction include shaking, headache, elevated temperature, back pain, confusion, and hematemesis.

34.   C: Professional Practice   T: Critical Thinking

1. The nurse follows agency policy about disclosure, but this is not her first priority.

2. The nurse informs the manager and prescriber (physician, extended role nurse, dentist, chiropractor), but that is not her first responsibility.

3. She must complete an incident report with the details after she makes sure the client is not in danger and has informed the appropriate agency personnel.

4. The nurse's first responsibility is to assess the client and make sure he is not in immediate danger.

35.   C: Professional Practice   T: Application

1. This is not appropriate unless the nurse knows why the client is restrained and the cost of a sitter has been negotiated with the unit manager or family.

2. Restraints should be tied with a quick-release tie rather than a knot for safety reasons.

3. Proper placement of the restraint, skin integrity, pulses, colour, and sensation of the restrained part should be assessed every hour or according to agency policy.

4. Reviewing the order for restraints should be done frequently but varies from agency to agency. Restraints may need to be reordered on a daily or weekly basis.

36.   C: Changes in Health   T: Knowledge

1. Normal oral temperature for an older adult is 36°C.

2. Infections in older adults may not present typically as they tend to have lower body temperatures, decreased pain sensation, and less immune response to infection. Older adults can often have advanced infection before it is identified.

3. The older adult has decreased pain sensation.

4. Constipation can be a common complaint in older persons due to a combination of many factors, such as impaired general health, use of medication, and decreased bowel motility and physical activity.

37.   C: Changes in Health   T: Application

1. It is not possible, nor is there any reason to restrain someone during a seizure.

2. Nothing should be inserted into the mouth of someone having a seizure.

3. Only put the client in a side-lying position if it is possible. This is usually possible only at the beginning of a seizure.

4. It is most important to protect the client from traumatic injury. They should make sure he is safe and protect him from injury by putting him on a flat surface and clearing the area of hazards.

38.   C: Changes in Health   T: Application

1. The Braden Scale measures sensory perception, moisture, activity, mobility, nutrition, and friction and shear, in an attempt to identify clients most at risk for pressure ulcers.

2. The Braden Scale is a risk assessment tool and does not identify interventions.

3. The Braden Scale does not only measure friction and shear. It also measures sensory perception, moisture, activity, mobility, and nutrition.

4. The Braden Scale is a risk assessment tool and does not identify preventive measures.

39.   C: Changes in Health   T: Application

1. Incentive spirometry is used to prevent or treat atelectasis in the postoperative client and should be used hourly while awake.

2. Leg exercises, including foot circles, dorsiflexion and plantar flexion, quadriceps setting, and hip and knee exercises, should be performed at least every two hours for five successive times while awake.

3. All postoperative clients are encouraged to use controlled rather than vigorous coughing to loosen and expectorate mucus that will have collected during and postsurgery in their lungs. Vigorous coughing may disturb the surgical site.

4. The client will likely have a chest tube but will probably not be on bed rest for long. Movement in bed as well as ambulation is encouraged to promote drainage from the pleural space and lung expansion.

40.   C: Changes in Health   T: Application

1. Palliative care is supportive treatment designed to relieve or reduce uncomfortable symptoms such as pain, nausea, and shortness of breath.

2. Palliative care should be supportive rather than curative. It should not postpone or delay death. Enteral feeds would postpone death.

3. Both client and family needs are the focus of any interventions.

4. The palliative care team offers bereavement support to families after the death of a client.

CHAPTER 6

Pharmacology and Nursing Practice

Leslie L. Brailsford, PhD, MS, MSc

Jennifer Cooke, RN, BScN

A major component within the scope of practice of registered nurses practising in Canada is the administration of medications and the care of clients receiving those medications. There is a legal responsibility on the part of the nurse to ensure a sound knowledge base of pharmacology. Nurses not only must master the physical skill of administering medications to their clients, but they are also responsible for the specific nursing interventions required in the administration of medications.

The nursing implications relating to the administration of medications are derived from a thorough understanding of the medications being administered and their actions, effects, side effects, both desirable and undesirable, contraindications, and normal dosage ranges. Only by being aware of the nature of medications, by making the appropriate assessments, and by initiating the appropriate actions prior to, during, and after the administration of medications can the nurse exercise professional responsibility and ensure the safe care of the client.

PHARMACOLOGY

Pharmacology is the study of drugs (chemicals) and how they affect living cells, the nature of those drugs, their biological activity on living cells, and their fate once they are absorbed into the body.

SOURCES OF DRUGS

There are many sources of drugs that are natural or synthetic products or a combination of both. Some of these sources are as follows:

- Plants (sources of heroin and digitalis)
- Soil (including Kaopectate from clay)
- Animals (including insulin and Premarin [conjugated estrogen])
- Minerals (such as iron)
- Synthesis in a laboratory provides better standardization of chemical characteristics: more

consistency of effects and a reduction in the potential for allergic reactions
- Semisynthesis – Naturally occurring substances are chemically modified to produce a drug (includes many antibiotics and some human insulins)
- Biotechnology – Drugs are produced through the manipulation of DNA and RNA and cloning (includes human insulin such as Humulin and Novolin and hepatitis B vaccine).

ROUTES OF ADMINISTRATION OF MEDICATIONS

The route of administration depends on the characteristics of the drug, the characteristics of the client, and the desired responses. The route also affects the action, absorption, and distribution of drugs.

See Table 7.1 for a comparison of different drug routes and absorption times.

Table 7.1 Drug Administration Routes and Absorption Rates

Drug Administration Route	Absorption Rate
1. Intravenous (IV)	• Most rapid and effective absorption and action
2. Intramuscular (IM)	• Certain preparations can produce drug action in a few minutes, and others have a slower action
3. Subcutaneous (SC)	• Slower than IM; faster than oral
4. Oral (PO)	• Absorption action is slower than the injectable routes that bypass the digestive system • Drugs with the fastest absorption rates are liquids, elixirs, and syrups • Drugs with the slowest absorption rates include enteric-coated tablets • Drugs undergo "first-pass" effects
5. Topical (Top) (skin and mucous membranes)	• Absorption and action vary according to drug form and application site • This is the slowest route of absorption for systemic applications compared with other parenteral routes

NAMING OF DRUGS

Chemical Name

This name describes the specific molecular structure and chemical composition of a drug and is used mainly by researchers (for example, 6-chloro-3,4-dihydro-2H-1,2,4-benzothiadiazine-7-sulfonamide 1,1-dioxide).

Generic (Nonproprietary) Name

The generic name is the one commonly used by health professionals that is created when a drug is ready to be marketed, for example, hydrochlorothiazide.

Brand/Trade (Proprietary or Trademark) Name

This name is owned by the manufacturer and can be created as soon as a generic name has been approved. The choice of name is motivated by marketing considerations (for example, HydroDIURIL).

Combination Drugs

These are drugs made up of a combination of two or more active drugs in a single tablet with complementary modes of action. They provide an additive, therapeutic effect with the possibility of decreasing side effects and increasing client compliance, and they reduce the number of prescriptions and administrative costs. For example, atorvastatin–amlodipine is a combination of two drugs, an anticholesterolemic and an antihypertensive agent, and treats two different major risk factors for coronary heart disease.

CANADIAN DRUG LEGISLATION

Food and Drug Act, 1953

This Act is administered by Health Canada, formerly the Department of National Health and Welfare of Canada. In the Act, a drug is defined as any substance or mixture of substances manufactured, sold, or represented for use in the diagnosis, treatment, mitigation, or prevention of disease, disorder, or abnormal physical state, or its symptoms, in human beings or animals, restoring, correcting, or modifying organic functions in human beings or animals or disinfection in premises in which food is manufactured, prepared, or kept.

The purpose of the law is to

- Govern the distribution and use of drugs in Canada
- Protect the consumer from unsafe drugs
- Investigate discrepancies
- Monitor the advertising and sale of drugs for treatment, prevention, and cure

- Divide drugs into specific categories (called schedules) depending on the classification of the drug, as follows:

Schedule F:

- Part 1: Prescription drugs (Pr) – Require prescription from a qualified physician or prescriber. (See Chapter 3, on professional practice, for the nurse practitioner's role in prescribing medications.)
- Part 2: Drugs obtained from a pharmacist without a prescription on request, or over the counter (OTC), such as Tylenol® #1
- Part 3: Drugs available in a pharmacy directly off the shelf, such as laxatives

Unscheduled Drugs: Drugs that can be purchased in any store, such as Tylenol® or Alka Seltzer®
Illicit Drugs: Drugs used or distributed illegally; includes drugs that may be obtained legally via a prescription but are distributed illegally (stolen or produced illegally by nonprofessionals)
Schedule G: Controlled drugs (habit-forming drugs), such as barbiturates
Schedule H: Restricted drugs (drugs producing dangerous side effects) that may be undergoing research (such as hallucinogens, lysergic acid diethylamide [LSD])

THE CONTROLLED DRUGS AND SUBSTANCES ACT 1997 (CDSA)

This Act outlines the legal control of addictive and habituating drugs and provides more extensive regulation and control over their possession, manufacture, sale, and distribution. It requires a specific type of prescribing and more stringent recording and record keeping.

The CDSA regulates the following categories of drugs:

- Opium poppy and its derivatives
- Cannabis and its derivatives (marijuana, hashish)
- Amphetamines, methylphenidate, LSD, methaqualone, psilocybin, and mescaline
- Sedative–hypnotics, such as barbiturates, benzodiazepines, and anabolic steroids

PHARMACODYNAMICS

The term "pharmacodynamics" describes the action of drugs on target cells and the changes occurring in body fluids as a result of the action of these drugs. The pharmacological effects of a drug on the body can be described as the local or systemic therapeutic effects, or both, as well as any side effects and any toxic effects.

TYPES OF ACTION

Most drugs combine with receptor sites on cells and are characterized by their mechanism of action upon those cells.

- Agonist – A drug that binds to a receptor, producing a biochemical response
- Antagonist – A drug that binds to a receptor, preventing an agonist from binding to that receptor, which results in no agonist biochemical response

FACTORS THAT AFFECT DRUG ACTION

- Drug dosage
- Route of administration
- Individual characteristics (age, gender, race, pathological condition)
- Drug–diet interaction
- Drug interactions
- Use of herbal and dietary supplements
- Genetic makeup

DRUG INTERACTIONS

- Potentiation (synergism) – The interaction between two drugs with the result that the overall effect is greater than if the drugs are given separately.
- Displacement – The effects of one drug are increased when its normal binding site on plasma protein within the blood is inhibited by another drug, thereby promoting more immediate action of the first drug.
- Antidotal effect – The toxic effects of one drug are reduced by a second drug that takes up the receptor sites of the first drug, thereby preventing a biochemical response.

NONPHARMACOLOGICAL EFFECTS OF A DRUG ON THE BODY

- Allergic reaction – An undesirable reaction to a drug (of protein origin) that is regarded by the body as an allergen; occurs after the second or subsequent dose of the drug
- Anaphylaxis – A severe, acute, systemic reaction to an allergen, causing massive vasodilation, dyspnea, and shock and requiring immediate emergency care
- Idiosyncratic reaction – An unexpected response to a drug by a specific client; commonly the result of genetic factors that cause the client to respond differently
- Teratogenic reaction – A reaction to a drug that may produce congenital defects if taken by a woman who is pregnant, such as thalidomide, which produced deformed limbs
- Drug tolerance – Resistance of the body to the action of a drug as a result of adaptation as a result of overuse; higher dosages are required in order to produce the desired effects

- Physical dependence – Dependence on a drug resulting in the body requiring a continuous supply in order to function normally; undesirable physical manifestations result if the drug is withdrawn
- Psychological dependence – A psychological dependence on the drug, where there is an overwhelming and uncontrollable desire for the drug that forces continued usage

PHARMACOKINETICS

Pharmacokinetics refers to how the body manages a drug: its absorption, distribution, metabolism (biotransformation), and excretion.

ABSORPTION

Absorption is the process that occurs from the time a drug enters the body until the time it enters the bloodstream. Factors that affect the absorption of a drug include the following:

- Size of the drug molecules
- Properties of the drug (such as lipophilic)
- Environmental temperature
- Membrane thickness
- Surface area of body
- Blood supply at absorption site
- Route of administration
- Presence of food or other drugs in the gastrointestinal (GI) tract
- Drug formulation (such as enteric or slow release)
- Bioavailability – How much of the drug actually enters the bloodstream to exert its effects on body cells; the route of administration is a major determinant
- Presence of disease

DISTRIBUTION

Distribution is the transport of drug molecules within the body. Factors that affect the distribution of a drug include the following:

- Blood circulation
- Plasma protein binding (drug inactivated temporarily while bound to the protein)
- Anatomical barrier (such as the blood–brain or blood–placental barrier)
- Presence of disease (such as peripheral vascular disease)
- Lipid solubility
- Storage in body tissues (the drug is inactive while in the storage site, such as in adipose tissue)

METABOLISM

An individual's metabolism determines how drugs are biotransformed by the body into simple, active, or inactive metabolites. For example:

- Lipid-soluble drugs are converted to water-soluble forms to be excreted by the kidney, which is achieved by enzyme systems in the liver, kidney, lungs, GI tract, red blood cells, and plasma mucosa.
- Toxic waste products can be produced if biotransformation is extremely rapid.
- Slow biotransformations result in lower drug dosages to cells.
- Factors that affect biotransformation include the following:
  - Immaturity of organs (infants)
  - Degeneration of organs (older adults)
  - Reduced circulation
  - A diet low in protein
  - Drugs that antagonized enzyme action
  - Disease (cirrhosis of liver)
  - Genetic factors

Excretion

- Elimination of a drug from the body
- Requires an adequately functioning cardiovascular system, kidneys, GI tract, lungs, and skin
- Prior to administering drugs, an assessment of adequate organ functioning needs to be made

DRUGS THAT AFFECT THE CENTRAL NERVOUS SYSTEM

Numerous classifications of drugs affect the nervous system. In general, there are two actions a drug can exert on the nervous system—stimulation or depression. Figure 7.1 shows the drug classifications and their

FIGURE 7.1
Drugs That Affect the Nervous System

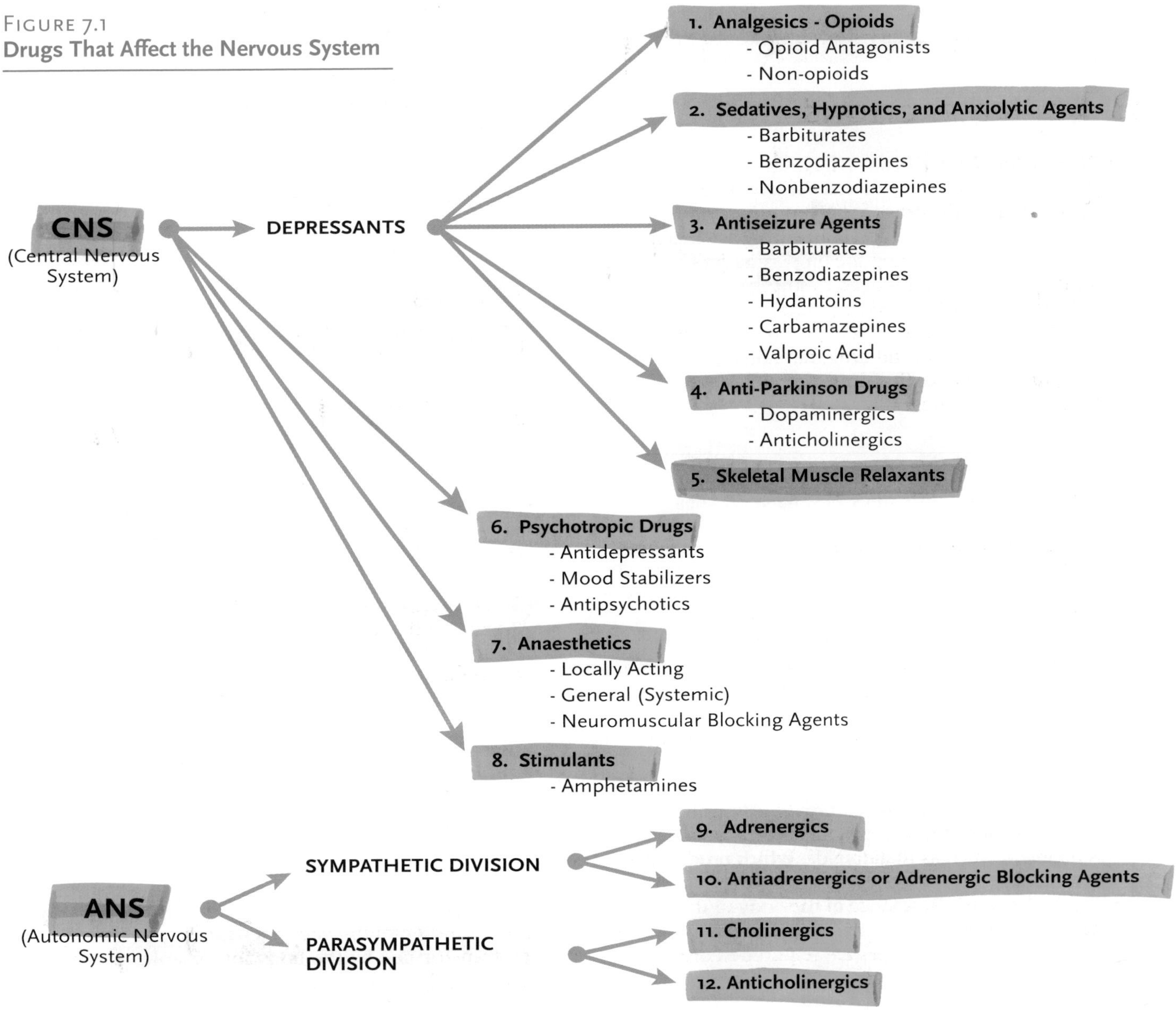
CNS
(Central Nervous System)
DEPRESSANTS
1. Analgesics - Opioids
- Opioid Antagonists
- Non-opioids
2. Sedatives, Hypnotics, and Anxiolytic Agents
- Barbiturates
- Benzodiazepines
- Nonbenzodiazepines
3. Antiseizure Agents
- Barbiturates
- Benzodiazepines
- Hydantoins
- Carbamazepines
- Valproic Acid
4. Anti-Parkinson Drugs
- Dopaminergics
- Anticholinergics
5. Skeletal Muscle Relaxants
6. Psychotropic Drugs
- Antidepressants
- Mood Stabilizers
- Antipsychotics
7. Anaesthetics
- Locally Acting
- General (Systemic)
- Neuromuscular Blocking Agents
8. Stimulants
- Amphetamines
ANS
(Autonomic Nervous System)
SYMPATHETIC DIVISION
PARASYMPATHETIC DIVISION
9. Adrenergics
10. Antiadrenergics or Adrenergic Blocking Agents
11. Cholinergics
12. Anticholinergics

therapeutic actions and effects on either the central nervous system (CNS) or the autonomic nervous system.

ANALGESIC AGENTS

Analgesics are used to relieve pain without causing loss of consciousness. There are two classifications of analgesics: opioids, prescribed for the treatment of severe pain, and non-opiate preparations, used for milder or more moderate pain. Many non-opioid preparations have both antipyretic and anti-inflammatory effects. The choice of analgesic will depend on the effectiveness of an agent, the route of administration to be used, the duration of action of the drug, the duration of the therapy, potential drug interactions (particularly if the client is receiving other depressant medications), and hypersensitivities that the client may have.

Although opioid analgesics are primarily prescribed for the treatment of pain, other therapeutic uses of specific types of opioid analgesics, such as codeine, include treatment to suppress a dry cough and severe diarrhea.

Opioid Analgesics

These are morphinelike substances that may be natural, derived from opium, or synthesized in the laboratory.

- Controlled under the CDSA
- Are associated with a high risk of dependence
- Are prescribed for treatment of moderate to severe pain, such as pain originating from visceral sources, such as surgery, myocardial infarction (MI), colic, and cancer pain

Table 7.2 Common Opioid Analgesics	
Opioid Analgesics	**Routes of Administration**
Morphine Sulphate	PO, IM, epidural, intrathecal, IV
Codeine Phosphate	PO, IM, SC
Fentanyl (Duragesic)	IM, IV, transdermal
Hydromorphone (Dilaudid)	IM, SC, IV, SUPP
Meperidine (Demerol)	IM, IV, SC, PO
Methadone (Metadol)	PO (not recommended for children)
Oxycodone (Oxyneo, others)	PO (not recommended for children under 12)
Tramadol and Acetaminophen (Tramacet)	PO (not recommended for children)

- Inhibit the release of substance P in the central and peripheral nerves, resulting in interference with the transmission of sensory nerve impulses to the brain from peripheral tissues
- Enhance the release of naturally occurring opioid-type chemicals within the body (enkephalin, dynorphins, and endorphins)
- Include effects such as the suppression of the CNS, preventing the sensation of pain within the CNS (the substantia gelatinosa, spinal cord, brainstem, reticular formation, thalamus, and limbic system)
- Modify the perception of pain
- Include additional actions and effects of opioids, such as the following:

  - Suppression of the cough reflex
  - Suppression of GI motility
  - Stimulation of the vomiting centre

Common Opioid Analgesics

The common opioid analgesics are listed in Table 7.2.

Analgesic Dosages
It is important to refer to a potency chart to ensure the correct dosage when changing the route of administration of an opioid. For example, 10 mg of morphine sulphate IM equals 30 mg morphine sulphate orally.

Adverse Effects of Opioid Analgesics

- Tolerance, physiological and psychological dependence (addiction)
- Nausea, vomiting, and constipation
- CNS depression, which may lead to respiratory depression
- Weakness, sedation
- Euphoria, disorientation, and hallucinations (particularly in older adults)

Contraindications of Opioid Analgesics

- Allergy
- Respiratory insufficiency (such as asthma)
- Elevated intracranial pressure
- Pregnancy

Nursing Considerations Relating to Opioid Analgesics

- Assess client need.
- Ask the client about his or her perception of the degree of pain; medication should be administered prior to the pain becoming too severe.
- Assess the client's history of opioid use.
- Check for the time of the last dosage.
- Assess the previous client response and adverse effects; antiemetics may be administered at the same time to avoid nausea and vomiting.
- Assess respiratory rate, depth, and rhythm prior to administration. Withhold the medication and report if

respiration is less than 10 per minute and shallow; an opioid blocker may be required.

- Frequently assess the client's vital signs, level of consciousness, alertness, and cognitive ability during therapy.
- Facilitate the effects of the analgesic administered by promoting an environment of rest, relaxation, peace and quiet, and physical comfort.
- Coughing exercises, deep breathing, and frequent moving help maintain normal functioning.
- Maintain careful documentation of administration of opioids, noting frequency. Observe for signs of dependence; opioids require frequent reordering by a physician or prescriber to minimize overuse and abuse.
- Monitor the client's intake and urine output for possible dehydration and urinary retention.
- Monitor bowel sounds and bowel functioning for signs of constipation.
- Client education includes knowledge relating to the nature of drug and usage, particularly in home use.
- Due to possible drowsiness, clients taking opioids at home should be cautioned to avoid situations requiring rapid reactions, including driving a car, the operation of dangerous machinery, and smoking.
- Care should be taken around the concurrent use of other CNS depressants, such as alcohol.

Agonist–Antagonist Agents

Agonist–antagonist combination drugs are narcotics with a narcotic antagonist added. They have the potency of an agonist but a lower potential for abuse than pure agonists and are commonly used to treat moderate to severe pain in clients with renal colic, burns, and cancer or as preoperative medication. Examples include the following:

- Buprenorphine (Subutex)
- Butorphanol (Stadol)
- Nalbuphine (Nubain)

Adverse effects of agonist–antagonists are similar to those of opioid agonists.

Opioid Antagonists

These drugs block the receptor sites of opioid analgesics or displace opiates occupying receptor sites.

- Act as an antidote to opioid agonists and agonist–antagonists
- Are used to relieve CNS and respiratory depression caused by an overdose of opioid analgesics
- Narcan (naloxone) – Used in the treatment of opioid overdoses
- ReVia (naltrexone) – Maintains an opiate-free state in clients addicted to opiates

Non-opioid Analgesics (Antipyretic/Anti-Inflammatory Agents)

These analgesics relieve mild to moderate pain, fever, and the inflammatory response. Common non-opioid analgesics are listed in Table 7.3.

Table 7.3 Common Non-opioid Analgesics

Classification	Action	Therapeutic Effects	Adverse Effects
Acetylsalicylic Acid, e.g., Aspirin	• Inhibits prostaglandin synthesis by binding to both forms of cyclo-oxygenase (COX-1 and COX-2)	• Mild analgesia • Antipyretic • Anti-inflammatory • Anticoagulant	• GI irritation • Tinnitus • Allergic reactions • Bleeding • Drowsiness, weakness, and dizziness
Acetaminophen, e.g., Tylenol®		• Mild analgesia • Antipyretic	• Liver and renal damage; not recommended for use in severe liver disease • Drowsiness, weakness, and dizziness
Ibuprofen, e.g., Advil®, Motrin®	• Inhibits prostaglandin synthesis by binding to both forms of cyclo-oxygenase (COX-1 and COX-2)	• Mild analgesia • Antipyretic • Anti-inflammatory	• Drowsiness, weakness, and dizziness
Celecoxib, e.g., Celebrex®	• Inhibits prostaglandin synthesis by binding cyclo-oxygenase (COX-2)	• Mild analgesia • Antipyretic • Anti-inflammatory	• Allergic reactions • Drowsiness, weakness, and dizziness
Naproxen, e.g., Naprosyn	• Inhibits prostaglandin synthesis by binding cyclo-oxygenase (COX-2)	• Mild analgesia • Antipyretic • Anti-inflammatory	• Drowsiness, weakness, and dizziness

Uses for non-opioid analgesics (antipyretics, nonsteroidal anti-inflammatory drugs [NSAIDs]) are as follows:

- Pain associated with muscles, joints, and connective tissue
- Treatment of pain and inflammation associated with osteoarthritis and rheumatoid arthritis (OA, RA) and rheumatic fever
- Fever
- Dysmenorrheal pain (especially ibuprofen)
- Headache

Nursing Considerations Relating to Non-opioid Analgesics (Antipyretics, NSAIDs)

- Clients should be monitored for bleeding and petechiae (ASA).
- Analgesics should be administered with food to reduce gastric irritation.
- Teaching for self-medicating clients:

  - Instruct clients not to exceed the recommended dosage and frequency.
  - Tell clients to avoid ASA if there is a history of gastric discomfort or bleeding tendency.
  - Clients should avoid activities that require alertness (driving) due to the sedating effects.
  - Clients should avoid other CNS depressants, such as alcohol.
  - Clients should seek medical attention if pain or fever persists >48–72 hr.

SEDATIVES, HYPNOTICS, AND ANXIOLYTICS

Classifications of sedatives, hypnotics, and anxiolytics include barbiturates, benzodiazepines, and nonbenzodiazepines. Irrespective of the classification of individual drugs, each has a calming, relaxing effect on the body by depressing CNS activity. Many of these drugs are strongly controlled, requiring a prescription; however, mild-acting drugs may be purchased OTC. Certain drugs may be used for sedation and relief of anxiety in low dosages, and in high doses, they would be prescribed to produce sleep.

Sedatives:
- Decrease the functional activity of the brain and response to stimuli without producing sleep
- Produce general CNS depression
- Are used to relax clients prior to procedures and for extreme anxiety (see the section on anxiolytic agents)

Hypnotics:
- Used to produce extreme sedation and sleep
- Act on the reticular activation system (RAS) to block the brain's response to incoming stimuli
- Are used to treat insomnia
- May be prescription drugs or OTC

Sedative–Hypnotics:
- Produce sedative or hypnotic effects, depending on the dose administered

Anxiolytics:
- Prescribed to produce relief of anxiety and panic disorder

Classifications of Sedatives, Hypnotics, and Anxiolytics

Benzodiazepines

These drugs act in the limbic and reticular activating systems to make gamma-aminobutyric acid (GABA), an inhibitory neurotransmitter, more effective.

Uses of Benzodiazepines

- To prevent mild to severe anxiety (including panic disorder) and insomnia
- To induce sleep
- For skeletal muscle relaxation
- As preoperative medication

Common benzodiazepines and their uses and dosages are outlined in Table 7.4.

Adverse Effects of Benzodiazepines

- Headache
- Drowsiness
- Blurred vision
- Benzodiazepines (contraindicated for pregnancy and lactation and severe respiratory, kidney, or liver disorders)

Common Nonbenzodiazepine Sedatives, Hypnotics, and Anxiolytics

Common uses and dosages of nonbenzodiazepines are outlined in Table 7.5.

Barbiturates

Barbiturates, derivatives of barbituric acid, act by inhibiting the conduction of nerve impulses within the CNS by promoting the inhibitory activity of GABA. They are less commonly used now for the treatment of anxiety, as sedatives, and for insomnia due to their side effects and strong addictive properties. The benzodiazepines and nonbenzodiazepines are the treatment of choice for these problems.

Barbiturates in common use today are as follows:

- Phenobarbital (Luminal), a long-acting barbiturate, used primarily as an anticonvulsant in conjunction with other anticonvulsants
- Pentobarbital, a short-acting barbiturate, used primarily as a preoperative sedative

Table 7.4   Common Benzodiazepines

Drug	Normal Dosage	Common Use
Alprazolam (Xanax)	0.25–0.5 mg tid PO	Anxiety and panic attacks
Diazepam (Valium)	2–10 mg bid PO 2–10 mg IM/IV	Mild anxiety Muscle relaxant
Clonazepate (Tranxene)	15 mg at bedtime, PO	Anxiety
Flurazepam (Dalmane)	15–30 mg at bedtime, PO	Insomnia
Triazolam (Halcion)	125–500 mcg at bedtime, PO	Insomnia
Chlordiazepoxide HCl (Librium)	PO/IM/IV 5–25 mg tid/qid	Mild to severe anxiety
Lorazepam (Ativan)	2–6 mg per day PO	Anxiety; sedation
Oxazepam (Serax)	10–30 mg tid/qid PO	Anxiety

Table 7.5   Common Nonbenzodiazepines

Drug	Dosage	Uses
Ethchlorvynol (Placidyl)	200 mg bid PO 500 mg, 1 g at bedtime, PO	Sedative, hypnotic
Chloral hydrate (Noctec)	500 mg, 1 g at bedtime, PO	Hypnotic
Meprobamate (Equanil)	400 mg, 3–4 times daily PO 400–800 mg, at bedtime, PO	Sedative, hypnotic, anxiolytic
Diphenhydramine (Sominex)	50 mg, at bedtime, PO	Antihistamine, mild hypnotic
Hydroxyzine (Atarax)	25–100 mg tid to qid per day 100 mg, IM	Sedative, anxiolytic
Sertraline (Zoloft)	50 mg daily PO	Anxiety and stress disorder

Nursing Considerations Relating to Sedatives, Hypnotics, and Anxiolytics

- Perform a careful assessment prior to administration, including vital signs, level of consciousness, other drugs being taken, health history, and any allergies.
- Instruct clients to avoid the concurrent use of these drugs with other CNS depressants (including alcohol).
- Take all precautions relating to drowsiness, dizziness, reduced awareness, and loss of coordination.
- Ensure that safety measures due to CNS depression are initiated to reduce the risk of injury.
- Clients should be assessed for side and adverse effects and observations charted and reported.
- Clients at home should be taught and cautioned about the following:

  - The risks of overuse, misuse, and dependence
  - The avoidance of dangerous behaviours, such as smoking
- These drugs should be restricted to short-term use only.

ANTISEIZURE AGENTS

Epilepsy is not a single disorder but a collection of conditions characterized by the sudden discharge of excessive electrical energy by brain cells. The goal of therapy is to effectively limit this uncontrolled firing of neurons and to control the spread of impulses. To achieve this goal, each client's treatment is based on the type of seizure he or she experiences.

The choice of drug therapy is dependent on the proper classification of the type of seizure. This classification is based on the client's clinical symptoms and electroencephalographic (EEG) pattern.

Types of Antiseizure Agents

Barbiturates

Barbiturates such as phenobarbital act to inhibit the conduction of nerve impulses within the CNS by promoting the inhibitory activity of GABA. This reduces the abnormal electrical activity within the brain that is causing seizure activity. Phenobarbital is the drug of choice for treating children with tonic–clonic seizures.

Benzodiazepines

Benzodiazepines such as diazepam (Valium) and clonazepam increase the GABA effect to inhibit neuron firing, thereby reducing abnormal electrical activity.

Hydantoins

The hydantoin class acts on the cell membrane of neurons in the cortex of the brain to stabilize nerve membranes, thus reducing voltage frequency and the spread of electrical discharges. Phenytoin (Dilantin) is the drug of choice for treating adults' tonic–clonic seizures.

Carbamazepines

Carbamazepine (Tegretol, Atretol), lamotrigine (Lamictal), and gabapentin (Neurontin) increase GABA activity and block sodium and calcium channels, thus reducing the nerve action potential. They are used for tonic–clonic and simple partial seizures.

Valproic Acid

Valproic acid (Depakene) increases the GABA effect, resulting in decreased electrical activity. It is used to treat absence, mixed, and complex seizures.

Adverse Effects of Antiseizure Medications

- Epigastric pain
- Nausea and vomiting
- Drowsiness
- Bradycardia
- Hypotension

Nursing Considerations Relating to Antiseizure Medications

- Prior to administration, an assessment of past and present health history for allergies, drug interactions, adverse effects experienced, and kidney, liver, and heart disease needs to be completed and vital signs taken.
- The drug should be given at the same time each day.
- Food to avoid GI irritation, nausea, and vomiting should be given.
- Clients should be informed of possible drowsiness that may occur initially.
- Clients should be cautioned to avoid taking antacids at the same time as medication.
- Clients should be cautioned about abruptly stopping medication.
- Clients should be advised to report any undesirable effects immediately.
- Clients should avoid other CNS depressants, such as alcohol.
- Perform an assessment of therapeutic blood levels for clients on long-term therapy.
- Liver function tests should be performed on a regular basis.
- Clients should be educated about the use of a MedicAlert bracelet as a protective measure.

ANTI–PARKINSON'S DISEASE AGENTS

Anti-Parkinson's pharmacotherapy is aimed at increasing or enhancing the action of dopamine in the brain (using dopaminergic agents) and inhibiting the action of acetylcholine (Ach) (with anticholinergic agents) for the purpose of restoring the balance between dopamine and Ach.

Dopaminergic Agents

These drugs increase the effects of dopamine at receptor sites in the substantia nigra. Since dopamine cannot cross the blood–brain barrier, drugs that act like dopamine or increase dopamine concentration are used.

- Levodopa (L-dopa) crosses the blood–brain barrier, where it is converted to dopamine. Large amounts are broken down to dopamine prior to passing through the blood–brain barrier and into the CNS. Levodopa given alone requires a high dosage to produce the desired effects.
- Carbidopa inhibits the breakdown of levodopa outside the CNS, allowing greater amounts of levodopa to enter the CNS. This effect results in a lower dosage requirement. Commonly, a levodopa–carbidopa combination drug is administered.
- Amantadine (Symmetrel) increases dopamine release and blocks the reuptake of dopamine into the presynaptic neuron.
- Selegiline decreases the breakdown of dopamine by monoamine oxidase B (MAO-B) inhibitors. (Monoamine oxidase is an enzyme that breaks down neurotransmitters.)
- Entacapone decreases the breakdown of dopamine by COMT (catechol O-methyltransferase, the enzyme that breaks down levodopa).

Adverse Effects of Dopaminergic Agents

- Nausea and vomiting
- Orthostatic hypotension
- Palpitations
- Dizziness

- Nervousness and agitation
- Muscle irritability

The beneficial effects of dopaminergic drugs are not seen until a few weeks after treatment begins. Vitamin B_6 facilitates the breakdown of levodopa, reducing levels outside the CNS and limiting the amount of dopamine reaching the brain.

Anticholinergic Drugs

These drugs oppose the effect of Ach at the receptor sites in the substantia nigra and corpus striatum, thus helping restore chemical balance in the area. They also help alleviate the tremors and rigidity associated with Parkinson's disease. Examples include benztropine (Cogentin) and trihexyphenidyl.

Adverse Effects of Anticholinergic Drugs

- Drowsiness
- Confusion
- Constipation
- Dry mouth
- Urinary retention
- Pupillary dilation

Nursing Considerations Relating to Anti-Parkinson's Drugs

- Prior to administration, perform an assessment of health history for CNS, GI, and urinary functioning and psychological state, such as swallowing, voiding patterns, constipation, peptic ulcer disease, prostate enlargement, depression, and so on, to identify possible contraindications or cautions.
- Administer following meals and at bedtime with a full glass of water.
- Encourage regular mouth care due to drying effects.
- Tell clients to avoid foods high in vitamin B_6 (such as spinach, bananas, liver, and sweet potato).
- Teach the importance of ingesting foods high in fibre to maintain regular GI functioning and avoid constipation.
- Teach clients that entacapone will produce a brownish discoloration of the urine that is normal.
- Observe for and chart desired and adverse effects experienced by clients.
- Encourage clients to report any undesirable effects that are experienced.

SKELETAL MUSCLE RELAXANTS

Skeletal muscle relaxants depress the CNS by blocking nerve impulses that cause muscle tone and contraction. The primary use is for the treatment of muscle spasm. The majority of muscle relaxants act on the CNS by depressing the system and indirectly relaxing the muscles. However, a few act directly by depressing the contraction of muscle fibres (such as dantrolene).

- Baclofen (Lioresal) is used to treat the spasticity of multiple sclerosis (MS) and spinal cord injury.
- Dantrolene (Dantrium) inhibits muscle contraction, relieving muscle spasticity and malignant hypertension. (The safety of these drugs for children 12 years and under has not been established.)
- Diazepam (Valium) is used for muscle spasm and inflammation.
- Methocarbamol (Robaxin) is used for muscle spasm and inflammation.

Nursing Considerations Relating to Muscle Relaxants

- Use all safety precautions relating to drugs that produce CNS depression.
- Teach clients about avoiding dangerous activities that require alertness and quick reflexes.

PSYCHOTROPIC DRUGS

Psychotropic drugs are used to treat clients who have lost the ability to cope with the normal activities of daily living due to changes in their mental state. An inability to cope with normal day-to-day functions can be the result of depression, changes in personality and mood, or psychotic behaviour. The three categories of drugs include antidepressants, mood stabilizers, and antipsychotics.

Antidepressants

Depression has no known external cause. It is theorized to be the result of decreased levels of the neurotransmitters norepinephrine (NE), dopamine, or serotonin in key areas of the brain. Older drugs, such as the tricyclic antidepressants (TCAs) and monoamine oxidase inhibitors (MAOIs), as well as newer drugs, such as the selective serotonin reuptake inhibitors (SSRIs), share the following characteristics:

- Relieve depression
- Must be taken for 2–4 weeks before depression symptoms improve
- Can be administered PO
- Are metabolized by cytochrome enzyme P-450 in the liver

Classifications of Antidepressants

Tricyclic Antidepressants (TCAs)

- TCAs reduce the uptake of serotonin and NE into nerves by inhibiting the presynaptic uptake; this, in turn, leads to increased levels in the synaptic cleft.
- Adverse effects of TCAs include the following:

  - Sedation
  - Sleep disturbances
  - Fatigue
  - Hallucination

- Visual disturbances
- Tremors
- GI problems
- Cardiac dysrhythmias

- Examples include imipramine (Tofranil), used to treat depression and childhood enuresis; amitriptyline (Novo-Triptyn), used to treat depression; and clomipramine (Anafranil), used to treat obsessive–compulsive disorder (OCD).

Monoamine Oxidase Inhibitors (MAOIs)

- Rarely prescribed today because of the requirement that clients have a specific diet free of tyramine, which produces drug toxicity
- Examples are phenelzine (Nardil) and tranylcypromine (Parnate)

Selective Serotonin Reuptake Inhibitors (SSRIs)

- The newest group of antidepressants
- Block the uptake of serotonin with little to no effect on NE; an increase in levels in the synaptic cleft promotes nerve impulse transmission and results in an antidepressant effect
- Examples include the following:

  - Fluoxetine (Prozac) – For treatment of depression, OCD, and bulimia nervosa
  - Fluvoxamine (Luvox) – For depression
  - Paroxeline (Paxil) – For depression, OCD, and generalized anxiety disorder
  - Sertraline (Zoloft) – For depression, OCD, and panic attacks
  - Citalopram (Celexa) – For depression

- Adverse effects of SSRIs include the following:

  - Fewer adverse effects are produced than with TCAs; however, because they bind significantly to plasma protein (with a half-life of 24–72 hr), accumulation within the body can occur when taken over a protracted period.
  - Anxiety
  - Dizziness
  - Seizures
  - GI effects
  - Must be used with caution in children and older adults

Mood Stabilizers

Lithium carbonate and lithium citrate, plus two lithium salts, are available for treatment and prevention of manic episodes. Lithium salts appear to alter sodium transport at nerve endings, inhibiting cyclic AMP formation in nerve cells and enhancing the uptake of NE and serotonin by nerve cells.

Lithium is not metabolized by the body and is entirely excreted by the kidneys; therefore, renal function assessment is necessary prior to treatment.

Cardiac and thyroid status should also be assessed prior to treatment due to the drug's potential adverse effects on these organs.

Sodium levels can affect the reabsorption of lithium; therefore, electrolyte levels should also be monitored. Lithium toxicity occurs at serum levels >2.5 mmol/L. Symptoms of toxicity include nystagmus, tremors, oliguria, and confusion.

- Examples include olanzapine (Zyprexa) – For treatment of mania and schizophrenia
- Carbamazepine (Tegretol) – To treat bipolar disorder (also an anticonvulsant)
- Valproic acid (Depakene) – To treat bipolar disorder (also an anticonvulsant)

Nursing Considerations Relating to Antidepressants or Mood-Stabilizing Drugs

- Do a careful assessment of clients' history of receiving antidepressant drugs.
- Assess for blood dyscrasias (such as leukopenia) and liver functioning.
- Monitor for extrapyramidal symptoms (EPSs) and cardiac dysrhythmias.
- Monitor the behaviour of clients with a history of suicidal attempts.
- Monitor vital signs: BP, pulse, and respiratory rates initially.
- Advise the client

  - That desirable effects may take several weeks to be established.
  - To take medication as prescribed and avoid missing or doubling dosages.
  - To take medication with food to avoid GI irritation.
  - Concerning the adverse effects of CNS stimulation.
  - To report to a doctor if adverse effects are experienced.
  - Not to discontinue prescribed medication independently.
  - To avoid taking other CNS-affecting drugs, such as alcohol, coffee, or tobacco.
  - To avoid exposure to direct sunlight and use sunscreen and protective clothing.

Antipsychotic Drugs

Neuroleptics or major tranquilizers are antipsychotic drugs. They are designed to bind to dopamine receptors and block the action of dopamine. These drugs are used primarily in the treatment of schizophrenia but may also be used to treat psychotic symptoms brought about by head injury, tumour, stroke, and other disorders.

Phenothiazines

This is the largest group of antipsychotic drugs and includes chlorpromazine (Largactil PO, IM), a prototype drug used in treating adults, older adults, and children.

Major side effects include sedation, extrapyramidal reactions, and moderate to high hypotension.

Thioxanthenes

These drugs cause fewer sedative and hypotensive effects than the phenothiazines but cause extrapyramidal effects. An example is thiothixene (Navane).

Atypical Agents

- These agents block both dopamine and serotonin receptors in the brain and relieve negative and positive symptoms of psychosis.
- Clozapine (Clozaril) is used as a second line of treatment for clients who do not respond well to the typical drugs.
- Risperidone (Risperdal) may be used as the first agent in the management of schizophrenia and inappropriate behaviour associated with dementia.

Nursing Considerations Relating to Antipsychotic Drugs

- Perform an assessment of clients' history of receiving antipsychotic drugs.
- Monitor for EPSs and cardiac dysrhythmias.
- Monitor the behaviour of clients with a history of suicide attempts.
- Monitor vital signs, including BP, pulse, and respiratory rates (for example, assess for postural hypotension).
- Monitor blood count and liver function.
- Advise clients

  - That beneficial effects may take several weeks to become evident.
  - To take medication as prescribed and avoid missing or doubling dosages.
  - Of the adverse effects of CNS stimulation.
  - To report to a doctor if adverse effects are experienced and not discontinue prescribed medication independently.
  - To avoid taking other CNS-affecting drugs, such as alcohol or coffee.
  - To wear sunscreen and protective clothing when outdoors or in direct sunlight.
  - To take the drugs with food or milk to avoid gastric problems.
  - Of possible sexual irregularities, such as enlargement of the breasts or menstrual irregularities.

ANAESTHETICS

Anaesthetics depress the CNS, producing loss of sensation. In the case of a local anaesthetic, the loss of sensation is to a particular area of the body; with a general anaesthetic, the result is loss of consciousness.

The overall action of an anaesthetic is suppression of nerve impulse conduction, causing loss of sensation. The primary purpose is to desensitize the client to pain.

Local Anaesthetics

Drugs in this classification are primarily used to eliminate sensation to a specific region to prevent discomfort. Dental surgery commonly uses local anaesthesia. It is also used to alleviate the discomfort of certain hospital procedures, such as the suturing of wounds, the insertion of certain therapeutic devices, and during certain diagnostic procedures. Clients need to be cautioned to protect the anaesthetized area until normal sensation returns to avoid injury or damage. A common local anaesthetic is lidocaine (Xylocaine).

General Anaesthetics

These preparations produce loss of consciousness, skeletal muscle relaxation, and suppression of reflexes. Deep general anaesthetics will depress respirations; thus, the client will require respiratory support. General anaesthetics are used most commonly for the performance of surgical procedures.

Commonly, a combination of anaesthetics is used: an intravenous short-acting CNS depressant to induce unconsciousness, followed by an anaesthetic gas to maintain unconsciousness for the duration of the surgical procedure. The administration of general anaesthetic drugs is carried out by an anaesthesiologist, who is responsible for the client's normal vital functioning during surgical procedures. Examples of general anaesthetics include ketamine or thiopental to induce anaesthesia and halothane or isoflurane—inhaled gases—to maintain general anaesthesia throughout a surgical procedure.

Clients require constant monitoring following surgery until full consciousness is re-established. This involves the following:

- Vital signs, especially respiratory rate and depth
- Positioning to avoid aspiration
- Warmth to maintain body temperature
- Suction apparatus placed at bedside
- Level of consciousness monitored frequently (q15min)

Neuromuscular Blocking Agents

These preparations promote extensive relaxation (paralysis) of skeletal muscles to facilitate the use of general anaesthetics. Using these agents permits a lower dose of the anaesthetic. Their mode of action prevents the depolarization of nerve plasma membranes by interfering with the action of Ach at the neuromuscular junctions. They may also be used to promote the effectiveness of mechanical ventilation by paralyzing the respiratory muscles and allowing the mechanical ventilator to function effectively. These preparations do not produce sedation, allowing clients to remain conscious and aware of their surroundings.

- Short-acting agents – For example, succinylcholine (Anectine)
- Intermediate agents – For example, rocuronium (Zemuron)
- Long-acting agents – For example, pancuronium (Pavulon)

The client requires constant care by trained nurses experienced with intensive care and CPR and airway skills. Caution needs to be taken with clients who suffer from renal or hepatic failure.

CENTRAL NERVOUS SYSTEM STIMULANTS

CNS stimulants are used to enhance nervous system activity. CNS stimulants can elevate mood, decrease perception of fatigue, increase alertness, decrease appetite, and improve motor function. Stimulants may be used improperly to maintain alertness in order to avoid sleep. One stimulant commonly used to maintain general alertness is caffeine. However, some CNS stimulants have the potential to produce tolerance and severe physiological and psychological dependence when used continuously. As a result, many are classified as controlled substances.

The main CNS stimulants in use today are the amphetamines, including dextroamphetamine (Dexedrine), amphetamine sulphate (Adderall), and methylphenidate HCl (Ritalin). These agents are prescribed primarily for the treatment of narcolepsy and attention deficit hyperactivity disorder (ADHD). They act by increasing the amount of neurotransmitters and dopamine—and possibly serotonin—in the system to promote mood elevation, increase alertness, and prolong wakefulness.

Nursing Considerations Relating to CNS Stimulants

- A careful physical and mental health history is essential, including other medications being taken and any self-medication with herbal remedies, such as ginseng.
- Observe for adverse effects relating to overstimulation of the CNS.
- Check for cardiovascular system effects, mental hyperactivity, and insomnia; report adverse effects immediately to a physician.
- Alert clients to the dangers of overuse and abuse.
- Instruct clients to take only the dosage and frequency prescribed.

DRUGS THAT AFFECT THE AUTONOMIC NERVOUS SYSTEM

The four categories of drugs that affect the functioning of this division of the nervous system can stimulate or suppress the sympathetic and the parasympathetic branches. An easy way to learn the general effects produced by each of the four groups of drugs is to recall the actions of the two systems and the effects they produce on the body. The following drugs will, in general, mimic these effects.

ADRENERGIC AGONISTS (SYMPATHOMIMETIC) DRUGS

Drugs belonging to this category stimulate the sympathetic nervous system. Many adrenergic drugs are used as emergency agents for treating cardiac arrest and cardiovascular collapse. Adrenergic agonists can stimulate both alpha adrenergic receptors (alpha agonists) and beta adrenergic receptors (beta agonists) of the autonomic nervous system (ANS). The action of these agonists mimics the actions of the sympathetic nervous system and the neurotransmitters NE and epinephrine, producing varied effects, including increased cardiac contractions, increased heart rate, bronchodilation, decreased gastric motility, decreased intraocular pressure, and pupil dilation.

Vasoactive Agents That Influence Blood Vessels

- Dopamine – Used to treat hypotension and shock
- Epinephrine (adrenaline) – Used to treat allergic reactions, cardiac arrest, hypotension and shock, bronchodilation, and cardiac stimulation
- Norepinephrine (Levophed) – Used to treat hypotension and shock

Adrenergic Agents Used to Treat Asthma and Bronchitis

These agents produce bronchodilation:

- Salbutamol (Ventolin)
- Epinephrine (adrenaline)
- Isoproterenol HCl

Adrenergic Agents That Suppress Appetite

Appetite suppressants include dextroamphetamine (Dexadrine).

Adrenergic Agents Used in Treating Glaucoma

These agents reduce intraocular pressure and dilate the pupil. They include tetrahydrozoline (Murine, Visine).

Adrenergic Agents Used As Nasal Decongestants

A common decongestant is pseudoephedrine (Sudafed).

ADRENERGIC BLOCKING AGENTS (SYMPATHOLYTIC) DRUGS

Adrenergic blocking agents inhibit or block the responses of adrenergic neurotransmitters at alpha and beta adrenergic receptor sites. In general, they block the action of the sympathetic nervous system.

Alpha blockers cause a decrease in BP and are used in treating headaches, hypertension, and peripheral vascular diseases. These agents promote blood flow to vasoconstricted areas. Examples include doxazosin (Cardura) and prazosin (Minipress).

Beta blockers also cause a decrease in BP. These agents decrease the heart rate and force of contraction, which decreases the load on the heart. Examples include the following:

- Propranolol (Inderol)
- Metoprolol (Lopressor)
- Atenolol (Tenormin)
- Sotalol (Betapace)
- Timolol (Blocadren)

CHOLINERGIC (PARASYMPATHOMIMETIC) DRUGS

In general, cholinergic drugs imitate the parasympathetic nervous system. Cholinergic drugs have limited use. Their primary uses are in the treatment of urinary retention and GI disturbances. Their actions mimic the neurotransmitter Ach. Examples include the following:

- Bethanechol (Duvoid) – Prescribed for the treatment of urinary retention
- Pyridostigmine (Mestinon), edrophonium (Tensilon), and neostigmine (Prostigmin) – Stimulate skeletal muscle contraction and are used in the treatment of myasthenia gravis. (These drugs are indirect-acting cholinergic agonists that react chemically with acetylcholinesterase [Ach-ase] in the synaptic cleft to prevent the breakdown of Ach.)
- Rivastigmine (Exelon) – Alzheimer's disease is associated with decreased Ach levels in the brain, and certain cholinergic agents can be employed to block Ach-ase.

Adverse Effects of Cholinergic Drugs

As previously stated, by recalling the effects of the parasympathetic nervous system, the adverse effects of cholinergic drugs can be identified. Pulmonary secretions, bronchospasm, respiratory depression, and respiratory paralysis are some of the potentially life-threatening adverse effects. Atropine sulphate should be close at hand to reverse the cholinergic effect in the event that a client experiences a cholinergic crisis. Also, prior to administering cholinergic agents, nurses should ensure that intubation equipment is readily available should respiratory depression or arrest occur.

ANTICHOLINERGIC (PARASYMPATHOLYTIC) DRUGS

These agents act by blocking Ach receptors. Their pharmacological action results in pupil dilation, decreased lacrimation, decreased heart rate, decreased GI motility, decreased salivation, and suppression of other physiological functions associated with Ach activity. Examples include the following:

- Atropine sulphate – This may be used as a preoperative drug to decrease GI and respiratory secretions. Atropine sulphate crosses the blood–brain barrier and in a sufficiently large dose will act as a stimulant. At toxic dose levels, it causes CNS depression.
- Hyoscine (Buscopan, Levsin) – This agent has both anticholinergic and antispasmodic effects. It is usually prescribed for GI spasms in irritable bowel syndrome and bladder spasms in clients with biliary or renal colic.
- Benztropine (Cogentin) and biperiden (Akineton) – These are used to treat the cholinergic disorder in Parkinson's disease.
- Flavoxate and oxybutynin – These agents are used for hyperactive urinary bladders.

Since antacids decrease the therapeutic effects of anticholinergic agents, the following precautions should be taken:

- Drugs should be administered at least 1 hr apart.
- Clients should be warned about undertaking activities that cause perspiration since anticholinergic agents inhibit perspiration, making clients susceptible to heat stroke.
- Clients should also be cautioned against using OTC drugs with antihistamine and drinking alcoholic beverages.

Nursing Considerations Relating to Sympathomimetic Drugs

- Maintain an awareness of sympathetic and parasympathetic nervous system effects on the body.
- Observations relating to sympathomimetics include tachycardia, elevation in BP, hyperactivity, sleeplessness, dry mouth, and pupillary dilation.
- Observations relating to sympatholytics will include bradycardia, decreased BP, sedation, weakness, lethargy, and dizziness.
- Observations relating to parasympathomimetics

will include bradycardia, hypotension, bronchoconstriction, increased salivation, perspiration, abdominal cramps, dizziness, and pupillary constriction.
- Observations relating to parasympathetic blockers include tachycardia, restlessness, confusion, pupillary dilation, blurred vision, urinary retention, dry mouth, and constipation.
- Vital signs should be monitored carefully.
- A relaxing environment should be promoted for clients on stimulant classifications of ANS drugs.
- Provide mouth care for dry mouth.
- Clients should be taught to report adverse effects.
- Clients on depressant classifications of ANS drugs should be cautioned concerning safety precautions, particularly driving or operating dangerous machinery.
- Anticholinergics may cause sensitivity to light due to pupillary dilation; use of sunglasses and avoidance of bright lights should be encouraged.
- Sympathomimetics and anticholinergics may cause urinary retention; clients should be taught to report urination problems

DRUGS THAT AFFECT THE CARDIOVASCULAR SYSTEM

The drugs that affect the cardiovascular system are outlined in Figure 7.2.

Agents Affecting Blood Coagulation

Two overall classifications of drugs affect blood coagulation: agents that inhibit blood coagulation and those that promote it. Classes of drugs that inhibit abnormal coagulation of blood (clot formation) may be divided into three general classifications: anticoagulants, antiplatelet agents, and thrombolytics. Agents that promote blood coagulation (to prevent abnormal blood loss) are called fibrinolytics.

Preliminary Tests

Before and during the administration of agents that affect the clotting of blood, a number of blood tests are used to assess the clotting processes within the body. These include the following (normal values are given in parentheses):

- Platelet count – (150,000–400,000 mm^3)
- Hemoglobin (Hgb) – (male: 8.7–11.2 mmol/L; female: 7.4–9.9 mmol/L)
- Hematocrit (Hct) – (male: 40–53%; female: 38–47%)
- Prothrombin time (PT) – (11–12.5 s)
- Partial thromboplastin time (PTT) – (28–35 s)
- Activated partial thromboplastin time (aPTT) – (30–40 s)
- International normalized ratio (INR) – 0.81–1.2

FIGURE 7.2
Drugs That Affect the Cardiovascular System

CVS
(Cardiovascular System)
BLOOD
BLOOD VESSELS
HEART
1. Anticoagulants
Heparin
Warfarin
Antiplatelet Drugs
2. Fibrinolytics
3. Antilipemics
4. Antianemics
5. Antihypotensives
6. Antihypertensives
7. Cardiotonics (Inotropics)
8. Antidysrhythmics
9. Anti–Angina Pectoris Drugs

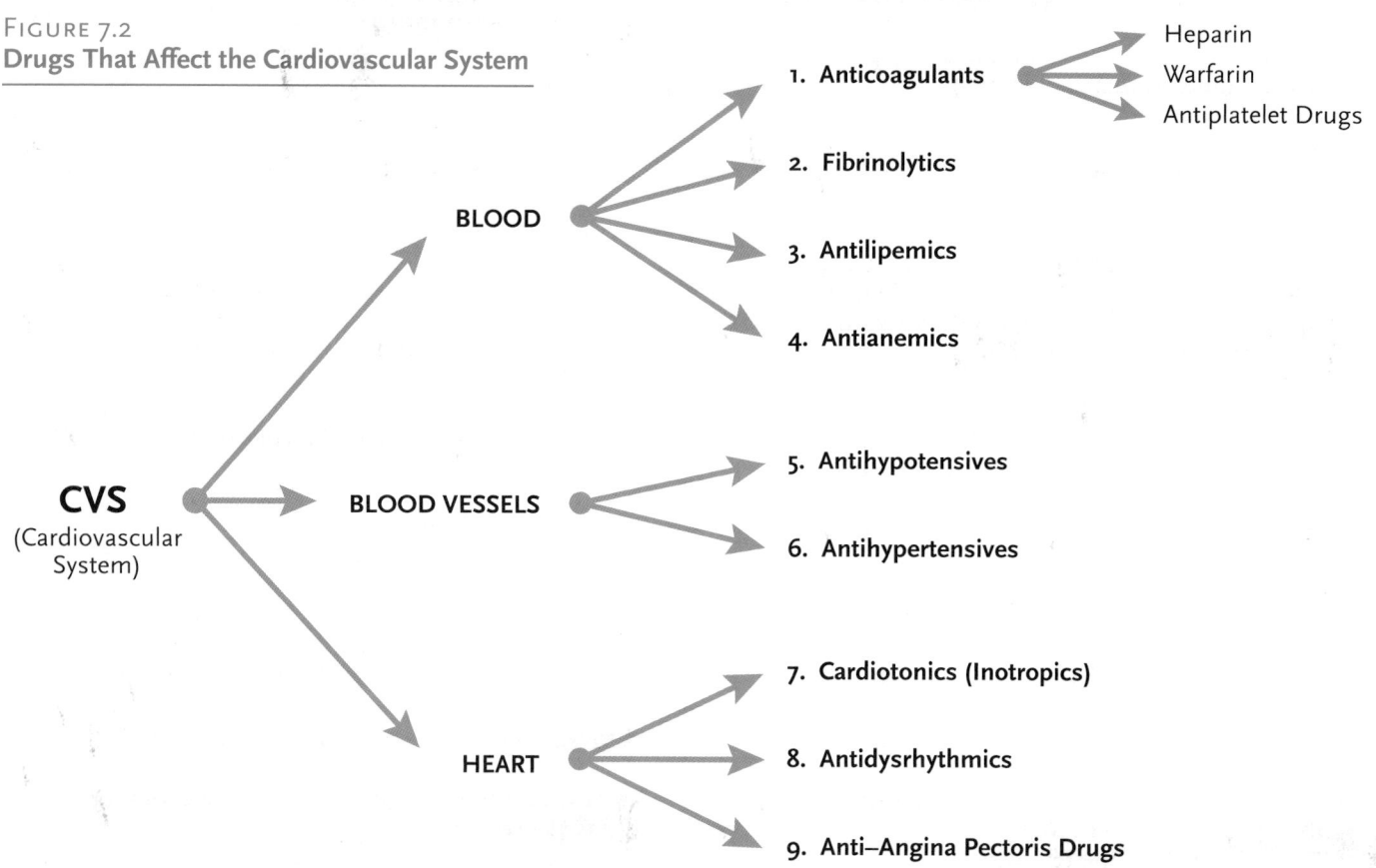

- For clients taking heparin, the aPTT or PTT is used to monitor the prescribed therapeutic range.
- For clients taking oral anticoagulants, PT or INR is used to monitor the prescribed therapeutic range.

Anticoagulants (Coagulation-Modifying Agents)

Anticoagulants prevent the formation of clots by inhibiting certain clotting factors and platelets. They are only given prophylactically as they have no direct effect on a blood clot that has already formed.

Common Uses

- Myocardial infarction (MI)
- Unstable angina pectoris
- Atrial fibrillation
- Emboli (pulmonary emboli)
- In-dwelling devices (pacemakers, mechanical valves)
- Pelvic surgeries (prostatectomy)

Primary Anticoagulants Prescribed

Heparin

- Heparin is commonly prescribed during the acute stage of a condition requiring anticoagulant therapy.
- Heparin activates antithrombin 3, causing neutralization of thrombin and inhibition of clot formation.
- Onset of action following SC injection is 20–60 min; duration of action is approximately 8–12 hr.
- Dosage is based on PTT or aPTT; therapeutic range is 1.5–2.5 times normal.

Warfarin (Coumadin)

- Warfarin is commonly prescribed after the acute stage of a condition requiring anticoagulant therapy to maintain therapeutic blood levels of anticoagulation.
- Warfarin interferes with production of vitamin K (necessary for clotting of blood). Vitamin K is necessary for the production of clotting factors 2, 7, 9, and 10.
- Onset of action is 2–7 days.
- Dosage is based on the PT and INR; the desirable therapeutic range is 1.5–2.5 times normal.

Antiplatelet Drugs

- These drugs interfere with the ability of platelets to aggregate during the process of blood clotting.
- Antiplatelet drugs are commonly prescribed to prevent arterial thrombosis and where a thromboembolism disorder exists, as in the prevention and management of conditions such as MI, cerebrovascular accident, and transient ischemic attacks.
- Bleeding time and PT are used to monitor the therapeutic effects of drugs.
- Examples include the following:

- Acetylsalicylic acid (ASA)
- Ticlopidine (Ticlid)
- Clopidogrel (Plavix)

Adverse Effects of Anticoagulant Drugs (Coagulation-Modifying Agents)

- Hemorrhage – Indicated by occult blood in stool, melena stool, petechia, bruising, bleeding from gums
- Gastric ulceration (ASA)

Nursing Considerations Relating to Anticoagulant Drugs (Coagulation-Modifying Agents)

- Observe for signs of hemorrhage, such as hematuria or black stool, and report.
- Administer oral medications with food to avoid gastric irritation.
- Administer SC heparin to avoid local bruising. Use a half-inch needle, do not aspirate the plunger, inject into the deep fatty tissue of the abdomen, withdraw carefully, and apply pressure to the site for several minutes; do not massage the site.
- Monitor blood tests for the degree of anticoagulation and report if abnormal for therapeutic dose.
- Use elastic stockings to promote circulation.
- Teach clients to exercise legs to promote circulation and prevent clot formation.
- Teach clients to avoid positions that impede blood circulation, such as dangling or crossing the legs or wearing restricting clothing.
- Maintain proper hydration to avoid hemoconcentration.
- Caution clients to avoid activities that may cause trauma or increase the tendency to bleed, including the following:

- Contact sports and other potentially risky activities
- Vigorous teeth-brushing or using a coarse-bristled toothbrush

- Remind clients to report abnormal bruising or unusual bleeding.
- Caution clients to avoid food high in vitamin K.
- Caution clients to avoid taking ASA if taking other anticoagulants.
- Instruct clients to take oral medications, particularly ASA, with food.
- Ensure that when a client is changed from heparin to a warfarin preparation, the client will remain on the heparin until the warfarin preparation achieves therapeutic levels in the blood.
- Carefully monitor PPT, aPPT (heparin), and PT and INR (warfarin) during therapy and when the client is changed from a parenteral to an oral preparation.

Fibrinolytic (Thrombolytic) Agents

- These agents act by converting plasminogen to plasmin (an enzyme that breaks down the fibrin in clots that have formed).

- Early initiation of therapy is required immediately after the condition develops to be effective.
- They are prescribed to act on clots that have formed in coronary artery occlusion (MI), pulmonary embolus, cerebral emboli (stroke), and deep vein thrombosis (DVT).
- They are administered by IV infusion
- Examples include streptokinase (Streptase), alteplase (Activase RT-PA), reteplase (Retavase), and tenecteplase (TNKase)

Adverse Effects of Fibrinolytics

- Lightheadedness, palpitations
- Hemorrhage
- Anemia

Nursing Considerations Relating to Fibrinolytic Drugs

- Clients receiving fibrinolytic drugs require care in the intensive care unit during therapy.
- Prior to administration, determine vital signs, hematocrit, platelet count, fibrinogen level, PTT, and INR to establish baseline and to indicate the safety of initiating therapy.
- Carefully observe for manifestations of hemorrhage (for example, in the GI tract or integumentary system).
- Avoid the use of anticoagulants while on therapy.
- Observe for possible allergic reactions.
- Monitor vital signs, ECG, and neurological status.

Reverse Anticoagulant Agents

These agents are used when an overdose of anticoagulant has occurred. Examples include the following:

- Protamine sulphate – Used in the case of heparin overdose; neutralizes heparin activity
- Phytonadione (AquaMEPHYTON, vitamin K) – Used for a warfarin overdose

Reverse Thrombolytic Agents

Agents such as aminocaproic acid (Amicar) and tranexamic acid (Cyclokapron) control bleeding caused by an overdose of thrombolytic therapy drugs.

ANTILIPEMICS (AGENTS USED TO TREAT HYPERLIPIDEMIA)

Antilipemic drugs are used to reduce lipid levels when dietary measures, weight loss, and exercise have been unsuccessful. Indication for treatment includes elevated plasma cholesterol, triglyceride, and low-density lipoprotein (LDL) levels.

Preliminary Tests

The following are the normal ranges for preliminary levels:

- Cholesterol: >5.2 mmol/L
- Triglycerides: 0.45–1.69 mmol/L
- LDL: <3.37 mmol/L

The choice of treatment depends on which type of lipid is elevated.

Bile Acid Sequestrants

These preparations combine with the bile acids in the intestine to form a nonabsorbable complex that is then excreted in the feces. This lack of reabsorption of bile forces the liver cells to metabolize cholesterol to produce more bile acids, thus reducing LDLs and total cholesterol levels. An example is cholestyramine resin (Questran).

HMG-CoA Reductase Inhibitors (Statins)

This is the most widely used classification of antilipemics in the treatment of hyperlipidemia. Statins block the formation of cellular cholesterol, causing a reduction in blood LDL and total cholesterol within weeks. Examples include the following:

- Lovastatin (Mevacor)
- Atorvastatin (Lipitor)
- Pravastatin (Pravachol)
- Simvastatin (Zocor)

Fibric Acids

These acids stimulate the breakdown and reduction in synthesis of very-low-density lipoproteins (VLDLs). Therapeutic effects include the lowering of VLDLs, the reduction of triglycerides, and the increase of high-density lipoprotein (HDL) levels. Examples include fenofibrate (TriCor) and gemfibrozil (Lopid).

Niacin (Vitamin B₃)

Niacin acts on liver cells to inhibit LDL and triglyceride production. It may be prescribed in combination with other antihyperlipidemic drugs.

Adverse Effects of Antilipemics

- The reduction of fat-soluble vitamins due to bile salts reducing their absorption
- The formation of gallstones (fibric acid preparations disturb the fat level of the blood)
- The effects of statins are usually mild; however, they should be used with caution in clients with liver and kidney impairment.
- Headache

- GI disturbances – Nausea, vomiting, distension, irritation, diarrhea, or constipation
- Myopathy (muscle aches) – Uncommon but significant (with statins)
- Flushing, skin rash, and itchiness (with niacin)
- Jaundice
- Antilipemics are contraindicated in liver and kidney disease.

Nursing Considerations Relating to Antilipemics

Client teaching:

- Stressing the importance of taking medication as prescribed
- Promptly complying with laboratory requests and physician appointments
- Reporting side effects to a physician (myopathy with statins, jaundice)
- Changing dietary habits; reducing fat intake
- Supplementing fat-soluble vitamins (A, D, E, K)
- Increasing dietary fibre and fluid intake
- The importance of moderate exercise and weight reduction
- Clients should not discontinue medications without consulting with a physician.
- Mild side effects usually dissipate after medication is established within the body.
- Do not take statins with grapefruit juice.
- Ensure that medication is taken with or without meals according to preparation.

ANTIANEMICS

There are many different classifications of anemia with differing causes, manifestations, and origins. Regardless of the type of anemia, the end result is a decrease in the concentration of circulating red blood cells or a low hemoglobin level.

Anemias result from a deficiency of nutrients necessary for the development of healthy red blood cells and hemoglobin (such as iron deficiency anemia (iron), fetal damage in pregnancy (folic acid deficiency), or pernicious anemia (vitamin B_{12} deficiency), or an abnormality of the bone marrow that produces the cells, such as marrow destruction as a result of radiation, or genetic deviation, such as sickle cell anemia or thalassemia. Refer to Table 7.6, which outlines the medications used to treat nutritional deficiency anemia.

Nutritional Deficiency Anemias

Nursing Considerations Relating to Antianemics

When taking dietary supplements for the treatment of nutritional deficiency anemia, clients should be

- Taught to take prescribed medications as required to maintain optimal blood levels.
- Encouraged not to discontinue medication without consultation with a physician.
- Observed for adverse effects and measures.
- Encouraged to take medication in the method prescribed.
- Encouraged to use natural dietary sources to complement prescribed medication.
- Taught not to break or crush preparations into a powder (many are coated to reduce irritation).

ANTIHYPOTENSIVE AGENTS

These agents are used to treat low BP and circulatory shock and to re-establish effective circulation and BP. Sympathomimetic drugs are the most common

Table 7.6 Nutritional Deficiency Anemia Drug Treatments

Preparation	Uses	Adverse Effects	Nursing Considerations
Iron • Ferrous fumarate • Ferrous gluconate • Ferrous sulphate	Iron deficiency anemia	• GI irritation • Discoloration of tooth enamel • Black stool • Drug allergy	• Oral preparations: give with food • Liquid preparations: drink with straw • IM: deep IM, Z-track technique to reduce tissue irritation
Folic Acid • Folvite	• Pregnancy • Megaloblastic anemia • Tropical sprue	• Rare • Discoloration of urine • Possible allergy	• Take with food
Vitamin B_{12} • Cyanocobalamin	• Pernicious anemia	In large doses • Diarrhea • Pruritis • Hypokalemia	• Take with food • Usually required for life

Table 7.7   Classifications of Antihypotensive Agents

Type	Drug	Action
Alpha Adrenergic Agents	• Norepinephrine (noradrenaline) • Phenylephrine (Neosynephrine)	• Constriction of vascular smooth muscle resulting in increased peripheral vascular resistance and increased BP
Beta Adrenergic Agents	• Dobutamine (Dobutrex) • Isoproterenol (Isuprel)	• Increases myocardial contractibility and heart rate, resulting in increased BP
Alpha and Beta Adrenergic Agents	• Dopamine HCl • Epinephrine (adrenaline)	• Causes constriction of vascular smooth muscle and stimulates cardiac contractibility • Increases blood flow to kidneys, preventing renal shutdown (dopamine) • Bronchodilation

classification of drugs used for the treatment of the above conditions and are effective in an emergency situation.

Classifications of Antihypotensive Agents

Table 7.7 summarizes the classifications and actions of antihypotensive agents.

Dopamine and epinephrine are the most commonly used agents for shock and hypotension.

- Dopamine is the drug of choice for treatment of cardiogenic shock because it increases blood flow to the kidneys and possibly prevents renal shutdown.
- Epinephrine is the drug of choice for management of anaphylactic shock. It is also used to manage other shocks because it increases BP and heart contractility and is the primary treatment for bronchospasm, which can occur in asthma.

Adverse Effects of Antihypotensive Agents

- Severe hypertension
- Hyperirritability and restlessness
- Tachycardia and palpitations
- Cardiac dysrhythmias
- Dry mouth
- Nausea and vomiting
- Headache

Nursing Considerations Relating to Antihypotensive Agents

- Frequent monitoring of vital signs (BP and heart rate) every 5–15 min during acute shock.
- Assess the following:

  - Therapeutic effect (systolic BP 80–100 mm Hg)
  - Dysrhythmias, abnormal BP changes
  - Urine output (intake and output q1hr)

- Provide emotional support for the client during a crisis

- Exercise extreme care regarding dosage when administering medication

ANTIHYPERTENSIVE AGENTS

Antihypertensive agents are usually prescribed for clients when diet, exercise, and other measures designed to reduce BP have failed to lower BP to a level that does not pose a health risk to the cardiovascular and renal systems. In general, to reduce BP, antihypertensive drugs either reduce blood volume (such as diuretics) or cause dilation of blood vessels (that is, they reduce peripheral resistance).

Treatment for hypertension depends on the severity of the disorder. Antihypertensive therapy for mild to moderate hypertension usually begins with a single medication, such as a thiazide diuretic. In the presence of moderate hypertension, in some clients, it may be necessary to give a combination of two drugs (for example, a thiazide diuretic in addition to one of a beta blocker, an angiotensin-converting enzyme [ACE] inhibitor, a vasodilator, a centrally acting antihypertensive agent, or an alpha blocker). For severe hypertension, a combination of drugs designed specifically for the client will be prescribed.

Classifications of Antihypertensive Agents

Table 7.8 summarizes the classifications and actions of antihypertensive agents.

Adverse Effects of Antihypertensive Agents

Adverse effects vary according to the category of drug prescribed. In general, adverse effects most commonly experienced are the result of vasodilation and reduced cardiac action, including the following:

- Hypokalemia (diuretics, such as thiazides)
- Muscle cramps (loop diuretics)
- Lightheadedness, dizziness, weakness, lethargy
- Orthostatic hypotension

Table 7.8   Classifications of Antihypertensive Agents

Type	Drug	Action
Diuretics (thiazide, loop, potassium sparing)	• Hydrochlorothiazide (HydroDIURIL) • Furosemide (Lasix) • Spirinolacone (Aldactone)	• Reduce circulating and interstitial fluid → reduce peripheral vascular resistance → ↓ BP
ACE Inhibitors	• Captopril (Capoten) • Enalapril (Vasotec) • Ramipril (Altace)	• Block enzyme that converts angiotensin I to angiotensin II → vasodilation → decrease peripheral vascular resistance → ↓ BP
Alpha Adrenergic Blockers	• Doxazosin (Cardura) (alpha$_1$) • Terazosin (Hytrin) (alpha$_1$) • Clonidine (Catapres) (alpha$_2$)	• Block stimulation of alpha adrenergic receptors in blood → vasodilation → decrease peripheral vascular resistance → ↓ BP
Beta Adrenergic Blockers	• Atenolol (Tenormin) • Metoprolol (Lopressor) • Propranolol (Inderal)	• Block beta adrenergic receptors within heart muscle → reduce strength and rate of cardiac contraction → decrease peripheral resistance → ↓ BP
Calcium Channel Blockers	• Nifedipine (Adalat) • Diltiazem (Cardizem) • Verapamil (Isoptin)	• Prevent the action of calcium at receptor sites, inhibiting smooth muscle contraction → vasodilation → decrease peripheral vascular resistance → ↓ BP
Centrally Acting Antihypertensives	• Clonidine (Catapres) • Methyldopa (Apo-Methyldopa)	• Stimulate the brain to modify the action of the sympathetic nervous system → reduce strength of cardiac activity and inhibit vasoconstriction → decrease peripheral vascular resistance → ↓ BP
Vasodilators	• Hydralazine (Apresoline) • Minoxidil (Rogaine)	• Produce vasodilation by acting directly on the arterial smooth muscle → decrease peripheral vascular resistance → ↓ BP

- Dehydration (diuretics)
- Urticaria (thiazide and loop)
- Photosensitivity (thiazide and loop)
- Headache (vasodilating effects)
- Gynecomastia (potassium sparing in men)
- Erectile dysfunction (thiazide)
- Menstrual irregularities (potassium sparing in women)

Nursing Considerations Relating to Antihypertensive Agents

- Observe for adverse effects related to specific medication prescribed (such as dehydration or electrolyte imbalance).
- Monitor vital signs—BP and pulse—lying and standing.
- Client teaching:

  - Dangers of uncontrolled hypertension
  - Reporting adverse side effects that may occur initially
  - Do not suddenly stop taking medication prescribed
  - Importance of taking medication as prescribed
  - Do not double up if a dose is missed
  - Take care when ambulating due to postural hypotension
  - Avoid very hot showers or baths due to vasodilating effects and dizziness that could result

- Ensure proper hydration; avoid becoming dehydrated, monitor fluid intake
- Avoid excess alcohol use since it is vasodilating and the effects produced interfere with drug metabolism and cause dehydration
- Monitor and report signs of swelling of lower extremities
- Keep physician and laboratory appointments for reassessments

- Stress the importance of the following:

  - Weight reduction
  - Balanced diet (restrict salt intake; potassium supplementation if on diuretics)
  - Stress reduction
  - Adequate rest

AGENTS USED TO TREAT HEART FAILURE

A variety of treatment regimens exist for the management of congestive heart failure. The following classifications of drugs may be prescribed to promote more effective cardiovascular functioning.

Vasodilators

Vasodilators decrease the workload of the heart and include ACE inhibitors, nitrates, and angiotensin II receptor blockers (used if ACE inhibitors are not tolerated well).

Diuretics

These drugs increase urine output and decrease sodium levels in the body. They are commonly used in combination with other medications to treat congestive heart failure and include thiazides and furosemide.

Beta Adrenergic Agonists

These agonists stimulate sympathetic nervous system activity to increase calcium flow into the cardiac muscle, resulting in increased contractility. Examples include dobutamine.

Cardiotonic (Inotropic) Drugs

This class of drug is widely used in the treatment of congestive heart failure. These drugs act by increasing the strength of cardiac contraction (positive inotropic effect), which results in increased cardiac output. The drug also slows the rate of cardiac contraction (negative chronotropic effect), leading to more effective heart action, an increase in renal output, and a decrease in rennin release results.

Cardiac Glycosides

- Have a narrow therapeutic index
- Are excreted from the body by the kidney (renal impairment may cause accumulation, leading to toxic levels)
- Dosages should be adjusted to prevent blood levels from becoming toxic.
- Examples include digitalis preparations, such as digoxin (Lanoxin).

Symptoms of Digitalis Toxicity

- Drowsiness, weakness, dizziness
- Confusion
- GI upset – Nausea, vomiting, diarrhea
- Visual disturbances (yellow-green distortion)
- Bradycardia or tachycardia
- Heart block

Digitalization
When a client is initially started on a digitalis preparation, a higher than normal dosage of the drug is commonly given to establish therapeutic levels as quickly as possible. The subsequent (maintenance) dosage is established to maintain the therapeutic level in the blood following the initial high dose. Careful monitoring of blood levels is undertaken to avoid possible toxicity and to establish the most effective maintenance dosage.

Nursing Considerations: Implications Relating to Digoxin

- Assess for adverse or toxic effects, reporting and charting immediately.
- Do not administer digoxin concurrently with the following drugs:

  - Antacids, which reduce absorption
  - Antimicrobial agents and calcium preparations, which may promote toxicity

- Monitor digoxin serum levels throughout treatment to detect toxic levels.
- Following each administration of the drug, charting should include indicating the apical heart rate at the time of administration.
- If the apical pulse rate is erratic, below 60 beats per minute in adults (<90 beats per minute in infants), or above 100–120 beats per minute, withhold the digoxin and report for additional assessment by the physician.
- Clients with hypokalemia, hypothyroidism, and acute MI should be monitored more frequently for toxic effects.
- Teach clients

  - To monitor for adverse effects, such as visual changes (colour perception)
  - How to monitor heart rate
  - To report concerns regarding the effects of the drug
  - To eat food high in potassium (due to loss through urine)
  - To avoid taking several medications if a drug interaction may occur
  - Not to take a double dose if a dose is missed

- The antidote for severe toxicity is digoxin immune fab (Digibind), which inactivates digoxin by drawing the drug from the tissues and binding to it.

Phosphodiesterase Inhibitors (PDIs)

- PDIs produce an inotropic effect on the heart as well as dilating arteries and veins.
- They increase the force of contractility of the heart muscles and decrease pre- and afterload on the heart.
- PDIs are administered intravenously.
- An example is milrinone (Primacor).
- Potential adverse effects of PDI administration include hypotension and dysrhythmias.
- Clients must be evaluated for BP, cardiac rhythm and rate, and cardiac output during and for several hours following administration.

ANTIDYSRHYTHMIC DRUGS

Antidysrhythmics are drugs used to treat dysrhythmias, to slow conduction of electrical impulses in the heart, to reduce spontaneous depolarization of myocardial cells, or to prolong the effective refractory period.

The Vaughan Williams classification of antidysrhythmic drugs, which is based on the effect that agents produce on action potential in the heart, list four classes of agents:

Class I: Sodium channel blockers (for example, quinidine, disopyramide, or procainamide)

Class II: Beta blockers (for example, sotalol or propranolol)

Class III: Potassium channel blockers (such as amiodarone, bretylium, and ibutilide)

Class IV: Calcium channel blockers (such as diltiazem and verapamil)

Other Drug Classifications

- Atropine for bradyrhythmias
- Digoxin for atrial fibrillation

These drugs, regardless of class, cause depression of the normal heart function.

Adverse Effects

- Quinidine – Disturbed hearing, giddiness, and impaired vision (cinchonism)
- Amiodarone can accumulate in tissue, causing photosensitivity rashes and lung problems
- See "Symptoms of Digitalis Toxicity," p. 194.

Precautions

- For quinidine (Cardioquin or Quinalan):

  - Monitor for toxicity.
  - Caution about diet that alkalinizes the urine.
  - Monitor for therapeutic range: 2–6 mcg/mL; toxicity results when levels exceed 8 mcg/mL.

Anti–Angina Pectoris Drugs

Anti-angina medications are prescribed to relieve angina pain and reduce the frequency of angina attacks. The drug helps restore oxygen supply to the heart by improving blood supply to the myocardium. This is accomplished by dilating coronary blood vessels, which, in turn, increase blood supply to the heart, relieving the hypoxia in myocardial cells.

Classifications of Drugs Used to Treat Angina Pectoris

Nitrates

Nitrates act by relaxing vascular smooth muscle, which dilates coronary blood vessels and increases blood flow to the myocardium. Examples are nitroglycerine (Nitrostat) and isosorbide mononitrate (Isordil).

Calcium Channel Blockers

These drugs act by relaxing vascular smooth muscle, which dilates the coronary blood vessels and increases blood flow to the myocardium. Examples include amlodipine (Norvasc), diltiazem (Cardizem), and nifedipine (Adalet).

Beta Adrenergic Blockers

Beta adrenergic blockers act to help reduce the risk of angina by decreasing the influence of the sympathetic nervous system on stimulating the myocardium, resulting in decreased cardiac output, reduced oxygen demand, and lower BP. Examples are propranolol (Inderal), atenolol (Tenormin), and nadolol (Corgard).

Adverse Effects of Anti–Angina Pectoris Medications

- Headache
- Flushing of skin
- Dizziness, weakness, and fainting

Nursing Considerations Relating to Anti–Angina Pectoris Medications

- Oral preparations and patches are used for the prevention of anginal attacks.
- Sprays and sublingual preparations are used for acute attacks.
- For treatment of acute anginal pain, the sublingual dose range for nitrate is 0.3–0.6 mg. The dose of nitrate may be repeated twice at five-minute intervals. If the pain persists, the client should seek medical attention immediately as the potential for MI exists.
- Clients should be taught

  - Techniques for administration.
  - To recognize adverse effects and report.
  - To rest while taking medication during an anginal attack.
  - To avoid swallowing for several minutes when administering sublingual preparations.
  - To store sublingual medications in a dry, cool, dark place.
  - To carry medication at all times.
  - To note and observe expiratory dates and replace.
  - That sublingual spray preparations should not be frozen, and prior to administration, priming of the pump is required.
  - That patches applied to the skin should be stored in a dry environment and applied to an area of skin without hair, the old patch is removed and the skin is cleansed, and the new patch is applied to a different area; apply at the same time each day.
  - To take oral preparations on an empty stomach.

- To avoid developing tolerance by removing the nitroglycerine patch for 8 hr overnight.

DRUGS THAT AFFECT THE GASTROINTESTINAL SYSTEM

The drugs that affect the GI system are outlined in Figure 7.3.

There are four common disorders of the GI system for which drugs are frequently prescribed: constipation, diarrhea, hyperacidity, and nausea and vomiting. Some of these disorders may be treated using OTC preparations, but for clients with serious conditions or those in institutions, the health care provider may prescribe the appropriate medication.

LAXATIVES

In this group, drugs are used to speed the passage of intestinal contents through the GI tract. They may be administered to prevent or relieve constipation (most common use), to prepare a client for lower GI tract procedures, to reduce the strain of defecation in clients with cardiovascular disease or hemorrhoids, to remove ingested toxic substances, or as treatment for parasitic infestations or other such conditions.

Classifications of Laxatives

Table 7.9 outlines the different classifications of laxatives, their actions, and their uses.

Adverse Effects Relating to the Use of Laxatives

- Diarrhea
- Abdominal cramps (can occur with the rapid-acting stimulant and saline laxatives and irritating stimulant laxative classifications)
- Flatulence
- Tolerance

FIGURE 7.3
Drugs That Affect the Gastrointestinal System

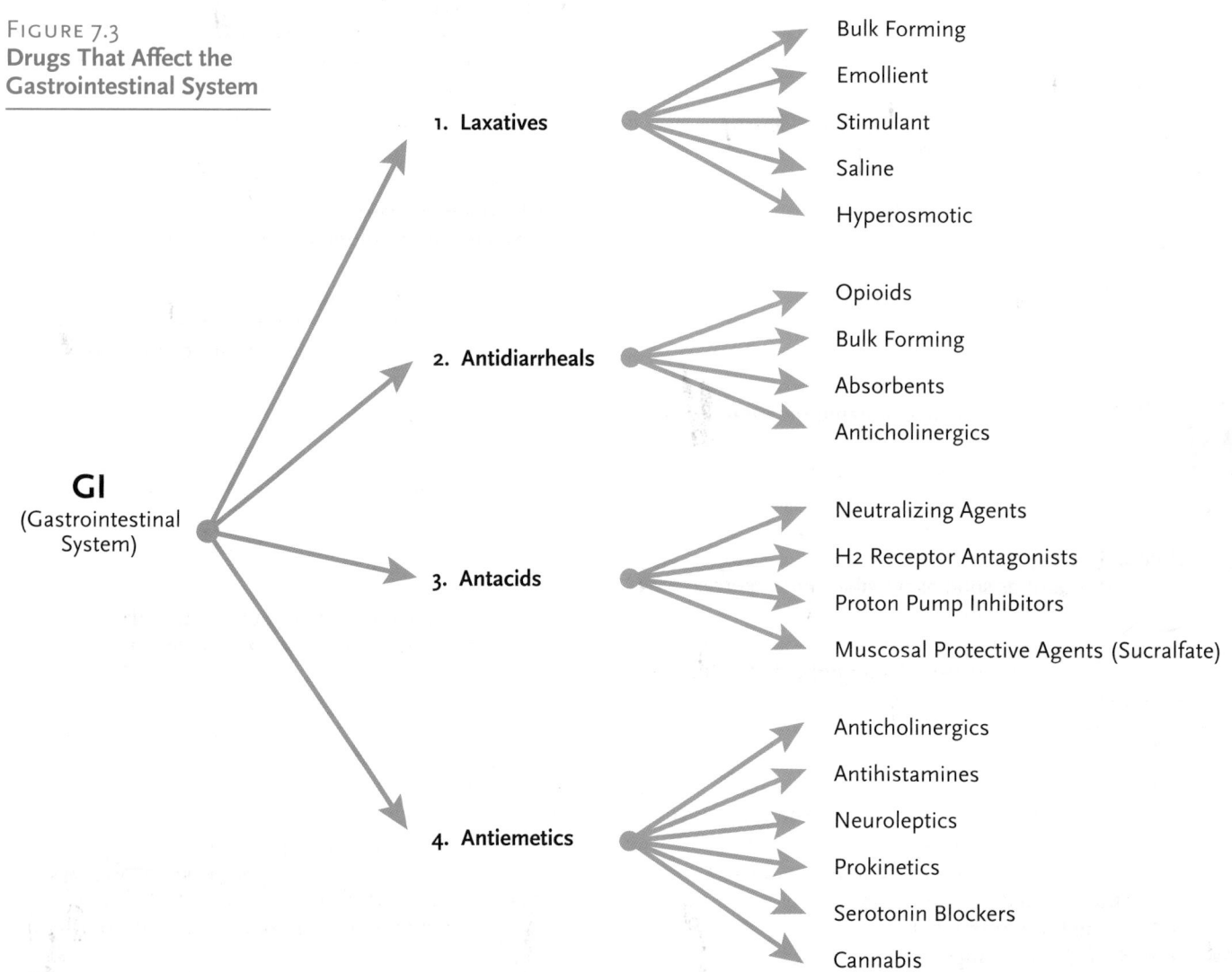

GI (Gastrointestinal System)

1. **Laxatives**
   - Bulk Forming
   - Emollient
   - Stimulant
   - Saline
   - Hyperosmotic

2. **Antidiarrheals**
   - Opioids
   - Bulk Forming
   - Absorbents
   - Anticholinergics

3. **Antacids**
   - Neutralizing Agents
   - H2 Receptor Antagonists
   - Proton Pump Inhibitors
   - Muscosal Protective Agents (Sucralfate)

4. **Antiemetics**
   - Anticholinergics
   - Antihistamines
   - Neuroleptics
   - Prokinetics
   - Serotonin Blockers
   - Cannabis

Table 7.9   Classifications of Laxatives

Type of Laxative	Action	Uses
Bulk-Forming Laxative • Psyllium (Metamucil)	• Acts by absorbing water into intestine ➔ increases bulk and distends bowel ➔ reflex bowel activity (peristalsis)	• Slow-acting (12–48 hr) • Long-term therapy for chronic constipation
Stimulant Laxative • Bisacodyl (Dulcolax)	• Irritates or stimulates the nerve plexus in the mucosa of small intestine and colon ➔ increasing peristalsis	• Rapid evacuation of bowel for diagnostic tests • Acute constipation
Saline Laxative • Magnesium citrate (Citro-Mag) • Magnesium hydroxide (Milk of Magnesia)	• Draws water into the bowel by osmotic action ➔ watery stool and distended bowel ➔ stimulates stretch receptors ➔ stimulates peristalsis	• Bowel cleansing • Acute constipation • Rapid onset
Emollient Laxative (stool softener) • Docusate sodium (Colace) • Mineral oil	• Detergentlike action that lowers surface tension of GI fluids ➔ water and fat absorbed into stool and increased peristalsis • Lubricates bowel for easier passage of stool	• Mild, gentle relief of constipation • Prevention of constipation
Hyperosmotic Laxative • Lactulose (Apo-Lactulose) • Polyethylene glycol (Miralax)	• Produces a hyperosmolar environment in bowel ➔ draws water from intestinal lining into bowel ➔ distension of bowel with added water ➔ stimulation of peristalsis	• Relieves acute constipation • Bowel preparation for diagnostic and surgical procedures • Very cleansing

- Bowel impaction or obstruction (with bulk-forming preparations)
- Electrolyte imbalances (with saline laxatives)

Nursing Considerations Relating to Laxatives

- Assessment of client need; evaluated record of bowel movements
- Contraindications include bowel surgery and bowel diseases.
- Observe and record therapeutic effects and adverse effects.
- Ambulate client as soon as possible since exercise promotes bowel action.
- Push fluids if not contraindicated.
- Provide a relaxed, unrushed, and private area for defecation.
- Client teaching:

  - Follow the directions indicated on the medication container (for example, take with the full glass of water; take before bedtime).
  - Increase fluid intake throughout the day if not contraindicated.
  - Increase fibre in the diet.
  - Reduce constipating foods in the diet.

  - Increase exercise.
  - Avoid overuse of medications as tolerance can develop.
  - If possible, use milder classifications such as stool softeners or bulk-forming laxatives.
  - Caution against overuse of bulk-forming laxatives, which can interfere with absorption of other medications and cause distension and possible obstruction.
  - Do not take prescribed medication if abdominal pain or nausea and vomiting are present.

ANTIDIARRHEAL AGENTS

Usually, the medication prescribed to treat diarrhea is given to treat the unpleasant symptoms or the underlying cause of the diarrhea. Some medications may be purchased without prescription and are available on pharmacy shelves or OTC, whereas others require a prescription because of the classification of the drug or the severity of the condition to be treated (such as opiate-related drugs).

Four general classifications of agents are used for the treatment of diarrhea: opioids, bulk-forming agents, absorbents, and anticholinergics. The type of drug prescribed depends on the cause and severity of the diarrhea.

Table 7.10   Classifications of Antidiarrheals

Classification	Action	Uses
Opioids • Codeine sulphate • Loperamide (Imodium) • Diphenoxilate + atropine (Lomotil)	• Suppress GI smooth muscle activity → ↓ GI motility, prolonging transit time → absorption of fluid and nutrients • Analgesic effect	• Acute diarrhea • Not usually recommended for diarrhea caused by infections as infectious agents may be retained within the bowel
Bulk-Forming Agents • Psyllium (Metamucil)	• Absorb water from large intestine → increase bulk → stool becomes less watery	• Symptomatic treatment of diarrhea
Absorbents • Bismuth subsalicylate (Pepto-Bismol) • Kaolin–pectin (Kaopectate)	• Absorb irritants and coat lining of the intestinal tract → inhibit irritation of the lining of intestines and absorb toxic substances for excretion in feces	• Diarrhea associated with intestinal infections and chronic bowel diseases, such as diverticulitis and ulcerative colitis
Anticholinergics • Belladonna	• Suppress parasympathetic nervous system activity of the intestinal tract → suppress peristalsis → reduce spasm and speed of passage of intestinal contents	• Require prescription; administered in conjunction with opioid preparation • Diarrhea associated with irritable and inflammatory bowel conditions

Classifications of Antidiarrheals

Table 7.10 outlines the different classifications of antidiarrheals, their actions, and their uses.

Adverse Effects Related to Antidiarrheal Agents

- Constipation
- Nausea and vomiting
- Dependency (with opioids)
- Sedation, drowsiness, weakness, lethargy (with opioids)
- Urinary retention (with atropine preparations and opioids)
- Clotting disorders (with bismuth preparations)
- Allergic reactions

Nursing Considerations Relating to Antidiarrheal Agents

- Assess the client's history relating to the diarrhea and established bowel patterns.
- Identify possible causes of the diarrhea.
- Adhere to established guidelines for administration of a specific preparation, such as the time to administer.
- Assess for contraindications.
- Increase fluid intake while diarrhea persists to prevent dehydration; monitor for electrolyte imbalances.
- Monitor client's intake and output.
- Client teaching:

  - Follow administration directives, including the correct dosage and when to take the medication.
  - Increase fluid intake to replace lost fluids.

- Monitor effects relating to relief of diarrhea.
- Maintain a record of the frequency and consistency of stools until normal bowel patterns resume.
- See a doctor immediately if diarrhea persists, manifestations increase in severity, or adverse effects develop (child: 24 hr; adult 2–3 days, depending on severity).
- Avoid irritating, gaseous foods that stimulate the bowel, such as cabbage, high-fibre foods, or psyllium fibre.
- Monitor weight for possible fluid deficits.
- Avoid overuse of opioid preparations due to possible development of dependence.
- Try to identify causes of the diarrhea for possible avoidance of a recurrence of the problem.
- Inform the client that sometimes the diarrhea facilitates the removal of undesirable substances from the body and antidiarrheals are not always necessary.
- Inform the client that bismuth preparations darken the stool and that this is no cause for alarm.

ANTACID AGENTS

Antacids form a large group of prescription and OTC drugs used to reduce the hyperacidity of the stomach. Certain alkaline drugs can directly neutralize the hydrochloric acid (HCl) secreted into the stomach (such as aluminum, magnesium, and calcium-containing drugs). Additives include simethicone, which reduces gaseous buildup and distension, and alginic acid, which protects the gastric lining and reduces the risk of acid reflux into the esophagus. Other classifications inhibit the production or release of HCl, which results in a reduction in the amount of HCl in the stomach, thereby relieving gastric irritation.

These drugs are used for the treatment of conditions such as mild gastritis, which is caused by indigestion and eating foods that cause "heartburn," gastroesophageal reflux disease (GERD), peptic ulcer disease, and hypersecretion disorders. A prescription for certain preparations may also be used as a preventive of stress ulcers caused by extreme traumatic events, such as extensive burns. The particular type of preparation prescribed is directed toward treating the specific condition.

Aluminum preparations may produce constipation, while magnesium preparations produce diarrhea; therefore, most products on the market today are a combination of products. Calcium preparations are fast-acting but are less commonly used due to the risk of developing renal calculi, acid rebound, and hypercalcemia. Sodium bicarbonate is fast and effective but highly soluble, resulting in absorption and the potential development of metabolic alkalosis.

Classification of Antacids

Table 7.11 outlines the different classifications of antacids, their actions, and their uses.

General Adverse Effects of Antacid Preparations

- Contraindicated in severe renal failure and GI obstruction
- Contraindicated in pregnancy and lactation; crosses barriers to infant

Nursing Considerations Relating to Antacid Preparations

- Administer at times indicated (such as pc, at bedtime, with food, 4–6 wk, and so on). However, sometimes

Table 7.11   Classifications of Antacids

Classification	Action	Uses	Adverse Effects
Neutralizing Agents • Aluminum Products (Amphogel) • Calcium Products (Tums, Rolaids) • Combination Products (Gelucil, Maalox, Diovol, Gaviscon)	• Neutralized HCl in the stomach, e.g., AlOH + HCl → AlCl + H_2O • Alginic acid – coating action of the stomach • Simethicone is added to some of these agents as an antiflatulent as it inhibits gas formation	• Treatment of acute irritation and inflammation of esophageal and gastric lining due to ingestion of certain foods and gastric reflux • Available in chewable tablets, powders, and liquid preparations • All preparations are available OTC	• Constipation (aluminum and calcium preparations) • Renal calculi (calcium preparations) • Systemic metabolic alkalosis (sodium bicarbonate) • Acid rebound hyperacidity (calcium preparations)
H_2 Receptor Antagonists • Cimetidine (Tagamet) • Ranitidine (Zantac) • Famotidine (Pepcid)	• Inhibit histamine stimulation of H_2 receptors within the parietal cells to produce HCl → reduce HCl secretion → reduce gastric acidity	• Peptic ulcer disease • GERD • Stress ulcers • Zollinger–Ellison syndrome*	• Lethargy, confusion (H_2 receptor antagonists) • Gynecomastia and erectile dysfunction (cimetidine) • Suppression of metabolic activities of the liver (cimetidine)
Proton Pump Inhibitors • Lansoprazole (Prevacid) (for *Helicobacter pylori* infections) • Omeprazole (Losec)	• Irreversibly bind to H^+/K^+ ATPase in parietal cells, preventing the movement of H^+ out of parietal cells → lowering HCl	• Erosive esophagitis • GERD • Active duodenal ulcers (short-term therapy) • Gastric hypersecretory conditions (Zollinger–Ellison syndrome*)	• GI infections due to decreased acid production (H_2 receptor antagonists, proton pump inhibitors)
Mucosal Protective Agents • Sucralfate (Sulcrate) • Bismuth	• Locally combine with HCl and proteins at ulcer site to form a thick paste that covers and sticks to the ulcer site → protect ulcer to allow for healing • Bismuth appears to stimulate prostaglandin and bicarbonate production	• Active peptic ulcers • Stress ulcers • Esophageal irritation	• Allergic reactions • Urticaria • Nausea • Constipation • Dry mouth

*Zollinger–Ellison syndrome: Nonendocrine pancreatic tumours that secrete gastrin, which in turn stimulates parietal cells within the lining of the stomach to secrete HCl and pepsin, resulting in the development of peptic ulcers.

clients may be prescribed low dosages of medication for extended periods.

- Observe for desired effects and adverse effects (such as constipation or diarrhea).
- Observe for occult blood or melena stool.
- Client teaching:

  - Take the medication according to the directions on the label.
  - Avoid overuse or long-term use.
  - See a physician if manifestations continue or if the medication is taken beyond the suggested duration.
  - Reduce possible causes of irritation or ulcer formation, such as stress.
  - Avoid alcohol and smoking.
  - Administer with a full glass of fluid to ensure absorption.
  - Take frequent small meals to maintain food within the stomach.
  - Avoid irritating foods or foods that stimulate acid production.
  - Remain sitting up for 1–2 hr following a meal to reduce the risk of acid reflux.
  - Monitor bowel movements for constipation, diarrhea, or black stool.

ANTIEMETICS

Antiemetics are agents used to prevent and treat nausea and vomiting. Conditions that precipitate nausea, vomiting, or both include GI irritation, infections occurring in many parts of the body (such as the brain), metabolic imbalances, severe pain, stress, fear and horror, motion imbalances that originate from the semicircular canals of the ear, or radiation therapy and drug toxicity within the body, such as the vomiting associated with chemotherapeutic agents for cancer.

Antiemetic agents suppress impulses travelling to the vomiting centre within the medulla oblongata of the brain to relieve the manifestation of nausea and vomiting.

Classification of Antiemetics

Table 7.12 outlines the different classifications of antiemetics, their actions, and their uses.

Adverse Effects Relating to Antiemetics

- Drowsiness, dizziness, weakness
- Orthostatic hypotension
- Visual disturbances (blurred vision)
- Dry mouth
- Urinary retention (with antihistamines, anticholinergics)
- Diarrhea (with prokinetics)

Nursing Considerations Relating to Antiemetics

- Administer medication as ordered: Dose, route, and time, such as ac, IV, IM, half an hour prior to nausea-producing treatment or event.

Table 7.12 Classifications of Antiemetics

Classifications	Action	Uses
Antihistamines • Dimenhydrinate (Gravol) • Anticholinergics • Scopolamine (Transderm V)	• Block Ach* receptors in vestibular region and reticular formation ➔ impulses blocked from stimulating chemoreceptor trigger zone (CTZ) ➔ CTZ prevented from stimulating the vomiting centre	• Prevention of nausea and vomiting due to motion sickness
Neuroleptics • Prochlorperazine (Stemetil) • Promethazine (Phenergan)	• Block dopamine receptors in CTZ ➔ CTZ prevented from stimulating the vomiting centre	• Nausea associated with inner ear disorders
Serotonin Blockers • Granisetron (Kytril)	• Inhibit stimulating effect of serotonin at receptor sites in GI tract and CTZ ➔ CTZ prevented from stimulating the vomiting centre	• Vomiting associated with chemotherapy
Prokinetic Agents • Metoclopramide (Apo-Metoclop)	• Stimulate release of Ach in GI tract ➔ speed gastric emptying ➔ decrease nausea and vomiting relating to gastric retention and distension • Block dopamine in CTZ	• Nausea and vomiting relating to gastric distension • Vomiting relating to migraine headache, chemotherapy, hiatus hernia
Cannabis	• Depresses reticular formation, thalamus, and cerebral cortex ➔ reduces sensitivity ➔ reduces nausea and vomiting	• Chemotherapy • Nausea and anorexia associated with HIV/AIDS

*Ach = acetylcholine

- Monitor and record effects and adverse effects.
- Implement safety precautions due to potential for drowsiness.
- Predict potential for vomiting and administer medication prior to occurrence.
- Withhold fluids until nausea is relieved.
- Offer fluids when nausea has been relieved, initially in small amounts.
- Monitor intake and output to maintain positive balance.
- Promote rest and relaxation when nausea occurs.
- Ensure that tissues and a kidney basin are available when the client is experiencing nausea.
- Provide mouth care during acute episodes of nausea and vomiting.
- Client teaching:

  - Take medications prior to nausea-producing event, such as motion sickness.
  - Avoid activities that require constant alertness (such as driving) when taking antiemetics.
  - See a physician if the nausea and vomiting persists beyond 24 hr.
  - Avoid food and situations that cause nausea and vomiting.

- Avoid activity and promote rest when nauseated.
- After nausea has subsided, initially take small amounts of clear fluids to determine tolerance.
- Recognize specific adverse effects of the classification of drug taken; report adverse effects.

DRUGS THAT AFFECT THE RESPIRATORY SYSTEM

The drugs that affect the respiratory system are outlined in Figure 7.4.

Several classifications of drugs are used to relieve disorders of the respiratory tract. These medications can relieve cough (antitussives), promote the removal of excess secretions from the respiratory passageways (expectorants, decongestants, and mucolytics), or facilitate the dilation of the respiratory passageways (antihistamines, corticosteroids, and bronchodilators).

ANTITUSSIVES

The classification of medications prescribed for the treatment of a cough depends on whether the cough is productive or dry. Productive coughs are usually treated

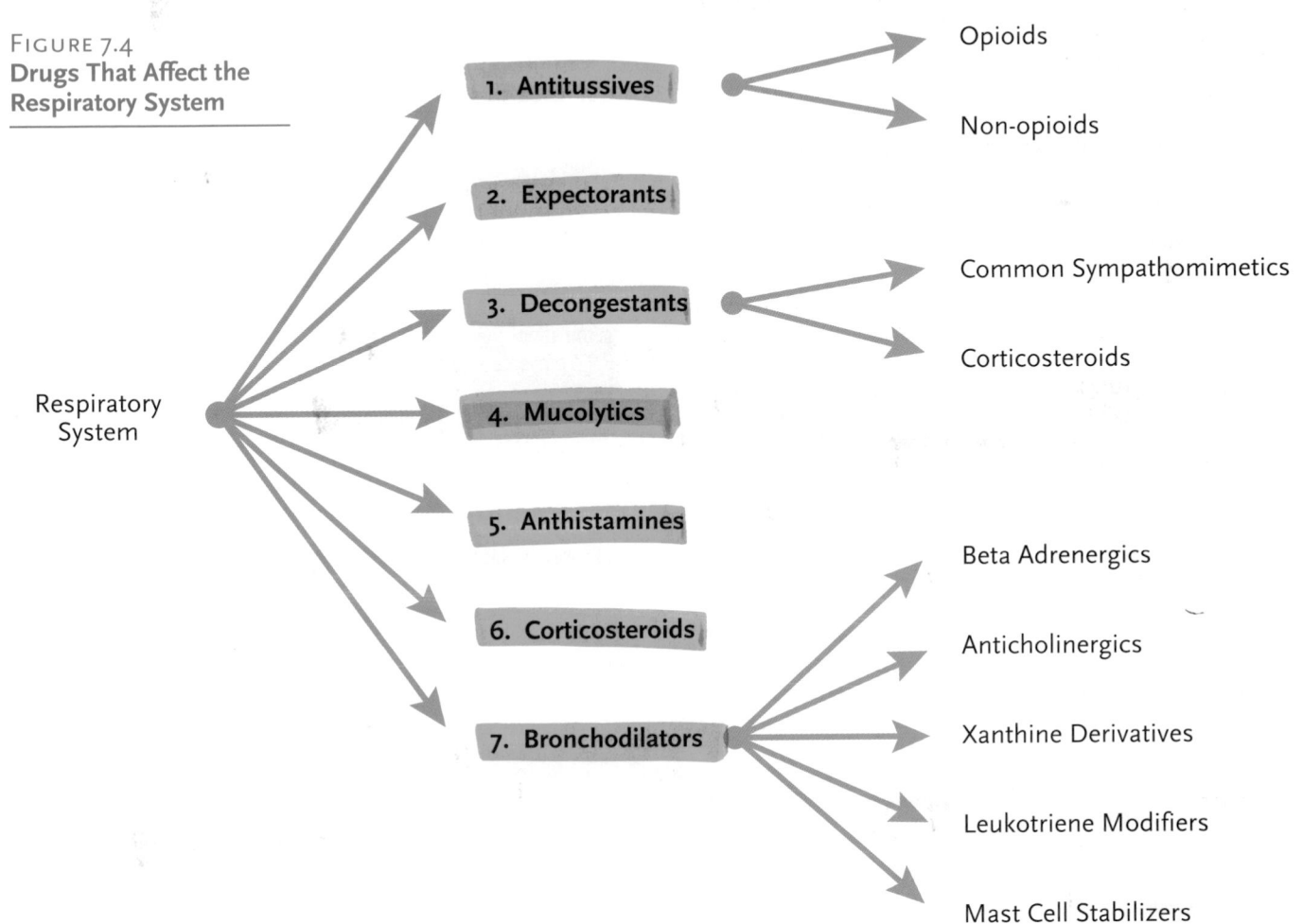

FIGURE 7.4
Drugs That Affect the Respiratory System

Respiratory System

1. **Antitussives** → Opioids / Non-opioids
2. **Expectorants**
3. **Decongestants** → Common Sympathomimetics / Corticosteroids
4. **Mucolytics**
5. **Anthistamines**
6. **Corticosteroids**
7. **Bronchodilators** → Beta Adrenergics / Anticholinergics / Xanthine Derivatives / Leukotriene Modifiers / Mast Cell Stabilizers

Table 7.13 Classifications of Antitussives

Classification	Action	Characteristics	Adverse Effects
Opioids • Codeine • Hydrocodone (Hycodan)	• Suppress the cough centre in the medulla oblongata ➔ suppress coughing • Suppress pain receptors ➔ analgesic effect ➔ ↓ cough reflex	• Low dosage reduces risk of addiction and excessive CNS depression • Commonly administered in syrup form in combination with expectorant	• Nausea and vomiting • Constipation • Weakness, dizziness
Non-opioids • Dextromethorphan (Benylin DM)	• Suppress the cough centre in the medulla oblongata ➔ suppress coughing	• No CNS depression or analgesic effects • Commonly administered in syrup form in combination with expectorant • Available OTC	• Drowsiness • Nausea

with expectorants and mucolytics, while dry coughs are treated with antitussives.

Antitussives (cough suppressants) are prescribed to decrease the intensity and frequency of the cough without obstructing the elimination of tracheo-bronchial phlegm. Since the cough reflex is required to clear the upper respiratory tract of obstructive secretions, antitussives are commonly given in combination with expectorants to prevent the congestion of respiratory secretions within the lungs.

Classifications of Antitussives

Table 7.13 outlines the different classifications of antitussives, their actions, and their uses.

Nursing Considerations Relating to Antitussives

- Ensure care regarding dosage and frequency.
- Observe for drowsiness and sedative effects.
- Client teaching:

  - Avoid activities that require constant alertness.
  - Report excessive drowsiness or sedation, headache, fever, and chest congestion.
  - Take only as directed by a prescriber or pharmacist.
  - Increase fluid intake to maintain hydration and liquefy respiratory secretions.
  - Take syrups undiluted.
  - Avoid intake of food or fluid for half an hour after administering the medication to promote local effects of syrup on throat.

EXPECTORANTS

Expectorants liquefy mucus by stimulating the secretion of natural lubricants from glands within the respiratory tract. This effect is achieved by the following:

- Reflex irritation of the respiratory passageways as a result of drug-induced irritation of the gastric lining,

which leads to stimulation of secretions to liquefy thick mucus
- Drug-induced irritation of the linings of the respiratory passageways stimulates secretions to liquefy thick mucus.
- Ciliary action and coughing expel the liquefied phlegm from the pulmonary system.
- Use includes the treatment of productive cough (in combination with an antitussive) and inflammatory conditions of the upper respiratory tract that produce excess secretions, such as pharyngitis and the common cold.

Common Preparations

- Guaifenesin (Robitussin, Benylin E)
- Potassium iodide

Adverse Effects of Expectorant Agents

- Minimal adverse effects
- Nausea and vomiting
- GI irritation
- Iodism (potassium iodide)

Nursing Considerations Relating to Expectorants

- Increase fluid intake to assist in liquefying mucus.
- Observe for adverse effects, including those relating to antitussives.

DECONGESTANTS

Decongestants are drugs used to relieve upper airway congestion, primarily nasal, which is caused by swollen mucous membranes irritated by conditions such as allergic rhinitis and the common cold. Many of these preparations may be obtained as OTC drugs. Preparations may be oral, inhalation sprays, or nose drops.

Common Decongestant Agents

Common Sympathomimetics

These products act by producing local vasoconstriction, which decreases blood flow to irritated and dilated capillaries in the mucous lining of the nasal passages and sinus cavities, widening airways for improved air entry and drainage. Examples include the following:

- Ephedrine (Vicks Vatronol)
- Oxymetazoline (Neosynephrine, Allerest, Dristan)
- Xylometazoline (Otrivin)
- Pseudoephedrine (Sudafed) – Oral

Topical Corticosteroids

Corticosteroids exert an anti-inflammatory action that reduces swelling and improves air entry. Examples are as follows:

- Beclomethasone dipropionate (Beclovent)
- Budesonide (Rhinocort)
- Dexamethosone (Decadron)

Adverse Effects of Nasal Decongestants

Usually, the dose remains topical; therefore, systemic effects are uncommon. Potential effects of sympathomimetics include the following:

- Headache
- Nervousness
- Dry mouth
- Palpitation
- Increased BP
- Urinary retention (as in prostatic hyperplasia)

Potential effects of corticosteroids include the following:

- Nasal irritation
- Nasal itchiness
- Dry mouth
- Oral fungal infections
- Cough

Nursing Considerations Relating to Decongestants

Client teaching:

- Caution use by clients who have hypertension, glaucoma, or cardiac disease.
- Clients should increase fluid intake to 2000–3000 mL per day unless contraindicated.
- Administer according to label instructions.
- Ensure correct dosage and frequency.
- Avoid prolonged use of OTC medications.
- If manifestations persist for longer than one week, a physician should be consulted.
- Prolonged use may result in rebound congestion.

- Clarify compatibility for use with other medications.
- Assess for adverse effects and report to a physician.
- Teach the client to observe for potential adverse effects and to discontinue the drugs and report to a physician.
- Teach correct methods for effectively administering nose drops or sprays:

  - Hyperextend the neck when instilling nose drops.
  - Breathe in while instilling spray.
  - Blow the nose gently prior to administering preparation into the nose.

MUCOLYTICS

Mucolytics are specific preparations prescribed to reduce the stickiness and viscosity of pulmonary secretions.

- Action focuses directly on the thick mucus plugs to liquefy and dissolve them, thereby promoting removal of the secretions by ciliary action, suction, postural drainage, and coughing.
- Mucolytics are prescribed for treatment of chronic bronchitis, emphysema, cystic fibrosis, and pneumonia.
- Examples include acetylcysteine (Mucomyst), inhaled by direct instillation or by nebulization, and dornase alfa, which exerts an enzyme action on thick mucus (used primarily for cystic fibrosis).

Adverse Effects of Mucolytics

- Drowsiness
- Rhinorrhea
- Bronchospasm (may occur during treatment)
- Nausea and vomiting

Nursing Considerations Relating to Mucolytics

- Assess the effectiveness of air entry prior to and after therapy.
- Follow directions regarding the preparation and administration of the product.
- Encourage increased intake of fluids to 2000–3000 mL per day.
- Encourage the client to cough deeply following treatment to remove secretions.
- Use suction equipment to remove excess liquefied secretions as necessary.
- Administer mouth care following treatment.

ANTIHISTAMINES

Antihistamines are used to treat a variety of disorders that result in an increase in capillary permeability, constriction of smooth muscle, and increased respiratory secretions. These effects result in swelling and obstruction of respiratory passageways and can occur with allergies.

These drugs act by opposing the action of histamine at the H_1 receptor sites, which leads to a decrease in capillary permeability, the relaxation of bronchial smooth muscle, and reduced secretions, resulting in more open passageways, reduced swelling, and, therefore, improved air entry.

Common Antihistamine Agents

First-generation preparations include the following:

- Diphenhydramine (Benadryl)
- Chlorpheniramine (Chlor-Tripolon)
- Promethazine ((Phenergan)

Second-generation preparations include the following:

- Loratadine (Claritin)
- Fexofenadine (Allegra)

Adverse Effects of Antihistamines

Effects vary depending on the preparation; second-generation preparations do not have as sedating an effect as those of the first generation. Possible effects include the following:

- Drowsiness
- Known drug allergies
- Dry mouth
- Urinary retention
- Dizziness, weakness, feeling faint
- Nervousness
- Nausea, vomiting
- Constipation or diarrhea
- Cardiac dysrhythmias, palpitations
- Headache
- Visual disturbances

Nursing Considerations Relating to Antihistamines

- Observe for desired effect and possible side effects.
- Note safety precautions relating to preparations with sedating effects and take caution with activities requiring constant attention.
- Client teaching:

  - Follow directions on dosage and frequency.
  - Administer with meals to avoid gastric discomfort.
  - Suck candies to relieve dryness in the mouth.
  - Report to a physician if manifestations of the condition persist.
  - Weakness and drowsiness may occur.
  - Consult with a physician before taking sedating products such as alcohol, sleeping pills, analgesics, and so on, which increase drowsiness and weakness.
  - Report to physician any unusual adverse effects.

CORTICOSTEROIDS

Corticosteroids exert their anti-inflammatory action on the respiratory passageways by suppressing airway inflammation, thereby reducing swelling within the bronchioles, as well as by decreasing mucus production, resulting in less airway obstruction.

These desirable effects are produced by inhibiting the production of histamine, which results in reduced capillary permeability and decreased production of tissue chemicals that cause inflammation. This leads to the suppression of the movement of protein, fluid, and blood cells into interstitial spaces, also reducing swelling and inflammation; corticosteroids also facilitate the action of beta$_2$ adrenergic agonists by increasing the sensitivity of their adrenergic receptors. This classification of drug is commonly prescribed for the treatment of asthma and any other conditions that cause bronchoconstriction.

Corticosteroids may be administered by inhalation, orally, or intravenously. They are not generally effective in relieving acute episodes. The drugs require several hours to produce their desirable effects.

Common Corticosteroid Agents

- Butesonide (Pulmicort) (inhalation)
- Fluticasone (Flovent) (inhalation)
- Hydrocortisone (Solu-Cortef) (IV)
- Prednisone (oral)

Adverse Effects of Corticosteroids

- Gastric irritation
- Hypertension
- Dry mouth
- Cough
- Oral fungal infections
- Adrenal failure at high doses (with systemic doses)
- Fluid retention

Nursing Considerations Relating to Corticosteroids

- Administer oral preparations with meals.
- Observe for desirable and adverse effects (optimal effects may take hours to days).
- Caution against prolonged use and abrupt stoppage of medication due to possible adrenal shutdown.
- Instruct clients to use inhalers as directed and only when necessary; they should avoid overuse.
- Have clients rinse their mouths following each treatment to prevent the development of infection.
- Teach clients to administer the corticosteroid inhaler approximately 15 minutes to half an hour following the use of other inhalers, such as bronchodilators.
- Instruct clients to shake the inhaler prior to administration.
- Client teaching:

- Employ the proper method for use of inhalers.
- Rest until relief of manifestations is achieved.
- Identify and avoid conditions that promote bronchoconstriction.
- Watch for possible adverse effects and report.
- Employ good mouth care to prevent oral infections.
- Drink plenty of fluids if not contraindicated.
- Do not suddenly discontinue a regularly prescribed oral preparation.
- Medications require a slow "weaning" process when discontinuing.

BRONCHODILATORS

Bronchodilators are used in the treatment of airway-obstructive diseases such as asthma. These agents relax the smooth muscles of the tracheobronchial tree, causing dilation of bronchioles and alveolar ducts, thereby decreasing the resistance to airflow.

Preparations are available in inhalation, oral, and IV forms. Inhalation and IV administration are used to treat acute attacks of bronchoconstriction; oral preparations are used for long-term prevention.

Inhalers

Inhalers or puffers release a small dose of medication into the lungs when discharged. They act topically on the lungs and require smaller doses than medications taken enterally.

Nebulizers

These devices pump compressed air through a solution of the drug, producing a fine mist that can be inhaled through a face mask.

Inhaled corticosteroids are used to prevent and treat asthma. This route reduces the need for oral corticosteroids as the inhaled versions have a direct, local effect on the inflammation in the respiratory system, with the result that systemic steroids are not required.

General Classifications of Bronchodilators

Table 7.14 outlines the different classifications of bronchodilators, their actions, and their uses. Some

Table 7.14   Classifications of Bronchodilators

Classification	Action	Uses	Adverse Effects
Beta Adrenergics • Salbutamol (Ventolin) • Epinephrine (Adrenalin) • Isoproterenol (Isuprel)	• Beta adrenergic agents (mainly beta$_2$-agonists) stimulate receptors in the muscle → smooth muscle relaxation within the respiratory tract → dilation of bronchial tree	• Acute attacks and long-term treatment of asthma	• Cardiac dysrhythmias, hypertension, and hypotension • Restlessness, nervousness • Hyperactivity, tremors • Dizziness • Insomnia • Headache • Hyperglycemia • Hypokalemia
Anticholinergics • Ipratropium bromide (Atrovent)	• Anticholinergics block the action of Ach in the muscles → smooth muscle relaxation in the respiratory tract → dilation of bronchial tree	• Primarily used to prevent bronchoconstriction • Long-term treatment of asthma	• Hyperactivity • Dry mouth • Dry cough • Dizziness • Insomnia • Anxiety • Gastrointestinal upset
Xanthine Derivatives • Aminophylline (Phyllocontin) • Theophylline (Theo-dur) • Oxytriphylline (Choledyl elixir)	• Act directly on smooth muscle of bronchi and blood vessels causing relaxation → dilation of bronchial tree • Inhibit release of slow-reacting substances of anaphylaxis (SRSA) and histamine → reduce bronchial swelling and narrowing caused by these two chemicals	• Acute attacks and long-term prevention of bronchoconstriction of asthma attacks	• Cardiac dysrhythmias and hypertension • Tachycardia • Restlessness, nervousness, hyperactivity • Insomnia • Headache • Nausea and vomiting • Gastroesophageal reflex (GERD)

Continued on next page

Table 7.14   Classifications of Bronchodilators (cont'd)

Classification	Action	Uses	Adverse Effects
Leukotriene Modifiers • Montelukast (Singulair) • Zafirlukast (Accolate)	• Act as leukotriene receptor antagonists by blocking receptors that control bronchoconstriction, vascular permeability, and mucus secretion → bronchodilation → ↓ frequency and severity of acute asthma attacks	• Long-term prevention of asthma attacks • Ineffective in the treatment of acute asthma attacks • Oral preparations	• Headache • Nausea and vomiting • Gastrointestinal upset • Liver damage
Mast Cell Stabilizers • Na cromoglycate (Intal) • Nedocromil (Tilade)	• Act by stabilizing and reducing the response of mast cells to irritating substances → ↓ release of substances that stimulate inflammation and smooth muscle constriction → maintenance of smooth muscle relaxation • Does not produce bronchodilation	• Prevention of acute asthmatic attacks • Ineffective in alleviating existing bronchospasm • Available in inhalation form	• Dizziness • Headache • Dry cough • Throat discomfort • Nasal inflammation

bronchodilators may be used in combination with corticosteroids for added and more prolonged effects.

Nursing Considerations Relating to Bronchodilators

- Administer specific medication according to directions (such as dosage, method of administration).
- Observe for desired effects, relief of respiratory distress, and reduced respiratory rate and chart.
- Observe for adverse effects relating to sympathetic nervous system stimulants, including beta adrenergics, anticholinergics, and xanthines.
- Instruct avoidance of caffeine, smoking, and OTC medications (xanthines).
- Use cautiously with clients who have cardiac, renal, or hepatic disorders.
- Provide a quiet, relaxing environment to reduce stimulation.
- Increase intake of fluids, if not contraindicated.
- When administering medication during an acute attack of bronchoconstriction, institute measures to promote optimal air entry into the lungs, such as a high Fowler's position.
- Client teaching:

  - Obtain basic knowledge regarding the nature of the condition: nature of the medications, dosage, time, and possible adverse effects.
  - Take the medication as prescribed by the prescriber and pharmacist.
  - Identify and reduce possible triggers that produce bronchoconstriction.
  - Demonstrate how to administer inhaled preparations correctly.
  - Take oral medications with food.

  - Try to relax and rest during acute attacks.
  - Contact a physician immediately if manifestations do not resolve.
  - Avoid drinking products that promote bronchoconstriction, such as caffeinated beverages.
  - Receive flu vaccinations each year to prevent respiratory manifestations.
  - Obtain prescriber advice prior to use of OTC medications.

ANTIMICROBIAL AGENTS

Figure 7.5 outlines the major antimicrobial agents. Antimicrobial agents are used to treat a variety of forms of pathogenic organisms capable of infecting the body. In addition to bacteria and viruses, there are a variety of pathogenic fungi, protozoans, and complex, multicellular organisms, such as worms.

Antimicrobial agents have been developed to destroy organisms or groups of organisms depending on the agent's specific chemical nature and action and the nature of the organism. Diagnosis of a particular infection, and the best antimicrobial agent to prescribe for its treatment, is commonly achieved by gathering a specimen from the client for culture and sensitivity tests. The laboratory identifies the organism and its sensitivity to the various antimicrobial agents.

ANTIBACTERIAL AGENTS

"Antibiotics" is the term commonly used to refer to antibacterial drugs. Agents that destroy living organisms are said to be bactericidal, while those that interfere with their development are bacteriostatic. Antibiotics are classified into broad categories based on their chemical structures—sulphonamides, penicillins, cephalosporins, macrolides, fluoroquinolones,

FIGURE 7.5
Antimicrobial Agents

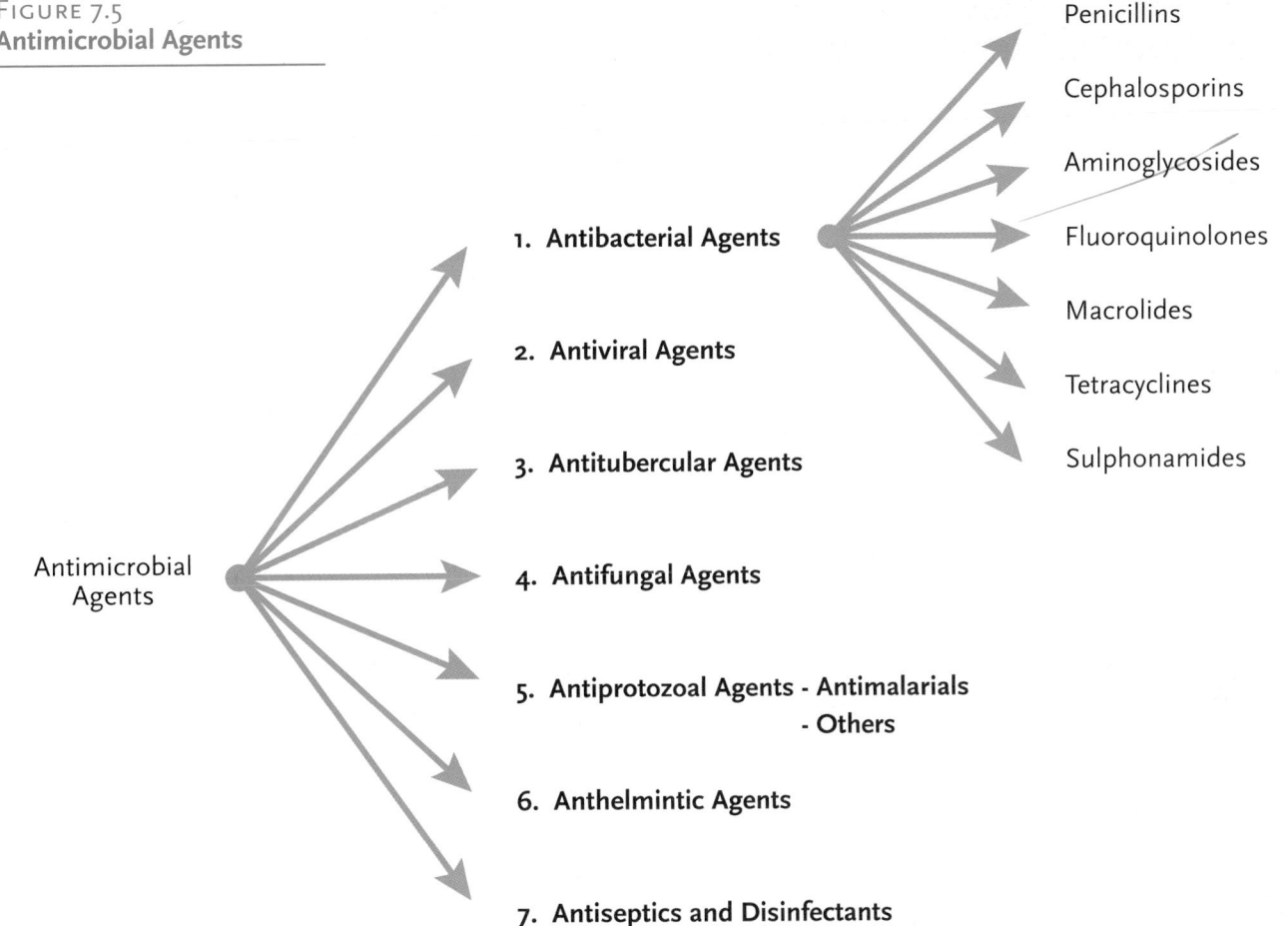

Antimicrobial Agents
1. Antibacterial Agents
2. Antiviral Agents
3. Antitubercular Agents
4. Antifungal Agents
5. Antiprotozoal Agents - Antimalarials
- Others
6. Anthelmintic Agents
7. Antiseptics and Disinfectants
Penicillins
Cephalosporins
Aminoglycosides
Fluoroquinolones
Macrolides
Tetracyclines
Sulphonamides

aminoglycosides, and tetracyclines—in addition to other miscellaneous categories, and their spectrum of activity (broad spectrum or extended spectrum).

The misuse and overprescription of antibiotics have resulted in strains of bacteria resistant to traditional antibiotic therapy. Such strains include the following:

- Methicillin-resistant *Staphylococcus aureus* (MRSA)
- Vancomycin-resistant *Enterococcus* (VRE)
- Extended-spectrum beta-lactamase-producing *E scherichia coli* (ESBL)
- Oxacillin-resistant *Staphylococcus aureus* (ORSA)

Classification of Antibiotics

Table 7.15 outlines the different classifications of antibiotics, their actions, and their uses.

Antiviral Agents

Viruses can only reproduce within the cells of a host because of their simple cellular structure (they contain only DNA or RNA). Antiviral agents act by inhibiting the entry of the virus into the host cell or by acting on the virus once it has entered the cell.

Antiviral agents most commonly inhibit the virus from replicating, and with the assistance of the body's normal immune system, destruction can then occur. Antiviral agents have been developed to target either DNA-containing viruses (antiviral agents) or viruses containing RNA (antiretroviral agents).

Vaccines and immunoglobulins are probably the best preventive for specific viral diseases. Postexposure prophylaxis (PEP) may protect persons who may have had direct contact with persons with conditions such as influenza A, HIV, or hepatitis B.

Commonly Used Antiviral Agents

- Acyclovir (Zovirax) – Herpes zoster, genital herpes
- Amantadine (Symmetrel) – Influenza virus
- Famciclovir (Famvir) – Herpes zoster, genital herpes
- Valganciclovir (Valcyte) – Cytomegalovirus
- Lapinovir (Combivir) – Prophylaxis (PEP)
- Ritonavir (Kaletra) – Prophylaxis (PEP)

Commonly Used Antiretroviral Agents

- Zidovudine (Retrovir) – HIV infections
- Tenofovir (Viread) – HIV infections

Table 7.15   Classifications of Antibiotics

Classification	Action	Characteristics	Adverse Effects
Penicillins Natural Penicillins • Penicillin G (IV and IM) • Penicillin V (PO) Amino Penicillins • Amoxicillin (Amoxil) Extended-Spectrum Penicillins • Piperacillin (IV, IM) (Tazocin) Penicillinase-Resistant Penicillins • Cloxacillin sodium (Nova-Cloxin)	• Interfere with the synthesis of bacterial cell walls	Bactericidal • Ear, nose, throat, and respiratory tract infections • Broad spectrum • Semisynthetic penicillin • Infections of the ear, nose, throat, respiratory tract, urogenital tract, and skin • Broad spectrum • *E. coli* and other pseudomonal organisms • Staphylococcal infections, except for MRSA*	• Hypersensitivity (allergic reactions): urticaria, respiratory difficulty, shock • Diarrhea • Thrombophlebitis (in clients receiving IV penicillin) • Superinfections
Cephalosporins • Structurally and pharmacologically related to penicillin • Derivative of cephalosporin C, produced by fungus and synthetically altered to produce an antibiotic • Cephalexin (Apo-Cephalex)	• Interfere with bacterial cell wall synthesis and bind to penicillin-binding proteins (PBPs) in bacteria cell walls	• Semisynthetic antibiotic • Broad spectrum • Bactericidal • Use with caution as an alternative if client has penicillin allergy • Urinary tract infections (UTIs), respiratory tract infections (RTIs), abdominal infections, septicemia, meningitis, and osteomyelitis	• Diarrhea • Thrombophlebitis • Hyperkalemia • Hypernatremia • Abnormal liver and renal function tests • Secondary infections: oral thrush, genital and anal pruritus, vaginitis, and vaginal discharge • Nephrotoxicity • Antacids, iron, and H_2 receptor antagonists may inhibit absorption

Aminoglycosides
• Natural antibiotics
  • Gentamicin (Alcomicin)
  • Neomycin (Mycifradin Sulphate)
  • Streptomycin
• Semisynthetic
  • Amikacin (Amikin)
	• Bind to ribosomes and thereby prevent protein synthesis within the bacteria	• Bactericidal
		• Poorly absorbed orally
		• Commonly used in combination with other antibiotics
		• Gram-negative bacteria that cause UTIs, wounds, and septicemias
		• Mainstay treatment of nosocomial infection
		• Reserved mainly for use in life-threatening infections
			• Dizziness
			• Headache
			• Skin rash
			• Fever
			• Renal failure
			• Hearing loss (ototoxicity)
			• Not favourable for long-term use

Fluoroquinolones • Norfloxacin (Noroxin) • Ciprofloxacin (Cipro)	• Inhibit activity of DNA gyrase, an enzyme necessary for replication of bacterial DNA	• Bactericidal • Excellent oral absorption • Used against wide variety of Gram-negative and selective positive bacteria • UTIs, sexually transmitted infections, and RTIs	• GI problems • Headache • Dizziness • Fatigue • Insomnia • Depression • Convulsions • Fever • Blurred vision • Tinnitus • Skin problems • Antacids decrease absorption • Contraindicated with cardiac problems

Continued on next page

Table 7.15   Classifications of Antibiotics (cont'd)

Classification	Action	Characteristics	Adverse Effects
Macrolides • Erythromycin (Erythrocin) • Azithromycin (Zithromax) • Clarithromycin (Biaxin) • Dirithromycin (Dynabac)	• Inhibit protein synthesis in susceptible bacteria	• Bacteriostatic • Bactericidal in high concentrations • Respiratory and GI tract infections • Sexually transmitted infections, when penicillin, cephalosporins, and tetracycline cannot be used	• GI irritation: nausea, heartburn • Palpitations, chest pain • Headache, dizziness, vertigo • Hepatotoxicity • Skin reactions • Tinnitus, hearing loss • Interacts with rifampin and rifabutin to reduce antibiotic effect and may increase adverse GI effects

Tetracyclines
• Natural tetracyclines
  • Tetracycline (Novo-Tetra)
• Semisynthetic tetracyclines
  • Doxycycline (Vibramycin)
	• Inhibit protein synthesis in susceptible bacteria by binding to a portion of the ribosomes and stopping bacterial growth	• Bacteriostatic
		• Inhibit growth of many Gram-positive and Gram-negative organisms, some protozoa
		• Treatment of sexually transmitted infections
		• Lyme disease
		• Rickettsia
		• Chlamydia
		• *Mycoplasma* organisms
			• Do not administer with milk, antacids, or iron salts
			• Contraindicated in pregnancy, allergies
			• Tooth discoloration in children (<8 yr)
			• Superinfections
			• Diarrhea, nausea, abdominal cramps, vomiting
			• Photosensitivity
			• Enhance the anticoagulant effect of warfarin

Sulphonamides • Trimethoprim–sulfamethoxazole (Co-Trimoxazole)	• Prevent synthesis of folic acid required by the bacteria for proper synthesis of purines and nucleic acid	• Bacteriostatic • Treat both Gram-positive and Gram-negative bacteria • UTIs, traveller's diarrhea, acute otitis media, and acute exacerbations of chronic bronchitis in adults	• GI irritation • Rash • Photosensitivity • Renal calculi

*MRSA = methicillin-resistant *Staphylococcus aureus*

ANTITUBERCULAR AGENTS

Tuberculosis is caused by *Mycobacterium tuberculosis,* an aerobic bacterium requiring high concentrations of oxygen in order to survive and replicate. The bacterium (tubercle bacillus) is very slow-growing and, after infecting the lungs, may become inactivated and encapsulated by fibrous tissue. Because of this slow growth, monotherapy with the usual antibiotics, such as streptomycin, does not provide effective treatment.

The treatment can be either monotherapy or combination therapy using first-line agents or second-line agents. The prescribed agent will depend on whether the goal is prevention or active treatment.

Common First-Line Agents for the Treatment of Tuberculosis

• Isoniazid (Isotamine)
• Ethambutol (Etibi)

• Rifampin (Rofact)
• Streptomycin (Streptocin)

Common Second-Line Agents for the Treatment of Tuberculosis

• Amikacin (Amikin)
• Levofloxacin (Levaquin)

Liver damage can result from long-term therapy. Clients should not drink alcohol while on therapy due to alcohol and drug interaction and resultant liver damage.

ANTIFUNGAL AGENTS

These drugs are used in the treatment of pathogenic fungal diseases, both systemic and local. Fungal diseases vary from superficial (skin, hair, and nail infections) to systemic (histoplasmosis and opportunistic mycotic diseases, such as aspergillosis and candidiasis).

Few mycotic drugs are available because most drugs that are effective in treating mycotic infections are toxic to human cells. Human cells are similar to fungal cells.

Common Examples of Antifungal Agents

- Amphotericin B (Fungizone) – Used to treat systemic infections (candidiasis and histoplasmosis)
- Nystatin (Mycostatin) – Used to treat candidiasis of skin and mucous membranes
- Tolnaftate (Tinactin) – Used to treat cutaneous mycosis, such as athlete's foot
- Terbinafine hydrochloride (Lamisil) – Used to treat athlete's foot (tinea pedis)
- Atovaquone (Mepron) – For treatment of *Pneumocystis* pneumonia
- Metronidazole (Flagyl) – For treatment of vaginal fungal infections

ANTIPROTOZOAL AGENTS

Antimalarial Agents

These agents are prescribed for the treatment of malaria. The agents are most effective when the malaria parasite is in its nonreproductive stage after entering the human body.

Common Antimalarial Agents

- Chloroquine (Aralen) – Used to treat an acute attack or as a preventive
- Primaquine (Aminoquinolone) – Effective against malaria in red blood cells and tissue
- Quinine sulphate (Quinine-Odan) – Used to treat chloroquine-resistant strains

Other Antiprotozoal Agents

Other protozoal diseases are common to tropical countries. Protozoal diseases encountered in Canada include trichomoniasis and toxoplasmosis. Treatment for these conditions includes the following:

- Atovaquone (Mepron) – For treatment of *Trichomonas* vaginitis
- Metronidazole (Flagyl) – For treatment of toxoplasmosis

ANTHELMINTIC AGENTS

These agents are used for the treatment of infections caused by worms, including pinworms, tapeworms, flatworms, and roundworms. These organisms are large in size, are sometimes visible to the naked eye, and commonly infest the GI tract. Systemic infections occur with some types of worms, particularly those from the tropics. Medications focus on the specific type of worm infection.

Common Anthelmintic Agents

- Praziquantel (Biltricide)
- Mebendazole (Vermox)

ANTISEPTICS AND DISINFECTANTS

Antiseptic Agents

Antiseptic agents may be applied locally for cleansing the skin and mucous membranes. Antiseptics inhibit microbial growth (carbolic acid is bacteriostatic) and at high concentration may kill microbes (for example, tincture of iodine is bactericidal).

Common Antiseptics

- Chlorhexidine gluconate
- Povidone
- Benzalkonium chloride

Disinfectant Agents

Disinfectants are agents that are applied to nonanimate objects, usually to destroy microorganisms; for example, glutaraldehyde (Cidex) has a bactericidal effect.

Common Disinfectants

- Iodine
- Hydrogen peroxide
- Formaldehyde

Nursing Considerations Relating to Antimicrobial Agents

- Perform a complete assessment of the client's history of taking antibiotics, including possible allergies, liver or renal disease, culture and sensitivity (C and S) reports, adverse effects previously experienced, and other drugs being taken.
- Take C and S specimens prior to administering the first dose of medication.
- Maintain awareness of contraindications and drug interactions with other medications being taken.
- Administer at the times indicated.
- Administer on an empty stomach if possible, with plenty of liquid.
- Administer for the length of time ordered.
- Monitor the desired effects, such as a reduction in fever or relief of manifestations.
- Monitor the client for possible allergic reactions (skin rash, shortness of breath, etc.) for at least two hours following administration.
- Hold medication and report if allergic reactions are observed.
- Monitor for development of superinfections.
- Observe for adverse effects, record, and report.
- Administer IM injections deep intramuscularly to reduce irritation and tissue damage.

- Administer IV preparations according to dilution ordered; monitor the drip rate carefully.
- Client teaching:

  - Report any adverse effects immediately.
  - Take medications at the times ordered.
  - Ensure that the complete prescription is taken to avoid recurrence of infection.
  - Take medication with at least one full glass of liquid.
  - Wear a MedicAlert bracelet if any allergies were experienced with past antimicrobial use.
  - Take medication with food if gastric manifestations occur.
  - Learn about potential adverse effects relating to specific preparations, such as photosensitivity with tetracyclines (avoid exposure to sun).
  - Avoid taking tetracyclines with dairy products.
  - Drink plenty of liquids when taking sulpha drugs to avoid renal calculi.

DRUGS THAT AFFECT THE URINARY SYSTEM

Drugs that affect the urinary system are outlined in Figure 7.6.

DIURETICS

Diuretics are drugs or substances that increase the production and excretion of urine by inhibiting the reabsorption of sodium and water from the nephron filtrate. Various diuretics differ in their chemical structure, the region within the kidneys in which they exert their actions, and their potency. Primary uses of diuretics include the following:

- Hypertension – A reduced circulating fluid volume decreases BP.
- Congestive heart failure – A decreased circulating fluid volume decreases the preload and afterload on the heart.

- Kidney failure – Stimulates optimal functioning of the damaged kidney and reduces retained fluid.
- Liver failure – Reduces retained fluid and wastes (ascites) by stimulating maximum functioning of the kidney.
- Increased intracranial pressure – Removes retained fluids within the brain to relieve pressure.
- For hormonal imbalances that result in the retention of fluid, such as during the premenstrual period and with corticosteroid use.

Classifications of Diuretics

Table 7.16 outlines the different classifications of diuretics, their actions, and their uses.

Combination Drugs

A combination diuretic is the potassium-sparing plus thiazide type, such as the following:

- Spirinolactone + hydrochlorothiazide (Aldactazide)
- Triamterene + hydrochlorothiazide (Dyazide)

Nursing Considerations Relating to Diuretics

- Perform a careful assessment of the following:

  - Hydration levels
  - Blood glucose levels
  - Serum electrolyte levels: Na^+, K^+, Cl^-
  - Vital signs
  - Urine output
  - Relief of fluid overload as manifested by edema and dyspnea

- Ensure that toilet facilities are readily available.
- Clients may require potassium supplementation based on the class of diuretic and potassium levels.

FIGURE 7.6
Drugs That Affect the Urinary System

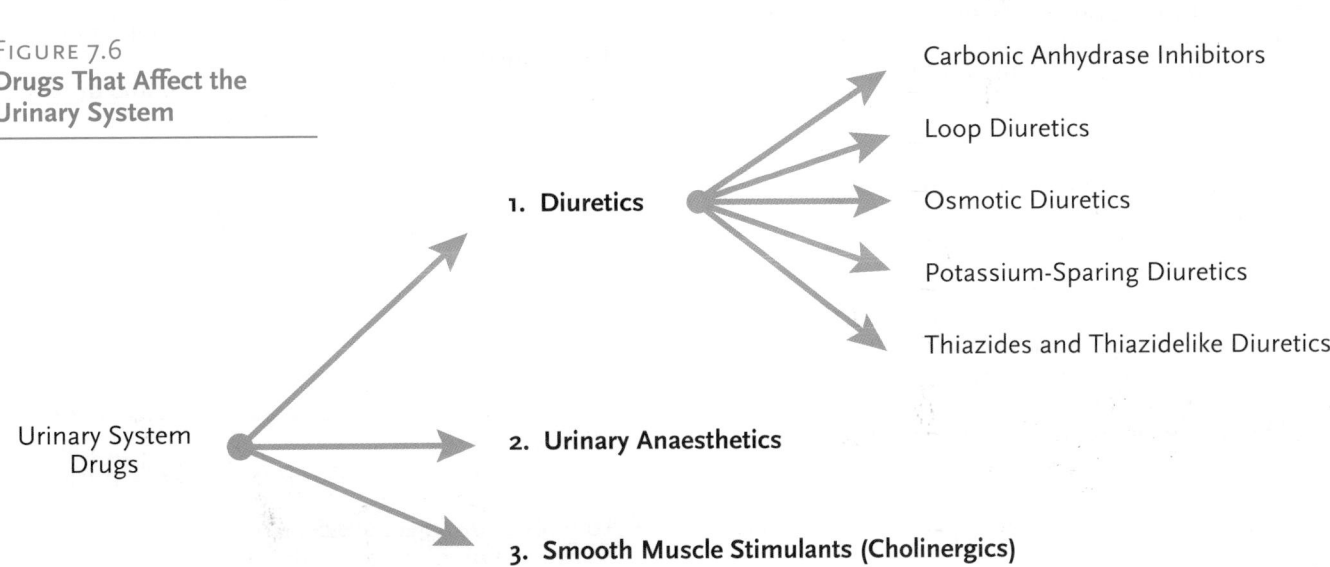

Urinary System Drugs

1. **Diuretics**
   - Carbonic Anhydrase Inhibitors
   - Loop Diuretics
   - Osmotic Diuretics
   - Potassium-Sparing Diuretics
   - Thiazides and Thiazidelike Diuretics

2. **Urinary Anaesthetics**

3. **Smooth Muscle Stimulants (Cholinergics)**

Table 7.16 Classifications of Diuretics

Classification	Action	Uses	Adverse Effects
Carbonic Anhydrase Inhibitors • Acetazolamide (Diamox) • Methazolamide (Neptazane)	• Inhibit the enzyme carbonic anhydrate from promoting the reabsorption of Na^+ from the proximal tubules → water remains in filtrate and is excreted	• Mild diuretic effect • Reduce intraocular pressure in glaucoma • Altitude sickness • Seizures (adjunct with other drugs)	• Drowsiness • Weakness • Visual disturbances • Hyperglycemia • Hypokalemia • Aplastic anemia • Crystalluria
Potent Loop Diuretics • Furosemide (Lasix)	• Block reabsorption of Na^+ and Cl^- in ascending loop of Henle → water remains in filtrate due to change in concentration gradient	• Provide potent and rapid diuresis • Heart failure • Liver failure • Renal disease • Hypertension	• Hypokalemia • Hypocalcemia • Hyperglycemia • Dizziness, headache, blurred vision • Nausea and vomiting • Abdominal pain
Osmotic Diuretics • Mannitol (Osmitrol)	• Filtered by glomerulus but are not reabsorbed → highly concentrated filtrate produced → inhibits reabsorption of water	• Produce large quantity of urine • Increased intracranial pressure • Acute renal failure • Situations requiring rapid reduction in water content, e.g., intraspinal pressure	• Lung congestion • Seizures • Thrombophlebitis • Headache • Visual disturbances • Tachycardia
Potassium-Sparing Diuretics • Spironolactone (Aldactone) • Triamterene (Dyrenium) • Amiloride (Midamor)	• Inhibit the exchange of Na^+ and K^+ in distal tubules independent of aldosterone → water and Na^+ are excreted; K^+ is retained	• Produce a mild diuretic effect • Hyperaldosteronism • Hypertension • Heart failure	• Dizziness, headache • Hyperkalemia • Abdominal cramps • Nausea, vomiting, and diarrhea • Gynecomastia in men (with long-term use)
Thiazides and Thiazidelike Diuretics • Hydrochlorothiazide (HydroDIURIL) • Chlorothiazide (Diuril) • Metolazone (Zaroxolyn)	• Block reabsorption of Na^+, K^+, and Cl^- in distal tubules → water is retained in tubules and excreted as urine • Arteriole smooth muscle relaxation → ↓ preload and afterload in heart	• Heart failure • Liver failure • Edema due to corticosteroid use or hormonal imbalance	• Hypokalemia • Hypocalcemia • Hyperglycemia • Dizziness, headache • Muscle spasm • Abdominal pain

• Administer with food to avoid gastric irritation.
• Monitor intake and output to assess effects. Client teaching:

- Eat foods high in potassium, such as bananas and orange juice.
- Take potassium supplements as ordered with food.
- Take medication in the morning to reduce the need for nocturnal voiding and loss of sleep.
- Fluid restrictions may be necessary.
- Avoid high-sodium foods.
- Avoid beverages with diuretic effects such as caffeine and alcohol as they may produce excess effects.
- Monitor blood glucose levels carefully if taking thiazide or loop diuretics.

- Use caution when rising from a lying to a sitting position due to possible postural hypotension.
- Keep scheduled physicians' visits to monitor progress.
- Report adverse effects immediately to a physician.
- Monitor weight carefully; increased weight is indicative of fluid retention.

URINARY ANAESTHETICS

These preparations produce relief of the discomfort produced by inflammation or infections of the bladder. They act by coating the lining of the urinary system, particularly the bladder, providing a local analgesic or anaesthetic effects; however, they have no antimicrobial properties.

- An example is phenazopyridine (Pyridium).
- It is important to inform the client that urine will become orange in colour (due to the drug's dye properties). This is normal.
- Clients should be aware of the importance of continuing the concurrent antimicrobial therapy as this medication has no antimicrobial properties.

SMOOTH MUSCLE STIMULANTS (CHOLINERGICS)

Specific cholinergic drugs may be prescribed to relieve urinary retention that is nonobstructive in nature. Cholinergics act by stimulating cholinergic receptors in the bladder, resulting in the contraction of the bladder smooth muscle and micturition. An example is bethanechol (Urecholine).

- Clients should be advised of cholinergic effects.
- Adverse effects include abdominal discomfort, bronchospasm, increased salivation, abdominal cramps, hypotension, and bradycardia.
- Clients should be advised to make position changes slowly to avoid postural hypotension.

ANTINEOPLASTIC AGENTS

Figure 7.7 outlines the major antineoplastic agents.

These agents, commonly referred to as chemotherapeutic agents, have been developed to treat various cancers. The specific agent used depends on the type of cancer present. Unlike other primary treatments for cancer, such as surgery, radiation, and laser therapy, chemotherapy using antineoplastic agents focuses not just on the primary site of the cancer but also on the entire system, attacking cancer cells from the primary tumour that have metastasized to different parts of the body. Antineoplastic agents are commonly used in conjunction with the other forms of therapy prior to or after surgical or radiation treatments to provide a multifaceted attack on cancerous tumours.

The pathology of cancer cells is similar, in many respects, to that of normal cells of the body. For this reason, it is a challenge to destroy the cancerous cells without destroying normal body cells.

As many chemotherapeutic agents exert their effects on cells that are undergoing mitosis, cells in the G_0 stage of their development (the resting stage) are minimally affected by the agents. This explains why the adverse effects of chemotherapeutic agents are primarily related to cells within the body that have active cell cycles, such as mucous cells, blood cells, and hair cells.

Sometimes the cancer cells become active and proliferate after chemotherapy has been completed. Another problem with cancer cells is their ability to develop resistance to chemotherapeutic agents. This ability explains why different forms of treatment and chemotherapeutic agents are required if further treatment is needed due to a return of cancer cells. Commonly, combination therapy is used to reduce toxicity and slow the development of resistance. Antineoplastic medications may be administered orally, parenterally, or by direct instillation.

GENERAL CLASSIFICATION OF CHEMOTHERAPEUTIC AGENTS

These agents interfere with the M phase and DNA synthesis (S) stages of the cell cycle and are effective against rapidly dividing cells.

Cycle Nonspecific Drugs

These drugs do not focus on one specific stage of the cell cycle. They are primarily used as a prophylactic treatment to suppress the proliferation of cancer cells.

FIGURE 7.7
Antineoplastic Agents

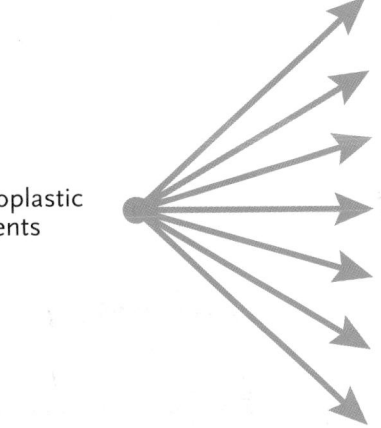

Antineoplastic Agents

- Alkylating Agents
- Antimetabolites
- Mitotic Inhibitors
- Antitumour Antibiotics
- Topoisomerase-1 Inhibitors
- Hormonal Antagonists
- Biological Response Modifiers

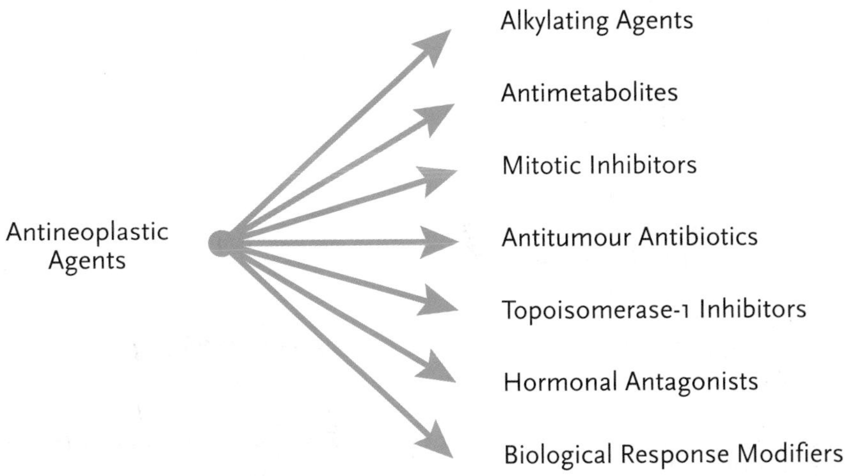

Table 7.17 Classifications of Antineoplastic Drugs

Classification	Action	Characteristics
Alkylating Agents • Busulphan (Myleran) • Cisplatin (Platinol) • Cyclophosphamide (Procytox)	• Inhibit tumour cell mitosis by interfering with the chemical structure of tumour cell DNA ➜ kill tumour cells or slow their growth	• Cell cycle nonspecific • Developed following chemical warfare during World War I
Antimetabolites • Methotrexate (Folex) • Mercaptopurine (Purinethol) • Fluorouracil (5-FU)	• Disrupt metabolic pathways of tumour cells by occupying spaces of normal building blocks ➜ tumour cells are unable to multiply	• Cell cycle specific (S phase) • Replaces normal building blocks required by cancer cells to survive
Mitotic Inhibitors • Vinblastine (Velban) • Vincristine (Oncovin) • Etoposide (VePesid)	• Interfere with tumour cells during mitosis	• Cell cycle specific (M phase)
Antitumour Antibiotics • Doxorubicin (Adriamycin) • Bleomycin (Blenoxane) • Dactinomycin (Cosmogen)	• Antibiotic destructive action on tumour cells by interfering with DNA or RNA synthesis ➜ destroy tumour cells	• Cell cycle nonspecific • Antibiotic effect
Topoisomerase I Inhibitors • Irinotecan (Camptosar) • Topotecan (Hycamtin)	• Inhibit normal functioning of tumour cell DNA during the S phase of the cell cycle ➜ tumour cell development is prevented	• Cell cycle specific • New class of antineoplastic • Plant alkaloid
Hormonal Antagonists • Tamoxifen (Nolvadex) (female specific) • Flutamide (Eulexin) (male specific)	• Alter hormonal environment required by tumour cells ➜ environment undesirable for growth and reproduction of tumour cells	• Cell cycle nonspecific • Prescribed for hormone-dependent tumours
Biological Response Modifiers • Interferon (IFN alpha 2a)	• Stimulate client's own immune system by enhancing the immunological functioning of the body	• Cell cycle nonspecific • Not specifically cytotoxic • Reduced adverse effects due to immuno-suppression

Classifications of Antineoplastic Drugs

Table 7.17 outlines the different classifications of antineoplastic drugs, their actions, and their uses.

ADJUVANT THERAPY

Adjuvent therapy agents are used in combination with chemotherapeutic agents as "rescue" drugs to combat certain adverse effects associated with specific chemotherapeutic agents.

Examples include mesna (Mesnex), which is used with antimetabolite agents, and leucovorin calcium (folinic acid), used with methotrexate and folic acid antagonists (antimetabolites).

Major Adverse Effects of Chemotherapeutic Agents

- GI ulceration
- Nausea and vomiting, diarrhea
- Anemia (erythrocytopenia)
- Infection (leukopenia)
- Hemorrhage (thrombocytopenia)
- Alopecia
- Thin, malformed, brittle nails

Nursing Considerations Relating to Antineoplastic Agents

- Educate the client and significant others regarding the nature and effects of the therapy.
- Promote a positive outlook and body image during therapy.
- Advise that adverse effects are temporary, including the following:

- Hair loss (discuss the use of wigs)
- Bleeding gums (encourage gentle cleaning of the mouth)
- Mouth ulcers (discuss available medications)
- Nausea and vomiting (discuss available medications to relieve discomfort)

FIGURE 7.8
Vitamins and Minerals

Vitamins
Fat-Soluble Vitamins
A
D
E
K
Water-Soluble Vitamins
B Complex
C
Common Minerals
Iron
Calcium
Phosphorus
Magnesium
Sodium
Potassium
Zinc

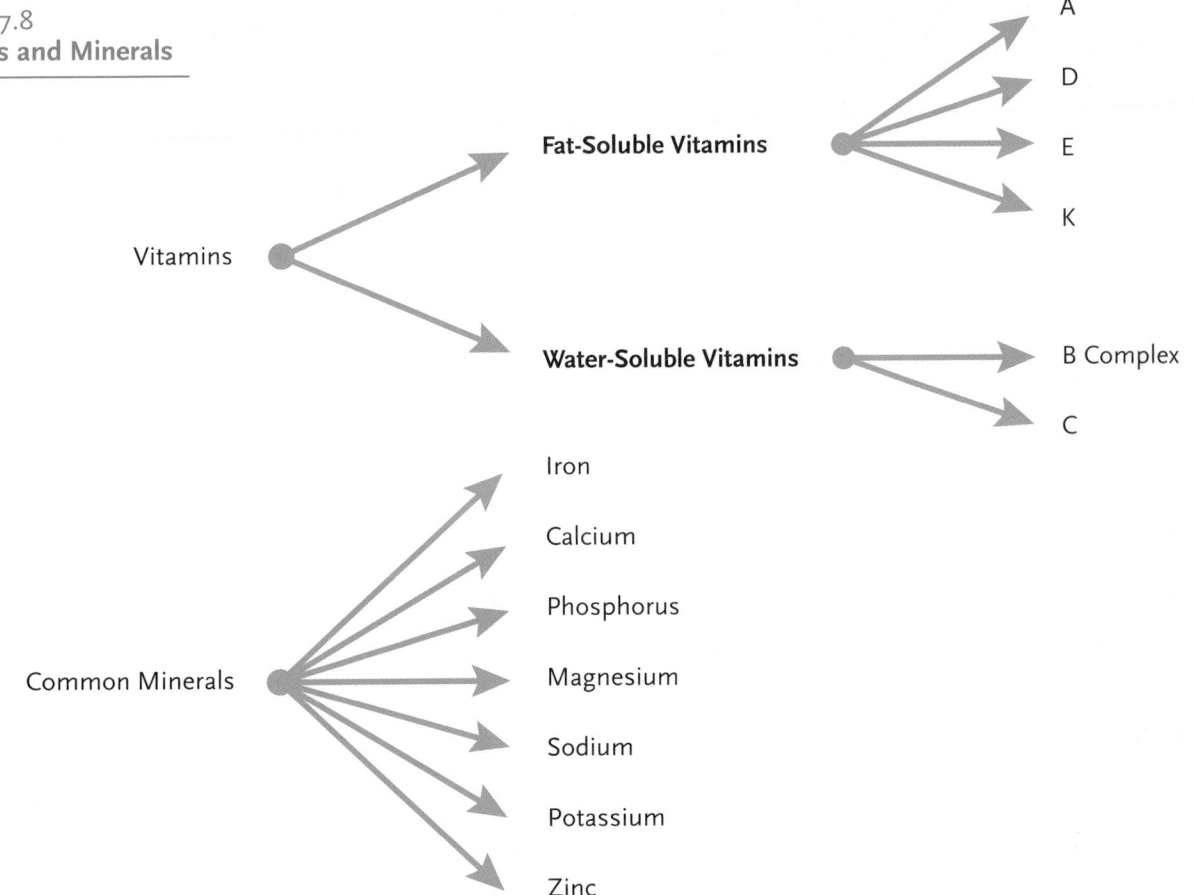

- Encourage clients to maintain regimen of treatment.
- Encourage clients to rest as required.
- Encourage a diet high in nutrients.
- Encourage clients to maintain hydration to avoid gastric irritation and acid fluids.
- Recommend that clients avoid crowds and visiting individuals with infections.
- Advise on the availability of support groups.
- Advise clients to avoid vaccinations during therapy.

VITAMINS AND MINERALS

Vitamins and minerals are outlined in Figure 7.8.

VITAMINS

Vitamins are complex chemical nutrients present in many foods and required in small amounts by the body to facilitate metabolic processes. Of the 13 major vitamins (A, B complex, C, D, E, and K), only D is made by the body. Vitamins function as coenzymes (except the vitamin B group) and as antioxidants (A, C, and E) to neutralize free radicals in the body.

VITAMIN USES

Vitamins are prescribed as supplements for clients with symptoms of vitamin deficiency or for older adults who may be at risk for deficiencies due to restricted diets. Older adults also may have impaired bowel function and high serum cholesterol levels, both of which can affect vitamin absorption. Vitamin D is prescribed for the treatment of osteoporosis.

VITAMIN DEFICIENCIES

Deficiencies may occur if intake is lower than the body's requirement. Shortages of the water-soluble vitamins (B and C) are more likely than of the fat-soluble vitamins (A, D, E, and K) because water-soluble vitamins are not stored in the body. Deficiencies of fat-soluble vitamins may occur in the absence of bile. Vitamin K can be depleted within about 10 days.

The body may also be unable to absorb and utilize nutrients. This malabsorption may be due to diseases, such as celiac disease, which affects the absorption of fat, or a lack of the intrinsic factor necessary for the absorption of vitamin B_{12}, causing pernicious anemia. A population also may have vitamin deficiencies due to poor food choices and low income.

Table 7.18 Classifications of Vitamins

VITAMIN	THERAPEUTIC DOSAGE	EFFECTS	ADVERSE EFFECTS
Water-Soluble Vitamins (cannot be stored by the body)			
Vitamin B₁ (thiamine)	5–30 mg/day	• Promotes carbohydrate, aerobic metabolism, transmission of nerve impulses	• Restlessness • Pulmonary edema • Hypersensitivity
Vitamin B₂ (riboflavin)	5–30 mg/day	• Acts as catalyst in oxidation of glucose and amino acid	
Vitamin B₃ (niacin)	50–100 mg/day	• Acts as catalyst in the reactions of cholesterol and fats • Causes vasodilation and treats pellagra	• Nausea, vomiting • Flatulence • Jaundice
Vitamin B₆ (pyridoxine)	2–10 mg/day	• Promotes protein, fat, and glucose metabolism and formation of neurotransmitters • Treats neuropathy • Pyridoxine supplements are used to relieve symptoms in women with premenstrual syndrome and neuritis due to treatment with isoniazid for tuberculosis	• Paresthesia • Seizure (these effects are rare)
Vitamin B₉ (folic acid)	IM, IV 0.25–1 mg/day	• Helps in protein synthesis and erythropoiesis	• Altered sleep patterns • Irritability • Depression • Anorexia
Vitamin B₁₂ (cyanocobalamin)	1000–2000 mcg/day	• Essential for cell growth and reproduction • Treatment for pernicious anemia	• Hypersensitivity
Vitamin C (ascorbic acid)	100–250 mg	• Antioxidant • Promotes collagen formation and tissue repair • High doses of vitamin C help prevent and treat common colds	• Rapid IV administration may lead to fainting • Overdose causes nausea, vomiting, gout attack, and renal stones
Fat-Soluble Vitamins (can be stored by the body)			
Vitamin A (retinol)	10,000–20,000 IU and up to 500,000 IU daily	• Derivates of vitamin A (retinoids) are used to treat severe acne	• Anorexia • Vomiting • Irritability • Muscle pain
Vitamin D (cholecalciferol)	400–600 IU daily	• Required for absorption and use of calcium and phosphorus by the body • Used to treat calcium deficiencies, e.g., osteoporosis	• Dehydration • Vomiting • Decreased appetite (anorexia) • Irritability • Constipation • Fatigue
Vitamin E (tocopherol)	60–75 IU daily	• Antioxidant	• Fatigue • Nausea • Blurred vision • Diarrhea
Vitamin K (phylloquinone, menaquinones)	90 mcg daily	• Necessary for normal clotting of blood • Used to treat deficiencies resulting in bleeding, petechiae, or bruising	• Can increase coagulation in clients taking warfarin

Table 7.18 outlines the different vitamins and their dosages, effects, and adverse effects.

Natural Sources of Vitamins

- Brewer's yeast is the best source of B-complex vitamins and many minerals and protects against vitamin D toxicity.
- Liver, beans, meat, eggs, wheat germ, yeast, and dairy products
- Fresh fruits are rich in vitamin C.

MINERALS

Minerals are essential in trace amounts for normal metabolic processes. They are usually obtained from a balanced diet. They function as structural components, helping to form healthy bones, teeth, and nails. In addition, minerals function as components of enzymes.

Other major functions for minerals include regulation of water metabolism, blood volume, cell membrane permeability, generation of nerve fibre action potentials, and maintenance of the acid–base balance. A mineral deficiency may be due to the inability to absorb minerals from the diet or a lack in the diet.

COMMON MINERAL AGENTS

- Ferrous gluconate, iron dextran injection, and ferrous sulphate may be used to treat iron deficiency anemia.
- Magnesium oxide, hydroxide, and sulphate are used to prevent and treat hypomagnesia, hypertension, and convulsion associated with toxemia of pregnancy or acute nephritis in children.
- Potassium chloride (Apo-K, K-Lyte, Slow-K, Micro-K) supplement is used to prevent and treat hypokalemia.
- Sodium chloride injections are given to treat hyponatremia.
- Zinc sulphate (A, D, E, K and pediatric drops) are used to prevent and treat zinc deficiency.
- Multiple mineral electrolytes such as Pedialyte are used to prevent and treat fluid and electrolyte deficiency.
- Calcium is used to treat deficiency and tetany in newborns.
- Phosphorus may be given to treat a deficiency, although this is rare.

Effects of Deficiency or Excess of Mineral Agents

- Hypernatremia (serum levels >145 mmol/L) causes electrolyte imbalance, nausea, and vomiting.
- Hyponatremia (serum levels <135 mmol/L) may cause nausea and abdominal cramps, as well as cerebral edema (mental deterioration).
- Hyperkalemia (serum levels >5.5 mmol/L) causes hypotension, muscle weakness, nausea, and diarrhea.
- Hypokalemia (serum levels <3.5 mmol/L) causes

cardiac arrhythmias, muscle weakness, nausea, vomiting, and delayed gastric emptying.
- Hypercalcemia (serum levels >2.75 mmol/L) may cause muscle weakness and headache, even confusion and coma.
- Hypocalcemia (serum levels <2.25 mmol/L) causes tetany, seizures, mental changes, and delayed ventricular repolarization.
- Excess iron causes diarrhea or constipation, vomiting, and dark stool.
- Iron deficiency causes tachycardia, brittle nails, and glossitis.

Nursing Considerations Relating to Minerals

- Iron should be administered with citrus or fruit juice to enhance absorption.
- When administering liquid iron preparations, have the client use a straw to avoid tooth discoloration.
- Encourage clients to take iron preparations with food to avoid gastric irritation.
- Phosphorus capsules should not be swallowed but broken to dissolve powder in water.
- Monitor clients' sodium and potassium serum levels for desired effects and overdose effects.

BIBLIOGRAPHY

Anderson, K. N. (1994). *Mosby's medical nursing and allied health dictionary* (4th ed.). Toronto: Mosby.

Canadian Pharmacists Association. (2006). *Guide to drugs in Canada* (Rev. ed.). Toronto: Dorling Kindersley Ltd.

Clayton, B. D., & Stock, Y. N. (2004). *Basic pharmacology for nurses* (13th ed.). Toronto: Elsevier Canada.

Cowan, M. K., & Talaro, K. P. (2006). *Microbiology: A system approach.* Toronto: McGraw-Hill.

Edmunds, M. W. (2006). *Introduction to clinical pharmacology* (4th ed.). Toronto: Mosby.

Fortinash, K. M., & Holoday-Worret, P. A. (2008). *Psychiatric mental health nursing* (2nd ed.). Toronto: Mosby.

Health Canada. (2007). *Drug product database (DPD).* Ottawa: Author. Retrieved January 17, 2013, from http://www.hc.gc.ca/dhp-mps/

Karch, A. M. (2008). *Focus on nursing pharmacology* (4th ed.). Philadelphia: Lippincott.

Lilley, L. L., Harrington, S., Snyder, J. S., & Swart, B. (2007). *Pharmacology and the nursing process in Canada* (2nd ed.). Toronto: Mosby.

McCuistion, E. L., & Gutierrez, K. (2007). *Saunders nursing survival guide: Pharmacology* (2nd ed.). Philadelphia: Saunders.

McKenry, L. M., & Salerno, E. (2001). *Mosby's pharmacology in nursing* (21st ed.). Toronto: Mosby.

Pommerville, J. C. (2004). *Alcamo fundamentals of microbiology* (7th ed.). Toronto: Jones and Bartlett Publishers.

Sizer, F. S., & Whitney, E. N. (2003). *Nutrition concepts and controversies* (9th ed.). Belmont, CA: Thomson Wadsworth.

Wilson, B. A., Shannon, M. T., Shields, K. M., & Stang, C. L. (2008). *Prentice Hall nurse's drug guide* (Rev. ed.). Chicago: Prentice Hall.

WEB SITES

Canadian Pharmacists Association (http//:www.pharmacists.ca): There are many useful medication-related resources on this site, which has sections for health professionals and for the general public.

Health Canada: Drug Products (http://www.hc-sc.gc.ca/dhp-mps/prodpharma/index-eng.php): This site has updated drug advisories, describes the drug regulation process, and contains other information for professionals and consumers.

Health Canada: Therapeutic Products Directorate (http://www.hc-sc.gc.ca/ahc-asc/branch-dirgen/hpfb-dgpsa/tpd-dpt/index-eng.php): This is the Web site of the government body that regulates therapeutic products, including drugs.

Saskatchewan Drug Information Service (http://druginfo.usask.ca/healthcare_ professional): This site has a vast amount of resources and links concerning drugs, immunization, and health and pharmaceutical organizations.

Practice Questions

Case 1

Mrs. Mabel Hawkins, 73 years of age, has been admitted to hospital with congestive heart failure (CHF). She is prescribed several medications, including digoxin (Lanoxin). Her condition is monitored to assess the effects of the drug therapy.

Questions 1–5 refer to this situation.

1. Mrs. Hawkins asks the nurse why her heart rate must be taken prior to giving her the "heart pill" (digoxin). Which of the following statements would be the nurse's best response?

    1. "I will make adjustments in the dosage of the drug depending on what your heart rate is."
    2. "I do not need to give you the drug if your heart rate is normal."
    3. "I will only give you half the dosage if your heart rate is less than 60 beats per minute."
    4. "I will not give the drug and report to the doctor if your heart rate is below the normal rate of 60."

2. Mrs. Hawkins is receiving the diuretic furosemide (Lasix), 40 mg by mouth daily. What is the most appropriate time of day to administer this medication?

    1. Just before bedtime
    2. Any time during the day but always at the same time in order to space the doses
    3. In the morning
    4. With food, preferably the midday meal

3. Mrs. Hawkins is ordered the potassium supplement Kaochlor liquid, 15 mL daily. What is the purpose of administering this medication?

    1. To replace potassium losses produced by the furosemide
    2. To promote the effects of the diuretic
    3. To help facilitate nerve impulse conduction within the heart
    4. To prevent adverse effects produced by digoxin

4. Mrs. Hawkins is scheduled for discharge from the hospital. She has been prescribed nitroglycerine in the form of a dermal patch and sublingual spray. Which of the following should the nurse teach Mrs. Hawkins concerning the correct use of nitroglycerine dermal patches?

    1. Apply a patch once a day for one hour to ensure that the medication gets absorbed through the skin
    2. Apply each patch daily to the same area of skin to maximize absorption
    3. Remove the old patch phd cleanse the area, then apply a new patch to a different area of skin

    4. Massage the area of skin around the patch to stimulate absorption of the medication

5. What directions should the nurse provide to Mrs. Hawkins regarding the use of her nitroglycerine sublingual spray when she experiences angina pectoris?

    1. Spray under the tongue at five-minute intervals. Continue the procedure until the pain subsides.
    2. Spray under the tongue. If pain continues, spray an additional time for better absorption.
    3. Spray under the tongue. If the pain is not relieved, apply a nitroglycerine patch to the skin to help facilitate the action of the spray.
    4. Spray once under the tongue at five-minute intervals to a maximum of three times. If the pain continues, seek medical attention.

Case 2

Leslie, a nurse educator in the diabetes clinic, is teaching new nurses on a medical unit about type 2 diabetes and the use of insulin. He provides client scenarios for the nurses and asks them to "brainstorm" answers as a group.

Questions 6 and 7 refer to this case.

6. The first client scenario involves Mr. B., a client who is taking regular and NPH insulin. Regular insulin has an onset of 30–60 min and a peak of 2–4 hr. NPH insulin has an onset of 1–2 hr, a peak of 6–12 hr, and a duration of action of approximately 18 hr. If Mr. B. is given a combination of regular and NPH insulin at 0730 hours, when might he require another injection of insulin?

    1. Noon
    2. Midmorning
    3. Midafternoon
    4. Bedtime

7. Another client scenario concerns Ms. A., who is receiving Novolin 30/70. Novolin 30/70 is a mixture of regular insulin (onset: 0.5–1 hr, peak: 2–4 hr, duration: 5–8 hr) and isophane insulin (onset: 1–3 hr, peak: 5–8 hr, duration: up to 18 hr). The nurse is concerned about hypoglycemia. When would hypoglycemia most likely occur?

    1. Between 0.5–1 hr and 2–3 hr after administering the insulin
    2. Between 2–4 hr and 5–8 hr after administering the insulin
    3. Between 5–8 hr and 18 hr after administering the insulin
    4. After 18 hr following the administration of the insulin

Case 3

Robert Melnick has been experiencing gastric discomfort for several months. His physician prescribes several medications, including H_2 receptor antagonists and simethicone, to alleviate the discomfort. The nurse teaches Mr. Melnick about his medications.

Questions 8 and 9 refer to this case.

8. The nurse is not familiar with H_2 receptor antagonists and asks the pharmacist for information. What would the pharmacist explain about the action of H_2 receptor antagonists?

   1. They neutralize excess hydrochloric acid (HCl) that has been secreted into the stomach
   2. They compete with histamine for binding sites on the surface of parietal cells and block hydrogen ion (H^+) secretion
   3. They inhibit the secretion of the digestive enzyme pepsin into the stomach
   4. They combine with, and convert, HCl in the stomach to a salt and water

9. What would the nurse explain to Mr. Melnick about the desirable effect of simethicone for the relief of gastrointestinal distress?

   1. It stimulates peristalsis
   2. It reduces gas distension
   3. It prevents diarrhea
   4. It absorbs excess hydrochloric acid (HCl)

Case 4

Francesca, a student nurse, has read about how overprescribing of antibiotics has led to multiple drug-resistant pathogens. She asks the RN for more information about antibiotics.

Questions 10 and 11 refer to this case.

10. Francesca asks the nurse, "What is meant by the term 'narrow-spectrum antibiotic agent'?" Which of the following would be a correct response by the nurse?

    1. An antimicrobial that is effective only against bacteria
    2. An antimicrobial that has a narrow therapeutic index
    3. An antimicrobial that can only be given in very small doses because of toxicity concerns
    4. An antimicrobial that is mainly effective against a few Gram-positive or Gram-negative bacteria

11. Francesca and the nurse discuss the treatment of infections for which antibiotics are not useful. For which of the following conditions is antibiotic treatment not indicated?

    1. Chlamydia
    2. *E. coli* infection
    3. Gonorrhea
    4. Influenza A and B

INDEPENDENT QUESTIONS

Questions 12–25 do not refer to a particular case.

12. Mr. Simmons has just developed acute renal failure. What is the safest action by the nurse regarding administration of his prescribed medications?

    1. Plan to administer lower doses of the medications due to the decreased ability of the kidneys to eliminate the drugs
    2. Consider administering higher doses of the medications to promote more effective elimination of the drugs
    3. Have his prescribed medications and doses reviewed by the prescriber and pharmacist prior to administering the drugs
    4. Do not administer any medications that are known to be eliminated through the kidneys

13. Which of the following nursing considerations should be addressed prior to the administration of morphine sulphate (morphine) to Mr. Shafikhani, who is experiencing pain associated with his terminal colorectal cancer?

    1. Assess the requirement for an antiemetic to be administered at the same time as the morphine to prevent nausea or vomiting, or both
    2. Administer the lowest dose of the range of morphine that has been prescribed by the physician
    3. Assess the client for any previous history of narcotic abuse prior to administering the medication
    4. Withhold administering the morphine if Mr. Shafikhani's respiratory rate is less than 15 respirations per minute

14. What should the nurse teach Ms. Porter about a possible adverse effect of taking an oral anticoagulant drug such as warfarin (Coumadin)?

    1. Bruising, or bleeding from her gums from hemorrhage
    2. Pain and edema in her lower legs from blood clots
    3. Shortness of breath from emboli formation
    4. Chest pain from a coronary thrombosis

15. What is the primary therapeutic goal of antilipemic therapy?

    1. To lower the serum LDL cholesterol levels
    2. To lower the serum HDL cholesterol levels

3. To raise the serum LDL cholesterol levels
4. To raise the serum HDL cholesterol levels

16. Mr. Michael, age 40 years, has been taking the antiadrenergic drug clonidine (Dixarit) for five months. His blood pressure has been normal for the last two months. He tells the nurse that he would like to stop taking the drug. What is the correct advice for the nurse to give him?

    1. "Since your BP is normal, you may stop the drug and watch for signs of hypertension."
    2. "You may stop the drug for a month and then return to your physician for a checkup."
    3. "You may stop the drug if you decide to exercise and restrict your salt intake."
    4. "This drug should not be stopped suddenly; let's discuss it with the prescriber."

17. Mr. Stavros is administered isoproterenol (Isuprel), a beta adrenergic agent, to treat circulatory shock resulting from trauma. What is the most significant adverse effect of the Isuprel that the nurse should monitor for?

    1. Suppressed gastrointestinal activity
    2. Hypotension
    3. Dysrhythmias
    4. Hyperactivity

18. Ms. Stellars has osteoarthritis and has heard that COX-2 inhibitors such as celecoxib would be beneficial for her. She believes she may be pregnant and asks the nurse whether she should take celecoxib. What should the nurse advise?

    1. "This drug is considered to be a nonsteroidal anti-inflammatory drug (NSAID) and is safe during pregnancy."
    2. "Celecoxib may cause gastrointestinal distress and so should be avoided during pregnancy."
    3. "Women must never take any drugs during the first three months of pregnancy."
    4. "COX-2 inhibitors such as celecoxib have definite risks for the fetus, so you should discuss this with your physician."

19. Ronnie, age 5 years, has been diagnosed with attention deficit hyperactive disorder (ADHD). His parents have resisted drug therapy, but his behavioural problems have brought them to the clinic to ask the nurse about "that drug that they give all the hyper kids." Which of the following medications is commonly used to treat ADHD?

    1. Chlordiazepoxide (Librium)
    2. Lithium (Carbolith)
    3. Methylphenidate (Ritalin)
    4. Phenobarbital (Luminal)

20. How would the action and effect of a drug that is metabolized by the liver be affected in a client with severe cirrhosis of the liver?

    1. The rate of the excretion of the drug will increase
    2. The duration of the action of the drug will decrease
    3. The action and effects of the drug on body cells will be blocked—hence no effect
    4. The action and effects of the drug on the body will be prolonged

21. A registered nurse works in a long-term care facility where she is the medication nurse for the residents. Which of the following factors will the nurse take into consideration when administering drugs to older adults?

    1. Older adults require higher dosages to compensate for degenerative changes in the liver
    2. Older adults require more frequent dose administration because of high levels of excretion by the kidneys
    3. Older adults require lower doses due to reduced function of body organs
    4. With older adults, the parenteral route is preferable due to less efficient absorption from the gastrointestinal system

22. Which of the following classifications of drugs would be prescribed for the treatment of depression?

    1. Barbiturates
    2. Antianxiolytics
    3. Selective serotonin reuptake inhibitors (SSRIs)
    4. Cholinergic agonists

23. Why do individuals who have been treated with cortisone preparations for an extended period of time have an increased risk of developing infections?

    1. Cortisone attracts microbes into the body
    2. Cortisone suppresses the body's normal immune response
    3. Cortisone therapy suppresses the body's natural bacteria
    4. Cortisone causes increased capillary permeability

24. Ms. Marina is taken to the sexual assault clinic at a local hospital after being a victim of rape. She believes the rapist may have been HIV-positive. Which of the following would be offered to Ms. Marina for postexposure prophylaxis (PEP)?

    1. Lopinavir (Combivir) and ritonavir (Kaletra)
    2. Amoxicillin (Amoxil) and E-Mycin
    3. Amantadine (Symadine) and acyclovir
    4. Acyclovir (Zovirax) and ganciclovir

25. Which of the following should be taught to a client who is taking isoniazid (INH)?

1. Urine and saliva may be reddish-orange in colour
2. Avoid alcohol to limit the danger of hepatic damage
3. Clients will need to have weekly chest X-rays
4. Take with an antacid to reduce gastric distress

Answers and Rationales for Practice Questions

1.   C: Changes in Health   T: Application

1. It is not within the role of the nurse to make adjustment in a drug dosage. Concerns need to be reported to the physician, who will make changes as necessary.
2. It is the physician's role to decide whether medications are to be given. Nurses do not withhold medications unless an order is written or they have a concern. If there is a concern, nurses consult with the physician or prescriber of the medication.
3. As a general rule, digoxin is withheld and reported if the heart rate is less than 60 beats per minute.
4. Withholding digoxin and reporting is the established procedure if the heart rate is less than 60 beats per minute. The physician will then determine whether the client is to receive the medication at that time.

2.   C: Changes in Health   T: Application

1. Furosemide will start to work within an hour, causing the client to awaken to void during the night and therefore to lose sleep.
2. While doses of furosemide should be spaced to maintain therapeutic levels, it should be administered in the morning to avoid nocturnal diuresis.
3. This is the correct time to administer a diuretic in order for diuresis to take place during the day prior to bedtime. This permits a restful sleep.
4. It is not necessary to take furosemide with meals.

3.   C: Changes in Health   T: Knowledge

1. Diuretics remove electrolytes, including potassium, putting the client at risk of developing hypokalemia. Supplements prevent this from occurring.
2. Potassium supplements do not facilitate the action of diuretics.
3. Although potassium plays a major role in the generation of a nerve impulse, potassium supplementation in this case is not for that purpose.
4. Potassium supplementation plays no significant role in preventing the adverse effects of digoxin.

4.   C: Changes in Health   T: Application

1. Patches should remain on the skin until a new dose is applied. The purpose of a dermal patch is to provide continuous, slow absorption of the medication throughout the day. Occasionally, patches may be removed overnight to reduce the development of tolerance.
2. Skin areas should be rotated to avoid skin irritation. Absorption will naturally occur in all areas of skin.

3. The patch should be removed and the skin cleansed to remove medication left on the skin; then the new patch is applied to a different area. Leaving the skin uncleansed may produce added dosage of the drug when added to the new dosage, causing undesirable effects.
4. This is incorrect as the patch is applied to provide slow, natural absorption. By massaging the site, absorption will occur more quickly, with the possibility of undesirable adverse effects.

5.   C: Changes in Health   T: Application

1. Only a maximum of three sprays should be taken. If pain persists, medical attention should be obtained immediately as a myocardial infarction may be occurring.
2. One spray may not be sufficient. Up to three sprays may be taken at five-minute intervals. Sublingual forms of nitroglycerine are destroyed by gastric secretions and will not be absorbed.
3. One spray may not be enough to relieve the pain. Up to three sprays may be administered. Patches are used as a preventive and have no effect on acute pain due to their slow absorption.
4. This is the correct method of using sublingual nitroglycerine sprays to relieve anginal pain. Three successive doses are acceptable, but persistent pain may indicate a myocardial infarction, and medical attention is required.

6.   C: Changes in Health   T: Application

1. At noon, regular insulin is at peak action, so no additional insulin is required.
2. At midmorning (about 1000 hr), regular insulin is near the peak level and NPH insulin is above the minimum effective concentration; therefore, no new dose is required.
3. At midafternoon (1500 hr), regular insulin has reached its minimum effective concentration level (MEC), but NPH insulin is at peak; therefore, no new dose is required.
4. By bedtime (2100–2200 hours), NPH insulin is present but will fall below the MEC soon after midnight.

7.   C: Changes in Health   T: Application

1. Between 0.5–1 hr and 2–3 hr after administering the insulins, the minimum effective concentration is reached for both types of insulin and blood levels are too low to cause adverse effects (hypoglycemia).
2. Between 2–4 hr and 5–8 hr after administering the insulins, the peak is reached for both types of insulin and the adverse effects occur at these peak levels.

3. Between 5–8 hr and 18 hr after administering the insulins, the minimum effective concentration is reached and adverse effects are unlikely.
4. After 18 hr, no adverse effect is likely because the MEC is passed.

8. C: Changes in Health   T: Knowledge

1. H_2 receptor antagonists do not act as bases. Only bases neutralize acids.
2. By blocking the receptor sites, H_2 receptor antagonists prevent histamine from binding to the surface of parietal cells, which prevents the cells from producing H^+. H^+ increases the stomach pH.
3. H_2 receptor antagonists have no effect on digestive enzymes.
4. Acid plus base converts to salt and water, but H_2 receptor antagonists are not bases.

9. C: Changes in Health   T: Knowledge

1. Stimulation of peristalsis is helpful in the presence of constipation, but it does not relieve gas.
2. Simethicone changes the surface tension of gas bubbles in the gastrointestinal tract, resulting in collection of one large gas bubble. This enables the individual to eructate or pass flatus.
3. Simethicone is not an antidiarrheal medication. Although simethicone relieves gaseous distension, it has no effect on the intestinal lining to prevent diarrhea.
4. Simethicone is not an absorbent. It does not absorb excess HCl.

10. C: Changes in Health   T: Knowledge

1. If an antimicrobial affects only bacteria, it is simply called an antibiotic.
2. The therapeutic index has to do with the safety of administration of a drug. A drug with a narrow therapeutic index means the therapeutic dose is very close to the toxic dose.
3. Spectrum is not related to toxicity.
4. The spectrum of microbial activity is the range of distinctly different types of microbes affected by an antimicrobial drug. Narrow-spectrum antibiotics treat effectively only a limited number of types of bacteria.

11. C: Changes in Health   T: Application

1. Chlamydia is a bacteria that can be treated with antibiotics.
2. E. coli is a bacteria that can be treated with antibiotics.
3. Gonorrhea is caused by a bacteria and can be treated with antibiotics.

4. Influenza A and B are viral infections. They are not susceptible to antibiotics but can be treated with antiviral drugs.

12. C: Changes in Health   T: Application

1. Mr. Simmons will possibly require lower doses of his medications, but it is not a nursing responsibility to independently change the dose.
2. He will likely need lower, not higher, doses.
3. Due to the renal failure, there is likely to be reduced excretion of some of the medications. It is the responsibility of the physician and pharmacist to decide if altered doses are required, depending on the particular drug and Mr. Simmons's condition.
4. It is not within the role of the nurse, in this situation, to independently withhold medications for Mr. Simmons.

13. C: Changes in Health   T: Application

1. Opioid analgesics are known to cause nausea and vomiting. Administration of antiemetics at the same time as administration of the morphine may prevent this side effect.
2. With the severe pain of colon cancer, this is an inappropriate choice. If the morphine is ordered with a range of dosing, the amount given should be based on the pain as rated by Mr. Shafikhani and previous doses that have resulted in therapeutic effects.
3. While a history of previous abuse is a nursing consideration in many cases of morphine administration, this is neither an important nor necessary assessment with a client who has severe pain from terminal cancer.
4. The morphine may need to be held if Mr. Shafikhani has a respiratory rate of less than 10/min.

14. C: Changes in Health   T: Knowledge

1. Warfarin suppresses vitamin K–dependent clotting factors, prolonging clotting time and leading to hemorrhage. This may be evidenced by excessive bruising and bleeding in the gums.
2. Warfarin is given to prevent, not promote, thrombus formation.
3. If there is a therapeutic level of warfarin, mobilization of blood clots is not likely.
4. With a therapeutic level of warfarin, there should be no thrombosis mobilization.

15. C: Changes in Health   T: Knowledge

1. A high level of LDL cholesterol is a major risk factor for cardiovascular disease (CVD); hence,

the goal of therapy is to lower it to the normal physiological level.

2. HDL is the "good" cholesterol. High levels are not a risk factor for CVD.

3. The goal of antilipemic therapy is to lower serum LDL cholesterol levels.

4. HDL cannot be effectively raised by drug therapy alone. Fibric acids used to treat a high triglyceride level do increase HDL but only slightly.

16. **C: Changes in Health   T: Application**

1. The blood pressure may be normal only because it is being effectively controlled by Dixarit. The BP would likely increase as soon as the client is off the medication.

2. This is not a safe option as the blood pressure is likely being controlled by the Dixarit.

3. Exercise and salt restriction are used to help control high blood pressure but may not be sufficient for many clients with stage I or stage II hypertension.

4. The decision has to be made by the doctor, who can diagnose and prescribe alternative therapy as the situation dictates.

17. **C: Changes in Health   T: Knowledge**

1. These preparations suppress parasympathetic activity and increase gastrointestinal motility. In a shock situation, this is not the priority observation.

2. The Isuprel should increase, not decrease, the BP. If the BP continues to decrease, further Isuprel will likely be ordered.

3. Agents used to treat shock include norepinephrine, isoproterenol, dopamine, and epinephrine. They may cause reflex bradycardia and tachycardia. Dysrhythmias may occur with any of the agents used to treat shock.

4. These drugs have a stimulant effect on the nervous system and tend to make the individual hyperactive. This is not a priority observation in a client with shock.

18. **C: Changes in Health   T: Knowledge**

1. COX-2 inhibitors are second-generation NSAIDs and are not considered to be safe in pregnancy.

2. COX-2 inhibitors may cause GI distress, but that is not the reason they should be avoided in pregnancy.

3. This is partly true but depends on the drug and the health problem. The risks for a pregnant woman taking particular medications must be determined by a physician.

4. COX-2 inhibitors are in FDA pregnancy category D. This means that they pose a definite risk to the fetus and that the risk versus benefit must be assessed by a physician.

19. **C: Changes in Health   T: Knowledge**

1. Librium is an anxiolytic that is not usually administered to children under 6.

2. Lithium is used for treating bipolar disorder and is not indicated for ADHD.

3. Ritalin is the drug of choice to treat ADHD. Its mechanism of action is not clear, but it helps children with ADHD focus on one activity for a longer period of time.

4. Phenobarbital is an antiepileptic drug not indicated for treatment of ADHD.

20. **C: Changes in Health   T: Knowledge**

1. The rate of excretion may be decreased because drugs metabolized by the liver may not be water soluble and therefore cannot be excreted in the urine.

2. The duration of action of the drug will increase due to the failure of the medication to be metabolized for excretion.

3. Only antagonist drugs, not liver disease, block receptors to produce no response.

4. When a drug is metabolized by the liver, inactive or active metabolites are produced. Inactive metabolites are usually removed by excretory organs, thus preventing drug accumulation. Active metabolites go to target cells and are subsequently inactive or excreted. If the drug is not metabolized by the liver because of cirrhosis, higher levels remain in the body for longer periods and produce actions and effects similar to a drug overdose.

21. **C: Changes in Health   T: Application**

1. Routine adult doses can cause toxicity since liver metabolism and renal excretion decline with age.

2. The frequency of drug administration is dependent on the drug's half-life, not the age of the recipient.

3. Body organs have fewer cells and reduced function with age; hence, the body requires a lower amount than the routine adult dose to produce the therapeutic effect.

4. Oral administration is easier, safer, and more practical than parenteral administration.

22. **C: Changes in Health   T: Knowledge**

1. Barbiturates promote drowsiness, which is not therapeutic for depression.

2. Antianxiolytics are used to treat anxiety, not depression.

3. Depressive symptoms are related to insensitivity of receptors and low serotonin levels. SSRI inhibitors work to promote the continued presence of serotonin in the synaptic cleft by inhibiting its uptake.
4. Cholinergic agonists have no effect on serotonin receptors.

23.   C: Changes in Health   T: Knowledge

1. Although cortisone limits the activity of white blood cells (WBCs), it does not attract microbes.
2. Higher than normal physiological levels of cortisone promote protein breakdown. Antibodies are composed of proteins. In addition, cortisone impairs the ability of antibodies to bind to cell surface receptors and so reduces cell-mediated response. The net result is lowering of the immune response.
3. Cortisone has no direct or indirect antibiotic activity.
4. Cortisone reduces cellular factors that lead to vascular permeability.

24.   C: Changes in Health   T: Knowledge

1. Kaletra and Combivir are the only two retroviral drugs potentially effective as prophylaxis against HIV infection.
2. Amoxicillin and erythromycin (E-Mycin) are used to treat bacteria infection and are of no use as prophylaxis for HIV.
3. Amantadine is a dopamine agonist with antiviral activity that is used to treat influenza.
4. Acyclovir and ganciclovir are used to treat herpes virus infection.

25.   C: Changes in Health   T: Knowledge

1. B-complex vitamins produce orange-coloured urine. INH may cause vitamin B deficiency.
2. INH is hepatotoxic, and liver function must be monitored carefully. Alcohol is not permitted while on INH, a factor that causes noncompliance in many cases.
3. While INH is used to treat and prevent tuberculosis, monthly X-rays are not necessary. If the disease is active, the client will be monitored by collecting sputum cultures.
4. Antacids interfere with the absorption of INH and should never be taken concurrently.

Medical–Surgical Nursing

Penny Davis, BScN, MEd

In Canada at present, nursing shortages are acute, and these shortages are likely to increase due to the aging of our nurses and that of our general population. More people are developing chronic illnesses and disabilities that require skilled nursing intervention. Nursing education requires students to synthesize and critically analyze knowledge in order to provide and promote holistic care to this growing sector of the population. With this point in mind, the following chapter provides a condensed summary of many medical and surgical topics to help students build on the knowledge and skills they will need to promote health, facilitate recovery from injury or illness, and provide support with coping with chronic illness and disability.

FLUID AND ELECTROLYTE IMBALANCES

Homeostasis

Homeostasis is the state of equilibrium in the internal environment of the body. Body fluids and electrolytes play an important role in homeostasis. Water is the primary component of body fluids and serves many functions:

- Transporting nutrients and oxygen
- Transporting waste
- Providing a medium for metabolic reactions
- Insulating and helping to regulate temperature
- Providing form and substance to body tissues
- Providing lubrication

Water accounts for 60% of body weight in an adult and 70–80% of body weight in an infant. Water content will vary with gender, body mass, and age. Fatty tissue has less water content. Insensible water loss is unavoidable, immeasurable water loss. Continuous water loss by evaporation occurs through the skin as insensible perspiration, a nonvisible form of water loss. Another example of insensible water loss is the water lost via respirations. Sensible water loss is observable and measurable, such as water lost in urine.

Electrolytes are substances that dissociate in solutions and are referred to as ions. Cations are positively charged electrolytes such as sodium (Na^+). Anions are negatively charged electrolytes such as chloride (Cl^-). Electrolytes help regulate water and the acid–base balance. They contribute to enzyme reactions and are essential to neuromuscular activity.

The following terms relate to the mechanisms controlling fluid and electrolyte movement:

- Diffusion and facilitated diffusion
- Active transport
- Osmosis, filtration, and osmotic pressure
- Tonicity, isotonic, hypertonic, and hypotonic
- Hypovolemia and hypervolemia
- Dehydration and edema

Fluid Shifting

Fluid in the body is divided into different compartments. See Table 8.1 for an explanation of body fluid compartments and fluid spacing.

The amount and direction of fluid movement within the capillaries are determined by the following:

- Capillary hydrostatic pressure
- Plasma osmotic pressure
- Interstitial hydrostatic pressure
- Interstitial osmotic pressure

Edema occurs when

- Fluid shifts from the plasma to the interstitial fluid.
- There is an elevation of capillary hydrostatic pressure.
- There is a decrease in plasma osmotic pressure.
- There is elevation of interstitial osmotic pressure.

Fluid is drawn into the plasma space when

- There is an increase in plasma osmotic pressure that causes the fluid to move from the interstitial space to the plasma.
- Osmoreceptors in the hypothalamus sense a fluid deficit or an increase in plasma osmolarity, or both, stimulating the primary regulator, thirst, and the release of antidiuretic hormone (ADH) from the posterior pituitary gland.
- The adrenal cortex releases the mineralocorticoid aldosterone, which has potent sodium-retaining and potassium-excreting capabilities.

The kidneys are the primary organs for regulating fluid and electrolyte balance. The kidneys selectively reabsorb or excrete water and electrolytes. The renal tubules are sites of actions for ADH and aldosterone. Pertaining to cardiac regulation, atrial natriuretic factor (ANF) is released by the cardiac atria in response to increased atrial pressure. ANF causes vasodilation and increased urinary excretion of sodium and water. ANF inhibits the kidneys from releasing the hormone renin.

The gastrointestinal (GI) tract receives most of the body's water intake, but only small amounts of water are eliminated by the GI tract. About 8 L of fluid is

Table 8.1   Body Fluid Compartments and Fluid Spacing

Body Compartment and Spacing	Description
Intracellular Fluid (ICF)	• ICF fluid is found within the cell. • ICF comprises about 42% of body weight and is about 30 L in total volume. • The most prevalent cation is potassium (K$^+$). • The most prevalent anion is phosphate (PO$_4^-$).
Extracellular Fluid (ECF)	• ECF fluid is the fluid that is found between cells (called interstitial fluid) and in the plasma space (called intravascular fluid). • Interstitial fluid bathes the cells and makes up two-thirds of ECF (ECF comprises about 15% of the body's total fluid volume). • The most prevalent anion is chloride (Cl$^-$). • The most prevalent cation is sodium (Na$^+$). • Intravascular fluid makes up the last third of the ECF, which is about 5% or 3 L of the body's total fluid volume.
Transcellular Fluid	• Transcellular fluid is a small but important fluid compartment and totals about 1 L. • Transcellular fluid includes cerebrospinal fluid, digestive secretions in the gastrointestinal tract, and fluid in the pleural spaces, synovial spaces, and peritoneal spaces.
First Spacing	• Normal distribution of fluid in ICF and ECF
Second Spacing	• Abnormal accumulation of fluid within the interstitial space, also known as edema
Third Spacing	• Fluid accumulates in a part of the body where it is not easily exchanged with ECF. • Fluid shifts from the vascular space into an area where it is not available for any physiological process. • Fluid is trapped and does not participate in normal functions of the ECF. • Weight does not change as the volume is not lost but is shifted to a nonfunctioning area. • This can lead to a decrease in the volume of the intravascular space. • Damage to tissues may result from the high fluid volume within the nonfunctioning space. • Treatment focuses on treating the underlying cause of the shift of fluid by removing the fluid from the third space, replacing fluid within the intravascular space, and maintaining adequate cardiac output.

moved in the bowel during an average day; however, only 100–200 mL is lost through feces. Insensible water loss, which occurs via vaporization from the lungs and the skin, accounts for about 900 mL per day. No electrolytes are lost with insensible water loss. However, excessive sweating could lead to the loss of both water and electrolytes.

Client History and Fluid and Electrolytes

Many conditions affect the fluid and electrolyte balance, such as diabetes or renal failure. The following conditions and topics should be discussed when taking a client history:

- Medications, such as diuretics, steroids, herbs, and total parenteral nutrition
- Abnormal fluid loss, such as vomiting, diarrhea, and polyuria
- Diet, whether prescribed or client initiated
- Present fluid intake history, including the client's ability to obtain fluids, mobility, and actual amount the client drank

EXTRACELLULAR FLUID VOLUME IMBALANCES

Hypovolemia

Hypovolemia can occur with the loss of normal body fluids, such as in the case of diarrhea, hemorrhage, decreased intake, or plasma loss due to interstitial fluid shift. The cause of the hypovolemia must be identified and treated. Once this is done, replacement fluid may be given either orally or intravenously (IV) with balanced solutions, isotonic chloride, or blood, depending on the cause of the hypovolemia.

Hypervolemia

Hypervolemia may result from the excessive intake of fluids, abnormal retention of fluids, or interstitial loss to plasma fluid shift. Treatment for hypervolemia will depend on the cause of the hypervolemia and may include diuretics, fluid restriction, and sodium restriction.

Nursing Management for Hypovolemia and Hypervolemia

Management for both hypovolemia and hypervolemia includes assessment and monitoring of the following:

- Strict intake and output
- Cardiovascular changes
- Respiratory changes
- Daily weights, which is the best way to monitor fluid balance over time
- Skin and mucous membranes
- Neurological status

Nursing Considerations for the Geriatric Client

Older adults are at significant risk for a fluid volume deficit, which can lead to dehydration and heat stroke. The risk is due to the following:

- The decrease in muscle mass in older adults leads to a decrease in total body water.
- The thirst response can be delayed in older adults.
- The skin of older adults has less elasticity, and there is sweat gland atrophy.
- A decreased ability to concentrate urine and possible kidney function changes
- Changes in the cardiovascular system and GI tract

Many common problems may affect older adults that can also affect fluid balance. These problems include dehydration, constipation with laxative abuse, and hyperthermia.

Nursing Considerations for the Pediatric Client

Most of the infant's body weight, 70–80%, is made up of fluid. Therefore, infants have a larger extracellular fluid (ECF) where water and electrolyte disturbances can occur more frequently and rapidly. Pediatric clients need more fluid intake and output relative to their size due to the large ECF volume and the following:

- Infants exchange more fluid across capillary membranes daily compared with adults.
- Infants have immature renal function and a greater body surface area, which together have an important effect on metabolism, heat production, and heat loss.

Infants exchange 50% of their body fluids per day, whereas adults exchange one-sixth of their fluids. Therefore, pediatric clients have smaller fluid reserves, and the balance can be upset more quickly. Note that an infant is less able to handle large quantities of solute-free water than an older child. Therefore, when an infant is being rehydrated, a solution with electrolytes should be used rather than plain water. Rehydration should proceed slowly with infants.

ELECTROLYTES

Sodium

Sodium (the normal, or reference, range is 135–145 mmol/L) plays a major role in electrolyte balance. This role includes its effect on ECF volume and concentration, the generation and transmission of nerve impulses, and the acid–base balance. Sodium is readily available in a balanced diet and is normally balanced within a healthy individual by the kidneys.

Hypernatremia

Hypernatremia (>145 mmol/L) is elevated serum sodium occurring with water loss or sodium gain. It is rarely seen in people with intact thirst mechanisms. Hypernatremia is caused by hyperosmolality leading to cellular dehydration. Clinical manifestations of hypernatremia include the following:

- Thirst
- Lethargy or agitation
- Disorientation
- Hallucinations
- Seizures
- Coma

Hypernatremia can be produced by nephrogenic diabetes insipidus. Management includes treating the underlying cause, as well as giving oral fluids or an IV solution of 5% dextrose in water, or hypotonic saline. Note that it is important that sodium levels be reduced gradually to avoid cerebral edema.

Hyponatremia

Hyponatremia (<135 mmol/L), a decreased level of serum sodium, can result from a loss of sodium-containing fluids or from excess water. Clinical manifestations include the following:

- Nausea, vomiting, or both
- Anorexia
- Muscle twitching
- Diminished reflexes
- Respiratory arrest
- Headache
- Confusion
- Seizures
- Coma

If hyponatremia is caused by water excess, fluid restriction is needed. If severe symptoms occur, small amounts of IV hypertonic saline solution (3% NaCl) are given. If hyponatremia is associated with abnormal fluid loss, fluid replacement with sodium-containing solution is required.

Potassium

Potassium (3.5–5 mmol/L) is necessary for the transmission and conduction of nerve impulses, the maintenance of normal cardiac rhythm, skeletal muscle contraction, and acid–base balance. Potassium is critical to the action potential of nerves. Normal renal function is needed for the maintenance of potassium balance because the majority of potassium is excreted from the body by the kidneys. The remaining potassium is lost through the bowel and perspiration. Potassium is plentiful in the normal diet of meats, fruits—particularly citrus fruits—green vegetables, and potatoes.

Hyperkalemia

Hyperkalemia (>5 mmol/L), the condition of an excessive amount of potassium in the body, can result from renal failure, potassium-sparing diuretics, an increased intake of potassium from foods high in potassium, tissue destruction, and acidosis. Clinical manifestations can include the following:

- Muscle weakness or paralysis
- Paraesthesias of the face, tongue, feet, and hands
- Nausea
- Ventricular fibrillation or cardiac standstill
- Impaired cardiac depolarization, resulting in a slow heart rate

Management focuses on elimination of the potassium source and potassium from the body through the use of potassium-wasting diuretics, Kayexalate, and dialysis. IV insulin may be administered to force potassium from ECF to intracellular fluid (ICF). IV calcium gluconate may be used to reverse the membrane effects of elevated ECF potassium.

Hypokalemia

Hypokalemia (<3.5 mmol/L) can result from the increased secretion of aldosterone, the use of loop diuretics, severe vomiting, or severe diarrhea and is associated with magnesium deficiency. Clinical manifestations include the following:

- Ventricular arrhythmias and impaired repolarization
- Muscle fatigue and weakness
- Cramps
- Decreased GI motility
- Altered airway responsiveness
- Impaired regulation of arterial blood flow
- Hyperglycemia

Management of hypokalemia focuses on replacement of the potassium, either orally or intravenously. In addition, it is important to teach preventive measures, such as eating foods containing adequate amounts of potassium or ingesting potassium supplements when dietary intake is not adequate.

Calcium

Calcium (2.25–2.75 mmol/L) is obtained through food sources. Calcium has an inverse relationship with phosphorus. The majority of calcium is stored in bones. Calcium blocks sodium transport and stabilizes cell membranes. Calcium functions include the transmission of nerve impulses, myocardial contractions, blood clotting, muscle contractions, and the formation of teeth and bones. Calcium is controlled by the parathyroid hormone (PTH). When this hormone is released, it stimulates calcium resorption from the bones. Calcitonin, secreted by the thyroid gland, inhibits the resorption of calcium from the bones. Vitamin D is needed to increase the intestinal absorption of calcium, which is excreted by the intestinal and urinary tracts.

Hypercalcemia

Hypercalcemia (>2.75 mmol/L) can result from hyperparathyroidism, malignancy, vitamin D overdose, and prolonged immobilization. Clinical manifestations of hypercalcemia include the following:

- Confusion, disorientation, and decreased memory
- Fatigue
- Decreased neuromuscular excitability, weakness, and decreased deep tendon reflexes

Management of hypercalcemia includes loop diuretics, hydration with isotonic saline, synthetic calcitonin, and client mobilization.

Hypocalcemia

Hypocalcemia (<2.25 mmol/L) can result from the decreased production of PTH, acute pancreatitis, multiple drug transfusions, alkalosis, and the decreased intake of calcium. Deficiency of vitamin D or insufficient exposure to the sun can cause reduced calcium absorption from the gut. Clinical manifestations include the following:

- Positive Trousseau's sign, indicating neuroexcitability; a positive sign is indicated if twitching of the hands and fingers occurs when a blood pressure (BP) cuff is inflated 10 mm Hg above the systolic pressure
- A positive Chvostek's sign also shows neuroexcitability, indicated if tapping the area below the temple with a finger causes muscle spasms of the mouth and cheek.
- Increased neuromuscular activity; tetany
- Laryngeal stridor, dysphagia, numbness, tingling around the mouth or extremities
- Decreased myocardial contractility

Management of hypocalcemia focuses on treating the cause, replacing the calcium, and ensuring that the intake of vitamin D is adequate.

Phosphate

Phosphate (0.97–1.45 mmol/L) is the primary anion in ICF and is essential for muscle and nerve function, as well as red blood cell (RBC) formation. Along with calcium, phosphate is important in the formation of bones and teeth. It is involved in the acid–base buffering system, adenosine triphosphate (ATP) production, and cellular uptake of glucose. A normal diet, including red meat, fish, poultry, eggs, milk products, and legumes, usually is sufficient for adequate phosphate absorption. However, vitamin D is needed in the absorption of phosphate. The kidneys are the major route of excretion for phosphate.

Hyperphosphatemia

Hyperphosphatemia (>1.45 mmol/L) can result from acute or chronic renal failure, chemotherapy, excessive ingestion of milk or phosphate-containing laxatives, and large doses of vitamin D. Clinical manifestations include the following:

- Hypocalcemia
- Muscle tetany
- Deposition of calcium–phosphate crystals in skin, soft tissue, cornea, viscera, and blood vessels
- Tingling of mouth and fingertips and numbness

Management focuses on identifying and treating the underlying cause, restricting foods and fluids containing phosphorus, and ensuring adequate hydration.

Hypophosphatemia

Hypophosphatemia (<0.97 mmol/L) can result from malnourishment or malabsorption, alcohol withdrawal, and the use of phosphate-binding antacids. Clinical manifestations include the following:

- Central nervous system (CNS) depression, confusion, delirium, and seizures
- Muscle weakness and pain
- Dysrhythmias, cardiomyopathy
- Acute respiratory failure (Acute RF)

Management includes phosphate replacement.

Magnesium

Magnesium (0.65–1.05 mmol/L) acts directly on the myoneural junction. It is also important for normal cardiac function. About two-thirds of the body's magnesium is stored in the bones, with the remaining one-third in the ICF. The kidneys are the primary route of excretion of magnesium, helping maintain a normal balance of magnesium within the body.

Hypermagnesemia

Hypermagnesemia (>1.05 mmol/L) can result from an increased intake or ingestion of products containing magnesium when renal insufficiency or failure is present. Clinical manifestations include the following:

- Lethargy, drowsiness, somnolence
- Peripheral vasodilation, causing flushing, warm skin, decreased BP, and rhythm disturbances with possible cardiac arrest
- Impaired reflexes
- Possible respiratory arrest

Management focuses on prevention, increased fluids, and IV calcium chloride or calcium gluconate.

Hypomagnesemia

Hypomagnesemia (<0.65 mmol/L) can result from prolonged fasting or starvation, chronic alcoholism, fluid loss, prolonged parenteral nutrition without supplementation, diuretics, osmotic diuretics, or high glucose levels. Hypomagnesemia is a common clinical problem. Clinical manifestations include the following:

- Hyperactive deep tendon reflexes, tremors, and seizures
- Cardiac dysrhythmias, increased heart rate and BP
- Confusion, convulsions, and disorientation

Management focuses on replacement of magnesium orally or intravenously. To prevent hypomagnesemia from occurring, adequate dietary intake of magnesium, including green vegetables, seafood, nuts, and grains, should be encouraged. Table 8.2 summarizes the major serum electrolyte concentrations and functions.

INTRAVENOUS FLUIDS

IV fluids are used to maintain fluid balance when oral intake is not adequate and to replace fluids and electrolytes when fluid losses have occurred and electrolytes are out of balance. The amount and type of fluid replacement depend on the client's daily maintenance requirements and on any imbalances identified through laboratory work.

IV solutions can be hypotonic, isotonic, or hypertonic. These types of IV solutions are listed in Table 8.3.

ACID–BASE BALANCE AND ARTERIAL BLOOD GASES

Regulating Mechanisms to Balance Acid–Base

The proper balance between the acids and bases in the human body is called acid–base homeostasis.

Table 8.2   Major Serum Electrolyte Concentrations and Functions

Electrolyte	Reference Range	International Recommended Units	Functions
Sodium (Na^+)	136–145 mEq/L	136–145 mmol/L	• Maintenance of plasma and interstitial osmolarity • Generation and transmission of action potentials • Maintenance of acid–base balance • Maintenance of electroneutrality
Potassium (K^+)	3.5–5.0 mEq/L	3.5–5.0 mmol/L	• Regulation of intracellular osmolarity • Maintenance of electrical membrane excitability • Maintenance of plasma acid–base balance
Calcium (Ca^{2+})	9.0–10.5 mg/dL	2.25–2.75 mmol/L	• Cofactor in blood-clotting cascade • Excitable membrane stabilizer • Adds strength and density to bones and teeth • Essential element in cardiac, skeletal, and smooth muscle contraction
Chloride (Cl^-)	98–106 mEq/L	98–106 mmol/L	• Maintenance of plasma acid–base balance • Maintenance of plasma electroneutrality • Formation of hydrochloric acid
Magnesium (Mg^{2+})	1.3–2.1 mEq/L	0.66–1.07 mmol/L	• Excitable membrane stabilizer • Essential element in cardiac, skeletal, and smooth muscle contraction • Cofactor in blood-clotting cascade • Cofactor in carbohydrate metabolism • Cofactor in DNA and protein synthesis
Phosphorus (Pi)	3.0–4.5 mg/dL	0.97–1.45 mmol/L	• Activation of B-complex vitamins • Formation of adenosine triphosphate and other high-energy substances • Cofactor in carbohydrate, protein, and lipid metabolism

Source: Ignatavicius, D. D., & Workman, M. L. (2010). Medical-surgical nursing: Patient-centered collaborative care (6th ed., p. 184, Table 13-4). St. Louis: Saunders. Data from Pagana, K., & Pagana, T. (2002). *Mosby's manual of diagnostic and laboratory tests* (2nd ed.). St. Louis: Mosby.

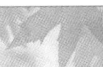

Table 8.3   Intravenous Fluids

Type of Solution	Description
Hypotonic Intravenous Solutions	• A solution that has fewer electrolytes and solutes than plasma and therefore dilutes the ECF • Osmosis moves the fluid from ECF to ICF, hydrating the cells. • An example of a hypotonic solution is 0.45% NaCl.
Isotonic Intravenous Solutions	• A solution that has the same tonicity as plasma • Is given to expand ECF only • Does not change ICF volume • Examples of an isotonic solution are 0.9% normal saline (NS) and Ringer's lactate.
Hypertonic Intravenous Solutions	• Hypertonic solutions contain more electrolytes or solutes than are normally found in plasma. • When IV hypertonic fluid is given, the osmotic pressure within the vessel increases, drawing fluid from the tissues into the vascular system, thereby decreasing fluid within the tissues and increasing fluid in the IV space. • An example of a hypertonic solution is 10% dextrose in water.

in other words, the body's pH, which must be maintained within a very narrow range. Arterial blood gases (ABGs) provide information about the various concentrations of the gases dissolved in the blood before the blood is distributed to the tissues. pH is the indirect measure of H^+ (hydrogen) ion concentration and measures the ratio of base bicarbonate (HCO_3) to acid carbon dioxide (CO_2). This ratio is normally 20:1. Acids give up (donate) H^+ ions, and bases pick up H^+ ions. The body maintains a slightly alkaline pH of 7.34–7.45 in arterial blood.

The three regulating mechanisms to maintain acid–base homeostasis are as follows:

- Chemical buffer regulators
- Respiratory regulators
- Renal regulators

Buffer Regulator System

The buffer system comprises the primary chemical regulators that act immediately. They are found in the blood and tissues and include bicarbonate, proteins, and hemoglobin.

Respiratory Regulator System

The respiratory system eliminates CO_2 (carbon dioxide) and water (H_2O), which, when joined, are carbonic acid (H_2CO_3), thus eliminating acid from the body through respiration. The respiratory centre within the medulla controls breathing. When the blood has too much carbonic acid in it, the respiratory centre will instruct the lungs to increase the respiratory rate in order to "blow off" the acid.

If the carbonic acid levels are low, the centre will instruct the lungs to decrease the respiratory rate in an effort to conserve carbonic acid. The respiratory regulating system works within minutes to hours to balance acid–base levels.

Renal Regulator System

The renal regulator system is the most powerful of the three systems. The kidneys secrete hydrogen ions and reabsorb bicarbonate ions. This activity is increased when the pH is acidotic and decreases when the pH is alkalotic. The renal system responds within hours to days to restore acid–base homeostasis.

Interpreting Blood Gases

Normal ABG values are as follows:

pH	7.35–7.45
$PaCO_2$	35–45 mm Hg (respiratory component)
HCO_3	21–28 mmol/L (metabolic component)
PaO_2	80–100 mm Hg
SaO_2	96–100% arterial O_2 saturation

When interpreting ABGs, the nurse must evaluate the pH and determine if it is acidotic or alkalotic. A value under 7.35 is acidosis; a value above 7.45 is alkalosis.

If there is an abnormality in the pH, the cause must be determined. Next, the respiratory component must be evaluated. If there is a high level of CO_2, above 45 mm Hg, this indicates an elevated level of carbonic acid ($H_2O + CO_2 = H_2CO_3$), and acidosis. If the level is low, below 35 mm Hg, this indicates a low level of carbonic acid and therefore alkalosis.

The metabolic component is determined by looking at the amount of base HCO_3. If there is a lot of base, indicated by a reading above 28 mmol/L, then the blood is alkalotic. If there is insufficient base, indicated by a reading below 21 mmol/L, the blood would be acidotic. See the blood gas summary in Table 8.4.

Table 8.4 Blood Gas Summary

Acid–Base Condition	pH Indicator	Respiratory or Metabolic Indicator
Respiratory Acidosis	pH is decreased	$PaCO_2$ is increased
Respiratory Alkalosis	pH is increased	$PaCO_2$ is decreased
Metabolic Acidosis	pH is decreased	HCO_3 is decreased
Metabolic Alkalosis	pH is increased	HCO_3 is increased

If both respiratory and metabolic components match the pH, a mixed complicated disorder may be present.

The body must maintain the correct pH. The body's regulatory systems will attempt to compensate for respiratory or metabolic problems by adjusting the levels of acid or base to bring the pH back to the normal range. Compensation is evident in ABGs if the pH is normal or near normal and the pCO_2 or HCO_3 is not within normal limits.

Respiratory acidosis occurs when the CO_2 is too high, causing the pH to be low (acidotic). This can be caused by hypoventilation, respiratory failure, pneumonia, pulmonary emboli, or long-standing chronic obstructive pulmonary disease (COPD).

Respiratory alkalosis occurs when the CO_2 is too low, causing the pH to rise above 7.45. It can be caused by the following:

- Hyperventilation
- Extreme anxiety
- High fever
- Sepsis
- Hypoxemia

Metabolic acidosis occurs when the HCO_3 is low, causing the pH to fall below 7.35. It can be caused by the following:

- Anaerobic metabolism
- Lactic acidosis

- Anoxia
- Poisoning
- Overdose

Metabolic alkalosis occurs when the HCO_3 is high, causing the pH to rise above 7.45. This can be caused by the following:

- Vomiting
- Poisoning or overdose
- Antacid ingestion (most common)

Mixed diagnoses do occur. This mixed picture occurs when the client has multiple system problems and experiences both respiratory and metabolic imbalances.

Hyperkalemia may occur in an acidotic state as the hydrogen ion drives the potassium ion out of the cell into the ECF. Once the acidosis is resolved, the hyperkalemia resolves. Acid–base imbalances are listed in Table 8.5.

IMMUNE SYSTEM DYSFUNCTION

Overview of the Immune System

The immune system has three lines of defence. Chemical and mechanical barriers such as the skin,

Table 8.5 Acid–Base Imbalances		
Common Causes	**Pathophysiology**	**Laboratory Findings**
Respiratory Acidosis • Chronic obstructive pulmonary disease • Barbiturate or sedative overdose • Chest wall abnormality (e.g., obesity) • Severe pneumonia • Atelectasis • Respiratory muscle weakness (e.g., Guillain-Barré syndrome) • Mechanical hypoventilation	• CO_2 retention from hypoventilation • Compensatory response to HCO_3- retention by kidney	• Plasma pH ↓ • PCO_2 ↑ • HCO_3- normal (uncompensated) • HCO_3- ↑ (compensated) • Urine pH <6 (compensated)
Respiratory Alkalosis • Hyperventilation (caused by hypoxia, pulmonary emboli, anxiety, fear, pain, exercise, fever) • Stimulated respiratory centre caused by septicemia, encephalitis, brain injury, salicylate poisoning • Mechanical hyperventilation	• Increased CO_2 excretion from hyperventilation • Compensatory response of HCO_3- excretion by kidney	• Plasma pH ↑ • PCO_2 ↓ • HCO_3- normal (uncompensated) • HCO_3- ↓ (compensated) • Urine pH >6 (compensated)
Metabolic Acidosis • Diabetic ketoacidosis • Lactic acidosis • Starvation • Severe diarrhea • Renal tubular acidosis • Renal failure • Gastrointestinal fistulas • Shock	• Gain of fixed acid, inability to excrete acid, or loss of base • Compensatory response of CO_2 excretion by lungs	• Plasma pH ↓ • PCO_2 normal (uncompensated) • PCO_2 ↓ (compensated) • HCO_3- ↓ • Urine pH <6 (compensated)
Metabolic Alkalosis • Severe vomiting • Excess gastric suctioning • Diuretic therapy* • Potassium deficit • Excess $NaHCO_3$ intake • Excessive mineralocorticoids	• Loss of strong acid or gain of base • Compensatory response of CO_2 retention by lungs	• Plasma pH ↑ • PCO_2 normal (uncompensated) • PCO_2 ↑ (compensated) • HCO_3- ↑ • Urine pH >6 (compensated)

*Commonly used diuretics such as thiazides and furosemide are known to produce mild alkalosis by affecting tubular excretion of electrolytes and bicarbonate.

Source: Lewis, S. M., Heitkemper, M. M., Dirksen, S. R., O'Brien, P., Bucher, L., et al. (2010). *Medical-surgical nursing in Canada: Assessment and management of clinical problems* (2nd Canadian ed., p. 384, Table 18-13). Toronto: Elsevier.

GI tract, and mucous membranes are the first line of defence. The second line is the inflammatory response, and the third line is the immune response. The immune response is slower to develop as it is more specific and can result in permanent protection.

Central lymphoid organs include the thymus gland and bone marrow. Peripheral lymphoid organs include the tonsils; gut-, genital-, bronchial-, and skin-associated lymphoid tissues; lymph nodes; and spleen (Lewis et al., 2010). The two immunity classifications are innate (natural) and acquired. Innate immunity is present in a person who has not been in contact with an antigen (a substance that elicits an immune response). Active acquired immunity is the consequence of an invasion of the body by foreign substances, such as microbes, and the subsequent development of antibodies and sensitized lymphocytes. Passive acquired immunity is one in which the host receives antibodies to an antigen, rather than synthesizing them, as with the immunoglobulins passed from mother to fetus.

Humoral immunity is made up of antibody-mediated immunity. This type of immunity is from antibodies that are produced in plasma (differentiated B cells). B lymphocytes, formed in the bone marrow, will differentiate into plasma cells when activated. These plasma cells will produce antibodies (immunoglobulins IgA, IgG, IgM, IgD, IgE) that will recognize and attack antigens. The primary immune response is seen four to eight days after the first contact with the antigen. When the individual is exposed to the antigen a second time, a secondary antibody response occurs. This response will occur faster, is stronger, and will last longer than the primary response (Lewis et al., 2010).

Cell-mediated immunity is initiated through specific antigen recognition by T lymphocytes, or T cells. T lymphocytes develop from cells that migrate from the bone marrow to the thymus, where they differentiate. These T cells respond directly to specific targets (antigens). T cytotoxic cells attack antigens on the cell membrane of the foreign pathogens, releasing cytolytic substances that destroy the pathogen. T helper lymphocytes (CD4s) and T suppressor lymphocytes (CD8s) play a role in the regulation of cell-mediated immunity and the humoral antibody response. Natural killer cells (NK cells) are not T or B cells but are large lymphocytes that do not require prior sensitization. NK cells recognize and kill virus-infected cells, tumour cells, and transplanted grafts. Cell-mediated immunity plays an important role against pathogens that survive inside cells, as well as in tumour immunity, fungal infections, the rejection of transplanted tissues, and contact hypersensitivity reactions.

Cells involved in the immune response include mononuclear phagocytes, lymphocytes, including B lymphocytes and all forms of T lymphocytes (T cytotoxic cells, T helper cells, and T suppressor cells), and NK cells. Cytokines are soluble factors secreted by white blood cells (WBCs) and a variety of other cells in the body that act as messengers between the immune cell types. There are over 100 cytokines, and they signal cells to change their proliferation, differentiation, secretion, or activity. See Table 8.6 for the types and functions of cytokines (Lewis et al., 2010).

INFLAMMATION

Inflammation provides protection against the effects of cell injury. Regardless of the injury, the response is the same. The inflammatory agent will be diluted and neutralized, necrotic materials will be removed, and an environment will be established that supports healing and repair. The inflammatory response can be caused by heat, radiation, trauma, chemical injury, microbial injury, ischemic injury, allergens, and normal body fluids. The intensity of the response depends on the extent and severity of the injury and the health of the injured or ill person. The inflammatory response comprises a vascular response and a cellular response.

Vascular Response

After cell injury, the following vascular changes occur:

- Arterioles in the area briefly undergo transient vasoconstriction.
- Histamines and other chemicals are released from the injured cells, resulting in vasodilation.
- Vasodilation and chemical mediators increase the capillary permeability, allowing fluid to move from the capillaries to the tissues.
- Initially, fluid is serous but later contains plasma proteins, primarily albumin, which exert oncotic pressure that draws additional fluid from the blood vessels.
- As the plasma protein fibrinogen leaves the blood, it is activated to form fibrin by products of the injured cells. This fibrin strengthens a blood clot formed by platelets. The purpose of the clot is to ensnare bacteria and prevent them from spreading. The clot also serves as a frame for the healing process (Lewis et al., 2010).

Cellular Response

In the cellular response to an injury, the following events occur:

- Blood flow through capillaries in the injured area slows.
- Neutrophils are first to arrive at the injury site (at 6–12 hr), and they phagocytize (engulf) foreign material and damaged cells.

Table 8.6 Types and Functions of Cytokines

TYPE	PRIMARY FUNCTIONS
Interleukins (ILs)	
IL-1	Augments the immune response; inflammatory mediator; promotes maturation and clonal expansion of B cells; enhances activity of NK cells; activates T cells; activates macrophages
IL-2	Induces proliferation and differentiation of T cells; activation of T cells, NK cells, and macrophages; stimulates release of other cytokines (α-IFN, TNF, IL-1, IL-6)
IL-3 (multicolony-stimulating factor)	Hematopoietic growth factor for hematopoietic precursor cells
IL-4	B-cell growth factor; stimulates proliferation and differentiation of B cells; induces proliferation of T cells; stimulates growth of mast cells
IL-5	B-cell growth and differentiation; promotes growth and differentiation of eosinophils
IL-6	Enhances the inflammatory response; B-cell stimulation; promotes differentiation of B cells into plasma cells; stimulates antibody secretion; induces fever; synergistic effects with IL-1 and TNF
IL-7	Promotes growth of T and B cells; increases expression of IL-2 and its receptor
IL-8	Chemotaxis of neutrophils and T cells; stimulates superoxide and granule release
IL-9	Acts as mitogen, supporting proliferation in absence of antigen; enhances T-cell survival; mast cell activation
IL-10	Inhibits cytokine production by T and NK cells; promotes B-cell proliferation and antibody responses; potent suppressor of macrophage function
IL-11	Is a multifunctional regulator of hematopoiesis and lymphopoiesis; osteoclast formation; elevates platelet count; inhibits proinflammatory cytokine production
IL-12	Promotes α-IFN production; induction of T helper cells; activates NK cells; stimulates proliferation of activated T and NK cells
IL-13	B-cell growth and differentiation; inhibits proinflammatory cytokine production
IL-14	Stimulates proliferation of activated B cells
IL-15	Mimics IL-2 effects; stimulates proliferation of T cells and NK cells
IL-16	Proinflammatory cytokine; chemoattractant of T cells, eosinophils, and monocytes
IL-17	Promotes release of IL-6, IL-8, G-CSF; enhances expression of adhesion molecules
IL-18	Induces α-IFN, IL-2, and GM-CSF production; important role in development of T helper cells; enhances NK activity; inhibits production of IL-10
IL-19	Similar to IL-10
IL-20	Similar to IL-10
IL-21	Similar to IL-2, IL-4, and IL-5
IL-22	Similar to IL-10

Continued on next page

Table 8.6 Types and Functions of Cytokines (cont'd)

TYPE	PRIMARY FUNCTIONS
Interleukins (ILs)	
IL-23	Similar functions to IL-12; promotes memory T-cell proliferation
IL-24	Similar to IL-10
Interferons (IFNs)	
Alpha-Interferon (α-IFN)	Inhibits viral replication; activates NK cells and macrophages; antiproliferative effects on tumour cells
Beta-Interferon (β-IFN)	
Gamma-Interferon (γ-IFN)	Activates macrophages, neutrophils, and NK cells; promotes B-cell differentiation; inhibits viral replication
Tumour Necrosis Factor (TNF)	Activates macrophages and granulocytes; promotes the immune and inflammatory responses; kills tumour cells; is responsible for extensive weight loss associated with chronic inflammation and cancer
Colony-Stimulating Factors (CSFs)	
Granulocyte colony-stimulating factor (G-CSF)	Stimulates proliferation and differentiation of neutrophils; enhances functional activity of mature PMN
Granulocyte-macrophage colony-stimulating factor (GM-CSF)	Stimulates proliferation and differentiation of PMN and monocytes
Macrophage colony-stimulating factor (M-CSF)	Promotes the proliferation, differentiation, and activation of monocytes and macrophages

NK, natural killer; *PMN*, polymorphonuclear neutrophils.

Source: Lewis, S. M., Heitkemper, M. M., Dirksen, S. R., O'Brien, P., Bucher, L., et al. (2010). *Medical-surgical nursing in Canada: Assessment and management of clinical problems* (2nd Canadian ed., p. 269, Table 15-3). Toronto: Elsevier.

- Monocytes arrive within 3–7 days after the onset of inflammation. They transform into macrophages, which are necessary for cleaning the area so that healing can occur. Unlike neutrophils, which have a short lifespan, macrophages have a long lifespan, can multiply, and may stay in the damaged tissues for weeks.
- Lymphocytes have a primary role related to humoral and cell-mediated immunity.
- Eosinophils are active during an allergic reaction, releasing chemicals that act to control the effects of histamine and serotonin, as well as phagocytizing allergen–antibody complexes.
- Basophils carry histamine and heparin, which are released during inflammation.
- Chemical mediators include histamine, serotonin, kinins, complement components, fibrinopeptides, prostaglandins, and leukotrienes, as well as cytokines.

The complement system is the primary mediator of the inflammatory response. The most important functions of this system are increased phagocytosis, increased vascular permeability, cellular lysis, and chemotaxis.

Prostaglandins are substances that can be produced from the phospholipids of the cell membranes of most body tissues, including blood cells. Prostaglandins are powerful vasodilators that cause increased permeability. Exudates made up of fluid and leukocytes move from the circulation to the site of injury. The nature and quantity of exudates depend on the type and severity of the injury and the tissues involved (Lewis et al., 2010).

Local clinical manifestations of inflammation include the following:

- Redness
- Heat
- Pain
- Swelling
- Loss of function

Systemic clinical manifestations include the following:

- Leukocytosis with a shift to the left
- Malaise
- Nausea
- Anorexia
- Increased heart rate and respiratory rate
- Fever

A concept map summarizing inflammation and its treatment is illustrated in Figure 8.1.

Human Immunodeficiency Virus Infection

Pathophysiology

The human immunodeficiency virus (HIV) is a fragile virus transmitted only through contact with blood, semen, vaginal secretions, and breast milk. The virus can be transmitted during sexual intercourse with an infected partner; through exposure to infected blood,

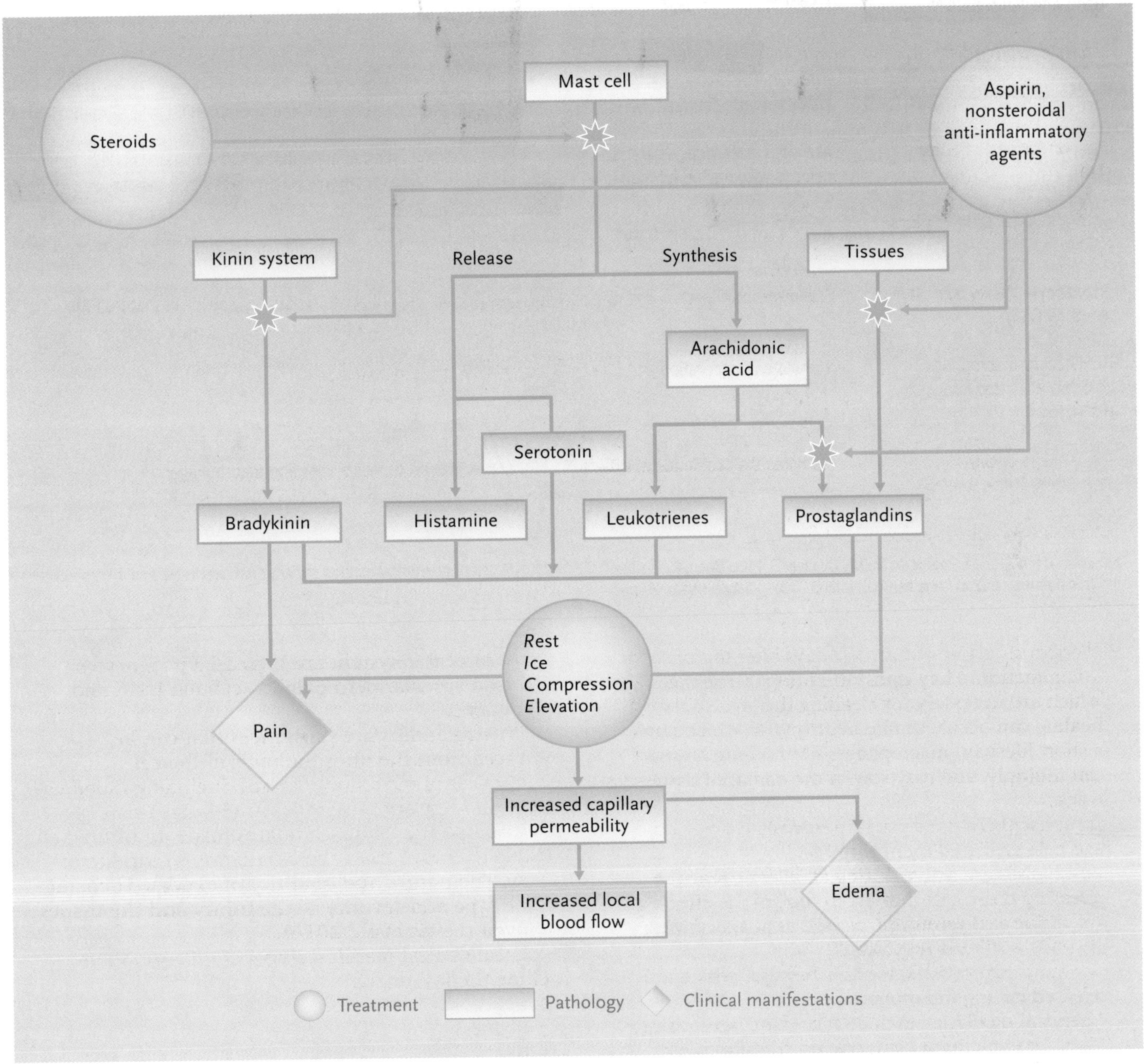
Mast cell
Steroids
Aspirin, nonsteroidal anti-inflammatory agents
Kinin system
Release
Synthesis
Tissues
Arachidonic acid
Serotonin
Bradykinin
Histamine
Leukotrienes
Prostaglandins
Rest
Ice
Compression
Elevation
Pain
Increased capillary permeability
Increased local blood flow
Edema
Treatment
Pathology
Clinical manifestations

FIGURE 8.1 **Understanding Inflammation and Its Treatments**

Note: The star (✳) symbols indicate the points at which treatment interrupts the progression of the inflammation process.
Source: Black, J. M., & Hawks, J. H. (2005). *Medical-surgical nursing: Clinical management for positive outcomes* (7th ed., p. 399). St. Louis: Saunders.

blood products, or needles; or via pregnancy and breastfeeding.

HIV is a retrovirus that binds to specific CD4 receptor sites on the surface of the lymphocytes (also referred to as T4 cells) in order to enter the cell.

- Once in the cell, reverse transcriptase, an enzyme made by the retrovirus, assists to make a single strand of viral DNA, making the viral genetic material the same as human DNA.
- This new viral DNA copies itself and incorporates itself into the cellular genetic makeup.
- All daughter cells from the infected cell will be infected with the virus.

After the initial infection, there is intense viral replication in the blood (viremia) and widespread dissemination of HIV throughout the body. In some situations, the level of HIV remains low and may continue to remain low for many years. During this period, there may be few clinical symptoms, ranging from none at all to severe flulike symptoms. At this stage, antibodies are not being developed yet, so the client will not test positive for the virus. By the time neutralizing antibodies can be detected, HIV is thriving in the host.

HIV causes immune dysfunction by destroying $CD4^+$ T cells (T helper cells), resulting in a high level of HIV and low CD4 counts in the blood, which are normally above 800 cells/microlitre. The client may now develop the following flulike symptoms:

- Fever
- Swollen lymph glands
- Sore throat
- Headaches
- Malaise
- Nausea
- Muscle and joint pain
- Diarrhea
- Rash

These manifestations usually occur three weeks into the acute phase. Figure 8.2 illustrates viral replication (Lewis et al., 2010).

gp120 proteins
Reverse transcriptase facilitates production of viral DNA using viral RNA as a template
CD4 receptor sites
Viral RNA
Single-stranded viral DNA
Double-stranded viral DNA
Receptor-mediated endocytosis
Incorporated into infected cell's DNA using integrase
Human DNA
Viral DNA
Human DNA
Viral RNA
Protease enzyme cleaves long strand of viral RNA
Assembly and release
Budding

FIGURE 8.2 **Viral Replication**

Source: Lewis, S. M., Heitkemper, M. M., Dirksen, S. R., O'Brien, P., Bucher, L., et al. (2010). *Medical-surgical nursing in Canada: Assessment and management of clinical problems* (2nd Canadian ed., p. 301, Figure 16-3). Toronto: Elsevier.

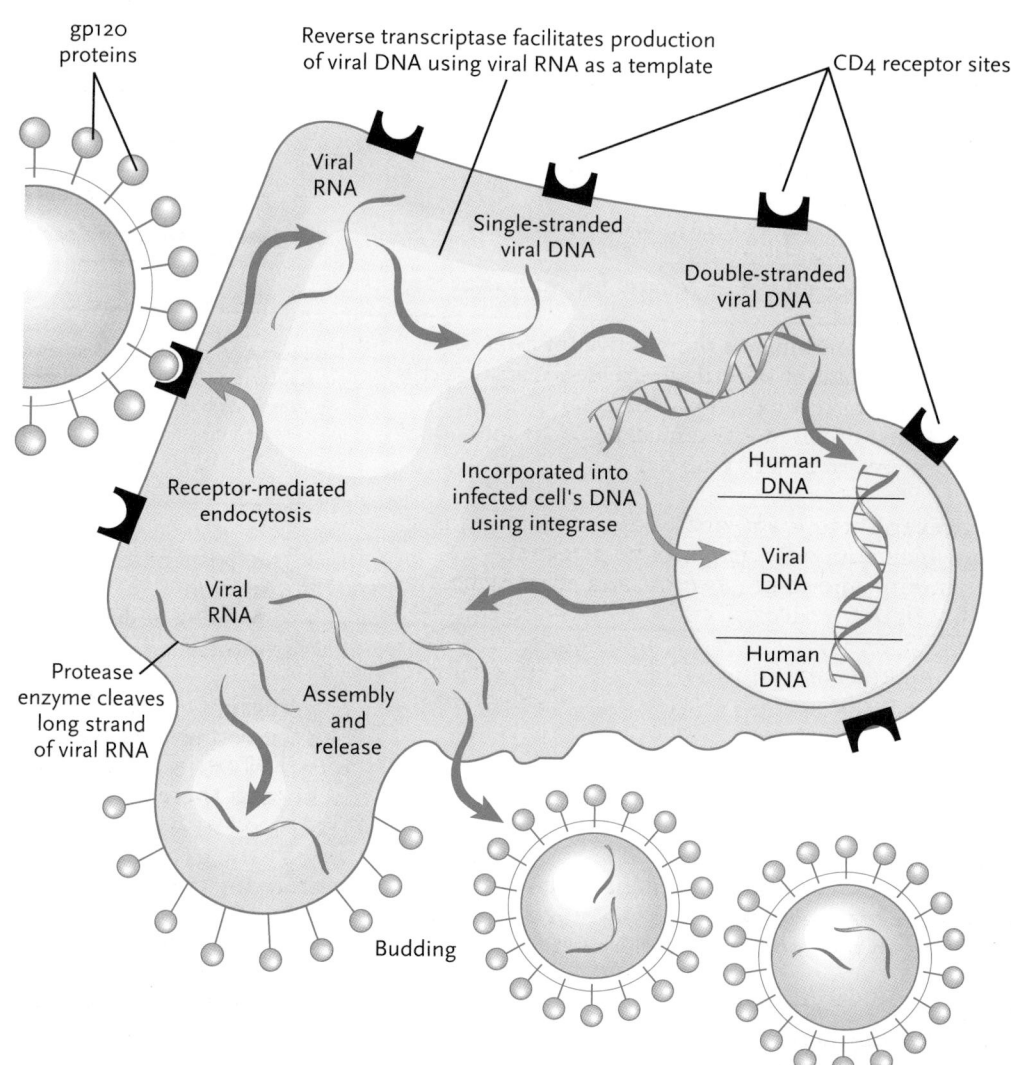

Clinical Manifestations

Early chronic infection can last about 10 years and is defined as the stage at which the CD4+ T-lymphocyte counts remain above 500 cells/microlitre. In this stage, the clients often feel relatively well, with symptoms ranging from none to headache, low-grade fever, and night sweats.

Intermediate chronic infection is marked by a drop in the CD4+ T-cell count to 200–500 cells/microlitre. Earlier symptoms become worse. Fever is persistent, night sweats are excessive, diarrhea may be constant, and fatigue is severe. With the CD4 count dropping, opportunistic diseases such as oral hairy leukoplakia, *Candida* infections, and Kaposi's sarcoma may develop.

Late chronic infection, or acquired immune deficiency syndrome (AIDS), has developed when the person infected meets the case definition set out by the Centers for Disease Control and Prevention, which includes HIV infection and a CD4 count below 200 cells/microlitre, or HIV infection with the presence of opportunistic infections. Box 8.1 outlines the diagnostic criteria for AIDS.

Diagnostics

Several screening tests are used to diagnose HIV infection, while other tests are used to assess the stage and severity of the infection. Screening tests for HIV-specific antibodies include the following:

- Enzyme immunoassay (EIA), formerly called enzyme-linked immunosorbent assay
- If the blood is found to be positive for antibodies, the test is repeated.
- If the blood continues to test positive for antibodies, the Western blot or immunofluorescence assay test is done to confirm seropositivity from the EIA test.
- If the blood proves positive in all tests, the individual is considered to be HIV positive.

However, there is a period of up to two months during which antibodies may not be detected.

To monitor the stage, severity, and effectiveness of treatment of the HIV infection, CD4+ T-cell counts as well as laboratory tests measuring viral activity are done throughout the course of the infection. Viral load testing counts the number of viral particles in a sample of blood.

Therapeutics

Protocols of care change often as new knowledge about both the infection and the treatment develop. However, collaborative management of the HIV-infected person still focuses on monitoring the following:

- HIV disease progression
- Immune function
- Acute retroviral treatment
- The development of opportunistic diseases
- Symptoms
- Preventing or decreasing the complications of treatment

There is no cure for HIV. Therefore, HIV continues for the rest of the client's life, causing increasing physical disability, impaired health, and eventual death. Although there is no cure, signs and symptoms can be managed with treatment.

Primary therapy for HIV infection includes three different types of antiretroviral drugs:

- Protease inhibitors, such as tironavir, indinavir, nelfinavir, and saquinavir
- Nucleoside reverse transcriptase inhibitors, such as zidovudine (AZT), didanosine, zalcitabine, lamivudine, and stavudine

Box 8.1 Diagnostic Criteria for AIDS

AIDS is diagnosed when an individual with HIV develops at least one of these conditions:

1. CD4+ T-cell count below 200 cells/microlitre.
2. One of the following opportunistic infections:
   - Fungal: candidiasis of bronchi, trachea, lungs, or esophagus; *Pneumocystis carinii* pneumonia (PCP); disseminated or extrapulmonary histoplasmosis, extrapulmonary cryptococcosis, disseminated or extrapulmonary coccidioidomycosis
   - Viral: cytomegalovirus (CMV) disease other than liver, spleen, or nodes; CMV retinitis (with loss of vision); herpes simplex, with chronic ulcer(s) or bronchitis, pneumonitis, or esophagitis; progressive multifocal leukoencephalopathy (PML)
   - Protozoal: toxoplasmosis of the brain, chronic intestinal isosporiasis; chronic intestinal cryptosporidiosis
   - Bacterial: *Mycobacterium* tuberculosis (any site); any disseminated or extrapulmonary *Mycobacterium*, including *M. avium* complex or *M. kansasii*; recurrent pneumonia; recurrent *Salmonella* septicemia
3. One of the following opportunistic cancers:
   - Invasive cervical cancer, Kaposi's sarcoma, Burkitt's lymphoma, immunoblastic lymphoma, or primary lymphoma of the brain
4. Wasting syndrome occurs. Wasting is defined as a loss of 10% or more of ideal body mass.
5. Dementia develops.

Source: Modified from Centers for Disease Control and Prevention (CDC). (1992). Recommendations and reports: 1993 revised classification system for HIV infection and expanded surveillance case definition for AIDS among adolescents and adults. *Morbidity and Mortality Weekly Report, 41*(RR-17), 1.

- Non-nucleoside reverse transcriptase inhibitors, such as nevirapine and delaviridine

These drugs are used in various combinations and are designed to inhibit HIV replication. The drugs can be toxic, and the client must be monitored for these toxicities. Other drug therapies used in AIDS include immunomodulatory drugs that are designed to boost the weakened immune system and antimicrobial and antineoplastic agents that are used to combat opportunistic infections and associated cancers.

The goals of drug therapy for those infected with HIV are to decrease the HIV RNA to an undetectable level, to maintain or increase CD4+ counts, to delay the development of symptoms of HIV/AIDS, and to maintain quality of life. Vaccines are in the developmental stages and are being tested in animals. Researchers will be investigating whether vaccines can boost the immune function of a person infected with HIV.

Health promotion focuses on prevention of HIV by decreasing the risks related to sexual practices, drug use, and perinatal transmission and by encouraging abstinence or safe-sex practices.

Early intervention promotes health and delays disabilities. The client diagnosed with HIV will likely experience panic, fear, guilt, depression, and denial and may have suicidal thoughts.

Multidrug therapy reduces viral loads but is complex, has interactions, and does not work for everyone. Antiretroviral therapy (ART) was introduced in 1987. Federal guidelines suggest that treatment be delayed until levels of immune suppression are observed. There is great debate about when to start ART. Adherence to drug regimens is critical to preventing disease progression and the development of opportunistic diseases and decreases the risk of viral drug resistance.

The client with HIV/AIDS is likely to develop infections and cancers that will have an effect on his or her ability to cope psychosocially and economically. Common opportunistic infections include *Pneumocystis carinii* pneumonia, cryptococcal meningitis, cytomegalovirus (CMV) retinitis, and *Mycobacterium avium* complex. A common opportunistic cancer is Kaposi's sarcoma.

As with most chronic diseases, most of the nursing care will take place in the client's home. Family members and those people caring for a client with HIV/AIDS need to understand that the client will be anxious, fearful, and depressed at times and may develop a variety of symptoms, such as diarrhea, pain, nausea, vomiting, and fatigue, throughout the course of his or her disease. Symptom management is important.

Some clients may develop metabolic disorders, such as hyperlipidemia, insulin resistance, and bone disease. The caregiver must be knowledgeable in assessing the client so that early detection and treatment can take place. Dementia often is present in the final stages of HIV.

AIDS dementia complex, also called HIV-associated cognitive motor complex, is caused by HIV infection in the brain or HIV-related CNS problems caused by lymphoma, toxoplasmosis, CMV, herpes virus, *Cryptococcus*, progressive multifocal leukoencephalopathy, dehydration, or drug side effects. This dementia may be reversible if a cause is diagnosed.

Nursing Considerations

Assessment is important in order to identify persons at risk for HIV. Individuals should be asked if they received blood products before 1985 or shared needles, syringes, or other injection equipment with another person. They need to be asked if they have had sexual experience with their penis, vagina, rectum, or mouth in contact with these areas of another person. Information regarding the client's history of diagnosed sexually transmitted infection is important.

Ongoing health and psychosocial assessment is paramount. Education about HIV should include what the infection is, how it is transmitted, treatment, preventing transmission, improving health, and family planning. Initially, the client may be in denial or shock, so the information needs to be repeated.

Assessment is dependent on the stage of the disease; focuses on prevention, treatment, or terminal-phase care; and must include social factors such as self-esteem, sexuality, family interactions, and finances.

The client should be encouraged to adhere to the drug regimens, to maintain a healthy lifestyle, to prevent opportunistic infections, and, most importantly, to prevent transmission to others. This plan requires developing supportive relationships, encouraging the client to maintain activity, and eventually to come to terms with issues related to living with HIV/AIDS and death and spirituality.

Dementia nursing considerations focus on safety, self-care, and helping caregivers support those activities. Prevent confusion by maintaining a consistent and familiar environment, frequent reorientation, and stress reduction measures. Emphasis should be placed on providing support to family members and significant others, who may have difficulty dealing with the client's mental and physical deterioration (Lewis et al., 2010).

In the terminal stages of HIV, palliative care is important to provide comfort and support to the client and the family. See the section on end-of-life care for further nursing considerations.

CANCER OVERVIEW

Pathophysiology

Cancer is an umbrella term for a group of disorders in which certain cells grow and multiply uncontrollably. Cancer cells are characterized by the loss of contact inhibition. They have altered recognition and adhesion and altered anchorage-dependent growth, have lost their restrictive point control, and keep on dividing. These cells do not stay put but invade other cells and are viable in blood and lymph fluid.

Cellular differentiation is normally an orderly process in which the cell progresses from a state of immaturity to a state of maturity. Malignant cells do not resemble their parent cells; they take on more of the appearance and some of the behaviours of fetal cells. The appearance of the cell and the degree of differentiation of the cell help classify the cancer. The less differentiated the cell is from the normal cell, the worse the grade of classification is. Normal cellular differentiation is illustrated in Figure 8.3.

Fertilized ova with potential to produce all the differentiated cells of the body
Endoderm
Mesoderm
Ectoderm
Differentiation
Differentiation
Differentiation
Mature cells of the • Trachea • Lungs • Epithelium
Mature cells of the • Muscles • Bones • Connective tissue
Mature cells of the • Brain • Skin • Glands

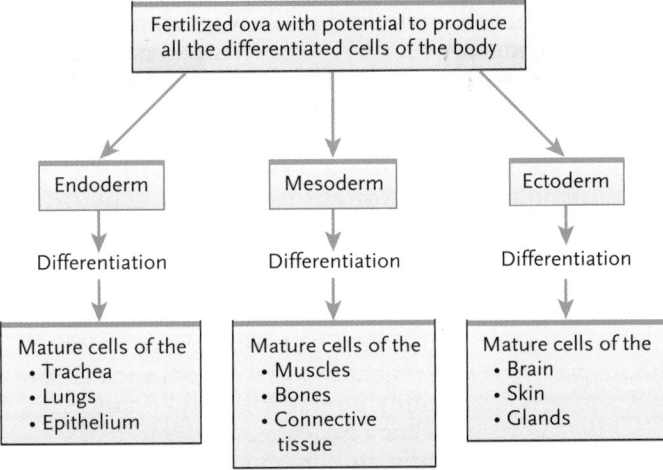

FIGURE 8.3 **Normal Cellular Differentiation**

Source: Kumar, V., Abbas, A. K., & Fausto, N. (2005). *Robbins and Cotran Pathologic basis of disease* (7th ed.). Philadelphia: Saunders.

Proto-oncogenes are normal cellular genes that are important regulators of normal cellular processes. Mutations that alter their expression can activate them to act as oncogenes, tumour-inducing genes that promote the development of cancer. Tumour suppressor genes help suppress the growth of tumours and render mutation inactive. Malignant tumours are able to metastasize, infiltrate, and expand; they frequently recur and have moderate to marked vascularity.

In many cases, the exact cause of cancer is unknown; however, specific factors have been implicated as causing genetic mutations. External stimuli include the following:

- Chemical carcinogens, such as tobacco smoke, arsenic, vinyl chloride benzene, exposure to viruses, and exposure to ultraviolet light
- A diet high in fat and low in fibre, which encourages the development of colon cancer
- Genetic abnormalities that affect the presence of oncogenes, proto-oncogenes, and tumour suppressor genes
- Chromosomal abnormalities, such as increased number (as in Down syndrome), deletion, translocation, and breakage of chromosomes, have been found to be present with cancer development.

Stages of Cancer Development

Cancer development follows a three-stage pattern: initiation, promotion, and progression.

First Stage: Initiation

The first stage begins with the "initiation," when the mutation of the cell's genetic structure first occurs. Carcinogens can initiate this mutation. This is the event that causes the change in the cell. The cell is still functioning normally but has the potential to develop into a clone of a neoplastic cell (Lewis et al., 2010).

Second Stage: Promotion

The promotion stage is characterized by the reversible proliferation of altered cells. A cancer cell is not a health threat unless it can divide. Lifestyle choices such as obesity, diet, and smoking can enhance promotion. If these behaviours improve, the promotion may be reversible. If not, the initial genetic alteration proceeds to clinical cancer (Lewis et al., 2010).

Third Stage: Progression

The progression stage is characterized by the increased growth rate of the tumour, as well as its invasiveness and metastasis. As progression continues, the malignant tumour will develop its own blood supply (angiogenesis). Figure 8.4 illustrates the process of this development.

The body's immune system will attempt to reject or destroy cancer cells if they are perceived as nonself. This attempt may be inadequate, however, as the cancer cells arise from normal human cells that the immune system may perceive as self. Some cancers cells have changes on their surface, called tumour-associated antigens (TAAs). The response to TAAs is termed immunological surveillance. Lymphocytes continually check cell surfaces and detect and destroy cells with abnormalities. Cytotoxic T cells, NK cells, macrophages, and B lymphocytes are involved. However, there are mechanisms by which cancer cells evade the immune system by suppressing factors that stimulate the T cells. Sometimes weak surface antigens allow cancer cells to "sneak through" surveillance. The cancer cells may develop a tolerance to the immune system. There may be a suppression of the immune response to products secreted by cancer cells, and antibodies that bind with TAAs may be blocked (Lewis et al., 2010).

Children develop different cancers than adults. Pediatric cancers are usually embryonic in origin or due to oncogenes. The child's immune system is less mature, and treatment protocols tend to be much longer than adult treatment protocols. See the section on cancer in Chapter 10, page 504.

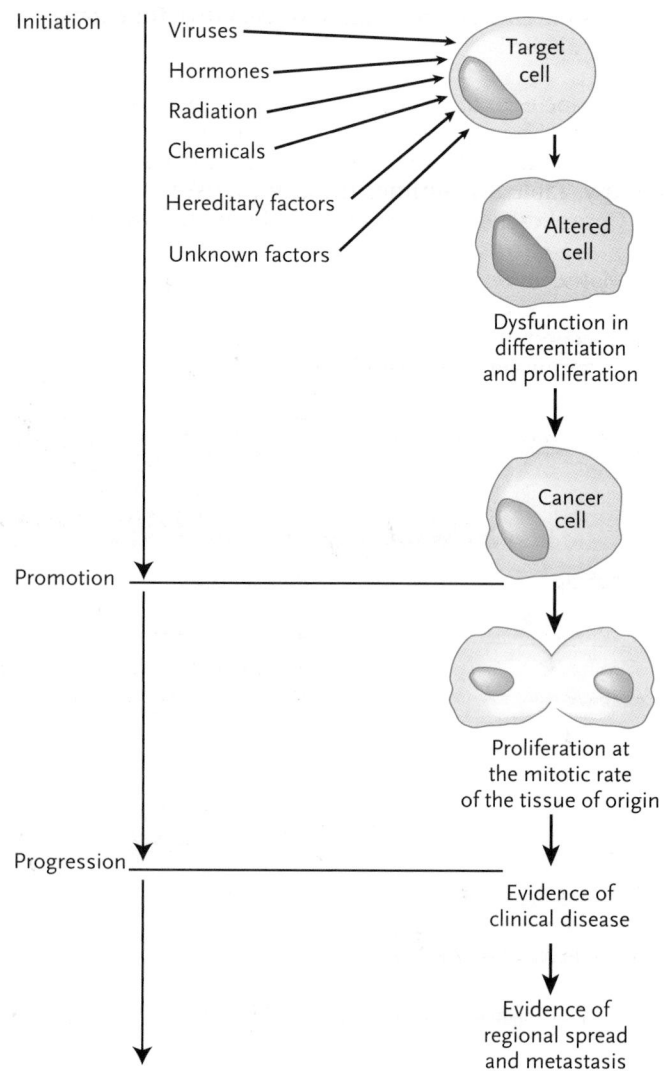

Initiation

Viruses
Hormones
Radiation
Chemicals
Hereditary factors
Unknown factors

Target cell

Altered cell

Dysfunction in differentiation and proliferation

Cancer cell

Promotion

Proliferation at the mitotic rate of the tissue of origin

Progression

Evidence of clinical disease

Evidence of regional spread and metastasis

FIGURE 8.4 **Process of Cancer Development**

Source: Lewis, S. M., Heitkemper, M. M., Dirksen, S. R., O'Brien, P., Bucher, L., et al. (2010). *Medical-surgical nursing in Canada: Assessment and management of clinical problems* (2nd Canadian ed., p. 326, Figure 17-3). Toronto: Elsevier.

Clinical Manifestations

Clinical manifestations are dependent on the type of cancer, the stage of its development, and its metastatic progression.

Diagnostics

Diagnosis involves the following:

- History and physical examination
- Blood work
- Tumour markers (oncofetal antigens)
- X-ray, computed tomography (CT), and magnetic resonance imaging (MRI)
- Ultrasonography and nuclear medicine
- Visualization via scopes

- Definitive diagnosis is done by biopsy. A biopsy of the suspected tumour is helpful only if the cancer is going to be treated.

Cancers are classified according to the following:

- Tissue of origin
- Anatomical site
- Degree of differentiation
- How closely the cancer cell resembles its parent cell

Some cancers are classified according to their receptor status, such as breast cancer; chromosomal abnormalities, including chronic myelogenous leukemia (CML), characterized by the Philadelphia chromosome; and tumour markers, such as those present in testicular cancer.

Therapeutics and Nursing Considerations

Cancer treatment goals include cure, in which the cancer is eradicated; control, in which containment of the tumour is attempted to prolong and improve quality of life; and palliation, which focuses on comfort and the relief of symptoms. Factors that determine treatment modality depend on cell type, location and size of the tumour, and extent of the disease. The physiological and psychological status of the client and his or her expressed needs must also determine treatment. Cancer treatment can involve one or more of the following:

- Surgery
- Radiation
- Chemotherapy
- Biological therapy

Surgical therapy is used to cure or control the disease process or for palliative reasons. When surgery is done, a margin of normal tissue surrounding the tumour will be removed, as well as the tumour itself. Preventive measures are used to reduce the risk of surgical seeding of the cancer cells. The usual sites of regional spread may also be removed.

Radiation therapy involves the use of high-energy particles or waves to treat the cancer. When radiation is used, many factors must be considered. The type of cell determines whether radiation will be beneficial. Malignant melanomas are not sensitive to radiation, whereas Hodgkin's disease is highly sensitive to radiation. The cycle of cell division also must be considered. Cells in the mitosis (M) and RNA synthesis (G_2) cycles are more sensitive to radiation than at other times within the cell division process. Well-oxygenated cells, as well as rapidly dividing cells, are more sensitive to radiation. The radiation breaks the chemical bonds in DNA, causing loss of the proliferative capacity. The radiologist will decide on a tumoricidal dose that can be delivered within the limits of tolerance of the surrounding tissues. Radiation is considered local therapy and will affect tissues directly radiated. Radiation can be delivered by external beam (teletherapy) or internal radiation (brachytherapy). Radiolabelled antibodies may also be used. The number of treatments will depend on the type of cancer, extent of the disease, area to be treated, dose, and fractionation, which is the administration of a course of therapeutic treatments planned as a series of fractions of the total prescribed dose. Side effects are related to damage to the normal cells in and around the treatment field. Factors affecting the development of side effects include the following:

- Tumour location
- Dose of radiation needed
- Method of delivery
- Individual factors

The destruction of the cells and the body's attempt to rid itself of the dead cells will cause fatigue. Anorexia may develop. Skin reactions may occur, and precautions should be taken in the proper care of the skin, such as using warm water, mild soap, and no antiperspirant or perfume.

The goal of chemotherapy is to reduce the number of cancer cells in the tumour site(s). Cancer cells are not sensitive to some chemotherapeutic agents when the cell is in the resting phase. Chemotherapy attacks rapidly dividing cells systemically. Because chemotherapy is systemic therapy, the side effects are different from the side effects of radiation. Some chemotherapeutic agents have known side effects, and these should be managed aggressively. Chemotherapeutic agents also have less common, unexpected toxicities, and the client should be carefully assessed to allow for early identification.

Chemotherapy may be administered by the following routes:

- Orally
- By injection
- Intravenously
- Intracavitarily
- Intrathecally
- Intra-arterially by perfusion
- By continuous infusion
- Subcutaneously
- Topically

Sometimes a chemotherapeutic agent is delivered directly into the tumour, allowing higher concentrations of the agent with fewer systemic effects.

Biological therapy involves the use of alpha-, beta-, or gamma-interferons, which are cytokines with antiviral, antiproliferative, and immunomodulatory properties. They cannot be delivered orally. Biological therapy will have side effects similar to those of radiation and chemotherapy. However, the main difference is that with biological therapy, a flulike syndrome may develop. Interleukins induce biological activities that activate the immune system or alteration in function of the cancer cells. Interleukins have toxic side effects, including the following:

- Capillary leak syndrome
- Specific organ toxicities
- Bone marrow suppression
- Possible changes in mentation (cognitive function)
- Anaphylaxis

Monoclonal antibodies, colony-stimulating factors, and hematopoietic growth factors such as erythropoietin and oprelvekin are also biological therapy. Table 8.7 outlines the clinical uses of cytokines. Complications of cancer include the following:

- Malnutrition
- Altered taste sensation
- Infection
- Superior vena cava syndrome

Table 8.7   Clinical Uses of Cytokines

Cytokine	Clinical Uses
Alpha-Interferon (Roferon-A, Intron A)	- Hepatitis B and C - Kaposi's sarcoma - Hairy cell leukemia - Lymphomas - Leukemias - Melanoma - Renal cell carcinoma - Multiple myeloma
Beta-Interferon - Interferon-1b (Betaseron) - Interferon-1a (Avonex, Refib)	- Multiple sclerosis
Colony-Stimulating Factors G-CSF, GM-CSF Filgrastim (Neupogen) Sargramostin	- Neutropenia
Soluble TNF Receptor Etanercept (Enbrel) (Soluble TNF Receptor)	- Rheumatoid arthritis
Interleukin-2 Aldesleukin (Proleukin)	- Renal cell carcinoma - Malignant melanoma - Lymphoma - Acute myelocytic leukemia
Erythropoietin (Epogen, Procrit)	- Anemia
IL-1 Receptor Antagonist Anakinra (Kineret)	- Rheumatoid arthritis

G-CSF, granulocyte colony-stimulating factor; *GM-CSF*, granulocyte-macrophage colony-stimulating factor; *IL*, interleukin; *TNF*, tumour necrosis factor.

Source: Lewis, S. M., Heitkemper, M. M., Dirksen, S. R., O'Brien, P., Bucher, L., et al. (2010). *Medical-surgical nursing in Canada: Assessment and management of clinical problems* (2nd Canadian ed., p. 270, Table 15-4). Toronto: Elsevier.

- Spinal cord compression
- Third space syndrome
- Syndrome of inappropriate antidiuretic hormone (SIADH)
- Hypercalcemia
- Tumour lysis syndrome
- Cardiac tamponade
- Carotid artery rupture

LEUKEMIA

Pathophysiology

Leukemia is a generalized term used to describe complex cancers of the blood that affect the blood and blood-forming tissues of the bone marrow, lymph system, and spleen. Leukemia results in an accumulation of dysfunctional cells because of loss of regulation in cell division. Most leukemias result as a combination of several genetic and environmental factors, including chromosomal factors, immunological factors, viruses, and exposure to radiation or certain chemicals.

The classification of leukemia is based on the type of WBCs involved and on whether the condition is acute or chronic. Acute leukemia is characterized by the proliferation of immature cells. Chronic leukemia involves more mature forms of WBCs, and the disease onset is more gradual. Acute and chronic leukemias are classified as lymphocytic or myelogenous according to the predominant cell type (Lewis et al., 2010). The four major types of leukemia are as follows:

- Acute myelogenous leukemia (AML)
- Acute lymphocytic leukemia (ALL)
- Chronic myelogenous leukemia (CML)
- Chronic lymphocytic leukemia (CLL)

Clinical Manifestations

The clinical manifestations of leukemia will vary. Essentially, symptoms relate to problems caused by bone marrow failure and the formation of leukemic infiltrates. The leukemic cells will crowd out normal WBCs, RBCs, and platelets, causing anemia with associated fatigue, dyspnea, pallor, frequent infections and flulike symptoms, and bleeding tendencies. As the abnormal WBCs continue to accumulate, they infiltrate the client's organs, leading to splenomegaly, hepatomegaly, lymphadenopathy, bone pain, meningeal irritation, and oral lesions (Lewis et al., 2010).

Diagnostics

The definitive test for leukemia is bone marrow aspiration and biopsy, which will determine the cell type, the type of erythropoiesis, and the maturity of the leukopoietic and erythropoietic cells.

A complete blood count (CBC) will show decreased hemoglobin and hematocrit, a low platelet count, and an abnormal WBC count. A physical examination may reveal lymph node enlargement.

Therapeutics and Nursing Considerations

Treatment of the leukemia is dependent on the type. When possible, treatment will focus on achieving remission. Systemic chemotherapy is used to eradicate leukemic cells and induce remission, restoring normal bone marrow function. The type of chemotherapy will vary with the type of leukemia present. Other treatments may include the following:

- Antibiotics, antifungals, and antivirals to control infections
- Platelet transfusions to prevent bleeding
- Blood or RBC transfusions to treat the anemia
- For some clients, bone marrow transplantation

HODGKIN'S DISEASE

Pathophysiology

Hodgkin's disease is a malignant lymphoma characterized by abnormal gigantic tumour cells called Reed-Sternberg cells, which are morphologically unique and thought to develop from immature lymphoid tissue. This lymphatic cancer initially develops in a single lymph node or chain of nodes. The disease then spreads in a predictable manner to nearby lymph tissue. If left unchecked, it will then spread to nonlymph tissue. All organs are susceptible to invasion as the disease progresses. The exact cause of Hodgkin's disease is unclear, although key factors, such as infection with the Epstein–Barr virus, genetic predisposition, and exposure to occupational toxins, could be possible causes (Lewis et al., 2010).

Clinical Manifestations

The onset of Hodgkin's disease is usually insidious. The initial development is most often painless enlargement of one or more lymph nodes. As the disease progresses, the client may experience the following symptoms:

- Pruritus
- Persistent fever
- Night sweats
- Fatigue
- Weight loss
- Malaise
- Headaches
- Changes in mentation
- Seizures (Lewis et al., 2010)

Diagnostics

Biopsy of the enlarged lymph nodes showing the presence of the Reed-Sternberg cell confirms the diagnosis. Other diagnostic tests should be done to rule out any infectious origin for the disease. A bone marrow biopsy will be done to identify the stage of the disease. Other tests will include a chest X-ray and a CT scan of the head, neck, chest, abdomen, and pelvis to look for possible spread of the disease.

Therapeutics and Nursing Considerations

Treatment will depend on the disease stage rather than the histological type and may include chemotherapy, radiation, or both. Radiation given to affected areas over four to six weeks can cure 95% of clients with stage I or II disease. Combination chemotherapy is used in some early stages in clients believed to have resistant or more advanced disease.

If the Hodgkin's disease does recur, high-dose chemotherapy and bone marrow or peripheral stem cell transplantation have proven to be successful in extending survival. Advances in treatment now enable some stage III and IV disease to be cured with high-dose chemotherapy and bone marrow or peripheral stem cell transplantation (Lewis et al., 2010).

RESPIRATORY SYSTEM DYSFUNCTION

ASTHMA

Pathophysiology

Asthma is a chronic reactive airway disorder that is characterized by chronic inflammation, bronchoconstriction, and bronchial hyper-responsiveness, causing increased mucus production. There is often a family history of asthma, and symptoms can occur seasonally. Asthma is commonly accompanied by nocturnal flare-ups.

Extrinsic asthma results from exposure to sensitizing agents such as pollen, animal dander, house dust, or mould. Intrinsic asthma may result from the following causes:

- Irritants
- Emotional stress
- Fatigue
- Endocrine changes
- Cold temperatures
- Exposure to noxious fumes

Other triggers of asthma include but are not limited to the following:

- Exercise
- Nonsteroidal anti-inflammatory drugs (NSAIDs)
- Upper airway infections
- Food dye

The triggers initiate the inflammatory response that contributes to the airway inflammation, mucus production, and bronchoconstriction, all of which cause airway obstruction.

Clinical Manifestations

Symptoms of asthma may include the following:

- Intermittent attacks of dyspnea and wheezing
- Tightness of the chest
- Coughing that is productive of thick, clear, or yellow sputum
- Tachypnea, with the result that the client needs to use the accessory respiratory muscles to breathe
- Orthopnea, with clients sitting upright with shoulders hunched forward

Clients in severe distress may experience diaphoresis, cyanosis, pallor, and diminished breath sounds. Between attacks, the client will breathe normally.

Diagnostics

A history and physical examination revealing dyspnea, wheezing, and coughing are highly suggestive of asthma. A chest X-ray may reveal hyperinflated lungs with air trapping during an attack. The lungs will look normal when the client is not having an attack. Pulmonary function tests are helpful in determining the extent of the client's asthma.

Therapeutics and Nursing Considerations

Treatment is usually tailored to each client and focuses on identifying and avoiding precipitating allergens and irritants. Primary drug therapy generally includes inhaled bronchodilators and steroids, either alone or in combination.

During an acute attack, respiratory function needs to be monitored closely while attempts are made to relieve the bronchoconstriction and expulsion of mucoid plugs. The client needs close supervision as he or she is likely to be frightened and needs to have constant reassurance. The nursing considerations are as follows:

- Encourage the client to sit in a semi- or high Fowler's position.
- Encourage the client to breathe using the diaphragm.
- Deliver oxygen via nasal prongs.
- Monitor for "silent chest," an indication that the client may be progressing to status asthmaticus.
- Perform a chest assessment before and after bronchodilator inhalations.
- Establish IV therapy to allow medications to be delivered quickly if necessary.
- For severe acute attacks, administer IV salbutamol and hydrocortisone (Solu-Cortef).

Chronic Obstructive Pulmonary Disease

Pathophysiology

COPD is an umbrella term that refers to emphysema, chronic bronchitis, and that is characterized by airflow obstruction. COPD patients may have asthma as well. Exposure to tobacco smoke is the primary cause of COPD. Other risk factors include recurrent or chronic respiratory tract infections, allergies, and familial or hereditary factors, such as alpha-antitrypsin deficiency.

Smoking causes the following complications:

- Nicotine acts as a sympathetic nervous system (SNS) stimulant, causing vasoconstriction and increased heart rate, BP, and cardiac workload.
- Smoking decreases ciliary activity and increases proteolytic enzymes that destroy elastin and collagen and cause cellular hyperplasia. This increases the production of mucus, reduces the airway diameter, and increases the difficulty in clearing secretions.

Emphysema is an abnormal permanent enlargement of the air space distal to the terminal bronchioles accompanied by destruction of their walls without obvious fibrosis. Figure 8.5 illustrates centrilobular emphysema. Emphysema pathology includes the following:

- Hyperinflation of the alveoli
- Destruction of alveolar walls (bullae development)
- Destruction of alveolar capillary walls
- Small airway collapse (air trapping)
- Loss of lung elasticity

Chronic bronchitis is diagnosed when an individual has had a productive cough for three or more months in each of two successive years. Figure 8.6 illustrates chronic bronchitis. Chronic bronchitis pathology includes the following:

- Hyperplasia of mucus-secreting glands in the trachea and bronchi
- An increase in the goblet cells

Panlobular emphysema (PLE)
Normal
Centrilobular emphysema (CLE)

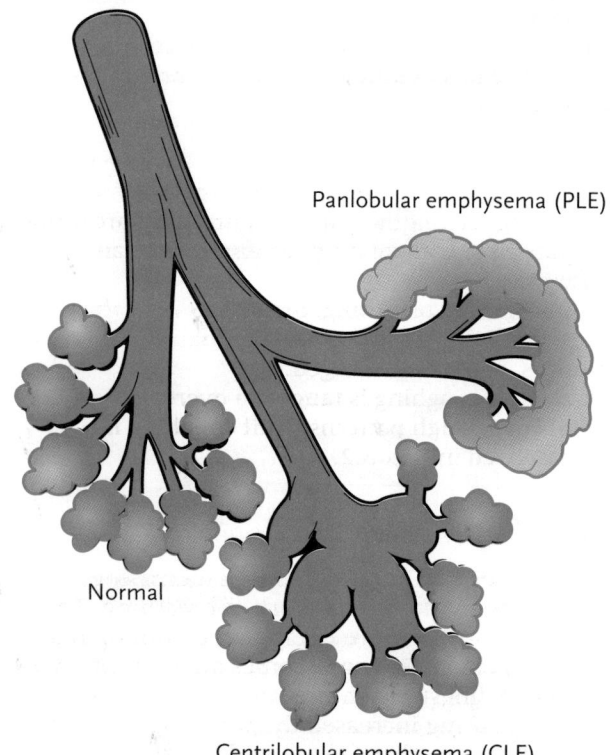

FIGURE 8.5 **Centrilobular Emphysema**

Source: Adapted from Lewis, S. M., Heitkemper, M. M., Dirksen, S. R., O'Brien, P., Bucher, L., et al. (2010). *Medical-surgical nursing in Canada: Assessment and management of clinical problems* (2nd Canadian ed., p. 694, Figure 30-9). Toronto: Elsevier.

Pulmonary artery
Cartilage
Submucosal gland
Mast cell
Basement membrane
Parasympathetic nerve
Smooth muscle
Bronchioles
Epithelium
Respiratory bronchioles
Goblet cell
Alveoli
Enlarged submucosal gland
Mucus accumulation
Mucous plug
Inflammation of epithelium
Hyperinflation of alveoli

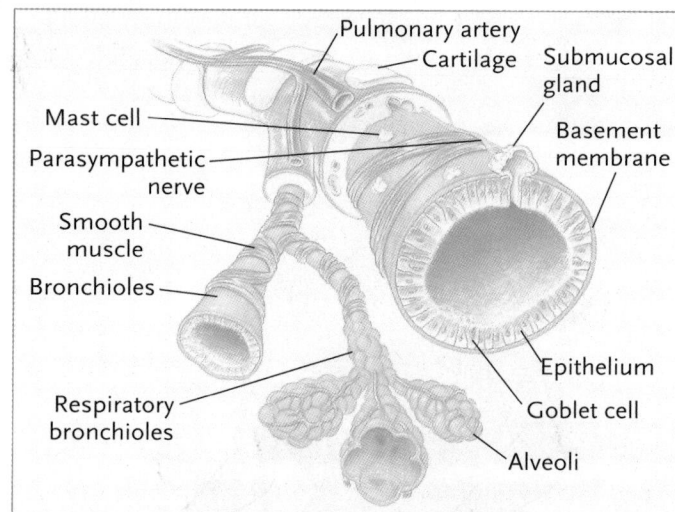

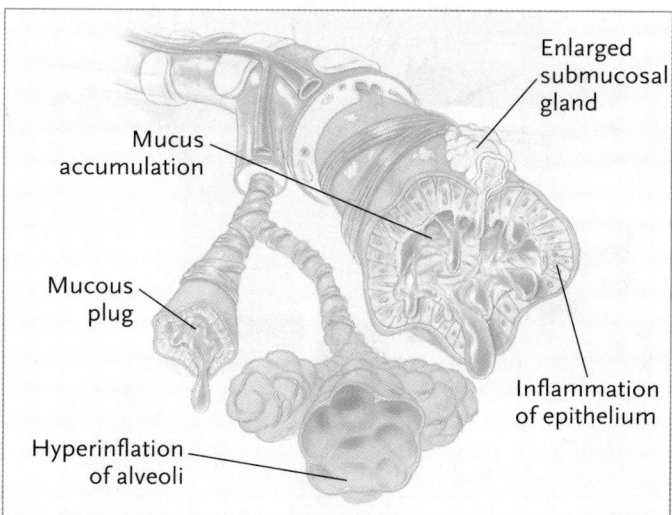

FIGURE 8.6 **Chronic Bronchitis**

Source: McCance, K. L., & Huether, S. E. (2006). *Pathophysiology: The biologic basis for disease in adults and children* (5th ed., p. 1221, Figure 33-10 A, C). St. Louis: Mosby.

- Disappearance of cilia
- Chronic inflammatory changes
- Altered alveolar macrophage function
- Normal alveolar structures and capillaries

Clinical Manifestations

Clinical findings may be absent in the early stages of COPD. As the disease progresses, various symptoms develop depending on the underlying disease entity. Regardless of this underlying entity, progressive airflow obstruction will eventually lead to poor ventilation–perfusion, resulting in hypoxia. The client may experience barrel chest, cyanosis, and clubbing of the fingers and nails. Dyspnea is usually the first symptom to develop. In chronic bronchitis, cough is usually the first symptom to develop. The typical posture of persons with COPD is illustrated in Figure 8.7. Complications may include the following:

FIGURE 8.7 **Typical Posture of Person With COPD**

Typical posture of person with COPD, primarily emphysema. The person tends to lean forward and uses the accessory muscles of respiration to breathe, forcing the shoulder girdle upward and causing the supraclavicular fossae to retract on inspiration.

- Polycythemia
- Acidosis
- Pulmonary hypertension
- Cor pulmonale
- Acute respiratory failure

Diagnostics

Diagnosis is based on the history and physical examination. A chest X-ray for a client with chronic bronchitis may show a flattened diaphragm, reduced vascular markings at the lung periphery, hyperinflation of lungs, and an enlarged heart. Pulmonary function tests may show an increase in residual volume, total lung capacity, and compliance, with decreased vital capacity, diffusing capacity, and forced expiratory volumes. Blood work may show polycythemia due to the hypoxia. A chest X-ray for a client with chronic bronchitis may show hyperinflation and normal or increased bronchovascular markings.

Therapeutics and Nursing Considerations

Treatment focuses on airway expansion and airway clearance with improved gas exchange. The treatments are as follows:

- Oxygen is administered at low-flow settings to treat hypoxia.
- Antibiotics are prescribed to treat infections.
- Avoidance of smoking or air pollutants is encouraged.
- Bronchodilators are prescribed to relieve bronchospasm and facilitate mucociliary clearance.
- Steroids may be prescribed to reduce inflammation.
- Breathing techniques, such as pursed-lip breathing, are taught to control dyspnea and reduce air trapping.
- Diaphragmatic breathing, breathing using the muscles of the diaphragm rather than the accessory muscles, is also encouraged.
- Often huff coughing is taught to overcome ineffective cough patterns. Huff coughing is summarized in Box 8.2.

Nursing Considerations

Clients with severe COPD expend an increasing amount of energy doing the work of breathing. They can expend 30–50% more energy on breathing than the average person. Eating becomes an effort as a result of dyspnea. A full stomach presses up on the flattened diaphragm, causing increased dyspnea and discomfort. It is difficult for the client to eat and breathe at the same time (Lewis et al., 2010).

- The client will need to be encouraged to rest prior to eating and again after eating.
- Small frequent meals are easier to tolerate than larger meals.

Box 8.2 Huff Coughing

1. The client assumes a sitting position with the neck slightly flexed, shoulders relaxed, knees flexed, forearms supported by a pillow, and, if possible, feet on the floor.

2. The client then drops the head and bends forward while using slow, pursed-lip breathing to exhale.

3. Sitting up again, the client uses diaphragmatic breathing to inhale slowly and deeply.

4. The client repeats steps 2 and 3 three to four times to facilitate the mobilization of secretions.

5. Before initiating a cough, the client should take a deep abdominal breath, bend slightly forward, and then huff cough (cough three to four times on exhalation). The client may need to support or splint his or her thorax or abdomen to achieve maximum effect.

Source: Lewis, S. M., Heitkemper, M. M., Dirksen, S. R., O'Brien, P., Bucher, L., et al. (2010). *Medical-surgical nursing in Canada: Assessment and management of clinical problems* (2nd Canadian ed., p. 705, Table 30-22). Toronto: Elsevier.

- Food that causes gas should be avoided.
- In some cases, puréed or blenderized food is easier for the client to tolerate.
- If there are no other medical conditions, the client should be encouraged to drink 3 L of fluid each day. Fluids should be offered between meals so that the client will eat a nutritious meal and then take the fluids.

COPD education focuses on the client maintaining the following:

- Effective airway clearance
- Effective gas exchange
- A balanced diet
- Adequate sleep
- Prevention of infection

In order to accomplish these, the client needs to be encouraged to be as physically active as his or her condition permits: walking each day, practising breathing exercises, and practising energy-conserving strategies, such as assuming the tripod position (elbows supported on table and chest flexed) when tired. Relaxation techniques can be very beneficial to relieve dyspnea. Appropriate use of medications prior to an activity is helpful. Long-acting theophylline or a long-acting bronchodilator medication may be needed to assist the client during sleep.

Many lifestyle changes may occur during the progression of COPD. Clients may go through the stages of grief as more and more of their normal activities may be lost (Lewis et al., 2010).

TUBERCULOSIS

Pathophysiology

Tuberculosis (TB) is an acute or chronic infection characterized by pulmonary infiltrates and formation of granulomas with caseation, fibrosis, and cavitation. TB is caused by *Mycobacterium tuberculosis* (*M. tuberculosis*). The prevalence of TB decreased in the 1940s and 1950s but resurged after 1985, coinciding with the spread of HIV infections. TB is more commonly found among individuals who are economically disadvantaged, homeless or living in crowded spaces, malnourished, immuno-compromised, or members of minority groups.

TB infection is spread to others via the following process:

- Droplet nuclei are released when the infected person coughs, sneezes, speaks, or sings.
- Droplets are inhaled by the recipient, and the bacilli are deposited in the lung.
- The immune system responds by sending leukocytes and macrophages to the area, ultimately resulting in encapsulation of the bacilli in the Ghon tubercle.
- At this stage, the client will demonstrate exposure to the TB bacilli via skin testing but does not have a TB infection.
- If the tubercle and inflamed nodes rupture, the infection contaminates the surrounding tissue and may spread through the blood and lymphatic circulation to distant sites such as the kidneys, epiphyses of bone, cerebral cortex, or adrenal glands.

Clinical Manifestations

- Clients in the early stages of TB are usually asymptomatic.
- Nonspecific symptoms such as fatigue, weakness, anorexia, weight loss, night sweats, and low-grade fever may develop as TB progresses.
- The client may experience cough, productive mucopurulent sputum, and chest pain.
- Hemoptysis develops in advanced cases.

Diagnostics

Definitive diagnosis is made by the following:

- Sputum cultures and stains
- Skin testing, which detects exposure to TB but does not distinguish between exposure and infection
- Chest X-rays, which may show nodular lesions, patchy infiltrates, cavity formation, scar tissue, and calcium deposits but which cannot distinguish between active or inactive TB
- Nucleic acid amplification, a new test that gives results within hours. However, this test does not replace smears and sputum cultures.

Purified protein derivative (PPD) of tuberculin is used primarily to detect the delayed hypersensitivity immune response of the individual. Two-step testing (the Mantoux test) is recommended for initial testing for health care workers. Once a two-step test has been done, follow-up testing only requires the one-step test (Lewis et al., 2010).

Therapeutics and Nursing Considerations

Prevention is very important. If the living conditions of the client cannot be changed, immunization with bacille Calmette-Guérin (BCG) may be given to prevent TB. This is commonly done in the Northwest Territories and Nunavut.

Treatment for TB includes the following:

- Antitubercular therapy, with daily oral doses of isoniazid (INH), rifampin, and pyrazinamide, with or without streptomycin and ethambutol (Myambutol), is administered for at least six to nine months.
- Combination therapy is used to increase the therapeutic effectiveness and decrease the development of resistant strains of *M. tuberculosis*.
- After two to four weeks of treatment, the client is no longer considered infectious and can resume a normal life while continuing to take his or her medications for six to nine months.
- Newer drugs that are sometimes used include ciprofloxacin (Cipro), ofloxacin (Floxin), sparfloxacin (Zagam), and rifapentine (Priftin), particularly when the client develops complications from one of the earlier antitubercular agents.

The client is taught health practices such as using tissues when coughing or sneezing, discarding the tissues in appropriate garbage containers, and washing hands after each cough and sneeze. Direct observation therapy (DOT) is now being used in many overcrowded areas to help ensure that the client takes the medications as instructed for the length of time they are needed. Noncompliance is a major factor in the emergence of multidrug resistance and treatment failures (Lewis et al., 2010). Individuals who have tested positive ("positive reactors") for *Mycobacterium* but do not have active disease are prescribed INH for six to nine months.

ACUTE RESPIRATORY DISTRESS SYNDROME

Pathophysiology

Acute respiratory distress syndrome (ARDS) is a form of pulmonary edema that can lead to acute respiratory failure. ARDS results from the following:

- Increased permeability of alveolocapillary membrane, causing the alveoli to fill with fluid and resulting in severe dyspnea

- Hypoxemia refractory to supplemental oxygen
- Reduced lung compliance
- Diffuse pulmonary infiltrates
- Can result from aspiration
- Infection or sepsis
- Lung trauma
- Head injury
- Embolism
- Oxygen toxicity
- Drug overdose of barbiturates
- Blood transfusion
- Smoke or chemical inhalation
- Pancreatitis uremia
- Near-drowning

Clinical Manifestations

The client will have rapid, shallow breathing, dyspnea, hypoxemia that does not respond to supplemental oxygen, tachycardia, intercostal and suprasternal retractions, crackles, and wheezing. The client will be restless, apprehensive, and then mentally sluggish, with motor dysfunction. As ARDS progresses, it is associated with profound respiratory distress requiring endotracheal intubation and positive pressure ventilation.

Diagnostics

The history and physical examination are important where risk factors can be ascertained. The following symptoms indicate ARDS:

- Acute onset of the distress
- Bilateral pulmonary infiltrates
- Clinical absence of heart failure

Therapeutics and Nursing Considerations

Treatment focuses on correcting the underlying cause of ARDS. Aggressive supportive care is usually required. The client with ARDS requires the following interventions:

- Intubation with volume ventilation with positive end-expiratory pressure (PEEP). The use of PEEP helps increase residual capacity and reverses alveolar collapse.
- May require a fluid-restricted diet and diuretics
- Correction of any electrolyte and acid–base imbalance
- May be sedated and neuromuscular blocking agents may be used to minimize the extreme anxiety of ARDS clients
- By minimizing the client's anxiety, oxygen consumption and carbon monoxide production may be reduced.
- Sodium bicarbonate may be administered to treat acidosis.

- Fluids and vasopressors may be needed to maintain the client's BP.
- Antibiotic therapy may be established.

Clients with ARDS are critically ill and require close monitoring and support.

ACUTE RESPIRATORY FAILURE

Pathophysiology

Acute RF occurs when the lungs no longer meet the body's metabolic needs. The partial pressure of oxygen in the arterial blood drops, and the partial pressure of carbon dioxide increases. Acute RF may develop from any condition that increases the workload of breathing and decreases the respiratory drive, such as alveolar hypoventilation and diffusion abnormalities. The causes of Acute RF include the following:

- Bronchitis and pneumonia, the most common precipitating factors
- Bronchospasm or accumulated secretions due to cough suppression
- Decreased respiratory drive due to brain injury
- Dysfunction of the chest wall due to neuromuscular disorders
- Dysfunction of the lung parenchyma due to trauma or pleural disease

Acute RF can also occur following major thoracic or abdominal surgery due to anaesthetic agents, analgesics, and sedatives.

Clinical Manifestations

Clients with Acute RF experience hypoxemia and acidemia affecting all body organs, especially the central nervous system (CNS), respiratory, and cardiovascular systems. Early signs of Acute RF are due to decreased oxygenation and include the following:

- Restlessness
- Fatigue
- Headache
- Dyspnea
- Tachycardia
- Increased BP

As the condition worsens, these symptoms become exaggerated. Accessory muscles will be used, and breath sounds will decrease.

Diagnostics

The history and physical examination are paramount. Blood gases and pulse oximetry should be obtained. Progressive deterioration in ABG levels and pH strongly suggests Acute RF, especially in clients with normal lung tissue. A chest X-ray may show atelectasis, pneumothorax, infiltrates, and effusions.

Therapeutics and Nursing Considerations

Acute RF is a medical emergency. If the client is in significant acidosis, mechanical ventilation through an endotracheal tube may be needed. Antibiotics, bronchodilators, and steroids may be administered. The client should always be monitored for the following:

- Changes in the respiratory pattern
- Altered mentation
- Cardiac arrhythmias
- Pulmonary hypertension
- Electrolyte and ABG levels and oxygen saturation

ATELECTASIS

Pathophysiology

Atelectasis is a condition of the lungs that may be acute or chronic and that is characterized by collapse of the alveoli. In atelectasis, a blockage impedes the passage of air to and from the alveoli. The trapped alveolar air becomes absorbed into the bloodstream, and without any replacement air, that area of the lung becomes airless and collapses.

The prognosis depends on prompt treatment, including removal of the airway obstruction, relief of hypoxia, and re-expansion of the collapsed area of the lung. Possible causes of atelectasis include the following:

- Bronchial obstruction by excessive secretions, a mucous plug, or a foreign object. This is the most common cause.
- Cancer
- Oxygen toxicity, pulmonary edema, and conditions that inhibit full lung expansion

Clinical Manifestations

Signs and symptoms are variable and may include the following:

- Cough, sputum production, and fever
- In acute atelectasis, respiratory distress is evident, and dyspnea, tachypnea, pleural pain, and central cyanosis may also be present.

Diagnostics

Decreased breath sounds and crackles during auscultation are indicators of atelectasis. A chest X-ray may be done. Pulse oximetry is usually found to be below 90%.

Therapeutics and Nursing Considerations

Strategies to prevent the development of atelectasis and to minimize or treat it by improving ventilation include the following:

- Frequent turning in bed, early ambulation, and deep-breathing exercises
- Coughing or suctioning may be needed to remove secretions that could be causing obstruction.
- Bronchodilators may be ordered to assist with removal of the secretions.
- If a pleural effusion is present, a thoracentesis may be needed to remove fluid from the lung.

PULMONARY EMBOLISM

Pathophysiology

A pulmonary embolism (PE) is an obstruction of a pulmonary artery or a branch of the artery by a thrombus that has developed in the venous circulation or right side of the heart from blood, amniotic fluid, air, fat, bone marrow, or foreign IV material.

- The most common source of the thrombus is the deep veins of the legs.
- The thrombus breaks loose and travels as an embolus until it lodges in the pulmonary vasculature.
- This thrombus can result in complete or partial occlusion of the pulmonary arterial blood flow.
- The lung tissue distal to the embolus is ventilated but not perfused.
- This ventilation–perfusion imbalance leads to an increase in pulmonary arterial pressure. This increases the work of the heart's right ventricle to maintain pulmonary blood flow, which could lead to right-sided heart failure.

Clinical Manifestations

The severity of clinical manifestations of PE depends on the size of the emboli and the size and number of blood vessels occluded. The most common manifestations of PE are as follows:

- Anxiety and the sudden onset of unexplained dyspnea and tachypnea
- Pleuritic chest pain that often mimics angina pain
- Cough, hemoptysis, and crackles
- Fever
- Changes in mentation

A massive embolus may produce sudden collapse of the client, with shock, pallor, severe dyspnea, and crushing chest pain. The pulse is likely to be rapid and weak, and the BP will be low. Death occurs in 60% of clients with massive PE, frequently within the first hour of symptom development.

Diagnostics

Diagnosis is based on the client's history and physical examination. The following tests are done to diagnose the embolism:

- Ventilation–perfusion scan
- Pulmonary angiography
- Chest X-ray
- Electrocardiography (ECG)
- Peripheral and arterial blood studies
- Plethysmography, depending on the amount of time available

Therapeutics and Nursing Considerations

Treatment should be instituted immediately. The objectives of treatment are to prevent further growth or multiplication of thrombi in the lower extremities, to prevent embolization from the upper or lower extremities to the pulmonary vascular system, and to provide cardiopulmonary support if indicated. The following treatments may be needed:

- Oxygen by mask or nasal cannula
- Mechanical ventilation
- Thrombolytic therapy may be used to dissolve clots.
- IV anticoagulant therapy will be initiated to prevent further clots from forming.
- Pulmonary embolectomy may be done in life-threatening situations.

Nursing care will focus on the following considerations:

- Minimizing the risk for more thrombi development
- Monitoring anticoagulation therapy and thrombolytic therapy
- Managing pain
- Managing oxygen therapy
- Relieving anxiety
- Monitoring for complications
- Educating the client and family regarding ways to prevent further thrombi formation

PNEUMOTHORAX

Pathophysiology

A pneumothorax is air in the pleural space. There is a resultant complete or partial collapse of a lung due to the accumulation of this air. Pneumothorax may be closed or open and, when associated with trauma, may be accompanied by hemothorax, a condition called hemopneumothorax. A closed pneumothorax has no associated external wound. The most common form is a spontaneous pneumothorax, which is accumulation of air in the pleural space without an apparent reason. It is caused by the following conditions:

- Rupture of small blebs on the visceral pleural space
- Trauma
- TB
- COPD
- Spontaneous pneumothorax may occasionally occur in lean adolescents and young clients with no apparent precipitating cause.

An open pneumothorax occurs when air enters the pleural space through an opening in the chest wall, such as a stab or gunshot wound. A penetrating chest wound is often referred to as a sucking chest wound. Tension pneumothorax is a pneumothorax with rapid accumulation of air in the pleural space causing severely high intrapleural pressures with resultant tension on the heart and great vessels. In tension pneumothorax, air that enters the pleural space during expiration does not exit during inspiration.

Clinical Manifestations

Pneumothorax may not produce symptoms in mild cases, but in moderate to severe cases, it may produce the following symptoms:

- Profound respiratory distress
- Weak rapid pulse, pallor, jugular vein distension
- Anxiety
- Severe chest pain accompanied by tachypnea
- Asymmetrical chest wall movement
- Dyspnea, cyanosis, decreased or absent chest sounds, or hyper-resonance on the affected side

Diagnostics

Diagnosis is made from a chest X-ray revealing air in the pleural space and a possible mediastinal shift. ABGs reveal hypoxemia and respiratory alkalosis. ECG changes may be present.

Therapeutics and Nursing Considerations

Treatment depends on the cause and severity of the pneumothorax.

- In mild cases, re-expansion can be achieved using a conservative approach, with bed rest, oxygen therapy, and close monitoring of the client's vital signs.
- In more severe cases, needle aspiration of the pleural space with a large-bore needle may be required.
- The most definitive and common form of treatment is to insert a chest tube and connect it to suction (usually 20 mm Hg suction). Repeated spontaneous pneumothorax may need to be treated surgically by a partial pleurectomy, stapling, or pleurodesis to promote adherence of the pleurae to one another.

Pneumonia

Pathophysiology

Pneumonia is an acute inflammation of the lungs that commonly impairs gas exchange. The inflammatory response causes fluid or blood to fill the lung tissue, creating an excellent environment for pathogens. The invading pathogen starts changing epithelial lung cells to allow it to adhere to the cell wall. The pathogen then destroys the macrophages that travel to the site, resulting in further congestion with decreased lung ventilation.

Pneumonia is more likely to result when

- Defence mechanisms are incompetent or become overwhelmed. Pneumonia is the leading cause of death in debilitated clients.
- There are infecting pathogens, either bacterial or viral, or chemical or other irritants, such as aspirated material.
- There are predisposing factors that increase the risk of pneumonia, including chronic illness, cancer, abdominal and thoracic surgery, atelectasis, aspiration, colds, COPD, smoking, alcoholism, malnutrition, chemotherapy, radiation, and immuno-suppressive therapy.
- There is onset in the community or within the first two days of hospitalization. This is referred to as community-acquired pneumonia.
- Hospital-acquired pneumonia occurs 48 hours or longer after admission.
- The abnormal entry of secretions into the lower airway causes aspiration pneumonia. There is usually a history of unconsciousness in which the gag and cough reflexes are suppressed. Gastrostomy tube feeding also carries a risk of aspiration pneumonia.

A less severe form of pneumonia is often termed "walking pneumonia." These clients often respond well to treatment at home.

Complications of pneumonia may include the following:

- Pleurisy
- Pleural effusion
- Atelectasis
- Delayed resolution
- Lung abscess
- Empyema
- Pericarditis
- Arthritis
- Meningitis
- Endocarditis

Clinical Manifestations

Clinical manifestations vary depending on the cause of the pneumonia. Symptoms may include fever, chills, tachypnea, tachycardia, dyspnea, cough with production of purulent sputum, hypoxemia, possible pleuritic chest pain, and possible confusion or stupor.

Diagnostics

Diagnosis is suspected by the history and physical examination and confirmed with a chest X-ray showing infiltrates. Blood cultures and sputum smears will define the causative agent.

Therapeutics and Nursing Considerations

Treatment focuses on clearing the infection and improving gas exchange and may include the following:

- Antibiotic therapy
- Oxygen for hypoxemia
- Analgesics for chest pain
- Antipyretics
- Influenza drugs
- Increased fluid intake
- Adequate caloric intake

LUNG CANCER

Pathophysiology

Lung cancer is the leading cause of cancer-related deaths in Canada. It most commonly occurs in individuals over age 50 with a history of cigarette smoking. Smoking is responsible for 80–90% of all lung cancers. Other risk factors for the development of lung cancer include genetic predisposition and exposure to carcinogenic industrial or air pollutants, such as asbestos, uranium arsenic, chromates, radon, nickel, iron, and iron oxides.

Ninety percent of lung cancers originate from the epithelium of the bronchus, developing squamous cell carcinoma. It takes eight to 10 years for a tumour to reach 1 cm, the smallest lesion detectable on X-ray. The lesions usually occur on segmental bronchi and the upper lobes of the lung. Pathological changes in the bronchial system result in hypersecretion of mucus, desquamation of cells, reactive hyperplasia of basal cells, and metaplasia of normal respiratory epithelium to stratified squamous cells.

Lung cancers metastasize by direct extension, blood circulation, and the lymph system. Common sites for metastatic growth include the following:

- Liver
- Brain
- Bones
- Lymph nodes
- Adrenal glands (Lewis et al., 2010)

Clinical Manifestations

Clinical manifestations appear late in the disease and depend on the type of primary lung cancer, location, degree of obstruction, and metastatic spread. The manifestations may include the following:

- Pneumonitis, persistent cough with sputum, and hemoptysis
- Chest pain
- Dyspnea
- Anorexia
- Fatigue
- Nausea and vomiting
- Hoarse voice
- Unilateral paralysis of diaphragm

Diagnostics

Diagnostic studies include a chest X-ray, which can detect a tumour two years before it becomes symptomatic, as well as the following:

- CT scans, MRI, and positron emission tomography (PET) to help find metastatic tumours
- Sputum specimens obtained from fibre-optic bronchoscopy, mediastinoscopy, and video-assisted thoracoscopy for cytological studies
- Biopsy of the tumour, to provide the definitive diagnosis and allow for staging of the cancer

Therapeutics and Nursing Considerations

Treatment involves combinations of surgery, radiation, and chemotherapy. However, surgery is contraindicated for small cell carcinomas. Squamous cell carcinomas, adenocarcinoma, and large cell cancer are likely treated with surgery. Radiation may be used prior to surgery to reduce the tumour size. If the tumour is nonresectable or other conditions, such as cardiac disease, exist, surgery is not an option. Radiation therapy is usually recommended for stage 1 and stage 2 lesions if surgery is contraindicated. Radiation can be used as an adjunct to surgery postoperatively.

Chemotherapy is the primary treatment for small cell lung cancer. Other therapies include biological therapy, prophylactic cranial therapy, bronchoscopic laser therapy, phototherapy, airway stenting, and cryotherapy.

Treatment focuses on providing comprehensive supportive care and client teaching to minimize complications and promote recovery from surgery, radiation, chemotherapy, or all of these. Overall goals include the following:

- Effective breathing patterns
- Adequate airway clearance
- Adequate oxygenation of tissues
- Minimal or no pain

- Providing psychological support and developing realistic attitudes toward treatment and prognosis

HEMATOLOGICAL HEALTH CHALLENGES

ANEMIA

Pathophysiology

Anemia is a decrease in the number of erythrocytes (RBCs), the amount of hemoglobin, or the volume of packed RBCs (hematocrit), all of which will result in a decreased amount of oxygen being delivered to the cells. Anemia is not itself a disease but rather is a clinical sign of an underlying disorder. Anemia can result from blood loss, impaired production of erythrocytes, or increased destruction of erythrocytes. The various types of anemia can be grouped according to a morphological (cellular characteristics) or an etiological (underlying cause) classification. A morphological classification gives information about the size and colour of the RBCs. Etiological classification is related to the underlying cause of the anemia.

Diagnostics

Laboratory assessment is needed to detect the type and size of RBCs as well as possible causes of the anemia. The following laboratory tests are used in the diagnosis:

- Hemoglobin, hematocrit, and reticulocyte counts
- Serum iron levels
- RBC indexes, particularly the mean corpuscular volume

Clinical Manifestations

Symptoms of anemia are caused by the body's response to the level of tissue hypoxia, which will depend on the severity of the anemia. When present, clinical symptoms may include the following:

- Palpitations
- Dyspnea
- Diaphoresis
- Pallor, due to reduced hemoglobin and reduced blood flow to the skin
- Jaundice, due to the increased hemolysis of RBCs, leading to increased concentrations of bilirubin
- Pruritus, due to an increased serum and skin bile salt concentration
- Cardiovascular manifestations of severe anemia result from additional attempts by the heart and lungs to provide adequate amounts of oxygen to the tissues
- Heart rate is increased in an attempt to maintain adequate cardiac output. Murmurs and bruits may develop due to the low viscosity of the blood.
- Angina, myocardial infarction (MI), and heart failure may develop due to the extreme increase in workload of the heart.
- Fatigue is common due to the increased heart rate and ineffective transportation of oxygen to the tissues.

Therapeutics and Nursing Considerations

Treatment of anemia is directed at correcting the cause of the anemia and maintaining adequate tissue perfusion. Acute interventions may include the following:

- Transfusion of blood or blood products
- Drug therapy, such as erythropoietin, vitamins, and supplements
- Oxygen therapy

Nursing considerations will be specific to the client's needs; however, all clients with anemia should be encouraged to balance rest with activity, eat a balanced diet rich in iron and folate, and be compliant with their drug therapy.

APLASTIC ANEMIA

Pathophysiology

Aplastic anemia is a deficiency of circulating RBCs due to failure of the bone marrow to produce these cells. Stem cells in the bone marrow, or the bone marrow matrix itself, are either injured or destroyed, resulting in pancytopenia (decrease in all blood cell types). The damaged marrow is replaced by fat, resulting in bone marrow hypoplasia (decreased hematopoiesis).

Aplastic anemia may be congenital, acquired, or idiopathic. Some causes of aplastic anemia may include the following:

- Adverse drug reactions to certain medications
- Exposure to toxic agents, such as benzene, inorganic arsenic, insecticides, and radiation
- Viral or bacterial infections, such as hepatitis

Clinical Manifestations

Clinical manifestations of aplastic anemia vary with the severity of the pancytopenia. Infection, bleeding tendencies, fatigue, pallor, and dyspnea are common.

Diagnostics

Diagnosis is confirmed by laboratory studies. RBCs, WBCs, and platelets will be decreased. Morphologically, aplastic anemia is considered normocytic, normochromic anemia. A bone marrow biopsy may show hypoplasia or aplasia, with cells being replaced by fat.

Therapeutics and Nursing Considerations

Management of aplastic anemia is based on identifying and removing the causative agent (when possible) and providing supportive care. The following treatments are used:

- Blood transfusions are the mainstay of treatment. Transfusions are discontinued once the bone marrow starts producing RBCs.
- Bone marrow transplantation is the preferred treatment of aplastic anemia for clients needing constant blood transfusions.
- A splenectomy may be performed when the spleen is destroying normal RBCs.

The prognosis for aplastic anemia is poor, with a mortality rate as high as 80–90%. Death may result from bleeding or infection.

SICKLE CELL ANEMIA

Sickle cell anemia is an inherited childhood disorder of autosomal recessive defects, characterized by the presence of an abnormal form of hemoglobin (called sickle cell hemoglobin, or HgbS) in the erythrocyte. This abnormal hemoglobin causes erythrocytes to become rigid and to take on a crescent shape in response to low oxygen levels, causing vaso-occlusive crises, and, over time, tissue hypoxia and necrosis. For more information on sickle cell anemia, see Chapter 10, page 499.

THROMBOCYTOPENIA

Pathophysiology

Thrombocytopenia is characterized by a deficiency of circulating platelets. Platelet disorders can be inherited or acquired due to deceased platelet production, increased sequestration in the spleen, or increased platelet destruction. Types of thrombocytopenia are as follows:

- Acquired thrombocytopenia may result from such drugs as nonsteroidal anti-inflammatory agents or antibiotic chemotherapeutic agents.
- In children, idiopathic thrombocytopenia is common.
- Transient thrombocytopenia may follow a viral infection such as Epstein–Barr virus or other infections.
- Immune (idiopathic) thrombocytopenic purpura (ITP) is an autoimmune disorder with platelet destruction.
- Thrombotic thrombocytopenic purpura (TTP) is a rare disease in which thrombi occlude small vessels.

The key factor with all types of thrombocytopenia is the low platelet level: below 100,000/mL of blood.

Clinical Manifestations

Many clients with thrombocytopenia are asymptomatic. When manifestations are present, the most common symptom is bleeding, usually noticeable only when the platelet count drops below 20,000/mL of blood. The major complication of thrombocytopenia is hemorrhage.

Diagnostics

Diagnosis is made by a laboratory test of platelets. The platelet count will be decreased. For any reduction below 150×10^9/L, thrombocytopenia should be suspected.

Therapeutics and Nursing Considerations

Treatment of thrombocytopenia depends on the etiology of the decreased platelet count. The underlying cause must be treated and may include the following:

- Splenectomy for hypersplenism
- Chemotherapy for acute or chronic leukemia
- Corticosteroids to enhance vascular integrity
- Steroids, danazol, or IV immune globulin for idiopathic thrombocytopenia
- Platelet transfusions for a count below 20×10^9/L
- Plasmapheresis (plasma is removed from the client and replaced with fresh frozen plasma) is the primary treatment for acute thrombocytopenia.

INGESTION, DIGESTION, ABSORPTION, AND ELIMINATION CHALLENGES

NAUSEA AND VOMITING

Nausea is a feeling of discomfort in the epigastrium with a conscious desire to vomit. Vomiting is the forceful ejection of partially digested food and secretions (emesis) from the upper GI tract. Nausea and vomiting can occur independently but usually are closely related and treated as one problem. A client can feel nauseated and vomit in response to many conditions. Some of these conditions include the following:

- Pregnancy
- GI disorders
- Infectious diseases
- Food poisoning
- CNS disorders
- Cardiovascular disorders
- Metabolic disorders and side effects of drugs
- Other triggers of nausea may include odours, intense activity or emotional stress, or certain types of food (Lewis et al., 2010).

Clinical Manifestations

Nausea is a subjective, unpleasant, wavelike sensation the client experiences in the back of the throat, epigastrium, or abdomen. This feeling may or may not lead to the urge to vomit.

Diagnostics

Diagnosis is arrived at via a client history and physical assessment.

Therapeutics and Nursing Considerations

The goals of management are to determine and treat the underlying cause of the vomiting, remove the cause, and provide symptomatic relief. Differentiation between vomiting, regurgitation, and projectile vomiting is important. The colour and odour of the emesis can supply important information. Fecal odour and bile indicate a lower obstruction of the bowel. The colour of the emesis aids in determining whether bleeding is taking place. Many different drugs can be used to treat nausea and vomiting. The exact drug therapy will depend on the cause. IV fluids may be needed to replace fluids and electrolytes. If vomiting is continuous, a nasogastric (NG) tube may be inserted to decompress the stomach. The client will be started on clear fluids when tolerated. The client will be encouraged to drink fluids between meals rather than with meals.

HIATUS HERNIA

Pathophysiology

Hiatus hernia is a protrusion of the stomach into the esophagus through an opening in the diaphragm. A sliding hiatus hernia occurs when the stomach slides through the gastroesophageal junction. A paraesophageal, or rolling, hiatus hernia occurs when the fundus or greater curvature of the stomach rolls up through the esophageal hiatus.

Many different factors may cause the development of a hiatus hernia. These include the following:

- A weakness in the muscles of the diaphragm
- Increased intra-abdominal pressure
- Obesity
- Pregnancy
- Ascites
- Tumour
- Heavy lifting
- Increasing age
- Trauma
- Poor nutrition
- Prolonged recumbent position

Potential complications of hiatus hernia are hemorrhage, obstruction, and strangulation.

Clinical Manifestations

Clinical manifestations are similar to those of gastroesophageal reflux disease (GERD) and are as follows:

- Pyrosis, dysphagia, reflux, and discomfort are associated with position.
- Bending over may cause pain.
- Large meals may cause pain.
- Smoking and alcohol may cause pain.
- Nocturnal symptoms of heartburn are common.
- Reflux symptoms are more common with a sliding hiatus hernia, and fullness is more typical in the paraesophageal hernia.

Complications that may occur with hiatus hernia include GERD, hemorrhage from erosion, stenosis of the esophagus, ulcerations of the herniated portion of the stomach, strangulation of the hernia, and regurgitation with tracheal aspiration (Lewis et al., 2010).

Diagnostics

Diagnosis of hiatus hernia begins with the history and a physical examination as well as barium swallow X-ray, endoscopic examination, or both, looking for any protrusion of the gastric mucosa through the esophageal hiatus or abnormalities in the mucosa.

Therapeutics and Nursing Considerations

Conservative care is attempted first and may include the following:

- Lifestyle modifications similar to those for GERD
- Elevation of the head of the bed to 30 degrees
- Use of antacids and antisecretory agents such as H_2 receptor blockers
- Weight reduction if the client is overweight

Surgical treatments attempt to reduce reflux by enhancing the integrity of the lower esophageal sphincter (LES). Different types of surgery all involve "wrapping" the fundus of the stomach around the lower portion of the esophagus in order to reduce the hernia, provide acceptable LES pressure, and prevent movement of the gastroesophageal junction. Postoperative care involves the following:

- Monitoring vital signs and airway and chest sounds
- Monitoring any chest tubes and possible respiratory distress
- Monitoring an abdominal incision for infection
- Monitoring the NG tube for patency and checking the abdomen for distension
- Always assessing clients for venous thrombus following these types of surgery

Education of the client will revolve around preventing respiratory complications by deep breathing and coughing frequently. Clients should be taught to prevent gas-bloat syndrome by slowing and progressively advancing their diet. Small, frequent meals will prevent overloading of the stomach. Carbonated drinks and gas-producing foods should be avoided (Black & Hawks, 2009).

Esophageal Cancer

Pathophysiology

Factors predisposing to the development of esophageal cancer include the following:

- Smoking and excessive alcohol use
- A diet low in fruits, vegetables, and certain vitamins and minerals, which increases the risk
- Achalasia (peristalsis is absent in the lower two-thirds of the esophagus), which results in delayed emptying of the lower esophagus; exposure to asbestos and metal; and a history of swallowing lye

Cancer of the esophagus is caused by malignant advancement into the esophageal area. If the malignancy spreads into the submucosa, the risk for metastasis and death increases drastically. The major types of esophageal cancers are adenocarcinoma and squamous cell cancers.

Complications with esophageal cancers include the following:

- Hemorrhage that may occur if cancer erodes through the esophagus and into the aorta
- Esophageal perforation with fistula formation into the lung or trachea
- Obstruction of the esophagus
- Spread of the cancer through the lymph system; the liver and lungs are common sites of metastasis

Clinical Manifestations

Symptoms appear late in the development, usually when the esophagus is 50–60% occluded, and include progressive dysphagia, pain in the epigastric area, substernally, or in the back, which may radiate to the neck and jaw. Other common symptoms may include a sore throat, choking and hoarseness, and weight loss.

Diagnostics

Diagnostic tests used to find esophageal cancer include barium swallow with fluoroscopy, which may show a narrowing of the esophagus at the site of the tumour. Endoscopy and biopsy are needed to make a definitive diagnosis and identify the malignant cells. A CT scan and MRI may be needed to assess the extent of the disease.

Therapeutics and Nursing Considerations

Since the disease is often not diagnosed until late in its development, the prognosis is poor. Treatments include the following:

- Surgery, which may include esophagectomy, removal of part or all of the esophagus
- Esophagogastrostomy, resection of a portion of the esophagus and anastomosis of the remaining portion to the stomach
- Esophagoenterostomy, resection of a portion of the esophagus and anastomosis of a segment of colon to the remaining portion
- Chemotherapy and radiation before or after the surgery

Palliative therapy consists of restoration of the swallowing function and maintenance of nutrition and hydration. Once the client is allowed to eat, he or she must be monitored for intolerance to feeding or leakage of the food into the mediastinum. Further palliative care focuses on pain management and maintaining as normal a lifestyle as possible.

Peptic Ulcer Disease

Pathophysiology

Peptic ulcer disease includes conditions characterized by erosion of the GI mucosa in the lower esophagus, stomach and duodenum, and jejunum. The ulcer may be acute with either superficial or minimal erosion. It can be of short duration and resolve quickly when the cause is identified and removed. A chronic ulcer is of long duration, eroding through the muscular wall with the formation of fibrous tissue. Peptic ulcers develop only in the presence of an acid environment. The stomach is normally protected from autodigestion and damage by the gastric mucosal barrier. When that barrier is damaged, acid–pepsin freely enters the mucosa, and cellular inflammation and destruction occur. The precise cause of peptic ulcers is not known; however, common risk factors include the following.

- *Helicobacter pylori* infection
- The use of NSAIDs, salicylates, or steroids
- Exposure to irritants, such as alcohol, coffee, and tobacco, increases the risk of peptic ulcer development.
- Other predisposing factors include emotional stress, physical trauma, and aging.

The major complications of peptic ulcers include hemorrhage, perforation, and gastric outlet obstruction. All three complications are considered emergencies requiring prompt medical treatment.

Clinical Manifestations

Clinical manifestations are variable. Those with gastric or duodenal ulcers often do not have any pain. When pain is present, it is described as burning or cramplike and most often is located in the midepigastric region. Eating or ingesting antacids often relieves the pain.

Diagnostics

Diagnostic testing includes the following:

- An upper GI tract X-ray will show abnormalities in the mucosa.
- A barium swallow examination can diagnose gastric outlet obstruction.
- Gastric secretory studies will show hyperchlorhydria.
- An upper GI endoscopy will confirm the presence of an ulcer.
- A biopsy will help rule out cancer.
- A serological or breath urea test is done to test for the presence of *H. pylori*.
- Stool may need to be tested for occult blood.

Therapeutics and Nursing Considerations

Treatment is essentially symptomatic, with an emphasis on drug therapy and rest. The following treatments are used:

- Antacids reduce gastric acidity. Proton pump inhibitors reduce gastric secretions in short-term therapy.
- Anticholinergics inhibit the vagus nerve effect on the parietal cells and reduce gastrin production and excessive gastric activity in duodenal ulcers.
- Antibiotic treatment may be used to reduce *H. pylori*.
- Physical rest promotes healing.
- Gastroscopy can facilitate coagulation of the bleeding site by cautery or laser therapy.
- If hemorrhage occurs, saline lavage, sclerotherapy, and angiography with vasopressin may postpone the need for surgery until the client stabilizes.

Surgery is indicated for clients with perforation or those unresponsive to conservative measures. Surgical procedures include vagotomy and pyloroplasty or distal subtotal gastrectomy.

Nutritional therapy identifies foods that cause distress, such as the following:

- Hot, spicy foods and pepper
- Alcohol
- Carbonated drinks
- Tea and coffee
- Foods high in roughage, which may irritate an inflamed mucosa
- Protein is considered the best neutralizing food, but it does stimulate gastric secretions.

- Milk can neutralize gastric activity and contains prostaglandins and growth factors.

Diet should consist of small dry feedings daily that are low in carbohydrates and that include a moderate amount of protein and fat. Fluids should not be taken during the meal. Clients are encouraged to rest for 30 minutes following every meal.

With an acute exacerbation when bleeding is occurring, the client often has increased pain with nausea and vomiting. The following treatment is required in this situation:

- An NG tube will be placed in the stomach with intermittent suction for 24–48 hours.
- Fluids and electrolytes will be replaced by IV infusion until the client is able to tolerate oral feedings without distress.

Management will be similar to that for upper GI bleeding. Blood, blood products, or both may be needed. The client will require the following nursing considerations:

- Careful monitoring of vital signs
- Monitoring of intake and output
- Laboratory studies
- Monitoring for signs of impending shock
- Endoscopic evaluation will reveal the degree of inflammation or bleeding as well as the location of the ulcer.

Perforation of the ulcer requires immediate action to stop spillage of gastric or duodenal contents into the peritoneal cavity and to restore blood volume. The following interventions are essential:

- An NG tube will be placed into the stomach as close to the perforation as possible.
- Circulating blood volume must be replaced.
- Packed RBCs may be needed.
- A central venous pressure line may be needed.
- An in-dwelling urinary catheter should be inserted and monitored every hour.

Surgery is not the usual method of treatment; however, it is indicated for such conditions as an intractable ulcer, history of hemorrhage, perforation, or obstruction. Surgical procedures done to treat ulcers include gastroduodenostomy (Billroth I), gastrojejunostomy (Billroth II), vagotomy, and pyloroplasty.

Postoperative complications include dumping syndrome, postprandial hypoglycemia, and bile reflux gastritis. The dumping syndrome is a direct result of surgical removal of a large portion of the stomach and pyloric sphincter. The syndrome results from the rapid emptying of gastric contents into the small bowel, which creates a fluid shift into the gut, resulting in abdominal distension. The client will feel dizzy and weak and complain of abdominal cramps.

GASTRITIS

Pathophysiology

Gastritis is not a disease but rather a condition of inflammation of the gastric mucosa. Acute gastritis is often due to the following:

- Eating foods contaminated with microorganisms or food that is highly seasoned.
- Chronic gastritis is sometimes associated with autoimmune disease, such as pernicious anemia.
- It can also be due to benign or malignant ulcers caused by *H. pylori* bacteria.

Gastritis occurs as a result of a breakdown in the gastric mucosal barrier. In gastritis, the mucous membrane becomes edematous and hyperemic and undergoes superficial erosion. This erosion may lead to hemorrhage.

Clinical Manifestations

Acute and chronic symptoms are the same and include anorexia, nausea and vomiting, epigastric tenderness, and a feeling of fullness. Hemorrhage is particularly common with alcohol abuse.

Diagnostics

Diagnosis is often suspected with a thorough history and physical examination where ingestion of drugs and alcohol may be discussed. Definitive diagnosis is made with an endoscopic examination and biopsy of the gastric mucosa from which a histological examination will occur. Upper GI radiographic studies may be ordered.

Therapeutics and Nursing Considerations

Treatment and management revolve around removal of the precipitating cause. Initially, the client will be nothing by mouth (NPO), with possible NG insertion to remove the causative agent. The client must be monitored for dehydration, which can occur quickly. Drug therapy focuses on reducing irritation of the gastric mucosa and providing symptomatic relief. Antacids and H_2 receptor blockers such as Zantac are helpful in reducing HCl secretion and in raising the pH to a more alkaline level. Nursing considerations will focus on promoting optimal nutrition, promoting fluid balance, relieving pain, and promoting self-care.

GASTROESOPHAGEAL REFLUX DISEASE

Pathophysiology

GERD refers to any clinically significant symptomatic condition of reflux of the gastric contents into the lower esophagus. There is no single cause for GERD. Predisposing factors include the following:

- Hiatus hernia
- Incompetent LES
- Decreased gastric emptying
- Pyloric stenosis

The acidic gastric secretions that reflux up into the lower esophagus result in esophageal irritation, inflammation, and corrosion.

Clinical Manifestations

Clinical manifestations include heartburn, described as a burning or tight sensation radiating to the neck. Clients with heartburn that occurs more than once a week, becomes more severe, or occurs at night and wakes the client from sleep should be investigated for GERD. Regurgitation is common and is frequently described as hot, bitter, or sour liquid coming into the mouth or throat.

Gastric symptoms may also include the following, which are related to delayed gastric emptying:

- Early satiety
- Postmeal bloating
- Nausea, vomiting

Diagnostics

Diagnosis of GERD is made by barium swallow or endoscopy to evaluate damage to the esophageal mucosa. Other tests may include biopsy with histological examination, esophageal manometric studies to monitor pH, and radionuclide tests to detect reflux and the rate of esophageal clearance.

Therapeutics and Nursing Considerations

Management focuses on lifestyle modifications and avoidance of situations that decrease LES pressure or that cause esophageal irritation. Nutritionally, clients are encouraged to avoid high-fat foods, avoid milk products at night, and avoid late-night snacking.

Drug therapy may include the following:

- H_2 receptor blockers
- Proton pump inhibitors
- Antacids
- Sucralfate
- Prokinetic drugs

If medical management is unsuccessful, fundoplication surgery (wrapping a portion of the gastric fundus around the sphincter of the esophagus) is performed. Nurses need to educate clients to

- Avoid factors causing reflux, such as smoking and acid-producing foods.

- Have the head of the bed elevated to about 30 degrees.
- Not lie down for two to three hours after eating.
- Take medications correctly.

GASTROENTERITIS

Pathophysiology

Gastroenteritis is an inflammation of the mucosa of the stomach and small intestine, resulting in vomiting and diarrhea. The condition usually is caused by infectious agents, such as the noroviruses and *Escherichia coli*. Most cases are self-limiting and do not require hospitalization. However, older adults and chronically ill clients may be unable to consume adequate fluids orally to compensate for fluid loss.

If symptoms are severe, or if the client is experiencing frequent watery stools, a culture for *Clostridium difficile* should be performed.

Clinical Manifestations

Clinical manifestations include the following:

- Nausea and vomiting
- Diarrhea
- Possible fever
- Abdominal cramping and distension
- Depending on the amount of fluid that is lost, the client may experience symptoms of hypovolemia.

Diagnostics

The history and physical examination of the client are usually diagnostic. However, Gram stain of stool specimens will confirm the causative agent.

Therapeutics and Nursing Considerations

Until vomiting stops, the client should be NPO. Thereafter, the client should have bland food and fluids as tolerated. Most gastroenteritis is managed at home. If the symptoms are severe, the following treatments may be needed:

- IV replacement therapy for dehydration
- Accurate monitoring of intake and output
- Potassium supplements
- Antibiotic, antimicrobial therapy, if the causative organism is identified
- Enteric precautions

Symptomatic nursing care is given for nausea, vomiting, and diarrhea. The nurse should assess complaints of pain, vomiting, and diarrhea as gastroenteritis is often confused with appendicitis.

APPENDICITIS

Pathophysiology

Appendicitis is an inflammation of the vermiform appendix, a narrow, fingerlike appendage found just below the ileocecal valve. Inflammation of the appendix usually occurs when the lumen is obstructed by fecal material, foreign bodies, or a tumour of the cecum. This obstruction can lead to distension, venous engorgement, and the accumulation of mucus and bacteria, which can, in turn, lead to gangrene and perforation of the appendix. If the appendix ruptures or perforates, the infected contents can spill into the abdominal cavity, causing peritonitis.

Clinical Manifestations

Appendicitis typically begins with periumbilical pain, followed by anorexia, nausea, and vomiting. The pain eventually will shift to the right lower quadrant and localize at McBurney's point, with rebound tenderness and muscle guarding. The client will probably want to lie still with knees flexed. Coughing aggravates the pain.

Diagnostics

Diagnosis of appendicitis can be difficult, so although the history and physical examination are important, further tests should be done, including the following:

- Rovsing's sign may be elicited by palpating the left lower quadrant.
- WBCs will be elevated, but this is not considered diagnostic.
- An ultrasonogram or CT scan of the abdomen is often needed to confirm the diagnosis.
- NeuroSpec imaging is a new technique that helps detect infection using a gamma camera and that can diagnose appendicitis within an hour.

Therapeutics and Nursing Considerations

Appendectomy is the only effective treatment for appendicitis. If the appendix has ruptured, treatment will also include insertion of an NG tube, IV fluids and electrolytes, and administration of antibiotics. Nursing care will focus on the following:

- Pain relief
- Maintaining fluid balance
- Support to reduce anxiety
- Maintaining skin integrity
- Monitoring and managing complications that may arise

DIVERTICULITIS

Pathophysiology

The diverticulum is a saccular outpouching of the mucosa through the muscular intestinal wall. Diverticulitis is an inflammation of the diverticular sacs, most commonly due to obstruction with fecal matter. Diverticula may occur at any point within the GI tract but are more commonly found in the sigmoid colon.

Diverticula in the sigmoid colon are thought to be associated with high luminal pressure from a deficiency in dietary fibre perhaps combined with a loss of muscle mass and collagen with the aging process. When diverticula form, the smooth muscle of the colon wall becomes thickened. Lack of dietary fibre slows transit time and more water is absorbed from the stool, making it more difficult for it to pass through the lumen. Decreased stool size raises intraluminal pressure, thus promoting diverticula formation.

Clinical Manifestations

The majority of people with diverticulitis are asymptomatic. When symptoms are present, they usually include the following:

- Abdominal pain localized over the involved area of the colon
- Fever
- Leukocytosis
- Sometimes a palpable mass

Complications of diverticulitis include perforation with peritonitis, abscess and fistula formation, bowel obstructions, ureteral obstruction, and bleeding.

Diagnostics

Diagnostic tests include CBC, urinalysis, and fecal occult blood test, as well as X-ray of the abdomen or ultrasound/CT scan to confirm diagnosis and evaluate the severity of the condition.

Therapeutics and Nursing Considerations

In acute diverticulitis, the goal of treatment is to allow the colon to rest and the inflammation to subside. Treatments include the following:

- Ensuring the client is NPO with IV therapy to maintain fluid and electrolyte balance
- Initiating broad-spectrum antibiotic therapy
- Monitoring the client for signs of peritonitis
- Surgery is reserved for clients with complications such as abscess or obstruction.

Nursing considerations focus on maintaining normal elimination patterns, relief of pain, maintaining fluid balance, and monitoring and managing potential complications. Teaching the client that diverticular disease can be prevented by a diet high in fibre and low in fats is important.

INFLAMMATORY BOWEL DISEASE

Inflammatory bowel disease consists of the immunologically related disorders of Crohn's disease and ulcerative colitis. Inflammatory bowel disease is characterized by chronic, recurrent inflammation of the intestinal tract. Clinical manifestations are varied for both conditions, but these often include long periods of remission interspersed with episodes of acute inflammation. Both diseases can be debilitating. The cause of inflammatory bowel disease is unknown; however, causes may include the following:

- Infectious agents
- Autoimmune reaction
- Food allergies
- Heredity

ULCERATIVE COLITIS

Pathophysiology

Ulcerative colitis is characterized by inflammation and ulceration of the colon and rectum. It may occur at any age but tends to peak between the ages of 15 and 25 years. It is equally prevalent in both sexes. The inflammation of ulcerative colitis usually starts in the rectum and moves in a continuous pattern toward the cecum. Ulcerative colitis is characterized by multiple ulcerations, inflammations, and shedding of the epithelium. The affected mucosa is hyperemic and edematous. The ulcerations destroy the mucosal epithelium, causing bleeding and diarrhea. This can lead to fluid and electrolyte losses, protein losses, and the development of pseudopolyps. Granulation tissue develops, and the mucosa musculature becomes thickened, shortening the colon. Intestinal complications include the following:

- Hemorrhage
- Abscess formation
- Perforation
- Toxic megacolon and colonic dilation
- Cancer

Toxic megacolon is the dilation and paralysis of the colon, which occurs in about 5% of clients and is often associated with perforation.

Clinical Manifestations

Clients with ulcerative colitis usually present with mild to severe acute exacerbations that occur at unpredictable intervals over many years. The major symptoms are bloody diarrhea and abdominal pain.

Diagnostics

Diagnosis of ulcerative colitis includes ruling out other diseases with similar symptoms and determining whether the client has ulcerative colitis or Crohn's disease. The following tests are done:

- CBC, serum electrolytes, and serum protein levels
- Stool will be examined for blood, pus, and mucus.
- Sigmoidoscopy and colonoscopy examination of the mucosa to look for inflammation, ulcerations, pseudopolyps, and strictures
- A double-contrast barium enema for areas of granular inflammation with ulceration

Therapeutics and Nursing Considerations

Goals of treatment include the following:

- Resting the bowel
- Control of inflammation
- Combating infection
- Correcting malnutrition
- Alleviating stress
- Symptomatic relief and improving quality of life
- Sulfasalazines are the principal drugs of choice. They are effective in the maintenance of remission.
- Other medications that may be used are corticosteroids, 5-ASA and 4-ASA, and immuno-suppressants such as Imuran.

Surgery is indicated if the client does not respond to medical treatment, has frequent or debilitating exacerbations, has massive bleeding or obstruction, or develops dysplasia or carcinoma. Surgical procedures include total proctocolectomy with permanent ileostomy, total proctocolectomy with continent ileostomy (Kock pouch), or total colectomy with rectal mucosal stripping and ileoanal reservoir.

Postoperatively, the nurse must monitor for the following:

- Stoma viability, mucocutaneous juncture, and peristomal skin integrity
- Signs of hemorrhage, abdominal abscess, small bowel obstruction, dehydration, and other complications

Diet is an important component in the treatment of ulcerative colitis. The goal is to provide adequate nutrition without exacerbating symptoms. This diet must correct and prevent malnutrition, replace fluid and electrolyte losses, and prevent weight loss. The diet should be

- High calorie
- High protein

- Low residue with vitamin and mineral supplements

Other nursing considerations include the following:

- Maintaining normal elimination patterns
- Relieving pain
- Promoting rest
- Reducing anxiety
- Preventing skin breakdown
- Enhancing coping mechanisms

CROHN'S DISEASE

Pathophysiology

Crohn's disease is a chronic nonspecific inflammatory bowel disorder of unknown origin that can affect any part of the GI tract from mouth to anus. Crohn's disease can occur at any age but usually presents between the ages of 15 and 30 years and affects both sexes equally.

Crohn's disease is characterized by inflammation of segments of the GI tract, and although the disease can affect any section, it is most often found in the terminal ileum. The inflammation of Crohn's disease affects all layers of the bowel wall. Eventually, deep ulcerations develop. There are also "skip lesions," in which segments of normal bowel occur between diseased portions. As the disease continues, the wall of the bowel thickens, and as strictures develop, the lumen of the bowel narrows. Severe diarrhea and malabsorption of nutrients result from the damaged bowel. Complications of Crohn's disease are similar to those of ulcerative colitis.

Clinical Manifestations

The onset of Crohn's disease is usually insidious, with nonspecific complaints of the following:

- Diarrhea
- Fatigue
- Abdominal pain
- Weight loss
- Fever

Diarrhea (non-bloody) and abdominal pain are usually the symptoms that cause the client to seek medical attention. As the disease progresses, the pain may increase in severity, abdominal distension may develop, and the client may develop arthritis and finger clubbing.

Diagnostics

Diagnostic studies are similar to those needed for ulcerative colitis, including barium studies, endoscopy with biopsy, blood work, and upper GI barium swallow.

Therapeutics and Nursing Considerations

The goals of treatment revolve around controlling the inflammatory process, relieving symptoms, correcting metabolic and nutritional problems, and promoting healing of the affected area.

Treatments include the following:

- Drug therapy similar to that used with ulcerative colitis. Sulfasalazines, corticosteroids, immunosuppressive agents, metronidazole, and infliximab may be used.
- Nutritional therapy, including elemental diets; parenteral nutrition when needed; and low-residue, low-roughage, low-fat, high-calorie, and high-protein diets are recommended.

The majority of clients will eventually require surgery at least once in the course of their disease. The disease is not cured by surgery, and the recurrence rate following surgery is high.

Nursing management is similar to that required for ulcerative colitis, with frequent rest periods and skin care. Client education is very important. Teaching includes the following:

- The importance of rest and diet management
- Teaching about the medications, what they are, why they are needed, and what they will do for the client helps clients be compliant with their medications. Clients should also be taught about possible side effects of their medications, as well as symptoms of disease recurrence.
- When to seek medical care
- The use of diversional activities to reduce stress

Colorectal Cancer

Pathophysiology

Colorectal cancer (CRC) is equally common in men and women. Nearly all CRCs are adenocarcinomas, most arising from adenomatous polyps. Tumours spread through the walls of the intestine and into the lymphatic system. Tumours commonly spread to the liver because venous blood flow from the colorectal tumour is through the portal vein.

CRC is the third leading cause of death from cancer in Canada. However, if diagnosed early, the cure rate is very high. Screening via colonoscopy for all persons over 50 years is now recommended.

The cause of CRC is unclear. However, risk factors for the development of CRC include the following:

- Familial tendencies
- Increasing age
- A diet high in fat and calories
- A history of inflammatory bowel disease

Clinical Manifestations

Clinical manifestations are nonspecific and may not appear until the disease is advanced. Most people with CRC have hematochezia (passage of blood through the rectum) or melena (black tarry stools) and abdominal pain or changes in bowel habits, or both. Occult bleeding and iron deficiency anemia lead to weakness and fatigue. The signs of CRC depend on the location of the tumour.

- Left-sided lesions tend to bleed. Clients tend to alternate between constipation and diarrhea, and they tend to have narrow, ribbonlike stools.
- Right-sided lesions are usually asymptomatic or cause vague abdominal discomfort.

In later stages, findings result from extension of the cancer to adjacent organs and reflect the symptoms of advanced cancer.

Diagnostics

Diagnostic studies include family history and physical examination, distal rectal examination, colonoscopy, endorectal ultrasonography, CT scan, fecal occult blood tests, and carcinoembryonic antigen. Only a biopsy will verify the presence of CRC.

Therapeutics and Nursing Considerations

Prognosis and treatment correlate with the pathological staging of the disease. Surgery seeks to remove the cancerous tumour and adjacent tissues, as well as lymph nodes that may contain cancer cells. Chemotherapy and radiation therapy are recommended for clients with positive lymph node involvement at the time of surgery or those who have metastatic disease. Chemotherapy and radiation may be the primary treatment when the CRC is nonresectable.

- A right hemicolectomy for advanced tumours of the cecum or ascending colon may include resection of the terminal segment of the ileum, cecum, ascending colon, and right half of the transverse colon with corresponding mesentery.
- A right colectomy may be done for tumours of the proximal and middle transverse colon, which includes the resection of the transverse colon and mesentery corresponding to midcolonic vessels.
- Alternatively, the surgeon may perform segmental resection of the transverse colon and associated midcolonic vessels.
- For sigmoid colon tumours, surgery is usually limited to the sigmoid colon and mesentery.
- Upper rectum tumours usually call for anterior or low anterior resection. A newer method, using a stapler, allows resection much lower than previously possible.

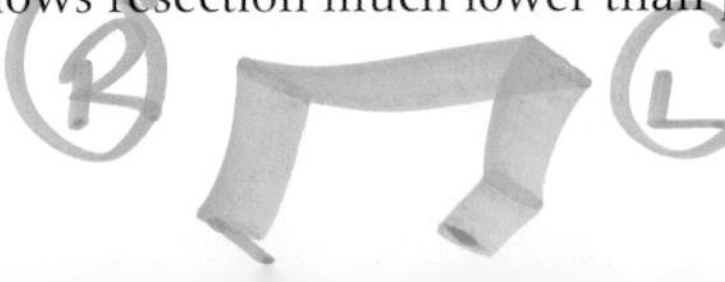

- For tumours in the lower rectum, abdominoperineal resection and permanent sigmoid colostomy are usually performed.

The overall goals for the client being treated for CRC are to attain normal bowel elimination patterns, maintain quality of life appropriate for the disease progression, be free of pain, and maintain feelings of comfort and well-being.

Other nursing considerations include the following:

- Providing emotional support
- Maintaining optimal nutrition
- Providing pain relief
- Providing wound care following a surgical procedure
- Educating about colostomy care, if applicable
- Supporting a positive image

Jaundice

Pathophysiology

Jaundice results from bilirubin diffusing into tissues and giving them a yellow or greenish-yellow tinge. In the spleen, during RBC destruction, the heme is separated from the globulin. The heme further breaks down to iron and biliverdin. The biliverdin then becomes unconjugated (lipid-soluble) bilirubin. In the blood, this unconjugated bilirubin joins with albumin, which makes it soluble in the blood. The bilirubin then travels via the blood to the liver. The hepatocytes within the liver join the unconjugated bilirubin with glucuronic acid, conjugating the bilirubin and making it water soluble. This conjugated bilirubin is excreted in bile, urine, and feces.

Jaundice is often the first and sometimes the only symptom of liver disease. In hepatitis, it is evident in the icteric phase as hyperbilirubinemia.

The three major types of jaundice are hemolytic, hepatocellular, and obstructive jaundice.

Hemolytic Jaundice

Hemolytic jaundice occurs when there is an increase in the number of RBCs destroyed, which increases the amount of unconjugated bilirubin in the blood. The liver cannot handle the increased load, and the increased unconjugated bilirubin remains in the blood and is not excreted in the urine or feces. Predisposing factors that may cause hemolytic jaundice are the following:

- Blood transfusions
- Anemia, especially sickle cell
- Reabsorption of extravascular blood found postoperatively or in hematomas
- Certain medications, such as chlorpromazine and penicillin

Hepatocellular Jaundice

Hepatocellular jaundice develops from damaged liver cells that are unable to clear bilirubin from the blood. There is impairment of uptake, conjugation, and excretion of bilirubin. Bile salts will deposit on the skin, and the client will have yellow discoloration. Predisposing factors for hepatocellular jaundice include hepatitis, cirrhosis, and liver cancer.

Obstructive Jaundice

Obstructive jaundice results from an obstruction to bile flow. Bile will back up into the liver and then into the blood. Urine will take on a deep orange colour. Stool will be light or clay coloured. Pruritus will be evident. Intrahepatic predisposing factors include the following:

- Swelling or fibrosis of the canaliculi and bile ducts in the liver
- Hepatitis
- Cirrhosis
- Tumours
- Medications

Predisposing extrahepatic factors include bile duct obstruction.

Clinical Manifestations

Body tissues including the sclera and skin become yellow or greenish-yellow tinged. The urine may be dark brown or brownish-red due to the presence of bilirubin. Depending on the cause of the jaundice, the client may experience the following symptoms:

- Loss of appetite
- Nausea
- Malaise
- Fatigue
- Weakness
- Pruritus
- Dyspepsia
- Intolerance to fatty foods

Diagnostics

The history and physical examination are important in diagnosing jaundice. Blood work including serum bilirubin, both direct and indirect, will assist in finding the cause of the jaundice. Liver function tests will give information regarding problems with the liver. Viral hepatitis testing may be needed.

Therapeutics and Nursing Considerations

Nursing management involves promoting the following:

- Acceptance of altered body image
- Control of pruritus

- Preventing skin irritation or injury
- Administering medications
- Monitoring clinical findings and laboratory data
- Providing distraction and rest

Adequate nutrition can be a challenge as the clients are often anorexic. Offering small frequent meals of foods that the client enjoys can be beneficial. Measures to stimulate the appetite, such as mouth care and antiemetics, should be included in the nursing plan. Rest is an important factor in promoting liver cell regeneration (Lewis et al., 2010). To treat the irritating pruritus, lanolin oil or oatmeal may be added to the bath. Skin irritation and injury can be prevented by keeping nails short or wearing mitts. Antihistamines may be prescribed in some situations.

Psychological and emotional rest is as essential as physical rest. Strict bed rest may produce anxiety and extreme restlessness in some clients, which may be more damaging than reasonable ambulation (Lewis et al., 2010). Educating the family is important so they understand what is happening to the client. Family can be very instrumental in supplying diversional activities.

Cholelithiasis

Pathophysiology

Cholelithiasis refers to stones in the gallbladder. Cholecystitis, or inflammation of the gallbladder, is usually associated with cholelithiasis. The stones vary in size, shape, and composition and may be lodged in the neck of the gallbladder or in the cystic duct and common bile duct. Cholelithiasis may be acute or chronic. The incidence is higher in multiparous women over the age of 40 years. Sedentary lifestyle, obesity, and family tendency also are risk factors.

The actual cause of the stone is unknown. The most common gallstones are formed from cholesterol, a major component of bile. The stones may remain in the gallbladder or migrate to the cystic duct or common bile duct. They cause pain as they pass through the ducts and may lodge in the ducts and produce an obstruction. Stasis of bile in the gallbladder can lead to cholecystitis.

Clinical Manifestations

Cholelithiasis may produce severe symptoms or none at all. Severity of symptoms depends on whether the stones are stationary or mobile and whether obstruction is present. When the stones are lodged in the cystic duct, the obstruction prevents the movement of bile, so the gallbladder becomes distended, inflamed, and possibly infected. This results in biliary colic with severe upper right abdominal pain that radiates to the back or right shoulder. Other symptoms may include the following:

- Tachycardia
- Diaphoresis
- Nausea and vomiting

Pain may last up to an hour, and when it subsides, a residual tenderness in the right upper quadrant is usually felt. The attacks frequently occur three to six hours after a heavy meal or when the client lies down. When total obstruction occurs, symptoms related to bile blockage are manifested, including steatorrhea, pruritus, dark amber urine, a tendency to bleed, and jaundice.

Diagnostics

The following tests are used in the diagnosis:

- Ultrasonography to diagnose gallstones
- CT scan to identify ductal stones
- Endoscopic retrograde cholangiopancreatography (ERCP) allows for visualization of the gallbladder, cystic duct, common hepatic duct, and common bile duct. Bile taken during the procedure is sent for analysis to identify any possible infecting organism.
- Percutaneous transhepatic cholangiography may be used to diagnose obstructive jaundice and to locate stones within the bile ducts.
- Laboratory studies may demonstrate liver function test abnormalities, elevated serum enzymes, pancreatic enzymes, increased WBCs, elevated direct and indirect bilirubin levels, and urinary bilirubin.

Therapeutics and Nursing Considerations

Cholelithiasis is most commonly treated by means of ERCP, which will clear the stones from the biliary tree. In some cases, surgical intervention is needed. Cholecystectomy is often the preferred surgical procedure. This can be done through laparoscopic surgery, in which the gallbladder is removed through one of four tiny punctures in the abdominal wall. Clients experience minimal postoperative pain and are usually discharged home the day of surgery or the day after surgery. Nonsurgical removal of gallstones involves dissolving the gallstones, using extracorporeal shock-wave lithotripsy or intracorporeal lithotripsy, but these methods have proven to be only temporary solutions. Drug therapy for gallbladder disease includes the following:

- Analgesics
- Anticholinergics
- Fat-soluble vitamins
- Bile salts
- Some pharmacological therapy can be used to dissolve small stones. This method of treatment is beneficial for clients unable to undergo surgery.

Nurses need to focus on the following considerations:

- Pain relief
- Improving respiratory status
- Promoting skin care
- Promoting biliary drainage
- Improving nutritional status
- Monitoring for potential complications
- Nutritional therapy for clients with cholelithiasis is a low-fat diet. If obesity is a problem, a low-calorie diet is also recommended.

HEPATITIS

Pathophysiology

Hepatitis is an inflammation of the liver marked by liver cell destruction, necrosis, and autolysis. In most clients, hepatic cells eventually regenerate, with little or no residual damage. However, advanced age and serious underlying disorders make complications more likely. Prognosis is poorer if edema and hepatic encephalopathy develop. The most common cause of hepatitis is viral infection.

Viral hepatitis may be caused by one of five viruses:

1. Hepatitis type A (HAV) is transmitted almost exclusively by the fecal–oral route, and outbreaks are common in areas of overcrowding and poor sanitation. Day care centres and other institutional settings are common sources of outbreaks. The incidence is also increasing in homosexuals and in people with HIV. HAV is the most common type of hepatitis worldwide.
2. Hepatitis type B (HBV) is transmitted by blood and blood products, by sexual intercourse, and through perinatal transmission.
3. Hepatitis type C (HCV) is transmitted by blood and blood products as well as sexual activity with an infected partner. HCV accounts for 45% of all cases of hepatitis and is the most common liver disease in Canada. Approximately 40% of people infected with HIV also have HCV.
4. Hepatitis type D (HDV) can cause an infection only if HBV is present; therefore, the routes of transmission are blood and blood products, as well as sexual intercourse with an infected partner.
5. Hepatitis type E (HEV) is transmitted by the fecal–oral route.

Infection with HAV or HBV provides immunity to that virus, but the client may still develop another type of viral hepatitis. Clients with HCV can be infected with another strain of hepatitis C.

Hepatitis may also be caused by CMV, Epstein–Barr virus, the herpes virus, coxsackievirus, and the rubella virus. Despite the different causative viruses, changes in the liver are usually similar in each type of viral hepatitis.

Liver damage is mediated by cytotoxic cytokines and NK cells that cause lysis of infected hepatocytes. In hepatitis, liver cell damage results in hepatic cell necrosis. This necrosis occurs in a spotty fashion, resulting in a piecemeal appearance. Many of the cells swell and rupture, while others shrink. Inflammation then occurs with proliferation and enlargement of the Kupffer cells. Inflammation of the periportal areas may interrupt bile flow, causing jaundice. Cholestasis may occur, as well as hepatomegaly and splenomegaly. Regeneration of liver tissue normally occurs alongside the death of liver cells. The ongoing necrosis, inflammation, and regeneration distort the normal structure and may interfere with blood and bile flow. If there are no complications, the liver cells will resume their normal appearance and function. Along with the hepatic changes, there may be some systemic effects, which may include rash, angioedema, arthritis, fever, and malaise.

Thirty percent of clients with HBV and 89% of clients with HCV are asymptomatic. Most clients with hepatitis recover completely, with no complications. The mortality rate is <1%. Complications due to hepatitis include fulminant hepatic failure, chronic hepatitis, cirrhosis, and hepatocellular carcinoma. Fulminant hepatitis is a clinical syndrome that results in severe impairment or necrosis of liver cells and potential liver failure. Fulminant hepatitis is rapid but rare. Chronic persistent hepatitis is the most common complication. It may be benign in HBV and HCV recovery and can be found with asymptomatic carriers.

Chronic active hepatitis is a persistence of symptoms of hepatitis and abnormal laboratory values for more than six months. A large percentage of those with HCV (85%) develop chronic active hepatitis, which is ongoing liver necrosis likely progressing to cirrhosis of the liver.

The characteristics of hepatitis viruses are summarized in Table 8.8.

Clinical Manifestations

The three phases of hepatitis are the preicteric phase, the icteric phase, and the posticteric phase. The preicteric phase is sometimes called the intestinal phase and may last from 1–21 days.

The preicteric phase is the period of maximal infectivity for HAV. This phase precedes the development of jaundice. The symptoms of this phase are as follows:

- Anorexia, nausea, and sometimes vomiting
- Abdominal discomfort, particularly the right upper quadrant
- Constipation or diarrhea
- Malaise and weight loss

Other symptoms may include the following:

- Headache
- Low-grade fever
- Arthralgias
- Skin rashes
- A distaste for dietary protein and cigarette smoke

Table 8.8   Characteristics of Hepatitis Viruses

Virus	Incubation Period	Mode of Transmission	Sources of Infection and Spread of Disease	Infectivity
Hepatitis A Virus (HAV)	15–50 days (average 28)	• Fecal–oral (fecal contamination and oral ingestion)	• Crowded conditions; poor personal hygiene; poor sanitation; contaminated food, milk, water, and shellfish; persons with subclinical infections; infected food handlers; sexual contact	Most infectious during 2 weeks before onset of symptoms; infectious until 1–2 weeks after symptoms start
Hepatitis B Virus (HBV)	45–180 days (average 56–96)	• Percutaneous (parenteral)/permucosal exposure to blood or blood products • Sexual contact • Perinatal transmission	• Contaminated needles, syringes, and blood products; sexual activity with infected partners; asymptomatic carriers • Tattoo/body piercing, bites	Before and after symptoms appear; infectious for 4–6 months; in carriers continues for client's lifetime
Hepatitis C Virus (HCV)	14–180 days (average 56)	• Percutaneous (parenteral)/permucosal exposure to blood or blood products • High-risk sexual contact • Perinatal contact	• Blood and blood products, needles and syringes, sexual activity with infected partners	1–2 weeks before symptoms; continues during clinical course; 75–85% go on to develop chronic hepatitis
Hepatitis D Virus (HDV)	2–26 weeks HBV must precede HDV; chronic carriers of HBV are always at risk	• Can cause infection only together with HBV; routes of transmission same as for HBV	• Same as HBV	Blood is infectious at all stages of HDV infection
Hepatitis E Virus (HEV)	15–64 days (average 26–42 days in different epidemics)	• Fecal–oral • Outbreaks associated with contaminated water supply in developing countries	• Contaminated water; poor sanitation; found in Asia, Africa, and Mexico; not common in Canada and the United States	Not known; may be similar to HAV

Source: Lewis, S. M., Heitkemper, M. M., Dirksen, S. R., O'Brien, P., Giddens, J. F., Bucher, L., et al. (2006). *Medical-surgical nursing in Canada: Assessment and management of clinical problems* (1st Canadian ed., p. 1112, Table 42-2). Toronto: Elsevier.

The icteric phase can last from two to four weeks and is characterized by jaundice. Symptoms in the icteric phase include pruritus and dark urine with light-coloured stools.

As the posticteric phase begins, the jaundice begins to disappear. This phase may last weeks to months, with the average being two to four months. Symptoms found in this phase include malaise and easy fatiguability. The disappearance of jaundice does not indicate recovery. Not all clients with viral hepatitis have jaundice; anicteric hepatitis does occur.

- In HAV, the onset of symptoms is acute, but the actual symptoms are a mild flulike manifestation.
- In HBV, the onset is insidious, and the symptoms tend to be more severe, with fewer GI symptoms.
- In HCV, the majority of clients are asymptomatic. HCV has a high rate of persistence and can induce chronic liver disease.

Diagnostics

Diagnosis of HBV will be confirmed by testing for the presence of hepatitis surface antigens and hepatitis B antibodies. These tests are as follows:

- Detection of an antibody to type A hepatitis confirms past or present infection with HAV.
- Detection of an antibody to type C hepatitis confirms a diagnosis of HCV.
- Viral load is measured by quantitative polymerase chain reaction assay and is useful in determining the need for treatment and monitoring therapy.
- The prothrombin time (PT) will be prolonged, indicating liver damage.
- Serum transaminase levels (alanine aminotransferase [ALT] and aspartate aminotransferase [AST]) will be elevated.
- Serum alkaline phosphatase will be slightly elevated.

- Serum and urine bilirubin levels are elevated.
- Serum albumin levels are low, and serum globulin levels are high.
- A liver biopsy and scan will show patchy necrosis.

Therapeutics and Nursing Considerations

There is no specific treatment for acute viral hepatitis. The following interventions are used:

- Most clients can be managed at home. Emphasis is on measures to rest the body and assist the liver in regenerating. Rest will help decrease the metabolic demands on the body and liver.
- Adequate nutrients and rest seem to be most beneficial for healing and liver cell regeneration. Dietary emphasis is on a well-balanced diet that the client can tolerate.

There is no specific drug therapy for viral hepatitis. Supportive drug therapy may include antiemetics, antihistamines, and sedatives, if needed.

Drug therapy for chronic hepatitis B is focused on decreasing the viral load, serum levels of AST and ALT, and the rate of disease progression. Alpha-interferons (Pegasys, PegIntron) and nucleoside analogues (Epovor, Hepsera) help suppress viral activity and decrease viral loads.

Drug therapy for chronic hepatitis C is directed at reducing the viral load, decreasing the progression of disease, and promoting seroconversion. Treatment includes a combination of ribavirin (Rebetol) and long-acting alpha-interferon (PegIntron).

Both hepatitis A vaccine and immune globulin are used for prevention of hepatitis A. The vaccine is used for pre-exposure prophylaxis, and the immune globulin can be used either before or after exposure. Immunization with hepatitis B vaccine is the most effective method of preventing HBV infection. For postexposure prophylaxis, the vaccine and hepatitis B immune globulin (HBIG) are used.

The diet needs to be adequate to assist hepatocytes to regenerate. The diet should be high in carbohydrates and calories. Protein may be limited if the liver is failing. Fat and sodium should be limited. Vitamin K supplements may be needed, and the client is encouraged to avoid drinking alcohol.

CIRRHOSIS

Pathophysiology

Cirrhosis of the liver refers to the chronic, progressive, irreversible, and widespread destruction of hepatic cells, with scar tissue (fibrosis) replacing healthy tissue. Cirrhosis can occur at any age but is more common in males between the ages of 40 and 60. Cirrhosis is the thirteenth leading cause of death in Canada, with alcohol ingestion being the most common cause. There are four major forms of cirrhosis:

- Alcoholic (Lannec's or portal/nutritional) cirrhosis results from malnutrition, especially protein deficiency and chronic alcohol intake. Alcohol alone has a direct hepatotoxic effect; it can produce necrosis of cells and fatty infiltrates.
- Postnecrotic cirrhosis is a complication of viral, toxic, or idiopathic hepatitis. Hepatitis C and alcohol are the two major causes of liver disease in Canada.
- Biliary cirrhosis results from bile duct disease.
- Cardiac cirrhosis is due to severe right-sided heart failure with cor pulmonale, prolonged constrictive pericarditis, and tricuspid insufficiency.
- Other forms of cirrhosis include nonspecific metabolic cirrhosis from infiltrating infections and cirrhosis due to inherited diseases such as hemochromatosis or Wilson's disease. Cirrhosis can be caused by drugs, toxins, and parasites. Nonalcoholic steatohepatitis (NASH) is found when fat builds up in the liver and eventually causes scar formation.

Pathophysiology of cirrhosis involves the destruction of hepatocytes. This hepatocyte necrosis leads to the development of scar tissue, which, in turn, disrupts blood and bile flow. This disruption then leads to an increase in pressure in the portal circulatory system, which causes portal hypertension. This hypertension damages more hepatocytes, resulting in loss of function and liver death.

Clinical Manifestations

Early manifestations of cirrhosis may be absent or minimal and then develop insidiously. These manifestations are as follows:

- Fatigue and weakness
- Decreased appetite and weight loss
- Nausea and vomiting
- Flatus
- Dull right upper quadrant discomfort due to swelling and stretching of the liver
- Possibly fever and pruritus

Later manifestations may include the following:

- Jaundice
- Skin lesions
- Hematological problems (thrombocytopenia, anemia, leukopenia)
- Endocrine disturbances (testicular atrophy, menstrual irregularities)
- Peripheral neuropathies
- Peripheral edema
- Infections

As the liver begins to fail, the normal functions of the liver also fail.

Diagnostics

Cirrhosis is typically advanced before it is diagnosed. The following tests are done to diagnose cirrhosis:

- A liver biopsy is the definitive test to diagnose cirrhosis.
- Blood work will show abnormal liver function, impaired clotting factors, thrombocytopenia, leukopenia, and anemia, as well as electrolyte imbalances due to an increase in aldosterone and ADH.
- A liver scan will show abnormal thickening and mass.

Therapeutics and Nursing Considerations

Treatment is aimed at removing or alleviating the underlying cause of the cirrhosis, preventing further liver damage, and preventing or treating complications. Complications that may result from cirrhosis are as follows:

- Portal hypertension
- Peripheral edema
- Ascites
- Varices
- Hepatic encephalopathy
- Hepatorenal syndrome [*atozemia. (kidney failure c cirrhosis)*]
- Fetor hepaticus [*peculiar odor of breath of people c liver disease*]

Portal hypertension can result in retention and pooling of visceral blood, which, in turn, causes congestion of adjacent viscera. The high portal venous pressure will shunt blood into the systemic circulation, causing esophageal, gastric, spleen, and rectal varices. These vessels are fragile and may rupture. Treatment for ruptured varices begins with finding the source of the bleeding and stopping it. Esophagoscopy may be done if possible to find and treat the bleeding. Gastric lavage, sclerotherapy, vasopressin injection, and an esophagogastric tamponade (Minnesota or Blakemore tube) may be used to stop the bleeding. Once stabilized, a portacaval shunt or a transjugular intrahepatic portosystemic shunt may be put in place. Fluid volume must be replaced. Vital signs must be monitored, assessing for any signs of shock.

[*Albumin = plasma Expander lowers not retention.*]

The failing liver impairs the synthesis of albumin. With the decrease in albumin, vascular oncotic pressure decreases, resulting in peripheral edema. Ascites develop due to the decreased hepatic synthesis of albumin, increased portal vein pressure, obstructed hepatic lymph flow, and increased serum aldosterone level. Ascites may be treated with sodium restriction, diuretics, and albumin. A paracentesis may be done to remove the excess fluid. A peritoneal venous shunt (LeVeen or Denver) may be inserted to remove fluid from the peritoneum to the superior vena cava. With the removal of fluid, the BP may drop, so the nurse must monitor the vital signs closely. Fluid replacement may be needed.

Hepatic encephalopathy is frequently a terminal complication. It is caused by increased levels of ammonia. Classic symptoms of hepatic encephalopathy include impaired attention span, irritability and restlessness, apathy, loss of interest, lethargy, somnolence, and coma. Hepatic encephalopathy is treated by identifying the precipitating cause and treating it with antibiotics, enemas, and lactulose. Lactulose will bind with the ammonia and help evacuate it via the bowel.

Hepatorenal syndrome results from functional renal failure with advancing azotemia, oliguria, and intractable ascites. The kidneys fail due to the redistribution of blood flow from the kidneys to the periphery and visceral circulation, or as a result of hypovolemia due to ascites. Vital signs need to be monitored closely.

Fetor hepaticus is a musty, sweetish odour detected on the client's breath. The odour is due to the accumulation of digested by-products. Additional complications of cirrhosis may include exhaustion, gallstones, complications with pharmacological therapy, and pruritus.

An important role of the nurse is educating the client about the general management of cirrhosis, which includes rest, avoidance of alcohol and anticoagulants, managing the possible complications, and ensuring adequate and appropriate nutrition.

PANCREATITIS

Pathophysiology

Pancreatitis is an inflammation of the pancreas that can be acute or chronic. The degree of inflammation varies from mild edema to severe necrosis. Pancreatitis can affect both men and women, but it is more commonly found in men. The prognosis is good when pancreatitis follows biliary disease but poor when it is a complication of alcoholism. The causes of pancreatitis are as follows:

- Alcohol is the number one cause of pancreatitis in Canada.
- Gallbladder disease is the next most common cause of pancreatitis.
- Other causes include viral infections, duodenal or peptic ulcers, pancreatic cancer, drugs such as glucocorticoids, metabolic disorders such as hyperparathyroidism and hyperlipidemia, and postsurgical trauma from ERCP.

In acute pancreatitis, the inflammation that occurs is caused by premature activation of digestive enzymes, which leads to autodigestion of the surrounding tissue. The pancreatic enzymes are activated while they are still in the pancreas rather than in the small intestine, so they digest pancreatic cells, causing severe edema, interstitial hemorrhage, and necrosis, which can lead to hypotension, shock, and disseminated intravascular coagulation (DIC).

Two major complications of pancreatitis are pseudocyst and pancreatic abscess. The pseudocyst is a cavity that develops around the pancreas that is filled with necrotic products and liquid secretions. If the cyst perforates, exudate inflames the surrounding tissues, causing peritonitis, followed by scar tissue. The pseudocyst may heal by itself or require draining. A pancreatic abscess is a large fluid-containing cavity within the pancreas that results from extensive necrosis of the pancreatic cells. This abscess may become infected and perforate.

Other complications of pancreatitis include pulmonary problems such as pleural effusion, atelectasis, and pneumonia. Cardiovascular problems such as hypotension and tachycardia may occur, and the client may develop tetany due to the low calcium levels in the blood.

Clinical Manifestations

Abdominal pain unrelieved by vomiting may be the first and only symptom of mild pancreatitis. A severe attack may cause a sudden onset of extreme pain in the left upper quadrant with possible radiation to the back. The pain is often described as severe, deep, piercing, and steady. The pain is aggravated by eating or drinking alcohol and does not subside with vomiting. Other manifestations may include flushing, cyanosis, edema, nausea, vomiting, low-grade fever, leukocytosis, jaundice, hypotension, and tachycardia.

Diagnostics

Diagnosis is made through the history and physical examination. Blood work may show elevated serum amylase levels, which rules out appendicitis, acute cholecystitis, perforated ulcer, and bowel infarction. Serum lipase, glucose, and WBC levels are likely to increase, while serum calcium levels are likely to decrease. An abdominal CT scan can help distinguish between cholelithiasis and pancreatitis.

Therapeutics and Nursing Considerations

Management of pancreatitis focuses on the following:

- Pain relief
- Maintenance of circulation and fluid volume
- Decreasing pancreatic enzymes
- Analgesics, vasodilators, and antispasmodics may be given. Dopamine may be needed for hypotension.
- The client will be NPO. An NG tube will be in place to remove secretions. IV therapy will be needed to maintain fluid volume. The client will be monitored for complications. Once the client is allowed food, small, frequent meals are offered. The diet should be high in carbohydrates and protein and low in fat.

Nursing considerations will focus on the following:

- Pain relief
- Improving breathing patterns
- Improving nutritional status
- Improving skin integrity
- Monitoring and managing any complications

The nurse will also be involved in client teaching about discontinuing alcohol, proper nutrition and rest, and ways to improve the client's general health.

Pathophysiology of Chronic Pancreatitis

Chronic pancreatitis develops from repeated attacks of pancreatitis. These repeated attacks cause scarring and calcification of the pancreatic cells, which leads to the permanent and progressive destruction of the pancreas. Both exocrine and endocrine functions of the pancreas are affected. Chronic obstructive pancreatitis results from inflammation of the sphincter of Oddi and is associated with cholelithiasis. Chronic calcifying pancreatitis is alcohol-induced pancreatitis.

Clinical Manifestations of Chronic Pancreatitis

Chronic pancreatitis manifestations include abdominal pain, usually described as a severe, heavy, gnawing feeling, burning, or cramplike pain. The client will experience malabsorption, constipation, steatorrhea, mild jaundice, and diabetes mellitus (DM).

Diagnostics for Chronic Pancreatitis

Diagnosis is the same as for acute pancreatitis.

Therapeutics and Nursing Considerations for Chronic Pancreatitis

Management of chronic pancreatitis focuses on prevention of attacks. During an attack, treatment is similar to that of acute pancreatitis. With chronic pancreatitis, the client needs to be taught about diet, pancreatic enzyme replacement, exogenous insulin, antacids, and cessation of alcohol intake. The client cannot tolerate fatty or rich foods. The DM is often "brittle" in response to insulin; therefore, the client may require frequent injections to control blood sugars. Client education is very important.

REGULATORY MECHANISM HEALTH CHALLENGES

ADDISON'S DISEASE

Pathophysiology

Addison's disease is the most common form of adrenal insufficiency. Although Addison's disease usually results from an autoimmune disorder, it can be caused by TB, histoplasmosis, adrenal hemorrhage, cancer, lymphoma, and certain drugs. Surgical removal of the adrenal glands and abruptly stopping long-term corticosteroid therapy can also cause Addison's disease. When the cause is autoimmune, antibodies against the client's own adrenal cortex destroy the adrenal gland's ability to secrete hormones.

Clinical Manifestations

Manifestations do not tend to become apparent until about 90% of the cortex has been destroyed. Manifestations that do develop do so insidiously and may include the following:

- Progressive weakness and fatigue
- Weight loss and anorexia
- Skin hyperpigmentation (bronze colouring) is a striking feature.
- The client also may have orthostatic hypotension, a weak irregular pulse, decreased tolerance for even minor stress, poor coordination, fasting hypoglycemia, a craving for salty foods, and amenorrhea.

Diagnostics

Diagnosis is made based on clinical features and decreased serum cortisol and sodium levels. Corticotrophin, serum potassium, and blood urea nitrogen levels are all increased. A failure of serum cortisol to rise following adrenocorticotropic hormone (ACTH) stimulation indicates primary adrenal disease.

Therapeutics and Nursing Considerations

Treatment of Addison's disease is focused on management of the underlying cause and replacement therapy.

- Hydrocortisone has both glucocorticoid and mineralocorticoid properties and is frequently used as replacement therapy.
- During periods of stress, the replacement therapy may need to be increased.
- In an adrenal crisis, the client may need prompt administration of dexamethasone, hydrocortisone, or both, and doses continue until he or she stabilizes.
- Vital signs must be monitored for signs of volume depletion and hypotension.
- Blood work needs to be monitored for altered electrolytes both before and during treatment.
- Blood glucose needs to be monitored as steroid replacement may alter insulin requirements.

Client education regarding medication compliance is essential.

CUSHING'S SYNDROME

Pathophysiology

Cushing's syndrome is a spectrum of clinical abnormalities caused by excess corticosteroids, particularly glucocorticoids. This adrenal hyperfunction can be caused by prolonged administration of high doses of corticosteroids, an ACTH-secreting pituitary tumour, or a cortisol-secreting neoplasm within the adrenal cortex that can be either carcinoma or adenoma.

Clinical Manifestations

Unmistakable manifestations of Cushing's syndrome include the following:

- Adiposity of the face (moon face) and neck (buffalo hump)
- Purple striae on the skin of the trunk, especially the abdomen
- Weight gain
- Muscle weakness and fatigue
- Thinning of the extremities with muscle wasting and fat mobilization
- Thin, fragile skin, ruddy complexion, hirsutism, acne, bruising, and impaired wound healing

Diagnostics

When Cushing's syndrome is suspected, a 24-hour urine collection test for free cortisol and a low-dose dexamethasone suppression test are done. If these tests are inconclusive, then a high-dose dexamethasone suppression test is done. Ultrasonography, CT scan, and angiography localize adrenal tumours. CT scan and MRI of the head help localize pituitary tumours.

Therapeutics and Nursing Considerations

The primary goal of treatment is to normalize hormone secretion. Radiation, drug therapy, or surgery may be needed to restore hormone balance and reverse Cushing's syndrome. Some examples of treatments are as follows:

- Trans-sphenoidal resection and radiation may be used for pituitary adenomas.
- Surgical removal or radiation may be used for an ectopic ACTH-secreting tumour.
- Nonendocrine corticotropin-secreting tumours require excision.
- Drug therapy with aminoglutethimide, etomidate, ketoconazole, myetyrapone mitotane, or trilostane decreases cortisol levels if symptoms persist or if the tumour is inoperable.

Before surgery, the client will require special monitoring and control of hypertension, edema, diabetes, and cardiovascular manifestations and to prevent infection. Glucocorticoid administration the morning of surgery can help prevent acute adrenal insufficiency during surgery. Nursing considerations will focus on the following:

- Decreasing risk for injury
- Decreasing risk for infection
- Encouraging rest and activity
- Promoting skin integrity
- Improving body image
- Improving thought processes
- Monitoring and managing complications

Clients with Cushing's syndrome require thorough ongoing assessment and supportive care, including emotional support, as the syndrome produces emotional lability. In some cases, sedation may be needed to help the client rest.

HYPERTHYROIDISM

Pathophysiology

Hyperthyroidism is a clinical syndrome in which there is a sustained increase in synthesis and release of thyroid hormones by the thyroid gland. The most common form of hyperthyroidism is Graves' disease (diffuse toxic goitre), an autoimmune disease that increases T_4 (thyroxine) production, enlarges the thyroid gland (goitre), and causes multisystem changes. In Graves' disease, a thyroid-stimulating hormone (TSH) receptor autoantibody stimulates the thyroid gland to produce high concentrations of T_3 (tri-iodothyronine) and T_4. Graves' disease has also been associated with the production of several autoantibodies formed because of a defect in suppressor T-lymphocyte function.

Thyrotoxic crisis (thyroid storm) is an acute, rare condition in which all hyperthyroid manifestations are heightened. This is a life-threatening condition for which aggressive measures must be taken to prevent death.

Clinical Manifestations

Classic manifestations of Graves' disease include the following:

- A diffusely enlarged thyroid
- Nervousness and insomnia
- Hair loss
- Fatigue and muscle weakness
- Edema
- Heat intolerance
- Weight loss and increased appetite
- Splenomegaly
- Hepatomegaly
- Sweating
- Diarrhea
- Tremor
- Palpitations
- Systolic hypertension
- Arrhythmias and atrial fibrillation
- Reproductive abnormalities
- Possible exophthalmos

Treatment is aimed at reducing circulating thyroid hormone levels and treating manifestations such as high fever with antipyretics, IV therapy for fluid replacement, and elimination of stressors.

Diagnostics

Graves' disease is diagnosed by the history and physical examination and laboratory tests finding decreased TSH and increased free T_4 levels. Radioactive iodine uptake test is needed to differentiate Graves' disease from other forms of thyroiditis. A thyroid sonogram helps distinguish cystic and solid lesions. A CT scan or MRI helps identify deep thyroid nodules.

Therapeutics and Nursing Considerations

The overall goal in the treatment of hyperthyroidism is to block the adverse effects of the thyroid hormones and stop their oversecretion. The primary forms of treatment for hyperthyroidism are as follows:

- Antithyroid drugs
- Radioactive iodine therapy
- Subtotal thyroidectomy

Choice of treatment will depend on the client's age, severity of the disease, client's present physical condition, and the client's preference.

- Propylthiouracil and methimazole block thyroid hormone synthesis.
- The administration of iodine in large doses rapidly inhibits synthesis of T_3 and T_4 and blocks the release of these hormones into the circulatory system.
- Beta-adrenergic blockers are used for symptomatic relief of thyrotoxicosis that results from increased beta-adrenergic receptor stimulation caused by excess thyroid hormone.
- Radioactive iodine damages or destroys thyroid tissue, thus limiting thyroid hormone secretion. This treatment is effective but leaves the client with hypothyroidism, requiring thyroid hormone replacement therapy.
- A subtotal thyroidectomy removes a significant portion (90%) of the thyroid gland and is needed for clients who do not respond to antithyroid therapy.

Nursing considerations focus on improving nutritional status, enhancing coping measures, improving self-esteem, maintaining normal body temperatures, and monitoring and managing any complications.

HYPOTHYROIDISM

Pathophysiology

Hypothyroidism is a state of low levels of serum thyroid hormones. Hypothyroidism may result from a number of causes but is mainly caused by the following:

- A thyroidectomy
- Radiation therapy
- Chronic autoimmune thyroiditis (Hashimoto's disease)
- Inflammatory diseases, such as amyloidosis

In primary hypothyroidism, thyroid hormone production is decreased due to decreased thyroid tissue. The pituitary gland will still secrete TSH, and a goitre may develop. In secondary hypothyroidism, the pituitary fails to synthesize or secrete adequate amounts of TSH, or target tissues fail to respond to normal blood levels of the thyroid hormone. Either type may progress to myxedema (an advanced form of hypothyroidism). This condition is considered a medical emergency.

Clinical Manifestations

Clinical manifestations of hypothyroidism will vary with the severity of the condition regardless of the cause. Symptoms develop insidiously and may include the following:

- Fatigue and lethargy
- Forgetfulness
- Slow speech
- Low exercise tolerance
- Weight gain
- Bradycardia
- Anemia
- Constipation
- Cool, dry, flaky skin; dry, sparse hair; and thick, brittle nails.

Symptoms of the life-threatening myxedema include progressive personality and mental changes moving toward stupor, hypoventilation, hypoglycemia, hyponatremia, hypotension, and hypothermia.

Diagnostics

The most common and reliable laboratory tests used to evaluate thyroid function are those that measure TSH and free T_4. When TSH levels are high, the defect is in the thyroid, and when the levels are low, the defect is in the pituitary or hypothalamus.

Therapeutics and Nursing Considerations

The goal of treatment for clients with hypothyroidism is replacement of the hormones by administering synthetic levothyroxine (Synthroid, Eltroxin). The nurse provides the following care:

- Routinely assesses the client to see if the medication is adequate or not.
- Encourages weight loss with a high-bulk, low-calorie diet.
- Encourages activity balanced with rest.
- Administers laxatives and stool softeners when needed.

Teach the client to watch for signs of hyperthyroidism, such as sweating, tachycardia, or rapid weight loss, and to always wear a MedicAlert bracelet or carry a MedicAlert card.

Syndrome of Inappropriate Antidiuretic Hormone (SIADH)

Pathophysiology

Syndrome of inappropriate antidiuretic hormone (SIADH) occurs when ADH is released despite normal or low plasma osmolarity. SIADH results from an abnormal production or sustained secretion of ADH and is characterized by fluid retention. The hyponatremia that can occur with SIADH can lead to cerebral edema. SIADH can occur due to malignant lung disease, infections, trauma, or medications that stimulate ADH release.

Clinical Manifestations

One of the chief clinical manifestations of SIADH is fluid retention; therefore, the client will gain weight and have a decreased urine output. The serum hyponatremia may cause the client to have the following symptoms as well:

- Muscle cramps, weakness, and muscle twitching
- Vomiting
- Seizures

If the hyponatremia progresses and sodium levels continue to decline, the client may experience cerebral edema, leading to lethargy, anorexia, confusion, headaches, seizure, and coma.

Diagnostics

The diagnosis of SIADH is made by simultaneous measurements of urine and serum osmolality. A serum osmolality of less than 280 mOsm/kg (280 mmol/kg) and a urine concentration greater than 100 mOsm/kg are indicative of SIADH.

Therapeutics and Nursing Considerations

Once SIADH is identified, the care is directed at the underlying cause of the condition. The immediate treatment is aimed at restoring normal fluid volume and osmolality. Fluid restriction may be all that is needed. If the hyponatremia is severe, hypertonic saline solutions may be administered cautiously as rapid administration could overload the heart.

DIABETES INSIPIDUS

Pathophysiology

Diabetes insipidus (DI) is a group of conditions associated with a deficiency of production or secretion of ADH (vasopressin) or a decreased renal response to ADH. DI may be familial, acquired, or idiopathic.

- It can be acquired as the result of intracranial neoplastic or metastatic lesions.
- Other causes may include hypophysectomy or other neurosurgery, head trauma, infection, granulomatous disease, vascular lesions, or autoimmune disorders.

Normally, the ADH is synthesized in the hypothalamus and stored in the posterior pituitary gland. When released, ADH works on the distal and collecting tubules of the kidneys, causing water to be reabsorbed. If ADH is absent or not released, the water is excreted in the urine. As a result, the client will void copious amounts of urine.

Clinical Manifestations

The classic sign of DI is polyuria, with amounts from 5–20 L and possibly up to 30 L/day. Polydipsia, increased thirst, may be present. Nocturia and fatigue are common, as well as dehydration with weight loss, poor tissue turgor, dry mucous membranes, constipation, muscle weakness, dizziness, tachycardia, and hypotension.

Diagnostics

A complete history and physical examination are needed to diagnose DI. Baseline vital signs and weight are taken, and urine and plasma osmolalities and specific gravity of the urine tests are usually performed. A urinalysis may reveal almost colourless urine with a low osmolality and low specific gravity. A water deprivation test confirms the diagnosis. The client will be denied water for 8–16 hours. The client will be anxious and thirsty and will require reassurance and support. Vital signs will be monitored closely, and the test will be stopped if the client develops orthostatic hypotension or body weight drops by 5%.

Therapeutics and Nursing Considerations

Determining the cause of DI is critical to its treatment. Hormone replacement of ADH is needed. Care of a client with DI resulting from nephrogenic problems includes a low-sodium diet and utilizing thiazide diuretics. The thiazides are able to slow the glomerular filtration rate (GFR), allowing the kidneys to reabsorb more water in the loop of Henle and distal tubules. If this does not work, indomethacin (an anti-inflammatory) may be prescribed.

Nursing management revolves around early detection, maintenance of adequate hydration, client teaching for long-term management, and encouragement and support while the client is undergoing diagnostic studies and treatment.

DIABETES MELLITUS

Pathophysiology

DM is a multisystem disease related to abnormal insulin production, impaired insulin utilization, or both. It is the leading cause of heart disease, stroke, adult blindness, and nontraumatic lower limb amputation.

Normally, insulin is produced by the beta cells in the islets of Langerhans of the pancreas. Insulin facilitates the normal glucose range of 3–7 mmol/L. Insulin is a storage hormone that promotes glucose transport from the bloodstream across the cell membrane into the cytoplasm of the cell. Ingesting food stimulates the release of insulin from the pancreas into the blood. Insulin stimulates the storage of glucose as glycogen and inhibits gluconeogenesis. Insulin also enhances fat deposition in adipose tissue and increases protein synthesis. Glucagon is a hormone produced in the alpha cells of the pancreas and functions by increasing blood glucose levels.

Type 1 DM was formerly known as "juvenile-onset" or "insulin-dependent" diabetes. Type 1 diabetes usually affects people under the age of 30, peaking at 11–13 years, but it can affect people older than 30 years of age. Type 1 diabetes involves the progressive destruction of pancreatic beta cells. Autoantibodies cause a reduction of 80–90% of normal beta cell function before manifestations occur. The causes of type 1 diabetes may be due to genetic predisposition or exposure to a virus. Manifestations develop when the pancreas can no longer produce insulin. Symptoms tend to be rapid in onset, and the client often presents to the emergency department with ketoacidosis. Other classic symptoms include weight loss, polyuria, polydipsia, and polyphagia. Diabetic ketoacidosis (DKA) occurs in the absence of exogenous insulin. It is a life-threatening condition that results in metabolic acidosis.

Type 2 diabetes accounts for 90% of clients with diabetes. It usually occurs in people over the age of 40; however, children are now being diagnosed with type 2 diabetes, usually due to obesity and a sedentary lifestyle. With type 2 diabetes, the pancreas continues to produce some endogenous insulin; however, the amount produced is either insufficient or is poorly utilized by the tissues. Insulin resistance is the key to type 2 diabetes, a situation in which the body does not respond to the insulin and hyperglycemia results. Some people experience glucose intolerance, in which the alteration in the beta cells is mild. In these situations, the blood glucose levels are higher than normal but are not high enough for a diagnosis of diabetes. Inappropriate glucose production by the liver is not considered a primary factor in the development of type 2 diabetes. Insulin resistance syndrome (syndrome X) is a cluster of abnormalities that act synergistically to increase the risk of cardiovascular disease. Type 2 diabetes typically has a gradual onset; the person may go many years with undetected hyperglycemia. See Table 8.9 for further characteristics of type 1 and 2 diabetes.

Diabetes can also develop during pregnancy, when it is usually detected at 24–28 weeks of gestation. With gestational diabetes, there is an increased risk for a caesarean delivery, perinatal deaths, and neonatal complications.

Diabetes can also develop secondary to another medical condition or the treatment of a medical condition. For example, there can be abnormal blood values in a client experiencing Cushing's syndrome or as a result of the use of parenteral nutrition.

Clinical Manifestations

Manifestations of type 1 diabetes include classic polyuria, polydipsia, and polyphagia. The client will also experience weight loss, weakness and fatigue, and ketoacidosis. Nonspecific symptoms include fatigue, recurrent infections, prolonged wound healing, and visual changes.

Diagnostics

Diagnosis of DM is made when fasting plasma glucose is greater than 7 mmol/L, a random plasma glucose measurement is greater than 11.1 mmol/L, or a two-hour oral glucose tolerance test (OGTT) is greater than 11.1 mmol/L when using a glucose load of 75 g. Tests used to evaluate glucose control and monitor for complications of diabetes include glycosylated

Table 8.9 Characteristics of Type 1 and Type 2 Diabetes Mellitus

Factor	Type 1 Diabetes Mellitus	Type 2 Diabetes Mellitus
Age at Onset	• More common in young persons but can occur at any age	• Usually age 35 yr or older but can occur at any age • Incidence is increasing in children
Type of Onset	• Signs and symptoms abrupt, but disease process may be present for several years	• Insidious
Prevalence	• Accounts for 5–10% of all types of diabetes	• Accounts for 90% of all types of diabetes
Environmental Factors	• Virus, toxins	• Obesity, lack of exercise
Islet Cell Antibodies	• Often present at onset	• Absent
Endogenous Insulin	• Minimal or absent	• Possibly excessive; adequate but delayed secretion or reduced utilization
Nutritional Status	• Thin, catabolic state	• Obese or possibly normal
Symptoms	• Thirst, polyuria, polyphagia, fatigue	• Frequently none or mild • Fatigue, blurred vision, and peripheral neuropathic pain in late diagnosis
Ketosis	• Prone at onset or during insulin deficiency	• Resistant except during infection or stress
Nutritional Therapy	• Essential	• Essential, possibly sufficient for glycemic control
Insulin	• Required for all	• Required for some
Oral Antihyperglycemic Agents	• Not indicated	• Usually beneficial
Microvascular/Macrovascular Complications	• Frequent	• Frequent

Source: Lewis, S. M., Heitkemper, M. M., Dirksen, S. R., O'Brien, P., Bucher, L., et al. (2010). *Medical-surgical nursing in Canada: Assessment and management of clinical problems* (2nd Canadian ed., p. 1336, Table 50-1). Toronto: Elsevier.

hemoglobin (hemoglobin A1c), lipid profile, blood urea nitrogen (BUN), serum creatinine, electrolytes, and TSH. Urine can be checked for glucose and acetone.

Therapeutics and Nursing Considerations

Goals for the treatment of DM include the following:

- Reducing symptoms
- Promoting well-being
- Preventing acute complications
- Delaying the onset and progression of long-term complications

Collaborative care includes five components: education, nutrition, medications, exercise, and self-monitoring of blood glucose.

Exogenous insulin is required for type 1 diabetes. It may be prescribed for clients with type 2 diabetes who cannot control their blood glucose by other means or when the client is under stress. Human insulin is the most widely used insulin; it is cost-effective, and there is less chance of the client developing an allergic reaction. Insulin can also be derived from beef and pork.

Insulin types differ in regard to onset, peak action, and duration. Different types of insulin may be used for combination therapy. Some common types of insulin are as follows:

- Lispro is a rapid-acting insulin.
- Regular and Toronto are short-acting insulins.
- NPH and Lente are intermediate-acting insulins.
- Ultralente and Lantus are long-acting insulins.

Insulin may be administered subcutaneously. At present, insulin cannot be taken orally; however, new research is finding alternative delivery methods, including aerosol, skin patches, oral spray, and pills. Problems with insulin therapy include hypoglycemia, allergic reactions, lipodystrophy, and the Somogyi effect.

Oral agents are not insulin. These medications work to improve the mechanisms through which insulin and glucose are produced and used by the body. These medications include the following:

- Sulfonylureas, meglitinides, biguanides
- Alpha-glucosidase inhibitors
- Thiazolidinediones
- Other drugs affecting blood glucose levels are beta-adrenergic blockers, thiazide, and loop diuretics.

Nutrition and Exercise in DM Management

Research has shown that within the context of an overall healthy eating plan, a person with diabetes can eat the same foods as a person who does not have diabetes. The overall goal of nutrition therapy is to assist people in making changes in nutrition and exercise habits that will lead to improved metabolic control.

- A type 1 DM meal plan is based on the individual's usual food intake and is balanced with insulin and exercise patterns.
- In type 2 DM, emphasis is placed on achieving glucose, lipid, and blood pressure goals. Calorie reduction is often needed.

Individual meal plans are developed with the assistance of a dietitian. The plan promotes a nutritional balance and does not prohibit the consumption of any one type of food. Alcohol can be included within the plan with the full understanding that alcohol is high in calories, promotes hypertriglyceridemia, and can cause severe hypoglycemia. The dietitian should provide instructions to the client and family or significant other.

Exercise is an essential part of diabetes management as it increases insulin sensitivity, lowers blood glucose levels, and decreases insulin resistance. Exercise also improves circulation and muscle tone, increases the resting metabolic rate, and alters blood lipids. The body considers exercise to be stress. In type 1 diabetes, the physiological decrease in circulating insulin that normally occurs with exercise cannot occur; therefore, clients with DM need to have small carbohydrate snacks every 30 minutes during exercise to prevent hypoglycemia. Exercise is best done after meals and should be individualized for every client. Blood glucose levels should be monitored before, during, and after exercise.

Self-monitoring of blood glucose (SMBG) enables clients to make self-management decisions regarding diet, exercise, and medications. SMBG is important for detecting episodic hyperglycemia and hypoglycemia. Client teaching is crucial. SMBG requires good visual acuity, fine motor coordination, cognitive ability, comfort with technology, willingness, and sufficient finances to pay for it.

Urine testing for glucose was a technique used before the development of SMBG. It is a less expensive technique, but it does not represent an accurate reading as the urine tested could have been in the bladder for a matter of hours. However, urine testing for ketones is essential when the client is ill.

Overall goals for the management of DM should include active participation of the client, no episodes of hypoglycemia or hyperglycemia, maintenance of normal blood glucose levels, prevention of complications, and lifestyle adjustments with minimal stress.

Acute Complications of DM

Acute complications pertaining to DM are hypoglycemia, DKA, and hyperosmolar hyperglycemic nonketotic syndrome (HHNK).

Hypoglycemia

Hypoglycemia is found in clients whose blood glucose level is abnormally below 3.3 mmol/L. Hypoglycemia may be caused by too little food or too much insulin. Symptoms of hypoglycemia include the following:

- Sweating
- Trembling

- Blurred vision
- Extreme tiredness and paleness
- Headache
- Hunger
- Mood changes
- Dizziness

To treat hypoglycemia, give 10–15 g of a fast-acting simple carbohydrate, such as three to four commercially prepared glucose tabs, 120–180 mL (4–6 oz) of fruit juice or a regular soft drink, or 6–10 hard candies. The blood should be retested after 15 minutes. If the blood glucose remains low, the carbohydrate intake should be repeated. When the level goes up, the client should be given a protein with a starch. An unconscious client can be injected with 1 mg of glucagon, either subcutaneously or intramuscularly. If this is not available, a source of glucose, such as corn syrup, honey, or icing, may be placed in the client's buccal pouch. After consciousness returns, the client should be given a protein or starch snack. Hypoglycemia is preventable. Clients with diabetes should always carry a simple sugar with them and have identification confirming their diagnosis. Family and friends need to know the signs and symptoms of hypoglycemia and what they can do to assist the client.

Diabetic Ketoacidosis

DKA is caused by an absence of insulin or a markedly inadequate amount. Clinical features of DKA include hyperglycemia, dehydration, and acidosis. DKA can be caused by a decreased or missed dose of insulin, an illness or infection, or undiagnosed and untreated diabetes. Clinical manifestations include the following:

- Blurred vision
- Weakness
- Headache
- Orthostatic hypotension
- Anorexia, nausea and vomiting, and abdominal pain
- Acetone breath
- Hyperventilation
- Possible mental changes

DKA is diagnosed with an elevated blood glucose, with levels varying from 14–44 mmol/L or higher. The severity of DKA is not necessarily related to the actual blood glucose level. Ketones will be found in the blood and urine, and the electrolytes may be low, normal, or high, depending on the level of dehydration.

Prevention of DKA is based on understanding the importance of food replacement during illness. A typical sick-day routine is as follows: Take insulin or oral antidiabetic agents as usual. Test blood glucose and urine for ketones every three to four hours. Report elevated blood glucose levels of 16 mmol/L or more or the presence of ketones in the urine to the health care professional. Treatment of DKA focuses on rehydration and balancing the electrolytes and pH. Clients receive potassium in the IV solution as long as they remain polyuric and hypokalemic. The acidosis is reversed

by administering insulin via an IV pump. Nursing management focuses on the following:

- Monitoring fluid and electrolyte balance
- Monitoring blood glucose levels
- Giving fluids, insulin, and other medications as ordered
- Ensuring renal function
- Monitoring for arrhythmias
- Monitoring vital signs
- Reassessing factors leading to the development of DKA

Hyperosmolar, Hyperglycemic Nonketotic Syndrome

HHNK includes hyperglycemia, dehydration, and hyperosmolality of the plasma, with the absence of ketones in the urine. HHNK differs from DKA in that HHNK does not cause fat tissue to break down; thus, ketones will not be released. Clinical manifestations include hypotension, profound dehydration, and tachycardia, with variable neurological signs. Medical and nursing management focuses on fluid replacement, correction of electrolyte imbalances, administering IV insulin, and monitoring fluid and electrolyte balance. Insulin is not used to treat acidosis in HHNK, but it is used to treat the hyperglycemia.

Chronic Complications of DM

Chronic complications of DM include microvascular and macrovascular complications and neuropathic complications. DM can cause macrovascular damage to the large blood vessels providing circulation to the brain, heart, and extremities. Dyslipidemia, hypertension, and impaired fibrinolysis have been found in uncontrolled DM.

Microvascular complications create abnormal thickening of the basement membrane in the capillaries by hyperglycemia. Hyperglycemia also disrupts platelet function.

- Retinopathy starts with small hemorrhages in the retinal capillaries. Neovascularization occurs, which can lead to proliferative retinopathy. People with DM have an increased risk of developing cataracts and open-angle glaucoma.
- Nephropathy accounts for over 36% of cases of end-stage renal disease (ESRD), with the characteristic lesion being glomerulosclerosis.
- Neuropathic complications can be found in 40–50% of those with diabetes; paraesthesia, autonomic complications, and sensory disturbances are common.
- Peripheral polyneuropathy involves both neuropathy and vascular problems. The real danger for the client with this condition is that the client cannot feel pain.
- Individuals with diabetes need to watch for any signs of infection. There is a defect in the mobilization of inflammatory cells and an impairment of WBCs in phagocytosis. Persistent glycosuria encourages bladder infections. There is a delay in healing due to decreased circulation as well as protein waste leading to poor wound healing.

Pancreas transplantation is done for clients with type 1 DM who have ESRD and have had or plan to have a kidney transplantation. The pancreas transplantation eliminates the need for exogenous insulin and eliminates hypoglycemia and hyperglycemia.

REPRODUCTIVE HEALTH CHALLENGES

BREAST CANCER

Pathophysiology

Breast cancer is the most diagnosed cancer in Canadian women. Genetic abnormalities account for 5–10% of breast cancers. *BRCA* gene carriers are also at risk of developing ovarian cancer. Having a first-degree relative with breast cancer increases the risk of developing breast cancer by one and a half to three times. Secondary risk factors include never giving birth, giving birth to a first child after the age of 30, prolonged hormonal stimulation, exposure to excessive ionizing radiation, and a history of endometrial, ovarian, or colon cancer.

Types of breast cancer are based on histological characteristics and growth patterns. Infiltrating ductal carcinoma is considered to be the most common form of breast cancer. The cancers generally arise from the epithelial lining of the ducts or from the epithelium of lobules. Breast cancer may be invasive or in situ. Most cancers that arise from the ducts are invasive. Factors affecting prognosis include the size of the tumour, axillary node involvement, tumour differentiation, DNA content, and estrogen and progesterone receptor status.

Ductal carcinoma in situ (DCIS) tends to be unilateral and progresses to invasive if untreated. Lobular carcinoma in situ (LCIS) appears to be more of a premalignant cancer. Women with LCIS have a greater risk of developing invasive breast cancer in the same or opposite breast.

Clinical Manifestations

Symptoms of breast cancer include the following:

- Detecting a lump or mass in the breast
- Changes in breast symmetry or size
- Changes in breast skin, such as dimpling
- Edema
- Skin ulcers
- Changes in nipples causing itching, burning, erosion, or retraction
- Skin temperature changes

The cancer often occurs in the upper outer quadrant; will present as hard, irregularly shaped, poorly delineated, and nonmobile; and will feel nontender when palpated. A serious complication of breast cancer is recurrence. Metastasis occurs primarily through lymphatic chains but can spread without invading axillary nodes.

Diagnostics

Diagnosis of breast cancer is based on biopsy and pathological evaluation of suspected tissue. Diagnostic studies used are lymph node dissection, axillary lymph node status, estrogen and progesterone receptor status, DNA content analysis, and cell proliferative indices.

Therapeutics and Nursing Considerations

Common surgical therapy involves breast conservation surgery (lumpectomy) with radiation therapy or modified radical mastectomy with or without reconstruction. Axillary node dissection is often performed regardless of treatment as it provides excellent prognostic data and helps develop further treatment.

Breast conservation surgery removes the entire tumour along with a margin of normal tissue. Radiation is delivered to the entire breast following surgery. Attempts are made to preserve as much of the breast as possible, including the nipple. A modified radical mastectomy removes the entire breast along with the axillary lymph nodes. The pectoral major muscle is preserved. This is done when the tumour is too large to excise with good margins. The client has the option of breast reconstruction.

Lymphedema, swelling caused by the localized retention of lymphatic fluid, can result from the excision or radiation of lymph nodes. This fluid can cause obstructive pressure. Lymphedema can be prevented by frequent and sustained elevation of the arms, performing arm exercises, and avoiding constrictive clothing.

The client will experience postmastectomy pain in the chest and upper arm. Tingling down the arm, numbness, and shooting or prickling pain are felt. Unbearable itching may also be present. This pain is treated with NSAIDs, antidepressants, topical lidocaine patches, EMLA cream (eutectic mixture of local anaesthetics), and antiseizure drugs.

Radiation is employed to destroy a cancerous tumour or as a companion to surgery. The radiation will shrink the tumour to an operable size. Radiation can be used for palliative care as well.

Chemotherapy is systemic therapy designed to destroy cells that have spread undetected to distant sites, as well as to decrease the primary tumour and suppress tumour growth.

Hormonal therapy will block and destroy estrogen receptors and suppress estrogen synthesis.

Biological therapy attempts to stimulate the body's natural defences to recognize and attack cancer cells.

Mammoplasty surgically changes the size and shape of the breast for cosmetic or reconstructive reasons. Possible complications include hematoma, hemorrhage, and infection. It is often done simultaneously with or after a mastectomy. When done simultaneously, reconstruction avoids surgery after scar tissue or adhesions develop. Mammoplasty can include breast implants and tissue expansions, or a musculocutaneous flap procedure may be done. This procedure involves using the client's own tissue, usually from the back or abdomen, to repair soft tissue defects if there is insufficient muscle after a mastectomy. Nipple and areolar reconstruction can also be done.

Ovarian Cancer

Pathophysiology

Ovarian cancer, malignant neoplasm of the ovaries, once was a cancer that occurred in women between the ages of 55 and 65 years. It is now affecting younger women, especially if there is a history of ovarian, breast, or colon cancer in the family. Risk factors are as follows:

- Nulliparity; women who have never been pregnant are at greater risk
- High-fat diet
- Increased number of ovulatory cycles
- Hormone replacement therapy (HRT)
- Use of infertility drugs

Oral contraceptives, breastfeeding, multiple pregnancies, and early age at birth of a first child are associated with lower risk.

Ninety percent of ovarian cancers are epithelial carcinomas. Germ cell tumours account for 10% of ovarian cancers. Ovarian cancer can metastasize directly by shedding malignant cells that often implant in the uterus, bladder, bowel, and omentum. The cancer can also spread via the lymph system.

Clinical Manifestations

Manifestations include general abdominal discomfort, a sense of pelvic heaviness, loss of appetite, feeling of fullness, and a change in bowel habits. As the malignancy grows, there can be an increase in the abdominal girth, bowel and bladder dysfunction, persistent pelvic or abdominal pain, menstrual irregularities, and ascites.

Diagnostics

There are no screening tests at present. A yearly bimanual pelvic examination should be done. Postmenopausal women should not have palpable ovaries. An abdominal or vaginal ultrasonogram can be used to detect ovarian masses. A combination of testing for the tumour marker CA-125 (ovarian antibody) and ultrasonography is recommended in addition to the pelvic examination. CA-125 is also used to monitor the course of the disease.

Therapeutics and Nursing Considerations

Treatment usually is a total hysterectomy and bilateral salpingo-ophorectomy. Abdominal and pelvic radiation, intraperitoneal radiation, and systemic combination chemotherapy may be done after tumour-reducing

surgery has been completed. Other surgical procedures include subtotal hysterectomy, panhysterectomy, simple and radical vulvectomy, vaginectomy, and radical hysterectomy. It is very important that the client and family participate in treatment decisions. Psychological support both preoperatively and postoperatively is necessary. The client will be encouraged to continue to practise cancer detection strategies postoperatively. A "second-look" procedure (laparoscopy or laparotomy) is performed a year after completion of primary treatment to confirm the absence or presence of the tumour.

Benign Prostatic Hyperplasia

Pathophysiology

Benign prostatic hyperplasia (BPH) is an enlargement of the prostate gland resulting from an increase in the number of epithelial cells and stomal tissue. It is the most common problem of the male reproductive system. It occurs in 50% of men over the age of 50. BPH does not predispose the client to the development of prostate cancer. The etiology is not really understood, but it is thought to result from endocrine changes as part of the aging process. Other theories suggest that BPH is due to the effect of chronic inflammation of the prostate gland. Research supports the theory that BPH results from a systemic hormonal (testicular androgen) alteration. As the prostate gland grows, it extends upward into the bladder and inward, narrowing the prostatic urethral channel. This obstructs urine flow.

Risk factors include family history, environment, and a diet high in zinc, butter, and margarine.

Clinical Manifestations

Symptoms usually appear gradually and include the following:

- Voiding symptoms, including a decrease in the calibre or force of the urinary stream, difficulty in initiating urination, intermittency, dribbling at the end of voiding, and incomplete bladder emptying
- Urinary frequency and urgency, dysuria, bladder pain, nocturia, and incontinence

Diagnostics

Diagnostic tests include a history and physical examination, urinalysis with culture, a prostate-specific antigen (PSA) level, serum creatinine levels, transrectal ultrasound scan (TRUS), uroflometry, and cystourethroscopy. A digital rectal examination should be done yearly.

Therapeutics and Nursing Considerations

The goal of treatment is to restore bladder drainage, relieve symptoms, and prevent complications. Pharmacological therapy includes finasteride (Proscar), which reduces the size of the prostate gland. Alpha blocking agents such as terazosin, doxazosin, and tamsulosin are given to constrict the prostate gland, reducing urethral pressure and improving urine flow. Improvement can be seen in two to three weeks. The side effects of these medications are orthostatic hypotension and dizziness. Some clients benefit from herbal therapy such as saw palmetto extract.

Invasive therapy is indicated when there is persistent residual urine in the bladder, acute urinary retention, or hydronephrosis causing decreased urine flow and discomfort. Urinary retention leaves residual urine in the bladder and creates a favourable environment for bacterial growth. Calculi may develop in the bladder due to alkalinization of residual urine. Hydronephrosis can cause renal failure. Pyelonephritis may develop, or the bladder could be damaged. Acute urinary retention is an indication for surgical removal in 25–30% of clients with BPH. Long-term catheter use is contraindicated because of the risk of infection. The choice of treatment depends on the size and location of the prostatic enlargement and the age of the client.

Transurethral resection of the prostate (TURP) removes the prostate tissue using a resectoscope inserted through the urethra. The enlarged portion of the prostate gland is then resected in small pieces.

Transurethral microwave thermotherapy (TUMT) delivers microwaves directly to the prostate in order to raise the temperature to 45°C, causing tissue death and relief of the obstruction. Postoperative urinary retention is common following the procedures. Transurethral needle ablation (TUNA) increases the temperature of the prostate tissue for localized necrosis. A low-wave frequency is used, and only the tissues that the needle touches are affected. Urinary retention, urinary tract infection (UTI), and irritative voiding symptoms may result. Laser prostatectomy delivers a beam that is used for cutting, coagulation, and vaporization of the prostatic tissue.

Goals for postoperative care include the following:

- The client is free of complications.
- The client has restored urinary control and complete bladder emptying.
- The client has satisfying sexual expression.

Clients will require teaching for adequate fluid intake, aseptic technique if using a catheter at home, medication information, and providing an opportunity to express concerns of alteration in sexual function.

Prostate Cancer

Pathophysiology

Prostate cancer is the most common cause of cancer in men. Ninety-five percent of prostate cancers are androgen-dependent adenocarcinomas that usually develop in the outer aspect of the gland. The cancer is usually slow-growing and metastasizes in a predictable pattern. Common sites of metastasis include the lymph nodes, bone marrow, pelvis, sacrum, and lumbar spine. Risk factors include the following:

- Increasing age
- Family history
- Being of African descent
- High-fat diet
- Exposure to certain chemicals

A history of BPH is not considered a risk factor.

Clinical Manifestations

The client is usually asymptomatic in the early stages. Eventually, symptoms similar to those with BPH develop, such as dysuria, hesitancy, dribbling, frequency, and urgency. Gross painless hematuria is the most common presenting symptom. The client may experience lumbosacral pain that radiates to the hips or legs. When these symptoms are coupled with urinary symptoms, metastasis should be considered.

Diagnostics

Diagnostic studies include a physical examination and history. A PSA blood test is likely to show elevated levels of PSA with prostatic pathology. Elevated levels of prostatic acid phosphatase (PAP) indicate prostate cancer. A direct rectal examination may find the prostate hard and enlarged with areas of indurations or nodules. A biopsy of the prostate gland is the only definitive diagnostic tool. A bone scan, CT, MRI, and TRUS are used to determine the location and extent of the spread of the cancer. Single-photon emission computed tomography (SPECT) can detect the spread of the cancer to pelvic lymph nodes.

Therapeutics and Nursing Considerations

Conservative treatment is recommended when life expectancy is less than 10 years, there is significant comorbid disease, or the cancer is a low-grade, low-stage tumour. Surgical treatment is a radical prostatectomy, in which the entire gland, seminal vesicles, and part of the bladder neck are removed. Retroperineal lymph node dissection is usually done for the most effective long-term survival. Complications of a radical prostatectomy include the following:

- Hemorrhage
- Urinary retention
- Infection and wound dehiscence
- Deep vein thrombosis (DVT)
- Pulmonary emboli

Sometimes nerve-sparing procedures are done to spare the nerves responsible for an erection. This type of surgery is done only when the cancer is contained in the prostate. Cryosurgery destroys cancer cells by freezing them and can be used as an initial or second-line treatment. Radiation therapy can be done by external and internal beam. External radiation is used to treat cancer confined to the prostate or the surrounding tissue. Brachytherapy includes implantation of radioactive seeds into the prostate gland. This spares the surrounding tissue and is best suited for stage A or B prostate cancers. Hormonal therapy focuses on androgen deprivation and can be used before surgery or radiation to reduce the tumour. The hormones commonly used are luteinizing hormone–releasing agonists, androgen receptor blockers, and estrogen. An orchiectomy (surgical removal of the testes) may be done in the advanced stages of prostate cancer. Chemotherapy is primarily limited to treatment for those with hormone-resistant tumours and prostate cancer in the late stages. The goal of chemotherapy is palliative.

The client is encouraged to actively participate in the therapeutic plan, which includes thorough discussion about possible sexual dysfunction.

TESTICULAR CANCER

Testicular cancer is the most common cancer in men 15 to 35 years of age. It is a highly treatable and usually curable cancer (Day, Paul, Williams, Smeltzer, & Bare, 2007).

Pathophysiology

The testicles can develop both germinal and nongerminal tumours. Germinal tumours are the most common form of testicular cancer. About half of germinal tumours are seminomas (tumours developing from sperm-producing cells of the testes). Seminomas tend to remain localized and therefore have a more favourable prognosis. Nonseminoma germinal cell tumours tend to develop earlier in the lifespan and grow quickly. Nonseminomas tend to metastasize quickly. A small percentage of testicular tumours develop in the supportive and hormone-producing tissues or stroma. Secondary testicular tumours have metastasized from other organs. Lymphoma is the most common cause of secondary testicular cancer (Day et al., 2007).

Clinical Manifestations

A painless mass or lump gradually appears on the testicle. Testicular cancer is rarely bilateral. The client may experience heaviness in his scrotum, inguinal area, or lower abdomen. Back pain, abdominal pain, weight loss, and general weakness suggest that metastasis has already occurred.

Diagnostics

Tumour markers are substances synthesized by the tumour cells and released into the circulation in abnormal amounts. Human chorionic gonadotropin and alpha-fetoprotein are tumour markers for testicular cancer. Benign testicular tumours do not elevate the levels of these markers. The markers can also be used to evaluate the responses to therapy for testicular cancer. Effective treatment drops the level of the markers. The persistence of elevated levels of markers after orchiectomy is evidence the client has metastatic disease. Other diagnostic tests could include CT of the abdomen and chest to assess for metastasis. Lymphangiography may be ordered to assess possible spread to the lymph system. Microscopic analysis is the definitive way to determine the presence of cancer.

Therapeutics and Nursing Considerations

Treatment selection is based on cell type and the extent of the disease. An orchiectomy is performed surgically to remove the cancerous testis. The client may also undergo a radical retroperitoneal lymph node dissection. Chemotherapy and radiation therapy may be indicated for clients who are high risk for metastasis.

Issues related to body image and sexuality need to be addressed. The client will require encouragement to maintain a positive attitude during the course of his treatment. Unilateral orchiectomy and radiation will not necessarily prevent the client from fathering children. The client will be encouraged to perform testicular self-examinations (TSE).

GENITOURINARY HEALTH CHALLENGES

URINARY TRACT INFECTIONS

Pathophysiology

UTIs are the second most common bacterial disease in women. Usually, the bladder and its contents are free of bacteria in the majority of healthy clients. A small minority of healthy individuals have colonizing bacteria in their bladder. This is called asymptomatic bacteriuria and does not justify treatment. *E. coli* is the most common pathogen causing UTIs. Clients who are immuno-suppressed, have diabetes, or have undergone multiple courses of antibiotics are vulnerable to developing UTIs.

UTIs may be classified as upper and lower, depending on their location within the urinary system:

- Infections of the upper tract involve the renal parenchyma, pelvis, and ureters.
- Lower tract infections involve the lower urinary tract, bladder, and urethra.

Pyelonephritis refers to infection of the renal parenchyma and collecting system, cystitis indicates inflammation of the bladder wall, and urethritis is inflammation of the urethra. Urosepsis is a UTI that has spread into the systemic circulation and is a life-threatening condition requiring emergency treatment.

UTIs may also be classified as uncomplicated and complicated infections. Uncomplicated infections occur in an otherwise normal urinary tract. Complicated infections occur with coexisting conditions, such as obstruction, stones, catheters, diabetes, or neurological disease, or are recurrent infections.

The physiological and mechanical defence mechanisms that help maintain the normally sterile condition of the bladder include the actual emptying of the bladder, normal antibacterial ability of the mucosa and the urine, the ureterovesical junction competence, and the peristaltic activity of the urinary tract. Alterations in any of these factors increase the risk of contracting a UTI. Organisms causing UTIs are usually introduced via the ascending route from the urethra. Less commonly, organisms can be introduced via the bloodstream or the lymphatic system. Gram-negative bacilli from the GI tract are the most common cause. Contributing factors that enhance development include urological instrumentation that allows bacteria present in the opening of the urethra to enter the urethra or bladder. Sexual intercourse promotes the "milking" of bacteria from the perineum and vagina. UTIs rarely result from the hematogenous route.

Clinical Manifestations

Symptoms of UTIs include the following:

- Dysuria, frequent urination, urgency, and suprapubic discomfort or pressure
- Urine itself may contain visible blood or sediment, giving it a cloudy appearance.
- Flank pain, chills, and fever are indicative of an upper UTI.

Diagnostics

Diagnostic studies include a urinalysis and urine for culture and sensitivity (C&S), following a complete history and physical examination of the client. Urine cultures may be obtained by clean-catch technique or catheterization or suprapubic needle aspiration. Sensitivity testing determines susceptibility to antibiotics.

Therapeutics and Nursing Considerations

Uncomplicated cystitis is treated by a short-term course of antibiotics. A complicated UTI requires a long-term treatment. Trimethoprim-sulfamethoxazole (TMP-SMX) and nitrofurantoin are frequently used to treat uncomplicated or initial infections. Pyridium is an over-the-counter drug that provides soothing effects on the urinary tract mucosa. The drug stains the urine a reddish orange colour that may be mistaken for blood; however, the drug is effective in relieving discomfort. Prophylactic or suppressive antibiotics are sometimes administered to clients with repeated UTIs.

Client teaching is important to help prevent UTIs, including the following:

- Emptying the bladder on a regular basis and wiping the perineal area from front to back
- Avoiding constipation
- Maintaining good fluid intake
- Drinking 236 mL of pure cranberry juice per day or taking essence of cranberry juice tablets

PYELONEPHRITIS

Pathophysiology

Acute pyelonephritis is a bacterial infection of the renal pelvis, tubules, and interstitial tissue of the kidney. It usually begins with colonization and infection of the lower tract via the ascending urethral route and is frequently caused by *E. coli*, *Proteus*, *Klebsiella*, or *Enterobacter* agents. Often pre-existing factors are present, such as vesicoureteral reflux or a dysfunction of the urinary tract by obstruction, stricture, or stones. Recurring episodes lead to scarred, poorly functioning kidneys and chronic pyelonephritis.

Clinical Manifestations

Symptoms will vary from mild fatigue to sudden onset of chills, fever, vomiting, malaise, flank pain, and lower urinary tract symptoms characteristic of cystitis. Costovertebral tenderness is usually present on the affected side.

Diagnostics

Diagnostic studies such as a urinalysis will show pyuria, bacteriuria, and varying degrees of hematuria. WBC casts indicate involvement of renal parenchyma. CBC will show leukocytosis with an increase in immature bands. Ultrasonography of the urinary system helps identify anatomical abnormalities or the presence of obstructing stones. Imaging studies also are helpful to assess for impaired renal function, scarring, chronic pyelonephritis, and abscesses.

Therapeutics and Nursing Considerations

Clients with severe infections may need hospitalization for control of nausea, vomiting, and dehydration. At home, clients are encouraged to drink an adequate amount of fluids, rest to increase comfort, and take their antibiotics until the prescription has been finished.

NEPHROTIC SYNDROME

Pathophysiology

Nephrotic syndrome is a condition characterized by marked proteinuria, hypoalbuminemia, hyperlipidemia, anasarca = generalized edema

and edema. Although nephrotic syndrome is not a disease itself, it results from a specific defect that makes the glomeruli more permeable to plasma proteins. Nephrotic syndrome usually is caused by an immune or inflammatory process. The increased glomerular permeability is responsible for a massive excretion of protein in the urine, especially albumin and immunoglobulin. This results in decreased serum protein, leading to decreased oncotic pressure with subsequent edema formation, which may include ascites and anasarca. The diminished plasma oncotic pressure also stimulates hepatic lipoprotein synthesis, which results in hyperlipidemia. Fat bodies commonly appear in the urine. Because of the loss of immunoglobulins, the immune response is affected, and infections can be serious complications. Hypercoagulability with thromboembolism is potentially the most serious complication of nephrotic syndrome. The renal vein is the most common site for thrombus formation. Pulmonary emboli are also a risk.

Clinical Manifestations

Characteristic manifestations may include massive proteinuria, hyperlipidemia and hypoalbuminemia, peripheral edema, possible third space shifting, foamy urine, orthostatic hypotension, malaise, and irritability.

Diagnostics

Diagnosis is made with a thorough history and physical examination. Urinalysis will reveal large quantities of protein and an increased number of hyaline, granular, and waxy, fatty casts.

Blood work shows the following:

- Increased cholesterol, phospholipid, and triglyceride levels
- Decreased albumin

Protein electrophoresis may be done to identify the type of protein lost in the urine.

Therapeutics and Nursing Considerations

Treatment aims at correction of the underlying cause if possible. Supportive treatment is aimed at protein replacement and relief of edema. Diuretics and a restricted sodium diet are ordered, with 1 g of protein per kilogram of body weight. Antibiotics may be given for infection. Some clients may need steroid medication; others may need lipid-lowering medications.

The nurse will pay particular attention to the relief of edema. Weigh the client daily. Accurate intake and output measurements are necessary. Abdominal girths may need to be measured. Edematous skin needs careful cleaning and care to protect it from trauma. Education regarding diet and fluid management is important.

GLOMERULONEPHRITIS

Pathophysiology

Glomerulonephritis is an inflammation of glomerular capillaries caused by an immunological process. It affects both kidneys equally and can lead to renal failure. The antigen–antibody complexes can be deposited in the glomeruli, causing obstruction. The kidney tissue itself may also serve as the antigen. Inflammation occurs within the glomeruli, followed by thickening and scarring of the glomerular membrane, which decreases glomerular filtration.

Clinical Manifestations

Clinical manifestations of glomerulonephritis include varying degrees of hematuria, proteinuria, and elevated serum creatinine and BUN. Other manifestations may include some degree of hypertension and edema.

Diagnostics

Diagnosis is based on the history and physical examination along with a urinalysis, CBC, BUN, creatinine, serum albumin, complement levels, and an antistreptolysin O (ASO) titre.

Therapeutics and Nursing Considerations

In most cases, recovery is complete following rest and symptomatic treatment. This includes diuretics for fluid retention and antihypertensives if the client is hypertensive. If progressive involvement occurs, the result is destruction of renal tissue and marked renal insufficiency.

RENAL CANCER

Pathophysiology

Renal cell carcinoma, also called adenocarcinoma, is the most common type of malignant kidney tumour. It usually starts in the proximal renal tubules. Local extension of kidney cancer into the renal vein and vena cava is common. The most common sites of metastases include the lungs, liver, and long bones. Some forms of renal carcinoma are inherited.

Clinical Manifestations

There are no characteristic early symptoms. The most common symptoms are hematuria, flank pain, and a palpable mass in the flank or abdomen. Other symptoms may be weight loss, fever, hypertension, and anemia.

Diagnostics

Diagnosis is made through the history and physical examination. An intravenous pyelogram (IVP) with nephrography or sonography is used to detect renal masses. Ultrasound helps differentiate between a tumour and a cyst. Angiography, percutaneous needle aspiration, CT scan, and MRI can also be used for diagnosis.

Therapeutics and Nursing Considerations

The treatment of renal cancer involves destruction or removal of the cancer. Radiofrequency ablation is a minimally invasive procedure that can be done to destroy the tumour. Nephrectomy (removal of a kidney) or radical nephrectomy, which is removal of the kidney, adrenal gland, surrounding fascia, part of the ureter, and draining lymph nodes, may be needed. Radiation therapy is used palliatively in inoperable cases and when there are metastases to the bone or lungs. Postoperative care focuses on the following:

- Monitoring for hemorrhage and adrenal insufficiency, which may cause hypotension
- Loss of urine output
- Changes in the level of consciousness (LOC)
- Pain management
- Fluid assessment
- Possible antibiotics and steroid replacement

The nurse needs to support the client and the family and share available resources with them.

POLYCYSTIC KIDNEY DISEASE

Pathophysiology

Polycystic kidney disease (PKD) is a common genetic disease. Cysts form in the renal tubules, and as they advance and increase in size, they fill the cortex and the medulla and destroy surrounding tissue by compression. The cysts are various sizes, involve both kidneys, and are filled with fluid, including blood or pus.

Clinical Manifestations

Symptoms appear when the cysts begin to enlarge. Often the first symptoms to appear are hypertension, hematuria, and feelings of heaviness in the back, side, or abdomen. On physical examination, palpable bilateral enlarged kidneys are often found. UTIs, urinary calculi, or both may be found, and chronic pain is common. The disease usually progresses to ESRD.

Diagnostics

Diagnosis is based on clinical manifestations, family history, IVP, ultrasonogram, and CT scan.

Therapeutics and Nursing Considerations

There is no specific treatment for PKD. A major aim of treatment is to prevent infections and to treat them promptly and effectively if they occur. Nephrectomy may be necessary if pain, bleeding, or infection becomes chronic. A kidney transplant may be the only cure.

Nursing management is the same as that used for the treatment and management of renal failure, namely diet modification, fluid restriction, medications, and helping the client accept the chronic disease process.

URINARY TRACT CALCULI

Pathophysiology

Nephrolithiasis refers to kidney stone disease. Urolithiasis (calculi) is stones in the urinary tract. Except for struvite stones, which are associated with UTI, stone disorders are more common in men than in women. The majority of clients are 20–55 years of age. Renal calculi may result from the following:

- Dehydration
- Infection
- Changes in urine pH
- Diet
- Immobilization
- Metabolic factors, such as hyperparathyroidism, cancers, and granulomatous disease

Calcium is the most common type of urolithiasis. Struvite stones are composed of magnesium, phosphate, and ammonium. Cystine and xanthine stones are associated with hereditary factors. Uric acid can also form stones. Different theories attempt to explain the development of stones in the urinary tract. One theory is that urinary constituents exceed their solubility. Keeping urine dilute reduces the risk of recurrent stone formation. Another theory is that the urinary pH affects the formation of stones. A higher pH is an environment that supports the development of calcium and phosphate stones. A lower pH supports the development of uric acid and cystine stones. Struvite stones usually form in the presence of a UTI with urea-splitting bacteria such as *Proteus* or *Klebsiella*.

Clinical Manifestations

Clinical manifestations of urinary stones occur because of the obstruction of urinary flow. Symptoms include a sudden onset of unilateral abdominal or flank pain. The type of pain is determined by the location of the stone. If the stone is not obstructing, there will not be any pain. Other symptoms include the presence of hematuria, urinary infections accompanied by fever, vomiting, nausea, and chills.

Diagnostics

Diagnosis is determined by an accurate history and physical examination. Urine pH will be checked. An X-ray of the abdomen and renal ultrasonography will reveal larger radiopaque stones. Ultrasonography can be used to identify radiopaque or radiolucent calculi in the renal pelvis, calyx, or proximal ureter. A CT scan will differentiate between a nonopaque stone and a tumour. IVP or a retrograde pyelogram localizes the degree and site of obstruction or confirms the presence of nonradiopaque stones (from cystine and uric acid). When stones are recovered, chemical analysis will be done to provide an indication of the underlying disorder.

Therapeutics and Nursing Considerations

The history and physical examination will reveal a family history of stone formation, nutritional assessment, activity pattern, a history of any prolonged illness with immobilization or dehydration, and a history of any condition or surgery involving the genitourinary or GI tract or endocrine disturbances.

Various medications are prescribed that prevent stone formation by altering urine pH, preventing excessive urinary excretion of a substance, or correcting a primary disease such as hyperparathyroidism.

Treatment for struvite stones requires control of infection. If the infection cannot be controlled, the stone will have to be surgically removed. Indications for surgical therapy include stones that are too large to pass through ureters, a client who cannot be treated medically, and a client with one kidney.

Calculi that are too large for natural passage may require surgical removal, percutaneous ultrasonic lithotripsy and extracorporeal shock wave lithotripsy (ESWT), or chemolysis.

Hematuria is common following lithotripsy procedures. Adequate fluid intake to prevent dehydration is encouraged prior to stone removal as an increase in fluids may exacerbate the colic associated with the episode. After the stone has passed, the client is encouraged to drink enough to ensure at least a 2 L output as this will dilute concentrations of minerals. Diet modifications may be needed to help prevent further stone formation.

Nursing considerations are listed below:

- Pain management and client comfort are primary nursing responsibilities when managing a person with an obstructing stone and renal colic.
- All urine voided by the client should be strained so it can be inspected for the stone.
- Ambulation with support is encouraged to promote movement of the stone.
- Client and family teaching is necessary regarding diet and fluid intake.
- Follow-up care should be discussed with both client and family.

RENAL FAILURE

Pathophysiology and Clinical Manifestations

Renal failure is a partial or complete impairment of renal function and is classified as acute or chronic. ARF has a rapid onset. Chronic renal failure (CRF) usually develops slowly over months or years.

Acute Renal Failure

ARF is a clinical syndrome characterized by a rapid loss of renal function with progressive azotemia (accumulation of nitrogenous wastes). Causes of ARF include conditions that reduce the blood flow to the kidneys, renal parenchymatous disease, and obstruction. Prerenal ARF is due to factors external to the kidney that reduce renal blood flow and lead to decreased glomerular perfusion and filtration. Prerenal causes are the most common cause of ARF and include the following:

- Hypovolemia
- Decreased cardiac output
- Decreased peripheral vascular resistance
- Vascular obstruction

Prerenal disease can lead to intrarenal disease (acute tubular necrosis) if renal ischemia is prolonged.

Intrarenal causes include the conditions that cause direct damage to the renal tissue (parenchyma), resulting in impaired nephron function. Intrarenal ARF is usually due to the following:

- Prolonged ischemia
- Nephrotoxins
- Rhabdomyolysis [old muscle tissue leads to release muscle fiber into blood.]
- Glomerulonephritis
- Complications of diabetes on the glomerular basement membrane

Causes of postrenal ARF involve obstruction of urinary outflow. The most common causes are as follows:

- Prostate cancer and BPH
- Urinary tract calculi
- Extrarenal tumours

ARF progresses through four phases: initiation, oliguric, diuretic, and recovery.

Initiation Phase: The initiation phase begins at the time of the insult. This phase continues until symptoms become evident.

Oliguric Phase: The oliguric phase reflects a reduction in the GFR that causes oliguria.

- The oliguric phase usually starts 1–7 days after the initiating event and lasts about 10–14 days.

- The longer the oliguric phase lasts, the poorer the prognosis is for complete recovery of renal function.
- Due to the decrease in urine in the oliguric phase, the client will have fluid retention.
- Fluid overload can lead to heart failure, pulmonary edema, and pericardial and pleural effusions.
- Metabolic acidosis results when the kidneys cannot synthesize ammonia, which is needed for the excretion of hydrogen ions.
- The client may exhibit Kussmaul breathing (rapid and deep) as the respiratory tract attempts to compensate and blow off carbon dioxide.
- Waste products are not eliminated and remain in the blood.
- Potassium levels rise in the blood as the kidneys are unable to eliminate potassium.
- The kidneys are unable to eliminate phosphate, so the calcium levels within the blood will drop.
- As the waste products build in the blood, the client may become anorexic and experience nausea and vomiting with bowel disturbances.
- Uremic breath may develop.
- The kidneys are unable to produce the active form of vitamin D, so absorption of calcium from the intestine is limited.
- Anemia occurs due to the kidneys' inability to produce erythropoietin.
- Hematological changes may result in GI bleeds and the development of stomatitis as the waste products damage the leukocytes, immunoglobulins, and platelets.
- Neurological changes can occur as nitrogenous waste products accumulate in the brain and other nervous tissue. Symptoms can be as mild as fatigue and difficulty concentrating or can escalate to seizures, stupor, and coma.

Diuretic Phase: The diuretic phase begins with the gradual increase in urine output. As this phase continues, the output may be as high as 3–5 L per day or more. The diuretic phase may last one to three weeks or more.

- The kidneys are starting to recover their ability to excrete waste and fluid.
- During this period, the client's acid–base, electrolyte, and waste product values are beginning to normalize.
- Because of the large volume of fluid and electrolytes lost during this phase, the client must be monitored closely for hypovolemia, hypotension, hyponatremia, and hypokalemia.

Recovery Phase: The recovery phase begins when the GFR increases and the BUN and creatinine levels plateau.

- Although major improvements occur in the first two weeks of this phase, renal function may take up to 12 months to stabilize.
- Many clients who survive ARF never regain a normal GFR.

Chronic Renal Failure

CRF refers to the progressive, irreversible destruction of nephrons, resulting in systemic damage to all organs. The causes are as follows:

- The most common cause of CRF is uncontrolled diabetes, followed closely by uncontrolled hypertension.
- Other causes may include glomerulonephritis, renal vascular disease, pyelonephritis, and polycystic disease.

CRF is insidious; symptoms do not become evident until the GFR has dropped to 20% of its norm. The clinical course progresses from decreased renal reserve, with 40–70% of renal function, to renal insufficiency, with renal function of approximately 40% and GFR of 70–125 mL/min.

As the condition worsens, the client becomes symptomatic, with increasing levels of BUN, creatinine, and other waste products, resulting in anemia.

A client with CRF exhibits the following changes:

- A GFR of 5–25 mL/min, with azotemia (high levels of BUN and creatinine)
- Metabolic acidosis
- Fluid retention
- Increased serum potassium, phosphate, and possibly sodium
- Decreased calcium
- Severe anemia
- Oliguria

Figure 8.8 illustrates the manifestations of this condition. The term *uremia* refers to the entire signs and symptoms of CRF.

In the final stage of CRF, renal function is 15% or less, and the GFR is less than 5 mL/min. This is ESRD. The client experiences uremic syndrome with severe metabolic acidosis and severe fluid and electrolyte imbalance. ESRD is fatal if clients do not receive dialysis or a kidney transplant.

Diagnostics

Diagnostic studies include a thorough history to determine the etiology of the failure.

Blood work shows the following:

- Elevated BUN and creatinine levels
- Elevated potassium and phosphate levels
- Acidic pH, with low levels of bicarbonate
- Hemoglobin and hematocrit

Urine specimens show the following:

- Casts, cellular debris, and decreased specific gravity, and in glomerular disease, proteinuria and urine osmolality close to serum osmolality
- The creatinine clearance test measures the GFR and is used to estimate the number of remaining functioning nephrons.

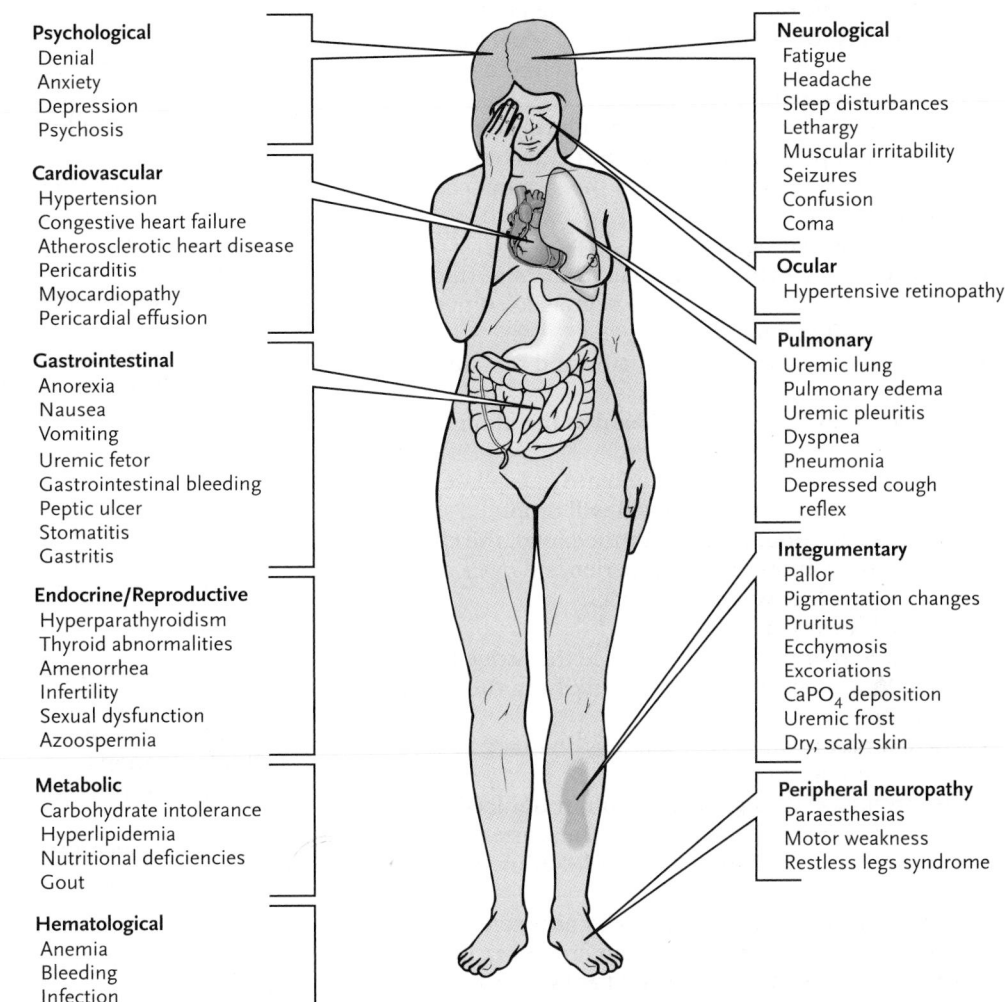

Psychological
Denial
Anxiety
Depression
Psychosis
Cardiovascular
Hypertension
Congestive heart failure
Atherosclerotic heart disease
Pericarditis
Myocardiopathy
Pericardial effusion
Gastrointestinal
Anorexia
Nausea
Vomiting
Uremic fetor
Gastrointestinal bleeding
Peptic ulcer
Stomatitis
Gastritis
Endocrine/Reproductive
Hyperparathyroidism
Thyroid abnormalities
Amenorrhea
Infertility
Sexual dysfunction
Azoospermia
Metabolic
Carbohydrate intolerance
Hyperlipidemia
Nutritional deficiencies
Gout
Hematological
Anemia
Bleeding
Infection
Neurological
Fatigue
Headache
Sleep disturbances
Lethargy
Muscular irritability
Seizures
Confusion
Coma
Ocular
Hypertensive retinopathy
Pulmonary
Uremic lung
Pulmonary edema
Uremic pleuritis
Dyspnea
Pneumonia
Depressed cough reflex
Integumentary
Pallor
Pigmentation changes
Pruritus
Ecchymosis
Excoriations
$CaPO_4$ deposition
Uremic frost
Dry, scaly skin
Peripheral neuropathy
Paraesthesias
Motor weakness
Restless legs syndrome

FIGURE 8.8 **Uremia: Clinical Manifestations of Chronic Renal Failure**

Source: Lewis, S. M., Heitkemper, M. M., Dirksen, S. R., O'Brien, P., Bucher, L., et al. (2010). *Medical-surgical nursing in Canada: Assessment and management of clinical problems* (2nd Canadian ed., p. 1284, Figure 48-5). Toronto: Elsevier.

- Other studies include ultrasonography of the kidneys, renal scan, CT scan, retrograde pyelography, MRI, and plain films of the abdomen, kidneys, ureters, and bladder (KUB).

Therapeutics and Nursing Considerations

The primary goal of treatment is to find the underlying cause of the ARF and eliminate it. Management of signs and symptoms and prevention of complications are also high priorities. Assessing for adequate cardiac output is mandatory. Diuretic therapy along with volume expanders may be used to prevent fluid overload. If ARF has already been established, conservative measures may be necessary until renal function improves. Fluid intake is closely monitored. Blood work is closely monitored for changes in potassium, sodium, bicarbonates, phosphates, blood gases, BUN, creatinine, and calcium.

The diet will be high in carbohydrates and low in protein until the diuretic phase begins. Restriction of potassium- and sodium-containing foods will be regulated according to the levels of these electrolytes in the blood. If potassium levels rise too high, the client may be given Kayexalate to rid the body of potassium, glucose, and insulin to help move the potassium into the cells or calcium gluconate to decrease the excitability of the cell membrane. In some situations, dialysis will be initiated.

Treatment of CRF is to find the precipitating cause and treat or manage it as well as treat the consequences of the progressive condition. Once CRF has progressed to ESRD, dialysis and renal transplantation are the only options. See Figure 8.9.

Dialysis

Dialysis is a technique in which substances move from the blood through a semipermeable membrane and into a dialysis solution (dialysate). Dialysis is used to correct fluid and electrolyte and acid–base imbalances and to remove excess waste products. The two main methods of dialysis include hemodialysis (HD) and peritoneal dialysis (PD). In PD, the peritoneal membrane acts as a semipermeable membrane. In HD, an artificial membrane is used as the semipermeable membrane and is in contact with the client's blood. Generally,

End-Stage Renal Disease (ESRD)
Client
Assess
Hiram Slovok
76-year-old African-American man who has called his physician with fatigue, loss of appetite, and swollen ankles.
Mr. Slovok has a history of
• High blood pressure for 30 years
• A cerebrovascular accident 5 years ago
When questioned, Mr. Slovok states that he
• Has occasional "palpitations of my heart"
• Is frequently bothered by dry skin and itching that "nothing seems to help"
• Experiences difficulty breathing with activity
• Has had nosebleeds for the past few months and seems to bruise easily
• Is urinating less frequently
Laboratory Results
Anemia
Hyperkalemia
Elevated serum creatinine
Elevated blood urea nitrogen
Hypertension (+)
Diabetes mellitus
Glomerulonephritis
African American (+)
Clinical manifestations
Central Nervous System
Lethargy/seizures (?)
Glove/stocking sensory changes (?)
Cardiovascular
Fatigue (+)
Cardiac dysrhythmia (+)
Peripheral edema (+)
Hematological
Fatigue (+)
Ecchymosis (+)
Epistaxis (+)
Respiratory
Shortness of breath (+)
Gastrointestinal
Weight loss (?)
Anorexia (+)
Skin
Pruritus (+)
Ecchymosis (+)
Renal
Oliguria (+)
Diagnostic Tests
Hemoglobin = 9 g
BUN = 120 mg
Serum creatinine = 5.5 mg
Serum potassium = 6 mEq/L
Assessment data
Nursing diagnoses
Nursing interventions
Client outcomes
* NIC Nursing Interventions Classifications
* NOC Nursing Outcomes Classifications
Analyze
Imbalanced Nutrition: Less than Body Requirements
Plan
Protein/potassium/sodium/phosphorus restriction
Vitamin supplementation
Refer to dietitian
NIC Nutrition Management
Evaluate
NOC Nutritional Status: Nutrient Intake
Excess Fluid Volume
Diuretics
Fluid restriction
NIC Fluid/Electrolyte Management
NOC Electrolyte & Acid–Base Balance
Fluid Balance
ACE inhibitors
Calcium channel blockers
Alpha/beta-adrenergic blockers
Vasodilators
Decreased Cardiac Output
NIC Hemodialysis Therapy
NOC Circulation Status
Risk for Infection
NIC Infection Protection
Dialysis Access Maintenance
NOC Hemodialysis Access
Risk for Injury
NIC Environmental Management: Safety
NOC Risk Control
Fatigue
Erythropoietin iron
NIC Energy Management
NOC Activity Tolerance
Energy Conservation
Anxiety
NIC Coping Enhancement
NOC Coping

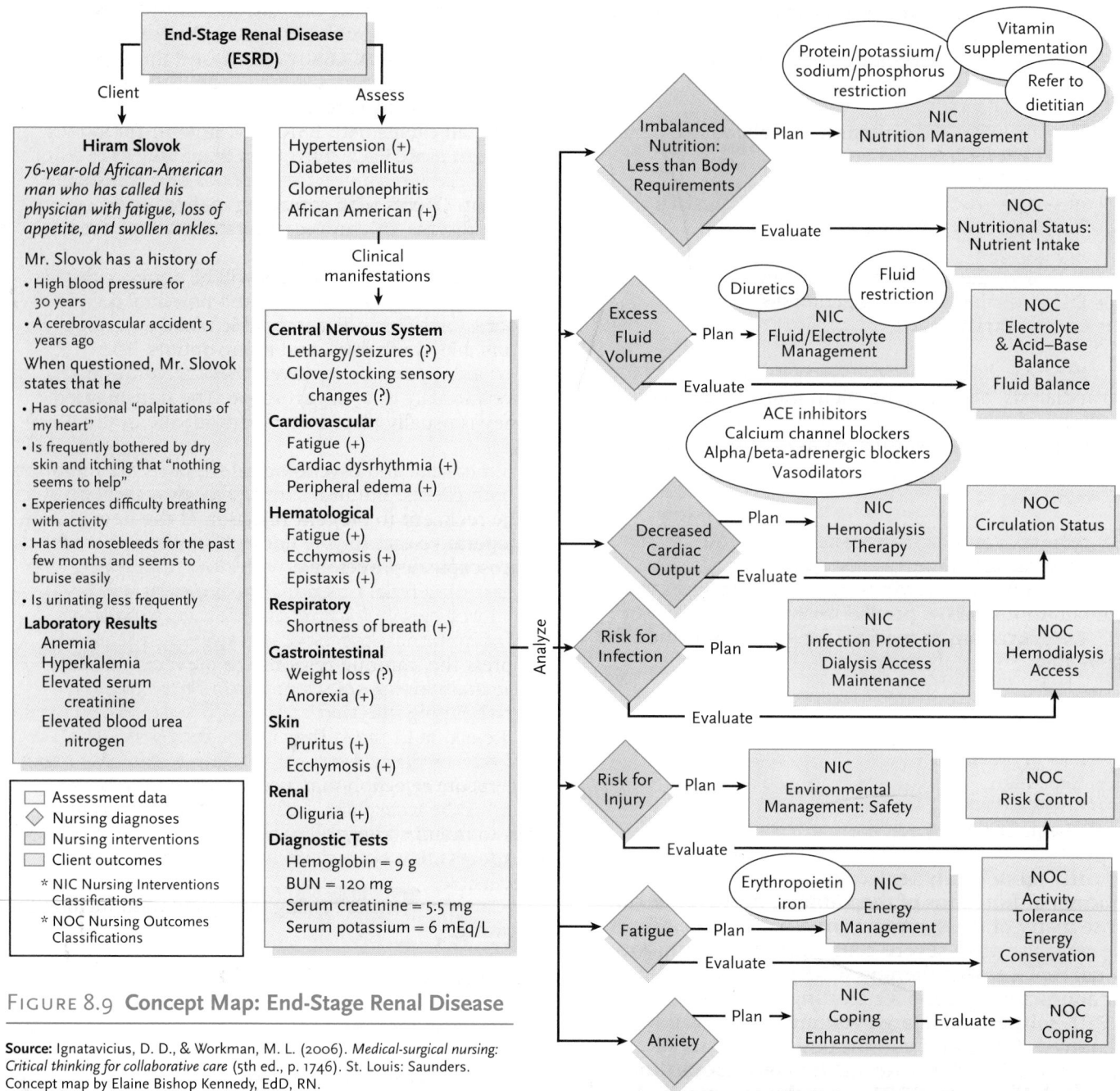

FIGURE 8.9 **Concept Map: End-Stage Renal Disease**

Source: Ignatavicius, D. D., & Workman, M. L. (2006). *Medical-surgical nursing: Critical thinking for collaborative care* (5th ed., p. 1746). St. Louis: Saunders. Concept map by Elaine Bishop Kennedy, EdD, RN.

dialysis is initiated when the GFR or creatinine clearance of the client is less than 15 mL/min (normal is 100–125 mL/min); however, these criteria can vary widely in different clinical situations. Certain uremic complications indicate an immediate need for dialysis and are as follows:

- Encephalopathy
- Neuropathies
- Uncompensated metabolic acidosis
- Uncontrollable hyperkalemia
- Pericarditis
- Accelerated hypertension

The general principles of diffusion, osmosis, and ultrafiltration are involved in both forms of dialysis.

Peritoneal Dialysis

With PD, a catheter is surgically placed through the anterior wall of the abdomen into the peritoneum. The catheter is stitched in place. Dialysis solutions are available commercially in 1–2 L plastic bags with glucose concentrations of 1.5%, 2.5%, or 4.25%. The electrolyte concentration is similar to plasma. There are two forms of PD: automated peritoneal dialysis (APD) and continuous ambulatory peritoneal dialysis,

(CAPD), as well as three phases: the inflow, the dwell, and the drainage.

Complications pertaining to PD include the following:

- Exit site infection, peritonitis, and abdominal pain
- Outflow problems and hernias
- Lower back problems
- Bleeding
- Pulmonary complications
- Protein loss
- Carbohydrate and lipid abnormalities
- Encapsulating sclerosing peritonitis
- Loss of ultrafiltration

Peritoneal dialysis is considered effective for short-term dialysis, allowing the client more independence and ease of travelling. There are fewer dietary restrictions for clients using PD as opposed to HD.

Hemodialysis

HD requires vascular access and incorporates shunts and internal arteriovenous fistulas and grafts. The HD dialyzers are basically long plastic cartridges that contain thousands of parallel hollow tubes or fibres.

Complications to monitor for with HD include the following:

- Hypotension
- Muscle cramps
- Loss of blood
- Hepatitis
- Sepsis
- Disequilibrium syndrome

HD cannot fully replace the metabolic and hormonal functions of the kidneys; however, it can ease many of the symptoms of renal failure and prevent the most severe complications. Continuous renal replacement therapy (CRRT) is an alternative or adjunctive method for treating ARF. With CRRT, solutes and a large volume of fluid can be removed slowly and continuously. CRRT can be used in conjunction with HD for continuous fluid removal. However, CRRT is not the technique of choice for life-threatening manifestations of uremia as it does not work quickly. There are two types of CRRT: continuous arteriovenous therapies and continuous venovenous therapies. CRRT provides continuous fluid removal versus the intermittent fluid removal utilized in HD. CRRT is more stable from a hemodynamic perspective than is HD and does not require constant monitoring or complicated HD equipment.

Kidney Transplantation

Kidney transplantation is the treatment of choice for clients with ESRD and is considered extremely successful, with a high survivor rate from both cadaver and live donors. Unlike dialysis, the transplanted kidney is able to reverse many of the pathophysiological changes associated with renal failure, eliminates the dependence on dialysis, and is less expensive than dialysis after the first year following surgery.

Not all clients with ESRD are suitable for kidney transplantation. Each transplant team will have criteria that the client must meet in order to be a transplant recipient. Clients with spreading malignancies, severe cardiac disease, or chronic respiratory failure are not suitable recipients.

Histocompatibility studies will be done to identify HLA antigens for both donors and potential recipients. Donor sources include compatible blood type cadaver donors, blood relatives, and living donors. The donor kidney will be removed (nephrectomy) either conventionally or by laparoscope. The transplanted kidney is usually placed extraperitoneally in the iliac fossa.

Emotional and psychological supports are important for both clients. Immunosuppressive drugs will be given to the recipient to prevent rejection of the new kidney. Postoperative care for the donor is similar to care for laparoscopic nephrectomy, with close monitoring of remaining renal function. The recipient will be monitored closely for fluid and electrolyte balances. The goal of immunosuppressive therapy is to adequately suppress the immune response to prevent rejection while maintaining sufficient immunity to prevent overwhelming infection.

Rejection of the kidney by the recipient is the antibody-mediated humoral reaction to the new organ. Hyperacute rejection may occur within minutes to hours of the transplant. Acute rejection can occur days to months after the transplant. Chronic rejection is a process that occurs over months to years and is irreversible.

Complications following transplantation include the following:

- Infection
- Cardiovascular disease
- Malignancies
- Recurrence of original renal disease
- Steroid-related complications

HEALTH CHALLENGES RELATED TO MOVEMENT AND COORDINATION

HEADACHE

Pathophysiology and Clinical Manifestations

Headaches (cephalalgia) are the most common type of pain experienced by humans. Headaches are classified as either primary, with no identifiable cause, or secondary, with an underlying cause. Primary classifications of headaches include tension-type, migraine, and cluster headaches.

The tension-type headache is the most common type, in which the client experiences bilateral feelings of pressure around the head caused by irritation of the pain-sensitive structures of the brain. There is no prodrome (symptom indicative of an approaching disease). Tension-type headaches have at least two of the following characteristics:

- The sensation of pressure or tightness
- Mild to moderate severity
- Bilateral location
- Worsening with physical activity
- Sensitivity to light (photophobia) or sound (phonophobia)

Diagnostics

To diagnose tension-type headaches, a careful history and physical examination, including a neurological examination, are needed. Routine laboratory studies may be done. CT of the sinuses, MRI, angiography, and electromyography (EMG) may be performed.

MIGRAINE HEADACHES

Pathophysiology and Clinical Manifestations

Migraine headaches are characterized by unilateral or bilateral throbbing pain caused by vasodilation of the dural blood vessels that then stimulate the trigeminal nerve pain pathway. Neuropeptides are released, which make the vasodilation worse. There is usually a family history of migraine headaches. The onset is usually in childhood or adolescence.

Migraine headaches may be preceded by an aura (sensation occurring before a disorder) and prodrome by days or hours. The prodrome can include psychic disturbances, GI upset, and changes in fluid balance. The headache itself may be triggered by the following:

- Stress
- Excitement
- Bright lights
- Menstruation
- Alcohol
- Certain foods

Migraine headaches are subdivided into migraine with aura and migraine without aura. A classic symptom of an aura is flashing lights in one quadrant of the visual field (scintillating scotomata).

Migraine without aura involves at least one of the following: nausea and vomiting, photophobia, and phonophobia. Migraine without aura is the most common type of migraine.

Symptoms of a migraine with or without an aura are as follows:

- Generalized edema
- Irritability
- Pallor
- Nausea and vomiting
- Sweating

Clients may seek shelter from noise, light, odours, people, or other stressors. They feel a steady, throbbing pain synchronous with the pulse.

Diagnostics

Diagnostic tests are the same as those for tension headaches.

CLUSTER HEADACHES

Pathophysiology and Clinical Manifestations

Cluster headaches are thought to be variants of migraine headaches and are characterized by repeated headaches that occur for weeks or months at a time, followed by periods of remission. Cluster headaches are considered one of the most severe forms of head pain. The etiology of cluster headaches is unknown. The pathophysiology of cluster headaches is similar to that of migraine headaches; however, the triggers are different in that cluster headaches can be triggered by alcohol, nicotine, and histamines.

Clinical manifestations of cluster headaches include the following:

- Severe unilateral orbital, supraorbital, or temporal pain
- Associated symptoms, including nasal congestion, lacrimation, rhinorrhea, and forehead and facial swelling

Cluster headaches do not cause nausea and vomiting. The onset of the headache is usually abrupt, without prodrome. It commonly occurs at night and may recur several times a day for several days. The pain is described as deep, steady, and penetrating but not throbbing. Clients with cluster headaches often pace the floor, cry out, and avoid being touched by others.

Diagnostics

Diagnostic tests are the same as those for tension headaches.

Therapeutics and Nursing Considerations

Drug treatments for headaches are as follows:

- Tension-type headache medications may include non-narcotic analgesics used alone or in combination with a sedative, muscle relaxant, tranquilizer, or codeine.

- Migraine headache drugs focus on terminating or decreasing the symptoms.
- Aspirin or acetaminophen may be effective for mild forms of the headache.
- Ergotamine is used when analgesics do not relieve the pain.
- Other medications may include serotonin receptor agonists, alpha- and beta-adrenergic blockers, tricyclic antidepressants, calcium channel blockers, and antiseizure drugs.
- Cluster headaches are treated with alpha-adrenergic blockers and vasoconstrictors. An acute treatment for cluster headaches is inhalation of 100% oxygen delivered at a rate of 7–9 L per minute for 15–20 minutes.

Overuse of analgesics can lead to chronic daily headache or drug-induced headache.

Client and family teaching regarding the medication regimen, nonpharmacological management, and stress reduction techniques can be very helpful. Alternative therapy such as heat or cold applications, acupuncture, or hypnosis has been found to be beneficial for many clients.

HEAD INJURY

Pathophysiology

Head injury is any trauma to the scalp, skull, or brain. Head trauma includes an alteration in consciousness, no matter how brief. There are many causes of head injury, such as firearm-related injuries, motor vehicle accidents, falls, assaults, sports-related injuries, and recreational accidents. There is a high potential for a poor outcome when the head is injured. Not all brain damage is evident at the time of the event.

Scalp lacerations are the most minor type of head trauma. The scalp is very vascular and therefore can bleed profusely. Trauma can result in an abrasion, contusion, laceration, or hematoma. The major complication from a scalp laceration is infection.

Skull fractures may be linear, comminuted, depressed or compound, closed or open. The type and severity of a skull fracture depend on the velocity, momentum, and direction of the injuring agent and the site of impact. The force of the damaging impact could be due to the mechanism of acceleration or deceleration. Specific manifestations of a skull fracture are generally associated with the location of the injury. The major potential complications of skull fractures are as follows:

- Intracranial infections
- Hematomas
- Meningeal and brain tissue damage

Minor head trauma includes concussions and postconcussion syndrome. A concussion involves a change in the LOC. Major head traumas are contusions and lacerations that involve severe brain

trauma. Contusions are bruising of brain tissue most commonly found at the site of impact (coup injury) or in the line opposite the site of impact (contrecoup injury). Lacerations involve the actual tearing of the cortical surface vessels, which may lead to secondary hemorrhage and cerebral edema and inflammation. Intracerebral hemorrhage can be associated with cerebral laceration. The prognosis is generally poor for the person with a large intracerebral hemorrhage.

When major head trauma occurs, many delayed or secondary responses can be seen, including the following:

- Hemorrhage and hematoma formation
- Seizures
- Cerebral edema

Complications of head trauma include an epidural, subdural, or intracerebral hematoma. An epidural hematoma results from bleeding between the dura and the inner surface of the skull. Laceration of the middle meningeal artery is the usual cause, and as such, the hematoma develops rapidly and requires immediate control of the bleeding and evacuation of the blood in the epidural space.

Subdural hematomas occur from bleeding between the dura mater and arachnoid layer of the meningeal covering of the brain and are usually venous in origin and much slower to develop into a mass large enough to produce symptoms. The accumulation of clots puts pressure on the brain surface and eventually displaces brain tissue.

An intracerebral hematoma can be due to a hemorrhagic stroke or ruptured aneurysm.

Clinical Manifestations

Signs of a concussion may include a brief disruption in LOC, amnesia, and headache. Symptoms are generally of short duration. The postconcussion syndrome can occur anywhere from two weeks to two months after the head injury and involves the following:

- A persistent headache
- Lethargy
- Personality and behaviour changes

With acute subdural hematoma, the client exhibits the following signs within 48 hours of the injury:

- Appears drowsy and confused
- Ipsilateral pupil dilates and becomes fixed

With a subacute subdural hematoma, symptoms take longer to appear, between two to 14 days after the injury.

- Failure to regain consciousness may be an indicator.

Chronic subdural hematomas develop over weeks or months after a seemingly minor head injury. The damaged area is filled with fluid rather than blood clots, and symptoms tend to be less acute.

Diagnostics

Diagnosis of a head injury includes the history and physical examination. A CT scan is considered the best diagnostic test to determine craniocerebral trauma. MRI, PET, cervical spine and skull X-ray series, and the Glasgow Coma Scale (GCS) are also used.

Therapeutics and Nursing Considerations

Care for the client with head trauma focuses on the following:

- Monitoring the neurological status and using the GCS
- Observing for cerebrospinal fluid (CSF) leak

The overall goals are to maintain adequate cerebral perfusion; to keep the client normothermic and free from pain, discomfort, and infection; and to attain maximal cognitive, motor, and sensory function. In some situations, craniotomy, craniectomy, cranioplasty, or burr-hole surgery is done to remove the hematoma.

Nursing considerations will focus on the following:

- Promoting good air entry
- Controlling intracranial pressure (ICP)
- Maintaining temperature control
- Monitoring fluid and electrolyte balance
- Preventing infection
- Assisting the client to resume normal activities
- Providing emotional support to the client and the family

INFLAMMATORY BRAIN DISORDERS

Bacteria, viruses, fungi, and chemicals can cause inflammatory brain disorders. Meningitis, encephalitis, and brain abscesses are among the most frequently occurring CNS infections. During an infection, infectious agents can enter the bloodstream. Once the organisms reach the brain, the CSF in the subarachnoid spaces and the pia-arachnoid membrane may become infected. The infection spreads quickly through the meninges and can invade the ventricles. This infectious process can cause serious long-term neurological deficits.

Bacterial Meningitis

Pathophysiology, Clinical Manifestations, and Diagnostics

Bacterial meningitis is a medical emergency with a high mortality rate. The inflammatory response increases CSF production and ICP. The major bacteria associated with bacterial meningitis are *Streptococcus pneumoniae* and *Neisseria meningitidis*.

Symptoms include fever, severe headache, nausea and vomiting, positive Kernig sign, positive Brudzinski sign, photophobia, decreased LOC, and signs of increased ICP. Seizures occur in 20% of all cases. The headache becomes progressively worse. Vomiting and irritability may accompany the worsening headache. Delirium and complete disorientation may develop quickly.

Rapid diagnosis is done by history and physical examination. A blood culture, lumbar puncture, and analysis of CSF are done. A head X-ray, CT scanning, and MRI may be done.

Therapeutics and Nursing Considerations

Antibiotic therapy is initiated after all necessary specimens are collected. The antibiotic needs to be able to cross the blood–brain barrier to be effective. The client is cared for while in a comfortable position in a darkened room to help prevent hallucinations. Pain medication is administered as needed. The client must be observed and treated for any neurological problems, such as seizures. Antipyretics should be given as needed. Hydration must be monitored and small, frequent meals offered. Aseptic technique must be utilized at all times. Progressive range-of-motion (ROM) exercises are required, and client activity should be increased as tolerated. The nursing considerations for all of the following inflammatory brain disorders are similar to those for bacterial meningitis.

Viral Meningitis

Pathophysiology, Clinical Manifestations, and Diagnostics

Viral meningitis is most commonly caused by enterovirus, arbovirus, HIV, or HSV. Viral meningitis, also known as aseptic meningitis, usually presents with a headache, fever, photophobia, myalgias, and a stiff neck. Diagnosis is done by the history and physical examination and a lumbar puncture with cultures done on CSF. In viral meningitis, the CSF will show lymphocytosis, but no organisms will be present in Gram stains or acid-fast smears.

Therapeutics and Nursing Considerations

Symptomatic management with full recovery should be expected. The nursing considerations for viral meningitis are similar to those for bacterial meningitis.

Encephalitis

Pathophysiology, Clinical Manifestations, and Diagnostics

Encephalitis is an acute inflammation of the brain that can be fatal. It can be caused by a number of viruses, including West Nile virus. Ticks or mosquitoes can transmit epidemic encephalitis. Advanced age is a risk factor for developing encephalitis. Most cases have mild flulike symptoms in addition to nonspecific symptoms, such as the following:

- Fever and headache
- Nausea and vomiting
- Stiff neck
- Declining LOC

Signs appear two to three days postinfection and may vary from minimal alterations to coma. Abnormalities in brain function are common in encephalitis. Diagnosis is done by the history and physical examination, MRI, PET, and tests for the IgM antibody to West Nile virus in CSF. Diagnosis between meningitis and encephalitis is based on brain function.

Therapeutics and Nursing Considerations

The treatment for encephalitis may include diuretics, corticosteroids, acyclovir (Zovirax), vidarabine (Vira-A) for HSV infection, and antiseizure drugs. Mosquito control may be used as a preventive measure. The nursing considerations for encephalitis are similar to those for bacterial meningitis.

Brain Abscess

Pathophysiology, Clinical Manifestations, and Diagnostics

Brain abscess is a purulent infection of the brain with an accumulation of pus within brain tissue. The infection may be due to an ear, tooth, mastoid, or sinus infection; skull fracture; brain trauma or surgery; or a complication of meningitis. *Streptococcus* and *Staphylococcus aureus* are the causative agents. The client will present with headache, fever, and nausea and vomiting and may show signs of increased ICP. The symptoms will reflect the local area of abscess. CT and MRI will be used for diagnosis.

Therapeutics and Nursing Considerations

Antimicrobial therapy is the primary treatment, as well as symptomatic treatment for any manifestation. The abscess may need to be drained or removed. If the abscess is left untreated, the client will not survive. The nursing considerations for brain abscesses are similar to those for bacterial meningitis.

MULTIPLE SCLEROSIS

Pathophysiology

Multiple sclerosis (MS) is a chronic, progressive, degenerative neuromuscular disease that is characterized by inflammation of the white matter of the CNS. The disease usually affects young to middle-aged adults, with onset between 15–50 years of age.

Women are affected more than men. The cause is unknown; however, it may be related to infectious, immunological, and genetic factors. Other autoimmune theories include the possibility that autosensitization occurring in response to an antigen on the myelin membrane or a cell-mediated immune reaction triggers the demyelination process. There is no cause-and-effect relationship between a pathogenetic agent and MS. Possible precipitating factors include the following:

- Infection
- Physical injury
- Emotional stress
- Excessive fatigue
- Pregnancy
- Poor state of health

The disease process consists of loss of myelin, disappearance of oligodendrocytes, and proliferation of astrocytes. Changes result in plaque formation, with plaques scattered throughout the CNS. Initially, the myelin sheaths of the neurons in the brain and spinal cord are attacked, but the nerve fibre is not affected. Clients may complain of noticeable impairment of function. Myelin can regenerate and symptoms disappear, resulting in remission, or myelin can be replaced by glial scar tissue. Nerve impulses slow down without myelin. With the destruction of axons, impulses are totally blocked, resulting in permanent loss of nerve function.

Clinical Manifestations

Vague symptoms can occur intermittently over months and years. The disease may not be diagnosed until long after the onset of the first symptom. Symptoms of MS are characterized by chronic, progressive deterioration in some clients, with remissions and exacerbations in others. Common signs and symptoms of MS include the following:

- Motor manifestations, which may include weakness or feelings of heaviness in the legs, paralysis of limbs, diplopia, hyper-reflexia and spasticity of muscles, and sensory, cerebellar, and neurobehavioural problems.
- Sensory manifestations can include numbness and tingling, blurred vision, vertigo, and tinnitus.
- Cerebellar manifestations include nystagmus, ataxia, dysarthria, and dysphagia.
- Neurobehavioural manifestations may include emotional lability.
- Other symptoms may include bowel and bladder dysfunction, optic neuritis, and fatigue. Sexual dysfunction can also occur with MS.

Diagnostics

Diagnosis is based primarily on the history, clinical manifestations, and the presence of multiple lesions over time as measured by an MRI. Laboratory tests will show an increase in activated T4 lymphocytes and IgG content.

Therapeutics and Nursing Considerations

The goal of treatment is to maintain the client's independence for as long as possible. Drug therapy for the treatment of MS includes the following:

- Corticosteroids, which are used to treat acute exacerbations by reducing edema and inflammation at the site of demyelination
- Immunosuppressive therapy is beneficial in clients with progressive relapsing, secondary-progressive, and primary-progressive types of MS.
- Immunomodulators include interferon-beta 1b (Betaseron), interferon-beta-1a (Avonex), glatiramer (Copaxone), natalizumab (Antegren), and mitoxantrone (Novantrone).
- Antispasmodics, CNS stimulants, anticholinergics, tricyclic antidepressants, and antiseizure medications may also be prescribed.

Surgical interventions, such as a neurectomy, rhizotomy, or cordotomy, or dorsal column electrical stimulation may be required if spasticity is not controlled with antispasmodics. Neurological dysfunction sometimes improves with physical therapy and speech therapy. Nutritional therapy prescribes a high-protein diet with supplementary vitamins. Clients will be encouraged to balance rest with activities and maintain optimal nutrition.

As the condition progresses, symptomatic treatment and assistance will be needed. Support groups for MS have been very beneficial for clients and their families.

PARKINSON'S DISEASE

Pathophysiology

Parkinson's disease is a disease of the basal ganglia characterized by slowing down in the initiation and execution of movement (bradykinesia), increased muscle tone (rigidity), tremor at rest, and impaired postural reflexes. The diagnosis of Parkinson's increases with age, with the peak onset being in the sixth decade. Parkinson's is more common in men than in women and is caused by the following conditions:

- Onset of Parkinson's before age 50 is usually due to a genetic defect.
- In many cases, the cause of Parkinson's is unknown.
- Some cases are caused by exposure to toxins from drugs and chemicals that destroy the cells in the substantial nigra of the brain.
- Other causes of Parkinson's include hydrocephalus, hypoxia, infections, stroke, tumour, and trauma.

Parkinson's affects the extrapyramidal system, which influences movement. A dopamine deficiency occurs in the basal ganglia. Reduction of dopamine in the corpus striatum upsets the normal balance between the dopamine (inhibitor) and acetylcholine (excitatory) neurotransmitters. Symptoms occur when affected brain cells can no longer perform their normal inhibitory function within the CNS.

Clinical Manifestations

Symptoms of the disease do not occur until 80% of neurons in the substantia nigra are lost. The classic triad of manifestations includes tremor, rigidity, and bradykinesia.

- Insidious tremor begins in the fingers (unilateral pill-roll tremor). The tremor is more prominent at rest and is aggravated by emotional stress or increased concentration.
- Rigidity is caused by sustained muscle contraction and consequently elicits complaints of soreness and feeling tired and achy. Rigidity inhibits the alternating contraction and relaxation in opposing muscle groups, slowing movement. The rigidity may be uniform or jerky (cogwheel rigidity). The client may have difficulty walking, with the gait lacking normal parallel motion. Bradykinesia (slow and retarded movement) is particularly evident.
- Other symptoms include a high-pitched, monotone voice, drooling, a masklike facial expression, slow, slurred speech, and dysphagia.

Complications of Parkinson's are caused by progressive deterioration and the negative impact this deterioration may have on the client. For example, dysphagia can lead to malnutrition. Dementia occurs in up to 40% of clients with Parkinson's.

Diagnostics

There are no specific tests for diagnosing Parkinson's. Diagnosis is based solely on the history and clinical features. A firm diagnosis can be made when at least two of the three classic symptoms are present. The ultimate confirmation of the disease is a positive response to antiparkinsonian drugs.

Therapeutics and Nursing Considerations

The drug therapy is aimed at correcting imbalances of neurotransmitters within the CNS. These drugs either enhance the release or supply of dopamine or antagonize or block the effects of acetylcholine. The drug treatments are listed below:

- Levodopa with carbidopa (Sinemet) is often the first drug used. Levodopa is a precursor of dopamine and can cross the blood–brain barrier. It is converted to dopamine in the basal ganglia. Carbidopa inhibits an enzyme that breaks down levodopa before it reaches the brain. The effect of Sinemet could wear off after a few years of therapy.
- Anticholinergics may be used in the management of Parkinson's.
- Antihistamines and antiviral agents are also used.

- As Parkinson's progresses, a combination therapy is often required.

Surgical procedures are aimed at relieving symptoms in clients who are usually unresponsive to drug therapy. Ablation therapy has largely been replaced by deep brain stimulation, which involves placing electrodes in the thalamus, globus pallidus, or subthalamic nucleus. Both ablation and deep brain stimulation procedures work by reducing the increased neuronal activity produced by the dopamine depletion.

Transplantation of fetal neural tissue into the basal ganglia provides dopamine-producing cells in the brains of clients with Parkinson's. This type of therapy is still experimental.

Since malnutrition and constipation can cause serious consequences, adequate nutrition is essential. Clients with dysphagia and bradykinesia need food that is easily chewed and swallowed. The client needs adequate roughage. Small, frequent meals are best to prevent fatigue. Ample time must be allowed for the client to eat and not become frustrated. Levodopa can be impaired by protein ingestion.

The goals of treatment focus on maximizing neurological function and maintaining independence in activities of daily living for as long as possible. Optimizing psychosocial well-being is very important.

SPINAL CORD INJURY

Pathophysiology

Spinal cord injuries (SCIs) are most common in males between the ages of 16–30 years. The causes of this injury include motor vehicle accidents, falls, violence, and sports injuries. Types of SCI include cord concussion, in which the cord is severely jarred, as in a sports injury. There may be cord contusion, in which compression of the cord results in bleeding into the cord, causing bruising and edema. The extent of the damage will depend on the severity of the inflammatory response. Cord laceration, in which there is an actual tear in the cord, results in permanent injury as the neurons of the CNS do not regenerate. Cord transection, either complete or incomplete, results in loss of neurological function below the site of the injury.

The extent of the neurological damage caused by an SCI results from the primary injury, which is the actual physical disruption of an axon, and the secondary injury damage due to ischemia, hypoxia, microhemorrhage, and edema. Secondary injury occurs over time; therefore, a prognosis of recovery is more accurate 72 hours after the initial injury. The secondary injury refers to the ongoing progressive damage that occurs after the initial injury. This ongoing injury can be due to free radical formation, uncontrolled calcium influx, ischemia, lipid peroxidation, or some combination of these.

Spinal shock can last days to months and is characterized by the following:

- Decreased reflexes
- Loss of sensation
- Flaccid paralysis below the level of injury, which is experienced by 50% of people with acute SCI (Lewis et al., 2010).

The six syndromes associated with incomplete cord lesions are summarized in Table 8.10.

Table 8.10 Incomplete Cord Lesion Syndromes

Syndrome	Cause and Results
Central Cord Syndrome	• Damage is to the central spinal cord, with the client experiencing motor weakness and sensory loss in both upper and lower extremities.
Anterior Cord Syndrome	• Damage is to the anterior spinal artery, resulting in motor paralysis and loss of pain and temperature sensation below the level of injury. • Position, vibration, and touch sensations remain intact.
Brown-Séguard Syndrome	• Typically results from a penetrating injury involving half of the spinal cord • Loss of motor function, position, and vibratory sense on the same side as the injury, with contralateral loss of pain and temperature sensation
Posterior Cord Syndrome	• Rare syndrome in which damage is to the posterior spinal artery, resulting in loss of proprioception. • Pain, temperature sensation, and motor function below the site of the lesion will be intact.
Conus Medullaris Syndrome and Cauda Equina Syndrome	• Damage is to the very lowest portion of the spinal cord (conus) and lumbar and sacral roots (cauda equina). • These types of syndromes result in lower motor neuron injury with flaccid paralysis of the bowel and bladder and loss of sexual function.

Spinal shock is manifested by the following:

- Decreased reflexes
- Loss of sensation
- Flaccid paralysis below the level of injury

These symptoms may last days to months and may mask postneurological function. In clients with spinal injuries at T6 or higher, return of the reflexes once spinal shock has been resolved may trigger the development of autonomic dysreflexia, which is a massive uncompensated cardiovascular reaction mediated by the SNS. Autonomic dysreflexia is life-threatening and usually occurs in response to visceral stimulation once the spinal shock is resolved. A distended bladder or rectum is the most common precipitating cause of autonomic dysreflexia. Manifestations of autonomic dysreflexia include the following:

- Extreme hypertension
- Blurred vision
- Throbbing headache
- Marked diaphoresis and flushed skin
- Piloerection
- Nasal congestion
- Nausea
- Anxiety (Lewis et al., 2010)

Clinical Manifestations

Clinical manifestations are generally a direct result of trauma. The manifestations are related to the level and degree of injury. With the incomplete lesion, there will be a mixture of symptoms.

A higher injury will have more serious manifestations. Sensory function closely parallels motor function at all levels. Disturbances of respiratory function in injuries below T6 are minimal. See Figure 8.10 for examples of patterns of injury. The following manifestations are common for upper level injuries:

- Hypoventilation can be a serious complication with a cervical injury. Mechanical ventilation is required. Atelectasis and pneumonia can easily develop, and the client may require an artificial airway.
- An injury above the T6 level greatly decreases the influence of the SNS, resulting in bradycardia, peripheral vasodilation, and hypotension.
- With spinal cord lesions, the client may experience urinary retention and bladder distension and may need an in-dwelling catheter.

When lesions involve lower motor neurons, flaccid muscle weakness or paralysis, loss of reflex activity, and atrophy of the involved muscles are usually evident. Any lesion that destroys or interferes with upper motor neurons initially results in muscle flaccidity and hyporeflexia. Gradually, the reflex arcs become reactive. Voluntary muscle function is lost, but hyper-reflexia of all cord segments occurs, with increased muscle tone and spasticity. Pressure sores can develop. Temperature regulation can be problematic as the client will have a decreased ability to sweat or shiver. Loss of body weight is common. DVT is common, with pulmonary embolism being one of the leading causes of death in clients with SCIs.

Diagnostics

SCIs are initially diagnosed on the basis of the presenting clinical manifestations. Diagnostic studies include complete spine films, CT scans, and MRIs.

Therapeutics and Nursing Considerations

The initial goals focus on sustaining life and preventing further cord damage. Knowing how the injury occurred and how the client perceives the extent of the injury immediately after the accident is very important.

Assessment of brain injury, sensory examination, musculoskeletal injuries, damage to internal organs, and evaluation and monitoring of respiratory, cardiac, urinary, and GI function need to be done. Refer to Chapter 4, Health Assessment Across the Lifespan, for the specific system health assessments.

Nonoperative stabilization involves traction and realignment. Surgery such as decompression laminectomy may be necessary to stabilize the spine, reduce secondary injury from cord compression, prevent neurological deficits, stabilize compound fracture of the vertebrae, stabilize bone fragments, and stabilize penetrating wounds of the cord or surrounding structures.

Drug therapy includes the early use of methylprednisone to decrease edema and improve blood flow. Tirilazad mesylate may be administered for 48 hours to improve motor recovery rates. Vasopressor agents may be used as adjuvants in the acute phase.

Proper immobilization of the neck is essential to stabilize the cervical spine. The nose should always be in line with the sternum to assist in correct alignment. The following nursing considerations are crucial:

- Traction will help stabilize cervical injuries.
- A body jacket or Jewett brace may be used for thoracic or lumbar injuries.
- Meticulous skin care is important.
- A client with a tracheostomy will require aggressive chest physiotherapy and adequate oxygenation.
- Pain management will also be needed.
- All systems should be regularly assessed and monitored for the development of complications, and if these are recognized, they must be treated promptly and aggressively.

As the client's condition stabilizes, retraining takes place. The client will require the following:

- A balanced diet with adequate calories and dietary fibre

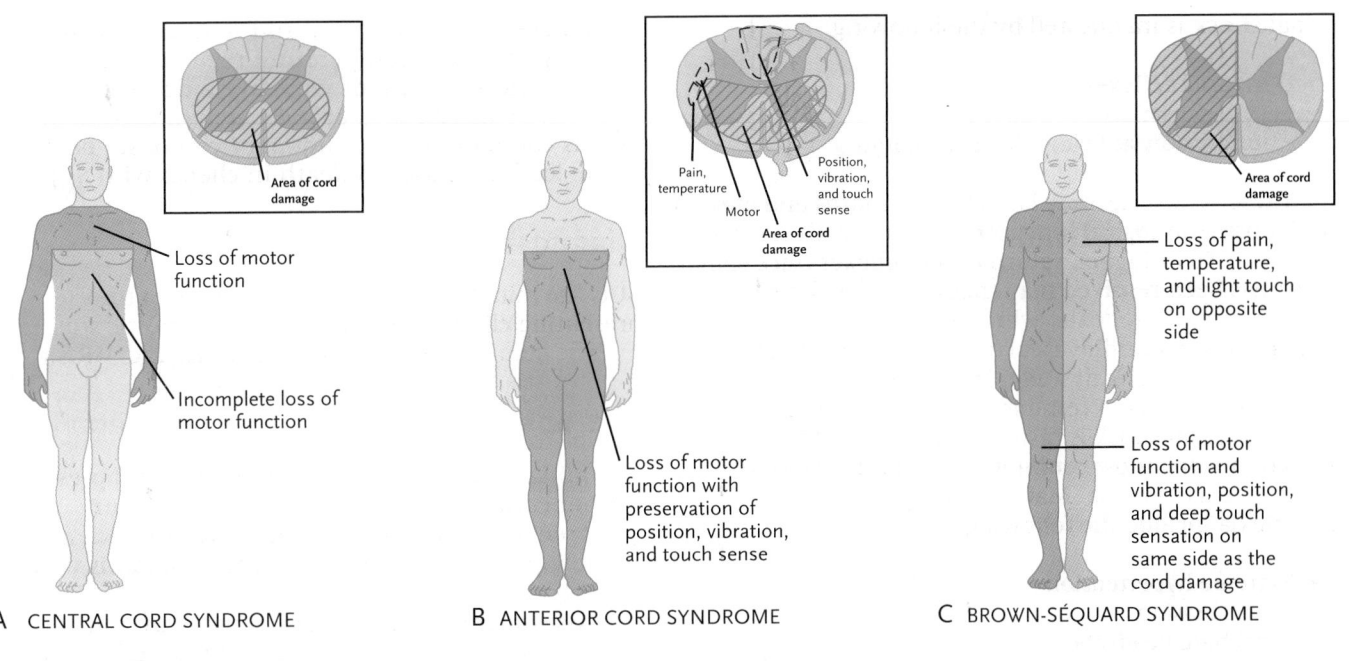

Area of cord damage
Loss of motor function
Incomplete loss of motor function
A CENTRAL CORD SYNDROME
Pain, temperature
Motor
Area of cord damage
Position, vibration, and touch sense
Loss of motor function with preservation of position, vibration, and touch sense
B ANTERIOR CORD SYNDROME
Area of cord damage
Loss of pain, temperature, and light touch on opposite side
Loss of motor function and vibration, position, and deep touch sensation on same side as the cord damage
C BROWN-SÉQUARD SYNDROME
Area of cord damage
T11
T12
L1
L2
Conus
Flaccidity of lower extremities
D CONUS MEDULLARIS SYNDROME
Area of cord damage
L2
L3
L4
L5
Cauda equina
Loss of sensation in sacral area
E CAUDA EQUINA SYNDROME

FIGURE 8.10 **Patterns of Injury Leading to Partial Paralysis**

Source: Black, J. M., & Hawks, J. H. (2009). *Medical-surgical nursing: Clinical management for positive outcomes* (8th ed., p. 1953, Figure 73-13). St. Louis: Saunders.

- May require an in-dwelling catheter or intermittent catheterization to regularly and completely empty the bladder to avoid UTIs
- A bowel training program
- Monitoring of the environment to maintain proper body temperature
- Respiratory rehabilitation, which may include a diaphragmatic pacemaker, ventilator care, assisted coughing, incentive spirometry, and deep-breathing exercises

Because the individuals who most commonly experience SCI are young, sexuality plays an important role. Reflexogenic erection is possible with upper motor neuron lesions. Drugs, vacuum devices, or surgery for erectile dysfunction may be done. Women usually

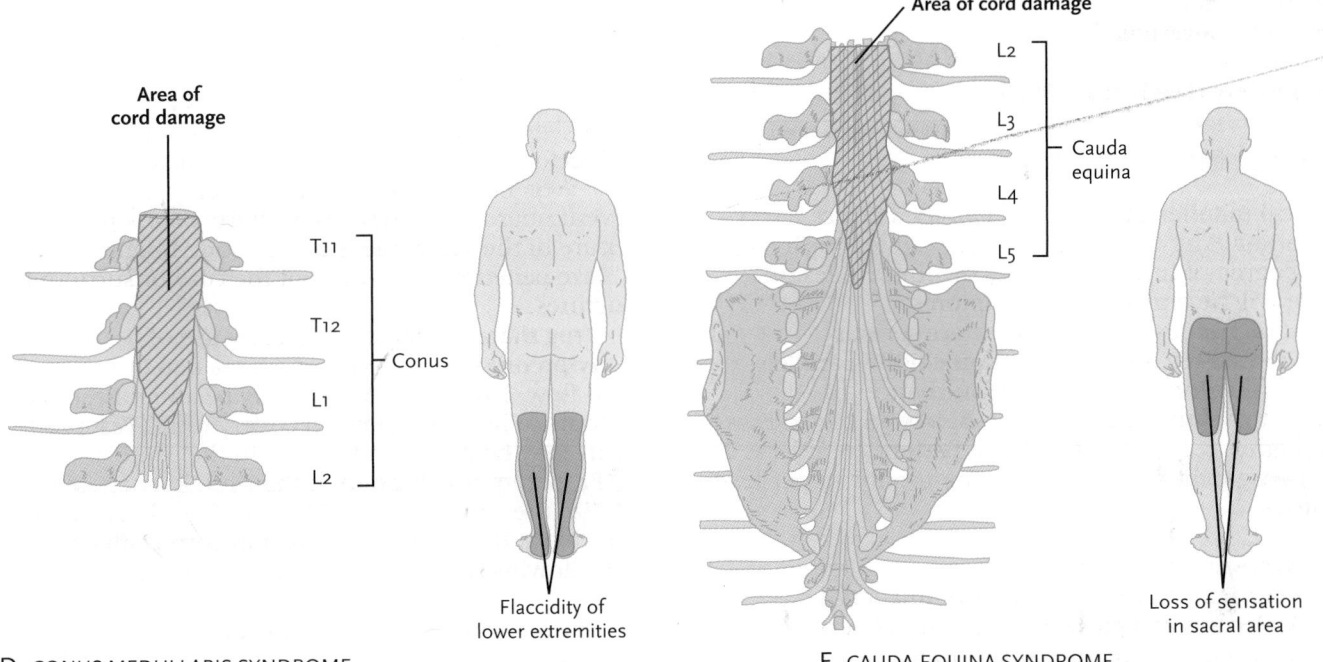

remain fertile; however, uterine contractions are not felt, and menses may cease for up to six months following injury. Open discussion with the client and partner is essential.

Grief and depression should be anticipated. The client may regress at different stages of recovery. Wide fluctuations of emotion should be expected. Mourning is normal and must be allowed. Assistance to obtain control during the anger phase is difficult but helpful. Above all, promotion of independence is critical.

OSTEOMYELITIS

Pathophysiology

Osteomyelitis is a severe infection of the bone, bone marrow, and surrounding soft tissue. The most common infection microorganisms are *S. aureus*, *Staphylococcus epidermis*, *E. coli*, and *M. tuberculosis*. Osteomyelitis is usually a bloodborne disease that affects rapidly growing children.

Common sites of infection include the lower end of the femur and the upper ends of the tibia, humerus, and radius. In adults, the most common sites are the pelvis and vertebrae. The infection causes tissue necrosis, breakdown of bone structure, and decalcification.

Acute osteomyelitis refers to an infection of less than one month in duration. Chronic osteomyelitis is rare and is characterized by multiple draining sinus tracts and metastatic lesions.

Clinical Manifestations

Clinical manifestations are both systemic and local and include the following:

- Fever
- Night sweats
- Chills
- Restlessness
- Nausea
- Malaise
- Constant bone pain that is unrelieved by rest and worsens with activity
- Swelling, tenderness, and warmth at the infection site
- Restricted movement of the affected part and possible drainage from the sinus tracts (later sign) with chronic osteomyelitis

Long-term and rare complications of osteomyelitis include septicemia, septic arthritis, pathological fractures, squamous cell carcinoma, and amyloidosis.

Diagnostics

Diagnostic studies include a bone or soft tissue biopsy, blood or wound cultures, or both; elevated WBC and erythrocyte sedimentation rate (ESR); bone scans; MRI; and CT.

Therapeutics and Nursing Considerations

Vigorous and prolonged IV antibiotic therapy is the treatment of choice for acute osteomyelitis as long as bone ischemia has not yet occurred. Cultures or bone biopsy should be done prior to drug therapy. If antibiotic therapy is delayed, surgical debridement and decompression are often needed. Clients are discharged to home care with IV antibiotics delivered via a central venous catheter or peripherally inserted central catheter (PICC).

Surgical treatment includes the removal of the poorly vascularized tissue and dead bone. Antibiotic-impregnated polymethylmethacrylate bead chains may be implanted at this time to aid in combatting the infection. After debridement, the wound may be closed and a suction irrigation system is inserted. Intermittent or constant irrigation of the affected bone with antibiotics may also be initiated. Protection of the limb or surgical site with casts or braces is frequently done.

Hyperbaric oxygen therapy of 100% oxygen may be administered in chronic osteomyelitis. Amputation of the extremity may be necessary to preserve life and improve quality of life.

Upon discharge, family members need to know their role in monitoring the client's health. Key points of client and family education include the following:

- Family members should be aware that symptoms of bone pain, fever, swelling, and restricted limb movement should be reported immediately.
- Immobilization may be indicated to decrease pain, and excessive manipulation should be avoided.
- Pain assessment and interventions need to be taught.
- Instructions concerning wound care with sterile management and frequent changes of open wound dressings, if present, are needed.
- The family needs to understand the infection is not contagious.
- Heat application and activities such as exercise should be avoided.
- Uninvolved joints and muscles should continue to be exercised.
- Care and management of the venous access device are needed, as well as instruction about antibiotic administration.
- The importance of continuing to take the antibiotics even after the symptoms have subsided needs to be strongly impressed upon the family.

The family should be advised that periodic home nursing visits will provide support and help reduce anxiety.

OSTEOPOROSIS

Pathophysiology

Osteoporosis is a chronic, progressive, metabolic bone disease characterized by low bone mass and structural deterioration of bone tissue. The rate of bone resorption accelerates as the rate of bone formation decelerates, resulting in decreased bone mass and the bones becoming porous and brittle. Osteoporosis occurs more frequently in the spine, hips, and wrists. Risk factors for developing osteoporosis include the following:

- Female gender
- Family history
- Being of European or Asian descent
- Being of small stature
- Excess alcohol intake
- Cigarette smoking
- Early menopause
- Anorexia
- Liver disease
- Oophorectomy
- Sedentary lifestyle
- Insufficient calcium intake
- Long-term use of corticosteroids

Clinical Manifestations

Osteoporosis is often referred to as the "silent disease" because there are no symptoms. Later manifestations include fractures, back pain, kyphosis, and loss of height.

Diagnostics

Diagnosis includes a history and physical examination as well as a bone mineral density test, quantitative ultrasonography, and dual-energy X-ray absorptiometry.

Therapeutics and Nursing Considerations

Treatment focuses on proper nutrition, with calcium supplements, exercise, medications, and prevention of fractures. The following treatments are recommended:

- Taking supplemental vitamin D
- Increasing nutritional intake of good sources of calcium, including milk and milk products, green leafy vegetables, seafood, almonds, and hazelnuts
- Encouraging exercise to build up and maintain bone mass
- Advising quitting smoking and cutting down on alcohol intake to decrease bone loss
- Drug therapy may include the following:

  - HRT and calcitonin to inhibit osteoclastic activity
  - Bisphosphonates to inhibit osteoclast-mediated bone resorption
  - Selective estrogen receptor modulators, such as Evista, may be ordered, as well as Forteo, which contains recombinant PTH.

Nursing plays an important role in health promotion and teaching how to optimize bone health and prevent osteoporosis.

FIBROMYALGIA SYNDROME

Pathophysiology

Fibromyalgia syndrome (FMS) is a widespread, nonarticular, musculoskeletal pain condition that causes fatigue and multiple tender points. The etiology is unknown, but there is a link between sleep disturbances, lack of exercise, and fibromyalgia, and multiple theories exist. Some include possible CNS involvement with serotonin and substance P, abnormal levels of norepinephrine, hyperfunctioning of the hypothalamic–pituitary–adrenal axis, an increase in cortisol, a decrease in ACTH, a dysfunction in the autonomic nervous system, viral illness or Lyme disease, a decreased amount of growth hormone, or simply a low pain threshold with increased muscle tenderness.

Clinical Manifestations

Clinical manifestations include widespread burning or gnawing pain that worsens and improves throughout the day. It is difficult to discriminate the origin of the pain.

- Head or facial pain may develop from a stiff neck and shoulder muscles and can accompany temporomandibular joint dysfunction.
- There is joint tenderness at 11 or more of the 18 specific tender point sites.
- The client has difficulty concentrating, has memory lapses, and often feels overwhelmed by multiple tasks.
- Depression, anxiety, numbness or tingling in hands or feet, restless legs syndrome, and irritable bowel syndrome frequently develop.
- The client often has difficulty swallowing, perhaps due to abnormalities in esophageal smooth muscle function.
- The client experiences urinary frequency and urgency and may experience dysmenorrhea with worsening of symptoms.

Diagnostics

Laboratory tests can rule out other suspected disorders. A muscle biopsy may have a nonspecific moth-eaten appearance or show fibre atrophy. Rheumatology classifies a client as having FMS when the following criteria are met: pain is experienced in 11 of 18 tender points on palpation and there is a history of widespread pain for at least three months.

Therapeutics and Nursing Considerations

Treatment focuses on restoring sleep and relieving pain. This consists of the following:

- Balancing rest with activity
- Using analgesics for pain relief

- Administering low-dose tricyclic antidepressants or skeletal muscle relaxants for stress, fatigue, and sleep disturbances. Selective serotonin reuptake inhibitors (SSRIs) may be used for depression and benzodiazepines for anxiety.
- Massage combined with ultrasound or application of alternating heat and cold to sore muscles is often beneficial.
- Practising gentle stretching, yoga, Tai Chi, or low-impact aerobics is encouraged
- Limiting the intake of sugar, caffeine, and alcohol is recommended.
- Vitamin and mineral supplements are suggested to assist the immune system.
- Relaxation strategies are discussed.

CHRONIC FATIGUE SYNDROME

Pathophysiology

Chronic fatigue syndrome (CFS) is characterized by unexplained debilitating fatigue and a variety of associated complaints lasting longer than six months. Immune abnormalities are also present. This syndrome is more common in women, with the usual onset between 25 and 44 years.

The precise cause is unknown, but viral infections such as herpes, Epstein–Barr virus, CMV, and retroviruses are suspected to be involved.

CFS often follows a cyclical course, alternating between illness and relatively symptom-free intervals. An abnormal immune function appears to be the central event, which leads to decreased immunoglobulin production, reduced NK cell activity, and altered cytokine production. CFS is sometimes referred to as a mental illness due to the mild to moderate depression that develops in these clients. CFS is often difficult to distinguish from FMS.

Clinical Manifestations

Clinical manifestations include sleep disturbances, low-grade fever, generalized musculoskeletal pain, fatigue, sore throat, cervical or axillary adenopathy, multijoint pain without swelling, and headaches.

Diagnostics

Ruling out other possible causes assists in the diagnosis. No specific laboratory test is used for diagnosis.

Therapeutics and Nursing Considerations

Treatment is aimed at controlling the symptoms. Education of the client with CFS focuses on managing the fatigue while improving functioning and quality of life. Management consists of informing the client about what is known about the disease and recognizing the fears and concerns of the clients as real. The treatments are as follows:

- NSAIDs for relief of pain and fever
- Treatment for any allergic symptoms
- Tricyclic antidepressants and SSRIs for mood and sleep problems
- Clonazepam for sleep disturbances or panic disorders
- Exercise to improve conditioning and restore energy, with gradual increases in intensity and duration
- Total rest is not advised as it can potentiate the client's self-image of being an invalid; rather, a carefully graduated exercise program is encouraged.
- Clients are taught to maintain a balanced diet as good nutrition is essential to producing adequate energy stores. Referrals to agencies and CFS groups are very helpful for the client.

OSTEOARTHRITIS

Pathophysiology

Osteoarthritis (OA) is a noninflammatory disorder of the diarthrodial (synovial) joints. It is slowly progressive, with 90% of adults being affected by age 40. After menopause, more women than men are affected by OA. OA may occur as an idiopathic (of unknown cause) or secondary disorder due to a previous infection, trauma, or skeletal deformity. Estrogen reduction at menopause, as well as genetic factors, seems to play a significant role. Modifiable risk factors include obesity and sedentary lifestyle.

OA causes deterioration of the joint cartilage and reactive new bone formation at the margins and subchondral areas. The progression of OA causes cartilage to gradually become softer, less elastic, and less able to resist wear with heavy use. Continued changes in the cartilage collagen lead to erosion of the articular surface. Uneven joint surfaces create an unequal distribution of stress across the joint, resulting in limited joint movement. Although inflammation is not characteristic of OA, a secondary synovitis may result when phagocytic cells try to rid the joint of small pieces of cartilage torn from the joint surface. These inflammatory changes contribute to the early pain and stiffness of OA. In later stages of OA, contact can occur between exposed bony joint surfaces after cartilage has completely deteriorated.

Clinical Manifestations

Clinical manifestations do not include systemic symptoms. The symptoms are as follows:

- Joint pain is the most common symptom and occurs particularly after exercise or weight-bearing.

- Joint pain may worsen as barometric pressures fall before inclement weather.
- Sometimes crepitation, a grating sensation caused by loose particles of cartilage, can be felt in the joint cavity.
- The joint pain is asymmetrical, and the client may experience early-morning stiffness, but this stiffness is usually resolved within 30 minutes.
- Joints that are commonly involved include the distal interphalangeal, proximal interphalangeal, and carpometacarpal joint of the thumb. Weight-bearing joints such as the hips and knees are commonly affected, as well as the metatarsophalangeal and the cervical and lower lumbar vertebrae.
- Heberden's nodes are deformities of the distal interphalangeal joint and indicate osteophyte formation. Bouchard's nodes are deformities found on the proximal interphalangeal joint. These deformities often appear red, swollen, and tender.

Diagnostics

Diagnosis is based on a history and physical examination. Bone scans, CT scans, MRIs, and X-rays are used to look for joint changes. Blood work would include ESR and CBC. Synovial fluid analysis will rule out an inflammatory arthritis.

Therapeutics and Nursing Considerations

There is no cure for OA; therefore, treatment is focused on the following:

- Management of symptoms of pain and inflammation
- Prevention of deformity and maintenance of joint function
- Rest and joint protection are encouraged.
- Heat and cold applications may help reduce pain and stiffness.
- Nutritional therapy
- Exercise
- Complementary and alternative therapies are discussed.
- Supportive devices such as braces can be used to protect the joint.

Drug therapy is based on the severity of the symptoms. Salicylates or NSAIDs are the first line of drug therapy. Corticosteroids, disease-modifying antirheumatic drugs (DMARDs), immunosuppressants, and antibiotics may be added depending on the client. As the pain worsens, non-opioid and then opioid medications may be added.

Education is a necessary element for the client. The client needs to know about medications and the treatment plan and be a full participant in his or her own care.

RHEUMATOID ARTHRITIS

Pathophysiology

Rheumatoid arthritis (RA) is a chronic, systemic disease characterized by inflammation of the connective tissue in the diarthrodial (synovial) joints and surrounding tissues. Systemic manifestations include pulmonary, cardiac, vascular, ophthalmological, dermatological, and hematological effects. RA typically has periods of remission and exacerbation. It affects all ethnic groups and can occur at any time of life; however, the incidence increases with age. Women are affected two to three times more than men. Smoking appears to play a role in the development of RA.

The cause of RA is unknown, although an autoimmune etiology is currently the most widely accepted theory. The unknown antigen triggers the formation of an abnormal IgG. RA is characterized by the presence of autoantibody, rheumatoid factor (RF). RF and IgG form immune complexes that initially deposit on synovial membranes or superficial articular cartilages in the joints, which leads to activation of complement and an inflammatory response. Joint changes from inflammation begin when the hypertrophied synovial membrane invades the surround cartilage, ligaments, tendons, and joint capsule. Pannus forms with the joint and eventually covers and erodes the entire surface of the articular cartilage. Inflammatory cytokines further contribute to cartilage destruction. The pannus scars and shortens supporting structures, causing joint laxity, subluxation, and contracture. A genetic predisposition appears to be important in the development of RA.

Anatomical changes of RA follow four stages:

- Stage 1 – Early: There are no destructive changes on X-ray, although there may be evidence of osteoporosis.
- Stage 2 – Moderate: X-rays reveal evidence of osteoporosis with or without slight bone or cartilage destruction. There is no joint deformity. Adjacent muscle will atrophy, and extra-articular soft tissue lesions may be present.
- Stage 3 – Severe: X-rays reveal cartilage and bone destruction in addition to osteoporosis. There will be joint deformity with extensive muscle atrophy, and extra-articular soft tissue lesions may be present.
- Stage 4 – Terminal: Fibrosis, bony ankylosis, or both are present, as well as all the criteria for stage 3.

Clinical Manifestations

The onset of RA is typically insidious. Nonspecific manifestations may precede the onset of arthritic complaints. These may include the following:

- Fatigue
- Anorexia and weight loss
- Generalized morning stiffness

Specific articular involvement of pain, stiffness, limitation of motion, and signs of inflammation develop. The joint symptoms occur symmetrically and frequently. The joints most frequently affected include the small joints of the hands and feet and the larger peripheral joints of the wrists, elbows, shoulders, knees, hips, ankles, and jaw. The cervical spine may also be involved. The client with RA will often experience joint stiffness after periods of inactivity. Morning stiffness may last from 60 minutes to several hours or more. Joints become tender, painful, and warm to the touch. Joint pain increases with movement, varies in intensity, may not be proportional to the degree of inflammation, and may make it difficult for the client to grasp things (tenosynovitis). The inflammation and fibrosis of the joint capsule and supporting structures may lead to deformity and disability.

RA can affect nearly every system of the body. The three most common complications include rheumatoid nodules, Sjögren's syndrome, and Felty's syndrome. Rheumatoid nodules develop in 25% of all clients with RA who have high titres of RF. Sjögren's syndrome affects 10–15% of clients with RA and can occur as a disease by itself or in conjunction with other arthritic disorders. Felty's syndrome occurs most commonly in clients with severe nodule-forming RA.

Diagnostics

Diagnosis depends on an accurate history and physical examination. RF can be found in 75–80% of clients with RA. ESR and C-reactive protein are indicators of active inflammation. X-rays are not specifically diagnostic in the early stages. A bone scan may detect early changes and confirm the diagnosis. Synovial fluid analysis will show increased volume and turbidity but decreased viscosity. The client might be slightly anemic with slight leukocytosis.

Therapeutics and Nursing Considerations

Treatment focuses on drug therapy, education, physical therapy, and occupational therapy. Drug therapy is the cornerstone of RA treatment and is as follows:

- DMARDs such as methotrexate, sulfasalazine, leflunomides, or combinations of these have the potential to lessen the permanent effects of RA.
- NSAIDs, salicylates, and steroids are also used.
- In some situations, antimalarials, gold sodium thiomalate, or antibiotics may be used.

The choice of drug depends on the disease activity, the client's level of function, and lifestyle considerations.

Other important treatments include the following:

- Balanced nutrition to control weight loss, which may result from loss of appetite and inability to shop for and prepare food.
- Corticosteroids or immobility may result in unwanted weight gain.
- Exercise reduces stress on arthritic joints. The client is encouraged to alternate rest and activity.
- Lightweight splints help rest inflamed joints and prevent deformity.
- Occupational therapists are helpful in teaching the client about work simplification techniques and time-saving joint protection devices.

Psychological support is important as clients are constantly threatened by problems of limited function and fatigue, loss of self-esteem, altered body image, fear of disability and deformity, and loss of sexuality.

The major goals of therapy for clients with RA include the following:

- Promoting comfort and satisfactory pain relief
- Promoting independence and self-care with minimal loss of functional ability of affected joints
- Reducing fatigue
- Maintenance of a positive self-image
- Preventing injury and promoting mobility and maintenance of activities of daily living.

SYSTEMIC LUPUS ERYTHEMATOSUS

Pathophysiology

Systemic lupus erythematosus (SLE) is a chronic multisystem inflammatory disorder of the connective tissue. SLE affects multiple organ systems, including the skin, and can be fatal. It mostly affects young women of African, Asian, or Aboriginal descent, although it does affect people of European descent as well. The etiology is unknown; however, genetic influences, hormones, environmental factors, and certain medications have been known to precipitate the disease. The onset of SLE usually occurs following menarche. The autoimmune reactions are directed at the body producing antibodies against components of its own cells, resulting in immune complex disease. Clients with SLE may produce antibodies against RBCs, neutrophils, platelets, lymphocytes, or any organ or tissue in the body.

Clinical Manifestations

Since SLE has multisystem involvement and characteristics of remission and exacerbation, the clinical manifestations can be many. These may include the following:

- Characteristic facial butterfly rash
- Photosensitivity
- Oral ulcers
- Arthritis

- Pleuritis
- Pericarditis
- Renal disorders (proteinuria)
- Neurological disorders (seizures, psychosis)
- Hematological disorders (hemolytic anemia, leukopenia, lymphopenia, thrombocytopenia)
- Immunological disorders and development of antinuclear antibodies

Diagnostics

There is no specific diagnostic test for SLE, which is primarily diagnosed on examination of criteria relating to client history, physical findings, and laboratory findings. Antinuclear antibodies are positive for 95% of clients with SLE.

Therapeutics and Nursing Considerations

Management of SLE revolves around drug therapy. The following drugs are utilized:

- NSAIDs
- Antimalarial drugs
- Steroid-sparing drugs
- Corticosteroids
- Immunosuppressive drugs

Since SLE is a chronic condition, the client's physical, psychological, and sociocultural problems should be assessed and managed. Pain and fatigue need to be monitored daily. The client needs to be educated regarding management of these ongoing issues. The overall goals for managing clients with SLE include satisfactory pain relief and compliance with the therapeutic regimen to achieve maximum symptom management. Other goals are to demonstrate awareness of and avoid activities that cause disease exacerbation and to maintain optimal function and a positive self-image.

With an acute exacerbation, it is important to record the severity of symptoms and the client's response to therapy. The client needs to be observed for the following:

- Fever pattern
- Joint inflammation
- Limitation of motion
- Location and degree of discomfort
- Fatigue
- Signs of bleeding
- Weight, fluid, and electrolyte anomalies need to be monitored if on corticosteroid therapy.
- Neurological disorders

The client will require support with explanations through the exacerbation. Once the exacerbation has ended, further client teaching needs to focus on adherence to the treatment plan and minimizing exposure to precipitating factors.

Low Back Pain

Pathophysiology

Low back pain is a common problem that affects about 90% of the population at least once and can result in significant economic and social costs. The lumbar region is susceptible to injury as this area bears most of the weight of the body and is the most flexible region of the spinal column. This region has poor biomechanical structure, and the nerve roots in the area are vulnerable to injury. Risk factors for developing low back pain are as follows:

- A lack of muscle tone
- Excess weight
- Poor posture
- Cigarette smoking
- Stress
- Repetitive heavy lifting
- Vibrations
- Prolonged periods of sitting

Low back pain is most often due to musculoskeletal problems, such as acute lumbosacral strain, instability of the lumbosacral bony mechanism, and OA of the lumbosacral vertebrae. Low back pain can also be due to intervertebral disc degeneration or herniation of the intervertebral disc.

Chronic back pain lasts for more than three months or is manifested in repeated incapacitating episodes. The causes of chronic back pain include the following:

- Degenerative disc disease
- Lack of physical exercise or prior injury
- Obesity
- Structural and postural abnormalities
- Systemic disease. OA of the lumbar spine is found in clients over the age of 50 years.
- Cold, damp weather can aggravate back pain.

Clinical Manifestations

Acute low back pain lasts four weeks or less and is usually associated with some activity that causes undue stress on the tissues of the lower back. The actual lower back pain with or without spasms will often appear later. Straight-leg raises will increase the pain.

Diagnostics

A thorough history and physical examination are needed to rule out serious conditions that may present as low back pain. MRI and CT scanning are not usually done unless trauma or systemic disease is suspected.

Therapeutics and Nursing Considerations

The client is cared for on an outpatient basis with the following treatments:

- Analgesics
- Muscle relaxants
- Massage
- Possible use of a corset to prevent rotation, flexion, and extension
- Rest may also be beneficial.

The client will be encouraged to avoid lifting, bending, twisting, and prolonged sitting. Most cases improve within two weeks.

Once an acute episode has resolved, health promotion is very important. Suggestions such as maintaining an appropriate weight, avoiding sleeping in the prone position, and using a firm mattress are beneficial. The client will be instructed not to lean forward without bending the knees, lift anything above the level of the elbows, stand in one position for a prolonged time, or exercise without consulting a health care professional. Treatment of chronic low back pain is similar to that for acute low back pain.

HERNIATED INTERVERTEBRAL DISC

Pathophysiology

A herniated intervertebral disc is often referred to as a "slipped disc." It is a protrusion of the nucleus pulposus between adjacent surfaces of vertebral bodies and may occur anywhere along the spine. It can result from trauma, a sharp or sudden movement, or natural degeneration due to age. The gelatinous centre of the disc may rupture, causing acute injury and back pain. Common sites of rupture include L4–L5, L5–S1, C4–C5, C5–C6, and C6–C7. Herniation of thoracic discs is less common.

Clinical Manifestations

Clinical manifestations of a herniated disc are dependent on the location and size of the herniation. Manifestations may include low back pain that radiates down the leg in dermatomal distribution. Lying down often relieves pain. Reflexes may be depressed or absent. Muscle weakness is found in the legs, feet, and toes. There may be incontinence and impotence.

Diagnostics

Diagnostic studies include X-ray, myelography, MRI, CT, epidural venography, discography, and EMG to determine the severity of nerve irritation and to rule out other pathological conditions.

Therapeutics and Nursing Considerations

Treatment involves limitation of extremes of spinal involvement; the local application of heat, ice, or both; ultrasound and massage; and traction and transcutaneous electrical nerve stimulation (TENS).

Drug therapy can include NSAIDs, short-term narcotic opioids, and muscle relaxants. Once symptoms subside, back-strengthening exercises are encouraged. The client should be taught the principles of good body mechanics.

Surgical therapy is needed when the client is unresponsive to conservative treatment or experiences consistent pain or there is a persistent neurological deficit. Several surgical procedures can be used to treat a herniated disc, which are as follows:

- Laminectomy, removal of a portion of the lamina, is the most common surgery for a herniated disc.
- A discectomy, removal of all or part of the herniated disc.
- A spinal fusion is done to stabilize two or more vertebrae by the insertion of bone grafts with or without the addition of rods, plates, screws, or other hardware.
- Decompression can also be done to release the pressure on the spinal roots by removing osteophytes, bone, or soft tissue.

After surgery, the client will be on a flat bed for one to two days, depending on the extent of the surgery. The client will be turned by log-rolling. Pillows will be placed under the thighs of each leg when the client is supine and between the legs when the client is in the side-lying position. The client is often fearful of any movement; therefore, explanation and reassurance are essential. IV narcotics will manage pain. Muscle relaxants may be prescribed. The client should be monitored for CSF leakage, which would manifest by a severe headache or the appearance of clear or slightly yellow fluid at the surgical site. Neurological assessment is ongoing, comparing the movement of the arms and the legs with preoperative movement. The client should be assessed for paraesthesia in all appropriate dermatomes. Movement and muscle strength of all extremities should be monitored. Wound care is done when needed. The donor site for a bone graft must be regularly assessed. The posterior iliac crest is the most common donor site. The donor site often produces more pain than the fused area. A pressure dressing may be needed to prevent excessive bleeding at the site.

Complications following surgery may include the following:

- Paralytic ileus and interference with bowel function
- Nausea, abdominal distension, and constipation; stool softeners may be ordered
- Bladder emptying may be altered due to limited activity, the use of narcotics, or anaesthesia.
- Loss of sphincter tone or bladder tone may indicate nerve damage.

The client will have to adjust to a permanent immobility at the graft or fusion site. The client and family will need education regarding proper body mechanics, avoiding standing or sitting for long periods of time, balancing rest with activity, and that bending, lifting, and stooping could be injurious. Walking should be encouraged. Twisting movements of the spine are contraindicated.

FRACTURES

Pathophysiology

A fracture is a disruption or a break in the continuity of the structure of a bone, usually due to a blow to the body, a fall, or another accident. Fractures are described and classified according to their type and anatomical location and whether there is communication or noncommunication with the external environment. Other classification categories include appearance, position, alignment of the fragments, classic names, and whether they are stable or unstable. Figure 8.11 illustrates various types of fractures.

Typical complete fractures include the following:

- Closed (simple) fractures are noncommunicating wounds between bone and skin.
- Open (compound) fractures are communicating wounds between bone and skin.
- Other types include comminuted, linear, oblique, spiral, transverse, impacted, pathological, avulsion, extracapsular, and intracapsular fractures.

Typical incomplete fractures include greenstick, torus, bowing, stress, and transchondral fractures.

Clinical Manifestations

Clinical manifestations of fractures include the client reporting a mechanism of injury resulting in immediate localized pain, loss of function, and obvious deformity. Other symptoms could include excessive motion at the site, crepitus, soft tissue edema in the area of injury, warmth over the injured

Avulsion
Comminuted
Displaced
Greenstick
Impacted
Interarticular
Longitudinal
Oblique
Pathological
Spiral
Stress
Transverse

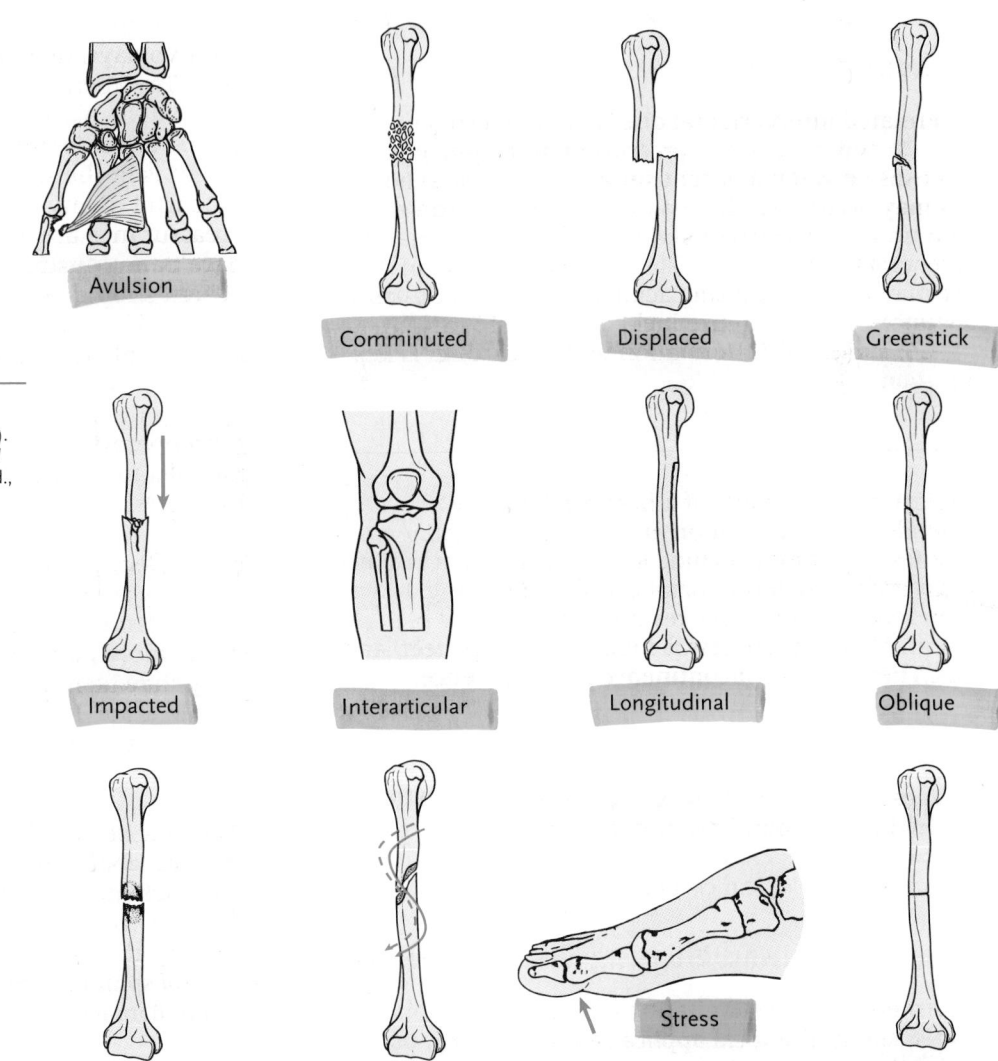

FIGURE 8.11 **Types of Fractures**

Source: Lewis, S. M., Heitkemper, M. M., Dirksen, S. R., O'Brien, P., Bucher, L., et al. (2010). *Medical-surgical nursing in Canada: Assessment and management of clinical problems* (2nd Canadian ed., p. 1739, Figure 64-6). Toronto: Elsevier.

area, ecchymosis of skin surrounding the injured area, paralysis, impairment or loss of sensation distal to the site of injury, signs of shock, and inability to bear weight on or use the affected part.

Therapeutics and Nursing Considerations

Fracture healing is a reparative process of self-healing (union) that occurs in the following stages:

1. Fracture hematoma
2. Granulation tissue
3. Callus formation
4. Ossification
5. Consolidation
6. Remodelling

Treatment focuses on anatomical realignment of fragments (reduction), immobilization to maintain alignment, and restoration of normal function. A closed reduction involves nonsurgical manual realignment. An open reduction is the correction of bone alignment through a surgical incision. Forms of immobilization include skin traction for short-term immobilization and skeletal traction for long-term immobilization.

Traction is the mechanism by which a steady pull is exerted on a part or parts of the body while countertraction pulls in the opposite direction. Traction is used to prevent or reduce muscle spasm, immobilize the limb, reduce the fracture, stretch adhesions, and correct deformities. Suspension is the use of traction equipment, such as frames, splints, pulleys, and weights, to suspend but not exert pull on a body part. Balanced suspension is often used with traction to allow the client more freedom.

Casts are considered temporary circumferential immobilization devices and are commonly used with closed reductions. There are many different types of casts.

External fixation uses metallic devices composed of pins that are inserted into the bone and attached to external rods. Internal fixation uses pins, plates, rods, and screws that are surgically inserted at the time of realignment.

Drug therapy for the treatment of fractures may include the following:

- Muscle relaxants
- Tetanus–diphtheria toxoid or immunoglobulins
- Bone-penetrating antibiotics, such as cephalosporin and analgesics as needed

The overall goals for treatment of the fracture include physiological healing with no associated complications, pain relief, and achievement of maximal rehabilitation potential. The following considerations are important:

- Neurovascular assessment of colour, temperature, capillary refill, peripheral pulses, edema, sensation, motor function, and pain should be ongoing.
- Fractures pose a risk of peripheral neurovascular dysfunction, pain, and infection.
- A high fluid intake and a diet high in bulk are important due to the immobility of the client.
- Traction equipment should be checked for proper functioning, and pin site care must be done.
- Too tight a cast can result in neurovascular complications; extremities must be checked frequently.
- If a cast is applied, the limb should be elevated above the level of the heart if possible when the client is resting.
- The client should be encouraged to exercise the joints above and below the cast to decrease muscle atrophy.
- Assistive devices such as canes, walkers, or crutches may be needed to help mobilize the client.

Complications of fractures include infections. Open fractures and soft tissue injuries have an increased risk of developing infections. Osteomyelitis may become chronic. If infection is present in an open fracture, surgical debridement may be necessary. Antibiotic therapy will be initiated.

Compartment syndrome is a condition in which elevated intracompartmental pressure within a confined myofascial compartment compromises the neurovascular function of the tissues within the space. This causes capillary perfusion to be reduced below a level necessary for tissue viability and is classified as acute, chronic or exertional, or crush. Two basic etiologies create compartment syndrome. There may be a decreased compartment size due to restrictive dressings, splints, or casts, or there may be increased compartment content due to bleeding or edema. Clinical manifestations of compartment syndrome include the following "six Ps":

- Paraesthesia
- Pain
- Pressure
- Pallor
- Paralysis
- Pulselessness

Clients may present with one or all of the six Ps. Absence of a peripheral pulse is considered an ominous late sign. Treatment requires prompt, accurate diagnosis. Early recognition is key. The bandage or cast should be removed and traction weight reduced, and the limb should not be placed above the heart, nor should it receive hot or cold applications. Surgical decompression (fasciotomy) may be needed.

Venous thrombus is another potential complication of fractures. Precipitating factors include venous stasis, caused by incorrectly applied casts or traction, local pressure on the vein, and immobility.

Fat embolism syndrome (FES) is characterized by the presence of fat globules in tissues and organs after a traumatic skeletal injury. The fractures that most often cause FES include fractures of the long bones, ribs, tibia, and pelvis. Tissues that are most affected are the lungs, brain, heart, kidneys, and skin. Symptoms will occur within 24–48 hours after injury and may manifest as interstitial pneumonitis, which may produce symptoms of ARDS (chest pain, tachypnea, cyanosis, decreased PaO_2, dyspnea, apprehension, and tachycardia). The course of FES is rapid, with an acute onset and feelings of impending doom, and the client may be comatose for a short while. Treatment is directed at prevention; careful immobilization of the bone fracture is the most important preventive factor.

STROKE (BRAIN ATTACK OR CEREBROVASCULAR ACCIDENT)

Pathophysiology

A cerebrovascular accident (CVA) occurs when there is a sudden interruption of circulation in one or more of the cerebral blood vessels, resulting in the death of brain cells. Functions such as movement, sensation, and emotion that were controlled by the affected area of the brain are impaired or lost. The severity of the loss of function varies according to the location and extent of involvement.

Nonmodifiable risk factors for developing a stroke include increasing age, male gender, female gender postmenopause, heredity, and being of African descent. Modifiable risk factors include the following:

- Poorly controlled DM
- Heart disease, arrhythmias, hypertension, hypercoagulability, and hyperlipidemia
- Obesity, sedentary lifestyle, smoking, and heavy alcohol use
- Sickle cell disease (if sickling episodes can be prevented)
- Oral contraceptives

Blood is supplied to the brain by two major pairs of arteries, the internal carotid arteries and the vertebral arteries. The brain requires a continuous supply of blood to provide the oxygen and glucose that neurons need to function. If blood flow to the brain is totally interrupted, neurological metabolism is altered in 30 seconds. Metabolism stops within two minutes, and cellular death occurs in five minutes.

Atherosclerosis is the major cause of stroke. It can lead to thrombus formation and contribute to emboli development. In response to ischemia, a series of metabolic events (ischemic cascade) occur, which include inadequate ATP production, loss of ion homeostasis, release of excitatory amino acids, free radical formation, and cell death. Around the core area of ischemia is a border zone of reduced blood flow where ischemia may be reversed. If adequate blood supply can be restored (in less than three hours), the ischemic cascade can be interrupted, with the result

that there is less brain damage and less neurological function is lost.

Transient ischemic attack (TIA) is a temporary focal loss of neurological function caused by ischemia. TIAs usually resolve with three hours but may last as long as 24 hours. TIAs may be due to microemboli that temporarily block the blood flow and are warning signs of progressive cerebrovascular disease.

Strokes are classified based on the underlying pathophysiological findings and are either ischemic or hemorrhagic in nature. Ischemic strokes result from inadequate blood flow to the brain from partial or complete occlusion of an artery. Ischemic strokes constitute 85% of all strokes and are due to either thrombus or emboli damage. Thrombotic stroke occurs in relation to injury to a blood vessel wall and subsequent formation of a blood clot that narrows the blood vessel, resulting in a decreased amount of blood delivered to the tissue. This is the most common type of stroke and is usually associated with hypertension, DM, or both. Thrombotic stroke is often preceded by a TIA.

Embolic stroke occurs when an embolus lodges in and occludes a cerebral artery. This results in no blood to the distal tissues, leading to infarction and edema. This is the second most common cause of a stroke. The majority of emboli originate in the inside layer of the heart, with plaque breaking off from the endocardium and entering the circulation. Clients with an embolic stroke commonly have a rapid occurrence of severe clinical symptoms that may or may not be related to activity. Clients experiencing an embolic stroke usually remain conscious, although they often have a headache. Recurrence is common unless the underlying cause is aggressively treated.

Hemorrhagic strokes account for about 15% of all strokes. They result from bleeding into the brain tissue itself or into the subarachnoid space or ventricles. Intracerebral hemorrhage is bleeding within the brain caused by a rupture of a vessel, usually during activity. Hypertension is the most common cause. The onset is sudden, with a progression of symptoms over minutes to hours due to ongoing bleeding. Manifestations include neurological deficits, headache, nausea, vomiting, hypertension, and decreased levels of consciousness.

Subarachnoid hemorrhage occurs when there is intracranial bleeding into the CSF-filled space between the arachnoid and pia mater. This bleeding is commonly caused by rupture of a cerebral saccular or berry aneurysm. The majority of aneurysms are in the circle of Willis. Clients often describe the pain as "the worst headache in [their] life."

Clinical Manifestations

Motor impairment is the most obvious effect of stroke and can involve the following:

- Mobility
- Respiratory function

- Swallowing, speech, and gag reflex
- Self-care abilities
- Loss of skilled voluntary movement
- Impairment of integration of movements and alteration in muscle tone
- Alterations in reflexes
- An initial period of flaccidity may last from days to several weeks and is related to nerve damage.
- Spasticity of the muscles follows the flaccid stage and is related to interruption of upper motor neuron influence.

- The client may experience aphasia (total loss of comprehension and language) when a stroke damages the dominant hemisphere of the brain.
- Many clients also experience dysarthria (impairments with pronunciation, articulation, and phonation).
- Dysarthria does not affect the meaning of communication or the comprehension of language, but it does affect the mechanics of speech. For various neurological deficits and their nursing considerations, see Table 8.11.

Table 8.11 Neurological Deficits of Stroke

NEUROLOGICAL DEFICIT	MANIFESTATION	NURSING CONSIDERATIONS AND CLIENT TEACHING APPLICATIONS
Visual Field Deficits		
Homonymous hemianopsia (loss of half of the visual field)	• Unaware of persons or objects on side of visual loss • Neglect of one side of the body • Difficulty judging distances	• Place objects within intact field of vision. • Approach the client from side of intact field of vision. • Instruct/remind the client to turn his or her head in the direction of visual loss to compensate for loss of visual field. • Encourage the use of eyeglasses if available. • When teaching the client, do so within the client's intact visual field.
Loss of peripheral vision	• Difficulty seeing at night • Unaware of objects or the borders of objects	• Avoid night driving or other risky activities in the darkness. • Place objects in centre of client's intact visual field. • Encourage the use of a cane or other object to identify objects in the periphery of the visual field.
Diplopia	• Double vision	• Explain to the client the location of an object when placing it near the client. • Consistently place client care items in the same location.
Motor Deficits		
Hemiparesis	• Weakness of the face, arm, and leg on the same side (due to a lesion in the opposite hemisphere)	• Place objects within the client's reach on the nonaffected side. • Instruct the client to exercise and increase the strength on the unaffected side.
Hemiplegia	• Paralysis of the face, arm, and leg on the same side (due to a lesion in the opposite hemisphere)	• Encourage the client to perform range-of-motion exercises to the affected side. • Provide immobilization as needed to the affected side. • Maintain body alignment in functional position. • Exercise unaffected limb to increase mobility, strength, and use.
Ataxia	• Staggering, unsteady gait • Unable to keep feet together; needs a broad base to stand	• Support client during the initial ambulation phase. • Provide supportive device for ambulation (walker, cane). • Instruct the client not to walk without assistance or supportive device.
Dysarthia	• Difficulty forming words	• Provide the client with alternative methods of communicating. • Allow the client sufficient time to respond to verbal communication. • Support the client and family to alleviate frustration related to difficulty in communicating.
Dysphagia	• Difficulty swallowing	• Test the client's pharyngeal reflexes before offering food or fluids. • Assist the client with meals. • Place food on the unaffected side of the mouth. • Allow ample time to eat.

Continued on next page

Table 8.11 Neurological Deficits of Stroke (cont'd)

NEUROLOGICAL DEFICIT	MANIFESTATION	NURSING CONSIDERATIONS AND CLIENT TEACHING APPLICATIONS
Sensory Deficits		
Paraesthesia (occurs on the side opposite the lesion)	• Numbness and tingling of extremity • Difficulty with proprioception	• Instruct the client to avoid using this extremity as the dominant limb due to altered sensation. • Perform range-of-motion exercises on affected areas and apply corrective devices as needed.
Verbal Deficits		
Expressive aphasia	• Unable to form words that are understandable; may be able to speak in single-word responses	• Encourage client to repeat sounds of the alphabet.
Receptive aphasia	• Unable to comprehend the spoken word; can speak but may not make sense	• Speak slowly and clearly to assist the client by modelling sounds.
Global (mixed) aphasia	• Combination of both receptive and expressive aphasia	• Speak clearly and in simple sentences; use gestures or pictures when possible. • Establish alternative means of communication.
Cognitive Deficits		
	• Short- and long-term memory loss • Decreased attention span • Impaired ability to concentrate • Poor abstract reasoning • Altered judgement	• Reorient the client to time, place, and situation frequently. • Use verbal and auditory cues to orient the client. • Provide familiar objects (family photographs, favourite objects). • Use noncomplicated language. • Match visual tasks with a verbal cue; holding a toothbrush, simulate brushing of teeth while saying, "I would like you to brush your teeth now." • Minimize distracting noises and views when teaching the client. • Repeat and reinforce instructions frequently.
Emotional Deficits		
	• Loss of self-control • Emotional lability • Decreased tolerance to stressful situations • Depression • Withdrawal • Fear, hostility, and anger • Feelings of isolation	• Support the client during uncontrollable outbursts. • Discuss with the client and the family that the outbursts are due to the disease process. • Encourage the client to participate in group activity. • Provide stimulation for the client. • Control stressful situations, if possible. • Provide a safe environment. • Encourage the client to express feelings and frustrations related to the disease process.

Source: Day, R. A., Paul, P., Williams, B., Smeltzer, S. C., & Bare, B. (2009). *Brunner & Suddarth's textbook of medical-surgical nursing* (2nd Canadian ed., p. 1900, Table 62-2). Philadelphia: Lippincott, Williams & Wilkins. Reprinted with permission.

Clients who suffer a stroke may have difficulty controlling their emotions, with the result that their emotional responses may be exaggerated or unpredictable. Depression and feelings associated with changes in body image and loss of function can make this worse. Clients may also be frustrated with immobility and communication problems.

Both memory and judgement may be impaired as a result of stroke. A left-brain stroke is more likely to result in memory problems related to language. Stroke on the right side of the brain is more likely to cause problems in spatial perceptual orientation, although this can also occur with left-brain stroke. Most problems with urinary and bowel elimination occur initially and are temporary. Manifestations for right-brain and left-brain stroke are summarized in Figure 8.12.

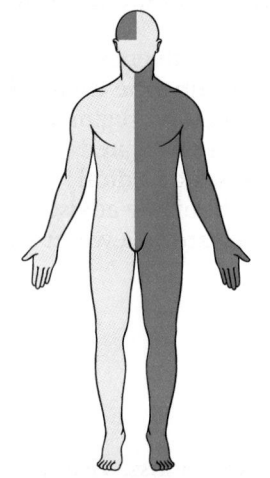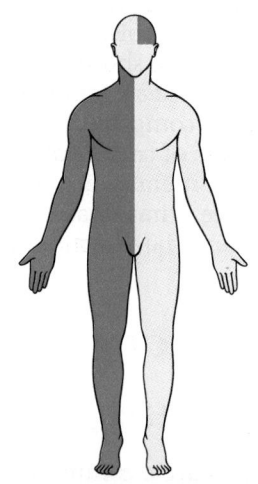

Right-brain damage	**Left-brain damage**
(stroke on right side of the brain)	(stroke on left side of the brain)
• Paralyzed left side: hemiplegia	• Paralyzed right side: hemiplegia
• Left-sided neglect	• Impaired speech/language aphasias
• Spatial–perceptual deficits	• Impaired right/left discrimination
• Tends to deny or minimize problems	• Slow performance, cautious
• Rapid performance, short attention span	• Aware of deficits: depression, anxiety
• Impulsive, safety problems	• Impaired comprehension related to language, math
• Impaired judgement	
• Impaired time concepts	

FIGURE 8.12 **Manifestations of Right-Brain and Left-Brain Stroke**

Source: Lewis, S. M., Heitkemper, M. M., Dirksen, S. R., O'Brien, P., Bucher, L., et al. (2010). *Medical-surgical nursing in Canada: Assessment and management of clinical problems* (2nd Canadian ed., p. 1606, Figure 59-4). Toronto: Elsevier.

Diagnostics

A CT scan is the primary diagnostic test used when stroke is suspected. The CT scan diagnoses either hemorrhage or ischemic stroke and thus assists in appropriate treatment. Brain scans reveal ischemia but may not be positive for up to two weeks after a stroke. Carotid ultrasonography may detect a blockage, stenosis, or reduced blood flow of the carotid arteries. Ophthalmoscopy may detect signs of hypertension and atherosclerosis in retinal arteries. Angiography can help pinpoint the site of occlusion or rupture. An electroencephalogram (EEG) may help localize the area of damage. Laboratory tests include CBC, platelets, PT, partial thromboplastin time (PTT), electrolytes, glucose, renal and hepatic studies, and lipid profile.

Therapeutics and Nursing Considerations

Goals for collaborative care during the acute phase of a stroke are to preserve life, prevent further brain damage, and reduce disability. The following interventions are critical:

- Airway patency must be ensured and adequate oxygen delivered.
- IV access must be obtained.
- Vital signs and neurological assessments are ongoing, including LOC, motor and sensory function, pupil size and reactivity, oxygen saturation, and cardiac rhythm.
- Thrombolytic therapy may be initiated to re-establish blood flow through a blocked artery to prevent death in clients with acute onset of ischemic stroke symptoms. There is a crucial "window of opportunity" of around three hours for thrombolytic therapy to be beneficial; after that time frame, brain damage has usually occurred.
- Surgical interventions for stroke include immediate evacuation of an aneurysm-induced hematoma or cerebellar hematoma >3 cm.

Rehabilitation care begins after the stroke has been stable for 12–24 hours. Collaborative care shifts from preserving life to lessening disability and attaining optimal function. Goals at this time include maintaining a stable or improved LOC, attaining maximum physical functioning, attaining maximum self-care abilities and skills, and maximizing communication abilities. A plan to prevent recurrence of stroke is developed with the client and family. Management of the following systems is very important, and considerations are listed below:

- The respiratory system is a priority as the client may be at risk for aspiration pneumonia and airway obstruction.
- The neurological system requires close monitoring for changes that might suggest an extension of a stroke.
- The cardiac system (vital signs and cardiac rhythm) also requires close monitoring due to the potential for a decreased cardiac reserve.
- Monitoring the lungs for sounds of fluid and the heart for the sound of murmurs is important for early detection of heart failure.
- Fluid and electrolyte balance is important.
- Proper positioning with appropriate supports and ROM exercises are needed to help prevent joint contracture and muscle atrophy.
- The skin of a client with stroke is susceptible to breakdown related to loss of sensation, decreased circulation, and immobility. This can be compounded by the client's age, poor nutrition, dehydration, edema, and incontinence. Pressure relief by proper turning and positioning is needed, along with good skin hygiene.
- Early mobility is helpful.
- Stress of the illness contributes to a catabolic state that can interfere with recovery. Good nutrition is

essential, but the client must be checked for an active gag reflex before oral feedings are initiated. Feedings should be followed by thorough oral hygiene.

- Constipation is a common bowel problem for clients with stroke. Physical activity will promote bowel function. Stool softeners and suppositories may be needed. Urinary incontinence is more common in the acute stage of the illness. Efforts should be made to promote normal bladder function and avoid the use of in-dwelling catheters.

It is imperative to meet the psychological needs of the client. The client will be assessed for the ability to speak and understand. Speaking slowly and calmly with simple words and sentences assists the client in speech improvement. Blindness in the same half of each visual field is a common problem after a stroke. Other visual problems may be diplopia, loss of the corneal reflex, and ptosis.

Explanations about what has happened to the client and about diagnostic and therapeutic procedures should be clear and understandable to the client and family.

HEALTH CHALLENGES RELATED TO ALTERED SENSORY INPUT

OTITIS MEDIA

Pathophysiology

Inflammation or infection of the middle ear is considered the most common cause of conductive hearing loss. It can be caused by viruses or bacteria, with *Streptococcus* infections being the most common causative factor in bacterial otitis media. An accumulation of fluid can build up behind the tympanic membrane, resulting in loss of movement of the membrane, which can prevent the ossicles from moving and result in temporary hearing loss (Lewis et al., 2006.)

Clinical Manifestations

Symptoms of otitis media vary according to the severity of the infection. They may include tugging at the ears, pain and irritability, poor sleeping, diarrhea, vomiting and fever, inability to hear soft sounds, fluid draining from the ear, and possibly loss of balance (Lewis et al., 2010). Refer to Chapter 10, Pediatric Nursing, for more information on otitis media.

Diagnostics

Diagnosis is made based on otoscopic examination, which reveals that the tympanic membrane is red and bulging (Lewis et al., 2010).

Therapeutics and Nursing Considerations

Treatment for this condition includes acetaminophen for pain and fever control and antibiotics specific to the infectious organism.

The nurse should monitor the effectiveness of the antibiotic and acetaminophen. Educating the client regarding compliance with the medication regimen, awareness of complications such as a perforated tympanic membrane, and when to seek medical assistance is important. The client should be advised not to fly until the infection has been cleared (Lewis et al., 2010).

CATARACTS

Pathophysiology

Cataracts are a common cause of vision loss. Vision is lost gradually due to the developing opacity of the lens or lens capsule of the eye. Cataracts commonly occur bilaterally but progress independently. They can be due to the following:

- Blunt force trauma
- Congenital factors
- Radiation and ultraviolet exposure
- Systemic corticosteroids
- Ocular inflammation

Most cataracts occur due to age-related changes in the lens and are called "senile cataracts." Frequent exposure to ultraviolet light may cause cataracts to occur earlier in life.

Clinical Manifestations

The client presents with a decrease in vision and abnormal colour perception. There may be whitening of the pupil, and the client may complain of halos around lights and a blinding glare from headlights at night. The client also is likely to experience glare and poor vision in bright sunlight.

Diagnostics

Diagnostic testing includes a detailed history and physical examination along with a visual acuity measurement. Ophthalmoscopy, slit lamp microscopy, and glare testing will confirm the diagnosis.

Therapeutics and Nursing Considerations

Nonsurgical treatment includes visual aids to compensate for the decreased ability to see. Surgical treatment consists of removal of the opaque lens and insertion of a prosthetic intraocular lens. The procedure is usually done on an outpatient basis. Postoperatively, the client requires antibiotic and anti-inflammatory eye drops and possibly an eye patch and may be advised against activities that increase intraocular eye pressure.

GLAUCOMA

Pathophysiology

Glaucoma refers to a group of disorders characterized by abnormally high intraocular pressure (IOP, fluid pressure in the eye), which can damage the optic nerve. Glaucoma occurs in three primary forms: open-angle (primary), acute angle-closure, and secondary to other causes. Risk factors for chronic open-angle glaucoma include genetics, hypertension, diabetes, aging, being of African descent, and severe myopia.

Acute angle-closure glaucoma (also called narrow-angle glaucoma) results from obstruction to the outflow of aqueous humour from anatomically narrow angles between the anterior iris and posterior corneal surface. It also results from shallow anterior chambers, a thickened iris that causes angle closure on pupil dilation, or a bulging iris that presses on the trabecular meshwork, closing the angle. Precipitating risk factors for acute angle-closure glaucoma include drug-induced mydriasis (extreme dilation of the pupil) and excitement or stress, which can lead to hypertension.

Secondary glaucoma may result from uveitis, trauma, steroids, diabetes, infections, or surgery.

Diagnostics

Ophthalmoscopic examination will show cupping and atrophy of the optic disc. Diagnostic studies include tonometry measurements of IOP, gonioscopy to examine the angle between the iris and the cornea, and peripheral and central vision tests.

Therapeutics and Nursing Considerations

Chronic open-angle glaucoma can be treated by drug therapy, cyclocryotherapy, argon laser trabeculoplasty, or trabeculectomy. Acute angle-closure glaucoma can be treated with miotics, hyperosmotic solutions, laser peripheral iridotomy, or surgical iridectomy. Secondary glaucoma is managed by treating the underlying problem and with antiglaucoma medications.

It is very important that the client is able to understand and comply with the treatment. The client's ability to react to sight-threatening disorders needs to be assessed. The expected goals of treatment are no progression of vision loss, the client and family understanding the disease process and treatment, the client's compliance with the treatment, and no postoperative complications.

MACULAR DEGENERATION

Pathophysiology

Age-related macular degeneration (AMD) is a degeneration of the macula, the central area of the retina, which results in varying degrees of central vision loss. AMD is divided into two classic forms: dry (atrophic), which is the most common, and wet (exudative), which is more severe. AMD is the most common cause of irreversible central vision loss in people over the age of 60.

AMD is related to retinal aging. Risk factors include the following:

- Family history is a major risk factor, and a gene responsible for some cases of AMD has been identified.
- Long-term exposure to ultraviolet light
- Hyperopia (farsightedness)
- Cigarette smoking
- Light-coloured eyes

In dry AMD, the client notices reading and other close vision tasks becoming more difficult. This form starts with the abnormal accumulation of yellowish coloured extracellular deposits called drusen in the retinal pigment epithelium. Atrophy and degeneration of macular cells then result, leading to a slowly progressive and painless vision loss.

Wet AMD is characterized by the growth of new blood vessels from their normal location in the choroids to an abnormal location in the retinal epithelium. As the new blood vessels leak, scar tissue gradually forms. Acute vision loss may occur in some cases due to this bleeding.

Clinical Manifestations

Symptoms include blurred and darkened vision, the presence of scotomata (blind spots), or metamorphopsia (distortion of vision).

Diagnostics

Diagnosis is based on the history and physical examination, visual acuity measurements, ophthalmoscopic examinations, an Amsler grid test, fundus photography, and IV fluorescent angiography.

Therapeutics and Nursing Considerations

When visual acuity is compromised, laser photocoagulation of abnormal blood vessels has been the therapy of choice, but it can also destroy the retinal pigment epithelium and photoreceptor cells. Photodynamic therapy is a newer therapy that results in fewer complications.

The permanent loss of central vision associated with AMD has serious psychological implications for nursing care. Uncorrectable vision impairment needs specific care and consideration.

HEALTH CHALLENGES RELATED TO OXYGEN PERFUSION

HYPERTENSION

Pathophysiology

Hypertension refers to an intermittent or sustained elevation in the diastolic or systolic BP. Essential (also known as primary or idiopathic) hypertension is the most common form. Secondary hypertension results from a number of disorders, such as coarctation of the aorta or renal disease. Malignant hypertension is a severe fulminant form of hypertension.

There is no single cause of hypertension, but there are numerous risk factors, including the following:

- Family history
- Being of African descent
- Males are more at risk than females, but the risk level reverses postmenopause.
- Stress
- Obesity
- High dietary fat and sodium intake
- Cigarette smoking
- Hormonal contraception
- Sedentary lifestyle
- Aging
- DM

Complications of hypertension target the heart, brain, kidneys, and eyes. Individuals with poorly controlled hypertension have an increased risk for developing the following diseases:

- Coronary artery disease, left ventricular hypertrophy, and heart failure
- Cerebrovascular disease and peripheral vascular disease
- Nephrosclerosis
- Retinal damage

Clinical Manifestations

Essential hypertension usually begins insidiously and progresses slowly. If left untreated, even mild cases can lead to major complications. Initially, the client is asymptomatic. As the disease progresses, the client may experience the following symptoms:

- Fatigue and reduced activity tolerance
- Palpitations, angina, and dyspnea
- Epistaxis
- Blurred vision

Diagnostics

Along with the client's history and physical examination, the following tests may identify underlying causes: urinalysis, blood glucose, CBC, lipid profile, BUN and creatinine, electrolyte levels, and ECG.

Therapeutics and Nursing Considerations

Treatment of primary hypertension focuses on lifestyle changes and drug therapy. Secondary hypertension is treated by treating the underlying cause. The goal of therapy is to reduce the overall cardiovascular risk factors and control the BP by the least intrusive means possible. Follow-up monitoring is very important, as is gaining the client's trust to help enhance adherence to therapy. Lifestyle modifications may include the following:

- Dietary changes to low-fat, low-sodium products
- Limitation of alcohol intake and avoidance of tobacco use are important.
- Regular physical exercise and stress management are encouraged.

If lifestyle modifications are not enough or the BP remains high, drug therapy will be initiated. Drug therapy is directed at reduction of systemic vascular resistance and a decreased volume of circulating blood. The types of medications used include the following:

- Diuretics
- Adrenergic inhibitors
- Direct vasodilators
- Angiotensin inhibitors
- Calcium channel blockers

See Chapter 7, page 192, for more specific information on hypertensive drugs. The client will be assessed weekly, then every second week, then every three months, and then every six months. Explanation and encouragement are necessary with every visit to encourage compliance with treatment.

In rare situations, a client may go into a hypertensive crisis, in which there is a severe, abrupt elevation in BP. This more commonly affects a client who is not compliant with the treatment. A hypertensive crisis puts the client at risk for developing renal insufficiency, heart failure, pulmonary edema, severe diaphoresis, and, in extreme cases, hypertensive encephalopathy. This is an emergency, and the client requires immediate medical assistance.

CORONARY ARTERY DISEASE

Pathophysiology

Coronary artery disease (CAD) refers to any narrowing or obstruction of arterial lumina that interferes with cardiac perfusion. Deprived of sufficient blood, the myocardium can develop angina pectoris, infarction, arrhythmias, heart failure, and sudden death. The vessels involved are the right coronary artery, the left coronary artery, and the left anterior descending artery.

The right coronary artery supplies blood to the right atrium, right ventricle, inferior portion of the left ventricle, and posterior walls of the septum. The left coronary artery branches off to form the left circumflex artery, which supplies blood to the left atrium, lateral and posterior walls of the left ventricle, and posterior intraventricular septum. The left anterior descending artery supplies blood to the anterior wall of the left ventricle. The majority of blood passes into the coronary arteries when the heart muscle is at rest (diastole).

Every myocardial cell has four unique properties: automaticity, excitability, conductivity, and contractility. When a blockage occurs in an artery, the cells distal to the blockage will suffer, and these unique properties will be damaged or destroyed. The ejection fraction (EF), the percentage of blood ejected from the ventricle per beat, will be affected when any property is compromised.

Risk factors for the development of CAD include the following:

- Family history
- Obesity
- Smoking
- A high-fat diet
- A sedentary lifestyle
- Stress
- Diabetes
- Hypertension
- Hyperlipidemia

Atherosclerosis begins as soft deposits of fat accumulate along the inner wall of an artery. As the atherosclerosis progresses, luminal narrowing is accompanied by vascular changes that impair the diseased vessel's ability to dilate. When oxygen demand exceeds what the diseased vessels can supply, localized myocardial ischemia develops. Transient ischemia can cause angina pectoris, a reversible change that can depress myocardial function. If untreated, actual tissue injury or necrosis (infarction) may result. Oxygen deprivation causes a shift to anaerobic metabolism in the myocardium, resulting in the formation of lactic acid. The accumulation of lactic acid—with a subsequent drop in pH—further impairs cardiac function and results in decreased cardiac output (CO). When occlusion of the coronary arteries occurs over a long period of time, there is a greater chance that collateral circulation will develop. Some clients have an inherited predisposition to developing new vessels.

Angina pectoris has three main forms. Stable angina refers to cardiac pain that is predictable in frequency and duration and can be relieved with rest and nitrates. Unstable angina is unpredictable, with increasing cardiac pain. Prinzmetal's angina is a variant of unpredictable angina that is caused by vasospasm.

MI occurs as a result of sustained ischemia causing irreversible cellular death. The degree of altered function depends on the area of the heart involved and the size of the infarct. A subendocardial infarct is found when the damage to the heart muscle has not penetrated through the entire thickness of the wall. This is also called a non–Q-wave infarct. A transmural infarct involves the entire thickness of the myocardium.

Within 24 hours of the infarct, leukocytes infiltrate the area of cell death. Enzymes are released from the dead cells, and proteolytic enzymes of neutrophils and macrophages remove all necrotic tissue by the second or third day. Collateral circulation improves areas of poor perfusion. The necrotic zone can be identified on the ECG and by nuclear scanning. Ten to 14 days following an infarct, scar tissue is developing but is still very weak. By six weeks, the scar tissue has replaced the necrotic tissue and the area is said to be healed. Ventricular remodelling is an attempt by the heart to compensate for the infarcted muscle and includes hypertrophy and dilation.

Complications of a MI include the following:

- Arrhythmias
- Heart failure (most common)
- Cardiogenic shock
- Papillary muscle dysfunction
- Ventricular aneurysm
- Pericarditis
- Dressler syndrome, which is pericarditis with effusion and fever that can develop one to four weeks post-MI
- Pulmonary embolism

Clinical Manifestations

Clinical manifestations of myocardial infarction include the following:

- Pain in the chest, neck, jaw, arms, or epigastric region
- Dyspnea
- Nausea and vomiting
- Cool, clammy, pale skin
- Low-grade fever within the first 24 hours
- Initially an increase in BP and heart rate, which may later drop due to decreased CO
- Decreased urine output

- Crackles
- Peripheral edema
- Fear with feelings of impending doom

Recent research has shown that women present differently than men. In women, severe fatigue prior to the MI is the most common complaint. Sleep disturbances, shortness of breath, and anxiety are also symptoms of CAD in women. Women can experience chest discomfort, but they are more likely to express discomfort in the diaphragm, neck, or jaw.

Diagnostics

Diagnosis will be based on the client's history and physical examination. Pain is the chief complaint and can be described as a heavy pressure on the chest, up the neck, along the arms, and in the back or as epigastric discomfort. The cardiac pain usually does not change with respiration or position change. An ECG can show ischemia with a "flipped" T wave, injury with ST elevation or depression, or an infarct with an elongated Q wave. Laboratory work will show elevation in the following blood work:

- Cardiac enzymes (troponin)
- Creatine phosphokinase (CPK)
- Cardiac isoenzyme (CK-MB)
- Lactate dehydrogenase (LDH)
- Aspartate aminotransferase (AST)

Coronary angiography can reveal coronary stenosis or obstruction. A stress ECG may provoke chest pain and signs of myocardial ischemia.

Therapeutics and Nursing Considerations

Treatment for angina consists of the following considerations:

- Rest to decrease the oxygen demand
- Nitrates
- Acetylsalicylic acid (ASA)
- Possible stent placement
- With some clients with angina, beta blockers or calcium channel blockers may be needed.

Invasive interventions may include percutaneous coronary interventions, atherectomy, laser angioplasty and myocardial revascularization with coronary artery bypass graft (CABG), or minimally invasive direct coronary artery bypass grafting (MIDCABG). The same management may be used for treating a client with an infarct, with the addition of thrombolytics to dissolve the clot and allow blood to pass. The main complications following thrombolytic therapy are bleeding arrhythmias and reocclusion. Medications used in the acute management of an infarct include the following:

- Oxygen
- Nitrates
- Morphine
- Antiarrhythmic drugs
- Beta-adrenergic blockers
- Angiotensin-converting enzyme inhibitors
- Stool softeners may also be used.

Once the acute phase has ended, the client will need cardiac rehabilitation to help him or her return to as normal a lifestyle as possible. This rehabilitation includes physical, emotional, and psychological assistance. Figure 8.13 provides a concept map for understanding MI and its treatment.

SUDDEN CARDIAC DEATH

Sudden cardiac death is unexpected death from cardiac causes. There is a disruption in cardiac function causing an abrupt loss of cerebral blood flow. Death usually occurs within an hour of the onset of symptoms and occurs secondary to natural causes. It is mostly caused by ventricular arrhythmia and accounts for about 50% of all deaths from cardiovascular causes.

DYSRHYTHMIAS

Pathophysiology

The normal electrical pattern of the heart begins at the sinoatrial (SA) node, which is considered the pacemaker of the heart. It is found in the right atrium and usually sets a rate of 60–100 beats per minute (bpm). The electrical signal spreads through the atria and then travels to the atrioventricular (AV) node, where it is held for a short period of time to allow the atria to contract. If there is interference with the SA electrical impulse, the secondary pacemaker nodes (AV and Purkinje fibres) will automatically activate to keep the heart contracting. The AV node is normally the only avenue of connection with the ventricles. If an impulse starts at the AV node, the rate is usually around 40–60 bpm. The impulse then travels down the bundle of His and spreads to the ventricles via the Purkinje fibres. Once all cells in the ventricle are stimulated, the ventricles contract. If the impulse is formed in the ventricle, the normal rate is around 20–40 bpm.

A dysrhythmia is an abnormal heartbeat. It is very important to assess how this abnormal rhythm is affecting the CO.

The ECG is a display of electrical activity of the heart. The ECG can detect rate, rhythm, and conduction abnormalities; left ventricular hypertrophy; electrolyte imbalance; and digoxin toxicity. The P wave represents atrial depolarization. The PR interval represents the time for the impulse to spread from the atria to the ventricles. The QRS complex represents the

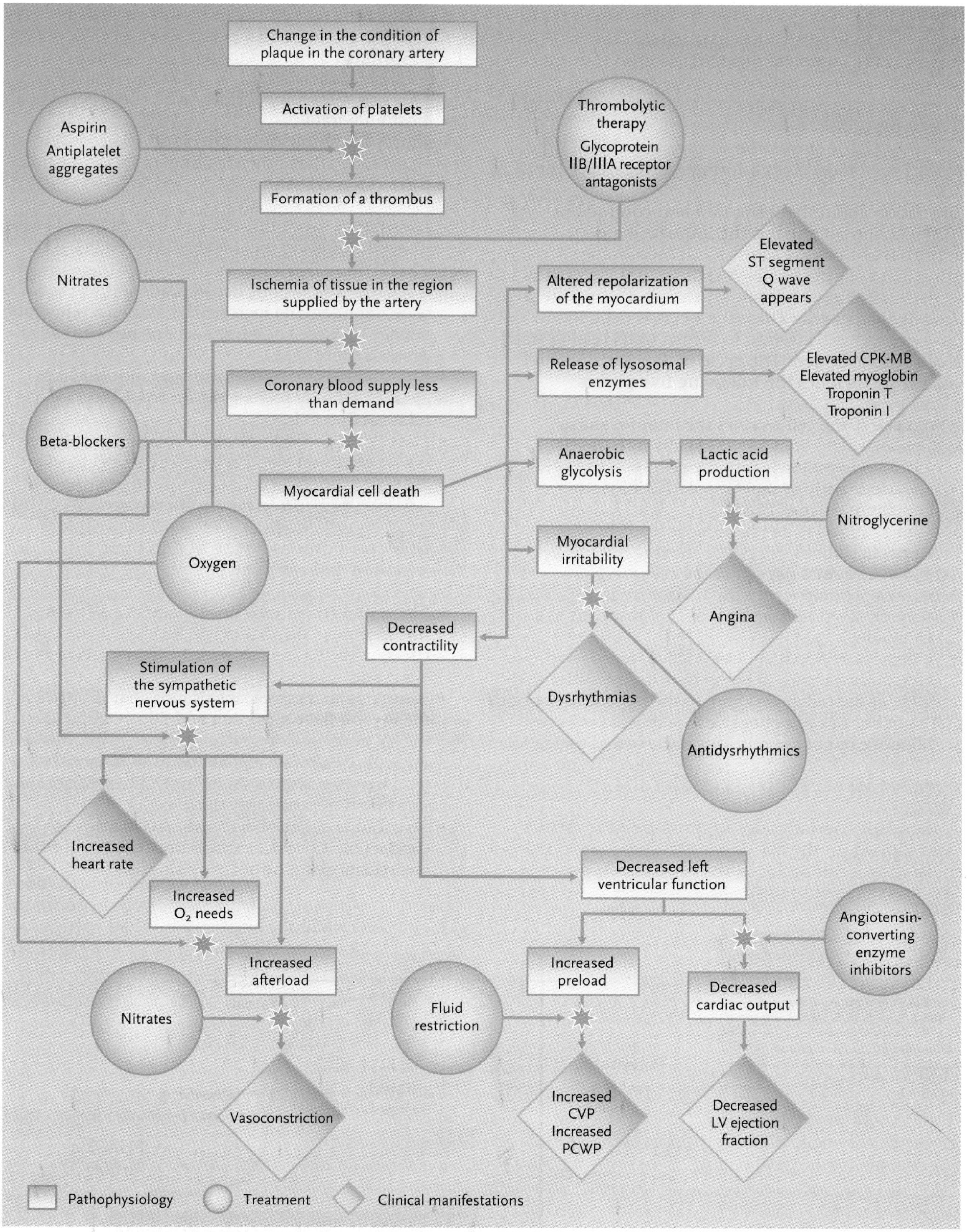
Change in the condition of plaque in the coronary artery
Activation of platelets
Aspirin
Antiplatelet aggregates
Thrombolytic therapy
Glycoprotein IIB/IIIA receptor antagonists
Formation of a thrombus
Nitrates
Ischemia of tissue in the region supplied by the artery
Altered repolarization of the myocardium
Elevated ST segment
Q wave appears
Coronary blood supply less than demand
Release of lysosomal enzymes
Elevated CPK-MB
Elevated myoglobin
Troponin T
Troponin I
Beta-blockers
Anaerobic glycolysis
Lactic acid production
Myocardial cell death
Nitroglycerine
Oxygen
Myocardial irritability
Angina
Decreased contractility
Stimulation of the sympathetic nervous system
Dysrhythmias
Antidysrhythmics
Increased heart rate
Increased O2 needs
Decreased left ventricular function
Angiotensin-converting enzyme inhibitors
Increased afterload
Increased preload
Decreased cardiac output
Nitrates
Fluid restriction
Vasoconstriction
Increased CVP
Increased PCWP
Decreased LV ejection fraction
Pathophysiology
Treatment
Clinical manifestations

FIGURE 8.13 **Concept Map for Understanding Myocardial Infarction and Its Treatment**

Source: Black, J. M., & Hawks, J. H. (2005). *Medical-surgical nursing: Clinical management for positive outcomes* (7th ed., p. 1710). St. Louis: Saunders.

ventricular depolarization and the atrial repolarization. The T wave indicates ventricular repolarization. The ST segment is the complete depolarization of the ventricles and the start of repolarization of the ventricles. The QT interval is electrical systole. The time between T and P waves is diastole.

The ECG also shows the voltage and duration of waves. The voltage gives information regarding the thickness of the chamber walls, and the duration gives information about the formation and conduction.

The action potential is the impulse generated by the movement of ions across a cell membrane. A cell is resting in a polarized state. A change in the electrical charge across the membrane causes an action potential, or cell depolarization. Once the heart is completely depolarized, it will attempt to return to its resting state via cell repolarization. The cycle of depolarizing and repolarizing includes the following five phases:

- In phase 0, the cell receives the impulse and is depolarized. Sodium moves rapidly into the cell, and calcium moves slowly into the cell.
- In phase 1, early or rapid repolarization occurs, and the sodium channel closes.
- In phase 2, a plateau phase, slow repolarization occurs. Calcium is still slowly moving into the cell, and now potassium flows out of the cell.
- In phase 3, rapid repolarization returns as the calcium channels are closed, and potassium flows out of the cell rapidly.
- In phase 4, the resting phase, active transport through the sodium–potassium pump returns potassium to the inside of the cell and sodium to the outside of the cell. The cell is now impermeable to sodium. Potassium can still move out of the cell. This is the end of the cycle, and the cell is ready for a new impulse. The cardiac action potential is shown in Figure 8.14.

Refractory periods refer to the stage of resistance to stimulation. In the absolute refractory period, no depolarization can occur. In the relative refractory period, a strong stimulus is needed to initiate an impulse. In the supernormal refractory period, only a mild stimulus is needed to initiate an impulse. Many dysrhythmias are triggered in the relative and supernormal refractory periods, with the T wave being the most vulnerable.

Antidysrhythmic drugs are classified according to the phase they affect. The classes of antidysrhythmic drugs are outlined below:

- Class I drugs block the influx of sodium into the cell in phase 0. These are sodium channel blockers.
- Class II drugs block the beta-receptors; therefore, they block the SNS, depress depolarization, slow the SA node impulses, and increase the AV nodal refractory period. They are considered general myocardial depressants.
- Class III drugs block the potassium movement in phase 3, thereby prolonging the repolarization and refractory periods.
- Class IV drugs block calcium in phase 2 and so are calcium channel blockers or slow channel blockers. They act to prolong conductivity and increase the refractory period and time at the AV node.

Other medications do not fit into these classifications and are listed below:

- Adenosine decreases conduction at the AV node.
- Atropine is an anticholinergic that blocks the vagal effect on the SA and AV nodes, thereby increasing the heart rate.
- Digoxin is an inotropic medication that strengthens the myocardial contraction and slows conduction at the AV node.
- Epinephrine acts on alpha- and beta-adrenergic receptor sites of the SNS, helping to restore normal sinus rhythm post–cardiac arrest.
- Magnesium sulphate decreases excitability and conduction. Table 8.12 shows drug therapy for stable angina and acute coronary syndrome.

FIGURE 8.14 **Cardiac Action Potential**

Source: Day, R. A., Paul, P., Williams, B., Smeltzer, S. C., & Bare, B. (2009). *Brunner & Suddarth's textbook of medical-surgical nursing* (2nd Canadian ed., p. 736, Figure 26-5). Philadelphia: Lippincott, Williams & Wilkins. Reprinted with permission.

PHASE 1
Rapid repolarization
PHASE 2
Plateau
PHASE 0
Rapid
depolarization
PHASE 3
Final repolarization
PHASE 4
Resting
Potential
(mV)
+40
+20
0
-20
-40
-60
-80
-100
Na+
Ca++
K+
Na+
K+
Cell membrane

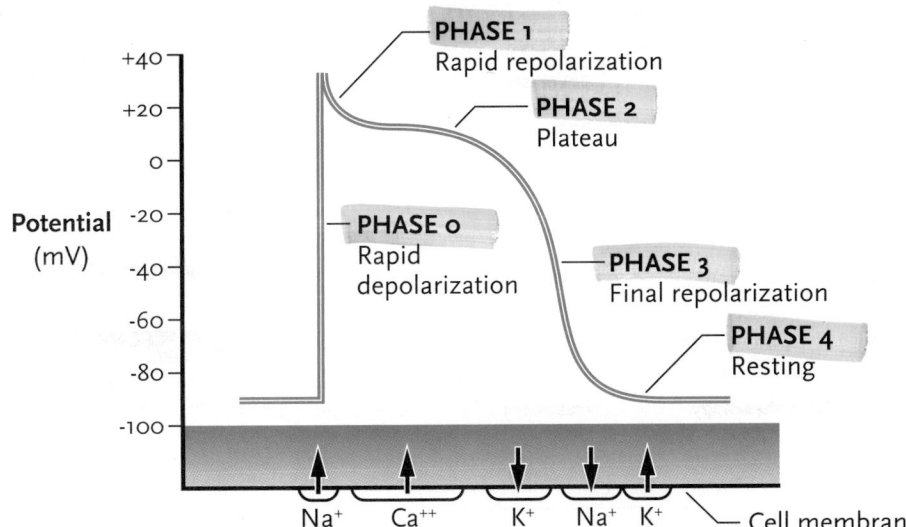

Table 8.12 Drug Therapy for Stable Angina and Acute Coronary Syndrome

DRUG	MECHANISM OF ACTION AND COMMENTS
Antiplatelet Agents Aspirin 325 mg (can be chewed) Low-dose ASA 81 mg	• Inhibit cyclo-oxygenase, which, in turn, produces thromboxane A_2, a potent platelet activator • Should be administered as soon as ACS is suspected
Beta-Adrenergic Blockers Metoprolol (Lopressor) Propranolol (Inderal) Esmolol (Brevibloc)	• Inhibit sympathetic nervous stimulation of the heart • Reduce both heart rate and contractility • Decrease afterload
Nitrates Sublingual nitroglycerine (Nitrostat, NitroQuick) Spray nitroglycerine (Nitrolingual) Transdermal nitroglycerine (Transderm-Nitro, Minitran) IV nitroglycerine (Nitro-Bid, Tridil) Long-acting formulations (isosorbide dinitrite [Isordil, Sorbitrate])	• Promote peripheral vasodilation, decreasing preload and afterload • Coronary artery vasodilation
Glycoprotein (GP) IIB/IIIA Inhibitors Abciximab (ReoPro) Eptifibatide (Integrilin) Tirofiban (Aggrastat)	• Prevent the binding of fibrinogen to platelets, thereby blocking platelet aggregation • Standard antiplatelet therapy in combination with aspirin for clients at high risk for unstable angina
Low-Molecular-Weight Heparin Dalteparin (Fragmin) Enoxaparin (Lovenox)	• Bind to antithrombin III, enhancing its effect • Heparin–antithrombin III complex inactivates activated factor X and thrombin • Prevent conversion of fibrinogen to fibrin
Direct Thrombin Inhibitors Bivalirudin (Angiomax) Lepirudin (Refludan)	• Bind directly to the receptor for thrombin, thus preventing the binding of thrombin and subsequent clot formation
Adenosine Diphosphate (ADP) Receptor Antagonists Ticlopidine (Ticlid) Clopidogrel (Plavix)	• Inhibit platelet aggregation • Alternative for client who cannot use aspirin
Fibrinolytic Therapy Recombinant plasminogen activator (rPA, reteplase [Retavase]) Streptokinase (Streptase) Tissue plasminogen activator (tPA, alteplase [Activase]) Tenecteplase (TNKase)	• Break up fibrin meshwork in clots • Used only in ST elevation MI
Calcium Channel Blockers Verapamil (Calan, Isoptin) Nifedipine (Procardia) Nicardipine (Cardene) Amlodipine (Norvasc) Diltiazem (Cardizem)	• Prevent calcium entry into vascular smooth muscle cells and myocytes (cardiac cells) • Coronary and peripheral vasodilation • ↓ AV conduction • ↓ Myocardial contractility
Morphine	• Acts as an analgesic and sedative • Reduces preload and myocardial O_2 consumption
Angiotensin-Converting Enzyme Inhibitors Captopril (Capoten) Enalapril (Vasotec)	• Prevent conversion of angiotensin I to angiotensin II • Decrease endothelial dysfunction • Useful with heart failure, tachycardia, MI, hypertension, and diabetes

ACS, acute coronary syndrome; *AV*, atrioventricular; *IV*, intravenous; *MI*, myocardial infarction.

Source: Lewis, S. M., Heitkemper, M. M., Dirksen, S. R., O'Brien, P., Bucher, L., et al. (2010). *Medical-surgical nursing in Canada: Assessment and management of clinical problems* (2nd Canadian ed., p. 863, Table 35-13). Toronto: Elsevier.

Dysrhythmias are triggered by internal forces such as acid–base imbalances, electrolyte imbalances, and hypoxia and by external forces such as illness, medication, and stress. Dysrhythmias are characterized by an alteration in impulse formation affecting the rate, rhythm, and development of entopic beats (those outside the normal pathway) or by alterations in conductivity, where failure or delay of impulse transmission may occur. The rhythms are classified according to the site of impulse formation and the degree of conduction block.

Sinus bradycardia is a slow sinus rhythm with a rate below 60 bpm. This rhythm can be normal in trained athletes. It becomes significant when CO is decreased and hypotension develops. Sinus bradycardia can predispose a client with an acute MI to develop escape arrhythmias and premature ectopic beats. If the bradycardia is compromising the CO, it can be treated with atropine.

Sinus tachycardia is a sinus rhythm with a rate over 100 bpm. It can cause dizziness and hypotension. The increased rate increases the oxygen consumption of the heart. It can create angina and extend the size of an infarct. Treatment depends on determining the underlying cause. Beta-adrenergic blockers are used to decrease heart rate and oxygen consumption.

Atrial flutter is an atrial tachyarrhythmia identified by recurring, regular, sawtooth-shaped flutter waves. It is usually associated with slower ventricular responses and is significant only when the ventricular response is elevated. There is a risk of clot formation with this rhythm. Treatment focuses on slowing the ventricular response by increasing the AV block. The client may require electrical cardioversion. Diltiazem, digoxin, and beta blockers may be used. Anticoagulant therapy is needed to prevent the formation of clots.

Atrial fibrillation (AF) is the total disorganization of atrial activity without effective atrial contraction. It may be chronic or intermittent, can result in decreased CO, and carries a risk for stroke. AF is sometimes found in clients experiencing heart failure. Treatment is the same as for atrial flutter.

First-degree AV block is found when every impulse is conducted to the ventricles, but the duration of the AV conduction is prolonged (elongated PR interval). Many consider this block benign, but it may lead to more serious blocks.

Second-degree AV block type 1 includes a gradual lengthening of the PR interval, which occurs because of a prolonged AV conduction time. This mostly occurs at the AV node but can occur in the His–Purkinje system as well. It is often due to an inferior MI or ischemia and can be a warning for a more serious block. Depending on the degree of block and the loss of CO, treatment may be atropine or insertion of a pacemaker.

Second-degree block type 2 is found when the PR interval is constant then followed with a sudden drop of a beat. This block almost always occurs when bundle branch block is present. A certain number of impulses from the sinus node are not conducted to the ventricles. This type of block often progresses to third-degree block. As a result of decreased CO, it usually leads to a decrease in BP. Treatment is the insertion of a pacemaker.

Complete heart block or third-degree heart block is found when no impulses from the atria are being conducted to the ventricles. The atria beats at a regular rhythm, and the ventricles beat independently in their own intrinsic slow rhythm. A ventricular rhythm is an escape rhythm and cannot sustain life. It results in a significant drop in CO. The client with this condition requires a pacemaker.

Premature ventricular contractions (PVCs) are contractions originating in an ectopic focus in the ventricles. The ECG will show a premature occurrence of a QRS complex. They can be multifocal (more than one site), unifocal (one site), ventricular bigeminy (one normal beat with one PVC), ventricular trigeminy (two normal beats followed by one PVC), couplets (two PVCs together), or triplets (three PVCs together). The PVC takes on a characteristic bizarre wide configuration. PVCs are considered benign in clients with a normal heart. In heart disease, PVCs may reduce CO and precipitate angina and heart failure. PVCs represent ventricular irritability. They may also occur in reperfusion post-thrombolytic therapy or follow plaque reduction after percutaneous coronary intervention. Treatment consists of assessing the hemodynamic status. Beta blockers, procainamide, amiodarone, or lidocaine may be used.

Ventricular tachycardia is a run of three or more PVCs. It is considered life-threatening because of decreased CO and the possibility of deterioration to ventricular fibrillation. It may cause a severe decrease in CO and pulmonary edema, shock, and cerebral ischemia. IV procainamide, amiodarone, or lidocaine may be used. Synchronized cardioversion may be used when drug therapy is ineffective, the rate is exceptionally high, and the client is symptomatic.

Ventricular fibrillation is a severe derangement of the heart rhythm characterized by irregular undulations of varying contour and amplitude. There is no effective contraction, so no CO is available. The client is likely to lose consciousness, be without a pulse, be apneic, and possibly have seizures. If untreated, the client may die. This is an emergency, and the client needs cardiopulmonary resuscitation (CPR) and advanced cardiac life support (ACLS) with drug therapy and defibrillation.

Defibrillation is the most effective method of terminating ventricular fibrillation. Ideally, it is performed 15–20 seconds after the onset of the arrhythmia. It involves the passage of a direct current of electricity through the heart to depolarize all cells with the intent of allowing the SA node to resume its normal role. The charge is started at 200 joules and moves up to 360 joules.

Cardioversion is used for hemodynamically unstable ventricular or supraventricular tachyarrhythmias. The charge is synchronized with the client's own QRS complex. This is done on a nonemergency basis. The client is conscious and must sign a consent form. The charge is started at 50 joules and may go up to 200 joules. The client will be sedated before the conversion occurs.

A pacemaker is a pulse generator that provides electrical stimulus to a heart that cannot conduct its own impulse in order to supply adequate CO. It can be used for transient or permanent conduction defects.

HEART FAILURE

Pathophysiology

Heart failure (HF) is an abnormal condition involving impaired cardiac pumping. It is not a disease but a syndrome. HF is often associated with long-standing hypertension and CAD. HF occurs when the heart is no longer able to pump an adequate amount of blood to meet the metabolic needs of the client. It is the most common reason for hospitalization in adults over age 65 years.

Risk factors for developing HF include the following:

- CAD
- Age
- Hypertension
- Obesity
- Cigarette smoking
- DM
- High cholesterol
- Being of African descent

Conditions that can precipitate or exacerbate HF include the following:

- Stress
- Dysrhythmias
- Infection
- Anemia
- Thyroid disorders
- Pregnancy
- Paget's disease
- Nutritional deficiency of B vitamins
- Pulmonary disease
- Hypervolemia

HF may be caused by any interference with normal mechanisms regulating cardiac output. CO depends on preload, afterload, myocardial contractility, heart rate, and metabolic rate.

Systolic failure is the most common cause of HF. The left ventricle loses its ability to generate enough pressure to eject blood into the body. The hallmark of systolic failure is a decrease in the left ventricular ejection fraction.

Diastolic failure is the impaired ability of the ventricles to fill during diastole and usually is the result of left ventricular hypertrophy. Pulmonary congestion results from diastolic failure, and there will be a normal ejection fraction until systolic failure develops.

There can also be mixed systolic and diastolic failure, as seen in dilated cardiomyopathy. This is known as biventricular failure. The ejection fraction in this case is extremely poor.

The four basic factors that cause HF are as follows:

- An increase in the volume of blood to be pumped
- An increase in the resistance against which the blood must be pumped
- A decrease in contractility
- A decrease in the filling of the cardiac chambers

Cardiac reserve refers to the heart's ability to increase CO in response to stress. A failing heart has limited ability to respond to increased demand.

There are three cardiac compensatory mechanisms: tachycardia, ventricular dilation, and ventricular hypertrophy. Systemic compensatory mechanisms involve the SNS, kidneys, and liver.

Clinical Manifestations

Clinical manifestations of HF depend on the specific ventricle involved, precipitating causes of the failure, the duration of the failure, and any underlying condition the client may have. One-sided failure eventually leads to biventricular failure.

Left-sided failure is the most common classification of HF. With this type of HF, blood backs up through the left atrium into the pulmonary veins, causing congestion and edema. Hypertension is the most common cause of left-sided HF, followed by cardiomyopathies, rheumatic heart disease, and CAD.

Right-sided failure results in the backward flow of blood to the right atrium and venous circulation, which creates venous congestion, peripheral edema, hepatomegaly, splenomegaly, and jugular venous distension. The primary cause of right-sided failure is cor pulmonale.

"Forward" or "backward" failure is based on the effect on circulation. Forward failure is the inability to propel blood forward, into the body. Backward failure is the inability to accommodate the volume of blood returning to the ventricle.

High-output failure occurs when a high-output CO or a normal CO is unable to meet the needs of the body. Thyroid toxicosis is often the cause of high-output failure. Low-output failure is when CO is depressed.

Complications of HF are pleural effusions, arrhythmias, left ventricular thrombus, and hepatomegaly.

Classifications of HF are based on the person's tolerance to physical activity. Classifications are as follows:

- Class 1 is no limitation of physical ability.
- Class 2 is slight limitation to physical ability.
- Class 3 is a marked limitation.
- Class 4 is the inability to carry on any physical activity without discomfort.

Manifestations of acute HF include the following symptoms:

- Agitation
- Pale, cyanotic skin and cold, clammy extremities
- Severe dyspnea and tachypnea

If untreated, the client may develop pulmonary edema. Chronic symptoms of HF include the following:

- Fatigue
- Dyspnea, orthopnea, and cough
- Tachycardia, pulse alterans, and AF
- Edema and nocturia
- Restlessness and confusion
- Chest pain
- Weight changes
- Skin may take on a dusky appearance
- Heart enlargement
- Cheyne-Stokes respirations

Death usually results from asphyxiation, pulmonary acidosis, shock, or dysrhythmias.

Diagnostics

Diagnostic studies are done to determine the underlying cause and extent of present failure, and they include the history and physical examination of the client. Chest X-ray, ECG, electrolytes, liver function tests, CBC, BUN and creatinine, and cardiac enzyme tests are performed. An echocardiogram with measurement of the ejection fraction may be done, along with stress testing and cardiac catheterization.

Therapeutics and Nursing Considerations

Treatment is focused on the following:

- Decreasing intravascular volume
- Decreasing venous return
- Decreasing the afterload
- Improving the gas exchange and oxygenation
- Improving cardiac function
- Reducing anxiety

Drugs that are frequently prescribed for HF include diuretics, beta blockers, nitrates, calcium channel blockers, and ACE inhibitors.

The client will be encouraged to be in a high Fowler's position with the legs down to help decrease blood return to the heart. Oxygen therapy is usually needed as the condition deteriorates. Symptom management is important. Teaching regarding the activity–exercise balance, nutrition with a low-sodium diet, medications, support systems, and possible psychological changes will be helpful for the client with HF.

VALVULAR HEART DISEASE

Pathophysiology

The heart contains two AV valves and two semilunar valves. The type of valvular heart disease depends on the valve or valves affected and the functional alterations, stenosis, or regurgitation.

With stenosis, the valve orifice is restricted, impeding the forward movement of blood. This creates a pressure gradient across the open valve. The degree of stenosis is reflected in the pressure gradient differences. Regurgitation involves the incomplete closure of the valve leaflets, which results in backward flow of the blood. Valvular disorders in children and adolescents usually occur because of congenital conditions; in adults, they are often the result of degenerative heart disease, commonly caused by rheumatic heart disease. See Chapter 10, page 494, for more information on pediatric valvular heart disease.

Clinical Manifestations

Clinical manifestations include the following:

- Dyspnea
- Palpitations from AF
- Fatigue
- Accentuated first heart sound, opening snap, and low-pitched, rumbling, diastolic murmur
- Hoarseness
- Chest pain
- Seizures
- May develop a stroke from emboli formed in the stagnant blood of the left atrium

Mitral Valve Disorders

Mitral valve patency depends on the integrity of the mitral leaflets, mitral annulus, chordae tendinae, papillary muscles, left atrium, and left ventricle. An abnormality of any of these structures can result in regurgitation. The majority of cases of mitral valve regurgitation can be attributed to the following:

- MI
- Chronic rheumatic heart disease
- Mitral valve prolapse
- Ischemic papillary muscle dysfunction
- Infectious endocarditis

An MI with left ventricular failure places the client at risk for rupture of the chordae tendinae.

Clients with mitral valve regurgitation may be asymptomatic for years until they develop some degree of heart failure. Initial symptoms may include the following:

- Weakness and fatigue
- Dyspnea gradually progressing to orthopnea

- Paroxysmal nocturnal dyspnea
- Peripheral edema
- May also have a brisk carotid pulse, auscultatory findings of accentuated left ventricular filling leading to an audible S_2, and a murmur

Mitral valve prolapse is a structural abnormality of the mitral valve leaflets and papillary muscles or chordae that allows the leaflets to prolapse into the left atrium during systole. It can occur in the presence of redundant mitral valve leaflets, elongated chordae tendinae, enlarged mitral annulus, or abnormally contracting left ventricular wall segments. Mitral valve prolapse is usually benign, but serious complications can occur, such as mitral valve regurgitation, infective endocarditis, sudden death, or cerebral ischemia.

Most clients are asymptomatic. Murmurs may develop due to insufficiency, which may get more intense through systole. There may be clicks during mid- to late systole that may be constant or vary beat to beat. Arrhythmias may develop, such as paroxysmal supraventricular tachycardia and ventricular tachycardia. Chest pain may be present but does not respond to antianginal treatment.

Aortic Valve Disorders

Aortic valve stenosis usually is discovered in childhood, adolescence, or early adulthood. If older adults develop it, rheumatic fever or senile fibrocalcific degeneration is usually the cause. Aortic stenosis results in the obstruction of flow from the left ventricle to the aorta during systole. This then causes left ventricular hypertrophy and increased myocardial oxygen consumption due to increased myocardial mass. This, in turn, leads to a reduced CO and pulmonary hypertension.

Clinical manifestations resemble the symptoms of angina pectoris. HF and syncope can develop. Auscultatory findings include a normal to soft first heart sound with a diminished or absent second heart sound. An examiner may hear a systolic crescendo–decrescendo murmur that ends before the second heart sound, with a prominent fourth sound. The prognosis is poor when the obstruction is not removed. Nitroglycerine is contraindicated as it reduces the preload that is necessary to free the stiffened valve so it can open.

Aortic valve regurgitation may result from disease of the aortic valve leaflets, the aortic root, or both. It can be caused by bacterial endocarditis, trauma, or aortic dissection. Chronic aortic regurgitation results from rheumatic heart disease, congenital bicuspid aortic valve, syphilis, or chronic rheumatic heart conditions.

With aortic regurgitation, blood flows back from the ascending aorta to the left ventricle, causing fluid overload. The heart tries to compensate by dilation and hypertrophy. Eventually, myocardial contractility declines and pulmonary hypertension occurs, leading to right heart failure.

Clinical manifestations may be a sudden manifestation of cardiovascular collapse, weakness, severe dyspnea, hypotension, distended pulses during systole, and quickly collapsing pulses during diastole. The first heart sound will be soft or absent, the third and fourth heart sounds will be audible, and there will be a soft, high-pitched diastolic murmur. There may be a systolic ejection murmur, an Austin-Flint murmur, or both. The client may be asymptomatic for years and then start to develop exertional dyspnea that gradually worsens and nocturnal angina with diaphoresis.

Tricuspid Valve Disorders

Tricuspid valve disease occurs almost exclusively in clients with rheumatic mitral stenosis. It can be found in IV drug users. In tricuspid valve disease, the right atrial output is obstructed, resulting in right atrial enlargement and elevated systemic venous pressure. If untreated, pulmonary hypertension develops, leading to right heart failure. Manifestations of tricuspid valve disease include peripheral edema, ascites, hepatomegaly, presystolic or midsystolic murmur, and a pansystolic murmur that may be heard during regurgitation.

Pulmonic valve disease is almost always congenital. However, it can be associated with other valvular disease.

Diagnostics

Diagnosis is done by history and physical examination, ECG, echocardiogram, and cardiac catheterization.

Therapeutics and Nursing Considerations

Treatment of valvular disease depends on the valve involved and the severity of the disease. The focus is on preventing the following complications:

- Exacerbations of HF
- Acute pulmonary edema
- Thromboembolism
- Recurrent endocarditis

Pharmacological therapy includes the following:

- Digitalis
- Diuretics
- Antiarrhythmics
- Beta blockers
- Anticoagulants

Percutaneous transluminal balloon valvuloplasty to split open the fuse commissures may be performed, or open surgery for valve repair or replacement may be required. Prosthetic valves can be either mechanical (Dacron or pyrolite carbon) or biological (tissue).

ABDOMINAL AORTIC ANEURYSM

Pathophysiology

An abdominal aortic aneurysm is an abnormal dilation in an arterial wall, commonly in the aorta between the renal arteries and iliac branches. Aneurysms commonly result from atherosclerosis, which weakens the aortic wall and gradually distends the lumen. Other causes include fungal infections, congenital disorders, trauma, syphilis, and hypertension.

Degenerative changes in the tunica media create a focal weakness, allowing the tunica intima and tunica adventitia to stretch outward. BP within the aorta progressively weakens the vessel walls and enlarges the aneurysm.

The most serious complication of an aneurysm is rupture. If it is a posterior rupture into the retroperitoneal space, bleeding may tamponade by surrounding structures, preventing exsanguination. If the rupture occurs anteriorly into the abdominal cavity, mortality is very high due to uncontained massive hemorrhage.

Clinical Manifestations

Clients are often asymptomatic. On physical examination, a pulsating mass is found in the periumbilical area. There may be a systolic bruit over the aorta, and the client may experience tenderness on deep palpation. Lumbar pain that radiates to the flank and groin can occur. If the aneurysm ruptures, there is severe, persistent, abdominal and back pain, often mimicking renal colic. Tachycardia, profuse diaphoreses, and hypotension can occur.

Diagnostics

Diagnosis is made by history and physical examination, chest X-ray, echocardiography, ECG, CT scan, and MRI.

Therapeutics and Nursing Considerations

The goal of management is to prevent rupture of the aneurysm. Early detection and prompt treatment are imperative. The aneurysm will be surgically removed and replaced with a Dacron graft. If the aneurysm is small and the client is asymptomatic, surgery may be delayed. Endovascular grafting may be used to repair an abdominal aneurysm. This is a minimally invasive procedure, in which a catheter with an attached graft is inserted through the femoral or iliac artery and advanced over a guide wire into the aorta. The graft is then positioned across the aneurysm. A balloon on the catheter expands, affixing the graft to the vessel wall. Figure 8.15 illustrates surgical repair of abdominal aortic aneurysm.

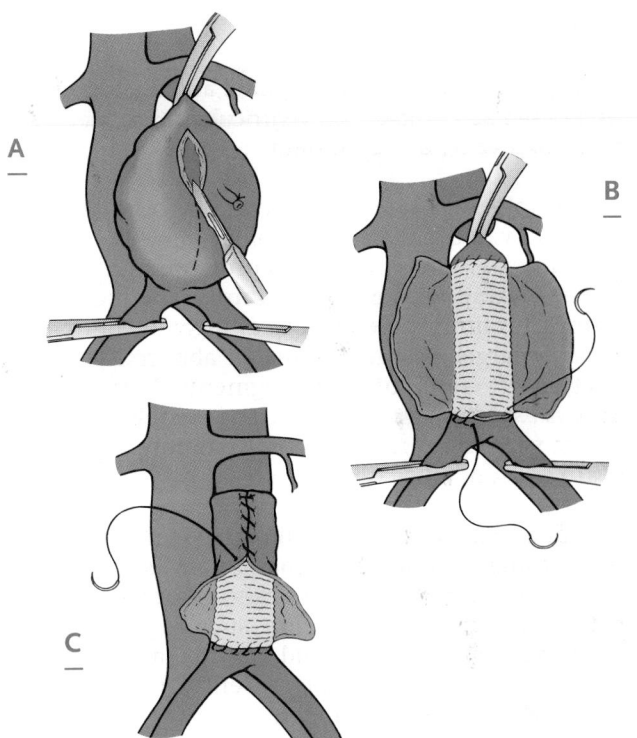

FIGURE 8.15 Surgical Repair of Abdominal Aortic Aneurysm

A, Incising the aneurysmal sac. B, Insertion of synthetic graft. C, Suturing native aortic wall over synthetic graft.

Source: Lewis, S. M., Heitkemper, M. M., Dirksen, S. R., O'Brien, P., Bucher, L., et al. (2010). *Medical-surgical nursing in Canada: Assessment and management of clinical problems* (2nd Canadian ed., p. 962, Figure 39-4). Toronto: Elsevier.

PERIPHERAL VASCULAR DISEASES

Pathophysiology

Peripheral vascular disease (PVD) is an imbalance between the supply and demand of blood and nutrients that results from the degeneration of the peripheral vascular system. PVD includes arterial insufficiency and occlusion and venous insufficiency and occlusion.

Peripheral arterial diseases (PADs) can affect any artery but tend to affect the aorta, iliac, femoral, popliteal, tibial, and peritoneal arteries. Risk factors for developing PAD include the following:

- Increasing age, smoking, diabetes, obesity, sedentary lifestyle, and stress
- Heredity
- Male gender
- Hyperhomocysteinemia
- CVD

There are two forms of PAD. Organic disease is caused by structural damage to the blood vessel with plaque or inflammation blocking blood flow. Functional disease is a reversible disturbance in the SNS. The vasospasm of Raynaud's disease is an example of functional disease.

Clinical Manifestations

The classic symptom of organic PAD is intermittent claudication, in which ischemic muscle ache or pain is precipitated by a constant level of exercise. The pain usually resolves within 10 minutes or less of rest. The pain is reproducible. Other manifestations may be as follows:

- Paraesthesia
- Thin, shiny, and taut skin
- Loss of hair on lower legs
- Diminished or absent pedal, popliteal, or femoral pulses
- Pallor
- Reactive hyperemia

Complications of PAD include the following:

- Atrophy of the skin and underlying muscles
- Delayed wound healing
- Wound infections
- Tissue necrosis
- Arterial ulcers

Diagnostics

Diagnostic studies include Doppler ultrasonography, ankle–brachial index, duplex imaging, or plethysmography. Invasive diagnostic tests are an angiogram, digital subtraction angiogram, or a lumbar sympathetic block.

Therapeutics and Nursing Considerations

Treatment focuses on preventing further damage to the vessel. The client is encouraged to do the following:

- Stop smoking
- Treat the hyperlipidemia, hypertension, and diabetes
- Exercise, as this improves oxygen delivery to the legs

Pharmacological therapy may include the following:

- ASA
- Ticlopidine (Ticlid)
- Clopidogrel (Plavix)
- Sulfinpyrazone (Anturane)
- Dipyridamole (Persantine)
- Pentoxifylline (Trental) or cilostazol (Pletal) may be prescribed for intermittent claudication.

If PAD progresses and the intermittent claudication becomes incapacitating, the client has pain at rest, or ulceration and gangrene develop, surgical intervention will be needed.

A percutaneous transluminal balloon angioplasty could be done. The most common surgical procedure is a peripheral arterial bypass operation with autogenous vein or synthetic graft material to bypass the lesion. An endarterectomy may need a patch graft. A sympathectomy may be done. When gangrene is present, amputation is needed. After surgery, the client will be on bed rest for 24–48 hours. While in bed, the client is encouraged to avoid flexing his or her knees.

Pathophysiology (Peripheral Venous Disease)

The most common peripheral disorder of the veins is venous thrombus, which is the formation of a clot in association with inflammation of the vein. Three important factors, known as Virchow's triad, are involved in the etiology of the clot formation. These factors are venous stasis, damage to the endothelium lining, and hypercoagulability of the blood. Some of the risk factors for developing either superficial or deep vein thrombosis include the following:

- Major abdominal surgery
- Pelvic or orthopedic surgery
- Oral contraceptives and HRT
- Obesity
- Pregnancy
- Heart disease
- Advanced cancer
- Coagulation disorders

Blood cells, platelets, and fibrin accumulate together to form the thrombus. A common site of clot formation is the cusps of the veins. An enlarged clot may occlude the lumen of the vein. Emboli can break away from the clot and lodge anywhere else in the body. The most serious complications of venous problems include pulmonary emboli and phlegmasia cerulea dolens (swollen, blue, painful legs).

Varicose veins are dilated tortuous subcutaneous veins that usually affect the saphenous system. Risk factors for developing varicosities include the following:

- Congenital defective valves
- Prolonged standing
- Obesity
- Systemic conditions such as pregnancy, ascites, heart disease, and abdominal masses

Clinical Manifestations

Clients with superficial thrombophlebitis may present with the following:

- A palpable, firm, cordlike vein
- Surrounding area may be red and tender and warm to touch
- A slight fever

Many clients with a DVT are asymptomatic. Those clients who are symptomatic experience the following:

- Unilateral leg edema
- Pain
- Warm, red skin

Varicosities present as prominent, superficial,

discoloured, tortuous veins. The client usually complains of the following:

- A dull ache or heaviness
- Fatigue
- Leg cramps and edema
- Some varicosities have nodular protrusions.

Diagnostics

Diagnoses can be made from the client's history and physical examination, blood work such as platelet count, bleeding time and international normalized ratio (INR), venous Doppler evaluation, duplex scanning, and venogram.

Therapeutics and Nursing Considerations

Treatment of superficial thrombophlebitis involves elevating the affected limb and applying warm moist heat to the area. ASA and acetaminophen (Tylenol®) may be used to relieve discomfort. NSAIDs may be used to treat the inflammation.

To prevent DVT development, early mobilization is encouraged. If the client is to remain in bed, frequent position changes are encouraged, as well as dorsiflexing the feet and rotating the ankles. Preventive measures such as compression stockings or support hose should be employed.

People with venous disorders should be encouraged not to cross their legs or ankles, not to stand in one place for long periods of time, and not to wear constrictive clothing.

If a DVT does develop, the client is usually started on anticoagulants to prevent the growth of the present clot and the development of any new clots. Unfractionated heparin, low-molecular-weight heparin, and warfarin (Coumadin) derivatives are the most commonly used anticoagulants. Coumadin requires 48–72 hours to have an effect on the PT; therefore, Coumadin is started before the heparin infusion is completed. A venous thrombectomy or insertion of a vena cava interruption device may be done to prevent pulmonary emboli. The client usually remains on prophylactic Coumadin.

Varicose vein management involves education concerning prevention, including lifestyle modifications, exercise, use of support hose, not standing for long periods, and reducing obesity. Surgical therapy for varicose veins may include sclerotherapy, ligation and stripping, or laser therapy for smaller varicosities.

CRITICAL HEALTH CHALLENGES

Burns

Pathophysiology

Burns occur when there is injury to the tissue of the body caused by heat, chemicals, electrical current, or radiation and can lead to many local and systemic problems. Burns are classified according to the depth, extent, and location of the burn, as well as the client's own risk factors. The depth of the burn is now categorized as a partial- or full-thickness burn, as follows:

- A superficial partial-thickness burn involves the epidermis.
- A deep partial-thickness burn involves the dermis.
- A full-thickness burn involves, fat, muscle, and bone.

Two commonly used guides for determining the total body surface damaged by burns are the Lund-Browder chart and the rule of nines, which are outlined in Figure 8.16.

A

Head	7
Neck	2
Ant. trunk	13
Post. trunk	13
R. buttock	2½
L. buttock	2½
Genitalia	1
R.U. arm	4
L.U. arm	4
R.L. arm	3
L.L. arm	3
R. hand	2½
L. hand	2½
R. thigh	9½
L. thigh	9½
R. leg	7
L. leg	7
R. foot	3½
L. foot	3½
TOTAL	100%

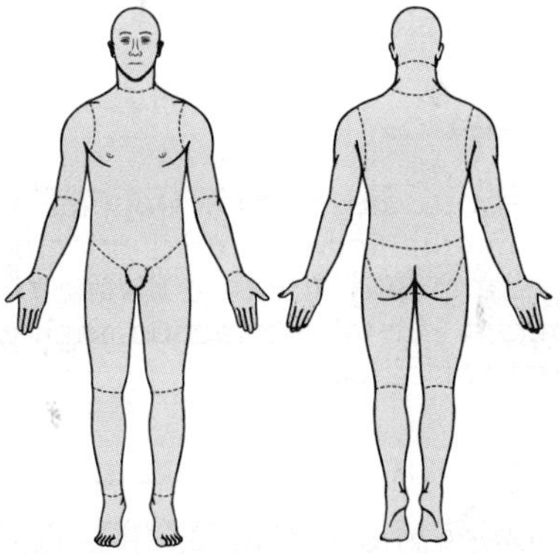

B

Head & neck	9%
Arms	9%
Ant. trunk	18%
Post. trunk	18%
Legs	18%
Perineum	1%
TOTAL	100%

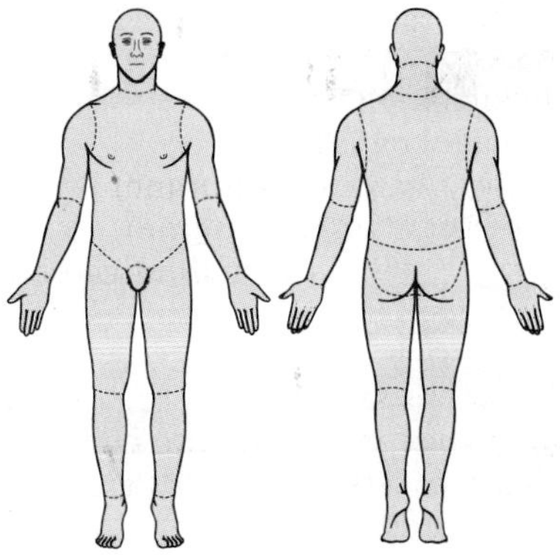

FIGURE 8.16 **A, Lund-Browder and B, Rule of Nines Charts for Body Surface Burn Assessment**

Source: Lewis, S. M., Heitkemper, M. M., Dirksen, S. R., O'Brien, P., Bucher, L., et al. (2010). *Medical-surgical nursing in Canada: Assessment and management of clinical problems* (2nd Canadian ed., p. 554, Figure 26-4). Toronto: Elsevier.

The location of the burn is related to the severity of the injury. Face, neck, and chest burns can result in respiratory complications. Circumferential burns of the extremities can cause circulatory problems and compartment syndrome. Older clients or clients who have pre-existing cardiovascular conditions, respiratory conditions, renal disease, diabetes, alcoholism, a history of drug use, or malnutrition are slower at healing from a burn.

Clinical Manifestations

Manifestations of burns are as follows:

- Shock
- Blisters
- Dynamic ileus
- Shivering
- Altered mental status

Many complications can result from burns and are listed below:

- Cardiovascular complications include arrhythmias, hypovolemic shock, edema, ischemia, necrosis, gangrene, and increased blood viscosity.
- Respiratory complications can be mechanical obstruction and asphyxia, interstitial edema, pneumonia, and pulmonary edema.
- Renal complications because of acute tubular necrosis can result in kidney damage.
- GI changes that can occur from burns include impairment of gastric mucosal integrity and motility. Paralytic ileus may develop. Abdominal distension can occur, and curling ulcer (acute ulcerative gastroduodenal disease) can develop.

Metabolic complications can include hypermetabolism, increasing body temperature, and increasing catabolic rates.

Skin complications occur due to the burn injury's disruption of the protective barrier of the skin, which increases the risk of infection.

Therapeutics and Nursing Considerations

Care begins at the time of the burn. The client must first be removed from the source of the burn. For smaller burns, cover the burn with a clean, cool, tap water–dampened towel. For larger burns, remove burned clothing and wrap the client in a clean sheet, without using any cool water or ice.

Emergent Phase

The emergent (resuscitative) phase is from the onset to two to five or more days following the burn. In the first 24–48 hours, the client will lose fluid and form edema until fluid mobilization and diuresis occur. At this time, the client is at risk for the following complications:

- Hypovolemic shock can occur due to the massive shift of fluid out of the intravascular space that results from increased capillary permeability.
- This shift causes intravascular depletion, edema, decreased BP, and increased pulse.
- Insensible water loss can increase from 30–50 mL per hour to 200–400 mL per hour.
- RBCs are hemolyzed by a circulating factor released at the time of the burn. Thrombosis occurs.
- Sodium shifts to the interstitial spaces and remains there until the edema formation ceases.
- A potassium shift develops because injured cells and hemolyzed RBCs release potassium into the extracellular space.
- Neutrophils and monocytes accumulate at the site of injury.
- Fibroblast and collagen fibrils begin wound repair within the first 6–12 hours after injury.
- The immune system is compromised as the skin barrier is destroyed and circulating immunoglobulins are decreased.

Initial management focuses on survival. Goals of management include the following:

- Securing the airway
- Supporting circulation by fluid replacement
- Keeping the client as comfortable as possible with analgesics
- Preventing infection
- Maintaining body temperature
- Providing emotional support
- Airway management may require mechanical ventilation.
- Fluid management is essential using colloidal solutions.
- Wound care is delayed until a patent airway, adequate circulation, and adequate fluid replacement have been established. When time permits, the wound should be cleansed by using a hydrotherapy tub, shower, or bed. Debridement is the removal of loose, necrotic skin and may require sedation. An open wound is covered with a topical antibiotic without a dressing. When dressings are used, they should be in the form of sterile gauze laid over the topical antibiotic. Dressings are changed two to three times per day initially and then less often as the wound heals.
- Allograft or homograft skin grafts are commonly used but are often rejected by the client's body.
- Routine blood work is important to monitor for electrolyte imbalance and homeostasis.
- Early ROM exercises help prevent contractures.
- Analgesics and sedatives are given, as well as a tetanus immunization.
- Antimicrobial agents, both topical and systemic, are used.
- Fluid replacement takes priority over nutritional requirements. Oral intake can be started once the bowel sounds return. Due to the increased metabolic

state, the client will need high-calorie meals with vitamin and mineral supplements.

Acute Phase

The acute phase begins with the mobilization of ECF and subsequent diuresis and ends when the burned area is completely covered by skin grafts or when the wounds are healed. Necrotic tissue will begin to slough off, and granulation tissue will form. A partial-thickness wound will heal from the edges. Full-thickness wounds must be covered by skin grafts. Partial-thickness wounds form eschar initially, and then epithelialization begins once the eschar is removed. Full-thickness wounds require debridement. The interventions required are as follows:

- Wound care in the acute phase includes daily observation, cleansing, and debridement.
- Appropriate coverage of the graft is needed. A fine mesh gauze is placed on the graft, followed by a middle and outer dressing. Sheet skin grafts must be kept free of blebs. Eschar is removed down to the subcutaneous tissue of fascia. Cultured epithelial autographs, grown from biopsies of the client's own skin, or artificial grafts may be used.
- Analgesics and sedation are needed.
- Passive and active ROM exercises should be performed.
- Splints help prevent deformities.
- A high-protein, high-carbohydrate diet helps meet the client's increased metabolic needs.

Rehabilitation Phase

The rehabilitation phase begins when the client's burn wounds are covered with skin or healed, and the client is able to resume a level of self-care activity. The burn wound will heal either by primary intention or by grafting. Layers of epithelialization begin rebuilding the tissue structure. Collagen fibres add strength to weakened areas. In about four to six weeks, the burn area becomes raised and hyperemic. Mature healing is reached in six months to two years. The skin will never completely regain its original colour. The following are nursing considerations:

- Skin and joint contractures are the most common complication in the rehabilitation phase.
- Both the client and the family become active learners regarding wound care.
- An emollient water-based cream is recommended.
- Cosmetic surgery may be needed.
- The client will require constant encouragement and reassurances. The family will need to understand the importance of re-establishing the client's independence while participating in client care. It is important to assess for psychoemotional cues and understand that psychiatric intervention may be needed.

SHOCK

Pathophysiology

Shock is a syndrome characterized by decreased tissue perfusion and impaired cellular metabolism. Cardiogenic shock or low-blood-flow shock involves systolic and diastolic dysfunction and compromised CO. The causes are as follows:

- MI, cardiomyopathies, and blunt cardiac injury
- Severe systemic or pulmonary hypertension
- Severe sepsis can cause cardiogenic shock.

Diastolic dysfunction results from the impaired ability of the ventricle to fill during diastole and a decrease in stroke volume. Early signs of cardiogenic shock include the following:

- Tachycardia
- Hypotension and narrowed pulse pressure
- Increased systemic vascular resistance (SVR)
- Increased myocardial oxygen consumption, tachypnea, pulmonary congestion, and crackles
- Since the CO is low, renal blood flow and urine output decrease.
- Lack of oxygen to the tissues can result in anxiety.

Hypovolemic Shock

Hypovolemic shock is loss of intravascular fluid, either an absolute or relative volume loss. Absolute hypovolemia can be due to the following:

- Hemorrhage
- GI loss
- Fistula drainage
- Diuresis

Relative hypovolemia occurs when fluid moves out of the intravascular space into an extravascular space (third spacing). With hypovolemic shock, the size of the vascular compartment is unchanged, and there is a decreased venous return to the heart, decreased preload, and decreased CO, which results in impaired cellular metabolism. If the loss of blood is more than 30% of total volume, blood replacement is needed.

Neurogenic Shock

Neurogenic shock occurs after SCI, at T5 or above. Neurogenic shock results in massive vasodilation, leading to pooling of blood in the vessels. Clinical signs include hypotension and bradycardia. Hypothalamic dysfunction is characteristic, with temperature dysregulation.

Spinal Shock

Spinal shock is manifested by decreased reflexes, loss of sensation, and flaccid paralysis below the level of injury. These symptoms may last days to months and may mask postneurological function. Once spinal shock has been resolved in clients with spinal injuries at T6 or higher, return of the reflexes may trigger the development of autonomic dysreflexia, which is a massive uncompensated cardiovascular reaction mediated by the SNS. Autonomic dysreflexia is life-threatening and usually occurs in response to visceral stimulation once the spinal shock is resolved. A distended bladder or rectum is the most common precipitating cause of autonomic dysreflexia. Manifestations of autonomic dysreflexia include extreme hypertension, blurred vision, throbbing headache, marked diaphoresis, piloerection, flushed skin, nasal congestion, nausea, and anxiety (Lewis et al., 2010).

Anaphylactic Shock

Anaphylactic shock is an acute life-threatening hypersensitivity reaction that causes massive vasodilation, increased capillary permeability, and release of mediators. This can lead to respiratory distress and circulatory failure. Sudden symptoms are anxiety, confusion, and a sense of impending doom.

Septic Shock

Septic shock is a systemic inflammatory response to infection. It is the leading cause of death in noncoronary intensive care units (ICUs). The primary causative agents are Gram-negative and Gram-positive bacteria. With septic shock, there is increased coagulation and inflammation. The decreased fibrinolysis results in the formation of microthrombi that can obstruct microvasculature. SVR will decrease, leading to hypotension. The client will be tachypneic and have temperature dysregulation, decreased urinary output, altered neurological status, GI dysfunction, and respiratory failure (Lewis et al., 2010).

Clinical Manifestations

Initial Stage of Shock

The initial stage of shock may not be clinically apparent. Metabolism changes from aerobic to anaerobic with lactic acid accumulation. Lactic acid must be removed by the blood and broken down in the liver, which requires oxygen that is not available.

Compensatory Stage

During the compensatory stage, the body attempts to re-establish homeostasis. Baroreceptors in the carotid and aortic bodies activate SNS in response to the decreased BP. The following actions happen as listed below:

- Peripheral vasoconstriction occurs to maintain blood to the visceral organs. Extremities will be cool and clammy, with the exception of the septic client, who will be warm and flushed.
- The decreased renal blood flow activates the renin–angiotensin system in an attempt to increase venous return to the heart and increase CO and BP.
- The impaired GI motility can lead to paralytic ileus.
- The decreased arterial oxygen levels cause increased respirations. SNS stimulation increases myocardial oxygen demand.

Progressive Stage

If the perfusion deficit is corrected, the client will recover with no residual sequelae; if the deficit is not corrected, the client enters the progressive stage, which begins when the compensatory mechanisms fail.

Aggressive intervention is needed to prevent multiorgan dysfunction syndrome. Decreased cellular perfusion and altered capillary permeability are hallmarks for the progressive stage of shock. With these hallmarks, the following events occur:

- Protein leaks into the interstitial space, and there is increased systemic interstitial edema.
- Anasarca results in fluid leakage to solid organs and peripheral tissues, as well as decreased blood flow to pulmonary capillaries.
- Fluid moves from the pulmonary vasculature to the interstitium, resulting in pulmonary edema, bronchoconstriction, and decreased residual capacity.
- Fluid moves into the alveoli, impairing gas exchange, decreasing compliance, and increasing tachypnea, crackles, and the work of breathing.
- CO fails, leading to decreased tissue perfusion, increased capillary permeability, weak peripheral pulses, and ischemia to distal extremities.
- Myocardial dysfunction develops, leading to arrhythmias, ischemia, MI, and deterioration of the cardiovascular system.
- The mucosal barrier of the GI tract becomes ischemic, leading to ulcers, bleeding, and a decreased ability to absorb nutrients.
- Liver failure leads to jaundice, elevated enzymes, loss of immune function, and risk for disseminated intravascular coagulation (DIC).

Refractory Stage

The refractory stage involves the exacerbation of anaerobic metabolism, accumulation of lactic acid, and increased capillary permeability. The client may be hypotensive and tachycardic and may experience both cardiac and cerebral ischemia, as well as hypoxia. In the refractory stage, failure of one organ will affect the other organs. Recovery at this stage is unlikely. Figure 8.17 illustrates the systemic effects of shock.

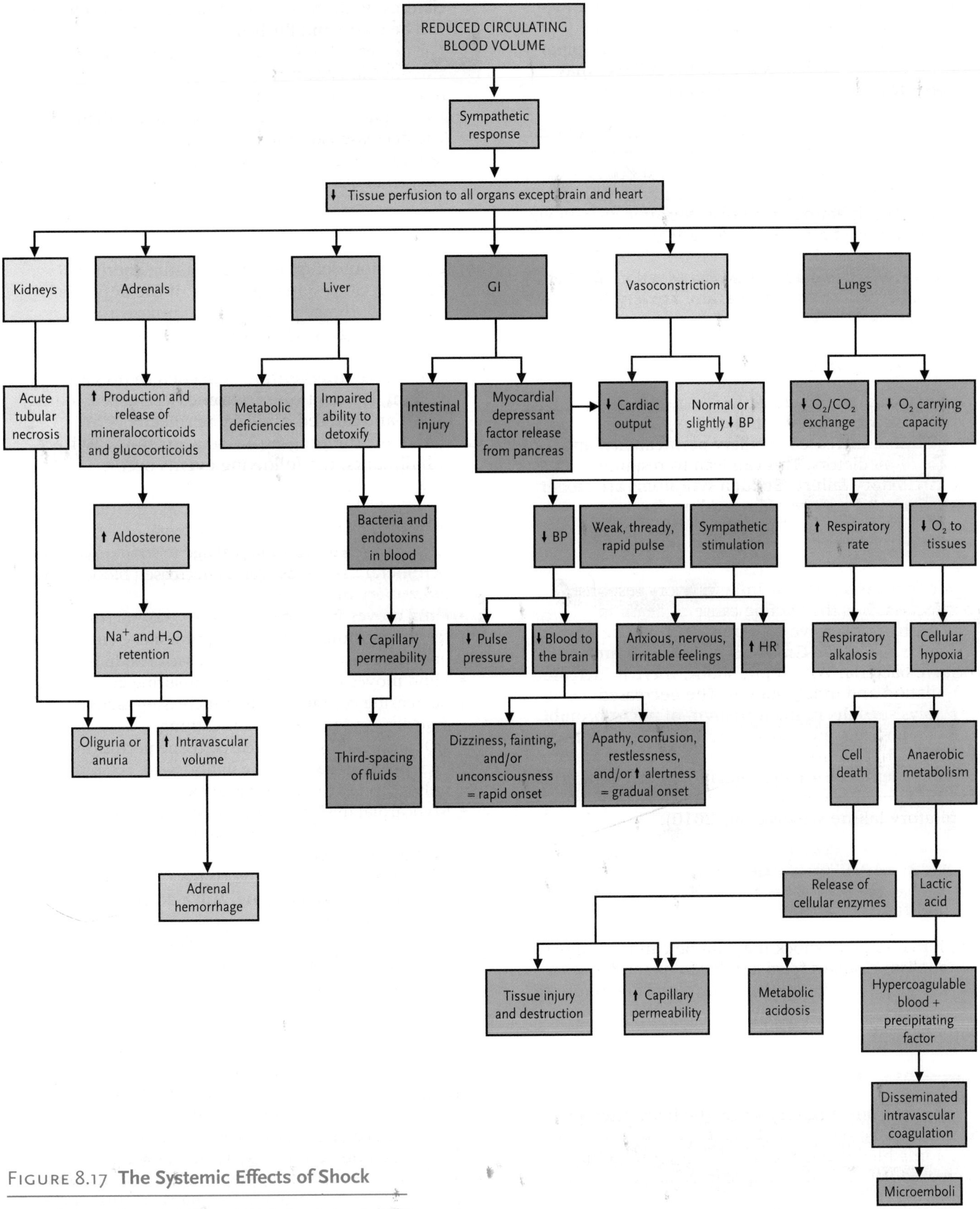
REDUCED CIRCULATING BLOOD VOLUME
Sympathetic response
↓ Tissue perfusion to all organs except brain and heart
Kidneys
Adrenals
Liver
GI
Vasoconstriction
Lungs
Acute tubular necrosis
↑ Production and release of mineralocorticoids and glucocorticoids
Metabolic deficiencies
Impaired ability to detoxify
Intestinal injury
Myocardial depressant factor release from pancreas
↓ Cardiac output
Normal or slightly ↓ BP
↓ O_2/CO_2 exchange
↓ O_2 carrying capacity
↑ Aldosterone
Bacteria and endotoxins in blood
↓ BP
Weak, thready, rapid pulse
Sympathetic stimulation
↑ Respiratory rate
↓ O_2 to tissues
Na^+ and H_2O retention
↑ Capillary permeability
↓ Pulse pressure
↓ Blood to the brain
Anxious, nervous, irritable feelings
↑ HR
Respiratory alkalosis
Cellular hypoxia
Oliguria or anuria
↑ Intravascular volume
Third-spacing of fluids
Dizziness, fainting, and/or unconsciousness = rapid onset
Apathy, confusion, restlessness, and/or ↑ alertness = gradual onset
Cell death
Anaerobic metabolism
Adrenal hemorrhage
Release of cellular enzymes
Lactic acid
Tissue injury and destruction
↑ Capillary permeability
Metabolic acidosis
Hypercoagulable blood + precipitating factor
Disseminated intravascular coagulation
Microemboli

FIGURE 8.17 **The Systemic Effects of Shock**

Source: Black, J. M., & Hawks, J. H. (2009). *Medical-surgical nursing: Clinical management for positive outcomes* (8th ed., p. 2160, Figure 81-3). St. Louis: Saunders.

Diagnostics

There is no single diagnostic test to determine shock. Integration of the physical examination and medical history is key.

Therapeutics and Nursing Considerations

Treatment focuses on interventions to control or eliminate the cause of decreased perfusion and to protect the organs from dysfunction. Multisystem care is needed, including the following:

- Ensuring a patent airway and optimizing oxygen delivery
- Possible blood transfusions or other fluid replacement therapy
- An in-dwelling catheter allows for frequent checks of output.
- Vital signs and ABGs must be monitored frequently.
- Vasopressor agents may be given for hypotension.
- Vasodilators may be given.
- Cardiac monitoring may be done.
- A pulmonary catheter may be used to monitor venous pressures.
- Chest and bowel sounds should be assessed frequently.

The goal for treatment is to provide adequate tissue perfusion, to restore normal BP, to recover organ function, and to have no complications.

Treatment for life-threatening autonomic dysreflexia includes the following:

- Raising the head of the bed to 45 degrees
- Immediate urinary catheterization if the bladder is distended
- A digital rectal examination with topical anaesthesia may be needed if the client is constipated.
- Constrictive clothing and tight shoes need to be removed to prevent excessive skin stimulation.
- Blood pressure must be closely monitored and treated with an alpha-adrenergic blocker or an arteriolar vasodilator (Lewis et al., 2010).

CONCEPTS IN NURSING PRACTICE

PREOPERATIVE CARE

Surgery can be described as the art and science of treating diseases, injuries, and deformities by operation and instrumentation. Surgery can be performed for purposes of diagnosis, cure, palliation, prevention, exploration, and cosmetic improvement. A surgery may be a planned event (elective surgery) or arise unexpectedly (emergency surgery).

Part of preoperative care includes interviewing the surgical client. The purpose of this interview is to obtain health information, determine client expectations, provide and clarify information about the surgery, and assess the emotional state and readiness of the client. During the interview and any other interactions, the use of a common language is important; therefore, translators may be needed.

Preoperative care also includes nursing assessment of the client undergoing surgery. The goals of the nursing assessment should include the following:

- Determining the client's psychological status in order to reinforce coping strategies
- Determining any psychological factors of the procedure that may contribute to risks
- Establishing baseline data
- Identifying medications and herbs taken that may affect surgical outcomes
- Identifying, documenting, and communicating results of laboratory and diagnostic tests
- Identifying cultural and ethnic factors that may affect the surgical experience
- Determining if the client has signed the informed consent for surgery

Psychosocial assessment is important as a magnified stress response can affect recovery. During this assessment, the nurse can identify any emotional reactions to hospitalization, allay anxieties or fears, assess coping mechanisms, and help restore self-esteem. The nursing assessment includes obtaining information on the following:

- The client's health history
- Medical conditions
- Previous surgeries
- Menstrual and obstetric history
- Familial diseases
- Reaction to anaesthesia
- Current prescribed medications and over-the-counter medications
- Herbs or homeopathic preparations used
- Vitamins
- Recreational drugs
- Alcohol
- Tobacco
- Allergies

There are different methods of performing the physical assessment; however, they should contain a review of the systems of the body: the cardiovascular, respiratory, nervous, urinary, GI, integumentary, musculoskeletal, endocrine, and immune systems. Other assessments include fluid and electrolyte status and nutritional status.

Preoperative teaching is very important. The client has the right to know what to expect during and after surgery. By having this knowledge, the client will have decreased anxiety and an increased sense of control. Instruction on postoperative deep breathing, coughing, and ambulation, and giving the client the rationale for these actions, increases the client's success and compliance in performing them. Methods of pain control should be discussed. The client and family should be informed about any tubes, drains, monitoring devices, or special equipment that might be present postoperatively. This knowledge will decrease client and family fears and anxiety. Information should be provided to the client and the family about fluid or food restrictions, the need for certain treatments prior to surgery, the need for a shower prior to surgery, and the need to remove jewellery and prosthetics prior to surgery.

Legal preparation is important. Ensure that all forms have been correctly signed and witnessed. These forms could include the informed consent form, a blood refusal form, if needed, an advance directive, a living will, and a power of attorney. With voluntary consent, the client must have a clear understanding and comprehension of what is going to happen prior to signing the consent form. An anaesthesiologist will assess the client for anaesthetic risk and discuss the type of anaesthetic that will be used. The surgeon is responsible for obtaining the client's consent on the agency consent form after the surgical procedure and risks have been clearly explained. The nurse may witness the signature. The client has the right to withdraw consent at any time. Legally appointed representatives of the family may give consent if the client is a child, unconscious, or mentally incompetent. Medical emergencies may override the need for consent. If no next of kin is available, the surgeon may document the necessity of the surgery.

On the day of surgery, the following nursing interventions are essential for any type of surgery:

- Preoperative teaching should be reinforced.
- Consent should be verified.
- Preoperative charting should be complete.
- Clients cannot wear any cosmetics.
- Dentures should be removed.
- Correct client identification and allergy bands must be in place.
- Valuables are given to the family or locked in a safe.
- The client is encouraged to void prior to surgery.

INTRAOPERATIVE CARE

The surgical suite is a controlled environment designed to minimize the spread of infection and to allow for the smooth flow of clients, personnel, and instruments or equipment. The operating room is geographically, environmentally, and bacteriologically controlled.

The basic surgical team includes the perioperative nurse, the circulating nurse, the scrub nurse, the surgeon, and the anaesthetist. The perioperative nurse ensures that the client is fully prepared for the surgery. The circulating nurse is not scrubbed, gowned, or gloved. The circulating nurse assists the scrub nurse with the surgical count, provides supplies as needed to the scrub team, assists the anaesthesiologist as needed, and documents the procedure. The scrub nurse follows a designated scrub procedure, participates in the surgical count, monitors blood loss and medications used during surgery, requests sterile supplies as needed, passes instruments and implements to the surgeon, and remains within the sterile field. The surgeon is the physician who performs the procedure. The anaesthesiologist administers the anaesthesia, maintains the client's physiological homeostasis, and monitors his or her physical status throughout the surgery.

Proper positioning of the client is important to provide accessibility of the operative site and for the administration of anaesthetic agents, the maintenance of the airway, and the correct skeletal alignment. The client should be protected from pressure on nerves and skin over bony prominences. The eyes should be protected. Adequate thoracic excursion should be provided. Arteries and veins should not be occluded. Modesty in exposure of the body should be respected. Any painful area or deformity should be recognized and respected. Client safety is a priority.

Anaesthetics are classified as general, local, conscious sedation, and regional. General anaesthetics provide loss of sensation with loss of consciousness, skeletal muscle relaxation, and analgesia. General anaesthetics can affect somatic, autonomic, and endocrine responses. General anaesthetics are usually given to clients who require significant skeletal muscle relaxation, must be placed in awkward positions, or require extended surgical time. These anaesthetics are also given to clients who are extremely anxious or refuse or have contraindications for a local or regional anaesthetic. General anaesthetics may be inhaled or administered by IV line. IV administration is rapid, quickly inducing a pleasant sleep. Inhalation agents enter the body through the alveoli and are excreted rapidly by ventilation. Complications of inhalation agents include coughing, laryngospasm, bronchospasm, increased secretions, and respiratory depression. Adjuncts to general anaesthetics include opioids, benzodiazepines, and neuromuscular blocking agents.

Local anaesthesia results in a loss of sensation without loss of consciousness. Local anaesthetics can be administered topically, intracutaneously, and subcutaneously. Local anaesthesia produces autonomic nervous system blockage and skeletal muscle paralysis in the area of the affected nerve. There is little systemic absorption, and recovery tends to be rapid, with little residual "hangover." Possible complications include discomfort, hypotension, and seizures.

Conscious sedation results in a minimally depressed LOC with maintenance of the client's protective airway reflexes. The goal with conscious sedation is to reduce the client's anxiety and discomfort and facilitate cooperation. A sedative–hypnotic and opioid are frequently used with conscious sedation.

The client is able to maintain his or her own airway and to respond to appropriate commands.

Regional anaesthesia results in loss of sensation in a body region without loss of consciousness, when the administration of a local anaesthetic blocks a specific nerve or group of nerves. Spinal anaesthesia and epidural blocks are a form of regional anaesthesia. The client will need to be monitored for autonomic nervous system blockage, bradycardia, hypotension, nausea, and vomiting.

Other management techniques that may be done during surgery include controlled hypotension, in which the BP is decreased during the administration of the anaesthetic to decrease blood loss during surgery. Hypothermia results from the deliberate lowering of the client's body temperature in order to reduce the demand for oxygen and anaesthesia. Cryoanaesthesia freezes a localized area to block pain impulses. Hypoanaesthesia is hypnosis to alter pain consciousness. Acupuncture decreases sensation to specific areas.

Catastrophic events that may happen in the operating room include anaphylactic reactions, which may be masked by the anaesthesia. Malignant hyperthermia is a rare metabolic disease that can be fatal. Hyperthermia with skeletal muscle rigidity can also occur. This is possibly due to exposure to succinylcholines. Other factors such as trauma, heat, and stress may be triggers of malignant hyperthermia. Some clients have inherited hypermetabolism of the skeletal muscles, resulting in altered control of intracellular calcium.

Manifestations of malignant hyperthermia include the following:

- Tachypnea
- Hypercarbia
- Hyperthermia
- Tachycardia
- Ventricular dysrhythmias, which can result in cardiac arrest and death

Postoperative Care

Care of the client in the postoperative (anaesthesia) care unit (PACU) includes the following:

- Monitoring and managing respiratory and circulatory function
- Pain
- Temperature
- Surgical site
- Airway patency, rate and quality of respiration, and auscultation of breath sounds in all fields will be assessed.
- Oxygen therapy may be established.
- Cardiac monitoring, including the rate and rhythm of the client's heartbeat, will be compared to preoperative findings.
- BP and temperature will also be compared to the previous baseline.
- Neurological assessment will include LOC, orientation, sensory and motor status, and size and equality of pupils.
- Intake and output will be monitored.
- Surgical sites and the condition of dressings will be noted, with the amount and type of drainage.

Because hearing is the first sense to return, it is essential to explain to clients that the surgery is over, where they are, whether the family has been notified, and who is caring for them. Figure 8.18 outlines potential problems in the postoperative period.

Clients who are particularly at risk for respiratory

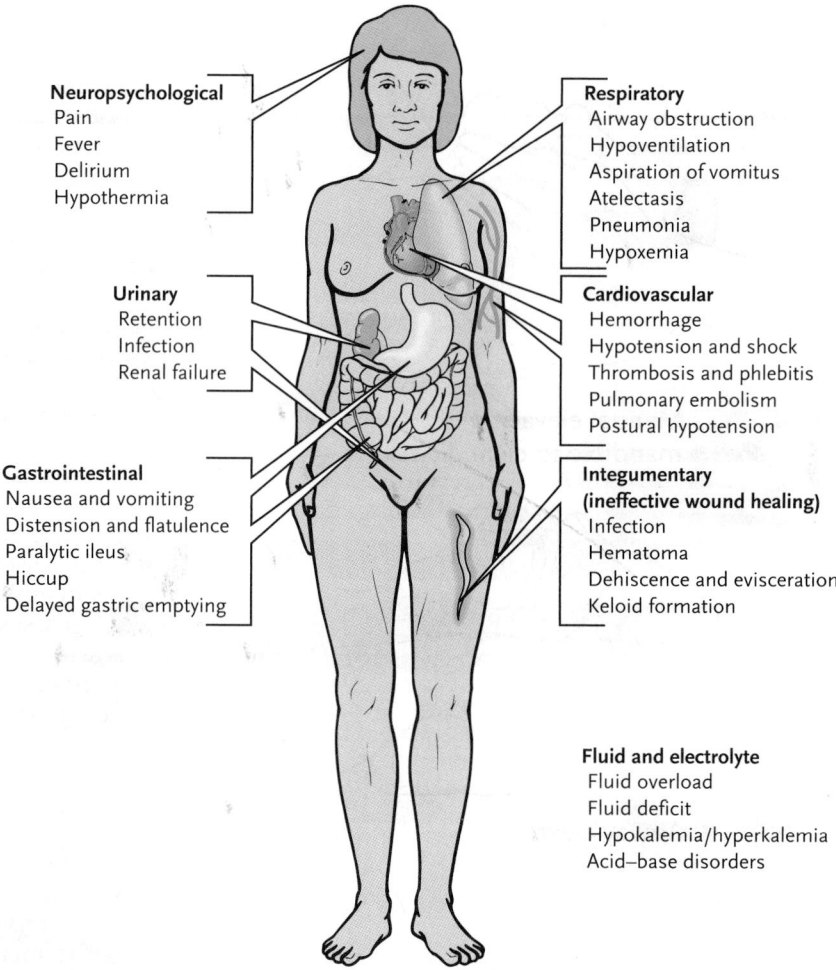

Neuropsychological
Pain
Fever
Delirium
Hypothermia
Respiratory
Airway obstruction
Hypoventilation
Aspiration of vomitus
Atelectasis
Pneumonia
Hypoxemia
Urinary
Retention
Infection
Renal failure
Cardiovascular
Hemorrhage
Hypotension and shock
Thrombosis and phlebitis
Pulmonary embolism
Postural hypotension
Gastrointestinal
Nausea and vomiting
Distension and flatulence
Paralytic ileus
Hiccup
Delayed gastric emptying
Integumentary
(ineffective wound healing)
Infection
Hematoma
Dehiscence and evisceration
Keloid formation
Fluid and electrolyte
Fluid overload
Fluid deficit
Hypokalemia/hyperkalemia
Acid–base disorders

FIGURE 8.18 **Potential Problems in the Postoperative Period**

Source: Lewis, S. M., Heitkemper, M. M., Dirksen, S. R., O'Brien, P., Bucher, L., et al. (2010). *Medical-surgical nursing in Canada: Assessment and management of clinical problems* (2nd Canadian ed., p. 433, Figure 21-1). Toronto: Elsevier.

problems include those receiving general anaesthesia, older adults, those who smoke heavily, those who are obese, and clients who are undergoing thoracic, airway, or abdominal surgery. Potential alterations in respiratory function include airway obstruction, hypoxemia, atelectasis, pulmonary edema, aspiration of gastric contents, bronchospasms, and hypoventilation. See Figure 8.19 for an example of airway obstruction.

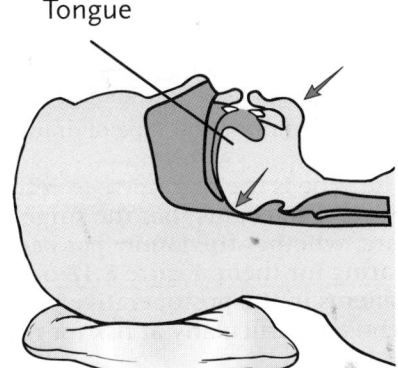

Tongue

Tongue occluding airway

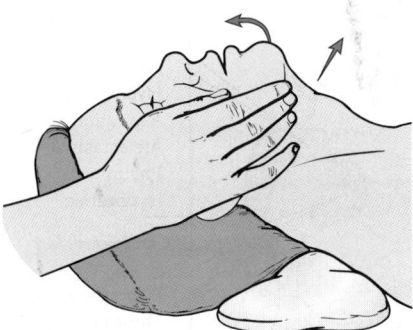

Manual elevation of mandible to clear airway

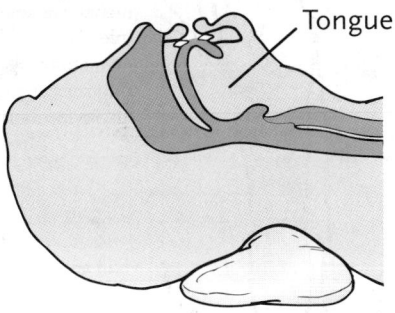

Tongue

Airway cleared

FIGURE 8.19 **Etiology and Relief of Airway Obstruction caused by Client's Tongue**

The etiology of an airway obstruction caused by the client's tongue and the method used to relieve it.

Source: Lewis, S. M., Heitkemper, M. M., Dirksen, S. R., O'Brien, P., Bucher, L., et al. (2010). *Medical-surgical nursing in Canada: Assessment and management of clinical problems* (2nd Canadian ed., p. 435, Figure 21-2). Toronto: Elsevier.

To prevent these potential respiratory problems, the client should be placed in the proper position to facilitate respiration and protect the airway. The lateral position is best unless contraindicated. Once conscious, the client will be allowed in the supine position with the head of the bed elevated. Deep breathing is encouraged to facilitate gas exchange and promote the return to consciousness.

The most common complications of cardiovascular function include hypotension, hypertension, and dysrhythmias. Clients at greatest risk for developing these complications are those with a previous cardiac history, older adults, and those who are debilitated or critically ill. To prevent these complications, the following interventions are performed:

- Frequent monitoring of vital signs
- Assessing skin colour, temperature, and moisture
- Notifying the anaesthetist if the systolic BP is <90 or >160, the pulse is <60 or >120, the BP is gradually increasing, irregular cardiac rhythms develop, or there is significant variation from preoperative readings

Management of these complications may include oxygen therapy, IV fluids, antidysrhythmic medication, analgesics, warming the client, and emptying the client's bladder.

Emergence delirium and delayed awakening are neurological complications that may develop. Emergence delirium or violent emergence can be manifested by restlessness, agitation, disorientation, thrashing, and shouting and may be caused by anaesthetic agents, hypoxia, bladder distension, pain, electrolyte abnormalities, or anxiety. Delayed awakening is usually due to a prolonged drug action. Frequently evaluating the respiratory function is essential as agitation could be due to hypoxia. Sedation may be required.

Pain and discomfort are common concerns for clients. Discomfort could be due to the surgical manipulation, positioning, or presence of internal devices. Discomfort also occurs when the client starts to ambulate following surgery. The nurse will need to assess the pain as to intensity, location, and characteristics. Analgesics could be in the form of IV narcotics, epidural catheters, patient-controlled analgesia (PCA), or regional anaesthetic blocks.

Hypothermia is diagnosed when the core body temperature drops to <36.0°C, signifying that heat loss is greater than heat production. Hypothermia may occur due to loss of heat from body organs exposed to the air or when the client is debilitated or intoxicated. Prolonged anaesthetic administration may lead to redistribution of body heat and increase the risk of hypothermia. Complications that may occur due to hypothermia include compromising the immune function, postoperative pain, bleeding, myocardial ischemia, and delayed drug metabolism. The nurse must monitor the temperature and the vital signs of the client. Passive rewarming raises the basal metabolic rate.

Active rewarming requires an application of warming devices such as blankets, heated aerosols, radiant warmers, forced air warmers, and warm IV fluids. When using external warming devices, the nurse will need to monitor the temperature at 15-minute intervals and monitor the skin to prevent burns.

Nausea and vomiting can be significant postoperative problems, causing increased discomfort, delays in discharge, and dissatisfaction with the surgical experience. To treat these symptoms, the nurse may give antiemetics or prokinetic drugs.

In order for the client to be discharged from the PACU, the client must be mobile, alert, and able to provide a degree of self-care. Pain, nausea, and vomiting should be controlled. The PACU nurse will give a report to the receiving nurse on the ward that summarizes the operative and postoperative periods. The client will be transferred to the bed, and then an in-depth assessment must be done, postoperative orders will be initiated, and ambulation may be encouraged.

Atelectasis and pneumonia are complications that may occur after abdominal and thoracic surgery (see Figure 8.20). There may be postoperative development of mucous plugs and decreased surfactant related to hypoventilation, a recumbent position, ineffective coughing, or smoking.

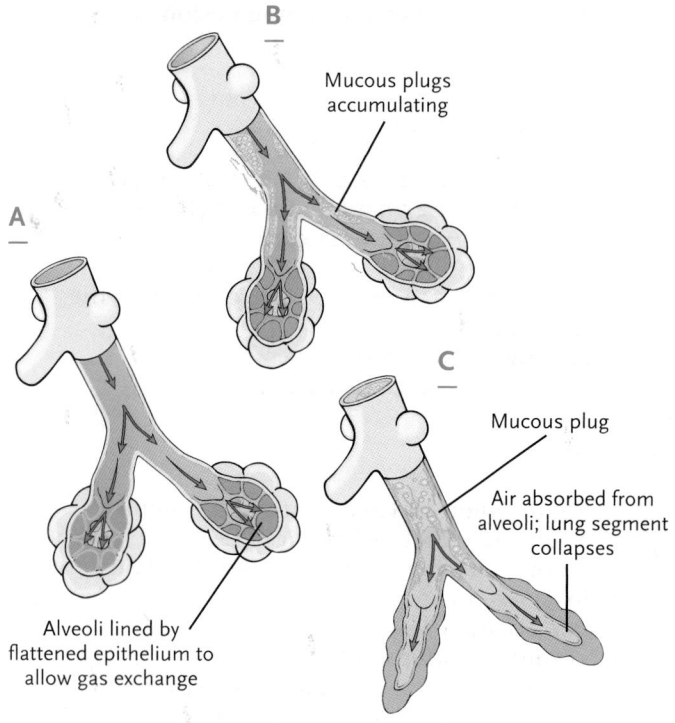

Mucous plugs accumulating

Mucous plug

Air absorbed from alveoli; lung segment collapses

Alveoli lined by flattened epithelium to allow gas exchange

FIGURE 8.20 **Postoperative Atelectasis**

Postoperative atelectasis. A, Normal bronchiole and alveoli. B, Mucous plug in bronchiole. C, Collapse of alveoli due to atelectasis following absorption of air.

Source: Lewis, S. M., Heitkemper, M. M., Dirksen, S. R., O'Brien, P., Bucher, L., et al. (2010). *Medical-surgical nursing in Canada: Assessment and management of clinical problems* (2nd Canadian ed., p. 435, Figure 21-3). Toronto: Elsevier.

To help prevent the development of atelectasis and pneumonia, the nurse will encourage the client to breathe deeply and cough. Other techniques to encourage full lung expansion include the use of incentive spirometry, splints, diaphragmatic breathing, and changing position every two hours.

Fluid and electrolyte imbalances may contribute to cardiovascular alterations. Fluid retention in the first two to five days could occur due to the stress response. Fluid overload may occur when IV fluids are administered too quickly, if chronic disease exists, or if the client is an older adult. Fluid deficits may result from inadequate fluid replacement, causing a decreased CO and tissue perfusion. Hypokalemia can result from urinary or GI losses.

The stress response can contribute to an increase in clotting factors, causing DVT or pulmonary emboli. Symptoms of a pulmonary embolus include the following:

- Tachypnea
- Dyspnea
- Tachycardia
- Chest pain
- Hypotension
- Dysrhythmias
- Heart failure
- Hemoptysis

Syncope can indicate deceased CO, fluid deficits, or deficits in cerebral perfusion.

Vital signs need to be monitored and compared with the preoperative status. Intake and output need to be assessed accurately. Laboratory work, especially electrolytes, needs to be monitored. Mouth care and leg exercises are also part of postoperative care of the client.

A low urinary output can be expected for the first 24 hours due to an increase in aldosterone and ADH levels in the client's body due to the stress response of surgery, fluid losses during surgery, drainage, and diaphoresis. The anaesthesia may depress the nervous system, allowing the bladder to fill to a greater than normal extent before the urge to void is felt. Anticholinergic and narcotic drugs may also interfere with the ability to initiate voiding. Fluid retention is more likely to develop with abdominal or pelvic surgery where pain may alter the perception of a full bladder. The recumbent position may also impair the ability to void. The normal urine output should be at least 0.5 mL/kg body weight per hour. This would mean about 30 mL/hr for an adult. If the client does not have a catheter, he or she should be able to void about 200 mL following surgery. To assist the client to void, place the client in the normal voiding position. Use techniques such as running water, pouring water over the perineum, or ambulation or use the bedside commode.

Nausea and vomiting may be caused by anaesthetic agents or narcotics, delayed gastric emptying, slowed peristalsis, or resumption of oral intake too soon after surgery. Abdominal distension results from a decreased peristalsis caused from the handling of the bowel during surgery or by the client swallowing air. Hiccups occur due to irritation of the phrenic nerve. The client will remain NPO until the gag reflex has returned and the client has bowel sounds. Bowel sounds indicate that peristalsis has resumed. Clear fluids are introduced first and advanced fluids added as tolerated. Regular mouth care is essential when the client is NPO. An NG tube may be inserted if the vomiting persists and to help decompress the abdomen. Early ambulation is helpful to prevent abdominal distension.

The surgical incision disrupts the skin barrier, and healing is a major concern during the postoperative period. Adequate nutrition is important to help fight the catabolic effect of the stress response and assist in wound healing. Wound infections may be caused by oral flora, intestinal flora, or exogenous flora on the skin or in the environment. The incidence of wound sepsis is higher in malnourished, immuno-suppressed, or older persons or those experiencing a prolonged hospital stay.

Wound infection usually is not apparent until the third to fifth postoperative day, when the following symptoms may appear:

- Local manifestations of redness
- Edema
- Pain and tenderness around the site
- Purulent drainage leaking from the surgical incision
- Systemic manifestations, including leukocytosis and fever

Accumulation of fluid in the wound may impair healing and may require a drain to be placed in the area. The nurse should note the type, amount, colour, and consistency of the drainage. Assessment of position changes on the drainage should also be noted. The physician should be notified of excessive or abnormal drainage.

Postoperative pain may be caused by traumatization of skin and tissues, reflex muscle spasms, and anxiety or fear. Analgesics should be administered on a timely basis to ensure effectiveness during activities and for comfort. The nurse should observe for behavioural clues of pain and ask clients about their pain, as well as assess for the location, intensity, and quality of the client's pain. The nurse should evaluate the effectiveness of any pain management technique that is utilized and notify the physician if alternative pain management orders are needed.

Anxiety and depression may be more pronounced with clients experiencing a poor prognosis. Attention to a history of neurotic or psychotic disorders is important. The client's response may be part of the grief process. Confusion and delirium may result from psychological or physiological sources, including the following:

- Fluid and electrolyte imbalances
- Hypoxemia
- Drug effects
- Sleep deprivation
- Sensory alteration or overload

Delirium tremors may result from alcohol withdrawal. The nurse must provide adequate support for the client. Listen and talk with the client, offer explanations, reassure, and encourage involvement of the significant other.

Planning for discharge begins in the preoperative period. The client is informed and prepared to gradually assume greater responsibility for self-care. The following client teaching topics should be covered:

- Information should be provided regarding care of the wound site and dressing.
- Information should be provided about the action and side effects of medications as well as when and how to take medications.
- Dietary restrictions or modifications should be explained.
- Describe any symptoms that should be reported.
- Explain where and when to return for follow-up care.
- Give written instructions to help in reinforcement and remembering.

The nurse should always allow plenty of time for the client to ask questions regarding postoperative care at home.

END-OF-LIFE CARE

End-of-life care refers to issues that relate to death and dying, the concluding phase of the normal lifespan. The three main goals of end-of-life care are as follows:

- Providing comfort and supportive care during the dying process
- Improving the quality of the remaining life
- Helping ensure a dignified death

Pathophysiology

Death occurs when all vital organs and systems cease to function. There will be irreversible cessation of circulatory and respiratory function. The body gradually slows down until all functions end. Generally, respirations cease first, with the heart stopping within a few minutes. Hearing and touch are the last senses to disappear. The vision may blur, the eyes may sink and gaze over, the blink reflex is absent, and the eyelids may remain half open. The skin of the hands, arms, feet, and legs becomes mottled and feels cold and clammy. There may be cyanosis on the nose, nail beds, and knees. A waxlike appearance of the skin suggests that death is imminent. Initially, there may be an increase in respiration, followed by Cheyne-Stokes respirations slowing down to terminal gaps of breathing until respirations cease. Urinary output will gradually decrease. The client may be incontinent of urine or be unable to urinate. The digestive functions slow, with a possible accumulation of gas, resulting in abdominal distension and nausea. The client may experience a loss of sphincter control. A bowel movement may occur before imminent death, at the time of death, or not at all. The client will gradually lose the ability to move, and the jaw will sag as facial muscle tone is lost. Swallowing can become difficult, as can maintaining body alignment. The gag reflex will be lost. The heart rate may increase and then slow with a weakening pulse. The cardiac rhythm often is irregular.

Brain death occurs when the cerebral cortex stops functioning or is irreversibly destroyed. The cerebral cortex is responsible for voluntary movements and actions as well as cognitive functioning.

Psychosocial manifestations include the following:

- Altered decision making
- Anxiety about unfinished business
- Decreased socialization
- Fear of loneliness
- Fear of pain

Often the client and family feel overwhelmed, helpless, powerless, and tired. End-of-life clients need time to ponder their thoughts, review their lives, and express their feelings.

Grief

Grief is the emotional and behavioural response to loss. Grief is an individual experience and can be manifested in many ways. The intensity of grief is driven by the individual's personality, the nature of the relationship with the dying person, concurrent life crises, coping resources, and the availability of support systems. Table 8.13 is a comparison of the different stages of grieving.

Table 8.13 Comparison of Stages of Grieving

Kübler-Ross (1969)	Martocchio (1985)	Rando (1993)
Denial	Shock and disbelief	Avoidance
Anger/bargaining	Yearning and protest	Confrontation
Depression	Anguish, disorganization, and despair	Accommodation
Acceptance	Identification of bereavement	
	Reorganization and restoration	

Source: Lewis, S. M., Heitkemper, M. M., Dirksen, S. R., O'Brien, P., Bucher, L., et al. (2010). *Medical-surgical nursing in Canada: Assessment and management of clinical problems* (2nd Canadian ed., p. 184, Table 11-4). Toronto: Elsevier.

Grief is a complex process in which an individual attempts to make sense of the loss. Not everyone experiences all stages of grief, nor do they progress through the stages in a linear fashion. Bereavement is a term used to describe an individual's response to the loss of a significant person. Bereavement may begin prior to the actual death. The normal grief process may take months to years. Goals for the grief process include the following:

- Resolving emotions
- Reflecting on the dying person
- Expressing feelings of loss and sadness
- Valuing what has been shared

Pathological grief refers to grief that has not lessened after the first year. Conflicted grief is when the bereaved person has not resolved ambivalent feelings toward the deceased. Absent grief is seen when the bereaved person appears to be coping by carrying on as if nothing has happened. Maladaptive or dysfunctional grief refers to prolonged, disruptive, or unresolved grief. Adaptive grief is a healthy response, in which the person comes to accept the reality of death. See Chapter 11, page 591, for further information on grief.

Canada is a very multicultural society; therefore, health professionals need to be aware of the variables that may affect end-of-life care. These variables include attitudes and beliefs, as well as cultural, religious, and family influences, and often the client's beliefs and attitudes are based on his or her culture and religion. However, health care professionals must be vigilant not to assume that a person from a certain culture will always hold a particular set of cultural, religious, and spiritual beliefs and values. Nursing assessment must be completed on an individual basis to avoid stereotyping.

Advance and Instructional-Living Directives

In Canada, it is recognized that all people have the right to make decisions regarding their health care, including the right to request or refuse life-sustaining treatment (Lewis et al., 2010). Advance directives give information about future medical care and treatments and include instructional-living wills or treatment directives and proxy directives. Instructional-living directives include living wills and treatment directives. Living wills give instruction about future medical care and treatments and specify whether the client would like to die without heroic or extraordinary measures. Living wills are an important form of communication when the client is unable to communicate verbally. Proxy directives are in the form of a power of attorney for personal care document. The power of attorney for personal care will list the person(s) who may make health care decisions on the client's behalf should the client become unable to make informed decisions on his or her own.

If a do not resuscitate (DNR) order is in place, CPR will not be attempted, but the DNR does not preclude the use of other forms of treatment. A new term that is being used to replace DNR or "no code" is "allow natural death" (AND). In this case, the client will still receive pain control and symptom management but no resuscitative treatment.

Ethical issues may arise regarding pain relief, in particular with clients who are terminally ill. According to the principle of nonmaleficence, the nurse is expected to prevent or reduce harm to the client and to provide adequate pain control to alleviate suffering in the terminally ill, even if a secondary effect of pain control is an earlier death. Euthanasia, in which a deliberate action hastens death, is not legal in Canada.

Palliative Care

The Canadian Hospice Palliative Care Association defines palliative care as the combination of active and compassionate therapies to comfort and support clients and families who are living with life-threatening illnesses. During illness and bereavement, palliative care strives to meet physical, psychological, social, and spiritual expectations and needs while remaining sensitive to personal, cultural, and religious values, beliefs, and practices (Lewis et al., 2010).

In Canada, the terms *palliative care* and *hospice* are often used interchangeably. Hospices exist to provide support and care for persons in the last phases of incurable diseases. This care is aimed at relief of suffering and improving the quality of life for these individuals. There are over 500 hospices in Canada, and they are organized under a variety of models. There are free-standing hospices, home hospice care, and hospital-based palliative care units. Hospices are run by a medically supervised interdisciplinary team of professionals and volunteers, the hospice nurse being an integral part of this team. The hospice nurse plays a key role in educating the client and family on pain and symptom management. Grief support is incorporated into the plan of care for the family members and significant others during the illness and after the client's death.

The decision to begin hospice care is sometimes difficult due to a lack of information about hospice palliative care, difficulty in accessing palliative care services, the attitudes of health care professionals, who sometimes regard palliation as a personal failure, and the fact that clients and families may regard palliative care as "giving up." Coordination of palliative care focuses on the needs of the client and his or her family and significant others, as well as on education, counselling, advocacy, and support. The goals of palliative care focus on ensuring that the client is able to express and share his or her feelings with others and that comfort measures and physical maintenance care are provided during the last stages of life.

Education of the palliative client and family involves providing ongoing information about the disease, the dying process, the care needed and offered, coping strategies, and barriers to grief.

Nursing Considerations

Nursing considerations for the dying client focus on comfort and improving the quality of life. Psychosocial care and physical care are interrelated for both the dying client and the family (Lewis et al., 2010). Anxiety is a feeling of uneasiness caused by a source that is not easily identified. Anxiety in end-of-life clients is frequently related to fear. Anxiety and depression may be exhibited during the end-of-life period and can be caused by pain that is not well controlled, psychosocial factors related to the disease process or impending death, altered physiological states, or the effects of drugs. Encouragement, support, and education can help decrease some of the anxiety. Pharmacological and nonpharmacological measures may also be used.

Fear is a typical feeling for palliative clients. Fear of pain, loneliness and abandonment, and meaninglessness are common fears. Clients and families fear pain as they often associate death with pain. There is no physiological evidence that death is always painful. Psychologically, pain may occur based on anxieties. Terminally ill clients should receive enough analgesic so that they are comfortable. They should not be in physical pain, nor should they be deprived of the ability to interact with others.

There can be a real fear of loneliness and abandonment if the clients fear their loved ones cannot cope and will abandon them. Palliative clients appreciate loved ones comforting and supporting them at this stage. Holding hands, touching, and listening are greatly valued. Simply providing companionship allows the dying person a sense of security.

Fear of meaninglessness often leads palliative clients to review their lives, often examining their intentions and actions. Some clients may express regret, but many clients are able to recognize the value of their lives. Nurses should encourage clients and families to identify the positive qualities of the client's life. Nurses should also respect and accept practices and rituals associated with the client's life review without being judgemental.

Physical care centres around physiological and safety needs. Symptom management is key. The palliative client deserves the same care as people who are expected to recover from their illnesses. See Table 8.14 for the nursing management of physical care at the end of life.

Therapeutic Communication

Therapeutic communication is an important nursing intervention that includes the essential components of empathy and active listening. Clients and their families should be allowed time to express their thoughts and feelings. Sometimes unusual communication by the

Table 8.14   Nursing Management: Physical Care at the End of Life

CHARACTERISTIC	NURSING MANAGEMENT
Pain • Pain may be a major symptom associated with terminal illness and is the most feared. • Pain can be acute or chronic. • Physical and emotional irritations can aggravate pain.	• Assess pain thoroughly and regularly to determine the quality, intensity, location, and pattern, as well as the contributing and relieving factors. • Minimize possible irritants such as skin irritations from moisture, heat or cold, or pressure. • Administer medications around the clock in a timely manner and on a regular basis. • Provide complementary and alternative therapies, such as guided imagery, massage, acupressure, heat and cold, therapeutic touch, distraction, and relaxation techniques, as needed. • Evaluate the effectiveness of pain relief measures frequently to ensure that the client is on an adequate drug regimen. • Do not delay or deny pain relief measures to a terminally ill client.
Delirium • Delirium is characterized by confusion, disorientation, restlessness, clouding of consciousness, incoherence, fear, anxiety, excitement, and often hallucinations. • It may be misidentified as depression, psychosis, anger, or anxiety. • The use of opioids, corticosteroids, or both (as well as many other medications) in end-of-life care may cause delirium. • The underlying disease process may contribute to delirium. • It is generally considered a reversible process.	• Perform a through assessment for reversible causes of delirium, including pain, constipation, and urinary retention. • Provide a room that is quiet, well lit, and familiar to reduce the effects of delirium. • Reorient the dying person to person, place, and time with each encounter. • Administer ordered benzodiazepines, sedatives, and antipsychotics as needed. • Stay physically close to a frightened client. Reassure in a calm, soft voice with touch and slow stroking of the skin.
Restlessness • This may occur as death approaches and cerebral metabolism slows.	• Assess for spiritual distress as a cause for restlessness and agitation. • Do not restrain. • Use soothing music and slow, soft touch and voice. • Limit the number of persons at the bedside. • Limit other stimuli and activity.
Dysphagia • This may occur because of extreme weakness and changes in level of consciousness.	• Identify the least invasive alternative routes of administration for drugs needed for symptom management. • Suction orally as needed. • Administer frequent oral care.
Dehydration • Dehydration may occur during the last days of life, but hunger and thirst are rare. • As the end of life approaches, clients tend to take in less food and fluid.	• Assess the condition of mucous membranes frequently to prevent excessive dryness, which can lead to discomfort. • Maintain complete, regular oral care to provide for comfort and hydration of mucous membranes. • Do not force the client to eat or drink. • Encourage the consumption of ice chips and sips of fluids or use moist cloths to provide moisture to the mouth. • Use moist cloths and swabs for unconscious clients to avoid aspiration. • Apply lubricant to the lips and oral mucous membranes as needed. • Reassure the family that reduced food and fluid intake is a natural part of the process of dying.
Dyspnea • This is a subjective symptom, often accompanied by anxiety and the fear of suffocation. • An underlying disease process can exacerbate dyspnea.	• Assess respiratory status regularly. • Elevate the head or position the client on his or her side, or both, to improve chest expansion. • Use a fan or air conditioner to facilitate the movement of cool air. • Administer supplemental oxygen as ordered.

Continued on next page

Table 8.14   Nursing Management: Physical Care at the End of Life (cont'd)

CHARACTERISTIC	NURSING MANAGEMENT
Dyspnea (cont'd)	• Administer drugs (depending on the underlying cause of the dyspnea) such as opioids, sedatives, diuretics, antibiotics, corticosteroids, and bronchodilators as ordered to relieve congestion and coughing and to decrease apprehension.
Pooling of Secretions • Coughing and expelling secretions become difficult.	• Perform gentle oropharyngeal suctioning as needed to remove accumulated secretions. • Position the client on his or her side supported with pillows with head down, or in a semiprone position if there are excessive secretions. • Use anticholinergic medications (scopolamine or glycopyrrolate [Robinul]) as ordered.
Weakness and Fatigue	• Assess the client's tolerance for activities. • Time nursing interventions to conserve the client's energy. • Assess the client to identify and complete valued or desired activities. • Provide support as needed to maintain positions in a bed or chair. • Provide frequent rest periods.
Myoclonus • This is mild to severe jerking or twitching, which is sometimes associated with the use of large doses of opioids. • Clients may complain of involuntary twitching of the upper and lower extremities.	• Assess for the initial onset and duration of this effect and any discomfort or distress experienced by the client. • If myoclonus is distressing or becoming more severe, discuss possible drug therapy modifications with the physician. • Changes in opioid medication may alleviate or decrease myoclonus.
Skin Breakdown • Skin integrity is difficult to maintain at the end of life. • Immobility, urinary and bowel incontinence, dry skin, nutritional deficits, anemia, friction, and shearing forces lead to a high risk for skin breakdown. • Disease and other processes may impair skin integrity. • As death approaches, circulation to the extremities decreases, and they become cool, mottled, and cyanotic.	• Assess the skin for signs of breakdown. • Implement protocols to prevent skin breakdown by controlling drainage and odour and keeping the skin and any wound areas clean and dry. • Perform wound assessments as needed. • Follow appropriate nursing management protocol for dressing wounds. • Consider the use of special pressure-relieving air mattresses. • Follow appropriate nursing management to prevent skin irritations and breakdown from urinary and bowel incontinence. • Use blankets to provide warmth; never apply heat. • Prevent the effects of shearing forces.
Bowel Patterns • Constipation can be caused by immobility, the use of opioid medications, a lack of fibre in the diet, and dehydration. • Diarrhea may occur as muscles relax or from a fecal impaction related to immobility, the use of opioids, or both.	• Assess bowel function. • Assess for and remove fecal impactions. • Encourage movement and physical activities as tolerated. • Encourage fibre in the diet if appropriate. • Encourage fluids if appropriate. • Use suppositories, laxatives, or enemas if ordered.
Anorexia, Nausea, and Vomiting • May be caused by complications of the disease process. • Drugs may contribute to nausea. • Constipation, impaction, and bowel obstruction can cause anorexia, nausea, and vomiting.	• Assess the client for complaints of nausea, vomiting, or both. • Assess possible contributing causes for nausea or vomiting. • Have family members provide the client's favourite foods. • Discuss modifications to the drug regimen with the health care team. • Provide frequent mouth care, especially if the client has vomited.

Source: Lewis, S. M., Heitkemper, M. M., Dirksen, S. R., O'Brien, P., Bucher, L., et al. (2010). *Medical-surgical nursing in Canada: Assessment and management of clinical problems* (2nd Canadian ed., pp. 191–193, Table 11-9). Toronto: Elsevier.

client may take place at the end of life. The client's speech may be confused, disoriented, or garbled. The client may even speak with family or friends who have predeceased them. At other times, the client may leave instructions for family members or speak of projects that have to be completed. Active careful listening allows identification of specific patterns in the client's communication and decreases the risk for inappropriate labelling of behaviours.

The resolution of grief is the primary focus of interventions for anticipatory and dysfunctional grief. Specific interventions for both types of grief are similar and include providing an environment that allows the client to express his or her feelings. Clients should be free to express feelings of anger, fear, or guilt without others' judgement. Both the client and the family need to understand that the grief reaction is normal. The client's privacy should be respected. Honesty in answering questions and giving information is essential. Families and clients need encouragement to continue their usual activities as much as possible. Planning for the future or for the funeral may be needed based on the client's or family's coping abilities. Anger must be recognized as a normal response to dying. When a client or family member acts out in anger, the nurse must not react on a personal level. Nurses need to encourage realistic hope within the limits of the situation. A sense of power can be restored for the client by encouraging him or her to identify goals and make decisions pertaining to his or her own care.

Care of the Body

After the client is pronounced dead, the nurse prepares or delegates preparation of the body for immediate viewing by the family. Considerations when preparing the body include cultural customs, provincial and territorial laws, and agency policies and procedures.

REFERENCES

Black, J. M., & Hawks, J. H. (2005). *Medical-surgical nursing: Clinical management for positive outcomes* (7th ed.). St. Louis: Saunders.

Black, J. M., & Hawks, J. (2009). *Medical-surgical nursing: Clinical management for positive outcomes* (8th ed.). St. Louis: Saunders.

Centers for Disease Control and Prevention (CDC). (1992). Recommendations and reports: 1993 revised classification system for HIV infection and expanded surveillance case definition for AIDS among adolescents and adults. *Morbidity and Mortality Weekly Reports, 41*(RR-17), 1.

Day, R. A., Paul, P., Williams, B., Smeltzer, S. C., & Bare B. G. (2007). *Brunner & Suddarth's textbook of medical-surgical nursing* (2nd Canadian ed.). Philadelphia: Lippincott, Williams & Wilkins.

Day, R. A., Paul, P., Williams, B., Smeltzer, S. C., & Bare, B. G. (2009). *Brunner & Suddarth's textbook of medical-surgical nursing* (2nd Canadian ed.). Philadephia: Lippincott, Williams & Wilkins.

Ignatavicius, D., & Workman, L. (2006). *Medical-surgical nursing: Patient-centered collaborative care* (5th ed.). St. Louis: Saunders.

Ignativicius, D., & Workman, L. (2010). *Medical-surgical nursing: Patient-centered collaborative care* (6th ed.). St. Louis: Saunders.

Kumar, V., Abbas, A. K., & Fausto, N. (2005). *Robbins and Cotran Pathologic basis of disease* (7th ed.). Philadelphia: Saunders.

Lemone, P., & Burke, K. (2004). *Medical-surgical nursing: Critical thinking in client care* (3rd ed.). Upper Saddle River, NJ: Prentice Hall.

Lewis, S. M., Heitkemper, M. M., Dirksen, S. R., O'Brien, P., Giddens, J. F., Bucher, L., et al. (2006). *Medical-surgical nursing in Canada: Assessment and management of clinical problems* (1st Canadian ed.). Toronto: Elsevier.

Lewis, S., Heitkemper, M., Dirksen, S., Bucher, L., et al (2010). *Medical-surgical nursing in Canada: Assessment and management of clinical problems* (2nd Canadian ed.). Toronto: Elsevier Canada.

McCance, K., & Huether, S. (2006). *Pathophysiology: The biologic basis for disease in adults and children* (5th ed.). St. Louis: Mosby.

Pagana, K., & Pagana, T. (2002). *Mosby's manual of diagnostic and laboratory tests* (2nd ed.). St. Louis: Mosby.

BIBLIOGRAPHY

Black, J. M., & Hawks, J. H. (2009). *Medical-surgical nursing: Clinical management for positive outcomes* (8th ed.). St. Louis, MO: Saunders.

Daniels, R., Nosek, L., & Nicoll, L. (2007). *Contemporary medical-surgical nursing*. New York: Thomson Demlar Learning.

Day, R. A., Paul, P., Williams, B., Smeltzer, S. C., & Bare, B. G. (2007). *Brunner & Suddarth's textbook of medical-surgical nursing* (1st Canadian ed.). Philadelphia: Lippincott, Williams & Wilkins.

Day, R. A., Paul, P., Williams, B., Smeltzer, S. C., & Bare, B. G. (2009). *Brunner & Suddarth's textbook of medical-surgical nursing* (2nd Canadian ed.). Philadephia: Lippincott, Williams & Wilkins.

Diepenbrock, N. (2011). *Quick reference to critical care* (4th ed.). Philadelphia: Lippincott.

Fischbach, F., & Dunnings, M. B. (2008). *A manual of laboratory and diagnostic tests* (8th ed.). Philadelphia: Lippincott.

Hannon, R.A., Pooler, C., & Porth, C. (2009). *Pathophysiology: Concepts of altered health states* (1st Canadian ed.). Philadelphia: Lippincott.

Hockenberry, M., & Wilson, D. (2012). *Wong's essentials of pediatric nursing* (9th ed.). St. Louis: Mosby.

James, S., & Ashwill, J. (2007). *Nursing care of children: Principles and practice* (3rd ed.). St. Louis: Saunders.

Karch, A. (2012). 2013 *Lippincott's nursing drug guide* (Canadian Edition). Philadelphia: Lippincott.

Lemone, P., & Burke, K. (2004). *Medical surgical nursing: Critical thinking in client care* (3rd ed.). Upper Saddle River, NJ: Prentice Hall.

Methany, N. (2000). *Fluid and electrolyte balance nursing considerations* (4th ed.). Philadelphia: Lippincott.

Potts, N., & Mandleco, B. (2011). *Pediatric nursing caring for children and their families* (3rd ed.). New York: Thomson Demlar Learning.

Price, S., & Wilson, L. (2003). *Pathophysiology: Clinical concepts of disease processes* (6th ed.). St. Louis: Mosby.

Walraven, G. (2010). *Basic arrhythmias* (7th ed.). Upper Saddle River, NJ: Prentice Hall.

WEB SITES

Canadian Nursing Index (http://www.nursingindex.com/): This Web site provides numerous links to Canadian nursing information on the Internet. This service gives general information on nursing in Canada with a multitude of resources. Some examples include Internet search engines and Internet indexes of nursing resources. There are also many links to nursing specialties, such as emergency and primary care nursing.

Health Finder (http://www.healthfinder.gov/): The Health Finder Web site is an official address for the United States Department of Health and Human Services. The site is a health library that has information on a wide variety of topics and an easy to use alphabetical search engine. An example of a topic for the general public is an article on how to prevent diabetes, which includes information in a variety of languages. It also includes a useful section on drug interactions.

Mount Sinai Hospital Department of Microbiology (http://microbiology.mtsinai.on.ca: The Mount Sinai Web site is a collaborative project between Mount Sinai and Toronto Medical Laboratories. This resource contains extensive material on laboratory tests, adult immunizations, and infection control. It also has an online laboratory manual.

National Center for Complementary and Alternative Medicine (http://nccam.nih.gov/): Part of the American National Institutes of Health, this site offers comprehensive health information on a large variety of herbs and other dietary supplements. It also includes alternative treatment modalities, such as acupuncture. In addition, it features clinical trials and research opportunities.

Public Health Agency of Canada (http://www.phac-aspc.gc.ca/a-z/index-eng.php): This health Web site is provided by the federal government of Canada and originates with Health Canada. It provides many resources on health promotion and health prevention, including specific disease conditions, immunizations, and educational publications.

CHAPTER 8

Practice Questions

Case 1

Ms. Peal, age 32 years, has just been diagnosed with breast cancer. Family history reveals that both Ms. Peal's mother and sister have had breast cancer. A modified radical mastectomy is scheduled for Ms. Peal. Following the surgery, she will have chemotherapy followed by radiation.

Questions 1–5 refer to this case.

1. Ms. Peal asks the nurse to explain to her the relationship between tumour size, node involvement, and prognosis. Which of the following statements would be most accurate?

   1. Smaller tumours with positive node involvement have the best prognosis
   2. Larger tumours with negative node involvement have the best prognosis
   3. Smaller tumours with negative node involvement have the worst prognosis
   4. Larger tumours with positive node involvement have the worst prognosis

2. Ms. Peal wonders if she should have breast reconstruction at the time of her mastectomy. She asks the nurse for her opinion. What should the nurse respond?

   1. "This is a personal decision you should make once you have all the information."
   2. "Reconstruction is not generally done until after chemotherapy and radiation."
   3. "Having the reconstruction at the time of the mastectomy will help with your body image."
   4. "There are very good breast prostheses now, so perhaps you should try them before you decide."

3. Ms. Peal has surgery and starts chemotherapy. She experiences severe vomiting. Which of the following is the most important nursing intervention for Ms. Peal?

   1. Provide a quiet darkened room with soft music
   2. Provide a light meal of nonirritating foods before treatments
   3. Offer dry crackers and carbonated fluids when she feels hungry
   4. Administer prescribed antiemetics one hour prior to her treatment

4. Ms. Peal is to have external radiation therapy on an outpatient basis once she recovers from the chemotherapy. Ms. Peal should be informed that she might experience which of the following with external beam radiation therapy of the breast?

   1. Diarrhea and abdominal discomfort
   2. Headaches and seizures
   3. Fatigue, skin changes, and breast edema
   4. Taste changes

5. Ms. Peal is at risk for developing lymphedema. What would the nurse advise Ms. Peal is the most effective strategy to reduce lymphedema?

   1. Wear sweaters or blouses with tight-fitting arms
   2. Try to keep her arms in an elevated position
   3. Perform hand and arm exercises daily
   4. Do not carry heavy parcels

Case 2

Ms. Zhang, who has a five-year history of lung disease, arrives at the emergency room experiencing dyspnea. She is provided with low-flow oxygen.

Questions 6 and 7 refer to this case.

6. The following are the results of Ms. Zhang's initial arterial blood gases:

pH	7.30
pCO_2	53 mm Hg
HCO_3	22 mmol/L
pO_2	96 mm Hg
O_2 saturation	95%

   The results indicate which of the following?

   1. Metabolic acidosis
   2. Metabolic alkalosis
   3. Respiratory acidosis
   4. Hypoxia

7. Over the next three hours, Ms. Zhang's condition deteriorates. She is experiencing significant dyspnea and an increased respiratory rate. She is pale and diaphoretic. Arterial blood gases are now as follows:

pH	7.18
pCO_2	68 mm Hg
HCO_3	32 mmol/L
pO_2	46 mm Hg
O_2 saturation	81%

   Based on this information, what action should the nurse take?

   1. None, as compensation has occurred
   2. Administer increased oxygen
   3. Have Ms. Zhang breathe into a paper bag
   4. Call the physician

Case 3

Fred Kingsley, a 52-year-old country and western singer, has been diagnosed with vocal cord polyps, requiring surgical laser removal.

Questions 8–10 refer to this case.

8. What is the nurse's priority assessment in Mr. Kingsley's immediate postoperative period?

1. Hemorrhage
2. Pain
3. Difficulty swallowing
4. Oral pharyngeal edema

9. What is the recommended postoperative position for Mr. Kingsley?

1. Prone with his head on a pillow
2. Reverse Trendelenburg with the neck extended
3. Semi-Fowler's with the neck flexed
4. Supine with his neck hyperextended and supported with a pillow

10. What nursing action can best alleviate Mr. Kingsley's throat discomfort?

1. Having him drink warm fluids
2. Giving him aspirin (ASA)
3. Giving him acetaminophen (Tylenol®), elixir or pills
4. Placing a heating pad around his throat

Case 4

Consuela Gomez, age 58, moved to Canada from Mexico 10 years ago. For the past few months, she has been experiencing fatigue, cough, and occasional blood-tinged sputum. The nurse administers a Mantoux tuberculin skin test, and Mrs. Gomez returns to the clinic for the test to be read.

Questions 11–14 refer to this case.

11. Mrs. Gomez's Mantoux test yields an induration area of 10 mm. What is the most accurate interpretation of a 10-mm result?

1. Active disease is present
2. She has been exposed to *M. tuberculosis* or has been vaccinated with BCG
3. The disease is not active, but preventive treatment should be initiated
4. The reaction is questionable and should be repeated

12. Which of the following tests is most reliable to confirm a diagnosis of tuberculosis (TB) for Mrs. Gomez?

1. A chest X-ray
2. Acid-fast bacilli in a sputum smear
3. A nucleic acid amplification test
4. Second-step Mantoux test with induration of 10 mm or greater

13. Mrs. Gomez is started on a multiple-drug regimen. The nurse teaches Mrs. Gomez about the medications. Which of the following drugs have side effects of ototoxicity and nephrotoxicity?

1. Ethambutol (Myambutol)
2. Isoniazid (INH)
3. Rifampin (Rifadin)
4. Streptomycin (Streptomycin)

14. The nurse discusses with Mrs. Gomez the importance of compliance with her medications. How long will Mrs. Gomez be required to take the pharmacological treatment for TB?

1. 1–2 months
2. 3–4 months
3. 5–6 months
4. 6–9 months

Case 5

Harold Hart is an 82-year-old man admitted to the coronary care unit (CCU), having experienced a myocardial infarction (MI). Mr. Hart has a history of hypertension.

Questions 15–18 refer to this case.

15. What laboratory tests will confirm the diagnosis of MI?

1. PT, PTT, INR
2. Troponin, CK-MB, LDH
3. Na, K, CK-BB
4. BUN, Cr, CK-MM

16. Mr. Hart is to receive the thrombolytic drug tenecteplase (TNKase). What complication does the nurse need to observe Mr. Hart for during and after this treatment?

1. Irregular pulse
2. Epistaxis
3. Chest pain
4. Ecchymosis

17. The nurse determines that thrombolytic therapy has been effective when Mr. Hart displays which of the following?

1. Stops having chest pain
2. Has a marked increase in the CK levels within three hours of therapy

3. Develops premature atrial contractions
4. Has an increased respiratory rate

18. Mr. Hart survives his MI. What is the most common complication following an MI?

1. Dressler syndrome
2. Ventricular septal defect
3. Pericarditis
4. Dysrhythmias

Case 6

Ms. Juliet Mathias, age 34, has been overweight most of her life. Because she began feeling light-headed and dizzy, she came to the health clinic for a checkup. She was diagnosed with essential hypertension following serial blood pressures of 150/100 mm Hg. The community nurse visits her in her home.

Questions 19–21 refer to this case.

19. Which of the following statements about essential hypertension is true?

1. It requires management by drug therapy
2. It has no identifiable cause
3. It is related to another underlying condition
4. Obesity is not a factor

20. Ms. Mathias is started on hydrochlorothiazide (HydroDIURIL) by the physician for her hypertension. Which dietary modification, related to the HydroDIURIL, would the nurse teach Ms. Mathias in order to prevent an electrolyte imbalance?

1. Increase potassium-containing foods
2. Decrease sodium-containing foods
3. Increase sodium-containing foods
4. Decrease potassium-containing foods

21. The nurse determines that Ms. Mathias's hypertension is not well controlled on the diuretic. She is referred back to the physician, who prescribes a calcium channel blocker. What would be priority teaching for her regarding this medication?

1. She should watch for decreased urine output
2. She may develop hair loss
3. She may develop high blood pressure
4. She may feel dizzy when she stands quickly

Case 7

Linda Hynes, age 52, is admitted to the hospital in preparation for surgery for an adrenal tumour that has caused Cushing's syndrome. A health assessment

reveals Ms. Hynes to be manifesting truncal obesity, thin arms and legs, a round face, and a "buffalo hump" on her upper back. She is irritable during the assessment and says she just wants to be left alone.

Questions 22–24 refer to this case.

22. In addition to the manifestations noted in the initial health assessment, which of the following, observed by the nurse, may be additional manifestations of Cushing's syndrome?

1. Petechiae and abdominal purplish red striae on the abdomen
2. Decreased axilla and pubic hair
3. Tachycardia and bulging eyes
4. Hypotension and hypoglycemia

23. Later in the day, Ms. Hynes apologizes for her irritability and tells the nurse she just does not like anyone examining her because she looks so bad. Which response by the nurse is most appropriate?

1. "You really shouldn't worry about how you look. It's what you are on the inside that counts."
2. "There are some really good ways to dress so that the changes wouldn't seem so noticeable."
3. "You are going to look much better right after your surgery."
4. "Most of the physical and mental changes caused by the disease will gradually improve after your surgery."

24. Ms. Hynes is scheduled for a bilateral adrenalectomy. The morning of surgery, the surgeon orders intravenous hydrocortisone (Solu-Cortef) to be started. What is the rationale for the use of Solu-Cortef?

1. Promotion of glucocorticoid response to the stress of surgery after removal of the adrenal glands
2. Stimulation of the inflammatory response to promote wound healing
3. Promotion of the effects of aldosterone to retain fluid postsurgery
4. Stimulation of bone resorption to increase calcium in the blood

Case 8

Brian Wilson, a 17-year-old student, sustains a mandibular fracture while playing rugby. There was no loss of teeth. His treatment includes intermaxillary fixation surgery.

Questions 25–27 refer to this case.

25. Postoperatively, how should the nurse position Brian?

1. Prone to facilitate lung expansion
2. On his side with his head slightly elevated to prevent aspiration
3. Supine with his head to the side to promote the drainage of secretions
4. Slight Trendelenburg to prevent aspiration of fluids

26. What is the most important postoperative goal for Brian?

1. Adequate nutrition
2. Jaw immobilization
3. Oral hygiene
4. Patent airway

27. Which of the following is the most important to be available at Brian's bedside?

1. Nasogastric suction tube
2. Nasopharyngeal suction catheter
3. Wire cutter
4. Oxygen cannula

Case 9

Mrs. Cheng, age 78 years, fell on the ice and injured her hip. She was transported to the nearest emergency department, where a fractured hip was diagnosed.

Questions 28–30 refer to this case.

28. Mrs. Cheng is on bed rest with immobilization of her hip while she is waiting for an operating room to be available for surgery later in the day. What assistive device will the nurse provide for Mrs. Cheng?

1. A urinary catheter as a bedpan may not be used
2. A trapeze to facilitate lifting movement
3. Side rails in the "up" position for Mrs. Cheng to use for moving herself
4. A "geri-chair" so Mrs. Cheng may sit up for meals

29. Mrs. Cheng has surgery to repair the intracapsular fracture with a hemiarthroplasty and is transferred for rehabilitation. The nurse at the rehabilitation unit assists Mrs. Cheng with which of the following to avoid displacing the femoral head prosthesis?

1. Sitting in chairs without arms to assist in rising to a standing position
2. Keeping her hip in adduction
3. Putting on socks and shoes
4. Placing a chair inside a shower or tub so that she remains seated while showering

30. It is determined that Mrs. Cheng has osteoporosis. Prior to discharge from rehabilitation, the nurse discusses measures to prevent further fractures.

Which of the following would be important to discuss with Mrs. Cheng?

1. Calcium supplements and prescribed bisphosphonate medication
2. Incorporating non–weight-bearing exercise into her daily routine when allowed by the physician
3. Vitamin D, 200 international units (IU)
4. Planning for a move from her residential home to an assisted living facility

Case 10

The nurse in a walk-in, ambulatory clinic assesses Sandra Procinski, 33 years old. She states she experienced a sore throat about a week ago but has not had any problems until today. This morning she awoke to find her face swollen, particularly around her eyes. She also has noted that her urine appears smoky.

Questions 31 and 32 refer to this case.

31. The nurse suspects that Ms. Procinski is manifesting symptoms of which of the following?

1. Urinary tract infection
2. Pyelonephritis
3. Nephrotic syndrome
4. Acute glomerulonephritis

32. What is the likely initial treatment for Ms. Procinski?

1. A diet low in potassium
2. Rest
3. Antihypertensives
4. Antibiotics

Case 11

Bernard Cowler, 36, arrived at the emergency department complaining of right-sided chest pain that is worse with inspiration. He is anxious, diaphoretic, and tachycardic, with a respiratory rate of 25. He states that he fell from a ladder one week ago.

Questions 33–35 refer to this case.

33. When Mr. Cowler asks the nurse what she thinks is wrong with him, what might the nurse respond?

1. "From your symptoms, it sounds as if you have a thoracic aneurysm, but the doctor must make the diagnosis."
2. "You are probably experiencing angina, a type of pain

that occurs when there is insufficient blood reaching your heart muscle."

3. "The fall from the ladder may have caused a pulmonary embolism, which is a blood clot in your lungs."

4. "With your history, the pain you are describing sounds like a hiatus hernia and can easily be treated."

34. Mr. Cowler is started on heparin (Hepalean) therapy. What blood test result does the nurse need to monitor closely?

1. International normalized ratio (INR)
2. Partial thromboplastin time (PTT)
3. Platelet function assay (PFA)
4. Prothrombin time (PT)

35. Several days later, the nurse transcribes a physician order for Mr. Cowler: "Discontinue heparin, start warfarin (Coumadin) at 5 mg OD each morning." What action should the nurse take?

1. Stop the heparin and notify the pharmacy to prepare Coumadin for Mr. Cowler
2. Stop the heparin and give Mr. Cowler his first dose of Coumadin
3. Question the doctor regarding the dose of Coumadin
4. Question the doctor about discontinuing heparin before therapeutic levels of Coumadin are reached

Case 12

The nurse interviews Arnold Hampton, age 69 years, at the clinic. He states he has been experiencing muscle cramps in his legs that are getting worse, and he is not able to walk as much as he once did. He tells the nurse the pain gets better when he sits but starts again shortly after he gets up and begins walking.

Questions 36–38 refer to this case.

36. When performing the physical assessment on Mr. Hampton, the nurse instructs him to abduct his leg. What does abduction mean?

1. Movement of part toward midline of body
2. Movement of part away from midline of body
3. Movement along longitudinal axis away from midline of body
4. Movement along longitudinal axis toward midline of body

37. The nurse and physician suspect Mr. Hampton may have peripheral arterial disease (PAD). What assessment would the nurse perform with a client with presumed PAD?

1. Assess for diminished or absent pulses in the extremities

2. Assess for pallor or blanching of the foot when in a dependent position
3. Assess for lower leg edema
4. Assess blood pressure in both thighs

38. What self-care activities would the nurse suggest to Mr. Hampton?

1. Use a heating pad to help him become comfortable while resting
2. Purchase support stockings to wear daily
3. Walk at least 30 minutes a day
4. Inspect his feet for redness once a week

Case 13

Arkady Sharapov, age 74 years, is admitted to the emergency department with a diagnosis of exacerbation of COPD. The nurse establishes low-flow oxygen therapy as per physician order.

Questions 39 and 40 refer to this case.

39. What is the most appropriate assessment to determine appropriate FiO₂ levels for Mr. Sharapov?

1. Arterial blood gases
2. Oxygen saturation
3. Normalization of vital signs
4. Change of skin tone from dusky or cyanotic to pink

40. Mr. Sharapov's condition is stabilized, and he is to be discharged on home oxygen therapy. What action by the nurse would best assist Mr. Sharapov in managing home oxygen therapy?

1. Provide a teaching session on the use of a portable oxygen compressor
2. Give Mr. Sharapov a pamphlet on oxygen therapy that he could refer to when he is at home
3. Arrange for a home consultation with a respiratory therapist or technologist
4. Make an appointment for Mr. Sharapov to have pulse oximetry one week after discharge

Case 14

Sarah Sawchuk is an 18-year-old female who is admitted to the hospital with severe diarrhea, anorexia, weight loss, and abdominal cramps. She is diagnosed with ulcerative colitis.

Questions 41–43 refer to this case.

41. What symptoms of fluid and electrolyte imbalance caused by ulcerative colitis should the nurse report immediately?

1. Thirst and dry, sticky mucous membranes
2. Extreme muscle weakness and tachycardia
3. Development of tetany and muscle spasms
4. Numbness and tingling of fingers, mouth, and toes

42. Ms. Sawchuk's condition deteriorates, and she requires an ileostomy. What would her postoperative care include?

    1. Removing rectal packing four hours after surgery
    2. Continuous, slow feedings via nasogastric tube
    3. Monitoring intake and output accurately
    4. Removing the nasogastric tube on arrival at the unit

43. The nurse teaches Ms. Sawchuk about nutrition related to her ileostomy. Which of the following foods may cause an obstruction and should be avoided by Sarah?

    1. Raw fruits and vegetables
    2. Beans and legumes
    3. Eggs
    4. Cheese

Case 15

Mrs. Edna O'Brien, age 90 years, lives in a retirement home. Although she is generally healthy, she has bilateral cataracts that she has been reluctant to have treated. Mrs. O'Brien is presently almost totally blind.

Questions 44 and 45 refer to this case.

44. The nurse instructs the dietary aide in assisting Mrs. O'Brien with her meals. What direction might the nurse give to the aide?

    1. Do not give Mrs. O'Brien sharp utensils
    2. Provide Mrs. O'Brien with finger foods that she can feel and pick up easily
    3. Help Mrs. O'Brien locate the food on her plate by comparing it to a clock; for example, say, "The toast is at nine o'clock."
    4. Stay with Mrs. O'Brien throughout the meal and feed her when necessary

45. Mrs. O'Brien consents to have her cataracts treated. At a local clinic, she has an initial right cataract extraction with intraocular lens implant and is discharged the same day. What discharge instructions would the nurse provide to Mrs. O'Brien?

    1. "I will give you a stool softener to prevent constipation."
    2. "You need to drink at least six glasses of water or fluids this evening."

3. "You will not be allowed to bathe until you return to see the doctor in two days."
4. "You are allowed to watch TV, but you should not read for the next 48 hours."

Case 16

Mrs. Gardner, age 84, was diagnosed with heart failure two years ago. She has been a pack-a-day cigarette smoker for over 50 years. She has never had a myocardial infarction. Mrs. Gardner arrives in the emergency department of her local hospital with severe shortness of breath and only able to speak in one-word sentences. She is pale, diaphoretic, and cool to the touch. Her pulse is rapid and irregular.

Questions 46–50 refer to this case.

46. What should the nurse anticipate would be the priority care requested by the physician?

    1. An ejection fraction thallium scan
    2. Administration of lorazepam (Ativan)
    3. Administration of furosemide (Lasix)
    4. Cardioversion

47. What position should the nurse encourage Mrs. Gardner to assume while being treated in the emergency department?

    1. Prone, to allow her to rest more effectively
    2. Semi-Fowler's, to allow her to breathe more easily
    3. Trendelenburg, to encourage drainage of fluids from the upper respiratory airway
    4. High Fowler's with legs down, to decrease preload

48. Mrs. Gardner is given furosemide (Lasix) to initiate urinary output. When she starts to void, what is the priority assessment?

    1. Electrolyte levels
    2. Blood pressure
    3. Hourly output
    4. Respiratory rate

49. It is determined that Mrs. Gardner has left-sided heart failure. Which of the following would the nurse assess for in Mrs. Gardner?

    1. Pitting edema
    2. Jugular venous distension
    3. Hepatomegaly
    4. Lung crackles

50. During Mrs. Gardner's hospitalization, blood work showed elevated BUN and creatinine levels, with reduced creatinine clearance. Chronic renal failure

was diagnosed, and she was placed on a renal diet. The nurse should teach Mrs. Gardner to avoid which of the following foods?

1. Red meat and shellfish
2. Potatoes and citrus fruit
3. Cookies and cake
4. Lean meat and chicken

INDEPENDENT QUESTIONS

Questions 51–80 do not refer to a particular case.

51. A nurse attends a summer pool party. One of the male guests dives into the shallow end of the pool and sustains a high neck fracture and spinal cord injury. The nurse suspects a C2 level injury. What priority first aid measure will the nurse likely need to provide until paramedics arrive?

1. Immobilize him on a firm board, such as a Styrofoam "flutter board"
2. Fashion a roll out of cloths to stabilize the neck
3. Maintain him in the pool without attempting to lift him out
4. Provide rescue breathing

52. Minh Tam Tran is a 16-year-old who has been diagnosed with asthma. She has been prescribed salbutamol (Ventolin) and beclomethasone (Beclovent) metered-dose inhalers. Minh asks the school nurse why she needs to take these medications. What is the nurse's most appropriate response?

1. "The Beclovent is a steroid, and the Ventolin is a bronchodilator."
2. "You take both of these so that you don't have another asthma attack."
3. "The Ventolin opens your airways, and the Beclovent decreases the swelling, so together they stabilize your asthma."
4. "You must be careful to take both of these inhalers exactly as they are prescribed to prevent another attack."

53. Which of the following is an indication for a permanent cardiac pacemaker?

1. Sick sinus syndrome
2. Premature ventricular beats
3. Atrial fibrillation with controlled ventricular response
4. First-degree AV block

54. Mr. Sanders visits the neurology clinic, where he receives a diagnosis of Parkinson's disease from the physician. The nurse sees Mr. Sanders following his meeting with the physician. What would be the most helpful approach by the nurse?

1. "I am really sorry about your diagnosis, but the drugs can keep you stable for a long time."
2. "What did the physician explain to you about your diagnosis of Parkinson's disease?"
3. "There is a lot of research about Parkinson's disease these days, so many new treatments may be available."
4. "I understand that you are upset by this very bad diagnosis. I will sit here with you for a while."

55. Ms. Singh has a hemoglobin of 6.2 mmol/L. What will be the most likely manifestation of her condition?

1. Headache
2. Bradycardia
3. Icteric sclera
4. Fatigue

56. Mrs. Angelina has experienced several weeks of diarrhea as a result of a viral gastroenteritis. Mrs. Angelina is at risk of being deficient in which of the following due to the diarrhea?

1. Magnesium
2. Calcium
3. Potassium
4. Sodium

57. Mr. Wheeler has symptoms of gastroesophageal reflux disease (GERD). What would the community nurse recommend while he is waiting for his appointment with the physician?

1. "I will refer you to a therapist who will evaluate and treat your swallowing difficulties."
2. "I recommend you place a heating pad on your stomach area to ease the pain."
3. "You might try an antacid preparation to soothe the heartburn."
4. "Eating small frequent meals will prevent nausea and vomiting."

58. Mr. Tibor, age 44 years, is brought to the emergency department by ambulance because of frank gastric bleeding. He has a history of peptic ulcer disease. What priority intervention should the nurse anticipate?

1. Sengesten-Blakemore tube insertion
2. An intravenous bolus of normal saline
3. Insertion of a nasogastric tube and saline lavage
4. Administration of oxygen

59. Which of the following is a manifestation of diverticulitis?

1. High fever
2. Chronic diarrhea
3. Epigastric discomfort
4. Left lower quadrant pain

60. Mr. Wilmox, age 45, is referred to the emergency department by his family physician because appendicitis is suspected. The nurse assesses Mr. Wilmox. Which of the following is a possible manifestation of appendicitis?

1. Increased abdominal pain with coughing
2. Esophageal reflux
3. High-grade fever
4. A negative Rovsing's sign

61. In a client with viral hepatitis, the nurse should closely monitor for indications of which of the following abnormal laboratory values?

1. Decreased vitamins C and E
2. Elevated serum potassium
3. Prolonged prothrombin time
4. Decreased calcium

62. During recovery from hepatic coma, a high-fibre diet is recommended. What is the primary rationale for recommending this diet?

1. To prevent hyperlipidemia
2. To prevent diarrhea
3. To decrease hypokalemia
4. To decrease serum ammonia

63. Mr. Hawkins has radical neck surgery for cancer of the larynx. Which of the following is the most important assessment postsurgery?

1. Pain
2. Temperature of 38°C
3. Stridor
4. Serosanguinous oozing from the operative site

64. Mrs. Cohen has primary adrenal insufficiency (Addison's disease). The nurse assessing Mrs. Cohen should anticipate which of the following manifestations?

1. Exophthalmos and goitre
2. Polydipsia and polyuria
3. Moon face and buffalo hump
4. Bronze pigmentation and hypotension

65. Which of the following is descriptive of cluster headaches?

1. Constant, squeezing tightness at the base of the skull
2. A throbbing, synchronous, pulsing pain commonly unilateral and anterior
3. Palpable neck and shoulder muscles, stiff neck, and tenderness
4. Severe "bone-crushing" pain radiating up and down from one eye

66. Mr. Gianopoulos, 35 years old, had just recovered from an upper respiratory infection when he suddenly experienced muscle weakness in his feet and lower legs. He sought medical assistance and was diagnosed with Guillain-Barré syndrome. Which of the following would be the priority of nursing care?

1. Treating the infection that triggered onset of the syndrome
2. Managing respiratory muscle dysfunction
3. Strengthening and stretching targeted muscles
4. Preventing major complications due to immobility

67. Mr. Andersson, age 32, experienced a cerebrovascular accident (CVA) resulting from a ruptured aneurysm with a subarachnoid hemorrhage. He is gradually improving; however, his family has been informed that he has apraxia as a result of the CVA. The family asks the nurse to tell them what apraxia means. What should the nurse respond?

1. "Apraxia is loss of comprehension of verbal or written language."
2. "Apraxia is the inability to use objects properly."
3. "Apraxia is an inability to recognize objects, sights, sounds, or other sensory stimuli."
4. "Apraxia is the loss of production of verbal or written language."

68. Mrs. Tetrault, an 83-year-old widow, has a history of type 2 diabetes and chronic arterial occlusive disease. She is hospitalized due to gangrene of all her right toes. The doctor has informed her that she will need a below-the-knee amputation. The nurse goes into Mrs. Tetrault's room and finds her crying about this upcoming procedure. How should the nurse respond to Mrs. Tetrault?

1. "Don't cry; this really isn't such a bad thing. They do wonderful things with prostheses now."
2. "I know you will be just fine. You are so strong you can get through this."
3. "I can see that you are upset. Would you like to talk about your concerns?"
4. "It's okay to be upset. This is devastating news. I'd be upset too."

69. The clinic nurse performs a physical examination on Mr. Fredericks, age 60. What assessment data would support the diagnosis of abdominal aortic aneurysm?

1. Epigastric discomfort
2. Pyrosis
3. Abdominal bruit
4. Tearing abdominal pain

70. Mrs. Olsen, age 84, is admitted to hospital from a nursing home due to extreme lethargy. Her hematocrit is 54% and sodium is 52 mmol/L. Which intervention should the nurse anticipate will be implemented?

1. Pushing oral fluids
2. Establishing an IV line of 10% dextrose solution
3. Starting an IV line of normal saline (0.9% NaCl)
4. Inserting a nasogastric tube for enteral feeding

71. Mr. Frank Ulrinski is a farmer who lives on the prairies. He is bald and spends most of his working day in the sun. The nurse performs a skin assessment. What type of skin cancer is Mr. Ulrinski most at risk for?

1. Adenocarcinoma
2. Basal cell carcinoma
3. Malignant melanoma
4. Spongioblastoma

72. Which of the following is presumed to be the most effective prevention for cancer of the cervix?

1. Routine Papanicoulaou (Pap) tests
2. Colposcopy
3. Human papillomavirus (HPV) vaccine
4. Laser treatment for genital herpes

73. Catherine Blinker, age 92, has osteoporosis. She is generally well but uses a walker frame to assist with mobility. What activity would the nurse recommend to improve her osteoporosis?

1. Swimming
2. Walking
3. Aerobics
4. Range-of-motion exercises

74. Brenda Chaisson is pregnant with her second child when she is diagnosed with multiple sclerosis. What manifestations is she likely to have initially experienced?

1. Sensory disturbances that include blurred vision and tinnitus
2. Bradykinesia, rigid muscle tone, tremors, and impaired postural reflexes
3. Fluctuating weakness of certain skeletal muscle groups
4. Unpleasant motor and sensory abnormalities (paraesthesias)

75. Georgio Mariani, age 16, is evaluated for a closed head injury following a snowboarding accident. Which of the following assessments would be of priority concern to the RN?

1. Headache
2. Vomiting
3. Tinnitus
4. Diplopia

76. What is the depth of a partial full-thickness burn?

1. Epidermis
2. Epidermis and some dermis
3. Epidermis, dermis, and subcutaneous tissue
4. Epidermis, dermis, subcutaneous tissue, fascia, and muscle

77. Mrs. Raiza has been diagnosed with low-grade non-Hodgkin's lymphoma. Her physician has offered the choice of two treatment options: chemotherapy or careful monitoring with no active treatment. Mrs. Raiza says to the nurse, "If you were me, which treatment would you choose?" What is the best response by the nurse?

1. "You need to discuss treatment options in more detail with the physician."
2. "I am not you, and everyone chooses the treatment that is best for them."
3. "It would not be professional of me to tell you what treatment to choose."
4. "Tell me what you understand about both treatment options."

78. Six hours following a transurethral resection of the prostate (TURP), Mr. Douglas experiences abdominal pain and distension. What action will the nurse implement?

1. Pain assessment
2. Flushing of the continuous bladder irrigation catheter
3. Decreasing the flow rate in the bladder irrigation
4. Notifying the physician

79. Mr. Fell is about to be discharged after having trans-sphenoidal surgery for a pituitary cyst. What specific instructions would the nurse include in discharge teaching?

1. Notify the physician if you feel tired
2. Do not blow your nose for two weeks
3. Observe for bleeding from the cranial incision site
4. Call the surgeon if you have clear fluid dripping from your ear

80. A nurse on the palliative care team is supporting the family of Mrs. Millar, who has chosen to die at home. The family asks the nurse how they will know death is imminent. What would the nurse respond?

1. "Her skin may become mottled."
2. "Her respirations will be slow and deep."
3. "Her pulse will increase."
4. "Her temperature will decrease."

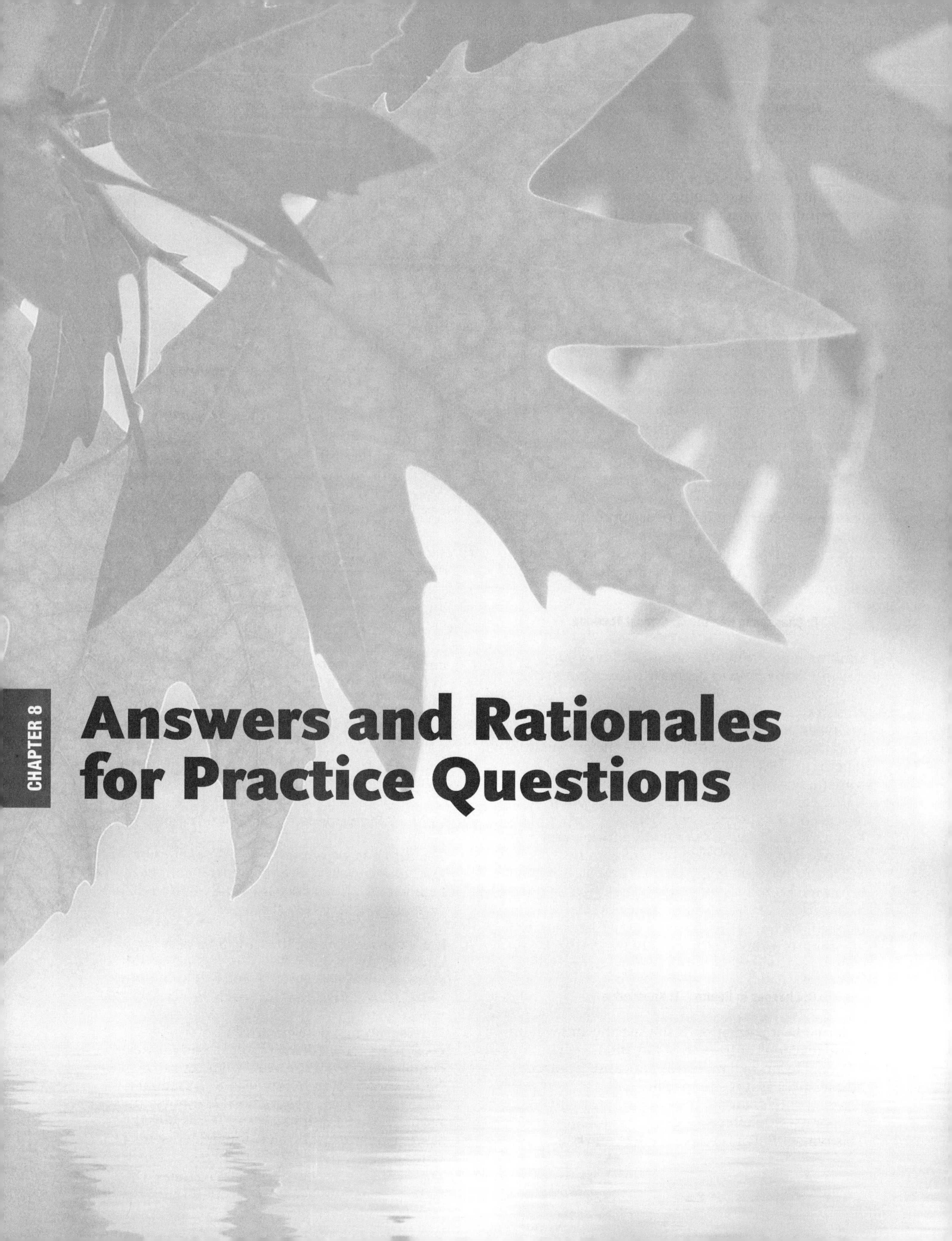

CHAPTER 8

Answers and Rationales for Practice Questions

1.   C: Changes in Health   T: Knowledge

1. Even though the tumour is small, with node involvement, there is a poorer prognosis.
2. While there is no node involvement, the tumour is large and not as likely to have the best prognosis.
3. Small tumours with negative node involvement have the best prognosis.
4. According to the TNM classification of breast cancer, the larger the tumour and the more nodes are involved, the worse the prognosis is.

2.   C: Nurse–Client Partnership   T: Critical Thinking

1. Ms. Peal needs to obtain all the information about the pros and cons of breast reconstruction at the time of mastectomy and then make an informed decision based on what she feels is right for her.
2. Depending on the type of cancer, breast reconstruction can be done just after the mastectomy. Not all centres in Canada offer this approach.
3. This may be true, but it is not as appropriate as choice 1.
4. This response provides Ms. Peal with more information, but it is not as appropriate as choice 1.

3.   C: Changes in Health   T: Critical Thinking

1. Limiting environmental stimuli and providing music therapy help to decrease nausea but are not as effective as antiemetics.
2. This strategy is helpful at times to prevent nausea, but when Ms. Peal is already experiencing severe vomiting, antiemetics will provide the greatest relief.
3. Antiemetics will provide greater relief.
4. Nausea and vomiting are the most commonly observed GI side effects of chemotherapy. Postchemotherapy nausea and vomiting and nausea without vomiting have major effects on quality of life, and it is essential that interventions be undertaken to manage this side effect in order to improve the client's experience. Antiemetic protocol includes the delivery of the antiemetic one hour prior to chemotherapy treatment.

4.   C: Changes in Health   T: Knowledge

1. External beam radiation is site specific and will only cause reactions at the site of radiation.
2. External beam radiation will not cause headaches and seizures as it is site specific.
3. Fatigue, skin changes, and breast edema may be temporary side effects of external radiation.
4. This type of radiation has no effect on taste.

5.   C: Changes in Health   T: Critical Thinking

1. This will help to reduce lymphedema but is not as effective as exercises.
2. This is true but not as effective as exercises.
3. Hand and arm exercises often help prevent or decrease lymphedema as they increase the lymph circulation.
4. As in choice 2.

6.   C: Changes in Health   T: Application

1. This is acidosis, but bicarbonate is within the normal range, so it is not metabolic. Also, it is known that Ms. Zhang has a respiratory problem, so that is a clue there is a respiratory basis to the acidosis.
2. The pH indicates acidosis, not alkalosis.
3. Respiratory acidosis is indicated by an elevated pCO_2 and low pH. She is also manifesting dyspnea, which indicates a respiratory origin to the acidosis.
4. The pO_2 and O_2 saturation levels are both normal.

7.   C: Changes in Health   T: Critical Thinking

1. Compensation has occurred to some degree, but Ms. Zhang's condition has worsened.
2. The nurse should increase Ms. Zhang's oxygen, but she is experiencing serious respiratory problems and requires treatment from a physician.
3. This is done for a low pCO_2. Ms. Zhang's pCO_2 is high.
4. This is the correct action. Ms. Zhang's O_2 is dangerously low, her pCO_2 is dangerously high, and her pH shows significant acidosis. Ms. Zhang may need additional ventilatory support.

8.   C: Changes in Health   T: Critical Thinking

1. The throat is a vascular area, and even with laser surgery, there is a recognized danger of hemorrhage. It may occur quickly and is the most immediately life-threatening postsurgical complication.
2. It is expected that the throat will be very sore after surgery. Around-the-clock analgesia with acetaminophen (Tylenol®), rather than aspirin (ASA), is administered. An ice collar may provide relief.
3. This is a normal postoperative finding.
4. Oral pharyngeal edema is a common postoperative complication from throat surgery resulting from trauma to the site. It may lead to a gradual increase in airway obstruction. The nurse must monitor Mr. Kingsley's airway status but, more immediately, must be alert for sudden signs of hemorrhage.

CHAPTER 8

9.   C: Changes in Health   T: Application

1. This position would encourage pooling of the secretions in the mouth and possibly cause choking, coughing, or aspiration.
2. This position would not encourage drainage of secretions out of the mouth.
3. Positioning the client in a semi-Fowler's with the neck flexed helps prevent pooling of secretions in the mouth and allows easier breathing and less chance of choking, coughing, and aspirating. Clients often put themselves into the high Fowler's position for comfort and ease of breathing.
4. This position would be uncomfortable and impossible for the client to remain in for very long.

10.   C: Changes in Health   T: Application

1. Clients are given cool, not warm, fluids once they are able to swallow. The coolness helps soothe the sore throat and decrease the chance of swelling. Coolness also reduces spasms in the muscles surrounding the throat.
2. Aspirin or any other medication that alters bleeding time is not given to postoperative clients.
3. Acetaminophen elixir or pills is the analgesic of choice and should be given around the clock. Sometimes rinsing the mouth out with viscous lidocaine is effective to decrease pain in the throat.
4. Ice collars rather than heating pads are used to help decrease swelling and pain. Heat may cause increased swelling and bleeding.

11.   C: Changes in Health   T: Application

1. Active disease is diagnosed by sputum cultures for acid-fast bacilli. Three consecutive sputum specimens collected on different days are obtained and sent for smear and culture. Material obtained from gastric washing, CSF, and pus from an abscess may also be examined.
2. This is a positive reaction. It indicates the presence of a TB infection but does not show whether the infection is active or dormant. People who have been vaccinated with BCG (bacille Calmette-Guérin) will have positive skin tests due to exposure to the vaccine.
3. Further studies need to be done before treatment is started. The health care professional needs to know if, in fact, the client has TB before initiating treatment.
4. Two-step testing is generally recommended only for initial testing for health care workers who require repeated testing and for those who have a decreased response to allergens. For these people, a second PPD test later may cause an accelerated response (booster effect), misinterpreted as a new PPD conversion.

12.   C: Changes in Health   T: Critical Thinking

1. Although the findings of a chest X-ray are important, it is not possible to make a diagnosis of TB solely on the basis of the X-ray. Other diseases can mimic the X-ray appearance of TB.
2. The demonstration of tubercle bacilli bacteriologically is essential for establishing a diagnosis.
3. This is a new rapid diagnostic test for TB that provides results within a few hours. It does not replace the routine sputum smears and cultures, but it offers a health care professional increased confidence in the diagnosis.
4. Repeated Mantoux testing will only show that the person has either been vaccinated with BCG or exposed to the mycobacterium. It does not mean that the person has contracted the disease.

13.   C: Changes in Health   T: Application

1. Side effects of ethambutol include skin rash, GI disturbances, malaise, peripheral neuritis, and optic neuritis.
2. Side effects of isoniazid include peripheral neuritis, hepatotoxicity, skin rash, optic neuritis, and vitamin B_6 neuritis.
3. Rifampin's side effects include hepatitis, GI disturbances, and peripheral neuritis.
4. Streptomycin's side effects include ototoxicity (affecting the eighth cranial nerve), nephrotoxicity, and hypersensitivity.

14.   C: Changes in Health   T: Application

1. This is too short a time.
2. As in choice 1.
3. As in choice 1.
4. A problem with compliance with therapy for TB has been the length of time medication must be taken. Six to nine months of therapy have proven to be effective.

15.   C: Changes in Health   T: Knowledge

1. PT, PTT, and INR are all tests that evaluate clotting time, not heart damage.
2. Troponin I and cardiac troponin T are proteins in myocardial tissue. When cardiac muscle is damaged, this protein is released into the blood within an hour of injury. CK-MB is one of the three isoenzymes that can be separated for creatine kinase (CK). CK-MB is released into the blood when cardiac tissue has been damaged. LDH refers to lactate dehydrogenase, which is released into the blood when tissues are damaged.

3. Sodium and potassium levels are important in that abnormal levels may hinder conduction, but they do not detect heart muscle damage. CK-BB is an isoenzyme separated from CK and shows when brain tissue has been damaged.

4. BUN and creatinine are kidney function tests. Elevated levels show that the kidneys are not functioning optimally. CK-MM is an isoenzyme separated from CK and shows when skeletal muscle tissue has been damaged.

16. C: Changes in Health T: Critical Thinking

1. Tenecteplase may cause dysrhythmias, but the major complication is bleeding.
2. Tenecteplase is a thrombolytic whose action is to dissolve clots within the body. Therefore bleeding is a major complication.
3. A complication may be re-occlusion of the vessel resulting in chest pain, but the major complication is bleeding.
4. Ecchymosis, or bruising, is not as acute a result of bleeding as epistaxis.

17. C: Changes in Health T: Application

1. The fact that Mr. Hart has stopped having chest pain suggests that his heart muscle is now receiving oxygenated blood; therefore, the clot has been dissolved, allowing blood to move into the damaged area.
2. A marked increase in the CK levels, in particular the isoenzyme CK-MB, suggests damage to the heart tissue. This damage is caused by loss of oxygenated blood.
3. Development of premature atrial contractions merely suggests that there are excitable foci in the atria triggering these premature beats. This has nothing to do with the clearing of the artery but may, in fact, reflect the irritability of the damaged area.
4. An increased respiratory rate does not reflect the effectiveness of tenecteplase. It may reflect pain, hypoxia, or fear but not the dissolving of any clots within the body.

18. C: Changes in Health T: Knowledge

1. Dressler's syndrome is characterized by pericarditis with effusion and fever that develops one to four weeks after an MI. This is a complication of MI but not the most common.
2. Ventricular septal defect results from the phagocytic action on the septum. This complication is usually found in the second week after an MI and requires emergency surgery. It is not the most common

complication. Ventricular septal defects are also congenital malformations.

3. Pericarditis is an inflammation of the pericardium that may result in cardiac compression, decreased left ventricular filling and emptying, and cardiac failure. It usually occurs two to three days post-MI. It is a complication but not the most common complication.
4. Dysrhythmias are the most common complication post-MI, found in 80–90% of clients with MI. Ventricular dysrhythmias can be fatal.

19. C: Changes in Health T: Knowledge

1. Essential hypertension may be managed by drugs, but lifestyle modifications will often be attempted initially to bring the pressure within normal range.
2. Essential hypertension, also known as primary hypertension, has no identifiable cause.
3. This answer refers to secondary hypertension, in which an identifiable cause can be determined.
4. Research has shown that blood pressure is related to obesity and that if Ms. Mathias were to decrease her weight, her blood pressure could be lowered.

20. C: Changes in Health T: Knowledge

1. HydroDIURIL may cause loss of potassium. Clients are encouraged to eat foods containing potassium, such as bananas, and monitor serum potassium levels.
2. While this is advised for clients who are hypertensive, it is not related to the HydroDIURIL.
3. High-sodium diets are contraindicated.
4. This may cause hypokalemia.

21. C: Changes in Health T: Application

1. Calcium channel blockers may cause polyuria in some clients.
2. Calcium channel blockers may cause skin rash, dermatitis, pruritus, and urticaria, but they do not cause hair loss.
3. Calcium channel blockers may cause hypotension, not hypertension.
4. Cardiovascular effects from the use of calcium channel blockers may include peripheral edema, hypotension, palpitations, bradycardia, tachycardia, and arrhythmias that may induce orthostatic hypotension.

22. C: Changes in Health T: Application

1. Clients with Cushing's syndrome may have thin, fragile skin, purplish red striae, petechial hemorrhages, bruises, facial plethora, acne, and poor wound healing.

CHAPTER 8

2. There is usually increased axilla and pubic hair. Hirsutism is commonly found with Cushing's syndrome.
3. Tachycardia and bulging eyes suggest hyperthyroid disease.
4. Hypertension and hyperglycemia are found with Cushing's syndrome.

23. C: Nurse–Client Partnership T: Application

1. This statement is patronizing and ineffective.
2. This statement does not address Ms. Hynes's concern.
3. Her appearance will change after surgery, but it will take time for all the physical and mental changes to occur.
4. The statement addresses Ms. Hynes's concern and gives accurate information.

24. C: Changes in Health T: Application

1. High doses of corticosteroids are administered IV during surgery and for several days afterward to ensure adequate responses to the stress of the procedure.
2. Because of the use of corticosteroids, the client will actually be susceptible to infection and delayed wound healing.
3. Aldosterone is a mineralocorticoid, not a glucocorticoid.
4. This statement refers to the role of the parathyroid hormone.

25. C: Changes in Health T: Application

1. Because the client is unable to open his or her mouth after surgery, the client must be closely monitored for airway obstruction and aspiration of vomitus. Lying on the stomach will not facilitate this.
2. Brian should be positioned on his side with his head slightly elevated to help drain secretions and prevent airway obstruction.
3. Lying on his back will not facilitate drainage of secretions and could result in airway obstruction.
4. Having the head slightly below the chest will encourage secretions to drain into the mouth, causing a potential for aspiration and choking.

26. C: Changes in Health T: Critical Thinking

1. Adequate nutrition is important but is not the priority postoperatively.
2. The jaw is immobilized by wiring the jaws together during surgery; therefore, it is not the nursing priority.

3. Oral hygiene is another important intervention but is not the priority immediately postoperatively.
4. Two major potential problems in the immediate postoperative period are airway obstruction and aspiration of vomitus. The nurse must observe for signs of respiratory distress.

27. C: Changes in Health T: Critical Thinking

1. Suctioning should be necessary only if the client vomits or chokes. The nasopharyngeal or oral route may be used, depending on the extent of injury and the type of repair. A nasogastric tube may be needed to remove fluids and gas from the stomach.
2. This is one method of suctioning if needed.
3. Wire cutters or scissors (for rubber bands) must be taped to the head of the bed and sent with Brian on all appointments and examinations away from the bedside. These may be used to cut the wires and elastic bands in case of an emergency.
4. Oxygen is required only if Brian experiences any respiratory distress.

28. C: Changes in Health T: Application

1. This is not necessary. Mrs. Cheng may use a slipper bedpan.
2. A trapeze suspended over Mrs. Cheng's bed will allow her to lift herself if she is uncomfortable or for use with the bedpan.
3. This would encourage a twisting motion, and the limb and joint must be maintained in alignment.
4. Mrs. Cheng will not be allowed to sit in a chair until after surgery. Moving her into a chair would cause pain and would not keep the leg in alignment.

29. C: Changes in Health T: Application

1. She should have chairs with arms.
2. She should keep her leg straight, not adducted.
3. She should have assistance to put on stockings and shoes.
4. Mrs. Cheng will be taught to be seated on a chair while showering, use elevated toilet seats, use a pillow between her legs for the first eight weeks postsurgery, to keep her hip in a neutral, straight position when sitting, walking, or lying, and to notify her surgeon if severe pain, deformity, or loss of function occurs.

30. C: Changes in Health T: Application

1. Bisphosphonate medication, such as risendronate (Actonel), inhibits bone resorption and absorbs calcium phosphate crystal in bone. Bisphosphonates are "front-line" drugs in the treatment of osteoporosis. Calcium supplements

are required to increase available calcium to the bone.

2. Weight-bearing exercises are recommended for osteoporosis as they help strengthen muscles around the bone and increase the strength of the bones.

3. Vitamin D is needed for regulation of calcium. Recommended levels for women of Mrs. Cheng's age are 1000 IU or greater; 200 IU is not sufficient.

4. This is a premature recommendation. There is no indication that Mrs. Cheng may require any assistance with activities of daily living postrehabilitation.

31.   C: Changes in Health   T: Application

1. Symptoms for urinary tract infections may include dysuria, frequency of urination, urgency, and suprapubic discomfort or pressure.

2. Pyelonephritis may manifest with symptoms of cystitis, flank pain, fever, chills, vomiting, and malaise.

3. Nephrotic syndrome may manifest with peripheral edema, massive proteinuria, hyperlipidemia, and hypoalbuminemia.

4. Acute glomerulonephritis may present with a variety of signs and symptoms, including edema, hypertension, oliguria, hematuria, and proteinuria. Fluid retention is usually first found in the low-pressure tissues, such as those around the eyes. Acute poststreptococcal glomerulonephritis develops 5–21 days after an infection of the pharynx or skin by group A beta-hemolytic streptococci.

32.   C: Changes in Health   T: Application

1. Management for acute glomerulonephritis focuses on symptomatic relief. If Ms. Procinski has a high potassium level, she will be instructed to eat foods low in potassium and to stay away from foods high in potassium. In some instances, the client will be given Kayexalate to remove potassium from the body.

2. For all cases of glomerulonephritis, rest is recommended until the signs of the glomerular inflammation subside.

3. If Ms. Procinski is hypertensive, she may be started on a short-term course of antihypertensives.

4. Glomerulonephritis is an antigen antibody immune situation resulting from a previous infection. Antibiotics will not correct the glomerulonephritis, although some doctors do prescribe antibiotics prophylactically.

33.   C: Changes in Health   T: Application

1. Although this must be ruled out, a thoracic aneurysm does not usually present with pain.

2. All chest pain needs to have a cardiac cause ruled out, but angina does not usually worsen with inspiration.

3. A pulmonary embolus can cause severe chest pain that often mimics cardiac pain. The severity of the pain will depend on the size and location of the embolus. The history of a fall from a ladder is significant.

4. Hiatus hernias are most often asymptomatic, but if symptoms do occur, they are usually similar to GERD, with pyrosis or heartburn.

34.   C: Changes in Health   T: Critical Thinking

1. INR is used to measure warfarin (Coumadin) action in the body.

2. PTT is used to measure heparin action in the body.

3. PFA is used to detect platelet dysfunction.

4. PT is used to measure Coumadin action in the body.

35.   C: Changes in Health   T: Critical Thinking

1. Heparin should not be stopped until a therapeutic level of Coumadin is attained.

2. As in choice 1.

3. Five milligrams of Coumadin is an appropriate dose.

4. A therapeutic level of Coumadin must be attained before heparin is stopped to maintain anticoagulant blood levels.

36.   C: Changes in Health   T: Knowledge

1. This refers to adduction.

2. This is the definition of abduction.

3. This refers to external rotation.

4. This refers to internal rotation.

37.   C: Changes in Health   T: Application

1. Diminished or absent pedal, popliteal, or femoral pulses are frequently noted in clients with PAD due to obstruction of the artery.

2. The foot will become pale on elevation. Clients with PAD will have reddened feet when they are in a dependent position.

3. Lower leg edema may be seen in venous, not arterial, obstruction.

4. Assessment requires more than just a blood pressure at the thigh. Segmental blood pressures are taken at the thigh, below the knee, and at ankle level while the client is supine. A fall-off in segmental pressure of more than 30 mm Hg indicates PAD.

38.   C: Changes in Health   T: Application

1. Heating devices should not be used on the feet of clients with vascular problems as the client may not be able to feel a burn injury.
2. Support stockings are used for venous problems.
3. Walking promotes the development of collateral circulation.
4. Feet should be inspected daily for redness.

39.   C: Changes in Health   T: Critical Thinking

1. Arterial blood gases are used as a guide to determine what FiO_2 level is sufficient and can be tolerated. They are the most accurate guides for determining titration of oxygen to the client.
2. Oxygen saturation is valuable but does not provide information concerning CO_2 levels and pH.
3. The nurse must monitor vital signs and would assess for improving pulse and respiratory rates, but these are not accurate for determining appropriate FiO_2 levels.
4. If the client is receiving an appropriate level of FiO_2, the skin colour should improve. However, skin colour does not indicate if the client is receiving too much oxygen, which would place him at risk for oxygen toxicity.

40.   C: Professional Practice   T: Critical Thinking

1. The nurse is not the most knowledgeable health care professional to teach about home oxygen therapy. It is also likely that Mr. Sharapov will require continual support when he is at home.
2. This is an appropriate educational tool but is not as effective as a consultation with a respiratory therapist or technologist.
3. This is part of the role of the respiratory therapist or technologist. An in-home consultation will provide the best information and support for correct use of home oxygen therapy.
4. Mr. Sharapov will require follow-up pulse oximetry to determine if the supplemental oxygen is required and is being administered at the correct rate. It is not a strategy to assist Mr. Sharapov to manage the home oxygen.

41.   C: Changes in Health   T: Knowledge

1. These are manifestations of hypernatremia.
2. Severe diarrhea can lead to excessive loss of potassium. Hypokalemia can lead to rapid arrhythmias, which, in turn, can lead to a cardiac arrest. Other symptoms include muscle fatigue, weakness and leg cramps, nausea and vomiting, polyuritis, and hyperglycemia.
3. These are manifestations of hyperphosphatemia.
4. These are manifestations of hypocalcemia.

42.   C: Changes in Health   T: Application

1. The rectal packing helps stop bleeding in the perineal area. It should not be removed right after surgery unless it is saturated with serosanguinous drainage.
2. Feeding of any kind would not be established until peristalsis has returned and drainage appears in the ileostomy bag.
3. In the first 24–48 hours after surgery, the amount of drainage from the stoma may be negligible. An ileostomy causes a loss of absorptive functions provided by the colon. Once peristalsis returns, there may be a period of high-volume bilious output, up to 1200–1800 mL per day. Fluid and electrolyte imbalance is a potential problem.
4. The nasogastric tube would not be removed until peristalsis has returned.

43.   C: Changes in Health   T: Application

1. Clients are encouraged to cook fruits and vegetables and limit their amounts in the initial postoperative period as there is the potential for these foods to cause obstruction.
2. Beans and legumes are gas forming.
3. Eggs are odour producing.
4. Strong cheese is gas forming.

44.   C: Changes in Health   T: Application

1. There is no reason Mrs. O'Brien cannot have sharp utensils. The aide should help Mrs. O'Brien locate the utensils on the meal tray.
2. Mrs. O'Brien does not require finger foods. She is able to use utensils. Finger foods would be more appropriate for the person who has dementia and experiences difficulty managing a knife and fork.
3. At mealtime, Mrs. O'Brien can be oriented to her meal by comparing her plate to a clock. This visual image will help her easily locate each item of food.
4. There is no indication that Mrs. O'Brien needs assistance with eating. She just needs assistance in finding food she cannot see.

45.   C: Changes in Health   T: Application

1. The nurse could offer a stool softener to prevent constipation. Straining at stool increases intraocular pressure and must be avoided post–cataract surgery.
2. There is no need to either increase or decrease fluids after cataract surgery.
3. Some physicians may restrict showers after cataract surgery, but there is no contraindication to baths.
4. Mrs. O'Brien's right eye will likely be patched, making watching TV or reading difficult. However,

there are no contraindications to reading or watching TV provided that there are no rapid head or eye movements.

46.   C: Changes in Health   T: Critical Thinking

1. Although a thallium scan is helpful to determine the ejection fraction, this treatment can be done at a later time. It is not the priority.
2. Lorazepam (Ativan) may be ordered later to help settle the client, but it is not the priority of care.
3. Furosemide would be ordered to help reduce the fluid in the lungs, which is the cause of her shortness of breath. This is the priority of care. Other medications that may be used could include vasodilators, which open the vessels, decreasing the pressure and encouraging fluid to move out of the lungs.
4. Since her pulse is rapid and irregular, a cardioversion may be done, but only after an ECG confirms that the client is experiencing atrial fibrillation. The priority of care is removing the fluid from her lungs.

47.   C: Changes in Health   T: Application

1. A prone position would encourage fluid buildup in the lungs, which is what is causing her shortness of breath.
2. A semi-Fowler's position is not adequate to help decrease fluid buildup in the lungs. In this position, the legs are level with the sacrum and encourage fluid return from the lower limbs.
3. This position would simply magnify the shortness of breath while encouraging fluid return from the extremities.
4. A high Fowler's position, sitting upright with legs dependent, promotes fluid retention in the legs, decreasing the fluid return to the heart and keeping the fluid in the bases of the lungs.

48.   C: Changes in Health   T: Critical Thinking

1. The electrolytes will need to be monitored but will not significantly change as quickly as the blood pressure.
2. Although all assessments are important, the priority of care is blood pressure. Once Mrs. Gardner starts to diurese volume from the intravascular space, BP can decrease drastically and result in hypotension.
3. Hourly output tells the nurse how much volume the client is voiding, but the more important determination is the effect the decreased volume has on the lungs. The nurse would monitor lung sounds to evaluate the decrease in crackles, signifying the loss of fluid in the lungs.

4. Monitoring the respiratory rate is important as a decreased rate will indicate improvement. Mrs. Gardner may have clear lung fields but be hypotensive; therefore, blood pressure is the priority.

49.   C: Changes in Health   T: Knowledge

1. This is a manifestation of left-sided heart failure.
2. As in choice 1.
3. As in choice 1.
4. Fluid in the lungs is symptomatic of left-sided heart failure.

50.   C: Changes in Health   T: Application

1. Clients with gout, not renal failure, are encouraged to limit purine in their diet. Purine is found in red meat, particularly organ meat and shellfish.
2. Failing kidneys do not excrete potassium efficiently; thus, a renal diet is low in potassium. Potatoes and citrus fruit such as oranges, grapefruit, and strawberries are high in potassium and should be avoided.
3. Cookies and cake are high in calories and low in nutritive value. Mrs. Gardner will be allowed to eat these but will be encouraged to include more complex carbohydrates.
4. Mrs. Gardner may need to limit protein; however, protein is necessary for tissue repair and maintenance of the immune system.

51.   C: Changes in Health   T: Critical Thinking

1. This is a good strategy to provide immobilization to the neck injury and can be done while the guest is still in the pool. However, breathing is the priority.
2. This is a possibly appropriate first aid measure but is not as urgent as providing rescue breathing.
3. This is appropriate as people who have sustained a spinal cord injury while swimming should not be lifted out of the pool until there is experienced help. Moving the guest may cause further damage. However, it is not as important as breathing.
4. Spinal cord injuries above C3 may cause respiratory paralysis. The priority action must be to provide rescue breathing until the paramedics arrive.

52.   C: Nurse–Client Partnership   T: Critical Thinking

1. While this is true, it is in language that she may not understand.
2. This is true, but it does not answer Minh's question.
3. This describes the action and the rationale in language that Minh will be able to understand.
4. This is true but does not answer Minh's question.

53.   C: Changes in Health   T: Application

1. Sick sinus syndrome occurs when the sinoatrial node is damaged and not able to fire its regular rhythm. When this happens, an impulse is not initiated; therefore, no P, QRS, or T waves are produced. This creates a pause. If the cause cannot be found, a pacemaker will be needed to generate a steady rhythm.
2. A premature ventricular contraction is an ectopic beat originating in either the left or right ventricle. PVCs are caused by ventricular irritability due to such things as stress, drugs, hypoxia, hypokalemia, or MI. Treating the underlying cause is the most important intervention.
3. In atrial fibrillation, there is chaotic impulse formation, producing impulses at a rate of 400 or more per minute. An irregular ventricular response occurs as a result. When the ventricular response (rate) is less than 100 bpm, a pacemaker is not required.
4. First-degree heart block occurs when the conduction between the atrium and ventricle is prolonged. All impulses do get through; it just takes longer. Since every impulse gets through, a pacemaker is not needed.

54.   C: Nurse–Client Partnership   T: Critical Thinking

1. This is an encouraging but not helpful comment. The nurse cannot predict how fast his Parkinson's disease will progress or whether drugs will be effective.
2. This is the first step of the nursing process: data collection. The nurse needs to find out, by using an open-ended question, what Mr. Sanders has been told by the physician and whether Mr. Sanders understands what was discussed. Once the nurse has this information, she may gauge his level of readiness for clarification of information and teaching about the disease.
3. This is true, but it is not the appropriate response at this time. It may downplay Mr. Sanders' worries and may not invite dialogue between Mr. Sanders and the nurse.
4. While this may be an appropriate action in some situations, it is not likely to be helpful initially with Mr. Sanders. If Mr. Sanders indicates to the nurse that he is neither able nor willing to talk at present, then the nurse might offer to sit with him quietly.

55.   C: Changes in Health   T: Knowledge

1. Neurological symptoms do not develop until the anemia is severe. Then the client may experience headaches, vertigo, irritability, depression, or impaired thought processes.
2. Bradycardia is not a manifestation of anemia. Tachycardia and palpitations occur even in mild anemia as the body attempts to compensate for the decrease in oxygen in the blood.
3. The eyes and skin are not affected until the anemia is severe. Then the client may experience pallor, jaundice, pruritus, icteric conjunctiva and sclera, retinal hemorrhage, and blurred vision.
4. With anemia, the body must work hard to get what oxygen it has to all tissues. Clients frequently complain of weakness, malaise, and being unable to accomplish normal activities.

56.   C: Changes in Health   T: Knowledge

1. Hypermagnesemia usually occurs only in renal insufficiency or failure.
2. Hypocalcemia can be caused by any condition that results in a decrease in the production of parathyroid hormone. Diarrhea does not cause hypocalcemia.
3. Hypokalemia, or low potassium, can result from abnormal losses of potassium due to a shift of potassium from ECF to ICF or, rarely, from a dietary deficiency of potassium. The most common causes of hypokalemia are abnormal losses via either the kidneys or the GI tract.
4. Hypernatremia, or high sodium, can be caused by an increase in insensible water loss, such as in diabetes insipidus, or osmotic diuresis. Hypernatremia is not a result of diarrhea.

57.   C: Changes in Health   T: Application

1. Swallowing difficulties, or dysphagia, are a manifestation of esophageal cancer. When difficulty swallowing occurs in clients who have had strokes or dementia, a therapist will evaluate the swallowing and recommend appropriate interventions.
2. Pain in the epigastric area is a manifestation of peptic ulcer.
3. Pyrosis (heartburn) is the most common manifestation of GERD and can be soothed by antacid preparations prior to H_2 antagonist treatment.
4. Nausea and vomiting are not necessarily manifestations of GERD.

58.   C: Changes in Health   T: Critical Thinking

1. This is a priority for bleeding from esophageal varices, not peptic ulcer disease.
2. Establishing an IV line is important so the nurse has access to a vein if volume replacement is required. However, it is not the priority.
3. A nasogastric tube will be established, followed by saline or water lavages until the returns are clear and the bleeding has stopped.
4. In many situations, oxygen is the priority. However, in this situation, the priority is to stop the

bleeding. There is no indication that Mr. Tibor is in respiratory distress.

59.   C: Changes in Health   T: Knowledge

1. A high fever would be present only if perforation had occurred.
2. Diverticulitis usually develops because of constipation rather than diarrhea.
3. Abdominal pain is localized over the involved area of the colon, usually the sigmoid colon, not the epigastric area.
4. The cause of diverticulitis is related to the retention of stool and bacteria in the diverticulum, forming a hardened mass called a fecalith. This causes inflammation and possible small perforations that may become edematous. The majority of clients with diverticulitis do not have any symptoms. Diverticuli may occur at any point within the GI tract but are most commonly found in the sigmoid colon; thus, lower left quadrant pain would be present when pain is present.

60.   C: Changes in Health   T: Application

1. Initially, pain is found around the periumbilical area. As appendicitis worsens, the pain becomes persistent and shifts to the right lower quadrant, localizing at McBurney's point. Coughing aggravates the pain.
2. Esophageal reflux is not symptomatic of appendicitis.
3. Clients may or may not present with low-grade fever, not a high-grade fever.
4. Clients may present with a positive Rovsing's sign when palpation of the left lower quadrant causes pain to the right lower quadrant.

61.   C: Changes in Health   T: Knowledge

1. The liver does not store vitamin C or E, so these would not be affected by hepatitis.
2. Potassium levels are not affected by hepatitis.
3. The liver may not be able to produce prothrombin and other factors essential for blood clotting. Therefore, the prothrombin time may be prolonged.
4. Calcium is not stored in the liver.

62.   C: Changes in Health   T: Application

1. A high-fibre diet helps reduce fat absorption.
2. A high-fibre diet helps decrease the risk of constipation.
3. A high-fibre diet does not affect potassium absorption.
4. A high-fibre diet helps trap ammonia in the gut before it is absorbed into the bloodstream.

63.   C: Changes in Health   T: Critical Thinking

1. Postoperative pain should be expected.
2. Low-grade fever is expected.
3. Stridor is a serious finding as it could indicate that inflammation is compressing the trachea. Mr. Hawkins should be placed in a semi-Fowler's position to decrease edema and limit tension on the suture line.
4. Serosanguinous drainage is expected initially.

64.   C: Changes in Health   T: Knowledge

1. This is seen in Graves' disease or hyperthyroidism.
2. These are manifestations of diabetes insipidus.
3. These are manifestations of Cushing's syndrome.
4. These are manifestations of Addison's disease.

65.   C: Changes in Health   T: Knowledge

1. This describes tension-type headache.
2. This describes migraine headache.
3. This describes tension-type headache.
4. These are manifestations of cluster headaches.

66.   C: Changes in Health   T: Critical Thinking

1. He has recovered from the upper respiratory infection.
2. Guillain-Barré syndrome may cause respiratory paralysis.
3. This will be done but is not a priority.
4. This is an aspect of care but is not the priority.

67.   C: Changes in Health   T: Knowledge

1. Refers to receptive (Wernicke's) aphasia.
2. Refers to apraxia.
3. Refers to agnosia.
4. Refers to expressive (Broca's) aphasia.

68.   C: Nurse–Client Partnership   T: Application

1. This statement does not value Mrs. Tetrault's feelings or concerns.
2. This statement is not helping her grief or suggesting ways to help her. It may be interpreted as being patronizing.
3. This response acknowledges Mrs. Tetrault's concern and allows her to vent and question without being judged.
4. Although this statement acknowledges the concern, the nurse talks about herself, not focusing on the client.

69.   C: Changes in Health   T: Knowledge

1. Refers to possible GI upset such as gastroesophageal reflux disease (GERD). People with abdominal aortic aneurysm (AAA) do not usually complain of pain.
2. Refers to heartburn, experienced by clients with GERD.
3. Abdominal bruit is symptomatic of AAA.
4. Refers to a dissecting AAA.

70.   C: Changes in Health   T: Application

1. Mrs. Olsen is extremely lethargic and will not be able to drink enough fluids to bring the sodium level to within normal limits.
2. A 10% dextrose solution is a hypertonic solution that will draw fluid from the tissues and increase diuresis in an already dehydrated client.
3. Establishing an IV line of an isotonic solution will help rehydrate Mrs. Olsen and bring the hematocrit and sodium levels within their normal limits.
4. Inserting a nasogastric tube will not bring the sodium and hematocrit to within normal limits.

71.   C: Changes in Health   T: Knowledge

1. Adenocarcinomas are malignant tumours arising from glandular organs.
2. Basal cell carcinoma is the most common human cancer, a malignancy typically found on skin exposed to sun or other forms of ultraviolet light.
3. Mr. Ulrinski is also at risk for malignant melanoma. Although the incidence is increasing, it is not as common as basal cell carcinoma.
4. Spongioblastoma is a glioma of the brain (a neoplasm or tumour composed of neuroglial cells) derived from spongioblasts.

72.   C: Changes in Health   T: Critical Thinking

1. Pap tests will discover abnormal cells but will not prevent cancer of the cervix.
2. Colposcopy will aid in diagnosis of cancer of the cervix but will not prevent it.
3. The HPV vaccine protects against human papillomavirus, which is considered to be the major causative factor in the development of cancer of the cervix.
4. Warts can be removed with lasers, but this is not preventative.

73.   C: Changes in Health   T: Application

1. Weight-bearing exercises are recommended for osteoporosis. Swimming is not a weight-bearing exercise.
2. The best exercises for osteoporosis are weight-bearing ones. Ms. Blinker will be able to walk using her walker.
3. While aerobics are beneficial for older adults for increased muscle strength, coordination, and osteoporosis, it is unlikely that if Ms. Blinker requires a walker, she would be able to participate in aerobic exercise.
4. This is not a weight-bearing exercise.

74.   C: Changes in Health   T: Application

1. Multiple sclerosis is a chronic, progressive, degenerative disorder of the CNS characterized by disseminated demyelination of nerve fibres of the brain and spinal cord. The initial manifestations are often vague and inconsistent but include sensory disturbances such as blurred vision and tinnitus.
2. Refers to Parkinson's disease.
3. Refers to myasthenia gravis.
4. Refers to restless legs syndrome.

75.   C: Changes in Health   T: Critical Thinking

1. Headache is common after a head injury and is not necessarily an urgent concern.
2. Vomiting is a sign of increased intracranial pressure, which must be immediately treated.
3. Tinnitus, or ringing in the ears, may occur after a head injury but is not necessarily an urgent concern.
4. Diplopia, or double vision, may occur after a head injury but is not necessarily an urgent concern.

76.   C: Changes in Health   T: Knowledge

1. This is the definition of a shallow partial-thickness, or superficial, burn.
2. This is the definition of a deep partial-thickness burn.
3. This is the correct definition of a partial full-thickness burn.
4. This is the definition of a deep full-thickness burn.

77.   C: Nurse–Client Partnership   T: Application

1. This is not the most therapeutic response as it directs Mrs. Raiza to go back to the physician and does not address her question.
2. This is true but may close off the conversation and not be therapeutic in assisting Raiza to come to a decision.
3. This is not a therapeutic answer.
4. This response invites dialogue with Mrs. Raiza. She may need more information about her options. The nurse would have the opportunity to clarify and expand on Mrs. Raiza's knowledge, which will help her choose a treatment.

78.   **C: Changes in Health   T: Application**

1. This is a component of postsurgical care and is not directly related to the manifestations of abdominal pain and distension.
2. Post-TURP with continuous bladder irrigation, it is common for blood clots to block the catheter, requiring the nurse to flush the catheter.
3. The catheter is likely blocked by clots. Decreasing the flow will not solve this problem.
4. The physician does not need to be notified unless flushing does not solve the problem.

79.   **C: Changes in Health   T: Application**

1. Feeling tired is a normal after-effect of any type of surgery.
2. Trans-sphenoidal surgery is performed through the nose and the sphenoid sinus in order to easily access the pituitary gland. Avoidance of sneezing, coughing, or nose-blowing helps heal the internal incision site.
3. The incision site is inside the nose, not the cranium.
4. This would be a worry if the clear fluid, cerebrospinal fluid, were dripping from the nose, not the ear.

80.   **C: Changes in Health   T: Application**

1. As death approaches, the skin becomes cool, clammy, and mottled due to diminished circulation.
2. Respirations are often rapid and shallow, progressing to Cheyne-Stokes respirations.
3. The pulse becomes weak, but the rate does not increase.
4. Although the skin feels cool to touch, body temperature often increases prior to death.

Chapter 9

Maternal—Newborn Nursing

Christine Barbetta, RN, BScN

In a woman's life, and within her family experiences, pregnancy and giving birth are profound, life-changing events influenced by many factors. These factors include the woman's health and well-being; her life experiences, beliefs, and culture; and the diverse Canadian society in which she lives. Family-centred maternal–newborn nursing reflects an evidence-informed practice that respects pregnancy and childbirth as a normal physiological event unique to each woman and her family.

This approach also acknowledges the complexity of the childbirth experience and the potential for health and social complications. Nurses respond by providing care through a collaborative relationship that is founded on respect and adaptation to the varied and changing needs of the family.

WELL-WOMAN CARE: HEALTH IN THE CHILD-BEARING YEARS

Although the child-bearing years begin with the onset of puberty and sexual maturation, a woman's lifetime supply of immature eggs is present in the ovaries at the time of her own birth. Puberty and menarche represent not only a time of rapid and multiple physical changes but also psychological and social development. Throughout a woman's child-bearing years, many health, societal, and personal issues will influence her decisions regarding sexual and reproductive choices and the lifestyle she chooses to live. Nurses need to consider the determinants of health within Canadian society, which also have an important influence on women's reproductive health and well-being.

PUBERTY

Physical sexual maturity and reproductive potential begin when the primary and secondary sexual characteristics develop during puberty in response to neuroendocrine hormonal changes. The timing of puberty varies widely, beginning about two years earlier for girls than for boys. For both, puberty is usually completed by the mid- to late teens. The psychological and cognitive developmental stages of adolescence also greatly affect an individual's identity and relationships with peers and family.

Female Manifestations

Between the ages of 8 and 14, the maturing brain begins to produce and secrete hormones that stimulate the ovaries and uterus of the young girl to mature in preparation for potential pregnancy. Growth hormones are also produced, which, over three to four years, bring about the characteristic physical changes in appearance and size that announce the transition from childhood into adolescence and early adulthood. These changes include the following:

- Reproductive changes – The uterus, ovaries, and vagina increase in size and blood supply, and hormones stimulate maturation of an ovum each month at the time of menarche. Menstruation may be irregular for the first year or two, and the first few menstrual cycles may be anovulatory (infertile).
- Ovulation marks the onset of fertility.
- Secondary sexual characteristics develop – Growth of pubic, leg, and axillae hair; breast development and growth; subcutaneous fat stores with characteristic curves and softness to body shape; sweat gland activity increases; and facial acne may develop.
- Skeletal changes – The pelvis widens, and there is sudden skeletal growth, with adult height typically reached at 2–2½ years after menarche.

Male Manifestations

Between the ages of 13 and 15, the maturing brain stimulates a marked increase in the production of androgens, the male sex hormones, especially testosterone. In boys, this stimulates the following changes:

- Reproductive changes – Testosterone stimulates sexual interest, the production of sperm, and the growth and maturation of the penis, scrotum, testes, prostate gland, and seminal vesicles. Onset of fertility begins with ejaculation of mature sperm and continues throughout life, with new sperm formed about every 10 weeks.
- Testosterone also stimulates rapid skeletal bone growth in length and bone density that continues until almost 18 or 20 years of age, widening of the shoulders, increased cellular metabolism, and increased red blood cell production.
- Secondary sex characteristics – Increased body hair on the face, chest, axillae, and pubic area; thickening of the vocal cords and deepening of the voice; enlargement and thickening of the muscles; and increased sebaceous gland activity and acne formation

Nursing Considerations

There are many important nursing considerations in regard to these developmental stages. These considerations include the following:

- Provide factual, nonjudgemental information.
- Be aware that teenagers may obtain inaccurate information from peers and be reluctant to discuss their concerns with adults.
- Recognize that both girls and boys may have body-image conflicts as they naturally gain weight and experience body changes.
- Offer reassurance and clarification of normal variations in puberty changes.

Chapter 10, pages 455–456, has more detailed information on adolescent growth and development.

THE MENSTRUAL CYCLE

The female reproductive cycle begins at puberty and ends at menopause. It is composed of the ovarian and endometrial cycles or phases, which are influenced by hormones released by the brain. All work in unison in preparation for a potential pregnancy. If pregnancy does not occur, hormone levels decrease, menstruation occurs, and the cycle repeats. A cycle typically lasts 28 days, plus or minus five days, but may vary and last as long as 38 days. See Figure 9.1 for an illustration of the female cycle.

The Ovarian Cycle

Follicular Phase

The follicular phase of the cycle occurs in the following sequence:

- The follicular phase occurs in the first half of the cycle, approximately 14 days prior to ovulation. In women who experience irregular menstrual cycles, the follicular phase varies in length.
- The anterior pituitary in the brain releases follicle-stimulating hormone (FSH) and luteinizing hormone (LH). FSH stimulates the ovarian follicle, and the immature oocyte grows. As the follicle matures, it releases estrogen. LH stimulates the final maturation of the follicle just prior to ovulation. A mature graafian follicle develops by the midpoint of the cycle under the influence of both FSH and LH.
- Under the influence of progesterone, body temperature increases 0.3°C to 0.6°C for 24–48 hr after the time of ovulation and remains elevated until menstruation begins.
- Ovulation usually occurs on the fourteenth day or midpoint of the cycle; the follicle ruptures, and the mature ovum is released.

Luteal Phase

The luteal phase of the cycle occurs in the following sequence:

- The luteal phase begins when the ovum leaves the follicle, which occurs between day 15 and day 28 of a 28-day cycle.
- LH influences the development of the corpus luteum from the ruptured follicle. As it reaches a peak, estrogen levels drop, and progesterone secretion begins.
- When fertilization occurs, the corpus luteum is maintained until weeks 10–12 of the pregnancy; it secretes human chorionic gonadotropin (HCG), estrogen, and progesterone to maintain the pregnancy until the placenta is mature.
- If fertilization does not occur, the corpus luteum degenerates, causing a decrease in estrogen and progesterone hormone levels, and menstruation follows by day 28 of the cycle.

The Endometrial Cycle

The Menstrual Phase

The menstrual phase of the cycle occurs in the following sequence:

- The menstrual phase occurs during days 1–5, when estrogen and progesterone levels are low.
- Menstrual discharge or uterine blood loss is dark red and may contain small clots.

The Proliferative Phase

The proliferative phase of the cycle occurs in the following sequence:

- On days 7–14, the proliferative phase of the endometrium corresponds to the follicular phase of the ovary.
- Estrogen causes the endometrial lining of the uterus to thicken in anticipation of the implantation of a fertilized ovum, and the cervical mucus becomes more hospitable to sperm: clear, thin, elastic, and alkaline.
- Mittelschmertz (midcycle abdominal pain), midcycle spotting, or both may occur as the ovum is released from the follicle at the time of ovulation.

The Secretory Phase

The secretory phase of the cycle occurs in the following sequence:

- The secretory phase occurs on days 15–26, corresponding to the luteal phase of the ovary.
- Estrogen decreases as progesterone levels remain high and the vascularity of the endometrium and uterus increases. If fertilization and implantation occur, the endometrium remains thickened and continues to develop.

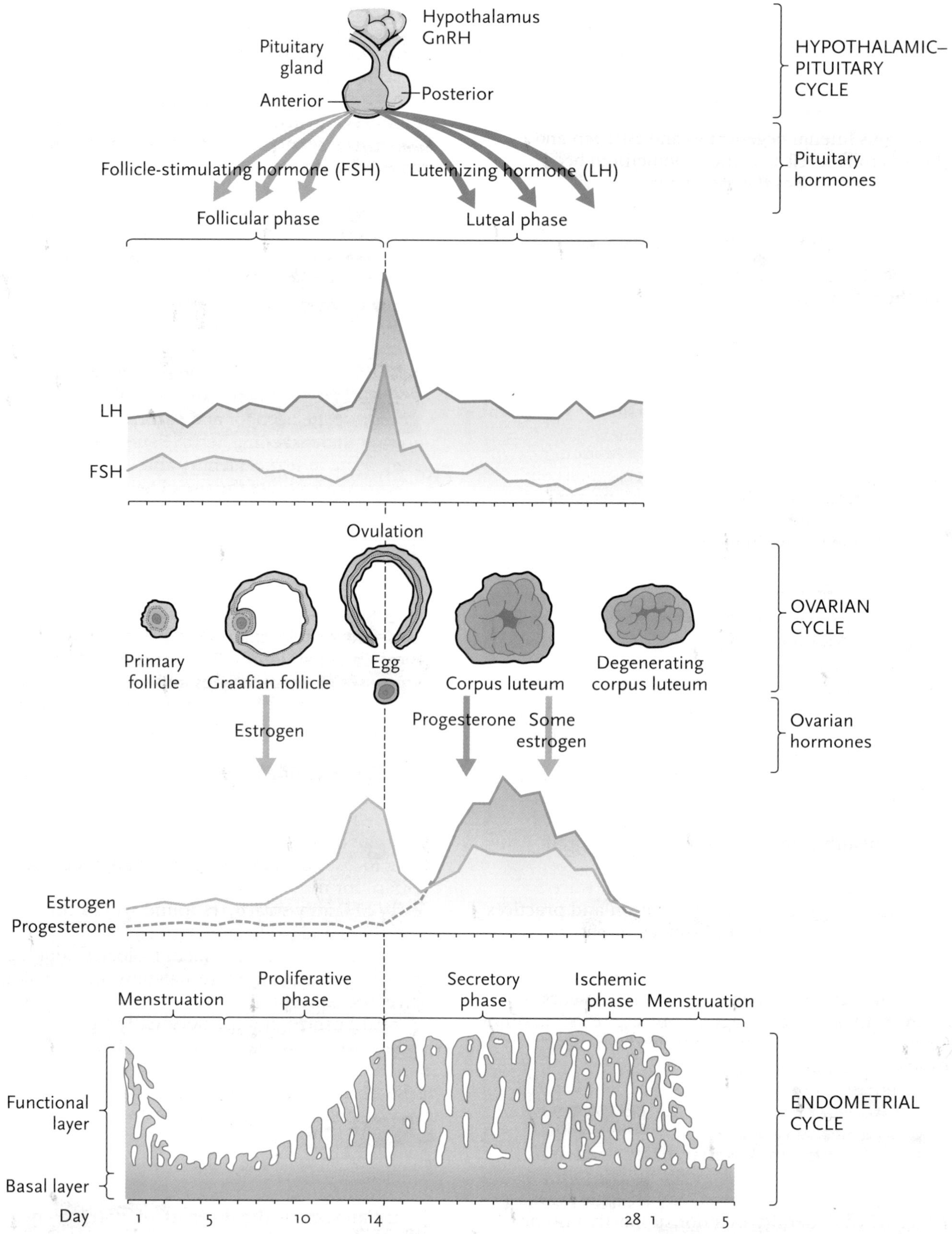
Hypothalamus
GnRH
Pituitary gland
Anterior
Posterior
HYPOTHALAMIC–PITUITARY CYCLE
Follicle-stimulating hormone (FSH)
Luteinizing hormone (LH)
Pituitary hormones
Follicular phase
Luteal phase
LH
FSH
Ovulation
Primary follicle
Graafian follicle
Egg
Corpus luteum
Degenerating corpus luteum
OVARIAN CYCLE
Estrogen
Progesterone
Some estrogen
Ovarian hormones
Estrogen
Progesterone
Menstruation
Proliferative phase
Secretory phase
Ischemic phase
Menstruation
Functional layer
Basal layer
ENDOMETRIAL CYCLE
Day
1
5
10
14
28
1
5

FIGURE 9.1 **The Menstrual Cycle: Hypothalamic–Pituitary, Ovarian, and Endometrial Cycles**

Source: Lowdermilk, D. L., Perry, S. E., Cashion, K., & Alden, K. R. (2012). *Maternity & women's health care* (10th ed., p. 68, Figure 4-7). St. Louis: Mosby.

The Ischemic Phase

The ischemic phase of the cycle occurs in the following sequence:

- On days 27 to 28, if fertilization does not occur, the corpus luteum degenerates and estrogen and progesterone levels fall. The endometrium becomes ischemic and pale as the vasculature constricts.

Nursing Considerations

Nursing considerations with regard to these stages include the following:

- Be aware of and sensitive to religious and cultural beliefs that may affect practices and behaviours at the time of menstruation.
- Basal body temperature and cervical mucus changes may be used in predicting ovulation.
- Include in health promotion teaching caution regarding the use of super-absorbent tampons and their association with the rare but serious condition of toxic shock syndrome.
- The best time for teaching and performing breast self-examination is following the menstrual phase, when hormonal levels are lowest.

LESBIAN HEALTH ISSUES

It is estimated that about 5–10% of women are self-described as being lesbian, gay, or homosexual. While women's health in general has gradually become an area of increasing research and interest, it is important for nurses to recognize that societal prejudice against a woman's sexual orientation may result in health concerns that are not well recognized or addressed within the health care community and professions. These issues may include the following:

Societal Bias and Discrimination: Disclosure to health professionals of sexual orientation and practices may be avoided out of fear of hostility or past negative experiences following disclosure of such information.

Routine Screening: About 15% of lesbian women avoid mammograms, Papanicolaou (Pap) smears, breast examinations, and regular physical examinations because they fear prejudicial attitudes from health care providers (Davis, 2000).

Health History and Assessment: While over 90% of lesbian women reported that they believed it was important for health care professionals to know their sexual orientation, less than half provided this information (Davis, 2000).

Adolescent Lesbians: Teens may struggle with and hide their sexual identity in a nonsupportive home or health environment. Mental health issues may be heightened; there is an increased risk for attempted suicide and intentional pregnancies to mask sexual identity, as well as emotional distress and a sense of isolation (Davis, 2000).

Pregnancy and Children: Many lesbian families include children through adoption, through donor insemination, or from previous heterosexual relationships. However, lesbians may be less likely to attempt to conceive due to a lack of societal or health-community support.

Assault and Sexual Abuse: Lesbians are at increased risk for antigay violence and verbal abuse. As with women in general, almost 40% of lesbians report a history of childhood sexual abuse (Davis, 2000).

Nursing Considerations

There are many nursing considerations in regard to these sensitive issues, including the following:

- Examine and be aware of your personal beliefs and prejudices regarding sexual orientation.
- Recognize the need for and participate in education toward understanding health issues and concerns as they relate to sexual identity and orientation.
- Obtain and promote the use of health histories that acknowledge sexual orientation in a language and format that is inclusive and bias-free.

CANADIAN FAMILIES

No one definition or example can accurately describe a typical Canadian family. The concept of "family" encompasses many meanings and values, some of which are influenced by social circumstances, ethnicity, culture, and the belief systems of each family unit. In the 2006 Canadian census, more than 200 ethnic origins were identified. Defining a "family" within a legal framework has also been a subject of intense societal debate and court challenges.

Despite these challenges, maternal–newborn nursing focuses on a family-centred approach. It is important for nurses to recognize and respect the diversity of family structures found within their communities and professional practices.

In addition to the traditional biological and legal definitions of family, in maternal–newborn nursing practice, the concept of family is identified by the social relationships that are personally significant and important to the woman. Understanding family within a framework that is broad and inclusive reflects an attitude of respect and responsiveness to the unique needs and structure of each family.

FAMILY DIVERSITY

In Canadian society, the diversity of maternal–newborn families is influenced by many factors, including culture, ethnicity, race, language, socioeconomic status, maternal age, delayed child-bearing trends, employment of women outside the family home, social supports, community resources, and isolation from extended families and support (Health Canada, 2000c). Refer to the definitions in Box 9.1, which capture this diversity of family forms in Canada.

Box 9.1 Family Forms

Nuclear Family: A nuclear family consists of two parents (married or common-law) and their children.

Extended Family: The extended family includes the nuclear family and other relatives (perhaps grandparents, aunts, uncles, cousins).

Step Family: The step family is formed when at least one child in a household is from a previous relationship of one of the parents.

Blended Family: The blended family is formed when both parents bring children from previous relationships into a new, joint living situation, or when there are children from both the current union and previous unions living together.

Lone-Parent Family: The lone-parent family consists of one parent (either father or mother) and one or more children. The lone-parent family is formed when one parent leaves the nuclear family because of death, divorce, or desertion, or when a single person decides to have or adopt a child.

Other Family Forms: These relationships include married and common-law couples without children, "skip-generation" families (grandparents caring for grandchildren), "non-families" (adults living alone), and homosexual couples (with or without children).

Source: Potter, P. A., Perry, A. G., Ross-Kerr, J. C., & Wood, M. (Eds.). (2010). *Canadian fundamentals of nursing* (Revised 4th ed., p. 277, Box 20-1). Toronto: Elsevier.

PRINCIPLES OF PROVIDING FAMILY-CENTRED CARE

Health Canada's principles of family-centred care (Health Canada, 2000c) include the following:

- Pregnancy and birth is usually a normal healthy process and a unique experience for each woman and her family.
- Care is based on research evidence and directed at maximizing the probability of a healthy woman giving birth to a healthy baby.
- Relationships between health care professionals, women, and their families are based on mutual respect and trust. Women are cared for within the context of their families, and within the childbirth experience, a woman defines her family and support system.
- To make informed choices, women and their families need knowledge about their care.
- Women have autonomy in decision-making and are empowered to take responsibility.

- Health care professionals have a powerful effect on women who are giving birth and their families. A woman's subjective experience is included in assessing the quality of care.
- Family-centred care includes many disciplines of practice, including registered nurses, midwives, physicians, doulas, and childbirth educators.
- Technology is used judiciously and appropriately and does not replace direct supportive care and observation.
- Language is important and should ease communication by conveying openness and appreciation for the importance of families (Health Canada, 2000c).

FAMILY COMPOSITION AND CHILDBIRTH TRENDS

National and regional trends in family composition and childbirth practices are relevant to maternal–newborn nursing as they influence the required resources, choices, needs, and even expectations of women and their families. The health care system and nurses who provide direct care must recognize and respond to the many significant changes taking place in Canadian families.

CHANGES IN CANADIAN FAMILIES

Factors Influencing Canadian Families

Fewer Babies Across the Country: The annual number of births continues to decline.

Delayed Motherhood: By 2003, nearly 50% of first-time mothers were aged 30 or older. The number of women giving birth after the age of 40 has increased by 53%. An exception to this trend is First Nations women, who tend to give birth at younger ages than the rest of the population (Canadian Council on Social Development [CCSD], 2006; Government of Canada, 2003).

Smaller Families: Large families are now rare; the number of families with three or more children has decreased. In addition, families have on average 1.8 children at home (CCSD, 2006).

Fewer Marriages and Divorces: Since 1994, the number of marriages has decreased by about 9%; divorces have decreased by about 10%. The number of Canadians who get married once by the age of 50 has decreased from 65% of men and women in 1981 to a rate of 51% of women and less than 50% of men in 2001 (CCSD, 2006).

More Common-Law and Blended Families: There are more than four times as many common-law families in Canada as there were 20 years ago. Younger children are more likely to live with common-law parents, especially in Quebec. Six percent of Canadian children under the age of 12 lived in blended families in 2000 (CCSD, 2006).

Same-Sex Families: It is estimated, and some say underestimated, that 0.5% (34,000) of the population is made up of same-sex couples. Three thousand of these families are raising children (CCSD, 2006).

More Lone Parents Raising Children: Twenty-seven percent of all Canadian families are lone-parent families, compared with 11% in 1961. Women head eighty-one percent of these families. Male lone-parent families are also increasing (CCSD, 2006).

Child Custody Arrangements: Increasingly, the courts are awarding joint-custody arrangements. Mothers are awarded custody more often in Quebec, Ontario, and British Columbia (CCSD, 2006).

Parental Employment: Increasing numbers of mothers participate in the workforce, especially those with young children under the age of 6. The proportion of employed women with children under the age of 16 has increased to 72%, and most of them work full time (CCSD, 2006).

Aboriginal Families: Half of Canada's Aboriginal population is under the age of 25, compared with about one-third of the rest of the Canadian population. The birth rate per thousand in Nunavut is more than double that of all the other Canadian provinces and territories (Statistics Canada, 2008). The size of the Aboriginal youth population living in urban areas, especially in western Canada, has more than doubled in the last 20 years. More Aboriginal children live in lone-parent or multiple-family households than do other Canadian children (Statistics Canada, 2008).

CHILDBIRTH CHOICES AND TRENDS

Within the philosophy of family-centred care, families have many options and decisions to make when planning for prenatal care, the birth of the baby, and the family's postpartum transition. These plans include the following:

- Prenatal education and birth preferences – Community or private classes and programs, specialized programs such as Lamaze, breathing techniques, hypnosis, therapeutic touch, acupuncture, medication and pain control options and preferences
- Family participation – Identifying participants and their roles at each stage of the birth experience, attendance of the father or other support persons at childbirth classes and during labour and birth, the involvement of siblings and extended family members
- Health care setting – Deciding upon home birth, a birthing centre, a community hospital, or a high-risk pregnancy hospital
- Health care providers and support – Doula, registered or nonregistered midwife, family general practitioner, obstetrician, registered nurses, lactation consultant
- Postpartum – Breast- or formula feeding, circumcision, early-discharge programs, in-home support and community follow-up, newborn and maternal assessment, family involvement

Nursing Considerations

Nursing considerations are many and include the following:

- Provide information on available pregnancy and birth choices in the community.
- Refer as appropriate to community and hospital resources.
- Consider and respect cultural beliefs and preferences when discussing choices with families.
- Recognize that when families are provided with current, accurate information regarding choices, they are the experts at understanding which options will best fit their beliefs, preferences, and needs.
- Provide counselling and support to families whose personal birth plans may require adaptation due to the need for specialized care or medical intervention.

MIDWIFERY

Historically, midwifery has a long and respected role as a childbirth option for families. Midwives, often working in teams of two, provide holistic care for the woman and family throughout the pregnancy and birth process. Birth options may include hospital, clinic, or home-birth settings. Postpartum care and support is an integral part of midwifery practice.

Access to regulated midwifery care varies across Canada as some provinces now offer publicly funded, legislated midwifery services, while other provinces and territories continue to study the issues and logistics of formally recognizing and regulating midwifery practice. Despite the growing demand for this childbirth option, there continues to be a lack of midwifery care available in some communities, and there are waiting lists in many communities that do provide this option. The Canadian Association of Midwives (CAM) and various provincial groups continue to be active in raising public awareness and lobbying governments to provide this option to all Canadian families.

- Midwives collaborate with other health care professionals, including nurses, as appropriate and as indicated by the needs of the mothers and families they care for.
- Ontario was the first province in 1994 to regulate and publicly fund midwives. Midwives are legislated under the *Regulated Health Professions Act* (RHPA).
- Midwifery as a legislated and regulated profession is currently available to families in British Columbia, Alberta, Saskatchewan, Manitoba, Ontario, Quebec, Nova Scotia, Newfoundland, and the Northwest Territories (CAM, 2012).
- The National Aboriginal Health Organization (NAHO) continues to lobby for Aboriginal midwifery to be recognized and supported as a safe and culturally sensitive birth option with a long and respected history within the Aboriginal community (NAHO, 2012).
- In some parts of Canada, Aboriginal midwives, trained in community-based programs, are exempt from midwifery regulations (NAHO, 2012).

ACCESS TO CARE: REGIONALIZATION

Regionalization of care refers to the coordination of the many facilities and professional services needed to provide optimal maternal–newborn care to families. Regions are catchment areas within defined geographical boundaries that are structured to provide all the necessary maternal–newborn services required for both uncomplicated and high-risk births. The provision of comprehensive services may be affected by challenges such as geography, funding constraints, and the availability of health care professionals. Despite these challenges, advantages to regionalization include lower maternal and newborn morbidity and mortality rates, improved reproductive outcomes, and more efficient, economical utilization of facilities and personnel. Regionalization uses the principles of risk assessment and referral to provide access to the care that is appropriate to the needs of the mother, baby, and family at a location that is as close to their home as possible.

THE GOALS OF REGIONALIZATION

The goals of regionalization are as follows:

- The provision of quality care for all women, newborns, and their families (preconception, pregnancy, birth, postpartum, newborn) and the provision of referral mechanisms
- The coordination of services, the appropriate use of personnel and facilities, the provision of professional education, and the incorporation of research and evaluation (Health Canada, 2000c)

REGIONAL CARE LEVELS

Three levels of care are directed at ambulatory prenatal care, labour and birth, and postpartum and newborn care.

Primary Level: Level 1

The primary level of care includes the following:

- Eighty-five percent of pregnancies, identified as uncomplicated normal, including healthy mothers and newborns, of a pregnancy or gestational age of 36 weeks or older, and newborns weighing more than 2.5 kg
- Facility and personnel are able to provide assessment, education, and monitoring of normal pregnancies, as well as identification of at-risk pregnancies with appropriate referrals.
- Able to provide and manage immediate care for emergency maternal and newborn complications, including stabilization until support from and transportation to a level 2 or 3 facility are possible (Health Canada, 2000c)

Secondary Level: Level 2

The secondary level of care includes the following:

- Twelve percent of pregnancies, identified as low to moderate obstetrical or neonatal risk
- Mothers with pregnancy greater than 32 weeks and newborns with gestational age greater than 32 weeks and weighing more than 1.5 kg
- Intensive care services available for mother with obstetrical risks and complications. Able to provide short-term (48 hr) assisted ventilation to newborns.
- Able to provide immediate and ongoing care of newborns with problems expected to resolve quickly, as well as care of stabilized newborns transferred from level 3 facilities
- Availability of neonatology expertise and follow-up in the form of neonatologists and advanced practice clinical nurse specialists (Health Canada, 2000c)

Tertiary Level: Level 3

The tertiary level of care includes the following:

- Three percent of pregnancies
- Provides level 1 and 2 services and also manages and provides all services required for very high-risk, complicated pregnancies, births, and newborns
- Includes intensive care services under the direction of neonatologists and advanced practice clinical nurse specialists, as well as specialized services and resources, including advanced diagnostics, specialty consultations, surgery, and follow-up care (Health Canada, 2000c)

FERTILITY CONTROL AND INFERTILITY HEALTH CHALLENGES

FERTILITY CONTROL

More than any other time in history, women today have many options by which they can exercise control over the planning and prevention of pregnancies. Men, too, share in the responsibility for fertility control. Despite this, Canadian statistics show that even in stable relationships, 45–50% of pregnancies are unplanned. In Canada, teenagers 14 years of age and older can obtain prescription birth control without parental consent (Picard & Cullen, 2005).

Each contraceptive method has associated advantages and disadvantages, and its success at preventing pregnancy varies. Birth control methods are most effective when used consistently and correctly all the time. Only total sexual abstinence is 100% effective in preventing pregnancy and the transmission of sexually transmitted infections (STIs). In educating women in making a choice of the best contraceptive method, several considerations must be taken into account. These considerations include the following:

- Key client teaching points:

  - Most birth control methods *do not* offer protection from STIs such as human immunodeficiency virus (HIV), *Chlamydia*, herpes, or gonorrhea. The use of a male condom, known as dual protection, is recommended in addition to the primary method of birth control.
  - Emergency hormonal contraceptive is available in Canada from a pharmacist without a medical pre-scription. It must be taken within 72 hours of unprotected sexual intercourse (Dunn & Guilbert, 2003).
  - Breastfeeding is *not* a reliable method of birth control unless accurately using the Lactational Amenorrhea Method (LAM). LAM is not recommended in North America because most breastfeeding mothers do not maintain the required feeding patterns.

- The woman's overall health status, sexual patterns and frequency, the number of sexual partners, if children are desired in the future, effectiveness, potential side effects and risks, and financial costs and availability
- Ease of use and comfort level with using the method
- Cultural beliefs and religious practices that may limit acceptable birth control options

COMMON METHODS OF CONTRACEPTION AND NURSING CONSIDERATIONS

Fertility Awareness Methods

- Sexual intercourse is avoided on the seventh day or later, when a woman with regular menstrual cycles is fertile.
- Awareness, knowledge, and careful monitoring of menstrual patterns, cervical mucus changes, and basal body temperature changes are required. Effectiveness can be 80% when used with considerable knowledge, motivation, and consistency.

Male Condoms

- Male condoms can be purchased without a prescription; this is a barrier method that blocks the sperm from reaching the ovum and protects against HIV and STIs.
- Effectiveness is 85–98%, depending on correct use and early application during sexual activity. Condoms are most effective when used with a vaginal spermicide.
- Oil- and petroleum-based lubricants can cause latex to break down, resulting in the condom tearing or breaking. Only water-soluble lubricants should be used if needed. Condoms should be made from latex or polyurethane; animal- or natural-product condoms have micro-openings that can allow HIV to be transmitted.

Female Condoms

- Effectiveness is 80–90% with this barrier method.
- Female condoms can be inserted up to 24 hours in advance of sexual intercourse; they offer protection against HIV and STIs.

Oral Contraceptives

- Oral contraceptives are commonly known as "the pill" and are taken daily. The pill contains the hormones estrogen and progestin, which suppress the release of the ovum. Effectiveness is 95–99%. The pill does not protect against HIV and STIs.
- Extended-cycle pills containing levonorgestrel/ethinylestradiol were approved in July 2007 by Health Canada and are taken for 12 consecutive weeks followed by one week of nonhormonal pills. This limits menstruation to four cycles per year, which can help manage endometriosis.
- Some antibiotics may interfere with effectiveness. Women who are prescribed antibiotics should be advised to use an additional method of birth control.
- In the province of Quebec, school and community health nurses may prescribe oral contraceptives to teenagers without a medical prescription or parental consent (Picard & Cullen, 2005).
- Women over 35 years of age or who smoke may be advised to choose an alternative method of birth control to minimize the known risks of high blood pressure, blood clots, and arterial blockage. The pill may be contraindicated in women with a history of blood clots or breast, liver, or endometrial cancers.

The "Mini" Oral Contraceptive

- The "mini-pill" contains only the hormone progestin and acts by thickening the cervical mucus so that sperm cannot reach the egg. In addition, if the egg does become fertilized, it is prevented from implanting in the uterine wall.
- The mini-pill may be an option for those women who cannot take estrogen-based contraceptives.
- Effectiveness is 92–99%, but only if taken at the same time each day.

Intrauterine Devices (IUDs)

- The device is placed inside the uterus, preventing sperm from reaching the egg, the implantation of the fertilized egg, or both. The device may use copper or the hormone progesterone as an active ingredient to prevent pregnancy.
- Effectiveness is 98–99%. The device must be replaced every year or every several years.

Depo-Provera

- This is an injection of the hormone progestin given every three months. Its effectiveness is 97%.
- Use of Depo-Provera is limited to two years due to a temporary side effect of bone-density loss.

Diaphragm, Cervical Cap

- These are barrier methods, used with spermicidal gel or foam prior to sexual intercourse. Both must be properly fitted to cover the cervix; if used correctly, they can be 85–91% effective.
- They must be left in place 6–8 hr after intercourse to prevent pregnancy and be removed no later than 24 hr after intercourse.

Surgical Sterilization

- Tubal ligation prevents the egg from reaching the fallopian tube and uterus and is a permanent method of birth control with 99.9% effectiveness.
- Vasectomy, with 99% permanent effectiveness, involves ligation, the removal of a piece of the vas deferens, or both, thereby eliminating sperm from the semen.

Emergency Contraception

- Emergency contraception is also referred to as the "morning-after pill." Hormones interfere with ovulation, and possibly implantation, preventing pregnancy from occurring. This pill can be used up to 72 hours after unprotected intercourse or contraceptive failure such as a broken condom, providing 75% effectiveness.
- This contraception is sold in Canada under the name "Plan B" and is available from pharmacists without a medical prescription.
- This pill does not prevent the transmission of HIV or STIs.
- Side effects may include nausea, vomiting, irregular vaginal bleeding, fatigue, headache, breast tenderness, and dizziness (Dunn & Guilbert, 2003).

PREGNANCY TERMINATION THROUGH INDUCED ABORTION

While induced abortions are legal in Canada and many countries in the world, they continue to be a source of controversy among those with strongly opposing views based on moral, religious, and ethical beliefs. Pregnancies may be ended by medical or surgical means depending on the gestational age, with the majority occurring in the first trimester of pregnancy. Factors influencing a woman's decision to choose to have an abortion may include the following:

- Contraceptive failure
- Diseases or a life-threatening medical condition affecting the mother or fetus
- Psychosocial factors, including distress due to the timing and circumstances of the pregnancy

Medical Abortion

Medical abortions are currently offered in the United States but are not available in Canada.

- Used during the first seven weeks of pregnancy, mifepristone, formerly known as RU-486, is administered in pill form during a medical office visit, followed two days later by an oral dose of the prostaglandin misoprostol.
- Mifepristone blocks the action of progesterone, making the endometrium unviable to a pregnancy. Prostaglandins administered orally or vaginally are used to induce contractions, causing expulsion of the embryo or fetus.

Surgical Abortion

- First trimester surgical methods include dilatation and curettage (D&C), vacuum suction or aspiration, and vacuum curettage.
- Second trimester surgical methods include dilatation and extraction, systemic or intrauterine prostaglandins, and intrauterine hypertonic saline administration.
- Risks and side effects include cramping, bleeding, perforation of the uterus, and laceration to the cervix.

Nursing Considerations

Nursing considerations include the following:

- Be aware of your own beliefs regarding elective induced abortion.
- Know the applicable and relevant rules and guidelines of the nursing regulatory body for your province or territory regarding providing nursing care for clients seeking or undergoing elective abortions.
- Provide accurate information regarding side effects to be expected following the abortion, including cramping, bleeding, and pain.
- Provide counselling or referral for follow-up psychological support and possible contraceptive planning.

INFERTILITY

Infertility, affecting 10–20% of couples trying to conceive, is diagnosed when pregnancy does not occur following a year without contraception. Primary infertility refers to a couple who has never conceived. Secondary infertility describes a couple who experiences fertility problems after having at least one previous conception. Sterility is an absolute inability to conceive. Many infertility issues may respond to interventions. The psychological impact on the couple dealing with infertility must not be underestimated and can be extremely challenging.

Female Infertility Factors

Female infertility factors include the following:

- Social – Delaying child-bearing until age 30 and beyond with corresponding lowered fertility

- Weight – Excessive weight gain or loss can decrease fertility levels.
- Reproductive organs – Tubal obstructions, cervical stenosis, infections, especially with pelvic inflammatory disease, scarring of the uterus, congenital anomalies, uterine fibroids, inhospitable cervical mucus, in utero exposure to diethylstilbestrol (DES), polycystic ovarian syndrome, antibodies to partner's sperm, and endometriosis
- Endocrine – Abnormal hormone production in the hypothalamus, anterior pituitary, ovary, thyroid, or adrenal glands
- Ten to fifteen percent of infertility is due to unknown causes

Male Infertility Factors

Male infertility factors include the following:

- Male factors account for 35–40% of infertility causes
- Social – Prolonged bicycling, hot tubs, malnutrition, or trauma
- Environmental – Testicular radiation; heavy marijuana, cocaine, or alcohol use
- Reproductive organs – Congenital anomalies, hypospadias, varicocele, cryptorchidism, infections, STIs, retrograde ejaculation, ejaculatory failure, impaired circulation, diabetes, obstructions, and faulty spermatogenesis
- Endocrine – Cushing's syndrome, pituitary tumour, or acromegaly
- Unknown causes – 10% of male infertility

Diagnostic Assessment

Diagnostic assessments include the following:

- Complete health and reproductive history respecting individual confidentiality issues
- Physical examination, which may also include tests for anatomical abnormalities, tubal patency, endometrial biopsy, transvaginal ultrasonography, laparoscopy to evaluate peritoneal factors such as endometriosis and tubal adhesions, Sims-Hubner's test, a postcoital examination of cervical mucus and the quantity and quality of sperm present, and basal body temperature monitoring
- Analysis of semen: volume, sperm count, motility
- Laboratory assessment for STIs and infections, hormonal analysis of endocrine and ovarian function, ovulation predictor kits or LH surge kits to detect ovulation

Therapeutics

Therapeutic interventions for infertility are directed at the underlying cause or causes.

Male Factors

- Sperm washing and assisted intrauterine insemination, use of donor sperm, antibiotic treatment for infections, androgen (testosterone) hormone therapy
- Referral to a urologist for treatment of reparable structural disorders

Female Factors

- Surgery for tubal occlusions, pelvic adhesions, fibroids, or reparable structural abnormalities
- Antibiotics for infections

Hormonal Therapy

- Clomid (cloimiphene citrate) - Stimulates the hypothalamus and anterior pituitary to induce ovulation. Side effects include ovarian hyperstimulation, ovarian cysts, and multiple births.
- Parlodel (bromocriptine mesylate) – Inhibits the secretion of prolactin in the anterior pituitary, thereby improving the production and actions of FSH and LH
- Pergonal (menotropins)(FSH and LH) – Follicular stimulation and ovum maturation
- Danazol (danocrine) – Used for 6–12 months in the treatment of endometriosis; suppresses ovulation and menstruation to allow for atrophy of the ectopic endometrial tissues
- Adverse effects of hormonal therapy include hyperstimulation of the ovaries, ovarian cysts, multiple births, nausea and vomiting, dizziness, and headache.

Assisted Reproductive Technologies (ARTs)

These technologies include any therapeutic intervention in which the sperm, eggs, or both are managed outside the body. There are several techniques, and the use of donor sperm and eggs may be part of the intervention. National guidelines have been established and position papers published recommending limitations to the use of ART techniques, including restrictions on the number of embryo transfers and implantations, given the higher incidence of maternal and fetal complications. Often multiple steps are required to prepare the woman's body for ART interventions. The medications used may have several adverse side effects. Extensive teaching and counselling support are essential. Artificial reproductive technologies include the following:

- In vitro fertilization (IVF) – The ovaries are stimulated with Pergonal, oocytes are collected by needle aspiration, and fertilization occurs in the laboratory with the partner's or donor's washed sperm. After 48 hours of growth, up to two or three fertilized embryos are implanted in the uterus.
- Therapeutic donor insemination with intrauterine insemination, bypassing the vagina and cervix
- Gamete intrafallopian transfer (GIFT) – May be used if the woman has at least one patent fallopian tube. Oocytes and sperm are combined, and the gametes are inserted at the opening of the fallopian tube.

Fertilization occurs naturally in the fallopian tube.
- Zygote intrafallopian transfer (ZIFT) – Oocytes are retrieved laparoscopically, followed by culture and insemination of the oocytes in the laboratory. Within 24 hours, the fertilized eggs are transferred to the fallopian tube.

Nursing Considerations

The nursing considerations surrounding infertility treatment include the following:

- Psychological support and counselling are essential when managing fertility problems as infertility issues are often accompanied by feelings of helplessness, frustration, and grief.
- Women need to be informed of and closely monitored for adverse side effects and risks when undergoing hormonal therapies and ART interventions. Maternal and fetal morbidity and mortality rates in pregnancy, birth, and postpartum are higher for ART interventions.
- Referral to adoption agencies should be included in infertility counselling information.

NORMAL PREGNANCY

A woman's body undergoes tremendous physiological changes as it adapts to the demands of supporting a pregnancy. This major life event inevitably also brings many developmental and psychosocial adjustments as roles and relationships change within a family. Whether in antenatal community health settings or labour birthing rooms, nurses play a significant role in educating and supporting a woman and her family during this profoundly important event.

CONCEPTION, FERTILIZATION, AND IMPLANTATION

The sequencing of these stages includes the following:

- At the time of ovulation, the ovum is released and swept up by cilia in the ampulla of the fallopian tube. The ovum is fertile and viable for about 24 hours after ovulation.
- Spermatozoa are viable and optimally fertile for 24 hours postejaculation, although they may survive and remain mobile in the cervical mucus for two to three days. Although 200–500 million sperm may be contained in the ejaculate, only one will penetrate and fertilize the ovum. Prostaglandins in the semen stimulate uterine smooth muscle contractions and help propel the sperm to the fallopian tube, where fertilization commonly takes place.
- Capacitation – Enzymes in the sperms' heads are released, changing the outer coating of the ovum to allow one sperm to penetrate the ovum.
- Zonal reaction – Once a sperm has penetrated the

ovum, cellular changes occur on the ovum's surface membrane, preventing other sperm from entering.
- At the time of fertilization, the nuclei of the sperm and ovum fuse and the 23 chromosomes from each combine to restore the diploid number of 46. Sex is determined by the twenty-third pair of chromosomes, the male contributing either an X chromosome for an XX (female) or a Y chromosome for an XY (male) chromosome pair.
- Chromosomal disorders may or may not be linked to hereditary causes. Hazards such as radiation or chemical exposure may also cause chromosomal defects.

Multiple Pregnancy

- Occurs naturally in about one in 80 pregnancies. Arises from two different processes:

  - Monozygotic or identical twins occur due to the spontaneous division of one fertilized ovum early in development. There are three distinct types, which may or may not share a common amnion and placenta, depending on time of start.
  - Dizygotic or fraternal twins occur when two or more separate ova are fertilized by two or more different spermatozoa. Fetuses have separate placentas and individual chromosomal genotypes.

- ART fertility treatments may produce multiple fertilized ovums. The Society of Obstetricians and Gynaecologists of Canada (SOGC) currently recommends implantation of no more than two or three zygotes, depending on maternal age and reproductive status, due to the increased maternal–fetal morbidity and mortality risks (Min, Claman, & Hughes, 2006).

EMBRYONIC AND FETAL DEVELOPMENT

Development is divided into three stages: the ovum, embryonic, and fetal stages. The amniotic cavity provides a climate-controlled environment for the developing fetus. The placenta is a key structure with multiple functions. As the uterus receives 10% of the maternal cardiac output, anything that impairs uteroplacental circulation will adversely affect the fetus. Knowledge of this relationship is crucial for nurses when assessing risk factors for maternal–fetal well-being.

Ovum Stage

- From conception to day 14. Characterized by cellular division, formation of the blastocyst and beginnings of the embryonic membranes, and differentiation of the primary germ layers.
- The two-celled zygote continues to undergo mitotic cellular division (also known as cleavage) while travelling through the fallopian tube toward the uterine cavity.

- With each mitotic division, two-, four-, and eight-celled groups called blastomeres form until a solid ball of 16 cells called a morula reaches the uterus and prepares to implant into the uterine wall.
- Inside the morula, development continues as a solid inner mass of cells called the blastocyst forms. This marks the first important differentiation from which specific structures will develop, including the embryo, which will develop into a fetus.
- Implantation occurs at 7–10 days after fertilization as chorionic villi on the blastocyst implant into the top one-third of the fundus of the uterine wall.
- Following implantation, the endometrium is now called the decidua.
- The chorionic villi then secrete the hormone HCG, maintaining the corpus luteum until the placenta develops enough to take over hormone production. HCG is the hormone detected in pregnancy testing.
- The primary germ layers form (ectoderm, mesoderm, and endoderm), from which all tissues and organs will develop.
- The ectoderm is the source of the central and peripheral nervous systems, sensory epithelium, tooth enamel, nails and hair, and lens of the eye.
- The mesoderm produces the skeletal bones and cartilage, muscles, connective tissue, cardiovascular and reproductive systems, kidneys, and spleen.
- The endoderm's lower layer forms the pancreas, liver, bladder, epithelial lining of the respiratory tract, and vagina.

Embryonic Stage

- The embryonic stage lasts from gestational day 15 until the embryo reaches a crown-to-rump length of 3 cm, or approximately to the end of the eighth week.
- This is a critical time of development of all organ systems and external body features and a high-risk time for teratogenic substances to interfere with and harm organ and tissue development.
- From the blastocyst, the amnion (innermost layer) and chorion (outermost layer) membranes form to protect the developing embryo.
- The amnion continues to grow, enclosing the developing embryo in a protective, fluid-filled cavity.
- The chorion becomes the fetal side of the placenta and contains the umbilical blood vessels—two arteries and one vein—surrounded by Wharton's jelly connective tissue.

Fetal Stage

- This stage begins at week 9 and lasts until birth or the end of the pregnancy.

Major developmental milestones are outlined in Table 9.1, and high-risk critical times of development are depicted in Figure 9.2.

Table 9.1   Essentials of Fetal Development by Pregnancy Trimester

FIRST TRIMESTER	SECOND TRIMESTER	THIRD TRIMESTER
Up to 12 weeks' gestation	13–24 weeks' gestation	25–40 weeks' gestation
Weight 45 g	Weight 60–780 g	Weight 900–3500 g
Heart beats at 28 days; fetal circulation complete; fetal heart beat (FHB) heard by Doppler; all body organs are formed; differentiation of sex glands; sex determination possible; fingers and toes are distinct; face appears human; eyelids closed; tooth buds appear; skin pink and smooth; palate has developed and closed; outlines of bones visible on ultrasonogram; lungs acquire shape; kidneys produce urine, contribute to amniotic fluid; able to move limbs	By 16 weeks, there is rapid growth; transparent skin; blood vessels visible; active movements present; sucking motions; meconium produced; sweat glands developing; skeletal system obvious At 20 weeks, mother feels fetal movement ("quickening"); lung alveoli appear; surfactant begins production; respiratory movements occur, called fetal breathing movements (FBM); eyes are closed; there is rapid growth By 24 weeks, eyebrows and lashes are formed; skin is red, wrinkled; there is little subcutaneous fat; fingerprints, footprints are present; vernix covers the body; lanugo is abundant; myelination of the spinal cord begins; fetal suck and swallow reflexes are present; peristalsis begins; teeth form; grasp reflex is present	By 28 weeks, weight 1200 g; eyes open and close; gas exchange possible; two-thirds of final size; testes descend; nervous system begins some regulation; germinal matrix of brain rich in blood, increasing risk of bleeding if born now By 32 weeks, weight 2000 g; CNS regulation rapidly developing, bones fully developed; iron stores begin; subcutaneous fat stores develop; skin less wrinkled and red; pupils react to light By 35 weeks, lung surfactant peaks, signalling lung maturity; lanugo and vernix decrease By 38 to 40 weeks, considered full term

Main Embryonic Period (in weeks)
Fetal Period (in weeks)
1
2
3
4
5
6
7
8
9
16
32
38
Period of dividing zygote, implantation, and bilaminar embryo
Embryonic disc
Morula
Amnion
Blastocyst
Embryonic disc
Not susceptible to teratogenesis
Death of embryo and spontaneous abortion common
Neural tube defects (NTDs)
Mental retardation
CNS
TA, ASD, and VSD
Heart
Amelia/Meromelia
Upper limb
Amelia/Meromelia
Lower limb
Cleft lip
Upper lip
Low-set malformed ears and deafness
Ears
Microphthalmia, cataracts, glaucoma
Eyes
Enamel hypoplasia and staining
Teeth
Cleft palate
Palate
Masculinization of female genitalia
External genitalia
Common site(s) of action of teratogens
Less sensitive period
Highly sensitive period
TA—Truncus arteriosus; ASD—Atrial septal defect;
VSD—Ventricular septal defect
Major congenital anomalies
Functional defects and minor anomalies

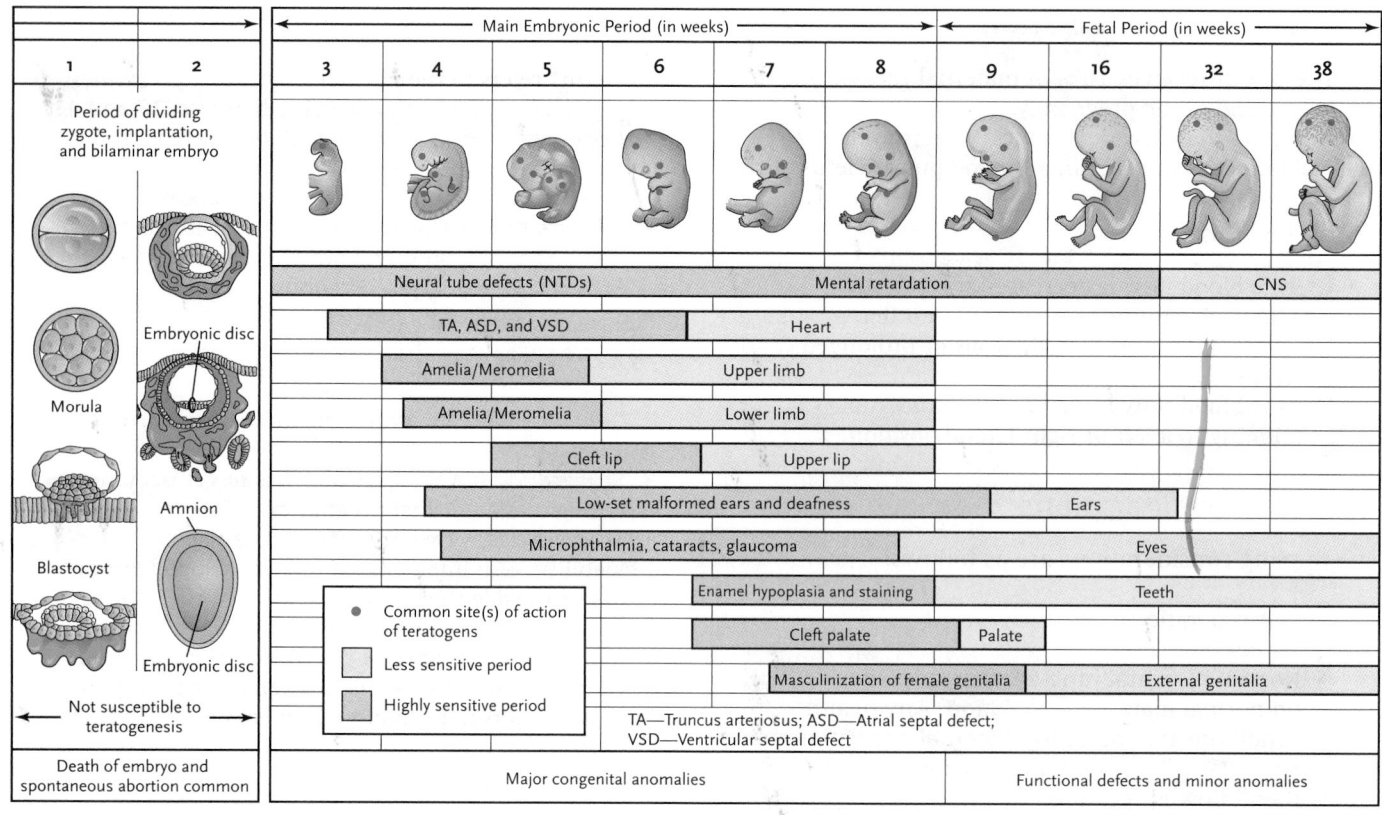

FIGURE 9.2 **Sensitive or Critical Periods in Human Fetal Development**

Source: Moore, K., & Persaud, T. (2003). *Before we were born: Essentials of embryology and birth defects* (6th ed.). Philadelphia: Saunders.

Amniotic Fluid

Amniotic fluid is derived initially from maternal blood filtrates and eventually consists mostly of fetal urine. Normal volume is 500 cc to a maximum of 1000 cc.

- Oligohydramnios is a volume of less than 300 cc, which impairs fetal movement and symmetrical growth and may be associated with fetal abnormalities, and if prolonged, does not allow for normal alveoli development.
- Polyhydramnios is a volume greater than 1.5–2 L and is also associated with fetal abnormalities.
- The amniotic fluid functions to control temperature, protect the fetus from trauma, and allow symmetrical growth, fetal breathing, and motor movements.

The Placenta

- The placenta is structurally complete by week 12 gestation; it continues to grow and expand until 20 weeks.
- Fetal and maternal blood are independent, although separated only by a thin layer of cells.
- Functions include gas exchange, heat transfer, antibody transfer, transportation of nutrients, excretion of metabolic wastes, and hormone production essential for maintaining the pregnancy.
- Most substances are of a molecular size that allows for transfer across the maternal circulation and into the fetal circulation. This can include protective maternal immunoglobulins but also harmful antibodies, viruses, most drugs, and other external teratogenic substances, including alcohol, nicotine, caffeine, and cocaine.

Hormone Production

- Estrogen is a steroid that stimulates growth of the uterus and breast tissue, increases in amount as the pregnancy reaches term, and helps stimulate uterine muscle contractility, thereby helping to stimulate the onset of labour.
- Progesterone is a protective hormone that may help maintain the pregnancy by decreasing uterine contractility. It also decreases smooth muscle contractions in maternal circulation and helps maintain the endometrium.
- HCG is detected by pregnancy tests, found in maternal serum and urine 8–10 days postconception, and maintains the function of the corpus luteum until the placenta is fully developed.
- Human placental lactogen (HPL) is a growth-type hormone that supports fetal growth by stimulating maternal metabolism and increasing the transport of glucose to the fetus. It also prepares the breasts for milk production and lactation.

Uteroplacental Circulation

- The uterus receives 10% of maternal cardiac output by the end of the pregnancy.
- Anything that adversely affects maternal circulation will impair placental function and put the fetus at risk.

Uterine Blood Flow

- Uterine blood flow is decreased by maternal hypotension, supine hypotensive disorder, prolonged labour contractions, and vigorous or prolonged cardio exercises.
- Uterine blood flow is increased by maternal positioning to a left or right lateral position.

Nursing Considerations

The nursing considerations are as follows:

- Key considerations:

  - Normal placental function depends almost entirely on normal maternal circulation. Any health conditions that decrease maternal circulation may adversely affect placental function.
  - Blood flow is decreased by maternal vasoconstriction related to diabetes, hypertension, either chronic or pregnancy induced (PIH), vasopressor medications, nicotine, and cocaine.

- Assess the learning needs of families and provide resources for understanding fetal growth and development. Assess the need for genetic counselling based on family history or teratogenic exposure and refer as appropriate.
- Teach the mother measures by which to maximize uteroplacental circulation throughout her pregnancy: avoiding unsupported supine position, following treatment plans for medical and circulatory problems, utilizing a left or right lateral sleeping and resting position, and avoiding excessive or prolonged cardio exercise practices.
- Maternal elevated core body temperature or a fever of 38.5°C or higher may increase the risk of harm in embryological development. Teach the mother the balance between benefits and risks regarding avoiding excessive body temperature overheating. For example, hot tubs and saunas should be avoided especially during the sensitive embryonic development stage to protect the embryo. Reducing fever with medications such as acetaminophen is a safely used fever reduction practice even in pregnancy.

Calculating Length of Pregnancy

- The length of a pregnancy is calculated from the first day of the last menstrual cycle or period (LMP). It can be described as approximately 280 days, 40 weeks, nine calendar months, or 10 lunar months. Nine calendar months are divided into three trimesters of three months each.
- "Term" refers to the normal length of a pregnancy, with labour and birth occurring between 38 and 42 weeks' gestation. "Preterm" refers to labour and birth between 20 and 37 weeks' gestation. Post-term is labour and birth after 42 weeks' gestation.
- Naegle's Rule – The estimated date of confinement (EDC, that is, labour and birth) is calculated as follows: EDC = LMP + 7 days – 3 months + 1 year.

PREGNANCY TERMS

- Gravida – Any pregnancy, including the current pregnancy
- Nulligravida – A woman who has never been pregnant
- Primigravida – A first pregnancy
- Multigravida – Two or more pregnancies
- Viability – An infant sufficiently developed enough to live outside the womb, technically after 20 weeks' gestation or weighting more than 500 g. True viability is more realistic after 23–24 weeks' gestation and would still require neonatal intensive care support.
- Para – Refers to birth after 20 weeks' gestation. The outcome or number of infants born is not taken into account.
- Nullipara – Has not given birth to an infant of viable age. Note that the woman may have been pregnant but may have had a spontaneous abortion (miscarriage) or induced abortion.
- Primipara – Has given birth at more than 20 weeks' gestation, regardless of outcome and regardless of how many infants were born (for example, twins count as one para event)
- Multipara – Two or more viable births
- TPAL (term, preterm, abortions, living) is a more accurate way of describing parity and outcome.
- See the Labour and Birth Processes section, pages 402–410, for additional terms.

PRECONCEPTION

Ideally, women of child-bearing age should have preconception access to information and health practices that will increase the likelihood of a healthy pregnancy. To improve healthy outcomes and lower risk factors, pregnancy health promotion should take place in the classroom, the public media, and any health care setting before a pregnancy is planned or occurs. Nurses, by virtue of their wide range of professional practice settings, are ideally situated to assess, counsel, and support women in all stages of pregnancy planning and care.

ANTENATAL HEALTH ASSESSMENT

This assessment includes nursing assessment, teaching, support, and referral in the following areas identified by Health Canada as variables that influence pregnancy outcomes (Health Canada, 2000b):

- Social support – Life stressors, economic status, stability of housing and accommodations, employment, community resources, quality and nature of relationships and available support, family defined
- Abuse and violence – There is an increased incidence of violence in intimate relationships during pregnancy.
- Female genital mutilation (FGM) – The diversity of the Canadian population and the worldwide prevalence of this cultural practice mean that nurses may provide counselling and care to women who have undergone FGM despite the practice being banned in Canada.
- Lifestyle practices – The type and amount of exercise and activity, as well as tobacco, alcohol, and medicinal and nonmedicinal drug use, are identified as potentially adverse lifestyle practices and support, education, and resources are provided.
- Exposure to environmental chemicals and toxic hazards – Previous and current exposure is identified, including that in home, recreational, and workplace settings. These exposures may include anaesthetic gases, radiation, lead, or pesticides.
- Health history – Past medical and family history, especially cardiovascular disease, diabetes, congenital disorders, genetic family history, STIs, past illnesses and hospitalizations, chronic conditions, mental health, bleeding disorders, surgeries, partner's health history, and family mortality and causes
- Current health status – Weight, age, occupation, current medications and herbal supplements, allergies, teratogenic exposure or risks, chronic conditions, nutrition and dietary patterns, and immunizations, especially rubella and varicella
- Cultural, spiritual or religious, and ethnic considerations and practices and language barriers
- Pregnancy and birth plan preferences, education, and family involvement and roles
- Psychological readiness for pregnancy, attitudes toward this pregnancy: excitement, ambivalence, anxiety, emotionally labile
- Gynecological and reproductive history – Age at menarche, STIs or other infections, menstrual cycle, last Pap smear, contraceptive history, infertility, past pregnancies, postpartum depression, TPAL, breastfeeding history, complications of past pregnancies or births, prenatal education, blood type, and Rh factor
- Current pregnancy – Calculating first day of LMP; pregnancy test results if known; weight gain; discomforts of pregnancy or complications such as spotting, cramping, or bleeding; any medications, vitamins, or supplements; attitude regarding this pregnancy; and family and support system

HIGH-RISK PREGNANCY SCREENING

High-risk screening identifies health or social issues that may adversely affect the mother or fetus during the pregnancy, labour, and birth. Early identification of these factors provides an opportunity to monitor, intervene, or make referrals promptly, thereby providing the best chance for a healthy pregnancy outcome.

Many provincial and territorial health systems utilize standardized antenatal risk screening assessment profiles to identify those at risk and needing referral for specialized monitoring or care. The assessment tool is completed at the first prenatal visit and updated at each visit. For example, pregnancy risk levels may be differentiated and defined as a healthy pregnancy with no predictable risk, a pregnancy at risk, or a pregnancy at high risk.

Social Risk Factors

There are many social risk factors, including the following:

- Low socioeconomic status and education level, housing problems, and social isolation
- Living in a high-altitude geographical location
- Extremes in weight – Obesity (>90 kg) or extreme underweight (<46 kg)
- Extremes in age – Adolescent (<16 years) or mature (>35 years)
- Lifestyle – Alcohol, tobacco, or recreational drug use
- Exposure to occupational or environment hazards or toxin exposure, past or present (Health Canada, 2000a)

Reproductive Health Risk Factors

- Past or pre-existing conditions, including cardiovascular disease, diabetes, thyroid disorders, blood or bleeding disorders, blood incompatibility or Rh sensitization, renal disease, mental health disorders, and congenital or genetic disorders
- Past and current obstetrical complications with pregnancy or birth – DES exposure; ectopic pregnancy; cervical insufficiency (premature dilation of cervix); surgeries; stillbirths; caesarian births; premature or prolonged rupture of membranes; multiple gestation; STIs or other infections, especially rubella, cytomegalovirus (CMV), herpes, and syphilis; abruption or placenta previa; PIH; or gestational diabetes
- Fetal or past neonatal complications of morbidity or mortality – Prematurity or postmaturity, teratogen exposure, small for gestational age (SGA) or large for gestational age (LGA), or fetal compromise

Initial Prenatal Physical Examination

In addition to a detailed history as described above, the physical examination will include vital signs, height, weight, weight gain, pelvic examination, including assessment of pelvic type and adequacy, and breast examination.

Initial Laboratory Assessment

- Blood work – Complete blood count (CBC), ABO and Rh typing, syphilis, HIV screening, gonorrhea, CMV, rubella titre, hepatitis B screen, glucose, sickle cell disease if parent is of African descent, thalassemia trait if parent is of Mediterranean descent

- Urinalysis
- Pap smear

Danger Signs of Pregnancy

At any time during the pregnancy, the following signs and symptoms should be reported at once:

- Cramping and uterine contractions, vaginal spotting or bleeding
- Persistent vomiting
- Painful, frequent urination or oliguria
- Temperature above 38°C
- Persistent or severe headache, edema of hands or face, dizziness, muscle irritability, epigastric pain related to PIH
- Unusual pain, especially abdominal or uterine pain, absence of fetal movement
- Signs of preterm or impending labour – Rupture of membranes, bloody show, uterine contractions that are regular and increasing in intensity and duration, expulsion of mucous plug

Nursing Considerations

The nursing considerations for antenatal assessment are as follows:

- Key client education point:

  - Teach the mother the danger signs and symptoms of pregnancy that should be reported immediately and provide health teaching for immediate interventions.

- Create an interview atmosphere that ensures privacy, safety, and sensitivity to encourage honest, open communication and responses. Ask direct questions, especially regarding abuse and risk factors for abuse.
- Women who have undergone FGM are at increased risk for complications throughout the pregnancy and postpartum experience and need support and education to manage any complications.
- Provide information and refer to community and professional services for any identified preconception and antenatal risks, including information about antenatal screening procedures and rationales for testing.
- Moderate exercise appears advantageous if already part of a women's prepregnancy lifestyle. Advise women about the avoidance of hot tubs, saunas, or strenuous, prolonged activity, which may cause overheating.

PERINATAL ASSESSMENT AND CARE

SUBSEQUENT HEALTH ASSESSMENT IN NORMAL PREGNANCY

Common health assessment routines for normal pregnancies are listed below:

- Every 4 weeks until 28 weeks' gestation
- Every 2 weeks until 36 weeks' gestation
- Every week until birth of the infant
- Routine assessment includes physical assessment, maternal weight and weight gain patterns, adjustment to pregnancy, discomforts of pregnancy, presence of edema, nutritional assessment, family life and psychosocial status, vital signs, urine testing, fundal height and uterine growth, fetal heart rate (FHR), and a pelvic examination at 36 weeks' gestation to assess for signs of impending labour.

SUBSEQUENT LABORATORY AND MATERNAL SCREENING

- First trimester combined screen (FTC) at 11–14 weeks, including ultrasound nuchal translucency and serum PAPP-A and free beta-HCG, which are proteins produced during pregnancy
- Urinalysis for protein, glucose, ketones; trace glucose may reflect normal alterations to renal function in pregnancy
- Maternal serum alpha-fetoprotein (MS-AFP) at 16–20 weeks for detection of neural tube defect
- Glucose tolerance testing at 24–28 weeks' gestation if there is excessive glucose in urine or a history of diabetes or gestational diabetes
- Indirect Coombs test on Rh-negative women at 28 weeks to assess for Rh sensitization
- Fetal ultrasonogram at 16–18 weeks
- Group B *Streptococcus* (GBS) at 35–37 weeks' gestation
- Maternal CBC at 28 weeks' gestation to assess for anemia
- Other fetal well-being tests may be used; see the Fetal Evaluation and Monitoring section, pages 400–402.

EXPECTED PHYSICAL ASSESSMENT FINDINGS IN NORMAL PREGNANCY

Vital Signs

- Temperature – 36.5–37.5°C
- Heart rate – 60 to 90 bpm; heart rate may increase by 10 bpm due to cardiovascular adaptations

- Blood pressure – 90 to 120/60 to 80 with a decrease in the second trimester due to smooth muscle relaxation of blood vessels

Fetal Heart Rate and Movement

- 110–160 bpm
- Detected at 10–12 weeks by Dopplerultrasonography, 16–20 weeks by stethoscope

Fundal Height

After 20–22 weeks' gestation, fundal height in centimetres for a woman of average weight corresponds approximately to the gestational age in weeks. Individual differences in growth make this inaccurate after 36 weeks' gestation.

Weight Gain

Women of normal prepregnancy weight can expect to gain an average of 11–14 kg (25–30 lbs) during a 40-week pregnancy. In addition to the fetal weight, expected increases in weight are due to increased blood volume, reproductive tissue growth, especially uterine growth, as well as the placenta, amniotic fluid, and products of conception. The trimester weight gain is as follows:

- First trimester – Approximately 1.5–2.5 kg (3–5 lbs), almost all of which is due to maternal physiological changes and growth
- Second trimester – Approximately 5.5–7 kg (12–15 lbs), due to a combination of maternal reproductive organ growth and fetal growth
- Third trimester – Approximately 5.5–7 kg (12–15 lbs), primarily due to rapid fetal growth

Nursing Considerations

The nursing considerations for normal pregnancies are as follows:

- Key consideration:

  - Weight gain of more than 1 kg (2 lbs) in one week may be a sign of excess fluid retention or hypertension and should be assessed further.

- Quickening or maternal awareness of fetal movement occurs at around 20 weeks' gestation, earlier in multiparas.
- Higher than expected fundal height may be related to polyhydramnios, or multiple gestation.
- Lower than expected fundal height may be due to oligohydramnios, a fetus that is SGA, and/or intrauterine growth restriction.
- Women may need to be reassured regarding body image and weight gain fears and be made aware of the risks of excessive weight gain or being underweight.
- Explain that the varied and changing emotional responses to pregnancy are normal and expected. Encourage discussion between partners regarding feelings of ambivalence, uncertainty, and insecurities regarding changing roles and body image. These feelings are an expected part of adapting to a major life change. If feelings continue beyond the first trimester to be a source of distress or conflict, encourage and offer resources and referral to appropriate counselling services. Also promote childbirth preparation classes in a group setting for health information and peer support.

Physical and Physiological Adaptations to Pregnancy

In order for the woman's body to accommodate the demands of a pregnancy, all body systems undergo normal changes. While the reproductive system undergoes the most significant and noticeable changes, all body systems adapt as necessary.

Reproductive System Changes

Reproductive body system changes are as follows:

- Uterus – Increased growth, elasticity, and enlargement of pre-existing muscles; increased vascularity and blood supply (10% of cardiac output by term); irregular Braxton Hicks contractions provide regulatory blood flow to placenta and are felt after the second trimester
- Cervix – Softer (Goodell's sign), shorter, especially as term approaches, closed by a protective mucous plug; increased vascularity makes it appear cyanotic on a prenatal examination (Chadwick's sign)
- Ovaries – May be enlarged on palpation in first trimester due to hormone-producing corpus luteum
- Vagina – There is an increase in vascularity, elasticity, and secretions, and the pH changes to alkaline with added risk of infections.
- Perineum – Increased vascularity (Chadwick's sign) and hypertrophy of tissues
- Breasts – Increased sensitivity, vascularity with more prominent veins, increased size of periareolar glands and areola, increased pigmentation in response to increased melanin production

Cardiovascular System Changes

Significant changes occur in the cardiovascular system as the body supports the added blood volume, flow, and transportation demands.

- Blood volume and flow – Increases 30–45% as plasma volume peaks at 22 weeks, with a marked increase in flow to the uterus and kidneys
- Blood constituents – Red blood cells increase by 10–15%, but not in proportion to the increase in plasma volume, creating the condition known as

physiological anemia. Hemoglobin should remain at or above 120 mmol/L or the client should be assessed for true anemia. Fibrinogen increases by 50% (to help prevent excess bleeding at birth and postpartum), and the erythrocyte sedimentation rate (ESR) increases.

- Cardiac output – Increases by 30–50%, peaking at 20–24 weeks' gestation
- Heart rate – Increases by 10–15 bpm. A systolic murmur may be heard.
- Blood pressure – Decreases slightly in the second trimester due to progesterone; may lead to postural hypotension or fainting

Respiratory System Changes

The respiratory system is also impacted by pregnancy and includes the following changes:

- Respiratory rate and tidal volume increase due to progesterone and slight respiratory alkalosis, 30–40% increased volume. Oxygen requirements increase 15–20%.
- The diaphragm is displaced upward, leading to shortness of breath as the pregnancy progresses; there is lateral expansion of the ribs and chest wall with increased elasticity and dilation of airways.
- Increased vascularity is secondary to estrogen; resulting nasal congestion and nosebleeds are common.

Gastrointestinal System Changes

The gastrointestinal system includes the following changes:

- Carbohydrate metabolism with insulin secretion increases, although its effectiveness is impaired by the action of hormones, and demand may exceed the pancreas's ability, resulting in symptoms of gestational diabetes. Fasting blood sugar decreases secondary to the accelerated utilization of glucose to meet fetal demands, and hypoglycemia may lead to fainting and dizziness.
- Gastric motility decreases with prolonged gastric emptying, slower peristalsis secondary to progesterone, and increased risk of constipation, hemorrhoids.
- Esophageal smooth muscle relaxation is secondary to progesterone and regurgitation.
- The gallbladder has decreased tone, distension, slower emptying, and increased risk for gallstone formation.
- The liver has increased alkaline phosphatase and cholesterol and decreased albumin.
- Gingivitis is secondary to increased estrogen.

Renal System Changes

The renal system has significant changes, including the following:

- Bladder has decreased tone, increased capacity, and urinary stasis with increased risk of urinary tract infections.

- Renal blood volume and flow changes the glomerular filtration rate, which increases 50%; kidneys receive one-fifth of cardiac output.
- Impaired reabsorption of glucose and nitrogen with excretion into urine

Integumentary System Changes

The skin system is also affected by pregnancy and includes the following changes:

- Increased melanin from the anterior pituitary, leading to linea nigra darkening down mid-abdomen, facial chloasma (mask of pregnancy) with brown patchy pigmentation over cheeks and forehead, darkening of areola and development of secondary areola
- Pruritis (itching) due to increased estrogen and liver changes
- Increased sweat and sebaceous gland stimulation with acne, perspiration, and night sweats
- Striae gravidarum, or stretch marks, are due to underlying connective tissue weakening and breakage; they are dark red or bluish during pregnancy and fade to silver.
- Spider nevi are fine red dilated arterioles over the face, neck, and thorax secondary to increased estrogen.

Musculoskeletal System Changes

The musculoskeletal system also exhibits many changes, including the following:

- Joints – Hypermobile secondary to the hormones relaxin and progesterone with increased risk for injury
- Postural changes – Accentuated lumbar spinal curvature, waddling gait

Metabolic System Changes

The differences in the metabolic rates are as follows:

- Basal metabolic rate increases by 15–20%.
- Carbohydrate metabolism – Insulin production increases, and fasting blood sugar decreases.

Endocrine System Changes

The endocrine system is affected by pregnancy as follows:

- Increased hormone production by hypothalamus–pituitary–ovarian axis – Menstruation ceases, and estrogen and progesterone increase.
- Adrenal cortex – Increased ADH, aldosterone, cortisol
- Pancreas – Increased insulin demand and production but increased maternal resistance to insulin
- Thyroid – Slight enlargement, increased T_4
- Light-headedness, fainting in early pregnancy secondary to hypoglycemia, postural changes

COMMON DISCOMFORTS OF PREGNANCY

Some of the changes noted above will lead to what are commonly referred to as minor or normal discomforts of pregnancy. Although minor from a health viewpoint, many pregnant women view these discomforts as a source of concern and distress. Nurses can use prenatal visits to educate their clients concerning what to expect and to help plan interventions for relieving these discomforts.

First Trimester Discomforts and Nursing Considerations

Discomforts of early pregnancy can include the following:

- Nausea and vomiting – 50–80% of women complain of nausea, with 50% of them also reporting episodes of vomiting
- Urinary frequency – Related to uterine pressure on the bladder until the uterus expands out of the pelvis
- Fatigue
- Breast tenderness – Secondary to progesterone and estrogen hormone changes
- Vaginal discharge – Leukorrhea
- Nasal congestion and nosebleeds – Secondary to increased estrogen

Recommend that pregnant clients do the following:

- Eat small, frequent meals, eat dry foods separate from liquids, and eat dry crackers early in the morning to help relieve nausea.
- Avoid large fluid intakes prior to sleep and void frequently during the day.
- Try to plan times for increased rest and naps.
- Wear a supportive bra, adjust it for increased breast size, and even wear a bra to bed if helpful.
- Shower daily and avoid douching.

Second and Third Trimester Discomforts and Nursing Considerations

Common discomforts of the second and third trimesters include the following:

- Heartburn and regurgitation of gastric contents
- Leg cramping due to imbalance in the phosphorus–calcium ratio and postural changes
- Varicose veins
- Hemorrhoids and constipation
- Backache
- Ankle edema – Related to poor venous return and increased sodium levels
- Carpal tunnel syndrome related to medial nerve compression, especially in the dominant hand
- Shortness of breath
- Sleep disturbances

Recommend the following to clients:

- Continue to eat small, frequent meals, avoid spicy, high-fat meals, and use extra pillows to elevate the head.
- Evaluate dietary intake and increase calcium intake, eat fewer phosphorus-rich foods, and increase fluids and fibre for constipation and hemorrhoids.
- Elevate legs; take frequent breaks when driving long distances or sitting for prolonged periods; wear supportive stockings and dorsiflex ankle to relieve cramping.
- When lightening occurs as the uterus moves lower in the pelvis in the primigravida, shortness of breath will be relieved; in bed, elevate the head with pillows.

PSYCHOLOGICAL TASKS OF PREGNANCY

Pregnancy involves a myriad of emotional responses and psychological adjustments as a new developmental role is undertaken and family members adjust to accepting a new member into their lives. In addition to the pregnant woman, all family members, including involved extended family such as grandparents, must adjust to the changes in their roles and responsibilities. This can be a time of both happiness and anticipation but also of ambivalence and stress. Nurses can help families in understanding the feelings and role changes and can provide support and reassurance.

The psychological tasks include the following:

- Planning the pregnancy
- Confirming the pregnancy through testing and medical confirmation
- Accepting the pregnancy; even planned pregnancies are associated with feelings of ambivalence and conflict
- Perception of fetal movements
- Accepting the fetus as an individual, role-playing, and fantasizing
- Birth – reconciling the imagined infant with reality
- Sensory interactions – seeing, touching, giving care (Merenstein & Gardner, 2006)

All family members, especially the woman and her partner, need the opportunity to discuss their emotions and adaptations to the pregnancy. Pregnancy, even when carefully planned for, represents a major developmental change for the woman and her partner. The challenges of integrating all the practical, physical, financial, and role changes into a relationship and family can threaten the stability a family may or may not have. The adaptations, conflicts, and changing roles need to be acknowledged. Community childbirth classes, prenatal programs, and prenatal visits provide an opportunity for open discussion, support, and, when needed, referral to counselling services. Many community programs also offer classes to prepare siblings for the changes that happen when a new family member arrives.

SEXUALITY IN PREGNANCY

Body image, sensuality, and sexuality are all affected by the demands and changes pregnancy brings—on both an individual and a relationship level. Concerns may include fear of harming the developing fetus, fear of miscarriage, and cultural beliefs and practices. Physical changes may also influence desire and comfort with sexual practices.

Contraindications

There are few absolute contraindications to sexual activity or intercourse during pregnancy. They include vaginal spotting or bleeding, premature rupture of membranes, active vaginal infection, uterine cramping, and a history of spontaneous abortions.

Nursing Considerations

- Assess for beliefs, fears, and concerns and offer reassurance and factual information.
- Assess for contraindications and offer support and alternative suggestions.
- First trimester – Sexual desire may be decreased due to nausea, fatigue, breast tenderness, psychological ambivalence, and fear of harming the fetus. Suggest alternatives to sexual intercourse if desire is decreased; reassure that unless risk factors are present, there is no risk of harming the fetus during sexual intercourse.
- Second trimester – Increased interest and satisfaction due to increased vaginal and perineal vascularity, lessening of the discomforts of the first trimester
- Third trimester – Increased size and discomfort may affect comfort level. Suggest changes in positions or alternatives to sexual intercourse that will offer closeness and intimacy.

PERINATAL NUTRITION

The anatomical and physiological changes of pregnancy result in increased daily requirements for energy, nutrients, and vitamins. Ideally, optimal nutrition is part of preconception planning for pregnancy. Meeting nutritional needs during pregnancy is an important factor in promoting healthy outcomes for both mother and infant. For many women, due to inadequate preconception dietary intake, special attention should be paid to ensuring that there is an adequate intake of calcium, vitamin D, folate, iron, and essential fatty acids.

CALORIES

- The demands of pregnancy require an average 100 kcal (400 kJ) increase per day in the first trimester and an average 300 kcal (1300 kJ) increase above the woman's daily requirements in the second and third trimesters (Health Canada, 1999).

- Actual calorie requirements will vary between individuals as differing activity levels, lifestyles, and basal metabolic rates are considered.

NUTRITIONAL SUPPLEMENTS

- A prenatal daily vitamin is recommended as it will contain the additional required minerals, vitamins, and folic acid supplements.
- Vitamin A – Consumed in excess, vitamin A is teratogenic in the early weeks of pregnancy. There is a known increased risk of birth defects at intakes of 10,000 IU daily. The recommended intake for vitamin A, 4355 IU, is easily met through dietary means; supplementation is therefore not recommended (Health Canada, 1999).
- Calcium and vitamin D are essential for the development and maintenance of bone mass both prior to and during pregnancy. Adequate intake is also needed for fetal skeletal development. Vitamin D is needed to enhance the intestinal absorption of calcium. The recommended daily intake for calcium during pregnancy is between 1200 and 1500 mg, depending on age. Vitamin D daily requirement is 200 IU or 5.0 micrograms (mcg). During the summer months in Canada, daily sun exposure of 15 minutes meets recommended requirements. From November to April, vitamin D production from sun exposure ceases due to low sunlight levels; therefore, additional supplements are required (Health Canada, 1999).
- Iron – Additional iron is needed to support the increase in maternal red blood cell production. Iron supplementation is recommended during the second and third trimesters based on the assumption that prepregnancy iron stores are inadequate in most women. Recommended iron intake increases from 13 to 18 mg in the second trimester and to 23 mg by the third trimester (Health Canada, 1999).
- Folate – Folate supplementation significantly reduces the risk of neural tube defects, which affect about one in 1000 babies born in Canada (live births and stillbirths). A supplement of 400 mcg daily in addition to dietary intake is recommended. A supplemental dose of 4000–5000 mcg is recommended for women at increased risk—compromised health, diabetes, obesity, or previous birth of baby with a neural defect, starting one month before pregnancy and through the first trimester.
- Essential fatty acids are important during pregnancy for proper fetal neural and visual development. The fetus is dependent on maternal sources, especially during the rapid growth period of the last trimester of pregnancy. Women are encouraged to increase dietary intake of foods rich in essential fatty acids, including nonhydrogenated vegetable oils, nuts, eggs, meat, and fatty fish such as wild salmon.

Nursing Considerations

- Assess and work to develop a plan toward optimal preconception and perinatal nutrition practices, including adequate caloric intake of nutrient-dense foods that meet the requirements of pregnancy and follow *Eating Well With Canada's Food Guide*.

- Be aware of and sensitive to the reality that dietary habits and practices are influenced by socioeconomic status, cultural diversity, and religious dietary practices and beliefs.
- When taking into account individual differences for caloric energy increases, suggest that women use appetite as a guide to satisfying hunger. Review strategies for managing nausea in the first trimester.
- Refer clients to dietary supplement programs sponsored by Health Canada and administered by local community agencies, such as the Canada Prenatal Nutrition Program (CPNP).
- Provide suggestions for dietary sources of foods rich in folate, calcium, and iron.
- Increase awareness and understanding of potential adverse effects of excessive use of some vitamins, especially vitamin A, and over-the-counter herbal supplements.
- Ensure that vegetarians understand sources for increased protein and iron dietary intake.
- Assess for risk factors for inadequate iron stores and probable need for supplementation, including a diet deficient in meat, fish, poultry, or vitamin C, as well as frequent consumption of tea or coffee close to meal time, multiple gestations, and parity of three or more (Health Canada, 1999).
- Include in teaching that there is increased absorption of iron from heme sources such as meat, poultry, and fish. Particularly for vegetarians, nonheme iron is found in vegetables, fruit, grains, nuts, eggs, iron-enriched cereals, and pastas. Vitamin C and meat, poultry, and fish enhance the absorption of nonheme iron. Iron absorption is inhibited when consumed with tea, coffee, whole grains, and calcium.
- Assess for risk factors of low calcium intake, including low socioeconomic status, pregnant adolescents, and vegetarians who do not consume milk products.
- Assess for risk factors for inadequate vitamin D production, including dark-pigmented skin, inadequate exposure to sunlight due to northern geographical location during the winter months (most of Canada), or consistent use of sunscreen products with limited exposure to sunlight (Health Canada, 1999).
- Promote the consumption of healthy essential fatty acids through increased dietary intake. Reassure women who may have misconceptions that all dietary fats are harmful.

MATERNAL HEALTH PROBLEMS AND PREGNANCY

In an ideal world, all women planning for or beginning a pregnancy would enjoy optimal health and well-being. In the past, women who had pre-existing health issues, especially those affecting the cardiovascular and renal systems, would be discouraged from becoming pregnant. In large part, this was because of the limitations of nursing and medicine to provide the level of expert care and intervention needed to maximize the chance for a healthy outcome for mother and infant.

With advances in technology, research, high-risk referral, and professional expertise, women with health concerns and their infants are experiencing better outcomes. It is essential, however, to recognize the very real risks and complications that are associated with many maternal health issues. Women need to be informed of the potential risks for increased maternal and fetal morbidity and mortality and educated on the early monitoring and intervention provided.

CARDIAC AND BLOOD DISORDERS

As previously discussed, the cardiovascular system is challenged during pregnancy to accommodate a 50% increase in circulating volume and an increase in cardiac output. For women with a pre-existing heart condition, the needed cardiac reserve to accommodate those changes may not be sufficient. Heart disease is a significant cause of maternal morbidity and mortality and puts a woman into a high-risk pregnancy classification.

Congenital Heart Defects

- If the defect has been surgically corrected and no episodes of cyanosis are present, pregnancy outcomes are generally positive.
- If the condition is associated with cyanosis and decreased systemic circulation, regardless of treatment, pregnancy should be avoided.
- If maternal oxygenation and systemic circulation are impaired, the fetus will suffer the effects of decreased uterine blood flow and hypoxia. This can result in fetal compromise, fetal death, SGA, or spontaneous abortion.
- Antibiotic prophylaxis may be recommended during labour and birth because of an increased risk of bacterial endocarditis.

Mitral Valve Prolapse

- Mitral valve prolapse occurs in about 3% of child-bearing women. Pregnancy is usually uneventful, although some may experience palpitations and dyspnea. Prophylactic antibiotics may be prescribed if regurgitation is present. Eliminating caffeine may reduce palpitations.

Sickle Cell Anemia

- While mortality is rare with this disorder, morbidity is increased, with a higher risk of respiratory and urinary tract infections, renal failure, and congestive heart failure. Risks to the fetus include prematurity and poor growth.
- During a sickle cell crisis, fetal death may occur secondary to ischemia and hypoxia.

Nursing Considerations

- A preventive approach to minimizing complications of known conditions is emphasized.
- Realistic information about the risks and a plan of care will enable the mother to participate in her care and reduce anxiety.
- Throughout pregnancy, labour, and birth, care is directed at minimizing cardiac workload for those clients at high risk for hypoxemia. Bed rest or restricted activity may be recommended. Cardiology referral and high-risk care will be required.
- Postpartum – The first hours following birth present a high-risk time as the body begins to remobilize the extra circulating blood volume acquired during pregnancy. This adds to the workload of the heart. Assess the client for signs of respiratory distress and pulmonary edema.
- In sickle cell anemia, care should be directed at preventing crises by avoiding maternal dehydration, infection, high altitude, and fever. Additional folic acid supplementation is required. Genetic counselling may be recommended.

INFECTIONS

During pregnancy, the woman's immune system is suppressed, leading to an increased risk of acquiring infections. TORCH infections (toxoplasmosis, other [such as hepatitis], rubella, CMV infection, herpes simplex, and syphilis) are those caused by a group of organisms that can cross the placenta. In the mother, symptoms may be flulike but may cause significant developmental problems in the fetus that increase the risk of illness and death.

Toxoplasmosis

- Detected in maternal serum antibodies, this infection can be acquired by handling cat feces or garden soil or through raw meat consumption. Abortion is common; surviving newborns may present with severe neurological problems, seizures, hepatic splenomegaly, jaundice, and mental retardation.
- Advise pregnant women to wear gloves while gardening and to avoid handling cat litter and eating raw meat products.

Other: Viral Hepatitis A and B

- Can be transmitted sexually or by droplet transmission. May result in spontaneous abortion. Encourage preconception vaccination, especially for high-risk populations: health care workers, travellers to southern climates and Asia, and those who engage in unprotected sexual behaviours.
- Hepatitis A – First trimester exposure can lead to stillbirth, cross-infection, and fetal anomalies.
- Hepatitis B – Infection occurs during birth, with increased risk if maternal infection occurs in the third trimester. Newborns receive immunoprophylaxis.

Rubella

- Exposure in the first trimester has a high incidence of spontaneous abortion and congenital anomalies, including heart, eye, ear, and brain defects.
- Preconception titre testing is recommended and vaccination with three months of contraception. Vaccine should not be given during pregnancy, but there have been no documented cases of congenital rubella syndrome when inadvertently given while pregnant (SOGC, 2008).

Cytomegalovirus (CMV)

Pregnant women may be asymptomatic, but the fetal effects can be severe. CMV is easily transmitted in all body fluids and crosses the placenta to infect the fetus. Fetal effects include microcephaly and severe intellectual and developmental problems, seizures, hydrocephaly, SGA, cerebral calcifications, and deafness.

Herpes Simplex Virus (HSV)

- Type 1 infections cause cold sores; type 2 infections are sexually transmitted. HSV-1 can seroconvert to type 2 following oral–genital contact. Transmission is via the birth canal; however, caesarian birth is recommended only when active lesions are present.
- Infection control and health teaching to limit transmission are essential.
- Fetal and newborn effects include microcephaly, severe intellectual and developmental impairment, patent ductus arteriosus, and eye defects.

Human Papillomavirus (HPV)

- HPV is the most common sexually transmitted virus and certain strains are correlated with precancerous lesions, which can lead to cervical cancer. Transmission to the fetus is unknown, but infection can result in respiratory tract papillomatosis.
- With Health Canada approval in 1996, a vaccine is available and recommended for all young women prior to becoming sexually active (Public Health Agency of Canada, 2007).

HIV and AIDS

- All pregnant women should be offered voluntary HIV screening and counselling at their first prenatal visit.
- Advances in the past 25 years now give pregnant women the opportunity to be treated with antiretroviral prophylaxis to effectively help prevent HIV transmission to the fetus, and treating the pregnant women decreases risk from 25% to 2%.
- Prophylaxis treatment of a triple multidrug regimen is started at 28 weeks' gestation for most women. Treatment options, including known and unknown risks of therapy, should be discussed.
- Birth by Caesarean section if viral load is >1000 copies/mL, avoidance of invasive procedures, and

avoidance of breastfeeding greatly reduce transmission to the infant.

- Complications of HIV and AIDS, including an increased risk of infections, should be managed on an individual basis.
- The importance of compliance with the antiviral treatment needs to be emphasized. A multidisciplinary team approach to care is essential for managing this complex disease.

Group B Streptococcus (GBS)

- GBS is a bacterial infection vertically transmitted from mother to infant.
- Maternal problems include preterm labour and preterm rupture of membranes.
- Fetal neonatal problems, including blindness, deafness, mental retardation, neonatal sepsis, and meningitis, may appear within 72 hours of birth with significant morbidity and mortality.
- Prenatal assessment and treatment intrapartum with penicillin is recommended.

Varicella (Chickenpox)

Maternal varicella infections can cause serious complications to the fetus or neonate. In first trimester exposure, fetal defects include microcephaly, skin, eye, and limb anomalies, and low birth weight. Third trimester infection may rarely result in neonatal complications. A varicella zoster immune globulin (VZIG) is available to exposed pregnant women. Varicella vaccine is recommended but cannot be given during pregnancy (SOGC, 2012).

Chlamydia

- This epidemic infection is the result of a parasitic transmission that occurs by direct sexual contact or exposure at birth. Infection, often asymptomatic in the mother, is associated with increasing infertility rates in Canada.
- Fetal and newborn effects are common and include prematurity, low birth weight, and stillbirth.
- Prophylaxis erythromycin eye treatment is given to all newborns at birth to prevent conjunctivitis and potential eye sequelae.

Gonorrhea

- This bacterial infection is spread by direct contact in the lower genital tract, causing only minor maternal symptoms but potentially serious infections.
- Fetal effects include preterm birth and the premature rupture of membranes. Newborns are at risk for pneumonia and eye infections. Prophylaxis erythromycin eye treatment is given to all newborns at birth to prevent conjunctivitis and potential eye sequelae.

Nursing Considerations

- Routine screening for STIs should be part of all

initial prenatal assessments. Nurses need to know reportable STIs.

- Thorough history-taking in a private setting with a nonjudgemental approach is important for honest disclosure of high-risk behaviours.
- Stress the importance of consistency and compliance with treatment protocols for infections.
- Refer to appropriate community resources for information and follow-up care.
- Administer prophylactic treatment to all newborns as indicated.

RESPIRATORY DISORDERS

Asthma

For unknown reasons, the incidence and severity of asthma during pregnancy may improve (30%), remain unchanged (50%), or worsen (22%) (Gardner & Doyle, 2004).

Infections

- Most upper respiratory tract infections are self-limiting and pose no added risk to the fetus.
- Bacterial pneumonia should be treated with antibiotics that are considered safe in pregnancy, including those in the penicillin family.

Nursing Considerations

- For all respiratory conditions, the approach to care centres around the prevention of hypoxemia in the mother. This includes promoting effective control of asthma attacks.
- Systemic steroid when used in the treatment of maternal asthma in the first trimester may be teratogenic.
- Over-the-counter cold and cough remedies cause vasoconstriction of blood vessels, which may elevate blood pressure and therefore should be avoided. Herbal treatments may have unknown side effects, including potential harm to the fetus, and should be avoided.
- Hypoxemia associated with acute respiratory distress or pneumonia may cause fetal compromise, and chronic hypoxia may increase the risk for SGA.

CONNECTIVE TISSUE DISORDERS

These diseases are characterized by an autoimmune-mediated abnormality and include rheumatoid arthritis, multiple sclerosis, scleroderma, myasthenia gravis, and systemic lupus erythematosus (SLE). SLE has the most significant and serious consequences for the mother, fetus, and infant.

Systemic Lupus Erythematosus (SLE)

- SLE affects any and all body systems and results in connective tissue inflammation in a disease that is marked by remissions and exacerbations.

- Maternal effects depend on whether the disease is in remission at the time of conception. Ideally, a remission period of six months or longer with normal renal function will result in a positive outcome in the vast majority of pregnancies. If conception occurs during a period of exacerbation, the disease tends to worsen and maternal complications increase.
- Maternal complications may include spontaneous abortion, hypertension, preterm labour and birth, and intrauterine death. Postpartum also presents an increased risk time for triggering and exacerbation of the disease.
- If the woman has compromised chronic circulatory or renal impairment from SLE, pregnancy is not advised as it can be life-threatening for the mother and often results in spontaneous abortion.

Nursing Considerations

- When health teaching, emphasize the importance of adequate rest, especially with the increased metabolic demands of pregnancy. Teach the mother to recognize the signs of preterm labour.
- Educate the woman as to the antenatal fetal well-being monitoring techniques.
- Ensure that the mother understands to immediately report the early signs of SLE flare-ups.

CANCERS

The occurrence of pregnancy and cancer together during the child-bearing years is relatively rare but represents a devastating time of fear and crisis for the woman and her family. Pregnancy is a growth event as the hormones of pregnancy work to prepare and sustain the woman's body to support the pregnancy and developing fetus. Hormone-responsive cancers may also experience accelerated growth as a result.

Breast Cancer

- Cancer may be difficult to diagnose in pregnancy due to breast growth, difficulty palpating masses, and avoidance of mammograms in pregnancy.
- Increased vascularity and estrogen hormones may accelerate tumour growth; estrogen receptor tumours are more common in pregnancy.
- The prognosis is often worsened because of advancement of the disease by the time a diagnosis is made.
- Radiation therapy is avoided due to teratogenic fetal effects. Surgery for tumour removal is often the treatment of choice. For advanced disease, chemotherapy may be used in the second or third trimester to improve maternal survival.
- Breastfeeding is contraindicated due to the unknown risk of transmission, and the increased vascularity in the unaffected breast may increase the risk of metastases.

Malignant Melanoma

- Although it is a relatively rare cancer in the child-bearing years, pregnancy may worsen melanoma due to the physiological effect of the increased production and release of melanocyte-stimulating hormone.
- It is recommended that women delay pregnancy for three years following surgical treatment for melanoma until the high-risk recurrence time has passed.
- Cancer therapy, especially in the embryonic and first trimester, can lead to fetal death, spontaneous abortion, and growth retardation, and chemotherapy is avoided until the second or third trimester if possible.

Nursing Considerations

- A multidisciplinary approach in collaboration with the family is essential in all stages of treatment and care.
- Decisions regarding treatment options and continuing with the pregnancy are deeply personal and need to be supported and informed by the best available research.
- Nurses need to recognize the importance of seeking support for themselves when working with families in these very difficult circumstances.

HYPERTENSION

Hypertension in pregnancy can be a pre-existing chronic condition or can be associated with the pregnancy itself. PIH, also known as pre-eclampsia and eclampsia, poses a more significant risk for the mother and the fetus.

PRIMARY HYPERTENSION

- Includes pre-existing chronic hypertension and chronic renal diseases
- Increases the risk for uteroplacental insufficiency and placental abruption
- May lead to intrauterine growth retardation

HYPERTENSIVE DISORDERS OF PREGNANCY

Predisposing Factors

- Primigravida
- Adolescent or advanced maternal age: younger than 18 years or older than 35 years
- Diabetes mellitus
- Chronic hypertension or chronic renal disease
- Multiple pregnancy
- Previous or family history of hypertensive disorders of pregnancy (HDP).
- Hydatidiform mole – Molar pregnancy with a proliferation of trophoblastic cells from the chorionic villi

Pathophysiology

Placental arteries do not widen as needed to increase placental perfusion, and the resulting ischemia leads to damage of all blood vessel walls. This damage results in generalized vasoconstriction, leading to poor tissue perfusion, elevated blood pressure and damage to cell wall permeability, and fluid leakage and loss. Other consequential changes include the following:

- A decrease in placental perfusion (placental vascular insufficiency), renal blood flow, glomerular filtration rate, and oliguria
- Hepatic changes with elevated alanine transaminase (ALT), aspartate transaminase (AST), and fluids shifting into the extracellular spaces, causing an increase in the hematocrit, and stretching of the hepatic capsule resulting from subcapsular hemorrhage in the liver
- Central nervous system (CNS) – Edema, cerebral hemorrhage, hyper-reflexia, and severe headache with progression to seizure activity
- HELLP syndrome – Hemolysis secondary to vasospasm, elevated liver enzymes, and low platelet count; may occur in 2–12% of cases where capillary wall damage leads to the deposit of fibrin and platelets

Clinical Manifestations

- Cardinal signs are hypertension, proteinuria, and obvious generalized edema after 20 weeks' gestation.
- Subjective signs – Complaints of headache, photophobia, blurred or double vision, oliguria, nausea and vomiting, epigastric or right upper quadrant pain, hematuria, and severe headache
- Pulmonary edema
- Manifestations quickly resolve following the birth of the infant within 48 hours.

Maternal and Fetal Risks

- Maternal – Placental abruption leading to hemorrhage or DIC, maternal seizures, pulmonary edema, stroke, renal failure, and ruptured liver
- Fetal – SGA, prematurity, fetal hypoxia or demise, neonatal hypocalcemia

Diagnostics and Therapeutics

Diagnostics

- Mild pre-eclampsia – Hypertension and proteinuria: diastolic blood pressure ≥90, and if systolic is ≥140, monitor closely for diastolic hypertension; generalized edema of the face or hands, 1+ proteinuria, 1–2+ deep tendon reflexes, and adequate urine output
- Severe pre-eclampsia – Blood pressure greater than 160–180/110, oliguria (less than 400 mL/24 hr), 2+ proteinuria, 3+–4+ deep tendon reflexes, visual disturbances, retinal detachment, severe headache, epigastric pain, pulmonary edema, generalized edema, weight gain of more than 1 kg in one week
- Eclampsia – Seizures or coma preceded by severe headache, visual disturbances, epigastric pain, or right upper quadrant abdominal pain (SOGC, 2008)

Therapeutics for Mild Pre-Eclampsia

- Therapeutics include rest; fetal antenatal monitoring, including ultrasonography, nonstress testing (NST), and intrapartum monitoring; laboratory work-up for liver, blood, clotting factors, and renal function. Magnesium sulphate may be administered.

Therapeutics for Severe Pre-Eclampsia

- Hospitalization with advanced hemodynamic monitoring, planned early birth if worsening of symptoms or fetal compromise, fetal monitoring
- Antihypertensive therapy and magnesium sulphate ($MgSO_4$) – A loading dose is given intravenously (IV) over 10–15 min, followed by a maintenance IV dosage to lower CNS irritability and seizure risk. Magnesium toxicity should be observed for, which includes loss of the patellar reflex, respiratory depression, and hypermagnesemia leading to hypocalcemia, hot flushing, sweating, and flaccidity. The antidote for $MgSO_4$ is calcium gluconate, given intravenously. Preparation for an early birth may be necessary.

Therapeutics for Eclampsia

- Maintain a patent airway and provide oxygen support.
- A bolus amount of $MgSO_4$ is given, as well as diazepam, if needed.
- A corticosteroid for fetal lung maturation may be given if early delivery is needed.
- Vaginal birth is preferred when the mother has been stabilized.

Nursing Considerations

- Assess for worsening cardinal and other manifestations through careful monitoring and teach the mother, if still at home, to assess blood pressure and urine protein.
- Diet should be high in protein and moderate in salt.
- Assess weight daily and carefully monitor fluid intake and output.
- Promote and teach methods to maximize uteroplacental circulation, including lying in the left or right lateral position.
- Administer $MgSO_4$ following unit protocols and observe for signs of toxicity, including respiratory depression below 12 breaths per minute (bpm), depressed reflexes, and blood serum levels exceeding 1.2 mmol/L. Have on hand the antidote of calcium gluconate.
- Monitor fetal well-being with fetal heart rate (FHR) monitoring and NST.

- Use seizure precautions as needed, protect the client from injury if seizures occur, and establish a patent airway; provide supplemental oxygen.
- Promote rest and a quiet environment to minimize distress from cerebral manifestations.
- Monitor for signs of HELLP or impending seizure activity: assess level of consciousness, reports of epigastric or shoulder pain, and loss of vision.
- Observe for signs of placental abruption and be prepared for an emergency birth.
- Provide psychological support to all family members.

DIABETES MELLITUS AND GESTATIONAL DIABETES

Pregnancy is a diabetogenic event. The normal carbohydrate and hormonal changes that occur in the body during pregnancy create a situation that challenges the pancreas to produce more insulin while some of the hormones of pregnancy make the cells more resistant to the effects of insulin. For a woman with pre-existing diabetes mellitus, pregnancy is a high-risk event requiring careful ongoing management. For other women, the manifestations of diabetes will become apparent only during the pregnancy. In this situation, a diagnosis of gestational diabetes is made. For the woman with gestational diabetes, the disease process stops after the birth of the infant, although she will carry a higher risk of developing type 2 diabetes later in life. In both types of diabetes, maternal risks are present, and the fetus and newborn are also at risk for complications and must be carefully monitored.

Pathophysiology

- Placental hormones cause an anti-insulin effect, allowing the fetus, in the first half of the pregnancy, to receive the increased amounts of glucose that it needs for growth and development. Maternal glucose crosses the placenta; maternal insulin does not.
- At around 20 weeks' gestation, the maternal pancreas is challenged to produce increasing amounts of insulin, which it normally does. A woman with pre-existing diabetes cannot meet this challenge, and her symptoms of diabetes will worsen. In other women, if the pancreas fails to match the increased demand for insulin, signs and symptoms of diabetes will appear.
- If the resulting hyperglycemia is not diagnosed or well controlled, the fetus will continue to receive high amounts of glucose, resulting in excessive growth. This creates added risk during labour and at the time of birth.
- The fetal pancreas produces increased amounts of insulin to match the high levels of glucose it is receiving. Following birth, the infant no longer receives high amounts of glucose, but the pancreas needs time to adjust and continues to produce large amounts of insulin. This can quickly lead to moderate to severe hypoglycemia in the newborn.

Clinical Manifestations

Maternal

- In the first trimester, hypoglycemia is present.
- At around 20 weeks' gestation, the development of hyperglycemia and glucosuria, ketonuria, increased risk for urinary tract infections due to glucosuria, increased risk of PIH and spontaneous abortion if there is pre-existing diabetes, risk of polyhydramnios, risk of postpartum hemorrhage due to increased macrosomia.

Fetal

Risks include increased growth, LGA (over 4 kg), risk of congenital anomalies, preterm birth, birth trauma, and hypoglycemia.

Diagnostics and Therapeutics

- Monitor for glucosuria and ketonuria at all prenatal visits. Perform glucose challenge test to test for gestational diabetes at 24-28 weeks and early in pregnancy if at high risk (SOGC, 2008).
- Normal values are a fasting glucose level of 5.8 mmol/L or less. If the result is abnormally high, a three-hour oral glucose tolerance test is done with an oral load of glucose. Blood glucose levels are taken hourly for three hours, which exceeds normal limits; a diagnosis of impaired glucose tolerance (IGT) is made.
- Management includes consultation between the pregnant woman, dietitian, endocrinologist, obstetrician, pediatrician, and nurse.
- Frequent monitoring of blood glucose levels, up to four times daily, and administration of insulin injections to maintain a normal glucose level. A dietary plan is developed with the dietitian.
- Additional, frequent prenatal visits and possible planned earlier delivery at 37–38 weeks' gestation, depending on NST results and maternal well-being. Morbidity and mortality are lowest if the birth takes place as close to term as possible.
- Fetal monitoring may include additional (AFP) ultrasonograms, NST, biophysical profile, amniocentesis, an alpha-fetoprotein test, and electronic fetal monitoring during labour.
- During labour and birth, the woman is kept nothing by mouth (NPO), and an IV with 5% glucose is used to maintain normal serum glucose levels. Insulin is given as needed. Postpartum, insulin requirements decrease, especially for the first 48 hours.
- Breastfeeding is encouraged as it lowers the amount of insulin required.
- The newborn is monitored closely for respiratory distress and hypoglycemia. IV dextrose is administered and adjusted according to frequent blood glucose levels. Care in a level 2 or 3 nursery may be required.

Nursing Considerations

- Because oral hypoglycemics cross the placenta, they are considered teratogenic and are not used in the first trimester. Glyburides are used in later trimesters.
- Teach the pregnant woman the manifestations of hyperglycemia and insulin reaction and measures to take for each.
- Support and encourage compliance with needed diligence for glucose testing, insulin self-administration, dietary control, balancing rest and activity levels, accurate record-keeping, and follow-up visits to specialists.
- Provide information and support for additional tests monitoring fetal well-being.
- Prepare the woman and family for a possible earlier planned birth and the potential need for a caesarian birth.
- Observe for signs of hypoglycemia in the newborn, including lethargy, jitteriness, poor sucking reflex, and a blood glucose level of less than 2–2.5 mmol/L.
- Observe the newborn for signs of respiratory distress, birth trauma, hypothermia, and possible congenital anomalies.
- Promote and support breastfeeding as the ideal feeding option for mothers with diabetes.

PREGNANCY COMPLICATIONS

ADOLESCENT PREGNANCY

The pregnancy rate for teenagers in Canada has been declining since 1994 with the exception of Nunavut and the Northwest Territories (Min et al., 2006). Pregnancy during the teen years presents many life challenges and interrupts the normal developmental tasks of adolescence. Pregnant adolescents and their newborns are at an increased risk for complications; the younger the teen, the higher the risk. All of the determinants of health need to be addressed during and after the pregnancy, and if the young mother chooses to raise her child, community support is essential.

Risk Factors

Obstetrical: Premature birth; high risk of PIH, anemia, and poor nutrition; lack of knowledge about the harm of using tobacco and alcohol; poor prenatal care if the pregnancy is hidden; cephalopelvic disproportion; SGA infants; postpartum hemorrhage

Psychosocial: Lack of partner and family support, interruption to education, feelings of isolation and fear, lack of knowledge and life experience to manage changes and transitions, risk of poor coping strategies, lack of community support in isolated areas with minimal resources, negative attitudes and judgement from others

Socioeconomic: Unless community support through services directed at adolescent parents is available and accessible, teen parents are at risk for not completing high school or progressing to postsecondary education, low earning potential, lack of affordable housing, continued social isolation, chronic stress and poor self-esteem, and increased risk of inadequate nutrition for themselves and their child.

Nursing Considerations

- Provide collaborative, early intervention and prenatal care that focuses on the young woman's strengths in a trusting and supportive environment of care. Assess the adolescent's maturity, coping strategies, health history, and support systems, both available and needed. Use a collaborative approach to decision making and planning for the birth of the baby and understanding the demands of the pregnancy.
- Identify the needs of adolescence and her obstetrical risk factors.
- Arrange referral to community resources and programs for teen mothers, including those sponsored by Health Canada. Needs may include programs for prenatal nutrition; healthy-baby programs; parenting programs; social services for housing, child care, and employment; and educational opportunities to finish high school.
- Provide counselling and nonjudgemental support to assist the new mother with postpartum decisions regarding appropriate birth control options.

SPONTANEOUS ABORTION (MISCARRIAGE)

A spontaneous abortion is the natural termination of the pregnancy before viability is established, which is usually at 20 weeks' gestation. Early miscarriage occurs in the first 12 weeks of pregnancy.

Pathophysiology

- Maternal factors – Infection, cervical insufficiency, failure of the placenta to develop or implant normally, trauma, teratogenic exposure
- Fetal factors – Genetic or developmental abnormality, faulty implantation into endometrium

Clinical Manifestations

- Threatened – No cervical dilatation, cramping, vaginal spotting or bleeding. The pregnancy may or may not terminate.
- Imminent or inevitable – Bleeding, cramping, with cervical dilatation
- Incomplete – Bleeding, expulsion of only some of the products of conception
- Complete – All products of conception are expelled.

- Missed abortion – Embryo or fetal death without cervical dilatation, cramping, or bleeding. No FHR is detected; pregnancy test is negative.
- Habitual – Three or more consecutive miscarriages

Diagnostics and Therapeutics

- Threatened – Rest, avoidance of sexual intercourse, restricted activities
- Incomplete – Outpatient day surgery for D&C
- Missed abortion – Vaginal or abdominal ultrasound, HCG hormone test, D&C to remove products of conception. If the missed abortion is between 16 and 20 weeks, induction of labour may be required with prostaglandins.
- Complete – No medical treatment is necessary; provide emotional support and follow-up.
- Habitual – Referral for infertility investigation, possible surgical intervention for incompetent cervix
- Grief reaction at the loss of the pregnancy includes shock, disbelief, sadness, anger, depression, and fear for fertility and the future ability to carry a pregnancy.

Nursing Considerations

- Provide a WinRho® injection to any woman who is Rh-negative to prevent a maternal immune antibody response.
- For each woman, a pregnancy has very individual meaning and significance. Support the woman's emotional reaction and response; dispel any feelings of blame or guilt.
- Teach what to expect with either natural completion of the miscarriage process or operative D&C procedure.
- Assess vital signs and vaginal bleeding; provide pain relief and emotional support.
- Refer as appropriate to community resources for follow-up counselling, including local grief support and infertility groups.

PLACENTA PREVIA

Pathophysiology

- The placenta implants in the lower uterus, at or near the internal os at the cervix, instead of the top one-third of the uterine fundus. The cause is unknown, but this condition affects about one in 300 pregnancies, and the following risk factors have been identified: multiparity, previous caesarian birth or uterine surgery, previous placenta previa, tobacco use, and maternal age greater than 35 years.
- Close to term, around 30 weeks' gestation or later, placental villi become separated from the uterine wall as the uterus contracts and the cervix thins and dilates.
- Placenta previa is classified by the position of the placenta:

- Total or complete – The placenta completely covers the internal os.
- Partial or incomplete – The placenta covers some of the internal os.
- Low-lying or marginal – The placenta reaches but does not cover the internal os.

Clinical Manifestations

- Painless, bright red vaginal bleeding with a uterus that is soft and relaxed or relaxes between contractions

Diagnostics and Therapeutics

- Many low-lying placenta previas are commonly detected on early antenatal ultrasonograms and resolve by term as the uterus elongates. Repeat ultrasonography in the third trimester is needed for confirmation of true placenta previa. The need for caesarian birth is determined by the classification of the previa, the amount of vaginal bleeding, and fetal well-being.
- In unconfirmed placenta previa, vaginal examination may be deferred until emergency operative interventions are in place.
- Decision to allow a vaginal birth is based on ultrasound findings, which locate the placenta.
- Outpatient management may be used if the woman is stable, home support is available, bed rest is an option, and there is close proximity to the hospital with readily available transportation and telephone access (Oppenheimer, 2007).
- If blood loss is significant or worsens, interventions must include maternal resuscitation for blood loss and shock. Immediate delivery must be done to treat fetal distress due to hypoxia.
- Blood typing, cross-match, and available blood products for maternal resuscitation are needed.

Nursing Considerations

- Reinforce the need for bed rest and accurate pad counts to monitor bleeding. Teach the client to report immediately any changes in condition.
- Ensure that women who are discharged home prior to labour and birth understand and are able to comply with outpatient management. Sexual intercourse is contraindicated.
- Observe for signs of shock and be prepared to insert a large-bore intravenous catheter to administer blood products and proceed to emergency operative birth.
- Provide emotional support and an opportunity to discuss fears and anticipatory grieving response.
- Monitor for fetal well-being and FHR and conduct an NST; birth will be delayed if possible to allow for fetal lung maturity. Steroids may be given to advance lung maturity.

PLACENTAL ABRUPTION

Placental abruption occurs when a normally implanted placenta prematurely separates or partially separates in the second half of pregnancy or during labour. Abruption is an emergency situation with a high risk of maternal and fetal morbidity and mortality.

Pathophysiology

- The exact cause or causes are unknown, but theories include the degeneration, necrosis, and separation of the placental arterioles at the site of implantation.
- The bleeding can be concealed (no vaginal bleeding) due to formation of retroplacental clot.
- Risk factors include primary hypertension or PIH, multiparity, abdominal trauma short umbilical cord, previous caesarian birth, large placenta, smoking, vasoconstrictive drugs, decompression of overdistended uterus, delivery of first twin, and older mothers.
- Complete abruption with massive hemorrhage can lead to complications including fetal demise, maternal shock, DIC, and death.

Clinical Manifestations

- Sudden, intense pain with or without bright red vaginal bleeding
- Concealed bleeding
- Uterus is hard; does not relax between contractions
- Sudden onset of acute, severe fetal compromise
- Signs of maternal shock with tachycardia, hypotension, cold clammy skin, pallor, loss of consciousness

Diagnostics and Therapeutics

- Often this is an obstetrical emergency, and interventions may be initiated based on clinical findings without confirmation by ultrasound, especially if maternal and fetal compromise is present. If maternal and fetal vital signs are stable, an ultrasound may be used to confirm bleeding, but not to diagnose concealed abruption.
- Immediate birth is planned for, vaginal or caesarian, depending on the stage and progression of labour.
- Nursing staff need to be prepared for the possible resuscitation of the mother and infant.

Nursing Considerations

- Key consideration:

  - Note the distinguishing difference between placenta previa (painless) and placental abruption (painful) bleeding in your immediate assessment.

- Initiate emergency measures to assist in prompt resuscitation efforts and emergency birth: establish an IV and administer volume expansion fluids, administer oxygen 6–8 L/min at 100%, monitor FHR continuously, perform ultrasonography if time and condition allow, cross-match and administer blood prn.
- Provide information and support to the mother and family members.

ECTOPIC PREGNANCY

An ectopic pregnancy occurs when the fertilized ovum implants itself in a location outside the uterine endometrium.

Pathophysiology

- Implantation can occur anywhere, including the abdominal cavity, but, overwhelmingly, implantation occurs in the fallopian tube, mainly on the right side, for reasons that are unknown.
- Risk factors – Fallopian tube damage secondary to pelvic inflammatory disease, STIs, structural abnormalities, tumours, scarring and partial obstruction, IUD contraceptive, endometriosis, history of ectopic pregnancy, tobacco use, maternal age >35 years

Clinical Manifestations

- Early rupture – Missed menstrual period or abnormal period, signs and symptoms of early pregnancy and positive pregnancy test, abdominal tenderness over lower abdomen
- Rupture – If the fallopian tube ruptures, acute lower quadrant abdominal pain occurs, often on the right side, along with referred shoulder pain, low-grade fever, and possible shock due to blood loss.

Diagnostics and Therapeutics

- Careful history-taking is important as manifestations mimic other conditions, including appendicitis, ovarian cyst, and urinary tract infection.
- Pelvic examination, ultrasonography to confirm, laparoscopic surgery to remove the products of conception, possible repair or removal of the fallopian tube, and control of bleeding
- Systemic methotrexate may be considered for unruptured or chronic ectopic pregnancies as it destroys the pregnancy over several weeks while preserving the fallopian tube.

Nursing Considerations

- Careful menstrual history-taking is essential; in particular, take note of missed or unusual menstrual periods, use of IUD, or past history of STIs or infections.
- Observe for signs of shock and prepare for surgery.
- Offer support and counselling as often the woman may not have been aware a pregnancy had occurred.
- Women with an Rh-negative blood type must

have WinRho® administered to prevent blood incompatibility antibody formation.

HYPEREMESIS GRAVIDARUM

This condition of severe, unrelenting nausea and vomiting occurs in about 1% of pregnancies and greatly impacts the quality of life of the women affected.

Pathophysiology

This condition is poorly understood and likely related to many factors. Theories have included high levels of circulating HCG. It is also associated with multiple gestation and hydatidiform molar pregnancy.

Clinical Manifestations

- Persistent vomiting that leads to a 5% prepregnancy weight loss with associated electrolyte balance and ketonuria (Arsenault & Lane, 2002)
- Psychosocial aspects – Anxiety, worry, exhaustion, and depression related to quality of life issues, including absence from employment and relationship and family stress. The severity of the personal impact has led some women to consider or undertake elective termination of the pregnancy.

Diagnostics and Therapeutics

- Diagnosis is made on the basis of history-taking and presenting manifestations, including confirmation by blood electrolytes and urinalysis and weight loss confirmation.
- Oral pharmacological interventions considered safe for use in pregnancy include doxylamine–pyridoxine combination as the standard of care. Other medications may be used for breakthrough episodes or as adjunct therapy.
- Corticosteroids are avoided in the first trimester due to their teratogenic effect.

Nursing Considerations

- Provide information and reassurance regarding current pharmacological interventions.
- Supportive therapies may include ginger, acupuncture, acupressure, and meditation.
- Encourage dietary and lifestyle changes that support the woman's choices in choosing foods that are appealing.
- Early recognition and prompt treatment to restore metabolic balance and quality of life
- Accurate intake and output; monitor weight, assess for fetal well-being
- Offer reassurance and counselling to address psychosocial distress, fears, and concerns.
- Refer to social services as appropriate if hospitalization is prolonged.

TERATOGENS AND SUBSTANCE ABUSE

A teratogen is any agent, drug, toxin, chemical, or infection that can harm the developing embryo or fetus. Depending on molecular size and fat solubility, many, if not most, substances cross the placenta. During the embryonic stage of development in the first trimester, exposure to teratogens can have devastating consequences for the developing embryo, resulting in spontaneous abortion, congenital defects, or death (see Figure 9.2). Even with over-the-counter and prescription medications, teratogenic effects are still poorly understood, and decisions to use medications must be made balancing the risks and benefits to maternal and fetal well-being. A few commonly used teratogenic substances and their effects are described below.

Alcohol

- The severity of fetal effects is influenced by development at the time of exposure, genetic sensitivity, and quantity of alcohol exposure. No safe amount of alcohol consumption is known.
- Adverse effects of fetal alcohol spectrum disorder (FASD) and fetal alcohol syndrome (FAS) include congenital defects, including craniofacial deformities, skeletal abnormalities, cardiac anomalies, moderate to severe intellectual and development delays, recurrent ear infections, behavioural problems including impulsivity, attention deficit hyperactivity disorder (ADHD), and short-term memory impairment. These abnormalities persist into adulthood with ongoing negative outcomes and adverse effects on quality of life.
- The newborn may exhibit irritability, a high-pitched cry, inconsolability, jitteriness, and poor sucking and feeding.
- Nursing considerations include careful antenatal assessment and teaching that no amount of alcohol is safe. Screen for alcohol use. Referral to community agencies and ongoing support to stop drinking should be provided. Referral should be made to FAS follow-up programs and provision made for long-term support for newborn effects.

Tobacco

- Nicotine in tobacco products, inhaled via smoking or exposure to second-hand smoke, is a powerful alkaloid vasoconstrictor that can affect uteroplacental blood flow.
- Fetal effects include prematurity, SGA, increased incidence of childhood asthma, and increased risk of sudden infant death syndrome (SIDS).

Cocaine

- A powerful vasoconstrictor that leads to decreased cardiac output, uteroplacental insufficiency, and an

increased level of fetal neurotransmitters
- Maternal effects include onset of premature labour, risk of spontaneous abortion, cardiovascular failure, hypertensive crisis, seizures, and placental abruption.
- Fetal complications – Prematurity, SGA, brain damage, cardiac anomalies, CNS abnormalities including cerebral infarcts, fetal compromise
- Neonatal complications – Neurobehavioural abnormalities at birth, including hyper-reflexia, high-pitched cry, extreme sensitivity to environmental stimuli, poor feeding, diarrhea, increased risk of SIDS

Pregnancy Risk Drug Categories

When pharmaceutical drugs are prescribed for a pregnant woman, consideration is given to the designated risk categories described below (Meadows, 2001).

Risk Category A: The drug is usually considered safe in pregnancy. Clinical information has failed to show risk in the first trimester, and there is no evidence of risk in later trimesters. Few drugs can meet these strict criteria for safety due to a lack of absolute certainty.

Risk Category B: Animal studies show no risk. There are no adequate clinical studies in women. Many prescribed drugs used in pregnancy fall into this category, such as penicillin antibiotics. Clinical trials cannot be done for ethical reasons, so risk is based on safety in animal studies and historical use in clinical settings.

Risk Category C: Animal studies do show risk. The potential benefit to a pregnant woman may outweigh the risks to the fetus.

Risk Category D: There is evidence of risk to human fetuses.

Risk Category X: Use is contraindicated. The risks outweigh the benefits.

FETAL EVALUATION AND MONITORING

ESSENTIALS OF FETAL EVALUATION

Some of the most frequently used tests to assess for fetal well-being in the antenatal and intrapartum periods are described below. Daily monitoring of fetal movememnts starting at 26-32 weeks should be done in clients at risk for adverse outcomes. Contraction stress test is used when biophysical profile is not accessible.

Nonstress Test (NST)

The brain is extremely sensitive to the amount of oxygen it receives. Any maternal condition that adversely affects blood and oxygen supply to the placenta can lead to fetal hypoxia and distress. A sign that the fetus is receiving enough oxygen for the CNS

to respond normally is seen when the FHR increases in response to fetal activity. This is considered a reassuring sign of fetal well-being. This ability to respond is assessed during an NST. When the fetus does not respond as expected, it may be an indication of acute or chronic conditions of hypoxia.

- Indications – Any high-risk maternal condition that may cause uteroplacental insufficiency, including hypertension, HDP, renal disease, diabetes, cardiac disease, or multiple gestation. Also, if the mother reports decreased fetal activity, an NST may be used along with ultrasound to assess well-being. This test is also part of the biophysical profile test.
- Procedure – An external FHR monitor is attached and a tocodynamometer is strapped over the woman's uterus to pick up uterine activity. Over a 20-minute period, the FHR changes in response to fetal activity are recorded on a monitoring strip. There are three categories of NST: normal, atypical, and abnormal. If no acceleration in a 40-minute period, follow up with a CST or biophysical profile.

Biophysical Profile (BPP)

This series of five tests, using real-time ultrasound imaging and FHR monitoring, is a noninvasive way of assessing for signs of fetal compromise from conditions that may be causing acute or chronic hypoxemia and asphyxia (Table 9.2). Ultrasound is used to assess the volume of amniotic fluid and fetal activity and breathing movements. Fetal monitoring assesses the increased FHR normally expected in response to fetal movement. A modified BPP, using only an NST and amniotic fluid volume, is also used. Using multiple test parameters to assess well-being is considered more accurate than assessing only one factor. A score of 8 to 10 is considered a reassuring measure of fetal well-being (Manning, 1999).

Nursing Considerations

- Counsel and educate the woman about the purpose and procedure; the test is completed in 30–45 minutes and is noninvasive and not painful.
- Occasionally, the fetus will be sleeping and nonactive. Otherwise, the test may have to be repeated. The mother should be reassured that this is not uncommon.

Ultrasonography

High-frequency sound waves are painlessly transmitted via a vaginal or abdominal transducer. Sound waves reflect different body tissue densities and are displayed on a monitor. This diagnostic tool is widely used to assess the status of the pregnancy and fetal growth and well-being.

Table 9.2   Biophysical Profile Scoring

Biophysical Variable	Normal Score = 2 points	Abnormal Response = 0
Fetal Breathing Movement	At least 1 episode, 30 seconds in duration in a 30-minute test	Absent or less than 30 seconds in a 30-minute test
Gross Body Movement	Three distinct body or limb movements in 30 minutes	Less than three movements
Fetal Tone	At least one active extension and flexion of limb or trunk	Slow, partial, or absent
Reactive Fetal Heart Rate (FHR)	At least two episodes of FHR acceleration >15 beats/minute, lasting 15 seconds in duration in 30 minutes	Less than two episodes
Qualitative Amniotic Fluid (AF) Volume	One or more vertical pockets of AF of at least 1 cm	Either no pockets of AF or <1 cm in two vertical planes

Source: Adapted from Manning, F. A. (1999). Fetal biophysical profile. *Obstetrics & Gynecology Clinics of North America, 26*(4), 557–577.

- First trimester indications – If used before 20 weeks' gestation, fetal gestational age can be calculated within three days' accuracy by measuring crown–rump length and biparietal skull diameters. Ultrasound at 8-12 weeks is most accurate. Other indications include confirmation of fetal demise, fetal heart beat, location of placenta, number of fetuses, obvious anatomical abnormalities, amniotic fluid volume, ectopic pregnancy diagnosis, and vaginal bleeding.
- Second and third trimester indications – Placental location, source of vaginal bleeding, and amniotic fluid volume, are less accurate in confirming gestational age and growth, polyhydramnios, congenital anomalies, fetal presentation and position
- Procedure – Before 20 weeks' gestation, the woman drinks enough fluids to have a full bladder to lift the uterus up out of the pelvis for better visualization. Gel is applied to the abdomen with the woman lying on her back. It takes about 20 minutes to complete the test.
- Ultrasonography is widely used because to date no harmful effects have been found. There is controversy over the use of ultrasonography for gender identification; this practice is not condoned or a legitimate indication for use in Canada. Ultrasonography may provide false reassurance that the fetus has no health issues or complications.

Amniocentesis

This is a test used to obtain a sample of amniotic fluid for biochemical and genetic analysis. It is performed at 15–17 weeks' gestation when enough amniotic fluid is available to sample. Clinical trials using early amniocentesis before 12 weeks' gestation showed increased risk of complications and spontaneous abortion; the test is not performed in Canada before 15 weeks.

- Indications – Maternal age over 35 years, karyotyping assessment for chromosomal abnormalities, bilirubin levels, alpha-fetoprotein levels, assessing fetal lung maturity by lethicin to sphingomyelin ratios (L:S); a 2:1 ratio indicates lung maturity, hemolytic disease if the mother's antibody titre is elevated
- Procedure – The woman is prepped and empties her bladder, and abdominal ultrasonography is used to locate a pocket of amniotic fluid and avoid fetal and placental structures. By needle aspiration, 15–20 cc of amniotic fluid is removed. The mother and fetus are monitored throughout the procedure.
- Complications are less than 1% but may include spontaneous abortion, hemorrhage, Rh iso-immunization, infection, fetal injury, leaking of amniotic fluid, and premature rupture of membranes. The woman may experience mild cramping postprocedure.
- WINRho is administered to Rh-negative women to prevent antibody formation.

Percutaneous Umbilical Blood Sampling

Also known as cordocentesis, a sample of blood from an umbilical vein is collected for evaluation.

- Indications – Blood sampling for chromosomal analysis, bilirubin levels, blood cultures to diagnose fetal infection, treatment for Rh blood incompatibility with exchange transfusion, diagnosis of blood type and blood disorders, blood gas analysis

- Procedure – Can be performed after 18 weeks' gestation. Ultrasound is used to visualize the needle placement into the umbilical vein near the placenta. FHR monitoring is used to assess for fetal compromise.
- Risks include fetal injury, leakage of amniotic fluid, and fetal distress during sampling or treatment

LABOUR AND BIRTH PROCESSES

The intrapartum period, composed of four stages, begins with the onset of regular, true contractions that result in cervical dilatation and end with the recovery and stabilization of mother and infant following the birth.

FACTORS THAT AFFECT THE LABOUR PROCESS

The four factors, also known as the 4 Ps, are the passage, the passenger, the powers, and the psyche of the mother.

The Passage

The passage is made up of the maternal structures of the pelvis and soft tissues that the fetus must navigate through in the process of being born.

- Bony pelvis – Of the four types of pelvis (android, anthropoid, platypelloid, and gynecoid), the gynecoid pelvis is the most common (50%) and is ideally suited in its shape and dimensions to accommodate the movements of the fetus toward birth.
- Soft tissues – The lower uterus, cervix, vaginal canal, and introitus (opening) must all thin, stretch, and open to allow the fetus to pass through.

The Passenger

The fetus, or passenger, travels through the passage with an ease or degree of difficulty that is influenced by several factors.

Fetal Head Size: The skull of the fetus is made up of bony plates connected by unfused suture lines and two fontanelles. The anterior and posterior fontanelles can be palpated vaginally to help determine the position and presentation of the fetus. The fetal skull can fit through the bony pelvis with the help of a slight overlapping of the bones, called moulding, during labour. Following birth, the head resumes its normal shape within a few days.

Fetal Lie: This describes the relationship between the long axis of the mother and the long axis of the fetus. Normal lie for a vaginal birth is longitudinal.

Fetal Presentation: The bony part of the fetus that presents or enters the pelvic inlet first. A cephalic, or head, presentation occurs in 97% of births. A breech presentation occurs in about 3%.

Fetal Attitude: The relationship of fetal body parts to each other. A normal attitude is one of moderate flexion, with the fetal chin tucked in toward the chest. A flexed attitude ideally allows for the smallest diameter of the head, the suboccipitobregmatic diameter, to enter the true pelvis. The biparietal diameter of the fetal head is the widest diameter.

Fetal Position: The relationship of the bony presenting part of the fetus to the four quadrants of the maternal pelvis. Using three letters, the position indicates if the presenting part (occiput, sacrum) is to the right or left of and anterior or posterior to the pelvis. ROA means that the occiput is facing toward the front and right of the pelvis. Posterior positions may result in persistent back pain during labour and a more prolonged labour.

Engagement: This occurs when the largest transverse diameter (usually the biparietal) of the presenting part has passed through the pelvic inlet and into the true pelvis. Engagement can be determined by vaginal examination. For the primipara, engagement may occur a few weeks before the onset of labour.

Station: Station is the relationship of the presenting part to the ischial spines of the maternal pelvis. The ischial spines are designated as station zero; above the spines is noted as a negative number from 1–5 cm and below is plus 1–5 cm. Station is assessed during a vaginal examination. Birth is imminent at +4 or +5 cm.

The Powers

Primary Powers

- These are the involuntary uterine contractions, measured by their frequency, duration, and intensity as they thin and dilate the cervix. Contractions are initiated by pacemaker points at the top of the fundus and radiate down over the uterus in rhythmic waves.
- The **relaxation phase** (minimum 60 seconds) between contractions is essential for restoring blood flow to the uterus and placenta.
- **Frequency** is measured as the time from the beginning of one contraction to the beginning of the next contraction. For example, contractions can be three minutes apart in frequency.
- **Duration** is the length a contraction lasts in seconds. Normal contractions last a maximum of 90 seconds in duration. After 90 seconds, there is a risk of fetal compromise and hypoxia.
- **Intensity** indicates the strength of the contraction, assessed by palpating the firmness of the uterus, and is recorded as mild, moderate, or strong.
- **Effacement** is measured as a percentage from 0–100%. During a contraction, the upper half of the uterus shortens and pulls up the lower uterine segment, stretching and thinning the cervix until only a thin edge can be palpated. In primiparas, effacement is quite advanced by the time contractions begin. In multiparas, effacement and dilatation occur together.

- **Dilatation** is the opening of the cervix and cervical canal from less than 1 cm to full dilatation, about 10 cm. Full dilatation marks the end of stage 1 of labour.

Secondary Powers

When the cervix is completely dilated, the secondary powers are an important aid in assisting with the descent of the fetus through the birth canal. When the presenting part of the fetus descends to the pelvic floor, the contractions become expulsive. The mother experiences the urge to "bear down," which is the secondary power and is additional help in expelling the fetus.

- Uterine contractions continue.
- The mother feels an overwhelming urge to bear down and push, contracting her abdominal muscles and diaphragm with each contraction.
- Maternal position can aid the secondary powers. Being in an upright or squatting position improves uterine blood flow and uses gravity to help with the descent and birth of the fetus.

The Psyche

This important factor encompasses all of the psychosocial influences, past experiences, preparation, hopes, and beliefs the woman brings to the labour and birth experience. This event and the support she receives will impact the memories and beliefs she will integrate into her life after the experience. Supporting, educating, and collaborating with the mother and family during all stages of the labour and birth process are essential parts of the nursing role.

PAIN MANAGEMENT DURING LABOUR AND BIRTH

Intrapartum pain is complex and has both physiological and psychological components. Uterine contractions cause visceral hypoxic pain, while traction, pressure, and stretching can also cause various pain sensations to be felt. The woman's previous experience with pain and her coping strategies, fears, support systems, and beliefs about her control over the pain will also influence her perception of pain. The goal of pain management is to collaborate with the mother in finding measures that provide comfort and superior pain relief that is safe and appropriate to the stage of labour. The need for pharmacological agents is often reduced when timely information is provided about the progress of labour and supportive comfort measures are used.

Alternatives to pharmacological pain relief can include breathing techniques, walking or rocking motions, warm showers, hypnosis, meditation, effleurage, transcutaneous electrical nerve stimulation (TENS), therapeutic touch, and acupuncture.

Pharmacological Interventions

- Systemic opioids such as morphine sulphate provide pain relief and mild sedation; however, they cross the placenta, causing fetal CNS depression. They are avoided if birth is anticipated within 2–3 hours.
- Barbiturates and tranquilizers are not recommended for use in labour as they cross the placenta, cannot be reversed, and have a long half-life that may lead to respiratory and CNS depression in the mother and newborn.
- General anaesthesia is used less often for emergency caesarian births. Maternal aspiration is a risk. Fetal CNS depression (including bradycardia, respiratory depression) may result from the drugs used and can be reversed with a narcotic antagonist.
- Regional anaesthesia usually provides very effective pain relief without affecting the woman's level of consciousness. Narcotic and anaesthetic agents are injected into a localized area and block the transmission of sensory nerve impulses to the brain. Limitations include only achieving partial pain relief, nerve damage (rare), and the need for skilled administration and careful monitoring for potential side effects.
- Regional anaesthesia methods include local infiltration of perineal tissues, pudendal block of perineal pain via local injection near the nerve plexus beside the ischial spines of the pelvis, and epidural block. In Canada, 45% of births used epidural anaesthesia, with regional differences ranging from 3% in Nunavut to almost 75% in Quebec (Canadian Institute for Health Information [CIHI], 2007).

Epidural Regional Anaesthesia

- The anaesthetic agent is usually administered when the mother is in active labour. Injection is performed by a skilled anaesthetist into the lumbar epidural space between L2 and L3 or L3 and L4. Dermatome testing is done to assess for pain and respiratory distress. Epidural anaesthesia can be used for vaginal or caesarian births.
- Preparation – Consent is obtained, an IV is established, and vital signs are recorded. A bolus of fluid is often given to increase maternal circulating volume and prevent hypotension. The mother is positioned in a curled side-lying or upright position leaning over to open the epidural spaces for maximum exposure. The nurse supports the mother in holding still during the needle insertion and alerts the physician to the onset of any contractions. If the catheter is left in place, it is securely taped to the woman's back.
- Monitoring – Pain relief is often obtained within 5–10 minutes, and the woman will experience a heaviness and numbness of the abdomen and legs. Turning the mother from one side to the other may help with even distribution of pain relief. Maternal vital signs and FHR are monitored frequently (q2–5 min initially) for hypotension and adverse effects.
- Complications, although very rare, may include inadvertent puncture of the dura with leakage of cerebrospinal fluid and respiratory distress. Injection into a vein rarely occurs but may result in seizures,

loss of consciousness, cardiovascular collapse, and even death.

Nursing Considerations

- Discuss and plan for comfort and pain management strategies early in the labour process based on assessment findings and the wishes of the mother.
- Effective support includes promoting open communication, providing anticipatory teaching, offering praise and encouragement, and providing information about the progress of labour.
- Prepare the mother for the administration of any pharmacological agents and continuously monitor the mother and fetus for any potential adverse effects. Document all findings.
- Assist with epidural block by positioning the client during the procedure, securing a continuous epidural line, establishing IV access, administering fluids, monitoring VS changes, especially hypotension, monitoring contractions and FHR, assessing the effectiveness of pain relief, assessing for bladder distension, and monitoring the progress of labour.
- Have emergency equipment and narcotic antagonists such as naloxone (Narcan) available to reduce the effects of CNS depression if narcotic analgesics have been used.
- Evaluate the effectiveness of the pain management plan and modify strategies as needed.

INTRAPARTUM FETAL MONITORING

Assessment of the FHR is the accepted standard of care to assess for fetal well-being and detect fetal compromise during active labour (Liston & Crane, 2002). FHR can be assessed using noninvasive periodic auscultation with a stethoscope or electronic transducer or via continuous electronic FHR monitoring devices. All have their advantages and disadvantages. The most appropriate and least invasive means is used to provide the information needed for optimal care of the mother and the fetus during labour.

Manual Auscultation of FHR

- This is the preferred method of FHR monitoring for women in active labour with no identified fetal or maternal risks (Liston & Crane, 2002). The FHR is heard best over the fetal back via Leopold's manoeuvre. Take the maternal pulse at the same time to ensure the fetal pulse is not the mother's.
- Fetoscope or Doppler transducer – Listen for one full minute; apply gel to the woman's abdomen when using a transducer to improve sound wave transmission.

Continuous Electronic FHR Monitoring

This method monitors the response of and relationship between the FHR and the uterine contractions.

- Indications – High-risk pregnancies with a risk of uteroplacental insufficiency, apparent signs of fetal compromise, oxytocin induction in labour
- External monitoring – A flexible disc attached to an elastic belt, called a tocotransducer, is strapped over the fundus to detect and monitor contractions, but does not accurately measure uterine intensity or resting tone. An intrauterine pressure catheter measures uterine pressure. A second transducer is placed over the fetal back to assess FHR.
- Internal (scalp clip) – This method is used when electronic fetal monitoring patterns are nonreassuring. The scalp clip can only be applied to the fetal scalp if the amniotic membranes are ruptured, the cervix is at least 2 cm dilated, and the fetal position and presentation are known.
- Advantages – Allows ongoing assessment and early intervention for signs of fetal distress during active labour; potential decrease in fetal morbidity and mortality
- Disadvantages – Potential interference with the labour process due to restriction on the mother's activity, inaccurate interpretation and increased risk for medical and surgical interventions, including caesarian birth, increased risk of infection with scalp clip monitoring, false reassurance, or increased fears and anxiety regarding fetal well-being

Baseline FHR Patterns

- Baseline FHR is 110–160 bpm over 10 minutes.
- Fetal tachycardia is considered to be a rate greater than 160 bpm over a 10-minute period. The tachycardia may be related to maternal anxiety, infection, or prematurity or may indicate distress if accompanied by other changes in FHR patterns, such as poor variability.
- Fetal bradycardia is a FHR of less than 110 bpm for 10 minutes. The bradycardia may be related to maternal hypotension, fetal hypoxia, placental separation, or cord compression. Bradycardia associated with poor variability and late deceleration patterns requires clinical assessment. May need scalp pH and prepare for early delivery.

Variability

FHR variability is the term used to describe the normal small fluctuations in heart beat rate observed over one minute. The average FHR variability is 6-25 bpm. Count maternal and fetus pulse. Variability that is absent or minimal (≤5 bpm) for 40 minutes is atypical and requires ongoing close monitoring. If this pattern continues for greater than 80 minutes, immediate intervention is needed.

Periodic Changes in FHR

The following periodic changes in FHR last less than two minutes and are in response to uterine contractions. They occur early, late, or variably during the course of the contractions.

- Accelerations – FHR normally increases with fetal activity 15 bpm for 15 seconds for term infant, and is a sign of normal sympathetic nervous system response.
- Early decelerations – Occur early in the contraction with a return to normal baseline by the time the contraction is over. They are repetitious. They are associated with head compression as labour progresses. They do not require intervention.
- Variable decelerations – Vary in duration, degree of severity, length of time, and timing during the contractions. They are associated with umbilical cord compression, and as the cord becomes compressed during or between contractions, the FHR drops and then recovers. These decelerations are considered ominous, with an immediate need for intervention if variability is also depressed and the decelerations are 60 bpm below normal baseline and last longer than 60 seconds in duration. Reduce maternal anxiety and coach to change breathing or pushing.
- Late decelerations – Occur late in the contraction, with recovery during the resting phase between contractions. They are associated with uteroplacental insufficiency as seen with maternal hypertension disorders, diabetes, or obstetrical emergencies such as placental abruption. Persistent, late decelerations are ominous, even if the FHR does not decrease dramatically, since they represent fetal compromise and hypoxia. If there is also poor variability, intrauterine resuscitation measures should be initiated promptly.

Nursing Considerations for FHR Monitoring

- Assess the most appropriate means of monitoring FHR. Provide explanations and answer questions regarding the use of electronic monitoring.
- Electronic fetal monitoring patterns should be documented with uterine contractions, every 15 minutes in the active phase of labour and every 5 minutes in the second stage of labour once pushing.
- Respond to changing situations in FHR patterns by providing the mother with information and ongoing rationales for actions.
- Initiate intrauterine resuscitation measures to correct early distress by increasing uterine blood flow and perfusion, decreasing umbilical cord compression, improving fetal oxygen supply, and allowing time for preparing for an emergency caesarian birth if needed.

Nursing Considerations for Intrauterine Resuscitation

- Change the maternal position to the left or right lateral position.
- Turn off any intravenous oxytocin or labour induction medications.
- Notify appropriate nursing and medical personnel, including the obstetrician, special care nursery, pediatrician, or neonatologist.

- Initiate maternal supplemental oxygen by nasal prongs, at 4 L/min, or face mask at 6–8 L/min.
- Increase maternal circulating blood volume by initiating or increasing IV fluids as per unit protocol.
- Assist with obtaining fetal scalp gases to assess for fetal acidosis.
- If abnormal uterine contraction patterns occur, administer tocolysis medications to stop labour and allow the uterus to rest. Tocolysis is the use of medications (terbutaline, magnesium sulphate, indomethacin, nifedipine) to suppress uterine contractions by promoting smooth muscle relaxation. Sublingual nitroglycerin puffs can also be successful.
- Prepare the client for immediate birth.

PREMONITORY SIGNS OF LABOUR

There are many theories concerning what triggers labour, including decreasing progesterone levels, increasing oxytocin and prostaglandins that stimulate contractions, and placental aging and uterine distension that irritate the uterus and stimulate contractions. The following list includes some of the most significant indicators that labour is imminent:

- "Lightening" – The perceived sensation that the fetus is lower in the pelvis. Occurs anytime in the last four weeks of pregnancy for the primipara and closer to or at the time of labour for the multipara.
- Braxton Hicks contractions – Involuntary uterine tightening becomes stronger and more frequent.
- Nesting instinct or a burst of energy may result from lowered progesterone levels.
- Diarrhea, loose stools
- Weight loss of 1–2 kg a few days before onset of labour
- Increased vaginal secretions or bloody show may indicate that the mucous plug has been expelled.
- Spontaneous rupture of membranes – Confirmed with nitrazine paper; amniotic fluid is alkaline and will fern on a glass slide; it should be clear and odourless.

STAGES AND MECHANISMS OF LABOUR AND BIRTH

First Stage of Labour

The first stage of labour is from the onset of regular uterine contractions to the full effacement and dilatation of the cervix. It is divided into three phases: latent, active, and transitional. Primiparas tend to labour longer than multiparas (20 hr versus 14 hr on average).

- Latent phase – Up to 3 cm dilatation, regular contractions, mostly progress in effacement
- Active phase: 4–7 cm dilatation, contractions every 2–5 minutes, descent of the fetus begins
- Transitional phase: 7 cm to full dilatation; contractions every two minutes are very intensely felt by the mother

Second Stage of Labour

- From complete cervical dilatation and effacement to the birth of the infant, up to two hours for a primipara, often much less time for a multipara
- Crowning – The widest diameter of the head is encircled by the introitus. Pushing is stopped to allow for controlled delivery of the head and to prevent perineal trauma.

Third Stage of Labour

- From the birth of the infant to the expulsion of the placenta, lasting up to 30 minutes
- The uterus maintains a contracted state, constricting the blood vessels and controlling bleeding.

Fourth Stage of Labour

The fourth stage is the immediate recovery and stabilization time, from the delivery of the placenta to 2–4 hours after the birth.

Mechanisms of Labour

Also known as the cardinal movements, these are the various positions the fetus assumes in a cephalic presentation as it moves through the confines of the pelvis and birth canal. See Figure 9.3.

- **Descent** – The fetus moves downward into the pelvic passageway.
- **Flexion** – The head flexes downward, chin to chest.

Posterior fontanelle
A
Posterior fontanelle
B
Posterior fontanelle
C
D
Posterior fontanelle
E
Posterior fontanelle
F

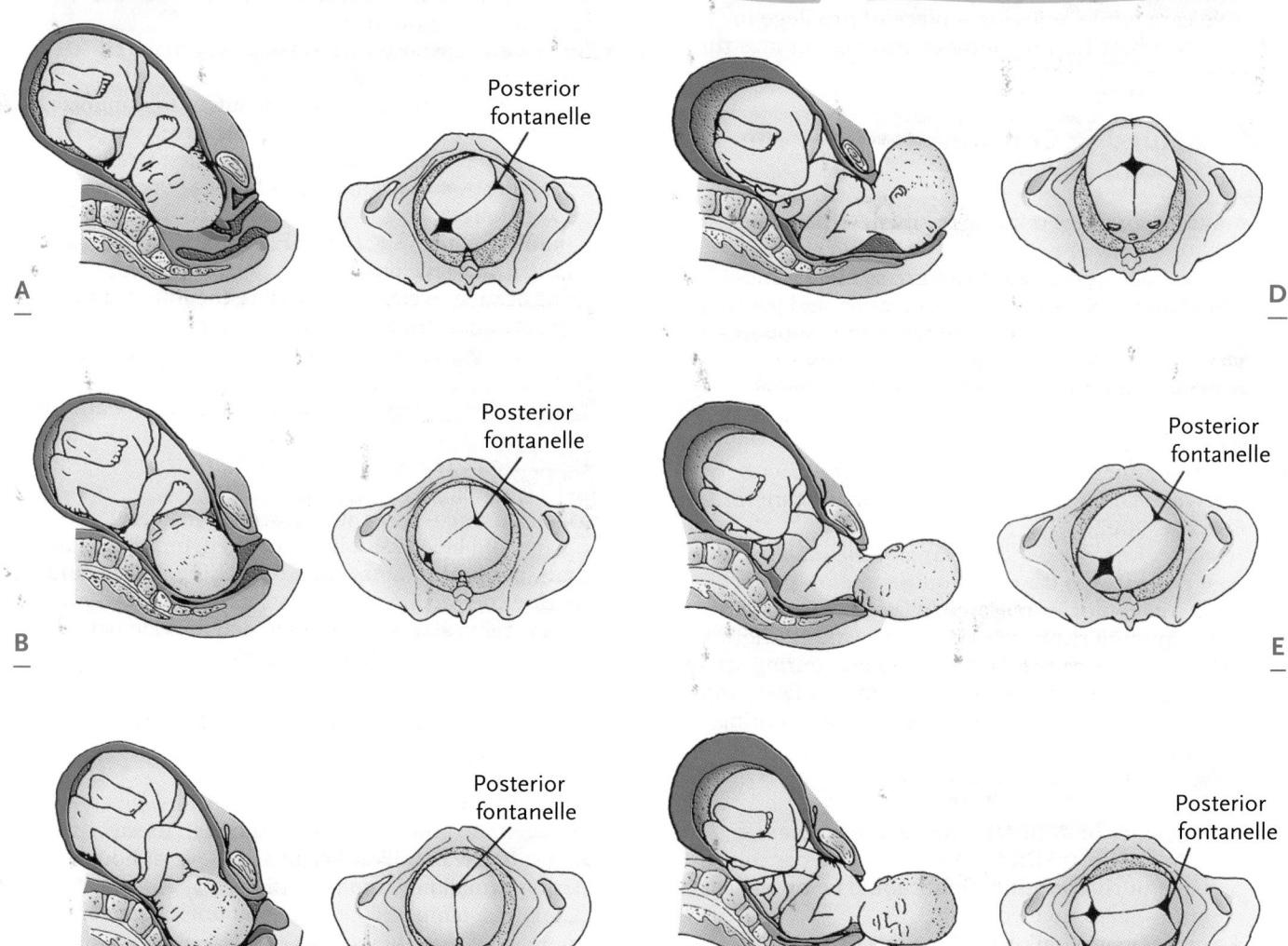

FIGURE 9.3 **Cardinal Movements of the Mechanism of Labour**

A, Engagement and descent. *B*, Flexion. *C*, Internal rotation to occipitoanterior (OA) position. *D*, Extension. *E*, External rotation beginning (restitution). *F*, External rotation.

Source: Lowdermilk, D. L., Perry, S. E., Cashion, K., & Alden, K. R. (2012). *Maternity & women's health care* (10th ed., p. 381, Figure 16-13). St. Louis: Mosby.

- **Internal rotation** – The head rotates 45 degrees.
- **Extension** – The head passes under the symphysis pubis and reaches the perineum.
- **External rotation** – The head rotates back to its original position (restitution), followed by shoulder rotation.
- **Expulsion** – The shoulders pass under the pubic arch and perineum; the body is delivered.

NURSING CONSIDERATIONS DURING LABOUR AND BIRTH

In a hospital birth, the nurse spends more time with the woman and her family during the labour and birth process than any other health care professional. This presents a significant responsibility to provide safe, effective care while enjoying a place of privilege in welcoming a new family member and person into the world.

Labour Nursing Considerations for the First Stage of Labour

- Maternal and fetal initial assessment – Includes past history, length of pregnancy, onset of labour and progression, spontaneous rupture of membranes, contractions, bloody show, preparation and plans for pain management and childbirth, family support, vital signs, FHR, gestational age, risk factors or complications, plans for infant feeding, vaginal examination for cervical dilatation, effacement, station, fetal presentation and position
- It is recommended that women in active labour receive ongoing support with 1:1 nursing care (Liston & Crane, 2002).
- Monitor the progress of labour and the maternal and fetal responses to labour according to unit protocols or more frequently as indicated by assessment findings. The minimum should be vital signs, vaginal show q1h, contractions and FHR q15–30 min during active labour and more frequent assessment of bloody show, contractions, FHR monitoring (q5–10 min) during transition.
- Monitor for bladder fullness, especially if an epidural block is used.
- Spontaneous or artificial rupture of membranes (AROM) – Assess FHR for distress due to possible cord prolapse or compression; fluid should be clear and odourless, with no meconium.
- Assess for complications of labour – Duration of contractions longer than 90 seconds, resting phase shorter than 60 seconds, FHR outside normal limits or periodic changes, maternal temperature above 38°C, rupture of membranes more than 24 hr before, foul-smelling amniotic fluid or maternal show, persistent dark or bright red vaginal bleeding, sustained abdominal pain with rigid abdomen
- Vaginal examinations are kept to a minimum to reduce the risk of infection. After the initial examination, a repeat examination may be done prior to giving additional pain medication or when the mother feels increased perineal pressure and the urge to bear down.
- Prepare for the birth when the multiparous woman reaches transition and when the nulliparous woman is fully dilated.

Nursing Considerations for the Second and Third Stages of Labour

- Prepare the mother by ensuring that her bladder is empty prior to pushing, assisting her into a birthing position, giving support for relaxing between contractions and pushing effectively during contractions, and monitoring contractions and FHR.
- Prepare for the infant by having warm, dry blankets available, a preheated radiant overhead warmer, and resuscitation equipment.
- Immediate newborn care – Assess and maintain a patent infant airway, use maternal–fetal skin-to-skin contact and immediately dry the infant to minimize hypothermia, note the time of birth, assess Apgar scores at 1 and 5 minutes, document first voiding or passing of meconium, assess for gestational age and obvious defects, provide resuscitation as needed, administer vitamin K (1.0 mg IM if birth weight >1500 g) and eye prophylaxis, verify and apply identification, weigh and measure the infant, and promote attachment with the mother and family through early breastfeeding, holding the infant, and interacting.
- Apgar scores – Used to assess adaptation to extrauterine transitions. Parameters are heart rate, respiratory effort, muscle tone, reflex irritability, and colour. A score of 8–10 is normal.
- Maternal care – Assist with placental delivery; obtain cord blood samples if required; monitor vital signs, perineal trauma, vaginal bleeding, lochia, and uterine contractility; administer oxytocin for uterine contractility; assess the bladder; and provide pain medication and a perineal ice pack.

Nursing Considerations for the Fourth Stage of Labour

- Assess for uterine contractility: Fundal height (midway between the umbilicus and symphysis); uterus rises to just below umbilical height after several hours; position (midline); and tone (firm)
- Assess perineum and lochia – Amount, character, presence of clots, hemorrhage
- Hemorrhage (blood loss greater than 500 cc) is suspected if uterine tone is soft and a perineal pad is saturated within 15 minutes. Assess the perineum for hematomas, swelling, and hemorrhoids; offer ice packs.
- Assess maternal vital signs, bladder tone, and ability to void.
- Promote early parental attachment and provide support for breastfeeding choice.

- Assess fetus for ongoing ease of transition to extrauterine life, monitor vital signs and responsiveness, and prevent heat loss.

ESSENTIALS OF LABOUR AND BIRTH COMPLICATIONS

Dystocia

Dystocia is defined as a prolonged, abnormal labour related to maternal (uterus or pelvis) or fetal factors (size, presentation, position, number of fetuses).

- Abnormal uterine contractions – Hypertonic contractions in the latent phase are abnormally painful and irregular but ineffective in effacing or dilating the cervix. Narcotic analgesia may allow the mother to rest and uterine patterns to revert to normal. Hypotonic contractions become ineffective or stop at the active phase. Oxytocin may be used to augment labour once fetal pelvic relationship problems have been ruled out.
- Precipitous labour – Lasts less than three hours, with increased risk of uterine rupture, amniotic fluid embolism, and postpartum hemorrhage. Fetal complications include distress and hypoxia.
- Pelvic dystocia relates to a pelvic shape that does not allow for descent of the fetus, leading to prolonged labour, increased risk of assisted birth with forceps or vacuum, risk of birth trauma, or caesarian birth.
- Cephalopelvic disproportion – Excessive fetal size causes problems with descent through the pelvis or under the pubic arch. Assisted birth with forceps, vacuum suction, or caesarian birth may be needed.
- Breech presentation occurs in 3% of presentations, with the sacrum (buttocks) most commonly presenting to the pelvis. There is an increased risk of birth trauma, prolonged labour, asphyxia, cord prolapse, and the need for caesarian birth.
- Multiple fetuses increase the risk of preterm labour, breech or shoulder presentation of one or more fetuses, cord prolapse, fetal compromise, and operative birth.

Induction or Augmentation of Labour

Methods, including AROM or medications, are used to initiate labour prior to the onset of spontaneous contractions.

- AROM usually stimulates contractions within 12 hr. Amniotic fluid is slowly released. The fetal head should be engaged to prevent cord prolapse. Nursing considerations include noting the time of rupture and the colour, amount, and presence of meconium and monitoring maternal temperature q2h as the risk of infection increases 24 hr after rupture of membranes.
- Cervical ripening methods include Foley catheter insertion into the cervix, cervical prostaglandin gel, and augmentation 24 hr later with oxytocin infusion.
- Oxytocin infusion – This method requires following a careful protocol for administering IV oxytocin with an infusion pump. The dosage should be increased no more frequently than q30 min followed by frequent maternal and fetal monitoring. Fetal monitoring is used and contractions are closely monitored for excessive uterine activity or tetanic contractions (>90 seconds). At any sign of maternal or fetal compromise, the oxytocin infusion is stopped until further assessment can be made (Crane, 2001).

Caesarian Birth

- Indications for a caesarian section are often related to preventing or intervening in situations of fetal compromise or maternal medical emergencies that require an immediate response or operative birth.
- Surgical incision is most commonly low segment transverse (bikini line) with improved healing and lower risk of hemorrhage or subsequent rupture. The classic and longitudinal incision increases the risks of hemorrhage, pain, healing time, and future uterine rupture is related to location of incision.
- Regional anaesthesia is the preferred method for pain management as the mother is awake and there are fewer complications than with general anaesthesia. General anaesthesia is primarily used when rapid birth is necessary in emergency situations.
- Maternal risks and complications include aspiration, infection, hemorrhage, anaesthesia complications, prolonged postpartum recovery, thrombophlebitis, pain, and immobility.
- Fetal risks include transient tachypnea with "wetter lungs" as fetal lung fluid was not removed during passage through the birth canal, as well as CNS depression from the general anaesthetic.
- Additional nursing considerations include postoperative vital sign monitoring, assessment of incision, pain management, extra assistance with infant care and feeding, monitoring for complications, and encouraging early ambulation.

Vaginal Birth After Caesarian (VBAC)

Following a caesarian birth, it may be possible for a woman to attempt to give birth vaginally in subsequent pregnancies. Recommended parameters for VBAC are the desire to have a vaginal birth, the absence of previous indications for caesarian section, uncomplicated pregnancy, fetal vertex presentation, normal labour, and a previous incision that was low segment transverse (Martel & MacKinnon, 2005).

Preterm Labour and Birth

Labour between 20 and 37 weeks' gestation with uterine contractions and cervical dilatation is considered preterm and presents the risk of premature birth of an immature fetus. Preterm labour is a common problem in pregnancy and is responsible for 75–85% of newborn deaths (Gilbert, 2007). Progesterone is used for preterm labour.

- Maternal risk factors include underweight (<45 kg), smoker, strenuous physical activity, physical abuse, no antenatal care, chronic illness, premature rupture of membranes, infection, multiple pregnancy (50% of twin gestations are premature), past history of preterm labour, maternal age less than 18 years, polyhydramnios, cervical insufficiency, cardiovascular disease, placental disorders, and unknown causes (Gilbert, 2007; SOGC, 2006).
- Therapeutic interventions include early risk screening, early detection of onset, stopping uterine contractions, and preparing for care of the premature infant. High-risk mothers should be knowledgeable and know how to immediately report all signs of preterm labour; activities may be restricted or admission to hospital indicated.
- Tocolytic intervention is used to halt labour, and indomethacin is used as a short-term tocolytic agent. Fetal well-being must be assessed during treatment. Maternal side effects include cardiovascular complications, which include the risk of pulmonary edema.
- All at-risk pregnant women between 24 and 34 weeks' gestation should be considered candidates for antenatal treatment with a single course of corticosteroids within seven days of preterm birth to hasten surfactant maturing. Treatment should be two doses, 12 mg IM of betamethasone 24 hr apart, or four doses of dexamethasone 6 mg IM 12 hr apart (Hui et al., 2007; Lowdermilk & Perry, 2007).
- If birth is inevitable, an episiotomy may be used to reduce the risk of intraventricular hemorrhage from pressure on the fragile premature skull. A pediatrician or neonatologist should be present to assist in the resuscitation and transportation of the newborn. Nursing considerations in addition to assisting with the birth include supporting the parents with factual information, avoiding false hope, acknowledging their concerns, taking photos if the infant is to be admitted to a newborn intensive care unit, and providing ongoing psychological support and information.

Perinatal Loss and Bereavement

When perinatal loss occurs during the course of a pregnancy, it is a tragedy and crisis for the parents and family. For many young families, it may be their first encounter with the death of a family member. Maternal newborn nurses and staff are also affected by the death of a fetus or newborn. Perinatal loss is unique in that it often occurs suddenly, with little warning, and interrupts the normal developmental processes of pregnancy and parenthood. Nurses need to understand the grief process as it applies to perinatal loss and provide skillful, sensitive care during this highly vulnerable time.

- Losses include stillbirths, prematurity, newborns with anomalies, and neonatal deaths.
- Grief is a personal experience of deeply felt sorrow at the loss of something highly valued. Grief occurs in stages, slowly over a period of time, allowing the individuals to work their way through the various defences the psyche uses to protect itself from the full impact of the loss. Grief does not follow a linear path—it is a dynamic process.

Stages of Grief

- Parents experience disbelief and shock as they cannot take in the reality of the news. In being overwhelmed, parents may appear not able to hear or understand what is being said to them; they may be immobile or emotionally numb in their initial reactions.
- Anger may be expressed as the reality of the situation is absorbed. Women often have more difficulty than men in expressing anger; this may result in depression and feelings of guilt. Anger may be directed at staff.
- Bargaining occurs when there is an understanding of the reality of the situation but hope that something can change it.
- Depression, overwhelming sadness, and withdrawal represent a greater level of acceptance of the impact of the loss.
- Acceptance is the process of integrating the experience and its meaning into one's life. Normal activities slowly resume, and memories of both sorrow and joy can be recounted.
- Acute grief reactions are intensely felt for 6–10 weeks, but the full process of grieving usually takes time, frequently over 1–2 years.

Behavioural and Physical Symptoms of Grief

- Somatic manifestations include weight gain or loss, nausea, hyperventilating, sighing respirations, tightening of the throat, heavy feeling in the chest, palpitations, headaches, loss of muscle strength, and extreme fatigue.
- Behavioural manifestations include preoccupation; nightmares; feelings of guilt, shame, apathy, loneliness, isolation, anger, sorrow, and irritability; decreased sexual interest; social withdrawal; crying; exhaustion; loss of concentration and motivation; and restlessness.

Nursing Considerations

- Promote an empathetic environment that openly acknowledges the death of the newborn and supports the reactions of the mother and family. Provide time for the parents to see, touch, and be with the infant. Take photos and collect as many mementos as

possible: locks of hair (requires parental permission), footprints, ID band, and weight and length information.
- Provide information about community resources on grief counselling, bereavement, and follow-up in the postpartum period.
- Be sensitive to and accommodate cultural and religious practices.
- Grieving parents are vulnerable to well-meaning but harmful comments and clichés that minimize their loss. Educate others as to why these comments are harmful. Offer suggestions for helping the family acknowledge and cope with the loss.
- Immediate and extended family members are all affected by the loss. Sibling responses will be dependent on their age and stage of development. Simple language that is honest and clear in its meaning and uses words such as "death" lessens confusion and fears.
- Nurses need to take the time to understand their own beliefs and reactions to loss and death in order to be emotionally available to others who are grieving. Finding ways to nurture oneself following these painful experiences is beneficial and important.

THE POSTPARTUM STAGE

Sometimes referred to as the fourth trimester, this six-week puerperium is when the mother's body returns to its prepregnant state, the newborn adapts to an extrauterine life, and family members begin to adjust to the many changes a newborn brings into their lives.

MATERNAL ADAPTATIONS

Physiological Changes

- Reproductive – The uterus remains firmly contracted and undergoes involution, descending from the height of the umbilicus about one fingerbreadth per day until it can no longer be palpated by days 10–14. By six weeks postpartum, the uterus has returned to its nonpregnant state. The cervix becomes thicker and firmer and contracts over several weeks to an elongated rather than a circular opening. The perineum remains swollen, perhaps bruised for a few days, and the vaginal rugae and tone return within 6–10 weeks.
- Sexual intercourse – Assuming there is no infection or complications, intercourse may resume when the woman feels physically and emotionally comfortable and ready. Appropriate methods of birth control should be discussed and planned for as part of postpartum teaching prior to discharge home.
- Lochia, or uterine discharge, changes over the course of about three weeks from lochia rubra (dark red, with small clots) for 3–4 days, to lochia serosa (pinkish, serosanguineous) from days 3 to 10, to lochia alba (whitish to clear, no odour) from day 10 to week 3.
- Breast changes – Colostrum is present at the time of birth, and breast milk is produced by the third or fourth day postpartum. Engorgement is common when milk production starts and lasts 24 hours. Newborn suckling and feeding stimulates prolactin, which stimulates more milk production. (see the section on newborn nutrition).
- Cardiovascular changes are significant as the circulating blood volume decreases rapidly and is lost through diuresis and diaphoresis (perspiration). Blood pressure remains stable; transient bradycardia (as low as 50 bpm) lasts up to three months.
- Renal – The glomerular filtration rate is elevated to help mobilize excess vascular volume; overdistension of the bladder and difficulty voiding in the first 24 hours are fairly common. A full bladder may displace the uterus in the early postpartum stages.
- Endocrine – Estrogen and progesterone drop rapidly following birth, and prolactin rises, reaching a peak at day 3, when breast milk production begins. Menstruation is often delayed with breastfeeding until 12–24 weeks postpartum. Menstruation returns for nonbreastfeeding mothers by 6–12 weeks postpartum.

Psychological Adaptations and Attachment

- The disruption to normal sleep patterns, the increased need for rest and recovery, the needs of a newborn, and changing roles and relationships all add to the stress of adapting to parenting in the postpartum period.
- The transition to parenting is aided by family and community support, positive past experiences, cultural beliefs and practices that promote attachment, and learned adaptive behaviours for coping with change.
- The term "attachment" is preferred to the older term "bonding" when describing the process by which the parents interact and form a relationship with their newborn. The newborn is more awake and sensitive to its surroundings in the first hour of life than it will be for the next two weeks, so it is an ideal time for interaction. While this time is ideal, parents should not feel guilty if circumstances do not allow for this first intimate contact to happen. Attachment is the reciprocal relationship that develops over time as parents and newborn interact with each other, using cues and responses to learn to understand each other and to connect on an emotional level.
- Most women experience postpartum blues, often on days 3–5, when milk production begins and prolactin levels surge. This condition is characterized by feelings of inexplicable sadness, letdown, and increased crying and usually resolves within 10 days.

MATERNAL COMPLICATIONS

Postpartum Hemorrhage

- Risk factors include polyhydramnios, multiple gestation, rapid labour, prolonged rupture of membrane, placenta previa, high parity, a history of coagulation disorder, uterine atony, retained placenta, and trauma.

- Early postpartum hemorrhage is a blood loss of 500 cc or more that occurs in the first 24 hr after giving birth. It is usually related to the uterus not contracting or staying contracted following delivery of the placenta, lacerations of the cervix or vagina, parts of the placenta being retained, or clotting disorders. It presents a greater risk of morbidity and mortality to the mother than does a late hemorrhage.
- Late postpartum hemorrhage occurs after 24 hr following birth and is most often related to retained placental fragments.

Nursing Considerations

- Assess uterine involution and teach the mother what to expect with vaginal discharge and what signs of complications to report, including fever >38°C, lochia that changes back to rubra or bright red bleeding, a pad that soaks through in 15 minutes, foul-smelling lochia or urine, or feelings of inability to cope and sadness that last more than one or two weeks.
- Inability to void and a full bladder may displace the uterus from its midline position, impairing the normal contractility and increasing the risk of hemorrhage. Assess the bladder frequently early in the postpartum period and encourage frequent voiding.
- Monitor the uterus and vaginal blood loss q15 min following birth for the first hour and as per unit protocol for the next 24 hr. Gentle massage of the uterus may stimulate uterine contractility, as will breastfeeding. Know the policy and procedure for responding to a postpartum hemorrhage.
- Following birth, is it recommended to administer oxytocin to promote uterine contractility and prevent postpartum hemorrhage. Effective protocols include 10 units IM, five to ten units by IV push, or 20–40 units per litre IV drip run at 150 mL/hr (SOGC, 2009).

Infection

Infection is a significant cause of maternal morbidity and may include the uterus, post–caesarian section incision, urinary tract, or breasts (mastitis).

Nursing Considerations

- Assess the mother for signs of infection including temperature of 38°C or higher, tachycardia, pain and tenderness, redness or swelling, nausea and feeling unwell, foul-smelling discharge, and excessive fatigue.
- Teach the mother how to recognize and report any signs of fever and infection. Teach the importance of taking all doses of antibiotics as prescribed. In the case of mastitis, continued breastfeeding or manual expressing of breast milk is recommended.

Postpartum Depression

Unlike those of the postpartum blues, the manifestations of depression continue and worsen over time. They include feelings of despair, hopelessness, inadequacy, ambivalence or apathy toward the newborn, inability to feel joy, and somatic symptoms of headache, appetite changes, sighing, excessive fatigue, or hyperactivity. This disorder is more common than thought or reported in the past and must be part of health teaching and follow-up care.

Nursing Considerations

It is essential that nurses teach the parents to be aware of the manifestations of depression and to seek support and medical help promptly. Depression is a disease process of neurochemical imbalance; it is not a personal failure or weakness. It is crucial to seek help, follow the treatment plan, and involve others who may provide support, including extended family and community programs.

NEWBORN ADAPTATIONS

Beginning with the process of labour, the fetus undergoes many changes on a physiological and developmental level. These transitional changes allow the newborn to adapt to life outside the uterine environment. While remaining dependent on others for nutrition, warmth, and a nurturing environment, the newborn is remarkably well equipped to interpret, respond to, and make known his or her needs.

Transition to Extrauterine Life

Transition is a critical time period in the first 6–24 hr of life, when many newborn anatomical and physiological changes occur, especially in the cardiovascular and respiratory systems. The fetus has three unique cardiac features that change during transition, beginning with the stimulation of labour and the newborn's first breath. External and internal stimuli initiate these changes. Nurses assess the newborn's ability to adapt during the different transitional periods of reactivity.

Respiratory Adaptations

- Lung maturity – By 35–37 weeks, the fetal lungs are structurally developed enough to do the work of breathing. Surfactant, a phospholipid that lubricates the lungs and helps keep them partially inflated after each breath, peaks, with an L:S ratio of 2:1.
- Fetal anatomical structures that change during transition as the newborn initiates breathing are the ductus venosus, ductus arteriosus, and foramen ovale.
- Stimuli that initiate respirations include chemical, mechanical, and sensory factors.

- Chemical stimuli – Uterine contractions temporarily decrease fetal oxygen supply, causing a mild acidosis that stimulates the respiratory centre of the brain to initiate breathing.
- Mechanical stimuli – Most of the lung fluid is squeezed out as the fetal chest is compressed in the birth canal. There is a passive intake of breath when the chest is born.
- Sensory stimuli – The abrupt change in environmental temperature at birth is a major stimulus to breathe, in addition to touch, light, sound, noise, and pain.
- After the first breath, pressure changes occur in the lungs and circulation. The lungs open and pulmonary vessels dilate, changing from a closed high-pressure system to an open low-pressure system.

Circulatory Adaptations

- Changes from a low-pressure to a higher-pressure system, causing the fetal circulatory structures to close
- The foramen ovale, located between the right and left atrium, closes as blood flow and pressure on the left side of the heart become greater than on the right side of the heart.
- The ductus venosus, located between the inferior vena cava and the umbilical vein, closes when the umbilical cord is clamped.
- The ductus arteriosus, located between the pulmonary artery and the aorta, closes when pulmonary blood flow and pressures increase. Rising oxygen levels are detected by chemoreceptor sites on the ductus, which also helps stimulate the ductus arteriosus to close.
- **Note:** These anatomical structures functionally close with 15–20 min, but a murmur may be heard for 6–12 hr in the newborn. If the infant is hypoxic or asphyxiated, the ductus arteriosus may open again. Refer to Figure 9.4, which illustrates fetal circulation.

Temperature Adaptation

- All newborns are at increased risk for heat loss (via convection, radiation, evaporation, and conduction) due to their large body surface compared to body mass, blood vessels close to the skin surface, an inability to shiver, and immature CNS temperature-control mechanisms. Newborns can also easily overheat if wrapped in too many layers of clothes.
- Maintaining a neutral thermal environment means that the newborn must use only minimum amounts of oxygen, glucose, and metabolic energy to keep warm.
- Newborns use nonshivering thermogenesis to metabolize their unique brown fat stores to generate body heat.

Renal Adaptations

- Full-term infants normally void in the first 24 hours of life. They have a limited ability to concentrate urine and may lose 10% of their body weight in the first three days of life due to fluid shifts and losses.

They will regain the weight within one week with normal feeding.
- **Note:** In the first week, a newborn that is receiving adequate hydration through feeding should have one heavy wet diaper for each day of life.

Gastrointestinal Adaptations

- The gut is sterile at birth, bowel sounds begin within the first few hours, the first meconium stool passes within 24 hours, and the newborn requires frequent feedings of 30–90 cc—or until satisfied at the breast—every few hours.
- There is an increased risk of bleeding in the first week of life, and vitamin K IM is routinely administered.
- The cardiac sphincter between the esophagus and stomach is immature, and regurgitation of feeding is common. Burping following feeding will help.
- Stool characteristics change from meconium (thick, sticky, black, passed in the first 24 hours) to transitional stools (thin, brownish-green). Breastfed stools are bright mustard yellow, loose, and frequent. Formula-fed stools are pasty, pale yellow, and less frequent. Elimination patterns may vary, from once to five or six per day in the first few weeks.
- Bilirubin and jaundice – The fetal liver is immature and unable to conjugate bilirubin well at term. Most preterm and 50% of full-term infants will experience physiological jaundice in the first week of life.
- **Note:** Physiological jaundice or hyperbilirubinemia (indicated by yellowed skin, mucous membranes, and eye sclera) appears after 24 hours of life in infants who are otherwise well, peaks at three days, and resolves itself by 10 days. Phototherapy may be used as ultraviolet light aids in conjugating bilirubin into a water-soluble form that can be excreted in urine and stools. Frequent feedings help resolve physiological jaundice.

Nursing Considerations

- Adequately hydrated newborns should wet 6–8 diapers each day.
- Monitor for physiological jaundice, encourage early and frequent feedings, and implement phototherapy as needed, covering eyes while exposing skin to ultraviolet lights. Phototherapy side effects include a sleepy newborn, loose stools, and an increased need for fluids of 10%.
- As newborns are obligate nose breathers from birth up until three months of age, ensure that nasal passages are clear.
- Closely monitor for expected vital signs and physical and behavioural adaptations.

- First period of reactivity:

  - Immediately after birth, tachypnea up to 80 breaths per minute with nasal flaring
  - Tachycardia up to 180 bpm
  - Murmur may be heard; hands and feet may appear blue (acrocyanosis) as peripheral circulation is sluggish

FIGURE 9.4 **Fetal Circulation**

Source: Moore, K. L., & Persaud, T. V. N. (2003). *The developing human: Clinically oriented embryology* (7th ed.). Philadelphia: Saunders.

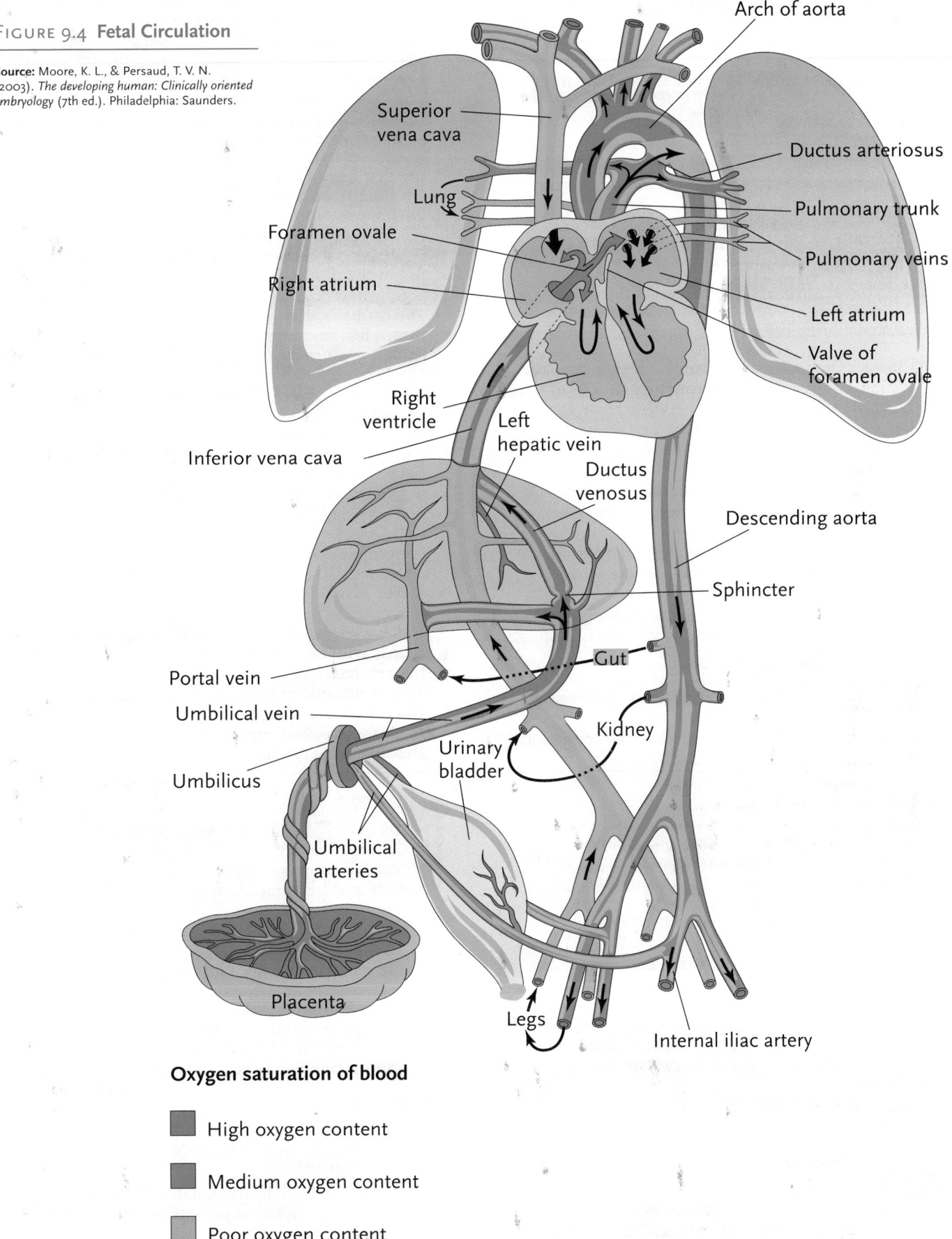

Arch of aorta

Superior vena cava

Ductus arteriosus

Lung

Pulmonary trunk

Foramen ovale

Pulmonary veins

Right atrium

Left atrium

Valve of foramen ovale

Right ventricle

Left hepatic vein

Inferior vena cava

Ductus venosus

Descending aorta

Sphincter

Gut

Portal vein

Umbilical vein

Kidney

Urinary bladder

Umbilicus

Umbilical arteries

Placenta

Legs

Internal iliac artery

Oxygen saturation of blood

High oxygen content

Medium oxygen content

Poor oxygen content

- Neurologically awake and alert
- Period of relative inactivity:

  - Heart and respiratory rate and effort decrease to normal range of heart rate 120–160 bpm
  - Respiratory rate of 30–50
  - Newborn falls asleep

- Second period of reactivity:

  - Very responsive and awake
  - Increased oral mucus may lead to gagging and cyanosis
  - May have tachycardia
  - Bowel sounds present; may pass meconium and void for the first time

- Monitor temperature frequently; prevent heat loss by drying newborn immediately, protecting from drafts

Essential Newborn Assessment

A systematic assessment of the full-term newborn reveals findings in appearance, reflexes, and responses to the environment that are normal, a variation on normal, or abnormal (Figure 9.5). These findings also vary depending on the gestational age of the newborn. Assessment should include the following:

- Vital signs – Temperature labile, prone to hypothermia due to large body surface area, not a reliable indicator of infection, 36.5–37°C, blood pressure 60/40 to 80/50, respiratory rate 30–60; listen for heart rate at apex for one full minute; 120–170 bpm when awake, 80–90 bpm when sleeping.
- Weight and length – Average weight is 3500 g; average length is 50 cm.
- Skin – Pink or ruddy, body fat present, acrocyanosis resolves after 12 hr waxy vernix is present in creases, lanugo (fine downy hair), erythema toxicum or newborn rash and milia on nose are common and resolve spontaneously. Birthmarks may be permanent, such as port wine stain, or resolve, as in strawberry hemangioma or "stork bite marks."
- Head – Appears large compared to flexed body; measure head circumference at the widest diameter of the occiput and over the eyebrows; average is 33–35 cm. Moulding resolves in the first week, anterior fontanelle is soft and pulsating and may be tense with crying, symmetrical facial features, outer edge of eye in line with top of the ear; eyes are slate blue and tearless and can focus 45 cm; ear cartilage springs back when folded. Palate in mouth is intact; may see Epstein's pearls (small white gum cysts) that look like teeth but disappear spontaneously.
- Chest – Chest moves in unison with abdomen when breathing, 32 cm circumference over nipple line, and engorged breasts are common due to maternal estrogen effect.
- Back and extremities – Flexed limbs; symmetrical, flexible, full-term nails extend beyond fingertips; back is smooth and straight; no dermal sinus or defect at base of spine; skin creases on soles of feet
- Abdomen – Cylindrical, protrudes, bowel sounds after 30 minutes, umbilical cord has two arteries and one vein and dries and falls off within seven days, patent anus passes meconium within 24 hours, voids within 24 hours, reddish-brick dust spots in urine are harmless urate crystals
- Genitals – In girls, the labia majora covers the minora, and pseudomenstruation is common due to the effect of maternal hormones; in boys, assess that both testes are in scrotum and full-term scrotum has rugae; inspect penis for central position of the urethra.
- Reflexes in full-term newborn include Moro (startle), rooting (turns head toward stroked cheek), grasp/palmar (grasps fingers around object), tonic neck (head turned to one side, same side arm and leg extend, opposite arm and leg flex), stepping (held upright, legs move as if stepping), and positive Babinski (when the sole of the foot is stroked upward, the toes extend outward).
- Behaviour states – These include crying, quiet and alert (ideal time to interact, assess, feed), deep sleep (tunes out environment, very still, regular respiratory rate), and active alert (irregular breathing, easily startled, eyes wide, may cry, turns from eye contact).

Nursing Care, Parent Teaching, and Follow-Up Considerations

- Safety – Teach the parents to never leave the newborn unattended in a bath, on a change table, or with a family pet. Also, Canadian law requires that all newborns be transported in an approved car seat. The safest position is rear-facing with the car seat in the back seat of the vehicle.
- A pinpoint bright red diaper rash that does not resolve within 24 hours may be caused by *Candida albicans* and should be assessed for antifungal skin treatment. Oral thrush (coated or red tongue and throat) will also require treatment.
- Sudden infant death syndrome (SIDS) – Newborns should sleep on their backs, in their own crib, on a firm mattress with no pillows or thick blankets in the crib.
- Following stabilization in the transitional stage, ongoing assessment at each shift and as needed includes monitoring of vital signs and skin colour and integrity; nutrition and elimination patterns; behavioural responses; and interactions with the mother and family.
- If not part of labour and birth procedures, administer vitamin K 1.0 mg IM within six hours of birth to prevent hemorrhagic disease of the newborn (into the middle one-third of the side of the thigh muscle—the vastus lateralis—using a 25-gauge needle) and eye prophylaxis (erythromycin ointment onto the lower lid of the eye).
- Hygiene – A sponge or tub bath daily or twice per week using mild soap is recommended. Prevent excess heat loss and assess water temperature (24°C) using a thermometer or dorsal part of the hand, not the fingers; do not use baby powder as particles may be

FIGURE 9.5 Common Variations in the Newborn

Source: See page 423 for source material.

A
B

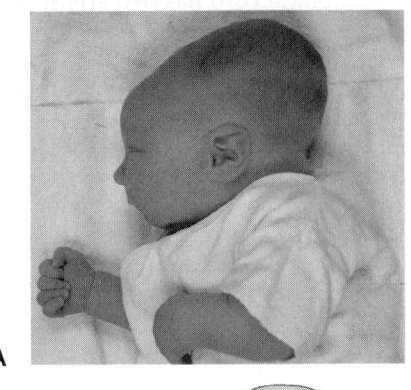

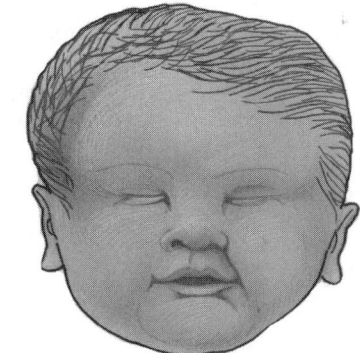

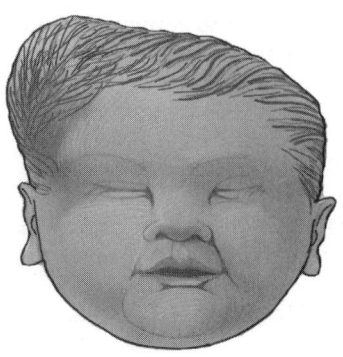

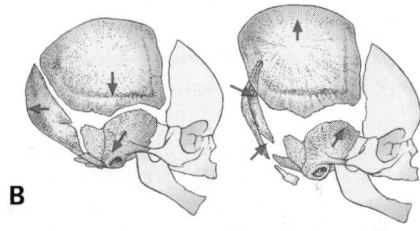

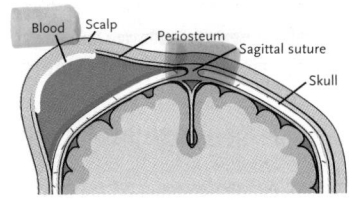

MOLDING
A. Significant molding, soon after birth.
B. Schematic of bones of skull when molding is present.

Swollen subcutaneous tissue
Blood
Scalp
Periosteum
Sagittal suture
Skull

CAPUT SUCCEDANEUM

Blood
Scalp
Periosteum
Sagittal suture
Skull

CEPHALHEMATOMA

Caput succedaneum (left) and cephalhematoma (right) are common birth injuries.

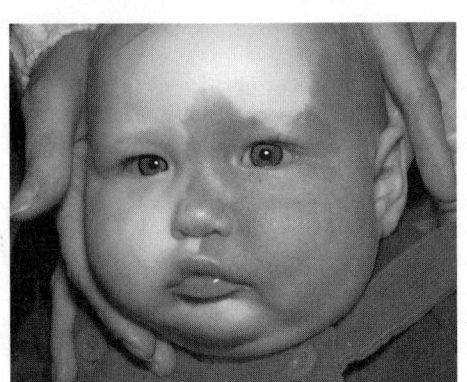

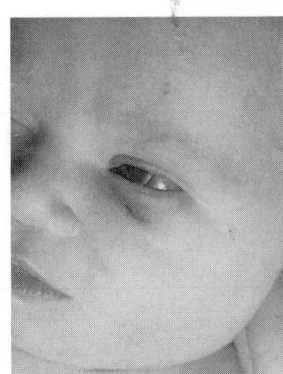

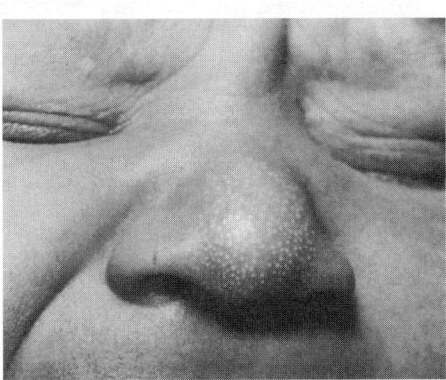

NEVUS FLAMMEUS
(Port-wine stain)

SUBCONJUNCTIVAL HEMORRHAGE

MILIA
(Vernix-filled sebaceous glands)

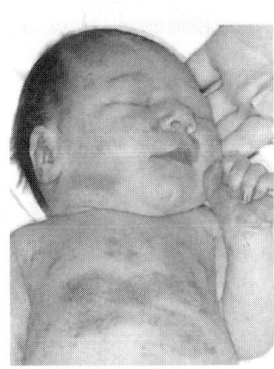

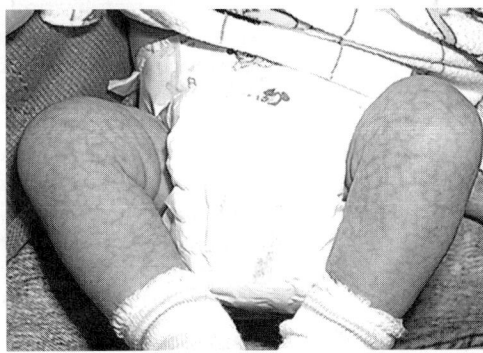

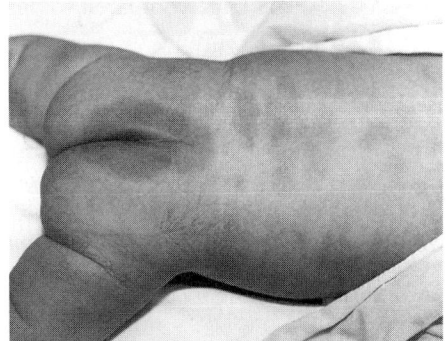

FORCEPS MARKS

CUTIS MARMORATA
(Mottling)

MONGOLIAN SPOT
Mongolian spots are common in dark-skinned children. These bluish skin discolorations should not be confused with bruises.

aspirated. Bathing prior to feeding will avoid the risk of regurgitation and promote alertness for better feeding success.

- Provide phone numbers and resources and teach parents to seek help if the newborn is experiencing difficulty breathing, not successfully feeding, not voiding 6–8 wet diapers per day, crying inconsolably, lethargic, or jaundiced or appears unwell.
- Everyone having contact with the newborn should first wash their hands and avoid contact if they are infectious as the newborn immune system is immature.
- Diaper rash may be treated with exposure to air (avoid cold stress), petroleum jelly or zinc oxide barrier products, and frequent diaper changes with each feeding.
- Umbilical cord care – The cord normally dries within 24 hours and falls off within seven days. Teach the mother to dry around the cord carefully and report any signs of bleeding, foul odour, or discharge.
- Holding and positioning – Newborns require interaction and nurturing, ideally during quiet alert states. They are consoled by being contained in a moderately flexed body posture with a receiving blanket and with skin-to-skin contact covered with a blanket. Newborn necks have weak muscles, and the heavy head must be supported at all times when holding the infant.
- Male circumcision is most often practised to comply with religious or cultural beliefs. Routine circumcision is not recommended (Fetus and Newborn Committee, 2007). If circumcision is performed, teach the parents to observe for first voiding and complications including bleeding (apply direct pressure and seek medical help) and infection. Pain medication should be used during the procedure.
- Upon discharge, ensure that the mother and family have a follow-up appointment usually at week 1 or 2 and then monthly. Provide information for breastfeeding or nutrition support, public health nursing, telephone help lines, and emergency contact numbers.

Newborn Nutrition

Newborns require adequate fluids and calories to promote hydration and growth. Breastfeeding is widely recognized and recommended as the ideal feeding method to meet the newborn's nutritional requirements. There are few contraindications to breastfeeding, and there are numerous health advantages. Nurses support the mother in meeting the newborn's nutritional needs by providing evidence-informed information, teaching, and practical support. Some mothers, for a variety of reasons, will instead use formula feedings, and their decision also needs to be respected and appropriate teaching and information provided.

Requirements

- A healthy full-term newborn requires about 100–120 kcal/kg/day. Expected rates of growth include a weight gain of 15 g/kg/day or an average of 1 kg per month for the first six months of life. Growth charts are used to monitor acceptable growth patterns.
- Newborns go through growth spurts at 2 weeks, 4–6 weeks, 3 months, and 6 months, and demands to be fed will increase accordingly.
- Fluoride supplementation is not recommended in the first six months of life.
- Breastfed infants need vitamin D supplementation of 400 IU/day, available in infant drops. In areas of Canada north of 55° latitude (such as Edmonton) or for dark-skinned infants, 800 IU/day is needed between October and April, when sunlight levels are low (Canadian Paediatric Society [CPS], 2007; First Nations, Inuit and Métis Health Committee, 2007).

Breastfeeding

- Exclusive breastfeeding is recommended for the first six months of life and can be continued for two years and beyond (CPS, 2007; Health Canada, 2005).
- Contraindications include mothers who are HIV positive, have undergone long-term chemotherapy, or have galactosemia, untreated active tuberculosis, or herpes simplex lesions on or near the nipple (Health Canada, 2005).
- Advantages – Breastfeeding is ideally suited to newborn metabolic needs and digestion and is associated with decreased infections, lower risk of SIDS, prevention of allergies, enhanced brain development, and lower costs for newborn feeding.
- Colostrum is available at the time of birth. It is rich in proteins, vitamins, minerals, and immunoglobulins. Breast milk is produced by day 3 or 4 postpartum under the influence of the hormone prolactin. Oxytocin hormone causes the letdown reflex that releases the milk when the baby begins to feed. The amount of milk produced is dependent on the breast being stimulated and emptied with frequent feedings. Mothers are encouraged to feed on demand. Newborns may initially feed 8–12 times in 24 hours.

Formula Feeding

- Commercial formulas that are cow's milk based and iron enriched are the most acceptable alternative to breast milk until 9–12 months of age.
- Soy-based formulas are recommended only if dairy-based milk is not used for health, religious, or cultural reasons, as in the case of a vegan lifestyle or infants with galactosemia.
- Water for formula should be boiled for at least two minutes and then cooled for infants under four months in order to remove pathogens (Health Canada, 2005).

Nursing Considerations

- Nurses have an important role in promoting and supporting breastfeeding as the optimal choice for infant nutrition; educate and support parents, create a supportive environment to learn breastfeeding techniques, and provide follow-up resources.

- Breast milk can be expressed and stored in glass bottles (or bisphenol A-free plastic) in the fridge for 24 hours or the freezer for 14 days. It is important not to microwave breast milk because it destroys the antimicrobial agents and vitamin C.
- Breastfeeding latching on – The newborn will feed best if correctly attached to or latched on to the breast. The mother should be comfortable and supported. Signs a baby is feeding well include a wide open mouth encircling the breast, movement of the baby's jaw, not just lips, the baby swallowing at regular intervals, the baby is content after feeding, the mother is not in pain, and the baby wets 6–8 diapers in a 24-hour period. Most newborns, properly latched, will empty the breast within 30 minutes. The mother should break the seal by placing a clean finger between the breast and the baby's mouth. Upright burping will help release any swallowed air. Small amounts of regurgitation are normal.
- Nutrient-rich solid foods can be introduced at 6 months of age in addition to breast milk or formula feedings, including iron-fortified cereals, meat, or other protein sources. To prevent newborn botulism, no honey or honey products should be given in the first year of life. Herbal teas are not recommended.
- Criteria for postpartum discharge should include demonstration of a clear understanding of feeding needs and techniques, written instructions, community resources and referrals, and at least two successful infant feedings independently performed by the mother. Professional follow-up within 48 hours of discharge is recommended to assess infant hydration, feeding, and the presence of jaundice (CPS, 2007).

NEWBORN COMPLICATIONS

Maturity and Size

Preterm or post-term newborns may be SGA (10th percentile), LGA (90th percentile), or average (AGA, 50th percentile), depending on their percentile score against weight and age categories on a growth assessment chart. SGA newborns score below the 10th percentile, meaning that 10% of other newborns weigh less than them and 90% weigh more. LGA babies should be investigated as infants of diabetic mothers. SGA newborns may be associated with conditions that impaired uteroplacental circulation during the pregnancy.

Preterm Newborn

Pathophysiology

- A preterm baby is one born after 20 weeks and before the end of 37 weeks' gestation, regardless of weight. Assessment tools to determine age include the Dubowitz and Ballard scoring systems.

- Cause is often unknown; leading cause of morbidity and mortality; see the risk factors in the section Preterm Labour and Birth, pages 408–409.
- Preterm complications are numerous depending on age and include an inability to establish and maintain independent respirations (respiratory distress syndrome [RDS]), heart murmurs, cold stress, electrolyte and calcium imbalances, increased risk of infection, poor skin integrity, hypoglycemia, risk of neurological impairment and bleeding, anemia, poor digestive ability and malnourishment, and retinopathy of prematurity.

Clinical Manifestations

Physical characteristics are dependent on gestational age but may include extended body position, fine downy hair on the head, soft pliable ear without cartilage, lack of body fat, tissuelike or gelatinous skin with visible veins, lack of rugae on the scrotum, labia minor and clitoris visible on female, no sole creases, fine downy lanugo hair widely distributed, and vernix covering the body.

Nursing Considerations

- Observe for signs of respiratory distress, including grunting, chest indrawing, nasal flaring, oxygen saturation of less than 85%, tachypnea, or apnea.
- Maintain a neutral thermal environment; monitor temperature, preventing cold stress using a hat and booties; and maintain skin integrity.
- Establish early frequent feedings to counter hypoglycemia. If the respiratory rate is >60, nasogastric feedings will be required. Carefully monitor intake and output and weight gains or losses.
- Support parents in understanding the needs of the preterm infant, especially if intensive care is required; allay feelings of guilt; and anticipate grieving and the need for open discussion.

Post-Term Newborn

Pathophysiology

- A post-term newborn is one born after 42 weeks' gestation, a condition associated with primiparas, past history of postmaturity, and congenital anomalies, including anencephaly (lack of brain development).
- Morbidity and mortality risks are associated with increasingly poor uteroplacental circulation and hypoxia and include meconium aspiration, pneumothorax, hypoglycemia, hypothermia, asphyxia, and birth trauma.

Clinical Manifestations

Physical characteristics include a long thin body with wasted appearance, little body fat, long nails, dry and cracked skin, meconium staining, and no vernix or lanugo.

Nursing Considerations

- Monitor for uteroplacental insufficiency with regular NST beginning at pregnancy term.
- Be prepared for complications at the time of birth and the need for respiratory support.
- Closely monitor respiratory rate and effort, observe for complications, prevent cold stress, monitor for hypoglycemia and establish frequent regular feedings, and provide information for follow-up care in the community and referral to a pediatrician if needed.

Birth Trauma

Most instances of birth trauma are temporary and self-resolve over time. Trauma may result from medical interventions, including forceps, or be related to pelvic or fetal dystocia factors. Examples include the following:

- Cephalohematoma – A well-defined, soft, localized swelling, an accumulation of blood between the skull and periosteum that does *not* cross the cranial suture lines. It emerges on day 2 or 3 following birth and then slowly disappears over weeks or months. There is a risk of jaundice secondary to the blood loss and reabsorption.
- Caput succedaneum – A poorly defined, localized soft tissue edema caused by cervical pressure on the fetal head, present at birth, crosses the suture lines, and disappears within hours or days
- Forceps injury – Facial bruising may be apparent over the cheeks from forceps application. Compression may cause one-sided facial nerve palsy, with one side of the newborn's face appearing asymmetrical, especially when crying. The bruising resolves within a few days. The facial paralysis is rarely permanent and usually resolves within a few hours or days.
- Brachial plexus injury is the most common nerve injury and is caused by traction on the nerves in the neck and head during birth. The affected arm is extended and limp, with absent reflexes. Recovery is within weeks with immobilization and physiotherapy. Some infants require surgical intervention. LGA infants with shoulder dystocia and breech infants are especially at risk.
- Fractured clavicle – Redness, swelling, or crepitus is noted over the collar bone, and the infant may be irritable and crying. The fracture is confirmed by X-ray and immobilized.
- Bruises and edema – The infant may have bruising and edema on the other parts of the body due to birth trauma, particularly in difficult deliveries, which disappears in a few days. These bruises can be mistaken for Mongolian spots. Mongolian spots are bluish-black areas of pigmented skin that can occur in babies of Mediterranean, Latin American, Asian, or African descent. They disappear eventually in months or years.

Hemolytic Disease

ABO and Rh blood incompatibilities in the fetus and newborn are caused by maternal immune reactions against blood group factors on the fetal red blood cells. While fetal and maternal blood supplies are separate, minute amounts of fetal blood cross into maternal circulation with placental breaks and at the time of birth.

Pathophysiology

- ABO incompatibility affects about 20% of pregnancies of group A or B infants with group O mothers. Group O mothers have natural anti-A or anti-B antibodies, or both, which initiate a hemolytic response against the fetal red blood cells.
- Rh incompatibility affects about 2% of pregnancies. The mother is Rh-negative, while the fetus is Rh-positive. During the first pregnancy, the hemolytic response is initiated when the mother's blood is sensitized and antibodies are produced. The first pregnancy may be unaffected, but unless treated, each subsequent pregnancy will result in a stronger immune hemolytic response with resulting destruction of fetal red blood cells and stimulation of the fetal liver and spleen to produce more red blood cells.
- Immunization and antibody formation can also occur with a spontaneous or induced abortion, amniocentesis, or ectopic pregnancy.

Clinical Manifestations

- ABO incompatibility – Neonatal jaundice in the first 24 hours, mild anemia, rarely enlarged liver or spleen
- Rh incompatibility – In affected pregnancies, jaundice in the first 24 hours, moderate to severe anemia, hepatosplenomegaly, cardiac or pulmonary failure, ascites, edema, or even stillbirth in severe cases

Diagnostics and Therapeutics

- ABO incompatibility – Diagnosis is via direct and indirect Coombs test (detecting maternal antibodies), bilirubin, and complete blood count (CBC). Usually resolves without complications using phototherapy.
- Rh incompatibility – Blood tests are the same as for ABO; may also test amniotic fluid for bilirubin levels or perform cordocentesis for fetal blood analysis.
- Provide Rh-immune prophylaxis (WinRho®) for all at-risk women to prevent and suppress the maternal antibody response.
- Exchange blood transfusion – The newborn's blood is replaced with type O blood, which will not react to the maternal antibodies. The newborn will revert back to its natural blood type over time without a subsequent hemolytic reaction.

Nursing Considerations

- Monitor antibody, bilirubin, and CBC levels in the mother and newborn.

- Provide information and teaching to the Rh-negative woman about the importance of receiving WinRho® prophylaxis in all high-risk situations. It is given at 28 weeks' gestation, within 72 hours postpartum, or following the at-risk episodes noted above.
- Antenatal fetal monitoring for Rh incompatibility, including ultrasonography and amniocentesis
- Assess the newborn for early-onset jaundice and implement appropriate treatment.

REFERENCES

Arsenault, M., & Lane, C. (2002). The management of nausea and vomiting of pregnancy [electronic version]. *Journal of Obstetrics and Gynaecology Canada, 24*(10), 817–823.

Beischer, N. A., Mackey, E. V., & Colditz, P. B. (1997). *Obstetrics and the newborn* (3rd ed.). Oxford: Baillière Tindall.

Bowden, V., Dickey. S., & Greenberg, C. (1998). *Children and their families: The continuum of care*. Philadelphia: Saunders.

Canadian Association of Midwives. (2012). *Midwifery in Canada*. Montreal: Author. Retrieved January 19, 2013, from http://www.canadianmidwives.org/

Canadian Council on Social Development. (2006). *The progress of Canada's children and youth*. Ottawa: Author. Retrieved January 19, 2013, from http://www.ccsd.ca/pccy/2006/

Canadian Institute for Health Information. (2007). *Analysis in brief and update: Giving birth in Canada: Regional trends from 2001–2002 to 2005–2006*. Ottawa: Author. Retrieved September 6, 2012, from http://secure.cihi.ca/freeproducts/childbirth_aib_070725_3.pdf

Canadian Paediatric Society. (2007, reaffirmed 2012). *Breastfeeding*. Ottawa: Author. Retrieved January 19, 2013, from http://www.cps.ca/caringforkids/babies/breastfeeding.htm

Crane, J. (2001). Induction of labour at term [electronic version]. *Journal of Obstetrics and Gynaecology Canada, 23*(8), 717–728.

Davis, V. (2000). Lesbian health guidelines [electronic version]. *Journal of Obstetrics and Gynaecology Canada, 22*(3), 202–205.

Dunn, S., & Guilbert, E. (2003). Emergency contraception [electronic version]. *Journal of Obstetrics and Gynaecology Canada, 25*(8), 673–679.

Eichenfield, L. F., Frieden, I. J., & Esterly, N. B. (2001). *Textbook of neonatal dermatology*. Philadelphia: Saunders.

Fetus and Newborn Committee. (2007). *Position statement: Neonatal circumcision revisited*. Ottawa: Canadian Pediatric Society. Retrieved January 19, 2013, from http://www.cps.ca/en/documents/position/circumcision

First Nations, Inuit and Métis Health Committee. (2007). Vitamin D supplementation: Recommendations for Canadian mothers and infants. [electronic version]. *Paediatrics & Child Health, 12*(7), 583–589.

Gardner, M., & Doyle, N. (2004). Asthma in pregnancy. *Obstetrics and Gynecology Clinics of North America, 28*(3), 385–413.

Gilbert, E. S. (2007). *Manual of high risk pregnancy & delivery* (4th ed.). St. Louis: Mosby.

Government of Canada. (2003). *The well-being of Canada's young children: Government of Canada report 2003* (RH64-20/2003). Ottawa: Minister of Public Works and Government Services Canada. Retrieved January 19, 2013, from http://publications.gc.ca/site/eng/2454010/publication.html

Health Canada. (2000a). *Chapter 2: Organization of services*. In *Family-centred maternity and newborn care: National guidelines* (4th ed.). Ottawa: Minister of Public Works and Government Services Canada. Retrieved January 19, 2013, from http://www.phac-aspc.gc.ca/hp-ps/dca-dea/publications/fcm-smp/fcmc-smpf-02-eng.php

Health Canada. (2000b). *Chapter 3: Preconception care*. In *Family-centred maternity and newborn care: National guidelines* (4th ed.). Ottawa: Minister of Public Works and Government Services Canada. Retrieved January 19, 2013, from http://www.phac-aspc.gc.ca/hp-ps/dca-dea/publications/fcm-smp/fcmc-smpf-03-eng.php

Health Canada. (2000c). *The guiding principles of family-centred maternity and newborn care*. In *Family-centred maternity and newborn care: National guidelines* (4th ed.). Ottawa: Minister of Public Works and Government Services Canada. Retrieved January 19, 2013, from http://www.phac-aspc.gc.ca/hp-ps/dca-dea/publications/fcm-smp/fcmc-smpf-01-eng.php

Health Canada. (2005). *Nutrition for healthy term infants—Statement of the joint working group: Canadian Paediatric Society, Dietitians of Canada and Health Canada* (H44-76/2005E-PDF). Ottawa: Minister of Public Works and Government Services Canada. Retrieved January 19, 2013, from http://www.cps.ca/en/documents/position/nutrition-healthy-term-infants

Hui, D., Lui, G., Kavuma, E., Hewson, S. A., McKay, D., & Hannah, M. E. (2007). Obstetrics: Preterm labour and birth: A survey of clinical practice regarding use of tocolytics, antenatal corticosteroids, and progesterone [electronic version]. *Journal of Obstetrics and Gynaecology Canada, 29*(2), 117–131.

Leifer, G. (2007). *Maternity nursing: An introductory text* (10th ed.). St. Louis: Saunders.

Liston, R., & Crane, J. (2002). Fetal health surveillance in labour [electronic version]. *Journal of Obstetrics and Gynaecology Canada, 24*(3), 250–262.

Lowdermilk, D. L., Perry, S. E., Cashion, K., & Alden, K. R. (2012). *Maternity & women's health care* (10th ed.). St. Louis: Mosby.

Manning, F. A. (1999). Fetal biophysical profile. *Obstetrics & Gynecology Clinics of North America, 26*(4), 557–577.

Martel, M.-J., & MacKinnon, C. (2005). Guidelines for vaginal birth after a previous Caesarian birth [electronic version]. *Journal of Obstetrics and Gynaecology Canada, 27*(2), 164–174.

Meadows, M. (2001). Pregnancy and the drug dilemma [electronic version]. *FDA Consumer Magazine, 35*(3), 16–20.

Merenstein, G., & Gardner, S. (2006). *Handbook of neonatal intensive care* (6th ed.). St. Louis: Mosby.

Min, J., Claman, P., & Hughes, E. (2006). Guidelines for the number of embryos to transfer following in vitro fertilization [electronic version]. *Journal of Obstetrics and Gynaecology Canada, 28*(9), 799–813.

Moore, K., & Persaud, T. (2003). *Before we were born: Essentials of embryology and birth defects* (6th ed.). Philadelphia: Saunders.

Moore, K. L., & Persaud, T. V. N. (2003). *The developing human: Clinically oriented embryology* (7th ed.). Philadelphia: Saunders.

National Aboriginal Health Organization. (2012). *Midwifery.* Ottawa: Author. Retrieved January 19, 2013, from http://www.naho.ca/midwifery.pdf

Oppenheimer, L. (2007). Diagnosis and management of placenta previa [electronic version]. *Journal of Obstetrics and Gynaecology Canada, 29*(3), 261–266.

Picard, A., & Cullen, C. (2005, April 27). School nurses can now prescribe the pill to Quebec teens. *The Globe and Mail*, p. A19. Retrieved January 19, 2013, from http://www.sogc.org/media/pdf/news/schoolnursescannowprescribethepillforquebecteens_april272005.pdf

Potter, P. A., Perry, A. G., Ross-Kerr, J. C., & Wood, M. (Eds.). (2010). *Canadian fundamentals of nursing* (Rev. 4th ed.). Toronto: Elsevier.

Public Health Agency of Canada. (2007). *Human papillomavirus (HPV) prevention and HPV vaccine: Questions and answers.* Ottawa: Author. Retrieved January 19, 2013, from http://www.phac-aspc.gc.ca/std-mts/hpv-vph/hpv-vph-vaccine_e.html

Society of Obstetricians and Gynaecologists of Canada. (2006). *Women's health information: Pregnancy: Preterm labour.* Ottawa: Author. Retrieved January 19, 2013, from http://www.sogc.org/health/pregnancy-preterm_e.asp

Society of Obstetricians and Gynaecologists of Canada. (2008). 806C Clinical Practice Guidelines: Rubella in pregnancy. *Journal of Obstetrics and Gynaecology Canada 30*(2), 152–168.

Society of Obstetricians and Gynaecologists of Canada. (2009). Clinical Practice Guideline: Active management of the third stage of labour to prevent postpartum hemorrhage [electronic version]. *Journal of Obstetrics and Gynaecology Canada, 31*(10), 980–993.

Society of Obstetricians and Gynaecologists of Canada. (2012). Management of varicella infection (chickenpox) in pregnancy. *Journal of Obstetrics and Gynaecology Canada, 34*(3), 287–292.

Statistics Canada. (2008). *Births and birth rate, by province and territory.* Ottawa: Author. Retrieved January 19, 2013, from http://www.statcan.gc.ca/daily-quotidien/070921/dq070921b-eng.htm

Statistics Canada. (2008). *2006 Census: Ethnic origin, visible minorities, place of work and mode of transportation.* Ottawa: Author. Retrieved January 19, 2013, from http://www.statcan.gc.ca/daily-quotidien/080402/dq080402a-eng.htm

Zitelli, B. J., and Davis, H. W. (2002). *Atlas of pediatric physical diagnosis* (4th ed.) St. Louis: Mosby.

BIBLIOGRAPHY

Anderson, C. (2007). Pre-eclampsia: Exposing future cardiovascular risk in mothers and their children [electronic version]. *Journal of Obstetric, Gynecologic, & Neonatal Nursing, 36*(1), 3–8.

Arsenault, M., & Lane, C. (2002). The management of nausea and vomiting of pregnancy [electronic version]. *Journal of Obstetrics and Gynaecology Canada, 24*(10), 817–823.

Association for Safe Alternatives in Childbirth. (2001). *Midwifery across Canada.* Edmonton: Author. Retrieved January 19, 2013, from http://www.asac.ab.ca/updatesMidwiferyCanada.html

Beck, C. (2003). Recognizing and screening for postpartum depression in mothers of NICU infants. *Advances in Neonatal Care, 3*(1), 37–46.

Benjamin, K. (2005). Distinguishing physical characteristics and management of brachial plexus injuries. *Advances in Neonatal Care, 5*(5), 240–251.

Bobak, I., & Jenson, M. (1993). *Maternity and gynaecologic care* (5th ed.). St. Louis: Mosby.

Boland, M. (2005). Exclusive breastfeeding should continue to six months [electronic version]. *Paediatrics & Child Health, 10*(3), 148.

Boucher, M. (2001). Mode of delivery for pregnant women infected by the human immunodeficiency virus [electronic version]. *Journal of Obstetrics and Gynaecology Canada, 23*(4), 48–50.

Brucker, P., & McKenry, P. (2004). Support from health care providers and the psychological adjustment of individuals experiencing infertility. *Journal of Obstetric, Gynecologic, & Neonatal Nursing, 33*(5), 597–603.

Callister, L. (2005). What has the literature taught us about culturally competent care of women and children? *American Journal of Maternal/Child Nursing, 30*(6), 380–396.

Campbell, S. (2003). Prenatal cocaine exposure and neonatal/infant outcomes. *Neonatal Network, 22*(1), 19–21.

Canadian Association of Midwives. (2012). *Midwifery in Canada.* Montreal: Author. Retrieved January 19, 2013, from http://www.canadianmidwives.org/

Canadian Institute for Health Information. (2004). *Giving birth in Canada: A regional profile.* Ottawa: Author. Retrieved January 19, 2013, from https://secure.cihi.ca/estore/productFamily.htm?pf=PFC415&lang=en&media=1

Canadian Institute for Health Information. (2007). *Analysis in brief and update: Giving birth in Canada: Regional trends from 2001–2002 to 2005–2006.* Ottawa: Author. Retrieved January 19, 2013, from http://secure.cihi.ca/freeproducts/childbirth_aib_070725_3.pdf

Canadian Nurses Association. (2005). *Nursing and genetics: Are you ready?* Nursing Now, 20. Retrieved January 19, 2013, from http://www2.cna-aiic.ca/CNA/documents/pdf/publications/NN_Genetics_05_e.pdf

Canadian Paediatric Society. (2007, reaffirmed 2012). *Breastfeeding; Vitamin D.* Ottawa: Author. Retrieved January 19, 2013, from http://www.cps.ca/caringforkids/babies

Carroll, J., Slobodzian, R., & Steward, D. K. (2005). Extremely low birthweight infants: Issues related to growth. *American Journal of Maternal Child Nursing, 30*(5), 312–318.

Centres for Disease Control and Prevention. (2000). Accutane®-exposed pregnancies – California, 1999 [electronic version]. *Morbidity and Mortality Weekly Report, 49,* 28–31.

Cherniak, D., Grant, L., Mason, R., Moore, B., & Pellizzari, R. (2005). Intimate partner violence consensus statement [electronic version]. *Journal of Obstetrics and Gynaecology Canada, 27*(4), 365–388.

Clemmens, D. (2004). Postpartum depression as profiled through the Depression Screening Scale. *The American Journal of Maternal/Child Nursing, 29*(3), 180–185.

College of Midwives of Ontario. (2007). *About midwifery.* Toronto: Author. Retrieved January 19, 2013, from http://www.cmo.on.ca/midwifery.asp

College of Nurses of Ontario. (2009). *Professional conduct: Professional misconduct.* Retrieved January 19, 2013, from http://www.cno.org/Global/docs/ih/42007_misconduct.pdf

Crane, J. (2001). Induction of labour at term [electronic version]. *Journal of Obstetrics and Gynaecology Canada, 23*(8), 717–728.

Davis, V. (2000). Lesbian health guidelines [electronic version]. *Journal of Obstetrics and Gynaecology Canada, 22*(3), 202–205.

Dunn, S., & Guilbert, E. (2003). Emergency contraception [electronic version]. *Journal of Obstetrics and Gynaecology Canada, 25*(8), 673–679.

Farine, D., Mundle, W. R., & Dodd, J. (2008). Technical update: The use of progesterone for prevention of preterm birth. *Journal of Obstetrics and Gynaecology Canada, 30*(1), 67–71.

Fetus and Newborn Committee. (2004). Routine administration of vitamin K to newborns [electronic version]. *Paediatrics & Child Health 2*(6), 429–431.

First Nations, Inuit and Métis Health Committee. (2007). Vitamin D supplementation: Recommendations for Canadian mothers and infants [electronic version]. *Paediatrics & Child Health, 12*(7), 583–589.

Fraser Askin, D. (2004). Intrauterine infections. *Neonatal Network, 23*(5), 23–31.

Gardner, M., & Doyle, N. (2004). Asthma in pregnancy. *Obstetrics and Gynecology Clinics of North America, 28*(3), 385–413.

Gilbert, E. S. (2007). *Manual of high risk pregnancy & delivery* (4th ed.). St. Louis: Mosby.

Gilliland, F. D., Berhane, K., McConnell, R., Gauderman, W. J., Vora, H., Rappaport, E. B., et al. (2000). Maternal smoking during pregnancy, environmental tobacco smoke exposure and childhood lung function. *Thorax, 55,* 271–276.

Government of Canada. (2006). *Chapter 3: The well-being of Canada's young children: Government of Canada report 2006.* Ottawa: Minister of Public Works and Government Services Canada. Retrieved Jaunary 19, 2013, from http://publications.gc.ca/site/eng/245490/publication.html

Greene, C. M., & Goodman M. H. (2003). Neonatal abstinence syndrome: Strategies for care of the drug-exposed infant. *Neonatal Network, 22*(4), 15–25.

Gregory, K. (2005). Update on nutrition for preterm and full term infants. *Journal of Obstetric, Gynecologic, & Neonatal Nursing, 34*(1), 98–108.

Hackman, P. (2001). Recognizing and understanding the cold-stressed term infant. *Neonatal Network, 20*(8), 35–41.

Hamelin, K., Saydak, M. I., & Bramadat, I. A. (1997). Interviewing mothers of high risk infants. What are their support needs? *Canadian Nurse, 93*(6), 35–38.

Health Canada. (2000). *Chapter 2: Organization of services.* In *Family-centred maternity and newborn care* (4th ed.). Ottawa: Minister of Public Works and Government Services Canada. Retrieved January 19, 2013, from http://www.phac-aspc.gc.ca/hp-ps/dca-dea/publications/fcm-smp/fcmc-smpf-02-eng.php

Health Canada. (2000). *Chapter 3: Preconception care.* In *Family-centred maternity and newborn care* (4th ed.). Ottawa: Minister of Public Works and Government Services Canada. Retrieved January 19, 2013, from http://www.phac-aspc.gc.ca/hp-ps/dca-dea/publications/fcm-smp/fcmc-smpf-03-eng.php

Health Canada. (2003). *Canadian perinatal health report 2003.* Ottawa: Minister of Public Works and Government Services Canada. Retrieved January 19, 2013, from http://www.phac-aspc.gc.ca/hp-ps/dca-dea/publications/fcm-smp/fcmc-smpf-01-eng.php

Health Canada. (2005). *Nutrition for healthy term infants – Statement of the joint working group: Canadian Paediatric Society, Dietitians of Canada and Health Canada.* Ottawa: Minister of Public Works and Government Services Canada. Retrieved January 19, 2013, from http://www.hc-sc.gc.ca/fn-an/pubs/infant-nourrisson/nut_infant_nourrisson_ term-eng.php

Health Canada. (2006). *Healthy living: Birth control;* and *Healthy living: Sexual health and promotion.* Ottawa: Minister of Public Works and Government Services Canada. Retrieved January 19, 2013, from http://www.hc-sc.gc.ca/hl-vs/sex/control/index-eng.php

Helewa, M., Levesque, P., & Provencher, D. (2002). Breast cancer, pregnancy, and breastfeeding [electronic version]. *Journal of Obstetrics and Gynaecology Canada, 24*(2), 164–171.

Higgins, L. (2005). Screen for abuse during pregnancy. *The American Journal of Maternal/Child Nursing, 30*(2), 109–114.

Hole, J. (1984). *Human anatomy and physiology* (3rd ed.). Dubuque, IA: Wm. C. Brown Publishers.

Hui, D., Lui, G., Kavuma, E., Hewson, S. A., McKay, D., & Hannah, M. E. (2007). Obstetrics: Preterm labour and birth: A survey of clinical practice regarding use of tocolytics, antenatal corticosteroids, and progesterone [electronic version]. *Journal of Obstetrics and Gynaecology Canada, 29*(2), 117–131.

Jarvis, C., Browne, A. J., MacDonald-Jenkins, J., Luctkar-Flude, M. (2009). *Physical examination and health assessment* (1st Canadian ed.). Philadelphia: Saunders.

Jones, M., & Bass, W. T. (2003). Follow-up of the high-risk infant: Fetal alcohol syndrome. *Neonatal Network, 22*(3), 63–70.

Keenan-Lindsay, L., & Yudin, M. (2006). HIV screening in pregnancy [electronic version]. *Journal of Obstetrics and Gynaecology Canada, 28*(12), 1103–1107.

Kenner, C., & Lott, J. (2007). *Comprehensive neonatal care: An interdisciplinary approach* (4th ed.). St. Louis: Saunders.

Kidner, M., & Flanders-Stepans, M. (2004). A model for the HELLP syndrome: The maternal experience. *Journal of Obstetric, Gynecologic, & Neonatal Nursing, 33*(1), 44–55.

Kim-Godwin, Y. (2003). Postpartum beliefs & practices among non-Western cultures. *The American Journal of Maternal/Child Nursing, 28*(2), 74–77.

Lachat, M., Scott, C. A., & Relf, M. V. (2006). HIV and pregnancy: Considerations for nursing practice. *The American Journal of Maternal/Child Nursing, 31*(4), 233–242.

Lawrence, E. (2006). Part I: A matter of size: Evaluating the growth-restricted neonate. *Advances in Neonatal Care, 6*(6), 313–322.

Lowdermilk, D., Perry, S., Cashion, K., & Alden, K. R. (2012). *Maternity & women's health care* (10th ed.). St. Louis: Mosby.

MacMullen, N., Tymkow, C., & Shen, J. (2006). Adverse maternal outcomes in women with asthma: Differences by race. *The American Journal of Maternal/Child Nursing, 31*(4), 253–268.

Magee, L., Helewa, L. A., Moutquin, J., & von Dadelszen, P. (2008). Diagnosis, evaluation, and management of the hypertensive disorders of pregnancy [electronic version]. *Journal of Obstetric, Gynecologic, & Neonatal Nursing, 30*(3), 9–24.

Manning, F. A. (1999). Fetal biophysical profile. *Obstetrics & Gynecology Clinics of North America, 26*(4), 557–577.

McManus, A., Hunter, L., & Renn, H. (2006). Lesbian experiences and needs during childbirth: Guidance for health care providers. *Journal of Obstetric, Gynecologic, & Neonatal Nursing, 35*(1), 11–23.

Meadows, M. (2001). Pregnancy and the drug dilemma [electronic version]. *FDA Consumer Magazine, 35*(3), 16–20.

Min, J., Claman, P., & Hughes, E. (2006). Guidelines for the number of embryos to transfer following in vitro fertilization [electronic version]. *Journal of Obstetrics and Gynaecology Canada, 28*(9), 799–813.

Money, D., & Dobson, S. (2004). The prevention of early-onset neonatal group B streptococcal disease [electronic version]. *Journal of Obstetrics and Gynaecology Canada, 26*(9), 826–832.

Murphy, P., & Chez, R. (2000). Management of nausea and vomiting in pregnancy: Alternative therapies. *Contemporary OB/GYN, 45*(4), 55–64.

National Aboriginal Health Organization. (2012). *Midwifery.* Ottawa: Author. Retrieved January 19, 2013, from http://www.naho.ca/midwifery.pdf

Olds, S., London, M., Ladewig, P., & Davidson, M. (2004). *Maternal-newborn nursing & women's health care* (7th ed.). Upper Saddle River, NJ: Pearson Prentice Hall.

Ontario Maternity Care Expert Panel. (2006). *Executive report of the Ontario Maternity Care Expert Panel: Emerging crisis, emerging solutions.* Toronto: Ontario Women's Health Council. Retrieved January 19, 2013, from http://www.cmo.on.ca/downloads/Executive_Report_FINAL.pdf

Oppenheimer, L. (2007). Diagnosis and management of placenta previa [electronic version]. *Journal of Obstetrics and Gynaecology Canada, 29*(3), 261–266.

Midwives Association of British Columbia. (2009). *What does a midwife do?* Vancouver: Author. Retrieved January 19, 2013, from http://www.bcmidwives.com/node/1

Parker, L. (2005). Early recognition and treatment of birth trauma: Injuries to the head and face. *Advances in Neonatal Care, 5*(6), 228–297.

Parker, L. (2006). Birth trauma: Injuries to the intra-abdominal organs, peripheral nerves, and skeletal system. *Advances in Neonatal Care, 6*(1), 7–4.

Perinatal HIV Guidelines Working Group. (2007). *Recommendations for use of antiretroviral drugs in pregnant HIV-infected women for maternal health and interventions to reduce perinatal HIV transmission in the United States.* Rockville, MD: AIDS*info.* Retrieved January 19, 2013, from http://www.aidsinfo.nih.gov/ContentFiles/PerinatalGL02112007901.pdf

Picard, A., & Cullen, C. (2005, April 27). School nurses can now prescribe the pill to Quebec teens. *The Globe and Mail,* p. A19. Retrieved January 19, 2013, from http://www.sogc.org/media/pdf/news/schoolnursescannowprescribethepillforquebecteens_april272005.pdf

Poole, J. (2003). Analgesia and anethesia during labor and birth: Implications for mother and fetus. *Journal of Obstetric, Gynecologic, & Neonatal Nursing, 32*(6), 780–786.

Potter, P.A., Perry, A.G., Ross-Kerr, J.C., & Wood, M. (2010). *Canadian fundamentals of nursing* (Rev. 4th ed.). Toronto: Mosby.

Public Health Agency of Canada. (2007). *Human papillomavirus (HPV) prevention and HPV vaccine: Questions and answers.* Ottawa: Author. Retrieved January 19, 2013, from http://www.phac-aspc.gc.ca/std-mts/hpv-vph/hpv-vph-vaccine_e.html

Roberts, S. (2006). Health care recommendations for lesbian women. *Journal of Obstetric, Gynecologic, & Neonatal Nursing, 35*(5), 583–591.

Schuurmans, N., MacKinnon, C., Lane, C., & Etches, D. (2000). Prevention and management of postpartum hemorrhage [electronic version]. *Journal of Obstetrics and Gynaecology Canada, 22*(4), 271–281.

Secco, M., Profit, S., Kennedy, E., Walsh, A., Letourneau, N., & Stewart, M. (2007). Factors affecting postpartum depressive symptoms of adolescent mothers. *Journal of Obstetrics and Gynaecology Canada, 36*(1), 47–54.

Sherman, T., Greenspan, S., St. Clair, N., Touch, S., & Shaffer, T. (2006). Optimizing the neonatal thermal environment. *Neonatal Network, 25*(4), 251–260.

Simpson, K. (2004). Monitoring the preterm fetus during labour. *The American Journal of Maternal/Child Nursing, 29*(9), 380–388.

Simpson, K. (2005). The context and clinical evidence for common nursing practices during labour. *The American Journal of Maternal/Child Nursing, 30*(6), 356–363.

Society of Obstetricians and Gynaecologists of Canada. (2008). Diagnosis, evaluation, and management of hypertensive disorders [Online]. *Journal of Obstetrics and Gynaecology Canada, 30*(3, Suppl 1), S1–S56.

Society of Obstetricians and Gynaecologists of Canada. (2004). SOGC clinical practice guidelines: Canadian contraception consensus. *Journal of Obstetricians and Gynaecologists of Canada, 26*(2):143–156. Retrieved January 19, 2013, from http://www.sogc.org/guidelines/public/143E-CPG1-February2004.pdf

Society of Obstetricians and Gynaecologists of Canada. (2012). Management of varicella infection (chickenpox) in pregnancy. *Journal of Obstetrics and Gynaecology Canada, 34*(3), 287–292

Spicer, K. (2001). What every nurse needs to know about breast pumping: Instructing and supporting mothers of premature infants in the NICU. *Neonatal Network, 20*(4), 35–41.

Statistics Canada. (2008). *Pregnancy outcomes by province or territory of residence—Live births;* and *Total pregnancies.* Ottawa: Author. Retrieved January 19, 2013, from http://www.statcan.gc.ca/pub/84f0210x/84f0210x2008000-eng.pdf

Statistics Canada. (2008). *2006 Census: Ethnic origin, visible minorities, place of work and mode of transportation.* Ottawa: Author. Retrieved January 19, 2013, from http://www.statcan.gc.ca/daily-quotidien/080402/dq080402a-eng.htm

Straight, B., & Harrison, L. O. (1996). *Maternal newborn nursing* (2nd ed.). Philadelphia: Lippincott.

Stringer, M. (2004). Nursing care of the patient with preterm premature rupture of membranes. *The American Journal of Maternal/Child Nursing, 29*(3), 144–150.

Thoyre, S., Shaker, C., & Pridham, K. (2005). The early feeding skills assessment for preterm infants. *Neonatal Network, 24*(3), 7–15.

Vieira, T. (2003). When joy becomes grief: Screening tools for postpartum depression. *AWHONN Lifelines, 6*(6), 506–513.

Wiseman, C., & Kiehl, E. (2007). Picture perfect: Benefits and risk of fetal 3D ultrasound. *The American Journal of Maternal/Child Nursing, 32*(2), 102–109.

Wyatt, S., & Rhoads, S. (2006). A primer on antenatal testing for neonatal nurses: Part 2: Tests of fetal well-being. *Advances in Neonatal Care, 6*(5), 228–241.

WEB SITES

Health Canada/First Nations and Inuit Health (http://www.hc-sc.gc.ca/fniah-spnia/famil/index-eng.php): This pregnancy Web site is part of the Health Canada/Healthy Living section. This part of the Web site is designed specifically for the First Nations, Inuit, and Aboriginal populations in regard to healthy pregnancy and baby care. There are links to government resources that are in place to help this population.

Health Canada/Healthy Living/Healthy Pregnancy (http://www.hc-sc.gc.ca/hL–vs/preg-gros/index-eng-php): The Health Canada Web site has an extensive healthy living segment that includes a healthy pregnancy window. This window has a variety of topics in a frequently asked question format on pregnancy and baby care. Some examples of question topics are prenatal nutrition, folic acid, exercise, smoking, and alcohol use. In addition, there is a health professional window.

Motherisk (http://www.motherisk.org/women): The Motherisk Web site is from The Hospital for Sick Children. This site is designed to provide information and guidance about the safety of or risk to the developing fetus or infant from maternal exposure to drugs, chemicals, diseases, radiation, and environmental agents. Different topics are available, such as HIV, morning sickness, drugs in pregnancy, breastfeeding in pregnancy, and herbal products. The site contains the Motherisk hotline numbers to get telephone advice.

Society of Obstetricians and Gynaecologists of Canada (http://www.sogc.org): This Web page has a women's health information section that includes pregnancy. The site features a video clip section on frequently asked questions. The focus of this site is on evidence-informed education. As well, there are many resources for health professionals.

Women's Health Matters (http://www.womenshealthmatters.ca): This Web site has been created by Women's College Hospital experts on women's health and has an English and a French version. It has a section on pregnancy and newborn care on such topics as prepregnancy planning, childbirth, multiple births, and life with a newborn. There is also a version of the Web site in French (http://www.femmesensante.ca).

FIGURE 9.5 **Common Variations in the Newborn**

Sources: (top left) Lowdermilk, D. L., Perry, S.E., Cashion, K., & Alden, K. R. (2012). *Maternity & women's health care* (10th ed., p. 542, Figure 23-8). St. Louis: Mosby. A, Courtesy Kim Molloy, Knoxville, IA; **(top right)** Bowden, V., Dickey. S., & Greenberg, C. (1998). *Children and their families: The continuum of care.* Philadelphia: Saunders; **(middle left)** Zitelli, B. J., and Davis, H. W. (2002). *Atlas of pediatric physical diagnosis* (4th ed.) St. Louis: Mosby; **(middle centre)** Beischer, N. A., Mackey, E. V., & Colditz, P. B. (1997). *Obstetrics and the newborn* (3rd ed.). Oxford: Baillière Tindall; **(middle right)** Beischer, N. A., Mackey, E. V., & Colditz, P. B. (1997). *Obstetrics and the newborn* (3rd ed., p. 599). Oxford: Baillière Tindall; **(bottom left)** Leifer, G. (2007). *Maternity nursing: An introductory text* (10th ed., p. 169, Table 10-1). St. Louis: Saunders; **(bottom centre)** Eichenfield, L. F., Frieden, I. J., & Esterly, N. B. (2001). *Textbook of neonatal dermatology.* Philadelphia: Saunders; **(bottom right)** Hockenberry, M. J., Wilson, D, Winkelstein, M, & Kline, N. (2003). *Wong's nursing care of infants and children* (7th ed.). St. Louis: Mosby.

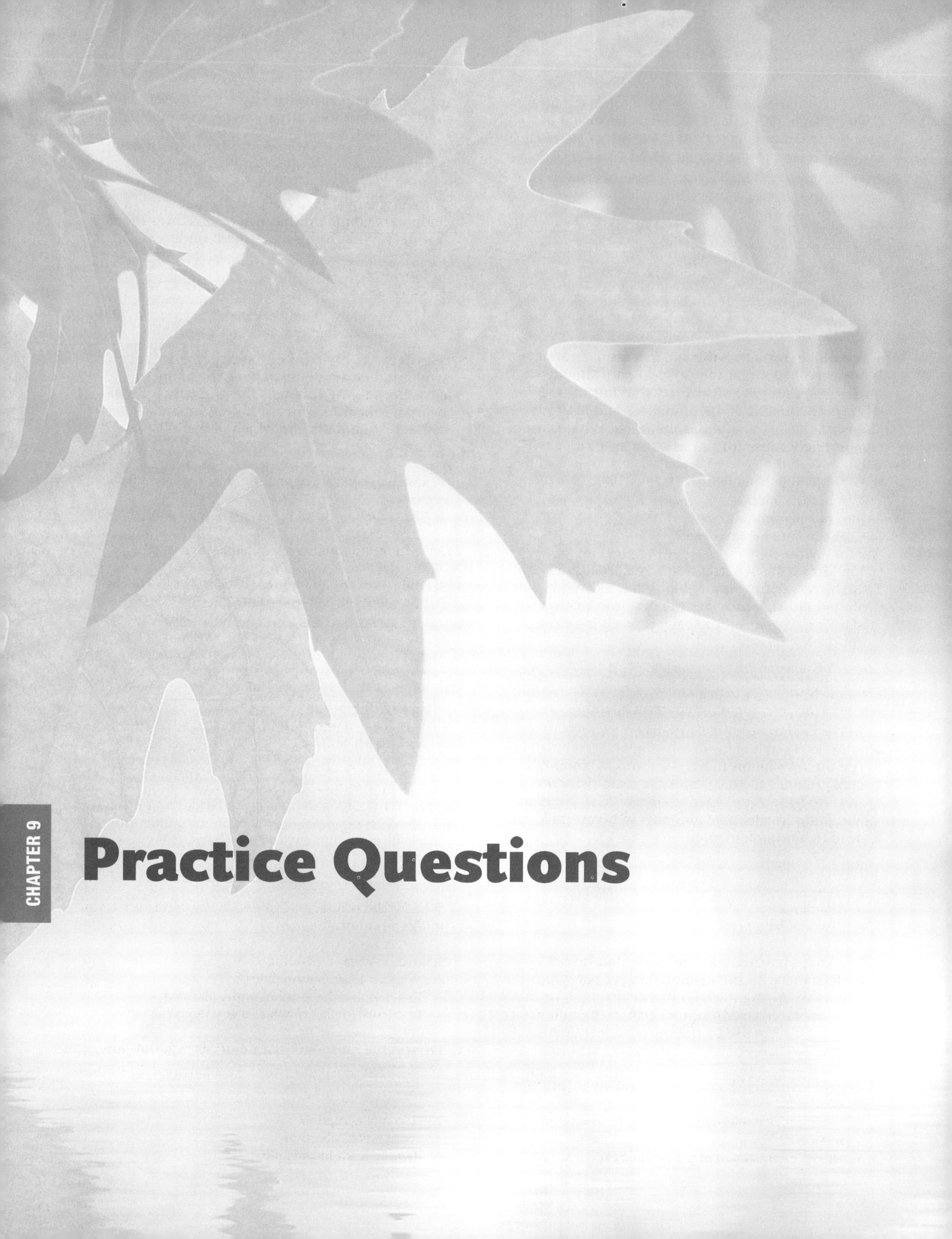

CHAPTER 9

Practice Questions

Case 1

Ms. Viraj gave birth to her first child 18 hours ago in an uncomplicated vaginal birth. She is preparing to be discharged home later today with her newborn son and her common-law partner. The baby has successfully breastfed several times since birth. The nurse is performing a postpartum assessment and preparing the family for discharge.

Questions 1–6 refer to this case.

1. The nurse notes that the lochia is a moderate amount of rubra on the perineal pad. She palpates Ms. Viraj's uterus and assesses that it is firm, 2 cm above the height of the umbilicus, and located toward the left side of the abdomen. What is the most likely cause for this assessment finding?

   1. Postpartum hemorrhage
   2. A uterine infection
   3. A full bladder
   4. Normal uterine involution

2. Ms. Viraj is concerned that she will not know if the baby is getting enough breast milk. Which of the following provides the best information for Ms. Viraj to assess if the baby is receiving enough nourishment?

   1. The baby sleeps for five or six hours between feedings
   2. The baby wets 6–8 diapers in a 24-hour period
   3. The baby's weight increases after each feeding
   4. The baby passes a stool each day

3. The nurse explains to Ms. Viraj that while breast milk provides the ideal nutrition, she will need to give the baby supplemental drops. What nutrients, not found in adequate amounts in breast milk, will need to be supplemented?

   1. Vitamin D
   2. Iron
   3. Vitamin A
   4. Essential fatty acids

4. Ms. Viraj's partner tells the nurse that he can't understand why she keeps talking about what happened during the labour and birth, telling the story over and over again. Which of the following is the best response by the nurse to Ms. Viraj's partner?

   1. "You seem tired. Perhaps you should try to get some extra rest."
   2. "I can provide referral information for counselling services."
   3. "It's an essential part of the bonding experience for her."

4. "Reliving the experience helps her with the reality of the experience and is a normal part of adjusting to parenthood."

5. The baby's physical assessment reveals a poorly defined, soft mass across the top of the head. The nurse explains to the parents that this is a temporary condition that will resolve over the next few days. What is this assessment finding called?

   1. Moulding
   2. Caput succedaneum
   3. Cephalohematoma
   4. Mongolian spot

6. Ms. Viraj and her partner have been discussing whether they are going to have their son circumcised. Ms. Viraj tells the nurse that she has heard it is healthier for the baby. The nurse's best response would include which of the following information?

   1. Circumcision should be performed only for religious reasons
   2. The nurse's personal beliefs regarding the need for circumcision
   3. Circumcision is not recommended as a routine practice
   4. There is clear evidence that circumcision is beneficial and should be performed in infancy

Case 2

Ms. Smitherman, age 42, gravida 1, para 0, is admitted to the labour unit at 33 weeks' gestation after she experienced painless vaginal bleeding that soaked through several sanitary pads. An ultrasonogram is ordered. Preparations are made for a possible early birth. Six hours later, Ms. Smitherman goes into premature labour and her vaginal bleeding worsens.

Questions 7–10 refer to this case.

7. What is the primary purpose for the ultrasonogram in this situation?

   1. To assess fetal well-being
   2. To detect fetal abnormalities
   3. To determine the location of the placenta
   4. To calculate fetal growth and gestational age

8. What is the most likely cause of Ms. Smitherman's painless vaginal bleeding in the third trimester?

   1. Placenta previa
   2. Placental abruption
   3. Spontaneous abortion
   4. Hemolytic Rh incompatibility

CHAPTER 9

9. The nurse prepares Ms. Smitherman for a caesarian birth. Corticosteroids are ordered in two doses, 24 hours apart. What is the purpose of administering corticosteroids?

1. To improve and accelerate fetal lung maturity
2. To reduce the risk of maternal postoperative complications
3. To reduce the severity of the vaginal bleeding
4. To provide regional anaesthesia via the epidural catheter

10. In the operating room, a neonatal team of physician, nurse, and respiratory therapist attends the premature infant when it is born. What is the most important assessment by the team after delivery?

1. Respirations
2. Apical heart rate
3. Colour
4. Identification of any congenital defects

Case 3

Mr. and Ms. Cane's full-term newborn son is three days old. Ms. Cane is recovering from a difficult birth. The baby has forceps bruising on his face and a cephalohematoma on the right side of his head. The morning assessment of the baby reveals that the sclera of the eyes, oral mucous membranes, and skin are yellowed. Blood work shows an elevated bilirubin. Phototherapy is prescribed for the baby.

Questions 11 and 12 refer to this case.

11. Mr. Cane asks the nurse if the baby has a liver disease that caused the jaundice. In explaining physiological jaundice to the parents, which explanation would best describe this condition?

1. It occurs after 24 hours in many babies who are in good health and will resolve in a few days
2. Physiological jaundice was caused by the bruising and cephalohematoma
3. Physiological jaundice occurs on the first day of life, and more tests will be needed
4. A blood exchange transfusion will be required to prevent brain damage

12. What side effect of phototherapy should the nurse teach the parents to expect?

1. Fluid requirements for the baby decrease by 10% while undergoing phototherapy treatment
2. The baby may experience constipation with fewer, firmer stools
3. The baby may be more awake, irritable, and difficult to settle

4. The baby's eyes will be covered for protection, but the majority of skin will be exposed and may darken temporarily

INDEPENDENT QUESTIONS

Questions 13–25 do not refer to a particular case.

13. Ms. Cooke is 39 weeks' gestation with her first pregnancy. She calls the obstetrician's office and tells the nurse she is having regular contractions seven minutes apart, but her membranes have not ruptured. What advice would the nurse provide?

1. Wait until her membranes have ruptured before going to the hospital
2. Have her partner drive her to the hospital
3. Walk around the house to see if the contractions become less regular
4. Come to the hospital when the contractions are four minutes apart

14. By what physiological mechanism do newborns stay warm?

1. Shivering
2. Metabolizing brown fat stores
3. Decreasing oxygen consumption
4. Keeping an extended body posture

15. Which of the following is an indicator used in assessing gestational age?

1. Weight
2. Head circumference
3. Ear cartilage
4. Body length

16. During the transitional changes at birth when the newborn breathes independently, what causes the foramen ovale to close?

1. Oxygen levels increase
2. The umbilical cord is clamped
3. Pressure in the left atria of the heart becomes greater than that in the right atria of the heart
4. Pulmonary blood vessels constrict, and pulmonary blood pressure increases

17. Ms. Morrissey, age 34, is in active labour and is 6 cm dilated. She has a history of chronic hypertension. Continuous electronic fetal heart rate monitoring reveals a baseline heart rate of 110 bpm with a variability of 16–18 bpm. What are these findings most indicative of?

1. Fetal well-being
2. Head compression
3. Umbilical cord compression
4. Uteroplacental insufficiency

18. Rh-immune prophylaxis treatment with WinRho® should be administered in certain situations to prevent maternal antibody formation. In which one of the following situations would WinRho® be administered to the mother?

1. Following the birth of an Rh-negative newborn
2. Following a spontaneous or induced abortion
3. Following all births regardless of blood type and Rh factor
4. Following an ABO-incompatible birth

19. Teaching parents ways to reduce the risk of sudden infant death syndrome (SIDS) is an important part of discharge planning. Which one of the following statements best reflects current recommendations?

1. Newborns should sleep in a bed with their mothers so they can be closely monitored
2. Newborns should sleep on their backs in their own crib on a firm mattress without a pillow
3. Newborns should sleep on their sides or stomachs after feeding to avoid aspiration
4. Newborns should be dressed in several layers and well covered to avoid cold stress

20. Which of the following represents the greatest risk for female infertility?

1. Ms. Cartwright, who has delayed child-bearing until after age 35 to improve her socioeconomic stability
2. Ms. Allbright, who is in a same-sex relationship
3. Ms. Abruzzon, who has had more than five sexual partners
4. Ms. Gusen, who experienced early onset of puberty and menarche, before the age of 13 years

21. Which of the following is a risk factor for the infant of a mother with gestational diabetes?

1. Hypoglycemia
2. Small for gestational age (SGA)
3. Hyperglycemia
4. Insulin resistance

22. A prescription drug, such as an antiepileptic medication, that is known to cause defects in animal studies may still be prescribed for a pregnant woman if the maternal need and benefits outweigh the risks to the fetus. Which risk category is assigned to these drugs?

1. Risk category A
2. Risk category B
3. Risk category C
4. Risk category X

23. The nurse at the community health centre is conducting a prenatal class on maternal nutrition in pregnancy. He tells the class that during pregnancy, the need for most nutrients increases. But he cautions that one nutrient taken in excessive amounts has been associated with teratogenic effects on the newborn. Which nutrient should not be taken in increased or supplemented amounts in pregnancy?

1. Calcium
2. Folic acid
3. Iron
4. Vitamin A

24. Systemic opioid analgesics, such as morphine sulphate, may be used for maternal pain management. Which statement best describes the nursing considerations for administering systemic opiate analgesics?

1. Systemic opioids are often administered up to the second stage of labour
2. An opioid antagonist such as naloxone (Narcan) should be administered to the mother to reverse the effects if birth is imminent
3. An opioid antagonist such as naloxone (Narcan) should be administered to the newborn if signs of CNS depression are present
4. Systemic opioids should not be used for postpartum pain management as these drugs cross into breast milk and may cause CNS depression in the newborn

25. A two-day-old 36-week gestation infant is receiving oxygen in the neonatal intensive care unit. He is not able to tolerate oral feeds as yet. His mother is upset as she had planned to breastfeed. What would be appropriate for the nurse to say to her?

1. "I will bring you the electric breast pump so that you may start pumping your breasts for when your baby can start feedings."
2. "Your baby will probably need feeds through an intravenous infusion for several weeks and perhaps after that you may be able to provide him with breast milk."
3. "It is best to give premature infants formula when they start feedings as the exact amounts of milk can be determined."
4. "As soon as the baby is out of oxygen, you will be able to put him to breast."

Answers and Rationales
for Practice Questions

1.   C: Changes in Health   T: Application

1. Early postpartum hemorrhage is most often associated with failure of the uterus to remain contracted and poor uterine tone on palpation.
2. There are no apparent signs of infection.
3. A full bladder will push the uterus higher in the abdomen and cause it to deviate away from the expected midline position. It is common for the bladder to become full in the first 24–48 hours postpartum due to swelling and trauma from birth and elimination of excess intravascular volume.
4. A normal uterine involution would mean that the top of the uterus could be found midline in the abdomen and about two fingerbreadths below the umbilicus.

2.   C: Changes in Health   T: Application

1. Newborns will demand feed frequently every 2–3 hours in the first weeks of life, and frequent feedings are encouraged.
2. Six to eight wet diapers in 24 hours indicate adequate hydration and nourishment.
3. It is impractical and unreliable to weigh a newborn as a sign of adequate feeding and nutrition.
4. Passage of stools for a breastfed or formula-fed infant is not a reliable or predictable indicator of adequate hydration.

3.   C: Changes in Health   T: Application

1. Breastfed infants need vitamin D supplementation of 400 IU/day, available in infant drops.
2. The breastfed newborn has adequate iron stores for the first six months of life.
3. Vitamin A supplementation is not recommended or required.
4. Breast milk contains all the necessary essential fatty acids.

4.   C: Nurse–Client Partnership   T: Application

1. While the partner might be tired, this answer ignores his question and does not provide useful information about the process of taking in the experience of labour and birth.
2. Referral for counselling is not indicated in this situation.
3. Attachment is a process that takes place over time. No one event or behaviour is essential. The term bonding is avoided as it implies a short-term process that may fail or succeed if feelings and behaviours are not quickly established.
4. Ms. Viraj's behaviour is a normal part of adaptation to parenting. Providing information to the partner about this expected behaviour would help address his concerns.

5.   C: Changes in Health   T: Knowledge

1. Moulding is a temporary overlapping of the cranial bones. The head appears pointed and elongated in shape.
2. Caput succedaneum is soft scalp swelling, commonly due to pressure on the head from the cervix. It is poorly defined and crosses the suture lines of the skull. It appears at or shortly after birth and resolves within a few days.
3. Cephalohematoma appears after 24 hours, is localized on one side of the head, and does not cross the suture lines of the skull. It is a collection of blood under the periosteum and takes several weeks to be reabsorbed.
4. A Mongolian spot is a darkened pigmentation of the skin located over the lumbar spine area.

6.   C: Changes in Health   T: Application

1. Circumcision is most often practised to comply with religious or cultural beliefs but may also be a personal preference and choice made by the parents.
2. The nurse's responsibility is to provide current, evidence-informed information so the parents can make an informed decision.
3. Routine circumcision is not recommended (Canadian Paediatric Society, 2007).
4. The evidence supporting or refuting the need for circumcision is not absolute or definitive in supporting routine circumcision in infancy.

7.   C: Changes in Health   T: Critical Thinking

1. Fetal well-being in this situation would be better assessed with the use of fetal heart monitoring.
2. Detecting fetal abnormalities by ultrasound would be part of an ultrasound assessment early in the pregnancy and is not a priority in this situation.
3. Ultrasound would be used to locate and confirm the position of the placenta to determine if it is implanted near the cervix.
4. These determinations are made in early ultrasonograms and would not be a priority in this situation.

8.   C: Changes in Health   T: Application

1. Placenta previa is manifested by painless red vaginal bleeding in the third trimester. Ms. Smitherman's advanced maternal age is also a known risk factor.
2. Placental abruption more often occurs during labour and is manifested by concealed or apparent vaginal bleeding and pain, with the uterus feeling hard, tense, and painful.
3. Spontaneous abortion occurs prior to 20 weeks' gestation.

4. Rh incompatibility is not indicated by these manifestations. The hemolytic process would affect the newborn only and does not result in painless vaginal bleeding in the third trimester.

9.   C: Changes in Health   T: Application

1. Women between 24 and 34 weeks' gestation who are at risk for a preterm birth should be considered for corticosteroid treatment to accelerate fetal lung maturity.
2. This intervention will not affect maternal risk factors for complications.
3. This intervention will not affect maternal bleeding.
4. Opioid agents, not corticosteroids, are used in epidural anaesthesia.

10.   C: Changes in Health   T: Critical Thinking

1. The priority assessment is ensuring spontaneous respirations so that the infant may be adequately oxygenated. If the infant is not breathing adequately, the infant will require supplemental oxygen, bagging, and possibly intubation with mechanical ventilation.
2. This would be an important assessment, but breathing is the priority.
3. Colour is part of the assessment related to breathing. A newborn at birth will likely be cyanosed, becoming pink centrally after spontaneous respirations or supplemental bagging is initiated.
4. This is part of the neonatal assessment but is not the priority assessment.

11.   C: Changes in Health   T: Application

1. Pathological jaundice associated with liver damage would occur at birth or in the first 24 hours. Physiological jaundice in a full-term, otherwise healthy infant occurs after 24 hours, peaks within 3–4 days, and resolves within a week.
2. The bruising and blood from the cephalohematoma may have contributed to the elevated bilirubin levels but are not the cause. An immature liver and limited ability to conjugate bilirubin lead to physiological jaundice.
3. Pathological hyperbilirubinemia occurs at birth or in the first 24 hours of life and requires investigation.
4. A blood exchange transfusion is not always required, especially for physiological jaundice.

12.   C: Changes in Health   T: Application

1. Fluid requirements increase by 10%, and more frequent breastfeeding should be supported.

2. Stools become looser and more frequent.
3. The baby will be drowsier and lethargic.
4. Skin exposure is important to maximize the benefit of the ultraviolet lights. Eyes must always be covered for protection.

13.   C: Changes in Health   T: Application

1. This is not a safe option. In many cases, the membranes do not rupture until shortly before delivery.
2. Regular contractions at seven minutes apart indicate the end of the latent phase of labour. It is not known how quickly Ms. Cooke's labour will progress; therefore, she should be assessed by a nurse or physician at the hospital.
3. Suggesting the pregnant woman walk when she feels contractions is often advised to distinguish between true and false labour. Ms. Cooke has indicated that the contractions are regular, so it is not likely that this is false labour. She should be assessed at the hospital.
4. Contractions that are four minutes apart occur during the active phase of labour. As it is not known how quickly the labour will progress, Ms. Cooke should not delay being assessed.

14.   C: Changes in Health   T: Knowledge

1. Infants do not possess the ability to shiver at birth.
2. Nonshivering thermogenesis uses the chemical breakdown of brown fat stores to generate heat.
3. Cold, stress, and heat production increase oxygen demands and consumption.
4. An extended body posture increases heat loss.

15.   C: Changes in Health   T: Knowledge

1. Weight is not used to assess gestational age as infants may be small, large, or average weight independent of their gestational age.
2. Head circumference is not a reliable indicator of gestational age. A newborn may be small, large, or average in growth regardless of gestational age.
3. Absence of ear cartilage is seen in prematurity, while the presence of ear cartilage is a sign of full-term gestational maturity.
4. Body length is influenced by growth patterns, and infants may be average, below, or above average in length regardless of gestational age.

16.   C: Changes in Health   T: Application

1. Increased oxygen levels cause the ductus arteriosus to constrict.
2. Clamping of the umbilical cord closes the ductus venosus.

3. When the pulmonary vessels open, more blood flows into the left atrium, increasing pressure and volume. This pressure becomes greater than the pressure in the right atrium, and the foramen ovale functionally closes.
4. During transition, the pulmonary blood vessels dilate and pulmonary blood pressure decreases.

17.   C: Changes in Health   T: Application

1. Fetal well-being is indicated by heart rate variability of 6–25 bpm, with a normal baseline heart rate of 110–160 bpm and no periodic decelerations.
2. Head compression is associated with early decelerations during labour near the time of birth.
3. Cord compression is associated with variable decelerations.
4. Periodic late decelerations are associated with uteroplacental insufficiency, which can occur when the placental supply of oxygen is reduced or interrupted, as in chronic hypertension.

18.   C: Changes in Health   T: Application

1. WinRho® is administered to Rh-negative mothers who give birth to an Rh-positive newborn. There will not be an immune response if the newborn is also Rh-negative; therefore, prophylaxis is not required.
2. WinRho® is given in this situation in case the embryo or fetus was Rh-positive and isoimmunization has occurred.
3. WinRho® is administered to Rh-negative mothers who give birth to an Rh-positive newborn or in situations where the Rh factor of the embryo or newborn is unknown, including ectopic pregnancies and spontaneous or induced abortions. Blood type is not a consideration.
4. WinRho® is not required in this situation as the incompatibility occurs with an O-positive mother who has anti-A and anti-B antibodies. WinRho® will not affect blood type incompatibilities.

19.   C: Changes in Health   T: Application

1. Bed sharing is not recommended by the Canadian Paediatric Society.
2. The incidence of SIDS is lowered when these guidelines are followed.
3. These positions are not required to prevent aspiration and are linked to an increased risk of SIDS.
4. Extra clothing layers and blankets are not needed or recommended.

20.   C: Changes in Health   T: Critical Thinking

1. Infertility increases in women who delay pregnancy until after the age of 30. Aging is a major contributing factor in increased infertility.

2. Being in a same-sex relationship does not necessarily affect female fertility. Same-sex female couples may choose to use a sperm donor and conceive either through intercourse or artificial insemination.
3. Sexually transmitted infections are known risk factors for infertility. Provided that safer sex with barrier methods was practised to prevent infections, more than five partners is not necessarily a risk for infertility.
4. The onset of puberty and menarche does not affect fertility over a woman's reproductive lifespan.

21.   C: Changes in Health   T: Knowledge

1. There is an increased risk of hypoglycemia as maternal glucose supply stops at birth, the newborn's pancreas continues to produce large amounts of insulin, and the infant, particularly if the child is large for gestational age (LGA), uses up glucose stores quickly.
2. Infants of mothers with gestational diabetes are at risk of being LGA due to the additional maternal glucose supply. SGA is a risk for people with type 1 diabetes who may experience chronic UTI.
3. There is an increased risk of hypoglycemia, not hyperglycemia. See rationale 1.
4. The fetal pancreas responds to increased glucose from the mother by producing large amounts of insulin in the first few days of life, resulting in temporary hyperinsulinism, not insulin resistance.

22.   C: Changes in Health   T: Knowledge

1. Risk category A drugs are considered safe, with no evidence of risk.
2. Risk category B drugs show no risk in animal studies only.
3. Risk category C drugs do show risk of teratogenic effects in animal studies, but maternal well-being and benefit may outweigh the risks to the fetus.
4. Risk category X drugs are contraindicated as there is evidence of harm to fetuses that outweighs potential benefits.

23.   C: Changes in Health   T: Knowledge

1. Calcium requirements increase to 1200–1500 mg per day depending on age.
2. A supplement of 400 micrograms (mcg) daily in addition to dietary intake is recommended.
3. Recommended iron intake increases from 13 to 18 mg in the second trimester and to 23 mg by the third trimester (Health Canada, 2007).
4. There is a known increased risk of birth defects at intakes of vitamin A of 10,000 IU daily. The recommended intake for vitamin A,

CHAPTER 9

4355 IU, is easily met through dietary means; supplementation is therefore not recommended (Health Canada, 2007).

24.   C: Changes in Health   T: Application

1. Systemic opioids are avoided if birth is anticipated within two hours and would therefore not be administered up to the second stage of labour.
2. Narcan is administered to the newborn to reverse the opioid effect, not to the mother.
3. Systemic opioids do cross the placenta to the fetus and may cause CNS depression in the newborn. Naloxone can be administered to the newborn to reverse the side effects.
4. Opioids are found in insignificant amounts in breast milk and will not cause adverse effects in the newborn. It is important to provide effective pain management for the mother so she is able to interact with and learn to care for her newborn.

25.   C: Changes in Health   T: Application

1. Human milk is the ideal food for preterm infants. Mothers of preterm infants should begin pumping their breasts with a hospital-grade electric pump as soon as possible after birth and should pump 10 times daily to establish milk flow.
2. The mother needs to start pumping her breasts as soon as possible. After several weeks, she may not be able to establish adequate milk flow.
3. Breast milk is more beneficial than formula for all infants. Breast milk can be measured to provide exact volumes for the infant.
4. Depending on the suck and swallow reflex, the behavioural readiness to take oral feedings, and the infant's physical condition, it is not known when the infant will be able to be put to breast.

Pediatric Nursing

Nancy McDonald, RN, BScN, MScN
Cheryl Sams, RN, BScN, MSN

This chapter on pediatric nursing encompasses the care of children of all ages, from newborns to adolescents, focusing on injury prevention and the promotion of optimal health in a variety of health conditions. An awareness of growth and development patterns in children, as well as the unique physical changes that occur at each stage of development, is essential to the delivery of quality pediatric nursing care.

Pediatric care is provided within the context of the family. Effective care is respectful of social and cultural differences and beliefs and involves the development of trusting and collaborative relationships between family members and the nurse.

FAMILY INFLUENCES ON CHILD HEALTH

The term "family" has been defined in many ways and is essentially defined by each individual. As a matter of policy and practice, the Vanier Institute of the Family considers that the concept of family is self-defined and promotes respect for and support to all types of families (Vanier Institute of the Family (n.d.)). Numerous social, cultural, religious, and economic factors influence the family and impact the health and well-being of the child.

Historically, families were excluded from the care of an ill child. A family-centred care model is now recognized to promote child health and well-being. In pediatric nursing, a thorough family assessment is essential and should include the collection of data concerning both family structure and family function.

FAMILY STRUCTURE

"The family structure, or family composition, consists of individuals, each with a socially recognized status and position, who interact with one another on a regular, recurring basis in socially sanctioned ways" (Hockenberry & Wilson, 2011). With the transition from the nuclear family to nontraditional family structures, the pediatric nurse is challenged to understand the influences each family structure has on the health and well-being of a given child.

Common Types of Family Structures

Traditional Nuclear Family: The traditional family is defined as a married couple and their biological children. Characteristics include the following:

• No other relatives or persons live in the household.
• The husband is the provider and the wife stays at home, but in some situations, this is reversed.
• Nursing considerations include respect for the caregiver at home as well as an awareness of the stresses and demands on the provider.

Nuclear Family: This family is defined as two parents cohabiting with their children; the parents may not necessarily be married. Characteristics include the following:

• Parent relationships and sibling relationships can be biological, step, adoptive, or foster.
• No other relatives or persons live in the household.
• Nursing considerations for a dual-income nuclear family include developing strategies for the family to meet the conflicting demands of career and child-rearing while promoting optimal health.

Blended Family: This family has at least one step-parent, step-sibling, or half-sibling. The number of blended families is increasing, from 200,000 (or 2.3% of all Canadian families) in 2001 to 231,000 (or 2.4% of all Canadian families) in 2006 (Statistics Canada, 2006). Nursing considerations include providing resources for families on parenting styles and strategies to reduce conflicts that can arise between the step-child and the step-parent.

Extended Family: In this type of family, household expenses and child-rearing responsibilities are shared with a couple and a grandparent or other relative. This type of family structure is common for recently immigrated families as well as working-class families. Nursing considerations include ensuring that resources are in place for aging family members participating in child-rearing, such as an older grandparent, who may have financial difficulties and increasing health problems.

Lone-Parent Family: This term describes a household led by one parent following death, divorce, separation, or illegitimacy. Characteristics include the following:

• These families are traditionally led by the mother, but there is an increase in father-led families.
• These families made up 2.4% of all Canadian families in 2001 and 2.8% in 2006 (Statistics Canada, 2006).
• Nursing considerations include focusing on resources for social, emotional, and financial support.

Binuclear Family: This term describes parents who continue their parenting roles with their biological children in two independent households (in a joint custody or co-parenting arrangement). Nursing considerations include ensuring consistency in health promotion teaching and guidance with each parent in the event of an acute or chronic illness in the child.

Gay or Lesbian Family: These families are headed by same-sex, gay, or lesbian adult(s). There is no evidence that children raised in this family structure are more dysfunctional than children raised by heterosexual parents (Ariel & McPerson, 2000). Nursing considerations include ensuring a non-judgemental approach when dealing with child or family health concerns.

FAMILY FUNCTION

"Family function refers to the interactions of family members, especially the quality of those relationships and interactions" (Hockenberry & Wilson, 2011). Assessment of family strengths and unique functioning styles is important for a pediatric nurse as these factors can promote a stronger family unit and will influence how a family copes with illness in their child.

PARENTING

Parents assume a leadership role in the family to guide children to learn acceptable behaviours. Ideally, parents instill beliefs, morals, and cultural values in their children in an effort to develop socially responsible and contributing members of society. The parenting style, along with the child's personality traits, will influence that child's developmental outcomes.

Parenting Styles

There are three main parenting styles. Families will generally display one style but may assume a different style in certain situations.

- Authoritarian Parents

  - Rules and standards of conduct are set by the parent and followed rigidly.
  - Children do not participate in family decision making.
  - Children develop with poor communication and negotiation skills.
  - Children are generally shy and self-conscious.

- Authoritative Parents

  - Firm controls and limits are set by the parent.
  - Children participate in open discussions on family issues and decisions.
  - Children develop a sense of high self-esteem and self-reliance.

- Permissive Parents

  - Parents exercise little or no control over their children.

  - Children are permitted to regulate their own activity as much as possible.
  - Children often control the parents and are disobedient, rebellious, and aggressive.

Parenting in Special Circumstances

Even in the most ideal circumstances, parents encounter many challenges when raising their children. When the family unit deviates from the norm, parents and children can face challenges that can potentially lead to family disruption.

Adoption

In 2009, Canadians adopted 451 children from China, the number one choice (Adoptive Parents of Canada, 2011).

Adoption is not merely a simple matter of the legal transfer of parental rights from one party to another but includes the social and emotional health of the adopted child, the birth parents, and the adoptive families. Nursing can support families by helping to identify sources of adoptive agencies, by assisting families in preparing other siblings for the arrival of the adoptive child, and by helping to integrate the adoptive child into the family system.

Divorce

In Canada, the divorce rate has increased dramatically following the introduction of the *Canadian Divorce Act* (Statistics Canada, 2008). Potential effects of divorce on children are as follows (Hockenberry & Wilson, 2011):

- Children may experience more emotional and behavioural problems.
- Factors that influence the impact include the age and sex of the child, the outcome of the divorce, the quality of the parent–child relationship, and parental care following the divorce.
- Children may experience two major phases post-divorce: a crisis phase lasting for a year or longer and characterized by emotional upheaval and an adjustment phase involving adaptation to the new family structure.
- Children may feel more loyal to one parent and may become the "message carrier" between the divorced parents.

GROWTH AND DEVELOPMENT

It is essential to understand the stages of growth and development when caring for children. As children progress through infancy to adolescence, their nutritional, cultural, and social situations will impact their development. Pediatric nurses integrate their knowledge of growth and development in each encounter with a child, and care is delivered in an age-appropriate manner.

Key terms for growth and development are as follows:

- **Growth** refers to increases in physical parameters, for example, height, weight, vital signs.
- **Development** refers to increases in capability or function, including motor, psychosocial, and cognitive function.
- **Cephalocaudal** means developmental progression from head to toe. For example, a child gains control of the head and neck before the trunk and limbs.
- **Proximodistal** means developmental progress that proceeds from the centre of the body outward to the extremities. For example, a child gains control of the hands before the fingers.

MAJOR THEORIES OF DEVELOPMENT

Many theorists have organized their observations of childhood development into stages based on these approximate age groups:

- Infancy: birth to 1 year
- Toddler: 1–3 years
- Preschool: 3–6 years
- School age: 6–12 years
- Adolescence: 12–18 years

A few of the major theories of childhood development include the following:

Freud's Theory of Psychosexual Development

Freud's theory suggests that sexual energy is centred in specific parts of the body at certain ages. Unresolved conflict and unmet needs at a certain stage lead to a fixation of development at that stage (Lerner, 2002).

Erickson's Theory of Psychosocial Development

Erickson's theory suggests that individuals progress through life experiencing developmental crises at certain stages in life. Critical developmental needs must be met at each stage in order to move on to future stages and prevent future maladaptive social relationships (Erickson, 1963).

Piaget's Theory of Cognitive Development

Piaget's theory suggests that children are greatly influenced by age, experience, and maturational ability. Children learn from new experiences by integrating these experiences into their learning base. The child will then manage new experiences through accommodation (Piaget, 1972).

The three theorists are summarized in Table 10.1.

Kohlberg's Theory of Moral Development

Kohlberg's theory explains the development of moral decision making and judgement. Older children and adolescents start to develop a value system that is autonomous from that of their parents and other authority figures. The theory has been controversial because of sexual bias and the lack of cultural sensitivity. See Table 10.2 for Kohlberg's theory (Ball & Binder, 2006).

Spiritual Development

Stages of spiritual development are listed in Table 10.3.

INFANCY: BIRTH TO ONE YEAR OF AGE

BIOLOGICAL CHANGES

Infancy is the most rapid period of growth, with increases in length, weight, and head and chest

Table 10.1 Developmental Theories of Freud, Erickson, and Piaget			
	Freud	**Erickson**	**Piaget**
Infancy (Birth–1 Year)	Oral stage	Trust vs. mistrust	Sensorimotor
Toddler (1–3 Years)	Anal stage	Autonomy vs. shame and doubt	Sensorimotor (ends at 2 years) Preoperational (begins at 2 years)
Preschool (3–6 Years)	Phallic stage	Initiative vs. guilt	Preoperational
School-Aged (6–12 Years)	Latency stage	Industry vs. inferiority	Concrete operational
Adolescence (12–18 Years)	Genital stage	Identity vs. role confusion	Formal operational

OAPLG   TAIII   SPCF

Table 10.2   Kohlberg's Theory of Moral Development

Preconventional (4–7 Years)	Decisions are based on the desire to please others and to avoid punishment.
Conventional (7–11 Years)	• A conscience or internal set of standards is based on beliefs and teaching of others, such as parents. • Rules are important and to be followed to please others and "be good."
Postconventional (12 Years and Older)	• Ethical standards on which to base decisions are internalized, and the child uses awareness of the common good and ethical principles rather than relying on the standards of others. • Social responsibility is identified.

Source: Ball, J. W., &, Binder, R. C. (2006). *Child health nursing: Partnering with children & families.* New Jersey: Pearson/Prentice Hall (pp. 138–139).

Table 10.3   Stages of Spiritual Development

Age Group	Spiritual Concepts
Toddler	• Children learn about God through the family and friends but cannot understand the concept or religious teaching because of immature cognitive system. • Can begin to associate God with family routines such as prayers before bedtime and draw comfort from these
Preschooler	• Develop a concrete concept of "their" God and give Him physical characteristics • Understand simple stories and memorize prayers but have a limited understanding of the concepts • Important to have children view their God as one who provides unconditional love rather than judging good or bad behaviour as they learn good behaviour to avoid punishments • Religious communities can help the toddler and the family cope with illnesses or crises.
School-Aged	• Visualize their God as a person and think of Him in concrete terms • Think of heaven and hell and going to hell as a punishment for not following the rules, which is important to children in this age group as they develop a conscience • Older children begin to realize that all of their prayers will not be answered by their God.
Adolescent	• More abstract thinking with spiritual and ideological aspects • More emphasis on internal aspects of religious commitments rather than the practices and rituals of organized religion

circumference and changes in fontanelles. Growth should be charted on standardized growth charts for boys and girls to observe for comparable gains in length, weight, and head circumference.

Length

- Increases in length occur in spurts rather than through slow and steady growth.
- Elongation of the trunk dominates, with height increasing by 2.5 cm per month during the first six months and then by 1.25 cm per month during the second six months.
- Length should increase by 50% by the end of the first year.

Weight

- Weight increases 680 g per month for the first five months, at which point, the birth weight is doubled.

- Weight increases at half this rate for the next six months, with an average of 340 g per month; by 12 months, the birth weight should have tripled.
- Breastfed infants tend to weigh slightly less than formula-fed infants during the second six months of life.

Head and Chest Circumference

- Head growth is rapid and is a major indicator of brain development.
- Head circumference increases on average 1.5 cm per month for the first six months then 0.5 cm per month for the next six months.
- By the end of the first year, head size has increased on average 33%.
- Chest circumference is normally 2 cm less than head circumference.

Fontanelles

◊ PT-AD

- The anterior (diamond-shaped) fontanelle typically measures 5 cm at birth and closes at between 12–18 months.
- The posterior (triangular-shaped) fontanelle typically measures 1 cm and closes at 1 month.

Vital Signs

Temperature

- Body temperature measurements differ in children based on the method used. See Table 10.4 for recommended routes.
- The rectal route gives the closest temperature to the core temperature.
- Rectal temperatures may lag behind a core temperature during rapid temperature changes.

- The axillary route is recommended unless a core temperature is necessary.
- For safety reasons, do not use an oral thermometer.
- Rectal thermometers should not be used in newborns under one month due to the risk of anal perforation.

For further information on temperature-taking, refer to Chapter 6, page 126.

Heart Rate

- Heart rate decreases as age increases.
- Most reliable is the apical impulse (heard through a stethoscope held to the chest at the apex of the heart).
- Count the apical rate for one full minute as young children may have irregularities in rhythm.

Table 10.4 Recommended Temperature Screening Routes in Infants and Children

Birth to 2 Years	• Axillary • Rectal if definitive temperature reading is needed for infants over 1 month
Over 2 Years to 5 Years	• Axillary • Tympanic • Oral • Rectal if definitive temperature reading is needed
Over 5 Years	• Axillary • Tympanic • Oral

Source: Adapted from Hockenberry, M. J., & Wilson, D. (2011). *Wong's nursing care of infants and children* (9th ed., p. 145, Box 6-11). St. Louis: Mosby.

Table 10.5 Comparison of Pediatric Differences in Vital Signs

	Temperature (°C)	Pulse (bpm)	Respirations (number per minute)	Blood Pressure (mm Hg)
Newborn	37.5	100–180	35	65–80/40–50
1–12 Months	37.7	80–150	30	95–110/60–70
1–3 Years	37.2	70–110	23–25	100–115/74–85
3–6 Years	37.0	70–110	21–23	105–115/63–75
6–12 Years	36.7	70–110	19–21	115–125/75–82
12–18 Years	36.8	55–90	16–19	125–132/82–86

Source: Hockenberry, M. J., & Wilson, D. (2011). *Wong's nursing care of infants and children* (9th ed., inside back cover). St. Louis: Mosby.

Respirations

- Rate decreases as age increases.
- Count for one full minute due to irregular movements.
- Monitor abdominal movements since respirations are primarily diaphragmatic.

Blood Pressure

- The most important factor in accurate assessment is use of an appropriately sized cuff that covers three-quarters of the upper arm.

See Table 10.5 for a summary of pediatric differences in vital signs.

GROSS AND FINE MOTOR DEVELOPMENT

Gross motor development includes maturation in posture, head balance, sitting, creeping, standing, and walking. Fine motor development includes the use of hands and fingers to grasp objects. Table 10.6 summarizes growth and development during infancy.

NUTRITION

Both the rate and the pattern of growth can be modified by nutrition.

Table 10.6 Growth and Development During Infancy

Age	Physical	Gross Motor Development	Fine Motor Development	Vocalization
1 Month		• Can turn head side to side when prone • Marked head lag when pulled from lying to sitting position	• Hands predominantly closed • Grasp reflex is strong	• Cries to express displeasure • Small throat sounds • Comfort sounds during feeding
2 Months	• Posterior fontanelle closed	• Less head lag	• Hands often open • Grasp reflex fading	• Vocalizes, distinct from crying • Coos • Vocalizes to familiar voices
3 Months	• Primitive reflexes fading	• Able to hold head more erect when sitting but still bobs forward	• Holds rattle but will not reach for it • Grasp reflex gone • Pulls at blankets and own hands	• Squeals aloud to show pleasure • Coos, babbles, chuckles
4 Months	• Drooling begins	• Balances head well in sitting position • Able to sit erect if propped up • Rolls from back to side	• Inspects and plays with hands • Tries to reach for objects but overshoots • Cannot carry objects to mouth	• Laughs aloud • Makes consonant sounds n, k, g, p, b • Vocalization changes according to mood
5 Months	• Beginning signs of tooth eruption • Birth weight has doubled	• Able to sit for longer periods of time with back supported • Can turn from abdomen to back	• Able to grasp objects voluntarily • Takes objects directly to mouth • Plays with toes	• Squeals • Makes cooing vowel sounds with interspersed consonants (i.e., ah-goo)
6 Months	• Growth rate may decrease • Teething may begin with two lower central incisors	• When supine, puts feet in mouth • When prone, can lift chest and bear weight on hands • Rolls from back to abdomen	• Grasps and manipulates small objects • Drops one cube when given another • Holds bottle	• Begins to imitate sound • Vocalizes to toys and mirror images • Enjoys hearing own sounds
7 Months	• Eruptions of upper central incisors	• Bears full weight on feet • Bounces when held in standing position • Sits erect momentarily	• Transfers objects from one hand to the other • Holds two cubes more than momentarily • Bangs cubes on table	• Produces vowel sounds and chained syllables (i.e., baba, dada, kaka)

Continued on next page

Table 10.6   Growth and Development During Infancy (cont'd)

Age	Physical	Gross Motor Development	Fine Motor Development	Vocalization
8 Months	• Begins to show regular bladder and bowel patterns	• Sits steadily unsupported • Readily bears weight on legs when supported and stands holding onto furniture	• Has beginning pincer grasp • Reaches for and pulls toys • Rings bell purposely	• Listens selectively for familiar words • Utterances signal emphasis and emotion
9 Months	• Eruption of upper lateral incisor may begin	• Creeps on hands and knees • Pulls self to standing position by holding onto furniture	• Uses thumb and index finger in crude pincer grasp • Shows preference for use of dominant hand	• Responds to simple commands • Comprehends "no-no"
10 Months	• Labyrinth righting reflex is strongest (when in prone or supine position, infant is able to raise head)	• Cruises by holding onto furniture • Can change from prone to supine position • Recovers balance easily while sitting	• Release of object from crude pincer grasp begins • Grasps bell by handle	• Says "dada" or "mama" with meaning • May say one word (i.e., hi, bye, no)
11 Months	• Eruption of lower lateral incisors may begin	• When sitting, will pivot to reach objects behind • Cruises or walks while holding onto furniture	• Examines objects more closely • Has neat pincer grasp • Drops object deliberately to be picked up	• Imitates definite speech sounds
12 Months	• Birth weight has tripled	• Walks with one hand held and cruises well • Can sit down from standing position without any help	• Can turn pages in a book, many at a time • Attempts to build two-block tower but fails	• Recognizes objects by name • Imitates animal sounds • Understands simple verbal commands (i.e., give it to me)

Source: Adapted from Hockenberry, M. J., & Wilson, D. (2011). *Wong's nursing care of infants and children* (9th ed., pp. 481–485, Table 12-3). St. Louis: Mosby.

- Breast milk is the most desirable, complete diet for infants during the first 12 months.
- Breastfed infants will feed on demand.
- Breastfed infants require a daily supplement of 10 mcg (400 IU) of vitamin D from birth until the equivalent amount is obtained from other dietary sources or until they reach 1 year of age. If the infant lives north of the fifty-fifth parallel, this level should increase to 20 mcg (800 IU) from all sources between October and April (Canadian Paediatric Society [CPS], 2007a; Health Canada, 2012a). Formula-fed infants receive vitamin D in formula but still require supplements of an additional 10 mcg (400 IU) if they live north of the fifty-fifth parallel. The CPS has recommended further research in response to studies that have shown that supplemental vitamin D levels may still be inadequate, particularly in at-risk populations such as First Nations, Inuit, and Métis in northern climates. The CPS is also recommending that pregnant and lactating women consult their physicans about taking up to 2000 IU of vitamin D daily to ensure adequate amounts (CPS, 2007a).
- An acceptable alternative to breastfeeding is a commercial iron-fortified formula.
- Formula-fed infants will take about 5–8 feedings every 24 hr.
- Boil all drinking water and water used for formula.
- Fluid requirements average 125–150 mL/kg/day from birth to 6 months of age and 120–135 mL/kg/day from 6–12 months.
- Use of a cup at 6–9 months will help reduce nursing bottle caries when diluted apple juice is introduced.
- Solids can be introduced at 6 months, starting first with rice cereal, which is easy to digest, contains iron, and rarely causes an allergic reaction.
- Introduce other cereals, fruits, vegetables, and finally meats one at a time and usually three days apart to test for possible food allergies.
- Finger foods such as toast, teething crackers, soft fruits, and cooked vegetables should be introduced at 6–7 months. Parents should be advised to monitor for choking.
- Chopped table food or commercially prepared junior food can be introduced around 9–12 months.
- Weaning from the breast or bottle to a cup may occur after 6 months and should be based on the readiness of the mother and infant.

SLEEP

- Sleep patterns vary greatly among infants.
- By 3–4 months, most infants will sleep 15 hours a day, of which 9–11 hours will be overnight.
- By 12 months, morning and afternoon naps are common.
- Breastfed infants will usually sleep for shorter periods than bottle-fed infants.

DENTAL

- Fluoride is an essential mineral to promote healthy teeth.
- Most Canadian municipalities add fluoride to drinking water.
- Primary teeth erupt around 6 months of age, beginning first with the upper central incisors.
- Parents should begin a routine of good dental hygiene before teeth are present by using a soft-bristled toothbrush or a damp cloth with water rather than toothpaste. Swallowing too much toothpaste containing fluoride can lead to fluorosis (CDA, 2012).

- To prevent dental caries, discourage breast- and bottle-feeding during sleep and avoid fruit juices in a bottle, particularly before 6 months of age.
- Foods with concentrated sugar should be used in limited quantity.
- Discourage the practice of coating a pacifier with honey; this can cause infant botulism.
- Discourage the use of hard-candy pacifiers, not only due to the sugar content but also as parts of the candy can break off and be aspirated.

IMMUNIZATIONS

See Table 10.7A–D for recommended Canadian immunization schedules (Public Health Agency of Canada, 2006).

Nursing Considerations

When administering immunizations,

- Ensure proper storage of the vaccine.
- Rotate sites and administer the injections as painlessly as possible.

Table 10.7A   Canadian Routine Immunization Schedule for Infants and Children

Age at Vaccination	DTaP-IPV	Hib	MMR	Var	HB	Pneu-C-13	Men-C	Tdap	HPV	Inf
Birth										
2 Months	●	❖				□	(◉)			
4 Months	●	❖			★	□	(◉)			
6 Months	●	❖			Infancy 3 doses	□	(◉)			6–59 months
12 Months			■	●		□ 12–15 months	◉			✪
					or					
18 Months	●	❖	■	●						1–2 doses
			or	or						
4–6 Years	●		■	●*						
12 Years					Preteen/teen 2–3 doses		◉		Females 9–45 Males 9–26 years 3 doses	
14–16 Years								▲		

Source for Tables 10.7A–D: Public Health Agency of Canada. (2013). *Canadian Immunization Guide*. Adapted and reproduced with permission from the Minister of Health, 2013.

Table 10.7B Routine Immunization Schedule for Children <7 Years of Age Not Immunized in Early Infancy

Timing	DTaP-IPV	Hib	MMR	Var	HB	Pneu-C-13	Men-C	Tdap	HPV
First Visit	⊙	❖	■	●	★	□	⊙		
2 Months Later	⊙	(❖)	■*		★	(□)			
2 Months Later	⊙			●*		(□)			
6–12 Months Later	⊙	(❖)			★				
4–6 Years of Age	(⊙)								
12 Years of Age							⊙		✹ Females 9–45 Males 9–26 years 3 doses
14–16 Years of Age								▲	

Table 10.7C Routine Immunization Schedule for Children ≥ 7 Years of Age Up to 17 Years of Age Not Immunized in Early Infancy

Timing	Tdap	IPV	MMR	Var	HB	Men-C	HPV
First Visit	▲	✚	■	●	★	⊙	✹
2 Months Later	▲	✚	■*	(●)*	(★)		✹ Females, ≥ 9 years
6–12 Months Later	▲	✚			★		✹
10 Years Later	▲						

Table 10.7D Routine Immunization Schedule for Adults (≥18 Years of Age) Not Immunized in Childhood

Timing	Tdap	Td	MMR	Var	Men-C	Pneu-C-23	HPV	Inf
First Visit	▲		■	●	(⊙)		✹	
2 Months Later		◫	(■)	●			✹ Females, 14-26 years	
6–12 Months Later		◫				(▣)	✹	(✪)
10 Years Later		◫						

Notes for Tables 10.7A–D

( ) Symbols with brackets around them imply that these doses may not be required, depending on the age of the child or adult. Refer to the *Canadian Immunization Guide* http://www.phac-aspc.gc.ca/publicat/cig-gci/p04-eng.php for further details on this vaccine.

* Symbols with an asterisk imply: or 2 doses of MMR-Var at least 6 weeks apart.

○ Diphtheria, tetanus, acellular pertussis, and inactivated polio virus vaccine (DTaP-IPV): DTaP-IPV($\pm$ Hib) vaccine is the preferred vaccine for all doses in the vaccination series, including completion of the series in children who have received one or more doses of DPT (whole-cell) vaccine (for example, recent immigrants). In Tables A and B, the 4–6 year dose can be omitted if the fourth dose was given after the fourth birthday.

❖ *Haemophilus influenzae* type b conjugate vaccine (Hib): The Hib schedule shown is for the *Haemophilus* b capsular polysaccharide-polyribosylribitol phosphate (PRP) conjugated to tetanus toxoid (PRP-T). For catch-up, the number of doses depends on the age at which the schedule is begun. Refer to the *Canadian Immunization Guide* for further details on this vaccine. Not usually required past age 5 years.

■ Measles, mumps, and rubella vaccine (MMR): A second dose of MMR is recommended for children at least one month after the first dose for the purpose of better measles protection. For convenience, options include giving it with the next scheduled vaccination at 18 months of age or at school entry (4–6 years) (depending on the provincial/territorial policy) or at any intervening age that is practical. In the catch-up schedule (Table B), the first dose should not be given until the child is ≥12 months old. MMR should be given to all susceptible adolescents and adults.

● Varicella vaccine (Var): Children aged 12 months to 12 years should receive one dose of varicella vaccine. Susceptible individuals ≥13 years of age should receive two doses at least 28 days apart.

★ Hepatitis B vaccine (HB): Hepatitis B vaccine can be routinely given to infants or preadolescents, depending on the provincial/territorial policy. For infants born to chronic carrier mothers, the first dose should be given at birth (with hepatitis B immunoglobulin); otherwise. the first dose can be given at two months of age to fit more conveniently with other routine infant immunization visits. The second dose should be administered at least one month after the first dose and the third at least two months after the second dose, but these may fit more conveniently into the four- and six-month immunization visits. A two-dose schedule for adolescents is an option. Refer to the *Canadian Immunization Guide* for further details on this vaccine.

□ Pneumococcal conjugate vaccine-13-valent (Pneu-C-13): Recommended for all children under 2 years of age. The recommended schedule depends on the age of the child when vaccination is begun. Refer to the *Canadian Immunization Guide* for further details on this vaccine.

◨ Pneumococcal polysaccharide-23-valent (Pneu-P-23): Recommended for all adults ≥65 years of age. Refer to the *Canadian Immunization Guide* for further details on this vaccine.

⊙ Meningococcal C conjugate vaccine (Men-C): Recommended for children under 5 years of age, adolescents, and young adults. The recommended schedule depends on the age of the individual and the conjugate vaccine used. At least one dose in the primary infant series should be given after 5 months of age, and one dose in early adolescence, preferably around 12 years old. Refer to the *Canadian Immunization Guide* for further details on this vaccine.

▲ Diphtheria, tetanus, acellular pertussis vaccine, adult/adolescent formulation (Tdap): A combined adsorbed "adult-type" preparation for use in people ≥7 years of age that contains fewer diphtheria toxoid and pertussis antigens than preparations given to younger children and is less likely to cause reactions in older people.

◫ Diphtheria, tetanus vaccine (Td): A combined adsorbed "adult-type" preparation for use in people ≥7 years of age that contains less diphtheria toxoid antigen than preparations given to younger children and is less likely to cause reactions in older people. It is given to adults not immunized in childhood as the second and third doses of their primary series and subsequent booster doses; Tdap is given only once under these circumstances as it is assumed that previously unimmunized adults will have encountered *Bordetella pertussis* and have some pre-existing immunity.

✳ Human papillomavirus (HPV): HPV vaccine is recommended for routine use in females between 9 to 45 and males 9 to 26 years old. The recommended schedule is 3 doses at 0, 2, and 6 months, with a minimum interval of one month between the first two doses.

✪ Influenza vaccine (Inf): Recommended for all children 6–59 months of age and all persons ≥65 years of age. Previously unvaccinated children <9 years of age require two doses of the current season's vaccine with an interval of at least 4 weeks. The second dose within the same season is not required if the child received one or more doses of influenza vaccine during the previous influenza season. Refer to the *Canadian Immunization Guide* for further details on this vaccine.

✜ IPV: Inactivated polio virus.

Source: Public Health Agency of Canada. (2013). *Canadian Immunization Guide.* Adapted and reproduced with permission from the Minister of Health, 2013.

- Consider use of topical anaesthestics such as EMLA cream to prevent a painful injection.
- Give acetaminophen prior to the injection; this will provide pain relief and make the child more comfortable after the immunization.
- Monitor for signs of allergic reaction.
- Ensure adequate penetration of the muscle when administering intramuscularly.
- Provide adequate information to parents on the risks and benefits of immunizations. See Chapter 5, page 107, for more information on vaccinations and risk communication.
- Maintain accurate documentation in an immunization record for parents to keep.

SAFETY

- Almost half of all deaths among children aged 1 to 4 years are due to injury (Health Canada, 2011).
- Some of the leading causes of injury include suffocation, choking, strangulation, drowning, falls, poisonings, burns, and motor vehicle accidents.
- As the infant develops fine and gross motor skills and begins to explore the environment, the risk of injury should be addressed with parents with appropriate injury prevention teaching. See Table 10.8 for hazards and how to prevent infant injuries.
- The Health Canada Web site provides consumer information on potentially hazardous products, particularly toys that present choking hazards and toxic compositions. This site also includes product recalls, for example, toys that are manufactured with unacceptable levels of lead paint. See the end of this chapter for additional Web sites that focus on child safety.

PLAY

- In infancy, play is mostly used for physical development and for gaining awareness of the environment.

Table 10.8 Preventable Hazards for Infants

Hazard	Nursing Considerations When Educating Caregivers
Falls	• Keep car seat or baby carrier on the floor rather than on a table or counter. • Always use safety straps in strollers and high chairs. • Always raise crib rails. • Never leave a child alone on a change table. Keep all supplies at hand. • Wheeled baby walkers, which have been banned in Canada since 2004, should not be used as they can cause serious injuries to children, including falls, head injuries, and burns. • A baby gate used at the top of stairs must be fastened to the wall with screws, not suction.
Burns	• Check the temperature of bath water and foods and liquids. • Keep hot items out of reach. • Place guards in front of fireplaces or heating devices. • Avoid hanging tablecloths as children may pull down hot items. • Avoid overexposure to the sun and use sunscreen if the infant is over 6 months of age.
 Motor Vehicle Accidents	• Motor vehicle crashes are the leading cause of preventable injury and death to children from birth to 14 years (Health Canada, 1997). • Every year about 10,000 children 12 years or under are injured, some fatally, in traffic collisions in Canada (Transport Canada, 2012). • The Transport Canada Web site provides information on child car seat requirements for individual provinces and territories. The site includes installation instructions, airbag safety tips, and recall alerts. • For children up to 20.5 kg, use rear-facing car seats. • For children over 20.5 kg, use forward-facing seats until they outgrow the seats. • For children who have outgrown forward-facing seats, use booster seats until the child weighs at least 36 kg and is 145 cm tall. • For children 36 kg or 145 cm tall and 9 years of age, seat belts need to be used. • The safest location for children 12 years or younger is in the back seat, away from airbags (Transport Canada, 2012).
  Drowning	• Drowning is the second leading cause of death for Canadian children (Safe Kids Canada, 2010). • Children can drown in as little as 5 cm (2 in) of water in just seconds. • Never leave an infant alone in a bath, even for a few seconds. • Avoid the use of a baby bath seat as it is not a safety device.

Continued on next page

Table 10.8 Preventable Hazards for Infants (cont'd)

Hazard	Nursing Considerations When Educating Caregivers
Poisoning	• Do not store toxic substances in food containers. • Keep medications locked up. • Do not administer medications as candy. • Keep the phone number of a poison control centre readily available. • Refer to Table 10.11 for the same poisoning risks.
Suffocation and Strangulation	• Position infants to sleep on their backs. • Do not place pillows, bumper pads, or stuffed toys in a crib. • Do not use plastic in a crib. • Avoid latex balloons. • In Canada, cribs made before 1986 are dangerous and should not be used as the part supporting the mattress can fall, entrapping an infant. • Crib bars should be no more than 6 cm (2³⁄₈ in) apart to prevent the infant's head from getting caught in the bars. • Keep the infant's crib away from windows as children have died when their heads got caught in the cords of blinds. • Do not use pacifiers with cords attached. • Do not use baby gates made before 1990 as children have died when their heads were trapped in the gates (these are usually gates with large diamond- or V-shaped openings).
Choking	• Hold infant for feeding and do not prop a bottle. • Use pacifiers with one-piece contraction and a loop handle. • Keep small objects such a buttons, beads, and small toys away from the infant. • Avoid the use of baby powder. • Use caution with toys and ensure that no small parts can come off and choke the infant.

- Play is basically solitary and will become more interactive during the first year.
- Toys should be simple to match the child's attention span.
- Toy safety is of primary concern, to prevent aspiration and injury.

See Table 10.9 for a list of suggested toys.

REACTIONS TO ILLNESS AND HOSPITALIZATION

The impact of hospitalization on an infant under 3 months is minimized if it is a short time period and there is a nurturing person who can meet the child's physical needs. At 4–6 months, the infant starts to recognize the parents as separate from itself and develops a fear of strangers, which can lead to separation anxiety if the child is hospitalized.

Nursing Considerations During Hospitalization

- Be present with the parents within sight of the infant to build a sense of safety in the child.
- Encourage parents to participate in the child's care as much as possible.
- Follow home routines as much as possible.
- Give the infant a sense of security by holding the child and moving gently, cuddling, talking, and responding to the child's reactions.
- Ensure that sensorimotor stimulation is provided.
- Provide physical care, comfort, and safety.
- Keep the infant warm and dry and plan treatments and tests around the home feeding schedule to prevent hunger and discomfort.
- Encourage breastfeeding or the use of the same type of formula used at home.
- Make sure crib rails are up and provide safe crib toys and an area to play in.
- Encourage cognitive stimulation through the use of various stimulating toys, such as rattles, mobiles, and music boxes with different textures.
- Encourage vocal stimulation and language development by talking to the infant and making sounds.
- Develop and maintain a relationship with the parents and encourage parent participation throughout the hospitalization whenever possible.
- Encourage the parents to voice their concerns and address them as much as possible.
- Try to keep the same core nurses as much as possible.

Table 10.9 Suggested Toys for Infants

Age	Visual Stimulation	Auditory Stimulation	Tactile Stimulation	Kinetic Stimulation
Birth–1 Year	• Nursery mobiles • Unbreakable mirrors • Contrasting coloured sheets	• Music boxes • Music mobiles • Crib dangle bells • Small-handled clear rattle	• Stuffed animals • Soft clothes* • Soft or furry quilt* • Soft mobiles	• Rocking crib or cradle • Weighted or suction toy • Infant swing
6–12 Months	• Coloured blocks • Nested boxes or cups • Books with rhymes and bright pictures • Strings of big beads • Simple take-apart toys • Large ball • Cup and spoon • Large puzzles • Jack-in-the-box	• Squeaky toys and animals • Rattles of different sizes, shapes, tones, and bright colours • Recordings with light, rhythmic music	• Soft, different-texture animals and dolls • Sponge toys • Floating toys • Squeeze toys • Teething toys • Books with textures, such as fur and zippers	• Activity box for cribs • Push-pull toys • Wind-up swing

*Toys must be removed from the crib when the infant is sleeping to avoid suffocation.

Source: Adapted from Hockenberry, M. J., & Wilson, D. (2011). *Wong's nursing care of infants and children* (9th ed., p. 480, Table 12-2). St. Louis: Mosby.

TODDLER: ONE TO THREE YEARS OF AGE

BIOLOGICAL CHANGES

Growth slows considerably during childhood. The toddler will experience steplike growth with spurts and lags versus the more linear growth of infancy.

Toddlers have the traditional pot-belly abdomen as a result of underdeveloped abdominal muscles. Legs will remain slightly bowed in appearance due to the weight of a comparatively large trunk.

Height

- The rate of increase in height slows, with an average increase of 7.5 cm per year.
- Increase occurs mainly in elongation of the legs rather than the trunk.
- Adult height is about twice the height of the child at age 2.

Weight

- Average weight gain is 1.8–2.7 kg per year.
- Birth weight is quadrupled by age 2½.

Head and Chest Circumference

Chest circumference surpasses head and abdominal circumferences, giving the toddler a taller, leaner appearance.

Vital Signs

See Table 10.5 for normal-range vital signs for the toddler.

Temperature

- Recommended routes include axillary, tympanic, and rectal (if a core temperature is required).
- Use of an oral thermometer is not recommended in children 4 years or younger.

Heart Rate

A satisfactory radial pulse can be obtained in children over 2.

GROSS AND FINE MOTOR DEVELOPMENT

- The major gross motor development of the toddler is locomotion.
- Fine motor development is demonstrated by increasingly skillful manual dexterity.

See Table 10.10 for the stages of toddler motor development.

NUTRITION

- As growth slows, so will the toddler's requirements for calories, protein, and fluids.
- By 12 months, most children will eat the same food prepared for the rest of the family.

Table 10.10   Toddler Growth and Development

Age	Physical	Gross Motor Development	Fine Motor Development	Language
12–15 Months	• Steady growth in height and weight	• Walks alone without help • Creeps up stairs • Assumes standing position without support	• Can grasp a very small object • Can drop a small object into a narrow opening • Repeatedly throws objects and retrieves them • Scribbles spontaneously with a crayon • Cannot insert a particular shaped object into a matching hole • Drinks from cup • Uses spoon but will rotate it	• Says 4–6 words • Asks for objects by pointing • Shakes head to denote "no" • Understands simple commands
18 Months	• Physiological anorexia from decreased growth needs • Anterior fontanelles closed • Physiologically able to control sphincters	• Tries to run but falls easily • Walks up stairs with one hand held • Jumps in place on both feet • Can throw a ball over head without losing balance	• Can build a tower of 3–4 blocks • Can insert a particular shaped object into the matching hole • Manages spoon without rotation	• Says 10 words or more • Forms word combinations • Points while naming the object
24 Months	• Chest circumference exceeds head circumference • May be ready to toilet train • Primary dentition of 16 teeth	• Walks up and down stairs on own	• Can build a tower of 6–7 blocks • Imitates a circular and a vertical line with a crayon • Turns door knobs and unscrews lids • Turns pages in a book one at a time	• Has a vocabulary of about 300 words • Uses pronouns I, me, and you • Refers to self by name • Talks continuously
2½ Years	• Quadruples birth weight • May have bladder and bowel control during the day • Primary dentition is complete at 20 teeth	• Can jump using both feet • Stands on one foot for a second or two • Can take a few steps on tiptoe	• Can build a tower of eight or more blocks • Holds a crayon with fingers rather than in fist	

Source: Adapted from Hockenberry, M. J., & Wilson, D. (2011). *Wong's nursing care of infants and children* (9th ed., p. 565, Table 14-2). St. Louis: Mosby.

- Parents should be encouraged to follow *Eating Well With Canada's Food Guide* for children 2 years of age and older. (See *Eating Well With Canada's Food Guide* in Chapter 5, page 101.)
- Toddlers will fully transition from the bottle to a cup by age 18 months, with some spilling.
- Proper control of a spoon is seen after 18 months of age.
- Emphasis should be placed on the introduction of a variety of foods and in developing healthy eating habits.
- Food should be presented in an appealing manner and served in small sizes; toddlers enjoy finger foods.
- By 18 months, most toddlers will display a phenomenon called physiological anorexia, evidenced by a decrease in nutritional needs and appetite.
- Toddlers become picky eaters and may eat voraciously one day and almost nothing the next; however, most toddlers will continue to consume enough nutrients for growth.

- A toddler may experience "food fads" or "jags," eating one particular type of food for several days in a row and then suddenly refusing to eat it again.
- Toddlers need to feel a sense of control.

SLEEP

- Total sleep decreases slightly during the second year, with an average of 12 hours per day.
- Most toddlers will require one nap per day and most often will give up napping by age 3.
- Toddlers will commonly experience difficulty going to bed and falling asleep as a result of separation anxiety.
- Parents should establish bedtime rituals with a consistent bedtime and the use of a transitional object such as a stuffed animal or a blanket for comfort and security.

DENTAL

- The Canadian Dental Association encourages the assessment of infants by a dentist within six months of the eruption of the first tooth or by 1 year of age (Canadian Dental Association, 2012).
- All 20 baby (or primary) teeth should erupt by 2 to 3 years.
- Dental hygiene includes brushing with a soft-bristled toothbrush and flossing.
- As with infants, avoid using toothpaste.
- Foods high in sugar should be limited.

IMMUNIZATIONS

See Table 10.7A–D for immunization schedules.

SAFETY

- Injuries are one of the major causes of death and morbidity for children and youth after the age of 1 (Health Canada, 2011).
- Leading causes of injury include suffocation, choking, strangulation, drowning, falls, poisonings, burns, and motor vehicle accidents.
- As the infant develops fine and gross motor skills and begins to explore the environment, injury prevention should be addressed with parents.

See Table 10.11 for a list of preventable toddler injuries.

Table 10.11	Preventable Hazards for Toddlers
Hazard	**Nursing Considerations/Parent Education**
Falls	• Due to a developing sense of balance, toddlers will quite often fall while climbing, jumping, or running. • Parents should continue to keep crib rails up, monitor the toddler around stairs, and secure windows and screens.
Burns	• Keep hot items well back from the edge of a countertop as with increased height, the toddler can easily reach for items on top of counters. • Turn pot handles in on stoves. • Avoid hanging tablecloths as children may pull down hot items. • Teach the toddler what "hot" means. • Check bath water and do not allow the toddler to play with the faucets. • Avoid overexposure to the sun and use sunscreen.
Motor Vehicle Accidents	• Rear-facing child seats are required for children up to 20.5 kg (45 lb), then front-facing seats are necessary until seats are outgrown. • Supervise the toddler at all times during outdoor play and teach the safety rules around roads and parked cars. • Head injuries are the number one cause of serious injury and death to children riding wheeled vehicles, including bicycles, in-line skates, scooters, etc. (Safe Kids Canada, 2008a). • Fit the toddler properly with a bike helmet that meets safety standards of the Canadian Safety Association (CSA).
Drowning	• Never leave a toddler alone in a bath, even for a few seconds. • Supervise the toddler around all sources of water at all times, including buckets. • Keep bathroom doors closed and toilet seats down.
Poisoning	• Poisonings by household chemical products, such as bleaches, paint thinners, ammonia, and abrasive cleaners, are among the top causes of injuries and deaths in children under the age of 5. • A small amount of a chemical product can be harmful to a child, and bad tastes and odours do not keep children away from chemical products. • Keep other harmful products, such as cosmetics, drugs, vitamins, and first-aid treatment products, out of the sight and reach of children.
Suffocation	• Remove draw strings from clothing. • Dispose of old appliances properly by removing doors. • Select safe toy boxes without heavy hinged lids. • Keep window covering cords out of the toddler's reach.
Choking	• Avoid foods that are choking hazards, such as whole hot dogs, large chunks of meat, fruit with pits, fish with bones, dried beans, chewing gum, nuts, popcorn, grapes, round candies, and marshmallows.

Play

- Toddlers engage in parallel play by playing alongside, but not with, other children.
- Toddlers will play freely and spontaneously without following rules.
- This is an active stage of development that involves intense exploration of the environment.
- Due to their short attentions spans, toddlers will change activities often.
- Appropriate toys will help develop locomotion (push–pull toys), imagination, language, and gross and fine motor skills. See Box 10.1 for a list of appropriate toddler toys.

Box 10.1 Appropriate Toys for the Toddler

- Dolls
- Play telephones, furniture, and dishes
- Puzzles with few, large pieces
- Pedal toys such as a riding truck or tricycle
- Push-pull toys
- Clay, sand box, crayons, finger paints
- Large blocks and pounding toys

Toilet Training

One of the major tasks for the toddler to master is toilet training.

See Box 10.2 for a summary of the factors involved in determining readiness to toilet train.

Box 10.2 Assessing Toilet Training Readiness

Physical Readiness

- Voluntary control of anal and urethral sphincters, usually by ages 22 to 30 months
- Ability to stay dry for 2 hr, decreased number of wet diapers, waking dry from naps
- Regular bowel movements
- Gross motor skills of sitting, walking, and squatting
- Fine motor skills to remove clothing

Mental Readiness

- Recognition of urge to defecate and urinate
- Verbal or nonverbal communication skills to indicate when child is wet or has the urge to defecate or urinate
- Cognitive skills to imitate appropriate behaviour and follow directions

Psychological Readiness

- Expressing willingness to please parent
- Ability to sit on toilet for 5–8 minutes without fussing or getting off
- Curiosity about adults' or older siblings' toilet habits
- Impatience when in soiled or wet diapers, desire to be changed immediately

Parental Readiness

- Recognition of child's level of readiness
- Willingness to invest the time required for toilet training
- Absence of family stress, such as a divorce, moving, new sibling, or imminent vacation

Source: Hockenberry, M. J., & Wilson, D. (2011). *Wong's nursing care of infants and children* (9th ed., p. 565). St. Louis: Mosby.

Reactions to Illness and Hospitalization

The toddler age group has a poorly defined body image and body boundaries. Painful and invasive procedures can cause extreme anxiety. Toddlers react to pain in a similar way to infants but also can recall previous painful experiences. Most toddlers have separation anxiety and look at hospitalization as being abandoned.

Toddlers respond to stressful situations by using regression as a coping mechanism. They can have a feeling of loss of control when they are physically restricted, if there is a disruption of routines and rituals, or when there is a fear of injury, pain, or dependency. The peak age for separation anxiety is 18 months (Ball & Binder, 2006). The following are the three stages of separation anxiety:

- Protest – This is the usual reaction to hospitalization. The child cries for the parents, verbally or physically attacks others, tries to find parents, clings to them, and is inconsolable.
- Despair – The child shows disinterest in surroundings and play, passive reactions, depression, loss of appetite.
- Detachment or denial – The child appears to adapt to surroundings, but the adaptation is superficial, and the child remains detached. This adaptation usually happens after a long period of separation.

Nursing Considerations Related to Separation Anxiety

- Encourage the toddler to protest.
- Encourage parents to stay if possible.

- Encourage the use of transitional or parent objects associated with the parents that can be left with the child.
- Request that parents leave the room only when the child is awake and truthfully tell the child their return time.
- Try to keep to home routines, such as bedtime rituals, and use the words that the child is familiar with, such as "bye bye," to promote security.
- Provide activities and a play area to enhance muscle development.
- Encourage self-care with assistance in feeding, toileting, dressing, and hygiene.
- Encourage sensorimotor learning by imitation.
- Promote language skills by reinforcing mastered vocabulary and using activities that require language.
- Provide simple explanations to prepare for treatments.
- Enhance the toddler's sense of autonomy by offering choices.
- Use parents' photographs and encourage parental visiting.

PRESCHOOL: THREE TO SIX YEARS OF AGE

The preschooler has a slow and uniform rate of growth. Preschool children tend to be slight, sturdy, and nimble and have improved posture.

The major milestone for a preschooler is to prepare to enter school. Achievements that prepare them for school include gaining control of bodily systems, experiencing brief and prolonged periods of separation, ability to interact cooperatively with other children and adults, use of language, increased attention span, and memory preparation (Hockenberry & Wilson, 2011).

BIOLOGICAL CHANGES

The rate of physical growth slows down and stabilizes:

- Increases in height remain steady at an increase of about 6.5–9 cm per year.
- Increases in weight continue to be steady as well at a rate of 2–3 kg per year.
- A typical 4-year-old will be 103 cm tall and will weigh an average of 16.5 kg.
- Boys and girls will have a similar body shape and size and may at times be distinguishable only by dress and hairstyle.
- Muscles and bones continue to mature as the preschooler gains strength by walking, running, and jumping.
- A balance of good nutrition, exercise, and rest is essential for growth and development.
- Blood pressure should be measured annually in children over 3 years of age.

GROSS AND FINE MOTOR DEVELOPMENT

Gross motor skills improve and become more refined:

- An average preschooler can hop, skip, and run, which can lead to the introduction of a sport such as soccer, skating, or swimming.
- Encouraging physical activity in children of this age will help create a pattern that may benefit them for the rest of their lives.

Fine motor skill advancement is most evident in improvements in the preschooler's ability to draw:

- The preschooler will begin to hold a pencil or crayon with the fingers rather than the fist.
- Drawings demonstrate advancements in perception of shape as well as developing fine motor skills.

See Table 10.12 for a summary of preschooler growth and development.

NUTRITION

As they do in the toddler, the nutritional and fluid requirements in the preschooler continue to decrease slightly, with the exception of protein requirements, which will increase.

- Follow the *Canada Food Guide* to determine the correct amount and portions of each food group. See Chapter 5, page 101, for *Eating Well With Canada's Food Guide*.
- Preschool children will change their eating patterns daily, and parents may find that the quantity consumed varies day to day.
- Parents should be concerned with the quality versus the quantity of food as children have the ability to self-regulate their caloric needs and intake. What they do not eat at one meal they will make up at the next.
- An average preschool child will consume slightly more food than a toddler, or about half an adult portion.
- Food habits such as fad foods and strong food preferences will continue in the preschool years.
- At age 4, the child may become more rebellious and refuse to try new foods.
- By age 5, the child will become more open to trying new foods and will enjoy being included in food preparation with a family member.
- Parents should introduce table manners but should be cautioned not to be too strict. The preschooler may find it difficult to sit still for long periods of time.

SLEEP

The preschooler will sleep an average of about 12 hours a night and very rarely naps during the day. It

Table 10.12   Growth and Development During Preschool Years

Age	Physical	Gross Motor	Fine Motor	Language
3 Years	• May have night-time control of bowel and bladder	• Rides tricycle, jumps off bottom step, goes up and down stairs using alternate feet, may dance, stands on one foot for a few seconds	• Builds tower of nine to 10 cubes, builds bridge of three cubes, copies a circle, imitates a cross, names what has been drawn, cannot draw stick figure	• Says 900 words, uses three- to four-word sentences, talks incessantly, asks many questions
4 Years	• Length at birth is doubled	• Skips, jumps, goes downstairs using alternate feet, catches a ball reliably, throws a ball overhead	• Uses scissors successfully to cut out picture following outline, laces shoes, copies a square, adds three parts to stick figure	• Says 1500 words, uses four- to five-word sentences, tells exaggerated stories, sings simple songs; questioning is at its peak
5 Years	• Permanent teeth may begin to erupt • Handedness is determined (90% are right-handed	• Skips and hops on alternate feet, throws and catches a ball well, balances on alternate feet well with eyes closed	• Ties shoe laces; uses scissors, simple tools, and pencil well; copies a diamond and a triangle; prints a few numbers, letters, or words such as first name	• Says 2100 words, uses six- to eight-word sentences, names four or more colours, knows days of the week and the months

Source: Adapted from Hockenberry, M. J., & Wilson, D. (2011). *Wong's nursing care of infants and children* (9th ed., pp. 593–594, Table 15-1). St. Louis: Mosby.

is common to see most sleep disturbances during the preschool years.

- Mastery of autonomy, separation, and object permanence can lead to sleep disturbances (Hockenberry & Wilson, 2011; Thiedke, 2001).
- Nightmares can occur and are typically defined as a scary dream followed by full waking. They typically occur in the second half of the night, when dreams are more intense. Once fully awake, the child will be aware of the parent's presence and can be comforted and reassured.
- Sleep terrors can also occur and are typically defined as a partial arousal from a deep sleep. They typically occur 1–4 hr after falling asleep. The child will not be aware of the parent's presence and hence is not easily consoled. The child should simply be observed during the sleep terror until it subsides and the child returns to a calm state. He or she should be guided back to bed if needed.
- Establishing good bedtime routines is essential to promote good sleep patterns.
- Behaviour that delays bedtime and is determined to be attention-seeking should be ignored by the parent.
- Preschoolers can be very active during the day, and slowing down before bedtime can lead to less resistance in going to bed.

DENTAL

The focus for preschoolers is on dental hygiene and prevention of decay:

- Encourage them to brush their own teeth, but they will require adult supervision of how well they manipulate the toothbrush.
- Professional care and routine follow-ups are encouraged every six months (Canadian Dental Association, 2012).
- Dental injuries are not uncommon at this age and should be examined by a professional.

IMMUNIZATION

See Table 10.7A–D for immunization schedules.

SAFETY

Preschoolers are less accident-prone than toddlers; however, injuries among children in this age group are common. The most common causes of injury in the home to children less than 5 years of age are falls from heights, burns and scalds, and poisonings (Health Canada, 2008).

- To reduce the risk of injury caused by falls from heights in this age group, ensure that there is a mechanism to prevent the child from falling down stairs or from opening windows more than 15 cm (LeBlanc et al., 2006).
- To reduce the risk of injury caused by burns and scalds, ensure that the maximum temperature of tap water is less than 54°C; cords do not dangle from the

kettle or other appliances in the kitchen; there is a stove guard to prevent a child from grabbing pots; and matches and lighters are well out of reach.
- To reduce the risk of injury by fire, ensure that the home has functioning smoke detectors and fire extinguishers (LeBlanc et al., 2006).
- To reduce the risk of injury caused by poisonings, ensure that all choking hazards in the home are out of reach of the child; all bathroom supplies, cleaning supplies, and medications are out of reach; all bathroom bottles and medications have child-resistant lids (especially grandparents' and visitors'); and a functioning carbon monoxide detector is in the home (LeBlanc et al., 2006).

PLAY

Preschoolers engage in associative play. This age group enjoys group play in similar activities but without rigid organization or rules.

- Activities should promote physical growth and motor skills and include running, jumping, and climbing.
- Toys that help develop muscles and coordination include tricycles, wagons, gym and sports equipment, sandboxes, and wading pools.
- Activities to help promote muscle strength and coordination include swimming, skating, and skiing.
- Large blocks, puzzles, crayons, paints, and simple crafts can help develop fine motor skills.

REACTIONS TO ILLNESS AND HOSPITALIZATION

Preschoolers still have poor differentiation between themselves and their environment. They still have a limited understanding of language and can see only one part of an object or situation at a time.

Preschoolers believe that unrelated events cause illness. They also have magical thinking that cause them to perceive illness as a punishment. There is also a fear of mutilation.

Reactions to hospitalization at this stage are primarily regression and a lack of cooperation as coping mechanisms for separation. Preschoolers can experience a loss of control because they feel a loss of their own power. Fear of injury and pain leads to a fear of mutilation and invasive treatments. They lack knowledge about the body. This creates, for example, a fear of castration from enemas or rectal thermometers or a fear that the insides of their body may leak out during the insertion of an IV line. They perceive hospitalization as a punishment and separation from parents as a lack of love.

Nursing Considerations for Separation Anxiety

- Use puppets and dolls to demonstrate treatments with an appropriate level of vocabulary.
- Use adhesive bandages to "stop the insides from coming out."
- Stay with the preschooler during treatments.
- Give rewards such as stars or stickers.
- Use hospital therapeutic play kits to work through anxieties.
- Help prevent a sense of guilt by reassuring the preschooler that he or she is not responsible for the illness.
- Provide motor stimulation and praise achievements.
- Promote autonomy by encouraging choices and self-care, such as a choice of clothing.
- Promote language skills by telling stories and teaching new words.
- Encourage parental involvement and visiting as well as contact with siblings and peers to decrease separation anxiety.

SCHOOL AGE: SIX TO TWELVE YEARS OF AGE

At this age, the child has a slow and uniform rate of growth. This is a generally healthy age group with fewer visits to the pediatrician and fewer immunizations.

- Focus on establishing good health habits, proper nutrition, and physical activity.
- There may be an increased risk of obesity at this stage.

BIOLOGICAL CHANGES

This is generally a period of gradual growth and development with a growth spurt at prepuberty.

- Height changes are slow and steady, adding 5 cm per year to gain about 30 to 60 cm.
- Weight will almost double, with increases of 2–3 kg per year.
- Boys and girls vary little during this phase, although girls will begin to surpass boys in both height and weight toward the end of the stage.
- At prepubescence (two years preceding adolescence), the difference in girls and boys in biological terms can be as much as two years, with girls starting prepubescence first.
- In girls, prepubescence is a period of rapid growth, with puberty beginning at approximately age 12.
- This may cause anxiety in girls who develop earlier or later than their peers.
- In boys, prepubescence is a period of steady growth, with puberty beginning at approximately age 14.
- Changes in height and weight will differ greatly among children; therefore, some may appear older physically than their behavioural, emotional, or mental development would indicate.
- Heart rate and respirations tend to decrease, whereas blood pressure will increase in this stage.

GROSS AND FINE MOTOR DEVELOPMENT

Generally, school-aged children are steadier on their feet and more graceful than those at the previous stage. Bodies will take on a more slender look, and certain activities, such as biking and climbing, will be easier.

Muscle mass will increase, but it is important not to overwork muscles to the point of fatigue. See Table 10.13 for a summary of growth and development in the school-age years.

NUTRITION

The focus for this age group is independence and forming good habits for the years to come. Children become more independent in their food choices at home and school, have strong likes and dislikes for foods, are exposed to choices of foods from vending machines, and are very influenced by friends and the media.

- Good choices and habits will lead to good nutrition and healthy weight gain, whereas poor choices and habits will lead to excessive weight gain and poor nutrition.
- Caloric needs tend to decrease.
- There are fewer stomach upsets, blood sugar levels balance out and are better maintained, and there is an increase in stomach capacity, meaning that food is retained for longer periods of time.

SLEEP

It is very important for school-aged children to have enough energy for school and other activities.

- They begin to take charge of bedtime routines; however, they will need reminders to go to bed.
- They no longer take naps and will sleep through the night with typically 8–12 hours of sleep.

DENTAL

Many changes to the mouth at this stage require regular visits to the dentist.

- Most children lose their first tooth by age 6 (usually the front).

Table 10.13   Growth and Development During the School-Age Years

Age	Physical	Gross Motor	Fine Motor	Language
6 Years	• Continues to grow slowly, loses first tooth, vision reaches maturity	• A very active age with constant activity • Demonstrates gradual increase in dexterity	• Likes to draw, print, and colour	• Develops concept of numbers, knows morning from the afternoon, defines objects in terms of use (i.e., fork, chair), knows left from right hand
7 Years	• Begins to grow at least 5 cm per year • Jaw begins to expand to accommodate permanent teeth	• More cautious approach to new performances • Repeats performances to master them	• Can copy a diamond	• Notices certain items missing from a picture, repeats three numbers backward, develops concept of time
8–9 Years	• Continues to grow at least 5 cm per year	• Dresses self completely • More limber, bones grow faster than ligaments • Always on the go and hard to quiet down	• Produces simple paintings and drawings	• Gives similarities and differences • Can count backward from 20 • Describes common objects in detail, not just by use
10–12 Years	• Slow growth in height and rapid weight gain, possibly leading to obesity • Posture more similar to that of an adult	• Reaches adult levels	• Continues to refine	• Writes brief stories • Writes occasional short letters to friends • Reads for practical information or own enjoyment

Source: Adapted from Hockenberry, M. J., & Wilson, D. (2011). *Wong's nursing care of infants and children* (9th ed., pp. 659–660, Table 17-1). St. Louis: Mosby.

- Eventually, they will lose all 20 deciduous teeth, and permanent teeth will begin to erupt.
- Permanent teeth appear large in proportion to the rest of the face, a stage that is sometimes known as the ugly duckling phase.
- The jawline elongates, and the new teeth move into their new positions.
- Regular flossing, brushing, and dental visits will promote good oral hygiene.
- Sweets and sugary snacks should be limited.

IMMUNIZATION

See Table 10.7A–D for the immunization schedules.

SAFETY

School-aged children tend to have frequent minor injuries, such as falls from bikes, skin rashes from environmental exposures, and bruises from ball sports.

- Due to the increasing need for independence, this age group tends to engage in activities without an adult. Therefore, teach about safety, risks, and consequences.
- Encourage the use of protective gear such as bike helmets.
- Ensure the use of seat belts.
- Put safety strategies into place for "latch key" children.
- Streetproofing and learning how to avoid abduction allow children to achieve independence and autonomy, safely.
- Parents may participate in community programs in which fingerprints and other identification systems are organized in case the child is missing.
- After-school programs keep children occupied during times when parents are unavailable to supervise.
- Emergency numbers and contact people need to be readily available to the child.

PLAY

Learning good physical activity habits will influence future involvement in an activity or sport. A proper amount of physical activity will help with weight control, encourage good socialization, help develop gross and fine motor skills, and give the child a sense of accomplishment.

- Play involves increased physical skill, intellect, and fantasy.
- Groups and cliques foster a sense of belonging to a team or club, which leads to a sense of importance.
- Games now have well-established rules, and knowing the rules means belonging (conformity and ritual will guide play).

- Increased interest in complex games and electronic games.
- Increased interest in reading.
- Quiet and solitary play is valued at this stage as school-aged children enjoy collecting objects and toys, which they tend to keep in disorganized piles.

MENTAL HEALTH

This is an age at which one's self-concept and self-esteem are developed (Ball & Binder, 2006).

- Self-concept is the mental idea one has of oneself.
- Self-esteem reflects a positive self-concept.
- The family has a great influence on the child's development of self-esteem and self-concept.
- Children at this age are beginning to form a concept of sexuality and need to have good information and openness to discuss ideas, questions, misconceptions, and fears.
- They are beginning to develop ways to problem-solve situations and develop solutions, for example, around doing homework, making choices, or setting limits.
- This is the concrete stage of cognitive development; therefore, when teaching, provide opportunities to touch, feel, and become engaged in learning.
- Three types of temperament categories in this stage are as follows (Ball & Binder, 2006):

  - Easy: Adapts readily to new situations
  - Slow to warm up: Uncomfortable with new situations and takes time to adapt
  - Difficult: Easily distracted and needs to be prepared for a situation.

REACTIONS TO ILLNESS AND HOSPITALIZATION

The school-aged child can be stressed by immobilization, fear of mutilation and death, and modesty. This child can also be stressed by necessary dependency, which gives a sense of loss of control. It may still be difficult for these children to be able to express themselves verbally, and they may be self-conscious with their care. However, they are curious about their body and are eager to learn about it.

Children at this stage think of illness as being caused by external forces. School-agers are aware of the implications of the different illnesses. They react to separation by exhibiting loneliness, boredom, isolation, and depression. They may show aggression, irritability, and inability to relate to siblings and peers.

Nursing Considerations for Illness and Hospitalization

- Encourage verbalization and reassure the child that it is acceptable to cry.

- It is important to promote autonomy, self-care, and choices with participation in care.
- Celebrate successes when the child succeeds at tasks in order to enhance feelings of accomplishment.
- Encourage peer interaction and use group teaching.
- Provide diversions that help with the development of fine motor skills, such as computer skills, as well as with stress control.
- Increase understanding of bodily functions and the illness and prepare for procedures using pictures to teach the child about the body.
- Work through emotions and stress by having the child draw how the illness impacts on his or her body.

ADOLESCENCE: TWELVE TO EIGHTEEN YEARS OF AGE

Adolescence is the second most rapid growth period. It is defined as the transition period between childhood and adulthood and is a time of development in which one makes educational and occupational choices for the future. It is common for adolescents to take chances and engage in risk-taking behaviour, which may lead to health concerns and injury.

BIOLOGICAL CHANGES

The period of development referred to as puberty involves complex biological, cognitive, psychological, and social changes—more so than any other time in life.

- Puberty involves a predictable series of hormonal and physical changes in both sexual maturation and physical growth.
- Puberty is triggered by a series of hormonal changes in the body controlled by the anterior pituitary gland in response to stimulus from the hypothalamus (Hockenberry & Wilson, 2011).

Changes in the Female

The primary sexual change in girls is the buildup of enough estrogen to force the release of an egg, or ovum, from the ovaries every 28 days.

- The Tanner Stages, a sequence of events divided into five stages, describe the development of secondary sexual characteristics (Hockenberry & Wilson, 2011).

Female Breast Development

- Stage 1: The prepubertal stage
- Stage 2: Characterized by the development of breast buds
- Stage 3: Characterized by the further enlargement of the breasts and areolae, with no separation of contours

- Stage 4: Characterized by projection of areolae and papillae to form secondary mounds
- Stage 5: Characterized by adult configuration

Pubic Hair Development (Male and Female)

- Stage 1: The prepubertal stage
- Stage 2: Characterized by sparse, long, straight, downy hair
- Stage 3: Characterized by darker, coarser, curly hair that is sparse over the entire pubis
- Stage 4: Characterized by dark, curly, and abundant hair in the pubic area only
- Stage 5: Characterized by an adult pattern

Changes in the Male

The primary male sexual characteristic is the development of viable sperm.

- Follicle-stimulating hormone (FSH) and luteinizing hormone (LH) act on testicular cells to stimulate the production of testosterone and viable sperm.
- The production of viable sperms tends to follow the boy's first ejaculation.

Male Genitalia Development

- Stage 1: Prepubertal stage
- Stage 2: Characterized by enlargement of the scrotum and testes and rugation and reddening of the scrotum
- Stage 3: Characterized by lengthening of the penis and further enlargement of the scrotum and testes
- Stage 4: Characterized by an increase in the length and width of the penis, development of the glans, and darkening of the scrotum
- Stage 5: Characterized by an adult configuration

GROSS AND FINE MOTOR DEVELOPMENT

In the adolescent, gross motor development reaches adult levels. Fine motor development continues to be refined.

NUTRITION

Puberty marks the beginning of accelerated physical growth, which can result in as much as double the adolescent nutritional requirements for iron, protein, zinc, and calcium.

Many factors influence an adolescent's nutrition, including growing independence, the need for peer acceptability, concerns over physical appearance, and an active lifestyle.

- It is common for the adolescent to choose snacks of "empty calories," those devoid of any appropriate vitamins and minerals.

- Adolescents are at increased risk for obesity, as well as for eating disorders such as anorexia and bulimia.

SLEEP

Adolescents commonly feel fatigued. Factors contributing to fatigue include rapid growth, overexertion, a tendency to stay up late, insufficient sleep, and poor nutrition. In an effort to catch up on missed sleep, many adolescents like to sleep in.

DENTAL

Continued dental hygiene must be encouraged, including proper brushing, flossing, and regular dental visits.

- Orthodontics are common and may lead to teasing and embarrassment.
- Encourage good snack choices and reduce exposure to empty calories.

IMMUNIZATION

See Table 10.7A–D for the immunization schedules.

SAFETY

Adolescents rarely consider the risk or consequence of their actions and often feel invulnerable.

- The use of safety devices decreases in this age group, resulting in increased injury, such as the failure to use helmets or seat belts.
- Health teaching should focus on managing peer pressure to engage in risky activities.

REACTIONS TO ILLNESS AND HOSPITALIZATION

For adolescents, hospitalization can have a significant impact, causing stresses due to issues around body image, separation from peers, and reduced independence due to necessary restrictions. In children up to 14 years, illness may still be viewed as a punishment.

Reactions to illnesses include the adolescent coping mechanisms of denial and displacement. A sense of a loss of control occurs because of dependency and loss of identity, causing the adolescent to react with rejection, uncooperativeness, self-assertion, anger, frustration, or possibly withdrawal, even from peers. Adolescents also fear mutilation and sexual changes, fears demonstrated by a lot of questioning, rejecting others, questioning adequacy of care, psychosomatic complaints, and sexual reactions. Separation, particularly from the peer group, may result in further withdrawal, loneliness, and boredom.

Nursing Considerations for Illness and Hospitalization

- Relate to adolescents at their level and be authentic.
- Allow them to wear their own clothes, keep their belongings, and decorate their rooms.
- Telephone access is important for family and peer interaction.
- Respect their privacy.
- Set limits.
- Teach about puberty-related issues such as personal hygiene, breast self-examination, testicular self-examination, sexuality and safe sexual practices, contraception, HIV, and other relevant topics.
- Provide clear explanations based on science.
- Encourage as much mobility and exercise as possible.
- Encourage the adolescent to participate and be an active decision maker in his or her own health care.
- Promote independence.
- Explore body image and self-esteem.
- Encourage family participation and support.
- Encourage the teen to keep up with schoolwork and in contact with teachers and encourage career goals.

THERAPEUTIC RELATIONSHIP

A therapeutic relationship with the child and the family is the foundation of pediatric nursing. See Chapter 3, page 20, for more information on this topic. The hallmarks of effective communication are as follows:

- Establish trust.
- Respect and maintain confidentiality.
- Be truthful.
- Convey respect.
- Implement appropriate communication strategies.

Inherent in every group of nursing considerations in this chapter is the importance of the nursing role in developing therapeutic relationships, encouraging clients and families to participate in their care and verbalize their concerns, being a client and family advocate, teaching disease prevention and health promotion, providing support and counselling, and making ethical decisions. The impact of hospitalization according to the age and stage of development is outlined in the previous sections. These principles should be referred to in relation to each of the following health challenges.

PAIN MANAGEMENT

Pain management is an important aspect of pediatric nursing care. Nurses perform pain assessments and provide nonpharmacological and pharmacological pain-relieving interventions that bring relief and comfort to children and their families.

Box 10.3 Developmental Characteristics of Children's Responses to Pain

Young Infant
- Generalized body response of rigidity or thrashing, possibly with local reflex withdrawal of stimulated area
- Loud crying
- Facial expression of pain (brows lowered and drawn together, eyes tightly closed, and mouth open and square-shaped)
- No association demonstrated between approaching stimulus and subsequent pain

Older Infant
- Localized body response with deliberate withdrawal of stimulated area
- Loud crying
- Facial expression of pain or anger
- Physical resistance, expecially pushing the stimulus away after it is applied

Young Child
- Loud crying, screaming
- Verbal expressions such as "Ow," "Ouch," "It hurts"
- Thrashing of arms and legs
- Attempts to push stimulus away before it is applied
- Lack of cooperation, need for physical restraint
- Requests termination of procedure
- Clings to parent, nurse, or other significant person
- Requests emotional support, such as hugs or other forms of physical comfort
- May become restless and irritable with continuing pain
- Behaviours occur in anticipation of actual painful procedure

School-Aged Child
- May exhibit all behaviours of young child, especially during actual painful procedure, but fewer in anticipatory period
- Stalling behaviour, such as "Wait a minute" or "I'm not ready"
- Muscular rigidity, such as clenched fists, white knuckles, gritted teeth, contracted limbs, body stiffness, closed eyes, wrinkled forehead

Adolescent
- Less vocal protest
- Less motor activity
- More verbal expressions, such as "It hurts" or "You're hurting me"
- Increased muscle tension and body control

Source: Hockenberry, M. J., & Wilson, D. (2011). *Wong's nursing care of infants and children* (9th ed., p. 180, Box 7-1). St. Louis: Mosby.

PHYSIOLOGICAL MEASURES OF PEDIATRIC PAIN

Physiological reactions to pain, particularly in the nonverbal younger age groups and children with communication and cognitive impairments, can help nurses assess the child's level of pain.

DEVELOPMENTAL CHARACTERISTICS OF CHILDREN'S RESPONSES TO PAIN

The response to pain depends on the child's developmental stage. Characteristics of pain response based on development are summarized in Box 10.3.

Table 10.14 Premature Infant Pain Profile (PIPP)

Ages of Use	Reliability and Validity	Variables	Scoring Range
28–40 Weeks' Gestational Age	• Internal consistency using Cronbach alpha = 0.75–0.59; standardized item alpha for 6 items = 0.71 • Construct validity using handling vs. painful situations: statistically significant differences (paired $t = 12.24$, two-tailed $p <0.0001$, and Mann-Whitney $U = 765.5$, $p <0.0001$) and using real vs. sham heelstick procedures with infants aged 28–30 weeks' gestational age ($t = 2.4$, two-tailed $p <0.02$, and Mann-Whitney $U = 132$, $p <0.016$) and with full-term males undergoing circumcision with topical anaesthetic vs. placebo ($t = 2.6$, two-tailed $p <0.02$, or nonparametric equivalent Mann-Whitney U test, $U = 145.7$, two-tailed $p <0.02$)	• Gestational age (0–3) • Eye squeeze (0–3) • Behavioural state (0–3) • Nasolabial furrow (0–3) • Heart rate (0–3) • Oxygen saturation (0–3) • Brow bulge (0–3)	0 = no pain; 21 = worst pain

Source: Stevens, B., Johnston, C., Petryshen, P., & Taddiom, A. (1996). Premature Infant Pain Profile: Development and initial validation. *The Clinical Journal of Pain, 12*(1), 13–22. Reprinted with permission.

Pain Tools

Nurses can use a variety of pain tools to help assess children's level of pain. These tools are adapted to the different developmental stages and include behavioural, physiological, or self-report measurements.

Pain Scale for Preterm Infants

A unique pain scale was developed for preterm infants, called the PIPP (Premature Infant Pain Profile). There is a higher pain score for infants with a lower gestational age. Sleeping infants also receive additional points for reduced reactions. See Table 10.14 for the PIPP scale.

Pain Scale for 1- to 5-Year-Olds

The CHEOPS scale, or Children's Hospital of Eastern Ontario Pain Scale, was developed for 1- to 5-year-olds by McGrath, Johnson, Goodman, and others in 1985 in collaboration with recovery room nurses. Six categories of behaviours are identified: cry, facial, verbal, torso, touch, and legs. See Table 10.15, which outlines the tool.

Pain Scale for 3- to 12-Year-Olds

The Wong-Baker FACES Pain Rating Scale is a self-reporting tool for children 3–12 years old. See Figure 10.1 and www.painsourcebook.ca for the FACES tool.

Pain Assessment in the Child With Communication and Cognitive Difficulties

Children with communication and cognitive difficulties present a significant challenge to nurses in accurately assessing their pain level. These children may not react in the usual way to pain. Parents are very important in helping nurses interpret the child's pain reactions. The most reported pain reactions in this type of child are as follows (Hockenberry & Wilson, 2011):

- Moaning, crying, or being irritable
- Being less active
- Seeking comfort

FIGURE 10.1
Wong-Baker FACES Pain Rating Scale

Source: Hockenberry, M. J., Wilson, D., & Winkelstein, M. L. (2005). *Wong's essentials of pediatric nursing* (7th ed., p. 1259). St. Louis: Mosby. Used with permission. ©Mosby.

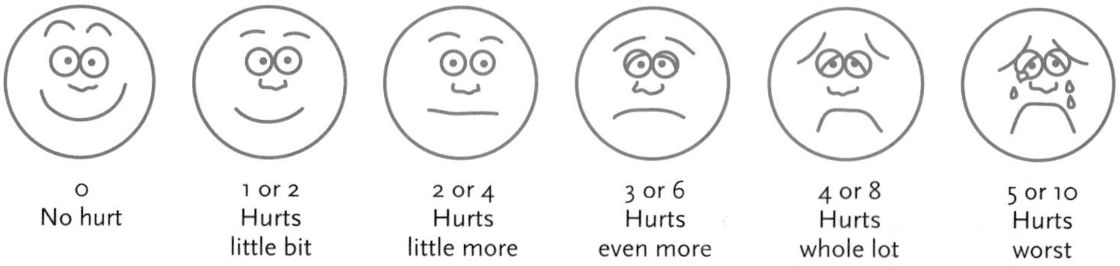

0 No hurt	1 or 2 Hurts little bit	2 or 4 Hurts little more	3 or 6 Hurts even more	4 or 8 Hurts whole lot	5 or 10 Hurts worst

Table 10.15   Children's Hospital of Eastern Ontario Pain Scale (CHEOPS)

Ages of Use	Reliability and Validity	Variables	Scoring Range
1–5 Years	• Interrater reliability = 90%–99.5% • Internal correlation = significant correlations between pairs of items • Concurrent validity between CHEOPS and visual analogue scale (VAS) = .91; between individual and total scores of CHEOPS and VAS = 0.50–0.86 • Construct validity with preanalgesia and postanalgesia scores = 9.9–6.3	Cry (1–3) Facial (0–2) Child verbal (0–2) Torso (1–2) Touch (1–2) Legs (1–2)	4 = no pain; 13 = worst pain

Source: McGrath, P. J., Johnson, G., Goodman, J. T., et al. (1985). The CHEOPS: A behavioural scale for rating post-operative pain in children. In H. L. Fields, R. Dubner, & F. Cervero (Eds.), *Advances in pain research and therapy* (p. 207). New York: Raven Press. Reprinted with permission.

• Not cooperating
• Being stiff, spastic, tense, or rigid
• Sleeping less
• Being difficult to satisfy or pacify
• Flinching or moving body part away and being agitated or fidgety.

NONPHARMACOLOGICAL STRATEGIES FOR PAIN MANAGEMENT

Many nonpharmacological strategies can be used to help children cope with pain. Some of these strategies are listed in Box 10.4.

PHARMACOLOGICAL STRATEGIES FOR PAIN MANAGEMENT

The following are routes used to deliver pain analgesics:

• Oral, sublingual, buccal, or transmucosal
• Intravenous
• Subcutaneous, continuous
• Patient-controlled analgesia (PCA), family-controlled analgesia, or nurse-activated analgesia
• Intramuscular
• Intranasal
• Intradermal
• Topical or transdermal

Box 10.4 Nonpharmacological Strategies for Pain Management

General Strategies

• Use nonpharmacological interventions to supplement, not replace, pharmacological interventions and use for mild pain and pain that is reasonably well controlled with analgesics.

• Form a trusting relationship with the child and the family.

• Express concern regarding their reports of pain and intervene appropriately.

• Take an active role in seeking effective pain management strategies.

• Prepare the child before potentially painful procedures but avoid "planting" the idea of pain.

• Use "nonpain" descriptors when possible, such as "It feels like heat" rather than "It is a burning pain." This avoids suggesting pain and gives the child control in describing reactions. Avoid evaluative statements or descriptions such as "It will hurt a lot."

• Stay with the child during a painful procedure.

• Allow parents to stay with the child if so desired by both child and parent and encourage the parent to talk softly to the child and to remain near the child's head.

• Involve the parent in learning specific nonpharmacological strategies and in assisting the child with their use.

• Educate the child about the pain, expecially when explanation may lessen anxiety, and ensure that the child understands he or she is not responsible for the pain.

Continued on next page

Box 10.4 (cont'd)

Specific Strategies

Distraction

- Employ play, music, computer games, singing, and rhythmic breathing.
- Have the child use deep breathing and blowing it out.
- Encourage the child to concentrate on yelling or saying "ouch."
- Have the child look through a kaleidoscope and concentrate on designs.
- Use humour by watching cartoons, telling jokes or funny stories, or acting silly with the child.
- Help the child read, play games, or visit with friends.

Relaxation

- Hold infant in a comfortable position and rock or sway back and forth.
- Repeat one or two reassuring words softly.
- Use relaxation techniques, such as going limp as a rag doll while exhaling or asking the child to yawn.

Guided Imagery

- During a painful episode, have the child identify and describe some pleasurable or imaginary experiences, including as many senses as possible.
- Write down or record a script.
- Combine the script with relaxation and rhythmic breathing.

Positive Self-Talk

- Teach the child positive statements to say when in pain.

Thought Stopping

- Identify positive facts about the painful event.
- Identify reassuring information.
- Condense positive and reassuring facts into a set of brief statements and have the child memorize them and repeat whenever he or she thinks about or is experiencing a painful event.

Behavioural Contracting

- May be used with children as young as 4 or 5, with stars, tokens, or stickers as rewards.
- Identify rewards or consequences that are reinforcing and goals that can be evaluated.
- Reinforce identified rewards or consequences.
- Use a formal written contract, dated and signed by all persons involved in any of the agreements.

Source: Adapted from Hockenberry, M. J., & Wilson, D. (2011). *Wong's nursing care of infants and children* (9th ed., p. 194). St. Louis: Mosby.

Groups of Drugs

Many types of drugs can be used in pediatric pain control. See Chapter 7, Pharmacology and Nursing Practice, for more specific information on the drugs listed here. For the pediatric population, the types of drugs that can be used are as follows (Hockenberry & Wilson, 2011):

- Nonsteroidal anti-inflammatory drugs (NSAIDs) approved for children
  - Indomethacin, ibuprofen, naproxen
- Acetaminophen
- Opioids formulated for children
  - Morphine, fentanyl, codeine, hydromorphone, hydrocodone and acetaminophen, levorphanol, meperidine, methadone, oxycodone
- Antidepressants
  - Amitriptyline, nortriptyline
- Anticonvulsants
  - Gabapentin, carbamazepine
- Anxiolytics
  - Lorazepam
- Corticosteroids
  - Dexamethasone
- Others
  - Clonidine, mexiletine

SKIN AND HAIR CARE

PEDICULOSIS CAPITIS

Pediculosis capitis, or head lice, is an infestation in the hair and is a common condition that can be difficult to eliminate. It can also spread to other family members. It occurs in all socioeconomic groups. Outbreaks can occur, particularly in elementary schools and day care facilities.

Pathophysiology

Head lice live only on humans and are transmitted by direct hair-to-hair contact or by sharing brushes, combs, towels, and so on. They can move quickly but do not jump. The female louse will lay her eggs along the hair shaft. The eggs, which stick to the hair and look like teardrops, hatch in 8 to 10 days.

Clinical Manifestations

The child will complain of severe itching of the scalp, and the scalp has the appearance of dandruff. Secondary infections can develop because of scratching lesions.

Therapeutics and Nursing Considerations

The CPS (2008a) recommends a topical insecticide shampoo treatment, which contains pyrethrins or permethrin. These pediculicides affect the lice but do not affect the nits (eggs); therefore, the treatment must be repeated to kill the hatched lice. Lindane shampoo may be used as a secondary treatment, but only with caution and not with children under 2 because of potential toxicity and resistance. A new noninsecticidal product has been recently approved that contains isopropyl myristate and cyclomethicone for use in children who are over 4 years old.

The nit bond can be loosened by vinegar, and the nits can be combed out with a fine-toothed comb. This homemade treatment has not been shown to be effective (CPS, 2008a).

DERMATITIS

Dermatitis is a skin inflammation that develops in response to various stimuli. The types of dermatitis that are the most common in children and adolescents are contact, diaper, seborrheic, and atopic, or eczema. A child's skin is sensitive, and it is important to keep the skin clean, moisturized, and protected from skin breakdown to prevent infections.

Contact Dermatitis

Contact dermatitis is an inflammatory reaction of the skin to an allergen or irritating substance. It commonly affects infants of 9–12 months.

Pathophysiology and Clinical Manifestations

The clinical manifestations are erythema, edema, pruritis, vesicles, or bullae that rupture, ooze, and crust over. Contact dermatitis is usually present only in the contact area, where fissures, dryness, scaling, and necrosis can also appear. Sometimes there is a rash that is distal to the originating area after about one week that can last about 3–4 weeks without treatment.

Irritants can cause an inflammatory response, and allergens can be absorbed into the skin, creating an initial sensitization. The allergen is carried to the T lymphocytes to create an immune memory. It takes repeated exposures to the allergen to create an allergic inflammatory reaction. The exception is poison ivy or poison oak, which requires only one or two exposures to elicit the immune reaction.

Therapeutics and Nursing Considerations

The treatment is to remove the irritant or allergen and wash the skin, decrease itching, and promote healing. The child may need patch testing for the allergen. Antihistamines, calamine lotion, wet dressings, or colloidal oatmeal–based bath products will help decrease the itching. Burow's solution soaks (aluminum acetate) will encourage drying. Topical corticosteroids after dressing soaks followed by an emollient will increase the absorption and decrease the itching. If the rash covers more than 10% of the body, oral corticosteroids may be required to decrease the inflammation and start the healing (Ball & Binder, 2006).

Diaper Dermatitis

Diaper dermatitis is caused by a skin reaction to urine, feces, moisture, or friction that causes abrasion.

Pathophysiology and Clinical Manifestations

The skin reacts to the irritants and becomes increasingly permeable to the irritants and microbes. Irritants such as urine and stool can lead to a rash and subsequent skin breakdown. Common diaper rash, or diaper dermatitis, occurs frequently and affects approximately one-third of infants. Breastfed babies have a lower pH, which helps decrease the occurrence of dermatitis (Ball & Binder, 2006).

The clinical manifestations are as follows:

- Red glazed plaques in the diaper area
- In most cases, the rash is not in the skin folds of the groin area but affects the rest of the diaper region.
- If the rash becomes severe, it is characterized by a raised, red, and confluent rash, and pustules may also occur.
- *Candida albicans* infection can occur as a primary or secondary infection and is indicated by red, scaly

plaques with sharp margins. Small papules and pustules can be present, including in the groin area.

Diagnostics

A skin scraping for microscopic testing with potassium hydroxide can diagnose *Candida* (Ball & Binder, 2006).

Therapeutics and Nursing Considerations

A barrier cream with zinc oxide paste can treat a mild dermatitis. Moderate or severe dermatitis can by treated with a mild hydrocortisone cream (0.25–1%) with each diaper change for five to seven days. For candidiasis, an antifungal cream such as clotrimazole can be added. Sometimes an oral antifungal drug may be used to decrease the candidiasis in the bowels (Ball & Binder, 2006).

It is important to teach the family how to prevent dermatitis. The following interventions can help (Ball & Binder, 2006):

- Using superabsorbent disposable diapers, change the child every two hours during the day and once at night.
- Cleanse skin with mild soap and use diaper barrier creams frequently.
- Do not use tight diapers or waterproof pants.

Seborrheic Dermatitis

Seborrheic dermatitis is an inflammatory skin condition that recurs.

Pathophysiology and Clinical Manifestations

This form of dermatitis is probably caused by an overgrowth of *Pityrosporum* yeast, which is generally found near sebaceous glands in the scalp (cradle cap), forehead, postauricular and periorbital regions, eyelids, inguinal area, skin neck folds, or nasolabial folds. It often occurs in infants and adolescent age groups. It presents with the following manifestations (Ball & Binder, 2006):

- A waxy, scaly rash with yellow-red patches
- Looks like dandruff

Therapeutics and Nursing Considerations

The treatment is as follows:

- In young babies, daily shampooing with a baby shampoo
- In the adolescent age group, antidandruff shampoo on the scalp with selenium sulphide or salicylic acid and baby shampoo on the eyes and eyebrows
- It often occurs on the scalp in the infant age group because parents may be reluctant to shampoo over the soft fontanelle. In this case, the scalp needs to be soaked with oil, and then the scales are gently combed out and the area is shampooed (Ball & Binder, 2006).

Eczema or Atopic Dermatitis

Eczema is a chronic, superficial inflammatory condition that is very itchy.

Pathophysiology and Clinical Manifestations

Eczema is due to a genetic predisposition and external triggers that cause T cells to activate and produce an excess amount of IgE. A child with eczema tends to have allergies and has an increased risk of developing asthma. Frequent triggers are dust mites, animal dander, pollens, food allergies, soaps, chemicals, hormonal changes, and emotional stress. Flare-ups tend to be related to high or low temperatures, perspiration, scratching, and irritant fabrics, such as wool. Severe atopic dermatitis in the infant age group tends to be related to food allergies (Ball & Binder, 2006; Hebert, Rakes, Loach, & Murphy, 1997).

The symptoms are as follows:

- Pruritis
- Erythematous patches with vesicles, exudate, and crusts
- Chronic symptoms include pruritis, dryness, scaling, and lichenification (thickening of the skin)
- Occurs most often in dry or cold weather and usually on the face, upper arms, back, upper thighs, and back of the hands and feet. Skin folds are frequently affected.

Diagnostics

Eczema is diagnosed by family history and through the presence of a generalized rash without any known exposure to an allergen. Culture of the skin may be done if there is a secondary infection. A food elimination test can be done to see if food allergies are a factor. Most often, cow's milk, wheat, eggs, soy, citrus, and peanuts are the food allergens (Ball & Binder, 2006).

Therapeutics and Nursing Considerations

- Wet dressings or colloidal oatmeal cleansing will help decrease the itching; lubricate with emollients while the skin is still moist to enhance moisture trapping.
- If there is oozing, Burow's solution soaks (aluminum acetate) will encourage drying.
- Topical corticosteroids after dressing soaks followed by an emollient will increase the absorption and decrease the itching.
- In the case of a severe flare-up, oral corticosteroids may be required to decrease the inflammation and start the healing.

- Immunomodulators that inhibit T-lymphocyte action are a second line of topical drug that is more often used on the face.

BURNS

Burns can range from a minor scald to a major, life-threatening deep tissue injury. In children under 5 years, burns comprised 54.3% of the injury cases reported to the Canadian Hospital Injury Reporting and Prevention Program (Health Canada, 2011). Thermal burns are the most frequent injuries, from scalding, flames, or contact with a heated object such as a hot cooking pot. Some of these burns are caused by child abuse. Because of the sensitivity of children's skin, they burn more quickly than adults.

Special age groups are at greater risk for certain types of burns, and they are as follows (Ball & Binder, 2006):

- Infants have mostly thermal burns from scalds and house fires.
- Toddlers have mostly thermal burns as a result of pulling hot liquids and grease onto themselves.
- Preschoolers are mostly burned by scalding or by hot objects such as irons or ovens.
- School-agers and adolescents are mostly injured by thermal burns (from matches or fireworks), electrical burns (due to climbing high-voltage towers and contact with electrical wires), and chemical burns (from combustion experiments).

Children are at more risk from the fluid and balance shifts and electrolyte imbalances that result with a burn because their bodies have a greater surface area. Refer to Chapter 8, pages 329–331, for burn treatment and nursing considerations. Burns can be devastating to a child, causing pain, scarring, decreased range of motion (ROM), and damage to self-image and self-esteem.

FLUID AND ELECTROLYTE IMBALANCES

The percentage of body water varies with the age of the child:

- In the infant age group, total body water constitutes 80% of the body weight.
- At age 3, a child's total body water constitutes about 65% of the body weight.
- At age 15, total body water constitutes about 60% of the body weight.

The daily maintenance fluid requirements are shown in Table 10.16.

Fluid and electrolyte imbalances occur more often and more quickly in infants and young children. They

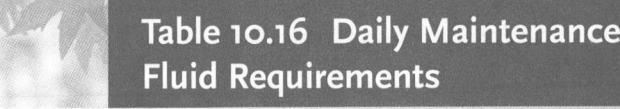

Table 10.16 Daily Maintenance Fluid Requirements

Body Weight	Amount of Fluid per Day
1–10 kg	100 mL/kg
11–20 kg	1000 mL plus 50 mL/kg for each kg >10 kg
>20 kg	1500 mL plus 20 mL/kg for each kg >20 kg

Source: Hockenberry, M. J., & Wilson, D. (2011). *Wong's nursing care of infants and children* (9th ed., p. 1055, Table 28-1). St. Louis: Mosby.

are more at risk for these imbalances because of the following:

- A greater body surface area permits a higher proportion of water to be lost through the skin.
- A higher metabolic rate increases the water turnover, and the body fluid needs to be replaced.
- The immature kidney function and buffer system in young children make it harder for them to regulate homeostasis.
- There is a higher proportion of fluid in the extracellular spaces.
- There are higher insensible water losses through the skin and respiratory system.
- Young children lack the ability to control body temperature by sweating or shivering.

DEHYDRATION

Dehydration is an excessive loss of water from the body tissues. It occurs in infants and children whenever total fluid intake is less than fluid output. It is caused by problems that result in an increase in water loss from the kidneys and gastrointestinal (GI) system and insensible water loss from the skin and respiratory tract. Possible causes include the following:

- Excessive vomiting and diarrhea
- Insufficient oral fluid intake
- Prolonged high fever
- Diabetic ketoacidosis (DKA)
- Extensive burns

Pathophysiology

A child can become dehydrated and can lose both fluid and electrolytes depending on the cause of the loss. Dehydration is categorized as isotonic, hypotonic, or hypertonic. For further information on fluid and electrolytes, see Chapter 8, pages 230–235.

The degrees of dehydration can be estimated by comparing the child's current weight with his or her weight before the illness. As with diarrhea, dehydration can be classified by severity, as follows (Hockenberry & Wilson, 2011):

Table 10.17 Clinical Manifestations of Dehydration

Manifestation	Isotonic (Loss of Water and Salt)	Hypotonic (Loss of Salt in Excess of Water)	Hypertonic (Loss of Water in Excess of Salt)
Skin • Colour • Temperature • Turgor • Feel	• Grey • Cold • Poor • Dry	• Grey • Cold • Very poor • Clammy	• Grey • Cold or hot • Fair • Thickened, doughy
Mucous Membranes	• Dry	• Slightly moist	• Parched
Tearing and Salivation	• Absent	• Absent	• Absent
Eyeball	• Sunken	• Sunken	• Sunken
Fontanelle	• Sunken	• Sunken	• Sunken
Body Temperature	• Subnormal or elevated	• Subnormal or elevated	• Subnormal or elevated
Pulse	• Rapid	• Very rapid	• Moderately rapid
Respirations	• Rapid	• Rapid	• Rapid
Behaviour	• Irritable to lethargic	• Lethargic or comatose; convulsions	• Marked lethargy with extreme hyperirritability on stimulation

Source: Hockenberry, M. J., & Wilson, D. (2011). *Wong's nursing care of infants and children* (9th ed., p. 1060, Table 28-4). St. Louis: Mosby.

- Mild is a loss up to about 5% of pre-illness weight.
- Moderate is a loss of 5–10% of pre-illness weight.
- Severe is a loss of more than 10% of pre-illness weight.

Clinical Manifestations

Clinical manifestations are summarized in Table 10.17.

Diagnostics

The following diagnostic tests are used to assess the level of dehydration:

- Abnormal values of serum electrolyte (Na^+, K^+, Cl^-)
- Decreased serum pH value if there is acidosis
- Increased hematocrit
- Increased blood urea nitrogen (BUN) level
- Urine is concentrated with a high specific gravity (>1.030) and high osmolarity
- Decreased urine sodium concentration

Therapeutics and Nursing Considerations

Nursing consideration goals are to correct fluid and electrolyte imbalances and to treat the underlying cause.

- Assess the child's health history, health assessment findings, and laboratory tests to help find the cause of the dehydration.
- Weigh the child to get an accurate initial weight and monitor weight changes indicating fluid balance increases and decreases.
- Administer oral rehydration solution (ORS) or other oral fluids in small quantities—about 30–60 mL (1–2 oz) every hour—and do not give a full diet to the child until the child's hydration has improved, the reason for the dehydration has been corrected, and the fluid balance is normal.
- If the child cannot drink enough fluid to rehydrate or has significant dehydration, start an IV line and administer an appropriate replacement solution, as prescribed. The ordered solution is usually a saline solution containing 5% dextrose. The selection of solution depends on the type and cause of dehydration. Sodium bicarbonate and K^+ may be additives to balance the pH and electrolytes if needed.
- Observe the IV site frequently for signs of infiltration.
- Do not add potassium to the IV solution until the child voids.
- Assess the child's level of hydration by watching the fluid balance and watching for signs of dehydration.
- Observe and record accurate intake and output and urine specific gravity values.

- Prevent infection by using aseptic technique to insert the IV line and keeping the skin clean at the site.
- Maintain good hand washing and isolation techniques, if required, to prevent spreading infection.
- Slowly increase the child's diet until a full diet is tolerated and chart the response.
- Provide family teaching and support for the following:

  - Oral fluid rehydration and diet increases
  - Care of a child with an IV line
  - Cause and signs and symptoms of dehydration
  - Education regarding hand washing and other hygiene techniques
  - Follow-up medical appointments as necessary after discharge

FEVER

Fever or hyperpyrexia occurs when there is an increase in the hypothalamic set point, the body's thermostat-like mechanism, and when the body's heat loss mechanism cannot dissipate excess heat production, leading to an abnormally elevated body temperature.

- Hyperthermia occurs when the body's set point is normal, but other internal or external conditions exceed the ability of the body to eliminate excess heat. These conditions could include heat stroke, aspirin toxicity, and hyperthyroidism (Hockenberry & Wilson, 2011).
- Frequent causes of pyrexia in pediatrics include otitis media, respiratory tract infections, general viruses, and enteric viral infections.
- More serious causes of fever include urinary tract infections (UTIs), bacteremia, meningitis, pneumonia, osteomyelitis, cancer, immunological disorders, septic arthritis, poisoning or drug overdose, and dehydration.

Pathophysiology

Fever most commonly results from interference with the hypothalamic set point as a result of allergy, infection, endotoxins, or tumour and leads to increased heat production and decreased heat loss. Clinical assessment of associated symptoms will help the nurse decide how serious the fever is. For example, infants, with their larger body surface, are at higher risk for fluid imbalances due to a fever.

Clinical Manifestations

- Temperature of 38.9–40.6°C by axilla. Refer to Table 10.5 for the differences in pediatric vital signs.
- Reddened skin with diaphoresis and chills
- Sluggishness or restlessness

Diagnostics

Laboratory tests and results will vary depending on the etiology of the fever.

Nursing Considerations

- Check the temperature as indicated. It is important for the nurse to remember that the degree of fever does not necessarily indicate the severity of the illness.
- Fever can be a serious concern, and the child needs immediate medical assessment in the following circumstances (Hockenberry & Wilson, 2011):

  - Infant is under 3 months of age
  - Fever is over 40.5°C
  - Child is appearing or acting very ill

- Administer antipyretics as prescribed if the child has pyrexia.
- As prescribed, administer acetaminophen instead of aspirin because of the association with Reye's syndrome. Acetaminophen is given as an antipyretic and to alleviate discomfort and can be given every four hours but not more often than five times per 24 hours.
- Administer NSAIDs, ibuprofen, if prescribed. Ibuprofen also is approved for reducing fever in children as young as 6 months.
- Loosening clothing, decreasing room temperature, applying a cool washcloth to the forehead, and increasing the amount of circulating air are effective measures if provided about one hour after an antipyretic drug, but only if the child is not shivering. Shivering increases the metabolic rate and can increase the core temperature.
- Teach parents how to take the child's temperature accurately and control fever.

FEBRILE SEIZURES

A febrile seizure is a seizure that is associated with an illness that has caused a fever. It is the most common seizure in children.

- Febrile seizure affects approximately 3–5% of children. It usually occurs after 6 months and before 3 years and is unusual after 5 years; the usual onset is between 18 and 22 months (Hockenberry & Wilson, 2011).
- Most children have only one seizure, but some will have recurrences, particularly if febrile seizure runs in families.
- The etiology is unknown, but it is usually associated with common childhood illnesses such as upper respiratory tract infections and UTIs.

Pathophysiology

Febrile seizure usually is a tonic–clonic seizure, associated with an acute febrile illness.

- Febrile seizure usually results when the child hits a peak temperature threshold over 38.8°C, and not from the rapid rise in temperature (Hockenberry & Wilson, 2011).

- It is considered benign if the electroencephalograph (EEG) is normal and other neurological and physical abnormalities are not found.

Clinical Manifestations

Seizure activity generally ceases by the time the child is brought in for medical attention. Most seizures are tonic–clonic and last less than one minute.

Diagnostics

Diagnostic tests to check for other underlying problems that contributed to the seizure include lumbar puncture to rule out meningitis and an EEG to rule out a seizure disorder. Computed tomography (CT) and magnetic resonance imaging (MRI) are other tests that may be performed.

Therapeutics and Nursing Considerations

- Observe for signs and symptoms of illness.
- Provide a safe environment in case of a seizure, have suction and oxygen ready, and roll the child on the side to maintain a patent airway.
- Prepare the client and family for procedures and provide emotional support.
- Use temperature-reducing interventions, as above.
- Educate parents on how to lower a fever and how to protect the child during a seizure.
- Administer anticonvulsant therapy as prescribed if the child is still seizing when he or she arrives at hospital.

Diarrhea

Diarrhea is defined as frequent, abnormally watery stools. Diarrhea can be mild, moderate, or severe. There is also acute or chronic diarrhea, which can be inflammatory or noninflammatory. Diarrhea is a very common childhood illness that can be life-threatening if the child becomes dehydrated and has an electrolyte imbalance with hypovolemia. The children who are most at risk are young, attend day care centres, and have poor sanitation at home.

Pathophysiology

- Acute diarrhea is caused by a rotavirus, which is the most common nonbacterial gastroenteritis. Bacterial causes include *Escherichia coli, Salmonella, Campylobacter,* and *Shigella. Clostridium difficile* may occur after antibiotic treatment.
- Chronic diarrhea is commonly related to malabsorption syndromes, immune deficiencies, allergies, and inflammatory bowel disease.

In cases of infectious diarrhea, the pathogens produce enterotoxins that attack the intestinal walls and cause an increase in fluid and electrolyte secretions.

Clinical Manifestations

The severity of the diarrhea and the category need to be determined, as follows (Ball & Binder, 2006):

- Mild is a slight increase in frequency with a liquid consistency.
- Moderate is several loose or watery stools, possibly accompanied by nausea, vomiting, or irritability, which resolves in one to two days.
- Severe is frequent or continuous stools with moderate to severe fluid and electrolyte imbalances, cramping, and irritability. The child may appear lethargic, with inappropriate responses, and may become comatose.

Diagnostics

A stool specimen can be sent for culture and sensitivity to confirm the presence of an infectious or parasitic agent. A stool pH of less than 6 and the presence of reducing substances suggest carbohydrate malabsorption or a lactase deficiency. In stools with a fatty or oily appearance, a three-day stool collection can determine fat malabsorption.

Stool positive for occult blood can be an indicator of irritation or inflammation.

It is important to also test for serum complete blood count (CBC), electrolytes, creatinine, and BUN.

Therapeutics

The fluid and electrolyte imbalances need to be corrected and the cause of the diarrhea treated. Premixed oral rehydration therapy (ORS) is the initial treatment for mild or moderate dehydration. If there is significant dehydration and electrolyte imbalance, IV treatment is started. Reintroduction of a normal diet is done gradually as tolerated by the dehydrated child (CPS, 2006). A child who is not dehydrated should be fed a normal diet.

Nursing Considerations

- Obtain an accurate history in order to identify the causative factor, such as travelling or eating contaminated foods.
- Assess the type of diarrhea.
- Assess for signs of dehydration, which are outlined in Table 10.17.
- ORS should be given frequently to the child with dehydration and the volume increased as tolerated.
- Check for specific gravity of urine and daily weights and maintain strict intake and output to monitor fluid balance.
- Administer prescribed parenteral fluid and antimicrobials if needed.
- Cleanse the skin area around the perineum and apply protective cream such as zinc oxide to prevent skin breakdown and reduce the potential for infection.
- Provide education to help the family assess the child's diarrhea and level of hydration and to know when to seek medical attention.

- Teach parents oral rehydration treatment with commercial products such as Pedialyte, Rehydralyte, Gastrolyte, Enfalyte, or Cera. It is important to instruct the family not to give the child water, fruit juices, carbonated beverages, gelatin, or any caffeine-containing products when rehydrating the child.
- Restart the child's normal nutrition, in particular breastfeeding and solids, unless the child has developed a lactose intolerance from the diarrhea. A lactose-free formula or half-strength lactose-containing product can be used briefly if there is intolerance until the bowel returns to normal.
- Teach proper handling of stools and hand hygiene to prevent the spread of infection.

SEPSIS

Sepsis is a generalized bacterial infection with a systemic inflammatory response. Infants within the first year of life, particularly if they are low birth weight, have a high risk of developing sepsis. All neonatal infections are potentially opportunistic, and any bacteria are capable of causing sepsis. Group B *Streptococcus* is the most common bacteria, and *E. coli* and *Listeria monocytogenes* are also common causes of sepsis (CPS, 2007b). The neonatal inflammatory and immune defence mechanisms are immature, which allows rapid invasion, spread, and multiplication of infecting microorganisms. The young infant is unable to localize infections.

Clinical Manifestations

The initial signs and symptoms may be subtle and may include temperature instability (the child may be hypo- or hyperthermic), tachycardia, poor peripheral perfusion with pallor, cyanosis or mottling, and respiratory distress. The manifestations may also include poor sucking and feeding, weak cry, lethargy, irritability, decreased pain response, hypotension, jaundice, dehydration, GI disturbances, seizures, hypotonia, tremors, full fontanelle, and cardiac arrest. Late-onset sepsis (up to age 4 months) usually appears with meningitis.

Diagnostics

- Blood culture, urine culture, and lumbar puncture for cerebrospinal fluid (CSF) analysis are done to try to determine the focal site of the infection.
- CBC with an elevated white blood cell (WBC) count with increased immature neutrophils indicates infection, and C-reactive protein (CRP) levels may or may not be elevated.
- A chest X-ray is done when the infant has respiratory symptoms.

Therapeutics

The infant is treated immediately with antimicrobials after the cultures have been collected. Ampicillin and gentamicin are usually prescribed and are based on drug sensitivities to the common organisms cultured from the infant with sepsis. If the cultures are negative in 48 hours, then the drug therapy can be discontinued (CPS, 2007b).

Nursing Considerations

Nursing management is focused on the following goals and is similar to that given to a high-risk newborn:

- It is very important to assess the newborn for signs and symptoms of onset infection and sepsis, particularly in infants having invasive procedures done that can elevate the risk of infection.
- Provide a neutral thermal environment due to the infant's immature abilities to regulate temperature.
- As prescribed, administer antibiotic therapy for 7–10 days if culture results are positive and discontinue therapy if culture results are negative (usually in two days).
- Monitor hydration and intake and output.
- Monitor the infant for signs of a worsening condition or shock (Ball & Binder, 2006).

MENINGITIS

Meningitis is an inflammation of the meninges caused by a bacterial or viral infection. Neonates and infants are at increased risk of developing bacterial meningitis, and it can be fatal if not treated immediately. Viral meningitis is less virulent. The outcome of the meningitis depends on the organism, as well as the child's age and response to treatment.

- Most cases occur between 1 month and 5 years, with infants under 12 months being the most susceptible to bacterial meningitis. The risk of mortality is higher in adolescents and young adults.
- *Haemophilus influenzae, Neisseria meningitidis,* and *Streptococcus pneumoniae* are the most common organisms to cause meningitis after the neonatal period. The *H. influenzae* type b vaccine has almost eliminated this type of bacterial meningitis in young children in countries where the vaccine is given regularly. The newer pneumococcal vaccine is also being given to the younger age group and will likely decrease the incidence of *S. pneumoniae* meningitis (Yoev & Guzman-Cottrill, 2005). *E. coli*, group B *Streptococcus,* and *Listeria monocytogenes* are the most common organisms in the neonate.
- Viral meningitis or aseptic meningitis is caused mainly by enteroviruses and less commonly by arboviruses, herpes simplex, and varicella zoster. It is a self-limiting disease lasting 7–10 days.
- In bacterial meningitis, the bacteria from a focal infection site, such as otitis media, enter the meninges through the bloodstream and spread through the CSF. The infection can also be introduced as the result of an invasive procedure or through a surgical or

trauma site. The bacteria toxin creates a meningeal inflammatory response and causes a release of purulent exudates that spreads the infection rapidly. The brain surface becomes covered in exudate and is edematous. The ventricles can then become obstructed by pus, fibrin, or adhesions, blocking the CSF flow and potentially producing increased intracranial pressure (ICP). Serious damage to the brain cells, some of which can be permanent, is caused by necrosis.

- Complications can include syndrome of inappropriate antidiuretic hormone (SIADH), disseminated intravascular coagulation (DIC), subdural effusion, septic arthritis, seizures, sensorineural hearing loss, hydrocephalus, behaviour problems, and learning problems (Ball & Binder, 2006).

Clinical Manifestations

The manifestations vary depending on the child's age, the type of bacterial infection, and the onset of the infection. Newborns have nonspecific symptoms that are different from those of older children. Symptoms in this age group may include poor sucking ability, vomiting, or diarrhea. Neonates with meningitis tend to have poor muscle tone with little movement and a weak cry. The fontanelle may be bulging, but this is a late sign. The newborn may be irritable, lethargic, jaundiced, and drowsy and have seizures, apnea or irregular respirations, cyanosis, fever (varies with level of maturity), and weight loss. If the infant is not treated, there is deterioration leading to cardio-vascular collapse, seizures, and apnea (Hockenberry & Wilson, 2011).

Infants who are between 3 months and 2 years of age show signs of fever, poor feeding, vomiting and a bulging or tense fontanelle and often have a high-pitched cry. Nuchal rigidity (resistance to neck flexion) and Brudzinski's and Kernig's signs are not usually present in children under 12 to 28 months of age. Older children may initially have respiratory or GI problems and then develop nuchal rigidity (stiff neck), headache, and tripod posturing. Kernig's sign is present with meningitis when the supine or sitting child's knee is flexed, and there is pain and resistance upon extension of the knee. Brudzinski's sign is present with meningitis when the supine child's head is flexed, and the hips and knees flex involuntarily. A petechial rash may also appear.

Diagnostics

- A lumbar puncture is done in order to diagnose meningitis. CSF may be cloudy, with an elevated WBC count, elevated protein level, and decreased glucose level. The CSF is cultured, and a Gram stain is done to determine the causative agent. A CT scan may be done before this test if increased ICP is present to prevent brain herniation.
- CBC reveals increased WBC count.

- Blood culture may pinpoint the causative agent as well.

Therapeutics

For children who are older than 6 weeks, the antibiotic treatment is a combination of vancomycin and a third-generation cephalosporin. Dextramethasone can also be used for suspected bacterial meningitis before or within one hour of the antibiotic dose in order to treat the inflammatory brain process (CPS, 2008b).

Nursing Considerations

Perform careful assessments to monitor the child for changes in illness and signs of complications.

- Monitor temperature, vital signs, and level of consciousness frequently, particularly for shock or respiratory distress.
- Accurately monitor intake and output and fluid and electrolyte balance; children with decreased levels of consciousness should receive nothing by mouth; others are allowed fluids and diet as tolerated.
- Assess neurological signs and level of consciousness, including signs of increased ICP. Measure head circumference to monitor for the development of subdural effusions and obstructive hydrocephalus.
- Administer antibiotics as prescribed (the type depends on the organism) and maintain IV line.
- Provide fever-reducing measures.
- Monitor for signs of a secondary infection.
- Steroids may be prescribed to relieve cerebral edema.
- Set up respiratory isolation for 24–48 hr after antibiotic administration begins.
- The child will be sensitive to sound and bright lights; keep the room as quiet as possible to decrease environmental stimuli.
- Assess the level of pain and give prescribed acetaminophen with codeine as needed.
- Position the child in a side-lying position without a pillow with the head of the bed slightly raised to increase comfort from neck stiffness (Hockenberry & Wilson, 2011).

PSYCHOSOCIAL AND MENTAL HEALTH CHALLENGES

CHILD MALTREATMENT

Child maltreatment refers to the harm, or risk of harm, that a child or youth may experience while in the care of a person whom he or she trusts or depends on, including a parent, sibling, other relative, teacher, caregiver, or guardian. Harm may occur through the direct actions by the person (acts of commission) or through the person's neglect to provide a component of care necessary for healthy child growth and development (acts of omission).

The five types of child maltreatment are as follows:

Physical Abuse (Assault): The application of unreasonable force by an adult or youth to any part of a child's body

Sexual Abuse: Abuse involving a child, by an adult or youth, in an act of sexual gratification, or exposure of a child to sexual contact, activity, or behaviour

Neglect: A failure by a partner or caregiver to provide the physical or psychological necessities of life to a child

Emotional Harm: Adult behaviour that harms a child psychologically, emotionally, or spiritually

Exposure to Family Violence: Circumstances that allow a child to be aware of violence occurring between a caregiver and his or her partner or between other family members

Child abuse is a very serious situation that has long-term implications for the child and the family. In 2003, an estimated 235,315 child maltreatment investigations were conducted, and in 49% of these cases, the child protection worker substantiated the abuse (Public Health Agency of Canada, 2002). Three characteristic factors put a child at increased risk of being abused: these factors can be grouped under the headings of the parents, the child, and the environment.

Parental Factors

- Severe punishment as children
- Poor impulse control
- Free expression of violence
- Social isolation
- Poor social–emotional support system
- Low self-esteem
- Substance abuse

Child Factors

- Temperament: doesn't "fit" as well into the family
- Illness, disability, or developmental delay
- Illegitimacy
- Hyperactivity
- Resemblance to someone the parent does not like
- Failure to bond
- Problem pregnancy, delivery, or prematurity
- Other siblings are not attached

Environmental Factors

- Involves all socioeconomic groups
- Chronic stress such as divorce or poverty
- Frequent relocation
- Substitute caregivers can be abusive (Hockenberry & Wilson, 2011)

To meet the legal definition, sexual abuse must be committed by a caregiver to the child for the use, persuasion, or coercion of a child to conduct sexually explicit acts. If the abuse is committed by a stranger, it is considered to be sexual assault. Sexual abuse includes incest, molestation, exhibitionism, child pornography, child prostitution, and pedophilia (Hockenberry & Wilson, 2011).

The following are characteristics of the abuser and the child:

- Anyone can be an abuser, but usually it is a male whom the child knows.
- Child maltreatment involves all socioeconomic groups.
- The abuser may be a prominent community member or someone who works with children, such as a teacher or coach.
- Pornography or prostitution can involve the parents or strangers.
- Stepfathers may put a child more at risk.
- The child is often a runaway.
- The child is often afraid to expose the abuser because of a fear of retaliation or that he or she will not be believed.
- Boys are less likely to report abuse (Hockenberry & Wilson, 2011).

Clinical Manifestations

Physical Abuse

Physical indicators of physical abuse are as follows:

- Skin injuries, such as bruising, with different stages of healing in unusual locations and often shaped like the object that was used
- Burns, such as cigarette burns
- Fractures, such as spiral fracture
- Head injuries, particularly in a young child
- Fatal intracranial trauma without signs of external injuries caused by violent shaking, especially in infants under 6 months (CPS, 2001)
- Subdural or retinal hemorrhages in the absence of external signs
- Traumatic eye injuries such as conjunctival hemorrhages
- Mouth injuries
- Poisonings
- Drowning
- Repeated accidents
- Child can be wary of adults and fearful of parents as well as afraid of going home
- Child suffers pain without crying
- Superficial relationships or overly friendly
- Child reports injury by parents
- Child exhibits attention-seeking behaviour (Hockenberry & Wilson, 2011)

Nursing Considerations

Nurses often identify potential or actual abuse situations. Any suspected child maltreatment must be immediately reported to the appropriate authorities, such as a hospital child abuse team or a children's aid society. The following interventions are critical to ensuring a child's safety, as well as helping the child and the child's family cope with the situation:

- Careful physical examination and history-taking for signs of abuse are essential.
- Accurate documentation is very important to preserve the facts.
- Encourage the child to verbalize concerns without any undue questioning.
- Encourage positive self-concept in the child.
- Use play to help the child work out stress.
- Collaborate with the interdisciplinary team and refer the family to social services.
- If the child has been apprehended, help the child cope with the loss of the family and ease his or her transition into foster care.

Emotional Abuse

Emotional abuse is a deliberate attempt to destroy a child's self-esteem or confidence.
   Indications:

- Failure to thrive, developmental delays
- Feeding problems
- Sleep problems
- Enuresis
- Habit disorders such as rocking, biting, or hair-pulling
- Withdrawn
- Unusual fearfulness
- Behaviour problems of extremes, either withdrawal or aggression
- Age-inappropriate behaviours
- Attempted suicide (Hockenberry & Wilson, 2011)

Neglect

The definition of neglect is to deprive a child of necessities.
   Physical indicators:

- Failure to thrive, malnutrition, constant hunger
- Poor hygiene and inappropriate clothing
- Bald patches on an infant's head
- Lack of adequate supervision, abandonment
- Poor health

Behavioural indicators:

- Dull, inattentive infant
- Begging or stealing food
- School attendance issues
- Use of drugs and alcohol
- Delinquency
- Child reports having no caretaker (Hockenberry & Wilson, 2011)

Sexual Abuse

Physical signs of sexual abuse:

- In many children, no obvious signs
- Difficulty walking or sitting
- Torn, stained, bloody underwear

- Gross evidence of trauma (genital, oral, anal), pain, itching, sexually transmitted infections, discharge
- Pregnancy
- Weight loss, eating disorder
- Vague somatic complaints

Behavioural indicators:

- Under age 5: Regression, feeding or toileting disruptions, temper tantrums, requests for frequent underwear changes, seductive behaviour
- Ages 5–10: School problems, night terrors, sleep problems, anxieties, withdrawal, refusal of physical activity, and inappropriate behaviours
- Adolescents: School problems, running away, delinquency, promiscuity, drug and alcohol abuse, eating disorders, depression, and other significant psychological problems, such as suicide attempts (Hockenberry & Wilson, 2011).

Munchausen's Syndrome by Proxy

This syndrome occurs when a parent, usually the mother, induces the symptoms of an illness, such as poisoning, in a child. It is very hard to verify.
   Indicators:

- The history does not match the clinical findings.
- Unexplained, prolonged, or extremely rare illness that does not respond to treatment and occurs only when the parent is present.
- The parent shows unusual interest in the health care team members and pays special attention to the child.
- Family members display similar symptoms (Hockenberry & Wilson, 2011).
- The child and family need to be referred to the child abuse team. There can be significant physical effects that can potentially cause serious physical illness and death. As well, significant emotional trauma can be caused to the child.

SUICIDE

Suicide is taking action to intentionally end one's life. Among Canadian youth, suicide follows motor vehicle accidents as the leading cause of injury death in males and females from ages 10–19 years (Public Health Agency of Canada, 1999). Almost 20% of the overall injury deaths were suicides. The First Nation and Inuit populations are at a significantly higher risk. The risk factors for suicide in this age group are as follows:

- Previous suicide attempts
- A friend who has tried to or has committed suicide
- School issues and grade changes
- Substance abuse
- Problems with a love relationship
- Depression, loneliness, and isolation
- Chronic family issues
- Chronic condition

- Change in behaviour or weight
- Family history of suicide
- Abuse—physical, emotional, sexual
- Low self-esteem
- Giving away possessions
- Access to guns and ammunition
- Minority sexual practice (Ball & Binder, 2006)

Clinical Manifestations

- Depression usually precedes suicide. Symptoms of depression may be obvious or subtle.
- Danger signs include lethargy, feeling unwell, insomnia or early-morning awakening, poor appetite or overeating, excessive crying, giving away important possessions, a preoccupation with death or death themes, and statement of intent.

Nursing Considerations

- Provide education for groups such as teachers, families, and youth about risk factors.
- Provide youth counselling, stress management, and problem-solving techniques.
- Assess if the child has a suicide plan.
- Arrange for counselling, crisis intervention, and hospitalization if necessary and refer the youth and family to a professional therapist.
- Provide counseling after a suicidal death for the adolescent's family and friends to help them understand and work through their bereavement.

ATTENTION DEFICIT HYPERACTIVITY DISORDER (ADHD)

ADHD is defined as developmentally inappropriate degrees of inattention, impulsiveness, and hyperactivity. Some symptoms are present before the age of 7 and must be present in at least two different settings, such as home and school.

ADHD is classified into three categories, as follows:

- The combined type, which is the most common: The child has six or more symptoms of inattention and six or more symptoms of hyperactivity/impulsivity that have lasted for at least six months.
- The predominantly inattentive type: The child has six or more symptoms of inattention but fewer than six symptoms of hyperactivity with impulsivity for at least six months.
- The predominantly hyperactive/impulsive type: The child has six or more symptoms of hyperactivity and impulsivity but fewer than six symptoms of inattention for at least six months.

For most children, ADHD disorder is relatively level through early adolescence, and in most individuals, symptoms subside between late adolescence and early adulthood. A few individuals have full ADHD symptoms into middle adulthood (Hockenberry & Wilson, 2011).

Pathophysiology

The cause of ADHD is uncertain. Many causes are likely to be involved, including organic, genetic, and environmental factors. There is speculation that the cause of ADHD is neurochemical, causing a developmental lag due to sensitivities to sucrose or food additives or exposure to toxins or illnesses. Many do respond to central nervous system (CNS) stimulants, suggesting a neurochemical link. Boys are diagnosed at a rate three times that of girls (Hockenberry & Wilson, 2011).

Clinical Manifestations

The behaviours of a child with ADHD are normal childhood behaviours, but the quality of the motor activity and hyperactivity differs. The manifestations vary in number and degree, and each child has a unique array. Most behaviours are seen at an early age, but learning disabilities may not become obvious until the child is in school.

Therapeutics

Different approaches are aimed at treating the child with ADHD. The combination of approaches of behavioural therapy, pharmacological therapy, and environmental manipulation can be effective in helping improve the child's ADHD symptoms and family life (McCord, 2011).

Behavioural therapy provides the following when the child and family are referred for family counselling:

- Strategies to teach parenting skills and coping mechanisms, such as positive reinforcement techniques, to help the child be successful in school and in everyday activities
- Pharmacological therapy utilizing psychostimulants, such as methylphenidate (Ritalin) or dextramphetamine (Dexedrine)
- Tricyclic antidepressants such as imipramine (Norpramin) and nortriptyline (Pamelor), used to block norepinephrine and serotonin at the nerve endings and increase the action of these substances in nerve cells

Nursing Considerations

The nurse is an active member of the health care team in managing a child with ADHD and acts as a link between other health care professionals and educators. In this role, he or she

- Encourages parents to express their concerns and express their emotions.

- Participates in child and family teaching, arranges referrals to support groups, and discusses school settings and classroom placement for special assistance.
- Provides information on the medication and treatment plan:

  - Teaches that some drugs take 2–3 weeks to have the maximum benefit and others are started at low doses and gradually increased until effective.
  - Gives information on potential side effects, such as sleeplessness, anorexia, and blurred vision.
  - If the child is prescribed methylphenidate, recommends small, frequent meals and snacks to help overcome potential anorexia and to monitor growth, which can be slowed by the drug.
  - Suggests administering methylphenidate earlier in the day to prevent drowsiness.
  - Provides information on the fact that tricyclics can cause dental caries, so careful dental hygiene and care are needed.
  - Recommends keeping the drugs out of reach of other children in the family.

Environment manipulation education is needed to help the family and the child. The use of organizational charts, decreasing distractions, and modelling positive behaviours in a consistent approach may help. Arrange for a referral if the child or another family member has anxiety or depression (McCord, 2011).

School Phobia

School phobia is described as an abnormal, persistent fear of attending school. Usually, it is related to separation anxiety or is a significant anxiety and fear of school-related activities such as bullying.

Clinical Manifestations

Common signs and symptoms include nausea, vomiting, anorexia, headache, leg pains, and stomachache. Symptoms tend to clear up quickly when the child is permitted to remain at home (Hockenberry & Wilson, 2011).

Nursing Considerations

- Work together with the child's parents, teacher, and school counsellor to uncover the underlying problem and problem-solve some strategies to solve it.
- Discuss the problem and possible strategies with the child.
- Implement plans to send the child back to school.
- Encourage the child to stay in school while working through the problem to decrease the feelings of low self-esteem, dependency, and lack of coping abilities.

The success of the treatment program can be evaluated when the child goes to school on a regular basis; feels comfortable freely sharing any issues with parents, teachers, or a school counsellor; and has no physical manifestations.

Autistic Spectrum Disorders

Autistic spectrum disorders (ASDs) are related to brain dysfunction with intellectual and behavioural deficits. These disorders are complex developmental disorders that fluctuate in the type and level of severity. ASDs occur in the United States in 1–2 in 500 children and are about four times more common in males than in females. The etiology of ASD is not known. The research evidence is pointing toward multiple biological causes. In the past, there were some reports that ASD may be caused by thimerosal-containing immunization vaccines or the measles-mumps-rubella vaccine, but this was not proven. Some associated conditions occur in conjunction with ASD, such as fragile X syndrome, tuberous sclerosis, metabolic disorders, fetal rubella syndrome, *Haemophilus* meningitis, and structural brain anomalies. There is a higher incidence of ASD in families with another child with autism. The cause may be an autosomal recessive gene defect, but this has not yet been identified (Bryant, 2007).

Clinical Manifestations

Deficits in social development are the major characteristic of the condition. Most children with ASD have some level of mental retardation that varies from mild to severe, with self-mutilation tendencies. More females than males have low test scores for intelligence quotient (IQ). Some children with ASD have a high level of functioning in specific areas, such as mathematics, music, art, and memory (Bryant, 2011). The manifestations include the following:

- Highly unusual characteristics, mostly in regard to social interactions, with communication and behaviour issues
- The inability to maintain eye contact
- Self-stimulating behaviour, for example, hand-flapping or head-banging
- Limited functional play, and the child may relate to toys in a strange way
- Inability to read social cues or respond to others' body language
- Frequent speech and language problems, such as echolalia and severe delays in meaningful verbal communication

Diagnostics

The following may indicate autism:

- Abnormal EEGs, seizures
- Developmental assessment testing, which may show delayed hand dominance, poor language and social

interaction abilities, and other developmental lags
- Metabolic abnormalities which may show increased serotonin levels
- Hypoplasia of the cerebellum in the vermis, which is involved in controlling motion and some parts of the memory (Bryant, 2011)

Therapeutics

Early diagnosis, referral, and concentrated intervention are critical for the child to progress and increase the level of social development. Some children can improve when language and communication skills can be acquired. Intensive behaviour modification programs with positive reinforcement strategies that emphasize social awareness and verbal communication and decrease negative behaviours seem to be the most effective.

Nursing Considerations

Children with autism do not adapt easily to new situations and require directed activities, minimal stimulation, established routines, and close supervision. It is important to encourage the family to stay with the child when hospitalization is required because of the difficulties surrounding new people and situations.

The child and the family require highly specialized care and treatment. They need to be referred to community treatment centres and support networks.

Autism is not caused by parenting or environmental factors. Families need support and education on how to manage the child at home. The treatments can be very expensive and can be a significant drain on the family's finances.

Anorexia Nervosa and Bulimia Nervosa

Anorexia nervosa is a potentially life-threatening eating disorder that affects mainly females. The peak incidence is at 12–13 years; there is another peak again at 17–18 years. Bulimia nervosa also occurs mainly in females and with a teenage onset. See Chapter 11, pages 588–590.

End of Life

Developmental Stages and Reactions to End of Life

Refer to the earlier sections on reactions to hospitalization, pp. 445, 449–450, 452, 454–455, and 456, for the different developmental stages.

Infants and Toddlers: There is currently no consensus as to whether this age group grieves or mourns. Children in this age group will perceive that the family is very upset and sad even though they do not understand why. Encourage the family members to stay with the dying child and provide physical comfort, such as cuddling and rocking. Establishing routines and rituals with familiar objects will give a sense of security.

Preschoolers: Children at this stage are familiar with the term "death" but see it as a going away or possibly as sleep. Preschoolers take statements literally; when family members tell a preschooler that they have put their dog to sleep, the child may fear sleeping. Death is equated with sleep and separation and is reversible.

- In the magical thinking of preschoolers, the dead can be alive and do things such as breathing, eating, and sleeping.
- Preschoolers who have a seriously ill sibling may feel that their own actions have caused the death and that the anger and sadness of the family are being directed at them; as a result, they may view the illness as a punishment for their actions and thoughts.
- Separation from parents is the biggest fear for this group, and the preschooler may feel that the parents will go away and not come back.
- Encourage the family to minimize separations, use concrete language, and be alert for a sense of punishment and guilt.

School-Aged Children: For these children, death is only temporary and is personified by figures such as the "bogeyman" or the devil. The child may think that death can be avoided by being good. There are degrees of being dead; therefore, people are not really dead; life and death are transposable. By 7 to 9 years, there is a deeper understanding that death is universal and irreversible, and the child will defy death and joke about it.

When the school-aged child or a sibling has a terminal illness, the child fears the unknown and loss of control, which leads to a decreased sense of security and self-confidence. Clear explanations of what is going to happen will give the child a sense of control and maintain his or her self-esteem. The child at this stage can appear to be uncooperative or rude but is trying verbally to gain some sense of control and power.

- Encourage the child to express his or her feelings and provide physical activities to relieve stress.
- Provide as much choice and control as possible.

Adolescence: Adolescents normally respond with appropriate grief and react to death with an almost adult understanding. This age group is starting to look for the meaning in death and religious meaning, such as life after death.

- Adolescents are unable to prioritize their losses; therefore, the loss of a friend may be just as upsetting as the loss of a parent.

- A loss due to death can interfere with the search for identity, and physical changes in the body of a terminally ill adolescent can be more devastating than the actual illness.
- The ill adolescent is often isolated from his or her peer group; encourage contact and communication with friends because the child may be unable to communicate with his or her parents and get support. Peer support groups can be helpful.
- The nurse can facilitate communication between these groups and provide as much independence and control as possible.

Clinical Manifestations

When evaluating a child's psychological state in relation to death and dying, assessment findings usually take into consideration the following:

- The developmental stage of the child
- Cultural and spiritual concerns
- Socioeconomic factors
- Support network and family connections
- Grief manifestations
- Unfinished business between parents and child
- Anticipatory grieving
- Dysfunctional grieving (Hockenberry & Wilson, 2011)

Nursing Considerations

The end of life is a very sensitive topic. The child and the family need guidance in understanding the process of death and dying and to maintain as healthy a grieving process as possible.
Nursing considerations:

- Encourage discussion of the child's past experiences with death and dying.
- Determine and develop strategies to help decrease anxiety.
- Determine comfort measures and objects and promote a sense of security.
- Encourage the use of the child's and family's rituals, routines, and customs.
- Provide a member of the clergy if the child and the family would like the referral.
- Encourage the child and the family to verbalize feelings and concerns.
- Refer the family to social services or community resources if the family needs financial assistance.
- Organize and help activate support systems.
- Refer the family to a grief counsellor if needed (Hockenberry & Wilson, 2011).

SUDDEN INFANT DEATH

- Sudden infant death syndrome (SIDS) is the sudden, unexplained death of any infant for whom a postmortem examination fails to determine the cause

of death. The death usually occurs during sleep. There is a lack of Canadian statistics on the rate of incidence of SIDS. In the United States, the SIDS incidence has dropped to a historical low of 0.07 per 1000 live births in 2002, which is a 40% drop from 1992 (American Academy of Pediatrics, 2003). The drop in rates may be due to how infants' deaths are classified, but likely it is mainly due to the changes in recommendations for safe sleeping positions for young infants.

The risk factors for infants are as follows:

- Sleeping position other than on the back
- Sleeping alone in a room
- Bed sharing with mothers who are cigarette smokers
- Bed sharing with an adult who is extremely fatigued or impaired by drugs or alcohol
- Use of soft bedding, a pillow, and covers that can cover the head
- Sleeping with an infant on a sofa, which is of particular high risk
- Bed sharing with other than parents or usual caregiver (CPS, 2008c)

Infants who are at higher risk of SIDS include the following groups:

- Infants requiring cardiopulmonary resuscitation or vigourous stimulation with a combination of apnea, colour change, marked change in muscle tone to limpness, and choking or gagging (ALTE, apparent life-threatening events)
- Preterm infants with apnea spells when discharged home
- Siblings of two or more SIDS occurrences
- Infants with certain types of diseases or conditions, particularly with central hypoventilation (Hockenberry & Wilson, 2011)
- The peak age for SIDS ranges from 2–4 months, with most cases occurring before 6 months.
- SIDS affects male infants more than females and usually occurs in winter.

Pathophysiology

The cause of SIDS is unknown, but the most accepted theory is an abnormality of the brainstem, the area that regulates the neurological system of cardiopulmonary control, which can cause sleep apnea, dysrhythmic breathing, and impaired arousal to increased carbon dioxide and decreased oxygen. However, sleep apnea does not cause SIDS. There may be a genetic predisposition. Maternal smoking may be an important factor in SIDS. Prone sleeping is also a major factor, one that can impair arousal, cause oropharyngeal obstruction and carbon dioxide rebreathing, and affect thermal balance. Soft bedding may prevent infants from turning their heads to the side, creating the same dangers as prone sleeping (Hockenberry & Wilson, 2011).

Clinical Manifestations

There are no characteristic findings before death. Usually, parents discover that the infant has died in the crib. The infant is often found with blankets over the head, face down, with frothy, blood-tinged secretions in the nose and mouth. The diaper usually has both urine and stool in it. The child's appearance causes acute distress to the family (Hockenberry & Wilson, 2011).

Diagnostics

No laboratory tests are diagnostic of SIDS.

Nursing Considerations

- Encourage the family to verbalize concerns and validate feelings.
- Assess the family's grieving patterns and ability to cope.
- Refer the family for counselling if needed. Bereavement counsellors and support groups are often very helpful.
- Provide a supportive environment and time for the family to say goodbye to the child.
- Offer a memory package with a lock of hair, foot and hand prints, and other important mementos.
- Teach families about the importance of positioning and other preventive SIDS protocols.

EAR DYSFUNCTION

ACUTE OTITIS MEDIA

Acute otitis media (OM) is the inflammation of the middle ear, with the signs and symptoms of acute infection, fever, and ear pain. It is the most common reason that antibiotics are prescribed. It is usually caused by *H. influenzae, Moraxella catarrhalis,* or *S. pneumoniae.* The viral cause is usually respiratory syncytial virus (RSV) and influenza. It occurs more commonly in boys. Seventy percent of all children will develop OM (Hockenberry & Wilson, 2011).

Pathophysiology

Infants and children more predisposed to OM are as follows:

- Children who have short, horizontally positioned eustachian tubes, which allow secretions to easily migrate into the middle ear
- Children with immaturely developed cartilage that lines the eustachian tube opening; this makes the tubes more likely to open up, allowing secretions to migrate into the middle ear
- Children have immature immune systems, which increases the risk of infection.

- Enlarged lymph tissue can block the eustachian tube openings.
- Breastfed infants have a lower incidence because of their semi-upright feeding position and immunity acquired from the mother, whereas bottle-fed infants who are fed in the supine position have a higher incidence of infection due to the possibility that formula may reflux into the eustachian tubes.
- Passive smoking is a factor, increasing inflammation and decreasing secretion drainage.

Treatment of OM with antibiotics remains controversial because of the risk of bacteria such as *S. pneumoniae* developing antibiotic resistance. Although controversial, antibiotic therapy is the main treatment, with amoxicillin being most frequently used, unless the child has been on antibiotics in the last month. Other antibiotics include amoxicillin–clavulanates, azithromycin, and cephalosporins. It is generally agreed that waiting up to 72 hours for the infection to clear in healthy children is acceptable, but for children under 2 years, caution is needed because of the risk of sepsis (Hockenberry & Wilson, 2011).

Possible complications include hearing loss, scarring of the tympanic membrane, tympanic perforation, chronic suppurative otitis media, mastoiditis, meningitis, and cholesteatoma, in which the epithelial lining forms scales and can destroy bone and middle ear structures.

Myringotomy tubes are tiny drainage tubes that may be inserted into the tympanic membrane to drain excess secretions in the middle ear and equalize pressure.

Follow-up is important to ensure that the antibiotic therapy has cleared the infection and that there are no complications, such as hearing loss.

Clinical Manifestations

Health history and physical assessment data may reveal the following:

- Irritability, pulling at the affected ear, and complaints of ear pain
- Fever
- Decrease in appetite
- Nasal congestion, rhinorrhea, cough, and vomiting and diarrhea, showing a concurrent infection
- Otoscopic findings, including erythematous tympanic membrane; bulging tympanic membrane, membrane with no visible landmarks, including no light reflex; or diminished tympanic membrane mobility and discoloured effusion
- Purulent discharge

Diagnostics

Culture and sensitivity tests may identify organisms in ear discharge. An audiology referral for hearing tests can be done if hearing impairment is suspected.

Nursing Considerations

- Reduce fever by administering antipyretics as prescribed and dressing the child lightly.
- Relieve pain with prescribed analgesics by offering soft foods to reduce chewing and through the application of local heat or warm compresses to the affected ear. Note that heat may aggravate the pain in some children. Ice packs on the affected ear may relieve pain by reducing edema.
- Facilitate drainage by having the child lie on the affected ear.
- Prevent skin breakdown by keeping the external ear clean and dry and by using a moisture barrier.
- Assess for hearing loss and recommend referral for audiological testing if indicated.
- Administer prescribed antibiotics; prophylactic antibiotic treatment may be prescribed for children with recurrent infections.

RESPIRATORY DYSFUNCTION

UPPER RESPIRATORY INFECTION

Upper respiratory tract infections include nasopharyngitis, pharyngitis, and tonsillitis.

Nasopharyngitis and Pharyngitis

Also called the common cold, nasopharyngitis is a viral infection of the nose and throat. It is usually caused by viruses such as rhinoviruses, RSV, adenoviruses, influenza, and parainfluenza viruses. Pharyngitis is an inflammation of the pharynx. Nasopharyngitis is the most common illness in infancy and childhood.

Pathophysiology

The disease course of upper respiratory tract infections is usually self-limiting and lasts from about four days and up to 10 days if there are complications. If the infection is caused by group A, beta-hemolytic *Streptococcus*, there is the potential for complications such as acute glomerulonephritis or rheumatic fever (Hockenberry & Wilson, 2011). Young children are more susceptible to catching these infections because of their immature immune systems.

Clinical Manifestations

The symptoms often include fever, irritability, restlessness, decreased appetite and fluid intake, and decreased activity. Rhinorrhea and nasal congestion can occur because of inflammation and can lead to skin irritation from wiping away secretions.

Therapeutics

- Antipyretics and other fever-reducing measures are given.

- The CPS (2007c) recommends saline drops to help clear nasal congestion. Over-the-counter decongestants and cough medicines may not be very effective and are not recommended for children under 3 years unless recommended by a physician or nurse practitioner.

Nursing Considerations

Teaching family members to care for their children at home is important; considerations are as follows:

- Elevate the head of the bed to help the secretions drain.
- Suction with a nasal bulb to clear congestion and use vaporization.
- Fluid intake is needed to prevent dehydration.
- Prevention of infection is difficult, but when possible, children should be kept away from infected people and encouraged to wash their hands frequently.

Tonsillitis

Tonsillitis is inflammation of the tonsils and often occurs with pharyngitis. In young children, the tonsils commonly are enlarged and become smaller as the child ages. The infection can be caused by bacteria or viruses.

Clinical Manifestations

The symptoms are caused by inflammation and include the following:

- Difficulty eating and swallowing because of swelling and pain. If the tonsils are very large, there can be breathing issues due to airway obstruction.
- The child's breath can have an odour, and he or she may have decreased ability to smell and taste.
- Frequent sore throats and ear infections can occur.
- There may be a muffled and nasal tone of speech if the adenoids are enlarged.
- Throat cultures may show streptococcal organisms; if so, the child needs to be treated with an antibiotic.
- Nonbacterial tonsillitis is mild and self-limiting. It is characterized by a gradual onset, low-grade fever, mild headache, sore throat, hoarseness, and a cough.
- Bacterial tonsillitis is marked by the rapid onset of high fever, headache, generalized muscle aches, and vomiting.

Nursing Considerations

- Tonsillectomy is not recommended unless there are recurrent, frequent streptococcal infections or a history of peritonsillar abscess (Hockenberry & Wilson, 2011).
- Treatment is focused on symptom relief: antibiotics if it is a bacterial infection, analgesics–antipyretics such as

acetaminophen or an opioid combination, salt–water throat gargles for older children, lozenges or hard candy, fluids or soft foods, and rest.

If surgery is required,

- Preoperatively: Prepare the child and family for hospitalization and surgery as with any procedure, with the teaching adapted to the child's developmental level. Explain that the child will have a sore throat after surgery but will be able to talk and swallow normally.
- Postoperatively: Observe for unusual bleeding; monitor vital signs; assess child's colour; be alert for restlessness, which can indicate hemorrhaging; help prevent bleeding by discouraging the child from coughing, clearing the throat, and blowing the nose; until the child is fully alert after the anaesthetic, position him or her on the side or the abdomen to facilitate drainage from the throat.

Clear fluids that are not red in colour, which could disguise bleeding, and that are cool or iced should be given first; milk products should not be used because they tend to coat the throat and cause throat-clearing; analgesics should be given on a regular basis (Hockenberry & Wilson, 2011).

- Postoperative teaching:
  - Avoid gargling and vigorous tooth-brushing.
  - Avoid persons with infections.
  - Provide a soft diet that does not include acidic, spicy, or other irritating foods.
  - Avoid coughing and clearing the throat and do not use straws.
  - Monitor the child for bleeding, especially immediately postoperatively and 5–10 days postoperatively, when tissue sloughing occurs. Return to hospital immediately if bleeding occurs.
  - Limit activity to decrease the risk of bleeding, including when the child returns to school.

PNEUMONIA

Pneumonia's main feature is an acute inflammation of the bronchioles, alveolar ducts and sacs, and alveoli that impairs gas exchange.

Pneumonia is classified according to the etiological agent and the location and extent of pulmonary involvement:

- Lobar pneumonia involves a large segment of one or more lobes; when both lungs are affected, it is called bilateral pneumonia.
- Bronchopneumonia begins in the terminal bronchioles, which become clogged with mucopurulent exudates, and then consolidates in patches in the nearby lobules.
- Interstitial pneumonia is an inflammation confined to the alveolar walls and peribronchial and interlobular tissues (Hockenberry & Wilson, 2011).

Pathophysiology

Pneumonia most commonly results from infection from viruses, bacteria, mycoplasma, or fungi. In children less than 5 years old, viral pneumonia is the most common type, including RSV, adenovirus, rhinovirus, influenza, parainfluenza, and enterovirus. Bacterial pneumonia in the newborn is commonly caused by group B *Streptococcus* and *Chlamydia trachomatis*.

- In children over 5, bacterial pneumonia is most common and is most often caused by *Staphylococcus aureus* and *S. pneumoniae*.
- In school-aged children, *Mycoplasma pneumoniae* is a common cause of pneumonia.
- It is anticipated that *H. influenza* type b and *S. pneumoniae* will decrease as causative agents as a result of current immunizations against these agents (Ball & Binder, 2006).
- Pneumonia typically begins with a mild upper respiratory tract infection. As the disorder progresses, lung inflammation occurs.
- Bacterial pneumonia flows through the bloodstream to the lungs, usually causing inflammation and edema with cellular debris and mucus, in turn leading to airway obstruction and consolidation within one lung.
- Viral pneumonia agents enter the lung through the upper respiratory system into the alveoli near the bronchi and spread to nearby lung tissue in a patch pattern. Infants' small airways make them vulnerable to atelectasis and edema.
- Aspiration pneumonia can be caused by a child aspirating formula or vomitus or experiencing gastric reflux and can cause chemical injury and an inflammatory response that leads to pneumonia as a secondary infection.

Clinical Manifestations

Manifestations vary depending on the causative agent. Common signs and symptoms in viral pneumonia include the following:

- Variations ranging from mild fever, slight cough, and malaise to high fever, severe cough, and prostration
- Nonproductive or productive cough with whitish sputum
- Wheezing or fine rales

Common signs and symptoms in bacterial pneumonia include the following:

- High fever
- Unproductive to productive cough with whitish sputum, tachypnea, wheezing, rales, dullness on percussion, chest pain, retractions, nasal flaring, pallor or cyanosis (depending on severity)

- Irritability, restlessness, lethargy
- Nausea, vomiting, anorexia, diarrhea, and abdominal pain (Hockenberry & Wilson, 2011)

Diagnostics

- Chest X-ray studies may show diffuse or patchy infiltrates, consolidation, disseminated infiltration, or patchy clouding, depending on the type of pneumonia.
- Blood tests may reveal an elevated WBC count.
- A causative agent may be grown in blood culture or Gram stain and culture of sputum.
- Positive antistreptolysin-O (ASO) titre is diagnostic of streptococcal pneumonia (Hockenberry & Wilson, 2011).

Nursing Considerations

Administer medication as prescribed.

- Viral pneumonia: Treatment is usually supportive, with fever and pain control, although antibiotic therapy may be recommended to reduce the risk of a secondary bacterial infection.
- Bacterial pneumonia: Antibiotic therapy is indicated; oral amoxicillin and clavulanate or a second-generation cephalosporin such as cefuroxime should be given if the child is not completely immunized for *H. influenzae*. Erythromycin is given to older children and adolescents until *M. pneumoniae* has been diagnosed.

If the child is hospitalized:

- Humidified oxygen, chest physiotherapy, and suctioning with deep breathing, as well as incentive spirometry may be helpful.
- Assess for respiratory distress by monitoring respiratory status and vital signs.
- Change the child's position frequently and elevate the head of the bed.
- Monitor fluid balance and encourage oral fluid intake to ensure hydration.
- Promote rest by maintaining bed rest and organizing nursing care to minimize disturbances.
- Provide client and family teaching.
- Discuss home care and follow-up measures.

ATYPICAL PNEUMONIA

Some children have an atypical type of pneumonia that is caused by *M. pneumoniae*. It occurs commonly in the school-aged child who is living in crowded conditions.

A serious new form of atypical pneumonia appeared in Asia in 2003, called severe acute respiratory syndrome (SARS). SARS is caused by a previously unrecognized coronavirus called SARS-CoV. Persons who are in contact with clients with SARS, or who have travelled in areas where SARS is present, are at risk of being infected. Strict isolation with a fitted respiratory mask is required. The clinical manifestations include the following:

- Fever higher than 38°C
- Headache
- Cough, shortness of breath, difficulty breathing
- A dry, nonproductive cough after 2–7 days
- Some require ventilation
- In the young child, milder symptoms and a runny nose and cough
- In the adolescent group, malaise, myalgia, chills, and rigour (Denison, 2005)

Treatment is mostly supportive, with no clear improvement from using steroids, antibiotics, or antivirals (Hockenberry & Wilson, 2011).

ASTHMA

Asthma is a chronic inflammatory respiratory disease that causes difficulty breathing following exposure to certain triggers. A trigger is anything that causes inflammation in the airways and is specific to the individual. Inflammatory triggers include dust mites, animals, cockroaches, moulds, pollens, viral infections, and certain air pollutants. Symptom triggers, which do not cause inflammation but instead provoke "twitchy" airways, include smoke, exercise, cold air, strong smells such as perfumes, food additives such as sulphites, air pollutants, moulds and mildew, dust, and intense emotions. Because it is a chronic condition, asthma must be monitored and controlled over a lifetime. Asthma is the most common cause of pediatric admissions to hospital in Canada.

Pathophysiology

In response to triggers, the following changes occur in the airways:

- Bronchoconstriction, which is tightening and narrowing of the circular muscles in the airway
- Edema of the airways as an inflammatory response
- Mucus production, which is also part of the inflammatory response to triggers

The result is a narrowing of the airways primarily on expiration, causing restricted airflow and subsequent respiratory distress.

Clinical Manifestations

Children typically present with signs of asthma between the ages of 3 and 8. In younger children, an attack usually follows a respiratory infection. Symptoms typically occur at night or in the early morning. Asthma can vary in symptoms from mild or moderate to severe and can vary from person to person.

- Wheezing on expiration is a classic sign.
- Suprasternal and substernal retractions
- Shortness of breath, dypsnea, increased respiratory rate
- Tightness in the chest
- Coughing that may be dry, nonproductive, or productive and that commonly occurs at night
- Diaphoresis, worried look, anxiety, pale skin
- Hunched shoulders, tripod position, refusal to lie down
- In more severe attacks, difficulty speaking, behavioural signs of hypoxia
- "Silent chest," an ominous sign of impending respiratory arrest

Diagnosis is typically determined on the basis of clinical manifestations, history, and physical examination. Generally, chronic cough in the absence of infection or diffuse wheezing during expiration is sufficient enough for a diagnosis.

Diagnostics

Peak flow measurements and spirometry test lung volumes and expiratory capacities. Pulmonary function tests are more comprehensive tests to determine airway parameters.

Therapeutics

- Controller medicines (usually inhaled steroids) stabilize the airways and decrease the inflammatory response. They are maintenance therapy and are of no use during an acute attack.
- Reliever medicines (usually inhaled bronchodilators) open the airways during attacks and are used prior to steroid inhalations to provide maximum airway dilation.
- Allergy desensitization has proven to be of little value.

Nursing Considerations

- Asthma can best be managed if an asthma plan is in effect. This plan is best formulated with the input of the health care team and family. The focus is on avoidance of triggers, appropriate and timely medication therapy, proper use of inhalers, avoidance of upper respiratory infections, symptom monitoring, involvement of the child and the family, and maintenance of a normal lifestyle.
- Ensure the proper use of inhalers as this is a frequent cause of poorly managed asthma. Use appropriate devices, such as a spacer, to improve medication delivery. Allow several minutes between bronchodilator inhalations.
- The child may benefit from using the bronchodilator prior to exercise or in cold weather.
- Advise the child to rinse the mouth following steroid inhalation.
- Teach parents when to bring the child to hospital for emergency care.

In hospital,

- Observe the chest, including size, shape, symmetry, and movement.
- Perform lung auscultation to assess for adventitious breath sounds.
- Take vital signs.
- Administer inhaled bronchodilator via a mask with compressed air or oxygen. Monitor the response to the inhalation.
- Maintain the child on clear and increased fluids.
- Extreme shortness of breath or the absence of breath sounds accompanied by a sudden rise in respiratory rate is an ominous sign indicating respiratory failure and imminent asphyxia.
- Support and reassurance are necessary as an asthma attack is very frightening for both the child and the parent.

RESPIRATORY SYNCYTIAL VIRUS (RSV) AND BRONCHIOLITIS

RSV is the most common respiratory pathogen for bronchiolitis and pneumonia among infants and children under 2 years of age. Approximately 80% of infants are infected with RSV during their first year of life, and virtually all children will have been infected by the age of 2 years (Hockenberry & Wilson, 2011). In many cases, RSV will cause symptoms similar to a cold; however, serious infection in the lungs can occur in premature infants, babies with chronic lung disease or congenital heart disease, or those infants who are immuno-compromised. The infection rate rises in the late fall, peaks midwinter, and decreases in frequency in the spring in countries with temperate climates, such as Canada. This highly contagious pathogen is typically spread from hand to eye, nose, or other mucous membranes. The virus will live on surfaces such as clothing, toys, countertops, and facial tissues for hours.

Pathophysiology

RSV affects the epithelial cells of the respiratory tract, causing obstruction due to accumulated debris from infected cells, mucus, and exudate. This leads to small airway obstruction, air trapping, poor gas exchange, increased work of breathing, and a characteristic expiratory wheeze.

Clinical Manifestations

The signs and symptoms of RSV will vary depending on the age and condition of the child and the severity of the infection. Peak incidence of RSV bronchiolitis is 2–5 months. The infection progresses as follows:

- Early: Runny nose, sneezing, pharyngitis, coughing, wheezing, and crackles. There may be intermittent fever.

- As illness progresses: Increased coughing and sneezing, shortness of breath, tachypnea and accessory muscle use, and cyanosis
- In severe illness: Tachypnea at more than 70 breaths per minute, listlessness, poor air exchange, significantly decreased breath sounds, and apneic spells, which may rapidly progress to respiratory failure
- Symptoms will appear 3–5 days after exposure and will last approximately 12 days.

Diagnostics

Positive diagnosis of RSV is based on the initial upper respiratory infection symptoms, the time of year (late fall to early spring), history of exposure, chest X-ray to rule out other respiratory conditions, and a nasal swab culture.

Therapeutics

RSV infections are treated symptomatically with high humidity, adequate fluids, and caloric intake and rest. Most children can be managed at home. Hospitalization is required for those with advanced symptoms of the illness or an underlying respiratory or cardiac disease. RSV immune globulin, or, less frequently, RSV monoclonal antibody, may be administered prophylactically for high-risk infants. Bronchodilators and steroids can be used but are controversial in terms of effectiveness (Hockenberry & Wilson, 2011).

Nursing Considerations

- Monitor for respiratory distress, noting respiratory rate and rhythm, breath sounds, and adventitious sounds, especially wheezing.
- Assess skin colour and hydration status.
- Take appropriate isolation precautions.
- Administer prescribed medications.
- Ensure high humidity with oxygen as prescribed; increase fluids to maintain adequate hydration, offering small amounts frequently to prevent aspiration.
- The child may need IV fluids if tachypnea creates a potential for aspiration.
- Maintain proper positioning to promote increased air exchange, usually high Fowler's.
- Provide support for parents.

Treatment with ribavirin:

- Note that use of this medication is controversial as it may cause toxic effects in health care workers who inhale the aerosol, and the effectiveness in children has not been definitely proved.
- Ribavarin may be used for high-risk children, such as premature or very young infants, and infants at increased risk for progressing from mild to severe disease.

- Delivery is by aerosol.
- Due to potentially toxic effects, pregnant health care workers should not provide care to children receiving ribavirin.
- Reduce environmental exposure to ribavirin (temporarily stop medication when the tent is open and administer the drug in well-ventilated rooms).

LARYNGOTRACHEOBRONCHITIS

Laryngotracheobronchitis (LTB), or croup, is an inflammation and narrowing of the laryngeal and tracheal areas. The cause is usually viral, and the common infectious agents are RSV, influenza viruses, parainfluenza viruses, adenoviruses, and measles virus. As a result of effective immunization campaigns, the number of *H. influenzae* LTB infections has decreased. LTB also may be of bacterial origin (as in diphtheria or pertussis).

LTB affects boys more than girls, usually between the ages of 3 months and 8 years, and peaks in the winter months (Hockenberry & Wilson, 2011).

Pathophysiology

LTB usually follows an upper respiratory infection, which may spread to the larynx, trachea, and sometimes the bronchi. The elastic larynx of a young child can go into spasm and can cause a significant airway obstruction. Severe airway edema can cause airway obstruction and seriously affect air exchange.

Clinical Manifestations

In spasmodic croup with rapid onset, the child wakes at night with a barklike or seal-like cough.

- Acute LTB: Gradual onset from upper respiratory tract infection, progressing to signs of respiratory distress with pallor or cyanosis
- Hoarseness, inspiratory stridor, indrawing, and possibly severe respiratory distress
- May have low-grade fever
- Restlessness and irritability
- Wheezing, crackles, and localized areas of diminished breath sounds

Therapeutics

Treatment is commonly humidity with cool mist via a croupette, despite the fact that it has not been shown to decrease subglottal edema.

- Racemic epinephrine, which causes vasoconstriction and decreases subglottal edema, is administered by nebulizer for children who are not improving.
- Steroids may be effective when administered orally or intramuscularly if oral steroid cannot be tolerated.

Nursing Considerations

- Assess for airway obstruction by evaluating respiratory status by colour, respiratory effort, evidence of fatigue, and vital signs.
- In severe cases of LTB, intubation to manage the airway may be necessary.
- Administer oxygen and increase humidity to decrease hypoxia if O_2 saturation is below 92%.
- Administer IV or oral fluids as prescribed to ensure good fluid balance.
- Reduce the child's anxiety by maintaining a quiet environment and promoting rest and relaxation.
- Provide parental support and teaching.
- Teach home management with cool moist air: for example, to decrease subglottal edema, take the child outside in the cool night air, to the basement, or to stand in front of a freezer.

EPIGLOTTITIS

Epiglottitis is an acute and severe inflammation of the epiglottis that causes a supraglottic airway obstruction. It is mainly caused by parainfluenza A and B, adenovirus, and RSV. *H. influenzae* immunizations have decreased the occurrence of that type of infection. Now it usually affects older children and is caused by viruses.

Pathophysiology

Swelling and inflammation of the soft tissue of the epiglottis cause life-threatening obstruction of the airway. Progressive obstruction results in hypoxia, hypercapnia, and acidosis, closely followed by decreased muscle tone, altered level of consciousness, and, if obstruction becomes complete, sudden death. Endotracheal intubation or tracheostomy usually is considered. IV antibiotics are initiated, and steroids may be used for edema.

Clinical Manifestations

- Sudden onset of fever, sore throat, dyspnea, and lethargy
- Restlessness and anxiety due to respiratory obstruction
- Hyperextension of the neck, drooling, severe sore throat with refusal to drink
- Stridor, hoarseness
- Rapid, thready pulse
- Child adopts characteristic "tripod" position: sitting upright, leaning forward with chin thrust out, mouth open, drooling, and tongue protruding
- Late signs of hypoxia: listlessness, cyanosis, brady-cardia, decreased respiratory rate with decreased aeration
- Child's throat is red and inflamed with a large, red, edematous epiglottis (Hockenberry & Wilson, 2011).

Diagnostics

- Lateral neck X-ray shows epiglottal enlargement.
- Elevated WBC count and increased bands and neutrophils may be seen on the differential count.
- Causative bacteria may be identified by blood cultures (Hockenberry & Wilson, 2011).

Nursing Considerations

If epiglottitis is suspected, throat examination should be by a specially trained person. Ensure that intubation and tracheostomy equipment is nearby as the throat examination may cause laryngospasm and precipitate a complete airway obstruction.

Provide care as for other respiratory conditions.

CYSTIC FIBROSIS

Cystic fibrosis (CF) is a chronic autosomal recessive hereditary disorder that affects the pancreas, respiratory system, GI tract, salivary glands, and reproductive tract. The majority of clients with CF are people of European descent with a 95% ratio compared with other ethnic backgrounds.

The gene responsible for CF was identified in 1989 on chromosome 7. The most common lethal inherited disease affecting children of European descent, CF occurs in about one in 1600 live births. Incidence is equal in both sexes. The median age of survival in Canada is the mid–30's, with almost 40% of clients being 18 or older. Advancements in treatments with gene and protein therapy, in addition to aggressive chest physiotherapy, inhalation therapy with antibiotics, and nutritional support, have improved the prognosis.

Pathophysiology

The underlying defect is in the *CFTR* gene, causing impaired chloride movement and abnormally viscous and thick mucus that obstructs bronchioles and ducts in the pancreas and other exocrine glands, creating multisystem problems. The child with CF has an increase in sodium and chloride in the saliva and sweat.

In the lungs, ciliary movement is slower and the thickened secretions accumulate, creating obstruction, air trapping, and infection. Respiratory infections recur and cause bronchiectasis and fibrotic scarring. The pancreas becomes obstructed and significantly decreases production of the digestive enzymes, leading to major malabsorption of proteins and fats. The small intestine can become obstructed.

Clinical Manifestations

Manifestations vary with severity and time of emergence; they may appear at birth or take years to develop. Children with CF often taste salty because of the high salt content of their sweat.

Respiratory signs and symptoms:

- Wheezing, dyspnea, cough, cyanosis
- Respiratory infections are usually caused by staphylococci, *Pseudomonas aeruginosa*, and, eventually, as the disease progresses, *Burkholderia cepacia*. The child can develop resistance to antibiotics.
- As CF progresses, atelectasis and generalized obstructive emphysema result from mucus blockage in the small airways, producing a barrel-shaped chest and finger clubbing.
- Chronic sinusitis, bronchitis, bronchopneumonia, or ear, nose, and throat problems

Gastrointestinal signs:

- Meconium ileus at birth; rectal prolapse (common); loose, bulky, frothy, fatty stools; large appetite; weight loss; marked tissue wasting; failure to thrive; distended abdomen; thin extremities; evidence of vitamin A, D, E, and K deficiencies

Reproductive signs:

- Females: Decreased fertility apparently from increased viscosity of cervical mucus, which blocks the entry of sperm
- Males: Sterility in 95%, which may be caused by blockage of the vas deferens with abnormal secretions or failure of the vas deferens tubes to develop (congenital bilateral absence of the vas deferens [CBAVD])

Cardiovascular signs:
Cor pulmonale, right-sided heart enlargement, and congestive heart failure resulting from obstruction of pulmonary blood flow (Hockenberry & Wilson, 2011).

Diagnostics

- Elevated chloride levels on the sweat test (iontophoresis with pilocarpine); chloride level is >60 mEq/L
- Absence of pancreatic enzyme activity
- Steatorrhea detected in stool analysis
- Generalized obstructive emphysema on chest X-ray
- Fetal diagnosis in utero (Ball & Binder, 2006)

Therapeutics

The child with CF receives aggressive treatments for respiratory infections from oral, inhaled, and IV antibiotics. Aminoglycosides, such as tobramycin and gentamicin, and cephalosporins are often used. Sputum cultures are required because clients with CF become colonized with *P. aeruginosa* and then the more antibiotic-resistant strain of *B. cepacia*, and antibiotics must match the sensitivity of the organisms. Clients with CF who are colonized with *B. cepacia* have a poorer prognosis. Inhaled bronchodilators, which may

include inhaled tobramycin, are used before daily chest physiotherapy sessions with postural drainage. Huff breathing techniques, positive expiratory pressure, use of a spirometer flutter valve, and high-frequency chest wall oscillation all help clear mucus and prevent infection. DNAse can also be given by nebulizer to help thin respiratory secretions. Exercise also helps clear the mucus.

Replacement pancreatic enzymes in the form of one to five capsules are given with meals to help improve digestion of food. Fat-soluble vitamins are needed because of the difficulty of digesting fat. Esophageal reflux is common and is treated as usual.

Breast milk or hydrolysate formula can be given. Lactulose may prevent early distal intestinal obstructions and prevent recurrence; abdominal obstructions are treated with Golytely. Constipation, which can contribute to obstruction, is treated as usual. A high-calorie, high-protein, and high-fat diet is important to prevent malnutrition (Ball & Binder, 2006).

Nursing Considerations

- Perform pulmonary mucus clearance to help increase sputum clearance, such as chest physiotherapy, postural drainage, inhalation treatments with bronchodilators, and breathing exercises.
- Monitor respiratory status.
- Encourage good nutrition with meals high in fat and protein. Increasing salt intake is important when the child experiences increased salt losses through the skin, as when he or she is in a hot environment or has a fever.
- Assess nutritional status by doing calorie counts, monitoring intake and output, and recording daily weights.
- Administer medications as prescribed, pancreatic enzymes with food, fat-soluble vitamins (A, D, E, and K), bronchodilators, and antibiotics when prescribed for infections, primarily of *P. aeruginosa* and *B. cepacia*.
- Promote growth and development by providing activities that enhance developmental stages.
- Monitor for signs of infection; prevent infection by promoting good health and hygiene practices, as well as by avoiding exposure to people with infections.
- Encourage adequate rest by organizing nursing activities around rest periods.
- Help the child maintain a positive self-concept by active listening, encouraging verbalization, and identifying strengths and coping strategies.
- Foster communication and allow the family and child to express their feelings about the chronic nature of the disorder and its long-term implications, the potential need for a lung transplant, and death and dying.
- Provide client and family teaching regarding pulmonary care, dietary instructions, medication dosage, administration and side effects, infection prevention, and the need for routine follow-up (Hockenberry & Wilson, 2011).

GASTROINTESTINAL SYSTEM DISORDERS

The GI system has numerous important functions. The major purposes are to break down and digest foods so that the nutrients may be absorbed through the digestive tract and waste products may be eliminated.

During fetal development, the GI system begins to form during the fourth week of the embryonic stage, starting with the mouth and anal tube. The GI tract becomes more mature in the last few weeks of development. If there is any interruption in normal fetal growth, then malformations can occur anywhere along the GI tract. Congenital anomalies of the GI tract can be present at birth or shortly after birth.

OBESITY

Pathophysiology

Increasingly, obesity is becoming a health concern in Canada and around the world. As childhood obesity rates rise, so do unusual childhood complications such as type 2 diabetes. There is widespread concern that children with obesity will have significant health issues as adults as a direct result of their condition. Childhood obesity is a predictor of adult obesity; therefore, prevention is the best intervention.

There are many reasons for increasing obesity rates, including the following:

- Parental overweight
- Overweight at birth
- Physical inactivity
- Irregular snacking
- Poor food choices
- Lack of availability of a variety of nutritious foods (Health Canada, 2012b)

Complications of obesity include the following:

- Decreased levels of growth hormone, prolactin in girls and testosterone in boys
- Increased rates of amenorrhea and dysfunctional uterine bleeding in girls
- Hyperlipidemia and hypertension
- Choledocholithiasis (gallstones)
- Slipped capital femoral epiphyses, Legge–Calvé–Perthes disease
- Obstructive sleep apnea and Pickwickian syndrome (increased daytime sleepiness and hypoventilation)
- Increased respiratory illness in toddlers under 2
- Psychosocial disturbances, such as low self-esteem, abnormal body image, difficulty developing peer relationships, social withdrawal, and isolation
- Adult obesity

Diagnostics

Tests include random blood glucose, thyroid-stimulating hormone (TSH) and thyroxine (T_4) levels (if short in stature), and urinalysis for glucose and lipid profile. In addition, in adolescent girls with amenorrhea or dysfunctional uterine bleeding, pelvic ultrasonography should be performed to rule out polycystic ovaries.

Therapeutics and Nursing Considerations

Goals of the treatment are family centred and are designed to modify behaviour so that more energy is used by the child for growth, activity, and metabolic processes than is consumed. Nurses play an important role in planning, teaching, and monitoring the child's progress.

Considerations include the following:

- Decreased caloric intake and making healthier choices using *Eating Well With Canada's Food Guide* (see Chapter 5, page 101)
- Increased exercise over time
- Decreased sedentary activities, such as watching television and playing video games
- Employing a population-based approach to prevent childhood obesity (Health Canada, 2012b)

Follow-up visits are necessary to monitor height and weight.

CLEFT LIP AND PALATE CONDITIONS

The most common craniofacial malformation is cleft lip (CL), with or without a cleft palate (CP). It occurs in approximately one in 700 live births (Hockenberry & Wilson, 2011). CL with or without CP occurs more commonly in males, and CP alone occurs more in females. There is an increased occurrence in relatives and in monozygotic twins.

Implications for the child and family involve feeding, speech, dentition, and body image (Murray, 2002).

Pathophysiology

CL occurs in the upper lip when the tissue does not completely close during the sixth week of fetal development. CL can occur unilaterally or bilaterally, with varying degrees of depth. CP occurs when the embryonic palate plates do not completely close at about the seventh and twelfth weeks of gestation. Cleft lip and palate conditions can occur separately, or both malformations may be present in a newborn.

See Figure 10.2 for variations in clefts of the lip and palate at birth.

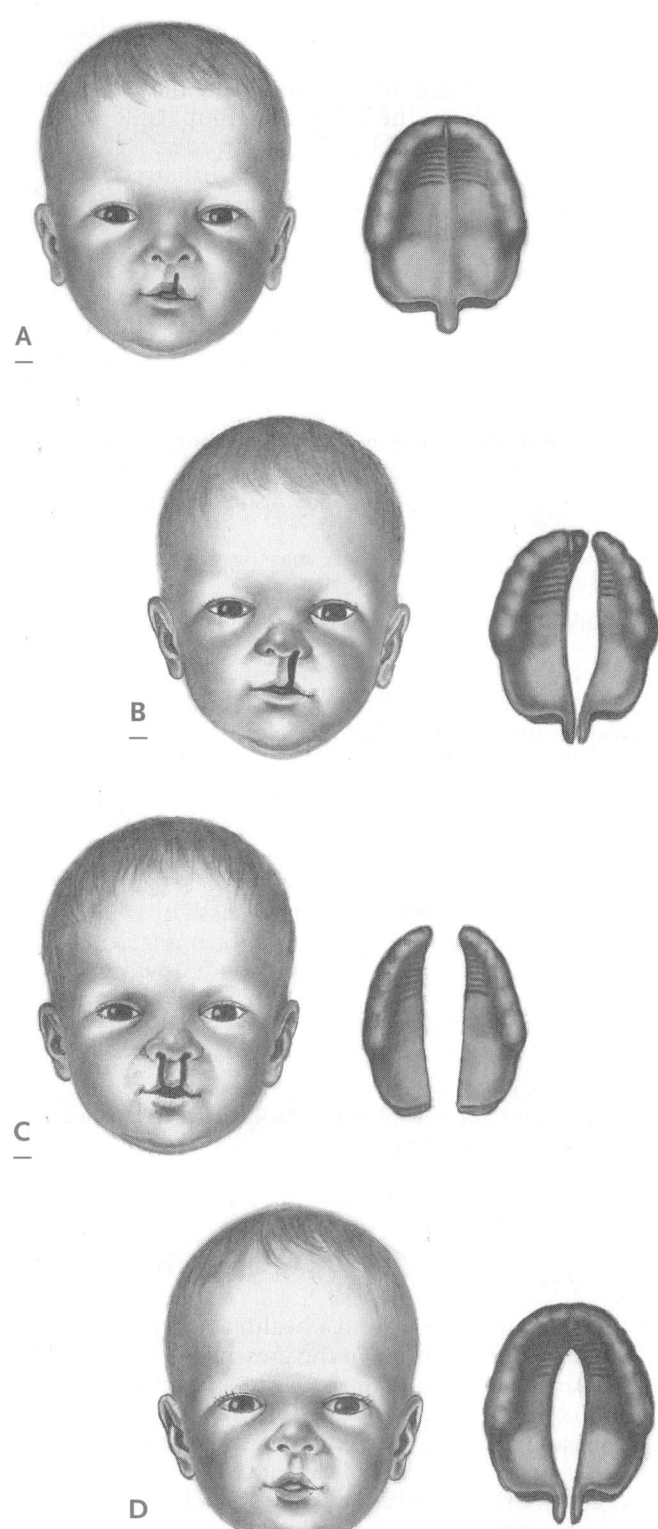

FIGURE 10.2
Variations in Clefts of Lip and Palate at Birth

A, Notch in vermillion border. *B*, Unilateral cleft lip and cleft palate. *C*, Bilateral cleft lip and cleft palate. *D*, Cleft palate.

Source: Hockenberry, M. J., & Wilson, D. (2011). *Wong's nursing care of infants and children* (9th ed., p. 429, Figure 11-16). St. Louis: Mosby.

Clinical Manifestations

The defects are present at birth. Other investigations need to be done to rule out other midline birth malformations.

Diagnostics

There are no specific tests to be performed.

Therapeutics

The treatment for CP and CL is surgical intervention.

- Early surgical correction of CL within one month permits a more normal sucking pattern and increases parental bonding. It also promotes a more normal speech pattern.
- For larger clefts, surgery for scar revision may be needed in the future.
- An extensive treatment plan developed by a multidisciplinary palate team is required for CP.
- The timing of surgical repair of the palate is controversial; it can be done in the neonate but is usually done at 12–15 months, before the incompletely fused palate can cause a speech impediment. A posterior pharyngeal flap is performed, and a bone graft may be done later to build up the palate density.
- The child with CP will have corrections performed in stages and usually requires speech therapy as well as orthodontics and prosthodontics to correct misaligned, missing, or malformed teeth.
- An obturator is a temporary appliance that blocks the defect in the palate until surgery is done, but it is controversial and may not be used.
- Ineffective eustachian tube function creates impaired drainage of the middle ear, with the result that recurrent bouts of OM can occur. Bilateral myringotomies may be required.
- There is the potential for damage to the child's self-image, particularly related to a speech impairment.
- Delayed development has also been observed.

Nursing Considerations

Potential concerns include feeding problems, airway compromise, frequent ear infections, major orthodontic work and self-image problems, and parental bonding.

Feeding Implications

- Openings in the palate make it difficult for the infant to suck. It is challenging for the child with CP to get enough pressure to adequately squeeze the nipple in the bottle or the areola of the breast.
- CL and CP babies may be more successful at breastfeeding than at using adaptive enlarged nipples, soft bottles, or syringes.
- During feeding, there is a risk of aspiration, so infants need to be held more upright and the milk directed

away from the cleft toward the side of the mouth.

- Ensure adequate nutritional intake by monitoring height and weight gain.
- Feed slowly and burp frequently to prevent excessive air swallowing and regurgitation.

Psychosocial Implications

- Encourage the family to express feelings and concerns to facilitate acceptance and bonding.
- Model acceptance of the child and the condition to the family members.
- Reassure parents that surgery usually is successful.
- Show the parents pictures of successful surgical repairs and refer them to a support group.

Postoperative Care

- Assess airway clearance and vital signs to monitor for edema and respiratory distress.
- Place an infant with CL in a baby seat or on one side to avoid contact with the surgical site. Position a child with CP prone to facilitate drainage.
- Cleaning the suture line and applying prescribed antibacterial ointment for CL will prevent infection and help prevent scarring.
- Apply elbow restraints to prevent rubbing of the suture line. Remove restraints every two hours to provide ROM exercises and give skin care.
- Feed the infant with adaptive devices such as droppers with a rubber tip, bulb syringes, Breck feeders, or soft bottle nipples, to help decrease pressure on the suture line.
- For older children, do not provide straws or sharp objects and try to keep them from rubbing the suture line with their tongue.
- Administer analgesics as prescribed to provide pain control.
- Check temperatures of warm liquids to prevent burns; the child with a new palate may lack nerve endings and sensation in the area.
- Mouth care is needed to prevent the mucous membranes from drying out due to the child tending to mouth-breathe.
- Family teaching requirements include care of the surgical wound; feeding strategies and positioning; prosthetic care if utilized; long-term follow-up with the multidisciplinary team services; referral to community services; and a genetic counselling referral, if requested.

GASTROESOPHAGEAL REFLUX AND GASTROESOPHAGEAL REFLUX DISEASE

Gastroesophageal reflux (GER) occurs when stomach contents flow back up the esophagus due to an incompetent or relaxed cardiac sphincter. Gastroesophageal reflux disease (GERD) is reflux into the esophagus or oropharynx, causing symptoms. Approximately one in 300 to one in 1000 children has

GERD (Hockenberry & Wilson, 2011). It usually does not require surgery unless it causes significant complications and continues into late infancy. This is the most common esophageal disorder in the infant age group. GER is often associated with other pediatric disorders, such as tracheoesophageal fistulas or esophageal atresia, neurological disorders, scoliosis, asthma, or cystic fibrosis.

Pathophysiology

The cause of GER is not known but may be related to immature lower esophageal neuromuscular function or hormonal control system.

- Cardiac sphincter incompetence allows reflux of stomach contents into the esophagus.
- Delayed gastric emptying may also be a cause of the reflux.
- Repeated episodes of reflux may harm the mucosal lining of the esophagus.
- Small amounts of reflux are considered normal in all age groups.
- Long-term problems with GER can cause esophageal strictures from a scarred esophagus and recurrent respiratory problems due to aspiration.
- Usually, infants improve by 12–28 months of age and respond to conservative treatment.

Clinical Manifestations

The most common sign in infants is passive regurgitation or vomiting; occasionally, hematemesis is seen. Other manifestations include the following:

- Weight loss and poor growth
- Aspiration and frequent respiratory infections
- "Blue spells" or apnea
- Esophagitis and bleeding due to gastric acid irritating the esophageal lining
- Melena stools
- Heartburn and abdominal pain

Diagnostics

- A history of vomiting and a health assessment examination can confirm the presence of GER.
- Barium swallow and upper GI radiology demonstrate reflux.
- An esophageal pH probe can measure the level of acidity, the timing of acid clearance, and the reflux amount. It can determine the impact of feedings and positioning.
- Intraesophageal pH monitoring measures reflux gastric acid from the stomach.
- Scintigraphy can detect delayed gastric emptying (Hockenberry & Wilson, 2011).

Therapeutics

Most infants are treated conservatively until the reflux disappears. Small, frequent feedings of thickened rice cereal using enlarged bottle nipples and frequent burping decrease the number and volume of emesis. Placing the infant in the prone position decreases reflux but is controversial due to an increased risk of SIDS in infants placed in this position (Hockenberry & Wilson, 2011).

- Pharmaceutical treatments include H_2 antagonists such as cimetidine (Tagamet), ranitidine (Zantac), and famotidine (Pepcid) to treat the esophagitis and proton pump inhibitors such as omeprazole (Prilosec), lansoprazole (Prevacid), pantoprazole, and rabeprozole to suppress gastric acid; as well, prokinetics such as bethanecol (Urecholine) and metoclopramide (Reglan) are often prescribed to promote esophageal peristalsis and increase gastric emptying, but they are of limited value. Antacids are not generally recommended for children due to the aluminum content of the formulations, possible neurotoxicity, and lack of research.
- Surgery is performed on children who have not responded to conservative measures or when there are contributing anatomical anomalies.
- The most common surgical procedure is called a Nissen fundoplication, which creates an antireflux valve by bringing a portion of the fundus of the stomach around the esophagus. Children with delayed gastric emptying may have a pyloroplasty.
- Fundoplications can result in complications including small bowel obstruction, no relief from GER, wrap hernia, retching, gas-bloat syndrome, and dumping syndrome (Hockenberry & Wilson, 2011).
- For children who require long-term tube feeding, an alternative to a plication is the insertion of a percutaneous gastrojejunostomy.

Nursing Considerations

- Manage acute and chronic pain.
- Assess hydration and the frequency, amount, and characteristics of the vomitus.
- Assess whether positioning, postfeed handling, or the type of activity affects the vomiting.
- Provide small, frequent feedings of thickened formula and burp often.
- Although positioning the infant upright after meals has not necessarily proven to be effective, it is generally used as a method to help prevent postfeeding reflux. Minimize handling of infants postfeeds and place children over 1 year in a left-sided position with the head of the bed elevated.
- Assess for signs of aspiration pre- and postfeeding.
- Monitor with a cardiac or apnea monitor if appropriate.
- Administer prescribed medications.
- Fundoplication requires routine abdominal postoperative care, including surveillance for wound infections, return of bowel motility, gagging, distension from gas, or intolerance of some foods, such as spicy meals. See Chapter 6, pages 154–156.
- Treatment may involve temporary gastric decompression by nasogastric (NG) tube and gradual clamping of the tube until the infant tolerates the feeds.

- Client and family teaching should relate to medications, hydration, nutrition, and feeding techniques.

HYPERTROPHIC PYLORIC STENOSIS

Hypertrophic pyloric stenosis (HPS) occurs when a narrowed circular pyloric sphincter obstructs the flow of gastric contents into the intestine. It requires a surgical pyloromyotomy to correct the constricted valve and the obstruction.

HPS is shown in Figure 10.3.

Pathophysiology

The narrowed pyloric sphincter leads to increasing hypertrophy of the valve. The pyloric canal narrows, leading to blockage of the pyloric sphincter, obstruction, gastric distension, and forceful vomiting. The cause

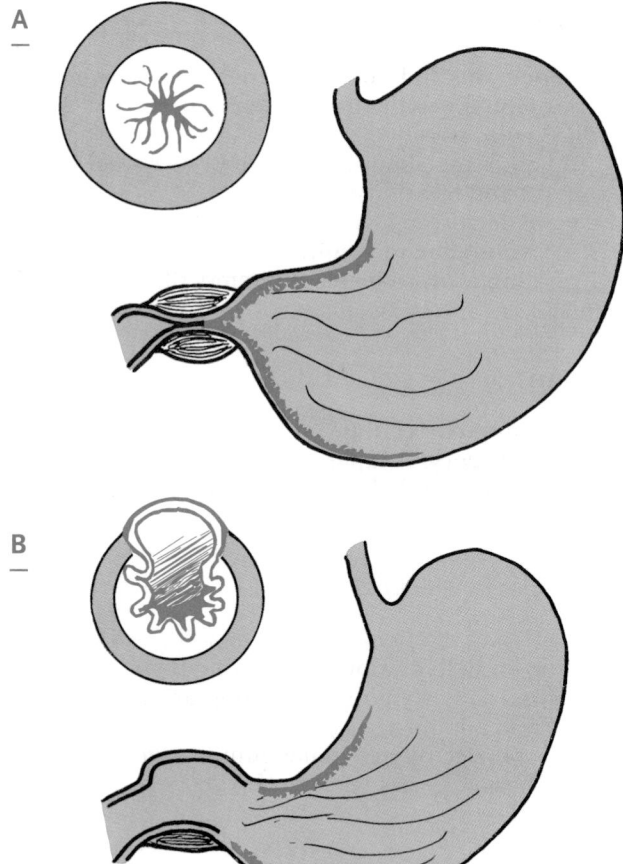

A
—

B
—

FIGURE 10.3
Hypertrophic Pyloric Stenosis

A, Enlarged muscular tumour nearly obliterates pyloric canal. *B*, Longitudinal surgical division of muscle down to submucosa establishes adequate passageway.

Source: Hockenberry, M. J., & Wilson, D. (2011). *Wong's nursing care of infants and children* (9th ed., p. 1322, Figure 33-6). St. Louis: Mosby.

is unknown but may be related to local innervation problems and can be associated with other conditions, such as intestinal malrotation and esophageal and duodenal atresia. HPS occurs more commonly in first-borns, boys, and full-term infants and has a tendency to run in families.

Clinical Manifestations

- Nonbilious vomiting usually begins at about three weeks but can vary.
- Vomiting increases in frequency and strength until it is projectile.
- Vomitus may be brown tinged from blood if gastritis develops.
- The infant is hungry and irritable.
- The condition progresses to dehydration, weight loss, and failure to thrive, with upper abdominal distension.
- Gastric peristalsis and the pylorus olive-shaped mass can be visible and palpable in the epigastrium to the right of the umbilicus.

Diagnostics

- Ultrasonograms and upper GI series show slowed gastric emptying with an abnormally stretched and thinned pylorus.
- The child has metabolic acidosis with increased serum pH and bicarbonate levels.
- There are decreased levels of serum chloride, sodium, and potassium due to vomiting.
- Dehydration leads to increased hemocrit, hemoglobin, and BUN levels.

Therapeutics

Rehydration and correction of electrolyte imbalance occur before surgery. A laparoscopic pyloromyotomy splits the pyloric muscle longitudinally. An NG tube may be inserted to decompress the stomach.

Nursing Considerations

- Maintain hydration and electrolyte balance by assessing for dehydration, monitoring intake and output and daily weights, evaluating urine specific gravity, and administering prescribed IV fluids of glucose and electrolytes (potassium is added to the IV fluid after voiding has occurred).
- Provide NG tube care if in situ. See Chapter 6, page 150.
- Provide mouth care and a pacifier when a child is on a nothing by mouth (NPO) order.
- Small amounts of clear fluids are started within 24 hours postsurgery; increase diet progressively, as tolerated, up to 48 hours postsurgery.
- Infants may be bottle- or breastfed for shorter than usual intervals.
- Feed slowly and burp frequently; place the child in a high Fowler's position on the right side after feeding.
- Administer analgesics as prescribed.
- Assess for wound infection as infants are more prone to wound healing problems.
- Encourage parent and family involvement in care; demonstrate feeding, positioning, and wound care.

Intussusception

Intussusception occurs when a portion of intestine invaginates, or folds into, an adjacent portion. This folding causes an obstruction that does not resolve and needs emergency medical intervention if the child is to survive.

Pathophysiology

Invagination usually begins close to or at the ileocecal valve. It can also occur in the ileum or the colon. Peristalsis pulls the invaginated section and causes edema and resulting obstruction that shuts off the flow of blood and lymph to the area. If intussception is untreated for more than 24 hours, bowel strangulation can occur and cause ischemia, perforation, peritonitis, hemorrhage from venous engorgement, mucus build-up, and shock.

The cause of intussusception is usually not known but may be connected to viruses, intestinal polyps, lymphoma, CF, and Meckel's diverticulum. It is one of the most common causes of bowel obstruction in children and usually affects children from 3 months to 3 years, most commonly between 5 and 9 months. It is twice as common in males as in females (Brandt, 1999). Figure 10.4 shows the invagination of the bowel in a child with intussusception.

Blood vessels drawn in between layers
Hepatic flexure
Intussusceptum
Ileocolic valve
Ileum
Appendix

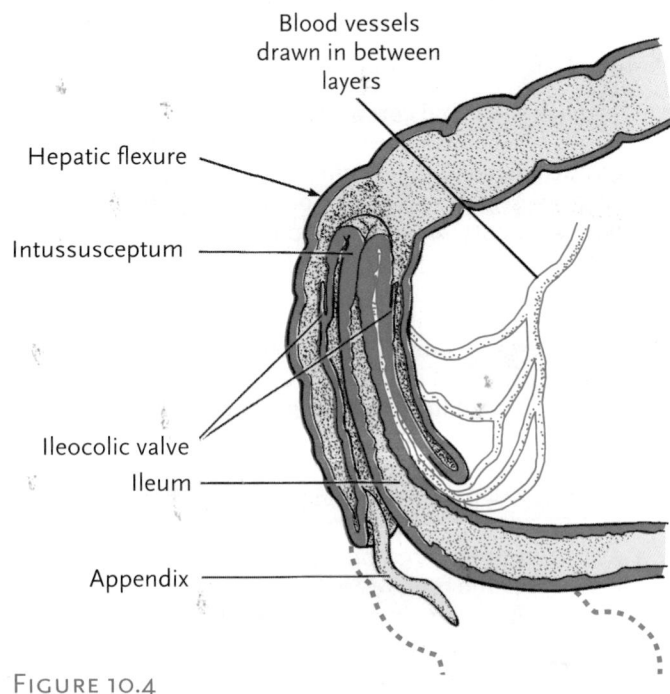

FIGURE 10.4
Ileocecal Valve (Ileocolic) Intussusception

Source: Hockenberry, M. J., & Wilson, D. (2011). *Wong's nursing care of infants and children* (9th ed., p. 1324, Figure 33-7). St. Louis: Mosby.

Clinical Manifestations

- Sudden, severe, spasmodic abdominal pain that causes the child to cry and draw the legs up to the abdomen.
- As intussusception progresses, the child will vomit gastric contents and blood will appear in the stools.
- The classical presentation of a tender, distended abdomen, with a possibly palpable sausage-shaped abdominal mass and "currant jelly" stools, occurs in 20% of children.
- The child may present with a more chronic picture of diarrhea, anorexia, weight loss, occasional vomiting, and periodic pain. The older child may have only pain.
- If the obstruction is not relieved, symptoms are lethargy, "currant jelly" stool (containing blood and mucus), bile-stained or fecal emesis, and shocklike syndrome, which can progress to death (Hockenberry & Wilson, 2011).

Diagnostics

- Initially, an abdominal X-ray is done to detect intraperitoneal air, which contraindicates a barium enema.
- A barium enema detects the obstruction to the flow of barium, confirming the diagnosis.
- A rectal examination produces mucus and blood and can detect a low intussusception.

Therapeutics

- IV fluids, NG decompression, and antibiotic therapy may be given before the enema.
- If there are no signs of shock or perforation, the initial barium enema is frequently replaced by air pressure and water-soluble contrast to prevent barium peritonitis and to reduce the intussusception by using hydrostatic forces.
- If the enema is unsuccessful in resolving the invagination, a surgical bowel resection is required.

Nursing Considerations

- Monitor vital signs, NG drainage, and signs of bowel bleeding.
- Postsurgery, encourage clear fluid intake and increase diet as tolerated.
- Monitor for signs of infection; assess wound healing for redness, swelling, and drainage; and monitor temperature.
- Perform pain assessment and management.
- Provide parental support and discharge teaching for diet and wound care.

APPENDICITIS

Appendicitis is the most common condition that requires surgery in the pediatric population. The vermiform appendix becomes obstructed, leading to increased lumen pressure and bacterial infiltration with subsequent necrosis, perforation, and peritonitis. Surgical removal of the appendix is required. Appendicitis occurs slightly more often in males and in older children, age 10–12 years. It is unusual in children under 4 years and is rare in infants less than a year. Perforation occurs more often in the younger child, possibly related to later detection.

Pathophysiology

The appendiceal lumen may become obstructed from a peritoneal skin fold, submucosal lymphoid tissue, fecaliths (hardened stool), foreign body, and parasites.

Clinical Manifestations

- The most common symptom is a spasmodic pain in the periumbilical area, which moves to the right lower quadrant near McBurney's point (located midway between the right anterior superior iliac crest and the umbilicus) with rebound tenderness.
- The pain causes difficulty with walking or when moving abdominal muscles over the inflamed area.
- Anorexia, nausea, and vomiting (common early sign but is less common in older children)
- Low-grade fever in the early stages; sharp rise with peritonitis
- Decreased or absent bowel sounds
- Constipation or small watery stools
- Irritability
- Complications can include perforation or peritonitis if appendicitis remains undiagnosed.
- Peritonitis leads to a sudden increase in fever, the release of and increase in pain, abdominal distension and guarding, tachycardia, and pallor.
- Can be difficult to diagnose and can mimic other common conditions.

Diagnostics

- There is no definitive test; diagnosis is based mainly on history and physical examination.
- Blood tests mirror other common conditions.
- WBC count is elevated but is similar to counts for other types of infections.
- Urinalysis is done to rule out UTI.
- Ultrasonography and CT of the abdomen will visualize the appendix and show fluid around it.

Therapeutics

- Treatment for dehydration and electrolyte imbalance with IV therapy
- NG tube decompression if vomiting
- Preoperative antibiotics
- Appendectomy through an incision in the right lower quadrant removes the appendix.

- If perforated, abdominal lavage is done; the suture line may be left open for a drain, and a catheter may be inserted to instill antibiotics.
- Ampicillin, clindamycin, metronidazole, or gentamicin for 7–10 days if perforated, with an elective appendectomy at a later date

Nursing Considerations

- Preoperatively: Monitor hydration levels, administer prescribed IV fluid and electrolytes, assess the level of abdominal pain, perform light palpation only, and observe for signs of shock.
- Postoperatively: Maintain NPO, administer IV fluids and electrolytes, assess for abdominal distension and signs of peritonitis, listen for bowel sounds and observe for normal bowel movements, and provide pain management.
- If a drain has been left in to prevent infection, monitor drainage, assess for wound healing and signs of infection and fever, and apply saline-soaked wet dressings.

CONSTIPATION AND ENCOPRESIS

Constipation is a common condition in pediatrics. Functional constipation occurs with disruption of the normal pattern of bowel movements, a change in regularity or consistency, or in how easy it is to pass stool. This type of constipation has no underlying problem and occurs because of a brief illness, holding stool in due to a negative experience, or as a result of a diet lacking in fluid and fibre. Diet changes, enemas, and mild stool softeners usually solve the problem.

Pathophysiology and Clinical Manifestations

Constipation is diagnosed when a child has not passed a stool for more than three days, stool is hard and can be blood streaked, bowel movements may be painful, and stool is retained with or without soiling.

All children have their own pattern of bowel movements.

Infants

- Meconium should be passed within 24–36 hours of birth.
- Meconium plugs that have less fluid can be removed digitally or with irrigation and may be caused by lack of innervation in the bowel, hypothyroidism, meconium ileus, or obstruction resulting from CF.
- Other causes include low fibre intake, mild cow's milk allergy, hard stools, infection of the perianal area, some antiseizure and diuretic medications, dehydration, CF, and anal or rectal anomalies.

Toddlers and School-Aged Children

- Passing painful, hard stools may cause the child to withhold stool for fear of pain. This causes further dilation of the colon and decreases the urge to defecate. Subsequently, the child avoids passing stool, creating even more constipation.
- Encopresis can occur when stool is withheld and stool leaks around the stool plug, causing incontinence and embarrassment.
- When the child enters school, there is a change in toileting patterns, such as new daily schedules and a lack of privacy in the school toilets, and children can be teased if they are incontinent.
- Constipation can be caused by physical problems such as disorders of the GI tract, neurological disorders, and decreased activity.

Diagnostics

The child needs to be assessed for any physical abnormalities or underlying psychological factors that are contributing to the constipation.

Therapeutics

- Mild constipation does not need treatment.
- Breastfed babies have fewer problems with constipation.
- Constipation usually improves when solids are introduced or fluids and fibre in the diet are increased.
- Stool softeners such as lactulose work well.
- Hard, impacted stool can be removed with suppositories, enema flushing, and occasionally propylene glycol electrolyte solution (Golytely) orally or by NG tube.
- Rectal stimulation is discouraged because it can be a negative experience and result in more constipation due to retention.
- Insitute regular toileting routines for bowel retraining.

Nursing Considerations

Client and family teaching should cover diet changes to increase fibre, instituting a toileting routine, and the administration of medications, bowel irrigations, or other stool evacuation procedures.

Psychological factors need to be explored and a plan devised by the client and family.

HIRSCHSPRUNG'S DISEASE

Hirschsprung's disease, or congenital aganglionic megacolon, is a lack of colon innervation that causes poor GI motility in the region of the colon or rectum and results in obstruction and dilatation. In rare cases, a child can be treated conservatively with stool softeners and enemas, but, generally, surgery is required to remove the aganglionic portion of the intestine. A temporary colostomy is created with a later pull-through procedure to close the colostomy.

Pathophysiology

Hirschsprung's disease is the absence of autonomic parasympathetic ganglia in one or many sections of the intestine. It may involve the entire intestine. As a result, intestinal contents collect in the abnormal part of the colon. The intestine then becomes distended because of the lack of GI motility and peristalsis.

Hirschsprung's disease is a congenital condition occurring in one in 5000 births and about four times as often in males than in females. It is found in children with the genetic trait and less commonly in children with trisomy, Down syndrome, GI malformations, and craniofacial defects. There may be an accompanying tight anal sphincter, which interferes with the evacuation of stool. Figure 10.5 illustrates the dilated colon in Hirschsprung's disease.

Clinical Manifestations

Clinical manifestations are variable depending on the age of the child when diagnosed.

In neonates, there are commonly symptoms of

- Failure to pass meconium stools and abdominal distension in the first 48 hours
- Poor feeding and vomiting that is bile-stained
- Irritability

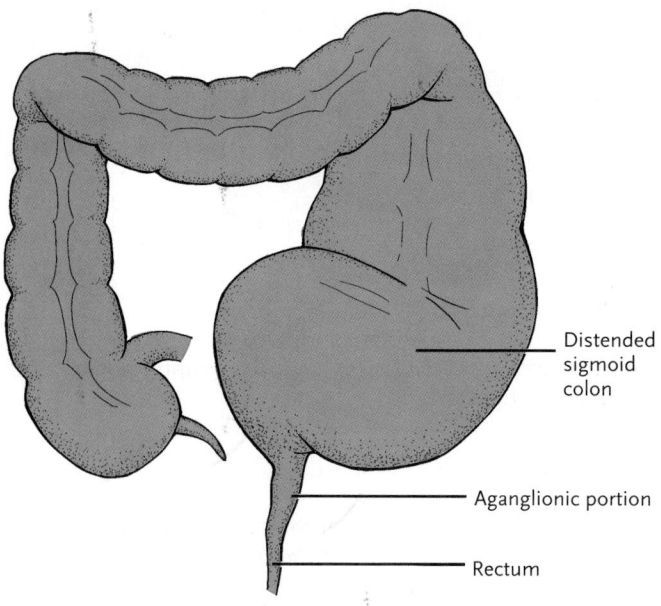

Distended sigmoid colon

Aganglionic portion

Rectum

Figure 10.5
Hirschsprung's Disease

Source: Hockenberry, M. J., & Wilson, D. (2011). *Wong's nursing care of infants and children* (9th ed., p. 1305, Figure 33-5). St. Louis: Mosby.

In infants, there can be symptoms of

- Poor weight gain
- Vomiting and bowel obstruction
- Abdominal distension, ribbonlike stools, constipation, and bouts of diarrhea

In older children, there are symptoms of

- Chronic constipation, ribbonlike, foul-smelling bowel movements, abdominal distension, palpable fecal mass, observable peristalsis, malnourishment, and anemia and hypoproteinemia

A complication of Hirschsprung's disease is enterocolitis. The symptoms include explosive, watery stools, fever, and severe prostration. This complication can be life-threatening.

Diagnostics

- Rectal examinations show a lack of stool in the rectal area with stool overflow and a tight anal sphincter.
- Barium enema shows a dilated megacolon and a narrow distal portion in children over 2 months.
- Rectal biopsy demonstrates aganglionic cells.
- Anorectal manometry measures a lack of reflex relaxation.

Therapeutics

The majority of the children affected with Hirschsprung's disease need to have surgical intervention. Very few can be managed with regular enemas and a low-fibre diet.

The surgery is usually very successful and is done in two stages. The bowel is resected, the aganglionic section is removed, and an ostomy is created. When the child has gained weight, a second-stage pull-through surgery eliminates the colostomy. If the bowel is not too distended, the ostomy may not be required. Some children who have a large part of the intestine involved may need a permanent ileostomy.

Following pull-through surgery, the child may have some incontinence or require bowel retraining or anal dilatation.

Nursing Considerations

Neonate: Observe bowel movements and prepare parents for the surgery and colostomy.

Child: Assess bowel history and patterns and observe for clinical manifestations of Hirschsprung's disease.

- If required, provide parental teaching regarding either pharmacy-prepared or correct homemade saline enemas.
- If the child is malnourished, the surgery may be delayed and managed with small, frequent, low-fibre, high-protein, and high-calorie meals; periodic

enemas; and, if severely malnourished, total parenteral nutrition.

- Observe the bowel movement patterns and stool characteristics.
- Administer stool softeners and enemas as prescribed.
- Elevate the head of the bed to decrease discomfort, change the child's position frequently, and assess for respiratory distress due to abdominal distension.
- Preoperatively, prepare the child and the family for the surgery and resulting colostomy.
- If enterocolitis develops, emergency care is required.
- Monitor the child's vital signs for signs of shock, check fluid balance and IV fluid and electrolyte therapy, administer blood derivatives if prescribed, and measure abdominal circumference and mark with a pen for accuracy.
- Assess for signs of bowel perforation: fever, increasing pain, irritability, dyspnea, and cyanosis.
- Postoperatively,

  - Perform NG tube decompression with suction and monitor fluid balance, including NG tube losses and stool from the ostomy.
  - Keep diapers below the suture line to prevent urine contamination.
  - Assess bowel sounds and bowel movements before oral fluids and solids are given.
  - Provide pain control.
  - Monitor wound healing and provide ostomy care.
  - Provide client and family teaching on ostomy care, signs of infection, wound care, monitoring bowel patterns and stool characteristics, signs of bleeding, and referral to home care for follow-up.

CELIAC DISEASE

Celiac disease is a gluten-sensitive enteropathy in which the child has a permanent intolerance to grain gluten and associated proteins. Exposure to gluten causes villous atrophy in the small bowel. The most serious complication can be an increased risk of developing a lymphoma, particularly in the region of the small intestine. Management of diet with restricted intake of gluten will decrease the symptoms and the lymphoma risk. The incidence is one in 3000–4000 people and is more common in women and people of European descent.

Celiac disease is the second most common cause of malabsorption; CF is the first (Dieterich, Esslinger, & Schuppan, 2003).

Pathophysiology

Celiac disease is a genetic immune condition that causes an inability to digest the gliadin part of gluten found in wheat, barley, rye, and oats. As a result, the amino acid glutamine accumulates and is toxic to the intestinal mucosal cells. The resulting villous atrophy leads to malabsorption of nutrients due to decreased absorptive surface area.

Clinical Manifestations

- Symptoms usually appear at the age of 1–5 years, a few months after pasta and beans become part of the solid diet.
- Poor fat absorption causes steatorrhea and very foul-smelling stools.
- Poor absorption of nutrients can cause failure to thrive, weight loss, anemia, and muscle-wasting.
- Chronic diarrhea with abdominal distension, anorexia, vomiting, irritability, and abdominal pain is common.
- A lack of vitamin K due to malabsorption can cause epistaxis, bruising, or melena.
- Celiac crisis can occur episodically with acute, severe, watery diarrhea and vomiting.

Diagnostics

- Duodenal biopsy showing villous atrophy and hyperplasia of the crypts
- Three-day fecal fat stool collection test
- Clinical improvement with removal of gluten from the diet
- Blood tests show antigliadin and antiendomysial immunoglobulin G (IgG) and IgA antibodies when the child is on a gluten diet, and these antibodies disappear when dietary gluten is removed (Murdock & Johnston, 2005).

Therapeutics

A gluten-free diet is necessary for life. In addition, supplemental vitamins, iron, and folate are needed until malnutrition is corrected.

Nursing Considerations

- Provide child and family teaching regarding a gluten-free diet.
- Avoid fibre until the bowel symptoms have improved.
- When the bowel is inflamed, the child may develop lactose intolerance.
- Provide a referral to a dietitian for nutritional counselling.
- For a celiac crisis, an NG tube is inserted for decompression, and IV fluid and electrolyte imbalances are corrected.
- Recognition by the family of early symptoms of celiac crisis is important.

HERNIAS AND HYDROCELES

A hernia occurs when part of the bowel protrudes through an abnormal hole in the abdominal wall. In the pediatric population, it occurs most often at the umbilicus and in the inguinal canal. Hernias can occur in association with other congenital anomalies. Inguinal hernias occur most often in males in a 5 to 1 ratio to girls and account for the majority of all hernias. A hydrocele occurs when abdominal fluid is trapped in the scrotal sac.

Pathophysiology

In an umbilical hernia, the umbilical ring is not completely closed and results in parts of the omentum and intestine protruding through the opening. The opening closes spontaneously by 3–5 years. Surgical intervention is needed if the opening does not close or if the herniated bowel becomes incarcerated.

Inguinal hernias occur because the processus vaginalis does not close between the abdomen and the scrotum (or uterus in females), and a section of the intestine pushes downward. Incarceration results when the lower section becomes trapped in the hernia sac and the blood supply is reduced.

Emergency surgical intervention is required when a hernia is incarcerated. A hernia that is not incarcerated may still require elective surgical intervention.

There are two types of hydrocele. At birth, a noncommunicating hydrocele occurs when some peritoneal fluid is caught in the lower section of the processus vaginalis (the tunica vaginalis) with no communication with the peritoneal space. Normally, the fluid is reabsorbed and disappears in the first few months without any intervention.

A communicating hydrocele is often present with an inguinal hernia due to lack of closure of the opening in the processus vaginalis from the scrotum to the abdominal space. Surgical intervention is undertaken if the fluid is not absorbed by 1 year of age.

Clinical Manifestations

Hernias

- An umbilical hernia manifests as a soft protrusion around the umbilical region and usually can be reduced or decreased by pushing gently with a finger.
- An inguinal hernia is a painless, soft protrusion in the inguinal region that can be reduced and increases with crying, straining, coughing, or standing for long periods.
- An incarcerated hernia manifests with irritability, tenderness, anorexia, abdominal distension, and difficulty having a bowel movement. It can lead to a complete abdominal blockage, and a lack of blood flow can cause gangrene.

Hydroceles

- A noncommunicating hydrocele is a soft protrusion that does not increase with activity and is easily transilluminated.
- A communicating hydrocele is an inguinal protrusion that changes in size depending on the child's position and is not reducable.

Nursing Considerations

- Teach the family to avoid ineffective and potentially harmful home remedies such as taping a hernia.
- Teach early recognition of an incarceration.
- Hernia repair is usually done as day surgery.
- Postsurgery family teaching: Change diapers as soon as they are damp, use an occlusive dressing to protect the incision and decrease the risk of irritation and infection, assess for signs of a wound infection, and administer analgesics as needed.
- Older children should avoid strenuous activity for about three weeks.

CARDIAC SYSTEM DISORDERS

Review of Circulation Changes at Birth

See Figure 10.6 for differences between prenatal and postnatal circulation.

CONGENITAL HEART DEFECTS

The rate of congenital cardiac defects is approximately 5–8 per 1000 live births, and these defects are the second major cause of death—after prematurity—within the first year (Hoffman & Kaplan, 2002). In the majority of cases, the cause of the congenital heart defect (CHD) is unknown. Children with CHD are more likely to have other associated defects, such as tracheoesophageal fistulas, which have occurred simultaneously in the developing fetus. Factors associated with the increased incidence of CHD include the following:

- Fetal and maternal infections in the first three months of gestation, especially rubella
- Chronic maternal illnesses, such as type 1 diabetes
- Exposure to toxins such as maternal use of alcohol or drugs with teratogenic effects
- Having a sibling or parent with CHD
- Chromosomal abnormality such as Down syndrome

CHDs are classified as acyanotic and cyanotic. These terms can be misleading because acyanotic cardiac conditions can also have cyanosis associated with the condition.

ACYANOTIC CARDIAC CONDITIONS

In acyanotic cardiac disorders, there is little or no reduction of blood flow to the lungs; therefore, deoxygenated venous blood does not enter the systemic arterial circulation. Defects that involve the left to right shunting of blood through an abnormal opening include patent ductus arteriosus (PDA), atrial septal defect (ASD), and ventricular septal defect (VSD). Malformations or lesions that obstruct or restrict ventricular outflow, such as aortic valvular stenosis, pulmonic stenosis, and coarctation of the aorta, are also acyanotic defects.

Superior vena cava
Patent ductus arteriosus
Descending aorta
Pulmonary artery
Foramen ovale
Pulmonary vein
RA
LA
A
RV
LV
Ductus venosus
Inferior vena cava
Ligamentum arteriosus
Tricuspid valve
Mitral valve
B
Aortic valve
Ligamentum teres
Pulmonic valve

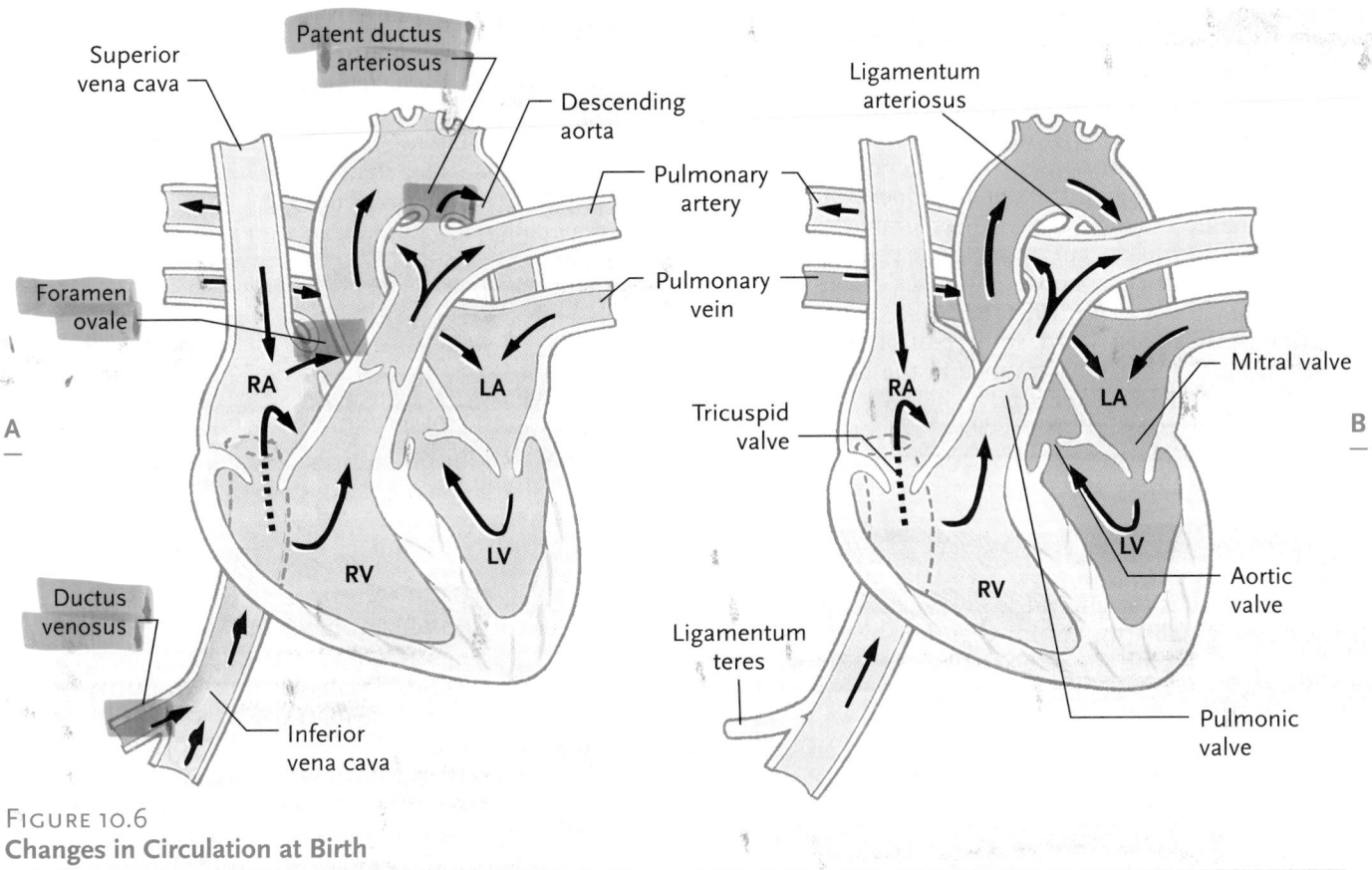

FIGURE 10.6
Changes in Circulation at Birth

A, Prenatal circulation. *B*, Postnatal circulation. Arrows indicate direction of blood flow. Four pulmonary veins enter the **LA**; for simplicity, only two are shown here. *LA*, left atrium; *LV*, left ventricle; *RA*, right atrium; *RV*, right ventricle.

Source: Hockenberry, M. J., & Wilson, D. (2011). *Wong's nursing care of infants and children* (9th ed., p. 1342, Figure 34-2). St. Louis: Mosby.

Pathophysiology and Clinical Manifestations

Patent Ductus Arteriosus Defect

PDA occurs when the ductus arteriosus remains open, instead of closing, at about 3–4 days after birth. As a result, blood flows from the aorta through the PDA and back to the pulmonary artery and lungs. It usually affects premature infants but is seen in 5–10% of all cardiac anomalies and is more frequent in females.

Clinical Manifestations

- Children with a small defect may be asymptomatic.
- A loud, machinelike murmur is common.
- The child may have frequent respiratory infections. The child may develop congestive heart failure (CHF) with tachypnea, failure to thrive, poor feeding, hepatosplenomegaly, and irritability.

Atrial Septal Defect

ASD occurs when atrial septal tissue does not fuse properly during fetal development, creating an abnormal opening. The pressure of blood within the heart is normally higher in the left atrium than in the right; therefore, blood shunts from the left to the right side of the heart through the abnormal opening. The right ventricle and pulmonary artery dilate because of the increased workload of more blood.

Clinical Manifestations

- Many infants are aymptomatic until early childhood, and up to 40% of defects close spontaneously by early school age.
- Symptoms vary depending on the size of the ASD.
- The usual symptoms are dyspnea and fatigue on exertion.
- Slow weight gain is also a common symptom.
- The child may have frequent respiratory infections.
- A characteristic systolic murmur is usually heard at the second intercostal space.

Ventricular Septal Defect

VSD is an abnormal opening in the ventricular septum that can vary from very tiny to a large defect, such as a missing septum. The higher pressure in the left ventricle causes the blood to flow through the abnormal opening to the right ventricle, leading to an increase in pulmonary vascular resistance and right heart enlargement.

- 20–25% of total cardiac anomalies are VSDs, making it the most common defect.

Clinical Manifestations

- Manifestations vary depending on the size of the VSD, the child's age, and the amount of resistance.
- The child is usually asymptomatic.
- Failure to thrive
- Excessive diaphoresis and fatigue
- May have increased respiratory infections
- May have signs and symptoms of CHF

Aortic Valvular Stenosis Defect

A narrowing of the aortic valve causes an obstruction to the flow of blood from the left ventricle into the aorta. The long-term result is a left ventricular hypertrophy. Restricted and poor blood flow to the myocardium can develop because the oxygen need of the hypertrophied left ventricle is not met.

Clinical Manifestations

- In infants with a severe defect, practitioners would expect to see decreased cardiac output, faint pulse, hypotension, tachycardia, and poor feeding.
- Older children may present with exercise intolerance, chest pain, and dizziness when standing for a long time.
- A characteristic systolic ejection murmur is heard at the second intercostal space.

Pulmonic Stenosis

Pulmonic stenosis is a narrowing at the entrance of the pulmonary artery from the right ventricle. The obstruction to blood flow increases right ventricular pressure. Over a period of time, right ventricular hypertrophy failure may result. Pulmonic stenosis occurs in 5–8% of all cardiac lesions, and many children have other associated cardiac anomalies.

Clinical Manifestations

- The child may be asymptomatic or have a mild cyanosis and signs of CHF.
- Characteristic systolic murmur may be heard over the pulmonic area, and a thrill may be felt if stenosis is severe.
- In a child with a severe defect, there is decreased exercise tolerance, dyspnea, pain in the precordial region, and generalized cyanosis.

Coarctation of the Aorta

Coarctation of the aorta (COA) is a narrowing of the aorta. The three types of COA depend on the location of the narrowing:

1. Preductal: Located proximal to the insertion of the ductus arteriosus
2. Postductal: Located distal to the ductus arteriosus
3. Juxtaductal: Located at the insertion of the ductus arteriosus

There is an increase in pressure proximal to the defect and a decrease in pressure distal to it. The narrowed aorta restricts the blood flow, causing an increase in left ventricular pressure, dilation of the proximal aorta, left ventricular hypertrophy, and possibly failure. Over a period of time, collateral blood vessels bypass the coarcted area and supply improved blood flow to the lower part of the body. COA occurs more often in males and makes up about 8% of cardiac anomalies.

Clinical Manifestations

- Child may be asymptomatic
- May have a marked difference in blood pressure and pulse quality between the upper and lower extremities. The upper extremity pulses are bounding with high blood pressure, and femoral pulses are weak or absent.
- May include epistaxis, headaches, fainting, and lower leg muscle cramps
- Risk of a stroke, aneurysm, and ruptured aorta
- A characteristic systolic murmur may be heard over the left anterior precordium and between the scapula posteriorly.

Diagnostics for Acyanotic Heart Defects

- Chest X-rays may show cardiac enlargement.
- Electrocardiograms (ECGs) may show an enlargement of the atria and ventricles, unclosed ductus arteriosus, size of shunts, and degrees of obstruction.
- Echocardiography can accurately detect specific cardiac conditions and may help the child avoid having to have a cardiac catheterization.
- Cardiac catheterization identifies defects and measures pressure variations.

Therapeutics

PDA

- This condition is managed either conservatively or surgically and has a risk of less than 1% mortality.
- Medical management includes administration of prostaglandin–synthetase inhibitors, such as indomethacin, to stimulate closure of the open ductus.
- In clients with uncomplicated PDAs, nonsurgical management involves placing coils via cardiac catheterization to block the PDA.

- Surgical management involves ligating or dividing the PDA via a thoracotomy or clipping the PDA via video-assisted thoracoscopic surgery.
- Surgery is performed at age 1 to 2 years, or in infancy if CHF is present.

ASD

- This condition is managed either surgically or nonsurgically, with less than 1% mortality.
- Nonsurgical treatment includes the placement via cardiac catheterization of a septal occluder for more centred and smaller defects.
- Surgical treatment includes the placement of a pericardial or Dacron patch, which requires a cardiopulmonary bypass and is usually done before school age.

VSD

- This condition is managed surgically or nonsurgically, with less than 2% mortality in uncomplicated VSDs.
- Nonsurgical treatment is currently being investigated, using closure devices via cardiac catheterizations.
- Surgical treatment includes suturing small defects or placing a Dacron patch via cardiopulmonary bypass if the defect is larger.
- Palliative care, used only in children with complex cardiac anomalies, involves banding the pulmonary artery to decrease pulmonary blood flow.

Pulmonary Stenosis

- This condition is managed surgically or nonsurgically and carries a mortality rate of less than 1%—slightly higher rate in neonates.
- The most common nonsurgical treatment is balloon angioplasty via cardiac catheterization. The balloon catheter is inserted into the narrowed valve, and the balloon is blown up and pulled back through the valve. The procedure dilates the pulmonary valve and improves blood flow.
- Surgical treatment consists of a pulmonary valvotomy, in which the valve is reconstructed via cardiopulmonary bypass.

COA

- This condition is managed surgically or nonsurgically, with less than 5% mortality.
- Nonsurgical treatment, usually used in older children, is the balloon procedure to dilate the narrowed portion of the aorta.
- Surgical treatment is used in infants of less than 6 months and in older children with a complex cardiac defect. The narrowed part of the aorta is removed, and the ends are reconnected. The alternative is to dilate the aorta using a prosthetic graft or a graft from a subclavian artery.

Nursing Considerations

Management of Hypoxia

- Assess for signs of tachypnea, cyanosis, bradycardia, tachycardia, restlessness, cyanosis, grunting, nasal flaring, cough, and syncope:
  - Place the child in a knee–chest position.
  - Administer oxygen as prescribed.
  - Administer medication as prescribed.

Management of Nutrition

- Good nutrition, especially an iron-rich diet, is needed in these clients for normal growth patterns and electrolyte balance and to prevent anemia and infections.
- Provide a balanced diet rich in iron and potassium and low in sodium.
- Give small frequent meals if the child tires easily.
- The duration of breast- or bottle-feedings may need to be limited, or it may be necessary to feed the child more often for shorter periods to avoid fatigue.
- Evaluate weight gain daily.
- Decrease the child's oxygen needs by organizing care around periods of rest, preventing crying, and providing quiet activities for the older child.
- Assess for signs of CHF.
- Observe for signs of bacterial endocarditis: fever, pallor, petechiae, anorexia, and fatigue.
- Antibiotics may be prescribed prior to dental work or before surgery or suturing repair.
- Observe for manifestations of thrombosis, including irritability, restlessness, seizure activity, coma, paralysis, edema, hematuria, oliguria, and anuria.
- To decrease the risk of thrombosis, keep the child well hydrated.
- Institute infection control measures.
- If the child is on potassium-losing diuretics, provide a high-potassium diet and administer potassium supplements when prescribed.
- Prevent anemia by supplying an iron-rich diet and iron supplements as prescribed.
- Encourage the child's self-esteem through self-care activities.
- Encourage activities within the child's exercise tolerance.
- Provide client and family education regarding hypoxic episodes, weight gain, exercise tolerance, avoiding infections, and medication management.
- Provide referrals to home care agencies, support groups, and follow-up care.

CYANOTIC CARDIAC CONDITIONS

Cyanotic cardiac conditions are heart defects in which deoxygenated blood enters the systemic arterial circulation. Cyanotic heart defects include tetralogy of Fallot, transposition of the great vessels, truncus arteriosus, and hypoplastic left heart syndrome. In each of these defects, cyanosis is caused by the right to left shunting of blood through abnormal cardiac openings, resulting in a mixing of oxygenated and deoxygenated blood. Most cyanotic conditions require complex surgery.

Pathophysiology, Clinical Manifestations, and Therapeutics

Tetralogy of Fallot

Tetralogy of Fallot is the most common cyanotic heart defect, consisting of four major abnormalities: VSD, right ventricular hypertrophy, pulmonic stenosis, and aorta overriding VSD. The combination of these defects results in the aorta receiving blood from both the right and left ventricles.

Clinical Manifestations and Therapeutics

- Manifestations depend on the size of the VSD and the degree of pulmonic stenosis.
- Some infants are cyanotic at birth; others gradually develop cyanosis over the first year, with an increase in the degree of pulmonic stenosis.
- It is common for infants to have cyanotic spells or "Tet spells," in which there is an acute cyanotic episode, especially during feeding or crying. These episodes can lead to a transient cerebral ischemia.
- After a cyanotic spell, there is a risk of emboli, seizures, and loss of consciousness.
- In older children, squatting is an adaption that decreases the return of venous blood from the lower parts of the body, increases systemic vascular resistance, and increases pulmonary blood flow.
- Failure to thrive
- Clubbing of the fingers, exertional dyspnea, fainting, or slowness due to hypoxia
- Characteristic pansystolic murmur heard at the mid–lower left sternal border
- The only treatment is surgery, either complete or palliative, if complete surgery cannot be done.
- A Blalock–Taussig shunt is inserted, which provides blood flow to the pulmonary arteries from the left or right subclavian artery via a tube graft. The shunt has the potential to distort the pulmonary artery.
- Complete repair is usually done during the first year, when there is an increasing level of cyanosis and Tet spells. A cardiopulmonary bypass and sternal entry are used. Improved techniques have reduced surgical mortality to less than 3%.

Transposition of the Great Vessels

The pulmonary artery and aorta exit abnormally from the opposite ventricle. This abnormality leads to two separate circulatory patterns, in which the right heart manages systemic circulation and the left heart manages pulmonary circulation. To survive, the child must have an associated defect that allows oxygenated and deoxygenated blood to mix in the heart chambers. These infants are often referred to as "blue babies." There are many serious potential complications, including CHF, endocarditis, brain abscess, and cerebrovascular accident resulting from hypoxia or thrombosis.

Clinical Manifestations and Therapeutics

- Varying degrees of cyanosis are seen, depending on the size of the associated defect.
- Cardiomegaly occurs within the first few weeks of birth.
- Severe cyanosis at birth
- In a child with associated defects, there is less cyanosis, but the child has CHF symptoms.
- Failure to thrive
- No murmur is evident, or there is a murmur characteristic of an associated defect.
- This condition requires surgical intervention.
- Initial treatment is to provide mixing of oxygenated and deoxygenated blood.
- The administration of prostaglandin E keeps the ductus arteriosus open.
- A balloon atrial-septostomy may be performed to enlarge the ASD in order to increase the mixing of oxygenated and deoxygenated blood.
- Surgical intervention in the first few weeks of life involves performing an arterial switch, which re-establishes normal circulation, with the left ventricle acting as the systemic pump.
- Mortality is less than 2%.
- Long-term problems include suprapulmonic stenosis and aortic dilation and regurgitation.

Truncus Arteriosus

This is a defect of a single blood vessel instead of a separate pulmonary artery and aorta. Newborns with this abnormality may initially appear normal, but as pulmonary vascular resistance decreases after birth, severe pulmonary edema and CHF usually develop.

Clinical Manifestations and Therapeutics

- Significant cyanosis, particularly when active
- Clinical manifestations of CHF
- Left ventricular hypertrophy, dyspnea, significant exercise intolerance, and failure to thrive
- Characteristic loud systolic murmur best heard at lower left sternal border and radiating throughout the chest
- Treatment is performed in the first month of life.
- The condition requires a complex surgery that involves closing the VSD and forming conduits to establish continuity between the right ventricle and pulmonary artery.

- Postoperative complications include persistent CHF, bleeding, pulmonary artery hypertension, dysrhythmias, and residual VSD.
- Mortality is higher than 10%.
- Conduits do not grow with the child and may require one or more replacements.

Hypoplastic Left Heart Syndrome

Hypoplastic left heart syndrome involves a variety of abnormalities, including an underdeveloped or hypoplastic left ventricle, aortic valve, mitral valve, and ascending aorta. In order for the child to survive, the ductus arteriosus must remain open. When the ductus closes, low cardiac output leads to hypoxia and inevitable death.

Clinical Manifestations and Therapeutics

- This condition is usually evident by 2 weeks of age.
- Mild cyanosis and CHF become more severe with closure of the ductus.
- Signs and symptoms of CHF
- Single S_2 heart sound
- Characteristic soft ejection murmur is present.
- Neonates require inotropes and stabilization with mechanical ventilation.
- Prostaglandin E is administered to maintain ductal patency and ensure adequate systemic blood flow.
- Complex two-stage surgical interventions are needed for the infant to survive.
- Prognosis for the first-stage operation varies widely, but survival rates have improved over the past 10 years.
- If surgeries are unsuccessful, or if the defect is profound, heart transplantation may be the only option.

CONGESTIVE HEART FAILURE

CHF results from an inability of the heart to produce enough cardiac output to meet the body's oxygen and metabolic needs. There is a decrease in myocardial contractibility, or the cardiac output is not sufficient to meet the needs of pathological conditions that require a higher cardiac output.

Pathophysiology

CHF is caused by volume or pressure overload, decreased contractility, or a need for high cardiac output. There are two types of CHF, right- and left-sided. Right ventricular failure occurs when the right ventricle is unable to pump effectively, causing pooling of systemic venous circulation and edema of the extremities. Cor pulmonale is the term for CHF resulting from obstructive lung diseases such as CF or bronchopulmonary dysplasia. Left ventricular failure occurs because the left ventricle is unable to pump blood effectively into the systemic circulation. This leads to lung congestion, increased pulmonary pressure, and pulmonary edema.

Causes of CHF

The primary cause in the first 3 years of age is CHD. Other causes include the following:

- Cardiomyopathies, arrhythmias, and hypertension
- Pulmonary embolism or chronic lung disease
- Severe hemorrhage or anemia
- Adverse effects of an anaesthetic or surgery, transfusions or infusions, or drugs such as doxorubicin
- Increased body demands resulting from conditions such as fever or infection
- Severe physical or emotional stress
- Excessive sodium intake

Clinical Manifestations

- It may be difficult to distinguish right- from left-sided ventricular failure because when one side of the heart is failing, it causes an impact on the other side.
- Weakness, fatigue
- Poor feeding, ascites, weight loss or weight gain from edema, and pleural effusions
- Irritability
- Pallor, cyanosis, and diaphoresis
- Dyspnea, tachypnea, orthopnea, wheezing, cough, weak cry, and grunting
- Tachycardia, cardiomegaly, and gallop rhythm
- Hepatomegaly and abdominal pain or distension
- Distended jugular, neck, and peripheral veins and edema

Diagnostics

- Chest radiology shows an enlarged heart and increased pulmonary vascular markings due to increased pulmonary blood flow.
- Blood values display dilution hyponatremia, hypochloremia, and hyperkalemia.
- Ventricular hypertrophy appears on an ECG.
- Echocardiology detects the cause of CHF, such as a specific CHD.

Therapeutics

The aim of the therapeutic management program for a child with CHF is to manage the CHF and stabilize the condition until the underlying cause can be treated.

- Angiotensin-converting enzyme (ACE) inhibitors reduce the afterload on the heart, making it easier for the heart to pump.
- Digoxin (Lanoxin) administered in an elixir or parenterally is the primary drug to improve myocardial contractility.

- Doses of digoxin must be exact and must be individually regulated for each client.

Nursing Considerations

- Monitor for signs of respiratory distress, suction as needed, administer oxygen as prescribed, keep the head of the bed elevated, and monitor arterial or capillary blood gas values.
- Monitor for signs of altered cardiac output, pulmonary edema, arrhythmias, including extreme tachycardia and bradycardia, and characteristic ECG and heart sound changes.
- Evaluate fluid balance by intake and output measurements, monitoring daily weights, assessing for edema and severe diaphoresis, and monitoring electrolyte and hematocrit levels, as well as maintaining fluid restrictions as prescribed.
- Prevent infections by using hand hygiene and keeping the child away from individuals with infections.
- Reduce cardiac demands by keeping the child warm, scheduling nursing interventions around rest periods, restricting infant feeding to less than 45 minutes at a time, and providing gavage feeding if the infant is fatigued or needs supplemental feeding.
- Help ensure adequate nutrition by feeding the child small, frequent, high-calorie, low-sodium meals as prescribed.
- Help decrease anxiety by providing developmentally appropriate explanations and encouraging parental involvement in the child's care as appropriate.
- Administer medications as prescribed: digoxin to increase cardiac performance; diuretics such as furosemide, hydrochlorothiazide, and spironolactone to reduce venous and systemic congestion; and iron and folic acid supplements to improve nutritional status.
- Monitor for digitalis toxicity: extreme bradycardia and increased serum levels are cardinal signs of toxicity; withhold digoxin if the child's heart rate falls below the normal range for his or her age.
- Provide referrals to follow-up community services as needed.
- Offer client and family teaching for signs and symptoms of CHF, nutrition and fluid restrictions, and the dosage, administration, and side effects of prescribed medications.

HEMATOLOGICAL AND IMMUNOLOGICAL SYSTEM DISORDERS

IRON DEFICIENCY ANEMIA

Iron deficiency anemia (IDA) is one of the most common nutritional disorders. IDA is most often caused by an insufficient quantity of iron in the diet, poor absorption of iron, or a significant loss of blood.

Premature infants, children between the ages of 6 months and 3 years, and adolescents are most at risk. Infants fed cow's milk can develop intestinal irritation and lose blood through the stools.

Pathophysiology

- IDA is caused by an insufficient supply of iron that is required for normal red blood cell (RBC) formation.
- Lack of iron leads to smaller cells, a reduced RBC mass (microcytic), a decreased hemoglobin concentration, and decreased oxygen-carrying capacity of the blood.
- Over time, the depleted RBC mass leads to a decreased hemoglobin concentration and reduces blood capacity.

Clinical Manifestations

- The child may be asymptomatic.
- Pallor, irritability, fatigue
- Pica or eating nonfood items
- Tachycardia and systolic heart murmur
- Headaches and dizziness
- Muscle weakness and delayed growth
- Developmental delay may occur.
- Nail deformities

Diagnostics

Diagnostic blood tests include the following:

- CBC: RBC is normal or slightly decreased; hemoglobin and hematocrit are low; mean corpuscular volume (MCV) is decreased (microcytic); and mean corpuscular hemoglobin (MCH) is decreased (hypochromic).
- Erythrocyte protoporphyrin (EP) is greater than 35 micrograms per decilitre.
- Low serum iron capacity
- Elevated total iron binding capacity

Therapeutics

- Treat the underlying etiology, if it can be corrected.
- Ensure adequate nutritional intake of iron; boost iron intake via breast milk, iron-fortified formula, and cereal.
- Provide oral supplements of elemental iron to create iron stores. Ferrous iron is usually used because it is absorbed easily. Iron has side effects of nausea, GI irritation, anorexia, diarrhea, and constipation.
- Parenteral iron, administered intravenously or intramuscularly, is reserved only for children who do not respond to oral supplements and iron-rich diets as it is painful and expensive.
- Reticulocyte count is done after about 10 days to evaluate the effectiveness of the therapy.
- Blood transfusions are administered only to children with severe anemia.
- Supplemental oxygen is administered if the tissue hypoxia is severe.
- Some children have vitamin B_{12} deficiency and require intramuscular B_{12} injections.

Nursing Considerations

- Encourage sufficient intake of iron-rich foods, including iron-fortified formula and cereals, lean meat, fish, leafy dark green vegetables, beans, and whole-grain breads.
- Discourage milk as the predominant food source when the child is on solid food.
- Administer intramuscular injections of iron, using the Z-track method.

Child and family teaching regarding iron:

- Administer an oral iron supplement by giving it in two to three divided doses in a small amount of vitamin C–containing liquid (such as orange juice) before meals to enhance absorption and minimize side effects.
- Administer iron with a dropper to an infant or through a straw to an older child to minimize staining of the teeth.
- Brush the child's teeth after administration to minimize teeth staining.
- Explain the side effects of nausea and vomiting, diarrhea or constipation, and dark green or black stools.
- Ensure safety precautions as iron is very toxic.

SICKLE CELL ANEMIA

Sickle cell anemia (SCA) is an inherited autosomal recessive disorder and a chronic, serious, hemolytic disorder found predominantly in Canadians of African descent. With each pregnancy, there is a 25% chance of the child having sickle cell disease when both parents carry the trait. The sickle cell trait is not usually symptomatic, unless there is an extreme or prolonged lower level of oxygen. SCA may lead to significant long-term complications. The major cause of death in children under 5 with SCA is bacterial sepsis. SCA is the most common of the group of sickle cell diseases in which hemoglobin S is a factor. Sickle cell C disease (HgbSC), the second most common SCA, is a variant of sickle cell disease in which both hemoglobin S (HgbS) and hemoglobin C (HgbC) are present.

Pathophysiology

Low oxygen and pH in the blood trigger HgbS to transform RBCs into a sickle (crescent) shape. Because of the sickle shape, the cells tend to clump, creating thrombosis, blockage of arteries, thickening of the blood, early breakdown of the cell, tissue anoxia, and necrosis. Acute and eventually chronic changes occur as the sickling progresses. Sickle cell crisis may be precipitated by infection, dehydration, fever, cold exposure, hypoxia, strenuous exercise, extreme fatigue, or extreme changes in altitude.

Clinical Manifestations

- Enlarged spleen because of clogging from sickled cells
- Enlarged liver, which causes pain due to poor blood flow
- Hematuria, inability to concentrate urine, enuresis, and occasionally nephritic syndrome, bone weakness, and

dactylitis (symmetrical swelling of the hands and feet)
- Pain, often severe, especially during a vaso-occlusive crisis

Complications include the following:

- Stroke
- Myocardial infarction (MI)
- Poor growth, delayed sexual maturation, decreased fertility, priapism
- Recurrent severe infections
- Splenic sequestration: a life-threatening condition in which the spleen collects a large amount of blood, causing a severe drop in blood volume and resultant shock. Symptoms include paleness, abdominal distension, pain and irritability, low blood pressure, and increased heart rate. Treatments are transfusions and splenectomy (Hockenberry & Wilson, 2011).

See Figure 10.7 for differences between normal RBCs and sickled RBCs and their potential impact on the child with SCA.

Diagnostics

Blood tests:

- The Sickledex screening blood test can identify if HgbS is present; however, hemoglobin electrophoresis is needed to differentiate between sickle cell trait and SCA.

Therapeutics

- Treatment varies depending on the specific complications for individual children.
- Standard immunizations for pneumococcal *H. influenzae* type b and meningococcal vaccine should be given.
- Prophylactic penicillin may be prescribed for the first five years to prevent life-threatening sepsis.
- Hydroxyurea decreases recurrent severe painful episodes by increasing the level of HgbF. This may reduce long-term complications and potentially reduce strokes (Gulbis, Haberman, DuFour, et al., 2005).
- During vaso-occlusive crises,

  - Ensuring good hydration levels by administering IV and oral fluid to increase the blood fluid volume will help prevent sickling and, potentially, blood clots.
  - Electrolyte replacement is used to offset the acidosis caused by hypoxia, which can increase sickling.
  - Oxygen therapy is used to offset hypoxia.
  - Blood transfusions decrease the viscosity of the blood and treat anemia.
  - Morphine is administered for pain control, often via PCA, which may be used in children as young as 5 years.
  - Acetaminophen and codeine-containing compounds are administered for mild pain.

A
B
Infarction
Pneumonia
Chest syndrome
Pulmonary hypertension
Atelectasis
Congestive heart failure
Hemolysis
Anemia
CVA (stroke)
Paralysis
Death
Retinopathy
Blindness
Hemorrhage
Avascular necrosis (shoulder)
Hepatomegaly
Gallstones
Splenomegaly
Splenic sequestration
Autosplenectomy
Hematuria
Hyposthenuria (dilute urine)
Avascular necrosis (hip)
Abdominal pain
Dactylitis (hand–foot syndrome)
Priapism
Pain
Osteomyelitis
Chronic ulcers (rare in children)
G. J. Wassilchenko

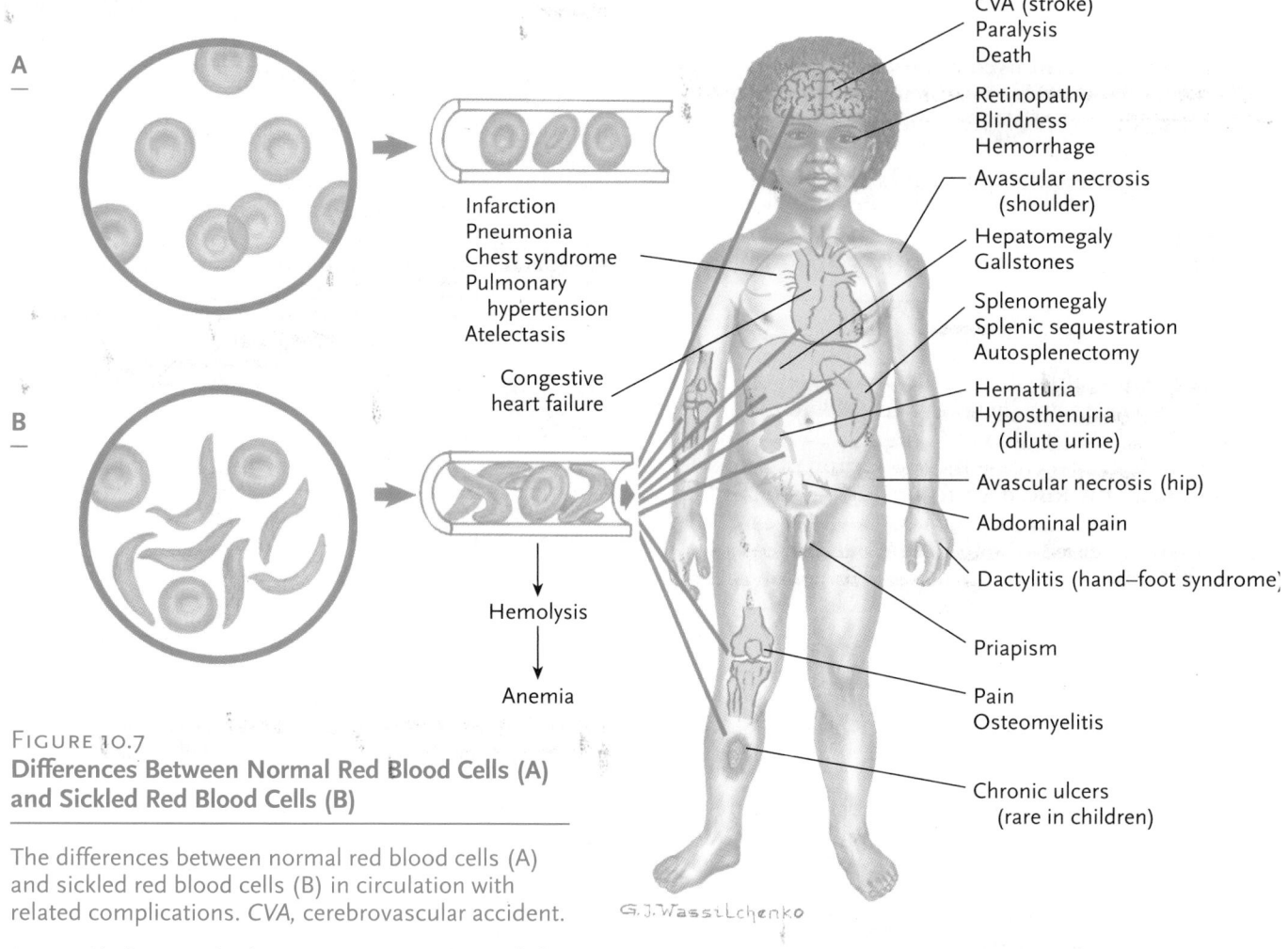

FIGURE 10.7
Differences Between Normal Red Blood Cells (A) and Sickled Red Blood Cells (B)

The differences between normal red blood cells (A) and sickled red blood cells (B) in circulation with related complications. *CVA*, cerebrovascular accident.

Source: Hockenberry, M. J., & Wilson, D. (2011). *Wong's nursing care of infants and children* (9th ed., p. 1428, Figure 35-4). St. Louis: Mosby.

Nursing Considerations

- Monitor vital signs when the child is at rest and when active, particularly when there is reduced tissue perfusion.
- Assess for signs of CHF.
- Monitor height, weight, and developmental status; growth can be delayed in children with SCA due to profound anemia.
- Carefully assess skin colour and mucous membranes, particularly in children with darker skin tones.
- Encourage bed rest or reduced activities as necessary to conserve energy and avoid overexertion to promote tissue oxygenation. Passive exercises promote circulation and ROM.
- Help the child develop coping strategies when under emotional stress and to increase oxygen perfusion.
- Perform pain assessment and management, with a PCA pump, if possible.
- Use pain control techniques such as heat to affected areas, relaxation, and meditation, as well as placing the child in the most comfortable position.
- Administer prescribed analgesics around the clock.
- Monitor for signs of dehydration and electrolyte imbalance and ensure adequate hydration by encouraging oral fluid intake or administering IV fluids; maintain strict intake and output and daily weight records.
- Provide a nutritionally balanced diet.
- Help the child avoid known sources of infection.
- Monitor for signs of infection and administer antibiotics as prescribed.
- Provide emotional support to the child and family, particularly in relation to issues around anger, self-esteem, positive body image, and the effects of chronic pain.
- Child and family teaching: Explain the disease process, genetic aspects, and early signs and symptoms of sickling crises and discuss home management measures for a mild crisis; how to avoid factors known to precipitate crises; the recognition of early signs of infection; the importance of regular health, dental, and eye examinations; and maintaining as normal a lifestyle as possible.
- Provide referrals for possible genetic counselling.

THALASSEMIA

Thalassemia is the term used to describe genetic blood disorders characterized by insufficient synthesis of specific globulin chains of the hemoglobin molecule. The most common thalassemia is beta-thalassemia. The most serious form is thalassemia major (beta-thalassemia, or Cooley's anemia) and usually is seen in children of Mediterranean descent, particularly those of Italian, Greek, or Asian backgrounds.

Pathophysiology

- In thalassemia, a problem in the production of specific globin chains (beta) in hemoglobin ultimately results in the destruction of RBCs.
- The body tries to increase the production of RBCs to cope with the RBC destruction, but these cells are immature and break down quickly. The excess iron that is released when the RBCs disintegrate is stored in different organs, causing a condition called hemosiderosis.

Clinical Manifestations

- Thalassemia minor usually creates mild to moderate anemia that may be asymptomatic and often goes undetected.
- Thalassemia major produces clinical manifestations around the age of 6 months, when the protective effect of the fetal hemoglobin diminishes.

The signs of thalassemia are listed below (Hockenberry & Wilson, 2011):

- Early signs include pallor, anemia, unxplained fever, poor feeding, poor weight gain, and an enlarged spleen or liver.
- Later signs include chronic hypoxia; headache; bone and precordium pain; decreased exercise tolerance; damage to the liver, spleen, heart, pancreas, and lymph glands from hemochromatosis, the excess storage of iron, which results in cellular damage in these organs; slight jaundice or a bronze skin colour; thick cranial bones with prominent cheeks and a flat nose; and growth retardation and delayed sexual development.
- Long-term complications result from hemochromatosis: splenomegaly, usually requiring splenectomy; skeletal complications, such as thickened cranial bones and an enlarged head; prominent facial bones, malocclusion of the teeth, and susceptibility to spontaneous fractures; cardiac complications, such as arrhythmias, pericarditis, CHF, and fibrosis of cardiac muscle fibres; gallbladder disease; cirrhosis; jaundice and brown pigmentation due to iron deposits; growth retardation; and endocrine complications, such as delayed sexual maturation and diabetes.

Diagnostics

- CBC shows abnormalities in hemoglobin and RBCs: decreased hemoglobin, hematocrit, and reticulocyte counts.
- Hemoglobin electrophoresis shows that HgbA and HgbF values are increased, confirming the type and severity of the hemoglobin variants.
- Increase in RBC precursors in bone marrow
- Folic acid insufficiency
- Prenatal screening by chorionic villus sampling or fetal blood cell analysis

Therapeutics

- Supportive therapy with transfusions to maintain sufficient hemoglobin levels, with the goal of preventing tissue hypoxia and promoting normal growth and development, more physical activity, decreased cardiomegaly and hepatosplenomegaly, and fewer bony changes and infections (Hockenberry & Wilson, 2011).
- Desferoxamine (Desferal), an iron chelator, is administered with transfusions to minimize hemosiderosis (excess iron in tissues).
- Home chelation therapy with desferoxamine is done 5–7 days a week via an IV infusion pump, usually during the night.
- Splenectomy may be necessary to decrease abdominal pressure from the enlarged spleen and increase the lifespan of RBCs.
- Amniocentesis sampling of fetal blood cells can diagnose thalassemia.
- Bone marrow transplantation (BMT) has been used with some success.

Nursing Considerations

- Administer blood transfusions and observe for complications of transfusions, which can lead to an overload of iron.
- Monitor for iron toxicity related to blood transfusions: abdominal pain, vomiting, bloody diarrhea, decreased level of consciousness, shock, and metabolic acidosis.
- Administer chelation therapy and monitor vital signs, observing for hypotension or allergic reaction; visual acuity (ocular toxic) and hearing (ototoxic); intake and output; and colour of urine (may turn red).
- Provide information regarding splenectomy, if applicable.
- Administer folic acid as prescribed.
- Monitor for signs of infection and avoid sources of infection.
- Encourage the child to be careful with physical activities and to avoid situations of risk in order to prevent fractures.
- Promote adequate rest and good nutrition.
- Help minimize dietary iron ingestion as much as possible.
- Assess for signs and symptoms of hepatitis and iron surplus.
- Support and educate the child and family as to coping strategies and how to deal with a chronic illness and treatment protocols.

- Refer to family support groups as appropriate.
- Provide instructions for home chelation therapy (Hockenberry & Wilson, 2011).

HEMOPHILIA

Hemophilia is a group of hereditary bleeding disorders in which there is a deficiency in a blood clotting factor. The most common types of hemophilia are factor VIII deficiency (classic hemophilia, hemophilia A) and factor IX deficiency (Christmas disease, hemophilia B). Eighty percent of hemophiliacs have factor VIII deficiency. Hemophilia is mainly an X-linked recessive disorder transmitted by females or caused by a gene mutation. The occurrence is about one in 5000 males.

Pathophysiology

Hemophilia is classified as mild, moderate, or severe, depending on the degree of coagulation involved.

- In hemophilia A, there is a defect in the clotting function, although the factor VIII molecule is present.
- In hemophilia B, there is an impaired ability to form a fibrin clot caused by a defect or deficiency of factor IX (Hockenberry & Wilson, 2011).

Clinical Manifestations

- Hemophilia is initially suspected in the case of a newborn with excessive bleeding from the umbilical cord or after circumcision.
- The manifestations of hemophilia include the following:

  - Bruising easily and prolonged bleeding from wounds
  - Nosebleeds
  - Spontaneous hematuria
  - Hemarthrosis (hemorrhages in the joints causing pain, swelling, and decreased ROM), which can be crippling

- Complications include the following:

  - Airway obstruction can occur due to bleeding into the neck, mouth, or thorax.
  - Bone changes, osteoporosis, and muscle atrophy from hemarthrosis
  - Intracranial bleeding is a very serious potential complication that can lead to death.
  - GI hemorrhage can lead to intestinal obstruction.
  - Bleeding into the spinal cord can result in paralysis (Hockenberry & Wilson, 2011).

Diagnostics

- The platelet count and bleeding time may be normal.
- Tests that evaluate clotting factor function, such as prothrombin time (PT), partial thromboplastin time (PTT), and whole blood clotting time, may be normal.
- Factor VII or IX level may be low.
- Prenatal diagnosis is done through amniocentesis and carrier identification.

Therapeutics

- Factor VIII concentrates acquired through genetic engineering or pooled plasma are used to replace the missing clotting factors. Home factor VIII treatments are taught to families and clients when children are old enough to perform self-administration.
- Corticosteroids are used to reduce joint inflammation and control hematuria.
- Anti-inflammatory drugs such as ibuprofen can be used for chronic synovitis but must be administered carefully because they inhibit platelets.
- Acetaminophen—with or without codeine—can be given for pain.
- Early intervention with home factor treatments is helping to prevent the severe joint damage from hemarthrosis that has occurred in the past. Exercise programs and physical therapy have also contributed to joint health.

Nursing Considerations

- Being vigilant for acute or chronic bleeding is very important, particularly for signs of internal bleeding, such as hypovolemia and black, tarry stools, and signs of cranial hemorrage, such as headache, slurred speech, vomiting, blurred vision, and decreased level of consciousness.
- Assessing for changes in neurological status is also important: vision, hearing, and neurological development.
- If there is bleeding into a joint from an injury, factor treatment and the RICE protocol (rest, ice, compression, and elevation) should be initiated immediately, followed by ROM exercises after the acute phase is over in order to prevent stressing and overstretching of the joint.
- Monitor for side effects of therapy.
- Implement a physical therapy program to help prevent joint dysfunction and injury.
- Encourage normal activities and noncontact sports.
- Support the child's self-esteem and positive self-image.
- Child and family teaching should include home factor administration and information on support groups such as the Hemophilia Foundation.
- Maintain good oral hygiene and avoid vigorous tooth-brushing, which might cause gums to bleed. Recommend that clients clean their teeth by wetting a very soft toothbrush or using a sponge-tipped swab or water irrigation device.

IDIOPATHIC THROMBOCYTOPENIC PURPURA

Idiopathic thrombocytopenic purpura (ITP) is an acquired hemorrhagic disorder in which the number of circulating platelets is reduced through the destruction of platelets (thrombocytopenia), there is purpura or bruising from petechiae, and the bone marrow, though normal, features an unusual number of large, young platelet cells. ITP occurs most frequently between the ages of 2 and 10 but may occur at any age. The etiology is unknown, but it is likely an autoimmune reaction and often occurs after an upper respiratory infection, measles, or chickenpox. The child usually recovers completely within six months. ITP can be either an acute illness, lasting six months or less (80%), or it can become a chronic illness that lasts longer than six months (20%) (Hockenberry & Wilson, 2011).

Pathophysiology

The number of circulating platelets is reduced as a result of the action of an antiplatelet antibody that is produced in the spleen. This results in bleeding into the tissues (purpura). It is self-limiting.

Clinical Manifestations

- The child bruises easily, with petechiae, hematomas, and blood in the mucous membranes, stool, or urine.
- The child does not look sick.

Diagnostics

- Platelet count drops below 20,000/mm³.
- Blood tests that depend on platelet function, such as bleeding time, as well as clot retraction and tourniquet tests, are not normal.
- Bone marrow aspiration needs to be done to rule out other conditions that cause low platelets, such as leukemia and lupus.

Therapeutics

- Treatment is supportive as ITP is usually self-limiting.
- Steroids can be prescribed for children at high risk for serious bleeding.
- Intravenous immunoglobulin (IVIG) may be used to increase platelet production.
- The anti-D antibody protects the platelets from destruction but can be used only if the child is not bleeding and meets specific criteria, such as having an Rh+ blood type.
- A splenectomy may be required if the child is unresponsive to treatment or if bleeding is severe (Hockenberry & Wilson, 2011).

Nursing Considerations

- Observe for bleeding and new areas of petechiae and bruises.
- Focus on safety and injury prevention until the platelet count returns to normal.
- Avoid aspirin or aspirin-containing products, rectal temperatures, and intramuscular injections.

- Teach the importance of follow-up care to monitor the child's platelet level, usually every one to two weeks.

HIV AND AIDS

HIV leads to a wide range of diseases and a variety of clinical courses. Acquired immune deficiency syndrome (AIDS) is the most serious condition of these diseases. Advances in treatments have been able to turn AIDS from a nonsurvivable disease into a chronic disease.

Pathophysiology

AIDS is caused by HIV, a retrovirus that infects a subset of T lymphocytes (CD4+ T cells) and suppresses the immune system, reducing the number of CD4+ T cells. Abnormal B-cell function can be detected early in pediatric HIV infection. The child with HIV cannot fight bacterial infections because helper T cells that control B-cell function have been reduced, decreasing cell-mediated and humoral immunity.

Modes of HIV transmission in children are as follows:

- Perinatally, mother-to-infant transmission occurs before or at birth and also through breastfeeding. Most infected children are born to families in which one or both parents are infected. The risk of infection for an infant whose mother is HIV-positive is 13–30% without medical intervention (Hockenberry & Wilson, 2011).
- Sexual contact from homosexual and heterosexual partners.
- Percutaneous exposure to contaminated needles can also transmit HIV.
- Transfusion of blood, blood components, or clotting factor concentrates is now a rare mode of transmission.
- There is dissemination of the virus throughout the lymphoid organ. At the same time, the virus suppresses the function of the T lymphocytes, which no longer function effectively in the peripheral bloodstream. The suppression of the CD4+ function creates an immune response that maintains the HIV plasma level. During the latency period, the virus does not increase in number, and in the adult population, this period can last at least 10 years.
- The incubation period of a symptomatic HIV infection ranges from months to years. Over this time period, the CD4+ cells gradually continue to decrease in number, and, eventually, the child will develop opportunistic infections that can lead to death. In infants infected perinatally, the median age for onset of symptoms is 3 years, with the disease progressing more quickly because of the immaturity of the immune system.

Clinical Manifestations

The common manifestations of HIV are as follows:

- Lymphadenopathy, hepatosplenomegaly, oral candidiasis, chronic or recurrent diarrhea, failure to thrive, developmental delay, and parotitis

The common manifestations for AIDS are as follows:

- *Pneumocystis carinii* pneumonia (PCP), lymphocytic interstitial pneumonitis (LIP), recurrent bacterial infections, wasting syndrome, candidal esophagitis, HIV encephalopathy, cytomegalovirus disease, *Mycobacterium avium intracellulare* complex infection, pulmonary candidiasis, herpes simplex disease, and cryptosporidiosis (Hockenberry & Wilson, 2011).
- Many children with AIDS have developmental disabilities, including problems with motor skills, communication, use of language, memory loss, and behaviour changes (Hockenberry & Wilson, 2011).

Diagnostics

- For children over 18 months, traditional enzyme-linked immunosorbent assay (ELISA) and Western blot assay tests are used.
- Accurate testing in infants is complicated due to the presence of maternal antibodies for up to 18 months; the result may be a false-positive ELISA. HIV cultures, detection of HIV–DNA sequences using the polymerase chain reaction (PCR), and identifying specific HIV antigens can be used for these infants. Most infants are diagnosed within 1–3 months of age.

Therapeutics

- There is currently no cure; management is primarily supportive, with treatment for opportunistic infections.
- Goals of therapy include slowing the growth of HIV, preventing and treating opportunistic infections, ensuring good nutritional support, and relieving symptoms.
- Medication regimens include combinations of the antiretroviral drugs that help prevent the production of new viral particles. There are different classifications of these drugs, including nucleoside reverse transcriptase inhibitors (such as zidovudine and didanosine), non-nucleoside reverse transcriptase inhibitors (such as nevirapine and delaviridine), and protease inhibitors (including indinavir and saquinavir). New antiretroviral drugs are being developed, and the use of these in combination, as well as strict adherence to the medication regimen, prevents the development of drug resistance (Anabwani, Woldetsadik, & Kline, 2005).
- Trimethoprim–sulfamethoxazole is prescribed as well as a prophylaxis drug of choice to prevent and treat PCP, the most opportunistic infection in this population, particularly in clients between 3 and 6 months of age.
- These children should be immunized with pneumoccocal and influenza vaccines as scheduled (Hockenberry & Wilson, 2011).

Nursing Considerations

- Observe blood and excretion precautions (use gloves to change dressings; clean up spilled body fluids with a 1:10 bleach solution; keep trash in a closed container; flush feces, urine, and other body fluids down the toilet; use proper containers for needles).
- Protect the child from infection, for example, by maintaining distance from people with infections, using hand hygiene, or through reverse isolation.
- Promote optimum nutrition.
- Administer antibiotics and other medications as prescribed.
- Assist the child in maintaining self-esteem, appropriate developmental tasks, and normalization of lifestyle.
- Assist with pain management.
- Provide health teaching concerning the disease and its transmission (particularly for sexually active adolescents); protection from infections; compliance with drug regimens, blood tests, and follow-up care; and referral to appropriate community agencies.
- Teach at-home body fluid precautions: avoid mixing the ill child's secretions with those of the family; have separate linens, a separate toothbrush, a separate razor, and separate eating utensils.

CANCER

Childhood cancer is a rare occurrence in Canada, and most will survive. However, it is the leading cause of death from disease in children over 1 month of age. In Canada, approximately 850 children are diagnosed yearly and one-sixth do not survive. The incidence rate of childhood cancer is not increasing, the mortality rate is decreasing, and today the five-year survival rate is over 82%. Improved diagnostic methods and better treatment plans have improved this rate (Canadian Cancer Society, 2008).

There are changing incidences for various cancers throughout childhood. In all groups, leukemia is the most common, at 26% of cases, causing 28% of deaths. Lymphomas are the next most common at 18%, and 8% of deaths. CNS cancers account for 16% of new cases and 24% of deaths (Canadian Cancer Society, 2008).

Cure criteria include cessation of therapy, continuous freedom from clinical and laboratory evidence of cancer, and minimal or no risk of relapse, as determined by previous experience with the disease. Time that must elapse ranges from two to five years (Hockenberry & Wilson, 2011).

Pathophysiology

Categories of malignant cells include the following:

- Embryonal: Cells that arise from embryonic tissue, such as blastomas
- Lymphomas: Cells arising from the lymphatic system
- Leukemias: Cells that arise from blood-forming organs

- Sarcomas: Cells derived from connective and supportive tissue, such as bone
- Carcinomas: Those derived from epithelial cells
- Adenocarcinomas: Carcinoma of glandular tissue, such as breast tissue (Hockenberry & Wilson, 2011)

Properties of tumour cells include the following:

- The growth rate usually is rapid.
- Anaplasia is the loss of differentiation and organization of cells for a specific function.
- Invasion: Cancer cells invade adjacent tissue and replace normal cells.
- Metastasis: Cancer cells spread to distant sites (via the blood or lymphatic system, or by iatrogenic methods, such as biopsy) to form colonies of malignant growth.
- Competition: Cancer cells compete with normal cells for essential nutrients.
- Expansion: Unrestricted growth of cancer cells compresses adjacent tissue and causes organ damage.
- Staging criteria and terminology are used.
- Criteria to describe and classify the extent of malignant neoplasms and their metastases depend on the specific tumour or treatment centre.
- Staging systems are used to guide therapy and evaluate progress (Hockenberry & Wilson, 2011).

Clinical Manifestations

Specific clinical findings vary depending on the particular body system involved. The cardinal signs and symptoms of cancer in children are as follows:

- Fever, night sweats
- Persistent, localized pain or limping
- Tendency to bruise easily
- Palpable mass
- Sudden changes in behaviour, gait, balance, or vision
- Sudden, unexplained weight loss and anorexia
- Unexplained paleness and fatigue

Diagnostics

- CBC, such as increased production of immature cells, chemistry, and urinalysis
- Bone marrow aspiration or biopsy and other tissue biopsies for definitive diagnosis of cancer
- Lumbar puncture to analyze CSF for leukemic cells, as well as brain tumours and other cancers
- Imaging techniques (CT, ultrasonography, MRI) to detect solid tumours and areas of metastases

Therapeutics

- Protocols may include the following therapies: surgery, chemotherapy, radiotherapy, immunotherapy, and BMT.
- Supportive therapy, such as nutritional supplements, is needed when serious damage occurs to normal cells as the result of cancer treatment.

- Complications that may occur from therapy include oncological emergencies, such as acute tumour lysis syndrome, obstruction, superior vena cava syndrome, and infections (Hockenberry & Wilson, 2011).

Nursing Considerations

- Childhood cancer has a significant impact on the family and profound psychosocial implications.
- The child and family need to adapt to living with the various phases of a life-threatening illness.
- The child's reaction largely depends on his or her age, the information the child is given, and the physical impact of the disease on his or her energy level and coping skills.

LEUKEMIA

Leukemia is the most common cancer found in children, affecting about one-third of all children with cancer. Leukemia may be diagnosed at any age but has a peak onset between 2 and 6 years. The etiology is unknown. Several genetic diseases have been associated with increased incidences of leukemia, including Down syndrome and Fanconi's hypoplastic anemia.

Leukemia is a proliferation of abnormal WBCs. There are different types of leukemia, based on the morphology of the cells and the course of the disease. Each type has a different prognosis and different characteristics.

Most leukemia in children is acute (97%), involving a proliferation of very immature WBCs, or blasts. Acute leukemia has a short history of symptoms and, without treatment, a rapidly declining course leading to death in 3–6 months.

The most common leukemia in children is acute lymphoblastic leukemia (ALL), at approximately 80% of cases; acute myelogenous leukemia (AML) occurs in 20%.

Pathophysiology

- Malignant leukemia cells arise from precursor cells in blood-forming elements.
- Cells accumulate and crowd out normal bone marrow elements, spill into peripheral blood, and eventually invade all body organs and tissues, depriving all body cells of nutrients necessary for survival.
- Replacement of normal hematopoietic elements by leukemic cells results in bone marrow suppression, marked by decreased production of RBCs, normal WBCs, and platelets.
- Bone marrow suppression results in anemia, decreased RBC production, the predisposition to infection due to neutropenia, and bleeding tendencies due to thrombocytopenia.
- Infiltration of reticuloendothelial organs (spleen, liver, and lymph glands) causes marked enlargement and, eventually, fibrosis.

- Leukemic infiltration of the CNS results in increased ICP.
- Other possible sites of long-term infiltration include the kidneys, testes, prostate, ovaries, GI tract, and lungs (Hockenberry & Wilson, 2011).

Clinical Manifestations

- Anemia from RBC suppression causes fatigue, tachycardia, and pallor.
- Bleeding from platelet suppression causes petechiae, purpura, hematuria, epistaxis, and melena stools.
- Immunosuppression from WBC suppression causes fever, infection, and poor wound healing.
- Reticuloendothelial involvement causes hepatosplenomegaly, bone pain, and lymphadenopathy.
- If CNS metastasis occurs, manifestations include headache, meningeal irritation, and signs of increased ICP.
- General symptoms include weight loss, anorexia, vomiting, and fever (Hockenberry & Wilson, 2011).

Diagnostics

- CBC findings show a normal, decreased, or increased WBC count with immature cells (blasts), decreased RBCs, and decreased platelets.
- Diagnosis is confirmed with bone marrow aspiration showing extensive replacement of normal bone marrow elements by leukemic cells.
- Lumbar puncture is performed to assess the migration of abnormal cells to the CNS.

Therapeutics

Therapy involves a combination of chemotherapy and possibly cranial irradiation therapy, provided at four levels:

1. Remission induction to eradicate the cancer cells: chemotherapy includes vincristine, prednisone, and L-asparaginase, with or without another drug such as doxorubicin for ALL. Doxorubicin, daunomycin, and cytosine arabinoside, as well as other drugs, may be added to treat AML.
2. Intensification or consolidation therapy, which further decreases the number of cancer cells not reached by remission induction. The therapy includes L-asparaginase, high-dose methotrexate or intermediate-dose methotrexate with leucovorin rescue, vincristine, doxorubicin, steroids, cytarabine, and 6-mercaptopurine.
3. CNS prophylactic therapy prevents leukemic cells from invading the CNS and usually consists of intrathecal administration of methotrexate, cytarabine, and hydrocortisone.

   - Radiation to the brain, spinal cord, or testis is rarely done unless it is a high-risk client or there is existing infiltration of the CNS.

- Prepubertal male clients may require androgen replacement therapy; sterility may also occur.

4. In the remission phase, maintenance therapy to decrease the risk of recurrence is given with daily oral 6-mercaptopurine, weekly methotrexate, and monthly pulses of vincristine and prednisone.

- If relapse occurs and leukemic cells appear in the bone marrow, reinduction therapy is prednisone and vincristine with a combination of other drugs not previously used. The prognosis worsens with each relapse.
- BMT, when successful, destroys leukemic cells and replenishes bone marrow with healthy cells. BMT is usually done following a second relapse with ALL and is considered in the first phase for AML, which has a poorer prognosis (Hockenberry & Wilson, 2011).
- There are three categories of BMTs:

   - Allogenic refers to tissue from a histocompatible donor, usually a sibling, but may also involve an unmatched donor.
   - Autologous refers to tissue that is collected from the child's own tissue, frozen, and sometimes processed to remove undesired cells.
   - Syngeneic refers to tissue that is identical to the child's tissue, which comes from an identical twin.

Nursing Considerations

Set realistic goals depending on the type of therapy prescribed:

- Prepare the child and family for diagnostic tests and treatments by assessing the child's level of understanding, addressing specific fears, providing information appropriate to the child's age and developmental level, and specifying what the child will see, smell, hear, and feel.
- Help prevent complications related to bone marrow suppression, such as infection, bleeding, and anemia.
- Promote optimal nutrition to maintain and rebuild healthy tissue.
- Promote adequate rest.
- Minimize the risk of infection secondary to diagnosis and chemotherapy: avoid contact with others who have infections, monitor the child's temperature every four hours, practise hand washing, and avoid live plants and uncooked fruits and vegetables, which may contain pathogens.
- Prevent injury secondary to thrombocytopenia and chemotherapy.
- Minimize injections; when necessary, apply pressure to sites for 3–5 minutes to stop bleeding.
- Avoid rectal temperatures.
- Monitor hemoglobin and hematocrit.
- Monitor and report hemorrhagic bleeding.
- Minimize nausea and vomiting secondary to chemotherapy by administering an antiemetic 30 minutes before chemotherapy begins, continuing

antiemetics as prescribed, and employing nonpharmacological measures such as visualization and music.

- Minimize discomfort from stomatitis secondary to chemotherapy by assessing the mouth frequently and providing mouth care every two hours using a soft toothbrush. Avoid potential irritants such as firm toothbrushes, commercial mouthwashes, and lemon–glycerine swabs, any of which can irritate the gums and mucous membranes; instead, offer cool, soothing, bland foods and liquids and administer anaesthetic mouthwashes.
- Minimize body image disturbances related to alopecia by reassuring the child that hair loss is temporary; educating him or her that the new hair may have different texture; using hats, scarves, and wigs; and avoiding the use of hair chemicals when hair grows back.
- Minimize other side effects of specific chemotherapeutic agents:

  - Vincristine (neurotoxicity): Foot drop, depression, ataxia, and vision changes
  - Methotrexate (nephrotoxicity): Renal failure, stomatitis, GI disturbances, and skin changes
  - L-Asparaginase (hepatotoxicity): Lethargy, confusion, and anaphylaxis; liver dysfunction
  - Daunorubicin and doxorubicin (cardiotoxicity): Changes in heart rate and rhythm
  - Prednisone (multiple side effects): Moon face, fluid retention, mood changes, gastric irritation, and increased susceptibility to infection (Hockenberry & Wilson, 2011)

- Support the child and family by encouraging verbalization of concerns, fostering family support systems, and using appropriate resources.

  - Provide palliative care counselling as appropriate and use appropriate resources.
  - Encourage normal growth and development by fostering activities appropriate for the child's age and condition.
  - Provide child and family teaching.
  - Refer to appropriate home care and follow-up services (Hockenberry & Wilson, 2011).

WILMS' TUMOUR (NEPHROBLASTOMA)

Wilms' tumour is a malignant neoplasm of the kidney, which is the most common intra-abdominal tumour in children and the most curable solid tumour. Wilms' tumour occurs most often in young children but may occur in adolescents. The median age at diagnosis is between 3 and 4 years, with 80% of cases under the age of 5. Siblings of children with Wilms' tumour have an increased risk of developing this cancer than do children in the general population (Hockenberry & Wilson, 2011).

Pathophysiology

- The tumour originates in the renal parenchyma.
- It is well encapsulated in the early stages but may later extend into the lymph nodes and the renal vein or vena cava and metastasize to the lungs and other sites. Wilms' tumours are classified into five stages, from stage 1 (confined to one kidney) to stage 5 (involving both kidneys).
- Usually, the tumour is unilateral and occurs with other abnormalities, such as an absent iris or genitourinary problems.
- This type of tumour has one of the highest survival rates of all childhood cancers (Hockenberry & Wilson, 2011).

Clinical Manifestations

- There may be no symptoms.
- Characteristics may include a firm, nontender upper quadrant mass, fever, abdominal pain, hematuria, anemia (due to hemorrhage within the tumour), hypertension (due to secretion of excess renin from the tumour), anorexia, weight loss, and lethargy.
- If the tumour has metastasized to the lungs, shortness of breath, cough, and chest pain may be present.

Diagnostics

- Blood studies may show anemia secondary to bleeding from the tumour.
- Abdominal ultrasonography, CT, and MRI may disclose a mass or evidence of metastasis.

Therapeutics

- Nephrectomy, with removal of regional nodes and any resectable regional tumour, as well as the adjacent adrenal gland.
- Chemotherapy using actinomycin D and vincrinstine may be used; doxorubicin and cyclophosphamide may be used for more advanced stages. The treatment lasts for six to 15 months and may be effective at all stages.
- Radiation may be used as well, but not for stages 1 and 2 (Hockenberry & Wilson, 2011).

Nursing Considerations

- Prepare the child for diagnostic tests and treatments.
- Help prevent rupture of an encapsulated tumour by avoiding abdominal palpation and by careful bathing and handling.
- Monitor bowel sounds and perform an assessment for signs and symptoms of intestinal obstruction resulting from abdominal surgery, vincristine-induced adynamic ileus, and radiation-induced edema.
- Help prevent infection by practising hand hygiene and limiting the child's exposure to persons with infections; observe for signs of infection.

- Monitor blood pressure.
- Help prevent postoperative pulmonary complications by providing frequent position changes and by encouraging coughing and deep-breathing exercises as well as ambulation.
- Provide child and family teaching as for a child with leukemia.

BRAIN TUMOURS

Brain tumours include astrocytoma, medulloblastoma, brainstem glioma, and ependymoma. CNS tumours account for about 20% of all childhood cancers.

Pathophysiology

- Tumours arise from anywhere in the cranium: glial cells (astrocytomas), nerve cells, neuroepithelium, cranial nerves, blood vessels, pineal gland, or hypophysis.
- About half are infratentorial, occurring primarily in the cerebellum or brainstem, and cause symptoms of increased ICP. The others are supratentorial and occur mainly in the cerebrum (Hockenberry & Wilson, 2011).

Clinical Manifestations

- Recurrent and progressive headache, especially on waking
- Loss of balance and coordination
- Increase in head circumference and tense fontanelles
- Behavioural changes such as irritability or lethargy
- Severe morning vomiting and failure to thrive
- Cranial nerve neuropathy
- Signs of increased ICP
- Seizures

Diagnostics

- MRI is used to diagnose brain tumours and assess the growth of the tumour before and after treatment.
- CT permits direct visualization of the brain parenchyma, ventricles, and surrounding subarachnoid space.
- Angiography provides information about the tumour's blood supply.
- A definitive diagnosis is made by biopsy during surgery.

Nursing Considerations

- Assess for signs and symptoms when a diagnosis of brain tumour is suspected.
- Prepare the child and family for diagnostic tests and protocols.
- Prevent postoperative complications by monitoring vital signs, positioning, regulating fluids, and administering medication.

- Monitor for signs of increased ICP and seizures.
- For chemotherapy, follow the planning and interventions used for leukemia.
- Provide child and family teaching as for a child with leukemia.

ENDOCRINE SYSTEM DISORDERS

The endocrine system regulates energy production, growth, fluid and electrolyte balance, response to stress, and sexual reproduction. Most endocrine disorders are chronic in nature and require ongoing care related to health maintenance, education, development, and psychosocial needs.

Diagnostics

- Blood chemistry, including thyroid function tests and hormone, calcium, phosphorus, alkaline phosphatase, and electrolyte levels
- Urine studies, to evaluate sodium, calcium, phosphorus, and glucose levels and specific gravity
- Radiographic studies to evaluate bone age and density and soft tissue calcification
- Genetic studies, to detect enzyme deficiencies, such as congenital adrenal hypoplasia (Hockenberry & Wilson, 2011)

Nursing Considerations

There are important psychosocial implications for a child and family with an endocrine disorder:

- Young children may interpret treatments, such as hormonal injections, as punishment for wrongdoing.
- Injections may be a source of fear and may enhance a child's body mutilation anxieties.

HYPOPITUITARISM

Hypopituitarism results from a diminished or deficient secretion of pituitary hormones, usually growth hormone (GH).

Pathophysiology

- Hypopituitarism may be caused by several conditions, including developmental disorders, lesions such as tumours, trauma, or certain hereditary or functional disorders, such as anorexia nervosa or dwarfism.
- The most frequent organic cause of undersecretion of GH is a tumour in the pituitary or hypothalamic region, especially a craniopharyngioma.
- More than half of the cases are idiopathic and related to GH deficiency.

Clinical Manifestations

- GH deficiency produces varied effects, depending on the degree of dysfunction, which include decreased linear growth, decreased muscle mass, thin hair, poor skin quality, delayed growth, excessive subcutaneous fat, hypoglycemia, and deficiencies of adrenocorticotropic hormone (ACTH), TSH, LH, and FSH, which produce effects related to the functions of these hormones.
- The chief presenting complaint is short stature.
- Children generally grow during the first year; then growth slows, remaining below the third percentile.
- Children with hypopituitarism appear younger than their chronological age.
- Premature aging is common later in life.
- Primary teeth usually appear when expected, but secondary tooth eruption is delayed.
- Sexual development is usually normal but delayed.
- Most children have normal intelligence.
- Emotional and academic problems are common.

Diagnostics

- Family history, including parental height, is an important predictor of the child's ultimate height.
- A history of the child's growth patterns and previous health status is required to rule out prenatal maternal disorders that affect growth, such as malnutrition, and to check for evidence of chronic illness in the child.
- Bone age is younger than chronological age.
- Definitive diagnosis is possible with a subnormal GH level.

Therapeutics

- Early diagnosis and treatment are crucial for children to achieve their genetic growth potential.
- The treatment of GH deficiency resulting from organic etiology is directed at correcting the underlying cause.
- Treatment for children with functional GH deficiency is replacement therapy using a biosynthetic GH agent, which succeeds about 80% of the time.
- Other hormone deficiencies also require replacement therapy.

Nursing Considerations

- Monitor children for growth curves below the third percentile on growth charts.
- Prepare the child for diagnostic tests and procedures; explain that endocrine studies may require multiple blood draws.
- Monitor for early signs and symptoms of hypoglycemia, particularly during provocative tests for GH. If hypoglycemia occurs, increase the child's blood glucose level rapidly by giving orange juice.
- Administer GH replacement therapy at the same time of day.
- Assess for GH overdose, indicated by initial hypoglycemia followed by hyperglycemia.

- Promote the child's self-esteem and a positive self-image related to short stature.
- Provide realistic expectations for the child's growth and the effectiveness of GH replacement therapy and encourage the family to provide normal growth and development activities.

DIABETES MELLITUS

Diabetes mellitus (DM) is a deficiency of pancreatic insulin, resulting in chronic high blood glucose levels and problems with fat and carbohydrate metabolism. The differential diagnosis of DM has become more complex and now includes type 1 DM (T1DM), type 2 DM (T2DM), and monogenic and secondary forms of diabetes. DM is either a complete deficiency (T1DM) or a partial deficiency (T2DM) of the hormone. Type 2 diabetes in children has previously been rare, but the incidence is increasing due to the rise in childhood obesity.

T1DM is the most common endocrine disease of childhood. When pancreatic beta cells (which produce insulin) are destroyed, a lack of insulin is the result. T1DM has two forms. The first form of T1DM results from an autoimmune reaction, causing the destruction of pancreatic beta cells. This occurs when a child with a genetic predisposition is exposed to a trigger, most often a virus. The second form of T1DM is rarer and idiopathic, with no known etiology. In children with T2DM, obesity and genetic predisposition are factors. Children of Aboriginal, African or Caribbean, Hispanic, or Asian descent are at particular risk for this form of DM (CPS, 2007d). See Chapter 8, pages 278–282.

Secondary forms of DM can be due to an underlying medical condition such as CF or Cushing's syndrome. Other secondary forms are caused by treatments such as steroid and L-asparaginase. The latter form can resolve itself when the underlying conditions are treated or the medication treatments are finished. Secondary forms of DM are on the increase. They are difficult to differentiate from T2DM and may also be related to obesity (CPS, 2007d).

Pathophysiology

Insulin, produced by the beta cells of the pancreas, is needed to support carbohydrate, protein, and fat metabolism and to facilitate the entry of these substances into cells. The destruction of 90% or more of the pancreatic beta cells leads to a cascade of metabolic events, including hyperglycemia (increased glucagon, epinephrine, GH, and cortisol levels), lipolysis, fatty acid release, and ketone production.

- Excessive ketone production can cause DKA, a life-threatening condition characterized by marked hyperglycemia, metabolic acidosis, dehydration, and altered level of consciousness ranging from lethargy to coma.

- See the section in Chapter 8, pages 278–282, on T1DM.

Clinical Manifestations

The classic symptoms of T1DM are the three Ps: polydipsia, polyuria, and polyphagia, along with fatigue. Other symptoms include weight loss, dry skin, and blurred vision. Some children present with an abrupt onset of DKA.

Diagnostics

- A fasting blood glucose level >6.5–7 mmol/L
- A level two hours postprandial of >7.8 mmol/L
- Glycosuria
- In DKA, there is hyperglycemia, acidosis, glycosuria, and ketonuria.

Therapeutics

Treatment for T1DM in the child involves an interprofessional approach to manage the complexity of the disease and to foster self-care.

- Insulin therapy: The dose is calculated individually for each child based on blood glucose levels and is administered via subcutaneous injection or an insulin pump. Doses will be adjusted during stress, illness, exercise, growth, and puberty. Future therapies may include nasal administration of insulin and islet cell or pancreas transplantation.
- Glucose monitoring: Blood sugar must be monitored daily. There are many easy-to-use glucometers for home use.
- Glycolysated hemoglobin measured every three months is the best method for assessing glucose control.
- Nutrition: Food intake should be planned according to blood sugar readings, exercise, insulin injection times, and food preferences. Although concentrated sweets are not advised, there are no longer any absolute rules about foods that are not permitted.
- Exercise is encouraged; children will need to learn about food and insulin adjustments during exercise.

Nursing Considerations

- These are similar to those found in Chapter 8, in the section on diabetes.
- Children are able to learn at a young age about self-care: glucose testing, injection of insulin, and diet.
- Teach according to the developmental age of the child and include the child in health teaching.
- Teach the child and family about the signs and treatment of hypoglycemia.
- Children may have periods of fluctuating blood sugars with difficulty achieving stabilization. Glucose needs to be monitored frequently, along with increased follow-up with the diabetes team.
- Adolescents may rebel at the need for injections,

glucose monitoring, and lifestyle changes. Parents and the health care team must be aware of the risk of noncompliance in these clients.

RENAL SYSTEM DYSFUNCTION

Kidney development is complete at the end of the first year. Glomerular filtration and absorption do not reach adult capabilities until between 1 and 2 years.

Kidney functions include maintaining body fluid volume, secreting erythropoietic stimulating factor (ESF), which stimulates the production of RBCs, and producing renin, which stimulates the production of angiotensin. Urine is formed in the nephron and then passes into the renal pelvis, through the ureter, into the bladder, and out of the body through the urethra.

URINARY TRACT INFECTIONS

UTIs lead to inflammation, usually caused by bacterial infections, of the urethra (urethritis), bladder (cystitis), ureters (ureteritis), or kidneys (pyelonephritis). Peak incidence occurs between 2 and 6 years, with increased incidence also noted in adolescents who are sexually active. Females have a 10–30 times greater risk of developing UTIs than do males (except in neonates).

Pathophysiology

- In uncomplicated UTI, inflammation usually is confined to the lower urinary tract.
- Recurrent cystitis may produce anatomical changes in the ureter that lead to vesicoureteral valve incompetence and resultant urine reflux, conditions that provide organisms with access to the upper urinary tract.
- Pyelonephritis usually results from an ascending infection from the lower urinary tract and can lead to acute and chronic inflammatory changes in the pelvis and medulla, with scarring and loss of renal tissue. Recurrent or chronic infection results in increased fibrotic tissue and kidney contraction.
- *E. coli* and other gram-negative organisms account for most UTIs.
- In the neonate, the urinary tract may be infected via the bloodstream; in older children, bacteria ascend the urethra.
- There is an increased incidence of UTI in females due to the shorter urethra and proximity to the anus.
- The incidence of UTI in male infants is often due to congenital malformations of the urinary tract and should be investigated.
- Contributing factors include urinary stasis, urinary reflux, poor perineal hygiene, pregnancy, noncircumcision, in-dwelling catheters, tight clothes or diapers, bubble baths, antimicrobial agents that alter normal urinary tract flora, local inflammation, such as vaginitis, and sexual intercourse.

Clinical Manifestations

Characteristics vary with age and the location of the infection. Approximately 40% of UTIs are asymptomatic.

Infants: Fever, weight loss, failure to thrive, vomiting, and diarrhea

Older children: Dysuria, frequency, urgency, incontinence, foul-smelling urine, abdominal pain, and possibly hematuria

Pylenonephritis: Fever, chills, flank pain, and costovertebral abdominal tenderness

Diagnostics

- Urinalysis: Urine is tested for hematuria, proteinuria, and pyuria.
- Urine characteristically has a foul odour, cloudiness, and strands of mucus.
- Diagnosis is confirmed by bacteria in urine culture.

Therapeutics

- Antibiotics such as penicillins, sulphonamides (including trimethoprim–sulfamethoxazole), cephalosporins, nitrofurantoin, and tetracyclines are prescribed to treat a current disease or to provide prophylaxis, depending on the sensitivity identified through urine culture.
- All antibiotics can eventually cause resistant strains.

Nursing Considerations

- Evaluate urinary status by observing the appearance and odour of urine and by noting signs and symptoms such as frequency, burning, enuresis, urinary retention, or flank pain. Follow-up urine cultures may be required.
- Maintain sterile technique when performing urinary catheterization.
- Provide comfort measures: analgesics, antipyretics, and urinary anaesthetics.
- Encourage increased fluid intake to reduce fever and dilute urine.
- Employ and teach preventive measures, including good perineal hygiene, cleaning a girl from the urethra back toward the anus, avoiding irritants such as bubble bath and tight clothing, wearing cotton underwear instead of synthetics such as nylon, maintaining adequate fluid intake, voiding regularly and completely emptying the bladder with each urination, and maintaining acidic urine by drinking beverages such as cranberry and blueberry juice.
- Drinking cranberry juice or blueberry juice helps prevent bacteria from sticking to the bladder and urethra walls, in turn minimizing the incidences of UTIs. Research now shows that acidic urine is not the reason for UTIs but rather the sticking of bacteria. This nonsticking effect works to prevent UTIs.
- For the sexually active adolescent, teach the importance of voiding both before and after sexual intercourse.

VESICOURETERAL REFLUX

Vesicoureteral reflux (VUR) occurs when there is a backward flow of urine in the urinary tract when voiding. The prevalence of VUR in healthy children is estimated at less than 1%. However, it is found in 29–50% of children following UTIs and is the most common radiographic abnormality associated with UTIs in children. Development of VUR may in part be genetic; siblings are 10 times more likely to develop it than other children (Hockenberry & Wilson, 2011).

Pathophysiology

- VUR usually occurs a result of an incompetent valvular mechanism at the ureterovesicular junction.
- VUR is graded according to the degree of reflux from the lower ureter to the kidney.
- VUR is a major cause of renal damage; refluxed urine ascending into the collecting tubules of nephrons initiates renal scarring from infective organisms.
- If the amount of refluxed urine is large, the child feels an urge to void shortly after having urinated.
- If the amount is small, it may remain in the bladder, causing urinary stasis and increasing the risk of infection.

Causes:

- Primary reflux results from congenital abnormalities at the point of insertion of the ureters into the bladder.
- Secondary reflux results from infection and ureterovesicular junction incompetency; it may also result from neurogenic bladder or progressive dilation of ureters following surgical urinary diversion (Hockenberry & Wilson, 2011).

Clinical Manifestations

- Dysuria
- Urinary frequency, urgency, and hesitancy
- Urine retention
- Cloudy, dark, or blood-tinged urine

Diagnostics

- Urinalysis may reveal RBCs or pyuria.
- Structural abnormalities may be detected by IVP, voiding cystourethrography, and cystoscopy.

Therapeutics

- Antibiotics and urinary antiseptics
- Possible antireflux surgery, involving the reimplantation of ureters

Nursing Considerations

- Administer or teach parents to administer prescribed medications, such as continuous low-dose antibiotics, usually given as nitrofurantoin or trimethoprim–sulfamethoxazole.
- Encourage increased fluids to dilute urine and develop a regular (three-hour) voiding plan.
- Encourage a high-fibre diet to prevent constipation in order to facilitate muscular relaxation, thereby helping to reduce residual urine.
- Some children with a lower grade reflux can have endoscopic correction instead of a surgical procedure.
- As appropriate, explain antireflux surgery, involving reimplantation of ureters.
- Provide preoperative and postoperative care after antireflux surgery:

  - Observe and protect urinary drainage tubes, indwelling catheters, suprapubic catheters, and ureteral stents.
  - Considerations are as in a child with UTI (Hockenberry & Wilson, 2011).

NEPHROTIC SYNDROME

Nephrotic syndrome is characterized by massive proteinuria, hypoalbuminemia, hyperlipidemia, altered immunity, and edema. The condition is of idiopathic origin 95% of the time. The prognosis is usually good for the most common type, called minimal change nephrotic syndrome (MCNS), which is self-limiting and usually responds to steroidal therapy.

Pathophysiology

- Pathogenesis in MCNS is not understood, but a disturbance in the membrane of the glomeruli causes an increased permeability to protein.
- Proteins, especially albumin, leak through the glomerular membrane and are excreted in the urine.
- Once the albumin is excreted, colloidal osmotic pressure decreases, allowing fluid to escape from the intravascular spaces to the interstitial spaces, resulting in ascites in the abdomen.
- The plasma volume decrease stimulates the antidiuretic hormone (ADH) and aldosterone to reabsorb water and increase the intravascular volume.
- Secondary nephrotic syndrome usually occurs after glomerular damage of known or presumed cause (for example, due to systemic lupus erythematosus, DM, or sickle cell disease).

Clinical Manifestations

- These manifestations may include periorbital, pedal, and pretibial edema initially, progressing to generalized edema (anasarca), weight increase, ascites, pleural effusion, decreased urine output, pallor, anorexia, fatigue, abdominal pain, and diarrhea.
- With significant edema, the child may appear pale and have respiratory distress.
- Blood pressure may be normal or slightly decreased.
- Children are more prone to infection from decreased immunity.

Diagnostics

- Urinalysis shows marked proteinuria, hyaline casts, few RBCs, and high urine specific gravity.
- The serum protein level is markedly decreased, especially the albumin level.
- A renal biopsy may be performed.

Therapeutics

- Diuretics such as loop diuretics, usually furosemide in combination with metolazone, are sometimes effective, and restrictions are placed on high-sodium foods and salt to manage edema.
- Prednisone is usually prescribed for three months to reduce proteinuria.
- Immunosuppressant therapy (usually cyclophosphamide) is recommended for the child who fails to respond to steroids. Immunosuppressants decrease the rate of relapse but can have long-term implications, particularly in terms of causing male sterility if used for more than two to three months.
- A broad-spectrum antimicrobial agent may be given if infection is present.
- Plasma expanders, such as salt-poor albumin, may be needed to manage severe edema (Hockenberry & Wilson, 2011).

Nursing Considerations

- Assess for a decrease in blood volume by monitoring for increased edema and by measuring abdominal girth, weight, intake and output, blood pressure, and pulse rate. Test urine for protein and specific gravity.
- Monitor for signs of infection and take precautions to prevent infection (the child is susceptible to secondary infection because immunoglobulin is lost in the urine).
- Promote skin integrity by checking areas of edema for skin breakdown, ensuring frequent position changes, using scrotal supports for boys, and providing good skin care.
- Provide a high-protein, high-calorie diet without added salt. Fluids may be restricted if severe edema is present.
- Conserve the child's energy by encouraging bed rest and quiet activities.
- Perform urine testing for albumin.
- Provide parent and child teaching such as monitoring for relapses and signs of infection, medication administration, urine testing, and signs of skin breakdown.

Acute Glomerulonephritis

Acute glomerulonephritis (AGN) is an immune complex disease that may be a primary condition or can be symptomatic of a systemic disorder. It is likely caused by an immune injury secondary to *Streptococcus*, pneumococci, and viruses. Recovery occurs in most cases.

Acute poststreptococcal glomerulonephritis (APSGN) is the most common form. APSGN can occur at any age but is usually seen in school-aged children, peaking at 6 to 7 years. It is uncommon in children under the age of 2.

The majority of infections do not cause AGN. A latent period of 10–14 days occurs between the infection—usually of the throat or skin—and the onset of clinical symptoms.

Pathophysiology

It is speculated that the original infectious organism releases material into the circulation that is antigenic, and antibodies are formed in response. Antibodies interact with antigens that remain in the glomeruli, leading to immune complex formation and tissue injury, a decrease in filtration, and reduced excretion of sodium and water (Hockenberry & Wilson, 2011).

Clinical Manifestations

- Manifestations appear approximately 10–14 days after an infection, although some children do not appear to have been ill. These include mild to moderate or high blood pressure, pallor, irritability, fatigue, lethargy, periorbital and generalized edema, weight gain, oliguria and hematuria (urine is brown—cola- or tea-coloured—and cloudy), costovertebral tenderness, and anorexia.

Diagnostics

- Urinalysis: Urine contains RBCs, epithelial cells, granular casts, WBCs, and protein.
- Serum chemistry: Elevated BUN and creatinine levels, elevated erythrocyte sedimentation rate (ESR), and elevated ASO titre and complement level (C3)
- Cultures of the pharynx are done on the child and family members, and if there is a positive culture of group A streptococci, all family members should be treated with an antistreptococcal agent.
- A renal biopsy is not usually performed unless an atypical nephritis is suspected.

Therapeutics

- Treatment usually includes medications to control hypertension, decrease fluid overload, and treat infection.
- Treatment for severe hypertension includes calcium channel blockers, beta blockers, or ACE inhibitors.
- Treatment for mild or moderate hypertension involves loop diuretics.
- Diuretics, usually furosemide, are given for edema and fluid overload if no renal failure is present.
- The diet is usually no added salt; if edema is present or the client is hypertensive, there may be moderate sodium restrictions. During periods of oliguria, potassium is also restricted. Protein is restricted only if severe azotemia has developed due to prolonged oliguria.
- Antibiotics are used to treat an existing streptococcal infection.
- Rarely, dialysis may be required to manage severe AGN or heart failure.
- Caloric intake may be increased to balance protein breakdown.
- Diuresis indicates the beginning of recovery.

Nursing Considerations

- Assess fluid status by monitoring intake and output, recording daily weights, and monitoring for edema.
- Closely monitor blood pressure and respiratory rate to identify early signs of complications.
- Administer medications and observe for side and therapeutic effects.
- Maintain adequate caloric intake and nutrition with any dietary restrictions.
- Provide child and family teaching on the need for medical follow-up for urine testing and blood pressure monitoring, as well as on home care measures, including activity and diet instructions, infection prevention measures, and the signs and symptoms of potential complications.

Enuresis

Enuresis is repeated involuntary urination, usually at night, in a child who should have bladder control (usually by age 4 or 5). Enuresis is primary when the child has never achieved continence and secondary if the child starts bedwetting after continence is achieved. Boys are affected more than girls, and night-time bedwetting usually stops between the ages of 6 and 8. Enuresis may have a familial component; 75% of children with enuresis have a first-degree relative with the problem (Hockenberry & Wilson, 2011).

Pathophysiology

Enuresis is primarily a problem of delayed or incomplete neuromuscular maturation of the bladder. Most children with enuresis sleep long periods as infants, have a family history of enuresis, and exhibit slower development up to 3 years of age. The condition is benign and self-limiting.

Therapeutics

- Bladder retention training, motivational therapy, or behaviour modification
- Drug therapy, such as imipramine (Tofranil), which has an anticholinergic effect on the bladder, or desmopressin (DDA VP) nasal spray, which decreases night-time output
- Urine-alarm mattresses, which sound an alarm when wet and can be very effective

Nursing Considerations

- Help the family accept the child's problem and avoid placing blame or adopting attitudes that may foster feelings of low self-esteem in the child.
- Discuss strategies to manage night-time incontinence, such as rubber sheets on beds. Suggest the use of incontinence "pull-ups," which do not look like diapers.

HYPOSPADIAS

Hypospadias occurs when the urethral opening is located below the glans penis or anywhere along the ventral surface (underside) of the penile shaft. The rate of occurrence is approximately one in 500 newborns. Testes are undescended in approximately 10% of boys with hypospadias, and inguinal hernias are a common associated finding.

Pathophysiology

- The urethral folds fail to fuse completely over the urethral groove.
- Ventral foreskin is lacking, and the distal segment looks like a hood.

Clinical Manifestations

- Abnormal placement of the meatus should be evident at birth.
- In mild cases, the meatus is just below the tip of the penis.
- In severe cases, the meatus is located on the perineum between the halves of the scrotum.
- Chordee (a ventral curve of the penis) results from the replacement of normal skin with fibrotic tissue and usually accompanies severe hypospadias.
- Severe hypospadias with undescended testes must be differentiated from ambiguous genitalia.

Therapeutics

Surgical repair improves the child's ability to stand when urinating and to urinate in a straight stream and improves the appearance of the penis, as well as preserving sexual adequacy. It is usually performed at 6–12 months of age to avoid issues with body image.

Nursing Considerations

- Inform the parents to avoid circumcision as the foreskin is usually used for surgical repair.
- Allow the parents to verbalize their feelings about the child's condition.
- Prepare the parents and child for the surgical procedures and the possibility of urinary diversion while the new meatus is being constructed.
- Prepare parents for the expected cosmetic result and show them pictures of successful repairs.
- Monitor intake and output and urinary patterns, encourage fluids, maintain patency, and prevent and observe for infection if the child is catheterized postoperatively.

MUSCULOSKELETAL AND NEUROMUSCULAR DYSFUNCTION

Bone growth occurs in diameter and length. Growth in bone length occurs at the epiphyseal plate, a vascular area of active cell division. These cells are highly sensitive to the impact of GH, estrogen, and testosterone. In adolescence, the epiphyseal plate turns to bone and growth stops.

In children, the epiphyseal plate represents an area of bone weakness that is prone to injury through fracture, crushing, or slippage. Injury to the epiphyseal plate can disturb bone growth. Because a child is still growing, some bony deformities due to injury can be remodelled or straightened over time. Conversely, this can also cause some deformities to worsen with growth.

Because a child's bones are more plastic than an adult's, more force is required to fracture a bone, and specific forces may produce different types of fractures. A child's bones generally heal much faster than those of an adult, often greatly reducing the time required for immobilization.

Pathophysiology

Physical activity is essential for the growth and development of bones and muscles. Conditions that may limit mobility include congenital defects, degenerative neurological disorders, integumentary disorders, musculoskeletal trauma, imposed bed rest to assist healing and restoration, and mechanical restraint as part of therapy.

Clinical Manifestations

General signs and symptoms of musculoskeletal disorders in children are as follows:

- Joint contracture and pain
- Muscular atrophy and weakness
- Fatigue
- Diminished reflexes

- Delayed healing
- Orthostatic hypotension
- Thrombus formation
- Shallow respirations
- Anorexia and constipation
- Renal calculi
- Urinary incontinence or signs of urinary infection
- Skin breakdown and pressure ulcers
- Sensory changes

Diagnostics

- Radiographs (the most common study to assess injury and healing)
- CT scan
- Bone scan
- Arthrography and arthroscopy
- Joint aspiration
- Electromyography (EMG)

Therapeutics

- Therapy is specific to the condition.
- Immobilization may be required to stabilize disrupted muscle or protect bone integrity.

Nursing Considerations Related to Immobilization

- Treatment for musculoskeletal problems often requires immobilization (casts, traction, or body frames), which can be frightening and painful.
- Play, social interaction, and self-care help the immobilized child gain self-esteem and independence and promote normal growth and development.
- Protect skin integrity by turning the child frequently and inspecting the skin for early signs of breakdown.
- Promote adequate hydration and nutrition by offering high-protein, high-calorie foods in small, frequent amounts.
- Promote bowel elimination by encouraging fluids and a high-fibre diet. Administer stool softeners as prescribed.
- Promote urinary elimination by encouraging fluids, monitoring intake and output, and assessing for bladder distension.
- Prevent respiratory complications by keeping the child well hydrated, changing the child's position frequently, and encouraging deep-breathing exercises.
- Protect the child from injury by moving and positioning the child carefully and by monitoring physical activities closely; postural hypotension and falling may result if the child resumes usual activities too quickly.
- Help prevent UTIs by keeping the child well hydrated, promoting frequent voiding, providing foods such as blueberry and cranberry juice, which prevents bacteria from sticking to the epithelium in the bladder area, and limiting high-calcium foods.
- Prevent contractures by maintaining proper body alignment and providing ROM exercises.

- Administer medications, which may include antibiotics to treat infection; diuretics to remove high levels of calcium; calcium-mobilizing drugs; anticoagulants to prevent clot formation; and stool softeners to prevent constipation. Be alert for the side effects of these medications.
- Be aware that preschoolers may view immobilization as punishment.
- Provide child and family teaching as appropriate, such as cast care, positioning, skin care, nutrition and hydration to repair bone and muscle damage and prevent constipation and UTIs, as well as how to observe for thrombus and circulatory problems and what medical follow-up is required.

DEVELOPMENTAL DYSPLASIA OF THE HIP (DDH)

Developmental dysplasia is a spectrum of hip abnormalities that may arise in the fetus, infant, or child. Hip instability may involve subluxations and dislocations, which, if uncorrected, will lead to permanent disability. The etiology of DDH is unknown, but predisposing factors may be categorized as physiological (lax joints due to maternal hormones), genetic (family history), and mechanical (breech birth). DDH occurs most often in females and most frequently in the right hip.

Pathophysiology

- Subluxation, the most common form of DDH, is defined as an incomplete dislocation, in which the femoral head remains in contact with the acetabulum, but a stretched capsule and ligament tears cause the head of the femur to be partially displaced.
- Dislocation describes the situation in which the femoral head loses contact with the acetabulum and is displaced posteriorly and superiorly over the fibro-cartilaginous rim.

Clinical Manifestations
"clunk" c̄ abduct
dislocate & adduct

- In the newborn: Ortolani's sign, Barlow's sign, asymmetrical gluteal folds, limited abduction of affected hip
- In older children: Limp, Trendelenburg's sign

drop pelvis when lift leg opp. to weak glut. muscle.

Diagnostics

- Radiographic examination is not reliable until between 3 and 6 months of age.
- Ultrasonography may be helpful in diagnosing dysplasia in the newborn.

Therapeutics

Newborn to 6 months: The infant is usually placed in a Pavlik harness, which centres the femoral head into

the acetabulum in flexion and deepens the acetabulum by pressure.

- The harness is worn continuously until the hip joint is clinically and radiographically stable.
- By 3 to 6 months, the child usually is transferred to a protective abduction brace, which is worn for less than a year.

Six to 18 months: The child is placed in traction for gradual reduction, followed by cast immobilization until the joint is stable. If soft tissue blocks reduction, an open reduction is performed, followed by a spica cast for 4–6 months. Then an abduction splint is worn.

Older children: Correction is difficult because secondary changes create complications.

- Surgical reduction is required.
- Successful reduction after 4 years of age is difficult and may require preoperative traction, tenotomy of contracted muscles, and an innominate osteotomy procedure and casting. Reduction is inadvisable after 6 years of age.

Nursing Considerations

- Provide care as for the immobilized child.
- Children may be prone to putting toys, food, and so on inside the cast.
- Petal cast edges with waterproof tape, particulary in the diaper area.
- Place a disposable diaper beneath the entire perineal opening in the cast.
- Provide child and family teaching regarding holding techniques, moving, feeding, care of restrictive devices, and signs and symptoms of complications such as increased temperature, pain or blood on voiding, and difficulty breathing.

CEREBRAL PALSY

Cerebral palsy (CP) is a group of neurological disorders caused by injury or insult to the brain either before or during birth or in early infancy. CP has an early onset, and there is abnormal muscle tone and coordination. CP is the most common permanent disability in childhood. Risk factors include prematurity, asphyxia, ischemia, perinatal trauma, congenital and perinatal infections, and perinatal metabolic problems, such as hyperbilirubinemia and hypoglycemia. Infection, trauma, and tumours can cause CP in early infancy. Approximately 80% of CP is caused by unknown prenatal factors (Krigger, 2006). The estimated occurrence in the United States is 1.2–3 of every 1000 births. CP can range from mildly hypertonic muscles to severe physical and neurological impairment (Hockenberry & Wilson, 2011).

Pathophysiology

- Disabilities usually result from injury to the cerebellum, the basal ganglia, or the motor cortex.
- CP is nonprogressive but may become more apparent as the child grows older.
- It can be difficult to establish the precise location of neurological lesions because with a few exceptions, there is no typical pattern of pathology. In some children with CP, there is gross brain malformation, and in others, there is vascular occlusion, neuron loss, and laminar degeneration.
- Anoxia appears to be an important factor in neurological damage.
- CP is often secondary to a wide range of causative factors (Hockenberry & Wilson, 2011).

Classification of CP

Spastic: This type is the most common and may involve one or both sides. It involves upper motor neuron muscular weakness with intact reflex arc, increased stretch reflexes, increased muscle tone, and often weak muscles. Hallmarks include hypertonicity with poor control of posture, balance, and coordinated movement; impairment of fine and gross motor skills; and active attempts at motion increase abnormal postures and the overflow of movement to other parts of the body. In the infant up to 1 year, hypotonia is present; then spasticity begins to develop.

Dyskinetic: This form is defined by abnormal involuntary movements that disappear in sleep and increase when the child is stressed; the major manifestation is athetosis (wormlike movement), in addition to dyskinetic movement of the mouth, drooling, dysarthria, and choreiform (jerky) movements.

Ataxic: The ataxic form is characterized by a wide-based gait, rapid, repetitive movements performed poorly, and disintegration of movements of the upper extremities when the child reaches for objects.

Mixed Type: This type features a combination of spasticity and athetosis (Hockenberry & Wilson, 2011).

Clinical Manifestations

- The most common clinical manifestation is universal delayed gross motor development.
- Additional typical manifestations include abnormal motor performance (early dominant hand preference, abnormal and asymmetrical crawl, poor sucking, feeding problems, and persistent tongue thrust), poor head control after 3 months, alterations of muscle tone (such as increased or decreased resistance to passive movements, the child feels stiff when he or she is being handled or dressed, difficulty in diapering, and opisthotonos), the child exhibits abnormal postures (such as scissoring the legs or persistent infantile posturing), and reflex abnormalities (persistent primitive reflexes, such as tonic neck or hyper-reflexia).

- Behavioural manifestations include extreme irritability, little interest in the environment, and sleeping for unusually long periods.
- Associated disabilities include intellectual delays, seizures, attention deficit disorder, and sensory impairment (Hockenberry & Wilson, 2011).

Diagnostics

- Perinatal history
- Persistence of primitive reflexes
- Neurological examination
- Related diagnostic tests, such as an MRI, to rule out other pathologies

Therapeutics

Although there is no cure, the child can be assisted to reach his or her optimum developmental potential.

- Therapeutic goals are as follows:

  - To establish locomotion, communication, and self-help
  - To gain optimal appearance and integration of motor functions
  - To correct associated deficiencies as effectively as possible
  - To provide educational opportunities based on the child's needs and abilities

- Successful therapy relies on a multidisciplinary approach and collaboration among health care team members to manage various aspects of treatment.
- The child may require orthotic devices, such as braces, splints, or casting.
- The child may use assistive and adaptive devices, such as walkers, scooters, motorized wheelchairs, communication boards, and computers.
- Medications for spasticity, pain, seizures, and constipation may be required.
- Adaptive education and learning programs and educational support services should be investigated.
- Speech and language therapy may be employed.
- Physical and occupational therapy may be recommended.
- Some children may require surgery, such as tendon transfers, to correct deformities and decrease spasticity (Hockenberry & Wilson, 2011).

Nursing Considerations

- Prevent injury by providing the child with a safe environment, appropriate toys, and protective gear (helmet, knee pads), if needed.
- Minimize physical deformity by ensuring the correct use of braces and other assistive devices and by providing ROM exercises.
- Promote mobility by encouraging the child to be involved with age- and condition-appropriate motor activities.

- Ensure good nutrition by providing a high-protein, high-calorie diet.
- Administer prescribed medications, which may include sedatives, muscle relaxants, anticonvulsants, and analgesics.
- Encourage self-care by urging the child to participate in activities of daily living (ADLs) that are appropriate for the child's age and condition; normalize as much as possible.
- Facilitate communication by talking to the child directly and slowly, using pictures to reinforce speech, and using communication devices.
- Encourage early speech therapy to prevent poor or maladaptive communication habits and to provide a means of articulate speech; technology, such as computer use, may help children with severe articulation problems.
- Seek referrals as necessary for corrective lenses and hearing devices to decrease sensory deprivation related to vision and hearing deficits.
- Help promote a positive self-image in the child by praising his or her achievements and appearance, setting realistic goals, and encouraging his or her involvement with age- and condition-appropriate peer group activities.
- Refer the family to support organizations, such as the Cerebral Palsy Support Foundation of Canada.
- Discuss with the parents that achievement of new tasks will require patience and help from caregivers.
- Encourage the family to seek appropriate functional, adaptive, and vocational education for the child.
- Encourage family members to achieve balance in their lives between caring for the disabled child and pursuing other family and personal interests.
- Facilitate respite care as appropriate (Hockenberry & Wilson, 2011).

DUCHENNE MUSCULAR DYSTROPHY

Duchenne muscular dystrophy (DMD) is the most common and severe form of a group of disorders that cause progressive degeneration and weakness of skeletal muscles. Half of all cases are X-linked, and males are almost exclusively affected. Muscle weakness is progressive, and the disorder is eventually fatal, usually in adolescence, due to infection or cardiopulmonary failure. The incidence is one in 3600 births.

Pathophysiology

DMD occurs when a gene mutation occurs in the gene that encodes dystrophin. Dystrophin, a protein product in skeletal muscle, is absent in the muscles of children with DMD. This lack of dystrophin leads to a gradual degeneration of muscle fibres and is characterized by progressive weakness and muscle wasting.

Clinical Manifestations

- Symptoms begin between the ages of 3 and 5, starting with weakness in the pelvic girdle.
- Key manifestations are delays in motor development; delayed walking and difficulties in running, riding a bicycle, and climbing stairs are among the first symptoms reported.
- Later, a waddling gait, lordosis, and problems with sitting and standing up appear as muscles degenerate.
- Gowers' sign may appear: From a supine position, the child rolls over, kneels, and presses his or her hands against the ankles, shins, knees, and thighs in a "climbing" action to rise to a standing position.
- Profound muscular dystrophy appears in later stages, commonly with deformities and contracture in the large and small joints; by age 12, children with the disorder are usually unable to walk.
- Eventually, the diaphragm and accessory muscles are affected and cardiomegaly usually appears. Respiratory or cardiac failure is often the cause of death.

Diagnostics

- Increased serum creatinine phosphokinase
- Muscle biopsy discloses degeneration of muscle fibres and a lack of dystrophin through DNA analysis. The DNA can also be tested for genetic problems by a serum sample.
- An ECG and pulmonary function tests may help diagnose compromise of heart and lungs.
- EMG results may show a decrease in amplitude and duration of motor unit potentials.

Therapeutics

Therapy is supportive to minimize deformity, prolong ambulation, and assist with ADLs.

Nursing Considerations

- Therapy is provided by an interprofessional team.
- Maintain optimal physical mobility by facilitating the maximum level of activity that the child can manage, including muscle strengthening and ROM exercises.
- Considerations are the same as those for the immobilized child.
- Monitor temperature when children with DMD receive an anaesthetic because they are at risk for malignant hyperthermia.
- Support the child and family in coping with this degenerative and fatal disorder.
- Refer the family to support agencies, such as Muscular Dystrophy Canada.
- Facilitate respite care for the family as required.
- Assist the family in obtaining genetic counselling.

SCOLIOSIS

Idiopathic scoliosis is a lateral curvature of the spine. It may result from leg length discrepancy, hip or knee contractures, pain, neuromuscular disorders, or congenital malformations but usually is idiopathic. Scoliosis is often of unknown cause and usually is seen in females. Evidence points to a probable genetic autosomal dominant trait or to multifactorial causes. The most common spinal deformity, scoliosis affects 3–5% of all children. The curvature can be minor, causing no disability, or severe.

Pathophysiology

- The deformity progresses during periods of growth, particularly during adolescent growth spurts, and stabilizes when vertebral growth is completed.
- As the spine grows and the lateral curve develops, the vertebrae rotate, causing rib asymmetry and thoracic hypokyphosis.
- The child attempts to maintain an erect posture, resulting in a compensatory curve.
- Vertebrae become wedge-shaped, and vertebral discs undergo degenerative changes.
- Muscles and ligaments either shorten and thicken or lengthen and atrophy, depending on the concavity or convexity of the curve.
- A hump may form as a result of the ribs rotating backward on the convex side of the curve.
- If the deformity is severe, the thoracic cavity becomes asymmetrical, leading to compromised respiratory function, decreased vital capacity, and potential pulmonary hypertension, cor pulmonale, and respiratory acidosis.

Clinical Manifestations

- If slight, scoliosis can be asymptomatic and can remain undetected until age 10.
- In more moderate to severe degrees of the condition, there may be a curve, asymmetry of the scapula and extremities, unequal distance between arms and waist, a pronounced hump, or twisting of the body.

Diagnostics

- Physical examination may detect scoliosis; when the child bends forward and dangles the arms, the curvature is apparent.
- Radiographic examination reveals the degree and location of the curvature.

Therapeutics

- Early detection is important to prevent a more severe curvature.
- Exercise and bracing are used in milder idiopathic scoliosis to slow the progression of the curvature until growth is completed. Devices such as the Boston and Wilmington braces are plastic shells that mould to the body, and the thoracolumbosacral orthotic brace is a plastic mould that fits under the arms.

- In more severe cases, surgery may be attempted for spinal realignment and straightening by external or internal fixation and instrumentation combined with bony fusion of the realigned spine. Several surgical techniques are used in the surgery, and different instrument systems are available, such as the Harrington, Dwyer, Zielke, Luque, Cotrel-Dubousset, Isola, Texas Scottish Rite Hospital, and Miami–Moss systems.

Nursing Considerations

- Nurses are often the first to diagnose scoliosis during health assessments of adolescent females.
- Evaluate the child's acceptance of any prescribed brace and exercise to determine his or her compliance level and the need for further teaching.
- Emphasize the positive aspects of wearing the brace, including improved posture and symptom relief. Encourage the child to verbalize any concerns about wearing the brace in relation to body image, which is very important to adolescent females.
- Teach skin care to children wearing a brace: ensuring its proper fit, wearing a cotton shirt under the brace, and early treatment of skin breakdown.
- Provide the child and family with information about scoliosis and its treatment, including equipment.
- See Chapter 6, pages 154–156, for postoperative care.

Fracture

Fractures are breaks in the continuity of a bone when more stress is placed on the bone than it can resist. The bone is realigned or reduced by closed or open reduction followed by immobilization with a splint, traction, or a cast.

Pathophysiology

The fracture types that are most commonly seen in children are as follows:

- Bend: The bone bends to the breaking point and will not straighten without intervention. These are most commonly in the ulna and fibula.
- Buckle: This fracture results from a compression of porous bone, with the bone telescoping on itself.
- Greenstick: The bone does not fracture completely through.
- Complete fracture: The bone divides into bone fragments that are subclassified as transverse, spiral, oblique, comminuted, or butterfly.

Common sites include the following:

- The clavicle
- The humerus (in supracondylar fractures, which occur when a child falls backward onto the hands with the elbows straight, there is a high incidence of neurovascular compromise due to the closeness of the brachial artery and nerves to the fracture site)
- Radius, ulna, and femur (often associated with child abuse)
- Epiphyseal plates (with the potential for growth deformity)

Precautions must be taken to prevent complications, such as cast syndrome, infections, and compartment syndrome. Fractures in children may be the result of falls, sports injuries, motor vehicle accidents, or child abuse.

Clinical Manifestations

Fracture manifestations vary, depending on the location, cause, and type of fracture. Usual symptoms are the five "Ps": pain, pulse, pallor, paraesthesia, and paralysis.

Other symptoms include deformity, swelling, bruising, muscle spasms, tenderness, pain, impaired sensation, loss of function, abnormal mobility, crepitus, shock, and refusal to walk or crawl (in small children).

Diagnostics

X-ray examination reveals the initial injury and subsequent healing progress. Ultrasonography, bone scan, and MRI might be required to further differentiate the injury.

Nursing Considerations

Emergency management includes the following:

- Assess the "five Ps."
- Determine the mechanism of injury.
- Immobilize the part, moving the injured parts as little as possible.
- Apply traction if circulatory compromise is present.
- Elevate the injured limb if possible.
- Apply cold to the injured area.

Later treatment includes the following:

- The child needs to be monitored for neurovascular status (circulation, sensation, and movement) and signs of compartment syndrome, edema and swelling, skin integrity, and signs of infection.
- Cast care needs to be done, including cast petalling, keeping the cast dry, and checking for foul odour and soft spots. It is very important to check for tightness of the cast when edema is present as it can decrease circulation and cause nerve damage.
- Pain management is another important consideration.
- Refer to the immobility section earlier in the chapter for further nursing considerations.

Osteomyelitis

Osteomyelitis is an infection of the bone, most commonly caused by *S. aureus*. It may occur acutely as a result of a bloodborne organism or infection through a break in the skin or as a chronic condition that may lead to dead bone tissue and orthopedic disability. Typically, the joints and long bones of the leg are involved.

Pathophysiology

- In acute hematogenous osteomyelitis, organisms from sites such as infected tonsils and abscessed teeth travel through the bloodstream and infect the bone.
- In exogenous osteomyelitis, there is a direct inoculation of the organism through trauma close to the bone, for example, a fracture or puncture wound.
- Chronic osteomyelitis occurs when the infection is resistant to treatment, which may lead to dead bone or bone loss.

Clinical Manifestations

- Fever, pain, and tenderness at the site of infection.
- There may or may not be signs of inflammation.

Diagnostics

- Cultures are ordered to identify the organism.
- Bone scans, CT scans, and MRIs are helpful in determining areas of infected bone.
- A bone biopsy may be done if necessary.

Therapeutics

- IV antibiotics are administered, usually for at least four weeks.
- Surgery may be required if there is a poor response to the antibiotics.

Nursing Considerations

- Positioning and support of the painful limb
- Weight-bearing activities should not be permitted until healing is established, to prevent stress fractures.
- Consider venous access devices for long-term IV antibiotic administration.
- Administer analgesics as required.
- Provide physical therapy and ROM exercises as indicated.
- Monitor for signs of improvement in the area of infection.

NEUROLOGICAL COGNITIVE DYSFUNCTION

INCREASED INTRACRANIAL PRESSURE

Increased ICP is excessive pressure from tissue or fluid volume within the rigid cranial vault that disrupts neurological function. While an infant's fontanelles are still open, the sutures can widen and expand slightly and compensate for some of the increased pressure.

Pathophysiology

- Normally, ICP remains relatively constant within a fluctuating range as a result of a system of compensatory mechanisms among the cranium's contents: the brain tissue, meninges, CSF, and blood.
- Any increase in the proportional volume of one component must be accompanied by an equivalent reduction in one or more of the others.
- After cranial sutures are fused, only two alterations can compensate for increasing intracranial volume: the displacement of CSF to the spinal subarachnoid space and increased CSF absorption.
- An increase in intracranial volume that exceeds the ability of these mechanisms to compensate produces clinical manifestations of increased ICP.
- Conditions that produce increased ICP include craniocerebral trauma, hydrocephalus, brain tumour, meningitis, encephalitis, and intracerebral hemorrhage.

Clinical Manifestations

- Early signs and symptoms of increased ICP usually are subtle.
- Manifestations in infants include the following:

  - A tense, bulging anterior fontanelle and separated cranial sutures
  - Increased occipital frontal circumference
  - "Setting sun" sign
  - Macewen's sign ("cracked pot sound")
  - Irritability and restlessness with a high-pitched cry
  - Changes in feeding habits
  - Crying when picked up or disturbed

- Manifestations in older children include the following:

  - Headache upon awakening that improves with emesis
  - Anorexia, nausea, and vomiting, usually projectile
  - Cognitive, personality, and behavioural changes, including irritability, restlessness, indifference, lethargy, decreased school performance, decreased physical activity and motor performance, drowsiness, increased sleeping, and inability to follow commands
  - Diplopia, blurred vision
  - Seizures

- Late manifestations of extremely high ICP include the following:

  - Confusion or decreased loss of consciousness (LOC), ranging from drowsiness to coma
  - Decreased motor response to commands
  - Decreased sensation to painful stimuli

- Decreased pupil size and reactivity
- Extension or flexion posturing
- Papilledema and strabismus
- Cheyne–Stokes respirations
- Bradycardia

Diagnostics

- ICP is measured by various devices, from a noninvasive transducer to the more commonly used invasive devices, such as a subarachnoid bolt, an epidural transducer, an intraventricular catheter transducer, and an anterior fontanelle pressure monitor.
- Normal pressure ranges are 0–15 mm Hg.

Nursing Considerations

- Assist in reducing intra-abdominal and intrathoracic pressures, which contribute to ICP, by elevating the head of the bed 15–30 degrees.
- Monitor for early changes in ICP by assessing vital signs (increased systolic blood pressure, wide pulse pressure, and bradycardia indicate increased ICP), LOC, respiratory status, motor activity, behaviour, and pupil size and reactivity.
- If appropriate, use a transducer to monitor ICP.
- Assist with treatments and supportive measures, such as hyperventilation, mechanical ventilation, and hypothermia.
- Prevent overhydration, which can lead to cerebral edema and can be fatal, and underhydration for adequate cerebral perfusion pressure; monitor intake and output, and impose fluid restrictions if prescribed.
- Avoid positions or activities that may increase the child's ICP, such as neck vein compression, flexion or extension of the neck, turning the head from side to side, painful or stressful stimuli, and respiratory suctioning or percussion. Use a pressure mattress to avoid skin breakdown and use sand bags to keep the head midline.
- Avoid a noisy environment that can raise ICP and use touch to help decrease ICP.
- Promote normal bowel elimination to prevent an intra-abdominal pressure increase from straining.
- As appropriate, prepare the child for surgical intervention to relieve the increased ICP, such as a subdural tap, ventriculotomy, epidural evacuation, placement of ventricular shunt, decompressive craniectomy, or tumour resection.
- Administer medications as prescribed, including corticosteroids to decrease cerebral edema, osmotic diuretics such as mannitol or urea, sedatives for combative children, and antiseizure agents if seizuring.
- Control hyperthermia from fever with antipyretics and cooling devices to decrease oxygen needs.

SEIZURE DISORDERS

Seizures are interruptions in normal brain function resulting from excessive and disorderly abnormal electrical discharges in the brain, which can cause LOC, involuntary body movements, and changes in behaviours, sensation, and the autonomic system. Seizures are more common before 2 years than at any other time. Up to 5% of all children experience at least one seizure by adolescence.

Pathophysiology

- Many conditions can cause seizures. They result from overly active and hypersensitive neurons in the brain that trigger excessive electrical discharges. Seizures are normally contained in a focal area, but if a specific trigger, such as hypoglycemia, is present, they can become generalized.
- The location of the hypersensitive cells and the pattern of discharges determine the clinical manifestations.
- There are three categories of seizures:

  - Generalized seizures involve both hemispheres of the brain, are bilateral and symmetrical, and do not have a local onset.
  - Partial, or focal, seizures involve a small area of the cerebral cortex and have a local onset; these seizures may be simple or complex.
  - Unclassified epileptic seizures, such as neonatal seizures, do not provide enough evidence to allow categorization, so they are put in this classification.

- Underlying possible causes include prenatal or perinatal hypoxia, infections, hemorrhages, allergies, syncope, congenital malformations, metabolic disturbances, lead poisoning, head injuries, drug abuse, alcohol misuse, or tumours.
- Most seizures are idiopathic.
- There is some evidence of a genetic etiological factor in which the seizure threshold is lower in affected individuals.

Clinical Manifestations

For generalized seizures:

- Tonic–clonic (formerly called grand mal): Tonic rigidity, extension of extremities, LOC, eyes roll up, fixed jaw and increased salivation, respiratory cessation, dilated pupils; clonic–rhythmic jerking of extremities, autonomic symptoms, possible incontinence
- Myoclonic: Sudden brief contractions of muscle groups, similar in appearance to an exaggerated startle reflex
- Atonic and akinetic: Sudden, brief loss of muscle tone and postural control, and child falls
- Infantile spasm: Brief flexion of the neck, trunk, or legs or, less frequently, extension
- Absence seizure (formerly called petit mal): Brief periods of unconsciousness, may have tonic or atonic phase or automatisms (such as lip-smacking); often mistaken for daydreaming

For partial seizures:

- Simple partial: Motor or sensory signs: consciousness is usually maintained; may include focal motor component (abnormal movement of leg); sensory component (tingling); autonomic (sweating) or psychic manifestations (déjà vu, anger)
- Complex (psychomotor): Begins as a simple seizure but progresses to unconsciousness
- Status epilepticus involves recurrent, continuous, generalized seizure activity with the danger of cardiac arrest and brain damage.
- Some children experience an aura prior to the seizures, which is actually a partial seizure that reflects the area of abnormal activity. The aura occurs prior to the seizures and may take the form of odd smells, hallucinations, or a feeling of déjà vu.

Diagnostics

- EEG is done to document abnormal activity.
- Long-term video-EEG is performed to correlate observed seizures with brain electrical activity.
- Blood tests are done to screen for infections and metabolic imbalances.
- MRI may be performed to rule out a brain tumour.
- A lumbar puncture can rule out meningitis.
- A full physical examination and history are necessary.

Therapeutics

- Anticonvulsant medications may be prescribed to raise the threshold of neuronal excitability in predisposed persons. A few of the commonly used agents are phenobarbital, phenytoin, carbamazepine, valproic acid, clonazepam, and gabapentin, with the dosage adjusted as the child grows. Drug levels must be measured.
- Surgery may be indicated to remove the area of involvement if the seizures are caused by a cerebral lesion. For children with incapacitating refractory seizures that cannot be controlled by medication, surgery may be performed.
- A therapeutic diet, such as a ketogenic diet (high-fat, low-carbohydrate, low-protein diet, to induce ketosis), may be recommended in children with absence or other kinds of seizures; this diet is very difficult to maintain.
- Vagus nerve stimulation may be recommended as an additional treatment in clients 12 years of age and older. A subcutaneous signal stimulates the left vagal nerve at the onset of a seizure.

Nursing Considerations

- Obtain a thorough clinical history (birth trauma, medications, injuries, illnesses, family history, seizure descriptions).
- Maintain safety; provide a helmet, pad the bed's side rails, and have oxygen and suction equipment at the bedside.
- During a seizure, do not restrain the child, do not place anything in his or her mouth, remove harmful objects from the area, extend the neck to maintain the airway, position the child on one side to allow secretions to flow from the mouth, loosen clothing, and screen the child for privacy if possible.
- Document all seizure activity and encourage the family to keep a seizure journal, including the following:

  - The apparent trigger, if known or suspected
  - The child's behaviour before the seizure and whether or not there was an aura
  - The time the seizure began and ended
  - The clinical manifestations of the seizure
  - The child's postictal seizure behaviour and symptoms

- Help prevent seizures by preventing the child's exposure to known triggers, such as emotional stress or blinking lights.
- Use precautions with anticonvulsant medications and observe for side effects, including the following:

  - Phenobarbital: Assess mental status, maintain safety precautions owing to sedation, and monitor levels as ordered.
  - Phenytoin: Provide mouth care, observe gums for inflammation, monitor levels as prescribed, and monitor CBC and liver function test values.
  - Carbamazepine: Monitor for bone marrow depression: frequent infections, bleeding, anemia, and CBC.

- Provide child and family teaching concerning the nature of the disorder and its possible triggers, seizure precaution measures, diagnostic tests and procedures, potential medication side effects, the importance of not discontinuing medication and of not switching to a different brand of the same medication, the need for periodic re-evaluation of medication effectiveness as well as follow-up and close monitoring of blood work, urinalysis, and vital signs; the importance of encouraging a normal lifestyle, activity limitations, the need to share information about the child's special needs with others, such as teachers and school nurses; adolescent needs, such as information about drugs and alcohol, peer pressure, dating, and getting a driver's licence.

NEURAL TUBE DEFECTS

Neural tube defects (NTDs) are a group of related defects of the CNS involving the cranium or spinal cord, which vary from mildly to severely disabling. NTDs include anencephaly, encephalocele, and spina bifida. Heredity and environmental factors have been implicated; NTDs have also been associated with the interaction of genetic predisposition and folic acid deficiency. In the United States, NTDs have decreased from 1.3 per 1000 births in 1990 to 0.3 per 1000 births after the mandatory addition of folic acid to certain foods in 1998 (Honein, 2001). One study suggested that the incidence of NTDs at birth has decreased related to early prenatal detection and the option to abort the pregnancy.

Pathophysiology

- During the third to fourth week of gestation, the embryonic neural plate closes to form the neural tube, which eventually forms the spinal cord and brain.
- The vertebral column develops, along with the spinal cord.
- Normally, the spinal cord and cauda equina are enclosed in a protective sheath of bone and meninges. If the sheath fails to close, leaving either a small opening or an opening the entire length of the spinal cord, this creates various degrees of defects.

The following are types of NTDs:

- Anencephaly: A severe defect involving the absence of both cerebral hemispheres. Many anencephalics are aborted or stillborn; living infants usually survive only a few hours.
- Encephalocele: Meningeal and cerebral tissue protrudes in a sac through a defect in the skull, with the occiput being the most common site; in mild forms, there is little or no residual neurological impairment.
- Spina bifida (SB): A defective closure of the vertebral column, SB is the most common defect of the CNS. The two categories of SB are occulta and cystica. The cystica category is further divided into the meningocele and myelomeningocele (meningomyelocele) types.

Clinical Manifestations

- Manifestations vary with the degree of the defect.
- The degree of neurological dysfunction is directly related to the anatomical location of the defect and thus to the nerves involved; sensory disturbances usually parallel motor dysfunction.
- Spina bifida occulta: The spinal cord usually is not affected; external signs may include nevi, hair tufts, or dimpling of the skin over a dermal sinus. The condition may go undetected, and most children do not have any neurological deficits; if they do occur, there usually is a motor or sensory deficit of the lower extremities associated with problems of the urinary system and bladder sphincter.
- Spina bifida cystica:

  - Meningocele: A sac containing meninges and filled with spinal fluid protrudes outside the vertebrae, usually in the lumbosacral area; the spinal cord is not involved; therefore, there is usually little to no neurological involvement.
  - Myelomeningocele: Similar to meningocele, but the spinal cord and accompanying nerve roots are

involved. Myelomeningocele is the most severe and most common NTD, occurring usually in the lumbosacral area, and involves significant sensorimotor deficits, urinary and bowel problems, and joint deformities such as club foot and DDH.

Diagnostics

- Diagnosis is made on the basis of a clinical examination; if the sac transilluminates, it usually is a meningocele.
- Other tests include ultrasonography, CT, MRI, and myelography.
- Prenatal detection involves ultrasonography and identifying elevated levels of alpha-fetoprotein in the amniotic fluid between 16 and 18 weeks. (AFP)

Therapeutics

- No treatment is indicated for spina bifida occulta unless there is neurological damage; if a dermal sinus is present, it may need to be closed surgically.
- Meningocele requires closure as soon after birth as possible; the child should be monitored for postoperative complications that could include hydrocephalus, meningitis, and spinal cord disruption.
- Myelomeningocele requires management by a coordinated interdisciplinary team, including neurology, neurosurgery, pediatrics, urology, orthopedics, rehabilitation, and nursing.
- Closure of the defect is performed within 24 hours, to a maximum of 72 hours, in order to minimize infection and prevent further damage or stretching of the spinal cord and nerve roots (Kaufman, 2004).
- Skin grafting may be required, and shunting is performed for hydrocephalus.
- Antibiotics are initiated to prevent infection.
- The child will need correction of musculoskeletal deformities and management of urological deficits and bowel control.

Nursing Considerations

For myelomeningocele:

- Before surgery, prevent infection by applying sterile, moist saline soaks to the sac or open lesion and keep them moist.
- Avoid placing a diaper or other covering directly over the lesion, to prevent infection from fecal contamination.
- Prevent trauma and tears to the sac by gently placing the infant prone in an isolette or warmer.
- The infant may require clean intermittent catheterizations if neurogenic bladder is present.
- Help prevent hip subluxation by positioning the legs in abduction with a pad between the knees and the feet in a neutral position with a roll under the ankles.
- Monitor vital signs, measure head circumference, and monitor neurological status, including signs of ICP.

- After surgery, place the child in a prone position if a side-lying position, which is permitted by many neurosurgeons, aggravates the hips.
- Refer parents to Spina Bifida and Hydrocephalus Canada for resources.
- Provide family teaching for associated problems in the growing child, such as neurogenic bladder and bowel, impaired mobility, skin breakdown, ICP, and possible neurological impairment related to hydrocephalus.
- Carefully assess the family's ability to care for the child and refer them for further assistance if needed.

HYDROCEPHALUS

Hydrocephalus is a condition caused by a blockage to the flow of CSF, or an imbalance in the production and absorption of CSF in the ventricular system. When production exceeds absorption, CSF accumulates, usually under pressure, creating ventricular dilatation. The condition occurs in three births in 1000. Hydrocephalus is caused by congenital defects, such as myelomeningocele, or acquired conditions, such as intraventricular hemorrhage or CSF infection.

Pathophysiology

- CSF flows from the lateral ventricles through the foramen of Monro to the third ventricle, then through the aqueduct of Sylvius into the fourth ventricle through the foramen of Luschka, and the midline foramen of Magendie into the cisterna magna. From there, it flows to the cerebral and cerebellar subarachnoid spaces, where it is absorbed.
- Causes of hydrocephalus are varied but result in either impaired absorption of CSF within the arachnoid space (communicating, or nonobstructive, hydrocephalus) or obstruction to the flow of CSF through the ventricular system (noncommunicating hydrocephalus).
- Most cases of noncommunicating hydrocephalus are the result of developmental malformations; others may be caused by tumours, infection, or trauma.
- Blockage to the normal flow can occur at any point in the CSF pathway, producing increased pressure and dilation of the pathways proximal to the site of blockage.
- Noncommunicating hydrocephalus can result from meningitis, prenatal maternal infections, meningeal malignancy (secondary to leukemia or lymphoma), arachnoid cyst, or tuberculosis.

Therapeutics

- Surgery is the preferred intervention to remove the obstruction.
- A shunt provides primary drainage of the CSF to an extracranial compartment, usually the peritoneum.
- Ventriculoperitoneal shunts consist of a ventricular catheter, a flush pump, a unidirectional flow valve,

and a distal catheter.
- Major complications of shunts are infections and malfunction; others include subdural hematoma caused by a too rapid reduction of CSF, peritonitis, abdominal abscess, perforation of organs, fistulas, hernias, and ileus.

Clinical Manifestations

In infants: The child's head grows at an abnormal rate; signs and symptoms include a bulging fontanelle, a tense anterior fontanelle, often bulging and nonpulsatile; dilated scalp veins; Macewen's sign ("cracked pot sound"); frontal bossing; setting sun sign; sluggish and unequal pupils; irritability and lethargy with varying LOC; abnormal infantile reflexes; and possible cranial nerve damage.

In children: Signs of ICP include headache on awakening with improvement following emesis; papilledema; strabismus; ataxia, irritability, lethargy, apathy, and confusion.

Diagnostics

- Ultrasonograms can diagnose hydrocephalus at 14 weeks' gestation.
- Cranial transillumination shows varying degrees of localized fluid accumulation.
- CT and MRI scans confirm fluid accumulation and enlarged ventricles.

Nursing Considerations

Preoperative considerations:

- Assess head circumference, fontanelles, cranial sutures, and LOC; also assess for signs of ICP: irritability, altered feeding habits, and high-pitched cry.
- Irritability, seizures, poor feeding, lethargy, and altered vital signs point to an advanced condition.
- Prepare the child and family for diagnostic procedures.
- Carefully support the head and neck when holding or repositioning the child.
- Provide skin care, particularly for the back of the head.
- Offer small, frequent feedings to decrease the risk of vomiting.
- Encourage parental participation in the child's care and promote bonding.

Postoperative considerations:

- Assess for signs of increased ICP.
- Measure head circumference daily; check the anterior fontanelle for size, tenseness, and fullness.
- Position the child on the side opposite the shunt to prevent pressure on the valve.
- Keep the child flat for the first 24 hours so as not to drain the CSF too quickly.
- Monitor dressings for bloody and clear drainage (the

presence of glucose in drainage indicates CSF).
- Monitor the fluid balance.
- Promote natural bowel elimination in children with ventriculoperitoneal shunts, who may have constipation.
- Administer antibiotics as prescribed, IV or intraventricular.
- Monitor for infection, particularly CSF or peritonitis; watch for abdominal distension, which can mean peritonitis from the shunt insertion, or postoperative ileus because of shunt catheter placement.
- Administer osmotic diuretics as prescribed to reduce increased ICP.
- Provide child and family teaching concerning ICP, possible neurological impairment, skin care, and the need for frequent follow-up care.

HEAD INJURY

A head injury is a pathological process that can involve the scalp, skull, or meninges. It can range from a mild injury to severe damage to the head.

Pathophysiology

- Pathophysiology and management are directly related to the force of the impact. Intracranial contents are damaged when the force is too great to be absorbed by the skull and the musculoskeletal support of the head.
- Types of head traumas include skull fractures, contusions, diffuse injuries, and hematomas.
- Head injury is one of the most common causes of disability and death in children.
- Head injury is most frequently caused by motor vehicle accidents, abuse, falls, and birth trauma, with the etiology related to the child's age.

Clinical Manifestations

Skull fractures: The type, extent, and accompanying symptoms depend on the velocity, force, and mass of the object; the area of skull involved; and the age of the child. Fracture types include the following:

- Linear: This is the most common type of fracture. It resembles a thin line and is from a low-velocity blow. Linear fractures are not often seen in children under 2 or 3 years. There are usually no signs other than those found on X-ray; the child is observed for neurological changes; the fracture heals on its own.
- Comminuted: This type has a "cracked eggshell" appearance and may also be categorized as depressed.
- Depressed: The skull is indented at the point of impact, which may cause compression on the brain, shifting of brain tissue, and intracranial damage; symptoms depend on the area damaged. This fracture may require surgery to lift the bone off the cerebrum. Bone fragments could also tear the dura and cause bleeding.
- Basilar: A linear fracture involving the basilar portion of the frontal, ethmoid, temporal, or occipital bones of

the skull, often resulting in a dura tear; classic signs are "raccoon eyes," "Battle's sign" (bruising behind the ear from bleeding into the mastoid sinus), and a possible blood or CSF leak into the ears, nasopharynx, or nose.

Brain injury: Signs and symptoms depend on location and severity; post-traumatic syndromes (seizures, hydrocephalus, focal neurological deficits), and metabolic complications (diabetes insipidus, hyponatremia or hypernatremia, hyperglycemic hyperosmolar states) may occur; all of these may occur up to two years after the injury.

Hematomas: Epidural (between the skull and the dura) and subdural (between the dura and arachnoid layer) are the most common types.

- Epidural: Life-threatening, with rapid onset, characterized by rapid deterioration, headache, seizures, coma, and brain herniation with compression of the brainstem
- Subdural: Occurs within 48 hours of injury, characterized by headache, agitation, confusion, drowsiness, decrease in LOC, and increased ICP; chronic subdural hematomas may also occur

General manifestations of minor head trauma are as follows:

- May or may not involve LOC
- Transient confusion
- Listlessness and irritability
- Pallor and vomiting

Signs of deterioration are as follows:

- Altered mental status
- Increasing agitation
- Significant changes in vital signs
- Reflexes hyporesponsive, hyperresponsive, or nonexistent

Diagnostics

Fractures may be visualized by X-ray; brain injuries and hematomas are viewed by CT or MRI.

Therapeutics

- Therapeutic interventions depend on symptoms, which must be closely observed and monitored.
- Surgical evacuation of hematomas may be needed and may be facilitated by burr holes for evacuation and relief of increased ICP; depressed skull fractures need to be elevated surgically.
- Scalp and dural lacerations may require sutures.

Nursing Considerations

- Promote prevention of injury, especially of falls.
- Promote safety practices, including the use of bike

helmets, seat belts, and protective sports equipment; encourage safe driving.
- Perform neurological assessments of cerebral functioning (alertness, orientation, memory, speech), vital signs (check for increased blood pressure, decreased pulse), pupils, and motor and sensory function.
- Assess for cervical and other injuries.
- To help decrease cerebral edema, and if there is no cervical injury, raise the head of the bed to 30 degrees.
- Monitor for complications, which can develop rapidly; monitor vital signs and neurological status frequently; and check for increased ICP and for drainage (of CSF or blood) from the nose and ears.
- Be aware that seizures may occur for up to two years after injury.
- The child may also require rehabilitation following an extensive brain injury.
- Provide child and family teaching:

  - Discuss complications and what to observe for in post-traumatic syndrome.
  - Refer family members to the Brain Injury Association of Canada.

INTELLECTUAL DISABILITY

Intellectual disability (ID), or cognitive impairment (formerly known as mental retardation), is part of a broad category of developmental disability. The condition is now defined by the American Association on Intellectual and Developmental Disabilities (AAIDD) as "a disability characterized by significant limitations both in intellectual functioning and in adaptive behavior as expressed in conceptual, social, and practical adaptive skills. This disability originates before the age of 18" (AAIDD, 2008).

Pathophysiology

- Pathophysiology depends on cause.
- Early diagnosis and prompt treatment may be particularly important in cases involving an identifiable and possibly correctable cause, such as hypothyroidism phenylketonuria, malnutrition, or child abuse.
- A diagnosis of ID cannot be made on the basis of intellectual ability alone; there must be both adaptive (personal independence and social responsibility) and intellectual impairment.
- Causes include infection and intoxication, trauma or physical agents, metabolic or nutritional abnormalities, gross postnatal brain disease, unknown prenatal conditions, chromosomal abnormalities, gestational disorders, psychiatric disorders with onset during the child's developmental period, such as autism, and environmental influences (Hockenberry & Wilson, 2011).
- Chromosomal disorders account for 20–25% of ID, with most related to Down syndrome; 25% of diagnoses are related to specific disorders; and

10–20% are related to CP, microcephaly, or infantile spasms.

Diagnostics

- Diagnosis usually is made after a period of suspicion, although it may be made at birth from recognition of a specific syndrome, such as Down syndrome.
- Diagnosis and classification are based on a variety of standardized IQ test scores.

Clinical Manifestations

Findings vary depending on the classification or degree of disability.

- Mild (50–70 IQ):

  - Preschool: Often the child is not noted as having a disability but is slow to walk, talk, and feed himself or herself.
  - School age: The child can acquire practical skills and learn to read and do arithmetic to a sixth grade level; with special education, the child achieves a mental age of 8–12 years.
  - Adult: Adults can usually achieve social and vocational skills, may need occasional guidance, and may handle marriage but have difficulty with parenting.

- Moderate (35–55 IQ):

  - Preschool: The child has noticeable delays, especially in speech.
  - School age: The child can learn simple communication, health and safety habits, and simple manual skills; he or she has a mental age of 3–7 years.
  - Adult: Adults can perform simple tasks under sheltered conditions and can travel alone to familiar places but usually need help with self-maintenance.

- Severe (20–40 IQ):

  - Preschool: The child exhibits marked motor delays and few communication skills; he or she may respond to training in elementary self-help, such as feeding.
  - School age: The child usually walks with difficulty, has some understanding of and may respond to speech, can respond to habit training, and has the mental age of a toddler.
  - Adult: Adults can conform to daily routines and repetitive activities but need constant direction and supervision in a protective environment.

- Profound (<20 IQ):

  - Preschool: The child exhibits gross intellectual disability, has some capacity for function in sensorimotor areas, and needs total care.

- School age: The child displays obvious delays in all areas; shows a basic emotional response; may respond to skillful training in the use of the legs, hands, and jaws; needs close supervision; and has the mental age of a young infant.
- Adult: A profoundly delayed adult may walk but has primitive speech and needs complete custodial care; he or she usually benefits from regular physical activity.

Therapeutics

- The treatment goal is to promote optimal development.
- Preventive measures include regular prenatal care, support for high-risk infants, rubella immunization, genetic counselling, education, and injury reduction.

Nursing Considerations

- Support the family at the time of the initial diagnosis.
- Facilitate the child's self-care abilities through an early stimulation program, self-feeding, independent toileting, and independent grooming.
- Promote optimal development by encouraging self-care goals and emphasizing the universal needs of children, such as play, social interaction, and parental limit-setting.
- Assist the family in planning for the child's future needs.
- Refer parents to appropriate community agencies.
- Discuss the need for patience with the child's slow attainment of developmental milestones.
- Discuss stimulation and safety.
- Demonstrate communication strategies; accentuate nonverbal cues, such as facial expressions and body language, to help cue speech development.
- Explain the need for discipline that is simple, consistent, and appropriate to the child's development.
- Review an adolescent's need for simple, practical sexual information.
- Discuss the importance of positive self-esteem, built by accomplishing small successes, in motivating the child to accomplish other tasks.

Down Syndrome

Down syndrome is the most common chromosomal abnormality. This condition occurs more in individuals of European descent than in other groups.

Pathophysiology

- Approximately 95% of cases may be attributed to an extra chromosome on chromosome 21—hence the name nonfamilial trisomy 21.
- About 4% of cases may be caused by translocation of chromosomes 15 and 21 or 22; this usually is hereditary and is not related to maternal age.

- Children with Down syndrome are born to parents of all ages.
- There is a higher statistical risk for mothers over age 35, but most are born to mothers under this age, likely due to prenatal screening for women in older age groups as well as the option of abortion.
- The level of cognitive and physical impairment is related to the percentage of cells with the abnormal chromosome makeup.

Clinical Manifestations

- The most common findings include separated sagittal suture, oblique palpebral fissures, small nose, depressed nasal bridge, high-arched palate, skin excess and laxity, wide space between the big and second toes, plantar crease between the big and second toes, hyperextensible and lax joints, and muscle weakness.
- Other common findings include a small penis, short, broad hands (with a transverse [simian] palmar crease), protruding tongue, small ears, Brushfield spots, and dry skin.
- Associated problems and features include the following:

  - Intelligence varies from severely disabled to low-normal but is generally within the mild to moderate range.
  - Social development may be two to three years beyond mental age; temperament range is similar to that of normal children, with a trend toward the "easy" child.
  - Forty to 45% have congenital heart disease, especially septal defects.
  - Other defects include renal agenesis, duodenal atresia, Hirschsprung's disease, tracheoesophageal fistula, and skeletal deformities.
  - Sensory problems include strabismus, nystagmus, myopia, hyperopia, cataracts and excessive tearing, and conductive hearing loss.
  - Other physical disorders may include altered immune function, respiratory infections, leukemia, thyroid dysfunction, and early aging.
  - Shortened stature with a tendency for rapid weight gain.
  - Sexual development may be delayed, incomplete, or both.
  - Male genitalia and secondary characteristics are underdeveloped; men are infertile.
  - Female breast development is mild to moderate with menarche at an appropriate age; women may be fertile.

Diagnostics

Diagnosis is made by physical examination and chromosomal analysis.

Therapeutics

- Surgery may be used to correct some accompanying defects.

- Behaviour modification may be recommended for dealing with negative behaviours.
- Developmental, social, and educational supports will likely be required.

Nursing Considerations

- Implement nursing care as with ID.
- Support parental genetic counselling.
- Explain hypertonicity and joint hyperextensibility to parents.
- Feeding can take longer in the infant due to the large tongue and weak suck.
- For the older child, use a small, straight-handled spoon to push food to the side and back of the mouth.
- Monitor for common associated congenital anomalies, especially cardiac.

COMMUNICABLE DISEASES OF CHILDHOOD

MEASLES (RUBEOLA)

Rubeola, or "red measles," is a communicable disease that has been largely eradicated in Canada. Occasional outbreaks are primarily related to people who have been inadequately immunized.

Pathophysiology

- Rubeola, or measles, is a communicable virus that is usually transmitted by direct contact with droplets.
- A vaccine prevents this disease.
- Incubation time is 10–20 days, and infected individuals are contagious from four days before to five days after the rash appears.

Clinical Manifestations

- Stage 1: The prodromal stage includes fever and malaise; 24 hours later, acute rhinitis, cough, conjunctivitis with photophobia, and Kolick spots (white spots in the mouth) develop.
- Stage 2: Three to four days after the prodromal stage, a rash appears, causing red maculopapular lesions on the face and spreading down toward the trunk and extremities. The rash changes to a browner colour in three to four days; fine peeling of the skin begins in the more severely affected regions.
- Potential complications include otitis media, pneumonia, laryngotracheitis, and encephalitis.

Diagnostics

- Assessment of rash
- Antibody titres

Nursing Considerations

- Provide comfort measures, including antipyretics, skin care with oatmeal, cleansing the eyes if conjunctivitis develops, and sunglasses and dim lights for the photophobia.
- Promote childhood immunization.

RUBELLA

Rubella, or "German measles," is a communicable disease that, like rubeola, is now largely eradicated in Canada. However, outbreaks are of concern to the public as this disease may cause severe birth defects if contracted by pregnant women.

Pathophysiology

- The rubella virus is transmitted by direct and indirect contact.
- The incubation period is 14–21 days.
- The child is communicable for seven days before to approximately five days after the rash appears.

Clinical Manifestations

- A reddish-pink maculopapular rash begins on the face and spreads downward to the trunk and extremities.
- The rash disappears first in the initial lesions.
- Symptoms also include a low-grade fever, malaise, and lymphadenopathy.
- Complications include possible damage to the fetus in a pregnant woman and, rarely, encephalitis, arthritis, or purpura.
- Rubella is preventable with a vaccine.

Diagnostics

Diagnosis is generally based on observation of rash and antibody titres.

Nursing Considerations

- Provide comfort measures for the child.
- Advise the parents of the danger to pregnant women of exposure to a communicable child.
- Promote childhood immunization.

CHICKENPOX (VARICELLA)

Chickenpox is an uncomfortable, communicable disease of children and adults. It may leave scars and create a significant health risk for the immuno-compromised child.

Pathophysiology

- Varicella zoster is the communicable agent.
- Infection is transmitted by direct contact and via contaminated objects.

- The child is communicable for one or two days before the rash appears and remains infectious until all of the lesions are crusted over.

Diagnostics

Diagnosis is based on assessment of rash and antibody titres.

Clinical Manifestations

- The prodromal stage involves low-grade fever, malaise, and loss of appetite.
- Rash starts on the face with macules that turn to papules, then vesicles, then pustules, and finally crusts. The rash then spreads to the proximal extremities, with fewer lesions in distal areas.
- Lesions can also appear on the mucous membranes.
- The lesions cause severe itching.
- Other symptoms include fever, lymphadenopathy, and irritability from itching.
- Complications are secondary infections, such as encephalitis, pneumonia, and hemorrhagic varicella in immuno-compromised children.

Nursing Considerations

- Strict isolation until vesicles are dry is necessary to prevent spread.
- Provide comfort measures: a cool environment, cool oatmeal baths to soothe itchy and irritated skin and decrease the risk of secondary infection and scarring from scratching, loose clothing, antihistamines, and antipyretics.
- Zoster immune globulin (ZIG) and acyclovir are given to children who are immuno-compromised.
- Varicella is preventable with vaccination.

Pertussis (Whooping Cough)

Pertussis is a potentially serious disease in the infant. Occasional outbreaks of pertussis occur in Canada despite adequate immunization.

Pathophysiology

- The infectious bacterium is *Bordetella pertussis.*
- The incubation period is 6–20 days, with an average of seven days.
- Stage 1: The catarrhal stage, when the child has signs of an upper respiratory infection; one or two weeks later, the hacking cough increases in severity.
- Stage 2: The paroxysmal stage, which usually lasts four to six weeks. The child has the classic paroxysmal "whoop" cough, which usually occurs at night; the child is flushed or has a cyanotic face, bulging eyes, and a protruding tongue and coughs until he or she coughs up a mucous plug, often vomiting afterward.

- Stage 3: The convalescent stage, in which the cough slowly decreases, vomiting stops, and strength returns.
- Complications include atelectasis, otitis media, seizures, hemorrhage, weight loss, and dehydration.
- In infants, apnea and respiratory arrest from a mucous plug can occur.
- Pertussis is preventable with a vaccine.

Diagnostics

Diagnosis is based on the characteristic cough and a throat swab for culture.

Nursing Considerations

- Maintain isolation.
- Use respiratory precautions.
- Provide a quiet environment, encourage fluids, and monitor for respiratory distress.

Mumps

Mumps is an infectious disease of the parotid glands. Occasional outbreaks occur in Canada despite adequate immunization.

Pathophysiology

- The infectious agent is paramyxovirus.
- Transmission is by direct contact or droplet.
- The incubation period is 14–21 days.
- The child is communicable immediately before the swelling occurs until immediately after.
- Symptoms of the prodromal stage are pyrexia, headache, and loss of appetite followed by earache, which worsens with chewing.
- The second acute stage occurs by the second day with parotid gland swelling, which is painful and peaks in one to three days.
- Complications include meningoencephalitis, orchitis, epididymitis, arthritis, and, rarely, sterility in males.

Diagnostics

Mumps is generally diagnosed by the characteristic facial swelling produced.

Nursing Considerations

- Ensure isolation and bed rest with respiratory precautions.
- Administer analgesics and fluids and provide warmth and support for orchitis.

References

Adoptive Parents of Canada. (2011). *Canadian adoption news and events.* Retrieved on January 19, 2013, from http://www.adoptiveparents.ca/adoptivenews.html

American Academy of Pediatrics. (2003). Task Force on Sudden Infant Death Syndrome: The changing concepts of sudden infant death syndrome: Diagnostic coding shifts, controversies regarding the sleeping environment, and new variables to consider in reducing risk. *Pediatrics 116*(5), 1245–1255.

American Association on Intellectual and Developmental Disability (2008). *Definition of intellectual disability.* Retrieved January 19, 2013, from http://www.aaidd. org/content_100.cfm?navID=21

Anabwani, M. G., Woldetsadik, E. A., & Kline, M. W. (2005). Treatment of human immunodeficiency virus (HIV) in children using antiretroviral drugs. *Seminars in Pediatric Infectious Disease, 16,* 116–124.

Ariel, J., & McPerson, D. W. (2000). Therapy with lesbian and gay parents and their children. *J Marriage Family, 26* (4), 421–432.

Ball, J. W., &, Binder, R. C. (2006). *Child health nursing: Partnering with children & families.* New Jersey: Pearson/ Prentice Hall.

Bjornson, C., Klassen T., Willamson, J., et al. (2004). A randomized trial of a single dose of oral dexamethasone for mild croup. *New England Journal of Medicine 351*(13), 1306–1313.

Brandt, M. L. (1999). Intussusception. In J. McMillan & R. Feigin (Eds.), *Oski's pediatrics: Principles and practice* (3rd ed.). Philadelphia: Lippincott, Williams & Wilkins.

Bryant, R. (2011). The child with cognitive, sensory, or communication impairment. In M. Hockenberry & D. Wilson (Eds.), *Wong's nursing care of infants and children* (9th ed., 908–945). St. Louis: Mosby, Elsevier.

Canadian Cancer Society, National Cancer Institute of Canada, Statistics Canada, Provincial/Territorial Cancer Registries, Public Health Agency of Canada. (2008). *Canadian cancer statistics 2008.* Retrieved January 19, 2013, from http://www.cancer.ca/Canada-wide/ About%20cancer/Cancer%20statistics

Canadian Dental Association. (2012). *Cleaning teeth.* Retrieved January 19, 2013, from http://www.cda-adc. ca/en/oral_health/cfyt/dental_care_children

Canadian Diabetes Association. (2012). *Children and type 2 diabetes.* Retrieved January 19, 2013, from http://www. diabetes.ca/diabetes-and-you/youth/type2/

Canadian Paediatric Society. (2006). Oral rehydration therapy and early refeeding in the management of childhood gastroenteritis. *Paediatric Child Health, 11*(8), 527–531.

Canadian Paediatric Society. (2007a). Vitamin D supplementation: Recommendations for Canadian mothers and infants. *Paediatrics & Child Health, 12*(7), 583–589. Reaffirmed March 2012.

Canadian Paediatric Society. (2007b). Management of the infant at increased risk for sepsis. *Paediatrics & Child Health, 12*(10), 893–898.

Canadian Paediatric Society. (2007c). *When your child is sick.* Author. Retrieved January 19, 2013, from http://www. caringforkids.cps.ca/whensick/otc_drugs.htm.

Canadian Paediatric Society. (2007d). *Canadian paediatric surveillance program non-type 1 diabetes mellitus in Canadian children.* January 19, 2013, from http:// web.cps.ca/English/Surveillance/CPSP/Publications/ highlights/2007/June.pdf

Canadian Paediatric Society. (2008a). Head lice infestations: A clinical update. *Paediatric Child Health, 13*(8), 692–696.

Canadian Paediatric Society. (2008b). Therapy of suspected bacterial meningitis in Canadian children six weeks of age and older – summary. *Paediatric Child Health, 13*(4), 309.

Canadian Paediatric Society. (2008c). Recommendations for safe sleeping environments for infants and children. *Paediatric Child Health, 9*(9), 659–663. Appendix. Reaffirmed January, 2012. Retrieved January 19, 2013,from http://www.cps.ca/en/documents/position/ safe-sleep-environments-infants-children

Denison, M. R. (2005). Severe acute respiratory syndrome: Coronavirus pathogenesis, disease and vaccines: An update, *Pediatric Infectious Disease Journal, 23*(11 Suppl.), S207–S214.

Dieterich, W., Esslinger, B., & Schuppan, D. (2003). Pathomechanisms in celiac disease. *International Archives of Allergy and Immunology 132*(2), 98–108.

Erickson, E. (1963). *Childhood and society.* New York: W.W. Norton.

Family Service Canada. (2012). *Who are we.* Retrieved January 19, 2013, from http://www. familyservicecanada.org/about/purpose-history

Gulbis, B., Haberman, D., DuFour, D., et al. (2005). Hydroxyurea for sickle cell children and for prevention of cerebrovascular events: The Belgian experience. *Blood, 205*(7), 2685–2690.

Health Canada. (1997). *For the safety of Canadian children and youth: From injury data to preventive measures.* Ottawa: Author.

Health Canada. (2011b). Healthy living: Injury prevention and safety. Retrieved January 19, 2013, from http:// www.hc-sc.gc.ca/hl-vs/securit/index-eng.php

Health Canada. (2012a). *Vitamin D supplementation of breastfed infants in Canada: Key statistics and graphics* (2009-2010). Retrieved January 19, 2013, from http://www. hc-sc.gc.ca/fn-an/surveill/nutrition/commun/prenatal/ vit_d_sup-eng.php

Health Canada. (2012b). *Clinical Practice Guidelines for Nurses in Primary Care - Pediatric and Adolescent Care.* Retrieved January 19, 2013, from http://www.hc-sc.gc. ca/fniah-spnia/services/nurs-infirm/clini/pediat/index-eng.php

Hebert, P. W., Rakes, G. P., Loach, T. C., & Murphy, D. D. (1997). Recognizing the young atopic child. *Contemporary Pediatrics, 14*(4), 131–139.

Hockenberry, M. J., & Wilson, D. (2011). *Wong's nursing care of infants and children* (9th ed.). St. Louis: Mosby.

Hockenberry, M. J., Wilson, D., & Winkelstein, M. L. (2005). *Wong's essentials of pediatric nursing* (7th ed.) St. Louis: Mosby.

Hoffman, J., & Kaplan, W. (2002). The incidence of congenital heart disease. *Journal of the American College of Cardiology, 39,* 1890–1900.

Honein, M. A. (2001). Impact of folic acid fortification of the US food supply and occurrence of neural tube defects, *JAMA, 285*(23), 2981–2986.

Johnston, M. K., & Kinsman, S. (2004). Congenital anomalies of the central nervous system. In R. E. Behrman, R. M. Kliegman, H. B. Jenson (Eds.), *Nelson textbook of pediatrics* (17th ed., 1983–1993). Philadelphia: Saunders.

Kaufman, B. A. (2004). Neural tube defects. *Pediatric Clinics of North America 51*(2), 389–419.

Krigger, K. W. (2006). Cerebral palsy: An overview. *American Family Physician 73*(1), 91–100, 101–102.

LeBlanc, J. C., Pless, I. B., King, W. J., Bawden, H., Bernard-Bonnin, A., Klassen, T., et al. (2006). Home safety measures and the risk of unintentional injury among children: A multicentre case-control study. *Canadian Medical Association Journal, 175*, 883–887.

Lerner, R. E. (2002). *Adolescence.* Upper Saddle River, NJ: Pearson Education.

McCord, S. S. (2011). Health problems of middle childhood. In M. Hockenberry & D. Wilson (Eds.), *Wong's nursing care of infants and children* (9th ed., 684–737). St. Louis: Mosby.

McGrath, P. J., Johnson, G., Goodman, J. T., et al. (1985). The CHEOPS: A behavioural scale for rating post-operative pain in children. In H. L. Fields, R. Dubner, & F. Cervero (Eds.), *Advances in pain research and therapy.* New York: Raven Press.

Murdock, A., & Johnston, S. (2005). Diagnostic criteria for celic disease: Time for change? *European Journal of Gastroenterology and Hepatology, 17*, 41–43.

Murray, J. (2002). Gene/environment causes of cleft lip and/or palate. *Clinical Genetics, 61*(4), 248–256.

Piaget, J. (1972). *The child's conception of the world.* Totowa, NJ: Littlefields Adams Co.

Public Health Agency of Canada. (1999). *Measuring up. A health surveillance update on Canadian children and youth.* Retrieved January 19, 2013, from http://www.ihe.ca/publications/health-db/geo/119/

Public Health Agency of Canada. (2002). *The family violence initiative, five year report.* Retrieved January 19, 2013, from http://www.publications.gc.ca/pub?id=256644&sl=0

Public Health Agency of Canada. (2002a). *Canadian incidence study of reported child abuse and neglect, final report.* Retrieved January 19, 2013, from http://www.phac-aspc.gc.ca/publicat/cisfr-ecirf/index-eng.php

Public Health Agency of Canada. (2013). *Canadian immunization guide.* Author: Ottawa.

Safe Kids Canada. (2010). *Drowning prevention.* Retrieved January 19, 2013, from http://www.safekidscanada.ca/Parents/Safety Information/Drowning-Prevention/Index.aspx

Safe Kids Canada. (2012a). *Car seats.* Retrieved OJanuary 19, 2013, from http://www.safekidscanada.ca/Parents/Safety-Information/Car-Seats/Index.aspx

Safe Kids Canada. (2012b). *Wheeled activities.* Retrieved January 19, 2013, from, http://www.safekidscanada.ca/Parents/Safety-Information/Wheeled-Activities/Index.aspx

Statistics Canada. (2006). *Families by family structure, Canada and regions.* Retrieved January 19, 2013, from http://www.statcan.gc.ca/pub/89-625-x/2007001/t/4054991-eng.htm

Statistics Canada. (2008). *Divorces by province and territory.* Retrieved January 19, 2013, from http://www.statcan.gc.ca/tables-tableaux/sum-som/l01/cst01/famil02-eng.htm

Stevens, B., Johnston, C., Petryshen, P., & Taddiom A. (1996). Premature Infant Pain Profile: Development and initial validation. *The Clinical Journal of Pain, 12*(1), 13–22.

Thiedke, C. C. (2001). Sleep disorders and sleep problems in childhood. *American Family Physician, 63*(2), 277–284.

Transport Canada. (2009). *Car seats, seat belts and your child.* Retrieved October 31, 2012, from http://www.tc.gc.ca/eng/roadsafety/safedrivers-childsafety-car-index-873.htm

Transport Canada. (2012). Child safety. Retrieved January 19, 2013, from http://www.tc.gc.ca/eng/roadsafety/safedrivers-childsafety-index-53.htm

Vanier Institute of the Family. (n.d.). *Definition of the family.* Retrieved January 19, 2013, from http://30645.vws.magma.ca/node/2

Yoev, R., & Guzman-Cottrill, J. (2005). Bacterial meningitis in children: Critical review of current concepts. *Drugs, 65*(8), 1097–1112.

BIBLIOGRAPHY

Jarvis, C. (2008). *Physical examination and health assessment.* St. Louis: Elsevier.

Muscari, M. E. (2005). *Pediatric nursing* (4th ed.). Lippincott's Review Series. Ambler, PA: Lippincott Williams & Wilkins.

Potter, P., & Perry, A. (2010). *Canadian fundamentals of nursing* (Revised 4th ed.). Elsevier Canada.

WEB SITES

About Kids Health (http://www.aboutkidshealth.ca): About Kids Health is a Web site that is designed by The Hospital for Sick Children to provide an electronic resource centre that provides specific information to families and children on pediatric conditions such as prematurity, cardiac defects, and seizure disorders. This site includes a fun and interactive window with games and contests that teach children how their bodies work.

Canadian Paediatric Society (http://www.cps.ca): The CPS Web site was created by Canadian pediatricians to provide child health care information for physicians and other interdisciplinary health professionals.

Caring for Kids (http://www.caringforkids.cps.ca/): Caring for Kids is a CPS site that provides child health and wellness information to families and children. There are many different topics, such as pregnancy and babies, immunizations, care for sick children, and the use of natural products.

Pediatric Clinical Guidelines for Nurses in Primary Care (http://www.hc-sc.gc.ca/fniah-spnia/services/nurs-infirm/clini/pediat/index-eng.php): The nursing pediatric guideline site is part of the larger Health Canada federal government site. The site includes pediatric clinical practice guidelines for nurses on different subjects, such as health assessment, prevention, fluid management, and child abuse.

Safe Kids Canada (http://www.safekidscanada.ca): The Safe Kids Canada site was founded by The Hospital for Sick Children with a large number of partners. The goal of the site is to provide evidence-informed material to communities, families, and children to prevent unintentional serious injuries. There are many safety topics, such as motor vehicles, wheeled activities, poisonings, and playing safely in playgrounds and at sports.

CHAPTER 10

Practice Questions

Case 1

Simon is a 6-year-old boy who is brought by his parents to the emergency department of a local hospital. The triage nurse assesses that Simon has tachypnea, wheezing, and diminished air entry. The physician diagnoses asthma.

Questions 1–5 refer to this case.

1. In addition to wheezing and tachypnea, Simon manifests other clinical signs of an acute asthma attack. Which of the following are signs of respiratory distress seen in childhood asthma?

   1. Tripod position with refusal to lie down
   2. Harsh, barking cough on inspiration
   3. Shallow breathing with periods of apnea
   4. Continuous respiratory stridor

2. Simon's initial treatment is salbutamol (Ventolin) by inhalation. During the inhalation, Simon begins to shake. What should the nurse do?

   1. Stop the inhalation immediately
   2. Reassure Simon that this is a side effect of the Ventolin
   3. Provide Simon with a warm blanket
   4. Reduce the flow of air or oxygen in the inhalation

3. Which of the following is an appropriate and appealing diet for Simon while he is experiencing respiratory distress?

   1. Ice cream
   2. Macaroni and cheese
   3. Clear beef soup
   4. Ice pops (Popsicles)

4. Simon's parents ask the nurse how they can prevent further episodes of asthma. What would be the most appropriate response by the nurse?

   1. "We can discuss developing a plan to manage the asthma."
   2. "It is difficult to prevent asthma attacks in children Simon's age, so you need to know how to treat each attack."
   3. "You need to find out what particular triggers cause Simon's attacks."
   4. "Simon needs to take his asthma medications all the time, even when he is not wheezing."

5. The nurse assesses that Simon's environment has many potential allergens, for example, pet dander, dust, and second-hand smoke. Prior to discharge, the nurse reviews strategies for Simon's parents to modify the environment in order to reduce these allergens. Before discharge home, which of the following is the most important action that can be immediately implemented by the parents?

   1. Remove Simon's dog from the home
   2. Stop smoking cigarettes in the car
   3. Have a high-energy particulate air (HEPA) filter installed
   4. Wet dust all floors and surfaces, particularly in Simon's bedroom

Case 2

Leah is a healthy 9-month-old infant brought to the community health clinic by her parents. The registered nurse performs an assessment and health teaching.

Questions 6–10 refer to this case.

6. Leah's parents ask the nurse what to do when their daughter has a "cold" with a low-grade temperature. What would the nurse respond?

   1. Take Leah to the doctor if the symptoms continue for two days
   2. Give her infant ASA (aspirin) as directed on the bottle
   3. If she is uncomfortable, give her pediatric acetaminophen (Tylenol) or ibuprofen
   4. Administer an over-the-counter cold remedy formulated for infants

7. Leah's parents ask for advice on toys that are best for developing her motor abilities. Which of the following are most appropriate for motor development?

   1. Putting her in an infant walker with rollers
   2. Giving her several types of baby rattles
   3. Reading a book to her at bedtime every night
   4. Letting her play with kitchen utensils, such as bowls and spoons

8. The nurse discusses infant safety with Leah's parents. Which of the following safety precautions would the nurse advise?

   1. Do not give Leah finger foods until she is 18 months of age
   2. Place pillows around Leah when she is in her crib
   3. Dress Leah in clothes with Velcro fasteners
   4. Check all toys for small movable parts

9. As part of Leah's assessment, the nurse reaches out to Leah to take her vital signs. Leah begins to scream and cling to her father. What should the nurse do?

   1. Remove Leah gently from her father
   2. Postpone the taking of vital signs for another visit
   3. Talk softly at eye level with Leah
   4. Hold her arms out and smile at Leah

10. The nurse discusses developmental milestones with Leah's parents. She asks them about Leah's ability to vocalize and understand language. What vocalization milestone is appropriate for a 9-month-old infant?

   1. Responds to simple verbal commands and understands "no no"
   2. Produces repetitive vowel sounds such as "baba" and "kaka"
   3. Begins to imitate sounds
   4. Says three to five words in addition to "mama" and "dada"

Case 3

A day care that provides care for children with health problems asks a community nurse for a consultation about safe health practices.

Questions 11–15 refer to this case.

11. One of the children who attends the day care centre has a severe peanut allergy. What would the nurse recommend to best prevent potential sources of peanuts from coming in contact with the children?

   1. Do not allow parents to bring homemade food to share with the other children
   2. Send home a letter to the parents informing them of a ban on foods containing peanuts
   3. Identify all children at the day care centre who have a documented allergy to peanuts
   4. Examine all food given to the children for sources of peanuts

12. Many of the children develop communicable diseases, particularly upper respiratory infections and diarrhea during the fall and winter seasons. The nurse is asked about best practices for caregivers to reduce the incidence of infectious diseases with the children. Which of the following would the nurse recommend?

   1. All workers should wash their hands with alcohol-based cleaner after changing diapers
   2. Child care staff should wash their hands several times throughout the day
   3. All equipment and toys should be washed with an antibacterial solution between uses by children
   4. Any child who develops signs of a communicable disease during the day should be immediately separated from the other children

13. Jayden is a 4-month-old infant with congestive heart failure secondary to a congenital heart defect. The nurse discusses optimal feeding strategies for Jayden with the day care workers. Which of the following should the nurse advise?

   1. Feed Jayden on an every-two-hour schedule
   2. Provide frequent rest breaks when feeding Jayden by bottle
   3. Dilute formula feeds so that excess energy is not required for sucking
   4. Gavage feed Jayden to conserve his energy

14. The nurse has heard that there is a community outbreak of chickenpox. She is concerned about the children in the day care centre as many are immuno-compromised. What immunization should the nurse ensure that each child has received?

   1. Varicella
   2. MMR
   3. Hib
   4. DTaP

15. Shobana, one of the children attending the day care centre, has been discovered to have head lice. What would the nurse recommend to the staff of the centre to control the spread of the head lice?

   1. Notify all families that Shobana has head lice and if their children have been playing with her, they should examine their children's hair
   2. Send a letter to all parents about the outbreak with instructions for examining their child's hair and recommended treatment
   3. Examine the hair of all children as they arrive at the day care centre and prohibit attendance if lice are found
   4. Treat all of the children with the recommended pediculicide shampoo

INDEPENDENT QUESTIONS

Questions 16–25 do not refer to a particular case.

16. James, age 2 months, has diaper dermatitis (diaper rash). What would the nurse recommend to the parents to treat this problem?

   1. Expose the diaper area to air whenever possible
   2. Use a hair dryer or heat lamp to dry the area
   3. Wash the area completely with commercial wipes after every diaper change
   4. Use talc on the diaper area to absorb moisture

17. A registered nurse arrives at the scene of a house fire involving children. The nurse assesses a child who has sustained burns involving denuded skin on his trunk and arms. What first aid should the nurse provide?

   1. Cool the burned areas using cold water, or ice if available
   2. Apply a clean cloth to the burned areas
   3. Treat the burns with a topical burn ointment obtained

from a first aid kit
4. Leave the burned areas open to the air

18. Mr. and Mrs. Kaplan are the parents of a newborn who has Down syndrome. They ask the nurse what to expect when they take their infant home. What potential problems might the nurse discuss with the parents?

1. Possible difficulty with feedings
2. An increase in infections due to a decreased immune system
3. An inability to respond to affection
4. A gradual deterioration in developmental milestones

19. Candace, age 16 years, is hospitalized during a vaso-occlusive sickle cell crisis. Which of the following is an appropriate nursing intervention?

1. Administer analgesics prn
2. Monitor intake and output
3. Promote exercise
4. Apply cold compresses to painful joints

20. A mother brings her 2-month-old infant to the health clinic, stating that the child has long episodes of crying with apparent abdominal pain and cannot be comforted. The infant is formula-fed. What would be an appropriate initial nursing intervention?

1. Obtain a detailed history of the infant's diet, daily routine, and description of the crying episodes
2. Suggest a change to another formula as the symptoms are likely colic caused by an allergy to cow's milk
3. Discuss the advisability of initiating breastfeeding using techniques to re-establish the production of breast milk
4. Tell the mother that her infant is displaying classic manifestations of colic, and burping him more often along with comfort measures will correct the problem

21. What are the most common forms of childhood malignancy in Canada?

1. Leukemias
2. Lymphomas
3. Central nervous system tumours
4. Renal tumours

22. Jamal, age 17 years, is a refugee who has recently arrived in Canada. He speaks with a male nurse in the clinic concerning an "embarrassing problem" he would like to have fixed. The nurse examines Jamal and finds he has hypospadias. What would the nurse explain to Jamal?

1. "A doctor can bring your testicles down into your scrotum, but you may be infertile."
2. "Your urethra opens on the top side of the penis and can probably be fixed by a surgeon."
3. "Your penis is small as a result of an inherited condition, but it can be enlarged."
4. "I will refer you to a urologist who will surgically repair the abnormal opening on the underside of your penis."

23. A registered nurse works on a pediatric surgical unit with children experiencing postoperative pain. Which of the following is correct concerning pain in children?

1. It is not possible to accurately assess pain in children
2. Use of narcotics in children is not recommended for pain control
3. Children are often undertreated for pain
4. Children always tell the truth about pain

24. The nurse must administer a suspension of oral prednisone to a toddler. The prednisone solution is known to have a bitter taste. The child spat out the previous dose and is refusing to take the medicine. What is the most effective action to administer the prednisone?

1. Have the parent assist the nurse in administering the prednisone
2. Ask the physician to change the liquid form to a suppository
3. Restrain the child and administer the prednisone via oral syringe
4. Mix the prednisone in applesauce

25. Arlene, age 14 years, is diagnosed with moderate idiopathic scoliosis. What is the most important nursing consideration when teaching Arlene about her treatment with a Wilmington brace?

1. Assessing Arlene's compliance with wearing the brace
2. Having Arlene demonstrate appropriate skin care
3. Reviewing a list of exercises for Arlene to perform when not wearing the brace
4. The importance of routine follow up appointments to assess if the brace is correcting the scoliosis

Answers and Rationales for Practice Questions

1.   C: Changes in Health   T: Application

1. The child adopts this position in an attempt to facilitate the use of accessory muscles of respiration. If the child is able to lie down, the asthma attack is not likely to be severe.
2. This is a manifestation of laryngotracheobronchitis (croup).
3. Children with asthma try to breathe deeply. There are rarely periods of apnea, unless the child is progressing to respiratory arrest.
4. This is a manifestation of laryngotracheobronchitis (croup).

2.   C: Changes in Health   T: Application

1. This is a recognized side effect of Ventolin. The inhalation should not be stopped.
2. Shaking is a recognized side effect of Ventolin and occurs especially with increased frequency of inhalations. Simon should be reassured that it is normal.
3. The shakes are not due to Simon being cold. A blanket will not help.
4. Air flow does not influence the side effect of shaking with Ventolin.

3.   C: Changes in Health   T: Application

1. Milk products tend to increase mucus secretions in the airways and so should be avoided in clients with respiratory distress.
2. Solid foods are not recommended during respiratory distress as they may increase the risk of vomiting and aspiration.
3. It is appropriate to have clear fluids, but a child would not be likely to choose beef soup.
4. Children with respiratory distress should have diets consisting of clear fluids. These are better tolerated, provide recommended fluids to help liquefy mucus secretions, and do not pose a risk for aspiration. Ice pops would be an attractive choice for a child.

4.   C: Changes in Health   T: Critical Thinking

1. Research has shown that children who have developed a comprehensive plan for asthma management with their health care professional have the best management of symptoms and the fewest hospitalizations.
2. This may be true, but it is not the most helpful answer.
3. This is true, but an asthma plan will help identify triggers.
4. While this is true for some children with asthma, it is not known if Simon will require this level of medication.

5.   C: Changes in Health   T: Critical Thinking

1. This may be necessary but would be distressing for Simon. Removal of pets should not be considered unless allergen testing proves Simon is allergic to dog dander.
2. Second-hand smoke is a definite trigger for asthma. Several Canadian provinces have enacted legislation preventing adults from smoking in cars with children.
3. This is a valuable strategy to help clean the air in Simon's home but is not the most important, immediate strategy.
4. Wet dusting is necessary to remove dust accumulation but is not as important or immediate as not smoking in the car.

6.   C: Changes in Health   T: Application

1. A visit to a physician for a "cold" is not necessary. She will need to see a physician if the fever continues for a week or if the illness becomes worse.
2. ASA should not be given to children due to the risk of Reye's syndrome.
3. Pediatric Tylenol and ibuprofen are appropriate analgesics and antipyretics for minor childhood conditions such as teething, colds, immunizations, and so on.
4. These medications are not recommended for infants and children and in some cases have been removed from pharmacies.

7.   C: Changes in Health   T: Application

1. Infant walkers are unsafe and not allowed for sale in Canada.
2. A baby rattle is more appropriate for an infant of 1 to 3 months.
3. Reading, while an excellent method of promoting bonding, literacy, and reading readiness, does not develop motor skills.
4. Manipulating these objects will assist in the development of fine motor skills.

8.   C: Changes in Health   T: Application

1. Provided that the finger foods are not hard and large (such as peanuts or carrots), finger foods are nutritious, help develop motor skills, and are well liked by older infants and toddlers.
2. This is not necessary. If the sides of the crib are in the raised position, Leah will not fall.
3. This is not realistic. Other closures such as zippers and snaps are safe.
4. Small movable parts may become dislodged from the toy and are a hazard to infants and toddlers.

9.   C: Changes in Health   T: Application

1. Leah is exhibiting stranger anxiety, which is developmentally normal at 9 months. Removing Leah from her father will frighten her.
2. This should not be necessary if the right approach is taken and Leah is given time to get used to the nurse.
3. This is the recommended approach as the soft voice is comforting and meeting the child at eye level makes the stranger appear smaller.
4. This is intrusive and is likely to frighten Leah.

10.   C: Changes in Health   T: Application

1. This is an appropriate developmental milestone for a 9-month-old infant.
2. This would be expected to be achieved by 7 months.
3. This becomes evident at 6 months of age.
4. This is appropriate to a developmental age of 12 months.

11.   C: Changes in Health   T: Critical Thinking

1. Peanuts may be used in many ingredients that may not be evident. A ban on all homemade foods (such as cakes and ice cream) will prevent inadvertent sources of peanut by-products from being ingested by the children. Many day care centres have enacted this practice.
2. This will communicate the peanut allergy problem to the parents but may not prevent food substances that contain peanuts from being available to the children. Parents may not be aware of which foods are likely to have traces of peanuts.
3. This will help the staff identify children at risk but will do nothing to prevent foods containing peanuts from being in the day care centre.
4. All sources of peanut, for example, peanut oil, may not be easily identifiable.

12.   C: Changes in Health   T: Critical Thinking

1. This is a safe practice but should be performed before changing diapers as well. It may not be effective in preventing airborne transmission of microorganisms.
2. Hand hygiene is the best infection control practice, but several times a day is not frequent enough to prevent transmission.
3. This is not practical in most day care settings.
4. Children with obvious signs of infection should be cared for at home. However, if they develop symptoms during the day, they should be isolated from the rest of the children.

13.   C: Changes in Health   T: Application

1. This is too frequent and will tire Jayden unnecessarily. There will not be sufficient rest time between feedings.
2. Feeding of the infant with congestive heart failure is similar to exercise in an adult. The infant often tires and may need frequent rest periods.
3. Infants with a congenital heart defect require feedings with increased caloric density in the formula or breast milk.
4. This may be necessary if it is found Jayden cannot tolerate bottle feedings. There may not be trained staff at the day care centre to competently gavage-feed infants.

14.   C: Health and Wellness   T: Knowledge

1. Varicella-zoster virus is the name of the herpes virus that causes the disease varicella, or chickenpox.
2. MMR is the vaccine that protects the child from measles, mumps, and rubella.
3. Hib is the *Haemophilus influenzae* type b (Hib) vaccine and protects the child primarily against bacterial meningitis and epiglottitis.
4. DtaP is a combination vaccine that provides immunity to diphtheria, tetanus, and pertussis.

15.   C: Changes in Health   T: Application

1. This is a breech of confidential information. The child with pediculosis (lice) does not have to be specifically identified. Shobana may not be the only child with head lice.
2. This alerts the families to the problem and provides practical information to examine and treat their children. Treatment at home will prevent transmission of the head lice at the day care centre.
3. It is not practical to examine the hair of every child on arrival and then to send the child home without prior notice to the parents. A useful alternative would be to screen all children early in the day, isolate those found to have lice, and then notify the families.
4. This is not the responsibility of the day care centre. Treatment should be provided in the home.

16.   C: Changes in Health   T: Application

1. Wet skin, especially if contaminated with urine and fecal irritants, promotes dermatitis. Exposure to air helps dry the skin.
2. Use of a hair dryer or heat lamp is not recommended as it may cause burns.
3. Overwashing, particularly with commercial wipes and perfumed soaps, may cause irritation.

4. Cornstarch rather than talc is recommended as it is more effective in reducing friction and tends to cake less than talc. There is also a danger that infants may aspirate talc.

17.   C: Changes in Health   T: Application

1. Burns with denuded skin should not be cooled as this could lead to a drop in core temperature.
2. The burns should be covered with a clean cloth to prevent contamination and alleviate pain by eliminating air contact.
3. The application of topical ointments, oils, or other home remedies is contraindicated.
4. Burns should be covered with a clean cloth, not left open to the air. Air contact may cause pain, and contaminants may be in the air.

18.   C: Changes in Health   T: Application

1. Infants with Down syndrome often have difficulty with feedings due to their large tongues and poor muscle control and coordination.
2. There can be decreased immunity with Down syndrome, but it is not a common finding.
3. Down syndrome infants and children are very receptive to affection.
4. There is a gradual increase, not deterioration, in developmental functioning.

19.   C: Changes in Health   T: Application

1. The continuous infusion of opioids provides better pain relief than does intermittent therapy.
2. During a sickle cell crisis, increased fluids are required to prevent further sickling and to delay the vaso-occlusion and hypoxia–ischemia cycle. The kidneys are not able to concentrate urine. Strict monitoring of intake and output is required.
3. While most children can gauge their tolerance for exercise, and strict bed rest is not required, children in a vaso-occlusive crisis should limit exercise to avoid additional tissue oxygen needs.
4. Cold compresses are not applied to the area because this may enhance vasoconstriction and occlusion.

20.   C: Changes in Health   T: Critical Thinking

1. This is the first step in the nursing process: data collection. The nurse needs more information about the diet and pattern of discomfort. The infant likely has colic, and the detailed history will assist the nurse to provide potential therapeutic measures to ease the infant's discomfort.
2. This is a possibility, but a thorough history is required initially.

3. Reestablishing breast milk may not be possible at this stage. Breastfed infants also develop colic.
4. This may be true, but in order to develop individualized and appropriate comfort measures, the nurse requires more information.

21.   C: Changes in Health   T: Knowledge

1. Leukemias are the most common form of childhood cancer in Canada, occurring at a rate of 32.2 cases per million children per year.
2. Lymphomas occur in children at a rate of 27.5 cases per million per year.
3. Central nervous system tumours occur in children at a rate of 26.8 cases per million per year.
4. Renal tumours occur in children at a rate of 6.8 cases per million per year.

22.   C: Changes in Health   T: Knowledge

1. This explanation relates to cryptorchidism, or undescended testicles.
2. This is epispadias.
3. Hypospadias is not a small penis, although men with the defect may also have a small penis as a result of the defect.
4. Hypospadias is a condition in which the urethral opening is localized anywhere along the ventral surface of the penis. Depending on the severity, it can generally be surgically corrected to improve appearance, to enable the client to urinate while standing, and to preserve sexual function.

23.   C: Changes in Health   T: Application

1. This is not true. There are a variety of pain rating scales and behavioural indicators that are useful for assessing pain in children. Children by the age of 4 can accurately point to the body area where they have pain.
2. Narcotics can be successfully and safely used with children. They are no more dangerous for children than for adults.
3. Several research studies have examined the pattern of pain medication in children compared with adults and have found consistently that many children are not medicated appropriately for their degree of pain.
4. Children may not admit having pain to avoid an injection or may not ask for analgesia because they believe adults know how they feel.

24.   C: Changes in Health   T: Application

1. Having the parent assist may help calm the child and achieve compliance with taking the

prednisone. The child is more likely to trust the parent than the nurse.

2. Prednisone does not come in suppository form. A suppository is inappropriate and invasive.

3. Children should never be restrained unless there is a medical order. Restraints would be frightening for the child.

4. This may sound like an attractive option, but the bitter taste of the prednisone would not be masked by the applesauce, and it is unlikely that the child would eat a sufficient amount to receive all of the prednisone. The child may be offered applesauce or another favourite food after the prednisone to help clear the mouth of the bitter taste.

25.   **C: Changes in Health   T: Critical Thinking**

1. Adolescents girls are very concerned about body image, therefore Arlene may not be compliant with wearing the brace.

2. This is important as skin breakdown can occur, but it is not as important as ensuring Arlene is wearing the brace.

3. Exercise will help to slow the progression of the curvature, but Arlene needs to wear the brace.

4. Follow-up appointments are important, but not as important as ensuring Arlene wears the brace.

Mental Health Nursing

P. Jane Milliken, RN, BScN, MA, PhD

Mental health, like physical health, affects a person's well-being. Often the two go hand in hand due to the complex relationships among biological, genetic, psychological, and social or environmental factors. People with mental illnesses frequently develop physical symptoms and vice versa. Mental illness does not discriminate among ages, cultures, or income or education levels. In Canada, 20% of people suffer from a mental illness during their lives (Canadian Institute for Health Information [CIHI], 2002).

Mental health and mental illness occur along a continuum, just as physical health and illness do. Consequently, just as we speak of health within illness, a person can have a mental illness but manage that illness in healthy ways. People, in general, may have varying qualities and experiences that could be designated as healthy or unhealthy, but only when the unhealthy outweighs the healthy will help be sought or required from a mental health professional. Nurses care for clients with mental health conditions in every type of setting and play an essential role in helping these clients and their families on the road to achieving their optimal level of health.

LEGAL, ETHICAL, AND INTERPERSONAL CONSIDERATIONS FOR MENTAL HEALTH NURSING

As professionals, nurses are bound by legal, moral, and ethical principles that govern their practice. Because laws, morals, and ethics are grounded in providing for the good of society, they offer guidelines that help nurses provide exemplary care for their clients. Sometimes, however, these guidelines are not completely clear, and often they can contradict one another. Ethical dilemmas occur when a practice decision must be made between two competing but imperfect and not completely desirable choices. Mental health practice challenges nurses to use their judgement to interpret the guidelines and make ethical decisions, often when the circumstances are ambiguous.

Canadian nurses are bound by the Code of Ethics of the Canadian Nurses Association (CNA, 2008), in which a nurse's responsibilities are defined under the following seven values:

Safe, Compassionate, Competent, and Ethical Care: Our professional obligation to our clients.

Promoting Health and Well-Being: Relates to nurses promoting their clients' optimal health and well-being.

Promoting and Respecting Informed Decision Making: Involves respect for individuals' right to be informed and autonomous in decision making.

Preserving Dignity: Promotes respect for the intrinsic worth of each person.

Maintaining Privacy and Confidentiality: Safeguards the personal, family, and community information obtained in the context of a professional relationship.

Promoting Justice: Safeguards human rights, equity, and fairness by promoting the public good.

Being Accountable: Holds nurses accountable for their actions and answerable to their profession.

The CNA Code of Ethics is discussed in more detail in Chapter 3. Refer to the CNA Web site, listed at the end of the chapter in the Web site section, for more information.

In Canada, health care is the responsibility of the provincial and territorial governments. Consequently, each province and territory has its own *Mental Health Act* outlining the regulations for voluntary and involuntary admission to hospital, consent for treatment, and the rights of (and safeguards for) mental health clients. Similarly, legislation defining guardianship and Substitute Decision Makers varies across the country. Federal laws that impact mental health clients include the Canadian Charter of Rights and Freedoms and the Criminal Code of Canada (Gray, Shone, & Liddle, 2000).

PATHOPHYSIOLOGY

Psychological, neurobiological, and genetic pathology cause mental disorders that result in disorganization and impairment of thinking, memory, mood, behaviour, or all of these. Consequently, people with mental illnesses suffer significant distress and difficulties in everyday functioning.

Impairments of cognition and emotion can interfere with an individual's ability to make appropriate decisions in his or her own best interest, or they may cause the client to make decisions or exhibit behaviours that interfere with the rights of others. Thus, the client's condition may require nurses to make ethical and legal choices between competing values. For example, in the case of psychotic clients, denying a client's right to autonomy may preserve his or her health or the rights and safety of others.

CLINICAL MANIFESTATIONS

Mental illness does not discriminate; anyone can suffer from a mental illness. The characteristics of different population groups may pose particular legal and ethical issues for mental health nurses. Here, issues related to different cultures and the homeless population are discussed.

Cultural Differences

Mental health care in Canada is decidedly influenced by Western ideology and practices, yet we are a multicultural society, and different cultures may define normal and abnormal behaviour differently. They may differ in thinking about when professional care is needed and what kind of care is acceptable. Because mental health nursing relies on communication, language can be a barrier. An interpreter needs to be able to convey both words and personal and cultural nuances. Thus, when available, a family member is often the most appropriate interpreter to use.

To be culturally sensitive and competent, mental health nurses need to do the following:

- Critically examine their personal cultural beliefs, values, and any ethnocentric tendencies
- Become familiar with a variety of different cultures and ethnic groups
- Plan culturally sensitive care after conducting a thorough cultural assessment
- Assess how cultural groups define mental illness and what methods of healing are acceptable
- Learn about cultural and religious rituals, protective symbols, and standards of modesty in various belief systems
- Respect a person's dietary restrictions and customs

Homelessness

The connections between mental illness and homelessness are many. The downsizing of mental hospitals over 40 years ago began a process of deinstitutionalization, when many people were discharged without appropriate community services and programs in place. The inability of many mentally ill persons to achieve high levels of education or full employment is coupled with reductions in social assistance eligibility. Fewer opportunities for unskilled work, the lack of affordable housing, and a propensity for substance abuse are also factors leading to poverty and homelessness. Estimates of the proportion of homeless people with mental illnesses vary widely across Canada, but in many places, they range from 45–75% (CIHI, 2007).

- The NIMBY syndrome ("not in my backyard") is a common social attitude. Canadians want homeless people off the streets but reject having services and housing for them located in their own neighbourhoods.
- For some, having a severe mental illness leads to being homeless; for others, the stress of being homeless leads to developing a mental illness.
- Mentally ill persons are particularly vulnerable to being victimized in inner-city areas.
- Health care services for mentally ill homeless people involve assertive outreach programs that provide medical and psychiatric care, social assistance, meals, temporary shelters and housing, vocational and life skills training, and advocacy.
- The values of dignity and justice in the CNA Code of Ethics guide nursing practice with homeless, mentally ill persons.

NURSING CONSIDERATIONS

Interpersonal Relationships With Mental Health Clients

Establishing a therapeutic relationship with a mental health client obligates the nurse to act in both ethical and legal ways. People with mental illnesses are very vulnerable; their relationships with care providers are often lengthy and very important to them. Conscientious nurses establish and maintain caring relationships but stay within their professional boundaries. Nurses must also be very aware of their relative power in those relationships and avoid abusing that power, while trying to balance a client's rights and safety with the societal rights of others.

Privacy and Confidentiality

- The CNA Code of Ethics states that personal, family, and community information must be protected and kept confidential. The only exceptions occur (a) when the nurse is legally required to disclose information and (b) when revealing information could prevent serious harm to the client or to others. In such cases, the nurse should try (where possible) to avoid actually identifying the client and to minimize any resulting stigma.
- If a client refuses to share information with family members, an ethical dilemma may arise, particularly if the family member is the person's primary caregiver outside the hospital.
- In most provinces, a family member must legally be notified when a client is admitted to or discharged from the hospital or scheduled to appear before a review board. The client nominates a family member or a near-relative (someone who the client has identified as being equivalent to family) as the person who should be notified in these cases.

Clients' Rights

In Canada, unlike the United States, there is no Client's Bill of Rights. Mental health clients, including those involuntarily admitted to hospital, are entitled to the same fundamental rights as all Canadians, under the Canadian Charter of Rights and Freedoms. All provincial and territorial *Mental Health Acts* must comply with the Charter (Gray et al., 2000).

Voluntary Admission to Hospital

- Most psychiatric clients in Canada are admitted voluntarily, by their own consent, under the same processes as other hospital clients.
- Voluntary clients may discharge themselves from the hospital when they wish.
- In most parts of Canada, for clients who are incapable of giving consent (such as a child or an incapable adult), consent may be provided by a parent, legal guardian, or Substitute Decision Maker nominated by the client while well. In such cases, clients may not discharge themselves without the consenting person's agreement.

Involuntary Admission to Hospital

Admission to a psychiatric facility without the client's consent is often called commitment and usually happens in response to a crisis or need for emergency care. Although admission without consent contradicts the ethical value of promoting and respecting informed decision making, a client may be admitted when all three of the following conditions are met:

- The client refuses to be admitted or is incapable of making that decision.
- The person appears to have a mental disorder.
- The illness is likely to cause harm or danger to the client or to others.

A physician completes a medical certificate that allows the person to be apprehended, transported to a mental health facility, and admitted for a specified period that varies across Canada from one to three days. Involuntary clients can only be admitted to hospitals that are defined by that province's *Mental Health Act* as mental health facilities.

If an individual meets these three criteria but refuses to see a doctor, the police may apprehend the person and take her or him to a hospital emergency department. There, a physician examines the person and completes the first certificate, if necessary.

To keep the client longer than the legally limited initial period, another physician or psychiatrist must complete a second certificate. In New Brunswick, however, the admission decision is made by a tribunal; in Quebec, by a judge; and in the Northwest Territories (NWT), by the Minister of Health. When the specified longer period of detention expires (between two and four weeks, depending on the jurisdiction), a renewal certificate must be completed or the client must be allowed to leave.

If an involuntary client wishes to be discharged, he or she (or a Substitute Decision Maker, if one is available) applies to a review panel. This board acts as a judge and can overrule the physician on the basis of evidence gathered. (In the NWT, this review takes place in court.) Review boards also meet at legally defined designated intervals for clients who are certified for long periods.

The Canadian Charter of Rights and Freedoms mandates that involuntary clients must be informed of their legal rights upon admission. Some provincial and territorial *Mental Health Acts* require this notification to be repeated each time a certificate is renewed. Clients must be informed of the following:

- Why they were admitted
- That they have the right to contact a lawyer
- That they can apply to a review board for a legal ruling on the involuntary admission (Gray et al., 2000).

Informed Consent

For consent to be informed, a person must be provided with the following information to consider:

- Information about the condition
- Information about the proposed treatment
- The benefits to be expected from the treatment
- The risks and side effects of getting the treatment
- Any alternative treatments or courses of action
- The consequences to be expected from not receiving the treatment

Nurses value the right of people to make their own decisions about health care and services, without coercion, and to have sufficient information upon which to base those choices.

- The CNA Code of Ethics stipulates that nurses must assist people to obtain complete current knowledge of their condition and also must respect a client's decision (or that of a legally approved Substitute Decision Maker), even if it differs from the nurse's own beliefs and opinions. This includes respecting the right to refuse consent or withdraw consent at any time.
- Further, a nurse is responsible for providing care that goes against his or her personal values, until a replacement care provider can be obtained.
- A person is considered incapable of providing consent if he or she cannot understand or appreciate the consequences of accepting or rejecting treatment.
- Involuntary admission does not necessarily mean that treatment can begin, although in some provinces or territories, the physician or facility director can authorize treatment. In others, a tribunal must meet

to approve treatment, and this may mean a delay lasting a few days.

- If the client has requested a review, no treatment can begin until the review panel upholds the involuntary admission, even if a Substitute Decision Maker has signed the consent for treatment.

Treatment in the Least Restrictive Setting

Aggressive behaviour is common with some mental illnesses. When mental illnesses are well controlled, however, there is no greater risk of violence than there would be from the general population. Violence is most common when the illness is poorly controlled, as in the case of a client who has stopped taking his or her medications.

Restraints and Seclusion

When a client or someone else is likely to be harmed or property may be destroyed, seclusion or restraint may be necessary. The following restraint principles must be followed:

- The client is always entitled to the least restrictive alternative that ensures safety.
- Restraints should be released and the client allowed out of seclusion as soon as he or she has calmed down.
- Restraints require a physician's order.
- Clients in restraints or seclusion must be closely monitored and all physical needs addressed, including safety, comfort, food, fluids, and elimination. Accurate and complete documentation is vital.
- Physical or chemical restraints (sedation) should not be used when a brief period of seclusion would suffice to calm the client and ease the situation.
- In most provinces and territories, the *Mental Health Act* provides legal protection for staff to give treatment or restrain individuals, if their health or safety is endangered or the safety of others would be compromised without that treatment or restraint (CIHI, 2007).
- Restraints and seclusion should never be used as punishment or for staff convenience.
- Seclusion and restraints are contraindicated for people who are clearly suicidal and for those with delirium or dementia, for whom decreased stimulation is likely to increase agitation.

Duty to Report

People who are mentally ill are vulnerable to abuse. Nurses are legally and ethically obliged to report suspected or confirmed cases to the appropriate authorities in the following circumstances:

Family Abuse: Child abuse, elder abuse, and partner abuse are criminal acts and must be reported to the police for investigation.

Abuse of Clients: Staff who abuse clients should be reported to management, and criminal charges may be laid. Professional staff should be reported to their licensing bodies. Nurses have a duty to report any nursing colleague who abuses clients to the college or nursing association that registers nurses in their province or territory.

Unsafe Nursing Practice: Nurses are also obligated to report unsafe nursing practices to management and to the body that registers nurses in their province or territory.

SPECIFIC COMMUNICATION AND THERAPEUTIC APPROACHES WITH THE MENTAL HEALTH CLIENT

To fully understand mental health, mental illnesses, and therapeutic approaches in mental health nursing, we review the functions of the brain and central nervous system (CNS).

PATHOPHYSIOLOGY AND SELECTED MANIFESTATIONS

Brain Structure and Function

The structure and function of the brain are illustrated in Figure 11.1.

Cerebrum

Two hemispheres are connected by the corpus callosum, where the pineal gland is located. The pineal gland regulates gonadal function and also produces melatonin, which influences the sleep cycle. Each hemisphere of the cerebrum contains the four lobes and other structures depicted in Figure 11.1. The following points describe the function of the structures within the hemispheres:

- Right hemisphere – Regulates creativity and intuition and controls the left side of the body
- Left hemisphere – Regulates logical, analytic thinking and controls the right side of the body
- Frontal lobes – Integrate and organize complex thinking for solving problems, producing speech, planning and making decisions, regulating arousal, and focusing attention. Abnormalities in these lobes are found in schizophrenia, attention deficit hyperactivity disorder (ADHD), and dementia.
- Parietal lobes – Interpret taste and touch and help with spatial perceptions and balance
- Temporal lobes – Interpret hearing and smell and support memory, language comprehension, and the expression of emotions
- Occipital lobes – Help coordinate and interpret speech and vision

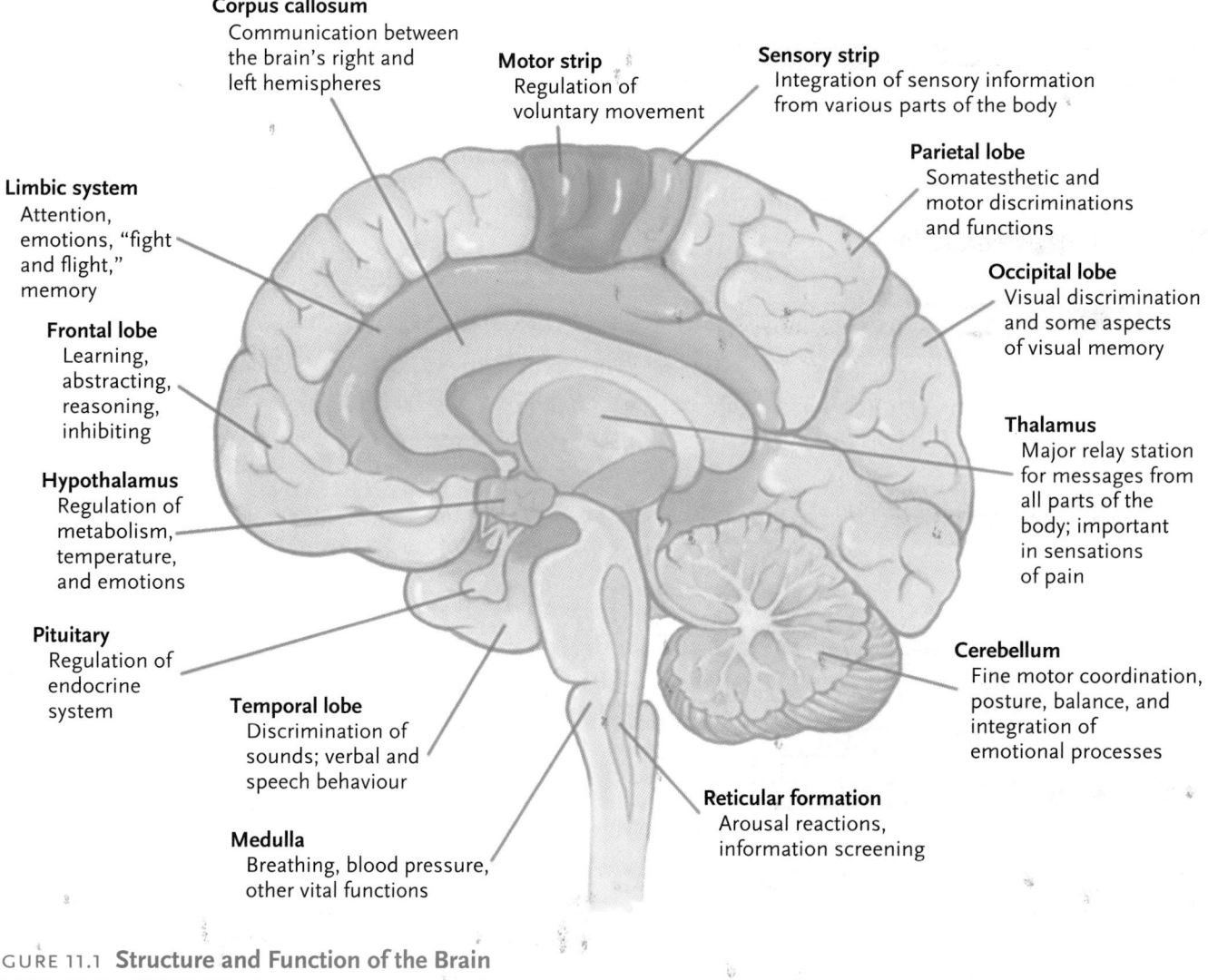

Corpus callosum
Communication between the brain's right and left hemispheres
Motor strip
Regulation of voluntary movement
Sensory strip
Integration of sensory information from various parts of the body
Parietal lobe
Somatesthetic and motor discriminations and functions
Occipital lobe
Visual discrimination and some aspects of visual memory
Thalamus
Major relay station for messages from all parts of the body; important in sensations of pain
Cerebellum
Fine motor coordination, posture, balance, and integration of emotional processes
Reticular formation
Arousal reactions, information screening
Medulla
Breathing, blood pressure, other vital functions
Temporal lobe
Discrimination of sounds; verbal and speech behaviour
Pituitary
Regulation of endocrine system
Hypothalamus
Regulation of metabolism, temperature, and emotions
Frontal lobe
Learning, abstracting, reasoning, inhibiting
Limbic system
Attention, emotions, "fight and flight," memory

FIGURE 11.1 **Structure and Function of the Brain**

Source: Carson, R. C., Butcher, J. N., & Mineka, S. © (2000). *Abnormal psychology and modern life* (11th ed.). Reproduced by permission of Pearson Education, Inc., Upper Saddle River, NJ.

Cerebellum

The cerebellum coordinates movement and balance. Damage to the cerebellum is implicated in Parkinson's disease and dementia.

Brainstem

The brainstem structures control the following:

- Medulla oblongata – Controls cardiac and respiratory function
- Reticular activating system – Controls sleep and consciousness and relays motor neuron impulses
- Locus ceruleus – Implicated in impulsive behaviour, related to stress and anxiety

Limbic System

The limbic system controls the following:

- Thalamus – Regulates mood, activity, and sensation
- Hypothalamus – Regulates temperature, appetite, hormones, and impulsive reactions, such as anger and excitement. The hypothalamus is involved in psychosomatic disorders and in stress response.
- Hippocampus and amygdala – Regulate emotions and memory
- Psychopathology of the limbic system includes dementia, mania, and other psychoses.

Ventricles

These spaces between the hemispheres and other structures are filled with cerebrospinal fluid (CSF), which cushions and nourishes brain structures. In many psychiatric disorders, enlarged ventricles imply the destruction and atrophy of surrounding brain structures.

FIGURE 11.2 **Neurotransmission**

Source: Stuart, G. W., & Laraia, M. T. (2005). *Principles and practice of psychiatric nursing* (8th ed., p. 94, Figure 6-7). St. Louis: Mosby.

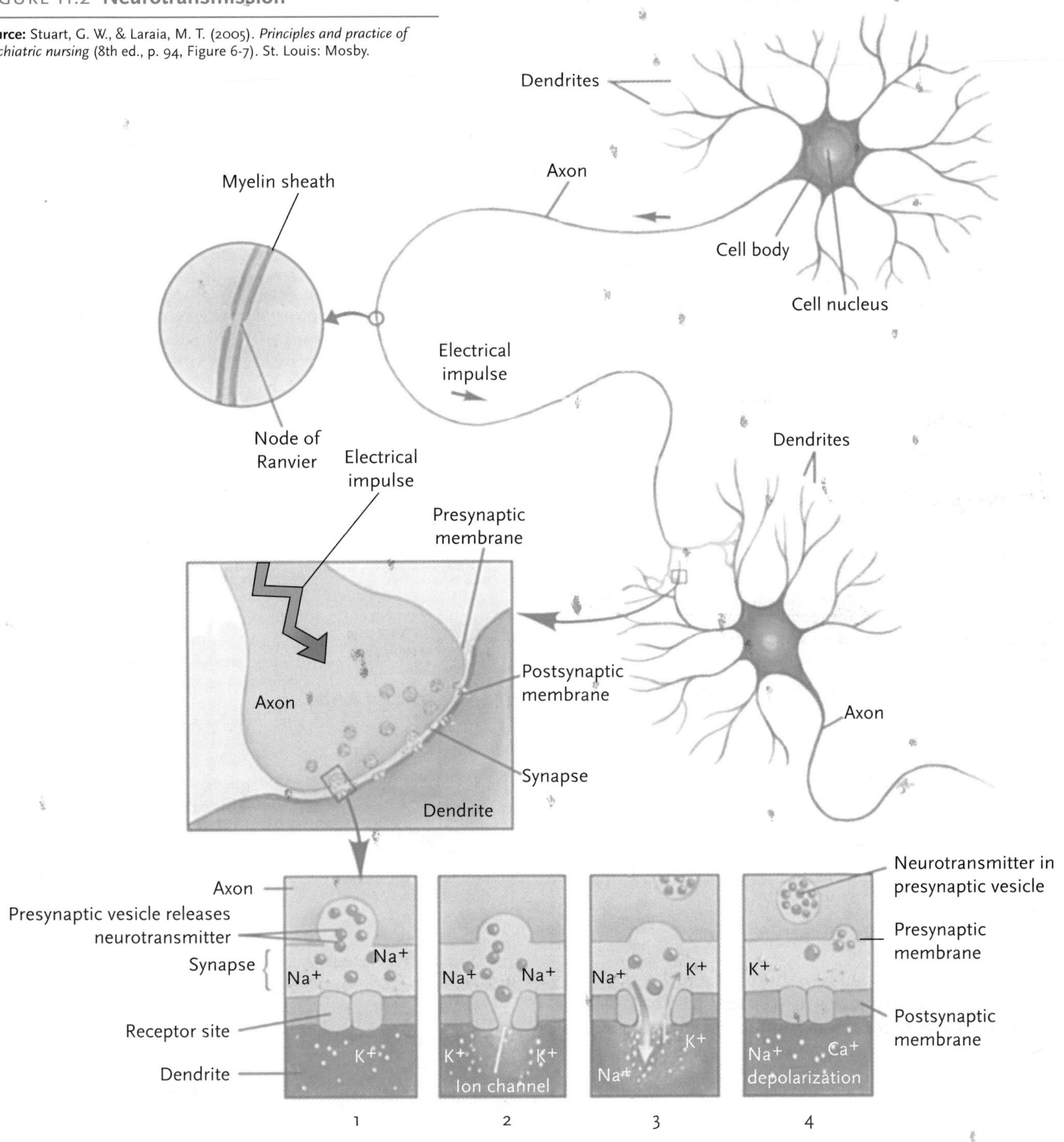

Dendrites
Axon
Myelin sheath
Cell body
Cell nucleus
Electrical impulse
Node of Ranvier
Electrical impulse
Dendrites
Presynaptic membrane
Postsynaptic membrane
Axon
Axon
Synapse
Dendrite
Axon
Presynaptic vesicle releases neurotransmitter
Synapse
Receptor site
Dendrite
Na+
Na+
K+
Na+
Na+
K+
K+
Ion channel
Na+
K+
K+
Na+
K+
Na+
Ca+
depolarization
Neurotransmitter in presynaptic vesicle
Presynaptic membrane
Postsynaptic membrane
1
2
3
4

Neural Structure and Function

Figure 11.2 illustrates the process of neurotransmission.

Neurotransmitters

Neurotransmission is the relaying of information in the synapse from neuron to neuron through electrical impulses and chemicals called neurotransmitters.

Neurotransmitters and their function play an important role in many mental health conditions, as follows:

- Reuptake – After the message impulse is transmitted to the receptor cells, neurotransmitters return to the axon for storage or, alternatively, are inactivated and metabolized by enzymes, primarily monoamine oxidase (MAO).
- Psychiatric illnesses – Abnormally high or low concentrations of certain neurotransmitters.
- Norepinephrine and epinephrine (noradrenaline

and adrenalin) – Found mainly in the brainstem, these chemicals control the stress response ("fight or flight") and influence the brain's reward system. Norepinephrine also helps regulate mood.

- Dopamine – Has mainly an excitatory effect upon movement, emotions, motivation, and cognition. Dopamine is involved in movement disorders such as Parkinson's disease, as well as in schizophrenia and other psychotic illnesses.
- Serotonin – Has primarily an inhibitory effect. Changing levels affect appetite, sleep cycles, pain and temperature control, and sexual and emotional behaviour. Serotonin is also connected to major symptoms of schizophrenia, including delusions, hallucinations, and social withdrawal.
- Acetylcholine – May be excitatory or inhibitory, affecting sleep and waking cycles, and signalling muscular activity. People with Alzheimer's disease have low levels of acetylcholine.
- Glutamate – Opens the calcium ion channel to allow electrical impulses through the synapse. Excessively high levels (such as those found in stroke, hypoglycemia, and ischemia and as a result of taking drugs such as PCP) are toxic to brain cells.
- Gamma-aminobutyric acid (GABA) – An inhibitory neurotransmitter that helps regulate other neurotransmitters. Benzodiazepines increase GABA to reduce anxiety and promote sleep.
- Endorphins and enkephalins – The brain's natural opiates. They have an inhibitory effect, reducing pain and stimulating pleasure by affecting the brain's reward system.
- Histamine – In addition to moderating allergic responses and reducing gastric and cardiac stimulation, histamine controls alertness. People with depression have low levels of histamine.

DIAGNOSTICS AND THERAPEUTICS

Diagnosis

Criteria for diagnosing all psychiatric disorders and illnesses are defined in the *Diagnostic and Statistical Manual of Mental Disorders*. The current version is called the DSM IV-TR (American Psychiatric Association [APA], 2000). Here, psychiatric diagnoses and other types of pertinent information are classified under five axes or categories:

Axis I: All major clinical psychiatric disorders, with the exception of mental retardation and personality disorders

Axis II: Mental retardation and personality disorders

Axis III: Medical conditions that may cause or contribute to a person's psychiatric condition (co-morbidities)

Axis IV: The psychosocial and environmental issues impacting on the client's mental illness or health. A related term is "the social determinants of health."

Axis V: The Global Assessment of Functioning (GAF), scored from 0–100 and used to rate a person's overall psychological functioning

Psychological Testing

Clinical psychologists administer many tests to measure intelligence and cognitive functioning, as well as aspects of personality, memory, impulse control, interpersonal behaviour, and self-concept. A common one is the Minnesota Multiphasic Personality Inventory (MMPI).

Electroencephalogram

Electroencephalograms (EEGs) are graphic tracings of the brain's electrical impulses, used to differentiate among neurological and psychiatric conditions and to evaluate various neurological symptoms, such as delirium, hallucinations, and altered states of consciousness.

Neuroimaging

Newer and more sophisticated technology for visualizing the brain includes the following:

- CT scans – Computed axial tomography uses X-rays and sometimes a contrast agent such as iodine to produce sharply defined images of a "slice" through body tissues.
- MRI scans – Magnetic resonance imaging uses magnetic energy to discriminate among different tissue densities. This technique is contraindicated in pregnancy and for people with metal in their bodies, including pacemakers, metal plates, and bone replacements.
- CT and MRI scans detect structural abnormalities, such as tumours and hematomas.
- PET scans – Positron emission tomography helps investigate brain function by measuring glucose consumption, that is, metabolic activity, in brain cells. Blood flow and synaptic activity can be distinguished.

More information is available on these neuro-imaging tests in Appendix D.

Pharmacotherapy

In general, medications used for psychiatric therapy regulate abnormal levels of specific neurotransmitters. Refer to Chapter 7 for medication action, side effects, and signs of overdose, with particular attention to the following classes of drugs:

- Antipsychotics – Typical and atypical
- Mood stabilizers – Lithium, antiepileptics
- Antidepressants – Tricyclic, selective serotonin reuptake inhibitors (SSRIs), MAO inhibitors (MAOIs), atypical antidepressants
- Antianxiety medications – Also called anxiolytics

The major drug interactions and incompatibilities are reviewed in Table 11.1.

Table 11.1   Interactions of Psychotropic Drugs and Other Substances

PSYCHOTROPIC CATEGORY	POSSIBLE INTERACTIONS
Antianxiety Agents *Benzodiazepines with*	
Central nervous system (CNS) depressants (alcohol, barbiturates, antipsychotics, antihistamines, cimetidine)	Potential additive CNS effects, especially sedation and decreased daytime performance
Selective serotonin reuptake inhibitors (SSRIs), disulfiram, estrogens	Increased benzodiazepine effects
Antacids, tobacco	Decreased benzodiazepine effects
Sedative–hypnotics with	
CNS depressants (alcohol, antihistamines, antidepressants, narcotics, antipsychotics)	Enhancement of sedative effects; impairment of mental and physical performance; may result in lethargy, respiratory depression, coma, death
Anticoagulants (oral)*	Decreased warfarin plasma levels and effect; monitor and adjust dose of warfarin
Antidepressants *Tricyclics (TCAs) with*	
Monoamine oxidase inhibitors (MAOIs)*	May cause hypertensive crisis
Alcohol and other CNS depressants	Additive CNS depression; decreased tricyclic antidepressant (TCA) effect
Antihypertensives* (guanethidine, methyldopa, clonidine)	Antagonism of antihypertensive effect
Antipsychotics and anti-parkinsonians	Increased TCA effect; confusion, delirium, ileus
Anticholinergics	Additive anticholinergic effects
Antiarrhythmics (quinidine, procainamide, propranolol)	Additive antiarrhythimic effects; myocardial depression
SSRIs*	Increased TCA serum level/toxicity through inhibition of cytochrome P-450 system
Anticonvulsants	Decreased TCA effect; seizures
Tobacco	Decreased TCA plasma levels
SSRIs with	
Clomipramine, maprotiline, bupropion, clozapine	Increased risk of seizures
MAOIs*	Serotonin syndrome
Barbiturates, benzodiazepines, narcotics	Increased CNS depression
Carbamazepine	Neurotoxicity: nausea, vomiting, vertigo, tinnitus, ataxia, lethargy, blurred vision
Aripiprazole	Fluoxetine and paroxetine lower levels
Risperidone	Fluoxetine and paroxetine may increase risperidone to toxic levels
Selegiline*	Hypertensive crisis; increased serotoninergic effects; mania
St. John's wort, naratriptan, rizatriptan, sumatriptan, zolmitriptan, tramadol*	Serotonin syndrome

Continued on next page

Table 11.1   Interactions of Psychotropic Drugs and Other Substances (cont'd)

PSYCHOTROPIC CATEGORY	POSSIBLE INTERACTIONS
Haloperidol	Decreased effect of either drug
Calcium channel blockers	Neurotoxicity; dizziness, nausea, diplopia, headache
Valproate	Decreased valproate serum concentration
Cimetidine, erythromycin, isoniazid, fluconazole	Somnolence, lethargy, dizziness, blurred vision, ataxia, nausea, increased carbamazepine levels
Clozapine*	Avoid due to increased risk of agranulocytosis
Aripiprazole	Increased blood levels of aripiprazole
Rifampin	Decreased carbamazepine levels
Antipsychotics With	
Antacids, tea, coffee, milk, fruit juice	Decreased phenothiazine effect
CNS depressants (narcotics, antianxiety drugs, alcohol, antihistamines, barbiturates)	Additive CNS depression
Anticholinergic agents (levodopa)*	Additive atropinelike side effects and increased anti-Parkinson effects
SSRIs	Increased neuroleptic serum level and extrapyramidal side effects (EPS)
Antipsychotics *Clozapine with*	
Carbamazepine*	Additive bone marrow suppression
Benzodiazepines*	Circulatory collapse, respiratory arrest
SSRIs*	Increased risk of seizures
*Potentially clinically significant	

Source: Adapted from Stuart, G. W. (2009). *Principles and practice of psychiatric nursing* (9th ed., pp. 505–506, Table 26-1). St. Louis: Mosby.

Common Psychiatric Treatments

"Psychotherapy" refers to various approaches to the psychological treatment of mental or emotional disorders, aimed at changing people's attitudes, feelings, and behaviour. These approaches are conducted by trained therapists.

"Talk Therapy" Approaches

- Psychoanalysis – Based on Freudian theory, this is a lengthy process of years of individual therapy aimed at uncovering repressed memories and other unconscious influences on thinking, behaviour, and relationships.
- Psychodynamic therapy – Also based on Freudian concepts but shorter in duration, lasting weeks or months. The focus is on developing insight on particular issues thought to be causing the client's distress.
- Interpersonal therapy – Used for examining past relationship patterns to reveal ways of achieving more positive personal and interpersonal interactions.

Behaviour-Oriented Therapy

Various techniques of behaviour modification focus on changing clients' behaviour patterns. Overall, positive behaviours are positively rewarded and negative behaviours are negatively rewarded. Examples include the following:

- Assertiveness training – Clients learn to express their wishes in a matter-of-fact way and to say no to unreasonable expectations without feeling guilty.
- Positive conditioning – Clients learn to associate

desirable behaviours and the sources of any phobias with pleasurable outcomes and relaxation.
- Aversion therapy – Undesirable behaviours are associated with painful or negative stimuli.
- Desensitization – Clients are gradually exposed to situations that they fear.
- Thought stopping and thought switching – Clients practise controlling fears by stopping the negative thoughts (for example, by using a verbal reminder) or switching to more positive ones.
- Token economy – Good behaviour is rewarded with tokens that clients can trade for privileges or desired objects.

Group Therapy

Small groups of people with similar problems meet together, facilitated by a therapist, to discuss and work through their concerns. In community settings, many groups focus on self-help, with members helping one another. Professionals do not usually attend. Instead, more experienced members are the facilitators.

Cognitive Therapy and Cognitive–Behavioural Therapy

There are two forms of cognition therapy:

- Cognitive therapy focuses on changing "irrational beliefs, faulty reasoning, and negative self-statements that underlie behavioral problems" (Stuart, 2005a, p. 656). Therapists help clients change their self-concept and coping skills by altering their thought patterns and behaviour.
- In cognitive–behavioural therapy, similar techniques of behaviour modification are used, along with strategies for cognitive restructuring and reducing anxiety (relaxation training, biofeedback, role-playing). Clients have homework assignments for practising between sessions.

NURSING CONSIDERATIONS

Communication Techniques

Therapeutic communication is the heart of mental health nursing. While nurses may focus on developing therapeutic verbal communication techniques, non-verbal communication is equally important. Nurses need to be aware of a client's nonverbal signals, just as clients are sure to be aware of the nurse's. Clients know when a nurse is being genuine, honest, and sincere. They can sense a nurse's respect and empathy (and they sense the opposite responses just as easily).

Managing therapeutic communication implies that nurses monitor all aspects of their own and their client's communication, such as movement, gestures, posture, facial expression, and body language. Be aware of vocal tone, pitch, and volume, as well as nervous habits, such as coughing or giggling. We also communicate a great

deal about ourselves and our regard for clients through touch. Always remember that cultural patterns of communication may be different, especially with regard to boundaries of personal space and touching.

When it is necessary to confront a client about undesirable behaviour or attitudes, be assertive, but not aggressive or angry. Point out discrepancies in a matter-of-fact way between a client's self-interpretation of behaviour and how others may view those same actions. In Table 11.2, you will find a summary of therapeutic communication techniques. Refer to Chapter 3, pages 20–21, for more ideas on how to develop therapeutic communication techniques and interviewing skills.

Assessing Mental Status

Evaluating the client's mental status is an important aspect of clinical assessment. Combining what the client can tell you with your own observations, the mental state assessment evaluates the client's current mental functioning, not his or her psychiatric history. Most organizations have a structured form to help the nurse recall the range of questions to ask and observations to make, to ensure that sufficient and appropriate information is collected. In general, assessing mental status includes describing the following characteristics:

- Appearance, speech, activity, and interaction in the interview
- Emotions: mood and affect
- His or her perceptions of personal experiences
- Thought content and thinking processes, including ability to concentrate
- Level of consciousness
- Memory
- Level of intelligence
- Evidence of judgement and insight

Further details on mental health assessment and neurological physical assessment are in Chapter 4.

Milieu Therapy

Nurses help create a therapeutic community or milieu on the inpatient unit, in which clients become part of a community where they can learn new social skills, improve their coping mechanisms, and develop healthy interpersonal relationships. Establishing this type of environment to aid in social rehabilitation is more difficult in today's context of relatively brief hospital stays; in outpatient settings, such as group homes, a therapeutic community is more easily established.

Family Therapy

Family nursing is important in mental health practice. Families are both the context within which the mentally ill client lives and clients in need of nursing care themselves. Often the family serves as caregiver

Table 11.2   Selected Therapeutic Communication Techniques

Technique	Definition	Example
Listening	An active process of receiving information, showing interest and acceptance	Maintain eye contact and convey positive nonverbal responses
Broad Openings	Asking questions that allow the client to select topics for discussion	"What are you thinking about?"
Restating	Repeating the client's main thought to have him or her validate what you heard and to emphasize important points	"You say that your mother left you when you were 5 years old."
Clarification	Asking the client to explain what he or she means, to help the client examine issues in more detail	"I'm not sure that I fully understand. Could you tell me about that again?"
Reflection	Directing back the client's ideas, feelings, questions, and content to signify empathy and validate the nurse's understanding	"You're feeling anxious, and it's related to your conversation with your husband last night."
Informing	Providing information for health teaching and self-care	"It's important for you to know how this medication works."
Focusing	Questions or statements that help the client expand on the topic, keeping the communication goal-directed	"I think we should talk more about your relationship with your father."
Sharing Perceptions	Asking the client to verify your understanding of his or her thoughts or feelings, to clear up confusion	"You're smiling, but I sense that you are really very angry with me."
Identifying Themes	Identifying issues or problems that the client repeatedly refers to in conversation, aimed at helping the client understand and explore important problems	"I've noticed that you have spoken often of being hurt or rejected by men with whom you have formed relationships."
Silence	Intentionally not initiating verbal communication, to allow time for thinking and reflection and to encourage the client to initiate communication	Sitting with the client to nonverbally communicate support and interest
Suggesting	Presenting alternative ideas for the client to consider in problem solving, to increase possibilities and choices	"Have you thought about responding differently to your boss when he raises that issue with you? For example, you could ask him whether a specific problem has occurred."

Source: Adapted from Stuart, G. W. (2009). *Principles and practice of psychiatric nursing* (9th ed., pp. 31–33, Box 2-8). St. Louis: Mosby.

and case manager for clients outside the hospital. Families need education about the client's illness and help with learning new patterns of interacting with the client. Different types of groups can help provide support to these families; these are outlined below:

- Psychoeducational groups for families provide support to families coping with a member who has a severe mental illness. Families are taught about the signs and symptoms of the illness, medications, other options for therapy, sources of community help, and how to recognize signs of a relapse. In these groups, family members can share their experiences and successful strategies for managing the client at home.
- Self-help groups for families can be accessed through voluntary organizations, such as the Canadian Schizophrenia Society and the Canadian Mental

Health Association. Such mutual aid groups empower families, reduce their isolation, and help them learn coping skills.

Community Mental Health Nursing

Because most people with mental illnesses are treated outside the hospital, roles for community mental health nurses are expanding. Community treatment focuses clients on recovery, with a goal of helping clients learn to manage their illness and incorporate any limitations into a satisfying life. Social and functional-living skills (and, where possible, employment skills) enable clients to cope while living as independently as possible.

As members of interdisciplinary teams, nurses work in several models for community mental health services. Community outreach programs aim to assist clients where they live. Other services are provided in offices where clients must make and keep appointments. Many programs are a combination. Outreach programs may provide specific services for mentally ill clients and their families, or they may refer clients to other programs in the community. Examples of these services include the following:

Assertive Community Treatment (ACT): A specific interdisciplinary team model for intensive community support. Community programs and services may include client identification, mental health care and counselling, medical care, dental care, crisis response, social assistance, financial management, community education and advocacy, rehabilitation, housing, family support, and case management.

Case Management: Case managers develop caring and supportive therapeutic relationships with complex clients. They may be attached to an ACT team or a hospital outpatient service.

Supported Housing: Varies, from apartments with a resident manager with some mental health knowledge to group homes. Some group homes follow the Club House model, where residents are members and collaborate with staff in running the house and its programs.

Community Mental Health Centres (CMHCs): Provide outpatient clinics, mental health programs, and support services.

Public Health: In rural areas, the public health nurse may be the only source of community mental health outreach. In more urban areas, public health nurses are more likely to focus on prevention, such as stress management and parenting classes, school programming, or screening for depression. They make referrals to mental health programs and agencies.

Addiction Services: Street nurses may be the first point of contact for mentally ill persons with substance abuse problems.

MOOD DISORDERS: DEPRESSION, MANIA, BIPOLAR DISORDER

Mood disorders are also called affective disorders, "affect" meaning the expression of a person's mood. Emotional ups and downs are normal features of living. Severe or prolonged changes in a person's mood may not be.

Abnormal mood ranges between two emotional extremes: depression and mania. Mania is an abnormally and persistently elevated mood state marked by hyperactivity, delusions, and lack of judgement. Depression is described below.

Usually, hospitalized clients have either a severe depression or a bipolar illness, in which their mood swings between depression and mania.

DEPRESSION

Depression, the most common psychiatric illness, affects approximately 8% of Canadian adults, and 4–5% suffer from major depression in a given year (CIHI, 2002). All age groups can be clinically depressed—even children. Depression is common in adolescents and very common in the older adult. Adult women are twice as likely as men to suffer from major depression; however, with aging, the incidence decreases for women but increases for men.

Pathophysiology

Neurological and genetic factors interact in complex ways to produce depression.

- Neurological factors – These include low levels of monoamines, such as serotonin and norepinephrine. Other neurotransmitters that are poorly regulated include dopamine, acetylcholine, GABA, and serotonin (5-HT). Serotonin also affects levels of growth hormone, cortisol, and prolactin, all of which are poorly regulated in people with depression.
- Brain scans – These can show decreased metabolic activity in the frontal and temporal lobes and increased blood flow to the amygdala.
- Genetic factors – People with a family history of depression have an increased incidence of depression. Genetic factors predispose people to develop depression when faced with environmental factors such as stressful life events.
- Endocrinology – Depression is commonly associated with Addison's disease, Cushing's syndrome, thyroid diseases, and abnormal estrogen levels. These hormonal imbalances disrupt the regulatory functions of the hypothalamus and pituitary glands. As well, seasonal depression (seasonal affective disorder [SAD]) may be linked to abnormalities in the hypothalamic control of circadian rhythms.
- Electrolytes – High levels of calcium, sodium bicarbonate, and either high or low levels of potassium are common with depression.

Clinical Manifestations

Depression is expressed as intense feelings of sadness, despair, and powerlessness, often as a consequence of loss. Depression can be brief and transient in the normal response to everyday disappointments or more prolonged, ranging through mild to moderate to severe chronic depression. Moderate depression (dysthymic disorder) and severe depression (major depressive disorder [MDD]) tend not to resolve without professional help.

People with depression share a number of common characteristics. They will tell you that they feel empty and extremely sad, with no hope for the future. Their pain is both emotional and physical, with diffuse aches and pains throughout their bodies. Previously enjoyable activities now provide no pleasure, and, not surprisingly, they can be irritable and socially withdrawn.

Normally, grief for a loved one is experienced as depression, with many of the same symptoms.

Overwhelming sadness and hopelessness are manifested in sleep disturbances, changes in appetite and weight, and inability to concentrate or carry out usual activities. Unlike those experiencing chronic depression, grieving people recognize the reason for their feelings. Gradually, acceptance develops, the depressive symptoms resolve, and normal coping mechanisms resurface.

Depression is a common response with major loss, including the loss of health experienced with a chronic illness. Other risk factors include stressful life events, poor social support, substance abuse, and having a history of depression. Several specific depressive disorders include the following:

Major Depressive Disorder (MDD)

Major depression is persistent and devastating. MDD can occur in a single episode, or more frequently as recurrent relapses, or a chronic condition lasting longer than two years. In some, the symptoms are severe enough to cause psychosis (a psychotic break from reality) with delusions, hallucinations, and psychomotor retardation to the point of catatonia. Almost 15% of untreated people with major depression commit suicide. MDD is characterized by the following symptoms:

- Feelings of sadness and emptiness, with crying
- Anhydonia – No interest in activities that were previously enjoyed
- Appetite changes, accompanied by either weight loss or weight gain
- Sleep pattern changes (insomnia, or sleeping during the day)
- Lack of energy, extreme fatigue
- Feelings of worthlessness or inappropriate and excessive guilt
- Psychomotor agitation (restlessness) or retardation (slowed movement)
- Inability to concentrate or make decisions, difficulty thinking
- Recurrent thoughts of suicide or death (APA, 2000)

Dysthymic Disorder

Dysthymia, less prevalent than major depression, is a chronic moderate level of depression. The somewhat milder symptoms are similar to major depression but chronic, persisting for at least two years. (For children and adolescents, the diagnosis may be made after one year.) Individuals feel depressed most of the time. When they are depressed, they also exhibit at least two of the other symptoms listed for major depression. Social and occupational impairment are significant.

Postpartum Depression

Some degree of depression affects more than half of all new mothers. Although most mothers experience "baby blues" in the week or two after the birth, postpartum depression is more severe and lasts longer. Women with limited social support, previous episodes of depression, or perinatal complications are most at risk.

Postpartum depression greatly reduces a woman's ability to care for her child, with negative consequences for both the mother's health and that of her baby. In severe cases, the mother can become psychotic and may harm herself or her child.

Seasonal Affective Disorder

Often called SAD, in this disorder, changes in mood occur in response to a reduced exposure to daylight. In fall and winter, people with SAD become clinically depressed. Depression generally resolves in the spring.

Diagnostics

Along with a full history and physical examination to identify symptoms and comorbid illnesses, several rating scales are available to assess depression. Three of the most common scales are as follows:

- Beck Depression Inventory (BDI) – A self-rating scale that clients complete
- Zung Self-Rating Depression Scale (ZSRD) – Another self-report scale
- Hamilton Rating Scale for Depression (HAM-D) – Completed by clinicians

Therapeutics

Pharmacotherapy is the predominant mode of treatment for mood disorders. Remember that medications may take several weeks to be effective. See Chapter 7, page 183, for more details about antidepressants, including drug classifications, actions, and side effects. Chapter 7 also includes nursing implications for these drugs.

Medications for Depression

- Tricyclic antidepressants – Side effects are significant; therefore, these are used less frequently now.
- SSRIs – Selective serotonin reuptake inhibitors
- MAOIs are usually reserved for hard-to-treat MDD clients due to their severe side effects.

Nursing Considerations

Nursing Assessment

Many clients with mood disorders never enter psychiatric settings. Therefore, nurses working in all health care, occupational, and community settings should be attentive to signs of mood disorders. When a disorder is first suspected, the client may be asked to complete a self-assessment scale.

Assessment of Depression

To assess for depression, the nurse determines whether the client

- Is psychotic
- Is on drugs or other substances
- Has comorbid medical conditions that may contribute to psychiatric symptoms
- Has ever had other mental health problems that may contribute to depression
- Is at risk of harming himself or herself or other people (see the section on psychiatric emergencies, pages 592–595)

If the client has a history of depression, find out what worked then and what did not. Discuss with the client his or her level of knowledge about depression and whether supportive family members are available. Finally, assess whether the client needs referral to a primary care provider (physician or nurse practitioner).

The Nurse–Client Relationship

The cornerstone of connecting with clients with mood disorders is spending time with the person to reinforce reality and provide support. Use a calm approach and moderate tone of voice—neither overly cheerful nor too serious—and active listening. Establishing rapport and communicating with people at either end of the mood spectrum present additional and different challenges, as outlined below:

- Be kind and compassionate – Just sitting with an isolated person is comforting and supportive.
- Use simple, direct language – To counteract slowed thinking processes
- Be patient – Allow extra time for the person to follow directions and respond.
- Offer observations – Instead of questioning an individual who is not talkative, point out characteristics of the person and the immediate environment, for example, "Your blue dress matches your eyes" or "Your son brought you some fruit."
- Avoid common expressions that can discount a client's feelings, such as "Oh, things will be better soon; it just takes time."

Pharmacotherapy

Be aware of and monitor for side effects, adverse reactions, and interactions of major medications used for mood disorders. Clients with mood disorders may object to taking medications; be sure to supervise as they swallow oral medications.

Antidepressants
Nursing implications for antidepressant drug side effects are discussed in Table 11.3.

Monoamine Oxidase Inhibitors (MAOIs)
MAOIs increase levels of serotonin, epinephrine, and norepinephrine in the brain. These medications can cause severe interactions with certain foods and medications:

- Over-the-counter cold medications – These interact with MAOIs, producing a hypertensive crisis, a life-threatening condition manifested by tachycardia, severe headache and nosebleeds, stiff neck, nausea and vomiting, and cold, clammy skin. Clients can develop chest pains or a stroke and die. Emergency treatment for hypertensive crisis involves the following:

  - Discontinue MAOI.
  - Keep the client's head elevated.
  - Reduce fever by external methods, such as fans, tepid baths, or ice packs.
  - Give a calcium channel blocker such as nifedipine sublingually.

- Other contraindicated drugs for people taking MAOIs include narcotics, tricyclic antidepressants, antihypertensives, sedatives, including alcohol, and legal or illegal stimulants, such as amphetamines and cocaine.

In order to prevent a hypertensive crisis, which is rare but potentially fatal, the client also needs to avoid certain foods, particularly those with high levels of tyramine, which are listed below:

- Instruct the client not to eat *any* of the following foods: aged cheeses (cream cheese and cottage cheese are safe); red wine, sherry, and liqueurs; over-ripe fruit; sauerkraut; pickled or smoked fish; beef and chicken liver; fava beans; brewer's yeast; monosodium glutamate; and all fermented products.
- Consume moderate amounts only of alcohol, beer, and white wine; beverages with caffeine; ripe avocado, yogurt, soy sauce, figs, raisins, ripe bananas, chocolate, and meat tenderizers.

Complementary and Alternative Medications
St. John's wort is a herbal product with proven effects against mild to moderate depression, SAD, and sleep disturbance. Melatonin supports circadian rhythm equilibrium, thus improving sleep. Many people place great trust in natural remedies and self-medicate for the less severe mood disorders. When prescription medications are required, clients should discontinue the herbal remedies. Interactions can either reduce or increase the action of prescribed drugs, potentially causing toxic effects. Clients should be given this information.

General Nursing Care

The following nursing considerations are also important:

- Maintain client safety – Observe closely for self-harm or suicidal thoughts. Remove belongings that could be used for self-harm.

Table 11.3 Nursing Considerations for Antidepressant Drug Side Effects

SIDE EFFECT Anticholinergic Side Effects	NURSING CARE AND TEACHING CONSIDERATIONS
Blurred Vision	Temporary; avoid hazardous tasks
Dry Mouth	Encourage fluids, frequent rinses, sugar-free hard candy and gums; check for mouth sores
Constipation	Increase fluids, dietary fibre and roughage, exercise; monitor bowel habits; use stool softeners and laxatives only if necessary
Tachycardia	Temporary, usually not significant (except with coronary artery disease), but can be frightening; eliminate caffeine; ß-blockers might help; provide supportive therapy
Urinary retention	Encourage fluids and frequent voiding; monitor voiding patterns; bethanecol; catheterize
Cognitive Dysfunction	Temporary; avoid hazardous tasks; adjust lifestyle; provide supportive therapy
Cytochrome P-450 inhibition*	SSRIs inhibit the liver isoenzyme cytochrome P-450, which is instrumental in the metabolism of a variety of drugs (TCAs, trazodone, barbiturates, most benzodiazepines, carbamazepine, narcotics, neuroleptics, phenytoin, valproate, verapamil). This effect can be potentially life-threatening because it increases serum concentrations as well as therapeutic and toxic effects of these drugs.
Dizziness/Lightheadedness	Have client dangle the feet; provide adequate hydration, elastic stockings; protect from falls
ECG Changes	Obtain complete cardiac history; obtain pretreatment ECG for clients over 40 and children; ST segment depression, T wave flattened or inverted, QRS prolongation; worsening of intraventricular conduction problems; do no use if recent myocardial infarction or bundle-branch block
Ejaculatory Dysfunction	Dose after sexual intercourse, not immediately before
GI Disturbances (Nausea, Diarrhea)	Take with meals or at HS; adjust diet if indicated
Hallucinations, Delusions, Activation of Schizophrenic or Manic Psychosis	Change to another antidepressant class of drug; initiate antipsychotics or mood stabilizers if appropriate
Hypertensive Crisis*	See the following discussion of MAOIs.
Hypotension	Obtain frequent BP; hydrate; provide elastic stockings; may need to change drug. For postural hypotension: obtain lying and standing BP, encourage gradual change of positions, protect from falls.
Insomnia	Dose as early in the day as possible; promote sleep hygiene; decrease evening activities; eliminate caffeine, relaxation techniques; sedative–hypnotic therapy
Memory Dysfunction	Temporary; encourage concentration, make lists, provide social support, adjust lifestyle
Perspiration (Excessive)	Suggest frequent changes of clothes, cotton or linen clothing, good hygiene; increase fluids
Priapism	Change dose, change drug
Psychomotor Activation	Take drug in morning rather than HS; adjust lifestyle
Sedation/Drowsiness	Administer drug at HS; avoid hazardous tasks
Serotonin Syndrome (SS)*	SS is a life-threatening emergency resulting from excess central nervous system 5-HT caused by combining 5-HT-enhancing drugs or administering SSRIs too close to the discontinuation of MAOIs. Symptoms are confusion, disorientation, mania, restlessness/agitation, myoclonus, hyper-reflexia, diaphoresis, shivering, tremor, diarrhea, nausea, ataxia, headache. Discontinue all serotoninergic drugs immediately; anticonvulsants for seizures; serotonin antagonist drugs may help; clonazepam for myoclonus, lorazepam for restlessness or agitation, other symptomatic care as indicated; do not reintroduce serotonin drugs

Continued on next page

Table 11.3 Nursing Considerations for Antidepressant Drug Side Effects (cont'd)

SIDE EFFECT Anticholinergic Side Effects	NURSING CARE AND TEACHING CONSIDERATIONS
Sexual Dysfunction	Dose after sexual intercourse; use lubricant if vaginal dryness is present; antidotes such as sildenafil, bupropion, or bethanecol
Tachycardia	See anticholinergic side effects
TCA Withdrawal Syndrome	Symptoms: malaise, muscle aches, chills, nausea, dizziness, coryza; when discontinuing drug, taper over several days or weeks
Tremors	Temporary; adjust lifestyle as indicated
Weight Gain	Increase exercise; reduced-calorie diet if indicated; may need to change class of drug

NOTE: Always educate the client and use the techniques in this table. Consider decreasing or dividing drug dose. Change drug only if necessary.
*Potentially life-threatening
BP, blood pressure; *ECG*, electrocardiogram; *GI*, gastrointestinal; *HS*, at bedtime; *5-HT*, serotonin; *MAOIs*, monoamine oxidase inhibitors; *SSRIs*, selective serotonin reuptake inhibitors; *TCAs*, tricyclic antidepressants.

Source: Adapted from Stuart, G. W. (2009). *Principles and practice of psychiatric nursing* (9th ed., p. 518, Table 26-11). St. Louis: Mosby.

- Maintain nutrition – Give small, frequent meals, taking preferences into account.
- Maintain elimination – Add high-fibre foods to counteract constipation.
- Assist with personal hygiene – Encourage the client to gradually resume self-care.
- Encourage social interaction – Provide reassurance and positive reinforcement for gradually joining group activities.

MANIA AND BIPOLAR DISORDER

In contrast to depression, about 1% of Canadians have bipolar illness, with the first manic episode usually appearing during adolescence or in the twenties (CIHI, 2002). A person has a bipolar illness if his or her mood alternates between mania and either depression or euthymia (mood level is neither "up" nor "down"). An older name for bipolar illness that you may still hear is manic depression.

Pathophysiology

A complex interplay of underlying biological factors also leads to the development of mania:

- Neurological – Neurotransmitter abnormalities, that is, high plasma levels of epinephrine and norepinephrine
- Brain scans – These show abnormalities in the white matter (fatty sheaths surrounding neurons), particularly in those areas of the brain responsible for emotions.
- Genetics – As with depression, higher rates of mania are found among first-degree relatives.

- Endocrinology – The biological clock is located in the hypothalamus. In mania, circadian rhythms are disrupted; sleep deprivation is common. Hypothyroidism is linked to bipolar illness.

Clinical Manifestations

Mood changes between mania and depression are called switching or cycling, sometimes with periods of normality between the episodes. The episode length may vary, although manic periods tend to be shorter than the depressions. Clients also vary in how frequently and quickly they cycle from "high" to "low" or vice versa; however, mania usually begins and ends more quickly than depression. Over four switches a year, usually without normal periods, constitutes a rapid-cycling bipolar illness. Bipolar disorder can persist for months and even years.

Symptoms of the depressive episodes are the same as those of major depression. In contrast, during a manic phase, clients' symptoms are as follows:

- Overly talkative, hyperactive (psychomotor agitation), and self-confident—so busy that they may not take time to eat or drink properly
- Effusively outgoing, overly friendly, and humorous
- Often engaged in money-making schemes or irresponsible spending, but with very little insight into their behaviour and how it affects others
- Rapid, often confusing, speech patterns; "pressured speech" or "flights of ideas"
- Disturbed sleep patterns—seemingly needing very little sleep
- Easily distracted
- Irritable and aggressive at times, especially if stopped from following impulses and desires

- Self-centred and overly involved in activities that are fun or risky
- High risk of suicide
- Mania can escalate to a psychotic state, with delusions and hallucinations.

Cyclothymia

Cyclothymia is a milder form of bipolar disorder with shorter and less extreme episodes. During hypomanic periods, individuals may excel in occupational and artistic achievements, but, ultimately, the unevenness of their behaviour and productivity tends to damage their careers and relationships. Self-medication with alcohol or other substances is common. Treatment is recommended because about one in three persons progress to a fully developed bipolar illness.

Diagnostics

Mania is diagnosed when at least three of the symptoms listed above persist for at least a week.

Along with a full history and physical examination to identify symptoms and comorbid illnesses, several rating scales are available to assess depression (see scale list under "Diagnostics," page 556).

Medications for Mania and Bipolar Disorder

- Lithium carbonate
- Anticonvulsants, such as carbamazepine (Tegretol), valproic acid
- Anxiolytics
- Antipsychotics – Typical and atypical

See Chapter 7, page 184, for more details in the mood stabilizers, antipsychotics, and anticonvulsants section, which include drug classifications, actions, and side effects. Chapter 7 also includes nursing implications for these drugs.

Nursing Considerations

Assessment of Mania and Bipolar Disorders

To assess for mania, the nurse determines whether the client

- Is a danger to himself or herself (exhaustion in severe mania can lead to death) or others (due to poor impulse control) and needs to be hospitalized
- Is spending money uncontrollably and engaging in overly risky behaviours
- Has comorbid medical conditions
- Has substance abuse problems
- Requires information about bipolar disorder, medications, and support groups for the client or family

Mania

- Try to maintain a calm, nonstimulating atmosphere on the unit.
- Convey self-confidence when setting limits on the client's behaviour.
- Guard against being manipulated and ensure consistency with the rest of the team in your response to manipulative behaviour or acting out.

Pharmacotherapy

In the case of bipolar disorder, the medication dosage must be delicately balanced. Monitor clients' responses carefully; antidepressants can induce manic symptoms and mood stabilizers may cause depression.

Lithium Carbonate
Because achieving an adequate level of lithium in the body takes weeks or months, other mood stabilizers, antidepressants, or atypical antipsychotics may also be used for mania until the therapeutic level of lithium is reached. Lithium toxicity is an abnormally high serum level of lithium. It can result from nonsteroidal anti-inflammatory drugs (NSAIDs), diuretics, vomiting, diarrhea, and other causes of fluid and electrolyte imbalance or from an overdose.

- Monitor clients for early signs of lithium toxicity: anorexia, nausea, diarrhea, drowsiness, muscle weakness, tremors, unsteadiness, and lack of coordination.
- If toxicity is suspected, monitor vital signs and level of consciousness. Push fluids.
- More severe signs—fever, decreased urine, low blood pressure, electrocardiogram (ECG) changes, irregular heartbeat, seizures, and loss of consciousness—can cause death.
- To prevent lithium toxicity, encourage fluid intake of 2–3 L daily and replace any fluid loss from exercise, vomiting, or diarrhea. If a dose is forgotten or late, skip that dose and resume with the next scheduled dose.

Anticonvulsants

- Action – These drugs stabilize mood by boosting the inhibitory effect of GABA on the stress response. Without inhibition due to GABA, high levels of epinephrine and norepinephrine heighten neural synapse activity.
- Kindling – The neurochemical sensitization of the brain due to stress, resulting in "automatic" initiation of the stress response, without a precipitating stressful event. This also may result from reduced GABA inhibition.
- Serious side effects – Carbamazepine can cause agranulocytosis. Divalproex (a valproic acid derivative) can cause thrombocytopenia. Overdoses can be lethal.
- Monitor blood test results and observe the client for evidence of bruising and bleeding.

General Nursing Care

- Maintain client's safety and that of other clients. Lock up sharp and hazardous possessions.
- Seclusion – Employ if necessary when the client is argumentative and annoying to other clients. Maintain close supervision and spend time with the client after he or she calms down, discussing his or her feelings and suggesting strategies to prevent future escalation of behaviour.
- Give emotional support and encourage rest periods.
- Set realistic limits on behaviour and reinforce socially appropriate conduct. For example, it may be necessary to impose controls on spending to prevent bankruptcy.
- Maintain nutrition and hydration – High energy levels require increased calories. Manic clients need reminders to eat and drink. Provide high-calorie finger foods between mealtimes and, if the client is on lithium, salty snacks.
- Assist with personal hygiene; promote self-care.
- Suggest activities that suit the client's short attention span.

ELECTROCONVULSIVE THERAPY

Electroconvulsive therapy (ECT) involves passing electrical current through the brain, producing a tonic–clonic seizure lasting about 30–60 seconds. Researchers have been unable to pinpoint exactly how ECT works, but the current speculation is that it improves brain chemistry in a manner similar to that of mood-disorder drug treatments. Muscle relaxants confine most seizure activity to the brain, almost completely eliminating contractions elsewhere in the body (unlike the depictions of ECT in the media). ECT remains the treatment of choice for a major depression that does not respond to antidepressants and for an acutely suicidal depressed client. Similarly, ECT can be used for acute mania, if lithium or other mood stabilizers have proven ineffective, or if the mania has escalated to dangerous behaviour or exhaustion, which are life-threatening.

ECT has risks, especially for those with cardiovascular disease. Most memory loss is temporary, although permanent loss can occur. The electrodes are now commonly placed unilaterally rather than bilaterally, thus reducing the level of memory loss that clients experience.

Commonly, a series of three treatments weekly is given for two to four weeks. Reassurance, empathy, and teaching are necessary to allay a client's fears. Nursing care, before and after the procedure, is similar to that required by any client undergoing a general anaesthetic. Nursing considerations for clients receiving ECT therapy include the following:

- Before ECT, educate the client and family about the procedure and effects and encourage them to express any concerns. Allow nothing by mouth for several hours prior to the treatment. Remove valuables and dentures. Clients should urinate before the procedure.
- During the procedure, assist with monitoring vital signs and the electroencephalography.
- After ECT, monitor vital signs and maintain the client's airway until fully awake. Assist with ambulation and reorientation. Give analgesics and antiemetics as necessary. Reinforce teaching and ensure that family members understand the client's initial confusion or memory loss.

THERAPIES AS ADJUNCTS TO MEDICATION

Therapies that are used as an adjunct to medications for treating depression and mania include the following:

Individual Psychotherapy: Aimed at improved social functioning; therapy may focus on a client's interpersonal relationships, developmental problems, and role transitions.

Group Therapy: Provides peer support and education after clients are no longer acutely ill. Groups may be facilitated by professionals or peers. Peer-led groups are usually in community settings, often through voluntary agencies, such as the Mood Disorders Society of Canada.

Family Therapy or Marital Therapy: Aimed at education and at restoring adaptive and functional family relationships.

Cognitive Therapy: Aimed at guiding clients to examine the validity of their thinking and at modifying any distorted perceptions.

Milieu Therapy: The nurse may need to provide seclusion for highly manic bipolar clients.

Phototherapy or Light Therapy for SAD: Regular exposure to broad-spectrum fluorescent lighting (which is of a higher intensity than normal indoor lighting) improves symptoms for most sufferers of SAD.

TEACHING AND LEARNING

For mood disorders, client and family teaching comes after ensuring the client's safety and addressing social needs. It is important to wait until the client is ready and able to learn.

Topics for the Family and Client Education

It is important for the nurse to educate the client and the family on the following topics:

- The illness, including the nature, causes, and symptoms of depression or bipolar disorder
- Medications, including the management of side effects and which side effects to report to the doctor. Emphasize the length of time required for medications to become fully effective, taking medications correctly and regularly, and diet restrictions for those on MAOIs. For people on lithium, highlight having regular blood tests and reinforce the symptoms of lithium toxicity.

- Techniques for stress management, assertiveness (for depression), and anger management (for bipolar disorder)
- Available support services, including support groups, suicide hotline, and legal and financial assistance

ANXIETY DISORDERS: PHOBIC, PANIC, OBSESSIVE–COMPULSIVE, POST-TRAUMATIC STRESS, GENERALIZED ANXIETY

Anxiety and fear are normal stress responses to threatening situations. When anxiety is mild or moderate, people may have adaptive coping abilities to alleviate their concerns and overcome or avoid stressors. In contrast, with severe anxiety or panic, individuals experience considerable distress, the perceptive field narrows, and reactions are quite likely to be maladaptive and disorganized.

Anxiety that is without a specific source or higher than expected for a given threat indicates an anxiety disorder. People with this disorder suffer excessive levels of "anxiety, fear, or worry, causing them either to avoid situations or to develop compulsive rituals that lessen the anxiety" (CIHI, 2002, p. 60). Many develop physical symptoms. In Canada, anxiety disorders are common, affecting 12% of the population (9% of men and 16% of women), with mild to severe impairment. Most can be treated successfully in primary health care settings (CIHI, 2002).

PATHOPHYSIOLOGY

The normal autonomic stress response is called "fight or flight" or the "general adaptation syndrome." It consists of three stages:

Alarm: The body prepares for defence or escape. The hypothalamus stimulates the adrenal glands to release adrenalin and norepinephrine for fuel and the liver to convert glycogen to glucose for cellular nutrition.

Resistance: The body adapts for survival, either by "fight or flight." The pupils dilate. Breathing and heartbeat accelerate, shunting highly oxygenated blood to the muscles. Once the person is out of danger, body responses relax.

Exhaustion: Unless resolved by adaptation during the resistance stage, emotional arousal continues until the body is depleted of stored energy, which will eventually cause death.

Anxiety disorders cause a prolonged and exaggerated stress response. Neurotransmitters of the limbic system (epinephrine, norepinephrine, dopamine, serotonin, and GABA) regulate anxiety. The biological mechanisms include the following:

- Excessive secretion of norepinephrine, which stimulates the cerebral cortex, the limbic system (especially the right temporal lobe), brainstem, and spinal cord, even without a source of fear
- Low levels of GABA – GABA inhibits the excitatory neurotransmitters norepinephrine and dopamine, thus lessening emotional arousal and preventing disorganized responses.
- Abnormal serotonin functioning and glucose metabolism are also implicated.
- Genetics – Anxiety disorders cluster in families, indicating a genetic component.
- Neuroimaging shows anatomical brain changes contributing to (or resulting from) chronic stress. These include smaller frontal and temporal lobes and abnormalities of the amygdala (which regulates fear, memory, and emotion) and the hippocampus (the site of emotion and memory storage). The hippocampus is smaller in people with post-traumatic stress disorder (PTSD).

CLINICAL MANIFESTATIONS

- All age groups are affected. In children, separation anxiety consists of an intense fear of losing their primary caregiver. Symptoms include refusing to attend school, fear of the dark and of going to sleep, stomachaches, headaches, nausea, and feeling faint. Other common anxiety disorders in children are social phobias, generalized anxiety syndrome, and obsessive–compulsive disorder (OCD).
- Seniors – There is a high prevalence of anxiety disorders in older adults, although the incidence is slightly less than in other age groups.
- The major anxiety disorders are outlined in Table 11.4.

Defence Mechanisms

People use defence mechanisms to cope with anxiety. For the most part, defence mechanisms are employed unconsciously to preserve emotional stability and a sense of self. Sometimes, however, defence mechanisms are overused, or they promote reality distortion and self-deception, hindering the person's ability to cope realistically and practically. Nurses can help clients learn appropriate problem-solving and more effective coping strategies. Some common defence mechanisms include the following:

- Repression – Unconsciously blocking awareness of anxiety-provoking or painful perceptions
- Suppression – Similar to forgetting. It may be conscious or unconscious.
- Denial – Rejecting the reality of threatening situations, even with confirming evidence
- Projection – Attributing one's emotions, thoughts, and impulses to another person
- Introjection – Adopting the values and attitudes of others without questioning them
- Reaction formation – Stating the opposite of what one actually feels and thinks

Table 11.4 Symptoms of Anxiety Disorders

Disorder	Symptoms
Post-Traumatic Stress Disorder (PTSD)	Recurrent flashbacks, dreams, and recollections of a life-threatening event, leading to impaired social functioning
Obsessive–Compulsive Disorder (OCD)	Intrusive and inappropriate thoughts and impulses that the person realizes are unreasonable but is nonetheless compelled to repeat
Phobias	Relentless, excessive, or unwarranted fears that interfere with daily life
Agoraphobia	Fear of being in crowds or of losing control or being unable to escape in any setting leads to staying at home to avoid anxiety-provoking environments
Panic Disorder	Short, isolated episodes of intense anxiety, with palpitations, diaphoresis, shakiness, hyperventilating, nausea, chest pain, fear of dying or choking, and distorted perceptions of reality
Generalized Anxiety Disorder	Extensive anxiety in many situations, with inability to concentrate, fatigue, irritability, tension, restlessness, and sleep disturbances

Source: Adapted from Frisch, N. C., & Frisch, L. E. (2006). *Psychiatric mental health nursing* (3rd ed., p. 195, Table 12-2). Clifton Park, NY: Delmar Learning.

- Displacement – Directing negative responses, such as anger, toward someone who is usually less threatening than the person who triggered the response
- Regression – Behaviour that characterizes an earlier developmental stage when the person may have felt more secure
- Withdrawal – Becoming passive and emotionally uninvolved

DIAGNOSTICS AND THERAPEUTICS

Diagnosis

Clients suffering from anxiety often present with the following concerns:

- They feel that they are doomed and likely to die.
- They have difficulties with problem solving and concentration.
- Their vital signs are indicative of the stress response: perspiring; increased blood pressure (BP), heart rate, and respirations; muscle tension; and dilated pupils.
- They exhibit somatic symptoms, for example, nausea, palpitations, frequent voiding or urgency, throat tightening, or a shaky voice.
- They complain of feeling tired and being short-tempered, disorganized, and unable to sleep.

While the above complaints clearly indicate anxiety, before concluding that it is a mental health problem, it is important to rule out whether the apprehension and worries stem from an underlying medical ailment. Medical illnesses causing anxiety may require urgent treatment. For example:

- Respiratory diseases such as chronic obstructive pulmonary disease (COPD), asthma, pulmonary edema, pulmonary embolism
- Cardiovascular diseases such as angina, congestive heart failure, hypertension, hypotension, arrhythmias
- Endocrine diseases such as hyperthyroidism and hypoglycemia
- Neurological diseases such as delirium, Parkinson's disease, postconcussion syndrome
- Metabolic diseases such as hypercalcemia, hyperkalemia, hyponatremia

Treatment

First, treat any comorbid medical conditions. Then consider

- Cognitive–behavioural therapy (CBT), including psychoeducation and cognitive restructuring
- Behavioural therapy, including relaxation, desensitization, response prevention, and thought stopping
- Psychotherapy, to help the client develop insight
- Pharmacotherapy, including anxiolytics (especially benzodiazepines), antidepressants, beta blockers, and antihistamines

NURSING CONSIDERATIONS

Nursing Assessment

Begin with a full health history and physical assessment to ascertain whether there are concurrent medical conditions associated with the heightened anxiety. Ask about social activities and any worries, fears, or feelings of nervousness, tension, or insecurity. Does the person talk about a past traumatic experience?

- Several rating scales for anxiety are available, for example, the Hamilton Rating Scale for Anxiety.
- Check vital signs (pulse, BP, respiratory rate, etc.), changes in appetite or weight, and other physiological symptoms, such as gastrointestinal (GI) upsets, fatigue, diaphoresis, and insomnia.
- Assess the risk of self-harm or suicide (see the section on psychiatric emergencies).
- Inquire about cognitive capacity (ability to concentrate, disorientation, illogical thinking, narrowed perceptual field, etc.).
- Probe for any reasons for heightened anxiety.

The Nurse–Client Relationship

Clients in any health care setting experience some level of anxiety. Reducing their anxiety to tolerable levels depends on a nurse's skill and patience in developing a trusting relationship. Be patient. There may not be much improvement for weeks or even months.

- Show respect by addressing your client using his or her preferred name.
- Use a calm, warmly accepting, and quiet approach.
- Encourage the client to talk about feelings and emotions.
- Convey compassion, empathy, and honesty.
- Speak slowly, wait patiently while your client responds, and then listen carefully.

Nursing Goals

- Maintain a restful, nonstimulating environment or move the client to a quiet place and always stay with any person who is experiencing high levels of anxiety.
- Speak slowly in clear, simple language, repeating as necessary.
- Reinforce reality where there are distortions in the client's perception and understanding.
- Listen for themes in the client's communication.
- Monitor and encourage self-care activities for those clients with ritualistic and obsessive–compulsive behaviours. Phobias and intense concentration on rituals can interfere with a client's personal hygiene and grooming, adequate nutrition and fluid intake, elimination, and sleep.
- Ensure client safety and protection from impulsive and destructive reactions based on fear.

Teaching and Learning

Teach relaxation techniques, either individually or in groups. Some examples of these techniques include the following:

- Deep muscle relaxation – Have the clients lie down and tense and relax voluntary muscles, progressing from the toes upward and focusing attention on each area in turn.
- Controlled breathing or meditation or both
- Guided imagery of places and situations that the person has previously experienced as peaceful and restful
- Systematic desensitization of anxiety-causing situations, either through visualization, role-play, or repeated real exposure, while also engaging in controlled breathing or deep muscle relaxation techniques
- Teach about anxiety and the client's specific diagnosis.
- Support services – Provide information about available community programs and services, such as support groups, crisis hotlines, and sources for individual psychotherapy.
- Medications – Teach clients and families about medications and their side effects, such as the following:

  - Warning them to avoid working with dangerous equipment
  - Warning them to avoid both alcoholic and caffeinated beverages. Alcohol can enhance the effect of the medication, and caffeine can reduce it.
  - Warning women to avoid pregnancy and breast-feeding when taking benzodiazepines
  - Teaching dietary restrictions for MAOIs
  - Warning that stopping the medications abruptly may cause withdrawal symptoms, such as tremors, convulsions, confusion, insomnia, irritability, and nervousness

SCHIZOPHRENIAS AND DELUSIONAL AND SCHIZOAFFECTIVE DISORDERS

Schizophrenia is "a devastating disease of the brain that affects a person's thinking, language, emotions, social behaviour and ability to accurately perceive reality" (Varcarolis, 2002d, p. 524). It is a common disorder with a lifetime prevalence of 1%, both in Canada and worldwide. The mortality rate for people with schizophrenia is twice that of the general population, and life expectancy is 20% shorter. Estimates of attempted suicide among people with schizophrenia vary from 30–50%. Ten percent of those with schizophrenia commit suicide; studies vary in estimating the suicide risk from 15–75 times that of the general population (Health Canada, 1994). Thus, for a substantial proportion of clients, schizophrenia is a terminal illness.

There are a number of related disorders, including schizophreniform disorder, schizoaffective disorder, delusional disorder, brief psychotic disorder, and shared psychotic disorder (sometimes called folie à deux). Although some people (and often the media) confuse multiple personality disorder (MPD) with schizophrenia, the two are distinctly different psychiatric illnesses, and MPD is a much rarer condition.

PATHOPHYSIOLOGY

Causation is complicated and involves many factors. Evidence is clear, however, that brain structure, balancing of neurochemical transmitters, and disrupted neural circuits underlie the development of schizophrenia. Although social and environmental factors may trigger the onset or exacerbation of schizophrenia symptoms, the psychosocial theories blaming dysfunctional families and parenting are both outdated and harmful. Some key factors include the following:

- Brain abnormalities – At the time of diagnosis, larger cerebral ventricles, atrophy of the cerebellum or frontal lobe, and a variety of other structural abnormalities can be seen; for example, the hippocampus may be smaller than normal. As the illness progresses, further degeneration is minimal. Abnormalities of the prefrontal cortex are associated with reductions in higher cognitive functions.
- Neurochemical transmitters – There is excessive dopamine activity. Serotonin, glutamate, and other neurotransmitters are also poorly regulated.
- Genetics – Decades of studies on twins provide ample evidence that inheritance is a factor. People with a parent or sibling with schizophrenia are at higher risk of developing schizophrenia. If both parents have schizophrenia, a child has almost a 50% risk of developing the disorder.
- Street drugs – These do not cause schizophrenia; however, when a person is genetically predisposed to schizophrenia, illegal substances may initiate symptoms earlier and with more severity than would occur otherwise.

CLINICAL MANIFESTATIONS

Schizophrenia affects men and women in equal numbers, although, on average, males are usually diagnosed in their late teens or early twenties, while women are often diagnosed during their mid-twenties. Males also tend to display more severe symptoms and more negative symptoms and be less responsive to pharmacological treatment, thus suffering a poorer outcome. Females, in contrast, are more likely to have a family history of schizophrenia but have less severe symptoms and cognitive impairment. Late onset, after the age of 40, occurs infrequently. Women and those with later onset tend to have better outcomes. Comorbid mental health conditions are common, especially depression and anxiety. As well, many people abuse substances, trying to relieve their symptoms through self-medication.

Schizophrenia is a lifelong illness for at least 95% of sufferers. Some people will have one severe episode for which they receive treatment but are then well stabilized on medications that they take for the remainder of their lives. A few are eventually able to function without antipsychotics. For many, however, the illness is marked by hospitalization during psychotic episodes interspersed with periods of community treatment. Over many years, the psychotic episodes may become further apart. A minority do not respond to antipsychotic medications and remain in psychiatric hospitals long term.

Symptoms of Schizophrenia

The symptoms of schizophrenia are categorized as either "positive" or "negative." Many symptoms are visible to others and become a source of stigma against the disease, the people affected, and their families. Clients are often withdrawn and socially isolated, either to hide their illness or in an attempt to feel safe. Social isolation also is brought about by the ridicule and rejection that they experience, stemming from the stigma surrounding the illness and misunderstanding on the part of the public.

Positive Symptoms

Positive symptoms are characterized by the exaggeration or distortion of normal functions. Sometimes positive symptoms are subdivided into psychotic and disorganized dimensions.

Psychotic Symptoms

- Hallucinations are distorted perceptions involving any of the five senses. Auditory hallucinations, in which the voices that clients hear are unusually threatening or disapproving, are particularly prevalent.
- Delusions are unrealistic and unfounded beliefs. Common delusions are of grandeur, of being persecuted, of being controlled, or of having one's mind read.

Disorganized Symptoms

- Bizarre appearance or behaviour that others define as "weird." When psychotic, the person's behaviour may be catatonic. Catatonia is defined as "a state of psychologically induced immobilization at times interrupted by episodes of extreme agitation" (Varcarolis, 2002b, p. G-3). Examples of catatonic behaviour include robotlike activity, complete immobility, or holding a position for long periods of time (waxy flexibility).
- Hostility and aggression, most often in response to paranoid and persecutory delusions. People who become violent while experiencing delusions are trying to defend themselves.
- Cognitive disturbances are problems in processing information. Clients are often bombarded so rapidly with ideas that focusing on anything or sorting out what is relevant from what is not becomes impossible. Thoughts are illogical and disconnected. Terms used for

cognitive disturbances include "thought disturbance," "loose associations," and "flight of ideas."

- Incoherent speech patterns reflect the disturbed thoughts and may be rapid, jumping from one topic to another. This is sometimes referred to as "word salad."

Negative Symptoms

- Inappropriate affect – People display emotions that are inconsistent with the occasion
- Flattened affect – Emotions or emotional responses are diminished
- Alogia – A lack of speech or inadequate communication caused by an interruption in the thought processes
- Poor attention span – Inattentiveness and impaired concentration
- Anhedonia – The inability to experience pleasure from activities or social relationships
- Apathy – Physical inertia
- Avolition – An inability to persist with activities, including grooming and hygiene

A summary of the signs and symptoms of schizophrenia is listed in Figure 11.3.

Related Disorders

Schizophreniform Disorder

A person with schizophreniform disorder has the symptoms of schizophrenia but for less than six months, during which there are periods of functional social and occupational activity.

Schizoaffective Disorder

People with schizoaffective disorder have schizophrenic symptoms and a concurrent major depressive or bipolar disorder, but no concurrent general medical disorder or substance abuse.

Positive Symptoms
• Hallucinations
• Delusions
• Disorganized speech (associative looseness)
• Bizarre behaviour
Negative Symptoms
• Blunted affect
• Poverty of thought (alogia)
• Loss of motivation (avolition)
• Inability to experience pleasure or joy (anhedonia)
Cognitive Symptoms
• Inattention, easily distracted
• Impaired memory
• Poor problem-solving skills
• Poor decision-making skills
• Illogical thinking
• Impaired judgement
Affective Symptoms
• Dysphoria
• Suicidality
• Hopelessness
All dimensions alter the individual's
• Ability to work
• Interpersonal relationships
• Self-care abilities
• Social functioning
• Quality of life

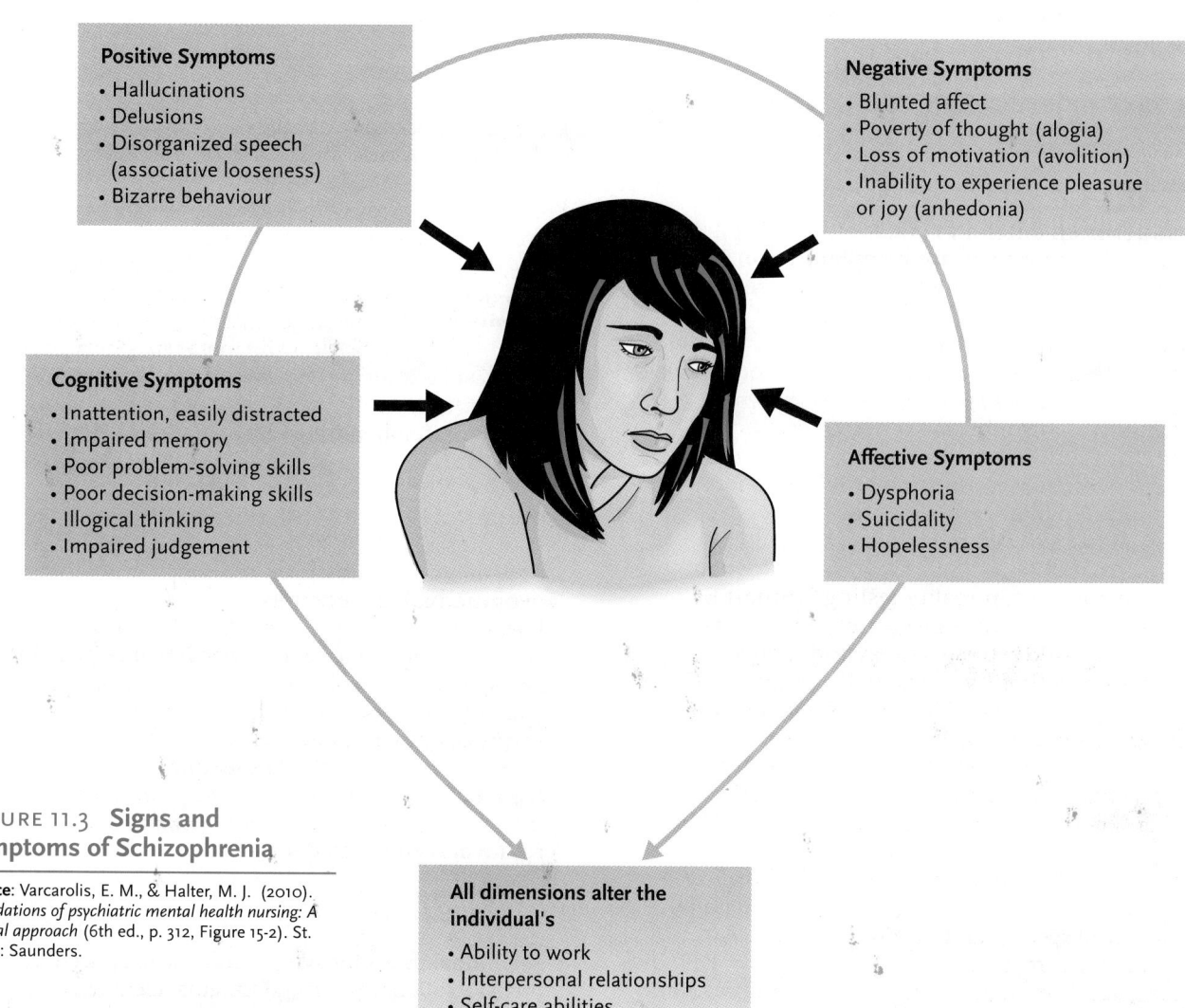

FIGURE 11.3 **Signs and Symptoms of Schizophrenia**

Source: Varcarolis, E. M., & Halter, M. J. (2010). *Foundations of psychiatric mental health nursing: A clinical approach* (6th ed., p. 312, Figure 15-2). St. Louis: Saunders.

Delusional Disorder

People with delusional disorder experience delusions for at least a month that could occur in real life (that is, they are not bizarre), such as jealousy, persecution, delusions of grandeur, or having an infection or a somatic illness. They are able to function socially and at work.

Brief Psychotic Disorder

Following a very stressful life event, psychotic and disorganized symptoms appear suddenly, lasting for one day to a month, after which the person returns to his or her usual functioning.

Shared Psychotic Disorder

This disorder is also called folie à deux. Here, a relative or close friend of a person who is psychotic begins to believe the delusions of the ill person and to act accordingly. In other aspects of life, the relative is able to function quite well. Cult beliefs are sometimes classified in this way.

DIAGNOSTICS AND THERAPEUTICS

Diagnosis

Clients suffer from different combinations of symptoms, and none of the symptoms are completely confined to schizophrenia. Most of the time, clients are at least partly in touch with reality and may be able to hide their symptoms, to avoid stigma or admission to the hospital. For these reasons, diagnosing schizophrenia is complex.

Commonly, schizophrenia is not diagnosed until the person has suffered at least one psychotic episode. Psychosis is defined as a psychological break from reality. Associated behaviours include "regressive behaviour, personality disintegration, reduced level of awareness, great difficulty in functioning adequately, and gross impairment in reality testing" (Stuart & Laraia, 2005, p. 867). Once diagnosed, care providers and families are able retrospectively to identify long-evident symptoms that have gradually escalated. Given that most people become ill in their late teens or early adulthood, many of the early symptoms are originally blamed on adolescent rebellion and immaturity.

Schizophrenia is diagnosed by three criteria, after other disorders have been ruled out:

- At least two of the five major symptom classifications last for at least one month: delusions, hallucinations, disorganized speech, grossly disorganized behaviour, and negative symptoms.
- There is marked social or occupational dysfunction, affecting interpersonal relations, work or education, or self-care.
- The illness persists for at least six months.

Research has shown that each time a client recovers from psychosis, the psychological and functional outcome is worse than the time before. Consequently, there is a new emphasis on identifying the illness and initiating treatment early, if possible before psychosis sets in. As a result, some people avoid psychosis altogether and are treated exclusively in the community. Long-term social and occupational prospects for these people are much more promising.

Neuroimaging

CT, MRI, and PET scans may be used to narrow down the diagnosis.

Treatment

Antipsychotic Medications

Antipsychotics are also called neuroleptics and major tranquilizers. There are two groups: the older typical antipsychotics and the newer atypicals (also called novel antipsychotics).

Typical Antipsychotics

- Action – Blocks dopamine postsynaptic receptors in the hypothalamus, limbic system, brainstem, basal ganglia, and medulla
- Effect – They provide some relief, primarily for the positive symptoms of schizophrenia.
- Major side effects include neuromalignant syndrome and movement disorders (extrapyramidal symptoms [EPSs]).
- Examples include chlorpromazine (Thorazine), thioridazine (Mellaril), trifluoperazine (Stelazine), thiothixene (Navane), loxapine (Loxitane), molindone (Moban), mesoridazine (Serentil), perphenazine (Trilafon), fluphenazine (Prolixin), and haloperidol (Haldol).

Atypical Antipsychotics

- Action – Blocks dopamine, serotonin, and other neurotransmitter receptors
- Effect – Eases both the positive and negative symptoms, thus markedly enhancing quality of life for people with schizophrenia
- Examples are clozapine (Clozaril), olanzapine (Zyprexa or Zydis), quetiapine (Seroquel), and risperidone (Risperdal). At the time of writing, only these four are available in Canada; however, drug trials are in progress, and future Health Canada approval is anticipated for others.

Other Medical Treatments

- Additional drugs for symptoms of schizophrenia include antidepressants, antimania agents, and benzodiazepines.
- ECT is used for psychotic depression and for people who do not respond to antipsychotics.

Nursing Considerations

Nursing Assessment

Nursing assessment for psychosis is complex, but before focusing on the symptoms, try to rule out whether a medical condition or substance use is implicated and think "safety first."

Hallucinations: Assess especially if the person is hearing voices that order self-harm or harming others. If so, are the voices accepted as real, and is there intent to follow the commands?

Delusions: Are there firm beliefs that are not reality based? Again, determine whether these could result in self-harm or harm to others and institute precautions if necessary.

Co-Occuring Mental Disorders: These might include depression, suicidal thoughts, anxiety, substance abuse, or violent acts in the past.

Medications: Has the individual been on any medications? If so, are they still being taken?

Family: Is the family involved? In what way? Are they caring? Overprotective? Hostile? Suspicious? Does the family understand psychosis, the need for medication, and about support or respite services?

Global Assessment Scale (GAF): Has global functioning been assessed (Varcarolis, 2002d, p. 536)?

The Nurse–Client Relationship

Particular challenges in caring for someone who is psychotic involve communicating when a person is out of touch with reality. Mastering the following suggested communication skills will help the nurse establish a relationship of trust with these clients (Varcarolis, 2002d, p. 541).

Communicating With a Client Experiencing Delusions or Hallucinations

- To overcome suspicion and gain trust, be present, straightforward, honest, and reliable.
- Ask directly about delusions and hallucinations, for example, "Who is trying to hurt you?" "Are you hearing voices?" "What do they say?"
- Observe for cues, such as the client's eyes searching around or staring at a particular empty space, and for events that appear to generate the delusions. Try to discuss these observations with the client.
- Do not argue with the voices and beliefs or react as though they are real. Instead, provide your own observations and encourage the client to talk about feelings. For example, "I can't see what you do, but it seems to be upsetting you," or "It must be frightening to think that people are against you."
- Divert attention back to reality: "Try not to listen to the voices so that we can talk now."
- If some aspect of the delusion or hallucination is real, validate that part, such as, "Yes, I heard Mr. Green talking on the phone, but he was discussing a movie

he had seen. He didn't refer to you" (Varcarolis, 2002d, p. 541).

Nursing Goals

Interventions for schizophrenia vary depending on the stage of the client's illness. The focus for treatment and professional collaboration during each phase of schizophrenia is described in Table 11.5.

Pharmacotherapy

Serious and sometimes permanent side effects occur with antipsychotic medications. In Table 11.6, the nursing implications for antipsychotic drug effects are described.

Drug Interactions

Be aware of potential interactions with other medications. Note the following examples:

- Cimetidine (Tagamet) – For acid indigestion. Promotes liver detoxification of antipsychotics, thus decreasing their effect.
- Other common antacids reduce absorption of oral antipsychotics. Take four hours before or after the antipsychotic.
- Anticonvulsants lower the blood levels of antipsychotics, interfering with their efficacy.
- Epinephrine can produce severe hypotension if given with chlorpromazine.
- Lithium occasionally can produce neurological impairment when combined with antipsychotics. Monitor clients closely for neurological signs and symptoms.
- Some cardiac drugs reduce the effectiveness of antipsychotics, increasing psychosis.

For more information on these drugs, see Chapter 7.

Engaging With Families

Having a family member with schizophrenia is emotionally painful, exhausting, and frightening. Relatives, often the main caregivers when the client is not in hospital, should be consulted in treatment planning and decision making. Family caregivers generally know the client best.

When a client is first diagnosed, however, education for relatives is essential. A family educational plan for understanding psychoses appears in Table 11.7.

Community Supports

Nurses should know what community resources and services are available and assist families to access these services. The following two major community agencies provide comprehensive programs.

Table 11.5 Treatment Focus at Different Phases of Schizophrenia

	PHASE 1		PHASE II	PHASE III
	Acute: Onset, Exacerbation, or Relapse	Subacute and Convalescent	Maintenance Adaptive Plateau	Stable Plateau
Clinical Focus	• Crisis intervention • Safety • Acute symptom stabilization	• Social supports • Stress and vulnerability assessment • Living arrangements • Daily activities • Economic resources	• Understanding and acceptance of illness	• Social, vocational, and self-care skills • Learning or relearning • Identification of realistic expectations • Adaptation to deficits

Intervention	• Acute psychopharmacological treatment
	• Limit setting
	• Supportive and directive
	• Psychiatric, medical, neurological evaluation
	• Meet with family
		• Psychosocial evaluation
		• Linkage with
		  • Social services
		  • Human service
		  • Community treatment agencies
		• Psychoeducational interventions with families
			• Support and teaching
			• Medication teaching and side effect management
			• Direct assistance with situational problems
			• Identification of prodromal and acute symptoms and signs of relapse
			• Continued psychoeducation work with families as needed
				• Attention to details of self-care, social, and work functioning
				• Direct intervention with family and employers
				• Cognitive and social skills enhancement
				• Medication maintenance
				• Continued psychoeducational intervention with families as needed

Professional Collaboration	• Inpatient treatment team • Residential alternative to hospitalization • Community crisis intervention • Internist • Neurologists	• Social work department • Health and human services • Day treatment or community support	• Community support staff • Family support groups • Group therapies and self-help groups • Behaviour therapies using educational models	• Group therapists • Social, vocational, and self-care providers • Family, employer, community support staff

Source: Adapted from Gabard, G. O. (2001). *Treatment of psychiatric disorders* (3rd ed.). Washington, DC: American Psychiatric Publishing, Inc.

The Schizophrenia Society of Canada

Provincial and local chapters are found across the country. Services and programs may include the following:

- Support groups and counselling services for family members; peer support for clients
- Monthly educational meetings and periodic conferences for family members
- Education programs for parents, siblings, and children of people with schizophrenia
- Public education programs for schools and other community agencies and service providers

The Canadian Mental Health Association

Services and programs may vary by location but may include the following:

- Educational programs for parents and families
- Community education programs
- Recreation and leisure opportunities for people with mental health challenges

- Peer options for connecting people with mental illnesses and reducing their isolation
- Supported housing
- Bereavement counselling

PERSONALITY DISORDERS

Personality is "a complex pattern of characteristics, largely outside of the person's awareness, that comprise the individual's distinctive pattern of perceiving, feeling, thinking, coping and behaving" (Limandri & Boyd, 2005, p. 421). Each person develops unique personality traits from his or her biological constitution, psychosocial experiences, and environment. Personality traits become deeply engrained and stable, exerting control over a person's attitudes and behaviour.

When a person's character and behaviour deviate markedly from social and cultural expectations, causing functional impairment and distress, the person may have a personality disorder (PD). PDs vary from mild to severe, and people can function quite well when symptoms are mild or intermittent. In fact, most people occasionally display maladaptive characteristics identified with a PD, and some people are clearly eccentric. Nurses should refrain from labelling people too quickly. To be pathological, inflexible and enduring views and behaviour patterns must impinge on a broad range of situations, causing problems for the person or others.

Canadian statistics on PDs are incomplete; however, American estimates show that 6–9% of the US population is affected. Most people can be treated in the

Table 11.6 Nursing Considerations for Antipsychotic Drug Effects

CNS SIDE EFFECTS	NURSING CARE AND TEACHING CONSIDERATIONS
Extrapyramidal Symptoms (EPSs)	General treatment principles: • Tolerance usually develops by the third month • Decrease dose of drug • Add a drug to treat EPSs, then taper after 3 months on the antipsychotic • Use a drug with a lower EPS profile • Give client education and support
Acute Dystonic Reactions: Oculogyric Crisis, Torticollis	Spasms of major muscle groups of neck, back, and eyes; occur suddenly; frightening; painful; parenteral medication works faster than PO; have respiratory support available; more common in children and young males and with high-potency drugs. Taper dose gradually when discontinuing antipsychotic drugs to avoid withdrawal dyskinesia.
Akathisia	Cannot remain still; pacing, inner restlessness, leg aches are relieved by movement; rule out anxiety or agitation; medicate
Parkinson's Syndrome: Akinesia, Cogwheel Rigidity, Fine Tremor	More common in males and older adults; tolerance may not develop; medicate with DA antagonist amantadine (must have good renal function)
Tardive Dyskinesia (TD)	Can occur after use (usually long term) of conventional antipsychotics; stereotyped involuntary movements (tongue protrusion, lip smacking, chewing, blinking, grimacing, choreiform movements of limbs and trunk, foot tapping); if using typical antipsychotics, use preventive measures and assess often; consider changing to an atypical antipsychotic drug; there is no treatment at present for TD
Neuroleptic Malignant Syndrome (NMS)*	*Potentially fatal: Fever, tachycardia, sweating, muscle rigidity, tremor, incontinence, stupor, leukocytosis, elevated creatine phosphokinase (CPK), renal failure; more common with high-potency drugs and in dehydrated clients; discontinue all drugs; supportive symptomatic care (hydration, renal dialysis, ventilation, and fever reduction as appropriate); can treat with dantroline or promocriptine; antipsychotic drugs can be cautiously reintroduced eventually
Seizures*	*Potentially life-threatening: Seizures occur in approximately 1% of people taking these drugs; clozapine has a 5% rate (in clients on 600 to 900 mg/day); may have to discontinue clozapine
Side Effects on Other Systems	
Agranulocytosis*	*This is an emergency: It develops abruptly with fever, malaise, ulcerative sore throat, and leukopenia. High incidence (1–2%) is associated with clozapine; must do weekly CBC and prescribe only one week of drug at a time; discontinue drug immediately; may need reverse isolation and antibiotics
Photosensitivity	Use sunscreen and sunglasses; cover body with clothing
Anticholinergic effects	Symptoms: constipation, dry mouth, blurred vision, orthostatic hypotension, tachycardia, urinary retention, nasal congestion; see Table 11.3 for nursing care
Weight gain	See Table 11.3 for nursing care

*Potentially life-threatening side effect
CBC, complete blood count; CNS, central nervous system; DA, dopamine; PO, oral tablet or capsule.
Source: Adapted from Stuart, G. W. (2009). *Principles and practice of psychiatric nursing* (9th ed., p. 528, Table 26-18). St. Louis: Mosby.

Table 11.7   Family Education Plan: Understanding Psychosis

Content	Instructional Activities	Evaluation
Describe psychosis	• Introduce participants and leaders • State purpose of group • Define terminology associated with psychosis	The participant will describe the characteristics of psychosis
Identify the causes of psychotic disorders	• Present theories of psychotic disorders • Use audiovisual aids to explain brain anatomy, brain biochemistry, and major neurotransmitters	The participant will discuss the relationship between brain anatomy, brain biochemistry, major neurotransmitters, and the development of psychosis
Define schizophrenia according to symptoms and diagnostic criteria	• Lead a discussion of the diagnostic criteria for schizophrenia • Show a film on schizophrenia	The participant will describe the symptoms and diagnostic criteria for schizophrenia
Describe the relationship between anxiety and psychotic disorders	• Present types and stages of anxiety • Discuss steps in reducing and resolving anxiety	The participant will identify and describe the stages of anxiety and ways to reduce or resolve it
Analyze the impact of living with hallucinations	• Describe the characteristics of hallucinations • Demonstrate ways to communicate with someone who is hallucinating	The participant will demonstrate effective ways to communicate with a person who has hallucinations
Analyze the impact of living with delusions	• Describe types of delusions • Demonstrate ways to communicate with someone who has delusions • Discuss interventions for delusions	The participant will demonstrate effective ways to communicate with a person who has delusions
Discuss the use of psychotropic medications	• Provide and explain handouts describing the characteristics of psychotropic medications that are prescribed for schizophrenia	The participant will identify and describe the characteristics of medications prescribed for self or family member
Describe the characteristics of relapse and the role of compliance with the therapeutic regimen	• Help the participants describe their own experiences with relapse • Discuss symptom management techniques and the importance of complying with the therapeutic regimen	The participant will describe behaviours that indicate an impending relapse and discuss the importance of symptom management and compliance with the therapeutic regimen
Analyze behaviours that promote wellness	• Discuss the components of wellness • Relate wellness to the elements of symptom management	The participant will analyze the effect of maintaining wellness on the occurrence of symptoms
Discuss ways to cope adaptively with psychosis	• Lead a group discussion focused on coping behaviours and the daily problems in living with psychosis • Propose ways to create a low-stress environment	The participant will describe ways to modify his or her lifestyle to create a low-stress environment

Source: Stuart, G. W. (2009). *Principles and practice of psychiatric nursing* (9th ed., p. 361, Table 20-9). St. Louis: Mosby.

community. Those who enter hospital are between ages 15 and 45 and stay for an average of nine and a half days (CIHI, 2002).

PATHOPHYSIOLOGY

Some evidence exists for neurobiological abnormalities, but as for most psychiatric disorders, no clear-cut cause for personality disorders has been identified. A complex interaction of genetics, brain functioning, and psychosocial, and environmental factors correlate with PD.

• Genetics – Some evidence exists for a genetic link for antisocial and criminal personality traits, as well as for schizotypal and paranoid PD.
• EEG evidence – Research evidence is mixed. Some studies show a relationship between PD and abnormal

temporal and frontal lobe waves, but others do not.
- Neurotransmitters – Low dopamine and serotonin levels are found in aggressive and impulsive behaviours, as well as in suicidality.
- Autonomic nervous system (ANS) – Dominance of parasympathetic over sympathetic impulses may amplify or jumble neural impulses, resulting in cognitive or affective problems.
- Limbic system – Because of controlling emotions, the limbic system (amygdala, hippocampus) and its connections to the thalamus and hypothalamus are also implicated in PD.

CLINICAL MANIFESTATIONS

PDs usually arise in adolescence and early adulthood. Thus, if there is a biological predisposition, the social and developmental challenges of this life stage, related to gaining independence and separation from family, may trigger a PD. Strong attachments to supportive family, peer, and community networks may protect people from PD by enhancing coping skills and personal growth. Conversely, a history of abuse or neglect in childhood puts people at risk.

PDs share features of other mental illnesses, but no single illness completely explains the long-standing maladaptive thinking and behaviour patterns of PD, some of which are as follows:

- Inappropriate emotions, with poor impulse and emotional control
- Disturbed self-concept and inappropriate perceptions of others and the environment
- Unhealthy or very limited personal relationships
- School or employment difficulties
- Often an associated depression or substance abuse, or both

PDs are classified into three groups or clusters. Two additional, but not yet categorized, diagnoses are depressive and passive–aggressive PDs.

Cluster A: Odd and Eccentric

Odd and eccentric behaviour patterns are characteristic of three personality disorders, in which people tend toward social and emotional withdrawal. Descriptions of these three disorders and their symptoms follow.

Paranoid Personality Disorder

- Suspicious and distrustful, misinterpreting others' motives as threatening, exploitive, or deceiving. These people often bear grudges.
- Detached and socially isolated
- Overreacts to threats – even with no actual evidence of malice. Hostile outbursts are common.
- Fears becoming close to others or confiding in anyone
- Hypervigilant and hyperactive—unable to relax
- Hypersensitive, irritable, often angry and jealous

Schizoid Personality Disorder

- A loner, detached from social and family relationships
- Emotionally detached; prefers solitary activities, although the person may be lonely
- Avoids intimacy; indifferent to the feelings or reactions of others
- Flattened affect

Schizotypal Personality Disorder

- Acutely uncomfortable in social relationships
- Eccentric and odd behaviour and appearance
- Strange beliefs or magical thinking (superstitions, clairvoyance, telepathy, distorted cognition, fantasies, and preoccupations) that is outside cultural norms
- Unusual patterns of speech (metaphorical, vague, very elaborate and flowery)
- Sometimes paranoid and may progress to schizophrenia

Cluster B: Dramatic and Emotional

These four PDs are distinguished by behaviour that is overly emotional, dramatic, and erratic.

Borderline Personality Disorder

- Instability of mood, interpersonal relationships, and self-image
- Impulsive, reckless behaviour that is often self-damaging, such as substance abuse, spending binges, heightened sexuality, or binge eating
- Uncontrolled, inappropriate, or frequent anger episodes
- Fear of rejection and being alone; feels empty; frantically tries to avoid being abandoned
- Behaviour undermines goal achievement, leading to job loss, chaotic relationships, and quitting education programs
- Self-injury and suicide threats are common

Narcissistic Personality Disorder

- Feelings of superiority; rude and arrogant
- Attention-seeking; requires constant admiration and special treatment
- Envies those with high status and pursues friendships with them
- Lacks empathy for others – It's all about me!
- Manipulative; driven to succeed; takes advantage of others to achieve personal goals

Histrionic Personality Disorder

- Wants to be the centre of attention; craves excitement and instant gratification
- Vain and arrogant; preoccupied with appearance, fearful of aging
- Impulsive and self-indulgent; lacks empathy for others

- Overly sensitive to criticism; reacts with anger
- Provocative and sexually inappropriate behaviour

Antisocial Personality Disorder

- Persistent disregard for the rights of others; contempt for other's feelings and rights
- Disregard for the law; frequent arrests. About 50% of prisoners have antisocial personalities.
- Lack of remorse
- Impulsive and irresponsible
- Deceitful; chronic lying and misrepresentation of self but can appear very charming
- Older diagnostic terms are psychopath and sociopath, referring to a lack of social conscience

Cluster C: Anxiety and Fear

The defining features of Cluster C are anxious and fearful behaviour.

Obsessive–Compulsive Personality Disorder

Avoid confusing obsessive–compulsive PD with obsessive–compulsive disorder, an anxiety disorder. The person with the PD desires perfection and order. In contrast, the true obsessions and compulsions of the anxiety disorder are more intense and compelling. Symptoms of obsessive–compulsive PD include the following:

- Rigid desire for perfection and control, coupled with ruthless self-criticism
- Overly attentive to rules and regulations, schedules, and discipline
- Indecisive and unable to complete tasks; afraid of making a mistake
- Inflexible with ethics, thriftiness, and moral values, but not necessarily religious
- Diligent work habits and difficulty delegating work; a "workaholic"

Avoidant Personality Disorder

- Low self-esteem; feelings of inadequacy and of being a failure
- Socially withdrawn; intensely shy and lonely
- Sensitive to criticism and rejection
- Avoidance of personal risks, new activities, or relationships

Dependent Personality Disorder

- Clinging behaviour; pervasive need to be taken care of; fears separation
- Indecision; requires excessive advice and reassurance; defers major responsibilities to others
- Craves approval and support; therefore unable to disagree with others
- Low self-confidence; unable to initiate activities
- Craves relationships; desperately seeks a new relationship when one has ended

Related Diagnoses

Depressive

This persistent pattern of sad, gloomy, and pessimistic cognitions and behaviour, like major depression but less severe, is often identified in relatives of people with major depression.

Passive–Aggressive

Sometime called negativistic PD, this disorder is defined by a negative attitude and passive resistance to social and occupational expectations. Passive–aggressive behaviours include procrastination, stubbornness, resentment of others, and efforts to undermine those in authority.

DIAGNOSTICS AND THERAPEUTICS

Diagnosis

Enduring but distressing behaviour patterns that deviate from cultural norms and that affect social and occupational functioning in a broad range of activities and social situations are identified. Diagnosis is challenging because of overlapping symptoms and the tendency for some people to have more than one PD. Initially, one must rule out other mental or medical disorders and treatment or medication side effects. PDs affect at least two of the following:

- Faulty cognitive schema – Misperceptions and interpretations of self, others, and social situations lead to dysfunctional responses
- Inappropriate emotions – Abnormal range, intensity, and emotionally labile responses
- Poor interpersonal functioning – Maladaptive behaviours, hard to get along with
- Poor impulse control

Treatment

Many PDs are difficult to treat because of the client's self-denial. Common treatments include intensive psychotherapy or group psychotherapy, along with psychopharmacology:

- Antipsychotics – For severe agitation or delusional thinking in paranoid, schizotypal, and borderline PD
- SSRIs, other antidepressants – For obsessive thoughts, anger, irritability, and unstable mood
- Anxiolytics – For Cluster C disorders
- MAOIs – To decrease self-harm and impulsive acts
- Lithium carbonate, propranolol – For antisocial PD with violent episodes

Nursing Considerations

Nursing Assessment

Some questions to ask when assessing for PDs are (Varcarolis, 2002c, p. 380):

- Could the PD symptoms arise from some other psychiatric or medical disorder?
- Are there suicidal or homicidal thoughts? If so, address this issue first.
- Would this behaviour be acceptable in this client's cultural, ethnic, or social milieu?
- Is there a recent bereavement or traumatic social event that could intensify symptoms?
- Is there a substance abuse problem?
- What is the client's view of the problem? Are others in agreement—family, police, and employer?
- How would the client like the problem resolved?
- How would you describe the client's emotional state and physical condition?
- What behaviours and defence mechanisms are displayed by the client (see below)?

The Nurse–Client Relationship

Nurses encounter PDs wherever they work, and establishing a therapeutic alliance challenges even very experienced nurses. These clients know just which "buttons to push." Pay special attention to professional boundaries and set realistic limits on the client's behaviour and your availability. Keep your communication clear and unambiguous, giving simple directions. Avoid power struggles or arguments, showing confidence in your abilities and decisions. Remember that for such enduring patterns of behaviour, improvement takes time.

Splitting behaviour, that is, setting staff members against one another, is common. Thus, professional teamwork is vital. Staff must support each other and be consistent with the client.

Nursing Goals

Nursing care of people with PD involves providing them with structure and clear expectations for their behaviour. A contract may be helpful for encouraging specific behaviours. Communicate respect for the person. The behaviour is the problem, not the client. Set mutually agreed-upon goals and stick to them. Help clients identify and voice their emotions. Some specific considerations for specific PDs follow.

Paranoid Personality Disorder

- Involve the client in planning care, thus helping the person feel in control.
- Teach clients to delay responding to others until they have validated their perceptions and assumptions. This helps them avoid acting on paranoid ideas.

Schizoid Personality Disorder

- Support the client's ability to function in the community (for example, provide a referral to social services to arrange supportive housing).
- These clients are likely to require case management, either a professional case manager or at least a family member who can arrange for services and assistance.

Schizotypal Personality Disorder

Assist with development of self-care and social skills.

Borderline Personality Disorder

- Ensure safety; negotiate a no self-harm contract with the client. The client agrees not to engage in injurious actions and to inform a nurse if he or she is losing control.
- Help the client identify moods, emotions, and situations that trigger self-harm activities and explore more effective coping strategies for those triggers.
- Provide structured daily activities that include health-promoting activities.

Narcissistic Personality Disorder

- Use a matter-of-fact approach as you try to gain the person's cooperation with treatment.
- Milieu therapy – Engage the individual in community activities (either the therapeutic community in the hospital or the larger community outside). Reinforce appropriate behaviour.

Histrionic Personality Disorder

Provide social skills training, with factual feedback about his or her behaviour.

Antisocial Personality Disorder

- Teach effective problem-solving and anger-management techniques.
- Confront the client when he or she oversteps acceptable limits on behaviour.

Obsessive–Compulsive Personality Disorder

- Cognitive restructuring – Explore and encourage the client to accept outcomes that are "good enough" or "satisfactory."
- Assist the client with decision making and completing tasks.

Avoidant Personality Disorder

- Promote self-esteem by providing support and reassurance.
- Cognitive restructuring – Try positive self-talk, reframing situations, and decatastrophizing (for example, ask, "What is the worst thing that could happen?" "How likely is that?").

Dependent Personality Disorder

- Encourage autonomy and self-reliance.
- Teach problem-solving and decision-making skills.

Depressive

- Protect from self-harm (see above under "Borderline Personality Disorder").
- Encourage involvement in activities.

Passive–Aggressive

Assist the client to identify feelings and express them directly.

SUBSTANCE ABUSE

Substance use and substance abuse refer to the consumption and excess consumption (by any route) of drugs and alcohol. Nurses often forget that the overuse of legally approved medications, both over-the-counter and prescription, also constitutes substance abuse.

Most Canadians use alcohol, some use illicit drugs, some use both, and many abuse these substances. Three-quarters of Canadians over 14 years consume alcohol. About one-third admit to heavy drinking (five or more drinks on one occasion) at least once a year; half of those do so at least monthly. Almost 13% use illegal drugs, although 10% only use cannabis (marijuana). Risk factors for dependence on drugs, alcohol, or both include youth, low income, less education, and being male (Tjepkema, 2004).

The comorbidity of mental illness and substance abuse (also called dual diagnosis) is common. Some people use substances to ease their psychiatric symptoms; for others, substance use and abuse may promote the development or severity of a mental illness. For this reason, many health authorities combine mental health and addiction services into one department.

PATHOPHYSIOLOGY AND CLINICAL MANIFESTATIONS

Addictive substances either depress or stimulate the CNS. Marijuana seems to do both. All interfere with neurotransmission and the limbic system, altering emotions and the brain's reward system.

Central Nervous System (CNS) Depressants

Drugs that depress the CNS produce drowsiness and sedation. They include alcohol, opioids, sedatives, anxiolytics, and probably inhalants. Alcohol, accepted in many cultures, is also the most commonly abused drug. People overuse these drugs because of the pleasant sensations of relaxation, euphoria, and reduced inhibition, commonly called being "high." Tolerance develops, such that higher and higher doses are required to produce the same effects, and eventually the person cannot function without the drug, experiencing cravings and physical dependence or addiction. Overdose can lead to respiratory or cardiovascular depression, coma, convulsions, and death.

Alcohol

- Alcohol, soluble in fat and water, is absorbed from the stomach and small intestine. It is quickly disbursed throughout the body and metabolized by the liver at the rate of one drink (one beer, five ounces of wine, or one ounce of hard liquor) per hour.
- Alcohol initially stimulates the release of naturally produced opioids (endorphins and enkephalins) and dopamine (the reward centres of the limbic system), producing feelings of pleasure. In higher concentrations, it is toxic to nerve cells, producing poor emotional control, reduced muscle coordination, and then mental confusion and loss of consciousness. At very high concentrations, it produces coma, respiratory depression, and eventual death.
- Chronic alcoholism produces general body damage. Complications are dementia, hepatitis and cirrhosis, cardiomyopathy, gastritis, peptic ulcers, pancreatitis, and peripheral neuropathy.
- Withdrawal produces neural excitation, with tremors, agitation and anxiety, irritability, insomnia, and sometimes delirium tremens (DTs) with hallucinations, seizures, and delirium. This is a medical emergency and, without treatment, can cause death. Symptoms include high fever, hypertension, tachycardia, and seizures.

Opioids

- Opium derivatives are narcotics. Many are legally controlled, but heroin is illegal.
- Taken intravenously (IV) or nasally (snorting), they act on the reward centres of the brain, reducing neuron excitability, especially of the pain neurotransmitters, and producing analgesia and euphoria (a "rush"). Other effects include respiratory depression, constricted pupils, and constipation.

Sedative–Hypnotics and Anxiolytics

- These include the benzodiazepines and barbiturates, taken orally or intravenously.
- Tolerance, dependence, and withdrawal usually do not develop if taken for under a month.
- Withdrawal symptoms can be avoided by gradually tapering the dosage under medical supervision.

Inhalants

- These volatile substances are inhaled and include fuels, solvents, thinners, propellants, and nitrates.

- Inhalants produce a cheap "high" and are mostly used by youth. However, side effects from high doses or prolonged use are serious, damaging the brain, liver, kidneys, heart, and lungs.

Date Rape Drugs

- These are given to unsuspecting victims prior to rape.
- They include rohypnon (roofies), GHB (gamma-hydroxybutyrate), and ketamine (vitamin K).
- Effects are reduced inhibition and sedation, often enhanced by mixing with alcohol. Overdose depresses respirations or causes seizures, coma, and death.
- Rohypnon also produces amnesia.

Central Nervous System (CNS) Stimulants

Stimulants produce alertness, excitation, and aggressiveness and reduce fatigue. Metabolism is increased, and appetite is suppressed. They include caffeine, nicotine, amphetamines, cocaine, and hallucinogens. The stronger drugs produce restlessness, overtalkativeness, anxiety, irritability, suspicion, paranoia, and hallucinations. Tolerance and dependence occur. Withdrawal symptoms, however, are less physiologically dangerous than those of alcohol or opiates. Withdrawal brings depressed mood, sleep disturbance, fatigue, and anhedonia (inability to experience pleasure).

Caffeine and Nicotine

- Caffeine (coffee, cola soft drinks) can cause nervousness, anxiety, and difficulty sleeping.
- Nicotine (tobacco) is highly addictive. It became less socially acceptable with the recognition of the negative health effects, particularly for bystanders exposed to second-hand smoke. Effects include relaxation, excitement, and decreased appetite. Quitting smoking is very difficult, producing withdrawal (mood changes, anxiety, irritability, restlessness, and hunger).

Amphetamines and Cocaine

- The initial effect is stimulation, but CNS depression follows. Both drugs produce marked euphoria, but dangerous cardiovascular effects (tachycardia, arrhythmias, hypertension, vasoconstriction) that can cause heart failure, myocardial infarction, strokes, and renal complications can occur. First-time cocaine users have died. Continued use leads, however, to tolerance and some decrease in cardiovascular side effects.
- These drugs are absorbed intravenously through mucous membranes (oral, nasal [snorted or smoked], or buccal membranes). Cocaine is the most addictive of all abused substances.
- Long-term sniffing causes ulcers in the nose and perforations of the septum; long-term smoking damages the throat, upper GI tract, and lungs.
- Crack cocaine is a purified, crystallized form. It is easily available and inexpensive, with an immediate but very short effect (5–7 minutes) followed by profound depression, and there is a strong drive to relieve the depression with another "hit." The result is that crack is extremely addictive.

Hallucinogens

- These include LSD (acid), MDMA (ecstasy), and mescaline.
- Effects are alterations in perception, including hallucinations with euphoria (a "trip") or frightening and depressing perceptions (a "bad trip"). People report awareness of themselves and surroundings but altered sensory perceptions of colours, time, arousal, body image, hearing, and so on.
- Sympathetic nervous system stimulation causes palpitations, increased blood pressure, blurred vision, dilated pupils, and sweating. A bad trip may induce dizziness, anxiety, and panic.
- Flashbacks occur, perhaps more often if hallucinogens are combined with other substances.

PCP (Angel Dust)

Effects include hyperactivity, aggressiveness, impulsivity, unpredictable behaviour, feeling superhuman, and sometimes psychosis. Dangerous respiratory and cardiovascular side effects can lead to seizures, coma, and death.

Marijuana

- Also called cannabis, hashish, THC (tetrahydro-cannabinol), pot, weed, grass, or Mary Jane.
- Marijuana has both CNS stimulant and CNS depressant effects, through its influence on a variety of neurotransmitters and neurochemicals.
- Common effects are euphoria, relaxation, drowsiness, heightened or altered sensory perceptions, reduced coordination, dry mouth, tachycardia, red eyes, disorientation, and appetite stimulation.

DIAGNOSTICS AND THERAPEUTICS

Diagnosis

During a complete history and physical examination, special attention is paid to the manifestations noted above. The clinician may note needle tracks and bruising along arm and leg veins, signs of malnourishment, teary and reddened eyes, a runny nose, or frequent swallowing, indicating a postnasal drip. Laboratory tests may include toxicology urine screening, blood alcohol levels, or both, in addition to a full workup for suspected complications. Denial is common with substance abusers, making history-taking challenging.

Substance abuse is recurrent substance use, leading to the following:

- Unsatisfactory performance at home, work, or school
- Impairment in hazardous situations (such as driving)

- Frequent legal issues or being arrested
- Ongoing social and interpersonal problems

Physical dependence on substances is diagnosed with evidence of the following:

- Tolerance – Needing increased amounts to achieve intoxication
- Withdrawal symptoms when the substance is stopped or unavailable
- Failing attempts to quit or cut down substance use. People often continue to use, while at the same time recognizing the problems being created.
- Avoiding social, occupational, or recreational activities in favour of substance use
- Increased time, effort, and money spent on substances or on recovering from intoxication

Treatment

Treatment depends on the severity of the client's condition. First, treat an overdose and then address withdrawal symptoms. Only after stabilization can one begin to address addiction. Pharmacotherapy for treating chemical dependency varies according to the particular substance being abused. Some of the major pharmacological treatments follow.

Alcohol

- Benzodiazepines for alcohol withdrawal
- Naltrexone and Antabuse (disulfiram) to help maintain abstinence
- Thiamine to help prevent major brain damage complications (Wernicke-Korsakoff syndrome) for long-term alcoholics

Other CNS Depressants

- Phenobarbital is given for withdrawal from sedative–hypnotics, benzodiazepines, and barbiturates.
- Methadone and clonidine are used to manage withdrawal from opiates. They reduce the severity of withdrawal symptoms by binding with opioid receptors.

CNS Stimulants

- Nicotine gum and nicotine patches replace smoking, with gradual tapering over time.
- Buproprion (Zyban, Wellbutrin) aids withdrawal from smoking by reducing cravings.
- Benzodiazepines and antipsychotics lessen psychotic reactions from hallucinogens and PCP.
- Naloxone (Narcan), an opioid antagonist, is used for narcotic overdose.
- Buprenorphine (Buprenex), an opioid analgesic, is used for withdrawal from narcotics. It is less addicting than other narcotics.
- Currently, no specific medications are available for cocaine withdrawal or addiction, although antidepressants may ease mood changes due to

abstinence; sedatives help with insomnia; and anxiolytics reduce symptoms of anxiety.

Treatment for chemical addiction is multifaceted and may include the following:

- Psychotherapy and counselling
- Education
- Cognitive–behavioural therapy
- Behaviour modification
- Motivational therapy
- Group therapy
- Peer support groups in the community, for example, Alcoholics Anonymous (AA). Newer programs, often modelled on the AA 12-step program, have been developed for other addictions and may be accessed, depending on community availability.
- For dual diagnosis, successful treatment of the co-morbid psychiatric diagnosis often reduces the individual's addictive behaviour.

Harm Reduction

Harm reduction is a relatively new and increasingly common approach to drug addiction, although it is not without political controversy. The first harm reduction programs were methadone maintenance programs in the 1960s and 1970s. Recognizing the compulsion underlying dependence and that abstinence is difficult to achieve, the goal of these programs is to minimize the damage of addiction to the individual and to society (Pauly, Goldstone, McCall, & Payne, 2007). By providing such things as clean equipment and education about safe practices, they aim to

- Decrease overdoses, infections, hepatitis B and C, tuberculosis, other diseases, such as HIV/AIDS, and deaths for injection drug users
- Reduce the violence and crime associated with the drug culture
- Reduce the use of impure street drugs that lack any quality control
- Provide access to community outreach, public health programs, education, detoxification programs, and other treatment
- Promote trust among drug users, their families, and health providers

Some examples include needle-exchange programs, methadone replacement, safe injection sites, and equipping automobiles with breathalyzer equipment that prevents ignition unless the driver "blows" below a specified alcohol level.

NURSING CONSIDERATIONS

Nursing Assessment

Nurses should supplement their assessment of a client's physical and mental health with screening for substance use, dependence, and abuse. Ask clients about their pattern of substance abuse and experiences of withdrawal. At the very least, determine the amount and frequency of alcohol or drugs used by clients. Some suggested questions include the following:

- Is the client interested in stopping the use of a substance?
- Are there any physical complications from addiction (AIDS, hepatitis, abscesses, tachycardia)?
- What community resources are available for safe detoxification, treatment, and client and family support? Are the client and family aware of how to access them?
- A common, easily remembered assessment tool for alcoholism that all nurses should know and use is the CAGE Questionnaire. If a client answers "yes" to two of the four questions, it is an indication for further assessment of probable alcoholism.

  - Cut down: Have you ever been told you should cut down on your drinking?
  - Annoyed: Has anyone annoyed you by criticizing your drinking?
  - Guilt: Have you ever felt guilty or bad about your drinking?
  - Eye-opener: Have you ever had a drink first thing in the morning to get over a hangover?

The Nurse–Client Relationship

In order to develop an effective therapeutic relationship with clients who are substance users, the nurse must examine his or her personal beliefs and overcome any prejudice toward them. Otherwise, the nurse should refer the client to another staff member who can accept the client more openly and with whom the client will feel safe to communicate openly and honestly. Interacting with substance users requires patience, honesty, persistence, and acceptance of the potential for relapses. Principles underlying interacting with substance users include the following:

- Abstinence – Negotiate a contract with the client to abstain from substance use.
- Individualized treatment and goals – Negotiate a plan addressing the client's personal issues.
- Set appropriate limits – Include in your contract the conditions under which you will work together. Outline behaviour that is acceptable and unacceptable.
- Anticipate defensive reactions – Address them by identifying or redirecting the behaviour and supporting appropriate responses.
- Patience – Acknowledge that recovery occurs in stages and that each stage takes time.
- Focus on the benefits of giving up substance use that make abstinence worthwhile.

Nursing Goals

When clients are ready for psychosocial interventions, that is, at the point at which overdose or withdrawal symptoms are stabilized, attention turns to overcoming addiction and maintaining abstinence.

Individual Interventions

Use all opportunities with the client to engage in brief interventions, aimed at motivating change and supporting healthy behaviours. A helpful acronym for recalling the elements of these encounters is FRAMES (Dyehouse & Sommers, 1998; Smith-DiJulio, 2002a):

- Feedback: Give personal feedback about client progress, including liver enzyme values.
- Responsibility: Emphasize that change is the client's responsibility, no one else's.
- Advice: Clearly provide supportive advice on the need to change. Avoid being judgemental.
- Menu: Allow clients to choose from a menu of addiction treatment options and programs.
- Empathy: Communicate warmth, respect, understanding, and support.
- Self-efficacy: Reinforce with the client that he or she has the ability to be successful.

Group Therapy

Encourage your client to attend group therapy, where available, but afterward be available to discuss and reinforce what clients learn about their addiction and themselves. Advantages of group therapy include mutual support and sharing of strategies for success. Interacting with other addicts who have maintained sobriety reduces isolation and encourages learning new social skills. Groups also offer opportunities for socializing that are not dependent on substance use.

Self-Help Groups

AA is the model for many other self-help groups that use the 12-step approach, for example, Narcotics Anonymous, Al-Anon for adult family members or friends of an alcoholic or chemically dependent person, and Alateen for teenage family members. (Some large urban centres also have Narc-Anon, specifically for families of those addicted to chemical substances.) Twelve-step programs require that members

- Admit to their powerlessness over the addictive substance and that they are unable to quit on their own, but require help from a power greater than themselves
- Accept responsibility for their own recovery
- Admit that no one and nothing else can be blamed for their addiction

In response to objections to the semi-religious nature of AA, the organization has altered references to God to either "a power greater than ourselves" or "God, as we understand Him."

Teaching and Learning

In addition to information about the types of substances abused, education for families and clients may include concepts such as tolerance, dependence, intoxication, withdrawal, flashbacks, dual diagnosis, co-dependency, and the social and physical complications of substance abuse. Even more important may be education on managing recovery. Some examples for topics are healthy nutrition, techniques for relaxation, stress relief, and problem solving, as well as the availability of community supports, including financial and legal assistance.

Relapse Prevention

Avoid becoming discouraged when a client succumbs to temptation and relapses. Most clients will relapse, even when they are determined to succeed with abstinence. You can help clients prevent relapses using the following strategies (Smith-DiJulio, 2002a, p. 771):

- Discuss difficult situations that the client has been able to handle relatively successfully.
- Discuss situations that he or she has had little success in handling and rehearse some possible management strategies.
- Help the individual recognize role models among his or her acquaintances.
- Group activities could include role-playing stressful situations to try out various solutions.

Engaging With Families

Substance abuse damages family relationships, and many family members experience "guilt, shame, resentment, insecurity, delinquency, financial troubles, isolation, fear, and violence" (Laraia & Jefferson, 2005, p. 505). Substance abuse can cause family break-up or become a self-sustaining pattern. Spouses and partners, if not already substance users, may become so, and many children learn patterns of addiction early. Many families, however, recognize the problems caused by substance abuse and seek education and help, whether or not the substance abuser wants to overcome the addiction.

Co-Dependency

Sometimes family dynamics evolve to enable the alcoholic or drug abuser to continue using. Family members try to preserve the peace, hoping that unconditional support will help the substance user become strong enough to quit. They may cover up dysfunctions to preserve the individual's or family's reputation and financial integrity. Two unintended consequences are as follows:

- Co-dependence – The family member's own needs for self-actualization and fulfillment are blocked in favour of catering to the needs and desires of the substance user.

- Enabling – Inadvertently, co-dependency reinforces substance abuse by protecting the addicted person from the consequences of his or her behaviour. Family members who assist a loved one to maintain an addiction need help to understand their own enabling behaviour patterns and to face the reality that the addict, alone, must assume responsibility for quitting.

Self-Help Groups for Partners and Families

Nurses must be aware of self-help organizations so they can refer family members. Most communities have local chapters of Al-Anon and Alateen for families of alcoholics. Where self-help groups for drug addiction are located, such as Narcotics Anonymous and Cocaine Anonymous, associated programs for family members are also usually available.

SOMATOFORM DISORDERS: CONVERSION, BODY DYSMORPHIC DISORDER, AND HYPOCHONDRIASIS

No nurse would argue that the mind and body are not connected. Emotional stress often results in psychosomatic symptoms, producing or intensifying a physical illness. Conversely, having a disease increases stress. The expected conversion of mental states and experiences into physical symptoms is called somatization. People have a somatoform disorder if

- Physical symptoms cannot be confirmed by laboratory tests or other medical evidence.
- They have significant psychological issues or conflicts.
- They are consciously unable to control the illness symptoms.

PATHOPHYSIOLOGY

Stressful psychophysiological responses were identified by Hans Selye as the general adaptation syndrome (GAS), or stress response (see the section on anxiety disorders). The physiological results of stress can be confirmed by pathological changes; for example, chronic stress is implicated in heart disease. Without confirming pathology, however, the symptoms are presumed to be due to a mental disorder. Nevertheless, health care professionals must guard against this assumption until after a completed physical workup as true somatoform disorders are relatively rare.

CLINICAL MANIFESTATIONS

Somatoform disorders include the following:

Somatization Disorder: Multiple symptoms are experienced. The illness may be acute, but it is more likely to be chronic, beginning around 30 years of age. Symptoms may be a combination of pain and neurological, gastrointestinal, and sexual complaints.

Conversion Disorder: The person suddenly loses sensory or motor functions, resulting in paralysis or blindness. Often the client seems less concerned than one would expect (termed la belle indifférence). In such cases, the deficit actually brings relief by preventing the client from participating in an anxiety-provoking activity. Neurological testing is negative.

Hypochondriasis: Clients become obsessed with the fear that they have a serious disease, often when they have misinterpreted minor symptoms.

Body Dysmorphic Disorder: These people are overly concerned about defects in their appearance. The imperfection may be either completely imagined or greatly exaggerated.

Pain Disorder: These clients suffer from pain that seems to be related to their psychological state and that cannot be relieved by analgesics.

Somatoform disorders do *not* include the following psychiatric disorders:

Malingering: Occurs when people fabricate physical symptoms for secondary gain. Either they want something (drugs, insurance payments), or they want to avoid something, such as going to work. The symptoms tend to dissipate after those hopes have been satisfied. This process of getting what they want is called receiving a secondary gain.

Munchausen's Syndrome: Also called factitious disorder. People with this syndrome intentionally create symptoms in order to gain attention. They may even inflict a self-injury. When a person harms someone else or causes another person to be sick (so that he or she can be rewarded for caring for or saving the other person), the disorder is called Munchausen's by proxy.

DIAGNOSTICS AND THERAPEUTICS

Diagnosis

Initially, a complete diagnostic workup is done to rule out medical conditions, reactions to substances, or other mental disorders (such as an anxiety disorder) that may be suspected from the client's symptoms. An in-depth medical and social history may help rule out malingering. After a somatoform disorder has been diagnosed, health care professionals must continue to observe for ongoing and new symptoms. There is a real danger of discounting legitimate medical conditions that the person may later develop and that require treatment.

Treatment

- Individual psychotherapy is aimed at helping clients gain insight into their stress and learn more adaptive coping strategies. Clients can be encouraged to discuss their feelings and conflicts rather than repress them.
- Periodic physical examination – When assessing the client, provide verbal reassurance of her or his positive

state of health.
- Cognitive therapy – Help clients appraise stressful situations realistically and reduce their attention on distorted body sensations and perceptions.

NURSING CONSIDERATIONS

Nursing Assessment

A thorough physical and psychological assessment is required. Because the client perceives the symptoms as real, carefully evaluate his or her daily living patterns. Some fabricated symptoms will interfere with basic needs, for example, nutrition, exercise, hygiene, rest, and so on. Evaluate how well clients are able to express their feelings. Estimate their level of stress and any opportunities for secondary gain through a full psychosocial assessment, including the following:

- Income
- Work
- Other daily activities
- Living arrangements
- Social support
- Self-care
- Stressful events
- History of physical and mental health symptoms, including prior treatment, outpatient treatment, and any significant symptoms that have not been treated (Varcarolis, 2002, p. 353)

The Nurse–Client Relationship

Caring for clients with somatoform ailments requires patience and understanding, to allow a trusting relationship to develop in which a client will be able to discuss his or her feelings and fears. Provide positive feedback when clients are able to express their feelings to others. Emphasize that you want to know your client as a person and not just about any physical symptoms. Acknowledge physical complaints but do not allow the person to dwell on them. Instead, try to promote insight by encouraging the person to tell you what causes stress in his or her life. Then together problem solve some ways of dealing with those stresses. Try to focus conversation on the positive aspects of the client's life and sources of satisfaction.

Nursing Goals

- Give physical nursing care and explain all procedures fully, until physical illness has been ruled out by laboratory tests and other diagnostic investigation.
- Once a somatoform diagnosis has been confirmed, reduce opportunities for clients to achieve benefits from sick behaviour; for example, persuade clients to get out of bed and dress for the day, eat in the dining area, interact with other clients, and so on.
- Journal – Encourage the client to keep a diary, describing activities and interactions, occurrences that

cause stress, and when symptoms appear. Help the client reflect on the relationship between stresses and symptoms. Explore other ways of achieving comfort and relieving symptoms rather than relying on medications and medical treatments.

- Encourage activities and exercise, both for promoting health and giving clients something to think about besides their complaints.
- Document any new physical complaints and report them to the medical staff for investigation.

Teaching and Learning

Client education focuses on learning about stress and about more adaptive coping strategies, including stress management techniques and establishing a healthy lifestyle. A client education plan (Stuart, 2005b, p. 292) may cover the following:

- Define and describe stress, having the client share associated feelings and behaviours.
- Ask clients to describe and role-play stressful situations. Talk about the behaviours that you observe. What are some of the adaptive and maladaptive coping mechanisms observed?
- Talk about events and experiences that are common stressors in everyday life. Try to have the client identify the elements in those experiences that heighten stress.
- Ask the client to choose one adaptive coping mechanism to practise for a day or a week and then review how it went at the end of the period and provide feedback.

Engaging With Families

Family education is essential. Once family members understand the reasons behind the client's symptoms, they can understand the importance of giving attention to the person when the client is *not* complaining of illness and reducing attention to their behaviour in the role of a sick person. Families and clients together can plan strategies for avoiding stress in the client's life and for reducing unavoidable stress. Family members may also need to learn the importance of expressing their feelings as repressing emotions may be a longstanding family dynamic that the client has learned.

COGNITIVE DISORDERS: DEMENTIAS, INCLUDING ALZHEIMER'S DISEASE, AND DELIRIUM

Cognition means "mental operations that relate to logic, awareness, intellect, memory, language, and reasoning powers" (Townsend, 2006, p. 934). Cognitive ability is, for many people, synonymous with their sense of self. Two major classifications of cognitive impairment are dementia and delirium. Both of these

conditions occur most often, although not exclusively, in older adults. With Canada's aging population, cognitive disorders will constitute an increasing proportion of nursing practice.

Many people assume that cognitive impairment is inevitable, that is, that all older adults become senile. Most nurses recognize this to be an ageist attitude. In older adults, although physiological changes in the brain result in some cognitive decline, general intellectual capacity remains intact. Older adults retain their ability to learn, although processing new information and retrieving memories may take a little longer. Some older adults are more easily distracted. Thus, for seniors, cognitive functioning varies, just as it does for younger people. Only where significant cognitive deficits are noted should the nurse suspect a cognitive disorder.

PATHOPHYSIOLOGY

Delirium

Although intellect is not markedly affected by age, the brain becomes less resistant to harm from factors such as electrolyte imbalance, medications, ischemia, hypoglycemia, and infections. The resulting cognitive impairment, called delirium, is also associated with many mental and physical illnesses, but, in general, the cognitive difficulties improve once the primary illness is resolved. Nurses on medical–surgical units frequently encounter delirium, especially following surgery or resulting from various other pathophysiological conditions that upset the biochemical balance of the CNS. In children and adolescents, the major causes are infection with a high fever, head trauma, drug toxicity, and brain tumours.

Dementias

In contrast, dementias involve progressive memory loss and are not, for the most part, reversible. Alzheimer's disease is the most common, accounting for 64% of all dementias in Canada, or almost 300,000 of the 450,000 cases of dementia. In 2007, two women for every man were estimated to develop a dementia, for a total of 97,000 new cases across the country (Alzheimer's Society of Canada, 2007). A minority of dementias can be reversed, including those caused by subdural hematoma, some brain tumours, cerebral vasculitis, and hydrocephalus.

The cerebral atrophy and deterioration of Alzheimer's disease are caused by the following:

- Senile plaques – Microscopic deposits composed of degenerated neuron cells
- Neurofibrillary tangles of the hippocampus that affect the memory and emotions
- Low acetylcholine levels resulting from insufficient levels of the enzyme necessary to produce acetylcholine, a major neurotransmitter
- A genetic defect involving at least four identified genes

CLINICAL MANIFESTATIONS

Delirium

Symptoms of acute confusion and disorientation with bizarre behaviour patterns develop quickly, often at night. The person may be highly agitated or dazed, with hallucinations and aggressive behaviour (anger and lashing out). Speech may become incomprehensible. Over a 24-hour period, symptoms may fluctuate in intensity.

Dementias

Dementias are chronic and progressive. Onset is slow, with gradual deterioration of the cognitive and physical neurological systems. In the early stages, symptoms are often attributed to aging, stress, or mild depression. Symptoms may include forgetting, difficulty concentrating, limited problem-solving ability, apathy or irritability, and some language disturbance, such as searching for words. Over time, cognitive abilities decline and individuals become increasingly distressed, depressed, and debilitated, needing progressively more physical care, support, and supervision. The eventual outcome is death.

In Alzheimer's disease, the course of the illness is about 8 to 12 years, divided into four stages. Diagnosis usually is made between 40 and 65 years, and, in general, the younger the person at diagnosis, the faster the deterioration. The stages are outlined in Table 11.8 (Varcarolis, 2002a).

DIAGNOSTICS AND THERAPEUTICS

Diagnosis

Diagnosing delirium usually involves diagnosing the underlying medical condition and identifying contributing factors, such as medications and substance

Table 11.8 Stages of Alzheimer's Disease

STAGE	HALLMARKS
Stage 1 (Mild) Forgetfulness	• Losses in short-term memory; loses things, forgets • Memory aids compensate: lists, routine, organization • Aware of the problem; concerned about lost abilities • Depression common, worsens symptoms • Not diagnosable at this time
Stage 2 (Moderate) Confusion	• Memory loss progressive; short-term memory impaired; interferes with all abilities • Withdrawn from social activities • Declines in instrumental activities of daily living (ADLs), e.g., money management, legal affairs, transportation, cooking, housekeeping • Denial common; fear of "losing my mind" • Depression increasingly common; frightened because aware of deficits • Cover-up for memory loss through confabulation • Problems intensified when stressed, fatigued, out of own environment, ill • Commonly need day care or in-home assistance
Stage 3 (Moderate–Severe) Ambulatory dementia	• ADL losses (in order): willingness and ability to bathe; grooming; choosing clothing; dressing; gait and mobility; toileting; communication, reading, and writing skills • Loss of reasoning ability, safety planning, and verbal communication • Depression resolves as awareness of losses diminishes • Difficult communication; increasing loss of language skills • Evidence of reduced stress threshold; institutional care usually needed
Stage 4 (Late) End stage	• Family recognition disappears; does not recognize self in mirror • Nonambulatory; little purposeful activity; often mute; may scream spontaneously • Forgets how to eat, swallow, chew; commonly loses weight; emaciation common • Problems associated with immobility, e.g., pneumonia, pressure ulcers, contractures • Incontinence common; seizures may develop • Most certainly institutionalized at this point • Return of primitive (infantile) reflexes

Source: Adapted from Hall, G. R. (1994). Caring for people with Alzheimer's disease using the conceptual model of progressively lowered stress threshold in the clinical setting. *Nursing Clinics of North America, 29*(1), 129–141.

abuse. Diagnosing dementia involves ruling out other illnesses and distinguishing among the various dementias. In addition to Alzheimer's disease, other dementia diagnoses include Lewy body dementia, Creutzfeldt-Jakob disease, Pick's disease, Huntington's disease, and vascular dementia. Dementia also occurs with advanced AIDS and Parkinson's disease.

Although delirium and dementias develop at different rates, symptoms overlap, and, not uncommonly, they are confounded. Postsurgical confusion is common in older adults, and too often, delirium goes unrecognized, and the confusion is blamed on dementia. Untreated, the delirium can result in permanent damage. As well, depression (common in both delirium and dementia) is also very common for seniors. Thus, diagnosing cognitive disorders can be tricky. Table 11.9 provides a comparison of the three Ds: delirium, dementia, and depression.

Table 11.9   Comparison of Delirium, Depression, and Dementia

	Delirium	Depression	Dementia
Onset	Rapid (hours to days)	Rapid (weeks to months)	Gradual (years)
Course	Wide fluctuations; may continue for weeks if cause is not found	May be self-limited or may become chronic without treatment	Chronic; slow but continuous decline
Level of Consciousness	Fluctuations from hyperalert to difficult to arouse	Normal	Normal
Orientation	Client is disoriented, confused	Client may seem disoriented	Client is disoriented, confused
Affect	Fluctuating	Sad, depressed, worried, guilty	Labile; apathetic in later stages
Attention	Always impaired	Difficulty concentrating; client may check and recheck all actions	May be intact; client may focus on one thing for long periods
Sleep	Always disturbed	Disturbed; excess sleeping or insomnia, especially early-morning waking	Usually normal
Behaviour	Agitated, restless	Client may be fatigued, apathetic; may occasionally be agitated	Client may be agitated or apathetic; may wander
Speech	Sparse or rapid; client may be incoherent	Flat, sparse; may have outbursts; understandable	Sparse or rapid; repetitive; client may be incoherent
Memory	Impaired, especially for recent events	Varies day to day; slow recall; often short-term deficit	Impaired, especially for recent events
Cognition	Disordered reasoning	May seem impaired	Disordered reasoning and calculation
Thought Content	Incoherent, confused, delusional, stereotyped	Negative, hypochondriac, thoughts of death, paranoid	Disorganized, rich in content, delusional, paranoid
Perception	Misinterpretations, illusions, hallucinations	Distorted; client may have auditory hallucinations; negative interpretation of people and events	No change
Judgement	Poor	Poor	Poor; socially inappropriate behaviour
Insight	May be present in lucid moments	May be impaired	Absent
Performance on Mental Status Examinations	Poor but variable; improves during lucid moments and with recovery	Memory impaired; calculation, drawing, and following directions usually not impaired; frequent "I don't know" answers	Consistently poor; progressively worsens; client attempts to answer all questions

Source: Modified from Holt, J. (1993). How to help confused patients. *American Journal of Nursing, 93*(8), 32; and Henry, M. (2002). Descending into delirium: Confusion, isolation, forgetfulness, lethargy. *American Journal of Nursing, 102*(3), 49.

Diagnostic Tests

No single test provides a definitive diagnosis for delirium or dementia, but laboratory findings can help ascertain the cause of delirium, guide treatment decisions, and rule out other diagnoses. Neuropsychological testing may be used for either delirium or dementias to assess mental status.

The following laboratory results may be indicative of delirium:

- Serum electrolyte levels – Low calcium, low potassium, abnormal sodium
- High blood urea nitrogen (BUN), high creatinine, protein in the urine – To assess renal function and fluid levels
- Elevated prothrombin time, low hematocrit, abnormal blood gases – To assess for anoxia and poor circulation
- Blood glucose, elevated aspartate transaminase (AST), and serum glutamic-oxaloacetic transaminase (SGOT) – To assess metabolism

Physicians will order many laboratory tests when ruling out other medical conditions before settling on the diagnosis of dementia, including electrolytes, vitamin B_{12} level, thyroid function tests, EEG, ECG, HIV testing, and vision and hearing evaluation. The diagnosis of dementia is usually confirmed through neuroimaging with CT scans, PET scans, an MRI, or some combination of these.

Treatment

Medical treatment of the underlying condition usually reverses delirium. All medication use in older adults should be carefully monitored for signs of overdose and side effects. This is vitally important to prevent both of the following:

- Drug interactions due to the high number of medications that many older persons routinely take (polypharmacy)
- Accumulation of toxic drug levels in the body due to less efficient and effective metabolism and excretion in older adults

Cholinesterase inhibitors (Aricept is a common one) are effective against some of the symptoms of Alzheimer's disease, slowing down the functional deterioration. By reducing the rate of acetylcholine metabolism, they may help preserve memory and learning and reduce anxiety. Other medications help ease behavioural symptoms, such as agitation (beta blockers, estrogen, anticonvulsants, SSRIs), anxiety (antidepressants, antipsychotics, benzodiazepines), aggression (anticonvulsants), depression (antidepressants), and psychotic symptoms (antipsychotics and SSRIs).

NURSING CONSIDERATIONS

Nursing Assessment

A number of assessment tools for evaluating a person's mental status are available. In many centres, nurses use the Mini-Mental State Examination. Refer to Chapter 4, page 47, for more information on mental status and neurological assessment.

Because of the acuity of most delirium and the temporary duration, assessment focuses primarily on the client's medical and mental condition. Monitor neurological status for fluctuating levels of consciousness. Ask the family about the client's normal cognitive status and whether there is a history of periods of confusion. Be alert for changes in medical signs and symptoms, monitoring vital signs, edema, intake and output, signs of jaundice, and pain level.

In contrast, much of the nurse's assessment for dementia is directed toward the client and family together. Determine the client's present cognitive functioning level, what medications are regularly taken, and the family's understanding of dementia. Discuss with family caregivers their concerns, coping abilities, safety issues in the home environment, and their knowledge of and access to community resources.

The Nurse–Client Relationship

Mental confusion is frightening to clients. Interaction, while challenging for the nurse, can be extremely frustrating for clients, who may search for words to communicate but often speak incomprehensibly. The nurse should approach clients calmly, speaking slowly and using simple language. Always introduce yourself at each contact and call the client by name, making certain that he or she can see your face. Ensure that clients who have hearing aids and glasses use them. Encourage them to tell you about themselves, their families, and their lives. Avoid arguing about their misperceptions and delusions; instead, reinforce what is real and gently try to change the subject. Distraction can help defuse anger and frustration, but always acknowledge the person's feelings. Above all, respect clients' humanity and never address them like children.

Nursing Goals

The overall goals in nursing care of people with cognitive disorders have been called the three Ps: protecting their dignity, preserving their functional status, and promoting their quality of life (Eliopoulos, 2000, pp. 946–947). Principles of caring for people with cognitive disorders include the following:

- Safety first – Close supervision is essential to prevent falls and other injuries or the client wandering away and becoming lost.
- Maintain nutrition and fluid balance – Malnutrition and dehydration promote confused states.

- Repeatedly orient the client to person, place, and time. Reinforce reality with aids such as a clock, a calendar, and pictures of family members.
- Provide a calm, restful environment – Lower the lights during the day and provide soft lighting at night, but be aware that shadows can be frightening.
- Promote adequate sleep at night – Try comfort measures such as warm milk or a backrub.
- Encourage independence with self-care. When assistance is required, take it slowly; give directions one step at a time.
- Restraints – Use restraints as an absolute last resort. Confused persons react to restraints with agitation and anxiety, both of which provoke unsafe behaviour.

Involving Families

For disoriented people, a familiar face can be soothing and help the individual to feel safe. If possible, a family member should stay while the client is in hospital to assist with the following:

- Reducing fear – Unfamiliar surroundings and strangers increase anxiety and agitation.
- Reducing disorientation – Even if the client is unable to recognize the family member, structuring the client's care in terms of personal preferences and routines is less disorienting. Informal caregivers know a person's idiosyncrasies and can help with care planning. Request that the family bring in some familiar objects from home.
- Safety – Constant supervision helps maintain safety and avoids the use of restraints.

Caring for the families and caregivers of confused people is integral to nursing care in cognitive disorders.

- Be honest with family members about the diagnosis and future outcomes.
- Invite family caregivers to talk with you about their fears and emotions.
- If the client rejects family members, compassionately explain that it is not intentional.
- Families may also need help with financial and legal affairs and accessing community resources.
- Families want to be helpful, but nurses must also remember that hospitalizing the client with dementia can provide respite for the primary caregiver. Encourage other family members to stay with the client to allow the primary caregiver frequent breaks and opportunities for rest.
- Help families identify and access community resources, for example, the Alzheimer's Society of Canada and its local branches, the Canadian Caregiver Network, the Canadian Mental Health Association, home care nursing services, home support services, respite care, Meals on Wheels, accessible transportation for disabled persons, support groups for caregivers, and so on. Consult with the community health liaison nurse, if your hospital has one.

- Express appreciation to family caregivers for their devotion and assistance.

DISORDERS OF SEXUALITY AND IDENTITY

Sexuality and identity are important sources of personality. Sexuality, sexual health, and reproduction contribute significantly to health and well-being throughout life. Nurses recognize that normal sexuality includes the curiosity and experimentation of children, as well as the need and desires for sexual relationships among older adults and people who are disabled, either cognitively or physically.

Sexual orientation includes heterosexuality (being straight), homosexuality (gay or lesbian), and bisexual attraction to both males and females. In the not too distant past, cultural and moral standards limited acceptable sexual behaviour to heterosexual relations, preferably within marriage. Now, variations in sexual orientation and behaviour are considered to be mental health disorders only if a client defines them as such or wants to change, or if the client's sexual behaviour impinges on the rights of another.

It is perhaps better to consider sexual responses not in terms of normality but rather as being adaptive or maladaptive. Adaptive sexual responses occur "between two consenting adults, [and are] mutually satisfying to both, not psychologically or physically harmful to either, lacking in force or coercion, and conducted in private" (Poorman, 2005, p. 539). In general, disorders of sexuality and identity can be divided into three categories:

- Sexual dysfunction
- Abnormal sexual fantasies and behaviours, known as paraphilias
- Disorders of sexual identity and preference

PATHOPHYSIOLOGY

Sexual identity is largely determined genetically and manifested as male or female anatomy and physiology, although psychosocial factors, in other words, how people perceive of themselves and behave in a sexual role, also influence gender. Another biological influence on sexual expression is hormonal, as evidenced by puberty and the fact that for both men and women, libido is related to testosterone levels or high serum prolactin. In addition, high levels of androgens are found in people who exhibit inappropriate sexual arousal and hypersexual behaviour.

Sexual function, or the sexual response cycle, consists of four stages: desire, excitement, orgasm, and resolution. Disturbance at any stage can result in a sexual dysfunction, as can pain experienced with sexual intercourse. Sexual functioning can also be affected by comorbid illness, physical injury, or the medications taken to contend with these.

- Depression, hypothyroidism, atherosclerosis, diabetes mellitus, and some urological infections and disorders, as well as neurological diseases such as epilepsy, multiple sclerosis, and Parkinson's disease, can negatively affect sexual functioning.
- Antihypertensives, antipsychotics, anxiolytics, anticonvulsants, antidepressants, and chronic alcohol or cocaine use may reduce levels of sexual desire and arousal.

CLINICAL MANIFESTATIONS

Sexual Dysfunction

Four subtypes of sexual dysfunction disorders follow. The first three are related to the sexual response cycle.

Sexual Desire Disorders

- Hypoactive sexual desire disorder, more common in women, is an absence or lack of sexual desires or fantasies.
- Sexual aversion disorder, or avoidance of sex, is often characterized by fear, disgust, and anxiety about intimacy and genital contact.

Sexual Arousal Disorders

- Female sexual arousal disorder, the inability to achieve and maintain excitement throughout sexual activity, may be related to physical limitations in lubrication or engorgement of the external genital organs, which sometimes occurs with menopause.
- Male erectile disorder (ED) is difficulty achieving or maintaining an erection.

Orgasmic Disorders

- Female orgasmic disorder is the inability to achieve orgasm.
- Male orgasmic disorder causes delay in ejaculation or the absence of an ejaculation.
- Premature ejaculation is a disorder of early ejaculation, with minimal stimulation or penetration.

Sexual Pain Disorders

- Dyspareunia, recurrent or persistent pain with intercourse, can affect either women or men. This may be caused by infection or prostate problems.
- Vaginismus is the unconscious constriction of the vagina, preventing penetration and intercourse.

Paraphilias

Paraphilias are characterized by sexual arousal resulting from fantasies and behaviours. Often the fantasies involve nonhuman objects, painful or humiliating sexual activity, or sex without mutual consent. Generally, such fantasies and behaviours lead to arousal and orgasm, often assisted by masturbation. Paraphilias include exhibitionism, fetishism, pedophilia, sexual masochism, voyeurism, and transvestite fetishism. People engage in paraphilias secretly to avoid social sanctions, with the result that they are likely underdiagnosed. As with many mental disorders, paraphilias may intensify when a person experiences stress.

Gender Identity Disorder

Gender identity relates to a person's awareness of being male or female. Gender identity disorder occurs when biological sex and gender identity differ. From the outset, children with the disorder prefer opposite-gender playmates. With maturation, they become increasingly less comfortable with their assigned gender role. Disapproval and rejection lead to low self-esteem and impaired family and social interactions. As adults, they may be asexual, heterosexual, or homosexual, preferring same-sex partners. Identifying with the opposite sex, they tend to engage in cross-gender roles and activities and often in cross-dressing. Wearing clothes of the opposite sex often helps decrease their anxiety and depression and may or may not be accompanied by sexual excitement.

An extreme version of gender identity disorder is transsexualism. Often depressed and anxious from pressure to conform to their assigned sex role, people with transsexualism may feel disgust toward their own bodies. Biological males may cross-dress and live as transvestites. Females who adopt masculine dress have become more accepted as a result of feminism. Transsexuals often enter the mental health system requesting sexual reassignment.

DIAGNOSTICS AND THERAPEUTICS

Diagnosis of sexual disorders requires a detailed general and sexual history and complete physical examination. The therapist probes for predisposing and developmental factors, as well as family and social history.

Treatment

Treatment for sexual disorders includes the following:

- Individual or group psychotherapy
- Couple therapy
- Behaviour modification
- Pharmacotherapy with antianxiety medications or antidepressants, as necessary

More specific treatments differ depending on the classification of the sexual disorder.

Sexual Dysfunction

- Pharmacotherapy – Antidepressants, including SSRIs, have been successful against rapid ejaculation. Viagra and Cialis are used for EDs.

- Medications for female sexual disorders are less available, although studies with Viagra have shown some success when there is no history of sexual abuse.

Paraphilias

- Cognitive–behavioural therapy
- Medications to lower testosterone levels, such as methoxyprogesterone, may be effective.

Gender Identity Disorder

- Hormone therapy for development of opposite-sex secondary sexual characteristics
- Clients may undergo sex-change surgery, after intensive psychotherapy, hormone therapy, and living as a member of the opposite sex for a significant period, usually at least two years.

NURSING CONSIDERATIONS

Nursing Assessment

Begin with a full health history, family history, and physical examination. Include the usual questions about sexual activity, number and sex of sexual partners, birth control, concern regarding HIV and other sexually transmitted infections (STIs), and whether there are any concerns about sexual functioning. Once you have established a relationship, you can ask more specific questions regarding the following:

- Sexual knowledge, family attitudes, and sexual experience during childhood and adolescence
- Cultural and religious beliefs regarding sexuality
- The client's concerns and depth of understanding of his or her sexuality
- Sexual fantasies, dreams, and use of erotic material
- Sexual patterns within or outside marriage
- Probes in regard to the individual's psychosexual diagnosis
- Self-esteem
- Anxiety and level of stress
- Social interaction
- Coping strategies

The Nurse–Client Relationship

Culture, family background, societal values, the media—all contribute to the taboos surrounding sexual conduct and what is considered to be "normal." Nurses need to examine their own attitudes and values regarding sexual expression and sexual behaviour, to minimize anxiety when discussing sexual matters. Awareness of one's personal attitudes, beliefs, and knowledge regarding sexuality is necessary before the nurse can set those issues aside to allow for an open and sensitive discussion, communicating warmth, acceptance, and positive regard. Because sexuality is one of the most private and personal aspects of our

lives, few people will volunteer information, leaving it to the nurse to introduce the topic and guide the conversation.

Caring for People With Sexual Disorders

Sexual therapy is not within the scope of practice for a newly qualified nurse. For intensive therapy, the nurse should make a referral to a qualified sex therapist. The regular nurse's role includes assessment, education, and support to a client being treated for a sexual disorder. Some basic approaches that are helpful to clients with sexual problems include the following:

- Active listening, allowing the client to explore sexual values and beliefs
- Helping the client set realistic goals
- Setting limits on the client's sexual behaviour
- Relaxation techniques for stress and anxiety reduction
- Assisting with the behaviour modification plan by implementing the agreed-upon consequences for maladaptive behaviour

Teaching and Learning

If the client has a stable sexual relationship, include the partner in client education. Explore whether there are differences in their sexual beliefs and expectations as these can lead to conflict and misunderstanding. For example, the client's dissatisfaction with sexual desire and arousal may be less a matter of his or her personal lack of response than it is of not being able to match his or her partner's expectations.

Topics for client and family education regarding sexual disorders (Townsend, 2006, p. 640) include the following:

- The sexual response cycle and what is considered to be normal and abnormal
- Sexual dysfunctions and paraphilias: types, causes, and symptoms
- Medications with side effects that contribute to sexual dysfunction
- The effect of alcohol use on sexual function
- Relaxation techniques
- STIs
- Available community resources for sexual therapy

Responding to a Client's Sexual Advances

One very difficult aspect of caring for clients with paraphilias is dealing with seductive advances and comments directed at the nurse. Sexually inappropriate behaviour toward nurses is not restricted to mental health settings but can be found in any health care environment. Inappropriate touching, asking for dates or personal contact information, and making explicit passes at the nurse cannot be tolerated, and the client must be so informed. The most professional response is to respond firmly and set clear limits.

EATING DISORDERS: ANOREXIA AND BULIMIA

Eating disorders are appetite disturbances. The continuum ranges from eating too little (anorexia nervosa), through disordered eating with binging and purging (bulimia nervosa), to chronic overeating causing obesity (binge eating disorder). In our culture, however, obesity is not always considered a mental health problem, and most treatment consists of diet therapy only. Binge eating disorder often goes unrecognized. Anorexia and bulimia often overlap, with about half of people with anorexia displaying bulimic behaviours at times or developing bulimia later in their lives. Eating disorders are primarily identified in women (85–90%). However, the prevalence of bulimia in men may be underestimated because of their reluctance to seek treatment.

PATHOPHYSIOLOGY

Normal appetite regulation is a function of the hypothalamus, through several mechanisms that produce sensations of either hunger or satiety (feeling full). Hunger is experienced when the hypothalamus is stimulated by

- Low blood glucose levels,
- Contractions of an empty stomach (and possibly stimulation of the vagus nerve), and
- High levels of neurotransmitters, such as serotonin.

Satiety is felt when the hypothalamus is suppressed. This occurs due to

- High levels of fat and amino acids in the blood,
- Slow emptying of the stomach and distension of the GI tract, and
- High cortisol levels (a physiologic reaction to stress).

CLINICAL MANIFESTATIONS

Eating disorders are closely related to body image and low self-esteem. Where thinness is admired and celebrated in all forms of the media, dissatisfaction with one's shape and size is widespread. Weight loss is big business, and some people engage in extreme measures to control their weight. Behaviours associated with eating disorders include the following:

- Binge eating – Consuming large amounts of food and excessive calories. The frequency of binging varies from occasionally to several times weekly or even many times each day.
- Dieting – Restricting food intake below what is necessary to maintain weight
- Fasting – Refusing to eat
- Purging – Inducing vomiting to lose weight or using over-the-counter laxatives or diuretics to stimulate fluid and waste excretion

Anorexia and Bulimia

The defining feature of anorexia is that body weight drops below 85% of the normal weight for a person's height. The typical person suffering from anorexia nervosa is an adolescent or young adult woman, very thin but preoccupied with food and her physical appearance. She equates attractiveness with being thin, perceiving herself as fat even when others see her as emaciated and refusing to admit that fasting and dieting are harmful. Often cold, she wears warm layers of clothing, even in hot weather. Sexually inactive and experiencing amenorrhea, she is obsessive, a perfectionist, and quite introverted. She fears gaining weight and tends to eat alone so that others cannot observe how little she eats. She may exercise incessantly, smoke or drink alcohol to stave off hunger, or purge. Eventually, she may become unaware of any appetite sensations.

In contrast, people with bulimia may be either slightly or grossly overweight, but often they manage to maintain normal weight by balancing their binging with purging and exercising excessively. They tend to be consumed with shame related to their eating habits and eat secretly to hide their binging from others. Menstruation may be absent or irregular, but bulimics are more sexually active than those with anorexia. Drug and alcohol abuse are common, as are self-mutilation and other behaviour problems.

Complications of Eating Disorders

Without treatment, eating disorders cause medical complications in many body systems. Serious complications of starvation and dehydration include hypokalemia and hypoalbuminemia leading to hypotension, cardiac arrhythmias, and heart and renal failure, which are life-threatening. Frequent vomiting can cause stomach and esophageal ulcers, GI bleeding, tooth decay, and gum erosion. Amenorrhea is related to estrogen deficiencies that may result in calcium deficiency and osteoporosis. Deaths from eating disorders are tragic and much too frequent!

DIAGNOSTICS AND THERAPEUTICS

Predisposing Factors

Risk factors for developing eating disorders are a complex combination of personal, social, cultural, and behavioural factors. Many of the personal risk factors can be identified in the description above of the characteristics of people with anorexia. Criticism or teasing about one's weight from parents or peers can damage self-esteem, as can other family dysfunctions and a history of sexual or physical abuse. Dieting is almost a cultural pastime. The drive for perfection, especially in vocations that demand a slim body, such as gymnastics, dance, acting, and modelling, sets many young women on the path to an eating disorder.

Treatment

Unless there is a medical crisis, clients can be cared for as outpatients in community clinics, day treatment, or partial hospitalization. Where possible, community care tends to be the best option, allowing clients to maintain autonomy while learning healthy self-control and a better lifestyle. Seriously malnourished clients are at risk of death, and hospitalization is required when the client's weight drops below 75% of normal. Other indications of crisis are severe dehydration, cardiac damage, low blood glucose, and electrolyte imbalance, or if the client becomes psychotic, suicidal, or severely depressed. Sometimes people with bulimia who cannot achieve control over their binging and purging also may be admitted to the hospital.

Once in hospital, medical treatment to stabilize physiological health is the first priority. Only then can more behaviourally oriented interventions be initiated. Treatment may include the following:

- A healthy diet, possibly with liquid supplements
- Vitamin and mineral supplements
- Pharmacotherapy with anxiolytics (helpful for those with obsessive–compulsive features), tricyclics, and SSRIs (to decrease mood swings, depression, irritability, and food and fat obsessions). Sometimes appetite suppressants are used for bulimia, but only until new eating patterns have been established.
- Individual or group psychotherapy
- Cognitive–behavioural therapy
- Behaviour modification therapy
- Family therapy
- Stress management and self-monitoring

NURSING CONSIDERATIONS

Nursing Assessment

Assessment of eating disorders begins with two simple screening questions (Frisch & Frisch, 2006, p. 478):

- Are you satisfied with your eating patterns? People with anorexia usually say "yes," but those with bulimia do not.
- Do you ever eat in secret? People with either anorexia or bulimia generally answer "yes."

Continue your assessment with a full health history, family history, and physical examination, placing emphasis on the following:

- Nutritional status and diet history, including food preferences, eating behaviours, and purging episodes
- Weight history, height and weight measurement
- Signs of fluid and electrolyte imbalance
- Menstrual history, especially amenorrhea
- Frequency, type, and amount of exercise
- Mood and emotional state, for example, depression, anxiety, distress
- Evidence of obsession or compulsion, especially regarding food
- Evidence of disturbed body image, low self-esteem, self-criticism
- Risk of suicide
- Frequency, type, and amount of exercise
- History of dysfunctional family relationships
- Level of insight and motivation for treatment

The Nurse–Client Relationship

People with eating disorders tend to be suspicious. They fear health professionals who want to ruin their lives by urging them to be "fat." Literally starving if anorexic, or shamed and frustrated if bulimic, they are often irritable. Strive to get to know your client well, not just the eating disorder. Establishing a trusting therapeutic relationship challenges nurses to overcome their frustration and need for control. Successful interpersonal strategies include being nonjudgemental, straightforward, and firm. Avoid power struggles with the client over food intake.

Nutritional Rehabilitation

The nurse encourages healthy eating by negotiating agreement on a target weight and a mutually determined recovery plan that includes the following:

- Adequate food intake
- Structured, time-limited meal times (for example, three small meals a day)
- Food preferences
- Nutritious snacks between meals

Monitor the client's eating and weight in an accepting and nonpunitive way.

- Stay with the client during meals and for an hour after to reduce opportunities for purging (in anorexia and bulimia) or stashing food (in bulimia and obesity).
- Ensure a pleasant and social atmosphere at mealtimes, discussing topics other than food.
- Encourage use of a food diary.
- Offer small amounts of food and drink frequently.
- Weigh the client daily in the morning, in the same clothing, after first voiding, and on the same scale. Be vigilant for attempts to artificially increase her weight, such as stuffing items into pockets or under clothes.
- Record intake and output.
- Assess for signs of dehydration: skin turgor, colour, and moistness of oral mucous membranes.
- Encourage rest times and appropriate exercise with supervision.

Teaching and Learning

Provide information about normal nutrition and balanced diet nutrients, such as teaching about normal growth and body development and that cutting out all fat is unhealthy. Discuss the nature of the illness (symptoms, causes, effects on the body) and the importance of expressing emotions and fears rather than holding them inside. What emotions and beliefs does the client associate with eating? Help people with anorexia set attainable goals. Commonly, their perfectionism leads them to setting unrealistic goals that result in failure and frustration. Regularly review the client's food journal and diet plan with her or him and explain how better nutrition will improve symptoms and prevent complications. Review the action, dose, and possible adverse effects of any mediation that the client is taking. Additional important components of teaching for clients with anorexia nervosa include the following:

- The physiologically damaging effects of dieting
- The identification and avoidance of triggers
- Techniques for self-monitoring
- Community resources (White, 2005, p. 510)

Additional important components of teaching for clients with bulimia include the following:

- The effects on the body of the binging and purging cycle
- Adequate hydration
- Self-monitoring and the avoidance of cues
- Learning to set limits and appropriate boundaries
- Assertiveness (White, 2005, p. 519)

Psychosocial Interventions

Behaviour Modification

- A nurse–client contract ensures that the client understands the illness and treatment involved and is committed to participating in making informed decisions to benefit his or her health.
- Agreed-upon consequences for not adhering to the contract terms, such as loss of privileges, should be imposed consistently and in a matter-of-fact manner and voice tone.
- Provide encouragement and positive reinforcement for adherence to the contract.
- Help the client identify any cues that stimulate harmful eating behaviour and explore ways of avoiding those situations or changing to a more adaptive response.

Body Image Perception

- Encourage your client to share his or her thoughts and feelings about body shape and weight.
- Avoid contradicting the client, but present alternative ideas and interpretations.
- Help the client reflect on and consider those alternative perceptions and explanations.
- Promote self-acceptance. Draw attention to positive physical characteristics.
- Imagery and relaxation may reduce body-related anxiety.

Low Self-Esteem

- Explore the client's desire for perfection and encourage acceptance of what is good enough.
- Explore family and relationship history and the impacts upon self-esteem and self-acceptance.
- Emphasize positive attributes and behaviours.

Interactions With Families

- Include families in treatment team meetings and in planning care, in both the hospital and community phases of treatment.
- Be emotionally supportive but also candid about the client's state of health.
- Advise families to make their visits social occasions and to talk about topics other than eating.
- Encourage families to become informed about nutrition and about eating disorders.

ADJUSTMENT DISORDERS

Abnormal behavioural or emotional reactions to an identifiable stressor, without an associated psychiatric diagnosis, constitute an adjustment disorder. All ages can be affected, often at times of major life transitions, such as starting school, adolescence, family breakup, loss of a job, financial problems, menopause, retirement, or the death of a spouse. People with poorly developed social skills or coping strategies or lacking supportive social networks may be particularly vulnerable. Symptoms begin within three months after the stressor appears and usually resolve over the next six months. If the stressor is ongoing, however, the adjustment disorder may also persist, accompanied by worsening financial problems or difficult relationships. Adjustment disorders are usually resolved with community treatment and seldom warrant hospitalization.

PATHOPHYSIOLOGY

No clearly defined biological causes or physiological changes are correlated with adjustment disorders, although when people exhibit depressive or anxiety-related behaviours, the expected pathophysiological changes for those conditions would be present. Theorists suggest that genetic factors may be implicated, at least for those persons with cognitive disorders or developmental challenges who respond poorly to stressful situations.

CLINICAL MANIFESTATIONS

The behavioural and emotional symptoms of adjustment disorders can negatively affect functioning at work or school, and clients typically use a variety of defence mechanisms. Six major types of adjustment disorders are identified:

- Adjustment disorder with depressed mood is the most frequent adjustment disorder. Depressed mood, crying spells, and feelings of hopelessness are characteristic symptoms of a mood disorder; however, they are less severe than major depression.

- Adjustment disorder with anxiety – Some people who have an adjustment disorder also display nervousness, worry, and anxious feelings and behaviour.
- Adjustment disorder with mixed anxiety and depressed mood – Here, both anxiety and depression affect the person's ability to adapt to stressful events.
- Adjustment disorder with disturbance of conduct – Acting out inappropriately defines this type. Adolescents with a history of skipping school, fighting, vandalism, rebelling against all forms of authority, and getting into trouble with the law are often diagnosed with this disorder.
- Adjustment disorder with mixed disturbance of emotions and conduct – As the name implies, this is a mixture of the above types.
- Adjustment disorder unspecified – People with this disorder do not display the above symptoms but may withdraw socially or develop physical symptoms.

DIAGNOSTICS AND THERAPEUTICS

Diagnosis

Diagnosing adjustment disorders requires a thorough personal history that shows a stressful event or social situation followed by the development of symptoms. These symptoms are more intense and last longer than usual, and all underlying physical or mental disorders have been ruled out. Risk factors include a dysfunctional family upbringing with overprotective or abusive parents, frequent moves as a child, living in poverty, and being involved in wars and violence. Sometimes delayed or prolonged grief is classified as an adjustment disorder.

Treatment

- Individual psychotherapy
- Family therapy
- Behavioural therapy
- Self-help groups
- Pharmacotherapy with antidepressants and anxiolytics

NURSING CONSIDERATIONS

Nursing Assessment

- Assess the level of anxiety or depression.
- Assess the client's support system, including family dynamics.
- Examine how the client perceives the problem or problems.

The Nurse–Client Relationship

- Convey empathy and support.
- Avoid minimizing the client's struggle with empty reassurances, such as "You'll be fine" and "Everything will work out."
- Encourage the person to recognize that a problem exists and that it is important to talk together about his or her emotional reactions.
- Provide positive reinforcement for desirable behaviour. This helps increase self-esteem.

Nursing Goals

- Have the client describe his or her life and lifestyle prior to the stressful event.
- Listen when the client expresses anger, fear, and other negative emotions.
- Encourage healthy self-care and lifestyle: eating well, adequate sleep, regular exercise, and enjoyable hobbies.
- Assist with problem solving, providing alternatives for the client to consider.
- Assist the client to identify family members and friends who can provide support.
- Encourage family and friends to provide strong support.

Teaching and Learning

- Teach stress management techniques.
- Involve family and friends in teaching and learning opportunities.

Caring for Persons With Unresolved Prolonged Grief

Explain to clients and families the following stages of grief:

- Numbness and shock – An inability to feel anything, sometimes alternating with extreme emotional outbursts
- Yearning and searching – Expressions of anger, intense sorrow, and weeping as the reality of the loss sets in. There are often moments of imagining that the loved one will reappear.
- Despair and disorganization – Characterized by emotions of hopelessness and acute loneliness, depression, and apathy
- Reorganization and acceptance – Finally, there is gradual restoring of the self and a return to regular activities. Memories of the loved one become more comforting and less painful.

The nursing responsibilities in assisting a person who is grieving include the following:

- Help the client identify his or her current stage of grief.
- Be accepting of expressions of anger. Accompany the client to a private and quiet area and stay with him or her.
- Try to engage the person in activities (keeping busy).

- Assess a client's spirituality and make a referral to a chaplain or minister, if that is desired.
- Refer the person to a grief support group.

PSYCHIATRIC EMERGENCIES: CRISIS, SUICIDE, VIOLENCE

In a highly stressful event or when confronted with a perceived threat for which the usual coping strategies are ineffective, people experience high levels of anxiety. This may escalate to a state of crisis. Crises may be developmental (such as adolescence, marriage, moving away from home to attend college) or situational (such as divorce or sudden unemployment). Extreme situational crises are sometimes called adventitious, indicating that the event is totally outside the person's control. Some examples include natural disasters, wars, or being the victim of a crime.

With no resolution of the crisis, behavioural reactions may continue to escalate. The most serious behavioural reactions include suicide and violence, neither of which are rare events. Shockingly, 2% of all Canadian deaths are due to suicide. Among young people aged 15–24, suicide accounts for one-quarter of deaths, and the rates are rising. The suicide death rate for men is four times as high as that for women, and men over 80 have the highest suicide rate of all. The most common psychiatric disorders associated with suicide are mood disorders, substance abuse, schizophrenia, and anxiety disorders (CIHI, 2002, pp. 92–95).

PATHOPHYSIOLOGY

- For a description of the stress response, refer to the section on anxiety disorders.
- The limbic system is responsible for regulating emotions and aggression. The amygdala is involved in distinguishing between aversive and rewarding stimuli. Rage can be activated in animals by stimulating the amygdala.
- There is a correlation between low levels of serotonin and aggressive behaviour.
- Abnormalities in the temporal lobe may be related to aggressive responses.
- Some people are prone to aggressive behaviour after a traumatic brain injury.

CLINICAL MANIFESTATIONS

Clients in crisis are overwhelmed by emotional pain and anxiety. After having attempted a number of solutions without success, they may reach the point of being "at their wit's end" and in a state of complete disorganization. Although people react to crises differently, common maladaptive behaviours include anger, apathy, somatic complaints, emotional outbursts, insomnia, fear, flashbacks, shock, hopelessness, helplessness, or substance abuse.

DIAGNOSTICS AND THERAPEUTICS

Diagnosis

Diagnosis is initially based on the client's behaviour and inability to control the source of extreme and intense anxiety. First, determine whether the person is suicidal or violent and initiate steps to ensure safety. Once safety is ensured, the nurse should try to identify the precipitating event or events. In psychiatric and community settings, the exacerbation of a mental illness often occurs when clients reject treatment. Apprehension under the *Mental Health Act* and certification for admission or treatment or both may be necessary (see the earlier section on the legal aspects of mental illness).

Nurses should know what services are locally available for crisis intervention and how to contact them. Some examples (CIHI, 2002) include the following:

- Medical treatment – Once available options are exhausted, admission to a psychiatric facility becomes necessary.
- Short-term crisis stabilization – Residential settings where clients receive protection and support
- Mobile crisis outreach – Services in which health care professionals and police together provide assistance at the scene of the crisis
- Walk-in crisis intervention centres
- Telephone or Internet crisis services

Treatment

Treatment varies depending on the root cause of the crisis. Treatment goals are to preserve the safety of the client and all those who could be exposed to danger, to prevent the client's anxiety from escalating, and to return the client to a pre-crisis state of being.

Psychopharmacology

Common medications for those prone to high levels of anxiety and impulsive behaviour include the following:

- Anxiolytics and sedative–hypnotics to manage agitation
- Antidepressants, especially SSRIs, to balance levels of serotonin
- Mood stabilizers to reduce aggressive behaviour
- Antipsychotics – The quick action of IM haloperidol combined with lorazepam is often used to calm people with escalating agitation. Atypical antipsychotics are given to reduce the incidence of violence in people at risk.

NURSING CONSIDERATIONS

Nursing Assessment

Assessment focuses on identifying the precipitating event, the client's interpretation of it, the client's coping resources, and the support systems available. Does the person in crisis require emergency psychiatric treatment or hospitalization? Whether you are a community nurse or in a hospital setting, your assessment will include several elements:

- Try to ascertain whether the person clearly understands the event that precipitated the crisis.
- What coping mechanisms may be helpful in this situation? Has the client used these coping strategies in the past?
- What or who are the client's current situational supports?
- Are there any cultural or religious beliefs or traditions that need to be taken into consideration?
- What is the appropriate level of intervention in this situation?

  - Primary intervention, such as education, changes in the environment, or new coping skills
  - Secondary, or crisis, intervention
  - Tertiary intervention, such as rehabilitation (Varcarolis, 2002d).

Suicide

Thoughts of suicide or suicide attempts should be suspected when clients appear alienated, disconnected, or in despair. In a kind but straightforward way, ask distressed clients if they are experiencing suicidal thoughts. If the answer is "Yes," ask whether the client has developed a plan. If so, evaluate whether the person has the ability and opportunity to carry it out.

Risk factors for suicide vary depending on the population group:

- Depressed adolescents with a family history of suicide and a personal history of legal trouble and substance abuse are at high risk.
- For older adults, high risk factors include a family member's death or having a serious or terminal illness.
- For depressed clients, times of greatest danger occur in the first few days following either admission to or discharge from the hospital. Clients are at high risk for suicide for the first few days following initiation of treatment with antidepressants or ECT. Psychomotor retardation improves before mood improves. Thus, early in treatment, the client remains severely depressed but now has regained the motivation necessary to follow through with suicidal thoughts. Following discharge, some clients are more at risk of suicide when they return home to find that the things that initially caused their depression have not changed.
- People with schizophrenia are at less risk for suicide when they are psychotic than when they begin to recover and become aware of having little hope for a satisfying life.
- Psychiatric clients who are at high risk for suicide are those who engage in self-directed harm, including self-mutilation to relieve tension, and those who stop taking their medications or are otherwise non-compliant with treatment.
- People who misuse substances are at high risk, as are those who have been recently separated, divorced, or bereaved.
- Be especially wary of a severely disturbed client who suddenly becomes calm and rational. When people see suicide as the only escape from an intolerable existence, and when they have thought through a plan and have the means to carry it out, they may feel comforted by knowing their struggles are nearly over.

Violence

Nurses should be able to distinguish between assertive and aggressive behaviour.

Assertive Behaviour: People who are assertive are direct, persuasive, and self-assured in their communications and interactions with other people. They convey respect for others.

Aggressive Behaviour: People who are aggressive exert their own rights at the expense of the rights of others. They tend to express anger. They fight to get what they want and expect others to approach interactions in the same way. Aggressive behaviour can escalate to violence, and nurses should be aware that setting limits on clients' behaviour is sometimes an antecedent of aggressive behaviour by hospitalized clients. On the one hand, aggression is more common in psychiatric clients with active psychosis and in those who abuse substances. On the other hand, people with schizophrenia and mania are no more violent than ordinary citizens as long as they are well controlled on their medications. The best predictor of a person becoming violent is past violent behaviour.

The Nurse–Client Relationship

Connecting with violent and aggressive clients is challenging. Some nurses worry that their own behaviour could trigger a client's angry response. If a client is verbally abusive, the nurse's first response should be to leave the room. Of course, it is always best to prevent angry outbursts if at all possible. For clients with a history of violence or who are otherwise deemed to be at risk for violence, reward appropriate behaviour by giving time and attention to the person.

Identify stressors and ways to avoid them and learn to recognize indicators that the client is becoming stressed. If so, the nurse draws on interpersonal skills for de-escalating the situation. Speak calmly and find out what the client needs or wants. If appropriate, help the client attain those wants. If not, then clearly state other more appropriate options from which the client might choose.

Be assertive and confident but also genuine and empathetic. Allow ample personal space between yourself and the client, continually assess for personal safety, and be certain that you have other nursing or security staff close by. Use medications for chemical restraint only when absolutely necessary and when less restrictive methods have been tried without success.

Nursing Goals

Relieving acute stress involves helping the client process the traumatic event, emotionally and cognitively, and improve coping mechanisms. Ensuring the client's safety in a supportive environment always takes precedence. When a client feels safe, his or her anxiety should diminish, enabling the person to engage with the nurse, reflect on the experience, and explore alternative, more adaptive responses.

Suicide

- Suicide precautions – When suicide risk is high, toxic substances and sharp objects should be removed from the client's environment. No belts, neckties, or other articles of clothing that could be used for self-destruction should be worn, and the client should be monitored closely, one to one. Communicate a caring presence and provide reassurance that you will help the client stay safe. Some clients will agree to a no self-harm contract, which is one way of helping clients begin to re-establish personal control. Encourage the client to express feelings and discuss ways for the client to manage those feelings and keep safe. If at all possible, provide for continuity of care as establishing an emotional bond with someone could be a turning point toward suicide prevention.

Violence

With violent clients, nurses must be hypervigilant of their own safety. A rule of thumb is to stay between the client and a door for escape. Call security to assist with violent episodes. Some behavioural strategies used with aggressive clients include the following:

Setting Limits: Nurses define for the client acceptable behaviour patterns and the consequences of unacceptable behaviour. All staff must agree to monitor the behaviour and apply the agreed-upon consequences consistently.

Behaviour Contracts: The nurse and client negotiate and sign a contract outlining rewards for acceptable behaviour and the consequences of unacceptable behaviour.

Time-Outs: Socially unacceptable behaviour results in a time-out, removing the client from an overstimulating environment to a quiet area or the client's room. If the client agrees to this and goes voluntarily when reminded by the nurse, it is not considered to be the same as seclusion.

Token Economy: Clients can earn tokens or points that they can barter for privileges. They lose tokens for unacceptable behaviour.

Teaching and Learning

Here are some ideas for teaching clients about anger and how it can be used appropriately.

- Focus on nonverbal expressions of anger, role-playing, and talking about angry feelings in the client's own words, allowing the client to demonstrate angry body language and facial expressions.
- Talk about situations where it is okay to feel angry and role-play those types of situations.
- Help clients identify real situations that cause anger. Role-play confronting the object or person that generates the anger. Give feedback on appropriate verbal and nonverbal responses.
- Give permission for the client to confront the real object of his or her anger. Provide a supportive presence if needed and debrief with the client afterward.

Families and Violence

Interpersonal violence and abuse in family contexts can affect all generations: children, intimate partners, and older adults. Each form of abuse is an instance of the abuser exerting control or power over the abused person (Alvarez, 2002).

- Forms of family abuse include physical abuse or neglect, forced sexual activity (including rape), psychological intimidation and threats, emotional maltreatment, and financial exploitation.
- Substance abuse – Alcohol and drug abuse often underlie violence and neglect within families.
- Nurses are ethically and legally responsible for reporting evidence of all types of family abuse to the appropriate legal authorities.

Intimate-Partner Abuse

- "The cycle of violence" refers to the pattern of four phases of intimate-partner violence. During phase one, tension builds. Phase two is the actual incident of battering. The couple reconciles in phase three, the honeymoon phase. The perpetrator vows that it will not happen again, with gifts and kindnesses to the victim as proof of love. Then the cycle begins again.
- Intimate-partner abuse is the most common form of family violence. Battered spouses tend to return and reconcile with their violent partner three times before they are able to leave permanently. Feminist theory suggests that patriarchy and sexual inequality make it difficult for women to maintain themselves independently, thus explaining the return to a dangerous home situation.
- Abusive partners are frequently pathologically jealous and prone to blame others for their own inadequacies.
- Victims suffer low self-esteem and feelings of helplessness and hopelessness and need help to make future plans. Nurses can teach victims of family

violence strategies for ensuring their safety. A safety plan for victims of domestic violence may include the following:

- Posting emergency numbers and teaching children to call 9-1-1
- Making a plan for at least two different places the client can go to be safe and storing extra clothes, cash, and copies of important documents there, even if the client hopes that the violence is over
- Providing a neighbour with a signal that will indicate he or she should call police
- If there is a restraining order, keeping it with the client at all times and giving a copy to a child's school or day care
- Connecting with a support group and with old friends

Child Abuse

- Abusive parents often were abused as children. They have poor impulse control and ineffective coping and parenting skills.
- Sexual abuse may be suspected when children display the following dysfunctional behaviour patterns: excessive aggression, sexual activity that is inappropriate for their developmental stage, social withdrawal, poor performance at school, sleep disturbances, and low self-esteem.

See Chapter 10, pages 468–470, for more details on pediatric abuse.

Elder Abuse

Older adults are prone to abuse as their physical and/or mental health deteriorates and they become dependent on their relatives. The types of elder abuse are listed below (Fishwick, Parker, & Campbell, 2005):

- Violation of individual rights
- Exploitation
- Physical abuse
- Psychological neglect and abuse
- Physical neglect

Caregiver stress can lead to abuse in families that are dysfunctional in other ways or when caregivers are also at risk for mental health issues. Some of the types of abuse are harder to pinpoint but are prevalent and must be reported to the appropriate legal authorities.

Recognizing Signs of Family Violence

Although the guidelines below refer specifically to clients who present in the emergency department, community nurses often will discover evidence of abuse during home visits or in ambulatory settings such as public health clinics. In any setting, signs of family stress could manifest as emotional and behavioural problems, including increased aggression, inability

to sleep, trouble in school, or being accident-prone. Pregnancy is a particularly vulnerable time for women. Abuse may be suspected when people present to the emergency department with internal injuries, multiple contusions (especially facial or head and neck), burns (especially from cigarettes) and scalds, perforated eardrums, or miscarriage. There is often evidence of bruising at various stages of healing and a history of multiple emergency department or clinic visits with diffuse and varied complaints. Psychological trauma, anxiety, depression, and severe stress may be evident, and often the explanations fall short of matching the extent or seriousness of the injury. The type of abuse or neglect may be physical, sexual, emotional, or even financial (Smith-DiJulio, 2002b).

Interviewing Victims of Violence

Feelings of shame, fear, and worries of how to survive outside the family may make it difficult for victims of abuse to admit truthfully to the causes of their injuries. A health care professional who suspects maltreatment of a client is obligated to report it but also to validate the concerns to the greatest extent possible. Interview the client in a nonthreatening way in private; convey concern and understanding; reassure the victim that he or she is not at fault; and encourage the client to tell the story by using open-ended questions that encourage a description of events. Some suggested questions are as follows (Smith-DiJulio, 2002b):

- Who looks after you? (In the case of dependent children and adults.)
- What does that person do when you do something wrong?
- How do you and your partner (or caregiver) settle arguments or differences of opinion?
- What arrangements do you have for child care when you are at work or when you go out?
- When the baby cries a lot, what do you do to get him or her to stop?
- What sorts of behaviour by your child do you find most upsetting?

If the answers confirm your suspicions, you should inform the client that you plan to make a referral to social services or the police, or both.

REFERENCES

Alvarez, C. (2002). Anger and aggression. In E. M. Varcarolis (Ed.), *Foundations of psychiatric mental health nursing* (4th ed., pp. 665–684). New York: Saunders.

Alzheimer's Society of Canada. (2007). *People with Alzheimer's disease and related dementias.* Toronto: Author. Retrieved January 19, 2013, from http://www.alzheimer.ca/english/disease/stats-people.htm

American Psychiatric Association. (2000). *Diagnostic and statistical manual of mental disorders* (4th ed. text revision). Washington, DC: Author.

Canadian Institute for Health Information. (2002). *A report on mental illnesses in Canada*. Retrieved January 19, 2013, from http://secure.cihi.ca/cihiweb/en/downloads/reports_mental_illness_e.pdf

Canadian Institute for Health Information. (2007). *Improving the health of Canadians: Mental health and homelessness*. Ottawa: Author. Retrieved January 19, 2013, from https://secure.cihi.ca/estore/productFamily.htm?pf=PFC871&locale=en&lang=en&mediatype=0

Canadian Nurses Association. (2008). *Code of ethics for Canadian nurses*. Ottawa: Author.

Carson, R. C., Butcher, J. N., & Mineka, S. (2000). *Abnormal psychology and modern life* (11th ed.). Upper Saddle River, NJ: Pearson Education.

Dyehouse, J. M., & Sommers, M. S. (1998). Brief intervention after alcohol-related injuries. *Nursing Clinics of North America, 33*(1), 93–104.

Eliopoulos, C. (2000). Cognitive disorders. In V. B. Carson (Ed.), *Mental health nursing: The nurse-patient journey* (2nd ed., pp. 924–972). Philadelphia: Saunders.

Fishwick, N., Parker, B., & Campbell, J. C. (2005). Care of survivors of abuse & violence. In G. W. Stuart & M. T. Laraia (Eds.), *Principles and practice of psychiatric nursing* (8th ed., pp. 798–815). St. Louis: Elsevier.

Frisch, N. C., & Frisch, L. E. (2006). *Psychiatric mental health nursing* (3rd ed.). Clifton Park, NY: Delmar Learning.

Gabard, G. O. (2001). *Treatment of psychiatric disorders* (3rd ed.). Washington, DC: American Psychiatric Publishing, Inc.

Gray, J. E., Shone, M. A., & Liddle, P. F. (2000). *Canadian mental health law and policy*. Toronto: Butterworths.

Hall, G. R. (1994). Caring for people with Alzheimer's disease using the conceptual model of progressively lowered stress threshold in the clinical setting. *Nursing Clinics of North America, 29*(1), 129-141.

Health Canada. (1994). *Suicide in Canada: Update of the report of the Task Force on Suicide in Canada* (H39-107/1995E). Ottawa: Health Programs & Services Branch.

Holt, J. (1993). How to help confused patients. *American Journal of Nursing, 93*(8), 32.

Henry, M. (2002). Descending into delirium: Confusion, isolation, forgetfulness, lethargy. *American Journal of Nursing, 102*(3), 49.

Laraia, M. T. (2005a). Biological context of psychiatric nursing care. In G. W. Stuart & M. T. Laraia (Eds.), *Principles and practice of psychiatric nursing* (8th ed.). St. Louis: Mosby.

Laraia, M. T. (2005b). Pharmacology. In G. W. Stuart & M. T. Laraia (Eds.), *Principles and practice of psychiatric nursing* (8th ed.). St. Louis: Mosby.

Laraia, M. T., & Jefferson, L. V. (2005). Chemically medicated responses and substance-related disorders. In G. W. Stuart & M. T. Laraia (Eds.), *Principles and practice of psychiatric nursing* (8th ed.). St. Louis: Mosby.

Limandri, B., & Boyd, M. (2005). Personality and impulse-control disorders. In M. Boyd (Ed.), *Psychiatric nursing: Contemporary practice* (3rd ed., pp. 420–469). Philadelphia: Lippincott, Williams, & Wilkins.

Moller, M. D. (2005). Neurobiological responses and schizophrenia and psychotic disorders. In G. W. Stuart & M. T. Laraia (Eds.), *Principles and practice of psychiatric nursing* (8th ed., pp. 386–422). St. Louis: Mosby.

Pauly, B., Goldstone, I., McCall, J., Gold, F., & Payne, S. (2007). The ethical, legal & social context of harm reduction. *Canadian Nurse, 103*(8), 19–23.

Poorman, S. G. (2005). Sexual responses and sexual disorders. In G. W. Stuart & M. T. Laraia (Eds.), *Principles and practice of psychiatric nursing* (8th ed., pp. 528–559). St. Louis: Elsevier.

Smith-DiJulio, K. (2002a). Care of the chemically impaired. In E. M. Varcarolis (Ed.), *Foundations of psychiatric mental health nursing* (4th ed., pp. 745–785). New York: Saunders.

Smith-DiJulio, K. (2002b). Family violence. In E. M. Varcarolis (Ed.), *Foundations of psychiatric mental health nursing* (4th ed., pp. 689–718). New York: Saunders.

Stuart, G. W. (2005a). Cognitive behavioral treatment strategies. In G. W. Stuart & M. Laraia (Eds.), *Principles and practice of psychiatric nursing* (8th ed., pp. 654–667). St. Louis: Elsevier.

Stuart, G. W. (2005b). Psychophysiological responses and somatoform and sleep disorders. In G. W. Stuart & M. T. Laraia (Eds.), *Principles and practice of psychiatric nursing* (8th ed., pp. 285–302). St. Louis: Elsevier.

Stuart, G. W. (2005c). Therapeutic nurse-patient relationship. In G. W. Stuart & M. T. Laraia (Eds.), *Principles and practice of psychiatric nursing* (8th ed., pp. 15-49). St. Louis: Mosby.

Stuart, G. W. (2009). *Principles and practice of psychiatric nursing* (9th ed.). St. Louis: Mosby.

Tjepkema, M. (2004). Alcohol and illicit drug dependence. *Supplement to Health Reports, 15*, 9–19. Ottawa: Statistics Canada.

Townsend, M. C. (2006). *Psychiatric mental health nursing: Concepts of care in evidence-based practice* (5th ed.). Philadelphia: F. A. Davis.

Varcarolis, E. M. (2002a). Cognitive disorders. In E. M. Varcarolis (Ed.), *Foundations of psychiatric mental health nursing* (4th ed., pp. 573–609). New York: Saunders.

Varcarolis, E. M. (2002b). Glossary. In E. M. Varcarolis (Ed.), *Foundations of psychiatric mental health nursing* (4th ed.). New York: Saunders.

Varcarolis, E. M. (2002c). Personality disorders. In E. M. Varcarolis (Ed.), *Foundations of psychiatric mental health nursing* (4th ed., pp. 373–409). New York: Saunders.

Varcarolis, E. M. (2002d). Schizophrenia and other psychotic disorders. In E. M. Varcarolis (Ed.), *Foundations of psychiatric mental health nursing* (4th ed., pp. 523-571). New York: Saunders.

Varcarolis, E. M. (2002e). Somatoform & dissociative disorders. In E. M. Varcarolis (Ed.), *Foundations of psychiatric mental health nursing* (4th ed., pp. 341-371). New York: Saunders.

Varcarolis, E. M., & Halter, M. J. (2010). *Foundations of psychiatric mental health nursing: A clinical approach* (6th ed.). St. Louis: Saunders.

White, J. H. (2005). Eating disorders. In M. A. Boyd (Ed.), *Psychiatric nursing: Contemporary practice* (3rd ed., pp. 492–523). Philadelphia: Lippincott Williams & Wilkins.

BIBLIOGRAPHY

Townsend, M. C. (2005). *Essentials of mental health nursing* (3rd ed.). Philadelphia: F. A. Davis.

Videbeck, S. L. (2004). *Psychiatric mental health nursing* (2nd ed.). Philadelphia: Lippincott.

WEB SITES

Canadian Coalition of Alternative Mental Health Resources (http://www.ccamhr.ca): This site contains resources about mental health services and organizations, including alternative treatment programs. It has a section for mental health news and policy research.

Canadian Mental Health Association (http://www.cmha.ca/bins/index.asp): This Web page provides information on many specific mental health conditions and explores ways in which to promote good mental health. This organization has offices and mental health services across Canada. The site hosts a variety of discussion groups about different mental health topics and a forum for sharing knowledge and giving support.

EMentalHealth.ca (http://www.ementalhealth.ca/site/ontario/index.php?m=1&ID=26): This Canadian mental health Web site provides a resource directory and event calendar with information relevant to both consumers and care providers. The site is an anonymous and confidential source of mental health information.

Mental Health Commission of Canada (http://www.mentalhealthcommission.ca/english/pages/default.aspx): This organization's goal is to integrate mental health services in Canada. The site follows the progress of the commission in terms of its projects and policies.

mindyourmind.ca (http://mindyourmind.ca): An innovative Canadian site with resources for youth about mental health disorders and managing stress and crises. It has a blog, a section for personal stories, a book list, and links.

Mood Disorders Society of Canada (http://www.mooddisorderscanada.ca): The site describes different mood and anxiety disorders and their diagnosis and treatment. It is primarily designed for clients and their families and links to resources that may be useful for health care professionals.

Public Health Agency of Canada: Mental Health Problems and Disorders (http://www.phac-aspc.gc.ca/mh-sm/problems-eng.php): This Health Canada site deals with mental health problems in the Canadian population, mental health services, and related policy. It provides documents that cover many issues relevant to both consumers and service providers.

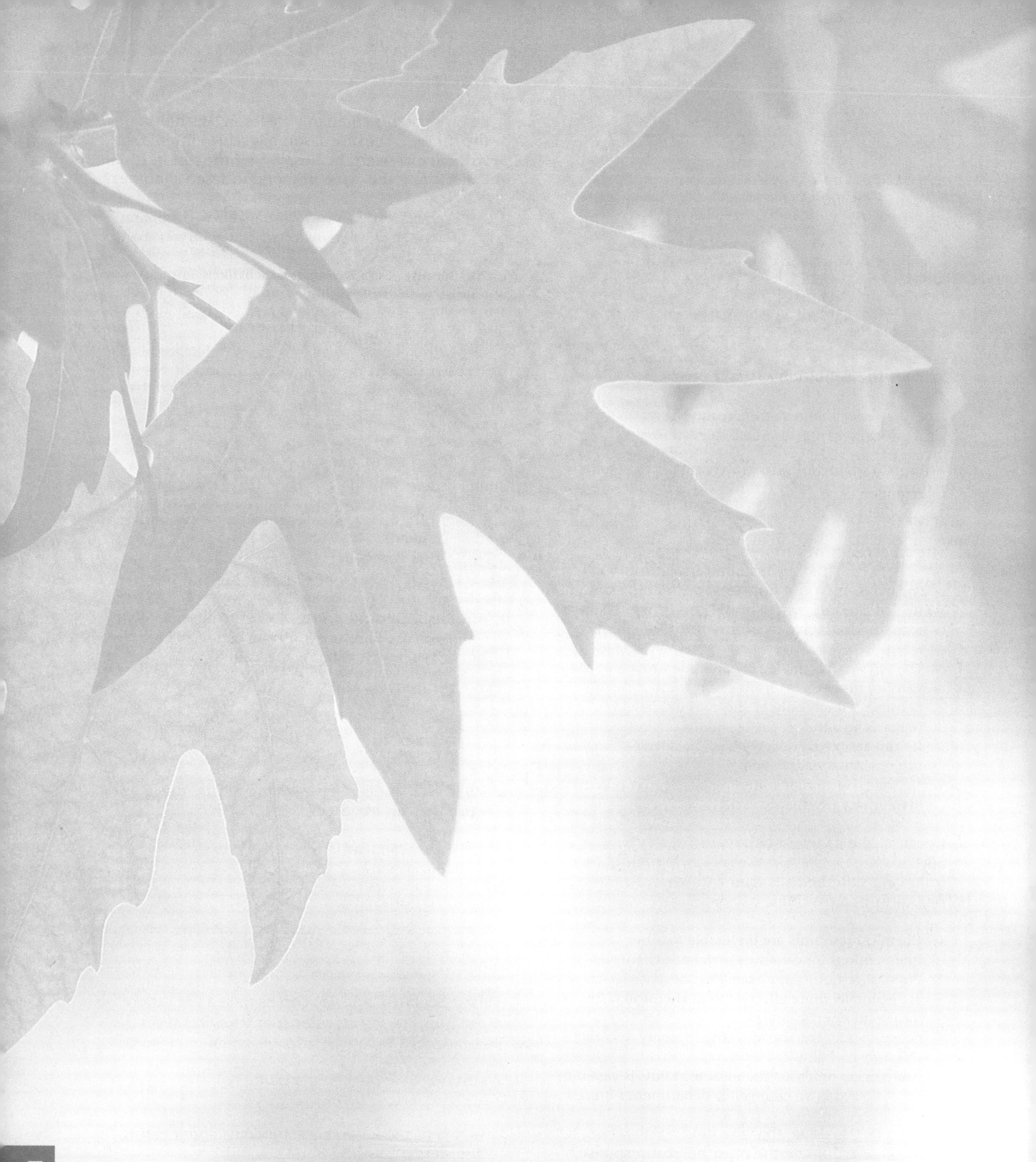

CHAPTER 11

Practice Questions

Case 1

Jason Beames, age 17 years, was brought to the emergency department by the police. His mother called the police after Jason violently attacked his father with no provocation. Jason is admitted to the psychiatric unit for investigation of his psychosis, with a provisional diagnosis of schizophrenia.

Questions 1–5 refer to this case.

1. What is the definition of psychosis?

   1. A psychological break from reality
   2. A group of mental disorders characterized by various anxiety symptoms
   3. A disturbance of consciousness and change in cognition
   4. Another term for schizophrenia

2. The emergency department physician completes a certificate designating Jason an involuntary client because Jason would not consent to admission. Which of the following should the nurse tell Jason concerning his rights as an involuntary client?

   1. The physician is not legally permitted to admit him without his consent
   2. Because Jason is only 17, he does not have the same rights as an adult
   3. He can apply to a review board for a legal ruling on his involuntary admission
   4. He has no legal rights since he has been certified as an involuntary psychiatric client

3. Because of his violent behaviour, Jason is administered a chemical restraint. Which of the following statements is true with regard to using restraints in a psychiatric setting?

   1. Chemical restraints are preferable to other interventions for calming a psychotic client
   2. Physical restraints, for example, two-point restraints, are generally more effective than chemical restraints for psychotic episodes
   3. Guidelines for the use of restraints apply to both chemical and physical restraints
   4. A physician order for chemical restraints is generally not required in an emergency department setting

4. Jason tells the nurse that the voices are yelling at him. What would be the most helpful response?

   1. "I don't hear the voices that you hear."
   2. "What are the people yelling at you?"
   3. "You realize there are really no voices yelling at you."
   4. "Why do you think you are hearing voices?"

5. Jason's parents come to visit Jason. His mother asks the nurse if, because Jason has schizophrenia, he will have to be in the hospital for the rest of his life. What might the nurse respond to Jason's mother?

   1. "I can refer you to the local Canadian Schizophrenia Society. They will provide education for you about Jason's disease."
   2. "Because Jason is young, he will likely not have any further serious psychotic episodes."
   3. "I don't really know. We will have to wait to see how he responds to his medications."
   4. "Schizophrenia is a lifelong disorder, but antipsychotic medications allow most people to live and be treated outside the hospital."

Case 2

Marty Steele, age 42, has been diagnosed with borderline personality disorder. He is admitted to a psychiatric unit.

Questions 6 and 7 refer to this case.

6. Mr. Steele tells the nurse, Jeremy, that one of the other nurses, Sarah, is lazy and is not as good a nurse as Jeremy. What is this called?

   1. Narcissistic behaviour
   2. Schizoid behaviour
   3. Splitting behaviour
   4. Dependent behaviour

7. What is the priority assessment for the nurse to conduct with Mr. Steele?

   1. Potential for harm to himself or others
   2. Hallucinations
   3. History of child abuse
   4. Sexual orientation

Case 3

Tiffany Scolfield, age 15, comes to see the school nurse because she stopped menstruating several months ago. The nurse suspects an eating disorder.

Questions 8–12 refer to this case.

8. Which of the following statements about eating disorders is true?

   1. People can die from anorexia but not from bulimia
   2. Men can suffer from bulimia but not from anorexia
   3. Women who recover from anorexia often develop bulimia later
   4. People with bulimia deny feelings of hunger

9. The nurse assesses Tiffany for medical complications associated with her eating disorder. Which of the following physical assessments would it be most important to perform while Tiffany was in her office?

   1. Complete skin survey for breakdown
   2. Abdominal palpation for constipation
   3. Oral examination for dental caries
   4. Blood pressure monitoring for hypotension

10. Tiffany talks to the nurse about her feelings. The nurse uses clarification as a form of therapeutic communication. Which of the following responses is an example of clarification?

    1. "I'm not sure what you mean. Could you tell me about that again?"
    2. "Can you tell me more about what is bothering you?"
    3. "What do you think is causing you to feel this way?"
    4. "You've mentioned many things. Let's go back to how eating makes you feel."

11. The nurse arranges for Tiffany to come to the health office at regular intervals to monitor her weight. What would the nurse be aware of regarding the process of weighing Tiffany?

    1. Tiffany may drink excessive fluids to increase her recorded weight
    2. She will probably refuse to be weighed
    3. Tiffany should be weighed wearing her street clothes and shoes
    4. The nurse must inform Tiffany's parents about the monitoring of her weight

12. Tiffany's weight decreases, and she is admitted to an eating disorders unit at a local pediatric hospital. What should be included in her care plan?

    1. Large meals at frequent intervals to improve her nutritional status
    2. Accurate input and output to monitor fluid status
    3. Leisurely meals to promote decreased stress while eating
    4. Segregation from other adolescents with eating disorders

Case 4

Nandini Balkan, age 48, is admitted to an inpatient psychiatric facility due to acute depression with suicidal ideation.

Questions 13–15 refer to this case.

13. With clients who have suicidal ideation, when is the most likely time for them to act on their suicidal impulses?

    1. On admission to a psychiatric facility
    2. On discharge from a psychiatric facility
    3. When symptoms of the depression are most severe
    4. As the symptoms and mood begin to improve

14. The nurse finds Ms. Balkan curled in a fetal position, crying. Through her tears, she says to the nurse, "I really can't go on. I just want to end it all. Please, won't you help me die?" What is the most appropriate response by the nurse?

    1. "I am sorry you are feeling so badly today. Perhaps you will feel better tomorrow."
    2. "I see that you are terribly unhappy today. But you know I cannot help you to die."
    3. "You are feeling very badly today. Would you like to tell me about it?"
    4. "This feeling is just temporary. Why would you want to die?"

15. Ms. Balkan is prescribed fluoxetine hydrochloride (Prozac). The nurse would advise Ms. Balkan of which of the following about this medication?

    1. She will likely feel better in about four weeks
    2. There is increased risk of suicide after therapy is well established
    3. Anxiety and nervousness will likely decrease in about two weeks
    4. St. John's wort, a herbal preparation, helps improve the therapeutic effect of Prozac

INDEPENDENT QUESTIONS

Questions 16–25 do not refer to a particular case.

16. Mr. Fraser is receiving high doses of haloperidol (Haldol). What adverse effects would require the nurse to consult with the physician about stopping the drug?

    1. Mr. Fraser tells the nurse he feels sleepy
    2. The nurse notices a yellow tinge to Mr. Fraser's skin and eye conjunctiva
    3. Mr. Fraser feels dizzy when he stands
    4. The nurse observes extrapyramidal symptoms in Mr. Fraser

17. Which of the following individuals are at the highest risk of suicide?

    1. Mrs. Hardacre, age 42, who has a history of alcohol abuse
    2. Mrs. Blatchfor, age 49, who is distressed because her children have moved away from home
    3. Mr. Tyrell, age 19, who is upset that his girlfriend has broken off their relationship
    4. Mr. Grimes, age 82, who is lonely after the death of his wife

18. A newly graduated nurse obtains employment at a psychiatric outpatient clinic. A young client in distress confides to the nurse that he has a gender identity disorder. He feels he is a female trapped in the body of a man. What is the most effective action taken by the nurse?

1. Provide him with relaxation exercises to decrease the anxiety associated with his distress.
2. Refer him to a qualified sexual therapist.
3. Enroll him in the clinic's sexual disorders psychotherapy group.
4. Perform a complete physical examination to determine any contributing physical problems.

19. Echolalia is often seen in clients with schizophrenia and autism. Which of the following is an example of echolalia?

1. Nurse: "Are you ready to eat?" Client: "Ready to eat, ready to eat, ready to eat."
2. Nurse: "Your family is in the waiting room." Client: "Have to go, I must go, must go, ready, set, go."
3. Client: "I went to bed, and I read, who should heart, be my part."
4. Client: "I live at . . . . I can't think of my address."

20. Which form of substance abuse is most common in Canada?

1. Narcotics
2. Alcohol
3. Marijuana
4. Inhalants

21. Which of the following is an important consideration when conducting a culturally sensitive mental health assessment?

1. Nurses must treat clients according to the established beliefs of their specific culture
2. Some cultures are not accepting of mental illnesses among their population
3. Nurses must facilitate verbal expressions of feelings in cultures in which this is not a common practice
4. Regardless of culture, all people react to adverse stressors with similar behaviours

22. The RN is unsure if Henry Picard, age 87, is manifesting symptoms of delirium or dementia. What question might he ask Mr. Picard's family?

1. "Do you think Mr. Picard has Alzheimer's disease?"
2. "How long has Mr. Picard shown confused thinking?"
3. "Do you have any family members with a history of dementia?"
4. "Has Mr. Picard ever been violent?"

23. Alex Carolis has been diagnosed with antisocial personality disorder. Which of the following comments by Mr. Carolis would be most typical of this disorder?

1. "I am feeling very anxious."
2. "I am going to buy myself a new top-of-the-line car today."
3. "I have learned never to cheat on an exam again."
4. "I have a responsibility to care for my younger brother."

24. Chandra Wasson, age 27 years, is an inpatient at a psychiatric facility. Her nurse, Sanjay, age 29 years, accompanies her to a local restaurant for coffee. Is this an appropriate behaviour for Sanjay?

1. It is appropriate if it is part of the care plan
2. It is appropriate if the friendship is mutual and non-sexual
3. It is not appropriate as Ms. Wasson is a client with a mental health diagnosis
4. It is not appropriate as it is never ethical for a registered nurse to be in a social situation with a client

25. An RN is unhappy and stressed with her work situation in a busy emergency department. She manifests these feelings with passive–aggressive behaviour. Which of the following might be an example of the nurse's passive–aggressive behaviour?

1. Yelling at clients
2. Written complaints to the unit manager about the work environment
3. Being chronically late for her shifts
4. Readily agreeing to work overtime

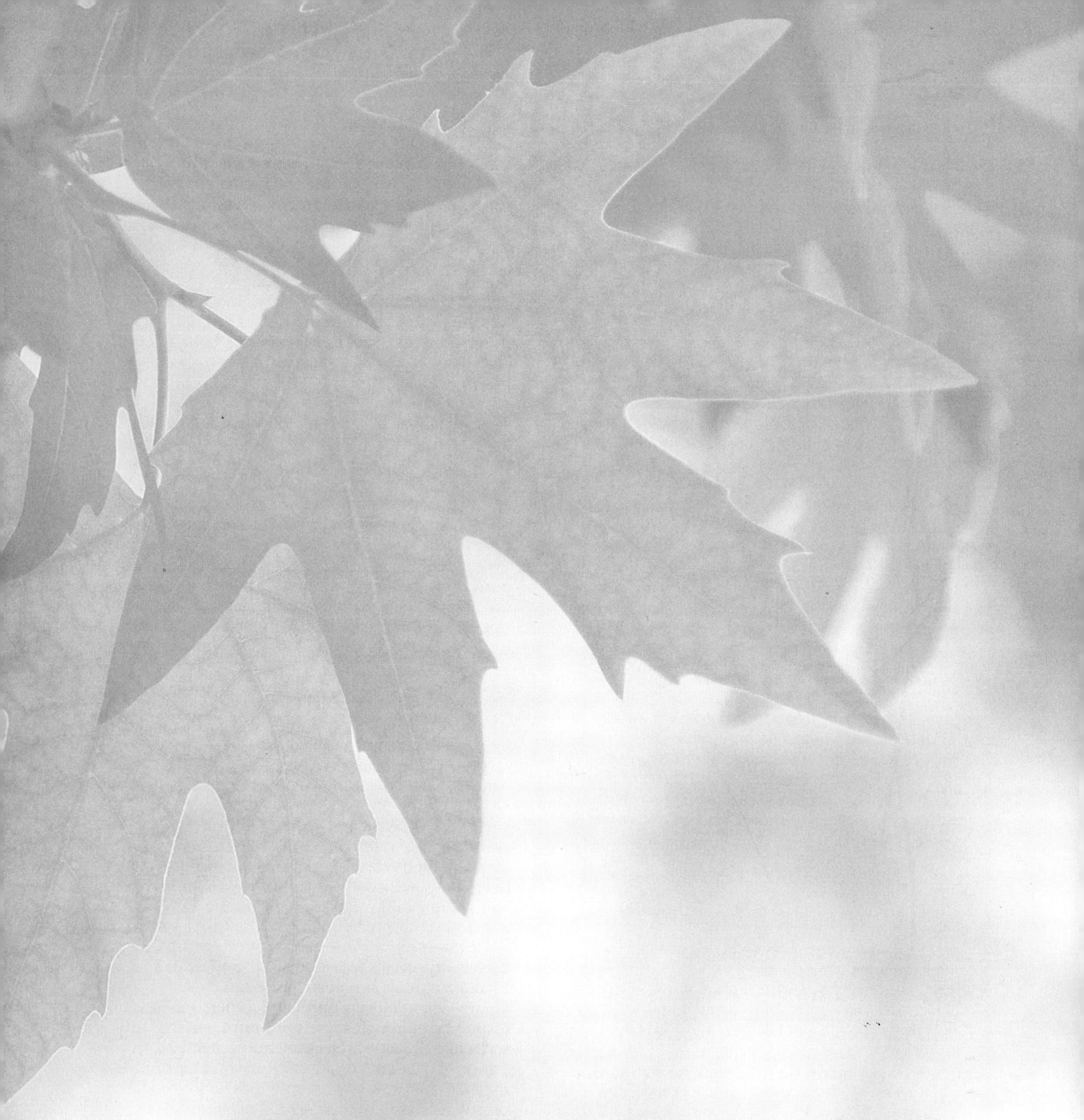

CHAPTER 11

Answers and Rationales for Practice Questions

1.   **C: Changes in Health   T: Knowledge**

1. This is the definition of psychosis.
2. This is the definition of neurosis.
3. This is the definition of delirium.
4. Schizophrenia is a psychotic illness but is not synonymous with psychosis. Psychosis may also occur in manic phases of bipolar disorder, substance abuse, delirium, organic mental disorders, post-traumatic stress disorder, and major depression.

2.   **C: Changes in Health   T: Application**

1. Emergency involuntary admission is permitted when a person is deemed in need of psychiatric treatment, presents a danger to self or others, or is unable to meet his basic needs.
2. Depending on the province or territory, there are different ages for consent. Many have an age of consent that is 16 years or younger. Regardless of his age or the age of consent of the jurisdiction, Jason has rights.
3. Under law, Jason may apply to a review board to review the involuntary admission.
4. Jason does have legal rights.

3.   **C: Changes in Health   T: Application**

1. Quiet seclusion may help some clients. Chemical restraints may not always be preferable.
2. In many cases, physical restraints increase violent behaviour and chemical restraints are preferable.
3. The policy of least restraint and guidelines for use of restraints apply equally to physical and chemical restraints.
4. The setting of an emergency department still requires a physician order for a chemical restraint as it is a medication.

4.   **C: Changes in Health   T: Application**

1. This is an honest and truthful response, which helps identify the voices as a unique experience for Jason but does not involve arguing reality with him.
2. Although it may be useful for the nurse to find out more about the hallucinations, it is not helpful to Jason to pretend to believe in them.
3. It is not helpful to Jason to argue with him about reality. The voices are real to him.
4. Hallucinations are a symptom of psychosis. It is neither helpful nor therapeutic to explore why Jason is hearing voices.

5.   **C: Changes in Health   T: Application**

1. This is a good suggestion but does not answer Jason's mother's question.

2. This may not be true.
3. This is a vague response and implies that the nurse is not competent to provide an answer.
4. This is the most complete and most correct response to Jason's mother's question.

6.   **C: Changes in Health   T: Knowledge**

1. People who exhibit narcissistic behaviour feel superior to everyone else and lack empathy for others. This is evident in narcissistic behaviour disorder.
2. People who exhibit schizoid behaviour, found in schizoid personality disorder, are loners. They display very little emotion and tend to be indifferent to the feelings of others.
3. Mr. Steele displays splitting behaviour, setting one person up against another. It is a type of manipulative behaviour common in people with borderline personality disorder and some other personality disorders.
4. People with dependent personality disorder are very dependent on others. They lack self-confidence and would be unlikely to say anything negative about Sarah or anyone else for fear of losing that person's support and approval.

7.   **C: Changes in Health   T: Application**

1. People with borderline personality disorder are impulsive. Self-injury and suicide threats are common with this disorder. When there are suicidal or homicidal thoughts, ensuring the safety of the client and others is a nurse's first priority.
2. Hallucinations are a sign of psychosis. Borderline personality disorder is not a psychotic illness.
3. While personality disorders may develop from a socially disrupted childhood, the nurse would not probe for such information until he or she is confident that the client is safe and until a relationship has been established.
4. Sexual orientation is unrelated to personality disorders, although some symptoms, such as low self-esteem, fear of rejection, and sensitivity to criticism, that are common in personality disorders may also be present in people if they are confused or not accepting of their sexual orientation.

8.   **C: Changes in Health   T: Application**

1. People with both anorexia and bulimia suffer complications in many body systems. In extreme cases, death can result from cardiac, GI, metabolic, or CNS complications.
2. Although eating disorders are much more common in women than men, men do suffer from both anorexia and bulimia.

3. About half the women with anorexia display bulimic behaviours or develop bulimia later in their lives.

4. People with bulimia may feel intense hunger and binge to satisfy this hunger. Appetite suppressants are sometimes used to help them control the hunger, until new eating patterns have become established.

9.   C: Changes in Health   T: Critical Thinking

1. Skin breakdown may occur secondary to inadequate nutrition but is not as important as blood pressure.

2. While constipation may occur with eating disorders, it is more logical to ask Tiffany about her bowel pattern rather than perform an abdominal palpation.

3. People with eating disorders often develop dental caries. While the nurse may examine Tiffany's mouth, it may not be possible to determine dental caries on inspection. It would be more efficient to refer Tiffany to a dentist or dental hygienist.

4. People with eating disorders often have a lower than normal blood volume, leading to hypotension.

10.   C: Nurse–Client Partnership   T: Application

1. This is an example of clarification. It helps clients clarify their own thoughts and maximizes mutual understanding.

2. This is the therapeutic technique of exploring, which examines experiences more fully.

3. This is reflecting, directing feelings and ideas back to the client.

4. This is focusing, which concentrates attention on a single point.

11.   C: Changes in Health   T: Application

1. Young women with eating disorders, particularly anorexia, may attempt to mask their weight loss by drinking excessive water (water loading) or hiding articles within their clothing prior to weighing.

2. Generally, most young women with anorexia are superficially compliant with weight monitoring.

3. It is more important that Tiffany be weighed wearing the same clothes at each occasion. It is preferable not to wear shoes or clothing where heavy articles may be hidden.

4. Depending on the provincial law, there may be no legal imperative to inform Tiffany's parents. This needs to be discussed between Tiffany and the nurse, and parental involvement should be encouraged.

12.   C: Changes in Health   T: Application

1. People with anorexia are not able to tolerate large meals. They should be offered small meals and frequent nutritious drinks and snacks, paying special attention to their likes and dislikes.

2. The nurse must record intake and output carefully as a measure of adequate hydration. Other indicators to be monitored are skin turgor and colour and moistness of oral mucous membranes.

3. Mealtimes should be time limited. To decrease stress while eating, ensure a pleasant atmosphere and conversation about topics other than food.

4. Adolescents with eating disorders generally respond well to group therapy. In addition, isolating the client provides more opportunities for secretive purging.

13.   C: Changes in Health   T: Application

1. When first admitted to a psychiatric facility, the client will more likely be distracted by and focused on the admission process.

2. People are often pleased about leaving the hospital, believing it is a positive step in their illness.

3. As depression deepens, the client has less motivation and physical energy to follow through on suicidal action.

4. Clients are at high risk for suicide for the first few days following initiation of treatment. Energy levels improve before mood improves. Thus, early in treatment, the client is still severely depressed but may now have the energy necessary to follow through with suicidal thoughts. Following discharge, some clients are more at risk of suicide when they return home to find that the things that caused their depression have not changed.

14.   C: Nurse–Client Partnership   T: Application

1. This is not a therapeutic response. It does not address Ms. Balkan's present feelings, and she may not feel better the next day.

2. This is not a therapeutic response as it does not invite Ms. Balkan to discuss her feelings.

3. This recognizes Ms. Balkan's feelings and invites her to discuss these feelings.

4. This is not therapeutic as it may appear to belittle Ms. Balkan's feelings, and it may not be true that the feeling is temporary.

15.   C: Changes in Health   T: Knowledge

1. Therapeutic effects may take up to four weeks to be achieved.

2. Although there have been reports of an increase in suicide after starting Prozac (fluoxetine hydrochloride), there is not a large body of research

to substantiate this. It is possible that in early treatment, there is an increased risk of suicide due to the fact that the clients are beginning to feel better.

3. Anxiety and nervousness are side effects of Prozac and may increase.
4. St. John's wort may have an additive effect with Prozac and should not be taken.

16.   C: Changes in Health   T: Application

1. This is a side effect that usually disappears after several weeks.
2. The yellow skin and conjunctiva indicate jaundice, which is a sign of liver damage. The drug should be stopped.
3. As in choice 1.
4. Extrapyramidal signs usually indicate that the dose of Haldol should be reduced. The Haldol is not stopped unless the extrapyramidal symptoms persist at the lower dose.

17.   C: Changes in Health   T: Critical Thinking

1. Mrs. Hardacre is at increased risk of suicide due to her alcohol abuse, but she does not have the highest level of risk of the four individuals.
2. Women attempt suicide more often than men, but more men are successful.
3. While men have a higher rate of successful suicide, it is in the 35–50 age group. Mr. Tyrell would be at risk if he had a concrete plan for taking his life.
4. Mr. Grimes is at the highest risk of suicide. There is a higher incidence of suicide than previously thought in the older adult. Older men have a much higher suicide rate than older women.

18.   C: Changes in Health   T: Critical Thinking

1. This is within the scope of practice for this nurse and may be helpful, but it is not the most effective option.
2. Gender identity disorders are complex and beyond the scope of practice of a new nurse. They require the skills of a qualified sexual therapist.
3. This may be advised by the sexual therapist.
4. This is best performed by the sexual therapist or physician.

19.   C: Changes in Health   T: Application

1. Echolalia is the automatic and meaningless repetition of another's words or phrases. It is often used as part of the diagnostic criteria for early autism.
2. This is perseveration, which is the involuntary and pathological persistent repetition of words,

ideas, and phrases regardless of the stimulus or its duration. It occurs in clients with brain damage.
3. This is clang association, a connection between dissociated ideas in speech because of similarity in the sound of words.
4. This is blocking, which occurs with thought disorganization when clients have difficulty articulating a response.

20.   C: Changes in Health   T: Knowledge

1. A very small percentage of Canadians use illegal narcotics, such as heroin and cocaine. A small percentage of people prescribed narcotics for medical treatment of pain become addicted.
2. Alcohol is the most common type of substance abuse in Canada. In a 2002 study, 35% of adults reported at least one episode of heavy drinking during the prior year, with the highest percentage (60%) occurring in the 20–24 age group.
3. Cannabis or marijuana is used by approximately 10% of Canadians.
4. Inhalants are hallucinogenic drugs. Altogether, 2.4% of Canadians abuse drugs such as cocaine, ecstasy, heroin, speed, and solvents (inhalants).

21.   C: Changes in Health   T: Application

1. While the nurse needs to be educated about the client's culture and provide culturally competent care, all clients should first be treated as individuals.
2. In some cultures, mental health disorders are considered shameful or frightening.
3. In some cultures, a discussion of feelings is neither acceptable nor comfortable. The nurse must interview in accordance with the comfort level of the client.
4. Manifestations of stress may vary from one culture to another.

22.   C: Changes in Health   T: Application

1. It is not likely that Mr. Picard's family will be able to distinguish between dementia and delirium. This question will not elicit the most important information.
2. Delirium tends to be of short duration and may be triggered by a specific condition. Dementia is a progressive cognitive disorder, occurring gradually over a period of time.
3. This may be an important question if it is determined that Mr. Picard has dementia.
4. Violent behaviour does not help distinguish between delirium and dementia.

23. **C: Changes in Health   T: Application**

1. People with antisocial personality disorder rarely feel anxious.
2. People with antisocial personality disorder tend to be impulsive with poor self-control.
3. People with this disorder tend not to learn from past mistakes or from punishment.
4. People with this disorder are generally self-centred and do not display responsibility toward others.

24. **C: Changes in Health   T: Application**

1. There are situations where the therapeutic plan includes monitoring and assistance in a social situation. If the outing is part of the agreed-upon care plan, it is appropriate. Sanjay must take care to keep the outing strictly professional.
2. It is not appropriate for a registered nurse to have a social relationship with a mental health client.

3. It is appropriate if it is decided upon by the health care team and is part of the care plan.
4. As in choice 3.

25. **C: Changes in Health   T: Application**

1. This is aggressive behaviour.
2. This is focused, positive behaviour in response to stress.
3. A feature of passive–aggressive behaviour is resistance to meeting the demands of others. Instead of voicing her unhappiness and stress, and taking positive steps to correct the situation, the nurse responds passive–aggressively by arriving late for work.
4. This is passive behaviour.

Practice Exam
Book One

Introduction to Practice Exams

The following practice examinations are designed to be similar to those you will encounter in the Canadian Registered Nurse Examination (CRNE). The exam is organized into two books that contain 130 multiple-choice questions each, for a total of 260 questions. You may want to write the practice exam in a group with fellow students to help replicate an actual exam situation.

INSTRUCTIONS

Read each question carefully and then choose the answer that you think is the best of the four options presented. If you cannot decide on an answer to a question, proceed to the next one and return to this question later if you have time. Try to answer all the questions. Marks are not subtracted for wrong answers. If you are unsure of an answer, it will be to your advantage to guess. Allow yourself three hours for each book.

When you have completed both practice exam books, tally your scores and calculate your percentage for the total examination. See Chapter 2 for more details on test-taking skills.

PRACTICE EXAM – BOOK ONE

CASE QUESTIONS

Case 1

Nada Wasson delivered a healthy, 3600-g baby boy, Sandu, a week ago. She attends the newborn infant clinic at her local hospital, where the nurse examines Sandu.

Questions 1–5 refer to this case.

1. The nurse takes Sandu's vital signs. Which of the following would be normal for a 1-week-old infant?

   1. Heart rate 100, respirations 26, blood pressure 44 mm Hg systolic
   2. Heart rate 165, respirations 65, blood pressure 94 mm Hg systolic
   3. Heart rate 140, respirations 40, blood pressure 70 mm Hg systolic
   4. Heart rate 130, respirations 32, blood pressure 100 mm Hg systolic

2. The nurse tests Sandu's Babinski reflex. What is the expected response by Sandu to the Babinski test?

   1. Dorsiflexion of the big toe
   2. Flexion and extension of the leg
   3. Flexion of the fingers
   4. Extension and adduction of extremities

3. The nurse obtains a weight of 3450 g for Sandu. Mrs. Wasson is concerned about the weight loss, telling the nurse that she is probably not producing enough milk. What would be the best response by the nurse?

   1. "This weight loss is normal in the first week. Continue breastfeeding at frequent intervals."
   2. "Although most newborns lose weight in the first week, you should probably supplement him with formula for the next few days."
   3. "This is not a significant weight loss, so don't be concerned."
   4. "To prevent further weight loss, you can increase your milk supply by drinking more liquids during the day."

4. Mrs. Wasson complains that her nipples are sore. What should the nurse suggest for care of the breasts?

   1. Air her nipples as much as possible
   2. Use a lanolin-based cream after every feeding
   3. Use plastic-lined breast pads
   4. Begin nursing with the breast that is most painful

5. Mrs. Wasson plans to express breast milk for use when she has a babysitter. She asks the nurse how she should instruct the babysitter to warm the bottle. What should be the nurse's response?

   1. Place the bottle in a pot of water and heat slowly on top of the stove
   2. Place the bottle in a microwave oven and heat at a low temperature
   3. Place the bottle in a bowl of lukewarm water
   4. Warming is not necessary as the bottle can be used directly from the refrigerator

Case 2

Edgar is a 14-year-old boy who was diagnosed with type 1 diabetes at age 4 years. His blood sugar control has been poorly maintained for the past two months. It is suspected that the lack of control is related to an adolescent growth spurt and possible poor compliance with blood glucose monitoring, nutrition, and insulin administration. Edgar has been admitted to a short-stay unit in hospital for stabilization.

Questions 6–10 refer to this case.

6. When Edgar was diagnosed at age 4, he exhibited the cardinal symptoms of the three "polys." What are these manifestations?

1. Polycythemia, polyuria, polymyositis
2. Polydipsia, polyelectrolyte, polyneuropathy
3. Polyopia, polyarthritis, polyphagia
4. Polyphagia, polydipsia, polyuria

7. The nurse reviews insulin action, dosage, and administration with Edgar. What is the optimum insulin regimen for most children with diabetes?

1. Twice-daily injections of rapid-acting and intermediate-acting insulins
2. Multiple daily injections of rapid- and long-acting insulins
3. Total dosage and percentage of regular- to intermediate-acting insulins determined individually
4. Ratio and dose determined by weight in kilograms

8. Edgar admits to the nurse he has been experimenting with alcohol and binge drinking on the weekends. He states that his parents are "heavy drinkers" and are not aware of his behaviour. What is the most critical issue concerning Edgar's drinking of alcohol?

1. Alcohol causes a rise in blood sugar, leading to a sustained period of hyperglycemia
2. Binge drinking can lead to inappropriate and dangerous behaviour
3. Alcohol causes a drop in blood sugar that could lead to severe hypoglycemia
4. Because Edgar's parents are "heavy drinkers," he is more likely to develop a dependency on alcohol

9. Edgar injects seven units of regular (Humulin R) insulin at 1600 hours. When should the nurse caution him to be alert for a possible hypoglycemic episode?

1. 1830 hours
2. 2030 hours
3. 2230 hours
4. 2400 hours

10. The nurse assesses that Edgar has been noncompliant with his diabetes management. What is the most appropriate nursing action to address Edgar's noncompliance?

1. Ask Edgar's parents to supervise him more closely
2. Provide education to Edgar and his family about the potential dangers of poorly controlled diabetes
3. In private, explore Edgar's feelings about diabetes and the treatment regimen
4. Suggest to Edgar that he join an adolescent diabetes support group

Case 3

A registered nurse works on an orthopedic surgery unit of a hospital. Many of the clients are older adults with increased risk for hospital-acquired, infections.

Questions 11–15 refer to this case.

11. Which of the following is the most important step for the nurse to protect her clients from hospital-acquired infections?

1. Identify clients who are at risk
2. Review hygiene practices with all clients
3. Restrict visitors
4. Lobby for the use of alcohol-based hand sanitizers

12. Mr. Carolis, age 81, has just had a total hip replacement. He has a history of poor nutrition. Postoperatively, he has an in-dwelling urinary catheter. Which of these factors puts Mr. Carolis most at risk for developing an infection?

1. Age
2. Poor nutrition
3. Surgery
4. In-dwelling urinary catheter

13. Mr. Carolis develops manifestations of an infection. Which of the following abnormal findings indicates that Mr. Carolis may have an infection?

1. Leukocytosis
2. Neutropenia
3. Thrombocytosis
4. Leukopenia

14. Mr. Carolis is ordered to have blood and urine cultures and then is started on intravenous antibiotics. What action should the nurse take with regard to the specimen collection and antibiotic administration?

1. Commence the antibiotics as soon as the medication is received from the pharmacy department
2. Ask the physician for the correct order for specimen collection and medication administration
3. Withdraw blood for the culture, take the urine sample from the in-dwelling catheter, and then commence the medication
4. Perform the blood culture, administer the antibiotics, and then collect the urine sample from the urinary collection bag

15. The nurse discovers that she has administered twice the ordered dose of a medication to Mr. Carolis. What is the most important initial action for the nurse to perform?

1. Complete an incident report
2. Notify the ordering physician
3. Assess Mr. Carolis for adverse effects of the overdose
4. Report the error to the nurse administrator

Case 4

Mr. Kassam has chronic renal failure, secondary to type 2 diabetes. He has been attending an outpatient renal clinic for several years, and, recently, his condition has deteriorated. The registered nurse sees Mr. Kassam in the clinic.

Questions 16–21 refer to this case.

16. Which of the following laboratory blood test results would be of most concern to the nurse?

1. Potassium: 7 mmol/L
2. pH: 7.37
3. Sodium: 142 mmol/L
4. Blood urea nitrogen (BUN): 6.8 mmol/L

17. Mr. Kassam is on erythropoietin therapy. What is the rationale for this therapy?

1. To treat the associated anemia
2. To control hypertension
3. To correct the acid–base balance
4. To increase perfusion in the kidney

18. An important component of conservative treatment for chronic renal failure is diet therapy. Which of the following would be an appropriate lunch menu for Mr. Kassam?

1. A 100-g cheese sandwich on whole wheat bread, a banana, and 200 mL of milk
2. Canned tomato soup, 250 mL, saltine crackers, and 400 mL of orange juice
3. Turkey, 60 g, on white bread with mayonnaise, an apple, and 250 mL of ginger ale
4. Grilled beefsteak, 300 g, a baked potato, cooked spinach, and chocolate milk

19. Mr. Kassam's chronic renal failure can no longer be managed conservatively. The physician, the nurse, and Mr. Kassam discuss the advantages and disadvantages of peritoneal dialysis and hemodialysis. What is a disadvantage of peritoneal dialysis?

1. There are increased dietary restrictions
2. It is not recommended for clients with type 2 diabetes
3. It is not as effective as hemodialysis
4. There is a risk of peritonitis

20. Following several months of dialysis, Mr. Kassam exclaims to the nurse, "I just can't do this anymore. I'd rather be dead!" What is the most therapeutic response by the nurse?

1. "You'd rather be dead?"
2. "This is very difficult treatment. Tell me about what is bothering you the most."
3. "Just hang on until we can get you a kidney transplant."
4. "Are you depressed?"

21. Mr. Kassam reveals to the nurse he has found an Internet site that provides kidney transplant surgery in another country for a significant amount of money. What is the nurse's professional responsibility in response to Mr. Kassam?

1. Tell Mr. Kassam it is illegal to buy or sell organs in Canada
2. Tell Mr. Kassam he must wait until he can receive a kidney in Canada
3. Ask Mr. Kassam for more details about the Internet site and details of the transplant service
4. Inform Mr. Kassam that he should not waste his money

Case 5

Mrs. Dhillon, age 58, is suspected of having ovarian cancer. She has been referred by her family physician to an oncologist. The registered nurse consults with cancer clients in the physician's office.

Questions 22–26 refer to this case.

22. What are the early manifestations of ovarian cancer?

1. Vague or mild symptoms of abdominal pressure and digestive problems
2. Painful menstrual periods with increased bleeding
3. Sharp pain and swelling in the area of the affected ovary
4. Swollen inguinal lymph nodes

23. The oncologist plans a biopsy via laparoscopy. Mrs. Dhillon asks the nurse about this test. What should the nurse explain to Mrs. Dhillon?

1. "A laparoscopy is the insertion of a large needle through the abdomen into the ovary to collect cells for biopsy."
2. "A laparoscopy is an operation done through a surgical incision in the abdomen and can be used to take a biopsy of ovarian tissue or to remove any visible cancer."
3. "A laparoscopy is the insertion of a flexible tube through a small cut in the abdomen, through which small biopsy samples can be taken."
4. "A laparoscopy is the insertion of air into the fallopian tubes to enable ovarian cells to be withdrawn via the tubes."

24. The results of the biopsy determine that Mrs. Dhillon has stage 3, grade 2 ovarian cancer. The nurse explains that these results help determine which treatment will be most effective for her. Which of the following is the correct interpretation of stage 3, grade 2?

1. The cancer has spread to tissues in the pelvis but is slow-growing
2. The cancer has spread to organs of the abdomen and lymph nodes but is spreading at a moderate rate
3. The cancer is confined to the ovaries but is highly likely to spread
4. The cancer has spread outside the abdomen to distant parts of the body and is growing quickly

25. The oncologist recommends surgery followed by chemotherapy to treat the cancer. Mrs. Dhillon telephones the nurse two days later, saying, "Surgery is too drastic, and the chemotherapy is poison that will destroy my body." She will, instead, try some special herbs she has heard about from a friend. What is the best response by the nurse to Mrs. Dhillon?

1. "These herbs have not likely been tested for safety or effectiveness, so it is not known whether they will harm you or be effective for your cancer."
2. "This is not recommended and will probably cause you to die sooner."
3. "At this stage, you are in denial, so call us back when you change your mind."
4. "You are right about the toxins in the chemotherapy, so it is a good idea to try the herbs first."

26. Mrs. Dhillon is experiencing difficulty deciding on a course of treatment for her cancer. She says to the nurse, "I am just so depressed. It doesn't matter what treatment I have; I'll die anyway." What is the most appropriate response by the nurse?

1. "Why do you feel this way?"
2. "Everyone diagnosed with cancer feels this way just after they receive their diagnosis."

3. "Everything will be fine as soon as you start your treatment."
4. "Let's talk about your prognosis and treatment options."

Case 6

A registered nurse works at a fitness centre. She has been employed to perform health assessments, health counselling, and first aid should the need arise.

Questions 27–32 refer to this case.

27. Reza Morhudi, age 32 years, has just run 10 km on a treadmill and asks the nurse to take his blood pressure. The nurse obtains a reading of 146/90 mm Hg in Mr. Morhudi's right arm. What is the appropriate nursing action in response to this blood pressure reading?

1. Tell Mr. Morhudi to rest for 20 minutes and reassess the blood pressure
2. Obtain a second blood pressure reading in his left arm
3. Ask Mr. Morhudi if he has any history of hypertension
4. Tell Mr. Morhudi this is a normal reading for a man of his age and fitness level

28. The nurse is called to see Valerya Dove, who is on the floor of the gym, crying and saying she has "twisted" her ankle. The nurse assesses that Ms. Dove has sprained her ankle. What interventions should the nurse perform?

1. Heat, passive range of motion (ROM), analgesics
2. Rest, ice, compression, elevation
3. Cool compresses, partial weight bearing, maintain joint in flexion
4. Immobilize the joint and send Ms. Dove to the emergency department for an X-ray

29. Mr. Lackraj introduces himself to the nurse as a new client to the fitness centre. He is 54, obese, and florid and appears short of breath. What should be the nurse's initial assessment question?

1. "What has been your past pattern of exercise?"
2. "What is your personal goal for an exercise plan?"
3. "Have you consulted your physician about an exercise plan?"
4. "Are you anticipating exercise will help you lose weight?"

30. The nurse is concerned about transmission of pathogens among the clients of the fitness centre as many people use the equipment during the day. What would be the most effective action to reduce the potential of transmission of communicable diseases?

1. Terminal cleaning of all equipment at the end of the day
2. Screening all clients for symptoms prior to use of equipment
3. Creating a poster board with information about communicable diseases
4. Installation of alcohol gel dispensers for client hand hygiene between uses of equipment

31. What additional advice might the nurse provide to her clients regarding "gym hygiene"?

1. Place a towel on any surfaces you will be touching with bare skin
2. Bring your own towel and launder it once every five visits
3. Do not use the showers at the gym
4. Dress in pants and long-sleeved clothing rather than shorts and sleeveless tops

32. The nurse has noticed that one of her adolescent clients, Bart Matthews, has developed acne and reduced body fat, with increased muscle size and strength. She suspects that he is using anabolic steroids to improve his sports performance. What would be the most appropriate approach for the nurse to initiate a discussion about the possible use of steroids?

1. "I've noticed that your muscle size has increased quite a bit and you have developed acne."
2. "Are you aware of the dangers of taking anabolic steroids?"
3. "Did you know that using anabolic steroids would disqualify you from sports competitions?"
4. "Are you taking any supplements to improve your performance?"

Case 7

Raize Manche is a 59-year-old woman who has been admitted to an inpatient psychiatric unit following a suicide attempt. She appears unkempt, lethargic, and tearful. She tells her primary nurse, "I am no use to anyone. There is no point in me going on." Her diagnosis is dysthymia with suicidal ideation.

Questions 33–36 refer to this case.

33. During an interaction, Ms. Manche tells the nurse that no one cares about her, but she does love her grandchildren. What would be the most therapeutic response by the nurse?

1. "Tell me more about your grandchildren."
2. "I am sure that your family does care about you."
3. "If you talk about your feelings, you will feel better and enjoy your grandchildren more."

4. "Your grandchildren would be very upset if you harmed yourself."

34. Ms. Manche has not been eating during her depression and tells the nurse she "just isn't hungry." What would be an appropriate intervention by the nurse to encourage adequate nutrition?

1. Have Ms. Manche's family bring in food from home
2. Consult with a dietitian about the most appropriate menu for Ms. Manche's anorexia
3. Offer Ms. Manche bland, high-protein foods
4. Ask Ms. Manche what foods and drinks she likes to eat

35. After being on the unit for several days, Ms. Manche is asked to join a patient discussion group. Ms. Manche states she does not want to go because she has "nothing to say." How should the nurse respond to Ms. Manche?

1. "You must go to the group, but you don't have to talk."
2. "Perhaps you could participate by talking about your grandchildren."
3. "You feel you have nothing to say?"
4. "The group will be very therapeutic for you."

36. Ms. Manche's physician orders a selective serotonin reuptake inhibitor, sertraline (Zoloft). Ms. Manche tells the nurse she doesn't want to take any drugs because they "won't fix anything." How should the nurse respond?

1. "No one likes to take drugs, but these might help you."
2. "Zoloft helps correct the flaw in brain chemistry in depression and should relieve many of your symptoms."
3. "You should speak with your psychiatrist about whether you can participate in psychotherapy without taking medications."
4. "Zoloft is one of the newer antidepressants and does not have many side effects."

Case 8

A registered nurse works in a long-term care facility, Sunset Acres. The clients are primarily adults over 80 years of age, with physical and cognitive disabilities.

Questions 37–41 refer to this case.

37. The nurse finds Ms. Abetiu, a client with Alzheimer's disease and dementia, on the floor by her bed. The nurse examines Ms Abetiu and finds no injuries. Throughout the day when she asks Ms. Abetiu if she has pain, Ms. Abetiu answers "No." The nurse documents the incident but takes no further action. The following day, the nurse notices Ms. Abetiu grimacing and occasionally crying out as if in pain. What is the most appropriate nursing action?

1. Contact the facility physician
2. Call an ambulance to transport Ms. Abetiu to the hospital
3. Ask Ms. Abetiu if she is experiencing any pain
4. Contact Ms. Abetiu's family to report the incident and present manifestations

38. Mrs. Ensoy is a newly admitted client with dementia. One morning, the nurse observes Mrs. Ensoy to be very agitated and aggressive. What action by the nurse may be of immediate help to manage Mrs. Ensoy's agitation?

1. Sit and talk with Mrs. Ensoy to find out what is bothering her
2. Orient Mrs. Ensoy to the reality of her new environment
3. Hand Mrs. Ensoy a cloth and ask her to dust the furniture
4. Administer the ordered medication, risperidone (Risperdal)

39. Many of the clients at Sunset Acres have urinary incontinence. Evidence-informed practice suggests that which of the following is most effective in reducing urinary incontinence in people with dementia?

1. Medication with cholinesterase inhibitors
2. Reducing total fluid intake, especially in the evening
3. Use of adult incontinence products, such as Attends or Depends
4. Scheduled toileting and prompted voiding

40. The nurse has just attended a conference on wound care and has samples of a new product that research has proven to be more effective than the products used by her agency. What should be the nurse's action with regard to wound care on her unit?

1. She should use the samples of the new products as the research has proven their efficacy
2. She should conduct her own research project comparing the new product and the product currently in use on her unit
3. She should discuss findings from the conference with her unit manager and lobby for a change to the new product
4. She should change the agency policy to comply with the new research on wound care

41. The nurse is aware that her clients are at high risk for skin breakdown. Which of the following clients would be most at risk for a sacral pressure ulcer?

1. Mr. Boston, age 92, who is fully ambulatory but has moderate dementia
2. Mrs. Colorado, age 85, who is on bed rest and limited ambulation following total hip replacement
3. Mrs. Carys, age 95, who has a fractured radius
4. Mr. Cleveland, age 75, who has paraplegia and uses a wheelchair

Case 9

Anusha Satgun immigrated to Canada from Southeast Asia yesterday after a 12-hour flight. She felt unwell during the night, and her worried family took her to the local hospital the following day. The registered nurse sees Mrs. Satgun in the triage area.

Questions 42–45 refer to this case.

42. Mrs. Satgun does not have private insurance, nor is she eligible for care through the *Canada Health Act*. What is the necessary action by the nurse?

1. She should refer to agency policies regarding provision of treatment to uninsured individuals
2. She should provide care based on professional humanitarian principles
3. She should advise Mrs. Satgun to arrange for health care insurance, after which care will be provided
4. She should refer Mrs. Satgun to the local community clinic that provides care for recent immigrants to Canada

43. The nurse conducts an initial health screening with Mrs. Satgun. What would be the most important question to ask Mrs. Satgun?

1. "What is your previous medical history?"
2. "Have you had any coughs, colds, or fever in the past week?"
3. "What medications are you presently taking?"
4. "Have you consulted a physician in the past year?"

44. Mrs. Satgun is assessed by the nurse and then referred to a physician due to a possible immobility-induced deep vein thrombosis (DVT). What symptoms is Mrs. Satgun likely to have manifested?

1. Severe, stretching-type pain in the inguinal area
2. Pain, swelling, and erythema in the affected calf
3. A dull ache and feeling of coolness in the affected thigh
4. A line of erythema stretching from the popliteal area to the groin

45. What is the most serious complication of DVT?

1. Gangrene in the affected limb
2. Pulmonary embolism

3. Varicose veins
4. Cerebral thrombosis

Case 10

Matthew is a 5-month-old infant who was born with a large ventricular septal defect. He has a co-diagnosis of failure to thrive related to the heart defect. He is admitted to hospital for evaluation and treatment of his symptoms.

Questions 46–51 refer to this case.

46. What is a ventricular septal defect (VSD)?

1. An area of scar tissue in the left ventricle of the heart
2. Failure of the aorta to develop, causing a stricture of blood flow in the ventricles
3. Right ventricular hypertrophy
4. An abnormal opening between the two ventricles of the heart

47. Due to his cardiac defect, Matthew has difficulty feeding and is severely malnourished. He is lethargic and exhibits poor sucking at the breast. What feeding methods might be recommended initially during the first few days of hospitalization?

1. Encourage Matthew's mother to breastfeed frequently
2. Provide breast milk or formula by a nasogastric tube, as ordered
3. Introduce solids by spoon
4. Feed Matthew formula by bottle

48. Matthew has a cardiac catheterization to help determine the extent of his VSD. During the procedure, cardiac output is determined. What is cardiac output?

1. The peak pressure in the left ventricle during systole
2. The amount of blood present in the left ventricle at the end of diastole
3. The amount of blood ejected from the heart in one contraction
4. The amount of blood ejected by the heart in one minute

49. Matthew returns to the unit after his cardiac catheterization. What assessment will be a priority for the nurse?

1. Level of consciousness
2. Pulses in both extremities
3. Pain
4. Temperature

50. Matthew has surgery to correct his VSD. After being in the intensive care unit for two days, Matthew is

admitted back to the cardiac unit. Matthew is alert and stable but has several intravenous infusions and monitoring wires. His parents are at the bedside when Matthew arrives. What might the nurse say to facilitate parental interaction with Matthew?

1. "You need time alone with Matthew. I'll check back later to see how you are."
2. "Matthew needs the comfort of being close to you. I'll help you to hold him."
3. "All the tubes and wires must be frightening. Try to stroke his skin where there are not any wires."
4. "Talk to him in a soothing voice so he knows you are here with him."

51. Matthew's parents, Mai Kassaye and Jerome Dime, are both 15 years old. They are in a common-law relationship and live with Jerome's parents. Who may legally provide consent for Matthew's care?

1. Both Mai and Jerome
2. Jerome
3. Jerome's parents
4. Mai

Case 11

A nurse works in a hospice for people terminally ill with HIV/AIDS. One of her clients is Georgia Wilcyska, an Aboriginal woman who became HIV-positive many years ago as a result of IV heroin use. She was noncompliant with her antiretroviral therapy and is now receiving palliative care for late chronic infection/AIDS.

Questions 52–57 refer to this case.

52. Ms. Wilcyska talks to the nurse about the days when she was "turned on" to heroin by a male friend. What feeling would Ms. Wilcyska describe as a result of injecting heroin?

1. Increased alertness
2. Euphoria
3. Insomnia
4. Increased sexual drive

53. Prior to being a heroin addict, Ms. Wilcyska was married with children and had a job. She states she "lost everything" because of her addiction. What is the most likely reason Ms. Wilcyska continued to take heroin in spite of the effects on her family life?

1. Neurophysical dependence
2. Uncomfortable withdrawal symptoms
3. Peer influence
4. Cultural factors

54. The nurse is aware that scientific evidence has shown that the practice of harm reduction reduces the financial and human costs of substance abuse. What might be included in harm reduction strategies?

1. Education targeted to abstinence from chemical substances
2. "Tough on crime" law enforcement approach to drug dealers and users
3. Supervised injection of illicit drugs in designated environments
4. Segregated hostels for people addicted to harmful street drugs

55. Ms. Wilcyska has two children who were taken into care by child welfare authorities many years ago due to her heroin addiction, neglect, and physical abuse. Ms. Wilcyska tells the nurse she regrets she was not a better mother. How should the nurse respond?

1. "I'm sure your children know you tried your best."
2. "You must feel your life has been wasted."
3. "Would you like me to help you write a letter to them?"
4. "Do they have problems now due to the abuse and neglect?"

56. Ms. Wilcyska was likely diagnosed with AIDS when which of the following conditions was present?

1. Her ratio of T helper cells to T suppressor cells increased to 2:1
2. She developed a persistent fever
3. The viral load, or viral burden, in her blood decreased
4. Her CD4+ T-cell count dropped below 200 cells/microlitre

57. The nurse is trained in therapeutic touch, which she uses as therapy for Ms. Wilcyska. What is therapeutic touch?

1. Rebalancing of energy through the hands of the practitioner to the person
2. A group of therapeutic procedures that help the client redirect physiologic responses
3. A type of therapeutic massage that increases blood flow and decreases tension
4. Directed attention to a single unchanging, repetitive stimulus to invoke relaxation

Case 12

Gabrielle French and her partner Jennifer Philips have conceived via in vitro fertilization. Ms. French has experienced an uneventful pregnancy and is now at 36 weeks' gestation. Ms. French and Ms. Philips plan to deliver their child at home with the assistance of a doula and a midwife.

Questions 58–63 refer to this case.

58. Ms. French's membranes spontaneously rupture at 36 weeks. After 12 hours, there are no contractions, and she becomes concerned. She contacts the midwife, who makes a home visit. Which classification of medication will the midwife most likely give her?

1. An antibiotic
2. An analgesic
3. An antipyretic
4. An oxytocic

59. Although Ms. French and Ms. Philips wish to stay at home, the midwife decides to admit Ms. French to the hospital as a precaution. Shortly afterwards, Ms. French commences labour. On the antenatal unit, Ms. French has electronic fetal heart monitoring. The nurse performing the monitoring notes a pattern of early decelerations. What is this most likely caused by?

1. Head compression
2. Cord compression
3. Placental insufficiency
4. Uterine contractions

60. Gabrielle French is anxious, apprehensive, and upset that she will not be able to have a home delivery. Ms. Philips says to the nurse, "I don't seem to be able to help Gabrielle as well as the nurses. Do you think I should leave?" What would be the best response by the nurse?

1. "As a woman you should understand that Gabrielle needs you very much now."
2. "This is difficult for you. Let me help you to support her."
3. "Yes, you should leave if you are feeling unsure of the situation. Why don't you relax in the waiting room and come back when you are feeling better?"
4. "It's probably best for you to take a break because you will transmit your anxiety to Gabrielle."

61. As a precaution, an intravenous infusion is inserted in Ms. French's left arm. What is the most appropriate method of helping her to put on a hospital gown with the IV in situ?

1. Disconnect the IV, quickly put on the gown, and reconnect the IV
2. Apply the gown through her right arm and drape the other sleeve over her right shoulder
3. Insert the IV bag through the sleeve from the inside of the gown
4. Apply the gown sleeves over both arms, keeping the tubing inside the gown

62. Gabrielle French delivers a 36-week male infant with a one-minute Apgar of 3. Which of the following manifestations would be most likely to be observed in the baby?

1. Muscle tone flaccid
2. Heart rate 126 bpm
3. Respirations 42
4. Blood pressure 60 systolic

63. Ms. French and Ms. Philip's baby is taken to the close observation nursery and placed under a radiant warmer. When the nurse assesses him at age 6 hours, she hears an audible expiratory grunt, a common early symptom of respiratory distress in premature infants. Grunting respirations are the body's attempt to do which of the following?

1. Remove fluid from the lungs
2. Trap carbon dioxide in the lungs
3. Decrease mucus obstruction
4. Open the alveoli

Case 13

A registered nurse works in a palliative care hospice. One of his clients is Mr. Morrissey, who has terminal pancreatic cancer. Mr. Morrissey is weak and has been unable to move from his bed for several days. He has stopped eating and is not able to drink more than a few sips of water every few hours.

Questions 64–68 refer to this case.

64. What is the most important factor for the nurse to consider when developing end-of-life care for Mr. Morrissey?

1. Cultural
2. Spiritual
3. Religious
4. Individual uniqueness

65. Mr. Morrissey has not completed an advance directive. When he is no longer able to make decisions regarding his care, who should be the Substitute Decision Maker (SDM)?

1. Mr. Morrissey's former spouse
2. Mr. Morrissey's eldest son
3. Mr. Morrissey's adult children
4. Mr. Morrissey's sister

66. Mr. Morrissey develops pain that is not adequately controlled by morphine. He moans and cries out. His family demands additional and more frequent doses of morphine, but the nurse is aware this may hasten his death. What is the most appropriate information for the nurse to communicate in this situation?

1. "I understand your distress. Let's discuss this."
2. "I will arrange a meeting with the pain team for us to find a solution."
3. "I will speak with the physician to ask him what to do."
4. "I am not allowed, as a registered nurse, to administer medication that will cause him to die more quickly."

67. Mr. Morrissey develops constipation. In consultation with the physician, what should be the nurse's initial intervention?

1. Administer a cleansing enema
2. Remove fecal impactions
3. Administer a bulk-forming agent, such as Metamucil
4. Administer a stool-softening suppository

68. In the last few days of his life, Mr. Morrissey becomes dehydrated. What should the nurse do?

1. Apply lubricant to his lips and oral mucous membranes
2. Arrange for intravenous fluid replacement
3. Obtain an order for fluids via hypodermoclysis
4. Insert a nasogastric tube to administer fluids

Case 14

During November, 5-month-old Sean is brought to the nursing station in a remote northern community by his parents. He appears to be in respiratory distress, with dyspnea, chest retractions, and nasal flaring. He has a nonproductive, paroxysmal cough. His oxygen saturation is 89%. His parents report that he has had a "cold" with a runny nose for the past few days. The nurse performs a chest assessment and hears wheezing, crackles, and decreased breath sounds.

Questions 69–72 refer to this case.

69. Based on his signs and symptoms, the nurse should suspect that Sean has which of the following infectious viral conditions?

1. Pharyngitis
2. Croup
3. Bronchiolitis
4. Epiglottitis

70. The nurse decides to treat Sean at the nursing station, where she can monitor his condition. What will care for Sean include?

1. Antiviral agents
2. Humidified oxygen

3. Cough suppressants
4. Antibiotic agents

71. The nurse has other clients at the nursing station. Where is the most appropriate location to place Sean?

1. With other infants his age
2. In a room by himself
3. With adults
4. Beside her at the desk in the nursing station

72. Sean's parents are upset concerning Sean's illness and tell the nurse they would like to stay with their son. What is the nurse's best response to this request?

1. "It is best for Sean if you take a break, go home, and get some rest."
2. "I will put a cot beside his bed so you may stay with him."
3. "It will help if you stay as I have so many other clients to care for."
4. "There is not enough room for both parents, so only the mother is allowed to stay."

INDEPENDENT QUESTIONS

Questions 73–130 do not refer to a particular case.

---

73. The registered nurse assists the physician to insert a peripherally inserted central catheter (PICC line) at the bedside of Mr. Blazevic. Immediately after the insertion, what should be the priority assessment?

1. Hemorrhage at the insertion site
2. Blood pressure monitoring
3. Circulation distal to the insertion site
4. Ability to withdraw blood from the catheter

74. The nurse teaches colostomy care to Mr. Singh following his colon resection surgery. Mr. Singh asks why he has to irrigate the colostomy. What should the nurse explain to him?

1. Similar to colonic irrigations, irrigating a colostomy removes toxins from the gastrointestinal tract
2. Irrigation helps regulate the evacuation of feces
3. Colostomy irrigations are necessary postsurgery to cleanse the surgical site
4. Routine irrigation prevents constipation

75. Post–caesarian section, Ms. Urquhart has her urinary catheter removed. Six hours later, she has not voided. What should be the nurse's first action?

1. Provide her with a bedpan and provide privacy
2. Assess her for abdominal distension

3. Re-catheterize her for residual urine
4. Assist her to the bathroom and encourage her to void

76. Mrs. Scales is experiencing a loss of peripheral vision. This is likely to be caused by which of the following eye conditions?

1. Glaucoma
2. Cataracts
3. Macular degeneration
4. Detached retina

77. Ms. Kyrios buys a home pregnancy test kit one week after her first missed menstrual period. What hormone will the kit test for to determine if she is pregnant?

1. Human chorionic gonadotropin (HCG)
2. Estrogen
3. Progesterone
4. Follicle-stimulating hormone (FSH)

78. A client in the intensive care unit pulls out his right-side chest tube. What is the immediate action by the nurse?

1. Place an occlusive dressing over the puncture site
2. Call for the on-site physician
3. Position the client on his right side
4. Place a saline dressing over the exit site

79. Mr. Gupta has a Mantoux skin test at a physician's office. The nurse reading the test obtains a result of 7 mm induration. What should be the next action by the nurse?

1. No action is required as this is a normal finding
2. The nurse should refer Mr. Gupta to a physician for further investigation
3. The nurse should inform Mr. Gupta that he requires prophylactic medications that will be ordered by a physician
4. The nurse should repeat the test as the result is inconclusive

80. The registered nurse finds a client, Lindsay Breakwell, covered in blood after slashing her wrists in a suicide attempt. What should be the immediate action to manage the bleeding?

1. Apply pressure to the laceration
2. Apply a tourniquet distal to the laceration
3. Determine if the bleeding is arterial blood
4. Elevate the arm

81. The registered nurse is about to administer vitamin K by intramuscular injection to newborn Jeremy. Which site should the nurse choose for the IM injection?

1. Vastus lateralis
2. Dorsogluteal

3. Deltoid
4. Rectus femoris

82. A public health nurse is concerned about the morbidity of tuberculosis in her city. Which of the following best defines the morbidity of tuberculosis?

1. The rate of tuberculosis infection in a population
2. The effect of tuberculosis on a defined group of individuals
3. The death rate from tuberculosis
4. The extent of communicability of tuberculosis within a community

83. Mr. Broadshaw has experienced an episode of renal calculi. The nurse teaches him dietary strategies to help prevent another attack. Which of the following should the nurse include in health teaching for this client?

1. To increase his intake of clear fluids
2. To increase his intake of dairy products
3. To increase his intake of tea and chocolate
4. To use antacids for indigestion and nausea

84. Matthew, age 2 years, has chronic otitis media and has been on antibiotics 8 times in the past year. What would the nurse be concerned about regarding the antibiotics?

1. He may develop antibiotic resistant microorganisms.
2. He may develop chronic diarrhea.
3. He will develop a hearing loss.
4. His immune system will become dependent on the antibiotics.

85. Mr. Bland has experienced a thrombolytic stroke and is receiving tissue plasminogen activator (t-PA). Which of the following assessments should be of the most concern to the nurse during this therapy?

1. Apical pulse of 80 bpm
2. Altered level of consciousness
3. Blood pressure of 130/90 mm Hg
4. Hematuria

86. Which of the following is the leading cause of cancer deaths in Canada?

1. Lung
2. Breast
3. Colorectal
4. Prostate

87. Mr. Shafikhani, age 25 years, has been recently diagnosed with epilepsy. The nurse speaks with him just after his physician tells him that he is no longer allowed to drive a motor vehicle. What is the most therapeutic statement to make to Mr. Shafikhani?

1. "Would you like a referral to the local Epilepsy Association?"
2. "How will not being able to drive affect your life?"
3. "I know this is difficult for you, but it is the safest option."
4. "Do you understand why you are not allowed to drive?"

88. Ms. Aubrey Gans, gravida 1, para 0, has a spontaneous abortion (miscarriage) at 10 weeks' gestation. Of the following, which is the most important question for the nurse to ask?

1. "Did you want this pregnancy?"
2. "Do you know if you are Rh-negative or Rh-positive?"
3. "Did you have difficulty becoming pregnant?"
4. "Did you take any medications while you were pregnant?"

89. The RN is performing oropharyngeal suctioning on Mr. Abernethy. Which of the following would be a nursing consideration during the suctioning?

1. Encourage Mr. Abernethy to cough out secretions during suctioning
2. Maintain sterile technique
3. Measure the catheter from the mouth to the ear to the xiphoid process
4. Moisten the catheter tip with a petroleum jelly lubricant

90. An agency nurse is working his first shift in a long-term care facility where he is to administer evening medications to the residents. Residents do not wear identification armbands. It is not possible to identify residents from pictures in the medication record as the pictures are of poor quality. What is the initial action by the nurse to ensure safe administration of medications?

1. Ask the resident their name and have them sign for the medication.
2. Refuse to administer the medications as it is not safe.
3. Contact the Director of Care for advice and directives.
4. Use a combination of the picture, clothing identification labels and resident self-identification.

91. The nurse must instill mineral oil eardrops bilaterally to Mr. Lewis every eight hours. She directs him to lie in a side-lying position. What action should the nurse take to ensure successful instillation?

1. Instill the drops in the right ear, insert a cotton swab, reposition him, and then instill drops in the left ear
2. Instill the drops in the right ear, and then eight hours later, instill drops in the left ear
3. Instill the drops in the right ear, have Mr. Lewis sit upright, and then instill drops in the left ear

4. Instill the drops in the right ear, wait 10 minutes, and have him turn to the other side for the left eardrop instillation

92. Ms. Samms has fatty liver disease, with resulting ascites. Which position would be best to assist her breathing?

1. Prone
2. Semi-Fowler's
3. Sims'
4. Supine

93. Harriet, an RN, discovers her nursing colleague, Angie, smoking in the stairwell of the psychiatric facility where they work the night shift. Angie tells Harriet that she cannot last an entire shift without a cigarette, and it is too cold for her to go outside. What should Harriet do?

1. Remind Angie that smoking is against agency policies and that unless Angie stops this behaviour, she will have to report this to nursing management
2. If Angie is on a scheduled break, Harriet has no responsibility to interfere with Angie's smoking
3. Caution Angie about the dangers of smoking in an unapproved area and the potential dangers to the clients of second-hand smoke
4. Discuss with Angie her addiction to cigarettes and provide support to establish a strategy that may assist her to quit smoking

94. A nurse suspects one of her colleagues has falsified her credentials as a registered nurse. What should the nurse do?

1. Talk with the colleague and ask to see her registration.
2. Report her suspicion, with rationale, to the nurse manager.
3. Report her suspicion to the provincial registration body.
4. Intervene to stop the colleague from performing nursing care.

95. Mrs. Verde experiences frequent urinary tract infections (UTIs). What should the nurse advise to decrease the incidence of these infections?

1. Drink orange juice daily
2. Do not wear cotton underpants
3. Use a lubricant and a condom during sexual intercourse
4. Treat vaginal yeast disorders promptly

96. Mrs. Brankston has had colon resection surgery due to Crohn's disease. Physician orders include "NPO until bowel sounds are heard." What is the rationale for this order?

1. There is a risk of emesis following gastrointestinal surgery
2. Bowel sounds are an indication that peristalsis has resumed

3. Eating any food will disturb the operative site
4. To prevent nausea associated with anaesthetic administration

97. The nurse notes early decelerations on the fetal monitor of Ms. Loates, who is in active labour. What should be the nurse's first action?

1. Notify the physician
2. Position Ms. Loates on her left side
3. Perform a vaginal examination
4. No action is required

98. Ms. MacLeod has received 760 mL of IV fluid and has had 140 mL of tea. She has voided 540 mL of urine and vomited 110 mL. What is Ms. MacLeod's fluid balance?

1. +900 mL
2. +250 mL
3. −650 mL
4. −110 mL

99. Which of the following is an example of the defence mechanism "displacement"?

1. Ms. Colm repeatedly tells her nurse, Reena, how much she admires her, when in fact Ms. Colm does not like Reena
2. Ms. Henry yells at the nurse after the physician is rude to Ms. Henry
3. Mr. Patrick forgets to make an appointment with his physician when he feels a lump on his testicle
4. Mrs. Miyagi refuses to believe that her sister has a diagnosis of terminal lung cancer

100. Mrs. Townsend is 20 weeks pregnant. She tells the nurse that she has twin girls at home but had a miscarriage prior to this pregnancy. What is her pregnancy classification?

1. Gravida 4, para 2
2. Gravida 3, para 3
3. Gravida 3, para 2
4. Gravida 2, para 1

101. Which of the following is an initial screening test for fetal neural tube defects?

1. Alpha-fetoprotein
2. Chorionic gonadotropin
3. Hegar's screen
4. Amniocentesis

102. Mr. Brendan asks the occupational health nurse why he always looks pale when he is cold. What should the nurse explain to Mr. Brendan?

1. When you are cold, you have less melatonin
2. In a cold environment, blood vessels in your skin constrict to save heat

3. If your skin looks pink in warm weather, it is likely because you have mild sunburn
4. In cold weather, surface capillaries dilate and make the skin appear whitish

103. A child at the Tiny Tots day care centre has been diagnosed with impetigo. What advice should the public health nurse provide to the centre's child care workers?

1. Place the day care centre under quarantine
2. Close the day care until complete cleaning has been performed
3. No special precautions are required
4. Suspend attendance for the infected child for 48 hours

104. Which of the following behaviours would be considered to be a boundary violation of the nurse–client relationship in a mental health setting?

1. Asking the client about his sexual history
2. Sharing coffee and cookies with the client during a therapeutic session
3. Nodding and smiling at the client
4. Honouring a request by the client to keep a secret from the health care team

105. Brad Shaw tells the nurse he has been finding bright red blood on the toilet paper when he has a bowel movement. What should be the nurse's first response to Mr. Shaw?

1. "Do you have abdominal bloating or cramping?"
2. "We need to book you for a colonoscopy."
3. "I will give you a test kit for fecal occult blood."
4. "Are your stools hard, or are you constipated?"

106. A first-year nursing student about to enter her first clinical practice experience has artificial nails. Her nursing professor tells her the policy states she must have the nails removed. What is the most appropriate rationale for this policy?

1. Artificial nails are too long and may injure the client
2. Artificial nails may accidentally be ripped off during client care, injuring the nurse
3. Artificial nails are not professional looking
4. Artificial nails may harbour microorganisms

107. Troy, age 16, tells the school nurse that he frequently feels tired during the day and sometimes falls asleep during his classes. What would be the most appropriate initial question for the nurse to ask Troy?

1. "Are you taking any medications that would make you drowsy?"
2. "How often do you exercise?"
3. "When was the last time you had a complete physical exam?"
4. "How much sleep do you get at night?"

108. Ms. Alexandra has 20/40 vision on the Snellen eye chart. She will most likely need which of the following assistive devices or services?

1. Large-print books
2. Instruction in Braille
3. Referral to an ophthalmologist
4. Corrective lenses

109. Which of the following is the most widespread sexually transmitted infection in Canada?

1. Gonorrhea
2. HIV/AIDS
3. Nongonococcal urethritis (NGU)
4. Chlamydia

110. Mr. Schloss, a client with congestive heart failure, is ambulating in the hall when he suddenly collapses. What is the priority assessment by the nurse?

1. Check for injuries caused by the fall
2. Take an apical pulse to assess cardiac status
3. Assess for breathing
4. Observe for or establish a patent airway

111. A physician has written the following order for pain relief for Mr. Madrigan: "meperidine (morphine), 10 mg, oral, q3–4h, prn." What is the appropriate nursing action?

1. Administer the meperidine after completing the five rights
2. Perform a pain assessment on Mr. Madrigan
3. Calculate that this is an appropriate dose of meperidine for Mr. Madrigan
4. Contact the physician for clarification of the drug

112. Jennie, age 18 months, is brought by her parents to the emergency department of her local community hospital. Jennie has bilateral otitis externa with enlarged tonsils and adenoids. She is mouth breathing and diaphoretic and appears febrile. What method should the nurse choose to take Jennie's temperature?

1. Tympanic
2. Axillary
3. Oral
4. Rectal

113. Mr. Rivers asks the nurse why he is being discharged home with community nursing care only three days after an uncomplicated appendectomy. What would be the nurse's best response?

1. "You do not require acute care facilities."
2. "Your condition is stable, so, with support, it is better to recover at home."
3. "It is too expensive to have people stay in hospital to recover after surgery."

4. "The trend in health care is to discharge clients as soon as possible."

114. The nurse tells Mr. Bartholomew, age 65, that his temperature is 36.6 degrees Celsius. He responds: "I only know Fahrenheit. Is 36.6 Celsius the same as 98.6 degrees Fahrenheit? Is it normal?" What should the nurse tell Mr. Bartholomew?

1. "Yes, it is the same as 98.6 degrees Fahrenheit."
2. "It is about 98, almost the same as 98.6 degrees Fahrenheit, and is normal."
3. "No, it is 99.7 degrees Fahrenheit and is slightly elevated."
4. "It is quite a bit lower than 98.6 degrees Fahrenheit and shows you are cold."

115. Mr. Constant, a client in a psychiatric unit, tells the nurse: "The voices are saying bad things about me." What would be an appropriate response?

1. "I do not hear the voices."
2. "I understand you are frightened by the voices, and I will stay with you."
3. "Why don't you sit with the other clients and watch TV?"
4. "Don't listen to what the voices tell you."

116. Prior to the infusion of antibiotics for cellulitis, Mrs. Collins tells the nurse she is allergic to penicillin. What should be the nurse's first action?

1. Place an allergy band on Mrs. Collins's wrist
2. Notify the prescribing physician of the allergy
3. Check that the ordered antibiotics do not contain penicillin
4. Ask Mrs. Collins what happens when she has penicillin

117. Teklie, age 2 years, has had two episodes of watery diarrhea. What should the nurse recommend to Teklie's parents?

1. Encourage constipating foods such as cheese
2. Administer an over-the-counter antidiarrhea medicine
3. Offer clear fluids, ice pops, and crackers
4. Continue with Teklie's normal diet

118. Mrs. Bennett requires transfer from her wheelchair to the commode. She tells the nurse usually 2 people perform this lift. The nurse has not previously cared for Mrs. Bennett, but assesses she can do the lift by herself. What should the nurse do?

1. Use a mechanical lift so she does not require 2 people.
2. Ask Mrs. Bennett for more details about why 2 people are required for the lift.

3. Find another co-worker to assist with the lift.
4. Begin the lift to see if how difficult she thinks it will be.

119. Mrs. Sheyer, age 87 years, is brought to the emergency department by her family because she has had a fever for several days. During the health assessment, the RN determines that Mrs. Sheyer is exhibiting early signs of delirium. What would be the most important step of data collection to determine the possible cause of the delirium?

1. Review Mrs. Sheyer's medication profile
2. Interview the family to determine cognitive function prior to admission
3. Assess Mrs. Sheyer's level of hydration
4. Take Mrs. Sheyer's temperature

120. An RN in a community mental health clinic is in the midst of a counselling session with Mr. Olan. Ms. Isabelle approaches the RN and asks to speak with her. How should the RN respond to this situation?

1. "What can I help you with, Ms. Isabelle?"
2. "Excuse me, Mr. Olan, I need to speak with Ms. Isabelle."
3. "Ms Isabelle, I am with Mr. Olan until 10. I will see you directly afterward."
4. "Ms. Isabelle, you should not interrupt Mr. Olan and me."

121. A nurse is grocery shopping when she observes a young toddler experience a tonic–clonic seizure. What is the nurse's first responsibility in this situation?

1. Call 9-1-1
2. Insert any safe object in the child's mouth to maintain an airway
3. Observe the seizure and protect the child from injury
4. Reassure the parents

122. Ten-year-old Nicholas has just been diagnosed with a brain tumour. His parents tell the nurse Nicholas is not to be informed about the tumour. What is the nurse's most appropriate response to this request?

1. "At Nicholas's age, he is not able to understand the diagnosis, so this is a wise decision."
2. "Let's talk about the reasons why you don't think he should be told."
3. "The policy of this hospital is that children have a right to age-appropriate information."
4. "Children are very intuitive, and Nicholas probably already knows about the tumour."

123. The charge nurse on a busy surgical unit must assign care for Mr. Michener, age 27, who is three days postsurgery from an appendectomy. Mr.

Michener's vital signs are stable, and the wound is approximated and shows no signs of infection. Mr. Michener is to be discharged the following day and requires health teaching. What category of health care worker is the most appropriate and cost-effective to be assigned to Mr. Michener?

1. Registered nurse (RN)
2. Registered/licensed practical nurse (RPN/LPN)
3. Expanded role nurse/nurse practitioner/clinical nurse specialist
4. Unregulated care provider (UCP)

124. Mrs. Fraser, a pale-skinned woman of European descent, age 59 years, comes to the clinic. What is the most important observation by the nurse when performing a skin assessment on Mrs. Fraser?

1. Areas of dry, flaky skin
2. A reduction in skin elasticity
3. A change in a mole or lesion
4. Senile lentigines

125. The nurse obtains a thermometer reading of 39.6 degrees Celsius on Nick, age 4 years. His previous temperature two hours ago was 36.3 degrees Celsius, he does not feel hot, and he states that he feels well. What is the appropriate nursing action?

1. Take the temperature again in another hour
2. Take a rectal temperature to obtain a core temperature
3. Administer the ordered antipyretic
4. Use a different thermometer to retake the temperature

126. Mrs. Ginger has an amputation of her left leg. The afternoon following surgery, the RN finds Mrs. Ginger lying in bed, in a fetal position, crying. What is the most appropriate documentation of this event?

1. "Lying in a fetal position, crying"
2. "Displaying manifestations of postsurgical depression"
3. "Grieving observed due to loss of leg"
4. "Client upset, manifesting sadness related to amputation"

127. Andre, age 6 years, is about to have an injected immunization. He is very tearful and apprehensive about how much the needle will hurt him. Which of the following would be the most effective method to reduce the pain of an injection for Andre?

1. Use of a topical anaesthetic cream
2. Distracting the child during the injection
3. Having the parent hold Andre during the injection
4. Postinjection analgesics, such as acetaminophen

128. A nurse manager is concerned about the incidence of work-related accidents on the unit, causing many staff nurses to be on long-term disability. What is the first action the manager should take to address these problems?

1. Compile a list of all data on staff accidents for the past 2 years
2. Tour the unit to observe hazardous workplace habits or environments
3. Interview all staff on long-term disability to find out how they were injured
4. Interview all staff for their opinions and observations about workplace hazards

129. Anita Forbes is a practical nurse who has worked on a medical–surgical unit for 10 years. Her nurse manager wonders if Anita should be a preceptor for a second-year RN student who will be on their unit. What should the manager consider in this situation?

1. Registered nurses and practical nurses have different scopes of practice; thus, it is not suitable for Anita to precept the student
2. The role of an RN includes supervision of practical nurses, so this would not be an appropriate preceptorship
3. Anita is an exemplary practitioner who is aware of the roles of the two categories of nurses; thus, Anita will be a professional preceptor
4. There are no contraindications for Anita to be a preceptor to any category of health care worker

130. During the influenza season, how should the nurse in a community walk-in health clinic best prevent transmission of the influenza virus to clients?

1. Place all clients with respiratory symptoms in a separate area and have them wear masks and wash their hands
2. Immunize all clients with the influenza vaccine as they arrive
3. Post a sign in the window of the clinic refusing care to people with symptoms of influenza
4. Keep all clients at least half a metre apart in the waiting room

Answers and Rationales for
Book One

1.   C: Changes in Health   T: Knowledge

1. These values are all low. See choice 3.
2. These values are too high. See choice 3.
3. Normal vital signs for a 1-week-old infant are heart rate 120–160 bpm, respirations 30–60 breaths per minute, and median blood pressure generally 65–80 mm Hg by Doppler (but can increase during crying or agitation).
4. Heart rate and respirations are within normal ranges, but blood pressure is too high.

2.   C: Changes in Health   T: Knowledge

1. The Babinski reflex is elicited by stroking the outer sole of the foot upward from the heel across the ball of the foot, causing dorsiflexion of the big toe and fanning of the toes.
2. This is the response from the dance, or step, reflex.
3. This is the expected response from the grasp reflex.
4. This is the part of the expected response from the Moro, or startle, reflex.

3.   C: Nurse–Client Partnership   T: Application

1. This response best addresses Mrs. Wasson's concerns. A weight loss of up to 10% is expected 3–4 days after birth. Adequate breast milk supply is best facilitated by frequent feedings.
2. It is well established that the use of supplemental formula feedings before breastfeeding is to be avoided.
3. This is true but does not answer Mrs. Wasson's concerns about milk production.
4. Increased fluids have not been proven to increase milk supply.

4.   C: Health and Wellness   T: Application

1. Airing the nipples as much as possible, and using heat, will help dry the nipples and decrease discomfort.
2. Creams and oils are to be avoided.
3. Plastic-lined breast pads may trap moisture, increasing the risk of skin breakdown.
4. Nursing should start with the least affected breast.

5.   C: Health and Wellness   T: Application

1. Breast milk or infant formula does not need to be heated.
2. It is unsafe and unnecessary to warm milk in the microwave because the heat is not evenly distributed. The bottle may remain at a cooler temperature than the liquid, and the liquid may burn the baby.
3. Warming a bottle in lukewarm water is sufficient to bring it to room temperature.

4. Infants are used to body temperature milk from the breast and may not adjust to cold milk.

6.   C: Changes in Health   T: Knowledge

1. Polycythemia, an increase in red blood cells, and polymyositis, inflammation of many muscles, are not manifestations of diabetes.
2. Polyelectrolyte (many charged electrolytes) and polyneuropathy (a disorder of the peripheral nerves) are not manifestations of diabetes.
3. Polyopia, a defect in sight, and polyarthritis, an inflammation of more than one joint, are not manifestations of diabetes.
4. Polyphagia, hunger (excessive eating), polydipsia (excessive thirst), and polyuria (excessive urination) are cardinal manifestations of type 1 diabetes.

7.   C: Changes in Health   T: Application

1. This is the conventional regimen and involves insulin administration in the morning before breakfast and before the evening meal. It may not suit all people with diabetes, particularly during illness, stress, growth spurts, and so on.
2. Some children require more frequent administration of insulin, with multiple injections during the day. After individual assessment, this may be the optimum regimen.
3. The precise dose of insulin and optimum regimen cannot be predicted and need to be individualized for every child. Insulin requirements do not remain constant, changing with growth, activity, and pubertal status.
4. Although many pediatric medication dosages are calculated per kilogram, insulin dosages are not.

8.   C: Changes in Health   T: Application

1. Alcohol causes a drop, not an increase, in blood sugar.
2. This could be a serious problem, but more significant is an immediate and severe drop in blood glucose.
3. Alcohol causes hypoglycemia. The manifestations of slurred speech and antisocial combative behaviour are similar to those of being intoxicated; thus, Edgar may not receive appropriate life-saving treatment.
4. There is a family pattern to alcohol dependence, but this is not the most critical issue at this time.

9.   C: Changes in Health   T: Application

1. The peak action for regular insulin is 2–4 hours after administration; therefore, a hypoglycemic episode may occur between 1800 and 2000 hours.

2. This is past the time of peak action.
3. The insulin would likely not be in the bloodstream at this time.
4. There should be no effects from the insulin at this time.

---

10.   **C: Nurse–Client Partnership   T: Application**

1. This may need to occur but is not the best initial approach.
2. Both Edgar and his parents may require more education, but an assessment of Edgar's needs and particular reasons for noncompliance must be explored first.
3. Prior to implementing interventions, the nurse must be aware of the reasons for Edgar's noncompliance. She should discuss this with him in private as he may speak more freely when his parents are not present.
4. This may be appropriate but does not address Edgar's individual needs with his present noncompliance.

---

11.   **C: Health and Wellness   T: Critical Thinking**

1. Clients who are at high risk, for example, those who are immuno-suppressed, need to be identified in order to implement appropriate precautions.
2. This may not be necessary with all clients.
3. In some facilities and in some situations, this may be necessary, but it does not need to be generally implemented.
4. Alcohol-based hand sanitizers are as effective as soap and water and aid in increasing the frequency of hand hygiene by health care workers but are not as important a step as the identification of at-risk clients.

---

12.   **C: Changes in Health   T: Critical Thinking**

1. Age is a risk factor as older adults generally have a decreased immune system; however, it is not as great a risk as a urinary catheter.
2. Poor nutrition may lead to poor immunity, but this is not as great a risk as a urinary catheter.
3. Surgery is a risk; however, the surgery should have taken place under strict sterile techniques.
4. An in-dwelling urinary catheter, even though it is a closed system, places Mr. Carolis at risk of a urinary tract infection and should be discontinued at the earliest opportunity.

---

13.   **C: Changes in Health   T: Application**

1. Leukocytosis is an abnormal increase in white blood cells and is indicative of an infection.

2. Neutropenia is an abnormal decrease in neutrophils. During an infection, there is an increase in neutrophils.
3. Thrombocytosis is an abnormal increase in platelets and may be indicative of malignancies or blood disorders.
4. Leukopenia is an abnormal decrease in white blood cells and may indicate bone marrow suppression.

---

14.   **C: Changes in Health   T: Application**

1. Antibiotics may interfere with accurate results from cultures.
2. It is not necessary to consult with the physician. This is nursing judgement.
3. This is the correct sequence. Culture specimens can be inaccurate if taken after antibiotics are given.
4. Sterile urine specimens must be taken from the catheter port, not the collection bag. The specimen must be taken before the antibiotics are administered.

---

15.   **C: Professional Practice   T: Critical Thinking**

1. Incident reports are specific agency documents. They are important for quality assurance purposes for the institution but are not the most important initial action for Mr. Carolis.
2. This must be done but is not the first action.
3. The immediate action must be to address client safety. Administration of medication that is twice the ordered dose could have severe effects, particularly in an older client, and the nurse's first responsibility must be to assess Mr. Carolis.
4. This must be done but is not the first action.

---

16.   **C: Changes in Health   T: Knowledge**

1. Hyperkalemia, caused by decreased excretion by the kidney, is the most serious electrolyte disorder associated with kidney disease. A level of 7 mmol/L could result in a fatal arrhythmia.
2. This is a normal value.
3. This is a normal value.
4. This is a normal value.

---

17.   **C: Changes in Health   T: Knowledge**

1. Administration of erythropoietin intravenously or subcutaneously is effective in treating the anemia that results from the decrease in erythropoietin production occurring with kidney failure.
2. An adverse side effect of erythropoietin may be hypertension.
3. Erythropoietin will not affect the acid–base balance.
4. Erythropoietin will not increase perfusion in the kidney.

18.   C: Changes in Health   T: Critical Thinking

1. Cheese has high sodium and high protein. Banana and milk are high-potassium foods. Sodium, protein, and potassium are restricted in renal failure.
2. Canned soups are high in sodium, as are saltine crackers. Orange juice is high in potassium. Fluids are restricted: 400 mL is too much fluid at one meal.
3. Nutrition therapy in renal failure is complex. It requires the expert determination by a nutritionist of menus that comply with guidelines of low sodium, protein, and phosphorus; restricted fluids; and unlimited carbohydrates and fats to ensure sufficient calories. Turkey, mayonnaise, bread, an apple, and ginger ale comply with these guidelines.
4. The beefsteak provides too much protein, and the baked potato, cooked spinach, chocolate, and milk are high in potassium.

19.   C: Changes in Health   T: Application

1. There are fewer dietary restrictions with peritoneal dialysis.
2. Peritoneal dialysis is preferable in clients with type 2 diabetes.
3. Although hemodialysis provides more rapid fluid and toxin removal, it is no more effective than peritoneal dialysis.
4. Peritonitis, caused by contamination of the dialysate or exit site infection, is a major complication of peritoneal dialysis.

20.   C: Nurse–Client Partnership   T: Application

1. This reply does not necessarily allow Mr. Kassam to discuss his feelings.
2. This open-ended response confirms Mr. Kassam's feelings and invites him to share them.
3. This response closes the conversation and does nothing to help develop coping strategies. Kidney transplant may not yet have been discussed with him.
4. This is not a therapeutic response and does not allow for Mr. Kassam to discuss his feelings.

21.   C: Professional Practice   T: Critical Thinking

1. Although this is true, it is not pertinent as the transplant surgery is being offered in another country.
2. It is neither the ethical nor the professional responsibility of the nurse to tell the client what he must do.
3. This response provides the nurse with more information about a potentially dangerous, illegal,

or unethical situation. It allows for a respectful discussion between the nurse and Mr. Kassam.
4. As in choice 2.

22.   C: Changes in Health   T: Knowledge

1. Ovarian cancer in its early stages may not cause symptoms, or they may include mild pressure in the abdomen, pelvis, or back of the legs. There may be abdominal swelling or gastrointestinal symptoms, such as indigestion, nausea, and bloating.
2. This is not a manifestation of ovarian cancer but more likely of uterine cancer. At age 59, Mrs. Dhillon would likely be postmenopausal and thus not menstruating.
3. This is not a manifestation of ovarian cancer.
4. This is not a manifestation of early ovarian cancer.

23.   C: Changes in Health   T: Application

1. This is a needle biopsy.
2. This is a laparotomy.
3. This is the correct definition of laparoscopy. It may be preferable to laparotomy as it is less invasive, is less painful, and only requires a local anaesthetic.
4. This is not the definition of laparoscopy.

24.   C: Changes in Health   T: Application

1. This is grade 2, stage 1.
2. This is the correct interpretation of grade 3, stage 2.
3. This is grade 1, stage 3.
4. This is grade 4, stage 4.

25.   C: Nurse–Client Partnership   T: Application

1. This is factual information that will assist Mrs. Dhillon to make an informed decision about her treatment.
2. The herbs are probably not recommended, but it is not a therapeutic response to tell Mrs. Dhillon that they will cause her to die sooner, especially as Mrs. Dhillon may not be aware of the possibility of a terminal diagnosis.
3. This is not a therapeutic response. It presumes she is in denial and presumes that she will change her mind. It does not provide information to assist her in making her decision.
4. This is an incorrect and potentially life-threatening response.

26.   C: Nurse–Client Partnership   T: Application

1. Mrs. Dhillon has a type of cancer that has a very poor prognosis. It is evident why she is depressed.

2. This is patronizing and does not address Mrs. Dhillon as an individual. It ends the conversation.
3. This is probably not true and would not encourage further discussion.
4. This is an open-ended response that invites further discussion with Mrs. Dhillon about her cancer and her feelings about the situation.

27.   C: Changes in Health   T: Application

1. Physical activity increases the cardiac output and thus increases the blood pressure. Twenty to thirty minutes of rest following exercise is indicated before a resting BP can be considered reliable.
2. This is not necessary. A BP in the left arm is likely to be the same as in the right arm.
3. This action would be indicated if, after resting, Mr. Morhudi's blood pressure remained elevated.
4. A normal blood pressure for Mr. Morhudi would be 120/80 mm Hg.

28.   C: Changes in Health   T: Application

1. Ice, not heat, is recommended for a muscle sprain. Heat may be applied after 24 hours. The ankle should be rested initially. Analgesics may be required once the RICE therapy has been initiated.
2. This is RICE treatment. Movement should be limited, cold is applied to produce hypothermia, compression with an elastic bandage limits swelling, and the limb is elevated to impede edema formation.
3. Ice is more effective than a cool compress. Ms. Dove will be encouraged to move the ankle joint once it is supported with a bandage. There is no rationale for maintaining the joint in flexion.
4. This is not necessary unless the nurse assesses there has been a possible fracture.

29.   C: Health and Wellness   T: Application

1. This is an appropriate question but is not the most important initial data collection.
2. As in choice 1.
3. Mr. Lackraj appears to have risk factors for cardiovascular disease. All clients should consult with their physician prior to initiating an exercise plan.
4. As in choice 1.

30.   C: Health and Wellness   T: Critical Thinking

1. This is neither practical nor possible.
2. This may help; however, many people are not symptomatic in the initial stages of many infections. It would be difficult for the nurse to screen all clients.

3. This may help, but people may not read the poster.
4. Hand hygiene is the most effective action to reduce the transmission of infectious diseases.

31.   C: Health and Wellness   T: Critical Thinking

1. Placing a towel on common surfaces will protect the skin from bacteria that may be on the bench. Do not use the underside of the towel after it has been placed on the bench.
2. It is safer for clients to bring their own towels, but they should be laundered after each visit.
3. There is no need to avoid the showers at the gym provided that plastic "flip-flops," or other waterproof barriers, protect feet. In fact, it is important to get out of sweaty clothes and shower after a workout.
4. Clients are less likely to contract a skin rash if they are wearing long sleeves; however, this is not practical advice

32.   C: Nurse–Client Partnership   T: Application

1. This initial answer is a statement of facts and does not accuse Mr. Matthews. It will likely lead to a discussion of the causes of his muscle bulk and acne.
2. This accuses Bart without any proof and will cause him to feel defensive.
3. As in choice 2.
4. This approach calls for a yes or no answer, is accusing, and is not likely to lead to a meaningful discussion.

33.   C: Nurse–Client Partnership   T: Application

1. The depressed client often has difficulty acknowledging any positive aspects of his or her life. By asking about the grandchildren that Ms. Manche loves, the nurse is reinforcing that she has worthwhile relationships.
2. This ignores Ms. Manche's feelings and closes off the discussion.
3. This provides false reassurance and applies pressure on Ms. Manche to talk.
4. This answer is not therapeutic as it may cause Ms. Manche to feel guilty.

34.   C: Health and Wellness   T: Application

1. This may be appropriate but does not consider Ms. Manche's preferences. She did not eat at home when these foods were available.
2. There is no need to consult with a dietitian at this time. When Ms. Manche's food preferences have been established, a dietitian may be consulted.
3. This does not consider Ms. Manche's preferences.
4. Ms. Manche is more likely to eat foods that she prefers.

35.   C: Nurse–Client Partnership   T: Application

1. While this reassures Ms. Manche that she does not have to talk, it does not lead to a therapeutic discussion.
2. This is a helpful response but may not lead to Ms. Manche exploring her feelings.
3. This allows the nurse to further explore Ms. Manche's feelings of low self-worth and may lead to a discussion about the therapeutic effects of the group discussion.
4. This response is autocratic, gives advice, and does not allow Ms. Manche to explore her feelings.

36.   C: Changes in Health   T: Critical Thinking

1. Ms. Manche has not said that she does not like to take drugs. This response makes the use of antidepressants appear to be of limited effectiveness.
2. Antidepressant therapy benefits about 65–80% of people with depression. This response is factual and explains that depression is a chemical problem.
3. The antidepressant is a first-line agent in the treatment of depression and should be combined with psychotherapy. This response negates the role of the nurse.
4. Ms. Manche has not asked about side effects; she has said she doubts the drugs will work.

37.   C: Professional Practice   T: Critical Thinking

1. Ms. Abetiu is manifesting symptoms of pain and needs to be assessed by a physician for any possible injury that could have occurred due to the fall.
2. The initial action is to contact the agency physician, if available, who should examine Ms. Abetiu. If there were no agency physician, the appropriate action would be to call for an ambulance for transport to a hospital.
3. People with dementia have difficulty communicating symptoms of health problems or pain. While the nurse could ask Ms. Abetiu if she is experiencing pain, it is not likely that Ms. Abetiu would be able to provide accurate information, especially considering that she had previously denied pain. Health care staff must take the responsibility for assessment and diagnosis.
4. This will be necessary but is not the most appropriate action at this time.

38.   C: Changes in Health   T: Application

1. This is not likely to calm Mrs. Ensoy's agitation. In an agitated phase, logical discussions about feelings and cause and effect are not likely to be successful.
2. While reality orientation is helpful with clients who have dementia, in the agitated state, this would not be effective.
3. Redirection is often helpful when dealing with difficult behaviour. Performing an activity such as dusting, which would be a familiar activity to Mrs. Ensoy, may calm her.
4. Risperidone is helpful in managing disruptive behaviour; however, nonpharmacological therapies should be attempted initially.

39.   C: Changes in Health   T: Application

1. These drugs do not affect urination or continence.
2. This practice is dangerous with older adults. It is necessary to ensure that older adults have sufficient fluid intake.
3. Use of these products helps manage urinary incontinence but does not reduce incontinence.
4. Evidence-informed practice has determined that behaviour modification, in the form of routine toileting and prompting the client to void, reduces urinary incontinence in people with dementia.

40.   C: Professional Practice   T: Application

1. The nurse should not vary from agency policy until it is approved.
2. There is no need to duplicate other research.
3. This is the most effective and professional approach to responding to recent research and implementing a change in agency policy.
4. The nurse may not change agency policy without authorization.

41.   C: Changes in Health   T: Application

1. People who are ambulatory have a low risk for pressure ulcers.
2. Mrs. Colorado is still able to change positions and ambulate.
3. A fractured radius will not lead to a pressure ulcer in the sacral area.
4. With paraplegia, there is decreased sensation and immobility, both of which are risk factors for pressure ulcers.

42.   C: Professional Practice   T: Critical Thinking

1. The most appropriate action is to refer to agency policies. There is likely to be an appropriate policy that will address ethical, financial, and legal implications of provision of treatment for nonresidents.
2. If Mrs. Satgun's condition were life-threatening, the humanitarian principle would be to provide emergency care.

3. Mrs. Satgun may not be able financially to obtain the necessary medical insurance. Her condition could potentially deteriorate during the time it takes to obtain the insurance.
4. This may ultimately be the solution; however, it is dependent on the policies of the agency.

43.   C: Health and Wellness   T: Critical Thinking

1. This is important but is not the most immediate concern.
2. This is the most important question, particularly as Mrs. Satgun has recently arrived in Canada from a foreign country. This question helps screen for recent communicable diseases, which may be a hazard to the rest of the clients and staff in the hospital and may require specific isolation precautions.
3. This is important to develop a profile of Mrs. Satgun's health status but is not the most important question.
4. This is important as it may reveal underlying conditions that are important for Mrs. Satgun's subsequent treatment; however, it is not as important as knowing her recent communicable disease status.

44.   C: Changes in Health   T: Knowledge

1. DVT, particularly after a long air flight in a confined space, is most likely to occur in the calf.
2. In this type of DVT, the inflammatory response causes pain in the calf and swelling, and the area feels warm.
3. Mrs. Satgun may feel a dull pain but is likely to feel warmth rather than coolness, and it is not likely to be in the thigh.
4. The swelling and erythema of DVT are generally not linear and are generally not in the popliteal–groin area.

45.   C: Changes in Health   T: Knowledge

1. If untreated, the DVT could lead to necrosis and gangrene, but this is neither the most likely nor the most serious complication.
2. Pulmonary embolism is a life-threatening complication of DVT.
3. Varicose veins are not caused by DVT and are not as serious as pulmonary emboli.
4. Cerebral thrombosis is serious and life-threatening; however, if the thrombus in the leg were to enter the venous circulation, it would first travel to the lungs.

46.   C: Changes in Health   T: Knowledge

1. This is not the definition of VSD. It is not scar tissue.

2. Coarctation of the aorta is failure of the aorta to develop, causing reduced systemic blood flow below the level of the defect.
3. A large VSD may cause right ventricular hypertrophy but is not the actual defect.
4. This is the definition of a VSD.

47.   C: Changes in Health   T: Critical Thinking

1. Children with heart defects often have limited energy for sucking. Putting the child to the breast more often will tire the child out more quickly.
2. If ordered, high-calorie feeds via a nasogastric tube will decrease the energy demands for the infant while providing adequate hydration and nutrition.
3. While infants with heart defects are often started on solids early, Matthew requires more immediate increased nourishment to correct his malnourished state.
4. While bottle-feeding requires less energy than breastfeeding, this is not the optimum method of providing increased nourishment to Matthew.

48.   C: Changes in Health   T: Knowledge

1. This is the definition of systolic left ventricular pressure.
2. This is the end-diastolic volume (EDV).
3. This is stroke volume.
4. This is the definition of cardiac output.

49.   C: Changes in Health   T: Critical Thinking

1. Matthew may need to be sedated for the procedure and may be sleepy, but this is not the priority assessment.
2. The catheter is inserted into either the femoral vein or the femoral artery. There is risk of vasospasm or thrombus formation, which could interfere with blood flow to the extremities. Thus, assessment of pulses is the priority assessment.
3. Matthew may be experiencing pain, but this is not the priority assessment.
4. Matthew may be somewhat hypothermic if the temperature in the catheterization laboratory is reduced. It is not, however, the priority assessment.

50.   C: Nurse–Client Partnership   T: Critical Thinking

1. This may not be safe, especially as Matthew has recently had heart surgery. The parents may be nervous to be alone with him.
2. This reinforces their role as parents of Matthew and that he needs them. Helping them manage the wires and tubes, which may be frightening for the parents, will facilitate interaction.

3. It would be best for the parents to hold their infant, not just stroke his skin. There is no reason why they should stroke his skin rather than hold him.

4. The soothing talk is likely to be comforting to Matthew, but holding by the parents will be more effective in facilitating interaction.

51.   C: Professional Practice   T: Application

1. Both parents have equal rights and are considered emancipated minors because they have a child.

2. Jerome has no greater rights to provide consent than Mai. Both are emancipated minors.

3. Jerome and Mai are emancipated minors and may provide consent for treatment for their son.

4. Mai does not have greater rights than Jerome.

52.   C: Changes in Health   T: Knowledge

1. Injection of heroin is more likely to cause detachment from the environment.

2. After injection of heroin, users feel a strong sense of euphoria.

3. Following the euphoria, users are more likely to feel drowsiness than insomnia.

4. Heroin users often have a decreased libido.

53.   C: Changes in Health   T: Critical Thinking

1. Current research shows that addictive drugs appear to increase the availability of dopamine in the pleasure area of the brain. Without the substance, the individual experiences depression, anxiety, irritability, and an intense craving for the drug. To feel "normal," the individual must take increasingly large doses of heroin.

2. While the withdrawal symptoms, such as nausea, pain, vomiting, and so on, are unpleasant, the physical addiction is the primary difficulty.

3. Peer influence is a documented influencing factor associated with drug abuse but is not as direct a factor as the physical addiction.

4. Cultural factors affect the incidence of substance abuse and are a documented health problem with people of First Nations descent. However, culture is not as direct a factor as physical addiction.

54.   C: Health and Wellness   T: Application

1. Abstinence is not part of a harm reduction strategy.

2. This is a societal view that seeks to punish those who use illicit drugs.

3. This is a part of a continuum of strategies that aims to reduce the adverse health and social effects of problematic drug use.

4. This is repressive.

55.   C: Nurse–Client Partnership   T: Application

1. This is patronizing and is unlikely to help Ms. Wilcyska.

2. This confirms to Ms. Wilcyska that she was a poor mother and is not therapeutic.

3. Reaching out to her estranged children may help Ms. Wilcyska. Writing letters to her children may bring the comfort of knowing that something of her may survive after her death.

4. This further emphasizes to Ms. Wilcyska that she was a poor mother and is not therapeutic.

56.   C: Changes in Health   T: Application

1. As the disease progresses, this ratio reverses from 2:1.

2. This is a manifestation of intermediate chronic HIV disease that has not progressed to late chronic HIV or AIDS.

3. In AIDS, the viral load increases.

4. This is a diagnostic criterion established by the Centers for Disease Control and Prevention (CDC).

57.   C: Health and Wellness   T: Application

1. With the hands of the practitioner either on the body or close to the body, energy flow is redirected and brings the person back into energy balance. It may be of value to reduce anxiety and pain.

2. This is biofeedback.

3. Therapeutic touch is not a type of massage.

4. This is meditation.

58.   C: Changes in Health   T: Knowledge

1. With ruptured membranes, there is a risk of ascending infection, particularly B Streptococcus. If the infant is not delivered, the risk of infection increases relative to the time that has passed since the membranes ruptured; therefore, antibiotics are given to the mother.

2. This is not indicated.

3. This is not indicated.

4. Labour will likely not be induced unless the infant is in distress.

59.   C: Changes in Health   T: Knowledge

1. Head compression may cause early decelerations.

2. Cord compression may cause variable decelerations.

3. Placental insufficiency will cause late decelerations.

4. Uterine contractions may cause fetal tachycardia.

60.   C: Nurse–Client Partnership   T: Application

1. This statement is judgemental and patronizing.
2. This acknowledges the fears of Ms. Philips. Both parents require additional support from the nurse at this time.
3. Ms. French needs the support of her partner at this time. Generally, partners will not be asked to leave unless they are in the way during the emergency.
4. This does not help Ms. Philips fulfill her role in supporting Ms. French and may make Ms. Philips feel that she is failing her partner.

61.   C: Changes in Health   T: Application

1. This is not safe as there is potential for introducing pathogens into the IV.
2. This would be uncomfortable for Ms. French.
3. This ensures that the bag and tubing are safely put through the arm of the gown, with no unsafe breaks in the system or tension applied to the tubing.
4. This would place the IV tubing inside the gown, where it is not in view, it may become kinked, and it may create tension on the insertion site.

62.   C: Changes in Health   T: Application

1. An Apgar score of 3 indicates severe distress. Of the listed manifestations, this is the only abnormal finding. It is given a score of 1 on the Apgar.
2. This is normal. With an Apgar score of 3, the heart rate would likely be lower.
3. This is normal and would likely be associated with an Apgar of 7 to 10.
4. Blood pressure is not a component of the Apgar score.

63.   C: Changes in Health   T: Application

1. There may be fluid in the lungs, but it is not removed by grunting.
2. The lungs require oxygen, not carbon dioxide.
3. There is no mucus obstruction in neonatal respiratory distress.
4. With neonatal respiratory distress, the alveoli collapse due to insufficient surfactant. Grunting is an attempt by the body to open up the alveoli.

64.   C: Nurse–Client Partnership   T: Critical Thinking

1. Cultural, spiritual, and religious factors will influence end-of-life care; however, each person is a unique individual.
2. As in choice 1.
3. As in choice 1.

4. Although a person's cultural, spiritual, and religious background must be included in end-of-life care, assumptions cannot be based on these factors. All people are unique.

65.   C: Professional Practice   T: Application

1. If they are no longer legally married, the former spouse cannot be the SDM unless Mr. Morrissey has designated her as the SDM.
2. There is no provision in the legislation that states that the eldest child, whether male or female, should be the SDM.
3. The adult children are the legal next of kin and will be the SDMs. The children should agree upon decisions, and in practice, the child who has been most involved with the parent may have more influence.
4. The sister is not the next of kin, unless she has been designated as the SDM.

66.   C: Professional Practice   T: Application

1. This is a patronizing answer and does not find a solution to the pain management problem.
2. This is an action-oriented response. It is the role of the palliative care team to appropriately manage pain and the ethics of increased morphine.
3. This implies that the nurse does not have a professional role in pain management.
4. Depending on the specifics of the situation, this may or may not be true. But it does not solve the problem of Mr. Morrissey's pain management.

67.   C: Changes in Health   T: Application

1. This should not be the initial action as it may be unpleasant for Mr. Morrissey and may not be necessary.
2. This may be necessary depending on a thorough assessment of the constipation. It would be a last resort for impacted feces that did not respond to a suppository.
3. Bulk-forming agents require the person to ingest larger amounts of fluids, which Mr. Morrissey is not able to do. They also require time to achieve results.
4. This is the most appropriate and comfortable initial action. The suppository may soften the stool so that Mr. Morrissey will be able to pass it with limited effort.

68.   C: Changes in Health   T: Application

1. Skin dryness can lead to discomfort. Lubricating the lips and mucous membranes is soothing.
2. This is likely not appropriate close to death, unless

he has requested an IV.

3. Injections of saline under the skin are not appropriate to maintain hydration, unless he or the family has requested it.
4. This is not appropriate unless requested.

69.   C: Changes in Health   T: Application

1. Clients with pharyngitis usually present with sore throat ranging in severity from "scratchy" to severe pain that makes swallowing painful. The pharynx is red and edematous, with or without patchy exudates.
2. Symptoms of croup include a barky cough with low-grade fever. The voice may be harsh, but the client is able to speak and swallow.
3. Bronchiolitis, most often caused by the respiratory syncytial virus (RSV), is common in infants during the fall and winter. It is frequently found in northern communities. It often begins with an upper respiratory infection. Symptoms include dyspnea, paroxysmal nonproductive cough, tachypnea with retractions and nasal flaring, and wheezing.
4. Epiglottitis is most commonly found in children between the ages of 2 and 5 years. Signs and symptoms include sudden onset of high fever, difficulty breathing, severe sore throat, difficulty swallowing, drooling, and muffled voice, but no cough.

70.   C: Changes in Health   T: Application

1. Antivirals are not used with this condition.
2. Mist therapy is generally combined with oxygen to alleviate the dyspnea and hypoxia.
3. Cough suppressants are not recommended for children.
4. Antibiotics are of no use with viral illnesses.

71.   C: Health and Wellness   T: Application

1. Respiratory syncytial virus (RSV) is very contagious, and Sean should not be with other infants.
2. Sean requires isolation to prevent transmission to others.
3. If there are no isolation rooms, placement with adults would be the next best choice as adults are not as severely affected by RSV.
4. The nurse may want to monitor Sean's condition by having him close by; however, he should be isolated.

72.   C: Nurse-Client Partnership   T: Critical Thinking

1. This is not the philosophy of family-centred care. It is not the nurse's role to tell the parents it is best for them to leave their son.

2. This is the appropriate response and validates family-centred care and the role of his parents in Sean's care.
3. The nurse should not imply she would not be able to adequately look after Sean if they do not stay. This will not promote trust in her nursing care.
4. There is no evidence that there is not enough room. Both parents should be able to stay. The nurse should not presume that if only one parent stays, it would be the mother.

73.   C: Changes in Health   T: Critical Thinking

1. This is the priority assessment. As with any invasive procedure, bleeding from an arterial access device carries considerable risk and could be life-threatening.
2. This is important but not a priority postprocedure. BP should be taken on the arm opposite the insertion site.
3. This is an important observation postinsertion and will need to be assessed at all times while the device is in situ. Immediately postprocedure, it is not the priority assessment.
4. This must be determined by the physician at the time of insertion and monitored thereafter by the nurse, but it is not the most critical assessment postprocedure.

74.   C: Changes in Health   T: Application

1. This is not true, either for colonic irrigations or colostomy irrigations.
2. The primary purpose of irrigating a colostomy is to promote regular bowel movements.
3. It is not necessary to cleanse the anastomosis site.
4. Constipation is not a common occurrence with a colostomy. Regular irrigation may help prevent constipation, but it does so by promoting regular bowel movements.

75.   C: Changes in Health   T: Critical Thinking

1. The inability to void may be due to residual effects from an anaesthetic. As well, voiding into a bedpan is not easy for many clients, so this would not be the optimal strategy, unless Ms. Urquhart is unable to ambulate.
2. This should be the first action. If Ms. Urquhart has a full bladder, further and more immediate action will be required. If the bladder is not distended, the situation is less urgent.
3. This may happen but is not necessary until the bladder is assessed for distension.
4. This should be done after Ms. Urquhart is assessed for bladder distension.

76.   C: Changes in Health   T: Knowledge

1. Glaucoma is manifested by loss of peripheral vision, producing "tunnel vision" and halos around lights.
2. With cataracts, vision loss is generally progressive blurring or haziness.
3. With macular degeneration, close vision tasks become difficult.
4. A detached retina may cause loss of vision in the affected area, blurring, or spots and flashes of light.

77.   C: Health and Wellness   T: Knowledge

1. This hormone is produced by the chorionic villi of the developing embryo and is present in the blood and urine of a pregnant woman.
2. Estrogen prepares the uterus for pregnancy. An elevation in estrogen occurs later in pregnancy and does not necessarily indicate pregnancy.
3. Progesterone helps maintain the pregnancy and prepare the breasts for lactation but is not the hormone detected in pregnancy tests.
4. Follicle-stimulating hormone (FSH) helps mature follicles but is not the hormone detected in pregnancy tests.

78.   C: Changes in Health   T: Critical Thinking

1. An occlusive dressing is needed to prevent air from entering the pleural space.
2. The physician will need to be notified to reintroduce the tube; however, the initial action must be to occlude the puncture site.
3. This will not be as effective as the occlusive dressing.
4. This will not prevent air from entering the pleural space.

79.   C: Health and Wellness   T: Application

1. Five to 10 mm of induration may be significant. This is not normal.
2. This is the appropriate action as it is the physician's responsibility to further interpret the results and decide on further diagnostics.
3. This is not a definitively positive test. It is presumptive to tell Mr. Gupta that he requires prophylactic treatment.
4. Although the protocol on repeating inconclusive tests varies among agencies, in this situation, it is not apparent that the nurse has the authority to repeat the test without consulting the physician.

80.   C: Changes in Health   T: Critical Thinking

1. This is the correct emergency action. Pressure to the site of bleeding will help control the bleeding.

2. This should not be done as it may compromise arterial blood flow.
3. This is important, but the priority is to control the bleeding.
4. Elevating the arm will help control the hemorrhage but is not as important as pressure at the site.

81.   C: Changes in Health   T: Application

1. The vastus lateralis is the best-developed muscle in infants and is the safest for intramuscular injections.
2. This is not a well-developed muscle in the infant.
3. As in choice 2.
4. As in choice 2.

82.   C: Health and Wellness   T: Knowledge

1. Morbidity refers to the incidence of disease within a defined population.
2. Morbidity does not refer to disease effects.
3. This is the definition of mortality.
4. This refers to the ability of an infectious disease to spread within a population.

83.   C: Changes in Health   T: Application

1. Calculi are more likely to form when the urine is concentrated. Increased fluids help dilute the urine.
2. Dairy products should be decreased as they contain calcium. Most kidney stones are calcium oxalate.
3. Tea and chocolate have high levels of oxalate and should be reduced in the diet.
4. Use of antacids is to be avoided as they contain calcium.

84.   C: Changes in Health   T: Critical Thinking

1. A concern about overuse of antibiotics is that they will lose their effectiveness and create drug-resistant strains.
2. Some antibiotics cause diarrhea, but they will not cause chronic diarrhea.
3. Hearing loss may occur due to the chronic otitis media, but not due to the family of antibiotics used for otitis.
4. Antibiotics do not cause dependence.

85.   C: Changes in Health   T: Critical Thinking

1. The heart rate should be monitored for trends, and particularly for bradycardia, but a rate of 80 bpm is not a concern.
2. It is likely that Mr. Bland has an altered level of consciousness (LOC) caused by the stroke. LOC

must be monitored but is not the most important concern during t-PA.
3. Blood pressure must be monitored carefully during therapy. This blood pressure is not of concern.
4. Hematuria is a sign of bleeding, which is a significant danger in fibrinolysis.

86.   C: Health and Wellness   T: Knowledge

1. In 2012, estimates from the Canadian Cancer Society are 20,100 deaths due to lung cancer, making it the leading cause of cancer deaths.
2. Breast cancer causes an estimated 5200 deaths per year.
3. Colorectal cancer is the second-leading cause of cancer deaths in Canada, at an estimated 9200 per year.
4. Prostate cancer causes an estimated 4000 deaths per year.

87.   C: Nurse–Client Partnership   T: Application

1. While a referral is a good option for Mr. Shafikhani, this does not address the immediate concern of not being able to drive.
2. This open-ended question deals practically and emotionally with the issue of a young male no longer being able to drive.
3. The nurse does not know Mr. Shafikhani's feelings. This sounds patronizing and does not invite therapeutic communication.
4. This is a closed question. The nurse may only get a yes or no answer. He may infer that she thinks he is not intelligent enough to understand.

88.   C: Nurse–Client Partnership   T: Critical Thinking

1. Emotional reactions to the pregnancy loss must be explored, but this question is inappropriate and insensitive.
2. Aubrey's Rh status must be identified. If she is Rh-negative, she will require administration of RhoGAM within 72 hours of the miscarriage to prevent antibody formation in future pregnancies.
3. This is an appropriate question but is not as important as determination of the mother's Rh status.
4. This may be an important question if Aubrey requires a D&C but is not important at this stage and may imply that Aubrey was at fault for the miscarriage.

89.   C: Changes in Health   T: Application

1. Coughing moves secretions from the lower airway into the mouth and upper airway and may decrease the amount of suctioning required.

2. Oral suctioning does not require sterile technique.
3. This is a measurement for a nasogastric tube.
4. Oil-based lubricants are not to be used as they are not water soluble and may be aspirated.

90.   C: Professional Practice   T: Critical Thinking

1. This is not a safe option as some residents may answer to any name.
2. This is not a professional option.
3. The Director of Care is responsible for policies and care in the agency and needs to be consulted regarding the safest option. This may involve the director administering the medications.
4. This may be safer than the photos or self-reporting alone, but does not necessarily guarantee the correct resident would receive the medication.

91.   C: Changes in Health   T: Critical Thinking

1. Cotton may be ordered post–eardrop instillation, but it will not prevent the mineral oil from flowing back out of the right ear during immediate instillation in the left ear.
2. This would be a medication error as the drops must be instilled in both ears every 8 hours.
3. This will not prevent the drops from flowing back out of the right ear.
4. This is the correct procedure. Mr. Lewis must remain in the side-lying position for at least 10 minutes in order for the drops to effectively be delivered to deeper ear structures.

92.   C: Changes in Health   T: Application

1. This may compromise her breathing.
2. The semi-Fowler's position reduces the pressure of the enlarged abdomen on the diaphragm.
3. This will assist breathing somewhat but is not the most effective.
4. This may compromise breathing.

93.   C: Professional Practice   T: Application

1. Angie's behaviour is unprofessional: smoking on health care premises is contrary to agency policies and most municipal by-laws. As well, Angie is placing the clients at risk from second-hand smoke. Harriet must report Angie's disregard of policies, the law, and client safety.
2. Angie is on agency property; whether she is on a scheduled break is not pertinent.
3. It is likely that Angie is already aware of agency policies and the dangers of second-hand smoke. This does not address her unprofessional behaviour.
4. This discussion may be held at a different time. The professional responsibility for Harriet is to stop and report the behaviour.

94.   C: Professional Practice   T: Critical Thinking

1. This is potential fraud and needs to be reported.
2. This is the appropriate chain of command. The nurse manager will investigate.
3. This will be done by the nurse manager.
4. This could be done, but only if the nurse views unsafe practice.

95.   C: Changes in Health   T: Application

1. Cranberry and blueberry juices, not orange juice, will help prevent UTIs.
2. Cotton, not synthetic, underpants are recommended.
3. Sexual intercourse can "milk" bacteria from the vagina and perineum into the urethra. Use of a lubricant will decrease the incidence of skin breakdown in the urethral area, and use of a condom may prevent the transmission of bacteria from her partner(s).
4. Vaginal yeast disorders do not predispose clients to UTIs, unless related itching causes skin breakdown.

96.   C: Changes in Health   T: Critical Thinking

1. There may be a risk of vomiting, but this is not the primary rationale. The answer must provide a rationale for both the NPO and the detection of bowel sounds.
2. Anaesthesia slows peristalsis. Hearing bowel sounds is an indication that peristalsis has returned. If Mrs. Brankston is fed when the bowel is not moving, the food would remain in the upper GI system, possibly leading to vomiting, obstruction, discomfort, and potential aspiration.
3. Unless there is peristalsis, it is not likely that any food will reach the operative site.
4. A side effect of anaesthesia is nausea; however, this is not a postoperative rationale for NPO until bowel sounds are heard.

97.   C: Changes in Health   T: Critical Thinking

1. There is no reason to contact the doctor. Early decelerations are a normal pattern.
2. This would be appropriate for late decelerations.
3. This is appropriate if Ms. Loates's membranes had ruptured.
4. No action is required. Early decelerations are a normal fetal heart rate pattern during labour.

98.   C: Changes in Health   T: Application

1. +900 mL: incorrect calculation
2. +250 mL: 760 mL + 140 mL = 900 mL total intake

540 mL + 110 mL = 650 mL total output
For fluid balance, subtract output from intake:
900 mL – 650 mL = 250 mL positive balance
3. –650 mL: incorrect calculation
4. –110 mL: incorrect calculation

99.   C: Changes in Health   T: Application

1. This is reaction formation.
2. This is the definition of displacement. Ms. Henry is displacing her anger at the physician toward the nurse.
3. This is repression.
4. This is denial.

100.   C: Changes in Health   T: Application

1. This would indicate four pregnancies, but Mrs. Townsend has been pregnant only three times.
2. This would denote three pregnancies, which is correct, but also three living children. Mrs. Townsend has only two living children.
3. Gravida 3 is correct: the present pregnancy, the pregnancy that resulted in twin births, and the previous miscarriage. Para 2 is correct: Mrs. Townsend has two living twin children.
4. This would indicate two pregnancies and one living child.

101.   C: Changes in Health   T: Knowledge

1. Elevated levels of alpha-fetoprotein (AFP) in maternal blood may indicate an open neural tube defect in the developing fetus.
2. This substance is the basis for the pregnancy test.
3. This is a presumptive sign of pregnancy.
4. Amniocentesis is an invasive diagnostic procedure that may be ordered following the detection of elevated AFP levels.

102.   C: Health and Wellness   T: Application

1. This is not necessarily true. Melatonin is increased in response to sun exposure, not when someone feels hot or cold. Also, people vary in the amount of melatonin they have naturally.
2. This is a physiological response to cold. The constriction of the blood vessels to conserve heat means that there is not as much blood close to the skin surface, with the result that the skin appears a paler colour.
3. This may occur, but this is not what Mr. Brendan asked.
4. This is the opposite of what occurs.

103.   C: Health and Wellness   T: Application

1. This is an extreme measure and not necessary.
2. Although thorough cleaning is necessary at any day care, in this situation, it is not necessary for the day care to close. Transmission is most likely via contact with the infected child.
3. This is not true. See choice 4.
4. Impetigo is an infection of the skin caused by *Streptococcus* or *Staphylococcus* bacteria and is transmissible to other children. The child with impetigo must be isolated from other children until 24–48 hours after treatment has started.

104.   C: Professional Practice   T: Application

1. This may be an important part of the client assessment, depending on the situation and client problem.
2. This may help put the client at ease.
3. This is a therapeutic response.
4. This is crossing a boundary. It implies a special relationship between the client and the nurse. The nurse must inform the client that all relevant information must be shared with other members of the health care team.

105.   C: Health and Wellness   T: Application

1. These are manifestations of irritable bowel disease, which does not cause rectal bleeding.
2. This may be necessary once hemorrhoids or constipation is ruled out as a cause for the bleeding.
3. This is not a necessary test as Brad has said the blood is visible.
4. The most common cause of minor rectal bleeding is tearing of the rectal mucosa due to constipation and hard stool.

106.   C: Professional Practice   T: Critical Thinking

1. Artificial nails may be trimmed to an appropriate length that would not scratch or injure a client.
2. This is possible, but not likely, and would not be the most appropriate reason for the policy.
3. Artificial nails, if kept well trimmed and without polish, may be professional in appearance.
4. Studies have shown that artificial nails, especially if not well maintained, may have crevices that enable microorganisms to flourish.

107.   C: Health and Wellness   T: Critical Thinking

1. This question could be asked as some prescription and nonprescription drugs cause drowsiness as a side effect. However, medications are not the most

frequent cause of adolescent fatigue.
2. Lack of exercise may lead to fatigue during the day but is not the most common cause of adolescent fatigue.
3. This may be important information to obtain but should not be the initial question.
4. The most common cause of daytime fatigue at all ages is inadequate sleep. Most teenagers do not know they need approximately nine hours of sleep each night.

108.   C: Changes in Health   T: Application

1. Large-print books are needed for people who have severe vision problems.
2. Instruction in Braille is not necessary. Vision of 20/40 is mild vision loss.
3. While an ophthalmologist can prescribe corrective lenses, generally, for simple near-sightedness, referral is not required.
4. A score of 20/40 indicates vision that will likely respond well to corrective lenses, either glasses or contact lenses.

109.   C: Health and Wellness   T: Application

1. This is a common STI in both sexes but is not the most prevalent.
2. This is not the most prevalent STI in Canada.
3. This is the most common STI in males but not in the general population.
4. Chlamydia is the most widespread STI in Canada.

110.   C: Changes in Health   T: Critical Thinking

1. Injuries occurring from the fall will need to be assessed, treated, and documented, but this is not the most important initial action.
2. Circulation is not the first priority.
3. Breathing is assessed after assessing for a patent airway.
4. The priority of assessment is according to the ABCs: airway, breathing, and circulation. A clear airway is necessary for breathing and must be the initial assessment.

111.   C: Professional Practice   T: Critical Thinking

1. Meperidine should not be administered as there is confusion concerning the correct drug.
2. This should not be done until the correct drug is clarified.
3. This could be done once the drug is clarified.
4. Meperidine is the generic name for Demerol, not morphine. The ordered dose is within the normal dosing range for morphine. The medication order must be clarified with the prescriber prior to any other action.

112.   **C: Changes in Health   T: Critical Thinking**

1. Tympanic thermometers should not be used with clients who have ear infections or ear pain.
2. An axillary temperature is not as accurate as tympanic, oral, or rectal temperature, but in this situation, it is the most appropriate approach. The thermometer should be kept under the axilla for five minutes.
3. Oral thermometers should not be used with an 18-month-old child. In addition, a child who is mouth breathing may not be able to keep his or her mouth closed for the required time, and this may lead to an inaccurate reading.
4. Rectal temperatures should not generally be used with children due to the risk of rectal injury and the discomfort and distress related to the procedure.

113.   **C: Nurse–Client Partnership   T: Application**

1. This does not answer Mr. Rivers's question.
2. This reassures Mr. Rivers that he is well enough to be discharged, he will have support by nurses in his home, and this is better for him.
3. This may be true but will not be reassuring for Mr. Rivers.
4. This is true but does not answer Mr. Rivers's question or reassure him.

114.   **C: Health and Wellness   T: Application**

1. It is not exactly the same, and the nurse has not answered that it is a normal temperature.
2. The conversion of 36.6 degrees Celsius to Fahrenheit is 97.9, or 98 degrees.

$$\frac{36.6 \times 9}{5} + 32 = 97.9$$

   This is considered a normal temperature. Many clients who were not educated in the metric system prefer to use the Fahrenheit scale.
3. This is an incorrect conversion and is not elevated.
4. It is lower, but not significantly, and is still considered to be a normal temperature.

115.   **C: Changes in Health   T: Application**

1. The voices are real to Mr. Constant, so this is not therapeutic.
2. The voices are real and frightening to Mr. Constant. Acknowledging this, and staying with him, demonstrates concern and may reduce his fears.
3. Mr. Constant will not be able to concentrate on the TV because of his fears.
4. Mr. Constant is not able to separate the voices from reality.

116.   **C: Professional Practice   T: Critical Thinking**

1. This will need to be done once the nurse assesses the type of allergic reaction.
2. As in choice 1.
3. This is important, but the nurse initially needs more information about the allergy.
4. It is important to first obtain more information from Mrs. Collins about the allergy. Some clients have a sensitivity reaction; with others, it may be anaphylactic.

117.   **C: Changes in Health   T: Application**

1. Milk-based foods are likely to irritate the gut and cause further diarrhea.
2. This is not appropriate in a child.
3. With mild diarrhea, clear fluids will maintain hydration and will not irritate the gut. Crackers are also appropriate and will decrease Teklie's hunger.
4. A normal diet may be resumed once the diarrhea has stopped.

118.   **C: Professional Practice   T: Critical Thinking**

1. This may help, but generally 2 people are required for a mechanical lift.
2. The nurse needs more data, as what the client is telling her is different from her assessment.
3. The nurse will probably have to obtain assistance, but it is best to find out first from Mrs. Bennett more information about the lift.
4. This could potentially be dangerous for both Mrs. Bennett and the nurse.

119.   **C: Changes in Health   T: Critical Thinking**

1. Medications can trigger delirium, but this is not the most important step in the data collection.
2. All of these responses are important when assessing the cause of Mrs. Sheyer's delirium. By obtaining a baseline understanding of Mrs. Sheyer's cognitive function, it can be better determined how, or if, her behaviour has changed and what particular triggers may have been involved.
3. Dehydration can cause delirium in an older client but is not the most important step in the data collection.
4. Fever or infection may trigger delirium, but this is not the most important step in the data collection.

120.   **C: Nurse–Client Partnership   T: Application**

1. This allows Ms. Isabelle to continue with inappropriate behaviour and is not therapeutic toward Mr. Olan.

2. As in choice 1.
3. This response is clear, provides exact information without appearing punitive toward Ms. Isabelle, and demonstrates respect for both clients.
4. This response is punitive.

121. C: Changes in Health   T: Critical Thinking

1. This is important; however, the nurse's expertise is needed with the toddler. It is more appropriate for the nurse to delegate another to call 9-1-1.
2. The nurse should observe for a patent airway, but this is not a safe option. It may cause damage to the mouth and teeth.
3. The safest option with a child is to observe the seizure, make sure the child is not injuring him- or herself, and ensure that they are maintaining a patent airway and not to actively intervene or attempt to restrain the child. These observations will be helpful when emergency medical personnel arrive at the scene.
4. This is not the priority action. It may be appropriate once the seizure is over.

122. C: Nurse–Client Partnership   T: Critical Thinking

1. This is not true. At age 10 years, Nicholas would have an understanding of the diagnosis.
2. This response opens up communication with the parents.
3. This may be true but closes communication.
4. This may be true but may upset the parents and may not encourage communication.

123. C: Professional Practice   T: Critical Thinking

1. This category of nurse is appropriate; however, the knowledge and skills of an RN would be more appropriately used for a more acutely ill, unstable client.
2. The RPN or LPN is the most appropriate caregiver as the practical nurse provides care to clients such as Mr. Michener, whose conditions are stable and whose outcomes are predictable. The practical nurse has the competency to perform discharge health teaching, and assigning this task to him or her is more cost-effective than assigning it to a registered nurse.
3. While this category of nurse is certainly competent to provide care, his or her knowledge and skills would be more appropriately used for an acutely ill or complex client; therefore, this is not the most cost-effective option.
4. The UCP would be appropriate to provide some basic care for Mr. Michener but would not have the knowledge to provide discharge health teaching or wound assessment.

124. C: Changes in Health   T: Application

1. This is a normal finding in the skin of a 59-year-old woman.
2. As in choice 1.
3. This could be a possible finding of skin cancer and should be further investigated.
4. These are more commonly known as "age spots" or "liver spots" and may be seen in adults starting in their late forties or fifties.

125. C: Professional Practice   T: Critical Thinking

1. There is no reason to wait an hour. The elevated temperature must be confirmed as soon as possible as temperatures in children can rise rapidly.
2. It is neither appropriate nor necessary to obtain a rectal temperature. The use of a rectal thermometer would be very upsetting and intrusive for a 4-year-old.
3. This action should not be taken until the temperature is confirmed. Other evidence suggests that Nick may not have a fever.
4. The second step of the nursing process is validation of data collected. Nick does not display manifestations of a fever; therefore, it is possible that the thermometer is malfunctioning or requires recalibration. The temperature should be confirmed using another thermometer.

126. C: Professional Practice   T: Application

1. This is factual documentation of observed behaviour.
2. This is an assumption and interpretation of behaviour. Documentation requires the inclusion only of observable facts.
3. As in choice 2.
4. As in choice 2.

127. C: Changes in Health   T: Critical Thinking

1. Topical anaesthetic creams are effective in preventing pain from immunization and may help prevent future fear of needles.
2. Distraction techniques may help decrease stress and minimize pain, but they are not as effective as the anaesthetic cream.
3. As in choice 2.
4. Postinjection analgesics are often prescribed but are most useful with children who develop swelling and fever postimmunization. They do not prevent the pain of injections but treat it after the fact.

128.   **C: Professional Practice   T: Critical Thinking**

1. All responses could be correct. This is the first action as the manager needs objective data: the number of accidents and types of accidents on the unit.
2. This is a good action, but is not as important as the actual accident statistics.
3. The manager should know this information. Not all accidents may cause staff to be on long-term disability.
4. As in Choice 2.

129.   **C: Professional Practice   T: Critical Thinking**

1. Although there is a difference in the scope of practice of registered nurses and practical nurses, at the level of a second-year student, an exemplary practical nurse would be a valuable preceptor. What is most important is the level of knowledge, expertise, and competence of the practical nurse.
2. It is not true of all jurisdictions that RNs supervise practical nurses.

3. As part of a collaborative practice model, practical nurses who are competent, familiar with the practice setting, aware of the differences in scopes of practice, and exemplary nurses are appropriate preceptors for student RNs.
4. There are contraindications only if the level of expertise, competency, and level of client acuity are not considered.

130.   **C: Health and Wellness   T: Critical Thinking**

1. Influenza is communicated primarily by droplet and contact transmission. Having symptomatic clients segregated, wearing masks, and performing hand hygiene will decrease the incidence of viral particles coming in contact with other clients.
2. This is not practical, and the vaccine requires up to two weeks to provide immunity.
3. This is not ethical. As well, people with influenza may be infectious before they have symptoms.
4. Droplet transmission is possible up to two metres from an infected person.

Practice Exam

Book Two

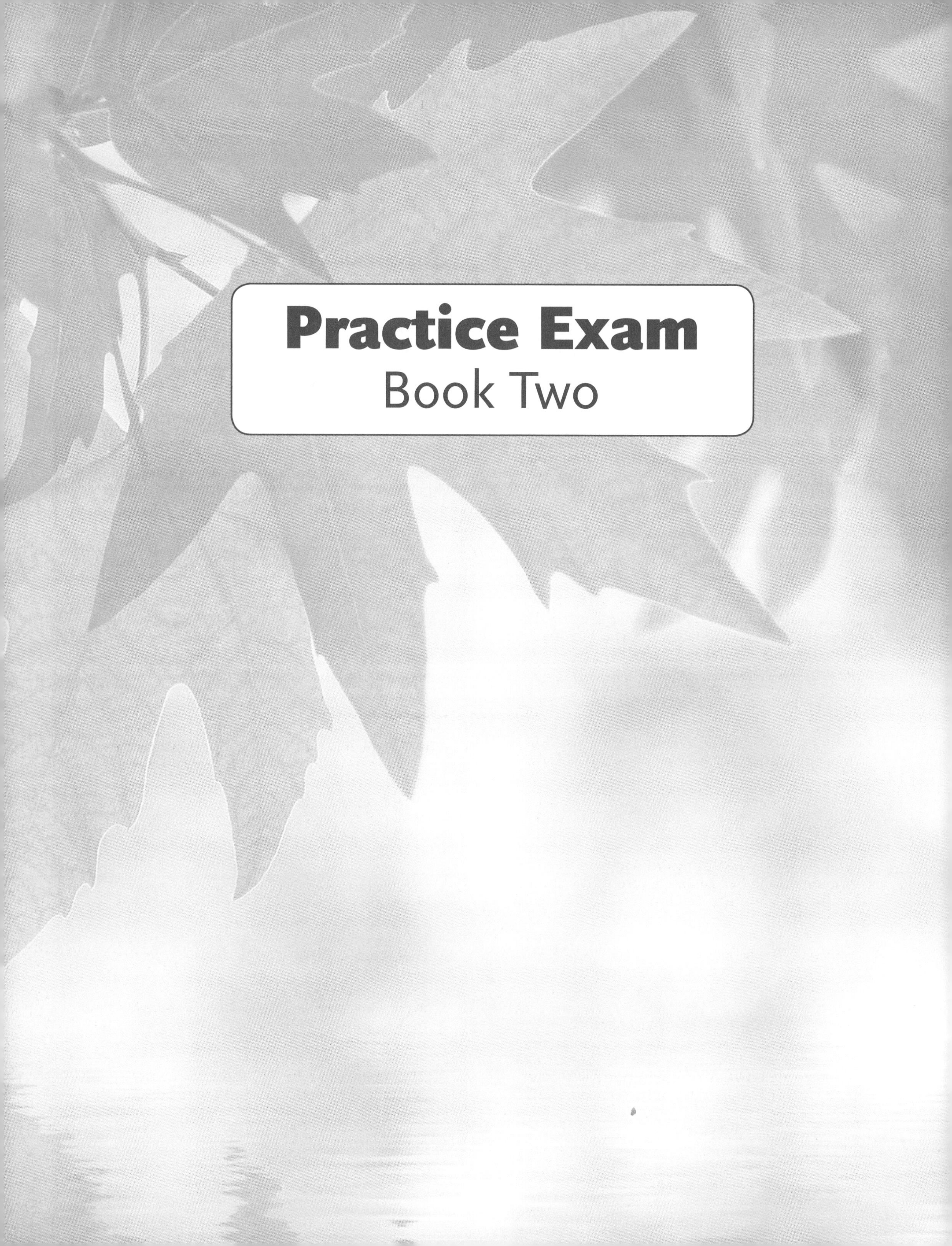

PRACTICE EXAM – BOOK TWO

CASE QUESTIONS

Case 1

A registered nurse is employed by a hospital-based palliative care team that includes a physician, a pharmacist, and a social worker. The nurse is the primary member of the team supporting the family of Mrs. Haliburton, who is terminally ill with stomach cancer and has chosen to die at home.

Questions 1–5 refer to this case.

---

1. The family asks the nurse how they will know Mrs. Haliburton's death is imminent. What should the nurse respond?

1. Her skin may become mottled
2. Her respirations will be slow and deep
3. Her pulse will increase
4. Her temperature will decrease

2. One morning when the nurse visits, he finds the family sitting around Mrs. Haliburton's bed, crying. They tell him that she stopped breathing 30 minutes ago. The nurse examines Mrs. Haliburton and finds no respirations, no heart rate, and no pupillary reaction, and her body is cooling. What should be the first action by the nurse?

1. Confirm to the family that Mrs. Haliburton has died
2. Pronounce death and document it in the health record
3. Call the physician for him to complete a death certificate
4. Notify the funeral home

3. Mrs. Haliburton's health record had been kept in her home during her palliative care. What should the nurse do with Mrs. Haliburton's health record after her death?

1. Leave it with the family
2. Put it in a sealed envelope for the physician
3. Take it to the agency that employs the palliative care team
4. Destroy the record as it is no longer needed

4. Several days later, the family calls the nurse to ask him what to do with Mrs. Haliburton's left-over morphine. What should the nurse say to them?

1. "Take it to your pharmacy."
2. "I will pick it up."
3. "Dispose of it in the biohazard container I left."
4. "Keep it just in case another family member requires morphine."

5. The nurse has been working in palliative care for several years and is surprised when he feels tremendous sadness at Mrs. Haliburton's death. What should the nurse initially do to cope with these emotions?

1. Examine his patterns of dealing with grief
2. Arrange for time off or a vacation
3. Reflect on the need to change to another specialty in nursing
4. Make an appointment with a psychiatrist who specializes in palliative care

---

Case 2

Jean Cetaine, age 68, is golfing with his friends when he develops severe chest pain and shortness of breath. His friends call an ambulance, and he is transported to hospital, where he is diagnosed with unstable angina.

Questions 6–9 refer to this case.

---

6. Upon Mr. Cetaine's arrival in the emergency department, which of the following is a "first-line" medication he will likely receive?

1. Nitroglycerine (Nitrolingual)
2. Propranolol (Inderal)
3. Tissue plasminogen activator (t-PA)
4. Captopril (Capoten)

7. Which of the following tests will best evaluate the extent of Mr. Cetaine's coronary artery disease?

1. Chest X-ray
2. Cardiac ultrasonography
3. Electrocardiography (ECG)
4. Angiography

8. It is decided that Mr. Cetaine requires coronary bypass surgery (CABG). What is the purpose of coronary artery bypass surgery?

1. To provide a new circuit for blood flow to get to the heart muscle
2. To repair damage to the heart muscle
3. To provide new vessels bringing blood to the right atrium
4. To provide a route for blood to flow past obstructions in the ascending aorta

9. Nursing care within the first three days postsurgery for Mr. Cetaine would include which of the following?

1. Complete bed rest
2. Care for two surgical sites

3. Administration of oxygen via nasal cannula at 3 L/min
4. Prn analgesia

Case 3

A nurse educator provides an orientation session about documentation to recently hired registered nurses.

Questions 10–13 refer to this case.

10. The nurse educator reviews the purpose of documentation. Of the following, which is the most important reason for client documentation?

    1. To facilitate communication concerning the client
    2. To demonstrate nursing accountability and professional practice
    3. To provide a source of data for evidence-informed practice
    4. To identify the type and amount of care clients require

11. The nurse educator presents a case scenario about a client who requests information from his health record. When care is provided through an agency, who owns and has access to the health record?

    1. The agency owns the health record, and the client has access only in exceptional circumstances
    2. The client owns the health record and must provide consent to agency staff for its use for purposes related to care
    3. The agency and the client co-own the health record, and both have equal access to the information
    4. The agency owns the health record, but the client has legal access to the information according to agency policies

12. The nurse educator cautions the nurses to only record care they personally provide. When is it acceptable to document care provided by another nurse?

    1. When the other nurse is not registered
    2. During an emergency when more than one nurse is involved
    3. When two or more nurses care for a client, only one nurse is required to document
    4. There are no exceptions to the practice of never documenting for another

13. The nurse educator presents another case scenario to the group. A postmastectomy client, Ms. Scharfe, has been crying, refuses to eat, and will not speak to her husband. The nurse educator asks the group to record this behaviour. What is the best documentation of this client situation?

    1. "Ms. Scharfe shows manifestations of depression."
    2. "Ms. Scharfe is upset due to her mastectomy."

3. "Ms. Scharfe is crying, refuses food, will not talk to her husband."
4. "Ms. Scharfe experienced an emotional postop day, with periods of weeping and anorexia due to pain and anaesthetic, and was ignoring her husband."

Case 4

Glen Martin has a history of alcohol dependence with a high daily intake of alcohol for 15 years. He has made several attempts to stop drinking, has attended Alcoholics Anonymous and private counselling, and has told his wife that he no longer drinks. She arrives home one day to find him confused, smelling of alcohol, and with hand tremors. She takes him to the local emergency department.

Questions 14–19 refer to this case.

14. The health care team tell Mrs. Martin that her husband is experiencing acute alcohol withdrawal and must be admitted to hospital. What is the most important reason alcohol-dependent people need to be monitored carefully while withdrawing from alcohol?

    1. Cardiac failure
    2. Acute organ failure
    3. Seizures
    4. Risk of suicide

15. Mrs. Martin says that she can't understand why her husband was drinking because he had promised her he had stopped. What should the nurse respond to Mrs. Martin?

    1. "Because of the effects of alcohol on the brain, he likely did not know what he was doing."
    2. "Why do you think he was lying to you?"
    3. "Your husband is trying to change a long-term habit, and lapses are sometimes to be expected."
    4. "He probably can't help himself."

16. After Mr. Martin's successful detoxification, the health care team notices that he has jaundice. Tests are ordered to confirm a diagnosis of cirrhosis of the liver. Which test should be ordered to confirm the level of jaundice?

    1. Alkaline phosphatase
    2. Serum bilirubin
    3. Alanine aminotransferase (ALT)
    4. Prothrombin time (PT)

17. Mrs. Martin asks the nurse why her husband is yellow. What would be the most appropriate answer by the nurse?

1. "Your husband has jaundice."
2. "There is inadequate hepatodetoxification of cellular metabolites resulting from scleroses related to alcohol."
3. "The effects of alcohol on the liver have interfered with the ability to remove a yellow pigment that is released when red blood cells break down."
4. "Pressure of the liver on the kidneys prevents them from filtering urine effectively, so it builds up in his system, causing the yellow colour."

18. The nurse teaches Mr. and Mrs. Martin about therapeutic nutrition related to cirrhosis. Which of the following breakfast menus should the nurse recommend?

1. Toast, margarine, and banana
2. Cheese omelette
3. Bagel and peanut butter
4. Ham, eggs, and hash brown potatoes

19. Mr. Martin is ready to be discharged home, with a referral to an outpatient alcohol rehabilitation program. He has refused alcohol aversion medications. Mrs. Martin is concerned that he will start drinking again. She states that she will consent to giving him disulfiram (Antabuse) but tell him that it is a vitamin. How should the nurse respond?

1. "Can you arrange to be made his Substitute Decision Maker so that you can consent to the Antabuse?"
2. "Mr. Martin cannot be given Antabuse without his consent."
3. "That would be helpful, but I don't think you would be allowed to consent for him."
4. "Perhaps you can get the doctor to order it for you and then give it to your husband."

Case 5

Mr. Ian Lewis is an 83-year-old man who has been referred to the respiratory clinic. He has chronic obstructive pulmonary disease (COPD) and asthma, with poor symptom control for the past few months. Mr. Lewis is frail but lives alone and independently.

Questions 20–23 refer to this case.

20. The nurse reviews Mr. Lewis's health history. She asks him about his use of over-the-counter (OTC) medications. What medication would be of most concern to the nurse?

1. Aspirin (ASA)
2. Acetaminopn (Tylenol®)
3. Ibuprofen (Advil®, Motrin®)
4. Loratidine (Claritin®)

21. Mr. Lewis reports that he takes a combination inhaler that contains a long-acting beta$_2$ agonist as well as a steroid. What is the therapeutic action of these two medications?

1. The medications act in combination to decrease airway inflammation
2. They work in combination to decrease airway bronchoconstriction
3. They provide bronchodilation and reduced airway inflammation
4. The two medications potentiate each other and provide longer-acting symptom control

22. The nurse asks Mr. Lewis to demonstrate the use of his aerosol metered-dose inhaler (MDI) and observes that he has difficulty using the MDI effectively. What should the nurse recommend to Mr. Lewis?

1. He should consult with the pharmacist about taking his medications in a form other than the inhaled route
2. There are oral forms of the medications that are just as effective and easier for him to take
3. A spacer used with the MDI is easier to use and will provide better delivery of medication to his airway
4. He will need to be re-educated in the use of inhaled medications

23. Mr. Lewis tells the nurse he becomes quite frightened when he has a "bad attack" of asthma. He becomes very short of breath, wheezes, and feels as if he is drowning. What should the nurse teach him about the first thing he should do for a serious acute episode of shortness of breath?

1. Take his combination inhaled drugs to relieve the bronchoconstriction
2. Call 9-1-1 to take him to the hospital for emergency respiratory therapy
3. Breathe cool, humidified air to liquefy secretions and open the airways
4. Use his "rescue inhaler" and wait for about 10 minutes to assess if it restores normal breathing

Case 6

A registered nurse is the manager of a busy family practice clinic. She supervises clinic staff, maintains client health records, and provides primary nursing care to clients.

Questions 24–27 refer to this case.

24. Ryan Fraser is a new client to the clinic. He brings his health record from his previous doctor and asks the nurse manager who will have access to his health record at this clinic. What should the nurse manager tell Mr. Fraser?

1. "Only the doctor has access to your record."
2. "Any of the staff working in the clinic may see your record."
3. "The doctor, clerical staff, and myself are able to view your health record."
4. "You may keep your record if you are concerned about confidentiality."

25. The nurse manager facilitates booking screening tests for clients. Which of the following clients should have priority in scheduling for a screening colonoscopy?

    1. Nonie Masseur, age 48, who has a sister recently diagnosed with colon cancer
    2. Norma Williams, age 36, who has hemorrhoids
    3. Nancy Morgan, age 42, who has irritable bowel syndrome
    4. Anne Daniels, age 29, who has tested positive for the *BRCA1* gene mutation

26. Miss Shannon has had disabling knee pain for several months and is booked to have magnetic resonance imaging (MRI) in several months. Miss Shannon does not want to wait this long and asks the nurse how she can get the test done earlier. What should the nurse respond?

    1. "Only clients with life-threatening illnesses can have immediate MRI scans."
    2. "You could call the MRI clinic to ask to be put on the cancellation list."
    3. "In Canada, there are not sufficient MRI machines, so you will have to wait until one is available."
    4. "It is not likely that your knee pain is serious, so be reassured that waiting will not contribute to a worsening of your condition."

27. The nurse performs an intramuscular injection on Mr. Gold. Mr. Gold says to the nurse, "Why did you pull back on the syringe before you pushed the plunger?" What would be the best response by the nurse?

    1. "Because that is how we were taught to perform injections."
    2. "Because best practice guidelines state the nurse should aspirate before injecting."
    3. "Because I want to make sure the plunger slides smoothly in the syringe."
    4. "Because I need to ensure the needle has not hit a blood vessel."

Case 7

Tom Rutlege, 63 years old, has had surgery for a ruptured aortic aneurysm. The repair was successful, and after stabilization in the intensive care unit, he is transferred to a cardiovascular surgical unit.

Questions 28–32 refer to this case.

28. The nurse takes and records Mr. Rutlege's vital signs on admission to the unit: temperature 36.4°C; BP 100/60 mm Hg; pulse 90 beats/minute; respirations 20 breaths/minute; oxygen saturation 96%. What should be the nurse's action in response to Mr. Rutlege's vital signs?

    1. Cover him with a warm blanket
    2. Increase the oxygen, within medical directives
    3. Continue to monitor the vital signs
    4. Call the surgeon

29. Which of the following would be of concern to the nurse when providing postoperative care to Mr. Rutlege?

    1. Urinary output of less than 30 mL per hour
    2. Absent bowel sounds
    3. Pain from the incision site
    4. Scant serosanguineous drainage from the incision

30. Mr. Rutlege has chest tubes attached to a Pleurovac drainage system. The nurse is aware that care of this type of chest tube drainage system includes which of the following?

    1. Ensuring continuous bubbling in the water seal chamber
    2. Taping the connection between the chest tube and drainage system
    3. Adding sterile water to the suction control chamber every eight hours
    4. Maintaining the system above waist level

31. Mr. Rutlege is ordered a type and cross-match prior to a blood transfusion. What is the purpose of the type and cross-match test?

    1. To determine if Rh agglutinins are present
    2. To determine if there is ABO incompatibility
    3. To determine the presence of A or O antigens
    4. To determine the compatibility of his blood with donor blood

32. Mr. Rutlege recovers from surgery and is to be discharged home. He will be caring for his incision himself. How should the nurse best evaluate his ability to perform incision care?

    1. Have him explain how to care for the incision
    2. Have him demonstrate how to care for the incision
    3. Ask him questions based on the instructional DVD he has viewed
    4. Ask him if he has any questions about the care of his incision

Case 8

Four-year-old Sam has fallen out of a tree. His mother calls a neighbour, who is a registered nurse, for help. The nurse observes Sam lying on the ground, moaning and crying. He has several abrasions and a 1 cm cut on his forehead.

Questions 33–37 refer to this case.

33. The nurse assesses Sam for injuries. What is the priority assessment?

1. Signs of head injury
2. Evidence of limb fracture
3. Sam's pulse
4. Other injuries that may not be visible

34. The nurse needs to examine Sam's left leg. What would be the most appropriate initial action to determine if there is a fracture?

1. Ask Sam to stand on his left leg
2. Rotate the leg and ankle
3. Ask Sam to point to where his leg hurts
4. Apply pressure to the injured area to assess for bone integrity

35. The nurse determines that Sam probably has a fracture close to or at the ankle. What is the most appropriate first aid to apply before transporting him to the hospital?

1. Wrap the leg in a soft blanket
2. Immobilize the foot, ankle, and lower leg in a rolled magazine
3. Splint the left leg against the right leg
4. Apply ice to the fracture site

36. At the hospital, Sam is seen by a nurse practitioner who orders tests to determine if Sam has a fractured bone in his leg. What test will the nurse practitioner most likely order?

1. X-ray
2. Bone scan
3. Bone densitometry
4. CT scan

37. It is determined that Sam has a fracture and his leg is encased in a plaster of Paris cast. Which of the following should be instructions to Sam's parents regarding cast care in the first 24 hours?

1. Wrap the cast in a plastic bag to prevent it from getting wet or dirty
2. Expose the cast to air until dry
3. Lift and support the wet cast with the fingertips
4. Use a hair dryer to speed the drying process

Case 9

Roberta Wilmot, age 54 years, has osteoarthritis. Ms. Wilmot, who admits to being overweight, is a postal worker who walks a route to deliver mail. She is the single mother of a disabled adult son and must work to maintain health benefits.

Questions 38–41 refer to this case.

38. Which of the following manifestations of osteoarthritis is Ms. Wilmot most likely to experience?

1. Pain in her knees
2. Sudden onset of pain in most joints
3. Swelling and erythema in her feet
4. Paraesthesia in her fingers

39. The nurse counselling Ms. Wilmot discusses lifestyle changes to help with the osteoarthritis. Which of the following should the nurse most appropriately recommend to Ms. Wilmot?

1. Change of job
2. Weight loss
3. Assistance with her disabled son
4. More exercise

40. Which of the following medications will be of greatest help to alleviate the symptoms of osteoarthritis?

1. Muscle relaxants
2. Nonsteroidal anti-inflammatory drugs (NSAIDs)
3. Antibiotics
4. Acetaminophen (Tylenol®)

41. An interprofessional team works with Ms. Wilmot to manage her osteoarthritis. In addition to the nurse and physician, which of the following health care workers would be most important to include on the team?

1. Pharmacist
2. Naturopath
3. Social worker
4. Physiotherapist

Case 10

Meredith Marshall is a 42-year-old woman who is 22 weeks pregnant with her fifth child. She attends the antenatal clinic, where she sees the registered nurse.

Questions 42–44 refer to this case.

42. What is the most important assessment for the nurse at this visit?

   1. Mrs. Marshall's blood pressure
   2. Presence of ketones in Mrs. Marshall's urine
   3. Estimate of fetal growth
   4. Weight gain or loss

43. It is determined that Mrs. Marshall has pre-eclampsia. What is the recommended treatment for mild pre-eclampsia?

   1. Complete bed rest in hospital
   2. Restricted activity at home
   3. Sodium-restricted diet
   4. Administration of magnesium sulphate

44. Which of the following questions related to pre-eclampsia should the nurse ask Mrs. Marshall?

   1. "Do you have headaches or visual disturbances?"
   2. "Are you constipated or bloated?"
   3. "Have you experienced any vaginal bleeding or mucus discharge?"
   4. "Have you felt any mild contractions or tightening in your abdomen?"

Case 11

Ross is a 14-year-old adolescent in foster care. Ross was diagnosed as HIV-positive when he was an infant. He has been generally well, except for occasional acute infections that have required hospitalization. Ross is compliant with his antiretroviral therapy. He attends the HIV clinic every two months. The clinic nurse notes that Ross's CD4 counts have been dropping over the past few months.

Questions 45–49 refer to this case.

45. When Ross has his appointment at the clinic, which of the following initial actions, specific to his HIV status, should the nurse implement?

   1. Performing hand hygiene
   2. Gloving when she examines Ross
   3. Placing him in a room separate from infectious clients
   4. Asking him if he has been taking his medications

46. The nurse weighs Ross and notes that he has lost 2 kg since his last appointment. What would be an appropriate initial comment to Ross about his weight loss?

   1. "What has your appetite been like in the past two months?"
   2. "Have you had any episodes of diarrhea?"
   3. "This may be a sign that your condition is getting worse."

   4. "It's good to see you are not one of these obese children we've been reading about."

47. Which of the following is an appropriate topic for the nurse to discuss with Ross at this clinic visit?

   1. Feelings and concerns about sexuality
   2. Pain management
   3. Education regarding transmission of HIV
   4. Stress management techniques

48. Which of the following is a principle of drug therapy for HIV infection?

   1. Clients with chronic HIV do not require treatment if they are asymptomatic
   2. Treatment regimens should be individualized depending on CD4 counts
   3. It is preferable to begin treatment with single-drug therapy
   4. Pediatric treatment is limited due to fewer antiretrovirals that are safe for children

49. The physician in the clinic discusses starting a new research medication with Ross. The nurse is not sure if Ross is able to consent to the research drug because he is 14 and in foster care. What knowledge should the nurse have in this situation?

   1. Ross is an emancipated minor and may provide his own consent for the research drug
   2. Foster parents are legally able to provide consent for minors
   3. Agency policies for consent guidelines regarding age and research drug protocols
   4. An assessment of Ross's understanding of the proposed treatment

Case 12

Mr. Red Ford has been seriously burned in an industrial fire. His condition is stabilized in hospital, but he is only able to manage small sips of fluid by mouth and is not able to maintain adequate nutrition. The physician orders total parenteral nutrition (TPN) of protein electrolyte, vitamin, trace elements, and fat emulsion via a peripherally inserted central catheter (PICC).

Questions 50–56 refer to this case.

50. The nurse practitioner inserts the single-lumen PICC line at Mr. Ford's bedside. What precautions are necessary for this procedure?

   1. A tourniquet placed around his upper arm
   2. Sterile conditions
   3. Intravenous infusion of midazolam (Versed) for light anaesthesia

4. Mr. Ford positioned with his head to the side to facilitate subclavian access

51. What must be done by the nurse prior to the first infusion of the TPN solution?

1. Ensure correct catheter placement is verified by chest X-ray
2. Educate Mr. Ford about the PICC line and TPN
3. Warm the solution for a minimum of three hours
4. Add ordered electrolytes and trace elements to the solution

52. Mr. Ford is ordered an intravenous antibiotic. How should the nurse administer this medication?

1. Add the antibiotic to the protein and electrolyte solution
2. Administer it in the fat emulsion solution
3. Administer it via Y-tubing to the PICC line
4. Commence an additional peripheral intravenous line in a separate vein

53. The nurse is aware she needs to observe many safety measures related to Mr. Ford's PICC line and the TPN infusion. Which of the following is a nursing action related to client safety?

1. Change all TPN tubing lines every 24 hours
2. Label the tubing and filter with the date and time they were changed
3. Change the dressing at the catheter insertion site once per shift
4. Send the tubing for culture once per week

54. How should the nurse best evaluate Mr. Ford's tolerance of the TPN?

1. Daily weights
2. Positive balance for intake and output
3. Improved healing of his burns
4. Laboratory values

55. Several days later, Mr. Ford tells the nurse he still doesn't really understand the PICC line and where it is in his body. What would be the most appropriate response by the nurse?

1. "Let me draw you some pictures of where the PICC line is in your body."
2. "The PICC line is a flexible catheter that sits inside the large vein leading to your heart."
3. "The manufacturer's monograph provides most of the information you need."
4. "The nurse practitioner who inserted the line will explain it to you."

56. Mr. Ford's TPN solution is stopped one day because he is off the unit for tests. He is behind a total of 500 mL of solution. The solution is running at 200 mL per hour. What should the

nurse do, in accordance with agency policies, in this situation?

1. Do not make up the 500 mL
2. Increase the ordered flow to 220 mL until the 500 mL is made up
3. Take the solution off the infusion pump and increase the rate to 300 mL per hour
4. Offer Mr. Ford increased fluids by mouth

Case 13

Jennifer and Ronald Buxton are clients at a family practice clinic. Mr. and Mrs. Buxton have lived together in a "stormy" relationship for 10 years. A registered nurse at the clinic has often suspected intimate-partner violence and has spoken with Mrs. Buxton about it, but Mrs. Buxton has denied any abuse.

Questions 57–61 refer to this case.

57. One day, the nurse receives a phone call from Mrs. Buxton, who is hysterical and crying, saying, "Ronnie is beating me up." What should be the nurse's first response to Mrs. Buxton?

1. "How long has he been abusing you?"
2. "You need to come to the doctor's office right away."
3. "How badly has he beaten you up?"
4. "Are you in a safe place?"

58. Mr. Buxton is arrested by the police and subsequently convicted of assault. His sentencing requires him to have mandatory counselling. During the first session with the counsellor, who is a mental health nurse, what is the nurse's most important initial therapeutic goal?

1. Establishing trust between himself and Mr. Buxton
2. Determining the causative factors involved in the abuse of Mrs. Buxton
3. Developing healthy and open patterns of communication
4. Ensuring that Mr. Buxton understands that counselling is mandatory

59. Mr. Buxton tells the nurse that he has absolutely no memory of hitting Mrs. Buxton. What defence mechanism is this an example of?

1. Splitting
2. Repression
3. Introjection
4. Compensation

60. Mr. Buxton eventually admits to abusing Mrs. Buxton. He tells the nurse that it is all because she "nags" him. What would be a therapeutic response by the nurse?

1. "That is no excuse to hit Mrs. Buxton."
2. "Does hitting Mrs. Buxton make her stop nagging?"
3. "I'm not sure what you mean; please explain that to me again."
4. "Why does Mrs. Buxton nag you?"

61. As the nurse learns more about Mr. Buxton, he finds that Mr. Buxton has some typical characteristics of abusers. Which of the following is most characteristic of perpetrators of abuse?

1. A history of alcohol abuse
2. Low socioeconomic status
3. Cultural factors
4. A family history of abuse and authoritarianism

Case 14

Aubrey Hudson and her partner Christof Peters are a couple in their thirties who have experienced fertility problems. After taking clomiphene (Clomid) for several months, Ms. Hudson becomes pregnant. An ultrasonogram at 8 weeks' gestation confirms that Ms. Hudson is expecting twins. A registered nurse provides prenatal care and counselling.

Questions 62–69 refer to this case.

62. Ms. Hudson is likely expecting fraternal twins. Which of the following is a characteristic of fraternal twins?

1. A single ovum has divided into two embryos
2. They will be the same sex
3. They are more likely to occur in younger women
4. There are two amniotic sacs

63. During her second trimester, Ms. Hudson asks the nurse what to do about constipation. What should be the first action the nurse recommends?

1. Increase fluids, fresh fruits, and vegetables in her diet
2. Increase her exercise
3. Use a natural laxative
4. Take a stool softener, such as docusate sodium (Colace)

64. Ms. Hudson will be monitored carefully during the pregnancy because of the previous fertility problems and multiple gestation. She will deliver in hospital rather than the birthing centre. Which of the following is a significant risk for women with fraternal twin pregnancy?

1. Preterm labour
2. Twin to twin transfusion

3. Conjoined twins
4. Oligohydramnios

65. During the latter half of the second trimester, the nurse reviews situations in the third trimester that require immediately notifying the physician. Which of the following would be a danger sign during a pregnancy?

1. Dyspnea
2. A weight gain of 0.5–0.75 kg in the third trimester
3. Leg cramps
4. Fewer than 10 fetal movements in 12 hours

66. Ms. Hudson has brown eyes, and her partner Mr. Peters has blue eyes. Ms. Hudson asks the nurse what colour the babies' eyes will be. What should be the nurse's response?

1. Both babies will likely have blue eyes
2. Both babies will most likely, but not certainly, have brown eyes
3. One baby will have brown eyes, the other will have blue eyes
4. Eye colour is genetically random, and it is not possible to predict

67. As the pregnancy progresses, Ms. Hudson develops edema in her ankles. What should the nurse recommend to reduce the edema?

1. Fluid restriction
2. Keeping her legs uncrossed
3. Elevating her legs
4. Range-of-motion exercises

68. Ms. Hudson tells the nurse that although she is happy to have twins, she is disappointed because she will not be able to breastfeed two infants. What should the nurse respond?

1. "You could breastfeed one and formula-feed the other."
2. "Perhaps if you are able to get pregnant again, you could breastfeed the next baby."
3. "It is very difficult to breastfeed twins, and most women are not successful."
4. "With planning and extra nourishment, you may be able to breastfeed both infants."

69. At 36 weeks, Ms. Hudson delivers twins by caesarian section. Each twin has a separate health care team in the delivery room. What is the first assessment each nurse would perform with the infants?

1. Heart rate
2. Temperature
3. Respirations
4. Blood pressure

Case 15

A nursing teacher is assisting student nurses who are conducting a blood pressure clinic at a local shopping mall.

Questions 70–72 refer to this case

70. The nursing teacher instructs a student nurse how to correctly perform blood pressure monitoring by auscultation. Which of the following should the teacher demonstrate as the proper technique?

1. Have the client lie down with the arm extended
2. Use a cuff width that is 80% of the length of the client's upper arm
3. Quickly inflate the cuff to 10% above the client's expected blood pressure
4. Place the bell of the stethoscope over the brachial artery

71. The nursing teacher instructs a student how to perform self–blood pressure monitoring using an electronic device. What would be the most effective evaluation of the teaching?

1. The student is able to correctly perform blood pressure monitoring on another student
2. The student is able to verbalize the correct procedure for blood pressure monitoring
3. The student is able to state normal blood pressure values
4. The student is able to demonstrate the technique on himself

72. One of the students takes Mr. Brown's blood pressure using the portable electronic blood pressure monitor and obtains a reading of 186/110 mm Hg. He retakes the blood pressure but obtains the same result. Mr. Brown tells the teacher and the student that although he takes antihypertensives, to his knowledge, his blood pressure has previously been within normal limits. What should be the nursing teacher's first action?

1. Retake the blood pressure with a manual device
2. Ask Mr. Brown to lie down and relax and then take the blood pressure again
3. Find out from Mr. Brown which antihypertensive medication he takes
4. Replace the batteries in the electronic monitor

INDEPENDENT QUESTIONS

Questions 73–130 do not refer to a particular case.

73. Which of the following drugs may depress a client's immune system?

1. Meperidine (Demerol)
2. Cefazolin (Ancef)
3. Prednisone (Apo-Prednisone)
4. Salbutamol (Ventolin)

74. What is the primary reason why registered nurses should be involved in social justice issues?

1. Socioeconomic and political issues have an impact on health
2. Social justice will improve the working conditions of nurses
3. Advocacy is part of the role of the nurse
4. Politicians will change laws based on nursing input

75. Ms. Hope, mother of five-month-old Isabelle, asks the nurse when Isabelle will be able to pull herself to a standing position. What should the nurse tell her?

1. "It should be any time now."
2. "Infants generally pull themselves up onto furniture at about six to seven months."
3. "Isabelle will probably stand holding onto a table by about eight to nine months."
4. "I don't think you should expect Isabelle to stand until about 11 to 12 months."

76. When are antilipidemic medications such as atorvastatin (Lipitor) most appropriately ordered?

1. In people over 65 years of age
2. In people who do not exercise sufficiently
3. In people for whom dietary measures have not lowered cholesterol
4. In people who have elevated cholesterol for over two months

77. Health Canada recommends that all women of child-bearing years take a folic acid supplement. What is the reason for this recommendation?

1. It helps prevents neural tube defects in the fetus should the woman become pregnant
2. It maximizes the nutritional status of the woman prior to becoming pregnant
3. It prevents the occurrence of cleft lip and palate, which occurs early in pregnancy
4. It is necessary for the adequate formation of estrogen and progesterone

78. What is the most frequent reason for hospitalization among the homeless population?

1. Wound infections
2. Respiratory problems
3. Mental illness
4. Cardiovascular disorders

79. A community nurse is concerned because many of her chronically ill clients do not have a primary care provider. What short-term solution should the nurse suggest to the clients?

1. Advise them to go to the local community walk-in clinic as necessary.
2. Provide them with a list of all the community physicians for them to call.
3. Advise them to call the provincial telephone health information line for advice.
4. Provide the clients with comprehensive health care to the best of her ability.

80. Manifestations of sickle cell disease may include which of the following?

1. Anemia
2. Fever
3. Vomiting
4. Bradycardia

81. Ms. Blatchberg has leukopenia. Which of the following should the nurse include in client teaching?

1. Her gums may bleed when she brushes her teeth
2. She should try to eat green leafy vegetables
3. She should ensure she receives the influenza vaccine
4. She should avoid people with communicable diseases

82. Mr. Skinner has sustained a gunshot wound and is in the early stages of hypovolemic shock, with a respiratory rate of 42 breaths per minute. When he arrives in the emergency department, which of the following is a priority nursing action?

1. Administer oxygen, as ordered, via nasal cannula
2. Place him in a semi-Fowler's position
3. Request a physician order for an IV bolus of normal saline
4. Perform a complete chest assessment

83. Ms. Benjamin, age 52 years, is scheduled for an elective hysterectomy. She has a prosthetic mitral valve and was advised by her physician to discontinue her daily dose of aspirin (ASA) prior to surgery. What property of aspirin forms the rationale for this action?

1. Analgesic
2. Antipyretic
3. Anti-inflammatory
4. Antiplatelet

84. A registered nurse reviews client data when she arrives on shift. She notes that one of her clients, Mr. Barry, routinely takes Advair, which is a combined inhaled steroid and bronchodilator. Which of the following would be a priority assessment for the nurse to perform on Mr. Barry?

1. Cardiovascular
2. Gastrointestinal
3. Neurological
4. Respiratory

85. Which of the following would be the correct procedure when taking the blood pressure of a hypertensive client who is monitored at the clinic once a week?

1. Ensure that the client has not had caffeine within the last five hours
2. Allow the client to rest for five minutes prior to taking the blood pressure
3. Use manual rather than electronic blood pressure devices
4. Alternate arms for each visit

86. Ms. Brette is voluntarily admitted, on a short-term basis, to a psychiatric unit for management of her anxiety disorder. She experiences a severe anxiety attack while she is in the client lounge. What should the nurse do?

1. Comfort Ms. Brette by holding and hugging her
2. Move Ms. Brette closer to other clients
3. Administer her ordered prn lorazepam (Ativan)
4. Take her to her room

87. A registered nurse is on an airplane flight and is asked to come to the aid of a fellow passenger. The nurse assesses a man who is approximately in his 60s, diaphoretic, and complaining of severe pain in his chest. What should be the nurse's first action?

1. Tell airline staff the passenger may be having a heart attack
2. Ask the man if he has any history of heart disease
3. Take the man's vital signs with equipment provided by the airline
4. Administer oxygen via passenger mask

88. Sepsis, or septicemia, causes many deaths in Canada. How is septicemia diagnosed?

1. Blood culture
2. Swab of the infected area
3. White blood cell count, specifically neutrophils
4. Lumbar puncture with cerebrospinal fluid (CSF) analysis

89. A registered nurse works at a provincially funded telephone health centre. She receives a telephone call from Mrs. Dunlop, who tells the nurse that her husband is experiencing chest pain and is sweating. Which of the following should the nurse recommend?

1. Call 9-1-1
2. Call 9-1-1 and give her husband an aspirin (ASA) if available

3. Call 9-1-1 and place her husband in a knee-chest position
4. Call 9-1-1 and cover her husband with a blanket

90. Dina Shpak, age 54, has chronic stable angina pectoris. Her physician orders nitroglycerine in the form of a spray (Nitrolingual sublingual spray). The nurse teaches Mrs. Shpak about the use of the spray. Which of the following should she include in teaching?

1. The aerosol should be inhaled as she takes a deep breath
2. If she experiences headache, she should immediately notify the physician
3. She will experience pain relief in approximately 30 minutes
4. Take the spray before exercise or stressful physical activity

91. Mrs. Wiesenthal, a client on a chronic care rehabilitation unit, has a positive test for *Clostridium difficile* (*C. difficile*). What organism-specific manifestation is she most likely to experience?

1. Fever
2. Vomiting
3. Chills
4. Diarrhea

92. After many years of symptoms and diagnostic tests, Ms. Drummond has been diagnosed with fibromyalgia. Which of the following is characteristic of this condition?

1. It is primarily a psychiatric diagnosis
2. There is no effective treatment
3. There are neither manifestations nor diagnostics specific to the disease
4. Pain and fatigue become progressively worse

93. A nurse wishes to join an organization to protest social and economic inequality. Another nurse asks what this has to do with health. What is the nurse's best response?

1. Economics is a social determinant of health.
2. People at the lower end of the socio-economic scale have proven poorer health than those at the upper end.
3. Health care must be equal and available to all.
4. Nurses have an obligation to be advocates for all levels of society.

94. Mr. Hardacre has just returned to the recovery room following tracheotomy surgery. What is the priority nursing action?

1. Observing for hemorrhage
2. Maintaining a patent airway

3. Performing frequent suctioning
4. Taking vital signs

95. Mr. Scott is diagnosed with hepatitis A after returning from a tropical vacation. He asks the nurse how he got the virus. What should the nurse respond?

1. "Did you have any sexual encounters when you were on vacation?"
2. "Because of the air circulation in planes, it is likely you got the virus on the flight."
3. "Hepatitis A is endemic to tropical countries."
4. "You most likely ingested contaminated food or water."

96. A nurse finds that she has difficulty sleeping after working a 12-hour night shift and feels chronically sleep-deprived. Which of the following may be a recommendation to help her obtain more sleep?

1. Eat a main meal consisting of high protein and low fat toward the end of the night shift
2. Wear dark sunglasses before leaving work after her night shift
3. Perform aerobic exercise for 30 minutes on her way home from working nights
4. Advocate for a minimum of 12 hours off between rotating from night to day shift

97. Mrs. Bedford, the mother of 4-month-old Garth, asks the nurse, "Which of my son's teeth are going to come in first?" What should the nurse respond?

1. The upper two teeth, the frontal incisors
2. The bottom two teeth, the central incisors
3. The two "eye teeth," or canine teeth
4. His primary molars

98. The nurse notes that Mr. Varcoe's nasogastric tube has not drained for several hours, and his abdomen appears distended. What should be the nurse's first action?

1. Irrigate the tube
2. Instill saline in the tube
3. Remove the tube
4. Notify the physician

99. Ms. Bacci is 10 weeks' gestation with her third pregnancy. She tells the nurse, "I make big babies. My other two were over 10 pounds when they were born." What screening test, related to this statement, would be most appropriate for Ms. Bacci?

1. Fasting blood glucose
2. Amniocentesis
3. Maternal nutrition analysis
4. Pelvimetry

100. A family visits the child health clinic. The father tells the nurse "I have read on several Web sites that there is scientific evidence vaccines are not effective so I will not consent to immunizing my child." What would be the best response by the nurse?

1. "Has your child, or any child you know, ever had a serious adverse effect after an immunization?"
2. "Do you have any cultural, religious, or personal beliefs regarding immunization?"
3. "Which vaccines have you read about that are not effective?"
4. "I agree there is much conflicting information. Can you tell me more about what you read?"

101. Ann Atkins's mother died several years ago of ovarian cancer at age 48. Ann is now 25 years old. Although she is healthy and is manifesting no symptoms of cancer, what screening test should she be advised to have?

1. Transvaginal ultrasonography
2. Mammography and clinical breast examination
3. Chest X-ray
4. Blood test for tumour marker CA-125

102. A pregnant woman has just received results indicating that she is HIV-positive. She says to the nurse, "How am I going to tell my boyfriend that I have AIDS?" What is the most appropriate response by the nurse?

1. "Is there a chance you got HIV from your boyfriend?"
2. "You do not have AIDS; let's talk about being HIV-positive."
3. "It is more important at this time to think about protecting your baby from HIV."
4. "He will have to know you are HIV-positive; let's talk about how to tell him."

103. A nurse works in a multilingual environment. In many instances he cannot communicate with his clients, and knows he is not providing optimal care. What is the nurse's best action for a long-term solution to this problem?

1. Communicate to all clients to bring a family member to interpret.
2. Advocate for the purchase of English translation dictionaries for the most common languages.
3. As part of his reflective practice, enroll in classes to learn the most common languages.
4. Speak with the agency representative regarding purchase of an on-site telephone or media interpreter service.

104. A registered nurse who works in a corrections facility has been called as a witness for an inquest into the death of an inmate. What is the purpose of a medical inquest?

1. To determine criminal liability in an unexpected medical event
2. To determine civil liability in a suspicious death
3. To prosecute persons or agencies suspected of neglect with regard to their clients
4. To make recommendations to improve the health care system in the future

105. Which of the following people, according to their body shape and body mass index (BMI), have the highest risk of cardiovascular disease (CVD) and type 2 diabetes?

1. Mark: apple shape, BMI 24
2. Consuelo: apple shape, BMI 31
3. Pedro: pear shape, BMI 27
4. Christa: pear shape, BMI 18

106. Aisha has anorexia nervosa. She has severely restricted fat in her diet. If Aisha were to eat 12 g of fat and a total of 1100 kcal per day, what percentage of her daily intake would be from fat?

1. 8%
2. 10%
3. 12%
4. 15%

107. Mrs. Carnegy is hospitalized for pneumonia. She tells the nurse that she would like to continue to take peppermint, an herbal preparation, which she finds is effective for her irritable bowel syndrome (IBS). What should the nurse do?

1. Consult with the health care team to see if they agree to include peppermint in the plan of care
2. Tell Mrs. Carnegy that herbal preparations cannot be administered while she is in hospital
3. Agree to provide Mrs. Carnegy with peppermint as it is a recognized complementary therapy
4. Recommend that Mrs. Carnegy consult with her physician about other prescription medications that may be more effective than peppermint

108. A nurse visits a seniors' residence in northern Saskatchewan. What would be an important safety precaution the nurse should suggest to the residents?

1. Stay inside during icy winter days
2. Place area rugs on bare floors
3. Use a stove to warm food rather than microwave ovens
4. Take over-the-counter cough preparations at the first sign of a chest cold

109. What is the most conclusive screening test for colorectal cancer?

1. Fecal occult blood
2. Sigmoidoscopy
3. Colonoscopy
4. Barium enema

110. A 2-year-old child in respiratory distress has the following physician order: "Give oxygen by face mask to keep the O_2 saturation above 95%." The nurse notes that the oxygen saturation has fallen to 80%. What should be the initial action by the nurse?

1. Double-check the order with the physician
2. Administer additional oxygen
3. Arrange for arterial blood gases to confirm the O_2 saturation reading
4. Perform a chest assessment

111. Mr. Patrick has had seasonal allergies for many years. Recently he has found his usual over-the-counter allergy medication is not working as effectively. He asks the nurse what he should do. What would the nurse initially suggest?

1. Speak with his pharmacist.
2. Make an appointment with the nurse practitioner.
3. Arrange for allergy testing with a medical allergist.
4. Discuss environmental controls with a respiratory therapist.

112. Mr. Price is admitted to hospital for investigation of abdominal pain. The nurse notes that one of Mr. Price's medications is clozapine (Clozaril), an antipsychotic. What action should the nurse take prior to administration of the Clozaril?

1. Ask Mr. Price why he is taking an antipsychotic medication
2. Look in the chart for information related to why he is on an antipsychotic drug
3. Perform an orientation to reality assessment on Mr. Price
4. Ensure that safety measures are in place prior to entering his room with the medication

113. What is a frequent complaint of older adults who are beginning to experience age-related hearing loss?

1. Ringing in the ears
2. Other people mumbling when they talk
3. They can't hear men's voices
4. They can't hear themselves speaking

114. Mr. Braham has been on the rehabilitation unit for two days. He has been identified by the nurses as being a "demanding" client. He rings the call bell frequently for what are felt to be minor concerns and complains he is not receiving enough attention. When Mr. Braham calls for his nurse the fourth time within one hour, what is the best intervention by the nurse?

1. Tell Mr. Braham that he is not allowed to ring the call bell more often than once an hour, unless it is an emergency
2. Sit with Mr. Braham and ask him to describe his feelings and concerns
3. Alternate care with the other RN on duty so that he feels he is receiving more attention
4. Set limits by telling Mr. Braham his physical condition does not require the attention he is demanding and his behaviour is not appropriate

115. Mr. Hill is a caregiver for his wife Verna, who has dementia. He expresses frustration to the nurse because of difficulties communicating with Verna. What communication technique would be most effective for the nurse to suggest to Mr. Hill?

1. Speak slowly and loudly
2. Use written rather than verbal communication
3. Speak in short, simple sentences
4. Repeat phrases several times

116. Ms. Enright, a client newly admitted to a mental health facility, says to the nurse, "Do you have a boyfriend?" What is the most appropriate response by the nurse?

1. "Let's talk about you. Do you have a boyfriend?"
2. "I am not allowed to tell you about my personal life."
3. "Yes I do. We have been together for three wonderful years."
4. "This interview is about you, not me."

117. Mr. Dovgan has just been admitted to the neurology unit. Mr. Dovgan is recovering from a brain injury and also has unstable bipolar disorder. When the nurse enters the room to assess Mr. Dovgan, he says to her, "Get out of here or I am going to kill you." What should be the primary action by the nurse?

1. Document and report to the nurse in charge the facts of the verbal abuse and threat
2. Recognize that the behaviour is related to Mr. Dovgan's diagnosis and not take the abuse personally
3. Implement safety strategies to protect herself
4. Obtain support from nursing colleagues who are involved in Mr. Dovgan's care

118. A registered nurse works at a suicide prevention telephone hotline. Which of the following callers would the nurse consider to be most at risk for suicide?

1. Lindsay, age 16, who says she is going to buy razor blades to cut her wrists

2. Ahmet, age 21, who tells the nurse he is going to use his gun to shoot himself
3. Florence, a 40-year-old woman who expresses the desire to overdose on antidepressants but has agreed to go to the hospital
4. Fred, a senior citizen who is recently widowed and says he no longer wants to live

119. Mrs. Scales is a resident of a long-term care facility. She has advanced dementia, no spontaneous mobility, and severe contractures of her hands. The family asks how often splints are applied to her hands. What is the most appropriate response by the nurse to their question?

1. The splints are ordered to be applied for 4 hours a day
2. The physiotherapist has recommended the splints be applied 4 hours a day
3. I have just assessed Mrs. Scales and she has the splints on
4. The nurse's documentation shows the splints are applied 4 hours a day from 8 in the morning to noon

120. The nurse is planning a teaching session about nutrition with a group of children. What must the nurse initially assess prior to the teaching session?

1. What the children know about nutrition
2. What the children normally eat
3. What the developmental level of the children is
4. What the learning outcomes should be from the session

121. Elizabeth O'Byron is a newly registered nurse who has started a job on a general medical unit at University Hospital. What should she put on her new nametag?

1. E. O'Byron, Registered Nurse
2. Elizabeth, RN
3. Ms. O'Byron, Nurse
4. Elizabeth O'Byron, Registered Nurse

122. Douglas, age three, has recently been diagnosed with autism. What is a priority goal for Douglas's development?

1. Provision of appropriate pharmacological treatment
2. Intensive early intervention and education therapy
3. Referral to a pediatric psychiatrist
4. Safety assessment of the home

123. Antonia Chaley, age 6, experiences frequent epistaxis, particularly in cold, dry weather. What should the nurse advise Antonia and her parents for first aid treatment?

1. Pinch both nostrils closed for about five minutes
2. Tilt the head back and hold the bridge of the nose

3. Blow the nose gently and repeatedly until the bleeding stops
4. Pack the nose with tissue or cotton balls

124. Martina is a preceptor for a fourth-year nursing student. The student has difficulty finishing her work before the end of the shift and has not been able to accurately assess client acuity. Martina has never been a preceptor before. What should be her initial action to address the situation with the student?

1. Discuss with the student her learning goals, present performance, and past experience
2. Consult with the faculty advisor concerning the expected level of performance for a fourth-year student
3. Discuss the student's performance with the unit nurse educator
4. Refer to written material, provided by the nursing school, concerning student and preceptor expectations

125. Ms. San asks her neighbour, Ms. Ryerson, a registered nurse, for advice about what she should take for aches, pains, and mild headaches. She tells Ms. Ryerson that she has always taken ibuprofen (Advil®) but now finds that it bothers her stomach. How should Ms. Ryerson, RN, respond?

1. Try naproxen (Aleve®)
2. Celecoxib (Celebrex®) will work for mild headaches
3. Acetaminophen (Tylenol®) is safe and effective for most people
4. Ms. Ryerson should not recommend any over-the-counter remedies

126. Liam Douglas is receiving intravenous fluids of 0.9% sodium chloride at 40 mL per hour. His nurse must hang a 2-L bag of IV fluid as no smaller bags are available. The nurse is not certain how long he can safely leave the bag hanging before he changes it. What is the most appropriate action by the nurse?

1. Change the bag of IV solution after 24 hours
2. Label the date and time of hanging the bag
3. Consult agency policies regarding IV solution "hangtimes"
4. Change the bag when it is empty

127. Mrs. Brown is brought to the emergency department by her husband George. She is 39 weeks' gestation and has been treated for pregnancy-induced hypertension. She is now experiencing severe abdominal pain, has heavy vaginal bleeding and a hard fundus, and is demonstrating signs of shock. What should be the first action by the nurse in the emergency department?

1. Notify the physician
2. Insert a fetal monitor
3. Prepare for a caesarian section
4. Reassure Mrs. Brown

1. 1008 kcal
2. 1936 kcal
3. 2231 kcal
4. 2420 kcal

128. Which of the following is an example of nursing evidence-informed practice?

1. Changing the fever treatment protocol as a result of meta-analysis of related studies in nursing journals
2. Performing cool sponge baths for clients with fever, based on agency protocol
3. Administering acetaminophen (Tylenol®) for fever, as ordered by the physician
4. Assessment of individual clients with fever and their requirements for fever treatment

129. A moderately active female requires 18 kcal per 0.45 kg to maintain an ideal weight. How many kilocalories would a 56-kg woman require per day?

130. Following hip replacement surgery, Ms. Cakebread, age 92, develops pneumonia. She is receiving intravenous antibiotics and oxygen via a nasal cannula. Which of the following manifestations would be of most concern to her nurse?

1. Respiratory rate of 20 breaths per minute
2. Productive cough
3. Restlessness
4. Arterial pO_2 of 90 mm Hg

Answers and Rationales for
Book Two

1.   **C: Changes in Health   T: Application**

1. As death approaches, the skin becomes cool, clammy, and mottled due to diminished circulation.
2. Respirations are often rapid and shallow, progressing to Cheyne-Stokes respirations.
3. The pulse becomes weak, but the rate does not increase.
4. Although the skin feels cool to the touch, body temperature often increases prior to death.

2.   **C: Professional Practice   T: Critical Thinking**

1. The nurse will need to perform all the listed actions. Because the family is right there, the first action is to confirm for them that Mrs. Haliburton has passed away. It would be inappropriate to document or make calls before speaking with the family. He can offer them time alone with the body while he performs other duties.
2. The nurse must do this after speaking with the family.
3. As in choice 2.
4. As in choice 2.

3.   **C: Professional Practice   T: Critical Thinking**

1. The health record does not belong to the family.
2. The physician is part of the palliative care team. He does not own the health record.
3. The health care record belongs to the agency, in this case, the agency that employs the palliative care team. The nurse must take the record to the agency for legally specified storage.
4. This is not legal. Records must be maintained by the agency for a length of time as specified in legislation.

4.   **C: Professional Practice   T: Application**

1. The morphine is the legal property of the Haliburtons. They have no means to dispose of it safely. Pharmacies will safely dispose of unused medications.
2. The nurse should not be transporting narcotics. This is not a nursing responsibility.
3. It is not optimum for a narcotic to be disposed of in a biohazard container.
4. This is not safe advice. One person should not use medications prescribed for someone else.

5.   **C: Professional Practice   T: Application**

1. The nurse's initial action should be to reflect on his coping mechanisms for grief and whether they have been effective in the past. Once he has

analyzed his reactions, he may choose one of the other options.
2. This may be an option after self-reflection.
3. Reflection may determine a need to change to another specialty.
4. This is not likely to be necessary at this stage, only if the nurse experiences further emotional difficulties.

6.   **C: Changes in Health   T: Application**

1. Nitrates are first-line therapy for treatment of acute anginal symptoms. They will dilate peripheral blood vessels and coronary arteries, increasing blood flow to the heart.
2. Beta adrenergic blockers reduce the heart rate and contractility and reduce afterload. They are not first-line drugs in emergency angina care.
3. This would be given only if the presence of thrombi were confirmed.
4. Angiotensin-converting enzyme inhibitors are useful with heart failure, tachycardia, myocardial infarction, and hypertension. They are not first-line drugs for stable angina.

7.   **C: Changes in Health   T: Critical Thinking**

1. An X-ray will be taken to assess cardiac enlargement, cardiac calcification, and pulmonary congestion. It does not allow for visualization of the coronary arteries.
2. Cardiac ultrasonography is not of significant use with angina.
3. An ECG is obtained to determine abnormalities of electrical function in the heart. In Mr. Cetaine's case, it will likely be used to rule out myocardial infarction but does not confirm the extent of angina.
4. Coronary angiography allows visualization of the coronary arteries and helps determine appropriate treatment.

8.   **C: Changes in Health   T: Knowledge**

1. The construction of new conduits beyond the coronary obstruction restores blood flow to the myocardium.
2. CABG cannot repair damage to the myocardium but can help prevent further damage.
3. CABG provides new blood vessels to the myocardium, not the right atrium.
4. The obstruction is in the coronary artery, not the aorta.

9.   **C: Changes in Health   T: Application**

1. Complete bed rest is rarely indicated postsurgery as it is likely to increase postoperative complications.

Mr. Cetaine likely would be permitted to gradually resume a limited degree of activity.

2. CABG requires a graft from another site, most often the saphenous vein, internal mammary artery, or radial artery; thus, there would be a chest and a graft site.

3. Oxygen will be ordered according to oxygen saturations. It may not necessarily be required.

4. Pain management is important, particularly if there is a thoracotomy. Narcotics are used; however, they are administered around the clock, not prn.

10.   C: Professional Practice   T: Critical Thinking

1. The primary purpose of documentation is to communicate client information among care providers. Documentation is communication that reflects the client's health and well-being, the care provided, the effect of care, and the continuity of care. All health care professionals need ongoing access to client information to provide safe and effective care and treatment.

2. Documentation does demonstrate nursing accountability and gives credit to nurses for their professional practice. However, the primary purpose is to communicate information about the client.

3. Health records can be a valuable source of data for research and quality assurance purposes; however, this is not the primary purpose.

4. Data from nursing documentation can identify the care and services provided to clients and the efficiency of the care. However, this is not the primary purpose of documentation.

11.   C: Professional Practice   T: Application

1. The agency does own the health record, but the client has the right of access to the information, not just in exceptional circumstances.

2. The client does not own the record. Consent for disclosure to agency staff for purposes related to care is implied upon admission.

3. Only the agency owns the record.

4. When care is provided by an agency, the actual record belongs to that agency. With very few exceptions, clients have right of access to their own records. Agencies generally have policies about what to do if clients ask for their charts.

12.   C: Professional Practice   T: Application

1. The term "nurse" is applied only to registered individuals. Although student nurses are not yet registered, and there may be others who have not yet received confirmation of registration, those people must document the care they provide.

2. This is the exception. The nurse who documents

the care provided by another nurse in such situations would have been involved and have had personal knowledge of the situation. This most frequently occurs in emergency or "code" situations, in which one nurse may be designated as the recorder.

3. This is not true. Both nurses are required to document the care they provided.

4. There is an exception, as noted in choice 2.

13.   C: Professional Practice   T: Application

1. This is a judgement and not fact.

2. As in choice 1.

3. This is an accurate description of the facts concerning Ms. Scharfe's behaviour. Information should be recorded concisely and accurately and focus on facts rather than assumptions.

4. This entry is too wordy and makes assumptions.

14.   C: Changes in Health   T: Critical Thinking

1. Alcohol withdrawal delirium, or delirium tremens (DTs), may lead to death caused by hyperthermia, peripheral vascular collapse, and cardiac failure.

2. This does not occur in alcohol withdrawal.

3. Seizures may occur but are not as serious as cardiac failure.

4. The client in alcohol withdrawal is unlikely to be able to commit suicide.

15.   C: Nurse–Client Partnership   T: Application

1. This is not likely. He would be aware of his drinking.

2. This is not a therapeutic response.

3. This is a factual response. It may help Mrs. Martin understand the disease and that support, although not acceptance, will be most helpful to her husband's recovery.

4. Alcohol is a strong addiction; however, if Mr. Martin wishes to stop drinking, he has the ability to help himself.

16.   C: Changes in Health   T: Knowledge

1. This is a test for liver enzymes.

2. Bilirubin metabolism abnormalities with cirrhosis are responsible for the deposit of yellow pigment in the skin (jaundice).

3. As in choice 1.

4. Prothrombin time is a reflection of clotting factors.

17.   C: Nurse–Client Partnership   T: Critical Thinking

1. This does not explain why Mr. Martin is yellow.

2. This is too complex an answer for Mrs. Martin.

3. This is the correct physiological rationale for the jaundice and is at a level that Mrs. Martin can understand.
4. This is not physiologically correct.

18.   **C: Changes in Health   T: Application**

1. Cirrhosis interferes with the liver's ability to eliminate ammonia. Protein is converted to ammonia; therefore, Mr. Martin requires a low-protein diet. This breakfast is low in protein.
2. This is a high-protein meal.
3. This is a high-protein meal.
4. This is a high-protein meal.

19.   **C: Nurse–Client Partnership   T: Application**

1. There is no reason to assume that Mr. Martin is not cognitively able to make his own treatment decisions.
2. This is a factual answer. Giving Mr. Martin Antabuse without his consent is unethical.
3. This implies that an unethical practice is condoned and that the nurse is not sure of the legal and ethical implications.
4. This is an unprofessional and unethical response.

20.   **C: Changes in Health   T: Application**

1. Aspirin can trigger asthma attacks in 20% of adults.
2. There are no contraindications for the use of acetaminophen (Tylenol®) in clients with asthma.
3. There are no contraindications for the use of ibuprofen in clients with asthma.
4. Many people with asthma have seasonal allergies and use antihistamines such as loratidine for symptom control. These drugs are not contraindicated except during an acute attack.

21.   **C: Changes in Health   T: Application**

1. Beta$_2$-agonists do not decrease airway inflammation.
2. Inhaled steroids do not decrease bronchoconstriction.
3. The long-acting beta$_2$-agonist provides bronchodilation for up to 12 hours. The inhaled steroid decreases inflammation. Combining the two medications provides a convenient dosing regimen for the client.
4. The medications do not potentiate each other, nor is it necessary to combine the drugs in one inhaler to provide longer-acting symptom control.

22.   **C: Changes in Health   T: Application**

1. Inhaled medications are the preferred therapy for asthma. Other forms are not as effective and may have increased side effects.
2. As in choice 1.
3. Many people have difficulty using the MDI properly. A spacer is a tube that attaches to the MDI. Drugs are inhaled from the tube, resulting in better delivery of the medications into the airway.
4. This is a possibility; however, the use of a spacer is easier for Mr. Lewis and is most likely to be successful.

23.   **C: Changes in Health   T: Critical Thinking**

1. The combination drugs need to be taken to stabilize and control chronic symptoms. They are not effective during an acute attack.
2. Mr. Lewis may need to do this if the rescue inhaler is not effective.
3. This is of value in croup but will not produce the bronchodilation necessary during an asthma attack.
4. Short-acting bronchodilators (also known as rescue medications) provide temporary relief of bronchospasm and should help restore normal breathing within 10 to 15 minutes. Another puff may be taken if optimum breathing does not resume.

24.   **C: Professional Practice   T: Application**

1. Any health care worker who provides care to Mr. Fraser has access to the record.
2. Only health care professionals who are caring for Mr. Fraser have access to his record.
3. These people are legally entitled to view the health record. While clerical staff may not be considered health care workers, they must view the chart in order to insert and maintain the information.
4. This is unrealistic. The family practice clinic is responsible for initiating and maintaining relevant information and maintaining confidentiality. Mr. Fraser may have copies if he wishes.

25.   **C: Health and Wellness   T: Critical Thinking**

1. There is a familial risk for close relatives of people who have been diagnosed with colorectal cancer. Ms. Masseur should have a screening colonoscopy to rule out tumours and identify colon polyps.
2. Hemorrhoids are not a risk for colorectal cancer. Screening colonoscopies are recommended for people age 50 and older.
3. Irritable bowel syndrome has manifestations similar to colorectal cancer but has not been shown to be a

risk for developing cancer.
4. This gene mutation contributes primarily to the development of breast and ovarian cancers. There is an increased incidence of familial colorectal cancer and breast or ovarian cancer, but Ms. Daniels will likely not require a colonoscopy screening as yet.

---

26.   C: Nurse–Client Partnership   T: Application

1. While this is true, it does not answer Miss Shannon's question.
2. If Miss Shannon asks the clinic to put her on the cancellation list, she may be able to take a spot that opens up, allowing her to have the scan earlier.
3. This is true, but Miss Shannon may be able to have the test earlier if she accesses the cancellation list.
4. This may not be true and does not advocate for Miss Shannon to be involved with her plan of care.

---

27.   C: Professional Practice   T: Critical Thinking

1. This is correct but does not answer Mr. Gold's question.
2. Although nurses should follow best practice guidelines, this does not answer Mr. Gold's question.
3. This is partially correct, but this should have been assessed prior to injecting Mr. Gold.
4. This answers Mr. Gold's question and provides a rationale for action.

---

28.   C: Changes in Health   T: Application

1. Mr. Rutlege's temperature is within normal limits. A blanket may be used for comfort if he wishes but is not necessary.
2. The oxygen saturation is within normal limits. There is no reason to increase the oxygen.
3. The vital signs are within normal limits for a postoperative client and should be monitored as per protocol.
4. There is no reason to contact the physician.

---

29.   C: Changes in Health   T: Application

1. An adult's urinary output should be a minimum of 30 mL per hour. Urinary output below this level may indicate inadequate perfusion of the kidneys, or urinary retention.
2. This is normal following abdominal surgery.
3. This is a normal finding postsurgery.
4. This is a normal finding.

---

30.   C: Changes in Health   T: Application

1. There should not be any bubbling in the chamber. This indicates a leak.
2. Taping connections prevents accidental disconnection.
3. Sterile water is added only as necessary to replace evaporation.
4. The system should be maintained below waist level.

---

31.   C: Changes in Health   T: Knowledge

1. Type and cross-matching determines more than Rh information.
2. Type and cross-matching determines more than ABO information.
3. Type and cross-matching determines more than ABO information.
4. Type and cross-matching provides a complete blood profile to determine the compatibility with donor blood.

---

32.   C: Nurse–Client Partnership   T: Critical Thinking

1. He may be able to explain the care but not able to actually perform care.
2. This is the most appropriate method to evaluate his ability to care for the incision.
3. This does not demonstrate competence.
4. This does not demonstrate competence. Most clients will not want to admit that they do not understand instructions and so may tell the nurse they do not have questions.

---

33.   C: Changes in Health   T: Critical Thinking

1. With a fall from a height, there is the danger of head injury. In view of the fact that Sam is moaning, and therefore can breathe, and there is no evidence of critical hemorrhaging from the small cut, the most important assessment is for signs of head injury.
2. This assessment would be made after assessing for head injury.
3. Because Sam is crying, this is evidence that he has an adequate, although likely elevated, pulse. The pulse should be taken, but it is not the priority.
4. These should be assessed after the level of consciousness.

---

34.   C: Changes in Health   T: Critical Thinking

1. This is not appropriate if there is a fracture as it may cause further injury.
2. The injured limb should be moved as little as possible.
3. The initial nursing efforts are directed at calming

the child. It is best not to touch children initially but to ask them to point to the painful area.

4. Sam will be frightened and upset. Applying pressure to the area will cause unnecessary pain and make the remainder of the assessment difficult.

35.   C: Changes in Health   T: Critical Thinking

1. It is better to immobilize the limb and joint in a rigid rather than a soft splint.
2. A rolled magazine may be used for a young child to form a rigid splint to keep the ankle in alignment and prevent further injury, especially to soft tissues.
3. This can be done if no splint is available.
4. This can be done, but it is more important to immobilize the area of fracture.

36.   C: Changes in Health   T: Knowledge

1. In this situation, the diagnosis can be easily and most cost-effectively determined with an X-ray.
2. A bone scan is isotope imaging and is not required for what is believed to be a simple fracture.
3. Bone densitometry is used to determine osteoporosis.
4. A CT scan is not necessary for a fractured limb.

37.   C: Changes in Health   T: Application

1. This will slow the drying process. The cast may be put in plastic after it is dry for purposes of bathing the child.
2. A plaster of Paris cast does not fully dry for up to 72 hours. Until then, it must be left exposed to the air to speed the drying process.
3. The cast should be handled with the palms of the hands rather than the fingers to prevent indentations.
4. Dryers are not to be used because they may cause the cast to dry on the outside but remain wet on the inside, thus becoming mouldy.

38.   C: Changes in Health   T: Knowledge

1. Osteoarthritis is a joint disorder primarily affecting weight-bearing joints such as the knees.
2. The onset of osteoarthritis is more gradual.
3. This occurs with osteomyelitis.
4. Paraesthesia, or a "pins and needles" feeling, occurs more often in rheumatoid arthritis.

39.   C: Health and Wellness   T: Critical Thinking

1. Ms. Wilmot may not be able to change her job as she needs the health insurance benefits.

2. A modifiable factor in Ms. Wilmot's osteoarthritis is reducing the weight on her knees.
3. There is no evidence that Ms. Wilmot needs assistance in caring for her son.
4. Ms. Wilmot obtains exercise by walking her postal route. She more likely may need rest during a period of acute inflammation.

40.   C: Changes in Health   T: Application

1. These are used for muscle spasms, not osteoarthritis.
2. NSAIDs have been shown to provide greater relief than acetaminophen (Tylenol®) in clients with knee pain from osteoarthritis.
3. Antibiotics are not useful in osteoarthritis.
4. NSAIDs provide greater pain relief than does acetaminophen (Tylenol®).

41.   C: Professional Practice   T: Critical Thinking

1. Unless Ms. Wilmot experiences difficulties or lack of therapeutic effect with her medications, there is no need for a pharmacist.
2. A naturopath would not necessarily be part of the team unless requested by Ms. Wilmot.
3. There is no evidence that at present Ms. Wilmot requires the services of a social worker.
4. Physiotherapy is useful in planning appropriate exercise programs and recommending necessary assistive devices.

42.   C: Changes in Health   T: Critical Thinking

1. Pregnancy-induced hypertension occurs after 20 weeks' gestation, more frequently in high-risk pregnancies. It can result in pre-eclampsia and eclampsia, which are dangerous to the mother and the fetus.
2. This is an indication of diabetes that is not controlled. The nurse would be testing for protein in the urine, a sign of pre-eclampsia.
3. This is important but not as vital as the blood pressure determination.
4. This may be important as an indication of fetal well-being but is not as important as the blood pressure.

43.   C: Changes in Health   T: Knowledge

1. Hospitalization is not necessary. Bed rest has proven to be controversial and may have adverse physiological outcomes.
2. Most women with mild pre-eclampsia may be managed at home with restricted activity and mild exercise.
3. Because pregnant women with hypertension

have lower plasma volume than do normotensive women, sodium restriction is not necessary.
4. Magnesium sulphate is used to prevent or control convulsions in women with eclampsia. It is not necessary in mild pre-eclampsia.

44.   C: Changes in Health   T: Application

1. These are signs of more severe pre-eclampsia.
2. Constipation is not related to pre-eclampsia.
3. This may be a sign of early labour, not pre-eclampsia.
4. These are signs of early labour, not pre-eclampsia.

45.   C: Health and Wellness   T: Critical Thinking

1. This is mandatory prior to all client care, not specific to clients with HIV.
2. Gloves are not necessary unless the nurse is handling blood or body fluids.
3. Ross is at risk of infection and thus must have restricted contact with persons who have infections.
4. This may be an appropriate question later on during the appointment, particularly as adolescents are often noncompliant with medications. It is not important initially.

46.   C: Nurse–Client Partnership   T: Application

1. Weight loss and a decrease in growth are potential complications in children with HIV/AIDS. Weight loss may also be part of normal adolescence. The initial question for data collection should be to determine the reason for the weight loss.
2. It may be that the weight loss is due to diarrhea, but this should not be the initial question.
3. This is insensitive and may not be true.
4. While a relatively high percentage of Canadian children are considered obese, this is not an appropriate comment to make with an HIV-positive client.

47.   C: Nurse–Client Partnership   T: Application

1. At Ross's age, he will have normal age-related concerns about sexuality. He needs to have anticipatory education about safe, healthy expressions of sexuality considering his HIV status.
2. There is no indication that Ross is experiencing pain.
3. At age 14, if Ross has had HIV for his entire life, he is likely well aware of the modes of transmission.
4. This may be appropriate, but Ross has not indicated to the nurse that he is experiencing stress.

48.   C: Changes in Health   T: Application

1. Guidelines for the use of antiretroviral agents in HIV-infected adults and adolescents recommend that asymptomatic HIV-positive clients should be treated.
2. Because rates of disease progression differ among individuals, treatment decisions should be individualized by the level of risk indicated by CD4 T-cell counts and plasma HIV RNA levels.
3. The most effective means to suppress HIV replication is by combination antiretroviral therapy.
4. Many drugs are available for pediatric use.

49.   C: Professional Practice   T: Application

1. Ross is not an emancipated minor.
2. In many cases, foster parents are not legal guardians and may not provide consent.
3. The nurse must know agency policies that will provide specific direction for investigational drugs and age of consent.
4. The physician is recommending the treatment; thus, it is the doctor's responsibility to provide the necessary information.

50.   C: Changes in Health   T: Application

1. A tourniquet helps the nurse practitioner examine the antecubital fossa to select a suitable vein but is not necessary.
2. Placement of a PICC line is performed under sterile conditions with preparation of the insertion site according to institution policy.
3. There is no need for light anaesthesia. A topical anaesthetic cream is usually used at the insertion site.
4. A PICC line is not inserted in the subclavian vein.

51.   C: Changes in Health   T: Application

1. An X-ray is necessary to confirm placement of the catheter in the superior vena cava prior to administration of the TPN.
2. Education is appropriate before insertion of the PICC line, not after.
3. The solutions are to be refrigerated until 30 minutes before use. Leaving the solutions at room temperature for longer encourages microbial growth.
4. The solutions are prepared by the agency pharmacy, and nursing staff make no additions.

52.   C: Changes in Health   T: Application

1. Once established for TPN, a single-lumen catheter is not to be used for administration of blood or antibiotics or the drawing of blood samples.
2. As in choice 1.
3. As in choice 1. Use of Y-tubing will infuse the antibiotic into the PICC line.
4. An additional IV line is required for the administration of antibiotics.

53.   C: Professional Practice   T: Application

1. This creates an unnecessary break in the system. Canadian Infection Control Guidelines recommend that all intravascular delivery system components up to the hub should be changed at 72-hour intervals and lipid emulsions every 24 hours.
2. This not only identifies the tubing but also is a reminder to other nursing staff when the tubing will need to be changed.
3. Dressing changes are per institution protocol and usually not more often than once every other day.
4. This is not necessary. Only if there are signs of infection is the tubing cultured.

54.   C: Changes in Health   T: Critical Thinking

1. Weight gain or loss may be an indication of fluid shift, edema, or diuresis and does not evaluate tolerance of the TPN.
2. This evaluates his hydration status, not his tolerance of the TPN.
3. This will be a result of the improved nutrition but is not an ongoing accurate assessment of tolerance of the TPN.
4. Blood glucose, electrolytes, urea nitrogen, complete blood count, and hepatic enzyme studies are performed at routine intervals. Assessment of these values will assist the nurse in evaluating Mr. Ford's tolerance of parenteral nutrition.

55.   C: Nurse–Client Partnership   T: Critical Thinking

1. Visuals, such as drawings and pictures, will increase Mr. Ford's understanding.
2. A picture, rather than a verbal description, would improve Mr. Ford's understanding.
3. Manufacturers' monographs are written at a technical level not suitable for most clients.
4. If the explanation were requested prior to insertion, the nurse practitioner would be responsible for the education in order to obtain informed consent. After insertion, the nurse has the knowledge to explain the PICC line.

56.   C: Changes in Health   T: Critical Thinking

1. If possible, the 500 mL should be made up to maintain normal blood values and nutrition.
2. The flow of parenteral solutions can be increased by no more than 10%; thus, this is an appropriate option to make up the lost amount.
3. TPN solutions should never be taken off an infusion pump and, due to their hypertonicity, may not run any faster than at 10% above the ordered rate.
4. Mr. Ford is not able to ingest sufficient fluids; therefore, this may not be possible.

57.   C: Health and Wellness   T: Critical Thinking

1. This is not the most important information at this time.
2. Mrs. Buxton may not be able to come to the doctor's office. Other information needs to be determined first.
3. This is an important question, but the nurse first needs to determine if Mrs. Buxton is safe.
4. The initial priority is Mrs. Buxton's safety. The nurse needs to determine whether she is somewhere that Mr. Buxton can find her and continue the beating.

58.   C: Nurse–Client Partnership   T: Critical Thinking

1. Establishing trust is essential when counselling any client.
2. This may come out later on in the counselling but is not the most important initial goal.
3. Communication is important, but it is an ongoing process and is likely to be facilitated by trust between the nurse and Mr. Buxton.
4. This puts the nurse in an authoritative rather than a therapeutic relationship.

59.   C: Changes in Health   T: Knowledge

1. Splitting is viewing people and situations as either all good or all bad.
2. Repression is the involuntary exclusion from awareness of a painful or conflictual thought, impulse, or memory. It is the primary ego defence. Mr. Buxton does not want to believe that he beats Mrs. Buxton.
3. Introjection is intense identification with another.
4. Compensation is a process by which a person makes up for a perceived deficiency by strongly emphasizing a feature thought of as an asset.

60.   C: Nurse–Client Partnership   T: Application

1. This is a punitive response.
2. This could be viewed as a sarcastic response.

3. This is the therapeutic communication technique called clarification. Attempting to put into words Mr. Buxton's unclear thoughts helps clarify his feelings, ideas, and perceptions.
4. This avoids the topic and is not therapeutic.

61. C: Health and Wellness   T: Application

1. Some abusers blame their behaviour on alcohol, but this is a myth. Abuse is a learned behaviour, not the result of the loss of inhibitions.
2. This may be a contributing factor, the hopelessness of poverty, but is not the most characteristic. Most people with a low socioeconomic status are not abusive.
3. While there are cultures that may appear to ignore or condone family violence, there are no specific cultural factors that are most characteristic of abusers.
4. This is the most frequent finding in perpetrators of family violence. There is a history of violence, neglect, or emotional deprivation. The role model is abusive.

62. C: Changes in Health   T: Knowledge

1. Identical twins begin with a single ovum that has been fertilized with one sperm and divides into two embryos.
2. Identical twins are the same sex. Fraternal twins may be the same or different sexes.
3. Older women are more likely to release two ova.
4. Fraternal twins are two ova that have been fertilized by two sperm. They develop as two fetuses and will have two amniotic sacs.

63. C: Changes in Health   T: Application

1. Fluids and roughage in fruits and vegetables increase the fluids in stool, making them softer and more easily passed through the colon.
2. Exercise does help constipation; however, because of the twin pregnancy, the physician should clear this. It would not be the first approach.
3. Laxatives, whether or not they are natural, should not be used without consulting the physician. They are not the first approach.
4. The first approach would not be taking a stool softener, and a physician must order it.

64. C: Changes in Health   T: Application

1. Women with a multiple gestation are at high risk for developing preterm labour.
2. This is a rare complication of twin pregnancy but occurs in monozygotic twins.
3. This is a rare occurrence in monozygotic twins,

when the division of the embryo occurs very late, causing incomplete cleavage.
4. With twin pregnancy, there is more likely to be hydramnios, or an excess of amniotic fluid. Oligohydramnios is a decrease in amniotic fluid and may be associated with fetal kidney disorders.

65. C: Changes in Health   T: Application

1. Dyspnea is a common discomfort, particularly in the latter half of the third trimester and in multiple births. It is caused by pressure of the enlarged uterus on the diaphragm.
2. This is normal weight gain.
3. Leg cramps are a common discomfort of pregnancy, caused by a calcium–phosphorus imbalance.
4. A decrease in fetal movement is an ominous sign that indicates a loss of vitality in one or both infants. In a twin pregnancy, this is a greater risk, and it may be difficult for the mother to determine if one or both infants are not moving or are moving less.

66. C: Changes in Health   T: Application

1. Blue eyes are a recessive genetic trait; therefore, it is not as likely for both infants to have blue eyes.
2. Brown eyes are a dominant trait; therefore, it is most likely that both infants will have brown eyes.
3. This is possible but not as likely as both infants having brown eyes.
4. Eye colour is not a random genetic trait. Brown eyes are dominant.

67. C: Changes in Health   T: Application

1. Fluids should not be restricted in pregnancy.
2. Legs should be uncrossed as much as possible to help prevent varicosities, but this is not likely to be of benefit for ankle edema.
3. Elevating the legs will help venous return and decrease ankle edema.
4. Range-of-motion exercises may be of limited benefit but are not as helpful as elevating the legs.

68. C: Health and Wellness   T: Application

1. This is a possibility but is not necessary. Both infants can be breastfed.
2. With Ms. Hudson's fertility problems, this may not happen, and they may not want more than two children. She is able to breastfeed twins.
3. It is more difficult to breastfeed twins, but it is not true that most women are not successful.
4. While breastfeeding twins does require planning and adaptation, mothers can successfully

breastfeed twins, either simultaneously or one at a time.

69.   C: Changes in Health   T: Critical Thinking

1. This would be the second assessment.
2. Because the infants are preterm, they have a greater risk for hypothermia. However, this is not the most important assessment just after birth.
3. Respirations are the most important initial assessment. Adequate respiratory effort is necessary for transition to extrauterine life.
4. Blood pressure is not a necessary assessment in the delivery room.

70.   C: Changes in Health   T: Application

1. It is not necessary for the client to lie down. He or she may sit, with the arm extended at heart level.
2. The cuff width should be at least 40% of the length of the client's upper arm.
3. The cuff should be inflated to 30% above the expected systolic pressure.
4. The brachial artery is used for blood pressure determination. The teacher will demonstrate palpation of the brachial artery and place the bell of the stethoscope over the pulse point.

71.   C: Professional Practice   T: Critical Thinking

1. This is a valuable step in learning how to manage the equipment, but being able to perform blood pressure monitoring on himself is more effective.
2. Verbalizing the procedure is not as effective as actually being able to demonstrate the skill.
3. This is important but is not an evaluation of the skill.
4. This is the most effective evaluation as the nursing teacher will be able to determine if the student can manipulate the equipment on himself.

72.   C: Professional Practice   T: Critical Thinking

1. The second step of the nursing process is to validate data. The best way to validate the high reading, and reassure Mr. Brown, is to take the blood pressure again using a manual device that is not dependent on correct calibration.
2. This would be the next step if the high BP were confirmed by the manual method.
3. This question should be asked but is not the first step.
4. This is likely required, but it may be that the monitor requires recalibration. Also, this will not quickly reassure Mr. Brown.

73.   C: Changes in Health   T: Knowledge

1. Demerol, an analgesic, does not depress the immune system.
2. Ancef, an antibiotic, will not depress the immune system.
3. Prednisone, a corticosteroid, has recognized immuno-suppressive effects.
4. Salbutamol, a bronchodilator, does not have immuno-suppressive effects.

74.   C: Health and Wellness   T: Critical Thinking

1. Developing an awareness of social justice involves socioeconomic and political issues that can contribute to poor health in disadvantaged populations.
2. This may occur but is not the primary reason.
3. This is true but does not answer the question of why nurses should be social justice advocates.
4. The purpose of advocacy in social justice is to improve conditions for all people. It does not necessarily involve changes in law. Nurses may influence politicians, but it is not a given that laws will be changed based on nursing input.

75.   C: Changes in Health   T: Application

1. This is too early for an infant to pull himself or herself to a standing position.
2. This is too early for most infants to pull themselves to a standing position.
3. While there is considerable variation among infants with regard to milestones, this is the approximate age at which an infant can pull himself or herself to a standing position holding onto furniture.
4. If a child is not able to pull himself or herself to a standing position by 11 to 12 months, he or she should be further evaluated.

76.   C: Changes in Health   T: Application

1. Lipid-lowering medications are ordered depending on lipid levels, not age.
2. Exercise is only one factor influencing lipid levels.
3. Generally, diet therapy is attempted prior to medications.
4. Only chronically elevated cholesterol levels with failure of conservative lifestyle measures require medications.

77.   C: Health and Wellness   T: Application

1. Folic acid is recommended to prevent neural tube defects during pregnancy. Women should take it

prior to becoming pregnant as it is necessary from the early stages, when the woman may not be aware she is pregnant.
2. This is not the role of folic acid.
3. As in choice 2.
4. As in choice 2.

78.   C: Health and Wellness   T: Knowledge

1. Individuals who are homeless are at risk for wound infections, but this is not the most frequent reason for hospitalization.
2. Homeless people are at risk for respiratory problems, but this is not the most frequent reason for hospitalization.
3. Statistics from the Canadian Institute for Health Information show that, in 2005–2006, mental illness was the reason for 52% of acute-care hospitalizations among the homeless.
4. Homeless people are at risk for cardiovascular problems, but this is not the most frequent reason for hospitalization.

79.   C: Professional Practice   T: Critical Thinking

1. The clinic will have health care providers who can manage chronic health problems.
2. This may take a long time and may not be successful.
3. The nurse will have better information on availability of physicians in the community.
4. The client may have needs beyond the scope of practice of the nurse.

80.   C: Changes in Health   T: Knowledge

1. Sickle cell disease, often termed sickle cell anemia, is a chronic inherited condition that results in abnormally shaped hemoglobin, resulting in anemia.
2. Fever is not a manifestation of sickle cell disease.
3. Vomiting is not a manifestation of sickle cell disease.
4. Children with sickle cell disease are more likely to be tachycardic, in response to red blood cell destruction and anemia.

81.   C: Changes in Health   T: Application

1. Thrombocytopenia, not leukopenia, causes gums to bleed.
2. There is no particular reason to eat these foods with leukopenia.
3. Clients with leukopenia should not be immunized except on the judgement of their physician.
4. Leukopenia is reduced white blood cells (WBCs). With fewer WBCs, the immune system

is depressed, causing the client to be at risk of a communicable disease.

82.   C: Changes in Health   T: Critical Thinking

1. Mr. Skinner's oxygenation and respiratory status is compromised, requiring immediate exogenous oxygen. This is an action that can be performed quickly, prior to the other actions.
2. This will assist his breathing but is not the first or most important action.
3. The physician should be notified immediately, after the oxygen has been applied. A bolus of saline will likely be ordered.
4. This should be performed close to the time that the physician is called.

83.   C: Changes in Health   T: Application

1. There would be no rationale for discontinuing an analgesic prior to surgery.
2. There would be no rationale for discontinuing an antipyretic prior to surgery. If she did have a fever, surgery would likely be cancelled.
3. There is no rationale for discontinuing an anti-inflammatory drug prior to surgery.
4. People with prosthetic heart valves are at risk for thrombus formation. Aspirin decreases platelet aggregation, preventing formation of thrombi. However, during surgery, there is an increased risk of hemorrhage if the client is taking an antiplatelet medication; thus, the medication should be stopped prior to surgery.

84.   C: Changes in Health   T: Critical Thinking

1. Although the bronchodilator has cardiovascular side effects, the priority assessment is respiratory.
2. These are respiratory drugs.
3. As in choice 2.
4. Advair, which is a combination of fluticasone (an inhaled steroid) and salmeterol (an inhaled bronchodilator), is commonly used on clients with asthma. A respiratory assessment would be a priority to form a baseline and to assess the therapeutic effects of the drugs.

85.   C: Changes in Health   T: Application

1. Caffeine can cause false elevations in blood pressure lasting up to three hours. There should be no effect after five hours.
2. Relaxation facilitates a more accurate blood pressure reading.
3. Electronic monitoring devices, if properly calibrated, are as reliable as manual devices. Care should be taken if interchanging the devices or if

the electronic reading shows significant variance in comparison with previous readings.
4. The same arm should be used at each visit.

86. C: Changes in Health   T: Application

1. This is an invasion of Ms. Brette's personal space and not an appropriate therapeutic technique.
2. This may prove to be too stimulating for Ms. Brette. She requires a calm, quiet environment.
3. Antianxiety medications are commonly used to bring the anxiety to a manageable level.
4. Ms. Brette may view this as punishment, unless she initiates moving to her room.

87. C: Changes in Health   T: Critical Thinking

1. Airline staff will need to know this information so a decision can be made regarding landing at the closest airport or obtaining on-ground medical advice. It is not, however, the priority action.
2. This is an important question, but it can be asked after oxygen is administered.
3. As in choice 2.
4. If the man is experiencing a myocardial infarction, the heart muscle is being deprived of oxygen. The oxygen supply to the heart must be increased immediately to prevent heart damage.

88. C: Changes in Health   T: Knowledge

1. Septicemia is a systemic infection in which pathogens spread from an infection in any part of the body to the bloodstream. It is diagnosed by culture of the blood. The organism is identified so that vigorous treatment with antibiotics can be provided.
2. This is done for an accessible area of potential infection. Septicemia is infection in the blood.
3. While a WBC will help diagnose an infection, it is not specific for septicemia.
4. This will diagnose an infection of the CSF or meninges.

89. C: Changes in Health   T: Critical Thinking

1. Mr. Dunlop is displaying manifestations of myocardial infarction; thus, 9-1-1 must be called. This is not the most complete answer.
2. This is the most complete answer. ASA is a fibrinolytic that may help break up thrombi that contribute to MIs. It is recognized to be part of appropriate first aid treatment if myocardial infarction is suspected.
3. There is no need to put Mr. Dunlop in a knee-chest position.

4. A blanket may provide increased comfort for Mr. Dunlop, but administration of ASA is more important.

90. C: Changes in Health   T: Application

1. The spray is directed under the tongue, not inhaled.
2. Headache is an expected side effect.
3. Pain relief should be within two minutes. If there is no significant relief within 15 minutes, she should notify her physician.
4. Exercise creates cardiovascular demand. Administration of nitroglycerine prior to physical activity will increase blood flow to the heart, increasing tolerance for the activity.

91. C: Changes in Health   T: Application

1. Fever is likely to be manifested, but it is not the classic symptom of *C. difficile* infection.
2. Vomiting sometimes, but not always, accompanies a *C. difficile* infection.
3. Chills often accompany the fever, but are not specific to *C. difficile*.
4. Overgrowth of *C. difficile* in the colon causes diarrhea that is usually watery and voluminous.

92. C: Changes in Health   T: Knowledge

1. Fibromyalgia is not a psychiatric disorder. Depression and anxiety may be involved, possibly due to living with chronic pain and fatigue.
2. While fibromyalgia cannot be cured, there are treatments, including antidepressants, physiotherapy, rest, and analgesics.
3. A definitive diagnosis of fibromyalgia is difficult to establish as there are no specific diagnostic tests. Often the diagnosis is achieved by ruling out other conditions. Manifestations may be similar to many other conditions.
4. The pain and fatigue are not progressive.

93. C: Professional Practice   T: Critical Thinking

1. True, but this does not answer the question.
2. This explains why nurses support political advocacy for social determinants of health.
3. This is part of the *Canada Health Act* but does not answer the question.
4. This is true but does not answer the question.

94. C: Changes in Health   T: Critical Thinking

1. This is an important nursing action but not the priority.
2. Maintaining a patent airway is the priority action based on the type of surgery and the ABC principles of critical care.

3. This is one action that will assist in maintaining the patent airway.
4. As in choice 1.

95.   C: Health and Wellness   T: Application

1. Hepatitis A is not transmitted by blood or body fluids.
2. Hepatitis A is not an airborne virus.
3. This does not explain the mode of transmission. While there may be more cases of hepatitis A in tropical countries, it is not necessarily considered endemic.
4. Hepatitis A is transmitted by the fecal–oral route, most commonly in contaminated food and water. It may be more prevalent in countries where there is a warmer climate and poor sanitation practices.

96.   C: Health and Wellness   T: Application

1. This meal should be eaten around 0100 of the night shift. Large meals eaten shortly before going to bed after a night shift do not facilitate sleepiness.
2. This may help prevent the circadian rhythm from being triggered by the morning light.
3. Because of its potentially stimulating effects, shift workers are advised to avoid strenuous activity just before bedtime.
4. A 24-hour time period is recommended between shifts for those who rotate shifts.

97.   C: Changes in Health   T: Application

1. These are generally the second set of teeth to erupt.
2. The lower central incisors are generally the first teeth to erupt, at about 6 to 8 months of age.
3. The canine teeth do not generally erupt until about 20 months.
4. The first molar does not generally erupt until 14–18 months.

98.   C: Changes in Health   T: Critical Thinking

1. The tube must be assessed for patency. Irrigating can be done by instilling, and then withdrawing, saline.
2. Instillation may not determine patency and may add to the residuals in the stomach.
3. The tube should not be removed as this may not be necessary and should not be done without a physician's order.
4. The physician does not need to be notified until the patency of the tube has been determined.

99.   C: Changes in Health   T: Application

1. Women with gestational diabetes often deliver large infants. It is important to determine the maternal baseline blood sugar level as early as possible.
2. Amniocentesis is not indicated for large infants unless there had been previous anomalies with the infants.
3. Maternal diet can be related to the size of the infant at term but is not the most important test at this time.
4. Pelvimetry will be important later in the pregnancy to determine if Ms. Bacci will be able to deliver a large baby vaginally.

100.   C: Nurse–Client Partnership   T: Critical Thinking

1. This is important to know but the nurse requires more information about what the father has read.
2. As in Choice 1.
3. As in Choice 2.
4. This response validates the father's findings and invites him to discuss with the nurse what he has read.

101.   C: Health and Wellness   T: Application

1. This test is done to diagnose or stage ovarian cancer and is not a screening test.
2. Women with close relatives, a mother or a sister, who have had ovarian cancer are at greater risk of breast, uterine, ovarian, and colorectal cancer. They should be screened at an earlier age than women with no familial history.
3. Chest X-ray may be used to diagnose or screen for other cancers, primarily lung cancer. There is no reported increase in lung cancer with a family history of ovarian cancer.
4. This test is performed when there are indications of ovarian cancer and is generally not a screening test.

102.   C: Nurse–Client Partnership   T: Application

1. This avoids the question and puts the blame on the boyfriend.
2. While this is true, the woman has expressed concern about telling her boyfriend, and this is the subject that needs to be discussed.
3. As in choice 2.
4. This introduces the legal and ethical implications of telling the boyfriend and encourages communication about how to approach the discussion.

103.   C: Nurse–Client Partnership   T: Critical Thinking

1. This may help in the short term but it is best not to use family.
2. This may help but there are too many languages and staff may not be able to effectively use a

written dictionary.
3. The nurse may want to learn the most common languages, but it is not reasonable to be fluent in all.
4. This is the best long-term option. Telephone and video link call centres with health care interpreters are available around the clock.

104.   C: Professional Practice   T: Knowledge

1. Inquests are not held to determine criminal liability, although evidence provided may lead to formal charges.
2. Inquests are not held to determine civil liability.
3. Inquests are not held to prosecute persons or agencies.
4. Inquests are held to provide recommendations that may be used to improve systems or practices in health care. They must answer how the person died and the manner of death.

105.   C: Health and Wellness   T: Application

1. A person with an apple body shape carries weight around the waist, which creates a higher risk of developing CVD and type 2 diabetes. However, Mark's BMI is within the normal range.
2. An apple-shaped person carries weight around the waist, which creates a higher risk of developing CVD and type 2 diabetes. A BMI above 25 indicates that Consuelo is overweight.
3. A pear shape indicates that the person carries weight around the hips and thighs and is not as unhealthy as someone who carries weight around the waist. The BMI indicates that Pedro is only slightly overweight.
4. Christa has a pear shape, but her BMI indicates that she is slightly underweight, which may not be a risk factor for CVD and type 2 diabetes.

106.   C: Changes in Health   T: Application

1. This is an incorrect calculation.
2. The correct calculation is 12 grams × 9 kcal/gram = 108 kcal. 1100 kcal divided by 108 kcal = 10.1, or 10%.
3. This is an incorrect calculation.
4. This is an incorrect calculation.

107.   C: Health and Wellness   T: Application

1. Nurses should consult with the health care team before starting a complementary therapy. If the team agrees, the peppermint may be added to the plan of care. The nurse is responsible for assessing the appropriateness of the complementary therapy and has sufficient knowledge of the action and effects of the therapy to assess the risks and benefits.
2. This is not true.
3. The nurse needs to consult with the health care team prior to providing Mrs. Carnegy with the peppermint.
4. Mrs. Carnegy has found the peppermint to be effective, so there may be no need to consult with the physician about an alternative medication.

108.   C: Health and Wellness   T: Application

1. Falls are the leading cause of injury in older adults. In icy winter conditions, there is a greater risk of falls with severe injuries.
2. Area rugs may be a safety hazard. Bare floors decrease the likelihood of tripping, falling, and slipping due to rugs that may not be firmly attached to the floors.
3. An open element on a stove is more dangerous than a microwave, provided that the microwave is properly used.
4. Over-the-counter cough medications are not recommended for children or older adults. These clients should, more appropriately, drink fluids and take acetaminophen for discomfort. The nurse or physician should assess them if their symptoms worsen.

109.   C: Health and Wellness   T: Critical Thinking

1. This is a useful screening test and is recommended for people over the age of 50. However, it is not as conclusive as a colonoscopy.
2. A sigmoidoscopy looks only at the sigmoid colon.
3. A colonoscopy is direct visualization of the entire colon from rectum to cecum. Because polyps and cancerous growths actually can be seen, colonoscopy is the recommended screening test.
4. A barium enema is an X-ray of the lower bowel following the insertion of barium contrast medium. It can be used to see areas of obstruction; however, it is not as conclusive as the colonoscopy.

110.   C: Changes in Health   T: Critical Thinking

1. This is not necessary as the order is clear to provide oxygen. The nurse may want to further consult with the physician regarding the child's decreasing O_2 saturation.
2. This is the first action as it is has been ordered by the physician, and the child is in need of supplemental oxygen.
3. This may occur but is not the initial action.
4. This should occur and will be ongoing; however, the first action is to provide additional oxygen.

111.   C: Professional Practice   T: Critical Thinking

1. The pharmacist has the specific scope of practice to best recommend effective over-the-counter antihistamines to Mr. Patrick.
2. The nurse practitioner may be able to recommend effective therapies, but the pharmacist would be the most appropriate first choice.
3. This may be an alternative, but it would be better for Mr. Patrick to first consult with a pharmacist concerning effective medications.
4. A respiratory therapist might be an appropriate referral if Mr. Patrick were experiencing breathing difficulties.

112.   C: Professional Practice   T: Application

1. Although, in some situations, it is appropriate to discuss with the client his or her medication regimen, the professional nurse must display knowledge of the rationale for the medications being administered. Having to ask Mr. Price may create a lack of trust in the nurse's knowledge.
2. This is the appropriate resource to determine the rationale for the antipsychotic. The nurse must have this knowledge prior to administration of the medication.
3. This may be part of the psychiatric assessment but is not the first action.
4. Because Mr. Price is receiving an antipsychotic medication, this is not a reason to assume that he will be violent or that the nurse will need safety measures when performing care.

113.   C: Changes in Health   T: Application

1. This is not a manifestation of presbycusis.
2. With age-related hearing loss, the ability to hear high-pitched consonants decreases, and sound becomes muffled. It seems to the person that others are not speaking clearly.
3. The higher-pitched sounds of women's voices are lost initially.
4. People are able to hear their own speech.

114.   C: Nurse–Client Partnership   T: Application

1. This is setting limits to behaviour, and in this case, it may make Mr. Braham more anxious. Demanding behaviour is often an attempt to decrease anxiety.
2. All behaviour has meaning. The nurse needs to determine what is causing Mr. Braham's demanding behaviour. By sitting with him and asking open-ended questions, she may be able to determine the underlying problems.
3. Maintaining continuity of care with one nurse is optimum to developing a trusting relationship between Mr. Braham and the nurse.

4. This is confrontational and will likely escalate the demanding behaviour. It is not a therapeutic response.

115.   C: Nurse–Client Partnership   T: Application

1. The person with dementia is not necessarily deaf, and Mr. Hill does not have to speak loudly.
2. The person with dementia will not understand written communication any better than verbal communication.
3. The person with dementia has lost some ability to interpret complex language. Short, simple sentences may enable the client with dementia to comprehend the spoken word.
4. Repeating the communication will not aid in comprehension of what has been spoken.

116.   C: Nurse–Client Partnership   T: Application

1. A nurse may or may not decide to answer a question that may be a natural conversational question for a client. If the nurse chooses to respond, it should be a brief answer. The most appropriate response, however, is to refocus the conversation to the client. In this scenario, Ms. Enright may be using the question to open the topic of her boyfriend.
2. This response indicates that rules rather than professional judgement direct her practice.
3. This response provides too much personal information about the nurse. It may be considered a boundary crossing.
4. This response may sound harsh and punitive to the client. There are better words to redirect the client.

117.   C: Professional Practice   T: Critical Thinking

1. This is necessary as most threats against health care workers are under-reported. It is not, however, the primary action.
2. This is true; however, it is not the primary action or consideration.
3. The nurse must first protect herself from verbal abuse that may turn to physical abuse. Once safeguards are in place, she may address documentation, support, communication with colleagues, and methods to provide care to Mr. Dovgan.
4. This is important to obtain support and assistance in devising methods for caring for Mr. Dovgan. It is not, however, the primary action.

118.   C: Changes in Health   T: Critical Thinking

1. Lindsay is asking for help, but she does not actually have the razor blades, so the suicide risk is not imminent.

2. Young men have a high risk of suicide, often by violent means. Ahmet has the gun and is able to act on his impulse immediately.
3. Florence has agreed to treatment.
4. Seniors are at risk for suicide, but Fred may be feeling a grief reaction that will improve. He has not formed a plan.

---

119.   C: Nurse–Client Partnership   T: Critical Thinking

1. This is the order, not what might be actually occurring.
2. This is the recommendation by the physiotherapist, but not what might be actually happening.
3. This is current, but may not be what occurs all the time.
4. Only this response specifically answers the family's question.

---

120.   C: Nurse–Client Partnership   T: Critical Thinking

1. This is an important assessment, but the developmental stage must first be determined.
2. As in choice 1.
3. Developmental level is essential in assessing children's ability and level of understanding. It must be determined prior to a teaching plan.
4. As in choice 1.

---

121.   C: Professional Practice   T: Application

1. Most nursing regulatory and professional bodies recommend that the nurse's full name and category of registration appear on a nametag.
2. As in choice 1.
3. As in choice 1.
4. Nurses are accountable to the public. One way to demonstrate this accountability is identification by full name and professional role within the health care team. Nurses cannot be anonymous due to the public nature of their work. If there are safety concerns about the use of a nurse's full name, safeguards may be implemented in specific situations.

---

122.   C: Changes in Health   T: Critical Thinking

1. Autism is not treated with medications, although some drugs appear to alleviate particular symptoms in individuals.
2. This is the cornerstone of treatment for autism and assists clients to achieve their potential.
3. Autism is not considered to be a psychiatric disease and cannot be helped with psychiatric treatment. In the past, it was viewed to be maladaptive parenting, which may have responded to psychiatric treatment.

---

4. While a safety assessment is important, it does not help achieve developmental goals.

---

123.   C: Changes in Health   T: Application

1. This is the most effective method for stopping a nosebleed.
2. The head should not be tilted back as the blood may flow down the back of the throat. Holding the bridge of the nose is ineffective.
3. This may increase the bleeding.
4. This is a last resort, and cotton balls should not be used.

---

124.   C: Professional Practice   T: Application

1. The initial step in any type of conflict is to discuss the situation with the people involved. By discussing the student's performance with her, it provides an opportunity to clarify both appropriate roles and expectations.
2. This is a correct action but should occur after the discussion with the student.
3. The nurse educator may be a valuable resource, but the initial action is for Martina to speak with the student.
4. Martina should have read this information prior to the beginning of the preceptorship.

---

125.   C: Professional Practice   T: Application

1. Naproxen may cause stomach irritation.
2. Celecoxib is used for pain related to arthritis.
3. Acetaminophen is generally considered to be a safe analgesic and is appropriate for mild aches, pyrexia, and headache.
4. It is within the scope of practice for Olivia as a registered nurse to recommend over-the-counter medications, provided that she takes responsibility for determining the appropriateness of the medication for Ms. San.

---

126.   C: Professional Practice   T: Application

1. This is not necessary.
2. This is an expected nursing action but does not answer when the bag will need to be replaced.
3. There are no recommendations by the US Centers for Disease Control and Prevention for the "hangtime" of IV fluids. It is the responsibility of each agency to develop policies, which the nurse will need to consult.
4. The bag will not be empty for several days. This may be contrary to agency policies.

127.   C: Changes in Health   T: Critical Thinking

1. Mrs. Brown is exhibiting manifestations of abruptio placentae with signs of severe hemorrhage and shock. This is a life-threatening condition. The physician must be notified immediately so that medical interventions may be initiated to save the lives of the fetus and the mother.
2. Although the heart rate of the fetus should be assessed, this will not be possible due to the severe maternal bleeding.
3. This will need to occur as soon as the doctor is notified.
4. It is an important nursing action to assure Mrs. Brown that action is being taken to handle the situation. However, the safest priority action is to notify the physician.

128.   C: Professional Practice   T: Application

1. Evidence-informed practice refers to the use of knowledge based on systematic research studies.
2. Agency protocol may rely on tradition, not clinical or evidence-informed practice.
3. If ordered by the physician, administering acetaminophen (Tylenol®) may not be the result of nursing research but of medical protocol.

4. Clinical assessment of individual clients may lead to evidence-informed practice but may not include systematic research studies as rationales for nursing practice.

129.   C: Changes in Health   T: Application

1. This is an incorrect calculation.
2. This is an incorrect calculation.
3. Correct calculation:

$$\frac{56 \text{ kg}}{0.45 \text{ kg}} = 124 \times 18 \text{ kcal} = 2231 \text{ kcal}$$

4. This is an incorrect calculation.

130.   C: Changes in Health   T: Critical Thinking

1. This is a slightly elevated respiratory rate and should be monitored.
2. A productive cough is expected and aids the lungs in clearing mucus.
3. Restlessness is a cerebral manifestation of hypoxia.
4. This may be normal in an older client but should be monitored.

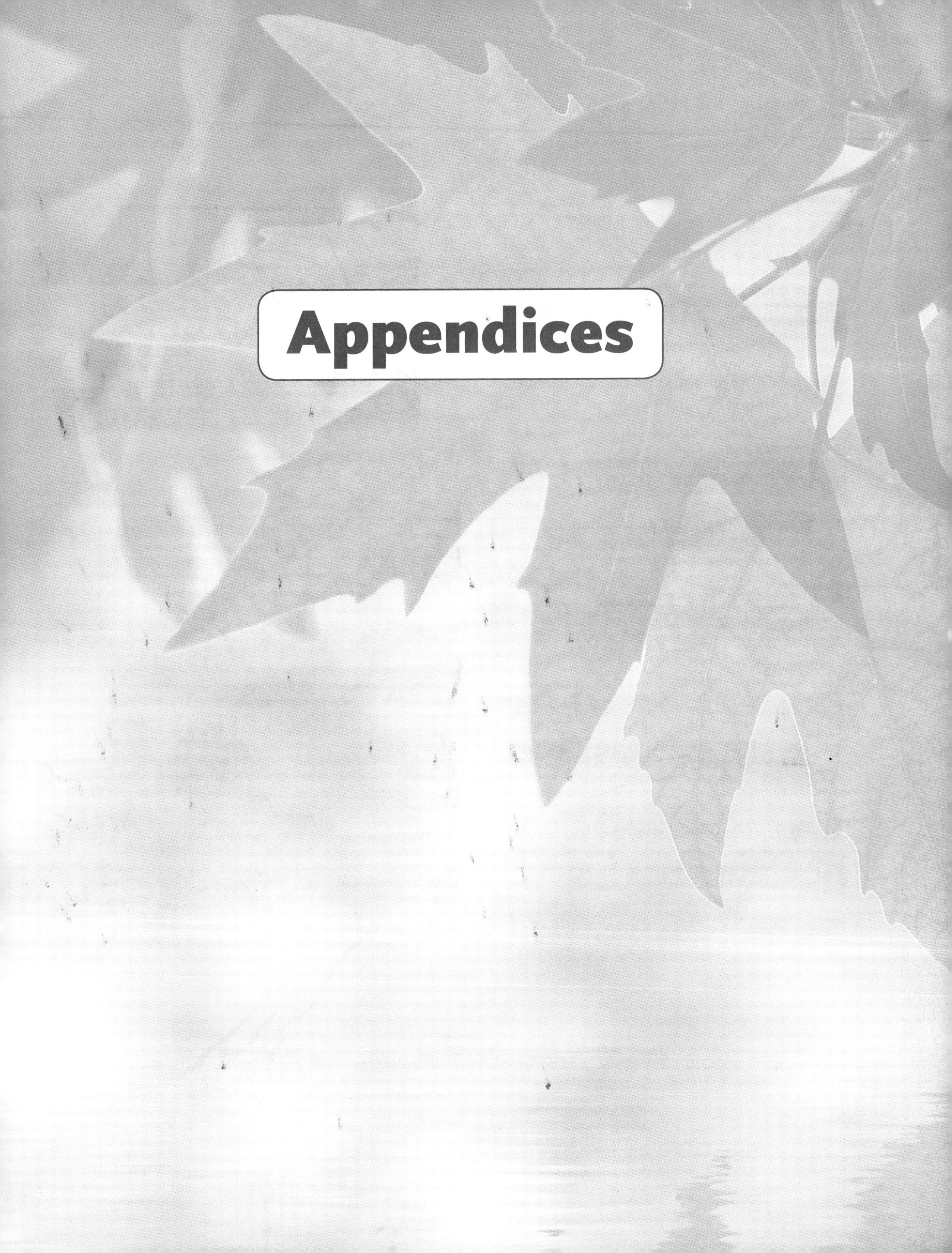

Appendices

APPENDIX A: THE CRNE COMPETENCIES

Assumptions

Throughout the development of the CRNE competencies, the following assumptions were established:

1. The CRNE competencies are directed toward the professional practice of the entry-level registered nurse in Canada.
2. Entry-level registered nurses practise in a manner consistent with:
    (a) professional nursing standards of the regulatory body;
    (b) nursing codes of ethics;
    (c) scope of nursing practice applicable in the jurisdiction; and
    (d) common law and provincial/territorial and federal legislation that direct practice. (Jurisdictional Collaborative Process, 2006)
3. The CRNE competencies are each of equal importance for safe, ethical, and effective practice of entry-level registered nurses.
4. The entry-level registered nurse is a generalist whose practice, autonomy, and proficiency will be enhanced by reflective practice, evidence-informed knowledge, and collaboration and support from registered nurse colleagues, other health care team members, and employers.
5. The entry-level registered nurse is prepared to practise safely and competently along the continuum of care in situations of health and illness across a client's lifespan.
6. The entry-level registered nurse and the client are partners in the decision-making process related to the client's health.
7. The CRNE competencies are grounded within the context of the client's health, the principles of primary health care, current and emerging health trends, determinants of health, the Canadian health-care system and professional nursing practice.
8. The practice environment of entry-level registered nurses can be any setting, program, or circumstance in which nursing is practised (e.g., hospitals, communities, homes, clinics, schools, industries, residential facilities, telehealth, correctional facilities). (Jurisdictional Collaborative Process, 2006).
9. The nursing process is used by registered nurses to think critically and to make sound and reasonable decisions (Potter, Griffin Perry, Ross-Kerr, and Wood, 2006) and is reflected throughout the competencies.
10. The entry-level registered nurse has a leadership role in the health care system. Leadership is not limited to formalized roles. (College of Registered Nurses of Nova Scotia, 2004; Jurisdictional Collaborative Process, 2006).
11. The entry-level registered nurse uses information and communication technologies to interpret, organize and utilize data to influence nursing practice, improve client outcomes and contribute to knowledge development in nursing. (Hebert, 2000).

1. Professional Practice

Registered nursing competencies in this category focus on personal professional growth, as well as intraprofessional, interprofessional, and intersectoral practice responsibilities. Each registered nurse is accountable for safe, compassionate, competent, and ethical nursing practice. Professional practice occurs within the context of the *Code of Ethics for Registered Nurses* (CNA, 2008), provincial/territorial standards of practice and scope of practice, legislation and common law. Registered nurses are expected to demonstrate professional conduct as reflected by the attitudes, beliefs, and values espoused in the *Code of Ethics for Registered Nurses*.

Professional registered nurse practice is self-regulating. Nursing practice requires professional judgement, interprofessional collaboration, leadership, management skills, cultural safety, advocacy, political awareness, and social responsibility. Professional practice includes awareness of the need for, and the ability to ensure, continued professional development.

This ability involves the capacity to perform self-assessments, seek feedback, and plan self-directed learning activities that ensure professional growth. Registered nurses are expected to use knowledge and research to build an evidence-informed practice.

Competency 1: Professional Practice

	The Registered Nurse
PP-1	Practises in a manner consistent with the values in the *Code of Ethics for Registered Nurses* (2008) (e.g., providing safe, compassionate, competent, and ethical care; promoting health and well-being; promoting and respecting informed decision-making; preserving dignity; maintaining privacy and confidentiality; promoting justice; being accountable). (CNA, 2008)
PP-2	Practises in a manner that recognizes and respects the intrinsic worth of clients (e.g., providing privacy, respecting diversity and vulnerabilities, relieving suffering, respecting and fostering cultural expression, appropriately using chemical and physical restraints, accepting a client's report of pain). (CNA, 2008)

Competency 1: Professional Practice (cont'd)

	The Registered Nurse
PP-3	Applies ethical and legal principles related to maintaining client confidentiality in all forms of communication: written, oral and electronic (e.g., blogs, social networking sites, camera phones, text messaging, e-documentation, electronic health records). (Jurisdictional Collaborative Process, 2006)
PP-4	Uses professional judgement when accessing, organizing, and using electronic resources (e.g., for own professional development, nursing practice, text messaging, personal digital assistant).
PP-5	Maintains clear, concise, accurate, objective and timely documentation.
PP-6	Uses established communication protocols within and across health care agencies and with other service sectors (e.g., preserving privacy, maintaining confidentiality, following appropriate channels of communication). (Jurisdictional Collaborative Process, 2006)
PP-7	Advocates for equitable treatment and allocation of resources for the client (e.g., assisting vulnerable and marginalized clients to gain access to quality health care, facilitating and monitoring the quality of care, facilitating appropriate and timely responses by health care team members, challenging questionable decisions).
PP-8	Demonstrates accountability for own actions and decisions.
PP-9	Practises within the scope of practice of the registered nurse.
PP-10	Articulates the registered nurse's scope of practice to others (e.g., the client, health care team members, the public, community leaders, politicians).
PP-11	Provides rationale for nursing actions and decisions based on professional judgment and theoretical and evidence-informed knowledge from nursing and related disciplines.
PP-12	Uses professional judgement when following agency policies, procedures, and protocols (e.g., when to use chemical and physical restraints, when to consult another member of the health care team).
PP-13	Uses professional judgement in the absence of agency policies, procedures, and protocols.
PP-14	Integrates continuous quality improvement into nursing practice (e.g., identifying and reporting when a policy, procedure, or protocol is unsafe, obsolete or unnecessary; participating in audits; participating in quality improvement committees). (Jurisdictional Collaborative Process, 2006)
PP-15	Uses evidence and critical inquiry to challenge, change, enhance, or support nursing practice (e.g., questioning accepted practice, participating in research).
PP-16	Takes action when aware of potential or actual abuse of the client by health care professionals, family, or others.
PP-17	Takes action when aware of potential or actual abusive situations to protect self and colleagues from injury (e.g., aggressive behaviours, bullying, workplace incivility, non-abuse policies). (Jurisdictional Collaborative Process, 2006)
PP-18	Recognizes and reports errors, near misses, and sentinel events, and takes action to minimize harm (e.g., client incorrectly identified, error in drug administration).
PP-19	Intervenes when unsafe practice of nursing colleagues and other members of the health care team is identified (e.g., talking to colleague, stopping the unsafe practice, reporting to appropriate authority).
PP-20	Uses conflict-resolution strategies.
PP-21	Implements strategies for continuing competence based on reflective practice, identified strengths, limitations, and learning needs.
PP-22	Is accountable when assigning nursing activities to other health care providers consistent with competence, expertise, education, role description/agency policy, legislation, and the client's needs (e.g., assessment, planning, implementation, and evaluation of workload assignment).
PP-23	Manages workloads effectively (e.g., time management, prioritizing, assignment).
PP-24	Seeks appropriate assistance when unsafe workload is identified.
PP-25	Collaborates and builds partnerships with nursing colleagues and other members of the health care team to provide health services.
PP-26	Understands the roles and contributions of other health care team members (e.g., scope of practice, role description, consultation).
PP-27	Shares knowledge and provides constructive feedback to colleagues (e.g., peer assessment, continuing competence, nursing students, mentorship, interprofessional rounds).
PP-28	Manages resources in an effective and efficient manner (e.g., human, material, technological, financial).

2. NURSE–CLIENT PARTNERSHIP

Registered nursing competencies in this category focus on therapeutic use of self, communication skills, nursing knowledge and collaboration to achieve the client's identified health goals. The nurse–client partnership is a purposeful, goal-directed relationship between nurse and client that is directed at advancing the best interest and health outcome of clients. The therapeutic partnership is central to all nursing practice and is grounded in an interpersonal process that occurs between the nurse and client (Registered Nurses' Association of Ontario, 2002). The nurse approaches this partnership with self-awareness, trust, respect, openness, empathy and sensitivity to diversity, reflecting the uniqueness of the client.

Competency 2: The Nurse–Client Partnership

	The Registered Nurse
NCP-1	Applies the principles of a therapeutic nurse–client relationship and responds appropriately (e.g., openness, nonjudgemental attitude, active listening, self-awareness).
NCP-2	Uses therapeutic verbal and nonverbal communication techniques with the client.
NCP-3	Establishes a therapeutic relationship with the client (e.g., maintaining professionalism, maintaining boundaries).
NCP-4	Fosters an environment that encourages questioning and exchange of information.
NCP-5	Analyzes the impact of personal values and assumptions on interactions with clients (e.g., cultural safety, ethical issues).
NCP-6	Applies principles of effective group processes (e.g., group roles, group phases, group dynamics, establishing group norms).
NCP-7	Demonstrates sensitivity to and respect for diversity in health practices and beliefs (e.g., sexual orientation, gender identity, childbirth practices, dietary differences, gender, beliefs, values, spirituality, culture, language).
NCP-8	Ensures that the client's informed consent has been obtained prior to providing nursing care, including involving others in the care (e.g., implied consent for nursing care).
NCP-9	Supports the informed choice of the client in making decisions about care (e.g., right to refuse, right to request care, right to choose, right to participate in research).
NCP-10	Facilitates and respects the client's informed choice to use alternative or complementary therapies (e.g., aromatherapy, acupressure, therapeutic touch, nutritional supplements, diets).
NCP-11	Collaborates with clients in developing strategies to accommodate or modify health practices (e.g., integrating traditional food into a diabetic diet, modifying built environments, promoting healthy choices in schools).
NCP-12	Provides care that is supportive to the client experiencing loss (e.g., loss of health, amputation, natural disaster, chronic illness, death).
NCP-13	Promotes the client's positive self-concept (e.g., supporting cultural and spiritual preferences, validating the client's strengths, promoting the use of effective coping techniques, building community capacity).
NCP-14	Uses principles/strategies related to teaching and learning to meet the client's learning needs (e.g., assessing readiness to learn, identifying strategies for change, establishing an environment conducive to learning, evaluating the learning process, using theoretical approaches, using social marketing).

3. HEALTH AND WELLNESS

Registered nursing competencies in this category focus on recognizing and valuing health and wellness. The category encompasses the concept of population health and the principles of primary health care. Registered nurses partner with clients to develop personal skills, create supportive environments for health, strengthen community action, reorient health services, and build healthy public policy. Nursing practice is influenced by continuing competency, determinants of health, life phases, demographics, health trends, economic and political factors, evidence-informed knowledge, and research.

Competency 3: Health and Wellness

	The Registered Nurse
HW-1	Collaborates with clients to identify priority areas for health promotion (e.g., healthy public policy, environmental health, stress management, social justice).

Competency 3: Health and Wellness (cont'd)

The Registered Nurse

HW-2   Assists clients in understanding links between health-promotion strategies and health (e.g., education programs regarding cancer risks, health fairs, anti-smoking campaigns, handwashing campaigns, ergonomics).

HW-3   Collaborates with key partners in health-promotion activities (e.g., community leaders, public- and private-sector organizations, special interest groups).

HW-4   Collaborates with clients to prioritize needs and develop prevention strategies (e.g., safe needle exchange, condoms in public places, reading nutritional labels).

HW-5   Collaborates with clients and other health care providers to respond to rapidly changing complex health risks (e.g., SARS outbreak, Norwalk virus, antibiotic-resistant organisms, pandemic).

HW-6   Collaborates with clients to identify appropriate groups and resources for mutual aid, support, and community action (e.g., poverty, homelessness, marginalized and vulnerable populations).

HW-7   Collaborates with other health care team members to implement strategies that prevent violence, abuse, and neglect (e.g., using screening tools, providing information).

HW-8   Collaborates with other health care team members in implementing strategies related to the prevention and early detection of prevalent diseases (e.g., cardiovascular disease, cancer, diabetes, communicable disease).

HW-9   Collaborates with other health care team members in implementing strategies related to the prevention of addictive behaviours (e.g., smoking, substance use, gambling).

HW-10   Collaborates with other health care team members in implementing strategies to promote mental health (e.g., stress management, support groups, coping strategies, public policy, crisis intervention).

HW-11   Coordinates activities with the client and others to facilitate continuity of care (e.g., cardiac rehabilitation, breastfeeding support, nutrition program).

HW-12   Promotes and utilizes safety measures to prevent injury to clients (e.g., accessibility of a call bell, supervision, diffusion of potentially violent situations, suicide prevention, least restraint, falls prevention, seat belts, bicycle helmets, smoke alarms, infant car seats).

HW-13   Promotes healthy lifestyle practices (e.g., physical activity and exercise, nutrition, rest/sleep, stress management, sexual health, family planning, contraception, hygiene, waste disposal, food preparation, infection prevention and control, smoking cessation, mental health).

HW-14   Implements strategies related to the safe and appropriate use of medication (e.g., overuse or underuse of antibiotics, polypharmacy, complementary medicine, over-the-counter medication, medication reconciliation).

HW-15   Takes action to address actual or potential risk factors related to health (e.g., food access, unsafe sexual practices, inactivity, smoking).

HW-16   Takes action to address actual or potential environmental risk factors (e.g., incidents and accidents, environmental contaminants, mechanical equipment, infectious diseases).

HW-17   Takes action to address actual or potential risks of abuse (e.g., intimate partner violence, older adult abuse, child abuse, sexual abuse, bullying, substance abuse, workplace incivility).

HW-18   Participates in preventive strategies related to workplace safety (e.g., occupational health and safety practice, latex sensitivity protocols, needleless systems, musculoskeletal injury prevention, protective equipment, WHMIS, managing aggressive and violent behaviour, pandemic planning, healthy workplace environment initiative).

HW-19   Incorporates determinants of health into the plan of care (e.g., adequate income, food and water safety, adequate housing and shelter).

HW-20   Incorporates research about health risks and risk/harm reduction to support evidence-informed practice (e.g., second-hand smoke, Pap smears).

HW-21   Uses the appropriate protocol when there is risk of communicable disease transmission (e.g., education on hand hygiene, isolation protocol, adhering to reporting protocols, encouraging needle exchange program, participating in immunization programs).

HW-22   Supports the client in role change and/or developmental transitions (e.g., parenting groups, retirement, job loss, puberty, menopause).

HW-23   Documents relevant data related to health promotion, risk reduction and injury and illness prevention (e.g., needs assessment, program planning, implementation, evaluation).

HW-24   Uses safety measures to protect self, colleagues, and clients from injury (e.g., nonscented products, harassment, psychological abuse, physical aggression, safe walking buddy system, falls prevention, workplace incivility).

Competency 3: Health and Wellness (cont'd)

	The Registered Nurse
HW-25	Provides education about immunization programs.
HW-26	Provides evidence-informed health-related information to clients (e.g., credible electronic sources, relevant and current information).
HW-27	Uses data collection techniques that are appropriate to the client and the situation (e.g., community assessment, assessment tools).

4. Changes in Health

Registered nurse competencies in this category focus on care across the lifespan of the client who is experiencing changes in health. The competencies in this category thus focus on health promotion and illness prevention activities, as well as on acute, chronic, rehabilitative, palliative, and end-of-life care. Such nursing actions may be delivered across a range of settings. Essential aspects of nursing care include critical inquiry, safety, solution-focused approaches, reflective practice, and evidence-informed decision-making. Registered nurses collaborate with clients and other health care professionals to identify health priorities and empower clients to improve their own health. In responding to and managing health situations, nurses promote optimal quality of life and development of self-care capacity and dignity during illness and during the dying and death process.

Competency 4: Changes in Health

	The Registered Nurse
CH-1	Collaborates with clients in a holistic assessment (e.g., physical, emotional, mental, spiritual, cognitive, developmental, environmental, meaning of health). (Jurisdictional Collaborative Process, 2006)
CH-2	Involves clients in identifying their health needs, strengths, capacities, and goals (e.g., the use of community development and empowerment principles, networking strategies, understanding of relational power, community capacity assessment).
CH-3	Collects assessment data from a range of appropriate sources (e.g., the client, previous and current health records, nursing care plans, collaborative plans of care, family members, significant others, substitute decision-makers, census data, epidemiological data, evidence-informed data, referrals, other health care providers).
CH-4	Uses appropriate assessment techniques for data collection. (e.g., observation, inspection, auscultation, palpation, percussion, selected screening tests, pain scales, interview, consultation, focus group, measuring, and monitoring).
CH-5	Validates data collected with the client and appropriate sources (e.g., medication reconciliation, health history, consultations, referrals).
CH-6	Analyzes data to establish relationships and draw conclusions from the various data collected (e.g., determining relationship between health assessment and laboratory values).
CH-7	Applies knowledge from nursing and other disciplines concerning current health situations (e.g., the health care needs of older adults, vulnerable and/or marginalized populations, health promotion and injury prevention, pain prevention and management, end-of-life care, addiction, blood-borne pathogens, traumatic stress syndrome). (Jurisdictional Collaborative Process, 2006)
CH-8	Applies knowledge from the health sciences (e.g., physiology, pathophysiology, psychopathology, pharmacology, microbiology, epidemiology, genetics, immunology, nutrition, sociology). (Jurisdictional Collaborative Process, 2006)
CH-9	Identifies actual and potential changes in health (e.g., pain management, disability, immobility).
CH-10	Collaborates with the client in developing and implementing the plan of care (e.g., setting priorities, establishing target dates, selecting relevant interventions, developing teaching plans, administration of insulin, home IV and TPN programs, referring to self-care groups).
CH-11	Incorporates the client's personal strengths and resources in meeting self-care needs (e.g., healthy habits, personal beliefs, complementary and alternative therapies, social supports, coping strategies).
CH-12	Uses evidence-informed knowledge to assist the client to understand interventions and their relationship to expected outcomes (e.g., possible risks and benefits, discomforts, inconveniences, costs).

Competency 4: Changes in Health (cont'd)

The Registered Nurse

CH-13	Individualizes the plan of care to apply interventions consistent with the client's capacities, identified priorities, and health situation (e.g., geriatric care, palliative care).
CH-14	Collaborates with the client during the care process to prepare for transfer and discharge (e.g., discharge teaching and planning, transfer of care).
CH-15	Documents nursing practice (e.g., assessment data, written plan, actual care, evaluation).
CH-16	Applies technology in accordance with available resources and the client's needs (e.g., relevant Web-based material, e-documentation, telehealth, patient lifts, home IV pumps).
CH-17	Supports the client through transitions related to health situations (e.g., new diagnoses, chronic illness, dying process).
CH-18	Facilitates physical, psychological, and psychosocial adjustment (e.g., therapeutic communication, counselling, appropriate referral, chronic disease management).
CH-19	Facilitates the involvement of family and significant others in collaboration with the client.
CH-20	Prevents and minimizes complications (e.g., turning and positioning, early detection and intervention).
CH-21	Evaluates changes in the client's health status (e.g., decreased oxygen saturation, decreased urine output).
CH-22	Manages multiple nursing interventions simultaneously (e.g., prioritizing and organizing interventions).
CH-23	Communicates accurate and relevant information about the client's health situation to appropriate health care team members.
CH-24	Intervenes in a timely manner to changes observed in the client's health situation.
CH-25	Evaluates the effectiveness of nursing interventions in collaboration with the client (e.g., learning needs, comparing actual outcomes to anticipated outcomes).
CH-26	Modifies plan of care based on an ongoing holistic assessment of the client's changing health situation.
CH-27	Initiates urgent inclusion of the health care team members in response to the client's changing health status (e.g., hemorrhage, imminent birth, low blood pressure, drug reactions).
CH-28	Coordinates activities with the client and other members of the health care team to promote continuity and consistency of care within and across settings (e.g., referrals, unit reports, community health centres, air and ground transport).
CH-29	Consults with other health care team members to analyze and plan care in complex health situations (e.g., obesity, comorbidities, chemical exposure, burns, cancer, complex family situations). (Jurisdictional Collaborative Process, 2006)
CH-30	Prepares the client for diagnostic procedures and treatments (e.g., explanation, evidence-informed information, tests, obtaining specimens).
CH-31	Provides preoperative and postoperative care.
CH-32	Promotes oxygenation (e.g., positioning, deep breathing and coughing exercises, oxygen therapy, oral and nasal suctioning).
CH-33	Promotes circulation (e.g., active or passive exercises, positioning, mobilization, cast care).
CH-34	Promotes and monitors fluid balance (e.g., intake and output, weight, noninvasive hemodynamic measurement, measuring abdominal girth).
CH-35	Promotes and manages adequate nutrition (e.g., burns, inflammatory bowel disease, diabetes, HIV/AIDS, infant gastric reflux, obesity, malnutrition).
CH-36	Administers and manages parenteral and enteral nutrition (e.g., TPN, nasogastric tube).
CH-37	Promotes and manages adequate urinary elimination (e.g., stoma care, bladder retraining, self-catheterization, bladder irrigation, bladder catheterization, pharmacological measures).
CH-38	Promotes and manages adequate bowel elimination (e.g., bowel retraining, ostomy care, enema, rectal tubes, pharmacological measures, dietary measures).
CH-39	Promotes and ensures a client's proper body alignment (e.g., proper positioning, external immobilizing devices).
CH-40	Promotes mobility (e.g., active and passive exercises, early ambulation, activities of daily living, prosthetic and mobilizing devices, use of ergonomics).
CH-41	Promotes and maintains tissue integrity (e.g., providing skin and wound care).
CH-42	Promotes and maintains comfort (e.g., the nurse's presence, warm and cold application, touch, positioning).
CH-43	Determines and implements appropriate sensory stimulation for the client's health situation (e.g., touch with unconscious client, minimizing environmental stimuli, sensory stimulation for premature infant in isolette, adolescent in isolation).

Competency 4: Changes in Health (cont'd)

	The Registered Nurse
CH-44	Evaluates safe use of prescribed and nonprescribed medication (e.g., safe dosage and route, food–drug interactions, drug–drug interactions, age, weight).
CH-45	Takes action with unsafe medication packaging and/or orders.
CH-46	Calculates medication dosage.
CH-47	Administers medication (e.g., right client, drug, dose, route and time; documentation; client's rights; right reason; allergies).
CH-48	Evaluates client's response to medication (e.g., desired effects, adverse effects, interactions).
CH-49	Assesses when a prn medication is indicated (e.g., analgesics, inhalers, antihypertensives, antianginals, laxatives, antianxiety agents).
CH-50	Takes action when desired responses to medication are not attained.
CH-51	Assists the client to manage pain with nonpharmacological measures (e.g., applying heat and cold, touch, massage, visual imagery, turning and positioning).
CH-52	Assists the client to manage pain with pharmacological agents or devices (e.g., non-opiates, opiates, epidural analgesia, patient-controlled analgesia [PCA]).
CH-53	Collects and communicates accurate medication information (e.g., medication reconciliation upon admission, at transfer of care, at discharge).
CH-54	Administers blood and blood products safely.
CH-55	Manages central venous access devices (e.g., implanted devices, PICC lines, infusion pumps).
CH-56	Manages drainage tubes and collection devices (e.g., chest tubes and vacuum drainages).
CH-57	Inserts, maintains, and removes nasogastric tubes.
CH-58	Inserts, maintains, and removes peripheral intravenous therapy.
CH-59	Applies routine/standard precautions.
CH-60	Intervenes in a rapidly changing health situation: acute cardiovascular event (e.g., myocardial infarction, unstable angina).
CH-61	Intervenes in a rapidly changing health situation: acute neurological event (e.g., brain attack [stroke], transient ischemic attack [TIA], seizure, head injury).
CH-62	Intervenes in a rapidly changing health situation: shock (e.g., hypovolemic, anaphylactic, neurogenic, cardiogenic, septic, and hemodynamic deterioration).
CH-63	Intervenes in a rapidly changing health situation: acute respiratory event (e.g., acute asthma, pulmonary embolus, pulmonary edema).
CH-64	Intervenes in a rapidly changing health situation: cardiopulmonary arrest.
CH-65	Intervenes in a rapidly changing health situation: perinatal (antepartum, intrapartum, postpartum, newborn).
CH-66	Intervenes in a rapidly changing health situation: diabetes crisis (e.g., diabetic coma, hyperglycemia, hypoglycemia, ketoacidosis).
CH-67	Intervenes in a rapidly changing health situation: mental health crisis (e.g., psychotic episode, neuroleptic malignant syndrome, suicide ideation, delirium, acute onset of extrapyramidal side effects).
CH-68	Intervenes in a rapidly changing health situation: trauma (e.g., burns, fractures).
CH-69	Intervenes in a rapidly changing health situation: postoperatively (e.g., malignant hyperthermia, hemorrhage, wound dehiscence).
CH-70	Intervenes in a rapidly changing health situation: acute renal failure (e.g., nephrotoxins).
CH-71	Provides supportive care to meet hospice, palliative, or end-of-life care needs of dying clients (e.g., symptom control, spiritual care, advocacy, family counselling, support for clients and significant others, advance care planning, grief and bereavement counselling). (Jurisdictional Collaborative Process, 2006)
CH-72	Intervenes to meet spiritual needs (e.g., assessing for spiritual distress, providing time for prayer or meditation, appropriate referral, cultural safety).
CH-73	Facilitates with the client to explore and access community resources (e.g., self-help groups, geriatric day programs, respite care, finances, transportation, social networks).
CH-74	Facilitates the client's development of independence and safety in activities of daily living (e.g., removal of scatter rugs, keeping essential furniture on one level of the house, raised toilet seat, ordering specialized equipment such as a walker and special utensils, consulting with other health care team members).

Competency 4: Changes in Health (cont'd)

	The Registered Nurse
CH-75	Facilitates social well-being of the client (e.g., encouraging and creating opportunities for social participation, encouraging development of new interests and support systems, facilitating of peer-to-peer helping model).
CH-76	Facilitates the client's reintegration into family and community (e.g., adaptation to role transitions, physical mobility, self-help groups).
CH-77	Provides supportive care to clients with chronic health situations (e.g., outpatient clinics, adult day care, respite care, pain management, symptom management, polypharmacy, group therapy, addictions counselling).
CH-78	Demonstrates understanding of organizational responses and appropriate nursing roles in emergency community disasters and emerging global health issues (e.g., mass casualty response, bioterrorism, pandemic, emergency preparedness/disaster planning, food and water safety).
CH-79	Takes appropriate nursing actions in disaster situations (e.g., mass casualty response, bioterrorism).

Source: *The Canadian Registered Nurse Exam Prep Guide* (5th ed., Appendix A, pp. 175–185). 2010, ©Canadian Nurses Association. Reprinted with permission. Further reproduction prohibited.

APPENDIX B: MEDICAL TERMINOLOGY

Jennifer Cooke, RN, BScN

An understanding of the distinct language used in the health sciences is of critical importance for safe nursing practice. Medical terminology can be simplified and better understood by analyzing the structural characteristics of the words.

Understanding the meaning of the basic prefixes and suffixes, and the definition of the root word, will allow you to derive the meaning of specific terms and greatly enhance your vocabulary.

ROOT WORD: The foundation word; directs us to the general, fundamental meaning of the word; e.g., cardio (pertaining to the heart) = cardiology (the study of the heart)

PREFIX: Added to the beginning of a word to specify a particular meaning of the root word; e.g., endo (within or inside) = endocardium (inner lining of the heart)

SUFFIX: Added to the end of a word to specify a particular meaning of the root word; e.g., itis (inflammation of) = endocarditis (inflammation of the inner lining of the heart)

Commonly Used PREFIXES in Medical Terminology

Prefix	Meaning	Example
a -	without/not	**a**pnea: absence of breathing
ab -	away from	**ab**duction (of arm): moving arm away from the centre of the body
ad -	toward	**ad**duction (of arm): bringing arm toward the centre of the body
ante -	before	**ante**natal: before birth
anti -	against	**anti**histamine: against (opposes) histamine
auto-	self	**auto**graft: grafting tissue from one part of the body to another part
brady -	slow	**brady**cardia: slow heart rate
contra -	against	**contra**ceptive: against conception
dorsi -	back	**dorsi**flexion: flexing a joint backward
dys -	faulty/difficult	**dys**pnea: difficulty in breathing
ecto -	outside	**ecto**pic pregnancy: embryo growing outside the uterus
endo -	inside	**endo**cardium: inner lining of the heart
exo -	outside	**exo**crine gland; gland that secretes onto an outside surface
eu -	normal	**eu**pnea: normal breathing
hemi -	half	**hemi**plegia: paralysis of half the body
hyper -	above/excessive	**hyper**tension: abnormally high blood pressure
hypo -	below/deficient	**hypo**thermia: below normal body temperature
infra -	below/beneath	**infra**mandibular: below the jaw
inter -	between	**inter**cellular: between the cells
intra -	inside	**intra**venous: inside the veins
macro -	large	**macro**cyte: an enlarged erythrocyte
mal -	bad	**mal**absorption: faulty absorption
micro -	small	**micro**cytic: small blood cell
neo -	new	**neo**plasm: new tumour growth
noct -	night	**noct**uria: urination during the night
para -	beside, near, resembling	**para**plegia: paralysis of the lower half of the body
peri -	around	**peri**cardium: around (outer layer of) the heart

Commonly Used PREFIXES in Medical Terminology (cont'd)

Prefix	Meaning	Example
pneum -	breathing	**pneum**onia: condition of abnormal breathing due to infection of the lungs
poly -	many	**poly**uria: excessive urine
post -	after	**post**operative: after surgery
pre -	before	**pre**ganglionic: before a ganglion
pro -	in front of, before	**pro**dromal: beginning, initial stages
retro -	behind	**retro**peritoneal: behind the peritoneum
sub -	below	**sub**chondral: below the cartilage
super -	above/excess	**super**sensitive: extra sensitivity
supra -	above	**supra**pubic: above the pubic region
tachy -	fast	**tachy**cardia: fast heart rate
trans -	across/through	**trans**membrane: across a membrane

Commonly Used SUFFIXES in Medical Terminology

Suffix	Meaning	Example
- ac	pertaining/relating to	cardi**ac**: pertaining to the heart
- al	"	abdomin**al**: pertaining to the abdomen
- ar	"	ventricul**ar**: pertaining to a ventricle
- eal	"	perin**eal**: pertaining to the perineum
- ic	"	opt**ic**: pertaining to the eye
- ose	"	adip**ose**: pertaining to fatty tissue
- ous	"	cutan**eous**; pertaining to skin
- algia	pain	neur**algia**: neural pain
- cele	sac/pouch/hernia	cysto**cele**: herniation of the bladder
- centesis	puncture into a cavity	thora**centesis**: puncture wound into thorax to remove fluid
- clasia	breaking up, division	osteo**clasia**: intentional fracture of a bone to correct abnormality
- ectomy	removal of	append**ectomy**: removal of appendix
- emia	condition of the blood	leuk**emia**: cancer of the WBCs
- genic	begin/generate/produce	patho**genic**: producing disease
- gram	a drawing or recording	cardio**gram**: a recording of the electrical activity of the heart
- graph	recording instrument	cardio**graph**: recording device that registers the electrical activity of the heart
- graphy	recording process	cardio**graphy**: recording and study of the electrical activity of the heart
- ia	condition/abnormal state	anem**ia**: condition of reduced RBCs
- ian/ist	specialist in field of study	pediatric**ian**: physician who specializes in the care of children
- iasis	formation/condition of	nephrolith**iasis**: formation of calculi (stones) in the kidney
- ism	condition of	alcohol**ism**: condition of excess alcohol intake
- itis	inflammation of	dermat**itis**: inflammation of the skin
- logist	specialist in area of study	patho**logist**: physician who specializes in the study of disease

Commonly Used SUFFIXES in Medical Terminology (cont'd)

Suffix	Meaning	Example
- logy	study of	cyto**logy**: the study of cells
- lysis	breaking down	hemo**lysis**: breaking down of blood cells
- megaly	enlargement	cardio**megaly**: enlargement of the cells
- oma	neoplasm or tumour	sarc**oma**: cancerous tumour of connective tissue
- parous	bearing or giving birth to	multi**parous**: pertaining to multiple births
- pathy	disease	nephro**pathy**: disease of the kidney
- penia	pathological reduction/ reduced amount	erythrocyto**penia**: abnormal decrease in the number of RBCs
- phile, - philia	an attraction to or abnormal tendency toward	lipo**philic**: attracted to fats
- phobia	fear of	hydro**phobia**: fear of water
- plasia	formation	hyper**plasia**: excessive formation of new cells
- plasm	a material that forms cells	neo**plasm**: new growth/tumour
- plasty	repair of/reconstruction	rhino**plasty**: reconstruction of the nose
- pnea	breathing	ortho**pnea**: difficulty breathing in recumbent position
- poiesis	formation of	erythro**poiesis**: formation of RBCs
- scope	instrument for visual examination	broncho**scope**: instrument that visualizes the bronchial tree
- scopy	examination using a scope	cysto**scopy**: procedure that uses a cystoscope to visualize the urinary bladder
- stasis	constancy, stillness, or stagnation	hemo**stasis**: arrested or halted blood flow
- stenosis	narrowing	pyloric **stenosis**: narrowing of the pyloric valve
- stomy	creation of artificial opening	colo**stomy**: an opening from the colon to the surface of the body
- therapy	treatment	cryo**therapy**: treatment of diseased body tissues by using extreme cold
- trophy	development; a certain type of growth	hyper**trophy**: increase in the size of a body structure or organ
- uria	condition of the urine	olig**uria**: abnormally low urine output

Commonly Used ROOT WORDS in Medical Terminology

Root Word	Meaning	Example
amnio -	amnion	**amnio**centesis: aspiration of fluid from the amniotic sac
angi -	vessel	**angi**ogram: X-ray of blood vessel
arter -	artery	**arter**iosclerosis: hardening of the arteries
arth -	joint	**arth**rectomy: removal of a joint
ather -	fatty material/plaque	**ather**osclerosis: fatty deposit causing hardening of an artery
audi -	hearing	**audi**ogram: a graphic recording of hearing
bronch -	bronchus	**bronch**oscopy: examination of the bronchi
carcin -	cancer	**carcin**ogen: cancer-producing substance
cardi -	heart	**cardi**ologist: heart specialist
cephal -	head	**cephal**opathy: disease involving the brain

Commonly Used ROOT WORDS in Medical Terminology (cont'd)

Root Word	Meaning	Example
cerebr -	brain	**cerebr**ovascular: blood vessel of brain
cervic -	neck of body or uterus	**cervic**itis: inflammation of uterine cervix
chem -	chemical	**chem**otherapy: drug therapy (for cancer)
cholecyst -	gallbladder	**cholecyst**ectomy: removal of gallbladder
chondr -	cartilage	**chondr**oma: tumour of cartilage
col -	colon	**col**onoscopy: examination of the colon
crani -	skull	**crani**otomy: opening in cranium
cutane -	skin	**cutane**ous: pertaining to the skin
cyst -	bladder	**cyst**ectomy: removal of the bladder
cyt -	cell	**cyt**ology: study of cells
derm -	skin	**derm**atitis: inflammation of the skin
dipl -	double	**dipl**opia: double vision
encephal -	brain	**encephal**opathy: disease of the brain
enter -	intestines	**enter**itis: inflammation of small intestine
erythr -	red	**erythr**ocyte: red blood cell
esophag -	esophagus	**esophag**itis: inflammed esophagus
gastr -	stomach	**gastr**ectomy: removal of stomach
gloss -	tongue	**gloss**itis: inflammation of the tongue
gly -	sugar	**gly**cosuria: sugar in the urine
gynec -	woman	**gynec**ology: study of diseases of women
hem -	blood	**hem**atoma: blood clot
hepat -	liver	**hepat**omegaly: enlarged liver
hydr -	water	**hydr**ophobia: fear of water
hyster -	uterus	**hyster**ectomy: removal of uterus
lapar -	abdomen	**lapar**oscopy: endoscopic examination of abdomen
laryng -	larynx	**laryng**itis: inflammation of larynx
leuk(c) -	white	**leuk**ocytosis: increased number of WBCs
lingu -	tongue	**lingu**al: pertaining to the tongue
mamm -	breast	**mamm**ogram: X-ray of the breasts
muc -	mucus	**muc**olytic: substance that breaks down mucus
my -	muscle	**my**opathy: muscle disease
myel -	spinal cord	**myel**ogram: X-ray of spinal cord
necr -	death	**necr**osis: tissue death
nephr -	kidney	**nephr**itis: inflammation of the kidney
neur -	nerve	**neur**ectomy: removal of a nerve
onc -	tumour	**onc**ology: study of tumours
ophthalm -	eye	**ophthalm**ologist: eye specialist
oste -	bone	**oste**oporosis: loss of calcium from the bones
ot -	ear	**ot**ic: pertaining to the ear

Commonly Used ROOT WORDS in Medical Terminology (cont'd)

Root Word	Meaning	Example
path -	disease	**path**ogen: disease-causing organism
p(a)ed -	child	**ped**iatrics: study of medical care and treatment of children
periton -	peritoneum	**periton**itis: inflammation of the peritoneum
pleur -	pleura	**pleur**al: pertaining to the pleura
pneum -	air, lungs	**pneum**onia: infection of the lungs
proct -	anus, rectum	**proct**itis: inflammation of the rectum
pulmon -	lung	**pulmon**ary artery: blood vessel leading to the lungs
ren -	kidney	**ren**al: pertaining to the kidneys
rhin -	nose	**rhin**oplasty: plastic surgery on the nose
seps -	infection	a**seps**is: absence of infection
thorac -	thorax	**thorac**otomy: surgical opening into the thorax
thromb -	clot	**thomb**us: blood clot attached to side of blood vessel obstructing blood flow
tox -	toxin	**tox**icology: study of poisons (toxins)
trache -	trachea	**trache**otomy: surgical opening into the trachea
ur -	urine	**ur**ology: study of the urinary system
ven -	vein	intra**ven**ous: into a vein

Common Directional Terms and Body Positions Relating to Medical Terminology

Term	Meaning
abduction	moving a body part away from the midline of the body
adduction	moving a body part toward the midline of the body
anterior	toward the front of the body
bilateral	both sides of the body
coronal (frontal)	lengthwise plane of the body; dividing the body into front and back halves
deep	interior of the body
distal	away from the centre of the body
dorsal recumbent	lying supine with knees bent
eversion	turning a body part outward
extension	straightening out a joint
flexion	bending a joint
inferior	lower; toward the feet
inversion	turning inward
lateral	to the side of the body
medial	toward the midline of the body
palmar	relating to the palm of the hand
plantar	relating to the sole of the foot
posterior	toward the back of the body

Common Directional Terms and Body Positions Relating to Medical Terminology

Term	Meaning
prone	lying on the stomach with legs extended
proximal	close to the centre of the body
sagittal	lengthwise plane dividing the body into front and back halves
Sims' position	lying on left side, left arm extended along back, chest forward, left knee slightly flexed, right knee highly flexed
superficial	on or near the surface of the body
superior	toward the head
supine	lying on the back, with legs extended
transverse (horizontal)	cross-section of body dividing it into upper and lower parts
Trendelenburg position	lying supine with the head lower than the feet
unilateral	applying to one side of the body

BIBLIOGRAPHY

Chabner, D. (2005). *Medical terminology – A short course*. St. Louis, Saunders.

APPENDIX C: APPROVED LIST OF ABBREVIATIONS

Abbreviation	Meaning	Abbreviation	Meaning
BP	blood pressure	mg	milligram(s)
bid	twice daily	min	minute(s)
°C	degrees Celsius	mL	millilitre(s)
cm	centimetre(s)	mm Hg	millimetres of mercury
h	hour	mmol/L	millimoles per litre
IM	intramuscular	P	pulse
IV	intravenous	po	orally
g	gram	prn	as needed
gtt	drops	qid	4 times daily
kg	kilogram(s)	q8h	every 8 hours
L	litre(s)	stat.	immediately
mcg	microgram	T	temperature
mEq	milliequivalent	tid	3 times daily

Source: Adapted from Canadian Nurses Association (2005). *The Canadian registered nurse exam prep guide* (4th ed, p. 350, Appendix B). Ottawa: Author. Reprinted with permission from the Canadian Nurses Association. Further reproduction prohibited.

APPENDIX D: COMMON LABORATORY AND DIAGNOSTIC TESTS

Jennifer Cooke, RN, BScN

LABORATORY VALUES ABBREVIATIONS

Abbreviation	Meaning	Abbreviation	Meaning	Abbreviation	Meaning
<	less than	L	litre	mm	millimetre
>	greater than	mcg or μg	microgram	mm Hg	millimetres of mercury
≥	greater than or equal to	μkat	microkatal	mmol	millimole
dL	decilitre	μL	microlitre	mOsm	milliosmole
EU	Ehrlich unit	μmol	micromole	ng	nanogram
fL	femtolitre	μU	microunit	nmol	nanomole
g	gram	mEq	milliequivalent	pg	picogram
IU	international unit	mg	milligram	pmol	picomole
kPa	kilopascal	mL	millilitre	U/L	units per litre

HEMATOLOGY

- Involves tests on whole blood
- Tests focus on the examination of the blood cells

Test	Normal Value	Interpretation
Complete Blood Count and Differential (CBC and diff.)	Screening of all blood cells, including Hgb, Hct, platelets and breakdown of WBC	
Erythrocyte Count (RBC)	Male: 4.7–6.1 million/mm³ Female: 4.2–5.5 million/mm³	• The number of circulating RBCs
Hematocrit (Hct)	40–54% (males) 38–47% (females)	• Percentage of RBCs to whole blood
Hemoglobin (Hgb)	8.7–11.2 mmol/L (males) 7.4–9.9 mmol/L (females)	• Measures hemoglobin on RBC of venous blood
Hemoglobin Electrophoresis	HgbA – 95–98% HgbA$_2$ – 2–5% HgbC – neg. HgbF – <1% HgbS – neg.	• Identifies presence of abnormal hemoglobin molecules, e.g., sickle cell • Anemia, thalassemia

Test	Normal Value	Interpretation
RBC Indices		
• Mean Corpuscular Volume (MCV)	82–98 fL (femtolitre)	• Average size of RBC
• Mean Corpuscular Hemoglobin (MCH)	27–33 pg	• Average Hgb weight of RBC
• Mean Corpuscular Hemoglobin Concentration (MCHC)	32–36%	• % of Hgb on RBC
• Erythrocyte Sedimentation Rate (ESR)	Male: <50 yrs –<15 mm/hr Male: >50 yrs –<20 mm/hr Female: <50 yrs –<20 mm/hr Female: >50 yrs –<30 mm/hr	• Measures the time it takes RBC to settle out on standing • Indicative of systemic inflammatory disease
White Blood Cell (WBC) Count	4000–11,000/mm³	• WBCs in venous blood

HEMATOLOGY (CONT'D)

Test	Normal Value	Interpretation
Differential WBC Count		
• Neutrophils	60–70%	• Bacterial infections
• Monocytes	0–9%	• Infection, inflammation
• Eosinophils	0–6%	• Allergic reactions, parasites
• Basophils	0–3%	• Inflammation
• Lymphocytes	9–36%	• Immune response

Test	Normal Value	Interpretation
Coagulation Tests		
Prothrombin Time (PT)	11–12.5 sec	• Used to measure degree of anticoagulation, therapeutic level: 2–3 min
International Normalization Ratio (INR)	0.81–1.2 min / 30–40 sec	• Standardized PT for clients on coumarin
Activated Partial Thromboplastin Time (aPTT)	60–70 sec	• Used for clients on heparin to measure degree of anticoagulation
Partial Prothrombin Time (PPT)	150,000–400,000/mm³	• Therapeutic level: 46–76 sec
Platelets (Thrombocytes)		• Necessary for normal clotting of blood in the early stages of the clotting process

BLOOD CHEMISTRY

• Measures noncellular components of the blood

Test	Normal Value	Interpretation
Arterial Blood Gases (ABGs)		
• Arterial pH	7.35–7.45	• Evaluates respiratory, cardiac, and renal functioning and determines acid–base balance
• Arterial PO_2	80–100 mm Hg	
• Arterial PCO_2	35–45 mm Hg	
• Bicarbonate HCO_3	21–28 mmol/L	
• O_2 Saturation	95–100%	
Cardiac Markers		
Cholesterol	<5.2 mmol/L / <3.4 mmol/L	• ↑ risk of coronary artery disease (CAD)
		• "Good cholesterol"
High-Density Lipoproteins (HDL) Low-Density Lipoproteins (LDL)	<3.37 mmol/L	• "Bad cholesterol"
Triglycerides	0.45–1.69 mmol/L	• Storage form of lipids
		• ↑ risk of CAD
Transaminases		
• Aspartate Aminotransferase (AST)	0–35 IU/L	• ↑ liver disease, pulmonary and myocardial infarctions
• Alanine Aminotransferase (ALT)	<40 IU/L	• ↑ liver disease, shock

BLOOD CHEMISTRY (CONT'D)

Test	Normal Value	Interpretation
Transaminases (cont'd)		
• Troponin T (TnT) • Troponin I (TnI)	<0.1 mcg/L <0.1–3.1 mcg/L	• Cardiac damage, renal failure • ↑ 3 hours following damage
• Creatine Kinase (CK)	Male: 55–170/mcL Female: 30–135 mcL	• ↑ Cardiac muscle, skeletal muscle, brain damage • ↑ 6 hours following damage
Lactate Dehydrogenase (LDH)	50–150 U/L	• Tissue damage, CHF, MI, liver disease, muscle damage
Gamma-Glutamyl Transpeptidase (GGT)	Adults >45 yr: 8–38 IU/L Females <45 yr: 5–27 IU/L	• ↑ MI; liver disease, pancreatic disease, CMV infections
Folic Acid	<60 yr: 4.1–20.4 nmol/L >60 yr: 1.2–12 nmol/L	• ↑ Pernicious anemia, vegan diet • ↓ Alcoholism, B_{12} deficiency, malnutrition, renal disease
Diabetic Markers		
Fasting Blood Glucose (FBG)	4–6 mmol/L	• ↑ Indicates hyperglycemia (diabetes mellitus)

Test	Normal Value	Interpretation
Two-Hour Oral Glucose Tolerance Test (OGTT)		
• After 1 hour postintake • After 2 hours postintake	<7.8 mmol/L <11.1 mmol/L	• Evaluates absorption of glucose into cells, assesses for diabetes mellitus or excess insulin secretion
Glycosylated Hemoglobin (HbA₁c) • Glycohemoglobin	HbA₁c: <6%	• Measures the average blood glucose levels over approx. 2 months. A high value indicates blood glucose level fluctuations (unbalanced diet).
Electrolytes		
• Sodium (Na⁺) • Potassium (K⁺) • Chloride (Cl⁻) • CO_2 content	135–145 mmol/L 3.5–5 mmol/L 95–105 mmol/L 21–28 mmol/L	• Required for normal fluid and electrolyte balance, acid–base balance, nerve impulse conduction, muscle contraction
Calcium		
• Total Calcium • Ionized Calcium	1.0–1.15 mmol/L 3.6–5.2 mmol/L	• Osteoporosis, hypo- and hyperparathyroidism

BLOOD CHEMISTRY (CONT'D)

Test	Normal Value	Interpretation
Calcium (cont'd)		
Serum Magnesium	0.56–1.05 mmol/L	• Required for ATP production, neuromuscular functioning • ↓ Malnutrition, alcoholism • ↑ Mg^{++} antacids, renal disease
Serum Phosphorus	Adult: 0.97–1.45 mmol/L Child: 1.45–2.1 mmol/L	• ↑ P = ↓ Ca^{++} • ↓ Hypercalcemia; chronic P-containing antacids, low dietary intake, alcoholism • ↑ Renal and liver failure, hypocalcemia, bone cancer
Iron		
• Serum Iron	Male: 14–32 µmol/L Female: 11–29 µmol/L	• ↓ Inadequate dietary intake, malabsorption, blood loss, neoplasms
• TIBC	45–82 µmol/L	
• Ferritin	Male: 12–300 mcg/L Female: 10–150 mcg/L	• ↑ Liver disease, hemochromocytosis, hemolytic anemias

Test	Normal Value	Interpretation
Liver and Renal Disease Markers		
Protein		
• Total • Albumin • Globulin	60–80 g/L 34–50 g/L 20–35 g/L	• Malnutrition, renal disease, liver disease, burns
Bilirubin		
• Total • Indirect • Direct	3.4–22 µmol/L 1.7–17 µmol/L 1.7–5.1 µmol/L	• Elevated with impaired liver functioning
Blood Urea Nitrogen (BUN)	44–144 µmol/L	• Liver and renal disease, protein catabolism
Creatinine	2.25–2.74 mmol/L	• Secreted by kidneys, result of creatine metabolism
BUN/Creatinine Ratio	6:25	• Measures liver and renal functioning • ↑ Creatinine – renal disease • ↓ BUN in liver disease • ↑ BUN in renal disease • ↑ Indicative of kidney disease

BLOOD CHEMISTRY (CONT'D)

Test	Normal Value	Interpretation
Uric Acid	Male: 268–387 µmol/L Female: 149–327 µmol/L	• End product of purine metabolism • High-protein diet, alcoholism, tissue destruction
Serum Amylase	30–220 U/L	• Assess for pancreatitis • ↑ Bowel obstruction and perforation, mumps
Thyroxine (T₄) free Triiodothyronine (T₃)	10–30 pmol/L 1.7–3.5 nmol/L	• Diagnosis of hypo- or hyperthyroidism
Viral Testing for AIDS		
Enzyme-Linked Immunosorbent Assay (ELISA)	Negative	• Identifies antibodies to HIV, not viral antigens; usually takes 2–12 weeks to develop
Western Blot Test	Negative	• Used to verify positive ELISA test, presence of viral genetic material in blood, viral load of less than 500 copies/mL is indicative of effective treatment
Viral Load	Undetected	
Polymerase Chain Reaction (PCR)	Negative	• Detects presence of virus

URINE CHEMISTRY

- Measures components of the urine
- General characteristics: clear, amber yellow, aromatic odour

Test	Normal Value	Interpretation
pH	4–8	• Alkaline urine: vegetarian diet, renal failure • Acidic urine: acidosis, starvation, diarrhea, fever
Specific Gravity (SG)	1.003–1.030	• ↑ (meaning a high specific gravity, above the high range given): dehydration, glycosuria, SIADH • ↓ (meaning a low specific gravity, below the low range given): overhydration, diabetes insipidus
Bilirubin	Negative	• Presence indicative of liver disease
Catecholamines		
• Epinephrine • Norepinephrine	<118 nmol/day <591 nmol/day	• ↑ Indicative of heart failure, pheochromocytoma • 24-hour specimen
Chloride (Cl⁻)	110–250 mmol/L	• 24-hour specimen • ↑ Addison's disease • ↓ dehydration, perspiration, burns, vomiting

URINE CHEMISTRY (CONT'D)

[handwritten: Myoglobin brd of muscle]

Test	Normal Value	Interpretation
Creatinine	7.1–17.7 mmol/day	• 24-hour specimen • ↓ renal disease • ↑ anemia, leukemia, atrophy
Creatinine Clearance	1.42–2.25 mL/sec	• 24-hour specimen • ↓ renal disease
Glucose	Negative	• Presence indicative of diabetes mellitus, stress, infection; low renal threshold for reabsorption of glucose
Ketone Bodies *[handwritten: fat bld]*	Negative	• Presence indicative of diabetes mellitus, excess protein in diet, starvation
Protein (single specimen)	Negative	• Presence indicative of heart disease, stress, renal disease
Protein (24-hour specimen)	<0.15 g/day	• Renal disease
Sodium (Na^+)	40–250 mmol/day	• 24-hour specimen • ↑ renal disease • ↓ hyponatremia
Schilling Test (Vitamin B_{12})	8–40% of radioactive vitamin B_{12} in urine in 24 hours	• Measured dose of vitamin B_{12} administered followed by 24-hour urine specimen • Identifies vitamin B_{12} deficiency • Lack of B_{12} in urine indicates malabsorption; lack of intrinsic factor
Uric Acid	1.5–4.5 mmol/day	• 24-hour specimen • ↑ gout, leukemia • ↓ renal inflammation
Urobilinogen	0.5–4 EU/day	• 24-hour specimen • ↑ Liver disease, hemolytic disease • ↓ Biliary obstruction

Microscopic Examination

• Red blood cells	0–2	• Presence indicative of infection, renal disease, trauma
• White blood cells • Casts • Crystals • Bacteria	0–4 Negative Negative Negative	• ↑ Indicative of infection • ↑ Glomerulonephritis • ↑ Infections, renal calculi • ↑ Infections

STOOL

Test	Normal Value	Interpretation
Occult Blood	Negative	• Intestinal bleeding that cannot be visualized directly • May indicate tumours, diverticulitis, ulcers, inflammatory bowel disease, oral or nasopharyngeal bleeding
Ova and Parasites	Presence of pathogenic organisms	• Intestines normally contain bacteria, e.g., *E. coli, S. aureus, Clostridium* • Overgrowth due to imbalance may cause disease • Ova = parasitic eggs

MISCELLANEOUS

Test	Normal Value	Interpretation
Cerebrospinal Fluid (CSF)	Clear, colourless RBC – negative WBC – 0–5 cells/L (adult) Organisms – negative Pressure: <20 cm H_2O	• Change → infection, tumour, hemorrhage, trauma
Sweat Chloride Test	<50 mEq/L	• ↑ Used to diagnose cystic fibrosis

DIAGNOSTIC PROCEDURES

Abdominal Paracentesis

This is a sterile procedure in which accumulated fluid from within the abdominal cavity is removed for client comfort or for analysis. The client first voids to avoid bladder injury and is then, in most instances, placed in a supine position for the procedure. A large-bore needle is inserted into the peritoneal cavity, and fluid is withdrawn into a syringe or drained into a vacuum bottle. Following the procedure, pressure to the inserting site is applied for several minutes, followed by a sterile dressing.

Amniocentesis

This sterile test involves the insertion of a needle trans-abdominally to remove a sample of amniotic fluid from the amniotic sac. The woman voids and is placed in a supine position with a towel under the right buttock to displace the uterus. A fetal monitor assesses the fetus during the procedure and a sonogram is used to direct the needle. The test is used to detect certain defects, such as chromosomal abnormalities, ABO and Rh incompatibilities, and disorders such as fetal anemia.

Angiography

An angiogram is an X-ray of blood vessels following the injection of a radio-opaque contrast medium. The contrast medium is injected via a percutaneous catheter. Images of the area being examined are visualized on a monitor and may be recorded on film. The contrast medium will outline abnormalities and obstructions.

Arthroscopy

This test is an invasive surgical procedure involving the insertion of a fibre-optic arthroscope into a joint space for the purpose of directly visualizing the internal structures of the joint. Abnormalities caused by injury or disease can be identified. In addition, boney debris can be removed and specimens obtained for laboratory examination.

Barium Enema

This test is an X-ray of the lower bowel following the insertion of a radio-opaque barium contrast medium enema. Preparation of the bowel with laxatives or enemas is required on the day prior to the examination to ensure that the lower bowel is clear of stool. The examination identifies any gross abnormalities, such as growths or obstructions.

Barium Swallow

8hrs NPO

X-rays are taken as the client swallows a radio-opaque contrast barium drink. X-rays can identify abnormalities of structure and motility in the pharynx, esophagus, and stomach. The client needs to be on NPO eight hours prior to the test, and all metal objects must be removed. To promote excretion of the barium, the client is encouraged to drink plenty of fluids following the test.

Bone Marrow Aspiration

This sterile test involves the removal of bone marrow cells from sites such as the iliac crest or sternum, for laboratory examination. Bone marrow cells are responsible for the production of blood cells (hematopoiesis), and, consequently, laboratory examination can identify defects in the cells and their formation. Specimens may be taken for the diagnosis of such conditions as anemias, blood carcinomas, lymphomas, and effects of chemotherapy.

Colposcopy

small bleed + θsex.

This procedure is used to locate suspicious areas of the cervix requiring biopsy. A colposcope is a macroscope containing a light source and magnifying glass that allows the physician to see abnormal areas of the cervix that would not be visible to the naked eye. It directs the physician more accurately to areas of tissue that need to be biopsied. After the specimen for cytological examination has been obtained, the cervix is cleansed with 3% acetic acid to remove cellular debris. Changes in epithelial tissues can more clearly be observed. Following the procedure, the client should be advised that a small amount of bleeding may occur if a biopsy was taken. Abstinence from intercourse is recommended until biopsy results have been obtained.

Bone Mineral Density (BMD)

The dual-energy X-ray absorptiometry (DEXA) procedure measures the mass of bone density per unit volume. Two X-rays of different energy levels measure the density of the bones being examined. The procedure measures the density of the bone in the specific areas of the hips, spine, and forearm. This test is commonly done on menopausal women to assess for osteoporosis.

Bone Scan

A bone scan is a nuclear medicine procedure used in the examination of bones. A radioactive contrast medium is injected, and then a scanner visualizes the condition of the bone. The procedure is used in the diagnosis of metastatic bone disease.

Bronchoscopy

Direct visualization of the upper respiratory passageways (tracheobronchial tree) is done through the use of a bronchoscope. The bronchoscope may be rigid or flexible. Specimens may be taken during the procedure for laboratory examination. The procedure may also be used for therapeutic purposes, such as removal of foreign bodies or obstructions. The client requires sedation and local anaesthesia to prevent activation of the choking reflex.

Cardiac Catheterization

NPO 8hrs.

This test is a sterile, invasive procedure that involves the insertion of a catheter through a vein or artery that is then passed into the heart chambers. Following injection of a radio-opaque dye through the catheter, X-ray images of the gross cardiac structures and coronary arteries can be visualized. For right-sided catheterization, the catheter is inserted into the femoral, brachial, or subclavian vein and passed into the structures of the right side of the heart. For left-sided heart catheterization, the catheter is inserted into the right femoral or brachial artery and then passed into the aorta and left heart chambers.

Cardiac catheterization is used to determine pressures within the heart structures, narrowing of coronary arteries, congenital abnormalities, and ventricular aneurysms and to perform angioplasty surgery. Clients require sedation and should be NPO for at least eight hours. An intravenous line is inserted for access should medications be required during the procedure. The client should void prior to the procedure.

Following the procedure, the client remains on bed rest for eight hours; a pressure dressing is applied to the catheter insertion site and monitored carefully for hemorrhage; the affected extremity remains extended and immobilized to ensure effective clotting at the catheter insertion site; and vital signs are monitored carefully.

bed rest 8hrs.

Cardiac Exercise Stress Test

This noninvasive test is used to evaluate cardiac functioning under physical stress. The client undertakes controlled exercise on a stationary bicycle or treadmill while an ECG (EKG), the heart rate, blood pressure, and development of chest pain are monitored. At regular intervals, the intensity of the exercise is increased in order to identify any abnormal changes that may occur as the exercise increases. The degree of intensity of the exercise is predetermined by the cardiologist based on the client's health, physical condition, and age. Abnormal changes in the ECG, heart rate, blood pressure, and development of pain indicate the inability of the coronary arteries to meet the demands of the heart, as in coronary artery disease. Stress testing is contraindicated in clients suffering from conditions such as unstable angina, severe congestive heart failure, recent myocardial infarction, certain chronic lung diseases, and so on.

Colonoscopy

Direct visualization of the colon is observed through the use of an endoscope. The endoscope is long and flexible and is inserted through the rectum, back through the colon to the cecum. The physician is able to visualize the lining of the colon for abnormalities and growths. On the day prior to the test, complete cleansing of the bowel is required through the prescription of strong cleansing laxatives or enemas. The client is also restricted to clear fluids. This ensures that the bowel can be visualized clearly.

Computed Tomography Scan (CT Scan)

A CT scan is a noninvasive, specialized computerized scanner that X-rays the body from different angles, providing a three-dimensional picture of the specific body part to identify abnormalities. The procedure uses ionized radiation as an energy source.

Cystoscopy

Direct visualization of the urethra and inner lining of the urinary bladder is observed through the use of a cystoscope. The procedure is usually performed with the use of a local anaesthetic. Abnormalities in the urethra, prostate, and bladder lining can be identified.

Biopsy

A biopsy involves the removal of a small sample of tissue for macroscopic and microscopic pathological examination. Biopsies may be taken by a needle inserted into the tissue and withdrawing a sample, excision of a small piece of tissue, a scraping from a surface of the tissue to be biopsied, or a punch that when placed on top of the tissue excises a sample. In some instances, local anaesthesia may be used to reduce discomfort. Tissue for biopsy is also commonly taken during surgical procedures under general anaesthetic.

Echocardiogram (Heart Sonogram)

This noninvasive ultrasound test uses sound waves to assess the structures of the heart and how they function. A transducer is moved over the chest wall emitting high-frequency sound waves that reflect off the heart structures and back to the transducer. The waves are then displayed on an oscilloscope, allowing for direct visualization of the heart shape, size, and thickness; activity of the heart valves; and related structures. Structural and functional abnormalities can be identified, such as atrial septal defects, valve disease, and aortic stenosis.

Electrocardiogram (ECG, EKG)

This noninvasive test provides a graphic recording of the cardiac cycle during depolarization and repolarization of the heart. Electrodes (leads) are placed on each of the client's limbs and at specific regions of the chest. The electrodes detect the activity of the heart from a variety of regions and can detect abnormalities in the electrical conduction of the intrinsic cardiac conducting system, such as cardiac arrhythmias or damage to myocardial tissue. An individual ECG using 12 leads provides a comprehensive recording of myocardial currents in two different planes. ECG monitoring may be continuous at the bedside, allowing for constant monitoring of cardiac activity, as in critical care units. In this situation, either three or five leads are usually applied to the chest.

Electroencephalography (EEG)

This test is a noninvasive electrophysiological procedure that evaluates the electrical activity within the brain. With the client in a sitting or supine position, approximately 10 electrodes are placed in specific positions around the head. Electrical records are then taken and produced on paper for analysis. Specific wave patterns indicate certain disorders, such as seizure activity, the presence of lesions, effects of certain toxic substances, inflammation, increased intracranial pressure, and the determination of death.

Endoscopy

The direct visualization of a hollow organ or a tubular structure within the body is achieved using a flexible fibre-optic scope or an inflexible scope. Endoscopy can be used to examine the bronchi, esophagus, stomach, colon, bladder, and so on. See the sections on bronchoscopy, gastroscopy, and cystoscopy

Endoscopic Retrograde Cholangiopancreatography (ERCP)

This test uses a fibre-optic endoscope to provide direct visualization of the pancreatic and biliary ducts. Injection of radio-opaque dye into the area allows for X-ray visualization of the pancreatic, common bile, and hepatic ducts. With the client sedated, the endoscope is inserted down the esophagus, through the stomach, and into the duodenum for examination of the area.

The endoscopic procedure also allows for gallstones to be removed from the common bile duct, drainage of bile in jaundiced clients, insertion of stents in areas that have become narrowed, and widening of the bile duct. Specimens of tissue may also be taken for pathological examination.

The client is on NPO from midnight of the day before and is administered sedation just prior to the procedure. Following the procedure, the client remains on NPO until the gag reflex returns.

Gastroscopy

Direct visualization of the lining of the stomach is observed through the use of an endoscope. The esophagus is also visualized during the procedure. Sedation is required to prevent choking.

Intravenous Pyelogram (IVP)

Following the intravenous injection of a radio-opaque contrast medium, a series of X-rays are taken as the dye is excreted in the urine, passing through the kidneys, ureters, and bladder. Obstructions and abnormalities can be identified. Care needs to be taken when using the dye as clients may have adverse reactions. The dye can also be nephrotoxic to the kidneys.

Laparoscopy

This procedure involves the insertion of a scope into the abdomen to directly observe the abdominal and pelvic organs. It is used to identify pathological conditions that are manifested by acute and chronic abdominal pain, such as cancerous lesions. Certain surgical procedures may also be performed using a laparoscope, such as cholecystectomy, appendectomy, tubal ligation, and hernia repair.

This procedure is performed under general anaesthetic and requires all the pre- and postoperative care precautions and nursing care.

Lumbar Puncture

This invasive test involves the insertion of a cannular needle into the subarachnoid space of the spinal column at the 3–4 lumbar space. The client is side-lying, the back rounded and knees flexed toward the abdomen. The client should be directed to remain still during the procedure and, following completion of the procedure, remain flat for approximately eight hours.

This test allows for measurement of CSF pressure by attaching a manometer to the needle. It also allows the removal of CSF for examination (colour, clarity, presence of RBCs, bacteria, malignant cells, protein, glucose, etc.). Medications can also be administered via this route, such as antimicrobials or anaesthetics.

Magnetic Resonance Imaging (MRI)

MRI is a noninvasive examination of a particular area of the body using magnetic and radio waves. A three-dimensional picture of the area is created, and abnormalities can then be identified. MRI does not use ionized radiation. All loose metal objects need to be removed from the client and procedure room.

Mammography

This test is a low-dose X-ray that reveals images and views of the breast from different angles. The breast is placed between two plastic plates that then gently compress and flatten the breast to provide a clearer image of the breast tissue. No preparation is required for this X-ray. Based on research, the Canadian Cancer Society suggests that under normal circumstances, women over the age of 40 have a yearly mammogram. Between the ages of 50–69, a mammogram every two years is suggested. The rationale for this change is based on the different types of breast cancer that develop in the different age groups.

Nuclear Scan

This test scans different areas of the body and involves the injection of a radionucleotide that is taken up by specific tissues. Gamma rays are emitted by the radionucleotide and detected by a scintillator. The scintillator converts the rays to an image of the body part.

Bone Scan

Abnormal bone tissue absorbs greater quantities of the radionucleotide, producing areas of concentration (hot spots). Bone scan is used in the diagnosis of such conditions as tumour growth, osteomyelitis, and arthritis.

Cardiac Scan

A radionucleotide identifies cardiac dysfunction, such as myocardial ischemia, myocardial infarction, myocardial dysfunction, and coronary artery perfusion.

Lung Scan

This test identifies changes in blood perfusion through the lungs, as well as pulmonary emboli.

Gallium Scan

Gallium is the radionucleotide used for scanning the entire body. The body is scanned at 24, 48, and 72 hours following the injection of the radionucleotide. Gallium scan is used to identify tumours (benign and malignant), inflammation, infection, and abscesses.

Positron Emission Tomography (PET) Scan

This type of scanning procedure is commonly used for evaluation of the brain and heart and in oncology. Radioactive chemicals are administered to the client that in turn become part of the normal metabolic processes of the particular organ.

Positrons are emitted from the radioactive chemicals and detected and converted by sensors and computed tomography to two- or three-dimensional images indicating a particular metabolic process at a particular site.

Pelvic Ultrasonography

A noninvasive procedure to confirm pregnancy and evaluate whether it is normal, abnormal, or multiple; the stage of development of the fetus; fetal position; or whether a tumour exists instead of a pregnancy.

A transducer is passed over the abdomen above the uterus, reflecting sound waves off the structures within the uterus back to the transducer. The waves are translated into pictures on an oscilloscope. Ectopic pregnancies, placenta previa, abruptio placentae, and tubal pregnancies can be identified.

Pulmonary Function Tests

These tests are prescribed to determine respiratory functioning: to assess for the presence and degree of lung disease, identify the type of lung disease, or assess for the effectiveness of therapeutic interventions for lung disease.

Tests include spirometry, lung volume and capacity, rates of airflow, and gas exchange. For the airflow rates and spirometry, the client breathes through a sterile mouthpiece, inhaling deeply and then forcibly exhaling several times. Calculations are made to assess for

- Forced vital capacity (FVC)
- Forced expiratory volume in one second (FEV_1)
- Peak inspiratory and expiratory flow rates (PIFR/PEFR)
- Maximum mid-expiratory flow (MMEF)
- Maximal volume ventilation (MVV) is calculated by having the client breathe deeply and frequently for 15 seconds.
- Expiratory reserve volume (ERV) is calculated by having the client breathe normally into the spirometer and then exhale forcibly.
- Inspiratory capacity (IC) is calculated by having the client breathe normally into the spirometer and then inhale forcibly.
- Total lung capacity (TLC) is calculated by having the client breathe normally into the spirometer.
- Gas exchange of the lungs is usually evaluated by having the client inhale CO and then determining the difference between the amount of CO inhaled and exhaled.

For these tests to be successful, the cooperation of the client is important. Directions given to the client need to be clear. For six hours prior to the test, the client should refrain from taking any bronchodilators or smoking tobacco.

Thoracentesis

This sterile test involves the insertion of a needle into the pleural cavity for the purpose of removing fluid that has accumulated within the pleural space. With the client sitting upright, a large-bore needle is inserted into the pleural space and fluid is then aspirated.

Following removal of the needle, pressure is applied to the insertion site followed by a chest X-ray to check for pneumothorax.

Tuberculin Skin Testing

This test is used to identify a tuberculosis infection. It does not, however, detect whether the infection is active or dormant. An intradermal injection of purified protein derivative (PPD) of the tubercle bacillus is administered into the arm. An individual who is infected will produce a reaction at the injection site as lymphocytes that have been activated by the original infection will react to the PPD. A reaction (induration, not redness) at the injection site of greater than 5 mm in diameter read 48–72 hours following the injection indicates a positive result. A second injection may be administered to an individual who is suspected as having been infected but was negative for the first injection.

Individuals who received BCG vaccine in the past will show a positive result even though they have not been infected with the tubercle bacillus.

Ultrasonography

High-frequency sound waves are passed into the body, echo off body organs, and are then translated into a picture. Ultrasonography helps identify abnormalities. Depending on the area of the body being examined, certain preparation of the client may be required, such as NPO.

Ultrasonography can be performed on many areas of the body, such as the cardiac, abdominal, and pelvic regions, as well as the breast, to identify abnormalities in structure and function.

BIBLIOGRAPHY

Lewis, S. M., Heitkemper, M. M., Dirksen, S. R. (2006). *Medical-surgical nursing in canada* (1st Canadian ed.). Toronto: Mosby.

Pagana, J. D., Pagana T. J. (2005). *Mosby's diagnostic and laboratory test reference*. St. Louis: Mosby.

Potter, P. A., Perry, A. G., Ross-Kerr, J. C., Wood, M. J. (2006). *Canadian fundamentals of nursing*. Toronto: Mosby.

APPENDIX E: MATHEMATICAL FORMULAE RELATED TO THE PRACTICE OF NURSING

Jennifer Cooke, RN, BScN

CALCULATION OF ORAL AND PARENTERAL DOSES OF MEDICATIONS

The **dosage ordered** refers to the dosage of the drug that has been prescribed for the client, for example, 500 mg, 2 g, or 30 UI. The **dosage available** is the dosage of the drug that is on hand, such as 250 mg or 0.5 g. The **drug form** is the form in which the available dosage is supplied, for example, tablets, capsules, or liquid.

Formula

$$\frac{\text{Dosage ordered}}{\text{Dosage available}} \times \text{Drug form} = \text{Amount of drug to administer}$$

Example 1

Your client is ordered Lanoxin (digoxin) 0.125 mg by mouth daily. You have Lanoxin available in 0.25 mg tablets. How many tablets should you administer daily to your client?

$$\frac{0.125 \text{ mg}}{0.25 \text{ mg}} \times 1 \text{ tablet} = \textbf{0.5 tablets} \text{ of Lanoxin}$$

Example 2

Your client is ordered Lasix (furosemide) oral solution 40 mg daily for edema due to renal failure. The label on the container indicates 20 mg per 5 mL. How many millilitres should you administer daily to your client?

$$\frac{40 \text{ mg}}{20 \text{ mg}} \times 5 \text{ mL} = \textbf{10 mL} \text{ of Lasix}$$

CALCULATIONS FOR PEDIATRIC DOSAGES OF ORAL AND PARENTERAL MEDICATIONS

Medications prescribed for infants and children require adjustments in the dosages to accommodate the differences in their weights and body surface areas; gastrointestinal, liver, and kidney functions; and metabolic activities. Much smaller doses of medications are required to avoid overdosage and toxicity.

The child's weight and height are often used to calculate the correct dosage for a child. In addition, dosages for young children are usually ordered in liquid form.

Calculating Pediatric Dosage Based on Body Weight

Formula

$$\text{Drug dosage per kg of body weight} \times \text{Weight of child (kg)} = \text{Dosage to administer}$$

Example

A 2-month-old infant with septicemia is ordered ampicillin 100 mg/kg/day every 8 hours intravenously. The infant weighs 4 kg. How many milligrams should be administered with each dose?

$$100 \text{ mg} \times 4 \text{ kg} = 400 \text{ mg of ampicillin daily (3 doses)}$$

$$400 \text{ mg} \div 3 = 133.3 \text{ mg per dose of ampicillin}$$

Calculating Pediatric Dosage Based on Body Surface Area

Body surface area (BSA) is calculated in square metres (m^2). In order to obtain the body surface area, a child's height and weight are required. Using a pediatric body surface area nomogram, the body surface area can be determined in m^2.

The prescriber orders the dosage of a medication based on milligrams of the drug per m^2. The actual number of milligrams to be administered will be determined by the specific child's body surface area.

Formula

$$\text{Dosage per } m^2 \times \text{BSA (in } m^2\text{)} = \text{Dosage to administer}$$

Example

A 7-year-old child with juvenile rheumatoid arthritis is prescribed intramuscular Rheumatrex (methotrexate) 5 mg/m^2/week in a single dose. The child is 120 cm in height and weighs 20 kg. His body surface area (BSA) is 0.90 m^2. What dosage should be administered?

$$5 \text{ mg} \times 0.90 \text{ } m^2 = 45 \text{ mg of Rheumatrex}$$

CALCULATIONS FOR INTRAVENOUS DRIP RATE

The amount of solution to administer is the quantity of fluid in millilitres that is to be administered during the shift. Intravenous tubing is selected according to the amount of fluid to be administered. The drip factor is the amount of fluid delivered by the specific tubing being used.

$$\frac{\text{Amount of solution to administer}}{\text{Time for infusion in hours}} \times \frac{\text{Drip factor of tubing}}{60 \text{ min}} = \text{Drip rate (gtts/min)}$$

Example 1

The client is receiving 1200 mL of 2/3 and 1/3 per 8-hr shift. At what rate should you set the drip rate if the intravenous tubing delivers 10 drops per minute?

$$\frac{1200 \text{ mL}}{8 \text{ hrs}} \times \frac{10}{60 \text{ min}} = 25 \text{ gtts/min}$$

Example 2

The client is receiving 50 mL of 5% dextrose in water per hour. At what rate should you set the drip rate if the intravenous tubing delivers 60 drops per minute?

$$\frac{50 \text{ mL}}{1 \text{ hr}} \times \frac{60}{60 \text{ min}} = 50 \text{ gtts/min}$$

UNITS OF MEASUREMENT

Canada adopted the International System of Measurements (Systeme Internationale d'Units or SI) Metric System of Measurement in 1970. It is used by most countries of the world.

Although this system of measurement has been universally adopted throughout the health care system, the Household System of Measurement occasionally appears due to long-term habit. It is therefore important for the nurse to be aware of the more common equivalents.

Liquid Measure

3 teaspoons (tsp)	=	1 tablespoon (tbsp)
2 tablespoons (tbsp)	=	1 fluid ounce (fl oz)

8 fluid ounces (fl oz)	=	1 cup (C)
2 cups (C)	=	1 pint
2 pints	=	1 quart
4 quarts	=	1 gallon (gal)

Mass Measure

16 ounces (oz)	=	1 pound (lb)

Linear Measure

12 inches (in)	=	1 foot (ft)
3 feet (ft)	=	1 yard (yd)

Conversion of Household Measure to SI Measure

Liquid Measure

1 teaspoon (tsp)	=	5 mL
1 tablespoon (tbsp)	=	15 mL
1 ounce (oz)	=	30 mL
1 cup (C)	=	240/250 mL
1 pint	=	500 mL
1 quart	=	1000 mL (1 L)
1 gallon (gal)	=	4000 mL

Mass Measure

2.2 pounds (lb)	=	1 kg

Linear Measure

1 inch	=	2.54 cm
39.4 inches	=	1 m

Measurement of Temperature

To Convert Celsius to Fahrenheit

$$^\circ\text{Celsius} \times 1.8 + 32 = \quad ^\circ\text{F}$$

To Convert Fahrenheit to Celsius

$$^\circ\text{Fahrenheit} - 32 \div 1.8 = \quad ^\circ\text{Celsius}$$

INDEX

Italicized numerals connote figures, illustrations, and tables.